CRITICAL ACCLAIM FOR

Jane Adams

The Greenway

'A haunting debut.' Minette Walters

'*The Greenway* lingered in my mind for days. It takes the psychological suspense novel into new realms of mystery.' Val McDermid, *Manchester Evening News*

'Adams's narrative has a simplicity that is misleading. The story is compellingly told and rich with psychological insight.' *The Independent*

'An assured first novel, with a strong cast and a plot which twists and turns without a glitch.' *Yorkshire Evening Press*

Cast the First Stone

'Adams's debut last year, *The Greenway*, hinted at a promising crime-writing talent; *Cast the First Stone* amply confirms that view.' Marcel Berlins, *The Times*

'A powerful and corrosive thriller about child abuse, suspicion and guilt. Gripping, scary, a wonderful read. She could rise to the top of the genre.' *Yorkshire Post*

'The grippingly edgy quality of this *policier* . . . is tautened almost unbearably.' *Sunday Times*

'Will keep you on the edge of your seat from the first few pages until the chilling climax.' *Stirling Observer*

Bird

'Jane Adams' first two novels of psychological suspense promised a major talent in the making. With *Bird* she amply fulfils that promise with assurance and style.' Val McDermid, *Manchester Evening News*

'The art of the truly great suspense novel, an art which Adams has mastered.' *Crime Time*

'I am a great fan of good commercial fiction, and it rarely comes better than Jane Adams's *Bird*. It is a haunting crime novel and psychodrama pulling all the right strings in all the right places.' *The Bookseller*

Bird

Jane Adams was born in Leicester, where she still lives. She has a degree in sociology, and has held a variety of jobs including lead vocalist in a folk rock band. She enjoys pen and ink drawing, two martial arts (Aikido and Tae Kwon Do) and her ambition is to travel the length of the Silk Road by motorbike. She is married with two children.

Bird is Jane Adams's third novel, following *The Greenway* and *Cast the First Stone*. *The Greenway* was nominated both for the Crime Writers' Association John Creasey Award for best first crime novel of 1995 and the Authors' Club Best First Novel award.

Her fourth novel, *Fade to Grey*, will be published by Macmillan in September 1998.

By the same author

The Greenway
Cast the First Stone

Bird

Jane Adams

PAN BOOKS

First published 1997 by Macmillan

This edition published 1998 by Pan Books
an imprint of Pan Macmillan Ltd
Pan Macmillan, 20 New Wharf Road, London N1 9RR
Basingstoke and Oxford
Associated companies throughout the world
www.panmacmillan.com

ISBN 0 330 36885 0

9 8 7 6 5 4 3

A CIP catalogue record for this book is available from the British Library.

Phototypeset by Intype London Ltd
Printed and bound in Great Britain
by Mackays of Chatham plc, Chatham, Kent

For my late father, with love,
and for Stuart's mam – wish you
could have been there.

Prologue

They told me what it was like, but I never did believe them. By the time we'd been there three days I knew they'd lied. It was worse, far worse.

Sun that burned so hot by day it dried the spit in your mouth and baked your eyes in their sockets. And then the sun went down and you froze to the bone. Weeks, we had of it.

I remember that night, Birdie. Remember it when I've forgotten so much else. The sky was so damned clear and so damned black. Black and silver with the stars all studded like diamonds in velvet and the moon so big it looked like I could reach out and hold it in my hands.

And then I looked down, Birdie. Looked down at the ground. At the dead and dying men, and I knew then that there was no God. No final judgement and no fucking order anywhere, Earth or Heaven.

I knew that no one gave a damn about the guilt of one man's heart when there was so much blood. Making the ground black like a spreading shadow.

I don't know how many of us had the woman before we killed her. I took my turn and, I'm shamed to say, I didn't even think about what we were doing or the rights and wrongs of it.

We'd decided they were guilty but there was no logic in it, Birdie. No logic. No mercy and no reason.

I heard her screaming while I tied the ropes. Winding the cord tight. Binding it round the body of the rope the way I taught you to bind a whip handle. Do you remember, Birdie?

Only this time, I left the loops free and didn't pull them through.

She didn't scream when they brought her to me. I think she was past that by then, only cried out, a little cry, like a shocked child, when she saw the others already dead.

And I didn't look into her eyes.

For me, it was like seeing Rebekkah all over again. Seeing her there, rope tight about her neck, like a dirty rag hanging against the moon.

Chapter One

'I knew you'd come, Bird.'

Marcie smiled again and patted the old man's hand. It was the third time he had said those words in the half-hour she had been sitting beside him. She perched awkwardly on Jack's bed, the toe of one foot resting on the floor, the other leg tucked beneath her, Jack's hand clasped carefully in both of her own.

'It's nice here,' Marcie said. Her voice too bright. Too fragile. The hospital visitor's voice, trying to be cheerful; in a desperate hurry to get away before the conversation runs dry.

She glanced nervously at Jack, hoping he hadn't noticed. Then sighed, deeply. Jack didn't notice much of anything these days.

He had closed his eyes as though wanting to sleep, but his fingers still curved around hers, so Marcie stayed where she was and waited.

Four days she had been back. Four days of sitting beside Jack, first at her grandmother's home and, for the last two, here at the hospice.

Four days, and yet each time he had seen her Jack had greeted her like a long-lost friend.

She looked around her. The truth was, it was really very pleasant here.

Four-bedded ward, two others of them occupied. A

large french window opening on to a pretty garden bordered by tall trees.

The sky beyond, summer bright, clear and full of promise.

Jack – the old Jack, not the one lying here in this neat and tidy room, in this hospital smoothed bed – had loved this time of year. His garden in full bloom, vegetables ready for the harvesting and his beloved trees heavy with fruit.

Already, Marcie missed the old Jack so much. She'd never called him Grandfather, even as a child. He'd always complained it made him feel too old.

And he'd never called her Marcie; she'd been 'Bird' from the moment her father had brought her home to live with his parents.

Jack's scrawny little Bird.

'Better here,' he said. 'Much better here.'

Marcie turned to look at him. 'I thought you'd gone to sleep,' she said.

Jack smiled. 'Sleep, my love, and miss all the bit of time I've got with you?' He smiled again, then, as though the effort was too much, his face went slack and he closed his eyes.

'Much better here, you know. They let the sunshine in.'

Marcie patted his hand. 'They let you out there yet?' she asked. 'Or are they scared you'll come over all bossy and tell them what needs pruning?'

With a great effort, Jack shook his head. 'When it's not so windy, Birdie, my love. They say I can sit out, when the weather gets a bit better.'

He turned his face away from her, gazing out at the tall trees. The mature limes and Lombardy poplars.

'All flying away for winter,' he said, softly.

'What are, Jack?'

He didn't seem to hear her. 'Know the winter's coming, don't they? Funny how they all know, my Bird. Flying away before it gets too cold.' He paused, the soft smile at the corners of his mouth creasing his lined face. Then he closed his eyes again, drifting this time into deep sleep.

Marcie watched the even rise and fall of Jack's chest beneath the light blankets.

She stroked his hand. The skin, dry and lifeless as parchment. Whitened by lack of sunlight and marked with purple blisters where the blood pooled beneath the surface.

Then she lifted her head and looked once more at the blue sky and tall trees outside the window.

When the wind dropped, Jack had said. Then he could go outside.

Marcie stared up at the stern poplars, stark, almost black against the brilliant blueness of the sky.

When the wind dropped, Jack had said.

Marcie watched, willing the trees to move.

But the day was calm and still. Not even the merest breath stirring the top-most branches.

Chapter Two

When Marcie arrived back at her grandparents' house Aunt Alice was standing on the doorstep wearing her dark blue house dress, a duster in her hand.

'I heard the car,' she said, 'so I came right down to let you in.'

Alice angled her cheek for Marcie's kiss, then took her arm and led her through to the kitchen.

'Sit yourself down and I'll pour you some tea. I've just made a fresh pot.'

Marcie watched as the older woman busied herself with the tea things. Alice. Granddad Jack's sister, a few years younger and very like him.

Like Jack, her once-dark-brown eyes had seemed to fade with time, becoming hazel with slight greenish lights as she had grown older. Her grey hair was still as thick, though, and she still wore it long, coiled on the back of her head and secured with a single pin. Marcie had watched her braid, coil and dress it hundreds of times and was still uncertain about how she managed to hold so much hair with just the one. It took Marcie all her time to coax her own hair into a tidy pony tail.

'Where's Gran?' she asked as Alice placed the china cups on the table.

'Gone to see your granddad. Your dad's taken her

over there, you must have passed them and not known it.'

'Ah.' Marcie nodded.

She picked up her cup and sipped the hot tea. It seemed funny to be using these flimsy china things again. They'd been part of childhood. Things Marcie had so consciously left behind. At home with Michael she used brightly coloured mugs, buying whatever took her fancy. Here, things had always been so correct. China cups painted with tiny forget-me-nots and delicately curling leaves. The table laid properly at every meal, and clean, crisp linen, spread over thick quilting to protect the polished table.

Marcie had almost forgotten just how precisely things were done, here, in this place that for sixteen years she had called her home.

She felt her stomach tighten in response to the memories. The pang, half of nostalgia, half of the fear that had first gripped her four days before and had renewed itself each and every time she re-entered the house.

The kitchen even smelt the same. The mixture of old-fashioned carbolic, of the breakfast toast, of polish and fresh laundry and, as her aunt reached across the table to take her hand, of fresh, scrubbed skin and baby powder.

Marcie felt the tightness spreading to her chest and throat, making it impossible to swallow her tea. The quiet, claustrophobic correctness of her childhood edging once more into her consciousness. Possessing her, even after all this time and all the things that lay between.

'Are you all right, Marcie, dear?'

She managed a stiff smile. 'I'm fine. Just thinking about Jack, that's all.'

Alice nodded, sympathy expressed in the downturn of her mouth; disapproval in the expressionlessness of her eyes.

'How was he this morning?'

'Much the same. He said he likes it there, at the hospice.' Marcie smiled, a little more honestly this time. 'He said they let the sunshine in and he could see the trees and the garden. That seemed to please him . . .'

She trailed off, realizing belatedly that she had said the wrong thing.

Alice sighed deeply and got up, taking her cup over to the sink and rinsing it with unnecessary thoroughness.

'Well, I'm sure that's nice for him. But we all did our best for him here, you know.'

Marcie got to her feet also and crossed to stand beside her aunt. 'Of course you did. I never meant . . .'

'No. No, I'm sure you didn't. It's just that . . .' She paused and snuffled into the folds of a clean white handkerchief. 'It's just, it's so easy for you to judge, Marcie, you haven't been here in all this time. There's been your gran and me trying to cope and your dad helping out when he could. And he's not been all that manageable, you know, your granddad.' She paused again, wiped her eyes once more on the white linen. Close to, she smelt of lavender, sweetly soapy and so very clean. Marcie put her arm around the older woman's shoulders.

'I never meant anything, Auntie. Nothing like that,'

she said. She hugged her aunt tightly, wanting, genuinely, to give some comfort.

Gently but firmly, Alice eased her arms away. 'The hospice have agreed to have Jack for at least a week, so I've put your things in the room he was in. No point you sleeping on that camp bed when there's a proper one to be used.'

'Thank you, Aunt Alice,' Marcie said meekly.

The woman patted her arm. 'Well, I'd better be getting on. They'll be hungry when they get back and lunch won't make itself.'

Marcie turned reluctantly and headed for the door. It was no good offering to help. Alice had made it clear from day one that she did things herself and in her own way. It was a pity, though, Marcie thought. She'd wanted to ask about the things Jack had been saying. About the woman he'd called Rebekkah, about the birds. About Jack's obsession with its being winter instead of high summer. She knew, though, with Alice in this mood, there'd be no chance for conversation. Alice hid herself behind a constant screen of busyness which nothing could penetrate unless she permitted it.

'Oh, I changed the sheets, of course,' Alice shouted from the kitchen. 'And I'm sure you're not going to be silly about things, are you?'

Marcie glanced back down the stairs. Her aunt had emerged from the kitchen, a glass in one hand and cloth in the other. 'I mean, he won't be back for at least a week.' She paused, as though waiting for some response from Marcie, then continued. 'And you won't be staying that long, will you, dear?'

She went back into the kitchen without waiting for a response. Marcie sighed and continued on up the stairs, aware that she'd been put well in her place.

You walked out on us, her aunt was saying. You went away and you've not been back more than twice in all this time, so you've no right to expect anything more.

Marcie pushed open the door to the spare room, the room Jack had been sleeping in, living in, for the last few months, and stepped inside.

She glanced around at the neatly made bed, the old-fashioned, heavy furniture, at her suitcase and travel bag placed on the straight-backed chair.

No. She had expected nothing else from them. Distant, disapproving courtesy and the occasional glimpse of affection, more, Marcie felt, for the child she'd been than for the woman she was now. It was strange and disturbing just how much like a wayward child they still made her feel.

The air in the room smelt close and musty. Over-breathed and unrefreshed. Marcie herself felt much the same. Very, very worn.

Her aunt's comments about the sheets brought a wry smile to her lips. Truth was, the very thought of sleeping in the bed that Jack had not long vacated made her feel sick.

Closeness by proxy. Infection through association. Whatever it was, she didn't want to sleep in that bed in this room tonight or any other night.

'Marcie, take a grip,' she told herself. 'And don't be so bloody stupid.'

She walked over to the bed and pulled the covers back, half expecting as she did so to see Jack's skeletal body lying there with its bone-thin limbs, flesh drawn so tight that it seemed barely able to cover his ribs and that obscenely bloated abdomen, soft and distended.

Marcie turned away from the bed, nauseated by the acutely, painfully remembered image, and crossed to the window, flinging it wide and looking out on to Jack's garden.

He'd packed so much into such a little space. Three small fruit trees. Cordoned blackberries, trained against the south-facing wall. Raised beds of sweet herbs and borders of bright flowers.

Only the tiny vegetable plot, with last year's pea sticks and its unweeded rows, showed the neglect of Jack's absence.

That and the raspberry canes, outgrown and bearing little fruit, and the unpruned roses, straggling on to the lawn.

Marcie leaned on the windowsill.

She'd grown up in this place, helped Jack with his garden, helped to dig and weed and to know when was the right time to plant and when to thin the growing seedlings. She'd taken as much pride and pleasure as he did in the growing and the fruit bearing. In the feeling of the moist earth, crumbling between her fingers with the sun warm on her back and the sweet, green scents rising up from the damp ground.

If she closed her eyes, Marcie could almost taste those other summers, the bright, safe days before everything had gone wrong and she had run away from Jack. From her father, from all of them.

Marcie could feel tears begin to prick at the corners of her eyes. She kept them closed, but the tears fell anyway, on to her hands as they gripped the sill. Sobs rose in her throat and she choked them into silence for fear of Alice hearing her.

Marcie breathed deeply, trying to control the conflicting emotions welling up inside her. She breathed the faint, sweet scents of the garden and the warm, dusty summer air, letting it ease and calm her mind.

And then she exhaled swiftly, forcing from her lungs the sudden, sour, decaying smell.

A slight sound behind her made her turn and that smell grew stronger. Close, overburdened air, suffused with half-identified odours of medication, soiled linen, the sourness of illness and decay.

Marcie retched, covering her mouth with her hands and willing herself not to be sick.

There was a movement, small but unmistakable, as though someone lying on the bed had tried to shift themself. The ghost of a movement in an empty bed.

Marcie shook herself angrily, crossed to the newly made bed and, this time, pulled the covers completely aside.

'No!'

She stared, her hands raised once more to her mouth. There it was. That slight but definite indentation as though someone had been lying there.

Willing herself to move, Marcie reached out and

touched the hollow where Jack's body would have lain.

Then snatched her hand away.

Where she had touched, the linen sheets had been warm.

Chapter Three

'What's the matter with Marcie?'

Her father's voice, strident and somewhat indignant, carried itself up the stairs. Marcie paused, strained to hear Alice's quieter reply.

'Blest if I know, love. She came racing downstairs this morning like she'd seen a ghost; went to see Jack and then spent the rest of the morning mooning about and getting under my feet.'

'Too much imagination, that one. Always did have.'

It was Gran who had spoken that time, her voice heavy with disapproval. 'Too much imagination' had always been one of Gran's favourite afflictions, an ill on which to blame most of the troubles of the world.

But she could be right, this time, Marcie owned. After all, what else but an overwrought, overtired imagination could have accounted for what she had seen? Or thought she'd seen?

She'd let herself get caught up in past regrets. Let her mind drift too far from the present, and scared herself stupid in the process.

But Marcie knew that she was lying to herself. What she'd seen in Jack's room had been so real and so intense there had to be more to it than an imagination working overtime.

When her father and grandmother had returned for

lunch she'd half expected news of Jack's death. That what she'd seen had been some sign that he was gone.

She could have accepted that. It would have made a kind of sense. But as it was . . .

Her father was speaking again, he sounded tired and impatient. Marcie listened. She felt no guilt at eavesdropping like this. Not with them. The younger Marcie had found that if she crept carefully out of bed and sat here, at the bend in the stairs, she could hear a great deal of what went on when she was meant to be fast asleep.

Jack had known. She was certain Jack had known.

But he'd never given her away.

That had been another of their secrets. Another thing that tied them so closely to each other.

'What did she have to come back for? I mean, what does she hope to prove?' Her father, weary now.

'She loved him.' Alice, strident and impatient, as though explaining to a stubborn child. 'For God's sake, Alec, it was your idea to contact her. You agreed that it was only fair they had a chance to make their peace.'

Alec sighed. Marcie couldn't hear the sigh, but she knew her father. Knew the way he would be pacing up and down the room, glass in hand. The way he'd let his shoulders sag slightly when he talked about her, as though the full weight of the problem, Marcie, rested upon them.

'Maybe I was wrong,' he said. 'Maybe we've all been wrong, wanting her back here, thinking we could change anything.' He paused for a moment, and when he spoke again his voice was louder, as though he'd moved closer to the door. Marcie placed a hand upon the banister, ready to take flight if he left the room.

'I don't know,' Alec said. 'I just thought she'd be different. More . . . I don't know, less like she used to be.'

'Ha!' That was Gran. 'Bad blood shows, you should have realized that, boy.'

'Bad blood! Oh, for God's sake, Mother, you sound like some Victorian melodrama. Bad blood!' Marcie could hear the shake of his head.

'You can't deny it,' Gran continued. 'She's not strong enough to cope with this any more than she could cope before. No backbone. That's why she ran away from us. And now she's back and you expect it to be all roses. Best thing you can do for Marcie is to pack her off home to her kids and let things be.'

'She loved him.' Alice's voice now, calm and dignified. She'd be seated, Marcie guessed, in the chair by the window. Sewing or knitting or some such, hands occupied as always, protecting her mind from too much thought.

'Loved,' Alec emphasized. 'Loved him in the past, Alice. But now? And you said yourself she was acting strangely.'

He paused again and Marcie could imagine him, standing by the window, looking out over the small, overgrown lawn. 'I should have let things lie,' he said at last.

'She's like her mother.' Gran's voice was harsh and petulant.

'You never even met her mother.'

'No. But I know what she was and I know what she did, and all we tried to do for Marcie couldn't make up for that, and you know that, Alec.'

She could hear them arguing but her mind had switched off to the words now. There was just the buzz of sound from the downstairs room. Another memory of childhood. This anger. This need to apportion blame for something they hadn't even been a part of. And this time there was no Jack to try to bring peace to the proceedings.

That's how she had known. Realized that he'd known about her listening. The way he tried so hard to protect her from their malicious words. From their secrets.

Marcie shifted up a step or two so that she could see herself in the mirror hanging above the first small landing.

Marciella Rose Whitney.

From the exotic to the sublimely ordinary.

What a name to be saddled with.

Marciella Rose Whitney, alias Marcie, alias Jack's Bird, stared at her reflection in the glass. She still looked younger than she was. At twenty-two she could pass for seventeen.

Black hair and dark brown eyes. Too-large eyes, and somewhat heavy brows that she resisted the urge to pluck or shape. A mouth that seemed always to be set in a faint half-smile, even when her mood was anything but happy, and a chin with a too-deep dimple and a funny, pointy look to it. Like a cat, her husband Michael always said. A curious, slightly puzzled cat.

The rest of her didn't fit the simile, though. Far from

being sleek or even elegantly slim, Marcie was small and slightly built, skinny almost to the point of boniness. After the twins had been born she'd lost so much weight that Michael had been truly worried, watching her eat, forcing her to drink milk until she was sick of the smell of it.

Eighteen months on and at least she'd got the curves back. She smiled faintly. Then frowned again as she thought about Michael and the twins. It would be another few hours yet before he would be home and she could phone him.

Marcie sighed.

Maybe Alec had been right. She shouldn't have come. Maybe she should pack her bags and head for home now. She could be there by the time Michael returned with the twins. It was clear that no one wanted her here.

No one but Jack.

Marcie shook her head and dismissed the thought of going home as quickly as it had been born. No, she had to stay, just a little longer. Make her peace and force Jack to make his.

Did he even remember why she had run away from him? If he did, he'd made no sign, spoken no word about it, just greeted her as though it was right and proper that she had come back to him, and talked, when he did talk, of things that Marcie didn't understand.

Marcie stiffened her shoulders and stood up, preparing to go downstairs and join the others. She'd spend another night here, or maybe two. Give Jack the chance to talk, try to get him to remember.

Marcie closed her eyes for a moment, focusing on that night more than five years before when she had left this house. Remembering Jack sitting in Aunt Alice's favourite chair and crying like a child, and Alice herself, hands clawlike on Marcie's shoulders, screaming at her.

'It never happened, Marcie! It never happened! You tell anyone and I'll swear you're lying. We'll all swear you're lying. An ungrateful and deceitful child, that's what you are, and there's no one here will say any different.'

Marcie opened her eyes once more, shivering slightly despite the heat.

'It never happened, Aunt Alice. Nothing ever happened, did it? Unless you all wanted it to. You spent sixteen years writing what you wanted me to see and making me see it.'

And now I'm back, Marcie thought. And you're the ones with the problem, because I know how it was, how all of it was, and I'm not about to let you turn me inside out a second time.

Chapter Four

It was one a.m. when Marcie signed herself in at the hospice reception and made her way to Jack's ward.

There was little of the hospital in this place. None of the drips and tubes and bleeping machines that Marcie had come to associate with sickness; nothing but that faint, distinctive smell, medicines and cleaning fluids, flowers left too long in cramped vases. Dying things.

The lights in the ward had been dimmed. Marcie stepped out of the brightly lit, picture-hung corridor and paused, letting her eyes adjust to the indoor twilight. The curtains had been left open over the french windows and a brilliant moon cast long shadows across the garden and on, into the ward itself. Tall trees, laying themselves down upon the four, darkened beds.

Jack seemed to be asleep. She sat beside him in the big green chair, watching his face as it twitched and grimaced, the slight fluttering of his hands lying outside the blankets, the little movements that told her he was still in pain despite the sedatives, the pain relief and the uneasy sleep.

Oh, Jack, Marcie thought. Why did it have to be this way? Couldn't it have been something quick and easy for you?

She had never realized until now that dying, this great act of uncreating, could take so much time and effort.

All for nothing.

'Would you like some tea, dear?' one of the night staff asked softly.

'Thank you.'

'You must be Jack's granddaughter?'

'Yes.'

'He's talked about you so much. His little bird, he says he calls you.'

Marcie managed to smile, embarrassed now, though she knew the woman meant no harm.

'Just like Piaf,' the nurse went on.

'Sorry?'

'Little sparrow, they used to call her. Do you sing, dear?'

Marcie gave a startled look, then comprehension dawned. 'Oh,' she said. 'Jack taught me songs when I was little. But that's not why . . .'

The woman was not really listening. 'How lovely, dear. I'll get you that tea.'

Marcie watched her go, amusement touching the corners of her mouth.

Little bird indeed. Hardly a songbird, Marcie thought. She could hold a tune, but her voice had no real strength to it.

Not like Jack's.

No, Jack called her Bird in memory of the first time he had seen her. Less than two months old and brought to his house by her father. Such a scrawny little thing and her mouth always open, wanting to be fed.

'It's good to see you smiling. Too many long faces round here.'

'I thought you were asleep,' she said.

Jack shook his head. A slight movement against the pillow. 'No, girl. Just hiding from her.' He gestured vaguely in the direction that the nurse had gone. 'Talk the legs off a donkey, she would. Worse than your gran.'

Marcie laughed, then stifled the sound quickly, looking around to make sure she had disturbed none of the real sleepers.

Jack grimaced, his mouth slack and toothless. He touched his tongue to his lips to moisten them before he spoke again.

'I won't be here much longer, girl. You know that, don't you?'

Marcie began to deny it. 'No, Jack, no, that's . . .'

'True, Bird, very true. And I don't much mind it, girl. I get tired, you know, and I can't do my garden like I used to.'

Marcie felt the tears beginning again. 'It's overgrown,' she said. 'I've never seen weeds in your garden before or the roses not pruned.'

'Forgotten how to do it, have you, Bird? Maybe you could do it for me, before the spring gets here. Too late when the sap begins to rise, they bleed then, you know. Bleed the life out of them if you do it in the spring.'

He closed his eyes again as though the conversation was too much and clutched at the sheets as a spasm of pain crossed his face.

Marcie reached out and covered his hand with her own.

'It isn't winter, Granddad Jack,' she told him. 'It's nearly September and it's warm outside.'

He returned her handclasp, the skin of his palms dry and oversmooth.

'Always were hot blooded, my Bird. Never felt the cold, did you?'

He opened his eyes wide for a moment and stared out of the window at the clear sky. 'Be a frost before morning, I shouldn't wonder, sky clear like that. Break up the ground well.' He moved, snapping his attention back to Marcie. 'Get your dad to help with that rough digging, girl. It's too much for you on your own. We'll have a week of frosts, I shouldn't wonder. If you did that far bed over now and let the frost lie on it we'll have an easier job preparing it come spring.'

Marcie bit her lip and nodded. 'Yes, Jack,' she said, 'I'll get it done for when you come back home.' There seemed no point in telling him again just how far away spring was. That there would be no frost tonight. Jack seemed satisfied and squeezed her hand.

'You're a good girl, Birdie,' he said, his voice cracked and whispery. 'Always told them that. A good girl.'

He closed his eyes and slept. The nurse arrived with the tea and Bird drank it, watching Jack's face, the slack mouth working even in sleep. It confused her. These moments of lucidity – like when he had talked about the nurse – followed so rapidly by disorientation and uncertainty.

She put the cup aside and, slipping her feet out of her shoes, drew them up on to the chair and wrapped her arms around her legs, resting her chin on her knees.

Watching Jack.

*

'Birdie.'

Marcie jerked herself out of sleep and looked around in confusion.

'Oh, Jack, I'm sorry. I must have gone to sleep.'

'Birdie!' There was a nervous edge to his voice now. 'Look, Bird, over there. She's followed me.'

'What?'

Marcie looked over to where Jack was pointing. His hand shook, but he seemed to be waving towards an empty chair that stood beside the opposite bed.

Marcie turned her gaze from the chair to Jack.

'There's no one, Jack,' she said. 'No one sitting there.'

He shook his head impatiently. 'Don't play games with me, Birdie, I don't have time.'

His voice had taken on a sudden sharpness; a strength that took her by surprise.

'She's followed me,' he said again. 'Never given up. Never given up.'

His voice trailed off, but his eyes continued to stare at the empty chair. Marcie could see his hands whiten as they clutched at the covers and the fear in his yellowed eyes.

This was not the time to argue what was real.

'Who is she, Jack?' she asked.

He glanced swiftly at her, relief showing on his face. 'You see her, don't you, Birdie?'

Marcie didn't answer.

'You see her,' he repeated, satisfied now. He eased himself back against the pillows and released his grip on the sheets. 'She comes to me,' he said. 'That damned rope round her neck and her hands tied, and she just looks. Looks at me. Those eyes, Bird. Those eyes.'

Marcie stared at the chair, then looked back at Jack. A half-memory of an earlier conversation wormed its way into her mind.

She felt herself grow cold, the hairs on her arms rising and a sudden chill clenching the muscles between her shoulders.

'Who, Jack?' she whispered softly. 'Who is she?'

At first he didn't answer. He had closed his eyes and his mouth began to work but no sound came out.

'Jack,' Marcie prompted. 'Is it the one you told me about? The woman in the desert?'

He shook his head, a small movement against the pillows.

'So cold,' he said. 'You wouldn't believe that, Bird, just how cold it was at night. Sky so clear and all the stars . . . You can see the moon so close it's like you could reach out and take a hold of it and it's so damned cold.'

Marcie nodded. She'd heard this before, about the moon, about the days full of heat and the nights cold enough for frost.

'In the war, Jack?'

He nodded. 'Out in the bloody desert. Cold, just like it is now, waiting for the frost. Like winter at night, it could be.'

He paused; Marcie waited but he didn't seem able to go on.

'Who was she, Jack?' she asked again, but he wasn't listening now. His mind was elsewhere. Detached from

Marcie, separate, even from the woman who sat in the chair and watched him.

'Who was she, Jack?' Marcie asked him for the final time. Then gave up. Jack was sleeping, his breath rasping in his throat and the bone-pale hands twitching as they lay on the cover.

Sharply, Marcie glanced back towards the empty chair. She rubbed her tired eyes.

'Stupid,' she muttered to herself. 'Just stupid.' Even so, she couldn't quite shake off the feeling that something had moved. That there had been a slight flicker at the corner of her vision, as though someone had risen to their feet and walked away.

Chapter Five

'You look like death,' Alec told her. 'Didn't you sleep?'

Marcie shook her head. 'Not well,' she said, 'and I was over with Jack most of the night.'

Alec snorted disapprovingly. He finished the rest of his tea and replaced the cup on the saucer with a loud chink. He pushed his chair back impatiently.

'Well,' he said. 'I've got to go. Some of us have work to do.' He looked sharply at his daughter. 'You'll run your gran over to see Jack when she wants to go?' he said.

Marcie nodded vaguely. She had woken feeling exhausted and horribly homesick. Almost packed her things then and there and fled back to Michael and the twins. The thought of doing so was still with her now. She was aware, suddenly, that Alec was staring at her as though waiting for something.

'I said,' he repeated, 'you'll run your gran over when she's ready.'

'Yes, yes. Of course I will.'

He nodded as though satisfied, but still frowned and did not move. 'Say much last night, did he?'

Marcie looked surprised, then shook her head. 'Not a lot, Da, you know how he is.' She laughed, weakly. 'He kept going on about one of the nurses. Said she talked too much.'

Alec allowed himself a half-laugh in return. He sounded relieved.

Marcie hesitated, then pressed on. 'He says he keeps seeing some woman. Someone he says keeps following him around and watching him.' She paused, gauging her father's expression. 'He's scared of her, Da.'

Alec frowned again. This was clearly something that he didn't want to hear.

'It's the drugs he's on, Marcie. You know that. They make him see things sometimes. And his mind wanders.' He paused. 'He's been ill for a long time. If we'd taken notice of half the crazy things he's ranted about we'd all be halfway round the twist by now.'

Marcie nodded weakly as Alec lifted his jacket from the back of his chair and slipped it on.

'I expect you'll be going soon,' he said. 'Get back to those kids of yours.'

Marcie poured her tea. 'He thinks it's winter,' she said softly. 'I keep telling him it's only the end of summer, but he's convinced it's winter.'

Alec looked angry this time. 'I've told you, it's the drugs he's on.' He shrugged his shoulders into his jacket, settling it better on his shoulders, and straightened his tie.

'Jack won't live to see another winter,' he said brusquely as he turned to open the door, 'so what the hell does it matter what season he thinks it is?' He glanced back and nodded at her. 'See you later, Marcie.' His voice was sharp and businesslike. Then he was gone, the door swinging shut behind him.

Marcie sipped at her tea, gazing absently at the wreckage of the morning's breakfast.

Slowly, she came to a decision.

She would stay today, and, yes, stay tonight. Pack her things late afternoon and spend the whole night over with Jack at the hospice. Then she'd go home. Tomorrow morning, she would go and never come back, not even for the funeral.

'I'm sorry, Jack,' she whispered softly, 'but no one wants me here and you hardly know whether I am or not.'

She put her cup down and got to her feet to carry the breakfast pots over to the sink.

'Then I'm going home, Jack,' she said softly. 'I'm going home.'

I was so proud of you today. Five years old already and so sweet in that pink dress and bows in your hair. I took so many pictures of you that your gran threatened to take the camera away.

But I don't care, my Birdie. She could lose a hundred cameras and every picture I've ever taken of you and I'd still remember.

She doesn't mean to be so hard, my Bird. Didn't mean to snap at you like that and spoil your special day. But she just believes in everything being proper. You know that, and those other children – well, Birdie, she doesn't see them as our sort.

I don't know, my Bird, she thinks I'm stupid sometimes. Thinks I indulge you too much and that isn't good for you. If she knew I wrote you these little letters, I don't suppose she'd understand, would she, darling. She'd have her reasons, too, I suppose. Maybe I do neglect her a little these days, but she makes it so hard. Always distant. Always so busy with things.

But you shouldn't fret, my Bird. There's you and there's your Granddad Jack, and there's nothing can come between.

Chapter Six

Marcie drove her grandmother to the hospice after lunch.

Both her grandmother and Aunt Alice had been very quiet that morning. Marcie had seen little of them. They had been closeted together in what had been her grandparents' room.

As Jack's illness had progressed they had moved him out, into Marcie's old room at the back of the house.

Passing by her grandparents' door, Marcie could hear the two women talking, something heavy being moved across the floor and, once, the sound of her grandmother crying quietly.

Feeling superfluous, Marcie had gone back to her room and slept in the chair.

They had eaten lunch together in almost total silence. Then left the clearing-away to Alice and gone out to the car.

'What's all that?' Marcie asked, noting a stack of bags beside the dustbin.

'The bin men come in the morning,' her grandmother replied. 'It seemed like a good time to clear the rubbish out.'

She seemed disinclined to say more. Marcie looked hard at the stack of 'rubbish'. 'Jack's things?' she asked quietly.

'He wanted to keep everything,' her grandmother

said. She sounded angry and more than a little hurt. 'I always told him, Jack, some of these things just have to go. You don't need them. But no. Insisted on keeping the whole damned lot.'

On keeping what? Marcie wanted to ask her, but the older woman had her lips pursed tight and a strained look about her eyes as though something pained her deeply.

'I'd like time with Jack on my own,' her grandmother said when they parked the car.

Marcie nodded. 'Sure, Gran. I'll take a walk.'

'A half an hour should do it. I can't think what I have to say will take longer.'

She marched off towards the reception, pushing through the swing doors and letting them close with a crash behind her.

Marcie watched her, puzzled. She saw her sign in at the desk, smooth her skirt and pat her hair back into place with the care of someone getting armed for battle.

She'd seen her grandmother in one of these moods before and always, this need to speak to someone alone. This careful mental preparation and physical ordering of herself presaged a row.

Marcie shook her head. What was the point of arguing with a dying man? Unless Gran caught him in one of his more lucid moods, it was unlikely Jack would even understand her.

Marcie turned away and walked across the car park. The sun felt warm on her back but the air had a dusty scent to it, like summer that has lasted just too long. She felt her restlessness growing, like the birds Jack talked about. She knew it was almost her time to fly.

When Marcie arrived on the ward it was plain that Jack and her grandmother had indeed been arguing. From the look of them the quarrel had been a violent one and was, despite the best efforts of staff to calm them both, still going on.

Her grandmother turned accusingly as Marcie walked in. Staring at the girl, she continued to talk to Jack, her words tight-lipped and over-precise, as though each one were designed for full effect. Then, as Marcie reached the bed, she rose to her feet.

'We're going now,' she said.

Marcie stared at her, ready to protest, but Jack reached out and clasped her hand.

'Best take her home,' he said. 'She's got herself in a state. There'll be no peace if you don't.'

'If you want me to,' she said, 'but, Jack—'

She broke off. Jack had slipped once more into his other world. He stared across the ward at some figure Marcie could not see. The grip on her hand tightened, fingers digging in like claws.

'Find her for me, Birdie,' Jack whispered. 'Find Rebekkah for me.'

The air was heavy with the scent of lilacs and the night warm for late April.

Jack stood at the end of his garden, as far from the

house as he could get without passing through the wooden gate and out into the street beyond.

His wife and sister stood close to the lighted window. Jack could see them behind the glass, the curtains still undrawn. They were pretending very hard not to watch him. Two shadow figures with the light behind them, casting furtive glances at the man outside.

Jack turned his back on them. The baby, cradled in his arms, had her eyes shut tight. Well fed and fast asleep, she cared nothing for any of the trio, set in their strange tableau.

She looked so peaceful, Jack thought. So tiny and so fragile in his arms.

'It's a beautiful night, my darling,' Jack told her softly. 'A beautiful night. Sky all full of stars and a great big moon shining down. And just smell those lilacs.' He breathed deep as though to encourage her. 'Blooming just for you.'

I love her already, Jack thought to himself. She's only been with me for this little time and yet I love her as though she'd been a part of me for ever.

He laughed suddenly as a thought struck him and the baby started slightly at the sudden sound. 'I didn't think he had it in him, that son of mine,' he said, his voice full of wonder. 'But here you are. Precious and beautiful and here to stay.'

He smiled down at the child. It wasn't often, he thought, that life gave anyone a second chance. A way to make amends, and yet here it was. This tiny bundle with the stupid name and some trace of his own blood flowing in her veins.

'Marciella,' he said, rolling the word around in his mouth as though getting used to the taste of it. 'Damned silly name, my love, but I suppose you're saddled with it now.' He sighed contentedly. Not that it mattered what they'd called her. She was his now. His little Bird. His to care for, to protect and to mould.

His to love and his to make things right again.

Chapter Seven

They drove back to the house in silence. Marcie tried to speak but her grandmother made no reply, just stared through the windscreen.

It wasn't until they reached the house that she spoke.

'We talked this morning,' she said, 'Alice and I. Then we told your father. We decided it would be best for all of us if you left this afternoon.'

'But why? I don't understand.'

The door opened. Alice stood on the step. Marcie could see her father behind, looking uncomfortable. They must have called him home from work, she thought.

She stood in the tiny hall between the three of them and listened while her father cleared his throat and tried 'to explain'.

'It's not that we don't want you here,' he told her. 'Just that it's harder than we all thought it would be to have you back. And it's upsetting Jack. Upsetting your gran, too.'

'How am I upsetting Jack?' Marcie demanded. 'And Gran? What have I done to bother you? I've tried to help out. Tried not to get in the way . . .'

'You don't know when to leave things alone,' her grandmother replied curtly. 'Jack was happy enough before you came back. Settled, he was. Not rambling on about all this nonsense he should have forgotten long ago. Not getting all upset and worrying his head about things that can't be changed. You never did know when to leave well alone,' she repeated.

She paused as though for breath, her shoulders squared indignantly. 'We've done our best for him all this time and not one word from you. And then you come back here, full of your ideas and your questions and your "I'm only sitting and listening to him" and make the lot of us look like we've never cared a damn. And he goes on about his Bird and how good she is to him . . .' She broke off, her lips trembling and her rigid spine beginning to bend under the payload of emotions. 'And it makes it sound like we've been nothing to him. Nothing!'

'It isn't like that,' Marcie told her hotly. 'You sent for me. You told me I'd better come, and, yes, I've sat and listened to Jack. Maybe you've been too busy to do that. Maybe you didn't want to hear what he had to say, I don't know. But he wanted to tell me things. Needed to tell someone and I just happened to be there.' She paused, not really wanting to argue like this. 'But, Gran, no one's suggesting you haven't done everything you could for him.'

'Oh, that's big of you,' her grandmother replied. 'It's nice to know you've noticed all the sacrifices we've been making for him. All the days we've been watching him get sicker and sicker and knowing he's going to die.'

Her voice failed her and she gulped air, trying to force back the tears.

Marcie tried to assimilate the mix of blame and pain in her grandmother's words. 'All right,' she said softly.

'I'll go. I'll go now, just as soon as I've packed my things. But you have to listen to him, Gran, Alice. There's something on his mind. Something that's bothering him and he can't sort it on his own. You have to listen to him.'

She looked from one to the other, but they stood in a tight-lipped, disapproving circle.

'I'll go and get my things,' Marcie said at last.

'We did it for you,' Alec told her. He reached behind him and lifted Marcie's bags from where they sat under the stairs.

Marcie stared open mouthed at this final insult. Then snatched the bags from his fingers.

The front door shut behind her as soon as she was through.

Marcie stood for a moment on the doorstep, confused and deeply hurt. Then she placed her luggage in the boot of her car.

'Damn them all,' she whispered. 'God damn them all.'

Her eye caught sight of the rubbish bags, loosely tied at the neck, sitting beside the bin. Curiosity and not a little anger took Marcie to them. She pulled at the neck of one, ripping the plastic and splitting down the side. Letters and photographs, books and old seed packets tumbled out and fell in a pathetic little heap at her feet.

Jack's things. Jack's memories. Fragments of Jack's life, thrown out as though they meant nothing, even before he was fully dead.

Marcie lifted some of the pictures. Most of them were of her. Marcie at five, blowing out candles on her cake. Marcie at eight in the school nativity play. Marcie as an awkward thirteen-year-old, all legs and skinny arms, standing uncertainly beside the front door.

'What are you doing? Just what are you doing!' Her grandmother's cry startled her to her feet.

'He isn't even dead yet!' Marcie spat at her. 'You've thrown all this away and he isn't even dead yet.'

Furious now, Marcie snatched the bags from where they lay beside the bin, piled them into her arms, spilling fragments of torn photographs and scraps of scribbled notes in her hurry.

She almost ran to the car, threw the armful into the boot and slammed the lid. Then turned again and scooped the remaining stuff, two boxes and another bag, into her arms.

Her grandmother was wrestling with the boot. Her father and Alice had come running from the house and joined the fray. Alec grabbed Marcie's arm as she thrust the remaining things into the back of the car and slammed the door. She pushed at him, hitting out at his face and kicking at his shins as he tried to stop her. She felt her foot make contact with bone. He yelled. Marcie followed through and kicked again; finding his shin once more, she ground down hard with the heel of her shoe, hitting him with her free hand.

'Haven't you taken enough of Jack already?' Gran shouted. 'It isn't yours. I'll have the police on you. I'll have you for assault.'

'Like fuck you will. Now let me go!'

She tore herself free of Alec, flailing and kicking like a spitting cat and almost knocking him to the floor, then scrambled into the car and locked the door. Behind her, she could hear her grandmother pounding on the boot, crying out in a voice that was flooded with tears. Alice was tugging at the driver's door.

'Marcie,' she was shouting. 'You're upset, we're all upset. Now open the door.'

Alec leapt forward as she started the car. For one crazy moment Marcie thought he would jump out in front of her. She revved the engine, dropped the clutch and spun the wheels, screeching away still in first with the engine protesting as she hit the red line.

Alec leapt aside.

Looking in the mirror, Marcie could see him staring helplessly as she drove away.

Watching him grow smaller and smaller in the mirror, Marcie began to laugh. Then, as she turned the corner, the laughter dissolved into a stream of angry tears.

Chapter Eight

Home was three hours away at normal speed.

But Marcie didn't drive at normal speed, at least not this time.

With the boxes and bags rattling about in the boot and tumbling from the seat in the back of the car, she made the distance in a little over two.

Middle-class suburbia gave way, first, to the sprawl of new industrial estates on the very outskirts of the city and then, when she skipped off the main roads, to a network of country lanes left almost unchanged by the centuries.

She slowed, just, for the villages, powered through the bends, foot flat against the floor. Regained the main roads just before the congestion of the rush-hour traffic would have forced her to slow her pace.

She remembered little of the journey. Grief and anger had combined to make her almost blind to the world beyond the confines of the car.

Turning into the side road that led to home and being forced suddenly to grab at the clutch in order to make the bend brought the madness of her journey back to her. A glance at her watch and a quick addition of the time was enough to have her shaking in her seat as she pulled up before the front door.

She sat, motionless, hands gripping the steering

wheel, feet welded to the pedals, for several minutes, before finally coming to enough to pull the handbrake on and switch off the engine.

Only then did Marcie begin to relax. She felt weak, almost light-headed, as she wriggled out of the car and crossed the short stretch of pathway to the front door, fumbling blindly for her keys.

Another hour, two at most, and Michael would be home with the twins.

Shaking now with fatigue and, she realized, good old-fashioned hunger, Marcie let herself in through the main door, made her way down the hall to their own front door at the end of the passage and went inside the muddled, comfortable little flat. She closed the door behind her and sat down on the floor, just inside, breathing in deeply the scent of baby powder and lemon polish, and the warm, indefinable smells that meant comfort. That meant safety. That meant home.

Michael arrived just before the rain began.

Marcie heard him crashing through the house door with the double buggy.

He must have seen the car because he shouted out to her, yelling at the twins, 'Mummy's home! Yeah! Let's go find her.'

Marcie flung open the door and threw herself at the three of them. The twins shrieked and wriggled against the pushchair straps. Michael grabbed at her and pulled her close to him, his arms full of shopping bags and disposable nappies.

'When did you get here?'

'About an hour ago.'

'Why didn't you phone? I didn't think you'd be here until at least tomorrow.'

He hugged her even closer, dropping the bags to the floor in an effort to get a tighter hold.

'I had problems,' she told him, her voice muffled against his chest. 'They didn't want me and I just couldn't take any more. I wanted to get home to all of you.'

The twins' yelling distracted them both. Marcie knelt down, undid their reins and picked them both up in one wriggling bundle of arms and legs and wet kisses.

'I did the washing-up,' she shouted back over her shoulder.

'No time this morning. I was at the centre for the early call.'

'We need shopping.'

'Go to the late-nighter now we've got the car back.' He folded the buggy, dumped it in a corner and shut the door with a crash, reaching out for Marcie and the twins again. 'God, but it's good to have you home. So tell me everything. How was it? Was it as bad as you thought it would be? What's that junk in the back of the car?'

Marcie laughed and deposited the twins on the floor, trying to keep hold of one of them long enough to remove his coat. Michael tackled the other.

'Lord, I'd almost forgotten. I should have brought it in, but I was in such a hurry just to get inside and close the door . . . It's stuff Aunt Alice and Gran threw away. I found it by the bin so I brought it with me.'

'Threw away? The bin?' He reached a hand to touch

her forehead, drew his finger back in mock surprise. 'God almighty, girl, we done get so poor we have to pick the rich folk's bins?'

She chased his hand aside. 'Don't be so daft,' she told him. 'It's all Jack's stuff. Pictures, letters. I don't know. I didn't really get a proper look. But I couldn't leave it there. Not just thrown out like that as though he didn't matter to anyone.'

She sighed and, as though suddenly deflated, flopped on to the sofa, watching the twins distractedly as they found their toys.

'I don't know what's in it, Michael. Three bags and a couple of boxes of stuff.'

She looked at him, suddenly shy. 'Thought you'd help me sort it out,' she said, hopefully. 'Find out just what it was they didn't want me to have.'

Chapter Nine

My Mary.

I could live for ever in that afternoon.

You didn't know your gran then. I know you don't always understand her, Marcie. And I guess she doesn't understand you. Not the way I do.

Oh, but you should have seen her then. That Sunday afternoon.

We'd gone walking. Down Swinhope Hill and along the bottoms out towards the mill.

She was eighteen, your gran. Eighteen, with this mane of long red hair and freckles scattered across her nose.

All dressed in white, with blue piping on the cuffs and collar and a big straw hat, perched on the top of her head, and a long blue ribbon trailing down her back.

Beautiful, she was, Birdie. Just beautiful.

I could live for ever in that afternoon.

It was several days before Marcie persuaded herself to sort through Jack's belongings. She was caught between a need to know what it was she had so impulsively brought with her and a half-fear of the memories stored away inside.

It was the call from Aunt Alice that finally prompted her. An angry, recriminatory phone call, made worse by Alice's inability to reach Marcie in the days before.

Marcie stood in the communal hall, listening to Alice's vitriol and trying to keep her answers calm. Twice, tenants from the upper floors passed by. Twice, Marcie was uncomfortably aware that Alice's voice could be plainly heard.

'You turn up,' Alice almost shouted, 'disrupt our lives, criticize the way we cared for Jack and then you steal from us! And when I try to be fair to you, try to talk to you and clear the air, you avoid my calls! Didn't you get my messages?'

Marcie doubted that there had been any messages. She knew of old that if she herself didn't get to the hall phone first, then Alice would simply ring off, try again later and complain about it.

'I've had no messages, Auntie, and I've hardly been here to receive them anyway. We both have to work, remember. And as to "clearing the air", my God, I think I've heard enough.'

Marcie didn't really listen to the rest of her aunt's complaints. She held the receiver loosely in her hand, gazing around distractedly at the dusty hall.

They had lived here, in this house, since that first night she had spent with Michael.

He'd had the attic room then or, rather, one of them. A cramped little bedsit with a two-ring stove, stuck high in the eaves of the Victorian house. The sloping roof oozed damp and there'd been a cracked pane in the window that must have been ages old. The line of the crack was filled with impacted grime.

A year on, they had moved down to a larger room on the first floor and then to ground level a few months before the twins had arrived.

At the end of the line, Alice's anger raged on. Gently, Marcie replaced the receiver on the rack and walked away.

Michael looked up as she re-entered the room. He was putting the twins to bed in what was laughingly called their bedroom. Marcie suspected it must have been a walk-in store cupboard, a butler's pantry or some such.

Now it had been converted into space enough for two drop-sided cots, an assortment of toys in plastic crates and the children's clothes, packed carefully in card-board boxes and old suitcases and slid beneath the cots.

A large blue curtain partitioned this 'room' from the rest of the living space. Their own bedroom, small but larger than the twins', led off the main living room and faced the front of the house. A cramped kitchen, hidden also by a faded curtain, was to the rear and the equally tiny bathroom without a bath – there was room, just, for a pink-tiled shower – was through another door to the side. Out at the back, there was a little yard.

'Aunt Alice,' Marcie said. 'Blazing.'

Michael grinned at her. 'That's what happens to witches,' he said.

'Hah! That's an insult to witches. No self-respecting coven'd want Aunt Alice.'

'Oh, I don't know,' he said. 'Useful for the odd exorcism, don't you think? I mean, who needs bell, book and candle when they've got an Aunt Alice?'

Marcie laughed nervously. 'What time are you due in tomorrow?'

'Not till two, so I'll be late back. You'll need to collect the twins.'

Marcie nodded. The temping agency had phoned earlier, to say they had some work for her, but tomorrow she was free. The twins usually went with Michael to the crèche at the law centre where he worked. Somewhere along the line the dreams of big-shot lawyerdom had fallen by the wayside as the need just to earn their keep had taken their place.

Michael put his training to good use, though, working at the centre five days a week. First as volunteer giving the odd hour and now as a paid worker.

Council-run, it was always under threat of closure and sometimes the insecurity of it worried Marcie.

But it, and they, somehow struggled through.

He crossed the room towards her, leaving the twins to grumble and chatter their way into sleep. He took her hands and drew her down beside him on to the sofa.

'She still talking about calling the police?' he asked.

'Nah, knew she wouldn't, though. It's all just talk. She's still yelling about me stealing Jack's things, but,' Marcie shrugged awkwardly, 'I mean, it's not right, is it? Chucking his things away like that.'

'And now, having rescued it all, it's going to stay there, stuffed in that cupboard, is it?'

Marcie laughed. 'No, I guess not. I just don't seem to have had the time since I got back.'

'Or the inclination?'

'That either.'

She paused, listening to the twins making sleepy noises. 'It's funny, you know. Going back and seeing him like that I thought I'd feel something . . . I don't know, something more. That there'd still be all the anger. But it wasn't like that. I just felt sorry for him. Sorry for them all, really.' She reached out and grasped his hand. 'They've spent a lifetime fighting, Michael. Fighting each other till their minds are raw, and you know? I still have no idea what it's all about. What they did to each other, or someone else did. Or what *I* did.'

She shook her head, the dark curls falling forward to half cover her face.

'And you're scared of finding out,' he said. 'Or is it that you're scared of me finding out?' He pounced on her suddenly, grabbing her just under the ribs, tickling her so that she fell back, giggling.

'Is that what you're worried about, Marciella Rose Whitney? Scared dis big black mon will find his momma's secrets?'

She fought him off, beating at his chest with her fists. 'Hush, you idiot, you'll wake the monsters.' She sat up, playfully straightening her hair and clothes. 'Anyway,' she said, 'you had all my secrets years ago. Nothing left to find out.'

'All of them? Oh, I'm disappointed now. I thought at least the odd one might have got away.'

Michael was a large man, grown heavier in the years since she had been with him. He worked out when time allowed, grew muscles almost by thinking about them and with the shoulder-length dreads he'd begun to grow three years ago, and the three rings in his left ear, he looked like the kind of man Aunt Alice would have warned her about.

He wasn't black, not exactly, a white mother had taken care of that, but his skin was richly dark and his eyes brown as melted chocolate.

Michael wasn't exactly the type that blended into the background.

'I suppose I should just take a quick look,' she said. 'Sort out what's in there.'

She looked and sounded so reluctant that Michael put his arm around her. 'Make some coffee,' he said. 'I'll drag the stuff out of the cupboard. You never know, we might find all you've got is kitchen scraps and dirty washing.'

Chapter Ten

' "I'm sorry about the kittens, Marcie, but really, it's the kindest thing . . ." '

'Kittens?' Michael frowned.

Marcie sat on the old sofa, the edge of the quilt pulled over her feet and her arms wrapped around her knees.

'I must have been about, oh, I don't know, eight,' she said. 'We had this big old cat. An old tabby Aunt Alice had adopted when her owners moved. Anyway, the cat had kittens. Five of them. Two black and white. One ginger and two this funny kind of tabby brown like their mother. And then, one morning, the mother cat got hit by a car . . .'

Marcie sat at the top of the stairs listening to the adults talking in the room below.

She didn't have to listen very hard. Gran was mad. Aunt Alice was calm but obviously annoyed, and this time even Jack didn't seem to be on her side.

At eight years old, Marcie knew already that there were rules for adults and other, often incomprehensible, ones for children.

'I can't abide cruelty to animals,' Aunt Alice had declared on more than one occasion. Marcie could clearly recall times when the wrath of Aunt Alice had fallen squarely on the heads of the local children if they teased a cat or ill-treated a dog. 'I can't abide cruelty to animals.'

If that were so, Marcie wondered, her mind confused and her eyes red with crying, if that were so, then why had she been so angry with Marcie over the kittens?

It had happened that afternoon.

Marcie ran through the events in her mind, trying to make more sense of them.

She had come home from school and gone into the garden to look for Jack. And then she'd seen him.

Seen him standing beside the water butt, his hands full of mewling, wriggling scraps of fur. As Marcie watched in horror, Jack plunged them, double-handed, into the water.

'Jack! They'll drown, Granddad Jack!'

Startled, Jack had turned, one hand lifting from the water as he swung around and looked at her. The kittens in his hand, dripping, mewling pitifully, struggling for breath.

'Jack!' Marcie screamed at him this time and ran towards him, arms outstretched, hands reaching to take the kittens from his grasp.

Jack swore and she halted. Watched in horror as he cast the little animals back into the water, cursing audibly now as he swung back towards her, reaching out his hand to grasp her arm.

Marcie snatched the arm away. She spun from him and ran towards the house, crying hysterically for her gran, for Aunt Alice, for anyone to come and stop him.

And then there'd been the lectures.

Three adults, their quiet world disrupted by an unruly child, telling her that it was kindest in the end. That the mother cat was dead and the kittens too small to fend for themselves. Too small even to lap milk.

'I'd have fed them,' Marcie whispered fiercely to herself. 'I would have done it. All of them.'

You couldn't do it, Aunt Alice had insisted. Not five kittens. Five hungry mouths to feed.

But she would have, Marcie told herself. She'd have fed them all with an eye-dropper, just like she had when they'd found the hedgehog with the broken leg in the vegetable garden.

Sitting on the stairs, snuffling miserably, Marcie heard her aunt moving towards the living room door.

She half rose, clinging to the stair rail, ready for flight.

'You should never have brought her here,' Gran was saying to her father. 'You should have left the child with her mother's people. Saved us all a lot of bother.'

'She had no people. Her parents were dead and I never did know where her brother had gone. There was no one.'

'And if there had been,' Jack was saying, 'who's to say what they would have been like? Her mother was unstable enough.'

'Just like the child.'

'Don't say that!' Jack's voice was sharp and angry. 'Not my Bird. She's sensitive, that's all, But she'll learn. It was just the shock made her act that way. You know how fond she was of that damned cat.'

Alice snorted irritably. 'She won't change and she

won't learn, Jack. Lives in a dream world and half the time I think you're there with her.'

Her voice grew louder and Marcie heard her cross the little bit of lino close to the door. She began to move then, slipping off up the stairs and back to her bedroom, trying to control the tears and the running nose and the tightness in her chest, and hoping, in spite of everything, that Jack would come up later. Come and talk to her. Make everything all right.

'I had a dream that night. A nightmare, really, and sometimes, even now, it comes back, even after all these years.' She paused and glanced across at Michael as though to make certain he was still listening.

'I dreamed I was in the garden, watching Jack. He was standing beside the water butt, with his hands in the water, and he was smiling.

'I moved closer to him, expecting to see the kittens. I can remember knowing that this was a dream and thinking that, maybe, in my dream, I could make things different.

'As I got nearer to him I could see that something struggled beneath his hands. He was holding something down in the water, keeping the pressure on tight so that even when the thing fought hard it didn't have a hope of getting free.'

' "There's nothing to be gained by keeping unwanted things alive, Birdie. Nothing at all."

'And then it was me,' she whispered, her eyes fixed and staring. 'It was me in the water. Me struggling to get free. Not able to breathe. I couldn't even cry out. The water flooded into my mouth when I tried and the bubbles frothed all around my eyes and in my hair and I couldn't get away.'

She shook herself as though to shed the dream, but her face was very pale.

'And still you couldn't hate him,' Michael said. He didn't question it, he understood too well that you cannot hate those who also love you. Not completely. Not for ever.

'Oh no,' Marcie whispered. 'I didn't hate him then. Oh no, that came much much later.'

I should have come up to you tonight, after you had gone to bed, and explained.

I'm sorry, Marcie. I feel I've failed you and, God knows, I'd never willingly do that.

Your gran says I should be tougher with you. That it's time you grew up and realized that the world is not always a gentle place. It seems to me you know that, my Birdie, and that it's me and not your gran that taught you.

I'm sorry about the kittens, Marcie, truly I am, but it's the kindest thing . . .

Chapter Eleven

Michael couldn't sleep.

They had gone to bed late and made love quietly and tenderly, glad to be back together. Marcie had fallen asleep curled up close to him, but Michael had lain awake long afterwards, unable to quiet his thoughts.

Finally, he had slipped out of bed, pulled on jogging bottoms and an old shirt and wandered back into the living room.

The twins were sound asleep. Michael drew back the curtain that divided their closet from the main room and stood looking at them. They were so different, Liam and Hanna, even when sleeping.

Liam lay on his side, his favourite soft toy clutched tightly by the ears. The covers neat and tidy, sheets still folded back. By contrast, Hanna was sprawled upon her back, arms and legs thrown outwards as though she had fallen from a great height. Covers thrust aside and escaping through the bars of her cot.

Smiling, Michael pulled them back over her plump little body, then moved swiftly away, knowing that, if she woke, that would be the last any of them saw of sleep that night.

He sat on the sofa, switched on the table lamp and picked up a handful of the letters and photographs he and Marcie had been looking through.

Much of Marcie's childhood seemed to have been contained in those anonymous black bags and battered cardboard boxes. Marcie's birthdays, Marcie's Christmases. Holidays and trips, fairgrounds and fireworks. Jack seemed to have catalogued practically all of it in snapshots – which spoke more of love than technique – and scribbled notes. And letters, some of them no more than a couple of lines, some spreading in awkward prose over six or seven pages. Letters, undelivered, but folded neatly into envelopes, sealed and dated, left that way until Marcie's grandmother and Alice had torn them open and read the thoughts inside.

There was no doubt that Jack had loved Marciella. Loved her with a fervour that bordered on the obsessive. Reading through Jack's 'letters', only half understanding the references made in them, looking at the fastidious detail with which Jack had noted down every important moment in Marcie's life, Michael could not help but feel some faint sympathy for Mary, Jack's wife, in her desire to rid herself of such memories.

Mary and Alice and even Alec, his son, were notable only for their absence in Jack's records. Of course, Michael thought, there must be other photographs, pictures of Jack's wife and sister and son, but they were not here. Maybe, Michael thought, Mary had chosen to keep those. But there seemed to be no group photographs either. No sense of family gathering or family unity. Jack had focused on Marcie, on his Bird, it seemed, to the exclusion of those with at least equal claim upon his love and attention.

Such absolute and total love – if it could be called

that – must have been suffocating to endure. Must have been painful and hurtful to witness and to be excluded from.

Michael wondered if Jack had once loved Alec in that way. If Alec's life, recorded piece by piece, lay treasured in a dusty box.

Somehow, he didn't think so.

There *were* images that were not of Marcie, many in faded black and white. Or even older, sepia toned and ragged edged. Michael gazed at these with keen interest.

'That one's of Jack just before he married,' Marcie had told him. 'And that's of all three of them. God! don't they look young?'

They *had* been young, Michael thought. Early twenties, maybe. Alice not even that. They were in the company of about a dozen others, all crowded close so they fitted into the frame, some perched high on a haywain, some standing in front or clinging to the sides.

All were in work clothes, the women in print dresses with dropped waists, the men in collarless shirts, sleeves rolled above their elbows. Harvest, Michael supposed. There had been horses hitched to the wain, but only their tails showed, the rest cropped from the scene. Michael found it hard to imagine that this was well within living memory. The time when horses still ploughed the fields and brought the harvest in. It was so remote from anything he knew.

He sighed and put the picture down, palmed his eyes to wipe the ache from them. He was tired now, ready to sleep. He was rising to his feet when a strange sound coming from the bedroom first froze him to the spot, then sent him diving across the room.

Marcie was choking, her breath wheezing through her teeth, her hands clutching at her throat as though to pull something free, her back arching up off the bed as she writhed from side to side, gasping and struggling.

'Marcie!' Michael shouted, forgetful for once of the sleeping twins. What the hell! Was it a fit? He grabbed at her wrists, easing them from her throat. The fingers were hooked as though around a tight and choking binding.

'Marcie!'

Hanna woke and began to cry. The crying of one twin woke the other. Michael pulled harder at Marcie's hands, at her arms bent rigidly against her body and her clawed fingers hooked against her throat.

The twins began to wail.

'Wake up, Marcie! God's sake, wake up!'

He was truly scared now. Her back arched like a full-drawn bow, suddenly her legs kicked out and she seemed to convulse, the breath rasping in her throat, her body jerking against the bed.

Then she opened her eyes. He shook her, pulling the hooked fingers and calling her name. She gulped air as if she'd almost drowned and stared up at him, her eyes wide and terrified.

'It's all right,' Michael was saying. 'Marcie, it's all right.' He stared back at her, his own eyes reflecting her fear and confusion. Behind them the twins were standing in their cots, Liam crying still and Hanna yelling for her dadda.

Michael didn't know who to comfort first, Marcie or the babies. He clasped his wife's hand for a moment, then went swiftly to the twins and lifted them both into his arms, carried them back to the bed.

'Are you all right?' he asked her. 'God, Marcie, I was so scared.'

She didn't reply, just sat up and reached out for Hanna, shaking her head, utterly confused.

'Dreaming,' she managed. 'I guess it was a nightmare . . . all that talk . . . Michael, what is it?'

He had frozen, half bending in the act of lowering Hanna on to the bed. As the child crawled free of his arm and landed herself in her mother's lap, he reached out slowly, a look of horror on his face, to touch the deep-bitten rope mark on Marcie's neck.

Chapter Twelve

The marks were still there the following morning, livid and angry, the twisting pattern of the rope clearly visible on her skin.

The rest of the night had brought little sleep. They had huddled together, all four of them, the twins taking up most of the bed.

'You can't go to work like that,' Michael said, watching Marcie apply concealer to the dark patches under her eyes. 'You've got to go and see the doctor.'

Marcie shook her head at him in the mirror. 'And tell him what?' she questioned. 'That I had a dream that strangled me with a rope and left the marks to prove it? He'll lock me up in a loony bin or have you arrested.'

Michael sighed. Marcie hated doctors anyway. And there was more than a little truth in what she was saying. He caught sight of himself behind her in the mirror. The image of a black Rasta trouble-maker reflected beside that of a small, scared-looking white girl. Even with his considerable skills and experience in dealing with the law, he felt he'd have one hell of a job proving that he'd had nothing to do with the marks on Marcie's neck, no matter what she said in his defence.

'Does it hurt?'

'Not as much as it looks like it ought to,' she said. 'It's a bit stiff and a bit sore, but that's about it.'

She dug around in the drawer for the tube of foundation cream she occasionally used and tried to apply it to the marks on her neck. 'Ow! That stings.'

'Best not to, love. You don't know how it'll react.'

She sighed and rummaged in her drawer once again, this time producing a blue silk scarf. She tied it, wrapped twice, around her neck. It covered most of the marks and didn't look too odd with her light summer suit.

'OK?' she asked him.

'Looks like you're hiding something,' he said, 'but yeah, I guess OK.' He paused for a moment, his eyes meeting hers in the mirror. She looked away first.

'We ought to be getting the monsters ready,' she said, moving towards the twins, who were still fast asleep on their parents' bed.

'Don't go today,' he said to her, reaching for her hands. 'We've got enough in reserve for you to miss a couple of days.'

'I have to, you know that. The trip to Jack's hasn't been cheap, and if I turn down work now at the last minute it's not going to look very good, is it?'

'OK,' he conceded, 'but take it easy. You feel sick or anything you come straight home.'

She smiled at him, squeezed his fingers lightly and then went to see to the twins.

Michael wandered out into the kitchen to start making breakfast. He was glad that he'd be driving her to work today. Dropping her off and taking the twins with him. She'd come to him at the law centre to get a lift home. He was frightened by what he had witnessed the night before, and it wasn't just the weird marks on her neck. At home, one of his foster sisters, Kate, had been epileptic. He'd seen her, several times, convulsed like that. Shaking and trembling and totally out of it. What if the stress of Jack's illness had triggered something like that in Marcie? It wasn't that the illness scared him. Kate had been just fine most of the time once they'd got her pills sorted out, but he knew how dangerous something like that could be if it went undiagnosed.

What if she had a fit while she was driving the car or crossing the road, or . . . ?

Marcie, entering the kitchen with the twins, put an end to his reverie. He managed to smile at her and lifted Hanna into her highchair.

Tonight he'd have another try at getting her to the doctor.

You haven't been here, my Birdie, not for days now. I keep asking for you, but your gran says you had to go away, tells me not to fret. Sometimes she says that I saw you yesterday, that I just forgot, but I know that's not true, my Bird. I've asked them, the doctors, the nurses, and they tell me the truth even when your gran tries to fool me.

You've got a husband, your gran says, and babies. Had to go back to them, I suppose. I can't see it, though, not you with babies or chained to some man. Your gran says you've married some big black fellow with too much hair, but I know she's just saying that. Knows how silly it sounds, but she says it anyway . . . and the winter's coming in so fast, you'd have no time to go off and get hitched up with anyone, my Birdie. Not with all the things you have to do, get the garden ready for the winter.

I wish I could help you. Wish I could be there just to watch, make sure you get things right.

We none of us always *get things right . . . and I have such dreams, my darling. Such nightmares.*

She comes back to me every time I close my eyes, and sometimes when I open them she's still standing there, mocking me with that rope tied round her neck and her hands fastened behind her back and her eyes never looking at the same place two seconds together. And sometimes, Birdie, sometimes, like in my dreams last night, she thinks to cheat me, thinks I won't do it to her if she changes the way she looks. But I know different, my sweetheart. I'd know her anywhere. Hang her just as high and watch her feet kicking at the stars. I'd know her, Birdie, even when she wears your face.

Chapter Thirteen

Friday was Sophie Lee's party.

They had stumbled through the last two days keeping themselves overly busy with work and children and the usual activities. They'd been afraid to sleep and watched old films on TV till late, finally falling asleep on the sofa. Nothing had happened. The marks on Marcie's neck were still there but were fading fast, and it was almost possible to accept the rather frantic explanations they had come up with.

'I must have scratched myself,' Marcie had said. 'Or maybe even got tangled in the sheets.'

'Psychosomatic,' Michael had stated emphatically.

That made her laugh. 'So I imagined it and made it happen?'

'Well, no, not exactly. But you remember that programme we watched, you know, on stigmata and that sort of thing? There was that case where that man suddenly got rope marks round his wrists. They said that his body must be remembering some previous trauma. Then found out he'd had something happen to him when he was a kid.'

'No one ever put a rope round my neck.'

'No, but with Jack so obsessed with that woman . . .'

They ran the problem ragged, then tried to forget about it. Michael was most relieved to find her so normal afterwards. No sign of the frightening seizure he had witnessed. She had slept fitfully for the last two nights, but without incident.

Maybe that was an end to it. Strange things happen to a stressed body, even stranger things to a stressed mind.

With a sense of rather cowardly relief, Michael let the matter slip, knowing Marcie wanted to do the same.

By Friday night they were both more ready for their beds than for a party. Michael had swapped an evening session for his usual Saturday morning slot, so at least he knew he could sleep late. And they were staying over at his foster mother's house, the one place in the world Michael knew that phantasms and fears would have no place. They'd be out on their ear in a blink.

Anyway, this was Sophie Lee's party. Michael would as willingly have missed this as he would chop off his hand.

Sophie Lee was Adele's mother. Adele was Michael's foster mother. Sophie Lee had been grandmother to all of Adele's children, those she'd fostered for a few weeks or those, like Michael and his brother Leroy, who'd been with her for years.

And today Sophie Lee was eighty. Maybe it was knowing about Jack's illness that brought it home to him, but Michael was acutely aware that there might not be too many birthdays left.

Adele's house was a large three-storey Victorian villa about a mile from where they lived. They were late arriving. Parking wasn't easy in Adele's road and they had walked from their flat after Michael had got home from work. The party was already lively. Music leaked out into the street and a warm blast of noise, perfume and the aroma of food enveloped them when Adele opened the front door. The twins had disappeared within minutes. Marcie glimpsed them in the front living room with some of the older kids dancing to Grand Master Flash, the heavy base beat clear enough even for the little ones to get the sense of. Sophie Lee was in the back room, shielded behind a heavy door that let only the base beat get through. Mantovani shimmered through the quieter air, helped along by the muffled rap. Mantovani with a base attitude, Marcie thought. She bent to hug Sophie and was pulled down beside the old woman, engulfed in arms that were as powerful as they were stick-thin, and a mix of three or four different perfumes. Presents, no doubt, Marcie thought. Sophie Lee would have had to try them all.

'Marciella, my love, and how are you?' Sophie Lee was asking her. 'And that grandfather of yours. How is he? He still living?'

Marcie glanced across at Michael and settled herself comfortably on the narrow sofa next to the old lady, preparing for a good long gossip. Michael smiled back, noting that the tension was gone from her for the first time in weeks. Since she'd first heard that Jack was ill.

'Leroy was lookin' for you,' someone shouted over. 'Think he's with Adele.'

Michael nodded thanks, bent to kiss and hug his grandmother, then went off to find his brother and Adele.

*

'The first time I came to this place,' Michael was saying, 'I was all of eight years old and felt like the weight of the whole world was landed on my shoulders.

'I can remember the smell of the place even now. Adele was cooking dinner and the air was full of rich, spicy scents drifting out on the heat from the kitchen. Leroy was holding on to my hand so tight our fingers had got slick and sweaty and the palms of our hands all sticky with what I hoped was just chocolate. Leroy was just five. Always poking his fingers into something and you never could tell.

'I remember looking up at this great big house with its top windows sticking out from the roof and wondering what it would be like and if, this time, we'd be staying.

'If we'd want to stay.

'This was the third place we'd been dumped in as many weeks. That might not sound fair, but it was the way we felt, Leroy and me. Like there was no one in the world gave a shit about us. And I'd made him this promise. Eight years old and I'd made the biggest promise I could ever think of making. We'll always stick together, I'd told him. Ain't no one goin' to take my bro away from me.

'I'd heard so many things about kids being split up and sent to different places and I was so worried that would happen to us. Just so scared.

'I knew Leroy's dad wasn't my dad. I knew as well that my mom'd spent the best part of the last two years trying to keep us one step away from him. I was just terrified they'd let Leroy go, to his real dad, and that would be it for the both of us.

'Then we came here, to Adele's place. She'd got other kids here and there wasn't that much space left so she asked us if we'd mind bunking in the top room, right up in the roof.

'Mind! That room was magic. She showed it to us, right up at the top of these narrow stairs. Easy to defend from anyone we didn't want, and off on the first landing down there was a door to the fire escape that led down the side of the building and out the back way. I knew then that if things did go wrong for Leroy and me, we could just flit out that way and through the yard. I could keep my promise.

'But it didn't do to look too eager. You know, look too eager and they know they've got you. So I looked round the little room, all casual, like, playing it real cool and I said, "Well, I guess it'll do," when really, deep inside, I was singing. This funny little room with its wooden floor and bright red rugs looked like the deck of a ship and with its twin beds pushed into the sloping corner under the eaves I knew me and Leroy could pretend like we were bears in a cave or pirates in a prison cell or anything else that we might want.

'But I still played it real cold and dumped our stuff on the floor next to the beds, looked all around me like I was inspecting the place, you know, swaggering about like I'd got a real big dose of attitude. The big man.

'Then Leroy here went and spoilt it all, tugging at my sleeve. "I wanna wee, Mikie. I need to do it now!"

'And there I was, Mr Cool, grabbing him by the hand

and yelling at Adele to tell me quick where the toilet was and as we went charging down the stairs trying to get you there before you peed yourself. And I could hear Adele and that social worker woman we'd come with – what was her name?'

'Mrs Simpson – call me Naomi,' Leroy supplied, mimicking the woman's clipped accent.

'Oh yeah, Naomi Simpson . . . I could hear the pair of them laughing at me and my face was getting real hot and . . .'

'You were mad as hell. Mr Cool! It was weeks before you eased up on Adele for laughing at you.'

Marcie giggled happily, her mood softened by a little too much wine and the atmosphere of Adele's house. She'd heard the story before, many times, slightly different versions from Adele and from Sophie Lee, but she was more than content to listen to it again.

She and Michael and his brother had planted themselves halfway up the first flight of stairs. The kids were still dancing in the front living room, Sophie Lee with them now, Hanna in her arms managing to be half asleep despite the Gangsta rap pounding through the floor.

The door to the second living room was open and Mantovani played on, his shimmering strings competing valiantly against the back-beat and the stomped-out lyrics.

Liam was dozing on Marcie's lap, his head lolling against her arm. She could barely hear it above the noise, but he was snoring contentedly.

She got up, a little unsteadily. 'Best put this one to

bed,' she said, turning to go up the stairs. 'See if you can prise Hanna away from Sophie, will you?'

'OK,' Michael said. He bent to kiss his son, then went off to face the music in the front room.

Hanna had taken longer to settle, objecting to the notion that she might be tired. 'Sophie party,' was still obstinately being declared even as her eyes were closing and her chubby limbs relaxing into sleep.

Marcie sat with the twins until she was certain they wouldn't wake. Then stayed a little longer to chat to Kate, Michael's foster sister, as she came in to lay her own small child in the other bed. A couple of the older ones, children of the generation just ahead of Michael, would be camping out on airbeds on the floor.

Judging by her previous visits here, Marcie doubted either she or Michael would get much sleep themselves. Sitting and talking well past the early hours was just something that happened when the clan gathered at Adele's house.

Later, she made her way back downstairs. The loud music in the front room had been muted now and altered in mood, the sounds drifting out through the half-closed door moody and romantic.

In the back room people were gathered in loose groups, chatting and laughing and teasing. Michael and Leroy sat next to Sophie Lee. A couple of others with whom they had shared bits of childhood had flopped on the floor close by.

Patrick Eaton, who was minister at the local Baptist

church, and a couple of neighbours Marcie knew by sight sat talking near the door.

Adele was seated at the now-cleared dining table, shuffling a pack of cards between her hands.

Marcie had once asked Adele just how many children she had fostered. Adele remembered them all in detailed order, even the ones who'd only been with her a week or so. She kept in touch with most, some only at a distance. Some, like Michael and his brother, had never quite moved out, even if they had moved away. And there'd been those who hadn't quite made it through, who'd slipped through the gaps even in Adele's tightly meshed net. One ended in prison. One turned up cold and swollen in the river. Others who'd just never pulled their lives together after a rocky start, even with Adele and Sophie Lee to help them.

She smiled at Marcie and beckoned her over to the table, spreading the cards in a perfect arc on the cloth.

'I am not seeing this, Adele,' Patrick Eaton said to her, his eyes laughing as he sipped at his drink.

'Don't you fret there, Patrick, you can save my soul again on Sunday.' She smiled at Marcie. 'Come and sit down, child. It's a long time since I read for you.'

'And the last time you did I had twins.' Marcie laughed.

She sat down at the table, not sure that she wanted this, but excited all the same. Adele's cards with their strange pictures held a fascination. Gran and Aunt Alice took a very dim view of anything that smacked of fortune-telling or the occult. They visited their church every Sunday, paid their debts to the unknown that way.

Anything else was, at best, frivolous and leading to idleness; at worst, probably even wicked.

Michael had once told Marcie that Sophie's mother had been an obeah priestess. Sophie Lee herself was a fervent Baptist, rejoicing with a completeness and pleasure that had, at first, shocked Marcie. And Adele, well, Adele managed to pick and choose and take the bits she liked.

With an expert movement, Adele swept the cards back into a neat pile and handed them to Marcie.

'I should be stopping you doing this,' Patrick said as Marcie, less expertly, shuffled the thick pack of cards.

'Ah, Patrick, this is nothing. I could be sitting here studying the entrails of a chicken, like my grandma used to. Then where would you be?'

'Hoping you'd roasted the rest of it,' Sophie Lee put in swiftly.

'Too true. Too true.'

Marcie spread the cards face down in a rather untidy arc across the table.

She'd wanted to go to a fortune-teller once. They'd been to the seaside and walked back through the funfair so that Marcie could ride the carousel. 'Descendant of Gypsy Rose Lee,' the sign had said, all painted up with roses and birth signs and with pictures of satisfied – *famous* satisfied – customers stuck in the window. A woman in 'Hollywood Gypsy' dress stood in the doorway.

'Please, Gran! Please!' Marcie had begged.

Gran had been outraged.

'You're really not old enough, Marcie,' Alice had said, trying to placate.

'Ha!' Gran had spat. 'Old or not, she's having nothing to do with bloody gypsies.'

Marcie had been fascinated to hear her grandmother swear.

'There were gypsies where we used to live,' Jack had said gently, a sadness in his voice.

'Gypsies!' Gran had repeated with an angry shake of her head. She had walked ahead then, scowling, and the carousel had been left behind, unridden and forgotten.

'Pick a card,' Adele was telling her. 'A card for where in your life you are now.'

Hesitantly, Marcie reached out and chose one, lay it face up in the centre of the table.

A horned figure with goat eyes looked back at her.

'Obsession,' Adele said slowly. 'The devil is a card of slavery, to an idea, a person, something you should have long ago outgrown.'

Marcie looked nervously at her, the rosy effects of the wine fading fast.

'Now cross the card and see the cause,' Adele said quietly.

'King of cups.'

'A man who draws you in with loving and fondness.' Adele shook her head. 'Alone, this would be a good card. Not the strongest of men, easily led and easily influenced, but loving and kind. Together with the devil card this is dangerous, my love.'

Marcie drew four more cards, placing them top and bottom, left and right, to form a cross.

'In your past was strength that went unquestioned,' Adele told her. 'See the emperor. Then came the tower and your world was rocked on its foundations, torn to the ground by an act of God.'

'That's close to blasphemy, Adele.'

'Is lightning not talked about as an act of God, Patrick? And here,' she held up the card. 'Lightning strikes the tower and brings it down. And now,' she continued, 'there are choices to be made. The lovers. The old ways and the new, and you must do the choosing. And the choice must be made swiftly and wisely. The sword and balance of justice is coming to or for you soon.'

'I don't think I like this, Adele.' Marcie looked across at the older woman, panic in her eyes.

'Just four more cards to lay,' Adele said soothingly. 'Let's see how you solve this, sugar.'

Reluctantly, Marcie drew the other cards. 'Death' came next.

'Great changes,' said Adele. 'At first you may not like them, but life is full of change.'

The two of swords. 'A divided house. Divorce and sadness. Cutting off the pain that lay in the past.'

Ace of swords. 'A new cycle begins. Something that absorbs you. That demands. That cuts through the bindings and forces you to see clearly.' She paused, then pointed to the final card.

'Judgement, Marcie. The rising of the dead. Ghosts that speak. Something must be finished before you can begin again.'

Marcie had grown pale. Maybe it was just the wine.

Maybe she was overtired, but suddenly this was too much. Too close to the events of the last few days.

'What's Michael told you?' she asked, her voice soft with the effort to keep it steady.

Adele shook her head. 'Michael has told me nothing, sugar, and remember, you chose each card yourself. I did nothing but tell you the meanings.'

Glancing across the room, Marcie met Michael's eyes and knew Adele was telling the truth. He looked just as baffled and she was painfully aware that she had become the focus for the whole room.

'It's Jack,' she whispered. 'There's this woman that keeps coming back, haunts him. I don't know if it's what you'd call a ghost or if it's just in his mind, but he says she hanged herself, or he was there when it happened.'

She paused, took a deep breath and glanced at Michael once more as though looking for approval, then unwrapped the blue silk from around her neck.

'Then a couple of nights ago,' she said, 'this happened to me.'

Chapter Fourteen

Strange how some things stay with you no matter what else in your life you might forget.

Some things remain fresh and clear in memory. Like that afternoon with her. That summer afternoon.

It had been so hot. Almost at the end of harvest and so many extra hands needed everywhere, it was easy to slip away. Everyone would just assume we had been somewhere else, helping in another field or another barn and it was so damned hot.

She stripped down to her petticoat and lay back in the dappled shade with her eyes closed and a half-smile curling across her mouth. I knew that she was watching me, dark eyes peeking out under those long lashes.

I felt awkward. Scared, almost. Like the first time we did it. Winter then, when we first made love in the darkest corner of Manx's barn. It was cold and I held her tight, my hands all over her, trying to keep her warm. The centre of us, where our bodies met, burning. Slick with sweat. My back and Rebekkah's arms rising in goose flesh.

Afterwards, we had to dress quickly. Then we lay there, my coat on the straw and hers spread over us, trying to stay warm.

But in the summer it was different.

She'd wait for me and catch me outside in the sunlight. Tease, with a touch of her tongue across her lip or a sideways look. And I went with her. God, I lost count of the times. I warned her, so many times I warned her that we should stop. But that wasn't Rebekkah's way. Oh no, the fear of someone finding out made it all the better. She would bite and tear at my flesh like she wanted to get inside me. Wear my skin. Take my bones for her own. Bite out my tongue and use it to speak my words for me.

I told her, that summer day, that it would be the last, and she just smiled.

'I'll dance at your wedding, Jack,' she said, 'but you needn't think it will change a thing between us.'

Then she took off her petticoat, slipping it from her shoulders, and let it fall to the floor. Stood there, naked and barefoot, with that black hair falling all around her face and on to her breasts and the sun golden on her skin.

'Come here, Jack,' she said, calling me to her like the witch she was. Beckoning. Her eyes laughed at me.

And then, God help me, I went to her.

It was Adele's Tarot that had led them back here. The talk had gone on long into the night. Questions and answers and speculations. Slowly, Marcie had begun to feel better. If people she liked and trusted could discuss all aspects of something very frightening in this easy, rational way then maybe it wasn't so crazy after all.

They had reached no conclusions, just come to the inevitable decision that Marcie must come back and talk to Jack – for her own peace of mind, and for Jack's. She had to end whatever needed ending before she could get on with her life. And, if it turned out that there was nothing to end, that all of this was caused by a sensitive imagination and love for an old man whose drugged mind was apt to ramble, well, then that would be that.

But if there were something more . . .

So. Sunday morning saw Marcie, Michael and the twins standing in the car park at the hospice, preparing to go inside.

'Their car isn't here,' Marcie said, glancing around. With luck, Alice and her gran would be at church and Alec, Marcie knew, rarely visited Jack alone.

'What if they've said something?' Marcie niggled. 'Told the desk I can't visit him?' She squared her shoulders and took the handles of the pushchair as though it offered some divine protection. 'Only one way to find out, I suppose.'

She need not have worried. Her grandmother's desire to save face had protected her from any problems. They recognized her at reception.

'Oh, he will be pleased to see you. And this is your family?' The woman smiled at Michael and bent to make a fuss of the twins. 'He's kept on asking for you, poor old soul. Though I expect you know that. Your grandmother said you didn't want to go, that you'd no holiday left.'

She cast a sympathetic look in Marcie's direction. 'So hard, isn't it, trying to balance everything when you've got so many demands?'

Marcie smiled and nodded as she signed them all in, writing down the registration of the car and their names.

'Is he still in the same place?' she asked.

'Yes, dear. You know the way, don't you?'

They made their way down the long corridor. It was bright with pictures and painted in a soft shade of peach. A thick green carpet dulled the sound of their feet.

'Doesn't look like a hospital,' Michael commented.

'It's not, really,' Marcie reminded him, 'but it is nice here.'

They turned into a side ward and Marcie paused. 'They've moved him next to the window,' she said. 'He'll like that.' For a moment she hesitated, then gripped the pushchair handles tighter and marched over to the bed.

Jack smiled, a wide, toothless grin that spread even wider as she lifted the twins on to the bed.

'Babies,' he whispered. 'Little tiddlers. Your gran said . . . but I didn't believe her.' He frowned suddenly as he caught sight of Michael. 'Who's he?'

'This is Michael, my husband,' Marcie said.

'Husband!' Jack almost spat the word, his face reddening slightly, his hands moving in agitation. He looked away deliberately, staring out at the tall trees and blue sky.

Marcie stiffened angrily. 'Jack, we've all come to see you,' she said, then waited uncertainly for the old man to give some clue that he had even heard, to make some response.

Then, 'They're pretty bairns,' he said reluctantly, adding with sudden strength, 'God, take them outside, man. It stinks of death and dying in here. You want them breathing that muck?'

Michael glanced at Marcie. He'd not expected a warm welcome, Marcie had told him of Jack's rather random prejudices. But unfriendly though the old man's greeting was, their reception could have been much worse.

The twins were already restless. Michael fished in the baby bag hanging on the pushchair and pulled out a soft red and yellow ball.

'We'll go into the garden,' he said. 'I won't go far.'

Marcie nodded and watched as Michael led the twins away.

'You're not being very polite, Jack.'

'Privilege of age,' he said. 'Anyway, why should I be? Got you pregnant, did he? Just like . . .'

'Jack! I said that was enough. I've not come all this way to argue. You want a fight, pick one with Gran.'

For a moment or two both were silent. 'You sound better,' Marcie said at last. 'More like your old self.'

'She said you'd had to go back to work,' Jack complained. 'Said you'd got kids and a husband. Just another of her lies.'

Marcie sighed. The fight that had brought colour to Jack's cheeks and a light back into his eyes seemed to have faded suddenly as though it took too much strength, and he had now slipped even further back.

'They need me, Jack. My family. Gran and Aunt Alice don't want me here. They think I upset you too much.'

'Upset me, Birdie? How could you upset me?'

He was drifting again, Marcie realized. For a moment

she glared suspiciously at him, wondering just how much of this present vagueness was for real or induced by drugs and illness. How much was just convenient for Jack? She leaned back in the chair and closed her eyes.

'I've been having some strange dreams, Jack,' she said quietly, deciding that she didn't have time to work around the problem.

'Always did, Birdie. Always did.'

'I dreamed . . . I dreamed about that woman, Jack. That woman you say comes to you. Watches you.'

Jack said nothing. Marcie opened her eyes and looked at him. He had turned his head away from her, was staring towards the entrance to the ward. Alec stood there, his face set and tense.

Marcie rose slowly, her eyes fixed on his. 'Good morning, Da.'

'What are you doing here?'

'Visiting Jack. You?'

Alec strode over to the bed and grabbed Marcie by the arm, drawing her aside. 'What right do you think you have?'

'Every right!' She shook him off. 'Oh, forget it, Da, there's no audience here now. You don't have to play the hero for them.'

She glanced back at the bed, but Jack seemed to be paying no attention to them. Marcie's anger bubbled into words.

'You treated me like shit, Da! You expect me to accept that?' she whispered furiously.

Alec glared at her. 'And you stole from us,' he returned. 'Those things weren't yours.'

'And they weren't yours either. Yours or Gran's or Alice's. They were *Jack*'s.'

'And that makes it all right, does it? Have you any idea how upset your gran was?'

'Do you know how little I care?'

She shook her head, aware that the last statement was at least a partial lie. Of course she cared. She'd had a whole childhood's worth of caring for what her family said and did and it was a habit hard to break.

'I'm sorry, Da,' she said softly, 'but what option did I have? I couldn't let her throw Jack's things away, just because he wasn't there to keep them.'

'Jack's things,' Alec repeated. He sounded sad and frustrated, she thought. 'Jack's this. Jack's that. God almighty, Marcie . . .' He broke off, frowning as a movement at the window caught his eye. 'Who's this?' he demanded, much as Jack had done.

Michael stepped into the ward, glancing back as he did so to check on the twins, who were picking daisies on the lawn. He'd tied his locks back with a band of yellow, red and green and wore a faded T-shirt and washed-out blue jeans with hi-top trainers.

'This is Michael,' Marcie told him. 'I'm married to him, remember?' She sighed deeply. 'Can we stop arguing for just a minute, Da, so you can say hello? Meet your grandkids?'

Startled by the thought, Alec stared out at Liam and Hanna, watching as their tiny fingers pulled the heads off daisies. It seemed suddenly to deflate him. He took a step forward as though to go outside. Then changed his mind.

'It's good of you to come,' he said to Michael, remembering his manners and determined to make an effort. 'I mean, yes, good of you to come. You'd better leave, though, Marcie. Your gran was going to get a lift from someone at church. I said I'd meet them here. I'm sure you want to be gone before they arrive.'

Marcie stiffened. 'I wanted to talk to Jack,' she said.

'Jack doesn't look like he's up to talking.'

Marcie looked across at the old man. He seemed to be sleeping, his mouth open, a tiny stream of spittle dribbling from the side. She knew her father was right. It would take time to learn anything from Jack, and, no, she didn't want to be around when her aunt and grandmother arrived.

'Who was Rebekkah?' she asked.

'What? Who was . . . ?' Alec was caught off-guard by her change of tack.

'She was someone Jack knew,' Marcie continued. 'In the war, perhaps. I think maybe she was hanged.'

'Oh!' Alec's face cleared. 'Her,' he said, as though it didn't matter. 'That didn't happen in the war, Marcie. That's just Jack off his head again. Rebekkah was someone Jack and your gran knew. She got herself murdered. Hanged by her husband, I believe.' He glanced back at where Jack lay. 'God! But he goes on. Hours at a time. Gets so you can't stand it.'

He shifted uncomfortably as though embarrassed by such an admission of weakness on his part. Then moved back on to more secure ground. 'Your gran and Alice were really upset by what you did.'

'Oh, belt up, Da. Isn't it time you owned up to how much you resent being under their thumbs?'

She said no more then, neither did she listen to Alec's half-hearted attempts to bluster. Michael stood in the doorway while Marcie got the twins and coaxed them back into their pushchair, accepting the daisy heads and stalks with an enthusiasm that blocked Alec out completely. Michael nodded curtly to Alec and followed his wife back down the ward.

Alec stood, arms limply at his side, and watched them go.

They think I don't hear them arguing. Think I don't know how much they quarrel amongst themselves or how much trouble I've been giving them, lying here like this, not doing my fair share.

I thought I heard my Birdie a little while ago, talking to me, telling me about her dreams the way she used to when she was just a little thing. Must have been Mary going on about babies. Must have dreamed about them being here. Little coffee-coloured bairns. Pretty as pictures, sitting on my bed.

It's late in life to be seeing angels. Dusky little angels with curly heads and big brown eyes. Just like my first-born. Brown eyes and curly hair and dead as my Rebekkah.

Sunlight on her skin like warm honey.

God above! But I'd never known such cold, not even in the deep of winter. Desert cold. Clear skies and stars like diamonds scattered on blue velvet. Like a rag doll, she was, hanging there. Hands tied so she couldn't fight it. The rope pulled tight around her neck.

It wasn't my fault, woman! No, no, I'd have set it right. Wasn't my fault the knot slid tight against your throat. I'd have set it right, one snap and that would have finished it.

Not left you choking with your feet kicking against the stars.

Kicking against the stars.

'Rebekkah?'

Mary halted beside the bed, her words of cheerful greeting frozen on her lips. Alec laid a hand on her arm.

'Mam, don't upset yourself. He doesn't know what he's saying.'

She turned away, pacing swiftly back down the ward, with Alec almost running behind her to keep up.

'He doesn't mean it, Mam. He sees her, she haunts him, Mam. It means nothing.'

'You're starting to sound like that daughter of yours,' Mary told him angrily, her voice stiff with unshed tears. 'And how should you know what your father means and what he doesn't? What does any of it mean to you?'

'Is it my fault if I don't understand? Well, is it? Tried talking to me, have you? Once in a while you might have thought about confiding in me. Letting me in instead of hiding behind this pretence that everything in the past is dead and gone and none of my concern.'

Mary looked at him, her eyes a mixture of pity and contempt. 'And so it is, boy,' she said.

'No!' Alec almost shouted at her. 'No, it's not, and neither is it none of my business, Mam.' She had halted for a moment and he reached out his hand, groping for hers. 'If it's all past and gone, why do you keep crying every time anyone mentions this woman? Keep pushing me away every time I try to help?' He paused, then said softly, 'Who was she, Mam? Who was she?'

Mary had allowed her hand to rest in his, had seemed to be listening to him, but now she snatched it away.

'It's none of your concern!' she snapped angrily. 'Not now, not ever.'

Chapter Fifteen

Rather than waste the rest of their Sunday they travelled some twenty miles further on, to the seaside.

This was a first for the twins. They spent the day building castles on the sand, paddling in the shallowest of water and finally, when the incoming tide brought a chill east wind, retreated to the fairground and hooked ducks to win furry monkeys that Marcie would not normally have given house room to.

On Sunday, Marcie buried her hurt and her anger in a day of very childlike pleasure. Monday was more difficult. Tuesday also, though the days passed reasonably enough. Work, home, play with the twins, the usual routines and actions, comforting in their demands. Nothing strange or frightening to disturb them, and the marks on Marcie's neck continued to fade.

Jack was barely mentioned. Alec and her aunt and grandmother not at all. Only once did she pick up the bundle of photographs – the oldest ones sorted from the others – finally gazing thoughtfully into the faces of those standing beside the haywain.

'I wonder if one of these is Rebekkah,' she said.

There were five women in the picture. Two they knew. A young Mary and an even younger Alice. The other three were just as youthful, just as hopeful, on that hot summer afternoon.

'It's a nasty way to die,' Michael commented, and Marcie nodded, looking into those forgotten faces, trying to imagine any one of them with a rope around her neck, an agony of fear in her eyes.

Wednesday, Marcie worked late, dashing home for a quick snack with Michael and telling him that she'd been offered overtime. Stocktaking, double time. They couldn't afford for her to turn it down.

Michael drove her back to work, then read to the twins and saw them into bed, tucking the Little Bear book that was Liam's current favourite in beside his small son.

Then he sat down to make some headway into the stack of case notes he had brought home with him from the law centre. People threatened with bankruptcy, eviction, trouble with neighbours, with landlords, with husbands and wives and local dogs.

Michael often pondered wryly at the way his once-cherished dreams of becoming a fully fledged QC had diminished into this morass of everyday problems. This never-ending stream of folk, out of their depth and needing vital but very often quite simple guidance. Sometimes he'd talk about getting his studies back on line, but the reality of their finances meant he didn't have the freedom to move from what he was doing.

He was buried in the minutiae of a tenancy agreement when Alec arrived.

'One of your neighbours let me in,' Alec said, as Michael opened the flat door and stared in amazement at the stocky figure standing on his threshold. 'Told me this was your door.'

'Marcie isn't here,' Michael told him. 'She had to work late tonight.'

'Oh,' Alec said. 'Oh, I never thought . . . should have rung first, I suppose, but it was, well, an impulse, I guess you'd call it.'

Michael raised an eyebrow. 'It's a three-hour drive,' he said. 'That was quite some impulse.'

Alec shuffled his feet, uncertain of his welcome. 'Maybe I should go,' he said. 'Do you know when . . . ?'

Michael shook his head. 'You'd better come in,' he told Alec, standing aside. 'Just keep the noise down, will you? Hanna sleeps real light.'

He went through to the kitchen to make coffee, standing with his back to the counter and his arms folded whilst the kettle boiled, wondering what on earth had brought Alec here. Considering whether he should be openly annoyed or let the other man take the lead first and see where the conversation went.

When he brought their coffee mugs through, Alec was standing with the curtain of the little alcove drawn aside, looking down at the sleeping children. His expression, the sadness of it, took Michael by surprise.

'I remember her as a baby,' he said, moving away and letting the curtain fall. 'Such a tiny, scrawny little mite. Jack thought she was the most wonderful thing in the world.'

He took the coffee and stood awkwardly as though uncertain of what to do with himself.

'Marcie told me her mother died in a car crash,' Michael said. 'That was why you brought her home to Jack.'

Alec nodded slowly, then sat down before speaking, curling both hands around the mug as though he felt the cold. 'She died,' he said stiffly. 'Took a bend too fast and fell close on a hundred feet on to the rocks.' He bowed his head sadly. 'Italy, up in the mountains. She should have known better, but she always did drive too fast. Marcie never really asked about her,' he added. 'Jack made sure of that. Never gave her space or need to know.'

'You could have told her,' Michael commented. 'She's your child.'

'My child,' he echoed. 'My child, was she? You don't know Jack.'

Michael regarded him thoughtfully for a moment. It occurred to him how little Marcie talked about Alec. When she had spoken of family, it had almost always been about Jack.

Alec drained the still-hot coffee then sat, staring down into his mug. He seemed to have given up on the conversation.

What had brought him here? Michael wondered again. He was clearly very disturbed about something. There was none of the semi-arrogant bluster Michael had witnessed on the previous Sunday. By contrast, he looked lost and bewildered.

The slight sound of Liam turning over attracted Alec's attention. He looked up. 'They're beautiful,' he said, with longing in his voice.

'I guess so was Marcie,' Michael said.

'Marcie,' Alec said, tilting his empty coffee cup towards him. 'Marcie. She was never mine, you know. Not from the moment I brought her home.'

'You made that choice.'

'Choice!' Alec almost shouted, then glanced guiltily towards where the twins were sleeping and dropped his voice. 'I had no choice. What else could I do? I knew nothing about babies. Nothing. And when her mother died . . . there was no one.'

He glanced up sharply, looking properly at Michael for the first time. Meeting the steadiness of his gaze. 'You don't think much of me, do you?'

'No,' Michael said shortly. 'I don't, but I don't think you rate yourself very highly either.'

'What do you know?' Alec bristled. But it was all posture with no muscle behind it. He leaned back in the chair and sighed. 'These days I don't even think about it much,' he said.

Michael watched the other man for a little longer, but he seemed unwilling to say more. He rose, went across and eased the cup from Alec's hand, then went to make more coffee. He started to talk while he reboiled the kettle, and measured sugar and coffee into the cups. Continued as he came back through to the living room.

'It was when she was pregnant, that's when she told me about that other baby and why she ran away from you and Jack. You did wrong by her, Alec. All of you. What had she done that was so bad? Fallen in love, or thought she had. Had sex with her boyfriend and been daft enough and innocent enough to end up pregnant. Did she do anything that deserved what you did to her?'

He paused, waited for an answer but got none. 'Just what did you hope to prove, Alec? Show her what big men you both were? God's sake! She was just a kid.

Scared out of her wits as it was and all you could do was treat her like she'd committed some terrible crime.'

'What she did was wrong. She let us down. We'd taught her better than that.'

'What she did was stupid. Misguided, maybe, but if we all have to pay so hard for the dumb things we do when we're no more than kids it's a poor future we've got, don't you think?'

'What do you know?' Alec fired at him again. It seemed to be a favourite phrase. 'We'd taught her better than that but she showed no self-respect or self-restraint. And that boy. Do you think a boy like that could ever be good enough for Marcie?'

'You're contradicting yourself, Alec,' Michael goaded. 'You can't have her on a pedestal *and* screwing in the gutters. Doesn't happen.'

Alec rose to his feet abruptly enough to spill the coffee in his newly filled mug. Whatever action he had planned was foiled by the rush of scalding liquid slopping over his hand.

'Damn and blast it.' He stared about him, distractedly.

He was more worried about the coffee spilling on the rug, Michael realized, than he was about the insults that had precipitated his reaction.

'Put your hand under the cold tap,' Michael said, pointing to the kitchen. 'I'll get a cloth.'

Mopping up gave them both a little breathing space. Alec seemed calmer when he sat down once more.

'It was Jack's idea,' Alec said, as though that explained it all.

'Don't suppose you thought to say no to him.'

'You don't say no to Jack. Or you didn't. And my mother . . . I never knew anyone refuse her. Lord!' he said, looking up sharply, 'that sounds pathetic, doesn't it?'

'A little, yes.' He caught Alec's expression and added swiftly, 'Hey, man, I ain't about to start badmouthin' you again. Too rough on Momma's carpets.'

He laughed, this time at Alec's expression. 'Look,' he said. 'It's not my place to pass judgement, only when that judgement affects Marcie. Then I think I got the right.'

Alec nodded slowly, then spoke softly, the words dragged painfully from memory.

'It was a cold night,' he said. 'We really thought, I guess, that we were doing the right thing . . .'

Just past Christmas and the nights had been very dark and very cold, full of snowclouds blocking out the stars.

Marcie had been sick for days, miserably so. Tummy bug, Aunt Alice had said, but even then Gran hadn't been too sure. Marcie, regular as clockwork, had missed her period.

It had taken several hours of argument, of anger and tears and threats of violence to get the truth from her.

'Who is he?' Mary had demanded over and over again, even before Marcie had finally admitted the truth.

'Once, I swear it, Gran, it was only once.'

'Once or many times. What does it matter? You sinned, girl. Sinned.'

'It's not a sin. It's not. I love him, Gran, I love him.'

'Love! You're a child. Fifteen years old. What do you know about love? I'll have the police on him. I'll have him in court and you'll have to tell all of them, judge and jury and everyone who cares to listen just what you've done.'

'I only did it once, Gran. Truly I did. I didn't think anything would happen. Not just once. I didn't even like it, Gran.'

They'd been empty threats, of course. Mary would have never faced the public humiliation involved in calling in the police, but Marcie had been too distraught to think of that. Finally the hours of harassment and anger had paid off. Marcie had given them the name of the boy and the places they had met and told them everything that they had ever done.

Mary had been doubly outraged. 'The Simpson boy! That good-for-nothing layabout. Why, Marcie? Why?'

'I love . . . I like him, Gran. He made me laugh. It was fun just . . . just fun going out with him and then it got serious, you know . . .'

Gran's expression told her that, no, she didn't know. *Wouldn't* know.

'You're old!' Marcie finally yelled at them. 'You don't remember what it's like to be young and to *feel* things.'

Mary had slapped her then, hard enough to send her spinning into the door. She fell to the floor winded and shocked, whimpering softly.

'Now go to your room,' Mary told her. 'Go to your room and don't come down until I say you can.'

Marcie had fled, racing up the stairs and slamming

her bedroom door before collapsing on the bed in tears. Even then there was no peace for her. Aunt Alice came up only moments later and began to empty Marcie's wardrobe and drawers.

'What are you doing?'

'Making sure you don't have any stupid ideas,' Alice said. 'Get your nightdress on and get into bed.'

She stood over her until Marcie had done as she was told, then left, taking her clothes and shoes away with her.

'You'll thank us for this one day,' she told her as she left the room.

Outside it was five below freezing, the sky still heavy with unfallen snow.

'You kept me shut away in that room for nearly five days,' Marcie said softly. 'Brought me food I couldn't eat and only let me out to be sick in the bathroom because Gran was scared I'd make a mess of my room. Then you let me get dressed that morning and put me in the car, took me away to that place where they didn't know or care whether or not I wanted to keep my baby.'

'You were too young,' Alec told her earnestly. 'Marcie, you were fifteen years old.'

'Old enough to get pregnant,' she said softly. 'Old enough to have talked about it.' She came closer to Alec, her eyes burning with a sadness and hatred that Michael had never seen before. 'How much did you pay them, Da, to do that to me without counselling or the proper consents?'

'You agreed to it,' Alec objected. 'You signed the forms, you agreed to it.'

'By that time, Da, I'd have agreed to anything just to get out of that room.' She shook her head slowly. 'I forgave you that. I know in your own minds you thought it was for the best, but you were wrong, Da. You were wrong.'

Michael got up from his seat and went over to kiss her. 'You hungry?' he asked. 'I'll make some tea.'

Alec had risen too, awkward now. The door was behind him and he'd not heard Marcie come in quietly, opening the door softly in case Michael had been having trouble getting the twins to sleep. She had stood, signing to Michael not to give her away, listening to Alec for several minutes, her father, staring at the floor, too tied up in his story to even notice her.

'You were wrong,' she repeated softly. 'What are you doing here?'

'I came to . . . I mean . . .' Alec shook his head. 'Been asking myself that all the way here.'

'Had a row with Gran?'

Alec started guiltily, telling Marcie that she'd hit the target.

He nodded. 'She's upset. About Jack. About you. I don't know, Birdie, I don't seem to be making a very good job of things lately.'

It was Marcie's turn to look startled. Only Jack had ever called her Bird. 'Only lately, Da?' she asked him. Seeing the intensity of hurt in his eyes, she relented a little. 'Does she know you're here?'

'God, no!' Alec's denouncement was almost comical.

'Still under Mummy's thumb,' Marcie said, then, 'Sorry, Da, I shouldn't have said that. She has got an awfully big thumb.'

Alec looked uncomfortable, but almost managed to laugh at his daughter's half-joke. 'I'll have to be getting back,' he said. 'It's a long drive.'

'There's a sofa,' Michael said, returning from the kitchen. Both Alec and Marcie looked at him in surprise.

'Thank you,' Alec said. 'But I ought to go.'

He sat down anyway and watched as Marcie checked on her children, covering Hanna gently. Michael poured tea into bright red mugs and offered biscuits. Marcie flopped down beside him on the sofa and closed her eyes, reaching automatically for Michael's hand. The atmosphere of intimacy that surrounded them took Alec by surprise. Casual touch and random affection were not something that had been on offer in his parents' house. Jack had tried, but he'd been bluff and male when Alec had really wanted tenderness and warmth – not that he'd readily put such feelings into thought. Mary had managed quick hugs and perfunctory kisses, seeing her more important duties as being those of housekeeper and maintainer of standards.

It was really only in his brief marriage that Alec had realized what he craved. Only in Jack's love of Marcie that he had really witnessed it.

'I loved your mother,' he said, blurting it out suddenly with all the force of a confession. 'Loved her so much it hurts even now to think about it.'

Marcie stared at him, not knowing what to say. It

was Michael who reached across the coffee table and clasped Alec by the hand.

'Of course you did,' he said quietly. 'That's one of the few things you've still got going for you.'

Chapter Sixteen

There were five of us – me, the Fisher brothers, Sam Nichols and Sergeant Mills – holed up in what was meant to be a safe house.

Her house.

I can remember, when she bent close to me to take my cup, the way she smelt. Clean and warm and her hair scented with sandalwood. Skin like honey, like my Becky had.

Then the shelling got closer. We heard the crashing and the screaming not more than a street away and the woman got shaky. Scared of us being found. Of what would be done to her if they discovered us in her house. So she took us out of there, her and that man she was with. Emile, I think they called him, though I never paid it that much mind . . . out into the dark, with me in the lead and Mills bringing up the rear.

She was scared-careful, I saw her checking that there was nothing left behind. I watched her as she put the cups we had been using back in the cupboard, setting everything neat. Every trace of us wiped clean away.

Backstreets that all looked the same. Tiny windows facing the world and dark gateways that led back into courtyards and alleyways. We kept to the shadows, moving like rats along the walls, nerves strung out by the fear of snipers hidden in the black gaps of the narrow windows.

There was a moon, but it was still low, hung behind the buildings. We caught glimpses of it between the broken walls where the shelling had laid open great wounds. And there was smoke, pluming up in the distance, dark against the dark, and a red glow where the fires were still burning. I remember thinking that the moon was rising over hell.

Like I said, there were five of us. If I think hard I can still recall their faces. Filthed-up and streaked with sweat. Sergeant Mills, regular soldier, big square hands, had a slow, steady way of moving like some big bull elephant. Purposeful, like he knew just where to go and what he planned to do once he'd got us there. Got to regroup, he said. Get back to what was left of our unit, like there was nothing to it, and no doubt we could manage it if we'd only just keep listening to him.

They took us to some bombed-out shell of a house, must have been five or six streets from where the woman lived, and we hid out in what was left of one of the back rooms. I could see the moon, shining down on us now through the gaps in the roof beams, bright enough so we could see each other's faces and for us to read the rough map Emile drew for us. A safe route, he said. Or safe as any place could be in a city of snipers. But they wouldn't take us further. Too scared of getting caught.

So we sat there in the half-light, waiting for the moon to set, hoping to make it out of that bloody little town between moonset and sunrise. Just sat there, listening to the shells falling, until our thoughts had been blasted into bits by the noise of shattered walls falling and the screams of those who couldn't get away. And the not knowing if it was our lot or theirs doing the most damage.

And the night moved on, ticking away so slow I could have sworn the moon had stopped and was just shining down, like the star of Bethlehem, pointing the way for them to find us.

Alec drove home in the early hours of the morning, drained and tired and deeply reluctant to go back.

I was fifteen when I left home, he reminded himself. Fifteen. Joined the navy. Did my time on the Ganges. Travelled the world and I was just a kid.

Marcie was right. He'd passed judgement on what was right for her when he himself had made decisions at the same age that now horrified him. He was still convinced that having a baby at that age would have been a crazy act, but they had handled things not just badly but probably with great cruelty.

Fifteen, he repeated to himself, and Jack had been at work on the farm a year younger than that.

And yet, they had been such children. Proto-adults, trying to find their way in a complicated world.

He drove along almost-empty roads. Even the motorway seemed thin and unfleshed by traffic. His mind drifted back to the night Marcie had confessed that she was pregnant and to the night not long after that when he and Jack had taken their revenge on the Simpson boy.

It had still been so cold and the snow had begun to fall again, blanketing the streets with a deadly purity. They had waited for him, waited for Patrick Simpson as he'd come out of the pub, said goodbye to his friends and set off across the park towards home.

Pat Simpson was just turned eighteen. A gangly, slightly pimply boy with overlong black hair and a reputation for making it easily with the girls. Alec couldn't see the attraction, but quite a slice of the female population seemed to find one. Older folk talked of him as something of a Jack the lad, but they did it fondly, as though that were something to be proud of, as though it made up for his lack of job and prospects.

Alec could remember clearly how they'd followed him. The night had been bitter. The boy had walked with his head uncovered, his collar turned up and his bare hands thrust deep into the pockets of his coat.

'We'll just talk to him,' Jack had said. 'Somewhere private, like. Make him see he's got to keep away from our Birdie.'

Even then, deep in disgrace, she was still Jack's Bird. Still on her pedestal even while rolling in the gutter, as Michael had said.

Alec had told himself that Jack meant what he said. That all they would do was talk. But following the boy across the park, moving like trackers from shadow to shadow, even Alec hadn't been able to keep up the pretence completely.

Then Jack had leapt at him, screaming like a maniac, arms strengthened by anger despite his years. He had wrestled the boy to the ground and begun kicking him in the head until the snow was stained with crimson and the boy lay still. Then even Alec had been forced to act.

He couldn't remember the words he had screamed at his father. They had seemed incoherent even then as he had struggled with Jack, pulled him way from the now unconscious Patrick Simpson.

'Oh, God! Oh, my God, you've killed him. You've fucking killed him, Dad!'

Jack glared, cat-like malevolence narrowing his eyes. 'Don't you swear at me, boy. Don't you ever swear at me!'

Then he'd bent down, grabbed mounds of snow in his bare hands and scrubbed the blood from his boots before marching away, his back rigid, arms swinging in strict time to his footsteps. When he moved his arm, Alec could almost see the rifle slung across his back.

'Oh, God. Oh, my God.'

He had bent down next to the body, certain that the boy was dead but too afraid of getting blood on his hands to test for a pulse. 'I could say I just found him. Walking in the park, and I just found him. Coming back from the pub. Yes, that's it. What if they know he's been seeing Marcie? What . . . ?'

There were voices coming from one of the other paths, people, concealed by the still-thick growth of evergreens, who might be heading his way.

With a skill that Jack would have been proud of, Alec slipped into the shadows. Backed down the path they had come in by, moving with a stealth born of sheer terror. Then, as the voices faded, he began to run.

Hampered by the thickly falling snow and by his heavy coat, it seemed to take for ever to reach the park gates.

Alec stood panting. The cold air was raw in his lungs. A telephone box. Oh, please let it be working. 'Yes, yes, I need the police, an ambulance. There's a dead body in the park down near the lake . . .'

He hung up, fought his way through the door, almost slipping on a patch of ice as he began to run again. They would know, they would know. The police would come for him. Be there when he reached home. They would know . . .

Alec shifted back from fifth gear as the final marker for his exit loomed, its white flashing stark and luminous as fresh snow.

There had been no police. No one knew. Marcie and Patrick had been careful, secretive enough in their meetings that there was nothing to connect them.

Patrick Simpson had been found two hours later, covered by a heavy blanket of snow that almost hid the body. His injuries, bloody though they were, would not have killed him. Had he been conscious. Had they found him sooner. As it was, the cold had killed him, wrapped him tight and frozen the life from him.

Marcie knew nothing about it, deprived of newspapers and television, even of the radio. Retreating to her room after returning from the hospital, refusing to eat, making *herself* ill, as Gran had insisted. It had been weeks before she went back to school and knew that anything had happened to Patrick Simpson.

Alec remembered vividly the night she had come

home with a vague story that Patrick had died of cold in the park on a winter's night.

'You did it to him, didn't you?' she challenged Jack. 'You did it to him.' Screaming with fury and despair.

Alec flicked the indicator late, almost losing his turn-off at the island. Remembering Marcie, one of Aunt Alice's kitchen knives clasped in her slim hand, flying at Jack with a wildness in her eyes that matched that in Jack's the night he had killed the boy.

Jack had thrown her aside easily, the knife grazing down his arm then cutting into the bicep as she fell.

And Marcie had seen the blood and her resolve had collapsed. Anger dissolving into fear.

'Oh, no, Jack. Oh, Jack, I'm sorry. Oh, Jack, Jack.'

And Jack had stared at her, then at his arm, and covered his face, blood draining from his features as though for the first time the shock of what he had done had come home to him.

'It was pandemonium after that,' Alec said to himself. 'Sheer pandemonium.'

He was heading back towards the city now, street lights marking his way, flicking by him far too fast. He dropped his speed, watching the needle of the speed-ometer fall from seventy back to forty-five.

He remembered Jack sitting in Aunt Alice's big chair, tears running down his cheeks, face screwed into wrin-kles, crying like a child.

And Alice, holding Marcie by the shoulders, shaking her, shouting at her. 'Nothing happened, Marcie! The baby, your relationship with that boy. Tonight. None of it happened. None of it! You hear me?'

None of it ever happened.

They moved out when the moon was low on the horizon.

The shelling had stopped and the streets were quiet but for sporadic bursts of gunfire far enough away to echo. They moved softly, keeping close to the walls, eyes everywhere and nerves strung so taut Jack fancied he could hear them snap.

Then it happened. Two shots and two men down. The others dived for cover as a third shot smashed into brick just inches above their heads. They hit the ground. Sergeant Mills had his rifle in his hands, scanning the building, a three-floored warehouse, from where the shots had come. But Jack was quicker. He'd caught the flash of the third shot and suddenly he was moving, avoiding Mills and his whispered orders, running at a crouch towards the warehouse and the shadow of a side door half hidden in a narrow alley.

The small door creaked as Jack pushed at it, jamming on the debris on the floor inside and opening just enough for Jack to consider sliding through. He shrugged free of his pack, lowered it to the ground, then squeezed through the door, the Lee Enfield held close to his body, sitting easy in his arms. Jack could see a broken stairway leading upwards, and a faint sound reached him from the upper floor.

He took the stairs in long strides, dust rising about

him and fragments of half-rotten wood flying from beneath his feet. He paused at the second flight, ears straining for the slightest sound. The sniper had heard him. Jack knew that; the faint sounds above him had completely ceased.

Jack knew he couldn't turn back. He knew there would be just one chance to get it right and only one if he didn't want to wind up dead.

Then he ceased to think of it.

Jack took the remaining flight at a run, then dived and rolled, firing from a half-crouch as he righted himself, then throwing himself sideways under the sniper's shot and through the open door.

It was pure luck that made the shot go wide, that and the insanity of Jack's run as though some instinct born of blind rage made him know how and when to move.

Jack's weight against the other man brought them both crashing to the floor and Jack had rolled free and fired before the other man could move, a close-range shot that blasted him wide open from groin to ribs, spreading his guts like so much waste across the floor, the stink of blood and shit rising from it to fill the dust-laden air.

It should have been enough, but Jack was beyond that kind of nicety. He moved forward and looked down into his enemy's face. A young face, filthy and grimed with sweat and dirt and, now, his own blood, and then Jack raised the gun once more, this time bringing the rifle butt down on the stranger's face with all his strength, feeling the bone and flesh smash and pulp, wanting to grind it into oblivion. For ever.

Chapter Seventeen

It was a small sound that woke Marcie. A small sound, but after weeks of night feeds, even more months of listening for her babies, Marcie was sensitive to such things.

She lay for a few moments in the dark, listening, trying to work out what it was that had awoken her. If it was nothing but one of the children turning over she didn't see the sense of getting out of a warm bed and maybe waking Hanna into the bargain.

Then the sound came again, the sound of sobbing, soft, as though whoever cried did not want to be heard.

Frightened, but also drawn to the sound, Marcie slipped from her bed, glancing back at Michael and wondering whether she had better waken him. Deciding against, she moved stealthily to the end of the bed, pulled her dressing gown around her shoulders and crept into the main room.

'Oh!' Marcie stopped in her tracks, a hand rising to her mouth to stop herself from crying out. There was no way, she told herself. No way this was real.

'What are you doing here? Get away from there. Get away from there!'

The curtain that covered the twins' tiny room was drawn right back, held by a woman in a white blouse and black skirt. Her dark hair fell down in soft waves over her shoulders and as she turned at Marcie's challenge Marcie could see the rope tied tight around her throat and the tears that ran freely down the woman's face.

Marcie almost flew across the room. 'Get away from there!' she screamed.

'Marcie!' Michael's voice behind her caused her to glance back for the merest instant. He was in the doorway behind her, staring not at her but at the woman standing beside the children's cots. Marcie turned back towards her enemy . . . but there was nothing there. The curtain hung partly drawn aside, otherwise nothing.

Michael was beside her now. 'It's all right,' he said. 'It's all right, she's gone now, Marcie. Gone.'

Weakly, sobbing with fear, Marcie allowed him to hold her, feeling that Michael too was trembling, his skin cold with shock. Then she stiffened.

'Hanna,' she whispered. 'Oh, Michael, Hanna. All the noise we were making. Why didn't Hanna wake up?'

Chapter Eighteen

Adele cuddled Hanna in her lap and let her help herself from the biscuit tin. Liam sat on his mother's knee drinking milk from one of the clown-printed mugs Adele kept specially for them. Both children as content and mischievous as they always were. It was their parents who were suffering, still shaken from the events of the night before.

Marcie and Michael had not slept for the rest of the night. They had spent some time just standing, watching their children, worried, at first, that the noise had not woken Hanna, holding on to each other and trying hard not to be quite so afraid.

Morning had found them camped, early, on Adele's doorstep, looking for sanctuary.

'You ask me if I believe in spirits,' Adele said quietly. 'In ghosts that come haunting the living.'

'Sure she does,' Sophie Lee put in. 'Like her grandmother, she sees ghosts and angels everywhere.'

Marcie laughed edgily, and Adele smiled across at her, then said more seriously, 'The babes were not hurt, honey. Could be that she meant no harm, only came to look.'

'But why, Adele?' Marcie shook her head. 'I don't believe in ghosts.'

'Then what name do you give to this not-a-ghost?' Sophie Lee asked her.

'I don't know. Imagination. Shock, seeing my dad turn up at our place. Something Jack put into my mind with all his talk about this dead woman.'

'But I saw her too,' Michael objected. 'I mean, I'm as sceptical as you are, but I saw her too.'

'I don't know,' Marcie said again. 'Maybe, maybe I saw her so strongly because of Jack, and I kind of projected her image to you. Maybe we shared a dream. I just don't know.'

'Excuse me if I'm wrong,' said Sophie Lee, 'but my calling her a ghost does seem a whole deal simpler than any of all that.'

'Yeah, I guess you're right.' Frowning, Marcie dragged out the photograph of the haywain once more and gazed intently at the picture. 'It's funny,' she said, 'but I always thought the one on the right, the small blonde one, might be Rebekkah, not that one.'

'You still don't know for sure,' Michael suggested. 'It could be that you just needed to give this apparition a face. That subconsciously you remembered the photograph and gave her one of the faces.'

Sophie Lee rolled her eyes dramatically. 'Oh, off we go again,' she said. 'Why do the young ones never go the simple way, huh? Tell me that.' She sighed. 'Look, my children. Marcie's granddad is dying. He's got something on his mind he don't want to face his maker with. Ain't no way he can sort it for himself, lying in that hospital bed, so his problem come to you to be sorted.'

Marcie stared at the old woman. 'But why me?' she asked. 'I don't even know who Rebekkah was, except that Jack and Gran knew her.'

'And she got herself killed,' Sophie Lee reminded her. 'Most ghosts die a violent death. Maybe Jack knew something about her dying that he didn't tell. Maybe she wants justice, Marcie.'

'I don't know. I don't even know how I'd find out. Jack rambles and I can't ask Aunt Alice or Gran.'

'There's Alec,' Michael reminded her. 'Seems to me he never did get around to telling you what he came for last night.'

Marcie sighed and reached for a piece of kitchen towel to wipe Liam's mouth.

She lifted her hand then to touch the almost-faded marks on her neck. That incident had upset her, but far less than last night. It had been Michael who had seen the image of the rope about her throat, seen her struggling for breath and trying to tear it free. For Marcie that night had been like a bad dream and, apart from the bruises and abrasions on her skin, it had faded in much the same way.

By contrast, last night's apparition reappeared with terrifying clarity each time she closed her eyes or let her thoughts wander.

'She was so young,' Marcie said quietly, looking at the photograph once more. Hugging Liam to her as though for protection, she re-ran the events, hoping that familiarity would somehow soften the image. De-focus it and make it bearable. A tiny gesture Rebekkah had made as she had turned came back to her. The way her hand had moved, touching her slightly swollen belly.

'She was pregnant,' Marcie said. 'When she died, she was carrying a child.'

Chapter Nineteen

They were forced to go to work, Michael and Marcie, and to put their problems aside for the needs of others. Michael installed the twins in the crèche, asking the young woman who ran it to keep a special eye on them, telling her that they had been a little unwell and had had a restless night.

She looked at him strangely as the pair had raced off with their usual show of energy. 'Looks like you're the one that had the bad night,' she said. 'Sure you feel OK?'

'I'm fine,' Michael assured her. 'Just fine.'

By ten he was on the phone to Marcie. She was in a meeting, they told him. Taking minutes. Could she call him back at lunchtime?

He put the phone down after thanking the woman, feeling stupid and ill at ease. Then turned with his work smile back in place, as his next problem of the morning came in through the office door.

Alec's day was no better. He was up for breakfast only a few short hours after getting home and left for work early, to avoid the awkward questions wrapped up in the disapproving looks from his aunt and mother. He closed the front door, more than a little ashamed that he felt unable to admit to them that he had been to see his daughter.

He sat outside his place of work for a good ten minutes before venturing inside and, when he did, he went straight to his boss's office.

Fifteen minutes later he was outside again, aware of the puzzled looks being cast at him from the first-floor window.

For more than twelve years Alec Armitage had been Mr Reliable. Never late, rarely absent. Conscientious and predictable. Booking the same two weeks every summer. The same extra days at Christmas and New Year.

And now, to come in like this, almost demand that he be given some of his annual leave. It must seem to them, thought Alec, that the world was about to end.

But they knew about Jack. Knew about the strain he must be under . . . or thought they did.

He started the car engine and began to drive slowly towards home. It was Thursday. Alice and his mother would be shopping from about ten until around midday. He waited two streets away until ten fifteen, then let himself into the house, packed a suitcase and left again. He tossed the case into the boot of the car and drove away, through the pretty tree-lined streets of nineteen-thirties suburbia.

He was waiting outside the house when Michael arrived with Marcie and the twins. Alec's mood had oscillated throughout the day between euphoria and despair. Just what did he think he was doing? Marcie would have every right to tell him to get the hell out of her life. What did he hope to prove by walking out without a word to Alice or his mother? Walking out and leaving them to cope with Jack.

Walking out. Yes! He was free. For the first time in years he was free. Though free to do what, Alec was not yet sure.

His emotions were on the turn when Michael's car pulled up in front of his. Alec practically leapt out on them.

'I want to take you to dinner,' he announced.

'Dinner?'

'Yes, all of you. I mean, they are old enough, aren't they?' He looked at the twins. 'Yes, of course they are.'

Marcie was staring at him in surprise, while Michael looked puzzled but amused.

'All right,' Michael said at last. 'I know of somewhere we can take the kids. Follow us in your car.' And he bent to re-strap the twins into their baby seats.

Alec got back in his car, his optimism failing once again. God, what was he doing here? Just what was he going to do?

The restaurant was Italian. Marcie and Michael had been there twice before, a birthday and an anniversary. Rare treats, saved for over weeks.

'I'm paying,' Alec reminded her again. 'Please, Marcie, do this for me, please.'

There were no highchairs, but the problem was solved happily enough with big cushions and white tablecloths tying the twins securely to their chairs. The children ate pizza, cut into little bites, and discovered just what breadsticks tasted like dipped into milk and anything else within reach.

The adults ate at first in silence, then slowly unwound over the antipasto. They were relaxed enough by the time the main course had arrived, fresh cooked and so hot it had to be eaten slowly, to begin talking.

'I don't mean to be rude, Da,' Marcie said to him at last, 'but just why did you come?'

Alec put down his fork and regarded the others sheepishly. 'It sounds so silly,' he said awkwardly, 'but I guess you could say that I've run away from home.'

'You've run . . . Oh, Da, you can't be serious.'

'You said you'd got a spare sofa,' Alec went on. 'I just hoped . . . Fact is, Marcie, I couldn't take it any more, Jack and Mam, and not being able to say a damned thing without she leaps down my throat, and I didn't have anywhere else to go.'

He paused, looking hopefully at her. 'Marcie, if you don't want me, I understand. I can't expect . . .'

Marcie looked away from him and spent several moments studying her plate.

'It will only be for the night,' he said. 'Or if you like, I'll book into a hotel.' He hesitated. 'I've got to find myself somewhere then, near to work. I've taken a few days off so I can look around. Get myself sorted out. Fact is, I'd like to talk, Marcie.'

She was slow to answer him and when she did her voice was thick with tears. 'No sense paying stupid hotel bills,' she said.

'Thank you,' Alec started to say. 'I really—'

'But if you want to talk,' Michael interrupted him, 'then we really do talk. Sort some things out. And to start with, we talk about what happened last night.'

'Last night?' Alec questioned. 'I don't understand.'

'No,' Michael told him quietly. 'Neither do we, Alec, that's the whole problem.'

Alec listened in silence as they rather hesitantly described to him the events of the night before. His first reaction was incredulity. 'Imagination,' he declared. 'Marcie's always—'

'Had too much for my own good. I know.'

'Oh, I didn't mean . . .' Alec said, suddenly contrite.

'Funny sort of imagination, Alec,' Michael reminded him. 'I saw it too. Saw her standing beside the cot as plain as I'm seeing you now. I could see every hair, every tear running down her face. She was real, Alec. Real . . .'

Alec shook his head slowly, trying to work it out. 'And you say she was in the picture.'

Marcie reached into her bag and withdrew the photograph. 'This one,' she said, pointing to the dark-haired woman. 'It was this one, Da.'

He stared thoughtfully at the photograph for a moment, then nodded. 'Yes,' he confirmed, 'that's her. God, I haven't seen this in years. It used to be in a frame, standing on the sideboard in the living room.' He pointed to the figures in turn. 'There's Jack in the striped work shirt, and there's your gran and Alice and that must be Joe right at the end there.' He shook his head. 'I used to know,' he said, 'used to know all their names. Mam still talked about them in those days. Then something changed and it was as if she wanted to forget them all. Rebekkah was suddenly "that woman", and you know Mam, she never did feel the need to explain.'

'Who's Joe?' Marcie asked him.

Alec looked puzzled. 'Oh,' he said, 'of course, you wouldn't know. Joseph Armitage was Jack's brother.'

'His brother!'

Alec nodded. 'Died years ago, so I understand. When I was still in the navy, I think.'

'Jack never talked about him,' Marcie said incredulously. 'Why did Jack never mention him to me?'

Alec sighed. 'There were a lot of things we never talked about,' he said, 'and to be honest, Marcie, I'm not sure there's much I can tell you. I know that's Rebekkah because I vaguely remember being told who everyone in the photo was. Like I said, it used to be framed and standing on the sideboard. But I know almost nothing about her.'

He sighed deeply once more. He seemed drained, as though the events of the day had begun to tell on him.

'I feel like a coward,' he said suddenly, 'just walking out like that. And you,' he looked across at Marcie. 'Why the hell should I expect you to care?'

'I don't know,' Marcie told him, returning his gaze steadily. 'But maybe, if we try hard enough, we can find a reason.'

We found them, the woman and the two men, hiding out on the upper floor. And, in the dust beside the window, marks where the sniper had knelt, looking down into the street. The bodies still lay there, dead and growing cold.

I've asked myself a hundred times, Marcie, why we didn't kill them then and there, and I still don't have the answer clear in my mind. Mills said we should have a trial, but what a farce that was. I don't know why we waited, Birdie, but it felt good, after all the death and killing and pain, to let our anger grow inside and plan the way to end it.

Darkness came and we moved out. Walked for what felt like hours, following Mills. Like a bloodhound, he was, knew where the others'd be almost like he could smell water. And we found them, what was left of our unit, camped out in an olive grove near a water-hole. A tiny village shadowed one side of the oasis, its buildings burnt out and deserted, but there was water there and others like us and it felt like coming home.

'Traitors,' Mills said. It was all he had to say. They were as good as dead.

Chapter Twenty

Alice phoned early on the Friday morning, demanding to know if Alec was there.

Michael, up first, took the call. He parried her questions as politely as he could; lied as convincingly as possible, resorting to half-truths that they had seen Alec but that he had stayed in a hotel somewhere. All of that seemed to take a very long time. Alice didn't question so much as interrogate, her next question forming before Michael had fully replied to the first.

Returning from the hall to the living room, Michael found Alec with Hanna planted in his lap. He was reading to her, making funny voices as the toy mouse squeaked and the big teddy waved his arms. He looked up, slightly embarrassed as Michael came back in.

'She woke up,' he said. 'And Marcie was so tired last night, it seemed a shame to get her out of bed before she had to.'

Michael smiled at him and bent down to take Hanna, who was now reaching out for her father. 'Thanks,' he said, then to Hanna, 'but we've got to wake your momma now, haven't we, sweetness? And I bet you want your breakfast.'

'Is there anything I can do?' Alec asked. He sounded anxious to be of use.

Michael nodded. 'Yeah, I'm sure there is. Always

rushing around like lunes this time of the morning. Oh, and that was Alice, by the way.' He turned towards the bedroom. 'Wanting to know if you were here.'

'What did you tell her?' Alec asked cautiously.

'That you'd gone to a hotel. That we'd seen you, but you'd left and I didn't know where to find you.'

'Thank you,' Alec said, almost fervently. 'I'll go and put the kettle on.'

The breakfast-time activity made Alec feel distinctly out of place. They were so busy, so purposeful. Feeding and dressing the twins, sorting things for the crèche, taking turns to watch the babies whilst the other showered and dressed. Alec did his best to help, but knew he was getting in the way. Finally he opted out and sat down on the old sofa, half hoping that Hanna would come and reclaim her book and her place on his lap.

He watched Marcie as she applied her rather minimal make-up and pinned her hair into something resembling order.

'I thought I'd go flat-hunting,' he said.

'Good idea.'

'Somewhere near to work.'

'Right.'

She turned to check that they had everything they needed in the twins' bag, automatically moving her lipstick out of range as Hanna reached up for it, then casting her glance about the room as though to make some assessment of their readiness.

'This isn't easy, Birdie,' Alec pleaded.

She straightened, looked at him. 'Did you expect it to be? Look, Da, we never were close, not even when I was this age.' She gestured almost angrily at Hanna.

'Jack . . .'

'. . . made it easy for you not to be a parent.'

'It wasn't like that.'

'Wasn't it?' She glanced quickly at her watch, then shook her head. 'Look, Da, we talked last night maybe more than we'd done in my first sixteen years. And I'm prepared to say that's good, you know.' She paused. 'Michael, we should be going now, love. Come on, sweetheart.' She scooped Hanna into her arms and went to persuade Liam away from his toy bricks.

'I'll be going too,' said Alec, lamely.

Marcie turned back to him, her dark eyes deeply troubled and, he thought hopefully, not without sympathy.

'I want us to make up for lost time, Birdie. I want to say I'm sorry.'

Her eyes hardened and for a moment she said nothing, then, as Michael appeared from the bedroom, she spoke. 'We go across to Adele's Friday nights. Come with us if you like, you'll be made welcome.'

Then she turned and headed for the door. Alec cast Michael a puzzled look. 'Adele?'

'My foster mum,' Michael told him. He reached into his pocket and withdrew a door key. 'Spare,' he said. 'Let yourself out when you're ready. OK? Don't forget to close the street door.'

'No. No, I won't,' Alec said, taking the key, feeling

somewhat bemused by this sudden kindness. 'Er, thanks,' he added as Michael followed Marcie and he heard the street door slam.

I remember it was late October and we'd had the first of the frosts. I'd been up in the top field checking on that bay gelding that had gone lame with a bruised tendon. We'd decided to bring him down into the stockyard. The swelling wasn't going down and I'd got a compress ready for it. Hog's lard and rye flour and camphorated wine. God, but it's a funny thing, Birdie, it's the hands that remember these things, not the head. It's the hands and the eyes that remember the measuring and the mixing and the feel of a good poultice. And the heat of it. Not so hot the fat and camphor would blister the skin, but hot enough to get into the cloth and bind well about the hoof.

I'd gone to get him from the top field. Put him out to grass, they'd said. Rest him, but they didn't know. Needed doctoring, poor old fellow. Getting past the work, you see. Too old for it.

I was leading him down, taking it careful along the back road, keeping him slow and easy. And there she was. Standing in the road and waiting for me.

Rebekkah. Black hair shining with those dark red lights dancing in it, though she looked pinched and sick with the cold . . .

*

'You've been avoiding me, Jack.'

'I told you, girl. It's over between us. This time for real, Becky.'

She came closer to him, laid a long slim hand on the rough cloth of his jacket. 'You don't mean that, Jack,' she said. 'You've said it many times before and never meant a word of it. You don't mean it now.'

'I mean it.' He patted her hand gently, squeezing the cold fingers before pushing them aside and tugging gently at the horse's leading rein. 'Walk on.'

'Jack! Jack, I've got to talk to you.'

'Nothing to say, Becky. It's over, I keep telling you that. I'm a married man now.'

She laughed at that. Bitter laughter that seemed to echo. 'That's never stopped you! A half-dozen times or more you've been with me since your wedding night. Disappoint you, did she, Jack?'

He turned sharply, hand raised as though to slap her. She had made to follow him but she stepped back now, her eyes shadowed with hurt.

'No more, Becky. No more! It's got to end and I'm ending it now. It was always crazy and now I've got too much to lose. Much too much.'

'Now?'

'Mary's pregnant,' he told her shortly. 'My wife is pregnant, Becky.'

She stared at him, her cheeks flushing and then growing pale.

'So am I, Jack,' she told him softly.

Chapter Twenty-One

Alec spent the morning trawling estate agents and the small ads in the local papers, managing to find Thursday's editions still in the town centre library. It had been a depressing task, places either too high in rent, or too small, or too far from where he worked . . . Or too close to home. By two he had found three possibles, all, it seemed to him, overpriced. He'd made appointments to view with the agents and signed on at an accommodation agency, a shabby basement office in the backstreets close to the university. It didn't inspire much confidence, but it was something else he could tell Marcie he had done, and it seemed important, somehow, to have positive things to tell her.

It's not easy, he told himself, to know that your daughter thinks you're a complete failure as a father and probably as a human being too.

He caught sight of himself in a shop window as he was leaving the last agent. The reflection startled him. He'd never been tall, but middle-aged thickening around his waist made him look even shorter, even stockier. And did he really brush his hair back over the bald patch quite that obviously? And when, oh when, for Pete's sake, did he go that grey?

Turning away abruptly, Alec tried to remember a time when he had actually felt good about himself.

He was still straining for the memory when he got back to his car. He ought to check on Jack, he decided. Take a chance on Alice and his mother's being there. He drove to the hospice still trying to think of the last really positive feeling he had had about his life. He recaptured the moment as he turned into the hospice car park. The night Marianne had agreed to be his wife. And when he had found one positive time, he was surprised at the others that followed quickly on its tail.

He was smiling as he signed himself in. Still smiling as he walked the length of the ward to Jack's bed, relieved beyond belief to find that his mother and Alice were absent. He sat down beside Jack and took the old man's hand as he had seen Marcie do.

'I've come to see you, Jack,' he said as his father turned to look at him. 'Come to talk to you.'

His father tried to smile, but the dry lips seemed ready to crack with the effort of it. Alec hesitated, his own smile fading as he looked at the old man's face, realized that Jack was much, much worse. Wondered what his mother had said about him and if he had been right to come back.

But it seemed that it was Alec's week for acting impulsively. He leaned forward, resting his elbows on the bed and bending his head close to Jack's. Breathing in the scent of dying and decay, he began to speak.

'I never told you, did I, about Marcie. Really told you about my . . . about my wife, about Marcie's mother. About how we met and about how beautiful she was. How much I loved her, Dad. How much she made me feel alive and wanted and so strong, just because she cared about me. Loved me, wanted to be happy with me. I never told you, did I? You only knew the bad parts, about how she died. How she got so depressed after Marcie was born and how we didn't realize just how serious it was.' He paused, looking intently into Jack's face. 'She drove too fast, Dad, but I've never believed she meant it. Never believed what Mam and Alice tried to push at me, that she'd taken her own life. You didn't know Marianne, Dad. If you had, you'd know it was all lies they made up about her to make them feel better. To make it seem right when they insulted her and I was too damned stupid to tell them no. I loved her, Dad. I don't care what she was or that she had nothing, or even that she went with other men. I loved her and she gave Marcie to me and that's all that matters now. All that really matters now.'

Jack's eyes flickered towards him and he moistened his lips with the tip of his tongue.

'Rebekkah,' he whispered, his voice cracked and arid like a whisper of dry autumn leaves.

It was not long after she'd told me she was pregnant. I knew her husband was away and it was pitch black when I crept round the back of their cottage and scratched on the window.

She'd hardly talk to me at first, was sly and bitter and only let me in for fear I'd make a row.

But I knew I could win her round if I just gave her time. Truth was, I liked the thought of it, two women with my bairns growing inside them. Yes, I have to say, I liked the thought.

She let me sit by the fire for a time, working me hard when I tried to make conversation. But I could tell she felt lonely in that house all on her own and needed someone to comfort her.

She didn't say no when I took her by the hand and led her upstairs, and didn't fuss either when I laid her on the bed and started unfastening her clothes.

Beautiful, she was, and now I knew about the baby I began to see the little changes in her, compared them to those I saw in Mary. Her breasts had grown heavier, the nipples huge and dark against the pale honey of her skin, and her belly was no longer flat. I stroked the slight swelling of it, gliding my hand down between her thighs.

'No, Jack,' she said, but she made no effort to stop me and when she cried afterwards I held her tightly, knowing that was what a woman needed at such a time.

Afterwards, I lit the lamp and set it on the wash-stand, stood behind her, watching her in the mirror while I brushed her black hair. Long slow sweeps of the brush down the length of it until it gleamed in the light.

In school we read a poem about a man who killed his lover with her own long hair, and I twisted Becky's in my hands, twining it about her throat and laughing at her in the mirror whilst I pulled it tight across her neck.

She lifted her hand to cover mine.

'You'd miss me, Jack,' she said, and her voice was sad. 'And I promise you, Jack, kill me and I'll never let

you be free. I'll be there always, even if you can't see me clearly. I'll be there, just off the corner of your eye or in the shadows waiting for you to fall asleep. Watching everything you ever do.'

She said it lightly, showing me I couldn't scare her, but I knew, even then, that she meant the words and I let her black hair fall. I stroked the soft skin of her throat gently with both my hands, watching her in the glass.

Chapter Twenty-Two

Saturday morning was bright and clear. They set off in Alec's car, leaving the twins with Adele and Sophie Lee. It seemed wrong to drag two small children on a longish journey that might well turn out to be a wild goose chase. Anyway, Marcie still felt shaken by the apparition she had seen standing beside the cots. Chasing after this thing, whatever it was, seemed bizarre and risky enough, without having to worry about its effect on her children.

In spite of everything, though, she still felt she had an obligation to Jack. More than that, the image of Rebekkah, standing beside her children's cots, preyed on her mind.

Finding out where Joseph Armitage, Jack's lost brother, was buried. Maybe finding someone who remembered him, had known Jack, even known Rebekkah, seemed their only way of finding the root to Jack's obsession. Adele had offered to have the twins and the agreement was that they would give up their weekend and possibly Monday to the project, Marcie having no work that day and Michael taking the precaution of swapping to the late call at the centre in case they needed the extra time. If they found nothing in that time, then they would consider it a lost cause.

Their journey took them north from the Midlands where Marcie had settled and back into Lincolnshire, where Jack and Mary had lived until just before Alec had been born.

'They moved just after they lost their first baby,' Alec said. 'Mam couldn't seem to rest after that and Jack was offered work so they uprooted and shifted to Harrelton. Been there ever since. Alice came to live with them when I was born. I think Mam was ill for quite a while.'

'I didn't know they'd lost a baby,' Michael said. 'That's really sad.'

Alec nodded. 'She was only a few days old.'

'When did Joe die?' Marcie asked.

Alec shrugged. 'I don't know,' he said. 'I was away for a long time. After I got back, I was told that he'd died, but your gran didn't seem inclined to talk and, well, you know what she's like. I never knew him anyway.'

'Did you never visit?' Michael asked.

'Not that I remember. There were Christmas cards, that sort of thing, but not much other contact. It's as if they wanted to sever all connections with the family. With everything.'

'Didn't that seem a bit odd?' Michael questioned.

'God, no,' Alec said. 'Perfectly normal. I think "keep ourselves to ourselves" was a phrase my mother invented.'

'So, where do we start?' Marcie asked.

'Louth, I think. It's a sizeable town and we take our bearings from there. I know they lived out at Ludford for a while when they first married and that my gran retired to a village called Binbrook. Mam moved back in with her during the war. Has some right horror stories to tell. It was surrounded by airfields, apparently.'

'They called it Bomber County,' Michael put in unexpectedly.

Alec shot him a surprised look through the rear-view mirror.

'Aw, bass, dis nigger boy know history,' Michael drawled at him.

'Sorry,' Alec said and flushed.

'I dare say we'll get used to each other.' Michael laughed.

Marcie shook her head at them. 'So, what are we looking for when we get there?' she asked. 'Someone with a memory like an encyclopaedia?'

'I guess so, Birdie,' Alec told her. 'I guess so.'

Mary was sitting at Jack's bedside.

'Everyone I've ever loved keeps leaving me. Not that there've been that many, Jack. Only, with you, it's like it's happening a second time. I knew about her, you know, but I told myself, Mary, he loves you. What does it matter what's past and gone?

'But it was never the same, was it? Not after our Margaret died. I felt you blamed me in some way for that, never quite forgave me for losing our baby. And when Marcie came to live with us, well, that was it, really, wasn't it? It was as if you didn't have enough love to go round. Never realized, did you, that love isn't sold in pound packages? You don't run out of it just because one person needs so much. There's still plenty left to go round, if you let it.

'And now Alec's gone too. Left us. Both my babies gone, it seems, and you getting ready to go with them.'

'Alec?' Jack's voice was cracked and hoarse.

'He's not here, love. There's only me. Only me.'

'Been dreaming. Long road and my horse . . . lame. Three parts hog's lard. Three parts . . . and camphorated wine . . .'

'It's all right, Jack, you were only dreaming. There've been no horses now, not for years.'

'Must be rye flour, Mary. Rye flour. Soaks up more, ground really fine so it's nearly black.'

'All right, Jack. I'll remember. I'll remember, love.'

'I told her, Mary, but the horse was lame and I couldn't leave him. Up ahead of me, standing there. Hair like soot with the fire dancing on it and I couldn't tell her no.'

'Jack, oh God, Jack, that's enough. Please, love, that's enough.'

She bent forward, her hands covering her face, weeping. Her tears falling on the neat, white linen sheets.

'I remember you,' Jack told her softly. 'Red hair and freckles on your nose and the sound of church bells. Lovely . . . got to be rye flour, promise. Wheat flour just won't do . . .'

Marcie had always thought of Lincolnshire as being flat. She'd been to the east coast a few times, crossing the fens to the seaside resorts, but she had never encountered the ridge of hills with their twisting, switchback roadways that formed the wolds.

'It's beautiful,' she said. 'Really gorgeous.'

'That's Louth, over there. See the church spire? I remember coming for picnics here when I was a little kid. A place called Hubbard's Hills. It's like a country park just on the edge of town. All trees and grass and not much else. Funny, though, I never realized that Mam and Dad came from around here, not for years.'

'Was it a market town?' Michael asked him.

'Hmm, yes. Must have been pretty wealthy too in its day. Let's find somewhere to have coffee then figure out where to start.'

It was ten in the morning and the streets were narrow and packed with pedestrians and too much traffic. Parking was difficult. Eventually they found a small café tucked away in a backstreet and settled themselves at a table by the large window.

Alec sat watching the passersby. His memories of Louth, apart from the quiet times spent in the hills above, were connected with the hustle and bustle of crowds pushing along the narrow streets. He remembered Jack talking about the place. One of the few times he could remember Jack talking freely and happily about his childhood.

'They held the hiring fairs here,' Alec said. 'Twice a year.'

'Hiring fairs?' Marcie asked.

'Most farm labourers were practically itinerant,' Alec said. 'They'd come here with their families and all their bits of possessions and stand in the market place with their . . . I don't know,' he laughed briefly, 'their CV, I suppose, pinned to their jackets. I remember Jack telling me about it. He'd come here with Joe and the uncle they lived with . . .'

It was spring. A year, almost to the week, since our folks had died in the last throes of the flu epidemic that had swept the country after the war. It had taken a few extra years to get itself our way, but in the end it had come north hard enough to take our parents.

This day, we'd gone to Louth with our Uncle William. He had chickens to sell and we'd piled on to the carrier cart, William up front with the drivers, me and Joe in the back. Mack's cart had wound its way from village to village. We were packed in the back with sacks of onions and casks of salted pork, Uncle Will's chickens squawking and fussing in a basket and me and Joe chucked in amongst the lot of it.

It was a warm day for April and we were still well stitched into our winter underwear. It was getting itchy and sweaty, but Aunt Emily wouldn't dream of letting us free of our winter clothes at least until the month end. We wore cord trousers and flannel shirts over the top and our oiled boots, newly hobnailed, which we clattered against the side of the cart, beating time with the horses' hoofs.

This was a special trip. First time we'd seen the hiring fair and the crowds of labourers and their kin vying with each other for work.

By the time we got to the market place and jumped down from the cart it was close to noon and Joe was complaining that he was hungry. The day was warmer, with some real heat in the sun, and I remember scratching and pulling at the thick woollen underwear and wishing that Aunt Em would let us out of it. But even that couldn't take the excitement away. It was a place that seemed made up of sounds and smells. The noise of cattle and fowl and voices announcing what they'd brought with them and the scents of spice and gingerbread all mixed up with the cow shit and the sweat of overwintered bodies.

I remember, we wandered through the narrow streets and crowded alleys, threaded our way across the market, filled with noise and heat and the crush of people. Eating the bits Aunt Em had packed up for us and backhanding the odd bit extra when anyone was careless enough not to be looking our way.

Life was good that day, secure and happy and sunny after a winter of hard graft and bad weather and months before that full of grieving when we'd lost kin.

I felt, and I swear that Joe felt the same, that we were coming out of a long, dark dream and that life was not so bad on that soft spring day.

There was a thing that happened, though, that brought all the pain and trouble back to us with such force.

We'd come to see the hiring fair, but in the interest of all the other things around us we'd almost forgotten that. Then we came upon it in a quiet corner close beside the church and the sight is one I swear I never will forget.

It marked me, Birdie, and I decided then and there

it would never be a part of my life, of my family's life, no matter what I had to do.

They stood there like so many head of cattle, their possessions crowded in a heap around them and their womenfolk and kids keeping to the background, silent and hopeful while their men sold themselves – or so it looked to me. They stood with their names and skills written on card, or scraps of paper, pinned to their jacket fronts for all to read. Stood solid and with as much pride as you could hope such a man could have while the foremen and the farmers and the petty landowners walked along the rows inspecting them. Reading what they had to say, examining their hands and barking questions about their past employ.

I expected, almost, that they'd make the men break into a trot, or that they'd open their mouths and look at their teeth to find their age.

Every so often, one would be called forward and sign his deed of contract, then leave with his new employer and a backward glance at those still left behind.

I know this was just the way of things, Birdie. That it had gone on, twice a year, for maybe hundreds of years. But it seemed to me hard not to feel degraded. That this way of doing things left a man with little worth or honour and I wondered, then, what would happen to those left behind at the end of the day. Where would they go, those who no one claimed? Would they just be swept away with the night's rubbish, like rotten cabbage and broken eggs at the end of a market?

We didn't watch for long, Joe and I. We went away then and tried to return to the excitement we had felt at having the day off. But it would not come back. I dreaded that I had glimpsed my future in those men. Standing with all they owned gathered at their feet, selling themselves to whoever would buy.

'I know it affected him,' Alec said. 'I was never certain what it was that bothered him so much. It was only like going to the job centre.'

Marcie laughed. 'There speaks a man who's been in the same job more years than he can remember,' she said.

Michael looked thoughtful. 'When Sophie Lee was a little girl,' he said, 'she met a woman who'd been born a slave.'

'It's hardly the same thing,' Alec argued, inexplicably uncomfortable with the analogy.

'No,' Michael agreed, 'it's not. But in real terms I wonder how much more choice those men really had. From what I understand, a lot of them were bonded labourers. They had no rights to even leave their employer until their time was up, however badly he treated them. It's not so far from slavery in my book.'

The thought sobered them. By the time they'd finished their coffee they had decided that maybe Louth was not going to be much help.

'They didn't actually live here, then?' Michael asked.

Alec shook his head. 'No, I just thought . . . Well, I guess this is the place I was most familiar with, but it's been years. I'm not sure this is such a good idea.

Binbrook's better. The last address we had for Joe was there.'

They left soon after, drove out past Alec's fondly remembered Hubbard's Hills and on up the switchbacks, the road twisting and turning like a snake across the backbone of hills.

The village of Binbrook, settled in a dip between hills, was quiet and small. They got out of the car, parked beside the walled garden of what looked to be an old manor house and scanned around, wondering where to begin. A couple of teenagers lounged inside the bus shelter, but otherwise the heart of the village seemed deserted. The kids glanced their way, their looks curious but unconcerned, then returned to talking.

Four roads led off a central open area, not quite a village square, more of an elongated triangle. A large pub, the Marquise, stood to the side of the apex. It was boarded up and deserted, Alec noted. The long wall of the manor house gardens ran along one full side, with a butcher's shop between the roads at the base, and other, smaller shops making up the third side.

The place had a prosperous, satisfied look to it that Alec recalled from childhood visits.

'There were two churches here once,' he remembered. 'Two churches and a chapel and at least two pubs. The Plough was the other one, I think.'

'Well, I guess we should look at both churchyards,' Marcie said.

'No need,' Alec told her. 'One burned down a long time ago. There's just St Mary's and St Gabriel's now.'

Michael glanced along the empty roadway, bleached white in the strong sunlight.

'The pub might be a good starting place,' he said, a trifle wistfully, Marcie thought.

'Later, maybe,' she said, smiling. 'We don't even know where to find that yet. We do know where the church is.'

They had passed the church on their way in, a walled graveyard visible to one side.

'We'd get more done if we split up,' she suggested. 'I'll take the shops, you and Michael try the churchyard.'

'All right,' Alec agreed. 'I wonder if it's still in use.'

'Well, you might find someone to tell you. Anyway, Joe died a while ago. Could be it was when he was here.' She flashed a quick smile in their direction and headed off towards the nearest shop.

Alec glanced at Michael. 'I think we're being organized,' he said.

Michael laughed. 'To the churchyard, Watson,' he said.

It did not take them long to realize that Joe wasn't buried there. The modern stones were easily recognizable; they checked the older-looking ones just in case, but there was no sign of a Joseph Armitage anywhere amongst them. They spent much of the remaining time on their knees deciphering moss-covered monuments decorated with the masonic equivalent of copperplate and reading the inscriptions on the airmen's graves, planted in a straight avenue of white behind the church, a reminder of the airfield so close by. Some had not even left their teens, Alec noted, remembering his own time in the forces, and, paradoxically, how happy he had been.

But there was no sign of Joe.

When Marcie appeared an hour later it was obvious from her expression that she had something important to tell. She hurried over to where they stood beside the churchyard's high north wall.

'You've found out something?' Alec questioned excitedly.

Marcie nodded. 'I tried everywhere, but there're quite a lot of new people. You know, been here less than a lifetime and still foreigners. Then I found an old lady at the post office, she overheard me asking the man behind the counter about Joe. Wanted to know why *I* wanted to know. Well, I told her who I was and that we were trying to find out where Joe was buried – made up a story about Jack wanting to be buried with his brother.'

'And?'

'And she thought it was hilarious. They were still having a laugh about it when I left.'

She paused, milking her story for all it was worth.

'And?' Alec asked again.

'Joe isn't dead,' she said. 'He's very old and not very well, but he was still alive two years ago and no one's heard about him being dead, so . . .'

'So where?' Michael demanded.

Alec looked shaken. 'Not dead,' he repeated.

'Lincoln. A sheltered housing place or something.'

'No clues to which one, I suppose? Lincoln must be quite a big place.'

'Something with "woods" in the name, that's all she could remember.'

'Still alive,' Alec said again. 'Why would they lie about something like that?'

Chapter Twenty-Three

I can remember her, Alec, when she was nine years old, how tall she'd grown, all long legs and long black hair. Pretty as a picture. We'd been on the beach all day. She was brown all over, long brown legs, long brown arms and that black hair. She wanted to ride the carousel. Always her favourite. Only horse she ever rode, painted and wooden with blue glass eyes.

Couldn't ever go lame, a horse like that.

Rye flour and camphor and . . . and I'll remember soon . . .

In the back seat of Alec's car, driving towards Lincoln, Marcie read from one of Jack's letters.

> I remember a day, my darling, when you were nine, when we'd been to the seaside.
>
> We'd played on the beach all that day, just you and me. The others had gone off somewhere, sightseeing. But the two of us, well, we'd played and paddled and got wet and dirty and sticky from all the bad things we shouldn't have been eating.
>
> Then your gran and the others came and found

us. Time to go back. Time for tea. You know what a stickler your gran is for time.

Well, I'd promised you a ride on the carousel. We'd picked out the horse. A big white brute painted with red and blue swirls on his flanks and neck and with glassy blue eyes and we made Gran promise that we could go there first.

Then you saw that damned woman. Gypsy Rose something or other, standing on the caravan steps, and you wouldn't be satisfied. Wanted to know your fortune. And your gran, so against all that sort of thing.

'Gypsies,' she said. 'Gypsies.' Wouldn't have you dealing with any gypsies.

Forgets the past, your gran. Rewrites it when it suits. All of us gypsies at one time. Dealers and horse-traders, all the old families. The villages were founded by the gypsy folk. But she doesn't like remembering that, my Mary. Too much of a lady to remember her past. So she changes it to suit.

But, then, I guess we're all a little guilty of that, aren't we, my Birdie?

Anyway, she marched us off, said it was time to go, right there and then. No arguing with your gran when she'd got the bit between her teeth. Not ever.

You never did get to ride the carousel . . .

Marcie blinked the tears away. 'I remember that day,' she said softly.

Always hoped I'd teach you to ride, Birdie. Ride for real. I could see you racing through my dreams on some great white horse, with eyes like blue glass.

I see her in you, Bird, see my Becky. The baby we'd have had if life had been kinder, if I could have found a better way . . . Must be rye flour, Birdie, remember that. Rye flour and camphorated wine and three parts hog fat.

Remembered it, didn't I? Memory in the hands and in the eyes, Birdie. In the hands and in the eyes, even when the words forget how it should go.

They arrived in Lincoln just before one thirty and parked up behind the castle. The early-afternoon sun shone brightly on the massive bulk of the stone walls and slanted through the narrow alleyways leading to the tourist centre around the cathedral square. They wandered, like tourists, admiring the mellowed stone and mish-mash of styles left by centuries of patchwork growth, feeling relaxed but somewhat bemused.

Where to start looking for one old man in an entire city?

Alec took them up on to the city walls. Looking out towards the cathedral, the sun hot on her bare head, Marcie gazed down on the beautiful, muddled roofline of the old city.

'I like this,' Michael said, gazing at the cathedral's twin towers. 'Look at the height of those things.' He glanced at Marcie. 'Think we'll have time to go in?'

Marcie shrugged, lethargic in the afternoon's heat.

'Oh, I should think so,' Alec said. 'I don't know about you pair, but I'm starving.'

They stifled hunger with ice-cream and then walked the rest of the walls, climbing the tower from where prisoners were hanged, the gibbet suspending them out over the walls in full view of the town.

'If you look down there,' Alec pointed, 'there's a pub, called the Strugglers. Offered the best seats in the house for an execution. Jack used to say they laid bets from there on how long the hanged man would keep twitching.' He grimaced as though the thought left a bad taste.

Marcie stared down at the pub sign as he spoke.

'They've changed the sign,' he continued. 'Now it's just somebody struggling with a barrel.'

'Too much reality,' Marcie said. 'Maybe bad for business.'

Alec snorted. 'I doubt it.'

The image of Rebekkah as she had seen her in their flat drifted once more into Marcie's mind, Rebekkah with a rope pulled tight about her throat. Rebekkah weeping over her own lost child.

Finally they climbed the many steps to the Lucy tower, the walled graveyard. Burial place for prisoners executed by hanging from the high tower. Even in death there was no liberty.

Marcie walked slowly between the stark rows. Graves marked with tiny slates, inscribed with no more than the initials of the dead and the year their lives had been ended. The whole overshadowed by a giant, spreading yew.

She shuddered with the cold that seemed to permeate the walled garden even in the heat of the afternoon.

'We're wasting time,' she said at last, squaring her shoulders in a fashion so reminiscent of her grandmother.

Alec nodded. 'Let's find some lunch,' he said, 'and think what we should do.' He shuddered in his turn as they left the stone-walled circle and retraced their steps. 'It's been a shock,' he said at last, 'finding out about Joe. Thrown me, rather.'

Marcie touched his arm. 'Yeah,' she said. 'I know it sounds daft, but I was almost counting on not being able to find anything. I sort of thought that if we tried and failed, well, that would be an end to it.' She looked sideways at him, the unease of her little confession showing on her face.

'I know what you mean,' Alec acknowledged. 'Nothing to let us off the hook now, I suppose. I feel,' he paused, trying to find the words, 'manipulated,' he managed at last. 'Just because one old man is dying and another hasn't. Cheap of me, isn't it?'

'No, Da, not cheap. It's just so hard to understand. Why tell you that his brother's dead? I mean, people lose touch all the time and no one thinks anything of it. They might regret it, but they don't generally lie.'

They walked back through the castle gates and across into the cathedral court. The two men waited for her there while Marcie found a telephone to call Adele. They said little. The afternoon lethargy seemed to have spread and even conversation seemed too much effort.

'There's no one there,' Marcie said when she came back.

'Probably shopping, or Adele's taken them to the park.'

'I had a quick look in the phone book. There're literally dozens of homes and sheltered housing set-ups.'

'Register of electors,' Michael said. 'That's our best bet. If he's been here a couple of years he should be on it.'

'Right! Of course.' She frowned. 'Where do we find that?'

'Police stations, post offices, some of the bigger libraries. It shouldn't be that hard.'

'It's Saturday afternoon,' Alec commented. 'Post offices will probably be closed. We could ask where the nearest library is at the tourist information back near the castle, but maybe the police station would be easier.'

'Though what do we tell them?' Alec worried. 'I mean, surely you can't just walk in and say you want to see the register.'

'Well, you can in theory,' Michael told him, 'but it might be best to have a reason.'

'Why not the truth?' Marcie asked. 'You two really are making this complicated.'

'The truth,' Alec considered. 'Jack is dying and he keeps seeing ghosts. Now he's got other people seeing them too. We want to get rid of them, so we're trying to find Jack's brother, who, until a couple of hours ago, we all thought was dead, in order to get a fix on this ghost so we can make it go away.' He paused. 'That do?'

Marcie laughed at him. 'No. I mean we just say that we're looking for your father's long-lost brother. That they quarrelled and lost touch and now Jack's dying he wants to kiss and make up before it's too late.'

'Flexible view of the truth you have,' Alec commented.

Marcie grinned wickedly. 'I had some very creative teachers.'

At the police station the desk sergeant listened thoughtfully to Marcie's explanation, then stood for a moment regarding them curiously. Alec shifted uncomfortably, suddenly aware of what an odd trio they must seem. He had quite forgotten his own first reaction to Michael. But the tall black man with his tied-back locks and faded jeans was part of his family now and was rather put out by the officer's scrutiny. Marcie was used to second looks. She slipped her hand into Michael's and smiled sweetly. 'We'd be really grateful if you could help us,' she said. 'We've come a long way today and if I could phone home and tell them that we've found Joe, it would be a real weight off my gran's mind.'

The sergeant smiled, and Alec glanced at his daughter, impressed at how glibly the half-truths slid off her tongue.

'Well, I'll see what I can do for you,' he said. 'But it might take a few minutes, all right?'

'Thanks,' Marcie said.

'Couldn't we look through the list ourselves?' Alec asked. 'I mean, we don't want to put you to any trouble.'

'We're computerized, mainly,' the sergeant explained. 'Provided he's filled in his registration forms and he's lived here more than, say, a year, we should be able to track him down for you.'

They waited in the reception area while the officer spoke to someone in an inner office. Waited quite a time longer watching the sergeant deal with a string of queries and complaints, document checks and lost motorists, feeling awkward and out of place, as though somehow they were awaiting judgement.

Eventually, a young WPC came through and handed the sergeant a slip of paper. He looked up at them. 'You're in luck,' he said. 'Sorry it took so long, but it appears the old boy moved earlier in the year and he hasn't been logged on the general register yet.' He gave them the same speculative look as before. 'Would you like me to phone the home for you? Make sure he's still there?'

It looked like the only way he was going to let go of the piece of paper, so Marcie nodded.

'That would be very kind,' Alec said. He stood up abruptly and fished his wallet out of his pocket. 'If you could tell them that Alec Armitage and his daughter and son-in-law would like to see him, I'd be very grateful.'

He laid his wallet open on the counter, to display his driving licence and the passport-size photo on the name tag he wore at work. 'I know you have to be careful,' he said softly. 'We could be anyone. But if you could just phone them.'

The sergeant scrutinized the documents for a moment, then nodded. 'All right, Mr Armitage,' he said. 'You just hold on and I'll give them a call.'

It took time, again, for the call to be put through, for someone in charge to be found to take it, for them to confirm that, yes, Mr Joseph Armitage was a resident at Hill Grove.

Finally the policeman put the phone down and spoke to Alec again. 'Mrs Silverman wants you to go over and see her, then she'll introduce you to Mr Armitage. He's not been well, she doesn't want to shock the old man, so she asks that you let her prepare him.'

'Yes,' Alec nodded. 'That's fine, more than fine.'

The desk sergeant took another sheet of paper, scribbled the address and some directions on it and talked through them, checking that Alec understood.

'Thank you,' Alec said. 'You've been a big help. I thought we were going to have to work our way through the phone book.' He laughed nervously, then waited for Marcie and Michael to follow him out, thanking the officer in their turn.

'God!' he said as he left and walked swiftly away from the big glass doors. 'I hate police stations. Make me feel as though I've committed a crime.' He coloured slightly and glanced at Michael, who looked back, his eyes non-committal.

'Thought I was the one with the right to have a complex,' he said.

Alec laughed again, just as nervously, and got into the car. 'Goes back to when I was about five or six,' he said. 'We still had this local station, couple of streets away from where we lived, it's part of the community rooms now. Anyway, there was this local bobby. Looked like Dixon of Dock Green but he had a voice that would cut steel and a way of talking that put the fear of God into me.'

He shifted into first and began to negotiate his way out of the overcrowded station car park.

'Mam used to threaten me with him. Bit like the bogeyman only far worse. The bogeyman lived miles away; PC Edwards was round in our street twice, maybe three times a day.'

'Sounds like good solid neighbourhood policing,' Marcie commented cynically.

Alec checked the road then pulled out, shifting into gear and driving down towards the lights, the first direction they'd been given.

'Yes, well, your gran, being your gran, she got on just fine with the old bugger. Cups of tea, cake, the works, and when I'd been a bit too much of a handful she'd threaten to call him, get him to lock me in the cells.'

'And did she?' Marcie asked.

'Damned right she did. I'd been playing her up or something. I don't even remember the reason. All I recall is coming home past the station and being dragged inside and her telling this big fat man who scared me so much that he was to lock me in his cell until I said sorry to her.'

Michael laughed, but it was a sound of disgust and disbelief. 'And did he?' he asked.

'Well,' Alec conceded, 'I'm not sure the place even had cells, but he shut me in this little room and left me there. I remember screaming the place down. Pulling on the handle and throwing myself at the wooden door trying to get out. I was convinced she'd just left me there and was never coming back. God, I was scared.'

Marcie stared at him with a mixture of recognition and sympathy. 'How long did she leave you?' she asked.

Alec shook his head. 'Look at those directions again, will you, Marcie? I think it's next left.'

He was silent as Marcie checked the scribbled instructions on the paper and relayed them back to him.

No, he thought, it probably hadn't been long. Ten minutes, maybe, but it had seemed like for ever and the panic had grown worse with every minute. At last he had become hysterical, beating against the walls with his fists, no longer even able to scream as his lungs locked tight and his head began to spin. Suddenly, he had felt the warm spurt of urine soaking the front of his shorts and flowing down his legs, forming a little puddle on the station floor. He had been even more terrified then, fearing his mother's continued anger, fed by the shame that he'd disgraced himself, disgraced her even further.

Alec remembered little more after that. Just the confused images of his own panic and desperation, blurring into a fog of pain, and his mother's voice, hot and angry, as PC Edwards finally opened the door to let him out.

Chapter Twenty-Four

Hill Grove was trying hard to live up to its name. Certainly, it was on the top of a small hill, and whoever owned it seemed to be attempting to construct the grove. Two mature trees in the front garden of the big Victorian house had been joined by younger, newly planted shrubberies and dense, overdressed flower borders. Everything appeared dusty and wilted in the summer heat. The grass was parched as a result of the hosepipe ban and even the brick pathway that led to an impressive black door with brass fittings was bleached and desiccated.

The front door stood slightly open to let what little breeze there was make its way into the hall. There was no one at the reception desk, but a bell sounded as Alec pushed the door wider, and a woman came through from what looked like a dining room; tables laid with check cloths and little vases of flowers could be seen through the open door behind her.

'Can I help you?' she asked, but she gave the impression that she knew already who they were and why they were here.

'I'm Alec Armitage,' Alec said. 'My daughter, Marcie, and my son-in-law, Michael Whitney.'

'Martha Silverman,' the woman said, extending her hand towards Alec. Then, 'I don't mean to be rude, but could you . . .'

'Of course,' Alec said. He produced his wallet once again and identified himself.

Michael reached into the pocket of his jeans and found his pass card for the law centre, giving his picture and his job description. 'You're a legal adviser?' the woman said. 'That must be a fascinating job. Is it like being a solicitor?'

She seemed satisfied then, not really waiting for Michael to reply and passing up on Marcie altogether.

'I'm sorry,' she said, 'but, you see, Joe has always told us that he has no family.'

'My father told me that Joe was dead a long time ago,' Alec said, as though to confirm this. 'They quarrelled, I understand. But Jack's dying now. He's not expected to last much longer and I think, well, I think he wants forgiveness.'

The woman regarded him thoughtfully, then she nodded. 'I told Joe you might be coming,' she said. 'I don't know if he took it all in but he's agreed to see you.'

They followed her out through the back of the house, through what had once been french doors – now widened and with a shallow ramp leading on to a terrace. A further shallow ramp with handrails on either side led down on to a broad, sun-parched lawn. More trees, more flowers, chairs and tables and an elderly man taking practice swings with a golf club and a tethered ball. The rear of the house had been added to, nicely, but with little reference to the original architecture. Two single-storey wings extended its width; living accommodation, Marcie guessed, with level patios running along the full length.

As they stepped on to the lawn a large tabby cat uncurled and stretched and looked up expectantly, then wandered off to find a better place in the sun, its tail in the air.

There was a quietness to Hill Grove, a sense of peaceable decay that both pleased and saddened. There must be, Marcie thought, far worse environments in which to spend your final years, but for all that it was melancholy.

Joe was seated at a small table under the shade of a massive lime tree. He wore a cardigan with leather buttons despite the day's heat, and a bright red Chicago Bulls baseball cap shading his eyes from the late-afternoon sun. A chess set, carved wooden pieces on a wooden board, was placed in front of him and he seemed to be concentrating on a half-finished game.

'Joe,' Martha Silverman said gently. 'These are the people I was telling you about.'

He looked up. It wasn't that their faces were all that alike, but the faded brown eyes that met Marcie's – their gaze curious and alert – could well have been Jack's.

'Joe,' Alec began, 'we've, er, come to . . .'

But Marcie stepped forward, her eyes fixed on the old man's, her hand fumbling inside her bag. Slowly, she removed the photograph of the summer harvest from her bag and laid it in front of him.

Chapter Twenty-Five

They drank tea and ate digestive biscuits, gathered around the tiny table. Alec had helped Mrs Silverman to get more chairs and she had brought the tea and biscuits on a tray, which Joe had insisted be placed on the ground and not on the table. 'I'm in the middle of a game,' he objected.

'You're always in the middle of a game, Joe.' She turned with a confidential air to the others. 'The trouble is, he has no one to play with here. He's beaten everyone who can play and now he says there's no opposition worth the name.'

'Well, there isn't,' he declared irascibly.

'I play,' Michael said.

Joe regarded him thoughtfully. 'Do you?' he said. 'I mean, do you *play*, or do you just know how to move the pieces?'

Michael was regarding the board carefully. He reached behind him and pulled up a chair, sitting down with his eyes still fixed on the board. 'White knight to king's bishop four,' he said, his hand hovering over the board. 'May I?'

Joe's eyes had lighted with sudden interest. 'Go ahead,' he said. 'Well, now. You pour the tea for us, there's a good girl,' he said to Marcie, rubbing his hands together in anticipation and studying the board with deep interest. 'Well, now,' he repeated. 'Looks like we may have ourselves a proper game here.'

Marcie rolled her eyes at Alec, then knelt down beside the tea tray and began to arrange the cups and saucers and pour the tea. Joe seemed almost to have forgotten them. For several minutes they sat in silence, watching the deliberations of the chess players and politely sipping tea. Marcie used the time to take a good look at her great-uncle.

Sitting down, it was hard to tell, but he looked to be about Jack's height and build. His hands were knotted by arthritis, blue veins stood out through the mottled, suntanned skin. His face was weathered with far more lines around the eyes than Jack had managed to collect, but there was a vibrancy in his movements, and especially in the brightness of his eyes and in his smile, that Jack had lacked, not just during his illness but for many years.

She found herself thinking back to her beloved, childhood, Jack. The one who could make the whole world right with a single word. The Jack who had arranged her birthday treats and taken her to the zoo, to the seaside. To see the latest Disney at the pictures. It occurred to her, not for the first time, just how rarely anyone else featured in these memories. Usually, it was just Jack and Bird, walking down the street hand in hand, the man's head bowed to hear the little girl's chatter. Gran and Aunt Alice and even her father had always been distant figures, watching from behind the curtained glass. Lips growing tighter and eyes sadder with the passing years and the exclusiveness of an old man's love.

Marcie looked across at Alec, meeting his eyes, seeing the tiredness in them as if for the first time.

There was so much bitterness in her heart directed at these others who had made her life with Jack less than perfect. She could not forgive them, any of them, Jack included, for all they had done. But she began to wonder, for the first time, just how much less than perfect had she in turn made their relationship with Jack. How much of their lives had Marcie swallowed whole and never realized. Never thought about until now.

Her reverie was interrupted by Joe clearing his throat, about to speak. With his hand still hovering over the board, still assessing his next move, he said, 'So, what have you found me for? Martha spun me some yarn about that brother of mine wanting to make peace, but I don't believe that.'

He made his move swiftly, his twisted hand swooping down with sudden agility and shifting his bishop two squares.

Marcie heard Michael whistle admiringly, but, glancing at the board, could only make a guess at who was ahead.

'What makes you so sure?' she asked him. 'Why shouldn't Jack want to be reconciled with you?'

The old man looked at her, his eyes shadowed beneath the peak of his cap. 'What makes you so sure I want to be reconciled with him?' he asked sharply. 'Believe me, my dear, I could see that so-called brother of mine burning in hell and I wouldn't even give him the grace of pissing on his balls.'

Marcie stared hard at the old man, who'd now turned

his interest back to his game. She looked at Alec; her father's round face wore a shocked expression that matched Marcie's own. Michael was laughing to himself. His eyes were fixed on the board and his face was admirably blank, but there was no mistaking the humour that shook his shoulders and twitched the corners of his mouth.

'I hadn't really thought of that,' Marcie said slowly. 'That you might not want to be contacted, I mean.'

Joe snorted rudely. 'Well, you know now,' he said. He cocked an eyebrow in Marcie's direction. 'And does he want to make peace? I mean, has he actually said so?'

'Well, no,' Marcie admitted. 'Not exactly.'

'So what is this all about, eh? I hear nothing from my so-called family for close on forty years and then three of you turn up out of nowhere and talk like UN peacemakers. I mean, lass,' he said, a smile easing the sternness from his question, 'you got to admit it's a bit of a conundrum.'

Marcie took a deep breath. 'It's a long sort of story, Joe,' she said, uncomfortable with the prefix of 'uncle'. 'I'm not too certain where I should begin.'

'Well,' he told her, the smile getting broader. 'Choose somewhere. If I need to go back a bit then I'll tell you. Be like Alice, begin at the beginning and carry on until you reach the end. Then this pair can help you fill in the gaps. Maybe you could start with how I've got myself a great-niece with a name like Marciella.'

'Italian mother,' she said with a smile. 'She died when I was just a baby and my da brought me home to live with Jack and Gran and Aunt Alice.'

Slowly, hesitantly, and with a great many interruptions from both Alec and Joe, Marcie pieced together the story of how she'd lived with her aunt, father and grandparents. And then the hardest part, trying to explain that Jack, this shadow-Jack who lay in some half-world of his own making, had found no peace in dying.

Instinctively, Marcie had not named the woman that haunted Jack's waking dream. Had kept the details sparse and made no reference to her own nightmares. Joe made no comment at this point, but, watching him, she could see his hands begin to tremble at each move he made on the board, and there was a curious, expectant tension in the set of his shoulders as he bent forward studying the game.

Marcie pushed the photograph towards him once again.

'The woman Jack keeps seeing,' she said. 'I think I know who she is. I know she died a long time ago. My father told me that much.'

Joe leaned back in his chair, his eyes fixed on the board as though still planning his move.

Not sure what to think, but knowing that the old man was deeply disturbed by what she had been saying, Marcie pointed to the woman in the picture.

'That's her,' she said, moving the image so that the dappled light, filtered by the spreading tree, illuminated Rebekkah's face. 'Her name's Rebekkah, Joe. We wondered, maybe. You must have known her. Do you know why Jack's so obsessed? What's eating him so much?'

Joe didn't look at the image she had set before him; instead he reached out and moved his queen, placing her to block the check that would have been Michael's next move.

'Oh, yes, I know her, lass. I know her. You see, Rebekkah was my wife.'

Chapter Twenty-Six

We moved to Naples after Monte Cassino. Days of being pinned down, flat on our bellies in the mud while the world exploded all around us.

Then Naples and the quiet shock of relative peace for a little while. The town clinging to the hillside with views of a calm blue sea and Capri on the horizon, beautiful and grey in the empty distance.

The thing I remember most, Birdie, was the kids. Dozens of the little mites, begging in the streets. There was one little thing, a little girl about six years old with great dark eyes and long black hair. She was just like Becky looked as a child and she had that way with her of looking at you. Young as a baby and old as the first woman ever born, and I knew that she was the one.

Jack watched the child.

He stood in the filthy street between narrow houses. The sky was an unearthly, polished blue and the sun beat down on the tiled roofs and battered, whitewashed walls.

The town might have been beautiful, Jack thought. At a different time and if his mind had not been so full of ugliness and dying. He could see with his eyes the loveliness that might have been there, even though he could not feel it in his heart. And there were signs here and there of the kind of normality that dominates even at the height of war. Someone had grown flowers in a stone jar by a door, and washing hung across the street, bright and clean, blowing upward towards the red-tiled roofs.

And the child, she seemed caught between war and non-war. Dancing her way down the dirty street, hopping and jumping, hopscotch without the numbers chalked upon the floor.

Bright and lovely she was, and untouched. The kind of child that he and Becky might have brought into the world.

But the world of war touched her as totally as it did Jack himself. Sullied the brightness he perceived in her. Earlier, as they had passed by, she had held out her hand and run along beside them. Two words of English she seemed to have by heart: 'Soldier give! Soldier give!'

These marching troops might be her parents' enemy, but her smile was bright and she had learned that few people could resist a pretty child.

They had stopped for a time then, sitting on the broken walls and smoking stubs of cigarettes, waiting to find out where they'd be camped. Jack wasn't sure what made him follow her a few brief steps as she ran back down the hill and disappeared into an alleyway that led towards the harbour.

Staring down at the way she had gone, Jack could see the clearer signs of passing war. Bombed-out buildings and charred ruins, stark and ugly against the clear blue of the sky and sea. And he lost sight of her, the dancing child, lost her amongst the confusion and rubble of broken buildings and blocked roads.

Her image danced in his mind, even as they were called to order and marched on.

And Jack smiled.

Chapter Twenty-Seven

They found bed and breakfast accommodation for the night a few streets away from Joe's home. It looked expensive, Marcie thought, here in this rather select and proper Victorian backwater.

'I'm paying,' Alec informed her abruptly. 'Least I can do.'

They were a little late if they wanted dinner, the woman at reception told them. It really needed to be booked, though she was certain something could be arranged.

Alec shook his head. 'No, we'll just get ourselves tidied up,' he said. 'Then probably go out for a while.'

The woman nodded, took his credit card details and signed them in.

'I'll meet you in the lounge,' Alec said. 'Say forty minutes. Give you time to get yourselves sorted out. Then we'll go and find somewhere to eat.'

Marcie flexed her tired muscles. The day seemed to stretch for ever behind them and she felt extraordinarily tired.

'I must phone Adele,' she said, suddenly pining for her children and wishing herself back at home.

As it happened, both Michael and Alec were ready early. Alec was sitting by the window reading the evening paper when Michael found him. He sat down opposite and gazed out of the window, listening to the soft rustle of pages as Alec read and the clatter, distant and comforting, of the other guests in the dining room.

'Marcie's just getting changed and calling home,' he told Alec. 'I think she plans to call the hospice as well.'

Alec nodded, then put his paper down and folded his hands comfortably in his lap.

'Do you think he killed her?' Alec asked. It hadn't seemed quite polite to ask the old man they'd just taken tea with if he'd killed his wife.

Anyway, the revelation had thrown them off balance.

'I don't know,' Michael said. 'He doesn't look like a murderer . . . but I suppose they don't, do they?'

Michael laughed, then stopped and looked at Alec strangely.

Alec went on.

'That boy I was telling you about. The one that made Marcie pregnant . . .'

Michael held up a hand to silence him. 'I don't want to know, Alec. Marcie told me all she could, long ago. Told me the official line was that he'd been attacked, mugged, probably, and died of hypothermia. She wasn't sure whether or not to believe it . . .'

'That's exactly it, Michael. I want to get this out into the open. All these years I've . . .'

'Then go to a priest. Go to the police. Salve your conscience elsewhere. That's not what I'm here for.' He paused and sighed. 'Look, Alec. I'm going along with this for Marcie. Given time I could even get to like you. But you've got to grow up, Alec. You can't make it better by piling your guilt on to someone else's lap. It's bad enough that Jack's doing that. I don't think we can handle your share as well.'

For a moment Alec was indignant. Then he nodded slowly. 'You're right, of course,' he said. 'But at the moment I don't know what to do.'

'Alec, you've done nothing all these years. A day or so won't make no difference.'

'And when I decide?'

'Decide what?' Marcie asked, coming up behind him.

'How's things?' Michael spoke as she bent to kiss him, covering for Alec's startled look.

'Twins are fine. They all went to the park this afternoon. Sophie Lee, Adele, Kate and her two and Leroy. Must have looked like a coach trip.' She faltered slightly.

'And Jack?'

Marcie shook her head. 'Much worse. They've got him on a morphine pump. He can't last much longer.' She looked helplessly at Michael, and he reached for her hand, gripping it tight.

'Well, then,' he said softly. 'We'd better get this right, hadn't we?'

Alice had stepped out into the hospice garden for a breath of air, leaving Mary alone. The day had been even hotter than expected, without even a breath of wind to stir the treetops or brush against the curtains.

It was eight thirty in the evening. The sky had begun to darken, but not with night blackness. 'There's going to be a storm, Jack,' Mary whispered, bending close to him but keeping her eyes fixed on the gathering clouds billowing iron-grey across the sky. 'You always loved to watch the rain. See the lightning and when the thunder cracked you'd count the seconds. Do you remember, Jack? Do you remember?

'Marcie must have been two years old. Such a tiny little thing, more like a baby doll than a toddler. That night the storm wrecked those climbing roses you loved so much. You held her in the window. Tiny little doll standing on the sill while the rain streamed down so fast that was almost all you could see through the glass. A world viewed through water and bright flashes opening up the sky . . .'

'She'll be scared, Jack, bring her off there.'

'No, she won't, not my Bird. Look at that, my darling, like fireworks. Just like fireworks.'

The child's eyes opened wide. She was trembling, whether with fear or with the chill coming off the glass Mary couldn't tell, but Jack held her tightly, his body pressed close to hers and one arm circling across her small, baby-plump body.

'Lights. Lights, Ganda Jack.'

'Yes, my darling, pretty lights.'

Mary had stepped back from them, watching. Excluded. As a child, Alec had been frightened of the storms. Had hidden under the table or behind a chair and never overcome Jack's disgust of such cowardice.

'Lights,' Marcie said again, small hand reaching out

as though to seize them, bring their brightness into the room.

Jack stroked her gently, his voice soft and full of praise, his face close to her dark curls.

A second small hand reached out for the lightning, the urgency of the child's desire transforming her entire body. She seemed to grow taller, bigger with the strength of it. Jack held her even tighter, his arms circling her as though he could never bear to let the moment go.

As if on cue a massive lightning flash crashed with full violence right outside the window. Mary cried out in fear and leapt instinctively towards her husband and grandchild.

Then she let her hands fall back to her sides and stood, still and despairing, watching them both. The crack of thunder followed swiftly on the lightning's tail and Mary watched, cursing her own despair. Her own unheeded need to love, as the child, hands still raised towards the heavens, laughed aloud.

'Your granddaughter just called,' the nurse told her, startling Mary back to the present.

'Are you all right, love? I didn't mean to make you jump.'

'Yes, yes, I'm fine.'

'I told her you were here, but she was in a payphone and didn't have much change.'

Mary nodded. 'Yes,' she said. 'I see. Thank you.'

She sighed deeply and reached across to take Jack's

bony white hand in her own. 'Even now,' she said softly. 'Even now, she's trying to take you away from me.'

They had found a pizza restaurant and been too tired to look for anything else. They ordered Pizza Margherita with extra toppings and salad from the salad bar. Marcie had eaten half of her salad and was wondering if she could sneak back for a second helping long before the pizza arrived.

'How come you don't get fat, eating the way you do?' Alec asked her.

Marcie shrugged. 'I get hungry. Normal, healthy appetite, that's all.'

'God, I can remember a time when we couldn't get a damn thing down you.'

He broke off, suddenly embarrassed. After the abortion, Marcie had just refused to eat. Even when she'd recovered a little and had gone back to school, she seemed to have no appetite. And then, when she had found out about Patrick Simpson, things had gone from bad to worse. Her emotional outbursts had become daily events. She refused to believe anything any of them said. Would barely even look at Jack, and her appetite had diminished to almost nothing once again.

Finally, she had fainted at school and they had had no choice but to get medical advice. The doctor had diagnosed eating problems, possibly anorexia. Had pressed for the family to let Marcie see a psychiatrist, wanted her to attend a special unit at the local hospital.

Outraged, and for once in harmony, Mary and Jack had refused.

Marcie had grown progressively worse. Underweight, lethargic but for the fierceness of her temper. Bitter. Then there had come the night when she had found the papers Jack had kept hidden in his garden shed. He'd bought and clipped out every report he could find about Patrick Simpson's death. Pasted each account into a scrapbook.

Marcie had brought the book up to the house.

The back door had slammed open, smashing against the kitchen counter. Eyes blazing, more life in her body than she had had in a long, long time, Marcie almost hurled herself through the living room door and threw the book into Jack's lap.

This was not like the time when she had first found out about Patrick Simpson. This time there was no hysteria, no rage, just a quiet despair

'Did you kill him, Jack? Did you? Did you?'

And Jack had stared at her, dumbfounded, as though even to think such a thing was madness.

'No, my Birdie. No, I swear to you. I never laid a hand on him.'

'You're lying to me, Jack, I know you are. Oh, Jack, I don't know what to think about you any more.'

She stood in front of him, dark eyes burning as though she had a fever, not wanting to believe. Begging Jack to explain, to tell her beyond doubt that it wasn't like that. That she could still salvage something of her old life.

Then there was Mary, holding Marcie in a fierce grip, her fingers digging deep into the thin flesh of her arms.

'He did nothing, Marcie, nothing. What do you think you're doing, bursting in here like this? Hysteria, girl, that's what it is.'

'I'm not . . .' Her voice rose as she began to protest. It was all the cue that Mary needed.

She slapped Marcie hard across the face, holding her steady with her other hand.

'I don't believe you,' the girl was whimpering now. 'Don't believe any of you. Oh, Jack, I want to believe.'

The following day Marcie was admitted to hospital. She had wandered into the emergency room in the early hours of the morning, clearly distressed, frozen. Dressed for bed with just a coat around her shoulders despite the bitter cold. She had been close to collapse. The hospital had informed the police, who had in turn contacted her family. Jack and Alec had rushed down, only to find their access denied.

'She doesn't want to see anyone,' they were told. 'You see, Mr Armitage,' the houseman told them carefully, 'your daughter is severely underweight, and possibly in a psychotic state. She's certainly very distressed. It's best if we go along with what she wants, for the moment, at least.'

Alec stared at him. It was the first and only time that anyone had addressed him, and not Jack, when they had talked about what was best for Marcie.

'I want to see her. When can I see her?'

The doctor shook his head. 'I'm sorry, Mr Armitage, but she doesn't want to see you. Any of you, I'm afraid, and we do what's best for our patients.'

Marcie had been sixteen and a half. It was almost a year since Patrick Simpson's death.

'You put yourself in hospital, didn't you?' Alec asked her now. It was something he had wanted to know for a long time. 'I mean, all that stuff about you being anorexic. It was just your way of getting back at us.'

Marcie didn't respond immediately. She stabbed viciously at a piece of new potato, heavy with mayonnaise.

'It got me away from all of you,' Marcie said at last. 'Anorexia, I don't know. Seems to me that's a word that labels a lot of problems and I saw a lot of kids that really couldn't help what they were doing. Me, I didn't want to eat. I didn't want to live. I certainly didn't want to be with any of you. It wasn't about the way I looked, I mean not even superficially about that. I'd given up thinking how I looked by then. It was about, I don't know, about what I didn't want to be.'

She looked across at her father. 'Look, Da, I don't think I'm ready for this now. We've other things to think about. Maybe another time, but not just now. I guess the reason I'm here, now, talking about this at all is because I want to move on. I can't, you know, not with Jack the way he is.' She paused, shook her head as though confused. 'I want to be free, Da. Free of all the things I think I owe the old Jack. The one I loved when I was a little kid. Stuff I owe all of you, I guess.'

Alec nodded slowly. 'Do you still love him?' he asked.

'What do you think? Oh, God, Da, you don't stop loving someone, not really. I've still got most of a lifetime tied up in memories of Jack. Memories of all of you.'

Alec said nothing. He felt that the last part had been added in deference to his feelings and wished it wasn't so. He was about to say more, but Michael, noting the tension in Marcie's voice, moved the conversation on.

'What do you think about Joe?' he asked.

There was silence for a moment, then, 'I think I could like him,' Marcie said.

'Do you think he killed her?'

Marcie shook her head. 'I don't know.'

'Jack always said that Rebekkah was killed by her husband. If Joe was her husband . . .'

'Jack also said that Joe was dead.'

'Well,' Alec went on as their pizza arrived, 'we see him tomorrow. Maybe we'll be able to talk about it then.'

'He plays a damned good game of chess,' Michael said, his voice admiring.

'Oh well, that's all right, then,' Marcie replied.

Michael smiled across at her, his look intimate. Alec watched them, feeling like an outsider. His mind drifted to Marianne, to the two short years they had had together. If she had lived, how would things have been? Would they have always been so happy? Would he always have felt as complete as he had back then?

Or would they have become like Jack and Mary? Disappointed and frustrated by a life that failed to deliver?

He thought of Joe, old and alone with only the memories of a woman long gone. A woman who had died by violence as great as that which had taken Marianne, but far more sinister.

Sighing, eating his meal with little awareness of how

it tasted, Alec thought of Joe as they had last seen him. An old, slightly awkward figure, walking with an ornately twisted stick, making his way across a parched lawn checkered by deep tree-cast shadows.

Alone. Alone for a long time now.

Alec shuddered suddenly as he found himself remembering the old man's face, and in his mind seeing not Joe's eyes but his own gazing back at him.

Chapter Twenty-Eight

It wasn't hard to get away. A few extra cigarettes slipped to the guard and that was it. They knew me. Knew I'd do the same for them some time.

I went back to where I had last seen the child disappear amongst the blasted rubble. It was a test, you see. If I hadn't found her that night, well, that would have been an end to it. Same, if Benny hadn't come back so soon, or that boy hadn't been there . . . A test, just circumstances.

But I knew the child would be there. Knew for certain.

I caught sight of her in the half-light, playing amongst the dirt and bricks and broken tiles, the moonlight bathing her skin so that already she looked ghostlike against the dark sky.

She looked up, scared at first, when she saw me. Then smiled widely as she realized who and what I was and came forward with her hands outstretched and her begging eyes fixed on mine.

I gave her money and the little bit of chocolate I had in my pocket and sat talking to her while she ate it.

Such a pretty little thing. And I could see Rebekkah, watching me all the time, standing in the shadows, just at the limit of my sight. Waiting for me.

I was sorry, you see, Bird, though I'll never get the

chance to tell you. Sorry for what had happened to her, and sorry, most of all, for the child that never got a chance to live. I knew she must be lonely.

So I knew she'd understand when I reached out and tried to smooth the tangle of curls back from the little girl's face, then took the comb from my pocket to ease away the cots. I knew Becky understood when she came closer so that I could see her clearly, and I knew she didn't mean me to stop, even though she held her hands out as though to hold mine still, her shadow blocking out the light as I tightened my grip around the child's throat.

Marcie drove. The roadways were twisting and narrow, at times with an almost alpine drop into deep green valleys.

Much of the road was over-arched with trees and the dappled shift of light through leaves confused Marcie's vision. Shadows took flight at the corner of her eye as the car sped by and she thought of Rebekkah, running with the shadows through the trees. Rebekkah, dancing with the shifting sunlight. Laughing, dreaming her dreams.

Rebekkah, dying in the cold darkness.

They took Joe to Ludford, but he had no wish to stop there, so they went on a mile or two and found a narrow place to park beside a little church set back from the road and sitting atop a bank. The bank was faced by local stone. Once, maybe, the graveyard had sloped down, level with the road, but the years of burials had built it high, and only the wall kept it from washing across the road in the winter storms.

Marcie couldn't guess how old the church was, but its stone was mellow and weathered and the path was shiny with the wear from centuries of feet. The church was locked and they couldn't get inside, but a notice in the porch gave the times of service. One Sunday in three a vicar could be spared for worship here, and this was not one of them.

Joe walked slowly, leaning on his stick. He wandered through the graveyard, Michael holding his arm when the going was hard. Joe pointed out the graves of people he had known or been related to. It was just past mid-morning, but already the day was growing warm. Joe wore the same thick, oatmeal-coloured cardigan with the leather buttons as he had the day before. It was buttoned closed, his only real concession to the heat the Chicago Bulls cap that shielded his eyes from the worst of the sun.

They made their way around to the back of the church. The graveyard, where it faced the road, had been well trimmed and the grass and plants cut back. At the back, the graves looked older and less ordered. Joe pointed to a place to the rear of the walled graveyard where long grass had not yet been cut and where brambles and nettles fought to dominate.

'She's buried there,' he said softly. 'My Becky.'

Michael helped him walk over the uneven grass towards the trees that bordered the graveyard.

'How long since you've been here?' he asked.

'Too long,' Joe told him sadly. He frowned in puzzlement, then shook his head. 'I can't quite remember. She's here somewhere, but I can't see.'

He edged closer to the overgrown foliage, his movements stiff and awkward. His distress that he couldn't pinpoint his wife's grave was serving to make him even more unsteady.

'Stand still,' Michael told him. 'I'll see what I can find.' He began trampling down the nettles, gingerly pulling the brambles aside.

'Should we be doing this?' Alec asked.

'Haven't noticed that you're doing anything,' Joe told him. 'Here, come and let me hold your arm. Here, girl.' He handed his walking stick to Marcie. 'Let him use this. I know she's there, my Becky. I know she's there.'

It took time for Michael and Marcie to clear the undergrowth away and expose the grave. Time in which Joe watched in excited silence and Alec glanced about him, fearful that they might be seen. At last, Marcie uttered a little cry of triumph. 'It's here, Joe!' she called out, as though until that moment she hadn't quite believed it.

She and Michael stood up, their hands covered in scratches from the brambles, their clothes stained with the ripening fruit. They held the long briars and runners aside for Joe to see beneath.

He stared in silence at the low mound of raised earth and at the simple headstone, muddied and stained.

'Read it to me,' he said as though he needed confirmation. Michael knelt, his fingers brushing away the dirt and grime, reading as much with his hand as with his eyes.

> Rebekkah Armitage. Born May 4th 1914. Died February 14th 1937, aged twenty-three. God enfold you in his arms.

He looked up at Joe as though expecting some response, but there was none. The old man's eyes had filled with tears, but he said nothing. Instead he took his stick from Marcie, reclaimed Michael's arm and pointed back the way they had come.

'Take me over there,' he demanded. 'I want to show you something else.'

The something else was a tiny grave marked by an equally tiny stone. The grass was clipped and neat and the headstone cleaned, the words easily visible.

'That's where Mary's child is buried,' he told them. 'It lived long enough to be given baptism. Margaret, they called her. Poor little bugger. Cursed before she was even born.'

'Cursed?' Marcie asked, wondering if he was speaking metaphorically.

Joe nodded sadly. 'They said that was what did it. I weren't here, of course. Locked me up by then, they had.'

Marcie shot a quick glance at her father, but Joe didn't pause in his narrative.

'It was Becky's mother cursed her. 'lizabeth. Took me years to find out what had happened and why she'd got it in for Mary and Jack. Then Jack told me and it started to make sense.'

He paused, shaking his head as if denying some memory. They almost held their breath waiting for him to go on.

Looking down once more at the tiny grave, Marcie frowned. The grass might have been clipped as part of a general measure to keep the front of the graveyard tidy and presentable, but that could not explain everything. Although Margaret died, the inscription said, in 1937, and her parents had long since moved away, fresh flowers in a little vase had been newly placed upon her grave.

Mary sat in Alice's big chair. She had moved it back from the window and sat in shadow, made deeper by the shaft of sunlight streaming through the window into the centre of the room.

She had been too hot, taken off her soft pink cardigan and sat down in the chair, her mind wandering. The cardigan lay in her arms now. She hugged it close, one hand stroking its softness as she rocked gently, singing a lullaby:

When you wake, you will have
all the pretty, little horses . . .

It had been a Sunday. Coming out of church on Jack's arm, the pleats of her best blue dress stretched tight over the swelling of her stomach. The baby kicking and squirming like a fish inside her.

So happy she had been. So very happy.

'Here, it's chilly, love, slip your coat on,' Jack had said. He'd been content lately and so attentive. Now the baby was almost due and the terrible events of the winter could be put aside.

Mary took his arm and they promenaded together down the churchyard path to the little gate, greeting friends, enjoying the watery spring sunshine glinting through the trees.

So happy, at peace, the man she loved beside her, showing her off to everyone. Proud, of her and of the child she carried.

Then out of nowhere she appeared. Elizabeth Lacey. Her black hair in tangles about her face, her clothes disordered and her youngest daughter tugging at her arm, trying to pull her away.

It was as if she owned the moment. The silence that fell all about her was unbroken but for her breathing, heavy and laboured, and her cry of pain as she caught sight of Jack.

'You!' she cried out. 'You. You killed her. You killed my Becky!'

Mary was stunned. She stood still beside Jack, clinging to his arm.

'Away with you, woman,' someone told her. 'Jack hadn't nothing to do with it.'

'You can't blame one brother for what another did, 'lizabeth.'

The vicar stepped forward trying to calm her, summoning help to assist her daughter, Ann, in easing Elizabeth Lacey away.

'She's mad,' Mary said. 'Mad or drunk.'

'Mad, am I?' Elizabeth hurled back at her. 'Drunk, is it? Let me tell you, I buried my child here in this churchyard. Mad with grieving if I'm mad at all. Drunk on it, I am.'

She broke free of those holding her and pointed a finger directly at Mary. 'And I'll tell you this, woman. You'll know what it's like to grieve for a lost one. That child of yours will not draw breath before you're burying it.'

A stunned silence fell once again over the gathered company. Mary stared, shocked. She placed her hands over her swollen belly as though to protect the unborn child.

'Mam, come away, Mam, please.'

People were protesting and trying to intervene.

'That was cruel, Elizabeth. Cruel and undeserved.'

'Mary, it's all right, love. It's like she said, the woman's mad with grief. She doesn't know what she's saying.'

Elizabeth was calmer now. She stood at the centre of a hostile circle, her eyes fixed on Mary.

Then she let Ann lead her away from the crowd, but she turned back towards them, looking over her shoulder, her eyes fixed on Mary's face.

'Mary? Oh, Mary, what is it, love?'

Alice set the tea tray down on the little table and went to her sister-in-law's side.

'Oh, sweetheart, please don't cry. Please don't, I think it's more than I could bear.'

She took her hands and pulled her from the chair and into her arms, folding her tightly.

'Oh, Mary. Mary, I know, my love, I know.' Tears flooded her own eyes then and ran unchecked down her face. Tears Marcie and the men of the house would never have been allowed to see.

'I was thinking about Margaret,' Mary sobbed. 'About my baby.' Her voice trailed off into a thin stream of crying. 'I could have loved her so much, Alice. So much, if there'd been room for me.'

Alice held her tightly, stroking her back and kissing her grey hair. 'I know, love, I know you could,' she said, uncertain if Mary still meant Margaret, or if she spoke of Bird.

'What did Jack tell you?' Marcie asked him at last, when she could bear the waiting no longer.

Joe closed his eyes for a moment. Then opened them again and looked back to where his wife was buried under the deep shadow of the ancient trees.

'About him and Rebekkah,' he said slowly. 'Always knew there was someone but I didn't know who. There were rumours, of course, all over the village about Becky being unfaithful. She had that look about her that men couldn't seem to resist and, God above, but she was beautiful. Black hair and dark eyes that could melt your heart, and skin like honey with the sun on it.'

'And Rebekkah and Jack . . .' Marcie whispered, beginning to understand. Understand a whole lot of things.

'They were lovers,' Joe said. 'And, likely as not, that baby she carried was his.'

'How can you be so certain?' Michael asked him.

'I can count, lad. Because when she got herself pregnant, I'd been away a month or more.'

He shook his head sadly. 'Things were bad. Work wasn't easy to find and I wanted the best for her. Not just a farm worker's wage. Often enough there wasn't even that. And if you couldn't work, you ended up on the parish given a pittance that wouldn't even pay the rent.

'I'd gone away after most of the harvest was brought in. A week or so after that picture you showed me, lass. That was taken early August. I was gone by the end of it. Two months without a break I was away, then I came home for a couple of weeks. She should have told me then. She must have known. But never a word.'

He sighed deeply and stared down at the baby's grave.

'Jack was full of it, how his Mary was in the family way . . . I should have come back at the Christmas, but I'd found a place on a merchantman. They needed unskilled hands. Hard work, long hours. But the pay was good. I came home on February the eighteenth. She'd been away, staying at her mam's since Christmas. Not well, everyone said, she'd seen no one. I went to fetch her from her mother's and then I realized why she'd kept herself hidden. Five months, she must have been, though she wasn't big with it. Barely eaten enough for one, let alone for two, and she could still almost hide it under her winter things.

'Everyone reckoned I must have found out she was pregnant and known that I wasn't its father.'

'And did you kill her?' Marcie asked gently.

Joe turned his gaze back on to her face, his faded brown eyes, so like Jack's, regarding her sadly.

'No, lass, I didn't. And I wouldn't have let on it wasn't mine. They'd have all known. Laughed behind my back for a bit, no doubt. But, you see, I loved her. I didn't care what she'd done. I knew how it was before I wed her. She'd have settled, given time. I knew right from the start that she loved me back. It was just temptation, getting in the way, and with me not there I should think she was lonely.' He shook his head. 'I loved her. I can't explain it away or make excuses for her. I loved her and that's the long and short of it.'

Alec looked quickly away, swallowing hard, his eyes fixed on the tall trees standing black against the summer sky.

'And if you'd found out earlier, about her and Jack?'

'Then they might well have found him hanging in a tree instead of her,' Joe said angrily, his jaw set and tense. 'One thing you've to understand. There's been no love lost between the two of us, Marcie. Right back from when we were kids, Jack was an evil bastard.'

Chapter Twenty-Nine

They took Joe to lunch in a little pub, then drove him back to Hill Grove. Michael spent the afternoon playing chess with him and they talked, but not about Jack and Rebekkah. Mostly, they chatted about the twins – Marcie had photographs of them – about Michael's job. About the dreams he had once had of being a QC. About Alec's time in the navy, and after, when he'd lived and worked in Greece and then in Italy.

Most of this was new to Marcie. 'I picked olives,' he told her. 'I caught fish. I worked two seasons in a taverna and I learned the language.'

Then in Italy he had found a job with a builder, managed to get permits and visas and he had settled, starting as a labourer and learning the trade from the foundations up.

'He restored churches,' Alec said, 'and built schools and houses. Even a railway station. I started off scraping bricks. Finished up doing his accounts.' He laughed. 'I'm not sure how I got from one to the other, it must have taken years, but now . . . it all crowds into a very small yesterday.' He looked across at his daughter, his rather bland face softened by a smile. 'Then I met your mother. Marco Benelli, the man I worked for, his daughter was getting married and Marianne was one of the extra workers they'd hired. And that was it. I followed her around all that night, pestered the life out of her until she agreed to go out with me.'

'I'd never figure you to be that determined,' Marcie said, smiling.

'Once upon a time I must have been,' Alec said quietly.

'So? What happened?' she pressed him, trying to keep her voice light in case he took offence.

'I don't know,' Alec told her wearily. 'I suppose I just gave up when she died. Gave up and came back home and it was all the same, just as if I'd never left.'

Thoresway was a tiny village hidden amongst a nest of hills where Jack and Joe had grown up and where Rebekkah had died.

The village ran along a single street. A few cottages, a church, a school now converted into a house with neat, arched windows, and a couple of larger houses, one of which looked to be the vicarage, half hidden by trees and almost neo-classical in design. It would not, thought Marcie, have been out of place on the set of *Gone with the Wind*.

They parked the car close to where a spring bubbled from beneath the hedges. Marcie reached down and dabbled her fingers in the water. It was cold and clear. Hot from travelling, she plunged both hands up to her wrists in the water, then lifted them to her face, watching the drips course their way down her arms and gather in the folded crook of her elbows.

Alec looked long at her, reminded of the infant daughter he had hardly known.

Joe had drawn a map for them and they walked back through the village, past the cottages and the white-washed house that enclosed a massive mill wheel. Then, turning through a gate at the other end, they trekked across fields up to the remote clump of trees Joe had marked on his rough map.

The hill was steep. Marcie found herself breathless. She thought of Rebekkah, pregnant and desperate, making the same climb. No one could have carried an unconscious woman up here, she told herself. If Rebekkah had been murdered, then it had been done here, on this ridge, with its backdrop of ash trees the only shelter from the open sky.

From the top of the hill, Marcie turned and looked back across the valley. Perspective seemed to be distorted; hills rose opposite and to the sides of them, billowing out, concealing features that could be clearly seen from lower down the slope.

'Down there,' Alec said, 'must be what they call Roman Hole. That's where the gypsies camped, in that hollow.'

'You've been here before?' Marcie asked in surprise.

'Must have been,' Alec confirmed. 'But I was just a child, I think. I have this memory of the place. Of Jack telling me about it and showing me different things, but I didn't connect until I saw the spring.'

Marcie nodded. Michael had gone further up the hill. He stood beside the grove of trees, Joe's sketch map in his hand, looking down towards the millhouse and the reservoir behind it half hidden by a small copse.

'Joe said it was an oak tree.' He frowned slightly. 'I don't know my trees very well, but these look like ash to me.' He glanced at Marcie. 'Sure we've got the right place?'

'Yeah,' she said softly. 'I'm sure.'

He sat himself down on a fallen branch and slipped a Pathfinder map from his pocket, glancing about him to get his bearings.

From the opposite hill, back across the road, two figures in bright clothes came hurtling down on mountain bikes. They didn't pause even as they crossed the road, instead came racing up the track, out of their saddles, heads down, legs pumping and bright clothing flashing in the sunlight. As they came closer Marcie could hear their breathing, laboured and excited, as they neared the top.

She moved aside to let them pass and looked down once more into the little village, noting, with amusement, Alec's anxious half-frown at the two children. She heard her husband ask them about the tree, knowing with a sudden intuition that Michael was sitting on all that remained of it.

Alec had moved closer to her. She half heard the conversation continue between Michael and the boys. They knew all about the 'hanging tree', revelled in the chance to share the story.

'It was her husband that killed her,' one of them said, with the certainty of common knowledge. 'And my granddad says no leaves ever grew on the branch she hanged from ever again.'

'Oh, that's stupid. It must have caught a disease or something,' said his friend.

'My granddad says it's the blood. Like that bit of fence that won't stand down in Roman Hole.'

'Don't talk wet, there's no blood when you hang . . .'

Marcie smiled across at Michael, who was encouraging them to tell him more. A good listener, was Michael, Marcie thought. Alec was speaking again, softly now as though not to attract attention.

'The fence,' he said, 'down at Roman Hole. They killed a child there. A baby.'

'Who did?' Marcie asked him.

'Gypsies, long ago. Some blood feud or other. A child had been murdered, I think, and this was the justice. They killed it and flayed it and hung its skin on the fence. Sent what was left back to its parents.'

He'd not intended the two boys to hear, but, of course, they did.

'My granddad says they skinned it alive. He says the doctor said if there'd been one scrap of skin on it then it would all have grown back. But they left nothing. Skinned it clean like a rabbit.'

'Aw, come off it. It would have died if you just took one bit of skin off. Like people do when they get burned. They lose body fluid,' the other finished triumphantly. He turned to Michael. 'That's right, isn't it?'

Marcie shuddered. 'I remember Jack telling me that,' she said softly. 'Gave me nightmares for weeks. I kept seeing this skin hanging on the fence and the poor child, bundled up like so much meat.'

She smiled wryly. 'For some stupid reason I had this idea it had been posted back through the letterbox. I tried it with my dolls, but only the Barbie would fit.'

Alec held her gaze.

'The dreams sort of changed then. I dreamed of this blood-soaked Barbie doll in the postman's bag, all wrapped up in brown paper and Aunt Alice finding it on the mat one morning and her saying to Gran that she'd forgotten to cancel the butcher's delivery that week.'

'God almighty! You were a strange child,' Alec told her. Then he reached out and touched her hand. 'I had nightmares about it too,' he confessed.

'Someone will see,' Jack whispered. 'For God's sake, Becky, get under the trees. You must be mad following me up here.'

She laughed, her dark eyes sparkling and her long hair lifting in the breeze. Then she sobered, sat down on the ground with her back against the oak and looked thoughtfully at him.

'Don't you ever get tired of sneaking around like this? Why can't we meet out open, Jack?'

'You're mad, Becky! My brother's wife. God! It would be close to murder round here the way our people would see it.'

She sighed and closed her eyes, tipping her head back to look through half-closed lids at the blue arc of sky.

'Do you never want to be away from here?' She

switched her gaze back to him abruptly. 'There's a whole world out there, Jack. So much to see. A whole big world and the two of us never been further than Lincoln.' She spat the word contemptuously.

'I ask you, Jack, what is there here? What future? I'm a wife, I'll one day be a mother. And what for? To breed another generation of farm workers and farm workers' wives.'

'You married Joe, you must have felt something for him.'

'Oh, I did! I do!' Her eyes softened in a way that turned him to water inside. 'He's a good man, that brother of yours, and one day I'll make him see sense and we'll be gone from here.'

Jack laughed out loud. 'If he's so good, then why is it that you're here with me? Joe's weak, always was. He'll never make anything of himself.'

'And you will? What's the great ambition, then? Foreman, maybe? Stockman? That the beginning and end of it, is it, Jack? And as for Joe being weak, when was the last time you took him in a fight?'

Jack looked away, angry with her. They both remembered the last time Jack had put Joe down.

Marcie watched as the two children hurtled back down the hill, yellow and orange streaks disappearing into the distance. Beside her she could feel Alec wince at the speed they were doing.

She moved into the shadow of the other trees, resting her eyes in the gloom, and stared hard at the fallen tree, trying to see where Rebekkah would have hung. Imagining her body, limp and lifeless, tied to the thick branches, her belly swollen. She saw in her mind the woman standing beside the twins' beds, one hand touching her abdomen in a way that both protected and despaired.

Joe said he'd played no part in Rebekkah's death, but he had refused to speak of it further. Marcie didn't blame him. Seeing him in the churchyard she had realized how much pain he still carried with him and she had no wish to add to it. He had convinced her that, whatever the courts might have said, he had not killed his wife.

'So,' Marcie asked herself, 'if Joe didn't kill you, then who?'

Only one name came to mind. One person who had so much to lose and whose conscience clearly burned him now . . .

In the afternoon Alec drove them home. It was a little later than they had intended and Michael decided he ought to go straight to the law centre. Alec took Marcie to collect the children from Adele's.

'She's, er, quite a character, Michael's foster mother,' Alec said, remembering his first meeting with Adele the Friday before.

Marcie nodded. 'One of the strongest women I've ever met,' she said. 'And one of the kindest.'

They arrived as Adele was cooking the evening meal. The kitchen was full of people helping and getting in the way. Liam and Hanna were at the table playing with dough – half of it seemed to be in their hair – and Sophie Lee was helping them to make pastry 'cakes', decorating them with bits of currant and chopped cherries.

They squealed at the sight of Marcie, demanding to be picked up. She hefted them both into her arms, trying vainly to keep the dough out of her own hair, and smothered them in kisses.

'Come along in,' Sophie Lee called out to Alec, who was standing nervously in the doorway. 'Leon, put the kettle on, my love.'

Alec sat down amid the chaos, looked around him with an air of bewilderment. The noise was incredible, everyone talking at once and asking questions and Adele calling out instructions.

'Is Michael not with you?' Leroy asked.

'No, he's gone straight to work.'

'Knives and forks on the table, if you please,' Adele called out. 'And how is your grandfather, Marcie?'

'A lot worse, Adele. They don't expect him to last much longer.'

'But you found the brother . . . ?'

'Oh yes,' Marcie said. 'We found Joe.'

'Stay the night here,' Adele invited. 'What point is there findin' a hotel or sleeping on a lumpy couch when we've got a good bed you can use?'

'Oh, I don't want to put you out,' Alec protested. 'Really.'

But Adele had made up her mind. 'Leroy, will you find clean sheets for me, please?' she said. 'There, now.

There's no bother and you can begin fresh in the morning.'

It was getting late and Alec had to admit that he was tired. They had talked for hours, both over the meal and after. Telling Adele and Sophie Lee about Joe, about the child's grave and about Jack and Rebekkah.

'It sounds like he has a guilty conscience,' Sophie Lee declared of Jack. 'You think he killed this woman who carried his child?'

'I don't know,' Marcie said. 'I don't want to think so, but it would explain so much.'

'I'm going back to Lincoln tomorrow,' Alec said. It was something he had decided as they had been talking. 'I've still got some time and I think we ought to find out what we can.'

'I don't think Joe will tell you much more,' Marcie said, frowning.

'No, maybe not, or at least not yet,' Alec agreed. 'I mean, he's trusted us with a great deal so far and I really don't want to push him. No, I thought I'd find the local newspaper offices, try and get a look at their archives. They're bound to have covered a murder trial.'

'I thought you were looking at a flat tomorrow?'

'Oh, damn, so I was. Well, I'll have to postpone it.'

Marcie looked at him thoughtfully. Alec had changed in these last few days, become more decisive, more in control. Even his manner of speaking was different. And it was odd, she noted, but Jack was no longer 'Dad', or 'my father', but merely Jack, as though he had removed himself in some way even while he chased the old man's interests.

'Why are you doing this?' she asked. 'I mean, there's no reason for you to do anything more.'

'No,' Alec agreed. 'I don't suppose there is. But it's like what you were saying the other night about unfinished business. Whatever happened between Jack and Rebekkah and Joe, and even my mother, it's affected us all ever since. It's embittered and frustrated and made lonely people who shouldn't have been that way.'

'There've been more victims in this than that poor girl and her baby,' Sophie Lee said, nodding sadly.

'Yes,' Alec agreed. 'We've all been victims. Jack and my mother. Joe. Me. Even Marcie. I'm not a superstitious man. I don't, if I'm honest, have the imagination for it. But it's as if Elizabeth Lacey's curse has lasted, right through the decades, and someone has to end it. Turn it back, or whatever it is you do with curses.'

Sophie Lee nodded wisely.

'Something I can't make fit,' Adele said. 'That woman Jack keeps talking about. The woman in the desert. Where does she fit into all these things?'

'I don't know,' Alec admitted. 'I'm afraid I never really listened to Jack when he went on about her. I've only what Marcie's told me.'

'Maybe he's got things confused. Maybe the woman in the desert was just a symbol.'

'I don't know, Birdie. I really don't. I remember him when he came back from the war. I didn't like him, not one little bit. I kept telling my mother to send the horrid man back.' He laughed harshly. 'Mam said he came back changed. He'd seen too much he couldn't forget. Kids begging for scraps, women and old people tortured and dying. And just so much death and destruction. He came back brutal and angry and I hated him. It took me years to realize that it might not have all been his fault. That he just couldn't cope with it, with being back, any more than we could cope with having him.'

Alec drove Marcie to the flat and helped her transfer the sleeping twins from the car and into their beds. It was late – Michael shouldn't be more than a couple of hours at most – but after Alec had gone the flat seemed to Marcie very quiet and terribly lonely.

She tried to watch the television, but nothing held her interest. She felt edgy and nervous, the slightest sounds making her jump. Finally, she went out into the hall, leaving the flat door open so that she could hear the twins, and phoned the hospice.

'There's been no change,' they told her. 'He's still hanging on, but he's barely conscious now.'

Marcie thanked the nurse and replaced the receiver. She stood in the darkened hallway, staring at the patch of light that flooded from her door, and tried to make sense of all the feelings she had about her father and about Jack. Alec seemed to be emerging from the shadows almost as fast as Jack was retreating into them. It was quite a revelation, after all this time, that she could actually like her father.

But what about Jack? What if she found out that Jack had killed Rebekkah?

She wandered back into the flat and, feeling suddenly cold, dug around in her drawer to find a sweater. In the bottom of the drawer was a folder, kept from schooldays, full of letters and cards and notes from friends, song lyrics. Even the odd picture, cut from magazines, of pop stars she'd once admired but whose names she could barely remember now. The usual debris of teenage years. It was the one thing she had taken with her when she had left her grandparents' house that night.

Marcie took it out of the drawer and looked inside. There was one other thing there. The clippings book, with its records of Patrick's death.

'I wanted to believe you, Jack,' she said softly. 'I don't want to think you did this, but now, I just can't be sure.'

'She never came back to us after that night,' Alec said. 'I know she ended up in some kind of hostel after she left the hospital, but that's about all.'

'Then why didn't you ask her?' Michael queried. 'It's no secret, Alec. When we first met she was seventeen and I was in my first year of uni. I'd worked a year before I went, tried to raise a bit of extra cash, so I was getting on for twenty by the time we met.'

Alec smiled wryly. 'You make twenty sound almost ancient,' he said.

Michael laughed. 'Did you never feel that old, Alec? Young enough to do anything and old enough to know the lot?'

'And you feel different now?' Alec asked.

'No, not so much. To be truthful, Alec, I hope I never do.'

He got up and crossed to the coffee maker, poured

them two cups of overbrewed but still warm coffee. 'Why did you come here?' he asked.

Alec took the coffee and stared into the black depths of it.

'Out of milk,' Michael told him. 'Sorry.'

'That's all right.' Alec glanced about him at Michael's tiny office in the law centre. Threadbare carpet, desk that looked like a badly put together flatpack and shelves laden down with books and files. A couple of spare chairs standing in the corner. He'd sat outside in the waiting room until Michael had seen the last of his clients, alone with his thoughts.

'I wanted to know,' he said. 'Where she went to. How you two met. What brought you together.'

'And what else?' Michael asked, his voice very gentle.

'It's about what I said to you the other night,' he said. 'No, it's all right, I'm not going to tell you. Not yet, anyway.'

Michael swirled the cooling coffee in the cup and regarded Alec thoughtfully. 'You must have guessed,' he said, 'that whatever you tell me here is confidential. I may not get to wear the fancy wig, but I don't betray a professional trust.'

'I did guess that. I know you wouldn't, but I can't do that to you. I just wanted to say that you were right. That I have to resolve this one on my own and do what, well, what my conscience tells me to.' He looked across at Michael, the pain in his eyes clear and unassumed. 'I've just begun to find my daughter, Michael, and I know I'm going to lose her again if she finds out what we did.'

Michael said nothing but listened closely, waiting for Alec to collect himself and carry on.

'I never laid a finger on that boy,' Alec said slowly, 'but I could have stopped him dying. I'm a coward, Michael, and for that I'm going to have to pay.'

For a moment the younger man said nothing, then he placed his empty cup on the table and leaned across towards Alec. 'You have to do what you feel is right,' he said. 'But one thing's for sure, you can't live with this any longer. You need to tell someone the truth.'

Jack heard Mary but the effort of showing it was beyond him. He was cocooned in a web of pain and drugs, his outer mind hazy and unresponsive. His inner mind raced and wove and built dreams.

In his dreams, Rebekkah called out to him as men held her down and raped her. Her fingers clutched sand. Her hair was filled with it, and as she struggled, throwing her head from side to side, the sand poured into her mouth, choking her until she could hardly breathe.

Becky! He wanted to call out, to make the dreams go away, but he was trapped inside with them. Inside this dope-filled, pain-racked cage.

'It's all right, Jack,' Mary whispered to him, feeling his restlessness as she clasped his hand, even though his body hardly moved. 'It's all right.'

Chapter Thirty

For more years than he could remember, Joe had kept his childhood in a wooden box tucked beneath his bed.

He bent awkwardly now, hooking it out with his stick and blowing the worst of the dust from its top, his mind resting on the day he had passed with Alec and Marcie and Michael, this strange assortment of family that had suddenly come into his life.

He sat down by the window with the box on his lap and his thoughts shifting to an earlier time and another family, long gone now but never really buried. He sat unmoving, watching through his window as the twilight deepened and all the ghosts Joe had collected in his long life gathered about him.

Finally, when the light beyond his window had faded into nothing, Joe reached out and switched on the blue-shaded lamp, then opened his wooden box.

He hardly needed the light to know the contents. The strange muddle of objects he had treasured when all else had been taken from him.

A photograph of his parents on their wedding day. Still and formal in their Sunday best. His father unsmiling and awkward and, by contrast, the wicked spark of humour in his mother's eyes.

Pressed flowers from his mother's wedding bouquet that his aunt had given him, sent to him in prison just before they'd finally locked him away. Pebbles, worn smooth, that he'd taken from the mill race where the water tumbled them, round and even, good to hold and twist in the hand. He'd kept them close to him, literal touchstones of freedom all the years he'd been confined. And there were the broken toys, cherished from a childhood that had little in the way of playthings.

He sorted through until he found what he was looking for. The only images he had now of his Becky. One staid photograph taken on their wedding day and one much older, taken of the entire school, all thirty or so of them, gathered in the school yard.

Boys in Norfolk jackets, worn and overworn by brothers and cousins before them. Tight collars, buttoned neatly to the throat, and hair severely combed, slicked down with water. And the girls, with their long hair fastened in ribbons, and aprons tied over their dresses to keep them clean. Most of them, Joe thought, would have only had the one dress. If they had a spare and one for Sunday they were considered well ahead of the game. He remembered his aunt washing out her daughter's clothes on a Saturday night after she had gone to bed and putting them to dry before the fire, her Sunday dress already ironed for the morning and her shoes given an extra brush.

They were all there. Himself and Jack, Mary and Alice and Rebekkah. She was standing in the third row, next to Mary and a half-head taller. Both looked directly into the camera, backs ramrod straight, both with silly, overlarge ribbons in their wavy hair. But there the resemblance ended. Mary, already aware of herself and the image she should project to the outside world, capable and stern and unyielding in the face of any adversity. And Rebekkah, lips parted slightly and a look in her eyes as though she questioned the photographer. Sought to look the other way through his long and awkward lens, see the world outside the little valley they inhabited.

'Never satisfied, were you, lass?' Joe said softly. 'I should have done what you wanted when we first wed. Taken you away from there. Emigrated, maybe. Canada or America. Made something for ourselves. But I was stubborn as Jack could be in my own way. Couldn't see it then that there might be a better life somewhere else, or that it could be for the like of us.'

He shook his head sadly at the thought, his gaze drifting from Becky's face and resting now on his brother, standing tall and stern in the back row. Given false height by the bench the boys had perched themselves upon so that they could be more easily seen. The old jacket he was wearing was stretched too tight across his shoulders and his collar did not quite meet where it should. His lips were pressed together in a tight grimace as he tried to look older than his years.

Joe recalled that day as clearly as the one he had just spent with Marcie and the others. It had burned itself into his memory. A point had been reached that day which, Joe felt, had set the pattern for the rest of their lives.

He looked again at the photograph, settling now on the little stretch of road running past the school and on a figure, shadowy and awkward, standing in the field beyond.

Benny.

It had been the last day of Benny's life, but no one had noticed him, standing in the background, gazing at the little group and the stranger come to freeze them all in time.

But, then, no one took much mind of Benny. The photographs had been printed and returned and two weeks had gone by before anyone even noticed he'd gone missing.

Two weeks and the flies had done their work well. They had not even tried to move the body, just dug a fire-break between the shack and the nearest trees and burned the lot to the ground.

The old man had lived in a tiny woodman's shack in the middle of one of the plantations about a mile from the village. The softwoods had been planted twenty years before Joe was born and he would see them felled the following summer. Interplanted with the oak and ash of the native woodland, the cover was thick. Poachers went there, Benny lived there, but that was all.

No one actively liked Benny. The adults tolerated him; he was considered mad but harmless and left alone. He didn't work, he had little to do with village life and he muttered constantly to himself as he walked along. The children laughed at him, following and calling names, and the women said that he was dirty, unclean.

How he kept himself fed and clothed was matter of great debate amongst the village children. Rumour had it that Benny had a treasure hidden somewhere in his dirty shack and even though they knew he fed himself by poaching and begged cast-offs to wear, the rumour was better. Much better.

On the day of the photograph, they had been let out of school early. A half-hour, no more, but it was free time. Not time for work or house chores. It had been Becky, always on the lookout for adventure, who had talked about the treasure.

'We could find it. Hide it till we're grown up, then all go away somewhere.'

'Like where?' Mary had asked disdainfully, but Joe could see the idea excited her.

'Travelling. Like our great-great grandkin used to. Oh, I don't mean like they did, fair to fair like the men do now. I mean across the sea. Maybe America! The New World. We could live there. Make our fortunes.'

Her eyes shone. They learned about America from the 'project readers' they studied in school. Books full of random chapters on history and maps and great battles, mixed without clear order into what were often dry essays. It had always seemed to Joe that these were books of fables. America might be as distant and mythical as the Golden Fleece, but to Becky it was something to be made real.

Her excitement was contagious. For a while they talked and argued. At not yet twelve Mary was already the realist. Becky, a little older, was still the dreamer and the rest vacillated between the two sides. Jack had been unusually silent. It was only after they had parted that he said to Joe, 'We could go and look. I mean . . . you don't know that he hasn't got a treasure hidden . . .'

They had argued about it before dinner while they'd

done their chores. Argued some more at bedtime, but it was clear Jack had made up his mind and equally clear that, as always, Joe would not choose to argue. He was far too afraid of Jack. The late night had found them creeping from the house and out of the village towards the plantation where Benny lived.

Sitting in his little room with the night shut out beyond his window, Joe recalled the tense excitement that had overtaken him then. The night sounds, familiar enough but so much louder this first time out so late without an adult. And the chill rising from the damp ground, making him shiver with more than cold.

They daren't speak much. The slightest noise seemed to carry in the stillness and it was not until they had reached the shelter of the plantation that Jack outlined his plan.

There was a good chance that Benny would be out. Poaching his supper and tomorrow's breakfast. If he was there, in the shack, then Joe would have to make a noise and lure him out.

'Why me?' Joe demanded.

'All right, I'll do it,' Jack stated angrily. 'Then you can be the one to go inside and search the place.'

Joe bit his lip and fell silent then. He was to wait outside, whatever happened, Jack told him. Keep watch and warn him if he heard Benny returning.

There was no sign of Benny. They stood holding their breath and listening for the slightest sound, but only the rising wind in the trees broke the silence. The door creaked as Jack crept inside. Joe watched through the tiny, dirty window as his brother crossed to the rough wooden table in the centre of the room and turned up the wick of the hurricane lamp Benny had left waiting for his return.

Jack looked up then and impatiently waved Joe away from the window. 'Go and keep watch!' he mouthed at him angrily.

Joe retreated into the darkness, reluctant to lose sight of the faint puddle of light spilling through the tiny window. He stood in the shadows, the night sounds growing louder all around him and the rising wind cracking the branches of the tall trees, willing Jack to hurry up and Benny not to return too soon.

Waiting seemed to last for ever and in the end Joe's watching did no good. Jack had intended for him to circle the shack, look all around for Benny's return, but Joe's nerve had failed him. The darkness seemed to grow more dark as he watched that bright flickering light against the window and the more he watched the light and the thicker the dark became the more reluctant Joe was to move.

'He won't come back, he won't come back,' he kept telling himself, willing it to be true.

But Benny did come back, rounding the side of the wooden shack, and the first Joe knew of it the door was opened wide, light spilling out on to the forest floor.

The breath rasping in his throat, Joe ran to the window and peered inside. The room had been torn apart in Jack's efforts to find Benny's treasure. He had thrown his bedding to the floor. Broken the few sticks of furniture Benny owned. Spilled food and water. Broken the wood-pile down and thrown the logs in all directions in his frantic search. And Benny stood there now, close behind the door, his shaggy head turning from side to side taking in the mess and destruction.

The low despairing moan rising from his throat clearly frightened Jack as much as it did Joe. The sound grew louder and Benny's arms began to move in time with the jerking of his head. He seemed, to Joe, to grow larger in the shifting light, his giant shadow thrown upon the wall.

He threw himself at Jack, knocking the boy off balance. Jack shouted something Joe could not make out and struggled to free himself from Benny's grip. Benny was shaking him now. Shaking him fiercely. Benny, throwing his head from side to side, his body following like some jerky marionette. His hands gripping Jack's arms, pinning them to his sides.

Joe stood frozen, knowing that he should help but unable to move.

Then the waiting was over. Jack pulled an arm free and hit out at the old man's head. Just for an instant Benny loosened his grip, but it was enough. Jack had something in his hand, Joe couldn't make out what, but it was a weapon. He hit Benny a glancing blow that sent him reeling.

Get out of there! Joe wanted to scream. Get out of there, we can lose him in the wood. But Jack had no intention of leaving now.

He raised his hands and Joe could see the piece of broken chair he held. He's scared, Joe told himself. He won't do anything, he's just scared.

Then Jack brought the weapon down on Benny's

head, smashing again and again into his head and shoulders until the old man lay still.

Joe stared. His feet were rooted. He couldn't believe what he had seen. Jack frequently got himself into fights, knocked Joe to the ground on a regular basis, but this . . . This was something else.

He was just scared, Joe told himself, didn't know when to stop. Just scared, that was all.

Then Jack turned towards the window as though he had known all along that Joe was standing there and he looked straight into his brother's eyes. A strange expression of exultation lit his face, demonic in the flickering light, and, as Joe watched, he saw his brother smile.

Chapter Thirty-One

I tied the rope, binding it well so the eyelet ran free and there was space enough for the rope to slide.

I can still recall the weight of it, the rope thinner than it should have been and coarser, too. I remember worrying about the way it would move against her skin, grazing the softness of her flesh when it pulled through, but it couldn't be helped. Some things just can't be perfect, can they, Bird?

And her long black hair, so soft as I placed the rope about her neck. The weight of blackness in my hands as I pulled it free so it wouldn't snag against the binding. But I didn't look into her eyes, my hands against the softness of her throat.

Dreaming, Jack remembered the texture of her skin against his hands. The scent of Becky as she lay against him. The child that had been Marcie sleeping in his arms.

The softness of her skin against his hands . . .

Marcie jerked herself out of sleep in sudden panic, her breath caught in her throat.

She gulped air, hungrily, forcing it into her lungs, her hands instinctively lifted to her neck and the marks, almost faded now but which had begun to burn with a new intensity.

The dream, so frightening and so vivid . . . She glanced about, nervously, realizing that she must have fallen asleep on the sofa waiting for Michael to come home.

Her fingers touching the burning places on her neck, Marcie crossed to the mirror. The marks were still there, no worse, visible but hardly more than dark stains on her skin. 'Only a dream,' she told her reflection, then she stiffened as the image of the other woman joined hers in the glass.

'Rebekkah?' She half turned, her eyes fixed on the reflection. She felt no fear this time, only a strange kind of kinship, as though she and the long-dead woman shared a relationship that she couldn't quite define.

Even as she watched, the image faded and by the time she turned fully, it had gone.

But even as she disappeared from view, Marcie had been certain that she saw Rebekkah smile.

Chapter Thirty-Two

Alec left for Lincoln early on Tuesday morning. The phone book gave him the address of the local paper and at ten o'clock he was standing in the reception area.

'You normally need an appointment,' the girl said. But she rang through to the archivist anyway and told him to wait.

An hour later Alec found himself in the records section. 'We're a bit short-staffed,' the archivist, a neat young woman in her early thirties, told him, 'so I'm going to have to leave you to it, I'm afraid.' She ran through the way the drawers were coded, showed him where he'd be most likely to find the relevant information and taught him how to use the microfiche.

Alec sat himself down with a pad and pen and wondered where to begin.

February 1937. He found the right drawer and carried it over to the viewer. February's section was somewhere close to the middle. He pulled out the first slide and put it in the viewer, then frowned in annoyance. He hadn't realized just how much information could be packed on to those little plastic sheets. Impatiently, he began to move it around under the viewer, getting hopelessly lost in the process. Finally he got the hang of it, deciding that he almost had to think backwards to find his position. There was, he guessed after looking at a couple, a complete edition of the paper on each plastic slide. At first it seemed that would make his task easier until he began to check the dates. Nothing seemed to be in order. February the third began the sequence, followed by the sixteenth and then the twelfth and then something from the middle of May.

Sighing, Alec realized that he would have to work his way through the whole month, note down the dates to be sure of not missing any, and hope that there were no absences.

Methodically, he set to work.

After only an hour of staring at the screen, his eyes were aching, but he was beginning to get somewhere. The first reports of Rebekkah's death had appeared and Alec was astonished by what he found.

'Thought you might appreciate a coffee,' the archivist said. 'Getting anywhere?'

'Thanks,' Alec said. 'Yes, I am, actually.' He pointed at the screen. 'This,' he said. 'This is what I'm looking for.'

' "Tragic suicide",' she read. ' "The body of a young woman was discovered this morning in the coppice known locally as Bale's Wood, close to the village of Thoresway." ' She glanced at Alec. 'A suicide? What's your interest, if you don't mind my asking?'

'She was a relative,' Alec told her. 'And I'd always been led to believe it was murder.'

Silently, Alec read through the article. Rebekkah Armitage, aged only twenty-three, had been found by a farm worker. He'd realized that she was dead and that nothing could be done for her and had run back to the closest farm to get help. The reporter gave a sad and graphic account.

> This young woman, pregnant with her first child. Her features now bloated and disfigured by the rope and mercifully hidden from full view by her thick black hair hanging like a curtain over her face. Her dress soaked with the morning dew . . .

The report went on to speak of the shame and tragedy of the event. Of the shock her husband of less than two years had displayed when he had come to the scene, his utter grief and despair. When they had cut the body down he had thrown himself on to it, crying out his wife's name.

'He probably didn't see a damn thing,' the archivist said.

'Sorry?'

'The reporter – probably wasn't even there. Certainly not in time to see the body cut down, even if he'd had a car.'

'I'm not sure I follow . . .'

'We've got so used to on-the-spot reports these days it's hard to remember that a lot of local news was gathered second hand back then. *The Echo* wasn't a massive paper. We probably got most of our news from the local bobbies.' She laughed. 'You read some of this stuff and you can tell a lot of it's not much more than gossip.'

'A murder, though, that would have got more coverage?'

'Well, yes, especially when it came to trial. People

don't change, everyone likes a good murder, but suicide's kind of, I don't know, something that people get all holier than thou over.'

She looked back at the screen. 'Poor thing,' she said. 'And pregnant, too. That's really sad.'

It was another couple of hours – and the archivist had told him she'd have to throw him out while she shut up for lunch – before Alec found the next stage of the story. Three days after Rebekkah Armitage had been found dead, her husband, Joseph Armitage, had been arrested for her murder. Media interest had suddenly hotted up.

Alec returned to *The Echo* immediately after lunch, impatient now to find out why Joe had been arrested. The bare facts were supplied by the first report. Alec remembered what the archivist had told him about hearsay evidence. That seemed to be the case here, the reporter going into great detail about Joe's arrest, despite the fact that the arrest had been made just after dawn as though there had been some need for secrecy.

The arrest had not been made easily. Despite the earliness of the hour, Joe had been awake and partly dressed and he had tried to run. 'A sure and certain indicator of his guilt,' the reporter had intoned, causing Alec a moment's pause. He remembered Joe as he was now, an old man with a lifetime of regrets, living out his final days quietly and peaceably. Like Marcie, he couldn't perceive of Joe as capable of killing in cold blood a woman and an unborn child. But maybe in a fit of rage?

Alec shook his head. Somehow, that didn't seem to fit. People got stabbed or shot or even – he swallowed nervously – kicked to death when their assailant was enraged. Did they really get themselves hung, from an oak tree in the middle of an open, hill-top field?

He scanned the report again, aware that at this stage there was no indicator of why Joe had been accused.

The police had come to Joe's cottage just after five. Three officers from the local constabulary based at Louth, the local officer, a part-timer, who did the job when he wasn't tending to his farm, and a half-dozen or so other men, dragged from their beds to assist.

It seemed like a large number to arrest just one man.

He read on. The reporter obviously fancied himself as more than just a local hack. He'd given life and soul to purple prose. Alec could almost imagine him beating his breast and declaiming his right to preach the truth.

> They came upon the cottage just as the first light of dawn was breaking. There were ten men in all, their grim faces lit by the lanterns they carried and the torches of the constables. They had been warned that Joseph Armitage might not let himself be taken easily and his reputation locally as a fighter, both inside and outside of the ring, led them all to be nervous of the task the law had appointed for them.

They had approached the cottage from both front and rear, two officers and an unnamed man climbing over the wall and into the cottage garden. A light had been on in one of the downstairs rooms. Joe, maybe unable to sleep, or, just as likely, getting himself ready for work.

He would not, Alec guessed, be a man willing to sit inside his house and grieve. He'd be far more likely to solve things by working. By keeping busy . . .

The local constable hammered on the door. 'Open up, Joe, we know you're there, open up now.'

There was no response from inside the cottage. The light burned steadily and, looking through the kitchen window, they could see a hurricane lamp in the centre of the table. But there was no sign of Joseph Armitage.

'Force the door.'

Two men hurled their combined weight against the front door. It was old but very thick and still fastened with a locking bar on the other side. Their first attempt made a loud noise, bruised arms and shoulders but had no perceptible effect. They tried again, the local constable shouting at the men in the cottage garden to be sure to be ready in case Joe made a break for it out the back way.

Unseen by them, Joe crouched low on the upstairs sill, looking down at the men below. The room behind him was in darkness.

Further down the road, he could see lights coming on, people opening their doors to see what all the noise was about. They'd be in the street next, ready to assist in case the felon should try to escape, he shouldn't wonder. All ready to do their bit for law and order . . .

The rumours had been spreading almost from the moment he'd come back – before, most likely – and at first he'd been the object of both village sympathy and ridicule. A child could have counted the months and known the infant Becky carried wasn't his. It was a tragedy. It was a joke, it was something everyone waited with bated breath to see resolved.

And then they'd found her dead. Killed by her own hand and taking the life of her unborn baby at the same stroke.

There was little to laugh over any more. No one knew what to say to him or what to do. He'd felt their fear and their confusion even as they offered him kindness. It was a small village, hard to cross the road to avoid another's pain, or escape the inadequacy of your own sympathies . . . but there were many that had done their best to try.

He'd heard them talking.

'It's a mercy, really . . .'

'Yes, but that poor little bairn.'

'Always the same, she was, all over the men. What Joe thought he was doing when he married her, Lord alone knows . . .'

And then the winds had changed direction. The rumours of another sort had begun and Joe had found himself shunned, the subject of questioning glances.

At first he hadn't noticed. Had been too wrapped up in his own thoughts to listen close to what rumours they were spreading. What guilt he'd been made to carry.

It had been Jack who had taken him aside and told him.

'They're saying you killed her, Joe. Saying there's a lump on the side of her head the size of a pigeon's egg.

That she was unconscious before . . . before, you know . . .'

'Before I strung her up!' Joe asked him angrily. 'God as my witness, Jack, I never laid a hand on her.'

Jack had nodded, patted his shoulder, but Joe could see the doubt even in his brother's eyes.

'You think I did it, don't you? Christ! You think I did it.'

'No, Joe, no, of course I don't, but there's plenty that will. Plenty. Maybe you should leave for a bit, go away. I've got a bit of money put away for when the baby arrives, but we'll give it to you. Best you go away.'

'No. I'm not running. If they've got something to say, something to charge me with, then let them come to me and say it. I'm ready for them.'

But that had been yesterday, when he'd been certain the rumours would blow themselves out. He'd been unable to comprehend how anyone could really think that he could hurt Rebekkah. Now, he was crouched on his bedroom windowsill, the bed he had shared with her taking up most of the tiny room behind him. The memories of her, of her laughter, of her love, the scent of her still clinging to the fabric of their home. Joe looked down at the men trying to break down his door and knew that they believed him guilty.

He knew he couldn't wait, he had to run, innocent or guilty. And the truth was that Joe wasn't certain any more just which was which. But he couldn't stay here. He had to run.

His cottage was the end one of three. To the right was a stone wall enclosing the side of his garden. Beyond that, fields and open space. Places to hide. Then he'd manage, somehow, to get to Jack. Ask him for the money. Ask him for help to get away. The window was not that high, the stone-built cottage being squat and settled into the ground, and it was set low in the upper wall above a supporting lintel.

And Joe was desperate.

He slipped the catch, balanced on the low sill, then, holding tight, lowered himself down and pushed off from the wall. Jumped almost over the heads of those still hammering at his door.

Pain in his ankle shot through his leg as he hit the ground, but it was nothing compared to his need to run. He pushed himself on, tearing down the road and towards the fields, but they were close behind. He could hear them, yelling and crying out. The hunt was on.

He fought as they came down on him. Felt the satisfying crunch as his fist met bone and was aware that his pursuers drew back. Confining him, but wary now. One man on the floor, with his hands covering a bloody face. Memories of the fights he'd won in his mind as he circled as best he could on his injured leg. His anger and grief fuelling the adrenaline that kept him on his feet.

'Come and take me then, ya bastards! Come and fucking get me!'

He hit out again as someone made a play for him, but it was only a feint meant to draw him on and the blow fell short, opening him up and throwing his balance for the merest instant. It was all they needed. Joe fell under the combined weight of three men, going down hard, his face grinding into the dirt as they dragged his hands behind his back and pinioned his arms tight.

'You'll fucking hang for this,' someone was saying to him, his voice muffled as his hands tried to divert the blood dripping from his nose.

'Oh, Becky,' Joe whispered. 'Oh, Becky, Becky. Why?'

Alec read the notes he had made out to them over the phone. Michael and Marcie huddled close, sharing the receiver, listening to the bare bones of the account Alec had managed to put down.

'Poor Joe,' Marcie said softly when he had finished. 'They'd found him guilty even before the trial. Have you talked to him, Da?'

'No, not yet. I'll try to go tomorrow. I've been at the newspaper offices all day. Finished when they finally chucked me out about an hour ago.'

'I saw her again,' Marcie told him. 'Rebekkah, I mean. She was here in the flat.'

'Are you all right?'

'Yes, yes. I'm fine. I had a bad dream and woke up with a real fright and . . . well . . . there she was. But the funny thing is, Da, I wasn't scared any more. Just sad for her, that was all.'

Michael hugged her to him. 'I wish we could help out,' he told Alec. 'I've switched shifts again for Friday, so we could maybe come over to Lincoln late afternoon.'

'That would be great, we'll take Joe out again. But look, I'll be back tomorrow night anyway and we'll talk about it then.'

'You want the sofa?'

'Thank you, but no. I'm still getting the lumps out of my back from the last time. Er, Adele's offered me a bed. I've told her thank you.' He paused awkwardly for a moment, then said, 'She's a nice lady, your Adele. Have you phoned the hospice?'

'Yes,' Michael told him. 'No change, Alec. I get the impression they're amazed he's hung on this long.'

'Right,' Alec replied. 'Well, I'll see you tomorrow night. Um, Marcie, kiss the babies for me, you know . . .'

He rang off then, leaving Marcie a little bemused.

'I want to like him,' she said. 'I *do* like him. There's just so much . . . I don't know, so much rubbish I've got to wade through.'

'I think he knows that,' Michael told her. 'I think there's a lot of his own dross he has to get rid of as well, you know. A lot of things he's not proud of.'

Marcie looked at him thoughtfully, then nodded. 'What is it they say in AA?' she asked. 'One day at a time?'

Joe ran, terrified of the look on Jack's face.

His only thought was that he had to get away. Hide before Jack turned on him.

Twice he fell, scraping his knees painfully on concealed branches. Twigs scratched at his face and tore across his eyes, dragged at his hair. In his mind it was Jack grabbing at him, pulling him down, grasping at his hair and clothes.

Jack trying to murder him.

He had no memory of fleeing Benny's shack, of leaving the wood or running back towards the village. Only the thought in his mind that he had to hide and that he dare not go back home.

The white shape of the wheelhouse loomed out of the darkness and in a moment Joe had wrenched the door open and was inside, his feet scrabbling across the narrow ledge behind the wheel and struggling to squeeze his body into the cramped space on the far side, the tiny work ledge used for maintenance.

He lay down on the ledge, willing himself small, struggling to control his breathing though his lungs burned and his throat was raw.

Joe closed his eyes, his body aching with shock. A little later he thought he heard Jack, his footsteps soft and steady, padding along the verge. He heard Jack's voice whispering his name before he passed by on his way home. But the way his mind was screaming with fear and pain it could have been a dog barking in the night. Or the wind, sounding through the wooden roof of the wheelhouse. Not his brother's voice at all.

Morning came, forcing itself through the cracks and under Joe's tight-closed eyes. He realized he must have fallen asleep despite his fear.

He had no idea of the time, but, since it was light, there would be people up and getting ready for work and Joe knew he had to move fast if he was to get away.

He squeezed his way back behind the wheel and pushed the door open, blinking in the sunlight, his eyes unfocused and his mind still confused. His uncle's roar brought him back to the present and a hand grabbing at his arms, fingers digging deep enough to bruise, made him yelp in pain.

'Stay out all night! Sneak out like a little thief and worry your aunt half to death! What do you think she thought when she went to wake you and there was no one there? I'll teach you what she thought.'

The beating was bad, but Joe had endured worse and he took it bravely, biting back the tears and apologizing to his uncle and his aunt for causing them distress. Clearly, they had put it down to some childish prank.

It was clear too that they had no notion Jack had been with Joe that night.

Glancing sideways under the shadow of his lashes, Joe could see his brother smirking at him from across the room.

Wednesday saw Alec back at the archive. The story of Rebekkah's death had remained in the news on an almost daily basis for the next ten days. Mostly a rehashing of events. Speculations in advance of the trial. Learned résumés from those who claimed to know both parties of what must have happened on the day Rebekkah died.

Items had been removed from the house that might have been used to strike Rebekkah. Common objects – pokers, rolling pins, a stone soda bottle. Things that could have been found anywhere. Others suggested that it must have been a blow from a fist or even a branch, citing the distance from the house to the hanging tree. A long way for even a strong man to carry an unconscious woman.

Alec thought about the loneliness of the spot. If Joe, if *someone*, had killed her – if Jack had struck that final blow, a thought he found unpleasant but, after Patrick Simpson, terribly possible – it would have been struck high on that lonely windblown hill. Not down in the valley where they would have been seen, or their raised voices overheard.

Joe and Becky had quarrelled. There were witnesses in plenty to that. But not on the day she'd died. When Joe had gone to his mother-in-law's house at Ludford and brought Rebekkah back to their cottage, her ill-kept secret had been impossible to keep hidden any more. They had quarrelled then, many people testified to that. But the next day Joe had been seen leaving the house early in the morning to work with Jack on the farm. From Rebekkah, even though many had knocked on her door, there had been only silence.

The morning after, she was dead.

Why, the paper asked, if Joe was innocent, why didn't he report his wife missing when he returned from work the night before? Was it, as he said, that he thought she had gone back to her mother's? That was why he had gone to Ludford that night, returning too late to continue his search.

The coverage grew less as nothing new was revealed. The trial date was set for almost a month distant and interest, though intense, could only be sustained for so long.

Alec moved his search to the trial date, then found himself backtracking again as something quite macabre turned up.

> Dr Fielding was asked by the preliminary hearing to ascertain the exact age of the child, or at least as close as such a judgement could be made. The doctor in question was also responsible for conducting the autopsy on the mother's body. It was Dr Fielding who discovered the large bruise at the side of Mrs Armitage's head that he believes at the least rendered her unconscious and unable to struggle when, it is alleged, her husband hanged her from the oak in Bale's Wood.

'Alleged,' Alec laughed to himself. Getting all legal and cautious, are we now?

> It is stated for the record that Mrs Armitage was underweight for a woman between the twentieth and twenty-fifth weeks of pregnancy and that it was impossible to tell from an external examination the exact state of advancement of the foetus. The doctor therefore undertook to remove the foetus from its mother's womb, to assess its maturity and to preserve it in case it should be required as evidence. The Prosecution's case hinges on the assumption that the murder was provoked by evidence of infidelity on the part of Mrs Armitage.
>
> This procedure was duly carried out, but was not at the time made public knowledge.
>
> On the evening of the twenty-sixth of March, the evening that this paper described this rather unfortunate necessity in its columns, person or persons unknown broke into Dr Fielding's surgery

> and from there gained access to his laboratory where the preserved remains of the foetus were stored. The doctor's laboratory was vandalised and many valuable items of experimental equipment smashed beyond use. Several preserved samples were stolen, including the unfortunate infant.
>
> It should be noted that the body of Mrs Armitage, which had been preserved for evidence in the ice house of the Stafford Hotel, is now being kept under guard.

It was, thought Alec, an extraordinary twist. Who would want to steal Rebekkah's child? And what else was taken? The report had spoken of several other preserved samples. He searched until in an edition two days later he found reference to them . . .

Dr Thomas Fielding swept broken glass from the Turkey carpet that covered his laboratory floor. Laboratory was too grand a word for a room that held books and microscopes and assorted samples pickled in jars on high shelves. But it was the way he thought about it and he tried always to work within the parameters of science. His search for knowledge was genuine and he was deeply upset by the scale of the vandalism. Glass vessels he had to order specially from London, often having to wait for weeks until they were delivered, smashed into tiny pieces and thrown on to the floor.

The family had been eating their evening meal at the time of the attack. He knew that, because he had been working until just before and returned immediately after. His laboratory was built, like the surgery, as an addition to the main house, separated by several walls and rooms from the dining room. They had heard nothing.

'You can take the rug now, Millie. Shake it carefully, though – there may be fragments caught up in the threads.'

'Yes, sir,' she replied, averting her eyes carefully from the tiers of preserved tissue, of tapeworms and tumours and animal remains stacked about the room.

She made her escape swiftly. Fielding rarely allowed the servants into this room and they were distinctly glad of it, he knew.

A polite cough made him turn. 'Ah, Sergeant Willis. Come in.'

Willis, a thick-set man with a music-hall moustache, stepped through the door and looked about him with wary interest, his hands behind his back as though he was afraid of knocking something over.

'That list, sir, you said you should have some idea by now of what else was taken.'

'Ah, yes. I've taken an inventory, but I don't think I've anything to add. Just the three jars.' He laughed grimly. 'I don't think whoever broke in here knew quite what they were looking for,' he said. 'There were three preserved samples: the foetus you're interested in; another from a miscarriage of a slightly earlier maturity, about twenty weeks. She died, poor woman. Pauper's grave – it was a useful teaching aid.'

The sergeant nodded gravely.

'The other was the embryo of a pig.'

'A pig, sir?'

Fielding nodded. 'Bears a strong resemblance at an early stage,' he said. 'Though by twenty-five weeks, of course, the foetus of a human looks human. Very un-porcine. My guess, sergeant, was that they took anything that had an umbilical cord and intended to sort out what was what later.'

'I see, sir,' he said, his large moustache twisting as he sought to keep the distaste from curling his lips. He found this cold discussion of what was, for him, the remains of a child, very unpleasant.

'They were in a hurry, I expect,' Fielding added.

'Not in too much of a hurry that they couldn't spare time to wreck the place.'

'No,' Fielding said heavily. 'That's why I think there must have been two of them. Anyway, the jars are heavy. Three would have been cumbersome to say the least. No. My guess is that you're looking for two people here. Though what the hell motive they might have is beyond me, Sergeant. The evidence has already been filed.'

'It could be the criminals didn't know that, sir.'

Three samples, Alec thought. He had only the most basic idea himself of the development of a twenty-five-week foetus. Would it look like a baby?

He thought back to recent hospital documentaries he had seen. There had been babies in a special unit that had been born at twenty-four weeks. And others at twenty-six. Even the slightly older ones had been fragile, wizened little things, with transparent skin and faces like aged monkeys. But yes, they had looked like babies.

It was puzzling. Had the thieves just taken anything that looked vaguely human? He shuddered slightly.

And then he thought of the teenage Marcie and the child she had been carrying.

Alec felt he had to get out. He packed away quickly, putting the film back in order and sliding the drawer away. He said goodbye to the archivist and left the building as quickly as he could.

Once out in the strong sunshine he felt better, more able to rationalize.

'I'm sorry,' he told his daughter, speaking out loud to her even though she was many miles away. 'I'm so sorry.'

The beating didn't stop him being sent to school. Joe walked in silence behind Jack, pretending Jack wasn't there, trying not to think about his bruises or the soreness of his backside.

He was still in shock from the night before, but an awareness was dawning that Jack would not let him off lightly. He had to act first, and make his actions good.

His chance came at lunchtime, when the class had gathered in the school yard. Jack was ready for him, as keyed up as Joe was himself. It took little goading to provoke him into fighting.

Within minutes a crowd had formed, arms linked to keep the fighters inside. The brothers were both known to be scrappers, but Jack, the elder and heavier, had never lost to Joe. Still, it might be a good fight . . .

The boys faced each other, taking a measure they already knew, feinting and tapping, goading the other to throw the first punch.

Deliberately, Joe waited, leading Jack on, pulling him around the circle until his anger made him strike. Joe took the first hit square across the side of the head and nearly fell under it, but he'd been ready, knowing Jack's way of fighting, and as he came up he hit Jack square on the point of his chin, the entire force of his body behind the punch – and the force of his fear and hatred following it through.

Jack fell like a pole-axed pig and Joe, his anger spent and his strength suddenly gone, fell beside him.

His uncle beat him again that night. Beat them both for fighting in the school yard, but Joe, lying supperless and aching in his bed, the split knuckles on his right hand heavily bandaged, knew it was worth every bruise.

It was not the last time they fought, but Joe had got the victory he wanted. The night of Benny's death was never mentioned between them, not even when his body was found.

Joe had earned his brother's respect, for a time . . .

Chapter Thirty-Three

'I read about you,' Alec told Joe. 'Back issues of *The Echo*. Quite a celebrity for a while.' He laughed nervously.

Joe eyed him thoughtfully, then reached for the metal teapot and poured for both of them.

'And what conclusions have you come to, then?' he asked. 'Is Joe Armitage guilty of murder or no?'

Alec took the proffered cup. His hands were shaking and he slopped tea into the saucer.

'Blast!'

'Nervous, aren't we?' Joe observed. 'Worried I've spiked your tea, Alec?' He chuckled wickedly, then sobered. 'So, Alec, did I do it?'

'Did you?' Alec shook his head. 'No, I don't believe you did, Joe. I think that maybe, in a fit of anger, you could kill. But I don't believe you killed your wife.'

He looked across at his uncle as though asking for confirmation.

Joe gave him none but busied himself rearranging the tea things on the aluminium tray.

'You tried to run away,' Alec went on. 'I mean, I don't understand. Why did you try to run away?'

'Bastards had decided I was guilty,' he said. 'Wasn't so sure by then they weren't right. I mean, had I driven her to it or summat? She were a high-strung lass, my Becky.'

Alec gazed at him sadly. Joe's voice was thick with emotion and the fall into dialect seemed evidence of his grieving.

'The lump on her head . . .' Alec pursued. 'They think she was struck first.'

'Ay, I know what they say. But I never hit her, Alec, and I never put that rope around her neck either.' He shook his head. 'I was there, remember. I was there listening at the trial to what they said about me. What they claimed about me and Becky.'

'And they found you guilty.'

Joe nodded slowly. 'Found me guilty and locked me away. But I didn't hang, though there was plenty of folk thought I should. The judge thought there was reasonable doubt. Allowed my lawyer to plead it was manslaughter. Or didn't your precious newspaper tell you that?'

'I didn't read that far,' Alec told him. 'Not yet.'

Joe sighed, then drained his cup and poured himself another before speaking. Alec glanced around the little room that Joe lived in at Hill Grove. Small and neat and tidy and almost devoid of personal possessions. Almost.

'The photo,' Alec pointed. A picture of Marcie's children in swimsuits, playing in an inflatable paddling pool, was propped up against the bedside lamp.

Joe's eyes softened. 'In the post this morning,' he said proudly. 'She said she'd send me one, but I didn't think she would.'

'She's a good girl,' Alec said, as though speaking of

Marcie as a child. The child he felt he had never really known.

'I let my lawyer make stuff up about what might have gone on. Present it as though it was truth,' Joe said. 'And I wasn't called to the stand, so I didn't have to lie. I was past caring then. Wanted to die, but they said no. I shouldn't die for something they weren't certain I'd done.'

'Then why not just acquit you?'

'Circumstantial evidence, they said. Too much of it and too many folk crying for blood.'

'So what did they say?'

'That I'd hit her. Not known my own strength, then realized that she was dead and panicked. Tried to make it look like she killed herself.' He paused. 'It was Elizabeth that made them do it. Made them doubt I was guilty, I mean.'

'Elizabeth?'

'Becky's mam. Said she didn't believe I'd killed her girl. I'd got an alibi for the day. Working up at Strawson's farm. I hadn't gone home that night. I couldn't face it. I'd gone to Ludford to see her mam. I wanted to know who she'd been seeing. I thought Elizabeth must know, but she wouldn't tell me.'

'Did she know?' Alec asked.

Joe nodded. 'I'm certain of it, but she wouldn't tell. She spoke up for me at the trial. Said I'd been with her that evening and that I'd been a good husband to Becky. But there was the travelling time. There and back. I'd seen no one and spoken to no one. I'd had time to kill her there or back and still make my journey. There'd have been no blood. Nothing to hide. But I'd have had to be a cold bastard, don't you think so, Alec? To kill my wife then go visiting her mother.'

'So they put in a plea of manslaughter.'

'Not everyone agreed, but the judge couldn't sentence me to hang and keep his conscience clear. That's what I was told, anyhow.'

'You were lucky,' Alec said.

'Was I? Fifteen years they kept me locked away. Then they let me out. Everywhere I went I had to explain where I'd been the past fifteen years. Who wants truck with a killer, Alec? Even one that's served his time.'

He pushed himself to his feet and reached for his stick. His arthritis was bad today and he limped slowly towards the cupboard beside the window.

When he came back to Alec he was carrying a large brown envelope, sealed up and addressed to 'Marciella' in large black letters.

'You'd better be off now, or you'll hit the traffic,' Joe said, handing the envelope to Alec. 'Tell them I'm glad they came. You too,' he added. 'Even if you are Jack's blood.'

Joe picked up the photograph of Marcie's twins and gazed fondly at the two children.

A small sound made him look up. She stood by the window, gazing out across the lawn.

'I thought you might come,' Joe said quietly. 'I've seen you, time to time, but I've always thought it was just me wishing till I found out others saw you too.'

Becky glanced across at him, smiling, though her eyes were still pained.

'It's nearly done now, isn't it, lass?' Joe asked her. 'Is it revenge you want, girl? If it is, I'd say you've got it. He'll lose her at the end, just as surely as I lost you.' He shook his head as though disbelieving. 'And even after all this time, Becky love, I can't find it in my heart to pity him.'

Alec took a wrong turn coming out of Lincoln and found himself, at five o'clock, trapped in the multi-lane tidal flow of traffic that led out of the city, heading down from the cathedral. It took a full half-hour, slipping the clutch, breathing a toxic mix of hot, summer air and traffic fumes, before he reached the final sweep of the hill and a clearer road – only to find that at some crucial point he'd failed to move into the correct lane and was headed out towards Melton, in the opposite direction from the one he wanted.

He found a phone box and called Marcie to let her know he'd be late.

She'd just arrived home. 'Couple of hours, I should think,' he told her. 'I've a lot to tell you both. Yes, yes, I talked to Joe. Look, I'm out of change. Talk to you soon.'

He got back into his car and pulled out his road map, not certain how to get himself back on the right route. The package Joe had given him earlier tumbled out with it. Alec picked it up. An ordinary A4 envelope, sealed up and obviously crammed full of something.

'I want her to open it when you're all together,' Joe

had told him. 'And I'll check up on you, Alec. You've been making decisions for that girl for far too long. I don't want you deciding which of these she should see and which she shouldn't.

'Tell them both, her and that black man, that I'm looking forward to seeing them on Saturday. And if they can bring those pretty children that would make me very happy.'

Alec glared at the brown envelope, wondering what the mystery was. He was suspicious of anything kept secret. There had been altogether too many secrets in this family so far. He sighed deeply as he realized there were still some that he himself was as yet unprepared to tell.

He spent a minute or two studying the map, then started the engine and resumed his journey, thinking of the reports he had read earlier that day and of what Joe had told him that afternoon.

He hadn't talked to Joe about the theft from Fielding's surgery. He wondered if Joe knew about it, but assumed that he must. It was hardly the sort of thing that could be kept quiet.

Who had taken the child? What had they done with it?

Alec tried to relax, wriggling his shoulders back into the driving seat and concentrating on the winding road ahead of him.

And how long, Alec wondered, did they leave Rebekkah's body lying in the hotel ice house? His mind wandered, imagining her lying there, skin blue with cold, the colour drained from her body, wrapped in a shroud waiting for burial.

It would have been so cold, lying there. Cold death, like that of Patrick Simpson, his blood reddening the snow.

'That's Jack's writing,' Marcie said.

'Doesn't look as if they were ever posted,' Michael commented, examining the envelopes. He flicked his long hair back from his face and detached the envelope from Liam's small hand. 'Can't have that, lovely. Not for Liam.'

'Joe mentioned that Jack gave them to him when he left prison,' Alec said. 'But he wouldn't tell me anything else. Just said we had to all be together when I opened the envelope.'

Marcie opened the first letter and looked at the date. 'August 1938,' she said. 'What's yours?'

'March '39.'

'Right, well, let's try to get them in order.'

'Delaying tactic?' Michael asked her.

Marcie frowned. 'Maybe.' She surveyed the mass of envelopes covering the little table and spilling over on to the floor. 'How many are there, for goodness' sake?'

They worked in silence but for the reading of dates, separating the letters from their envelopes and fastening them with paperclips. Sorting them into date order.

When they had finished, Marcie picked up the first one. She glanced nervously at the others. 'It must have been written just after they moved.' She read aloud from the faded page:

I wrote and gave you our new address, not that you write much, but in case you want to be in touch. It's pleasant here, Joe, but it's not what we're used to. Never thought I'd be able to settle in a town, but Mary couldn't bear it back there. Too many memories.

I don't need to tell you about memories, do I? I think of you, inside that place. You, who couldn't bear to be inside for more than an hour, and I could weep.

Always the gypsy, weren't you? The wanderer. You'd never have been a husband to her. Not in the real sense. You'd have been like our granddad, always on the move, following the fairs in summer and the auctions all winter. Coming home long enough to get his wife pregnant again and then off on the road. Was that any life for a woman like Rebekkah? She needed you there. Needed a man to care for her. I suppose that's the only excuse I can make for what I did, Joe.

Fact is, I can't live like this, keeping the secret from you. A man has a right to know. So, I came to a decision today. I'll write to you about all the things I want you to know and tell you about our lives and our news. Imagine I can keep you in touch with the outside, ready for when they let you go. And they will, Joe. One day you'll be a free man again. And we can forget all of this, put it behind us.

She broke off. 'He thought Joe could forgive him,'

she said, incredulous. 'That he could confess his sins and everything would go on as though it didn't matter.'

'No wonder Joe wants nothing to do with him.'

Michael nodded slowly. 'Confession can be a very dangerous thing,' he said softly.

Mary sat with Alice beside Jack's bed and talked about the past and the people they had once known.

'Do you recall Mother Atrie?' she asked. 'More than eighty, and travelled all her life. Only came home when she knew she was going to die.'

'Yes, I remember,' Alice said. An old woman with a wizened face, skilled in the arts of healing and brewing and birthing. 'But she'd had a good life, Mary. That's one woman went with nothing to regret.'

Mary's face was softened by a smile. 'You know what she said? "I want to be at me own wake," she told everyone and, my goodness, she managed it too. Drank everyone else under the table and died with an empty glass in her hand.'

She'd been kin to Jack and Joe, Mary thought, calling to mind how they'd come to give their blessings to her once she'd gone. Joe had been sixteen then and Jack a few years older. Both almost grown and already working all hours God sent.

'Joe fought that afternoon,' Alice said. 'Put three men twice his size to the ground. Tough as any of the travelling folk.' She stared into the middle distance, picturing that hot afternoon, the men bathed in sweat and Jack cheering his brother on – and taking bets on the side.

And at the end of it, Joe's eye half closed and the bruise rising. Spitting blood from cut lip and loosened teeth.

Mary laughed suddenly. 'Oh, and how the old folks glared at him in church the next day. Coming in with his face all bruised and his knuckles looking like some great dog had chewed them raw.' Her laughter faded as she remembered Rebekkah's face when she had looked at Joe, admiration in her eyes.

'They weren't like the rest of us,' she said aloud, knowing Alice would need no explanation. 'They were fey and wild, like. Not like Jack and you and me. I was glad of the choice I'd made when I married him. An honest, hard-working man, I thought.' An honest man . . . until I found out about Jack and that woman. Joe, coming out of jail and thinking the world owed him an explanation. Lord, but I thought they'd be fighting again that night, Joe as mad as he was. But even then, knowing about them, I swallowed my pride and stood by you, Jack. And here I am, still beside you . . .

She gave herself a little shake, aware that Alice was speaking again.

'They burned her wagon that night. Flames higher than the trees. And I remember a funny thing, Mary. I remember Joe looking at Jack in that odd way and saying to him it was like that time old Benny died. They burned that shack he lived in after he was gone. It seemed such an odd thing to talk about, I thought, and Jack looked so angry at Joe. I never did understand why.'

Chapter Thirty-Four

Alec returned to Lincoln on Thursday and spent the day at the archive. He telephoned Marcie and Michael in the evening, but his call did little more than confirm what Joe had told them about the trial.

Marcie's own day had been long. She had worked overtime and had not arrived home until close on eight o'clock. Michael, after work, had been involved with the twins. The main portion of Jack's letters still remained unread.

'I'm working until three tomorrow,' Marcie told him. 'Michael finishes at two. He's doing an extra evening session next week to make up for the Saturday. We should be with you just after five.' She hesitated, then added, 'It's going to be an expensive weekend, Da. And I'm not sure about that bed and breakfast place, with the twins.'

'Already sorted,' Alec told her. 'I drove out to the coast this afternoon, managed to get a chalet at a place called Anderby Creek. It's a bit out of the way, but it's right on the sea front. The french doors open practically on to the beach.'

'Sounds great, but how did you manage it at this time of the season?'

'It took some doing,' Alec confirmed, 'but I phoned around a bit and this place had a last-minute cancellation. It's cheaper than bed and breakfast and a lot more practical. Anyway, you let me worry about that. Oh, and I've bought buckets and spades, is that all right?'

Marcie laughed. 'Just great,' she said.

They arranged to meet at the chalet after Alec gave them directions. Marcie was smiling as she put the receiver down.

While her optimistic mood still held, she called the hospice. Yesterday was the first time she had missed in the last three weeks. Her feelings towards Jack had been severely challenged in these past few days, and yesterday she had felt so choked by them that her daily call had been left unmade. Dialling the number, she was afraid, guilty. What if Jack had died and no one had told her? What would the receptionist and nursing staff say to her? Would they hold it against her that she'd neglected him?

Angrily, she shook herself. 'Don't be such a prat, Marcie.' Forced a smile as the reception answered the phone and put her through to the ward.

'He's much the same, dear. Your gran and aunt have hardly left him, so if you've tried to get them at home . . . It must be hard for you, being so far away.'

'Yes,' Marcie agreed automatically. 'It is hard.'

'To be really honest, dear, we're surprised he's hung on this long.'

'I might be away for a couple of days,' Marcie told her on impulse, 'but I can give you a number to leave a message, if that's all right?' Marcie gave Adele's number. 'I'll call her a couple of times a day,' she said. 'And I'll phone you from here as well.'

She was aware she sounded over-anxious, but presumably the nurse was used to that. She must see so much pain, thought Marcie, so many anxious relatives and friends, afraid to miss the end.

She rang off, but stood looking at the telephone, wondering if she should have asked to speak to Mary or to Alice. Then decided that she could face neither of them. When Jack died she would try to make her peace. But that, she felt, would be soon enough.

The nurse told Mary and Alice that Marcie had called when she came to check on Jack. The morphine pump sighed and wheezed spasmodically. Jack never moved. He lay still, his eyes almost closed and his lips parted, a crust of salt grooved at the corners.

The nurse clasped Mary's hand soothingly. 'Why don't you go home and get some rest?' she said. 'Or if you'd rather, we can make up a bed for you. People often do, you know. You look worn out.'

'I'll be all right,' Mary told her. 'Thank you, but I'm fine just here.'

She sat in the high-backed chair, Alice in another beside her. Alice, her hands never idle, knitted with blue wool, the needles clicking softly against the silence.

'What's he waiting for?' Mary whispered, gazing at Jack's face with a mixture of love and resentment. 'Why is he hanging on like this?'

'Marcie,' Alice almost sighed the name. 'He's waiting for Marcie.'

'Then he'll wait a long time,' Mary said harshly. 'She'll not be back now.'

Alice said nothing, her hands pausing briefly while she counted her stitches, then continuing.

Children of my own, a house, a husband, work maybe, she was thinking. I could have had those things. Mary could have enjoyed those things. But it wasn't too late for them to live their own lives instead of just enduring Jack's. He would be gone soon . . . and then what?

She shifted her thoughts away briskly, packing them carefully as though afraid another might hear them and know. Tell Jack. Tell Mary.

The silence closed about them, and the women waited.

Friday seemed to drag, the last hour of work extending impossibly. Three o'clock and Marcie made her escape.

'Have a good weekend,' her supervisor told her. 'We've put in a request to have you back again, by the way, so we'll probably see you next week.'

'Thanks,' Marcie grinned. 'Nice weekend.'

Michael was already outside, illegally parked and watching out for traffic wardens. 'Hi,' he said. 'I was just thinking I'd have to go around the block again.'

She kissed him and glanced into the back of the car at the twins. 'Sleeping?' she said, surprised. Hanna and Liam rarely napped mid-afternoon.

'Morning in the park playing havoc with the ducks,' Michael said. 'Hanna got chased by a goose and yelled all the way back to the crèche. Gwen said that Liam joined in as well, just to be included, so they've worn themselves out.'

'Did it hurt her?' Marcie asked, turning around to examine the sleeping child.

'No, she'd been feeding it. It thought she'd still got more, I suppose, but she's just fine now.'

'Did you have a good morning?'

'Not bad, but I'm glad to be away.'

They drove in silence then for a time, each busy with their own thoughts. It would be another hour or so, Marcie knew, before Michael's attention shifted from the work he'd left behind. Her own thoughts were occupied by Joe and by Jack and the letters crammed into her bag. She reached down and fished them out. They had read no more than the first few, the night Alec had brought them home. Jack talked at length in them about himself and Rebekkah. Spoke of their meetings and their love-making. He phrased his telling as confessional, but that did nothing to mitigate the cruelty as he unfolded the depth of his relationship with his brother's wife.

To come out of prison, hoping to begin again, and then be faced with this, Marcie thought. The sensible thing would have been for Joe to burn the letters as soon as he realized their content. But he had kept them, read every one – from the number of folds in them, probably read them many times – unable to put them aside. Ordinary human curiosity would have been enough to make him look at each page, open each sealed envelope; the self-destructive side of Joe, which Marcie recognized in her own make-up. In Jack. Maybe in everyone, that tendency to probe wounds, see if they still cause pain, would have been enough to keep him reading, and remembering.

But he had never ceased to love his wife. Only learned to hate Jack.

She turned back to the letter she had begun.

'Read it to me,' Michael said.

'It's about something that happened when they were both kids, I think,' she said. 'But I can't make much sense of it.'

> I know you were angry with me about George, but there was nothing to be done about it. He was old and wouldn't have lasted much longer. I know we argued, Joe. That you believed he was in no pain and should be allowed to finish his life naturally, but what use was he? He couldn't hunt, he was stiff and arthritic and just costing food to eat. It's not merciful to keep useless things alive.
>
> I did feel for him, though, you must know that. He'd been around since we were babies, the pair of us, but he was fourteen. Old and had a lifetime of work behind him. I hanged the cat when he went blind and got too old to catch anything. But I couldn't kill the dog that way. I felt for him, you see, though you could never understand that. I got old Bill Haines to put a bullet in his head, then buried him up in the top field.
>
> Merciful, really. No sense keeping useless things alive.

Marcie shuddered as she folded the letter and looked at Michael.

'He hanged the cat, had the dog shot,' Marcie said slowly, her voice echoing her disgust. 'He drowned the kittens. Did he kill Rebekkah?'

'Horrible as it is, Marcie, it's quite a step from an animal to a woman he claimed to be in love with.'

'You don't think he could do it?'

'Do you? Look, darlin', I don't know about your granddad. I don't believe Joe's capable of it, but Jack?' He glanced sideways at her, noting the change of expression on her face. The sadness about her eyes and mouth. 'What are you thinking of?'

'About Patrick Simpson,' she said. 'About not knowing about him. About what I accused Jack of doing to him.'

Michael said nothing. He stared at the road ahead, silent, afraid to say too much and yet not wanting to lie to her, if only by omission.

Damn Alec, he thought. Damn him for what he's almost told me. For making me share in his secrets. For taking this circle of lying and deceit and making me carry it on.

Chapter Thirty-Five

Joe was captivated by Liam and Hanna. His eyes flooded with tears as Marcie brought them into his little room.

'You've brought them with you,' he said. 'I got your photograph. Look.'

Alec glanced across at the picture, enthroned now in a cheap gilt frame. 'This little lady's Hanna,' he said, 'and the quiet one is Liam. He has to get used to you first, but Hanna's ready to create chaos any time.'

Marcie laughed. 'We thought we'd take you out, if you like,' she said. 'It's a beautiful day.'

'I'd like that,' he said, his eyes still fixed on the twins. 'I don't get out much.' He looked up quickly. 'Can we go to the cathedral? I haven't been there in years.'

'Sure.'

'I'll take you in my car,' Alec said. 'There's more room in the front. Marcie's packed a picnic, is that all right?'

'Perfect,' Joe told him. 'Give me your arm, lad,' this to Michael. 'I'm ready when you are.'

Liam was reaching to be picked up. Marcie swept him into her arms and, not to be outdone, Hanna clung to Alec's trouser leg. 'Granddad, up,' she demanded.

Alec swung her high into the air and she squealed and shouted, 'Again!' He felt devastatingly happy. Almost able to believe that this was an ordinary family outing with an ordinary family that had more than blood kinship in common.

He glanced back as they went out to the cars. Michael and Joe were deep in conversation and, as she watched, the younger man threw back his head and laughed. The sound was free and unrestrained.

Alec sighed and cuddled Hanna close, suddenly afraid that this interval in a lifetime of strife was going to be all too short. That he was going to lose everything even before it was properly begun.

'I love you, sweetheart,' he whispered to Hanna, astonished to find just how much he meant it.

By the time they arrived at the cathedral, Hanna had decided that Joe was all right. She insisted on holding his free hand as he leaned heavily on his stick and walked slowly into the great nave.

Progress this far had been slow. Joe liked to walk, he said. He was fine if he wasn't rushed, but the brief distance from the car park to the cathedral close had taken them almost half an hour.

'The ankle didn't mend right,' he said. 'I broke it jumping from that bloody window and then ran about a quarter-mile on the blasted thing. It's given me strife ever since. Hadn't been for that then I'd have been home free.'

'Then what, Joe?' Marcie asked him.

'Oh, I dare say I'd have boarded a ship somewhere down the coast. They didn't make the checks then they do now. You could sign on as an unskilled hand and no one asked for papers. Just an honest day's work. Course, it was illegal to carry on like that even then, but no one bothered. Another year, of course, and we were winding up towards the war. Things must have got tighter then.' He shrugged awkwardly. 'I missed that show, not like Jack.' He turned a sharp glance upon Marcie. 'You read those letters yet?'

'Not all of them. I don't know if I want to read them all, Joe.'

'But you will,' he predicted. 'You will. Like me, you see, you have to know. Otherwise, why would you have come looking?'

He paused again, gazing up at the high vault of the ceiling arching over their heads. 'We used to sing here,' he said. 'In the choir, Jack and me. Beautiful voice, Jack had, sang solo. I hated it, but our mam and dad thought it was an honour. They never came themselves, mind.' He chuckled at the memory. 'It was the war that finished it for Jack, I'm convinced of that. Oh, he was mad enough before, but the war really brought it out in him. Made it all right.' He shook his head. 'You read about that poor woman yet?'

Marcie nodded. 'Last night,' she said. 'I could hardly sleep, Joe. It was a dreadful thing to do, to have to see.'

Joe looked sideways at her. 'War's full of dreadful things. The death camps were a dreadful thing. The blitzkrieg. The firebombing of Tokyo and the Burma railway, all dreadful things. I don't doubt there were precious, honourable, decent things came out of it too, but I'd have a hard time naming any far as Jack was concerned.' He led Hanna to a seat left from the last service and eased himself into it. 'Your Uncle Joe's got aching feet, my lamb,' he said. 'Have you the letter with you?' he asked.

Marcie dug into her bag and gave it to him. 'He gets her mixed up in his head, Joe. She'd got tangled up with Rebekkah in his mind. I don't know if he can tell the difference any more.'

Joe said nothing. He slid his glasses from his jacket pocket and perched them on his nose, held the letter at arm's length and peered thoughtfully at it. 'It was this one told me he'd really lost it,' Joe said. 'I wondered before if he'd killed her. It would have been the best thing, far as he was concerned. Get rid of her for good before I knew what he'd done.'

'He offered her money to go away,' Marcie said slowly. 'One of his other letters says so.'

Joe nodded. 'Just like he offered it to me under the guise of brotherly love,' he said.

'Maybe he meant it?' Marcie asked.

'My brother never offered me anything that didn't profit himself,' he said. 'No, not Jack.' He looked back at the letter. 'One death amongst so many,' he said. 'He felt it wouldn't matter.'

'It played on his mind,' Michael pointed out. 'Otherwise, why write about it?'

'Trouble shared is a trouble halved. That what you mean?'

Slowly, Michael shook his head. 'No,' he said. 'I don't mean that.' He thought of Alec. No, he definitely didn't mean that.

' "The night was so cold, you wouldn't believe it," ' Joe read slowly, and the stars were so bright it reminded me of those cold nights waiting for the lambs to be born. Huddled in the shack, back of the crew yard, keeping warm among the sheep. When you looked outside and the sky was so clear, hanging with frost, you could see right the way to heaven. She hung there, Joe, her feet kicking the stars like Becky had done, and for a minute I thought I was seeing it again. They'd not set the rope properly, see. Left it to pull tight across her throat instead of slipping the eyelet close beside her ear. It took her time to die, kicking the stars, Joe. Kicking at the stars.

Joe broke off and turned bright eyes on Marcie. 'You said you'd read this thing,' he said.

Marcie looked at him sadly, the implications of it sinking in for the first time. ' "Like Becky had done",' she repeated. 'He was there. There when she died.'

'Seems like it to me,' Joe said. Then, 'I'm sorry, love. Maybe I should never have shown you this. Maybe it's better to doubt than to know for certain.'

Marcie didn't know what to say to him. She swallowed and got to her feet, walking away from the others. Was it better to doubt? She had suspected Jack of many things, of killing Patrick Simpson, of murdering Rebekkah and her child. But always, there had been space to excuse, to let the love she still had for Jack worm him free of her questions and her accusations.

She walked slowly down the length of the nave, through the angel choir. There was a chapel set aside, which she had seen before, set with large stoneware pots like Ali Baba jars. They were filled with sand and set with candles lit in prayer. Marcie found herself there almost without realizing it, staring at the candles, her tears reflecting and refracting each tiny flame, transforming into hundreds the light of dozens.

Joe's footsteps behind her, the tapping of his stick marking the rhythm of his steps, made her wipe away the tears. He came to stand beside her, the letter rolled up and clasped in his hand.

'Why did you tell no one, Joe? You could have cleared your name,' she managed, her voice shaky and uncertain.

'Why? I don't know, lass, I don't know. Maybe I thought no one would care any more. Maybe, I don't know, maybe I thought there'd been enough suffering over this. Enough for Alice and Mary. Why take Alec's father from him?'

He reached out, the letter rolled up in his hand, and planted it like a candle in the sand. Took a small white candle from the box and offered it towards a flame, then turned it to the letter.

'No!' Marcie laid a hand on his. 'No. It'll change nothing, Joe. It's too late for that and I won't let you do it.'

Gently, she took the letter from the sand, smoothed it out and placed it back in her bag. Then she took the candle from Joe's hand and lit another from the same flame. 'For Rebekkah,' she said, 'and for Patrick.'

'Patrick?'

'Something else I couldn't quite believe,' Marcie told him.

Chapter Thirty-Six

It was hard to put things back on the level after that, but they tried. Alec suggested they went back to the chalet and Joe agreed enthusiastically. They drove back and spent the rest of the day on the beach, Joe resting in a beach chair at first, then, to please Liam, rolling up his trouser legs and paddling in the shallows, listing somewhat as his walking stick sank in the wet sand.

Marcie left the men to play with the children and busied herself with setting out the picnic, making tea and cold drinks, stealing the time taken by simple tasks to get her thoughts under control.

Just like Alice, she thought wryly. Maybe that was how it had begun. A way of stealing time for thought. Or time to be absent from it. She ran through what she knew.

Fact one was that Jack had killed Patrick Simpson. She no longer had any doubt about that.

Fact two, Rebekkah had been another victim, her baby too. He had killed them both that night, then stood aside, prepared to let Joe take the blame.

What if Joe had hanged for the crime? Would Jack have let it go that far? The thought made Marcie shiver despite the heat. She felt like winter inside.

Abandoning thoughts of Jack, she looked out across the beach, watching the others. Joe had Liam by the hand, who was kicking the water, watching the sunlit spray as it sparkled in the brilliant light and squealing with pleasure. Michael and Hanna played near by, though she refused to hold anyone's hand. Both hands and feet were in the water as she crawled through it on all fours. Alec stood a little apart, shoes still firmly in place, standing on the drier sand further up the beach. He was laughing, looking relaxed and happy. Away from Jack, she thought. Away from Mary and her demands. Away from everything.

Poor Mary. The thought came almost unbidden into her head. When had she found out about Rebekkah? Had she read the letters, or had Joe confronted his brother in her presence? Marcie had no doubt that her gran had known. Her reaction every time Rebekkah's name was mentioned, the sudden removal of the harvest photograph that Alec had said once resided on the sideboard, told her that. Joe must have shown her the letters when he came out of prison.

Marcie sighed. Why does anyone stay married? Maybe she still loved Jack in spite of everything. Looking at her own, mixed-up feelings for her grandfather, Marcie could sympathize with that.

She thought of Alec's sister, the baby that had died, and the carefully tended grave in the little churchyard. Who placed fresh flowers there and, after all this time, why?

There was, she remembered, a service at the church that Sunday, the one in three for which a vicar could be found.

Crossing the beach to call the others in to eat, Marcie decided that the next day that was where they'd be.

They brought her to me and I slipped the rope around her neck. She was shaking and crying and her eyes seemed to look everywhere at once, unable to focus on anyone.

I tried not to look into her face and I wanted to tell her that it would be quick. That I knew well how to do these things, had learned to do them properly.

The hands, remember, Birdie. The hands know.

I eased her black hair free of the noose, stroking down the length of it past her shoulders. They had torn her clothes and left her shoulders bare. The skin was soft beneath my fingers, the roughness of my own hands dragging against its smoothness.

I wanted it to be easy for her, the way it should have been for Becky, but the preparation should be slow, Birdie. Death is a thing the senses should be a party to, not a thing to be rushed.

But Mills didn't understand that and he grabbed her from me before I had a chance to set the eyelet right beneath her jaw and they threw the rope across the tree branch and hauled on it until her feet came off the ground and her body jerked and twisted like a puppet dancing, kicking at the sky.

It wasn't easy to find somewhere to park. Cars had been pulled up on to the grass verge, but what little space there was had been almost filled. They were glad that they had chosen to cram everyone into the one car, Marcie wedged not terribly comfortably between the twins' car seats.

The Sunday service had already begun by the time they arrived. They slipped quietly inside, aware of the curious stares as the congregation turned to look at the latecomers. The vicar smiled, indicated them to sit down and carried on with his announcements. They had arrived in time for the first hymn and, just as they had seated themselves, had to rise to their feet again.

Marcie didn't know the tune. Vainly she tried to match words to melody but in the end she gave up and turned her attention to Liam, who was eating a hymn-book and Hanna, who was trying to escape by sliding through the little gap in the wooden pews.

'Monster,' Marcie whispered, as she removed the book from Liam's mouth and ducked down to pull Hanna out of her hole. She tried to remember the last time she had been in a church like this. It had been a Sunday tradition all through childhood, but the last time . . . it was well before she had finally run away from home.

Since then she had been with Sophie Lee on odd occasions, enjoying the singing and the pure pleasure the congregation had taken in praising. But she had no religious feelings these days. None at all.

The hymn ended and they sat down, Michael with Liam on his lap and Hanna on a hassock on the floor, her fingers twisting the fringing, watching it spring unwound again. Marcie carefully lowered the baby bag on to the floor so that Hanna could reach the toys, checking to make certain nothing too noisy had found its way inside.

Then she took the time to look around, her mind wandering while the minister intoned the lesson for the day.

There were no more than twenty people in the church besides themselves. Mostly elderly, but with a few young people and three or four kids, sitting quietly with their parents. Fresh flowers decorated the altar and the side chapel, and light streamed in through high windows, broken into tiny diamonds by the glass.

Was one of these people the one who put flowers on Margaret's grave? she wondered, playing games with herself, imagining the elderly lady in the black hat kneeling to pluck weeds from the close-cropped grass, or the young man in the blue suit arranging the tiny vase of flowers. The old couple sitting with linked arms halfway down the row – were they the ones?

The service dragged. The hour that Marcie had been used to every Sunday, seated without thought of complaint between her grandparents, now seemed to stretch into eternity.

Finally it came to an end, with a hymn that Marcie actually remembered. She sang this time, fervently as though in apology for her inattention. Hanna decided that she would join in too. She climbed back on to the seat and stood beside her mother seriously intoning 'Baa, Baa, Black Sheep' against a background of 'There's a Wideness in God's Mercy'.

Marcie let it go. Beside her, Michael was trying hard

not to laugh. Alec stared, eyes strictly forward, pretending not to hear.

'I loved your version,' the vicar told Hanna as they left the church. 'You sang with real feeling.'

Hanna stared at him, then hid her face in her mother's skirt.

'Are you on holiday here?' he asked.

'Just up for the weekend,' Marcie replied. 'Our family came from around here. In fact, you've my father's little sister buried in the churchyard over there.'

'Really?'

Marcie pointed to the child's grave.

'Oh,' he said. 'Little Margaret Armitage, now isn't that interesting? You'll want to talk to Helen.' He called out to a young woman shepherding her children towards the door.

'Helen, these are relatives of Margaret Armitage.' He turned to Marcie. 'Helen's on our committee. We try to keep things up to the mark here. The committee split the work. Margaret Armitage is one of Helen's charges, isn't she? Always makes sure there are flowers. So sad, a child's grave, especially with no family living near by.'

Marcie's heart sank. So that was the solution. Just a church committee to keep the graveyard tidy, and a kind-hearted woman who could not bear to see a child's grave neglected.

The young woman was smiling at her and holding out her hand. 'I'm pleased to meet you,' she said. 'I hope you like what we've been doing?'

'Oh, I think it's lovely,' Marcie managed. 'Have you been doing it for long?'

'Oh, yes,' Helen said. 'I enjoy it.' They moved slowly towards the little grave, her children trailing behind, calling out to friends who were now leaving the church.

'It's odd, really, but my family have always looked after this grave, and when the vicar suggested we got a committee together, well, I couldn't let anyone else do it, so I took this section over.'

'Always?' Marcie asked her, puzzled.

'Well, yes, though I don't really know how it came about.' She smiled, looking slightly embarrassed. 'My gran used to do it and then my mum. I couldn't let it get overgrown, it wouldn't be right somehow.' She glanced curiously at them and asked, 'If you don't mind, how are you related to Margaret?'

'She was my sister,' Alec said quietly. 'My parents moved from here the year after she was born.'

'Oh, really? I hope you don't mind, then. I mean, after all, she was your sister . . .'

'Please,' Alec said hastily. 'I think you've done a marvellous job, just marvellous. Er, if you'll let me contribute towards flowers . . .'

'Oh no,' Helen told him. 'Mostly they're from my garden anyway. I'm sure the vicar would be grateful if you want to send something to the church.' She turned back to Marcie. 'You might like to remember me to your grandparents,' she said. 'Tell them the grave's looked after. They must have known my gran and my mum. Tell them, let me see, they would know my gran's name, that was Lacey. Elizabeth Lacey.'

*

It was time then to go back to Joe. They had talked further to Helen, but it had been obvious that Rebekkah's story was not familiar to her, though she knew the name. 'Oh yes,' she'd said. 'I think she died in childbirth. Quite common then, my mum says.'

They found Joe as they had first seen him, in the garden with the chess board set out in front of him.

'I know,' he said, as Marcie confronted him with what they had been told. 'Or at least I knew that Elizabeth tended the grave. It's good that someone still does.'

'But why?' Marcie asked him. 'Did she feel guilty, or what?'

It seemed as though Joe didn't want to answer, then he sighed deeply and said, 'She couldn't bear it. Bad enough that her daughter was dead, but to cut her open like that, you know . . . The police wanted to know for certain how far gone she was. They kept it quiet, like, as long as they could, but then some newspaperman let it slip that the child had been preserved in case they needed it for evidence. That's what they said, anyway. But I ask you, Marcie, they could have looked at the poor little bugger, figured out how old it was and let it go at that. Given it a decent burial. Bad enough she couldn't bury her girl, but to think of her grandchild, pickled like a side of pork in brine, it was more than Elizabeth could take.'

'The break-in at Dr Fielding's,' Alec said.

Joe nodded. 'She came to me, told me about it. Got special permission to see me in the jail. Desperate, she was, and I was scared as hell that she might get herself caught. But she was a determined woman, Elizabeth. She took someone with her, I believe, though she didn't tell me who, and they broke in through a back window. Took the child away.'

'What happened to it?' Alec asked.

'They buried it in Margaret's grave, didn't they, Joe?' Marcie said.

Joe nodded again. 'That's right, lass, they did. Seemed just, somehow. Two innocents buried together. It wasn't hard, she eased the turf from off the top and then dug down. It didn't take much of a hole. Took the spare earth and scattered it in a new-dug grave. Watered the turf back down again.'

'And Elizabeth knew about Jack?' Alec asked.

'She knew. Becky told her when she realized she was pregnant. Thought she could get Jack to leave his wife and go off with her, but he wouldn't have it. She felt she couldn't tell me. That it was Jack's baby, I mean. Then when I found out, I went to her. Wanted to know the truth and that's when she told me. All of it. She told no one else. I'm certain of that.'

'And she believed that Jack was guilty of the murder?' Alec asked him.

'Believed that all along,' Joe confirmed. 'Spoke up for me in court, but she could prove nothing about Jack, you see. She'd only Becky's word. And there were plenty willing to call Becky a whore. She didn't want her name dragged further through the mud than it had to be.'

'Did you show her the letter?'

'Yes.' Joe nodded slowly. 'I was mad as hell. Took it and showed her. She said the same as you, that I should try to clear my name with it, but I'd no faith in the law and no money to fight my case anyhow. It was lost before I even started.'

'Oh, Joe,' Marcie whispered, taking the old man's hand. 'What a waste. What a terrible waste.'

Chapter Thirty-Seven

'They say we should go now, if we want to be there,' Marcie said. She sounded undecided, as though going back to see Jack would be too hard.

'Then you'd better be on your way,' Joe said. The last letter Jack had sent to him, the one he had chosen not to let the others see, burned in his waistcoat pocket, folded tight. He had read it so many times he knew the words by heart: *The night she died was so clear and so cold . . .*

He had carried it there so long, unable to act, to change anything. He blamed Jack. Jack had taken Becky from him. Taken much of his life, too.

'You'd best go to him,' he said, and this time Marcie nodded.

'We'll be back, Uncle Joe,' she said, kissing him sadly.

Joe smiled. 'I know you will,' he said contentedly. 'I know you will.'

He watched them walk away across the parched lawn and smiled again. The one thing Jack had truly valued, truly loved, he thought, looking at Marcie, and he'd lost her.

Joe patted the letter in the pocket of his waistcoat and nodded, satisfied. He could have shown it to her.

But he chose not to. Something was owed, Joe felt, and Marcie and her family would well do in payment.

As Marcie turned to go up the ramp and into the house she paused, stepped back and then stood still as though something had caught her eye. Joe followed her gaze.

Beneath the trees, where the children had played a little time before, a figure stood in half-shadow. Black hair fell about her face and a hand protectively touched her swollen belly.

'Becky,' Joe whispered. 'Becky.'

He looked back sharply to where Marcie stood and their eyes met for a moment, and he knew that she had seen her too. Then she turned and walked away.

When he looked towards the trees there were only shadows. Long branch shadows, laying themselves across the dried-out grass.

Marcie had expected trouble when she reached the hospice; had expected that Alice and her grandmother would deny her wish to see Jack. But nothing happened. Mary and Alice had grown too tired to argue. They joined Alec and Michael in the waiting room and Marcie went to Jack's bedside alone.

'I've talked to Joe,' she told him without preamble. 'And he showed me the letters you sent to him, about you and Rebekkah.' She paused, finding words hard. 'How could you, Jack? How could you do that to someone you loved?'

Jack could barely open his eyes. He felt so tired, and the light, dim as it was, hurt. But he didn't need to look to know that Marcie was there or to hear her voice.

Becky, he thought. She was talking about Rebekkah.

'How could you kill her?' Marcie said. 'She was pregnant, Jack, pregnant with your baby. What was it, too inconvenient for you? Did you think she would tell Joe whose baby it was? Were you scared of him? Scared enough to kill them both and pin the blame on your brother?'

She shook her head, still half disbelieving, the enormity of Jack's crime overwhelming her. 'How could you, Jack? How could you . . . ?'

And then there was Patrick, Marcie thought, and her own ruined teenage years and the hurt he had caused to Alec and to Mary and to Lord alone knew who else.

Marcie found she couldn't bear to be there, beside him, any more.

In his half-conscious state Jack could hear Marcie's words.

No, he wanted to tell her. It wasn't like that. It wasn't like she said, but they were all there now, crowded round his bed. All hating him and judging him for what he'd done and what he'd been.

They were all there, Becky and the child and the woman he'd seen hanged on a cold desert night in some place he could barely remember. And that boy who'd got Marcie into trouble.

Jack knew they were waiting for him, but the fear of losing Marcie was the worst of all.

It wasn't like that, he wanted to say, as he saw Becky take the child by the hand and slowly walk away. It wasn't like that . . . as the others faded slowly from his vision, leaving empty space filled only with Marcie's voice.

'I'm going now, Jack,' she said slowly. 'I'm sorry, Jack, but you must understand that I have to go.'

Joe held Jack's final letter in his hand. The letter he had decided Marcie would never see.

> The night she died was so clear and so cold and there was a bright moon, two-thirds towards full. I'd missed you, Joe, up at the farm, and so I'd kept watching the house, waiting for you to come home. It wasn't hard. We could see the corner of your place and the road you'd come by from the kitchen window and I'd sat there, reading while Mary prattled away, keeping a lookout.
>
> It was Mary's idea. We'd hardly seen you since you got back and she wanted you to come in for supper. Family, like. Rebekkah, too, if she had to. I'd told her we should stick together, show solidarity.
>
> I thought it would soon pass. The trouble, I mean, and the village gossip. It wouldn't be the first child born with an awkward birthday and folk forget in time, or at least put their memories away.
>
> It was a strange thought I had as I watched

the door open and Becky slip through, that at least the child would be family. It made me smile and I had to take care that Mary didn't see and wonder why. She could be sharp at the oddest moments.

But I admit I was scared. What if Rebekkah had told someone about us? What if you found out in some way? A moment's carelessness or anger and that would be that.

When I saw her go out I took a chance. I wanted to talk to her. To make certain that things would stay secret. Mary was a good match. I loved her. Not like I loved Rebekkah, but still, I loved her. And her family were not people to offend.

So I made an excuse about trying to meet you on the road and I slipped out after Rebekkah.

I almost lost her. I'd been carrying a hurricane lamp, but turned it low as I'd left the village, afraid she'd see the light. There was something in the way she moved that made me feel strange and I was worried, anyway, that we might be seen if we stopped too close to the houses.

But she never looked back. Just walked with her eyes fixed straight ahead and her coat collar pulled up high. She carried no light and moved like an awkward shadow.

I almost lost her when she turned off the path. I'd gone by the gate and kept on up the road, thinking she was ahead of me where the road bent. But then, when I reached the straight and had a full view of the road as it went on up the hill, I knew she'd left it and cut across country.

So I went back.

There was a gate about a quarter of a mile back up the road leading off to Bale's field. She must have gone through, there was no other place. I climbed the gate and skirted the field, following her.

Joe sat in his favourite place by the window, watching the evening creep across the lawn, Jack's final letter to him clutched in his hand.

He looked up as she came into the room and he saw this time that the smile reached her eyes.

'Becky.'

She sat down opposite him, leaning back in the chair with a sigh, her hands resting lightly on the chair arms. She looked satisfied with herself, he thought. Happy after all this time.

'She's left him, then,' Joe said, his eyes soft as he smiled back at her.

Chapter Thirty-Eight

Marcie waited outside for Alec, aware that he couldn't just abandon Gran and Aunt Alice at a time like this, but feeling herself apart from it all now.

She watched Michael playing catch – or, usually, miss – with their children and thought . . . nothing. Her mind felt numb and tired. She wanted to go home and there was still luggage left at the chalet to collect. It would be as easy to drive back there tonight as to go home and make the longer trip the following day.

Alec came out eventually with his mother holding his arm.

'We've sorted things out here,' he said. 'They don't think Jack will last the night.'

Marcie nodded.

'You'll do all the arrangements for us, won't you, Alec?' Mary said to him, a touch of her old control returning.

Alec shook his head. 'If I can,' he said. 'If not, you'll have to ask Marcie and her husband if they'd mind giving you a hand.'

Mary was clearly dumbfounded.

Alec didn't give anyone the chance to question. Instead, he looked straight at Marcie and continued to speak, his tone calm and unhurried.

'There's something I have to do,' he said, 'and I don't quite know how it'll go.'

Marcie gave him a puzzled look. 'I don't follow you, Da.'

'It's about Patrick Simpson,' Michael ventured.

Alec nodded. 'You were right,' he said. 'I have to grow up some time. Decide things for myself.'

Marcie hesitated, looking from her husband to her father. Then she reached out and took her father's hand.

'This time we're coming with you,' she told him.

With Rebekkah beside him in the dimly lit room, Joe read on.

> I didn't see her until I'd reached the top of the hill and then I knew. She was standing there on that low branch, her arms around the trunk, and I remember thinking how hard it must have been for her to climb up there with her belly swollen and throwing her balance the way it must. But it had always been a good climbing tree, that one. Even a child could do it.
>
> Then she threw the rope over the higher branch and I understood. She'd thought it out well, made a loop in the other end, so all she had to do was thread the noose end through and pull it tight, and I remembered how I'd showed her how to bind a whip handle with thick cord, pulling it through so it made a noose, then hauling the free end to make it neat and safe. She'd bound

her death noose the same way. Made it secure so it wouldn't fail her.

You know, Joe, I remember I was proud of her then. Not many women would have gone to such trouble to get it right.

I had to respect her choice, Joe, you do know that. I had to let her go.

I sent you that letter, Joe. Told you, but you did nothing, so I knew you understood. What else was there to do?

But she haunts me, Joe, and I know she's waiting for me. Like that other one. They've found each other, stand each side of my bed and wait.

She saw me. She saw me. Just as I came over the rise and she'd already got the rope round her neck, was standing there, her feet planted on that big branch and her hands resting on the trunk to steady her.

She saw me, Joe. Looked straight into my eyes and there was this look, like she'd hoped I'd come. Not thought I would, but hoped I'd come. That I'd want her so much that I'd somehow know what she had in mind and come and make it right. Make it possible for her to go on living.

Tell me you'll leave her. Tell me you love me. You want me. Her eyes, fixed on mine, they said all those things, but I couldn't, Joe. I couldn't lose everything, she must have seen that.

Next moment, she'd thrown herself forward, her hands reaching for me and her skirts and hair billowing around her like a wave. Just for an instant, she seemed to be held there against a starry sky, beautiful as an angel, her hands reaching out in blessing.

Then the rope jerked her back. The force of it yanked her head sideways and cracked it against the tree. Then it was all over. Just her legs dancing some obscene dance and her body swaying in the wind, like a rag blowing across the moon.

Fade to Grey

By Jane Adams

What follows here are the opening scenes from Jane Adams's new novel, *Fade to Grey*, which reintroduces Detective Inspector Mike Croft and retired detective John Tynan.

It is published in hardback by Macmillan (priced £16.99) in September 1998.

Jane Adams

Prologue

She took a good photograph, anyone would say so. She had that look about her, that little bit of self doubt, or not quite innocence, that men found so appealing. Some men.

She'd always resisted Jake's attempts to make her look even younger than she was. The schoolgirl look or the baby doll just wasn't her style, she said. Though it was amazing what you could do with the right software package these days.

In the end he'd turned her out pretty much any way he wanted and she hadn't said a word about it.

He turned the pages of the latest magazine. Computer porn might be the new thing, but personally, he preferred the finished article to be one he could roll up and carry in his pocket.

Which he did now, tucking the magazine into the inside pocket of his coat.

It would be a collector's item, before long. This edition. In certain circles anyway. Those that were in the know . . .

Not because it was anything harder than you could pick up from the top shelf of any news-stand. Nothing more than soft porn in this edition – the other stuff, the stuff he could have been arrested for if he'd been caught prancing round town with it. That was elsewhere. Already distributed on the multi-media wave.

No, it wasn't the content that made this little package rare, but the scarcity of the commodity.

There would be no more centrefolds, not of this little lady. Not unless, of course, you liked your meat well done . . .

Chapter One

Stacey hesitated before squeezing through the next to the park gates. It was dark in there but it was also the quickest way of getting home. Besides, turning around and walking back the way she'd come would mean running into Richard again and she just knew he'd be standing around, waiting for her to come back to him. And Stacey wasn't going to apologize for anything. Let him stew for a while.

Once inside the park she stopped and groped in her bag for the little penlight torch she had attached to her keyring. The thin beam of light showed her only a few yards of the muddy path before it was swallowed by the thick darkness. She slid her finger through the ring, posting the key in between her fingers the way the man in the self-defence class had told them to. Nervous now, her mind niggling about those reports in the papers.

Maybe, after all, she should go back and find Richard. Not apologize exactly, just open the discussion enough for him to give her a ride home.

She glanced back over her shoulder one more time startled by what sounded like a footstep.

'Richard? Is that you?' No reply. 'Richard. Oh for Christ's sake, if that's you . . .'

She shone the torch back through the wrought-iron

gates but could see nothing, no one at all walking along the lonely street.

Stacey walked swiftly down what she could see of the slimy, leaf-covered path. The silence seemed to close in all around her, only the heels of her boots clacking with a reassuringly steady beat as she walked and the jingle of loose change in her pocket breaking the quiet.

Stacey shivered. It had begun to rain and the air was damp and clammy against her skin. Thinking she would be driven home she had only worn her denim jacket and left her umbrella on the table in the hall. She quickened her pace now, as the rain fell more heavily, desperate to be home.

And then it happened, footsteps, the sound of someone running making her look behind. Richard's name half spoken before one hand was clamped around her mouth and a second hand grabbing at her breasts, the man's body pressed tight against her back. Then he had shifted sideways and she was on the floor even before she realized that she was falling. The hand away from her mouth now, Stacey screamed in fear, then pain as the fist came crashing down at the side of her head.

Only half conscious she still tried to wriggle away from him. Felt the sudden chill of air on her legs and stomach as he wrenched her skirt up above her waist. Hard fingers bruising as they grabbed between her legs.

Stacey tried to scream again, but he was on top of her, his body heavy on her chest and breath hot in her face. He was saying something but Stacey was too stunned to understand the words.

The torch, the keys, somehow she had managed to

keep hold of them, the ring still tight around her finger. She brought her right hand up, striking into the man's face. Her left hand reaching up and grabbing at his hair, winding her fingers tight and pulling as hard as she could. Adrenalin and fear had overcome the pain of her bruised and bleeding head and half-closed eye.

The man was yelling now, loosening his grip on her just for an instant. Stacey hit out at him again, fighting for her life as he came back at her, his hands tightening on her throat.

Mike sat uneasily between Maria and her sister Josie watching as three wise men, bearing gold-wrapped boxes, slow marched across the stage. Enthusiastic music, played on a slightly off-key piano helped to keep them in time, left feet, right feet, lifted in unison like a dissociated caterpillar making its way towards the manger.

He tried desperately not to fidget, the hard plastic of the chair was digging into his back and there was no room to stretch out his long legs. A tall man who liked space to move around, Mike felt over large and over conspicuous wedged in between proud parents and grandparents. His body cramped and his mind overwhelmed by remembrance of another time when his son Stevie had been one of the three kings. Wearing his father's old plaid dressing gown and holding his gift high as he presented it to the little girl cuddling the baby doll.

'Doesn't she look lovely?'

It was Maria, smiling happily at her niece. Little Essie was grinning so much she almost forgot her words. Her thick black hair, braided tightly and threaded with blue and yellow beads, swung around her face as she strutted forward with her arms outstretched to take the presents from the kings. Mike didn't have to look sideways to know that Josie dabbed at tears, watching her little girl up on the stage.

He tried hard to smile, knowing he should feel grateful to be included in such a family event, but it brought back so many morbid thoughts and, since Stevie had died, he'd always found it hard to cope with this pre-Christmas rush of emotion.

The angels were just about to break into a new song when the beeping started. Mike grabbed at his pocket to silence it, aware of Maria's glare as he peeked a look at the number on the LCD screen. He unfolded himself awkwardly from the little plastic chair, trying hard not to catch her eye as he headed for the door, apologizing as he went and horribly conscious of every inch of his six-foot-two frame.

Maria caught up with him at the outer door.

'I thought I told you to leave that bloody thing behind.'

'Well no, actually it was the phone you told me to leave behind . . .' He smiled sheepishly, 'it's work,' he said.

'Isn't it always?'

'Um, I need the car keys, the phone . . .'

She sighed in exasperation and dug into her pocket for the keys. 'You'd better take the car,' she said. 'I'll get a lift back with Josie.'

'Thanks.' He paused, wondering if he should risk

a kiss goodbye. He reached out and caught her hand instead.

'I'm really sorry.'

'You're always really sorry.' Marie shook her head. 'God! Never get yourself involved with a policeman. Well, what's keeping you? Phone's in the car.'

He watched her as she stalked away, shoulders set. This was the third time in as many already scarce evenings off that he'd been called away. He could understand her getting mad at him. Mike was relieved when she glanced back from the door, not quite smiling, but her expression softened enough to let him know he was off the hook . . . almost.

Then he got into the car, rummaged in the glove compartment for the phone and called the office. 'DI Mike Croft.' He listened in silence as they told him about this latest attack.

'They've taken her to the Royal and District, Mike. Price is interviewing the boyfriend.'

'Is she badly hurt?'

"Bruising, shock. They'll be keeping her overnight though. You'll want to speak to the boyfriend?'

Mike signed off and turned the ignition key, listening to the low purr of the engine for a moment or two before pulling away, his mind already cataloguing the new information, he turned the car towards the hospital.

JANE ADAMS

The Greenway

Pan Books £5.99

Even in her dream Cassie could feel the exertion of that run . . . Then, the sudden shimmer, like a displaced heat haze; the feeling of heaviness cloaked around her shoulders, the ground shifting beneath her feet. Dimly, as she fell, she heard Suzie's distant voice calling her name.

Cassie Maltham still has nightmares about that day in August 1975 when she and her twelve-year-old cousin Suzie took a short cut through The Greenway, an ancient enclosed pathway steeped in Norfolk legend. For somewhere along this path Suzie simply vanished . . .

Haunted also is John Tynan, the retired detective once in charge of Suzie's case, still obsessed by the tragic disappearance he failed to solve.

Then another young girl goes missing at the entrance to The Greenway. And Cassie's nightmares take on a new and terrifying edge . . .

JANE ADAMS

Cast the First Stone

Pan Books £5.99

Ellie Masouk never knew who cast the first stone, but suddenly and inexplicably her world descended into madness . . .

Life in Portland Close was pleasantly uneventful for Ellie and her neighbours – until Eric Pearson moved in. For within just a few short weeks he had become the focus of violent intimidation.

Pearson claims he is being persecuted because he has the journal of the late Simon Blake JP, which details some sinister crimes. Crimes that could topple powerful figures . . .

Detective Inspector Mike Croft is asked to investigate, although at first it seems Pearson's allegations are simply the work of a bitter, obsessed man.

But then a terrible discovery is made on the outskirts of Bright's Wood . . .

'For months I lay in bed and plotted how to kill my ex-husband. But I knew I'd bungle it and get caught, so I wrote it in a book instead.'

Thus began the twin careers of Sue Grafton and Kinsey Millhone. In 1982 Sue Grafton was a twice divorced screenwriter, mother of three, with visions of homicide dancing in her head. Now she is the creator and alter-ego of one of America's most popular private investigators, Kinsey Millhone, star of the renowned 'alphabet' novels.

She was born in Louisville, Kentucky in 1940, her father the mystery writer, C. W. Grafton, whose own work gave his daughter the initial inspiration to write herself. Since then, Sue Grafton has moved to Santa Barbara, where she writes full time.

Also by Sue Grafton in Pan Books

'B' is for Burglar
'C' is for Corpse
'D' is for Deadbeat
'E' is for Evidence
'F' is for Fugitive
'G' is for Gumshoe
'H' is for Homicide
'I' is for Innocent
'J' is for Judgment
'K' is for Killer
'L' is for Lawless
'M' is for Malice
'N' is for Noose

Also available as Pan Triples:

'D' is for Deadbeat
'E' is for Evidence
'F' is for Fugitive

Sue Grafton

'A' IS FOR ALIBI

PAN BOOKS

The author wishes to acknowledge the invaluable assistance of the following people: Stephen Humphrey, Roger Long, Alan Tivola, Barbara Stephens, Marlin D. Ketter of Investigations Unlimited and Joe Driscoll of Driscoll and Associates Investigations, both of Columbus, Ohio, and William Christensen, Police Caption, City of Santa Barbara.

First published in Great Britain 1986 by Macmillan London

This edition published 1993 by Pan Books
an imprint of Pan Macmillan Ltd
Pan Macmillan, 20 New Wharf Road, London N1 9RR
Basingstoke and Oxford
Associated companies throughout the world
www.panmacmillan.com

ISBN 0 330 31582 X

27 29 28 26

A CIP catalogue record for this book is available from the British Library.

Typeset by Selectmove Ltd., London
Printed and bound in Great Britain by
Mackays of Chatham PLC, Chatham, Kent

For my father
Chip Grafton,
who set me on this path

1

My name is Kinsey Millhone. I'm a private investigator, licensed by the State of California. I'm thirty-two years old, twice divorced, no kids. The day before yesterday I killed someone and the fact weighs heavily on my mind. I'm a nice person and I have a lot of friends. My apartment is small but I like living in a cramped space. I've lived in trailers most of my life, but lately they've been getting too elaborate for my taste, so now I live in one room, a 'bachelorette'. I don't have pets. I don't have houseplants. I spend a lot of time on the road and I don't like leaving things behind. Aside from the hazards of my profession, my life has always been ordinary, uneventful and good. Killing someone feels odd to me and I haven't quite sorted it through. I've already given a statement to the police, which I initialed page by page and then signed. I filled out a similar report for the office files. The language in both documents is neutral, the terminology oblique, and neither says quite enough.

Nikki Fife first came to my office three weeks ago. I occupy one small corner of a large suite of offices that house the California Fidelity Insurance Company, for whom I once worked. Our connection now is rather loose. I do a certain number of investigations for them in exchange for two rooms with a separate entrance and a small balcony overlooking the main street of Santa Teresa. I have an answering service to pick up calls when I'm out and I keep my own books. I don't earn a lot of money but I make ends meet.

I'd been out for most of the morning, only stopping by the office to pick up my camera. Nikki Fife was standing in the corridor outside my office door. I'd never really met her but I'd been present at her trial eight years before when she was convicted of murdering her husband, Laurence, a prominent divorce attorney here in town. Nikki was in her late twenties then, with striking white-blonde hair, dark eyes, and flawless skin. Her lean face had filled out some, probably the result of prison food with its high starch content, but she still had the ethereal look that had made the accusation of murder seem so incongruous at the time. Her hair had grown out now to its natural shade, a brown so pale that it appeared nearly colorless. She was maybe thirty-five, thirty-six, and the years at the California Institute for Women had left no visible lines.

I didn't say anything at first; just opened the door and let her in.

'You know who I am,' she said.

'I worked for your husband a couple of times.'

She studied me carefully. 'Was that the extent of it?'

I knew what she meant. 'I was also there in court when you were being tried,' I said. 'But if you're asking if I was involved with him personally, the answer is no. He wasn't my type. No offense. Would you like coffee?'

She nodded, relaxing almost imperceptibly. I pulled the coffee-pot from the bottom of the file cabinet and filled it from the Sparkletts water bottle behind the door. I liked it that she didn't protest about the trouble I was going to. I put in a filter paper and ground coffee and plugged in the pot. The gurgling sound was comforting, like the pump in an aquarium.

Nikki sat very still, almost as though her emotional gears had been disengaged. She had no nervous mannerisms, didn't smoke or twist her hair. I sat down in my swivel chair.

'When were you released?'

'A week ago.'

'What's freedom feel like?'

She shrugged. 'It feels good, I guess, but I can survive the other way too. Better than you'd think.'

I took a small carton of half-and-half out of the little refrigerator to my right. I keep clean mugs on top and I turned one over for each of us, filling them when the coffee was done. Nikki took hers with a murmured thanks.

'Maybe you've heard this one before,' she went on, 'but I didn't kill Laurence and I want you to find out who did.'

'Why wait this long? You could have initiated an investigation from prison and maybe saved yourself some time.'

She smiled faintly. 'I've been claiming I was innocent for years. Who'd believe me? The minute I was indicted, I lost my credibility. I want that back. And I want to know who did me in.'

I had thought her eyes were dark but I could see now that they were a metallic gray. Her look was level, flattened-out, as though some interior light were growing dim. She seemed to be a lady without much hope. I had never believed she was guilty myself but I couldn't remember what had made me so sure. She seemed passionless and I couldn't imagine her caring enough about anything to kill.

'You want to fill me in?'

She took a sip of coffee and then set the mug on the edge of my desk.

'I was married to Laurence for four years, a little more than that. He was unfaithful after the first six months. I don't know why it came as such a shock. Actually, that's how I got involved with him . . . when he was with his first wife, being unfaithful to her with me. There's a sort of egotism attached to being a mistress, I suppose. Anyway, I never expected to be in her shoes and I didn't like it much.'

'According to the prosecutor, that's why you killed him.'

'Look, they needed a conviction. I was it,' she said with the first sign of energy. 'I've just spent the last eight years with killers of one kind or another and believe me, the motive isn't apathy. You kill people you hate or you kill in rage or you kill to get even, but you don't kill someone you're indifferent to. By the time Laurence died, I didn't give a damn about him. I fell out of love with him the first time I found out about the other women. It took me a while to get it all out of my system . . .'

'And that's what the diary was all about?' I asked.

'Sure I kept track at first. I detailed every infidelity. I listened in on phone calls. I followed him around town. Then he started being more cautious about the whole thing and I started losing interest. I just didn't give a shit.'

A flush had crept up to her cheeks and I gave her a moment to compose herself. 'I know it looked like I killed him out of jealousy or rage, but I didn't care about that stuff. By the time he died, I just wanted to get on with my own life. I was going back to school, minding my own business. He went his way and I went mine . . .' Her voice trailed off.

'Who do you think killed him?'

'I think a lot of people wanted to. Whether they did or not is another matter. I mean, I could make a couple of educated guesses but I don't have proof of anything. Which is why I'm here.'

'Why come to me?'

She flushed again slightly. 'I tried the two big agencies in town and they turned me down. I came across your name in Laurence's old Rolodex. I thought there was a certain kind of irony hiring someone he had once hired himself. I did check you out. With Con Dolan down at Homicide.'

I frowned. 'It was his case, wasn't it?'

Nikki nodded. 'Yes, it was. He said you had a good memory. I don't like having to explain everything from scratch.'

'What about Dolan? Does he think you're innocent?'

'I doubt it, but then again, I did my time so what's it to him?'

I studied her for a moment. She was forthright and what she said made sense. Laurence Fife had been a difficult man. I hadn't been all that fond of him myself. If she was guilty, I couldn't see why she would stir it all up again. Her ordeal was over now and her so-called debt to society had been taken off the books except for whatever remaining parole she had to serve.

'Let me think about it some,' I said. 'I can get in touch with you later today and let you know.'

'I'd appreciate that. I do have money. Whatever it takes.'

'I don't want to be paid to rehash old business, Mrs Fife. Even if we find out who did it, we have to make it stick and that could be tough after all this time. I'd like to check back through the files and see how it looks.'

She took a manila folder out of her big leather bag. 'I have some newspaper clippings. I can leave those with you if you like. That's the number where I can be reached.'

We shook hands. Hers was cool and slight but her grip was strong. 'Call me Nikki. Please.'

'I'll be in touch,' I said.

I had to go take some photographs of a crack in a sidewalk for an insurance claim and I left the office shortly after she did, taking my VW out the freeway. I like my cars cramped and this one was filled with files and law books, a briefcase where I keep my little automatic, cardboard boxes, and a case of motor oil given to me by a client. He'd been cheated by two con artists who had 'allowed' him to invest two grand in their oil company. The motor oil was real enough but it wasn't theirs; just some Sears thirty-weight with new labels pasted on. It had taken me a day and a half to track them down. In addition to the junk, I keep a packed overnight case back there, too, for God knows what emergency. I wouldn't work for anyone who wanted me *that* fast. It just makes me feel secure to have a nightgown, toothbrush, and fresh underwear at hand. I have my little quirks I guess. The VW's a '68, one of those vague beige models with assorted dents. It needs a tune-up but I never have time.

I thought about Nikki as I drove. I had tossed the manila folder full of clippings on the passenger seat but I really didn't need to look at them. Laurence Fife had done a lot of divorce work and he had a reputation as a killer in court. He was cold, methodical, and unscrupulous, taking any advantage he could. In California, as in many states, the only grounds for divorce are irreconcilable differences or incurable insanity, which eliminates the trumped-up adultery charges that were the mainstay of divorce attorneys and private eyes in the old days. There is still the question of property settlements and custody – money and children – and Laurence Fife could get his clients anything. Most of them were women. Out of court, he had a reputation as a killer of another kind and the rumor was that he had mended many a broken heart in that difficult period between interlocutory and final decrees.

I had found him shrewd, nearly humorless, but exact; an easy man to work for because his instructions were clear and he paid in advance. A lot of people apparently hated him: men for the price he extracted, women for the betrayal of their trust. He was thirty-nine years old when he died. That Nikki was accused, tried and convicted was just a piece of bad luck. Except for cases that clearly involve a homicidal maniac, the police like to believe murders are committed by those we know and love, and most of the time they're right –

a chilling thought when you sit down to dinner with a family of five. All those potential killers passing their plates.

As nearly as I could remember, Laurence Fife had been having drinks with his law partner, Charlie Scorsoni, the night of his murder. Nikki was at a meeting of the Junior League. She got home before Laurence, who arrived about midnight. He was taking medication for numerous allergies and before he went to bed, he downed his usual capsule. Within two hours, he was awake – nauseated, vomiting, doubled over with violent stomach cramps. By morning, he was dead. An autopsy and lab tests showed that he'd died as a result of ingesting oleander, ground to a fine powder and substituted for the medication in the capsule he took: not a masterly plot, but one employed to good effect. Oleander is a common California shrub. There was one in the Fifes' backyard as a matter of fact. Nikki's fingerprints were found on the vial along with his. A diary was discovered among her possessions, certain entries detailing the fact that she'd found out about his adulteries and was bitterly angry and hurt, contemplating divorce. The District Attorney established quite nicely that no one divorced Laurence Fife without penalty. He'd been married and divorced once before and though another attorney had handled his case, his impact was evident. He obtained custody of his children and he managed to come out ahead financially. The state of California is scrupulous in its division of assets, but Laurence Fife had a way of maneuvering monies so that even a fifty-fifty split gave him the lion's share. It looked as if Nikki Fife knew better than to try disentangling herself from him legally and had sought other means.

She had motive. She had access. The grand jury heard the evidence and returned an indictment. Once she got into court, it was simply a question of who could persuade twelve citizens of what. Apparently the D.A. had done his homework. Nikki hired Wilfred Brentnell from Los Angeles:

a legal whiz with a reputation as the patron saint of lost causes. In some sense, it was almost like admitting her guilt. The whole trial had a sensational air. Nikki was young. She was pretty. She was born with money. The public was curious and the town was small. It was all too good to miss.

2

Santa Teresa is a southern California town of eighty thousand, artfully arranged between the Sierra Madres and the Pacific Ocean – a haven for the abject rich. The public buildings look like old Spanish missions, the private homes look like magazine illustrations, the palm trees are trimmed of unsightly brown fronds, and the marina is as perfect as a picture postcard with the blue-gray hills forming a backdrop and white boats bobbing in the sunlight. Most of the downtown area consists of two- and three-story structures of white stucco and red tile, with wide soft curves and trellises wound with gaudy maroon bougainvillaea. Even the frame bungalows of the poor could hardly be called squalid.

The police department is located near the heart of town on a side street lined with cottages painted mint green with low stone walls and jacaranda trees dripping lavender blossoms. Winter in Southern California consists of an overcast and is heralded not by autumn but by fire. After the fire season come the mud slides. And then the status quo is restored and everything goes on as before. This was May.

After I dropped the roll of film off to be developed, I went into the Homicide Department to see Lieutenant Dolan. Con is in his late fifties with the aura of the unkempt: bags under his eyes, gray stubble or its illusion, a pouchy face, and hair that's been coated with some kind of men's product and combed across a shiny place on top. He looks like he would smell of Thunderbird and hang out under bridges throwing up on his own shoes. Which is not to say he isn't very sharp. Con Dolan is a lot smarter than the average thief. He and killers run about neck and neck. He catches them most of the time and only occasionally guesses wrong. Few people can out-think him and I'm not sure why this is true, except that his powers of concentration are profound and his memory clear and pitiless. He knew why I was there and he motioned me back to his office without a word.

What Con Dolan calls an office would do for a secretary anywhere else. He doesn't like being shut away and he doesn't much care for privacy. He likes to conduct his business tipped back in his chair with his attention half-turned to what's going on around him. He picks up a lot of information like that and it saves him needless talk with his men. He knows when his detectives come and go and he knows who's been brought in for questioning and he knows when reports aren't being done on time and why.

'What can I do for you?' he said, but his tone didn't indicate any particular desire to help.

'I'd like to look at the files on Laurence Fife.'

He arched an eyebrow at me ever so slightly. 'It's against department policy. We're not running a public library here.'

'I didn't ask to take them out. I just want to look. You've let me do that before.'

'Once.'

'I've given you information more times than that and you know it,' I said. 'Why hesitate on this?'

'That case is closed.'

'Then you shouldn't have any objections. It's hardly an invasion of anyone's privacy.'

His smile then was slow and humorless and he tapped a pencil idly, loving, I imagined, the power to turn me down cold. 'She killed him, Kinsey. That's all there is to it.'

'You told her to get in touch with me. Why bother with it if you don't have a doubt yourself?'

'My doubts have nothing to do with Laurence Fife,' he said.

'What then?'

'There's more to this one than meets the eye,' he said evasively. 'Maybe we'd like to protect what we've got.'

'Are "we" keeping secrets?'

'Oh I got more secrets than you ever dreamed about,' he said.

'Me too,' I said. 'Now why are we playing games?'

He gave me a look that might have been annoyance and might have been something else. He's a hard man to read. 'You know how I feel about people like you.'

'Look, as far as I'm concerned, we're in the same business,' I said. 'I'm straight with you. I don't know what kind of gripes you have with the other private investigators in town, but I stay out of your way and I've got nothing but respect for the job you do. I don't understand why we can't cooperate with one another.'

He stared at me for a moment, his mouth turning down with resignation. 'You'd get more out of me if you'd learn to flirt,' he said grudgingly.

'No I wouldn't. You think women are a pain in the ass. If I flirted, you'd pat me on the head and make me go away.'

He wouldn't take the bait on that one but he did reach over and pick up the phone, dialing Identification and Records.

'This is Dolan. Have Emerald bring me the files on Laurence Fife.' He hung up and leaned back again, looking at me with a mixture of speculation and distaste.

'I better not hear any complaints about the way you handle this. If I get one call from anyone – and I'm talking about a witness who feels harassed or anyone else, including my men or anybody else's men – you're up shit creek. You got that?'

I held up three fingers beside my temple dutifully. 'Scout's honor.'

'When were you ever a Scout?'

'Well, I was a Brownie once for almost a week,' I said sweetly. 'We had to paint a rose on a hanky for Mother's Day and I thought it was dumb so I quit.'

He didn't smile. 'You can use Lieutenant Becker's office,' he said when the files arrived. 'And stay out of trouble.'

I went into Becker's office.

It took me two hours to sort through the mass of paperwork but I began to see why Con had been reluctant to let me look because just about the first thing that came to light was a series of Telexes from the West Los Angeles Police Department about a second homicide. At first, I thought it was a mistake – that communiqués from another case had been inadvertently sandwiched into the wrong file. But the details nearly leapt off the page and the implications made my heart go pitty-pat. An accountant named Libby Glass, Caucasian, female, age twenty-four, had died from ingesting ground oleander four days after Laurence Fife died. She had worked for Haycraft and McNiece, a business-management firm representing the interests of Laurence Fife's law firm. Now what the hell was that about?

I flipped through copies of investigators' reports, trying to piece together the story from terse departmental memorandums and penciled summations of telephone calls flying back and forth between the Santa Teresa and West Los Angeles police departments. One memo noted that the key to her apartment had been found on the key ring in Laurence Fife's office desk drawer. A lengthy interview with her parents didn't add anything. There was an interview with a surly-sounding ex-boyfriend named Lyle Abernathy, who seemed convinced that she was romantically involved with a 'certain unnamed Santa Teresa attorney,' but no one had pinned it down much beyond that. Still, the connection was ominous enough and it looked like Nikki Fife's alleged jealous rage might have included the object of her husband's philanderings as well as the man himself. Except that there wasn't any proof.

I made notes, jotting down last-known addresses and telephone numbers for whatever good that might do after all these years, and then I pushed my chair back and went to the door. Con was talking to Lieutenant Becker but he must have known what I wanted because he excused himself, apparently satisfied that I hadn't missed the point. I leaned on the doorframe, waiting. He took his sweet time ambling over.

'You want to tell me what that was about?'

His expression was bemused but there was an air of bitterness about it. 'We couldn't make it stick,' he said flatly.

'You think Nikki killed her too?'

'I'd be willing to bet on it,' he snapped.

'I take it the D.A. didn't see it that way.'

He shrugged, shoving his hands in his pockets. 'I can read the California Evidence Code as well as the next man. They called off my dogs.'

'The stuff in the file was all circumstantial,' I said.

'That's right.'

I shut my mouth, staring off at a row of windows that badly needed to be cleaned. I didn't like this little turn of events at all and he seemed to know that. He shifted his weight.

'I think I could have nailed her but the D.A. was in a big hurry and he didn't want to jeopardize his case. Bad politics. That's why you didn't like being a cop yourself, Kinsey. Working with a leash around your neck.'

'I still don't like that,' I said.

'Maybe that's why I'm helping you,' he said and the look in his eyes was shrewd.

'What about follow-up?'

'Oh we did that. We worked on the Libby Glass angle for months, off and on. So did the West LAPD. We never turned up anything. No witnesses. No informants. No fingerprints that could have placed Nikki Fife at the scene. We couldn't even prove that Nikki *knew* Libby Glass.'

'You think I'm going to help you make your case?'

'Well, I don't know about that,' he said. 'You might. Believe it or not, I don't think you're a bad investigator. Young yet, and sometimes off the wall, but basically honest at any rate. If you turn up evidence that points to Nikki, I don't think you'd hold that back now, would you?'

'*If* she did it.'

'If she didn't, then you don't have anything to worry about.'

'Con, if Nikki Fife has something to hide, why would she open this whole thing up again? She couldn't be that kind of fool. What could she possibly gain?'

'You tell me.'

'Listen,' I said, 'I don't believe she killed Laurence in the first place so you're going to have a hell of a time persuading me she killed someone else as well.'

The phone rang two desks over and Lieutenant Becker held up a finger, looking over at Con. He gave me a fleeting smile as he moved away.

'Have a good time,' he said.

I scanned the file again quickly to make sure I hadn't overlooked anything and then I closed it up and left it on the desk. He was deep in conversation with Becker again when I passed the two of them and neither looked up at me. I was troubled by the idea of Libby Glass but I was also intrigued. Maybe this was going to be more than a rehash of old business, maybe there was more to be turned up than a trail that was eight years cold.

By the time I got back to the office, it was 4:15 and I needed a drink. I got a bottle of chablis out of my little refrigerator and applied the corkscrew. The two coffee mugs were still sitting on my desk. I rinsed out both and filled mine with wine tart enough to make me shudder ever so slightly. I went out onto the second-floor balcony and looked down at State Street, which runs right up the middle of downtown Santa Teresa, eventually making a big curve to the left and turning into a street with another name. Even where I stood, there were Spanish tile and stucco arches and bougainvillaea growing everywhere. Santa Teresa is the only town I ever heard of that made the main street narrower, planted trees instead of pulling them up, and constructed cunning telephone booths that look like small confessionals. I propped myself up on the waist-high ledge and sipped my wine. I could smell the ocean and I let my mind go blank, watching the pedestrians down below. I already knew that I would go to work for Nikki but I needed just these few moments for myself before I turned my attention to the job to be done.

At 5:00 I went home, calling the service before I left.

Of all the places I've lived in Santa Teresa, my current cubbyhole is the best. It's located on an unpretentious street that parallels the wide boulevard running along the beach. Most of the homes in the neighborhood are owned by retired folk whose memories of the town go back to the days when it was all citrus groves and resort hotels. My landlord, Henry Pitts, is a former commercial baker who makes a living now, at the age of eighty-one, by devising obnoxiously difficult crossword puzzles, which he likes to try out on me. He is usually also in the process of making mammoth batches of bread, which he leaves to rise in an old Shaker cradle on the sunporch near my room. Henry trades bread and other baked goods to a nearby restaurant for his meals and he has also, of late, become quite crafty about clipping coupons, declaring that on a good day he can buy $50.00 worth of groceries for $6.98. Somehow these shopping expeditions seem to net him pairs of pantyhose, which he gives to me. I am halfway in love with Henry Pitts.

The room itself is fifteen feet square, outfitted as living room, bedroom, kitchen, bathroom, closet and laundry facility. Originally this was Henry's garage and I'm happy to say that it sports no stucco, red Spanish tile or vines of any kind. It is made of aluminium siding and other wholly artificial products that are weather-resistant and never need paint. The architecture is completely nondescript. It is to this cozy den that I escape most days after work and it was from here that I called Nikki and asked her to meet me for a drink.

3

I do most of my hanging out in a neighborhood bar called Rosie's. It's the sort of place where you look to see if the chair needs brushing off before you sit down. The plastic seats have little rips in them that leave curls of nylon on the underside of your stockings and the tables have black Formica tops hand-etched with words like *hi*. To the left above the bar, there's a dusty marlin, and when people get drunk, Rosie lets them shoot rubber-tipped arrows at it with a toy gun, thus averting aggressions that might otherwise erupt into vicious bar-room snits.

The place appeals to me for a couple of reasons. Not only is it close to my home but it is never attractive to tourists, which means that most of the time it's half-empty and perfect for private conversations. Then, too, Rosie's cooking is inventive, a sort of devil-may-care cuisine with a Hungarian twist. It is with Rosie that Henry Pitts barters baked goods, so I get to eat his breads and pies as a dividend. Rosie is in her sixties with a nose that almost meets her upper lip, a low forehead, and hair dyed a remarkable shade of rust, rather like the color of cheap redwood furniture. She also does tricky things with an eyebrow pencil that make her eyes look small and suspect.

When Nikki walked in that night, she hesitated, scanning the place. Then she spotted me and moved through the empty tables to the booth where I usually sit. She slid in across from me and eased out of her jacket. Rosie ambled over, eyeing Nikki with uneasiness. Rosie is convinced that I do business with Mafia types and drug crazies and she was probably trying to determine the category into which Nikki Fife might fit.

'So are you eating something or what?' Rosie said, getting straight to the point.

I glanced at Nikki. 'Have you had dinner?'

She shook her head. Rosie's eyes moved from Nikki to me as though I might be translating for a deaf-mute.

'What have you got tonight?'

'It's a veal porkolt. Veal cubes, lotta onion, paprika, and tomato paste. You'll love it. You'll go nuts. It's the best kinda stew I make. Henry's rolls and everything, and on a plate I'm gonna put some good soft cheese and a coupla gherkins.'

She was already writing the order down as she spoke, so it didn't require much from us in the way of consent. 'You gonna have wine too. I'll pick the kind.'

When Rosie had left, I related the information I'd picked up in the files about the murder of Libby Glass, including the telephone calls that had been traced to Laurence's home phone.

'Did you know about her?'

Nikki shook her head. 'I heard the name but it was through my attorney, sometime during the trial, I think. I can't even remember now what was said.'

'You never heard Laurence mention her? Never saw her name written down anyplace?'

'No little love notes if that's what you mean. He was meticulous about that sort of thing. He was once named as co-respondent in a divorce action because of some letters he wrote and after that, he seldom put anything personal in writing. I usually knew when he was involved with someone but never because he left cryptic notes or telephone numbers on matchbook covers or anything like that.'

I thought about that one for a minute. 'What about phone bills though? Why leave those around?'

'He didn't,' Nikki said. 'All the bills were sent to the business-management firm in Los Angeles.'

'And Libby Glass handled the account?'

'Apparently she did.'

'So maybe he called her on business matters.'

Nikki shrugged. She was a little less remote than she had been but I still had the feeling that she was one step removed from what was happening. 'He was having an affair with *someone.*'

'How do you know?'

'The hours he kept. The look on his face.' She paused, apparently thinking back. 'Sometimes he would smell of someone else's soap. I finally accused him of that and afterwards he had a shower installed at the office and used the same kind of soap there that we used at home.'

'Did he see women down at the office?'

'Ask his partner,' she said with the faintest tinge of bitterness. 'Maybe he even screwed 'em on the office couch, I don't know. Anyway it was little things. It sounds stupid now, but once he came home and the edge of his sock was turned down. It was summer and he said he'd been out playing tennis. He had on tennis shorts and he'd worked up a sweat all right, but not out on a public court. I really zapped him that time.'

'But what would he say when you confronted him?'

'He'd admit it sometimes. Why not? I didn't have any proof and adultery isn't grounds for divorce in this state anyway.'

Rosie arrived with the wine and two paper napkins wrapped around some silverware. Nikki and I were both silent until she'd departed again.

'Why did you stay married to him if he was such a jerk?'

'Cowardice I guess,' she said. 'I would have divorced him eventually, but I had a lot at stake.'

'Your son?'

'Yes.' Her chin came up slightly, whether from pride or defensiveness I wasn't sure. 'His name is Colin,' she said. 'He's twelve. I have him in a boarding school up near Monterey.'

'You also had Laurence's kids living with you at the time, didn't you?'

'Yes, that's right. A boy and a girl, both in school.'

'Where are they now?'

'I have no idea. His ex-wife is here in town. You might check with her if you're curious. I don't hear from them.'

'Did they blame you for his death?'

She leaned forward, her manner intense. 'Everyone blamed me. Everyone believed I was guilty. And now I take it Con Dolan thinks I killed Libby Glass too. Isn't that what you were getting at?'

'Who cares what Dolan thinks? I don't think you did it and I'm the one going to work on this thing. Which reminds me. We ought to get the financial end of it clarified. I charge thirty bucks an hour plus mileage. I'd like to have at least a grand up front. I'll send you an itemized accounting from week to week indicating what time I've put in doing what. Also, you have to understand that my services are not exclusive. I sometimes handle more than one case at a time.'

Nikki was already reaching into her purse. She took out a checkbook and a pen. Even looking at it upside down, I could see that the check was for five thousand dollars. I admired the carelessness with which she dashed it off. She didn't even have to check her bank balance first. She pushed it across the table to me and I tucked it into my purse as though I disposed of such matters as casually as she.

Rosie appeared again, this time with our dinner. She put a plate down in front of each of us and then stood there until we began to eat. 'Mmm, Rosie it's wonderful,' I said.

She wiggled slightly in place, not yielding her ground.

'Maybe it don't suit your friend,' she said, looking at me instead of Nikki.

'Marvelous,' Nikki murmured. 'Really it is.'

'She loves it,' I said. Rosie's gaze slid across to Nikki's face and she finally seemed satisfied that Nikki's appreciation of the dish was equaled only by my own.

I let the conversation wander while we ate. Between the good food and the wine, Nikki seemed to be letting down her guard. Under that cool, unruffled surface, signs of life were beginning to show, as though she were just wakening from a curse that had rendered her immobile for years.

'Where do you think I should start?' I asked.

'Well I don't know. I've always been curious about his secretary back then. Her name was Sharon Napier. She was already working for him when he and I met, but there was something not right about her, something in her attitude.'

'Was she involved with him?'

'I don't think so. I really don't know what it was. I could just about guarantee they didn't have any sexual ties, but something had gone on. She was sometimes sarcastic with him, which Laurence never tolerated from anyone. The first time I heard her do it, I thought he'd cut her down, but he never batted an eye. She never took any guff from him at all, wouldn't stay late, wouldn't come in on weekends when he had a big case coming up. He never complained about her either, just went out and hired temporary help when he needed it. It wasn't like him, but when I asked him about it, he acted as if I were crazy, reading significance into the situation when there wasn't any. She was gorgeous, too, hardly the run-of-the-mill office type.'

'Do you have any idea where she is now?'

Nikki shook her head. 'She used to live up on Rivera but she's not there now. At least, she's not listed in the telephone book.'

I made a note of her last-known address. 'I take it you never knew her well.'

Nikki shrugged. 'We had the customary exchanges when I called the office but it was just routine stuff.'

'What about friends of hers or places she might hang out?'

'I don't know. My guess is she lived way beyond her means. She traveled every chance she could and she dressed a lot better than I did back then.'

'She testified at the trial, didn't she?'

'Yes, unfortunately. She'd been a witness to a couple of nasty quarrels I had with him and that didn't help.'

'Well, it's worth looking into,' I said. 'I'll see if I can get a line on her. Is there anything else about him? Was he in the middle of any hassles when he died? Any kind of personal dispute or a big legal case?'

'Not that I knew. He was always in the middle of something big.'

'Well, I think the first move is to talk to Charlie Scorsoni and see what he has to say. Then we'll figure it out from there.'

I left money on the table for the dinner check and we walked out together. Nikki's car was parked close by, a dark green Oldsmobile ten years out of date. I waited until she'd pulled away and then I walked the half block to my place.

When I got in, I poured myself a glass of wine and sat down to organize the information I'd collected so far. I have a system of consigning data to three-by-five index cards. Most of my notes have to do with witnesses: who they are, how they're related to the investigation, dates of interviews, follow-up. Some cards are background information I need to check out and some are notes about legal technicalities. The cards are an efficient way of storing facts for my written reports. I tack them up on a large bulletin board above my desk and stare at them, telling myself the story as I perceive it. Amazing contradictions will come to light, sudden gaps, questions I've overlooked.

I didn't have many cards for Nikki Fife and I made no attempt to assess the information I had. I didn't want to form a hypothesis too early for fear it would color the entire course of the investigation. It did seem clear that this was a murder where an alibi meant little or nothing. If you go to the trouble to substitute poison for the medication in someone's antihistamine capsules, all you have to do afterward is sit back and wait. Unless you want to risk killing off others in the household, you have to be sure that only your intended victim takes that particular prescription, but there are plenty of pills that would satisfy that requirement: blood-pressure medication, antibiotics, maybe even sleeping pills. It doesn't matter much as long as you have access to the supply. It might take your victim two days or two weeks but eventually he'd dose himself properly and you could probably even manufacture a reasonable facsimile of surprise and grief. The plan has a further advantage in that you don't actually have to be there to shoot, bludgeon, hack up, or manually strangle your intended. Even where the motivation to kill is overpowering, it'd be pretty distasteful (one would think) to watch someone's eyes bug out and listen to his or her last burbling cries. Also, when done in person there's always that unsettling chance that the tables might be turned and you'd wind up on a slab in the morgue yourself.

As methods go, this little oleander number was not half bad. In Santa Teresa, the shrub grows everywhere, sometimes ten feet tall with pink or white blossoms and handsome narrow leaves. You wouldn't need to bother with anything so blatant as buying rat poison in a town where there are clearly no rats, and you wouldn't have to sport a false mustache when you went into your local hardware store to ask for a garden pest control with no bitter aftertaste. In short, the method for killing Laurence Fife, and apparently Libby Glass as well, was inexpensive, accessible and easy to use. I did have a couple of questions and I made notes of those before I turned out the light. It was well after midnight when I fell asleep.

4

I went into the office early to type up my initial notes for Nikki's file, indicating briefly what I'd been hired to do and the fact that a check for five thousand dollars had been paid on account. Then I called Charlie Scorsoni's office. His secretary said he had some time free midafternoon, so I set up an appointment for 3:15 and then used the rest of the morning to do a background check. When interviewing someone for the first time, it's always nice to have a little information up your sleeve. A visit to the county clerk's office, the credit bureau, and the newspaper morgue gave me sufficient facts to dash off a quick sketch of Laurence Fife's former law partner. Charlie Scorsoni was apparently single, owned his own home, paid his bills on time, did occasional public-speaking stints for worthy causes, had never been arrested or sued – in short, was a rather conservative, middle-aged man who didn't gamble, speculate on the stock market or jeopardize himself in any way. I had caught glimpses of him at the trial and I remembered him as slightly overweight. His current office was within walking distance of mine.

The building itself looked like a Moorish castle: two stories of white adobe with windowsills two feet deep, inset with wrought-iron bars, and a corner tower that probably housed the rest rooms and floor mops. Scorsoni and Powers, Attorneys-at-Law, were on the second floor. I pushed through a massive carved wooden door and found myself in a small reception area with carpeting as soft underfoot as moss and about the same shade. The walls were white, hung with watercolors in various pastels, all abstract, and there were plants here and there; two plump sofas of asparagus green wide-wale corduroy sat at right angles under a row of narrow windows.

The firm's secretary looked to be in her early seventies, and I thought at first she might be out on loan from some geriatric agency. She was thin and energetic, with bobbed hair straight out of the twenties and 'mod' glasses replete with a rhinestone butterfly on the lower portion of one lens. She was wearing a wool skirt and a pale mauve sweater, which she must have knit herself, as it was a masterpiece of cable stitches, wheat ears, twisted ribs, popcorn stitches and picot appliqué. She and I became instant friends when I recognized the aforementioned – my aunt having raised me on a regiment of such accomplishments – and we were soon on a first-name basis. Hers was Ruth; nice biblical stuff.

She was a chatty little thing, full of pep, and I wondered if she wasn't about perfect for Henry Pitts. Since Charlie Scorsoni was keeping me waiting, I took my revenge by eliciting as much information from Ruth as I could manage without appearing too rude. She told me she had worked for Scorsoni and Powers since the formation of their partnership seven years ago. Her husband had left her for a younger woman (fifty-five) and Ruth, on her own for the first time in years, had despaired of ever finding a job, as she was then sixty-two years old, 'though in perfect health,' she said. She was quick, capable, and of course was being aced out at every turn by women one-third her age who were cute instead of competent.

'The only cleavage I got left, I sit on,' she said and then hooted at herself. I gave Scorsoni and Powers several points for their perceptiveness. Ruth had nothing but raves for them both. Still her rhapsodizing hardly prepared me for the man who shook my hand across the desk when I was finally ushered into his office forty-five minutes late.

Charlie Scorsoni was big, but any excess weight I remembered was gone. He had thick, sandy hair, receding at the temples, a solid jaw, cleft chin, his blue eyes magnified by big rimless glasses. His collar was open, his tie askew, sleeves rolled up as far as his muscular forearms would permit. He was tilted back in his swivel chair with his feet propped up against the edge of the desk, and his smile was slow to form and smoldered with suppressed sexuality. His air was watchful, bemused, and he took in the sight of me with almost embarrassing attention to detail. He laced his hands across the top of his head. 'Ruth tells me you have a few questions about Laurence Fife. What gives?'

'I don't know yet. I'm looking into his death and this seemed like the logical place to start. Mind if I sit down?'

He gestured with one hand almost carelessly, but his expression had changed. I sat down and Scorsoni eased himself into an upright position.

'I heard Nikki was out on parole,' he said. 'If she claims she didn't kill him, she's nuts.'

'I didn't say I was working for her.'

'Well it's for damn sure nobody else would bother.'

'Maybe not. You don't sound too happy about the idea.'

'Hey listen. Laurence was my best friend. I would have walked on nails for him.' His gaze was direct and there was something bristly under the surface – grief, misdirected rage. It was hard to tell what.

'Did you know Nikki well?' I asked.

'Well enough I guess.' The sense of sexuality that had seemed so apparent at first was seeping away and I wondered if he could turn it off and on like a heater. Certainly his manner was wary now.

'How did you meet Laurence?'

'We went to the University of Denver together. Same fraternity. Laurence was a playboy. Everything came easily to him. Law school, he went to Harvard, I went to Arizona State. His family had money. Mine had none. I lost track of him for a few years and then I heard he'd opened his own law firm here in town. So I came out and talked to him about going to work for him and he said fine. He made me a partner two years later.'

'Was he married to his first wife then?'

'Yeah, Gwen. She's still around town someplace but I'd be a little careful with her. She ended up bitter as hell and I've heard she's got surly things to say about him. She has a dog-grooming place up on State Street somewhere if that's any help. I try to avoid running into her myself.'

He was watching me steadily and I got the impression that he knew exactly how much he would tell me and exactly how much he would not.

'What about Sharon Napier? Did she work for him long?'

'She was here when I hired on, though she did precious little. I finally ended up hiring a girl of my own.'

'She and Laurence got along okay?'

'As far as I know. She hung around until the trial was over and then she took off. She stiffed me for some money I'd advanced against her salary. If you run into her, I'd love to hear about it. Send her a bill or something just to let her know I haven't forgotten old times.'

'Does the name Libby Glass mean anything to you?'

'Who?'

'She was the accountant who handled your business down in L.A. She worked for Haycraft and McNiece.'

Scorsoni continued to look blank for a moment and then shook his head. 'What's she got to do with it?'

'She was also killed with oleander right about the time Laurence died,' I said. He didn't seem to react with any particular shock or dismay. He made a skeptical pull at his lower lip and then shrugged.

'It's a new one on me but I'll take your word for it,' he said.

'You never met her yourself?'

'I must have. Laurence and I shared the paperwork but he had most of the actual contact with the business managers. I pitched in occasionally though, so I probably ran into her at some point.'

'I've heard he was having an affair with her,' I said.

'I don't like to gossip about the dead,' Scorsoni said.

'Me neither, but he did play around,' I said carefully. 'I don't mean to push the point, but there were plenty of women who testified to that at the trial.'

Scorsoni smiled at the box he was drawing on his legal pad. The look he gave me then was shrewd.

'Well, I'll say this. One, the guy never forced himself on anyone. And two, I don't believe he would get himself involved with a business associate. That was not his style.'

'What about his clients? Didn't he get involved with them?'

'No comment.'

'Would *you* get in bed with a female client?' I asked.

'Mine are all eighty years old so the answer is no. I do estate planning. He did divorce.' He glanced at his watch and then pushed his chair back. 'I hate to cut this short but it's four-fifteen now and I have a brief to prepare.'

'Sorry. I didn't mean to take up your time. It was nice of you to see me on such short notice.'

Scorsoni walked me out toward the front, his big body exuding heat. He held the door open for me, his left arm extending up along the doorframe. Again, that barely suppressed male animal seemed to peer out through his eyes. 'Good luck,' he said. 'I suspect you won't turn up much.'

*

I picked up the eight-by-ten glossies of the sidewalk crack I'd photographed for California Fidelity. The six shots of the broken concrete were clear enough. The claimant, Marcia Threadgill, had filed for disability, asserting that she'd stumbled on the jutting slab of sidewalk that had been forced upward by a combination of tree roots and shifting soil. She was suing the owner of the craft shop whose property encompassed the errant walkway. The claim, a 'slip and fall' case, wasn't a large one – maybe forty-eight hundred dollars, which included her medical bills and damages, along with compensation for the time she'd been off work. It looked like the insurance company would pay, but I had been instructed to give it a cursory look on the off-chance that the claim was trumped-up.

Ms Threadgill's apartment was in a terraced building set into a hill overlooking the beach, not that far from my place. I parked my car about six doors down and got my binoculars out of the glove compartment. By slouching down on my spine, I could just bring her patio into focus, the view clear enough to disclose that she wasn't watering her ferns the way she ought. I don't know a lot about houseplants, but when all the green things turn brown, I'd take it as a hint. One of the ferns was that nasty kind that grow little gray hairy paws that begin, little by little, to creep right out of the pot. Anyone who'd own a thing like that probably had an inclination to defraud and I could just picture her hefting a twenty-five-pound sack of fern mulch with her alleged sprained back. I watched her place for an hour and a half but she didn't show. One of my old cohorts used to claim that men are the only suitable candidates for surveillance work because they can sit in a parked car and pee discreetly into a tennis-ball can, thus avoiding unnecessary absences. I was losing interest in Marcia Threadgill and in truth, I had to pee like crazy, so I put the binoculars away and found the nearest service station on my way back into town.

I stopped in at the credit bureau again and talked to my buddy who lets me peek into files not ordinarily made public. I asked him to see what he could find out about Sharon Napier and he said he'd get back to me. I did a couple of personal errands and then went home. It had not been a very satisfying day but then most of my days are the same: checking and cross-checking, filling in blanks, detail work that was absolutely essential to the job but scarcely dramatic stuff. The basic characteristics of any good investigator are a plodding nature and infinite patience. Society has inadvertently been grooming women to this end for years. I sat down at my desk and consigned Charlie Scorsoni to several index cards. It had been an unsettling interview and I had a feeling that I wasn't done with him.

5

Living with the climate in Santa Teresa is rather like functioning in a room with an overhead light fixture. The illumination is uniform – clear and bright enough – but the shadows are gone and there is a disturbing lack of dimension. The days are blanketed with sunlight. Often it is sixty-seven degrees and fair. The nights are consistently cool. Seasonally it does rain but the rest of the time, one day looks very much like the next and the constant, cloudless blue sky has a peculiar, disorienting effect, making it impossible to remember where one is in the year. Being in a building with no exterior windows gives the same impression: a subliminal suffocation, as though some, but not all, of the oxygen has been removed from the air.

I left my apartment at 9:00, heading north on Chapel. I stopped for gasoline, using the self-service pump and thinking, as I always do, what a simple but absurd pleasure it is to be able to do that sort of thing myself. By the time I found K-9 Korners, it was 9:15. The discreet sign in the window indicated that the place opened for business at eight. The grooming establishment was attached to a veterinarian's office on State Street just where it made the big bend. The building was painted flamingo pink, one wing of it housing a wilderness supply store with a mummy bag hanging in the window and a dummy, in a camping outfit, staring blankly at a tent pole.

I pushed my way into K-9 Korners to the accompaniment of many barking dogs. Dogs and I do not get along. They inevitably stick their snouts right in my crotch, sometimes clamping themselves around my leg as though to do some kind of two-legged dance. On certain occasions, I have limped gamely along, dog affixed, their masters swatting at them ineffectually, saying 'Hamlet, get down! What's the matter with you!?' It is hard to look such a dog in the face, and I prefer to keep my distance from the lot of them.

There was a glass showcase full of dog-care products, and many photographs of dogs and cats affixed to the wall. To my right was a half door, the upper portion opening into a small office with several grooming rooms adjoining. By peering around the doorjamb, I could spot several dogs in various stages of being done up. Most were shivering, their eyes rolling piteously. One was having a little red bow put in its topknot, right between its ears. On a worktable were some little brown lumps I thought I could recognize. The groomer, a woman, looked up at me.

'Can I help you?'

'The dog just stepped on that brown lump,' I said.

She looked down at the table. 'Oh Dashiell, not again. Excuse me a minute,' she said. Dashiell remained on the table, trembling, while she grabbed for some paper towels, deftly scooping up Dashiell's little accident. She seemed pretty good-natured about it. She was in her mid-forties with large brown eyes and shoulder-length gray hair, which was pulled back and secured with a scarf. She wore a dark wine-colored smock and I could see that she was tall and slim.

'Are you Gwen?'

She glanced up with a quick smile. 'Yes, that's right.'

'I'm Kinsey Millhone. I'm a private investigator.'

Gwen laughed. 'Oh Lord, what's this all about?' She disposed of the paper towel and moved over to the half door and opened it. 'Come on in. I'll be right back.'

She lifted Dashiell from the table and carried him into a back room just off to the left. More dogs began to bark and

I could hear a blower being turned off. The air in the place was dense with heat, scented with the smell of damp hair, and the odd combination of flea syrup and dog perfume. The brown linoleum tile floor was covered with assorted clippings, like a barber shop. In the adjoining room, I could see a dog being bathed by a young girl who worked over an elevated bathtub. To my left several dogs, beribboned, were waiting in cages to be picked up. Another young woman was clipping a poodle on a second grooming table. She glanced at me with interest. Gwen returned with a little gray dog under her arm.

'This is Wuffles,' she said, half clamping the dog's mouth shut. Wuffles gave her a few licks in the mouth. She pulled her head back, laughing, and made a face.

'I hope you don't mind if I finish this up. Have a seat,' she said affably, indicating a metal stool nearby. I perched, wishing I didn't have to mention Laurence Fife's name. From what Charlie Scorsoni had told me, it would rather spoil her good humor.

Gwen began to clip Wuffles's toenails, tucking the dog against her body to prevent sudden moves. 'You're local, I assume,' she said.

'Yes. I have an office downtown here,' I said, pulling out my I.D. automatically. I held it toward her so she could read it. She gave it a glance, apparently accepting it without much suspicion or concern. It always amazes me when people take me on faith.

'I understand you used to be married to Laurence Fife,' I ventured.

'Yes, that's right. Is this about him? He's been dead for years.'

'I know. His case is being opened up again.'

'Oh, *that's* interesting. By whom?'

'Nikki. Who else?' I said. 'The Homicide Department knows I'm looking into it and I have their co-operation, if that helps you any. Could you answer some questions for me?'

'All right,' she said. Her tone was cautious but there was also a note of interest, as though she considered it a curious inquiry but not necessarily bad.

'You don't sound that surprised,' I said.

'Actually I am. I thought that was finished business.'

'Well, I'm just starting to look into it and I may come up with a blank. We don't have to talk here if it's inconvenient. I don't like to interrupt your work.'

'This is fine with me, as long as you don't mind watching me clip a few dogs. I really can't afford a time-out right now. We're loaded today. Hold on,' she said. 'Kathy, could you hand me that flea spray? I think we missed a few here.'

The dark-haired groomer left the poodle long enough to reach up for the flea spray, which she passed over to Gwen. 'That's Kathy, as you might have gathered,' Gwen said. 'The one up to her elbows in soapsuds is Jan.'

Gwen began to spray Wuffles, turning her face away to avoid the fumes. 'Sorry. Go ahead.'

'How long were you married to Fife?'

'Thirteen years. We met in college, his third year, my first. I'd known him about six months I guess.'

'Good years? Bad years?'

'Well, I'm mellowing some on that,' she said. 'I used to think it was all a big waste but now I don't know. Did you know Laurence yourself?'

'I met him a couple of times,' I said, 'just superficially.'

Gwen's look was wry. 'He could be very charming if he wanted to, but at heart he was a real son of a bitch.'

Kathy glanced over at Gwen and smiled. Gwen laughed. 'These two have heard my version about a hundred times,' she said by way of explanation. 'Neither has ever been married so I tend to play devil's advocate. Anyway, in those days I was the dutiful wife, and I mean I played the part with a dedication few could match. I cooked elegant meals. I made lists. I cleaned the house. I raised the kids. I'm not saying I'm anything unique for that, except that I took it awfully to heart. I wore my hair up in this French roll, not a pin out of place, and I had these outfits to put on and take off, kind of like a Barbie doll.' She stopped and laughed at the image of herself, pretending to pull a string from her neck. 'Hello, I'm Gwen. I'm a good wife,' she burbled in a kind of nasal parrot tone. Her manner was rather affectionate as though she, instead of Laurence, had died but was remembered fondly by dear friends. Part of the time she was looking at me, and part of the time she combed and clipped the dog on the table in front of her, but in any event her manner was friendly – hardly the bitter, withdrawn account I'd expected.

'When it was over, I was pretty angry – not so much at him as at myself for buying into the whole gig. I mean, don't get me wrong. I liked it at the time and it suited me fine, but there was also a form of sensory deprivation going on so that when the marriage blew up, I was totally unequipped to deal with the real world. He managed the money. He pulled the strings. He made the major decisions, especially where the kids were concerned. I bathed and dressed and fed them and he shaped their lives. I didn't realize it at the time because I was just running around anxious to please him, which was no easy task, but now that I look back on it, it was really fucked.'

She glanced up at me to see if I'd react to the language, but I just smiled back.

'So now I sound like all the other women who came out of marriages in that era. You know, we're all faintly grumpy about it because we think we've been had.'

'You said you'd mellowed some,' I said. 'How did that come about?'

'Six thousand dollars' worth of therapy,' she said flatly.

I smiled. 'What made the marriage blow?'

Her cheeks tinted slightly at that but her gaze remained just as frank. 'I'd rather save that for later if you're really interested.'

'Sure, fine,' I said. 'I didn't mean to interrupt anyway.'

'Well. It wasn't all his fault,' she said. 'But it wasn't all mine either and he hosed me with that divorce. I'm telling you, I got beat up.'

'How?'

'How many ways are there? I was scared and I was also naïve. I wanted Laurence out of my life and I didn't care much what it cost. Except the kids. I fought him tooth and nail over them, but what can I tell you? I lost. I've never quite recovered from that.'

I wanted to ask her about the grounds for the custody battle but I had the feeling it was touchy stuff. Better to let that slide for the moment and come back to it later if I could. 'The kids must have come back to you after he died, though. Especially with his second wife going to prison.'

Gwen pushed at a strand of gray hair with a capable-looking hand. 'They were almost college age by then. In fact, Gregory had left that fall and Diane left the year after. But they were very messed-up kids. Laurence was a strict disciplinarian. Not that I have any quarrel with that – I think kids need structure – but he was a very controlling person, really out of touch with anything emotional, rather aggressive in his manner of dealing with anyone, the kids in particular. So the two of them, after five years of that regime, were both withdrawn and shut-down. Defensive, uncommunicative. From what I could tell, his relation to them was based on attack, being held accountable, much like what he had done with me. Of course, I'd been seeing them alternate week-ends and that sort of thing, and I had the usual summer visitation. I just didn't have any idea how far it had gone. And his death was a kick in the head to them on top of that. I'm sure they both had a lot of feelings that were never resolved. Diane went straight into therapy. And Gregory's seen someone since, though not regularly.' She paused a moment. 'I feel like I'm giving you case histories here.'

'Oh no, I appreciate your candor,' I said. 'Are the kids here in town too?'

'Greg's living south of Palm Springs. Salton Sea. He has a boat down there.'

'What sort of work does he do?'

'Well, he doesn't have to do anything. Laurence did provide for them financially. I don't know if you've checked on the insurance yet, but his estate was divided equally between the three kids – Greg, Diane, and Nikki's son, Colin.'

'What about Diane? Where is she?'

'She's in Claremont, going to school. Working on another degree. She's interested in teaching deaf children and she seems to do very well. It worried me some at first because I suspect, in her mind, it was all tied up – my divorce, Nikki, Colin and her responsibility – even though it had nothing to do with her.'

'Wait a minute. I don't understand what you mean,' I said.

Gwen glanced up at me with surprise. 'I thought you'd already talked to Nikki.'

'Well, I talked to her once,' I said.

'Didn't she tell you Colin was deaf? He was deaf from birth. I don't really remember what caused it, but there was nothing they could do about it apparently. Diane was very upset. She was thirteen, I think, when the baby was born and maybe she resented the intrusion. I don't mean to be so analytical at every turn but some of this came out with her psychiatrist and it seems pertinent. I think now she can articulate most of it herself – in fact she does – so I don't think I'm violating any confidence.'

She selected a couple of strands of ribbon from about twenty spools hung on pegboard on the wall above the grooming table. She laid a blue and an orange on Wuffles's head. 'What do you think, Wuf? Blue or orange?'

Wuffles raised her (I assumed) eyes and panted happily, and Gwen chose the orange, which I must admit made a certain jaunty sense against Wuffles's silver-gray mop of hair. The dog was docile, full of trust, loving every move even though half of Gwen's attention was turned to me.

'Gregory was into drugs for a while,' Gwen said conversationally. 'That's what his generation seemed to do while mine was playing house. But he's a good kid and I think he's okay now. Or as okay as he'll ever be. He's happy, which is a lot more than most of us can say – I mean, *I'm* happy but I know a lot of people who aren't.'

'Won't he get tired of boating?'

'I hope so,' Gwen said lightly. 'He can afford to do anything he wants, so if the leisure begins to pall, he'll find something useful to do. He's very smart and he's a very capable kid, in spite of the fact that he's idle right now. Sometimes I envy him that.'

'Do you think it would distress the kids if I talked to them?'

Gwen was startled at that, the first time she'd seemed disconcerted by anything. 'About their father?'

'I may have to at some point,' I said. 'I wouldn't like to do it without your knowledge, but it might really help.'

'I suppose it would be all right,' she said, but her tone was full of misgivings.

'We can talk about it later. It may not be necessary at all.'

'Oh. Well. I don't see how it could hurt. I must say, I don't really understand why you're into this business again.'

'To see if justice was done, I guess,' I said. 'It sounds melodramatic, but that's what it amounts to.'

'Justice to whom? Laurence or Nikki?'

'Maybe you should tell me what you think. I'm assuming there was no love lost between you and them, but do you think he got his "just deserts"?'

'Sure, why not? I don't know about her. I figure she had a fair trial and if that's the way it came out, well she must have done it. But there were times I'd have done it myself if I had thought of some way.'

'So if she killed him, you wouldn't blame her?'

'Me and half a dozen others. Laurence alienated a lot of people,' she said carelessly. 'We could have formed a club and sent out a monthly newsletter. I still run into people who sidle up to me and say "Thank God he's dead." Literally. Out of the corner of their mouths.' Gwen laughed again. 'I'm sorry if that sounds irreverent but he was not a nice man.'

'But who in particular?'

She put her hand on her hip and gave me a jaded look. 'If you got an hour, I'll give you a list,' she said.

I laughed then. Her humor seemed irrepressible or maybe she was only feeling ill at ease. Talking to a private eye is often unnerving to people.

Gwen put Wuffles in an empty cage and then went into the other room and led out a big English sheepdog. She lifted its front feet first, placing them on the table, and then she heaved its hind legs up while the dog whined uneasily.

'Oh come on, Duke,' she snapped. 'This one is such a sissy.'

'Do you think we could talk again soon?' I asked.

'Sure, I'd like that. I close up here at six. If you're free then, we can have a drink. By the end of the day, I'm ready for one.'

'Me too. I'll see you then,' I said.

I hopped down off my stool and let myself out. When the door closed, she was already chatting with the dog. I wondered what else she knew and how much of it she was willing to share. I also hoped to hell I could look that good in another ten years.

6

I stopped off at a pay phone and gave Nikki a call. She picked up on the third ring.

'Nikki? This is Kinsey. I have a request. Is there any way I can get into the house where you and Laurence lived?'

'Sure. I still own it. I'm just leaving to drive up to Monterey to bring Colin back but it's en route. I can meet you there if you like.'

She gave me the address and said she'd be there in fifteen minutes or so. I hung up and headed for my car. I wasn't sure what I was after but I wanted to walk through the place, to get a feel for what it was like, living as they lived. The house was in Montebello, a section of town where there are rumored to be more millionaires per square mile than in any other part of the country. Most of the houses are not even visible from the road. Occasionally you can catch a glimpse of a tiled roof hidden away in tangles of olive trees and live oak. Many parcels of land are bordered by winding walls of hand-hewn stone overgrown with wild roses and nasturtiums. Towering eucalyptus trees line the roads, with intermittent palms looking like Spanish exclamation marks.

The Fifes' house was on the corner of two lanes, shielded from view by ten-foot hedges that parted at one point to admit a narrow brick driveway. The house was substantial: two stories of putty-colored stucco with white trim. The façade was plain and there was a portico to one side. The surrounding land was equally plain except for patches of California poppies in shades of peach and rich yellow, gold and pink. Beyond the house, I could see a double garage with what I guessed was a caretaker's quarters above. The lawns were well tended and the house, while it had an unoccupied look, didn't seem neglected. I parked my car on the portion of the drive that circled back on itself to permit easy exit. In spite of the red-tiled roof, the house looked more French than Spanish: windows without cornices, the front door flush with the drive.

I got out of my car and walked around to the right, my footsteps making no sound on the pale rosy bricks. In the rear, I could see the outline of a swimming pool and for the first time, I felt something chill and out of place. The pool had been filled to the brim with dirt and trash. An aluminium lawn chair was half-sunk in the sod, weeds growing through the rungs. The diving board extended now over an irregular surface of grass clippings and dead leaves, as though the water had thickened and congealed. A set of steps with handholds disappeared into the depths and the surrounding concrete apron was riddled with dark splotches.

I found myself approaching with uneasiness and I was startled out of my concentration by the sound of malicious hissing. Waddling toward me with remarkable speed were two huge white geese, their heads thrust forward, mouths open like snakes with their tongues protruding, emitting a terrifying sound. I gave a low involuntary cry and began to backtrack toward my car, afraid to take my eyes off them. They covered the ground between us at a pace that forced me into a run. I barely reached my car before they caught up with me. I wrenched the door open and slammed it again with a panic I hadn't felt in years. I locked both doors, half expecting the viperous birds to batter at my windows until they gave way. For a moment they balanced, half lifted, wings flapping, black eyes bright with ill-will, their hissing faces even with mine. And then they lost interest and waddled off, honking and hissing, pecking savagely at the grass. Until that moment, it had never even occurred to me to include crazed geese among my fears, but they had suddenly shot straight to the top of the list along with worms and water bugs.

Nikki's car pulled in behind mine. She got out with perfect composure and approached as I rolled my window down. The two geese appeared again around the corner of the house, making their flat-footed beeline for the flesh of her calves. She gave them an idle glance and then laughed. Both raised up again, short wings flopping ineffectually, their manner suddenly benign. Nikki had a bread bag in her hand and she tossed them some crumbs.

'What the hell *are* those things?' I eased out of the car cautiously but neither paid the slightest attention to me.

'That's Hansel and Gretel,' she said amicably. 'They're Embden geese.'

'The geese part I could tell. What happened? Did somebody train them to kill?'

'It keeps little kids off the property,' she said. 'Come on in.' She inserted a key in the lock and the front door swung open. Nikki stooped to pick up some junk mail that had been pushed through the slot. 'The mailman gives them saltines,' she said as an afterthought. 'They'll eat anything.'

'Who else had keys to this place?' I asked. I noticed an alarm-system panel, which was apparently turned off.

She shrugged. 'Laurence and me. Greg and Diane. I can't think of anyone else.'

'Gardener? Maid?'

'Both have keys now but I don't think they did at the time. We did have a housekeeper. Mrs Voss. She probably had one.'

'Did you have a security system then?'

'We do now but that's only been in the last four years. I should have sold the place years ago but I didn't want to make decisions like that when I was in prison.'

'It must be worth a lot.'

'Oh sure. Real-estate values have tripled and we paid seven hundred and fifty thousand at the time. He picked it out. Put it in my name for business reasons, but it never did appeal to me much.'

'Who did the decorating?' I asked.

Nikki smiled sheepishly. 'I did. I don't think Laurence knew any better, but I took a subtle revenge. He insisted that we buy the place so I left all the color out.'

The rooms were large, ceilings high, and plenty of light came in. The floors were dark-stained tongue and groove. The layout was very conventional: living room to the right, dining room to the left, with the kitchen behind. There was a sitting room beyond the living room and a long glassed-in porch along that side, running the length of the house. There was a curious air to the house, which I assumed was because no one had lived there for years, like a department-store display of especially elegant appointments. The furniture was still in place and there was no sign of dust. There were no plants and no magazines, no evidence of ongoing activity. Even the silence had a hollow tone, barren and lifeless.

The whole interior was done in neutral tones: grays and oyster whites, hazel and cinnamon. The couches and chairs were soft upholstered pieces with rounded arms and thick cushions, a sort of art deco look without any attempt at flash. There was a nice blend of modern and antique and it was clear that Nikki knew what she was doing even when she didn't care.

Upstairs, there were five bedrooms, all with fireplaces, all with bathrooms of remarkable size, deep closets, dressing rooms, the whole of it carpeted in thick fawn-colored wall-to-wall wool shag.

'This is the master suite?'

Nikki nodded. I followed her into the bathroom. Fat chocolate towels were stacked near the sink. There was a sunken tub, the surrounding ceramic tile a pale tobacco shade. There was a separate glassed-in shower that had been outfitted as a steam room. Soap, toilet paper, Kleenex.

'Do you stay here?' I asked as we came down the stairs.

'I haven't as yet, but I may. I have someone come in every two weeks to clean and of course there's a gardener on the premises all the time. I've been staying at the beach.'

'You have another house out there?'

'Yes. Laurence's mother left it to me.'

'Why you and not him?'

She smiled slightly. 'Laurence and his mother didn't get along. Would you like some tea?'

'I thought you had to hit the road.'

'I have time.'

I followed her out to the kitchen. There was a cooking island in the center of the room with a big copper hood above the burners, a wide expanse of chopping block counter, and all manner of pans, baskets, and kitchen implements hanging on a circular metal rack that extended from the ceiling. All of the other counters were white ceramic tile; a double stainless-steel sink was sunk into one. There was a regular oven, a convection oven, a microwave, a refrigerator, two freezers and impressive storage space.

Nikki put some water on to boil and perched herself on a wooden stool. I took up a stool across from her, the two of us sitting in the center of the room, which looked as much like a chem lab as a cook's dream.

'Who have you talked to so far?' she asked.

I told her about my conversation with Charlie Scorsoni.

'They seem like an odd pair of friends to me,' I said. 'My recollection of Laurence is a little hazy, but he always struck me as very elegant and cerebral. Scorsoni's very physical. He reminds me of a guy in an ad for chain saws.'

'Oh Charlie's a real scrapper. From what I hear, he came up the hard way, bulldozing his way past all obstacles.

Kind of like the blurb on a paperback: "stepping over the bodies of those he loved . . ." Maybe Laurence liked that. He always talked about Charlie with grudging respect. Laurence had everything handed to him. Of course Charlie thought Laurence could do no wrong.'

'That seemed clear enough,' I said. 'I don't suppose he had any motive for murder. Did you ever think he might have had a hand in it?'

Nikki smiled, getting up to take out cups, saucers and tea bags. 'At one time or another, I've considered everyone, but Charlie seems unlikely to me. He certainly didn't benefit financially or professionally . . .' She poured boiling water into both cups.

'As far as the eye can see,' I said, dunking my tea bag.

'Well yes, that's true. I suppose there might have been some kind of hidden dividend, but surely that would have come to light at some point in the last eight years.'

'One would think.' I went on to tell her about my interview with Gwen. Nikki's cheeks went ever so faintly pink.

'I feel bad about her,' she said. 'By the time they divorced, Laurence really hated her and I tended to fan the flames a bit. He never could take any responsibility for the failure of that marriage and as a result, he had to blame her and punish her. I didn't help. At first I really believed what he was saying about her. I mean, I personally thought she seemed like a capable person and I knew Laurence had been very dependent on her but it was safer to wean him away by feeding his bad feelings. You know what I mean? In some ways, his hating her so strongly was no different from his loving her, but it made me feel more secure to widen the breach. I'm ashamed of that now. When I fell out of love with him myself and he began to turn on me, I suddenly recognized the process.'

'But I thought you were the downfall of that relationship,' I said, looking at her carefully through the steam rising from my teacup.

Nikki ran both hands into her hair, lifting it away from her head and letting it fall again, giving her head a slight toss. 'Oh no,' she said, 'I was his revenge. Never mind the fact that he'd been screwing around on her for years. He found out she was having an affair so he had me. Nice, huh? I didn't realize all this until much later, but that's how it was.'

'Wait a minute. Let me see if I got this straight,' I said. 'He found out *she* was involved with someone, so he gets involved with you and then divorces her. From what I understand she got reamed.'

'Oh yes. That's exactly what he did. The affair with me was his way of proving he didn't care. Taking the kids and the money was her punishment. He was very vindictive. It was one reason he made such a good attorney. He identified passionately with anyone who'd been wronged. He'd whip himself into a frenzy over the least little thing and then he'd use that as a driving force until he'd ground the opposition down. He was merciless. Absolutely merciless.'

'Who did Gwen have the affair with?'

'You'd have to ask her that. I'm not sure I ever knew. It was certainly something he never talked about.'

I asked her about the night Laurence died and she filled me in on those details.

'What was he allergic to?'

'Animal hair. Mostly dogs but cat dander too. For a long time he wouldn't tolerate pets in the house but then when Colin was two, someone suggested that we get him a dog.'

'I understand Colin's deaf.'

'He was born deaf. They test newborns' hearing so we knew right away, but nothing could be done for him. Apparently I had a mild case of German measles before I even realized

I was pregnant. Fortunately that was the only damage he seemed to suffer. We were lucky to that extent.'

'And the dog was for him? Like a guard dog or something?'

'Something like that. You can't watch a kid night and day. That's why we had the pool filled in. Bruno was a big help too.'

'A German shepherd.'

'Yes,' Nikki said and then hesitated slightly. 'He's dead now. He got hit by a car right out there on the road, but he was a great dog. Very smart, very loving, very protective of Colin. Anyway, Laurence could see what it did for him, having a dog like Bruno, so he went back on the allergy medication. He really did love Colin. Whatever his faults, and he had lots of them, believe me, he did love that little boy.'

Her smile faded and her face went through an odd alteration. She was suddenly gone, disengaged. Her eyes were blank and the look she gave me was empty of emotion.

'I'm sorry, Nikki. I wish we didn't have to go into all of this.'

We finished our tea and then got up. She removed the cups and saucers, tucking them into the dishwasher. When she looked back at me, her eyes were that flat gun-metal gray again. 'I hope you find out who killed him. I'll never be happy until I know.'

The tone of her voice made my hands numb. There was a flash in her eyes like the one I'd seen in the eyes of the geese: malevolent, unreasoning It was just a flicker and it quickly disappeared.

'You wouldn't try to get even, would you?' I asked.

She glanced away from me. 'No. I used to think about that in prison a lot but now that I'm out, it doesn't seem that important to me. Right now, all I want is to have my son back. And I want to lie on the beach and drink Perrier and wear my own clothes. And eat in restaurants and when I'm not doing that, I want to cook. And sleep late and take bubble baths . . .' She stopped and laughed at herself and then took a deep breath. 'So. No, I don't want to risk my freedom.'

Her eyes met mine and I smiled in response. 'You better hit the road,' I said.

7

I stopped off at the Montebello pharmacy while I was in the neighborhood. The pharmacist, whose name tag said 'Carroll Sims,' was in his fifties, medium height, with mild brown eyes behind mild tortoiseshell frames. He was in the midst of explaining to quite an old woman exactly what her medication was and how it should be taken. She was both puzzled and exasperated by the explanation but Sims was tactful, answering her flustered inquiries with a benign goodwill. I could imagine people showing him their warts and cat bites, describing chest pains and urinary symptoms across the counter. When it was my turn, I wished I had some little ill I could tell him about. Instead, I showed him my I.D.

'What can I do for you?'

'Did you happen to work here eight years ago when Laurence Fife was murdered?'

'Well, I sure did. I own the place. Are you a friend of his?'

'No,' I said, 'I've been hired to look into the whole case again. I thought this was a logical place to start.'

'I don't think I can be much help. I can tell you the medication he was taking, dosage, number of refills, the doctor who prescribed it, but I can't tell you how the switch was made. Well, I can tell you that. I just can't tell you who did it.'

Most of the information Sims gave me I already knew. Laurence was taking an antihistamine called HistaDril, which he'd been on for years. He consulted an allergist about once a year and the rest of the time the refill on the medication was automatically okayed. The only thing Sims told me that I hadn't known was that HistaDril had recently been taken off the market because of possible carcinogenic side-effects.

'In other words, if Fife had just taken the medication for a few more years, he might have gotten cancer and died anyway.'

'Maybe,' the pharmacist said. We stared at one another for a moment.

'I don't suppose you have any idea who killed him,' I said.

'Nope.'

'Well, I guess that's that. Did you see any of the trial?'

'Just when I testified. I identified the pill bottle as one of ours. It had been pretty recently refilled but Fife himself had done that and we'd chitchatted at the time. He'd been taking HistaDril for so long we hardly needed to talk about that.'

'Do you remember what you did talk about?'

'Oh, the usual things. I think there was a fire burning across the backside of the city about that time and we talked about that. A lot of people with allergies were bothered by the increase in air pollution.'

'Was it bothering him?'

'It bothered everyone a little bit but I don't remember him being any worse off than anyone else.'

'Well,' I said, 'I thank you for your time. If you think of anything else, will you give me a buzz? I'm in the book.'

'Sure, if I think of anything,' he said.

It was midafternoon and I wasn't meeting Gwen again until 6:00. I felt restless and out of sorts. Bit by bit, I was putting together background information, but nothing was really happening yet, and as far as I knew nothing might ever come of it. As far as the state of California was concerned, justice had been served and only Nikki Fife stood in contradiction of this. Nikki and the nameless, faceless killer of Laurence Fife who had enjoyed eight years of immunity from prosecution, eight years of freedom that I was now being hired to violate. At some point, I was bound to tread on someone's toes and that someone was not going to be happy with me.

I decided to go spy on Marcia Threadgill. At the time she tripped on that crack in the sidewalk, she had just come from the craft shop, having purchased items necessary to make one of those wooden purses covered with assorted shells. I imagined her decoupaging orange crates, making clever hanging ornaments out of egg cartons festooned with plastic sprigs of lily of the valley. Marcia Threadgill was twenty-six years old and she suffered from bad taste. The owner of the craft shop had filled me in on the projects she had done and every bit of it reminded me of my aunt. Marcia Threadgill was cheap at heart. She turned common trash into Christmas gifts. This is the mentality, in my opinion, that leads to cheating insurance companies and other sly ruses. This is the kind of person who would write to the Pepsi-Cola bottling plant claiming to have found a mouse hair in her drink, trying to net herself a free case of soda.

I parked a few doors down from her apartment and got out my binoculars. I slouched, focusing on her patio, and then sat up. 'Well I'll be damned,' I breathed.

In place of the nasty brown withered fern was a hanging plant of mammoth proportions, which must have weighed twenty pounds. Now how had she lifted that up to attach to a hook high above her head? A neighbor? Boyfriend? Had she done it herself perchance? I could even see the price tag stuck to one side of the pot. She'd bought it at a Gateway supermarket for $29.95, which was quite a price considering that it was probably full of fruit flies.

'Shit,' I said. Where was I when she hoisted that mama up? Twenty pounds of glossy plant and moist soil on a chain at shoulder height. Had she stood on a chair? I drove straight over to the nearby Gateway supermarket and headed back to the produce department. There were five or six such plants – Dumbo ears or elephant tongues, whatever the damn things are called. I lifted one. Oh my God. It was worse than I had thought. Awkward and heavy, impossible to manage without help. I picked up some film in the Ten Items or Less, No Checks line and loaded my camera. 'Marcia, you little sweetheart,' I cooed, 'I'm gonna nail your ass.'

I drove back to her apartment and got out my binoculars again. I'd no more than settled down on my spine, glasses trained on her patio, than Ms Threadgill herself appeared, trailing one of those long plastic hoses, which must have been attached to her faucet inside. She misted and sprayed and watered and carried on, poking a finger down into the dirt, plucking a yellowing leaf from another potted plant on the patio rail. A real obsessive type by the look of it, inspecting the underside of leaves for God knows what pests. I studied her face. She looked like she'd spent about forty-five dollars having a free makeup demonstration in some department store. Mocha and caramel on her eyelids. Raspberry on her cheekbones. Lipstick the color of chocolate. Her fingernails were long and painted the approximate shade of cherry syrup in the sort of boxed candies you wish you hadn't bitten into so eagerly.

An old woman in a nylon jersey dress came out onto the patio above Marcia's and the two had a conversation. I guessed that it was some kind of complaint because neither looked happy and Marcia eventually flounced away. The old lady yelled something after her that looked dirty even in pantomime. I got out of the car and locked it, taking a clipboard and legal pad.

Marcia's apartment was listed on the register as 2-C. The apartment above hers was listed under the name Augusta White. I bypassed the elevator and took the stairs, pausing first outside Marcia's door. She was playing a Barry Manilow album full-blast, and even as I listened she cranked up the volume a notch or two. I went up another flight and tapped on Augusta's door. She was there in a flash, her face thrust forward through the crack like a Pekingese, complete with bulging eyes, pug nose, and chin whiskers. 'Yes?' she snapped. She was eighty years old if a day.

'I'm in the building next door,' I said. 'We've had some complaints about the noise and the manager asked me to look into it. Could I talk to you?' I held up my official-looking clipboard.

'Hold on.'

She moved away from the door and stomped back into her kitchen to get her broom. I heard her bang on the kitchen floor a few times. From below, there was a mighty thump, as though Marcia Threadgill had whacked on the ceiling with a combat boot.

Augusta White stomped back, squinting at me through the crack. 'You look like a real-estate agent to me,' she said suspiciously.

'Well, I'm not. Honest.'

'You look like one anyway so just go on off with your papers. I know all the people next door and you aren't one.' She slammed the door shut and shot the bolt into place.

So much for that. I shrugged and made my way back down the stairs. Outside again, I made an eyeball assessment of the terraces. The patios were staggered in a pyramid effect and I had a quick flash of myself climbing up the outside of the building like a second-story man to spy on Marcia Threadgill at close range. I had really hoped I could enlist someone's aid in getting a first-hand report of Ms Threadgill, but I was going to have to let it slide for the moment. I took some pictures of the hanging plant from the vantage point of my car, hoping it would soon wither and perish from a bad case of root rot. I wanted to be there when she hung a new one into place.

I went back to my apartment and jotted down some notes. It was 4:45 and I changed into my jogging clothes: a pair of shorts and an old cotton turtleneck. I'm really not a physical fitness advocate. I've been in shape maybe once in my life, when I qualified for the police academy, but there's something about running that satisfies a masochistic streak. It hurts and I'm slow but I have good shoes and I like the smell of my own sweat. I run on the mile and a half of sidewalk that tracks the beach, and the air is usually slightly damp and very clean. Palm trees line the wide grassy area between the sidewalk and the sand and there are always other joggers, most of them looking lots better than I.

I did two miles and then called it quits. My calves hurt. My chest was burning. I huffed and puffed, bending from the waist, imagining all kinds of toxic wastes pumping out through my pores and lungs, a regular purge. I walked for half a block and then I heard a car horn toot. I glanced over. Charlie Scorsoni had pulled in at the curb in a pale blue 450 SL that looked very good on him. I wiped the sweat trickling down my face on an upraised shirt sleeve and crossed to his car.

'Your cheeks are bright pink,' he said.

'I always look like I'm having an attack. You should see the looks I get. What are you doing down here?'

'I felt guilty. Because I cut you short yesterday. Hop in.'

'Oh no.' I laughed, still trying to catch my breath. 'I don't want to get sweat all over your seats.'

'Can I follow you back to your place?'

'Are you serious?'

'Sure,' he said. 'I thought I'd be especially winsome so you wouldn't put me on your "possibly guilty" list.'

'Won't help. I'm suspicious of everyone.'

*

When I came out of the shower and stuck my head around the bathroom door, Scorsoni was looking at the books stacked up on my desk. 'Did you have time to search through the drawers?' I asked.

He smiled benignly. 'They were locked.'

I smiled and closed the bathroom door again, getting dressed. I noticed that I was pleased to see him and that didn't sit well with me. I'm a real hard-ass when it comes to men. I don't often think of a forty-eight-year-old man as 'cute' but that's how he struck me. He was big and his hair had a nice curl to it, his rimless glasses making his blue eyes look almost luminous. The dimple in his chin didn't hurt either.

I left the bathroom, moving toward the kitchenette in my bare feet. 'Want a beer?'

He was sitting on the couch by then, leafing through a book about auto theft. 'Very literate taste,' he said. 'Why don't you let me buy you a drink?'

'I have to be somewhere at six,' I said.

'Beer's fine then.'

I uncapped it and handed it to him, sitting down at the other end of the couch with my feet tucked up under me. 'You must have left the office early. I'm flattered.'

'I'll go back tonight. I have to go out of town for a couple of days and I'll have to get my briefcase packed, tidy up some loose ends for Ruth.'

'Why take time out for me?'

Scorsoni gave me a quizzical smile with the barest hint of irritation. 'God, so defensive. Why not take time out for you? If Nikki didn't kill Laurence, I'm as interested as anyone in finding out who did it, that's all.'

'You don't believe she's innocent for a minute,' I said.

'I believe you believe it,' he said.

I looked at him carefully. 'I can't give you information. I hope you understand that. I could use any help you've got and if you have a brainstorm, I'd love to hear it, but it can't be a two-way street.'

'You want to lecture an attorney about client privilege, is that it? Jesus Christ, Millhone. Give me a break.'

'Okay, okay. I'm sorry,' I said. I looked down at his big hands and then up at his face again. 'I just didn't want my brain picked, that's all.'

His expression relaxed and his smile was lazy. 'You said you didn't know anything anyway,' he pointed out, 'so what's to pick? You're such a goddamn *grouch*.'

I smiled then. 'Listen, I don't know what my chances are on this thing. I don't have a feel for it yet and it's making me nervous.'

'Yeah and you've been working on it – what – two days?'

'About that.'

'Then give yourself a break while you're at it.' He took a sip of beer and then with a small tap set the bottle on the coffee table. 'I wasn't very honest with you yesterday,' he said.

'About what?'

'Libby Glass. I did know who she was and I suspected that he was into some kind of relationship with her. I just didn't think it was any of your business.'

'I don't see how it could make any difference at this point,' I said.

'That's what I decided. And maybe it's important to your case – who knows? I think since he died, I've tended to invest him with a purity he never really had. He played around a lot. But his taste usually ran to the moneyed class. Older women. Those slim elegant ones who marry aristocracy.'

'What was Libby like?'

'I don't really know. I ran into her a couple of times when she was setting up our tax account. She seemed nice enough.

Young. She couldn't have been more than twenty-five or twenty-six.'

'Did he tell you he was having an affair with her?'

'Oh no, not him. I never knew him to kiss and tell.'

'A real gentleman,' I said.

Scorsoni shot me a warning look.

'I'm not being facetious,' I said hastily. 'I've heard he kept his mouth shut about the women in his life. That's all I meant.'

'Yeah, he did. He played everything close to his chest. That's what made him a good attorney too. He never tipped his hand, never telegraphed. The last six months before he died, he was odd though, protective. There were times when I almost thought he wasn't well, but it wasn't physical. It was some kind of psychic pain, if you'll excuse the phrase.'

'You had drinks with him that night, didn't you?'

'We had dinner. Down at the Bistro. Nikki was off someplace and we played racquetball and then had a bite to eat. He was fine as far as I could tell.'

'Did he have the allergy medication with him then?'

Scorsoni shook his head. 'He wasn't much for pills anyway. Tylenol if he had a headache, but that was rare. Even Nikki admitted that he took the allergy cap after he got home. It had to be someone who had access to that.'

'Had Libby Glass been up here?'

'Not for business as far as I know. She might have come up to see him but he never said anything to me. Why?'

'I don't know. I was just thinking that somebody might have dosed them both somehow at the same time. She didn't die until four days later but that's not hard to explain if the caps were self-administered.'

'I never heard much about her death. I don't even think it hit the papers here. He was down in Los Angeles though, I do know that. About a week and a half before he died.'

'That's interesting. I'm going down there anyway. Maybe I can check that out.'

He glanced at his watch. 'I better let you go,' he said, getting up. I got up and ambled to the door with him, oddly reluctant to see him go.

'How'd you lose the weight?' I said.

'What, this?' he asked, slapping his midsection. He leaned toward me slightly as though he meant to confide some incredible regimen of denial and self-abuse.

'I gave up candy bars. I used to keep 'em in my desk drawer,' he murmured conspiratorially. 'Snickers and Three Musketeers, Hershey's Kisses, with the silver wrappers and the little paper wick at the top? A hundred a day . . .'

I could feel a laugh bubble up because his tone was caressing and he sounded like he was confessing to a secret addiction to wearing pantyhose. Also because I knew if I turned my face, I'd be closer to him than I thought I could cope with at that point.

'Mars Bars? Baby Ruth?' I said.

'All the time,' he said. I could almost feel the heat of his face and I slid a look up at him sideways. He laughed at himself then, breaking the spell, and his eyes held mine only a little longer than they should. 'I'll see you,' he said.

We shook hands as he left. I didn't know why – maybe just an excuse to touch. Even a contact that casual made the hairs stand up along my arm. My early-warning system was clanging away like crazy and I wasn't sure how to interpret it. It's the same sensation I have sometimes on the twenty-first floor when I open a window – a terrible attraction to the notion of tumbling out. I go a long time between men and maybe it was time again. Not good, I thought, not good.

8

When I pulled up in front of K-9 Korners at 6:00, Gwen was just locking up. I rolled down my car window and leaned across the seat. 'You want to go in my car?'

'I better follow you,' she said. 'Do you know where the Palm Garden is? Is that all right with you?'

'Sure, that's fine.'

She moved off toward the parking lot and a minute later she pulled out of the driveway in a bright yellow Saab. The restaurant was only a few blocks away and we pulled into the parking lot side by side. She had stripped off her smock and was brushing haphazardly at the lap of her skirt.

'Pardon the dog hair,' she said. 'Usually I head straight for a bath.'

The Palm Garden is located in the heart of Santa Teresa, tucked back into a shopping complex, with tables outside and the requisite palms in big wooden tubs. We found a small table off to one side and I ordered white wine while she ordered Perrier.

'You don't drink?'

'Not much. I gave that up when I got divorced. Before that I was knocking back a *lot* of Scotch. How's your case?'

'It's hard to tell at this point,' I said. 'How long have you been in the dog-grooming business?'

'Longer than I'd like,' she said and laughed.

We talked for a while about nothing in particular. I wanted time to study her, hoping to figure out what she and Nikki Fife had in common that both of them had ended up married to him. It was she who brought the conversation back around to the subject at hand. 'So fire away,' she said.

I curtsied mentally. She was very deft, making my job much easier than I'd thought she would. 'I didn't think you'd be so co-operative.'

'You've been talking to Charlie Scorsoni,' she said.

'It seemed like a logical place to start,' I said with a shrug. 'Is he on your list?'

'Of people who might have killed Laurence? No. I don't think so. Am I on his?'

I shook my head.

'That's odd,' she said.

'How so?'

She tilted her head, her expression composed. 'He thinks I'm bitter. I've heard it from a lot of different sources. Small town. If you wait long enough, anyone's opinion about you will be reported back.'

'It sounds like you'd be entitled to a little bitterness.'

'I worked that through a long time ago. By the way, this is where you can reach Greg and Diane if you're interested.' She pulled an index card out of her purse with the two names, addresses and telephone numbers.

'Thanks. I appreciate that. Any advice about how they should be approached? I was serious when I said I didn't want to upset them.'

'No, no. They're straight shooters, both of them. If anything, you might find them a LITTLE *too* up front.'

'I understand they haven't kept in touch with Nikki.'

'Probably not, but that's too bad. Old business. I'd much rather see them let that go. She was very good to them.' She reached back then and pulled the scarf out of her hair, shaking her hair slightly so that it would fall loose. It was shoulder-length, an interesting shade of gray that I didn't imagine had been tampered with. The contrast was nice . . . gray hair, brown eyes. She had strong cheekbones, nice lines around her mouth, good teeth, a tan that suggested health without vanity.

'What did you think of Nikki?' I asked, now that the subject had been broached.

'I'm not really sure. I mean, I resented the hell out of her back then but I'd like to talk to her sometime. I feel like we might understand each other a lot better. You want to know why I married him?'

'I'd be interested in that.'

'He had a big cock,' she said impishly and then laughed. 'Sorry. I couldn't resist that. Actually he was awful in the sack. A regular screwing machine. Terrific if you like your sex depersonalized.'

'I'm not crazy about that kind myself,' I said dryly.

'Neither was I when I figured it out. I was a virgin when I married him.'

'Jesus,' I said. 'That's a bore.'

'It was an even bigger bore back then but it was all part of the message I was raised on. I always thought the failure was mine in terms of our sex life . . . ' She trailed off and the faintest tint came to her cheeks.

'Until what,' I ventured.

'Maybe I should have wine too,' she said and signaled to the waitress. I ordered a second glass. Gwen turned to me.

'I had an affair when I turned thirty.'

'Shows you had *some* sense.'

'Well, yes and no. It only lasted about six weeks but it was the best six weeks of my life. In a way, I was glad to see it end. It was powerful stuff and it would have turned my life around. I wasn't ready for that.' She paused and I could see her reviewing the information in her head. 'Laurence was always very critical of me and I believed I deserved it. Then I ran into a man who thought I could do no wrong. At first I resisted. I knew what I was feeling for this man but it went against the grain. Finally I just gave in. For a while I told myself it was good for my relationship with Laurence. I was suddenly getting something I'd needed for a long time and it made me feel very giving with him. And then the double life began to take its toll. I deceived Laurence for as long as I could but he began to suspect something was going on. I got so I couldn't tolerate his touch – too much tension, too much deceit. Too much good stuff somewhere else. He must have felt the change come over me because he began to probe and question, wanted to know where I was every minute of the day. Called at odd hours in the afternoon and of course I was out. Even when I was with Laurence, I was somewhere else. He threatened me with divorce and I got scared so I 'fessed up. That was the biggest mistake of my life because he divorced me anyway.'

'As punishment.'

'As only Laurence Fife knew how. In spades.'

'Where is he now?'

'My lover? Why do you ask?'

Her tone was instantly guarded, her expression wary.

'Laurence must have known who he was. If he was punishing you, why not punish the other guy too?'

'I don't want to cast suspicion on him,' she said. 'That would be a lousy thing to do. He had nothing to do with Laurence's death. I'll give you a written guarantee.'

'What makes you so sure? A lot of people were mistaken about a lot of things back then and Nikki paid a price for it.'

'Hey,' she said sharply, 'Nikki was represented by the best lawyer in the state. Maybe she got a few bad breaks and maybe not, but there's no point in trying to lay the blame on someone who had nothing to do with it.'

'I'm not trying to blame anyone. I'm just trying to come up with a direction on this thing. I can't force you to tell me who he is . . . '

'That's right and I think you'd have a hell of a time finding out from anyone else.'

'Look, I'm not here to pick a fight. I'm sorry. Skip that for now.'

Two patches of red appeared on her neck. She was fighting back anger, trying to get control of herself again. I thought, for a moment, she would bolt.

'I'm not going to press the point,' I said. 'That's a whole separate issue and I came here to talk to you. You don't want to talk about that then it's fine with me.'

She still seemed poised for flight so I shut my mouth and let her work it out for herself. Finally I could see her relax a little and I realized then that I was as tense as she. This was too valuable a contact for me to blow.

'Let's go back to Laurence. Tell me about him,' I said. 'What were all the infidelities about?'

She laughed self-consciously then and took a sip of wine, shaking her head. 'Sorry. I didn't mean to get upset but you took me by surprise.'

'Yeah, well that happens now and then. Sometimes I surprise myself.'

'I don't think he liked women. He was always expecting to be betrayed. Women were the people who did you in. He liked to get there first, or at least that's my guess. I suspect an affair for him was always a power relationship and he was top dog.'

'"Do unto others before they do unto you."'

'Right.'

'But who had an ax to grind with him? Who could have hated him that much?'

She shrugged and her composure seemed restored. 'I've thought about that all afternoon and what's odd is that when it comes right down to it, I'm not sure. He had awful relationships with a lot of people. Divorce attorneys are never very popular, but most of them don't get murdered.'

'Maybe it wasn't related to business,' I suggested. 'Maybe it wasn't an irate husband pissed off about alimony and child support. Maybe it was something else – "a woman scorned."'

'Well, there were a lot of those. But I think he was probably very slick about breaking things off. Or the women themselves were sufficiently recovered to recognize the limits of the relationship and move on. He did have an awful affair with the wife of a local judge, a woman named Charlotte Mercer. She'd have run him down in the street given half a chance. Or that's what I've heard since. She wasn't the type to let go gracefully.'

'How'd you find out about it?'

'She called me up after he broke off with her.'

'Before your divorce or afterwards?'

'Oh afterwards, because I remember thinking at the time that I wished she'd called sooner. I went into court with nothing.'

'I don't understand,' I said. 'What good would it have done? You couldn't have gotten him on adultery even back then.'

'He didn't get *me* on that either but it sure would have given me a psychological edge. I felt so guilty about what I'd done that I hardly put up a fight except when it came to the kids, and even then he beat me down. If she'd wanted to cause trouble, she could have been a big help. He still had his reputation to protect. Anyway, maybe Charlotte Mercer can fill you in.'

'Wonderful. I'll tell her she's my number-one suspect.'

Gwen laughed. 'Feel free to mention my name if she wants to know who sent you. It's the least I can do.'

After Gwen left, I looked up Charlotte Mercer's address in the telephone book by the pay phone in the rear. She and the judge lived up in the foothills above Santa Teresa in what turned out to be a sprawling one-story house with stables off to the right, the land all dust and scrub brush. The sun was just beginning to go down and the view was spectacular. The ocean looked like a wide lavender ribbon stitched up against a pink-and-blue sky.

A housekeeper in a black uniform answered the bell and I was left in a wide cool hallway while 'the missus' was fetched. Light footsteps approached from the rear of the house and I thought at first the Mercers' teenage daughter (if there was one) had appeared in Charlotte's place.

'Yes, what is it?'

The voice was low and husky and rude and the initial impression of adolescence gave way rapidly.

'Charlotte Mercer?'

'Yes, that's right.'

She was petite, probably five-four, maybe a hundred pounds if that. Sandals, tank top, white shorts, her legs tawny and shapely. Not a line on her face. Her hair was a dusty blonde, cut short, her makeup subdued. She had to be fifty-five years old and there was no way she could have looked that good without a team of experts. There was an artificial firmness to her jaw and her cheeks had that sleek tucked-up look that only a face-lift can provide at that late date. Her neck was lined and the backs of her hands were knotted with veins but those were the only contradictions to the appearance of slim, cool youth. Her eyes were a pale blue, made vivid by the skillful application of mascara and an eye shadow in two shades of gray. Gold bracelets jangled on one arm.

'I'm Kinsey Millhone,' I said. 'I'm a private investigator.'

'Goody for you. What brings you here?'

'I'm looking into Laurence Fife's death.'

Her smile faltered, sinking from minimal good manners into something cruel. She gave me a cursory inspection, dismissing me in the same glance. 'I hope it won't take long,' she said, and looked back. 'Come out to the patio. I've left my drink there.'

I followed her toward the back of the house. The rooms we passed looked spacious and elegant and unused: windows sparkling, the thick powder-blue carpeting still furrowed with vacuum-cleaner tracks, fresh-cut flowers in professional arrangements on glossy tabletops. The wallpaper and drapes were endless repetitions of the same blue floral print and everything smelled of Lemon Pledge. I wondered if she used it to disguise the mild scent of bourbon on the rocks that wafted after her. As we passed the kitchen, I could smell roast lamb laced with garlic.

The patio was shaded by latticework. The furniture was white wicker with bright green canvas cushions. She took up her drink from a coffee table of glass and wrought iron, plunking herself down on a padded chaise. She reached automatically for her cigarettes and a slim gold Dunhill. She seemed amused, as though I'd arrived solely to entertain her during the cocktail hour.

'Who sent you up here? Nikki or little Gwen?' Her eyes slid away from mine and she seemed to require no response. She lit her cigarette, pulling the half-filled ashtray closer. She waved a hand at me. 'Have a seat.'

I chose a padded chair not far from hers. An egg-shaped swimming pool was visible beyond the shrubs surrounding the patio. Charlotte caught my look.

'You want to stop and have a swim or what?'

I decided not to take offense. I had the feeling that sarcasm came easily to her, an automatic reaction, like someone with a smoker's cough.

'So who sent you up here?' she said, repeating herself. It was the second hint I had that she wasn't as sober as she should have been, even at that hour of the day.

'Word gets around.'

'Oh, I'll bet it does,' she said with a snort of smoke. 'Well, I'll tell you this, sweetie pie. I was more than a piece of ass to that man. I wasn't the first and I wasn't the last but I was the fucking *best*.'

'Is that why he broke it off?'

'Don't be a bitch,' she said with a quick sharp look, but she laughed at the same time, low in her throat, and I suspected I might have gone up in her estimation. She apparently played fast and loose and didn't object to a cut now and then in the interest of a fair game. 'Sure he broke it off. Why should I have secrets these days? I had a little wingding with him before he divorced Gwen and then he came back around a few months before he died. He was like some old tomcat, always sniffin' around the same back porch.'

'What happened this last time?'

She gave me a jaded look as if none of it seemed to matter much. 'He got involved with somebody else. Very hush-hush. Very hot. Screw him. He discarded me like yesterday's underpants.'

'I'm surprised you weren't a suspect,' I said.

Her brows shot up. 'Me?' She hooted. 'The wife of a prominent judge? I never even testified and they knew damn well that I was involved with him. The cops tiptoed around me like I was a fussy baby taking an unexpected nap. And who asked 'em to? I would have told 'em anything. Hell, I didn't give a shit. Besides, they already had their suspect.'

'Nikki?'

'Sure, Nikki,' she said expansively. Her gestures were relaxed, the hand with the cigarette waving languidly as she spoke. 'You ask me, she was way too prissy to kill anyone. Not that anyone cared much what I thought. I'm just your Mrs Loud-Mouth Drunk. What does she know? Who's going to listen to her? I could tell you things about anybody in this town and who'd pay attention to me? And you know how I find out? I'll tell you this. You'll be interested in this because that's what you do, too, find out about people, right?'

'More or less,' I murmured, trying not to interrupt the flow. Charlotte Mercer was the type who'd barge right on if she didn't get sidetracked. She took a long drag on her cigarette, blowing smoke through her nose in two fierce streams. She coughed, shaking her head.

'Pardon me while I choke to death,' she said, pausing to cough again. 'You tell secrets,' she went on, taking up from where she left off. 'You tell the dirtiest damn thing you know and nine times out of ten, you'll net yourself something worse. You can try it yourself. I say anything. I tell stories on myself just to see what I get back. You want gossip, honey, you came to the right place.'

'What's the word out on Gwen?' I asked, testing the waters.

Charlotte laughed. 'You don't trade,' she said. 'You got nothing to swap.'

'Well no, that's true. I wouldn't be in business long if I didn't keep my mouth shut.'

She laughed again. She seemed to like that. My guess about her was that it made her feel important to know what she knew. I was hoping she liked to show off a little bit too. She might well have heard about Gwen's affair but I couldn't ask without tipping my hand so I just waited her out, hoping to pick up what I could.

'Gwen was the biggest chump who ever lived,' she said without much interest. 'I don't like the type myself and I don't know how she held on to him as long as she did. Laurence Fife was one cold cookie, which was why I was so crazy about him if you haven't guessed. I can't stand a man who *fawns*, you know what I mean? I can't stand a man sucking up to me, but he was the kind who took you right on the floor and he didn't even look at you afterwards when he zipped up his pants.'

'That sounds crude enough,' I said.

'*Sex* is crude, which is why we all run around doing it, which is why I was such a good match for him. He was crude as he was mean and that's the truth about him. Nikki was too refined, too lah-de-dah. So was Gwen.'

'So maybe he liked both extremes,' I suggested.

'Well now, I don't doubt that. Probably so. Maybe he married the snooty ones and fooled around with flash.'

'What about Libby Glass? Did you ever hear about her?'

'Nope. No dice. Who else?'

God, this woman made me wish I had a list. I thought fast, trying to milk her while she was in the mood. I had the feeling the moment would pass and she'd turn sullen again.

'Sharon Napier,' I said, as though it were a parlor game.

'Oh yeah. I checked that one out myself. The first time I ever laid eyes on that little snake, I knew something was off.'

'You think he was involved with her?'

'Oh no, it's better yet. Not her. Her *mother*. I hired a private dick to look that up. Ruined her life and Sharon knew about it, too, so up she pops years later and sticks it to him. Her parents broke up over him and Mommy had a nervous breakdown or turned to drink, some damn thing. I don't know all the details except he fucked everyone over but good and Sharon collected on that for *years*.'

'Was she *blackmailing* him?'

'Not for bucks. For her livelihood. She couldn't *type*. She barely knew how to spell her own name. She just wanted revenge, so she shows up every day for work and she does what she feels like doing and thumbs her nose at him. He took anything she dished out.'

'Could she have killed him?'

'Sure, why not? Maybe the gig wore thin or maybe just taking his pay from week to week wasn't good enough.'

She paused, pushing the ember out on her cigarette with a number of ineffectual stabs. She smiled over at me with cunning.

'I hope you don't think I'm rude,' she said with a glance at the door. 'But school's out. My esteemed husband, the good judge, is due home any second now and I don't want to sit around and explain what you're doing in my house.'

'Fair enough,' I said. 'I'll let myself out. You've been a big help.'

'I'll bet.' She got to her feet, setting her drink down on the glass-topped table with a resounding crack. There was no harm done and she recovered herself with a long slow look of relief.

She studied my face briefly. 'You're gonna have to get your eyes done in a couple of years. Right now, you're okay,' she pronounced.

I laughed. 'I like lines,' I said. 'I earn mine. But thanks anyway.'

I left her on the patio and went around the side of the house to where my car was parked. The conversation wasn't sitting that well with me and I was glad to be on my way. Charlotte Mercer was shrewd and perhaps not above using her drunkenness for its effect. Maybe she'd been telling the truth and maybe not. Somehow the revelation about Sharon Napier seemed too pat. As a solution, it seemed too obvious. On the other hand, the cops are sometimes right. Homicide usually isn't subtle and most of the time, you don't have that far to look.

9

It took me a day and a half to come up with an address on Sharon Napier. By means I'd just as soon not spell out, I tapped into the Department of Motor Vehicles computer and discovered that her driver's license had expired some six years back. I checked with the Auto Title Department, making a quick trip downtown, and found that a dark green Karmann Ghia was registered in her name with an address that matched the last-known address I had for her locally, but a side note indicated that the title had been transferred to Nevada, which probably meant that she'd left the state.

I placed a call to Bob Dietz, a Nevada investigator whose name I looked up in the National Directory. I told him what information I needed, and he said he'd call me back, which he did that afternoon. Sharon Napier had applied for and had been issued a Nevada driver's license; it showed a Reno address. His Reno sources, however, reported that she'd skipped out on a big string of creditors the previous March, which meant that she'd been gone for approximately fourteen months. He'd guessed that she was probably still in the state so he'd done some further nosing around. A small Reno credit company showed requests for information on her from Carson City and again from Las Vegas, which he thought was my best bet. I thanked him profusely for his efficiency and told him to bill me for his time but he said he'd just as soon trade tit for tat at some point, so I made sure he had my address and home phone if he needed it. I tried Information in Las Vegas, but there was no listing for her so I called a friend of mine down there and he said he'd check around. I told him I'd be driving to Los Angeles early in the week and gave him the number so he could reach me there in case it took him a while to pick up a lead on her.

The next day was Sunday and I devoted that to myself: laundry, housecleaning, grocery shopping. I even shaved my legs just to show I still had some class. Monday morning I did clerical work. I typed up a report for Nikki and put in another call to the local credit bureau just to double-check. Sharon Napier had apparently left town with a lot of money owed and a lot of people mad. They had no forwarding address so I gave them the information I had. Then I had a long talk with California Fidelity on the subject of Marcia Threadgill. For forty-eight hundred dollars, the insurance company was almost ready to settle with her and move on, and I had to argue with as much cunning as I could muster. My services on that one weren't costing them anything out of pocket and it pissed me off that they were halfway inclined to look the other way. I even had to stoop so low as to mention principles, which never sits that well with the claims manager. 'She's cheating your *ass*,' I kept saying, but he just shook his head as though there were forces at work that I was too dim to grasp. I told him to check with his boss and I'd get back to him.

By 2:00, I was on the road to Los Angeles. The other piece of the puzzle was Libby Glass and I needed to know how she fitted into all of this. When I reached L.A., I checked into the Hacienda Motor Lodge on Wilshire, near Bundy. The Hacienda is not even remotely hacienda-like – an L-shaped, two-story structure with a cramped parking lot and a swimming pool surrounded by a chain-link fence with a padlock. A very fat woman named Arlette doubles as manager and switchboard operator. I could see straight into her apartment from the desk. It's furnished, I'm told, from her profits as a Tupperware lady, a little hustling she does on the side. She leans toward Mediterranean-style furniture upholstered in red plush.

'Fat is beautiful, Kinsey,' she said to me confidentially as I filled out the registration card. 'Looka here.'

I looked. She was holding out her arm so that I could admire the hefty downhang of excess flesh.

'I don't know, Arlette,' I said dubiously. 'I keep trying to avoid it myself.'

'And look at all the time and energy it takes,' she said. 'The problem is that our society shuns tubbos. Fat people are heavily discriminated against. Worse than the handicapped. Why, they got it easy compared to us. Everywhere you go now, there are signs out for them. Handicapped parking. Handicapped johns. You've seen those little stick figures in wheelchairs. Show me the international sign for the grossly overweight. We got rights.'

Her face was moon-shaped, surrounded by a girlish cap of wispy blonde hair. Her cheeks were permanently flushed as though vital supply lines were being dangerously squeezed.

'But it's so unhealthy, Arlette,' I said. 'I mean, don't you have to worry about high blood pressure, heart attacks . . .'

'Well there's hazards to everything. All the more reason we should be treated decently.'

I gave her my credit card and after she made the imprint she handed me the key to room #2. 'That's right up here close,' she said. 'I know how you hate being stuck out back.'

'Thanks.'

I've been in room #2 about twenty times and it is always dreary in a comforting sort of way. A double bed. Threadbare wall-to-wall carpeting in a squirrel gray. A chair upholstered in orange plastic with one gimpy leg. On the desk, there is a lamp shaped like a football helmet with 'UCLA' printed on the side. The bathroom is small and the shower mat is paper. It is the sort of place where you are likely to find someone else's underpanties beneath the bed. It costs me $11.95 plus room tax in the off-season and includes a 'Continental' breakfast – instant coffee and jelly doughnuts, most of which Arlette eats herself. Once, at midnight, a drunk sat on my front step and yelled for an hour and a half until the cops came and took him away. I stay there because I'm cheap.

I set my suitcase on the bed and took out my jogging clothes. I did a fast walk from Wilshire to San Vicente and then headed west at a trot as far as Twenty-sixth Street, where I tagged a stop sign and turned around, jogging back up to Westgate and across to Wilshire again. The first mile is the one that hurts. I was panting hard when I got back. Given the exhaust fumes I'd taken in from passing motorists on San Vicente, I figured I was about neck-and-neck with toxic wastes. Back in room #2 again, I showered and dressed and then checked back through my notes. Then I made some phone calls. The first was to Lyle Abernathy's last-known work address, the Wonder Bread Company, down on Santa Monica. Not surprisingly, he had left and the personnel office had no idea where he was. A quick check in the phone book showed no listing for him locally, but a Raymond Glass still lived in Sherman Oaks and I verified the street number I had noted from the police files up in Santa Teresa. I placed another call to my friend in Vegas. He had a lead on Sharon Napier but said it would take him probably half a day to pin it down. I alerted Arlette that he might be calling and cautioned her to make sure the information, if she took it, was exact. She acted a little injured that I didn't trust her to take phone messages for me, but she'd been negligent before and it had cost me plenty last time around.

I called Nikki in Santa Teresa and told her where I was and what I was up to. Then I checked my answering service. Charlie Scorsoni had called but left no number. I figured if it was important he'd call back. I gave my service the number where I could be reached. Having tagged all those bases, I went next door to a restaurant that seems to change nationalities every time I'm there. Last time I was in town, it was Mexican fare, which is to say very hot plates of pale brown goo. This time it was Greek: turdlike lumps wrapped in leaves. I'd seen things in roadside parks that looked about that good but I washed them down with a glass of wine that tasted like lighter fluid and who knew the difference? It was now 7:15 and I didn't have anything to do. The television set in my room was on the fritz so I wandered down to the office and watched TV with Arlette while she ate a box of caramel Ayds.

In the morning, I drove over the mountain into the San Fernando Valley. At the crest of the hill, where the San Diego Freeway tips over into Sherman Oaks, I could see a layer of smog spread out like a mirage, a shimmering mist of pale yellow smoke through which a few tall buildings yearned as though for fresh air. Libby's parents lived in a four-unit apartment building set into the crook of the San Diego and Ventura freeways, a cumbersome structure of stucco and frame with bay windows bulging out along the front. There was an open corridor dividing the building in half, with the front doors to the two downstairs apartments opening up just inside. On the right, a stairway led to the second-floor landing. The building itself affected no particular style and I guessed that it had gone up in the thirties before anybody figured out that California architecture should imitate southern mansions and Italian villas. There was a pale lawn of crab and Bermuda grasses intermixed. A short driveway along the left extended back to a row of frame garages, with four green plastic garbage cans chained to a wooden fence. The juniper bushes growing along the front of the building were tall enough to obscure the ground-floor windows and seemed to be suffering from some peculiar molting process that made some of the branches turn brown and the rest go bald. They looked like cut-rate Christmas trees with the bad side facing out. The season to be jolly, in this neighbourhood, was long past.

Apartment #1 was on my left. When I rang the bell, it sounded like the br-r-r-r of an alarm clock running down. The door was opened by a woman with a row of pins in her mouth that bobbed up and down when she spoke. I worried she would swallow one.

'Yes?'

'Mrs Glass?'

'That's right.'

'My name is Kinsey Millhone. I'm a private investigator. I work up in Santa Teresa. Could I talk to you?'

She took the pins out of her mouth one by one and stuck them into a pin cushion that she wore on her wrist like a bristling corsage. I handed her my identification and she studied it with care, turning it over as though there might be tricky messages written in fine print on the back. While she did that, I studied her. She was in her early fifties. Her silky brown hair was cut short, a careless style with strands anchored behind her ears. Brown eyes, no makeup, bare-legged. She wore a wraparound denim skirt, a washed-out Madras blouse in bleeding shades of blue, and the kind of cotton slippers I've seen in cellophane packs in grocery stores.

'It's about Elizabeth,' she said, finally returning my I.D.

'Yes. It is.'

She hesitated and then moved back into the living room, making way for me. I picked my way across the living-room floor and took the one chair that wasn't covered with lengths of fabric or patterns. The ironing board was set up near the bay window, the iron plugged in and ticking as it heated.

There were finished garments hanging on a rack near the sewing machine on the far wall. The air smelled of fabric sizing and hot metal.

In the archway to the dining room, a heavyset man in his sixties sat in a wheelchair, his expression blank, his pants undone in front, heavy paunch protruding. She crossed the room and turned his chair around so that it faced the television set. She put headphones on him and then plugged the jack into the TV, which she flipped on. He watched a game show whether he liked it or not. A couple were dressed up like a boy and girl chicken but I couldn't tell if they were winning anything.

'I'm Grace,' she said. 'That's her father. He was in an automobile accident three years ago last spring. He doesn't talk but he can hear and any mention of Elizabeth upsets him. Help yourself to coffee if you like.'

There was a ceramic percolator on the coffee table, plugged into an extension cord that ran back under the couch. It looked as if all the other appliances in the room were radiating from the same power source. Grace eased down onto her knees. She had about four yards of dark green silk spread out on the hardwood floor and she was pinning a handmade pattern into place. She held a magazine out to me, opened to a page that showed a designer dress with a deep slit up one side and narrow sleeves. I poured myself a cup of coffee and watched her work.

'I'm running this up for a woman married to a television star,' she said mildly. 'Somebody's sidekick. He got famous overnight and she says he's recognized even in the car wash now. People asking for his autograph. Has facials. Him, not her. He was poor, I hear, for the last fifteen years and now they go to all these parties in Bel Air. I do her clothes. He buys his on Rodeo Drive. She could, too, on the money he makes but it makes her feel insecure, she says. She's much nicer than he is. I already read in the *Hollywood Reporter*,

"New Two You," him and somebody else "pulling up steaks at Stellini's". She'd be smart to put an expensive wardrobe together before he leaves her if you ask me.'

Grace seemed to be talking to herself, her tone distracted, a smile warming her face now and then. She picked up a pair of pinking shears and began to cut along the straight edge, the scissors making a crunching sound against the wood floor. For a while I didn't say anything. There was something hypnotic about the work and there seemed to be no compulsion to converse. The television flickered, and from an angle I could see the girl chicken jumping up and down, hands to her face. I knew the audience was urging her to do something—choose, pass, change boxes, take what was behind the curtain, give back the envelope, all of it taking place in silence while Libby's father looked on from his wheelchair incuriously. I thought she should consult her boy-chicken mate but he just stood there self-consciously like a kid who knew he was too old to be out in costume on Halloween. The tissue-paper pattern rustled as Grace removed it, folding it carefully before she laid it aside.

'I sewed for Elizabeth when she was young,' she said. 'Once she left home, of course, she only wanted store-bought. Sixty dollars for a skirt that only had twelve dollars' worth of wool at most, but she did have a good eye for color and she could afford to do as she pleased. Would you like to see a picture of her?' Grace's eyes strayed up to mine and her smile was wistful.

'Yes. I'd appreciate that.'

She took the silk first and placed it on the ironing board, testing the iron with a wet index finger as she passed. The iron spat back and she turned the lever down to 'wool'. There were two snapshots of Libby in a double frame on the windowsill and she studied them herself before she handed them to me. In one, Libby was facing the camera but her head was bent, her right hand upraised as though she were hiding her face. Her blonde hair was sun-streaked, cut short like her mother's but feathered back across her ears. Her blue eyes were amused, her grin wide, embarrassed to be caught. I couldn't think why. I'd never seen a twenty-four-year-old look quite so young or quite so fresh. In the second snapshot, the smile was only partially formed, lips parted over a flash of white teeth, a dimple showing near the corner of her mouth. Her complexion was clear, tinted with gold, lashes dark so that her eyes were delicately outlined.

'She's lovely,' I said. 'Really.'

Grace was standing at the ironing board, touching up folds of silk with the tip of the iron, which sailed across the asbestos board like a boat on a flat sea of dark green. She turned the iron off and wiped her hands briefly down along her skirt, then took the pieces of silk and began to pin them together.

'I named her after Queen Elizabeth,' she said and then she laughed shyly. 'She was born on November 14, the same day Prince Charles was born. I'd have named her Charles if she'd been a boy. Raymond thought it was silly but I didn't care.'

'You never called her Libby?'

'Oh no. She did that herself in grade school. She always had such a sense of who she was and how her life should be. Even as a child. She was very tidy – not prissy, but neat. She would line her dresser drawers with pretty floral wrapping papers and everything would be arranged just so. She liked accounting for the same reason. Mathematics was orderly and it made sense. The answers were always there if you worked carefully enough, or that's what she said.' Grace moved over to the rocking chair and sat down, laying the silk across her lap. She began to baste darts.

'I understand she worked as an accountant for Haycraft and McNiece. How long was she there?'

'About a year and a half. She had done the accounts for her father's company – he did small-appliance repair – but it really didn't interest her, working for him. She was ambitious. She passed her CPA exam when she was twenty-two. She took a couple of computer courses, too, in night school, after that. She made very good grades. She had two junior accountants working under her, you know.'

'Was she happy there?'

'I'm sure she was,' Grace said. 'She spoke of going to law school at one point. She enjoyed business management and finance. She liked working with figures and I know she was impressed because that company represented very wealthy people. She said you could learn a lot about someone's character by the way they spent money, what they bought and where – whether they lived within their means, that kind of thing. She said it was a study of human nature.' Grace's voice was tinged with pride. It was hard for me to reconcile the idea of this prim-sounding CPA with the girl in the photographs who looked pretty, animated, bashful, and rather sweet, hardly a woman with a hard-driving purpose in life.

'What about her old boyfriend? Do you have any idea where he is now?'

'Who, Lyle? Oh, he'll be around in a bit.'

'Here?'

'Oh my, yes. He stops by every day at noon to help me with Raymond. He's a lovely boy but of course you probably knew she broke off her engagement with him a few months before . . . she passed on. She went with Lyle all through high school and they both attended Santa Monica City College together until he dropped out.'

'Is that when he went to work for Wonder Bread?'

'Oh no, Lyle's had many jobs. At the time Lyle left school, Elizabeth was in her own apartment and she didn't confide much in me but I feel she was disappointed in him. He was going to be a lawyer and then he simply changed his mind. He said law was too dull and he didn't like details.'

'Did they live together?'

Grace's cheeks tinted slightly. 'No, they didn't. It may sound odd and Raymond thought it was very wrong of me, but I encouraged them to move in together. I sensed that they were drifting apart and I thought it would help. Raymond was like Elizabeth, disenchanted with Lyle for quitting school. He told her she could do much better for herself. But Lyle adored her. I thought that should count for something. He would have found himself. He had a restless nature, like many boys that age. He would have come to his senses and I told her so. He needed responsibility. She could have been a very good influence because she was so responsible herself. But Elizabeth said she didn't want to live with him and that was that. She was strong-willed when she wanted to be. And I don't mean that as criticism. She was as nearly perfect as a daughter could be. Naturally I wanted whatever she wanted but I couldn't bear to see Lyle hurt. He's very dear. You'll see when you meet him.'

'And you have no idea what actually caused the breakup between them? I mean, could she possibly have been involved with someone else?'

'You're talking about that attorney up in Santa Teresa,' she said.

'It's his death I'm looking into,' I said. 'Did she ever talk to you about him?'

'I never knew anything about him until the police came down from Santa Teresa to talk to us. Elizabeth didn't like to confide her personal affairs, but I don't believe Elizabeth would fall in love with a married man,' Grace said. She began to fuss with the silk, her manner agitated. She closed her eyes and then pressed a hand to her forehead as though checking to see if she'd contracted a sudden fever. 'I'm sorry. Sometimes I forget. Sometimes I pretend she got sick. The other makes me cringe, that someone might have done that to her, that someone could have hated her that much. The police here don't do anything. It isn't solved but no one cares anymore so I just . . . I simply tell myself she got sick and was taken. How could someone have done that to her?' Her eyes welled with tears. Her grief rolled across the space between us like a wash of salt water and I could feel tears form in my own eyes in response. I reached out and took her hand. For a moment, she clutched my fingers hard and then she seemed to catch herself, pulling back.

'It's been like a weight pressing on my heart. I will never recover from it. Never.'

I phrased my next question with care. 'Could it have been an accident?' I said. 'The other man – Laurence Fife – died from oleander, which someone put in an allergy capsule. Suppose they'd been doing business together, going over accounts or something. Maybe she was sneezing or complaining about a stuffy nose and he just volunteered his own medication. People do that all the time.'

She considered that for a moment uneasily. 'I thought the police said the attorney died before she did. Days before.'

'Maybe she didn't take the pill right away,' I said, shrugging. 'With something like that, you never know when someone will take a doctored capsule. Maybe she put it in her purse and swallowed it later without even realizing there was any jeopardy. Did she have allergies? Could she have been coming down with a cold?'

Grace began to weep, a small mewing sound. 'I don't remember. I don't think so. She didn't have hay fever or anything like that. I don't even know who'd remember after all these years.'

Grace looked at me then with those large, dark eyes. She had a good face, almost childlike, with a small nose, a sweet mouth. She took out a Kleenex and wiped her cheeks. 'I don't think I can talk about it anymore. Stay for lunch. Meet Lyle. Maybe he can tell you something that would help.'

10

I sat on a stool in the kitchen and watched Grace make tuna fish salad for lunch. She had seemed to shake herself, as though wakening from a brief but vital nap and then she had put on her apron and cleared the dining-room table of the rest of her sewing paraphernalia. She was a woman who worked with care, her movements restful as she assembled placemats and napkins. I set the table for her, feeling like a well-behaved kid again while she rinsed lettuce and patted it dry, placing a layer on each plate like a doily. She neatly pared thin ribbons of skin from several tomatoes and coiled them like roses. She fluted a mushroom for each plate, added two thin spikes of asparagus so that the whole of it looked like a flower arrangement. She smiled at me timidly, taking pleasure in the picture she had created. 'Do you cook?'

I shook my head.

'I don't have much occasion to myself except when Lyle's here. Raymond wouldn't notice and I probably wouldn't bother at all if it were just for *me*.' She lifted her head. 'There.'

I hadn't heard the truck pull into the driveway but she must have been tuned to Lyle's arrival. Her hand strayed unconsciously to a strand of hair, which she tucked back. He came in through a utility room off to the left, pausing around the corner, apparently to take off his boots. I heard two thunks. 'Hey, babe. What's for lunch?'

He came around into the dining room with a grin, giving her cheek a noisy buss before he caught sight of me. He halted, the animation flickering off and on, then draining out of his face. He looked at her hesitantly.

'This is Miss Millhone,' she said to him.

'Kinsey,' I filled in, holding out my hand. He reached out and shook my hand automatically, but the central question still hadn't been answered. I suspected that I was intruding on an occasion that ordinarily admitted no variation. 'I'm a private investigator from Santa Teresa,' I said.

Lyle moved over to Raymond without another glance at me.

'Hey, Pops. How's it going today? You feeling okay?'

The old man's face registered nothing, but his eyes came into focus. Lyle took the headphones off, turning the set off too. The change in Lyle had been immediate and I felt as if I'd just seen snapshots of two different personalities in the same body, one joyful, the other keeping watch. He was not much taller than me and his body was trim, his shoulders wide. He had his shirt pulled out, unbuttoned down the front. His chest muscles were spare but well formed like those of a man who's been lifting weights. I guessed him to be about my own age. His hair was blond, worn long and faintly tinted with the green of a chlorinated swimming pool and hot sun. His eyes were a washed-out blue, too pale for his tan, his lashes bleached, his chin too narrow for the breadth of his cheeks. The overall effect was of a face oddly off – good looks gone slightly askew, as though under the surface there were a hairline crack. Some subterranean tremor had caused the bones to shift minutely and the two halves of his face seemed not quite to match. He wore faded jeans slung low on his hips and I could see the silky line of darkish hair pointing like an arrow toward his crotch.

He went about his business, ignoring me completely, talking to Grace while he worked. She handed him a towel, which he tucked under Raymond's chin, and then he proceeded to lather and shave him with a safety razor, which he rinsed in a stainless-steel bowl. Grace was taking out bottles of beer, removing the caps, pouring liquid into tulip glasses which she set at each place. There was no plate prepared for Raymond at all. When the shaving process had been completed, Lyle brushed Raymond's thinning white hair and then fed him a jar of baby food. Grace shot me a satisfied look. See what a dear he is? Lyle reminded me of an older brother caring for a toddler so that Mom would approve. She did. She looked on affectionately while Lyle scraped Raymond's chin with the bowl of the spoon, easing the drooling vegetable puree back into Raymond's slack mouth. Even as I watched, a stain began to spread across the front of Raymond's pants.

'Hey, don't worry about it, Pops,' Lyle crooned, 'we'll get you cleaned up after lunch. How's that?'

I could feel the muscles in my face setting with distaste.

During lunch, Lyle ate quickly, saying nothing to me and very little to Grace.

'What sort of work do you do, Lyle?' I said.

'Lay brick.'

I looked at his hands. His fingers were long and dusted with mortar gray that had seeped down into the crevices of his skin. At this range, I could smell sweat, overlaid with the delicate scent of dope. I wondered if Grace noticed at all or if, perhaps, she thought it might be some exotic aftershave.

'I've got to make a run up to Vegas,' I said to Grace, 'but I'd like to stop back on my way up to Santa Teresa. Do you have any of Libby's belongings?' I was relatively certain she did.

Grace consulted Lyle with a quick look but his eyes were lowered to his plate. 'I believe so. There are some boxes in the basement, aren't there, Lyle? Elizabeth's books and papers?'

The old man made a sound at the mention of her name and Lyle wiped his mouth, tossing the napkin down as he got up. He wheeled Raymond down the hallway.

'I'm sorry. I shouldn't have mentioned Libby,' I said.

'Well that's all right,' she said. 'If you'll call or come by when you get back to Los Angeles, I'm sure it'd be all right if you looked at Elizabeth's belongings. There isn't much.'

'Lyle doesn't seem to be in a very good mood,' I remarked. 'I hope he doesn't think I'm intruding.'

'Oh no. He's quiet around people he doesn't know,' she said. 'I don't know what I'd do without him. Raymond is too heavy for me to lift. I have a neighbor who stops by twice a day to help me get him in and out of his chair. His spine was crushed in the accident.'

Her conversational tone gave me the willies. 'Do you mind if I use the bathroom?' I said.

'It's down the hall. The second door on the right.'

As I passed the bedroom, I could see that Lyle had already lifted Raymond into bed. There were two straight-backed wooden chairs pushed up against the side of the double bed to keep him from falling out. Lyle was standing between the two chairs, cleaning Raymond's bare ass. I went into the bathroom and closed the door.

I helped Grace clear the table and then I left, waiting in my car across the street. I made no attempt to conceal myself and no pretense at driving away. I could see Lyle's pick-up truck still parked in the driveway. I checked my watch. It was ten minutes to one and I figured he must be on a limited lunch hour. Sure enough, the side door opened and Lyle stepped out onto the narrow porch, pausing to lace his boots. He glanced over at the street, spotting my car, and seemed to smile to himself. Ass, I thought. He got into his truck and backed out of the driveway rapidly. I wondered for a moment if he intended to back straight across the street and into the side of my car, crushing me. He wheeled at the last minute, though, and flung the truck into gear, taking off with a chirp of rubber. I thought maybe we were going to have a little impromptu car chase but it turned out he didn't have that far to go. He drove eight blocks and then pulled into the driveway of a modest-sized Sherman Oaks house that was being refaced with red brick. I guessed it was a status symbol of some sort because brick is very expensive on the West Coast. There probably aren't six brick houses in the whole city of L.A.

He got out of his truck and ambled around to the back, tucking in his shirt, his manner insolent. I parked on the street and locked my car, following him. I wondered idly if he intended to smash my head in with a brick and then mortar me into a wall. He was not pleased with my arrival on the scene and he made no bones about that. As I rounded the corner, I could see that the owner of the house was disguising his little cottage with a whole new façade. Instead of looking like a modest California bungalow, it would look like certain pet hospitals in the Midwest, real high-rent stuff. Lyle was already mixing up mortar in a wheelbarrow in the back. I picked my way across some two-by-fours with crooked rusty nails protruding. A little kid would have to have a lot of tetanus shots after falling on those.

'Why don't we start all over again, Lyle,' I said conversationally.

He snorted, taking out a cigarette, which he tucked into the corner of his mouth. He lit it, cupping crusty hands around the match, and then blew out the first mouthful of smoke. His eyes were small and one of them squinted now as the smoke curled up across his face. He reminded me of early photographs of James Dean – that defensive hunched stance, the crooked smile, the pointed chin. I wondered if he was a secret admirer of *East of Eden* reruns, staying up late at night to watch on obscure channels piped in from Bakersfield.

'Hey, come on. Why don't you talk to me,' I said.

'I don't have nothin' to say to you. Why stir up all that shit again?'

'Aren't you interested in who killed Libby?'

He took his time about answering. He picked up a brick, holding it upright while he applied a thick layer of mortar to one end with a trowel, beveling the soft cement as if it were a gritty gray cheese. He laid the brick on the chest-high line of bricks where he'd been working and gave it a few taps with a hammer, bending down then to pick up the next brick.

I cupped my right hand to my ear. 'Hello?' I said, as if I might have gone temporarily deaf.

He smirked, cigarette bobbing in his mouth. 'You think you're real hot shit, don't you?'

I smiled. 'Listen, Lyle. There's no point in this. You don't have to tell me anything and you know what I can do? Spend about an hour and a half this afternoon finding out anything I want to know about you. I can do it in six phone calls from a motel room in West Los Angeles and I've even got someone paying me for my time, so it's nothing to me. It's fun, if you really want to know the truth. I can get your service records, credit rating. I can find out if you've ever been arrested for anything, job history, library books overdue . . .'

'Go right ahead. I got nothin' to hide.'

'Why put us through all that stuff?' I said. 'I mean, I can go check you out but I'll just come back around here tomorrow and if you don't like me now, you ain't gonna like me any better then. I might be in a bad mood. Why don't you just loosen up?'

'Aw, I'm real loose,' he said.

'What happened to your plans to go to law school?'

'I dropped out,' he said sullenly.

'Maybe the dope smoking got to you,' I suggested mildly.

'Maybe you can go get fucked,' he snapped. 'Do I look like a lawyer to you? I lost interest, okay? That's no fuckin' crime.'

'I'm not accusing you of anything. I just want to figure out what happened to Libby.'

He flipped the ash off the cigarette and dropped it, chunking it into the dirt with the toe of his boot. I sat down on a pile of bricks that had been covered with a tarp. Lyle glanced over at me through lowered lids.

'What makes you think I smoke dope anyway?' he asked abruptly.

I tapped my nose, letting him know I'd smelled it on him. 'Also laying brick doesn't seem that interesting,' I said. 'I figure if you're smart, you gotta do something to keep from going nuts.'

He looked at me, his body relaxing just a little bit. 'What makes you think I'm smart?'

I shrugged. 'You went with Libby Glass for ten years.'

He thought about that for a while.

'I don't know anything,' he said, almost gruffly.

'You know more than I do at this point.'

He was beginning to relent, though his shoulders were still tense. He shook his head, going back to his work. He took the trowel and moved the damp mass of mortar around like cake icing that has gone all granular. 'She dumped me after she met that guy from up north. That attorney . . .'

'Laurence Fife?'

'Yeah, I guess it was. She wouldn't tell me anything about him. At first, it was business – something about some accounts. His law firm had just hooked up with the place she worked and she had to get all this stuff on the computer, you know? Set up to run smoothly from month to month. It was all real complicated, calls goin' back and forth, things like that. He came down a few times and she'd have drinks when they finished up, sometimes dinner. She fell in love. That's all I know.'

He took out a small metal brace at right angles and hammered it into the wooden siding on the house, placing a mortar-laden brick on top.

'What's that do?' I asked out of curiosity.

'What? Oh. That keeps the brick wall from falling away from the rest,' he said.

I nodded, halfway tempted to try laying brick myself.

'And she broke up with you after that?' I asked, getting back to the point.

'Pretty much. I'd see her now and again, but it was over and I knew it.'

He was beginning to drop the tension in his tone and he sounded more resigned than angry. Lyle buttered another brick with soft mortar and set it in place. The sun felt good on my back and I settled on my elbows, leaning back on the tarp.

'What's your theory?' I asked.

He looked at me slyly. 'Maybe she killed herself.'

'Suicide?' The thought hadn't even crossed my mind.

'You asked. I'm just tellin' you what I thought at the time. She sure was hung up on him.'

'Yeah, but enough to kill herself when he died?'

'Who knows?' He lifted one shoulder and let it drop.

'How did she find out about his death?'

'Someone called her and told her about it.'

'How do you know that?'

'Because she called me up. At first she didn't know what to make of it.'

'She was grieving for him? Tears? Shock?'

He seemed to think back. 'She was just real confused and upset. I went over there. She asked me to come and then she changed her mind and said she didn't want to talk about it. She was shaky, couldn't concentrate. It kind of made me mad that she was jerking me around, so I left. Next thing I knew, she was dead.'

'Who found her?'

'The apartment manager where she lived. She didn't show up for work for two days and didn't call in, so her boss got worried and went over to her place. The manager tried peeping in the windows but the drapes were shut. They knocked some, front and back, and finally got in with a passkey. She was lying on the bathroom floor in her robe. She'd been dead for three days.'

'What about her bed? Had it been slept in?'

'I don't know. The police didn't give that out.'

I thought about that for a minute. It sounded like she might have taken a capsule at night, just as Laurence Fife had. It still seemed to me it might have been the same medication – some kind of antihistamine capsule in which someone had substituted oleander.

'Did she have allergies, Lyle? Was she complaining of a head cold or anything like that when you saw her last?'

He shrugged. 'She might have, I guess. I don't remember anything like that. I saw her Thursday night. Wednesday or Thursday of that week when she heard that attorney was dead. She died on Saturday night late, they said. That much they put in the paper when it happened.'

'What about this attorney she was involved with? Do you know if he kept anything at her place? Toothbrush? Razor? Things like that? Maybe she took medication that was meant for him.'

'How do I know?' he said testily. 'I don't stick my nose where it doesn't belong.'

'Did she have a girl friend? Someone she might have confided in?'

'Maybe from work. I don't remember anyone in particular. She didn't have "girl friends".'

I took out my notebook and jotted down the telephone number at my motel. 'This is where I can be reached. Will you give me a call if you think of anything else?'

He took the slip of paper and tucked it carelessly into the back pocket of his jeans. 'What's in Las Vegas?' he asked. 'How does that tie in?'

'I don't know yet. There may be a woman down there who can fill in some blanks. I'll be back through Los Angeles toward the end of the week. Maybe I'll look you up again.'

Lyle had already tuned me out, tapping the next brick into place, troweling away the excess mortar that had drooled out between the cracks. I glanced at my watch. I still had time to check out the place where Libby Glass had worked. I didn't think Lyle was telling the whole truth, but I had no way to be sure. So I let it slide – for the time being anyway.

11

Haycraft and McNiece was located in the AVCO Embassy building in Westwood, not far from my motel. I parked in an expensive lot adjacent to the Westwood Village Mortuary and went into the entranceway near the Wells Fargo Bank, taking the elevator up. The office itself was just to the right as I got off. I pushed through a solid teak door, lettered in brass. The interior was done with polished uneven red-tile flooring, mirrors floor to ceiling, and panels of raw gray wood, hung here and there with clusters of dried corn. A receptionist sat behind a corral to my left. A placard reading 'Allison, Receptionist' sat on the corral post, the letters burned into the wood as though by some charred stick. I gave her my card.

'I wonder if I might talk to a senior accountant,' I said. 'I'm looking into the murder of a CPA who used to work here.'

'Oh yeah. I heard about her,' Allison said. 'Hang on.'

She was in her twenties with long dark hair. She wore jeans and a string tie, her western-cut shirt looking like it had been stuffed with many handfuls of hay. Her belt buckle was shaped like a bucking mustang.

'What is this? A theme park or something?' I asked.

'Huh?'

I shook my head, not willing to pursue the point, and she clopped away in her high-heeled boots through some swinging doors. After a moment, she returned.

'Mr McNiece isn't in but the man you probably want to talk to is Garry Steinberg with two *r*'s.'

'B-e-r-r-g?'

'No, G-a-r-r-y.'

'Oh, I see. Excuse me.'

'That's okay,' she said. 'Everybody makes that mistake.'

'Would it be possible to see Mr Steinberg? Just briefly.'

'He's in New York this week,' she said.

'What about Mr Haycraft?'

'He's dead. I mean, you know, he's been dead for years,' she said. 'So actually now it's McNiece and McNiece but nobody wants to have all the stationery changed. The other McNiece is in a meeting.'

'Is there anybody else who might remember her?'

'I don't think so. I'm sorry.'

She handed me my card. I turned it over and jotted down my motel number and my answering service up in Santa Teresa.

'Could you give this to Garry Steinberg when he gets back? I'd really appreciate a call. He can make it collect if I'm not at the motel here.'

'Sure,' she said. She sat down and I could have sworn she eased the card straight into the trash. I watched her for a moment and she smiled at me sheepishly.

'Maybe you could just leave that on his desk with a note,' I suggested.

She leaned over slightly and came up again, card in hand. She speared it on a vicious-looking metal spike near the phone.

I looked at her some more. She took the card off the spike and got up.

'I'll just put this on his desk,' she said and clopped off again.

'Good plan,' I said.

I went back to the motel and made some phone calls. Ruth, in Charlie Scorsoni's office, said that he was still out of town but she gave me the number of his hotel in Denver. I called but he wasn't in, so I left my number at the message desk. I called Nikki and brought her up to date and then I checked with my answering service. There were no messages. I put on my jogging clothes and drove down to the beach to run. Things did not seem to be falling into place very fast. So far, I felt like I had a lapful of confetti and the notion of piecing it all together to make a picture seemed very remote indeed. Time had shredded the facts like a big machine, leaving only slender paper threads with which to reconstruct reality. I felt clumsy and irritable and I needed to blow off steam.

I parked near the Santa Monica pier and jogged south along the promenade, a stretch of asphalt walk that parallels the beach. I trotted past the old men bent over their chess games, past thin black boys roller-skating with incredible grace, boogeying to the secret music of their padded headphones, past guitar players, dopers, and loiterers whose eyes followed me with scorn. This stretch of pavement is the last remnant of the sixties' drug culture – the barefoot, sag-eyed and scruffy young, some looking thirty-seven now instead of seventeen, still mystical and remote. A dog took up company with me, running along beside me, his tongue hanging out, eyes rolling up at me now and then happily. His coat was thick and bristly, the color of caramel corn, and his tail curled up like a party favor. He was one of those mutant breeds with a large head, short body, and little bitty short legs, but he seemed quite self-possessed. Together, we trotted beyond the promenade, past Ozone, Dudley, Paloma, Sunset, Thornton and Park; by the time we reached Wave Crest, he'd lost interest, veering off to participate in a game of Frisbee out on the beach. The last I saw of him, he had made an incredible leap, catching a Frisbee midflight, mouth turned up in a grin. I smiled back. He was one of the few dogs I'd met in years that I really liked.

At Venice Boulevard I turned back, running most of the way and then slowing to a walk as I reached the pier again. The ocean breeze served as a damper to my body heat. I found myself winded but not sweating much. My mouth felt dry and my cheeks were aflame. It hadn't been a long run but

I'd pushed myself a little harder than I normally did and my lungs were burning: liquid combustion in my chest. I run for the same reasons I learned to drive a car with a stick shift and drink my coffee black, imagining that a day might come when some amazing emergency would require such a test. This run was for 'good measure,' too, since I'd already decided to take a day off for good behavior. Too much virtue has a corrupting effect. I got back in my car when I'd cooled down and I drove east on Wilshire, back to my motel.

As I unlocked the door to my room, the phone began to ring. It was my Las Vegas buddy with Sharon Napier's address.

'Fantastic,' I said. 'I really appreciate this. Let me know how to get in touch when I get down there and I'll pay you for your time.'

'General delivery is fine. I never know where I'll be.'

'You got it. How much?'

'Fifty bucks. A discount. For you. She's strictly unlisted and it wasn't easy.'

'Let me know when I can return the service,' I said, knowing full well that he would.

'Oh, and Kinsey,' he said, 'she's dealing blackjack at the Fremont but she's also hustling some on the side, so I hear. I watched her operate last night. She's very sharp but she's not fooling anyone.'

'Is she stepping on someone's toes?'

'Not quite, but she's comin' close. You know, in this town no one cares what you do as long as you don't cheat. She shouldn't call attention to herself.'

'Thanks for the information,' I said.

'For sure,' he said and hung up.

I showered and put on a pair of slacks and a shirt, then went across the street and ate fried clams drowned in ketchup with an order of french fries on the side. I got two cups of coffee to go and went back to my room. As soon as the door shut behind me, the phone began to ring. This time it was Charlie Scorsoni.

'How's Denver?' I asked as soon as he identified himself.

'Not bad. How's L.A.?'

'Fair. I'm driving up to Las Vegas tonight.'

'Gambling fever?'

'Not a bit. I got a line on Sharon.'

'Terrific. Tell her to pay me back my six hundred bucks.'

'Yeah. Right. With interest. I'm trying to find out what she knows about a murder and you want me to hassle her about a bad debt.'

'*I'll* never have occasion to, that's for sure. When will you be back in Santa Teresa?'

'Maybe Saturday. When I come back through L.A. on Friday, I want to see some boxes that belong to Libby Glass. But I don't think it will take long. What makes you ask?'

'I want to buy you that drink,' he said. 'I'm leaving Denver day after tomorrow, so I'll be in town before you. Will you call me when you get back?'

I hesitated ever so slightly. 'Okay.'

'I mean, don't put yourself out, Millhone,' he said wryly.

I laughed. 'I'll call. I swear.'

'Great. See you then.'

After I hung up, I could feel a silly smile linger on my face long after it should have. What was it about that man?

Las Vegas is about six hours from L.A. and I decided I might as well hit the road. It was just after 7:00 and not dark yet, so I threw my things in the backseat of my car and told Arlette I'd be gone for a couple of days.

'You want me to refer calls or what?' she said.

'I'll call you when I get there and let you know how I can be reached,' I said.

I headed north on the San Diego Freeway, picking up the Ventura, which I followed east until it turned into the Colorado Freeway, one of the few benign roads in the whole of the L.A. freeway system. The Colorado is broad and sparsely traveled, cutting across the northern boundary of metropolitan Los Angeles. It is possible to change lanes on the Colorado without having an anxiety attack and the sturdy concrete divider that separates east- and westbound traffic is a comforting assurance that cars will not wantonly drift over and crash into your vehicle head-on. From the Colorado, I dog-legged south, picking up the San Bernardino Freeway, taking 15 northeast on a long irregular diagonal toward Las Vegas. With any luck, I could talk to Sharon Napier and then head south to the Salton Sea, where Greg Fife was living. I could complete the circuit with a swing up to Claremont on my way back for a brief chat with his sister, Diane. At this point, I wasn't sure what the journey would net me but I needed to complete the basics of my investigation. And Sharon Napier was bound to prove interesting.

I like driving at night. I'm not a sightseer at heart and in travels across the country, I'm never tempted by detours to scenic wonders. I'm not interested in hundred-foot rocks shaped like crookneck squash. I'm not keen on staring down into gullies formed by rivers now defunct and I do not marvel at great holes in the ground where meteors once fell to earth. Driving anywhere looks much the same to me. I stare at the concrete roadway. I watch the yellow line. I keep track of large trucks and passenger vehicles with little children asleep in the backseat and I keep my foot pressed flat to the floor until I reach my destination.

12

By the time Las Vegas loomed up, twinkling on the horizon, it was well after midnight and I felt stiff. I was anxious to avoid the Strip. I would have avoided the whole town if I could. I don't gamble, having no instincts for the sport and even less curiosity. Life in Las Vegas exactly suits my notion of some eventual life in cities under the sea. Day and night mean nothing. People ebb and surge aimlessly as though pulled by invisible thermal currents that are swift and disagreeably close. Everything is made of plaster of Paris, imitative, larger than life, profoundly impersonal. The whole town smells of $1.89 fried shrimp dinners.

I found a motel near the airport, on the outskirts of town. The Bagdad looked like a foreign legion post made of marzipan. The night manager was dressed in a gold satin vest and an orange satin shirt with full puffed sleeves. He wore a fez with a tassel. His breathing had a raspy quality that made me want to clear my throat.

'Are you an out-of-state married couple?' he asked, not looking up.

'No.'

'There's fifty dollars' worth of coupons with a double if you're an out-of-state married couple. I'll put it down. Nobody checks.'

I gave him my credit card, which he ran off while I filled out the registration form. He gave me my key and a small paper cup full of nickels for the slot machines near the door. I left them on the counter.

I parked in the space outside my door and left the car, taking a cab into town through the artificial daylight of

Glitter Gulch. I paid the cabbie and took a moment to orient myself. There was a constant stream of traffic on East Fremont, the sidewalks crowded with tourists, hot yellow signs, and flashing lights – THE MINT, THE FOUR QUEENS – illuminating a complete catalogue of hustlers: pimps and prostitutes, pickpockets, corn-fed con artists from the Midwest who flock to Vegas with the conviction that the system can be beaten with sufficient cunning and industry. I went into the Fremont.

I could smell the Chinese food from the coffee shop and the odor of chicken chow mein mingled oddly with the perfumed jet trail left by a woman who passed me in a royal blue polyester print pantsuit that made her look like a piece of walking wallpaper. I watched idly as she began to feed quarters into a slot machine in the lobby. The blackjack tables were off to my left. I asked one of the pit bosses about Sharon Napier and was told she'd be in at 11.00 in the morning. I hadn't really expected to run into her that night, but I wanted to get a feel for the place.

The casino hummed, the croupiers at the craps tables shoveling chips back and forth with a stick like some kind of tabletop shuffleboard with rules of its own. I once made a tour of the Nevada Dice Company, watching with something close to reverence as the sixty-pound cellulose nitrate slabs, an inch thick, were cured and cut into cubes, slightly bigger than the finished size, hardened, buffed and drilled on all sides, a white resinous compound applied to the sunken dots with special brushes. The dice, in process, looked like tiny squares of cherry Jell-O that might have been served up like some sort of low-cal dessert. I watched people place their bets. The Pass line, the Don't Pass line, Come, Don't Come, the Field, the Big 6 and the Big 8 were mysteries of another kind and I couldn't, for the life of me, penetrate the catechism of wins, losses, numbers being rattled out in a low chant of intense concentration and surprise. Over it all there hung a pale cloud of cigarette smoke, infused with the smell of spilled Scotch. The darkened mirrors above the tables must have been scanned by countless pairs of eyes, restlessly raking the patrons below for telltale signs of chicanery. Nothing could escape notice. The atmosphere was that of a crowded Woolworth's at Christmas, where the throngs of frantic shoppers couldn't be trusted not to lift an item now and then. Even the employees might lie, cheat and steal, and nothing could be left to chance. I felt a fleeting respect for the whole system of checks and balances that keeps so much money flowing freely and allows so little to slip back into the individual pockets from which it has been coaxed. A sudden feeling of exhaustion came over me. I walked back out to the street again and found a cab.

The 'Middle Eastern' decor of the Bagdad halted abruptly at the door to my room. The carpet was dark green cotton shag, the wallpaper lime-green foil in a pattern of overlapping palms, flocked with small clumps that might have been dates or clusters of fruit bats. I locked the door, kicked off my shoes, and pulled down the chenille spread, crawling under the covers with relief. I put a quick call through to my answering service and another to a groggy Arlette, leaving my latest location with the number where I could be reached.

I woke up at 10:00 A.M., feeling the first faint stages of a headache – as though I had a hangover in the making before I'd even had a drink. Vegas tends to affect me that way, some combination of tension and dread to which my body responds with all the symptoms of incipient flu. I took two Tylenols and showered for a long time, trying to wash away the roiling whisper of nausea. I felt like I'd eaten a pound of cold buttered popcorn and washed it down with bulk saccharin.

I stepped out of my motel room, the light causing me to squint. The air, at least, was fresh and there was, by day, the sense of a town subdued and shrunken, flattened out again to its true proportions. The desert stretched away behind the motel in a haze of pale gray, fading to mauve at the horizon. The wind was mild and dry, the promise of summer heat only hinted at in the distant shimmering sunlight that sat on the desert floor in flat pools, evaporating on approach. Occasional patches of sagebrush, nearly silver with dust, broke up the long low lines of treeless wasteland fenced in by distant hills.

I stopped off at the post office and left a fifty-dollar money order for my friend and then I checked out the address he had given me. Sharon Napier lived in a two-story apartment complex on the far side of town, salmon-pink stucco eroding around the edges as though animals had crept up in the night to gnaw the corners away. The roof was nearly flat, peppered with rocks, the iron railings sending streaks of rust down the sides of the building. The landscaping was rock and yucca and cactus plants. There were only twenty units, arranged around a kidney-shaped pool that was separated from the parking area by a dun-colored cinder-block wall. A couple of young kids were splashing about in the pool and a middle-aged woman was standing in front of her apartment up on the landing, a grocery bag wedged between her hip and the door as she let herself in. A Chicano boy hosed down the walks. The buildings on either side of the complex were single-family dwellings. There was a vacant lot across the street in back.

Sharon's apartment was on the ground floor, her name was neatly embossed on the mailbox on a white plastic strip. Her drapes were drawn, but some of the hooks had come loose at the top, causing the lined fabric to bow inward and sag, forming a gap through which I could see a beige Formica table and two beige upholstered plastic kitchen chairs. The telephone sat on one corner of the table, resting on a pile of papers. Beside it was a coffee cup with a waxy crescent of hot-pink lipstick on the rim. A cigarette, also rimmed with pink, had been extinguished in the saucer. I glanced around. No one seemed to be paying any particular attention to me. I walked quickly through a passageway that connected the courtyard to the rear of the apartment building.

Sharon's apartment number was marked on the rear door, too, and there were four other back doors at intervals, the rear entrances emptying into little rectangles surrounded by shoulder-high cinder-block walls designed, I suspected, to create the illusion of small patios. The trash containers were lined up on the walkway outside the wall. Her kitchen curtains were drawn. I eased onto her little patio. She had arranged six geraniums in pots along the back step. There were two aluminium folding chairs stacked against the wall, a pile of old newspapers by the back door. There was a small window up on the right and a larger window beyond that. I couldn't judge whether it might be her bedroom or her neighbor's. I looked out across the vacant lot and then eased out of the patio, turning left along the walk, which opened out onto the street again. I got back in my car and headed for the Fremont.

I felt as if I'd never left. The lady in royal blue was still pasted to the quarter slot machine, her hair sculpted into a glossy mahogany scrollwork on top of her head. The same crowd seemed to be pressed to the craps table as though by magnetic force, the croupier pushing chips back and forth with his little stick as if it were a flat-bottomed broom and someone had made an expensive mess. Waitresses circulated with drinks and a heavyset man, whom I guessed to be plainclothes security, wandered about trying to look like a tourist whose luck had gone bad. I could hear the sounds of a female vocalist in the

Carnival Lounge, singing a slightly flat but lusty medley of Broadway show tunes. I caught a glimpse of her, emoting to a half-deserted room, her face a bright powder pink under the spotlight.

Sharon Napier was not hard to find. She was tall, maybe five ten or better in her high-heeled shoes. She was the sort of woman you noticed from the ground up: long shapely legs looking slender in black mesh hose, a short black skirt flaring slightly at the tops of her thighs. She had narrow hips, a flat stomach, and her breasts were pushed together to form pronounced mounds. The bodice of her black outfit was tight and low-cut, her name stitched above her left breast. Her hair was an ashen blonde, pallid under the houselights, her eyes an eerie green, a luminous shade I guessed to be from tinted contact lenses. Her skin was pale and unblemished, the oval of her face as white as eggshell and as finely textured. Her lips were full and wide, the bright pink lipstick emphasizing their generous proportions. It was a mouth built for unnatural acts. Something about her demeanor promised cool improvisational sex for the right price and it would not be cheap.

She dealt cards mechanically, with remarkable speed. Three men were perched on stools ranged around the table where she worked. No one said a word. The communication was by the slightest lift of a hand, cards turned over or placed under substantial bets, a shoulder shrugged as the up card showed. Two down, one up. Flick, flick. One man scraped the edge of his up card against the surface of the table, asking for a hit. On the second round, one man turned up a blackjack and she paid off – two hundred and fifty dollars' worth of chips. I could see his eyes take her in as she flicked the cards back, shuffling quickly, dealing out cards again. He was thin, with a narrow balding head and a dark mustache, shirt sleeves rolled up, underarms stained with sweat. His gaze drifted down across her body and back up again to the immaculate face, cold and clean, the green eyes blazing. She paid no particular attention to him, but I had the feeling the two of them might do some private business later on. I retreated to another table, watching her from an easy distance. At 1:30, she took a break. Another dealer took her place and she crossed the casino, heading toward the Fiesta Room, where she ordered a Coke and lit up a cigarette. I followed.

'Are you Sharon Napier?' I asked.

She looked up. Her eyes were rimmed with dark lashes, the green taking on an almost turquoise hue in the fluorescent light overhead.

'I don't think we've met,' she said.

'I'm Kinsey Millhone,' I said. 'May I sit down?'

She shrugged by way of consent. She took a compact out of her pocket and checked her eye makeup, removing a slight smudge of shadow from her upper lid. Her lashes were clearly false, but the effect was flashy, giving her eyes an exotic slant. She applied fresh lip gloss, using her little finger, which she dipped into a tiny pot of pink. 'What can I do for you?' she asked, glancing up briefly from her compact mirror.

'I'm looking into the death of Laurence Fife.'

That stopped her. She paused, her whole body going still. If I'd been taking a picture, it would have been the perfect pose. A second passed and she was in motion again. She snapped the compact shut and tucked it away, taking up her cigarette. She took a long drag, watching me all the while. She flicked an ash. 'He was a real shitheel,' she said brusquely, smoke wafting out with each word.

'So I've heard,' I said. 'Did you work for him long?'

She smiled. 'Well, you've done your homework at any rate. I bet you even know the answer to that.'

'More or less,' I said. 'But there's lots I don't know. Want to fill me in?'

'On what?'

I shrugged. 'What it was like to work for him? How you felt about his death . . .'

'He was a prick to work for. I felt terrific about his death,' she said. 'I hated secretarial work in case you haven't guessed.'

'This must suit you better,' I said.

'Look, I got nothing to discuss with you,' she said flatly. 'Who sent you up here anyway?'

I took a flyer on that one. 'Nikki.'

She seemed startled. 'She's still in prison. Isn't she?'

I shook my head. 'She's out.'

She took a moment to calculate and then her manner became somewhat more gracious. 'She's got bucks, right?'

'She's not hurting, if that's what you mean.'

She stubbed out her cigarette, bending the live ember under and mashing it flat. 'I'm off at seven. Why don't you come out to my place and we can chat.'

'Anything you'd care to mention now?'

'Not here,' she said.

She rattled out her address and I dutifully jotted it down in my notebook. She glanced off to the left and I thought at first she was lifting a hand to greet a friend. Her smile flashed and then faltered and she glanced back at me with uncertainty, turning slightly so that my line of sight was blocked. I peered back over her shoulder automatically but she distracted my attention, touching the back of my hand with a fingernail. I looked at her. She towered over me, her expression remote.

'That was the pit boss. End of my break.'

She told lies the way I do, with a certain breezy insolence that dares the listener to refute or contradict.

'I'll see you at seven then,' I said.

'Make it seven forty-five,' she said easily. 'I need time to unwind from work.'

I wrote out my name and the name of my motel, tearing a sheet from my notebook. She made a sharp crease and tucked the slip into her cigarette pack under the cellophane wrapper. She walked away without a backward glance, hips swaying gracefully.

The mashed butt of her cigarette was still sending up a drift of smoke and my stomach emitted a little message of protest. I was tempted to hang around, just to keep an eye on her, but my hands were feeling clammy and I longed to lie down. I didn't feel good at all and I was beginning to think that my flu symptoms might be more real than reactionary. The headache was creeping up again from the back of my neck. I walked out through the lobby. Fresh air helped some but only momentarily.

I drove back to the Bagdad and bought a 7Up from the vending machine. I needed to eat but I wasn't sure anything would stay down. It was early afternoon and I didn't have to be anywhere until well after suppertime. I put the Do Not Disturb sign on my door and crawled back into my unmade bed, pulling the covers around me tightly. My bones had begun to ache. It was a long time before I got warm.

13

The telephone rang with startling shrillness and I awoke with a jolt. The room was dark. I had no idea what time it was, no idea what bed I was in. I groped for the phone, feeling flushed and hot, shoving the covers away from me as I propped myself up on one elbow. I flicked on the light, shading my eyes from the sudden harsh glare.

'Hello?'

'Kinsey, this is Sharon. Did you forget about me?'

I looked at my watch. It was 8:30. Shit. 'God, I'm sorry,' I said. 'I fell asleep. Will you be there for a while? I can be right over.'

'All right,' she said coolly, as though she had better plans. 'Oh, hang on. There's someone at my door.'

She put the phone down with a clack and I pictured it resting on the hard Formica surface of the tabletop. I listened idly, waiting for her to come back. I couldn't believe I'd overslept and I was kicking myself for my stupidity. I heard the door open and her muffled exclamation of surprise. And then I heard a brief, nearly hollow report.

I squinted, sitting up abruptly. I pressed my ear to the phone, pressing my hand over the receiver. What was going on? The receiver was picked up on her end. I expected to hear her voice and I nearly spoke her name but some impulse made me clamp my mouth shut. There was the sound of breathing in my ear, the sexless hushed tones of someone slightly winded. There was a whispered 'hello' that chilled me. I closed my eyes, willing myself to silence; an alarm had spread through my body in a rush that made my heart pound in my ears. There was a small breathy chuckle and then the line went dead. I slammed the phone down and reached for my shoes, grabbing my jacket as I left the room.

The jolt of adrenaline had washed my body clean of pain. My hands were shaking but at least I was in motion. I locked the door and went out to the car, my keys jingling as I tried to hit the ignition switch. I started the car and backed out rapidly, heading toward Sharon's apartment. I reached for the flashlight in my glove compartment, checking it. The light was strong. I drove, anxiety mounting. She was either playing games or dead, and I suspected I knew which.

I pulled up across the street. The building showed no particular signs of activity. No one was moving about. There were no crowds gathered, no police cars parked at the street, no sirens wailing an approach. There were numerous cars parked in the slots, and the lights in the building had been turned on in almost every apartment that I could see. I reached around in the backseat, removing a pair of rubber gloves from my locked briefcase. My hand touched the short barrel of my little automatic and I desperately longed to tuck that in my windbreaker pocket. I wasn't sure what I'd find in her apartment, wasn't sure who might be waiting for me, but the notion of being discovered there in possession of a loaded gun wouldn't do at all if she was dead. I left the gun where it was and got out, locking my car, tucking the keys into my jeans.

I moved into the front courtyard. It was dark, but several outdoor spots were placed strategically along the walk, six more green and yellow spots shooting upward along the cactus plants. The effect was more gaudy than illuminating. Sharon's apartment was dark and the gap in the drapes had been pulled tight. I tapped at the door. 'Sharon?' I kept my voice low, scanning the front of the place for any signs of lights coming on. I pulled on the rubber gloves and tried the knob. Locked. I tapped again, repeating her name.

There was no sound from inside. What was I going to do if someone was in there?

I moved along the short stretch of walk that led around the building to the rear. I could hear a stereo playing somewhere in one of the upstairs apartments. The small of my back ached and my cheeks felt as hot as if I'd just gotten back from a run, though whether it was from flu or fear I couldn't say. I moved quickly and silently along the rear walkway. Sharon's kitchen was the only one of the five that was dark. There was an outside bulb burning above each back door, casting a shallow but clear light onto each small patio. I tried the back door. Locked. I tapped on the glass.

'Sharon?' I strained for sounds inside the apartment. All was quiet. I scanned the rear entrance. If she had an extra set of keys outside, they would be hidden someplace close. I glanced back at the small panes of glass in her back door. If all else failed, I could always break one out. I slid my fingers along the top of the doorframe. Too narrow for keys. All the flowerpots seemed straight and a quick search revealed nothing tucked down in the dirt. There was no doormat. I lifted the pile of old newspapers, giving them a little riff, but no keys clattered out. The surrounding cinder-block patio wall was made of one-foot-square decorative 'bricks', each design of sufficient intricacy to provide an ample, if not original, hiding place for a key. I hoped I wasn't going to have to check every single one. I glanced back at the small panes of glass, wondering if it might not be more to the point to pop one out with a padded fist. I looked down. There was a green plastic watering can and a trowel in one corner right up against the wall. I crouched, sliding my right hand into each of the decorative whorls of concrete. There was a key in one.

I reached up and gave the bulb above her back door a quick twist to the left. The patio was immersed in shadow. I fitted the key into the knob lock and opened the door a crack.

'Sharon!' I whispered hoarsely. I was tempted to leave the apartment in darkness but I had to know if I was alone. I held the flashlight like a club, groping to my right until I found a switch. The recessed light above the sink went on. I saw the switch to the overhead kitchen light on the opposite wall. I crossed the room and flipped it on, ducking down and out of sight. I hunkered, holding my breath, my back against the refrigerator. I listened intently. Nothing. I hoped like hell I wasn't making a colossal fool of myself. For all I knew, the noise I'd heard was the popping of a champagne cork and Sharon was in the darkened bedroom performing illicit sexual acts with a little show dog and a whip.

I peered into the living room. Sharon was sprawled out on the living-room floor in a kelly green velour robe. She was either dead or sound asleep and I still didn't know who else might be in that apartment with me. I crossed to the living room in two steps and pressed myself up against the wall, waiting a moment before I peered back out into the darkened hallway. I couldn't see shit. I found a light switch just to my left and flipped it on. The hall was ablaze with light and the portion of the bedroom I could see seemed unoccupied. I felt for the bedroom switch and flipped it on, peering around quickly. I guessed the open doorway off to my right was the bathroom. There was no indication that the place had been ransacked. The sliding closet doors were shut and I didn't like that. From the bathroom, there was a faint metallic sound. I froze. My heart gave a thud and a half and I crouched. Me and my flashlight. I wished like hell I'd brought the gun. The little metallic squeak picked up again, assuming a rhythm that suddenly took on a familiar tone. I crept over to the door and flashed the light in. There was a goddamn little mouse going round and round in an exercise wheel. The cage sat on the bathroom counter. I flipped the light on. The bathroom was empty.

I crossed to the closet doors and slid one open, half waiting to get my head bashed in. Both sides of the closet were empty of anything but clothing. I let out the long breath I'd been holding and then did a second quick search of the place. I made sure the back door was locked, pulling the kitchen curtains across the window above the sink. And then I went back to Sharon. I flipped on the lamp in the living room and knelt down beside her. She had a bullet hole at the base of her throat, looking like a little locket filled with raw flesh instead of a photograph. Blood had soaked into the carpet under her head and it had darkened now to the color of uncooked chicken liver. There were small slivers of bone in her hair. I guessed that her spine had been shattered by the bullet on impact. Nice for her. No pain. She seemed to have been knocked straight back, arms flung out on either side of her body, her hips turned slightly. Her eyes were half open, the luminous green color looking sour now. Her blonde hair looked gray in death. If I'd gotten there when I was supposed to, she might not be dead, and I wanted to apologize for my bad manners, for the delay, for being sick, for being too late. I wanted to hold her hand and coax her back to life again but there was no way and I knew, in a quick flash, that if I'd been there on time, I might be dead myself.

I ran my gaze around the room with care. The carpeting was a high-low, matted with wear, so there were no shoe prints. I crossed to the front window and readjusted the drapes, making sure no crack appeared to afford a view from outside now that the lights were turned on. I made a brief tour again, taking in details this time. The bed was unmade. The bathroom was littered with damp towels. Dirty clothing bulged out of the hamper. An ashtray sat on the rim of the tub with several cigarette butts stubbed out, folded over and mashed flat in the manner I'd seen her use. The apartment was basically only those three rooms –

living room with the dining table near the front windows, kitchen, and bedroom. The furniture looked as if it had been ordered by the boxcarload, and I assumed that little of it was actually hers. Whatever the disorder on the premises, it seemed to be of her own making – dishes in the sink, trash unemptied. I glanced down at the papers under the phone, a collection of past-due notices and bills. Apparently her penchant for financial chaos hadn't changed since her days in Santa Teresa. I picked up the whole batch and shoved them into my jacket pocket.

I could hear the little metallic squeak again and I went back to the bathroom, staring down at that foolish little creature. He was small and brown, with bright red eyes, patiently making his way around and around, going nowhere. 'I'm sorry,' I whispered, and tears stung my lips briefly. I shook my head. It was misplaced sentiment and I knew it. His water bottle was full but the plastic food dish was empty. I filled it with little green pellets and then I went back to the phone and dialed the operator, asking for the Las Vegas police. Con Dolan's warning sounded dully in my memory. All I needed was the LVPD holding me for questioning. One of those gravelly officious voices came on the line after two rings.

'Oh hello,' I said. My voice had a tremor in it and I had to clear my throat quickly. 'I, uh, heard some noise in my neighbor's apartment a little while ago and now I can't seem to get her to answer my knock. I'm worried that she's hurt herself. Is there any way you could check that out?'

He sounded irritated and bored, but he took down Sharon's address and said he'd send someone.

I checked my watch. I'd been in the apartment less than thirty minutes, but it was time to get out of there. I didn't want the phone to ring. I didn't want somebody knocking at the door unexpectedly. I moved toward the back, turning out lights as I went, unconsciously listening for sounds of someone approaching. I didn't have a lot of time to spare.

I glanced back at Sharon. I didn't like to leave her that way but I couldn't see the point in waiting it out. I didn't want to be linked to her death and I didn't want to hang around Las Vegas waiting for the coroner's inquest. And I certainly didn't want Con Dolan to find out I'd been here. Maybe the Mafia had killed her, or maybe some pimp, or maybe the man at the casino who'd looked at her with such hunger when she counted out his two hundred and fifty bucks. Or maybe she knew something about Laurence Fife that she wasn't supposed to tell.

I moved past her. Her fingers were relaxed in death, looking graceful, each tipped with a long rose-polished nail. I caught my breath. She had taken the slip with my name and motel jotted on it and had tucked it into her cigarette pack. But where was it? I looked around quickly, heart racing. I didn't see it on the Formica tabletop, though there was a cigarette that had apparently burned down to nothing, leaving only a perfect column of ash. There was no cigarette pack on the arm of the couch, none on the counter. I checked the bathroom again, listening acutely for sounds of the police. I could have sworn I heard a siren some distance off and I felt a ripple of alarm. Shit. I had to find that note. The bathroom trash was full of Kleenex and a soap wrapper, old cigarette butts. No cigarette pack on the bedtable. None on the dresser top. I went back to the living room and looked down at her with distaste. There were two generous side pockets in the green velour robe. I gritted my teeth, feeling gingerly. The pack was on the right-hand side, with maybe six cigarettes left, the sharply creased slip of paper bearing my name still visible under the cellophane. I tucked it hastily into my jacket.

I turned out the remaining lights and slipped to the back door, opening it a crack. I could hear voices remarkably close. A garbage can lid clattered near the apartment to my right.

'You better tell the manager her light's burned out,' a woman commented. She sounded as if she was standing right next to me.

'Why don't you tell *her*?' came the slightly annoyed reply.

'I don't think she's home. Her lights are off.'

'Yes she is. I just saw the lights on a minute ago.'

'Sherman, they're off. The whole place is dark. She must have gone out the front,' the woman said. The wailing siren was very loud, its tone winding down like a phonograph.

My heart was pounding so hard it was making my chest burn. I eased out onto the darkened patio, pausing to tuck the keys back into the little crevice behind the plastic watering can. I hoped like hell it wasn't my car keys I was hiding there. I slipped out of the patio, turning left, moving toward the street again. I had to force myself to walk casually past the patrol car that was now parked out front. I unlocked my car and got in, pushing the lock down hastily as though someone were in pursuit. I stripped off the rubber gloves. My head was aching fiercely and I felt a flash of clammy sweat, bile rising up in my throat. I had to get out of there. I swallowed convulsively. The nausea welled up and I fought an almost irresistible urge to heave. My hands were shaking so badly I could hardly get my car started but I managed, finally, and pulled away from the curb with care.

As I drove past the entranceway, I could see a uniformed patrolman move around to the back of Sharon's apartment, hand on the gun at his hip. It seemed somewhat theatrical for a simple domestic complaint and I wondered, with a chill, if someone else had placed a call with a message more explicit than mine. Half a minute more and I'd have been trapped in that apartment with a lot of explaining to do. I didn't like that idea at all.

I went back to the Bagdad and packed, cleaning the place of fingerprints. I felt as if I were running a low-grade fever. All I really wanted to do was roll up in a blanket and go back to sleep. Head throbbing, I went into the office. The manager's wife was there this time, looking like a Turkish harem girl – if the word 'girl' applied. She was probably sixty-five, with a finely wrinkled face, like something that had been left in the drier too long. She wore a pale satin pillbox perched on her gray hair, veils draped provocatively over her ears.

'I'll be on the road at five in the morning and I thought I'd get my bill squared away tonight,' I said.

I gave her my room number and she sorted through the upright file, coming up with my ledger card. I was feeling restless, anxious and sick, and I wanted to be out on the road. Instead, I had to force myself, brightly, casually, to deal with this woman who moved in slow motion.

'Where you headed?' she asked idly, totting up the charges on the adding machine. She made a mistake and had to do it all over again.

'Reno,' I said, lying automatically.

'Any luck?'

'What?'

'You win much?'

'Oh yeah, I'm doing pretty good,' I said 'I really surprised myself.'

'Better than most folk,' she remarked. 'You won't be making any long-distance calls before you leave?' She gave me a sharp look.

I shook my head. 'I'm going to hit the sack.'

'You look like you could use some sleep,' she said. She filled out the credit-card charge slip, which I signed, taking my copy.

'I didn't use the fifty dollars' worth of coupons,' I said. 'You might as well have those back.'

She put the unused coupons in the drawer without a word.

Within minutes, miraculously, I was out on Highway 93, heading southeast toward Boulder City, where I took 95 south. I got as far as Needles and then I had to have relief. I found a cheap motel and checked in, crawled under the covers again, and slept for ten hours straight. Even that far down in oblivion, I felt an awesome dread of what had been set in motion and a pointless, aching sense of apology to Sharon Napier for whatever part I'd played in her death.

14

In the morning, I felt whole again. I ate a big breakfast in a little diner across the road from the motel, washing down bacon, scrambled eggs and rye toast with fresh orange juice and three cups of coffee. I had the car filled up with gas, the oil checked, and then hit the road again. After Las Vegas, the desert drive was a pleasure. The land was spare, the colors subdued: a mild very pale lavender overlaid with fine dust. The sky was a stark, cloudless blue, the mountain ridges like crushed velvet, wrinkled dark gray along the face. There was something appealing about all that country unconquered yet, miles and miles of terrain without neon signs. The population was reduced to races of kangaroo rat and ground squirrel, the rocky canyons inhabited by kit fox and desert lynx. At fifty-five miles an hour, no wildlife was visible but I had heard the cries of tree frogs even in my sleep and I pictured now, from my speeding car, the clay and gravel washes filled with buff-colored lizards and millipedes, creatures whose adaptation to their environment includes the husbanding of moisture and an aversion to hot sun. There are parasol ants in the desert that cut off leaves and carry them as sunshades over their backs, storing them later like beach umbrellas in the subterranean chambers where they live. The idea made me smile, and I kept my mind resolutely from the recollection of Sharon Napier's death.

I found Greg Fife in a little gray humpbacked camper outside Durmid on the eastern shore of the Salton Sea. It had taken me a while to track him down. Gwen had said that he lived on his boat but the boat had been pulled out of the water for paint and repair and Greg was temporarily lodged in an aluminium trailer that looked like a roly-poly bug. The interior was compact with a folding table hooked flat against the wall, a padded bench that became a single bed, a canvas chair that completely blocked passage to the sink, a chemical toilet and a hot plate. He opened two bottles of beer, which he'd taken from a refrigerator the size of a cardboard box, located under the sink.

He offered me the padded bench, unfolding the small table between us. A single leg flopped down to give it support. I was effectively hemmed in and could only get comfortable by turning sideways. Greg took the canvas chair, tilting back so he could study me while I studied him. He looked a lot like Laurence Fife – lank dark-brown hair, a square-cut smooth face that was clean-shaven, dark eyes, bold dark brows, square chin. He looked younger than twenty-five but his smile had the same touch of arrogance that I remembered from his father. He was darkly tanned, cheekbones tinted with sunburn. His shoulders were wide, his body lean, his feet bare. He wore a red cotton turtle neck and cutoffs that were ragged at the bottom, nearly ruffled with bleached threads. He took a sip of beer.

'You think I look like him?'

'Yes,' I said. 'Does that suit you?'

Greg shrugged. 'Doesn't matter much at this point,' he said. 'We weren't anything alike.'

'How so?'

'God,' he said facetiously, 'let's just skip over the preliminaries and get right down to the personal stuff, why don't we.'

I smiled. 'I'm not very polite.'

'Neither am I,' he said.

'So what do you want to talk about first? The weather?'

'Skip it,' he said. 'I know what you're here for so get to the point.'

'You remember much about that time in your life?'

'Not if I can help it.'

'Except for shrinks,' I suggested.

'I did that to please my mom,' he said and then smiled briefly as though he recognized the fact that the phrase 'my mom' sounded too boyish for him at his age.

'I worked for your father a couple of times,' I said.

He began to peel a strip of label with his thumbnail, feigning disinterest. I wondered what he'd heard about his father and I decided, on impulse, not to give Laurence Fife any posthumous pats lest I sound condescending or insincere.

I said, 'I've heard he was a real bastard.'

'No shit,' Greg said.

I shrugged. 'I didn't think he was that bad myself. He was straight with me. I suspect he was a complicated man and I don't think many people got close to him.'

'Did you?'

'No,' I said. I shifted slightly in my seat. 'How'd you feel about Nikki?'

'Not that good.'

I smiled. 'Try to keep your answers short so I can get 'em all on one line,' I said. He didn't bite. I drank beer for a while, then rested my chin on my fist. Sometimes I just really do get sick of trying to coax information out of people who aren't in the mood. 'Why don't you fold up the table and we'll go outside,' I said.

'What for?'

'So I can get some fresh air, fucker, what do you think?'

He chuckled suddenly and moved his long legs out of my way as I slid out of the seat.

I'd surprised myself, getting snappish with him, but I get tired of people being cute or sullen or cautious or tight-lipped.

I wanted straight answers and a lot of them too. And I wanted a relationship based, just once, on some sort of mutual exchange instead of me always having to connive and manipulate. I walked aimlessly, Greg at my heels, trying to cool myself down. It wasn't his fault, I knew, and I'm suspicious of myself anyway when I'm feeling righteous and misunderstood.

'Sorry I snapped at you,' I said.

The trailer was about two hundred yards from the water's edge. There were several larger trailers nearby, all facing the sea, like a queer band of animals that had crept down to the water to drink. I pulled off my tennis shoes and tied the laces together, hanging them around my neck. The Salton Sea has a mild to nonexistent surf, like an ocean that has been totally tamed. There is no vegetation visible in the water and few if any fish. It gives the shore a curious air, as though the tides had been brought to heel, becalmed, the life forms leached away. What remains is familiar but subtly changed, like a glimpse into the future where certain laws of nature have been altered by the passage of time. I placed a drop of water on my tongue. The taste of salt was fierce. 'Is this ocean water?'

Greg smiled, apparently unperturbed by my former outburst. In fact he seemed friendlier. 'You want a lesson in geology,' he said, 'I'll give you one.' It was the first time his voice had contained any sign of enthusiasm.

'Sure, why not?'

He picked up a rock, using it like a piece of chalk as he drew a crude map in the wet sand. 'This is the California coastline and this is Baja. Over here is Mexico. Right at the tip of the Gulf of California is Yuma – southeast of here, more or less. This is us here,' he said, pointing. 'The Colorado River curves right up through here and then up past Las Vegas. That's Hoover Dam. Then it goes up here and over into Utah and then to Colorado, but we can skip that part. Now,' he said, tossing the rock aside. He began to draw with his fingertip, glancing up at me to see if I was listening. 'This area in here is called the Salton Sink. Two hundred and seventy-three feet below sea level – something like that. If it weren't for the Colorado River forming a kind of natural dam right here, all this water from the Gulf of California would have spilled into the Salton Sink years ago – all the way up to Indio. God, that gives me the willies when I think of it. Anyway, the Salton Sea came from the Colorado River itself, so it was originally fresh water. Overflowed in 1905 – the river did, billions of gallons of water pouring in over a two-year period. It was finally controlled with rock and brush dams. The salt, which has been gradually saturating the water, was probably from prehistoric times when all of this area was submerged.' He stood up, brushing wet sand off his hands, apparently satisfied with his summary.

We began to walk – he on the beach side, me scuffling my bare feet through the shallows. He tucked his hands in his back pockets. 'Sorry if I was a pissant before,' he said lightly, 'I've been in a bad mood with my boat out of the water. I was never meant to be on land.'

'You sure snapped out of it quick enough,' I remarked.

'Because you said "fuck." I always get tickled when women say that. Especially you. It was the last thing I expected to come out of your mouth.'

'What do you do down here?' I asked. 'Fish?'

'Some. Mostly sail. Read. Drink beer. Hang out.'

'I'd go nuts.'

Greg shrugged. 'I started out nuts so I'm getting sane.'

'Not really "nuts",' I said.

'Not certifiable, no.'

'What kind then?'

'Don't make me tell all that stuff,' he said mildly. 'I get bored with myself. Ask me something else. Three questions. Like magic wishes.'

'If I have to limit myself to three questions, I might as well go home,' I said, but basically I was willing to play the game. I looked over at him. He was looking less like his father and more like himself. 'What do you remember from the period just before he died?'

'You asked me that before.'

'Yeah, and that's just about the time you turned all surly on me. I'll tell you why I'm asking. Maybe that will help. I'd like to reconstruct the events just before his death. Maybe as far back as the last six months before he was killed. I mean, maybe he was involved in some kind of legal hassle – a personal feud. Maybe he fought with a neighbor over a property line. Somebody did it, and there had to be a sequence of events.'

'I wouldn't know about that stuff,' he said. 'I can tell you just family events, but the other I wouldn't know.'

'That's okay.'

'We came down here that fall. That's one of the reasons I came back.'

I wanted to prompt him with another question but I was afraid he'd count it as one of my three so I kept my mouth shut. He went on.

'I was seventeen. God, I was such a jerk and I thought my father was so impossibly perfect. I didn't know what he expected of me but I figured I'd never measure up, so I was a pissant. He was supercritical and he hurt my feelings a lot, but I'd just stonewall him. Half the time I hung on his every word and the rest of the time I hated his guts. So when he died, I lost the chance to square myself with him. I mean, for all time, you know? That's it. I've got no way to take care of any old business with him, so I'm stuck. I figured if I was stuck in time, I might as well be stuck in place, too, so that's why I came here. We were out on the beach once – and he had to go back to the car for something and I remember watching him walk. Just looking at him. He had his head bent and he was probably thinking about anything but me. I felt like I should call him back, really tell him how much I loved him, but of course I didn't. So that's the way I remember him. That whole business really screwed me up.'

'It was just the two of you?'

'What? No, the whole family. Except Diane. She got sick and stayed with Mom. It was Labor Day weekend. We drove to Palm Springs first, just for the day, and then came on down here.'

'How'd you feel about Colin?'

'Okay I guess, but I didn't see why the whole family had to revolve around him. The kid had a handicap and I felt bad about that, but I didn't want my life to focus on his infirmity, you know? I mean, Jesus, I would have had to develop a terminal disease to compete with him. This is me at seventeen, you understand. Now I'm a little more compassionate, but back then, I couldn't cope with that stuff. I didn't see why I should. Dad and I were never bosom buddies, but I needed time with him too. I used to have these fantasies of what it would be like. I'd really tell him something important and he'd really listen to me. Instead, all we talked about was bullshit – just *bull*shit. So six weeks later he's dead.'

He glanced at me and then shook his head, smiling sheepishly.

'Shakespeare should have done a play about this stuff,' he said. 'I could have done the monologue.'

'So he never talked to you about his personal life?'

'That's number three, you know,' he remarked. 'You sneaked in that little question about whether it was just Dad and me down here. But the answer is no. He never talked to me about anything. I told you I couldn't be much help. Let's knock it off for a while, okay?'

I smiled and tossed my shoes up on the beach, starting to jog.

'Do you jog?' I called back over my shoulder.

'Yeah, some,' he said, catching up. He began to trot at my side.

'What happens if I work up a sweat?' I asked. 'Can we get cleaned up?'

'The neighbors let me use their shower.'

'Great,' I said and picked up the pace.

We ran, not exchanging a word, just taking in sun and sand and dry heat. The whole time, the same question came up over and over again. How could Sharon Napier fit into this scheme? What could she possibly have known that she didn't live long enough to tell? So far, none of it made sense. Not Fife's death, not Libby's, not Sharon's death eight years later. Unless she was blackmailing someone. I glanced back at the little trailer, still visible, looking remarkably close in the odd perspective of the flat desert landscape. There was no one else around. No sign of vehicles, no boogeymen on foot. I smiled at Greg. He wasn't even panting yet.

'You're in good shape,' I said.

'So are you. How long do we keep this up?'

'Thirty minutes. Forty-five.'

We chunked along for a while, the sand causing mild pains in my calves.

'How about I ask you three?' he said.

'Okay.'

'How'd you get along with your old man?'

'Oh great,' I said. 'He died when I was five. Both of them did. In a car wreck. Up near Lompoc. Big rock rolled down the mountain and smashed the windshield. Took them six hours to pry me out of the back. My mother cried for a while and then she stopped. I still hear it sometimes in my sleep. Not the sobs. The silence after that. I was raised by my aunt. Her sister.'

He digested that. 'You married?'

'Was.' I held up two fingers.

He smiled. 'Is that for "twice" or question number two?'

I laughed. 'That's number three.'

'Hey, come on. You cheat.'

'All right. One more. But make it count.'

'You ever kill anyone?'

I glanced over at him with curiosity. It seemed like a strange follow-up. 'Let's put it this way,' I said. 'I did my first homicide investigation when I was twenty-six. A job I did for the public defender's office. A woman accused of killing her own kids. Three of them. Girls. All under five. Taped their mouths, hands, and feet, then put them in garbage cans and let them suffocate. I had to look at the glossy eight-by-ten police photographs. I got cured of any homicidal urges. Also any desire for motherhood.'

'Jesus,' he said. 'And she really did it?'

'Oh sure. She got off, of course. Pleaded temporary insanity. She might be back on the streets again for all I know.'

'How do you keep from getting cynical?' he asked.

'Who says I'm not?'

While I showered in the trailer next door, I tried to think what else I might learn from Greg. I was feeling restless, anxious to be on the road again. If I could get to Claremont by dark, I could talk to Diane first thing in the morning and then drive back to Los Angeles after lunch. I toweled my hair dry and dressed. Greg had opened another beer for me, which I sipped while I waited for him to get cleaned up. I glanced at my watch. It was 3:15. Greg came into the trailer, leaving the door open, sliding the screen door shut. His dark hair was still damp and he smelled of soap.

'You look poised for flight,' he said, getting himself a beer. He popped the cap.

'I'm thinking I should try to get to Claremont before dark,' I said. 'You have any messages for your sister?'

'She knows where I am. We talk now and then, often enough to keep caught up,' he said. He sat down in the canvas chair, propping his feet up on the padded bench next to me. 'Anything else you want to ask?'

'Couple of things if you don't mind,' I said.

'Fire away.'

'What do you remember about your father's allergies?'

'Dogs, cat dander, sometimes hay fever but I don't know what that consisted of exactly.'

'He wasn't allergic to any kind of food? Eggs? Wheat?'

Greg shook his head. 'Not that I ever heard. Just stuff in the air – pollens, things like that.'

'Did he have his allergy capsules with him when the family came down here that weekend?'

'I don't remember that. I would guess no. He knew we'd be out in the desert and the air down here is usually pretty clear even in late summer, early fall. The dog wasn't with us. We left him at home, so Dad wouldn't have needed the allergy medication for that, and I don't think there was anything else he needed it for.'

'I thought the dog got killed. I thought Nikki told me that,' I said.

'Yeah, he was. While we were gone as a matter of fact.'

I felt a sudden chill. There was something odd about that, something off. 'How'd you find out about it?'

Greg shrugged. 'When we got home,' he said, apparently not attaching much to the fact. 'Mom had taken Diane over to the house to pick something up. Sunday morning I guess. We didn't get back until Monday night. Anyway, they found

Bruno lying out on the side of the road. I guess he was pretty badly mangled. Mom wouldn't even let Diane see him up close. She called the animal-shelter people and they came and picked him up. He'd been dead awhile. All of us felt bad about it. He was a great beast.'

'Good watchdog?'

'The best,' he said.

'What about Mrs Voss, the housekeeper? What was she like?'

'Nice enough, I guess. She seemed to get along with everybody,' he said. 'I wish I knew more but that's about it as far as I can tell.'

I finished my beer and got up, holding out my hand to him. 'Thanks, Greg. I may need to talk to you again if that's okay.'

He kissed the back of my hand, pretending to clown but meaning something else, I was almost sure. 'Godspeed,' he said softly.

I smiled with unexpected pleasure. 'Did you ever see *Young Bess*? Jean Simmons and Stewart Granger? That's what he says to her. He was doomed, I think, or maybe she was – I forget. Ripped my heart out. You ought to watch for it on the late movie some night. It killed me when I was a kid.'

'You're only five or six years older than me,' he said.

'Seven,' I replied.

'Same smell.'

'I'll let you know what I find out,' I said.

'Good luck.'

As I pulled away, I glanced back out of the car window. Greg was standing in the trailer doorway, the screen creating the ghostly illusion of Laurence Fife again.

15

I reached Claremont at 6:00, driving through Ontario, Montclair and Pomona; all townships without real towns, a peculiar California phenomenon in which a series of shopping malls and acres of tract houses acquire a zip code and become realities on the map. Claremont is an oddity in that it resembles a trim little midwestern hamlet with elms and picket fences. The annual Fourth of July parade is composed of kazoo bands, platoons of children on crêpe-paper-decorated bikes, and a self-satirizing team of husbands dressed in Bermuda shorts, black socks and business shoes doing close-order drills with power mowers. Except for the smog, Claremont could even be considered 'picturesque' with Mount Baldy forming a raw backdrop.

I pulled into a gas station and called the number Gwen had given me for Diane. She was out, but her room-mate said she'd be home at 8:00. I headed up Indian Hill Boulevard, turning left onto Baughman. My friends Gideon and Nell live two doors down in a house with two kids, three cats and a hot tub. Nell I've known since my college days. She's a creature of high intellect and wry humor who's learned never to be too amazed by my appearances on her doorstep. She seemed pleased to see me nevertheless and I sat in her kitchen, watching her make soup while we talked. I called Diane again after supper and she agreed to meet me for lunch. After that, Nell and I stripped down and soaked in the hot tub out on the deck, with icy white wine and a lot more catching up to do. Gideon graciously kept the children at bay. I slept on the couch that night with a cat curled up on my chest, wondering if there was any way I could have such a life for myself.

I met Diane at one of those brown-bread-and-sprout restaurants that all look the same: lots of natural varnished wood and healthy hanging plants, macramé and leaded-glass windows and waiters who don't smoke cigarettes but would probably toke on anything else you've got. Ours was thin with receding hair and a dark mustache, which he stroked incessantly, taking our order with an earnestness that I don't think any sandwich ever deserved. Mine was avocado and bacon. Hers was a 'vegetarian delite' stuffed in pitta bread.

'Greg says he really treated you like shit when you first got down there,' she said and laughed. Some sort of dressing was leaking out through a crack in her pitta bread and she lapped it off.

'When did you talk to him? Last night?'

'Sure.' She took another unwieldy mouthful and I watched her lick her fingers and wipe her chin. She had Greg's clean good looks but she carried more weight, wide rump packed into a pair of faded jeans, and an unexpected powdering of freckles on her face. Her dark hair was parted in the center and pulled up on top with a broad leather band, pierced through with a wooden skewer.

'Did you know Nikki was out on parole?' I asked.

'That's what Mom said. Is Colin back?'

'Nikki was just on her way up to get him when I talked to her a couple of days ago,' I said. I was struggling to keep my sandwich intact, thick bread breaking with every bite, but I caught the look in her eye. Colin interested her. Nikki did not.

'Did you meet Mom?'

'Yes. I liked her a lot.'

Diane flashed a quick, proud smile. 'Daddy was really an asshole to dump her for Nikki if you ask me. I mean, Nikki's okay, but she's kind of cold, don't you think?'

I murmured something noncommittal. Diane didn't seem to be listening anyway. 'Your mother said you went into therapy right after your father died,' I said.

Diane rolled her eyes, taking a sip of peppermint tea. 'I've been in therapy half my life and my head's still not on straight. It's really a drag. The shrink I got now thinks I should go into analysis but nobody does that anymore. He says I need to go into my "dark" side. He's into this real Freudian horsehit. All those old guys are. You know, they want you to lie there and tell 'em all your dreams and kinky fantasies so they can whack off mentally at your expense. I did Reichian before that but I got sick of huffing and puffing and pulling on towels. That just felt dumb to me.'

I took a big bite of sandwich, nodding as if I knew what she was talking about. 'I've never been in therapy,' I murmured.

'Not even *group*?'

I shook my head.

'God, you must really be neurotic,' she said respectfully.

'Well I don't bite my nails or wet the bed.'

'You're probably the compulsive type, avoiding commitments and shit like that. Daddy was like that some.'

'Like how?' I said, skipping right over the reference to my character. After all, it was just a wild guess.

'Oh. You know. Fucking around all the time. Greg and I still compare notes on that. My shrink says he was just warding off pain. My granny used to manipulate the shit out of him so he turned around and manipulated everyone else, including Greg and me. And Mom. And Nikki, and I don't even know who else. I don't think he ever loved anybody in his life except Colin maybe. Too threatening.'

She finished her sandwich and spent a few minutes wiping her face and hands. Then she folded the paper napkin carefully.

'Greg told me you missed the trip to Salton Sea,' I said.

'What, before Daddy died? Yeah I did. I had the flu, really grisly stuff, so I stayed with Mom. She was great, really poured on the TLC. I never slept so much in my life.'

'How did the dog get out?'

She put her hands in her lap. 'What?'

'Bruno. Greg said he got hit by a car. I just wondered who let him out. Was Mrs Voss staying at the house while the family was gone?'

Diane looked at me with care and then away. 'I don't think so. She was on vacation, I think.' Her eyes strayed to the clock on the wall behind me. 'I've got a class,' she said. Her face was suffused with pink.

'Are you okay?'

'Sure. Fine,' she said, casually gathering up her purse and books. She seemed relieved to have something to do. 'Oh, I nearly forgot. I've got something for Colin if you're going to see him.' She held out a paper bag. 'It's an album I put together for him. We had all those pictures in a box.' She was all business now, her manner distracted, her attention disengaged. She gave me a brief smile. 'I'm sorry I don't have any more time. How much is my part of the lunch?'

'I'll take care of it,' I said. 'Can I drop you someplace?'

'I've got a car,' she said. All the animation had left her face.

'Diane, what's going on?' I said.

She sat down again abruptly, staring straight ahead. Her voice had dropped about six notes. 'I let the dog out myself,' she said, 'the day they left. Nikki said to let him have a run before Mom picked me up so I did but I just felt like shit. I lay down on the couch in the living room to wait for Mom and when she honked, I just grabbed my stuff and went out the front. I never even thought about the dog. He must have been running around for two days before I remembered. That's why Mom and I drove over there. To feed him and let him in.'

Her eyes finally met mine and she seemed close to tears. 'That poor thing,' she whispered. The guilt seemed to take possession of her totally. 'It was my fault. That's why he got hit. Because I forgot.' She put a trembling hand against her mouth, blinking. 'I felt awful about it but I never told anyone except Mom and nobody ever asked. You won't tell, will you? They were so upset that he got killed that nobody ever even asked me how he got out and I never said a word. I couldn't. Nikki would have hated me.'

'Nikki's not going to hate you because the dog got killed, Diane,' I said. 'That was years ago. What difference does it make now?'

Her eyes took on a haunted look and I had to lean forward to hear what she was saying. 'Because someone got in. While the dog was out. Someone got into the house and switched the medication. And that's why Daddy died,' she said. She fumbled in her purse for a Kleenex, her sobs sounding like a series of gasps, involuntary, quick, her shoulders hunching helplessly.

Two guys from the next table looked over at her with curiosity.

'Oh God, oh God,' she whispered, her voice hoarse with grief.

'Let's get out of here,' I said, grabbing up her belongings. I left too much money on the table for the check. I took her by the arm, propelling her toward the door.

By the time we got out to the parking lot, she was almost in control of herself. 'God, I'm sorry. I can't believe I did that,' she said. 'I never fall apart that way.'

'That's okay,' I said. 'I had no idea I'd set you off like that. It was just something that stuck in my mind after Greg mentioned it. I didn't mean to *accuse* you of anything.'

'I couldn't believe you said it,' she said, tears rising again. She looked at me earnestly. 'I thought you knew. I thought you must have found out. I never would have admitted it otherwise. I've felt so awful about that for so long.'

'How can you blame yourself? If someone wanted to get into the house, he would have let the dog loose anyway. Or killed it and made it look like an accident. I mean, who's going to get upstairs with a goddamn German shepherd barking and snarling?' I said.

'I don't know. Maybe so. It could be, I guess. I mean, he *was* a good watchdog. If he'd been in, nobody could have done anything.'

She let out a deep breath, blowing her nose again on the damp twisted Kleenex. 'I was so irresponsible in those days. They were always on my case, which just made things worse. I couldn't tell 'em. And nobody seemed to make the connection when Daddy died except me and I *couldn't* admit it then.'

'Hey, it's over,' I said, 'it's done. You can't beat yourself to death with it. It's not as if you did it deliberately.'

'I know, I know. But the result was the same, you know?' Her voice lifted up and her eyes squeezed shut again, tears running down her cheeks. 'He was such a shit and I loved him so much. I know Greg hated his guts, but I just thought he was great. I didn't care if he screwed around. That wasn't his fault. He was just so messed up all his life. He really was.'

She wiped her eyes with the wad of Kleenex and then took another deep breath. She reached in her purse for a compact.

'Why don't you skip your class and go home?' I said.

'Maybe I will,' she said. She looked at herself in the mirror. 'Oh God, I'm a wreck. I can't go anywhere looking like this.'

'I'm sorry I triggered this. I think I feel worse than you,' I said sheepishly.

'No, that's all right. It's not your fault. It's mine. I guess I'll even have to tell my shrink now. He'll think it's cathartic. He loves that shit. I guess everyone will know now. God, that's all I need.'

'Hey, I may or may not have to mention it. I really don't know yet, but I don't think it matters now. If someone was determined to kill your father, it would have been done one way or the other. That's just a fact.'

'I guess so. Anyway, it's nice of you to say that. I feel better. Really. I didn't even know it was still weighing on me, but it must have been.'

'You're sure you're okay now?'

She nodded, giving me a little smile.

We said our good-byes, which took a few minutes more, and then she walked to her car. I watched while she drove off and then I tossed the album for Colin in the backseat of my car and pulled out. Actually, though I hated to admit it, she was probably right. If the dog had been in the house, no one could have messed with anything. With the dog in or out, dead or alive, it certainly wouldn't have protected Libby Glass. And at least one piece of the puzzle now fitted. It didn't seem to mean much, but it did seem to establish the approximate date of entry to the house, if that's how the killer had effected the switch. It felt like the first blank I'd really filled in. Small progress but it made me feel good. I drove back to the San Bernardino Freeway and headed for L.A.

16

When I got back to the Hacienda, I went into the office to check for telephone messages. Arlette had four, but three of them turned out to be from Charlie Scorsoni. She leaned an elbow on the counter, munching on something sticky and dark brown enclosed in cookie dough.

'What is that thing?'

'Trimline Diet Snack Bar,' she said. 'Six calories each.' Some of the filling seemed to be stuck to her teeth like dental putty and she ran a finger along her gums, popping goo into her mouth again. 'Look at this label. I bet there's not one natural ingredient in this entire piece of food. Milk powder, hydrogenated fat, powdered egg and a whole list of chemicals and additives. But you know what? I've noticed real food doesn't taste as good as fake. Have you noticed that? It's just a fact of life. Real food is bland, watered-down-tasting. You take a supermarket tomato. Now it's pathetic what that tastes like,' she said and shuddered. I was trying to sort through my messages but she was making it hard.

'I bet this isn't even real flour in this thing,' she said. 'I mean, I've heard people say junk food just has empty calories, but who needs full ones? I like 'em empty. That way I figure I can't gain any more weight. That Charlie Scorsoni sure kept in touch, didn't he? He called once from Denver and then he called from Tucson and last night from Santa Teresa. Wonder what he wants. He sounded cute.'

'I'll be in my room,' I said.

'Well all right. Good enough. You want to return those calls, you just give me a buzz up here and I'll put you through.'

'Thanks,' I said.

'Oh yeah, and I gave your telephone number in Las Vegas to a couple of people who didn't want to leave messages. I hope that's okay. You didn't say I couldn't refer calls.'

'No, that's fine,' I said. 'Any idea who it might have been?'

'Male and female, one each,' she said airily.

When I got to my room, I kicked my shoes off and called Charlie Scorsoni's office and talked to Ruth.

'He was supposed to get back last night,' she said. 'But he didn't plan to come in to the office. You might try him at home.'

'Well, if I don't get him there, would you tell him I'm back in Los Angeles? He knows where to reach me here.'

'Will do,' she said.

The other message was a bonus. Apparently Garry Steinberg, the accountant at Haycraft and McNiece, had come back from New York a few days early and was willing to talk to me on Friday afternoon, which was today. I called and talked to him briefly, telling him I'd be there within the hour. Then I called Mrs Glass and told her I should be out at her place shortly after supper. There was one more call I felt I should make, though I dreaded the necessity. I sat for a moment on the edge of the bed, staring at the phone and then I said to hell with it and dialed my friend in Las Vegas.

'Jesus, Kinsey,' he said through his teeth. 'I wish you wouldn't do this to me. I get you the lowdown on Sharon Napier and next thing I know she's dead.'

I gave him the situation as succinctly as I could but it didn't seem to ease his anxieties. Or mine. 'It could have been anyone,' I said. 'We don't *know* that she was shot because of me.'

'Yeah, but I got to cover myself anyway. Somebody remembers that I was asking around after this lady and then she's found with a bullet in her throat. I mean, how does that look?'

I apologized profusely and told him to let me know anything he found out. He didn't seem that eager to keep in touch. I changed clothes, putting on a skirt, hose and heels, and then I drove to the Avco Embassy building and took the elevator to the tenth floor. I was feeling bad about Sharon Napier all over again, guilt sitting in my gut like a low-level colic. How could I have missed that appointment? How could that have happened to me? She knew *something* and if I'd gotten there on time, I might be wrapping this investigation up instead of being where I was – which was nowhere in particular. I made my way back into the imitation barnyard of Haycraft and McNiece, staring at the dried corn on the wall while I whipped myself some more.

Garry Steinberg turned out to be a very nice man. I guessed him to be in his early thirties, with dark curly hair, dark eyes and a small gap between his front teeth. He was probably five feet, ten inches and his body looked soft, his waist puffing out like rising bread dough.

'You're noticing my waist, am I right?' he asked.

I shrugged somewhat sheepishly, wondering if he did or did not want me to comment. He motioned me into a chair and then sat down behind his desk.

'Let me show you something,' he said, lifting a finger. He opened his top desk drawer and took out a snapshot, which he handed to me. I glanced at it.

'Who's this?'

'Perfect,' he said. 'That was the perfect response. That's me. When I weighed three hundred and ten pounds. Now I weigh two-sixteen.'

'My God,' I said and looked at the picture again. Actually I could see now that in the old days he had looked a bit like Arlette might if she decided to cross-dress. I'm crazy about 'before-and-after' shots, an avid fan of all those magazine ads showing women pumped up like tires and then magically thin, one foot arranged in front of the other, as though weight loss also involved the upsurge of charm and modeling skills. I wondered if there was anyone left in California not obsessed with self-image.

'How'd you do it?' I asked, handing the snapshot back.

'Scarsdale,' he said. 'It was a real honest-to-God bitch but I did it. I only cheated once – well, twice. Once was when I turned thirty-five. I figured I was entitled to a bagel and cream cheese with a birthday candle. And one night I binged because my girl friend got mad at me and kicked me out. I mean, lookit, when I was three-ten I never even had a girl. Now I'm having fits when she throws me out. We made up again though, so that turned out all right. I've got twenty-five pounds to lose yet but I'm giving myself a break. Strictly maintenance. Have you ever done Scarsdale?'

I shook my head apologetically. I was beginning to feel I'd never done anything. No Scarsdale, no therapy.

'No alcohol,' he said. 'That's the hard part. On the maintenance diet, you can have like a small glass of white wine now and then, but that's it. I figure the first fifty pounds I lost was from that. Giving up booze. You'd be surprised how much weight that adds.'

'Sounds a lot better for you,' I said.

'I feel good about myself,' he said. 'That's the important thing. So. Enough of that. What do you want to know about Libby Glass? The receptionist says you came about her.'

I explained what I was up to and how I came to be involved in the matter of her death. He took it all in, asking occasional questions. 'What can I tell you?' he said, finally.

'How long had she handled Laurence Fife's account?'

'I'm glad you asked me that because that's one thing I looked up when I knew you were coming over. We handled his personal finances first for about a year. The law firm of Fife and Scorsoni had only been with us six months. Actually a little less. We were just putting in our own computer system and Libby was trying to get all the records straightened out for the changeover. She was a very good accountant by the way. Real conscientious and real smart.'

'Were you a good friend of hers?'

'Pretty good. I was El Blimpo back then but I had a crush on her and we kind of had this brother-sister relationship – platonic. We didn't date. Just had lunch together once a week, something like that. Sometimes a drink after work.'

'How many accounts did she handle?'

'All together? I'd say twenty-five, maybe thirty. She was a very ambitious girl and she really knocked herself out . . . for all the good it did.'

'Meaning what?'

He got up and closed the door to his office, pointing significantly to the wall of the office next door.

'Listen, old man Haycraft was a petty tyrant, the original male chauvinist pig. Libby thought if she worked hard, she'd get a promotion and a raise, but no such thing. And these guys aren't much better. You want to know how I get a raise? I threaten to quit. Every six months I threaten to quit. Libby didn't even do that.'

'How much was she paid?'

'I don't know. I could maybe look that up. Not enough to suit her, I can tell you that. Fife and Scorsoni was a big account – not the biggest, but big. She didn't feel it was fair.'

'She did more work for Fife than Scorsoni, I assume.'

'At first. After that, it was half and half. A lot of the purpose of our taking over their business management was to keep track of all the estate work. That was a big part of their ongoing business from what she said. The dead guy,

Fife, did a lot of messy divorce work, which paid big fees but didn't require that much in the way of bookkeeping. Also, we did accounts receivable for them, paid their office bills, kept track of profits from the firm, and made suggestions about investments. Well, at that point, we weren't doing much in the way of investment counseling because they hadn't been with us that long but that was the object of the exercise eventually. We like to hold off some until we see where our clients stand. Anyway, I can't go into details on that but I can probably answer any other general questions you might have.'

'Do you know anything about where the money from Fife's estate went?'

'The kids. It was divided equally among them. I never saw the will but I helped settle the estate in terms of disbursements after probate.'

'You don't happen to represent Scorsoni's new law firm, do you?'

'Nope,' Garry said. 'I met him a couple of times after Fife died. He seemed like a nice man.'

'Is there any way I could look at the old books?'

'Nope,' he said. 'You could do it if I had Scorsoni's written permission but I don't know what good that would do you anyway unless you're an accountant yourself. Our system isn't that complicated, but I don't think it'd make sense to you.'

'Probably not,' I said, trying to think what else I wanted to ask him about.

'You want coffee? I'm sorry, I should have asked you sooner.'

'No thanks. I'm fine,' I said. 'What about Libby's personal affairs. Is there any chance that she was sleeping with Laurence Fife?'

Garry laughed. 'Now that I don't know. She'd been going with some creepy little guy ever since high school, and I knew she'd broken up with him. On my advice, I might add.'

'How come?'

'He came in to apply for a job here. I was in charge of screening all the applicants. He was just supposed to messenger stuff back and forth but he didn't even look that smart. He was belligerent, too, and if you want my honest opinion, he was high.'

'You wouldn't still have his application on file, would you?' I asked, feeling a faint surge of excitement.

Garry looked at me. 'We're not having this conversation, am I right?'

'Right.'

'I'll see what I can find,' he said promptly. 'It wouldn't be here. It'd be over in the warehouse. We have all the old records stored there. Accountants are real pack rats. We never throw anything away and everything gets written down.'

'Thanks, Garry,' I said. 'I can't tell you how much I appreciate this.'

He smiled happily. 'And maybe I'll look for the old Fife files as long as I'm over there. It won't hurt to take a peek. And to answer your question about Libby, my guess would be no. I don't think she was having an affair with Laurence Fife.' He glanced at his watch. 'I got a meeting.'

I shook his hand across the desk, feeling good. 'Thanks again,' I said.

'No problem. Stop by again. Anytime.'

I got back to my motel room at 3:30. I put a pillow on the plastic chair, set my typewriter up on the wobbly desk, and spent an hour and a half typing up my notes. It had been a long time since I sat down to do paperwork but it had to be caught up. By the time I pecked my way through the last paragraph, I had a pain in my lower back and another one right between my shoulder blades. I changed into my running clothes, my body heat resurrecting the smell of old sweat and car fumes. I was going to have to find a Laundromat soon. I jogged south on Wilshire, just for variety, cutting across to San Vicente at Twenty-sixth Street. Once I got on the wide grassy divider, I could feel myself hit stride. Running always hurts – I don't care what they say – but it does acquaint one with all of one's body parts. This time I could feel my thighs protest and I noticed a mild aching in my shins, which I ignored, plodding on gamely. For my bravery, I netted a few rude remarks from two guys in a pick-up truck. When I got back to the motel, I showered and got back into my jeans and then I stopped by McDonald's and had a Quarter Pounder with cheese, fries, and a medium Coke. By then, it was 6:45. I filled up the car with gas and headed over the hill into Sherman Oaks.

17

Mrs Glass answered the door after half a buzz. This time the living room had been picked up to some extent, her sewing confined now to a neatly folded pile of fabric on the arm of the couch. Raymond was nowhere in sight.

'He had a bad day,' she said to me. 'Lyle stopped by on his way home from work and we put him to bed.'

Even the television set was turned off, and I wondered what she did with herself in the evenings.

'Elizabeth's things are in the basement,' she murmured. 'I'll just get the key to the storage bin.'

She returned a moment later and I followed her out into the corridor. We turned left, past the stairway back to the basement door which was set into the right-hand wall. The door was locked and after she opened it, she flipped the light switch at the top of the stairs. I could already smell the dry musty scent of old window screens and half-empty cans of latex paint. I was about two steps behind her as we made our way down the narrow passageway, wooden stairs taking a sharp right-hand turn. At the landing, I caught a glimpse of concrete floor with bins of wooden lathing reaching to the low ceiling. Something wasn't right but the oddity didn't really register before the blast rang out. The light bulb on the landing shattered, spraying us both with thin flakes of glass and the basement was instantly blanketed in darkness. Grace shrieked and I grabbed her, pulling her back up the stairs. I lost my balance and she stumbled over me. There must have been an outside exit because I heard a wrenching of wood, a bang, and then someone taking the concrete steps outside two at a time. I struggled out from under Grace, jerking her up the stairs with me and then I left her in the corridor, racing out through the front and around the side of the building. Someone had left an old power mower in the driveway and I tripped in the darkness, sprawling forward on my hands and knees, cursing savagely as I scrambled back to my feet again. I reached the rear of the building, keeping low, my heart pounding in my ears. It was black-dark, my eyes just beginning to adjust. A vehicle started up one street over and I could hear it chirp out with a quick shift of gears. I ducked back, leaning against the building then, hearing nothing but the fading roar of a vehicle being driven away at high speed. My mouth was dry. I was drenched in sweat and belatedly I felt a shudder go through me. Both my palms stung where the gravel had bitten into the flesh. I trotted back to my car and got out my flashlight, tucking the little automatic into my windbreaker pocket. I didn't think there was anyone left to shoot but I was tired of being surprised.

Grace was sitting on the doorsill, her head hanging down between her knees. She was shaking from head to foot and she'd started to weep. I helped her to her feet, easing open the apartment door.

'Lyle knew I was picking the stuff up, right?' I snapped at her. She gave me a haunted, pleading look.

'It couldn't have been him. He wouldn't have done that to me,' she whimpered.

'Your faith is touching,' I said. 'Now sit. I'll be back in a minute.'

I went back to the basement stairs. The beam from the flashlight cut through the blackness. There was a second bulb at the bottom of the stairs and I pulled the chain. A flat dull light from the swinging bulb threw out a yellow arc that slowed to a halt. I turned off the flashlight. I knew which bin belonged to Mrs Glass. It had been smashed open, the padlock dangling ineffectually where the lathing had been broken through. Cardboard boxes had been torn open, the contents strewn about in haste, forming an ankle-deep mess through which I picked my way. The emptied boxes all bore the name 'Elizabeth,' obligingly rendered in bold Magic Marker strokes. I wondered if we'd interrupted the intruder before or after he'd found what he was looking for. I heard a sound behind me and I whirled, raising the flashlight instantly like a club.

A man stood there staring at me with bewilderment.

'Got a problem down here?'

'Oh fuck. Who are you?'

He was middle-aged, hands in his pockets, his expression sheepish. 'Frank Isenberg from apartment three,' he said apologetically. 'Did somebody break in? You want me to call the police?'

'No, don't do that yet. Let me check upstairs with Grace. This looks like the only bin that's been damaged. Maybe it was just kids,' I said, heart still thudding. 'You didn't have to sneak up on me.'

'Sorry. I just thought you might need some help.'

'Yeah, well thanks anyway. I'll let you know if I need anything.'

He stood there surveying the chaos for a moment and then he shrugged and went back upstairs.

I checked the basement door at the rear. The glass had been broken out and someone had pulled back the bolt by reaching through. The door was wide open of course. I shut it, pushing the bolt back into place. When I turned around, Grace was creeping timidly down the stairs, her face still pale. She clung to the railing. 'Elizabeth's things,' she whispered. 'They spoiled all of her boxes, all the things I saved.'

She sank down on the steps, rubbing her temples. Her large dark eyes looked injured, perplexed, with a touch of something else that I could have sworn was guilt.

'Maybe we should call the police,' I said, feeling mean, wondering just how protective of Lyle she intended to be.

'Do you really think?' she said. Her gaze flitted back and forth indecisively and she took out a handkerchief, pressing it against her forehead as though to remove beads of sweat. 'Nothing might be missing,' she said hopefully. 'Maybe nothing's gone.'

'Or maybe we won't know the difference,' I said.

She pulled herself up and moved over to the bin, taking in the disastrous piles of papers, stuffed animals, cosmetics, underwear. She stopped, picking up papers randomly, trying to make stacks. Her hands still trembled but I didn't think she was afraid. Startled perhaps, and thinking rapidly.

'I take it Raymond is still asleep,' I said.

She nodded, tears welling up as the extent of the vandalism became more and more apparent. I could feel myself relent. Even if Lyle had done it, it was mean-spirited, a violation of something precious to Grace. She had already suffered enough without this. I set the flashlight aside and began to pile papers back into the boxes: costume jewelry, lingerie, old issues of *Seventeen* and *Vogue*, patterns for clothing that Libby had probably never made. 'Do you mind if I take these boxes with me and go through them tonight?' I asked. 'I can have them back to you by morning.'

'All right. I suppose. I can't see what harm it would do now anyway,' she murmured, not looking at me.

It seemed hopeless to me. In this jumble, who knew what might be missing? I'd have to go through the boxes and see if I could spot anything, but the chances weren't good. Lyle couldn't have been down there long – if it had been him. He knew I was coming back for the stuff and when he'd been there earlier, Grace probably told him exactly what time I expected to arrive. He'd had to wait until dark and he probably thought we'd spend more time upstairs before coming down. Still, he was cutting it close – unless he simply didn't care. And why didn't he break in during the three days I was gone? I thought back to his insolence and I suspected that he might take a certain satisfaction in thwarting me, even if he was caught at it.

Grace helped me cart the boxes to the car, six of them. I should have taken the stuff the first time I was there, I thought, but I couldn't picture driving to Vegas with the entire backseat filled with cardboard boxes. Still, the boxes would have been intact. It was my own damn fault, I thought sourly.

I told Grace I'd be back first thing in the morning and then I pulled out. It was going to be a long night.

I bought two containers of black coffee across the street, locked the door to my motel room, and closed the drapes. I emptied the first carton onto the bed and then I started making stacks. School papers in one pile. Personal letters. Magazines. Stuffed animals. Clothing. Cosmetics. Bills and receipts. Grace had apparently saved every article Elizabeth had touched since kindergarten. Report cards. School projects. Really, six cartons seemed modest when I realized how much there was. Tax returns. The accumulation of an entire life and it was really only so much trash. Who would ever need to refer to any of this again? The original energy and spirit had all seeped away. I did feel for her. I did get some sense of that young girl, whose gropings and triumphs and little failures were piled together now in a drab motel room. I didn't even know what I was looking for. I flipped through a diary from the fifth grade – the handwriting round and dutiful, the entries dull. I tried to imagine myself dead, someone sorting carelessly through my belongings. What was there really of my life? Canceled checks. Reports all typewritten and filed. Everything of value reduced to terse prose. I didn't keep much myself, didn't hoard or save. Two divorce decrees. That was about the sum of it for me. I collected more information about other people's lives than I did about my own, as though, perhaps, in poring over the facts about other people, I could discover something about myself. My own mystery, unplumbed, undetected, was sorted into files that were neatly labeled but really didn't say much. I picked through the last of Elizabeth's boxes but there was nothing of interest. It was 4:00 in the morning when I finished. Nothing. If there had been anything there, it was gone now and I was irritated with myself again, berating myself for my own poor judgment. This was the second time I'd arrived too late – the second time some vital piece of information had slipped away from me.

I began to repack boxes, automatically rechecking as I went, sorting. Clothes in one box, stuffed animals tucked into the spaces along the sides. School papers, diaries, blue books in the next box. Back it all went, neatly catalogued this time, compulsively arranged, as though I owed Elizabeth Glass some kind of order after I'd pried into the hidden crevices of her abandoned life. I rifled through magazines, held textbooks by the spine, letting the pages fly loose. The stacks on the bed diminished. There weren't that many personal letters and I felt guilty reading them, but I did. Some from an aunt in Arizona. Some from a girl named Judy whom Libby must have known in high school. No one seemed to refer to anything intimate in her life and I had to conclude that she confided little or else that she had no tales to tell. The disappointment was acute. I was down to the last pile of books, mostly paperbacks. Such taste. Leon Uris and Irving Stone, Victoria Holt, Georgette Heyer, a few more exotic samples that I guessed had been from some literature survey course in college. The letter slipped out of the pages of a dog-eared copy of *Pride and Prejudice*. I nearly tossed it in the box with the rest of the stuff. The handwriting was a tightly stroked cursive on two sides in dark blue ink. No date. No envelope. No postmark. I picked it up by one corner and read it, feeling a cold pinching sensation begin at the base of my spine.

> Darling Elizabeth . . . I'm writing this so you'll have something when you get back. I know these separations are hard for you and I wish there were some way I could ease your pain. You are so much more honest than I am, so much more open about what you feel than I allow myself to be, but I do love you and I don't want you to have any doubts about that. You're right when you say that I'm conservative. I'm guilty as charged, your Honor, but I'm not immune to suffering and as often as I've been accused of being selfish, I'm not as reckless of others as you might think. I would like to take our time about this and be sure that it's something we both want. What we have now is very dear to me and I'm not saying – please believe me – that I wouldn't turn my life around for you if it comes to that. On the other hand, I think we should both be sure that we can survive the day-to-day absurdities of being together. Right now, the intensity dazzles and it seems simple enough for us both to chuck it all and make some kind of life, but we haven't known each other that long or that well. I can't afford to risk wife, kids and career in the heat of the moment though you know it tempts me. Please let's move slowly on this. I love you more than I can say and I don't want to lose you – which is selfish enough, I suppose, in itself. You're right to push, but please don't lose sight of what's at stake, for you as well as me. Tolerate my caution if you can. I love you. Laurence.

I didn't know what to make of it. I realized, in a flash, that it wasn't just that I hadn't believed in an affair between

Laurence and Elizabeth. I hadn't *wanted* to believe. I wasn't sure I believed it yet but why the resistance? It was so neat. So convenient. It fitted in so nicely with what I knew of the facts and still I stared at the letter, holding it gingerly by one corner as I read it again. I leaned back against the bed. What was the matter with me? I was exhausted and I knew I'd been through too much in the last few days but something nagged at me and I wasn't sure it had so much to do with the letter as it did with myself, with something in my nature – some little niggling piece of self-illumination that I was fighting hard not to recognize. Either the letter was real or it was not, and there were ways to verify that. I pulled myself together wearily. I found a large envelope and slipped the letter inside, being careful not to smudge fingerprints, already thinking ahead to Con Dolan, who would love it since it confirmed all his nastiest suspicions about what had been going on back then. Was this what Sharon Napier had figured out? Was this what she could have corroborated if she'd lived long enough?

I lay on the bed fully dressed, body tense, brain wired. Who could she have hoped to blackmail with this information if she'd known? It had to be what she was up to. It had to be why she'd been killed. Someone had followed me to Las Vegas, knowing that I would see her, knowing that she might confirm what I hadn't wanted to believe. I couldn't prove it, of course, but I wondered if I was getting close enough to the truth to be in danger myself. I wanted to go home. I wanted to retreat to the safety of my small room . . . I wasn't thinking clearly yet, but I was getting close. For eight years, nothing had happened and now it was all beginning again. If Nikki was innocent, then someone had been sitting pretty all this time, someone in danger of exposure now.

I saw, for an instant, the look that had flashed in Nikki's eyes, unreasoning malevolence, a harsh irrational rage. She had set all this in motion. I had to consider the possibility that Sharon Napier was blackmailing *her*, that Sharon knew something that could link Nikki to Libby's death. If Sharon had dropped out of sight, it was possible that Nikki had hired me to flush her out and that Nikki had then eliminated any threat with one quick shot. She might also have followed me back to Sherman Oaks for a frantic search through Libby's belongings for anything that might have linked Libby to Laurence Fife. There were pieces missing yet but they would fall into place and then maybe the whole of it would make sense. Assuming I lived long enough myself to figure it out . . .

18

I dragged myself out of bed at 6:00 a.m. I hadn't slept at all. My mouth felt stale and I brushed my teeth. I showered and dressed. I longed to run but I felt too vulnerable to jog down the middle of San Vicente at that hour. I packed, closing up my typewriter, shoving the pages of my report into my briefcase. I loaded the boxes into my car again, along with my suitcase. The lights in the office were on and I could see Arlette taking jelly doughnuts out of a bakery box, putting them on a plastic plate with a clear dome lid. Water was already heating for that awful, flat instant coffee. She was licking powdered sugar from her fingers when I went in.

'God, you're up awful early,' she said. 'You want breakfast?'

I shook my head. Even with my penchant for junk food, I wouldn't eat a jelly doughnut. 'No, but thanks,' I said. 'I'm checking out.'

'Right now?'

I nodded, almost too tired to talk. She finally seemed to sense that this was the wrong time to chat. She got my bill ready and I signed it, not even bothering to add up the charges. She usually made a mistake but I didn't care.

I got in my car and headed for Sherman Oaks. There was a light on in Grace's kitchen, which I approached from around the side of the building. I tapped on the window and after a moment, she came into the service porch and opened the side door. She looked small and precise this morning in an A-line corduroy skirt and a coffee-colored cotton turtleneck. She kept her voice low.

'Raymond's not awake yet but there's coffee if you like,' she said.

'Thanks, but I've got a breakfast meeting at eight,' I said, lying without much thought. Whatever I said would be passed on to Lyle and my whereabouts were none of his business – or hers. 'I just wanted to drop the boxes off.'

'Did you find anything?' she asked. Her gaze met mine briefly and then she blinked, glancing first at the floor and then off to my left.

'Too late,' I said, trying to ignore the flush of relief that tinted her cheeks.

'That's unfortunate,' she murmured, placing a hand against her throat. 'I'm . . . uh . . . sure it wasn't Lyle . . .'

'It doesn't matter much anyway,' I said. I felt sorry for her in spite of myself. 'I packed everything back as neatly as I could. I'll just stack the boxes in the basement near the bin. You'll probably want to have that repaired when you get the basement door fixed.'

She nodded. She moved to close the door and I stepped back, watching her pad back into the kitchen in her soft-soled slippers. I felt as if I'd personally violated her life somehow, that everything was ending on a bad note. She'd been as helpful as she knew how and she'd gotten little in return. I had to shrug. There was nothing I could do at this point. I unloaded the car, making several trips, stacking boxes just inside the damaged bin. Unconsciously, I listened for Lyle. The light in the basement was cold and gray by day, but aside from the splintered lathework and the shattered window, there was no other evidence of the intruder. I went out the back way on the last trip up from the basement, checking idly for smashed cigarette butts, bloody fingerprints, a small printed business card perhaps, dropped by whoever broke in. I came up the concrete stairs outside, looking off to the right at the path the intruder had taken – across the patchy grass in the backyard, over a sagging wire fence, and through a tangle of bushes. I could see through to the next street where the car must have been parked. It was early morning yet and the sunlight was flat and still. I could hear heavy traffic on the Ventura Freeway, which was visible in glimpses through the clumps of trees off to the right. The ground wasn't even soft enough to absorb footprints. I moved around the building to the driveway on my left, noting with interest that the power mower had now been pulled off to one side. My palms were still ripped up in places, two-inch tracks where I'd skidded across the gravel on my hands. I hadn't even thought to use Bactine and I hoped I wouldn't be subject to raging gangrene, perilous infections or blood poisoning – dangers my aunt had warned me about every time I skinned my knee.

I got back in my car and headed for Santa Teresa, stopping in Thousand Oaks for breakfast. I was home by 10:00 in the morning. I wrapped myself up in a quilt on the couch and slept for most of the day.

At 4:00, I drove out to Nikki's beach house. I had called to say I was back in town and she invited me out for a drink. I wasn't sure yet how much I would tell her or how much, if anything, I would hold back, but after my recent gnawing suspicions about her, I wanted to test my perceptions. There are moments in every investigation when my speculations about what's possible cloud and confuse any lingering sense I have of what's actually true. I wanted to check out my intuitions.

The house was situated on a bluff overlooking the ocean. The lot was small, irregular in shape, surrounded by eucalyptus trees. The house was tucked into the landscaping – laurel and yew, with pink and red geraniums planted along the path – its exterior made of cedar shingles, still a raw-looking wood brown, the roofline undulating like an ocean swell. There was a large oval window in the front, flanked by two bow windows, all undraped. The lawn was a pale green, tender blades of grass looking almost edible, curls of eucalyptus bark intermingled like wood shavings. White and yellow daisies grew in careless patches. The whole effect was subtle neglect, a refined wilderness untended but subdued, curiously appealing with the thick scent of ocean overlaid and the dull thunder of waves crashing down below. The air was moist and smelled of salt, wind buffeting the ragged grass. Where the house in Montebello was boxy, substantial, conventional, plain, this was a whimsical cottage, all wide angles, windows, and unpainted wood. The front door had a tall oval leaded-glass window in it, filled with tulip shapes, and the doorbell sounded like wind chimes.

Nikki appeared at once. She was wearing a celery-green caftan, its bodice embroidered with mirrors the size of dimes, the sleeves wide. Her hair was pulled up and away from her face, tied with a pale-green velvet ribbon. She seemed relaxed, her wide forehead unlined, the gray eyes looking light and clear, her mouth faintly tinted with pink, curving upward as though from some secret merriment. The languidness in her manner was gone and she was animated, energetic. I had brought the photograph album Diane had given me and I handed it to her as she closed the door behind me.

'What's this?' she asked.

'Diane put it together for Colin,' I said.

'Come see him,' she said. 'We're making bread.'

I followed her through the house. There were no square rooms at all. The spaces flowed into one another, connected by gleaming pale wood floors and bright shag rugs. There were windows everywhere, plant, skylights. A free-form fireplace in the living room looked as if it had been constructed from buff-colored boulders, piled up randomly like the entrance to a cave. On the far wall, a crude ladder led up to a loft that overlooked the ocean. Nikki smiled back at me happily, placing the album on the glass coffee table as she passed.

The kitchen was a semicircle, wood and white Formica and luscious healthy houseplants, windows on three sides looking onto a deck with the ocean stretching out beyond, wide and grey in the late afternoon. Colin was kneading bread, his back to me, his concentration complete. His hair was the same pale no-color shade as Nikki's, silky like hers where it curled down on his neck. His arms looked wiry and strong, his hands capable, fingers long. He gathered the edges of the dough, pressing inward, turning it over again. He looked like he was just on the verge of adolescence, beginning to shoot up in height but not awkward yet. Nikki touched him and he turned quickly, his gaze sliding over to me at once. I was startled. His eyes were large, tilted slightly, an army-fatigue green, his lashes thick and dark. His face was narrow, chin pointed, ears coming to a delicate point, a pixie effect with the fine hair forming a point on his forehead. The two of them looked like an illustration from a faerie book – fragile and beautiful and strange. His eyes were peaceful, empty, glowing with acute intelligence. I have seen the same look in cats, their eyes wise, aloof, grave.

When I spoke to Nikki, he watched our lips, his own lips parting breathlessly, so that the effect was oddly sexual.

'I think I just fell in love,' I said and laughed. Nikki smiled, signing to Colin, her fingers graceful, succinct. Colin flashed a smile at me, much older than his years. I felt myself flush.

'I hope you didn't tell him that,' I said. 'We'd probably have to run off together.'

'I told him you were my first friend after prison. I told him you needed a drink,' she said, still signing, eyes resting on Colin's face. 'Most of the time we don't sign this much. I'm just brushing up.'

While Nikki opened a bottle of wine, I watched Colin work the bread dough. He offered to let me help and I shook my head, preferring to watch his agile hands, the dough developing a smooth skin almost magically as he worked. He made gruff, unintelligible sounds now and then without seeming aware of it.

Nikki gave me chilled white wine in a glass with a thin stem while she drank Perrier. 'Here's to parole,' she said.

'You look much more relaxed,' I said.

'Oh I am. I feel great. It's so good to have him here. I follow him everywhere. I feel like a puppy dog. He gets no peace.'

Her hands were moving automatically and I could see that she was translating for him simultaneously with her comments to me. It made me feel rude and clumsy that I couldn't sign too. I felt as if there were things I wanted to say to him myself, questions I wanted to ask about the silence in his head. It was like charades of some kind, Nikki using body, arms, face, her whole self totally involved, Colin signing back to her casually. He seemed to speak much more quickly than she, without deliberation. Sometimes Nikki would halt, struggling for a word, remembering, laughing at herself as she relayed to him her own forgetfulness. His smile in those moments was indulgent, full of affection, and I envied them this special world of secrets, of self-mockery, wherein Colin was the master and Nikki the apprentice. I couldn't imagine Nikki with any other kind of child.

Colin placed the smooth dough in the bowl, turning it once to coat its pale surface with butter, covering it carefully then with a clean white towel. Nikki motioned him into the living room, where she showed him the photo album. Colin settled on the edge of the couch, leaning forward, elbows on his knees, the album open on the coffee table in front of him. His face was still but his eyes took in everything and he was already engrossed in the snapshots.

Nikki and I went out onto the deck. It was getting late but there was still enough sunlight to create the illusion of warmth. She stood at the railing, staring out at the ocean that rumbled below us. I could see tangles of kelp just under the surface in places, dark strands undulating in waves of paler green.

'Nikki, did you talk to anyone about where I was and what I was up to?' I asked.

'Not at all,' she said, startled. 'What makes you ask?'

I filled her in on the events of the last few days – Sharon Napier's death, my talks with Greg and Diane, the letter I'd found among Libby Glass's effects. My trust in her was instinctive.

'Would you recognize his handwriting?'

'Sure.'

I took the manila envelope out of my purse, carefully removing the letter, which I unfolded for her. She glanced at it briefly.

'That's him,' she said.

'I'd like you to read it,' I said. 'I want to see if it coincides with your intuitions about what was going on.'

Reluctantly her gaze dropped back to the pale blue pages. When she finished, she seemed almost embarrassed. 'I wouldn't have guessed it was that serious. His other affairs weren't.'

'What about Charlotte Mercer?'

'She's a bitch. She's an alcoholic. She called me once. I hated her. And she hated him. You should have heard what she said.'

I folded the letter carefully. 'I didn't get it. From Charlotte Mercer to Libby Glass. That's quite a leap. I assumed he was a man of taste.'

Nikki shrugged. 'He was easily seduced. It was his own vanity. Charlotte *is* beautiful . . . in her own way.'

'Was she in the process of divorcing? Is that how they met?'

Nikki shook her head. 'We socialized with them. Judge Mercer was a sort of mentor of Laurence's at one point. I don't imagine he ever found out about the affair – it would have killed him, I think. He's the only decent judge we've got anyway. You know what the rest are like.'

'I only talked to her a short time,' I said, 'but I can't see how she could be involved. It had to be somebody who knew where I was and how could she have come by that kind of information? Somebody had to have followed me up to Las Vegas. Sharon's murder was too closely timed to have been coincidence.'

Colin appeared at Nikki's side, placing the open photograph album up on the railing. He pointed to one of the snapshots, saying something I couldn't understand at all, an indistinct blur of vowels. It was the first time I'd heard him speak. His voice was deeper than I would have imagined for a twelve-year-old.

'That's Diane's junior-high-school graduation,' Nikki said to him. Colin looked at her for a moment and then pointed again more emphatically. He put his index finger in front of his mouth and moved it up and down rapidly. Nikki frowned.

'"Who" what, honey?'

Colin placed his finger on the picture of a group of people.

'That's Diane and Greg and Diane's friend, Terri, and Diane's mother,' she said to him, enunciating carefully and signing at the same time.

A puzzled smile formed on Colin's face. He spread his hands out, putting his thumb against his forehead and then his chin.

Nikki laughed this time, her expression as puzzled as his.

'No, *that's* Nana,' she said, pointing to a snapshot one page back. 'This is *Diane's* mother, not Daddy's. The mother of Greg and Diane. Don't you remember Nana? Oh God, how could he,' she flashed at me. 'She died when he was a year old.' She looked back at him.

Colin made some guttural sounds, something negative and frustrated. I wondered what would happen to his temper when puberty really caught up with him. Again the thumb against the forehead, then the chin. Nikki shot me another look. 'He keeps saying "Daddy's mother" for Gwen. How do you explain "ex-wife"?' She signed again patiently.

Colin shook his head slightly, suddenly unsure of himself. He watched her for a moment more as though some other explanation might be forthcoming. He took the album and backed away, eyes still fixed on Nikki's face. He signed once more, flushing uncomfortably. Apparently, he didn't want to look foolish in front of me.

'We'll go through those together in a minute,' she signed to him, translating for me.

Colin moved slowly back through the sliding glass doors, pushing the screen door shut.

'Sorry for the interruption,' she said briefly.

'That's all right, I've got to go anyway,' I said.

'You can stay for supper if you like. I've made a big pot of beef bourguignon. It's great with Colin's bread.'

'Thanks but I've got all kinds of things to do,' I said.

Nikki walked me to the door, signing our final chitchat without even being aware of it.

I got in my car and sat for a moment, puzzled by Colin's puzzlement over Gwen. That was odd. Very odd.

19

When I got back to my apartment, Charlie Scorsoni was sitting on my doorstep. I felt grubby and unprepared and I realized with embarrassment that I'd been entertaining a fantasy of how we'd meet again and it wasn't like this.

'God, don't get all excited, Millhone,' he said when he saw the expression on my face.

I got out my key. 'I'm sorry,' I said, 'but you catch me at the worst possible times.'

'You have a date,' he said.

'No, I don't have a date. I look like shit.' I unlocked the door and flipped on the desk lamp, letting him follow me in.

'At least I caught you in a good mood,' he said, making himself at home. He sauntered out to the kitchen and got out the last beer. The familiarity in his manner made me cross.

'Look, I've got laundry to do. I haven't been to the grocery store for a week. My mail is piled up, the whole place is covered with dust. I haven't even shaved my legs since I saw you last.'

'You need a haircut too,' he said.

'No I don't. It always looks like this.'

He smiled, shaking his head. 'Get dressed. We'll go out.'

'I don't want to go out. I want to get my life in shape.'

'You can do that tomorrow. It's Sunday. I bet you always do shit like that on Sunday anyway.'

I stared at him. It was true. 'Wait a minute. Here's how it's supposed to go,' I said patiently. 'I get home. I do all my chores, get a good night's sleep, which I could sorely use, then tomorrow I call you and we see each other tomorrow night.'

'I gotta be at the office tomorrow night. I have a client coming in.'

'On Sunday night?'

'We've got a court appearance first thing Monday morning and this is the only thing we could work out. I just got back into town myself Thursday night and I'm up to my ass.'

I stared at him some more, wavering. 'Where would we go? Would I have to dress up?'

'Well I'm not going to take you anywhere looking like *that*,' he said.

I glanced down. I was still wearing jeans and the shirt I'd slept in but I wasn't ready to back down yet. 'What's wrong with this?' I asked perversely.

'Take a shower and change clothes. I'll pick up some stuff at the grocery store if you give me a list. By the time I get that done, you'll be ready, yes?'

'I like to shop for my own stuff. Anyway, all I need is milk and beer.'

'Then I'll take you to a supermarket after we eat,' he said, emphasizing every single word.

We drove down to the Ranch House in Ojai, one of those elegant restaurants where the waiter stands at your table and recites the menu like a narrative poem.

'Shall I order for us or would that offend your feminine sensibilities?'

'Go ahead,' I said, feeling oddly relieved, 'I'd like that.' While he and the waiter conferred, I studied Charlie's face surreptitiously. It was strong and square, good jawline, visible dent in his chin, full mouth. His nose looked like it might have been broken once but mended skillfully, leaving only the slightest trace just below the bridge. His glasses had large lenses, tinted a blue-gray, and behind them, his blue eyes were as clear as sky. Sandy lashes, sandy brows, his thick sandy hair only beginning to recede. He had big hands, big bones in his wrists, and I could see a feathering of sandy hair at the cuff. There was something else about him, too, smoldering and opaque, the same sense I'd had before of sexuality that surfaced now and then. Sometimes he seemed to emit an almost audible hum, like a line of power stations marching inexorably across a hillside, ominous and marked with danger signs. I was afraid of him.

The waiter was nodding and moving away. Charlie turned back to me, obscurely amused. I felt myself go mute, but he pretended not to notice and I felt dimly grateful, faintly flushed. I was overcome with the same self-consciousness I'd felt once at a birthday party in the sixth grade when I realized that all the other little girls had worn nylon stockings and I was still wearing stupid white ankle socks.

The waiter returned with a bottle of wine and Charlie went through the usual ritual. When our glasses were filled, he touched his rim to mine, his eyes on my face. I sipped, startled by the delicacy of the wine, which was pale and cool.

'So how's the investigation going?' he asked when the waiter had left.

I shook my head, taking a moment to orient myself. 'I don't want to talk about it,' I said shortly and then caught myself. 'I don't mean to be rude,' I said in a softened tone. 'I just don't think talking about it will help. It's not going well.'

'I'm sorry to hear that,' he said. 'It's bound to improve.'

I shrugged and watched while he lit a cigarette and snapped the lighter shut. 'I didn't know you smoked,' I said.

'Now and then,' he said. He offered me the pack and I shook my head again. He seemed relaxed, in possession of himself, a man of sophistication and grace. I felt doltish and tongue-tied, but he didn't seem to expect anything of me, talking on about inconsequential things. He seemed to operate at half speed, taking his own time about everything.

It made me aware of the usual tension with which I live, that keyed-up state of raw nerve that makes me grind my teeth in my sleep. Sometimes I get so wired that I forget to eat at all, only remembering at night, even then not being hungry but wolfing down food anyway as though the speed and quantity of consumption might atone for the infrequency. With Charlie, I could feel my time clock readjust, my pace slowing to match his. When I finished the second glass of wine, I heaved a sigh and only then did I realize that I'd been holding myself tensely, like a joke snake ready to jump out of a box.

'Feel better?' he said.

'Yes.'

'Good. Then we'll eat.'

The meal that followed was one of the most sensual I ever experienced: fresh, tender bread with a crust of flaky layers, spread with a buttery pâté, Boston lettuce with a delicate vinaigrette, sand dabs sautéed in butter and served with succulent green grapes. There were fresh raspberries for dessert with a dollop of tart cream, and all the time Charlie's face across the table from me, shadowed by that suggestion of caution, that hint of something stark and fearful held back, pulling me forward even while I felt myself kept in check.

'How'd you end up in law school?' I asked him when coffee arrived.

'Accident I guess. My father was a drunk and a bum, a real shit. Knocked me around a lot. Not seriously. More like a piece of furniture that got in his way. He beat my mother too.'

'Doesn't do much for your self-esteem,' I ventured.

Charlie shrugged. 'It was good for me actually. Made me tough. Let me know I couldn't depend on anyone but myself, which is a lesson you might as well learn when you're ten. I took care of me.'

'You worked your way through school?'

'Every nickel's worth. I picked up money ghosting papers for jocks, sitting in on tests, writing C minus answers so no one would suspect. You'd be surprised how tricky it is to miss just enough questions to look genuine. I had regular jobs, too, but after I watched half a fraternity get into law school on my smarts, I figured I might as well try it myself.'

'What'd your father do when he didn't drink?'

'Construction till his health broke down. He finally died of cancer. Took him six years. Bad stuff. I didn't give a shit and he knew it. All that pain. Served him right,' he said and shook his head. 'My mother died four months after he did. I thought she'd be relieved he was gone. Turns out she was dependent on the abuse.'

'Why do estate law? That doesn't seem like you. I picture you doing criminal law, something like that.'

'Listen, my father pissed away everything he had. I ended up with nothing – less than nothing. It took me years to pay off his hospital bills and his fucking debts. I had to pay for my mother's death, too, which at least was quick, God bless her, but hardly cheap. So now I show people how to outwit the government even in death. A lot of my clients are dead so we get along very well and I make sure their greedy heirs get more than they deserve. Also when you're executor for somebody's estate, you get paid on time and nobody calls you up about your bill.'

'Not a bad deal,' I said.

'Not at all,' he agreed.

'Have you ever been married?'

'Nope. I never had time for that. I work. That's the only thing that interests me. I don't like the idea of giving someone else the right to make demands. In exchange for what?'

I had to laugh. I felt the same way myself. His tone throughout was ironic and the look he laid on me then was oddly sexual, full of a strange, compelling male heat as though money and power and sexuality were all somehow tangled up for him and fed on one another. There was really nothing open or loose or free about him, however candid he might seem, but I knew that it was precisely his opacity that appealed to me. Did he know that I was attracted to him? He gave little indication of his own feelings one way or the other.

When we finished our coffee, he signaled for the waiter without a word and paid the check. Conversation between us was dwindling anyway and I let it lie, feeling watchful, quiet, even wary of him again. We moved through the restaurant, our bodies close but our behavior polite, circumspect. He opened the door for me. I passed through. He'd made no gesture toward me, verbally or otherwise, and I was suddenly disconcerted, lest my sense of his pull turn out to be something generated in me and not reciprocal. Charlie took my arm briefly, guiding me up a shallow step but as soon as we were on smooth pavement again, he dropped his hand. We went around to my side of the car. He opened the door and I got in. I didn't think I'd said anything flirtatious and I was glad of that, curious still about his intentions toward me. He was so matter-of-fact, so removed.

We drove back to Santa Teresa, saying little. I was feeling mute again, not uncomfortable but languid. As we approached the outskirts of town, he reached over and took my hand noncommittally. It felt like a low-voltage current was suffusing my left side. He kept his left hand on the steering wheel. With his right hand, he was carelessly, casually rubbing my fingers, his attitude inattentive. I was trying to be as casual as he, trying to pretend there might be some other way to interpret those smoldering sexual signals that made the air crackle between us and caused my mouth to go dry. What if I was wrong, I thought. What if I fell on the man like a dog on a bone only to discover that his meaning was merely friendly, absentminded or impersonal? I couldn't think about anything because there was no sound between us, nothing said, not anything I could react to or fix on – no way to divert myself. He was making it hard to breathe. I felt like a glass rod being rubbed on silk. Out of the corner of my eye, I thought I saw his face turn toward me. I glanced at him.

'Hey,' he said softly. 'Guess what we're going to do?'

Charlie shifted in his seat slightly and pressed my hand between his legs. A charge shot through me and I groaned involuntarily. Charlie laughed, a low excited sound, and then he looked back at the road.

Making love with Charlie was like being taken into a big warm machine. Nothing was required of me. Everything was attended to with such ease, such fluidity. There were no awkward moments. There was no holding back, no self-consciousness, no hesitation, no heed. It was as though a channel had been opened between us, sexual energy flowing back and forth without impediment. We made love more than once. At first, there was too much hunger, too much heat. We came at each other with a clash, an intensity that admitted of no tenderness. We crashed against one another like waves on a breakwater, surges of pleasure driving straight up, curling back again. All of the emotional images were of pounding assault, sensations of boom and buffet and battering ram until he had broken through to me, rolling down again and over me until all my walls were reduced to rubble and ash. He raised himself up on his elbow then and kissed me long and sweet and it began all over again, only this time at his pace, half speed, agonizingly slow like the gradual ripening of a peach on a limb. I could feel myself go all rosy, turn to honey and oil–a mellowing ease filtering through me like a sedative. We lay there afterward, laughing and sweaty and out of breath and then he encompassed me in sleep, the weight of his big arms pinning me to the bed. But far from feeling trapped, I felt comforted and safe, as though nothing could ever harm me as long as I stayed in the shadow of this man, this sheltering cave of heat and flesh, where I was tucked away until morning without waking once.

At 7:00, I felt him kiss me lightly on the forehead, and after that the door closed softly. By the time I'd stirred myself awake he was gone.

20

I got up at 9:00 and spent Sunday taking care of personal chores. I cleaned my place, did laundry, went to the supermarket and had a nice visit in the afternoon with my landlord, who was sunning himself in the backyard. For a man of eighty-one, Henry Pitts has an amazing set of legs. He also has a wonderful beaky nose, a thin aristocratic face, shocking white hair, and eyes that are periwinkle blue. The overall effect is very sexy, electric, and the photographs I've seen of him in his youth don't even half compare. At twenty and thirty and forty, Henry's face seems too full, too unformed. As the decades pass, the pictures begin to reveal a man growing lean and fierce, until now he seems totally concentrated, like a basic stock boiled down to a rich elixir.

'Listen, Henry,' I said, plunking down on the grass near his chaise. 'You live entirely too idle a life.'

Sin and degradation,' he said complacently, not even bothering to open his eyes. 'You had company last night.'

'A sleep-over date. Just like our mamas warned us about.'

'How was it?'

'I'm not telling,' I said. 'What kind of crossword puzzle did you concoct this week?'

'An easy one. All doubles. Prefixes — "bi," "di," "bis," "dis." Twin. Twain. Binary. Things like that. Try this one: six letters, "double impression".'

'Already, I give up.'

'"Mackle." It's a printer's term. Kind of a cheat but the fit was so nice. Try this. "Double meaning." Nine letters.'

'Henry, would you *quit* that?'

'"Ambiguity." I'll leave it on your doorstep.'

'No, don't. I get those things in my head and I can't get 'em out.'

He smiled. 'You run yet?'

'No, but I'm on my way,' I said, hopping up again. I crossed the grass, glancing back at him with a grin. He was putting suntan oil on his knees, which were already a gorgeous shade of caramel. I wondered how much it really mattered that there was a fifty-year difference in our ages. But then again, I had Charlie Scorsoni to think about. I changed clothes and did my run. And thought about him.

Monday morning, I went in to see Con Dolan at Homicide. He was talking on the phone when I got there, so I sat down at his desk. He was tipped back in his chair, feet jammed against the edge of the desk, the receiver laid loosely against his ear. He was saying, 'uh-huh, uh-huh, uh-huh,' looking bored. He scanned me with care, taking in every detail of my face, as though he were memorizing me all over again, running me through a computer file of known felons, looking for a match. I stared back at him. In moments, I could see the young man in his face, which was sagging now and worn, pouches beneath his eyes, hair slicked down, cheeks turning soft at the jawline as though the flesh were beginning to warm and melt. The skin on his neck had collapsed into a series of fine folds, reddened and bulging slightly over his starched shirt collar. I feel an ornery kind of kinship with him, which I never can quite identify. He's tough, emotionless, withdrawn, calculating, harsh. I've heard he's mean, too, but what I see in him is the overriding competence. He knows his business and he takes no guff and despite the fact he gives me a hard time whenever he can, I know he likes me, though grudgingly. I saw his attention sharpen. He focused on what was being said to him and it made his temper climb.

'All right now, you listen here, Mitch, because I've said all

I intend to say. We're getting down to the short strokes on this and I don't want you fuckin' up my case. Yeah, I know that. Yeah, that's what you said. I just want it clear between us. I gave your boy all the breaks I mean to give so either he co-operates or we can put him right back where he was. Yeah, well you talk to him again!'

Con dropped the phone down from a height, not exactly slamming it but making his point. He was done. He looked at me through a haze of irritation. I put the manila envelope on his desk. He put his feet on the floor.

'What *is* this?' he said snappishly. He peered in through the flap, removing the letter I'd found in Libby Glass's effects. Even without knowing what it was, he held it by the edges, his eyes raking the contents once and then going back again with caution. He glanced up at me sharply. He tucked it back in the envelope.

'Where'd you get it?'

'Libby Glass's mother kept all her stuff. It was shoved in a paperback book. I picked it up Friday. Can you have it checked for fingerprints?'

The look he gave me was cold. 'Why don't we talk about Sharon Napier first?'

I felt a spurt of fear, but I didn't hesitate. 'She's dead,' I said, reaching for the envelope. He smacked his fist down on it and I drew my hand back. We locked eyes. 'A friend of mine in Vegas told me,' I said. 'That's how I knew.'

'Horseshit. You drove up there.'

'Wrong.'

'God damn it, don't lie to me,' he snapped.

I could feel my temper flare. 'You want to read me my rights, Lieutenant Dolan? You want to hand me a certification of notification of my constitutional rights? Because I'll read it and sign it if you like. And then I'll call my attorney, and when he gets down here, we can chat. How's that?'

'You've been on this business two weeks and somebody shows up dead. You cross me up and I'll have your ass. Now you give it to me straight. I told you to keep out of this.'

'Uh-uh. You told me to keep out of trouble, which I did. You said you'd like a little help making the connection between Libby Glass and Laurence Fife and I gave you that,' I said, indicating the manila envelope.

He picked it up and tossed it in the trash. I knew it was just for effect. I tried another tack.

'Come on, Con,' I said. 'I had nothing to do with Sharon Napier's death. Not in any way, shape or form. What do you think? That I'd run up there and kill somebody who might be of help? You're crazy! I never even went to Vegas. I was down at the Salton Sea talking to Greg Fife and if you doubt my word, call *him*!' I shut my mouth then and stared at him hotly, letting this bold admixture of truth and utter falsehood penetrate his darkened face.

'How'd you know where she was?'

'Because I spent a day and a half on a trace through a Nevada P.I. named Bob Dietz. I was going to drive to Vegas after I talked to Greg. I put a call through first and found out somebody'd put a bullet in her. How do you think *I* feel about that? She might have filled in a few blanks for me. I've got it tough enough as it is. This goddamn case is eight years old, now give me a break!'

'Who knew you intended to talk to her?'

'I don't know that. If you're implying that somebody killed her to keep her from talking to me, I think you're wrong but I couldn't swear to that. She was stepping on a lot of toes up there from what I hear. And don't ask me the particulars because I don't know. I just hear she was treading on somebody's turf.'

He sat and stared at me then and I guessed that I must have hit a vein. The rumors my friend in Vegas had passed on must have lined up with whatever the Las Vegas Police

Department had turned up. I was personally convinced that she'd been killed to shut her mouth, that someone had followed me and had gotten to her just in time, but I was damned if I was going to have a finger pointed at me. I couldn't see what purpose it would serve and it would only prevent me from getting on with my own inquiries. I still wasn't entirely easy about the fact that someone else had probably tipped off the Las Vegas PD about the shooting. One more minute in her apartment and I'd have been in a real jam, which might have closed down my investigation for good. Whatever regret I felt for my involvement with her death wasn't going to be expiated by my being caught up in the aftermath.

'What else have you found out about Libby Glass?' he asked me then, his tone shifting slightly along with the subject.

'Not a lot. Right now, I'm still trying to make a few pieces fall into place, and so far I'm not having much luck. If that letter really was written by Laurence Fife, then at least we can nail that down. Frankly, I hope it wasn't, but Nikki seems to think the writing is his. There's something about it that doesn't sit well with me. Can you let me know if the prints match?'

Con pushed impatiently at a stack of files on his desk. 'I'll think about that,' he said. 'I don't want us to get buddy-buddy over this.'

'Believe me, we will never be close friends,' I said, and for some reason his expression softened slightly and I almost thought he might smile.

'Get out of here,' he said gruffly.

I went.

I got in my car and left the downtown area, taking a left on Anaconda down to the beach. It was a gorgeous day –

sunny and cool, with fat clouds squatting on the horizon. There were sailboats here and there, probably planted by the Chamber of Commerce to look picturesque for the tourists who straggled along the sidewalk taking snapshots of other tourists who were sitting in the grass.

At Ludlow Beach, I followed the hill upward and then branched off onto the steep side street where Marcia Threadgill lived. I parked and got out my binoculars, scanning her patio. All of her plants were present and accounted for and they were all looking healthier than I liked. There was no sign of Marcia or the neighbor she feuded with. I wished she would move so I could take pictures of her lugging fifty-pound cartons of books down to a U-Haul van. I'd even settle for a glimpse of her coming back from the grocery store with a big double bag of canned goods ripping across the bottom from the weight. I focused in on her patio again and noticed for the first time that there were actually four plant hooks screwed into the wooden overhang of the patio above. On the hook at the near corner was the mammoth plant I'd seen before, but the other three hooks were empty.

I put the binoculars away and went into the building, pausing at the landing between the second and third floors. I peered down through the stair railing. If I situated myself correctly, I'd be able to focus my camera at just the right angle to pick up a nice view of Marcia's front door. Having ascertained that much, I went out to my car again and drove to the Gateway supermarket. I hefted a few houseplants potted in plastic and found one that was just right for my purposes – twenty-five pounds of sturdy trunk with a series of vicious swordlike leaves protruding at intervals. I picked up some prettied gift ribbons in a fire-engine red and a get-well card with a sentimental verse. All of this was taking up precious time that I would have preferred devoting to Nikki Fife's business, but I have my rent to account for and I felt like I owed California Fidelity for at least half a month.

I went back to Marcia's apartment and parked in front. I checked my camera, tore open the packaged ribbons, and stuck several of them to the plastic pot in a jaunty fashion and then tucked the card down inside with a signature scrawled on it that even I couldn't read. I hoisted plant, camera and myself with a slightly thudding heart up the steep concrete stairs, into the building, and up to the second floor. I set the plant down near Marcia's doorsill and then went up to the landing, where I checked my light meter, set up the camera and adjusted the focus on the lens. Nice angle, I thought. This was going to be a work of art. I trotted back down, took a deep breath and rang Ms Threadgill's bell, racing back up the stairs again at breakneck speed. I picked up the camera and checked the focus again. My timing was perfect.

Marcia Threadgill opened her front door and stared down with surprise and puzzlement. She was wearing shorts and a crocheted halter and in the background the voice of Olivia Newton-John boomed out like an audible lollipop. I hesitated a moment and then peered over the rail. Marcia was leaning over to extract the card. She read it, turned it over, and then studied its face again, shrugging with bewilderment. She glanced down the hallway to her left and then moved forward and peered down the stairwell as though she might catch sight of the delivery person. I began to click off pictures, the whir of the thirty-five-millimeter camera obscured by the record being played too loudly. Marcia padded back to her doorsill and bent casually from the waist, picking up twenty-five pounds of plant without even bothering to bend her knees as we've all been instructed to in the exercise manuals. As soon as she'd trucked the plant inside, I raced back down the stairs and out to the street, focusing again from the sidewalk below just as she appeared on the patio and placed the plant up on the rail. She disappeared. I backed up several yards, attaching the telephoto lens, waiting then with my breath held.

Back she came with what must have been a kitchen chair. I clicked off some nice shots of her climbing up. Sure enough, she picked up the plant by the wire, heaving it up to shoulder height, muscles straining until she caught the wire loop on the overhead hook. The effort was such that her halter hiked up and I got a nice shot of Marcia Threadgill's quite large bosom peeping out. I turned away just in time, I suspect, catching only the inkling of her quick look around to see if anyone else had spotted her exposure. When I glanced back casually she was gone.

I dropped the film off to be developed, making sure it was properly dated and identified. Still photographs were not going to be much good to us, especially without a witness to corroborate my testimony as to the date, time and circumstance, but the pictures might at least persuade the claims manager at California Fidelity to pursue the case, which was the best I could hope for at this point. With his authorization, I could go back with a video outfit and a real photographer and pick up some footage that would stand up in court.

I should have known he wouldn't see it that way. Andy Motycka is in his early forties and he still bites his nails. He was working on his right hand that day, trying to gnaw off what remained of his thumb. It made me nervous just to look at him. I kept expecting him to rip loose a big triangle of flesh at the corner of his cuticle. I could feel my face set with distaste and I had to stare just over his shoulder to the left. Before I was even halfway through my explanation, he was shaking his head.

'Can't do it,' he said bluntly. 'This chick doesn't even have an attorney. We're supposed to get a signed release from the doctor next week. No deal. I don't want to mess this one up. Forty-eight hundred dollars is chicken feed. It'd cost us ten grand to go into court. You know that.'

'Well, I know, but—'

'But nothing. The risk is too great. I don't even know why Mac had you check this one out. Look, I know it frosts your ass, but so what? You set her off and she'll go straight out and hire a lawyer and next thing you know, she'll sue us for a million bucks. Forget it.'

'She'll just do it again somewhere else,' I said.

Andy shrugged.

'Why do I waste my time on this shit,' I said, voice rising with frustration.

'Beats me,' he said conversationally. 'Let me see the pix, though, when you get 'em back. Her tits are huge.'

'Screw you,' I said and moved on into my office.

21

There were two messages on my answering service. The first was from Garry Steinberg. I called him back.

'Hey, Kinsey,' he said when I'd been put through.

'Hi, Garry. How are you?'

'Not bad. I've got a little piece of information for you,' he said. I could tell from his tone that he was feeling satisfied with himself, but what he said next still took me by surprise.

'I looked up that job application on Lyle Abernathy this morning. Apparently he worked for a while as an apprentice to a locksmith. Some old guy named Fears.'

'A locksmith?'

'That's right. I called the guy this morning. You'd have loved it. I said Abernathy had applied for a job as a security guard and I was doing a background check. Fears hemmed and hawed some and finally said he'd had to fire the kid. Fears was getting a lot of complaints about missing cash on jobs where Lyle had worked and he began to suspect he was involved in petty thievery. He never could prove it, but he couldn't afford to take the chance, so he let Lyle go.'

'Oh God, that's great,' I said. 'That means Lyle could have gotten into the Fifes' house anytime he wanted to. Libby's too.'

'It looks that way. He worked for Fears for eight months and he sure picked up enough information to give it a try, judging from what Fears said. Unless they had burglar alarms or something like that.'

'Listen, the only security system they had in effect was a big German shepherd that got hit by a car six weeks before

Laurence Fife died. He and his wife and kids were away when the dog was killed.'

'Nice,' Garry said. 'Nothing you could prove after all this time, but it might put you on the right track at any rate. What about the application? You want a copy?'

'I'd love it. What about Fife's accounts?'

'I've got those at my place and I'll look at 'em when I can. It's a lot of stuff. In the meantime, I just thought you might want to know about that locksmith stint.'

'I appreciate your help. Jesus, what a shmuck that guy is.'

'I'll say. Hey, I got another call coming in. I'll be in touch.' He gave me his home phone in case I needed him.

'You're terrific. Thanks.'

The second message was from Gwen at K-9 Korners. One of her assistants answered and I listened to assorted dogs bark and whine while Gwen came to the phone.

'Kinsey?'

'Yeah, it's me. I got your call. What's happening?'

'Are you free for lunch?'

'Just a minute. I'll check my appointment book,' I said. I put my palm against the mouth of the receiver and looked at my watch. It was 1:45. Had I *eaten* lunch? Had I even eaten breakfast today? 'Yes, I'm free.'

'Good. I'll meet you at the Palm Garden in fifteen minutes if that's okay for you.'

'Sure. Fine. See you shortly.'

My glass of white wine had just arrived when I glanced up to see Gwen approaching from across the courtyard: tall and lean, her gray hair slicked away from her face. The blouse she wore was a gray silk, long full sleeves nipped in at the wrist, the dark gray skirt emphasizing her trim waist and hips. She was stylish, confident – like Nikki in that – and I could see where both women must have appealed to Laurence Fife. I guessed that once upon a time Charlotte Mercer fitted the same mold: a woman of stature, a woman of taste. I wondered idly if Libby Glass would have aged as well had she lived. She must have been much less secure at twenty four, but bright – someone whose freshness and ambition might have appealed to Laurence as he neared the age of forty. God save us all from the consequences of male menopause, I thought.

'Hello. How are you,' Gwen said briskly, sitting down. She removed the napkin beside her plate and ordered wine as the waitress passed. Close up, her image softened, the angularity of her cheekbones offset by the large brown eyes, the purposeful mouth tinted with soft pink. Most of all, there was her manner: amused, intelligent, feminine, refined.

'How are all the dogs?' I said.

She laughed. 'Filthy. Thank God. We're swamped today, but I wanted to talk to you. You've been out of town.'

'I just got back Saturday. Have you been trying to get in touch?'

She nodded. 'I called the office on Tuesday, I think. Your answering service said you were in Los Angeles so I tried to reach you there. Some total nitwit answered — '

'Arlette.'

'Well, whoever it was, she got my name wrong twice so I hung up.'

The waitress arrived with Gwen's wine.

'Have you ordered yet?'

I shook my head. 'I was waiting for you.'

The waitress got out her order card, glancing at me.

'I'll have the chef's salad,' I said.

'Make that two.'

'Dressing?'

'Blue cheese,' I said.

'I'll have oil and vinegar,' Gwen said and then handed both menus to the waitress, who moved away. Gwen turned her attention to me.

'I've decided I should level with you.'

'About what?'

'My old lover,' she said. Her cheeks had flushed mildly. 'I realized that if I didn't tell you who he was, you'd be off on some wild-goose chase, wasting a lot of time trying to find out his name. It really amounts to more mystery than it's worth.'

'How so?'

'He died a few months ago of a heart attack,' she said, her manner turning brisk again. 'After I talked to you, I tried tracking him down myself. His name was David Ray. He was a schoolteacher. Greg's, as a matter of fact, which is how we met. I thought he should know that you were asking questions about Laurence's death, or at any rate that your curiosity might lead you to him.'

'How'd you find him?'

'I'd heard that he and his wife had moved to San Francisco. Apparently he was living in the Bay Area, where he was a principal of one of the Oakland public schools.'

'Why not tell me before?'

She shrugged. 'Misplaced loyalty. Protectiveness. That was a very important relationship and I didn't want him involved at this late date.'

She looked at me and she must have read the skepticism in my face. The flush in her cheeks deepened almost imperceptibly.

'I know how it looks,' she said. 'First I refuse to give you his name and then he's dead and out of reach, but that's exactly the point. If he were still alive, I don't know that I'd be telling you this.'

I thought that was probably true, but there was something else going on and I wasn't sure what it was. The waitress arrived with our salads and there was a merciful few minutes in which we busied ourselves with melba rounds. Gwen was rearranging her lettuce but she wasn't eating much. I was curious to hear what else she had to say and too hungry to worry about it much until I'd eaten some.

'Did you know he had heart trouble?' I asked finally.

'I had no idea, but I gather he was ill for years.'

'Did he break off the relationship or did you?'

Gwen smiled bitterly. 'Laurence did that but I wonder now if David might have engineered it to some extent. The whole affair must have complicated his life unbearably.'

'He'd told his wife?'

'I think so. She was very gracious on the phone. I told her that Greg had asked me to get in touch and she played right along. When she told me that David had died, I was . . . I didn't even know what to say to her but of course, I had to babble right on – how sorry, how sad . . . like some disinterested bystander making the right noises somehow. It was awful. Terrible.'

'She didn't mention your relationship herself?'

'Oh no. She was much too cool for that, but she did know exactly who I was. Anyway, I'm sorry I didn't tell you to begin with.'

'No harm done,' I said.

'How's it going otherwise?' she asked.

I felt myself hesitate. 'Bits and pieces. Nothing concrete.'

'Do you really expect to turn up anything after all this time?'

I smiled. 'You never know. People get careless when they're feeling safe.'

'I guess that's true.'

We talked briefly about Greg and Diane and my visits with them, which I edited heavily. At 2:50 Gwen glanced at her watch.

'I've got to get back,' she said, fishing in her purse for her billfold. She took out a five-dollar bill. 'Will you keep in touch?'

'Sure,' I said. I took a sip of wine, watching her get up. 'When did you last see Colin?'

She focused abruptly on my face. 'Colin?'

'I just met him Saturday,' I said as though that explained it. 'I thought maybe Diane might like to know he's back. She's fond of him.'

'Yes, she is,' Gwen said. 'I don't know when I saw him last myself. Diane's graduation, I guess. Her junior-high-school graduation. What makes you ask?'

I shrugged. 'Just curious,' I said. I gave her what I hoped was my blandest look. A mild pink patch had appeared on her neck and I wondered if that could be introduced in court as a lie-detecting device. 'I'll take care of the tip,' I said.

'Let me know how it goes,' she said, all casual again. She tucked the money under her plate and moved off at the same efficient pace that had brought her in. I watched her departure, thinking that something vital had gone unsaid. She could have told me about David Ray on the phone. And I wasn't entirely convinced she hadn't known about his death to begin with. Colin popped into my head.

I walked the two blocks to Charlie's office. Ruth was typing from a Dictaphone, fingers moving lightly across the keyboard. She was very fast.

'Is he in?'

She smiled and nodded me on back, not missing a word, gaze turned inward as she translated sound to paper with no lag time in between.

I stuck my head into his office. He was sitting at his desk, coat off, a law book open in front of him. Beige shirt, dark brown vest. When he saw me, a slow smile formed and he leaned back, tucking an arm up over the back of his swivel chair. He tossed the pencil on his desk.

'Are you free for dinner?' I said.

'What's up?'

'Nothing's up. It's a proposition,' I said.

'Six-fifteen.'

'I'll be back,' I said and closed his office door again, still thinking about that pale shirt and the dark brown vest. Now *that* was sexy. A man in a nylon bikini, with that little knot sticking out in front, isn't half as interesting as a man in a good-looking business suit. Charlie's outfit reminded me of a Reese's Peanut Butter Cup with a bite taken out and I wanted the rest.

I drove out to Nikki's beach house.

22

Nikki answered the door in an old gray sweatshirt and a pair of faded jeans. She was barefoot, hair loose, a paintbrush in one hand, her fingers stained the color of pecan shells.

'Oh hi, Kinsey. Come on in,' she said. She was already moving back toward the deck and I followed her through the house. On the other side of the sliding glass doors I could see Colin, shirtless, in a pair of bib overalls, sitting cross-legged in front of a chest of drawers, which the two were apparently refinishing. The drawers were out, leaning upright along the balcony, hardware removed. The air smelled of stripper and turpentine, which mingled not incompatibly with the smell of eucalyptus bark. Several sheets of fine sandpaper were folded and tossed aside, creases worn white with wood dust, looking soft from hard use. The sun was hot on the railings and newspapers were spread out under the chest to protect the deck.

Colin glanced up at me and smiled as I came out. His nose and cheeks were faintly pink with sunburn, his eyes green as sea water, bare arms rosy, there wasn't even a whisper of facial hair yet. He went back to his work.

'I want to ask Colin something but I thought I'd try it out on you first,' I said to Nikki.

'Sure, fire away,' she replied. I leaned against the railing while she dipped the tip of her brush back into a small can of stain, easing the excess off along the edge. Colin seemed more interested in the painting than he was in our exchange. I imagined that it was a bit of a strain to try to follow a conversation even if his lip-reading skills were good or maybe he thought adults were a bore.

'Can you remember offhand if you were out of town for any length of time in the four to six months before Laurence died?'

Nikki looked at me with surprise and blinked, apparently not expecting that. 'I was gone once for a week. My father had a heart attack that June and I flew back to Connecticut,' she said. She paused then and shook her head. 'That was the only time, I think. What are you getting at?'

'I'm not sure. I mean, this is going to seem far-fetched, but I've been bothered by Colin's calling Gwen "Daddy's mother." Has he mentioned that since?'

'Nope. Not a word.'

'Well, I'm wondering if he didn't have occasion to see Gwen at some point while you were gone. He's too smart to get her mixed up with his own grandmother unless somebody identified her to him that way.'

Nikki gave me a skeptical look. 'Boy, that *is* a stretch. He couldn't have been more than three and a half years old.'

'Yeah, I know, but a little while ago I asked Gwen when she saw him last and she claims it was at Diane's junior-high-school graduation.'

'That's probably true,' Nikki said.

'Nikki, Colin must have been fourteen months old at the time. I saw those snapshots myself. He was still a babe in arms.'

'So?'

'So why did he remember her at all?'

Nikki applied a band of stain, giving that some thought. 'Maybe she saw him in a supermarket or ran into him with Diane. She could have seen him or he could easily have seen her without any particular significance attached to it.'

'Maybe. But I think Gwen lied to me about it when I asked. If it was no big deal, why not just say so. Why cover up?'

Nikki gave me a long look. 'Maybe she just forgot.'

'Mind if I ask him?'

'No, go ahead.'

'Where's the album?'

She gestured over her shoulder and I went back into the living room. The photograph album was sitting on the coffee table and I flipped through until I found the snapshot of Gwen. I slipped it out of the four little corners holding it down and went back out to the deck. I held it out to him.

'Ask him if he can remember what was happening when he saw her last,' I said.

Nikki reached over and gave him a tap. He looked at her and then at the snapshot, eyes meeting mine inquisitively. Nikki signed the question to him. His face closed up like a day lily when the sun goes down.

'Colin?'

He started to paint again, face averted.

'The little shit,' she said good-naturedly. She gave him a nudge and asked him again.

Colin shrugged her off. I studied his reaction with care.

'Ask him if she was here.'

'Who, Gwen? Why would she be here?'

'I don't know. That's why we're asking him.'

The look she gave me was half doubt, half disbelief. Reluctantly, she looked back at him. She signed to him, translating for my benefit. She didn't seem to like it much.

'Was Gwen ever here or at the other house?'

Colin watched her face, his own face a remarkable mirror of uncertainty and something else – uneasiness, secrecy, dismay.

'I don't know,' he said aloud. The consonants blurred together like ink on a wet page, his tone conveying a sort of stubborn distrust.

His eyes slid over to me. I thought suddenly of the time in the sixth grade when I first heard the word *fuck*. One of my classmates told me I should go ask my aunt what it meant. I could sense the trap though I had no idea what it consisted of.

'Tell him it's okay,' I said to her. 'Tell him it doesn't matter to you.'

'Well it certainly does,' she snapped.

'Oh come on, Nikki. It's important and what difference does it make after all this time?'

She got into a short discussion with him then, just the two of them, signing away like mad – a digital argument. 'He doesn't want to talk about it,' she said guardedly. 'He made a mistake.'

I didn't think so and I could feel excitement stir. He was watching us now, trying to get an emotional reading from our interchange.

'I know this sounds weird,'I said to her tentatively, 'but I wonder if Laurence told him that – that she was his mother.'

'Why would he do that?'

I looked at her. 'Maybe Colin caught them embracing or something like that.'

Nikki's expression was blank for a moment and then she frowned. Colin waited uncertainly, looking from her to me. Nikki signed to him again. He seemed embarrassed now, head bent. She signed again more earnestly. Colin shook his head but the gesture seemed to come out of caution, not ignorance.

Nikki's expression underwent a change. 'I just remembered something,' she said. She blinked rapidly, color mounting in her face. 'Laurence did come out here. He told me he brought Colin out the weekend I was back east. Greg and Diane stayed at the house with Mrs Voss. Both had social plans or something, but Laurence said the two of them – he and Colin – came out to the beach to get away for a bit.'

'Nice,' I said with irony. 'At three and a half, none of it

would have made much sense to him anyway. Let's just assume it's true. Let's assume she was out here—'

'I really don't want to go on with this.'

'Just one more,' I said. 'Just ask him why he called her "Daddy's mother". Ask him why the "Daddy's mother" bit.'

She relayed the question to Colin reluctantly but his face brightened with relief. He signed back at once, grabbing his head.

'She had gray hair,' she reported to me. 'She *looked* like a grandmother to him when she was here.'

I caught a glint of temper in her voice but she recovered herself, apparently for his sake. She tousled his hair affectionately.

'I love you,' she said. 'It's fine. It's okay.'

Colin seemed to relax but the tension had darkened Nikki's eyes to a charcoal gray.

'Laurence hated her,' she said. 'He *couldn't* have—'

'I'm just making an educated guess,' I said. 'It might have been completely innocent. Maybe they met for drinks and talked about the kids' schoolwork. We really don't know anything for *sure*.'

'My ass,' she murmured. Her mood was sour.

'Don't get mad at me,' I said. 'I'm just trying to put this together so it makes some sense.'

'Well I don't believe a word of it,' she said tersely.

'You want to tell me he was too nice a man to do such a thing?'

She put the paintbrush on the paper and wiped her hands on a rag.

'Maybe I'd like to have a few illusions left.'

'I don't blame you a bit,' I said. 'But I don't understand why it bothers you. Charlotte Mercer was the one who put it into my head. She said he was like a tomcat, always sniffing around the same back porch.'

'All right, Kinsey. You've made your point.'

'No, I don't think I have. You paid me five grand to find out what happened. You don't like the answers. I can give you your money back.'

'No, never mind. Just skip it. You're right,' she said.

'You want me to pursue it or not?'

'Yes,' she said flatly, but she didn't really look at me again. I made my excuses and left soon after that, feeling almost depressed. She still cared about the man and I didn't know what to make of that. Except that nothing's ever cut-and-dried–especially where men and women are concerned. So why did I feel guilty for doing my job?

I went into Charlie's office building. He was waiting at the top of the stairs, coat over one shoulder, tie loose.

'What happened to you?' he said when he saw my face.

'Don't ask,' I said. 'I'm going to try to get a scholarship to secretarial school. Something simple and nice. Something nine-to-five.'

I came up level with him, tilting my face slightly to look at him. It was as though I had suddenly entered a magnetic field like those two little dog-magnets when I was a kid–one black, one white. At the positive poles, if you held them half an inch apart, they would suck together with a little click. His face was so solemn, so close, eyes resting on my mouth as though he might will me forward. For a full ten seconds we seemed caught and then I pulled back slightly, unprepared for the intensity.

'Jesus,' he said, almost with surprise, and then he chuckled, a sound I knew well.

'I need a drink,' I said.

'That's not all you need,' he said mildly.

I smiled, ignoring him. 'I hope you know how to cook because I don't.'

'Hey listen, there is one slight kink,' he said. 'I'm house-sitting for my partner. He's out of town and I've got his dogs to feed. We can grab a bite to eat out there.'

'Fine with me,' I said.

He locked the office then and we went down the back stairs to the small parking lot adjacent to his office building. He opened his car door but I was already moving toward mine, which was parked out on the street.

'Don't you trust me to drive?'

'I'm courting a ticket if I stay parked out here. I'll follow you. I don't like to be stuck without my own wheels.'

'"Wheels"? Like in the sixties, you refer to your car as "*wheels*"?'

'Yeah, I read that in a book,' I said dryly.

He rolled his eyes and smiled indulgently, apparently resigned. He got in his car and waited pointedly until I had reached mine. Then he pulled out, driving slowly so that I could follow him without getting lost. Once in a while, I could see him watching me in his rearview mirror.

'You sexy bastard,' I said to him under my breath and then I shivered involuntarily. He had that effect.

We proceeded to John Powers's house at the beach, Charlie driving at a leisurely pace. As usual, he was operating at half speed. The road began to wind and finally his car slowed and he turned left down a steep drive, a place not far from Nikki's beach house, if my calculations were correct. I pulled my car in beside his, nose down, hoping my handbrake would hold. Powers's house was tucked up against the hill to the right, with a carport dead ahead and parking space for two cars. The carport itself had a white picket fence across it, the two halves forming a gate, locked shut, with what I guessed to be his car parked inside.

Charlie got out, waiting as I came around the front of my car. As with Nikki's property, this was up on the bluff, probably sixty or seventy feet above the beach. Through the carport, I could see a patchy apron of grass, a crescent of yard. We went along a narrow walkway behind the house and Charlie let us into the kitchen. John Powers's two dogs were of the kind I hate: the jumping, barking, slavering sort with toenails like sharks' teeth. They reeked of bad breath. One was black and the other was the color of moldering whale washed up on the beach for a month. Both were large and insisted on standing up on their hind legs to stare into my face. I kept my head back, lips shut lest wet, sloppy kisses be forthcoming.

'Charlie, could you help me with this?' I ventured through clenched teeth. One licked me right in the mouth as I spoke.

'Tootsie! Moe! Knock it off!' he snapped.

I wiped my lips. 'Tootsie and Moe?'

Charlie laughed and dragged them both by neck chains to the utility room, where he shut them in. One began to howl while the other barked.

'Oh Jesus. Let 'em out,' I said. He opened the door and both bounded out, tongues flapping like slivers of corned beef. One of the dogs galummoxed into the other room and came trotting back with a leash in its mouth. This was supposed to be cute. Charlie put leashes on both and they pranced, wetting the floor in spots.

'If I walk them, they calm down,' Charlie remarked. 'Sort of like you.'

I made a face at him but there seemed to be no alternative but to follow him out the front. There were various dog lumps in the grass. A narrow wooden stairway angled down toward the beach, giving way in places to bare ground and rock. It was a hazardous descent, especially with two ninety-five-pound lunkheads doing leaps and pirouettes at every turn.

'John comes home at lunch to give 'em a run,' Charlie said back over his shoulder.

'Good for him,' I said, picking my way down the cliffside, concentrating on my feet. Fortunately, I was wearing tennis shoes, which provided no traction but at least didn't have heels that would catch in the rotting steps and pitch me headfirst into the Pacific.

The beach below was long and narrow, bounded by precipitous rocks. The dogs loped from one end to the other, the black one pausing to take a big steaming dump, backside hunched, eyes downcast modestly. Jesus, I thought, is that all dogs know how to do? I averted my gaze. Really, it was all so *rude*. I found a seat on a rock and tried to turn my brain off. I needed a break, a long stretch of time in which I didn't have to worry about anybody but myself. Charlie threw sticks, which the dogs invariably missed.

Finally, the dog romp at an end, we staggered back up the steps together. As soon as we were inside, the dogs flopped happily on a big oval rug in the living room and began to chew it to shreds. Charlie went into the kitchen and I could hear ice trays cracking.

'What do you want to drink?' he called.

I moved over to the kitchen doorway. 'Wine if you have it.'

'Great. There's some in the fridge.'

'You do this often?' I asked, indicating the pups.

He shrugged, filling ice trays again. 'Every three or four weeks. It depends,' he said and then smiled over at me. 'See? I'm a nicer guy than you thought.'

I twirled an index finger in the air just to show how impressed I was, but I did, actually, think it was nice of him to sit the dogs. I couldn't imagine Powers finding a kennel to keep them. He'd have to take them to the zoo. Charlie handed me a glass of wine, pouring a bourbon on the rocks for himself. I leaned against the doorframe.

'Did you know that Laurence had an affair at one time with Sharon Napier's mother?'

He gave me a startled look. 'You're making a joke.'

'No I'm not. Apparently it happened some time before Sharon went to work for him. From what I gather, her "employment" was a combination of extortion and revenge. Which might explain the way she treated him.'

'Who told you this stuff?'

'What difference does that make?'

'Because it sounds like crap,' he said. 'The name Napier never meant anything to me and I knew him for years.'

I shrugged. 'That's what you said about Libby Glass,' I replied.

Charlie's smile began to fade. 'Jesus, you don't forgive a thing, do you?' He moved into the living room and I followed. He sat down in a wicker chair, which creaked beneath his weight.

'Is that why you're here? To work?' he asked.

'Actually, it's not. Actually, it's just the opposite.'

'Meaning what?'

'I came out here to get away from it,' I said.

'Then why the questions? Why the third-degree? You know how I feel about Laurence and I don't like to be used.'

I felt my own smile fade, my face setting with embarrassment.

'Is that what you think?' I asked.

He looked down at his glass, speaking carefully. 'I can appreciate the fact you have a job to do. That's fine with me and I'm not complaining about that. I'll help you where I can, but I can do without the interrogation at every step. I don't think you have any idea what it's like. You ought to see the change that comes over you when you start talking homicide.'

'I'm sorry,' I said stiffly. 'I don't mean to do that to you. I get information and I need to have it verified. I can't afford to take things at face value.'

'Not even me?'

'Why are you doing this?' I said, and my voice seemed to have dropped to a hush.

'I'm just trying to get a few things clarified.'

'Hey. You were the one who came after me. Remember that?'

'Saturday. Yes. And you were the one who came after me today. And now you're pumping me and I don't like that.'

I stared down at the floor, feeling fragile and mortified. I didn't like being smacked down and it was pissing me off. A lot. I began to shake my head. 'I had a hard day,' I said. 'I really don't need this shit.'

'I had a hard day too,' he said. 'So what?'

I set my wineglass on the table and grabbed up my purse. 'Fuck off,' I said mildly. 'Just go fuck yourself.'

I moved toward the kitchen. The dogs raised their heads and watched me pass. I was hot and they lowered their eyes meekly as though I had communicated that much at any rate. Charlie didn't move. I banged out the back door and got into my car, starting it up with energy, peeling back up the driveway with a chirp. As I backed out onto the road, I caught a glimpse of Charlie standing near the carport. I put the car into first and pulled away.

23

I've never been good at taking shit, especially from men. It was an hour after I got home before I cooled down. Eight o'clock and I still hadn't eaten anything. I poured myself a big glass of wine and sat down at my desk. I took out some blank index cards and began to work. At 10:00 I had dinner – a sliced hard-boiled-egg sandwich, which I ate hot on wheat bread with a lot of mayonnaise and salt, popping open a Pepsi and a package of corn chips. By then I'd consigned all the information I had to the index cards, which I'd tacked up on my bulletin board.

I sketched the story out, allowing myself to speculate. I mean, why not? I didn't have much else to go on at this point. It seemed likely that someone had broken into the Fifes' house the weekend the German shepherd was killed, while Nikki and Laurence were off at the Salton Sea with Colin and Greg. It also seemed likely that Sharon Napier had come up with something after Laurence died – which was (maybe) why she had gotten herself killed. I started making lists, systematizing the information I had, along with the half-formed ideas that were simmering at the back of my head. I typed up my sheets and arranged them in alphabetical order, starting with Lyle Abernathy and Gwen.

I didn't dismiss the idea that Diane and Greg were possibly involved, though I couldn't make any sense of the notion that either could have killed him, let alone Libby Glass. I included Charlotte Mercer on my list. She was spoiled and spiteful and I didn't think she would spare any energy or expense in seeing that the world was arranged exactly as she wanted it. She could have hired someone if she didn't want to go to the trouble of murdering him herself. And if she killed him, why not Libby Glass? Why not Sharon Napier, if Sharon had figured it out? I decided it might be smart to check with the airlines to see if her name appeared on any of the passenger lists for Las Vegas at the time Sharon died. That was one angle I hadn't thought of. I made a note to myself. Charlie Scorsoni was still on my list and the realization had a disturbing effect.

There was a knock at the door and I jerked involuntarily, adrenaline shooting through me. I glanced at my watch: 12:25. My heart was thumping so hard it made my hands shake. I crossed to the door and bent my head.

'Yes?'

'It's me,' Charlie said. 'Can I come in?'

I opened the door. Charlie was leaning against the frame. No jacket. No tie. Tennis shoes with no socks. His square handsome face looked solemn and subdued. He searched my face and then looked away. 'I came down on you too hard and I'm sorry,' he said.

I studied his face. 'You had a legitimate complaint,' I said. I knew that my tone of voice was unrelenting, regardless of the content, and I knew that my purpose was punitive. He only had to look at me to guess my real attitude and it frosted him some.

'Jesus Christ, could we just talk?' he said.

I glanced at him briefly and then moved away from the door. He came in, closing it behind him. He leaned on the door, hands in his pockets, watching me prowl the room, circling back to my desk, where I began to take cards down, packing papers away.

'What do you want from me?' he said helplessly.

'What do you want from *me*?' I snapped back. I caught myself and raised a hand. 'I'm sorry. I didn't mean to use that tone.'

He stared down at the floor as though trying to figure out where to go next. I sat down in the upholstered chair near the couch, flinging my legs over the padded arm.

'Want a drink?' I asked.

He shook his head. He moved over to the couch and sat down heavily, leaning his head back. His face looked lined, his brow furrowed. His sandy hair looked as though he'd run a hand through it more than once. 'I don't know what to do with you,' he said.

'What's to do?' I asked. 'I know I'm a bitch sometimes, but why not? I'm serious, Charlie. I'm too old to take any guff from anyone. And truly, in this case, I don't know who did what to whom. Did you generate that fight or did I?'

He smiled slightly. 'Okay, so we're both touchy now and then. Is that fair enough?'

'I don't know from fair anymore. I don't know from any of this stuff.'

'Haven't you ever heard of compromise?'

'Oh sure,' I said. 'That's when you give away half the things you want. That's when you give the other guy half of what's rightfully yours. I've done that lots of times. It sucks.'

He shook his head, smiling wearily. I stared at him, feeling stubborn and belligerent. He'd already given more than I, and I still couldn't bend. He regarded me skeptically.

'Where do you go when you look at me that way?' he asked. I didn't know what to say so I kept my mouth shut. He reached over and waggled my bare foot as though to get my attention.

'You know you keep me at arm's length,' he said.

'Really? Saturday night you think I did that?'

'Kinsey, sex was the only time you let me get close. What am I supposed to do with that? Chase around after you with my dick hanging out?'

I smiled inside, hoping it wouldn't show on my face. He read it anyway in my eyes. 'Yeah, why not?' I said.

'I don't think you're used to men,' he said, not making eye contact, and then he corrected himself. 'Not men,' he said. 'I don't think you're used to having anyone in your life. I think you're used to being freewheeling. And that's okay. Essentially I live the same way, but this is different. I think we should be careful of this.'

'This what?'

'This relationship,' he said. 'I don't want you shutting me out. You're not that hard to read. Sometimes you disappear like a shot and I can't cope with that. I will try to tread easy. I'll try not to be a horse's ass myself. I promise you that. Just don't run off. Don't back away. You do this kind of knee-jerk retreat, like a clam —' He broke off then.

I softened, wondering if I'd misjudged him. I was too tough, too quick. I am hard on people and I know that.

'I'm sorry,' I said. I had to clear my throat. 'I'm sorry. I know I do that. I don't know who was at fault, but you ticked me off and I blew.'

I held my hand out and he took it, squeezing my fingers. He looked at me for a long time. He took my fingertips and kissed them lightly, casually, looking at me the whole time. I felt like a switch was being turned on at the base of my spine. He turned my hand over and pressed his mouth into my palm. I didn't want him to do that but I noticed I wasn't pulling my hand away. I watched him, hypnotically, my senses dulled by the heat that was raging way down, way deep. It was like a pile of rags beginning to smolder, some dark part of me hidden away under the stairs, something firemen had warned us about in grade school. Paint cans, jars of gasoline – fumes in compression. All it needed was a spark, sometimes not even that. I could feel my eyes close, mouth coming open against my will. I sensed that Charlie was moving but I couldn't take that in and the next thing I was aware of, he was on his knees between mine, pulling the neck of my T-shirt down, his mouth on my bare breast. I clutched at him convulsively, slid down and forward against him and he half lifted me, hands cupped under my ass. I hadn't known how much I wanted him until then, until that point, but the sound I made was primitive and his response was fierce and immediate and after that, in the half-light, with the table pushed aside, we made love on the floor. He did things to me that I'd only read about in books, and at the end of it, legs trembling, heart thudding, I laughed and he buried his face against my belly, laughing too.

He was gone again by 2:00 A.M. He had work to do the next day and so did I. Even so, I missed him as I brushed my teeth, smirking at my own reflection in the bathroom mirror. My chin was pink from whisker burn. My hair seemed to be standing straight up on end. There is nothing quite as smug as the self-congratulation that abounds when one has been thoroughly and proficiently screwed, but I was a little bit embarrassed with myself nevertheless. This was not good, not cool. As a rule, I scrupulously avoid personal contact with anyone connected with a case. My sexual wrangling with Charlie was foolish, unprofessional, and in theory, possibly dangerous. In some little nagging part of my head, it didn't feel right to me, but I did love his *moves*. I couldn't think when I'd last run into a man quite so inventive. My reaction to him was gut-level chemistry – like crystals of sodium flung in a swimming pool, throwing off sparks, dancing across the water like light. I had a friend once who said to me, 'Wherever there is sex, we work to create a relationship that's worthy of it.' I thought about that now, sensing that soon I would do that with him – start to bond, start to fantasize, start to throw out emotional tendrils like snow peas curling up a string. I was wary of it too. The sex was very good and very strong but the fact remained that I was still in the middle of an investigation and he still had not been crossed off my list. I didn't think our physical relationship had clouded my judgment about him, but how could I tell? I couldn't really afford to take the chance. Unless, of course, I was just rationalizing my own inclination to hold back. Was I *that* careful with myself these days? Was I really just sidestepping intimacy? Did I long to relegate him to the role of 'possible suspect' in order to justify my own reluctance to take a risk? He was a nice man – smart, caring, responsible, attractive, perceptive. What in God's name did I want?

I turned the bathroom light out and made up my bed, which really just amounted to a quilt folded lengthways on the couch. I could have opened out the sofa bed and done it right – sheets, pillow case, a proper nightgown. Instead I'd pulled the same T-shirt over my head and tucked myself into the fold of the quilt. My body heat was making a sexual perfume waft up from between my legs. I turned out the lamp on the desk and smiled in the dark, shivering with the recollection of his mouth on me. Maybe this wasn't the time to get analytical, I thought. Maybe this was just a time to reflect and assimilate. I slept like the dead.

In the morning, I showered, skipping breakfast, reaching the office by 9:00. I let myself in and checked with the service. Con Dolan had called. I dialed the Santa Teresa Police Department and asked for him.

'What,' he barked, already annoyed with the world.

'Kinsey Millhone here,' I said.

'Oh yeah? What do you want?'

'Lieutenant, you called me!' I could hear him blink.

'Oh. Right. I got a report here from the lab on that letter. No prints. Just smudges, so that's no good.'

'Rats. What about the handwriting? Does that match?'

'Enough to satisfy us,' he said. 'I had Jimmy go over it and he says it's legitimate. What else you got?'

'Nothing right now. I may come in and talk to you, though, in a couple of days if that's okay.'

'Call first,' he said.

'Trust me,' I replied.

I went out on the balcony and stared down at the street. Something wasn't right. I'd been half convinced that letter was a fake but now it was confirmed and verified. I didn't like it. I went back in and sat down in my swivel chair, tipping back and forth slightly, listening to it creak. I shook my head. Couldn't figure it out. I glanced at the calendar. I'd been working for Nikki for two weeks. It felt like she'd hired me a minute ago and it felt like I'd been on the case all my life. I tilted forward and grabbed a scratch pad, totaling the time I'd put in, adding expenses on top of that. I typed it all up, made copies of my receipts, and stuck the whole batch in an envelope, which I mailed to her out at the beach. I went into the California Fidelity offices and shot the shit with Vera, who processes claims for them.

I skipped lunch and knocked off at 3:00. I stopped on the way home and picked up the eight-by-ten color photographs of Marcia Threadgill and I sat in my car for a moment to survey my handiwork. It isn't often that I have such a captivating spectacle of avarice and fraud. The best shot (which I might have called 'Portrait of a Chiseler') was of Marcia standing up on her kitchen chair, shoulders strained by the weight of the plant as she lifted it up. Her boobs, in the crocheted halter top, sagged down like flesh melons bursting through the bottom of a string bag. The image was so clear that I could see where her mascara had left little black dots on her upper lids like tracks of some tiny beast. Such a jerk. I smiled to myself grimly. If that's the way the world works, then let me not forget. I was resigned by now to the fact that Ms Threadgill would have her way. Cheaters win all the time. It wasn't big news but it was worth remembering. I slid all the pictures back into the manila envelope. I started the car and headed toward home. I didn't feel like running today. I wanted to sit and brood.

24

I pinned the photograph of Marcia Threadgill up on my bulletin board and stared at it. I kicked my shoes off and walked around. I'd been thinking all day and it was getting me nowhere, so I took out the crossword puzzle Henry had left on my doorstep. I stretched out on the couch, pencil in hand. I did manage to guess 6 Down – 'disloyal', eight letters, which was 'two-faced', and I got 14 Across, which was 'double-reed instrument', four letters – 'oboe'. What a whiz. I got stuck on 'double helix', three letters, which turned out later to be 'DNA', a cheat if you ask me. At 7:05, I had an idea that jumped out of the dim recesses of my brain with a little jolt of electricity.

I looked up Charlotte Mercer's telephone number and dialed the house. The housekeeper answered and I asked for Charlotte.

'The judge and Mrs Mercer are having dinner,' she said disapprovingly.

'Well, would you mind interrupting please? I just have a quick question. I'm sure she won't mind.'

'Who shall I say is calling?' she asked. I gave her my name.

'Just one moment.' She put the receiver down.

I corrected her mentally. *Whom*, sweetheart. *Whom* shall I say is calling . . .

Charlotte answered, sounding drunk. 'I don't appreciate this,' she hissed.

'I'm sorry,' I said. 'But I need a piece of information.'

'I told you what I know and I don't want you calling when the judge is here.'

'All right. All right. Just one thing,' I said hurriedly before she could hang up. 'Do you happen to remember Mrs Napier's first name?'

Silence. I could practically see her hold the receiver out to look at it.

'Elizabeth,' she said and slammed down the phone.

I hung up. The piece I was looking for had just clicked into place. The letter wasn't written to Libby Glass at all. Laurence Fife had written it to Elizabeth Napier years ago. I was willing to bet on that. The real question now was how Libby Glass had gotten hold of it and who had wanted it back.

I took out my note cards and went back to work on my list. I had deliberately deleted Raymond and Grace Glass. I didn't believe either of them would have killed their own child, and if my guess about that letter could be verified, then it was possible that Libby and Laurence had never been romantically involved. Which meant that the reasons for their dying had to be something else. But what? Suppose, I said to myself, just suppose Laurence Fife and *Lyle* were involved in something. Maybe Libby stumbled on to it and Lyle killed them both to protect himself. Maybe Sharon got wind of it and he'd killed her too. It didn't quite make sense to me from that angle, but after eight years much of the real proof must have been lost or destroyed. Some of the obvious connections must have faded by now. I jotted down a couple of notes and checked the list.

When I came to Charlie Scorsoni's name, I felt the same uneasiness I'd felt before. I'd checked him out two weeks ago, before I'd even met with him and he was clean, but appearances are deceptive. As squeamish as it made me feel, I thought I'd better verify his whereabouts the night Sharon died. I knew he'd been in Denver because I'd called him there myself but I wasn't really sure where he'd gone after that. Arlette said he'd left messages from Tucson and again from Santa Teresa but she only had his word for that. When it came to Laurence Fife he did have opportunity. From the first, this had been a case where motive and alibi were oddly overlapped. Ordinarily, an alibi is an account of a suspect's whereabouts at the time a crime was committed and it's offered up as proof of innocence, but here it didn't matter where anyone was. With a poisoning, it only mattered if someone had *reason* to want someone else dead – access to the poison, access to the victim, and the intent to kill. That's what I was still sorting through. My impulse was simply to take Charlie off my list but I had to question myself on that. Did I really believe he was innocent or did I simply want to relieve myself of my own uneasiness? I tried to think about something else. I tried to move on, but my mind kept drifting back to the same point. I didn't think I was being smart. I wasn't sure I was being honest with myself. And suddenly, I didn't like the idea that my thinking might not be clear. The whole set-up gave me a sick feeling down in my bones. I looked up his home phone number in the telephone book. I hesitated and then I shook myself free and dialed. I had to do it.

The phone rang four times. I thought he might be out at Powers's house at the beach but I didn't have that number. I was rooting for him to be out, gone. He picked up on the fifth ring and I felt my stomach churn. There was no point in putting it off.

'Hi, it's Kinsey,' I said.

'Well hello,' he said softly. The pleasure in his voice was audible and I could picture his face. 'God, I was hoping I'd hear from you. Are you free?'

'No, actually I'm not. Uh, listen, Charlie. I'm thinking I shouldn't see you for a while. Until I get this wrapped up.'

The silence was profound.

'All right,' he said finally.

'Look, it's nothing personal,' I said. 'It's just a matter of policy.'

'I'm not arguing,' he said. 'Do what you want. It's too bad you didn't think about "policy" before.'

'Charlie, it's not like that,' I said desperately. 'It may work out fine and it's no big deal, but it's been bothering me. A lot. I don't do this. It's been one of my cardinal rules. I can't keep on seeing you until I understand how this thing ties up.'

'Babe, I understand,' he said. 'If it doesn't feel right to you, then it's no good anyway. Call me if you ever change your mind.'

'Wait,' I said. 'God damn it, don't do that to me. I'm not rejecting you.'

'Oh really,' he said, his tone flat with disbelief.

'I just wanted you to know.'

'Well. Now I know. I appreciate your honesty,' he said.

'I'll be in touch when I can.'

'Have a good life,' he said and the phone clicked quietly in my ear.

I sat with a hand on the phone, doubts crowding in, wanting to call him back, wanting to erase everything I'd just said. I'd been looking for relief, looking for a way to escape the discomfort I felt. I think I'd even wanted him to give me a hard time so that I could resist and feel righteous. It was a question of my own integrity. Wasn't it? The injury in his voice had been awful after what we'd been through. And maybe he was right in his assumption that I was rejecting him. Maybe I was just being perverse, pushing him away because I needed space between me and the world. The job does provide such a perfect excuse. I meet most people in the course of my work and if I can't get emotionally involved there, then where else can I go? Private investigation is my whole life. It is why I get up in the morning and what puts me to bed at night. Most of the time I'm alone, but why not? I'm not unhappy and I'm not discontented. I had to freeze up until I knew what was going on. He would just have to misunderstand and to hell with him until I got this goddamn case nailed down and then maybe we could see where we stood – if it wasn't too late. Even if he was right, even if my breaking with him was an excess of conscience, a cover for something else – so what? There were no declarations between us, no commitments. I'd been to bed with him twice. What did I owe him? I don't know what love is about and I'm not sure I believe in it anyway. 'Then why so defensive?' came a little voice in reply, but I ignored it.

I had to push on. There was no other way to get out of this now. I picked up the phone and called Gwen.

'Hello?'

'Gwen. This is Kinsey,' I said, keeping my voice neutral. 'Something's come up and I think we should talk.'

'What is it?'

'I'd rather talk to you in person. Do you know where Rosie's is, down here at the beach?'

'Yes. I think I know the place,' she said with uncertainty.

'Can you meet me there in half an hour? It's important.'

'Well sure. Just let me get my shoes on. I'll be there as soon as I can.'

'Thanks,' I said.

I checked my watch. It was 7:45. I wanted her on my turf this time.

Rosie's was deserted, the lights dim, the whole place smelling of yesterday's cigarette smoke. I used to go to a movie theater when I was a kid and the ladies' rest room always smelled like that. Rosie was wearing a muu-muu in a print fabric that depicted many flamingos standing on one leg. She was seated at the end of the bar, reading a newspaper by the light of a small television set, which she'd placed on the bar, sound off. She looked up as I came in and she set the paper aside.

'It's too late for dinner. The kitchen is closed. I gave myself the night off,' she announced from across the room. 'You want something to eat, you gotta fix it yourself at home. Ask Henry Pitts. He'll do you something good.'

'I'm meeting someone for a drink,' I said. 'Big crowd you got.'

She looked around as though maybe she'd missed someone. I went over to the bar. She looked as though she'd just redyed her hair because her scalp was faintly pink. She was using a Maybelline dark brown eyeliner pencil on her brows, which she seemed to draw closer together every time, coquettishly arched. Pretty soon, she could take care of the whole thing with one wavy line.

'You got a man yet?' she asked.

'Six or eight a week,' I said. 'Do you have any cold chablis?'

'Just the crummy stuff. Help yourself.'

I went around behind the bar and got a glass, taking the big gallon jug of white wine out of the refrigerator under the bar. I poured a tumblerful, adding ice. I went over to my favorite booth and sat down, preparing myself mentally like an actor about to go on stage. It was time to stop being polite.

Gwen arrived forty minutes later, looking crisp and capable. Her greeting to me was pleasant enough, but under it I thought I could detect the tension, as though she had some inkling of what I was about to say. Rosie shuffled over, giving Gwen a brief appraising look. She must have thought Gwen looked okay because she honored her with a direct question.

'You want something to drink?'

'Scotch on the rocks. And could I have a glass of water, too, please?'

Rosie shrugged. She didn't care what people drank. 'You want to run a tab?' she said to me.

I shook my head. 'I'll take care of it now,' I said. Rosie moved off toward the bar. The look Gwen and I exchanged inadvertently indicated that both of us remembered her first reference to drinking Scotch in the days long past, when she was married to Laurence Fife and playing the perfect wife. I wondered what she was playing now.

'I revert now and then to the hard stuff,' she said, picking up my thought.

'Why not?' I replied.

She studied me briefly. 'What's up?'

The question was brave. I didn't think she really wanted to know, but she'd always struck me as the type to plunge right in. She probably whipped off big pieces of adhesive tape, too, with the same decisive thrust, just to get it over with.

'I talked to Colin,' I said. 'He remembered you.'

The modification in her manner was slight and a look, not of apprehension, but of wariness flickered in her eyes.

'Well that's nice,' she said. 'I haven't seen him for years, of course. I told you that.' She reached into her purse and took out a compact, checking her reflection quickly in the mirror, running a hand through her hair. Rosie came back with her Scotch and a glass of water. I paid the tab. Rosie tucked the money in the pocket of her muu-muu and wandered back to the bar while Gwen took a sip of water. She seemed to be holding herself in check, not trusting herself to pick up the conversation where we'd left off. I bumped her along for the sake of surprise.

'You never mentioned that you had an affair with Laurence,' I said.

A laugh burbled out. 'Who, me? With him? You can't be *serious*.'

I had to interrupt her merriment. 'Colin saw you out at the beach house that weekend when Nikki was out of town. I don't know all the details, but I can make a guess.'

I watched her compute that and shift gears. She was a very good little actress herself, but the slick cover she'd constructed was getting shabby from disuse. It had been a long time since she'd had to play this game and her timing was slightly off. She knew all the right lines, but the pretense was hard to sustain after an eight-year gap. She didn't seem to recognize the bluff and I kept my mouth shut. I could almost see what was happening inside her head. The terrible need to confess and be done with it, the pressure to spill it all out was too tempting to resist. She'd gone a few rounds with me and she'd pulled it off beautifully but only because I hadn't known which buttons to push.

'All right,' she blurted out rebelliously, 'I went to bed with him once. So what? I ran into him at the Palm Garden as a matter of fact. I nearly told you the other day. He was the one who told me Nikki was out of town. I was shocked that he'd even speak to me.' She switched to the Scotch, taking a big drink.

She was fabricating as fast as she could and it sounded nice but it was like listening to a record album. I decided to skip the cuts I didn't want to hear. I bumped her again.

'It was more than once, Gwen,' I said. 'You had a full-blown affair with him. Charlotte Mercer was screwing his head off back then but he broke it off with her. She says he was into something very hush-hush. "Very hot," to quote her. I think it was you.'

'What difference does it make if we had an affair. He'd been doing that for years.'

I let a little time elapse and when I spoke I kept my voice low, leaning forward slightly just to give her the full effect.

'I think you killed him.'

The animation drained out of her face as though a plug had been pulled. She started to say something but she couldn't get it out. I could see her mind working, but she couldn't put anything together quickly enough. She was struggling and I pressed.

'You want to tell me about it?' I said. My own heart was pounding and I could feel damp rings of sweat forming under my arms.

She shook her head but that was all she could manage. She seemed transfixed. Her face had changed, taking on that look people get in their sleep when all the guards are down. Her eyes were luminous and dark and two bright patches of pink appeared now in the pale of her cheeks, a clownish effect, as though she'd applied too much blusher in an artificial light. She blinked back tears then, propping her chin on her fist, looking off beyond me, fighting for self-control, but the last defense was breached and the guilt was pushing against that gorgeous façade. I'd seen it happen before. People can hold out just so long and then they fold. She was really an amateur at heart.

'You got pushed too hard and you broke,' I said, hoping I wasn't overplaying my hand. 'You waited until he and Nikki left town and then you used Diane's keys to get into the house. You put the oleander capsules in his little plastic vial, being careful to leave no prints, and then you left.'

'I hated him,' she said, mouth trembling. She blinked and a tear splashed on her shirt like a drop of rain. She took a deep breath, words coming out in a rush. 'He ruined my life, took my kids, robbed me blind, insulted, abused – oh my God, you have no idea. The *venom* in that man . . .'

She snatched up a napkin and pressed it to her eyes. Amazingly, Rosie didn't seem to notice her distress. She sat at the bar, probably reading Ann Landers, thinking *At Wit's End* should have turned hubby in for the obscene calls he made, while a customer confessed to murder right under her nose. To her right, the little television set flickered a Muppets rerun.

Gwen sighed, staring down at the tabletop. She reached over and picked up her glass, taking in a big slug of Scotch, which made her shudder as it went down. 'I didn't even feel bad about it, except for the kids. They took it hard and that surprised me. They were far better off with him gone.'

'Why the affair?' I probed.

'I don't know,' she said, folding and refolding the paper napkin. 'I guess it was my revenge. He was such an egotist. I knew he couldn't resist. After all, I'd insulted the hell out of him by having an affair with someone else. He couldn't tolerate that. I knew he'd want his own back. It wasn't even that hard to engineer. He wanted to prove something to himself. He wanted to show me what I'd passed up. There was even a certain amount of jazz to the sex for once. The hostility was so close to the surface that it gave us both a sick charge. God, I loathed him. I really did. And I'll tell you something else,' she said harshly. 'Killing him once just wasn't enough. I wish I could kill him again.'

She looked at me fully then and the enormity of what she was saying began to sink in.

'What about Nikki? What did she ever do to you?'

'I thought they'd acquit her,' she said. 'I never thought she'd go to jail, and when the sentence was handed down I wasn't going to stand up and take her place. By then it was too late.'

'So what else?' I said and I noticed that my tone was getting sullen. 'Did you kill the dog too?'

'I had nothing to do with that. He got hit Sunday morning. I drove Diane over there because she'd remembered that she'd left him out and she was upset. He was already lying in the street. My God, I wouldn't run over a *dog*,' she said emphatically, as though I should appreciate the delicacy of her sentiments.

'And the rest just fell into place? The oleander in the yard? The capsules upstairs?'

'One capsule. I doctored *one*.'

'Bullshit, Gwen. That's bullshit.'

'It's not. I'm telling the truth. I swear to it. I'd thought about it for a long time but I couldn't see a way to make it work. I wasn't even sure it would kill him. Diane was a wreck about the dog anyway so I drove her to my place and put her to bed. As soon as she was asleep, I took her keys and went back and that's all it was.' She spoke with an edge of defiance, as though having opened up this far there was no point in mincing words.

'What about the other two?' I snapped. 'What about Sharon and Libby Glass?'

She blinked at me, pulling back. 'I don't know what you're talking about.'

'Oh the hell you don't,' I said, getting up. 'You've lied to me since the first minute we met. I can't believe a goddamn word you say and you know it.'

She seemed startled by my energy. 'What are you going to do?'

'Give the information to Nikki,' I said. 'She paid for it. We'll let her decide.'

I moved away from the table, heading toward the door. Gwen grabbed her jacket and purse, keeping pace with me.

Out on the street, she snatched at my arm and I shook her off.

'Kinsey, wait . . .' Her face was remarkably pale.

'Blow it out your ass,' I said. 'You'd better hire yourself a hot attorney, babe, because you're going to need one.'

I moved off down the street, leaving Gwen behind.

25

I locked the door to my place and tried dialing Nikki out at the beach. The phone rang eight times and I hung up, pacing the room after that with an unsettled sensation in my chest. There was something off. There was something not right and I couldn't put my finger on what was bothering me. There was no feeling of closure. None. This should have been the end of it. The big climax. I'd been hired to find out who killed Laurence Fife and I had. The end. Finis. But I was left with half a case and a lot of loose ends. Gwen's killing of Laurence had been part premeditation and part impulse, but the rest of it didn't seem to fit. Why wasn't everything falling into place? I couldn't picture Gwen killing Libby Glass. Gwen had hated Laurence Fife for years, titillating herself perhaps with ways of killing him, maybe never even dreaming that she'd actually do it, never imagining that she could actually pull it off. She'd come up with the oleander scheme and suddenly she'd seen a way to make it work. A perfect opportunity had presented itself and she'd acted. Surely Libby Glass's death couldn't have been that easy to arrange. How did Gwen know about her? How did she know where she lived? How could she have gotten into that apartment? And how could she have counted on her taking medication of any kind? I couldn't picture Gwen driving to Vegas either. Couldn't imagine her shooting Sharon in cold blood. For what? What was the point? Killing Laurence had wiped out an old grudge, satisfied an ancient and bitter hatred between them, but why kill the other two? Blackmail? Threat of exposure? That might account for Sharon but why Libby Glass? Gwen had seemed truly self-righteous in her bewilderment. Like her denial of any responsibility for killing the dog. There was just that odd note of genuine outrage in her voice. It didn't make sense.

Unless there was someone else involved. Someone else who killed.

I felt a chill.

Oh my God. Lyle? Charlie? I sat down, blinking rapidly, hand across my mouth. I'd bought into the notion that one person killed all three, but maybe not. Maybe there was another possibility. I tried it out. Gwen had murdered Laurence Fife. Why couldn't someone else have spotted the opening and taken advantage of it? The timing was close, the method the same. Of course it was going to look like it was all part of the same set-up.

I thought about Lyle. I thought about his face, the strange imperceptibly mismatched eyes: sullen, watchful, belligerent. He said he'd been with Libby three days before she died. I knew he'd heard about Laurence's death. He was not a man who possessed a giant intellect, but he could have managed that much, imitating the cunning of someone else – even stoned.

I called my answering service. 'I'm going down to Los Angeles,' I said. 'If Nikki Fife calls, I want you to give her the telephone number of the Hacienda motel down there and tell her it's important that she get in touch. But no one else. I don't want it known that I'm out of town. I'll check in with you often enough to pick up whatever calls come in. Just say I'm tied up and you don't know where I am. You got that?'

'All right, Miss Millhone. Will do,' she said cheerfully and then clicked off. God. If I'd said to her, 'Hold the calls. I'm slitting my throat,' she'd have responded with the same blank good will.

*

The drive to Los Angeles was good for me – soothing, uneventful. It was after nine and there wasn't that much traffic on the darkened road south. On my left, hills swelled and rolled, covered with low vegetation – no trees, no rocks. On my right, the ocean rumbled, almost at arm's length, looking very black except for a ruffle of white here and there. I passed Summerland, Carpinteria, passed the oil derricks and the power plant, which was garlanded with tiny lights like a decorative display at Christmastime. There was something restful about having nothing to worry about except having a wreck and getting killed. It freed my mind for other things.

I had made a mistake, a false assumption, and I felt like a novice. On the other hand, I'd made the very assumption that everyone else had made: same M.O., same murderer. But now I didn't think that was true. Now it seemed to me the only explanation that made any sense was that someone else had killed Libby Glass – and Sharon too. I drove through Ventura, Oxnard, Camarillo, where the state mental asylum was located. I've heard that there is less tendency to violence among the institutionalized insane than there is in the citizenry at large and I believe that. I thought about Gwen without surprise or dismay, my mind jumping forward and back randomly. Somehow I was more offended by the minor crimes of a Marcia Threadgill who tried for less, without any motivation at all beyond greed. I wondered if Marcia Threadgill was the new standard of morality against which I would now judge all other sins. Hatred, I could understand – the need for revenge, the payment of old debts. That's what the notion of 'justice' was all about anyway: settling up.

I went over the big hill into Thousand Oaks, with traffic picking up; tract housing stretched out on either side of the road, then shopping malls packed end to end. The night air was damp and I kept the windows rolled down. I felt over into the backseat for my briefcase and fumbled with the catch. I tucked my little automatic into my jacket pocket, encountering a wad of papers. I pulled them out and glanced down. Sharon Napier's bills. I'd stuck them in my windbreaker on the way out of her place and I hadn't thought about them since. I'd have to go through them. I tossed them on the passenger seat and looked at my watch by the icy wash of highway light. It was 10:10 – forty-five minutes of driving left, maybe more given traffic on the surface roads once I got off the freeway. I thought about Charlie, wondering if I'd blown a perfectly nice relationship. He didn't seem like the type to forgive and forget, but who knew. He was a lot more yielding than I was, that was for sure. My thoughts rambled on disjunctively. Lyle had known I was driving to Vegas. I wasn't sure how Sharon connected, but I'd figure that out. Blackmail still seemed like the best bet. The letter I couldn't figure at all. How had Libby come by that? Or had she? Maybe Lyle and *Sharon* were in cahoots. Maybe Lyle got the letter from her. Maybe he was *planting* the letter among Libby's effects, not trying to take it away. It was certainly to his advantage to reinforce the idea of Libby's romantic tie to Laurence Fife. He had known I was stopping back through to pick up her boxes. He could have made it back to Los Angeles well in advance of me since I'd stopped for the night to see Diane. Maybe he had deliberately timed it closely to incite my curiosity about what might have been tucked away there. My mind veered off that and I thought about Lieutenant Dolan with a faint smile. He was so sure Nikki had killed her husband, so satisfied with that. I'd have to put a call through to him when I got back. I thought about Lyle again. I didn't intend to see him that night. He wasn't as smart as Gwen, but he might be dangerous. *If* it was him. I didn't think I should jump to conclusions again.

I checked into the Hacienda at 11:05, went straight to room #2, and put myself to bed. Arlette's mother was on the desk. She is twice as fat.

In the morning, I showered and got back into the same clothes, staggering out to the car to retrieve the overnight case I kept in the crowded backseat. I went back to my room and brushed my teeth – oh blessed relief – and ran a comb through my hair. I went down to a delicatessen on the corner of Wilshire and Bundy, where I ordered scrambled eggs, sausage links, a toasted bagel with cream cheese, coffee and fresh orange juice. Whoever invented breakfast really did it good.

I walked back up to the Hacienda to find Arlette waving a massive arm out the office door for me. Her round face was flushed, her little cap of blonde curls in a flyaway state, her eyes squeezed almost to invisibility by the heavy cheeks. I wondered when she'd last seen her own neck. Still, I liked her, irksome as she was at times.

'There's someone on the phone for you and she sounds real upset. I told her you were out but I said I'd flag you down. Thank goodness you're back,' she said to me, out of breath and wheezing hard.

I hadn't seen Arlette so excited since she found out that pantyhose came in queen-size. I went into the office with Arlette hard on my heels, breathing heavily. The receiver was on the counter and I picked it up.

'Hello?'

'Kinsey, this is Nikki.'

Why the dread in her voice, I thought automatically. 'I tried calling you last night,' I said. 'What's the matter? Are you okay?'

'Gwen's dead.'

'I just talked to her last night,' I said blankly. Killed herself. She'd killed herself. Oh shit, I thought.

'It happened this morning. Hit-and-run driver. I just heard it on the news. She was jogging along Cabana Boulevard and someone ran her down and then skipped.'

'I don't believe it. Are you sure?'

'Positive. I tried calling you and the service said you were out of town. What are you doing in L.A.?'

'I've got to check out something down here but I should be back tonight,' I said, thinking fast. 'Look, would you see if you can find out the details?'

'I can try.'

'Call Lieutenant Dolan at Homicide. Tell him I told you to ask.'

'Homicide,' she said, startled.

'Nikki, he's a *cop*. He'll know what's going on. And it may not be an accident anyway, so see what he has to say and I'll call you as soon as I get back.'

'Well, okay,' she said dubiously, 'I'll see what I can do.'

'Thanks.' I hung up the phone.

'Is someone dead?' Arlette asked. 'Was it someone you knew?'

I looked right at her but I drew a blank. Why Gwen? What was happening?

She followed me out of the office and toward my room.

'Is there anything I can do to help? Do you need anything? You look awful, Kinsey. You're pale as a ghost.'

I closed the door behind me. I thought about that last image of Gwen, standing on the street, her face white. *Could* it have been an accident? Coincidence? Things were moving too quickly. Someone was beginning to panic and for reasons I still couldn't quite understand.

A possibility flashed into my head and out. I stood stock-still, running it by me again like an old film clip. Maybe so. Maybe yes. It was all going to come together soon. It was all going to fit.

I threw everything into the backseat of my car, not even bothering to check out. I'd mail Arlette the damn twelve bucks.

*

The drive to the Valley was a blur, the car moving automatically, though I paid no attention whatever to road, sun, traffic, smog. When I reached the house in Sherman Oaks where Lyle was laying brick, I saw his battered truck parked out front. I didn't have any more time to waste and I didn't want to play games. I locked the car and went up the drive, going around the side of the house to the back. I caught sight of Lyle before he caught sight of me. He was bending over a pile of two-by-fours: faded jeans, work boots, no shirt, a cigarette in the corner of his mouth.

'Lyle.'

He turned around. I had the gun out and trained on him. I held it with two hands, legs apart, meaning business. He froze instantly where he stood, not saying a word.

I felt cold and my voice was tight, but the gun never wavered an inch. 'I want some answers and I want them now,' I said. I saw him glance to his right. There was a hammer lying on the ground but he made no move.

'Back up,' I said, stepping forward slightly until I was between him and the hammer. He did as instructed, the pale blue eyes sliding back to mine, hands coming up.

'I don't want to shoot you, Lyle, but I will.'

For once, he didn't look sullen or sly or arrogant. He stared straight at me with the first sign of respect I'd seen from him.

'You're the boss,' he said.

'Don't fuckin' smart-mouth *me*,' I snapped. 'I'm not in the mood. Now sit down in the grass. Out there. And don't move a muscle unless I tell you to.'

Obediently, he moved out to a small stretch of grass and sat down, eyes on me the whole time. It was quiet and I could hear birds chirping stupidly but we seemed to be alone and I liked it that way. I kept the gun pointed right at his chest, willing my hands not to shake. The sun was hot and it made him squint.

'Tell me about Libby Glass,' I said.

'I didn't kill her,' he shot back uneasily.

'That's not the point. I want to know what went on. I want to know what you haven't told me yet. When did you see her last?'

He shut his mouth.

'*Tell me!*'

He didn't have Gwen's poise and he didn't have her smarts. The sight of the gun seemed to help him make up his mind.

'Saturday.'

'The day she died, right?'

'That's right, but I didn't do anything. I went over to see her and we had a big fight and she was upset.'

'All right, all right. Skip the build-up. What else?'

He was silent.

'Lyle,' I said warningly. The muscles in his face seemed to pull together like a drawstring purse and he started to weep. He put his hands up over his face pathetically. He'd kept it in for a long time. If I was wrong about this, I was wrong about everything. I couldn't let him off the hook.

'Just tell me,' I said, tone dead, 'I need to know.' I thought he was coughing but I knew what I heard were sobs. He might have been nine years old, looking squeezed up and frail and small.

'I gave her a *tranq*,' he said with anguish. 'She asked for one and I found this bottle in the medicine cabinet and gave it to her. God, I even gave her a glass of water. I loved her so much.'

The first rush subsided and he dashed at the tears on his face with a grubby hand, leaving streaks of dirt. He hugged himself, rocking back and forth in misery, tears streaming down his bony cheeks again.

'Go on,' I said.

'I left after that but I felt bad and I went back later and that's when I found her dead on the bathroom floor. I was afraid they'd find my fingerprints and think I'd done something to her so I wiped the whole place down.'

'And you took the tranquilizers with you when you left?'

He nodded, pressing his fingers into his eye sockets as though he could force the tears back. 'I flushed 'em down the toilet when I got home. I smashed up the bottle and threw it away.'

'How'd you know that's what it was?'

'I don't know. I just knew. I remembered that guy, the one up north and I knew he'd died that way. She might not have taken the goddamn thing if it weren't for me, but we had that screaming fight and she was so mad, she shook. I didn't even know she had any tranqs till she asked for one and I didn't see anything wrong with that. I went back to apologize.' The worst of it seemed to be over with and he sighed deeply, his voice almost normal again.

'What else?'

'I don't know. The phone was unplugged. I plugged it back in and wiped that down too,' he said woodenly. 'I didn't mean any harm. I just had to protect myself. I wouldn't poison her, I wouldn't have done that to her, I swear to God. I didn't have anything to do with that or anything else except I cleaned the place. In case there were fingerprints. I didn't want anything pointing to me. And I took the bottle the pills were in. I did that.'

'But you didn't break into the storage bin,' I said.

He shook his head.

I lowered the gun. I'd half known but I had to be sure.

'Are you going to turn me in?'

'No. Not you.'

I went back to the car and sat blankly, wondering in some vague irrational way if I really would have used the gun. I didn't think so. Tough. I'm tough, scaring the shit out of some dumb kid. I shook my head, feeling tears of my own. I started the car and put it into gear, heading back over the hill toward West L.A. I had one more stop and then I could drive back to Santa Teresa and clean it up. I thought I knew now who it was.

26

I caught sight of my reflection in one of the mirrored walls across from the entrance to Haycraft and McNiece. I looked like I was ready for the last round-up: seedy, disheveled, mouth grim. Even Allison, in her buckskin shirt with the fringes on the sleeves, seemed alarmed by the sight of me, and her pre-rehearsed receptionist's smile dropped from sixty watts to twenty-five.

'I have to talk to Garry Steinberg,' I said, my tone apparently indicating that I wouldn't take much shit.

'He's back in his office,' she said timidly. 'Do you know which one it is?'

I nodded and pushed through the swinging doors. I caught sight of Garry walking down the narrow interior corridor toward his office, slapping a batch of unopened mail against his thigh.

'Garry?'

He turned, his face lighting up at the sight of me and then turning hesitant. 'Where'd you come from? You look exhausted.'

'I drove down last night. Can we talk?'

'Sure. Come on in.'

He turned left into his office, gathering up a stack of files on the chair in front of his desk. 'You want some coffee? Can I get you anything?' He tossed the mail on the file cabinet.

'No, I'm fine but I need to check out a hunch.'

'Fire away,' he said, sitting down.

'Didn't you tell me once upon a time—'

'Last week,' he inserted.

'Yeah, I guess it was. You mentioned that Fife's accounts were being put on computer.'

'Sure, we were converting everything. Makes it a hell of a lot easier on us and it's better for the client too. Especially at tax time.'

'Well what if the books had been fiddled with?'

'You mean embezzlement?'

'In a word,' I said with irony. 'Wouldn't that have shown up pretty quickly?'

'Absolutely. You think Fife was milking his own accounts?'

'No,' I said slowly, 'I think Charlie Scorsoni was. That's part of what I need to ask you about. Could he have skimmed money out of the estates he was representing back then?'

'Sure. It can be done and it's not that hard,' Garry said appreciatively, 'but it might be a bitch to track. It really depends on how he did it.' He thought for a moment, apparently warming to the idea. He shrugged. 'For instance, he could have set up some kind of special account or an escrow account for all his estates – maybe two or three phony accounts within this overall account. A large dividend check comes in, he diverts a percentage of the check from the estate it's supposed to be credited to, and he credits it to a phony account instead.'

'Could Libby have realized something was wrong?'

'She might have. She had a head for that kind of thing. She'd have had to trace the dividends through Moody's Dividend Book, which gives the amount of each dividend by company. Then if there was some kind of discrepancy, she might have asked for records or documentation – bank statements, canceled checks, stuff like that.'

'Yeah, well Lyle told me last week that there were lots of phone calls back and forth, some attorney driving down for dinner. It finally occurred to me that Charlie might have engineered an affair with her in the hopes that she'd cover for him . . .'

'Or maybe he offered her a cut,' Garry said.

'Oh God, would she have done that?'

Garry shrugged. 'Hey, who knows? Would *he*?'

I stared down at his desk top. 'Yeah, I think so,' I said. 'You know, everybody kept saying that she was involved with some Santa Teresa attorney and we all assumed it was Fife because both died the same way. But if I'm right about this embezzlement business then I need proof. Are the files still at your place?'

'No, I've got 'em right here as a matter of fact. I thought I'd take a look at 'em during my lunch hour. I've been having cottage cheese but I don't think that counts as food so I thought I'd do without. I brought 'em in yesterday and then I got tied up. Now that you mention it, I do think she was working on that account when she died, because the cops found her briefcase at her place,' he said. He gave me a curious look. 'How'd you fix on him?'

I shook my head. 'I don't know. It just popped into my brain and it fitted. Charlie told me that Fife made a trip to Los Angeles sometime in the week before he died, but I don't think that's true. I think probably Charlie made the trip himself and it would have been within a day or two after Laurence died. Libby had a bottle of tranqs and I think he doctored some – who knows, maybe all of 'em. We'll never know about that.'

'Jesus. He kill Fife too?'

I shook my head. 'No, I know who killed Fife. My guess is that Charlie saw a way to bail himself out. Maybe Libby wouldn't play ball with him or maybe she'd threatened to turn him in. Not that I've got any evidence one way or the other.'

'Hey, it'll come,' he said soothingly. 'If it's there, we'll find it. I'll start on the files this afternoon.'

'Good,' I said, 'I'd like that.'

'Take care.'

We shook hands across the desk.

I drove back to Santa Teresa, resolutely refusing to think of Gwen. Thinking about Charlie Scorsoni was depressing enough. I would have to check his whereabouts at the time Sharon died, but he could easily have checked out of the hotel in Denver and flown straight to Las Vegas, picking up my location from the answering service, finding my motel, and then following me to the Fremont. I thought about Sharon – that moment in the coffee shop when I thought she'd seen someone she knew. She'd said it was the pit boss signaling the end of her break, but I was sure she was lying. Charlie may have put in an appearance then, pulling back when he spotted me. Maybe she thought he had shown up to pay her off. I was relatively certain she'd been leaning on him for bucks, but then again, I'd have to pin that down. Sharon must have known that Fife was never involved with Libby Glass sexually. It was Charlie who'd been making the trips down to Los Angeles to discuss the accounts. Sharon must have kept her mouth shut during the trial, watching the whole tale unfold, biding her time, eventually cashing in on whatever information she had. It was also possible that Charlie Scorsoni hadn't known where she was – that I'd led him straight down the path to her door. I was aware, as I went over the sequence of events, that much of it sounded like a lot of fancy guesswork, but I felt I was headed in the right direction and I could probe now for corroborating evidence.

If Charlie had killed Gwen in that hit-and-run accident, there were bound to be ways to trace it back to him: hair and fibers on the fender of his car, which probably sustained some damage that would have to be repaired; paint flakes and glass fragments on Gwen's clothes. Maybe even a witness somewhere. It would have been much wiser if Charlie'd never made a move – just held tight and kept his mouth shut, lying low. It probably would have been impossible to put a case together against him after all these years. There was an arrogance in his behavior, a hint that he considered himself too smart and too slick to get caught. No one was *that* good. Especially at the rate he'd been operating these days. He had to be making mistakes.

And why not just go down for the count on the original embezzlement? He must have been desperately trying to cover for himself in Laurence Fife's eyes. But even if he'd been exposed, even if he'd been caught, I didn't believe Laurence would have turned him in. As sleazy as Fife had been in his personal life, I knew he was scrupulously honest in business matters. Still, Charlie was his best friend and the two went a long way back together. He might have warned Charlie off or smacked his hand – perhaps even dissolved the partnership. But I didn't think Charlie would have gone to jail or been disbarred from the practice of law. His life probably wouldn't have been ruined and he probably wouldn't have lost what he'd worked so hard to achieve. He would have lost Laurence Fife's good opinion and his trust perhaps, but he must have known that when he first put his hand in the cookie jar. The ludicrous fact of the matter is that in this day and age, a white-collar criminal can become a celebrity, a hero, can go on talk shows and write bestselling books. So what was there to sweat? Society will forgive just about anything except homicide. It was hard to shrug that one off, hard to rationalize that one away and whereas before, Charlie might have come out somewhat tarnished but intact, he was in big trouble now and things just seemed to be getting worse.

I didn't even address myself to the matter of his relationship to me. He'd played me for a sucker, just as he'd done with Libby Glass, and she, in her innocence, at least had a better excuse for the tumble than I did. It had been too long since I'd cared about anyone, too long since I'd taken that risk and I'd already invested too much. I just had to slam the gate shut emotionally and move on, but it didn't sit well with me.

When I reached Santa Teresa, I went straight to the office, taking with me the sheaf of bills from Sharon Napier's apartment. For the first time, I was beginning to think those might be significant. I went through them with an abstract curiosity that felt ghoulish nevertheless. She was dead and it seemed obscene now to note that she'd bought lingerie that had gone unpaid for, cosmetics, shoes. Her utilities were a month behind, with dunning notices from several small businesses including her tax man, a chiropractor and a health spa membership renewal. Visa and Mastercharge had gotten churlish and American Express wanted its card back in no uncertain terms, but it was her telephone bill that interested me. In the area code that included Santa Teresa, there were three calls in the month of March, not an excessive number but telling. Two of the calls were to Charlie Scorsoni's office – both on the same day, ten minutes apart. The third number she'd called I didn't immediately recognize but the Santa Teresa exchange was the same. I picked up my Cross-Reference Directory. The number was for John Powers's house at the beach.

I dialed Ruth, not allowing myself to hesitate. Surely Charlie hadn't told her I'd broken with him. I couldn't picture him confiding his personal affairs to anyone. If he was there, I'd have to think fast and I wasn't sure what I intended to say. The information I needed was from her.

'Scorsoni and Powers,' she sang.

'Oh hi, Ruth. This is Kinsey Millhone,' I said, heart in my throat. 'Is Charlie there?'

'Oh hi, Kinsey. No he's not,' she said with a hint of regret in my behalf. 'He's in court up in Santa Maria for the next two days.'

Thank God for that, I thought, and took a deep breath. 'Well maybe you can help me instead,' I said. 'I was just going over some bills for a client and it looks like she was in touch with him. Do you happen to remember someone calling him a couple of times maybe six, eight weeks ago? Her name was Sharon Napier. Long-distance.'

'Oh, the one who used to work for him. Yes, I remember that. What did you need to know?'

'Well I can't quite tell from this if she actually got through to him or not. It looks like she called on a Friday – the twenty-first of March. Does that ring a bell?'

'Oh yes. Absolutely,' Ruth said efficiently. 'She called asking for him and he was out at Mr Powers's house. She was very insistent that I put her through but I didn't feel I should give out the number without checking with him, so I told her to call me back and then I checked with him out at the beach and he said it was fine. I hope that's all right. I hope she hasn't hired you to pester him or anything.'

I laughed. 'Oh heavens, Ruth, would I do that to him? I did see the number for John Powers and I just thought maybe she talked to him instead.'

'Oh no. He was out of town that weekend. He's usually gone around the twenty-first for a couple of days. I have it right here on my calendar. Mr Scorsoni was taking care of his dogs.'

'Oh well, that would explain it,' I said casually. 'God, that's been a great help. Now the only other thing I need to check is that trip to Tucson.'

'Tucson?' she said. Doubt was beginning to creep into her voice, that protective tone secretaries sometimes take when it suddenly occurs to them that someone wants something they're not supposed to get. 'What is this about, Kinsey?

Maybe I could be of more help if I understood what this has to do with a client of yours. Mr Scorsoni's pretty strict about things like that.'

'Oh no, that's something else. And I can check that out myself so don't worry about it. I can always give Charlie a buzz when he gets back and ask him.'

'Well, I can give you his motel number in Santa Maria if you want to call him yourself,' she said. She was trying to play it both ways – helpful to me if my questions were legitimate, helpful to Charlie if they weren't – but in any case, dumping the whole matter in his lap. For an old lady, she was adroit.

I jotted the number down dutifully, knowing I'd never call him but glad to get a fix on him anyway. I wanted to tell her not to mention my call but I didn't see how I could do it without tipping my hand. I just had to hope that Charlie wouldn't check in with her anytime soon. If she told him what I'd been asking about, he would know like a shot that I was on his tail and he wouldn't like that a bit.

I put in a call to Dolan at Homicide. He was out but I left a message, 'important' underlined, that he should call me back when he got in. I tried Nikki at the beach and got her on the third ring.

'Hi, Nikki, it's me,' I said. 'Is everything okay?'

'Oh yeah. We're fine. I still haven't quite recovered from the shock of Gwen's death, but I don't know what to do about that. I never even knew the woman and it still seems a shame.'

'Did you get any of the details from Dolan? I just tried to call him and he's out.'

'Not a lot,' she said. 'He was awfully rude. Worse than I remember him and he wouldn't tell me much except the car that hit her was black.'

'Black?' I said with disbelief. I was picturing Charlie's pale blue Mercedes and I'd fully expected some detail that would tie that in. 'Are you sure?'

'That's what he said. I guess the detectives have been checking with body shops and garages but so far nothing's turned up.'

'That's odd,' I said.

'Are you coming out for a drink? I'd love to hear what's going on.'

'Maybe later. I'm trying to clean up a couple of loose ends. I'll tell you what else I need. Maybe you can answer this. Remember the letter I showed you that Laurence wrote—'

'Sure, the one to Libby Glass,' she broke in quickly.

'Yeah, well I'm almost sure now that the letter was written to Elizabeth Napier instead.'

'Who?'

'I'll fill you in on that later. I suspect that Elizabeth Napier was the one he got involved with when he was married to Gwen. Sharon Napier's mother.'

'Oh, the *scandal*,' she said, light breaking. 'Oh sure, it could well be. He never would tell me much about that. Messy business. I know the story because Charlotte Mercer filled me in on that, but I was never really sure of the name. God, that would have been way back in Denver, just after his law-school days.'

I hesitated. 'Can you think who else would have known about that letter? Who could have had access to it? I mean, could Gwen?'

'I suppose so,' she said. 'Certainly Charlie would. He was working as a law clerk in the firm that represented the husband in that divorce and he lifted the letter from what I heard.'

'He what?'

'Stole it. Oh I'm sure that's the one. Didn't I ever tell you the end of that? Charlie snitched the letter, just cleaned out all the evidence, and that's why they ended up settling out of court. She didn't do that well but at least it got Laurence off the hook.'

'What happened to the letter? Could Charlie have kept the letter himself?'

'I don't know. I always assumed it had been destroyed but I guess he could have hung on to it. He never did get caught and I don't think the husband's attorney ever figured it out. You know how things disappear in offices. Probably some secretary got fired.'

'Could Gwen have testified to any of this?'

'What *am* I, the district attorney's office?' she said with a laugh. 'How do I know what Gwen knew?'

'Well, whatever it was, she's quiet now,' I said.

'Oh,' she said and I could tell her smile had faded fast. 'Oh, I don't like that. That's a terrible thought.'

'I'll tell you the rest when I see you. If I can get out there, I'll call first and make sure you're home.'

'We'll be here. I take it you're making progress.'

'Rapidly,' I said.

Her good-byes were puzzled and mine were brief.

I hauled out my typewriter and committed everything I knew to paper in a lengthy and detailed report. Another piece had fallen into place. The night the storage bin was broken into, it was Charlie, not Lyle, who was planting the letter among Libby's belongings, hoping I'd find it, hoping he could shore up his own tale about Laurence Fife's 'affair' with Libby Glass. Which probably also explained the key to her apartment that had been found on Laurence's key ring in the office. It wouldn't have been hard for Charlie to plant that one too. I typed on, feeling exhausted but determined to get it all down. In the back of my mind, I kept thinking of it as a safeguard, an insurance policy, but I wasn't sure what kind of coverage I needed. Maybe none. Maybe I didn't need protection, I thought. As it turned out, I was wrong.

27

I finished my report and locked it in my desk drawer. I went out to the parking lot and retrieved my car, heading north toward Charlie's house on Missile Avenue. Two doors down from his place was a house called Tranquility for reasons unknown. I parked in front of it and walked back. Charlie's house was a two-story structure with a painted-yellow-shingle exterior and a dark shingled roof, a bay window in front, a long narrow driveway to the left. It was the sort of house that might appear in an establishing shot for a television family show, something that might come on at 8:00 P.M., everything looking regular and wholesome and suitable for kids. There was no sign of his car in the drive, no sign of occupants. I eased along the driveway toward the garage, looking back over my shoulder as I went. There weren't even any nosy neighbors peering out at me. When I reached the one-car garage, I went around to the side, cupping my hands so that I could peer into the window. It was empty: a woodworking bench along the back wall, old lawn furniture, dust. I looked around, wondering whose black car it was and why the cops hadn't gotten a line on it yet. If I could fill in that blank, then I'd have something to talk to Con Dolan about. I was going to get back in touch with him anyway, but I wanted to have something concrete.

I walked back up the drive to my car and sat, a favorite occupation of mine. It was getting dark. I glanced at my watch. It was 6:45 and that startled me. I desperately longed for a glass of wine and I decided to drive on out to Nikki's. She had said she'd be home. I turned the car around, making an illegal U-turn, and drove back down Missile to the freeway, heading north. I got off at La Cuesta, heading toward the beach by way of Horton Ravine, a large sprawling expanse of land that is known as 'a luxury residential development'. Horton Ravine once belonged to one family, but it is now divided into million-dollar parcels to accommodate the housing of the nouveau riche. In Santa Teresa, Montebello is considered 'old' money, Horton Ravine the 'new' – but nobody really takes the distinction seriously. Rich is rich and we all know what that means. The roads through Horton Ravine are narrow and winding, overhung with trees, and the only difference I could see was that here some houses are visible from the road whereas in Montebello they are not. I came out at Ocean Way and swung left, the road running parallel now to the bluffs, with a number of elegant properties tucked into the selvage of land that lay between the road and the cliffs.

I passed John Powers's house, almost missing the place since I'd come at it before from the other direction. I caught a quick glimpse of the roof, which was almost level with the road. I had a sudden thought and I slammed on the brakes, pulling over to the side. I sat for a moment, heart thudding with excitement. I turned the key off and stuck my little automatic in my jeans, taking the flashlight out of the glove compartment. I flicked it on. The light was good. There were very few streetlamps along this stretch and those I could see were ornamental, as dim and misty-looking as a lithograph, casting ineffectual circles of light that scarcely penetrated the dark. I got out of the car and locked it.

There were no sidewalks, just tangles of ivy along the road. The houses were widely spaced with wooded lots in between, ratcheting now with crickets and other night-singing insects. I walked back along the road to the Powers's place. There were no houses at all across from it. No cars in either direction. I paused. There were no lights visible in the house. I headed down the driveway, shining the light in front of me.

I wondered if Powers was still out of town, and if so where the dogs were. If Charlie was going to be up in Santa Maria for two days he wouldn't have left them unattended.

The night was still, the ocean pounding, a recurrent thunder like a storm about to break. There was only a faint crust of moon against the hazy night sky. It was chilly, too, the air smelling lush and damp. The flashlight cut a narrow trail down the drive, illuminating in a sudden band of white the gateway across the carport. Beyond it was John Powers's car, face-in, and even from where I stood I could see that it was black. I wasn't surprised. The white picket fencing that comprised the gate was padlocked but I eased around to the left of the carport toward the front of the house. I shone the light on the car. It was a Lincoln. I couldn't tell what year but the car wasn't old. I checked the fender on the left-hand side and it was fine. I could feel my heart beginning to thump dully with dread. The right-hand fender was crumpled, the headlight broken out, metal rim crimped and pulled away, bumper indented slightly. I tried not to think of Gwen's body at the moment of impact. I could guess what it must have been like.

I heard an abrupt squealing of brakes on the road above, the high whine of a car backing up at high speed. There was a sudden wash of bright light as a car pulled into the drive. I ducked automatically, flicking out the flashlight. If it was Charlie, I was dead. I caught a glimpse of blue. Oh shit. He'd called Ruth. He was back. He knew. The Mercedes's headlights were directed straight into the carport, with only Powers's vehicle shielding me from complete exposure. I heard the car door slam and I ran.

I flew across the yard, fairly skimming the rough cut grass. Behind me, almost soundlessly, came the low scuffling of the dogs in long loping strides. I started down the narrow wooden steps to the beach, my vision inky after the harsh glare of the headlights. I missed a step and half slid my way down to the next, groping blindly. Above me, only yards away, the black dog grumbled and started down, panting, toenails scrambling on the steps. I glanced up and back. The black one was just above my head. Without even thinking about it, I reached back and grabbed at one of his long bony forelegs, yanking abruptly. The dog let out a yelp of surprise and I shoved it forward, half flinging it down the steep rocky embankment. The other dog was whining, a ninety-five-pound sissy, picking its way down the stairs with trepidation. I nearly lost my balance but I righted myself, loosened soil tumbling down into the darkness in front of me. I could hear the black dog lunging at the cliffside but he couldn't seem to get a purchase, prowling back and forth restlessly. I was nearly lying on my side as I slid down the last few feet, tumbling onto the soft sand. The gun popped out of my hand and I scrambled frantically until my fingers closed over the butt again. The flashlight was long gone. I didn't even remember when I'd lost my hold on it. The black dog was loping toward me again. I waited until he was almost on me and then I lifted a foot, kicking viciously, bringing the gun down on his head. He yelped. He'd clearly never been trained to attack. My advantage was that I knew he was a danger to me and he was just beginning to figure out how treacherous I was. He backed off, barking. I made a quick choice. North along the beach, the steep cliffs continued for miles, interrupted only by Harley's Beach, which was too isolated for sanctuary. North, the dog was blocking my path. The beach to my right would eventually straggle past the town and it couldn't be more than a couple of miles. I began to move backward, away from the dog. He stood there, head down, barking vigorously. The waves were already washing up over my shoes and I began to lift my feet, trudging backward through the surf. I turned, holding the gun up, beginning to wade. The dog paced back and forth, barking only occasionally now. The next big surge of waves crashed against my knees, drenching me to the waist. I gasped from the shock of cold, glancing back with a burble of fear as I caught sight of Charlie at the top of the cliff. The outside lights were on now, his big body sculptured in shadow. his face blank. He was staring straight down at me. I propelled myself forward, nearly flinging myself through the waist-high water, edging toward the rocks at the extreme southern limits of the beach. I reached the rocks, slippery and sharp, a mass of granite that had broken loose from the cliff and tumbled into the sea. I scrambled across, hampered by my soggy jeans, which clung to my legs, by my shoes weighted down with water, hampered by the gun, which I didn't dare relinquish. Jagged barnacles and slime alternated under me. I slipped once and something bit into my left knee, right through my jeans. I pushed on, reaching hardpacked sand again, the beach widening slightly.

There was no sign of the Powers house around the bend. No sign of either dog. I had known they couldn't follow this far even if they'd tried, but I wasn't sure about Charlie. I didn't know if he'd come down the wooden stairs and trail me along the beach or simply wait. I glanced back with dread, but the hill projected, obscuring even the light. All he had to do was get back in his car. If he took a parallel path to mine, he could intercept me easily on the other end. Eventually we'd both end up at Ludlow Beach, but I couldn't turn back. Harley's Beach was worse, too far from streetlights and residential help. I began to run in earnest, uncertain how far I had to go yet. My wet clothes stuck to me, clammy and cold, but my prime concern was the gun. I'd already dropped it once and I knew sea water had curled up toward it as I crossed the rocks. I didn't think it had gotten wet but I wasn't sure. I could see somewhat better now, but the beach was littered with rocks and kelp. I prayed I wouldn't twist an ankle. If I couldn't run, then Charlie could track me at his own pace and I'd have no way out. I glanced back: no sign of him, sound masked by the breaking surf. I didn't think he was there. Once I got to Ludlow Beach, there were bound to be other people, passing motorists. As long as I was running, the fear seemed contained, adrenaline driving out every sensation except the urge to flee. The wind was down, but it was cold and I was wet to the bone.

The beach narrowed again and I found myself running in shallow water, slogging my way through the churning surf. I tried to get my bearings but I'd never been up this far. I caught sight of a wooden stairway zigzagging up the cliff to my left, the wind-bleached railing showing white against the dark tangle of vegetation clinging to the cliff. I followed the line up with my eyes. I guessed that it was Sea Shore Park, which ran along the bluff. Parking lot. Houses across the road. I grabbed the rail and started up, knees aching as I climbed, chest heaving. I reached the top and peered over the rim, heart stopping again.

Charlie's 450 SL was parked above, headlights raking the fence. I ducked back and started down the stairs again, a mewing sound in my throat that I couldn't control. My breathing was ragged, my chest afire. I hit the sand again and ran on, accelerating my pace. The sand was sluggish now, too soft, and I cut to my right, searching out the wet sand that was packed hard. At least I was getting warmer now, wet clothes chafing, water dripping from strands of hair matted with salt. My left knee was stinging and I could feel something warm ooze through my pantleg. The beach was interrupted not by rocks this time but by the sheer face of the cliff, jutting out like a pie-shaped wedge into the black of the sea. I waded out into the waves, undercurrent tugging at me as I rounded the bend. Ludlow Beach was visible just ahead. I nearly wept with relief. Painfully. I began to run again, trying for a pace I could live with. I could make out lights now, dark patches of palm against gray sky. I slowed to a jog, trying to catch my breath. I stopped finally, bending from the waist, my mouth dry, sweat or salt water streaking down my face. My cheeks were hot and my eyes stung. I wiped my mouth on the back of my hand and moved on, walking this time, fear creeping up again until my heart was battering my ribs.

This stretch of beach was gentle and clean, looking pale gray, widening to the left where the high cliff finally dwindled away into sloping hillside, slipping down to the flat of the sand. Beyond, I could see the long stretch of parking lot and beyond that, the street, well lighted, empty and inviting. The beach park closed at 8:00 and I thought the parking lot would probably be chained and locked. Still the sight of Charlie's pale blue 450 SL was a jolt – that single vehicle in the whole expanse of empty asphalt. His car lights were on, slanting forward into the palms. There was no way I could cut across the sand to the street without his seeing me. The darkness, which had seemed to lift before, now felt like a veil. I couldn't see clearly. I couldn't pick out anything in that smoky wash of darkness. The streetlights at that distance seemed pointless and whimsical and cruel, illuminating nothing, marking a path to safety that I couldn't reach. And where was he? Sitting in his car, his eyes scanning the park, waiting for me to crash through to him? Or out among the palms much closer to the beach?

I moved to the right again, wading out into the ocean. The icy water was making my blood congeal but I crept on, waves splashing against my knees. Out here, I would be harder to spot and if I couldn't see him, at least he couldn't see me. When I was out far enough, I sank down, half walking, half drifting through the undulating depths beyond the breakers. It cost me everything to keep the gun up. I was obsessed with that, arm aching, fingers numb. My hair floated around my face like wet gauze. I watched the beach, seeing little, searching for Charlie. Car lights still on. Nothing. No one. I had moved perhaps two hundred yards past the far-left extreme of the parking lot, almost even now with the concession stand: a small oasis of palms and picnic tables, trash cans, public telephones. I put my feet down, easing into a standing position, still angling to the right. He could be anywhere, standing in any shadow. I waded toward the shallows, waves curling at knee height, washing forward then across my shoes. Finally I was on wet sand again, moving quietly toward the lot, straining through the darkness for sight of him. He couldn't be looking everyplace at once. I crouched, shifting my gaze to the left. Now that I was forced into immobility, the fear took up where it had left me, ice spreading across my lungs, pulse beating in my throat. I slipped out of my wet jeans and shoes – lightly, quietly.

The concession stand was dead ahead: squat structure of cinder block, windows boarded over for the night. I moved to the right, through powdery sand, sinking down to my ankles, working harder on land than I had in the water. I jumped. There he was – just a flash to my left. I dropped to a crouch again, wondering how visible I was. I eased down flat on my belly, pulling myself forward on my elbows. I reached the dark shade of the palms, which even at this hour cast clear shadows against the gray of night. I peered to the left, spotting him again. He wore a white shirt, darker pants. He disappeared into the shadows, passing into the grove of palm trees where the picnic tables were set out. Behind me, the ocean was hushed, a sibilant backdrop to our little cat-and-mouse. To my right, there was an oblong metal trash bin, chest-height with a hinged metal lid. I heard Charlie's car start up and I glanced back with surprise. Maybe he was leaving. Maybe he thought he had missed me and was moving now to intercept me farther down the beach. As he swung back to turn around, I darted toward the trash bin, lifted the lid, with one thrust, and pulled myself over the metal lip into the crush of paper cups, discarded picnic sacks, debris. I wrestled out a place for myself with my backside, shifting my bare legs down into the garbage, wrinkling my nose with disgust. My right foot was touching something cold and gooey and the trash beneath me felt warm, like a compost heap, smoldering with bacteria. I pushed up slightly and peered over my shoulder through the crack, the metal lid tilted slightly ajar by the mountain of accumulated trash. Charlie's car was moving toward me, headlights slicing straight across my hiding place. I ducked down, heartbeat making my eyes bulge.

He got out of the car, leaving the lights on. I could still see a slice of light reflected from where I crouched. He slammed the car door. I could hear his footsteps scratch across the concrete.

'Kinsey, I know you're here someplace,' he said.

I tried not to move. Tried not to breathe.

Silence.

'Kinsey, you don't have to be afraid of me. My God, don't you know that?' His tone was insistent, gentle, persuasive, hurt.

Was I just imagining everything? He sounded like he always did. Silence. I heard his footsteps moving away. I eased up slowly, peering out through the crack. He was standing ten feet away from me, staring out toward the ocean, his body still, half turned away. He started back and I ducked down. I could hear footsteps approaching. I shrank, pulling the gun up, hands shaking. Maybe I was crazy. Maybe I was making a fool of myself. I hated hide-and-seek. I'd never been good at that as a kid. I always jumped right out when anyone got close because the tension made me want to wet my pants. I felt tears rising. Oh Jesus, not *now*, I thought feverishly. The fear was like a sharp pain. My heart hurt me every time it beat, making the blood pound in my ears. Surely he could hear that. Surely he knew now where I was.

He lifted the lid. The beams from his headlights shone against his golden cheek. He glanced over at me. In his right hand was a butcher knife with a ten-inch blade.

I blew him away.

The Santa Teresa police conducted a brief investigation but in the end no charges were filed. The folder on Laurence Fife contains the report I sent to the chief of the Bureau of Collection and Investigative Services regarding the discharge of my firearm 'while acting within the course and scope' of my employment. There is also a copy of the refund check I sent to Nikki for the unused portion of the $5000 she advanced on account. All together, I was paid $2978.25 for services rendered in the course of that sixteen days and I suppose it was fair enough. The shooting disturbs me still. It has moved me into the same camp with soldiers and maniacs. I never set out to kill anyone. But maybe that's what Gwen would say, and Charlie too. I'll recover, of course. I'll be ready for business again in a week or two, but I'll never be the same. You try to keep life simple but it never works, and in the end all you have left is yourself.

Respectfully submitted,

Kinsey Millhone

Sue Grafton
'B' is for Burglar £5.99

The expensively wrapped client didn't look the type who was longing for a family reunion when she asked Kinsey to find her sister. It looked routine, but routine jobs still pay the bills.

The missing sister had gone missing headed for Florida in a $12,000 lynx coat. When Kinsey got to Florida, the case that looked routine was filled with fire-raising, burglary and murder.
Not so routine after all . . .

Tough, fetching Kinsey Millhone in swirling Florida water of murder and arson. "A" was for Alibi and on the evidence to date the rest of the Grafton alphabet could be well worth waiting for' THE OBSERVER

Sue Grafton
'C' is for Corpse £5.99

'Violent death is like a monster. The closer you get to it, the more damage you sustain . . .'

The doctors could do something about the damage to Bobby Callahan's body – but not for the broken bits of his brain. The car crash was no accident. Somebody wanted him dead and he can't remember who or why . . .

Three days later, whoever was trying to kill Bobby Callahan came up with the winning ticket. Kinsey Millhone had never worked for a dead man before, and she didn't need the money. But she cared . . . cared enough to try and make sense of the whole savage joke . . .

'E is for excellent, Ms Grafton' THE SUNDAY TIMES

'Quiveringly alive' DAILY TELEGRAPH

'C is for classy, strong characterisation and a tough cookie heroine' TIME OUT

'Private Eye-ette Kinsey Millhone gets more interesting by the book' THE TIMES

Sue Grafton
'D' is for Deadbeat £5.99

'Dawn was laid out on the eastern skyline like water colours on a matt board: cobalt blue, violet and rose bleeding together in horizontal stripes . . .'

Kinsey thought the job was cut and dried . . . until the client's cheque bounced. Daggett was about as worthless as his cheque. An ex con, inveterate liar, chronic drunk . . . and deader than his credit rating.

Accidental death, according to the cops. But Kinsey finds a long line of could-be killers. A long-suffering wife and daughter; a lady who *thought* she was his wife (and had the bruises to prove it); out-of-pocket drug dealers; and the families of five victims of horror death crashes . . .

'Classy . . . D is for deft and diverting' THE GUARDIAN

'Kinsey Millhone has a lot more than the alphabet going for her' THE OBSERVER

Sue Grafton
'E' is for Evidence £5.99

'I could feel my face heat, the icy itch of fear beginning to assert itself. I said. "This isn't the report I saw . . ." '

It was a routine job – and it was Christmas. All things considered, a neutral verdict looked a good bet.

But when a mystery well wisher weighs in with an unmarked bank deposit for $5,000, Kinsey Millhone's suspicions are finally aroused.

Too late to avoid the set up – and fighting for her life against the oldest trick in the book . . .

'A woman to identify with . . . a gripping read' PUNCH

'Kinsey Millhone is going to have herself a bright literary future' STANLEY ELLIN

All Pan Books are available at your local bookshop or newsagent, or can be ordered direct from the publisher. Indicate the number of copies required and fill in the form below.

Send to: Macmillan General Books C.S.
Book Service By Post
PO Box 29, Douglas I-O-M
IM99 1BQ

or phone: 01624 675137, quoting title, author and credit card number.

or fax: 01624 670923, quoting title, author, and credit card number.

or Internet: http://www.bookpost.co.uk

Please enclose a remittance* to the value of the cover price plus 75 pence per book for post and packing. Overseas customers please allow £1.00 per copy for post and packing.

*Payment may be made in sterling by UK personal cheque, Eurocheque, postal order, sterling draft or international money order, made payable to Book Service By Post.

Alternatively by Access/Visa/MasterCard

Card No. | | | | | | | | | | | | | | | | |

Expiry Date | | | | | | | | | | | | | | | | |

Signature ______________________________

Applicable only in the UK and BFPO addresses.

While every effort is made to keep prices low, it is sometimes necessary to increase prices at short notice. Pan Books reserve the right to show on covers and charge new retail prices which may differ from those advertised in the text or elsewhere.

NAME AND ADDRESS IN BLOCK CAPITAL LETTERS PLEASE

Name ______________________________

Address ______________________________

____

____

____

8/95

Please allow 28 days for delivery.
Please tick box if you do not wish to receive any additional information. ☐

The Body on the Beach

Simon Brett worked as a light entertainment producer in radio and television before taking up writing full-time in 1979. As well as writing the much-loved Mrs Pargeter novels and the Charles Paris detective series, he is also the author of the radio and television series *After Henry*, the radio series *No Commitments* and the best-selling *How to be a Little Sod*, which was adapted by BBC TV and featured Rik Mayall. His novel *A Shock to the System* was filmed starring Michael Caine.

Married with three children, he lives in an Agatha Christie-style village on the South Downs.

The Body on the Beach is the first novel in The Fethering Mysteries series. The second, *Death on the Downs*, is now available in Macmillan hardback.

'I stayed up until three in the morning and chewed off two fingernails finishing this delightful, thoroughly English whodunnit . . . And the good news, for those of us longing for the next instalment of gossip, is that this is only the first of an entire series of Fethering mysteries.'

Daily Mail

'Pure pleasure from beginning to end.'

Birmingham Post

'The yin/yang relationship of the women is both mysterious and wholly believable, and the sea coast setting is so vivid you can taste the salty air. For late-summer beach reading, this is a cracking good choice.'

Publishers Weekly

'A clever story told in a sprightly style about a pair of feisty heroines whose future adventures I look forward to reading.'

The Scotsman

'Aficionados of the elegant, well-turned mystery will find much cause for delight in the inauguration of this series.'

Crime Time

'Simon Brett comes up trumps yet again . . . an excellent thriller but also a well-observed social commentary.'

Irish News

'One of the exceptional detective-story writers around.'
Daily Telegraph

'[Brett is] highly commended for atmosphere and wit.'
Evening Standard

'Simon Brett is a man of many talents . . . totally engrossing and unusually funny.'
London Life Magazine

Also by Simon Brett in Pan Books

A Shock to the System
Dead Romantic
Singled Out

Mrs Pargeter novels

A Nice Class of Corpse
Mrs, Presumed Dead
Mrs Pargeter's Pound of Flesh
Mrs Pargeter's Package
Mrs Pargeter's Plot
Mrs Pargeter's Point of Honour

Simon Brett

The Body on the Beach

A Fethering Mystery

PAN BOOKS

First published 2000 by Macmillan

This edition published 2001 by Pan Books
an imprint of Pan Macmillan Ltd,
Pan Macmillan, 20 New Wharf Road, London N1 9RR
Basingstoke and Oxford
Associated companies throughout the world
www.panmacmillan.com

ISBN 0 330 37696 9

5 7 9 8 6 4

A CIP catalogue record for this book is available from the British Library.

Phototypeset by Intype London Ltd
Printed and bound in Great Britain by
Mackays of Chatham plc, Chatham, Kent

TO KEITH
who knows this
part of the world
(and many others)

Chapter One

Fethering is on the South Coast, not far from Tarring. Though calling itself a village, Fethering isn't what that word immediately brings to the minds of people nostalgic for an idealized, simpler England. Despite the presence of many components of a village – one church, one shop, one pub, one petrol station, and a whole bunch of people who reckon they're the squire – Fethering is in fact quite a large residential conurbation.

The core is its High Street, some of whose flint-faced cottages date back to the early eighteenth century. The peasant simplicities of these buildings, sufficient for their original fishermen owners, have been enhanced by mains drainage, gas central heating, sealed-unit leaded windows and very high price tags.

Out from the High Street, during the last century and a half, have spread, in a semicircle whose diameter is the sea, wave after wave of new developments. The late Victorians and Edwardians added a ring of solid, respectable family homes. Beyond these, in the 1930s, an arc of large, unimaginative slabs sprang up, soon to be surrounded by an infestation of bungalows. In the post-war period some regimented blocks of council housing were built in an area to the north of the village and named, by planners devoid of irony, Downside. Then in the late 1950s there burgeoned an expensive private estate of vast houses backing on to the sea. This compound, called Shorelands, was circumscribed by stern walls and sterner regulations. From that time on, stricter planning laws and a growing sense of its own exclusivity had virtually stopped any further development in Fethering.

The roads into the village are all regularly interrupted by speed humps. Though tourism plays a significant part in the local economy, strangers to the area are never quite allowed to feel welcome.

Because of its seaside location, the village boasts a Yacht Club, a cluster of seafront cafés and a small but tasteful amusements arcade. During the winter, of these the Yacht Club alone remains open, and to members only. But open all the year round along the front are the rectangles of glass-sided shelters, havens by day to swaddled pensioners killing a little time, and by night to amorous local teenagers. In spite of the overpowering gentility of the area, and ferociously deterrent notices about vandalism, the glass of the shelters gets broken on a regular basis.

Fethering is set at the mouth of the Fether. Though called a 'river', it would be little more than a stream but for the effects of the tides, which twice a day turn a lethargic trickle into a torrent of surprising malevolence. A sea wall, stretching out beyond the low-water mark, protects the beach from the Fether's turbulence. This wall abuts the Fethering Yacht Club, which controls access to the promenade on top. Only

Yacht Club members, and some local fishermen who keep their blue-painted equipment boxes there, are allowed the precious keys which give access to this area. Against the wall, on the beachward side, is the cement ramp down which the boats of the Fethering Yacht Club flotilla reach the water.

The sea goes out a long way at Fethering, revealing a vast, flat expanse of sludge-coloured sand. When the tide is high, only pebbles show, piled high against the footpath and the wooden breakwaters that stretch out from it like the teeth of a comb. Between the path and the start of the houses, lower than the highest part of the beach, is a strip of tough, short grass. At spring tides, or after heavy rain, pools of water break up the green. The road which separates this grass from the start of the houses is rather imaginatively called Seaview Road.

At regular intervals along the beach are signs reading:

NO CYCLING AT ANY TIME

POOP SCOOP AREA

CLEAN IT UP.

Though hardly separated from the coastline sprawl of Worthing, Fethering believes very strongly in its own identity. People from adjacent areas even as close as Tarring, Ferring or Goring-on-Sea are reckoned to be, in some imprecise but unarguable way, different.

Fethering is its own little world of double-glazed windows and double-glazed minds.

Carole Seddon had always planned to retire there. The cottage had been bought as a weekend retreat when she had both a job and a husband and, though now she had neither, she never regretted the investment.

Carole had enjoyed working for the Home Office. The feeling of having done something useful with her life fitted the values with which she had grown up, values which at times verged on the puritanical. Her parents had lived a life without frills; perhaps the only indulgence they had shown her was the slightly frivolous 'e' at the end of her first name. So Carole felt she had earned a virtuous retirement – even though, she could never quite forget, it had come a little earlier than anticipated.

Ahead of her, she imagined, until time finally distressed her body beyond repair, lay perhaps thirty years of low-profile life. Her Civil Service pension was at the generous end of adequate; the mortgage was paid off; there would be no money worries. She would look after herself sensibly, eat sensibly, take plenty of long sensible walks on the beach, perform a few unheralded acts of local charity for such organizations as the Canine Trust and be, if not happy, then at least content with her lot.

Carole Seddon did not expect any changes in the rest of her life. She had had her steel-grey hair cut sensibly short and protected her pale-blue eyes with rimless glasses which she hoped were insufficiently fashionable ever to look dated.

She bought a sensible new Renault, which was kept immaculately clean and regularly serviced, and in which she did a very low mileage. She had also acquired a dog called Gulliver, who was as sensible as a Labrador is capable of being, and she had kitted herself out with a sensible wardrobe, mostly from Marks & Spencer. Her only indulgence was a Burberry raincoat, which was well enough cut not to look ostentatious.

If her clothes were older than those usually worn by a woman in her early fifties, they represented sensible planning for the future. Carole was happy to look older than her age; that accorded with the image of benign anonymity she sought.

And someone who wished to slip imperceptibly into old age could not have chosen a better environment than Fethering in which to complete the process.

As she took her regular walk on the beach before it was properly light that Tuesday morning in early November, these were not, however, the thoughts going through Carole Seddon's brain. They were old thoughts, conclusions she had long ago reached and fixed in her mind; they never required reassessment.

But new, disturbing thoughts cut through the early-morning sounds, through the hiss of the gunmetal sea, the wheeze of the wind, the resigned complaint of the gulls, the crunch of sand and shingle on to which Carole's sensible gumboots trod. The new thoughts centred round the woman who, the previous day, had arrived to take possession of the house next door. It was called Woodside Cottage, though there wasn't a wood in sight. But then Carole's own house was called High Tor and it was a good 200 miles to the nearest one of those. That, however, was the way houses were named in Fethering.

Despite its High Street location, Woodside Cottage had been empty for some time. Buyers were put off by the amount of modernization the property required. Its former owner, an old lady of universal misanthropy, had been dead for eighteen months. Carole's initial neighbourly overtures, when she first started weekending in the area, had been snubbed with such ferocity that no further approaches had been made. This lack of contact, and the old lady's natural reclusiveness, had meant it was like living next door to an empty house. Death, turning that illusion into reality, had therefore made no difference to Carole.

But the prospect of having a real, living neighbour did make a difference. A potential variable was introduced into a life from which Carole Seddon had worked hard to exclude the unexpected.

She hadn't spoken to the newcomer yet. She could have done quite easily. The woman had been very much up and down her front path the previous day, the Monday, volubly ushering in and directing furniture-laden removal men. She had even engaged hitherto-unmet passers-by in conversation, exchanging cheery words with Fethering residents who, Carole knew, were deliberately taking the long route back from the beach to check out the new arrival.

Her name, the woman readily volunteered to everyone she spoke to, was 'Jude'. Carole's lips shaped the monosyllable with slight distaste. 'Jude' had about it an over-casual air, a studied informality. Carole

Seddon had never before had a friend called Jude and she wasn't about to start now.

The woman's relentless casualness was the reason why her neighbour hadn't engaged her in conversation. Though, as she sat by her open kitchen window, Carole had heard Jude's exchanges with other residents, she'd had no wish to be identified with the communal local nosiness. Her early-morning walk with Gulliver completed before the new resident and the removal vans arrived, she had had no further need to leave the house that day except for a quick mid-afternoon dog-relieving visit to the waste ground behind. Carole would find a more appropriate, more formal occasion on which to introduce herself to her new neighbour.

But she didn't see theirs ever becoming a close relationship. The newcomer's casualness extended to her dress, an assemblage of long skirts and wafty scarves, and also to her hair, blonde – blond*ed*, surely – and coiled into a loose bird's-nest, precariously pinned in place. That could of course have been a temporary measure, the hair pushed untidily out of the way of the inevitable dust generated by moving house, but Carole had a feeling it was the regular style. Jude, she knew instinctively, wasn't her sort of person.

She felt the prickle of small resistances building up within her. Carole Seddon had spent considerable time and energy defining her own space and would defend it against all encroachments.

She was shaken out of these sour thoughts by Gulliver's bark. The dog was down near the water's scummy edge, running round a bulky figure who was walking across the flat grey sand towards his mistress. This was surprising, given the early hour. There weren't many local walkers as driven and disciplined as Carole.

The figure was so hunched against the wind into a green shiny anorak that it could have been of either gender. But even if Carole had been able to see enough face to recognize someone of her acquaintance, she still wouldn't have stopped to talk.

There were social protocols to be observed on an early-morning walk along the beach at Fethering. When one met another human being – almost definitely proceeding in the opposite direction: everyone walked at the same pace; there was very little over taking – it was bad form to give them no acknowledgement at all. Equally, to have stopped and engaged in lengthy conversation at that time in the morning would have been considered excessive.

The correct response therefore was 'the Fethering Nod'. This single abrupt inclination of the head was the approved reaction to encounters with mild acquaintances, bosom friends, former lovers, current lovers and complete strangers. And its appropriateness did not vary with the seasons. The nod was logical in the winter, when the scouring winds and tightened anorak hoods gave everyone the face of a Capuchin monkey, and when any attempts at conversation were whisked away and strewn far across the shingle. But it was still the correct protocol on balmy summer mornings, when the horizon of the even sea was lost in a mist that promised a baking afternoon. Even then, to respond to anyone with more than 'the Fethering Nod' would have been bad form.

For other times of day, of course, and other venues, different protocols obtained. Not to stop and chat with a friend met on an after-lunch stroll along the beach would have been the height of bad manners. And Fethering High Street at mid-morning was quite properly littered with gossiping acquaintances.

Such nuances of social behaviour distinguished the long-time residents of Fethering from the newly arrived. And it was the view of Carole Seddon that anyone privileged to join the local community should be humble enough to keep a low profile until they had mastered these intricacies.

From what she'd seen of the woman, she rather doubted whether 'Jude' would, though.

Nor did the figure who passed her that morning seem aware of what was required. With an averted face and not even a hint of 'the Fethering Nod', he or she deliberately changed course and broke into a lumbering – almost panicky – run up the steep shingle towards the Yacht Club.

Gulliver's barking once again distracted Carole. Quickly bored with the unresponsive figure in the anorak, the dog had rushed off on another of his pivotal missions to rid the world of seaweed or lumps of tar-stained polystyrene, and disappeared round the corner of a breakwater. Invisible behind the weed-draped wooden screen, he was barking furiously. Beyond him, the sea, having reached its twice-daily nadir, was easing back up the sand.

Carole wondered what it would be this time.

Gulliver's 'sensibleness' went only so far. A crushed plastic bottle or a scrap of punctured beach ball could suddenly, to his eyes, be transformed into a major threat to world peace. And, until forcibly dragged away, he would continue trying to bark the enemy into submission.

But that morning it wasn't a bottle or a scrap of beach ball that had set Gulliver off. As Carole Seddon saw when she rounded the end of the breakwater, it was a dead body.

Chapter Two

He was maybe in his fifties, though his pallor made it difficult to tell. The flesh of his face, framed by matted greying hair and the sharp separate stubble of a three-day beard, was bleached the pale beige of driftwood. It seemed to Carole a mercy that his eyes were closed.

His mouth, though, hung open. To the right of the bottom jaw, a tooth was missing. It had been missing a long time.

The inside of one exposed wrist was pockmarked with old and new scar tissue.

The body was hunched uncomfortably against a barnacled wooden stanchion of the breakwater. At first sight the man might have crawled there for protection, but the unnatural conformation of his limbs denied that supposition. He hadn't got there by his own efforts. He had been manipulated and abandoned by the sea.

His clothes – jeans and a grey jumper – were soaked heavy. The sea had borne away one of his trainers, exposing a poignantly vulnerable sports sock, ringed in blue and red. Laced round his upper body was an orange life-jacket, stamped in faded black letters 'Property of Fethering Yacht Club'.

Instinctively, Carole looked up towards the small white-balconied clubhouse at the top of the beach by the sea wall. In front of it, guarded by a stockade of white railings, were drawn up rows of sailing boats, securely covered for the winter. She knew that if she moved closer, she would be able to hear the incessant clacking of rigging against metal masts. But there'd be nobody at the club so early in the morning. The first-floor bar-room's dark expanse of window looked out blankly to the sea.

Despite his life-jacket, any theory that the man had been the victim of a sailing accident was belied by the two wounds in his neck. Washed blood-free by the sea, they were thin, like the lines of a butcher's cleaver in dead meat, exposing the darker flesh beneath.

Never for a moment did it occur to Carole Seddon that the man was not dead. She felt no urge to kneel by the body and feel for pulses. It wasn't just squeamishness. There was no point.

Anyway, it was better to leave the corpse undisturbed for the police to examine.

Carole was distracted by more barking. Having drawn her attention to it, Gulliver had immediately lost interest in the body. He'd found a supplanting fascination in the sea itself and was now trying to catch the waves, fighting them back with all the optimism of a canine Canute. He'd managed to soak his body through in the process.

One sharp call was enough to bring the dog to

heel. He dissociated himself from the sea, looking round innocently as if he'd only just noticed its vast expanse. Carole stood back as he shook the tell-tale brine out of his coat. Then he rolled over in a mass of seaweed and something else more noxious. Carole registered dully that Gulliver would need a bath when they got home.

She gave one last look to the dead man by the breakwater, then started resolutely up the beach, Gulliver trotting maturely at her side.

It was only half-past seven when they got back to High Tor. Carole had woken early that morning, slow to adjust to the recent change from Summer Time, and got up briskly, as she always did. Thinking too much at the beginning of the day could so easily become brooding. It had been dark, the night's full moon invisible, when she and Gulliver left for their walk, and it was still gloomy when they returned, the kind of November day that would never get properly light. And never warm up either.

Carole bathed the dog before calling the police, splashing him down with a hose outside the back door. She knew, if she didn't, the house would smell of rotting seaweed for weeks. Gulliver never made a fuss about being bathed. He seemed positively to enjoy the process. Maybe it was the intimacy with his mistress he valued. Carole Seddon was not given to sentimental displays, least of all to animals, so Gulliver enjoyed the ration of contact he received from the necessary scrubbing and drying. In the cold weather she was particularly careful to get the last drop of water out of his coat.

When the dog was shining clean and snuffling into sleep by the Aga, and when Carole had mopped up the inevitable wet footprints he had left on the kitchen floor, it seemed natural for her to continue cleaning the kitchen. As a result, it was after nine before she went into the sitting room to confront the telephone.

She had gone through the walk back from the beach, as well as the mechanical processes of bathing Gulliver and cleaning the kitchen, without allowing herself to think about what she had seen. She had kept an equally tight control on her body, not permitting it the slightest tremor of reaction to the shock. As she had done frequently before in her life, Carole Seddon kept everything firmly damped down.

She dialled 999 and asked for the police. In simple, unemotional sentences, she gave them the necessary information. She described her actions precisely, the direction of her walk, the time she had returned, the fact that she had bathed her dog and cleaned the kitchen. She pinpointed the exact position where the body had been found and gave her considered estimate as to how long it would be before the returning tide reached that point. She gave her address and telephone number, and was unsurprised when told that someone would be round to talk to her.

Carole Seddon put the phone down and sat in an armchair. She did not collapse into an armchair. She sat in one.

And then she heard the strange noise from outside. Perhaps it had just started. Or it could have been going on unheard for some time, so intense had been her concentration on the task in hand.

The sound was a rhythmic dull thudding, something being hit repeatedly. Carole rose from her chair and moved tentatively towards the front-facing window. Through it, she saw Jude in the adjacent front garden. Her new neighbour had spread a slightly threadbare rug over a structure of boxes and was beating it with a flat besom brush. Though still wearing a trademark long skirt, Jude had removed her loose-fitting top to reveal a bright yellow T-shirt. Her large bosom and chubby arms shuddered with the efforts of her carpet-beating. In spite of the cold, her cheeks were red from the exercise.

Carole's instinctive reaction was one of disapproval. There was something old-fashioned in Jude's carpet-beating. The scene could have come from a film of back-to-back terraced houses in the 1930s. *Northern* terraced houses. The possibility, suddenly occurring to Carole, that Jude might come from 'the North' prompted a visceral recoil within her. 'The North' still conjured up images of unwanted intimacy, of people constantly 'dropping in', of back doors left unlocked to facilitate this 'dropping in'. It wasn't the kind of thing that happened in Fethering.

Back doors were kept firmly locked. Approaches to people's houses were made strictly from the front. And, except for essential gardening and maintenance, the only part of a front garden that was used was the path. Even if the space caught the evening sun, no one would dream of sitting in their front garden. And it certainly wasn't the proper place to do anything domestic, like beating a carpet. Passers-by, seeing someone engaged in such activities, might be forced into conversation.

In Fethering, except for chance meetings in the High Street, social encounters were conducted by arrangement. It was inappropriate to meet someone without having received planning permission. A prefatory phone call – ideally a couple of days before the proposed encounter – was the minimum requirement.

These thoughts were so instinctive that they took no time at all to flash through Carole Seddon's mind, but they still took long enough to allow something appalling to happen. Jude, taking a momentary respite from her efforts with the besom, had turned and caught sight of her neighbour framed in the window. Eye contact was unavoidable.

For Carole then to have repressed a half-smile and little flap of the hand would have been the height of bad manners. Her minimal gesture was reciprocated by a huge wave and a cheery grin.

If she had left the contact there, Carole knew she would have appeared standoffish. And, though standoffish she undoubtedly was, she had no wish to appear so. She found her hand and face doing a little mime of 'I'll come out and say hello.'

'My name's Carole Seddon. Welcome to Fethering. If there's anything I can do to help out, please don't hesitate to tell me.'

'Thanks very much.' Carole found her hand grasped and firmly shaken. 'My name's Jude.'

'Yes . . .' Carole awaited the gloss of a surname, but wasn't given one. 'You'll find we're a friendly lot round here,' she lied.

'Good.' Jude chuckled. It was a warm, earthy sound. 'I get along with most people. Most people do, don't they?'

Carole granted this alien concept a thin smile. 'Well, if I can tell you where things are . . . shops, dry-cleaners, you know . . . I'm only next door, so just ask.'

'Thanks. I'm sure I'll find my way around pretty quickly.'

'Mm . . .' Carole found the openness of Jude's dreamy brown eyes slightly disconcerting.

'Equally,' her neighbour said, 'if there's anything I can do to help you out, you'll say, won't you?'

Carole nodded this offer token gratitude, however incongruous might be the idea of her suddenly turning for assistance to someone she didn't know. The woman had only just moved to Fethering, for goodness' sake. Any support being offered should go from the established resident to the newcomer, not the other way round.

Surely Jude didn't imagine her neighbour was about to confide in her? Carole was hardly likely suddenly to start spilling the beans to a stranger about what she'd seen on the beach. But even as she had the thought, she was surprised how much she did want to talk about the shock she had received that morning. And there was something in those brown eyes that invited confidences.

'Anyway – ' Carole shook herself back on track – 'better get on. Things to do.'

'Yes.' Jude grinned easily. 'Me too. House is crammed full of boxes. God knows how long it'll take me to sort it all out.'

'Moving's always a nightmare.'

'Still, I can do it at my own pace. No hurry.'

Carole smiled as if she endorsed this view. But she didn't. Of course there was a hurry. One couldn't live in mess. One had an obligation to get one's house tidy as soon as possible. If people weren't aware of the necessity for hurry in life, society would break down completely.

'See you soon then.' Jude gave a relaxed wave and hefted her besom for a renewed assault on the carpet.

'Yes. Yes,' said Carole, turning in slight confusion back towards her front door.

Inside the house, she berated herself for how little solid fact she had got out of the conversation. She wasn't that interested, of course, but there were things one ought to know about a new neighbour.

She hadn't even elicited a surname, for goodness' sake. Jude. Just Jude. That wasn't very satisfactory. And then again, what was the woman's status? What was her age? Was she married, single, divorced? Was there a regular man on the scene? Carole realized that, uncharacteristically, she hadn't even checked out Jude's ring finger. Something compelling about those big brown eyes made it difficult to divert one's gaze elsewhere.

Did Jude have a job? A private income? A pension? Carole knew none of these things. Not that she was interested, but it was the kind of information that might be important at some stage.

Good heavens, Carole realized, she hadn't even found out whether or not Jude came from 'the North'.

Chapter Three

'So why were you walking on that part of the beach, Mrs Seddon?'

Carole didn't like Detective Inspector Brayfield's tone. She was the one who'd reported the body, after all. If anything, she deserved congratulation. Certainly not this hint of suspicion in her interrogator's voice.

Also, why were there two of them? Not just the Inspector in his almost dandyish single-breasted black suit. There was also the uniformed WPC, Juster, who hadn't said much but was clearly taking everything in. She sat on a straight-backed chair, tensely alert. Was there some new directive that the police always had to work in twos, even for routine inquiries? Maybe it was a gender thing. Allegations of sexual harassment would not be risked if a male police officer was never left alone with a female witness.

But the explanation didn't seem adequate. Carole still had the feeling that their encounter was adversarial, as if the police were expecting more from her than mere corroboration of what she'd already said over the telephone. She had dealt with a great many police officers in the course of her work at the Home Office but had never before felt this aura of mistrust.

'I always go for an early-morning walk along the beach. I have a dog.' Gulliver hadn't provided a visual aid when the police arrived. He was still sleeping off his walk at the foot of the Aga. As a guard dog he was hopeless. His first instinct was not to deter entry, but to give any new arrival at the house a fulsome welcome. 'And I always take my dog on the beach first thing.'

' "First thing" was rather early this morning, wasn't it, Mrs Seddon? Can hardly have been light when you set off.'

'I woke early. It always takes me a bit of time to adjust when the clocks change.'

'I understand,' said the Inspector, who clearly didn't. 'So why did you go to that particular part of the beach this morning?'

'It wasn't a *particular* part of the beach. It was just where I happened to be walking.' Exasperated by the scepticism in Detective Inspector Brayfield's eye, Carole went on. 'There are only two directions in which you can go along the beach. Off Seaview Road there's a path which goes down by the Yacht Club. At the end of that you're on the beach and you have the choice of turning left or turning right. Left you go virtually straight into the sea wall, so this morning, like most mornings, I decided to turn right.'

She wasn't meaning to sound sarcastic, but she knew that's how the words were coming out.

'For any particular reason?'

What was it with that word 'particular'? 'No,' Carole snapped. 'For no particular reason.'

'Are you sure you're all right?' It was WPC Juster

this time, her voice showing the professional concern of someone who's done a counselling course.

'Yes, I'm quite all right, thank you!' Why were they treating her like some semi-invalid?

'How old are you, Mrs Seddon?' Juster went on.

'I don't really see that it's any business of yours, but I'm fifty-three.'

'Ah,' said the WPC.

'Ah,' the Inspector echoed, as if that explained everything.

What was this – some kind of medical assessment? Had they written her off as a menopausal hysteric? Surely not. She had told them everything in a manner that was unemotional to the point of being dull. What were they trying to insinuate?

Though these questions ran through her mind, being Carole Seddon, of course she didn't voice any of them. Instead, she took the initiative. 'Presumably,' she said, 'when a body like that is found, it's photographed *in situ* first, and then taken off for forensic examination?'

Detective Inspector Brayfield, stroking the knot of his brightly coloured silk tie, agreed that that would be the normal procedure. But he wasn't to be deflected from his dissection of her story.

'You say there were cuts on the man's neck and scar tissue on the inside of his wrist?'

'Yes.'

'Which might suggest he had been an intravenous drug user?'

'Quite possibly.'

'Do you know much about intravenous drug users, Mrs Seddon?'

'No, I don't. But I do know enough to recognize that that was a possible explanation of the scars.'

'From things you've seen on television?'

'I suppose so, yes.'

Brayfield nodded, as if this too was of profound relevance. Then he said, 'Could we just recap once again exactly what happened this morning?'

'Oh, for heaven's sake!' She couldn't help herself. But, feeling the intense scrutiny of the two police officers after her outburst, she took a deep breath before saying, 'Yes, yes, of course.'

'Was there anyone else around on the beach this morning when you took your walk?'

'Apart from the dead body?'

'Apart indeed from the dead body. Do you recall seeing anyone else?'

'No, I don't think I did . . .' She screwed up her eyes with the effort of recapturing the scene. 'Ooh yes, yes, there was someone.'

Carole was aware of WPC Juster tautening in her chair and realized how guilty she must sound, first forgetting, then remembering. But she was damned if she was going to feel guilty. She had nothing to feel guilty about. She was just doing her duty as a public-spirited citizen. Never again, though. Next time she found a dead body, she'd walk away and leave some other unfortunate passer-by the task of breaking the news to the police.

'So who was this?' asked Detective Inspector Brayfield evenly. 'Who did you see?'

'It was someone in a shiny green anorak with the hood tied up tight. They were walking into the wind, you see. They hurried straight past me.'

'Hurried?'

'Almost ran.'

'Uh-huh. And was it a man or a woman?'

'I couldn't tell.'

'Really?' Though deliberately ironing out the intonation, he still couldn't remove the last wrinkle of scepticism. 'You didn't speak to this person?'

'No. I just gave them a nod.'

'And did they speak to you?'

'No.'

'Or give you a nod?' Carole shook her head. 'That's a pity, isn't it?'

'Why?'

'Well, obviously if we had any means of tracking down this other person on the beach, then we might have another witness of your dead body, mightn't we?'

'Yes.'

'Which might be very useful.' Before Carole had time to say anything, the Inspector moved abruptly on. 'So you came straight back here from the beach?'

'As I told you, yes.'

'But before calling the police, you bathed your dog?'

'Yes.'

'Why?'

'Because he was covered with seaweed and soaked with salt water. If I hadn't given him a bath, the whole house'd smell.'

'Hm. And then, after washing the dog, you cleaned

your kitchen.' The Inspector ran a hand over his chin, as if checking the quality of his morning's shave. 'You don't often find dead bodies on the beach, do you, Mrs Seddon?'

'No, of course I don't!'

'So, given the fact that it's an unusual – and probably rather a shocking – thing to happen to you, can you understand why I'm surprised that you bathed your dog and did some of your housework before reporting it?'

'I can see that, with hindsight, it may sound rather odd, but at the time it seemed the perfectly logical thing to do.'

'Did it?'

'Maybe I was in shock. Maybe I needed to do something mechanical, something mundane, to calm myself down.'

'Or maybe, Mrs Seddon, you just needed time to work things out.'

'Work what out?'

'What you were going to say when you rang the police.'

'I didn't need to work that out. I just had to say exactly what I'd seen.'

'The body on the beach?'

'Precisely.'

'And to direct us to where that body was lying?'

'Yes.'

'Well, Mrs Seddon, everything you've told us this morning makes perfect sense.'

'I'm glad to hear it.'

'We followed your directions to the letter. They

were very clear.' Carole nodded in acknowledgment of the compliment. 'We went down to the breakwater you described and everything was absolutely fine . . . except for one small detail.'

'And what was that?'

'When we got to the breakwater, there was nothing there. There was no body on the beach, Mrs Seddon.'

Chapter Four

Carole Seddon felt upset after the police's departure. They had come to the house with an agenda; their semaphore of little nods and eyelid flickers had been prearranged. Having arrived believing her to be a hysterical attention seeker, nothing she could say was going to make them leave with any change in their attitude.

That's what hurt – that they had thought her anything less than sensible. Throughout her career in the Home Office, Carole Seddon had prided herself on being a safe pair of hands. Male colleagues had paid her the ultimate compliment of appearing unaware of her gender. Even at times of crisis, when she returned to work after the birth of her son, when her marriage to David was turning horribly sour, she had never let her emotions show in her professional life.

And here she was faced with a detective and a WPC being *understanding* about her mental state.

There was nothing wrong with her mental state. Certainly nothing wrong with her hormonally. What stage she was at with her menopause was nobody's business but her own. And yet the attitude of the two police officers had undermined her confidence. She knew she wasn't a hysteric, but the fact that someone could imagine her to be a hysteric upset the carefully maintained equilibrium of her life.

The unease didn't dissipate during the course of the day. She went through the motions of her normal routine. Did a bit of housework for the rest of the morning. Forced down some soup and a hunk of granary bread at lunchtime, then settled to the regular mental aerobics of the *Times* crossword. But her brain was sluggish, slow to dissect words into their component parts, slow to make connections between them. She completed one corner, but could fill in only a few stragglers on the rest of the grid. The crossword, usually finished within half an hour, was set aside for completion later in the day.

Round four, she took Gulliver out for a shorter walk, through the back gate to do his business in the rough ground behind the row of cottages. Jude and her carpet were no longer in their front garden, but, Carole noted with disapproval, the structure of boxes still was. Her new neighbour would have to learn. People in Fethering didn't leave anything in their front gardens, except for staddlestones, tasteful statuary and – in one rather regrettable instance – gnomes.

Gulliver seemed to have caught his mistress's mood, sloping along by her side with none of his usual frenetic attacks on invisible windmills. The light too was depressing. True to its early promise, the day had never felt like day, and its leaden sky was now thickening into a November night. The cold stung her exposed cheeks and she shivered. Her circulation hadn't got properly going all day.

Still Carole Seddon couldn't lose the unpleasant aftertaste of her morning's visitation by the police.

Despite the sour mood they'd engendered, the thought did not for a moment occur to her that she might be in the wrong. There was no doubt that she had seen the body on the beach. The fact that the police hadn't found it was down either to their incompetence or – more likely – to the interference of some outside agency. Maybe they'd taken too long, arriving after the tide had come in far enough to move the body on. Maybe someone had moved it deliberately.

Once the body had been found – as she knew it would be – Carole Seddon was determined to get a very full apology from the West Sussex Serious Crimes Squad. Public-spirited citizens should not be treated like criminals.

Though the prospect of receiving some ultimate moral compensation was a comforting one, when she returned home Carole still felt unsettled. As she put on the lights and drew the curtains, she even asked herself if she was over-reacting, if she actually *was* in an emotional state. Maybe a delayed response to the shock of seeing the dead body and to the implications of the wounds on its neck?

Uncharacteristically, she wanted to talk to someone about the whole incident. For a brief, irrational moment, she even contemplated confiding in her new neighbour. She couldn't forget the unusual quality of empathy she'd seen in those wide brown eyes.

But that was ridiculous. Even if Carole Seddon had been the kind of person who talked to her neighbours about anything more weighty than the weather, she didn't even know this woman.

These uncharacteristic thoughts were interrupted when the doorbell rang.

She had received no early warning over the previous couple of days. No acquaintance was due to come round for tea. It must be someone selling something, Carole concluded as she approached the front door. Probably one of those men with a zip-up bag full of dishcloths, oven gloves and plastic storage boxes who would flash some laminated card of authorization. If it was, she'd send him off with a flea in his ear. There was a consensus view in Fethering that all such visitors were lookouts for criminal gangs. Carole Seddon wasn't about to have her joint cased for the benefit of burglars.

By the time she opened the door, she had built up a healthy head of righteous steam against the expected salesman and was surprised to be confronted by a thin, haunted-looking woman she had never seen before.

'Did you find a body on the beach this morning?'

Now Carole knew why she had let the woman in. Her instinct was always to get rid of unexpected callers – particularly callers in grubby jeans and purple quilted anoraks. But something in the woman's eyes had indicated that her visit was serious, maybe even important. Carole had ushered her stiffly into the sitting room, sat her down and waited till the reason for her presence was explained.

Now she knew she'd done the right thing. In the same armchair where Detective Inspector Brayfield had sat that morning, disbelieving her story of having found a body on the beach, here was a woman actually asking about her discovery.

'What makes you think I did?' Carole responded cautiously.

'I know you did.' The voice was uneducated South Coast, not from the more discriminating purlieus of Fethering. 'It was a woman with a beige raincoat and a Labrador,' she went on. 'You fit the description.'

'Whose description?'

'Never mind that. Look, I know it was you, so we can cut out the bullshit.'

Carole Seddon appraised the woman in front of her. The face had about it a deadness the colour and texture of papier mâché. The hair was flat and dull like tobacco. Only the eyes were alive, burning with a desperate energy.

'The police have been to see me this morning,' said Carole evenly. 'According to them, when they looked, there was no body on the beach.'

'I'm not interested in the police. You know and I know there was a body on the beach this morning. Down at the end of the breakwater.'

While it was gratifying to have her story corroborated, Carole still wanted to know where the woman had got her information. 'Were you watching me? Was it you who I saw walking away from the body?'

'I didn't go on the beach this morning.' The woman dismissed these irrelevant details and hurried on to what really concerned her. 'Did you take something from the body? Something out of his jacket pocket?'

'No, I certainly didn't. I didn't touch it.' Carole spoke with the affront of someone whose upbringing did not countenance theft, least of all from the dead.

'Are you sure?'

'Of course I'm sure!'

'Listen, it's important.'

'It may be important, but the fact remains that I did not take anything from the body I found on the beach this morning!'

'There wasn't no knife?'

'Knife? I didn't see any knife.'

This answer seemed to provide a moment of reassurance. The woman was silent, her eyes darting from side to side as she considered the next tack to take. 'Do you know where it went?' she asked eventually.

'The body?'

'Of course the body.'

'I've no idea.'

'After you seen it, did you see anyone else go near it?'

'No. I went home and rang the police. And – as I've just told you – when they finally came to see me, they said they hadn't been able to find the body.'

This news too seemed to reassure the woman, but only for a moment. Her tone changed. There was overt aggression in her next question. 'What were you doing down on the beach, anyway?'

'I was taking my dog for a walk.'

'Oh yes?' The woman could do scepticism just as

well as Detective Inspector Brayfield. Then, abruptly, she asked, 'Did the police say they'd come back?'

'To see me again? No.'

'If they do come back, you're not to tell them anything about it.'

Carole was getting exasperated. 'About what, for God's sake?'

'About what you seen on the beach. About you seeing anyone moving the body.'

'I've told you! I didn't see anyone moving the body!'

'If you're lying and I find out you snitched to anyone about what you seen, there'll be trouble.'

'What kind of trouble?' asked Carole, almost contemptuously.

'This kind of trouble,' said the woman with a new, sly menace in her voice.

As she spoke, she reached inside her quilted anorak and pulled out a gun.

Chapter Five

Carole was too affronted to feel any fear. 'Put that thing away!' she ordered. 'What on earth do you think you're doing? This is Fethering, not Miami Beach.'

The woman waved the gun threateningly. 'You shut up! I think you'd better cooperate with me.'

Carole rose from her seat and moved towards the telephone. 'I'm going to call the police.'

'Do that and I'll shoot you!'

The words stopped her in her tracks. Carole turned to look at the woman, assessing the risk of the threat being carried out.

Something she saw in the wild, darting eyes told her that the danger was real. The woman's expression wasn't natural. Perhaps she was under the influence of some drug. Indeed, that would make sense of her erratic behaviour since she'd arrived at the house. She wasn't entirely in control of her actions.

Which being the case, she was quite capable of using the gun. Carole returned silently to her seat.

'So tell me what you did see,' the woman demanded.

'I didn't see anything other than what I've told you about.'

Apparently coolness wasn't the best response. It seemed only to inflame the woman more. Waving the gun with increasing – and rather disturbing – abandon, she said, 'Cut the crap. You're nothing in this. You get shot, it doesn't matter. So long as the police never find out who moved the body.'

Her speech was slurring now, becoming something of a ramble. But that didn't make its content any less disturbing. Being shot by someone coherent or being shot by someone rambling didn't make a lot of difference, Carole realized. You were still dead.

'They'll never find out from me,' Carole said calmly, 'because I don't know who moved the body.'

The woman looked puzzled. 'Whose body? My son's body? My son's not dead.' Then, with another worryingly casual wave of the gun, she slurred, 'You could be lying.'

'Yes, I could be, but I'm not.'

'Does this gun frighten you?'

'Of course it does. I'm not stupid.'

'Sometimes,' the woman maundered on, 'people get shot just to keep them quiet. To make sure they don't say anything.'

This is ridiculous, thought Carole. I am sitting in my own sitting room – in Fethering of all places – and a woman I've never seen before is threatening to shoot me with a gun. People will never believe me when I tell them. On the other hand, of course, I may not be around to tell them.

Though her brain was working fast, her body was paralysed. Carole could do nothing. The gun was still pointing straight at her and a new, dangerous focus had come into the woman's eyes when . . . the front doorbell rang.

There was a momentary impasse. Then the woman hissed, 'Don't answer it.'

'But everyone knows I'm here. The lights are on. If I don't answer, they'll get suspicious and call the police.'

The barrel wavered while the woman weighed this up. Then she relented. Flicking the gun towards the door, she said, 'See who it is. Don't invite them in, though.'

'All right. I won't.'

As she went towards the front door, Carole reflected wryly on Gulliver's qualities as a guard dog. Two people – one at least of whom was carrying a gun – had rung her front doorbell in the previous half-hour. And Gulliver hadn't even stirred from his cosy doze by the Aga.

Carole opened the front door. The frost had set in fiercely while she'd been indoors and the cold air scoured her face. In the cone of light spreading from the overhead lamp stood Jude. Her blonde hair was covered by a floppy hat and she appeared to be wearing some kind of poncho.

'Carole, hi. I wondered whether you fancied going down to the Crown and Anchor for a drink?'

Under normal circumstances, the knee-jerk response would have been, 'No, thank you. I'm afraid I'm not a "pub person".' But the presence of a gun-toting, possibly drug-crazed woman in her sitting room disqualified the circumstances from being normal. 'Well . . .'

But that was all she had time to say. There was the clatter of a door behind her. Carole rushed back to find her sitting room empty. The sound of the back door slamming shut drew her through into the kitchen. That too was empty. From his position at the foot of the Aga, Gulliver looked up blearily. A real help, he was.

She moved with caution towards the window over the sink and peered into the encroaching darkness. There was no sign of the woman, but the gate at the end of the garden flapped open.

Carole turned back to see Jude framed in the kitchen doorway. That wasn't the Fethering way, her instincts told her. To come into someone's house without being invited, that wouldn't do at all.

'So what about a drink?' asked Jude casually.

To her surprise, Carole Seddon found her lips forming the words, 'Yes. Yes, what a good idea.'

Chapter Six

Carole wasn't a 'pub person' and it was a long time since she had been to the Crown and Anchor. When they first bought the cottage, while she still had a husband, they had gone once or twice for a drink before Sunday lunch. But that period of cohabitation with David in Fethering hadn't lasted, and pub-going didn't seem appropriate to her single status. Except for a couple of visits on those rare occasions when her son came to see her, Carole hadn't stepped inside the Crown and Anchor for at least five years.

To someone who didn't know Fethering, it might seem strange that there was only one pub. Though the Crown and Anchor had been adequate for a fishermen's village, the residential sprawl that had developed seemed to demand more watering holes. But they had never appeared. The Victorians were puritanical about drinking and later residents had been drawn to Fethering by the attractions of its privacy rather than its communal amenities. When the Downside Estate developed, plans were submitted for a new pub up in that area, but traditionalist influences prevailed and the applications were repeatedly rejected. By then the residents of Fethering were determined to ring-fence their village and prevent further expansion of any kind.

Besides, a short country drive to the east, to the west, or north into the Downs gave access to a wide range of characterful hostelries. There was no need for more pubs in Fethering.

Carole certainly hadn't been in the Crown and Anchor since the new management took over. Though established for nearly three years, in Fethering they were still known as the 'new' management. And even though there was only one of them, that one was always referred to as 'they'.

In fact, it was a 'he', and he was one of the reasons why Carole hadn't been in the pub recently. Ted Crisp had arrived with a reputation, and since his arrival in the village it had been amplified by local gossip.

Carole knew him by sight. His hair was too long, he had a scruffy beard and shuffled around in jeans and sweat shirts. She had from time to time vouchsafed the most minimal of 'Fethering Nods' when meeting him in the village shop, but had never exchanged words. The reputation Ted Crisp carried did not endear him to her.

There was the drinking, for a start. An occupational hazard for publicans, everyone knew, but in Ted Crisp's case it was rumoured sometimes to get out of hand. Not all the time, to be fair, but every now and then he was said to go on major benders.

Reports of his behaviour towards women were also exchanged in hushed voices among the lady residents of Fethering. Though the village was hardly at the sharp end of the political-correctness debate, Ted

Crisp's attitude was not approved of. It was one thing for a quaint elderly gentleman to call a lady 'love' or chivalrously to tell her not to worry her pretty little head about things that didn't concern her. It was something else entirely for a man hardly even into middle age to make coarse comments of an overtly sexual nature.

And, according to Ted Crisp's burgeoning reputation, that was what he did. No doubt that kind of thing went down well enough with the younger women, who would snap back at him in kind. But then what did you expect from girls who thought nothing of going into pubs on their own? There was probably no objection from the older brassy divorcees in the village either. But sexual innuendo wasn't the sort of attention that someone of Carole Seddon's background and character would appreciate. Her state of shock might have driven her into the Crown and Anchor that evening, but that did not mean that she was about to engage in vulgar badinage with its landlord.

Jude appeared to be untrammelled by such inhibitions. With an, 'I'll get these', she gestured Carole to a table, bustled up to the bar and greeted Ted Crisp as if she'd been a regular for years. Carole looked around the bar with some surprise. She'd expected something more garish, with flashing slot machines. Instead, she could have been in a comfortable family sitting room. And there was no piped music – a surprise, and a blessing.

'How're you then, young Jude?' Ted Crisp asked, with what Carole categorized as a lecherous leer.

'Not so bad, Ted,' came the easy reply, reinforcing

the impression that they'd known each other for years. Maybe they had, thought Carole. Maybe theirs was a relationship which went back a long way. Maybe there was even a 'history' between them.

But the landlord's next words ruled out that supposition. 'And how are you liking the upright citizens of Fethering? Or am I the only one you've met yet?'

'I've talked to a few people.' Jude gestured across to the table. 'You know Carole, of course?'

There's no 'of course' about it. He doesn't know me, thought Carole. He knows who I am, but he doesn't *know* me. All he knows is that I've never been in his pub before. Could this be a moment of awkwardness?

It wasn't. Ted Crisp extended a beefy arm in a wave and called, 'Evening, darlin' ' across the bar. Carole felt a little frisson of embarrassment. She wasn't anyone's 'darlin' '. Still, the bar was fairly empty. She could recognize nobody there likely to spread to other Fethering residents the news that Carole Seddon had allowed herself to be called 'darlin' ' by Ted Crisp.

'So what're you going to get pissed on tonight?' the landlord asked.

'Two white wines, please,' said Jude.

'Large ones?'

'Oh yes.'

Carole had a momentary urge to remonstrate. Whenever given the choice between large and small – whatever the commodity on offer – she instinctively opted for small. But she did feel rather shaken and trembly this evening. Maybe it was one of those moments when she needed a large glass of wine.

For the first time she let her mind address itself to what had recently happened in her sitting room. Locking up the house and maintaining small talk with Jude as they walked to the Crown and Anchor had effectively blocked off the encounter. Now she allowed the shock to assert itself.

The main shock was not the behaviour of the woman with the gun but her own reaction to it. Carole Seddon had just been the victim of a serious threat, almost an assault, in the privacy of her own home. It was not the kind of incident that should go unreported. If nothing else did, her long experience in the Home Office told her that the police should be informed as soon as possible about unhinged people wandering the countryside with guns.

And yet Carole felt no urgency to contact the police. This morning's interview had put her off them in a big way. She didn't relish further scepticism, further aspersions being cast on the state of her hormones.

Besides, when she thought about it, she realized she had as little corroborative evidence for the second incident as she had had for the first. The body on the beach had disappeared. There was only her word for the fact it had ever existed. And exactly the same applied to the woman with the gun. Carole was the only witness of the woman's arrival, of what she'd said in the sitting room and of her departure. Carole didn't even know whether her new neighbour had heard the closing of the doors when she arrived at the house. Jude certainly hadn't said anything about it.

And that was the way things should stay, for the moment at least. There was no point in asking Jude whether she'd heard anything. It would lead only to further questions and explanations. Carole needed time to work out her next move. Whatever had happened was her business, possibly even her problem. It wasn't something in which she needed to involve anyone else.

There was a roar of raucous laughter from the bar. Ted Crisp had just made a joke which seemed to have amused both Jude and the man slumped on a bar stool beside her. His grey hair was thinning and the way he attacked his large Scotch suggested it wasn't his first of the evening.

Now she could see his half-turned face, Carole knew who the man was. He'd been living in Fethering longer than she had. Rory Turnbull. Dentist with a practice in Brighton. Lived with a sour-faced wife in one of those huge houses on the Shorelands Estate. Carole knew the couple well enough to bestow upon them more than 'the Fethering Nod'; she would actually talk if she met them. But the conversations they shared never strayed on to any subject more contentious than the weather.

'It's the only philosophy worth a fart,' Ted Crisp was saying. 'Eat, drink and be merry . . .'

'Don't waste time with the eating,' said the dentist. 'Drink, drink and be merry – ' the landlord chuckled as Rory Turnbull went on ' – for tomorrow we die.'

There was a change of tone in his last words, as if

he were suddenly aware of their meaning, and that broke the conviviality of the moment. Jude moved away from the bar, cradling the two large glasses of wine and two packets of crisps.

Right, thought Carole, forget the body, forget the woman, now's my opportunity to find out something about my new neighbour. I don't know anything. Here's my chance to fill in the gaps.

Jude placed the wine glasses and dropped the crisps on to the table. 'I'm starving,' she said. 'Takes it out of you, hoicking all that stuff round the house.'

'I'm sure it does.' Carole wondered whether she should repeat her offer of help, but didn't.

'I'll probably order something to eat soon,' Jude went on. 'Haven't begun to get my kitchen up and running yet.'

'Takes time, doesn't it?' Life in Fethering had refined Carole's skill in the deployment of meaningless platitudes.

'If you fancy joining me in a bite . . .'

'No, no, I'll be eating later,' said Carole quickly.

But the thought of food was appealing. Suddenly very hungry, she opened her bag of crisps and put a greedy handful into her mouth. The lunchtime soup and bread seemed an age ago. She took a long swallow of wine.

'You look as if you could do with that,' said Jude.

'What?' Surely the woman wasn't suggesting she had a drink problem? But when she looked into the big brown eyes, Carole saw no criticism, only concern.

'You look like you've had a bit of a shock.'

'Well, yes, I suppose I have,' Carole found herself saying.

Jude was silent. She didn't ask any question, she offered no prompt, and yet Carole found herself ineluctably drawn to further revelation. 'The fact is,' she said, 'I did have rather a shock when I went for my walk on the beach this morning . . .'

And it all came out. The body. The interview with Detective Inspector Brayfield and WPC Juster. Not only the facts either. She told Jude exactly how diminished the police had made her feel.

And Jude simply responded. She didn't push, she didn't probe, she didn't even appear to be waiting for more. Carole could have stopped at any moment.

But she didn't. She went on. She went on to tell of the woman who'd arrived on her doorstep earlier that evening. Of their conversation. Of the gun. Of the woman's disappearance.

'You didn't hear anything? It was just after I opened the door to you.'

Jude shook her head. Blonde tendrils hanging from the bird's-nest of hair tickled her shoulders. It must be blonded, Carole thought again. She must be my age. Well, nearly. It can't be natural.

'No, I didn't hear anything,' said Jude. 'Not a thing.' Surely she's not disbelieving me too, thought Carole. But the panic was quickly allayed. 'Then, you get to know the sounds of your own house, don't you? You hear things other people wouldn't notice.'

'Yes, that's true.'

For the first time since the revelations had started,

Jude asked a question. 'You say the woman appeared as if she was on drugs?'

'Yes. Well, she was certainly odd. She was on *something*. I mean, I don't know much about drugs, except for what I see on the television . . .'

'No.'

' . . . but she did seem to be out of control. Which was why I was so worried about what she might do with the gun.'

'I'm sure you were.' And then Jude expressed her first opinion of the evening. 'I should think drugs are probably behind the whole thing.'

'What do you mean?'

'The body on the beach. The woman with the gun. There's a lot of drug business down here. Long tradition of smuggling on the South Coast. Once it was brandy, silks and tobacco. Now it's cannabis, cocaine and heroin.'

Carole chuckled. 'You seem to know a lot about the subject.'

'Yes,' said Jude.

Chapter Seven

The pub door clattered open, making both of the women look up. The newcomer was a short man of about seventy. The dark-blue reefer jacket and neat corduroy cap bestowed a deliberately naval air. A wispy white beard on the point of his chin gave his head the shape of some root vegetable newly plucked from the soil.

'Evening, mine host,' he said as he strode towards the bar.

Carole recognized Bill Chilcott, another High Street resident. He hadn't noticed her as he came in. She wouldn't have minded if things stayed that way. Since Carole Seddon wasn't a 'pub person', she didn't want the impression to get round that she was. Anything observed by Bill Chilcott would immediately be passed on to his wife, Sandra, and soon all Fethering would know.

'Evening, Bill.' Ted Crisp reached for the pump handle. 'Your customary half?'

'Yes, thank you. And my customary half-hour away from the little woman. Actually, Sandra's deep into some programme about neighbours redecorating each other's front rooms, so she's as happy as a pig in . . .

in its element.' He chuckled at his careful euphemism, then noticed the other man at the bar. 'Rory. How're you doing?'

'Been better,' the dentist grunted.

'Still, at least you didn't get breathalyzed, eh?'

'No, no.' His face twisted ironically before he said, 'Thank you for that.'

Ted Crisp handed Bill Chilcott his customary half. 'What's all this about the dreaded breathalyzer then?'

'The Bill was staking out Seaview Road last night. Stopped Sandra and me on our way back from line-dancing. I was fine, hadn't had a drop, but on the way home I saw Rory's car coming towards me, so I flashed him down to warn him there was a trap ahead. Of course,' Bill Chilcott went on innocently, 'I had no idea whether you'd been drinking or not . . .'

'No.'

'So what did you do, actually?'

'Parked the car by the Yacht Club and walked home. Last thing I need at the moment is trouble with the police.'

'Last thing any of us need.' Bill Chilcott shook his head ruefully. 'I think it's a bit much, the police breathalyzing right down here in Fethering. Up on the main road, that's fine, but here . . . Nanny state gone mad, eh? Mind you, if you want my opinion . . . the police shouldn't be wasting their time harassing respectable motorists. They should be concentrating on the young people round here. There's so much vandalism. I hear there've been more break-ins at the Yacht Club.'

'Have there?' Rory Turnbull looked shocked.

'Who'd you hear that from?' asked Ted. 'The Vice-Commodore?' He said it teasingly, deliberately prompting a predictable reaction.

It came. Bill Chilcott's tuber face turned purple with anger. 'You know I don't give the time of day to that old idiot! No, it was something Sandra heard along the grapevine, from one of our regular swimming group at the Leisure Centre. So no doubt the police'll soon be inspecting down the Yacht Club . . . too late. As ever, shutting the stable door after the horse has gone. If you want my opinion . . .'

But on this occasion the Crown and Anchor was spared another of Bill Chilcott's opinions. Rory Turnbull's stool had clattered against the counter as he rose to leave. 'Better be off,' he announced brusquely.

'Back to the lovely Barbara, eh?' said Ted Crisp.

'Yes, back to the lovely Barbara,' the dentist echoed in a doom-laden voice.

'See you soon, eh?'

'Oh yes. I'll be back.' He made it sound like a death sentence as he fumbled to get his arms into the sleeves of his padded coat.

Carole looked down at their wine glasses. Unaccountably, they'd both become empty.

'Think we need another of those,' declared Jude, rising to her feet.

Carole was out of practice with pub etiquette. 'No, I'll get them,' she said, a little late, following Jude to the bar.

The outer door clattered shut behind Rory Turnbull.

'Wouldn't like to be his first appointment in the morning,' Ted Crisp observed.

'Why? What's he do?' asked Jude.

'Dentist.'

'Oh.' She turned towards the closed door. 'I should've talked to him. I need to register with a dentist down here.'

'If you take my advice, go for one with a steadier hand. I'm afraid friend Rory's been knocking it back a bit the last few months.' Ted Crisp chuckled. 'I'd say you saved his bacon with that warning about the breathalyzer, Bill. Rory seems well marinated in the Scotch these days.'

''Fraid so.'

'Sorry, Bill, should have introduced you. You know Carole, don't you?'

'Of course.'

Was she being hypersensitive to detect a slight raising of one white eyebrow? Oh dear. Her presence in the Crown and Anchor would be all round Fethering the next morning.

'And this is Jude, who's just moved in to the High Street too.'

'Oh, hello. Bill Chilcott.' He flashed her a row of too-perfect dentures. 'You must be in Woodside Cottage.'

'That's right.'

'Needs a lot of work, doesn't it?'

'In time. No rush.'

Carole empathized with the old-fashioned reaction he gave to this laxity.

'Poor old Rory, though,' Ted Crisp went on. 'Mind

you, don't blame him. Must be a bloody depressing business, looking at rotten molars and breathing in everyone's halitosis all day.'

'Presumably the money's some compensation,' Carole observed drily. 'You don't see many poor dentists, do you?'

The landlord shook his head, bunching his lips in a silent whistle of disagreement. 'Don't you believe it. Living from hand to mouth, the lot of them.'

'They're certainly not. They're—'

But the sound of Jude and Bill Chilcott's laughter stopped Carole.

' "Hand to mouth". Dentist joke,' Ted Crisp explained.

Carole said nothing. She'd never been very good at recognizing jokes.

'Anyway, from the amount he's been putting back in here recently, I'd say Rory Turnbull was not a happy man. Sorry, I'm forgetting I'm here to work. Two more large white wines, is it?'

'Yes,' replied Jude, and Carole didn't even feel the slightest instinct to ask for a small one. 'Rory Turnbull?' Jude mused. 'And you said his wife's name's Barbara?'

'That's right.'

'Why, do you know her?' asked Bill Chilcott.

'No. Just I had a card through the letter box yesterday. From a Barbara Turnbull. Asking me to go to some coffee morning tomorrow. As a new resident of Fethering. Something connected with All Saints.'

'That'd be Rory's wife,' Carole confirmed.

'And I think, if you go, you'll have the pleasure of

meeting my wife, Sandra, there in the morning. She'll be going after our swim.'

'Oh, good.'

'Barbara Turnbull's very active in the church locally. She and her mother, Winnie. Very devout.'

'That's probably what drives old Rory in here,' said Ted. 'Needs to swill out the odour of sanctity with a few large ones. So you going to this coffee morning then, Jude?'

'Oh yes.'

'Joining the God squad, eh?'

'Not sure about that. I just want to find out everything about Fethering. A new place is always exciting, isn't it?'

Though not sure that she agreed, Carole didn't raise any objection as they settled back at their table with the refilled glasses. But realizing she'd been given a good cue to find out a bit more about her neighbour, she asked, 'Are you religious?'

Jude let out a warm chuckle. 'Depends what you mean by religious.'

'Well . . . church-going?'

The chuckle expanded into laughter. 'Good heavens, no.'

Having elicited one small piece of information, Carole pressed her advantage. 'I don't know anything about you, actually . . . Jude.' She managed to say the name with only a vestigial hint of quotation marks around it. 'Are you married?'

'Not at the moment. What about you?'

'Have been. Divorced.' Carole still felt a slight pang when she said the word. It wasn't that she regretted the loss of her married status or that she wished David was still around. Very much the opposite. She knew she was much better off without him. But being divorced still seemed to her to carry an overtone of failure.

'How long ago?' asked Jude.

'Ooh, ten years now. No, twelve. How time flies.'

'Any children?'

'One son. Stephen. He's nearly thirty. I don't see a lot of him. What about you?'

Jude looked at her watch, seeming not to hear the return question. 'I'm really starving,' she said. 'I've got to order something to eat. Are you sure you're not going to?'

'Well,' said Carole.

They both ended up ordering fish and chips. By then, Bill Chilcott, having made his customary half of bitter last exactly his customary half an hour, had left the pub with a hearty, 'Cheerio, mine host.'

The two women's conversation for the rest of the evening moved away from their personal details. Jude was intrigued by the two dramatic events of Carole's day and kept returning to the body on the beach and the woman with the gun, offering ever new conjectures to explain them. Only once had Carole managed to get back to her neighbour's domestic circumstances.

She'd said, 'So you're not married at the moment?'

'No.'

'But is there someone special in your life?'

But this inquiry had prompted only another throaty chuckle. 'They're all special,' Jude had said.

Carole's recollections of the end of the evening

were a little hazy. Of course, it wasn't just the alcohol. She may have drunk a little more wine than she usually did – quite a lot more wine than she usually did, as it happened – but it was her shocked emotional state that had made her exceptionally susceptible to its effects.

She comforted herself with this thought as she slipped into stupefied sleep.

The other thought in her mind was a recollection of something her new neighbour had said. Carole couldn't remember the exact words, but she felt sure Jude had suggested their working together. If the police weren't going to show any interest in doing it, then the two of them should find out who killed the body on the beach.

Chapter Eight

Carole was woken by Gulliver's barking. This was unusual. Normally, when she went downstairs to make herself a cup of tea, he was still comatose in his basket by the Aga. And the idea that he might have been barking to alert her to some intruder in the house was laughable. Such behaviour was not in Gulliver's nature.

As she looked around her bedroom, Carole realized something else was odd. The curtains were not drawn and thin but bright daylight was trickling through the windows. She raised an arm to check her wristwatch, but couldn't see the hands without her glasses. She fumbled and found them on the far edge of the bedside table, not neatly aligned on the near side where she left them every night.

She squinted to focus on the watch. A quarter to ten! Good heavens!

She sat up sharply, and then realized how much her head was aching.

Carole hurried into some clothes and rushed Gulliver out on to the open ground behind the house. The grass was still dusted with frost and her ears tingled in the cold air.

The speed and relief with which the dog squatted at the first opportunity made her realize what a narrow escape her kitchen floor had had.

She couldn't blame the dog. He'd been very good, exercising all the control of which he was capable, while his mistress overslept. She couldn't blame anyone but herself.

Except of course for her new next-door neighbour. It was Jude who'd led her into self-indulgence at the Crown and Anchor. Maybe Jude wasn't such a suitable companion after all. Carole decided that any future communication between them should be strictly rationed.

She felt a little tremor of embarrassment. She had talked far too much the previous evening, confiding things that she had never confided to anyone else.

No, Jude was definitely a bad influence. Carole couldn't remember when she'd last had a hangover.

At first she'd decided she wouldn't take anything for the pain, just brazen it out. But after an hour or so, ready to succumb, she had gone to the bathroom cabinet, only to find it empty of aspirin. Oh well, that was meant. Serve her right. She couldn't take anything.

Half an hour after reaching that conclusion, though, she had decided she'd have to go to the shop to get some aspirin.

As she set out, neatly belted up in her Burberry, Carole heard a heavy regular thudding which she knew didn't come from inside her own head. There must be some construction work happening somewhere in the Fethering area. Whatever it was, the noise didn't make her headache feel any better.

The shop was not a village shop in the old sense of the expression, though it occupied the site where a proper village shop had once stood. That old shop, incorporating a post office, had been run by an elderly couple and very rarely had in stock anything anyone might need. But that didn't matter. The people of Fethering drove in their large cars to do their major shopping at the nearby out-of-town Sainsbury's or Tesco's. They used the village shop only when they'd run out of life's little essentials – milk, bread, cheese, ketchup, cigarettes or gin – and to collect their pensions. Many of them went in to buy things they didn't need, just so they'd have the opportunity for a good gossip.

But that was no way to run a business and in the late 1980s, when the elderly couple retired, the old shop was demolished, replaced by a rectangular glass-fronted structure and called a supermarket. It was one of a local chain called Allinstore – a compression that someone in a meeting must once have thought was a good idea of 'All-in-store'. This verbal infelicity was untrue under the Trades Description Act (in fact, the store's local nickname was 'Nowtinstore'), but it was also symptomatic of the lacklustre style which epitomized Allinstore management. The only detail the new shop had in common with the old one was that it very rarely had in stock anything anyone might need, but people still went in to buy things they didn't need, just so's they'd have the opportunity for a good gossip.

In the transformation of Fethering's shopping facilities the village had also lost its post office, which led to a lot of complicated travel arrangements on pension days. And Allinstore had become an outlet for the National Lottery, thus enabling the residents of Fethering to shatter their hopes and dreams on a weekly basis.

The architect who'd designed the new supermarket (assuming such a person existed and the plans hadn't been scribbled on the back of an envelope by a builder who'd once seen a shoebox) had placed two wide roof-supporting pillars just in front of the main tills. Whether he'd done this out of vindictiveness or had simply been infected by the endemic Allinstore incompetence was unknowable, but the result was that many shopping hours were wasted and much frustration caused by customers negotiating their way around these obstructions. Mercifully Allinstore did not supply its shoppers with trolleys, only wire baskets, but many of its elderly clientele brought in their own wheeled shopping containers and these added to the traffic mayhem around the pillars.

Carole, aspirin packet in hand, was stuck behind one of them, out of sight of the tills, when she heard a familiar male voice say, 'Apparently they found a dead body on the beach this morning.'

She craned forward, encroaching on the elderly lady with a wheeled basket in front of her, and saw Bill Chilcott.

'Really?' said the girl behind the till, with the same

level of interest she would have accorded to the news that there were no more toilet rolls on the shelf.

'Oh yes,' he asserted. 'Heard it on the BBC local news this morning.'

Carole leaned over the elderly lady in front of her. 'Morning, Bill.'

'I don't know,' he said, unnecessarily loudly and with what he imagined to be a lecherous grin. 'Crown and Anchor last night, Allinstore this morning. We can't go on meeting like this. People will start to talk.'

'Yes.' Carole dismissed the pleasantry with a curt smile. 'What's this about dead bodies?'

'I heard it on the radio when Sandra and I came back from our swim at the Leisure Centre. A dead body found washed up on Fethering beach.'

'Did they say who it was? Or what had happened to him?'

'They didn't even say whether it was a "him". Probably be more on the lunchtime news. Mind you, if you want my opinion . . .' It was a mystery why Bill Chilcott always made this proviso; he was going to give his opinion anyway. 'I should think it's one of those *weekend sailors*.'

He loaded the words with contempt. Though the precise details of Bill Chilcott's naval background were ill-defined, he never missed an opportunity of saying that seafaring should be left to the professionals. 'Some idiot who took out a pleasure boat without sufficient knowledge of local conditions and *got what was coming to him*. If you want my opinion, they should impose some kind of regulations on the kind of people who're allowed to take boats . . .'

But as Bill Chilcott's hobbyhorse gathered momentum, Carole stopped listening. In spite of her headache, she felt a glow of vindication. She looked forward to grovelling apologies from Detective Inspector Brayfield and WPC Juster. There had been a body on the beach.

Chapter Nine

Jude found the Shorelands Estate rather spooky as she walked through on the way to Barbara Turnbull's coffee morning. It took a lot to cast down her spirits. The frosty greyness of the morning hadn't done it. Nor had she had any adverse reaction to the wine of the night before. She'd drunk no more than a usual evening's intake. But Jude had a feeling that spending any length of time in Shorelands could bring her spirits down very quickly indeed.

Though laid out on lavishly spacious lines, the predominant feeling the estate gave her was one of claustrophobia. The main entrance gates looked as if they were never closed, but they were nonetheless gates. The '20 mph' speed signs and the 'CRIME ALERT IN OPERATION' notices on lampposts gave Jude the feeling of being under surveillance.

This was reinforced by the contents of a display board which she stopped to read. Behind glass, under a neatly painted wooden sign reading 'Shorelands Estate', was a list of regulations for residents. Since these included orders as to how visibly washing could be hung out to dry and times at which lawn-mowing was permitted, Jude felt relieved that Shorelands was a part of Fethering way out of her price range.

Though of massive proportions and, in most cases, with much-sought-after sea-backing locations, none of the houses appealed to her either. The estate was far too upmarket to go for uniformity. Each house was very positively different from all the others, and each failed to appeal to Jude in a different way. Every conceivable architectural style was represented, but in a manner that seemed more parody than homage. Whether with Tudor beams, tall Elizabethan clusters of chimneys, geometric Georgian windows, Alpine chalet gables, thatched roofs or the turrets of French châteaux, all the houses seemed firmly rooted in the time of their construction, the unglamorous 1950s.

The architectural style echoed in the Turnbulls' home was Spanish. The wrought-iron gates in the high white-painted walls might have led into the vineyards of some well-heeled Andalusian grandee, were it not for the coy metal name-plate with a squirrel motif which revealed that the house was called Brigadoon. And the authentic Spanishness of the frontage, with its heavily embossed door, terracotta pots in niches and gratuitous curlicues of wrought iron, was also let down by two quaint Victorian lampposts and by the metal expanse of the double garage's up-and-over door.

The house into which Jude was admitted had been recently 'improved' by an expensive interior designer. No attempt had been made to continue the Spanish theme inside. The carpets toned with the walls; the walls were suitably complemented by the discreet pastel patterns of the curtains. Each item of furniture knew its place. The strain of all this tastefulness was almost tangible. To Jude the interior of Brigadoon had the homely charm of an intensive care unit.

But her impression of the decor was only fleeting. As ever, she was much more interested in people than in things, and immediately focused on the woman who had opened the door to her with a brisk, 'Ah, hello, you must be the new owner of Woodside Cottage. I'm Barbara Turnbull. I'm sorry, I didn't know your name, so I hope you didn't mind my just addressing the card to "The New Resident". But you said on the phone you're called "Jude".'

'That's right.'

'Jude . . . er . . .?' the hostess fished.

'Just Jude's fine.'

Barbara Turnbull was in her fifties and was one of those women who'd spread sideways. She walked with a slight swaying motion, but carefully, as if afraid her bulk might knock things over. Her hair, dyed a copper-beech colour, had been recently cut short. She wore a broad green skirt and little matching waistcoat over a blouse with an ivy design. Her stout legs ended in improbably small, flat blue shoes with decorative buckles. There were a lot of rings on her hands. Uniform beige make-up covered her face, and her lips were highlighted by lipstick of an only slightly darker beige.

'I'm afraid the house is a complete tip,' she said, as she hung up Jude's coat and led her through the hall. Barbara Turnbull's remark was completely at odds with the evidence. The house looked as if individual motes of dust were removed with tweezers every hour on the hour. 'My cleaning lady, Maggie, couldn't come in this morning. Just called five minutes before she was due to arrive to say she'd got some problem with her son. Honestly, people are so inconsiderate.'

'Her son couldn't help being ill, could he?' Jude suggested.

'That's not the point. Maggie should have had some contingency plan ready for that eventuality. Anyway, I'm not sure he was ill. Some other problem, I wouldn't be surprised. He's very neurotic, from all accounts. Maggie seems to have no control over that boy of hers. Psychological problems . . . But then . . . *single parent.*' Barbara spoke the words as though no further explanation were needed. Jude might have taken issue with her, but they had reached the door of the large front sitting room and she was ushered inside.

'Now, hello, everyone,' said Barbara loudly. 'This is "Jude", who's recently moved in to Woodside Cottage in the High Street. I'll just tell you who everyone is.'

'Don't bother.' Jude knew she'd never remember a whole catalogue of anonymous names. She'd do much better talking to the other guests individually, matching names with personalities. 'I'll work it out as we—'

Too late. Barbara Turnbull was determined to go through the full list. There were about a dozen, all women, with an average age of well over sixty. Jude got the impression that few of them had ever had jobs beyond looking after husbands and children. They were dressed as though their lives had become one long stationary cruise. Most of the faces looked deterrent, one or two more approachable. All of them wore too much make-up.

'. . . and this is my mother, Winnie.' Barbara Turnbull's guided tour finished on the smallest and oldest person present. 'Winnie Norton. Now, "Jude", why don't you sit and have a chat to Mummy while I get you some coffee. How do you like it?'

'Just black, please.'

'Any sweetener?'

'No, thanks.'

'Right you are, "Jude". Just black it is.'

'So how do you like Fethering?' asked Winnie Norton. Her hair, a blue that was picked up by the veins on the back of her hands, had been engineered into a rigid structure like spun sugar. The eyes were black and unashamedly curious. From the Yorkshire terrier on her lap peered another pair of black and unashamedly curious eyes. They took in Jude, not liking what they saw, and a low growl rumbled from the tiny silken body.

Winnie Norton wore a tweed suit whose dominant colour was turquoise. There were even more rings on her hands than on her daughter's, but they hung loosely on the thin talons.

'Seems fine from what I've seen of it so far,' Jude replied.

'Did you know the area before you moved here?'

'Not well.'

'Well, you'll find Fethering's very welcoming,' said Winnie Norton. The dog, unwilling to endorse this view, yapped petulantly. 'Quiet, Churchill.' She tapped his nose gently before going on, 'Yes, very welcoming . . . to the right sort of person.'

'Ah.'

'Of course, in the old days, before the war, only the right sort of person moved here, but since they developed that Downside Estate . . . well, something of an *element*'s crept in.' The little black eyes scrutinized Jude, trying to gauge the risk of her being an 'element'.

The smaller set of black eyes on her lap had already made up their mind. Jude was definitely an 'element'. He yapped ferociously, baring his vicious little teeth.

'Now do be quiet, Churchill,' said his mistress mildly. 'We have to be on our best behaviour for a coffee morning, don't we?'

The yapping subsided into a malignant rumbling.

'Have you lived here long, Mrs Norton?' asked Jude.

'All my life in the area, yes.'

'But not all that time here at Shorelands?'

'Oh, I don't live on the estate. No, when I sold the big house after my husband died, I bought one of those new flats near the Yacht Club. Spray Lodge – do you know where I mean?'

'Sorry. Still getting my bearings.'

'It's a very nice block. The residents do have a degree of control over who moves in.'

'Ah.'

'Well, you have to these days, don't you?' Winnie

Norton chuckled. 'All kinds of people have got the *money* to move into somewhere like Fethering now.'

'Yes.' Jude realized that, if she didn't quickly move the subject in another direction, she'd come to blows with the old lady. 'Do you have any grandchildren, Mrs Norton?'

'No. Barbara and Rory didn't want children.'

'Ah.' Churchill barked approval of this situation, while Jude looked around the vast sitting room. 'So it's just the two of them living in this house, is it?'

'Rory does very well,' said his mother-in-law, as if that answered the question. And perhaps, Jude reflected, by Winnie Norton's standards, it did. Rory Turnbull was making a lot of money as a dentist; therefore it behoved him to buy a large house on the Shorelands Estate. That was a fact of life, nothing to do with how much space he and Barbara actually needed. 'Of course,' the old lady went on, 'he never really was our sort, but Barbara's done wonders with him.'

Jude began to understand why Rory Turnbull needed his intravenous drip of whisky down at the Crown and Anchor. But Winnie Norton was prevented from casting down more of her poisoned pearls of wisdom by the arrival of her daughter with Jude's coffee.

'Now you mustn't monopolize our guest, Mummy. Incidentally, "Jude" – ' like Carole, Barbara Turnbull still couldn't quite say the name without a penumbra of quotation marks (a fact which amused its owner hugely) – 'we are hoping that Roddy himself will drop in later.'

'Roddy?'

'Canon Roderick Granger, to give him his full title. He's the vicar of All Saints'. A tower of strength locally.' Barbara lowered her voice and gave the newcomer a look whose beadiness matched her mother's and Churchill's. 'You are a believer, aren't you, Jude?'

'Oh yes.'

The easiness of the reply brought visible relief to Barbara Turnbull's face. 'Thank goodness for that. In these benighted times there are lots of people who don't even put "C of E" on forms.'

'I didn't say I was a believer in the Church of England,' Jude pointed out.

Her hostess looked horror-struck. 'You're not Catholic, are you?'

'No, I'm not.'

Another sigh of relief. 'There are a lot of them down here, you know. Arundel's quite a centre for the Rock Cakes.'

'Is it?'

'Mm. It's a Catholic cathedral there, you know.' Barbara moved on. 'You'll find All Saints' is a friendly church, with quite a lot of social activities. Roddy's very keen on that side of things. He always says it's too easy for church-goers to get po-faced about religion.' A little chuckle. 'He's such an amusing man.'

If what she'd just heard was an example of the vicar's wit, Jude wasn't convinced. What was clear, though, was that, in her hostess's eyes, Canon Roderick Granger could do no wrong. She was almost coquettish when she talked about him. It was quite possible that the Canon was held up to her husband as an exemplar of all the things that Rory Turnbull wasn't.

'Anyway,' Barbara went on, 'if you don't see him this morning, you'll catch him at the morning service on Sunday. Roddy's sermons are quite something. Lots of jolly good laughs on the way, but a real core of serious truth.'

'I'm not a church-goer,' said Jude.

'Oh.'

'I don't want you to get the wrong impression. I accepted your invitation because I wanted to meet some local people, not because I'm ever likely to step into All Saints'.'

Barbara Turnbull gaped like a beached fish.

'But I've nothing against the Church of England,' Jude reassured her with a huge smile. 'Everyone should be allowed to believe in what they want to believe in – don't you agree?'

Barbara's expression showed that she certainly didn't agree. Allow everyone to believe in what they want to believe in? That, her look seemed to say, is a short cut to anarchy.

But her transparent thoughts remained unvoiced. 'Do let me introduce you to some other people, "Jude".' This time she managed to get a double set of quotation marks round the name.

With the newcomer in her wake, Barbara bore down on a bird-like woman with spiky white hair who was saying, 'And this is meant to be a civilized country. I ask you, is it civilized to park a boat trailer so that the mast goes over the hedge into one's neighbour's garden by a full three inches? I mean, is that the action of a civilized human being? I'd say it was the action of a boorish lout, if you want my opinion.'

'Sorry to interrupt,' Barbara Turnbull cooed, 'but I'd like to introduce you to someone who's a very near neighbour of yours, Sandra.'

The bird-like eyes darted to take in Jude and form an instant opinion of her.

'This is Sandra Chilcott.' It was said in best hostess manner. 'And here's the new owner of Woodside Cottage, whose name is . . .'

'Jude,' said Jude, taking Sandra Chilcott's thin hand in hers.

'Jude, of course! I've heard all about you from Bill. Though, of course, being a man, he didn't tell me anything very interesting. I really do think men walk around with their eyes closed, don't you, Jude? They never notice anything.' She smiled slyly. 'Didn't take you long to find your way to the Crown and Anchor, though, did it?'

Jude was then introduced to the two women either side of Sandra, who'd acted as audience for the diatribe about her neighbour. 'Well, "Jude",' one of them asked, 'have you come down to Fethering in search of the quiet life?'

'No, not really. I think quietness is an internal thing, don't you?'

The two women looked at her in some puzzlement, as Sandra took her cue. 'If it's quietness you're after, I'm not sure that you've come to the right place.

You'll find quite a lot of exciting things happen in Fethering.'

'Really?'

'Oh yes.' Sandra Chilcott warmed to her task as news-bearer. 'For example, this morning a dead body was found on the beach.'

Chapter Ten

'Yippee!'

Carole gave her visitor an old-fashioned look. Her head was still aching and she still blamed Jude for leading her astray. It was a bit premature for her new neighbour to arrive again so soon at her door – and unannounced. And particularly shouting, 'Yippee!' That wasn't the way things were done in Fethering.

'What is the cause of your celebration?' Carole asked, rather frostily.

Jude was blithely unaffected by the deterrence in her tone. 'You were right. There was a body on the beach. I met Bill Chilcott's wife, Sandra, at Barbara Turnbull's – and she'd heard about it on local radio.'

'Yes, I heard too. I met Bill in Allinstore.'

'So you're vindicated, aren't you?'

'Well . . .'

They'd been standing on the doorstep almost long enough for the situation to become awkward. Carole would have to either invite her neighbour in or quickly invent some excuse and get rid of her.

But Jude solved the social dilemma before it developed. 'Anyway, I was thinking there's bound to be something about it on the local news at lunchtime.'

She looked at her watch, a huge white dial which appeared to be tied on to her chubby arm with a broad velvet ribbon. 'In two minutes. So I think we ought to watch that.'

'Yes.' Carole had been intending to do so anyway. But before she had time to say, 'Thank you very much for the reminder. I'll see you later', and close the door, Jude had grabbed her by the hand.

'So come on, let's go and watch it at my place.'

'What?'

'I'll knock up something for lunch. And we can open a bottle of wine.'

'In the *daytime*?' Carole responded instinctively.

'Sure, why not?'

'I think I probably had quite enough wine last night.'

'Oh, feeling the effects, are you?' There was no judgement, only sympathy in the way the question was posed. 'In that case you definitely need a hair of the dog.'

'That reminds me. I was going to take Gulliver out for—'

'Come *on*!' And Carole's hand, still being held, was given a quite definite yank.

'But I haven't got my coat!' wailed Carole.

'We're only going about five yards.'

As she locked her front door and followed Jude down the symmetrical flags of her garden path, Carole managed to convince herself she was going simply because it would be good to talk about her traumatic discovery of the day before, and not because she wanted to have a snoop inside Jude's home.

Her neighbour's front path was an ill-fitting jigsaw of uneven red bricks, through whose interstices moss and weeds protruded. 'Got into a terrible state, hasn't it?' Carole observed. 'You'll have to get this sorted, won't you?'

'Oh, I quite like it like that.' The breeziness with which Jude committed this blasphemy to the standards of Fethering suggested that it wasn't said for effect, that she really meant it.

She pushed the dark-wood front door open with an elbow and beckoned Carole to follow her inside. Good heavens, she hadn't even locked it. The fact that Jude had gone only next door didn't excuse this lapse. Suppose Carole had invited her in? Fethering High Street was a Neighbourhood Watch Area and, as everyone locally knew, the average burglary took less than three minutes.

And, dear oh dear, as she passed through the hall, Carole noticed that Jude's voluminous handbag was on a table right by the front door. Where had Jude come from to have such a cavalier attitude to the serious business of security? The thought reminded Carole once again that she still didn't know where Jude had come from. In fact, she knew very little more about her neighbour than she had the moment they first met.

The sitting room into which she was ushered was low and, because the old leaded windows hadn't yet been replaced by sealed double-glazing units, rather dark. Though Carole had never been inside Woodside Cottage during its previous occupancy, she'd assumed that the old lady would have had more of the basic modernization done. There was no evidence of central heating radiators, though an open fire crackled cheerfully from the grate (without a fire-guard in front of it, Carole noted, awarding her neighbour another black mark for domestic security).

Jude snapped on a couple of lights with dangly paper shades and illuminated what appeared to be an overstocked junk shop. She crossed to a portable television perched on a pile of old wooden wine-crates and switched it on. 'News is on One,' she said. 'Fiddle with the aerial if the picture's fuzzy. I'll go and open the wine.'

And she disappeared into the kitchen before Carole could say that she didn't really need wine at this time of day. As the television came to life with a picture that was indeed fuzzy and as she moved the aerial on top of the set around to improve it, Carole took in the crammed contents of the room.

No surface was unlittered. There were piles of books and papers and knick-knacks everywhere. And there didn't seem any theme or coherence to what was on display. Carved African animals jostled with brass handbells and green marble-stoppered bottles. Silver-framed photographs of stiff Victorians consorted with china cats and glass candlesticks. Eggs of exotically veined stone lay beside Russian dolls and spinner's bobbins.

Snuggled in the midst of this chaos were a small sofa and two armchairs. It was impossible to tell whether they were a matching set, though their varied outlines under the brightly patterned throws that covered them suggested otherwise. Further pieces of furniture were also hung with gratuitous drapery. The room was like the nest of a kleptomaniac magpie.

One must make allowances, thought Carole magnanimously. The poor woman moved in only a couple of days ago. She's just had everything dumped in here. When she's got the stuff distributed around the house, this room'll look a lot tidier.

'Do sit down,' said Jude, bustling in from the kitchen. One hand held a bottle of red wine, the other two glasses and a corkscrew that she was busily plying. As she slumped into one of the heavily draped armchairs, she looked around with satisfaction. 'At least I've got this room done,' she said.

Carole's jaw dropped. The decor was *intentional*. The confusion expressed how Jude *wanted* the room to look. But, even if Carole had been so ill-mannered as to say anything, there wasn't time. Jude sprang up again and shoved the wine and glasses into her neighbour's hands. 'Here, you pour this.'

Then she crossed to the still-fuzzy television and, with a cry of, 'Come on, behave yourself, you little bastard!', gave it a resounding thump on the side. The picture immediately resolved itself into crystalline clarity.

Her timing had been perfect. The local news had just started. It was fronted by the kind of gauche female newsreader who makes you realize that, bad though network presenters may be, there remain unimaginable depths of the television barrel yet to be scraped.

But Carole and Jude didn't notice the girl's incompetence; they were too caught up in what she was actually saying.

'A body was found on the beach at Fethering this morning by a woman walking her dog.'

'Only a day late,' Jude chuckled.

'It wasn't me,' Carole objected.

'The body,' the newsreader droned on, 'has been identified as that of sixteen-year-old – ' Carole's jaw dropped – 'Arran Spalding . . .'

As the name was mentioned, a picture of the dead boy filled the screen. One of those school photographs, posed against a vague cloud-like backdrop. The caption showed that, though it had been pronounced 'Arran', his name was spelt 'Aaron'. Aaron Spalding, with his floppy blond fringe and cheekily crooked grin, looked nearer twelve than sixteen. Probably he had been when the picture was taken. Self-conscious adolescents don't like being photographed; what showed on the screen was perhaps the most recent image available. But the innocent wickedness of his face added a poignancy to the fact of the boy's death.

The newsreader's voice continued drably: ' . . . who lived in Fethering and who had been missing for the past twenty-four hours. The cause of death has not yet been established, but the police have not ruled out foul play.'

Then, with one of those awkward jump-cuts beloved of local newsreaders, she moved on to the allegation that a recent spate of deaths among ducks in the area had been caused by ferrets.

The two women looked at each other in amazement. Carole noticed with even more amazement that half the contents of her wine glass had somehow disappeared.

'But it's . . . I mean . . .' she spluttered. 'It was a middle-aged man, the body I saw. No way could it have been mistaken for a teenager.'

'It wasn't mistaken for a teenager,' said Jude firmly. 'There have been *two* bodies on the beach. First the middle-aged man you saw, then this poor kid.'

'You don't think there's any connection between them, do you?'

Jude cocked her head thoughtfully to one side. 'There's no reason why there should be. It'd be a remarkable coincidence if they were connected. Then again, it's already a coincidence that two dead bodies have appeared on consecutive days. Logic dictates that the two incidents have nothing to do with each other, but my instinct says they have. And,' she concluded mischievously, 'in a straight fight between logic and instinct, I'd go for instinct every time.'

'Hm . . .' Carole might have called the odds rather differently. 'Well, this poor boy's death is nothing to do with me. It's not as if I even found the body. Some other woman with a dog. I wonder who it was . . . And, as for the first body, the police don't even believe that existed.'

'But it did!'

Jude sounded aggrieved, almost as if it was *her* story that was being doubted. Carole realized, with a sudden warm feeling, that her neighbour had never for a moment questioned her account of what she had found.

'Since that body did exist,' Jude went on, 'there are

two rather important questions which have yet to be answered. One – whose body was it? And, two – where is the body now?'

Carole shrugged. 'Two questions to which, I'm afraid, we can never know the answer.'

'Don't you believe it.' Jude rose determinedly and switched off the television. Then she picked up the bottle and refilled the glasses, which had both unaccountably become empty. 'I think we should find out the answers to those two questions.'

'Us?' said Carole. 'But surely murder – if it is murder – that's a job for the police.'

'Have you been impressed by how the police have reacted so far?'

'No, but . . .'

There was a gleam in Jude's big brown eyes. 'I think this could be rather fun.' Then, briskly, she announced, 'I'll get us some lunch. There's a sort of Turkish salad I do in the fridge. Aubergines and yoghurt and what-have-you. That sound all right?'

'Sounds great,' Carole replied. 'Are you vegetarian?'

'Sometimes,' said Jude easily, as she disappeared into the kitchen, leaving Carole to wonder when she'd found the time to buy aubergines. There was no way that Allinstore's stock would have aspired to anything so exotic.

The Turkish salad was excellent and somehow, by the time they'd finished it, the wine bottle was empty too. Carole felt very warm and cosseted in the draped sofa in front of the glowing fire. She yawned.

'Wiped out?' asked Jude.

'A bit. At least my headache's gone, though.'

'Never fails.' Jude chuckled. 'Go and have a little sleep.'

Carole was shocked. 'During the *day*? But I'm not ill.'

Her neighbour shrugged. 'Please yourself.' Then she looked thoughtful. 'I wonder who your body was . . .'

'No idea.'

'No, but we're going to find out.'

'Were you serious? What you said before lunch? About *us* investigating this?'

'Of course I was. Why, don't you think it's a good idea?'

To her astonishment, Carole found her lips forming the words, 'Yes, I think it's a very good idea.'

'Excellent. So where do we start?'

Carole looked blank. 'Don't know. I'm afraid I haven't got much of a track record as an investigator.'

'No, but you have a track record as an intelligent woman who can work things out for herself.'

'Maybe.'

'So what information do we currently have about your body on the beach?'

Carole stretched out a dubious lower lip. 'All we have, I suppose, is the fact that he was wearing a life-jacket that was printed "Property of Fethering Yacht Club".'

'Right.' Jude clapped her hands gleefully. 'Then it seems pretty obvious to me that the first thing we should do is go down to Fethering Yacht Club.'

'But we can't do that,' Carole objected.

'Why not?'

'Because we're not members.'

'Oh, for heaven's sake!' said Jude.

Chapter Eleven

In the snugness of Woodside Cottage they hadn't noticed the weather worsening, but when they emerged the afternoon had turned charcoal grey and relentless icy rain swirled around them. The wind kept animating new puddles on the pavement into flurries of spray. The cold wetness stung their faces.

'Sure you wouldn't rather have that sleep?' Jude suggested teasingly.

'No,' came the crisp reply. Affront at the idea of sleeping during the daytime, though unspoken, remained implicit. 'I'll just get my coat and we'll go to the Yacht Club.'

Carole hardened her heart against Gulliver's pathetic appeals to join them – he'd go for a walk in any weather – and wrapped her Burberry firmly around her. Soon she and Jude were striding into the horizontal rain towards the Fethering Yacht Club.

Fixed to the gatepost of one of the High Street houses they passed was a plastic-enclosed notice which read, in professionally printed capitals, 'THIS FRONT GARDEN IS PRIVATE PROPERTY. TRESPASSING, AT ANY LEVEL, IS STRICTLY FORBIDDEN.'

'What the hell does that mean?' asked Jude.

Carole chuckled. 'It's the Chilcotts.'

'Bill and Sandra?'

'The very same. They're having a feud with their next-door neighbour.'

Jude recollected the fag-end of conversation she'd heard at Barbara Turnbull's. 'About where he parks his boat?'

'About that or about anything else they happen to think of. It's a battle that's been running for years.'

'And does the neighbour respond in kind?'

By way of answer, Carole pointed to a notice, hand-written in marker-pen capitals, which was pinned to the gatepost of the next house. It read, 'ALL TRESPASSERS WILL BE TREATED WITH RESPECT AND COURTESY – SO LONG AS THEY'RE NOT THE PETTY-MINDED COUPLE FROM NEXT DOOR.'

Jude giggled. 'Sounds as if the people this side have at least got a sense of humour about it.'

'I'm not so sure,' said Carole. 'I think it's all in deadly earnest on both sides.'

Jude looked into the garden. The trailer of a sailing dinghy with a fitted cover was parked diagonally across the cemented area in front of the garage. Its flattened mast missed the shared hedge between the feuding households by fractions of an inch. 'So who's the sailor?' she asked.

'Denis Woodville. It's quite possible we'll meet him at the Yacht Club. He's rather a big noise there, so I've heard. Incidentally, Jude – ' Carole was finding, the more she said the name, the less pronounced were the virtual quotation marks with which she enclosed it – 'what are we going to say when we get there? I mean, shall I say that I saw one of the club's life-jackets on the body I found?'

'No, no, no. Don't mention the body – that'll only cause a lot of unnecessary follow-up questions.' Jude looked thoughtful for a moment, then clapped her gloved hands together as she found the solution. 'Yes! Everyone round here seems totally obsessed by security, so that's going to be our way in. We'll say we saw some kids on the beach playing with a Fethering Yacht Club life-jacket and we wondered if it'd been stolen . . . You know, whether the club's had any kind of break-in recently?'

'But that's not true,' Carole objected.

Jude's brown eyes took on a new vagueness. 'True? Truth is such a relative concept, though, isn't it, Carole? And telling the truth, the whole truth and nothing but the truth is the surest way of completely screwing up your life, wouldn't you agree?'

Carole certainly would not agree. Telling the truth, the whole truth and nothing but the truth to everyone had been one of the guiding principles of her life. It was an approach which had caused occasional awkwardnesses, moments when confrontations could have been avoided by a little tactful finessing of that truth. Indeed, if she'd been less strict in her adherence to the principle, she might still have been married. But Carole Seddon had never given in to the way of compromise. She had always told the complete truth and faced up to the consequences of her actions.

So she didn't give any answer to Jude's question.

* * *

Rather than going straight down the High Street and turning left on to Seaview Road, they cut along one of the side lanes and approached the Yacht Club along the banks of the Fether. Though it was hardly a day for sightseeing, Carole wanted to show Jude another aspect of the village.

There was a high path along the side of the river, the top of the defences which, further on by the Yacht Club, joined up with the sea wall. Cars were kept off this pedestrian area by serried rows of concrete bollards. Near the path a rusted Second World War mine had been converted into a collecting box for some maritime charity.

It was low tide. The Fether was a truculent sliver of brown water between swollen mudflats, which looked bleakly malevolent in the driving rain.

'Wouldn't fancy falling down there,' said Jude.

'No, I think you could have a problem getting out again. Everything sinks into that lot.'

Carole pointed out a row of public moorings, pontoons loosely attached to tall posts which rode up and down the water level with every tide. The rectangles of slatted wood lay on the mud, as did a few motor launches, stranded at asymmetric angles. 'One of those belongs to Bill Chilcott, I think.'

'What's that noise?' asked Jude.

Once again Carole was aware of the heavy thumping which had done so little to help her headache that morning. As they turned a bend of the path, they saw its source. On top of the sea wall, beyond the gates controlled by the Fethering Yacht Club, a cluster of builders' vehicles was gathered. There were a crane, two small vans and a JCB. Huge sheets of corrugated metal were piled by the blue fishermen's chests, and a lot of men in fluorescent yellow jackets and hard hats milled around.

Rising from the centre of this activity, at the edge of the Fether, stood a tall pile-driving machine. The rhythmic thumping sounded as it forced the metal sheets deep down into the mud. Gulls protested overhead, intrigued by the commotion.

'Repairs to the sea wall,' Carole explained. 'I'd heard it was due to be done some time.' She shivered. 'What a day for them to start.'

From inside the Fethering Yacht Club, but for the dull thudding of the pile driver, you wouldn't have known about the repair work taking place only fifty yards away. The building equipment was as invisible as everything else beyond the windows of the bar. The way the wind whipped the rain about in every direction, sitting in the Fethering Yacht Club that afternoon was like being in a car-wash.

Carole's conjecture had proved right and it was Denis Woodville who let them in. He was a tall, angular man with a high domed head surrounded by a little frill of white hair that gave the impression of a joke-shop tonsure. His nose was beaky and he had the sagging, papery skin of a heavy smoker. A politically incorrect Gauloise drooped from yellow-stained fingers and he kept sucking at it, as if desperate to tar up the last few unpolluted cells of his lungs. He perched on a stool and had gestured his visitors to sit on two others. Beside him, on the shelf that ran the length of the sea-facing window, was a balloon of brandy from which he took sips between drags of his cigarette. The bar-room was punctiliously neat and – the adjective could not be avoided – shipshape.

'Wouldn't surprise me at all if they'd nicked one of our life-jackets,' he said after Jude had glibly produced her lie. 'Lot of bloody kids always trying to break into this place.'

Denis Woodville's accent was unusual, upper class on the surface but very carefully spoken, as if he was afraid he might at any moment betray a less cultured voice beneath.

'And into the boats,' he continued, gesturing outside.

Though the windows were blinded with rain, Carole and Jude had seen what he was talking about as they approached the clubhouse. Rows of dinghies on trailers were regimented on a cement rectangle in front of the building, all zipped up to the necks of their masts in sturdy fitted covers.

'Bloody awful times we live in,' Denis Woodville went on. 'Nobody has any respect for property any more. Kids aren't brought up with any respect for anything, that's the trouble. May not be a fashionable sentiment, but bring back National Service, I say. A couple of years of doing what they're told, thinking about other people rather than themselves for a change – that'd bring the little buggers into line.'

His taking a reflective swallow of brandy enabled Carole to ask, 'Is this clubroom open right through the winter?'

'Yes. Every day. Normally a few regulars come in at midday, but when the weather's like this . . .' He shrugged. 'Won't put off the evening crowd, though, I'm sure. Actually, just as well there's no one in this lunchtime, because we've recently lost our barmaid – finished work on Friday. And you can't really have the Vice-Commodore pulling pints, can you?' He chuckled at the incongruity of the idea.

'So are you actually the Vice-Commodore?'

The note of awe that Jude had injected into her voice had the right effect. Denis Woodville preened himself as he replied, 'Yes. I am. Hotly contested election for the post last year, but I won through. Members of this club still appreciate the old-fashioned values of integrity and common sense, you know.'

'I'm sure they do. Are there a lot of members?' Jude asked ingenuously.

'Couple of hundred. Not all very active. Some're London folk who're just weekenders down here. We tend to be a bit careful about the kind of people we let in. Open the doors too wide and you could end up with all kinds of riff-raff, eh?'

'I suppose you could,' said Jude, in a manner that might have implied agreement.

'And it's all run by volunteers, is it?' asked Carole. 'You don't have any permanent staff?'

'We club officials give our services free,' the Vice-Commodore replied grandly. 'Obviously, expenses taken when required by the Treasurer and so on. That's Rory Turnbull, he's our Treasurer. Dentist chap. You know him, don't you, Mrs Seddon?'

'Yes.'

'He's got problems at the moment, you know . . .'

'Oh? Problems with what?'

'Club accounts. Don't tally, I'm afraid. It's the bloody accountant's cock-up. Honestly, these days you can't even trust the professionals. Just scrape through their bloody exams and then reckon they've got a meal-ticket for life. And when they get their sums wrong, it's the client who has to pay, of course. Do you know, the accountant who looks after the club has managed to mislay over a thousand quid somewhere during the last year. Rory's on to the case and it's getting sorted, but even so . . . it all takes time, doesn't it? In the old days, if you employed a professional, you could rely on getting a professional job done. Not any more.'

'No,' Carole apparently agreed. 'It's rather impressive that this whole set-up's run without any paid employees.'

'Well, of course, we pay the casual workers . . . cleaners, bar staff . . .'

'Except,' said Jude, 'you say you haven't got any bar staff at the moment.'

'No. Tanya finished Friday, as I said. Did you know her?' Carole shook her head. 'Rather large girl. No thing of beauty, and got this great industrial rivet punched through her nose, but polite enough to the members. And didn't drink the profits, just cup after cup of coffee all day.

'Well, anyhow, she suddenly reckons in her wisdom that this place was "too far from Brighton", so she's going to look for something closer to home. I don't know, young people nowadays just don't stick at anything. She'd got a perfectly good job here, done six months, members getting to know her, doing very well, and suddenly she decides a twenty-minute train journey is too much for her. Kids've got no tenacity these days.'

'So will you be advertising for a replacement barmaid?' asked Jude.

'Yes, have to get round to it. Why, you looking for a job?'

'Might be.'

This reply, as well as amazing Carole, seemed to release some warmth in Denis Woodville. He smiled into Jude's brown eyes as he said, 'If you want to pursue it, let me have a CV, and maybe I can put in a word with the committee.'

'I might just do that.'

Did she mean it, Carole wondered. Could she possibly mean it? People who had cottages in the High Street of Fethering didn't work behind bars. Once again she realized how little she knew of Jude's background. Maybe her neighbour actually did need a job and maybe she wouldn't be above working as a barmaid. Once again, Carole determined to get a few basic facts about Jude's life sorted out.

The relaxation of Denis Woodville's formality continued. 'Would either of you like a drink, by the way?'

'No, thank you,' replied Carole firmly, before Jude could once again succumb and lead her further astray.

'Oh.' The Vice-Commodore looked wistfully down at his empty brandy balloon. 'Well, I'd better not have another one either. Better get back home, I suppose.'

The prospect didn't appeal to him. 'Yes, better close up. Open again at six. The six o'clock regulars never miss a night, come hell, high water or both.'

'I gather from Carole,' said Jude, 'that we're neighbours, Mr Woodville.'

'Please . . .' He raised a veined hand in admonition. 'Don't call me Mr Woodville.'

'All right, if you—'

'Vice-Commodore'll do fine.'

'Oh. Very well, Vice-Commodore.'

'And we're neighbours you say? How's that?'

'I've just moved into Woodside Cottage in the High Street.'

'Oh, right. Really? Place needs a hell of a lot of work, doesn't it?'

'I quite like it as it is.'

'Do you?' Denis Woodville scratched his bald dome in disbelief. 'Good heavens.'

'And you're just down nearer the sea? Carole showed me. The house with the dinghy in the front garden.'

'That's the one, yes.'

'Next door to the Chilcotts.' Jude was apparently unaware of the clouding of the Vice-Commodore's expression as she chattered on. 'I've only met Sandra and Bill briefly. I look forward to getting to know them better.'

'I wouldn't get too excited about the prospect,' said Denis Woodville darkly.

'Oh? Is he a member of the club here?'

Carole couldn't decide whether Jude had calculated the effect of her innocent inquiry, but it was certainly explosive.

'Bill Chilcott? A member of the Fethering Yacht Club? Oh, for heaven's sake! We do have quite strict requirements for entry here, you know. The last thing we want is the kind of jumped-up little creep who talks about boats and sailing all the time and in fact doesn't know a blind thing about any of it.'

'Ah.'

'This is a serious Yacht Club, you know.'

'Yes, of course.'

'The likes of Bill Chilcott have to moor their boats up on the public moorings. Bloody *weekend sailors*!'

The Vice-Commodore seemed belatedly to realize that this diatribe wasn't the approved method of welcoming a new resident. Swallowing his spleen, he announced formally, 'Anyway, I do hope you'll be very happy in Fethering.' And then, in apparent contradiction of much he'd already said, he went on, 'You'll find people round here are very friendly . . . I'm sorry, I didn't get your name when you came in . . .'

'Jude.'

'Ah. Jude what?'

'People just call me Jude.' Carole had a little inward seethe at another missed opportunity to get more information, and was surprised to hear Jude go on, 'Did you hear about that poor boy who drowned, Vice-Commodore?'

'What? Oh yes, of course I did. Another "Fethering Floater".'

'Sorry, what does that mean?'

'Bit of local folklore you could call it. Based on a

peculiarity of the tides round here. Fether's not much more than a stream really, but it's got a nasty kick at high water. Moves pretty damn fast. Strange thing is, though, you'd have thought it'd take a body out a long way to sea. But no. Anyone who's so unfortunate as to fall into the Fether – or so damn stupid as to jump into it – some cross-current gets them, and they usually turn up on Fethering beach within twenty-four hours. They're your "Fethering Floaters". Name goes back hundreds of years, I've been told. A bit ghoulish . . . Still, nice to have a few local traditions, eh? Something for the tourists to get their teeth into.'

The Vice-Commodore seemed unaware of any potential bad taste in his remarks, given Aaron Spalding's recent death. He looked at his watch and said for the second time, 'Anyway, ladies, I think I'd better be closing up for the afternoon. So, if you'll excuse me . . .'

'Yes, of course.'

Carole and Jude stood up.

Outside the weather had, if anything, worsened. The rain had turned to stinging sleet and the day was dwindling into darkness. It was also bitterly cold. Soon the sleet would stop and a major freeze-up set in. Denis Woodville let the two women through the small gate beside the clubhouse and reached into his pocket for the key to its padlock.

'So, if you see any more Fethering Yacht Club property round the place, you let me know. And I'll get on to the police sharpish. These little buggers have got to be caught and taught some sense of responsibility. They've got to learn to respect other people's property, and if it took horse-whipping to achieve that end . . . well, you wouldn't hear any complaints from me. What about you?'

Gracefully, Carole avoided answering the question by saying, 'Thank you so much for your time, Vice-Commodore. If we all work together, I'm sure we can make Fethering a much more secure place to live in.'

'Absolutely certain we can. May I accompany you back up to the High Street, ladies?'

'Well, since we're all going the same—'

'That's very kind,' said Jude, 'but in fact we were going to have a walk along the beach before it gets completely dark.'

'Were we?'

'Yes,' Jude informed Carole firmly.

Chapter Twelve

'Are you really looking for a job as a barmaid?' Carole couldn't help asking as they pressed on into the icy gloom.

'Good heavens, no,' Jude replied. 'I just said that to keep the old boy sweet.'

'So what, do you have a job or are you retired?'

'Ah, you mean what do I live on?'

Carole wouldn't have put it quite that crudely, but she admitted that yes, that was more or less what she meant.

Jude chuckled. 'Like the rest of us, I live on money. And money comes and money goes, doesn't it?'

This did not come within Carole's definition of an adequate answer, but she had no time to probe further as her sleeve was snatched and Jude's voice hissed in her ear, 'It's all right. He's gone.'

'What?'

A gloved hand waved up towards the top of the beach. 'Our Vice-Commodore. He's out of sight.'

'So?'

'*So* he can't see what we're doing.' And, tugging on

Carole's arm, Jude pulled her round, so that they were both walking back the way they came.

'I wish you'd tell me what we *are* doing,' Carole complained.

'We're going back to where you found the body on the beach. The water's far enough out for us to see.'

'But we're not going to see anything. The tide's washed over the area a good few times by now.'

'That's not the point.'

However, Jude granted her no more information until they were standing at the foot of the breakwater, where, in what seemed like another lifetime, a dead man with a missing tooth had lain. Out of sight now in the encroaching darkness, the relentless thudding of the pile driver continued, eerily echoing off the sea.

Jude looked at the water-filled indentation at the foot of one of the breakwater's worn stanchions. 'It was here?'

'Yes. Exactly here.'

Scrunching up her eyes, Jude looked across the rain-slicked sand to where the pebbles started. 'And you say the tide was coming in?'

'Yes.'

'So how far was it away from the breakwater when you found the body? How far did it have to come in to reach here?'

'About twenty yards.'

'Hm.' Jude nodded thoughtfully. 'Well, there's no way the body was swept out to sea again.'

'How can you be so sure?'

'Because if the incoming tide was going to

move him at all, it'd move him *further up* the beach. He wouldn't be swept out till after the tide had changed. And the police came to see you too soon after they hadn't found the body for that to have happened.'

The deduction was undeniably true. Carole was surprised to encounter this new, logical streak in her neighbour.

'So . . .' Jude spun on her booted heel and looked around the semicircle towards the village. She stopped, facing the Fethering Yacht Club. 'I think we go back up there.'

'Hm?'

'For anyone who wanted to hide a body, it's the nearest place, isn't it?'

'But who wanted to hide a body?'

'We don't know that yet, do we?'

It was nearly dark when they got back to the side gate to the Yacht Club. Jude looked around but could see no one in the enveloping gloom. 'OK, give me a leg-up.'

'But we can't break in. I mean, particularly after what Denis Woodville was saying.'

'Nobody's going to see us, Carole. And if he does find any evidence of our intrusion, he's going to put it down to the local youngsters. "Kids these days just have no respect for property," ' she announced in an uncannily close echo of the Vice-Commodore's tones. 'Come on, give me a leg-up.'

With Carole's help, Jude negotiated her long skirt over the gate and then helped her neighbour to join her inside the compound. 'Now, let's have a look at all of these boats.'

'What are we looking for?'

'A loose cover. A sign that one of them's been broken into.'

'You think the body might have been hidden in one of the boats?'

Jude looked around. 'See anywhere else suitable?'

In the last threads of daylight, they felt their way along the rows of dinghies, Carole starting from one end, Jude from the other. On most, the blue covers were firmly battened down, either fixed with cleats or pulled tight by threaded cords. Above the two women, the wind sang in rigging and steel halyards clattered endlessly against metal masts.

'Could be something here!' Carole called out.

Jude was quickly by her side.

'Look!' Carole pointed to the rim of a boat cover, where a piece of rope dangled loose.

'Pity we haven't got a torch. It's really hard to see.'

'I have got a torch,' said Carole, trying to keep the smugness out of her voice. 'I always carry one in my raincoat pocket. There's no streetlighting on the High Street.'

'Isn't there? I hadn't noticed.'

Carole reached into her Burberry pocket and the beam of light was quickly focused on the trailing rope. It ended in a sharp right angle.

'Been cut through,' said Jude.

The severed cord had been rethreaded through the

eyelets of the cover in an attempt to hide the break-in. Jude started quickly to unpick it.

'Should we be doing this?' asked Carole plaintively.

'Course we should. We are doing it anyway. And nobody can see us.'

It was true. The wet darkness around them suddenly seemed total. The floodlights focused on the sea-wall repairs were only fifty yards away but looked pale, distant and insubstantial. Someone would have to be very close to detect their tiny torch-beam.

Freeing a corner of the cover, Jude flipped it back like a bedspread from the stern of the boat. 'Shine the torch here,' she said. 'No, here!'

The thin stream of light picked out a name in gold lettering: *Brigadoon II*.

'I wonder,' said Jude. 'Do you think there's a kind of person who would give their boat the same name as their house?' She didn't wait for an answer. 'Come on, let's get the rest of this cover off and have a look inside.'

'What are you expecting to find in there? The body?'

'It's a possibility.'

Carole shivered. The possibility was macabre. But she couldn't deny that it was also exciting.

When they had peeled the cover right back, however, they found no body. Just the moulded fibre-glass interior of a dinghy's hull. In the central channel a rectangle of trapped water gleamed against the torch-light. Its surface was frozen hard.

But the ice didn't stop an acrid smell from rising

to their nostrils. 'Standing water,' Carole observed. 'It's been leaking in for some time.'

She ran the beam of the torch carefully over the inside of the boat. It revealed nothing they wouldn't have expected to find there.

'Just check if there's anything under the water.'

Putting a foot on one of the trailer wheels, Jude hoisted herself with surprising ease over the side and into the dinghy. With a gloved fist, she hammered through the sheet of ice. Then, removing her right-hand glove and supporting herself on the other arm, she felt down into the bottom of the boat. She winced at the cold of the water.

'Something here.' She produced a nut and bolt, rusted immovably together, and handed them to Carole. 'Don't think that helps us much.'

She reached down again through the cracked ice into the fetid water and felt her way systematically along the trough. 'I think that's probably it. Be too easy if we – Just a minute . . .'

Carole craned over the side of the boat, trying desperately to see what her neighbour had uncovered. Jude's dripping hand raised her trophy into the torch-beam. 'Look at that,' she said with triumph.

It was a large, robust Stanley knife, clicked in the open position. The light gleamed on the shiny triangle of its blade.

'Wonder how long that's been there . . .?'

'Not very long,' said Carole. 'Blade like that would rust very quickly. And . . .'

'What?'

'The woman who drew a gun on me wanted to know if I'd found a knife.'

'Yes. So she did.'

Jude slowly turned the knife over in her hand. On the other side of the handle words had been printed in uneven white paint-strokes. They read: 'J. T. CARPETS'.

Chapter Thirteen

'So what have we got?' asked Jude.

They were back in Carole's house, sitting in front of her log-effect gas fire. She had chosen the system because she knew it would be a lot more sensible than an open fire. None of that endless business of filling coal scuttles, loading log baskets and sweeping out grates. But for the first time, with her new neighbour installed in a sofa in front of her virtual fire, Carole felt a little wistful for a grate glowing with real flames.

She had felt uncertain about inviting Jude in for a cup of tea, but the unalterable rules of reciprocal hospitality dictated that she should. The trouble was, when you invited someone in, you never knew how long they were going to stay. A drink with Jude in the Crown and Anchor had escalated, without apparent effort, into supper and a lot more drinks in the Crown and Anchor. With someone like Jude, who could say what 'a cup of tea' might escalate into?

And once inside the house, with Gulliver greeted and fed, the unalterable rules of reciprocal hospitality dictated that Carole should at least suggest the option of something other than 'a cup of tea'. In Jude's house she'd been offered wine, so when she returned from the kitchen to the sitting room, she said, 'I've put the kettle on, but if you'd rather have a glass of wine . . .'

This had prompted a quick glance at her large watch-face from Jude and a, 'No thanks, I don't want anything. Bit early for me to start on the wine, anyway. But don't let me stop you.'

The response had caught Carole on the back foot, seeming to imply that if anyone had an over-enthusiasm for alcohol it was her. But Jude's brown eyes contained no censure or patronage. Carole was coming to the conclusion that her new neighbour was a very unusual person. Certainly in Fethering.

'We've got the knife,' said Carole, picking up from Jude's question. 'But whether that has any relevance to the body on the beach, we just don't know, do we?'

'Let's start from the other point of view,' said Jude. 'If we assumed that the knife *did* have something to do with the body . . . would that help?'

'It depends *what* it had to do with the body.'

'All right. Well, your woman with the gun mentioned a knife, so that's a start. But suppose it actually belonged to the dead man . . . that it dropped out of his pocket while he was hidden away in the boat?'

'We don't know he *was* hidden away in the boat,' Carole objected.

'No, but let's assume that too. Think about it. Where else could the body have been hidden where the police wouldn't see it?'

'The boats are the obvious place, I agree. Or I suppose there are those chest things on the sea wall, where the fishermen keep their stuff. They're kept padlocked, but if someone was prepared to break into a boat, they'd be equally ready to cut through a padlock.'

'Yes.'

'Surely, though, if the police were looking properly for the body I told them about, then they'd have gone up to the Yacht Club, wouldn't they?'

'Ah, but were they looking properly? Or had they already marked you down as a hysterical fantasist before they got to the scene?'

Carole was affronted. 'I don't see how they could possibly have done that. When I rang them, I was extremely unemotional and controlled.'

'But you did say that you'd bathed Gulliver before calling them.'

'Yes. Yes, I think I did.'

Jude shrugged. 'That was probably what did it.'

'How? But . . .' Carole didn't pursue the objection. 'All right, *assuming* the body was hidden in the boat after I found it, that does raise a few other questions, doesn't it?'

'Like who hid it there?'

'Certainly.'

'And, more to the point, Carole, who removed it from the boat before we looked under the cover this afternoon?'

'Yes. And, still maintaining all the assumptions about there being a connection, the only clue we have to help us answer those questions is the Stanley knife . . .'

'Which might have belonged to the dead man . . . or might have belonged to the person who left the body there . . .'

'Or might have belonged to anyone else in the world,' Carole couldn't help saying.

'Ssh. Ssh.' Jude spoke very soothingly, as if she were some kind of therapist. 'We're just letting our ideas flow. Hold back on the logic for a little bit longer.'

'All right.'

Jude's brows wrinkled as her mind focused. 'Anyway, the knife couldn't have belonged to anyone else in the world. There are geographical limitations, logistical limitations . . . No, when you come right down to it, there are very few people to whom that Stanley knife could have belonged. Hm . . .' She twirled a tendril of blonde hair thoughtfully between finger and thumb. 'I suppose in fact the most likely person to have dropped the knife – is the boat's owner . . .'

'Who *might* be Rory Turnbull . . . assuming we go along with the theory that he would give the same name to his boat as his house.'

'Let's go along with that for a moment.' As she concentrated, Jude seemed to go in an almost trance-like state.

'Well,' said Carole with no-nonsense practicality, 'easy enough to find out who owns the boat. We simply ask our friend the Vice-Commodore.'

Jude dragged herself back to reality. 'Alternatively, I haven't registered with a dentist down here yet. Now I've met Barbara Turnbull and her mother, I'd like to know more about Rory.'

'All right. He's a bit of a sad case, as you saw in the pub. Anyway, you pursue that line of inquiry.' Carole moved into the delegating mode which had served her so well during her Home Office career. 'Meanwhile, I'll find out about J. T. Carpets. Start with *Yellow Pages*, then see where I go from there.'

'Good,' said Jude. 'That sounds very good.' Then, with another look at the moon-face of her watch, she stood up. 'I must be off.'

And within a minute she was out of the house, leaving Carole to wonder why she had to be off so suddenly. And to realize that, after all her worries about Jude staying too long, she wouldn't have minded her staying a little longer.

The red light on the answering machine was flashing when Jude got back to Woodside Cottage. Just one message. From Brad, saying he hoped she'd settled in all right to her new home and lots of luck for the next stage of her life. And it'd be good to see her.

Yes, she thought, it'd be good to see Brad too. Been a while. She'd call him later. First, though, she dialled a local number.

'Hello?' The voice was politely deterrent.

'Barbara, it's Jude.'

'Oh?'

'Jude from the coffee morning. New resident of Woodside Cottage.'

'Of course. How nice to hear from you.' The words were entirely automatic, invested with no element of sincerity.

'It was such a pleasure to meet you and your mother.' Jude's words, though completely untrue, sounded sincere. 'Thank you so much for inviting me.'

'We always like to make newcomers welcome here in Fethering . . . in the hope we're going to swell the All Saints' congregation.' The reproof in the voice, at Jude's failure to espouse the Church of England, was hardly disguised.

'Well, I just wanted to say that I appreciated it, and thank you for going to all that trouble.' Jude knew she was being over the top. Providing coffee and biscuits for a dozen people was hardly the most onerous assignment since records began.

But apparently it had seemed so to Barbara Turnbull. 'Yes, well, one likes to make an effort. And I've just about finished clearing it up now. I told you I'm completely without help, didn't I?'

'Sorry?'

'Maggie, my – ' Barbara had the usual middle-class difficulty with how one referred to staff – 'my "lady who does", didn't come in today.'

'Oh yes, you did say.'

'And what's more, I've just heard from her to say she won't be in tomorrow either. Still some problem with her son. I don't know, it's so thoughtless. I told her, in no uncertain terms, that she couldn't assume that the job at Brigadoon would stay open for ever. Have you found someone?'

The abrupt change of direction threw Jude. 'Sorry? Found someone?'

'To do your cleaning.'

This prompted a peal of laughter. 'Oh, really, Barbara! I'm not going to have a cleaner. Can't afford to, apart from anything else. And I think I can probably manage myself. Woodside Cottage is absolutely tiny.'

'Yes.' There was a wealth of nuance in the monosyllable, as Barbara Turnbull moved her new acquaintance a few more notches down her social ranking system. 'Well, it was a pleasure to meet you and I do appreciate your ringing.'

But Jude wasn't yet ready to have the conversation terminated. 'One thing I wanted to ask . . .'

'Yes?'

'I'm not registered with a dentist down here and I wondered whether your husband—'

'Rory isn't taking on any new National Health patients,' his wife asserted quickly.

'No, I wasn't imagining I could get a National Health dentist down here. I just wondered if you could give me the number of his practice.'

Unable to find any fault with the concept of getting her husband more work, Barbara Turnbull gave the number. Jude, in a spirit of devilment, then brought her own end to the conversation. 'And I hope that you'll let me repay your hospitality and that you'll come and have coffee here with me at Woodside Cottage one morning.'

'Yes. That'd be delightful. I'll look forward to it,' said Barbara Turnbull, meaning the exact opposite.

Chapter Fourteen

It was still office hours, so Jude rang through to the surgery number Barbara Turnbull had given her. She explained that she had just moved to the area and was looking for a dentist with whom to register. Once it had been established that she was prepared to pay for her treatment, the woman at the surgery became much more accommodating and asked when Jude would like to make an appointment. As soon as possible. Well, they had actually had a cancellation for the following morning.

Jude said that would be absolutely fine, couldn't be better. 'And that will be Mr Turnbull I'll be seeing, will it?'

'Sorry?' For the first time the voice sounded a little fazed.

'Mr Turnbull. He was the dentist that was recommended to me. My appointment is with him, is it?'

'Possibly.' But the voice was cagey. 'It may be one of his partners. We tend to allocate new patients according to who's free.'

'Surely the appointment is with one dentist or the other?'

But the voice did not wish to pursue this.

'See you in the morning. Thursday the 8th, ten-twenty. Goodbye.'

Bit odd. Still, at least she wasn't going to have to wait long for her appointment. Jude smiled softly to herself and then keyed in Brad's familiar number.

The first bit of Carole's research also went smoothly. J. T. Carpets were listed in the *Yellow Pages*, with an address not far away in East Preston. When she rang, the phone was answered by a voice which implied that it was very near the end of the working day and she had been about to get off home.

'My name's Mrs Seddon and I'm ringing because I found something which I believe is your property.'

'What's that then?'

'It's a knife . . . a Stanley knife . . . and it says "J. T. CARPETS" on it.'

'If it says "J. T. CARPETS" on it, then there's a strong chance that it does belong to J. T. Carpets, I'd have said.' The girl's voice was poised just the right side of insolence. But only just. 'Did one of our fitters leave it in your house?'

'No. I found it . . . on the beach.' No need to be too specific.

'Oh, all right. So why're you telling me?'

'I just thought you might want it back.'

'Not that bothered,' said the girl. 'I mean, it's only a Stanley knife. Not like it's the only one in the building.'

'Oh.'

Some residual compassion in the girl responded to the disappointment in Carole's tone. 'I mean, if you're passing the office, drop it in by all means,' she conceded magnanimously.

'But none of your staff has reported the knife missing?'

'Oh, come on, if they've lost company property, they're hardly going to go shouting to the boss about it, are they?'

'No, I suppose not. So you have no idea which member of your staff might've mislaid the—'

'Listen, lady. You drop it into the office, that'd be very public-spirited of you. If you don't, the company's not going to go to the wall – right? And, since it is now after half-past five, I'll say thank you very much for calling and *goodbye*!'

The phone was put down with some vigour. Carole felt uncomfortable. The patronizing tone been all too reminiscent of Detective Inspector Brayfield's. And Carole was also left with the feeling that she had a lot to learn about being a detective.

Jude's appointment turned out not to be with Rory Turnbull. She was told when she arrived at the smart reception area that she'd be seen by a Mr Frobisher. While she waited, Jude was aware of much toing and froing among the receptionists and dental nurses, as though the impact of some offstage crisis was being minimized for the watching patients.

The man who greeted her when she was ushered into his surgery was about forty and fit-looking, with an unreconstructed Australian accent. He was immaculately clean in white coat and rubber gloves, and his surroundings matched him. All the equipment was shiny and new. Even his dental nurse looked as though she'd been recently delivered and only just removed from her wrappings.

'I was put on to this practice by Barbara Turnbull,' said Jude, as she was settled into the chair and floated into a prone position.

'Oh yes?' said Mr Frobisher, without much interest.

'So I thought I might be seen by Mr Turnbull.'

'There are three of us in the practice. We tend to share out the new patients. I hope that's all right with you . . .'

'Yes, yes. Absolutely fine. So is Mr Turnbull in today?'

'No, he isn't, as it happens.' Was Jude being hypersensitive in detecting a slight resentment in Mr Frobisher's reaction to his colleague's absence? He sat astride his mobile stool and focused the overhead light on her face. 'So, Mrs—'

'Please call me "Jude". Everyone does.'

'Very well then, Jude . . . any problems with your teeth?'

'No, I just wanted to get registered.'

'Fine. Well, I'll have a quick look and confirm everything's OK.'

For the next few minutes, Mr Frobisher's probing around her mouth made further conversation impossible. He called out a few notes to the dental nurse, who clicked them in on a keyboard.

There was an interruption when one of the receptionists entered with a sheaf of printed papers. Some silent semaphore with Mr Frobisher caused him to break away from his examination of Jude's teeth. With an 'Excuse me a moment', he crossed to look at what the receptionist had brought in.

'No, that has to be wrong.'

'It's in black and white, Frobie.'

'Must be a misprint. Tell them I'll come and have a word in a couple of minutes, OK?'

He crossed back to his patient as the receptionist left the surgery. 'Sorry about that. We're having an inspection by the RDO – that's the Regional Dental Officer. Routine stuff, but they always manage to disrupt the whole place.'

'What is it that they—'

'Now, open wide again please.'

So Jude was unable to find out more about the workings of Regional Dental Officers. And Mr Frobisher gave her little opportunity for further conversation when the examination was concluded.

'Good. No serious problems at the moment. Couple of places where the gums're looking a bit red, though. Look after your gums and it makes my job of looking after your teeth a lot simpler.'

'Yes,' said Jude contritely.

'Make an appointment to see one of our hygienists on your way out, will you?'

'Sure. I—'

'Now, if you'll excuse me, I'd better go and sort out this RDO.'

She couldn't make him stay. And even if she had been able to make him stay, Jude wasn't sure what questions she would have wanted to ask Mr Frobisher.

'Tell reception to apologize to the next appointment,' he told the nurse as he left the room. 'Only be about five minutes.'

On the coastline train that rattled through an unbelievable number of small stations and rattled past an even more unbelievable number of bungalows on its way back to Fethering, Jude tried to comfort herself with the fact that there was nothing wrong with her teeth. But the predominant feeling in her mind was one she shared with Carole – that she had a lot to learn about being a detective.

Chapter Fifteen

The Crown and Anchor was on the way back from Fethering Station. Jude knew she shouldn't really, but the thought of grabbing a bite to eat there rather than knocking something together at home was appealing. She could be an excellent cook when she felt like it, but she very rarely did feel like it.

Jude knew she shouldn't really spend the money either. But what the hell? Tomorrow would be soon enough to start her economy regime. She went into the pub.

There were maybe half a dozen people scattered around the sitting room that was the Crown and Anchor's interior. Most were tucked away in alcoves, their presence betrayed by a glimpse of elbow or a murmur of chatter. The room looked comforting, as did the lugubrious grin Ted Crisp gave her from behind the bar.

'Couldn't keep away from me, eh, young Jude? My old animal magnetism doing its stuff?'

'Something like that.'

'So what can I do you for? Or are you just after my body?'

'I was thinking of lunch.'

He accepted this philosophically. 'First things first. And first thing's got to be a drink, hasn't it? Wodger fancy – apart from me, of course?'

'Glass of white wine.'

'Large, I take it?'

'Why not? And something to eat. Nothing very big. Do you do sandwiches?'

'We not only do sandwiches, we also do baguettes. Bread rolls with delusions of grandeur, no less. List of fillings on the board.'

Jude looked at the selection written out in multi-coloured chalk. 'I'll have the tuna and sweet corn, please.'

'You won't regret it. Good choice, that. One tuna and sweet corn baguette!' he shouted out towards the kitchen. 'Normally write the orders down. Not when we're slack like this, though.'

'Who've you got cooking today?'

'No idea. She's a woman. Knows her place. Never comes out of the kitchen.'

Jude could sense a degree of calculation in his words. Ted Crisp was sizing her up, testing the level at which she'd be offended.

She denied him the satisfaction of a response. 'You ever been married, Ted?'

'Used to be. You can tell. I'm still round-shouldered. Didn't take, though.' The landlord shook his shaggy head gloomily. 'Like an unsuccessful heart transplant. My body rejected it.' He was silent for a moment. 'Actually, that's not true. My body didn't reject her. She rejected me. Walked out after three months. With a double-glazing salesman. "But he's so transparent," I said. "Can't you see right through him?" She didn't listen. Said she wanted the security. Wanted to be with someone who didn't always come staggering in at four in the morning . . .'

'Having been out drinking?'

'Having been out *working*, I'll thank you very much, young Jude. And maybe a bit of drinking after the working. But the human body is like an old clock, you know. It needs to unwind.'

'So what did you do that kept you out till four every morning?'

'Stand-up. I was on the circuit. When I moved here was the first time I'd ever been in a *downstairs* room in a pub.'

'That explains a lot, Ted.'

'Like what?'

'Your jokes. They sound like they come from someone who *used* to be a comedian.'

He screwed up his face in a mock-wince. 'Ooh, you know how to hurt, don't you? Anyway, you're right. I wasn't a huge success on the circuit. It's a business where you're only as good as your last joke, and, as you've so diplomatically pointed out, my last joke was bloody terrible. So . . . about four years too late, I saw the wisdom of what my former wife'd said and went for security. Sold up the house, borrowed far too much from the brewery to get this place and . . . here I am.'

'Do you miss it?'

'Stand-up?' He screwed his lips into a little purse of disagreement. 'Nah. No different here. As a pub landlord, I still get heckled and shouted at and have glasses thrown at me by a bunch of drunkards.'

'Not in Fethering, surely?'

'Don't you believe it. Come Saturday night, they've all tanked up at home on the old Sanatogen Tonic Wine, they've got their pensions in their pockets and evil in their hearts. I tell you, you can hardly move in here for the flying zimmer frames. Ooh, here's your baguette.' He reached out through the hatch to a disembodied hand from the kitchen. 'Get outside of that and you won't hurt, young lady.'

There was a clatter from the front door and Jude turned to see Rory Turnbull making a clumsy entrance. He hadn't shaved that morning and looked unkempt.

The dentist weaved his way up to the bar. 'Large Scotch please, Ted.'

'If you're sure . . .'

The note of warning in the landlord's voice hit a raw nerve. 'Of course I'm bloody sure! Otherwise I wouldn't have bloody asked you for it, would I?'

As Ted Crisp turned to get the drink, Jude ventured a, 'Hello. We sort of met in here the other night, didn't we?'

'Hm?' Rory Turnbull's eyes had difficulty in focusing on her.

'And actually I went to your surgery this morning. Mr Frobisher looked after me.' Just as well it wasn't you, thought Jude, or my mouth'd be bearing the scars. 'Your wife put me in touch.'

'My wife?' He seemed puzzled by the alien concept.

'Yes, Barbara.'

'Oh, *that* wife.' He let out a bark of laughter, as though this were some huge joke. 'Thanks, Ted.' He took a long swallow from the glass.

'Why, you got another wife, Rory?' asked the landlord. 'Little totty tucked away somewhere?'

The dentist smiled slyly. 'I should be so lucky. Don't think you can get away with that kind of thing in Fethering.'

'Don't you believe it.' Ted Crisp struck his forehead in a mock moment of revelation. 'I just realized. Jude! You suddenly appear here in Fethering, nobody has a clue who you are, why you're here . . . You're Rory Turnbull's bit of stuff, aren't you?'

She smiled ruefully. 'Sorry. I'm afraid my only connection with Rory is professional – not even that, actually, because I saw his partner rather than him.'

'And you say my wife put you in touch?'

'Yes. Everyone needs a dentist, don't they?'

This struck Rory Turnbull as very funny. 'I'll say. Oh yes, everyone needs a dentist. Everyone needs someone with a steady hand to probe around their smelly mouth. Everyone needs that frisson of lying in a high-tech chair and just waiting to be *hurt*. And nobody thinks what the dentist needs. Nobody thinks how much it costs him to be there in the surgery every morning, there with the steady hand and the fixed grin and the knowledge that what he's doing is so stressful it's lopping the years off his life, one by one. How many dentists get to enjoy the wonderful pensions they salt away so much for through their working lives? Very few, very few. Because they drop dead, you see. Or if they don't drop dead, they top themselves. Did you know that dentists have one of the highest suicide rates of any profession? And why do you think that is? It's because what they do manages to be both deadly boring and agonizingly stressful at the same time. It's because being a dentist combines—'

But here the maudlin aria was interrupted by a voice from across the pub. 'Rory. I only just noticed you were in here. I wonder if you could . . .'

It was Denis Woodville. He was standing next to an alcove where, unnoticed by Jude, he had been lunching with a large young woman dressed in black, who had also risen to her feet. On the seat behind her, where it had been cast off, lay the semicircle of a green anorak.

'No, sorry, Vice-Commodore,' said Rory Turnbull. 'Can't stay. Have to finish my drink – ' he gulped down what remained in one 'and do some very important things.' Shovelling a pocketful of small change on to the bar counter, he set off unsteadily towards the door, repeating to himself, 'Very important things.'

'But what I need to talk about's important too!' Denis Woodville turned back to his guest as he made for the door. 'Sorry, Tanya. Be with you in a moment.'

The girl had risen from her booth, a lumpen creature in black sweat shirt, leggings and Doc Martens. Hair dyed reddish and cut short, a lot of silver dangling from the perforations in her ears. A silver stud in her nose. She looked anxious.

'It's all right, Tanya, love,' Ted Crisp called across.

'The Vice-Commodore'll be back. You won't be left to pick up the tab.'

'I hope not.' Her voice had those slack local vowels which sound uninterested even at moments of excitement. She drifted uneasily towards the bar.

'Though it's not like our Denis to be pushing the boat out like this,' Ted went on. 'Bit of a tightwad usually.'

'Lunch is on Fethering Yacht Club expenses,' the girl explained. 'He wanted to say thank-you now I've left, and since I didn't have anything else on today, I thought, "Well, it's a free lunch." '

'No such thing,' said Ted Crisp.

'Sorry?' The girl looked at him curiously.

'A free lunch. No such thing.'

'What?'

He spelled it out. 'There's no such thing as a free lunch.'

'No. You have to pay. In a pub or a restaurant, you always have to pay.'

Ted Crisp recognized he wasn't getting anywhere. Tanya was unaware of the reference. 'You like some coffee, would you? Seem to remember when you worked behind the bar here, you were virtually on an intravenous drip of coffee.'

The girl wrinkled her nose, a manoeuvre which the silver stud made look hazardous. 'No, thanks.' She looked across to the door. 'I hope he's all right.'

The landlord chuckled. 'I think the Vice-Commodore can look after himself in the face of drunken dentists. Don't you worry. He'll be back in a minute.'

No sooner had he said the words than Denis Woodville returned. He was lighting up another Gauloise and looked rather miffed. 'Tanya, I'll just sort out the bill for this lot and then we'll be off – all right?'

'Fine,' said the girl without interest.

The Vice-Commodore reached into a pocket for an envelope full of petty cash. 'Right, Ted, what's the damage?'

While he settled up, Jude attacked her baguette, which was excellent. After the unlikely couple, thin septuagenarian and broad twenty-year-old, had left, she said, 'You said Tanya used to work for you too, Ted?'

'That's right. Not of the brightest, as you might've gathered from our exchange about free lunches. No, Tanya's not a bad girl. Been in care, had a tough time when she was growing up, I gathered. But she did the job all right. And a good barmaid is hard to find.' His eyes narrowed as he looked across at Jude. 'Don't suppose you fancy doing the odd shift in here, do you?'

She chuckled. 'Not at the moment. Maybe, if I get desperate . . .'

'Yeah, nobody works for me unless they're desperate.' He sighed. 'Nobody does anything for me unless they're desperate.'

'Talking of desperation, Ted . . .'

'Hm?'

'How long's Rory Turnbull been drinking like that?'

'Only the last few months. Well, only the last few months he's been drinking like that in *here*. Maybe in the privacy of the Shorelands Estate he's been doing it for years.'

'Can't see the lovely Barbara being too keen on that.'

'No, nor the old witch, her mother.' He shuddered. 'That Winnie. One of the best arguments for misogyny I've ever encountered.'

'Do you know them well?'

'Hardly. Only by reputation, gossip, what-have-you. You hear a lot stuck behind the bar of a pub.'

'I bet you do.'

'And not much of it's very charitable.'

'No. So what have you heard from Rory Turnbull while you've been stuck behind the bar?'

'Well, it's all the same, really. You heard the full routine today. Goes on and on round the same things – how miserable life is, what hell it is being a dentist, what hell it is being married . . . usual cheery stuff. Tell you, after an evening spent with Rory, my own life seems a bed of blooming roses.'

A new thought struck Jude. 'Ooh, and he has a boat, doesn't he?'

'That's right. Called *Brigadoon*. Same as his house.'

Good, thought Jude. At least one of our conjectures has proved to be right.

But it still doesn't prove any link between the owner of *Brigadoon II* and the body on the beach.

Chapter Sixteen

Carole Seddon had woken that Thursday morning with a change of attitude. In Jude's company, caught up in the excitement Jude generated, the idea of playing at detectives had seemed a seductive one. Finding an explanation for the body on the beach had been imperative. On her own, though, Carole found it less compelling. Life, she reflected, is full of loose ends. There are many questions that will never be answered, and a sensible person will recognize that fact and get on with things.

So that morning Carole got on with things. She re-established the routine of her life that her discovery of the body and her meeting with Jude had briefly interrupted.

The weather was better, though still astringently cold and heavily overcast. She took Gulliver for his early-morning walk on the beach, striding resolutely past Woodside Cottage without a sideways glance. On her way back up the High Street, she did slow for a moment by the gate, contemplating a brief call to see if Jude's thinking had progressed at all. But, in spite of the ambient gloom, there were no lights on, so

Carole went straight into her own house and started a major cleaning offensive.

The telephone didn't ring all morning. This was not unusual, but that particular morning Carole kept half expecting it might.

She was very sensible and virtuous. She even emptied out the fridge and defrosted it.

After her morning of hard work, she felt she deserved an omelette and a glass of mineral water with the lunchtime news. There was nothing much on the international front. Reports of atrocities in the Balkans or Africa, where she got confused about which side was which – who the aggressors, who the victims – had little power to engage her interest.

The weatherman promised more of the same. The apparent improvement of that morning had been an illusion. More frost was coming. More wind. More gloom as the evenings darkened earlier and the year spiralled down to its close.

At the start of the strident signature tune of the local news, Carole reached for the remote control. But before she pressed the off-button, she heard the voice-over menu of headlines: 'Drowned boy's mother blames drug culture.'

Carole's button-finger froze.

Another newsreader who'd never make it on to national television appeared in shot. 'The mother of teenager Aaron Spalding' – once again the name was pronounced 'Arran' – 'today blamed the ready accessibility of drugs to young people on the South Coast for her son's death.'

A woman's distraught face filled the screen. 'Aaron

was a good boy. Then he got mixed up with a crowd who was doing a lot of drugs and I'm sure that's what caused his death. He was a good boy . . .' Her mouth wobbled as the tears took over.

But it wasn't what was said that kept Carole frozen in her chair. It was the fact that she'd seen the woman before.

In that very sitting room. Holding a gun.

Chapter Seventeen

Any thoughts of giving up trying to be a detective evaporated as if they'd never been there. Now there was something positive to link the two fatalities. The woman who'd come to Carole's house to ask her about the body she'd found on the beach was the mother of the boy whose body had been found on the beach the following day. Also she'd asked about a knife. There had to be a connection.

Carole rushed out of High Tor, not even bothering to lock the front door, and hurried up the garden path of Woodside Cottage. When the bell prompted no response, she hammered on the dark wooden door.

But there was no one in. For a moment she contemplated going down to the Crown and Anchor to see if Jude was having lunch there (which would have been a very good idea, because that was precisely what Jude was doing). But Carole's sensible side prevailed. If she didn't find Jude, she reasoned, then she'd have to stay in the Crown and Anchor and have a mineral water to justify her going in there. And if she did that, there was a real danger it might appear to the other residents of Fethering that she'd become the kind of woman who went into pubs on her own.

(The option of just going in and asking Ted Crisp if he'd seen Jude did not occur to her.)

So Carole left a message on Jude's answering machine, asking her to phone back as soon as possible. And then she sat waiting in an agony of frustration, once again made aware of how little she knew about Jude's life. Her neighbour could be anywhere. Maybe she did have a job and was off at work? Maybe she was visiting a family member . . . or a long-term lover? Maybe she owned a second home and had gone there? The possibilities were infinite.

To speed up the passage of time, Carole went to her bookshelves and consulted her reference library. Various works of criminology reflected different Home Office initiatives in which she had been involved. The volume she was looking for had come her way when she had been investigating police training methods. It was a manual about scene-of-crime techniques.

Carole looked dispassionately at the rows of photographs of those who'd come to violent ends. There was nothing gruesome about the task; this scientific layout of wounded bodies detached them from any humanity of which they might once have been part.

At the same time Carole focused on the image of the body she had found on Fethering beach. In particular, on the two cuts that she had seen on the man's neck.

She compared the picture in her mind with the picture on the page, and it confirmed a tiny doubt which had stayed with her since she first saw the corpse.

The two cuts on the man's neck were not deep enough. They were little more than flesh wounds and had not reached any major arteries. He might even have received the injuries post-mortem.

Whatever had killed the man, it hadn't been the wounds to his neck.

Carole had hardly reached this conclusion before there was a furious ringing at her doorbell. Jude was back from the Crown and Anchor.

'We've got to talk to her.'

'But, Jude, she'll be in a terrible state. She's only recently lost her son.'

'She's also only recently threatened you with a gun. Anyway, I'd have thought the one thing anyone would want to know if they've just lost their son is how it happened. We may be able to help her answer that question.'

'She may know already.'

'If she does, she can tell us. And also maybe tell us the connection between her son's death and the body you found. Come on, we've got to get to the bottom of what happened, haven't we?'

'Yes, of course we have.' Carole had by now completely forgotten her morning's doubts about the wisdom of pursuing the case. 'So how're we going to find her?'

'If she's local, she might be in the phone book.

The dead boy's called Aaron Spalding, so let's assume she's a Spalding too. Do we have a first name for her?'

Carole screwed up her pale-blue eyes with the effort of recollection. 'There was a caption up over the bit of interview they showed. Um . . . began with a "T", I think. Yes, it's coming. Theresa. That's right – Theresa.'

'Though presumably,' said Jude, grabbing the Worthing Area telephone directory and flicking through it, 'the entry would be in her husband's name.'

'If she's got a husband. You never know these days, do you?'

There were ten Spaldings, none of them with the initial T. Carole and Jude took turns to phone them all and ask to speak to Theresa. None had anyone of that name on the premises. And all of them seemed to regard a wrong number as an infringement of their human rights.

'So where do we go next?' asked Jude. 'Ring the television company who did the interview?'

'No, local paper,' said Carole firmly. 'Comes out today. Always on a Thursday. There's no way they wouldn't cover a story like this.'

They negotiated the pillars of Allinstore to buy a copy of the *Fethering Observer*, and didn't have to search far to find what they were looking for. The front page was dominated by the headline: 'TRAGEDY OF DROWNED TEENAGER'. Beside it, the boyish school photograph of Aaron Spalding appeared again.

'Wonder why it's spelt "Aaron" and pronounced "Arran"?' Jude mused.

'Maybe it's a local variation. Influenced by living so near the Arun Valley.'

'Maybe. Oh, look, there's the address. It says, "Mrs Theresa Spalding, of Drake Crescent, Fethering." Where's that?'

'Up on the Downside Estate, I'm sure. A lot of the roads there are named after famous Elizabethans. Marlowe . . . Sidney . . . Raleigh . . . Meant to give a bit of class when they were built. Mind you, I think it's the only bit of class they've still got left.'

'Not the most desirable part of Fethering then?'

A wrinkle of Carole's nose gave all the answer that was required. 'So,' she said, 'when do we go up to Downside and try to talk to Mrs Theresa Spalding?'

'No time like the present,' replied Jude. 'How do we get there?'

'In my car. Unless you want to go in yours . . .'

'Haven't got one.' Jude grinned. 'Never felt the need.'

Chapter Eighteen

Fethering doesn't have an underbelly in the way that, say, Los Angeles has an underbelly, but the Downside Estate is as near as it gets.

The houses there betrayed signs not of real deprivation but of diminishing willpower and ever-tightening budgets. The Downside Estate had been built as council housing, but cut after cut in local authority spending over the years meant that maintenance had been pared to the bone. The buildings had all reached the age when serious structural refurbishment was required, not short-term making-good repairs. Their late-1940s brickwork needed repointing. Windows needed painting, even those where the original frames had been replaced by soulless double glazing. Tiny front gardens were unkempt and littered. Depressed cars crouched against the pavements on failing suspension.

The drab November weather did not add to the estate's charms, as Carole navigated her sensible and immaculately clean Renault towards Drake Crescent. She tried to bite back her instinctive snobbishness, but the compartmentalizing habit of her mind was too strong. Here was a place, she decided, where cultural aspiration stopped at the *Sun* or the football, and hope existed only in the form of the National Lottery.

On the side of every house a satellite dish perched like a giant parasitic insect, leeching away more profits for Sky TV. In Downside no attempt had been made to hide them, whereas on the Shorelands Estate a visible satellite dish would have constituted a social lapse more terrible than walking around with one's flies undone.

'Pretty grim place to live,' Carole observed, as she turned off Grenville Avenue.

'Oh, I don't know. I've lived in worse,' said Jude, adding yet another to the list of questions that Carole must at some point put to her neighbour.

But this wasn't the moment. 'How do we know which house it is?' she asked as the car crawled along Drake Crescent. Unable to disguise her distaste, she added, 'Stop and ask someone?'

Jude chuckled. 'It wouldn't be such a bad thing to have to do. The people round here are human, you know.'

'Oh, I didn't for a moment mean—'

'Yes, you did,' said Jude cheerfully. 'Anyway, I don't think we're going to have to ask anyone. I'd say it's the house with the television crew outside.'

Sure enough, there was a blue and white van bearing the regional station's logo. A couple of dour technicians were rolling up cables and stowing them in the back. An effete young man stood awkwardly by, feeling he should offer to help, but not knowing how.

Jude jumped out as soon as Carole had parked the

car and went straight up to the young man. 'Is this Theresa Spalding's house?'

'Yes,' he said.

'Have you just been doing a news interview with her?'

'Not news, no. For a documentary. We're doing an in-depth analysis of the teenage drug problem on the South Coast.'

'Oh, that'll be interesting,' lied Carole, who'd come up to join them. All local documentaries, she knew, were ruined by inadequate budgets, sketchy research and inept presenters. 'And you were talking to Mrs Spalding about her son's death?'

'Yes. She's obviously very cut up about it.'

'I'm not surprised,' said Jude, starting up the short path that led to Theresa Spalding's front door.

'I'm not sure that she really wants to talk to anyone else at the moment,' said the young man. 'Unless, of course, you're social workers.'

'That's right,' Jude called breezily over her shoulder as she pressed the doorbell.

In amazement, Carole followed her neighbour. The young man, seeing his colleagues had finished packing the van, got inside.

It was a moment or two before the front door was opened, and then only halfway. The woman was undoubtedly the one who'd come to Carole's house, but her face had drained down to a new pallor. The darting eyes were raw with weeping and a hand flickered across in front of her as if warding off some unseen attacker.

'What do you want? I don't want to talk to no one.'

'We may be able to help you find out how Aaron died,' said Jude, pronouncing the name 'Arran' as everyone else had.

'I don't care *how* he died. My boy's dead – that's all that matters to me. I don't want to talk about it.'

She made as if to close the door, but Carole's incisive words stopped her. 'Then perhaps you do want to talk about why you drew a gun on me . . .'

The door-closing movement stopped. Through the remaining crack the woman's eyes took in the speaker's face.

'Unless you want the police to talk to you about why you drew a gun on me.'

Reluctantly, the crack of the door widened.

'You better come in then.'

Theresa Spalding lived in a maisonette. Whether the house had been built like that or subsequently converted into two dwellings was hard to tell. The sitting room, into which Carole and Jude were grudgingly ushered, was dominated by a huge television screen. Throughout their interview, some American sitcom full of overacting teenagers was running with the sound off.

Theresa Spalding gestured to a couple of broken-down chairs, stubbed out the remains of a cigarette and, with trembling hands, shook another out of a packet. She remained standing while she lit the new one. She took a drag, as though gulping in oxygen on the top of Everest.

'Look, I don't know what you want, but I've already got enough grief.'

The room was full of traces of her son. A poster of the Southampton football team. A Playstation with a scattering of CD-ROM games by the television. Stephen Kings and similar paperbacks littered on a shelf, along with a neat row of horror videos. A grubby pair of trainers left by the sofa, exactly where he'd kicked them off.

Jude took the lead. There had been no discussion between them, but instinctively they fell into their roles. If Carole, with her threats of police involvement, was the Bad Cop, then Jude was going to be the Good Cop.

'Yes, Mrs Spalding, I understand—'

'It's not "Mrs". I never been married. But if you think that means I didn't bring up Aaron right—'

'We're not saying that . . . Theresa. Can I call you "Theresa"?'

Carole knew she could never have got away with it, but the woman snorted permission to Jude for her first name to be used. There was something in Jude's manner which made such things possible.

'Thank you. I'm Jude, and my friend's called Carole.'

This first use of the word 'friend' gave Carole a warm feeling. She wasn't sure whether she was ready yet to reciprocate the compliment, but it was still nice to know that Jude thought of their relationship in that light.

'And we're both desperately sorry about what happened to Aaron.'

'Why? What business is it of yours?'

'It wouldn't be our business,' Carole responded sharply, 'if you hadn't come to my house and threatened me with a gun.'

'You needn't have worried. It wasn't a real gun.' Theresa Spalding crossed to a dresser and pulled the weapon out of a drawer. She chucked it across into Carole's lap for inspection. No parts of the gun's mechanism moved except for the trigger. A moulded replica. 'Just a thing Aaron bought.'

'Why did he buy it?' asked Carole.

'Not to do any harm!' Theresa snapped. 'He'd never have done an off-licence with it. He wasn't like that. Aaron was just a little boy and little boys like playing with guns. That's just a toy. He bought it as a toy!'

'Yes.' Jude's voice smoothed down the flare-up. 'But you can see why your use of the gun got us interested. What was so important to make you go to the house of someone you'd never met before and pull a gun on them – even if that gun was just a replica?'

Theresa was sullenly silent.

Carole picked up the baton of interrogation. 'What interests me even more is the fact that you mentioned the body that I'd found on the beach that morning. How did you know about that?'

Again there was no response.

'Did Aaron tell you about the body?' suggested Jude gently. 'Had he seen it down there?'

'Aaron didn't have anything to do with that bloke dying! Aaron was a good boy . . .' Once again, as in her television interview, these words unleashed a flood of tears from Theresa Spalding.

Jude rose and, with an arm around her, led the woman to sit down. 'Cry,' she murmured. 'It's good. You need to cry.'

Then, crouched beside the chair, she rocked the woman in her arms, crooning words whose sound was more important than their meaning. Carole watched the calming process with surprise and a degree of envy, knowing that she did not possess such skills.

Gradually, the shudderings of Theresa Spalding's body became tremors, which twitched away to nothing. She reached into the pocket of her jeans for a crumpled tissue and rubbed it against her nose.

'Ready to talk?' asked Jude.

The woman nodded. To her surprise, Carole found Jude was looking at her, indicating that she was to take over for the next bit.

'Right.' Carole had taken her glasses off and was rubbing the lenses on the end of her scarf. It was a mannerism of which she was entirely unaware, but which had been noticed by all her Home Office colleagues, a little ritual she went through before any important interview. 'We weren't suggesting that Aaron had anything to do with the death of the man I found on the beach. We just want to know why you were so concerned about that body.'

Theresa Spalding said nothing. Jude had calmed her, she didn't mind Jude, but she was still resistant to the Bad Cop.

'It was nothing to do with me. I didn't even see the body. I had no connection with it.'

'Apart from the connection through Aaron?' said Jude.

For a moment the woman's face contorted. If the suggestion had come from Carole, she would have shouted some defiant response. Because Jude had spoken, though, she accepted it.

'Yes. OK.'

Carole picked up again. 'You were particularly concerned about something in the dead man's pocket.'

Theresa nodded, still calm. 'Yes. Aaron had told me about it. I was just afraid, if the police found it, they'd make the connection with him and come after my boy.'

'What was it? What was in the man's pocket?'

She couldn't face answering this question without another cigarette. Carole and Jude watched in silence while she fumbled with the packet and lit up again.

'I don't know what it was, but it was something with Aaron's name on it. They all had to put their names on something. It was part of the test.'

The Bad Cop and the Good Cop exchanged glances. The understanding passed that Jude should take over again. 'Who's "they"?' she asked softly.

'The other lads. The ones he was with when they found the body.'

'Did they find the body at the Yacht Club?'

Theresa nodded. 'Aaron got in about four that morning. I started to bawl him out, but I could see what a bad way he was in. He'd been doing some stuff, I could tell. Weed, I suppose – maybe something stronger. Bit of smack perhaps. He was crying just like a kid. Wasn't much more than a kid, really. Got in with the wrong company, that was all that was wrong with Aaron. What chance did he have, living with me, no man around . . . well, no man around for long? And me always on some medication for the depression and the panic attacks. I did try to look after him. He never got put into care. Times they wanted to, but I wouldn't let them. I brought him up on my own, all on my own.'

Jude nodded, soothing, commending the achievement. 'So what did Aaron tell you?'

'He said they'd been drinking. He didn't say they'd been doing stuff too, but I knew they had. And then they decided to break into the Yacht Club . . . I don't know what for . . . maybe a bit of thieving or just to smash the boats up. It wasn't Aaron's idea, it was the others. And they broke into one boat and they found this man's body . . . He was dead. He was definitely dead before they found him. And they . . . I don't know what they did to the body, or exactly what they put in his pockets, but it was some test . . . some kind of test . . .'

'A test to prove how hard they were?' Jude suggested. 'How tough they were?'

'Perhaps. I don't know. Aaron's been into a lot of this horror stuff, you know, books and films and stuff. A lot of that age are. Black magic stuff, you know. Maybe what they done to the body was something to do with that. You know what kids that age are like – terrified, but it doesn't do to show they're terrified, so they egg each other on to show how brave they are, and they do stupid things. Anyway, whatever they actually did, it ended up with them chucking the body over the sea wall into the Fether. That's all Aaron told me, but he was in a bad way, a really bad way. He'd scared himself something terrible. He kept saying that the body would come back to life, that it was one of the Undead or some such crap, and that it'd come after him. And then he was afraid too the police was going to come and get him as soon as the body was found. I tried to calm him and put him to bed . . . Then I slept for a couple of hours, and Aaron was here when I woke up round eight . . . but later in the morning I went down the shops . . . and when I come back, he was gone . . .' A sob came into her voice. 'And that was the last time I saw my boy.

'I still thought he was coming back then, but I wanted to do a kind of damage-limitation thing – stop anyone who knew anything about the body talking to the police. That's why I come round your place with the gun.

'But Aaron didn't come back.' She swallowed down the sob welling up in her throat. 'It was the drugs. He got into bad company and they started him doing drugs . . . and Aaron couldn't cope . . . not with that and the other things they done. I think he just couldn't take it any more. He was convinced this Undead body was going to come after him and get him . . . so he must've jumped into the Fether at high tide Tuesday night . . . and that was the end.'

She didn't burst into tears this time, but stood, her body shaking with dry sobs.

'Did you tell all this to the police?' asked Carole.

'No, not the half of it. I don't want them thinking my boy'd been messing around with dead bodies.'

'So why did you tell us?'

'To stop you telling the police about the gun.' There was a naked appeal in the bloodshot eyes she turned on Carole. 'That was the only reason I turned it on you. I was trying to frighten you, so's you wouldn't tell the police what Aaron'd done. You won't tell them, will you?'

'No. We won't tell them.'

'What about his friends?' asked Jude. 'The ones he was with?'

'Friends!' Theresa Spalding spat out the word. 'You don't call someone who gets a sixteen-year-old boy into drugs a "friend", do you?'

'No, you don't. But who were they?'

'I don't know for definite. There's a bunch that gets together. Could have been any of them. But there's one who I'm sure was involved. Older boy. Aaron worshipped him, thought he was the business all right. Asked him round here once or twice, but I turfed him out. I can always spot a bad 'un. I'm sure it was him who got Aaron into drugs.'

'What's his name?'

'Dylan.'

'Surname?'

'Don't know. Never heard it.'

'Any idea where he lives?'

Theresa Spalding shook her head. 'Somewhere local. Went to the same school as Aaron. Few years older, though, like I said. He's left the school. Think he's got a job now.'

'Doing what?'

'Carpet-fitter.'

Chapter Nineteen

'What could be more logical,' asked Carole, 'than that someone who has just moved into a new home should be looking to have it carpeted?'

'Fine.' Jude nodded cheerfully. 'I'll just think of it as an acting job.'

'Have you ever acted?'

'Oh yes,' said Jude.

'What – professionally?'

'Sort of.'

'Oh?' But, frustratingly, no further information was forthcoming. Carole swung the Renault into a parking bay.

J. T. Carpets was a flat, rectangular building on a retail estate just outside East Preston. Nearby was a Sainsbury's, a Do-It-All, a Halfords, a Petsmart, an MFI and a Toys 'R' Us. Here the devoted homemaker could find everything he or she required – provided he or she possessed a car in which to cart it all away. (And in many cases, the devoted homemakers round the Fethering area arrived in huge four-wheel-drive off-road vehicles – essential equipment to negotiate the notorious gradients of the retail estate's car parks.)

Inside the outlet (on retail estates what used to

be called 'shops' had all become 'outlets'), they were greeted by the distinctive smell of rope and rubber which rises on the air wherever new floor coverings foregather. Variegated rolls and piles of carpets were laid out across the floor area. Sample books spread over tables. Small displays of corners of room demonstrated to the unimaginative how some of the carpets would look with furniture on them.

There were few customers. Late afternoons in November were not a favourite time for buying carpets. With the run-up to Christmas, people had other purchases on their minds.

As a result, there were plenty of staff available, and the two women were quickly accosted by a young man in a sharp suit and cartoon-character tie.

'Good afternoon, ladies. What can I do for you?'

Jude was straight into her cover story. 'Yes, I'm looking for a hard-wearing carpet for my landing and staircase,' she announced.

'Certainly, madam. What sort of quality had you in mind?'

'It's not so much the quality that concerns me as the price. On a tightish budget, I'm afraid.'

'Yes. Aren't we all?' He chuckled automatically. 'Well, with carpets as with most things, you get what you pay for, but we do have some very competitive offers which you'll find—'

'Excuse me, do you have a toilet?' Carole broke in.

'What?' The young man was totally thrown.

'A toilet. I need to go to the toilet.'

'Oh. Well, we don't have public toilets.'

'You must have staff facilities.'

'Yes, but—'

'I'm desperate. It's my age.'

The young man was so embarrassed by this that he immediately called over one of his female colleagues. Jude hid her grin as Carole was escorted out to the office area at the back.

'Now, your cheapest option,' the young man continued, blanking out the interruption, 'would be a hard-wearing cord . . .'

Jude listened, occasionally throwing in doubts and questions. She moved easily – and with some relish – into the role of a dithery little woman unable to make up her mind. She invented a husband called Kevin whom she'd have to consult about the various options. Had Carole not returned from the lavatory at that point, she would soon have invented a couple of children and an ageing grannie whose opinions also required canvassing.

'Better?'

'Much better, thank you,' said Carole, showing Jude a covert thumbs-up sign. 'It's awful when you get taken suddenly like that, isn't it? So embarrassing.'

'Oh yes.'

'How're you doing?'

'This young man has been extremely helpful. He's showed me all kinds of possibilities. I think what I'd better do now is go home and discuss them all with Kevin.'

'Good idea,' said Carole. It wasn't until they were back in the car that she asked, 'Who the hell's Kevin?'

'A necessary fiction. But never mind him. Have you found out what you wanted to?'

'Yes. Dylan is scheduled to be fitting carpets in a house on the Shorelands Estate tomorrow morning. For a Mrs Grant-Edwards. House is called Bali-Hai. I've memorized all the details.'

'How did you find out?'

'There was a duty-schedule board up in the office. Wipe-clean calendar thing with staff names and addresses where they were going to be working. I thought there would be,' Carole concluded smugly.

'Well, congratulations. Very convincing. For a moment back there I thought you really did want to go to the loo.' Jude was silent for a moment. 'Mind you, they might have told you where to find him if you'd just asked.'

'Yes,' Carole agreed. And then she did something that she did very rarely. She giggled. 'But the way I did it was much more fun.'

It was six o'clock and the Crown and Anchor had just opened. Carole had initially demurred at the idea of having a drink, but Jude had insisted they needed to talk to Ted Crisp as part of their investigation.

He was going round, wiping down the tables and emptying ashtrays into a bucket.

'Have to do everything yourself, I see,' Jude observed.

'That's right. It's tough at the top. Bar staff don't come on till seven during the winter.'

'And in the summer?'

'Summers I'm open all day. That's when I make my money. From all those dads sneaking off and leaving the mums on the beach with the kiddies.' He took up his post behind the bar. 'What can I do you for? Two large whites, is it?'

'Yes, please,' said Jude, and Carole didn't even make a token murmur of dissent. Instead, she moved straight to the purpose of their visit. 'Ted,' she began, and paused for a nanosecond of shock at the knowledge that she, Carole Seddon, was actually standing at the bar of the Crown and Anchor and calling the landlord 'Ted', 'you heard about that poor boy who was drowned the other day?'

'That Aaron Spalding? Course I did. Couldn't miss it. All over the telly, for a start. And lots of the old farts in here was talking about it and all . . . moaning on about young kids today getting messed up with drugs . . . and saying that kind of thing wouldn't happen if they brought back National Service.'

Carole wondered for a moment whether it had been Denis Woodville repeating his opinion, but decided it was probably a universal sentiment among the old codgers of Fethering.

'Did you know him at all? Aaron? Did he ever come in here?'

'Well, he shouldn't have done, because he was underage, but yes, I seen him in here a few times. He'd come in with a bunch of them. They'd sit in that dark corner over there, hoping I wouldn't clock them, and send up the one who looked oldest with a shipping order for drinks. They tried it on a few times, but I was wise to them. I'm not going to risk my licence for a bunch of kids.'

'Had you seen them in here recently?'

'Yes, three of them was in one evening this week. Monday, I think.'

The night they went on to the Fethering Yacht Club and found the body in Rory Turnbull's boat, thought Carole. 'Who were the other two?' she asked.

'One I'd never seen before. Young kid, looked even younger than Aaron. But I know the one they sent up for the drinks.' He spoke without enthusiasm. 'He comes in here quite often. Eighteen, nineteen I guess, so he can drink legally. But when he comes up and asks for three pints of lager on Monday night, I says to him, "I'll pull one for you, no problem, but it's going to be soft drinks for your two underage mates over there." Then he gets dead stroppy and starts swearing at me, so I tell him to get out. He's a nasty bit of work, that one. Deals a bit in drugs and all. I can do without that sort in here.

'Anyway, out they go, no doubt straight down to Nowtinstore, where he buys a dozen cans perfectly legally and they go off and drink them in one of the shelters on the front. At least they wasn't doing it on my premises. I hope they froze their bollocks off out there.'

'The police haven't come and asked you whether you saw Aaron, have they?'

'No, but presumably if they was retracing his movements they'd be interested in the next night, wouldn't they? Not the Monday. His body was found on the Wednesday morning, wasn't it?'

'That's right,' Carole agreed thoughtfully.

'So who was this older boy?' asked Jude. 'Do you know his name?'

'Don't know his second name, but his first name's Dylan.'

'Ah.' The two women exchanged significant looks. 'What does he look like?'

'Tallish. Thin. Short bleached hair. One big earring.'

'Sounds a real charmer,' Carole observed frostily.

Jude looked down at her large watch-face and her expression suddenly changed. 'Oh, Lord!' she cried. 'I'd completely forgotten! I've got a friend coming round this evening! I must dash!'

'So we'll go to the Shorelands Estate first thing?'

'Yes, fine. Communicate in the morning!' And, having gulped down the remains of her wine, Jude rushed out of the pub.

Carole finished her drink more sedately, as Ted Crisp chatted inconsequentially of this and that. She didn't feel relaxed alone with him. Carole Seddon would never really be a 'pub person'.

She tried not to be interested in who Jude's 'friend' might be. They were only neighbours, after all. There was no reason why they should know everything about each other's lives.

'Another one of those?' asked Ted Crisp, as she sipped down the last of her wine.

'No, thanks. I must get back home.' But at the door she did manage to stop and say, 'Good night, Ted.' Just like a regular 'pub person' might have done.

Chapter Twenty

It was after eight the following morning, the Friday. Gulliver had been duly walked and Carole still hadn't heard anything from Jude. They'd agreed to go to the Shorelands Estate early and intercept Dylan when he arrived for work at Bali-Hai. According to the duty roster Carole had snooped at, all fitters were meant to pick up their carpets from the depot at eight in the morning and be at the properties where they were scheduled to lay them by nine.

Her hand reached for the telephone to call Jude, but then she thought, this is stupid, the woman's only next door and I must make an effort to be a little less formal. Something in Jude's casual approach to life was secretly appealing. Carole knew that the ramparts of inhibition she had built around herself would never allow her to progress far down that road, but maybe she could take a few tentative steps.

Going round to Woodside Cottage rather than telephoning would be one such step. So Carole Seddon put on her Burberry and went to knock on her next-door neighbour's door.

To her considerable amazement, it was opened by a man. He had a head of black curly hair, more of which sprouted out of the top of his Guernsey sweater. Between was heavy dark stubble. He had jeans, trainers, blue eyes and a huge grin.

'Morning,' he said cheerily. 'I'm Brad. You must be Carole.'

'Yes, yes, I am.'

'Do come in. Jude's just dressing. She won't be a moment.'

'Oh, thank you.' In a state of bewilderment, Carole followed the man through the cluttered sitting room into the kitchen.

He indicated a plate of toast and marmalade. 'I was having some breakfast. Would you like a coffee or something?'

'No, thank you. I've just had some.'

'Well, excuse me if I continue munching.'

'Of course.'

'Do sit down,' said Brad, as he lowered himself on to a chair and took a bite of toast.

'Yes, thank you.' Carole knew she sounded ridiculously formal. 'So, Brad, have you known Jude long?'

'Oh yes. We go way back.'

'Ah.' Bubbling to the surface of Carole's mind were a whole lot of other questions she wanted to ask. How far back? Where did you meet? Where do you live? Are you a fixture in Jude's life? *What is the precise nature of your relationship*?

'Great place she's got here, hasn't she?' said Brad.

'Yes, yes, it's very nice. Needs a bit of work, of course.'

He didn't seem to hear the second part of this

response. 'No, good old Jude,' he said with easy admiration. 'Always lands on her feet.'

'Does she?'

'Oh yes.'

At that moment the subject of their conversation swept into the room in her customary swirl of drapery. She was twisting the blonde hair into a knot on top of her head. 'Morning, Carole,' she called out blithely. 'Brad's introduced himself, I hope.'

'Yes.'

'Sorry I wasn't ready. You know how it is.'

Carole didn't know how it was, and wouldn't have minded a few background details to tell her how it was. But she didn't get any.

'We'd better be off then,' said Jude. She leant across the table and planted a smacking kiss on Brad's marmalady lips. 'Don't know how long we'll be, but if you're not here when I get back, it's been good to see you.'

'You too. Always is.'

'The door's on the latch. Just click the thing up and close it behind you.'

'Sure. Nice to meet you, Carole.'

'And you, Brad.' Though she didn't feel that she'd met him at all.

In the immaculate Renault, as they drove off, Carole said, 'Brad seemed very pleasant.'

'Yes, he's good news.'

'He said you and he go way back . . .'

'That's right. He's a good friend.'

And Jude snuggled back into her seat, leaving Carole desperately in need of a definition of the word 'friend'. But Jude didn't volunteer one, and Carole couldn't see any way of getting one, short of actually asking straight out what her neighbour's relationship with Brad was. And she would never in a million years have done that.

The Shorelands Estate house which was receiving the benefit of J. T. fitted carpets was an Elizabethan pastiche with tall windows and bunches of thin, imaginatively topped chimneys. With the inappropriate nomenclature which seemed *de rigueur* in Shorelands, its name, Bali-Hai, was spelled out in rustic pokerwork on an asymmetrical piece of driftwood. In the driveway, behind closed railings, a large green Jaguar squatted, toad-like.

'I think we're in time,' said Carole, as she brought the Renault to a halt opposite the house. 'No sign of a van yet.'

She looked at her watch. Ten to nine. They'd just sit and wait. And chat. Maybe she'd find out a little more about Jude's visitor.

'Brad was the friend you rushed back from the pub to see last night, was he?'

'That's right, yes.'

'So he stayed over?'

'Yes. Well, it's a long way back for him.'

Back *where*? Though desperate to know the answer, that was another question Carole could never have brought herself to ask.

'He seemed very at home, Jude.'

'It's nice when friends feel relaxed staying with you, isn't it?'

'Yes.'

Jude looked across and gave Carole a sweet smile. Was there a trace of irony in it? Was Jude actually teasing her, deliberately withholding information, knowing how desperate she was to know about the relationship with Brad? It was impossible to tell.

Jude smiled inwardly. She *was* having a little game with her neighbour. If Carole had come out with direct questions, she'd have answered them. Jude had no secrets. But if she wasn't asked, it had never been her habit to volunteer information.

She felt good, though. It was always a pleasure to see Brad, catch up on what he was doing. Old friends, Jude found, became more valuable with the passage of the years.

There was a sudden tapping at the passenger side window. Jude wound it down.

'I don't know what you think you're doing parked here! This is a Neighbourhood Watch area and . . . Oh. Oh, Jude, good morning.'

The righteous resident of Shorelands bending down to the car window turned out to be Barbara Turnbull, her large frame swaddled up in an expensive tweed coat.

'Barbara, how nice to see you. You know Carole?'

'Yes. Yes, of course we know each other. Morning, Carole.'

'Morning.'

'I'm very sorry to have spoken to you like that, Jude, but you can't be too careful. There's been quite a spate of burglaries here in Shorelands and, since there's a bit of an *element* in Fethering these days, we've all been encouraged to accost anyone we see lurking around.'

'Sorry. I didn't realize we were *lurking*,' said Jude.

'No, obviously you weren't. But it's an unfamiliar car and, since I didn't know who was in it, it did look as though someone was lurking. Apparently, these criminal gangs send people down to check out potential targets. "Casing the joint", I believe they call it.' Having shared this piece of underworld know-how with her acquaintances, she straightened up. 'Anyway, I was just off to my mother's for a cup of coffee and to take her dog for a walk. First chance I've had to get out for days. Been tied up with housework. But thank goodness my cleaning lady's deigned to come back this morning.' Barbara Turnbull put a large smile in place over her features. 'So nice to see you both.'

'And you, Barbara,' said Carole. 'How's Rory?'

The smile froze in position. 'Rory's absolutely fine,' asserted Barbara Turnbull, daring anyone to contradict her. 'Goodbye.'

And with that she navigated her large, top-heavy body off down the road.

'Funny,' Jude observed. 'When she didn't know who we were, she thought we might be criminals lurking. As soon as she recognizes us, her suspicions cease. How does she know we're not "casing the joint"?'

'Because we're Fethering residents,' replied Carole stoutly.

'Still, I think it's good . . .' Jude mused.

'What's good?'

'All this security-consciousness. All this Neighbourhood Watch stuff.'

'I didn't think you'd approve of that.'

'Why not?'

'Because you seem to have rather a hippyish attitude to property' was the answer that came instinctively to Carole's mind. But all she said was, 'I thought you'd regard it as snooping.'

'Oh, I do. And that's the beauty of it. Everyone in Fethering seems to snoop. I'm sure it's impossible to do anything in this place without *someone* having seen you at it . . .'

'Well . . .'

'Which makes me very optimistic that we're going to find out how our two bodies came to end up on the beach. Someone must've seen what happened. It's just a matter of finding out who that someone is. And I think we—'

'Ssh! Look.'

A yellow Transit van had just drawn up outside Bali-Hai. Lettering on the side read 'J. T. CARPETS'.

'Here we go,' said Carole, her hand tightening round the Stanley knife in her raincoat pocket.

Two men got out of the van and went round to open the doors at the back. Both were middle-aged, one almost completely bald, the other with grizzled grey hair.

Jude shook her head ruefully. 'Neither of those looks like Dylan.'

'No.'

'Maybe you read the duty roster wrong?'

Carole was offended. 'I did not! There were three of them allocated to this job. Dave, Ken and Dylan.'

'Well, there go Dave and Ken.' Jude watched the two men, now carrying toolboxes, open the gates to Bali-Hai and go up to the front door. 'Looks like Dylan's called in sick.'

But, as she spoke, they were aware of the sound of a car approaching fast. It was a Golf Gti, a good ten years old, tarted up with extra chrome and decals. The way it was being driven gave two fingers to the demure '20 mph' signs of Shorelands.

'I think this could be our quarry,' said Carole, as she opened the car door.

They were both standing in front of Bali-Hai's railings by the time the boy emerged from his Golf. He fitted Ted Crisp's description perfectly. Bleached hair, single earring, 'a nasty bit of work'.

He looked through them as he came up to the gates.

'Are you Dylan?' asked Carole.

'What if I am?'

'I've got something that belongs to you.'

'Oh yes?'

Carole took the Stanley knife out of her pocket and held it in her open palm, with the painted 'J. T. CARPETS' uppermost. Both women watched the boy closely. Though he quickly covered it up, his first reaction was undoubtedly one of shock.

'Oh, well, thanks,' he said casually, reaching out for the knife. 'I can take it in to work with me.'

Carole withdrew her hand. 'Don't you want to know where we found it?'

'Not particularly.' After the initial giveaway response, his manner had become cocky, on the edge of insolence.

'We found it in a boat at the Fethering Yacht Club,' said Jude.

A flicker of the eyelid showed he hadn't been expecting that. But again he recovered quickly. 'Wonder how it got there . . .'

Carole took over the attack. 'We know that you were there on Monday night with Aaron Spalding and another boy.'

Dylan's lip curled. 'You know a lot. Nosy pair of old tarts, aren't you?'

'Being offensive isn't going to help, Dylan. This is serious. And you know it's serious. Aaron Spalding's dead.'

'Yes, I do know that. Stupid kid. Should have known better than to muck around on the banks of the Fether, shouldn't he?'

'And he's not the only one who's dead.'

The young man's face became a rigid mask. 'Don't know what you're talking about. I've got to get to work.' And he made to push past them.

Jude put her hand on his sleeve. 'The police might be very interested to talk to you about what happened on Monday night.'

'Oh yeah?'

'We have proof that you were with Aaron,' Jude went on, lying through her teeth.

Dylan turned back to look her straight in the face. 'All right, yes, I was with Aaron. That's not a crime, is it?'

'No.'

'We went down the Crown and Anchor, but that tight-arsed bastard of a landlord wouldn't serve the other two, so we pissed off down Nowtinstore and got some cans. We sank a few in one of them shelters on the front and Aaron asked me if I'd lend him my Stanley knife. So I did.'

'What did he want it for?'

'I don't know, do I?' Dylan replied, with a shrug of aggrieved innocence. 'And then I went home. I didn't go down the Yacht Club. What the other two done after I gone, I've no idea.'

'I think the police would want a rather fuller explanation than that, Dylan.'

But Carole's bid to frighten him didn't work.

'Maybe they would. But you're not the police, are you?' he sneered. 'And I don't quite honestly think the police'd be that interested in what a pair of old biddies like you have to say.'

Carole and Jude were rather afraid he was right. Their bluff had been called.

'Now, if you'll excuse me, I do have work to do.' Dylan put his hand on the railings of Bali-Hai's gates.

'Don't you want your knife back?' asked Carole.

'Not that bothered. We get through a lot of those. Tools of the trade.'

'Then I'll keep it . . .'

'Please yourself.'

' . . . as evidence.'

'Evidence of *what?*' Suddenly he'd seized the lapel of Carole's raincoat and brought his face close up to hers. Her nostrils were filled by a sickly musk-flavoured aftershave. 'You two harass me any more and things could get very unpleasant for you. I've seen you around. Fethering's a small place. Wouldn't be that hard for me to find out where you live. I'd advise you both to get off my bloody back!'

There was no doubting the reality of the threat in his last words. He raised his free hand to Carole's face. She flinched. Dylan chuckled and touched her cheek. Just one touch, very brief, very gentle and very menacing. Then he let go of her coat and turned towards Bali-Hai.

'Who was the third boy?' asked Jude.

'Who indeed?'

'There was you, and Aaron Spalding, and somebody else.'

'Spot on.'

'Who was it?'

'That's for you to find out. Mind you, I don't think you will.'

'Why? Is he dead too?' Jude called after the retreating back as Dylan strode up the drive.

But there was no answer. And the Stanley knife remained in Carole's hand.

'He's lying,' Jude hissed, the first time that Carole had seen her angry. 'He was with them at the Yacht Club.'

'I know.'

'But how're we going to prove it?'

'That,' said Carole pompously, 'has been the problem with crime investigation since records began.'

'Yes.'

'Having an instinct for what's happened, having a

flash of inspiration – that's the easy bit. It's when you try to make the charges stick that most cases collapse.'

Jude nodded thoughtfully. Then a slow smile spread across her broad features.

'What is it?' asked Carole.

'You talked about flashes of inspiration. I think I've just had one.'

'About what?'

'About finding the third boy. I may be wrong, but at least I've an idea where we can start looking.'

Chapter Twenty-one

They didn't have far to go through the Shorelands Estate to reach Brigadoon. The front garden's Victorian lampposts continued to look incongruous in their mock-Spanish surroundings.

'I still don't understand,' Carole complained as they approached the studded door. 'We know Barbara won't be there. We know her mother won't be there. And Rory'll be at work in Brighton.'

'It's not them we've come to see,' said Jude firmly, as she pressed the doorbell.

The woman who came to the door was probably late forties and could have been attractive in different circumstances. She wore jeans and a faded sweat shirt; her greying hair was scraped back into a rubber band at the nape of her neck and her face had the taut, drained look of total exhaustion.

'Good morning,' she said, in a surprisingly cultured voice, and waited for them to state their business.

Jude took the initiative. 'Good morning. This is Carole and I'm Jude. We're both friends of Barbara Turnbull and—'

'I'm afraid Mrs Turnbull isn't in.'

'No, we know that. You're Maggie, aren't you?'

'Yes,' the woman conceded cautiously.

'It was you we wanted to have a word with.'

Her face closed over. 'You're nothing to do with the Social Services, are you?'

'No, no, we're not. I promise.'

But that didn't resolve her suspicions. 'I'm sorry. I'm working.' She reached to close the door, but Jude's next words stopped her.

'We wanted to have a word about your son.'

A new wave of exhaustion flooded the woman's body. Her shoulders drooped. There was a note of fatalism in her voice as she asked, 'What's he done?'

'That's what we want to find out.' Jude pressed home her slight advantage. 'In particular what he was doing last Monday night.'

This did frighten the woman. Her spoken response, that she had no idea what they were talking about, was belied by a wildness in her eyes.

Some instinct told Carole this was the moment once again to produce the Stanley knife from her raincoat pocket. The woman's eyes grew wilder.

'What's that? Where did you find it?'

The telephone on the hall table rang. Indecision flickered in Maggie's frightened eyes. She didn't want to invite them in, but equally she didn't want to let them go until she knew as much as they knew. The phone rang on. It was clearly not going to be picked up by anybody else or by an answering machine. 'Wait there,' she said. 'I'll just be a moment.'

She picked up the phone and gave the number. 'What? Oh yes. Yes, he is here. I'll get him to the phone.' She crossed to the foot of the stairs and called up, 'Mr Turnbull! Telephone!'

She put the receiver down and crossed back to the women at the front door.

'I thought Mr Turnbull would be at work,' said Carole.

'He's not well.' Dismissing the detail quickly, Maggie came closer and addressed them with a quiet urgency. 'Look, I can't really talk now. But I do want to talk.' Then, with a mixture of dread and pleading in her voice, she said, 'You haven't spoken to anyone else about Nick, have you?'

'No,' replied Jude reassuringly.

'Not yet,' added Carole, who thought their level of menace should be maintained. Maggie had something to tell them; having hooked her, they didn't want to lose her.

'Carole. Good morning. What're you doing here?'

Rory Turnbull was coming down the stairs. He wore a shapeless towelling dressing gown. He looked raddled, hungover and haunted.

Carole improvised wildly. 'We were just calling about a Labrador charity I'm involved in. The Canine Trust.'

'If you're looking for a handout, I'm afraid dogs come fairly low down my pecking order of good causes.'

'No, we were just . . .' Not wishing to get tangled up in details of her fictitious charity call, Carole moved on. 'You met my new neighbour, Jude, in the pub, didn't you?'

'Did I?' Rory Turnbull's bloodshot eyes showed no

recognition but took Jude in, as though he were memorizing her features for future reference. 'You will excuse me.' He turned to Maggie and asked gracelessly, 'Who did you say was on the phone?'

'The BMW garage. Something about a bill or—'

'I'll take it in the study.' Without a word to the two women still standing on his doorstep, Rory Turnbull left the hall.

The urgency remained in Maggie's voice as she said, 'Listen, I can't talk now. I'm through here at twelve. Could we meet after that?'

'Sure,' said Jude. 'Where?'

'You'd better come round to my place. It's not far. Spindrift Lane – do you know it?'

Carole nodded. 'I do.'

'Number 26. Say half-past twelve. I'll be back by then.'

'Fine.'

'And please don't say anything to anyone.' There was a naked appeal in Maggie's eyes as she echoed Theresa Spalding's words. 'Nick's a good boy. He is, really.'

'I'm wondering why Rory came down,' Carole mused as she drove them back to the High Street. 'They must have a phone upstairs in a house that size. In their bedroom certainly.'

'Come to that, why didn't he answer it in the first place?'

'Asleep? He looked pretty crumpled when he did come downstairs.'

'Yes. Alternatively, he may just have been curious as to who was at the door. He heard our voices and came to have a snoop.'

'He certainly subjected you to a rather searching look, didn't he?'

Jude nodded and gave a little shudder. 'Uncomfortably searching. There's something very strange happening with that man, isn't there? He doesn't seem to be behaving like the pillar of society a Fethering dentist should be.'

'Certainly not. He's behaving like an alcoholic.'

'Or someone who's in the throes of a nervous breakdown?'

'Maybe. Still, poor old Rory's not really our concern. Except for the fact that his boat was possibly used as a temporary morgue, I can't see that he has anything to do with our body on the beach.'

'No, I guess not.'

'Though Maggie clearly does have something relevant to tell us. How on earth did you know that she would, Jude?'

'It was just a guess. Intuition, if you like. Barbara Turnbull had said something about Maggie's son having psychological problems and . . . I put two and two together. You know, sometimes you just have a sense of things being connected, don't you?'

'No,' replied Carole, who never did.

'Bad luck. Oh, here we are.'

Carole brought the Renault to a halt outside Woodside Cottage. She looked at her watch. 'Spindrift Lane's only five minutes' walk away. Hardly worth taking the car. Shall I knock on your door about twenty past twelve?'

'That'd be fine.'

Carole couldn't help herself from fishing a little. 'So you'll have time for a nice cup of coffee with Brad . . .'

'No,' said Jude breezily. 'I'll have to empty a few more boxes upstairs, I'm afraid. Brad's car's not here. He's gone.'

'Oh.' Carole couldn't for the life of her have left it there. 'But I dare say you'll be seeing him again . . .'

'I dare say,' Jude agreed, with an infuriating, but probably not deliberate, lack of specificity.

Carole parked the car in her garage. As she was doing so, she noticed on the mat a little scrape of mud left by Jude's boot. She got out the dustpan and brush which was used only for the car and swept it up.

Chapter Twenty-two

Spindrift Lane was part of the residential network which spread out from Fethering High Street. While not aspiring to the wealth-proclaiming grandeur of the Shorelands Estate, the houses there bore witness to lives well spent and money well invested. Paintwork gleamed and anything that could be polished had been polished. Even in November, no front grass was allowed to grow ragged and weeds had been banished from the interstices between flagstones in garden paths. The area was a testament to bourgeois values, which are, for the most part, financial values.

Number 26 Spindrift Lane, however, fell short of these values. The front lawn was unkempt, the paint on the window-frames blistered and split. The garden gate sagged, maintaining only a tenuous contact with its hinges. Carole and Jude exchanged looks as they pushed through and approached the front door.

Maggie had changed out of her working clothes into a navy woollen suit. With hair neatly brushed, her appearance matched the educated accent which had seemed so discordant earlier in the morning. As she ushered her two visitors into the sitting room, her mouth was tight with anxiety. Their welcome was polite – she had been well brought up – but not warm.

Carole and Jude were sat down on a sofa in a room that was sparsely furnished and, like the exterior of the house, could have done with being decorated. The grate in the fireplace was bleakly empty. The bunched curtains in the bay window had faded unevenly. There was a portable television, but no video recorder. The room boasted few ornaments, but those there were looked to be of good quality. The two watercolour seascapes on the wall made Carole want to know the artist's name. On the mantelpiece stood a pair of rather fine brass candlesticks and a photograph of a boy aged about fourteen. It was a school one, posed against a cloudy background, like the picture of Aaron Spalding featured in the *Fethering Observer.*

Maggie stood in front of the fireplace and confronted them. 'All right. What is all this? What's Nick being accused of?'

'We're not accusing your son of anything,' Jude replied calmly. 'May I call you Maggie?'

'Maggie . . . Mrs Kent . . . I don't care. Just tell me what you know.'

'You've heard about the death of that boy Aaron Spalding?' A curt nod of acknowledgement. 'Well, we have reason to believe that Aaron Spalding, with two other youths, was messing around on the seafront here at Fethering on Monday night.'

'How do you mean, "messing around"?'

'They had a few drinks and then they broke into the Fethering Yacht Club.'

Maggie Kent didn't say anything. She still watched and waited, gauging how much they knew.

'We know that one of the other youths was called Dylan. He's training as a fitter with J. T. Carpets . . .'

Carole decided that Jude's gentle approach was too much Good Cop, so she came in heavily in her Bad Cop persona. 'And we have reason to believe that the third youth was your son, Nick.'

For the first time in their acquaintance, Jude turned a look of reproof on her neighbour. They were going too fast. Maggie Kent didn't look like a woman who'd crumple in the face of bullying. They needed to play her very carefully if they were going to get anything out of her.

Maggie was silent for a moment. The women on the sofa watched her, each afraid that Carole had blown it.

Eventually she spoke. Her voice was quiet and measured. It was costing her a lot to achieve, but she was in control. 'Are you suggesting that my son had anything to do with Aaron Spalding's death?'

'No,' Jude hastened to assure her. 'Certainly not. Whatever happened to Aaron happened on the Tuesday night. We're concerned about events on the Monday.'

'Why? Why are you concerned about them?'

Carole took this on. 'Because I have reason to believe that a crime was committed that night.'

Anger blazed in Maggie Kent's eyes. 'And you think Nick did it?'

'No. I'm not quite sure what the crime was and I certainly have no idea at this point who did it. We're just trying to piece together the events of Monday night.' There was a silence, before Carole went on, 'I've spoken to the police about this, but they seem unwilling to take me seriously.'

'Oh? So your aim is not to turn all your information over to the police?'

'No. Not until we know precisely what happened and have a completely watertight case. I'm not going to be treated like a hysterical woman a second time.'

'Hm . . .' Maggie Kent nodded, taking in what she'd been told. Something Carole had said had relaxed her. The tension across her shoulders had lessened. She moved restlessly over towards the window and looked out into the November coldness. Then, seeming to reach a decision, she turned back and lowered herself into an armchair.

'All right.' There was a new complicity in her voice. 'I want to know what happened on Monday night at least as much as you do. But tell me first how you know Nick was involved. Were there witnesses?'

Jude shook her head. 'Not so far as we know. It was guesswork and a bit of luck, really. I'd had coffee with Barbara Turnbull and she'd been complaining about how her cleaning lady couldn't come in because of some problem with her son. I just made the connection.'

Maggie Kent's lip curled. 'And I bet the lovely Barbara was really sympathetic about the situation?'

'From your tone, I don't get the feeling I need to answer that.'

'No. I hope she's not a great friend of yours . . . In fact, I don't much care if she *is* a great friend of yours.

So far as I'm concerned, Barbara Turnbull is 100 per cent British cow.'

Carole had expected Jude to agree with this and was surprised to hear only a demure, 'I don't really know her that well.'

'Right. Fine. Well, I've been working for her for seven or eight months and I do know her – quite well enough. I wouldn't put up with her patronizing poison if I had any alternative.'

'Aren't there many jobs round here?' asked Jude innocently.

'Not many that don't involve travelling. I don't have transport these days. And I don't want to take on anything full-time yet. I still feel I should be around for Nick . . . you know, when he comes home from school.' She bit her lip. 'Not that it seems my being around for him is doing that much good.'

'Adolescence has always been pretty much purgatory.'

Not for the first time, Carole was struck by Jude's instinctive ability to get on someone's wavelength and say exactly the right thing. Maggie Kent nodded, coaxed into confidences. 'Yes, and he lost his father at a very difficult time.'

'I'm sorry. I didn't realize that—'

'Oh, I didn't mean "lost" in that sense. Nick's father's still alive – at least, I assume he is, I haven't heard anything to the contrary – but for all the use he is to his son – or to me, come to that – he might as well be dead.' She sighed, before launching into a potted history she'd delivered many times before. 'Sam – that's my husband – lost his job about three years ago. He worked in the printing industry – managerial job, good salary, all the accessories that go with a nice middle-class lifestyle. House in a desirable part of Fethering, two cars, son at private school, little wife needn't go out to work – all sorted. Then suddenly there's a takeover. Big German conglomerate buys up Sam's company and there's major reorganization, restructuring, redeployment, and all those other words beginning with "re-" which mean basically that people lose jobs. And Sam's out with a year's money.

'He wasn't good at being out of work. Sam was always one of those men who felt defined by his job. That was his status, his sense of identity. Take it away and – as I discovered – there wasn't a lot else there. At first Sam just pretended it hadn't happened, made no changes to the way we lived our lives, kept Nick on at the private school, all that. He seemed to think something was going to happen, some *deus ex machina* was going to swoop down from the skies with a large chequebook and make everything all right again.

'Well – surprise, surprise – that didn't happen. Sam realized rather belatedly that, unless he did something about it, nothing *would* happen. So he applied for a few jobs, but he wasn't good at selling himself. His confidence was so shot to pieces by then, he was going into interviews virtually telling them that he wasn't what they were looking for. Which – all too readily – they believed.

'From then on, it just got worse. The money ran out, Sam started drinking and, to make things even worse, he got into drugs. Cannabis at first – "to dull the pain", he kept saying – but pretty soon he was on to the hard stuff. Heroin. Under those circumstances, the marriage didn't stand a chance. Rows over money, rows about . . . about anything. Soon we stopped bothering with subjects to have rows about, we just cut straight to the row.

'And then my dear husband walked out. In about eighteen months Sam'd gone from executive to dosser. I don't know where he is now. Living rough somewhere, I imagine. I wouldn't dare look too closely in shop doorways along the Strand or on street corners in Brighton, in case I recognized my husband . . . assuming of course that I ever went to London or Brighton, and didn't spend all my time incarcerated in bloody Fethering!'

Gently, Jude eased the conversation on. 'And you say all this had a bad effect on Nick?'

'Of course it did. Devastating. For a start, he'd always worshipped his father, and suddenly there's this pathetic wreck around the house all the time. And Mum and Dad, who'd always seemed to get on so well, stop getting on well at all. And all Nick's friends are going off on expensive holidays and we can't afford to. And then one day there's not even a pathetic wreck round the house. His father's upped and gone.'

'And he hasn't been back since?'

'Not while Nick's been around, no. Sam did come back here a few times the first few weeks, but it was only to try and get money off me. Steal money from me if I wasn't here. He took virtually everything in the house that had any value and sold it off to feed his heroin habit. Even took his passport one time – no doubt he managed to get a few quid for that from illegal-immigrant racketeers. He's just gone.' Maggie Kent let out a defeated sigh. 'When he started going downhill, I felt dreadful, kept thinking I could save him from himself, that I *should* save him from himself. Now, I haven't got the energy even to think about him. So far as I'm concerned, Sam no longer exists.'

'But Nick must've been in an awful state when his father left,' Jude persisted gently.

'Oh yes, it was terrible for him. And Sam's departure coincided with running out of money for the school fees, so suddenly Nick's changing schools. I'm not saying anything against state education . . . well, yes, I am, actually. You grow up middle class and your mind rides along certain tracks for so long that it's almost impossible to derail it. Nick was much better taught at his private school than he is now, and he mixed with a much less damaging bunch of kids than he does now. There, I've said it! Deeply politically incorrect and I don't give a damn!'

The outburst had exhausted her further. Maggie Kent sagged in her chair, the anger drained out of her.

'I don't know. I suppose I should move out of here – I'll have to move out of here soon, anyway, the building society will see to that – and buy a little flat somewhere cheaper, and get Nick back into a decent school for his A-levels and . . .' She sighed. 'But I seem to lack the will. I keep thinking something'll happen, to sort out this whole bloody mess. Maybe I'm not so different from Sam, after all.' She slumped back, defeated.

'So, going back to Monday night,' Jude prompted tentatively, 'what time did Nick get home?'

'I don't know exactly. Not that late – one, two, I suppose. I was aware of him coming in, but I didn't see him. Quite honestly, I get so sick of all the rows about the time he comes in that if I can duck one I do.

'But he went out again early the next morning and it was what happened then that really affected him. The phone rang when I was hardly awake. Someone wanted to speak to Nick. Young voice, one of his mates I assumed, so I gave the lad an earful about ringing at that hour and got Nick to the phone. I don't know what was said, but it sure scared the hell out of my son. He threw some clothes on and rushed straight out of the house. I don't know where he was going, he wouldn't tell me, but he was shaking like a leaf.'

'What time would that have been?' asked Carole.

'Ooh . . . Five past seven, say.'

'Uh-huh.'

'Anyway, I was worried sick. Though Nick's given me quite a few nasty frights over the last few months, I'd never seen him in that kind of state. But of course I was due up at Brigadoon to be a dutiful Mrs Mop to the lovely Barbara . . . so I wait around as long as I can. And then, just when I'm about to leave, Nick comes back. He was in a worse state than ever, sobbing like a baby. No, worse than a baby. He was hysterical.'

'Did he tell you the reason?'

'No. Oh, I got bits out of him . . . that he'd been out with Dylan and Aaron the night before . . . that they'd had a few drinks . . . I think they did some drugs too. He didn't admit it in so many words, but

I'm pretty sure they did. And apparently they were talking about black magic, some gobbledegook I didn't understand, but which seemed to have got Nick pretty scared. Anyway, he told me that they broke into the Yacht Club . . . said it was just a lark, that they didn't do any harm.'

'But you reacted this morning when I showed you the Stanley knife,' Carole pointed out. 'He must've said something about that.'

'Yes, Nick mentioned it. He said that Dylan, who works as a carpet-fitter, had his knife with him. But then he seemed to regret saying that and clammed up. I asked if any of the boats had been vandalized and he assured me they hadn't.'

'But Dylan was definitely with Nick and Aaron when they broke into the Yacht Club?'

'Oh yes.'

Carole and Jude exchanged a look. Neither of them had believed Dylan's disclaimer at the time he said it.

'That was all the night before,' said Jude thoughtfully. 'But it's Nick's trip the following morning that seems really to have upset him. Did you find out anything about that?'

'Nothing. Not a thing. He kept saying he couldn't tell anyone about it. That he couldn't tell me, of all people.'

' "You, of all people" because you were his mother or because what happened had something to do with you?'

Maggie Kent shrugged helplessly at Jude's question. 'I haven't a clue. All I know is that my son was in a terrible state of shock . . . Oh, and I did notice he had sand on his trainers.'

'So he'd been on the beach.' Carole stated the obvious. 'The boy who phoned him that morning, are you sure you didn't recognize the voice?'

'I'd never heard it before. I mean, I could tell it was someone round Nick's age. They all talk ridiculously gruffly. Partly street cred and partly because they haven't got used to their voices having broken. But this wasn't one I recognized.'

'Could it have been Aaron Spalding?'

'Possibly. But I never heard Aaron Spalding speak, so I wouldn't know.'

There was a silence. Carole and Jude's minds were racing.

'You're sure there wasn't anything else, Maggie?' asked Jude.

'No, sorry. Nick clammed up again. That was all I could get out of him.'

'But he didn't go to school on the Tuesday?'

'He was in no state to go anywhere. I stayed here with him, tried to calm him down a bit. Wednesday he stayed here again, but he was more his old self. Then we heard about Aaron's death and I'm afraid Nick just cracked up again.'

'Is he at home now?' asked Carole.

Maggie shook her head. 'He said he felt up to school this morning. So he went there, and I went to the Shorelands Estate to be patronized by Barbara bloody Turnbull.'

'So you really have no idea what the three of them got up to at the Fethering Yacht Club?'

'No, but it was something pretty horrifying, if the effect it had on my son is anything to go by . . .'

'Not to mention the effect it had on Aaron Spalding,' Jude murmured.

'What do you mean?'

'There seems a very strong chance that Aaron Spalding killed himself.'

Maggie Kent nodded slowly, taking this in. It wasn't an entirely new thought to her. 'Yes.' Panic flared in her eyes. 'I hope to God Nick's all right!'

'He will be . . . He will be.'

'If only he'd tell me what happened.'

'You still haven't got anything beyond the fact that the three of them broke into the Yacht Club?'

'No, not a thing. And, God knows, it's not for want of trying.'

'Do you think,' Jude suggested diffidently, 'he might tell more to someone who wasn't his mother?'

'He might well, but I think it'd rather depend on who it was who asked him.'

'What about me?' asked Jude. 'Do you think he might tell something more to me?'

Maggie Kent looked at the blonde-haired stranger on her sofa with amazement, which gave way to deliberation and then assent. 'Do you know,' she said, 'I think he might.'

Chapter Twenty-three

Carole knew Jude was right about seeing Nick on her own, but that didn't take away her sense of frustration. It wasn't jealousy – in the short period of their acquaintance, Carole had come to accept her new neighbour had people skills that she lacked – it was more annoyance at being excluded from any part of the investigation. The feeling brought home to Carole how totally absorbed she had become by the body on the beach. In less than a week the imperatives of her normal, sensible routine had been swept away by the overwhelming need to explain its mystery.

Still, she wasn't going to let her frustration have completely negative effects. Gulliver at least should benefit from her enforced idleness. She would take him for a long walk on the beach.

The dog responded enthusiastically to her attention, making Carole feel guilty that he'd suffered from her recent preoccupations. He scampered about on the sand, scurrying back and forth, covering four times as much ground as his mistress. She walked along parallel to the sea, just below the pebble line, while Gulliver made his sudden, quixotic forays to challenge the unknown foes of flotsam and jetsam.

It was a beautiful afternoon. The weather, as if in apology for its recent bad behaviour, put on a perfect display – white winter sun, evenly pale-blue sky, the full works. It still felt cold – the lack of cloud cover ensured that – but the wind had dropped and the air no longer stung the cheeks. The heavy frosts of the previous days seemed a distant memory. Carole didn't think the night ahead would drop below freezing.

As she walked along, her restlessness eased. Life wasn't so bad after all, she reflected. Looking up to the crystal-clear contours of the South Downs in one direction and, the other way, across the beige sea to the distinct line where it became blue sky, Carole Seddon thought how lucky she was to live in such a beautiful place as Fethering. Amidst the crude cacophony of gulls, she heard the cry of a single curlew, like a piece of tape being wound backwards.

She seemed to see everything with new eyes. The seaweed clusters, stranded along the pebble line, weren't a uniform dull brown; they were a tangle of russets and copper, with the occasional unexpected burst of pimento red and fresh spinach green. Even the reminders of man's presence did not spoil the picture. An abandoned winching mechanism, encrusted with flaking rust and leaning drunkenly sideways, had its own beauty too.

Carole couldn't explain why she was thinking like this. She had many fallibilities, but lyricism was not among them. Yet somehow the combination of the sparkling afternoon, the susurration of the sea and Gulliver's ecstatic barking brought her to a feeling as near peace as her tightly constrained mind ever admitted. She had a feeling the mystery was nearing some kind of resolution.

Carole Seddon looked at her watch. It was nearly four. In a couple of hours, Jude had suggested, they should meet in the Crown and Anchor and she'd bring Carole up to date. Meanwhile, any moment now, less than half a mile away, Jude would be confronting Nick Kent.

'He's coming,' Maggie Kent hissed.

She was looking out of the window in Spindrift Lane. Jude rose from the sofa to join her. Three boys in dark trousers and navy anoraks, school bags hanging single-strapped from their shoulders, were running down the middle of the road, tossing a plastic American football between them. They were red-faced from the cold and the exertion.

'I always tell him he mustn't play in the street.' But Maggie spoke indulgently; she didn't sound too angry about it. 'Not that there's that much traffic down here.'

One of the boys stopped by the sagging gate of number 26. He was holding the ball, which he tossed with some unheard but raucous comment to one of his mates. He received a cheerful gibe back and grimaced some response. Jude recognized the face from the photograph on the mantelpiece, though it was at least two years out of date. Nick Kent's features had thickened since and his hair darkened a few shades, but he still looked a child.

As he parted from his friends and turned in at the

gate, his persona changed. Quick as the flick of a switch, the jokey face-pulling gave way to an expression of deep anxiety.

There was the sound of the front door opening and slamming shut, the thump of his school bag dropped on the hall floor and the thud of footsteps starting up the stairs.

'Hi, Nick. Could you come in here a minute?'

'Just going to the loo,' he called back to Maggie's summons. His voice was roughened by the local accent and the gruffness which his mother had mentioned.

The footsteps thundered on upstairs. A door opened and closed. After what seemed a long time, a lavatory flushed. The door opened and, with seeming reluctance, the footsteps dawdled back down again.

The boy stood in the doorway, registering shock at the unexpected visitor in the sitting room. 'What is this?' he asked on a note of panic.

'Nick, this is Jude.'

'Oh?'

'She wants to talk to you.'

'Well, I don't want to talk to her!'

He turned to bolt, but was stopped by Jude's even voice saying, 'I want to talk to you about this knife, Nick.'

He wheeled slowly round on his heel, unwillingly drawn to the Stanley knife that Jude held out towards him. When he saw it, his worst fears seemed to be confirmed. The colour left his face and tears welled in his eyes. He collapsed on to the sofa. 'Is she from the police?' he asked dully.

'No.' Maggie Kent looked as though she wanted to rush across and cradle her son in her arms, protect him from all the evil in the world. But she restrained herself.

'No,' Jude confirmed. 'I'm not from the police. I'm not trying to cause any trouble for you. In fact, I want to save you from trouble. I want to find out what happened on Monday night. I want to find out what it was that got you so upset on Monday night and Tuesday morning. I think you'll feel better if you talk about it.'

Maggie Kent listened with increasing surprise. There was a strange, almost hypnotic quality in her visitor's voice. It relaxed her own tensions a little, and seemed to be having the same effect on her son.

The boy on the sofa was silent, but his crumpled face betrayed complex emotions. He did want to talk, he wanted to end the pain he was going through, blot out the memories which were causing him such anguish. But at the same time he was afraid of the consequences that confession might unleash.

'Where did you get that knife?' he asked finally, his voice clotted with confusion.

'I found it in the bottom of a boat at Fethering Yacht Club. A boat called *Brigadoon II*.'

There was a long silence. Nick looked drained, his will sapped.

'I think you'd better tell me about it,' said Jude.

'I can't . . .'

'Or perhaps I should take this knife to the police . . .'

Threatening wasn't her usual style but at that

moment seemed justified. Its instantaneous effect proved her right. Nick Kent broke down, shedding about five years along with the tears that coursed down his cheeks. Jude could feel the urge within Maggie to go and hug her son, but restrained her by a little shake of the head. With difficulty, the mother stayed where she was.

'So, will you tell me?' Jude gently maintained the pressure.

'I can't . . .' The emotion had eroded the roughness of his voice. His accent now matched his mother's. 'I can't . . . not with Mummy here.'

Jude looked into Maggie's eyes and could see the hurt there. It was only a small rejection, but Nick was definitely rejecting her.

Maggie Kent, however, was a brave woman, and she accepted the priorities of the situation. 'Right. I'll go and put the kettle on.' She crossed to the door. 'Give me a call when I can come in again.' She managed to exclude sarcasm, but she couldn't keep the pain out of her voice.

The door shut behind her. 'So, Nick . . .'

'How much do you know?' The tears had stopped. He seemed to have accepted the inevitability of talking.

'I know what you told your mother . . . and a bit more that we worked out for ourselves.'

'Who's "we"?'

'I've been investigating this with a friend of mine called Carole Seddon.'

The name meant nothing to him, but it brought a new anxiety. 'She's not with the police either?'

'No. If anything, she's extremely anti the police.' Another silence. 'Come on, Nick. I know you were with Dylan and Aaron. I know you had some beers. I think you probably had some drugs too . . .'

'It was only cannabis,' he retorted, his use of the botanical name rather than any slang term making him sound younger than ever. 'Dylan had it with him.'

'I thought he might have done.'

'And he, Dylan, was getting at Aaron and me. Saying we were just kids, that we were mother's boys, that we were chicken . . .'

'Chicken of doing what?'

'Smoking the . . . the cannabis . . . the weed.'

'But you did that. So what else did he say you were scared of doing?'

'Breaking the law. He said we were goody-goodies.'

'He said that, for instance, you wouldn't dare break into the Yacht Club?'

There was a hesitation before Nick Kent admitted that this was indeed what Dylan had said.

'And you proved him wrong, and you broke in – or just climbed over the railings, that wasn't too difficult – and you chose a boat at random, which happened to be *Brigadoon II*, and Dylan got out his knife and cut through the rope holding down the cover—'

'How do you know all this?' Panic flared again in the boy's eyes. 'You didn't see us, did you?'

'No, I didn't see you. But you told most of that stuff to your mother.'

Nick nodded, partially reassured.

'Of course, what you didn't tell your mother was what you found in the boat.'

'No.' For a moment he looked defiant. 'And there's no reason why I should tell you either!'

'No reason, I agree. Though of course I could still take the Stanley knife to the police.'

This time the threat wasn't so potent. 'So, you take it to the police! That doesn't prove anything.'

'No,' Jude agreed softly. 'Not until they find the body.'

This really did shock him. 'How did you know about the body?' he murmured in horrified fascination.

Jude heaved a mental sigh of relief. He'd fallen for it. He'd conceded that there had been a body in the boat. She went on, 'A man's body I think it was you found in *Brigadoon II*. The body of a man in his fifties. But it's what you did with the body that interests me.'

'We were horrified when we found it. There was just moonlight – the moon was full that night – and – ' he shuddered – 'we could only see this outline. But we knew he was dead. And then Dylan . . .'

'Was Dylan as surprised to see the body as you and Aaron were? Or did he know it was going to be there?'

Nick Kent gave a decided shake of his head. 'He was shocked, just like us. Pretended not to be, pretended he was Mr Cool, but it got to him all right. And then . . .'

The boy was having second thoughts about continuing, so Jude repeated coaxingly, 'And then?'

He made up his mind to go on. 'And then Dylan had this mad idea. He's into all this occult stuff, you know, black magic, the Undead, all that kind of thing . . . and he said that if Aaron and I wanted to show we were really hard . . .'

'Yes?'

Nick flinched, as though he were trying to flick something off his face. 'No, no, I can't tell you.'

'Was it something to do with the knife?' asked Jude.

The boy slumped back, resistance gone. The woman seemed to know everything anyway. He might as well tell her. 'Yes,' he agreed flatly. 'He said if Aaron and me were really hard . . . he said cutting a dead man's flesh under a full moon, it'd make us strong . . . and then if we wrote our names in our own blood and left them on the body . . . we'd have special powers . . . if we did it . . .'

'And you believed him?'

'We'd had a lot to drink. And the weed . . . the cannabis, you know. We weren't thinking straight. And Dylan kept saying we were cowards and mother's boys and . . . and then he took the knife and made a cut in the man's neck. And then Aaron took the knife and he made a cut . . .'

'And did you, Nick?'

The boy looked away in embarrassment. 'No. I couldn't. I . . . Dylan said I was chicken, and I wouldn't get the power that he and Aaron were going to get, but I . . . I just couldn't . . .'

The boy shuddered, too overcome by the recollection to speak.

'And what about writing the names in blood?'

'Aaron did that. He wrote his name. He wanted to have special powers. There's a girl at school he fancies – he fancied. He wanted to have power over her.'

'So he wrote his name and put it in the dead man's pocket?'

'Yes.'

'What about Dylan? Did he write his name?'

'No, he said he didn't need to. Because he was the leader and the power would come to him automatically.'

Anger seethed within Jude, anger against Dylan. The older boy had egged on the others, probably making up his black magic mumbo-jumbo as he went along. But he wasn't going to incriminate himself by leaving his name around the scene of the crime. He'd allow the gullible Aaron Spalding to do so, though – and no doubt build up the boy's natural paranoia with garish tales of the Undead. Dylan, Jude felt sure, was directly responsible for Aaron's suicide. But she felt equally sure the older boy would never be called to account for it.

Her only comfort was the fact that it was Dylan who'd been careless enough to drop his Stanley knife in the boat. Without that she and Carole would never have made the connection to him.

'And what about you, Nick? Did you write your name?'

'No. Dylan said if I was too chicken to cut the man's flesh, then I didn't deserve to have any special powers. And they both laughed at me. Said I was just a kid and . . .' The memory of his humiliation still festered.

'And then what happened, Nick?'

'We . . . I don't know. We suddenly panicked when we realized what we'd done.'

'But you personally hadn't done anything.'

'I'd broken into the club. I'd handled the dead body. We were all in a terrible state. I think the booze and the weed made it worse. Even Dylan lost his bottle. We didn't want to leave any signs, any evidence, so we took the body out of the boat and we . . . and we . . .'

'And you threw it over the sea wall into the Fether.'

'How do you know all this?' He was sobbing again. 'You said you didn't see us.'

'I didn't. And then you all went your separate ways home that night – yes?'

'Yes.'

'But Aaron rang you the next morning. What did he say?'

'He said he'd woken up early and he'd panicked about us having left some clue to what we'd done down at the Yacht Club . . . and he'd gone down to the beach . . .'

'And found the body washed up by the tide.'

'Yes.'

Finally, there was corroboration for what Carole had seen on the Tuesday morning.

'He was in a terrible state. He said the evil was coming back to haunt him, that the body was one of the Undead, and it was coming after him. So I went down to the beach and met Aaron,' Nick went on, 'and it was still nearly dark and we thought if we put the body back in the boat, then nobody'd ever know that we'd been there . . .'

'And that's what you did?'

'Yes.'

Huge sobs were shuddering through the boy's frame. Jude reckoned she had got everything she was going to get out of him. 'One final question . . . Your mother said it was after you'd come back in the morning that you were in the really bad state, not the night before . . .'

'She didn't see me the night before, did she? Anyway, I was still full of the booze and the cannabis . . . I just passed out. But the next morning . . . the shock hit me. I knew it wasn't a dream. I knew we'd actually done it. I knew what I'd done.'

Something prompted a renewed outburst of emotion, more powerful than any that had come before. The boy's jaw trembled and his whole body shook uncontrollably.

'What is it?' pleaded Jude. 'What is it? What was so terrible?'

For a few moments he was incapable of framing any words, just mouthing hopelessly. Finally he managed to control himself. Nick Kent sounded like a very young child as he admitted, 'I'd never seen a dead body before.'

Chapter Twenty-four

'Well, behaviour of that kind,' concluded Carole, sitting back on her barstool in disgust, 'is all too typical of the youth of today.'

'That's a very Fethering thing to say,' said Jude.

'What do you mean?'

'It's the kind of remark I'd have expected from some old codger whose skin's already turned to tweed. Not from someone your age.'

'I'm not young,' Carole protested. But she was flattered by the implication.

'You're too young to start sounding off about "the youth of today".'

'But what Nick Kent and the others did was appalling.' She lowered her voice as she catalogued: 'Illegal drinking, taking drugs, breaking and entering – probably with intent to burgle – and then mutilating a corpse.'

'He wasn't involved in that.'

'No, but he was in everything else. Really, Jude, am I supposed to condone that kind of behaviour?'

'No, of course you're not. But you didn't see the boy. You didn't see how much he was suffering.'

'From what you've told me, he deserves to suffer. You're not making excuses for him, are you?'

'No, no. I'm just saying that Nick Kent has had a rough deal. And, OK, he drank and smoked dope, and OK, he gave in to peer pressure and behaved disgustingly, but at least you can understand why. Seeing his father fall apart before his eyes can't have been easy.'

'Huh,' Carole snorted. 'I'm sorry. If you're trying to win me round to some woolly liberal idea that there's a psychological explanation for everything, and criminals should take their shrinks to court with them to ensure that they get off with light sentences . . . well, you're not going to convince me. If there's one thing I learned from all my years in the Home Office, it's that there is such a thing as evil within man. And that every criminal who is not technically insane has to take responsibility for his or her own actions.'

Jude took a long swallow from her wine glass before replying. This was the nearest during their brief acquaintance that she and Carole had come to a row. It demonstrated how little they knew of each other's attitudes and politics. 'I'm not excusing the boy's behaviour,' she said calmly. 'I'm just saying, from the pain in his eyes, he'd hurt himself by what he'd done much more than he'd hurt anyone else. Now let me get you another drink.'

She waved at the unfamiliar girl behind the counter, who came to sort out their needs. There were only the three of them in the bar. 'Two large white wines, please. Ted not in tonight?'

'He's in the office out the back, talking to some people who came round.'

'Ah.'

'Well, I say "people",' the girl insinuated. 'In fact it's the police.'

'Really? What've they come for?'

'I've no idea. I'm not one to pry,' the girl replied righteously, as though it were Jude who'd initiated the speculation.

'Some problem with the licence?' suggested Carole, though that wasn't what she was thinking.

The pub door clattered behind them and they turned to see an agitated Denis Woodville approaching the bar.

'Evening, Vice-Commodore.'

'Oh, hello, ladies. Is Ted in?' he asked the barmaid.

'He's out the back, talking to some people.'

'The police, actually,' said Jude, upstaging any second attempt from the barmaid to cast aspersions on her boss.

'Is that so?' The news seemed to be of significance to Denis Woodville.

'Can I get you a drink, sir?'

'Oh yes, all right. A large brandy, please.'

'Soda or anything with that?'

'Just on its own, thanks.'

'No more break-ins at the club?' asked Carole.

'What?' He seemed distracted. 'No, no, I don't think so. Though in fact it does seem that we have been the victim of criminal activity.'

He might have elaborated on this portentously delivered hint had not Ted Crisp at that moment appeared through the door behind the bar. He looked as scruffy as ever, but unflustered. If the police presence had had anything to do with his own illegal activities, he wasn't going to let it get to him.

'Evening, Jude . . . Carole . . . Denis . . .' His eyes moved along from face to face. 'What're you all looking at me like that for?'

Denis Woodville voiced what the two women would have been too polite to raise. 'I gather you've had the police with you . . .'

'Yes. But don't get the wrong impression. I haven't done anything they could touch me for. My record is as driven snow-like as any of Cliff Richard's.'

'I wonder if they came to see you for the same reason they came to see me.'

The landlord cocked an interrogative eye at the Vice-Commodore. 'Missing person, was it?'

'Yes.'

The barmaid hovered, all ears. 'Oh, love,' said Ted, 'could you go and get us some tomato and orange juices from round the back? I noticed we was getting low.'

With very bad grace, the girl slunk out of the bar. She needn't have worried, though. It was only a temporary delay. She'd hear all the dirt soon enough. The Fethering grapevine was extremely efficient.

'Look, if you both know, you might as well tell us,' said Jude impatiently. 'Come on, what's it all about?'

Ted Crisp saw no point in secrecy. 'The police came in asking if I'd seen Rory Turnbull recently. Same with you, Denis?'

'Yes.'

'But we only saw him this morning,' Carole protested. 'Up at his house.'

'Well, maybe you'd better tell the police that,' said Ted. 'Though in fact they do know he was still at home at twelve, because he paid the cleaning lady when she left.'

So the police must already have been out to Spindrift Lane to talk to Maggie. Jude wondered what effect their arrival must have had on the terrified Nick Kent.

'Sometime after twelve, however,' the landlord went on, 'our Rory buggered off in the BMW. His wife got home round two and immediately raised the alarm.'

'What? Was she afraid he'd run off with another woman?' suggested Jude.

Denis Woodville's bald head was firmly shaken. 'Can't think so. There's never been any talk of that kind of thing with Rory.'

'It's always the quiet ones. These things happen.'

'Not in Fethering they don't,' said Carole tartly, before continuing, 'But why did Barbara raise the alarm? Surely there's no harm in a grown man going off for a drive in his own car when he feels like it?'

'Not usually, I agree, there isn't,' said Ted. 'But there is when he leaves a suicide note.'

Chapter Twenty-five

A silence followed Ted Crisp's words. Then Jude said thoughtfully, 'He certainly had the air of a man who was tired of life.'

'Well, comes of being a dentist – living from hand to mouth all the time.'

'You've already used that line, Ted.' Carole may not have been much good at spotting the humour of jokes, but she could certainly recognize one she'd heard before.

'Sorry. One of the hazards of a publican's life. You've only got so many jokes, and you keep forgetting who was in the bar when you last told them.'

'Mind you,' Jude went on, as though this exchange hadn't happened, 'there's a difference between being tired of life and actually ending it. What kind of major event is needed to push someone over the brink like that?'

'It needn't be a major event,' said Carole. 'When I worked for the Home Office, I was involved in a survey on suicides in prison. If a victim gets really depressed, often the tiniest reverse or setback will make them do it. They're not rational at that point.'

'No, but I'm sure something must've changed in

Rory Turnbull's life. I mean, he hated being a dentist. Apparently, he hated his wife too. And I'm certain he hated his mother-in-law. But he'd put up with all of that for years. Why is it suddenly now that he can't take any more?'

'I could tell you one reason . . .' Denis Woodville spoke with the sly confidence of someone who had secret information to impart. He allowed himself a pause, sure of his audience's attention, then went on, 'Did I mention, ladies, when you came to see me at the club, that we'd had a bit of a problem with last year's accounts?'

Carole nodded. 'Yes, you said the accountant had made a mistake.'

'So I thought. The discrepancy involved was a little over a thousand pounds. Well, I had a meeting with the accountant yesterday and he took me through everything. It wasn't their error. I'm afraid I had to eat rather a lot of humble pie for having even suspected them. No, it turned out that someone had actually been siphoning funds out of the club's bank account.'

'Really?'

'The only registered signatories for Fethering Yacht Club cheques are the Commodore, the Vice-Commodore and the Treasurer. Well, the Commodore has been abroad for the last four months, during which time most of the cheques were drawn. I can assure you I haven't been putting my hand in the till – might have helped me out a bit if I had, but I haven't. So that leaves the Treasurer.'

He paused for dramatic effect, and was visibly

miffed when Carole came in impatiently and upstaged him. 'Who is, of course, Rory Turnbull.'

'Yes,' a tight-lipped Denis Woodville conceded. 'So that might give him one reason for doing away with himself. He knew I was meeting the accountants yesterday. I imagine he just didn't want to face the music.'

'So he got into his BMW,' Ted Crisp speculated, 'drove up into the Downs, fixed a tube from the exhaust into the car's interior—'

'We don't know that's what happened, do we?' asked Jude. 'The police didn't say they'd found him, did they?'

'No,' the landlord agreed. 'But from what they were saying, it's pretty clear that's what they were expecting to find.'

'But *why* would he have done it?' demanded Carole. 'Put his hand in the Yacht Club till? For a thousand pounds? I mean, a thousand pounds would be very nice – none of us would say no to it . . .'

'Certainly not.' Denis Woodville's agreement was heartfelt.

' . . . but for someone in Rory Turnbull's position – dentist's salary, big house on the Shorelands Estate – a thousand pounds isn't much. Certainly not enough for him to risk public humiliation and possible criminal proceedings. *Why* would he have done it?'

'You'd be amazed.' Ted Crisp shook his shaggy head at the recurrent follies of humankind. 'Happens all the time – particularly in a place like Fethering. Somebody gets a position of power locally – only in the Cricket Club or the Yacht Club or something tinpot like that – ' he went on, apparently unaware of the

Vice-Commodore's bristling – 'and they have access to another chequebook, and they suddenly think, "Ooh, I can get something out of this." And they milk the funds. Just for the odd hundred they'll do it. I don't know why, but it certainly keeps happening.'

'I suppose everyone needs money,' Carole concluded. 'People may look like they've got plenty, but we can't see inside their bank accounts, can we? We can't know what demands there are on their resources, what foolish investments they may have made, what reckless loans they've taken on. It's one of the last taboos in this country, people actually talking about their financial affairs.'

'You're right.' Ted Crisp looked at their glasses. 'Come on, let's have another drink. This round's on me.'

'That's no way to make a profit,' Carole observed.

The landlord turned on her in mock anger. 'Are you saying no? Are you saying you don't want to take a drink from me?'

She smiled graciously. 'No, I'm not. Thank you very much indeed, Ted.'

As she pushed her wine glass forward, she felt another little frisson from the knowledge that she, Carole Seddon, was in the Crown and Anchor, exchanging banter with the landlord and calling him by his first name. She'd come a long way in a week.

'Of course, people develop expensive habits too,' Ted ruminated, as he poured the drinks. 'Rory Turnbull was getting through the Scotch in here like there was no tomorrow.'

'But on his income presumably he could afford an alcohol habit.'

'He could afford an *alcohol* habit, yes, Carole.'

She was quickly on to the slight pressure he'd put on the word. 'What do you mean? Are you saying he had another expensive habit? Are you saying Rory Turnbull was into drugs?'

But either Carole had mistaken his intonation or the landlord had decided he didn't wish to amplify the hint. He just said, 'Hardly. Don't somehow see him in the role of crazed junkie, do you?' He punctuated the end of such speculation by plonking the two replenished wine glasses on the counter. 'There you are – compliments of the management. Treasure this moment. Record it on the mental video cameras of your minds. Because I can assure you, it doesn't happen very often!'

When the round of thank-yous had subsided, Jude looked thoughtful. 'It's odd, though, isn't it? Two suicides in a week . . .'

'Two?' asked the Vice-Commodore.

'That boy Aaron Spalding.'

'Was that suicide?'

Jude caught Carole's eye and read caution in it. What they had been investigating was private, between the two of them, at least for the time being.

'Well, that's certainly been suggested,' said Jude, making her tone more generalized. 'I don't know whether there's been an inquest yet. OK, not two suicides – two unnatural deaths. All I'm saying is that for someone like me, who's lived here less than a week, that seems rather a high number. Or is it the usual pattern in Fethering?'

'By no means,' Denis Woodville replied. 'There's probably a higher death rate here than in most other parts of the country, but that's simply because of the average age of the residents. Two unnatural deaths like this is most unusual.'

Jude's brown eyes signalled to Carole not to worry, she was only floating an idea to see if it got any response, before she asked ingenuously, 'Makes one wonder whether there could be any connection between the two.'

The suggestion produced a snort of laughter from the Vice-Commodore. 'A connection between a highly respected middle-aged man living on the Shorelands Estate and some teenager from Downside? I would think not.'

'No,' said Jude.

'Hardly,' said Carole.

But they were both increasingly convinced that there was a connection.

There was the clatter of the bar door opening and a voice said, 'Evening, mine host.'

Bill Chilcott had arrived for his nightly half.

Denis Woodville stiffened and downed the remainder of the brandy Ted Crisp had bought him. 'Sorry, I must be off,' he said. 'Suddenly a rather nasty smell around this place.'

And, as if his next-door neighbour didn't exist, the Vice-Commodore stalked out of the Crown and Anchor.

Chapter Twenty-six

'It was in Rory Turnbull's boat,' said Carole, as they reached the gate of Woodside Cottage. The evening was mild. The frost would probably hold off that night. 'The body was put in *Brigadoon II*. That's the only thing we've got linking Aaron Spalding's death and Rory Turnbull's suicide.'

'It's not much,' said Jude.

Carole sighed despondently. 'Maybe there is no connection. Maybe it's just an unfortunate coincidence.'

Jude shook her head. 'No, there's a link between them. They are connected.'

So strong was the conviction in her voice that Carole didn't argue. Instead, characteristically, she moved on to practicalities. 'Well, I think we need to know more about Rory Turnbull. What he was like, what was happening in his life, what pushed him over the edge.'

'And whether he did have anything to do with drugs.'

'You noticed that too? When Ted hinted at something and then clammed up?'

'Oh yes. I'll follow up on the drugs thing tomorrow.'

'How?'

'Let's say I have an idea of where to start.'

'And I,' Carole announced confidently, 'will make it my business tomorrow to find out more about Rory Turnbull.'

'How'll you do that?'

'Let's say I have an idea of where to start,' came the lofty reply.

Carole Seddon could also play mysterious when she needed to.

Carole wasn't a dog person. When she left the Home Office, she'd taken on Gulliver for purely practical reasons. He would give a purpose to the many walks with which she had planned to fill the longeurs of her retirement. Being accompanied by a dog, she would avoid unwelcome questions and speculation. And anyway, people with dogs never look lonely.

It was the same kind of sensible thinking that had made her join the Canine Trust. She didn't feel particularly strongly about the civil liberties of dogs, but she recognized that volunteering for the charity might provide occasional useful work to fill a little more of her time.

The demands were not onerous. She helped out with the Canine Trust local branch's summer fête; twice a year she contributed to their bring-and-buy coffee mornings and she distributed raffle tickets.

Carole discharged these duties punctiliously, as she did everything, but she found her involvement in the charity increasingly dull. In fact, when the latest batch of raffle tickets arrived in the post a few weeks before, she had contemplated ceasing to be a volunteer.

But on the Saturday morning, clutching them in her hand as she walked down the High Street towards the Fethering Yacht Club, Carole positively blessed the raffle tickets. Nothing could have given her a better excuse to call on Winnie Norton.

And the reason why in the past she had tried to avoid calling on Winnie Norton with raffle tickets – because the old lady insisted on inviting her in and subjecting her to a minimum half-hour dose of the Winnie Norton view of the world – was on this occasion a positive advantage.

Spray Lodge was the nearest residential building to the river. Some eight storeys high, its most valued flats looked out, over the Yacht Club and the sea wall which separated the Fether from the beach, all the way to the distant horizon where the water melted into the sky. Normally, Spray Lodge was one of the most desirable of Fethering locations. But when the sea wall was being repaired, the block was uncomfortably close to the monotonous thud of the pile driver. Carole heard the noise increasing as she neared her destination.

Carole no longer took Gulliver on her raffle-ticket-selling excursions. The first time she'd thought he might be useful to establish her credentials as an authentic dog lover, but she had not repeated the experiment. The Fethering residents whom Canine Trust directives instructed her to target were, by definition, other dog owners, and Gulliver's noisy enthusiasm – not to mention combativeness – on greeting their pets had made for slow and uncomfortable progress. Since the first time, therefore, he had remained at home when his mistress went out with her raffle tickets.

Winnie Norton was a dog owner, and presumably therefore a dog lover – assuming she was capable of loving anything other than her daughter. She was the owner of Churchill, whom Jude had encountered at Brigadoon. Carole didn't really count Yorkshire terriers as dogs. They were too small, too silky, too yappy, a kind of bonsai mutant of what, to her mind, a dog should be.

When she buzzed through on the entryphone, she heard Churchill before she heard his owner. He was yapping, as ever. Then Winnie Norton's carefully enunciated tones inquired, 'Yes, who is it?'

'It's Carole Seddon. I've got the Canine Trust raffle tickets.'

'Oh, splendid. Do come up.' And the entryphone box buzzed admission.

Winnie Norton's second-floor flat was relatively small, but every item in it was exquisite. Carole knew that if she referred to any piece of furniture or ornament, her hostess would say, 'Oh yes, well, when I sold the big house after my husband died, I had to get rid of a lot of beautiful stuff. Phillips auctioned it, and I've kept only the best, the very best.' Then she would chuckle and continue, 'There are museums all over the world who'd give their eyeteeth for what's in this room.'

And Carole knew if she referred to the sea view,

Winnie Norton would say, 'Oh yes, well, you see it best from here on the second floor. The people in the flats below just look out over the Yacht Club, and those above get a much less good angle on the horizon. When I sold the big house after my husband died, I insisted that I had to have the best flat in the block with the best view.' And then she'd chuckle and continue, 'I may be slumming, but at least I'll slum in style.'

That Saturday morning Carole was determined to avoid commenting on either the furniture or the sea view.

When she opened the front door of the flat to let Carole in, Winnie Norton was revealed in a cherry-coloured woollen suit with gold braiding and buttons. Her hair, still bearing a bluish tinge, was fixed like stiff meringue on top of her head. With her spare hand, she held Churchill up to her chest. He was once again yapping furiously.

'There, you lovely boy,' Winnie cooed. 'Look who's come to see you – it's Carole. Look how pleased to see you he is, Carole.'

The dog's little eyes glinted a look of pure malevolence at the visitor. Don't worry, you revolting little mutt, thought Carole, it's mutual.

'Now, you do have time to stop for a coffee, don't you, dear?'

It was said defensively, almost challengingly. The last few times Carole had called, she'd managed to wriggle out of staying. This time, however, she gave the right answer.

'Oh, excellent. Now do sit down on the sofa, dear.

The kettle's just boiled. Barbara's bought me one of those new-fangled cafetières, so I'm getting quite "with it". But I must confess, it does make delicious coffee. Oh, and I'll just say the one apology now for that dreadful thumping from the sea wall.'

'Don't apologize. You can hear it all over Fethering.'

'Yes, but it's much worse from here. I tell you, I've had a splitting headache for days. It keeps going through the night, you know.'

'That's because of the tides.'

'Huh. I suppose it has to be done. And, in theory, it's all going to be finished by Monday. Mind you,' said Winnie Norton darkly, 'I'll believe that when it happens. Now, I won't be a moment getting the coffee. You stay and talk to Carole, there's a good boy.'

Winnie Norton poured Churchill down on to the carpet and went through to the kitchen. The dog leapt forward towards Carole, then stopped about a yard away from the sofa, his body tensed backwards. He growled.

'Get lost, you little rat!' Carole hissed.

The dog understood the sentiment, if not the words. He started up his high-pitched yapping again.

'Oh, shut up!'

Again she kept her voice down, but this time the injunction had an effect. With a final look of undiluted hatred, Churchill slunk off behind the sofa.

Carole looked out at the sea. Even though she was determined not to say so in Winnie's presence, the view was undeniably magnificent. She rose and went closer to the picture window. No, from here Winnie couldn't see the end of the breakwater where the dead man had lain. Because of the Yacht Club building, her view of the low-tide beach started further down.

'Wonderful view, isn't it?' Carole heard from behind her.

'Mm,' she agreed, as she turned to help Winnie with the coffee tray.

'Oh yes, well, you see it best from here on the second floor. The people in the flats below just look out over the Yacht Club, and those above . . .'

Damn, out came the whole routine. Winnie Norton didn't need prompting from anyone else. She was self-priming.

While the familiar words were rehearsed yet again, Carole reflected that her hostess wasn't acting like someone whose son-in-law had just committed suicide. Maybe she didn't yet know the news. Maybe Barbara Turnbull had kept it from her mother out of kindness until the facts had been confirmed.

Carole was determined to find out. She waited dutifully for the chuckle and the, 'I may be slumming, but at least I'll slum in style', before saying, 'I heard a dreadful rumour about Rory in Allinstore this morning.' (She certainly wasn't going to tell Winnie Norton that she'd heard it in the Crown and Anchor. Everyone in Fethering knew that Carole Seddon wasn't a 'pub person'.) 'I do hope it's not true.'

The light that blazed in Winnie Norton's eye revealed that she knew all the details. And also revealed that she was at least as proficient as her dog at looks of pure malevolence. 'It's true, all right. And absolutely typical of the man! Selfish to the end!'

If Rory Turnbull's suicide had been an attempt to

make people feel guilty and realize how much they'd undervalued him during his lifetime, the gesture had clearly failed with his mother-in-law.

'But it's definite, is it? I mean, they've found the body?'

'No, not yet. The police're still looking. Typical of Rory again – wasting police time like that. That man's never thought of anyone but himself from the moment he was born. I always told Barbara he was a dubious factor. Not our class of person at all. I could see that from the day I first met him.

'Barbara is, needless to say, distraught,' Winnie went on. 'What a terrible thing to happen to her. And, if it's confirmed as a suicide, that could well invalidate all the life insurance policies. Selfish, selfish, selfish. What's more, everyone in Fethering will assume that there was something wrong with their marriage.'

'And wasn't there?' asked Carole.

'There were faults on his side certainly. The only thing Barbara did wrong in that marriage was choosing an unsuitable man in the first place. But she knows it's a wife's duty to stay by her man. She's discussed her situation with Canon Granger – you know, Roddy – and he has nothing but admiration for the way Barbara has coped. She's behaved like a saint throughout . . . in spite of all the dreadful things Rory did.'

'What kind of things?' Carole decided it was going to be quite easy to get the information she was after. Such was the level of spleen Winnie Norton harboured for her son-in-law, the old woman didn't stop to consider why she was being asked all these questions.

'Well, he was always boorish. Had no manners. Someone brought up in the gutter never quite loses the tang of it, you know. Rory was a product of state education, as you could probably tell. Jumped-up little oik from a secondary modern who managed to scrape into a university and somehow get his dental qualifications. As I said, always a dubious factor. Barbara did all she could to make something of him, but . . . well, you know the proverb about silk purses and sow's ears . . .'

'But what kind of things specifically did Rory do?' Carole persisted. 'Was he unfaithful to Barbara?'

'Good heavens, no. Even he wouldn't have dared do that. No, it was more mental cruelty, I suppose you'd call it. He collected pornography, you know.'

'Did he?'

'Oh yes. Poor darling Barbara found boxes of the stuff when she was looking through their loft. And that was only the part of it.' Winnie Norton shook her head in shocked disapproval. 'Rory was up to all kinds of other things as well . . .'

'Like?'

'Like staying out late. Like getting into fights.'

'Getting into fights?'

'He came back in the small hours only a couple of months ago and he'd had a tooth knocked out, would you believe? Well, imagine how difficult it was for Barbara to maintain appearances when her husband was walking around looking like a prize-fighter. And then there was the drinking . . .'

'Had he always drunk? Right through their marriage?'

'He'd always had it in him,' Winnie Norton replied portentously. 'But it was only the last few months it'd got out of hand. And it wasn't just drink . . .'

'What do you mean?'

'Drugs.'

'Really?'

'Oh yes.' The old lady nodded vigorously. While she did so, her sculpted hair made no independent movement. 'Barbara had suspected something of the kind was going on, and I found some stuff in Rory's study.'

In other circumstances Carole might have asked what Winnie Norton was doing snooping round her son-in-law's study, but she didn't want to stop the flow.

Winnie seemed to anticipate the thought anyway. 'Maybe I shouldn't have been looking into his affairs, but I couldn't go on seeing my daughter suffer like that. So I took things into my own hands, and I found . . . this stuff.'

'What kind of stuff? Are you an expert on drugs?'

'Of course I'm not!' Winnie Norton snapped. 'But I watch television. There's hardly a drama on these days that doesn't show people taking drugs. So I recognized it when I saw it. In Rory's desk drawer I found a syringe, and some metal foil, and a little packet of white powder. I think he was spending all their money on drugs.'

There were a lot of follow-up questions she could have asked, but Carole decided to bide her time until she'd talked to Jude. She'd already been given more than she had dared hope for.

'Well, I'm distressed to hear all that, Winnie,' she

said blandly. 'Do give my condolences to Barbara, won't you?'

If she'd thought this traditional formality would be met by an equally formal response, she was disappointed.

'Condolences!' Winnie Norton spat out the word. 'Barbara doesn't need condolences. She needs congratulations. Twenty-eight years of misery and now finally she's shot of him.'

'Yes,' said Carole. 'Of course. Now, about these raffle tickets . . .'

'The Canine Trust, yes, yes, yes.' Winnie rose with surprising agility from her chair. 'Just get my chequebook.' She crossed to a writing desk decorated with intricate marquetry designs. 'This is a charming piece, isn't it? You see, when I sold the big house after my husband died, I had to get rid of a lot of beautiful stuff. Phillips auctioned it, and I've kept only the best, the very best.' She chuckled, then continued, 'There are museums all over the world who'd give their eyeteeth for what's in this room.'

Carole smiled graciously. Churchill emerged from behind the sofa and started yapping at her.

Chapter Twenty-seven

As she'd mentioned, Jude had done some acting in her time. She'd done a lot of things in her time. Hers had been a rich and varied life.

On the Saturday morning, while Carole went off to do her bit with Winnie Norton, Jude decided she'd have to call on her acting skills to further her own research. She rang through to J. T. Carpets. Even if no carpet-fitting went on at the weekend, the showroom was bound to be open. And there must be someone working in the office.

There was. Jude put on a voice of excruciating gentility (school of Barbara Turnbull) and went into her prepared spiel. 'Good morning. I'm trying to contact one of your carpet-fitters. Named Dylan.'

'I'm sorry. The fitters don't work at the weekend.'

'Well, could you give me his home address and phone number?' she demanded imperiously.

'I'm afraid it's not company policy to give out our employees' private details over the telephone.'

'Then in this case you must make an exception to company policy. My name is Mrs Grant-Edwards.' Jude was taking a risk that the girl in the office had never spoken directly to the real Mrs Grant-Edwards. And perhaps less of a risk in assuming that the real Mrs Grant-Edwards would talk the way she was talking. 'I live in a house called Bali-Hai on the Shorelands Estate, where your people have just been fitting a carpet.'

'Oh yes?'

'And one of the fitters was this young man called Dylan.'

'You haven't found anything missing, have you?'

The anxiety in her voice was a real giveaway. Clearly Dylan didn't have a reputation as the most trustworthy of employees. Jude wondered how many little pilferings had occurred in the houses where he had fitted carpets. And wondered how much longer he would keep his job.

'No, no, it's not that. It's rather the reverse. I've found something of his in the house.'

'What?'

Jude had thought long and hard what her cover story should be. She wasn't going to get anywhere with a complaint about Dylan. Inventing some domestic crisis was too risky; his employers were bound to know more about his family circumstances than she did. What was needed was something urgent, but unthreatening, something that would sound as though Mrs Grant-Edwards was actually doing him a good turn. Jude felt pleased with the solution she'd finally come up with.

'It's a wallet containing his credit cards. And since he hasn't come back to our house looking, I assume he doesn't know where he left it. Well, I know how tiresome it can be to lose one's credit cards. It happened to me last year and caused an awful kerfuffle. So I just wanted to ring him to put his mind at rest.'

The approach worked with the girl at J. T. Carpets. 'That's very kind of you, Mrs Grant-Edwards.'

'If we don't all help each other out in this life, what will become of us?'

'What indeed? Right, just a moment. I'll find Dylan's home number for you.'

The girl gave it. Jude had asked for his address too, but she couldn't justify pressing for that. Her cover story didn't require her knowing where he lived. So she just thanked the girl for her help and put the phone down.

The number had a Worthing code, which meant it was local, and the first two digits were the same as Jude's own, which meant it was very local. Dylan probably lived in Fethering. But whether with his family, a girlfriend or on his own she had no means of knowing.

The next call was going to need a change of persona and she had to get it right. Jude made herself a cup of peppermint tea while she focused on the role she was about to play. In spite of her floaty dress style, Jude was far from being a superannuated hippy, but she had met plenty of the breed. Indeed, during the time she'd lived on Majorca, people who didn't know her well might have reckoned her as one of their number. Most of her acquaintances from that period of her life had long since settled into the worlds of domesticity and employment, often as school-teachers or in the social services. They remained harmless idealists, benignly ineffectual, posing no threat to society at any level. True, they did break the law on a regular basis, but the one they broke Jude didn't think should be a law anyway.

She concentrated on getting the voice right. Laid-back, lazy, full of trailing vowels, that was it. And she'd use her mobile phone, so that the precise location she was calling from wouldn't be revealed if Dylan checked 1471.

She waited till half-past eleven, which she reckoned gave a lad-about-Fethering – assuming that's what Dylan was – time to wake up after the excesses of Friday night, and keyed in his number. She was in luck. He was at home.

'Hi.' He managed to invest the single syllable with insolence and menace.

'Is that Dylan?' Jude got exactly the right relaxed diffidence into her voice.

'Yeah. Who wants him?'

'I was given your name by someone. I want to get hold of some gear.'

'What kind of gear?'

'Pot.' She knew that's what most users of her generation would still call it. 'Cannabis.'

Dylan laughed harshly. 'So you're after some weed, eh? And what makes you think I might be able to help you?'

'I told you. A friend gave me your name.'

'I think you'd better tell me who the friend is. Otherwise I might suspect this is some kind of set-up.'

Jude took the risk. If Dylan didn't bite, then she knew she'd have lost him. She backed her hunch. 'Rory Turnbull.'

The silence lasted so long she thought she must've miscalculated. Then Dylan repeated, 'Rory Turnbull, eh? Our fine upstanding dentist?'

He didn't mention the fine upstanding dentist's recent disappearance. Which was good news, because it almost definitely meant he didn't know about it. When he did, he'd be on his guard, knowing the inevitability of police investigations into all aspects of Rory Turnbull's life.

'Yes. He said he was a customer of yours.'

'Not much of a customer. He bought very little from me. Just a bit of weed on a couple of occasions.'

'Oh?'

'I don't carry the stuff he was after.'

'He wanted hard drugs?'

'Yes. Smack. I gave him the name of a contact in Brighton and didn't hear from him again. So I guess that's where he took his business.'

'Who was that contact?'

Jude realized she had been over-eager even before Dylan responded. 'Hey, just a minute, just a minute. I thought you said it was weed – or was it "pot"? – you were after.'

'Yes,' she agreed contritely. 'Can you help me?'

'Maybe. It depends how much you're prepared to pay.'

He quoted her prices for the various grades of goods he had available. She agreed his terms without haggling, and he fixed to meet her in the seafront shelter nearest to the Fethering Yacht Club at seven o'clock that evening.

'How will I recognize you?' he asked.

'I'm very tall, nearly six foot. Thinnish, black hair. I'll be wearing a long brown leather coat and a brown fur hat.' Jude felt fairly safe with this anti-description of herself. And, for ethical reasons, her wardrobe contained nothing made of either leather or fur.

'OK. And a name? Or at least something you can identify yourself by, in case there's more than one tall bird in a leather coat down on the seafront tonight.'

'Caroline,' said Jude.

'OK, Caroline. See you later.'

And he put the phone down. As she switched off her mobile, a little tremor of distaste ran through Jude's body.

One thing she knew for certain, though. She would not be anywhere near a Fethering seafront shelter at seven o'clock that evening.

For a moment she contemplated ringing the police and suggesting they make a rendezvous with Dylan at a Fethering seafront shelter at seven o'clock that evening.

But no. Deep though her hatred for the boy was, shopping him to the authorities would have been a very unJude thing to do.

Chapter Twenty-eight

That afternoon, over a cup of tea at Carole's, the two women pooled the information they had gleaned. Both had a lot to tell. They had unearthed pretty convincing evidence that Rory Turnbull had been a heroin user. That expensive habit might well have led to his embezzling the funds of the Fethering Yacht Club.

And yet, when they had told each other all their findings, both Carole and Jude were left feeling flat. They had found reasons why Rory Turnbull might have wanted to take his own life, but they'd found nothing that linked him with the body Carole had found on Fethering beach. True, the dentist had had contact with Dylan the drug dealer, and Dylan had been the initiator of the black magic mutilation of the corpse in *Brigadoon II*, but that still did not provide a direct connection. They had no proof that Rory Turnbull knew the body was in his boat, and there seemed no obvious way of getting any.

As they shuffled through the possibilities, even Jude's customary good-natured calm gave way to despondency. All they were left with was that it had been a bad week for the Fethering body-count. Three deaths, and though Aaron Spalding's might well have been prompted by guilt for what he'd done to the unnamed corpse, Rory Turnbull's seemed to stand on its own.

'Of course, we don't actually know it's a death yet, do we?' reasoned Carole.

'No, not till they've found his body.'

'Yes, and who knows how long that'll take? He might have driven out to some disused barn, or into the woods, or driven the car into a pond or into the sea . . .' Carole sighed hopelessly.

'Right.' Jude screwed up her eyes and tapped with irritation at her furrowed brow. 'Is there something obvious we're missing? Some information we have that we haven't followed through?'

They both concentrated. There was a long silence, then Carole said, 'Theresa Spalding!'

'What about her?'

'I've suddenly realized there's something I should have asked her and didn't.'

'Hm?'

'I was concentrating too much on Aaron, and I forgot to ask her why she came here in the first place. How did she know I'd found the body? She said I "matched the description". She must've talked to someone who saw me. Who though?'

'Hey!' A smile slowly irradiated Jude's features. It was a great improvement. Gloom didn't suit her. 'Of course! Why on earth didn't we think of that at the time? Come on, let's go and ask her now!'

They went straight up to Downside in the Renault. The estate didn't look any more welcoming in the dark than it had in daylight and Carole was glad there were two of them in the car. In spite of the cold, a bunch of early teens loitered in Drake Crescent, sorting out plans for where they'd go for their Saturday night – or where they could go for their Saturday night without any money.

A car stopping in the road seemed to qualify as an excitement. The kids moved closer, watching the women get out and approach Theresa Spalding's front door. Two of them leaned against the Renault's doors, their exaggerated outlines menacing in puffa jackets. They watched in silence as Carole repeatedly pressed the bell. Only when she banged on the door did one of the kids shout out, 'She's not there. They've taken her away.'

'Who's taken her away? Where to?'

They all seemed keen to pitch in with information.

'An ambulance come.'

'They took her to where the crazy people go.'

'She'd totally lost it.'

'She's in the nuthouse.'

'In the looney bin.'

Carole and Jude exchanged rueful looks. They'd got the impression that Theresa Spalding's level of neurosis was pretty high at the best of times. She'd spoken of always being 'on some medication'. It was no surprise that her son's death should have destabilized the woman's precarious sanity.

They went back to the car. The two kids in puffa jackets stayed, insolently leaning against the doors till the last possible moment, then eased themselves upright and slouched away. As she started the engine, Carole heard some raucous remark at their expense, followed by a burst of derisive laughter. She shivered.

The Saturday evening and the Sunday compounded their frustration. Both of them kept contemplating calling round next door to discuss their investigation further. But both of them knew there was nothing else to say.

So Carole watched Saturday evening television, which only went to confirm her opinion that there never was anything on the television on Saturday evening. On the Sunday she took Gulliver out for longer walks than usual and virtuously tidied the cupboard under the stairs, packing into bin liners a lot of what she now designated rubbish. These activities, preparing a couple of plain meals and reading the Sunday papers served to fill the void of the day.

It was like any other Sunday. As if none of the excitements of the previous week had happened.

Next door, Jude unpacked a couple of boxes of books and stacked them upright in old wine-crates in her bedroom. She did her yoga. She cooked a rather adventurous prawn curry for her one meal of the day, taken round four o'clock. With it she drank half a bottle of wine. She drank the other half during the evening, much of which she spent reading in an aromatic bath, her toe reaching out every now and again to top up the hot water.

Though it was not in her nature to be as uptight as Carole, Jude too felt the tension of unfulfilment.

Nothing could happen until Rory Turnbull's suicide was confirmed to have taken place.

Chapter Twenty-nine

It was a different receptionist at the Brighton dental surgery the following morning, and Jude was directed to a different waiting room for her appointment with the hygienist. The plate on the closed door read 'Holly Draper', and from inside came sounds of girlish chatter.

Jude sat and read a woman's magazine of the kind she didn't know still existed. There was even a special offer for knitting patterns. She wondered how long it had been there.

Then the door opened and the previous appointment was ushered out by a woman who must be Holly Draper. A short unnatural blonde with large honey-coloured eyes, she wore a white overall and latex gloves. A disposable face-mask had been pulled down beneath her chin, perhaps to enable her to talk, though from the way she *was* talking it looked like it'd take a lot more than a face-mask to stop her.

'But that kind of thing seems to happen all the time these days, doesn't it? I mean, who can you trust? You read about all these MPs putting their hands in the till, and they're meant to be our elected representatives, aren't they? And then there are solicitors and . . .'

Jude instantly identified Holly Draper's conversational method. It involved firing out a fusillade of questions and giving her collocutor no time to answer any of them. Perhaps this derived from the fact that most of the people she spoke to in her professional life had their mouths so full of metalwork and saliva-siphons that they couldn't have replied even if they'd wanted to.

Whatever its cause, Holly Draper's monologue style was excellent news for Jude. Just get her on to the right subject.

And even that might not prove to be too difficult. As her previous appointment sidled along the wall in desperate hope of escape, the hygienist was saying, 'Well, you'd never have thought it to look at him, would you? Still, it's often the quiet ones, isn't it? Mind you, I can't imagine doing that to myself, can you? Well, I've never wanted to, as it happens. Just as well, isn't it? Have you ever—Oh, right, if you have to be off. Give those notes in at reception and make another appointment for three months' time – all right?'

She turned and flashed a hygienic smile at her next appointment. 'Well, hello. You must be—'

'Everyone calls me Jude.'

'Oh, right you are. I'm Holly. Jude as in "Judith", is that right? It's nice. Nicer that "Judy", isn't it? So many Judys around, aren't there? If you'd just like to come through into my little room . . . Lovely. And make yourself comfortable in the chair, will you?

And I'll just have a glance at your notes, if I may? Hm, ooh, Mr Frobisher says we've got a bit of inflammation round our gums, haven't we? Dear oh dear, aren't we a naughty girl? Right, well, I'd better have a look, hadn't I?'

Turning to pick up her examination mirror and toothpick brought a fractional pause, into which Jude managed to insert a line. 'Dreadful news about Rory Turnbull, wasn't it?'

'You heard about that, did you? Did you know him?'

Jude once again leapt into the minimal breech. 'I've just moved to Fethering and I did meet him briefly.'

'Ooh yes, well, as you can imagine, everyone here was gobsmacked when we heard the news – absolutely gobsmacked. Weren't you?'

'I didn't know him that well.'

'Didn't you? Still, after what's happened, we're all asking ourselves if any of us knew him that well, aren't we? It's a terrible thing for someone to do, isn't it?' Before Jude could offer an opinion on the ethics of suicide, silverware approached her mouth. 'Now if you could just open for me, could you? And can we pop this in? Could you just hold it, yes? We don't want our mouth filling up with saliva, do we?'

Further conversational prompts would be difficult. But Jude reckoned, having got Holly on to the right rails, the hygienist, in a state of permanently wound-up readiness, could be allowed to run.

'Ooh yes, a few places here where the gums are a bit red. Do you floss at all?' Jude let out a strangled response. Whether it was in the affirmative or negative didn't seem to affect Holly Draper's flow. 'Well, you should, because if your gums are healthy then there's a much better chance of your teeth being healthy, isn't there? Now I'm just going to go round and pick out a bit of the muck you've got between your teeth. OK? I'll try not to hurt, but round some of the inflamed bits, I may not be able to avoid it. All right with you?'

Praying that the hygienist's diversion into the professional hadn't derailed her train of thought, Jude gave a gurgled assent to being hurt.

She needn't have worried. While the point of her pick probed away, Holly Draper continued seamlessly, 'I mean, I'd never thought Rory was a particularly happy man, had you? And it was no secret that his marriage wasn't made in heaven, was it? But I'd never in a million years have thought he was the kind to do away with himself, would you? Mind you, you never know with people, do you?

'And, after what came out last week, well, it was perhaps a little less surprising, wasn't it? I mean, he must've known the Dental Estimates Board at Eastbourne would catch up with him in time. And when the Regional Dental Officer came to inspect on Thursday, it was clear something was seriously wrong and—' An uncharacteristic moment of caution stopped her. 'Maybe I shouldn't be talking about this . . . Could you just shift your chin down a bit please?'

Jude took the opportunity of this movement to manufacture a choking fit. As she spluttered, Holly swiftly removed the plastic tube from her mouth, pulled her upright and patted her back. 'Ooh, sorry about that. All right, are we? Take a rinse, why don't you? There, good. Spit it out, mm?'

Jude did as she was told and took advantage of another narrow window in Holly's monologue. She decided the best way to get further information would be to pretend more knowledge than she had. 'Yes, somebody in Fethering was talking about the Regional Dental Officer's inspection. I was really surprised to hear about that.'

It had been the right approach. The hygienist picked up her cue perfectly. 'Well, it was the scale of it that was so amazing, wasn't it? I mean, getting on for ten thousand pounds of dental work he'd claimed for, but never carried out. He was never going to get away with that in the long term, was he?'

'It doesn't seem as though he was thinking in the long term.'

The fact that Jude had managed to slip another line in made Holly Draper realize she shouldn't have left her patient's mouth empty for so long. 'Right, could you hold this in place again? There, good. And I'll just keep working round the ones at the back, shall I? Then, when I've finished this, we'll give them a nice clean, shall we?'

Jude was momentarily anxious that the hygienist wouldn't get back to the subject, but once again she needn't have worried. 'I mean, it makes you wonder what Rory could possibly have needed all that money for, doesn't it? There's been talk round here of drugs, but he didn't seem the type, did he? You don't associate that with middle-class dentists, do you? And you'd have thought he and his wife'd be very well set up, wouldn't you? Apparently, they've got this great big house over at Fethering – but you probably know that, don't you? And they don't have any kids, so where did all that money go? Maybe it was drugs. What do you think? Or perhaps he had another "secret vice", eh? Another woman? Ooh, I don't think so, do you?

'Mind you, we shouldn't really be surprised that he did away with himself. I've been told that dentists are one of the highest-risk professions for suicide. Did you know that?' She giggled. 'Not hygienists, though. We aren't daft, are we? Right, now we'll just give them all a nice clean-up, shall we?'

She turned to an articulated drill-like machine and fitted a small circular brush into its socket. This she dipped into a tub of paste. These actions did not for a moment interrupt her monologue.

'No, I don't think he was a bad man, though it was difficult to get close to him. Could you put your teeth together please? OK, take that out. Now this'll taste orangy and it may tickle a little bit. All right? No, as I say, Rory wasn't a bad man. He did some charity work, I believe. One of the girls on reception said he sometimes did free dentistry for down-and-outs out of hours, but he never talked about it. And he could be generous. There was this girl he quite often used to give a lift back to Fethering after work.'

'Who was that?' Fortunately Holly had just moved the electric brush away to get a different angle on Jude's mouth.

'Oh, I don't know. Girl about twenty, I suppose.

Short hair, sort of hennaed. I think she worked evenings in Fethering, which was why he sometimes gave her a lift. Well, she'll have to find someone else to do it for her now, won't she?

'There, all done, nice and clean, lovely. Look in the mirror. Doesn't that look better, eh? But now I'm going to be a real bully and give you a big lecture about flossing. All right? Can you cope? Are you feeling strong enough?'

Carole's frustration mounted through the Monday morning. What really annoyed her was knowing that the discovery of Rory's body might already have been made but she'd have to wait till the news filtered through to her. Though the Fethering grapevine, based on interconnecting substations like Allinstore, All Saints' Church and the Crown and Anchor, was extremely efficient, it wasn't the same as having a direct line to the police computers.

Still, within the guidelines of Fethering protocol, there was one approach she could make which might lead to further information. She looked up the number in the local directory and rang it.

'Hello?' The voice contrived to sound suspicious and malicious at the same time. In the background something yapped.

'Winnie, it's Carole Seddon.'

'Hello, dear.'

'I was just ringing to say thank you so much for the coffee on Saturday morning.'

'Oh, it was nothing. A pleasure to see you. Be quiet, Churchill, it's only your friend Carole.'

'And I just wondered . . . is there any sign of an end to poor Barbara's ordeal?'

'Poor Barbara's ordeal gets worse by the minute. Do you know what she's discovered now? That so-called husband of hers has virtually ruined her financially. Do you know, he'd remortgaged the house without telling her. And goodness only knows where all the money he raised has gone. There's nothing in any of the savings accounts. It's almost as if he was deliberately trying to make life difficult for Barbara. And then to commit suicide, so that she doesn't even get any of the insurance . . . Huh, I always said he was a dubious factor.'

'Oh, how awful, Winnie. But when you talk about suicide, I mean, that is definite now, is it? They've found his body?'

'Not yet, but it's only a matter of time. Typical of him to do away with himself somewhere inconvenient, though, isn't it? That man never gave a thought to another human being from the moment he was born. I mean, to have left Barbara destitute . . . Thank goodness my poor little baby's got my money to fall back on. There's my investment income and then, needless to say, I made quite a lot when I sold the big house after my husband died. That's when I started slumming down here, you know – though, mind you, I do like to think I slum in some style.' She chuckled, but then her tone darkened as she said, 'Thank goodness I never made any of my money over to that man, or no doubt he'd have squandered that too to feed his disgusting habits.'

'Did Rory ever ask you to make money over to him?'

'Not in so many words,' Winnie replied, with a wealth of implied subtext.

'Oh. Well, look, I hope you do get some good news soon.'

'The only good news I can get is the confirmation that that man is dead.'

'Wouldn't it be better news to hear that he's still alive – that he hasn't killed himself?'

Winnie Norton was rather stumped by that question. It caught her between the opposite pulls of the polite usages of Fethering society and her own seething hatred. The conventionally humanitarian response she managed to patch together left no doubt as to the true state of her feelings.

Chapter Thirty

'It's all too easy,' Jude announced.

They were walking along the beach on the Monday afternoon. The tide was low, the soft sand, sucking at their feet, made progress hard and slow. Gulliver scampered around them, off on more of his terribly important fool's errands. The two women had brought each other up to date on their individual researches.

'What do you mean, Jude?'

'Look, forget the body you found for the moment. Forget Aaron Spalding and the other boys. Let's just concentrate on Rory Turnbull. Now, the assumption is that he's committed suicide . . .'

'And it seems a very reasonable assumption. He left a note, for a start, saying that that was what he intended to do. And the more we discover about his circumstances, the more impossible his situation seems to have been. His marriage must always have been unhappy – certainly if Barbara had the same kind of attitude to him as his mother-in-law has. And his finances were getting totally out of control. I mean, now we've discovered he'd remortgaged the house and he had no savings left. He must've been really desperate to start fiddling the Yacht Club accounts. And making false claims for dental work on the NHS, that had to be a short-term thing. He knew he'd get found out in time.'

'And why was he doing all this? Why did he need all that money?'

'To feed his heroin habit.'

'And on what basis do we say he had a heroin habit?'

'Come on, Jude. You got that from Dylan, didn't you?'

'Not really. All I got from Dylan was the fact that he gave Rory a contact name for hard drugs. Rory came to him because he was the Fethering local drug dealer – well known to be, Ted Crisp told us as much. Didn't take us long, did it? Two not-very-streetwise women, and we get on to Dylan straight away, don't we? And all we actually know is that Rory bought a bit of weed from Dylan, and then asked for a contact name to get hold of the smack. We have no proof he ever followed up on that contact.'

'But we do. Rory's mother-in-law found evidence – she found the drug equipment in his study. Oh, come on, Jude, we can't argue with this. It all stacks up.'

'Yes, it all stacks up.' Jude stopped and narrowed her brown eyes to look out over the sea. Now the weather had changed, there was even a trace of blue in the waves. 'And I think it all stacks up too conveniently.'

'What do you mean?'

'I've known a few drug addicts in my time,' said Jude, 'and the one thing that distinguishes them is secrecy about their habit. Not when they're with other junkies perhaps, but they don't want the outside world to know. And yet we're being asked to believe that a middle-class dentist leaves evidence of his drug habit round the house where his mother-in-law can find it. And where his wife could easily have found it if his mother-in-law hadn't. Winnie told you that Barbara snooped around in the loft and found the pornography he'd stashed away – and he'd made a much bigger effort to hide that. So Rory knew full well that anything left round his house was a serious security risk.'

'But surely—'

Jude seemed unaware of the interruption as she went on, 'Besides, what Winnie found was so obvious. What – a syringe, some tinfoil and a packet of white powder?'

'That's what she said.'

'And she also said that she recognized what it was because she'd seen stuff like that on television. What she saw was like an identikit shorthand for drug addiction – something that even a genteel, middle-class lady in her seventies was bound to recognize. No, I'm sorry, I don't buy it. There's something going on here.'

'But what?'

Jude let out a wry little laugh. 'If we knew that, wouldn't life be simple? The only thing I do know, though, is that Rory Turnbull isn't dead.'

'How do you know that? All the evidence points to the fact that he definitely is dead.'

'And that's how I know it. There's too much evidence. I detect a bit of overkill in the planning here.'

'Whose planning?'

'Rory Turnbull's, I would imagine. Though what he was planning and why, I have no idea.'

'Well, even if he's not dead,' said Carole, 'it's no surprise that he's off the scene right now, is it?'

'How do you mean?'

'Retribution was getting dangerously close. He must've known when the Regional Dental Officer would be coming to make his inspection. And when Denis Woodville would be talking to the accountants, come to that.'

'Yes.' Jude rubbed her chin thoughtfully. 'It might in fact have been better from Rory's point of view if those things had come out *after* his apparent suicide. I wonder . . .'

'What?'

'Dunno. Just wonder if he had to change his plans for some reason. But since we don't know what his plans were, such speculation becomes rather difficult. Oh, what the hell? I'm going to paddle.'

And suddenly Jude was running down to the sea's edge.

'You're not going to take off your shoes, are you?' Carole called after her. 'The water'll freeze your toes off.'

'No, no, these boots are supposed to be waterproof!'

Jude jumped into the shallows and kicked about in frustration, raising flurries of spray around her. Gulliver, identifying the kind of game he never got to play with his owner, leapt into the water to join her, barking joyously. Carole stood a few yards above the tide mark, looking old-fashioned.

She gave covert looks along the beach in both directions and up towards the pebbles. There was no one in sight. Thank goodness. Flamboyance of the kind Jude was manifesting wasn't quite the thing in Fethering. Carole reminded herself how glad she was that she wasn't prone to such childish displays. But still she felt a little wistful.

'It's not true!' Jude called out through the spray.

'What's not true?'

'The manufacturer's claim for these boots. They're not waterproof.'

'Oh. Well . . .' Carole couldn't think of a response that wouldn't sound smug, so she said nothing.

Jude came out of the sea with a broad grin across her face. 'There,' she said. 'Feel better for that.'

Gulliver followed her out. Stopping alongside, he shook himself, covering her with fine spray.

'Gulliver, you naughty boy!'

'It's all right, Carole. I'm so wet already, it doesn't matter. Stay cool.'

Carole wasn't sure that she'd ever been cool, so staying cool might have been a problem. But again she didn't say anything.

Jude stood at the sea's edge, unaware of the wavelets lapping away at her heels. She looked up towards Fethering and her brow wrinkled. 'I'm sure the solution's very simple . . . if only we could work it out.'

'Huh.' Carole turned to face in the same direction, but stayed in front of Jude. Although her gumboots were infallibly waterproof, she didn't want to get them wet.

Jude looked across towards the Yacht Club. Behind

it, the men who'd been repairing the sea wall were dismantling their site. The cranes had already gone and other equipment was being loaded on to large flatbed trucks. The builders' work had been done. The wall was shored up and the quick-flowing Fether once again properly contained.

'Let's just think about your body,' she said. 'What we know of the movements of your body.'

'All right. Well, how it got there we have no idea, but we do know that it was lying in *Brigadoon II* on the Monday night when it was found by Dylan, Aaron Spalding and Nick Kent . . .'

'Then they did their black magic ritual with it and chucked it into the Fether . . .'

'But, true to form, it became a "Fethering Floater" and was washed up on the beach the next morning, where I found it . . .'

'Though the "someone else" you saw walking away from the breakwater may have found it before you did.'

'Possibly.'

'And then Aaron Spalding found it, presumably after you did.'

'I imagine so.'

'He rang Nick Kent and together the two boys manhandled the body back to where they'd found it. By the time the police started looking, the body was back in *Brigadoon II*.'

'Yes, though it wasn't there on the Wednesday afternoon when we looked inside the boat.'

'No.' Jude tugged pensively at an errant strand of her blonde hair. 'So, given the fact that moving dead bodies around during the daytime tends to attract attention, it seems reasonable to assume that the body was moved out of the boat on the Tuesday night.'

'The same night that Aaron Spalding jumped – or fell – into the Fether.'

'Yes. Are those two events connected? Hm . . .' Jude tapped her chin in frustration. 'So where did the body go? Where, come to that, is the body now?'

Her eyes moved restlessly across the horizon of Fethering, and stopped focused on a high thirties house with glass-fronted top floor. As she looked a flash of reflected sunlight caught on something behind the glass. 'Who lives there?'

'What?'

'That tall house, Carole. Who lives there?'

'Old bloke. I don't know his name. He's completely housebound, I think.'

'But from the top of that house, he can see everything that happens on the beach.'

'Well, yes, he probably can, but—'

'Come on!' And Jude had started running up the sand, her wet shoes squelching protests at every step. Gulliver, having recognized another game, also ran, barking enthusiastically.

'But, Jude,' Carole wailed, 'we can't just burst into his house!'

'Why not?'

'Because we don't know him.'

'Oh, Carole! For heaven's sake!'

Chapter Thirty-one

The house that overlooked the beach must once have been in single ownership but had been divided into flats, one on each of its four storeys. Assuming a correlation between the flats and the entryphone buttons, Jude boldly pressed the top one.

There was no response. She was about to press again when an electronic voice from the little speaker said, 'Hello?'

'Good afternoon. Are you the gentleman in the top flat?'

'Yes.'

'We wondered if we could come and talk to you.'

'Might I ask who you are?'

'My name's Jude, and I'm with my friend Carole Seddon. We both live in Fethering. In the High Street. Please. We would like to talk to you.'

'About what?' the voice crackled back.

'About things you may have seen on the beach over the last week.'

'Uh-huh.' There was a silence while the voice seemed to assess the proposition. Then it went on, 'So you are asking me, an elderly, housebound cripple, to open my door to two people I've never seen before . . .'

'Yes.'

'. . . in spite of the fact that the majority of crimes against the elderly are committed by malefactors who have infiltrated themselves into pensioners' houses on some spurious pretext?'

'Yes,' said Jude, with less confidence.

'Come on up,' the voice from the box intoned. Then the door buzzed its release. Jude pushed and held it, while Carole sorted out Gulliver. He wasn't going to enjoy being tied by his lead to a garden seat – particularly when he reckoned he was being taken out for a walk – but there was no alternative. As they went inside the building, he gave a couple of reproachful barks at the eternal perfidy of women.

The entrance was at the back, at the foot of a tower which housed a lift and had presumably been added at the time of the conversion into flats. Without the lift, surely no one in a wheelchair would live on the top floor.

'But we don't even know his name,' Carole complained as they rose up through the building.

'Then we'll ask him what it is.' Jude's tone came as near as it ever did to exasperation.

They emerged on to a small landing. Framed in the doorway opposite, which he had opened ready for them, was a small man in a wheelchair.

Perhaps he wouldn't have looked small if he could have stood up, but, crumpled down as he was, there seemed to be very little of him. He was partially paralysed, his head propped back at a strange angle. His left hand was strapped against the arm of his chair, while his right hovered over a control panel of buttons and levers. He wore a crested blazer and a cravat high around his neck. On his head was an incongruous navy corduroy cap.

'Good afternoon . . . Carole and Jude, was it?'

When he spoke, they realized that not only the entryphone had made his voice sound electronic. He talked through some kind of voicebox. The cravat must have been there to hide a tracheotomy scar.

'Come on in,' he said, flicking a control and going into sharp reverse. 'Close the door behind you.'

'Isn't that a risk?' asked Jude, as they came into his sitting room. 'If we were going to rob you or beat you up, nobody would hear your cries.'

Carole gave her neighbour a reproving look. What appalling bad taste. Had Jude no sense of the right remark for the right occasion?

But apparently it was exactly the right remark for their host. He let out a bark of electronic laughter and said, 'I'm prepared to take my chance with you two. I know appearances can be deceptive, but you don't project the traditional image of teenage tearaways.

'My name's Gordon Lithgoe, by the way. I'd offer to make you tea, but I'm so cack-handed, you'd be better off doing it for yourself. The makings are over there.'

'No, thank you. We don't require tea.' Carole didn't want the atmosphere to become too relaxed. When they started asking him questions, Gordon Lithgoe might decide to throw them out.

'This is a pretty stunning little eyrie you've got here,' said Jude.

It was. The window that took up the entire front

wall dominated the space, as if the sea were part of the decor. The original thirties metal-framed panes were still intact, but outside a more modern set of sliding windows protected them from the worst of the weather. The glow of the bright November afternoon permeated the whole room. There was little furniture; someone in a wheelchair had more use for space than armchairs and sofas. On the walls were pinned large-scale maps of shorelines, creeks and channels; there were a few plaques commemorating various ships; and in rows of bookcases stood the serried blue spines of books that looked as if they must have something to do with navigation.

Most interesting, though, from the point of view of the two women, was the area directly in front of the window. A platform had been built up there, and from it a ramp led down for the wheelchair. On the platform stood a telescope on a tripod. Two pairs of powerful binoculars lay on a nearby table, as well as an open ledger with a fountain pen lying down its middle crease. Some notes were written on the left-hand page.

'Very nautical flavour,' Jude went on. 'Were you in the Navy?'

'No, no,' said Gordon Lithgoe. 'No chance of someone like me passing the medical. So I've always had to remain as just an interested amateur.'

'Still – ' Jude looked around the room again – 'this is a wonderful place.'

'Just as well,' his voice crackled back, 'since the only times I leave it these days is to have operations.' There was another rasp of laughter. 'Apropos of which, ladies, sorry about the cap, but it's prettier than the scars underneath.'

'Yes, I'm sure it is,' said Carole, ever ready with the required Fethering platitude.

Her recourse to what passed locally for good manners reminded him of his own. 'Do sit down.' He pointed to two upright kitchen chairs. 'Sorry, not very comfortable, but then I have few visitors. The woman who brings my meals never stays. Otherwise, it's the nurse, the occasional social worker, very rarely the doctor and, even more rarely, the odd friend. Have to be odd to come and see someone like me – half man, half electronic gadget – wouldn't they?'

There was not a nuance of self-pity in his words. There hadn't been in anything he had said. He seemed, if anything, amused by his plight.

'Anyway,' he said, signalling the end of social niceties, 'you are here for a purpose. I saw you deciding to come up here.'

'You saw us?' said Carole.

'Oh yes.' He suddenly spun the chair on its wheels and shot like a rocket towards the platform by the window. He seemed to be going up the ramp far too fast, but, rather than smashing into the telescope, he came to a neat halt inches away from it. He'd practised the trick many times before.

He didn't need to move the telescope. It was already focused. He edged the wheelchair a fraction closer and his eye was at the lens. 'I could see you just like you were in the room with me. Pity I can't lip-read. But anyway your body language told me you'd decided to come up here.'

'Do you spend most of the day watching the beach?' asked Jude.

Again, Carole wouldn't have put the question so bluntly, but Gordon Lithgoe still didn't seem offended. 'No, I'm basically looking for shipping. That's what interests me.' His working hand fell on to the ledger by his side. 'Make a log of all their comings and goings.'

'And what about the people on the beach?' Jude maintained her direct approach. 'Do you make a log of their comings and goings too?'

He spun the wheelchair round and faced them. Against the brightness of the window, it was impossible to see his expression, and from the even signal of his voice, impossible to gauge his emotion.

'Some,' he said. 'Not all.'

'We're interested in the events of Monday night last week,' said Carole. 'And then through Tuesday and Wednesday.'

There was a moment's stillness, and they were both afraid he was going to clam up. Then, suddenly releasing a brake, he glided the wheelchair down the ramp and swung gracefully round to come to rest beside them. They could now see his face. It was smiling.

'Why do you want to know this?'

Carole replied, 'We think there's been something criminal going on.'

'And you're not police. Otherwise, as soon as you'd arrived, you'd have flashed that fact at me – along with your ID, wouldn't you?'

'Yes.'

'So what are you?'

'Just two people who want to get to the truth of what happened.' Even as she said the words, Carole knew how pompous they sounded.

'Oh, hurrah, hurrah.' Gordon Lithgoe's sarcasm made itself felt through the electronic crackle. 'How very noble. Truth-searchers, eh? Where would this great country of ours be without people who have a sense of public duty?'

'Do I gather you don't have a sense of public duty?'

Again Jude's lighter tone struck the right note. 'Not in the obvious way,' he replied. 'I've seen a lot of things in my life that were probably criminal, and I've never reported any of them. I've seen my role throughout as essentially that of an observer.'

'But if someone were to come and ask you? If the police were to come and ask you?'

'That would be entirely different. I would certainly cooperate and tell anything I knew – if asked. But I wouldn't just volunteer information. However – ' he drummed his right hand lightly on his sunken chest – 'in this case the police haven't come and asked me. They didn't make the deduction that I might have seen something, while you two ladies did make that deduction and have arrived on my doorstep . . .'

'So you'll tell us what you saw?' asked Jude very softly.

'Yes. Of course I will. I assume what you're interested in is the dead body which you – Carole, is it? – found on the beach on Tuesday morning?'

'How did you know it was me?'

'I told you. That telescope enlarges the face of

someone on the beach as if they're here in the room with me. I recognized you, anyway. I didn't know your name, but I'd seen you taking your dog for a walk every morning for the last three or four years.'

It was uncomfortable to know that she'd been being observed for such a long time. Not, of course, that Carole had ever done anything on the beach of which to be ashamed, but all the same . . .

'What we want to know is what happened to the body after I found it.'

'Yes. It was rather active, wasn't it – for one so dead? I'll find the relevant log.' He spun the wheel-chair across the room to a shelf and selected one from a pile of ledgers. Carole and Jude both marvelled at the extent of his record-keeping. The ledger by the window was half full, but he had to go to another one for events of less than a week before.

He flicked through the book with his good hand till he found the place, then, pressing it to his knee, wheeled himself back towards them. He looked down at his notes. 'I was first aware of the body at 6.52. That was first light. But, given where he was on the breakwater, and the fact that the tide had gone all the way out and was on its way back in, he could have been there for a couple of hours before that.'

'And I found him about seven, I should think.'

'7.02. Then you went back home with your dog.' Again, Carole felt a little shiver from the knowledge that she'd been watched. 'At 7.06 a boy climbed over the railings of the Yacht Club and raised the cover of one of the boats. He didn't like what he saw inside, I suppose, because he came running out and along the sea wall, looking down into the Fether. Then he ran down on to the beach, and he found the body at 7.21. He ran back up the beach – don't know where he went to, I couldn't see – but about a quarter of an hour later he came back . . .'

'With another boy?' Jude breathed.

'Yes. The two of them manhandled the body up the beach, over the railings into the Yacht Club and put it into the boat, the same boat the first boy had looked in.'

'And then?'

'And then the boys ran off. Out of vision of my telescope at 7.47. At 10.12 the police arrived, looked along the beach – not very hard – and then they left.'

'But what about the body?' asked Carole.

'That's it. That's all I can offer you. Great telescope I've got there, but it doesn't have night sights. If I could afford one with those, I'd get it tomorrow.'

'Oh, I don't know.' Jude chuckled. 'You've got to sleep sometime.'

'I don't sleep that much,' said Gordon Lithgoe.

'So . . .' Carole sighed despondently. 'It looks as though the body was removed on the Tuesday night, under cover of darkness. But by whom and where to, we have no means of knowing.'

'Where would you put a body, Mr Lithgoe?'

There was a scrape of electronic laughter. 'I'm glad to say, Jude, that's not a problem I've ever had to address. However, where you'd put a body depends on where you think people are going to look for it.'

'Ye-es. With you so far.'

'And, among the multiplicity of pastimes available

to the human species, carrying dead bodies around is one of the most hazardous. If you get caught doing it, you're facing a hell of a lot of uncomfortable explanations. What I'm saying is that, unless you've got transport, you don't want to move a body far. So if, say, you're hiding a body in a boat, and you think there's a strong chance someone might look in that boat, then you move it to somewhere close by where they're not going to look.'

'Into another boat?'

'Possibly. Except if one boat's a security risk, maybe they all are.'

'Where else then?'

'Come and have a look.' Gordon Lithgoe powered his wheelchair back up the ramp. His right hand slightly reangled the telescope and adjusted the focus. 'I don't know. It's a possibility. Have a butcher's.'

Carole looked first. She had to arch her back to get down low enough. The telescope was trained on the top of the sea wall, where the repairs had been taking place for the previous few days. The heavy machinery had all gone, as had the workers.

Revealed were the two blue-painted low chests used by local fishermen to store their bait and equipment.

'Bit big,' said Gordon Lithgoe, 'but otherwise it's the right shape for a coffin, isn't it?'

'Jude, have a look. And of course,' Carole went on thoughtfully, 'if whoever it was put the body in there just as a temporary measure . . . and they didn't know what was about to happen . . . their plans would have been really screwed up by the builders coming in.'

'Yes.' Jude rose from the telescope. 'They would, wouldn't they?'

'Are you off to have a snoop?' asked Gordon Lithgoe eagerly. 'I'd love to watch your exhumation through the telescope. But hurry – while the light lasts.'

'Yes, we must go. Mr Lithgoe, I can't thank you enough—'

'Please call me Gordon.'

'No, but you've been so generous with your time.'

'Time is not a commodity I need to ration. I have far too much of it. Any visitor is a welcome diversion. As I said there are people who come and see me occasionally, but—'

'Theresa Spalding,' said Jude with one of her sudden insights.

'What?' asked Carole.

'Theresa Spalding used to come and see you, didn't she, Gordon?'

'Yes, yes, she did.'

'And you mentioned the body on the beach to her?'

'That's right.'

'And described Carole?'

'Yes.'

'Which explains why she came to your house, Carole.'

'It must do, yes.'

'But, Jude, you said she *used* to come and see me. Is she not coming again?'

'I hope she is, Gordon. But she's not well at the moment. Did you hear, her son died? She's taken it very badly and she's in hospital.'

'Ah.' The news seemed to bring him deep sadness. 'I hope she'll be all right. She's had a lot to cope with, that girl.'

'Yes.'

'Anyway,' Carole broke in briskly, 'we must be on our way. Can't thank you enough for—'

'Carole, there's something we're forgetting!'

'What, Jude?' She spoke testily. She wanted to be on her way. Gulliver had been left tied up in the garden for far too long.

'The person you saw on the beach before you found the body.'

'Oh, my goodness, yes.'

'Ah,' said Gordon Lithgoe, 'I wondered if you'd ask about that.' He referred again to his ledger. 'That'd be the one who saw the body at 6.57.'

'Around then it must have been, yes.'

'In a shiny green anorak.'

'Yes. Who was he?'

'Wasn't a "he". It was a "she".'

'Really?'

'Young girl. It was hardly light, so I couldn't see when she actually came on to the beach, but she was running down from the direction of the Yacht Club. Seemed to be in a panic, until she found the body.'

'What did she look like?' asked Jude.

'Couldn't see the colour of her hair, because she had her anorak hood done up tight. Large young woman, though. And I could see one thing . . . She had a silver stud in her nose.'

Chapter Thirty-two

When they got out of the building, Gulliver provided an excellent illustration for the meaning of the word 'hangdog'. He was very reproachful.

'I'll have to take him home before we do anything else,' said Carole. 'Anyway, I don't want him present if there is going to be an exhumation.'

'No.'

They set out back towards the High Street, keeping on Seaview Road, which was firmer underfoot than the beach.

'We've got to talk to Tanya,' said Jude.

'She's not the only young woman in the world with a silver nose-stud.'

'No, but she's the only one who has a connection to Fethering Yacht Club. If only we could also find a connection between her and Rory Turnbull . . .'

'Well, he was Treasurer of the club, so she must've met him there.'

'Ye-es. Have we got anything else, though?'

'Hm . . . Ooh, just a minute, we might have. What about the girl your dental hygienist mentioned?'

'Well done, Carole. How stupid of me! I should've remembered that. Of course! Denis Woodville said she lived in Brighton, so if she was coming to do an evening shift at the club bar, then the timing would be absolutely right for Rory to give her the occasional lift to work when he'd finished at the surgery.'

The two women exchanged looks as they strode along. Carole's pale eyes sparkled behind their glasses. 'Then we definitely need to talk to Tanya.'

'Before we go into the exhumation business?'

'Yes.' Carole shuddered. 'And I certainly don't think we should do the exhumation bit alone.'

'You're not suggesting calling in the police, are you?'

'Certainly not! Not till we've confirmed that the body's there. I can just imagine the expression on Detective Inspector Brayfield's face if we got him to help us burglarize one of those fishermen's chests and found nothing in it except for boathooks and rotting bait. No, I think we should ask Ted Crisp to help us.'

'Oh?'

'You sound surprised, Jude. Don't you think it's a good idea?'

'I think it's a very good idea. My only surprise is that you were the one who suggested it.'

And it was surprising, when she came to think about it. The Carole of a week before would never have dreamed of making the suggestion.

As they took the left turn into the High Street, Jude went on, 'I'll give Ted a call. I'm sure he can slip away from the pub for half an hour.'

'It's got to be this evening.'

'Hm?'

'When we look for the body.' Carole went through

the logic. 'If Gordon Lithgoe's idea is correct and the body was moved as a temporary measure, then tonight's the first opportunity whoever moved it will have to retrieve it. The building workers have been there all the time since Wednesday.'

Jude nodded, then stopped. They were outside Denis Woodville's cottage. Its paintwork and paths were immaculately clean. The dinghy on its trailer was still in front of the garage. On his gatepost a new, meticulously hand-printed felt-tip notice read, 'BEWARE! WEEKEND SAILORS IN VICINITY! NEXT DOOR!' And a large arrow pointed towards the Chilcotts' house.

On their gatepost was a new printed notice. In a choice selection of fonts, it read, 'DANGER! LITTLE HITLER NEXT DOOR! YOU HAVE BEEN WARNED!' And an arrow pointed back at Denis Woodville's.

'I'd have thought these two were getting a bit close to the libel laws,' Jude observed.

'Only if one of them chooses to sue. And I think, deep down, both of them enjoy the game so much that they're not going to risk putting an end to it by court procedures.'

Jude chuckled. 'You're probably right. Anyway, I'm just going to see if Denis is in . . .'

'To get a contact number for Tanya?'

'That's right. You take Gulliver back. I'll be round in a minute.'

The Vice-Commodore was in, though on his home territory he seemed diminished, less assured than he had been in the surroundings of the Fethering Yacht

Club. Jude sensed in him a reluctance to invite her in, which was overcome only by ingrained good manners.

When he ushered her through to his sitting room, she could see why. In marked contrast to the neatness of its exterior, the house's interior was distinctly shabby. Some months had elapsed since the sitting room had experienced even the most cursory of cleaner's attentions. In the air, as well as stale Gauloise smoke, hovered the sickly smell of rotting fruit.

Denis Woodville's awareness of, and embarrassment about, the state of his home suggested he very rarely had visitors. 'I'm sorry, bit of a tip,' he barked, with an attempt at bluffness. 'Fact is, I was never up to much on the domestic front and, since my wife passed away, I . . . Not that I spend any longer here than I have to . . . Busy at the club a lot of the time anyway . . .'

Escaping to the club, Jude translated. The squalor of the room brought home to her the emptiness of the old man's life.

'Do take a seat.' He gestured vaguely to a selection of subsiding armchairs, none of which looked particularly inviting.

'No, I'm fine. If you could just find that number . . .'

'Yes, yes, of course.' Moving aside an ashtray and a couple of smeared beer mugs from a dresser, he riffled through a pile of dusty newspapers and unopened letters. 'I've got it here somewhere.' He had shown no surprise at being asked for Tanya's number and no curiosity as to why it might be wanted. 'Tell the young lady when you do get through to her that, if she's changed her mind, she can have her job back.

I haven't found a replacement yet . . . that is, unless of course you were serious about wanting to do it?'

Jude grimaced. 'Still finding my feet round here, actually. Bit early for me to commit myself to anything.'

'Yes, yes, of course. Damn, it doesn't seem to be here. Maybe it's in this lot.' He moved across to attack another pile of detritus on a coffee table.

'Nice-looking dinghy you have in the front there,' said Jude, to make conversation.

'Yes, she's a Mirror.'

'Ah.' This meant nothing to her. 'I'm surprised you don't keep it down at the Yacht Club.'

'Well, I used to, but, erm . . . well, times change . . .' Jude suddenly understood. Denis Woodville was saying that he could no longer afford to keep his dinghy at the Yacht Club. 'I probably won't keep her that much longer. Dinghy like that's a bit of a handful. I'm thinking of selling her . . . and getting something else . . . more suitable for my advanced years,' he added, with an unconvincing flourish of bravado.

'Good idea,' said Jude, not believing a word of it.

'Damn, it's not here. I know I've got the number down at the club.' The very mention of the word seemed to raise his spirits. He looked at his watch. 'Should be opening up there soon anyway.' The confidence in his voice mounted as the moment of leaving his squalid home drew closer. 'Damned place can't function without the Vice-Commodore, you know. If you wouldn't mind coming along with me . . .'

There was a little knot of elderly cronies already waiting for Denis Woodville to unlock the clubhouse.

They called out raucous comments about his timekeeping and did not let the fact he had a woman with him pass unremarked. The Vice-Commodore glowed in their attention.

Inside the bar-room, with the lights switched on, he whispered to Jude, 'Have to get their drinks sorted out first or I'll never hear the end of it. Can I get you a little something?'

Jude refused, anxious to get away. She had a sense that the pace of the investigation was accelerating.

Denis Woodville lit up another Gauloise and then made a great meal of pouring the drinks, with constant comments about how unsuitable it was for the Vice-Commodore to be involved in such menial tasks. Though it was clear he'd been doing it every night since Tanya left.

None of the others moved to help him. They just sat and pontificated on the appalling state of the world and how much better everything would be if they were in charge. One of them harked back to when he'd been stationed out in Singapore and pretty well ran the show out there. If the half of what these elderly gentlemen said was true, Jude was privileged to be in the company of the finest political and logistical brains in the entire world.

Eventually everyone was supplied with a drink. Denis Woodville took a long swig of his brandy and said, 'Now, let's find that phone number for you . . .'

He turned to a neat address book by the telephone. Whatever chaos might reign in his home, here at the Fethering Yacht Club the Vice-Commodore kept everything shipshape. As he picked up the book, he noticed the message light flashing on the answering machine. 'Excuse me. Better just check this. Might be the coastguard,' he said importantly.

The message wasn't from the coastguard. It was the voice of a bored young woman. 'Vice-Commodore, it's Tanya, calling on Monday afternoon. First, I wanted to say thanks for the lunch last week . . .'

Though spoken with total lack of enthusiasm, this still prompted ribald comments from the cronies round the bar.

' . . . and the other thing is, could you let me know whether those repairs on the sea wall have been finished yet? It's just, um . . . well, I was thinking of coming for a walk to Fethering and I didn't want to if the building's still going on, you know . . . Could you call me on . . .'

Jude scribbled the number down on the back of an envelope. 'And could I have her address please?'

'How very odd,' said the Vice-Commodore, as he passed the address book across. 'What on earth does the girl want to know about the sea wall for?'

Jude had a potential answer to that question. An answer that might make a connection she'd been seeking for some time. The girl's reason for wanting the information had been so clumsily fabricated that Jude felt a little charge of excitement.

'It's in code,' one of the Fethering Yacht Club members announced. 'It all has special meanings for the Vice-Commodore, eh? That's how he and Tanya have managed to keep their affair secret all these years.'

The remark was greeted by some token joshing,

but soon the old men moved on to more serious matters. When Jude slipped away from the clubroom, Denis Woodville was launching into his views on how the Northern Ireland problem should be solved. His recipe required rather lavish use of a reintroduced death penalty, but 'in the long run, it would only be being cruel to be kind . . .'

The Vice-Commodore was in his pomp. Jude felt sure none of his surrounding pontificators had ever seen him in the drabness of his home surroundings.

'Have you talked to Ted Crisp?'

It was the first thing Jude asked when she arrived and Carole was proud to be able to say, 'Yes. He's game for a bit of body-hunting . . . round seven.'

'Good.' Jude pulled out her mobile phone. 'I'll see if Tanya's there now.'

'You can use my phone.'

'Mm?' She was already keying in the numbers. 'Oh, it's OK.'

'But using a mobile is a lot more expensive.'

'Is it?' asked Jude, as though the idea had never occurred to her. 'Ah, hello, is that Tanya? My name's Jude. I don't know if you remember, we met in the Crown and Anchor at Fethering on Friday. Yes, that's right. Well, I wanted to talk about a body that got washed up on the beach here last week . . .'

With a rueful expression, Jude turned to Carole. 'Maybe the direct approach isn't always the best one. She hung up on me.'

'Ah. Still, wouldn't you say that's a sign of guilt or

complicity or something? If she had no idea what you were talking about, she'd have said so, not hung up.'

'You could be right.' Jude looked down at the envelope on which she'd written Tanya's address and phone number. 'I think I'd better go and see her.'

'In Brighton?'

'Yes. I know she's at home, don't I? At least at the moment.'

'How will you get there? I'd offer to drive you over, but if I'm meeting Ted at seven, I—'

'No, no, don't worry. I'll get a cab.'

'A *cab*?' Carole was shocked. 'All the way to Brighton?'

'It's not far, is it?'

'It may not be far, but it'll certainly cost you. Depends what kind of budget you're working to, of course.'

'Budget?' Jude savoured the unfamiliar word.

'Yes, budget. You know what it means, don't you?'

'I know what it means, of course,' said Jude mischievously, 'but I've never really come to terms with the *concept*.'

Carole looked blank. But then everyone looks blank when they try to converse with someone who speaks a different language.

Jude raised her mobile phone again. 'I'll give her another try. Maybe now Tanya's had time to think, she will want to talk to me.'

And so it proved. Guilt, anxiety or maybe simple curiosity had done their work, and Jude set off shortly after in a cab to Brighton.

* * *

Carole felt tense, but the anticipation was not unpleasurable. At least something was happening in her life. Searching for dead bodies might not be sensible, but it sure beat the hell out of most other Fethering residents' pastimes.

When the phone rang at twenty-five past six, she felt a little pang of potential disappointment. It would be Ted Crisp, calling off their seven o'clock tryst.

It wasn't.

'Carole, it's me, Jude. I'd just got to Brighton and paid off the cab when my mobile rang. It was Maggie Kent. Nick's gone missing!'

Chapter Thirty-three

'You have called the police, have you?'

'Yes.' Maggie Kent's voice on the telephone was tight with the effort of controlling her emotion. 'At first they weren't that interested. They said lots of kids come home late from school, and it had only been an hour, and Nick was sixteen for goodness' sake, and . . . Then I told them he'd been with Aaron Spalding the night before Aaron died and they began to take me a bit more seriously.'

'So they are out looking for him?'

'That's what they say. And I'm sure they are, though at what level of urgency I don't know. But I can't just sit here doing nothing. The thought that Nick's out there somewhere, confused, needing me – perhaps not needing *me*, but needing someone . . . It's so awful, I . . .' The dam on her emotions was cracking. Maggie Kent took a deep breath and evened out her voice as she went on, 'I rang your friend Jude, because I thought Nick might have confided something to her when they talked last week.'

'And had he?' Had Jude told the mother of her son's presence at the mutilating of a corpse?

'She told me a few bits and pieces I didn't know.

But I was really interested in what Nick and Aaron might have said to each other. Nick was in such a dreadful state over the weekend. He hardly slept at all, or ate come to that. There's something really terrible gnawing away at him and I'm scared. I'm scared he'll do what Aaron did.'

'You mean kill himself? Has it been confirmed that that's what Aaron did? Because there hasn't been an inquest yet, has there?'

'No, but the police told me. Aaron was seen by a courting couple in a car – they've only just come forward. He was up on the railway bridge over the Fether in the early hours of Tuesday morning. There seems no question he jumped in deliberately.

'And the thought that my Nick might have done the same thing is just too . . .' This time no floodgates would have been adequate to stop the flow of tears.

Carole waited till the note of the sobbing changed and then asked, 'So what are you going to do in the short term?'

'I don't know. I'll go mad if I just sit around here. And I feel I should be out by the railway bridge, looking for Nick. But I'm scared, if I go out and join the search, then the phone might ring and I wouldn't be here . . .'

'I'd go out if I were you. Good news'll keep.'

'And what about bad news?'

'Generally speaking, that'll keep too,' Carole replied grimly.

She had her own ideas of where she'd start looking for the boy. And, with a bit of luck, she'd have Ted Crisp there to help her. Carole Seddon took a large rubber-covered torch out of the cupboard under the stairs, and put on her Burberry.

Tanya lived in a Kemptown bedsit which, because it boasted its own bathroom, the landlord had the nerve to call a studio flat. There was a two-ring gas hob by the sink, but it didn't look as if it got used much. The walls had once been white but were pockmarked with Sellotape scars and Blu-Tack stains where previous tenants had taken down their posters and other decorations. Tanya seemed to have put up nothing of her own. Double bed, television, video, CD player – that was all she appeared to need to express her identity.

Quite loud in the background, when she let Jude in, was the clinical voice of some pop diva, draining the emotion out of yet another song. Tanya closed the door behind her guest and, with no attempt at social graces, demanded, 'What is all this then?'

'I was rather hoping you could tell me that.'

'Why should I? Particularly 'cause I don't know what you're talking about.'

Perhaps Tanya could on occasion be attractive, but in this aggressive mode she wasn't. She looked massive, stolid and resentful, her face already set into a kind of middle-aged disappointment. As she had been in the Crown and Anchor, she was dressed in black, whether the identical clothes or another similar set Jude couldn't tell. The black laced-up Doc Martens were certainly the same.

Recognizing that there was no chance of being offered a chair, Jude plonked herself down into one the landlord must have picked up at a house-clearance dealers. 'As I said on the telephone, I'm talking about a body that was washed up on Fethering beach last Tuesday morning. The body of a middle-aged man. We know you saw it.'

'How do you know?'

'The usual way. Someone saw you.'

'And told you about it?'

'Exactly.'

The girl sniffed. Then suddenly she said, 'I got to go to the toilet.' Pausing only by the CD player to turn up the diva even louder, she crossed the room and disappeared into the bathroom, shutting the door behind her.

Jude wondered whether turning up the music had been a gesture of delicacy, a recognition that embarrassing noises from the lavatory might otherwise be heard in such an enclosed space.

Certainly Tanya seemed to be doing something major in the bathroom. She was in there for a long time. Jude wondered whether the girl was fortifying herself for the interview ahead with a few drugs. The flush on her cheeks when she finally did return would have supported that hypothesis.

The first thing Tanya did after firmly shutting the bathroom door was to flick a switch on the CD and stop the diva in mid-wail. Plumping herself down on the edge of her bed, she began quickly, 'All right, about this body . . . Yeah, OK, I was going for a walk on the beach at Fethering and I saw it. And I didn't tell no one, 'cause if you ever been in care, you know that anything where the police is involved is just going to cause you a lot of grief and hassle.'

'And did you see anyone else on the beach that morning?'

'No. Oh yes. There was some old girl taking her dog for a walk.' Jude wasn't convinced Carole would have liked the description.

'And that was the only person you saw?'

'Yeah.'

'But what were you doing on Fethering beach at that time in the morning, anyway?'

'I got a job down there at the Yacht Club.'

'No, you haven't. You finished that on the previous Friday. And the Yacht Club isn't open before seven in the morning.'

'Well, I, er . . .' Tanya wasn't a very good liar. Lying needs a flicker of brightness, which she didn't have. Caught out in her lies, she turned to anger instead. 'Look, why you going on at me? It's my own bloody business where I go and what I do. I'm not in care any more, you know! I lead my own independent life!' She seemed to be trying to convince herself as much as Jude.

'Yes, of course. Going back to the body . . .'

'What?'

'Did you recognize it?'

'How d'you mean?'

'Had you seen the man before? Either dead or alive?'

'Bloody hell!' She looked deeply affronted. 'Seen him dead – what do you take me for? You imagine

I'm the sort of person who spends her time with dead bodies?'

'I'm not suggesting that.'

'I should bloody hope not. So far as I'm concerned, he's just some poor bugger who fell off a boat or something and got washed up on Fethering beach. Why?' Tanya looked at Jude with a new curiosity and cunning in her eye. 'Do you know who he was?'

Chapter Thirty-four

There was no sign of Ted Crisp by the entrance gate of the Fethering Yacht Club, where they had agreed to meet. Carole looked at her watch and saw with irritation that it was already ten past seven. She had never been late for anything in her life and she couldn't understand why everyone couldn't be like her. There was nothing difficult involved. It was simply a matter of leaving enough time – in fact, a matter of being organized.

Her earlier prejudices about Ted Crisp started bubbling back to the surface. The landlord of the Crown and Anchor certainly wasn't organized. No doubt, over a few drinks with his regulars, he'd completely forgotten the arrangement he'd made to meet Carole. The last thing you could expect from someone with a background as a stand-up comedian was reliability.

Still, she comforted herself, it might be just as well there was only one of them doing the first bit of her search. More than one might attract too much attention. When she fixed to meet Ted Crisp, she had forgotten that at seven o'clock in the evening the Vice-Commodore and his cronies would be setting the world to rights in the Fethering Yacht Club bar. She had once or twice peered covertly upwards and been relieved to see no one actually sitting in the window. Hopefully, on a winter's evening, they'd all be clustered round the bar counter. But there were undoubtedly members up there, and they did represent a security hazard.

Of course, there was nothing to stop her from marching upstairs and telling the Vice-Commodore what she proposed to do. She wasn't planning anything illegal – rather the reverse, it was a very public-spirited act. But such an approach to Denis Woodville would be too public. Carole didn't want to raise a hue and cry. In the unlikely event of her actually finding Nick, she didn't want him to be frightened off by too many people. The boy was in a very fragile emotional state . . . if he was still alive . . . and Carole had to make herself believe that he was still alive.

She lifted the latch on the white gate that led into the Yacht Club's forecourt. It seemed to make a disproportionately loud click in the winter night and an equally loud one when she closed it. The sea was a long way down the beach, its rustling muted. The only sound seemed to be the harsh scrape of Carole's boots on the cement.

She could have found her way to the right boat blindfold. The events of the previous week, and the images they had spawned, led her inexorably towards *Brigadoon II*. She trembled a little as she approached. The chill she felt had nothing to do with the weather.

Carole stopped, and the whole world seemed very still. She cocked an eye up towards the bar-room's broad window, but her luck held. There was still no outline of anyone observing her.

It was when she took the next step that she heard the noise.

A low keening, like that of some small, injured animal.

And it definitely came from inside *Brigadoon II*.

Carole knew how pivotal her next actions would be. She couldn't be sure what she would find inside the boat, but she had a good idea of what it might be. She must be very cautious.

She remembered exactly how Jude and she had turned the end of the cover over the previous Wednesday. She didn't want to use the torch, but her eyes were becoming accustomed to the gloom. The cut rope had not been repaired. Everything was as it had been.

Carole held the switched-off torch high in her right hand, estimating the direction of its beam. At the moment she flipped back the boat's cover, she pressed the on-button.

Blearily frozen in its beam was Nick's face. He looked about ten years old. Tears coursed down his cheeks and still the low, thin wail poured painfully out of him. He was curled in a foetal position against the fibreglass of the hull. What had been hard ice was now a pool of water which had soaked through his school uniform.

'Nick,' said Carole, as gently as she knew how. Jude would be doing this better, her mind kept saying. Jude has a better touch. I'm not good with people.

She forced herself to banish these thoughts. They

weren't relevant. Jude might do it better, but Jude wasn't there. Carole Seddon was the one facing the terrified boy. Carole Seddon was the one who would have to cope with the situation. There was no alternative.

'Nick,' she murmured again.

The boy squinted into the light. 'Who are you?' he sobbed.

'My name's Carole. I'm a friend of Jude, who you talked to last week.' He made no response. 'Your mother's been terribly worried. She really wants to see you, Nick.'

But this was the wrong thing to say. A new tremor of sobbing came over the boy. Through it, Carole could hear him saying, 'No, I can't see her. I can't see Mummy. Not after what I've done.'

'You haven't done anything so terrible,' said Carole, feeling in her words for the soothing timbre she'd heard in Jude's voice. 'Nothing that can't be forgiven.'

'You don't know what I've done.'

'True. All I know is that you need to go home. To see Mummy.'

She stretched out her hand over the transom of the boat and, to her huge gratification, saw the boy slowly uncurl himself, rise and step towards her. He put his icy hand in hers. Carole braced herself to take the strain, as Nick stepped on to the back of the boat, preparing to jump down. Maybe I'm not so bad at this people business after all, thought Carole with a little glow of pride.

It happened in a split second. Still in the air between boat and cement, he shook his hand free and landed facing away from her. He hit the ground running and weaved his way through the rows of boats towards the Fether.

'Help!' shouted Carole up towards the clubroom. 'Help!' Now she wished she'd brought every member of the Yacht Club with her to trap the boy and seal off his escape.

Dropping her torch in confusion, she ran as fast as she could, but Nick had a start and was a lot faster. She saw him vault over the far fence and rush towards the sea wall.

By the time Carole, panting with effort, reached the railings, Nick Kent was standing swaying on one of the blue fishermen's chests on the sea wall. Is that coincidence, Carole wondered, or does he know something about the whereabouts of the body?

Such speculation would have to wait. She heard behind her the clatter of feet down wooden steps and men shouting, as she called out, 'It's all right, Nick! Don't panic! Everything's all right!'

But the hue and cry she'd feared had started. One of the Yacht Club members had found a powerful spotlight, which he focused on the trembling boy.

That was the final straw. Nick Kent recoiled from the beam, as if the light had the physical power to push him.

Then he turned away and, trailing a thin scream, disappeared over the sea wall into the Fether.

Chapter Thirty-five

'I still want to know,' said Jude calmly, 'what you were doing on Fethering beach before seven in the morning.'

'And why should I tell you?' Tanya sneered. 'You're not police or anything. I don't have to answer your questions.'

'No, you don't. On the other hand, you did invite me to come here and the only possible reason for that is because I said I wanted to talk about the body on the beach. But now I'm here, you don't seem to want to talk about it.'

'Maybe I've changed my mind.'

'You see, I think you do know more about the body than you're saying. The person who saw you on the beach said you had come running down from the direction of the Fethering Yacht Club. I happen to know that the body you found had been stowed there overnight. In a boat called *Brigadoon II*.'

There was an involuntary intake of breath from Tanya. Jude knew more details than she was expecting.

'A possible interpretation of your actions would be that you knew the body had been put in the boat, but when you went to the Yacht Club to check on it – or possibly to move it – you found it had gone. That's what made you panic and run off down the beach, where fortunately you found the missing corpse against the breakwater. So maybe then you went off to get help to move it.'

'You're talking a load of rubbish.' But it was only a token defiance. Jude could see from the sulky set of the girl's chin that at least part of her conjecture had been correct.

'What I still don't know, though, is *how* you came to be involved with the body on the beach. What did it have to do with you, Tanya?'

Carole was well ahead of the others in reaching the sea wall. As she peered fearfully down over the side, the smell and the realization hit her at the same time. The Fether was at low tide and in the thin evening light the mudflats on either side took on the sheen of rotting meat.

Nick Kent had landed in the mud some feet away from the sea wall. The impetus of his jump had planted him up to his thighs in the ooze. His thin arms flailed around, like the wings of a moth caught on wet paint, as he tried in vain to get a purchase on the slime around him.

There was the hiss of a large wave washing up the channel from the sea. The level of the Fether was rising fast. And, even as Carole watched, Nick's body seemed to jolt sideways, sinking deeper into the mire.

She didn't think. She acted instinctively. There was

a gleaming new metal ladder against the sea wall, which had been fixed in place by the workmen doing the repairs during the previous week. Encumbered as she was by her raincoat, Carole swung herself round to take a foothold on the top rung and shinned quickly down.

The ladder stopped about a yard above the mud. 'It's all right, Nick. It's me, Carole,' she called out to the terrified boy.

In the gloom he seemed aware of her for the first time. 'Go away!' he shouted. 'I want to die.'

'No, you don't. What you've done can't be so terrible.'

'You don't know anything about it.'

Carole had hooked one arm around a ladder rung and stretched the other out, but was still half a yard short of the boy's hands. She undid the belt of her Burberry, slid it out of the loops and tried to flip it across the void.

Suddenly there was a flood of light from above. The Fethering Yacht Club regulars had arrived at the edge of the sea wall. 'We'll get a rope to him!' shouted Denis Woodville's voice, authoritative and confident. It was in times of crisis that Vice-Commodores came into their own.

But his authority was not unquestioned. There came a rumbling of other elderly voices, offering a wide variety of alternative rescue plans. One of them made comparisons with a similar incident that had happened while he'd been stationed out in Singapore.

Now that she could see where she was aiming, Carole made another throw with her belt. The buckle landed right by Nick Kent's hand. He could easily have taken hold of it and had at least some link to the dry land.

But he didn't. His hands stayed resolutely on the mud.

He meant what he had said. He wasn't going to do anything to help himself. He did want to die.

The metal ladder boomed and shook as someone else came down to join her. 'We can get this rope to him,' said an elderly male voice she didn't recognize from somewhere above her head.

Carole squinted upwards. 'You'll have to lasso it round him. He's not cooperating.

'Damn it,' said the voice. 'I'll go and get some duckboards. Perhaps we can get across the mud to him.' The ladder shuddered again as he clambered back up and started shouting, 'Get some duckboards! Bloody kid's on a kamikaze mission! Won't help himself!'

These orders prompted more shouting from other elderly male voices. One advocated ringing the coastguard. One recommended a boathook under the boy's collar. A third said he remembered something similar happening when he'd been stationed out in Singapore. Denis Woodville could be heard saying he'd go to the nearest boat and try saving the boy from the water.

The reasons why managers need to go on management training courses were all too apparent. There was a serious plethora of chiefs, and a serious deficit of Indians.

Carole tried another flick across the void with her

Burberry belt. It slipped out of her cold fingers and lay, a dead snake, on the mud between them.

She couldn't see Nick's expression. While the old men above argued about the optimum escape plan, they had forgotten about keeping the light pointing down on to the mud.

But Carole could see less of Nick, there was no question about that. He was now embedded in the ooze up to his chest and had to hold his arms up to keep them free of its embrace. The tide was sending ever stronger waves against the outflow of the Fether, and, with each hissing onrush, the water level crept closer to the stranded boy.

Carole slipped out of her precious Burberry. 'Nick!' she called out, as softly as she dared against the rush of the water. 'Grab hold of my coat. Then I can hang on until help comes.'

She flipped the Burberry out, in the manner patented by Sir Walter Raleigh. It landed, chequered-lining down, flat against the slime. Demonstrating once again that the mind has scant regard for the gravity of situations, Carole found herself thinking of cleaning bills and wondering whether dry-cleaning would remove the waterproof qualities of the material.

The hem of the Burberry was almost touching Nick. He could easily have reached out and grabbed hold, taken a strong purchase on the cloth and given himself a chance.

Still, he did nothing.

'For God's sake, Nick!' Carole shouted in exasperation. 'Is this really how you want to die?'

'I don't care how it happens, so long as I die!' came back the petulant reply.

Carole took a deep breath. Once again, the thought came to her that Jude would do this better. But Jude wasn't here. Carole Seddon was the only person who could make the boy change his mind and start participating in his own rescue. And Carole Seddon was bloody well going to do it.

'If you die now, Nick,' she began in a firm, no-nonsense way, 'what would your father think?'

'Don't talk about my father!' he shrieked.

'Why not? I know he's not around at the moment . . .'

'You can say that again!'

' . . . but you used to be close. And if he comes back to find that you gave away your life in such a pathetic way as this, what's he going to think?'

'He's not going to come back! Can't you understand – he'll never come back! He's gone for good!'

Carole changed tack. 'All right. Say that's true . . . Say he never does come back . . . That means your mother will have lost one of the two men in her life for ever, and you're about to deprive her of the other. Think of her. Think what this'll do to Mummy.'

'It's better than telling her,' the boy countered doggedly. 'It's better than her finding out what happened.'

'For God's sake, Nick, she's your mother! Mothers were put on the earth to forgive their children – whatever they've done.'

'Not this.'

'Yes, even this, whatever it may be. The one thing a mother won't forgive is herself, if she allows one of her children to take his own life. She'll blame herself for that throughout the rest of her days. Is that the fate you want to condemn your mummy to?' There was silence. 'The fate that Aaron Spalding's mother's condemned to?'

Carole knew it had been a risk, and the boy definitely flinched at the name. At the same moment, a rogue wave, a bit ahead of itself, broke noisily behind him. The slap sent up a little column of spray which came down over his head, flattening his hair to a shiny skullcap.

Whether it was the imminent reality of his demise or Carole's arguments which swayed him, she would never know. All that mattered was that suddenly, convulsively, Nick Kent grabbed hold of the hem of the Burberry. Carole could feel the shock of his weight, the socket-wrenching tug on the arm that grasped the raincoat's collar, and the equally painful strain on the arm that was hooked round the ladder.

'OK, we're coming with the duckboards!' a self-important voice announced from the top of the sea wall. 'Easy does it. We'll just – oh, bugger!'

Carole heard something heavy rushing through the air, then a sound like a small fart as the object flumped into the mud. A slatted rectangle of duckboarding stuck upright at an angle out of the ooze. It was a good three yards away from both the ladder and the sinking boy.

Again, Carole's mind, with its poorly developed sense of occasion, demanded why, in a crisis of this kind, when the best help available was required, the rescue mission seemed to be in the hands of Dad's Army or the Keystone Cops?

From above, she could hear more argument. One pompous elderly voice was saying that duckboards weren't the answer, they should be throwing down a lifebelt. Another argued back that duckboards were the answer, but they needed to be lowered down on ropes. A third announced that a similar thing had happened when he'd been stationed out in Singapore.

'For Christ's sake!' Carole bawled upwards. 'Throw down a lifebelt, you stupid old fools!'

This prompted some huffing and puffing of the 'Not very ladylike' variety, but after a few seconds there was a cry of, 'Mind your heads!', and a halo of plastic-covered cork whirled down through the air.

With a squelch, the lifebelt came to rest on the mudflat, between the capsized duckboarding and the stranded boy. Though less than a yard away from him, Nick Kent could no more have reached it than he could have flown. Each inward swirl of water was now lapping over his shoulders.

There was another, 'Bugger!' from above, then, 'Let's see if we can work it round.'

Manipulating the lifebelt with its rope, an attempt was made to flip it nearer to the boy. The ring rose in the air, complaining against the suction of the mud, and then flopped down again, a yard nearer to the sea wall.

Carole couldn't reach it. Still she clutched desperately at her Burberry, feeling the dead weight at the other end. She longed to change her hold, unhook her other arm from the ladder and get a two-handed grip on the coat, but she didn't dare. There was no hope of pulling him out with the Burberry, but at least they were in contact.

Another bumptious wave came along and broke right over the boy's head. She heard him splutter as he got a mouthful of water. Coughing, he said, 'It's not going to work. I'm going to die here.'

'No, you're not,' said Carole firmly. 'Anyway, a few moments ago that's what you said you wanted to happen.'

'Not now.'

'Good.'

'We'll get you out of this,' Carole announced, though she wouldn't have liked to have the provenance of her confidence investigated.

There was another splutter from the boy as a new wave caught him. Either because of further slippage into the mud or because of the rising water, only his head was now visible, and that got covered by the crest of each incoming wave.

Above them on the sea wall, old men, reliving distantly remembered wartime actions, shouted and countermanded each other's orders. If they ever did get to the point of agreeing a course of action, it would be far too late for Nick Kent.

Carole was aware of the sound of a boat's motor putt-putting closer. Craning round from her Burberry tug-of-war posture, she saw a small wooden launch approaching. There were two men in it, though she could not identify them in the gloom.

The boat was certainly aiming for Nick, but looked unlikely to get there in time. The boy's head was now only intermittently visible between the waves. No more sounds of spluttering or protest came from his submerged mouth. Only the continuing tension on the Burberry told Carole he was still alive. But for how much longer?

There was a splash from the approaching boat and she was aware of something moving through the water. It was a man swimming.

Just as the swimmer approached the spot where Nick had been, Carole felt a jolt through her body. The countertension on the Burberry was gone. Nick Kent had let go.

The swimmer was splashing around in the water, fixing something. Then he shouted back to the boat. 'All right, he's breathing through the snorkel. Chuck the rope down!'

Carole knew the voice, but in the tension of the moment could not put a name to it.

The man on the launch did as he was told. There was a rattle of anchor cable and the note of the motor changed to idling. The swimmer kept bobbing beneath the surface, near where the boy had last been seen.

'OK,' the swimmer called out. 'Take the strain!'

It's hopeless, thought Carole. For one thing, the boy's probably already dead. For another, no elderly member of the Fethering Yacht Club is going to be strong enough to pull a body up against the suction of that mud.

But she had reckoned without a winch. As soon as she heard the clank of gearing and the screech of ratchets, she knew there was a chance.

The man on the launch worked the machinery,

the swimmer kept the boy's snorkel upright, as he eased the body out of its clammy prison. Winching and manhandling, they flipped the inert mass over the stern of the boat. At that moment there was a cheer from the armchair admirals on top of the sea wall. With remarkable agility, the swimmer then pulled himself up on board as well.

'Is he all right?' Carole called across the void. 'Is Nick all right?'

'Will be,' called the swimmer's familiar voice. 'Just get the water out of his lungs. He'll be fine.'

As the tension drained out of her, Carole realized that she had no strength left in her arms. It was all she could do to cling on to the ladder. The challenge of climbing back up it was insuperable.

'Hey!' she shouted. 'Could someone give me a hand up the ladder?'

This request seemed set to start a new debate as to which Fethering Yacht Club member should take on the task, and what would be the best way of approaching it, but fortunately a rough voice cut through the cackle. 'I'll get her.'

Carole felt the ringing through the tubes of the ladder as a heavy body descended. When she felt his strong arms safely cradling her, she said tartly, 'You were supposed to meet me at seven, Ted Crisp.'

'Oh, really? I thought you said eight.'

'Honestly!'

'Why? Did I miss much?'

There are some questions, Carole thought, that aren't worth answering.

Looking down at the Burberry still gripped firmly

in her hand, Ted Crisp said, 'Aren't you going to chuck that filthy old thing?'

'Certainly not! Ooh, and could you manage to reach the belt down there?'

By swinging ape-like from the bottom rung and trailing his large foot across the mud, he managed to hook up the belt. He handed it across to her. 'There you are, madam. Your natural elegance restored.'

'Thank you.'

'Though it's about to be shot to pieces again by me giving you a fireman's lift.' And he slung her over his shoulder.

Carole got a little cheer from Dad's Navy when she was dumped unceremoniously on top of the sea wall. But her immediate concern was what was happening in the boat below.

One of the Fethering Yacht Club members proved he could do something right by turning the broad beam of his torch down to the little launch.

The bedraggled figure of Nick Kent looked very unsteady, but at least he was upright. He gave Carole a wave and a sheepish little grin.

Standing either side of him were Denis Woodville and, soaked to the skin but triumphant, Bill Chilcott.

Chapter Thirty-six

'My friend Carole and I have been working it out, you see,' Jude explained. 'We've got these two deaths and a disappearance. There's the body you found, Tanya – the one you refuse to tell me more about. There's Aaron Spalding, who committed suicide. And then there's the dentist, Rory Turnbull, who we're meant to think has committed suicide.'

The girl had looked frankly bored throughout the speech, but the last words lit a spark of interest. 'What do you mean by that?'

'You know Rory Turnbull, don't you, Tanya?'

'Sure.' She was about to say more, but changed her mind. Sullenly, she went on, 'He was Treasurer down the Yacht Club. I saw him there quite often.'

'And he sometimes gave you a lift from Brighton to Fethering for your evening shifts, didn't he?'

She was surprised. 'How'd you know that?'

Jude shrugged. 'You can find out most things if you ask around enough. Tanya, when did you last see Rory Turnbull?'

The girl coloured. 'I don't know. I finished working at the Yacht Club Friday before last . . . Round then, I suppose.'

'You're sure you haven't seen him since?'

'No. Where would I have seen him?'

The answers sounded clumsy, but then the girl's normal manner was clumsy. Jude couldn't be absolutely certain that she was lying.

'Anyway,' Tanya went on, 'I couldn't have seen him the last few days, 'cause he gone missing, hasn't he?'

'How do you know that?'

'It's common knowledge.'

'Common knowledge in Fethering. I wouldn't have thought it got talked about much in Brighton.'

'I'm still in touch with people from Fethering. Denis Woodville told me.'

'I see.'

Petulantly, the girl kicked at the carpet with one black-booted foot. 'Anyway, what's all this about? Where's it all leading? Is there something you definitely know about this body I saw on the beach?'

'There are two things I definitely know. One is that there is a connection between the body on the beach and Rory Turnbull. And the other is that Rory Turnbull is still alive.'

'Well, you're right in at least one of those.'

The bathroom door had opened silently and there was a third person in the room.

Rory Turnbull.

Chapter Thirty-seven

Maggie Kent arrived at the sea wall just after Carole had been deposited there by Ted Crisp. Which was probably just as well. In time she would hear the details of how close her son had come to death, but at least she had not had to witness the agony of the previous half-hour.

Moments later, the three from the motor launch disembarked at the floating jetty a little further upstream and Nick Kent, with a grubby blanket wrapped around him, was led by Denis Woodville and Bill Chilcott towards the waiting group. Carole and Maggie hurried forward to greet him. The mother, oblivious to the filth in which he was covered, threw her arms around her son. Both of them sobbed.

'You two did brilliantly,' said Carole to the rescuers. 'Amazing bit of cooperation and coordination.'

'Only did it because my boat was the closest,' said Bill Chilcott gruffly.

The Vice-Commodore's reaction was equally ungracious. 'Yes, in an emergency you can't choose the people you have to work with.'

There was a silence. A moment of potential rapprochement between the two sides of the feud . . .?

It seemed not. 'I must get this incident entered in the club log.' Denis Woodville turned abruptly on his heel and set off towards his cronies.

'And I must get out of these wet clothes.' Equally abruptly, Bill Chilcott turned in the opposite direction and strutted off squelching on his way back home.

Carole moved across to the muddy embrace of mother and son. Nick had stopped sobbing, but his breath was coming out in little jerky wheezes. 'Should I call an ambulance, Maggie, or get him to a doctor?'

'No, I don't want him to get caught up in hospitals and all that. Nick's freezing cold and he's had a terrible shock. I just want to get him home, get him into a hot bath and clean him up. Then, if there's anything wrong with him, I'll call the GP.' Maggie Kent looked dubiously at the crowd of elderly campaigners still clustered by the Yacht Club. 'Wish I could smuggle him away without talking to anyone.'

'I'll give you a lift,' said Carole.

She fixed a meeting point and five minutes later was back in the Renault to pick them up. Carole hadn't even wiped the mud off her own shoes and she made no demur as the slime-covered boy in his filthy blanket was laid across the precious upholstery of her back seat.

Maggie Kent ushered Carole into the bleak front room. 'Would you like a coffee or something? I'd offer you a real drink, but I'm afraid I don't have anything.'

'Don't worry. You just go and sort Nick out.'

'Yes. He's gone up to start the bath. There's lots of hot water. I'll give him a good scrubbing.'

'And, Maggie . . .'

'Yes?'

'It's not my business, but if I were you I wouldn't ask him about what happened. He'll tell you when he wants to.'

The mother nodded. 'I'd already decided that.'

'Good.'

'But would you mind staying till I've put him to bed? I'd like to hear your account of what happened.'

Carole couldn't say no, could she? 'That's fine.' She took a look at her watch. 'But may I use your telephone?'

It was the moment after Rory Turnbull had appeared from the bathroom, before Jude had had time to recover from her surprise and say anything, that her mobile rang. She snatched the phone immediately out of her pocket. 'Hello?'

'Jude, it's Carole. Nick Kent's all right.'

'Thank God. Listen, I've found—'

But the mobile was ripped from her hand and switched off. 'I don't think you need tell anyone what you've found,' Rory Turnbull said coolly.

As someone who'd never possessed a mobile phone, Carole's image of their technology was out of date. They were unreliable machines, prone to constant loss of signal and other breakdowns. So she wasn't that surprised to have been cut off.

She used the last-number redial on Maggie's phone. The ringing went on for some time, then a bloodlessly polite voice informed her that the caller was not responding, but she had the option of leaving a message.

There didn't seem much point. Jude had definitely heard her say that Nick was all right. That was the important news. Anything else would keep.

Odd, though. One moment Jude was answering her phone; a moment later, even though their conversation had been unfinished, she'd switched it off.

Maybe another vagary of mobile-phone technology . . . The explanation gave Carole reassurance. Partial reassurance.

Three-quarters of an hour had elapsed before Maggie Kent came back downstairs. 'I've got the worst of it off him. It'll take another few weeks of baths – or possibly a course of sandblasting – to get it all out of his pores, but he's OK.'

'You don't need to call the doctor?'

'I think all Nick needs is a lot of sleep. He's tucked up in bed and I've given him one of my sleeping pills. I'll get him a hot-water bottle. But he did want to have a word with you – just to say thank you.'

'Fine.' Carole rose to her feet, but Maggie still lingered in the doorway, not yet ready to lead her upstairs. 'What is it?'

'It's just . . . tell me . . . did Nick really try to kill himself?'

Carole answered with complete honesty. 'He thought that's what he wanted to do, yes. But when he got close to the reality, he changed his mind. He thought of the effect it would have on you and he couldn't allow himself to do it.'

'Good.' Some of the tension eased from Maggie Kent's shoulders and a warmth came into her tired face. 'Let's go up and see him.'

The decor of Nick Kent's room was the perfect illustration of a life poised uneasily between the pulls of the child and the adult. A poster of the Manchester United football team on one wall was having a face-off with the pouting images of the latest girl band on the other. A copy of *GFH* lay on top of an *Asterix*. Flashy deodorants and 'men's toiletries' stood side by side with Coca-Cola bottles.

Nick was propped up on pillows under a duvet with a Manchester United cover. He looked exhausted but calm. His scrubbed face bore the soft glow of childhood. His eyelids flickered. He would soon be asleep.

'I just wanted to say thank you very much,' he slurred. 'Wanted to thank you . . . should've thanked the men who pulled me out . . . didn't thank them properly . . .'

'Don't worry. There'll be plenty of time to do that.'

There was a shelf of treasures by the boy's bedhead and on it Carole saw something which unleashed a landslide of explanations. Among Subbuteo footballers, swimming certificates and snaps of leering boys from some long-past school trip stood a framed photograph.

It showed a smiling, grey-haired man in his late forties. Undoubtedly the missing Sam Kent.

And also undoubtedly, in spite of the fact that in the photograph he had no tooth missing, the man whose body Carole Seddon had found on Fethering beach.

Chapter Thirty-eight

'Well, thank you,' said Jude, 'for interrupting my phone call.'

Rory Turnbull put the turned-off mobile down on a table. 'Some people believe it's bad manners to take calls on mobiles in other people's homes.'

'Possibly. But that's not why you switched it off, was it?'

'No.' He moved to stand, almost protectively, behind Tanya's chair.

Jude took in the pair of them. The dentist looked less raddled than he had when she last saw him in the Crown and Anchor. For the first time, there was some confidence about him, the successful professional in his early fifties. Beside him, the lumpen girl in her crumpled black, surprisingly, did not look out of place.

'So you two are an item,' said Jude.

Rory looked as if he might have denied it, but Tanya responded instantly, 'Yeah, all right, and what if we are? He's a good man, first man I ever met who actually cares about me, isn't just trying to use me. What's wrong with that?'

'Nothing. There's nothing wrong with love.'

'Then why are you here . . . what's your name – Jude?' asked Rory.

'Jude, yes. There could be a lot of answers to why I'm here, but let's start with the fact that everyone who knows you thinks you've committed suicide. You did leave a note to that effect. The police have been searching for you for days.'

'I know.'

'Well, wouldn't you say that justifies a degree of curiosity? Why does someone want to stage his own death? And what might that deception have to do with the body that was found on Fethering Beach last Tuesday? I assume I don't have to explain to you which body I'm talking about? I'm taking it for granted you were listening from behind the bathroom door?'

'You're right. I encouraged Tanya to get you talking to find out how much you knew.'

A couple of details at least were explained – why Tanya had changed her reaction the second time Jude had phoned and the girl's long absence in the bathroom early on in their interview.

'And how much do you reckon I do know?' asked Jude coolly. She recognized that her situation was uncomfortable but was trying to work out whether or not it was dangerous.

'You tell me,' Rory replied. 'You've clearly made some connections. The fact that you're here and the fact that you're talking about the body demonstrate that. But how much else have you pieced together?'

'Well . . .' She hadn't pieced much together until that moment, but suddenly certain conclusions became glaringly obvious. 'If, on the one hand, you have a middle-aged man who, with maximum publicity, has declared he is about to commit suicide . . . and, on the other hand, you have the body of a second middle-aged man of similar build . . . I might suspect some substitution of bodies was being contemplated.'

There was a sharp breath from Tanya, but Rory neither confirmed nor denied the conjecture. He waited to see what else Jude was going to say.

'I don't know how the apparent death would be staged. In a car, I imagine. But not exhaust fumes. No, it has to be a method that would disfigure the corpse sufficiently to make identification difficult. Fire would probably be best. Body wearing Rory Turnbull's clothes found in burnt-out car belonging to Rory Turnbull, body must belong to Rory Turnbull. God knows the poor man had enough reasons to do away with himself. The heroin habit that was ruining him financially, leading him to remortgage his house, put his hand in the till at the Yacht Club, try to cheat the Dental Estimates Board . . . Many men have killed themselves to avoid lesser ruin than that little accumulation. Open and shut case.'

Rory Turnbull nodded slowly. 'Yes. You have done well, haven't you?'

Tanya had been silent too long. 'All right, so what's wrong with all that? It hasn't done anyone any harm, has it?'

'What about Rory's wife, Barbara?'

'That frigid bitch deserves everything that's coming to her! She's never given Rory anything all the time they've been married, just sucked out his lifeblood. And she'll be cushioned by her mother's money, whatever happens. She's not suffering from this.'

'All right, Tanya, putting Barbara on one side . . . what about the dead man? The one who would so obligingly pretend to be Rory? Are you telling me he didn't suffer either?'

'Only the suffering he brought on himself,' the girl snapped. 'He was a waster, out of his head on heroin, who just hung around the beach all the time. And then one day – Monday before last – he took an overdose and Rory just happened to be the one who found the body.' She looked at her lover with devout admiration. 'At that moment Rory saw a way out of all our troubles. It was then the whole substitution plan came into his mind and he brought the body back here.'

'But surely—'

'Tanya!' said Rory firmly. 'I think we could do with something to drink.'

'There's some white wine in the fridge.'

'No. Whisky.' He reached for his wallet and extracted a twenty-pound note. 'Could you go down to the off-licence and get a litre of Grouse?'

'But—'

'Now.'

She didn't argue any more, but rose to her feet. Putting his arms gently on her broad shoulders, Rory planted a little kiss on her forehead. 'Take care.'

'And you.'

Tanya flipped her shiny green anorak off a hook on the back of the door and left the bedsitter.

'She's pregnant, isn't she?' said Jude.

'Yes. How did you know?'

'I should have worked it out earlier from the fact that she'd gone off coffee, but what made me certain was the way you touched her just then, your concern for her, as if she was very fragile.'

'All right. So she's pregnant. What have you got to say about that?'

'Nothing. Except I assume that's the reason why you set this whole thing up?'

'The final reason, yes. The other reasons had been building for years.'

'Rory, men leave their wives for younger women every day of the week. Very few of them bother to set up mock-suicides to cover their tracks. Why didn't you just talk to Barbara, tell her you wanted out?'

'I couldn't do that!' A pallid transformation came over the dentist's face and Jude realized the extent of the terror he felt for his wife. 'Barbara would never have let me get away. And if she thought I was still alive, anywhere in the world, she'd come and find me. No, I've always known I'd only be safe if she thought I was dead.'

'So you really reckoned you could start over?'

'Not reckon*ed* – reckon. It's still going to happen. Tanya and I are going to live together in France and bring up our babies there. I've been salting away the money for months.'

The gleam in Rory's eyes showed Jude how much he was caught up in his fantasies, how long he'd been nursing them, and how potent to the middle-aged was the chimera of one last chance, the opportunity to wipe the slate clean and make a fresh start. It also showed Jude that the man she was dealing with was not entirely sane.

'Tanya was meant to come into my life,' he went on. 'It's been a long time coming, and there's been a lot of shit along the way, but she was meant to happen to me. She's wonderful. She's the first woman I've ever known who hasn't expected anything from me. Anything I give her she regards as a bonus. She has no *aspirations* for me.'

The fervour with which he said the word bore witness to the agony of the years Barbara and her mother had spent trying to 'make something' of Rory Turnbull. Part of Jude could empathize with his need to take action, do anything that would break him out of that straitjacket, out of the suffocating aspirational gentility of the Shorelands Estate.

'Me and Tanya,' Rory Turnbull concluded proudly, 'is a love match.'

And Jude could see how it was. Two damaged people who had asked for very little and been more abundantly rewarded than they'd ever dared to hope.

Appealing though this image was, it did not change the facts. 'I'm sure it is a love match,' said Jude, 'but does that justify murder?'

He gave her a pained look. 'Tanya told you. The man died of an overdose.'

'No. Tanya may well believe that, because it doesn't occur to her to question anything you tell her, but it doesn't work for me. The logic isn't there. This whole business has taken months of planning. Your cheating the NHS, your fiddling the Yacht Club accounts, planting the idea of your heroin habit, that's all long-term stuff. I'm afraid I don't believe you set it all up, on the off chance that, when the time came – the Monday before last – you'd stumble across a body the right age and shape who'd just conveniently died of an overdose. Sorry, call me old-fashioned, but I don't buy that. You'd targeted the man for months.'

'All right.' He made the confession lightly. 'Yes, I saw him first in the summer, down by the pier when I went for a walk one lunchtime. He asked me for money. I gave him some and thought how wretched he was – a man about my age, about my size, and he was reduced to that. And then I thought that, though I'd got all the things he hadn't – the money, the job, the house – I was even more wretched than he was. It was round the time I'd started seeing Tanya. I was still at that stage trying to behave correctly, trying to *do the decent thing* – and it was tearing me apart.

'I saw the man a few times after that – just walked past him, maybe gave him money, maybe didn't – but it was only when I knew Tanya was pregnant that the plan began to form in my mind. And, the more I thought about it, the more it started to obsess me.'

Yes, thought Jude, that's the word – obsess.

'And, of course, because Tanya was pregnant, there was a time pressure. There were a lot of time pressures.'

'The Dental Estimates Board, the Fethering Yacht Club accountants . . .'

'All that.'

'So how did you kill him? Where did you kill him?'

'Here. I'd sent Tanya out to the cinema. She loves movies – particularly weepies. I'd given him the money for a lot of heroin. He'd had a hit. He was feeling good. I smothered him – ' he gestured to the bed – 'with that pillow.' Rory read disapproval in Jude's expression. 'Go on, he died happy. Better than the way it would have happened otherwise. Contaminated drugs . . . a fight with another addict . . . an infected needle . . . with someone like that it was only a matter of time. He was already lost.'

'No one's lost, Rory. Not even at the very end. Anyway, didn't you think who he was?'

'I didn't know who he was.'

'He was a human being.'

'He didn't matter.'

She was silent for a moment before asking, 'And what made you change your plans?'

'Change my plans?'

'Yes. For your plan to work, the suicide in the car had to be staged as soon as possible after the man had died. The longer you left it, the more the body would decay and the more open your deception would be to exposure by forensic examination. Why didn't you do it the night you killed him?'

Rory Turnbull grimaced. 'Because of the bloody police.'

'What? Surely they didn't know what you were up to?'

'No. The trouble was I wanted to leave it fairly late, so that there wouldn't be many people around. But he'd died about six and—'

'You mean you'd killed him about six.'

'Whatever. There's a garage in this block that's hardly used – that's where my car is at the moment, actually. By midnight, which was the time intended to take the body down there, it had started to stiffen up.'

'Rigor mortis.'

'Yes. I'd meant to put him in the boot, but I didn't want to risk giving the body any unexplained injuries by bending the joints, so I just laid him on the back seat with a coat over him. I left Tanya here, as we'd agreed – we were going to meet in France a week or so later – and I set off. Just on the outskirts of Fethering, a car came towards me, flashing its lights.'

'Bill Chilcott.'

'Yes. I thought driving off at speed would draw more attention than stopping, so I stopped. Bill was just being charitable. He told me there were police staking out Seaview Road and stopping every car that came along. Random breath-tests – Sussex Police are very hot on drink-driving. Well, that really got me scared, because there's no other way to the Shorelands Estate except via Seaview Road.'

'But why did you have to go home?'

'Because that's how I'd planned it!' he snapped petulantly. 'The petrol and the rags and stuff I was going to use were all in the garage at Brigadoon.'

'Were you actually planning to stage your suicide in your own home?'

'Yes. On the paved area in front of the house.' A vindictive light burned in his eye. 'Very fitting – show all the tight-arsed snobs of the Shorelands Estate what Barbara and her bloody mother had driven me to. I thought that'd be very funny. A social indiscretion on that scale . . . they'd really find hard to live down.'

No, thought Jude, I am not dealing here with someone who's even mildly sane.

'Anyway, I panicked. I daren't risk the police looking inside the car. I decided I couldn't go through with the plan that night, so—'

'So you hid the body inside your boat at the Fethering Yacht Club.'

'Yes, I – How the hell did you know that?'

'Call it educated guesswork. And did you put the life-jacket on it?'

'Yes.'

'Why?'

'I don't know. I just thought, if anyone found the body, it might look more like an accident. I wasn't thinking straight.'

'You certainly weren't,' said Jude coolly. 'My next educated guess, incidentally, would be that you went home and the following morning early, terrified that someone might have found the body overnight, rang Tanya and asked her to go to Fethering and check it was where you'd left it.'

The dentist looked bewildered. 'Did she tell you this?'

'No. I think Tanya looked and the body was missing. But shortly afterwards she found it washed up on the beach. She went to ring you and tell you what had happened. Then two small boys—'

'What?' He turned pale. 'How do you know all this stuff? Are you psychic?'

'A bit,' said Jude, with a self-effacing grin, 'though, as it happens, that's not how I know. So, did Tanya see the boys had put the body back in the boat?'

'Yes.'

'Which meant your plan was all set to happen again, a mere twenty-four hours late. Body back in place, no police breathalyzer traps . . . Why didn't you do it on the Tuesday night?'

'Because I was disturbed by somebody. I'd just got the body out of the boat when I heard a noise. There was someone snooping around. A boy.'

'Do you think he saw you?'

'Yes. Just as I was lifting the body out of the boat. I was holding it in front of me and I came face to face with the boy. He screamed.'

Yes, he would have done, thought Jude. Poor Aaron Spalding, his head filled with half-digested stories of black magic and the Undead. The boy, tortured by guilt, had come back to check the scene of his crime and seen the dead body apparently moving. The Undead had come back to claim its victim. That could easily have been enough to unhinge the terrified Aaron, to make him throw himself into the Fether. Unless, of course . . . 'You didn't harm the boy, did you, Rory?'

'No, of course I didn't! I don't know what happened to him. He ran off along the river bank. He'd got me rattled, though, so I put my plans off for another twenty-four hours.'

'But because other people knew the body had been stowed inside *Brigadoon II*, you moved it to another hiding place.'

Once again he gave her a look as if she had unnatural powers. 'Are you sure Tanya didn't tell you all this?'

'Positive. Don't worry, she'd never betray you.'

'More educated guesswork then?'

'If you like. I'd say you put the body inside one of those blue fishermen's boxes near the Yacht Club . . .' A hissed intake of breath told her she'd hit another mark ' . . . little knowing that the next morning that whole area would be cordoned off and under the blaze of spotlights while the workmen carried out repairs on the sea wall.'

Rory's expression acknowledged the accuracy of this conjecture too.

'So, what with one thing and another,' Jude concluded lightly, 'it wasn't really that great a plan, was it?'

She'd caught him on the raw. 'It was a brilliant plan!' he spat back.

'Oh, I don't think you can use the word "brilliant" for any plan that has to be aborted.'

'This one's not going to be aborted.'

'You mean you're still thinking of going ahead with it?'

'Oh yes. I'm going ahead with it. Tonight. Only this time, Jude . . .' He savoured the name as if it had an unfamiliar but not unpleasant taste ' . . . you're going to be part of the plan.'

Chapter Thirty-nine

When Carole got back home from Maggie Kent's house, she felt quite shaken. Having garaged the Renault – and not even considered cleaning its interior until the morning – she found she was shivering as she walked the short distance to the house. Inside, even before attending to Gulliver's needs, she turned up the central heating and lit the log-effect gas fire. Then, once the dog was sorted, she poured herself an uncharacteristically large Scotch from the bottle which she kept for guests and which sometimes went untouched from one Christmas to the next.

It wasn't only her physical ordeal that had shaken her up. It was the discovery she had made in Nick Kent's bedroom. Now she knew the identity of the body she'd found, she could understand the reasons for the boy's mental collapse. To have been involved in a black magic ritual with a corpse was bad enough, but to discover in the cold light of the following morning that the body you had seen mutilated was that of your idolized father would have unhinged the most stable of adults. The effect it had had on a confused adolescent was all too predictable.

Thank God at least that Nick had held back from wielding the Stanley knife himself.

Carole hadn't said anything to Maggie. The awful truth would have to be faced at some point, but it should wait until the body had once again been found. And then the news should be broken to the unknowing widow by the proper authorities.

Carole was reminded that she had intended to spend that evening with Ted Crisp trying to find the body, but after all she been through another visit to the sea wall in search of a week-old corpse held little appeal. While the body on the beach remained anonymous, there had been an almost game-like quality to the investigations she and Jude had undertaken. But now the dead man possessed an identity and a family context, the idea of further probing became distasteful.

She decided she'd done quite enough for that evening. Maybe Jude would ring her or call round when she got back from Brighton. In the meantime, however, Carole Seddon was going to have a very long soak in a very hot bath.

Jude lay on the back seat of the BMW, where the body she did not know to be that of Sam Kent had lain a week before.

When Tanya had returned to her bedsitter with the whisky, Rory had got her to help tie Jude up. With soft scarves, over her clothes, so as not to leave any marks on her body.

Then Rory and Tanya had manhandled her down

to the garage and into the BMW. More scarves had been used to tie her wrists and ankles to the armrests, so that she couldn't sit up and attract attention to herself when they were driving. Rory had not bothered to gag her. The car was soundproof.

Jude had been left in the garage for nearly an hour, while the two conspirators presumably went through the final details of their forthcoming elopement, their separate journeys and their blissful reunion in France.

As she lay immobile in the dark, Jude could not feel optimistic. Assessing the feasibility of escape did not take long. Once she'd given up on that, she tried, with limited success, to focus on more spiritual matters. But anger kept getting in the way. This was neither the time nor the manner in which Jude wanted to die.

Bill Chilcott appeared in the Crown and Anchor a little later than usual that evening for his customary half. And, also uncharacteristically, he brought his wife with him. He looked sleekly bathed, the white bits of his turnip head gleaming from a recent shampooing. Sandra was also carefully groomed and both looked smug. They had clearly come to receive the plaudits of a grateful nation.

Over in the Fethering Yacht Club, Ted Crisp reckoned, Denis Woodville would also be reliving his triumphant part in the rescue. And no doubt being upstaged by other ideas of how it should have been done and recollections of similar incidents out in Singapore.

Bill Chilcott was a little miffed to find the Crown and Anchor bar rather empty. And no evidence of anyone who knew about his heroism.

Ted Crisp did his best to make up the deficiency. 'Full marks for what you done out there, Bill. What is it – your "customary half"? Or will you go mad and make it a pint?'

'Well, as it is a rather special occasion . . .'

'Sure. Have this on me. And what about you, Sandra?'

'Ooh, a dry sherry, please, Ted.'

'None the worse for your adventure, Bill?'

'Good heavens, no. Sandra and I do work hard on our fitness. All that regular swimming down at the Leisure Centre has certainly paid off tonight.'

'Not to mention our line-dancing.'

'No, no, don't let's forget the line-dancing. No, Sandra and I don't give in to *anno domini*. Did you hear how that dreadful man Denis Woodville was wheezing during the rescue? And he didn't swim. He only worked the mechanical winch.'

'Well, he smokes like a chimney, doesn't he, Bill?'

'Yes, Sandra, filthy habit. So unhealthy. All his arteries must be totally furred up. If you want my opinion, he'll just keel over one day.'

'And good riddance, that's what Bill and I say!'

'Thought you might,' Ted Crisp murmured. 'But the boy was all right, was he? None the worse for his ordeal?'

'I don't know,' Bill Chilcott replied. 'He went off with his mother in Carole Seddon's car.'

'Oh, is that what happened?' The landlord scratched his chin through the thickets of his beard. 'You know, I might just give Carole a call to see that the lad's OK . . .'

When Rory Turnbull finally did return to his prisoner in the car, he seemed blithe, almost euphoric. He was alone. He opened the garage doors, drove the BMW out and closed them again, before setting off at a steady pace west out of Brighton.

At least Jude could speak. She could try to reason for her life. Anything was worth trying. Without much hope, she announced, 'It won't work, you know, Rory.'

'Oh, it will.'

'The body's been dead a week.'

'But the weather's been on my side. Below freezing most of the last few days.'

'It'll still be obvious he died a week ago. The most basic of post-mortems'll show that – regardless of how much the body's disfigured by the fire.'

'I'm sure you're right. No, it wouldn't work . . . if fire was the method I was going to use.'

'You're not?'

'No. Change of plan, due to change of circumstances. Always pays to be flexible in one's planning, you know.' There was a heady, almost manic, confidence about him now. 'By the time the body's found, nobody'll be able to give a precise date of death. All they'll have to identify him by will be the fact he's in my car, he's wearing my clothes . . . and, of course,' he concluded smugly, 'they'll be able to check his dental work.'

'My God! The missing tooth. Did you . . .'

'Oh yes.' He was very full of himself now. 'I told you, I've been planning this for a long time. I don't know how he'd lost his tooth, but as soon as I noticed it I knew what I had to do.'

'You actually took out one of your own teeth?'

'Not difficult for someone of my profession. I made up some story to Barbara about having been in a fight, which fitted in well with the image of general social collapse that I was creating. And then I had a rather distinctive chromium cobalt denture made for me by our usual lab. They always put their own identification mark on all the stuff they make, so there'd be no question it was mine. And the plate also fits into the dead man's mouth well enough.'

Remembering something that Holly the hygienist had said in what seemed like a previous incarnation but was in fact only that morning, Jude murmured, 'You actually had him in your surgery to check that it fitted?'

'Yes. It was a risk, but I did it after hours. Pretended I was helping him out of charity. He didn't care. So long as I gave him a bit of money to buy heroin, he'd have done anything I wanted, anything. When I offered him money for his passport, he found it and handed it over like a lamb.'

'That's how you set up savings accounts, isn't

it? In his name. You used the passport for identification.'

'Oh yes,' he said smugly.

'You've really put a lot of planning into this, haven't you, Rory?'

'I certainly have.' Oblivious to her irony, he took it as a straight compliment, and the way he spoke stole away Jude's last shred of hope. Rory Turnbull was impervious to logic. His elaborate scheme would almost definitely not work, his subterfuges would be unmasked by scientific examination, but that didn't matter. He was so caught up in the fantasy of his plan that he was going to go through with it regardless of anything.

'You said,' Jude began with trepidation, 'you weren't going to use fire . . .'

'No. Not fire. The wreckage'd be found too quickly, which might prove . . . forensically embarrassing. No, I want the car to be discovered in a few weeks' time . . . after the fish have taken some of the flesh off the bodies.'

'Bod*ies*?' she echoed softly.

'Yes. I'm afraid, my dear Jude, you know far too much about what I've been up to for me to let you survive. But, fortunately, there has been a rumour around during the last week that I might have had another woman . . .' A rumour that Carole and I helped to foster, thought Jude bitterly, as Rory went on, 'Tanya heard about it from old Denis Woodville. And Ted Crisp in the pub suggested last week that you and I might be an item.'

'He was joking.'

'Many a true word . . . Or at least that's how it'll seem in retrospect. The doomed love affair. The suicide pact. The only way the two of them could be together. Which was of course why Rory Turnbull drove himself and his lover to their deaths off the sea wall at Fethering.'

Chapter Forty

The night was still and colder now. A thin moon diffused its watery glow over the snug houses of Fethering, in which, one by one, the lights were being switched off.

The BMW stopped outside the gates that led to the Yacht Club launching ramp and gave access to the sea wall. Rory Turnbull calmly got out and opened the lock with his member's key. Back in the car, he said, 'I'll close the gates when I leave. On foot. And, I'm sorry to say, alone.'

He edged the car forward till it was alongside one of the fishermen's chests. He was eager now and leapt out, leaving the door ajar.

Jude could not see as Rory took out his keys. Nor could she see him insert one into the new padlock he'd substituted for the one sawn off the previous Tuesday night. The padlock opened and he slipped it out of the hasp that held the chest's top down.

As he raised the lid, he caught a foul whiff of decay, but he was too near to his goal to be put off by such a detail. Reaching into the chest, he took a grip on the Fethering Yacht Club life-jacket which was still fixed around the torso of the late Sam Kent.

With sudden strength and in one movement, Rory Turnbull lifted the body out. For a moment he held the putrid flesh against his own body, almost as if it were a lover. Then he laid the body flat on the cement. With both hands, he forced the stiff dead jaws apart. He reached inside his own mouth and removed his dental plate. He fixed it inside the dead man's mouth.

The body had bloated and was bursting out of its clothes, but that did not stop the dentist from starting to remove them. The dead man's clothes would be destroyed and he himself would dress in a spare set he had in the car boot. He had thought it all through. For his plan to work – his precious plan that he had been nurturing for so long – the body when found must be dressed as Rory Turnbull.

'What are you doing, Rory?'

Ted Crisp rose over the side of the sea wall like an avenging fury from the ladder to which he had been clinging. At the same time Carole appeared from the shadows of the Yacht Club. When the landlord had phoned, her curiosity had proved stronger than her exhaustion.

Hearing voices, Jude shouted for help.

'You bastard! I'm not going to be stopped now!'

Rory Turnbull launched himself ferociously at the landlord. The initial impetus caught Ted off balance. For a moment he swayed, about to topple back into the Fether.

But somehow he regained his equilibrium and enfolded the furious dentist in a bear hug. Rory's elbows worked like pistons as he slammed punches into Ted's substantial paunch. The two men weaved around like one crazed four-legged creature on the edge of the sea wall.

Carole meanwhile had freed Jude from the armrests and manoeuvred her out of the BMW to release her other bonds. As soon as her hands were free, Jude threw her arms around her friend. They stood for a moment, instinctively hugging each other. Then Jude reached into the front seat of the car for her mobile phone. 'I'm calling the police!' she said.

There was a grunt and the two fighting men were suddenly apart. Rory Turnbull swung a wild haymaker of a punch, which by pure chance caught Ted Crisp on the tip of the chin and sent him flying across the cement.

Freed, the dentist rushed to pick up his precious body. Grasping it under the arms, he dragged it across to the BMW. Carole and Jude watched in amazement as he opened the passenger door and jammed the corpse into its seat. He slammed the door shut and hurried round to the other side.

'You're mad, Rory!' Jude shouted. 'You'll never get away with it!'

'Yes, I will!' he shrieked back. 'I've got it all planned out! I told you – I've got it all planned out!'

He started the engine and the BMW screeched in reverse back through the Fethering Yacht Club gates. In a howl of tyres he turned it round and shot off fast down the quayside road.

Far too fast. Rory Turnbull misjudged the corner and bounced off a concrete bollard. The BMW spun crazily before smashing into the Second World War mine that was used as a charity collecting box. With the impact, the car burst into flames.

When the wreckage was examined by the police, their first impression was that there were two near-identical bodies in the burnt-out car. In the mouth of one of them was a dental plate which had been specially made for Rory Turnbull.

Detailed post-mortem examination, however, revealed that the body with the dental plate had been dead for at least a week before the crash which killed the dentist.

Chapter Forty-one

'The ironical thing is,' said Ted Crisp, 'that because Rory died in a car crash, rather than in an apparent suicide, Barbara will actually benefit from his insurance policies.'

'And presumably inherit all that money he'd salted away,' said Jude.

'Except,' Carole pointed out, 'all that money is in accounts that he'd opened using Sam Kent's passport and so probably in Sam Kent's name.'

'Does that mean the Kents'll benefit? That'd be wonderful news. At least they'd get something positive out of the whole ghastly experience.'

But Carole threw a wet blanket over Jude's optimism. 'No. The accounts would have been set up illegally. I'm sure it'll all go back to Barbara in the end.'

Ted Crisp shook his shaggy head. 'Whole thing'll take one hell of a lot of sorting out. Still, I should think Barbara and Winnie are ecstatic. They've got shot of Rory and the details of what he was up to will never become public knowledge. Their version of events will become the official version. As Winnie will continue to say to anyone who'll listen, Barbara was just very unlucky in her choice of husband.'

Jude picked up the train of thought. 'The poor woman worked valiantly to "make something of him", but sadly "you can't make silk purses out of sow's ears". Barbara and Winnie's image of middle-class gentility will survive untarnished. The high values of the Shorelands Estate will be maintained.'

The landlord shuddered. 'When I think what that poor bastard Rory must've suffered in that marriage. Being diminished all the time, having every last shred of confidence removed by those two harpies.' Another tremor went through him. 'Sorry, it's a man thing. You two haven't got the physical equipment to understand what it's like to be systematically emasculated.'

'No,' Jude agreed softly, 'but we can empathize. Anyone who's been in a relationship where one partner blames the other for their own inadequacies knows the kind of pain involved. Strange how it keeps happening. There are enough unpleasant people out there in the world to cut you down to size. What everyone needs at home is someone to support and bolster them.'

Carole had got so used to these enigmatic references to Jude's past that she no longer felt a burning urge to ask the instinctive supplementary questions. Well, that is to say, she still felt the urge, but now automatically curbed it.

A week or so had passed since the dramatic events on the sea wall. Carole was wearing her freshly cleaned Burberry. The dry-cleaning, she was delighted to find, had not affected its waterproof qualities at all.

'Have you seen Maggie again, Jude?'

'Yes. I dropped in this afternoon.'

'How's she coping?'

Jude grimaced. 'It's going to be tough, but she'll come through it.'

'Yes.'

'And Nick?'

'He's being brilliant, she said. He's a good, bright boy. Whatever else all this has done, it's certainly brought those two closer together.'

'Excellent.' Carole wondered whether the boy would ever tell his mother the worst part of his nightmare, witnessing the mutilation of what he later found to be his own father's body. Probably not, she thought. But that would be Nick Kent's own decision, and she reckoned that when the time came he'd be mature enough to make it.

Carole considered whether she herself should call on Maggie. No, probably not. Jude was the one with people skills, after all. 'And any news been heard of Tanya?'

Jude shook her head. 'I haven't heard anything. Ted?'

'Nothing definite. Denis Woodville said he'd tried ringing and got someone else on her number. New tenant. So no idea where she's gone.'

They were silent, all wondering whether the poor kid had actually set off to France, to wait for the lover who would never now be coming to join her. They imagined Tanya becoming disillusioned and deciding that no men really cared, whatever they said, whatever they promised, whatever plans they made for you. And then her baby would be born, another child with a single parent, another statistic with limited prospects.

'It'll be tough for Tanya.' Jude shook her head sadly. 'It's always tough to bring up a kid on your own.'

Her sympathy sounded so heartfelt that Carole wondered whether that too came from personal experience. Had Jude been a mother? Carole still knew almost nothing about her neighbour's background. Whenever they got on to personal matters, however much she tried to resist the temptation, Carole always seemed to end up talking about herself.

And there does come a point when you know someone too well to be able to ask about the basic facts of their life. Carole had decided she'd have to set up a dinner party for Jude and a couple of the nosier denizens of Fethering. The village was rich in the expertly curious. Yes, if she invited people who hadn't met the newcomer before, they might be able to winkle out all the details that Carole had so signally failed to uncover. It remained deeply frustrating for her to know so little.

Recognizing that she wasn't going to get any more of Jude's history at that point, Carole moved the conversation on. 'What's sad about the whole Rory Turnbull story is that his plan was so preposterous. The chances of it working even first time round were minimal. I'm sure a basic post-mortem would have revealed the burnt-out body wasn't his. And by the time the corpse was a week old, he had no chance of getting away with it.'

Jude shook her head grimly. 'But by then he was so caught up in his plan that he couldn't let go.'

'He'd already committed murder, apart from anything else,' said Ted. 'He had to go through with it.'

'But why go through all that rigmarole? Why on earth didn't he just dump his wife and go off with a younger woman – like thousands of other married men before him?' asked Carole, with the bitterness of experience.

'You underestimate the hold Barbara had on him. I asked him that very question in Tanya's flat and I've never seen a man's face lose colour the way his did. He was literally terrified of his wife.'

Another tremor passed through Ted Crisp's body. 'Sorry. Man thing again.'

They heard the pub door open. Spot on cue, Bill Chilcott appeared. As ever, he was dressed in quasi-nautical style. And there was a smug smile on his root vegetable face. 'Evening, mine host.'

'Evening, Bill.' There was a mumble of greetings from the others. 'Your customary half?'

'I thank you kindly. And my customary half-hour away from my other half – from the little woman, that is.' Bill Chilcott chuckled, then turned to Jude. 'Or is it politically incorrect to make such a remark in the presence of a liberated woman *de nos jours*?'

'I can assure you, it's no more politically incorrect than anything else I've heard you say.'

Carole held her breath, but Jude's accompanying sweet smile somehow convinced Bill Chilcott that what she'd said was a compliment. 'Oh well, there you go. Of course, I've never spoken a word of criticism of

Sandra. She's extremely attractive and highly intelligent – for a woman.'

Over Bill's chuckle, Ted passed across the 'customary half'. 'You seem remarkably chipper this evening.'

'Yes, well, I do have the satisfaction of having achieved a small victory.' He beamed, waiting to be prompted to his revelation.

Carole obliged. 'This wouldn't have anything to do with Denis Woodville, by any chance, would it?'

'As a matter of fact it would. A small matter of trespass. I have warned the old fool often enough. He can't claim to be surprised by what's happened.'

'So what did happen?' Carole asked dutifully.

'You know he's had that wretched dinghy cluttering up his front garden for months?'

'Yes.'

'Apparently he's trying to sell it now. Fallen on hard times, I'm afraid, our Mr Woodville. Insufficient pension arrangements.' The complacency with which this was said left no doubt that Bill and Sandra Chilcott's pension arrangements were immaculate. 'Can't even afford to pay for the boat's space at the Yacht Club. That's rather funny, isn't it? Calls himself Vice-Commodore and puts on airs and excludes perfectly qualified yachtsmen from Fethering Yacht Club membership – ' he spluttered at the recollection, but quickly recovered himself – 'and yet he can't afford even to keep his own boat there.'

'So what happened?' asked Carole, keen to cut through the gloating to the facts.

'Someone came to see the dinghy this afternoon

with a view to buying it and, in the course of the potential purchaser's inspection, the boat got moved around a bit.' Bill Chilcott snickered in anticipation of his pay-off. 'In fact, it was left with six inches of the mast projecting over the hedge into our garden. Which, as I have made clear to Mr Woodville on numerous occasions, constitutes an act of trespass. Well, you'll never guess what I did . . .'

No one gave him the satisfaction of a response, so he had to deliver his punchline unprompted. 'I got a hacksaw . . . and I cut off the offending six inches of mast!' He looked round for response. 'Then I threw the offcut into Mr Woodville's front garden. Result – end of trespass!'

He rubbed his hands together gleefully and burst out laughing at the extent of his own cleverness. As he laughed and laughed, his tuber face took on the aspect of a white-rooted beetroot.

Carole, Jude and Ted Crisp didn't share the joke. They exchanged looks, and all their thoughts went along the front to the Fethering Yacht Club. There they imagined the plotting of revenge by the Vice-Commodore and his band of cronies. Wartime parallels would be being drawn, cunning deeds of sabotage recalled to provide the means for Denis Woodville to get his own back. And no doubt someone would be recalling a similar incident that happened while he was stationed out in Singapore.

The feud between Bill Chilcott and the Vice-Commodore would go on until one or other of them died, and even then the badmouthing would continue until all three – including Sandra – were dead. The two old men's cooperation to save Nick Kent might never have happened.

The old ways of Fethering had reasserted themselves. As they always did. As they always would. Senior citizens would continue to weave their strange square dance around the pillars of Allinstore. Bill Chilcott would appear in the Crown and Anchor at the same moment every evening for his 'customary half'. And in the Fethering Yacht Club the Vice-Commodore and his cronies would detail how much better a place the world would be if only they were in charge of it.

And Dylan, or someone like him, would be there as a hazard to the young people of the area. And peer pressure and consumerism would work their evil, and most of the young would survive them, and develop into adults no worse and no better than the current residents of Fethering.

But there'd be a few casualties. Like Aaron Spalding. And Sam Kent.

And Rory Turnbull. A dreamer, consumed – literally – by the fantasy that he could change everything in his life by one final throw of the dice.

For the remainder of his customary half-hour in the Crown and Anchor that evening, Bill Chilcott continued to recapture details of his triumph, unaware of, or unworried by, the lack of response from those around him. Then, having rationed his half-pint by the minutest calibrations of sips, he looked at his watch. 'Still, better go back to the little woman. Time, tide and Sandra wait for no man, eh?' He chortled. 'So . . . cheerio, ladies. And cheerio, mine host.'

'Good night,' Ted Crisp called out to the closing door, adding without enthusiasm, 'See you tomorrow.'

'God,' said Carole, 'it's so petty. Why don't they just stop the whole feud?'

'Because they enjoy it,' replied Jude. 'Only thing that keeps them alive – well, together with the line-dancing and the swimming in the Chilcotts' case.'

'Yes, you're probably right. Depressing, isn't it?'

A melancholy had settled on them. Ted Crisp tried to break it with forced geniality. 'Hold it right there – as the bishop said to the actress. What we all need is another drink. What d'you reckon? Landlord's treat again.'

'Really?' Jude grinned. 'You know, you always say that as if it's rarer than a total eclipse of the sun. And yet you keep on doing it. You keep on buying us drinks. Your trouble, Ted, is that beneath that gruff exterior, you're a total pussycat.'

He looked at her belligerently. 'If you wasn't a woman, you wouldn't get away with saying that. Now do you want this bloody drink or not?'

'Oh, certainly. I'll seize the moment while it lasts. Large white wine, please.'

'Carole?'

She looked at her watch. 'No, thanks, Ted. Better get back. I'm expecting a phone call.'

'If you're not there, they'll call back some other time, won't they?' As Carole rose from her seat, Jude grinned one of her big, easy grins.

Carole was torn. There was no phone call she was expecting. All that lay ahead of her was an evening watching television with Gulliver. She knew there'd be nothing much on. Nothing of any interest apart from the news, really. And that was becoming less interesting, as world powers mired themselves ever deeper in crises they did not understand and could not solve.

'Come on, Carole. Like I said, landlord's treat. Large white wine, isn't it?'

'Oh, very well, Ted.' She sank back into her seat. 'Thank you very much.'

Of course, Carole Seddon would never be a natural 'pub person', but it didn't do any harm to behave against character . . . just once in a while.

SIMON BRETT

Death on the Downs

A Fethering Mystery

It was not the sudden rain shower that made Carole Seddon's walk on the West Sussex Downs so distressing. Nor was it the barn in which she takes shelter. No, it was the human skeleton she discovers there, neatly packed into two fertiliser bags.

So begins the second investigation for strait-laced Carole and her more laid-back neighbour Jude. This time their enquiries take them away from their seaside village of Fethering to the small downland hamlet of Weldisham. There they witness how quickly the village gossip-mill can be set in motion – for, on the basis of very little evidence, the locals quickly and readily identify the corpse . . .

Now available in Macmillan hardback

The opening scene follows here

Chapter One

The bones didn't look old, but then what did Carole Seddon know about bones? Her work at the Home Office had brought her into contact with forensic pathologists from time to time, but she didn't lay claim to any of their arcane knowledge. She was just an ordinary member of the public – in retirement an even more ordinary member of the public.

But any member of the public who'd done the rudiments of anatomy at school, who'd watched television, or been to the cinema, would have recognized that the bones were human.

Carole saw them as she picked herself up off the floor of the barn. When the rain had showed no immediate signs of relenting, she had tried to make herself comfortable on a pile of roughly cut planks. They were dark green with the slime of ages, but her trousers and Burberry raincoat were already so mud-spattered and wet that more dirt would make little difference. She planned to spread out a newspaper over the immaculate upholstery of her Renault when she got back to the road where it was parked.

Maybe it was the slime, maybe it was the fact that they had recently been moved, but the planks proved an unstable seat. When Carole had put her full weight on them, they had tipped forward, spilling her unceremoniously on to the hard earth floor of the barn. Their collapse revealed the bright-blue fertiliser bags, out of one of which protruded the unmistakable ball joint of a human femur.

The barn was not on one of Carole Seddon's regular walking routes. Indeed, she rarely went on to the Downs. Gulliver, her dog, was too easily distracted up there, overexcited by the smells of cattle, rabbits and other smaller but infinitely intriguing species of wildlife. Given the luxury of all that space, it would have been cruel to keep the dog on a lead, but she didn't trust him to return from his manic forays into the Downs. Despite impeccable Labrador breeding, Gulliver wasn't a natural country dog. He was at home on Fethering Beach; he knew it well, and always returned safely to his mistress from quixotic tilts at seagulls, breakwaters, or the fascinating detritus that the tide brought in. Carole even reckoned he could, if necessary, find his own way back from the beach to her cottage, High Tor, in Fethering High Street.

But a sortie on the beach was the reason why Gulliver wasn't with his mistress that February afternoon on the Downs. The week before, with customary bravado, he'd attacked a seaweed-shrouded potential enemy, only to back off limping from a gash to his forepaw. His quarry had proved to be a rusty can with a jagged edge. An immediate visit to the vet, injections and bandaging had left Gulliver a mournful housebound creature, who snuffled piteously by the Aga, pressing his nose and teeth against the intransigent dressing on his leg. The bandages had to be swaddled in polythene to keep out the damp when he hobbled off with Carole on the essential toilet outings, which were the only social life the vet's instructions allowed him for a fortnight.

That was why Carole was up on the Downs. Without Gulliver's curiosity to worry about, she told herself positively, she had the freedom to roam. But in her heart she knew another reason for her choice of walking route. She was likely to meet less people on the Downs. In Fethering, Gulliver was her prop. If she was seen walking alone on the beach, she might look as if she was lonely.

She had parked the Renault on the outskirts of Weldisham, a village on the foothills of the South Downs that looked from the outside as though it hadn't changed much since the days when Agatha Christie might have set a murder there. The squat tower of a Saxon church rose above the naked trees. There presumably the aristocracy, the gentry and the commonalty might meet, casting suspicious glances from pew to pew after the dirty deed had been done. In the village pub, the Hare and Hounds, old men with rough-hewn accents might become indiscreet over foaming pints of ale, letting drop conveniently vital clues.

Weldisham offered a couple of homes substantial enough to host house parties at which crimes could be committed. A scattering of smaller dwellings might accommodate those local professionals – the doctor, the solicitor, the vicar – who didn't quite cut the social mustard, but who could prove invaluable as suspects and witnesses.

There were two old barns whose agricultural purpose was unspecified, but which would provide ideal venues for the discovery of the second murder victim impaled by a pitchfork. And then there were small, flint-faced cottages to house the peasantry - the farm workers, the gardeners and wheelwright – one of whose quaint dialect testimony would provide the final piece of the jigsaw, allowing the visiting sleuth to bring another malefactor to the unforgiving justice of the scaffold.

Though that was how Weldisham may still have looked to the uninformed observer, at the turn of the new millennium it housed a very different set of characters. The church looked no different, though its congregation could usually be counted without recourse to a third hand. And the Hare and Hounds, after many and varied refurbishments, was now owned by a chain, whose corporate mission was to maintain the authenticity and individuality of idiosyncratic country local hostelries.

A few estate cottages remained as estate cottages, though the farm workers who lived in them these days drove in closed tractors with heaters and music systems. Manual workers not employed by the estate couldn't begin to afford Weldisham prices. The other cottages had been made over into bijou residences for the retired or for London-based weekenders. Solicitors and doctors, now rather higher up the social pecking order than they had been in Christie's day, still inhabited the middle-range houses, from which they made their short commute to local offices and surgeries. Some hardened souls resolutely travelled up to London on a daily basis, their constant assertions that they had found 'quality of life' undermined by the fact that for half the year they left and arrived back at their country idylls in pitch blackness.

Carole Seddon didn't know Weldisham well. She had been to the Hare and Hounds once when her son Stephen had made one of his rare visits to the South Coast. The pub hadn't made much impression. It was too like every other idiosyncratic country hostelry whose authenticity and individuality had been maintained by a pub chain.

But she had no friends in Weldisham and that afternoon, after parking the Renault, she'd set off very firmly in the opposite direction from the village. The horizon seemed infinite, as though the undulations rolled into each other for ever. Carole felt she could walk for days before she saw another human being.

The prospect did not worry her. Carole Seddon had trained herself to be on her own, certainly after the collapse of her marriage and, according to the uncharitable view of her former husband, for a long time before that. Loneliness, like dependence on other people, was a luxury she did not allow herself.

But she couldn't deny that she was missing her next-door neighbour. Jude had been away for nearly two weeks, having departed suddenly with a characteristic lack of specificity as to where she was going, who she was going with or what she would be doing there. Only in Jude's absence did Carole realize how much she had come to rely on their occasional contacts, the spontaneous knocks on her door inviting her to share a bottle of wine. Though their views differed on many subjects – indeed on most subjects – it was comforting to have someone to talk to.

Still, Jude was away from Fethering for an undefined length of time. No point in brooding about it. Carole had been brought up with the philosophy that one just got on with things. She pulled her knitted hat down over short steel-grey hair. Through rimless glasses her pale-blue eyes looked determinedly at the track ahead of her.

The weather was sullen and threatening truculent clouds ready to unburden themselves of more rain.

After some half hour's walk, Carole had reached what she thought to be a summit, from which she would be able to look down over the flat coastal plain, with its shining threads of glasshouses, to the sulky gleam of the English Channel.

But when she got there, another level shut off her sea view. In front of her, the track rolled downwards to a declivity in which trees clustered like hair in a body crevice. At the bottom stood an old flint-faced tiled barn, structurally sound, but with an air of disuse. One of its doors was gone, the other hung dislocated from a single hinge. Outside an old cart lay shipwrecked in waves of grass.

Past the barn the track climbed up again to the top of the new level, from which the sea might perhaps be visible. Or from which only another prehistoric hump of Downs might be revealed.

Carole decided she'd walked enough. Forget the sea. She could see it from Fethering, if she was that desperate. When she got back to the car, she'd have been out an hour. That was quite long enough. Anything that needed to be proved would by then have been proved. She could get back to the comfort of her central heating.

Even as she made the decision and turned on her muddy heel, it began to rain. Not a rain of individual drops, but a deluge as if, in a fit of pique, some god had upturned a celestial tin bath.

Within seconds, water was dripping off her woollen hat, insidiously finding a route inside the collar of her Burberry to trickle down her neck. It cascaded off the bottom of the coat, quickly seeping through the thick fabric of her trousers.

She was half an hour from car. The barn offered the only possible shelter in the bleak winter landscape. She ran for it.

The inside of the building was fairly empty, though tidemarks of discoloration up the high walls bore witness to the crops that had once been housed there. And, though the roof looked in need of maintenance, it was surprisingly watertight. Here and there the shingles had slipped and water splashed down vertically into hollows made by previous rain. These irregular spatterings provided a rough melody to ride above the insistent drumming on the roof.

The thought struck Carole that she had put herself into a West Sussex minority. She was one of the few who'd actually been inside a barn, as opposed to the many who'd been inside barn conversions. The idea amused her.

She waited ten minutes before looking for somewhere to sit. But the deluge showed no signs of abating. The relentlessly sheeting water had made the day dark before its time. She checked her watch. Only quarter past three. She could give the rain half an hour to stop, and still in theory get back to the Renault in daylight. Assuming of course that daylight ever returned.

So Carole sat on the pile of planks. And the pile collapsed. And the blue fertiliser bags were revealed.

Once she had identified the human femur, taking a large swallow of air and holding her breath, she leant forward to look inside the sacks.

The bones were free of flesh, a greyish white and, when Carole did have to take another gulp of air, appeared not to smell at all. A cursory glance suggested that she was looking at the remains of one complete human body.

Inside the two stridently blue sacks, the bones had been neatly stacked and aligned like a self-assembly furniture kit.

PRAISE FOR

Andrea Badenoch

'A first novel of chilling intensity, a mystery which also happens to be a dissection of desire, friendship and obsession.' Ian Rankin

'First rate first novel . . . There is a talented writer on show here.' Mike Ripley, *Daily Telegraph*

'Terrific thriller . . . suspenseful.' *She*

'A great first crime novel.' *Eva*

'An excellent, gripping read.' *The Big Issue*

'The crime thriller is thriving . . . and invigorated with new blood in Andrea Badenoch's debut novel.' *Marie Claire*

'This is the best debut crime novel I have read for years . . . Compelling and original.' *Wimbledon Guardian*

'There has been a good crop of new talent emerging this year. Well worthy of mention is the excellent *Mortal.*' *Books Magazine*

'Grim and beautifully written, *Mortal* explores a dark terrain where love turns to grief, and grief turns to disillusion . . . it is a powerful, assured and in many ways profound novel. Strongly recommended.'
Andrew Taylor, *Tangled Web*

'A great read and full of surprises for those who like a straightforward but gripping thriller.' *Bath Chronicle*

'A gritty and compelling thriller.' *Bolton Evening News*

'The friend of a murdered girl discovers rather more than the identity of the killer in the suspenseful *Mortal*.'
She Magazine

'Violent thrills from the streets.' *19*

Driven

Andrea Badenoch lives in Newcastle. She lectures part-time and co-edits *Writing Women*, an annual anthology of new voices. Her first novel, *Mortal*, was published in 1998 and is also available in Pan Books.

Her new novel, *Blink*, a hauntingly resonant novel set in the early sixties, will be published in Macmillan hardback in March 2001 (priced £10).

Also by Andrea Badenoch in Pan Books

MORTAL

Andrea Badenoch

Driven

PAN BOOKS

First published 1999 by Macmillan

This edition published 2000 by Pan Books
an imprint of Pan Macmillan Ltd
Pan Macmillan, 20 New Wharf Road, London N1 9RR
Basingstoke and Oxford
Associated companies throughout the world
www.panmacmillan.com

ISBN 0 330 36926 1

'Do Wah Diddy Diddy' words and music by Jeff Barry and Ellie Greenwich, 1963, Trio Music Co Inc. Lyric reproduction by kind permission of Carlin Music Corp., Iron Bridge House, 3 Bridge Approach, Chalk Farm, London NW1 8BD.

3 5 7 9 8 6 4 2

A CIP catalogue record for this book is available from the British Library.

Phototypeset by Intype London Ltd
Printed and bound in Great Britain by
Mackays of Chatham plc, Chatham, Kent

For Jay, Miriam and Naomi

Acknowledgements

Several friends were generous with their time and expertise and helped me research details for this book. I am very grateful to Barry Stone. Thanks also to Mick Cook, Ian Jordan, Fiona Kearns, Steve Manchee, Paul Miller and Sean O'Brien.

We have done with Hope and Honour, we are lost to
Love and Truth,
We are dropping down the ladder rung by rung;
And the measure of our torment is the measure of
our youth.
God help us, for we knew the worst too young!

Rudyard Kipling

Prologue One

Jasmine was chopping up a half-rotten stable door when she saw the car approaching. It was red and determined looking and it bounced along the uneven track to the farm. She called the dogs and shut them inside the house, because they were noisy and aggressive with strangers.

The ground had been frozen solid for more than two weeks and there was no firewood, apart from that salvaged from the decaying buildings. Jasmine intended to use the door and then the roof of the derelict stable in order to light the kitchen stove and heat some water.

She saw two ladies inside the approaching vehicle. It was a Fiat Uno, she decided, not particularly new. They stopped and parked carefully, beyond the deep ruts of hard mud that were the yard. Then they picked their way gingerly in their city shoes towards the house. Jasmine held her axe and regarded their pale legs, their neat suits with coats over the top, their leather shoulder bags. One of them had a clipboard and a biro. The other held a small tape recorder.

Jasmine knew they were social workers. She'd read their letters. When they'd telephoned, she'd insisted her mam was indisposed. Her tone suggested chronic sickness but in fact Lola, her mother, was watching videos and drinking cheap Spanish wine in bed, running an electric fan heater in her room which Jasmine knew they couldn't afford. She wasn't ill, but she'd stayed in bed all winter, her hair matted, her nightdress and woolly jumper malodorous, expecting Jasmine, her eldest daughter, to do all the work.

'Good afternoon, dear,' said one of the ladies loudly. She was the sterner of the two. 'I believe you are all expecting us?' She made her way purposefully towards the front door. She had the air of someone used to getting her own way.

Jasmine jumped sideways into the dilapidated porch, blocking their entrance. She knew she must prevent them going in at all costs. 'You can't go in,' she said, without apology.

'You must be Jasmine,' said the kinder-looking official.

Jasmine frowned. She was very small for her age. Her pale freckled skin was stretched tight over her face, emphasizing her pointed features. Her thin red hair was dragged into a skinny plait. She was thirteen years old but this lady spoke to her as if she was about six.

The tape recorder clicked.

Jasmine had lived on this ruined smallholding for as long as she could remember. They were near Teesside, a few miles from Middlesbrough on a polluted rural-urban fringe known only for its ugliness. Her mother, Lola, was an ageing hippy, tired now of what she called 'the good life' but too lazy to move on. She'd spent the last fifteen years grazing a few sickly animals and raising organic vegetables, downwind of ICI. What hope that had ever been invested in this project had long since disappeared. She couldn't even remember her old optimism or ideals.

Different men, attracted by Lola's voluptuous body, had arrived, tried to help, become discouraged and then moved on. Now, as well as looking after the farm, Jasmine cared for her feckless, drunken mother and the twins, Peony and Mimosa. They were in the grip of a hard winter. All she wanted to do was leave. She resented her mother's idleness, the stale smell of her bed, the growing pile of unwashed crockery and empty bottles littering the floor of her room.

'I can't talk to you now,' she insisted. 'I've got to . . .' She was about to say 'find something for the dinner', but changed it to 'do my homework'.

The ladies each gave her a hard look. 'None of you go to school,' the strict one said.

'Oh, the twins are at school,' Jasmine lied. She took a deep breath. 'A special bus comes and picks them up at the end of the lane.' She prayed that the two girls would not suddenly appear, filthy and giggling. They never went to school. They hadn't been for years. She imagined them running over and grabbing the tape recorder and the clipboard, possibly even the shoulder bags. They were out of control, like wild animals. Their antics made her tired. 'They'll be late tonight,' she added quickly. She didn't want these nosy parker social workers to stay, hanging around, waiting to see her sisters. She had a bizarre thought, which she expressed. 'They're at their violin lesson.'

'Do you go to school?'

Jasmine hadn't been to school for eighteen months. 'Oh yes, but I'm off today. I had a bilious attack.' She knew she was undersized but otherwise a picture of health. She paused. 'Last night. Spewed up everywhere. Dodgy frozen scampi. It's OK though, I'm better now.'

The questions continued. Jasmine fielded them as best as she could. Yes, the twins were healthy. No, her mother was perfectly all right, she was fine. No, no one else lived with them. A man? No, there was no man. Yes, they had welfare benefits and they knew about free school meals. Of course they had a washing machine.

'We would like to see inside.' The strict lady moved towards the door.

Jasmine knew her rights. Holding up her axe, she stood firm. But she also knew that these ladies could take the twins away and put them into care. They could do the same to her. The three of them could end up fostered or, even worse, in a children's home. She pictured the inside of their dwelling; its empty larder, the long-abandoned freezer, the broken lavatory, the dismal, leaky attic room where she slept next door to the twins. She knew her mother was probably drunk and asleep in her stuffy, darkened lair, her electric fire burning away money they didn't have. 'No.' She sounded very definite. 'It's not convenient.'

The tape recorder was switched off. The younger lady filled in a laborious form. She had started to shiver. 'Well then,' she said. She sneezed. 'We'll be going.'

'Is that it?'

'For the moment.'

The strict one sighed. 'We'll be back,' she threatened. They began to walk away.

Jasmine watched them, relieved but her face completely impassive.

They stopped and looked up at the pockmarked roof, the crumbling chimney. One of them pointed at a rusting transit van. As they stood there, a chicken emerged from its window and fluttered to the lifeless ground. They shook their heads and got into their Fiat.

Jasmine noticed that the winter sky was stained both black and orange. A few white flakes appeared from nowhere. She scanned the fields, her anxiety moving away from the visitors and focusing on the whereabouts of the sheep. She hoped it wouldn't snow again. She had dug them out of a drift earlier in the week.

The car disappeared slowly along the track, its tail lights blinking as it joined the road. She went back to her chopping block, raising her axe above her head. At that moment a clod of frozen dung hit the side of her neck. She heard girlish laughter and scuffling. Mimosa and Peony appeared, dressed in long velvet skirts and lacy shawls, stolen from their mother's wardrobe.

Jasmine put down her axe. 'Look at you both,' she said, exasperated.

The twins' faces were smeared with jam. They had straw and peacock feathers in their straggly hair. Mimosa offered the same chicken that had recently emerged from the van. Its neck hung lifeless and broken. Peony held out a wizened turnip she'd found in the barn. 'Dinner,' they suggested, in unison.

'Go and light the stove,' ordered Jasmine.

'Light it yourself,' said Mimosa.

'We're going down to Mam's,' insisted Peony, meaning their mother's room. 'We're cold.'

'It's telly time,' insisted her twin. 'It's *Rug Rats*.'

'It's *Blue Peter*, later.' They joined hands, shrieking and jumping for joy, then they went inside.

*

At six o'clock, the stove blazing and the chicken roasting, Jasmine stood at the sink, peeling the turnip. She'd dug some frozen carrots and cut off the black bits. She'd made herself tea but there was no milk.

Suddenly, there was a commotion outside. The dogs were barking frantically, but in a way that indicated pleasure. Jaz went to the door. Another car was coming along the track. Like the dogs, she recognized the sound of the engine. It was a vintage Ford Escort. She felt a rush of pleasure which was immediately replaced by annoyance. She went back to her duties at the sink.

The front door banged and there was a blast of air. A tall, fat man appeared noisily in the kitchen. He was red-faced and jovial. He sniffed the air appreciatively then held up a Tesco's carrier bag. 'I went shopping,' he said cheerfully.

Jasmine smiled but refused to acknowledge him. She kept her back turned.

This was Lola's current boyfriend. His name was Blow and he was a used car dealer from Sunderland. He'd been around for about three years, part-time, and although he was kind and generous he was also unreliable. Jasmine liked him, not least because he was patient with the twins, but she knew he would never ease her burden. He was too weak, too indecisive and too lazy to be of much help.

For reasons Jasmine couldn't understand Blow shared her mother's bed and referred to her as his 'Queen'. He dumped the bag on the table, raising a cloud of chicken feathers. With big gestures he produced frozen pizzas, breakfast cereal, baked beans, three bottles of wine. 'Howzat!' he declared, as proud as a child.

Jasmine opened a can of beans and emptied it into a

pan. Blow uncorked a bottle and poured a glass for her mother. 'You were supposed to get food two days ago,' she said to him. Her voice was sulky, quiet. 'What am I supposed to do? Magic tricks?'

He moved towards the door, still grinning widely. He was wearing a suede car coat and a back to front baseball cap. His round cheeks were shining and his stomach protruded over the top of his trousers. He gave her a friendly wink.

Jasmine was suddenly furious. 'I've told you,' she shouted, 'and I'm not telling you again. I'm sick of this. You promised to get shopping. You're two days late and there's nothing here.' She pointed to the items on the table. 'What've you done with the child benefit? You had a hundred pounds to spend.'

Blow turned around, put the glass of wine on the mantelpiece then came over and tried to stroke Jasmine's cheek. 'What's bugging you, little baby?' he crooned. 'What's bugging little Jazzy Razzy?'

'Don't start that,' she yelled in his face. She backed away, dumping the pan of beans on the stove then opening its door, throwing in more wood. 'I've had enough. Those Authorities have been here. Those nosy parker ladies. What can I tell them? And there's no hay left. There's no chicken meal. The twins are almost starving. I give you all our money and you come back with fucking wine. Fucking pizzas . . .'

Blow opened his hands in a gesture of apology. He shrugged and smiled. 'I've sold that Roadster. The MG you polished up – I told you I would.' He blew her a series of kisses. 'I've got money . . .'

Jasmine picked up the pan of boiling carrots and hurled it at him. He jumped aside and it hit the wall.

There was an upward rush of steam and a clatter. The twins appeared in the doorway, whooping and yodelling.

'I'm out of here!' Jasmine yelled. 'All of you. You bastards. D'you hear me?' She took a deep breath. 'D'you really hear me?'

'Bastards!' repeated Mimosa, rushing in and stamping hard on the scattered, half-cooked carrots. 'Fucking pizzas!'

'Fucking bastard pizzas!' repeated Peony, running and sliding through the squashed vegetables and spilt water.

'I'm going to London. I tell you. I'm going away!'

'London!' screamed Mimosa, careering into the table, raising more feathers and overturning the wine.

'London! Fucking bastard London!' screeched Peony even louder, pushing over her sister, fists flailing. 'LUN DUN! LUN DUN! LUN DUN!'

Blow leaned against the mantelpiece, laughing. He clutched his sides.

Jasmine would not allow herself to cry. She tossed her apron into the sink full of peelings and water. She kicked the stove. She was white and shaking with anger as she slammed out of the room.

Prologue Two

The headlines were everywhere – blazing from newsstands, jumping out from TV screens in shop windows, moving fast, high up on a glass wall, from right to left, right to left, where they were broken only by the time, 18.36, and the temperature, 34. The words kept repeating 'Bonfire Bodies. Bonfire Bodies – More Human Remains.'

Jaz, formerly Jasmine, saw all this but averted her eyes. She heard the same message through her headphones, crackling on Capital Radio as she jogged down Shaftesbury Avenue. She imagined a burnt, blackened hand and immediately turned off her Walkman. She pictured suburban wasteland, somewhere beyond the city, with a petrol can and someone's charred cotton skirt. She sniffed the London air and could detect only car fumes, doughnuts and drains. She was relieved to be in the centre of things, amongst the crowds. Here, it was safe and anonymous.

Jaz was hot and her sports bag bulky. She stopped and bought a can of Dr Pepper, rubbing its damp coolness across her brow. As usual, the busy street made her feel invisible. She could sense people's eyes focused elsewhere, not meeting hers. She loved the anonymity when she ran around London, the impersonal bustle. No one was interested in her. After a childhood with only her family for company, miles from anywhere, this new life gave her a sense of freedom.

Later, Jaz sat outside a pub near the Strand, underneath a blue and yellow umbrella which advertised Pernod. The atmosphere wasn't French – there was too much traffic and the pavement was rather narrow. Nevertheless, the weather was warm and the huddles of London office workers, liberated at the end of Friday, were cheerfully making the best of things.

The golden light cast long shadows. Cars and buses moved through a shimmer of exhaust. Overhead, a helicopter beat and hovered like an insect against the deep, clear blue. The evening air was gentle and from a nearby café there wafted a smell of onions.

It's like being on holiday, Jaz thought to herself. She was with her two best friends, Harmony, who was known always as Harm, and Tracy, whose name they usually shortened to Trace.

Harm was brown-skinned with crinkly Afro-Caribbean hair, rolled into dreadlocks. She had an hourglass figure which she emphasized with cheap, fashionable clothes which were both too short and too tight. Trace was tall and lanky with cropped blonde hair. She always wore jeans. She had the sort of face which was both beautiful and ugly at the same time, the kind often seen in the more avant garde style magazines, but if it was ever suggested to her that she might try modelling, she simply snorted with derision.

Jaz was sipping canned orange slowly through a straw whilst her friends drank double Bacardis which were half price because of Happy Hour. 'He's given me a straw,' said Jaz, scowling through the open door at the barman.

'That's because you look about twelve,' answered Harm.

Harm and Trace, like Jaz, were sixteen years old. All three were runaways and had been surviving homelessness and unemployment in London for some time. At present, they were staying in a hostel in Tower Hill run by the Little Sisters of Hope, which was known by inmates simply as the Little Sisters. They'd been there for six months. Today, their discussion was mainly centred on the relative merits of moving out and moving on. They tried to take decisions together. They believed in standing by each other.

'I hate that young Little Sister,' said Harm. 'You know, the one with the moles.'

'Sister Teresa? She's a stupid cunt,' agreed Trace. This was an expression she'd picked up recently from another girl at the hostel and she'd begun using it indiscriminately, pleased by its power to shock.

'She got big personal problems,' giggled Harm, 'and one of them's her fat arse.'

'Problems?' said Jaz. 'She's giving me problems. No one speaks to me like that.' She sounded defiant. She was still smarting from a barrage of Sister Teresa's self-righteous abuse, delivered only that morning, in the refectory. 'I won't have anyone talking to me like that. Not any more. Who does she think she is? I'm telling you, I'm out of there.' She kicked her sports bag, indicating that she'd already left.

'She thinks we should be grateful,' commented Harm. 'For the charity.' She drained her glass. 'I have to say, I quite like the showers. And the breakfasts. There's a lot to be said for the breakfasts.'

'I'm not going back.' Jaz had made up her mind. 'She can stuff her fucking charity. And her showers. I'd just as soon take my chances on the streets.' Adamant, she gave her leftover vouchers to her two friends. Not for the first time, she thought that within the threesome she was the outsider, the one most likely to break away.

Harm and Trace, as inseparable as ever, decided not to decide. Then they thought they might stay a few more days, perhaps another week. Neither wanted to settle permanently in the Little Sisters' place, they said, becoming long-term charity cases. They dismissed such an existence as sad. They agreed that hostel dwellers were generally losers but saw themselves as free. 'We're just bumming along, using the facilities,' Harm insisted.

'We'll stick around,' said Trace. 'Like, you know. Take advantage. Do our laundry.'

'We'll catch up with you later,' agreed Harm, shrugging. 'Next week.' She sighed. She sounded more worldly, more mature than her sixteen years. 'It's one day at a time in the big bad city.'

A man on the next table held a copy of the *Evening Standard* in front of his face. The familiar headlines glared. 'Bonfire Bodies – New Lead.' After a while he folded the paper and placed it next to his pint. He leaned back and looked at the girls in an interested way. Jaz gave him a hostile glance but Harm smiled. 'Have you got a light, mister?' she asked, even though her own lighter was obvious. The man stretched out his arm, holding a match. He was about thirty-five, with longish dark hair combed behind his ears, an earring, and side-burns. He was slightly overweight and wore jeans and a tight white T-shirt which strained across his belly.

Harm bent forwards and whispered something to him. He smiled and shook his head. Jaz and Trace pretended not to notice. They both knew that Harm went with men, briefly and routinely, for quick money. She never missed a chance. It was something she'd always done and they'd given up trying to stop her.

The man was not embarrassed. 'Would you all like a drink?' he asked confidently. He had a London accent. He stood up, his expression open and friendly. 'Why don't I buy us all a round?'

'Thanks,' said Harm, in no way offended by his refusal. 'Two large rum and blacks and a Fanta.'

Jaz was relieved, both by the man's unwillingness to go with Harm and by his manner, which was reassuring and ordinary. She decided he was OK. She noticed his Millwall FC anorak, slung across the back of his chair. When he returned, she mentioned the team's prospects.

'I'll join you,' he said, pleased, and somehow innocent, moving his chair next to Jaz. 'So where're you from, darling? You new here?'

The daylight ebbed away and the sky turned purple. The office workers left and were replaced by tourists and two rich-looking couples in evening dress. The traffic died. A police car sped past, its siren wailing, and empty buses accelerated and rattled. An old man wearing sandwich boards shouted something about the end of the world.

Jaz chatted to the man. She described her mother's smallholding but didn't say that she'd run away from

Teesside. She told him she'd been staying in a hostel but didn't intend going back. She tried to give the impression that she'd come to London for work. 'Do you work near here?' she asked.

He shook his head. 'On the buildings, but not here. Down the East End.'

She noticed that his teeth were uneven and pointed.

Harm and Trace were drunk. They giggled over the problem page in *Sugar*, leaning together like children. Trace had never learned to read. 'Go on,' she said to Harm, 'go on, read me some more.'

Harm waved her cigarette wildly. She carried on reading from the magazine. Her voice became louder and emphatic. ' "I'm in love with my biology teacher." Christ, listen to this!' She laughed, holding the page away from her face, spilling some of her drink. 'Listen to this, Trace. It genuinely says this, no joke.' Her words were slurred. 'This is the frigging headline, right? "Classroom Love." This is unbelievable.'

Trace spoke to Harm in a loud stage whisper. 'Do you think this girl's like, you know . . .' she giggled, her hand over her mouth, 'a stupid cunt?'

Harm continued, adopting a soppy voice. 'It's the real thing. I love him and he loves me. I know we're made for each other. The problem is I'm only fifteen and I've missed my period.'

Trace laughed. 'I don't get this.' She was always a bit slow on the uptake.

Harm continued reading. ' "We've only done it standing up. We do it in the technology room during the breaks. He says because we're doing it standing up, I can't get pregnant." ' She dropped the magazine on the table. 'Can she be serious? This girl, she signs herself "Boyzone Fan". Is she for real?'

Trace laughed too. 'She's definitely a stupid cunt.'

'Biology!' spluttered Harm. She put her drink down.

Both Harm and Trace's laughter was now out of control. 'The technology room!' squeaked Harm.

'The stupid cunt!' shouted Trace. They held onto each other for a moment, rocking in their seats. The other customers on nearby tables looked over quizzically. Some of them seemed offended. The magazine slid to the ground.

Jaz didn't smile. She examined a beer mat.

'You don't drink?' asked the man, gently.

She shook her head.

'Not at all?' His mouth was near her ear. He was ignoring the others.

She was conscious of his attention. He was now very close, too close. She wondered if he was about to kiss her. She had decided she liked him, not least because she felt she already knew him. It was something to do with his big build that made him familiar. He reminded her of Blow. She could smell his aftershave and the beer on his breath. She shook her head again. She never discussed alcohol.

'I'll get myself another pint.' He stood up.

Harm, still laughing, gestured towards the table top, which was full with glasses. 'Two large thingies and a . . .'

The man smiled. 'Sure,' he agreed, disappearing inside the bar.

Harm took a deep breath and almost recovered her composure. 'He's nice,' she said, gesturing, pretending to admire his backside. 'Fat, but quite good looking.'

'You've scored there, Jaz,' added Trace, still gasping a little for air. 'He's got money.'

'Don't forget to do it standing up,' added Harm loudly.

Trace's laughter pealed out again. 'Find a technology room. You've got to find a technology room.'

The man reappeared and walked towards them. He carried another pint and two more Bacardis.

'Hey you!' Harm waved both her arms again. 'You can only do it to Jaz if you do it in a technology room.' She was swaying in her seat. 'It's the only safe way. Standing up. I read it somewhere!'

'Shut up,' said Jaz quietly. 'Just shut up, you two. If you don't go soon, you'll be locked out by those nuns.'

Harm and Trace stood up, holding onto each other, steadying themselves with the table, making sure they swallowed the drinks which had just arrived. 'She's right. We have to go. We're going to a technology room in Tower Hill. It's got showers. It's got bloody Little Sisters.'

'They're all stupid cunts,' offered Trace.

The man looked at Jaz. 'You going?'

'No.'

'You want to come with me? I've got space.'

'Maybe.'

'I'll finish my pint.'

Fifteen minutes later, after her friends had staggered off, Jaz picked up her sports bag and prepared to leave with the man.

As she stood up, he was clearly surprised by her size. 'You're very small, aren't you?'

'I'm eighteen.'

'I'm Keith.' He winked. His face was kind.

Jaz thought that he was quite attractive, but certainly old. She wasn't sure what to say.

They walked together down a side street. He didn't put his arm around her or stand too near. 'I did a trial for Millwall's youth squad,' he said, clearly pleased that she knew about his team. 'Trouble is, I never had the ankles.'

'The ankles?' repeated Jaz.

'Dodgy Achilles.'

There seemed to be no adequate response to this, so Jaz stayed quiet.

'I've got a car along here.'

'A car?' Jaz was surprised. She didn't know anyone in London who had a car. 'What kind of a car?'

'Mark II Zephyr. Nineteen sixty,' he said proudly. 'Canary yellow and cream.' He gave her a strange, sidelong stare, as if she might have some objection to the idea.

Jaz was pleased. She remembered the succession of old cars she'd watched Blow restore. 'I love old cars,' she said reassuringly. 'I'm a car freak.' With relief, she realized they had something in common.

The hot day had turned into a heavy, oppressive night. Jaz was conscious of dampness under her arms, a weight which seemed to press down from the dark buildings on either side, and the smell of refuse coming from the back of restaurants.

'Here we are,' said Keith, turning into a narrow rear entrance. His car was parked in a tight bay, between buildings. It was covered in a tarpaulin, as if he'd been expecting rain. He dragged this off and the Zephyr was illuminated in the glow from a street lamp.

Jaz let out a low whistle. 'Amazing,' she enthused. She

was genuinely impressed. 'Beautiful.' It was one of the best she'd ever seen.

'Highline,' Keith pointed out.

'I can see that.' Jaz took a few steps backwards.

'I prefer the highlines.'

'You've had the headlamp cowls chromed?'

He nodded, clearly pleased. 'Yeah. And the wheel arches – see them?' He paused. 'Rebuilt.'

Jaz walked around the vehicle, then surveyed it again from the front. The Zephyr had big chrome bumpers and a shiny grille with a period AA badge. She dropped her bag, put her hands on her hips and shook her head slowly. 'It's terrific. It's totally . . . fab.'

He unlocked the passenger door. 'Get in,' he said.

Jaz threw her sports bag in the back and slid over the bench seat. She took a deep, appreciative breath. It was a unique smell of old plastic and leather. Keith climbed in next to her and she realized again why he was so familiar. His height, his bulk, his long wavy hair and now his car – everything about him reminded her of Blow. As he turned the key in the ignition she was suddenly back on the farm, sitting next to Blow, admiring his latest acquisition, talking cars.

'Just listen to that,' he said. The engine gave a low growl.

'Straight six,' she offered.

'Needs a new clutch.' There was a slight judder as they moved off. 'I've got one ordered, though.' He paused. 'It's under control.'

They drove along Fleet Street, the car purring like a cat. Jaz noticed there was a collection of tax discs neatly secured behind the one displayed on the windscreen.

He'd kept them all. Blow had always done this with his best cars. It was a sign of fanaticism.

Soon Jaz caught a glimpse of the river. She realized they were heading east when she saw the dome of St Paul's. 'There's St Paul's,' she said, making conversation. Every time they turned a bend, she slid towards him on the slippery leather seat, so that their arms touched. She let this happen. She took another deep breath, this time for courage. 'Do you mind if I drive?'

Jaz loved driving. She had learned in her mother's tractor on the farm when she was eight. Then when Blow arrived, with his succession of second-hand vehicles, he let her manoeuvre them around the fields, the lanes, then, later, the quiet country roads. She was a good, instinctive driver. Blow said she was a natural. She considered driving to be her best talent, her greatest skill – the one of which she was most proud.

Keith pulled over. 'Why not?' he asked. 'Watch that clutch. It's tricky.'

Jaz got out and went around to the driver's door. Keith slid across onto the passenger side. She felt a flutter of excitement in her chest. She hadn't driven a vehicle since she'd left home, two and a half years before. She turned the key and started cautiously, slowly, waiting for the clutch to rebel. She got the measure of the engine. There was virtually no traffic but she'd never been on a main road in her life. The speedo said twenty. She was nervous. They crawled along. She was wary of the pedals. Gingerly, and in order to avoid a stationary bus, she moved out into the middle lane. After a few more minutes her confidence grew. She realized she'd already passed the hostel run by the Little Sisters of Hope. 'I was living around here,' she said, 'until very recently. Where are we going?' She accelerated to get through an amber light. 'This is great,' she added. 'This is totally brill.'

She saw a taxi rank ahead on her right and then the unmistakable figures of Harm and Trace. They were talking to a trio of drivers. She slowed and waved, proud to be driving.

'What's up?' asked Keith.

Jaz hooted at her friends. They turned and saw her.

'Come on,' said Keith. 'Never mind them.'

Jaz drove past the taxi rank and was aware of Harm and Trace coming out onto the road and then waving and running behind her. 'They're drunk.' She shrugged and accelerated away.

Keith gave her some directions. They were now in the East End. Jaz saw a sign saying East London Tabernacle. After about fifteen minutes, they entered a warren of small streets. 'Slow down,' he instructed. 'See these lock-ups?' They were adjacent to a row of railway arches. 'Stop here.'

Jaz got out of the car.

Keith unlocked a door, then parked the Zephyr out of sight. 'It's not far,' he assured her. 'My gaff's just up the road.' They set off, again walking two feet apart. For the first time, Jaz felt scared. They had come a long way and this was an area unfamiliar to her. Groups of Asian teenagers stood around on street corners outside grocery shops and video rental outlets which were still open. A sign said Wedding Saris. There was a smell of foreign food and occasional noisy bursts of car stereos.

'Let me take that,' said Keith, grabbing and then shouldering Jaz's sports bag. He started singing 'I'm turning Japanese, Oh yes, I'm turning Japanese, I really think so.' He sounded jolly and a little old-fashioned, like someone's dad.

Jaz was silent again. They walked for what seemed like a long time. The streets and alleys became more and more empty. The road had potholes and cracked drain covers. They passed large buildings, like hospitals, which were deserted, with stained bricks and broken windows. The dark purple-orange sky faded to black at the edges. Jaz was aware of pools of urine, gaping pavements, uprooted cobbles. She wished she hadn't come.

'Not far now,' Keith assured her.

Jaz hesitated at a small junction.

He turned around and looked down at her. 'Don't worry,' he said, reading her mind. 'I don't like sex.' He noticed a squashed drinks can in the gutter and flicked it up with his foot, bounced it on his knee then shot it expertly across the road. A dog started barking. Jaz noticed a group of drunks arguing in a pub doorway. As they turned a bend, she could see open space and several bunches of homeless men grouped around bonfires. Keith walked in the direction of the first blaze.

Jaz followed him. She was aware of bottles being shared and the familiar mixture of old and young, destitute and ordinary, alcoholic and sober. There was the usual combination of laughter, argument and weary silence. They regarded Keith and Jaz with interest, but didn't speak. She glanced at their faces, feeling the heat. It wasn't a cold night, it was close and warm, but she knew they lit fires from habit and from the strong need to make a focal point in the urban wilderness. She'd joined such a group herself, in the past, on more than one occasion.

There was no one amongst them that she knew. It

occurred to her again that she was a long way from her own patch. Keith carried on walking. Further on and around another corner Jaz saw more fires and more huddles. One or two makeshift shelters were already housing individuals who'd settled for the night.

Keith continued up the street but suddenly stopped. 'Here,' he said.

Jaz looked about. There were tall tenement blocks on either side, most of which seemed unoccupied. Their doors were boarded up with wood and corrugated iron, as if they were scheduled for demolition. She tried to get her bearings. At the end of the row, about thirty yards away, was the second patch of wasteland they'd crossed, with its glowing fires. She wanted to remember the way they'd come. She didn't like being lost.

Keith turned directly into a narrow slit between the flats. It was pitch black, and Jaz paused. He grabbed her arm. He pulled her roughly and she stumbled against him.

'Easy,' he said harshly. 'Steady on.'

Jaz could see nothing. She was conscious of his tight fingers and his breathing which had become a little heavy. There was rubble under her feet. They stopped. A hinge creaked and her eyes started to adjust. She could see a tiny green metal entrance inserted in a much larger, older wooden door. She was reminded of a tannery which had frightened her in a Middlesbrough back street when she was very small. They stepped inside.

Keith still had hold of her arm. 'Home sweet home,' he said in a gruff voice.

Jaz blinked. 'What is this?' She was afraid. She felt a change in Keith's manner. He had become threatening, even rough.

He dropped Jaz's bag. She picked it up with her free hand. Then, still holding her, he pushed the small door shut, wedging a short plank under it to keep it closed. His hand groped for a light switch. There was a click and a pale glimmer shone from a low watt bulb strung between some rafters. Jaz looked around. The building was old and damp with crumbling walls. There was a strong smell of mice, mould and rotting plaster. In a corner were new bags of cement, sand and a pile of bricks.

Keith propelled her down a corridor. 'Come and have a look at this,' he said. After a moment she was aware of emerging into a big dark space. He pressed another switch, illuminating a decorator's lamp which hung from a pair of step ladders.

Jaz gasped. Before them was the foyer of an old cinema. It was spacious and had once been very grand. There were marble stairs curving away upwards bound by iron balustrades hung in places with dusty cobwebs. There were ornate rococo walls and ceilings, a wooden booth under a sign saying tickets, framed, stained prints of long dead stars. The tiled floor was broken and in places dug up. The air was musty and stale. Again, there were signs of building work – trestles, planks, cement and other evidence of repairs or a conversion which had been abandoned.

'What is this place?' Jaz's voice was small and scared.

'It's empty,' muttered Keith. 'Bricked up. Been empty for years. Supposed to be the Calcutta Road bloody Arts Centre.' He sniffed aggressively. 'The Lottery never coughed. Bastards. Not a good enough cause. Not good enough for those bloody Lottery sods.' He mimicked someone on television. 'Just come on down.' His tone suggested resentment, anger, disappointment.

'You worked here, didn't you?' Jaz stared into his face. He met her eye and she realized his face had become strange, almost distorted. His eyes were staring and his mouth compressed in fury. He looked mad. He lifted a hand, his finger pointing into the air. He raised his voice. 'I still work here. And I'm not leaving.'

Jaz was aware of her heart beating. She'd imagined she'd been heading for a cheap rented room, or a temporary, anonymous bed and breakfast with old furniture, a dirty cooker, a lumpy settee. She'd stayed in many such places in London.

In the pub he'd seemed nice and friendly and quite good looking. She'd wanted him to fondle her, undress her, make a small fuss of her. She'd expected brief love-making, then a hot drink, a blanket and a safe place to sleep. She'd imagined waking up, having breakfast, kissing him lightly, moving on. He would have given her money, maybe arranged to meet her again. It was the usual pattern. It's what had happened every other time.

This place, this derelict old cinema miles from her usual area, and Keith's tight grip, his fanatical expression, were not at all what she'd expected. The situation was weird. This meant it was unpredictable and therefore dangerous. She knew she was in trouble. She looked around. There was a thick, looped chain and a padlock across what must have been the main entrance to the building.

'Come on,' he said.

Don't panic, she told herself. He pushed her through a new fire door into a room which had been recently constructed at the side of the ticket booth. It had ceiling spotlights, rows of new blue chairs which had become white in places with mildew, a rolled carpet, still in polythene, and a life-size cardboard cut-out of the men from *Reservoir Dogs*. At the front there was a small screen. A tiny cinema had been created within the vast body of the original, decaying building, and then left to deteriorate.

'You said an Arts Centre . . .' Jaz turned round in time to see Keith disappearing. In a couple of seconds he'd closed the door, locked it and extinguished the lights. She was alone and in the dark.

'You're shut in,' Keith confirmed. His voice was very muffled, from behind the soundproof barrier. 'What a shame.'

Jaz experienced a rush of fear. Her head swam and her knees went weak. She had a sensation as if her heart was leaping in her chest. She bit her lip, willing herself not to faint. He's a weirdo, she thought frantically. I'm a goner. She tried hard to see in the blackness and reached out, taking two nervous steps forward in order to hold onto the back of a chair.

After a while, there was a whirring noise and something appeared in front of her. She blinked, realizing it was a beam of projected light, shining on the small screen. A bright rectangle about four feet by six took shape and then diminishing numbers flashed up inside. She realized she was looking at the start of a film. She glanced behind her. Above her head, a projector shone the white triangle down into the room, and Keith stood behind it. He spoke again. 'I'm going to kill you, little girl.' His voice was quiet. He was no longer behind the soundproofing. He was very close. He spoke softly and menacingly. 'Yes, I am.'

Jaz felt sweat break out all over her body. First it was

hot, but it immediately became cold. She shivered, and looked at the screen.

A young Princess Margaret appeared, pale and grainy, wearing a pink suit and matching shoes. She shook hands elegantly, smiled and waved, received flowers, walked alongside a crowded pavement.

Jaz realized, with a shock, that the amateur film had almost certainly been shot in the street outside the building which now held her prisoner. She could see the flats, the old cinema façade, with the name Essoldo, and at the end of the road, the open stretch of wasteland where tonight there burned bonfires.

'I'm going to kill you,' Keith repeated. 'I'm going to do you like I did all the others. Then I'll put you on a fire.'

Bonfire Bodies, thought Jaz. She remembered the news headlines which had tried to intrude into her consciousness all day. She'd ignored them but had been unable to shut them out completely. Bonfire Bodies. They're here, she thought, those murders. They're not miles away. They're here, in London. Keith's doing it. He's using those bonfires. They're lit by the neighbourhood homeless, and then he uses them to get rid of the girls he's murdered.

'No one knows you're here,' said Keith. He sounded almost reasonable. 'No one knows I'm here. They won't look for anyone in this old place. No one comes here now. You won't be found.' He paused, then chuckled. 'Until you're roasted meat.'

Jaz took several deep breaths. She understood from the tone of his voice that he was enjoying this. He was excited by her fear. He doesn't like sex, she remembered. This is what turns him on. He gets off on this. This is his thing – the terror, the panic, the desperation of young girls.

A sensation rose up in her chest which was stronger than any of those feelings. She was aware of it growing and feeding greedily on the adrenalin which pulsed through her body. This new emotion took the place of her fear. It was anger. Keith's sadism was making her angry. 'Fucking bastard,' she said.

'What's that, girlie-wirlie?' he replied. 'What's that?'

Jaz was furious. Her fury took over, took control. She felt it welling up and spilling out, just as it always did. 'I hate you, you fucking bastard.' She shouted at him in a way that suggested she'd never known fear. Then she swallowed and lowered her voice. 'What's the matter with you anyway?' There was a silence, broken only by the fan spinning quietly on the projector.

Jaz then forced a laugh – deliberate, disparaging. Her anger made her hate him. She wanted to mock him. 'I think I know. I know exactly what your problem is, fat boy.' There was a pause. 'We just . . . freak you out, don't we? Us girlie-wirlies. You can't cope. Can't manage it, can you? Ugly old wanker. That's what's wrong with you. Your dick doesn't work.'

He didn't answer.

'You hear me? Wanker?'

The film in front of her flickered, then went off. The room was in total darkness again. Jaz imagined Keith coming back downstairs, maybe with a weapon. She was too angry to be afraid. Her anger was her defence, her courage. She was ready for him. She shouldered her bag and clenched her fists.

The screen became illuminated for a second time. She glanced up and behind. His outline was still visible.

'What've you got up there, arsehole? Porno films?'

A still image in black and white appeared. It was an old photograph of the cinema, looking huge and impressive. Painted on the side wall of the building was the word 'talkies'. Passers-by were dressed in old-fashioned clothes. Several other slides clicked into view. They were all of the cinema, taken at different times in its history. There were street vendors, crowds, trams, horses and carts. It was clear that in the past the area had been a lot more prosperous and populated than it was today. One or two photographs showed the interior of the building. It had contained mirrors and painted murals.

Jaz heard a noise. It was the key in the lock. The slide carousel continued to rotate upstairs, but Keith had returned. He opened the door and a chink of light shone through. He stepped inside, leaving the door ajar. Jaz prepared herself for a struggle, but he didn't come towards her. Instead he moved into the centre aisle and gestured at the screen. 'It could have been like this again,' he said, almost conversationally, 'if only they'd had the vision.'

At that moment there was a clatter and the babble of raised voices. Keith jumped, visibly surprised. Jaz instinctively took a few quick steps towards the door and flung it open. Keith lunged, then stopped in his tracks.

The dimly lit foyer was filling with people. There were shouts and jostling. Jaz blinked and emerged amongst them, her eyes smarting. Two women grabbed her. She realized, in a dazed instant, that they were Harm and Trace. They started dragging her towards the corridor which she knew led to the unlocked side door. She looked back at the surprising crowd. It milled and pushed its way into the new, small cinema, where briefly Jaz had been held prisoner. There were thirty or forty men and they seemed united, determined. Some of them were unkempt and dirty. Others were wearing blankets. Jaz couldn't take it in. The scene was surreal. Who are these people? she thought. Some of them waved sticks, others broken bottles. They surged, in a mob, towards the room where Keith was trapped. I know them, she suddenly decided. They're the men from the bonfires, the same people I passed on the way here. She tried to stop, to wait, wondering what would happen, but her friends continued to pull her towards the exit.

In a few seconds the girls were outside. 'Come on,' Harm insisted. 'Don't worry, they know. They know everything. He's been using their fires. Me and Trace, we know two of them. They used to doss in Stamford Street, last winter. We told them he'd brought you here.' She took Jaz's bag. 'Don't you see? All his victims were homeless. Runaways. There's a lot of angry stuff going down around these parts. We asked them for help. The posse was ready – they just needed info.'

'Yes,' Trace agreed. 'They thought this place was empty.'

'That creep's had it,' Harm continued. 'We have to get away.'

Jaz, led by her friends, one holding each hand, retraced her earlier footsteps back to the spot where Keith had hidden his car. Surprisingly, it seemed to take no time at all.

The streets were deserted. A single police car cruised past, unaware and nonchalant, then disappeared. As they approached the lock-up, Jaz saw that a black cab was idling. The driver grinned and looked at his watch. Jaz recognized him. He was one of Harm's regulars – someone from the taxi rank, the one she'd passed earlier, near the Little Sisters of Hope on Tower Hill. Jaz knew he routinely traded rides with Harm, in return for blow jobs. She turned to her friends. 'You're amazing,' she said.

They jumped inside. The cab moved off. Jaz lay back and closed her eyes. She heard the engine climb through its gears and felt the vehicle gain speed. She let out a huge sigh. 'Oh God,' she whispered. 'Thank Christ you got here.'

'Of course we got here,' said Harm gently. 'We've got to stick together. We shouldn't have separated.'

'How did you . . .'

'Don't ask.'

'I'm asking.'

'We saw you waving . . .' began Harm.

'We were worried . . .' Trace stroked Jaz's sleeve. 'Poor Jaz.'

'Saw you going past us, near the Little Sisters. At that taxi rank. Really slow. Like a snail. Then you speeded up. We jumped in the taxi and followed you here. Then we tailed you on foot.'

'We saw you,' interjected Trace. 'Waving. You were in a fancy car, with that bloke.'

'So?' Jaz was bewildered.

'You don't know?' Harm turned to Trace. 'I told you she didn't know.'

'Know what?' whispered Jaz.

'It's been all over the news, all day.' Harm was insistent. 'The man they want to question about those fires. The bodies in the East End. He drives a shiny yellow old car, a Ford Zephyr. It was on the news. In the papers. I can't believe you went and climbed into it, with that pig. Willingly.' She whistled. 'You got in it with him and went for a drive.' She turned to Trace. Her voice was a mixture of exasperation and relief. 'What's it with this girl? What exactly does she think she's doing? Is Jaz dumb, or what?'

Trace pursed her lips and looked out of the window. There was a bright star visible in the dead-night city sky, between the buildings. 'It's obvious what she is. She's a stupid cunt.'

Chapter One

Much later, when it was all over, after she'd been away on holiday and come back again, Jaz told everyone that she'd celebrated her twenty-first birthday at the best hotel in London. She said it with a smile and a shrug, but it was true. Her party was held in a luxury hotel, but not in the glowing dining room or the sumptuous lounge. It took place in a tiny scullery off the side of the kitchen. She crouched on the floor there, almost hidden by an industrial dishwasher and a trolley of stacked plates. Trace and Harm were the guests and they sat alongside and toasted her birthday with champagne, sipped from antique crystal glasses. Jaz joined in with chilled tomato juice, the colour of blood. She never drank alcohol. This was still one of the many rules which she used to run her life.

'These little gobfuls are nice,' said Harm, scooping up exquisite hors d'oeuvres from a polished platter and stuffing them into her mouth.

'I'll find some more,' offered Trace vaguely. 'There's loads of them, somewhere.' Trace was helping out at the hotel, off the record, no questions asked, cash in hand. What this meant was that every weekend and sometimes during the week, she took charge of the dishwasher, the crockery trolleys and sink-loads of precious metal and glassware that required 'hand rinsing'.

She stood up, wearing her regulation overall and hairnet. She went into the kitchen with confidence, smiling, mingling with foreign chefs, their stressed sous-chefs and calm, overtrained waiters in red cummerbunds. They all ignored her. She pushed another trolley of dirty dishes towards the scullery, this time bringing a half empty bowl of salmon mousse, more hors d'oeuvres and a paper carton, containing olives. Jaz and Harm dug into the glass bowl with silver spoons. 'These black things are weird,' said Trace, handing around the olives, 'but you get used to them. Better than the snails.'

Jaz was happy. This, she decided, was one of the best birthday celebrations she'd ever had. She was glad Trace had organized this, pleased she had such good, reliable friends. She pursed her lips thoughtfully, sipped her drink, remembered another good party when she was eleven. Blow had come back to the farm that morning in an open-topped Armstrong Siddeley. The chrome was crazed and pitted and the hide seats were mildewed but he pulled up outside the door hooting the horn and giving a mock gentleman's wave. Jasmine and her sisters were excited. They climbed all over the bonnet. 'I've just bought this from a duchess.' He grinned. 'Go and borrow your ma's finery. We're all going for a drive.'

Jasmine, her mother and her two little sisters searched through the big old bedroom wardrobe for hippy Indian cotton, lace, feathers, velvet and fur. They found leather boots and costume jewellery. They tried on hats. Blow squeezed into an old dinner suit. The family drove to Middlesbrough in his new old car where they turned heads and stopped traffic. They had tea in Burger King and Blow said they should eat as much as they liked, because it wasn't every day that someone special was eleven.

Jaz chewed on an olive and refilled her friends' glasses with champagne. Around the corner from their scullery, the kitchen was now busy. Even the waiters were running and raising their voices, but in their own special, private party corner, it seemed peaceful, wrapped in its cloudy, damp, dishwasher air. Harm burped quietly and announced that she'd had enough to eat. She eased her back away from a hot water pipe, sighed and stood up. 'S'pose I better go outside,' she suggested, 'for a ciggie?'

'Yes,' agreed Trace. 'This is a smoke-free zone.' She laughed. 'You could go and sit in the lounge.' She cleared their dishes from the floor, stacked some expertly in her sink, packed the rest in her dishwasher, closed it and switched it on. The jets roared.

'It's been nice,' said Jaz. 'Thanks.' She stood a little stiffly as Trace bent down and kissed her cheek.

'It's OK,' said Trace, stepping back and wiping her damp brow with the back of her hand. 'It's not every day your mate turns twenty-one.'

'What about that champagne?' asked Jaz.

Trace smiled. 'Come with me.' The three friends walked through the jostling kitchen. Harm ducked the flailing meat cleaver in the raised hand of an assistant's assistant. Instructions were shouted in French. There was sizzling and a flash of flame and Jaz closed her eyes for a second as two live lobsters were dropped into a steaming cauldron. 'Come on,' insisted Trace, catching both her friends by the arm, but not one of the kitchen staff bothered them.

They went down a corridor which led to the back of

the reception desk. Computer monitors winked, white on green. Above, on the marble counter, enormous vases of lilies were mixed with white roses. Only one uniformed receptionist was on duty and she was talking on the telephone. She giggled and swivelled from side to side on her high stool. Beyond her stretched the wide, glittering lobby lit by a dazzle of chandeliers. A group of guests in dinner suits talked and smoked. Two small children ran from the staircase towards the open door of a lift. Outside, a row of taxis idled. 'Wait here,' Trace said.

Harm and Jaz stood in the shadows. Trace slipped unnoticed in front of a computer and tapped for a moment on its keyboard. The receptionist didn't turn round but laughed again down the phone. 'You dirty beast!' she exclaimed.

Jaz turned to Harm. 'I didn't know Trace understood computers,' she murmured. 'She can't even read.'

Harm smiled. 'She understands what she needs to understand,' she replied. 'Never underestimate Trace.'

Their friend returned. 'You better go now,' she said.

'What've you done there?' asked Harm, pointing to the monitor.

'Taken care of the champagne,' Trace whispered. She smoothed her overall over her thin hips. 'I've just put it on Dustin Hoffman's room service account.'

Jaz and Harm stepped out, laughing, into the warm night. Harm lit a cigarette. Her mobile phone rang and she took it out of her bag. She exchanged a few words. Jaz knew it was Wesley, her current pimp. He had a client waiting for her in Belgravia.

Harm sighed. 'Time to earn a crust. I'll be going.' Her

words were slurred and soft. 'See you later, alligator.' She grinned. 'Happy Birthday.' She blew out a stream of smoke. Steadying herself against a lamp-post, she bent down and kissed the top of Jaz's head, then wandered away into the darkness. Jaz listened to her stilettos clicking for a moment above the hum of distant traffic.

She looked up at the BT tower and noticed that behind it, the moon was as full as an eye. The streets were empty, comfortable and strange. She passed several doorways where street people had bedded down under cardboard for the night. A ragged man came into view, then lurched past, pulling a tiny handcart. She switched on her Walkman, adjusted her headphones then set off at a steady jog in the direction of Tottenham Court Road. She imagined that she was one of the few people left on earth. The city is mine, she thought. She was happy.

Jaz lived in south London. For the last six months she'd been staying with Fat Andy, a friendly car thief, sharing his council flat in the badlands near Peckham Rye. She'd reminded him about her birthday, two nights before. They were in bed and she'd caressed his big stomach in a way she knew he liked. He was drinking Tia Maria from a plastic tumbler and reading *What Car?* magazine.

'You thought about my present?' she'd asked.

'What d'you want?'

'You know,' she murmured. She moved her hand downwards, gently. 'You know what I want.' She licked around his mouth, delicately, then her tongue probed inside his lips.

He tossed aside his magazine, put his drink down and

rolled heavily onto his back. 'Don't tell me.' He sighed. 'I know.'

'I know you know.' She climbed on top of his bulk and pulled on the child's nightdress, which was covered in pictures of Minnie Mouse. He'd bought it for her and it was the one he most liked her to wear.

Her body was small and thin, like a young girl's. 'I want to drive your car. You know I do. All around London. I want to drive it like I'm going to drive you.'

Andy rolled her pink nipples in his fingers, groaning slightly. Jaz was almost as flat-chested as a ten-year-old. 'Like what?' he asked, 'you sexy little baby.'

'Like crazy,' she laughed.

He kneaded her bony hips for a moment then raised his head. She knew the routine. She turned, leaned forwards and slipped a nipple between his lips. He sucked it greedily then fell back on the pillow. He always said the same things. 'Little baby, do it to me. Do it nice.'

'OK?' she said, as she guided him between her legs.

He shuddered and sighed. 'Nice. That's nice.'

Her hands pressing on his shoulders, she moved her hips quickly up and down. 'On my birthday?' she insisted. 'The Lotus Cortina? Is that a deal?'

Jaz jumped off a bus and ran lightly towards the estate. Her good mood was evaporating. Fat Andy hadn't come home last night and she'd waited on her own most of the day. She knew he might not keep his promise, but the thought of driving his car for the first time had kept her in a state of excitement for hours. Eventually, she'd admitted to herself that he wasn't coming. Her anticipation turned to anger. She'd tried his mobile for the tenth time but it was still switched off.

When Jaz had left the flat to meet Trace and Harm at the Savoy, she'd been furious with Andy. Now she was no longer emotional, just resigned. It's time to move on, she thought, running across the concrete courtyard. This wasn't the first time she'd decided to leave him, but she felt a stronger resolve than usual. She'd had enough.

I'm sick of living with a man I hardly know, she told herself. I'm sick of this feeling that I don't really understand him. Jaz felt close to only part of him. He wanted her to pretend to be much younger than she really was, and this had become a tiring game. He was secretive and evasive about many things. He'd forgotten her birthday.

Jaz felt a sense of relief at the prospect of change. Maybe he's back, she thought. If he's back, I'll drive the Lotus Cortina, but afterwards, I'll leave him anyway.

She pictured the shiny car, ermine white with its green flash and polished chrome, and the image led her to thoughts about Blow. He too had been big and fat with great old cars, and he too was unreliable. For some reason, she suddenly felt a pang of regret about leaving home and Blow and her sisters. This was followed by another feeling she couldn't name. What do I want? she thought. She decided at that moment to quit London and return to Teesside. Having a plan made it easier to dispel unwanted emotions and regrets. It gave her a sense of purpose. Only for a visit, she thought. I'll just stay for a while. See how they're getting on. Blow would let her drive his car, she was sure. He'd let her do anything she liked. He'd let her drive all his cars.

She remembered how in the months before she'd left,

he'd come into her bed a few times, late at night after her mother was asleep. He made the springs creak. He'd liked exactly the same things that Fat Andy liked. She'd been thirteen years old. She'd sat on top of him in the moonlight and she had worn a little girl's nightdress. He said he loved her. She never told tales. She never told anyone. Because of this, she knew he'd never deny her anything.

Slightly breathless from running, but not tired, Jaz entered the flats through the underground car park. It was twelve thirty. The Lotus Cortina was parked, gleaming and sleek on its low suspension, in Fat Andy's bay. He was back. A few teenagers stood around, sharing a joint, but Jaz knew they wouldn't touch the car. Fat Andy was known and respected on the estate.

Inside the building there was a sour odour and the strip lights were harshly bright. Jaz waited for the lift then decided it wasn't working. She started on the stairs, two at a time. From the doors she could hear televisions and arguments and a baby crying. The sourness was replaced by the smell of frying onions. Her trainers tapped quickly and evenly as she maintained a rhythm. She glanced at her watch. She was three seconds within her normal time. On the twelfth floor she stopped to catch her breath. A Vietnamese man passed her on his way down. He smelled of garlic and carried an extra large bottle of gin. He did not meet her eye. Jaz continued her rapid ascent. On the sixteenth floor, breathless, she began to unlock Fat Andy's door, but it swung open against the pressure of her hand.

It was oddly quiet in the flat. She'd been expecting

television or loud music or the jangle of Fat Andy's banjo. There were no lights on. 'Andy?' she called, pressing the switch in the hall. The small table by the door was overturned and the telephone was on the floor. Jaz picked them up and restacked the directories. 'Andy?'

She turned on the kitchen light and glanced inside. Her heavy breathing steadied but she was tense and wary. She went into the living room. The computer monitor was on and it cast an eerie glow. She walked over, pressed a key and examined the words that came up on the screen. It was an e-mail. 'Vinnys NOT a happy man', she read. 'Vinny says he wants his proparty back STRATE away. He wants his disk. Allrite? Allrite you Peckham git?'

Something bad had happened here. Jaz felt her pulse quicken again, but with the ugly, irregular flutter of uncertainty and fear. She looked around. The room was a mess. The sofa was on its side and a chair was broken in pieces. CDs and computer disks were scattered. Cups, plates and playing cards were strewn across the floor. Glasses were broken. A framed photo of Andy and his previous girlfriend, Princess, was smashed on the hearth. There was a smell of whisky and Jaz saw a bottle had been flung against a wall, streaking it brown. Andy's banjo was lying face down in the debris. She swallowed hard. This wasn't a burglary. Nothing was missing and no one on the estate would ever bother Fat Andy.

She went into the bedroom. It was in complete darkness. Jaz paused, aware that her brow was sweaty but not because she'd been running. Her whole body was suddenly clammy with a sense of dread. Something very bad had happened. This is scary, she thought to herself. This is very scary. Her fingers felt for the string that turned on the light. She couldn't find it. There was a strange smell and a chilly, nameless kind of quiet that was unnatural and new to the room. At last her groping fingers located the cord and the bed was suddenly illuminated. 'Andy?' she whispered.

He lay on his back, his boots dangling, toes pointing inwards. One hand was above his head, the other below his throat. Blood had oozed through his fingers and coagulated. It covered, thickly and glutinously, his neck, chest, waist, arm and half the bed. It had run down and made a large, sticky-looking pool which hadn't entirely sunk into the carpet. Jaz stared. She had seen blood before but never so much. It smelled strongly, salty, like fresh meat. She felt the urge to scream and cry out but held a hand over the bottom half of her face. The cold stillness of the room and the blood that had stopped flowing meant one real, definite thing. Fat Andy was dead. She went over and touched his raised hand. It was ice cold. It didn't feel like human flesh. His face was ghastly white, his eyes half closed, his mouth slightly open as if in surprise. His cheeks were like sunken, grey dough. Jaz couldn't move. She examined with her eyes the gash in his neck which reminded her, at that moment, of a woman's sexual parts. 'Andy?' she said.

Later, thinking about this night, Jaz would find it strange, remembering how quick and decisive she'd suddenly become. She turned and left Andy, left him lying there, left the bedroom, turning off the light. She was able, temporarily, to dismiss both shock and outrage. For the next fifteen minutes, her only thoughts were that she'd made a big mistake by being here and that it was necessary, imperative to get away. Far away. She shouldn't have come back tonight. She should never have stayed in this flat, lived here. She'd been trapped. She'd abandoned her freedom. For six months she'd been a fool. I'm a mug, was all she could think. What have I got myself into? Jaz, you're a mug. You're a stupid idiot.

She searched the rooms for her few possessions and packed them in her sports bag. From the mantelpiece, she took an old photograph of her twin sisters, Peony and Mimosa, which was undamaged. She picked up the smashed frame from the hearth and extracted the picture of Fat Andy and Princess. She decided to keep it as she had no other to remind herself of him. She found his jacket in the living room and took a fold of money and small change. She pocketed his leather driving gloves and his Filofax. For ten seconds she held the keys to the Lotus Cortina, staring at them, tempted, before tossing them aside.

She knew that her departure needed to be speedy, silent and unremarkable. She wasn't going to take the car. Not now. Not yet. She had to become the same homeless, unacknowledged shadow she'd previously been. She didn't want trouble. She didn't want the attention that would come from driving Andy's car. For a few mad months she'd broken her code. Living in a proper flat, with the same man, day in day out, had been an error of judgement. It wasn't her style. Now she would resume her former life where invisibility and safety were the same thing. She didn't want to be noticed. She certainly didn't want to be caught up in the glare that follows the discovery of a murder.

She locked the outside door. She ran down the stairs and across the deserted courtyard. She sprinted towards

Camberwell New Road. She ran and ran, heading instinctively towards the river. At Blackfriars she stopped and leaned against a wall. She was at last exhausted. She knew of a wide doorway nearby which was draught-free. She was relieved to find it unoccupied. Before settling down she found a phone box. She dialled 999 but hung up when asked for her name. Instead, she phoned the police station on Peckham High Street. 'Don't ask me anything,' she insisted. She gave the address of the flat and checked it was recorded correctly. 'Fat Andy's dead,' she then added. 'Get round there now.'

'What was that, Madam?'

'Fat Andy's dead.' As she said these words again the tears started flowing. She realized she was in shock. There was a pain in her chest which was nothing to do with running such a long way. She was on the verge of losing control. 'Andy,' she sobbed. 'My Andy. Someone's done him in.'

Chapter Two

The early morning traffic woke Jaz at four thirty. She'd become unaccustomed to sleeping outside, so despite feeling very free, she was also stiff and cold. A thin sun glimmered from below the skyline. She stood up, stretched and then remembered. Her life in Peckham had come to an abrupt close. She had been ready to end it herself, but she'd wanted merely to disappear. Such violence, such a brutal snuffing out of Fat Andy's life was unbelievable. She was appalled.

Jaz had lived on the streets for a long time and witnessed lots of unpleasant scenes, but seeing Andy like that, a person who was normally warm and cuddly and alive – seeing him like a butchered animal spread over their bed – this was the worst thing she'd ever had to deal with. An unfamiliar emotion spread from a pain at the centre of her chest and through her undersized frame, before lodging in her mind. She considered this sensation, deciding the only word to describe it was grief. Grief mixed with yesterday's shock. Her mind was racing and her body was trembling.

She picked up her sports bag, put on Andy's gloves and her Walkman and set off, across the river. The Thames was liquid silver streaked with grey. The sky was changing from orange-mauve to blue and overhead a helicopter hammered and swooped, frightening a flock of gulls. Jaz was the only person on the bridge and she walked quickly, then even quicker, before breaking into a gentle jog. The morning air was at its freshest, before the cars poisoned the day. She breathed evenly, concentrating on maintaining a rhythm. She increased her pace. As she sped up Farringdon Road, the exertion of running had its usual effect. All thoughts of Fat Andy and the carnage at his flat disappeared temporarily from her mind. She remembered instead that only yesterday, on the night of her birthday, she'd decided to return to Teesside. Now, this idea was compelling. She wanted to get as far away as possible from the flat, from Peckham, from London.

Ahead, on a bend, a vast hoarding advertised a building society. A delicate child was shown, ten times life-size, surrounded by apple blossom and cradling a dove. Suddenly, sentimentally, Jaz felt a desire to see the twins. Her sisters would make her feel better, she was sure. She remembered their small bodies, their silky cheeks and long eyelashes. It didn't occur to her that they must be seventeen years old. She still thought of them as young children. For the first time in years, she missed them. She thought of the way their golden hair lay across their brows, ragged and uncombed, hanging down in strands, hiding the innocent smoothness of their little-girl necks, their bony shoulders. She could imagine them only as they had once been. Peony and Mimosa existed forever in her mind as nine-year-olds, together and inseparable, playing carelessly amongst the mud and debris of their mother's ruined farmyard.

Jaz approached the Angel and slowed to walking pace. A group of women wearing overalls emerged from the

Tube station. They were cheerful and smiling, extending to her the complicity of early morning workers. London is a secret at five a.m., Jaz thought to herself – a precious secret known only to a handful of its inhabitants. She avoided their gaze. There was no way she wanted to belong to London now; be a Londoner. Instead, she needed to escape.

Jaz spent the day walking and running, covering several miles. She tried to contact Trace at the hotel, to tell her what had happened, but the receptionist said she knew no one of that name. Then she rang Harm's mobile and left a message, merely saying she was going away for a while, and not to worry. She was concerned that they would hear of Fat Andy's death and start panicking. She resolved to keep trying them until she could explain what had happened at the flat.

She sat in a park, ate a sandwich, then slept for a while on a bench. She hitched a couple of rides. Later, at a service station somewhere on the M11, acting out of habit she decided to ask someone for money. It was eleven p.m. She glanced around the lobby but couldn't see a woman. She went over to the café, but the diners were all men, lorry drivers and travelling salesmen. Even the staff, serving behind the hot counters in red waistcoats and bow ties, were male. She noticed two young men in overalls who were about to leave. They walked towards her at the entrance, each sipping a can of Pepsi.

'Hello, boys,' Jaz said too loudly and with confidence, 'I've got no money. Going to give me some?' She looked them in the eyes, in turn, and stood too close, using her sports bag to block their path. They stopped, surprised.

Automatically, politely, one searched in his pockets for change. He became flustered and embarrassed. Without examining it, he handed her a crumpled note. He didn't meet her gaze.

Jaz stepped into the restaurant and grinned. She smoothed out the cash. It was ten pounds. At least I can still hustle for money, she thought. I haven't lost my touch. She hadn't done this for a long time, but she knew that in the near future she might have no choice. Everything was uncertain. She was homeless again. The days and weeks ahead had an unknown quality that might demand anything – not least the use of her old street skills.

The café was called the Planet Suite and it was air conditioned. The low light fittings were ringed orbs. The ordinary food was imaginatively named. Using the ten pounds Jaz bought a large coffee, a Saturn Burger and a Milky Way ice cream. As she sat down she noticed that her plastic table top was a map of Mars. Outside was the straight corridor of the motorway, the thrum-thrum of lighted cars, empty fields and the real moon, hanging in the distance like a dirty plate. Jaz stirred her cup and glanced around. She thought to herself, this place is just a universe of lonely souls.

A few men studied tabloids, drank tea, slapped the bottoms of sauce bottles. For an instant each one was known to her – there was a neighbour from Peckham, a teacher from her school, a social worker she'd had sex with at the hostel in Hammersmith – but then, at each moment of recognition, their unfamiliar features focused and she knew she was amongst strangers. I'm tired, she thought a little bleakly. It's night-time. And there's miles and miles still to go.

After finishing her food, Jaz bought a second cup of coffee. The men around her arrived, left and arrived. They glanced at her without curiosity. She took the blotting paper doilies from between her cups and saucers and tore them into thin shreds. Sitting quietly, but restless, it was impossible not to think about Andy, lying with his throat cut on the bed where she'd slept with him for the last six months. She remembered a long smear of blood, brown and thick, across the blue pillowcase. The image of him dead kept cutting across thoughts of him alive. She tried to think of him settled in his armchair, drinking Scotch, big and jolly, always pleased to see her, but the grisly corpse in the bedroom kept returning to her mind.

She remembered the e-mail message on the computer screen. 'Vinnys NOT a happy man.' Reluctantly, Jaz thought about what this could mean. It was a threatening statement. Vinny from the Island was dangerous if he was unhappy. People tried to keep him happy at all costs.

Vinny dealt in cars. His legitimate business was run from a wide-fronted, brash showroom and its adjoining forecourt, both filled with new and second-hand Mazdas, all acquired legally. However, his legendary wealth was the result of another enterprise. Vinny employed a team of thieves who operated throughout east London and the City. His expertise lay in changing the identity of stolen cars and then selling them abroad. He specialized in Jaguars and BMWs, stolen to order, but he was prepared to handle any car that was new, gleaming and expensive. He paid well but demanded total loyalty. Fat Andy had worked for him for several years, supervising all the work on the streets. This meant he recruited and fired the thieves, specified which cars they were to steal, and handed out their wages.

Jaz drained her cup. She had worked for Vinny too, but not recently. She'd met Andy in a queue outside a Chinese takeaway and admired his Lotus Cortina. They started chatting about classic cars. That night, they arranged to meet again and once she had discovered his line of work, Jaz persuaded him to take her on. For a while she was his star thief, earning special commendations and a bonus. When she decided to quit an unsatisfactory squat in Kensington, Andy suggested she stay at his flat. After they started sleeping together, he'd asked her to stop stealing cars and reluctantly, she agreed. He said it was unsuitable work for a woman. What he meant was, he didn't like his girlfriend doing it. Vinny understood. He knew he had to let Jaz go. Vinny was familiar with the nuances and etiquette of male pride, and Fat Andy was not only proud but indispensable. Or at least he had been.

Jaz thought about the tiny office at the back of Vinny's showroom with its girlie calendars and battered desk. Vinny, she knew, sat there for hours, wiry and energetic in his dark suits, talking rapidly down the phone in his Greek accent, fixing deal after lucrative deal. He had contacts all over Europe. He had gold rings on his small, hairy hands, a compact, muscular body and dark eyes, one of which had a habit of wandering sideways, out of control, giving him a stupid look. But Jaz knew that Vinny from the Island was no fool. He was ruthless and clever and not a person to offend. She wondered what Andy had done. He'd said Vinny was ungrateful. He'd said he wanted a better deal, more money and responsibility. He wanted to be cut into the operation as a partner rather than a lackey. Whatever had happened between them, Andy had ended up dead.

Vinny was not a happy man. He wanted his property back. Andy had a disk belonging to him and because of this and probably other reasons, he had killed Andy or ordered him killed. Jaz was in no doubt: Vinny had done it. Of this, she was absolutely certain.

After another half hour, Jaz walked over to a games machine and fed the slot with her few remaining coins. Trying to be animated, she pressed several buttons and a stream of lucky silver cascaded to her feet. She was aware that all the men in the café were staring. She collected the coins together and went into a phone booth.

She checked in Andy's Filofax, then pressed the numbers of Vinny's mobile. It was twelve forty-five but she knew he suffered from insomnia. He was hyperactive and a gambler. Fat Andy had told her of his habits. He would be sucking Rennies for his heartburn. He was probably playing roulette at a down-market Chinese casino off the East India Dock Road.

The phone was answered immediately.

'Vinny! Companero!' She always called him this. 'You fucking Greek bastard, it's Jaz.' She pressed her hand against the pain in her chest.

There was a pause. 'Hello darlink,' he replied. His voice was always unnaturally high, making him sound effeminate. 'How yous keeping?'

Her voice became very cold. 'Why did you do it? You're a complete shit, you know that?'

'What you mean, darlink? What you want?'

'Vinny, don't piss about. I've left London. You can't find me. D'you think I won't shop you? Turn you in? You evil fucker. I know what's gone down in Peckham. D'you think I won't contact the Old Bill?' Jaz hung up. She wanted to make Vinny's sleep patterns even more troubled. She felt a rush of pleasure. She'd never liked him. Now there was nothing to stop her from harassing Vinny on his mobile, any time she felt like it. She decided to ring him again the next day.

Outside, the exit road curved away like a dark snake. Jaz needed to hitch a lift but felt reluctant to face the night. She picked up her bag and stepped out into the warm wind, then jogged across the car park. A mother and father unloaded two sleeping toddlers from the back of a Ford Escort. Jaz noted their roof-rack loaded with luggage and their window stickers showing previous holiday destinations. She thought of her own family and of Peony and Mimosa and how they'd never been anywhere on holiday apart from a day trip to Redcar sands. I'm going home, she thought to herself.

She ran past the petrol station and down the slip road towards the motorway's convoy of lorries, its buzz of anxious cars. I'm going home, she thought again. She stopped and turned around. The family with the sleeping children entered the service station. It shone like a friendly island in the sea of night. Jaz stood on the grass verge, hesitated, then loosened her hair, letting the wind stir it around her face. She felt smaller than ever in the darkness. She stood casually for a moment, her thin hip jutting, then she stretched out her arm.

A car stopped immediately. It was a new Mondeo, red and throaty. It throbbed lustily at her side. The driver leaned over and opened both the passenger and the rear door. There was a blare of music. She threw her bag on the back seat then climbed in next to him. As she clipped together her seat belt he turned down the volume of the

CD. Jaz noted that he was about twenty-seven, smart and smelled of scent. He smiled, accelerated and cruised over into the sparse but fast moving outside lane. Jaz inspected his suit, his gleaming collar, a faint shadow on his jaw, a nervous pulse in his temple.

'Michael,' he said. 'I'm only going as far as Cambridge.'

Jaz smiled and took off Fat Andy's driving gloves, turned round and tucked them into her sports bag. She recognized his flat friendly accent. She'd heard it in hostels all over London.

'Call me Mike,' he added self-consciously. 'I'm from Leeds.'

Jaz decided at that moment she could do with a bit of short-term help from Mike. She was in no hurry and she was tired. In an instant she had assessed both Mike's affluence and his susceptibility. He's not a weirdo, she thought to herself. He's ordinary and safe. He won't give me any trouble.

'Hi Mike,' she replied, moving closer and placing her right arm behind his head rest in a gesture that was both innocent and seductive.

With a strained roar from the engine he overtook a BMW. He was trying to impress her. Jaz decided he was a good driver but not as good as Fat Andy and definitely not as good as herself. One thing she'd learned from Blow was not to overwork a car.

Mike took a cigarette out of a packet on his lap and pressed the dashboard lighter. 'It's a dangerous game,' he said, 'thumbing lifts.' He inhaled. There was a silence. 'D'you always travel this way then?'

Jaz adopted a slightly breathless, babyish tone. It was one she'd sometimes used with Andy when she wanted her own way. She exaggerated her northern accent. 'Only with nice lads. Nice lads with decent cars.' She sounded at least six years younger than she actually was. She sounded under-age.

'Your mam and dad. They know where you are, luv?' He changed gear and his hand brushed her knee. He pretended it was an accident.

'That's all right,' Jaz murmured softly.

The Mondeo ate up the miles. A cool breeze blew on Jaz through the vent at her side and Mike played a Levellers album. Soft guitar music filled the small space. She was suddenly sleepy and for a moment wished more than anything that they were the only two people in the universe. Travelling at high speed in a fast car, late at night on the motorway was one of her favourite things in the world. She closed her eyes, pretending she was in a space rocket, circling the earth. It was so peaceful, she wanted it to go on for ever.

After a while, Jaz told Mike that she loved animals and that when she left school she wanted to study veterinary science. She invented an elderly godmother in Leeds. She could read Mike. He was excited by her presence in his car and pleased and flattered. He thought she was a wayward child. She built up the fiction. 'My older sister's a lesbian. She's sixteen. She's got fat legs.'

'You got a boyfriend, then?'

'No. 'Fraid not.'

'Good.'

'Is it?'

'Yeah.'

Jaz dozed again, almost happy. She woke up as the car curved, slowing, leaving the steady rhythm of the motorway. Instantly alert, she took in road signs, an all-night pizzeria, a double-decker bus. 'Where are we?' she mumbled, pretending to be confused.

They paused at a roundabout. 'I'm not going much further,' Mike said.

Jaz straightened, yawned, reached for her bag. 'Best drop me here then,' she said in a neutral voice, 'so's I can get another lift.'

'I can always take you to my place,' Mike offered, very hesitant. He pulled into a lay-by and turned towards her, his empty palms upward in a gesture of honesty and helplessness. 'It's no trouble.'

Jaz pretended to be shy. Her hair fell forward hiding her face. 'OK,' she agreed, sounding like a little girl.

'You sure?'

'I'm sure.'

Later, in Mike's bed, Jaz stared at the brown walls, the chrome alarm clock, the single plain white bathrobe hanging on the back of the door. This wasn't a woman's room. She held her hands over her nipples. Mike was next to her, propped on pillows, talking to Japan on the phone. The bed was soft and clean. Jaz wished that he was speaking to a wife or even a girlfriend. She felt almost sorry for him. She leaned over and stroked his thighs.

Mike put the phone down, switched off the light and turned towards her. Jaz's mind immediately moved to that distant place which makes feigned sexual interest possible. Out of habit, her expert hands travelled over his body. She held him and kissed his neck. She rubbed her chest against his and wrapped her legs around him. He was fleshier than she expected and at first his gentle passivity encouraged her. She kissed his lips fiercely, her hand travelling down his back, finding the crack in his buttocks. After a few more moments she realized he was not responding. 'What's the matter?' she whispered.

He rolled over onto his back. 'I'm sorry,' he said finally.

'It's OK.'

'No it's not. It's never OK.' He sounded desperate. 'I thought you'd be . . .' He paused.

'What?'

There was another awkward silence. Outside a siren announced an ambulance.

Jaz suddenly realized the nature of the problem. 'You thought I'd be a virgin,' she supplied. She'd been acting a part, but she'd not acted the right one for Mike. He'd wanted a naive and innocent female, not one who was experienced and knowing.

She stared at the space around the window blind where the orange light from a street lamp gleamed dully. When she heard him crying, she pretended to be asleep.

The alarm clock said seven a.m. Jaz touched Mike's cheek, checking he was still unconscious.

He breathed deeply and regularly. She slipped out of bed and with practised stealth, dressed in silence. She combed her hair with his comb and removed forty pounds from his jacket. She took the loose change from his trouser pocket. A box on the mantelpiece contained some gold cufflinks which she removed. Finally, without disturbing him, she slid his watch off the bedside table.

In the hall she was relieved to see that the burglar

alarm was not switched on. There was no complicated locking mechanism on the front door. In an instant, she was outside in the street where the morning rush hour was starting to build.

Chapter Three

Jaz had never been to Cambridge before. She wandered around, mingling with the crowds. A lot of people carried cameras and guidebooks. She wondered what it must be like to be a tourist and go somewhere on holiday. She thought again how she'd never been on holiday in her life.

After leaving another message for Harm, she bought a postcard showing two students in a punt and scribbled on the back 'Going up north for a visit, don't worry,' and sent it to Trace, care of the kitchen at the hotel. Jaz wasn't confident she'd receive it. It was likely that she had moved on to other casual employment by now.

It was hot in the bright sunshine and she bought an ice lolly. At one point, near some traffic lights, she thought she saw Mike in his red Mondeo but realized immediately that the registration number was different. Thinking of him with a mixture of pity and distaste, she found a shop with a sign in the window saying 'We Buy gold' and sold his watch and cufflinks for two hundred and fifty pounds.

Jaz had lunch in McDonald's, ordering a McChicken Sandwich and a strawberry milk shake. As she sat munching, she watched diners come and go and thought about how people from all walks of life ate at McDonald's, even men who were almost certainly university dons. She tried to keep her mind occupied but, inevitably, thoughts of Fat Andy came crowding in. The now familiar pain spread across her chest and she placed a hand on the centre. She could feel a rhythmic pulse. My heart is breaking, she thought. I was going to leave him, but now he's dead. I'm suffering. If only I'd stayed in and waited for him. If only I hadn't insisted that he come back for my birthday. If only I'd never met him. She repeated this new phrase in her mind. My heart is breaking.

She remembered Andy using the same words. They'd just had a row. She leaned her head in her hand, sipping her milk shake, picturing the scene in the flat. Andy didn't like Harm and Trace. He didn't like Jaz going out in the evening without him.

'They're my best mates,' she'd argued.

'They're slappers.'

'They saved my life!' Jaz was very angry. Not for the first time with Andy she felt trapped. 'We've been through all sorts together, us three. We're the nearest any of us has to family. They're more like my sisters than my real sisters. Who the hell do you think you are? I've only known you a few weeks.'

The quarrel ebbed back and forth.

'First you make me give up my job . . .'

'Nicking cars isn't a job . . .'

'Then you start telling me who I can and can't see . . .'

'I'm only saying . . .'

Jaz picked up her sports bag and went into the bedroom and stuffed it with clothes. She returned. 'I'm out of here,' she said. 'I'm not listening to any more of this fucking shit, you telling me what to do.' She took one of the photos off the mantelpiece. It was the picture of

Peony and Mimosa, dressed as angels. She packed it away. 'I'm going.' She pulled the zip and shouldered the bag. 'Pissing right off out of here.' She walked towards the door. 'Goodbye.'

Fat Andy was sitting in the armchair, his head in his hands, leaning forwards. He peeped at her between his fingers. As she opened the door he raised his head. Jaz turned and saw that his face was wet. He looked very sad. 'My heart's breaking,' he said.

Jaz was amazed. She stopped in her tracks. 'What?'

'My heart. You're breaking my heart.'

She put down her bag. She was pleased. He'd told her he loved her, but only in bed, when he wanted certain things. She hadn't believed him. She went over and wrapped her arms around his head, pressing his face to her chest. 'It's fine,' she said repeatedly, 'I'm sorry, everything's fine.' Her anger had vanished. His heart was breaking. She was at a loss for words. 'It's fine. Really. It's fine.'

Jaz stirred her milk shake with her straw and pressed her hand even harder against her chest. It occurred to her that she had never felt grief like this before and that the pain was physically sharp. Tears pricked her eyes but refused to fall. She wondered what had happened between Andy and Vinny and how things could have got so very bad between them. Andy must have pushed Vinny too far. He was never any kind of match for Vinny – he wasn't devious or clever enough and he wasn't cruel. In any case, Vinny never let anyone push him. Never. He demanded total loyalty. He demanded respect.

She finished her meal and went outside, into a phone

box. She dialled the number of Vinny's line in his garage but he didn't answer and she was asked to leave a message. She spoke angrily but quietly. 'Companero? You greasy pile of shite? Guess who? You'll not get away with this. You'll not, I repeat, not get away with this. I'll do you. I'm going to do you. You evil fuck. You Greek bastard.' Until yesterday, she'd never dared speak to Vinny like this. She realized she'd always wanted to. She wondered what the point of it was, but she hung up the phone feeling a tiny bit better.

Later, Jaz boarded a tourist bus and sat on the open-air top deck. She stayed there for an hour and a half, going round and round the town, listening to the same recorded commentary. It was reassuring to do such a predictable, innocent thing. It made her feel more like other people.

She remembered the first time she'd sat on such a bus. It was a cold, dark night in Sunderland and they'd driven there in one of Blow's old cars. It was late, a time she'd normally be in bed. She was with the twins. They parked, got on the bus and climbed the stairs. It was breezy and Blow wrapped the three of them together in an old blanket from the stable. The memory of the rough wool and the rank horse-smell was still with her. The bus drove in the darkness to the promenade but there was no moon and the sea was as black as the sky. Jaz remembered the sharp jabs of the twins' elbows and the way Blow had leaned towards them, his arm along the back of their bench, his breath sour with beer. The invisible sea rolled to and fro and they waited, unsure what was happening. Suddenly the air around them burst into a blinding dazzle of light. Peony screamed, and Jasmine's heart lurched in her chest. There was an explosion of colour. A brass band, somewhere below them, blew out the national anthem in a deafening, resounding blast. The bus started to move, driving slowly along, and above them were flashing Santas and snowflakes and the glare of a million light bulbs. 'It's the Illuminations,' exclaimed Blow, excited. 'Aren't they something, girls? You've just seen 'em switched on.'

Jaz sat on the bus, her mind wandering. She tried to imagine olden times, when the students wore gowns and worked within these ancient colleges with dusty books and quill pens, but thoughts of Fat Andy kept returning. She remembered the horrible quiet in the bedroom where the body had lain, the dreadful stillness of the corpse. She recalled the scent, the chill of death, the blood on the carpet.

I am a free person now, she reminded herself. I can do exactly as I please, just like in the old days. I was going to leave him anyway. I know what I'm doing. I know what I want. I'm going home. She was surprised that these realizations did not make her feel better. She got off the bus and jogged in the direction of a big modern hotel which she'd noticed earlier in the day.

She checked in and hung a 'Do Not Disturb' sign on the outside of her door before closing it firmly. Jaz loved hotels and even feeling as bad as she did, she went through her routine of lying down on the first bed, then bouncing on the other, like a child. She pressed a button which raised and lowered an external shutter and then she tinkered with the controls of the air conditioning. She made herself a cup of coffee, drank it then took a shower using the complimentary gel and shampoo. She wrapped herself in thick white towels and switched on the TV. She drank several non-alcoholic beverages from the mini-bar. There was nothing about the murder in the news. She rang Harm's mobile again. This time she answered.

'Look Harm, no questions, but I'm in Cambridge. Andy's been killed . . .'

'Jesus Christ, Jaz! What's happened?'

'Fat Andy's been killed. Murdered. I don't want to talk about it. I'm going home to Teesside, just for a bit. Tell Trace. Don't worry. I'm OK.'

She hung up, then picked up the phone again and rang room service to request three newspapers and a bacon sandwich. She combed through the papers but there was nothing about Fat Andy. Evidently a murder on a south London council estate was not remarkable enough to interest the national dailies. Jaz drew her curtains and climbed into bed. She knew she had enough cash to stay in the hotel for a while but was conscious of wasting resources. She decided to continue on her journey home the following day.

She picked up the phone again. Slowly and remembering the number whole, like a familiar place name, she pressed each separate digit carefully, her anticipation and fear growing with each electronic beep. She hadn't phoned home in years. When the ringing tone began, she almost hung up. Her heart was hammering and her mouth was dry. She pictured the empty hallway with its bare and rotting boards, the crazy lean of the dilapidated porch, the old-fashioned bakelite phone, dusty on the windowsill. She imagined the bell, echoing up the dead, damp space of the stairwell and the clatter of the twins' boots.

'Yes,' answered her mother. 'Who is it?'

Jaz's stomach lurched. Her mother never answered the phone. She'd expected Blow, or one of the girls. 'Lola?' she said. 'It's Jasmine.'

There was the briefest of pauses. The line hummed with a thousand ghostly conversations linking south and north. 'Well then,' her mother said. She sounded discouraged, just like she'd always done, but surprisingly sober. 'Well then.'

Jaz explained that she was on her way home.

'You've just caught me,' her mother said, as if she was at the start of an errand.

'I'll be a day or two yet,' Jaz explained, almost apologetic.

'That's not what I mean.' Her mother went on to say that she was leaving the farm, going the next day. Everything was sold. The fields were to be built over with starter homes.

Jaz listened to this, barely able to comprehend. Her mother's words buzzed in her head like a fly.

'And not a minute too soon,' said her mother. She sounded weary but at the same time more decisive than she'd ever been before.

'What about,' Jaz whispered, then paused. 'What about the others?'

Her mother's tone didn't change. 'What others?'

'The twins . . . Are they . . .'

'Peony's in town with a good-for-nothing labourer and twin baby boys. Mimosa's at Newcastle College making sculptures out of papier mâché.'

'And Blow . . .?'

There was a silence. Her mother sighed. 'Well of course. You wouldn't know.'

'Know what?'

'Blow's no longer with us.'

'You mean he's left?'

She sniffed, then coughed. 'Dead.' She paused. 'Crashed his car the same night as Princess Diana.'

Jaz gasped. There was another stab of pain in her chest, the same as before. She pressed her hand to the spot once again. 'What . . . what on earth was he doing in . . . Paris?'

'Don't be bloody stupid. He crashed on the A1, just north of Leeming Bar. He lost control, caused a pile-up, and everything caught fire. They had to use dental records to identify him.' She coughed again, then sighed.

Chapter Four

Jaz held the phone away from her face and stared at it in disbelief.

'Hello?' she heard her mother say. 'Hello?'

Purposefully, slowly, she replaced the receiver.

A few minutes passed. She watched the numbers on the clock radio change: 20.45, 20.46, 20.47, 20.48.

Blow is dead, she thought. Fat Andy is dead. She fiddled with the TV remote, turning the set off, then on again, without the sound. She got up and filled the kettle and switched it on, then forgot about it. After a while, she lay flat on the bed, clutching the pillows to her stomach. 'Oh, no,' she said aloud. It came out as a groan. 'Shit, shit, shit.'

A few tears ran down the sides of her face and into her ears. She sat up and wiped her nose. Outside, below in the street, a succession of emergency vehicles raced by, their sirens sounding.

Both of them, she thought. Both Blow and Fat Andy. Both dead. It seemed beyond all reason. She picked up the phone, intending to call Harm, but replaced it without dialling.

She realized, not for the first time, that the two of them – Fat Andy and Blow – were, in a curious way, the same person. They were very alike and she'd loved them.

She ran this word through her mind a few times. Love. She'd loved them. Yes, she loved them but never desired them. She'd loved them even though they'd let her down. The pattern had repeated itself.

I thought the world of them, she said to herself, realizing that this quaint expression was one she'd learned long before, but never in connection with her own feelings. She said it aloud, 'I thought the world of them.' She'd never admitted this, or even considered it, when they were alive. Love was a subject she never acknowledged, an emotion she always suppressed – but she felt it now. They were loved. Both Fat Andy and Blow, as if they were one. She pressed her hand again onto the place in her chest where she felt the wound. It was the pain of an empty space. It was an acute sense of loss.

She climbed back into bed but couldn't sleep. Instead, she kept imagining a scene where either Blow, or Fat Andy, or sometimes both of them curiously merged, were repairing the sills on a white, ex-police Ford Capri. Lying on their backs, heads partially hidden, they were drilling holes, then filling them with Waxoyl to keep the metal rust-free. 'How's it going?' she pictured herself asking, several times, always placing a steaming cup of tea on the ground.

'It's a right bastard,' they each said resignedly. 'This gunge. It's terrible when it drops in your hair.'

At two a.m. she sat up and tried to watch a Sky movie but couldn't understand the storyline. It was very complicated. The gangster in the sharp suit who was killing everyone reminded her of Vinny. He was bigger and better looking, and had an American accent, but he had the same mean, squinty stare. Suddenly she pictured Vinny, dressed in the gangster's clothes with the same machine gun, mowing down Blow and Fat Andy, as if they were nothing. Then, in her mind, she saw him with a knife at Andy's throat. She blinked. She saw a quick, nasty image of the neck wound, but the next moment she imagined him speeding up the A1 in his new Mazda 626 and, in a fit of road rage, deliberately running Blow off the carriageway.

Vinny's to blame, she thought. It's all Vinny's fault. She dozed off then, leaving the lights and the TV switched on.

She woke at five with a stiff neck and an angry sensation growing in her stomach. Anger was taking the place of grief. In an instant she remembered. Blow and Fat Andy were both dead. That fucking Vinny, she thought. She stood up and looked at herself, naked in the mirror. She clenched her fists. That evil spivvy bastard. I'm going to get him for this. He's not getting away with it. She picked up a damp towel from the floor and hurled it towards the bathroom. 'Vinny,' she said aloud. 'You shit. I'm going to get even with you, if it's the only worthwhile thing I ever do.'

She went back to bed and turned things over in her mind. Her anger made her feel strong. She wasn't afraid of Vinny. She had been once, but not any more. She knew he was clever, but then so was she. His viciousness and power could be matched by her determination. She was in a better place to take him on than Andy had been, not least because he wouldn't take her seriously. She wasn't sure how she was going to damage him, but she was determined to make him suffer.

A few certainties began to take shape in her mind.

Number one, Fat Andy and Blow were dead. Number two, Vinny was going to face the consequences. Number three, Harm and Trace were her very good friends and could be called on for help if necessary. This is what I'm going to do, she thought. I'm going to sort out the Greek bastard. She felt a little better. Things suddenly seemed very clear.

She was reminded of a phrase of Fat Andy's. It was one he'd used a lot and he'd repeated it to her endlessly when he was training her to steal cars. 'Stay calm,' he used to say. 'Stay focused. Stay cool.' She said this aloud several times. 'Stay calm, stay focused, stay cool.' She knew that she had to return to London. She wanted revenge. She would go in the morning, quickly, without wasting any time.

Chapter Five

At seven o'clock, Jaz ate a light breakfast, sitting alongside a few silent businessmen. They eyed her curiously over their newspapers whilst ordering extra coffee. Later, in the hotel lobby, she peeled off a few bank notes – part of the proceeds from the sale of Mike's jewellery – and paid her bill.

In the car park, she was pleased to discover there were no surveillance cameras. She walked around, weighing things up. Finally, she selected a 1994 VW Golf with a sticker in the back window which said 'Countryside Campaign'. Jaz was unsympathetic to this pressure group, despite her semi-rural childhood. She believed in the Right to Roam and thought fox-hunting was a sick joke.

She picked up a loose half brick from the edge of the paving. Leaning against the vehicle, her body shielding her action, she broke a quarter light and lifted up the button on the driver's door. She slid inside the car, rummaged in her bag for a pair of screwdrivers, then tossed her belongings onto the back seat.

She waited for a moment as two Japanese men with briefcases walked through the car park and disappeared. She looked at her watch before hitting the steering cowl hard, cracking it open. She threw the brick out of the window, levered the cowl with the large screwdriver, broke it cleanly then discarded the plastic pieces. Using both hands she stabbed the implement into the ignition, leaning against it, ramming it with the weight of her chest until she felt the soft metal around the keyhole open like a wound. Quickly, using the smaller screwdriver, she inserted its blade into the damaged inner barrel and moved it gently up and down. The soft alloy disintegrated, some of it falling to the floor at her feet. She leaned to the side and squinted into the hole she'd created. Satisfied, she repositioned the small screwdriver inside the mechanism and turned it carefully. The engine coughed and awoke with a guilty sigh. Jaz glanced at her watch again. Two minutes. Not bad, she thought.

At that instant, a hotel receptionist arrived and braked her Fiesta at the entrance to the car park. She was yawning, stretching, about to start her shift. She pressed her remote and raised the security barrier.

Jaz drove forward, towards the exit, as if she was in a hurry.

Politely, the young uniformed woman beckoned to the Golf, indicating that it should have priority.

Jaz gave her a thumbs-up as she turned out into the traffic.

The journey south was uneventful, if slow. The motorway was busy. Jaz opened the glove compartment and listened to a few CDs. She found a pair of Versace sunglasses which she put on and decided to keep.

In London, she took the advice of a radio presenter and turned off the main road early, only to get held up near Wood Green for half an hour because of a burst water main. Frustrated, she abandoned the Golf near Archway, took a Tube to London Bridge and changed to a train for Queen's Road. She put on her headphones and jogged steadily in the direction of the estate where she'd lived with Fat Andy. It was only very recently, she thought. It was not that long ago.

She'd decided to take Andy's Lotus Cortina. She couldn't manage without wheels if she was going to get even with Vinny. Her plans were still a bit vague, but she was certain that she'd need a car. Andy's Lotus Cortina was the only one she really wanted and he couldn't stop her driving it now. He's dead, she kept thinking as she ran towards the estate. Fat Andy's dead.

She paused for breath at a bus stop on the main road. It was another hot sunny day. She wiped her sunglasses then replaced them and rubbed her brow with the back of her sleeve. A homeless mother, whose headscarf and sallow skin suggested eastern Europe, begged for coins outside a launderette. Two women with deep, fake tans walked past with pushchairs, ignoring her. Jaz noticed for the first time that the seats at the bus stop were broken and the perspex of the shelter was scored with a thousand cigarette burns. Old newspaper stirred along the pavement, listless in the heat, a lazy dog scratched itself and a group of children, skiving off school, giggled in the doorway of an abandoned hairdresser's, passing around a magazine.

A middle-aged man lurched across the road, muttering. One of his arms was inside a metal hospital crutch and his other hand held a carrier bag full of empty bottles. Jaz recognized him as a former neighbour but avoided his eye. The homeless woman called out to him but he seemed not to hear.

Jaz hesitated, wondering if her reasons for coming here were more complicated than just taking the car. Maybe it was something to do with the place being home. She felt confused. It was, after all, the only proper home she'd had since leaving Teesside more than seven years before. I was living here, she reflected again with sadness. Only recently. Not that long ago. She blinked her eyes rapidly to avoid tears. Last week, she thought, everything was normal. She pressed against the pain in her chest with the palm of her hand.

She was unwilling to make her way towards the estate. Without wanting to, she imagined the final scene in the flat. She remembered the way Fat Andy's dead feet had pointed inwards, toes together, helpless and sad. She couldn't go there and there was no one she wanted to see. She examined her watch. The sun was bright and high and her pale face smarted in its strong urban rays. There was a smell of soft tarmac, drains and a whiff of an Indian takeaway.

A silver Mercedes drove past slowly. Three men lounged inside, behind the darkened windows – two of them black, the other white. There was the flash of gold jewellery, the impression of expensive sports clothes. Jaz watched as it circled the block, disappearing, then reappearing from behind the flats. It made another leisurely circuit then paused twenty yards from the bus stop. She knew these men were drug dealers and that they were involved in estate-based crime. She also knew their car – Fat Andy had supplied it, via Vinny, in return for cash, and she herself had stolen it to order the previous year.

A window of the Mercedes glided down and there was a sudden blast of rap. One of the black men looked at Jaz but her eyes were hidden by her sunglasses and she pretended not to notice. He was holding a phone. He pursed his lips in a kiss then spat confidently. She still didn't respond. He grinned then shrugged. The window was raised, extinguishing the music. With indifference, Jaz lifted, then quickly plaited her thin sandy hair in a tight braid, knotting it at the ends. The car cruised away.

She took another long hard look at the flats. This estate, she knew, was different from the real world. It was more extreme, more bizarre. It was a place where a young mother, crazy on drink and drugs, had thrown her three-year-old daughter out of a sixth-floor window. It was a place where an old man had lain dead and undetected in his bedroom for two years. It was a place where a teenage boy had been set alight and left to burn in a stairwell.

Jaz moved her sports bag from one shoulder to another. The rows of windows glittered symmetrically. The concrete oblongs were grouped together like strangers around their tract of empty wasteland. The forecourt and walkways seemed deserted. Jaz took a deep breath and purposefully walked over. 'Stay calm,' she said aloud. 'Stay focused.' She entered the dark and malodorous space beneath the flats that led to the underground car park.

Fat Andy's car was still there. She saw it immediately, gleaming in the half light. One of its back tyres was a little flat, but otherwise it was perfect. She wanted it and was determined to take it. It had been Fat Andy's and he never let her drive it, but it was no use to him any more. She walked towards it. Hello, you shining beauty, she thought. I want you. You're rare and gorgeous. You're mine.

She didn't have the right key but she knew that this wasn't a problem. Despite its superb styling, its spunky Lotus twin cam engine, its mint condition, it had useless sixties Ford locks which could be picked with a hairpin. Jaz pulled a large keyring out of her sports bag and selected an old double-sided chrome key which she wiggled in the lock of the driver's door. At first it wouldn't work. She turned to a pillar behind her and rubbed both sides on the concrete, filing it down. She tried again and this time she was successful. She unlocked the door, inserted the key in the ignition and turned it. The engine rattled then died. The battery was flat.

At that moment the Mercedes reappeared. It stopped about twenty yards away and reversed into a parking space. Jaz knew she had to ask for help. She went over to the car and smiled shyly at the white man, who was now sitting alone in the front. He opened the door.

Jaz sniffed. There was a smell of marijuana.

'Hi, doll. How you? You OK?' He was thin and young with a shaved head and a weasel-like expression. He had a conversational style which avoided the use of verbs.

'Elvis.' This was his real name. 'I need a jump start. Can you give me a hand?'

'No worries, doll.'

He drove over, got out and handed her the leads. Between them they had the Lotus Cortina firing in a minute.

'Sorry about Andy,' he said.

'Yeah, well. He fell out with that fucking bastard, Vinny.'

'His boss?'

'Yeah. Vinny from the Island. That Greek bastard.'

Elvis gave her a quizzical look.

'The police must think it was you lot. I bet they do. They blame you for everything. You and Peppy and Big Boy.'

He spat on the ground. 'Those coppers on the High Street? Pure harassment, doll. Intimidation.' He slapped the roof of the Mercedes. 'The Old Bill? Me in there twice, overnight, in a cell.' His mouth became a thin line. 'A victim, me. Police brutality. My brief? Complaint to the whatsisname. The Ombudsman. Ongoing, doll. Ongoing. What else? Big Boy's brief? Racism.'

Jaz closed the bonnet of the Lotus Cortina, slid inside and revved the engine a little. She checked the oil pressure. She raised her voice. 'I'm going to tell them it was Vinny. I think they'll pull Vinny. It won't stick but it might give you a break.'

Elvis took his jump leads and got back into the Mercedes. 'All right, him, that Andy,' he mused. 'An OK bloke. Never, you know, not Andy . . . Us? Knife in the neck? Not us.' He raised both hands in a gesture of innocence. 'You know? Straight up, doll.'

Jaz took her foot off the accelerator and let the engine idle. She looked into his hard south London face. It revealed generations of criminality. His eyes were like black pebbles. His mind was full of deals, coercion, cash, violence. He had no hobbies apart from drugs, no friends outside the gang and no family that he bothered with. She knew he'd kill anyone as soon as look at them, if there was a reason. But Fat Andy had never given him a reason.

'I know it wasn't you,' she said. She didn't like him. She wanted him to go away.

He gestured towards Fat Andy's car. 'His motor? You?'

'Yep. I need wheels. Been thinking about going on

holiday. Soon.' She shrugged, dismissing him. 'Cheers, mate.'

Elvis set the Mercedes in motion. 'Help with that flat tyre? Yes or no?'

She shook her head.

'Well, you around, I expect. Yeah?' He reparked, locked the Mercedes and slouched away, his hand raised in farewell.

Jaz changed to the spare, turned the Lotus Cortina then drove out, emerging into the late morning sun. For a few minutes, driving again, getting the feel of the car, she was elated. She put on her shades and headed towards the police station on Peckham High Street. It was twelve a.m.

Inside, within the stuffy anonymity of the waiting room, she gave a false name and an address which was a few doors away from where she'd been living with Fat Andy. When she was asked for a date of birth, she invented one which indicated she was only fifteen years old. 'It's about that killing,' she said, adopting a London accent. 'That fat geezer with his throat cut.'

After a short wait she was taken to an interview room by a plain-clothes officer who was working on the case. He was surly and wordless, as if he expected her to waste his time. He gestured to a chair, then seated himself behind a desk.

Jaz stared at him as he slowly copied her details onto another form. He was very clean, with a pale blue shirt and patterned tie. He was young, too young. His nails were manicured. His hair was shiny and shaped in a way that suggested he'd just been to the hairdresser. She pictured him in a department store, selecting expensive cologne. She wondered if he sat behind a desk, writing, all of the time. Maybe writing was his job. He didn't look like he fought any kind of war on the streets. 'Well?' he said.

She felt irritated by his unfriendly manner, his clerk's hands. She could feel her anger growing. She took off her sunglasses and put them in the top pocket of her denim jacket. 'I don't have to hang around here,' she told him.

'I'm sorry?' He pretended to look puzzled. He thought she was a child.

She stood up. 'This is frigging public spirit, mate, wasting time, coming here. This is my citizen's duty. I've got better things to do, me. This is neighbourhood bleeding watch.'

He frowned. His eyes were the same colour as his shirt. 'Why aren't you at school?'

Jaz returned his gaze, then shrugged. She glanced at the door, as if she was thinking of leaving.

He suddenly smiled, nervous, as if remembering some training he'd sat through once, ages ago, on interpersonal skills. 'How can I help?' he said, his tone more polite. He fiddled with his pen.

'That fat bloke. He was my neighbour. You came and spoke to my mum. She didn't know nothing, but I knew him.'

The policeman raised his eyebrows. 'Drugs?' he suggested casually.

'Nah, nothing like that. It was cars. He used to nick cars for a living. It was Vinny what did him. He's the one. He had a grudge, like. They'd argued.' She was insistent. 'Vinny from the Island.' She gave the address of Vinny's garage on the Isle of Dogs.

He looked unimpressed.

'Well write it down, then.'

He began writing. He said lazily, 'Just bring me up to speed. Run that past me again.'

Jaz repeated the address. She spoke quickly. 'It wasn't a drug thing. It wasn't, see? I know there's been a lot of all that going down on the estate, but this was different. The fat bloke, he wasn't into drugs. Not dealing. Nothing big time. Sure he smoked a bit of grass, but he mostly stayed away from the bad guys.' She had a sudden vision of Andy, big in his armchair, rolling a joint on the back of an old Jimmy Hendrix album cover. Fat Andy was an old hippy. He was a pacifist. He supported CND. 'He hated guns, knives, all that shit. He didn't like violence. It wasn't his scene.'

'That's not what we've heard.'

There had been two other murders and one stabbing on the estate in the last few months. They were all drug-related crimes. Elvis had been 'harassed' about these matters too. The police clearly thought, with Fat Andy's death, that they were tramping over familiar ground. Jaz knew they saw the flats as a no-go area, where everyone who was killed or injured probably had it coming.

'Listen to me, will you?'

He pursed his lips.

'You must have fingerprints, forensic stuff.'

'Yeah,' he agreed, 'like telly.' He smirked. '*Prime Suspect*. *Crimewatch UK*. Nick Ross, Jill Dando.'

Jaz wanted to hit him. She pressed on. 'Vinny's got a record. You'll have his dabs here somewhere, on your computer. I'm telling you, he was in that flat, that night. He killed the fat guy.'

'You saw him?'

She took a deep breath. 'Sure I saw him,' she lied. 'I saw him on the stairs.'

He wrote hurriedly for a few moments.

'Covered in blood,' she added for good measure. She knew she had his attention at last.

'Why haven't you come forward before?'

'I'm here now, aren't I, smart arse?'

'We'll need to take a statement.' He picked up the phone. He sounded excited. 'I've got something here,' he said. 'A witness.' He replaced the receiver and stood up. 'Wait here please,' he glanced at his notes. 'Miss Smith.' He walked to the door. 'I'll be back in a minute.'

Jaz counted to ten, then left the room, retracing her steps to reception. The duty sergeant was arguing with an old black woman who was surrounded by plastic carrier bags, apparently full of rubbish.

Jaz's heart was beating fast. She left the police station and ran off lightly in the direction of the supermarket car park, where she'd immobilized the Lotus Cortina. She stopped at a phone box and dialled Vinny's number at the garage. She heard him pick up the receiver. She imagined his small, monkey-like hands. 'I've shopped you, Companero. I've told the police. This is Jaz and I've only just fucking started. But don't worry, I'll keep in touch.'

Chapter Six

Jaz didn't believe that Vinny would actually be arrested for Fat Andy's murder. He might be picked up and questioned; he might even be held. This was as much as she could hope for. Vinny's tracks were always well covered and in any case he might not have done the deed himself. He sat at the centre of a complicated web of crime, giving lots of orders. He employed two minders, a pair of brothers, known behind their backs, jokingly, as Reggie and Ronnie.

She had a sudden, unwanted vision of the pool of blood at the side of Fat Andy's body, the way it had thickened, like packet soup. Is it possible that the brothers did it? she wondered. Jaz knew these brothers slightly. She'd met them a few times when she'd worked in Vinny's racket. She remembered introducing them to Harm, who'd become a favourite of theirs for a while. They were both big and bald and wore gold bracelets and expensive tracksuits. They had exceptionally good manners and were always quiet and polite. When they weren't working for Vinny they managed a gym on the Mile End Road.

Fat Andy liked Ronnie and Reggie. He referred to them as his mates. He drank with them regularly in a pub in Limehouse. He said they tried to persuade him to join the gym and work out on the machines but he'd always laughed at this idea. He was too lazy to exercise, too fat to make the effort. He told her he always changed the subject. Jaz had wondered, but never asked, what the three of them talked about. Andy said they were hard, but fair. He insisted that they were very sound and had their own moral code. Jaz wasn't sure what this meant, but it didn't seem likely that it covered slashing the throat of an old friend. It was more likely to be Vinny himself, she reasoned. Everyone knew he was vicious. It was rumoured he'd stabbed his two cousins in order to get control of the business. This may or may not have been true.

Jaz knew that the police would follow up her information. It had been too blunt and unambiguous for them to ignore. Officers would appear, with clear directives, asking questions at Vinny's garage.

She pondered the likely scenarios. Perhaps he would buy them off. He'd been doing this for years, in connection with his car exporting racket. Alternatively, he'd throw up some kind of effective smoke screen and they'd quickly resume their enquiries in Peckham, trying to nail Elvis and his gang. Jaz knew she mustn't underestimate Vinny. He'd been operating an illegal business for many years and no one had stopped him. All she could hope for was that things might become unpleasantly hot for him, for a while. It would serve him right, but it wasn't enough. It wasn't the answer. The bastard had to be properly punished. She needed a better plan.

Jaz got back into the Lotus Cortina. She drove slowly up the Old Kent Road, acclimatizing herself to the car's needs and possibilities. It seemed old-fashioned at first, a little stiff but, within its limits, responsive. It took her a while to get used to the clutch. Initially the pedals seemed soft, but after a couple of miles they were OK. This was a car without any modern refinements. Jaz realized that it didn't allow for excuses or half measures. She was in complete contact with the road and with the engine. There was no padding, no nannying, no leeway. The gear box had strong opinions. Any sloppiness on her part was immediately noticeable. She was aware of sharpening up her technique, of doing things properly. It didn't tolerate anything less than superb driving. After a while she realized that, well handled, the car drove like a dream. The engine purred like a cat or roared like a tiger at exactly the right moments. This was real driving. On a clear stretch of road, approaching the river, she let out an excited cry. She was exhilarated. She understood all at once why Fat Andy, who could have possessed and driven any car in Britain, had chosen this model. He'd loved it for more than its beauty. It was a car-lover's car. It was the real thing. It was perfect.

Jaz crossed the Thames at Blackfriars and went up into Clerkenwell. She stopped outside a newly improved, luxury development, where under the internal courtyard, there was a private car park. She opened Fat Andy's Filofax, then turned the car down the slope and tapped the resident's code into a key pad on the security barrier. Inside were alarms and surveillance cameras. Here, the car would be safe. Jaz didn't know how Andy had come by this number but it was always a useful place to leave the Lotus Cortina. He had made a list of such havens. She left her sports bag and jacket, taking only Andy's

Filofax and the wad of banknotes she'd acquired in Cambridge.

She went into a café and took off her sunglasses. It was quiet but the waiters were tense and speedy as if limbering up for a sudden rush. The food looked complicated, so she ordered a risotto from the blackboard. She turned down a free glass of house wine. The Spanish posters on the walls and the background music made her think again about holidays. Spain, she thought. The rain in Spain falls mainly on the plain. She pictured a dusty, rainless plain with cacti, cattle and a pair of flamenco dancers holding castanets. In the distance were mountains.

After she'd finished eating, Jaz called Harm's mobile from a payphone on the wall. Wesley answered. He sounded pleased to hear from her. Jaz remembered how good-natured and warm he was and not for the first time wondered about his career choice. She pictured his round, shiny black cheeks, his toothy grin. He seemed too kind and too gentle to be a pimp. He was into personal development and vegetarianism. Perhaps Harm's clients behaved well because he always set a good example. Jaz asked him if he knew about Andy.

'I'm sorry, honey. I didn't know the guy but I'm truly sorry. This is one mean, sad old town.' He sighed. 'One real messed up universe.'

'Can I speak to Harm?'

'She's working. She's in a hotel on Kingsway, then next stop, Portland Place.'

It occurred to Jaz that Harm had come a long way since turning tricks in back alleys and taxis when she was sixteen. 'Wesley, listen. Tell her to meet me at five in that pub in Covent Garden. You know, the one where the old guy in the bowler hat plays the piano? It's important.'

'Sure now. And you take care of yourself, honey. Shed some tears, of course, but stay, you know, centred. Staying centred, that's the karmic thing.'

'Bye then, Wesley.'

'Remember I love you, honey.'

Jaz sat outside in Covent Garden, at a pub table in the shade, watching jugglers and a fire eater entertain the tourists. One hand was pressed against her chest. Blow is dead, she thought. Andy is dead. They are both dead. She imagined their flesh disintegrating and falling off the skeletons underneath. She thought of worms, maggots. She closed her eyes.

Next to her, half hidden in a doorway, a group of ragged, dirty men passed a bottle to and fro, ignoring the jollity. They were arguing drunkenly amongst themselves, locked into their own world. Inside the pub, the pianist played Beatles' tunes.

At exactly five o'clock, Harm emerged from a black cab and clip-clopped towards the pub across the cobbles. It was still sunny and she cast a long shadow. She was wearing a leopard skin print lycra dress, very short, which hugged her generous curves. She was just, but only just, voluptuous, rather than too fat. Her heels were very high, at least six inches, and as she walked, her breasts bounced. Her Afro hair, newly plaited and oiled, was caught on top of her head in a big gold clip. She waved at Jaz and smiled, showing the gap between her front teeth.

Jaz saw people looking at Harm. The homeless men

ignored her, too lost in their own concerns, but other male eyes travelled up and down her body. Their womenfolk glanced with hostility before turning away. Jaz stood up and waved back.

Harm called out loudly, 'You still having trouble getting served, little one? I'll go in myself.' She emerged with an elaborate, decorated cocktail and a bottle of Perrier for Jaz. 'Got you a whole bottle. Those glassfuls are just a rip-off.'

'How's business?'

Harm shrugged. 'I got your messages. Sorry to hear about your bloke.' She examined Jaz's face for a moment. 'You upset or what?'

'Vinny did it.'

'Vinny from the Island?'

Jaz nodded. She was suddenly angry again. She put on her sunglasses, then took them off. Her voice was tense. 'There was some problem between them. Andy felt he wasn't getting a big enough piece. Wanted to be cut in properly, something like that. Aggro was building up.' She stopped and thought. 'I know they argued a few times. Andy wasn't happy. He talked about setting up on his own.' She hesitated. 'Although I doubt if he ever would. He wasn't . . . energetic. He wasn't driven.'

She had a vision of Fat Andy in bed in the mornings, half awake, his big hand silencing the alarm. He hated getting up. He always groaned and dozed, demanding a cup of tea. It took him an hour to pull himself together. She helped him on with his socks. Made his breakfast. He moved slowly around the flat, like a lumbering bear.

'Anyway, when I got back that night, there was this e-mail. The night he was killed. Andy must have taken something of Vinny's because it said something about

Vinny wanting his property back. Whatever it was, he ended up dead.'

Harm reached over and placed her dark, round hand, covered in rings, on top of Jaz's sleeve. 'I'm sorry.'

Jaz leaned back, disengaging herself. She had problems receiving sympathy. 'So am I. Life's a shit. You told Trace?'

'Of course. We've been worried. Not knowing where you were.' She paused. 'How're you feeling?'

'OK.'

'You don't seem OK.'

'I'm fucking angry.'

'You're always angry. You let anger hide your real feelings.' She reached out and briefly touched Jaz's arm again. 'Right?'

Jaz sighed. 'You're starting to sound like Wesley.' She changed the subject. 'You know those brothers that work for Vinny? . . . You know, Vinny's boys, Ronnie and Reggie?'

Harm stifled a laugh. 'Christ, don't let them hear you calling them that.'

'You remember them?'

'How could I forget? Those were the bad old days. I'm doing better than them now.'

'D'you think they kill people? Could it have been them?'

'What d'you mean?'

'Vinny. D'you think he ever gets them to kill people? Could they be the ones?'

Harm paused, sipping her cocktail then opening and closing its little paper umbrella. She lit a cigarette. 'Doubt it. Mind you, they never talked to me about their work. But they were quiet. Polite. Mostly it seemed, if they wanted something, they just turned up together, stood around looking threatening and that was enough. They didn't seem violent. They were more like window dressing. Vinny's reputation always went before him. No one crossed Vinny. Ever. As far as they were concerned, they did their job, quietly. Ran their gym. They seemed to care for nobody, except each other.'

'I thought they quite liked you.'

Harm raised her eyebrows, giving Jaz a pitying stare. 'What?'

'Well, you were round there often enough.'

Harm pursed her lips. 'Business is business.' She sounded annoyed.

'Look, Harm,' Jaz said hurriedly. 'I'm sorry, but I want a favour. I want you to talk to them.'

Harm exhaled heavily. 'Oh God, please . . . give me a break.'

'Yes, Harm. Do it for me. Go on. Find out what you can. Please.'

'What for?'

Jaz hesitated. 'Vinny killed Andy. I know he did. I've told the police, but they'll just go through the motions. I want to pay him back.'

'Keep out of it, Jaz.' Harm frowned. 'Just keep out of it.'

'No. I'm not going to keep out of it. I owe it to both of them. To Andy and to . . .'

'What the hell do you think you can do?' Harm was exasperated. 'So Vinny killed Andy. OK, I buy that. It's possible. He's a bastard. He'll stop at nothing, everyone knows that. He's unforgiving. That's what I've always heard. But what are you going to do about it? You'll end up in big trouble, Jaz. I mean it. Stay out of it. Vinny's bad news. He's one mean, nasty guy.' She stubbed out her half-smoked cigarette.

There was a silence. Harm finished her drink and went inside to get another. She sat down again without speaking. She looked serious and disapproving.

'If you don't go and talk to them, I'll go myself.' Jaz swigged some Perrier from the bottle.

Harm sighed and rested her head in one of her hands. She thought for a moment. 'I guess you will. And there's nothing I can say to stop you.'

They sat together for a moment in mutual recognition of this fact.

Harm stared at her colourful drink. Then she looked at Jaz. 'Remember that time you got kidnapped by that nutter and locked up in an old cinema? He was one mean motha.'

Jaz stared at the table.

Harm waited a moment. She sighed. 'What do you want me to ask them?'

Jaz relaxed a little and smiled at her friend. 'Facts. Ask about Fat Andy. What happened with Vinny. What went wrong and why. Maybe even . . . why Vinny killed him.'

Harm flashed her lighter at another cigarette. She was irritated again. 'For heaven's sake. Can you remember who we're dealing with here? They're not going to tell me anything, are they?'

'Just find out anything you can. Use, you know . . .' She gestured at Harm's large breasts. 'Your feminine charm.'

Harm picked a slice of orange from the rim of her glass and sucked it. 'I hoped I'd never see them again.

They were downmarket. East End trash. I was well out of there.'

'Just this once.'

Harm sighed heavily. 'Two conditions.'

'Being?'

'Number one, you stay away from them. You stay away from Vinny.'

'For the moment. I'll promise that. Just for the moment.'

Harm nearly protested, then stopped herself. 'Number two.'

'Yeah?'

'You don't tell Wesley.'

'Wesley won't go with you?'

Harm smiled fondly. 'Wesley couldn't handle it. Wesley handles . . .' she paused, 'a different kind of client.'

'OK.'

Harm fished in her bag and produced a couple of mobile phones. She handed one to Jaz. 'Here. Keep this. You've got my number. Use it. Stay in touch. I'll ring you if I find out anything.'

'Where's Trace?'

'She's chamber-maiding for a few weeks. A place on Bayswater Road.' She rummaged for a pen and wrote down a number. 'The Grand Bahama.' She smiled for the first time. Jaz was relieved. Harm had a beautiful smile. 'The Grand Banana. She's living in. You can ring her there.'

'Thanks, Harm.'

'Stay centred.'

Jaz laughed. 'Stay centred yourself.' She took another swig of Perrier and got up to leave.

Chapter Seven

Jaz slept in the car, parked up in another safe haven near Parliament Square. The next morning she bought a bacon sandwich from a street vendor and ate it hungrily, studying Fat Andy's road atlas. She wanted to go to a place called Hartley Wintney. It turned out to be much farther from London than she'd imagined. She discovered it was necessary to go west past Richmond and then get on the M3, which would take her down through Surrey. It'll be like going on holiday, she thought.

She found a garage and filled the tank. The Lotus Cortina was thirsty. With a sense of setting out on a journey into uncharted lands, she bought more sandwiches, chocolate, a packet of Eccles cakes and two bottles of Evian. She also bought an inflatable cushion and blew it up, because the driver's seat was very low. She took out the photograph of Andy and Princess and the one of Peony and Mimosa dressed as angels, examined them and put them on the passenger seat. Then she put on Andy's driving gloves but after a couple of miles took them off again, as they were much too big for gear changing.

The trip across London was slow. It was a very hot day. She needed the noisy fan to cool the car's interior, and drowned it out by listening to the Lightening Seeds on her Walkman.

As she expected, the car attracted attention. Because it was so immaculate, so old and so classic, it turned heads. Highly polished, the bodywork and chrome were dazzling. Dawdling along, hemmed inside the dull, sleek caravan of contemporary European motor-style, snaking its way through Chiswick, Twickenham, then Richmond, Andy's Lotus Cortina purred like a sex symbol and shone like a star.

Some drivers, awe-struck, hooted in appreciation. At other times, stationary for a moment at traffic lights and junctions, Jaz was aware of closer scrutiny, a kind of voyeurism. Usually, this came from middle-aged men. Jaz knew these were the true aficionados. Cortina-crazy in their youth, they suddenly recognized the model they'd always wanted, but never managed to possess. This car, this fabulous construct of metal and glass, had once been their dream. Their mouths gaped. They wound down their windows. Some tried to speak. Jaz didn't look at them. She tapped on the wooden rim of the steering wheel and sang a tune to herself. She hid behind her sunglasses. She knew their eyes would be grazing the car's lines, its perfectly preserved curves. Some might be reaching through their windows, their hands empty and gesturing, unable to touch what had never been attainable. Deliberately, she stepped on the accelerator as soon as she was clear. She knew she was leaving them disorientated, shocked, almost weeping. For the whole of the rest of their day, they would be alone with her after-image, wracked by nostalgia, regret, lust.

*

Once she'd reached the motorway, Jaz thought about her reasons for making this trip. She was on her way to see Princess, who up until a year, maybe eighteen months ago had been Andy's steady girlfriend. She picked up the photograph again, studied it, then threw it back on the seat. She'd decided during the night that it was necessary to break the news of Andy's death. People should be told. His passing had been too insignificant, she thought. He needs more than one mourner. She pressed her hand to her chest. I'm not enough, on my own. I didn't even know him well or for long. Jaz cruised down the outside lane, trees, fields and pylons flashing by. She knew that she wanted Fat Andy to be mourned in an appropriate way. He might have been a petty criminal but he'd mattered to her. He'd mattered . . . She thought of nights she'd lain by his side with the wind roaring round the high rise and police sirens blaring and the sound of screaming somewhere down the stairwell. He'd slept like a giant baby and the mound of him next to her, peaceful and oblivious – this had made her feel safer. Not safe, but safer. It had been the same with Blow. He'd offered a kind of security. 'Andy.' She said his name aloud. 'Andy.' She wanted his life to have meant something. This was another thing she had to do. It was another purpose, another reason for sticking around.

Jaz had never met Princess but she'd seen old videos, and the photo that was now beside her had sat until that final night on Andy's mantelpiece, alongside her own of Peony and Mimosa. Princess had smiled warmly at her in Andy's flat every day for six months.

Princess was a large blonde woman with a pretty face and small gold spectacles. In some ways she reminded Jaz of her mother. She had the same tawdry rock-chick glamour. Developed by Lola and her contemporaries in the early seventies, it was a combination of femininity, loucheness and rebellion. Princess was simply a more up-to-date version. Jaz had spoken to her on the phone. She had a braying voice which Andy referred to as her posh school gush. He mentioned her often, without rancour but with a kind of resigned sadness.

Jaz had never felt jealous. She considered this now. She decided she'd not minded the ever-present ghost of Princess in the flat. She hadn't been threatened or made insecure by another woman's taste, her property, or by her smiling mouth on the mantelpiece. Andy had been Princess's lover. He hadn't been hers. For Jaz, Andy had been a protector and a friend rather than a lover.

This was an interesting moment of self-analysis. She understood it had been the same with Blow. Blow had been her mother's lover, not hers. As far as Jaz was concerned he'd been protector and friend.

She let her mind wander over this realization as she drove south. She'd relished the security these men had offered her, but finally found it wanting. In both cases, she'd felt close to them for a while, but ended up being let down.

She hadn't cared for the sex. They'd liked it because of the games she'd played – not only looking like a child, but behaving like a child. They'd been turned on by those fantasies, all that role-play. They'd liked dominating her, pretending she was very young. They'd liked her wearing childish clothes, her hair in bunches, talking in a baby voice. She'd done this to please them, when they wanted sex. It hadn't seemed like much, she hadn't really minded. But she hadn't enjoyed it. Not when she was thirteen and not when she was twenty.

Her relationships with both had foundered whenever she asserted herself, tried to get her own way. She wondered how these men related to their real partners. Her mother and Princess were fully grown, buxom, loud-mouthed women – the exact opposite of the part she'd played.

She stayed in the outside lane and maintained a steady seventy. The Lotus Cortina drove like a dream. The inside and middle channels were full of heavy lorries and coaches of tourists. The road had become straight and boring and now the suburbs on either side were dull.

Jaz considered the fact that everyone who had been important to her was part of a twosome. Andy had never really got over Princess. Blow loved her mother. Peony and Mimosa were like one person, as were Harm and Trace. She seemed to exist as a hanger-on, a spare part, a surplus number three.

She asked herself if she would ever fall in love, like people did on television, and have a proper relationship. This would presumably involve equality, desire, quarrels, holidays, trips to the supermarket. Maybe she'd have children of her own and a solid pine kitchen in a proper house, with a tumble drier. The idea was ridiculous.

She wondered if she'd ever meet a man who wanted her because she was a real woman, rather than a little girl. Will I ever have a normal life, like other people? she thought. Is this what I really want? She expertly manoeuvred the car through the middle lane and off onto the slip road near a place called Bagshot. Will I ever be happy?

*

Princess had lived with Fat Andy for a long time. She was a few years older than him, maybe almost forty. When she met him, she was unemployed and staying temporarily with her father. Andy had gone to their house in Weybridge to pick up a BMW which Vinny was acquiring legally. Her father was away on business at the time. Andy often told the story of his first meeting with Princess – it was his favourite anecdote.

When he arrived there was a collection of cars outside in the street and on the drive. He wondered how he was going to get the BMW out, as it was probably blocked in the garage. He noticed a straggly, slightly embarrassed-looking group of men outside the front door. They were weighed down by camera equipment. He walked past them and rang the bell. After a delay, Princess opened it. She was completely naked. She told him to come in, and he followed her into the kitchen where she gave him a Heineken. He said afterwards that he'd tried to act cool, as if everything was totally normal, but he was, for once, at a loss for words. He watched her apply mascara and hairspray. After a while she disappeared out the front door. He next saw her in the back garden leaning against a tree. Her long blonde hair partially hid her large breasts and stomach. The photography club surrounded her in a semicircle, clicking and fiddling with lenses. Andy joked that they never had film in their cameras, although he said that Princess always hotly denied this, insisting they were serious artists.

Fat Andy ended the story by saying that he waited until the men had left in order to drive away the BMW. Princess eventually reappeared, wearing a caftan, and Andy gave her Vinny's cheque. She said she was bored and after a brief flirtation on her father's driveway, agreed to accompany him back to London. She arrived at the flat with no luggage, but stayed for six years.

He'd told Jaz that there'd been a lot of arguments, mainly about money. Like him, Princess was extravagant, but she was less lucky when it came to acquiring cash. She worked as a travel agent, a bank clerk, a doctor's receptionist. Andy said she got the sack more times than all the people he'd ever known in his life, all counted together. She was discontented. She didn't enjoy working, but she didn't like being at home. Eventually, whilst employed by an upmarket osteopath in Highgate, she met a wealthy client – a South African diamond importer, called Pillay, who had a bad back. In what Fat Andy described as 'no time', she'd married him and settled in Hartley Wintney.

In the village, Jaz stopped at a corner grocery where an Asian woman in a sari was adding water to a bucket full of cut flowers in the doorway. 'Hi there,' said Jaz in her friendliest tone, 'how much are these?' She picked up a colourful bouquet.

As she was paying, she asked innocently, 'Do you know Princess Pillay?' The name conjured up an image of a bejewelled Eastern temptress.

The woman handed over her change and deftly wrapped the blooms. Her eyes met Jaz's for the first time.

Jaz showed her the photo.

The shopkeeper glanced at Princess's toothy English smile.

'I've been employed to find her.'

The woman was wary, a little frightened. She glanced again at the picture. 'Find her?' she repeated. 'Is she in some trouble?'

'Oh, no,' replied Jaz, breezily. 'She's inherited money.

A long-lost aunt. The probate's being held up, and until the solicitor finds her, the estate can't be divided.' Jaz had heard these comments once on a TV film and memorized them, knowing they would come in useful. 'She's a beneficiary. She's married to a South African, that's all I know.'

The woman smiled nervously. She looked Jaz up and down and decided because she was so small, she wasn't threatening. 'At the end of this road, turn left. You'll see high rails with gold tops. Big house. Nice one.'

'Cheers,' said Jaz. She turned to leave.

'Excuse me, miss.' The woman was holding out a newspaper. 'Can you please take this? My delivery girl never turned up this morning.'

The house was single storey, mock-Georgian with a triple garage. It was expensive looking, with dead windows. It stood back from the road, surrounded by gilded railings and a collection of low, gloomy trees.

Jaz sat in the car, eating her lunch, wondering what she was going to say. She saw the curtains twitch a few times. After a while, the front door opened and a woman appeared. At first Jaz assumed she must be at the wrong house. If this was Princess, she certainly looked a lot different from the old days. She walked down the drive towards the car. Her face was hidden by a wide-brimmed straw hat and she wore a silk floral dress with a matching fitted jacket – the kind of outfit Jaz associated with weddings. She carried a bulky clutch bag.

Jaz rolled down the window.

The woman had stopped in her tracks. 'Oh, I thought . . .'

'You thought I was Fat Andy.' Jaz examined the face under the hat.

The woman was middle-aged. Her face was dull and plump, covered in thick foundation.

'Are you Princess?'

'Who's asking?'

Jaz recognized her voice. She was totally different from her photo. She'd not put on weight, but the formality of her clothes, the expensive tailoring, the matching shoes and bag, made her matronly and staid. She wasn't wearing her little hippy glasses and this revealed the lines around her eyes. Her lips were painted suburban pink.

Jaz opened the car door. She tapped the side of the Lotus Cortina. 'This is Andy's car.'

'I know it is. Who the hell are you?'

'Jaz. We've talked. On the phone. I've brought you these.' She picked up and handed her the newspaper and the bouquet. 'Can I come in?'

Princess seemed completely nonplussed. She held the flowers and paper to her breast. Her mouth had a slack look.

Jaz wondered if she was just surprised, or maybe drunk, or even tranquillized. 'Look,' she said more insistently, 'we need to talk. Were you going out somewhere? Can I give you a lift?'

Princess glanced over her shoulder at the house. She seemed afraid. 'You can't go in there. It's not possible. My husband, he isn't . . .' She paused. 'He isn't . . .good with visitors.' She hesitated. 'Just a minute.' She walked back to the house and disappeared briefly. Then she came out again, closed the front door and walked towards the road. She'd left the newspaper but still carried the flowers. 'You can take me if you like. I'm going to Basingstoke, to a Conservative ladies' luncheon. William Hague is speaking.' She tittered. 'I do what I'm told these days.'

Jaz opened the passenger door. Princess put the flowers and her hat on the back seat, climbed into the front and sighed. 'I haven't been in this car for . . .' She eased the seat belt across her substantial bosom and clicked it together like an expert. She stroked the dashboard approvingly. 'Where is he?' She glanced back at the house. A shadow crossed the window. Her voice changed. She was suddenly urgent. 'Quick. Let's get out of here.'

Jaz drove down the road then followed a sign indicating the M3. She eyed Princess curiously. Not that long ago she'd had a pert face and her body had been soft and inviting. Now things were reversed. She seemed corseted and restricted and her face had completely lost its tone. It was doughy, with soft jowls. Her hair was still long but it was rolled into a bun. There were streaks of grey at her temples. She wasn't attractive any more and her new style didn't suit her. She'd lost her freshness, her excited vitality that Jaz had noticed on Andy's home movies. She'd become bourgeois and defeated. Princess sighed, and Jaz thought she sounded depressed. Her breath smelled of gin.

'I'm afraid I've got some bad news,' Jaz said.

'Don't tell me. He's left you.'

'No, it's not that. He's . . .'

'You've left him and pinched the car.' Suddenly she laughed, a little wildly. They joined the motorway. 'Yippee!' Princess called out. 'Let's go!'

Her words sounded forced, even false, as if she was trying to recapture some long-lost pleasure. There was definitely something wrong with her, Jaz decided. She was drunk and miserable. She was possibly mad.

'You've taken his car! The fat bastard probably had it coming. I want to go faster!'

Jaz took a deep breath and stepped hard on the accelerator. The road was very quiet. 'He's dead.'

Princess looked straight ahead. 'Let's go faster! Faster!'

'Fat Andy's dead.' Jaz paused for effect. 'Vinny cut his fucking throat.' Jaz had not intended to be brutal, but Princess was so strange and distant she didn't know how to communicate with her. She had a sudden vision of the blood on Andy's shirt, a clot of it in his chest hair. She remembered the smell in the bedroom. Stay calm, she reminded herself. Stay focused.

She looked at the speedo. They were doing eighty and the engine was humming. She took it even higher. 'I'm sorry. It's a shock. I'm sorry to tell you like this. Maybe I should've phoned.'

'Faster,' Princess said. 'I want to go faster!' Jaz accelerated again. She overtook a lorry. On either side of the motorway, trees flashed past and there was a slight smell of burning coming from the hot road. 'Oh God,' Princess shrieked, 'it's just like the old days.' Jaz noticed she was crying. Her make-up was streaked by two black lines coursing through heavily powdered beige. They were going at a hundred miles an hour. It was too fast. Jaz saw a sign advertising a Little Chef and pressed on the brake. They slowed rapidly. Princess sighed again, either in relief or disappointment. Her emotions were all exaggerated. They turned up a slip road and into the car park.

Princess sniffed and took a handkerchief and powder compact out of her bag. Her excitement waned as quickly as it had arisen. 'That was great,' she said flatly, as if she'd been bored.

'Are you hearing me?' Jaz asked, pulling into a bay.

'Andy's dead. That's what I've come to tell you.' She could feel herself getting angry. The woman wasn't listening.

Princess patted her cheeks with a powder puff, mopping up the tears but making her face look even more caked. 'No he's not.'

Jaz sat back and stared at the horizon. There was a grim suggestion of distant factories and office blocks. Flags flapped listlessly outside the café, advertising kiddie meals.

Princess put away her powder and took a small bottle from her bag. It was a quarter of gin. She took a substantial swig then put it away.

Jaz felt at a loss. 'What can I say to you?' she asked.

'That fat bastard's not dead because he's on the telly every night. He's doing really well for himself. Typical, isn't it? I stuck with him for the best years of my life and what was he? He was a small-time car thief with no real money, dodgy friends, a grotty flat. He was nowhere.' She paused for emphasis. 'I had to work myself, you know, to pay the bills.' She sniffed again, self-pityingly, got the bottle out and drained it. She swayed slightly towards Jaz. 'I left him and now what's happened? He's suddenly on the telly. It's the nine o'clock news and big black cars and Downing Street. He's in the papers. What is he now?' She turned to Jaz enquiringly. 'Is he some sort of bodyguard?'

Jaz knew, from her experiences with Lola, that Princess was now very drunk. She might stay quiet and incoherent, or she might not. She might shout or get violent. She might be sick. She wanted to get her out of the Lotus Cortina. Fat Andy's old girlfriend might not dress like Lola any longer, but she was behaving like her. Jaz remembered the misery of her childhood. Her mother had been like this – unpredictable, out of control. Jaz didn't like it. Princess was making her nervous. She wanted rid of her. 'Why don't I call you a taxi?' she asked gently.

'A taxi?' Princess was suddenly angry. 'Why would I want a taxi? You're taking me to Basingstoke!'

Jaz didn't want a scene. Princess was big, but unsteady. It might be possible to bundle her out of the car and dump her here, but this would leave Jaz feeling guilty. She still wanted to do right by Andy. 'OK,' she whispered. She drove back out onto the M3. A sign said 'Basingstoke 5 miles'.

They continued in silence. When they got to the town Princess gave monosyllabic directions. They slowed outside a featureless building near an ugly shopping centre. 'Take me to an off-licence,' Princess demanded. 'I can't face this lot without a drink.'

They found a small shop which sold wine and spirits. Jaz waited while Princess bought more gin. When she got back in the car, her mood had swung again. She was cheerful. 'Take a look at these, if you don't believe me.' Opening her bag she produced a bundle of newspaper cuttings and tossed them onto Jaz's lap.

Jaz removed an elastic band and spread them out. They were a collection of photos, torn from the *Telegraph* and *The Times*. At first they seemed to be straightforward press shots of the Home Secretary. Some were very recent and had been taken at the party conference. One was at Heathrow. Another was at a press briefing, about the problem of homelessness in the capital.

Princess leaned over. Her finger jabbed into Jaz's knee. 'There he is,' she said.

Jaz held the picture and turned it towards the light.

She realized what Princess meant. Standing behind the man who was the focus of the photograph, half out of frame, was a large male chest in a double-breasted suit.

'That's him,' said Princess, pointing again.

Jaz examined a second picture. Again, in the background was a bulky figure. This time she could make out his double chin, the outline of a ponytail. This shadowy figure was very similar to Fat Andy. She picked up a third cutting. Here, the man in question was at the front of the picture, as if hurrying to get out of shot. He was immaculately dressed, his long hair was carefully groomed and secured, he looked confident, even complacent, rubbing shoulders with the country's leaders – but he definitely resembled Fat Andy. It was clear that Princess had been deluding herself with this fantasy for a long time. Jaz leafed through the pictures. She'd collected them for more than six months.

'Well,' Jaz said. 'It looks like him, but . . .'

Princess picked up the pile, rolled it tightly, then stuffed it back into her clutch bag. 'So, he's too good for both of us now,' she said, almost conspiratorially. 'He's cruising around in limousines, not even doing his own driving. What's he up to? What's he doing? D'you think he's shacked up with some lady MP?'

Jaz felt the pointlessness of trying to argue. She started the car and drove her passenger to her destination.

Princess seemed to be aware, even through the haze of too much gin, that Jaz was unconvinced by her collection of pictures. 'You get yourself in front of a telly,' she insisted. 'Just watch the news. He'll be on for the next few nights, with this new vagrancy White Paper everyone's talking about. There'll be press conferences and meetings. Watch him get in and out of those cars. He's usually got a label hanging on a chain around his neck.' She opened her new half litre of Gordon's, took another long swig, then squeezed the bottle into her handbag.

Jaz felt suddenly irritated – overwhelmed with a sense of having wasted her time and energy. She had been unsuccessful in her mission. Fat Andy still had no mourners apart from herself. She put her hand on Princess's arm, detaining her, then let go, slightly repelled. 'He never mentioned family,' she said. 'Did he, I mean does he have family?'

Princess reached into the back for her hat. She jammed it on her head, pushing loose strands of hair inside. 'You mean you've never met his mother? That hideous old bat in Pimlico?'

Jaz picked up a pen from the parcel shelf beneath the dashboard, then pulled out Andy's Filofax from under the driver's seat. 'Is her address in here?'

Princess looked puzzled.

'Just write down the address, will you?'

Princess scribbled across two pages. She burped quietly. 'I think this is right. It's something like this.'

Jaz watched as she walked towards the Conservative club offices, tottering slightly, her bulging bag under her arm, her other hand holding her hat which was caught in a spiteful breeze.

Chapter Eight

Jaz spent the night in a lay-by on the A30. She didn't care for parking on the road – the Lotus Cortina was an ostentatious vehicle to sleep in and its locks weren't safe. She feared being surprised by a passing weirdo. However it was the best possible option, other than a hotel, and she didn't want to waste more money. She had a meal in the Little Chef then found a suitably quiet spot, parked and slept in the back, with her head on the inflatable cushion. She was unconscious for six hours. When she awoke, stiff but refreshed, she drove back to London, thinking about Hartley Wintney and her unsuccessful attempt to find a mourner for Fat Andy. At least I've got his mother's address, she thought. Princess was a disaster, but tomorrow, I'll go and see the mother.

At nine o'clock she hid the car in a side street on the Isle of Dogs, overlooking the Thames. It was a bright morning and the sun, still low on the skyline, cast long, cool shadows. She stared at the glittering water and the Millennium Dome which crouched on the opposite bank like a pale, sleepy beetle.

Stay calm, she reminded herself. Stay cool. There was a lot to be done. Her life had suddenly become full of purpose. She pressed the pain in her chest. It burned, this morning; it was worse. Vinny will be punished, she assured herself, and Fat Andy will be mourned.

She polished the dashboard and the steering wheel of the Lotus Cortina with her sleeve. The interior was immaculate. A small air freshener in the shape of a pine tree swung from the fan switch. Andy had forbidden smoking and eating in the car. Guiltily, she picked up some crumbs and dropped them out of the window. I'm living here, she reasoned. Andy never actually lived in the Lotus Cortina, so it was easier for him. However, I must look after it as best I can.

She remembered several Cortinas from her childhood. Back in the eighties, Blow was nostalgic for them and bought and restored three or four. 'The car of my youth,' he used to declare, whenever he appeared with another one. 'We loved these. Had them in all colours. Knew them inside out, back to front. I spent more time with Cortinas than with my girlfriend. Or family. We were all the same. All the lads. Cortina crazy.'

Jaz remembered a cold autumn day, not long before she ran away from home. She'd just finished seeing to the hens and she was leaning against Blow's latest Cortina in the yard outside the farmhouse, worried about her sisters. She shivered and pulled Lola's old fur jacket around her thin frame. Just then, she heard a shriek and turned and saw the twins. She was relieved. They were fine. Peony and Mimosa had tied their ankles together and grasping each other's wrists, had formed their bodies into a giant loop. They steadied themselves like gymnasts, and as Jasmine watched they began rolling in a slow circle down the grassy slope, away from the house. Steadily and without losing their balance, they turned as one, gathering momentum. All at once, Jasmine felt lonely. They never include me, she thought. They're one person. They're one girl in two bodies.

Blow appeared, grinning. He opened the bonnet of the car, excited about his latest acquisition. 'Sixty-nine Mark II 1600 GT,' he informed her. 'It's the two-door. Rare as hen's teeth. See the colours?'

Jasmine stepped back and examined the white bodywork with the green stripe. She could hear the twins' laughter, but didn't look round at them again.

'Not a real Lotus Cortina,' he continued regretfully, half disappearing into the engine, 'but it's the nearest I could find. Lotus colours.' He tinkered with a spanner. 'I never had a Lotus Cortina. Never. None of us did. We all wanted one. Like a dream.'

After a moment, as she expected, he started singing. Do wah diddy diddy, dum diddy do. He always sang this when he talked about Cortinas and his friends in younger days. There she goes, justa walking down the street. He turned a spanner. Singing Do wah diddy diddy, dum diddy do.

Jasmine joined in, hoping the twins would hear. She looks good, she looks fine, canna really make her mine? She always imagined this song was about a Cortina. The song and the car were linked in Blow's mind. Do wah diddy diddy, dum diddy do. She believed this to be the kind of song they always sang in the sixties. It sounded innocent, friendly and full of hidden meaning.

Blow stopped singing suddenly. 'Damn!' he said.

Jasmine looked.

He pointed to the near-side inner wing.

'What's wrong with it?'

'See that rubber? That's the top bush. Suspension's bulging like a hernia.'

'What does that mean?'

'It means I'll have to remove the strut and replace the effing bush. That, or wobble like jelly on the bends.' He sighed. 'These struts are rock solid.' He leaned on the car and bounced the wing. He shook his head. 'Road holding, I won't get. Not unless I do it.'

Jaz sat for a while, thinking. Cortina crazy. She pictured Blow and Fat Andy as teenagers. Blow was young in the sixties. Andy was young in the seventies. She imagined a happy, simple time with open roads, jolly policemen on bicycles, steam trains, women with chiffon headscarves tied over candyfloss hair. A gentle, predictable world, she thought, compared with today. A world where everyone knew who they were and where they were going. Not like now. I'll take the car on holiday, she decided, when all of this is over. I'll go somewhere nice, with Harm and Trace. Somewhere old-fashioned, a long way from London. We'll be Cortina crazy too.

She crossed her arms over the steering wheel and leaned forwards, trying to direct her thoughts towards the moment. Pull yourself together, she told herself. Stay focused. She tried to recall times recently when Fat Andy had appeared troubled. After he'd insisted she leave the gang, she'd become largely out of touch with what went on at the garage. Fat Andy had never been one to share his problems. However, he'd complained about Vinny. Jaz imagined him pacing across the living room at the flat, a glass of Scotch in his hand. It was rare to see him in a bad humour, but this had happened several times.

He'd said that Vinny didn't realize his true worth. He'd said that without himself there'd be no gang and without the gang there'd be no stolen cars. 'He pays me well,' Andy had said to her. 'It's not the money. It's just that he doesn't listen to me. He keeps me right out on a limb.'

Another time he'd come home late at night, pale-faced and angry. Jaz sat up in bed, alarmed. She'd opened her arms to him and he'd lain down next to her, upset, still in his clothes. 'That Vinny,' he whispered. 'He's too much. Sometimes he really is too much . . .'

'What's happened?'

'You know Davey, in the gang? PhD drop-out? Gob full of long words? He got nicked this morning. Lifting a Megane Scenic. God knows what he was up to. You know his head's always in the clouds. Anyway, he's banged up now in Brixton. Vinny sent the boys over to his gaff, told them to break in, look for anything incriminating, anything that might link him to the garage. They came back with his dog.'

'You mean Blackie?'

'Yeah. That's the one. Well, the boys brought it back with them. For why? Because there was no one to feed it or look after it, that's why. An act of kindness. Well, what does Vinny do? Vinny took one look at it . . .' He paused, horrified. 'You know what he did? Guess what Vinny went and did?'

'What?'

'Snapped its little neck, that's what. In one move. Killed it. Like he'd done it lots of times before. Took him three seconds.' Andy was disgusted. 'The Greek bastard.'

'You're kidding!'

'I wish I was. I've got to go and tell Davey tomorrow. Vinny said it would teach him a lesson. Teach him not to be so careless.' He was silent for a minute. 'Snapped its poor little neck . . . little Blackie. Then he got in his car and drove away.' He brushed away a tear. 'Davey's finished, of course. Sacked. And now he's got no dog either. Have you ever known such a sadistic bastard as that Vinny?'

Jaz got out of the car. Vinny's legitimate workforce had been busy for at least an hour. She crossed the road. Behind the showroom, separated by a back alley, were the workshops. Sweet fumes emerged from the paint shop where cars, both legal and otherwise, were given new clothes.

Jaz didn't want to meet Vinny accidentally. Her plans weren't entirely clear yet, but she couldn't see any value in a confrontation. She walked past a hooded, spraying figure, lost behind a mist of blue. Further along was the repair shop. She peeped inside. Nearest the door, a few yards away, a mechanic lay underneath a VW Passat. She knew by his long legs and big boots that this was Pete. The place was too noisy to attract his attention so she picked up a small stone from the street and aimed it at his crotch. She didn't hear him curse but he emerged in an instant.

Jaz beckoned to him urgently. 'Sorry,' she mouthed.

Pete grinned, stood up and joined her outside. 'Make it quick, Jaz, I'm on time and a half. Another customer in a hurry.'

Jaz looked up at him. He was very tall. 'Vinny there?'

'I don't think so. Why?'

'Go and have a look, will you?'

Pete loped off in the direction of the shabby cubbyhole which was Vinny's office. He reappeared, shaking his head. Jaz regarded him appreciatively. He was lanky with long ginger hair, like her own, only his was thicker, a richer colour and more shiny. He wore stained blue overalls unbuttoned on his chest. Both his ears were pierced. He had a self-conscious, modern walk, which suggested he knew his sexual value. His young face was chiselled and bony. His complexion was like porcelain. Jaz had always thought his features belonged to a concert pianist or a poet rather than a mechanic. Similarly, his hands, although always dirty, were elegant and beautifully moulded.

Jaz whistled as he approached. 'You just get more and more tasty, Pete.'

He blushed, taken by surprise.

'Licking you all over wouldn't be hard.'

He looked at the ground and muttered, 'What for . . . I mean why d'you want Vinny?'

'I don't. You heard about Fat Andy?'

He nodded, raising his eyes to meet hers. 'Yeah. I heard he got done in, like.' He paused. 'Sorry. No one here knows nothing. No details.' He leaned in the doorway, trying to regain his composure, struggling to look casual. He scratched his balls and pretended to yawn.

Jaz knew he was nervous, but he wanted to appear cool. He was only eighteen. She was just about to tell him that Vinny had killed Fat Andy, then changed her mind. If he didn't believe her, then she'd lose him as a contact.

'How about a drink tomorrow night?' he said hesitantly and blushed again. He was doing his best.

'Well, you're not wasting any time.' She smiled at him.

She'd always fancied Pete. He had a nice body, his face was as pretty as a girl's and more importantly, now, he might prove useful. Whatever revenge she planned for Vinny, she'd need an insider. She took a step towards him, reached up and placed her index finger on his chest, in the gap of his overalls. 'Where?' His skin was hairless. She ran her finger lightly up and down.

His face was now bright red, but he was pleased. He suggested a time and a pub on Poplar High Street. 'It's karaoke night,' he said. 'Good laugh.'

He moved backwards, away from her, grinning shyly, then turned and lowered himself onto his trolley. Jaz noticed that his flush had extended from his face over his neck and onto his pale chest. She waited for him to disappear under the VW Passat.

She looked about. The coast was clear. She dodged behind a Skoda then ran across the floor of the workshop to the corner where Vinny had his office. The door was open and she went inside. A poster of Pamela Anderson wearing ragged bikini and handcuffs was blue-tacked to the back of the glass. A calendar, showing a woman wearing nothing, hung on the wall. Jaz wondered about this choice of decoration. Everyone knew Vinny was gay.

There was a lingering smell of aftershave, mixed with kebabs. The light on the answerphone was flashing and there was a pile of new faxes. Jaz looked at Vinny's computer. It was old. There was no modem. She slid the floppy out of the disk drive. She opened a drawer of the desk and found a plastic rack holding a dozen more disks: customer orders and repairs. She removed these, then took a small screwdriver from her sports bag and used it to unscrew the cover from the chassis of the computer. She glanced round the door. There was no one nearby. Working quickly, she located, then unfastened the hard disk. She took it out and examined it. Then she put everything in her sports bag including the faxes. She wiped the messages off the answerphone, then pressed record. 'Hi there, slimeball,' she hissed. 'Companero? It's me again. I've fucked up your computer here. I've got your files.' Unobserved, she left the building.

Later, at West India dock, she parked the Lotus Cortina, put on her Versace sunglasses and walked over to the side of the wharf. It had become a hot, breezy day and tourist boats ploughed back and forth. A group of children waved at her and some of them raised cameras. She could hear the recorded commentary, pointing out the sights of the capital. I'm going on holiday, she reminded herself, when this is all over.

The Thames was high, lapping against the sides, the water blue-grey and oily. Jaz dropped the faxes into the current and watched them swirl away. She tossed the floppy disks as far as she could and they scattered then sank. She threw the hard disk way out into the river. You've seen nothing yet, she thought to herself. She pressed her chest. The pain had eased slightly. You've messed with me, you fucking bastard, Vinny. And this is just the beginning.

Later, Jaz drove over to Peckham. Vinny's disks had reminded her of the e-mail she'd discovered on Fat Andy's computer just before finding his body. It hadn't been sent from the garage. Vinny must have a computer at home, she thought. She could remember the message almost word for word. 'Vinnys not a happy man. Vinny wants his proparty back strate away.'

She pictured the disks disappearing in the Thames. She was reminded of Fat Andy talking about a computer disk which contained the details of Vinny's illegal car exporting racket – his contacts in Europe, their specific orders, details of the ringed cars with both their old and new identities. I wonder if I threw it in the river? she thought. It seemed unlikely that it would be unprotected, in a desk drawer.

Andy had always joked that with this disk he could set up on his own, making a clean line between the thefts and the export, cutting Vinny out of the middle. Jaz had never taken him seriously, but now it suddenly seemed more than likely that Andy had stolen the disk. This must be the 'proparty' which Vinny wanted back so badly. He needed to protect his contacts and he wouldn't want this evidence of his covert business dealings to fall into the wrong hands. Jaz tried to remember the scene at the flat. There had been signs of a struggle but the place wasn't ransacked. She remembered that Andy's computer disks and CD roms had been strewn across the floor. She knew that if Andy had stolen Vinny's valuable disk, he wouldn't have left it lying around. She had a good idea where he might have hidden it.

Jaz stopped the Lotus Cortina near the estate where Fat Andy had died. She sat and considered. She still didn't want to go back to the flat. She had a key, but she knew it would be boarded up. It was, after all, the place where an unresolved murder had been committed, very recently. She brought to mind police programmes from the TV. She pictured yellow scene-of-crime tape, sealing off the area, possibly even a police guard. She imagined a body bag on a stretcher and forensic experts with tweezers and plastic bags, picking over the dirty carpet. In any case, she thought, I couldn't go back in there. I couldn't face it. It was too horrible. A vision of Fat Andy's dead, staring eyes flashed before her. His eyes had been the worst thing. They were unlike real eyes. In death, Fat Andy's eyes were more ghastly than anything she'd ever dreamed of.

She waited. She ate a bar of chocolate and drank a can of Dr Pepper. I could do with a shower, she thought. She watched two teenage boys drag a sobbing toddler up the street. A third followed behind with his pushchair. The wind had dropped and it was too hot. A dog tore open a bin liner and started rummaging. A woman, over-dressed in a raincoat, pulled a shopping trolley towards the launderette. The homeless mother in the headscarf was still in position with her baby, her supplicating hand outstretched. She made low, inarticulate sounds. Next to her was a young boy who held a piece of cardboard. 'Work-less and hungry', he'd written in red felt tip pen.

Jaz plaited her hair tightly and pinned it in a small clump on the back of her head. She looked in the mirror. Her fringe was too long. It hung in dry stands. The sun had caught her face, creating a rash of freckles. Her eyelids were pink.

Eventually the silver Mercedes came into view. As usual, it was moving at twenty miles an hour. Elvis always drove slowly around the estate and its neighbouring streets. It was a statement of ownership. One day, Jaz thought, he'll start giving a regal wave, like a member of the royal family.

She followed the Mercedes into the underground car park and drew up alongside it. Big Boy and Peppy got out immediately. Peppy staggered. He seemed disorientated and weaved towards the lift. Big Boy noticed Jaz and raised a hand in greeting. Jaz nodded. He followed behind Peppy, his large backside wobbling inside silky jogging bottoms. He disappeared.

Jaz stepped out of the Lotus Cortina and slid into the back seat of the Mercedes. Elvis was in the driving seat, wearing a set of headphones. The tinny sound suggested something heavy and rhythmic. Elvis moved his skinny body up and down in time to the beat. Jaz looked at the spots on the back of his neck, his shaved head. He was wearing a white shirt. She tapped him on the shoulder. He turned round defensively, pulling off his headphones. When he saw Jaz he smiled. He switched off the engine. 'Doll. How do!'

'Elvis, listen. Will you do me a favour?'

'Maybe.' Despite his clean, pressed shirt, he looked as if he hadn't slept for days. His skin was shiny and grey and his breath smelled of chemicals.

'Can you get into Andy's flat?'

He laughed. 'Your make-up, yeah? Doll? That it? Or your birth control pills?'

'Are the police still there?'

'They's not here now. 'Cept for harassment of course. 'Cept for Peppy's intimidation and false arrest. 'Cept for . . .'

'Can you get in?'

Elvis pursed his lips. 'Board on door. New. Padlocks.'

'What about the window?'

'Sixteenth floor. Yes or no?'

'Can you get in, Elvis? I'm serious.' She explained what she wanted and where to look. She told him about the loose polystyrene tile on the bathroom ceiling.

Elvis reached over and lifted her T-shirt. His mean little eyes met hers. 'Is it worth a shag? One now and one later?'

Jaz nodded. Stay calm, she thought. Stay cool. She slipped out of her jacket, pulled her T-shirt off and undid the button of her jeans.

Chapter Nine

The next day, on Oxford Street, Jaz approached a man selling the *Big Issue*. 'Hi, Davey.'

Davey was the ex-student, turned car thief, who was sacked by Vinny after getting caught by the police. Fat Andy had paid him off, cleared his fines and treated him generously. Davey had remained grateful. Jaz knew he was still in touch with the other members of the gang who worked the streets. She bent down and stroked his new dog. It was another collie, similar to Blackie.

'How's tricks?' Davey enquired. He grinned down at her, showing toothless gums.

Jaz was half expecting this friendly unconcern. Some news travelled on the grapevine, other news didn't. For some reason, no one seemed to know about Fat Andy's murder. She couldn't explain why. 'Fat Andy's dead.'

Davey took a shocked step backwards, jerking his dog's lead. The magazines slid from his grasp but he caught them before they dropped.

'I knew you didn't know. No one knows. I don't get it.'

Under the street grime, Davey's face had lost its colour. 'Hey man, it's nothing I've heard about. How the hell . . .?'

'I knew you'd be surprised.'

He took a tissue out of his trouser pocket and blew

his nose. 'Surprised? I'm gutted.' He sat down on his haunches, placing his magazines on the pavement.

Jaz bent towards him. 'Murdered.'

Davey was astonished. 'Murdered? Bloody hellfire!'

Jaz didn't hesitate. 'Vinny did it. Vinny killed him.'

'Never?'

'Yep.'

'You sure?'

Jaz was ready for this. 'I was there,' she lied. 'I saw everything.'

Davey paused, then said angrily, 'Why?'

'Dunno. Prestige? Power? Andy wanted more. Thought he deserved more.'

Davey was silent. Then he whispered, 'That Vinny was always a complete bastard.' He looked as if he might faint. He paused. 'Mephistopheles,' he muttered. 'A man without morals.'

'Yep.'

'I can't believe it.'

Jaz straightened up. 'Well, believe it. Put the word out. I don't know who's paying the boys now, doing Andy's job. But you make sure you tell them. Andy always did right by them. You tell all the boys.' She turned and walked away.

'They won't work for Vinny,' Davey called out, 'once they know about this.'

Jaz smiled to herself grimly. I know that, she thought. The gang's finished.

Later, sitting in the Lotus Cortina and using the mobile phone, Jaz rang the number she'd been given for Trace. She'd already been to Pimlico and discovered that the address of Fat Andy's mother supplied by Princess was that of a block of mansion flats, respectable and staid, which appeared to be occupied by well-to-do elderly people who had cleaners and chauffeurs and help with their shopping. Andy had never mentioned his mother. He'd never talked about his family.

The phone rang for a long time. Eventually it was answered by a foreign-sounding woman. 'Yes, please?'

'I would like if possible,' Jaz spoke very slowly, 'to speak to Trace.'

'Who?'

'Trace. One of your chambermaids.'

There was a silence. 'Who is this, please?'

'I'm Jaz. I'm a friend of hers.'

'Ah, OK, OK. Tracy. Yes, one moment please.'

Jaz waited for several minutes. Eventually Trace picked up the phone. 'Hello, Tracy speaking.'

'Hi, Trace, it's Jaz.'

Trace gasped. 'Jaz! We've been so worried! Where are you? Where've you been?'

'I'm OK. Listen. When are you free?'

'I'm sort of free now.'

'Will you do me a favour? Meet me in Churchill Gardens, off Grosvenor Road?'

'Why?'

'I'll tell you when you get here.'

'OK. I'll be . . . three quarters of an hour.'

Sitting in the car, perspiring gently in the heat, Trace listened in silence to Jaz's account of the events on the night of her birthday. She'd already heard a version from Harm, but she wanted to hear it from Jaz herself. When

Jaz had finished, Trace sat for a moment with her head in her hands. 'That's so terrible,' she whispered.

Jaz knew she would cry. Trace hadn't really known Fat Andy, but she was empathic and very sensitive. Jaz waited until she composed herself. 'I have to tell his mother. This is really important to me, Trace.'

''Course it is.'

'Andy's been done in and no one seems to know. No one seems to care.'

'We care, Jaz. We both care.'

'I'm not even sure if there's going to be a funeral or whatever. The murder wasn't in the papers. It's as if it doesn't matter. Just another killing on the estate. As if it was . . . ordinary. I've got to tell people. Andy would want everyone to know. He'd want a big production number. He'd want his people there for him.'

'Where, Jaz? At the funeral?' Trace glanced over at Jaz. She looked confused.

'No, not a funeral. That would be meaningless. I mean, he'd want people to be hurt for him. He'd expect concern, discussion. He'd want people to be angry and upset and bothered. And no one is. It's really getting to me. I mean . . . he had a life. He was a person with a life . . .'

'Of course he had a life, Jaz. He had . . . a beautiful life.' Trace wiped her eyes.

'That's right. And I want to tell his mother that it's ended. She may not know. It's right and proper that she should know. I want you to come with me.'

Trace was sympathetic but bewildered. Jaz waited patiently for a while, then explained again. It was always necessary to run things past Trace more than once. She was slow on the uptake, but once she'd absorbed something, she never forgot it.

'Why do you want me to come, Jaz? I mean, I'll come, but wouldn't it be better for you to see her, you know . . . one to one?'

After the episode with Princess, Jaz knew that she didn't want to go alone. 'I just do, OK? I want you to come.'

'OK.'

'And there's another thing.'

'What?'

'I need a shower. Can I come back with you to that hotel afterwards, and use a bathroom?'

'No problem.'

Jaz parked near the mansion block and took off her sunglasses. She fed the meter. She was just about to ring the bell when the main door opened and a maid emerged with a shopping trolley. She nodded and let the two of them through without question. The hall inside was dark, with wood panelling and a coloured, tiled floor. A grandfather clock ticked patiently. A vase of sweet, droopy roses scented the air. It was the kind of place where old people waited to die.

Jaz took the marble stairs two at a time with Trace at her heels. They went up to the third floor. The lobby was thickly carpeted and a large, elegant window gave a view of neighbouring rooftops.

Jaz rang the bell.

'What are we going to say?' Trace whispered.

'I don't know. We'll play it by ear.'

There was no reply. Jaz rang again. 'Shit, I hope she's in.'

After a while, there was a rattling and the door opened a fraction on a security chain.

'Hello,' Jaz said loudly. 'Hello. This is Jaz. I'm Andy's girlfriend. Your son, Andy. I'm with a friend. We want to speak to you.'

'Go away,' said a voice from inside. It was a woman speaking. She sounded very discouraging.

'No, we're not going away. Let us in. It's important. About your son.'

'No one comes in here.'

'We won't be long.' Jaz felt desperate. 'How about if we just talk to you in the hall?'

There was a long silence. Then to Jaz's relief, the chain was dropped and the door opened.

Jaz was expecting an old lady. The woman in the hallway was very tall and slim. Her pale hair was elaborately dressed in a sixties style, rolled in a bun on top with a deep pleat at the front, like a nurse's cap. She wore silk trousers with a matching tabard and a long string of beads. The first impression was one of glamour. 'Come in,' she said. She now sounded resigned. Jaz and Trace followed her down the hallway. Jaz realized she was, in fact, old. She walked stiffly, her back was bent and she had an old woman's elbows.

They entered a dark room which smelled of urine, overlaid with sandalwood. One table lamp was illuminated but it was draped in a coloured scarf. There were several low sofas and tables and wall hangings which seemed to depict scenes from the Kamasutra.

'Sit.'

Jaz and Trace sat down together.

The woman was indistinguishable in the shadows. She switched on another dim lamp, her back turned, then lit a stick of incense.

Jaz took in an oriental rug and cushions, an elephant carved in ivory, a hookah. The impression was one of an eastern bazaar.

Andy's mother faced them, then crouched awkwardly on a small leather pouffe. It was a young movement, but executed with difficulty. Her face, too, was disturbing. She had once been beautiful but her cheeks had fallen into low, baggy folds and her neck was a concertina of creases. Her mouth and eyes were surrounded by deep lines. Onto this ruined canvas, she had applied a great deal of make-up. Her lips were pearly pink, her eyes decorated with false lashes so long and black they looked like insects. She smiled. Her teeth were false and badly fitting. Jaz was reminded of a ghoul in a horror film.

'We're sorry to bother you,' said Jaz. She was nonplussed. She felt Trace grope for her hand and squeeze it.

The woman grasped her knees, tilted her head to one side and smiled. She appeared to be posing. After a few moments she said, 'I don't have visitors. Not these days.' She sighed theatrically. She had a posh, actressy voice.

There was a silence. 'It's, er, a nice day,' said Trace shyly. 'Like, you know . . . sunny.'

'Oh, I never go out.' The woman gestured at the heavy brocade curtains which blocked all natural light. 'I haven't been out since 1987.'

There seemed to be no reply to this. Jaz decided to dispense with small talk. 'I was Andy's girlfriend,' she began.

The woman's pencilled brows lifted in surprise. The furrows in her forehead were like a ploughed field. 'I don't know you,' she said. 'I only know that plump girl with the little round glasses. Princess. The one who won't work.'

Jaz was relieved. At least this was the right flat. At least this crazy-looking woman was talking sense.

'No, she went away. I was with Andy for the last six months,' she paused, 'of his life.'

Her response was immediate. She was sharp, Jaz realized. 'What do you mean "of his life"?'

'Andy's dead.'

Her mouth fell open and she raised a hand to cover it. 'He can't be. I saw him on the television.'

Jaz realized that she'd seen the same lookalike that had confused Princess. 'No, that wasn't him. I don't know who that is. Forget him. Andy was killed at the flat in Peckham. He was murdered. I'm sorry to have to tell you like this. Why weren't you informed? Through . . . you know . . . the usual channels?'

The woman stared, her hand at her mouth, her painted eyes wide with shock.

'Can I get you anything?' asked Trace timidly. 'Cup of tea?'

The woman nodded. She gestured and Trace disappeared in the direction of the kitchen.

'The usual channels don't apply,' she said. 'Not with me.'

'I'm sorry,' said Jaz. This was very difficult. She half wished she hadn't come.

'Are you quite sure?' Her voice had become a croak.

Jaz nodded.

'I told him he was mad, living down there amongst all those gangsters. Drug addicts. I told him he should move out of London. It would have been possible, in his line of work. I mean, computer programming . . . You can do that anywhere, can't you?'

Jaz decided not to contradict her. There was no point in telling her about Vinny. It wouldn't help.

'He was a good boy.'

'When did you last see him?'

'Oh, I don't know. I lose track of time. It was before Christmas.'

Jaz wasn't sure how to keep the conversation going, but she knew she couldn't just leave. 'The police haven't been to see you? What about a funeral?'

'No, no one's been here. Only my charlady.' She stood up shakily, then lowered herself onto a sofa nearer Jaz. She sank into the cushions and leaned back. 'I can't go to a funeral,' she whispered. 'I never go out.'

'It's OK.' Jaz wanted to reassure her. 'I just wanted to tell you, that's all. Andy would have wanted you to know.' She saw two tears trickle down the woman's cheeks making streaks in her foundation.

There was a silence between them. A whistling kettle sounded, then stopped. Jaz could hear a neighbour's radio and the faint hum outside that was the noise of London. She stared at the floor. The carpet, once beautiful, was old and stained.

Trace came back in holding a tray. She plonked it heavily on a table, rattling the cups. 'This is beautiful china,' she said. 'Spode. They've got some at the Dorchester, but it's not as nice as this.' She poured the tea.

The woman sniffed and blotted her face with the back of her hand. 'He was adopted,' she said suddenly, bending forward to pick up her cup. 'Taken away.' Her hand shook a little. 'I had them both adopted privately. Both boys. Jason and Justin. That's what I called them.' She smiled at the memory. She gazed away into nothing. 'They were darlings.'

'Both of them?' asked Jaz. 'What do you mean, both of them?'

Trace blew on her tea noisily.

'They were twins.' The woman's voice had become dreamy, almost sentimental.

'Andy had a twin?'

She sighed again. 'They were separated. Adopted separately. Cruel, but that's how it was. I was desperate.'

'What happened?'

She settled back on her sofa, composed now, as if she had told the story many times. She continued to stare into space, nursing her cup and saucer. 'I was with Mickey first,' she said, 'before he met Marianne.' She smiled to herself. The memory appeared to have replaced all emotion about Fat Andy. 'They were wild times. Paparazzi. Night clubs. Parties.'

Jaz watched as Trace spooned sugar into her cup.

'I'd been modelling,' the woman continued, 'a few commercials, a few walk-on parts at the Old Vic. I was the Revlon Girl back in 'sixty-two. Mickey was very sweet. Not at all like they tried to make out in the papers. I was a lot older than him, of course.'

'What's she on about?' asked Trace in a loud whisper.

'Shh!' said Jaz.

'I'd been engaged twice. Once to Neddy, he was the son of a Duke. Then to Mario. He was a top hairdresser. Mickey swept me off my feet. He was so . . . real.' She turned her head and stared at a framed photograph on a side table. It was a signed print of the Rolling Stones.

Jaz followed her gaze and the penny dropped. 'She means Mick Jagger,' she whispered. She stared at the woman. Her voice, she decided, had a brittle, false note. She didn't believe her.

'It was a while before I met Brian. When I did, it was love at first sight.'

'Brian?' queried Jaz, humouring her.

'Brian Jones. You must remember him. He was the original rhythm guitarist. Before Ronnie Wood.'

Jaz shook her head. It seemed rude to say she wasn't even born then, that her own mother was still a child. She glanced at Trace. She knew she'd probably never heard of the Rolling Stones. She had no sense of history.

The woman continued. 'He was the one who drowned. In his swimming pool.'

Jaz saw Trace's expression change. She was so empathic about calamity. She stared, horrified. 'His swimming pool! Really? What happened?'

The woman clearly wanted to tell her story in her own way. 'Brian and I were together for a few months. Let me tell you, dears, they were the happiest months of my life.' She paused. 'I was a mother to him, in a way. But he treated me so well.' She held out a hand. It was long and bony, like a claw, and on it sat a huge diamond. 'He bought me this.' She turned her hand towards herself and admired it. 'He bought me a lovely car. An E-Type Jaguar.'

'Roadster or hard-top?' asked Jaz automatically.

'Oh, yes.'

'All-synchromesh gearbox?'

The woman looked offended.

'What year was it? Have you still got it?'

'No, of course I haven't. Anyway. As I was saying.' She drank some of her tea, then returned the cup and saucer to the tray. 'We were in love. He went away on a tour and I did a very silly thing.'

'Crashed the E-Type?'

Trace elbowed Jaz in the ribs.

'I started seeing this boxer. He was a black fellow from the United States. Very handsome. He was as gentle as a lamb, but his people. Oh, my dears!'

'Oh, no, poor Brian,' sympathized Trace, as if she knew what was coming.

The woman smiled. She began directing her words towards Trace. 'Yes. You're right, dear. It was a mess. I was a fool.' She sighed. 'A silly young fool.'

'He drowned.' Trace said this in a way that made her sound familiar with the whole story, but Jaz knew she wasn't. She was just sad about the tragedy.

'There were horrid scenes when I went back to Brian. I just wanted the boxer to get on with his prize fight or whatever it was and go back home.' She sighed. 'But he was in love with me.'

'Oh, no!' exclaimed Trace. Her sympathies were now being pulled the other way.

'It was a love tangle.' The woman stopped talking and picked up a magazine.

Jaz realized she was at the end of her narrative. 'Brian Jones drowned.' She wanted to get back to the subject of Fat Andy.

The woman nodded.

'It wasn't an accident?'

She shook her head.

'That's awful,' said Trace.

'And you were pregnant,' added Jaz.

The woman's head sank onto her chest. She looked defeated, vulnerable. 'I was told they were twins. I didn't know what colour they would be. The boxer disappeared after the swimming pool incident. There was a big fuss. The official version was an accident, but everyone on the inside blamed me. No one would speak to me. I got no invitations any more. The phone never rang. I was persona non grata. I moved in here and became a ghost, dears. When the boys were born I couldn't cope. I got depressed. I mean, how was I supposed to know what to do with two babies? I just wasn't equipped. I was a celebrity, not a mother.'

'You said adopted?' Jaz prompted.

'Two private adoptions. An old school friend arranged it. I rang her up, absolutely desperate. She provided the childless couples. They paid well.' She thought for a moment. 'The right sort of people, of course.'

'The twins were separated?'

'Yes, I told you. Justin went to Bournemouth. Jason went to Highgate. I thought I'd never see them again. I never did see Jason again, but Justin turned up about four years ago. He'd traced me somehow and said his name was Andy. He had all sorts of papers and documents. I thought he wanted something, but he didn't. He was a good boy, a good-natured boy, a computer programmer. He was a surprise. He was rather ordinary, but I thought that was probably a good thing. He came to see me from time to time.'

'Andy's dead,' reminded Jaz. She didn't want to be brutal, but she thought the woman's grasp on reality was a little thin. She didn't want their visit to be a waste of time.

'Dead,' repeated the woman sadly. 'First lost. Now dead.'

Trace slid from her seat, kneeled in front of the

woman and stroked her hand. 'We're very sorry,' she murmured.

Jaz stood up abruptly and pulled Trace to her feet. 'We've got to go,' she said. 'We'll see ourselves out.' She made for the door, pulling Trace's arm. In moments they were outside in the street.

'She was sad,' said Trace. 'We shouldn't have just left her there like that.'

Jaz walked quickly towards the car, with Trace following. She unlocked the Cortina, got inside and slammed the door. As Trace climbed into the passenger seat, Jaz put on her sunglasses then started the ignition with a furious gesture. 'I didn't like her,' she said. 'Talking all that shit about the Rolling Stones. And she sold those babies, probably to the highest fucking bidder.' She paused. 'And she was very ugly. She had false teeth. She gave me the creeps.'

'You know something?' said Trace. 'You swear too much.'

Jaz fired the engine.

Trace was silent. Then she said, 'You know that woman on *Absolutely Fabulous*? The blonde one?'

Jaz turned out into the traffic and, still angry, quickly wound down her window.

Trace considered again for a moment. 'She'll look like Andy's mum one day. The way she carries on, that's where she's heading.'

'Trace,' said Jaz. 'Shut up. Start giving me directions, like now. I've got to have a shower.'

Chapter Ten

The hotel in which Trace worked illegally was more like a private health club. It was called Hotel Grand Bahama. Behind its regency exterior there was a fitness suite, chiropody and massage rooms, a beauty salon and a warm turquoise pool surrounded by palm trees. Middle-aged women wandered around in white towelling robes and mud packs.

Jaz had been expecting a quick, lukewarm shower in a maid's attic. Instead, in the luxurious staff quarters, Trace handed her a yellow overall with a tiny palm tree embroidered on the chest, white tights and a pair of white lace-up shoes. 'Put these on,' she said. 'We all wear these.' Jaz examined the unfamiliar garment as Trace pulled off her clothes and wriggled into her own overall. Then Jaz transferred her attention to Trace. Her hemline was very short because her legs were so long. Jaz undressed and donned hers. She hadn't worn a skirt for years. It was much too big and came halfway down her calves. 'I've got a date tonight,' she confided.

Trace giggled. 'Who with? Anyone I know?'

'Yes. He's called Pete. Do you remember him? You met him once or twice. He's a mechanic at the garage where Andy worked. Where I used to work.' It occurred to Jaz again that Pete might be a very useful ally. 'He lives near there. On the Isle of Dogs.'

Trace considered. 'Yeah . . . He's that tall, pretty boy . . . Nice.' She glanced at Jaz. 'You ought to get your hair done while you're here. I'll take you to the salon.'

'What exactly do you do here?' Jaz enquired.

'Clean the rooms, of course. But we wear the same uniform as the nurses and hairdressers and everyone.' She grinned. 'The manageress reckons we're just one big, happy family.'

'Until they don't need you any more,' exclaimed Jaz impatiently, 'until the job centre coughs up, or someone answers their advert in the *Evening Standard* and they have to start paying National Insurance.'

Trace frowned. 'Don't be like that,' she said, 'it's nice here. I like it. Except for the food. The guests pay hundreds of pounds and all they get to eat is leaves.'

Jaz wandered around. In her uniform, she immediately blended in. She went back to the staff quarters and had a shower. In the laundry room, she ran her own clothes through the washer-dryer. She ate a salad in the dining room next to a table full of large ladies discussing carbohydrate. Then she went down to the pool and sat naked in the jacuzzi.

Jaz found the onslaught of probing bubbles a strange sensation. She lay back and opened her limbs like a starfish. It was pleasant, she decided, sensual. She thought about sex and closed her eyes, imagining Pete stroking her thighs, his gestures both caressing and firm. She touched herself between her legs, excited, as a jet of warm water played against her body then inside it. She sighed with pleasure, but at that instant, unable to help herself, her fantasy switched to Fat Andy and to Blow.

Their faces and their insistent fingers, merged as one single, needy person, filled her thoughts. 'Little baby,' they whispered, handling her. With a splash she stood up, cupping water into her face, trying to free her mind of the image. She stepped out of the pool. I don't like this, she thought.

Later, egged on by Trace, she went into the hair and beauty parlour. The decor here, unlike the pastel reassurance of the rest of the premises, was modern and stark. Even the floor was made of chrome. Because it was a slack period, the therapist, Kayleigh, wearing the same uniform as her own, trimmed and styled Jaz's hair. She was very talkative. She urged Jaz to use conditioner. She said she was from the Isle of Wight.

Kayleigh was the mistress of a thousand potions. They were kept in a glass cabinet, locked with a key. She suggested a facial and then an eyebrow wax. Jaz drew the line at a top-to-toe fake bronzing, but her new friend persuaded her to have her contours defined with blusher, her cheekbones highlighted and her eyelids outlined with pencil. She coated her lips in orange gloss, then gave her the small tube. 'Keep this and use it,' she said.

As they were finishing, Trace appeared. She was holding Jaz's sports bag. 'Jaz. Your phone was ringing.'

The two of them went back to the staff quarters. Jaz put on her own clothes and phoned Harm. Wesley answered. He sounded upset. 'You better get over, Jaz,' he said. 'We're in a very, very negative energy field here.'

'Where's Harm? What's happened?'

'Harm's been harmed,' he said. He wasn't joking. He sounded as if he'd been crying. He sniffed a couple of times and hung up.

'What's up?' asked Trace anxiously.

'Come on,' said Jaz. 'Something bad's happened to Harm.'

Trace gave a little cry. In an instant she dragged off her overall, tights and shoes. She wasn't wearing a bra or knickers. Not for the first time, Jaz admired her gawky beauty. She wriggled into her jeans, a clean belly top and her flip flops. She yanked her fingers through her short, thick hair. In under a minute they were away, running towards the Lotus Cortina. In three minutes they were on the road, heading for Wesley's place in Shepherd's Bush.

Wesley had a spacious studio flat above a pork butcher. A homeless man was crouching in the doorway, holding out his hat, but in their hurry Jaz and Trace merely stepped over him. Wesley opened the door wordlessly and gave them a bleak stare. They followed him in. There was a strong smell of cooking meat coming from below. Trace grimaced. Like Wesley, she was a vegetarian.

Harm lay on the settee wearing a pink cellular blanket. Her face was bruised and swollen. Her bottom lip was split and blood, now dry, had collected in the corner of her mouth. One of her eyes was blackened and half closed. When she saw her two friends, she attempted to smile. Trace leaped towards her and then knelt at her side, burying her face in the blanket. Jaz sat at Harm's feet. Wesley disappeared to make coffee.

'My, my, Jaz, you look like Miss World,' joked Harm. Her voice sounded muffled. She could hardly open her mouth. 'You're wearing make-up!'

'I've a date,' Jaz muttered. 'You remember Pete from the garage? Lives in Poplar?' She paused. 'Shit,' she said, staring at Harm's injuries. 'Look at you. Who did this?' There was a lead weight in her stomach. She knew the answer.

Trace, her face still hidden, started to sob.

'Wesley?' Harm called out. 'Wesley? Can you come here?'

Wesley reappeared. He seemed desolate. He was carrying a tray with four mugs of instant coffee.

'Be a good Wesley,' said Harm. 'Go and get me a milk shake from McDonald's. Banana flavour. With a straw. I can't drink coffee. It just makes my bladder ache.'

Wesley looked miserable. He said nothing.

'Take Trace with you.'

He pulled on a bomber jacket.

Trace was still crying. 'Shut up, Trace,' said Jaz aggressively.

'Come on, Trace,' said Wesley. They both went out.

'This was my fault, wasn't it?' Jaz inserted one of Harm's cigarettes between her damaged lips and lit it.

Harm inhaled gratefully. 'Forget blame,' she said. 'We made a mistake, that's all.' She raised her hand with difficulty and flicked her cigarette ash onto the floor.

Jaz picked up an ashtray from the table and put it into her other hand. 'Ronnie and Reggie.' It was a statement rather than a question. 'Mile End Road.' Jaz stood up, paced across the room, then back again. She clenched and unclenched her fists. I'll fucking kill them, she thought. I'll kill Vinny. Her mouth felt very dry. She bent down and picked up her mug. She watched Harm smoke, noticing that her knuckles were grazed.

'They took me to an Indian restaurant,' said Harm. 'They were all right at first. We chatted and had a curry and a couple of beers. Then they took me back to the gym, paid me and we did the business. It was just like the old days. One watching the other, straight fucking, no extras. Then swapping around. It was afterwards, when I mentioned your bloke, that things turned heavy.'

'What did you say?' asked Jaz.

'I said he'd been murdered. I told them I hardly knew the guy, but that you were upset. I asked them if Vinny was behind it. I didn't cut corners, I just came out with it.'

Jaz stamped across the room and back, twice.

'They wanted to know where you're living,' Harm continued. 'Said they were looking for you. Wouldn't believe me when I said I didn't know. Jaz is a homeless person, she just stays anywhere, I said. You know that, boys. You know Jaz – what she's like. She's gone back to her old ways.' Harm sucked on her cigarette again, then extinguished it. 'They weren't having any of it. They tried to beat it out of me.'

'A mistake,' said Jaz. 'Going there was my mistake.'

'It was all a mistake. I shouldn't have gone. They're cheap. Always were cheap. They're not nice people.' She thought for a moment. 'And I know them. Another mistake. These days I only do business with men I don't know. Avoiding repeats. I don't want to get to know them. I don't want to talk to them. I shouldn't have gone back to the Mile End Road. Too much history there, too much baggage. It was another life.'

'I'm sorry, Harm.' Jaz drained her coffee and dumped the mug on a table. She was too angry to feel guilty. Guilt would come later.

'I'll recover. Worse things have happened. But you need to watch out, Jaz. They're after you.'

Jaz thought for a moment. 'They think that Andy took something belonging to Vinny.'

'Maybe they think you have it.'

'Did they say so?'

'Not exactly . . .'

'Do you think they killed Fat Andy?'

'They didn't answer questions, they asked them.' She grinned ruefully.

Jaz felt frustrated by the lack of information. She was not only angry, she was impatient. 'Yes, but what do you think?'

'I think they might have done, if Vinny told them to. They're Vinny's heavies, after all. If Vinny wanted Andy dead, then . . .' she paused, pursing her lips. 'They were the ones. Stay away from them, that's what I'm telling you.'

The front door slammed.

Harm spoke hurriedly. 'Remember that cinema weirdo who was going to kill you when you were sixteen. Remember the mess you were in that time. Don't do anything stupid.'

Wesley and Trace came in. He handed Harm her milk shake then left the room. The atmosphere was charged.

Trace resumed her place at Harm's side, her cheek on the blanket. 'A bad man,' she muttered. 'They're all of them bad men.'

Jaz paced back and forward again. She punched the air. 'The bastard,' she muttered. 'That fucking bastard Vinny.'

'A bad bastard,' Trace repeated vaguely. She sat up on her haunches and reached for a mug of coffee. 'You'll get killed one day, doing this awful job.'

Harm sipped through the straw. 'Where are you staying, Jaz, anyway? Just out of interest.'

Jaz shrugged. 'Fat Andy's car.'

'Don't take that batmobile anywhere near Stepney, that's all I can say. You'll stick out like the Boy Wonder.' She drank the milk shake steadily. 'You know what was funny? Typical of them? They beat me up, then called me a taxi. They even helped me on with my coat. They're vicious thugs, but they've got like . . . you know . . . perfect manners.'

Jaz moved towards the door. She needed to get outside. 'Come on, Trace.'

'Be careful, Jaz,' said Harm. 'Forget that Pete. Stand him up. Just stay away from the East End.'

Jaz dropped Trace back at her hotel then, disregarding Harm's advice, set off for Poplar High Street. She was supposed to be meeting Pete and she was late.

It was a beautiful evening. The light was soft and mellow and it was warm. The sky was high and blue. London seemed unlike itself, bathed in gentle, almost southern sunshine, its colours continental, its pedestrians wearing shirtsleeves and skimpy dresses, cheerful and relaxed.

Jaz thought of Italy, Portugal and Greece. She remembered everything she'd ever absorbed about such places on TV holiday programmes. Fat Andy laughed at her for watching them. 'I'll take you there,' he'd said once. 'I did all that stuff in the seventies. On the Magic Bus. But I'll take you, if you want.' Jaz suddenly remembered the way his hair, on that last evening, was matted and dead, like an animal run over on the road – thick and full of blood.

About half a mile from her destination, Jaz parked the car at the side of a police station. Fat Andy had always said that if there was nowhere else, it was a reasonably safe place. Jaz wasn't confident but then she remembered that she herself had never stolen a car from outside a police station. Not once.

She checked herself in the mirror. She wasn't sure about the make-up but decided to leave it on. She applied a little more lipstick from the free sample she'd been given. She sniffed her hair. It smelled of coconuts. It was straightened and with the extra benefit of Kayleigh's protein treatment, it hung in deep, smooth curves to her shoulders. It looked thicker and more glossy. The kinks and dry wisps had been eased away. Her fringe was even and manicured. Jaz decided at that moment to put her anger and frustration and revenge plans temporarily to one side. She was out on a proper date and she was almost pretty. She looked like a woman rather than a child.

As an extra precaution, she immobilized the car. She jogged the half mile to the pub, not too fast, to avoid getting sweaty. The place was large, on a corner. It had an excess of overflowing window boxes which cascaded garish flowers down its walls. A few tables were occupied outside and the sound of karaoke came from within. Someone was attempting an old Kate Bush hit, but they couldn't reach the high notes.

Jaz paused and smoothed her T-shirt. She had brought her sports bag but had left her jacket in the boot of the car. She checked her jeans pocket. The photo of her twin sisters was folded inside. She still had a roll of money, left over from her trip to Cambridge.

Pete was sitting alone. Jaz paused at the bar and looked at him. She ordered a lemonade. He was wearing a baggy black shirt and a green silk waistcoat. His hair was held in a ponytail. He looked more New Age than she was expecting. As she walked towards him she noticed that his white jeans were clean but deliberately ripped and frayed at the knees. His ankles were white and bony above black plimsolls. He saw her but didn't smile. She was ninety minutes late.

'Sorry,' said Jaz lightly. 'My friend Harm's been beaten up. I was at her bedside. You know, helping.'

Pete frowned. 'Harm?'

'I think you've met her. She used to hang out with those brothers on the Mile End Road. The big ones who work for Vinny.' Jaz was thirsty. She drained her glass.

Pete thought for a minute. 'Black girl? On the game?'

'Yep.'

'Occupational hazard, I should think.' Pete turned the long words slowly over his tongue.

There was a sudden blast of music. Jaz turned to the stage. An elderly Chinese man picked up the microphone and started dancing stiffly, like a puppet. He sang the opening to the Spice Girls' 'Wannabe'.

Pete finished his pint. He stood up to go to the bar. 'Want anything?'

Jaz shook her head.

He smiled. She knew she was forgiven. 'Never drink, do you?'

'No. My mother's a drunk.' She paused. 'An alcoholic.'

Pete nodded sympathetically.

When he returned, Jaz moved next to him on the bench seat. He rested his arm along the back, behind her, in a gesture that was both casual and enclosing. 'You don't mind me drinking?'

'Oh, I don't care what other people do.' She laughed. 'I need a few friends, you know.'

'Your hair looks nice,' he said.

'I had it done in a really posh place. My friend Trace works in this hotel. Called the Grand Bahama.'

'The Grand Banana?'

'Bahama,' Jaz laughed. 'People go there to lose weight.'

They chatted about various things. Jaz was surprised to discover he didn't share her enthusiasm for cars. He said when you fix other people's cars all day you don't want to think about them in your spare time. Jaz could see his point. Both Blow and Fat Andy had spent a lot of time fixing cars, without their passion becoming dimmed, but then they weren't doing it day in day out, non-stop, for other people, for a wage.

She changed the subject. They discovered they both liked football. Jaz expected him to be a Millwall fan but he supported Palace. They discussed Sunderland's new Stadium of Light. 'I never go back up there,' said Jaz. 'I was going to but . . .'

'But what?'

'My sisters have moved on. Grown up.' She took out the photo of Peony and Mimosa, dressed as angels, and showed it to him.

He smiled.

She folded it and put it away. 'My mother had a farm, but it's been sold . . .' She was going to mention Blow, but stopped herself.

'I'm sorry about Andy,' Pete said, as if reading her mind.

'So am I.'

'I hope you don't think . . .' He stopped, then tried again. 'I hope you don't think . . .'

'That you're taking advantage of the situation? No I don't. I don't. OK?'

'It's just that . . .'

'It's OK, Pete, honest.' She paused. 'Being on my own all the time doesn't help.'

He picked up her hand and kissed it, looking into her eyes. His touch was like an electric shock. Jaz hoped he hadn't felt her jump. She realized that his confidence had grown. He was no longer shy. She smiled and withdrew her hand. She was beginning to feel a little out of control.

'Where're you staying?' he asked.

Jaz didn't want to tell him she was homeless. She had a feeling that he wouldn't approve. 'With friends,' she lied.

He got up to go to the bar. Jaz watched his small rear and noticed that his lovely hair was tied back with coloured braid. He had young arms. She felt a surge of desire. What am I doing, she thought, with Blow dead, and Fat Andy dead? Why am I with someone else? She turned the question over in her mind. She placed her hand on the centre of her chest. The pain was still there. She was still grieving, but the situation with Pete was quite different and separate from anything that had happened with Andy or Blow. This had nothing to do with them. Then she remembered Fat Andy telling her to loosen up. He was a hedonist and he'd found her tightly strung and unadventurous. Enjoy yourself, girl, he'd kept saying. Find some pleasure in life! She looked at Pete, buying the drinks. He had bony, boyish shoulders. He was young and because of this he made her feel mature. She wanted him.

Andy would have approved, she thought. He would have found this need more normal and acceptable than my usual cold style. She smiled to herself. Maybe I just needed to find the right person.

Pete came back with half a pint for himself and a lemonade. Then he walked over to the stage. He was joining in the karaoke. He selected a song. He climbed up as the opening bars of Simply Red's 'Stars' started playing. Jaz was worried, and grasped a beer mat. She started shredding it, but immediately he began singing she realized everything was fine. He had a great voice. He sounded just like Mick Hucknall. He was a gentle New Age man. He turned to face her, singing something about falling from the stars and landing in her arms. People turned to stare at Jaz. She was embarrassed but very pleased.

It was dark outside. The window boxes gave off a faint, summery perfume. They walked away from the pub, down the warm, deserted street, holding hands. Pete carried her bag. The sky had turned purple. His flat was a short distance away. It was medium rise with balconies covered in plants. He tapped a keypad outside the entrance and the big glass door swung open. The lobby was brightly lit and a uniformed man sat behind a screen like a bank clerk. He saluted as they passed by, on their way to the lift.

'What is this place?' asked Jaz.

'It was a council gaff,' he replied, 'but it was bought out by a private company. They put the rents up, did a bit of decorating. They made the entrance more secure and hired that con-serge.'

'Who?'

'That con-serge. That bloke. He stops the troublemakers from coming in. It used to be hell before. Kids, winos, homeless dossers, beggars. Now it's sort of OK.'

Jaz coughed.

They got into the lift. 'Have you been here long?'

'All my life. My mum died and I stayed on.' A bell rang and the door opened. Jaz noticed that they were on the third floor.

Pete's living room was spartan but clean. Jaz was surprised. She'd expected his mother's old furniture, floral wallpaper and carpet. Instead, the walls were white, the floor sanded and the sofa and chair were black cotton. A small lamp was already burning by the window. He turned on the CD player and went into the kitchen to make tea. Jaz looked around. There was a framed print of the Zodiac on the wall and a poster with paintings of various weeds. On closer inspection, these turned out to be herbal remedies. She examined a row of books. There were a few crime novels but they were mostly concerned with astrology, herbalism and homoeopathy. There was a music magazine with a cover picture of the Verve. She looked out of the window. This was the back of the building but she couldn't quite see the river. They were surrounded by blocks of flats of varying heights. There was a deserted market place below, the stalls empty of their goods and awnings. Dominating the skyline, symmetrical and proud, glowed Canary Wharf, as elegant as a space rocket, as huge as a mountain. A plume of white vapour drifted from its tip, revealing then obscuring its upper outline, before being blown into the night air.

Pete returned, holding two mugs. They sat down and chatted about astrology. Jaz privately thought it was nonsense but she played along with it. She told him she was a Gemini and he looked up her date and time of birth in one of his books. He told her that her ascendant was Leo, which was the same as his.

'Does that mean we get along?' she asked, 'or the opposite?'

He replied by stroking her hair. 'You look different,' he said. 'You look kind of . . . softer.'

'I'm wearing make-up,' she replied. 'Do you like it?'

'I don't usually dig it, but it looks nice on you.' He laughed. 'I was worried about tonight.' He paused, searching for words. 'Because you're older than me and everything. But when I saw that you'd put make-up on and had your hair done, just for me, just for my benefit, I felt . . .' He laughed again. 'Flattered.' He leaned towards her and kissed her cheek. His hand fingered the waistband of her jeans. His other arm encircled her and drew her close. He kissed her tenderly, on the lips, on her neck, on her forehead. 'Your hair smells wonderful,' he whispered. 'What is it?'

'Coconut oil.'

His lips returned to hers and he slipped his tongue inside her mouth, probing gently. He undid the button of her jeans and slid down the zip.

Jaz felt very relaxed. She was enjoying his attention. She was passive, lying back in his arms, responding, but in a minimal way. As he kissed her she realized what was different. He wasn't expecting her to actively please him. In fact, the reverse was true.

Jaz had been with lots of men but usually in return for something – money, accommodation, a favour, a meal. This meant that she had to do what they wanted, maybe even going as far as pretending to be someone she wasn't. In bed with Fat Andy she'd been required to be a little girl. In any event, she'd always concentrated on the needs of these men rather than her own. Now, with Pete, he seemed to want nothing except to be with her. He was only interested in pleasing her.

Gently, he removed her jacket, then her T-shirt. His

hands brushed over her nipples and he kissed the hollow above her collarbone. Jaz realized that she was excited. She felt desirable. She was being properly appreciated, for herself. She concentrated on the sensations of being fondled. I like this, she thought. The relief of not having to focus on his needs, or on her own hard-won techniques, gave way to a languid sense of relaxation. Her mind drifted to a distant place which allowed her body to enjoy and respond to physical sensation. His lips grazed her neck. Gently he sucked her ear lobe. His hands stroked her back. 'Is that nice?' he whispered. 'Do you like that?'

She sighed and opened her eyes. He was smiling at her. 'Do you want to go to bed?' he murmured. He pulled her hand and she stood up and followed him into the next room. She helped him slide off her jeans and pants. Kneeling on the floor in front of her, he buried his face in the hair between her legs. The room was dark but the bed cover gleamed. Jaz held his head against her body then carefully stepped backwards, sitting then lying on the bed. He continued to kiss her – his mouth exploring her stomach and inner thighs then returning to the delicate folds between her legs. Jaz spread both her arms and her legs wide in this act of surrender that she had never dared allow herself before. She held her breath as an acute sensation built up, swept through her body and was then discharged. She made a small, involuntary cry.

There was a brief pause as he drew back but she held up her arms and gathered him towards her in a gesture that signified both gratitude and relief. 'You're beautiful,' she heard him whisper. 'I've always thought so.'

Pete had a single bed. They lay on their sides facing

each other, talking and giggling. His youth was refreshing. Jaz found herself being genuinely childish, rather than pretending. She told some silly jokes. She made rude noises with her hands and armpits. He laughed immoderately and talked about school.

She explored his body and discovered it was hard and thin with clearly defined muscles and bones. After a while, she climbed on top of him, gently coaxing him with her hands towards orgasm. Then, turning over, she let him enter her for his release. They made love again, dozed a little then continued. He was so young he had lots of energy and wasn't at all worried about having to get up early the next day. After several hours she snuggled backwards into the concave line of his body and slept. When she awoke, light shone through the thin curtains and she discovered he had gone.

Jaz stretched across the narrow bed and sighed. She felt wetness ooze from her vagina. She held up the covers and sniffed the scent of sex. They hadn't used condoms. She did a rapid calculation and decided that this was OK. She looked around the room. The painted floorboards were covered in a thin, colourful Indian rug. In a corner, there was a rowing machine and a pile of weights. There was a print of a famous painting of water lilies, which she couldn't name. The room was clean and bare, but pleasing. She sighed contentedly.

After a while her thoughts inevitably returned to Fat Andy and Blow. Despite her night with Pete, the pain of their loss was still there, physically manifested in her chest. She pressed it with her hand. She thought again how both the dead men would approve of her new relationship. This was comforting.

Her mind moved on to the question of Vinny. This

forced her out of bed. She washed, retrieved her scattered clothes and dressed. Her hair had returned to its normal thin-looking, flyaway state, so she plaited it tightly. She turned on the television in the living room. The Home Secretary was making a speech about the government's plans to deal with homelessness and begging. He called it the new deal on Clean Cities. Jaz half listened, cynically, dismissing his concerns as platitudes. She'd heard this kind of talk before. Not only his solutions, but even his definitions of the problem had nothing to do with the reality of life on the streets. She'd been there and knew it well. What do you know about hardship, she thought, you fat cat, you tosser? You designer dressed, feather-bedded wanker. As she was about to switch off the TV the camera panned and she froze in surprise. 'Andy!' she said aloud.

A man stood near the Home Secretary. As the politician moved off the platform, he followed him down some steps. In two seconds they were both gone. The bland face of the morning newsreader appeared. Fucking hell, she thought, it couldn't be . . . She remembered the comments of both Princess and Fat Andy's mother. Was it possible? It had to be. The likeness was uncanny. There was only one explanation. This had to be Fat Andy's twin! She switched off the television and closed her eyes, trying to bring an after image of the man to mind. He had Andy's exact profile, with its triple chin, soft cheeks and slightly hooked nose. His hair was long like Andy's, and the same colour, but straighter and smooth, drawn back tightly into a ponytail. He had the same bulk, the same enormous stomach but he was very smartly dressed in a suit with a white shirt and patterned tie. As Princess had suggested, he wore an identity badge on a long chain around his neck. She took a deep breath. Why had Andy never mentioned him? But then she remembered she knew nothing about Fat Andy's life. She hadn't known about his mother, about his glamorous if curious origins. That information had been shared with Princess, but not with her.

She realized that she had to speak to this man. He would be a proper mourner. He would be the chief mourner. He would understand. She paced back and forth across the room. Both Princess and Andy's mother had responded to the news of his death in a less than satisfactory way. A twin brother would be different. Jaz knew about twins. Twins were one person in two bodies. She would find him and tell him his twin was dead. She owed it to Fat Andy. This was absolutely clear.

She made the bed and opened the bedroom curtains, letting the bright sunshine flood in. There was a leafy balcony, covered in pot plants. This room overlooked the street. She glanced down. Her heart lurched. Two men were standing on the opposite pavement. One was leaning against a lamp-post, the other paced slowly to and fro. Their bald heads gleamed. It was Ronnie and Reggie.

Jaz bunched the edge of the curtain in her fist. Her mind was racing. A surge of adrenalin expelled the last of the calm, contented feeling that had been with her upon waking. She felt her muscles adopt their customary tense, ready state. Her mouth became a thin line, her eyes narrowed. A series of options flashed across her mind. She had to get out without being seen. She had to retrieve the car. She had to disappear. Another thought crowded in. That bastard Pete had betrayed her. He'd set her up.

Vinny and his gang were onto her, and they'd used Pete as a trap.

She strode around, angry, looking for something to steal. There was nothing that was both valuable and portable. She made a note of the phone number and then walked out of the flat, leaving the door wide open. The hi-fi and television were clearly visible from the landing. The room, with its modern decor, venetian blind and rubber plant, looked inviting, even prosperous. 'You shit,' she muttered. 'I hope this place is fucking stripped when you get home.'

She ran along the corridor. The only way out seemed to be down. The back of the building was inaccessible from the public areas. It was a line of closed doors.

She went up the stairs two at a time. On the next floor, halfway along the corridor next to the rubbish chute, there was a narrow metal staircase leading up to a hatch. This was secured with a small padlock. Breathing heavily, Jaz climbed the steps and rummaged in her bag for her smallest screwdriver. She swore to herself. An old woman emerged from a flat opposite and looked up, hands on hips. She examined Jaz quizzically as if expecting to see a naughty child. Holding onto the handrail, Jaz leaned out and towards her. She flicked open her small wallet, pretending to show ID. 'Satellite TV,' she said huskily. 'Service agreement.'

The woman frowned and disappeared without a word.

Jaz prised away the screws holding the catch on the exit. In seconds she was on the roof.

There was a stiff breeze and the sun was already hot on the back of her neck. The street was quiet. She walked over to the low parapet and looked down. The flats were not very high, but without protection the drop seemed dizzying. She could just make out the bald head of either Ronnie or Reggie, still at his post. His shoulders had the resigned droop of someone who was prepared to wait all day.

A helicopter swooped overhead and she felt the disturbance in the air. Combined with the wind, this gave her the feeling of being blown too hard towards the edge. She stepped backwards. The next-door building was two storeys down. Jaz considered staying on the roof until Vinny's men had given up and gone home. She looked around. There were a few satellite dishes, cables, pipes and a large, rusty water tank. It would be possible to sit it out. Just then she heard a shout. Turning, she saw a man emerging from the hatch. His bulky shoulders were through, and then, awkwardly, his stocky legs. He was wearing a purple silk tracksuit and new trainers. He spoke into a walkie-talkie and gestured to her to come towards him. He shouted again, but his words were indistinct, carried away by the wind. It was Ronnie or Reggie. He'd made his way up from the street.

Jaz looked down again. The building next door had a fire escape on the back. She swallowed hard. Maybe. I could jump it. Just. She didn't allow herself time for reflection. Hugging her bag she ran towards the man as if answering his call. He was a purple blur. When he was only yards away and without missing a beat she swung round on one heel and accelerated back towards the edge. She heard him shout again. The wind whistled in her ears and her heart pounded. She looked up at the clear blue sky and then across the rooftops. Without losing speed and without looking down, she felt one foot touch the parapet as she flung herself into space. The free fall was terrifying.

She landed on her feet. A sickening jolt surged from her ankles up through her thighs. She toppled forward onto her knees, winded. Her stomach felt like water. She breathed heavily for a few seconds, her eyes tight shut. She'd made it. She was on the roof of the building next door and she'd put a huge gap between herself and her pursuer. Drawing in a few more sharp breaths she stood up, testing her ankles. Stay calm, she told herself. Stay cool. She was shaking but she was OK.

Turning she saw Ronnie or Reggie waving from above, his walkie-talkie clasped to his ear. He looked small and helpless now, gesturing wildly. She ran over to the fire escape. It was old and rusty but as she gingerly stepped on it, she sensed it was secure. In a couple of minutes she was down and in the back street. She crossed the market place where traders were setting up for the day and entered a maze of narrow passageways between flats, then ran in what she hoped was the direction of the car. Emerging she saw a sign for the Blackwall tunnel and heard the roar of the main road. She felt hot, sticky and red-faced. A group of young Asian children, on their way to school, eyed her curiously and smiled. 'Good morning,' said one of them politely.

She bought a can of Coke from a corner shop, set off at a brisk walking pace, then a steady jog, hoping she was approaching the police station where she'd left the car. She found it without too much difficulty. There were two leaflets under the windscreen and a dollop of bird mess down the passenger door. Otherwise it was as she'd left it. She got in, recovered her breath and massaged her ankles. I must wash this car, she thought. She put on her sunglasses. Within a few seconds she was away. I need a plan, she decided. She wasn't going to let them beat her. She wanted revenge.

Chapter Eleven

Jaz spent another night in the car, parked in a secure covered area reserved for barristers in Lincoln's Inn Fields. This was another one of Fat Andy's safe havens for the Lotus Cortina, where he'd somehow managed to familiarize himself with the security measures. He'd recorded the information in his Filofax.

She lay on the back seat, her head on the inflatable pillow. She found it hard to sleep, not just because of the discomfort but because her mind was full of her night with Pete. She kept remembering things they'd done and what she'd said to him – revealing things, silly things – and now she felt humiliated. She loathed herself for confiding in him. She'd been a fool. She'd been off her guard and now she felt ridiculous. She vowed to herself that such a thing must never, ever be allowed to happen again. Sex was a means to an end, that was all. She didn't need it and she didn't want it, for any reason other than convenience. Pete would suffer for tricking her. She would have to think of a way of paying him back – the only thing was, her list of enemies was growing. He'd have to take his place in the queue.

She deliberately changed her memories to ones of Fat Andy. She pressed her hand on her chest and felt the pain. She recalled a night out in a pub in New Cross with all the members of the gang. They'd just completed an order from Denmark and stolen and delivered twelve BMW 750s. However, this wasn't the reason for the celebration. Andy had suggested a drink because one of the boys, Lem, had exchanged contracts on a house in Blackheath.

'It's something and a half,' Lem told everyone. 'Original features. Fireplaces and that. Plus it's got a bidet and a power shower.' Lem was a short, weasly thirty-year-old who at one time had been a professional boxer. 'It's a step up,' he told everyone, 'from a council house off Southwark Park Road.'

'We'll all come round,' suggested Fat Andy, 'when you've had a chance to settle in.'

Lem took Andy's hand and shook it formally. 'I owe it all to you,' he said.

Andy chuckled and called for another round of drinks. He was always very generous in pubs.

'I mean it,' insisted Lem. 'Now I can move me old mum and me sister and kiddies. Down there, it's like paradise. There's the park and there's no beggars or riff-raff. The air's clean.' He looked close to tears. 'It's heaven.'

Andy took him in his arms and hugged him. Lem seemed like a little boy, squashed against that massive chest.

'I mean it,' he repeated, as he was released. 'You've set me up, Andy mate, in this job. This is the best job I ever had. I'm flying high.' He paused. 'You're the guv'nor, you are, Andy.'

There was a murmur of approval. They all raised their glasses. 'To Andy!' they called in unison. Jaz was pleased and proud.

Fat Andy was flushed. He slapped a few backs. 'Let's

go through,' he announced, pointing to the back room. 'I've got the landlady to put on a spread.'

At nine a.m. the next day, Jaz called on Trace at the Hotel Grand Bahama and borrowed a leotard and trainers from the staff room.

'I wish I knew what you were up to,' said Trace, holding the lycra garment against Jaz's back, to check the size.

'Fat Andy's dead,' replied Jaz. 'I've a few things to sort, that's all.'

'Since that fat man was killed,' Trace offered reflectively, 'you've been running around like a . . . pea in a pod.' She sighed. 'No . . . I mean a bug in a rug. What do I mean?'

'What do you mean, Trace? That's a very tricky question.' Jaz sounded impatient.

Trace continued, her good temper intact. 'What happened to that other one, that Pete? At least he's nice looking. Gorgeous. And he's been asking about you.'

Jaz was just about to leave, but stopped in her tracks. 'Pete? How do you know about Pete?'

'You told me about him. He's the reason you had your hair done.' She paused for a moment. 'You know something? His hair's the same as yours.'

'He's been here?'

Trace nodded.

'What?' Jaz was aghast.

'Early today. About eight o'clock. He was looking for you. He thinks you're staying with friends. I told him you're sleeping in the car.'

Jaz clenched her fists. Her voice was angry. 'He had

no right . . . Coming here . . . the bastard.' She turned on Trace, her voice raised. 'Tell him nothing, right? Don't tell him a thing. I don't want him to know anything about me. I don't want to see him.' She felt close to tears and struggled to control herself. 'Trace, are you listening to me? What did he want? He has no right to hassle my friends.'

Trace was puzzled. 'He was really nice. He said you two were, you know, going out. I knew he meant shagging, but he was being polite and he was really concerned. He said he wanted to get hold of you, reckoned you'd left his door open and all his stuff was nicked . . . But he wasn't angry. More worried.'

'Tell him nothing!' Jaz was shouting. 'Nothing! He's a wanker and a liar!'

Trace put a finger to her lips. 'Shh!' she said urgently. She looked towards the door. 'Do you want to get me the sack?' she whispered.

Jaz hesitated. She swallowed hard. She looked at Trace's kind, mystified face and felt guilty. 'Why don't we meet up later?' she asked, struggling to get her voice back to normal. 'I'm sorry. I didn't mean to shout. I'm a bit strung out. I'll ring you. We could catch up on . . . news.'

Jaz knew that she'd not only been neglecting both Trace and Harm, she'd also been putting them in danger. Harm had been beaten up. Pete was now bothering Trace. It was a mess. The whole thing was a mess and it was her fault. The three friends didn't usually have secrets from one another. But she'd told them only a tiny bit of the truth. 'How's the invalid?' she asked.

Trace sighed. 'Pretty good, considering. Up and about. I just wish she'd stop . . . you know . . . what she does.'

'She's not going to, is she? Not now she's making real money.'

'You're right. She's not. But she takes such chances.' Trace paused. 'And she thinks cleaning hotels is a mug's game.'

Jaz squeezed her arm briefly, then left.

She set off immediately for Ronnie and Reggie's gym on the Mile End Road. She parked at the rear then crossed the road, watching the front of the building. People were waiting impatiently. At ten fifteen a woman in sports clothes appeared and opened up. She was followed inside by three beefy-looking men, two small teenagers who looked like jockeys and a gaggle of women wearing shorts and sweat bands. Cautiously, Jaz joined them as they climbed the stairs. At the top, the woman with the keys stood behind a desk. She smiled apologetically at the customers. Jaz approached her, forcing a grin. 'I'm new here,' she said. 'Can you explain things?'

The woman yawned, then smiled. She was young and pretty with long magenta hair loosely tied up on the top of her head. She was either tanned or dark-skinned, although her black eyes suggested origins which were not British. 'Sorry,' she said. 'I've been run ragged this morning. I'm behind. What can I tell you? You can sign up for a year's membership, pay by instalments and use all the facilities. I can show you around later. Or you can pay three quid and join in the aerobics class. It's just about to start. It should have started at ten.'

'I'll join the class. See if I like it.' Jaz paid the money and followed the woman in the direction of the changing rooms.

'Any health problems? Heart? That kind of thing?'

'No.'

'Done this before?'

'No, but I'm very fit. I run a lot.'

'If you have any problems, just stop and rest. It's not a test. Work at your own pace.'

'Don't worry. I'll be fine. Are you leading the class?'

'Yes.' She pushed open a door. Women were wriggling into leotards or skin-tight leggings with brief midriff-revealing tops. Some were applying make-up. They were mostly tanned and toned, although two outsiders, each standing in a corner, were overweight. They pulled on baggy T-shirts, to conceal their flab.

The instructor peeled off her tracksuit, revealing pert muscles and perfect curves.

'How well do you know the owners?' Jaz asked.

There was a rueful grin. 'Fairly. Why?'

Jaz stepped out of her jeans. 'Are they likely to be around this morning?'

The instructor moved towards the door, followed by her eager protégées. 'No. They're never in before three. They mostly cover evenings because that's when we get the boxers in – and the footballers.' She grinned. 'I'm Kormal, by the way.'

Jaz felt self-conscious in her yellow leotard with its embroidered palm tree. It was big and wrinkly. She thought it looked stolen. In the exercise studio she faced a floor-to-ceiling mirror where everyone stood, unsmiling, critically regarding themselves and each other. Several of the women were old. They had crêpey necks and thin, backcombed hair, but their figures were perfect. Jaz looked at her own thin legs, her flat chest. Why had she been so stupid as to imagine that Pete desired her? She didn't look like a woman. She looked undersized and prepubertal. She hated herself for being small. She hated herself for being duped. Even more, she hated him. You bastard, she thought. Just stay away from me. Stay away from my friends. She tried to push these angry thoughts aside as the music started.

The first movements were gentle and repetitive. Jaz stepped to the left, then backwards and forwards making small arm movements. This is for pensioners, she thought.

The instructor had her back to the group and everyone copied her. She moved gracefully like a dancer. Jaz noticed that her breasts and bottom were quite big but they were very firm. I'd give anything to look like that, she thought. Maybe I'll get into body-building. Maybe I need a high protein diet. Maybe I'll take steroids.

The music was very loud and it gathered pace. Jaz felt her heart beating and her breathing quickened. She struggled to follow the steps which were becoming slick and complicated. Sweat ran from her brow into her eyes. Her leotard was sticking to her chest and back and her shoes felt moist. She was required to kick her legs high and spin round. Her arms dipped and flailed like windmills. She glanced at the older women. They were bouncing at high speed from one end of the room to the other, following the impossible movements like robots. They were perfectly composed. Jaz started to gasp and her head felt light. She drove herself on. Her muscles were protesting with fatigue. Her chest was bursting. At the very point where she felt it was impossible to continue, the tempo eased slightly. They were cooling down. She felt shaky. She was relieved. She struggled to breathe normally, mopping her face with her hands. She looked in the mirror. Her skin was red and blotchy. My God, she thought, these women go through this torture maybe two or three times a week. They're amazing.

Back in the changing rooms most of them stripped off and disappeared into the showers. Jaz sat on a bench, recovering. 'I thought I was fit,' she said.

Kormal rubbed herself briskly with a towel then got back into her tracksuit. She wasn't even tired. There was a faint sheen on her brow, but otherwise she looked normal. 'You are. That was high impact. An advanced class. Most newcomers wouldn't attempt it, or they'd stop halfway through. You did very well.' She disappeared to answer the phone.

Jaz rested for a while as the other women prepared themselves for the outside world. One by one and in groups, they gradually disappeared. Jaz had a shower and dried herself with one of the towels provided. As she was leaving the cubicles, she saw a handwritten notice, sellotaped to the wall. 'Please look after your Proparty. Management not Responsable.' She recognized the spelling. Ronnie or Reggie had written it. They'd also sent Fat Andy the e-mail on the night of his death. The style was unmistakable. She paused, staring at the sign. She remembered in an instant why she'd come.

Back in reception, clutching the phone to her bosom, Kormal was pacing backwards and forwards alongside the desk. 'I just can't,' she said into the receiver, exasperated. 'What can I do? Damn! Why does it have to be like this?' She put the phone down. She looked close to tears.

'Problems?' asked Jaz.

'I've got to go. That was the blasted receptionist, phoning in sick. Again. But I can't stay. I've got to pick my little girl up from playgroup in a few minutes. I'm already late so I'll have to close the gym.' She seemed scared. 'I'll have to tell those men in the weights room to go home. The bosses will go off it . . .'

'Why don't you get the little one, then come back? How long will you be? I don't mind sitting here for a while.'

Kormal looked very doubtful.

'Don't worry. I know Ronnie and . . .' She swallowed hard. She adopted a cockney accent. 'I mean the owners. Your bosses. They're my cousins. Their old Mum, well, she's my Great Auntie May. I was only saying to her the other day . . .'

Kormal glanced at her watch. She seemed very harassed. She looked at the desk drawer.

Jaz had seen the cash box when she arrived. 'Go on. I won't touch anything. You can trust me.' She pointed to the opening times and the schedule of fitness classes displayed on the wall. 'I can answer the phone. If anything comes up that I can't handle, I'll ask them to ring back.'

Kormal was both desperate and convinced. She ran off down the stairs. 'Forty minutes,' she called out.

Jaz answered two phone enquiries then peeped into the weights room. The beefy men were pumping iron. Next door, one thin teenager was pedalling and the other was running on a treadmill. There was a smell of sweat and talcum powder.

Various acts of sabotage ran through Jaz's mind. She knew she could cut off the electricity supply in such a way that it would take a trained electrician a whole day to repair. She was also capable of damaging the plumbing. The phone system could be ruined, the security alarms confused. It was all possible. The thing was, she didn't want to get Kormal into trouble. If anything went wrong, she'd probably be held responsible. She was nice and a bit desperate and she probably needed the work.

Instead, Jaz spent the time examining the premises thoroughly and making a detailed mental sketch plan. She discovered that a back entrance led onto a fire escape and the door was wedged open with a chair, to create a through-draught. Below, there was a car park where she could see the Lotus Cortina. Two of the women who had been in the class appeared with some shopping, got into a red Polo and drove off. She went back into reception and made a note of the gym's phone number. Switching on the computer, she printed out a list of the members' names and addresses, folded it and put it in her pocket, then stole a couple of sheets of headed notepaper. She rummaged through the drawer of the desk and found a set of Mazda keys and a remote on a chrome ring. A paper label was tied to this, on which was written the words 'spairs'. She left these, but opened the computer's e-mail box and typed in a few lines. Remembering the details of the message to Fat Andy, which they'd sent before he was murdered, she decided to emulate the style. 'Jaz is not a happy girl. Jaz has got Vinny's property and she's going to give it to the police. You Stepney gits.'

Chapter Twelve

Jaz waited in a sandwich bar near Victoria coach station. She'd phoned the Hotel Grand Bahama on the mobile.

It was a very hot day and Trace arrived wearing denim cut-offs and a skimpy white top which revealed her flat stomach. Sensitized by her experience at the gym, Jaz admired her long, lean figure, her strong jaw, her wide mouth. 'I know I've said this before, Trace, but you could be a model.'

Trace slid behind the table and grabbed a gulp of Jaz's milk shake through the straw. She raised her eyes to the ceiling in an expression which said 'I've heard it all before!'

Jaz studied her perfect skin, her thick, badly cut blonde hair, the slant of her oval eyes and the jut of her cheekbones which were almost oriental. She knew, of course, that Trace couldn't handle modelling on her own. Her IQ was too low. 'I'll tell you what, I'll be your manager.' She was more than half serious. It suddenly seemed like a good idea. 'You just stand around in purple lippie and posh frocks and I'll look after the business side.'

'Shut up, Jaz.'

'You've got a foreign-looking face. You know that?' She was aware that Trace had been brought up by a series of foster parents. 'Do you think your real mum could have been Chinese?'

Trace didn't smile. 'My mother was from Leytonstone. She left me in a dustbin at the back of a betting shop.'

'That doesn't mean she wasn't Chinese.'

Trace picked up the pepper pot then slammed it down hard. 'She wasn't Chinese. Right?'

'OK, OK.'

'She wasn't Chinese. Have you got that?'

Jaz thought for a moment. 'There's nothing wrong with being Chinese.'

'Just shut up, won't you?'

Jaz drained her glass. The straw made funny, gurgling noises which she deliberately prolonged.

Trace laughed. She was always entertained by childish things. Her good humour was restored. 'I suppose my dad might've been a chinky,' she offered, chuckling to herself. 'But no one ever said.'

Trace ordered an all day vegetarian breakfast with double soy sausages and extra fried bread. She always ate as if she hadn't seen food for days. 'That bloke came back,' she said, sucking up a forkful of baked beans. 'Again. You know you said to tell you if he did? What's wrong with him, exactly? The girls at the hotel think he's after me. They got all giggly.'

Jaz frowned. She'd thought about telling Trace about Ronnie and Reggie and her need to avenge Fat Andy's death, but she'd dismissed the idea whilst waiting for Trace to arrive. She didn't like lying to her and keeping her in the dark but she knew she wouldn't be able to handle it. Trace hated violence. Also, she had a tendency to get muddled. Unless things were spelled out to her in great detail, several times, she made mistakes. Jaz decided that the less Trace knew about her current problems, the better.

'He's not nice,' she stressed. 'He let me down. He's only pretending to be interested in me.'

Trace cut up a sausage and chewed for a moment. 'You sure? He seemed pretty keen to me. He was carrying a new telly in a box and said it was your fault it got pinched . . .'

'What did you tell him?' She remembered she'd told Trace to tell Pete nothing.

Trace thought for a moment. 'That you'd said to tell him nothing, absolutely nothing at all, that you don't want to see him, that he has no right to bother your friends and that he's a wanker and a liar. That's what you said, isn't it?'

Jaz squeezed Trace's hand. 'Word for word.'

'He's really upset.'

'I don't care.'

'He said again that you left his door open and all his stuff was nicked.'

Jaz smiled. 'That why he's upset?'

'No. I think it was the "wanker and liar" bit. I thought he was going to cry.'

'Good.'

Trace shrugged. 'We all thought he was looking sexy in those overalls.'

Later, they strolled along the Embankment. Jaz put on her Versace sunglasses. 'How's it going at the hotel?' She asked. 'Any chance of a permanent job?'

Trace shook her head. She was eating a KitKat. 'Don't want one.'

The river glittered and a tourist boat ploughed past, its loudspeakers announcing the Oxo Tower and the South Bank. The air shimmered in the heat and two tiny aeroplanes, high above, trailed white spume.

'I like moving around because I've always moved around. My foster parents were all short term, till I ran away, then there were the children's homes. You know I don't like being tied down – it's what I'm used to.'

'You know what I was thinking the other day? I was driving along in the car and I wondered if I'd ever get married. Have a life, like normal people in adverts. You know, a fitted kitchen, cook-in sauces, stuff like that.'

Trace snorted.

'I'm serious. I'm twenty-one. You're twenty. What have we got to show for anything? I've got a car and a change of clothes and no boyfriend. What've you got? I mean, what exactly is the point of it all?'

'It's not even your car,' Trace agreed. She stopped and leaned on the railing looking out at the water. A flock of gulls circled and landed, bobbing on the current like ducks. She thought for a moment. 'I've got Harm and you,' she murmured gently.

Jaz said nothing. Sometimes, Trace made her feel humble.

'I'm OK, you know? I don't have any plans. That suits me.'

Jaz picked up a flat pebble and skimmed it across the water. It skittered near a gull. Disturbed, the bird flapped its wings, rose, then settled again.

'Be careful of that poor seagull, Jaz.'

'Why haven't you got a boyfriend?' Jaz had always wanted to ask Trace this, but had always felt too inhibited.

Trace gripped the railing and squinted her eyes

against the sun. She sighed. 'I don't want one. I had a lot of . . .' She paused. 'I had a lot of trouble . . . with a man in a children's home. It went on for three years. One of the senior staff. I was only little. It sort of put me off.'

'You mean you were abused?'

Trace said nothing but her silence was affirmative.

'My mother's boyfriend used to mess around with me,' Jaz confided. 'Have I ever told you that?'

'Yes,' said Trace. 'You mentioned it once.'

'The thing was, I didn't mind. I liked it. I hated my mother and I felt I was getting my own back. Also, he was nice. He was kind to us. He taught me to drive.'

'That's OK then. If you didn't mind. Not minding makes it sort of all right, I guess.'

'Actually, looking back, I think he was the reason I shacked up with Fat Andy. I didn't know it at the time, but Blow and Fat Andy were really very alike.'

Trace linked Jaz's arm. 'You see, the thing was with me, I like . . . minded a lot. I really minded, I hated it. He always hurt me but then he told me it was my own fault. He said I made him do it and I believed that for a long time. I blamed myself for feeling bad. It made me feel like . . .' She stopped.

'What?'

There was a long silence.

'Nothing.'

'Nothing?'

'Worth nothing.'

They continued walking. The trees drooped in the heat. A woman led a small girl by the hand who was licking a melting ice cream. She was dressed in a broderie anglaise pinafore and her little socks were trimmed with white frills.

'I can't think of myself as, you know . . .'

'Attractive?'

'Right.'

There was a silence as they continued their stroll. There was a frown on Trace's brow, as she remembered.

A man on a unicycle approached them on the pavement. Jaz saw him first. 'Look!' she called out. He came closer. He had a bald head and a very serious expression. His hands were clasped behind his back. He nodded without smiling as he sped by.

Trace laughed delightedly.

Jaz was relieved. 'You know the other day? We went to see Andy's mother?'

'Yep,' answered Trace. 'She was mega-sad.'

'You know she talked about twin sons?'

'Yep. Do you think it was all, like, made up? Just lies?'

Jaz considered. 'No. I mean I reckon the bit about Brian Jones and the Rolling Stones was fantasy. But I do think she had twin sons. And I want to try and find him. Fat Andy's twin.'

'You want to tell him about Andy being murdered and everything?'

'Like I told his mother. It's important to me. I feel . . .'

'It's your duty?'

'Something like that. It's something to do with what I was saying earlier. Like . . . what's the point of everything? What am I doing with my life? Since Fat Andy died, I've had a kind of . . . purpose.'

'Probably best if the brother didn't know. You thought of that? Maybe he doesn't even know he had a twin.'

'No. He should be told. I know about twins. I bet he sort of realizes already that something's wrong and it'll be driving him crazy. Like he's lost his shadow or something.

Whatever he knows, he'll feel bad. He'll feel . . . loss. He just needs to have it confirmed.'

'Is that so?'

'Yeah. Twins are like that. Sort of psychic. They know about each other. Once my sister Mimosa fell down an old well on the farm and her twin Peony was half a mile away and she still came running to raise the alarm. Another time, Mimosa was at a swimming gala and Peony was at school. They hardly ever went to school so this must've been when they were very young. Anyway, Peony was given the belt by this mean old cow who taught religious studies. It was probably illegal, you know? At the exact moment it happened, Mimosa swam to the side, got out of the water, went and got changed and walked back to school. The teacher tried to stop her, but she wouldn't be stopped. "My sister needs me," is all she would say. You see, that's the thing about twins. They're sort of linked. It's really very, very weird.'

Trace thought for a moment. 'How're you going to find him?'

'I've seen him on the television.' Jaz carefully explained to Trace about the Fat Andy lookalike who seemed to accompany a famous politician every time he appeared. 'It's him,' she insisted. 'No doubt.'

Trace was bewildered. Patiently, Jaz ran through it all again.

'I don't see how you're going to meet him,' argued Trace. 'You can't just go up to him outside ten Downing Street or somewhere and talk to him. You'll get arrested.'

'That's where you come in.'

Trace raised her eyebrows. 'Me? What can I do?' She thought for a minute. 'I know. Why don't you send him an e-mail? At the Houses of Parliament or something? Or you could ring them up at *News At Ten* and ask Trevor McDonald to pass on a message.'

Jaz smiled. Her own suggestion sounded just as unlikely, but she thought it would work. 'Trace, I want you to get a job in the Home Office. Like that one you had last year in Kensington Palace. Cleaning windows. Remember?'

'Of course I do.'

'Suss out who he is. Check out if he's got an office somewhere.'

Trace was silent.

'Please. It means a lot to me.' She handed Trace the photo of Fat Andy and Princess. 'He's a dead ringer for Andy.' She paused. 'Bad pun.'

Trace took the picture wordlessly.

Jaz knew that Trace's history in the black economy, with all her hundreds of contacts, made her employable almost anywhere. She'd worked in Harrods, Lambeth Palace, the Harbour Club, London Central Mosque. She worked for cash in hand, filling in, and no kind of security screening ever seemed to apply. She'd done Bill Clinton's laundry. She'd replenished the toilet rolls in the hotel bathroom of Michael Jackson. She once sat at the feet of Tony Blair, looking for his contact lens in the carpet.

'What about the Grand Bahama?' Trace was sulky.

'Fuck the Grand Banana,' replied Jaz. 'If they didn't need you they'd dump you tomorrow without batting an eye.'

Later Jaz drove over to Peckham. She sat around for a while in the car, feeling very hot. There was no sign of the silver Mercedes. She immobilized the Lotus Cortina and went up to the flat she'd shared with Fat Andy for six months. She stood outside for a while holding her chest where the pain was located. The entrance was boarded over and on it some joker had spray-painted the words 'Dead Cunt'.

Downstairs, she knocked at the armoured door of the flat which Elvis shared with Big Boy and Peppy. There was no reply. An old woman shuffled by carrying four bags of shopping. Jaz offered to help but she was too suspicious to agree. She held the bags closer defensively.

'D'you know where the boys might be? The ones who live here?'

The woman was clearly relieved that Jaz wasn't a mugger. 'Try the Duke of Salisbury,' she suggested. 'If not, then Jiggers or Riggers or whatever they call it now. The one that used to be the Old King's Head.'

Jaz crossed the estate. A group of homeless people stood around a scorched patch of earth where the remains of a settee smouldered, giving off black fumes. The sun was hot and their grouping at the fire seemed more from habit than necessity. Jaz recognized one of the women. She was holding a bottle of Lilt and talking dully to herself. Jaz remembered she was Joan. She was from Scotland and she was nice. They'd once doubled in a hostel room and Joan generously shared her food, her blankets, her money, without being asked. Jaz went over and tapped her on the arm. 'Hello,' she said, gently. It would be nice to pay Joan back, she thought.

The woman was startled and took two steps sideways, cradling her bottle. She glared at Jaz without recognition. She looked older and tired. She carried on muttering. Jaz glanced around the group. It was impossible to break in. Everyone seemed too dispirited to talk or make eye contact. It was like a scene from a war, she decided, where people had lost so much, there was nothing left to do or say.

Jaz continued on her way and went into the first pub. There was a thin haze of smoke and the rattle of a pinball machine. The place seemed almost deserted but she saw Big Boy's gigantic back partially concealed in an alcove. The three friends were hunched over soft drinks looking tired and ill. Elvis leaned back when he saw Jaz and blew a desultory smoke ring. 'Hi, doll,' he said, indicating a chair. 'A pew.'

Jaz bought them each a Coke and a Kaliber for herself. She sat down. 'Have you managed to get that . . . property?'

Elvis forced a grin. 'Maybe,' he said.

Big Boy nudged Peppy, they picked up their drinks and cigarettes and with a nod to Jaz they retreated to the pool table in a far corner.

'What's the matter with you three? You look like party time at the morgue. You're not telling me the drugs are finally catching up with you?'

Elvis sighed. 'A bit of bother,' he offered.

'Police harassment?' enquired Jaz.

'No. Trouble at Felixstowe. Consignment impounded. Those thieving customs bastards. Then the Merc. Torched down New Cross. Serious combat, doll. The art of war. Yes or no?'

Jaz thought about their beautiful car. 'Oh, no! What a waste!'

There was a silence. They swallowed their drinks. Elvis sighed again. He felt in the pocket of his jacket and produced a box of matches. Then he pulled out an envelope. 'Yours?' he asked.

Jaz glanced inside. It was a computer disk. 'Where d'you get it? Hidden where I said?'

Elvis nodded.

'How did you manage to get in there? That flat's so tight it looks like Rampton Special hospital.' She paused. 'Like your place.'

He shrugged.

'Thanks, Elvis.' There was an awkward pause. Jaz knew she'd promised him more sex, in payment. 'Do you want to do it?'

He leaned back, swinging his chair, and looked at her with narrowed eyes. Then he grinned. His teeth were bad and his gums were blackish and unhealthy. 'Fact. In total confidence, doll, I's shattered,' he whispered. 'I's depressed. Get it up? Not today.' He paused. 'Another time, definitely.'

Jaz carefully froze her face into a neutral expression in order not to display relief. She took the disk out of the envelope and examined it, then finished her drink. 'Thanks,' she said.

Elvis regarded her for a moment. 'Peppy hallucinate Fat Andy the other night. Down the basement, at the flats. A friggin' ghost. After his old car.'

'Too many drugs,' replied Jaz.

'Peppy's brain full of holes.' He sighed. 'A ghost, doll. A spectre.' He paused. 'Something for us?' he said thoughtfully.

'Yeah?'

'Wheels. We nothing in this fight without wheels.'

Jaz considered this. She was pleased. She was running low on funds. 'What had you in mind?'

'A Jag? An Audi? Big enough. Fast. Reasonably flash.' He paused. 'Not white, though. Bad luck. Bad *feng shui*.'

'You'll leave it up to me, then?'

'Yeah, doll. You's more the motor girl than us.' He reached into his pocket again, pulled out a roll of notes and handed it to her. 'Five hundred,' he said. 'Another five delivery.'

'When?'

'Yesterday.'

Jaz parked in the safe place in Lincoln's Inn Fields, put on her headphones and jogged down Holborn towards the City. Traditionally, this had been her most well trodden beat when she'd worked for Vinny as a car thief. She slowed to a dawdle. She felt a little nervous and realized that to some extent she'd lost her nerve. Like anything, car crime is perfect only with practice, she thought to herself. Apart from the ride back from Cambridge and the liberation of the Lotus Cortina she'd been out of action for a long time. She wasn't entirely sure what the manufacturers were doing now to stop thieves. They were constantly improving their systems. She wasn't on top of it. This was worrying.

She walked around the City, feeling out of place amongst the male suits, the briefcases, the expensive sandwich outlets, the bijou boutiques selling shoes and contact lenses. She saw a few appropriate vehicles – new, fast, expensive – but they were very exposed. After an hour she wandered in the direction of the river and crossed it at London Bridge. She felt hot. She pulled her T-shirt out from her jeans and wafted it up and down. Stay cool, she told herself. She was carrying her denim jacket and sports bag which contained her tools. Elvis's roll of money was making her hip pocket bulge. Stay calm, stay focused. She knew that if she lost her self-assurance, then she would fail. She bought a can of Dr Pepper and sat on a bench to drink it. She thought about holiday destinations. Malaga. She rolled the name around her mouth. Morecambe Bay. Montreal.

She glanced across the road. At that moment, her heart lurched and her limbs changed from hot to icy cold. A brand new Mazda sports car had pulled up opposite. Two men emerged simultaneously, struggling from the small interior cabin. Both had shiny bald heads and pastel coloured linen suits. They each smoothed the creases in their jackets and shook their baggy trouser legs. They were Ronnie and Reggie. A third, smaller man eased himself out, very slowly, from the tiny space which was normally a parcel shelf in the back. He was wearing a conventional dark suit and tie and carrying a briefcase. He placed this on the pavement, stretched like a monkey, grimaced in mock discomfort, then laughed. Jaz noticed his wandering, squinty eye. It was Vinny.

He picked up his case and spoke into an entryphone on the nearest doorway. In a moment, the brothers followed him into the narrow, dilapidated building. Immediately they climbed some stairs. She drained her can and tossed it into the shrubbery, then crossed the road. There was a row of brass and chrome plates outside the decaying offices advertising the names of insurance agents and mortgage brokers. On the ground floor there was a cranial osteopath.

She examined the car. It was a demonstration Mazda MX5, racing bronze, low and sporty. It was gleaming and desirable. 'You lovely little thing, you,' she said under her breath. She walked around it. Alloy wheels, she thought, front air dam skirt, contoured headlights. She whistled aloud, 'Just let me have you, you sexy little baby.'

She looked at her watch then opened the buttoned top pocket of her jacket and carefully removed a spent match and a used piece of gum. She chewed on the gum briefly, then checking that the coast was clear of pedestrians, she placed a tiny piece on the end of the matchstick and inserted it into the lock of the driver's door. She bent down, pretending to adjust a shoelace. She manoeuvred the chewing gum until it held open the little metal flap inside, then, carefully, she removed the matchstick. She stood up and waited as three Indian women in saris passed by. The traffic on the road was busy but drivers were looking ahead to a series of lights and she was confident they wouldn't notice her. She felt in another pocket and produced a yellow tennis ball, cut in half. She placed this over the lock and keeping her body very still, she whacked it silently with the bottom of her right hand, forcing the air from the half ball into the lock. Nothing happened. She tried again. On the third attempt, the central locking of the car disengaged with a quiet clunk. She glanced up the stairs of the office building. There was no sign of anyone.

She waited a few seconds, watching the traffic. Then she heard it. 'Yes!' she said aloud. She was in luck. A fire engine was approaching, its lights flashing and sirens blaring. She opened the driver's door, setting off the alarm. She tossed her jacket and half ball onto the passenger seat and in a quick gesture reached inside, pulling the lever to open the bonnet. The fire engine was passing, its noise drowning out the Mazda's frantic wail. Alongside the engine, tucked away but still visible she located the shiny case of the alarm and using all the strength she possessed, ripped it out. It was silenced as the fire engine turned left at the lights. She closed the bonnet and glanced again up the stairs. A couple of teenagers walked past looking at her quizzically. She got into the car. She was breathing rhythmically and sweat had broken out on her brow. Mazda, she thought to herself. Mazda, Mazda. Stay cool. Stay focused. I know. I know it's the same system as BMW. She put her hand into the well in front of the passenger seat, prodded up behind the fascia and dragged down a spaghetti of wires. She examined them briefly, pulled four apart with her pliers, then connected them in a different sequence. It was tricky. She disconnected a fuse. Let that be right, she thought. Stay focused. Stay cool.

She opened her bag and took out the larger screwdriver. Then she broke off the steering cowl and penetrated the ignition. 'Come on, baby,' she murmured, 'come on.' She felt it give, like soft putty. Once inside and with the smaller implement she turned the exposed, inner mechanism. This is the moment, she thought. Stay calm. The car started gently. She sighed and moved the seat forward, then checked the time: two hundred and thirty seconds. Not bad, she thought. Not my best, but then the stresses were huge.

She drove east, through Southwark. She felt enclosed, like being in the cockpit of a plane. The gearstick had a slick, short throw action which she liked. The suspension was taut, the acceleration positive. She listened with pleasure to the throaty rasp of the exhaust. She played with the electric windows and listened to Capital Radio.

A while later, Jaz checked into a guest house on Lambeth Palace Road and parked in the enclosed yard at the rear. The owner was a large Jamaican woman who Jaz had found, on several other occasions, to be kind but not inquisitive. She was happy for her to have a long, deep bath and to lend her a dressing gown while she laundered her clothes. She cooked up a skillet of spicy food and the two of them sat quietly in the back yard, alongside the Mazda and the dustbins and the washing line, eating chicken and yams and drinking homemade lemonade. 'That's a darling little car,' she said to Jaz.

'Isn't it?' she agreed. 'Isn't it just fab? Not for long though. I'm getting rid of it tomorrow.'

Later, upstairs in her room, Jaz used the mobile to phone Vinny's garage. She was connected to the showroom. 'Tell that fucking Vinny I've got the demonstration MX5,' she told the bewildered salesman. 'The bronze one. Tell the companero that Jaz has got it and she might sell it tomorrow. Sell it or torch it, or drive it into the river. Tell him Jaz hasn't fucking decided what to do with it yet. But she will.' She hung up.

She rang Trace. 'What's happening about the Home Office? Any luck?'

'I can do the House of Lords. Floor buffing and brasswork.'

'No good.'

'Thought not.'

'Get onto it, Trace, will you?'

'I am onto it. I'm definitely onto it.'

'You know you can do it.'

'I'll do it. Right?'

'Thanks, Trace. I appreciate it.'

Trace sniffed. 'Where're you staying?'

'Lambeth. Trevor McDonald's place.'

Trace laughed. She knew the place. 'Mrs McDonald's?'

'Yeah.'

'In the attic?'

'Tell Harm, will you? You know she worries.' She hesitated. 'Not that Pete! Is that clear? Tell that bastard nothing.'

'I know, I know.' Trace spoke as if she was rehearsing. 'Whenever he shows up, tell the pretty ginger boy nothing. Nothing at all.'

Chapter Thirteen

Jaz was aware that she couldn't deliver the Mazda to Elvis unless it was repaired. For this, she needed spares. She lay on her bed in the narrow attic room in Lambeth, waiting for dark and studying Fat Andy's Filofax. One of the codes he'd listed would disarm the security at Vinny's garage. She thought she knew which was the right one. She wished she could ring Pete to check. She felt fresh outrage about his double-crossing hypocrisy. He could have been really useful to her, if he hadn't turned out to be such a rat. As it was, she was determined to get even with him, as soon as she had the time.

It was risky, but she felt more confident about stealing spares from Vinny than she did about trying to negotiate unfamiliar premises. She knew where to go inside Vinny's storeroom and she knew where everything was kept. When she was working for him, Andy had always insisted that she help make good the damage which the team inflicted on stolen cars. He said he trusted her to do it well and that it was a question of having pride in the job.

Because of this, she knew what to expect – there were cameras at Vinny's, and sirens, but no razor wire, nor Alsatian dogs nor helmeted men with truncheons waiting around in vans.

At midnight, she borrowed a door key from her obliging landlady, jogged to the safe haven, collected the Lotus Cortina and set off for the Isle of Dogs. It was a warm, cloudless night with a sliver of white moon. She listened to an All Saints CD on her Walkman and drove with the windows open. The city was quiet, even subdued. She had a sense of London's massive energy, calmed and somnolent, enjoying the balmy stillness of the air, preparing itself for tomorrow and another hectic day.

At Vinny's place, the forecourt was closed for the night, but the showroom, with its rows of gleaming Mazdas, was brightly lit. Jaz drove into the narrow cobbled road behind. She got out and glanced around. The alley was dark and deserted. There was a smell of engine oil and paint. She took the number plates of the stolen sports car from the boot of the Lotus Cortina and looked around again. She could hear a train in the distance, river sounds and the raucous shouts of nearby drunks, but she was unobserved.

Vinny's paint shop, his body shop and parts storeroom were linked single-storey buildings, across the lane from the back of the main garage. The doors were covered by metal security shutters and the windows had grilles – except, she hoped, for a single one. She walked to the corner. As expected, a tiny window was accessible. It was on the end of the body shop, and she knew it led into the overused lavatory. Quickly and stealthily, using the handle of her large screwdriver, she broke its glass. Immediately, there was a pungent smell of urine. With her jacket wrapped around her arm, she cleared the frame of shards. The access was very limited but she hoped she could struggle through. She went in feet first, holding aloft the Mazda's plates. Her shoulders got stuck, but with a few wriggles she was inside. As she opened the door there was a whirr and the bright pop-pop of photographic flashes. Then the alarm went off. She ran across the line of the camera and then beyond it, blinking, struggling to see. The noise was deafening. She said a quick, heartfelt prayer, hoping the security system hadn't changed. She located it inside a cupboard in a corner of the room. Holding the plates under one arm, she tapped in the code, memorized from Andy's Filofax, straining to see the worn numbers printed on the illuminated plastic pad. Suddenly the noise and flashing camera were extinguished. The blackness and the silence were like a fog. Jaz's heart was beating hard and her stomach felt knotted and tight. 'Stay calm. Stay focused,' she whispered, 'stay cool.' Her ears were ringing, as if they'd been punched. You've done it, she thought, groping for a light switch. Jaz, you're a lucky bastard. You've done it and you're in.

In the storeroom Jaz paused at the small vinyl-topped counter, at the side of which was a computer. She remembered that during the day a thin, bored man with greasy hair usually stood here, resting on his elbows, chewing gum and reading the *Sun*. He wore a baggy grey overall coat which was never washed. When necessary he tapped listlessly on the keyboard and sold Mazda spares to the public. As well as this, unhelpful and slow, he secured necessary parts for both Fat Andy and the legitimate mechanics in the garage. He was called Mr Slipper. No one called him by his first name because no one liked him. Once Pete had said he had a personality disorder. She recalled complaining to Andy when, without speaking, he'd repeatedly rubbed his crotch against her body in the confined space between the racks. Andy must have had a word with him because he never did this again. However, he'd continued to be patronizing, as if she understood nothing about cars.

She noticed that the place had been tidied and the racks redesigned. In fact the place looked cleaner and more sterile than a dentist's surgery. Mr Slipper must have quit, she decided. Someone else was in charge, with a passion for order. There was nothing littering the floor. Two body shells in grey primer were hung from the ceiling like modern works of art.

On the computer, Jaz brought up the parts she wanted, one by one, noting down the reference numbers. It took a moment to locate the new ignition, immobilizer, door locks, keys and steering cowl within the new system. The whole place had been streamlined. Then, using the familiar numbers of the combination lock, she opened the old-fashioned safe under the counter. On the top shelf she found a box of unallocated registration documents for new cars. She took one which referred to a Mazda MX5. Underneath were sets of plates. She found the ones which matched the documentation and swapped them for the plates taken from the stolen car. She took a deep breath. She was a little calmer now. She decided, on impulse, to take two extra documents and sets of plates, for good measure. Both referred to the Mazda 626 which she knew was an upmarket saloon. They might come in useful, she reasoned. They would be missed, eventually, but with some luck no one would notice for a while.

Having obtained everything she needed, she wrapped it all in her jacket and dropped it outside in the lane, then went back and reset the alarm. It made a long low drone until she closed the lavatory door. Standing on the edge of the stinking bowl, she forced her shoulders through the window. As she climbed out, a needle of glass pierced her knee. She picked up her booty and got back into Fat Andy's car, then rested for a moment, breathing steadily, rubbing her face with her hands. She thought about fixing the damage to the stolen Mazda. She would do it in Lambeth tomorrow, in daylight. Then she would drive over to Peckham and collect another five hundred from Elvis. The car had only one hundred and seventy-five miles on the clock. It was worth over sixteen thousand pounds. He better be grateful, she thought. He owes me. I'll never need to have sex with him again after this. Thank God.

She wound up the windows of the Lotus Cortina. She was just about to drive off when she realized this was an opportunity missed. She remembered the three thugs in their designer suits, struggling from the Mazda MX5 earlier in the day. They'd killed Fat Andy. They'd slit his throat like a helpless animal. She pictured the brothers pinning him down while Vinny wielded the blade. They'd left him bleeding to death on his bed. On her bed. The bed she'd shared with him for six months.

His lifeless face came into her mind. His mouth had been open in surprise or because of a partially spoken protest. It was like the mouth of a dead fish, formless but rigid. Not me, he seemed to say. Not me. Not now. I'm not ready. Tears came to her eyes. He wasn't ready, she thought. He definitely wasn't ready. Not many people enjoyed life as much as Fat Andy.

And all for a computer disk, which they'd then failed to find. They'd taken his life for a few contacts, names of a bunch of dodgy characters over in Holland or Germany. For the lousy details of a string of hot vehicles.

Nicking cars is one thing, Jaz reasoned. But killing people is in a different league. It was not on. It was unacceptable. It demanded punishment. She crossed her hands on the steering wheel and leaned her head in her arms. This was very clear.

The pain in her chest was suddenly worse. It was like a knife. A hot, burning knife. 'Andy should be properly avenged,' she said aloud. 'I owe it to him.' She had never been so sure of something, so directed, so purposeful. It was almost enjoyable, this conviction, this belief.

Another thing was obvious. Stealing a car, even a neat sports car like the MX5, from a crooked motor dealer was hardly an adequate response. He'd been mildly inconvenienced, that was all. Everything she'd done to Vinny, so far, was pathetic. She had to do more. Andy would expect more. Anything else was weak and cowardly. She took a deep breath and, repeating the whole process, went back inside.

She turned on one light in the body shop but still managed to crunch her shin on an engine which had been removed from a front-ended saloon. She swore and glanced inside. Out of habit, she was looking for bloodstains on the upholstery.

At the far end of the building was the paint shop. She made her way there, having decided on a plan. She turned on the lights. There were no vehicles, just a wide open space with three pairs of ghostly overalls hanging on hooks along one wall. She went over to the oxyacetylene gear and, awkwardly at first, attempted to open the twin bottles. The valves were stiff and the key hurt her fingers. She licked her hand and rubbed it on her jeans. With a second attempt she was successful. She glanced around the room again and went over to the large drum of cellulose thinners in a corner. She began overturning it. It was one third full. As she lowered it onto its side, the contents slopped out, clear, like water. She felt the coldness of the liquid as it splashed her legs and a sting as it touched her cut knee. She dropped the drum and jumped back as it spread across the floor. The sharp, addictive smell was both choking and heavenly.

Quickly, she dragged the oxyacetylene bottles in their metal frame away from the spilt thinners, into the doorway. She turned the circular valves to open the gun and flicked the flint lighter. Adjusting the oxygen level, she made the flame small, blue and pointed. Holding the torch aloft, she felt a rush of adrenalin. Her jeans and boots were wet. One false move and she could burst into flames. She turned, looking behind her. She knew she had a straight run out, through the body shop to the lavatory window. She would have a minute, maybe two. Without pausing to consider, she tossed the torch, flinging it the entire length of its tubing onto the edge of the puddle. As she turned to run, there was a bright flash behind her and a roar.

In seconds, with the level of human energy which is only ever produced by fear, she was out of the window, into the Lotus Cortina and accelerating away. In her rear-view mirror she could see a glow. As she raced down the deserted Manchester Road there was a huge bang. She smiled. The acetylene bottle had exploded. The fire must have really taken hold.

Jaz parked the car by the river at Blackwall. She felt elated. She grasped the steering wheel and laughed out loud. The smell of the thinners from her jeans and her feet was heady and overpowering. She wondered if it was making her high. She opened the driver's door to get some fresh air.

She was reminded of a night at home, on the farm in Teesside, a few weeks before she decided to leave. Her mother was shouting and she'd gone to listen outside her bedroom door. Lola was drunk and in bed. She was yelling at Blow. 'You're a lousy provider,' she'd accused him, 'a lousy, rotten provider.' She kept repeating the phrase, as if she was proud of it. 'That's the long and the short of it. A lousy, rotten provider.'

Blow murmured softly, trying to calm her down. It wasn't working.

'You should get rid of those cars. Never mind polishing the buggers, just sell them. Sell them and bring some money in. Why should I keep you? You lousy, rotten provider.'

Jasmine heard Blow continue to speak in a placatory way. He was trying to be patient. He pointed out that the farm was losing money. He said his car dealing was subsidizing the farm and they still needed hay. They needed chicken meal.

'Don't you blame me! Sell that Austin Healy!' Lola had screamed. 'Why d'you want it? Who d'you think you are? James bloody Bond?' She was far gone on cheap Chianti and couldn't listen to reason.

Later, Jasmine heard Blow calling her name. She was skinning and gutting a rabbit on the kitchen table. His head appeared around the door. 'Give me a hand out here,' he said, 'soon as you've got that critter on the stove.'

After a while, she lit the gas under the saucepan and went out to the porch. The dull light of the miserable

November afternoon was slowly fading. The sky was purple and grey. It was very cold. A few starving chickens huddled together out of the wind which blew mournfully across the fields. The farm looked sad and hopeless. Blow was dragging an old gate into the barn. Jasmine pulled on her wellingtons and a disintegrating fur jacket which had belonged to Lola. He pointed towards a disused pig sty. 'Bring the wood from that into the barn,' he called to her.

The two of them laboured together for an hour. They built a bonfire out of rotten buildings and gates, fence posts, a roll of old lino and an abandoned armchair. When it was twelve feet high, Blow told her to get a can of petrol.

'It won't work,' said Jasmine knowingly, 'if you use petrol. Insurance men aren't daft.'

Blow scratched his head and considered. 'OK. We'll do it the Boy Scout way, then. Get some dry leaves, some twigs, a box of matches.'

As the fire caught hold, the twins appeared from nowhere. They shoved chicken feathers in their hair and ran around whooping, pretending to be Red Indians. Blow pulled straw bales and disintegrating trestles from the sides of the building. 'Keep away!' he shouted at them desperately.

They went suddenly quiet and stood together, holding hands. 'What's he doing?' asked Peony.

'What's he doing?' repeated Mimosa.

The fire licked along planks and bales towards a wooden wall.

They were subdued. 'He's burning down the barn,' whispered Peony, in an awestruck voice. She looked worried.

'Does Mam know?' asked Mimosa. 'Does Mam know he's burning down her barn?'

Jasmine took them each by an arm and led them outside. The three of them stood silently on an incline above the structure and watched as it caught alight. After a while Blow appeared, his face blackened by smoke and sweat. Breathing heavily, he joined the girls who were huddled together in the cold wind. Then, as the flames flickered towards the roof and the first crossbeam fell inwards, the heat began to warm them and the twins' excitement returned. Clinging together they started jumping up and down. 'One man went to mow,' they sang, irrelevantly. 'Went to mow his meadow. One man and his dog, went to mow his meadow!'

The fire soared and roared, turning the dark sky orange. In the distance, the penned animals cried out in fear. The smoke billowed like fast time-lapse clouds and the twins' song became a rhythmic chant. 'One man went to MOW! One man went to MOW!'

Jasmine felt a lump in her throat. She was angry, tense but also pleased. The way the barn was collapsing into this inferno of her own making was both strangely beautiful and satisfying. Blow stood slightly apart, his hands in his pockets. 'That's one hell of a blaze, Jasmine,' he said.

As Jaz sat in the Lotus Cortina, gazing at the river and the lights and the dark brown of the London night, a bright shower like a giant red firework suddenly burst upwards then cascaded down on the limits of the roofline. After a few moments, flames reached up above the buildings and the stark outlines of the cranes, illuminating the sky. Sparks flew like fireflies. It took her a moment to realize that this was her own handiwork. Vinny's repair shop was burning.

She licked her lips but her mouth was very dry. Sirens announced a convoy of engines speeding towards the blaze. Soon, a helicopter swooped above her, then inwards, over the Island.

Jaz thought about the heat that had come from the burning barn, up on the farm on Teesside, eight years before. She stared at the distant glow, pretending that she could feel its warmth, smell its acrid smoke, see the roof beams and walls implode. Just then she thought she heard the twins' raised voices, united in song. They sang one brief verse. Then, 'That's one hell of a blaze, Jaz,' someone seemed to say, close to her ear. She was startled. The imaginary, approving voice was not that of Blow. It was Fat Andy. He was grateful.

Chapter Fourteen

At some point during the night Jaz fell asleep in the car. When she awoke the sky was a blend of grey and orange, but in the spot above Vinny's garage, a black smudge proved that her fire was still burning. She got out and stretched and realized that her cut knee was stiff and painful.

Jaz drove back to Lambeth. She was no longer elated, but she was satisfied. It was a Saturday and still early, so everywhere was quiet. She parked the Lotus Cortina in the lane behind Mrs McDonald's yard. As she got out of the car, she knew something was wrong. The gates were open. When she looked inside, the Mazda MX5 was gone. Her heart jolted. She glanced around and cursed. She hadn't disabled it in the way she would have done her own car. In fact, she hadn't taken any precautions at all. She herself had dismembered the manufacturer's anti-theft devices. She'd left it completely vulnerable. Any halfwit with a screwdriver could have driven it away. One of the local lads had stolen it, she decided. You stupid cow, she said to herself. You cretin. You look after the Cortina like a precious baby but then go and neglect a real flash and dazzle car that would tempt any teenage joyrider.

She walked through the yard to the back door. She

could see her landlady through the kitchen window. She was holding a scrubbing brush and standing on a wet floor. She'd paused in her labours to speak to someone on the phone. Jaz went in.

'Here she is now,' said Mrs McDonald. 'I call you all back.'

Jaz shrugged and composed her features into a resigned expression. She didn't want to upset Mrs McDonald. 'It's my own fault,' she muttered.

The large woman carefully replaced the receiver. Her lips were puckered into a dismayed 'O'. She gestured for Jaz to sit down and she lowered herself onto a seat, dropping her brush. 'Very bad things with men happen here,' she said. 'Car thiefs come last night. But honey, I manages to get my three sons. That's them, in Birmingham. They says sit tight and they come down. Just as soon as their market finish. They packs up their stall, comes down, sorts it all out for you. No one bothers my guests. Not here. In my own house . . .'

'Who was here?' Jaz interrupted.

'Bad men. They steals your darling little car.'

'What did they look like?'

She thought for a minute, her face impassive. 'They're white boys. Brothers, I says.'

'Big? Bald? Fancy suits?'

'They dress like . . .' She pulled at the air with her hand as if trying to find words in it.

'Footballers?'

She frowned.

'Matching tracksuits?'

She shook her head.

'Fancy pale-coloured suits?'

'That's right.'

'Thirty-five? Look like bodyguards?'

Mrs McDonald nodded.

'Shit, shit, shit!'

'They says they look for you. I'm not worried at first except it's late. Come back tomorrow I says. She isn't here.'

Jaz stood up and started pacing back and forth. Her mind was racing. 'How did they know I was here?'

Mrs McDonald pointed at the kettle. 'Cup of tea, honey?'

'What did they say exactly? Can you remember exactly what happened? What time?'

Mrs McDonald filled the kettle, plugged it in and sat down again. Her gestures were apologetic. 'Just after you leave. Minutes after. They comes to the front door. They says they's looking for you and waiting. They goes round the back and comes in. You forget to bolt the gates. They sits outside bold as two canaries on the bonnet of your car. I don't know – I thought they just wait. I go out there and they says not to worry, us just waiting. I watch telly. Drink my cocoa. Then! What happen? They drives off! Thieve your car! Very fast. As if it emergency . . .'

'They probably had a phone call about the fire . . .'

'What fire?'

Jaz's pulse was beating like a drum. She suddenly realized she had to leave as soon as possible. Ronnie and Reggie might be back. She felt guilty about exposing her kind landlady to this intrusion. 'Did they threaten you? Scare you?'

She shrugged, palms upwards. 'No. Not at all. They is extra polite. Like proper gentlemen.'

'Mrs McDonald. I'm sorry you've had this trouble. Please don't worry. You don't know anything so they can't hurt you. It'll be all right. I'm going now.' Jaz pulled out Elvis's money and peeled off some notes. She put them on the kitchen table. 'Forget you've seen me.'

'But my boys come. They says they get the car back, if it anyone around here. They grows up here. They knows everyone. I tell them you just a young, defenceless child, in my home, with no one to look after you . . . No mum, no dad . . .'

Jaz backed towards the hall and ran upstairs to collect her things.

'Hey now, don't you want your cup of tea?'

Later, parked again in Lincoln's Inn Fields, Jaz tried to collect her thoughts. She couldn't imagine how Ronnie and Reggie had found her this time, but she'd underestimated them. She thought that having ditched Pete, she'd be able to punish Vinny from a position of safety, but his boys were cleverer than she'd expected.

She mused for a moment. Perhaps the Mazda had been electronically tagged. Fat Andy had told her about this worrying trend and how his thieves on the street overcame it. It hadn't occurred to her to check. In truth, she didn't know what such a device looked like. Her skills were dated. She sighed. Whatever had gone wrong, she needed to be more careful from now on. She took the mobile out of her pocket and fingered it.

Yes, she thought, vigilance was important. She almost put the phone away but instead dialled the gym on the Mile End Road. It was too early for it to be open and she heard the answerphone pick up. 'It's Jaz,' she said, 'with a message for Piggy and Porky. You've got your car back, you fat wankers, but don't think you've won this round, because I haven't finished.'

Later, she went to Boots, bought a packet of sandwiches and a bottle of Evian, some antiseptic and a bandage. Back in the car, she ate one sandwich then tried to dress her knee. The results were less than satisfactory. She took the photo of Peony and Mimosa out of her jeans pocket and examined it. It was becoming rather creased and worn, but the twins still stared out at her, truculent and beautiful, their cardboard haloes out of place, their faces unusually clean.

She tried to imagine Fat Andy as a small boy with a twin brother, but this was impossible. Fat Andy was the kind of person who'd never had a childhood. He never once mentioned his early life. She thought about their times in bed and how he liked to pretend she was a young girl. Sometimes he'd talked in a baby voice and played childish games. Unlike her sisters, he'd been cruelly separated from his natural playmate. Perhaps that was it, she thought to herself, perhaps with her, he'd been trying to create something he'd always missed.

She started the car and drove west to Shepherd's Bush, listening to the news on the local radio. She was disappointed when there was no mention of the fire.

At Wesley's flat, the homeless man was still crouched in the doorway of the pork butcher, wrapped in a travel rug. He was young and reasonably healthy looking, but his face was pale, mournful and detached. When Jaz stopped to ring the bell he took out a penny whistle and began to play. She gave him her spare sandwich, waited for a while, then rang the bell for a second time. Eventually the door opened a crack. It was Harm.

'I'm sorry,' said Jaz. 'Where's Wesley? Did I get you out of bed?'

'Come in, Jaz,' said Harm. 'Quickly. I'm a lot better. I don't want people to see me like this.'

Jaz studied her face. The bruises on her sallow skin had turned purple and yellow in a spectacular way, but the swelling and the cuts seemed much improved. 'You look both better and worse.'

'I look like hell. Hell on earth. That's the truth.'

They went upstairs. Harm was wearing a baggy T-shirt and fluffy slippers. The living room was untidy. She was still sleeping on the sofa and the covers were strewn around. The floor was littered with cups, magazines and ashtrays and the TV was on high volume, showing a morning chat show. Jaz remembered that Wesley's flat was normally spotless.

'Where's Wesley?'

'Oh, he's out somewhere. Gone to see his therapist or something.' She lit a cigarette.

'You going to stay here?' Like Jaz and Trace, Harm had no permanent address.

Her answer was a listless shrug. She seemed depressed.

Jaz sat on the arm of a chair. Harm lowered the sound of the television and flopped down on the sofa.

'I'm sorry about what happened, Harm. It was my fault. I shouldn't have asked you to do it. It was a bad mistake.'

Harm avoided her eye. She stared at the TV.

'Hey, we are still friends, aren't we?' Jaz bit her lip.

There was a strange, unrelaxed atmosphere in the room, which was unusual. Harm was normally so full of fun.

Harm turned and stared at Jaz. 'You staying away from those two heavies?'

Jaz paused. 'Yes,' she lied.

'You better be. Don't forget that time Trace and I had to rescue you from that psychopath in the East End. What was his name again?'

'Keith.'

Harm lit a cigarette and kneaded the flesh of one of her thighs. 'I'm getting fat, lying around here all day.' She met Jaz's eyes. 'You stay away from those guys. Right?'

'Right.' Jaz thought how ordinary Harm looked without make-up and without her glamorous clothes.

'Whatever they did to your bloke, it's not worth getting involved. You know that?'

Jaz tried to smile.

'It's not worth it.'

Jaz pointed to Wesley's desk. 'Can I use the computer for a minute? It's a car thing.'

Harm nodded. She changed channels irritably.

Jaz switched on the machine and slid in the disk provided by Elvis. She felt a flutter of excitement. As she scrolled down the screen she realized it was what Andy had talked about – it was a record of Vinny's illegal transactions and his shady European contacts. She licked her lips. Bloody great, she thought. She extracted the disk and pocketed it, then switched off the machine.

Harm was still watching TV.

Jaz crossed the room and picked up a book from the seat of the chair, turning it over absently. It was a paperback entitled *Psychosynthesis – Counselling in Action*. 'This Wesley's?'

Harm snorted. 'Well, it's hardly likely to be mine, is it?' She paused. 'You listening to me, Jaz? About those men?'

'Yeah, yeah, I've got the message.' Jaz dropped the book and stood up. 'Coffee?' She went into the kitchen and reappeared with two steaming mugs. 'I'm concentrating on finding his brother. Fat Andy had a twin brother.' She handed a mug to her friend. She had decided not to tell Harm about Vinny and her revenge tactics, but explained her need to find a mourner for Fat Andy.

Harm nodded. 'Trace has told me some of this,' she said.

Jaz described the man on television, behind the Home Secretary. 'It's important,' she insisted. 'It's hard to explain, but this is something I really have to do.'

Harm frowned. 'I don't know, kid. I wish you'd drop it, I really do. Wesley would say you're trying to meet your own subconscious needs. Whatever's driving you.'

'Well, maybe I am. It's to do with twins and family and trying to do something right for a change. I can see that.' She hesitated. 'It's about having some kind of a purpose. You know Trace is helping me. She's going to get a new job and help me to track down the twin brother.'

'She told me. She'll do it too. Trace will do anything for you. You know that.'

Jaz had a sudden brainwave. 'Harm, you ever worked in the House of Commons?'

Harm sipped her drink. She giggled.

Jaz was relieved by the return of her good humour.

Harm inhaled deeply. 'You mean have I done the business with MPs and suchlike?'

'That's exactly what I mean.'

Harm grinned. She lay back cradling her mug and looked at the ceiling.

'Really, this is important. Have you?'

'Of course I have. It's a goldmine. They're away from home, they work late nights, they're terrified of getting into anything semi-legit with a secretary or someone, in case the papers pick up on it. I'm in and out of there all the time.'

'What? The actual building?'

'Sure.'

'Harm, I don't believe you!'

'It's true! Don't ask who, though. Wesley will go off it if I talk. He's already pretty worried as it is. He keeps getting his calculator out and working out how much money we're losing, per day, per hour, per bloody minute.'

Jaz explained how this connection might be useful. 'Harm, I know I messed up last time, but if you can help me get to this twin brother character . . . will you?'

Harm was suddenly serious. 'As long as you stay away from those guys in the East End.'

'OK.'

'Anything else I can do that doesn't interfere with my own interests, I'll do. Within reason.' She sighed. 'But I wish you'd drop it. The fat guy's dead.' She sniffed. 'Get a life.' She picked up the TV remote and flicked channels. 'What happened to the pretty ginger boy? The one I used to know at the garage? Trace said you'd pulled him.'

'I sort of went off him.'

'OK. So what happened about your idea of going up north, for a visit?'

Jaz shrugged. 'I'm thinking of taking a holiday, when all of this is over.'

'Do something. Get your mind off this heavy stuff. It doesn't suit you.'

Later, towards evening, Jaz left the car in the safe space, put on her headphones and sunglasses and jogged at a medium pace to Mile End Road. Her knee was hurting but after the first mile it went numb. She checked around the back of Ronnie and Reggie's gym. As she'd expected, there was a brand new Mazda 626 in the staff car park. It was dark blue and elegant. Jaz suddenly remembered the specifications given by Elvis. He wanted something large enough for himself, Big Boy and Peppy. It had to be flash, and he didn't want white. The sports car she'd stolen last time around wouldn't have been suitable anyway. It had been too small. Jaz walked around the Mazda. It wasn't what Elvis had in mind, but it would do. It was a four-door saloon, with long, low contours. Classic lines, Jaz thought. They're back in fashion. It was a top of the range model with a rear spoiler, body-coloured bumpers and tinted glass. Jaz glanced around. Painted on the wall in front of it were the words 'Managers – Resurved'. Above, the door at the top of the fire escape was wedged open with a chair, as it had been before. She took out the mobile and pressed the numbers to connect her with reception inside. She knew that Kormal would have gone home hours before. A man answered.

'Are the bosses there?' she asked huskily, trying to disguise her voice.

'They're busy. Urgent, is it?'

'It can wait. What they doing?'

'Working out. Weight training.'

'Best not to disturb them?'

'That's right. Who is this anyway?'

'Courtesy call.' Jaz hung up. She ran up the fire escape and entered the back of the gym. Taking off her sunglasses, she stopped for a moment to get her bearings then entered a storeroom. Here there were bales of toilet rolls wrapped in polythene, mounds of freshly laundered towels, a Hoover and other cleaning equipment – and what she was looking for: a pile of maroon sweatshirts each in a plastic bag, with the name of the gym printed on the front. She opened one which said 'small' and put it on. She filled a bucket with hot water from a sink and taking this and two J-cloths, she went to reception. She was very nervous. She took a deep breath. A man was lounging in the swivel chair behind the desk, reading the *Evening Standard*. He was young, stocky and tattooed and wore a cutaway vest and shiny red shorts. His hair was shaved into bristles. He looked bored.

'Hello,' Jaz said innocently. 'I've been told to valet the Mazda.'

The young man sat up and tossed his paper down onto the desk. He looked her up and down and appeared unimpressed.

'I'm new,' she continued. 'There's not much doing. No ladies here. The bosses said to valet the Mazda.'

He looked at her steadily.

She forced a smile. 'Afterwards I've got to clean the showers.'

He grinned. 'Great, isn't it? You get a job as a fitness instructor and end up answering the phone . . .'

Jaz picked up the cue. 'Or swilling out the bogs, or washing towels . . .'

'Or going to the deli for pastrami on rye . . .'

She gave him what she thought was her most

appealing little-girl smile. She dropped the cloths in the bucket, fished around for them and squeezed them out. 'I'm Jaz, by the way.'

He turned towards her on the swivel chair and did something to his arms which made his muscles more erect and defined. 'I'm Baz. Hey, that's good! Baz and Jaz!'

She pursed her lips, lowered her chin and opened her eyes very wide. 'Where are the keys?'

He smiled. He had an even, dark tan and no body hair. 'What?'

'The spare keys to the Mazda, silly. I've got to do the inside and be careful of the leather trim. I've got to valet the boot.'

He opened a drawer and tossed her the labelled chrome ring holding a key and a remote.

As he did so, she dropped the cloths back in the bucket. She caught the ring and held it aloft. 'Thanks, mate.'

'Do mine afterwards if you like. Mine's the Honda Civic.'

'Piss off.' She turned to go down the stairs.

'See you later, Jaz. Mind you give it a good polish.'

'Make sure you fill up the drinks machine.'

She could hear him chuckling as she left the building.

Jaz took the Mazda 626 to Lincoln's Inn Fields. She parked it next to the Lotus Cortina and changed its plates for a pair she'd taken from Vinny's garage. She examined it thoroughly, but couldn't see anything which resembled a tracking device. Stay calm, she repeated to herself, like a mantra. Stay focused. Stay cool. She rubbed the bodywork lightly with a cloth, then drove it over to Peckham. She left it in the underground car park beneath the flats. A group of teenagers watched her. They were leaning on a barrier, gossiping and yawning. She went over to them. 'See that blue car?' she said. 'That's Elvis's new motor. You know what I think? I think you should keep an eye on it for him. Make sure it comes to no harm.'

Upstairs she banged and kicked on the armoured door of the flat. Eventually, she was invited to speak into the entryphone. 'Open up, for Christ sakes. It's Jaz. I've been out here for ten bloody minutes.'

Peppy opened the door. He looked better than he had in recent days. He smiled. 'It's little Jaz!' he exclaimed, pleased. He coughed. 'Er . . . we're busy in here. Business meeting. Can't ask you in.'

'Tell the man I've got the wheels.'

After a couple of minutes, Elvis appeared.

'You coming down to see it?'

'Nah, not now. *Stars in Their Eyes*? On the telly?' He pointed in the direction of the living room. Jaz could hear someone singing Madonna's 'Material Girl'. Elvis glanced backwards into the flat, then turned to her and handed over a wad of notes. 'Five hundred.' He blew her a kiss. 'You's the best, doll. Number one.'

'It's a Mazda six-two-six. Top of the range. Loads of Jap gadgets. A lighty-up ashtray and mirror, air conditioning, tilting seat, telescopic steering column . . .'

'Yeah, yeah.' Elvis looked over his shoulder again. He was worried about missing his favourite programme.

Jaz handed him the keys and the registration document which matched the plates. 'Send this paper to Swansea. You'll have to get new glass because the windows are etched . . .'

'Yeah, yeah.'

'Elvis, listen. I mean it. Get new glass off that dodgy guy in East Lane. He'll rip you off but if you don't the car is traceable . . .'

'Yeah, yeah.' She was sure he wasn't paying attention. He was straining to hear the TV.

'Get – new – glass!' Jaz started to walk away, pocketing the money. 'If you don't you'll get even more police harassment.'

Elvis stepped out onto the balcony and gave her the thumbs-up. He smiled widely, showing his rotten teeth. He'd been listening to her after all. 'Star quality, doll,' he called out. 'You? What you got, doll? Friggin' star quality.'

Chapter Fifteen

Jaz decided, after all the excitement of the last two days, to lie low for a brief spell. She checked into a big, modern hotel near Charing Cross and hung the 'Do Not Disturb' sign on her door. After a good night's sleep, she gathered up a pile of magazines removed from the foyer, a copy of *Radio Times* to check the TV scheduling and the room service menu, and spent the next day reading about celebrities, health and beauty tips, and home renovation on a budget. She familiarized herself with the Paris styles for autumn and the most fashionable new eye shadow colours. In between, she watched five soaps, three game shows and several live discussions where audience members interacted with a panel and argued about released paedophiles, Viagra, the future of Tellytubbies, and the problem of chewing gum stuck to city pavements. At regular intervals she ordered small but appetizing meals from room service. They were grilled and decorated with things like radish spirals, rocket, mango wedges and something called coulis. In the bathroom she showered and experimented with the free, fruit-scented detergents. She washed her knee and changed the bandage. She used all the towels. For a few hours she forgot her responsibilities.

She remembered that Fat Andy had introduced her

to the joys of spending money on hotel rooms. He stayed in hotels when he was away on business and he enjoyed emptying the minibar, making long distance phone calls, having his clothes laundered or dry cleaned, then charging the inflated bill to Vinny at the garage.

Andy, she thought. Oh, Andy. She pressed her chest. The pain was there, less obvious than the throbbing in her knee, but still bothersome. Neither places are healing, she decided. Not my knee, nor my heart. She blinked. In an instant she was back in the bedroom with Andy's corpse. There had been blood on the wall, she remembered. It must have sprayed upwards from his neck in an arc, like water spurting from a hose, and splattered the wall in a wide, dark curve. She closed her eyes and took some even breaths. Yes, Fat Andy had loved hotels, she told herself again, and the blood disappeared, replaced by a vision of him basking in the deep suds of a hotel tub, singing and splashing and soaping his armpits.

She smiled. Unlike herself, Fat Andy had indulged his voluptuous nature all the time. To her amazement, when she moved in, she discovered he ate takeaway or restaurant meals every day. 'But you've got a flat,' she'd exclaimed, 'you've got a cooker!' He also drank bottles of whisky without suffering any ill effects and spent money wildly whenever he got the chance. In the short time they were together, he'd bought a saxophone, a camcorder, a 1100cc Yamaha and a part share in a racehorse. All of these he'd given away. She knew he'd once spent hundreds on flying lessons and he'd had a top of the range whirlpool spa fitted in the dim and tiny bathroom. He wasn't a materialist, he didn't value possessions, but he was hedonistic. He believed in self-indulgence and having fun. Jaz knew she was the opposite. Apart from her occasional binges, her nature was essentially frugal.

I have my moments, she thought. She picked up the phone and ordered a glass of alcohol-free wine and honey-glazed kumquats in a brandysnap basket with chantilly cream. Her thoughts strayed to the pleasures of her night with Pete, but like the memory of Andy's body, she put these away. Pete's a bastard, she told herself. She took a deep breath. He's a bastard like Vinny. She picked up the hotel phone. She felt a sudden need to let Vinny know she was responsible for his troubles. It was a kind of vanity. Anonymous revenge wasn't good enough. She wanted a bit of limelight. Just like in the old days when she worked hard to prove to Vinny that she was the best of Andy's car thieves, now she wanted him to understand that he was up against her own brand of urban terrorism, and she was dangerous. She imagined him standing amidst the smouldering rubble of his repair shop shaking his head, overwhelmed by the force pitched against him.

She dialled Pete's number at the flat. 'Hi, it's Jaz.'

'Jaz! Where've you been? I've been trying . . .'

'Listen, you tosser. You probably haven't even got a job any more . . .'

'Too right I haven't, the whole place has been . . .'

'Burned down.'

'Right.' There was a pause. He sounded excited. 'Have you seen it on the telly? I went down there today and I couldn't believe . . .'

Jaz raised her voice. 'I didn't need to see it on the telly. I saw it myself when it happened.' She paused. She sounded both menacing and triumphant. 'I bloody started it!' There was a silence and then some electronic interference on the line. 'Did you hear me?'

'Hell, Jaz, what're you playing at? Whatever made you . . .'

'I'm not playing, right? This isn't a game. This isn't TV. This is revenge. You tell my companero, that greasy little bastard, your boss, that I haven't finished. I'm just getting started. You tell those joke cockney gangsters to lay off me and my friends. Or I'll burn more than a fucking outbuilding.' She hung up. Her heart was beating hard. She decided that leaving messages for Vinny was the best part of the whole exercise. She only wished she could be there to see his face.

Later, whilst watching *Going Places*, Jaz promised herself again that when the fallout from Fat Andy's death had finally settled, she would take the Lotus Cortina and go with Harm and Trace on holiday. She watched a report on English seaside resorts. Torquay, she thought, why not? Or Bridlington, or maybe Margate. They could eat candyfloss, walk on the prom, play pinball and sit in deck chairs listening to a brass band. In her mind's eye, the three of them were wearing big plastic sunglasses and unlikely sixties-style dresses with handbags and baby stilettoes, like Jacqueline Kennedy. Do wah diddy diddy, she hummed to herself. Dum diddy do.

She remembered spending a day in Redcar with her family, a few months before she'd run away to London. It was a hot, fine morning and Blow announced a picnic on the beach. Jasmine made the sandwiches, Blow tinkered with his car, the twins, incoherent with excitement, searched the outbuildings for an old bucket and spade while Lola complained about the heat.

They travelled to the coast in a Jaguar Mark II 3.8 which Blow had fixed and resprayed. Peony had a pet duck in a cardboard box which she refused to leave behind. Her mother was grey-faced but insisted the sea air would do her good. However, immediately after they parked, as close as possible to the sands, she disappeared into the nearest pub. Peony and Mimosa introduced the duck to the sea and it bobbed around happily, eyeing some distant seagulls with mistrust. Jasmine spread out a blanket and the twins ate their sandwiches and crisps and fought over a bottle of lemonade. After a while they decided to go shoplifting in the town. 'Look after Deirdre duck,' they called in unison as they climbed up the breakwater, heading for Woolworths and WH Smith.

Blow retrieved a tennis racquet from the car and he and Jasmine played French cricket. The wide, golden beach, despite the sunshine, was almost deserted. The sky was cloudless apart from the vapour from two tiny aeroplanes. Jasmine could feel the heat pricking her bare shoulders and arms. After a while Blow bought them each a raspberry-topped ice cream and he laughed as it melted and ran down his wrist. He sat on the blanket and read his newspaper. Jasmine took the twins' bucket and spade and built a sandcastle on the shoreline. It had turrets and a moat and each time a big wave broke it was surrounded by water. She sat next to it for a while, hypnotized by the steady, soft rhythm of the sea. The twins came back with throat sweets, pencil sharpeners, mascara and a pair of bathroom scales. They removed their clothes and joined Deirdre, splashing in the shallows. Eventually, as the sun sank in the sky, Blow went to find Lola and told the three of them to pack away. Mimosa carried the duck in her box back to the car. Peony dragged the blanket. Jasmine lingered on her own, on the beach, tidying the carrier bags and hunting for her sisters' shoes. She was tired and her skin was burnt but she knew it was the happiest day of her life.

In the evening, Jaz asked room service to provide her with a laptop computer. She typed a letter on Ronnie and Reggie's headed notepaper, addressed to their members, informing them that the gym was closing immediately for essential repairs and renovation. She said this was a result of fire regulations and the Health and Safety At Work Act. She apologized and recommended that all members attend another gym where good service would be provided. She then checked in Yellow Pages and named a rival establishment, not far away, on Commercial Road. When she'd finished, she phoned the hotel desk again and requested that they make seven hundred and fifty photocopies and provide envelopes. She then began the long and laborious task of addressing the letters to Ronnie and Reggie's customers.

She lay on the bed, intending to watch *Wild at Heart* on Channel Four. She heard a strange noise which she first thought was an alarm, until she realized her mobile phone was ringing.

It was Trace. 'Jaz, I got this number off Harm. Where you at?'

Jaz explained where she was staying and outlined how she'd spent her day. 'Tell Harm,' she said again. 'You know how she worries.'

'Sold a car or something?'

'Yep.'

'That's good news, Jaz.'

'Yep.'

Trace was speaking from a phone box, Jaz could tell from the special tone in the background. 'Listen, I think I've got it all sorted at the Home Office.'

Jaz sat up sharply, scattering letters. 'Bloody great.' She glanced at the TV on the wall. Someone was being brutally murdered. 'What exactly are you doing there?'

'I'm night relief tea lady'.

Jaz laughed. 'Straight up? What's night relief?'

'No, Jaz, it's not night relief. It's night – dot – relief. Some people work late here. That means I'm night shift, four to twelve, and I'm relief, which means I help out. Depending how busy it is. If it's not busy I'm supposed to be in a canteen somewhere, collecting and washing crockery. I haven't done that yet.'

'Bloody great, Trace,' Jaz repeated.

'The money's awful and the work's out to contract. That means everyone in an overall is probably an illegal immigrant. In the Home Office. Funny, right? It's a horrible building. I've got to use a payphone and there's no facilities. It's not the Grand Banana.' She sounded a little low.

'Where you staying?'

'That's the other thing, Jaz. It's a problem. What can I do? I'm back at the hostel, but only because they know me. You know it's supposed to be for under eighteens.'

'You showed anyone that photo yet?'

'Give me a chance. I've only just got my overall.'

'Keep in touch.'

'Will do.'

Jaz remembered Elvis and his TV programme. 'You've got star quality, Trace. You know that? Star quality.'

'I've got a trolley and an urn.'

Jaz had difficulty relaxing after Trace's call. It had returned her to the world and as far as Fat Andy's brother was concerned, she didn't have a clear plan. She thought about ringing him up at work, and telling him about the murder, but this seemed too brutal. She would have to arrange a meeting, as she'd done with Princess and Andy's mother. Trace would be the link.

She turned off the television and made herself a cup of instant coffee. Then she paced about the room and considered checking out, but the alternative was aimless driving, so she decided to stay put. She spent hours addressing the envelopes and rang down for someone to collect and mail them. She returned the laptop and managed to get a couple of hours' sleep.

At six forty-five the mobile rang again. 'Hi, Jaz. It's Trace. You asleep?'

'Yes.'

'Sorry. I'm ringing from the hostel. There's been a big fight here. Everyone's awake. The good news is I may have something. I asked around at the Home Office last night, showed the photo. Most people just laughed. I think it's because he needs a shave in the photo and his hair's a bit, well . . .'

'Messy?'

'Yeah. Well anyway. I explained I wasn't looking for him, I was after his brother. This made a difference. Apparently he's the spitting image of someone called Charles Merchant. He's like a main man there. Important. You know, fitted carpet, real coffee. He's a political adviser or something. Works with the Home Secretary.'

Jaz was excited. 'That's right. That's him, Trace.'

There was a pause. Trace put another coin in the hostel payphone. There was the sound of shouting, a door being slammed and a girl crying. 'Well?'

'Well what?'

'What d'you want me to do now?'

Jaz hesitated. 'Are you going to meet him?'

Trace laughed. 'I don't know. There's millions of us catering staff here, right? And it's like mega-big, this place. Chances of me bumping into him must be like winning the lottery. I'll try and get on his coffee rota. But what if I do? What'll I say?'

Jaz thought for a moment. 'I tell you what. Ask around. Get the gossip. Find out what he does. Maybe where he lives. You know, snoop about. I need to think about this.'

'OK, Jaz.'

'Thanks, Trace.'

After a full English breakfast, Jaz went outside. Beyond the air conditioning of the hotel lobby, London was hot, airless and cloudy. She jogged to Oxford Street to see Davey, the ex-student *Big Issue* vendor. Her knee was worse, but she tried to ignore it. She was aware that she was running with a limp.

Davey was in his usual place although looking less sad and dishevelled – he was wearing a bright red cotton shirt and he'd had a wash and a haircut. Even his dog appeared more cheerful and stood up and wagged his tail when Jaz stroked his head.

'Hi, Davey. How's it going?'

He smiled, showing his toothless gums. 'Can't complain.' He handed a magazine to a passer-by and pocketed the pound. 'Thanks, mate.'

Jaz stood for a moment, watching the swelling tide of Oxford Street. A familiar feeling overtook her. The compelling business of the real world, the routine and bustle, the morning repopulation of shops and offices, the whole complicated mechanism of capitalism – it had nothing to do with her. She lived on a different planet. She was a perennial outsider. She took a deep breath. 'What happened when you spread the word amongst the gang?'

'About Fat Andy?'

'Who else?'

He was suddenly sad. 'Shock and dismay, little Jaz. Shock and dismay. He was well liked. Always did right by us, did Andy. He cared about us. Not like that bastard, Vinny.' Davey turned his head to one side and spat on the pavement, reinforcing his point.

'You told them Vinny was responsible?'

'Sure.'

'What happened?'

Davey drew himself up to his full height. 'I called a meeting. They all remember me, of course, and they all came. They wouldn't have it at first. Argued. Didn't believe it. Said they'd seen Fat Andy and Vinny laughing and joking together only days before. Said business was good. They'd had an order for five Citroën Xsaras and eight Renault Lagunas from Holland. And the luxury class of car is still in demand – pulling high prices too, seeing as how they've made them so bloody difficult to steal. Vinny was on a roll . . .'

'Well? What happened? Did you tell them what I said?'

Davey turned and looked her in the eye, missing a potential magazine sale. 'Of course I did.'

'They remember me?'

'Remember? You kidding? You were one of the best.'

Jaz didn't smile. 'I was the best.'

'OK. You were the best. I told them you saw it happen. Told them little Jaz saw Vinny do it.'

'And?'

'He's finished – on the illegal side, that is. Hasn't got a gang any more. They just melted away. Gone. Disgusted. That's the only way to describe it. Disgusted.'

'So what's happening?'

Davey shrugged. 'Nothing's happening. What's he going to do? Fat Andy took care of the streets, recruited the boys. Vinny doesn't know how to put a gang together. Not a class act like Andy's. He hasn't got the contacts. He hasn't got the interpersonal skills.'

Jaz let out a relieved sigh. 'That's great, Davey. Thanks.'

'That squint-eyed little sod had it coming.' Davey grinned. 'Without Andy there was only trouble, apparently. No bonuses, no incentives, no job security. No one liked working for Vinny.'

'I'll bet.'

'How you feeling now, Jaz? All shook up?'

'Angry,' Jaz confided. 'I want to drive Vinny off the Island. I want to finish him.'

'That's a tall order.'

'I'm going to do it. I'm paying him back for Andy's murder. It's compulsive.'

Dave regarded her seriously. He thought for a moment. 'Let's make us medicine of our great revenge,' he quoted, 'to cure this deadly grief.'

Jaz set off back to the hotel, choosing back streets to avoid the growing crowds. A group of dishevelled teenagers blocked her way, waiting behind a big restaurant.

They were hot and quarrelsome. Jaz knew what they were doing. She'd been there herself a few years ago. Very soon, the refuse would appear from the night before. The manager was sympathetic. The edible food would be bagged or wrapped in foil, and they would scuffle amongst themselves and grab it and run off with it, like hungry dogs.

Jaz thought she might stay at the hotel for another couple of days, waiting to see if Trace contacted Fat Andy's twin. She was just about to push the heavy revolving door, when she saw two men sitting in the reception lounge. She stepped to the side, allowing the uniformed doorman to assist an old lady with her luggage. She peeped in again. There was no mistake – Ronnie and Reggie were waiting for her.

They hadn't seen her. She ran around to the back of the hotel, checked the underground car park to make sure the Lotus Cortina was still there, then jogged towards the service entrance. She was tired. She wished she'd not run all the way from Oxford Circus. Her limbs were heavy and protesting, like they'd been during the aerobics class at the gym, and her knee was agony. She ran up the back stairs to reception. She had to cross a corner of this wide lobby to get to the main flight up to her room. She put on her sunglasses and waited until her pursuers were facing each other, exchanging words, then she flashed through. Within four minutes she'd accessed her room, picked up her few belongings and was back down. As she entered reception again one of Vinny's men looked up. Her eyes met his. He jumped to his feet. She swerved across the marble floor, making for the service stairs. A guest, standing at the desk, let out a small scream.

Jaz felt panic. She practically fell down the concrete

steps. She crashed through the swing doors and bounded the seventy yards to her car. She fiddled in her pocket for the keys, found them and with shaking hands inserted one in the driver's door. Stay calm, she thought. She wasn't calm. It wouldn't turn. It was sticking, reluctant, in the way it had done several times before.

Jaz paused, took a deep breath, wiped the sweat off her hands and tried again. 'Come on, baby,' she whispered desperately. 'Please. Come on.' She wiggled the key gently. Forcing it would only bend it.

There was a slap-slap from the doors and a shout. She looked over. Ronnie and Reggie were pointing at her. 'Hold it!' one of them shouted. 'We just want to talk to you!'

Jaz rubbed her forehead with her sleeve. She fumbled again in her jacket pocket and found the small silver tube given to her by the beauty therapist at the Grand Bahama. Stay focused. Her hands were shaking but she managed to smear a line of lipstick on the edge of the key. She dropped the tube and willing her hands to a degree of steadiness tried for a third time to open the door. Come on, she thought. Don't let me down. She felt the lock release. You angel. Oh, thank you. Thank you. She opened the car and slid in. Dumping her bag in the back, she slammed the driver's door, turned on the ignition and threw the car into reverse. The engine roared and the Lotus Cortina jumped backwards. She dragged the wheel hard through both hands and swerved. She was suddenly facing Vinny's men who were almost upon her. Stay cool.

They stopped, their expressions contorted and surprised, and held up their arms in front of their chests, their palms towards her. 'No,' she saw them mouth. 'No, no.'

She changed gear and stepped on the accelerator, pushing it to the floor. With a furious snarl the car leaped forwards, heading directly for them. Jaz didn't flinch or alter the steering. She drove straight at them. Her breath was coming in painful short bursts. Fear and anger had sent her heart and brain into overdrive. I'll kill you bastards, she thought. Just let me run you down.

They each dived sideways, almost comically, like rugby players. Jaz's tyres squealed in protest as she spun the car towards the exit. In seconds she was out and away. She glanced behind several times but she wasn't being followed. In minutes, taking back alley short cuts, she disappeared into the hubbub of central London.

Chapter Sixteen

Jaz drove fast, then was forced to slow in dense traffic. When she found herself on a four-lane highway, she speeded up again. She had no particular destination in mind. She concentrated on her driving, her eyes flicking between road and mirrors, the interaction of hand and eye, her face set and her body recovering from both fright and exertion. Her knee was throbbing rhythmically. It was hot and the air smelled of exhaust and tarmac. The sun bounced off the hard surfaces of road and bonnet with a glare that her sunglasses couldn't ease. Her sweaty skin stuck to the seat and her mouth still tasted of fear but she felt freedom in this unnatural motion. She enjoyed the car. She felt in control. The Lotus Cortina drove like a dream, its engine purring and growling like a haughty pedigree cat. She felt connected to it. After a while, as well as sensing the disturbances in her own body, she became aware that the left front suspension was wallowing slightly on sharper bends. She remembered Fat Andy mentioning that it leaked fluid. When all of this is over, she decided, I must give the Lotus Cortina a proper going over. The works.

Fifty minutes passed and she was somewhere in north London. She turned down a leafy residential street. The moment she turned off the engine, the memory of

Vinny's heavies, both running towards her in the car park, returned with dazzling clarity. She buried her face in her arms and took several gulps of air. She wanted to cry but fought the impulse. After a while she sat up and noticed the street name and looked it up in Fat Andy's *A–Z*. She was in Haringey.

She lay back in her seat and closed her eyes. She had evaded her enemies again but next time she might fail. Her mind kept returning to the same question. How did they find me? She decided she'd been careless. The call to Pete had been reckless and stupid. She'd used the hotel phone and hadn't withheld the number. It was easy to match the number with the hotel and he'd clearly passed this on to the brothers. She thought about the letters she'd sent out to the members of the gym. They'd be delivered tomorrow, probably franked with the name of the hotel. In due course, Ronnie and Reggie would put two and two together and realize that as well as everything else, she'd been responsible for this act of sabotage.

Gradually she grew calmer. She reviewed recent events and felt a sense of pride. A lot had been achieved and she was still in one piece. She had never been so purposeful, so directed, so driven. More must be done to punish Vinny, but maybe soon she would be able to stop. She pressed her chest with the palm of her hand, then pressed gently on her injured knee. Stay calm, she thought. Stay focused, stay cool. A few more days. Maybe a week. I'll suggest the seaside trip to Harm and Trace. I'll spend the rest of the summer on holiday, taking a well-earned rest. She opened Fat Andy's road atlas and decided to pick a resort. She closed her eyes and pointed at the map of Britain. She lowered her hand, opened her eyes. She smiled. Her finger had landed in the sea, but the nearest coastal town was Weston-super-Mare. That'll do, she thought. We'll take the car and we'll go there. Weston-super-Mare. What a crazy name. In her imagination she could taste a salty tang and hear the gentle splish-splosh of waves. Children, not unlike the twins, ran back and forth across the shoreline, filling a hole with water. An old couple walked arm in arm, their clothes hitched up above the swirling foam. These people inhabited a safe, predictable world. They were happy. Overhead, sunlit birds wheeled and dived.

Jaz immobilized the Lotus Cortina and walked up the road. She passed a big garage. It was another dealership for Mazda – just like Vinny's place. The same line-up of new models gleamed in the showroom. She noted down the name and address. Afterwards, she had a meal in a café, then used the mobile to phone Harm. 'It's Jaz,' she said. 'D'you fancy a trip to the coast? Stay for a while, eat fish and chips, go to funfairs?'

'What?'

'You heard me.'

'You mean go on holiday?'

'Yeah. We never go on holiday. Why's that? Other people go on holiday. It's what people do in the summer.'

Harm hesitated. 'Are you all right, Jaz?'

'What d'you mean, am I all right? Of course I'm all right. Why should I not be all right? I'm just asking a simple question. Do you want to go on . . .'

Harm interrupted. 'You sound pretty strung out to me.'

Jaz was indignant. 'Well maybe I am! Fat Andy's had his throat cut, two gorillas are trying to kill me, I've got a sore knee that's turning septic . . .'

'Two gorillas? What happened?' There was a silence. 'You've broken your promise!'

Jaz raised her voice. 'No I haven't and I don't want to even bloody discuss it, right?' People on surrounding tables turned to stare. She spoke more quietly. 'Do you want to go on holiday? Yes or no?'

There was an angry silence, then Harm sighed, exasperated. Jaz heard her light a cigarette and inhale. 'I wouldn't mind going to the Costa del Sol.'

'I want to go to Weston-super-Mare.'

'Where the hell's that?'

'I'm not sure. But I've got a road map. I'll drive, Trace can sit in the front and play the record machine and you can map-read in the back. It'll be great. Honest, it will, Harm. It'll be fab. We'll sit in deck chairs and go on the pier.'

'OK.'

'What?'

'I said OK.'

Jaz was delighted. 'Great. That's great, Harm. We'll have to make a list. You know, of things to take . . .'

'You've had contact with those two guys? Be honest. Those brothers?'

'No,' Jaz lied.

'What did you mean when you said . . .'

'I didn't mean anything.'

'You sure?'

Jaz sighed, in mock exasperation. 'I'm sure.'

'OK, then.'

'One more thing. I've got to see a man in Haringey about something. A car thing. How's your poor face? Are you presentable? Will you come with me?'

'Why?'

'I just want you to.'

'If you like. I'll look normal again in two days.'

Jaz felt very cheerful about the prospect of the holiday. Her mood became positive. She consulted the *A–Z* and drove to the Whittington Hospital. She sat in the waiting room for two hours then watched in horror as a young, dark-skinned doctor anaesthetized her knee and with gentle-fingered care and dexterity, dug out a piece of glass. 'Where are your mother and father?' he asked.

'I haven't the faintest idea.'

He gave her a nervous, appraising glance.

'I'm twenty-one.'

'I see,' he said, clearly disconcerted. He cleaned and dressed the wound and gave her a prescription for antibiotics.

'I don't do them,' Jaz told him.

'I'm sorry?'

'I don't do them. I don't do drink, drugs or antibiotics.'

He raised his girlish eyebrows. 'Is it a religious thing?' he asked.

'You could say that.'

He smiled, shrugged and tore up the form.

'It's not infected. I think it was helped by paint thinners. They're antiseptics.' She smiled at him. 'I'm very grateful,' she insisted. 'Don't get me wrong.'

Her knee felt better. She jogged tentatively across the car park. As she was getting back into the Lotus Cortina the mobile phone rang. It was Trace.

'Listen, Trace. I've got this great idea. Harm and I have decided to go on holiday. We thought all three of us should go. Weston-super-Mare. We'll go in the car and stay in a guest house. Like, you know, a bed and breakfast. We could sit on the beach and eat candyfloss . . .' She paused. 'What d'you think?'

Trace coughed. She sounded afraid. 'I don't know, Jaz. I've never been out of London.'

'What? Never?'

'No.'

'Even more reason to go then.'

Trace laughed in an unconvinced way. 'I've met someone who says she can help you,' she said.

'In what way?'

'She's a temp. Maternity leave replacement, from an agency. She works for Charles Merchant. The only trouble is she says she wants paying.'

'How much?'

'She's got some papers she says are valuable. She wants four thousand pounds.'

'Trace, I'm not after leaked documents. Who does she think I am? Kenneth fucking Starr? I just want to find the guy Merchant and talk to him. No big deal.'

'I told her that.'

'Tell her I'll buy her a meal at Planet Pizza, Euston Road. We'll take it from there.'

Jaz heard the muffled sounds of Trace relaying this offer.

'You're on,' she confirmed. 'I can't come, though. I'm on duty. You'll have to see her on your own.' She described the woman.

Jaz gave a time and started the car.

*

Jaz had suggested an early meeting to avoid the rush. She sipped a glass of mineral water and played with the menu. Trace's contact was late but she was instantly recognizable. She was short, with dyed blonde hair, very ordinary, about fifty and wearing a red wool blazer with gold buttons, despite the warmth of the evening. Her shoes matched her bag and she carried a raincoat and some Marks & Spencer shopping. Jaz signalled with her menu and she approached with small, jaunty steps.

'Hello, dear,' she said cheerfully.

Jaz was reminded of social workers from her childhood.

A waitress appeared to take orders for drinks. 'I don't drink,' said Jaz. 'I'll have more water. Do you want wine?'

The woman smiled and nodded. She had careful, lacquered hair and pencilled eyebrows. 'A carafe of house red.' She started chatting amiably about the weather, the length of her journey back to High Wycombe and the fact that the train service was deplorable. She was middle class and effusive. She had the kind of voice people mistakenly describe as 'having no accent'. She was wearing a lot of costume jewellery. When her wine arrived she ordered minestrone and a four seasons pizza.

Jaz asked for a mixed salad.

The woman mentioned her new kitchen and conservatory. She said her husband, Malcolm, was retired but super-fit as a result of playing golf. When she started talking about her niece's exam results Jaz interrupted.

'D'you mind if we get down to business?'

She looked offended. 'Certainly,' she said huffily. 'Of course.'

The food arrived. Jaz picked up an oily leaf in her fingers. 'You know Charles Merchant. I want to arrange a meeting with him. It's personal. I have news for him which would be best delivered in person. Family business.'

The woman was still ruffled. 'Why don't you go through a solicitor?'

This hadn't occurred to Jaz. She thought for a moment. It wasn't a bad idea, except she never trusted professionals. She preferred straightforward transactions where clear needs were instantly met. 'I'm going through you, aren't I? Can you help or not?'

The woman tipped her bowl and chased the last slippery noodles with her spoon. She nodded. Within seconds her pizza arrived and she carefully cut a small piece and chewed it. Her table manners were restrained and prissy.

Jaz waited. 'Well?'

The woman suddenly put down her knife and fork, frowned and became less housewifely. Jaz looked into her eyes and, with a shock, realized she was intelligent. She was also shrewd. She'd underestimated her.

'I can tell you things about him which are reasonably well known. I can tell you things about him which are relatively unknown. I can tell you where he lives and where he eats and drinks. I know what club he belongs to. All this will cost you a hundred pounds. As well as this, I can show you something else which is not in the public domain, but which is very interesting. The last item is only a few days old. It hasn't been offered elsewhere. It will cost you four thousand pounds.'

Jaz imagined this apparently inoffensive, but self-important little woman eavesdropping, poking around in drawers, reading people's e-mails while they nipped out for a cigarette. She pictured her sitting at a word processor, printing off confidential documents whilst pretending to type minutes in a mindless way. She was the opposite of what she seemed.

Jaz was impressed. She could relate to this kind of duplicity. Because she herself looked ineffectual, she also gave people the impression of being harmless, when really she was very strong. They had this in common. 'I think I just want the hundred pound deal,' she said. 'That'll do me for now.' She smiled.

Jaz didn't doubt the woman's information. She'd learned through Trace's access to places of wealth and power that security was no more than expensive tokenism. It only worked if everyone believed in it, and this was never the case. Too many people were needed to service and maintain the rich and the successful. They came and went like an invisible conscripted army. They were low paid, resentful, and usually devoid of loyalty. Because of them, secrets were leaked and the mighty went unprotected more or less all of the time.

'All I want to do is speak to him.' She touched Elvis's roll of money in her hip pocket, then took it out and peeled off five twenties. 'I can't get through to him on the phone.'

'His calls are filtered three times, by three different people. You'll never get him at work.' The woman proceeded to talk for forty minutes, finishing her food and wine. She became more animated as she worked her way through the carafe.

Jaz tore a strip off the paper tablecloth and made a few notes. She learned that Charles Merchant was elusive and publicity shy. His boss, the Home Secretary, was a polished and handsome TV performer, who'd spent a lot on cosmetic dentistry and image consultation. However, it was Merchant, the political adviser, who had the brains and the imagination to make policy. Merchant was envied and feared. He seemed oblivious to sycophancy, flattery or intimidation. He had no known vices or skeletons in his cupboard. The woman compared him to other key figures in the government and used the word 'machiavellian'. 'He's perhaps the most brilliant of them all,' she added. 'He's a politician. An unelected politician. The most gifted of the age.'

Jaz disliked this hyperbole. 'I don't like any of them,' she said. 'None of them know what's really going on. I pay no attention to them at all.'

Her companion was undaunted. 'I think you're underestimating him. Merchant is a man with a mission,' she said. 'He calls it his new deal on Clean Cities. He wants to clean up the streets. Literally and metaphorically.' She gestured out the window. Huddled together in the soft evening, beyond the neon lit plate glass of the café, a young boy and girl in ragged overcoats held out their hands for coins.

'He wants to outlaw vagrancy, expand the prison population, make it illegal to sleep rough. He wants to quadruple hostel accommodation in big cities and raze all no-exit housing estates to the ground. He wants to overturn care in the community and reopen mental hospitals. He wants to tighten up pub licensing laws. He's got an agenda on defeating car crime. He's seriously anti-drugs. He's even devising innovative policies on refuse recycling. He says he wants everything neat and tidy in post-millennium Britain.' She swigged her wine. 'No litter, no riff-raff. Abolition of the underclass.'

Jaz snorted. It wasn't often she heard of a political programme which might affect her own lifestyle. 'Come on.' She laughed. 'That's just a joke.'

'At the very least he wants to hide it from view.'

Jaz smiled and shrugged. 'Hot air,' she muttered. She checked the details of where she might find him. 'Can I get back to you if I have problems?'

'You're dealing with a very powerful man here,' her new friend repeated. 'Some would argue he's more important than the PM. He trusts no one. He never talks to journalists, never gives interviews. He's a workaholic. He won't see you willingly. His private life's a mystery.'

'Look, I'm just not interested in him. He can try and clean up the whole damned planet, for all I care. That'll keep him busy. I just want to tell him something personal, right? It'll take five minutes. Then I'll go away.' Jaz attracted the attention of the waitress and paid the bill. She felt a little irritated by her companion's wine-fuelled fervency. 'Thanks for your help. I've got to go now.' She stood up abruptly and left the woman checking her lipstick in a handbag mirror. 'See you.'

In the car, Jaz dialled the number of Charles Merchant's club, spoke to a receptionist and left a message, giving the number of the mobile. She rang his home and a BT answering service asked her to leave the same information. She said it was a family matter and asked him to contact her. She then dialled his cellphone but it was switched off. She felt disappointed. She drove round to the address she'd been given, which turned out to be a private mews in Chelsea. She bribed the porter with ten pounds and wrote down her details on a memo pad. 'Give him this. I don't want anything except to speak to him, in person, for five minutes. Ask him to ring me. Tell him it's about his brother.' She decided to wait outside in the quiet street, in the Lotus Cortina, to see if he returned. She sat for several hours, her eyes on the entrance to his building. A long, dark limousine pulled up at about two a.m., driven by a chauffeur. A tall woman in an evening dress emerged, fishing in a gold net bag for some keys. Jaz decided it was Naomi Campbell. After this everything was quiet and deserted. At three o'clock she knew she was about to fall asleep. She realized she'd slept in the car a lot lately. She wondered if Charles Merchant meant to make this illegal too.

As she drifted in and out of consciousness, not entirely comfortable, her head on the inflatable pillow, dazzled by the lights of passing cars, Jaz remembered where she'd been living before Fat Andy took her in.

She'd been in a church crypt in Camberwell, with Trace, where temporary beds were set up during very cold weather. This service was run by volunteers, who were generous and nice, but a group of drug addicts from Edinburgh had arrived and spoilt everything.

Trace's few possessions were stolen and she decided, yet again, to go back to the Little Sisters of Hope in the East End. Jaz moved into a squat in Kensington where Harm had been living for three months, using the room of a cellist who was in police custody. It was a beautiful old house, full of paintings and delicate, threadbare carpets. Jaz slept on the floor of the living room where a skinhead chopped up valuable-looking furniture for firewood. There was no gas, electricity or running water. When the outside temperature dropped to minus fifteen, he began demolishing the ornate carved staircase. He suggested burning the cello. Harm became discouraged and went to stay with Wesley for a few days. Then she moved into a small hotel in Vauxhall. The Australian owner let her stay there rent free, in return for what Harm called professional services.

Jaz mentioned to Fat Andy that she had nowhere to live. First he offered her the settee in his living room. He was attentive and kind. He treated her like a child, sitting her on his knee and telling her stories. Within two days, he'd bought the Minnie Mouse nightdress and she was sharing his bed. He persuaded her to give up stealing cars.

Huddled in the back of the Lotus Cortina, Jaz thought to herself, I'm back to square one. I've got nowhere to live. But at least I'm unpredictable. Vinny can't find me if I keep moving.

As she drifted into sleep, Jaz dreamed that she was living in a lighthouse. The sea broke and sighed around her and the black sky was empty and calm. She lay in a strange curved bed, moulded against the round wall. The light flashed regularly and the steady beat of its mechanism was soothing and safe. It was lonely but peaceful. It was like being the only person in the world.

Chapter Seventeen

In the morning, Jaz immobilized the Lotus Cortina and left it outside the Chelsea mews. She dropped all her change into a parking meter and went to get some breakfast. Walking up the King's Road she caught the scent of an upmarket coffee shop. She went inside and ordered a baguette, a croissant and a cafetière of Colombian. She fingered her knee. It was almost better. She pressed her chest. The pain was still there.

She sipped her drink. She was immediately reminded of Sunday mornings with Fat Andy. He always drank a pot of coffee in bed, reading the *News of the World*. It was a ritual. She remembered cuddling up to his vast body as he cradled his mug. 'Little baby,' he said to her tenderly. Then her imagination suddenly veered to the blood-soaked bedclothes, the chill of the room on that final night and one of his limp, dead hands, open above his head, cupped as if asking for mercy. In the corner of her mind's eye, a leg of Vinny's sharp suit, and his gold-ringed monkey hand, holding the dripping knife, moved out of frame.

Hastily, she picked up a complimentary broadsheet. There was a picture of the Home Secretary on the front page. He was smiling, tanned and appeared even younger than usual. He was due to attend a Cabinet meeting that day. She scrutinized the edges, but there was no sign of Charles Merchant. Not even his fat arm or a button on his oversized jacket.

The accompanying column inches said a package of reforms called the new deal for Clean Cities would almost certainly be announced in the coming week. The government's waning popularity would be given a boost by the strong new direction to be taken in home policy. Jaz remembered her companion's comments the previous evening. She turned to a feature article on an inside page where the headline read 'New Deal for Homeless Angers Speculators'. Three paragraphs were full of conjecture but they seemed to be suggesting that as well as expanding prisons and reopening mental hospitals, the government had plans to sequestrate empty offices in big cities and turn them into temporary housing for street people. Even new buildings would not escape if they were unoccupied. They would become shortlife hostels and night shelters. Not surprisingly, many vested interests were unimpressed by this idea. The journalist was suggesting that the Home Secretary would have a fight on his hands, although he was likely to receive support from both the party and the country.

Jaz folded the newspaper and put it to one side. She leaned back, sipping from her oversized cup. The coffee was strong and fragrant. She thought about Charles Merchant. This was Fat Andy's brother. He was an innovator with a vision. He was both shadowy and clear. Instead of being self-seeking and egocentric, like elected politicians, he seemed to be driven by a personal view of how things should be.

Jaz decided there was something admirable about this. He seemed to have genuine ideas that were designed to help people. It is nice, she thought, identifying with him, to be absolutely sure about your aims. She felt that like Merchant, she too had goals. She was just as determined to carry them out. Hers were less grand but no less pressing. It was good to have direction.

Slowly she ate her breakfast. She wondered what Charles Merchant would be like and how he would behave when she finally tracked him down. She was intrigued, even a little excited. She felt less dismissive of his policies than she had the previous evening. She imagined telling him about her life on the streets and offering him insights and suggestions. She wanted to convince him that homelessness was as much about choice or luck or fate as it was about deprivation, that nothing was straightforward and big cities could never be tidy places. She pictured him questioning her, agreeing and disagreeing, quoting her in Ministerial speeches. She felt connected to him in a curious way, as if the two of them were somehow destined to know each other. She wondered if he shared Fat Andy's hedonism and specific sexual tastes. For a brief moment she thought about leaning against him, tucked under his heavy arm in the back of a swift moving government Daimler, her fingers teasing open the buttons of his hand-made Italian shirt.

Jaz tried Charles Merchant's numbers several times. She spoke to the day porter at the mews, bribed him as she had his evening colleague and left another message. He thought that no one had been back to the house, and intimated that it was often unoccupied. All in all, she spent a frustrating couple of hours. She felt at a loose end, unable to make progress.

Jaz hated this feeling. She decided to go for a run. It was a cloudy day, but hot. She took the bandage off her knee and found that it had healed in a satisfactory way. Putting on her sunglasses, she jogged up the King's Road, crossed the river and circled the lake in Battersea Park, where she stopped for ten minutes to eat an ice lolly. She hadn't pushed herself hard but the effort had boosted her circulation and cleared her mind of repetitive thoughts. She set off back at a steady jog, through Nine Elms and Vauxhall. Eventually she found herself in Westminster. She was tired now and her knee was aching. She slowed to walking pace, realizing that since she'd been driving Fat Andy's car she'd allowed herself to get out of condition. For years she'd averaged a ten-mile run every day. Since taking the car, she'd done much less. This had to change. She resolved to stay fit. It was important to be in tip-top physical shape. It was part of her personal code and necessary for self-preservation.

She wondered about going up to the Home Office, near St James's Park and having a look round outside. She might catch a glimpse of Charles Merchant or even get the opportunity to speak to him. She knew this was unlikely, but she was curious and anxious to make contact. As she proceeded up Whitehall she became aware of a gaggle of reporters, photographers and a TV crew. A road was cordoned off and half a dozen policemen were on duty. She realized she was at the end of Downing Street. She drew level as a shout went up from the small crowd. Three men with cameras broke away towards a string of long black cars. Without thinking, Jaz followed them, breaking into a fast sprint. The vehicles were moving sedately and behind there was an explosion of flash guns. Without effort, she outran the press pack and caught up with the cavalcade. One of them slowed in a leisurely sweep, before turning out into the main road. Jaz looked inside. A man in the back seat glanced up, startled, and for a moment stared into her face. Through the bluish tinted window she could see him clearly. It was the Home Secretary. Her damp palm slapped against the glass, in a decisive gesture, before the driver was able to accelerate away.

Later, when Jaz got back to the Lotus Cortina, she could hear the mobile ringing in the glove compartment. It was Trace. She was excited. 'I've seen him!' she squeaked. She explained she was in a phone booth in the Home Office building. 'I've seen him and he's exactly like your fat bloke. I can't believe it. It *must* be his brother!'

'Tell me slowly.'

'Well, actually, he's sort of fatter and I think his hair's a darker colour, but otherwise he's the same. Apart from the suit and the shiny shoes and suchlike. I wasn't expecting to see him. I got such a shock, I nearly wet myself!'

'Did you speak to him?'

'Get real. He was surrounded by a mob of flunkies holding clipboards and briefcases. He sort of swept past, out the door and into a big car.'

'Did he notice you?'

'I doubt it. There's just been a Cabinet meeting and he's off to speak to the Home Secretary. To discuss business. He's what we call NTG, here, straight down from the very top floor.'

'What's NTG?'

'Next to God. Hey, but listen, Jaz. I've got something else for you. A fax number and an e-mail address. There's a directory here. My friend Shirl looked him up.'

Jaz wrote these down. 'Trace. You've got to try and speak to him. Can't you go up there tomorrow with a plate of biscuits or something?'

Trace laughed. 'Sure, Jaz. I'll do my best.' She sounded very cheerful.

'Do you like it a bit better?' Jaz was tentative. 'Have you made some new friends?'

'Oh yes. There's two lovely women here. Iris and Shirl. They're a great laugh. I've joined a lottery syndicate . . .' She continued chatting about this for a minute or two.

Jaz was relieved. When she hung up, she reflected, not for the first time, on Trace's endless capacity to make the best of things. Wherever she lived or worked, her innocent friendliness and ability to see the good in people meant that she was OK. It wasn't a quality that Jaz envied, but she was touched by it, nevertheless. She thought about Trace's damaged past and her fear of sex. When this is over, she told herself, and we go to Weston-super-Mare, we'll all three of us be happy. We'll be Cortina crazy. She remembered Blow's old cars and his descriptions of his youth. She hummed his song to herself. Do wah diddy diddy, dum diddy do. We'll make our own sandwiches, wrap them in newspaper and eat them on the beach. We'll make flasks of tea. We'll hire deck chairs. We'll meet some nice, ordinary men who aren't perverts and go to the pictures. We'll queue up for the matinee. She let her mind linger on this. We'll hold their hands in the Ghost Train. We'll let them kiss us in the Tunnel of Love.

*

Jaz phoned Harm at Wesley's flat. 'Can I come over and use Wesley's computer again?'

Harm was suspicious. 'What for?'

'To send an e-mail. I want to use his fax. It'll only take a minute.'

Harm sighed. 'Jaz, why do I think you're not confiding in me? What's going on?'

'I'll tell you when I get there. Promise.'

'Wesley isn't here. He's gone to a conference. At the South Bank University.'

'A conference? What about?'

'It's called "Experiencing the 'I'. Psychosynthesis in Action." ' There was a pause and then a giggle. 'Don't ask.'

'Don't worry, I'm not going to. That Wesley's amazing. He's something else.'

Jaz arrived at the flat and gave a thumbs-up to the homeless penny whistle player in the doorway of the pork butcher. He didn't respond. He looked depressed. She dropped fifty pence into his hat.

Upstairs in the flat she was just in time to catch the news headlines. She held up her hand to silence Harm. 'Just let me see this, will you?'

There was film of Cabinet members leaving 10 Downing Street and getting into a waiting line of cars.

'Watch this,' said Jaz.

As the cars pulled away it was possible to see policemen and onlookers and then an untidy crowd of photographers and journalists which broke into a run. Suddenly, in an instant, Jaz appeared.

Harm let out a small cry.

Jaz was shown, dashing ahead of the rest, pursuing, then gaining on the lead car as it slowed at the junction. She looked like a pint-sized autograph hunter.

'That was you!'

The picture on the screen reverted to the newsroom and the next item.

Jaz laughed.

'It was you!' Harm turned to Jaz, her eyes wide. 'What the hell are you up to, Jaz? What's going on? I've just had Trace on the phone. She's obeying your orders as usual. She's tracked down this VIP bloke in Whitehall – the one you think's the fat man's twin. Does this let me off the hook at the House of Commons?' Anxiously she drew on her cigarette, stubbed it out, lit another. Her hands were shaking slightly. She fired questions like bullets. 'This whole thing, it's like the movies. You better tell me more about what's going on. I don't like this. I don't like mysteries. I'm worried about Trace. What are you getting her into? When have we ever had secrets from one another?'

Jaz slumped into an armchair, still grinning but suddenly tired. 'Stay calm,' she murmured. She looked around. The room was even more untidy than the last time she'd visited. The sofa was a tussle of twisted blankets and pillows. Clothes, underwear and tissues were strewn around and there was a tottering heap of partially empty boxes which had held pizzas and Chinese takeaway. Dirty cups were everywhere, and an overflowing make-up bag, full ashtrays and Wesley's CDs, all out of their boxes, littered the floor. 'It looks like a bomb's hit this place.' She glanced at Harm. 'Although you're looking better.'

Harm sat on the arm of the settee. She was wearing an outsize black T-shirt and black and gold leggings. She flicked open a mirror compact and studied her face, applying more lipstick. She was heavily made up, but looked almost normal.

'How d'you feel now?'

Harm sighed. She stared at Jaz, as if not expecting any answers. 'I'm OK. More or less. I'm staying off work till Wesley gets back.' She folded away the compact, threw it on the floor and placed her hands on her hips. 'Are you going to tell me what's going on, or not?'

'Can I use the computer first?'

Harm nodded.

Jaz switched on the machine, pressed a few keys and composed a message to Charles Merchant. It said 'Please make sure Mr Merchant gets this. It's personal. It's about his long-lost, deceased twin brother. It's important that I speak to him.' She added her name and the number of her mobile phone, then sent the message via fax and e-mail, using the information provided by Trace. 'Can I have a wash now, Harm?' she asked. 'You can talk to me while I'm having a soak.'

Harm led the way into the bathroom. She drew down the window blind, put the plug in and turned on both taps. She opened a long-necked bottle and poured green liquid into the gush. There was an immediate billow of foam and a smell which was sharp, pungent and uplifting. 'Get in. I'll make you a coffee.'

Jaz breathed deeply and stepped out of her clothes. She turned off the taps and lay down gratefully in the hot water. She was caressed by bubbles. The scent was wonderful, like an unpeopled Scottish hillside.

She was reminded of another bath, years before, when she'd smelled this same out-of-doors, woodland perfume. She remembered lying in the vast, old-fashioned bath in her mother's house, taking deep, exhilarated breaths. Cardboard was stuffed into a broken window and the steam condensed in thick clouds in the freezing air. To her left was the ancient lavatory with its rusting cistern high on the wall. An expanse of scored, worn linoleum lay between her and the door. She felt the water warm through to her bones.

She was going to a party. Earlier in the day she'd been trudging through the fields, cradling an armful of frost-bitten turnips, when she'd heard the sound of an engine. Hurrying to the front of the farm, she'd seen a motorbike with a sidecar bouncing away down the rutted track. She ran inside and dumped the vegetables in the sink. Blow appeared in the doorway. He seemed flushed and happy. 'That was the curate,' he said. 'I don't know why, but he's invited you girls to the Sunday School Christmas party.' He paused. 'It's a disco.'

The twins appeared. They'd been listening on the stairs. They were wearing matching bobble hats and filthy outsize woollens over their nightdresses. Their bare legs and feet were stained with manure. 'We're not going,' they said in unison. 'We don't like Sunday school, or Monday school, or Tuesday school.'

'We don't like Wednesday, Thursday or Friday school, either,' added Mimosa.

'We don't like discos,' agreed Peony. 'We only like classic West Coast rock.'

Blow looked concerned. 'I said you'd go.' His voice was plaintive. 'I said you'd be pleased.'

'I'll go,' said Jasmine. She was excited. 'I've never been to a party.'

Blow built a big fire and pulled down the damper to heat a tankful of water. He led Jasmine upstairs. In the bathroom he put the plug in the old, cracked porcelain tub and turned on the stiff taps. Jasmine struggled out of her layers of clothing. She hadn't had a proper bath for years. Shyly, Blow produced something from his trouser pocket. It was a small foil cube with a picture of a tree. 'I took this from your mother's dressing table,' he offered. He unwrapped it and crumbled the white block into the water. The dense air was immediately filled with perfume. It was a thrilling smell – the scent of pine forests. Jasmine stepped out of her oversized knickers and Blow's hands stroked her chest and bottom before she slid into the sweet depths. 'I'll wash my hair,' she offered.

Later, wearing a torn, net party dress, stolen from the back of Lola's wardrobe, and a pair of elastic-fronted plimsolls, Jasmine drove Blow's car in the direction of the village. She was cold and Blow fiddled with the heater. She steered carefully, moving up through the gears. He currently owned a well-preserved Hunter GT which was perfectly tuned and smelled of leather and oil. 'I'm going to see a man about a car,' he said, as she pulled up outside the church hall. He climbed into the driving seat. 'Pick you up in three hours.' He squeezed her arm. 'Have a great time.'

Inside, Jasmine hesitated in the corridor. There was the sound of pop music and teenage laughter. The walls were painted a dingy cream and she stared at a notice-board which mentioned Girl Guides and the church roof appeal. There was a smell of Lysol and something else which Jasmine couldn't name. Instinctively, she felt it as piety, conformity, restriction. She knew she was in the wrong place. She went back outside. It was sleeting heavily and Blow had gone.

She forced herself to go into the hall. A man was

sitting at a table in the entrance. He wore a clerical collar and a leather jacket and had a pop singer's haircut. He gave her a big smile. 'You're very welcome,' he said. He handed her a leaflet. It was about a new Bible study group for young people.

Wordless, Jasmine edged inside. It was dark. At the far end of the room a semicircle of coloured lights haloed a man at a record deck. He spoke into a microphone but his words were distorted. He put on another song and waved his arms in the air.

A group of girls began dancing in the centre of the floor. All of them, even those as young as Jasmine, were wearing miniskirts, tight sweaters and clumpy shoes. Their hair was long, shiny and loose and they tossed it about as they swayed and twisted in the gloom. Boys wearing trainers and tracksuits stood around in groups, drinking Coca-Cola from cans and watching the girls.

Jasmine didn't know anyone. She had seen all this before, but only on television. She remembered that Blow had talked about a disco. A disco must be a dance. She realized her expectations of party games and paper plates with cake were both childish and misjudged. She retreated into the darkest corner, fingering the hard mesh of her mother's net dress. It was black and long, almost to her feet. It had a baggy sequinned bodice, cut low and trimmed with moulting feathers. It smelled of mothballs and ancient patchouli oil. Lola called it her Deep Purple dress, because years before she'd seduced a member of the band when she'd been wearing it. Jasmine knew now that it was ridiculous. She was furious with Blow, who had supplied it, telling her it looked all right. She felt like a clown.

Two girls walked by. They were wearing white jeans

and white tops which glowed eerily in the peculiar light. They glanced at Jasmine and sniggered. She felt tears spring to her eyes, but she blinked them away. Her rage was growing. She was angry with Blow for bringing her here, she was angry with the curate for inviting her, she was angry with her sisters for being more aware than herself. Most of all, she was angry with Lola because she was drunk and in bed and had never taken her to a party or bought proper clothes or told her about discos. I hate my mother, she thought.

She edged towards the door. Another group of leggy girls arrived. They had bare arms, shimmering tights and tinsel in their hair. They giggled together and pushed one another. As the curate handed them their leaflets, Jasmine slipped unnoticed outside.

It was snowing and there was a strong wind. The sky was dark, with no moon. She closed the door, extinguishing the music. On a building opposite, a pub sign swung and creaked, but the place was in darkness. There was a rush-rush of turbulent trees. The snowflakes swirled, fell, then melted on the wet road. No vehicles approached in either direction. Jasmine shivered, her canvas shoes soaking up water. The cold air struck her naked arms and chest like a blade, raising her stiff skirt like beetles' wings. She swore to herself and looked around. The curate's motorbike was parked off the road, half behind the corner of the church hall. She approached it, glancing about, then examined it. He's got a nice taste in bikes, she thought. It was a twenty-five-year-old Ariel Redhunter. It was well cared for, with unpitted chrome. She opened the sidecar and found a pair of leather gauntlets and a soft pouch containing tools. She slammed the door and turned her attention to the immediate problem.

Selecting a thin screwdriver she pressed it hard into the lock and tried to turn it. It was no good. She tried again and again, but she couldn't penetrate it far enough. She found a pair of pliers, then tossed the rest of the tools aside. She picked up a broken brick and smashed it down on the ignition. She yanked out the wires and joined them, using the pliers. She mounted the saddle and, with all her strength, tried to drive the kickstart down. She slipped and there was a searing pain as cold steel tore the skin off her ankle. She shut her eyes, and held her mouth tight to prevent herself crying. She was determined. Pulling hard against the handlebars, just able to reach, she repeated the movement. The engine rumbled, turned over, then roared. The sensation between her legs reminded her of sex. She put it in gear and turned the throttle. As the combo moved forwards, she changed up. Gathering momentum, she put on the gloves.

Speeding along the road, away from the village, straddling the big machine like a pantomime midget, Jasmine became unaware first of her arms, then her shoulders and then her neck. They froze. Her feet and knees were numb. Her face was a stiff mask and the moisture that leaked from her half-shut eyes turned to ice. A strand of hair cut into her cheek but she was unwilling to leave go of the controls. She took the bike up to top gear. The engine was well maintained, responsive. On a straight stretch she checked the speedometer. She was doing eighty. The combo bounced and roared, following the dipping and soaring arcs of its yellow headlamps as they illuminated hedgerows, stone walls, telegraph poles. With a swerve and a shower of stones she turned onto the track to the farm. The bike climbed the steep slope, willing and still lively.

Lights glimmered in the distance signalling the farmhouse. Three quarters of the way up, she stopped. To the right of the track, the land fell steeply away and below this, a rocky precipice scarred the hillside. She knew that at the bottom was a boulder-strewn stream and the lowest reaches of her mother's barren fields. She stopped and dismounted, the engine ticking over.

Jasmine had no real love of motorbikes and the curate had to be punished. She manoeuvred the machine near the edge of the drop, then she gathered four big stones and wedged them under the section where the sidecar and bike were bolted together, lifting the back wheels above the ground. She put the bike in gear and watched its rear wheel spin. She removed the petrol cap. Then she took off Lola's dress, lassooed it around the stones and dragged them away. The combo moved forwards, driving itself towards the drop. After three seconds, its front wheels found only air and slowly, reluctantly, it tipped. Jasmine ran to the brink and watched it bang and clatter, its crazy lights veering, jumping, blinking. Within moments it was lost to the cold north wind, the snow, the blackness of the night. She waited. She didn't hear it hit bottom, but after a few seconds there was a dull bang and a flash of flame.

The next morning, Jasmine lay under her blankets, her mother's muddy party dress on the floor by her side. Her ankle was hurting. The telephone rang. She heard Blow arguing and she tiptoed to the landing. 'OK then, you tell the police,' he said assertively. 'She's twelve years old. She's barely four feet tall. You really think they'll believe you?'

*

Jaz lay in Wesley's bath, savouring the warmth. Harm reappeared with a mug of coffee for her friend and a bottle of Bacardi Breezer.

'OK,' said Jaz, taking her coffee, 'listen to this.'

Harm sat on the toilet, her feet propped on the side of the bath, tipping the pink bottle to her mouth and smacking her lips.

Jaz explained again about her need to find mourners for Fat Andy. She mentioned Princess and the woman in Pimlico and how they'd both been unsatisfactory. 'The thing is, Harm, like I said before, a man's died and it's like . . . well, it's not nothing. See? It's simply not nothing. I'm sick of it being seen as nothing. I'm sick of no one caring. Something has to be done. It's up to me. And this bloke Charles Merchant has got to be his twin. He's physically identical. The trouble is, I can't get hold of him. He's like . . . he's inaccessible.'

'No one's inaccessible,' said Harm. She thought for a moment. 'You've got Trace in the Home Office, cleaning bloody toilets or something . . .'

'Making tea.'

'Whatever. You asked me the other day if I turn tricks at the House of Commons. You've asked both of us to help you.'

'You said you'd help me if you could. Does that still hold?'

Harm hesitated. 'I guess so. What do you want me to do?'

Jaz pursed her lips. 'I'll think of something.' She picked up a bar of soap and washed her feet. 'Thing is, he's not returning my calls or messages. It's like people are screening me out. I'm not getting through to him.'

'Could be his decision. Maybe he doesn't want to talk

to you, doesn't want contact with his past. Maybe he wants to keep his past sealed up, like in a box. A lot of people feel that way.'

Jaz considered this for a moment. 'I don't buy that.'

'Why not?'

Jaz paused. 'It's a twin thing. He was an identical twin. He'll feel something's wrong. He must want to find out what it is. They always do, they're psychic. I know about twins.'

Harm shook her head. 'Let it go, Jaz. This murder has made you nuts. What's the matter with you, anyway?'

Jaz continued. 'I grew up with twins and they made me feel left out all my childhood. Always together. In bed, the bath, everywhere. You asked one of them a question and they'd answer, "We think this . . . We want that . . ." They had one mind in two bodies. They were inseparable.'

'So you think he's got to be interested?'

' I don't know. Something's happened. I feel different. I've just got to do this. I feel as if for the first time in my life I've got something that I believe in.'

Harm snorted.

'Don't laugh.' Jaz sipped her scalding drink. 'I've been thinking about this a lot lately. This whole thing has changed me. I feel as if I've got a job to do, a responsibility over and beyond just looking after myself.'

Harm stared. She took another long swig from her bottle.

Jaz put her mug on the windowsill, submerged herself then rubbed shampoo into her hair. 'I mean, what've we got, the three of us? All we've ever been clear about is what we don't want.' She thought for a moment. 'That, and getting money.'

Harm considered. 'You're right. I want to make enough money to do exactly as I please. So that I don't answer to anyone. Do my own thing. Make my own decisions.'

'Don't you see, Harm? That's my point exactly. All we've ever been concerned about is our own survival.' She suddenly thought about Charles Merchant and his agenda for change. 'What I'm saying is, maybe there's more. Maybe we should be concerned about what we're doing for other people.'

Harm stood up. 'God, Jaz.' She put her empty bottle on the side of the bath and flicked her hand in a dismissive gesture. 'What are you on about? I spend my whole life doing things for other people. I'm an object who's used by other people, for heaven's sake.' She paused. 'I'm concerned about getting more for me. They want me, they pay. They'll pay enough and finally, in the end, I can escape.'

Jaz hesitated. She lay back and washed the soap from her hair, then sat up again. There seemed no reply to this. She knew Harm had missed the point, but she felt unable to argue. 'I owe it to Fat Andy,' was all she could offer. 'I'll get this sorted, I promise. I'll get it all fixed. Then we'll go on holiday. We'll go on holiday and everything will be . . . it'll be . . .'

'It'll be what?'

Jaz stood up. Water cascaded from her small frame. Her fists were clenched. 'I don't know. We'll go to Weston-super-Mare and it'll be . . .'

'*What?*'

Jaz took a deep breath and stepped out of the bath. She thought of Blow again and his nostalgia for a simpler world. 'It'll be like . . .' She nearly said the words Cortina crazy. She thought for a moment. Blow's song came into her mind. Do wah diddy diddy, dum diddy do. 'I don't know. Everyone will have a smile on their face.'

Harm handed her a towel. 'Oh, yeah?'

Chapter Eighteen

Later, Harm fried some eggs and made sandwiches with tomato ketchup. 'I still can't see the point of causing all this trouble for yourself,' she said. She hesitated then handed Jaz her plate. 'You may not like this, but I phoned the ginger boy from the garage. I had a chat with him.' She paused nervously and lit a cigarette, then immediately extinguished it. She sounded guilty. 'I was worried about you.'

'You did *what?*'

Harm was clearly on thin ice. 'Trace said he'd been looking for you. That he was concerned. She gave me his number because he's been trying to find you. I remember you said you'd gone off him, but I told him you were coming here. He cares about you, Jaz, and he seems a very nice person.' She paused. 'I know you like being independent and everything, but we thought . . .' She stopped.

Jaz put down her sandwich. There was a silence. The atmosphere was tense. 'Who? Who are we talking about here? Who thought what exactly?' Her voice was cold. She waited a few seconds. 'Well?'

'Trace and me.' Harm spoke quickly. 'We discussed it. We never realized the fat bloke was such a good influence. He looked after you, didn't he? And you were more relaxed when you were with him. Less wired. Less driven. We thought maybe that's what you need. You know. A boyfriend.'

Jaz jumped to her feet and grabbed her jacket. 'Are you nuts? I don't want to see him. He's one of Vinny's boys. Fuck, Harm, why are you screwing things like this? I told Trace I never wanted to see him again!'

Harm looked anxious. 'I'm sorry. It's just that he seems . . . sweet. You know. Caring . . .'

'He was a shag. Have you got that? He was nothing. How would you like it if I started telling your fucking punters your address? Some of those weird, kinky ones? Just how would you like that?' Jaz was very angry. She was shouting. 'I can't believe you've fucking done this. What's fucking happening? You told him I was coming here? Are you mad, or what?'

'Stop swearing at me, Jaz.' Harm started to cry.

Jaz pulled on her jacket and made for the door. 'I'm out of here. And you tell that Pete to go fuck himself.'

Jaz slammed the door as she left. Below, the homeless man had disappeared but the pork butcher greeted her cheerily as he locked up his shop. She ignored him. It was growing dark outside and the sky was streaked with red. The air was still and warm. She kicked a can into the gutter. As she approached the Lotus Cortina she saw someone alongside it, leaning against a street sign. His long, thin legs and casual ponytail were unmistakable. It was Pete. He was reading a folded newspaper and his posture indicated he'd been waiting for some time. He hadn't noticed her.

Jaz swore at length under her breath. She stepped behind a parked van. This is too much, she thought, I don't believe this. She crossed the road and hid in a doorway. She put on her sunglasses and looked around. Ronnie and Reggie were probably staked out somewhere, waiting for her to make a move towards the car. She imagined Vinny, his mouth a thin line, clicking the joints of his small, hairy fingers, waiting in a Mazda in a lay-by, his Japanese air conditioning turned on, expecting his phone to ring. Stay calm, stay focused, she thought. On impulse, she pulled the mobile from her pocket and dialled his number.

It was answered. 'Vinny Stasinopoulos speaking.' His voice was even higher and more effeminate than usual. He sounded stressed.

'Companero?'

'Jaz?'

'Vinny, you lousy slimeball. Just tell your ugly gorillas they've lost me. I'm out of there by miles. I'm way off base. I'm in Milton Keynes. I'm in Tavistock. I'm in fucking Doncaster.'

'Jaz? It is you? One moment . . .'

'Fucking Doncaster. Right?' She hung up.

The street lamps came on and the rose-pink sunset wash was eclipsed from the evening, replaced by the usual city glare. Two young boys sauntered past. 'Got a light?' one of them asked, trying to sound hard. He was the same size as her.

Jaz stepped backwards. She felt the money in her pocket. 'I'll give you a hundred quid for your jacket and cap.'

The boy sniggered.

'I mean it.' She pulled out her money, thumbed through the notes and proffered a bundle. 'Now. Just do it. Do it now or forget it.'

He tried to appear in control. Whistling, he unzipped

his nylon jacket and handed it over. He removed his cap. In a sudden gesture, he grabbed the cash.

'Now piss off,' muttered Jaz.

The boys melted away.

She pulled on the garment, over her own. She looked at the cap. They were both blue and white and bore the words 'Toronto Blue Jays'.

The street was almost deserted. Pete still leaned patiently, reading, picking his ear. A wino raked through a rubbish bin, talking to himself. A bus went past, almost empty, followed by a taxi cab.

Jaz fastened the jacket higher than her chin. It smelled of cigarettes and sweat. She twisted her hair and covered it with the cap, pulling the front down low. She walked up the street, away from the Lotus Cortina at a fast pace and turned a corner into an alley.

Suddenly, she felt a pressure against her back. Her breath was forced out of her chest. She toppled forwards, aware of two pairs of feet behind her. A heavy, rough cloth smelling of petrol was thrown across her head, obscuring her vision. Strong arms encircled her, hurting her, then she was lifted off her feet. 'Let her have it!' she heard. She tried to scream. She struggled. She heard a car pull up and realized she was being tipped sideways and bundled inside. She struggled and kicked until a heavy weight pressed her down. Someone was sitting on her. Her cheek was pressed against leather. She fought desperately for air.

Chapter Nineteen

Jaz's mind swam into consciousness. I must have passed out, she thought. She took a deep breath. Her mouth and nose were now free but the air smelled bad. She became aware, slowly, that she was in a car and she was tied up. Her ankles and wrists were bound tightly and her hands and feet were numb. The motor throbbed, idle, its gears in neutral. It was dark and she was alone. She had a sense of being inside a building. She blinked and squinted at the illuminated numbers on the dashboard and to the side, the tiny flash of red that meant the security was engaged.

She tried to turn around. The tail lights illuminated the brick walls of a confined space, the back of a metal door. She was in a small garage. You bastard, Vinny, she thought. You evil fuck. I'm in a lock-up. She struggled against the twine which tied her.

The car spluttered an instant, then resumed its rhythmic judder. She concentrated on the dash. There was a tank full of petrol and the windows were all open an inch. Already, the air was thick and heavy. She squirmed and wriggled but she was trussed like a dead bird. She was drowning in exhaust fumes. Her captors had left her here to die.

The realization made her cough. She gagged and

choked. Her lungs wanted to explode. She twisted and thrashed and sweat broke out on her brow. She was light-headed. Lying on her back and raising her legs, she swung her feet over the passenger seat. The toes of her trainers thumped against plastic as she tried to locate the ignition key. From this position she could see nothing but the roof of the vehicle. She attempted to use the steering column as a guide. Failing, her feet awkwardly tied together, she kicked out wildly. There was a sudden burst of noise. She froze in surprise. The reception was poor but it was a man's voice. She'd turned on the radio. Without meaning to, she listened. Hearing his muffled but reassuring tones, she relaxed. Her brain was turning sleepy. Her muscles, starved of oxygen, were suddenly unwilling to move. The man was making a speech. It was the Home Secretary. Jaz recognized his soft, Northumbrian burr. 'Homelessness and destitution are the scourge of our cities,' he said. 'Hopeless, demoralized individuals, frequently young, have completely lost their way.'

We've lost our way, thought Jaz. We're hopeless and fucking demoralized. She forced herself to think. I've got to get out of here. Unless I get out of here, I'm a goner. With a big effort, she kicked again. Her shin hit something hard and her shoulders began slipping off the back seat. Her neck felt like it was breaking. With each breath, her brain was foggier. The air was now poison, like pure vapourized gasoline.

'Directionless,' he continued, 'they lie around our streets, begging, untidy, frequently intoxicated . . .'

The words had a sense beyond their meaning. They were seductive. Jaz eased backwards. Her feet dropped back to the floor. Again, she stopped struggling and slumped sideways. Intoxicated, she thought. The car seat felt welcoming – her head seemed to sink into it and then sink still further. She wanted to sleep, to drift, to lie still. Her body felt leaden, her mind cloudy with gas. She couldn't resist. The man's voice was calm, measured. Jaz thought it was the most beautiful voice she'd ever heard. The words blurred and became mere sounds. Their gentle resonance seemed in time with the car's heartbeats. I'll just lie here, she thought, I'll just lie here and go to sleep. It's peaceful here. She had a sense of spinning, then floating.

Suddenly, she was aware that the man's tone had changed. For some reason, he was angry. Jaz pulled herself back into consciousness. She forced herself to listen. He was haranguing his audience. What was he telling her?

'We are not, I repeat not, prepared to tolerate this. This situation is a criminal waste of resources. It squanders our education system, it drains our health service. It is a waste of the gift of life itself.' He paused. 'This government needs to act and I can assure you, it will act. We will gather, we will unite, we will stand up, we will confront this evil . . .'

The Home Secretary was excited now. Jaz remembered being overpowered, dragged into the car. Let her have it, someone had said. That bastard Vinny. Her old fury welled up. That murdering son of a bitch. She struggled to sit. We will gather our strength, confront the evil. Just like the man on the radio had told her to. 'We will not rest until we've won . . .'

Something was glinting on the floor. The air was too foul to gulp so she held her breath. She slid onto her belly, manoeuvred her head downwards and picked up the heavy object in her teeth. It was a tyre lever. Stay calm, she thought. The cold, metallic taste, along with her anger, somehow cleared her mind. Stay focused. With new energy she shoved the lever between her knees and rubbed her wrist bindings against its chipped metal edge. I'm out of here, she thought, you fucking bastards. I'm not staying here to die. We will not rest until we've won. One strand of twine broke, then two. She felt life flowing back into her hands. She unravelled the rest then shook her arms. She unfastened her ankles, lunged forwards and struggled into the driver's seat. She slammed the car straight into reverse and stamped on the accelerator. It leaped backwards and smashed against the door. There was a crash, a tinkle of glass, a groan of metal. The engine roared. She jerked forward a couple of feet then reversed hard again. She looked over her shoulder. The door bulged and buckled, coming off its hinges. She backed into it a final time and it gave way, bouncing and catapulting out into the road. Vinny, you evil shite, she thought, I'm not ready to die. I'm not wasting the gift of life itself. She almost smiled. Stay cool.

The Home Secretary, in agreement, concluded his speech. 'We will go on, and then we will go on!'

Jaz backed the car into the street, winding down the window. We will go on, she agreed. The outside world flowed around her like sweet wind. She coughed, retched, doubled up, spat, coughed again. She filled her aching lungs. She rammed the gears into first and pulled the car round. She'd driven one of these before. It was a Citroën Xantia. That's strange, she thought. It's not a Mazda. Vinny must be desperate. He's buying in extra help.

Chapter Twenty

Jaz looked up the street. She was disorientated. She also had a sense of déjà vu. She put both down to carbon monoxide poisoning. There was no traffic and it was night. The air was still warm and motionless. She looked at her watch. It was two a.m. She leaned over the steering wheel, fighting nausea. She massaged her wrists, then her ankles. She felt in her pocket. She still had her roll of money. A group of Asian youths walked by on the other side of the road. They looked at her curiously, but passed without comment, circling the damaged door in the road. She saw an all-night grocer's, an Indian video rental shop, a swiftly moving grey cat. There was a smell of foreign food. A black cab went by, its 'For Hire' sign extinguished. It was then she remembered. Shit, she thought, I really have been here before. I'm not imagining things. She clenched her fists. The cobbles had been recently covered in tarmac, the buildings were even more dilapidated than before, but it was the same place. She'd been brought here by a weirdo called Keith, five years ago. She'd been just sixteen. He'd parked his two-tone Zephyr in one of these lock-ups. A Mark II, she remembered. Spotless chrome. Highline. Canary yellow over cream. Then he'd taken her to an old cinema, showed her films and threatened to kill her. He said he was going to put her body on a bonfire.

Jaz opened the car door and was sick in the road. How could Vinny have known, she kept thinking as her stomach heaved and expelled its contents. How could he possibly have known? She wiped her mouth on her sleeve. Stay calm, she told herself, but she felt anything but calm. She was shaking and full of fear.

Stay focused. I am focused, she told herself. She turned on the lamps full beam and revved the engine until it screamed. Her feet were juddering on the pedals. Her knees knocked together. Keith's smiling face seemed to gaze at her through the windscreen. She hadn't thought about him seriously for a long time. She remembered his Millwall anorak, his small pointy teeth. He's been locked away, she reminded herself. The posse of tramps beat him senseless in the cinema after putting out both his eyes. He was taken off in an ambulance and ended up at the Old Bailey where the judge threw away the key. She hadn't given evidence. She'd stayed out of it, not wanting to be involved, but he was convicted anyway. Broadmoor. Indefinite period. She shoved the gear lever forwards and stepped on the accelerator. The car lurched and took the corner on two wheels. There was a bright flash as metal hit stone, a clatter as the broken rear bumper disengaged, a stench of burning rubber and the roar of the abused engine as the car took off like a rocket.

Jaz felt she was taking control. She drove at high speed, bursting through red lights, racing into roundabouts, junctions, right-hand bends. She scattered a band of revellers, her hand hard down on the horn. She forced a taxi onto a pavement, swerved round roadworks, sped illegally up one-way streets. For reasons she couldn't understand, she headed towards Peckham. When she got to the estate where she'd lived with Fat Andy, she squealed to a halt in front of the flats. There was no one about. She looked up at the window of the room she'd shared with him.

In an instant, she was back inside. She was standing by Andy's body touching his cold, lifeless hand. She remembered it had felt like wax on the point of setting. She had drawn away her own hand, repelled. She had stared at his neck. It was open, like a vagina in a pornographic magazine.

She shook her head, trying to dispel these images. She looked at her watch. It was still the middle of the night. She left the key in the ignition, the driver's door wide open, the attention-seeking radio on.

She felt better. She jogged off in the direction of Camberwell. First there'll be joyriders, she decided, sixteen-year-olds, skiving off school in the morning. They'll spend the day hotrodding around the estate practising their handbrake turns. Then, after dark, their younger brothers will use it to ram a sports goods shop on the High Street, smashing the plate glass. The shop will be looted and they'll drive off with their haul of stolen Air Max trainers, Kappa jackets and Adidas popper pants. Later it'll be abandoned and the hyenas will arrive. This will be the fathers and uncles. First to go will be the stereo, then the wheels. The engine will be stripped down quicker than Pete could do it. Quicker than Andy could have done it. Someone, unaccountably, will decide to make use of the seats. By the next morning it'll be an unrecognizable shell and some little kids will set it on fire.

*

Jaz sat in an all-night café near Ruskin Park listening to the conversations of three elderly black men who'd come off night shift in St Thomas's hospital. They were eating breakfast. She still felt sick and drank two mugs of hot, strong tea. It was very early. She took out the mobile phone and tried Charles Merchant again, on his various numbers. There was no reply and she didn't bother leaving more messages. She was still frightened. She turned to the overweight, cockney proprietor who wore a greasy white coat and a collapsed chef's hat. 'You remember that guy, a few years ago, in the East End who was killing homeless girls and putting them on bonfires?'

The man pushed back his hat and scratched his head. 'Can't say I do, darling.' He grinned. 'Jack the Ripper?' He was making sandwiches for the lunch-time rush. Despite his fat, short fingers, his chopping knife moved at the speed of light. He called over to his regulars. Cheerfully, he repeated Jaz's question.

'Have they let him out?' she enquired.

The three men turned around and smiled at Jaz. 'Fred West?' replied one.

'No man, he was down Devon. Or was it Somerset? Or Gloucester? Fred West. He hung himself. She means Dennis Nilsen. He didn't put them on bonfires. He flushed them down the pan.'

'No, not him,' said the third. 'This was another one. Out east. Stepney way. He was killed by vigilantes. Hell's Angels.'

Jaz gave up. They remembered nothing. She nodded politely, stood up and left. She ran swiftly to London Bridge and got on a train. She was worried about the car.

*

As she walked from Shepherd's Bush station to Wesley's flat, it started to rain. The air was hot and humid and the sky grew so dark it was as if dawn hadn't broken. Large drops fell straight down and bounced on the pavement. Within seconds, Jaz was soaked. This isn't English rain, she thought. There was a smell of wet dust and the traffic swished by listlessly. People huddled in shop doorways, their thin summer clothes sticking to their flesh. The Lotus Cortina came into view. Jaz sprinted towards it. It was undamaged and gleaming, but the water was no longer running off its bonnet in wormy droplets. She was relieved. It needs a polish, she thought. Poor thing. Its front grille and quarter bumpers greeted her like a wide grin. She stroked its pale roof. There was a piece of sodden paper on the windscreen. Jaz picked this off, got into the car and closed the door. Her sports bag was still on the back seat. She unfolded the disintegrating sheet and saw the blurred signature 'Pete'. His words, however, scrawled in felt tip, were unreadable. The ink had run together in purple streaks. She opened a window, made a ball of the note and threw it outside.

I've got to be very careful now, she thought. She remembered Keith again. Get real. It wasn't him. He's locked up and safe. It was that bastard Vinny, and he tried to kill me. I nearly died. She pressed her chest. The pain was still there as well as a curious tightness which was the result of the gas.

She took out the mobile and pressed Vinny's number. He didn't answer. She left a message. She forced herself to sound light, even jolly. 'Hey, companero? Jaz here. I'm just checking in. The Citroën's stripped in Peckham. I'm still here, fine and dandy, and I'm not fucking finished with you yet.'

The car started without effort. She drove past Wesley's flat. The penny whistle player was sheltering with two *Big Issue* vendors. She wondered about visiting Harm and trying to make it up with her, but decided it was far too early. Harm never got up before eleven.

The relentless downpour drummed on the roof and the wipers beat time slavishly. It was the first occasion she'd driven this car in rain. She felt secure in its familiar interior. Her wet clothes were steaming up the windows and she turned on the blower. She increased speed. Five and a half J wheels, she thought to herself. Michelins. There was no problem with grip on the bends but the leaf springs sometimes made the back end skippy. She slowed back down to thirty-five, concentrating solely on the car. Servo-assisted brakes. Fat Andy said they were responsive but they needed to be respected in the wet. She remembered seeing him in Vinny's repair shop with a high pressure airline, blowing clouds of asbestos dust out of the rear drums. She'd stepped back, worried about her lungs.

The rain started to come down even heavier. It was a wall of water. The more cowardly cars pulled up on verges and pavement kerbs. The road ran like a river and the noise inside the Lotus Cortina was deafening. Two small boys, almost naked, ran up the rushing, flooded gutter, screaming with joy.

Jaz thought of the twins. With one hand, she smoothed out their creased photo on the passenger seat. She remembered a heavy rainstorm on the farm when a broken gutter on the gable end had sent a cascade of water into the yard. Peony and Mimosa had raced in and out, cradling their pet duck, first removing their shoes, ankle deep in mud, then their coats, then their cardigans and dresses, then their underwear.

She ploughed on slowly, her wheels churning up waves that washed against the underside of the vehicle. Fat Andy had taken off the old underseal when he'd done the restoration. She made a mental note to check below for rust. When all this is over, she thought again, I'll give this car the service it deserves.

After a few minutes the rain eased. The traffic became dense and slow and the sky cleared. It was all at once sunny and hot again. Outside, the world began to steam. Jaz switched off the wipers and the blower and everything was curiously quiet. She sat in a jam. She took off the nylon bomber jacket and threw it in the back. She put on her sunglasses, avoiding the curious and admiring glances of other drivers. The mobile phone rang.

It was Trace. She was in a payphone and she sounded agitated. 'Jaz, you won't believe this. I've got the sack! This spotty bloke with a wig and tweed jacket's just been down from personnel. He said I'm a security risk.'

'What's happened?'

'I've not been paid, that's what's happened.' She broke off. Jaz could hear her voice muffled as she talked to someone else. 'Jaz, I'm going to take the money from the trolley. There's thirty pounds here in change from the teas and snacks. My friend Shirley says take the lot and scarper. She says she'll cover for me. She says she's never known the like.' Trace was excited and upset. There was more muffled conversation. 'She says the wig man has never been that abrupt with anyone before . . .'

'Tell me what happened,' Jaz interrupted.

Trace paused to collect her thoughts. 'Well, I did exactly what you said. Honest. Exactly as you said.'

'Go on.'

'I went into the fat bloke's office with tea and biscuits, although they weren't ordered. A china cup for the NTG. Top floor. Chocolate biscuits in silver paper instead of plain. Sugar in a bowl, milk in a jug. Not those little packets. I did it all right. I did it properly . . .'

'Get on with it.'

'He was in there, standing next to a filing cabinet. I just walked in. "My friend wants to talk to you," I said to him. "About your twin brother." I gave him his tea on a tray. He put it on the desk then took three biscuits and put them in his pocket. "She wants you to ring her. Write her number down," I said to him.'

'Did he do that?'

'No. He just stood there and sort of stared. He looked surprised. Then he turned around and walked out the door. I followed him but he'd disappeared. He didn't say a word. It was dead weird. I went back to my trolley downstairs and an hour later, what happens? I get the sack. It must have been him. He reported me. I don't know what I did that was so terrible. All I said was . . .' Trace was beginning to sound tearful. 'It's just so unfair . . .'

'Never mind,' said Jaz, trying to be reassuring. 'You might get back in at the Grand Banana.'.

At that moment, Trace's money ran out and she hung up. As Jaz stared at the phone in her hand, inching along in the car, her foot poised above the clutch, it rang again. 'I'll meet you tonight,' said Trace. 'In the Planet Pizza. Where you were before, with the temp. Eight o'clock.' She hung up for a second time.

Frustrated by her lack of progress, Jaz turned down a side road. Poor Trace, she thought. She's upset and it's my fault. But it'll be OK. Very soon, we'll go to Weston-super-Mare. Me, Harm and Trace. She imagined a row of pastel-coloured guest houses with bright flowers in their front gardens, chintz sofas, china tea cups and plates of bread and butter. We'll go there, as Cortina crazy as can be. We'll have a good time and be happy and together again, just like we were before.

Jaz's mind kept returning to the harsh words she'd flung at Harm. She felt guilty and insecure. Life was too precarious to fall out with her friends. After all, she reasoned with herself, Harm was only trying to help. She was wrong, but her motives were pure. She dialled Harm's number at Wesley's flat.

The phone rang for a long time. Eventually Harm answered. She sounded sleepy.

'Harm? It's Jaz. Look, I'm sorry for blowing you out.' Jaz swallowed. She never found apologies easy. 'I'm sorry, right?'

Harm yawned. She didn't say anything.

'You listening? I've just said I'm sorry.' There was a silence. 'That's three times, now, altogether.'

Harm sniffed. 'It's OK.' She sounded non-committal.

Jaz's mind was buzzing. 'Listen. You remember you talked about that nutter in the East End who took me to that cinema a few years ago and threatened to kill me?'

'How could I forget?'

'They haven't let him out, have they?'

'Why?'

Jaz paused. 'I dreamed about him.'

'There's been nothing on the telly. Not while I've been off work. I would've seen it.'

'Thought not.' Jaz chewed the end of her ponytail. Several ghostly electronic voices echoed down the line.

She coughed. 'I know you think I should drop the Fat Andy thing . . .'

'Too right I do. I've never known you be so strung out, so driven, so bad tempered . . .'

'Harm, I've nearly finished. I'm nearly there. I've had a great idea. Two great ideas. I need your help.'

Harm yawned again. 'What time is it? God, it's early. What d'you mean by waking me up at this time?'

'Two ideas. Ready? I want you to come with me to see the man in the garage in Haringey. Be nice to him. You know, wear a short skirt, that kind of thing.'

Harm was suspicious. 'What for?'

'It's nothing dangerous. We'll just give him some information. A computer disk, that's all. He's a Mazda dealer. He'll use the disk to prove to the Japs that Vinny's crooked and Vinny will lose the Mazda concession. It's simple. Then it's bye-bye Vinny. No garage. No repair shop. No team of car thieves. He'll be finished. That'll be the end of the Vinny thing.'

'What about those gorillas? His bodyguards?' Harm was anxious.

'This won't involve them, I promise. We'll be nowhere near them. Or him. There's no danger.'

Harm thought for a moment. 'Why d'you need me?'

'He won't listen to me. My appearance is against me. I'm too small. He won't take me seriously.'

Harm thought for a while. 'All right, then. What's the other thing?'

'I still haven't contacted Fat Andy's twin. Trace tried but she's had no luck. You remember you said you had clients in the House of Commons? He's got an office there. Maybe you could get a message to him somehow.'

Harm sighed. 'I wish you'd drop it, really I do.'

'A few more days. I promise. Vinny'll be sorted. I'll have a mourner for Fat Andy. I'll have done it all. Then we'll go on holiday to Weston-super-Mare.'

Harm laughed. 'I saw something about it on the telly. It's . . . well, it's not Fuengirola.'

'It'll be brill. I'm really looking forward to it.' Jaz paused. 'Are you going to help me or not?'

Harm sighed and drew on her cigarette. 'Guess so.'

Jaz gave her the address in Haringey. 'I'll meet you at three, OK?'

Chapter Twenty-One

Harm arrived in Haringey in a taxi. It was very hot. She wore a skimpy white cotton top which was low-cut with hidden underwiring. Her cleavage was spectacular. Below, she had on a tight white leather mini-skirt and her legs were bare. On her feet were patent stiletto sandals. Jaz examined her face. The swelling had disappeared. Any faint bruising was now merged with her normal dusky colour. Below each plucked eyebrow, and on each ear lobe, she'd stuck tiny silver sequins. Her lips were thick crimson gloss and her braided hair was secured in a loopy bun.

The two girls went into the Mazda showroom. There was a smell of polish and new car interiors. A young man in a suit appeared. He stared at Harm as if she was an apparition.

'We want to see the boss,' said Jaz. 'Now. Immediately. No bullshit. Take us straight through.'

Still open-mouthed, glancing at Harm out of the corner of a nervous eye, he led the way to an office. He knocked on the door, gestured to two chairs in the lobby and ran off. They didn't sit down.

'Stay cool,' whispered Jaz.

After a couple of minutes the door opened. The owner looked at Harm, blinked, tried to appear composed, then smiled. He gestured for her to enter. 'What can I do for you?' he asked. His voice was practised in politeness. He seemed unaware of Jaz, as if she was a child. He sat behind his desk.

Harm grinned, showing the gap in her teeth. 'D'you mind if I sit?'

Jaz watched the manager force his eyes from her breasts to her face. He blushed. He was trying to be professional. 'No, please, go ahead.'

Harm sat down and crossed her legs. Her skirt almost disappeared.

He was a large man, about thirty-eight, overweight with a garish tie. His shirtsleeves were rolled up and his jacket was draped over the back of his chair. Two semicircles of sweat soaked below his armpits.

'Do you know Vinny Stasinopolous on the Isle of Dogs?' Jaz remained standing. She was abrupt, business-like.

The man turned to her. 'I know of him, yes. Not personally.'

'He's a crook. Bent as they come. I can prove it. You show the evidence to Mazda, they'll close him down. They'll pull the plug on him.' She paused. 'You'll have it all your own way up here, with this dealership.' She gestured towards him, palms upwards. 'You listen to me and you can take out the competition in a single stroke.'

He smiled automatically, tried to shrug, unsure of how to react. Then he looked into her eyes and realized she was serious. He was caught off guard. He had no pat phrase or cliché suitable to act as a reply.

'Are you interested in success?' Jaz went on. She held his gaze. 'Are you interested in making money?' She removed the computer disk from her pocket. 'I'm holding your future in my hand.'

The man turned helplessly to Harm.

She grinned again. 'Don't underestimate our little friend here. She knows exactly what she's talking about.'

'Er, what . . . what is it exactly that you have there?' He stared at the disk.

Jaz took a step forward and slid it into the disk drive on the computer next to him. She switched on the machine and pressed a few keys. Columns and rows of numbers appeared. The man took a pair of half-rim spectacles from a case and put them on.

Jaz picked up a pencil and used it to point to the screen. 'These are the Dutch accounts.' She tapped knowingly.

The man inched forward, interested.

'Look,' said Jaz. 'These are cars. Here's the original registration numbers and alongside are the new ones. The cars were stolen and given new identities. The new identities came from write-offs. All the details are here. Every single one. Model and engine numbers, colours. The next column is the date they were shipped. This column here shows how much Vinny's Dutch contact paid for them. Further on is evidence of these sums being deposited into one of Vinny's bank accounts.' She scrolled down the screen. 'It's all here. Look, these are the names, addresses, phone numbers and e-mail addresses of each of Vinny's shady associates in Europe. There's evidence relating to four separate illegal operations in four countries.'

The man's eyes began to gleam. His mouth twitched expectantly.

Jaz went to the end of the disk. 'This is the best bit.

It's a record of faxes and e-mails sent via the computer for a period of six months last year. They've been saved. They have the address of the garage, everything. The names of everyone involved at the place on the Isle of Dogs.' She slapped the top of the computer. 'This is watertight, mister. You can't go wrong with this. Get this to Mazda. Download it today.'

'It'll cost you three thousand,' chipped in Harm.

Jaz turned and stared at Harm, alarmed. She hadn't intended to ask for money. She looked back at the garage owner. He hadn't flinched. He continued to stare at the screen. 'Is this genuine?' he muttered, with difficulty. He sounded as if his throat had gone tight and dry.

'Of course it is. I stole it off Vinny myself.'

He stood up and took off his glasses. He adjusted the waistband of his trousers on his belly. He suddenly become more decisive. 'Right!' he said, looking from one to the other.

Harm took a damp cigarette from between her breasts and held it up to her mouth.

The man fiddled in his pocket, produced a lighter, leaned over and lit it for her. 'Three thousand? I'll get it.'

Later, giggling and shrieking and pushing each other, the girls climbed into the Lotus Cortina. Jaz drove and Harm counted the money again. There was three thousand in new fifties. 'I didn't even have to take my clothes off!' she exclaimed. 'Bloody great!'

Jaz wound down her window and put on her sunglasses. 'One man went to mow,' she started singing, unaccountably. 'Went to mow a meadow. One man went to mow, went to mow a meadow.' She laughed again.

'Harm, you must take half the dosh. I couldn't have got in there without you.'

'Nicking things and flogging things. It's your line of work, not mine. You keep it. You deserve it.'

Jaz remembered Trace's phone call. 'Fancy an Italian meal later?'

'Sorry, I'm meeting Wesley. It's back to the grindstone. It's the funeral directors and crematorium operatives conference at Earl's Court. Opening night tonight. He's got me a full schedule. It'll be a busy couple of days.'

At ten past eight, Trace still hadn't shown up. Jaz took out the mobile phone and rang Vinny.

'Yes?' he answered, sounding weary.

'Is that you, slimeball?' asked Jaz. 'My little companero? Guess what? Mazda's got your disk. The one Fat Andy pinched, with all your fucking European contacts. The one you killed him for.' She paused. 'Have a nice evening.' She hung up.

The waitress arrived and she ordered a pizza margherita, tomato salad and a Kaliber. At eight thirty, Jaz saw Trace's head bobbing behind a queue at the door. She beckoned and waved. Trace walked towards her, tall and gawky. She was accompanied, two steps behind, by the temp from Charles Merchant's office, who was still wearing her red blazer, but appeared less purposeful. Neither of them smiled. They sat down. Trace looked anxious and the woman had a guarded, impassive expression, as if she had no desire to be in their company, but would rather be on a train, returning to Malcolm in

High Wycombe. Unlike the last time, she pushed the menu away, declining food and wine.

'We've both got the sack,' said Trace.

Jaz looked at the woman.

She stared at the paper tablecloth. Her lips were tight.

'They know you talked to me?' Jaz was curious.

The woman shook her head.

'It's not that,' interrupted Trace, 'I think they're clamping down on temporary staff . . .'

'It's bigger than both of you,' said the woman suddenly. 'This is bigger than any little cat and mouse game you two have decided to play. There's something going on here. It involves at least two people at the highest level of government. It's to do with Charles Merchant's policy ideas and his new deal for Clean Cities. Something's happened which is holding things up. I know. I made . . . certain discoveries.'

'Why did you get the push?' asked Jaz.

Her reply was hasty and defensive. 'I sent two e-mails, that's all. Two e-mails to a lobby correspondent. Nothing directly incriminating. Next thing I know, I'm out on my ear. No references. I'm finished at the agency. I've got no job and my house is ransacked.'

'Oh, no!' exclaimed Trace, as empathic as ever. 'Really? I didn't know that last bit. I'm sorry . . .'

'I phoned my husband half an hour ago. He was out playing golf. Came home to absolute chaos. Nothing's been taken, no valuables. It's a warning.' She stood up. 'I've got to go.'

'Thanks for telling me,' said Jaz mildly. She wasn't sympathetic. She felt sure the woman had been observed pilfering documents. It never pays to get caught, she thought. Careless. There was nothing mysterious about her dismissal. Jaz looked at her. She wasn't really interested in her problems. Her mind was full of what she'd done today to Vinny.

'You stay out of this,' the woman warned Jaz. 'That's why I've come here with your friend tonight. If anyone asks, you've never met me. You never gave me money. Keep your distance. There's something dangerous in the air.' She pushed a piece of paper across the table towards Jaz. 'That's my contact at the House. He used to drink with Charles Merchant occasionally at their club. Apparently, they were at university together. I don't want it. I'm well out of all this.' In an instant, she'd disappeared.

'I think I'll have a pizza,' said Trace, staring at the menu. She hadn't been listening. She seemed unconcerned. Now that the woman had gone, she'd forgotten her. She was shedding her experience at the Home Office like a discarded skin. 'Have you got any money, Jaz? I didn't take the trolley money in the end. It seemed like stealing. I'm skint and I'm starving. The food in here smells so nice. Have you got enough for a deep pan vegetarian deluxe? And garlic bread? And a tiramisu?'

Chapter Twenty-Two

Jaz spent the night in the car in Lincoln's Inn Fields. She didn't sleep much. The near-death experience in the Citroën had made her nervous. She knew she should be anonymous and untraceable, but her enemies were cunning. Harm had promised never to speak to Pete again, but the thought of him made her jumpy.

Early next morning, Jaz went for a run. The exertion, combined with the soft light, the gentle murmur of London stirring from sleep, the faint breeze rippling the grey silk of the river – all of this made her happy. She jogged along the embankment, her hand pressed to her chest. The pain was still there, she decided, it still ached. She knew that if she concentrated hard and brought to mind the images of Fat Andy and Blow, then she could still feel sad and abandoned. However, her fury was ebbing. With each act of revenge against Vinny, the anger had shrunk. It was like closing windows against a storm.

Later, she drove east. She parked two streets away from Ronnie and Reggie's gym and approached it cautiously. At the back, there were no vehicles in the car park. The door above the fire escape was closed and padlocked. She walked around the front. The glass entrance was locked and barred with metal grilles. A notice in familiar handwriting was taped to the window.

It said 'Shut Temparrarily'. She stared at it, unable to resist a grin.

A passer-by stopped and spoke. 'Been closed a day or two,' he offered.

Jaz turned to him.

He was tall and black and wearing a football strip. He carried a Head bag. 'I got a letter.' He shrugged. 'Everyone got one. We're all going to another place, down on Commercial Road. It's better, as it happens. Try it. More machines. More staff.' He nodded and carried on his way.

Jaz got back in the car and headed south-east, down to the Isle of Dogs. As she approached Vinny's garage, she slowed. A huge transporter was parked on the forecourt and three men in yellow overalls were driving the brand new Mazdas out of the showroom and up its metal ramps. They're here, she thought. They didn't waste time. The space was already almost cleared. Two salesmen in suits stood by helplessly. They looked perplexed. One attempted to remonstrate, but quickly gave up. Jaz was cautious, but there was no sign of Vinny.

He's finished, she decided. She pressed her chest. Yes, the pain was definitely going. She turned into the alley behind the main building. The repair and body shops were a blackened shell without a roof. There was a lingering smell of burning, and sooty flakes drifted in the air. Jaz wound up her window, wrinkling her nose. A small boy rode a bicycle across the cobbles. She moved over to avoid him and he gestured obscenely. You too, Jaz muttered at him. You too, sonny. She smiled at the ruined buildings. And all the rest of you. You fucking bastards.

*

Jaz bought a bacon sandwich from a kerbside vendor and parked up beside the Thames to eat it. On the opposite bank, cranes dipped and swivelled. The Millennium Dome squatted like a bug, its thin insect legs at rest. Small, buzzing launches and tugs busied about. There was a squeal of gulls and a low, occasional boom coming from down river. Jaz had heard this sound many times, but couldn't identify it. It was too deep to be explosives, too irregular to be any kind of a warning. It was something mysterious, to do with shipping, she decided. Commerce. Trading. Work. It was something from the real world.

Her mind wandered. She recalled an afternoon on the farm when she was thirteen years old. It was towards the end of her time there, in April, but spring, always late on that inhospitable hillside, was more delayed than usual. The ground was hard, still frozen in sheltered places, and the weather had been unusually dry. The grass was sparse and any buds on the wind-damaged trees were brown and firmly closed. It was cold and dreary. The seasons held their breath. The countryside was bound in chains.

Jasmine trudged along, checking the sheep. She was wearing worn-out wellingtons and an old car coat of Blow's. Her hair was tousled and pushed inside her collar. She carried a hazel wand. The sky was patchy with broken cloud and a thin, reluctant sun touched the desolate fields. It glittered on the back windows of the hilltop farmhouse. There were no birds, except for a solitary crow, hovering above the chimney pots. Lambing was almost over. She'd managed it on her own. A few remaining ewes were still in the shed and she went in to water them. It was warm inside and dark with the smell of animals and hay. A shuffling alerted her. One of the sheep was giving birth. She stood alongside, watching the bluish-red slimy lamb emerge from its mother. Half-way, it stopped. The ewe moaned a little and stamped. Jasmine tugged on the lamb gently and it came away, plopping onto the straw. There was a smell of blood and dung. She knew immediately that it wasn't right. It had an odd, twisted shape and its face was tight shut. It didn't move. She picked it up and there was no breath, no pulse of life. It was deformed and stillborn. Jasmine put it to one side and went to a neighbouring pen. Here the sheep had twin lambs. She picked up one of them and carried it over, giving it to the unlucky ewe. The baby bleated for an instant, then began suckling, whilst the blank face of the bereaved mother showed nothing but resignation.

Leaving the shed, Jasmine tossed the corpse onto a pile of debris behind the abandoned stable. She heard an engine and spotted a Royal Mail van swirling in a hasty U-turn outside the front door of the house. It skidded, then tore down the track towards the road, hooting at Peony and Mimosa. Jasmine watched as it disappeared in the direction of the village.

Later, as the pale sun started to sink in the sky, there was the sound of an explosion. It was too low and too long to be gunshot. Then there was another. Jasmine hurried towards the twins. They were down the track, out on the ridge at the same spot where Jasmine had once sent the curate's motorcycle over the drop. She knew what they were doing. They were throwing bombs.

Peony and Mimosa had a pile of their mother's old wine bottles, a bucket and a siphon. One by one, they were filling the bottles with liquid from the bucket, then hurling them into space, where they took several seconds to plummet towards the boulders of the scanty stream. As each bottle fell they yelled a strange incantation. 'Un-tah, un-tah, billie rosie ply,' they called in unison. When it hit the earth, it shattered and a ball of flame rose eerily, before dying. Then there was a deep, dull boom. 'Yes-sah, yes-sah, yes-sah,' they called as the ghostly and terrifying disturbance rent the still air.

Jasmine watched them. She knew they'd mixed weed-killer with sugar and that the unstable concoction was very dangerous, but it was pointless telling them to stop. They were exorcizing their own private demons in their own determined way. They drained the dregs into the last bottle. Peony threw it and unlike the others it climbed high into the air. At that moment there was a scream. It came from the house. Jasmine turned and ran up the slope, the twins following. Behind them, the final bomb burst noisily in the dying afternoon. As they entered the yard there was a succession of wild calls from within. It was Lola.

Jasmine crashed into the kitchen, the twins hard on her heels. Lola was standing at the sink, the sharp carving knife aloft. Her stained nightdress was undone. In her other hand was a letter. She screamed again. The cry was hysterical, forced, over-dramatic.

'Put that knife down,' said Jasmine in an authoritative tone.

Lola turned and saw her three children. Her eyes changed. They had been dead and lifeless. Suddenly they went black, hard and full of something that Jasmine could not name. She screamed again and this time her voice was full of pain. It was a wail of hopelessness and despair.

Jasmine took a step forwards. Lola spun in a pirouette, wielding the knife. She slapped her letter down on the table. Glancing at its logo, Jasmine could tell it was from the bank. Her eyes fixed on her mother's face. There was a frozen moment when no one made a sound. The wall clock ticked and some embers shifted in the stove.

'Mam,' said one of the twins.

'Stop it, Mam,' added the other. They sounded scared.

Lola screamed again and with a strange twisting gesture thrust the knife in and through her long, tangled hair. A clump of it came away like a matted, dead creature. She threw this on the floor then dashed to her bedroom. The girls followed, to find her breathless, frantic, slashing the grubby sheets, the down-filled coverlet, the pillows. The overheated air was filled with a billow of fake snow.

Jasmine grabbed each of her sisters by the hand. She dragged them forwards. Together, they pounced on Lola, forcing her forwards onto the bed. Jasmine grabbed the knife. 'Sit on her!' she ordered. She ran into the hall, grabbed a bottle from the cupboard under the stairs and threw it onto the bed. 'Right, come on!'

The twins jumped down, linked hands and made for the door. Swearing under her breath, Jasmine bundled them into the hall, grabbed the key and locked the door from the outside. They leaned together in a huddle, panting. After a while, Lola started crying. They heard her pour herself a drink.

'Where's Blow?' whispered Peony.

'We need him,' agreed Mimosa.

'He's coming,' Jasmine assured them. She tried to sound normal. 'He'll be back. He'll sort her out.'

*

In the Lotus Cortina, Jaz's mobile phone rang. It was Harm. 'I've moved into a hotel in Earl's Court. Just for a while. Wesley's little place was making me depressed. It's called the Kyle of Lockalsh.' She sounded breathless. 'I've managed to get discount from the owner. He's a Scotsman, only he's from Birmingham. He's called Mr McTavish and he's very friendly. Plays the bagpipes.'

'Right,' said Jaz, her mouth full of food. She jotted down the address and telephone number.

'It's really handy at the moment,' added Harm, 'you know, business-wise. The Exhibition Centre's booked solid for weeks.'

Jaz swallowed. 'Harm, when you've got time, and if you happen to be in the vicinity of . . .'

'I know,' Harm interrupted, 'the House of Commons. I haven't forgotten. Charles Merchant. Check him out and tell him you want to talk to him.'

'I don't think you'll get to him, Harm. Honest. He's just not . . . accessible.'

'I'll try.'

Jaz sighed. 'I don't think he's into vice.'

Harm thought for a moment. Jaz heard her light a cigarette. 'What is he into? He must be into something.'

'Changing the world.'

Harm was silent.

'I'll tell you what. Try this guy.' Jaz gave her the name of the lobby correspondent supplied by the sacked temp the previous night in Planet Pizza. 'He's an old friend of Merchant's. He might help.'

There was a pause while Harm made a note of this. Jaz imagined her writing the name in biro on her wrist. 'By the way,' Harm added, 'our Trace is here.'

'Where?'

'This hotel, where I'm staying. She's living in, full board. I recommended her. She's assistant breakfast chef and relief waitress. She's got to wear a kilt.' Harm laughed. 'She's just been trying it on, looks a right dickhead. See you, Jaz. Bye bye.'

Later, Jaz drove over to Earl's Court. She found the hotel without too much difficulty and parked in the small space reserved for patrons at the rear. She was still hungry, so without checking in, she went to find a McDonald's where she ate a Happy Meal and drank Coke. Afterwards, she picked up her sports bag from the car and entered reception. The place had a mock-Highland atmosphere with tartan sofas and curtains, travel posters of Loch Lomond and a moth-eaten deer's head, with antlers, mounted on the wall. A tape played a keyboard version of 'Mull of Kintyre'. She rang the bell.

Suddenly, there was a menacing, low growl. Jaz took two steps backwards. A huge dog appeared from around the desk, its hackles raised. Her heart began pounding. She grasped her sports bag in front of her and held out a hand to fend it off. 'Go away,' she whispered. The dog's lips moved back revealing rows of enormous teeth. Saliva hung from its jaws. It was as high as her elbow with a chest like a barrel. It advanced towards her, its growl deepening.

'Rocky!' A man appeared. He was grinning. 'Rocky, come away!'

The dog glanced at him and wagged its tail. It looked Jaz in the eye conspiratorially, and its tongue lolled out in friendly greeting.

Jaz placed her bag on the floor.

Mr McTavish was burly and Scottish-looking with a

full ginger beard. 'Sorry about Rocky,' he grinned. 'He's an actor.'

Jaz smiled weakly.

'He went to animal drama school in Haslemere. Been on lots of telly. *The Bill*, *EastEnders*. He was quite a star, a while back. He's retired now but he still likes to tread the boards, so to speak. Trying to appear hard.'

'Mr McTavish?' Jaz picked up her bag and motioned towards the register. She was relieved to discover that he was wearing ordinary clothes. There was no sign of his bagpipes. She checked in, making sure she had her own bathroom, and he handed her a key.

Upstairs, she found that her room was tiny and plain, but very neat. There were framed prints of Ben Nevis and a small plaster bust of Robbie Burns. She closed the curtains, undressed and using the complimentary bath gel washed her underwear, socks and T-shirt, hanging them on the towel rail to dry. She showered and changed her clothes. She flicked through the TV channels, but there was nothing worth watching. She dried her hair then opened the curtains and looked at the Lotus Cortina, parked below at the back. She decided it too was in need of attention. One of its quarter bumpers was at a slightly low angle. Also, it wasn't absolutely clean. She borrowed a couple of towels from her bathroom. Back downstairs, she found Trace hoovering the lobby.

'Where's your kilt?' she asked.

Trace grinned, switching off the machine. 'I don't wear it for cleaning, it's for waiting on tables, at breakfast. I've got a tartan hat as well. It's quite nice. The man's just been showing me how to make real porridge.' She yawned. 'He says it's an art rather than a science. What're you doing here?'

'I'm a guest. I just passed the initiation test. I've met the dog.'

Trace laughed.

'I need to wash the car. Can you bring me out a bucket of hot soapy water in about fifteen minutes?'

Outside, Jaz rummaged in the boot. Fat Andy had kept it well supplied. She sprayed WD40 behind the chrome bumper bolts and worked the nuts free. Using a small hydraulic jack, placed on a block of wood for height, she pressed the bumper back into position and fastened the nuts. She walked around the car. The rubbers around the front and rear windscreens were dull and grey. She scrubbed them vigorously with T-Cut then ran the cloth over the glass. Andy had told her not to do this, but she'd always found it brought them up to a shine.

Trace arrived with the hot water. 'Can't stop hoovering,' she said. 'I'm trying to make a good impression.'

Using a hotel towel, Jaz splashed the suds onto the rubbers and washed off a layer of slime. She then soaped the windows, rubbing them thoroughly, before washing and rinsing the whole car. The bird shit she'd picked up in the East End had burned into the cellulose paint. This was upsetting, but, she decided, hardly noticeable. Using the second towel, she dried the car quickly, avoiding smears. She then applied Turtle Wax to the rubbers and they came up black and glossy. Using a soft cloth from the boot, she polished the entire vehicle, buffing up the chrome until it dazzled. When she'd finished, the car shone like a jewel. She stood back, satisfied. A young man walking on the pavement behind the parking area called out, 'Brilliant nick.'

Jaz nodded to him, pleased. Replacing the tins, cloth and jack in the boot, she came across a chrome pipe. She realized it was a tail pipe extension which Fat Andy had never fitted to the exhaust. She shoved it on and tightened the nut. It looked shiny and neat. She walked around the Lotus Cortina several times. 'I love you, baby,' she said.

Chapter Twenty-Three

At seven o'clock, Jaz leaned against the mantelpiece in the small TV room off the reception area, watching *Wheel of Fortune*. The atmosphere smelled of pipe tobacco and air freshener. She picked up a small plastic dome and shook it. Inside, fake snow whirled around a garish model of a highland piper, standing alongside a bright blue loch. The words Fort William were inscribed on the base. She replaced it and turned towards the outside door as it swung open then banged closed.

Harm came in with a client. She saw Jaz and pulled a rueful face. She held up all her fingers twice to indicate that she would be twenty minutes. She pressed the buttons on the lift. Jaz noticed her companion was sombre. He wore a dark, old-fashioned suit and carried a hat. He's probably an undertaker, she remembered.

Her mind leaped to an image of Fat Andy in an outsize coffin. He was muffled in a white shroud, his hands arranged as if in prayer, but blood, insistent and bright, soaked through the draperies at his neck. His face was waxen, his eyes closed. He looked very unlike the corpse in the flat in Peckham. Somewhere in the background, in shadowy, religious darkness, hymns were playing. She pressed her chest. 'Andy,' she muttered aloud. He didn't seem real.

Jaz went to find Trace. She was drinking tea and eating ginger snaps in the kitchen with Mr McTavish. At seven forty-five the three girls met in the lobby. They linked arms and, giggling, piled out into the street. 'Let's get the Lotus Cortina,' suggested Jaz. 'I've just cleaned it. It looks fab.'

'Let's go up west,' agreed Trace.

Harm relaxed in the back, the inflatable cushion behind her head, smoking and dabbing her armpits and chest with French perfume. Trace fiddled with the radio, tuning into a disco beat. It was a Celine Dion dance mix. She shook her arms and shoulders. 'Let's go clubbing,' she suggested. She rapped on the dashboard. 'Party! Party! Party!'

Driving up the Brompton Road towards Knightsbridge, Jaz felt excited. She put on her sunglasses. The car purred contentedly. Its steady rhythms were almost sexual. Her feet caressed the pedals in an effortless heel-toe. Her left hand grazed the gear change like a lover. She felt her skin prickle and her heart thud with anticipation. This is just like old times, she thought. This is the old days. In a place in her brain beyond the jangle of the car radio, she heard Blow's song. Do wah diddy diddy, she hummed to herself. Dum diddy do.

Harm reapplied her make-up and sprayed her dreadlocks with glitter.

'Watch the headlining!' said Jaz. 'Bloody hell!'

Trace sang along to the Bee Gees, getting the words wrong. Complaining of the heat, they both took their tops off. Jaz glanced at them appreciatively. Harm now wore a black silk bustier embroidered with pearls. Trace sported a blue cotton crop top which revealed her long, concave stomach above the waistband of her jeans.

All the windows were open and the warm evening carried both the smell and the light of the city. The sun dropped low over Hammersmith. This is why I came here, Jaz thought, this is why I ran away. For a moment she forgot Fat Andy, Blow, Vinny and the rest. She was more than happy.

They parked in Soho and Jaz disabled the Lotus Cortina. Harm rummaged in her bag for some dangly earrings and put them in. Trace took off her shoes and left them in the car because the pavements were hot and smooth. Two young beggars approached them warily. They were wearing Manchester United strips and their faces were tanned. Harm gave them a pack of cigarettes.

They walked up Old Compton Street, holding hands. Harm waved cheerfully at a group of gay friends. They went into a bar. Harm ordered cigarettes, strawberry daiquiris, vodka tonics and a jug of lime and soda for Jaz. She paid with a hundred-pound note from inside her bra. 'This is undertaker's money,' she told the barman. 'This is proceeds from a brass-trimmed oak coffin.' He smiled at her with tolerance and bewilderment. He gave her a free bowl of tortilla chips.

After half an hour they moved to a café, then a pub, then another bar, then another. Harm and Trace's taste for exotic cocktails seemed to grow. They ordered blue fizzy ones, purple fruity ones, and tall ones decorated with plumage and pomegranate slices. Jaz stuck to soda water. At ten o'clock, in Wardour Street, they jostled into a Greek restaurant and squeezed around a window table. Here, they mopped up oily feta cheese, olives and sweet tomatoes with hunks of warm bread. Harm called for Retsina. She was quite drunk and loud but the waiters encouraged her. They brought her a leather bottle with tassles, on which was inscribed, incongruously, 'A Present From Barcelona'. She stood up, trying to drink by throwing back her head and squirting the wine into her mouth. It went everywhere, soaking her hair and bare shoulders. Trace shrieked and Jaz pretended to cover her face with her hands. It seemed like the whole restaurant was looking at them, grinning. A Greek man with an accordion came across to their table and Trace clapped her hands in time to his folk tunes. When he finished she shouted, 'Do you know this one?' She started singing huskily. The song was something about innocence, guilt and road rage. Harm latched onto this and started up the chorus with Trace, her voice a high, trilling soprano. The waiters started singing, the accordion player picked up the tune and the people on the next table started swaying, holding up their glasses, chanting in unison. The atmosphere was electric.

Jaz stood up and made for the toilets. As she passed through the tables she heard tipsy couples in the queue join in the song. Smiling, her mind full of the catchy chorus, she turned a corner and then stopped in her tracks. Her heart missed a beat. Tucked away out of sight, behind a dense artificial palm, his head propped in his monkey hands, sat Vinny. Instantly she moved out of his line of vision. Stay calm, she murmured. She took in the scene. He was oblivious to the hilarity at the other end of the room. He was wearing an oyster linen suit with a diamond tiepin and his hair was slicked back and oily, but he seemed tired and worn, his face grey, thin, lined. The deep channels down the sides of his cheeks looked gouged out by tears. He appeared shrunken and ill.

He was accompanied by a teenage boy of such

exceptional beauty that Jaz at first thought he was a girl. He had black curly hair, jutting cheekbones and a full, pouting mouth. He was wearing a matador's embroidered bolero. He looked bored. Vinny was talking, his voice low, his gestures intense. His companion hid a yawn behind his elegant hand.

At that moment, Vinny's mobile rang. It lay on the table next to his sleeve. He stared at it anxiously.

Jaz stood very still, smiling. He thinks it's me, she thought.

Vinny picked up the phone and seemed relieved. He issued a couple of orders and stood up to leave. Jaz stepped into an alcove. Vinny dropped two banknotes on the table and emerged. 'I'll see you later, back at the flat,' he said to the boy. Jaz noticed his wandering, squinty eye. He smoothed the sides of his head with both hands and nodded to a waiter. 'Put it on my account,' he said. He disappeared out the door.

Jaz watched the boy. Stay focused, she thought. He picked up the tenners then dropped them again. He seemed unhappy and resigned. She approached his table and sat down. He glanced at her and hastily pocketed the money. He looked suspicious.

'Hi,' Jaz grinned. Stay cool, she told herself. 'You don't remember me, do you?'

The boy shook his head. She noticed his eyes were large and brown, his lashes long. His strong cleft chin was unshaven.

'We met at a wedding or something,' she lied. 'Not long ago. Why don't you come and join me and my friends?' She gestured towards the noisy end of the restaurant. 'We're just relaxing after a hard day's work.' She stood up and he followed through the narrow spaces between tables. 'I'm Jaz, by the way.'

If the name meant anything to him, it didn't show in his face. He was impassive. 'I'm Pedro,' he offered, 'but you can call me Trevor.' He had a cockney accent.

Jaz pulled over a chair for him. Harm and Trace had stopped singing and the accordion player resumed his normal repertoire. Harm called for another bottle and another glass. The restaurant was even more noisy and crowded than before. In the opposite corner, a birthday gathering fired party poppers and opened champagne.

'This is Trevor,' Jaz said. She introduced her two friends.

Trace regarded him with interest. 'I like your Spanish waistcoat,' she said.

Later, standing outside in the street, a faint breeze warming their skin like a kiss, the foursome discussed what to do. Harm leaned drunkenly against Jaz, smoking a cigarette, her arm round her neck. Trace held onto a road sign with Trevor politely supporting her elbow. 'Lessgo dancing,' she suggested. 'I wanna dansh with this bullfighter.'

In the end they went to a club below the pavement, somewhere off Piccadilly. Harm knew the doormen and they got in for free. She pointed at Jaz. 'She's twenty-one,' she insisted.

Inside, Harm ordered grappas, Pernods and a jug of watery Sangria. 'Come on,' insisted Trace, dragging Trevor onto the dance floor. They disappeared in a press of bodies and flashing lights.

'Trace seems quite keen on him,' Jaz shouted above the music.

'She never follows through,' Harm replied. 'Just you watch.'

At about four a.m. Harm was asleep, snoring, lying out on the red plush bench seat. Trace was slumped forwards, her head in her arms, in a puddle on the table.

'Know Vinny well?' Jaz asked Trevor.

'Quite well,' he answered tonelessly. He looked at his watch. 'Shit,' he muttered.

'You late for Vinny?' Jaz persisted.

'Yeah.'

'Why don't you forget fucking Vinny and come home with us?'

Trevor tried to laugh. 'No can do.'

'Owns you, does he?'

He scowled and stared into his half empty glass. He looked at Jaz. 'Who are you anyway?'

'I'm Vinny's bad fairy.' She paused. 'I'm trouble.' She gave him a hard stare. 'I'm Jaz.' She stood up and delved in the front pocket of her jeans, then drew out a wad of money rolled in a brown envelope. It was the pay-off from the Mazda garage in Haringey. 'There's three thousand here. You can have it if you come home with us. If you dump Vinny. That is, permanently.'

Trevor's big eyes opened very wide.

Jaz peeled off the envelope, revealing a bundle of notes. 'You want it or not?'

He reached out his hand tentatively.

Jaz pulled the mobile phone out of the pocket of her denim jacket. She pressed a few numbers and waited. A lazy ballad played on the jukebox. 'Vinny? Companero?'

She gave a short laugh. 'Jaz here. Listen, you slimeball. I've got someone with me who wants to speak to you.'

She passed the phone to Trevor. He looked uncertain. He held it in the palm of his hand, as if unsure what to do with it.

'Go on, tell him.' She put the money on the wet, crowded table next to Trace and moved it a little towards him.

'Vin?' Trevor said. 'It's Pedro. I'm in a night club.' There was a silence as Vinny responded. He grimaced as if in pain. 'That's the thing, Vin. You've got it there, mate. I'm not coming back.' He looked at Jaz and shrugged. 'No, I'm not. That's just how it is. Sorry and all that.' He leaned back in his chair, scratching his balls, feigning unconcern. Jaz imagined Vinny remonstrating in his ear. Trevor picked up the money in one hand, weighed it in his fingers, fanned it, then in a deft gesture, folded it. 'And you,' he said firmly into the phone. 'You too, mate.' He switched off the phone and handed it back to her. His expression was unreadable. He pocketed the money. 'Right,' he exclaimed, his face brightening. He stood up. 'Let's get these two sleeping beauties into a cab or something. Where are we headed, exactly?'

Chapter Twenty-Four

The next day, Trace had a bad hangover. She offered to clean the hotel windows as penance for missing the breakfast rota. Mr McTavish said it was just as well he liked her, or she would have been out on her ear. Jaz, without confidence, took Rocky for a walk. Harm and Trevor each stayed in their rooms all day. Harm slept with her phone turned off and Trevor watched Sky Sports.

Jaz tried to ring Charles Merchant a few times, with no success. She drove over to the Chelsea mews and talked to the porter again. He was sympathetic but unable to help. She left another note then sat around waiting outside in the car for a few hours. He didn't show.

She opened her sports bag and took out her photo of the twins. For the umpteenth time she noted how their angel costumes did nothing to disguise the wilfulness in their eyes. Peony looked ready for anything. Mimosa held onto the hem of her sister's dress, clearly trying to suppress a giggle. I miss you, Jaz thought. She wondered who had cast them in the nativity play. They hardly ever went to school. That teacher, she decided, whoever she was, clearly had a sense of humour.

Jaz went back to Earl's Court, dispirited. She wished she'd given Trevor less money. She'd been over-generous, but then she hadn't known if he'd rise to the bait. She still had some of Elvis's cash, but it was leaking away. She didn't want to be facing penury. She'd had too much of that when she'd arrived in London. Bread-line poverty was difficult. It presented far too many challenges.

She knocked on the door of Trevor's room. She didn't intend asking for the money back, but she wanted to be sure he was keeping his side of the bargain. 'Come in!' Trace called.

Jaz was surprised to see Trace sitting in the window, swathed in a towel, having her hair cut. Trevor stood behind her, holding a silver tail comb and scissors, snipping at her shapeless wet locks. He looked confident and professional. He tilted her head forwards. Jaz noticed that he was tall and lean, wearing Levis and an acid yellow shirt which made his perfect complexion glow.

'Trevor's been telling me his life story,' Trace said. 'He was a trainee stylist.'

'I should never have left.' He paused, snipping carefully. 'Soho was a bad scene,' he added. 'Old men with old dicks. Everybody on the make.'

Jaz looked around. The room was full of half unpacked clothes, CDs, and hairdressing magazines. She was relieved. He'd moved in. 'You're not going back to Vinny then? It's bye-bye, Soho?' She hesitated. 'Bye-bye, Pedro?'

'Bye-bye, Pedro,' echoed Trace.

'I've made up my mind.' He bent his knees and manoeuvred his scissors around Trace's ears. 'I'm going back to hairdressing. I've got creative urges. I'll learn tinting and perming.' He said this without irony.

Jaz realized in an instant that he was a simple soul. Despite his sensational beauty, he was straightforward and honest, like Trace. He wasn't devious. He would keep his word. This meant Vinny was now without his lover. Vinny had lost everything. She turned to leave the room.

'There's been some people here looking for you,' said Trevor.

She stopped in her tracks. 'Who?'

'First of all, a tall guy. He looked familiar. I think I saw him working as a mechanic at Vinny's garage.'

'Oh, him!' Trace snorted. 'He's always after her!'

'Was it him, Trace?'

'Dunno. I didn't see him. Did he have ginger hair?'

'Ginger ponytail. I was careful, Jaz. I always am. I told him you'd left. He said he'd seen the car and jumped into a taxi and followed it. He'd tried every guest house in the road.'

Jaz felt a rush of panic. Pete had betrayed her so often. 'So he knows I'm here.'

'No. I was quite clear. You were here, but you'd left.'

'Is he going to go back to Vinny and tell him where you are? Is Vinny going to come and get you?'

'No, calm down. Definitely not. He didn't know me. I'm not sure he's ever seen me before. I just remember him, in his overalls. I was waiting for Vinny in the office once, watching him under the bonnet of a car. I thought he was sexy.'

'He is,' agreed Trace, 'but silly old Jaz thinks he's a wanker and a liar.'

Jaz gulped. 'Who else was here?'

'Two heavy-looking guys.'

'Oh, my God. Brothers? Bald heads? Flash clothes?'

'No . . .' Trevor thought for a moment. 'One was fair, the other dark. They were wearing jeans and bomber jackets.'

'Well, who the hell were they?'

'No idea. I didn't like the look of them. I told them I'd never heard of you.'

The next morning, Trace served Jaz with porridge in the dining room. She was wearing her Scottish outfit.

'Take your hat off a minute,' suggested Jaz. 'Let's see your hair.'

It was very short and stylishly rumpled.

'Fantastic,' said Jaz enthusiastically.

'He's good,' agreed Trace. 'He trained with Antoine at Fabio's.' She frowned, puzzled. 'Whoever that might be.'

'Are you two . . . you know . . .' Jaz waggled her hand suggestively.

Trace blushed. She picked up her tray. 'Sort of . . .' she offered, very embarrassed. 'We haven't done anything yet. You know. Apart from kissing. Trevor says we have too many wounds which need time to heal.'

Jaz nodded seriously.

'He says we should take time to get to know each other. To establish absolute equality and trust.' She repeated these words like an innocent child.

'I'm sure he's right.' Jaz stirred her porridge vigorously. 'You should speak to Wesley.'

Trace went back to the kitchen.

Mr McTavish appeared. 'Excuse me, madam.' His eyes twinkled. 'You're wanted on the phone.'

It was Harm. Jaz heard her yawn. 'Is it really morning?' she asked. 'I'm at the House of Commons with Wesley. I've had quite a heavy night.' She sounded tired. 'Turns out, would you believe, Wesley actually knows this lobby correspondent person. I mentioned it to him, and then, when I was through with my last client, I found them together in the bar. They used to play squash or something. We've all been having a drink.' She yawned again. 'They've just been discussing how their jobs are exactly the same.' She sighed. 'It's all a bit above my head.'

Jaz was excited. 'Have you asked him about Charles Merchant?'

'Not really, but he's prepared to see you.'

'When?'

She heard a muffled exchange. 'He's going to get his head down for a bit. He'll meet you at two. His house.' She gave Jaz the address.

Jaz parked the Lotus Cortina at the end of a row of polite, tiny Victorian houses in Lambeth. She glanced along the terrace. The restored shutters, the immaculate paintwork, the cultivated postage stamp gardens all suggested gentrification. So close to central London, these bijou residences were probably all worth a fortune.

She tugged the old-fashioned bell-pull of number fourteen. She took off her sunglasses. A small, dapper man answered the door. His automatic smile was immediately replaced by a look of astonishment.

'I think you're expecting me,' Jaz said.

He stood aside to let her in. He was only two or three inches taller than herself, and clearly surprised by her appearance.

Jaz had seen this consternation many times. She knew he assumed she was very young. He thinks I'm about fourteen, Jaz thought. She decided to gamble on this misconception. If he thinks I'm a child, she reasoned, he won't find me threatening. Stay calm, she thought. He'll think I'm innocent and this will help me get to

Merchant. 'I'm glad you've agreed to see me,' she chirped in her pretend, little-girl voice. She sounded slightly breathless. 'I won't take up too much of your time.'

They went into the living room. It was sparsely furnished in bachelor style, with leather furniture, a good hi-fi, black wooden shelving units and matching coffee table.

'Would you like a drink?'

'Got a can?'

'Coke? Lemonade?'

'Anything.'

He disappeared and returned with a glass, a can of lemonade and a large gin and tonic for himself. 'Sit down.'

Jaz sat on the sofa and studied him for an instant. Stay focused, she told herself. He was about forty-five, very boyish, with an unexceptional face and a neat, undersized body. His fair hair was thinning and he wore gold wire glasses. He seemed uneasy.

'Wesley's a friend of yours, is he?' she said, making conversation.

He shrugged and smiled, then took a big swig from his glass.

Jaz poured her drink and tossed the can into a metal waste bin. There was a noisy clatter. She decided to get straight to the point. 'I want to speak to Charles Merchant. It's no big deal, but it's a personal matter. I need to see him face to face. Half an hour, fifteen minutes, maybe, that's all, then I'll disappear. I've not been able to get in touch with him. I was hoping you might be able to help.'

He was staring at her.

'As I said, it's a personal matter. It's nothing to do with his job, Home Office policy, any of that kind of stuff . . .'

He removed some newspapers from the sofa and sat down next to her, even though there were two empty armchairs. He smelled of gin and scent. Jaz resisted the urge to slide along the seat, away from him.

'Can you help me or not?'

He gave her a sideways glance. 'That depends,' he muttered. 'Wesley told me you're a friend of . . . what's her name? Harm?'

'That's right.'

'Are you . . .?' He hesitated. 'In the same line of work?'

Jaz felt a lead weight sink to her stomach. Stay cool, she told herself. She wasn't going to prise anything out of him for free. She thought about getting up and walking out, but then she remembered Vinny, his unattractive squint, and how close she was to ending this whole damned thing. I'm nearly there, she thought, I'm just about finished. It's nearly over. Very soon I'll be on holiday. She imagined the repetitive wash-wash of the sea, the clean air, the ribbed, glittering sand.

She took a deep breath. 'Yes,' she lied.

He leaned over and cautiously put his arm around her.

'How old are you?'

'Old enough,' she piped childishly. Let's get it over with, she thought. She stood up, grasped his hand and pulled him to his feet.

Wordlessly, he led her to the bedroom. He closed the curtains and turned to face her in the gloom.

Quickly, she took off her clothes and climbed in between the bed covers. He joined her, fully dressed. 'I never expected . . .' he whispered, 'I never expected anyone like you.' He sounded as if he might burst into tears. 'You're the answer to all my prayers . . . That is . . . Yes . . . sorry . . . I mean that. My prayers.'

Jaz lay motionless, trying to get the measure of the situation. 'What were you expecting?'

'Oh, you know, someone older. Harder. Too much make-up. I hadn't intended . . . I hadn't intended . . .' He was unable to speak.

Jaz remembered Mike, with the red Mondeo in Cambridge. He seemed like a long time ago. She had destroyed his illusions by appearing too experienced. She turned towards the lobbyist but didn't touch him. 'You hadn't intended to do this?'

'No.' He sighed and ran his hands over her body. They felt nervous and cold. 'Just let me hold you,' he whispered. He cradled her in his arms. There was a silence.

Jaz felt the hardness of his erection inside his stiff cotton trousers. His shoulder bone dug into her cheek. 'What d'you want?' she said eventually.

'Nothing,' he murmured. 'Nothing.' Then he volunteered, 'I haven't seen Charles for a while. We used to meet regularly for a drink and a game of chess. No one's seen him socially, as it happens. In fact, no one's seen him at all, recently, apart from his Home Office lackeys. And, of course, his boss. But it's only odd to those who don't know him well. I'm not surprised. You see, the policies are so controversial . . .'

There was another silence. Jaz listened to a clock ticking. She rolled over onto her back and his hand slid onto her stomach.

'So controversial, Charles won't be taking any chances. There are some very powerful interests, deeply upset by what he wants to do with his new deal on Clean

Cities. Property developers. Financiers. Charles could ruin speculative office and city leisure development at a stroke.' He paused. 'At a stroke! I mean, what an idea!' He took a deep breath. 'Can you imagine all those lofty billion-dollar buildings, with their glass and steel atria, their fig trees and modern art . . ' He sighed, ' . . . those Roman inspired plunge pools, those air-conditioned, high-tech, twentieth-century palaces – all filled up with dirty riff-raff and drunken tramps?'

Jaz digested this question but didn't reply.

'He's lying low. I know him. He doesn't want to be pestered by journalists and lobbied by interest groups. There's even talk of him being in some kind of danger. He doesn't want to be deflected or side-tracked or bothered. He's busy, determined. He'll wait for the storm to break, weather it, and then move on to the next stage of his vision. The Home Secretary will deflect the flak and absorb the shock – that's what he's good at. They both know the party and the country are behind them. Charles knows what he's doing. He's masterminding this thing. And at the moment he's just keeping an even lower profile than usual.'

Jaz hesitated. 'So he's not seeing anyone?'

'Not even me. And I've known him over twenty years.'

'So you can't help me?'

'I'm advising you to wait.'

Jaz felt her body go tense. 'I can't wait.' She brought to mind her vision of the Lotus Cortina bowling down the M4 in the inside lane, heading for Weston-super-Mare with Harm and Trace, a picnic hamper and an antique plastic transistor radio blaring tunes from Manfred Mann. 'I can't wait,' she burst out emotionally. 'That's just it. I've got to finish this thing. Now.'

'Shush, shush, little one.' He leaned over and she could smell his gin and tonic breath, his armpits. 'Shush.' He stroked her thighs.

'I can't wait,' she repeated, more calmly.

His fingers moved between her legs and deftly penetrated her. He was insistent but gentle. 'You know who you're just like?' he murmured. 'My little sister. Little Jennifer.'

So that's it, Jaz thought. Oh, well. She turned back on her side, facing him, without dislodging his hand. 'Help me, please,' she whispered. 'You know how I rely on you.'

He propped himself up on one elbow, gently withdrew his fingers and licked them.

Jaz's eyes were now accustomed to the dim light in the room and she could see his face.

He smiled at her dreamily. 'OK. Listen to me. He has a Turkish bath twice a week. Tuesdays and Thursdays.' He mentioned an address in Southwark. 'It used to be a public wash house. Fabulous tiled interior with great gushing taps. Upmarket now, of course, private. He's there at seven a.m., twice a week. Never varies. Don't you dare tell him I told you.'

'Thanks.'

There was another long silence. Jaz was unsure what to do. 'You'd better go back to your own room now,' he murmured, forgetting himself.

Without speaking, she got up and got dressed. He stayed in bed. She went downstairs and let herself out of the front door.

Chapter Twenty-Five

Worried about her unexpected visitors at the hotel, Jaz decided not to return immediately. She phoned and spoke to Mr McTavish. 'Let my room go,' she told him, 'but tell the others I'll be back soon.'

'Are you all right?' he asked kindly.

'Yes. Why?'

'There were a couple of men here, asking for you. Trev said they'd been before. We didn't like the look of them. I told them I'm the proprietor and that you've never stayed here. I was most insistent. Rocky came out and he earned an Oscar.' He chortled. 'I hope I did the right thing.'

'Thank you. I don't want to cause you any trouble.'

'What's living without a little trouble?'

'I'll be back soon, OK?'

She decided, as a precaution, to spend the night in the car, parking it in another of Fat Andy's safe havens – an enclosed area reserved for medical waste at the back of Guy's Hospital. It was completely out of sight of the road. She felt nervous. I'll just get this over with, she thought, I'm almost finished, then I'll be away.

An occasional porter, topping up the bins with plastic sacks, regarded her without interest. She watched a constant plume of smoke from an incinerator inside the building and tried not to think about body parts, disease and death. She tried not to think about the corpse in the flat.

Before dark, she got out of the car, did some warm up exercises then went for a brisk run around the narrow, Dickensian streets, knowing that this exertion would help her lose consciousness.

She awoke at five o'clock. The windows were cloudy with condensation. A refuse wagon roared into the space alongside her. The noise and the smell were overwhelming. She wound up her window. Men in orange overalls swarmed over the bulging bins.

Her limbs were stiff, and because her inflatable cushion had slipped onto the floor during the night, she had a crick in her neck. She climbed into the driving seat feeling bad-tempered. She backed out and parked in a narrow bay which said 'Consultants Only', but it proved to be impossible to get back to sleep.

At six thirty she set off for the bathhouse. It was on the edge of a high-rise estate. She got out, wearing the Toronto Blue Jays bomber jacket and cap, traded in Shepherd's Bush just before she was kidnapped. She pushed her hair out of sight. She wanted to look male. She was about to disable the Lotus Cortina when a small boy, no more than nine years old, smoking a cigarette, sauntered up to her. 'Can I watch your car, mister?'

Jaz understood that to refuse would probably mean damage to the paintwork, at the very least. 'Watch it or wash it?'

'It don't need no washing. What's it anyhow? Antiques Roadshow?'

Jaz placed her hand on the roof. She took a deep breath. 'This, you ignorant little shit, is one of the most respected saloon sports ever made. This is a Mark I, twin cam, Lotus Cortina. But you wouldn't know it because you're a sad, small person and you understand nothing. I feel very sorry for you. That's why I'll give you this.' She fished in her pocket, pulled out a two-pound coin and flipped it in his direction.

He caught it with the minimum of movement, blowing a triple smoke ring.

Jaz smiled. 'Now piss off.'

He stamped his cigarette butt under his heel and regarded her steadily. 'Mister, what I am, right, is a man of my word.' He paused. 'Yes? You've paid me, so to speak, so I'll guard this useless heap of old junk as if it's really worth something.'

'Suit yourself.'

Apprehensive about her appearance, Jaz approached the baths and went inside. There was a sign for the Turkish suite, pointing downstairs to the basement. She read the information. Tuesdays and Thursdays were 'men only' sessions. She paid at the desk without being challenged and descended the marble staircase. So far so good, she thought. I wonder what the dress code is.

At the bottom were a pair of heavy velvet curtains. She took a deep breath and went through. She found herself alone in a small room. It was thickly carpeted and luxurious, with heavy floral wallpaper, a battered leather sofa, an arrangement of gilded salon chairs and a hookah. On the walls were ornate framed mirrors and pictures of partially clad maidens bathing or reclining in classical settings. Neatly folded newspapers were available in a rack. She passed through and down a corridor which opened into a large, blue tiled space. It was warm and damp, smelling vaguely of sandalwood. The ceiling was a serrated, coloured dome. A horseshoe of curtained cubicles elegantly circled two huge marble slabs. An overhead fan turned slowly. Jaz thought of sultans, harems and jewelled, curved daggers.

A black man with bulging cheeks, wearing a white buttoned jacket and trousers, dozed next to a pile of fresh linen. Jaz coughed quietly. He opened one eye and handed her two towels and a rubber wristband with a key.

'Istanbul,' she said thoughtfully, looking upwards.

'Constantinople,' he corrected her, in a deep, lazy voice. He didn't question her gender. He closed his eye.

She went into a cubicle which contained a bed, chair, basin, mirror and a wooden locker. I could live in here, Jaz thought. On a table were a hairdryer and a white hand towel spread open with a razor in a sterile wrapper, a shaving brush and soap. Behind the door hung a silk dressing gown. She took off her clothes, keeping on the ridiculous cap to hide her hair. She wrapped herself in a towel, then peeped around the curtain. The attendant still slumbered and there were no other customers.

She lay down on the bed and slept for a short while. It was soporific, with the drip-drip of plumbing in the distance and the quiet whirring of the fan.

She awoke to the sound of voices. Her heart started beating very fast. She opened the curtain a chink. Two naked men walked past, their towels draped over their arms. They were followed by a third. Jaz gasped. The vast back with its folds of flesh, the sagging buttocks, the rope of tawny hair caught roughly in an elastic band – they were almost as familiar as her own body. She nearly cried out. He's identical, she thought. It's incredible. He's Fat Andy's double. It's the same freakish cloning as it was with Peony and Mimosa.

Jaz waited a couple of minutes, then followed, clutching her towel above her nipples. She walked down another corridor and felt the temperature rise. The tiles under her bare feet became hotter. She opened a door and gasped. She tried not to cough. The room was dense with steam. She breathed in steam. Steam filled her eyes. The door swung shut and she sat on a wooden bench. It was almost impossible to see in the thick mist. She took deep then shallow breaths, unsure of the effect of the wet heat on her lungs. She started sweating.

The three men faced her. She pulled down the peak of her cap and looked out from under it. Her eyes adjusted to the gloom. Charles Merchant was in the middle, but his companions sat close on either side as if they were bodyguards. She studied him. His jowls were sunk onto his chest and his eyes were closed. His penis dangled below the edge of the bench and above it hung his big belly. He had the same sparse chest hair as Fat Andy, the same ham-like hands spread out on his knees. It's incredible, Jaz thought. The only difference seemed to be his expression. Fat Andy had an alert, cheerful look. He was always smiling. This man was careworn. His mouth was pulled down as if his mood was permanently morose. His colour was poor, probably from spending too much time indoors.

The four of them sat for a while. Jaz felt she'd never been so hot in her life. Sweat ran down her face. She licked her lips and they tasted of salt. I'm melting, she decided. Suddenly, Charles Merchant raised himself to his feet. He wrapped a towel around his waist and lumbered towards a second door. Instantly, the two others followed. Jaz waited a minute then pursued them. Beyond, the next room was well lit and dry. At first it was a relief but after a few seconds it was even hotter than the steam room. The three men had resumed their positions. Charles Merchant seemed again to be asleep. Jaz thought of deserts, parched trees and the bones of long dead animals.

After several moves between wet and dry, dry and wet, Jaz felt both sleepy and debilitated. Finally, she discovered Merchant spread out on a marble slab next to the cubicles. She stared at him, trying not to think about Andy in a coffin, a mortuary or on a pathologist's table. This was difficult, because the still body of Merchant looked like a monstrous corpse. The black attendant had woken up. He came over and began kneading the fat. The minders had disappeared into the sitting room, each wearing a silk dressing gown. Jaz went into her cubicle. She put on her robe and rubbed her head and neck with a towel. She looked in the mirror. Her face was bright red and the oversized garment and baseball cap looked very eccentric together. It's now or never, she decided. She emerged and stood next to the masseur.

Charles Merchant was face down, his tangled hair covering his features. Jaz watched the black hands pummel and vibrate his off-white flesh. 'Mr Merchant,' she said with fake confidence, 'there is a private matter I need to discuss with you. It's nothing to do with your job.' There was a slap-slap and a small groan. Jaz waited, breathing in the scent of exotic oil. 'Well?'

With difficulty, the fat man raised himself on his elbows. His hair hung forwards hiding his expression, his face. The masseur stepped aside and re-oiled his hands. 'I'll meet you tonight in Chelsea,' Merchant whispered. His voice was urgent and hoarse. 'You know the address. Eleven o'clock. Now get out of here. Quick.' He collapsed down again and the black man resumed.

Jaz slipped into her cubicle, triumphant.

Outside, the car had gone. Her elation evaporated and was replaced by a feeling of panic. Several women walked by with pushchairs, leading school-age children by the hand. She set off on foot towards the estate, cursing her own carelessness. That little bastard, she kept thinking. His legs were barely long enough to reach the pedals. She wandered around pointlessly, overheated from the baths, with the sun beating down and the windless air giving no relief. She asked a couple of teenagers if they'd seen the Lotus Cortina but they only shrugged and stared. Suddenly, she heard a voice. 'Hey mister! Hey! Over here!'

She turned. The small boy was sitting on a wall, enjoying another cigarette. As she approached him he winked and gave her a thumbs-up.

'Where's my car?'

'I moved it, so to speak. It's all right.' He jumped down. 'Come with me.'

She followed his jaunty, self-important little body down through an avenue of municipal trees, past a burnt-out community centre and through a courtyard reserved for overflowing wheelie bins. The Lotus Cortina was half hidden by shrubbery and refuse. It was undamaged.

Jaz felt in her pocket for the keys.

'There were these geezers much too interested,' the boy said, lighting up again. 'Walking round, staring.'

'What sort of geezers?'

'No one from round here.'

'Did they go into the baths?'

'Yep. Shortly after you.'

'Three of them?'

'Yep. The other one, he stayed outside, staring at your car. Walking round it. Kicking the tyres. Interested. Who knows why. Then he got back into this bloody great limo they'd come in and started talking on his phone. I thought to myself, this twat's up to no good, so to speak. I thought better safe than sorry. So I moved the heap of old junk. Out of there, so to speak. Over here.'

Jaz looked inside. The ignition was undamaged.

'Do me a favour,' he said, understanding her concern. 'What am I? An amateur? You left a window open. This old banger's easier to rob than shit. I was under the bonnet hot-wiring it in twenty-three seconds. No, I tell a lie. Nineteen. Four seconds to drive it away.'

Jaz grinned. 'You did good.' She fished in her pocket.

The boy held up a palm in refusal. 'I've been paid,' he said.

On impulse, Jaz bent down and kissed the top of his head.

He jumped back as if electrocuted. He drew on his cigarette. 'Hey, mister,' he said, 'what are you, so to speak? You one of those pervs?'

Jaz got into the car. She took off her cap and let her damp hair fall around her shoulders. 'I'm just a girl,' she said. She started the engine. 'Thanks very much.'

Chapter Twenty-Six

Jaz parked outside the Chelsea mews at ten forty-five. There was a warm, dust-laden wind and the street was deserted. She was hot. She leaned out of the window and stared at the skyline. A cat ran across the road and she knew she'd seen it several times before. Her long vigils had made the area very familiar. Just before eleven, she went inside. The porter gave her a silent thumbs-up then muttered on the intercom. After the exchange of a few words, he motioned Jaz towards the houses.

Charles Merchant answered the door. His hair was loose and dishevelled and his tie and top button were undone. He wore a silk-backed waistcoat and his shirt-sleeves were pushed up, exposing his massive freckled forearms. He didn't smile. He looked tired and depressed.

Jaz followed him into the living room. It was decorated in a spare and expensive style with a pale wooden floor, discreet lighting and modern bucket chairs covered in cream and gold brocade. A large abstract painting dominated one wall. Merchant picked up a glass of Scotch and sat down heavily. He sighed, but did not speak. A CD played classical music in the background.

'Are you alone?' asked Jaz.

He met her eye for a second, then looked away. He nodded.

'I've been trying to get hold of you for ages. You're better protected than royalty.' She felt uncomfortable. He hadn't asked her to sit down. She perched on the arm of a chair.

He took a gulp from his glass.

She wondered if he was drunk. Just get it over with, she said to herself. This isn't a social call. She got straight to the point. 'There's something you need to know. It's not good news, but I feel I've got to tell you. You know you had a twin brother?'

His eyes met hers again. They were the same colour as Andy's but they had a defeated, blank look.

She raised her voice slightly. 'Do you know this or not?'

He nodded again.

'Is that a yes?'

'Yes,' he muttered.

Jaz hesitated. 'Well, I'm sorry to have to tell you, but he's dead.'

He jumped visibly. He was shocked. Scotch splashed from his glass onto his arm and over his chair. He put the glass down on the floor. Jaz noticed that the little colour he possessed had completely drained away. He suddenly leaned forwards and hid his face in his hands, resting his elbows on his knees. 'What?' His voice was a strangled whisper.

Jaz decided to press on with her story. Sympathy's never been my strong point, she thought to herself. Stay calm. Just tell him and get the hell out of here. Her voice was confident. 'Your brother Andy was my boyfriend. We lived together for six months, over in Peckham. On the nineteenth of June, my birthday, I got back to the flat late at night. Andy was lying on the bed with his throat cut. He'd been killed that evening. The police more or less dismissed it as an estate-based drugs crime and they've done nothing. But Andy didn't do drugs. Not seriously. He was murdered by his boss. A criminal from the Isle of Dogs.' She paused and tried to swallow. Her mouth was dry.

Charles Merchant's hands still covered his face. He opened his fingers and looked out at her. The effect was a little comical, but she didn't feel like laughing. Her heart was beating fast. She'd waited a long time for this moment and all at once, she wanted both to leave the place and to cry. She positioned her hand on her chest, over the spot where she'd consistently felt the pain. There was more to say. 'It's because you're a twin,' she went on. She was less controlled now and her words started coming out in a rush. 'I knew I had to tell you. You see, I know about twins. I used to have . . . I mean . . . I've got . . . twin sisters. I understand what you're like, you twins. I mean, I know you weren't in touch, or anything, I know you were separated when you were little, but I know that identical twins are like . . . one person.' She stopped. Tears were running down her cheeks. She sobbed. 'You see, what it is . . . what I'm really trying to say is I know how you feel about Andy because I really miss him too—I feel the same . . . I miss Andy . . . and Blow . . . I really miss Blow . . . and my two sisters. I miss my sisters terribly. I miss everybody.'

Merchant slid his hands to the sides of his face, cupping his head. His cheeks were wet and doughy. His knee jerked involuntarily. He was in shock.

Jaz cried unrestrainedly. Seconds, then minutes passed. He didn't move and she found she couldn't stop. There was a box of tissues next to the television and she got up and pulled out a handful. She mopped her face and blew her nose. 'I'm sorry,' she said. She rubbed her face. 'This is fucking hard,' she whispered.

Merchant suddenly lay back, his eyes staring at the ceiling. He was suddenly more composed, almost resigned. 'Cry,' he said. 'You cry. It's all right. I don't mind.'

Jaz struggled for control of herself and, after a while, succeeded. 'The thing is, I wanted Andy to be mourned. I mean, properly mourned. I didn't think I was enough . . . I sort of felt that I wasn't good enough, or somehow not able . . . I wanted a real, proper mourner. I told his old girlfriend but she was too drunk and I told his old mother but she was too mad, so the only person left . . . was you.' She fought back more tears. 'I'm sorry,' she continued, 'I'm sorry about your brother.'

Merchant picked up his glass and drained it. He stood up and poured himself another whisky, then held it up to the light. 'I know I can't tempt you,' he said, his voice dull, sad. 'Not ever . . . not even for medicinal purposes.' He glanced over, shook his head then sat down again heavily. The chair creaked. 'It's good stuff this,' he added thoughtfully. 'Government issue. Single malt.'

Jaz stared at him. She swallowed hard. 'How do you know I don't drink?' she asked, her voice quiet. 'How could you know that . . .?'

He looked at her. His face was still morose and drawn.

She held his gaze. 'Tell me. Who told you I don't drink? Who've you been talking to? Who do you know who knows me?'

There was a long silence. The ornate mantel clock ticked. The classical music rose and fell in melodious cadences. A video recorder whirred as it switched itself off. Outside, two drunks chanted 'Here we go, here we go, here we go,' in desperate unison. Jaz listened to their voices recede in the hot night. Her fist tightened around her ball of wet tissue. 'Well?'

He sighed. His expression changed and became confiding. 'Why wouldn't I know?' he said eventually. 'You said it. We lived together for six months.'

Jaz let these words sink in. Her heart started beating very hard. She felt something rise from her chest into her throat. 'What?' she asked, 'what?' Her hand strayed back to her breastbone. 'What d'you mean?' His words and all the crying had released something. The pain had gone.

He opened his arms in a welcoming gesture. His wet face and his posture suddenly reminded her of Fat Andy and the time she'd threatened to leave him in Peckham. He'd cried and talked her out of it. 'You're breaking my heart,' he'd said then.

'Andy?' she said, her voice a small quaver. 'Andy? Is it you?' She stood up and uncertainly moved towards him. 'Is it really you?'

'Yes,' he replied simply.

She stood before him and he encircled her in his arms. He felt comfortable like Andy had always done and the smell of his skin, the spirits on his breath and the rough texture of his hair on her cheek, as she bent towards him, were all more than familiar.

'Little baby,' he murmured into her shoulder. 'My little sexy baby's here. She's come all the way here and found me.'

She crouched down on her haunches and stared into his face. They looked at each other for a while, without speaking. Jaz felt enormous relief. Impulsively, she leaned forwards, held him around his vast waist and squeezed him.

He chuckled. His mood had suddenly changed, just like it did in the old days. He struggled to his feet, picking her up. Clasping her to his belly he took a few steps then spun her around. He'd done this many times before. He put her on her feet and pressed a button on the hi-fi. There was a sudden burst of Boyz 2 Men. 'Let's dance,' he growled, taking both her arms and pulling her gently. He moved her around the room a few times. He was a good dancer, light on his feet.

'Hang on a minute,' Jaz said suddenly. She stopped and struggled, freeing herself. She reached over and switched off the music.

He was smiling broadly now and his colour had improved. The old twinkle had returned to his eye. 'Turn that back on,' he said. 'This bloody place is bugged.' He pressed a button and returned to the violin concerto. He adjusted a speaker. 'I couldn't believe it when I saw you at the Turkish baths. It's supposed to be men only. I wanted to laugh but it would have been suicide. I kept changing rooms. I couldn't get rid of you.'

Jaz stood upright, stiff, her arms by her sides. 'Andy, you tell me what's going on. Tell me now.'

He shrugged. 'We better both sit down.' He picked up his glass. He was a little breathless. He paused. 'It all started one day recently . . . as you said . . . it was your birthday.'

Jaz sat opposite him and listened, concentrating hard. Her eyes were fixed on his sleeve.

Fat Andy began talking. He explained how he'd been on his way home from the garage, driving the Lotus Cortina. 'How is it by the way? I saw it outside the baths.

It's got a bird-shit burn on the paintwork. How's it running?'

'It's running fine. It's outside.'

'I called at the flats one night to check on it. It wasn't there. I saw Peppy. He said you'd taken it.'

'Tell me what's going on.'

'Imagine this, right. I'm driving along, as normal. Then there's this Daimler. Big, black. Two guys in neat haircuts and designer shades are following me. It's like a bloody American movie. I pull over, thinking where's the cameras? Where's Andy Garcia? I get in their motor and ask them what their problem is.' He went on to detail an extraordinary conversation. He'd been told that his twin brother, whom he hadn't seen since infancy, was now a big shot political adviser. He was influential, apparently, successful. He was calling the tune in government policy. He was enormously powerful, well off, a key player in the administration. 'The only trouble was,' Andy continued, 'they said he'd had some sort of nervous breakdown. They said he'd gone to a sanatorium near Geneva, to recover his health.' There was a pause.

'So?' asked Jaz

'They said this nervous breakdown was like embarrassing deep-shitsville for the Home Secretary. For everybody. They asked me to sort of . . . stand in for him for a while. Like, pretend to be him. Follow his routines. They offered me a wad. More money than I've ever earned in my life, all together. I'm telling you, compared to working for Vinny, stealing lousy cars, it was an offer I couldn't refuse. They also threw in this place.' He gestured around the room. 'Restaurants, booze, a chauffeur-driven limo . . . the works. They said it would only be for a few weeks. Until my brother recovered. They didn't want any publicity. Things were too delicate at the moment, politically, and important new legislation was about to be announced. They were very, well, persuasive.'

'I can't believe you're telling me this.'

'Didn't you get my letter?'

'Letter?'

'I gave them a letter to give to you, and cheque for two grand. It was made out to you. I told you to hang on in there in Peckham and pay the rent. I told you to chill out, said I'd be back and then we'd both be a lot richer.' He scratched his head and sighed. 'Of course you didn't get it. Bastards, bastards, bastards.' He leaned back in his chair and stared into his glass. After a moment he continued. 'What I've been doing is . . . hiding. When they needed me to wander past a journalist or a TV crew I've done it. I've been driven around in flash cars, here and there, not knowing what the hell's going on. I was given a cupboard full of fancy suits and told to keep my trap shut.'

'What do you think's going on?'

He shook his head. 'Dunno. I'm out of my depth here, by fathoms. These guys have threatened me. I swear I've had a gun in my ribs.' He looked at her. 'No kidding. A gun. And I didn't like it, not one bit.'

'I bet.'

'I've never been famous for bravery.' He paused and gave her an appraising glance. 'Unlike you.' He sighed. 'Now, I act like a robot, obeying orders.'

Jaz described the scene at the flat, the night of her birthday. 'It was a nightmare,' she whispered. 'I thought it was you. It must have been . . .'

Fat Andy let out a deep sigh. He wiped his eyes again. 'The poor bastard. He was never ill. There was no nervous breakdown. That was all lies. He'd never been ill. They wanted him out of the way.'

'Why?'

Fat Andy shrugged. 'I don't know, I really don't. I'm a prisoner here. But one thing I've known from the start is these guys aren't working in my brother's interests.' He looked very unhappy. 'And now you tell me they went and killed him. He's been dead all along.' He sniffed and rubbed his face.

'What're they doing, exactly?'

'Blocking the changes he wanted to make, of course. They've nobbled civil servants. Bribed junior ministers, God knows who else. The Home Secretary's just a free-loading prick, in with them, you know, deep. Up to his lousy sun-tanned neck.' He paused. 'He wasn't before, but now the wind's changed, now these bad guys are making the running, he's backing off from Charles's new policies. You wait. There'll be a classic U-turn any day now.'

'Who are these guys?'

'High-class heavies. Ronnie and Reggie, only with degrees in economics. But it's the guys they represent who matter. Big businessmen, property speculators, financial manipulators. Men who stay well behind the scenes. They're the ones who want to stop Charles's proposals, his new deal on Clean Cities. They won't have their property requisitioned, won't have anyone interfering with their investments. And I tell you, those bastards will stop at nothing. It's not public yet, but in the back rooms, the policy's already as dead as a dodo.' He swigged his drink, finished it, poured another and sat down again. 'I'm supposed to be Charles Merchant and in a few days it'll seem to the world that he's backed down. He never would have backed down. Never in a million years. He was strong and he was shrewd and he had it all practically airborne. The whole goddamned thing was ready to fly. But not now. They got rid of him. And there's nothing I can do. I'm just their mouthpiece. As I said, I'm completely out of my depth.' He sighed again. 'You know me. Show me dodgy car documents, I'm your man. Show me a pair of stolen plates, I'm laughing. But show me White Papers, shite papers . . .' He sighed. 'I haven't got a bloody clue.'

'So it was them who killed him.' Jaz was thoughtful. She chewed the end of her ponytail. 'The heavies with degrees.'

'Must have been.'

'They frightened off a woman, a temp at your office. She helped me and then . . .'

'Oh, definitely,' Andy interrupted. 'She was over curious. Suspicious of me. She went through my jacket pockets and found an old wallet – Visa slips, my driving licence. Made photocopies. She was onto it. She knew.'

'They shut her up.'

Andy was silent for a moment. 'They will have done.' He paused. 'Oh, God . . .'

'The heavies with degrees.' Jaz's mind was spinning.

'Degrees and black Daimlers. FBI collars and ties. Gun holsters.' Fat Andy's face registered more pain. 'I didn't know they'd killed him. Charles. Not until you told me just now. But it makes sense. Complete sense. And no one knows. No one's interested. In the eyes of the world, a small-time car thief dies in a bedroom on a no-exit council estate. Who cares? Did it even make the South London Press? I think not.'

Jaz shook her head. She felt relieved, unburdened, even elated with the knowledge that the body in the flat, lying grotesque and bloodstained on their bed, had not been Andy, after all. Instead, it had been an unlucky stranger, a person she'd never met. She took several deep breaths. The crying had been cathartic. She felt better than she had for a long time. Her chest, her head, her whole body felt lighter, looser, calmer. She stared at her former lover. You're alive, she thought. You fat, lucky bastard. She almost smiled. Andy's predicament was serious, he was way out of his league, but at least he wasn't dead.

Images from the recent past jostled for attention in her thoughts. She remembered Princess, Andy's former girlfriend and the old woman, his mother, both of them lonely and desperate. She thought of the black masseur in the Turkish bathhouse and the lobby correspondent in Lambeth with his unrealizable desires. She pictured Andy's tormentors, cool and aggressive in their leather bomber jackets and fascist haircuts. She remembered, suddenly, the choking fumes in the Citroën, inside the lock-up in the East End, her nausea, her own brush with extinction. She concentrated on this. Her eyes narrowed. Her mind shifted, then steadied, like the gears of a car. 'They tried to kill me,' she said.

Fat Andy didn't reply. There was a silence. She looked at him. She'd seen this expression on his face many times before. He was trying to muster innocence.

A realization formed in her mind. 'They tried to kill me. The heavies with degrees.' She paused. 'Your heavies.'

Andy attempted a smile. His cheeks formed cherubic mounds, then collapsed.

Jaz's sense of calm ebbed away. In its place, her heart was thumping. 'You told them about the lock-up, about that shit-head Keith who wanted to murder me in the cinema when I was sixteen.' A hot feeling formed in her brain and in her stomach. It was anger.

Andy's lips formed a closed circle and he whistled, quietly and tunelessly.

Jaz raised her voice. 'You did. It must've been you. It was the same place. It was the garage where he kept his Ford Zephyr. I showed it to you more than once. We went there. I told you the whole story.'

He looked at the floor.

'You told them about that lock-up. Where it is. You told them that was the place that would really scare me. Really do my head in.'

'No.'

Jaz bent down and met his evasive eyes. He caught her glance unwillingly, then looked away. He was furtive. She knew he was lying. 'Bastard.' Her heart, light for that one brief moment, gained weight again and sank like a stone in her chest. It's the same old thing, she thought, horrified. He's unreliable, he's selfish. He's unthinking. He only ever worries about himself. And this time he's stepped so far out of line it's almost unbelievable. 'I might have died,' she added.

He pulled himself into a more upright position. He still looked shifty. 'They wouldn't have killed you, Jaz,' he said in unacknowledged admission. 'They were only trying to scare you off. They wanted you out of their hair because you were irritating them.'

Jaz remembered the lock-up, the foul air, the tight bindings on her wrists and ankles, her near collapse into unconsciousness in the carbon monoxide smog. She looked him up and down. He was overweight, perspiring and half-drunk. He was weak, floundering. He'd betrayed her, ignoring the consequences, in order to make life easier for himself. I used to love you, she thought. She turned this over in her mind. I must have been mad.

In an instant, she was in exactly the same place she'd been on the night of her birthday, before she found the body. Her love for him, as she'd known back then, was misplaced, founded on the wrong needs and reasons, and in any case, it was over. It was past tense. Finished. He was unworthy of her. He was undeserving. He had no values. Her anger evaporated at that moment because she knew he wasn't worth it. 'The car's outside,' she said coldly. 'Why don't I drop you somewhere?'

He sighed, almost luxuriantly. His stomach moved down then up. He was glad she'd changed the subject. 'No.' He paused. 'Don't worry, I'm leaving. I'm out of here. But not yet. I've got a plan, but it's got to be watertight. Two of us are working something out – me and the chauffeur.' He tried to force a laugh.

Jaz held out her hand in a gesture of friendship which she didn't mean.

Andy shook it formally. 'We're planning something James Bond-ish,' he said. 'Car chases, stunts, private aeroplanes . . .'

Jaz looked for the gleam in his eye, but it wasn't there. He was frightened. They both knew he was treading water, slowly sinking, slowly drowning.

Jaz gestured towards the window. 'I'm going to Weston-super-Mare.'

He levered himself to his feet. He was a little unsteady and held onto her arm. 'Do you think we might ever . . . you and I . . .'

In your dreams, thought Jaz. You betraying bastard. 'Don't think about it,' she said. 'Not now. Concentrate on the moment, the problem in hand.' She formed her mouth into a smile. 'You know what you always used to tell me when I was out on the streets, nicking BMWs?'

He shook his head. 'What?'

'Stay calm, stay focused, stay cool.' She stared briefly into his eyes then moved towards the door.

Chapter Twenty-Seven

Back at the hotel, the next day, Jaz found her two friends lounging in the small TV room, watching the Jerry Springer show. It was a confrontation entitled 'Keep your hands off – he's mine'.

Harm was painting her toenails purple. A cigarette was wedged in the corner of her mouth. Trace had her head on Trevor's shoulder. He was leafing through *Hair Today*, studying the photos. The air was thick with the smell of varnish. Rocky, the old Rottweiler, was asleep in a triangle of sunlight on the faded carpet. His jaws and feet twitched as he dreamed of mock combat and stardom.

Trace and Trevor moved along the sofa and Jaz sat next to them. There was another person in the room, sitting in an armchair, half concealed by the open door. It was Pete.

She froze, giving him a cold, hostile stare. 'You don't give up,' she said.

'Give the boy a break,' murmured Trevor lazily.

Pete leaned forward, clasping and unclasping his hands. 'Whatever you thought I did, I never,' he said. 'I never did anything to piss you off.'

'You left his door open,' said Trace mildly. 'His flat was stripped bare.'

'He'd have a job today,' agreed Trevor, 'if it wasn't for you.'

Jaz stared at Pete. His pale, poet's face was as handsome as ever. His long, delicate fingers were clean of oil and his nails were manicured. His hair was shining like a halo, wavy and loosely tied back. She remembered desiring him. She remembered what they'd done in his bed. 'You set those two goons onto me,' she spat out, despite herself. 'Vinny's heavies. You told them where I was. You kept telling them. They might have killed me.'

Pete's mouth dropped open. He gasped. 'I never! Jaz, I never did!'

Jaz's hands were clenched into fists, one on each knee. 'Well, some fucker did.' She thought about her recent nightmare days. Ronnie and Reggie had pursued her and found her several times. The kidnapping in the Citroën, she now knew, was the work of Fat Andy's heavies and they'd almost found her here. But Ronnie and Reggie had also come close to tracking her down. They'd been after her and they'd been persistent.

'Everywhere I went, those brothers turned up. I had something they wanted.' She glanced over at Harm but she was concentrating now on her fingernails, apparently not listening.

Trace sat up. 'Two brothers?' she asked innocently. She picked up the TV remote and switched off the set. There was a silence, broken only by the dog's snores. 'Two big guys in sports clothes? Baldy heads? Look like boxers?'

'That's them,' said Pete.

'Oh,' said Trace, suddenly dismayed. Her hand covered her mouth. 'That was me.'

Jaz stood up and faced her. 'What d'you mean?' She was astonished. 'Trace?'

'Whoops,' said Trace. The colour drained from her face.

'Tell me.'

Trevor picked up Trace's other hand in a gesture of support. He squeezed it tenderly, then raised it to his lips.

'Two brothers,' repeated Trace. She thought for a moment. Her voice was hesitant, uncertain. Her eyes were scared and fixed on Jaz. 'They came to the Grand Banana lots of times and the Little Sisters as well. They were looking for you. They said they'd seen the car.'

'What, the Lotus Cortina?'

Trace nodded. She bit her lip. 'They'd seen you leave in it, the first day you came to the Grand Banana. A classic Ford, or something. They were looking everywhere for you, Jaz, and were nice and polite and friendly and everything. They said you had a piece of property and they wanted to buy it off you. Said they'd give you a good price.' She paused. Her voice became a whisper. 'They meant the car.' She was ready to cry. 'Didn't they?'

'No,' said Jaz. Her voice was ice. 'They were after a computer disk.'

Trace swallowed then responded quickly. 'I don't know anything about a computer disk. I thought it was the car they were interested in, that one you're driving.' She was frightened. 'You're always selling people cars, Jaz. That's what you do. You sell cars.' She paused. 'Not computer disks . . . Why would they have wanted . . .' Her voice wavered then trailed away. She looked around desperately. 'I didn't mean to cause trouble for you, Jaz. Or anything like that. Were they bad men? What have I done?' Tears brimmed up in her eyes then rolled down her cheeks. Trevor stroked the back of her hand. 'I kept telling them where you were. With Pete. At Mrs McDonald's. At that flashy hotel in Charing Cross. So you could talk to them about it. About the car.'

Jaz stared down at Trace. 'Why didn't you tell me?'

Trace's lower lip trembled. More tears fell. 'I don't know, I think I forgot. It wasn't important, it was only a car. You told me not to tell him anything.' She pointed at Pete. 'So I didn't . . . I did exactly what you said, Jaz.' She was insistent. 'I always do what you tell me to do. Always.' She rubbed her face with the back of her hand.

'Sshh, sshh,' whispered Trevor consolingly.

There was another silence. Rocky awoke, eased himself up and glanced around. He growled menacingly, fixing Pete with a mean stare. He lifted his top lip, revealing his yellow set of teeth. Pete slid back in his chair nervously, lifting his feet and clasping his long legs in his arms. Satisfied, Rocky turned and left the room.

'The brothers aren't such bad guys,' said Pete after a while, breaking the silence. He sounded young. 'They're harmless. If they've got a problem, they throw Vinny's money at it. You had something of theirs?'

Jaz nodded.

'They would have paid you off. That's their style. They're not violent.'

Harm coughed. Jaz looked over at her. She screwed the top on her bottle of nail varnish and met Jaz's eye. 'OK,' she muttered. 'I lied.'

Jaz clenched her fists. She took a deep breath.

'I'm sorry. It wasn't the brothers who beat me up and I never went to see them. I lied to you.'

Jaz was speechless.

'I was done over by an American country and western singer in the Savoy. I won't say who, but he's very famous.' She pulled a face and admired her nails. 'D'you want to hear about it?'

No one spoke. 'Get this.' Harm took a deep breath. She was trying to make her voice light, anecdotal, hoping to improve the atmosphere. 'He comes out the bathroom wearing a woman's dress. He's a big macho guy, but you know, nothing surprises me. I'm cool. He plays music, very loud. He yells at me.' She shrugged, indicating she'd seen it all before. She lit another cigarette. 'I start to get a bit worried. Wesley's outside chatting to the PR woman and the guy's agent, but he never hears a thing. This guy, he punches me out and all his fingers are covered in rings. They come busting in eventually and rescue me. The guy's out of his head on crack. He thinks I'm his mother.' She laughed, unconvincingly. 'They got us out of there double quick, I can tell you. Paid us plenty to keep our mouths shut. Wesley's still devastated. He blames himself.'

Jaz tried to swallow. 'Why did you tell me it was . . .?'

Harm interrupted, her voice harsher now and more serious. 'To try and stop you, of course. Your boyfriend gets killed and you're in a state, understandably. You're in shock. But you needed to recover, not run around like a nutter, trying to get revenge. It was a mad idea you had, and I kept thinking about the time you nearly got murdered in the East End when you were sixteen, and I could see it happening again. Your judgement isn't good, Jaz. You're too rash. I thought if I told you it was Ronnie and Reggie who'd beaten me up, then you'd stay away from them.' She looked at Trace. 'I guess, between us, we really screwed up because you got completely the wrong idea about them. Screwed up right and proper.'

Pete uncurled himself and got to his feet. He tentatively put his arm around Jaz's shoulders. She stood mute and unresisting. 'I've ruined Vinny,' she said to no one in particular. 'Vinny's finished and I did it.'

'Vinny had it coming,' said Pete, kindly but firmly. 'No one misses Vinny.'

'Why didn't he try to stop me?' Jaz whispered. 'Are you telling me he wasn't even angry?'

Trevor leaned forwards. His voice was knowing. 'No,' he said, 'Vinny gave up when Andy died. He'd lost the illegal business because it was nothing without Andy and his gang. Vinny was finished. He knew that. All the rest was only ever pocket money. Just a front.'

'What's he going to do now?'

'He's going back to Greece,' answered Trevor confidently. 'He decided that ages ago. He wanted me to go with him. His mum owns a souvenir shop in Corfu and he says it could expand. It's got potential.'

Pete led Jaz out of the room. 'Let's go upstairs,' he whispered. He pressed the button of the lift.

Jaz lay in bed with Pete regarding the little motes of dust which floated in the beam of sunlight penetrating the crack in the curtains. Her head rested on his smooth chest and his gentle hands caressed her back and neck. She let him stroke away the tension, the anger and the fear. 'I had a pain in my chest,' she whispered, 'but it went away.'

Fragments of recent events were competing for attention in her thoughts. She saw the small boy outside the

Turkish baths, the dashboard of the Citroën when she'd been tied up and choking, the attractive aerobics instructor at Ronnie and Reggie's gym.

Pete had questioned her a little, but she'd not been forthcoming. They made love several times and this was better than talking.

She rolled against him and he rubbed the insides of her thighs. She stroked his penis until it stiffened again. She pressed her body against his, feeling both tenderness and relief. He kissed her deeply then moved on top of her. Downstairs the dog started barking. He laughed into her hair.

Epilogue

Jaz sat in the driving seat of the Lotus Cortina, studying Fat Andy's road atlas. She'd spent the previous day servicing the twin cam and she was confident it was running at its best. Now, she was illegally parked outside the hotel, as Wesley loaded Harm's heavy suitcases into the boot. 'You're going on holiday,' she heard him laugh, 'not emigrating.'

Harm opened a rear door and slipped inside the car. She was wearing hot pants, a halter top and the kind of zany sixties sunglasses which had featured in Jaz's imagination in recent weeks. She smelled of deodorant. She lit a cigarette.

Trace appeared in the hotel doorway, stuffing a large bottle of Ambre Solaire into a small duffel bag. This was her only luggage. She kissed Trevor goodbye and got in the front next to Jaz. She was giggling with apprehension. Trevor handed her a pile of cassettes. 'For the journey,' he suggested.

Jaz put on her Versace shades and slipped the car in gear. She eased into the traffic. Her window was wound down and she rested her elbow on the warm metal. As she pulled away she glanced in the rear-view mirror. Wesley, Trevor and Pete were framed together, standing on the pavement, grinning and waving. Mr McTavish appeared behind them, holding Rocky by the collar. He raised one arm in salute as the Lotus Cortina accelerated and turned right at the lights.

Somewhere on the M4, stuck in a long and winding jam, Trace switched off the tape and tried to tune into the traffic report. She was wearing Harm's sunglasses. It was hot. Harm was asleep in the back, her head on the inflatable cushion. The sun beat down mercilessly on the roof of the car. Jaz swigged some water from a bottle and handed it across. The news came on the radio. 'Leave that,' she said.

She listened to the main story about a by-election in Birmingham. The government had lost the seat, with a huge percentage swing to the opposition. The political correspondent gave his opinion. 'The expected reforms from the Home Secretary have, on announcement, proved to be negligible and disappointing,' he said. 'The electorate feels like a balloon let down. Huge promises have turned into hot air. Unless he can pull a rabbit out of his hat at this late stage, then the days of this administration seem numbered.' Jaz visualized a rabbit and a balloon and pursed her lips.

The second item was even more interesting. The presenter talked more rapidly. 'News is just in about a plane crash in Sussex. At about ten this morning a light aircraft plunged to the ground in flames in a field on the outskirts of Aldeburgh. Locals believe that two bodies were recovered but as yet there is no official statement. Witnesses describe a mystery car, a Daimler, without number plates, speeding through the quiet country lanes in quote, such a dangerous manner that some residents alerted police.

Two men were seen abandoning the car and boarding a plane which crashed immediately after take-off. Our correspondent Anna Smythe is at the scene.'

The announcer was replaced by a woman speaking to the studio by telephone. She was excited.

'Yes, Gary,' she said, 'the plane crash was preceded, apparently, by an amazing car chase, ending at a small private airfield near the coast. I'm there now.' Her voice was definite and clear. 'I can just see the wreckage in the distance but the site is cordoned off. There is a big black car, two of its doors open, on the runway. Earlier, an ambulance removed two body bags from the wreckage, but we can only speculate about casualties at this stage. One local witness, out walking his dog, describes a Daimler, without number plates, travelling at high speed. At one point it collided with a pillar box. Police gave chase, I'm told, with their lights flashing and their sirens sounding, but the lead car burst through a locked and chained gate onto the field, tore across the tarmac, then stopped beside a small waiting aircraft. Two men hurried on board and the plane took off within a minute. As it left the ground it is said to have exploded and burst into flames.'

'What exactly is happening there now, Anna?'

'Well, Gary, it's not entirely clear. The police seem as confused as the rest of us. As you said yourself, there has been no statement. The owner of the airfield, a local man, is quoted as saying it has been disused for two years and the flight was completely unauthorized. There is a rumour, I have to say unsubstantiated, that one of the men, attempting what seems to have been a spectacular getaway, was allegedly none other than Charles Merchant, the elusive political adviser to the Home Secretary.

But that's just hearsay, Gary. It's caused quite a stir, I have to say, and more journalists are arriving by the minute. The lanes are blocked and no one can move. We'll have to hang on for the official explanation. It's wait and see, I'm afraid. Now it's back to the studio.' There was a beep and the start of a record.

'Any connection with the sensational by-election result, do you think, Anna?' said the presenter hurriedly, speaking over the link.

'It's interesting to speculate, isn't it, Gary? That's one theory being discussed here at the moment. It's certainly possible.' She was faded out, replaced by Simon and Garfunkel.

Jaz glanced at her friends. They were both asleep. She changed up and accelerated gently as the traffic began to inch forwards. She pressed her hand on her chest. There was no pain. She was calm and relaxed. Fat Andy was dead and Blow was dead but it no longer felt like her business.

She pictured the burning aircraft and Blow's burning car on the motorway. They were both consumed by fire, cremated, obliterated. Up in flames, she thought, envisaging twisted metal; glare; heat; peeling, blistered paint; a pall of black smoke, curling towards the sky.

Her mind wandered to a flat, wide, imaginary beach where the tide was so far out, the sea was invisible. In this daydream, the sand was wet and fine, like grey mud, and there was heavy, low cloud. She was standing by the Lotus Cortina which was stationary on the beach, its doors open and its engine running. In the distance, Harm and Trace wandered off, arms linked, in the direction of the town.

Jaz pictured herself with a can of petrol, dousing the

car. She was alone and the light was fading. She stood back and tossed a roll of burning rags into its interior. There was a flash and a roar as it caught alight and she felt the heat as it was engulfed in fire. The dull scene was illuminated by the blaze and a flock of seagulls screamed overhead, their wings beating angrily, their beaks like razors. Goodbye, Blow, Jaz imagined herself saying, as the car burned. Goodbye Andy. So long, cheerio, adios, you fat bastards. I'm rid of you at last.

Later, with the jam behind them, the three girls hurtled along the outside lane of the motorway, overtaking coach-loads of tourists. A sign above them said Bristol, Exeter and the South West. 'What!' shrieked Trace delightedly. 'What does that one say?'

Later, another sign said Somerset and Devon. 'Somerset and Devon,' read Harm, excited. She handed out some sandwiches. 'We're nearly there.'

'Somerset and Devon,' yelled Trace, as high as a child. 'Oh, my gosh! Somerset and Devon! I can't believe it. We're on holiday!'

Jaz concentrated on driving. She felt connected to the Lotus Cortina. Her arms and the steering wheel were one smooth movement. The rhythm of the engine matched her own steady pulse. The muscles in her feet were held at exactly the same tension as the pedals. She felt in control. Her mind was blank except for an autonomic response to curve, speed, incline. I'll keep the car, she thought. It's mine now.

Trace fiddled with the radio. Blow's song, his joyful Cortina anthem, emerged from Jaz's subconscious and began to throb. Do wah diddy diddy, dum diddy do. It repeated several times, then disappeared. A pale glimmer on the horizon, almost blue, suggested open sea. It was then that the pure line of ocean and sky combined together in her line of vision, in her mind and in her heart. Her eyes flicked towards the hard shoulder and she braked, crossing lanes to reach the slip road. Weston-super-Mare, she'd noticed. Three miles. She smiled to herself. She was happy.

Blink

by Andrea Badenoch

It is 1962. The Beatles have released 'Love Me Do' and John Glenn has orbited the Earth. But in this pit village in County Durham, everyone is looking back towards the traditions of the past . . .

Except for Gloria, the local hair stylist. With her narrow skirts, low block heels and her Mini Cooper, Gloria is a modern woman – until she's found dead, floating in the coal-polluted shallows of a nearby pond.

Gloria's young cousin, Kathleen, finds the body but refuses to accept the suicide explanation embraced by the village. Gloria had everything to live for. Twelve-year-old Kathleen is shy and innocent but her mouse-like wordlessness makes her invisible. She is therefore an ideal witness . . .

Andrea Badenoch's new novel, *Blink*, is published in Macmillan hardback in March 2001, priced £10. The opening scenes follow here.

Chapter One

Kathleen walked gingerly down the rough, coal-strewn track towards the pond, her wellingtons slipping on the loose stones. It was windy and her coat collar was buttoned against the driving cold. Over one shoulder she carried a bulky square camera case on a strap. Under her other arm, she held a flat rectangle. This was a long-playing record which she'd borrowed - without asking her Auntie Joyce. It was called 'Please Please Me'. Her small Jack Russell terrier totted ahead. His name was Nosey and his eyes and ears were alert with excitement.

Kathleen was a slight figure on the monocrome slope and her little plaits blew behind her like micetails. Dying fireweed, its cotton puffs recently shed, stirred stiffly at the sides of the path and dust eddied on the black faces of the pit heaps which rose in high, steep mounds on all sides. Below, the surface of the water was uneasy. The sky was unbroken grey and the sullied landscape was colourless and bleak.

Beyond the pond, a lonely house came into view. This was her destination, the home of her school friend, Petra. Surrounded on all sides by mountains of waste from the pit, it resembled an outpost; a place of grim survival. Smoke puffed from its squat chimney and was immediately carried away. A light shone from between the half-closed kitchen curtains. It looked desolate and unwelcoming.

Kathleen approached the pond. She watched the wind form oily ripples which rolled then broke, sluggishly. The dog sniffed the air then barked. Here, nothing grew, not a blade of grass – not even fireweed. Polluted by the mine, the once legendary sweet waters had for decades been thick and lifeless. Formed in a natural fissure, the pool was deep – some said bottomless – but it was scummy now and stank of coal.

Kathleen's eyes narrowed. She stopped and peered through her spectacles. Still clutching the LP she took off her glasses, breathed on the lenses, rubbed them on her coat, then replaced them. In the distance, on the water's edge next to an ancient, ruined barn, something shone red. It was bright and startling. The dog barked again. A beachball, Kathleen thought. Maybe a lost umbrella. Intrigued, she left the track and walked towards the barn which tottered doorless on the far shore. Her feet sank into the black mud, leaving oozing footprints.

'Nosey!' she called, as he raced ahead, his tail erect and quivering. As she neared the red blotch, she could see it wasn't round at all – now it looked like fabric. It's a bedcover, she decided, blown off Petra's mam's washing line. It was caught between two rotting posts which emerged from the shallows like broken fingers.

She drew alongside the barn. Nosey was running to and fro, by the water's edge, yapping furiously. She gasped. She could see it clearly now – the red cloth was a jacket.

*

Kathleen laid the long-playing record on the ground, unfastened the heavy case and took out Da's old box brownie. She steadied herself, holding the camera firmly upright at waist height, in order to take a portrait shot. The wind was blowing against her and she leant forwards, balancing herself. Peering through her spectacles into the viewfinder she trapped the exact image and with her right thumb carefully pressed the lever on the side that released the shutter. There was a loud click as the mechanism moved, then the lever clicked back to the 'up' position. Carefully, she returned the brownie to its case, then stepped into the foul pond, the cold filling her wellingtons.

She waded forwards. She was afraid. The icy coldness rose up her thighs. The skirt of her coat floated then dragged. She lifted her feet from the slimy bottom to stop them sinking. She grasped one of the posts. The discoloured water was black on the surface but a few inches underneath it was a rusty orange which was both malodorous and dense. She looked again. Above the half-submerged red jacket there were floating tendrils of short blonde hair. She took off her glasses and rubbed her eyes. She saw what was unmistakably a rigid hand, an arm. She polished the spectacles on her shoulder and put them on again. She thought of posed plaster mannequins she'd seen in shop windows on her rare trips to town. Her heart turned over and she grasped the sodden jacket, tugging it hard. The stiff figure was freed from its mooring. Grotesquely, it turned over and reared up.

It was a dead body. A drowned person.

It had a yellowish-cream waxy face and eyes that met hers and stared. Its hair was stuck down, its mouth was open with water streaming out. Its lips were drawn back in a frozen grimace from which teeth protruded. Kathleen cried out and released it. With a gentle splash it sank below the surface.

Kathleen stepped back, unbalanced. She staggered then fell at the pond's edge. The dog barked hysterically. Soaked and filthy from her chest downwards, she struggled to her feet. One of her wellingtons came off and was lost. She gasped for breath in uneven sobs. She picked up the camera then half ran back to the track. The Jack Russell overtook her, excitedly. She turned to look behind. The body was no longer visible but she knew it hadn't been a bad dream. She moved her short-sighted gaze upwards to the pale cloud. There was no break in the flat canopy; not a sliver of blue, not a single bird. Nearby, a hidden train shunted and rattled. Her sobs steadied to a heavy, even rasp. She tried, but failed to remember some religious words. 'Gloria,' she managed to gasp, after a moment. Recovering her voice she shouted loudly: 'GLORIA!'

This wasn't a prayer directed at a godless sky. It was the name of her cousin. Her cousin Gloria was lifeless, waterlogged, dead. She lay drowned in Jinny Hoolet's pond.

Kathleen hammered on the side door of the isolated house of her friend. 'Mrs Koninsky!' she yelled. 'Petra! Open up!' She banged with both fists.

Petra peered through the gap in the kitchen curtains. The electric light made her sallow and suspicious. She opened the door. 'Where's the records?' she demanded. 'Where's Billy J. Kramer and the Dakotas? Where's John, Paul, George and Ringo?'

'Phone the police,' Kathleen muttered, leaning in the entrance, water forming a pool at her feet. 'Phone the doctor.' Dismayed, she realized as she spoke that she'd lost her Auntie Joyce's LP somewhere near the pond. She pushed past Petra into the dim kitchen where the pot-bellied stove smoked and gave off practically no heat.

'You're all wet,' was the reply. 'You're dirty.'

With uncustomary boldness, Kathleen walked through and opened the door into the hallway. The Koninskys were one of the few families in the area with a private telephone. 'Where's your Mam and Dad?'

'In bed. It's Sunday.'

'There's a body in the pond.'

Petra was suddenly wide-eyed and impressed. Her mouth fell open into a silent 'O'.

Kathleen picked up the smooth black handset and listened, tentatively, to the tone. 'What do you do with this? What do you do again?'

Her friend grabbed the receiver. She wanted to take charge. 'Nine, nine, nine,' she said with authority. 'I'll do it. We need to dial nine, nine, nine.'

Wearing only Petra's unwashed dressing gown, Kathleen stood on the edge of the bath and looked out of a small top window. Below, the police had put up a screen which blew like a sail in the wind. Two Alsatians were being led from a van, parked on the hard surface of the track. One uniformed constable was measuring the ground with a tape, another stood hands on hips, his helmet pushed back, gazing across the impassive pond.

'Let me look now, let me LOOK,' insisted Petra from the landing. 'It's my turn!'

They had been told to stay inside. Kathleen ignored her. She wondered what the adult Koninskys were doing. She blinked. She craned her neck as the flashing lights of another police car became visible on the road at the top of the hill.

Petra held Nosey, Kathleen's dog, under her arm. She was on the landing outside the bathroom door. The dog struggled a little because he didn't like her. She clamped him harder. 'Stop it!' she whispered, urgently. 'Keep still, you little bastard.' With her free hand she took a cigarette lighter from her pocket. It was gold with a single diamond in the centre and yesterday she'd stolen it from her mother. She flicked it open, creating a small flame and this she moved towards the dog's front paws. He wriggled frantically and freed himself, falling at her feet. Before she had time to back away he bared his teeth, bit her ankle then raced away down the stairs.

'It's MY TURN!' shouted Petra again, to Kathleen. She was angry. 'Get off there, will you, and let me have a look!'

Kathleen returned downstairs. Her clothes were still damp but she put them on anyway. She pushed a foot into her single wellington and located her camera. She called for Nosey but he didn't appear. She wasn't worried because he knew his way home. She ran a tap, rinsed a glass and drank some water. The sink was stained brown and there was dirty crockery piled up. She noticed cobwebs in the grey net curtains. She glanced around. The room was sombre and the worn linoleum was scuffed and grubby with bits of trampled food.

'Goodbye,' she called loudly and went outside.

Mrs Koninsky, praying fervently, stepped aside to let her pass. Kathleen paused and looked at the ambulance which was perched on the top of the track, its driver clearly unwilling to negotiate the steep, rough slope. Its siren was extinguished but its light was still flashing. Over at the barn, a burly older man wearing a trilby and an overcoat, wrote in a notebook. He had a red face and earlier he'd spoken briefly to Kathleen. He was nice, she decided, and he seemed to be in charge.

Just then a stretcher, carried by two ambulancemen, appeared from behind the flapping screen. Mrs Kóninsky, oblivious, her eyes half-closed, intoned in Latin. Kathleen removed her camera from its case and turned the film advance key on the left-hand side counter clockwise to wind on the film. She checked the little red window at the back – she had five pictures left. She held the box brownie sideways in both hands, waist height, to get a landscape shot. She squinted behind her spectacles and tried to stay as still as possible. Gloria's body was covered in a white aertex hospital blanket. Her feet were sticking out the end, toes erect, her legs stiff in death. As the stretcher passed Kathleen centred it in her viewfinder and took another photograph. Gloria was still wearing her black patent court shoes, Kathleen noticed. They were the latest fashion with a thick heel rather than a kitten stiletto. Kathleen was suddenly very, very sad. 'She only just got them shoes,' she murmured to the entranced, chanting woman behind her. 'She loved them. She got them from Dolcis, all the way up in Newcastle. She drove up there specially in her car. They cost her forty-nine and eleven.'

Later, in the dim warmth of Nana's gleaming kitchen, a pot bubbled on the range and the banked up fire cast shifting shadows around the walls. Nana's long body rocked energetically and her knitting needles clacked. She was in her usual place, at the side of the hearth, patchwork cushions heaped behind her to ease the pain in her joints. Nosey was asleep against the fender, his little legs twitching as he dreamed of rabbit hunts across the fields. Joyce, Nana's daughter, leaned over the table, her long hair thick, dishevelled and russet in the red light from the fire. Her uniform was partly undone revealing the dark line of her cleavage, the mound of her breasts. Her little pillbox hat was by her elbow. She heaped sugar into a cup of tea and stirred it vigorously. Nana's rocking chair creaked steadily, the old wall clock ticked and the coals shifted contentedly in the grate.

Kathleen sat half-hidden on her cracket, that is her low wooden stool, in a dark alcove. Her hands were folded over the camera in her lap. She was motionless, watching, listening. She'd put her damp clothes in the laundry basket in the wash-house and she was wearing her school uniform. She had nothing else, except pyjamas. Her glasses occasionally glinted from the gloom of her corner, but Nana and Joyce ignored her.

'It's a bad business,' said Nana, finally. She rocked more furiously for an instant, then suddenly placed both feet on the mat and stopped. She laid her knitting aside. 'It's a disgrace.'

Joyce sighed. She spoke softly. 'I saw it coming.' She slurped tea noisily from her cup.

Nana stood up abruptly, grasped her stick and lurched towards the dresser, her long legs stiff and unbending. She retrieved two glasses and a chipped cut-glass decanter half full of amber liquid. She poured an inch into each glass and handed one to her daughter. 'We'll be the talk of the neighbourhood.' Awkwardly, she sat down again, hooking her stick on to the mantelpiece. 'Never mind secondhand,' she said, mysteriously, 'that damned hussy, she was twenty-secondhand.'

Kathleen didn't move but there were tears welling in her eyes. 'Poor Gloria was a nice person,' she thought to herself. She remembered an expression often used by her teacher at school, although never about herself. 'She's got a very good brain. That's it,' she mused. 'Gloria had a very good brain.' She watched Nosey's little heart beating as he groaned and rolled over without waking. 'She was a brain-box.'

Joyce pushed her tea aside and swallowed her whisky in one gulp. She suppressed a burp. The clock struck the half hour. 'Miss High and Mighty,' she said. 'That was her. OK, I know she was a sort-of cousin, and everything, but I'm not pretending. I didn't like her and that's all there is to it. She gave herself airs. Thought herself Lady Muck.' She began to fasten her overall. She was soon to go to the local cinema where she worked as an usherette. 'Anyway, she was a mess, wasn't she? I'm not surprised she's done herself in. Didn't eat anything . . . much too thin . . .' She placed her pillbox hat on the back of her head. 'Mind you. Da will be upset.'

Kathleen listened attentively. Both women knew she had discovered the body earlier, but their concern had been minimal.

'That business must be worth something,' said Nana reflectively. 'And that flat. That flat will have to be sold.'

Kathleen thought about Gloria's neon-lit salon, with its row of overhead driers, its pink ruched curtains. She'd been a hairdresser – the only one in the village. She'd been planning a refurbishment.

'Da must be the beneficiary,' Nana said. Da was her second husband, not Joyce's father. She sipped from her glass and pulled a face, as if she was drinking medicine. 'That flat and that car will have to be sold.' She licked her lips. 'That's for sure.'

Joyce stood up and pulled on a wide, old-fashioned fur jacket. Her uniform strained against her hips. 'All those shoes,' she said spitefully. 'Those stupid little white boots. Lipstick like chalk. All that bloody Mary Quant. Not much good to her now, are they?'

Kathleen stood up and stepped into the pool of light in front of Nana's chair. 'Poor Gloria's dead,' she said simply. The tears that had been threatening to flow now spilled down her cheeks. She took off her glasses, rubbed her eyes then put them on again.

'Yes, and you'll be dead,' said Joyce sharply, 'if you don't find my Beatles long player. It'll be coming off your pocket money for bloody years.' She opened the dresser, poured herself another finger of Nana's whisky and downed it in one quick movement. She put down the glass and moved towards the door. 'Right? All right, Kathleen?'

Kathleen waited for the back door to slam then slipped upstairs to the airing cupboard. Her coat was still damp but she put it on. She jammed her feet into her school shoes and tied the laces. Silently, she went out. 'I wonder where Da is,' she thought. It was still early but the afternoon had faded to a damp, grey October evening. The winding wheel at the mine was drawing up pitmen at the end of their shift. 'I wonder if he knows.' The street lights at that moment flickered and came on, dimly. Kathleen paused for a second and blinked.

*

Da had been called away by the deputy. The news was broken softly to him, but in very few words. Now he stood in his work clothes and heavy boots, black from head to foot, his soft cap clutched in both hands, his head bowed. He was tall for a miner but the bright, white-tiled cleanliness of the mortuary, with its high ceiling, seemed to diminish him. He was sad and hunched and helpless as the trolley was wheeled towards him. The blanket was drawn slowly from Gloria's face, revealing its pallor, its staring expression, its ghastly, toothy grin. Da shuddered, stepped back and closed his eyes. The attendant muttered something consolatory. He looked again, but this time at a silver chain around his sister's neck. It was entwined with a black strand of debris from the pond. 'Is that . . . Is that . . .?' he stuttered.

The mortuary attendant was calm but helpful. 'Yes, sir?'

'Is that a St Christopher? Around her neck?'

Carefully, the man lifted the jewellery. A little pendant swung between his fingers.

'It's her,' said Da, his voice a dull sigh.

Her camera over her shoulder, Kathleen set off down the street where the neighbours had already drawn their curtains against the coming night. She cut through a cobbled lane to the centre of the village. All was quiet, the shops shut up for Sunday, except Gloria's hair salon. It shone brightly, tragically, its neon lights aglow, with two police cars parked outside. A tall PC filled the entrance. Kathleen glided unnoticed to the plate glass window and peered in through the nylon. A group of policemen, one the big man in the hat and overcoat, sat around, incongruously, under the driers. They were drinking tea from flasks. A young one had placed his helmet in a basket of plastic rollers which stood on a stand. Another leaned against a basin.

Kathleen slipped round to the back, entered the yard, located the key, quietly unlocked and pushed open the rear door. She stepped into the tiny storeroom where Gloria had sipped Tizer and read fashion magazines whenever business was slack. There was rumble of laughter from the men. Kathleen took a deep breath. The smell of the perming chemicals reminded her unbearably of her cousin. She peeped into the salon. At that moment she realized that Nosey was snuffling at her feet. He'd followed her. 'Go home!' she whispered fiercely.

The older, thick-set man had put his cup on the floor and was writing again in his notebook. Kathleen followed his gaze. He was copying some words which were inscribed large, on a wall mirror. The script was wobbly and written in what looked like dark red lipstick. Kathleen glanced down at a jar of combs in disinfectant and two oversized bottles of shampoo. She stared up again. 'DON'T LOOK FOR ME' the message read.

CRITICAL ACCLAIM FOR

Deborah Crombie

Leave the Grave Green

'A superbly engrossing whodunnit.'
BOOKLIST

'Absorbing . . . works well on every level.'
MOSTLY MURDER

'Deborah Crombie's quality shows in *Leave the Grave Green.*'
PETERBOROUGH EVENING TELEGRAPH

A Share in Death

'You'll enjoy some cosy bloodletting.'
DAILY TELEGRAPH

'For its style, characterization and plotting, *A Share in Death* deserves consideration for the year's major mystery awards.' MOSTLY MURDER

'Deborah Crombie has a bright future ahead of her.'
BIRMINGHAM POST

'A thoroughly entertaining mystery with a cleverly conceived and well-executed plot.' BOOKLIST

All Shall Be Well

'Written with compassion, clarity, wit and precision, this graceful mystery amply fulfils the promise of Crombie's debut novel, *A Share in Death*.'
PUBLISHERS WEEKLY

'Satisfying and almost poignant in its total impact.'
BIRMINGHAM POST

'As a murder and mystery devotee, I was delighted to be introducted to Deborah Crombie. *All Shall Be Well* is an entertaining read.' THE LADY

Leave the Grave Green

Deborah Crombie has had a lifelong interest in English mysteries and her debut, *A Share in Death*, was published in 1993 to international critical acclaim.

She grew up in Dallas, and has lived in Scotland and England, but now makes her home in North Texas.

Leave the Grave Green is the third novel in her Duncan Kincaid/Gemma James series.

Also by Deborah Crombie in Pan Books

A Share in Death

All Shall Be Well

Mourn Not Your Dead

Dreaming of the Bones

Deborah Crombie

Leave the Grave Green

PAN BOOKS

First published in Great Britain 1996 by Macmillan

This edition published 1996 by Pan Books
an imprint of Pan Macmillan Ltd
Pan Macmillan, 20 New Wharf Road, London N1 9RR
Basingstoke and Oxford
Associated companies throughout the world
www.panmacmillan.com

ISBN 0 330 34883 3

5 7 9 8 6 4

A CIP catalogue record for this book is available from the British Library.

Typeset by CentraCet Limited, Cambridge
Printed by Mackays of Chatham PLC, Chatham, Kent

For my dad, whose creativity and
enjoyment of life continue to inspire me

Acknowledgements

I'd like to thank Stephanie Woolley, of Taos, New Mexico, whose beautiful watercolours provided the model for Julia's portraits. I am also grateful to Brian Coventry, head cutter at Lilian Baylis House, who took time from his extremely busy schedule to show me LB House and introduce me to the mysteries of Making Wardrobe; and to Caroline Grummond, assistant to the orchestra manager at the English National Opera, who was kind enough to show me both front- and back-of-house at the Coliseum.

My agent, Nancy Yost, and my editor, Susanne Kirk, provided their usual expert advice, and thanks are, as always, due to the EOTNWG for their reading of the manuscript.

Last, but by no means least, thanks to my daughter, Katie, for helping our household run smoothly, and to my husband, Rick Wilson, for his patience and support.

Prologue

'Watch you don't slip.' Julia pushed back the wisps of dark hair that had snaked loose from her ponytail, her brow furrowed with anxious concern. The air felt dense, as thick and substantial as cotton wool. Tiny beads of moisture slicked her skin, and larger drops fell intermittently from the trees to the sodden carpet of leaves beneath her feet. 'We'll be late for tea, Matty. And you know what Father will say if you've not done your homework in time for practice.'

'Oh, don't be so wet, Julia,' said Matthew. A year younger than his sister, as fair and stocky as she was thin and dark, he'd physically outstripped her in the past year and it had made him more insufferably cocksure than ever. 'You're a broody old hen. "Matty, don't slip. Matty, don't fall," he mimicked her nastily. 'The way you carry on you'd think I couldn't wipe my own nose.' His arms held shoulder-high, he balanced on a fallen tree trunk near the edge of the swollen stream. His school rucksack lay where he'd dropped it carelessly in the mud.

Clutching her own books to her thin chest, Julia rocked on the balls of her feet. *Serve him right if he caught it from Father*. But the scolding, even if severe, would be brief, and life in their household would return quickly to normal – normal being that they all behaved, to quote Plummy when she felt particularly exasperated with him, 'as if the sun rose and set out of Matthew's backside'.

Julia's lips twitched at the thought of what Plummy would say when she saw his muddy bookbag and shoes. But no matter, all would be forgiven him, for Matthew possessed the one attribute her parents valued above all else. He could sing.

He sang effortlessly, the clear, soaring treble falling from his lips as easily as a whispered breath. And singing transformed him, the gawky, gap-toothed twelve-year-old vanishing as he concentrated, his face serious and full of grace. They would gather in the sitting room after tea, her father patiently fine-tuning Matthew on the Bach cantata he'd be singing with the choir at Christmas, her mother interrupting loudly and often with criticism and praise. It seemed to Julia that the three of them formed a charmed circle to which she, due to an accident of birth or some inexplicable whim of God, was forever denied admittance.

The children had missed their bus that afternoon. Julia, hoping for a private word with the art mistress, had delayed too long, and the loaded bus had rumbled by them, splattering dark freckles of mud on their calves. They'd had to walk home, and cutting across the fields, had caked their shoes with clay until they had to lift their heavy feet deliberately, like visitors from a lighter planet. When they reached the woods, Matthew had caught Julia's hand and pulled her, slipping and slithering through the trees, down the hillside to the stream nearest their house.

Julia shivered and looked up. The day had darkened perceptibly, and although the November afternoons drew in early, she thought the lessening visibility meant more rain. It had rained heavily every day for weeks. Jokes about the forty days and forty nights had long since grown stale; now glances at the heavy sky were followed by silent and resigned head-shaking. Here in the chalk hills north of the Thames, water leached steadily from the saturated ground and flowed into already overburdened tributaries.

Matty had left his tightrope-walking on the log and squatted at the water's edge, poking about with a long stick. The stream, in ordinary weather a dry gully, now filled its banks, the rushing water as opaque as milky tea.

Julia, feeling increasingly cross, said, 'Do come on, Matty, please.' Her stomach rumbled. 'I'm hungry. And cold.' She hugged herself tighter. 'If you don't come I shall go without you.'

'Look, Julie!' Oblivious to her nagging, he gestured towards the water with the stick. 'There's something caught under the surface, just there. Dead cat, maybe?' He looked round at her and grinned.

'Don't be disgusting, Matty.' She knew her prim and bossy tone would only fuel his teasing, but she was past caring. 'I really will go without you.' As she turned resolutely away she felt an unpleasant cramping sensation in her abdomen. 'Honestly, Matty, I don't feel—'

The splash sprayed her legs even as she whipped around. 'Matty! Don't be such an—'

He'd fallen in, landing on his back with his arms and legs splayed awkwardly. 'It's cold,' he said, his face registering surprise. He scrabbled towards the bank, laughing, shaking the water from his eyes.

Julia watched his gleeful expression fade. His eyes widened, his mouth formed a round *o*.

'Matty—'

The current caught him, pulling him downstream. 'Julie, I can't—' Water washed over his face, filling his mouth.

She stumbled along the bank's edge, calling his name. The rain began to fall in earnest, big drops that splashed against her face, blinding her. A protruding stone caught her toe and she fell. She picked herself up and ran on, only vaguely aware of the pain in her shin.

'Matty. Oh, Matty, please.' Repeated again and again, the words formed an unconscious incantation. Through the muddy water she could see the blue of his school jacket and the pale spread of his hair.

The ground descended sharply as the stream widened and turned away from her. Julia slid down the incline and stopped. On the opposite bank an old oak teetered precariously, a web of roots exposed where the stream had undercut the bank. Here

Matthew's body lodged, pinned under the roots as if held by a giant hand.

'Oh, Matty,' she cried, the words louder now, a wail of despair. She started into the water, a warm metallic saltiness filling her mouth as she bit through her lower lip. The cold shocked her, numbing her legs. She forced herself to go on. The water swirled about her knees, tugging at the hem of her skirt. It reached her waist, then her chest. She gasped as the cold bit into her ribs. Her lungs felt paralysed from the cold, unable to expand.

The current tugged at her, pulling at her skirt, shifting her foothold on the moss-covered rocks. With her arms held out for balance, she inched her right foot forward. Nothing. She moved a few feet to one side, then the other, feeling for the bottom. Still nothing.

Cold and exhaustion were fast sucking away her strength. Her breath came in shuddering gasps and the current's grasp seemed more insistent. She looked upstream and down, saw no easier crossing. Not that access to the other side would help her – it would be impossible to reach him from the steep bank.

A little moan escaped her. She stretched her arms towards Matty, but yards separated them, and she was too frightened to brave the current. Help. She must get help.

She felt the water lift and drag her forward as she turned, but she plunged on, digging her heels and toes in for purchase. The current slacked and she clambered out, standing for a moment on the muddy bank as a wave of weakness swept over her. Once more she looked at Matty, saw the outline of his legs twisting sideways in the current. Then she ran.

The house loomed through the dark arches of the trees, its white limestone walls eerily luminous in the dusk. Julia bypassed the front door without thinking. On around the house her feet took her, towards the kitchen, and warmth, and safety. Gasping from the steep climb up the hillside, she rubbed at her face, slick with rain and tears. She was conscious of her own breathing, of the squelching sound her shoes made with each step, and of the heavy wet wool of her skirt scratching her thighs.

Julia yanked open the kitchen door and stopped just inside, water pooling around her on the flags. Plummy turned from the Aga, spoon in hand, her dark hair dishevelled as always when she cooked. 'Julia! Where have you been? What will your mother have to say . . .?' The good-natured scolding faded. 'Julie, child, you're bleeding. Are you all right?' She came towards Julia, spoon abandoned, her round face creased with concern.

Julia smelled apples, cinnamon, saw the streak of flour across Plummy's bosom, registered in some compartment of her mind that Plummy was making apple pudding, Matty's favourite, for tea. She felt Plummy's hands grasp her shoulders, saw her kind and familiar face draw close, swimming through a film of tears.

'Julia, what is it? What's happened? Where's Matty?'

Plummy's voice was breathy now with panic, but still Julia stood, her throat frozen, the words dammed behind her lips.

A gentle finger stroked her face. 'Julia. You've cut your lip. What's happened?'

The sobs began, racking her slight body. She squeezed her arms tight to her chest to ease the pain. A stray thought flickered disjointedly through her mind – she couldn't remember dropping her books. *Matty. Where had Matty left his books?*

'Darling, you must tell me. What's happened?'

She was in Plummy's arms now, her face buried against the soft chest. The words came, choked out between sobs like a tide released. 'It's Matty. Oh, Plummy, it's Matty. He's drowned.'

Chapter One

From the train window Duncan Kincaid could see the piles of debris in the back gardens and on the occasional common. Wooden planks, dead branches and twigs, crushed cardboard boxes and the odd bit of broken furniture – anything portable served as fair game for Guy Fawkes bonfires. He rubbed ineffectually at the grimy window-pane with his jacket cuff, hoping for a better view of one particularly splendid monument to British abandon, then sat back in his seat with a sigh. The fine drizzle in the air, combined with British Rail's standard of cleanliness, reduced visibility to a few hundred yards.

The train slowed as it approached High Wycombe. Kincaid stood and stretched, then collected his overcoat and bag from the rack. He'd gone straight to Marylebone from the Yard, grabbing the emergency kit he kept in his office – clean shirt, toiletries, razor, only the necessities needed for an unexpected summons. And most were more welcome than this, a political request from the AC to aid an old school chum in a delicate situation. Kincaid grimaced. Give him an unidentified body in a field any day.

He swayed as the train lurched to a halt. Bending down to peer through the window, he scanned the station carpark for a glimpse of his escort. The unmarked panda car, its shape unmistakable even in the increasing rain, was pulled up next to the platform, its parking lights on, a grey plume of exhaust escaping from its tailpipe.

It looked like the cavalry had been called out to welcome Scotland Yard's fair-haired boy.

'Jack Makepeace. Sergeant, I should say. Thames Valley CID.' Makepeace smiled, yellowed teeth showing under the sandy bristle of moustache. 'Nice to meet you, sir.' He engulfed Kincaid's hand for an instant in a beefy paw, then took Kincaid's case and swung it into the panda's boot. 'Climb in, and we can talk as we go.'

The car's interior smelled of stale cigarettes and wet wool. Kincaid cracked his window, then shifted a bit in his seat so that he could see his companion. A fringe of hair the same colour as the moustache, freckles extending from face into shiny scalp, a heavy nose with the disproportionate look that comes of having been smashed – all in all not a prepossessing face, but the pale blue eyes were shrewd, and the voice unexpectedly soft for a man of his bulk.

Makepeace drove competently on the rain-slick streets, snaking his way south and west until they crossed the M40 and left the last terraced houses behind. He glanced at Kincaid, ready to divert some of his attention from the road.

'Tell me about it, then,' Kincaid said.

'What do you know?'

'Not much, and I'd just as soon you start from scratch, if you don't mind.'

Makepeace looked at him, opened his mouth as if to ask a question, then closed it again. After a moment he said, 'Okay. Daybreak this morning the Hambleden lock-keeper, one Perry Smith, opens the sluicegate to fill the lock for an early traveller, and a body rushes through it into the lock. Gave him a terrible shock, as you can imagine. He called Marlow – they sent a panda car and the medics.' He paused as he down-shifted into an intersection, then concentrated on overtaking an ancient Morris Minor that was creeping its way up the gradient. 'They fished him out, then when it became obvious that the poor chappie was not going to spew up the canal and open his eyes, they called us.'

The windscreen wiper squeaked against dry glass and Kincaid realized that the rain had stopped. Freshly ploughed fields rose on either side of the narrow road. The bare, chalky soil was a pale brown, and against it the black dots of foraging rooks looked like pepper on toast. Away to the west a cap of beech trees crowned a hill. 'How'd you identify him?'

'Wallet in the poor sod's back pocket. Connor Swann, aged thirty-five, brown hair, blue eyes, height about six feet, weight around twelve stone. Lived in Henley, just a few miles upstream.'

'Sounds like your lads could have handled it easily enough,' said Kincaid, not bothering to conceal his annoyance. He considered the prospect of spending his Friday evening tramping around the Chiltern Hundreds, damp as a Guy Fawkes bonfire, instead of meeting Gemma for an after-work pint at the pub down Wilfred Street. 'Bloke has a few drinks, goes for a stroll on the sluicegate, falls in. Bingo.'

Makepeace was already shaking his head. 'Ah, but that's not the whole story, Mr Kincaid. Someone left a very nice set of prints on either side of his throat.' He lifted both hands from the wheel for an instant in an eloquently graphic gesture. 'It looks like he was strangled, Mr Kincaid.'

Kincaid shrugged. 'A reasonable assumption, I would think. But I don't quite see why that merits Scotland Yard's intervention.'

'It's not the *how*, Mr Kincaid, but the who. It seems that the late Mr Swann was the son-in-law of Sir Gerald Asherton, the conductor, and Dame Caroline Stowe, who I believe is a singer of some repute.' Seeing Kincaid's blank expression, he continued, 'Are you not an opera buff, Mr Kincaid?'

'Are you?' Kincaid asked before he could clamp down his involuntary surprise, knowing he shouldn't have judged the man's cultural taste by his physical characteristics.

'I have some recordings, and I watch it on the telly, but I've never been to a performance.'

The wide sloping fields had given way to heavily wooded hills, and now, as the road climbed, the trees encroached upon it.

'We're coming into the Chiltern Hills,' said Makepeace. 'Sir Gerald and Dame Caroline live just a bit further on, near Fingest. The house is called Badger's End, though you wouldn't think it to look at it.' He negotiated a hairpin bend, and then they were running downhill again, beside a rocky stream. 'We've put you up at the pub in Fingest, by the way, the Chequers. Lovely garden in the back, on a fine day. Not that you're likely to get much use of it,' he added, squinting up at the darkening sky.

The trees enclosed them now. Gold and copper leaves arched tunnel-like overhead, and golden leaves padded the surface of the road. The late afternoon sky was still heavily overcast, yet by some odd trick of light the leaves seemed to take on an eerie, almost phosphorescent glow. Kincaid wondered if just such an enchanting effect had produced the ancient idea of 'roads paved with gold'.

'Will you be needing me?' Makepeace asked, breaking the spell. 'I'd expected you to have back-up.'

'Gemma will be here this evening, and I'm sure I can manage until then.' Seeing Makepeace's look of incomprehension, he added, 'Gemma James, my sergeant.'

'Rather your lot than Thames Valley.' Makepeace gave something halfway between a laugh and a snort. 'One of my green constables made the mistake this morning of calling Dame Caroline "Lady Asherton". The housekeeper took him aside and gave him a tongue-lashing he'll not soon forget. Informed him that Dame Caroline's title is hers by right and takes precedence over her title as Sir Gerald's wife.'

Kincaid smiled. 'I'll try not to put my foot in it. So there's a housekeeper, too?'

'A Mrs Plumley. And the widow, Mrs Julia Swann.' After an amused sideways glance at Kincaid, he continued, 'Make what you will of that one. Seems Mrs Swann lives at Badger's End with her parents, not with her husband.'

Before Kincaid could form a question, Makepeace held up his hand and said, 'Watch now.'

They turned left into a steep, high-banked lane, so narrow that brambles and exposed roots brushed the sides of the car. The sky had darkened perceptibly towards evening and it was dim and shadowed under the trees. 'That's the Wormsley valley off to your right, though you'd hardly know it.' Makepeace pointed, and through a gap in the trees Kincaid caught a glimpse of twilit fields rolling away down the valley. 'It's hard to believe you're only forty miles or so west of London, isn't it, Mr Kincaid?' he added with an air of proprietary pride.

As they reached the lane's high point, Makepeace turned left into the darkness of the beech woods. The track ran gently downhill, its thick padding of leaves silencing the car wheels. A few hundred yards on they rounded a curve and Kincaid saw the house. Its white stone shone beneath the darkness of the trees, and lamplight beamed welcomingly from its uncurtained windows. He knew immediately what Makepeace had meant about the name – Badger's End implied a certain rustic, earthy simplicity, and this house, with its smooth white walls and arched windows and doors, had an elegant, almost ecclesiastic presence.

Makepeace pulled the car up on the soft carpet of leaves, but left the engine running as he fished in his pocket. He handed Kincaid a card. 'I'll be off, then. Here's the number at the local nick. I've some business to attend to, but if you'll ring up when you've finished, someone will come and collect you.'

Kincaid waved as Makepeace pulled away, then stood staring at the house as the still silence of the woods settled over him. Grieving widow, distraught in-laws, an imperative for social discretion . . . not a recipe for an easy evening, or an easy case. He squared his shoulders and stepped forward.

The front door swung open and light poured out to meet him.

'I'm Caroline Stowe. It's so good of you to come.'

This time the hand that took his was small and soft, and he found himself looking down into the woman's upturned face. 'Duncan Kincaid. Scotland Yard.' With his free hand he pulled his warrant card from his inside jacket pocket, but she ignored it, still grasping his other hand between her own.

His mind having summed up the words *Dame* and *opera* as *large*, he was momentarily taken aback. Caroline Stowe stood a fraction over five feet tall, and while her small body was softly rounded, she could by no stretch of the imagination be described as heavy.

His surprise must have been apparent, because she laughed and said, 'I don't sing Wagner, Mr Kincaid. My speciality is bel canto. And besides, size is not relevant to strength of voice. It has to do with breath control, among other things.' She released his hand. 'Do come in. How rude of me to keep you standing on the threshold like some plumber's apprentice.'

As she closed the front door, he looked around with interest. A lamp on a side table illuminated the hall, casting shadows on the smooth grey flagstone floor. The walls were a pale grey-green, bare except for a few large gilt-framed watercolours depicting voluptuous, bare-breasted women lounging about Romanesque ruins.

Caroline opened a door on the right and stood aside, gesturing him in with an open palm.

Directly opposite the door a coal fire burned in a grate, and above the mantel he saw himself, framed in an ornate mirror – chestnut hair unruly from the damp, eyes shadowed, their colour indistinguishable from across the room. Only the top of Caroline's dark head showed beneath the level of his shoulder.

He had only an instant to gather an impression of the room. The same grey slate floor, here softened by scattered rugs; comfortable, slightly worn chintz furniture; a jumble of used tea things on a tray – all dwarfed by the baby grand piano. Its dark surface reflected the light from a small lamp, and sheet music stood open behind the keyboard. The bench was pushed back at an angle, as though someone had just stopped playing.

'Gerald, this is Superintendent Kincaid, from Scotland Yard.' Caroline moved to stand beside the large rumpled-looking man rising from the sofa. 'Mr Kincaid, my husband, Sir Gerald Asherton.'

'How nice to meet you,' Kincaid said, feeling the response inappropriate even as he made it. But if Caroline insisted on treating his visit as a social occasion, he would play along for a bit.

'Sit down.' Sir Gerald gathered a copy of the day's *Times* from the seat of an armchair and moved it to a nearby end table.

'Would you like some tea?' asked Caroline. 'We've just finished, and it's no trouble to boil the kettle again.'

Kincaid sniffed the lingering scent of toast in the air and his stomach rumbled. From where he sat he could see the paintings he'd missed when entering the room – watercolours again, by the same artist's hand, but this time the women reclined in elegant rooms and their dresses had the sheen of watered silk. A house to tempt the appetites, he thought, and said, 'No, thank you.'

'Have a drink, then,' Sir Gerald said. 'The sun's certainly over the yardarm.'

'No, I'm fine. Really.' What an incongruous couple they made, still standing side by side, hovering over him as if he were a royal guest. Caroline, dressed in a peacock-blue silk blouse and dark tailored trousers, looked neat and almost childlike beside her husband's bulk.

Sir Gerald smiled at Kincaid, a great, infectious grin that showed pink gums. 'Geoffrey recommended you very highly, Mr Kincaid.'

By Geoffrey he must mean Geoffrey Menzies-St John, Kincaid's assistant commissioner, and Asherton's old schoolmate. Though the two men must be of an age, there any outward resemblance ended. But the AC, while dapper and precise enough to appear priggish, possessed a keen intelligence, and Kincaid thought that unless Sir Gerald shared that quality, the two men would not have kept up with one another over the years.

Kincaid leaned forward and took a breath. 'Won't you sit down, please, both of you, and tell me what's happened?'

They sat obediently, but Caroline perched straight-backed on the sofa's edge, away from the protective curve of her husband's arm. 'It's Connor. Our son-in-law. They'll have told you.' She looked at him, her brown eyes made darker by dilating pupils. 'We can't believe it's true. Why would someone kill Connor? It doesn't make sense, Mr Kincaid.'

'We'll certainly need more evidence before we can treat this as an official murder inquiry, Dame Caroline.'

'But I thought . . .' she began, then looked rather helplessly at Kincaid.

'Let's start at the beginning, shall we? Was your son-in-law well liked?' Kincaid looked at them both, including Sir Gerald in the question, but it was Caroline who answered.

'Of course. Everyone liked Con. You couldn't *not*.'

'Had he been behaving any differently lately? Upset or unhappy for any reason?'

Shaking her head, she said, 'Con was always . . . just Con. You would have to have known . . .' Her eyes filled. She balled one hand into a fist and held it to her mouth. 'I feel such a bloody fool. I'm not usually given to hysterics, Mr Kincaid. Or incoherence. It's the shock, I suppose.'

Kincaid thought her definition of hysteria rather exaggerated, but said soothingly, 'It's perfectly all right, Dame Caroline. When did you see Connor last?'

She sniffed and ran a knuckle under one eye. It came away smudged with black. 'Lunch. He came for lunch yesterday. He often did.'

'Were you here as well, Sir Gerald?' Kincaid asked, deciding that only a direct question was likely to elicit a response.

Sir Gerald sat with his head back, eyes half closed, his untidy tuft of grey beard thrusting forward. Without moving, he said, 'Yes, I was here as well.'

'And your daughter?'

Sir Gerald's head came up at that, but it was his wife who answered. 'Julia was here, but didn't join us. She usually prefers to lunch in her studio.'

Curiouser and curiouser, thought Kincaid. *The son-in-law comes to lunch but his wife refuses to eat with him.* 'So you don't know when your daughter saw him last?'

Again the quick, almost conspiratorial glance between husband and wife, then Sir Gerald said, 'This has all been very difficult for Julia.' He smiled at

Kincaid, but the fingers of his free hand picked at what looked suspiciously like moth holes in his brown woollen sweater. 'I'm sure you'll understand if she's a bit . . . prickly.'

'Is your daughter here? I'd like to see her, if I may. And I will want to talk to you both at more length, when I've had a chance to review the statements you've given Thames Valley.'

'Of course. I'll take you.' Caroline stood, and Sir Gerald followed suit. Their hesitant expressions amused Kincaid. They'd been expecting a battering, and now didn't know whether to feel relieved or disappointed. They needn't worry – they'd be glad to see the back of him soon enough.

'Sir Gerald.' Kincaid stood and shook hands.

The watercolours caught his eye again as he turned towards the door. Although most of the women were fair, with delicate rose-flushed skin and lips parted to show small glistening white teeth, he realized that something about them reminded him of the woman he followed.

'This was the children's nursery,' Caroline said, her breathing steady and even after the three-flight climb. 'We made it into a studio for her before she left home. I suppose you might say it's been useful,' she added, giving him a sideways look he couldn't interpret.

They'd reached the top of the house and the landing was unornamented, the carpeting threadbare in spots. Caroline turned to the left and stopped before a closed door. 'She'll be expecting you.' She smiled at Kincaid and left him.

He tapped on the door, waited, tapped again and listened, holding his breath to catch any faint sound. The echo of Caroline's footsteps had died away. From somewhere below he heard a faint cough. Hesitating, he brushed his knuckles against the door once more, then turned the knob and went in.

The woman sat on a high stool with her back to him, her head bent over something he couldn't see. When Kincaid said, 'Uh, hello,' she whipped around towards him and he saw that she held a paintbrush in her hand.

Julia Swann was not beautiful. Even as he formed the thought, quite deliberately and matter-of-factly, he found he couldn't stop looking at her. Taller, thinner, sharper than her mother, dressed in a white shirt with the tail out and narrow black jeans, she displayed no softly rounded curves in figure or manner. Her chin-length dark hair swung abruptly when she moved her head, punctuating her gestures.

He read his intrusion in her startled posture, felt it in the room's instantly recognizable air of privacy. 'I'm sorry to bother you. I'm Duncan Kincaid, from Scotland Yard. I did knock.'

'I didn't hear you. I mean, I suppose I did, but I wasn't paying attention. I often don't when I'm working.' Even her voice lacked the velvety resonance of Caroline's. She slid off the stool, wiping her hands on a bit of rag. 'I'm Julia Swann. But then you know all that, don't you?'

The hand she held out to him was slightly damp from contact with the cloth, but her grasp was quick and hard. He looked around for somewhere to sit, saw nothing but a rather tatty and overstuffed armchair which would place him a couple of feet below the level of her stool. Instead he chose to lean against a cluttered workbench.

Although the room was fairly large – probably, he thought, the result of knocking two of the house's original bedrooms into one – the disorder extended everywhere he looked. The windows, covered with simple white rice-paper blinds, provided islands of calm in the jumble, as did the high table Julia Swann had been facing when he entered the room. Its surface was bare except for a piece of white plastic splashed with bright daubs of paint, and a Masonite board propped up at a slight angle. Before she slid onto the stool again and blocked his view, he glimpsed a small sheet of white paper masking-taped to the board.

Glancing at the paintbrush still in her hand, she set it on the table behind her and pulled a packet of cigarettes from her shirt pocket. She held it towards him, and when he shook his head and said, 'No, thanks,' she lit one and studied him as she exhaled.

'So, Superintendent Kincaid – it is Superintendent, isn't it? Mummy seemed to be quite impressed by the title, but then that's not unusual. What can I do for you?'

'I'm sorry about your husband, Mrs Swann.' He tossed out an expected opening gambit, even though he suspected already that her response would not be conventional.

She shrugged, and he could see the movement of her shoulders under the loose fabric of her shirt. Crisply starched, buttons on the left – Kincaid wondered if it might have been her husband's.

'Call me Julia. I never got used to "Mrs Swann". Always sounded to me like Con's mum.' She leaned towards him and picked up a cheap porcelain ashtray bearing the words *Visit the Cheddar Gorge*. 'She died last year, so that's one bit of drama we don't have to deal with.'

'Did you not like your husband's mother?' Kincaid asked.

'Amateur Irish. All b'gosh and b'gorra.' Then she added more affectionately, 'I used to say that her accent increased proportionately to her distance from County Cork.' Julia smiled for the first time. It was her father's smile, as unmistakable as a brand, and it transformed her face. 'Maggie adored Con. She would have been devastated. Con's dad did a bunk when Con was a baby . . . if he ever had a dad, that is,' she added, only the corners of her lips quirking up this time at some private joke.

'I had the impression from your parents that you and your husband no longer lived together.'

'Not for . . . ' She spread the fingers of her right hand and touched the tips with her left forefinger as her lips moved. Her fingers were long and slender, and she wore no rings. 'Well, more than a year now.'

Kincaid watched as she ground out her cigarette in the ashtray. 'It's a rather odd arrangement, if you don't mind my saying so.'

'Do you think so, Mr Kincaid? It suited us.'

'No plans to divorce?'

Julia shrugged again and crossed her knees, one slender leg swinging jerkily. 'No.'

He studied her, wondering just how hard he might push her. If she were grieving for her husband, she was certainly adept at hiding it. She shifted under his scrutiny and patted her shirt pocket, as if reassuring herself that her cigarettes hadn't vanished, and he thought that perhaps her armour wasn't quite impenetrable. 'Do you always smoke so much?' he said, as if he had every right to ask.

She smiled and pulled out the packet, shaking loose another cigarette.

He noticed that her white shirt wasn't as immaculate as he'd thought – it had a smudge of violet paint across the breast. 'Were you on friendly terms with Connor? See him often?'

'We spoke, yes, if that's what you mean, but we weren't exactly what you'd call best mates.'

'Did you see him yesterday, when he came here for lunch?'

'No. I don't usually break for lunch when I'm working. Ruins my concentration.' Julia stubbed out her newly lit cigarette and slid off the stool. 'As you've done now. I might as well quit for the day.' She gathered a handful of paintbrushes and crossed the room to an old-fashioned washstand with basin and ewer. 'That's the one drawback up here,' she said, over her shoulder, 'no running water.'

His view no longer blocked by her body, Kincaid straightened up and examined the paper taped to the drawing board. It was about the size of a page in a book, smooth-textured, and bore a faint pencil sketch of a spiky flower he didn't recognize. She had begun to lay in spots of clear, vivid colour, lavender and green.

'Tufted vetch,' she said, when she turned and saw him looking. 'A climbing plant. Grows in hedgerows. Flowers in—'

'Julia.' He interrupted the rush of words and she stopped, startled by the imperative in his voice. 'Your husband died last night. His body was discovered this morning. Wasn't that enough to interrupt your concentration? Or your work schedule?'

She turned her head away, her dark hair swinging to hide her face, but when she turned back to him her eyes were dry. 'You'd better understand, Mr Kincaid. You'll hear it from others soon enough. The term "bastard" might have been invented to describe Connor Swann.

'And I despised him.'

Chapter Two

'A lager and lime, please.' Gemma James smiled at the barman. If Kincaid were there he would raise an eyebrow at the very least, mocking her preference. So accustomed to his teasing had she become that she actually missed it.

'A raw evening, miss.' The man set the cool glass before her, aligning it neatly in the centre of a beer mat. 'Have you come far?'

'Just from London. Beastly traffic getting out, though.' But the sprawl of western London had finally faded behind her, and she left the M40 at Beaconsfield and followed the Thames Valley. Even in the mist she had seen some of the fine Victorian houses fronting the river, relics of the days when Londoners used the upper Thames as a playground.

At Marlow she turned north and wound up into the beech-covered hills, marvelling that in a few miles she seemed to have entered a hidden world, dark and leafy and far removed from the broad, peaceful expanse of the river below.

'What are the Chiltern Hundreds?' she asked the

barman. 'I've heard that phrase all my life and never known what it meant.'

He set down a bottle he'd been wiping with a cloth and considered his answer. Approaching middle age, with dark, wavy, carefully groomed hair and the beginning of a belly, he seemed happy enough to pass the time chatting. The lounge was almost empty – a bit early for the regular Friday night customers, Gemma supposed – but cosy with a wood fire burning and comfortable tapestry-covered furniture. A buffet of cold pies, salads and cheeses stood at the bar's end, and she eyed it with anticipation.

Thames Valley CID had certainly been up to the mark, booking her into the pub in Fingest and giving her precise directions. When she arrived she'd found a stack of reports waiting for her in her room, and having attended to them, she had only to enjoy her drink and wait for Kincaid.

'The Chiltern Hundreds, now,' said the barman, bringing Gemma sharply back to the present, 'they used to divide counties up into Hundreds, each with its own court, and three of these in Buckinghamshire came to be known as the Chiltern Hundreds because they were in the Chiltern Hills. Stoke, Burnham and Desborough, to be exact.'

'Seems logical,' said Gemma, impressed. 'And you're very knowledgeable.'

'Bit of a local history buff in my spare time. I'm Tony, by the way.' He thrust a hand over the bar and Gemma shook it.

'Gemma.'

'All the Hundreds are obsolete now, but the Stewardship of the Chiltern Hundreds is still a nominal office under the Chancellor of the Exchequer, the holding of which is the only reason one is allowed to resign from the House of Commons. A bit of jiggery-pokery, really, and probably the only reason the office still exists.' He smiled at her, showing strong, even, white teeth. 'There, I've probably told you more than you ever wanted to know. Get you a refill?'

Gemma glanced at her almost-empty glass, deciding she'd drunk as much as she ought if she wanted to keep a clear head. 'Better not, thanks.'

'You here on business? We don't let the rooms much this time of year. November in these hills is not exactly a drawing point for holiday-makers.'

'Quite,' said Gemma, remembering the fine drizzle under the darkness of the trees. Tony straightened glassware and kept an attentive eye on her at the same time, willing to talk if she wanted, but not pushing her. His self-assured friendliness made her wonder if he might be the pub's owner or manager, but in any case he was certainly a likely repository for local gossip.

'I'm here about that drowning this morning, actually. Police business.'

Tony stared at her, taking in, she felt sure, the curling ginger hair drawn back with a clip, the casual barley-coloured pullover and navy slacks. 'You're a copper? Well, I'll be . . .' He shook his head, his wavy hair not disturbed a whit by his incredulity. 'Best-looking one I've seen, I must say.'

Gemma smiled, accepting the compliment in the

same good humour as it was given. 'Did you know him, the man who drowned?'

This time Tony tut-tutted as he shook his head. 'What a shame. Oh, everyone around here knew Connor. Doubt there's a pub between here and London where he hadn't put his head in once or twice. Or a racetrack. A real Jack the Lad, that one.'

'Well liked, was he?' asked Gemma, fighting her prejudice towards a man on such good terms with pints and horses. Only after she'd married Rob had she discovered that he considered flirting and gambling as inalienable rights.

'Connor was a friendly sort of bloke, always had a word and a pat on the back for you. Good for business, too. After he'd had a couple of pints he'd buy rounds for everybody in the place.' Tony leaned forward against the bar, his face animated. 'And what a tragedy for the family, after the other.'

'What other? Whose family?' Gemma asked, wondering if she'd missed a reference to another drowning in the reports she'd read.

'Sorry.' Tony smiled. 'It is a bit confusing, I'm sure. Connor's wife Julia's family, the Ashertons. Been here for donkey's years. Connor was upstart Irish, second generation, I think, but all the same . . .'

'What happened to the Ashertons?' Gemma encouraged him, interested.

'I was just a couple of years out of school, back from trying it out in London.' His white teeth flashed as he smiled. 'Decided the big city wasn't nearly as glamorous as I'd thought. It was just about this time of year, as a matter of fact, and wet. Seemed like it had rained for months on end.' Tony paused and pulled a half-pint mug from the rack, lifting it towards Gemma. 'Mind if I join you?'

She shook her head, smiling. 'Of course not.' He was enjoying himself thoroughly now, and the longer she let him string out the story, the more detail she'd get.

He pulled a half-pint of Guinness from the tap and sipped it, then wiped the creamy foam from his upper lip before continuing. 'What was his name, now? Julia's little brother. It's been twenty years, or close to it.' He ran his fingers lightly over his hair, as if the admission of time passing made him conscious of his age. 'Matthew, that was it. Matthew Asherton. All of twelve years old and some sort of musical prodigy, walking home from school one day with his sister, and drowned. Just like that.'

The image of her own son clutched unbidden at Gemma's heart – Toby half-grown, his blond hair darkened, his face and body maturing from little-boy chubbiness, snatched away. She swallowed and said, 'How terrible. For all of them, but especially Julia. First her brother and now her husband. How did the little boy drown?'

'I'm not sure anyone ever really knew. One of those freak things that happen sometimes.' He shrugged and drank down half his Guinness. 'Quite a hush-hush at the time. Nobody talked about it except in whispers, and it's still not mentioned to the family, I suppose.'

A draught of cold air stirred Gemma's hair and swirled around her ankles as the outer door opened. She turned and watched a foursome come in and settle at a corner table, waving a familiar greeting to Tony. 'Reservations in half an hour, Tony,' one of the men called. 'Same as usual, okay?'

'It'll be picking up a bit now,' Tony remarked to Gemma as he began pouring their drinks. 'Restaurant usually fills up on a Friday night – all the locals out for their weekly bit of fun, minus the kiddies.' Gemma laughed, and when the air blew cool again against her back she didn't turn in anticipation.

Light fingers brushed her shoulder as Kincaid slid onto the barstool beside her. 'Gemma. Propping up the bar without me, I see.'

'Oh, hullo, guv.' She felt the pulse jump in her throat, even though she'd been expecting him.

'And chatting up the locals, I see. Lucky bloke.' He grinned at Tony. 'I'll have a pint of . . . Brakspear, isn't it, that's brewed at Henley?'

'My boss,' Gemma said in explanation to Tony. 'Tony, this is Superintendent Duncan Kincaid.'

'Nice to meet you, I'm sure.' Tony gave Gemma a surprised glance as he put out a hand to Kincaid.

Gemma studied Kincaid critically. Tall and slender, brown hair slightly untidy, tie askew and tweed jacket beaded with rain – she supposed he didn't look like most people's idea of a proper Scotland Yard superintendent. And he was too young, of course. Superintendents should definitely be older and weightier.

'Tell all,' Kincaid said, when he'd got his pint and

Tony had busied himself serving drinks to the customers in the corner.

Gemma knew that he relied on her to digest information and spit the pertinent bits back out to him, and she rarely had to use her notes. 'I've been over Thames Valley's reports.' She nodded towards the rooms above their heads. 'Had them waiting for me when I got in, very efficient.' Closing her eyes for a moment, she marshalled her thoughts. 'They had a call at seven-oh-five this morning from a Perry Smith, lock-keeper at Hambleden Lock. He'd found a body caught in his sluicegate. Thames Valley called in a rescue squad to fish the body out, and they identified him from his wallet as Connor Swann, resident of Henley-on-Thames. The lock-keeper, however, once he'd recovered from the shock a bit, recognized Connor Swann as the son-in-law of the Ashertons, who live a couple of miles up the road from Hambleden. He said the family often walked there.'

'On the lock?' Kincaid asked, surprised.

'Apparently it's part of a scenic walk.' Gemma frowned and picked up the thread of her story where she'd left off. 'The local police surgeon was called in to examine the body. He found considerable bruising around the throat. Also, the body was very cold, but rigor had only just begun—'

'But you'd expect the cold water to retard rigor,' Kincaid interrupted.

Gemma shook her head impatiently. 'Usually in drowning cases rigor sets in very quickly. So he thinks it likely that the victim may have been strangled before he went in the water.'

'Our police surgeon makes a bloody lot of assumptions, don't you think?' Kincaid selected a bag of onion-flavoured crisps from a display and counted out the proper coins to Tony. 'We'll see what the post-mortem has to say.'

'Nasty things,' said Gemma, eyeing the crisps distastefully.

Mouth full, Kincaid answered, 'I know, but I'm starving. What about the interviews with the family?'

She finished the last of her drink before answering, taking a moment to shift mental gears. 'Let's see . . . they took statements from the in-laws as well as the wife. Yesterday evening, Sir Gerald Asherton conducted an opera at the Coliseum in London. Dame Caroline Stowe was at home in bed, reading. And Julia Swann, the wife, was attending a gallery opening in Henley. None of them reported having words with Connor or having any reason to think he might be worried or upset.'

'Of course they didn't.' Kincaid pulled a face. 'And none of this means a thing without some estimate of time of death.'

'You met the family, didn't you, this afternoon? What are they like?'

Kincaid made a noise that sounded suspiciously like 'hummmph'. 'Interesting. Might be better if I let you form your own impressions, though. We'll interview them again tomorrow.' He sighed and sipped his pint. 'Not that I'll hold my breath waiting for a revelation. None of them can imagine why anyone would want to kill Connor Swann. So we have no motive, no suspect, and we're not even sure it's murder.' Raising his glass, he made her a mock toast. 'I can't wait.'

A good night's sleep had imbued Kincaid with a little more enthusiasm for the case. 'The lock first,' he said to Gemma over breakfast in the Chequers' dining room. 'I can't get much further along with this until I see it for myself. Then I want to have a look at Connor Swann's body.' He gulped his coffee and squinted at her, adding, 'How do you manage to look fresh and cheerful so early in the morning?' She wore a blazer the bright russet colour of autumn leaves, her face glowed, and even her hair seemed to crackle with a life of its own.

'Sorry.' She smiled at him, but Kincaid thought her sympathy was tinged with pity. 'I can't help it. Something to do with genes, I expect. Or being brought up a baker's daughter. We rose early at my house.'

'Ugh.' He'd slept heavily, aided by one pint too many the night before, and it had taken him a second cup of coffee just to feel marginally alert.

'You'll get over it,' Gemma said, laughing, and they finished their breakfast in companionable silence.

They drove through the quiet village of Fingest in the early morning light and took the lane leading south, towards the Thames. Leaving Gemma's Escort in the carpark half a mile from the river, they crossed the road to the path. A chill wind blew into their faces as they started downhill, and when Kincaid's shoulder accidentally bumped against Gemma's, he felt her warmth even through his jacket.

Their path crossed the road running parallel to the river, then threaded its way between buildings and overgrown shrubbery. Not until they emerged from a fenced passage did they see the spread of the river. Leaden water reflected leaden sky, and just before them a concrete walkway zigzagged its way across the water. 'Sure this is the right place?' Kincaid asked. 'I don't see anything that looks like a lock.'

'I can see boats on the far side, past that bank. There must be a channel.'

'All right. Lead on, then.' He gave a mock-gallant little bow and stepped aside.

They ventured out onto the walkway single file, unable to walk abreast without brushing the tubular metal railing which provided some measure of safety.

Halfway out they reached the weir. Gemma stopped and Kincaid came to a halt behind her. Looking down at the torrent thundering beneath the walkway, she shivered and pulled the lapels of her jacket together. 'Sometimes we forget the power of water. And the peaceful old Thames can be quite a monster, can't it?'

'River's high from the rain,' Kincaid said, raising his voice over the roar. He could feel the vibration from the force of the water through the soles of his feet. Grasping the railing until the cold of the metal made his hands ache, he leaned over, watching the flood until he began to lose his equilibrium. 'Bloody hell. If you intended to push someone in, this would be the place to do it.' Glancing at Gemma, he saw that she looked cold and a little pinched, the dusting of freckles standing out against her pale skin. He placed a hand lightly on her shoulder. 'Let's get across. It'll be warmer under the trees.'

They walked quickly, heads down against the wind, eager for shelter. The walkway ran on another hundred yards or so past the weir, paralleling the bank, then turned abruptly to the left and vanished into the trees.

The respite proved brief, the belt of trees narrow, but it allowed them to catch their breath before they came out into the open again and saw the lock before them. Yellow scene-of-crime tape had been stretched along the concrete aprons on either side of the lock, but not across the sluicegates themselves. To their right stood a sturdy red-brick house. The small-paned windows were symmetrical, one on either side of the door, but the one nearest them sported such a thatch of untrimmed green creeper that it looked like a shaggy-browed eye.

As Kincaid put a hand on the tape and bent to duck under it, a man came out of the door of the house, dodging under stray twigs of creeper, and shouted at them. 'Sir, you're not to go past the tape. Police orders.'

Kincaid straightened up and waited, studying the man as he came towards them. Short and stocky, with grey hair bristle-cut, he wore a polo shirt bearing the Thames River Authority insignia, and carried a steaming mug in one hand. 'What was the lock-keeper's name?' Kincaid said softly in Gemma's ear.

Gemma closed her eyes for a second. 'Perry Smith, I think.'

'One and the same, if I'm not mistaken.' He pulled his warrant card from his pocket and extended it as the man reached them. 'Are you Perry Smith, by any chance?'

The lock-keeper took the card with his free hand and studied it suspiciously, then scrutinized Kincaid and Gemma as if hoping they might be impostors. He nodded once, brusquely. 'I've already told the police everything I know.'

'This is Sergeant James,' Kincaid continued in the same conversational tone, 'and you're just the fellow we wanted to see.'

'All I'm concerned with is keeping this lock operating properly, Superintendent, without police interference. Yesterday they made me keep the sluicegates closed while they picked about with their tweezers and little bags. Backed river traffic up for a mile,' he said, and his annoyance seemed to grow. 'Bloody twits, I tell you.' He included Gemma in his scowl and made no apology for his language. 'Didn't it occur to them what would happen, or how long it would take to clear up the mess?'

'Mr Smith,' Kincaid said soothingly, 'I have no intention of interfering with your lock. I only want to ask you a few questions' – he held up a hand as Smith opened his mouth – 'which I'm aware you've already answered, but I'd prefer to hear your story directly from you, not second hand. Sometimes things get muddled along the way.'

Smith's brow relaxed a fraction and he took a sip from his mug. The heavy muscles in his upper arm stood out as he raised it, straining against the sleeve-band of his knitted shirt. 'Muddled wouldn't be the half of it, if those idiots yesterday set any example.' Although he seemed unaware of the cold, he looked at Gemma as if seeing her properly for the first time, huddled partly in the shelter of Kincaid's body with her jacket collar held closed around her throat. 'I suppose we could go inside, miss, out of the wind,' he said, a bit less belligerently.

Gemma smiled gratefully at him. 'Thank you. I'm afraid I didn't dress for the river.'

Smith turned back to Kincaid as they moved towards the house. 'When are they going to take this bloody tape down, that's what I'd like to know?'

'You'll have to ask Thames Valley. Though if the forensics team has finished, I shouldn't think it would be long.' Kincaid paused as they reached the door, looking at the concrete aprons surrounding the lock and the grassy path leading upriver on the opposite side. 'Doubt they'll have had much luck.'

The floor of the hall was covered in sisal matting and lined with well-used-looking rubber boots, the walls hung with working gear – oilskin jackets and hats, bright yellow slickers, coils of rope. Smith led them through a door on the left into a sitting room as workaday as the hall.

The room was warm, if spartan, and Kincaid saw

Gemma let go of her collar and take out her notebook. Smith stood by the window, still sipping from his mug, keeping an eye on the river. 'Tell us how you found the body, Mr Smith.'

'I came out just after sunrise as always, have my first cuppa and make sure everything's shipshape for the day. Traffic starts early, some days, though not so much now as in the summer. Sure enough, upstream there was a boat waiting for me to operate the lock.'

'Can't they work it themselves?' asked Gemma.

He was already shaking his head. 'Oh, the mechanism's simple enough, but if you're too impatient to let the lock fill and drain properly you can make a balls-up of it.'

'Then what happened?' prompted Kincaid.

'I can see you don't know much about locks,' he said, looking at them with the sort of pity usually reserved for someone who hasn't learned to tie their shoelaces.

Kincaid refrained from saying that he had grown up in western Cheshire and understood locks perfectly well.

'The lock is kept empty when it's not in operation, so first I open the sluices in the head gate to fill the lock. Then when I opened the head gate for the boat to enter, up pops a body.' Smith sipped from his cup, then added disgustedly, 'Silly woman on the boat started squealing like a pig going to slaughter, you've never heard such a racket. I came in here and dialled nine-nine-nine, just to get some relief from the noise.' The corners of Smith's eyes crinkled in what might have been a smile. 'Rescue people fished him out and tried to resuscitate the poor blighter, though if you ask me, anybody with a particle of sense could see he'd been dead for hours.'

'When did you recognize him?' asked Gemma.

'Didn't. Not his body, anyway. But I looked at his wallet when they took it out of his pocket, and I knew the name seemed familiar. Took me a minute to place it.'

Kincaid moved to the window and looked out. 'Where had you heard it?'

Smith shrugged. 'Pub gossip, most likely. Everyone hereabouts knows the Ashertons and their business.'

'Do you think he could have fallen in from the top of the gate?' Kincaid asked.

'Railing's not high enough to keep a tall man from going over if he's drunk. Or stupid. But the concrete apron continues for a bit on the upstream side of the gate before it meets the old towpath, and there's no railing along it at all.'

Kincaid remembered the private homes he'd seen upstream on this side of the river. All had immaculate lawns running down to the water, some also had small docks. 'What if he went in further upstream?'

'The current's not all that strong until you get close to the gate, so if he went in along there,' – he nodded upstream – 'I'd say he'd have to have been unconscious not to have pulled himself out. Or already dead.'

'What if he went in here, by the gate? Would the current have been strong enough to hold him down?'

Smith gazed out at the lock a moment before

answering. 'Hard to say. The current is what holds the gate closed – it's pretty fierce. But whether it could hold a struggling man down . . . unlikely, I'd say, but you can't be sure.'

'One more thing, Mr Smith,' Kincaid said. 'Did you see or hear anything unusual during the night?'

'I go to bed early, as I'm always up by daybreak. Nothing disturbed me.'

'Would a scuffle have awakened you?'

'I've always been a sound sleeper, Superintendent. I can't very well say, now can I?'

'Sleep of the innocent?' whispered Gemma as they took their leave and Smith firmly shut his door.

Kincaid stopped and stared at the lock. 'If Connor Swann were unconscious or already dead when he went in the water, how in hell did someone get him here? It would be an almost impossible carry even for a strong man.'

'Boat?' ventured Gemma. 'From either upstream or down. Although why someone would lift him from a boat downstream of the lock, carry him round and dump him on the upstream side, I can't imagine.'

They walked slowly towards the path that would take them back across the weir, the wind at their backs. Moored boats rocked peacefully in the quiet water downstream. Ducks dived and bobbed, showing no concern with human activity that didn't involve crusts of bread. 'Was he already dead? That's the question, Gemma.' He looked at her, raising an eyebrow. 'Fancy a visit to the mortuary?'

Chapter Three

The smell of disinfectant always reminded Kincaid of his school infirmary, where Matron presided over the bandaging of scraped knees and wielded the power to send one home if the illness or injury proved severe enough. The inhabitants of this room, however, were beyond help from Matron's ministrations, and the disinfectant didn't quite mask the elusive tang of decay. He felt gooseflesh rise on his arms from the cold.

A quick call to Thames Valley CID had directed them to High Wycombe's General Hospital, where Connor Swann's body awaited post-mortem. The hospital was old, the mortuary still a place of ceramic tiles and porcelain sinks, lacking the rows of stainless-steel drawers which tucked bodies neatly away out of sight. Instead, the steel gurneys that lined the walls held humped, white-sheeted forms with toe tags peeping out.

'Who was it you wanted, now?' asked the attendant, a bouncy young woman whose name-tag read 'Sherry' and whose demeanour seemed more suited to a nursery school.

'Connor Swann,' said Kincaid, with an amused glance at Gemma.

The girl walked along the row of gurneys, flicking toe tags with her fingers as she passed. 'Here he is. Number four.' She tucked the sheet down to his waist with practised precision. 'And a nice clean one he is, too. Always makes it a bit easier, don't you think?' She smiled brightly at them, as if they were mentally impaired, then walked back to the swinging doors and shouted, 'Mickey,' through the gap she made with one hand. 'We'll need some help shifting him,' she added, turning back to Kincaid and Gemma.

Mickey emerged a moment later, parting the doors like a bull charging from a pen. The muscles in his arms and shoulders strained the thin fabric of his T-shirt, and he wore the short sleeves rolled up, displaying an extra inch or two of biceps.

'Can you give these people a hand with number four, Mickey?' Sherry enunciated carefully, her nursery-teacher manner now mixed with a touch of exasperation. The young man merely nodded, his acne-inflamed face impassive, and pulled a pair of thin latex gloves from his back pocket. 'Take all the time you want,' she added to Kincaid and Gemma. 'Just give me a shout when you've finished, okay? Cheerio.' She whisked past them, the tail of her white lab coat flapping, and went out through the swinging doors.

They moved the few steps to the gurney and stood. In the ensuing silence Kincaid heard the soft expulsion of Gemma's breath. Connor Swann's exposed neck and shoulders were lean and well formed, his thick straight hair brown with a hint of auburn. Kincaid thought it likely that in life he had been one of those high-coloured men who flushed easily in anger or excitement. His body was indeed remarkably unblemished. Some bruising showed along the left upper arm and shoulder, and when Kincaid looked closely he saw faint dark marks on either side of the throat.

'Some bruising,' Gemma said dubiously, 'but not the occlusion of the face and neck you'd expect with a manual strangulation.'

Kincaid bent over for a closer look at the throat. 'No sign of a ligature. Look, Gemma, across the right cheekbone. Is that a bruise?'

She peered at the smudge of darker colour. 'Could be. Hard to tell, though. His face could easily have banged against the gate.'

Connor Swann had been blessed with good bone structure, thought Kincaid, high wide cheekbones and a strong nose and chin. Above his full lips lay a thick, neatly trimmed, reddish moustache, looking curiously alive against the grey pallor of his skin.

'A good-looking bloke, would you say, Gemma?'

'Probably attractive, yes . . . unless he was a bit too full of himself. I got the impression he was quite the ladies' man.'

Kincaid wondered how Julia Swann felt about that – she hadn't impressed him as a woman willing to sit at home meekly while her husband played the lad. It also occurred to him to wonder how much of his desire to see Connor had to do with assessing the physical evidence, and how much to do with his personal curiosity about the man's wife.

He turned to Mickey and raised a questioning eyebrow. 'Could we have a look at the rest?'

The young man obliged wordlessly, flipping the sheet off altogether.

'He'd been on holiday, but I'd say not recently,' Gemma commented as they saw the faint demarcation of a tan against belly and upper thighs. 'Or maybe just summer boating on the Thames.'

Deciding he might as well imitate Mickey's non-verbal style of communication, Kincaid nodded and made a rolling motion with his hand. Mickey slid both gloved hands beneath Connor Swann's body, turning him with an apparent ease betrayed only by a barely audible grunt.

Wide shoulders, faintly freckled; a thin pale band on the neck bordering the hairline, evidence of a recent haircut; a mole where the buttock began to swell from the hollow of the back – all trivial things, thought Kincaid, but all proof of Connor Swann's uniqueness. It always came, this moment in an investigation when the body became a person, someone who had perhaps liked cheese-and-pickle sandwiches, or old Benny Hill comedies.

'Had enough, guv?' Gemma said, sounding a bit more subdued than usual. 'He's clean as a whistle this side.'

Kincaid nodded. 'Not much else to see. And nothing does us much good until we've traced his movements and got some estimate of time of death. Okay, Mickey,' he added, as the expression on the young man's face indicated they might as well have been speaking in Greek. 'I guess that's it. Let's look up Sherry Sunshine.' Kincaid looked back as they reached the door. Mickey had already turned Connor's body and tidied the sheet as neatly as before.

They found her in a cubbyhole just to the left of the swinging doors, bent industriously over a computer keyboard, cheerful as ever. 'Do you know when they've scheduled the post?' Kincaid asked.

'Um, let's see.' She studied a typed schedule stuck to the wall with Sellotape. 'Winnie can probably get to him late tomorrow afternoon or early the following morning.'

'Winnie?' Kincaid asked, fighting the absurd vision of Pooh Bear performing an autopsy.

'Dr Winstead.' Sherry dimpled prettily. 'We all call him that – he's a bit tubby.'

Kincaid contemplated attending the post-mortem with resignation. He had long ago got over any sort of grisly thrill at the proceedings. Now he found it merely distasteful, and the ultimate violation of human privacy sometimes struck him as unbearably sad. 'You'll let me know as soon as you schedule it?'

'Quick as a wink. I'll do it myself.' Sherry beamed at him.

Out of the corner of his eye Kincaid saw Gemma's expression and knew she'd rag him about buttering up the hired help. 'Thanks, love,' he said to Sherry, giving her his full-wattage smile. 'You've been a great help.' He waggled his fingers at her. 'Cheerio, now.'

'You're absolutely shameless,' said Gemma as soon as they were through the outer doors. 'That poor little duck was as susceptible as a baby.'

Kincaid grinned at her. 'Gets things done, though, doesn't it?'

After a few unplanned detours due to her unfamiliarity with High Wycombe's one-way system, Gemma found her way out of the town. Following Kincaid's directions, she drove southwest, back into the hidden folds of the Chiltern Hills. Her stomach grumbled a bit, but they had decided that they should interview the Ashertons again before lunch.

In her mind she ran through Kincaid's and Tony's comments about the family, her curiosity piqued. She glanced at Kincaid, a question forming on her lips, but his unfocused gaze told her he was somewhere else entirely. He often got like that before an interview, as if it were necessary for him to turn inward before bringing that intense focus to bear.

She concentrated again on her driving, but she suddenly felt extraordinarily aware of his long legs taking up more than their share of the room in her Escort's passenger compartment, and of his silence.

After a few minutes they reached the point where she had to make an unfamiliar turning. Before she could speak, he said, 'Just here. Badger's End lies about halfway along this little road.' His fingertip traced a faint line on the map, between the villages of Northend and Turville Heath. 'It's unmarked, a shortcut for the locals, I suppose.'

Ribbons of water trickled across the pavement where a stream bed ran down through the trees and intersected the narrow road. A triangular yellow road sign warned DANGER: FLOODING, and suddenly the story Gemma had heard of Matthew Asherton's drowning seemed very immediate.

'Hard left,' Kincaid said, pointing ahead, and Gemma turned the wheel. The lane they entered was high-banked, just wide enough for the Escort to pass unscathed, and on either side thick trees arched until they met and intertwined overhead. It climbed steadily, and the high banks rose until the tree roots were at eye level. On the right, Gemma caught an occasional flash through the foliage of golden fields dropping down to a valley. On the left the woods crowded, darkly impenetrable, and the light filtering through the leafy canopy over the lane seemed green and liquid.

'Sledging,' Gemma said suddenly.

'What?'

'It reminds me of sledging. You know, bobsleighing. Or the Olympic luge.'

Kincaid laughed. 'Don't accuse me of poetic fancy. Careful now, watch for a turning on the left.'

They appeared to be nearing the top of the gradient when Gemma saw a gap in the left-hand bank. She slowed and eased the car onto the leaf-padded track, following it on and slightly downhill until she rounded a bend and came into a clearing. 'Oh,' she said softly, surprised. She'd expected a house built with the comfortable flint and timber construction she'd seen in the nearby villages. The sun, which had chased fitfully in and out of the cloud bank, found a gap, making dappled patterns against the white limestone walls of Badger's End.

'Like it?'

'I'm not sure.' Gemma rolled down the window as she turned off the engine, and they sat for a moment, listening. Beneath the silence of the woods they heard a faint, deep hum. 'It's a bit eerie. Not at all what I imagined.'

'Just wait,' said Kincaid as he opened the car door, 'until you meet the family.'

Gemma assumed that the woman who answered the door must be Dame Caroline Stowe – good quality, tailored wool slacks, blouse and navy cardigan, short, dark, well-cut hair liberally streaked with grey – everything about her spoke of conservative, middle-aged good taste. But when the woman stared at them blankly, coffee mug poised halfway to her mouth, then said, 'Can I help you with something?' Gemma's certainty began to waver.

Kincaid identified himself and Gemma, then asked for Sir Gerald and Dame Caroline.

'Oh, I'm sorry, you've just missed them. They've gone down to the undertakers for a bit. Making arrangements.' She transferred the coffee mug to her left hand and held out the right to them. 'I'm Vivian Plumley, by the way.'

'You're the housekeeper?' Kincaid asked, and Gemma knew from the less-than-tactful query that he'd been caught off guard.

Vivian Plumley smiled. 'You might say that. It doesn't offend me, at any rate.'

'Good.' Kincaid, Gemma saw, had recovered both aplomb and smile. 'We'd like a word with you as well, if we may.'

'Come back to the kitchen. I'll make some coffee.' She turned and led the way along the slate-flagged passage, then stepped back and let them precede her through the door at its end.

The kitchen had escaped modernization. While Gemma might sigh over photographs of gleaming space-age kitchens in magazines, she knew instinctively that they provided no emotional substitute for a room like this. Nubby braided rugs softened the slate floor, a scarred oak refectory table and ladder-backed chairs dominated the room's centre, and against one wall a red-enamelled Aga radiated warmth and comfort.

'Sit down, why don't you,' said Vivian Plumley, and gestured towards the table. Gemma pulled out a chair and sat, feeling tension she hadn't been aware of flow out of her muscles. 'Some biscuits?' added Vivian, and Gemma shook her head quickly, fearing they'd lose control of the interview entirely, seduced by the room's comfort.

Kincaid said, 'No, thank you,' and seated himself, taking the chair at the table's end. Gemma took her notebook from her bag and cradled it unobtrusively in her lap.

The drip coffeemaker worked as quickly as its expensive looks implied. It was only a few moments before the smell of fresh coffee began to fill the room. Vivian put together a tray with mugs, cream and sugar in silence, a woman enough at ease with herself not to make small talk. When the coffeemaker had finished its cycle, she filled the mugs and brought the tray to the table. 'Do help yourself. And that's real cream, I'm afraid, not dairy substitute. We have a neighbour who keeps a few Jerseys.'

'A treat not to be missed,' said Kincaid, pouring generously into his cup. Gemma smiled, knowing he usually drank it black. 'Are you not the housekeeper, then?' he continued easily. 'Have I put my foot in it?'

Vivian clinked her spoon around twice in her coffee cup and sighed. 'Oh, I'll tell you about myself, if you like, but it always sounds so dreadfully Victorian. I'm actually related to Caroline, second cousins once removed, to be exact. We're as close to the same age as never-mind, and we were at school together.' She paused and sipped from her cup, then made a slight grimace of discomfort. 'Too hot. We drifted apart, Caro and I, once we'd finished school. We both married, her career blossomed.' Vivian smiled.

'Then my husband died. An aneurysm.' The palms of her hands made a slapping sound as she brushed them together. 'Just like that, he was gone. I was left childless, with no job skills and not quite enough money to get by. This was thirty years ago, mind you, when not every woman grew up with the expectation of working.' She looked directly at Gemma. 'Quite different from your upbringing, I'm sure.'

Gemma thought of her mother, who had risen in the early hours of the morning to bake every day of her married life, then worked the counter in the shop from opening till closing. The possibility of *not* working never occurred to Gemma or her sister – it had been Gemma's driving ambition for the work to be of her own choosing, not something done purely for the necessity of putting food on the table. 'Yes, very different,' she said, in answer to Vivian Plumley's statement. 'What did you do?'

'Caro had two toddlers and a very demanding career.' She shrugged. 'It seemed a sensible solution. They had room, I had enough money of my own not to be totally dependent on the family, and I loved the children as if . . .'

They were your own. Gemma finished the sentence for her, and felt a rush of empathy for this woman who seemed to have made the best of what life had dealt her. She ran her fingers along the tabletop, noticing faint streaks of colour embedded in the wood's grain.

Watching her, Vivian said fondly, 'The children did everything at this table. They had most of their meals in the kitchen, of course. As much as their parents travelled, formal family dinners were a rare treat. School assignments, art projects – Julia did her first paintings here, when she was at grammar school.'

The children this . . . the children that . . . It seemed to Gemma as if time had simply stopped with the boy's death. But Julia had been there afterwards, alone. 'This must all be very difficult for Julia,' she said, feeling her way into the subject delicately, 'after what happened to her brother.'

Vivian looked away, grasping the table's edge with one hand, as if she were physically restraining herself from getting up. After a moment, she said, 'We don't talk about that. But yes, I'm sure Con's death has made life more difficult than usual for Julia. It's made life difficult for all of us.'

Kincaid, who had been sitting quietly, chair pushed back a bit from the table, mug cradled in his hands, leaned forward and said, 'Did you like Connor, Mrs Plumley?'

'Like him?' she said blankly, then frowned. 'It never occurred to me whether or not I should like Connor. He was just . . . Connor. A force of nature.' She smiled a little at her own analogy. 'A very attractive man in many ways, and yet . . . I always felt a little sorry for him.'

Kincaid raised an eyebrow but didn't speak, and Gemma followed his cue.

Shrugging, Vivian said, 'I know it sounds a bit silly to say one felt sorry for someone as larger-than-life as Con, but Julia baffled him.' The gold buttons on her cardigan caught the light as she shifted in her chair. 'He could never make her respond in the way he wanted, and he hadn't any experience with that. So he sometimes behaved . . . inappropriately.' A door slammed in the front of the house and she cocked her head, listening. Half-rising from her chair, she said, 'They're back. Let me tell—'

'One more thing, please, Mrs Plumley,' Kincaid said. 'Did you see Connor on Thursday?'

She sank down again, but perched on the edge of her seat with the tentative posture of one who doesn't intend staying long. 'Of course I saw him. I prepared lunch – just salad and cheese – and we all ate together in the dining room.'

'All except Julia?'

'Yes, but she often works through lunch. I took a plate up to her myself.'

'Did Connor seem his usual self?' Kincaid asked, his tone conversational, but Gemma knew from his still concentration that he was intent on her answer.

Vivian relaxed as she thought, leaning back in her chair again and absently tracing the raised flower pattern on her mug with her fingers. 'Con was always teasing and joking, but perhaps it seemed a bit forced. I don't know.' She looked up at Kincaid, frowning. 'Quite possibly I'm distorting things after the fact. I'm not sure I trust my own judgement.

Kincaid nodded. 'I appreciate your candour. Did he mention any plans for later in the day? It's important that we trace his movements.'

'I remember him glancing at his watch and saying something about a meeting, but he didn't say where or with whom. That was towards the end of the meal, and as soon as everyone had finished I came in here to do the washing up, then went to my room for a lie-down.

You might ask Caro or Gerald if he said something more to them.'

'Thank you. I'll do that,' Kincaid said with such courtesy that Gemma felt sure it would never occur to Vivian Plumley that she'd just told him how to do his job. 'It's strictly a formality, of course, but I must ask you about your movements on Thursday night,' he added almost apologetically.

'An alibi? You're asking me for an alibi for Connor's death?' Vivian asked, sounding more surprised than offended.

'We don't yet know exactly when Connor died. And it's more a matter of building known factors – the more we know about the movements of everyone connected with Connor, the easier it becomes to see gaps. Logic holes.' He made a circular gesture with his hands.

'All right.' She smiled, appeased. 'That's easy enough. Caro and I had an early supper in front of the fire in the sitting room. We often do when Gerald's away.'

'And after that?'

'We sat before the fire, reading, watching the telly, talking a little. I made some cocoa around ten o'clock, and when we'd finished it I went up to bed.' She added with a touch of irony, 'I remember thinking it had been a particularly peaceful and pleasant evening.'

'Nothing else?' Kincaid asked, straightening up in his chair and pushing away his empty mug.

'No,' Vivian said, but then paused and stared into space for a moment. 'I do remember something, but it's quite silly.' When Kincaid nodded encouragement, she continued. 'Just after I'd fallen asleep I thought I heard the doorbell, but when I sat up and listened, the house was perfectly quiet. I must have been dreaming. Gerald and Julia both have their own keys, of course, so there was no need to wait up for them.'

'Did you hear either of them come in?'

'I thought I heard Gerald around midnight, but I wasn't properly awake, and the next thing I knew it was daybreak and the rooks were making a god-awful racket in the beeches outside my window.'

'Couldn't it have been Julia?' Kincaid asked.

She thought for a moment, her brow furrowed. 'I suppose it could, but if it's not terribly late, Julia usually looks in on me before she goes up.'

'And she didn't that evening?'

When Vivian shook her head, Kincaid smiled at her and said, 'Thank you, Mrs Plumley. You've been very helpful.'

This time, before rising, Vivian Plumley looked at him and said, 'Shall I tell them you're here?'

Sir Gerald Asherton stood with his back to the sitting room fire, hands clasped behind him. He made a perfect picture of a nineteenth-century country squire, thought Gemma, with his feet spread apart in a relaxed posture and his bulk encased in rather hairy tweeds. He even sported suede elbow patches on his jacket. The only things needed to complete the tableau were a pipe and a pair of hunting hounds sprawled at his feet.

'So sorry to have kept you waiting.' He came towards them, pumped their hands and gestured them towards the sofa.

Gemma found the courtesy rather disarming, and suspected it was meant to be.

'Thank you, Sir Gerald,' Kincaid said, returning it in kind. 'And Dame Caroline?'

'Gone for a bit of a lie-down. Found the business at the undertakers rather upsetting, I'm afraid.' Sir Gerald sat in the armchair opposite them, crossed one foot over his knee and adjusted his trouser leg. An expanse of Argyle sock in autumnal orange and brown appeared between shoe and trouser cuff.

'If you don't mind my saying so, Sir Gerald,' Kincaid smiled as he spoke, 'it seems a little odd that your daughter didn't take care of the arrangements herself. Connor was, after all, her husband.'

'Just so,' answered Sir Gerald with a touch of asperity. 'Sometimes these things are best left to those not quite so close to the matter. And funeral directors are notorious for preying on the emotions of the newly bereaved.' Gemma felt a stab of pity at the reminder that this burly, confident man spoke from the worst possible personal experience.

Kincaid shrugged and let the matter drop. 'I need to ask you about your movements on Thursday night, sir.' At Sir Gerald's raised eyebrow, he added, 'Just a formality, you understand.'

'No reason why I shouldn't oblige you, Mr Kincaid. It's a matter of public record. I was at the Coliseum, conducting a performance of *Pelleas and Melisande.*' He favoured them with his large smile, showing healthily pink gums. 'Extremely visible. No one could have impersonated me, I assure you.'

Gemma imagined him facing an orchestra, and felt sure he dominated the hall as easily as he dominated this small room. From where she sat she could see a photograph of him atop the piano, along with several others in similar silver frames. She stood up unobtrusively and went to examine them. The nearest showed Sir Gerald in a tuxedo, baton in hand, looking as comfortable as he did in his country tweeds. In another he had his arm around a small dark-haired woman who laughed up at the camera with a voluptuous prettiness.

The photograph of the children had been pushed to the back, as if no one cared to look at it often. The boy stood slightly in the foreground, solid and fair, with an impish gap-toothed grin. The girl was a few inches taller, dark-haired like her mother, her thin face gravely set. This was Julia, of course. Julia and Matthew.

'And after?' she heard Kincaid say, and she turned back to the conversation, rather embarrassed by her lapse of attention.

Sir Gerald shrugged. 'It takes a while to wind down after a performance. I stayed in my dressing room for a bit, but I'm afraid I didn't take notice of the time. Then I drove straight home, which must have put me here sometime after midnight.'

'Must have?' Kincaid asked, his voice tinged with scepticism.

Sir Gerald held out his right arm, baring a hairy wrist for their inspection. 'Don't wear a watch, Mr Kincaid. Never found it comfortable. And a nuisance taking it off for every rehearsal or performance. Always lost the bloody things. And the car clock never worked properly.'

'You didn't stop at all?'

Shaking his head, Sir Gerald answered with the finality of one used to having his word taken as law. 'I did not.'

'Did you speak to anyone when you came in?' Gemma asked, feeling it was time she put an oar in.

'The house was quiet. Caro was asleep and I didn't wake her. I can only assume the same for Vivian. So you see, young lady, if it's an alibi you're after,' he paused and twinkled at Gemma, 'I suppose I haven't one.'

'What about your daughter, sir? Was she asleep as well?'

'I'm afraid I can't say. I don't remember seeing Julla's car in the drive, but I suppose someone could have given her a lift home.'

Kincaid stood. 'Thank you, Sir Gerald. We will need to talk to Dame Caroline again, at her convenience, but just now we'd like to see Julia.'

'I believe you know your way, Mr Kincaid.'

*

'Good God, I feel like I've been dropped right in the bloody middle of a drawing room comedy.' Gemma turned her head to look at Kincaid as she preceded him up the stairs. 'All manners and no substance. What are they playing at in this house?' As they reached the first landing, she stopped and turned to face him. 'And you'd think these women were made of glass, the way Sir Gerald and Mrs Plumley coddle them. "Mustn't upset Caroline . . . mustn't upset Julia,"' she hissed at him, remembering a bit belatedly to lower her voice.

Kincaid merely raised an eyebrow in that imperturbable manner she found so infuriating. 'I'm not sure I'd consider Julia Swann a good candidate for coddling.' He started up the next flight, and Gemma followed the rest of the way without comment.

The door swung open as soon as Kincaid's knuckles brushed it. 'Bless you, Plummy. I'm star—' Julia Swann's smile vanished abruptly as she took in their identity. 'Oh. Superintendent Kincaid. Back so soon?'

'Like a bad penny,' Kincaid answered, giving her his best smile.

Julia Swann merely stuck the paintbrush she'd had in her hand over her ear and stepped back enough to allow them to enter. Studying her, Gemma compared the woman to the thin, serious child in the photo downstairs. That Julia was certainly visible in this one, but the gawkiness had been transmuted into sleek style, and the innocence in the child's gaze had been lost long ago.

The blinds were drawn up, and a pale, watery light illuminated the room. The centre worktable, bare except for palette and white paper neatly masking-taped to a board, relieved the studio's general disorder. 'Plummy usually brings me up a sandwich about this time,' Julia said, as she shut the door and returned to the table. She leaned against it, gracefully balancing her weight, but Gemma had the distinct impression that the support she drew from it was more than physical.

A finished painting of a flower lay on the table. Gemma moved towards it almost instinctively, hand outstretched. 'Oh, it's lovely,' she said softly, stopping just short of touching the paper. Spare and sure in design, the painting had an almost oriental flavour, and the intense greens and purples of the plant glowed against the matte-white paper.

'Bread and butter,' said Julia, but she smiled, making an obvious effort to be civil. 'I've a whole series commissioned for a line of cards. Upscale National Trust, you know the sort of thing. And I'm behind schedule.' Julia rubbed at her face, leaving a smudge of paint on her forehead, and Gemma suddenly saw the weariness that her smart haircut and trendy black turtleneck and leggings couldn't quite camouflage.

Gemma traced the rough edge of the watercolour paper with a finger. 'I suppose I thought the paintings downstairs must be yours, but these are quite different.'

'The Flints? I should hope so.' Some of the abruptness returned to Julia's manner. She shook a cigarette from a pack on a side table and lit it with a hard strike of a match.

'I wondered about them as well,' Kincaid said. 'Something struck me as familiar.'

'You probably saw some of his paintings in books you read as a child. William Flint wasn't as well known as Arthur Rackham, but he did some marvellous illustrations.' Julia leaned against the worktable and narrowed her eyes against the smoke rising from her cigarette. 'Then came the breastscapes.'

'Breastscapes?' Kincaid repeated, amused.

'They are technically quite brilliant, if you don't mind the banal, and they certainly kept him comfortably in his old age.'

'And you disapprove?' Kincaid's voice held a hint of mockery.

Julia touched the surface of her own painting as if testing its worth, then shrugged. 'I suppose it is rather hypocritical of me. These keep me fed, and they supported Connor in the lifestyle to which he'd become accustomed.'

To Gemma's surprise, Kincaid didn't nibble at the proffered bait, but instead asked, 'If you dislike Flint's watercolours, why do they hang in almost every room in the house?'

'They're not mine, if that's what you're thinking. A few years ago Mummy and Daddy got bitten by the collector's bug. Flints were all the rage and they jumped on the bandwagon. Perhaps they thought I'd be pleased.' Julia gave them a brittle little smile. 'After all, as far as they're concerned, one watercolour looks pretty much like another.'

Kincaid returned her smile, and a look of understanding passed between them, as if they'd shared a joke. Julia laughed, her dark hair swinging with the movement of her head, and Gemma felt suddenly excluded. 'Exactly what lifestyle did your husband need to support, Mrs Swann?' she asked, rather too quickly, and she heard an unintended note of accusation in her voice.

Propping herself up on her work stool, Julia swung one black-booted foot as she ground the stub of her half-smoked cigarette into an ashtray. 'You name it. I sometimes thought Con felt honour-bound to live up to an image he created – whiskey, women and an eye for the horses, everything you'd expect from your stereotypical Irish rogue. I wasn't always sure he enjoyed it as much as he liked you to think.'

'Were there any women in particular?' Kincaid asked, his tone so lightly conversational he might have been inquiring about the weather.

She regarded him quizzically. 'There was always a woman, Mr Kincaid. The particulars didn't concern me.'

Kincaid merely smiled, as if refusing to be shocked by her cynicism. 'Connor stayed on in the flat you shared in Henley?'

Julia nodded, sliding off the stool to pull another cigarette from the crumpled packet. She lit it and leaned back against the table, folding her arms against her chest. The paintbrush still positioned over her ear gave her an air of slightly rakish industry, as if she might be a Fleet Street journalist relaxing for a brief moment in the newsroom.

'You were in Henley on Thursday evening, I believe?' Kincaid continued. 'A gallery opening?'

'Very clever of you, Mr Kincaid.' Julia flashed him a smile. 'Trevor Simons. Thameside.'

'But you didn't see your husband?'

'I did not. We move in rather different circles, as you might have guessed,' said Julia, the sarcasm less veiled this time.

Gemma glanced at Kincaid's face, anticipating an escalating response, but he only answered lazily, 'So I might.'

Julia ground out her cigarette, barely smoked this time, and Gemma could see a release of tension in the set of her mouth and shoulders. 'Now if you don't mind, I really must get back to work.' She included Gemma this time in the smile that was so like her father's, only sharper around the edges. 'Perhaps you could—'

'Julia.'

It was an old interrogation technique, the sudden and imperative use of the suspect's name, a breaking down of barriers, an invasion of personal space. Still, the familiarity in Kincaid's voice shocked Gemma. It was as if he knew this woman down to her bones and could sweep every shred of her artifice away with a casual flick of a finger.

Julia remained frozen in mid-sentence, her eyes locked on Kincaid's face. They might have been alone in the room.

'You were only a few hundred yards from Connor's flat. You could have stepped out for a smoke by the river, bumped into him, arranged to meet him later.'

A second passed, then another, and Gemma heard the rustle as Julia shifted her body against the work-table. Then Julia said slowly, 'I could have. But I didn't. It was my show, you see – my fifteen minutes in the limelight – and I never left the gallery at all.'

'And afterwards?'

'Oh, Trev can vouch for me well enough, I think. I slept with him.'

Chapter Four

'Division of labour,' Kincaid told Gemma as they stopped for a quick lunch at the pub in Fingest. 'You see if you can confirm Sir Gerald's alibi – that'll allow you a night or two at home with Toby – and I'll tackle Henley. I want to go over Connor Swann's flat myself, and I want to have a word with – what did Julia say his name was? Simons, that was it – Trevor Simons, at his gallery. I'd like to know a bit more about Julia's movements that night,' he added, and Gemma gave him a look he couldn't interpret.

They finished their sandwiches under Tony's watchful eye, then Gemma ran upstairs to pack her bag. Kincaid waited in the gravelled carpark, jingling the change in his pockets and drawing furrows in the gravel with his toe. The Ashertons were very plausible, but the more he thought about it, the more difficult it became to make sense of what they had told him. They seemed to have been on close terms with a son-in-law their daughter barely tolerated, and yet they also seemed to go to great lengths to avoid confrontation with Julia. He made a *J* in the gravel with his shoe, then carefully raked it over again. How had Julia Swann really felt about her husband? In his mind he saw her again, her thin face composed and her dark eyes fixed on his, and he found he didn't quite buy the tough persona she wore so successfully.

Gemma came out with her case, turning back for a moment to wave goodbye to Tony. The sun sparked from her hair, and it was only then that Kincaid realized it had ventured out from the clouds that had hidden it through the morning.

'Ready, guv?' asked Gemma as she stowed her things in the boot and slid behind the wheel of her Escort. Kincaid put his speculations aside and got in beside her. She seemed to him refreshingly uncomplicated, and he offered up a silent thanks, as he often did, for her competent cheerfulness.

Leaving the hills behind, they took the wide road to Henley. They had a glimpse of the river beneath the Henley Bridge, then it vanished behind them as the one-way system shunted them into the centre of town. 'Can you get back to the pub all right, guv?' Gemma asked as she pulled up to let Kincaid out in Henley's marketplace.

'I'll ask the local lads for a lift. I could pull rank and requisition a car, of course,' he added, grinning at her, 'but just now I think I'd rather not be bothered with parking the bloody thing.'

He stepped out of the car and gave the door a parting thump with his hand, as if he were slapping a horse on its way. Gemma let up on the brake, but before nosing back into the traffic she rolled down the

Escort's driver's-side window and called to him, 'Mind how you go.'

Turning back, he waved jauntily to her, then watched the car disappear down Hart Street. The sudden note of concern in her voice struck him as odd. It was she who was driving back to London, while he merely intended an unannounced interview and a recce of Connor Swann's flat. He shrugged and smiled – he'd quite grown to like her occasional solicitousness.

Henley Police Station lay just across the street, but after a moment's hesitation he turned and instead climbed the steps to the Town Hall. A cardboard sign taped to the wall informed him that Tourist Information could be found downstairs, and as he descended, he wrinkled his nose at the standard public building accoutrements – cracked lino and the sour smell of urine.

Fifty pence bought him a street map of the town, and he unfolded it as he walked thankfully back out into the sun. He saw that his way lay down Hart Street and along the river, so tucking the map in his jacket and his hands in his pockets, he strolled down the hill. The square tower of the church seemed to float against the softly coloured hills beyond the river, and it drew him on like a lodestone. 'St Mary the Virgin,' he said aloud as he reached it, thinking that for an Anglican church the syllables rolled off the tongue with a very Catholic resonance. He wondered where they meant to bury Connor Swann. Irish Catholic, Irish Protestant? Could it possibly matter? He didn't yet know enough about him to hazard a guess.

Crossing the busy street, he stood for a moment on the Henley Bridge. The Thames spread peacefully before him, so different from the thunder of water through Hambleden Weir. The river course wound north for a bit after Henley, curved to the east before it reached Hambleden, then meandered northeast before turning south towards Windsor. Could Connor have gone in the river here, in Henley, and drifted downstream to Hambleden Lock? He thought it highly unlikely, but made himself a mental note to check with Thames Valley.

He took a last look at the red-and-white Pimm's umbrellas beckoning temptingly from the terrace of the Angel pub, but he had other fish to fry.

A few hundred yards beyond the pub he found the address. Next door to the tearoom a discreet sign announced THE GALLERY, THAMESIDE, and a single painting in an ornate gilded frame adorned the shop window. The door chimed electronically as Kincaid pushed it open, then clicked softly behind him, shutting out the hum of sound from the riverside.

The silence settled around him. Even his footsteps were muffled by a thickly padded Berber carpet covering the floor. No one seemed to be about. A door stood open at the back of the shop, revealing a small walled garden, and beyond that another door.

Kincaid looked round the room with interest. The paintings, spaced generously around the walls, seemed to be mostly late nineteenth- and early twentieth-century watercolours, and most were river landscapes.

In the room's centre a pedestal held a sleek bronze

of a crouching cat. Kincaid ran his hand over the cool metal and thought of Sid. He had made arrangements with his neighbour, Major Keith, to look after the cat when he was away from home. Although the major professed to dislike cats, he looked after Sid with the same gruff tenderness he had shown to the cat's former owner. Kincaid thought that for the major, as well as himself, the cat formed a living link to the friend they had lost.

Near the garden door stood a desk, its cluttered surface a contrast to the spare neatness he saw everywhere else. Kincaid glanced quickly at the untidy papers, then moved into the second small room which lay a step down from the first.

He caught his breath. The painting on the opposite wall was a long narrow rectangle, perhaps a yard wide and a foot high, and it was lit by a lamp mounted just above it. The girl's body almost filled the frame. Dressed in shirt and jeans, she lay on her back in a meadow, eyes closed, hat tilted back on her auburn hair, and beside her on the grass a basket of ripe apples spilled over onto an open book.

A simple-enough composition, almost photographic in its clarity and detail, but it possessed a warmth and depth impossible to capture with a camera. You could feel the sun on the girl's upturned face, feel her contentment and pleasure in the day.

Other paintings by the same artist's hand were hung nearby, portraits and landscapes filled with the same vivid colours and intense light. As Kincaid looked at them he felt a sense of longing, as if such beauty and perfection existed forever just out of his reach, unless he, like Alice, could step through the frame and into the artist's world.

He had bent forward to peer at the illegibly scrawled signature when behind him a voice said, 'Lovely, aren't they?'

Startled, Kincaid straightened and turned. The man stood in the back doorway, his body in shadow as the sun lit the garden behind him. As he stepped into the room, Kincaid saw him more clearly – tall, thin and neat-featured, with a shock of greying hair and glasses that gave him an accountant-like air at odds with the casual pullover and trousers he wore.

The door chimed as Kincaid started to speak. A young man came in, his face white against the dead-black of his clothes and dyed hair, a large and battered leather portfolio tucked under his arm. His get-up would have been laughable if not for the look of supplication on his face. Kincaid nodded to Trevor Simons, for so he assumed the man who had come in from the garden to be, and said, 'Go ahead. I'm in no hurry.'

Rather to Kincaid's surprise, Simons looked carefully at the drawings. After a few moments he shook his head and tucked them back into the portfolio, but Kincaid heard him give the boy the name of another gallery he might try. 'The trouble is,' he said to Kincaid as the door chimed shut, 'he can't paint. It's a bloody shame. They stopped teaching drawing and painting in the art colleges back in the sixties. Graphic artists – that's what they all want to be – only no one tells them there aren't any jobs. So they come out of art college like this wee chappie,' he nodded towards the street, 'hawking their wares from gallery to gallery like itinerant peddlers. You saw it – fairly competent air-brushed crap, without a spark of originality. If he's lucky he'll find a job frying up chips or driving a delivery van.'

'You were courteous enough,' said Kincaid.

'Well, you have to have some sympathy, haven't you? It's not their fault they're ignorant, both in technique and in the realities of life.' He waved a hand dismissively. 'I've nattered on long enough. What can I do for you?'

Kincaid gestured towards the watercolours in the second room, 'These—'

'Ah, she's an exception,' Simons said, smiling. 'In many ways. Self-taught, for one, which was probably her salvation, and very successful at it, for another. Not with these,' he added quickly, 'although I think she will be, but with the work she does on commission. Stays booked two years in advance. It's very difficult for an artist who is successful commercially to find the time to do really creative work, so this show meant a lot to her.'

Realizing the answer even as he asked and feeling an utter fool, Kincaid said, 'The artist – who is she?'

Trevor Simons looked puzzled. 'Julia Swann. I thought you knew.'

'But . . .' Kincaid tried to reconcile the flawless but rather emotionally severe perfection of Julia's flowers with these vibrantly alive paintings. He could see similarities now in technique and execution, but the outcome was astonishingly different. Making an attempt to collect himself, he said, 'Look. I think perhaps I ought to go out and come in again, I've made such a muddle of things. My name's Duncan Kincaid' – he extended his warrant card in its folder – 'and I came to talk to you about Julia Swann.'

Trevor Simons looked from the warrant card to Kincaid and back again, then said rather blankly, 'It looks like a library permit. I always wondered, you know, when you see them on the telly.' He shook his head, frowning. 'I don't understand. I know Con's death has been a dreadful shock for everyone, but I thought it was an accident. Why Scotland Yard? And why me?'

'Thames Valley has treated it as a suspicious death from the beginning, and asked for our assistance at Sir Gerald Asherton's request.'

Kincaid had delivered this with no intonation, but Simons raised an eyebrow and said, 'Ah.'

'Indeed,' Kincaid answered, and when their eyes met it occurred to him that he might be friends with this man under other circumstances.

'And me?' Simons asked again. 'Surely you can't think Julia had anything to do with Con's death?'

'Were you with Julia all Thursday evening?' Kincaid said, pushing a bit more aggressively, although the note of incredulity in Simons's voice had struck him as genuine.

Unruffled, Simons leaned against his desk and folded his arms. 'More or less. It was a bit of a free-for-all in here.' He nodded, indicating the two small rooms. 'People were jammed in here like sardines. I suppose Julia might have popped out to the loo or for a smoke and I wouldn't have noticed, but not much longer than that.'

'What time did you close the gallery?'

'Ten-ish. They'd eaten and drunk everything in sight, and left a wake of litter behind like pillaging Huns. We had to push the last happy stragglers out of the door.'

'We?'

'Julia helped me tidy up.'

'And after that?'

Trevor Simons looked away for the first time. He studied the river for a moment, then turned back to Kincaid with a reluctant expression. 'I'm sure you've seen Julia already. Did she tell you she spent the night? I can't imagine her being silly enough to protect my honour.' Simons paused, but before Kincaid could speak he went on. 'Well, it's true enough. She was here in the flat with me until just before daybreak. A small attempt at discretion, creeping out with the dawn,' he added with a humourless smile.

'She didn't leave you at any time before that?'

'I think I would have noticed if she had,' Simons answered, this time with a genuine flash of amusement, then he quickly sobered and added, 'Look, Mr Kincaid, I don't make a habit of doing this sort of thing. I'm married and I've two teenage daughters. I don't want my family hurt. I know,' he continued hurriedly, as if Kincaid might interrupt him, 'I should have considered the consequences beforehand, but one doesn't, does one?'

'I wouldn't know,' Kincaid answered in bland policemanese, all the while thinking, *Does one not, or does one consider the consequences and choose to act anyway?* The image of his ex-wife came to him, her straight flaxen hair falling across her shuttered face. *Had Vic considered the consequences?*

'You don't live here, then?' he asked, breaking the train of thought abruptly. He gestured towards the door across the garden.

'No. In Sonning, a bit further upriver. The flat was included in the property when I bought the gallery, and I use it mainly as a studio. Sometimes I stay over when I'm painting, or when I've an opening on.'

'You paint?' asked Kincaid, a little surprised.

Simons's smile was rueful. 'Am I a practical man, Mr Kincaid? Or merely a compromised one? You tell me.' The question seemed to be hypothetical only, for he continued, 'I knew when I left art school I wasn't quite good enough, didn't have that unique combination of talent and luck. So I used a little family money and bought this gallery. I found it a bit ironic that Julia's opening also marked the anniversary of my twenty-fifth year here.'

Kincaid wasn't inclined to let him off the hook, although he suspected his curiosity was more personal than professional. 'You didn't answer my question.'

'Yes, I paint, and I feel insulted if I'm referred to as

a "local artist" rather than an "artist who paints locally". It's a fine distinction, you understand,' he added mockingly. 'Silly, isn't it?'

'What sort of things do you paint?' Kincaid asked, scanning the paintings on the walls of the small room.

Simons followed his gaze and smiled. 'Sometimes I do hang my own work, but I haven't any up just now. I've had to make room for Julia's paintings, and frankly I've other things that sell better than mine, although I do paint Thames landscapes. I use oils – I'm not good enough yet to paint in watercolour, but one day I will be.'

'Is what Julia does that difficult, then?' Kincaid allowed himself to study Julia's lamplit painting, and discovered that he had been deliberately resisting doing so. It drew him, as she did, in a way that felt both familiar and perilous. 'I always thought that one just made a choice, watercolours or oils, depending on what one liked.'

'Watercolour is much more difficult,' Simons said patiently. 'In oil you can make any number of mistakes and just as easily cover them up, the more the merrier. Watercolour requires a confidence, perhaps even a certain amount of ruthlessness. You must get it right the first time.'

Kincaid looked at Julia's paintings with new respect. 'You said she was self-taught? Why not art college, with her talent?'

Simons shrugged. 'I suppose her family didn't take her seriously. Musicians do tend to be rather one-dimensional, even more so than visual artists. Nothing else exists for them. They eat, sleep and breathe music, and I imagine that to Sir Gerald and Dame Caroline, Julia's paintings were just amusing dabs of colour on paper.' He stepped down into the lower room and walked over to the large painting, staring at it. 'Whatever the reason, it allowed her to develop in her own way, with no taint of graphic mediocrity.'

'You have a special relationship,' Kincaid said, watching the way Trevor Simons's slender body blocked the painting in an almost protective posture. 'You admire her – do you also resent her?'

After a moment Simons answered, his back still to Kincaid. 'Perhaps. Can we help but envy those touched by the gods, however briefly?' He turned and the brown eyes behind the spectacles regarded Kincaid candidly. 'Yet I have a good life.'

'Then why have you risked it?' Kincaid said softly. 'Your wife, family . . . perhaps even your business?'

'I never intended it.' Simons gave a self-mocking bark of laughter. 'Famous last words – I never meant to do it. It was just . . . Julia.'

'What else didn't you intend, Trevor? Just how far did your loss of judgement take you?'

'You think *I* might have killed Connor?' His eyebrows shot up above the line of his spectacles and he laughed again. 'I can't lay claim to sins of that magnitude, Mr Kincaid. And why would I want to get rid of the poor bloke? Julia had already chewed him up and spat out the partially digested remains.'

Kincaid grinned. 'Very descriptively put. And will she do the same to you?'

'Oh, I expect so. I've never been able to delude myself sufficiently to think otherwise.'

Pushing aside an untidy stack of papers, Kincaid sat on the edge of Simons's desk and stretched out his legs. 'Did you know Connor Swann well?'

Simons put his hands in his pockets and shifted his weight in the manner of a man suddenly territorially displaced. 'Only to speak to, really. Before they separated he came in with Julia occasionally.'

'Was he jealous of you, do you think?'

'Con? Jealous? That would be the pot calling the kettle black! I never understood why Julia put up with him as long as she did.'

A passer-by stopped and peered at the painting in the window, as had several others since Kincaid had come into the gallery. Beyond her the light had shifted, and the shadows of the willows lay longer on the pavement. 'They don't come in,' Kincaid said as he watched her move towards the tea shop and pass from his view.

'No. Not often.' Simons gestured at the paintings lining the walls. 'The prices are a bit steep for impulse buying. Most of my customers are regulars, collectors. Though sometimes one of those window-shoppers will wander in and fall in love with a painting, then go home and save up pennies out of the housekeeping or the beer money until they have enough to buy it.' He smiled. 'Those are the best, the ones that know nothing about art and buy out of love. It's a genuine response.'

Kincaid looked at the illuminated painting of the girl in the meadow, her eyes gently closed, her faintly freckled face tilted to the sun, and acknowledged his own experience. 'Yes, I can see that.'

He stood and regarded Trevor Simons, who, whatever his sins, seemed a perceptive and decent man. 'A word of advice, Mr Simons, which I probably shouldn't give. An investigation like this moves out in ripples – the longer it takes the wider the circle becomes. If I were you I'd do some damage control – tell your wife about Julia if you can. Before we do.'

Kincaid sat at the table nearest the window in the tea shop. The tin pot had leaked as he poured, and his cup sat in a wet ring on the speckled plastic tabletop. At the next table he recognized the woman who had stopped at the gallery window a few minutes before – middle-aged, heavyset, her greying hair tightly crimped. Although the air in the shop was warm enough to form faint steamy smudges on the window-panes, she still wore a waterproof jacket over her bulky cardigan. Perhaps she feared it might rain unexpectedly inside? When she looked up, he smiled at her, but she looked away, her face frozen in an expression of faint disapproval.

Gazing idly at the river again, he fingered the key in his trouser pocket. Gemma had acquired Connor's key, address and a description of the property from Thames Valley along with the initial reports. Until a year ago Julia and Connor had lived together in the flat he thought must be just along the terrace, near the willow-covered islands he could see from the window.

Julia might have stopped in here often for a morning coffee or a cup of afternoon tea. He imagined her suddenly, sitting across the booth from him in a black sweater, smoking jerkily, frowning in concentration. In his mind she rose and went out into the street. She stood before the gallery for a moment, as if hesitating, then he heard the door chime as she opened it and went in.

Shaking his head, Kincaid downed the remains of his tea in one gulp. He slid from the booth and presented his soggy bill to the girl behind the counter, then followed Julia's phantom out into the lengthening shadows.

He walked towards the river meadows, gazing alternately at the placid river on his left and the blocks of flats on his right. It surprised him that these riverside addresses weren't more elegant. One of the larger buildings was neo-Georgian, another Tudoresque, and both were just a trifle seedy, like dowagers out in soiled housecoats. The shrubbery grew rankly in the gardens, brightened only by the dark red dried heads of sedum and the occasional pale blue of Michaelmas daisies. But it was November after all, Kincaid thought charitably, looking at the quiet river. Even the kiosk advertising river trips and boats for hire was shuttered and locked.

The road narrowed and the large blocks of flats gave way to lower buildings and an occasional detached house. Here the river seemed less separate from the land, and when he reached the high black wrought-iron fence he recognized it from the scrawled description in his pocket. He grasped two of the spiked bars in his hands and peered through them. A commemorative ceramic plaque set into the wall of the nearest building informed him that the flats were quite recently developed, so perhaps Julia and Connor had been among the first tenants. They were built to look like boathouses, in a soft-red brick with an abundance of white-trimmed windows, white deck railings and white peaked gables adorned with gingerbread. Kincaid thought them a bit overdone, but pleasantly so, for they harmonized with both the natural landscape and the surrounding buildings. Like the Prince of Wales, he found most contemporary architecture to be a blight upon the landscape.

Dodging an array of parked boats and trailers, Kincaid walked along the fence until he found a gate. The flats were staggered behind a well-tended garden, and none was quite identical to the next. He found the house easily, one of the three-tiered variety, raised above the ground on stiltlike supports. Feeling suddenly as if he were trespassing, he fitted the key in the lock, but no one called out to him from the adjacent decks.

He had expected black and white.

Illogically, he supposed, considering the intensity of colour Julia used in her paintings. This was a softer palette, almost Mediterranean, with pale yellow walls and terra-cotta floors. Casually provincial furniture filled the sitting room and a fringed Moroccan rug softened the tile floor. On a tiled platform against one wall stood an enamelled wood-burning stove. A small painted table in front of the sofa held a chess set. Had Connor played, Kincaid wondered, or had it been merely for show?

A sports jacket lay crumpled over the back of a chair, an untidy pile of newspapers spilled from sofa to floor and a pair of boat shoes peeked from beneath the coffee table. The male clutter seemed incongruous, an intrusion on an essentially feminine room. Kincaid ran his forefinger across a tabletop, then brushed off the resulting grey fuzz against his trouser leg. Connor Swann had not been much of a housekeeper.

Kincaid wandered into the adjoining kitchen. It had no windows, but opened to the sitting room with its view of the river. Unlike the sitting room, however, it looked immaculate. Cans of olive oil and coloured-glass bottles of vinegar stood out like bright flags against the oak cabinets and yellow countertops, and a shelf near the cooktop held an array of well-thumbed cookbooks. *Julia Child*, read Kincaid, *The Art of Cooking. The Italian Kitchen. La Cucina Fresca.* There were more, some with lavish colour photographs that made him hungry just looking. Glass jars filled with pasta lined another open shelf.

Kincaid opened the fridge and found it well stocked with condiments, cheeses, eggs and milk. The freezer held a few neatly wrapped and labelled packages of meat and chicken, a loaf of French bread, and some plastic containers of something Kincaid guessed might be homemade soup stock. A pad beneath the telephone held the beginnings of a grocery list: *aubergines, tomato paste, red-leaf lettuce, pears.*

The descriptions Kincaid had heard of Connor Swann had not led him to expect an accomplished and enthusiastic cook, but this man had obviously not resorted to zapping frozen dinners in the microwave.

The first floor held a master bedroom and bath done in the same soft yellows as the ground floor, and a small room which apparently served as an office or study. Kincaid continued up the stairs to the top floor.

It had been Julia's studio. The wide windows let in a flood of late afternoon light, and over the willow-tops he could see the winding Thames. A bare table stood in the centre of the room, and an old desk pushed against one wall held some partially used sketch pads and a wooden box filled with odds and ends of paint tubes. Curious, Kincaid rummaged through them. He hadn't known that professional watercolours came in tubes. *Winsor Red. Scarlet Lake. Ultramarine Blue.* The names ran through his mind like poetry, but the tubes left the fine dust of neglect on his finger-tips. The room itself felt empty and unused.

He slowly retraced his steps, stopping once more at the door to the bedroom. The bed was hastily made, and a pair of trousers lay thrown over a chair, belt dangling.

The sense of a life interrupted hung palpably in the air. Connor Swann had meant to shop for groceries, prepare dinner, put out the newspapers, brush his teeth, slide under the warmth of the blue-and-yellow quilt on the bed. Kincaid knew that unless he came to an understanding of who Connor Swann had been, he had little hope of discovering who had killed him, and he realized that all his knowledge and perceptions of him were filtered through Julia and her family.

This was Julia's house. Every room bore her imprint, and except for the kitchen, Connor seemed to have only drifted across its surface. Why had Julia left it, like a commander who held all the advantages retreating from the citadel?

Kincaid turned from the bedroom and went into the study. The room contained nothing but a desk and chair facing the window, and a wing-backed chair with a reading lamp. Sitting in the straight-backed chair, he turned on the green-shaded desk lamp and began picking desultorily through the clutter.

A leather-bound appointment book came first to hand. Starting with January, Kincaid flipped slowly through it. The names of the racetracks jumped out first – Epsom, Cheltenham, Newmarket . . . They rotated regularly through the months. Some had times written beside them, others sharp exclamation points. A good day?

Kincaid went back to the beginning, starting more carefully. In between races he began to see the pattern of Connor's social life. Dates for lunch, dinner, drinks, often accompanied by a name, a time and the words *Red Lion. Bloody hell*, thought Kincaid, *the man had kept up an exhausting social schedule.* And to make it worse, pubs and hotels called the Red Lion were as common as sheep in Yorkshire. He supposed the logical place to start would be the plush old hotel here in Henley, next to the church.

Golf dates appeared often, as well as the notation

Meet with J., followed by a dash and varying names, some cryptic, some, like Tyler Pipe and Carpetland, obviously businesses. It looked as though these weren't all social engagements, but rather business appointments, entertaining clients of some sort. Kincaid had assumed that Connor lived off the Asherton income, and nothing in the Thames Valley reports had led him to think otherwise, but perhaps that hadn't been the case. He closed the book and began shuffling through the papers on the desktop, then had a thought and opened the diary again. *Lunch at B.E.* appeared every Thursday, regular as clockwork.

The stack on the desktop resolved itself into ordinary household bills, betting slips, a set of racing-form books, a corporate report from a firm in Reading, and an auction catalogue. Kincaid shrugged and continued his inventory. Paperclips, paper knife, a mug emblazoned with HENLEY ART FEST, which held a handful of promotional pens.

He found Connor's cheque book in the left-hand drawer. A quick look through the register revealed the expected monthly payments, as well as regular deposits labelled *Blackwell, Gillock and Frye.* A firm of solicitors? wondered Kincaid? An interesting pattern began to form – he returned to the beginning of the register, double-checking. The first cheque written after every deposit was made out to a K. Hicks, and the amounts, although not the same, were always sizeable.

Lost as he was in speculation, it took a moment for the soft click from downstairs to penetrate Kincaid's consciousness. He looked up. Dusk had fallen as he worked. Through the window the outline of the willows showed charcoal against a violet sky.

The sounds were more definitive this time – a louder click, followed by a creak. Kincaid slid from the chair and moved quietly out into the hall. He listened for a moment, then went quickly down the stairs, keeping his feet carefully to the outside of the treads. When he reached the last step, the light came on in the sitting room. He listened again, then stepped around the corner.

She stood by the front door, one hand still on the light switch. The glow from the table lamps revealed tight jeans, a fuzzy pink sweater in a weave so loose it revealed the line of her bra, impossibly high heels, blonde hair permed into Medusa-like ropes. He could see the quick rise and fall of her chest beneath the sweater.

'Hullo,' he said, trying a smile.

She took one gulping breath before she shrieked 'Who the bloody hell are you?'

Chapter Five

Disoriented, Gemma reached out and touched the other side of the double bed, patted it. Empty. Opening her eyes, she saw the faint grey light brightening the wrong side of the room.

She came fully awake. New flat. No husband. Of course. Sitting up against the pillows, she pushed the tangle of hair away from her face. It had been months since she dreamed of Rob, and she had thought that particular ghost well laid to rest.

The hot water had just begun to gurgle through the radiator pipes as the automatic timer switched on the central heating. For a panicked moment she wondered why the alarm hadn't gone off, then relaxed in relief. It was Sunday. She closed her eyes and snuggled down into the pillows, feeling that luxurious laziness that comes with waking early and knowing one doesn't have to get up.

Sleep, however, refused to be coaxed back. The thought of the interview she'd managed to schedule later in the morning at the Coliseum niggled at her consciousness until finally, with a yawn, she swung her feet from under the duvet. The opera had seemed the logical place to start checking out Gerald Asherton's story, and she found herself looking forward to her day with a tingle of pleasure.

When her toes touched the floor they curled involuntarily from the cold, and she fumbled for her slippers as she shrugged into her dressing gown. At least she could take advantage of the time before Toby awakened to have a quiet cup of coffee and organize her thoughts for the day.

A few minutes later the flat was warming nicely and she sat at the black-slatted table in front of the garden windows, cradling a hot mug in her hands and questioning her sanity.

She had sold her house in Leyton – three bedrooms, semi-detached with garden, a symbol in brick and pebbledash of Rob's unrealistic plans for their marriage – and instead of buying the sensible flat in Wanstead she'd had in mind, she'd leased . . . this. She gazed round the room, bemused.

Her estate agent had begged, 'Just have a quick look, Gemma, that's all I ask. I know it's not what you're looking for, but you simply must see it.' And so she had come, and seen, and signed on the dotted line, finding herself the surprised tenant of the converted garage behind a square detached Victorian house in a tree-lined street in Islington. The house itself was unexpected, standing as it did between two of Islington's most elegant Georgian terraces, but it occupied its space with the confidence of good breeding.

The garage was separate from the house, and lower than the garden, so that the hip-high windows which lined one entire wall of the flat were actually ground level on the outside. The owners, a psychiatrist who worked from a shed in the garden, and his wife, had done up the garage in what the agent described as 'Japanese minimalist' décor.

Gemma almost laughed aloud, thinking of it. An exercise in 'minimalist living' would be a fitting description of what it had become for her. The flat was basically one large room, furnished with a futon and a few other sleek, contemporary pieces. Cubbyholes along the wall opposite the bed contained kitchen and water closet, and a storage room with a small window had become Toby's bedroom. The arrangement didn't allow much privacy, but privacy with a small child was a negligible quality anyway, and Gemma couldn't imagine sharing her bed with anyone in the foreseeable future.

Gemma's furniture and most of their belongings had been stored in the back of her parents' bakery in Leyton High Road. Her mum had shaken her faded red curls and tut-tutted. 'What were you thinking of, love?'

A quiet, tree-lined street with a park at its end. A green, walled garden, filled with interesting nooks and crannies for a little boy to hide in. A secret place, filled with possibilities. But Gemma had merely said, 'I like it, Mum. And it's nearer the Yard,' doubting her mother would understand.

She felt stripped clean, pared down to essentials, serene in the room's black-and-grey simplicity.

Or at least she had until this morning. She frowned,

wondering again what had made her feel so unsettled, and the image of twelve-year-old Matthew Asherton came unbidden to her mind.

She rose, put two slices of brown bread in the toaster that stood on the tabletop and went to kiss Toby awake.

Having deposited Toby at her mum's, Gemma took the tube to Charing Cross. As the train pulled away, the rush of wind down the tunnel whipped her skirt around her knees and she hugged the lapels of her jacket together. She left the station and entered the pedestrian mall behind St Martin-in-the-Fields, and rounding the church into St Martin's Lane she found the outside no better. A gust of north wind funnelled down the street, flinging grit and scraps of paper and leaving tiny whirlwinds in its wake.

She rubbed her eyes with her knuckles and blinked several times to clear them, then looked about her. Before her on the corner stood the Chandos Pub, and just beyond it a black-and-white vertical sign said LONDON COLISEUM. Blue and white banners emblazoned with the letters ENO surrounded it and drew her eyes upwards. Against the blue-washed canvas of the sky, the ornate white cupola stood out sharply. Near the top of the dome, white letters spelled out ENGLISH NATIONAL OPERA rather sedately, and Gemma thought they must be lit at night.

Something tugged at her memory and she realized she'd been here before. She and Rob had been to a play at the Albery Theatre up the street, and afterwards had stopped for a drink at the Chandos. It had been a warm night and they'd taken their drinks outside, escaping the smoky crush in the bar. Gemma remembered sipping her Pimm's and watching the opera-goers spill out onto the pavement, their faces animated, hands moving with quick gestures as they dissected the performance. 'It might be fun,' she'd said rather wistfully to Rob.

He had smiled in his condescending way and said, light voice mocking, 'Old cows in silly costumes screeching their lungs out? Don't be stupid, Gem.'

Gemma smiled now, thinking of the photo she'd seen of Caroline Stowe. Rob would've fallen over himself if he'd come face-to-face with her. Old cow, indeed. He'd never know what he had missed.

She pushed through the lobby doors, feeling a small surge of excitement at her own entrance into this glamorous fairy-tale world. 'Alison Douglas,' she said to the heavy grey-haired woman at the reception desk. 'The orchestra manager's assistant. I've an appointment with her.'

'You'll have to go round the back, then, ducks,' the woman answered in less than rarefied accents. She made a looping motion with her finger. 'Round the block, next to the loading bay.'

Feeling somewhat chastened, Gemma left the plush-and-gilt warmth of the lobby and circled the block in the indicated direction. She found herself in an alleylike street lined with pub and restaurant delivery entrances. With its concrete steps and peeling paint, the stage entrance to the London Coliseum was distinguished only by the increasingly familiar ENO logo near the door. Gemma climbed up and stepped inside, looking around curiously at the small lino-floored reception area.

To her left a porter sat inside a glass-windowed kiosk; just ahead another door barred the way into what must be the inner sanctum. She announced herself to the porter and he smiled as he handed her a sign-in sheet on a clipboard. He was young, with a freckled face and brown hair that looked suspiciously as if it were growing out from a Mohawk cut. Gemma looked more closely, saw the tiny puncture in his earlobe which should have held an earring. He'd made a valiant effort to clean up for the job, no doubt.

'I'll just give Miss Alison a ring,' he said as he handed her a sticky badge to wear. 'She'll be right down for you.' He picked up the phone and murmured something incomprehensible into it.

Gemma wondered if he'd been on duty after last Thursday evening's performance. His friendly grin augured well for an interview, but she had better wait until she wouldn't be interrupted.

Church bells began to ring close by. 'St Martin's?' she asked.

He nodded, checking the clock on the wall behind him.

'Eleven o'clock on the dot. You can set your watch by it.'

Was there a congregation for eleven o'clock services, Gemma wondered, or did the church cater solely to tourists?

Remembering how surprised she'd been when Alison Douglas had agreed to see her this morning, she asked the porter, 'Business as usual here, even on a Sunday morning?'

He displayed the grin. 'Sunday matinée. One of our biggest draws, especially when it's something as popular as *Traviata*.'

Puzzled, Gemma tugged her notebook from her purse and flipped quickly through it. '*Pelleas and Melisande*. I thought you were doing *Pelleas and Melisande*.'

'Thursdays and Saturdays. Productions—'

The inner door opened and he paused as a young woman came through, then continued to Gemma, 'You'll see.' He winked at her. 'Alison'll make sure you do.'

'I'm Alison Douglas.' Her cool hand clasped Gemma's firmly. 'Don't mind Danny. What can I do for you?'

Gemma took in the short light brown hair, black sweater and skirt, platform shoes, which didn't quite raise her to Gemma's height, but Alison Douglas's most notable characteristic was an air of taking herself quite seriously.

'Is there somewhere we could talk? Your office, perhaps?'

Alison hesitated, then opened the inner door, indicating by a jerk of her head that Gemma should precede her through it. 'You'd better come along in, then. Look,' she added, 'we've a performance in just under three hours and I've things I absolutely must do. If you don't mind following along behind me we can talk as we go.'

'All right,' Gemma agreed, doubting she'd get a better offer. They had entered a subterranean maze of dark green corridors. Already lost, Gemma followed hard on Alison Douglas's heels as they twisted and turned, went up, down and around. Occasionally, she looked down at the dirty green carpet beneath her feet, wondering if she recognized the pattern of that particular stain. Could she follow them like Hansel and Gretel's breadcrumbs? The smells of damp and disinfectant made her want to sneeze.

Alison turned back to speak to her, stopped suddenly and smiled. Gemma felt sure her bewilderment had been entirely visible, and thought for once she ought to be grateful her every emotion registered on her face.

'Back-of-house,' Alison said, her brusque manner softening for the first time. 'That's what all the unglamorous bits are called. It's quite a shock if one's never been backstage, isn't it? But this is the heart of the theatre. Without this' – she gestured expansively around her – 'nothing happens out front.'

'The show doesn't go on?'

'Exactly.'

Gemma suspected that the key to loosening Alison Douglas's tongue was her work. 'Miss Douglas, I'm not sure I understand what you do.'

Alison moved forward again as she spoke. 'My boss

– Michael Blake – and I are responsible for all the administrative details of the running of the orchestra. We—' Glancing at Gemma's face, she hesitated, seeming to search for a less complicated explanation. 'We make sure everything and everyone are where they should be when they should be. It can be quite a demanding business. And Michael's away for a few days just now.'

'Do you deal directly with the conductors?' Gemma asked, taking advantage of the opening, slight as it was, but the corridor turned again and Alison pushed aside the faded plush curtain which barred their way. She stepped back to allow Gemma to pass through first.

Gemma stopped and stared, her mouth open in surprise. Beside her, Alison said softly, 'It is rather amazing, isn't it? I begin to take it for granted until I see it through someone else's eyes. This is the largest theatre in the West End, and it has the largest backstage area of any theatre in London. That's what allows us to put on several productions simultaneously.'

The cavernous space bustled with activity. Pieces of scenery belonging to more than one production stood side by side in surreal juxtaposition. 'Oh,' Gemma said, watching a huge section of stone wall roll easily across the floor, guided by two men in overalls. 'So that's what Danny meant. Thursdays and Saturdays Sir Gerald conducts *Pelleas and Melisande* – Fridays and Sundays someone else is doing . . . what did he say?'

'*La Traviata.* Look.' Alison pointed across the stage. 'There's Violetta's ballroom, where she and Alfredo sing their first duet. And there – ' she gestured towards the section of stone wall, now slotted neatly into a recess – 'that's part of King Arkel's castle, from *Pelleas*.' She looked at Gemma, studied her watch, looked once again at Gemma and said, 'There are a few things I simply must see to. Why not have a look round here while I get things in hand? After that I'll try to manage a quarter of an hour in the canteen with you.' She was already moving away from Gemma as she finished, the soles of her platform shoes clicking on the wooden floor.

Gemma walked to the lip of the stage and looked out. Before her the tiers of the auditorium rose in baroque splendour, blue velvet accented with gilt. The chandeliers hung from the dome high above her like frosted moons. She imagined all the empty seats filled, and the expectant eyes upon her, waiting for her to open her mouth and sing. Cold crept up her spine and she shivered. Caroline Stowe might look delicate, but to stand on a stage like this and face the crowd required a kind of strength Gemma didn't possess.

She looked down into the pit and smiled. At least Sir Gerald had some protection, and could turn his back on the audience.

A thread of music came from somewhere, women's voices carrying a haunting, lilting melody. Gemma turned and walked towards the back of the stage, straining to hear, but the banging and thumping going on around her masked even the sound's direction. She didn't notice Alison Douglas's return until the woman spoke. 'Did you see the pit? We jam a hundred and nineteen players into that space, if you can imagine that, elbow to—'

Gemma touched her arm. 'That music – what is it?'

'What – ?' Alison listened for a moment, puzzled, then smiled. 'Oh, that. That's from *Lakme*, Mallika's duet with Lakme in the high priest's garden. One of the girls in *Traviata* is singing Mallika next month at Covent Garden. I suppose she's swotting by listening to a recording.' She glanced at her watch, then added, 'We can get that cup of tea now, if you like.'

The music faded. As Gemma followed Alison back into the maze of corridors she felt an odd sadness, as if she'd been touched by something beautiful and fleeting. 'That opera,' she said to Alison's back, 'does it have a happy ending?'

Alison looked back over her shoulder, her expression amused. 'Of course not. Lakme sacrifices herself to protect her lover, in the end.'

The canteen smelled of frying chips. Gemma sat across the table from Alison Douglas, drinking tea strong enough to put fur on her tongue and trying to find a comfortable position for her backside in the moulded plastic chair. Around them men and women dressed in perfectly ordinary clothes drank tea and ate sandwiches, but when Gemma caught snippets of conversation it contained such obscure musical and technical terms that it might as well have been a foreign language. She pulled her notebook from her handbag and took another sip of tea, grimacing at the tannin's bite. 'Miss Douglas,' she said as she saw Alison touch the face of her wristwatch with her fingertips, 'I appreciate your time. I'll not take up any more than necessary.'

'I'm not sure I understand how I can help you. I mean, I know about Sir Gerald's son-in-law. It's an awful thing to happen, isn't it?' Her forehead creased as she frowned, and she looked suddenly very young and unsure, like a child encountering tragedy for the first time. 'But I can't see what it has to do with me.'

Gemma flipped open her notebook and uncapped her pen, then laid both casually beside her teacup. 'Do you work closely with Sir Gerald?'

'No more so than with any of the conductors – ' Alison paused and smiled – 'but I enjoy it more. He's such a dear. Never gets in a tizzy, like some of them.'

Hesitating to admit she didn't understand how the system worked, Gemma temporized with, 'Does he conduct often?'

'More than anyone except our music director.' Alison leaned over the table towards Gemma and lowered her voice. 'Did you know that he was offered the position, but declined it? This was all years ago, way before my time, of course. He said he wanted to have more freedom to work with other orchestras, but I think it had something to do with his family. He and Dame Caroline started with the company back at Sadler's Wells – he would have been the obvious choice.'

'Does Dame Caroline still sing with the company?

I would have thought . . . I mean, she has a grown daughter . . .'

Alison laughed. 'What you mean is that she's surely past it, right?' She leaned forward again, her animated face revealing how much she enjoyed teaching the uninitiated. 'Most sopranos are in their thirties before they really hit their stride. It takes years of work and training to develop a voice, and if they sing too much, too soon, they can do irreparable damage. Many are at the peak of their careers well into their fifties, and a few exceptional singers continue beyond that. Although I must admit, sometimes they look a bit ridiculous playing the *ingénue* parts when they get really long in the tooth.' She grinned at Gemma, then continued more seriously. 'Not that I think that would have happened to Caroline Stowe. I can't imagine her looking ridiculous at any age.'

'You said "would have happened". I don't—'

'She retired. Twenty years ago, when their son died. She never sang publicly again.' Alison had lowered her voice, and although her expression was suitably concerned, she told the story with the relish people usually reserve for someone else's misfortune. 'And she was brilliant. Caroline Stowe might have been one of the most renowned sopranos of our time.' Sounding genuinely regretful, Alison shook her head.

Gemma took a last sip of tea and pushed her cup away as she thought about what she'd heard. 'Why the title, then, if she stopped singing?'

'She's one of the best vocal coaches in the country,

if not the world. A lot of the most promising singers in the business have been taught, and are still being taught, by Caroline Stowe. And she's done a tremendous amount for the company.' Alison gave a wry smile, adding, 'She's a very influential lady.'

'So I understand,' said Gemma, reflecting that it was Dame Caroline's influence, and Sir Gerald's, that had dragged the Yard into this investigation in the first place. Seeing Alison straighten up in her chair, Gemma asked, 'Do you know what time Sir Gerald left the theatre on Thursday evening?'

Alison thought for a moment, wrinkling her forehead. 'I really don't know. I spoke to him in his dressing room just after the performance, around eleven o'clock, but I didn't stay more than five minutes. Had to meet someone,' she added with a dimple and a lowering of her lashes. 'You'll have to ask Danny. He was on duty that night.'

'Did Sir Gerald seem upset in any way? Anything different about his routine that night?'

'No, not that I can think—' Alison stopped, hand poised over her teacup. 'Wait. There was something. Tommy was with him. Of course, they've known each other practically forever,' she added quickly, 'but we don't often see Tommy here after a performance, at least not in the conductor's dressing room.'

Feeling the sense of the interview fast escaping her, Gemma said distinctly, 'Who exactly is Tommy?'

Alison smiled. 'I forgot you wouldn't know. Tommy is Tommy Godwin, our Wardrobe Manager. And it's not that he considers one of his visits akin to a divine blessing, like some costume designers I could name – ' she paused and rolled her eyes – 'but if he's here at the theatre he's usually busy with Running Wardrobe.'

'Is he here today?'

'Not that I know of. But I expect you can catch him tomorrow at LB House.' This time Gemma's bewilderment must have been evident, because before she could form a question, Alison continued. 'That's Lilian Baylis House, in West Hampstead, where we have our Making Wardrobe. Here.' She reached for Gemma's notebook. 'I'll write down the address and phone number for you.'

A thought occurred to Gemma as she watched Alison write in a looping, schoolgirl hand. 'Did you ever meet Sir Gerald's son-in-law, Connor Swann?'

Alison Douglas flushed. 'Once or twice. He came to ENO functions sometimes.' She returned the pen and notebook, then ran her fingers around the neck of her black sweater.

Gemma cocked her head while she considered the woman across the table – attractive, about her own age, and single, if her unadorned left hand and the date she'd alluded to were anything to go by. 'Shall I take it he tried to chat you up?'

'He didn't mean anything by it,' Alison said, a little apologetically. 'You know, you can tell.'

'All flash and no substance?'

Alison shrugged. 'I'd say he just liked women . . . he made you feel special.' She looked up, and for the first time Gemma noticed that her eyes were a light, clear brown. 'We've all talked about it, of course. You know what the gossip mill's like. But this is the first time I've really let myself think . . .' She swallowed once, then added slowly. 'He was a lovely man. I'm sorry he's dead.'

The canteen tables were emptying rapidly. Alison looked up and grimaced, then bustled Gemma back into the dark green tunnels. Murmuring an apology, she left Gemma once again in Danny the porter's domain.

''Ullo, miss,' said Danny, ever cheerful. 'You get what you came for?'

'Not quite.' Gemma smiled at him. 'But you may be able to help me.' She pulled her warrant card from her handbag and held the open case where he could see it clearly.

'Crikey!' His eyes widened and he looked her up and down. 'You don't look like a copper.'

'Don't get cheeky with me, mate,' she said, grinning. Resting her elbows on the counter-sill, she leaned forward earnestly. 'Can you tell me what time Sir Gerald signed out last Thursday evening, Danny?'

'Ooh, alibis, is it?' The glee on Danny's face made him look like an illustration in an Enid Blyton novel.

'Routine inquiries just now,' Gemma said, managing to keep a straight face. 'We need to know the movements of everyone who might have had contact with Connor Swann the day he died.'

Danny lifted a binder from the top of a stack and

opened it at the back, flipping through the last few pages. 'Here.' He pointed, holding the page up where Gemma could see. 'Midnight on the dot. That's what I remembered, but I thought you'd want – what is it, corroboration?'

Sir Gerald's signature suited him, thought Gemma, a comfortable but strong scrawl. 'Did he usually stay so long after a performance, Danny?'

'Sometimes.' He glanced at the sheet again. 'But he was last out that night. I remember because I wanted to lock up – had a bird waiting in the wings, you might say.' He winked at Gemma. 'There was something, though,' he said more hesitantly. 'That night . . . Sir Gerald . . . well, he was half-cocked, like.'

Gemma couldn't keep the surprise from her voice. 'Sir Gerald was drunk?'

Danny ducked his head in embarrassment. 'I didn't really like to say, miss. Sir Gerald always has a kind word for everybody. Not like some.'

'Has this happened before?'

Danny shook his head. 'Not that I can remember. And I've been here over a year now.'

Gemma quickly entered Danny's statement in her notebook, then closed it and returned it to her bag. 'Thanks, Danny. You've been a great help.'

He passed over the sign-in sheet for her initial, his grin considerably subdued.

'Cheerio, then,' she said as she turned towards the door.

Danny called out to her before she could open it.

'There's one other thing, miss. You know the son-in-law, the one what snuffed it?' He held up his ledger and pointed to an entry near Sir Gerald's. 'He was here that day as well.'

Chapter Six

Eggs, bacon, sausage, tomatoes, mushrooms – and could that possibly be kidneys? Kincaid pushed the questionable items a little to one side with the tip of his fork. Kidneys in steak-and-kidney pie he could manage, but kidneys at breakfast were a bit much. Otherwise the Chequers had done itself proud. Surveying his breakfast laid out on the white tablecloth, complete with china teapot and a vase of pink and yellow snap-dragons, he began to think he should feel grateful for Sir Gerald Asherton's influence. His accommodations when out of town on a case were seldom up to these standards.

As he'd slept late, the more righteous early risers had long since finished their breakfasts and he had the dining room to himself. He gazed out through the leaded windows at the damp and windy morning as he ate, enjoying his unaccustomed leisure. Leaves drifted and swirled, their golds and russets a bright contrast against the still-green grass of the churchyard. The congregation began to arrive for the morning service, and soon the verges of the lanes surrounding the church were lined with cars parked end to end.

Wondering lazily why a parish church would draw such a crowd, he was suddenly struck by the desire to see for himself. He pushed a last bite of toast and marmalade into his mouth. Still chewing, he ran upstairs, grabbed a tie from his room and hastily knotted it on his way back down.

He slipped into the last pew just as the church bells began to ring. As he looked around it occurred to him that this was most likely the Ashertons' church. He wondered who knew them and if some of those gathered had come out of curiosity, hoping to see the family.

None of the Ashertons were in evidence, however, and as the peaceful order of the service settled over him, he found his mind drawn back to the previous evening's revelations.

It had taken him a few minutes to calm her down enough to get her name – Sharon Doyle – and even then she'd taken his warrant card and examined it with the intensity of the marginally literate.

'I've come for me things,' she said, shoving the card back at him as if it might burn her fingers. 'I've a right to 'em. I don't care what anybody says.'

Kincaid backed up until he reached the sofa, then sat down on its edge. 'Who would say you didn't?' he asked easily.

Sharon Doyle folded her arms, pushing her breasts up against the thin weave of her sweater. 'Her.'

'Her?' Kincaid repeated, resigned to an exercise in patience.

'You know. Her. The wife. *Julia,*' she mimicked in an accent considerably more precise than her own. Hostility seemed to be triumphing over fright, but although she moved nearer him, she still stood with her feet planted firmly apart.

'You have a key,' he said, making it a statement rather than a question.

'Con gave it to me.'

Kincaid looked at the softly rounded face, young beneath the makeup and bravado. Gently, he said, 'How did you find out Connor was dead?'

She stared at him, her lips pressed together. After a moment her hands dropped to her sides and her body sagged like a rag doll that had lost its stuffing. 'Down the pub,' she answered so quietly that he read her lips as much as heard her.

'You'd better sit down.'

Folding into the chair across from him as if unaware of her body, she said, 'Last night. I'd gone round to the George. He hadn't rung me up when he said, so I thought, I'm bloody well not going to sit home on my own. Some bloke'd buy me a drink, chat me up – serve Con bloody well right.' Her voice wavered at the last and she swallowed, then wet her lips with the pink tip of her tongue. 'The regulars were all talking about it. I thought they were havin' me on, at first.' She fell silent and looked away from him.

'But they convinced you?'

Sharon nodded. 'Local lad came in, he's a constable. They said, "Ask Jimmy. He'll tell you."'

'Did you?' Kincaid prompted after another moment's silence, wondering what he might do to loosen her tongue. She sat huddled in her chair, arms folded again across her breasts, and as he studied her he thought he saw a faint blue tinge around her lips. Remembering a drinks trolley he'd seen near the wood-stove as he explored the room, he stood and went over to it. He chose two sherry glasses from the glassware on the top shelf, filling them liberally from a bottle of sherry he found beneath.

On closer inspection he discovered that the stove was laid ready for a fire, so he lit it with a match from the box on the tiled hearth and waited until the flames began to flicker brightly. 'This will take the chill off,' he said as he returned and offered the drink to Sharon. She looked up at him dully and lifted her hand, but the glass tipped as she took it, spilling pale gold liquid over the rim. When he wrapped her unresponsive fingers around the stem, he found them icy to the touch. 'You're freezing,' he said, chiding her. 'Here, take my jacket.' He slipped off his tweed sports jacket and draped it over her shoulders, then circled the room until he found the thermostat for the central heating. The room's glass-and-tile Mediterranean look made for a pleasant effect, he decided, but it wasn't too well suited for the English climate.

'Good girl.' He sat down again and lifted his own glass. She'd drunk some of hers, and he thought he saw a faint flush of colour on her cheeks. 'That's better.

Cheers,' he added, sipping his sherry, then said, 'You've had a rough time, I think, since last night. Did you ask the constable, then, about Connor?'

She drank again, then wiped her hand across her lips. 'He said, "Why d'you want to know, then?" and gave me this fishy-eyed look, so I knew it was true.'

'Did you tell him why you wanted to know?'

Sharon shook her head and the blonde curls bounced with the movement. 'Said I just knew him, that's all. Then they started a slanging match about whose round it was, and I slipped out the door by the loo.'

Her survival instincts had functioned well, even in shock, Kincaid thought, a good indication that she'd had plenty of experience looking after herself. 'What did you do then?' he asked. 'Did you come here?'

After a long moment she nodded. 'Stood about outside for hours, bloody well freezing it was, too. I still thought, you know, maybe . . .' She put the fingers of both hands over her mouth quickly, but he'd seen her lip tremble.

'You had a key,' he said gently. 'Why didn't you come in and wait?'

'Didn't know who might come in here, did I? Might tell me I hadn't any right.'

'But today you got up your courage.'

'Needed my things, didn't I?' she said, but she looked away, and Kincaid fancied there was more to it than that.

'Why else did you come, Sharon?'

'You wouldn't understand.'

'Try me.'

She met his eyes and seemed to see in them some possibility of empathy, for after a moment she said, 'I'm nobody now, do you see? I thought I'd never have another chance just to be here, like . . . we had some good times here, Con and me. I wanted to remember.'

'Didn't you think Con might have left you the flat?' Kincaid asked.

Looking down into her glass, she swirled the few remaining drops of sherry. 'Couldn't,' she said, so quietly that he had to lean forward to hear.

'Why couldn't he?'

'Not his.'

The drink didn't seem to have done much in the way of lubricating her tongue, Kincaid thought. Getting anything out of her was worse than pulling teeth. 'Whose is it, then?'

'Hers.'

'Connor was living in Julia's flat?' He found the idea very odd indeed. Why hadn't she booted him out and stayed herself, rather than going back home to her parents? It sounded much too amicable an arrangement for a couple who had supposedly not been speaking to one another.

Of course, he added to himself as he considered the girl sitting across from him, it might not have been true. Perhaps Connor had needed a handy excuse. 'Is that why Connor didn't have you move in with him?'

His jacket slipped from Sharon's shoulders as she shrugged, re-exposing the pale swell of her breasts through the weave of the pink fuzzy sweater. 'He said it wasn't right, it being Julia's house and all.'

Kincaid hadn't imagined Connor Swann being a great one for moral scruples, but then Connor was proving to be full of surprises. Glancing at the open-plan kitchen, he asked, 'Do you cook?'

Sharon looked at him as if he had a slate loose. 'Course I can cook. What do you take me for?'

'No, I mean, who did the cooking here, you or Connor?'

She thrust her lower lip out in a pout. ''E wouldn't let me touch a thing in there, like it was a bloody church or something. Said fry-ups were nasty, and he'd not have anything boiled in his kitchen but eggs and water for the pasta.' Still absently holding her glass, she stood and wandered over to the dining table. She traced a finger across its surface. ''E cooked for me, though. No bloke ever did that. Nobody ever cooked anything for me but me mum and me gran, come to think of it.' Looking up, she stared at Kincaid as if seeing him for the first time. 'You married?'

He shook his head. 'I was once, a long time ago.'

'What happened?'

'She left. Met someone else.' He said the words flatly, with an ease born of years of practice, yet it still amazed him that such simple sentences could contain such betrayal.

Sharon considered that, then nodded. 'Con made me supper – "dinner," I mean – he'd always remind me to say "dinner". Candlelight, best dishes. He'd make me sit while he brought me things – "Try this, Shar, try that, Shar." Funny things, too.' She smiled at Kincaid. 'Sometimes I felt like a kid playing dressing-up. Would you do things like that for a girl?'

'I've been known to. But I'm afraid I'm not up to Con's standards – my cooking runs more to omelettes and cheese on toast.' He didn't add that he'd never been inclined to play Pygmalion.

The brief animation that had lit Sharon's face faded. She came slowly back to her chair, empty glass trailing from her fingertips. In a still little voice she said, 'It won't happen to me again.'

'Don't be silly,' he scolded, hearing the false heartiness in his voice.

'Not like with Con, it won't.' Looking directly at Kincaid, she said, 'I know I'm not what blokes like him go for – always said it was too good to be true. A fairy tale.' She rubbed the sides of her face with her fingers, as if her jaws ached from unshed tears. 'There's not been anything in the papers. Do you know about the . . . arrangements?'

'No one in the family's rung you?'

'Rung me?' she said, some of her earlier aggression returning. 'Who the hell do you think would've rung me?' She sniffed, then added, mincing the names, 'Julia? Dame Caroline?'

Kincaid gave the question serious consideration. Julia seemed determined to ignore the fact that her husband had existed, much less died. And Caroline? He could imagine her performing a distasteful, but necessary, duty. 'Perhaps, yes. If they had known about you. I take it they didn't?'

Dropping her gaze to her lap, she said a little sullenly, 'How should I know what Con told them? I only know what he told me.' She pushed the hair from her face with chubby fingers, and Kincaid noticed that the nail on her index finger was broken to the quick. When she spoke again the defiance had gone from her voice. 'He said he'd take care of us – little Hayley and me.'

'Hayley?' Kincaid said blankly.

'My little girl. She's four. Had her birthday last week.' Sharon smiled for the first time.

This was a twist he hadn't expected. 'Is she Con's daughter, too?'

She shook her head vehemently. 'Her dad buggered off soon as he knew I was going to have her. Rotten swine. Not heard a word from him since.'

'But Con knew about her?'

'Course he did. What do you take me for, a bloody tart?'

'Of course not,' Kincaid said soothingly, and, eyeing her empty glass, unobtrusively fetched the bottle. 'Did Con get on with little Hayley, then?' he asked, dividing the last of the sherry between them.

When she didn't answer, he thought perhaps he'd gone over the mark with the sherry, but after a moment she said, 'Sometimes I wondered . . . if it was really her he wanted, not me. Look.' Digging in her handbag, she pulled out a worn leather wallet. 'That's Hayley. She's lovely, isn't she?'

It was a cheap studio portrait, but even the artificial pose and tatty props couldn't spoil the little girl's beauty. As naturally blonde as her mother might have been as a child, she had dimples and an angelic, heart-shaped face. 'Is she as good as she looks?' Kincaid asked, raising an eyebrow.

Sharon laughed. 'No, but you'd never think it to look at her, would you? Con called her his little angel. He'd tease her, call her names in this silly Irish voice. "Me little darlin'",' she said in a credible Irish accent. 'You know, things like that.' For the first time her eyes filled with tears. She sniffed and wiped the back of her hand across her nose. 'Julia didn't want any kids. That's why he wanted the divorce, but Julia wouldn't give it to him.'

'Julia wouldn't divorce Connor?' Kincaid asked, thinking that although no one had actually said, that wasn't the impression he'd had from Julia or her family.

'When the two years were up he was going to divorce her – that's how long it takes, you know, to obtain a divorce without the other party's consent.' She said the last bit so precisely Kincaid thought she must have memorized it, perhaps repeating something Connor had said in order to comfort herself.

'And you were going to wait for him? Another year, was it?'

'Why shouldn't I have done?' she said, her voice rising. 'Con never gave me reason to think he wouldn't do what he said.'

Why indeed? thought Kincaid. *What better prospect*

had she? He looked at her, sitting back a little in her chair now, with her lower lip pushed out belligerently and both hands clasped around the stem of the sherry glass. Had she loved Connor Swann, or had she merely seen him as an attractive meal ticket? And how had such an unlikely union taken place? He certainly doubted that they had moved in the same social circles. 'Sharon,' he said carefully, 'tell me, how did you and Connor meet?'

'In the park,' she said, nodding towards the river. 'Just there, in the Meadows. You can see it from the road. In the spring, it was. I was pushing Hayley in the swings and she fell out, skinned her knee. Con came over and talked to her, and before you knew it she'd stopped her bawling and was laughing at him.' She smiled, remembering. 'Him and his Irish blarney. He brought us back here to look after her knee.' When Kincaid raised an eyebrow at that, she hurried on. 'I know what you're thinking. At first I was afraid he might be . . . well, you know, a bit funny. But it wasn't like that at all.'

Sharon looked relaxed now, and warm, sitting with her feet in their preposterous shoes stretched out in front of her, sherry glass cradled in her lap. 'What was it like?' Kincaid asked softly.

She took her time answering, studying her glass, the fan of her darkly mascaraed lashes casting shadows on her cheeks. 'Funny. What with his job and all, it seemed like Con knew everybody. Always lunches and dinners and drinks and golfing. Busy, you know, important.' She raised her eyes to Kincaid's. 'I think he was lonely. In between all those engagements, there wasn't anything.'

Kincaid thought about the desk diary he'd seen upstairs, with its endless round of appointments. 'Sharon, what was Con's job?'

''E was in advertising.' Wrinkling her brow, she said, 'Blakely, Gill . . . I can never remember. In Reading, it was.'

That certainly made sense of the diary. Remembering the deposit stubs, he recited, 'Blackwell, Gillock and Frye.'

'That's it.' Pleased at his cleverness, she beamed at him.

Kincaid ran back through the cheque book register in his mind. If Connor had helped Sharon out financially, he had done it on a cash basis – there had been no cheques made out in her name. Unless he had passed the money through someone else. Casually, he asked, 'Do you happen to know someone called Hicks?'

'That Kenneth!' she said furiously, sitting up and sloshing what remained of her drink. 'Thought you were him, didn't I, when I first came in and heard you upstairs. Thought he'd come for what he could get, like a bloody vulture.'

Was that why she'd been so frightened? 'Who is he, Sharon? What connection did he have with Con?'

A little apologetically, she said, 'Con liked the horses, see? That Kenneth, he worked for a bookie, ran Con's bets for him. 'E was always hanging about, treated me like I was dirt.'

If that were the case, Connor Swann had not played

the ponies lightly. 'Do you know what bookmaker Kenneth Hicks worked for?'

She shrugged. 'Somebody here in the town. Like I said, he was always hanging about.'

Remembering all the Red Lion notations in the diary, Kincaid wondered if that had been their regular meeting place. 'Did Con go to the Red Lion Hotel often? The one next to the chur—?'

Already shaking her head, she interrupted, 'All tarted up for the tourists, that one. A posh whore, Con called it, where you couldn't get a decent pint.'

The girl was a natural mimic, with a good memory for dialogue. When she quoted Con, Kincaid could hear the cadence of his voice, even the faint hint of Irish accent.

'No,' she continued, 'it was the Red Lion in Wargrave he liked. A real pub, with good food at a decent price.' She smiled, showing a faint dimple like her daughter's. 'The food was the thing, you know – Con wouldn't go anywhere he didn't like the food.' Putting her glass to her lips and turning it end up, she drained the last few drops. ''E even took me there, a few times, but mostly he liked to stay at home.'

Kincaid shook his head at the contradictions. The man had lived a boozing, betting, life-in-the-fast-lane, by all accounts, but had preferred to stay at home with his mistress and her child. Connor had also, according to his diary, had lunch with his in-laws every single Thursday for the past year.

Kincaid thought back to the aftermath of his own marriage. Although Vic had left him, her parents had somehow managed to cast him as the villain of the piece, and he had never heard from them again, not so much as a card at Christmas or on his birthday. 'Do you know what Con did on Thursdays, Sharon?' he asked.

'Why should I? Same as any other day, far as I know,' she added, frowning.

So she hadn't known about the regular lunch with the in-laws. What else had Connor conveniently not told her? 'What about last Thursday, Sharon, the day he died? Were you with him?'

'No. 'E went to London, but I don't think he'd meant to, beforehand. When I'd given Hayley her supper, I came over and he'd just come in. All wound up he was, too, couldn't sit still with it.'

'Did he say where he'd been?'

Slowly, she shook her head. 'Said he had to go out again for a bit. "To see a man about a dog," he said, but that was just his way of being silly.'

'And he didn't tell you where he was going?'

'No. Told me not to get my knickers in a twist, that he'd be back.' Slipping off her high-heeled sandals, she tucked her feet up in the armchair and rubbed at her toes with sudden concentration. She looked up, her eyes magnified by a film of moisture. 'But I couldn't stay, 'cause it were Gran's bridge night and I had to see to Hayley. I couldn't . . .' Wrapping her arms around her calves, she buried her face against her knees. 'I didn't . . .' she whispered, her voice muffled by the fabric of her jeans, '. . . wouldn't even give him a kiss when he left.'

So she had been pouting, her feelings hurt, and had childishly snubbed him, thought Kincaid. A small failing, an exhibition of ordinary lovers' behaviour, to be laughed about later in bed, but this time there could be no making up. Of such tiny things are made lifetimes of guilt, and what she sought from him was absolution. Well, he would give whatever was in his power to bestow. 'Sharon. Look at me.' Slipping forward in his chair, he reached out and patted her clasped hands. 'You couldn't know. We're none of us perfect enough to live every minute as if it might be our last. Con loved you, and he knew you loved him. That's all that matters.'

Her shoulders moved convulsively. He sat back quietly, watching her, until he saw her body relax and begin a barely perceptible rocking, then he said, 'Con didn't say anything else about where he was going or who he meant to see?'

She shook her head without lifting it. 'I've thought and thought. Every word he said, every word I said. There's nothing.'

'And you didn't see him again that night?'

'I said I didn't, didn't I?' she said, raising her face from her knees. Weeping had blotched her fair skin, but she sniffed and ran her knuckles under her eyes unselfconsciously. 'What do you want to know all this stuff for, anyway?'

At first her need to talk, to release some of her grief, had been greater than anything else, but now Kincaid saw her natural wariness begin to reassert itself. 'Had Con been drinking?' he asked.

Sharon sat back in her chair, looking puzzled. 'I don't think so – at least he didn't seem like it, but sometimes you couldn't tell, at first.'

'Had a good head, did he?'

She shrugged. 'Con liked his pint, but he wasn't ever mean with it, like some.'

'Sharon, what do you think happened to Con?'

'Silly bugger went for a walk along the lock, fell in and drowned! What do you mean "What happened to him?" How the bloody hell should I know what happened to him?' She was almost shouting, and bright spots of colour appeared on her cheekbones.

Kincaid knew he'd received the tail end of the anger she couldn't vent on Connor – anger at Connor for dying, for leaving her. 'It's difficult for a grown man to fall in and drown, unless he's had a heart attack or is falling-down drunk. We won't be able to rule those possibilities out until after the post-mortem, but I think we'll find that Connor was in good health and at least relatively sober.' As he spoke her eyes widened and she shrank back in her chair, as if she might escape his voice, but he continued relentlessly. 'His throat was bruised. I think someone choked him until he lost consciousness and then very conveniently shoved him in the river. Who would have done that to him, Sharon? Do you know?'

'The bitch,' she said on a breath, her face blanched paper-white beneath her makeup.

'What–'

She stood up, propelled by her anger. Staggering,

she lost her balance and fell to her knees before Kincaid. 'That bitch!'

A fine spray of spittle reached his face. He smelled the sherry on her breath. 'Who, Sharon?'

'She did everything she could to ruin him and now she's killed him.'

'Who, Sharon? Who are you talking about?'

'Her, of course. Julia.'

The woman sitting beside Kincaid nudged him. The congregation was rising, lifting and opening hymnals. He'd heard only snippets of the sermon, delivered in a soft and scholarly voice by the balding vicar. Standing quickly, he scrabbled for a hymnal and peered at his neighbour's to find the page.

He sang absently, his mind still replaying his interview with Connor Swann's mistress. In spite of Sharon's accusations, he just didn't think that Julia Swann had the physical strength necessary to choke her husband and shove him into the canal. Nor had she had the time, unless Trevor Simons was willing to lie to protect her. None of it made sense. He wondered how Gemma was getting on in London, if she had found out anything useful in her visit to the opera.

The service came to a close. Although the congregation greeted one another and chatted cheerfully as they filed out, nowhere did he hear Connor or the Ashertons mentioned. They glanced curiously and a little shyly at Kincaid, but no one spoke to him. He followed the crowd out into the churchyard, but instead of returning to the hotel, he turned his collar up, stuck his hands in his pockets and wandered among the headstones. Distantly, he heard the sounds of car doors slamming and engines starting, but the wind hummed against his ears. Leaves rustled in the thick grass like small brown mice.

He found what he had been looking for behind the church tower, beneath a spreading oak.

'The family,' said a voice behind him, 'seems to have been more than ordinarily blessed and cursed.'

Startled, Kincaid turned. Contemplating the headstone, the vicar stood with his hands clasped loosely before him and his feet spread slightly apart. The wind whipped his vestments against his legs and blew the strands of thinning, grey hair across his bony skull.

The inscription said simply: MATTHEW ASHERTON, BELOVED SON OF GERALD AND CAROLINE, BROTHER OF JULIA. 'Did you know him?' Kincaid asked.

The vicar nodded. 'In many ways an ordinary boy, transformed into something beyond himself by the mere act of opening his mouth.' He looked up from the headstone and Kincaid saw that his eyes were a fine, clear grey. 'Oh yes, I knew him. He sang in my choir. I taught him his catechism, as well.'

'And Julia? Did you know Julia, too?'

Studying Kincaid, the vicar said, 'I noticed you earlier, a new face in the congregation, a stranger wandering purposefully about among the headstones, but you did not seem to me to be a mere sensation seeker. Are you a friend of the family?'

In answer Kincaid removed his warrant card from his pocket and opened the case. 'Duncan Kincaid. I'm looking into the death of Connor Swann,' he said, but even as he spoke he wondered if that were now the entire truth.

The vicar closed his eyes for a moment, as if conducting a private communication, then opened them and blinked before fixing Kincaid with his penetrating stare, 'Come across the way for a cup of tea. We can talk, out of this damnable wind.'

'Brilliance is a difficult enough burden for an adult to bear, much less a child. I don't know how Matthew Asherton would have turned out, if he had lived to fulfil his promise.'

They sat in the vicar's study, drinking tea from mismatched mugs. He had introduced himself as William Mead, and as he switched on the electric kettle and gathered mugs and sugar onto a tray, he told Kincaid that his wife had died the previous year. 'Cancer, poor dear,' he'd said, lifting the tray and indicating that Kincaid should follow him. 'She was sure I'd never be able to manage on my own, but somehow you muddle through. Although,' he added as he opened the study door, 'I must admit that housekeeping was never my strong suit.'

His study bore him out, but it was a comfortable sort of disorder. The books looked as if they might have leaped off the shelves, spreading out onto every available surface like a friendly, invading army, and the bits of wall space not covered by books contained maps.

Setting his mug on the small space the vicar had cleared for him on a side table, Kincaid went to examine an ancient-looking specimen which was carefully preserved behind glass.

'Saxton's map of the Chilterns, 1574. This is one of the few that show the Chilterns as a whole.' The vicar coughed a little behind his hand, then added, out of what Kincaid thought must be a lifetime's habit of honesty, 'It's only a copy, of course, but I enjoy it nonetheless. It's my hobby – the landscape history of the Chilterns.

'I'm afraid,' he continued with an air of confession, 'that it takes up a good deal more of my time and interest than it should, but when one has written a sermon once a week for close on half a century, the novelty pales. And these days, even in a rural parish like this one, for the most part our work is saving bodies, rather than souls. I can't remember when I've had someone come to me with a question of faith.' He sipped his tea and gave Kincaid a rather rueful smile.

Kincaid, wondering if he looked as though he needed saving, smiled back and returned to his chair. 'You must know the area well, then.'

'Every footpath, every field, or close enough.' Mead stretched out his legs, exhibiting the trainers he had slipped into upon returning to the house. 'My feet must be nearly as well travelled as Paul's on the road to Damascus. This is an ancient countryside, Mr Kincaid – ancient in the sense the term is used in landscape history, as opposed to planned countryside. Although these hills are part of the calcareous backbone that underlies much of southern England, they're much more heavily wooded than most chalk downlands – this, and the layer of clay with flints in the soil, kept the area from extensive agricultural development.'

Kincaid cradled his warm mug in both hands and positioned his feet near the glowing bars of the electric fire, prepared to listen to whatever dissertation the vicar might offer. 'So that's why so many of the houses here are built from flints,' he said, remembering how incongruous the pale smooth limestone walls of Badger's End had seemed, glowing in the dusk. 'I'd noticed, of course, but hadn't carried the thought any further.'

'Indeed. You will also have noticed the pattern of fields and hedgerows in the valleys. Many can be traced back to pre-Roman times. It is the "Immanuel's Land" of John Bunyan's *Pilgrim's Progress*, ". . . a most pleasant mountainous country, beautiful with woods, vineyards, fruits of all sorts; flowers also with springs and fountains; very delectable to behold."

'My point, Mr Kincaid,' continued the vicar, twinkling at him, 'lest you grow impatient with me, is that although this is a lovely countryside, a veritable Eden, if you will, it is also a place where change occurs slowly and things are not easily forgotten. There has been a dwelling of some sort at Badger's End since medieval times, at the least. The façade of the present house is Victorian, though you wouldn't think it to look at it, but some of the less visible parts of the house go back much further.'

'And the Ashertons?' Kincaid asked, intrigued.

'The family has been there for generations, and their lives are very much intertwined with the fabric of the valley. No one who lives here will forget the November that Matthew Asherton drowned – communal memory, you might say. And now this.' He shook his head, his expression reflecting a genuine compassion unmarred by any guilty pleasure in another's misfortune.

'Tell me what you remember about that November.'

'The rain.' The vicar sipped his tea, then pulled a crumpled, white handkerchief from his breast pocket and gently patted his lips. 'I began to think quite seriously about the story of Noah, but spirits sank as the water rose and I remember doubting my parishioners would find a sermon on the subject very uplifting. You're not familiar with the geography of the area, are you, Mr Kincaid?'

Kincaid assumed the question to be rhetorical, as the vicar had gone to his desk and begun rooting among the papers even as he spoke, but he answered anyway. 'No, Vicar, I can't say that I am.'

The object of the search proved to be a tattered Ordnance Survey map, which the vicar unearthed with obvious delight from beneath a pile of books. Opening it carefully, he spread it before Kincaid. 'The Chiltern Hills are a legacy of the last Ice Age. They lie across the land at a horizontal angle, from the northeast to the southwest, do you see?' He traced a darker green oblong with his fingertip. 'The north side is the escarpment, the southern the dip-slope, with valleys running down it like fingers. Some of these valleys bear rivers – the Lea, the Bulbourne, the Chess, the Wye, and others – all tributaries of the Thames. In others the springs and surface-flow only break out when the water table reaches the surface – during the winter or other times of particularly heavy rain.' Sighing, he gave the map a gentle tap with a forefinger before folding it again. 'Hence their name – winterbournes. It's quite pretty, isn't it? Very descriptive. But they can be treacherous in flood, and that, I'm afraid, was the downfall of poor young Matthew.'

'What exactly happened?' asked Kincaid. 'I've only really heard the story secondhand.'

'The only one who will ever know exactly what happened is Julia, as she was with him,' said the vicar, with an attention to detail worthy of a policeman. 'But I'll do my best to piece it together. The children were walking home from school and took a familiar shortcut through the woods. The rain had given us a brief respite, for the first time in days. Matthew, indulging in some horseplay along the bank of the stream, fell in and was caught by the current. Julia tried to reach him, going dangerously far into the water herself, and, failing, ran home for help. It was too late, of course. I think it quite likely that the boy had stopped breathing before Julia left him.'

'Did Julia tell you the story herself?'

Mead nodded as he sipped his tea, then set his mug down and continued. 'In bits and snatches, rather less than coherently, I'm afraid. You see, she was quite ill afterwards, what with the shock and the chill. No one thought to see to her until hours later, and she'd been soaked to the skin. Even that was Mrs Plumley's doing – the parents were entirely too distraught to remember her at all.

'She developed pneumonia. It was touch and go for a bit.' Shaking his head, he held his hands out towards the electric fire, as if the memory had made him cold. 'I visited her every day, taking it in turn with Mrs Plumley to sit with her during the worst of it.'

'What about her parents?' asked Kincaid, feeling the stirrings of outrage.

Distress creased the vicar's gentle face. 'The grief in that house was as thick as the water that drowned Matthew, Mr Kincaid. They had no room in their minds or hearts for anything else.'

'Not even their daughter?'

Very quietly, almost to himself, Mead said, 'I think they couldn't bear to look at her, knowing that she was alive and he was not.' He met Kincaid's eyes, adding more briskly, 'There, now, I've said more than I should. It's been a long time since I've thought of it, and Connor's death has brought it all back.'

'There's more you're not telling me.' Kincaid sat forward in his chair, not willing to let the matter drop.

'It's not my place to pass judgement, Mr Kincaid. It was a difficult time for everyone concerned.'

Kincaid translated that as meaning that Mead thought the Ashertons had behaved abominably, but wouldn't allow himself to say so. 'Sir Gerald and Dame Caroline are certainly solicitous of their daughter now.'

'As I said, Mr Kincaid, it was all a very long time ago. I'm only sorry that Julia has had another such loss.'

A movement at the window caught Kincaid's eye. The wind had raised a dervish of leaves on the vicar's lawn. It spun for a moment, then collapsed. A few leaves drifted towards the window, lightly tapping the panes. 'You said you knew Matthew, but you must have come to know Julia quite well, actually.'

The vicar swirled the dregs of his tea in his mug. 'I'm not sure anyone knows Julia well. She was always a quiet child, watching and listening where Matthew would plunge into things. It made the rare response from her all the sweeter, and when she took an interest in something it seemed genuine, not merely the latest enthusiasm.'

'And later?'

'She did talk to me, of course, during her illness, but it was a hotchpotch, childish delirium. And when she recovered she became quite withdrawn. The only time I had a glimpse of the child I knew was at her wedding. She had that glow that almost all brides have, and it softened the edges.' His tone affectionate, the vicar's smile invited Kincaid's understanding.

'I can almost imagine that,' Kincaid said, thinking of the smile he'd seen when Julia had opened the door to them, thinking it was Plummy. 'You said you married them, Vicar? But I thought—'

'Connor was Catholic, yes, but he didn't practise, and Julia preferred to be married here at St Barts.' He nodded at the church, its distinctive double tower just visible across the lane. 'I counselled Connor as well as Julia before the wedding, and I must say I had my doubts, even then.'

'Why was that?' Kincaid had developed a considerable regard for the vicar's perceptions.

'In some odd way he reminded me of Matthew, or of Matthew as he might have been had he grown up. I don't know if I can explain it . . . he was perhaps a bit too glib for my liking – with such outward charm it's sometimes difficult to tell what runs beneath the surface. An ill-fated match, in any event.'

'Apparently,' Kincaid agreed wryly. 'Although I'm a bit confused as to who wouldn't divorce whom. Julia certainly seems to have grown to dislike Connor.' He paused, weighing his words. 'Do you think she could have killed him, Vicar? Is she capable of it?'

'We all carry the seeds of violence, Mr Kincaid. What has always fascinated me is the balance of the equation – what factor is it that allows one person to tip over the edge, and another not?' Mead's eyes held knowledge accumulated over a lifetime of observing the best and worst of human character, and it occurred to Kincaid once again that their callings were not dissimilar. The vicar blinked and continued, 'But to answer your question, no, I do not think Julia capable of killing anyone, no matter what the circumstances.'

'Why do you say "anyone", Vicar?' Kincaid asked, puzzled.

'Only because there were rumours at the time of Matthew's death, and you are bound to hear them if you poke long enough under rocks. Open accusations might have been refutable, but not the faceless whispers in the dark.'

'What did they say, the whisperers?' Kincaid said, knowing the answer even as he spoke.

Mead sighed. 'Only what you might expect, human nature being what it is, as well as being fuelled by her sometimes obvious jealousy of her brother. They insinuated that she didn't try to save him . . . that she might even have pushed him.'

'She was jealous of him, then?'

The vicar sat up a bit in his chair and for the first time sounded a bit irascible. 'Of course she was jealous! As any normal child would have been, given the circumstances.' His grey eyes held Kincaid's. 'But she also loved him, and would never willingly have allowed harm to come to him. Julia did as much to save her brother as anyone could expect of a frightened thirteen-year-old, probably more.' He stood up and began collecting the tea things on the tray. 'I don't possess the temerity to call a tragedy like that an act of God. And accidents, Mr Kincaid, are often unanswerable.'

Placing his mug carefully on the tray, Kincaid said, 'Thank you, Vicar. You've been very kind.'

Mead stood, tray balanced in his hands, gazing out of the window at the churchyard. 'I don't profess to understand the workings of fate. Sometimes it's best not to, in my business,' he added, the twinkle surfacing again, 'but I've always wondered. The children usually took the bus home from school, but they were late that day and had to walk instead. What kept them?'

Chapter Seven

Kincaid reshuffled the files on his desk and ran a hand through his hair until it stood up like a cockscomb. The late Sunday afternoon lull at the Yard usually provided the perfect time to catch up on paperwork, but today concentration eluded him. He stretched and glanced at his watch – past teatime, and the sudden hollow sensation in his stomach reminded him he'd missed lunch altogether. Tossing the reports he'd managed to finish into the out tray, he stood up and grabbed his jacket from the peg.

He'd go home, look after Sid, repack his bag, perhaps grab a Chinese take-away. Ordinarily the prospect would have contented him, but today it didn't ease the restlessness that had dogged him since he left the vicarage and caught the train back to London. The image of Julia rose again in his mind. Her face was younger, softer, but pale against the darkness of her fever-matted hair, and she tossed in her white-sheeted bed, uncomforted.

He wondered just how much political clout the Ashertons wielded, and how carefully he need tread.

It was not until he'd exited the Yard garage into

Caxton Street that he thought of phoning Gemma again. He'd rung periodically during the afternoon without reaching her, although she must have been finished with her interview at the ENO hours ago. He eyed the cellular phone but didn't pick it up, and as he rounded St James's Park he found himself heading towards Islington rather than Hampstead. It had been weeks since Gemma moved into the new flat, and her rather embarrassed delight when she spoke of it intrigued him. He'd just pop by on the off-chance he'd catch her at home.

When he remembered how carefully she had avoided inviting him to her house in Leyton, he pushed it to the back of his mind.

He pulled up in front of the address Gemma had given, studying the house before him. A detached honey-coloured stone, it was one of a hotchpotch of houses lying rather incongruously between two of Islington's Georgian crescents. Its two bow-fronted windows caught the late afternoon sun, and an iron fence surrounded the well-tended garden. From the front steps two large black dogs of indeterminate breed regarded him alertly, ready to protest if he should cross the bounds of the gate. Remembering Gemma's description, he left the car in the nearest space and walked round the corner, following the garden wall.

The garage doors were painted a cheerful daffodil yellow, as was the smaller door to their left. Above it a discreet, black number 2 satisfied him that he had indeed found the right place. He knocked, and when no one answered, he sat down on the step leading up to the garden, eased his back into a comfortable position against the bars of the narrow gate and prepared to wait.

He heard her car before he saw it. 'You'll get a ticket, parking on the double-yellows,' he said as she opened the door.

'Not when it's my own garage I'm blocking. What are you doing here, guv?'

She unbuckled Toby's seat belt and he clambered across her, shouting with excitement.

'Nice to be appreciated,' Kincaid said, slapping Toby's palm, then lifting him up and tousling the straight, fair hair. 'Your engine's developing a bit of a knock,' he continued to Gemma as she locked the Escort.

She grimaced. 'Don't remind me. Not just yet, anyway.' They stood awkwardly for a moment, Gemma clutching a bouquet of pink roses to her chest, and as the silence lengthened he grew ever more uncomfortable.

Why had he thought he could breach her carefully maintained barriers without consequence? His invasion seemed to stand between them, tangible as stone. He said, 'I'm sorry. I'll not come in. It's just that I couldn't reach you, and I thought we should connect.' Feeling more apologetic by the second, he added, 'I could take you and Toby for something to eat.'

'Don't be daft.' She dug in her handbag for her keys. 'Do come in, please.' Smiling at him, she unlocked the door and stood back. Toby darted between them with a whoop. 'This is it,' she said as she entered behind him.

Her clothes hung on an open rack beside the door. Brushing against a dress, he smelled for an instant the floral scent of the perfume she usually wore. He took his time, looking around with pleasure, considering. The simplicity surprised him, yet in some way it did not. 'It suits you,' he said finally. 'I like it.'

Gemma moved as if released, crossing the room to the tiny closet of a kitchen, filling a vase with water for the roses. 'So do I. So does Toby, I think,' she said, nodding at her son, who was busily yanking out drawers from the chest beneath the garden windows. 'But I've had a particularly severe thrashing from my mum this afternoon. She doesn't think it a suitable place for a child.'

'On the contrary,' he said, wandering about the room on a closer tour of inspection. 'There's something rather childlike about it, like a playhouse. Or a ship's cabin, where everything has its place.'

Gemma laughed. 'I told her my granddad would have loved it. He was in the navy.' She placed the roses on the small coffee table, the splash of pink the single accent in the black and grey room.

'Red would have been the obvious choice,' he said, smiling.

'Too boring.' Two pairs of cotton knickers, a bit faded and frayed about the elastic, hung suspended in front of the radiator. Flushing, Gemma snatched them down and tucked them away in a drawer beside the bed. She lit lamps and closed the blinds, shutting out the twilit garden. 'I'll just get changed.'

'Let me take you out.' He still felt he needed to make amends. 'If you don't already have plans,' he added, giving her an easy out. 'Or we'll have a quick drink and catch up, and I'll be on my way.'

She stood for a moment, jacket in one hand and hanger in the other, looking around the room as if assessing the possibilities. 'No. There's a Europa just round the corner. We'll pick up a few things and cook.' She hung the jacket up decisively, then pulled jeans and a sweater from a chest beneath the rack.

'Here?' he asked, eyeing the kitchen dubiously.

'Coward. All it takes is a bit of practice. You'll see.'

'It does have its limitations,' Gemma admitted as they pulled chairs up to the half-moon table. 'But you learn to adapt. And it's not as though I have time to do much fancy cooking.' She looked pointedly at Kincaid as she filled his wineglass.

'Copper's life. You'll get no sympathy from me,' he said with a grin, but in truth he admired her determination. With its long, unpredictable hours and heavy caseload, CID was a tough proposition for a single mother, and he thought Gemma managed remarkably well. It didn't do to let his compassion show, however, as she bristled at anything she could construe as special treatment.

'Cheers.' He lifted his glass. 'I'll drink to your adaptability any time.' They'd cooked pasta on the gas ring and served it with ready-made sauce, a green salad, a loaf of freshly baked French bread and a bottle of fairly respectable red wine – not bad fare from a kitchen the size of a broom closet.

'Oh, wait. I almost forgot.' Gemma slipped out of her chair and rummaged in her handbag, retrieving a cassette tape. She popped the tape into the player on the shelf above the bed and brought the case to Kincaid. 'It's Caroline Stowe, singing Violetta in *Traviata*. It's the last recording she made.'

Kincaid listened to the gentle, almost melancholy strains of the overture. As they shopped, he had told Gemma about his encounter with Sharon Doyle and his visits to Trevor Simons and the vicar, and Gemma had related her interviews at the Coliseum. She'd given her usual attention to detail, but there had been an added element in her recital, an interest which stretched beyond the bounds of the case.

'This is the drinking song,' she said as the music changed. 'Alfredo sings about his carefree life, before he meets Violetta.' Toby banged his cup enthusiastically on the table in time to the rollicking music. 'Listen, now,' Gemma said softly. 'That's Violetta.'

The voice was darker, richer than he'd expected, and even in the first few phrases he could hear its emotional power. He looked at Gemma's rapt face. 'You're fascinated by all this, aren't you?'

Gemma sipped her wine, then said slowly, 'I suppose I am. I never would have thought it. But there's something . . .' She looked away from him and busied herself cutting Toby's pasta into smaller pieces.

'I don't think I've ever seen you at a loss for words, Gemma,' Kincaid said, a little amused. 'You're more likely to be guilty of the opposite sin. What is it?'

She looked up at him, pushing a stray copper hair from her cheek. 'I don't know. I can't explain it,' she said, but her hand went to her chest in a gesture more eloquent than words.

'Did you buy this today?' he asked, tapping the cassette case. A younger Caroline Stowe looked back at him, her delicate beauty accentuated by the nineteenth-century costume she wore.

'At the ENO shop.'

He grinned at her. 'You're converted, aren't you? A proselyte. I'll tell you what – you interview Caroline Stowe tomorrow. We still need a more detailed account of her movements on Thursday evening. And you can satisfy your curiosity.'

'What about the post-mortem?' she asked, wiping Toby's hands with a cloth. 'I'd expected to go with you.' She patted Toby on the bottom as she scooted him out of his chair with a whispered, 'Jammy time, love.'

Watching her, Kincaid said, 'I'll manage it myself this time. You stay in town until you can see Tommy Godwin, then drive to Badger's End and tackle Dame Caroline.'

She opened her mouth to protest, but closed it again after a moment and returned to collecting salad on her fork. Attending post-mortems was a particular point of honour with her, and Kincaid felt surprised she hadn't offered more of an objection.

'I've put Thames Valley on to tracing Kenneth

Hicks,' he said, pouring a little more wine into his glass.

'The bookie's runner? Why would he want to get rid of his source of cash? They'll never collect anything from Connor Swann now.'

Kincaid shrugged. 'Maybe they wanted to make an example of him, start a few rumours among the big gamblers – this is what's in store if you don't pay up, mate.'

Gemma finished her pasta and pushed her plate away, then picked up another piece of bread and buttered it in an absent-minded way. 'But he did pay up, regularly. A bookie's dream, I should think.'

'They could have had an argument over a payment. Maybe Connor found Kenneth was skimming off the top, threatened to tell the boss.'

'We don't know that he was.' Gemma stood up and began clearing the table. 'We don't know much of anything, for that matter.' Setting down the stack of plates again, she ticked off on her fingers. 'We need to map out Connor's day. We know he had lunch at Badger's End, and that he was meeting someone, but we don't know who. Why did he go to London? Who did he see at the Coliseum? Who did he go that night, after he came back from London? Who did he see then?'

Kincaid grinned at her. 'Well, that at least gives us somewhere to start,' he said, viewing a return of her usual combativeness with relief.

After Gemma had put Toby to bed, he tried to help with the washing up, but the kitchen would not hold more than one at a time. 'Sardines?' Kincaid suggested as he squeezed in behind her to put away the bread. The top of her head fitted just under his chin, and he was suddenly aware of the curves of her body, aware of how easy it would be to put his hands on her shoulders and hold her against him. Her hair tickled his nose and he stepped back to sneeze.

Gemma turned and gave him a look he couldn't read, then said brightly, 'Try the chair while I finish up.'

Eyeing the curving chrome and black leather article dubiously, Kincaid said, 'Are you sure it's not an instrument of torture? Or a sculpture?' But when he lowered himself gingerly into it, he found it enormously comfortable.

His expression must have given him away, because Gemma laughed and said, 'You didn't trust me.'

She pulled a dining chair near him and they chatted amiably, finishing their wine. He felt at peace, free of the restless tension that had disturbed him earlier, reluctant to manoeuvre himself out of the chair and go home. But when he saw her smother a yawn, he said, 'Early start for both of us. I'd better be off.' She didn't demur.

It was only as he drove home that he realized he hadn't told her of Sharon Doyle's accusations that Julia Swann had killed her husband. Hysteria, he thought, shrugging. Not worth recounting.

A small voice reminded him that neither had he told her of Julia's illness after her brother's death, and his only excuse for this omission was that telling the vicar's story smacked of betrayal in a way he couldn't explain.

Backstage at the Coliseum should have prepared Gemma for Lilian Baylis House, but Alison's description had misled her. 'A big old house, a bit difficult to get to. Used to be a recording studio for Decca Records.' From that Gemma envisaged a genteel place, set back in a large garden, populated by ghosts of rock stars.

'Bit difficult to get to' had proved to be more than an under-statement. Not even her well-thumbed *London A to Z* prevented her from arriving half an hour late for her appointment with Tommy Godwin, flustered, her hair escaping from its clip and her breath coming hard after a three-block sprint from the only available parking space. She felt the beginnings of a blister where her new shoe rubbed her heel.

The dark blue sign with its white ENO legend identified the house easily enough, which was just as well, as it bore no resemblance whatsoever to Gemma's fantasy. A square, heavy house with soot-darkened red brick, it stood sandwiched between a dry cleaners and an auto-parts shop in a busy shopping street just off the Finchley Road.

Squelching the thought that she might not have become so hopelessly muddled if she'd had her mind on her driving instead of Kincaid's visit the previous evening, she tucked a stray hair into place and pulled open the door.

A man leaned against the door jamb of the receptionist's cubicle, chatting with a young woman in jeans. 'Ah,' he said, straightening up and holding a hand out to Gemma, 'I see we won't have to send your colleagues out searching for you, after all, Sergeant. It is Sergeant James, is it not?' He looked down the considerable length of his nose at her, as if assuring himself he hadn't made a mistake. 'Had a bit of trouble getting here, I'd say, from the look of you.' As the young woman handed Gemma a clipboard similar to the one Danny had used at the Coliseum, he looked at her and shook his head. 'You really should have warned her, Sheila. Not even London's finest can be expected to navigate the wilds north of the Finchley Road without a snag.'

'It was rather dreadful,' Gemma said with feeling. 'I knew where you were, but I couldn't get here from there, if you see what I mean. I'm still not quite sure how I did.'

'No doubt you'd like to powder your nose,' he said, 'before you have your wicked way with me. I'm Tommy Godwin, by the way.'

'So I'd gathered,' retorted Gemma, escaping gratefully to the loo. Once safely behind the closed door, she surveyed her reflection in the fly-specked mirror with dismay. Her navy suit, Marks and Sparks best, might as well have been jumble sale beside Tommy Godwin's casual elegance. Everything about the man, from the silk of his jacket to the warm shine of his leather slip-on shoes, spoke of good taste, and of the money spent to indulge it. Even his tall, thin frame lent itself to the act, and his fair, greying hair was sleekly and expensively barbered. A swipe of lipstick and a comb provided little defence, but Gemma did the best she could, then squared her shoulders and went out to regain charge of her interview.

She found him in the same relaxed posture as before. 'Well then, Sergeant, feeling better?'

'Much, thank you. Is there somewhere we could have a word?'

'We might steal five uninterrupted minutes in my office. Up the stairs if you don't mind.' He propelled her forward with a light hand upon her back, and Gemma felt she'd once again been outmanoeuvred. 'This is officially the buying office, the costume co-ordinator's domain,' he continued, ushering her through a door at the top of the stairs, 'but we all use it. As you might guess.'

Every available inch of the small room seemed to be covered – papers and costume sketches spilled from the worktables onto the floor, bolts of fabric leaned together in corners like old drunkards propping one another up, and shelves on the walls held rows of large black books.

'Bibles,' said Godwin, following her gaze. Gemma's face must have registered her surprise, because he smiled and added, 'That's what they're called, really. Look.' He ran his finger along the bindings, then pulled one down and opened it on the worktable. 'Kurt Weill's *Street Scene*. Every production in rep has its own bible, and as long as that production is performed the bible is adhered to in the smallest possible detail.'

Gemma watched, fascinated, as he slowly turned the pages. The detailed descriptions of sets and costumes were accompanied by brightly coloured sketches, and each costume boasted carefully matched fabric swatches as well. She touched the bit of red satin glued next to a full-skirted dress. 'But I thought . . . well, that every time you put on an opera it was different, new.'

'Oh no, my dear. Productions sometimes stay in rep as long as ten or fifteen years, and are often leased out to other companies. This production, for instance' – he tapped the page – 'is a few years old, but if it should be done next year in Milan, or Santa Fe, their Wardrobe will be responsible for securing this exact fabric, down to the dye lot, if possible.' He sat on the edge of a stool and crossed his long legs, displaying the perfection of his trouser crease. 'There are some up-and-coming directors who insist that a show they've originated mustn't be done without them, no matter where it's performed. Upstarts, the lot of them.'

Making an effort to resist the fascination of the brightly coloured pages, Gemma gently closed the book. 'Mr Godwin, I understand you attended last Thursday evening's performance at the Coliseum.'

'Back to business, is it, Sergeant?' He drew his brows together in mock disappointment. 'Well, if you must, you must. Yes, I popped in for a bit. It's a new production, and I like to keep an eye on things, make sure one of the principals doesn't need a nip here or a tuck there.'

'Do you usually drop in on Sir Gerald Asherton after the performance as well?'

'Ah, I see you've done your homework, Sergeant.' Godwin smiled at her, looking as delighted as if he were personally responsible for her cleverness. 'Gerald was in particularly fine form that night – I thought it only fitting to tell him so.'

Growing increasingly irritated by Tommy Godwin's manner, Gemma said, 'Sir, I'm here because of the death of Sir Gerald's son-in-law, as you very well know. I understand that you've known the family for years, and under the circumstances I think your attitude is a little cavalier, don't you?'

For an instant he looked at her sharply, his thin face still, then the bright smile fell back into place. 'I'm sure I deserve to be taken to task for not expressing the proper regret, Sergeant,' he said, clicking his tongue against his teeth. 'I've known Gerald and Caroline since we were all in nappies.' Pausing, he raised an eyebrow at Gemma's look of disbelief. 'Well, at least in Julia's case it's quite literally true. I was the lowest of the lowly in those days, junior assistant to the women's costume cutter. Now it takes three years of design school to qualify for that job, but in those days most of us blundered into it. My mother was a dressmaker – I knew a sewing machine inside out by the time I was ten.'

If that were the case he'd certainly done a good job of acquiring his upper-middle-class veneer, thought Gemma. Her surprise must have shown, because he smiled at her and added, 'I had a talent for copying as well, Sergeant, that I've put to good use.

'Junior assistant cutters don't fit the principals' costumes, but sometimes they are allowed to fit the lesser luminaries, the has-beens and the rising stars. Caro was a fledgling in those days, still too young to have mastered control of that marvellous natural talent, but ripe with potential. Gerald spotted her in the chorus and made her his protégée. He's thirteen years older – did you know that, Sergeant?' Godwin tilted his head and examined her critically, as if making sure he had his pupil's attention. 'He had a reputation to consider, and oh, my, tongues did wag when he married her.'

'But I thought—'

'Oh, no one remembers that now, of course. It was all a very long time ago, my dear, and their titles weren't even a twinkle in the Queen's eye.'

The hint of weariness in his voice aroused her curiosity. 'Is that how you met Caroline, fitting her costumes?'

'You're very astute, Sergeant. Caro had married Gerald by that time, and produced Julia. She'd sometimes bring Julia to fittings, to be fussed and cooed over, but even then Julia showed little evidence of being suitably impressed.'

'Impressed by what, Mr Godwin? I'm not sure I follow you.'

'Music in general, my dear, and in particular the whole tatty, overblown world of opera.' Sliding from the stool, he walked to the window and stood, hands in his pockets, looking down into the street. 'It's like a bug, a virus, and I think some people have a predisposition for catching it. Perhaps it's genetic.' He turned and looked at her. 'What do you think, Sergeant?'

Gemma fingered the costume sketches lying loose on the table, thinking of the chill that had gripped her as she heard *Traviata*'s finale for the first time. 'This . . . predisposition has nothing to do with upbringing?'

'Certainly not in my case. Although my mother had a fondness for dance bands during the war.' Hands still in his pockets, he did a graceful little box-step, then gave Gemma a sideways glance. 'I always imagined I was conceived after a night spent swinging to Glenn Miller or Benny Goodman,' he added with a mocking half-smile. 'As for Caroline and Gerald, I don't think it ever occurred to them that Julia wouldn't speak their language.'

'And Matthew?'

'Ah, well, Matty was a different story all together.' He turned away again as he spoke, then fell silent, gazing out of the window.

Why, wondered Gemma, did she meet this stone wall every time she brought up Matthew Asherton? She remembered Vivian Plumley's words: 'We don't talk about that,' and it seemed to her that twenty years should have provided more solace.

'Nothing was ever the same after Caro left the company,' Godwin said softly. He turned to Gemma. 'Isn't that what they always say, Sergeant, the best times of one's life are only recognized in retrospect?'

'I wouldn't know, sir. It seems a bit cynical to me.'

'Ah, but you've contradicted yourself, Sergeant. I can see you do have an opinion.'

'Mr Godwin,' Gemma said sharply, 'my opinion is not in question here. What did you and Sir Gerald talk about last Thursday night?'

'Just the usual pleasantries. To be honest, I don't remember. I can't have been there more than five or ten minutes.' He came back to the stool and leaned against the edge of its seat. 'Do take the weight off, Sergeant. You'll go back to your station and accuse me of dreadful manners.'

Gemma kept firmly to her position, back against the worktable. She was finding this interview difficult enough without conducting the rest of it on a level with Tommy Godwin's elegant belt buckle. 'I'm fine, sir. Did Sir Gerald seem upset or behave in an unusual way?'

Glancing down his long nose, he said with mild sarcasm, 'As in dancing about with a lampshade on his head? Really, Sergeant, he seemed quite the ordinary fellow. Still a bit charged up from the performance, but that's only to be expected.'

'Had he been drinking?'

'We had a drink. But it's Gerald's custom to keep a bottle of good single-malt whisky in his dressing room for visitors, and I can't say I've ever seen him any the worse for it. Thursday night was no exception.'

'And you left the theatre after your drink with Sir Gerald, Mr Godwin?'

'Not straight away, no. I did have a quick word with

one of the girls in Running Wardrobe.' The coins in his pocket jingled softly as he shifted position.

'How long a word, sir? Five minutes? Ten minutes? Do you remember what time you signed out with Danny?'

'Actually, Sergeant, I didn't.' He ducked his head as sheepishly as an errant schoolboy. 'Sign out, that is. Because I hadn't signed in, and that's quite frowned upon.'

'You hadn't signed in? But I thought it was required of everyone.'

'In theory it is. But it's not a high-security prison, my dear. I must admit I wasn't feeling entirely sociable when I arrived on Thursday evening. The performance had already started when I came in through the lobby, so I just gave one of the ushers a wink and stood at the back.' He smiled at Gemma. 'I've spent too much of my working life on my feet, I suppose, to feel comfortable staying in one position for very long.' As if to demonstrate, he left the stool and came to stand near Gemma. Lifting a swatch of tartan satin from the table, he ran his fingers over its surface. 'This ought to do nicely for *Lucia*—'

'Mr Godwin. Tommy.' Gemma's use of his first name caught his attention, and for an instant she saw again the stillness beneath his surface prattle. 'What did you do when the performance finished?'

'I've told you, I went straight to Gerald's—' He stopped as Gemma shook her head. 'Oh, I see what you mean. How did I get to Gerald's dressing room?

It's quite simple if you know your way around the warren, Sergeant. There's a door in the auditorium that leads to the stage, but it's unmarked, of course, and I doubt anyone in the audience would ever notice it.'

'And you left the same way? After you spoke to Sir Gerald and – ' Gemma paused and flipped back through her notes – 'the girl in Running Wardrobe.'

'Got it in one, my dear.'

'I'm surprised you found the doors still unlocked.'

'There are always a few stragglers, and the ushers have to tidy up.'

'And I don't suppose you remember what time this was, or that anyone saw you leave,' Gemma said with an edge of sarcasm.

Rather contritely, Tommy Godwin said, 'I'm afraid not, Sergeant. But then one doesn't think about having to account for oneself, does one?'

Determined to break through his air of polished innocence, she pushed him a little more aggressively. 'What did you do when you left the theatre, Tommy?'

He propped one hip on the edge of the worktable and folded his arms. 'Went home to my flat in Highgate. What else, dear Sergeant?'

'Alone?'

'I live alone, except for my cat, but I'm sure she'll vouch for me. Her name is Salome, by the way, and I must say it suits—'

'What time did you arrive home? Do you by any chance remember that?'

'I do, actually.' He paused and smiled at her, as if

anticipating praise. 'I have a grandfather clock and I remember it chiming not long after I came in, so it must have been before midnight.'

Stalemate. He couldn't prove his statements, but without further evidence she had no way to disprove them. Gemma stared at him, wondering what lay beneath his very plausible exterior. 'I'll need your address, Mr Godwin, as well as the name of the person you spoke to after you saw Sir Gerald.' She tore a page from her notebook and watched as he wrote the information in a neat left-handed script. Running back through the interview in her mind, she realized what had been nagging her, and how deftly Tommy Godwin had sidestepped.

'How well did you know Connor Swann, Mr Godwin? You never said.'

He carefully capped her pen and returned it, then began folding the paper into neat squares. 'I met him occasionally over the years, of course. He wasn't exactly my cup of tea, I must say. It baffled me that Gerald and Caro continued to put up with him when even Julia wouldn't, but then perhaps they knew something about him that I didn't.' He raised an eyebrow and gave Gemma a half-smile. 'But then one's judgement of character is always fallible, don't you find, Sergeant?'

Chapter Eight

The High Wycombe roundabout reminded Kincaid of a toy he'd had as a child, a set of interlocking plastic gears that had revolved merrily when one turned a central crank. But in this case five mini-roundabouts surrounded a large one, humans encased in steel boxes did the revolving, and no one in the Monday morning crush was the least bit merry. He saw an opening in the oncoming traffic and shot into it, only to be rewarded by a two-fingered salute from an impatient lorry driver. 'Same to you, mate,' Kincaid muttered under his breath as he escaped gratefully from the last of the mini-roundabouts.

A hold-up on the M40 had delayed him, and he arrived at High Wycombe's General Hospital half an hour late for the post-mortem. Kincaid tapped on the door of the autopsy room and opened it just enough to put his head in. A small man in green surgical garments stood facing the stainless-steel table, his back to Kincaid. 'Dr Winstead, I presume?' Kincaid asked. 'Sorry I'm late.' He entered the room and let the door swing shut behind him.

Winstead tapped the foot switch on his recorder as

he turned. 'Superintendent Kincaid?' He edged the microphone away from his mouth with the back of his wrist. 'Sorry I can't shake,' he added, holding up his gloved hands in demonstration. 'You've missed most of the fun, I'm afraid. Started a bit early, trying to catch up on the backlog. Should have had your fellow done Saturday, yesterday at the latest, but we had a council housing fire. Spent the weekend identifying remains.'

Tubby, with a mop of curly, greying hair and boot-button black eyes, Winstead lived up to his sobriquet. Kincaid found himself thinking that his vision of Pooh Bear with scalpel in hand hadn't been too far off the mark. And like many forensic pathologists Kincaid had come across, Winstead seemed unfailingly jolly. 'Find anything interesting?' Kincaid enquired, just as glad that Winstead's body blocked part of his view of the steel table. Although he'd grown accustomed to the gaping Y-incision and peeled-forward scalp, he never enjoyed the sight.

'Nothing to jump for joy over, I'm afraid.' He turned his back on Kincaid, his gloved hands again busy. 'One or two things to finish up, then we could nip over to my office, if you like.'

Kincaid stood watching, the cold air from the vents blowing in torrents down the back of his neck. At least there wasn't much smell to contend with, cold water and refrigeration having done a good bit towards retarding the body's natural processes. Although he could look at almost anything, he still had to fight the gag response triggered by the odour of a ripe corpse.

A young woman in scrubs came in, saying, 'Ready for me, Winnie?'

'I'll just leave the tidying up to my assistant,' Winstead said over his shoulder to Kincaid. 'She likes to do the pretty work. Don't you, Heather darling?' he added, smiling at her. 'Gives her a sense of job satisfaction.' He peeled off his gloves, tossed them in a rubbish bin and scrubbed his hands at the sink.

Heather rolled her eyes indulgently. 'He's just jealous,' she said *sotto voce* to Kincaid, 'because I'm neater than he is.' She slipped on a pair of gloves and continued. 'This chap's mum would be proud of him by the time I've finished, isn't that so, Winnie?'

At least Connor Swann's adoring mum had been spared admiring Heather's handiwork, thought Kincaid. He wondered if Julia would defy convention to the extent of avoiding the mortuary and the funeral.

As Winstead ushered Kincaid from the room he said, 'She's right, I'm afraid. I get the job done, but she's a perfectionist, and her hand is much finer than mine.' He led Kincaid down several halls, stopping on the way to retrieve two coffees from a vending machine. 'Black?' he asked, pushing buttons with familiarity.

Kincaid accepted the paper cup and sipped, finding the liquid just as dreadful as its counterpart at the Yard. He followed Winstead into his office and stopped, examining the human skull which adorned the doctor's desk. Attached to the facial surface by pins were small cylinders of rubber, each of varying height with a black number inked on its tip. 'Voodoo or art, Doctor?'

'A facial reconstruction technique, lent to me by an anthropologist chum. A guess as to sex and race is made by measuring certain characteristics of the skull, then the skin depth markers are placed according to information from statistical tables. Clay is added to a thickness that conforms to the markers, and Bob's your uncle, you have a human face again. It's quite effective, actually, even if this stage does look like something from *Nightmare on Elm Street*. Heather is interested in forensic sculpture, and with her hands I don't doubt she'd be good at it.'

Before Winstead wandered too far on the subject of the lovely Heather's attributes, Kincaid thought he had better redirect him. 'Tell me, Doctor,' he said as they settled into worn leather chairs, 'did Connor Swann drown?'

Winstead knitted his brows, an exercise which made him look comical rather than fierce, and seemed to bring himself back to the body in question. 'That's a pretty problem, Superintendent, as I'm sure you very well know. Drowning is impossible to prove by autopsy. It is, in fact, a diagnosis of exclusion.'

'But surely you can tell if he had water in his lungs—'

'Do hold on, Superintendent, let me finish. Water in the lungs is not necessarily significant. And I didn't say I couldn't tell you anything, only that it couldn't be proved.' Winstead paused and drank from his cup, then made a face. 'I'm an eternal optimist, I suppose –

I always expect this stuff to be better than it is. Anyway, where was I?' He smiled benignly and took another sip of his coffee.

Kincaid decided Winstead was teasing him deliberately, and that the less he fussed the faster he'd hear the results. 'You were about to tell me what you *couldn't* prove.'

'Gunshot wounds, stabbing, blunt trauma – all fairly straightforward, cause of death easily determined. A case like this, however, is a puzzle, and I like puzzles.' Winstead uttered this with such relish that Kincaid half-expected him to rub his hands together in anticipatory glee. 'There are two things which contradict drowning,' he continued, holding up the requisite fingers. 'No foreign material present in the lungs. No sand, no nice slimy river-bottom weeds. If one inhales great gulps of water in the act of drowning, one usually takes in a few undesirable objects as well.' He folded down one finger and waggled the remainder at Kincaid. 'Secondly, rigor mortis was quite delayed. The temperature of the water would account for some degree of retardation, of course, but in an ordinary, garden-variety drowning the person struggles violently, depleting the ATP in their muscles, and this depletion speeds up the onset of rigor considerably.'

'But what if there was a struggle before he went in the water? His throat was bruised – he might have been unconscious. Or dead.'

'There are several indications that he died quite a few hours before his body was discovered,' Winstead admitted. 'The stomach contents were only partially digested, so unless your Mr Swann ate a very late supper indeed, I'd guess he was dead by midnight, or as close to it as makes no difference. When the analysis of the stomach contents comes back from the lab you may be able to pinpoint that last meal.'

'And the bruising—'

Winstead held up a hand, palm out like a traffic warden. 'There is another possibility, Superintendent, that would account for Mr Swann having been alive when he went in the water. Dry drowning. The throat closes at first contact with the water, constricting the airway. No water gets into the lungs. But, as the laryngospasm relaxes after death, it is impossible to prove. It would explain, however, the lack of foreign matter in the lungs.'

'What causes a dry drowning, then?' Kincaid asked, willing himself again to be patient and let the doctor have his bit of fun.

'That's one of nature's little mysteries. Shock would probably be your best catch-all explanation, if you must have one.' Winstead paused and drank from his cup, then looked surprised that it hadn't miraculously improved in the interval since his last tasting. 'Now, about this throat business you're so keen on. I'm afraid that's inconclusive as well. There was some external bruising – I understand you visited the morgue?' When Kincaid nodded, he continued, 'You'll have seen it, then – but there was no corresponding internal damage, no crushing of the hyoid processes. Nor did we find any occlusion of the face or neck.'

'No spots in the eyes?'

Winstead beamed at him. 'Exactly. No petechiae. Of course, it's possible that either by accident or design, someone put enough pressure on his carotid arteries to render him unconscious, then shoved him in the river.'

'Could a woman exert that much pressure?'

'Oh, a woman would be quite capable physically, I should think. But I would have expected more than just bruising – fingernail marks, abrasions – and there were none. He was clean as a whistle. And I doubt very much if a woman could have rendered him unconscious without her hands suffering some trauma from the struggle.'

Kincaid digested this for a moment. 'So what you're telling me is' – he touched the tip of one index finger to the other – 'that *a*: you don't know how Connor Swann died, and if you can't give me *cause of death*, I have to assume that *b* follows: you won't hazard a guess as to *manner of death*.'

'Most drownings are accidental, and often alcohol-related. We won't know his blood alcohol until the report comes back from the lab, but I'd be willing to bet it was quite high. However' – up came the traffic warden hand again as Kincaid opened his mouth to speak – 'if you want my off-the-record opinion . . .' Winstead sipped from his coffee again, although Kincaid had long since abandoned his, finding an inconspicuous spot for the cup among the litter on Winstead's desk. 'Most accidental drownings are also fairly straightforward. Bloke goes out fishing with his friends, they all have a few too many, bloke falls in and his friends are too pissed to pull him out. Corroborating stories from several witnesses – end of case. But in this instance' – the intelligent boot-button eyes fixed on Kincaid – 'I'd say there are a good deal too many unanswered questions. No indications of suicide?'

Kincaid shook his head. 'None.'

'Then I'd say there's not much doubt he was helped into that river in one way or another, but I'd also say you're going to have a hell of a time proving it.' Winstead smiled as if he'd just delivered a welcome pronouncement.

'What about time of death?'

'Sometime between when he was last seen and when he was found.' Winstead chortled at his own humour. 'Seriously, Superintendent, if you want my intuitive stab at it, I'd say between nineish and midnight, or perhaps nine and one o'clock.'

'Thank you, I think.' Kincaid stood up and held out a hand. 'You've been . . . um, extremely helpful.'

'Glad to be of service.' Winstead shook Kincaid's hand and smiled, the Pooh Bear resemblance more pronounced than ever. 'We'll get the report to you as soon as the lab work comes back. Can you find your way to the front? Cheerio, then.'

As Kincaid left the office he glanced back. The skull seemed to be superimposed upon Winstead's chubby form, and as Winstead waved Kincaid could have sworn the skull grinned a little more widely.

*

Kincaid left the hospital feeling little further forward than before. Although now more certain of the fact, he still had no concrete proof that Connor had been murdered. Nor had he a plausible motive, or any real suspects.

Hesitating when he reached his car, he glanced at his watch. Once Gemma had managed to track down Tommy Godwin, she would be on her way to interview Dame Caroline, and as long as she was looking into the Asherton end of things, he had better concentrate on Connor. Connor was the key – until he knew more about Connor nothing else would fall into place.

It was time he did a little prying into the part of Connor's life that did not seem to be connected to the Ashertons. Using his phone, he ascertained the address of Blackwell, Gillock and Frye, then took the road south to Maidenhead and Reading.

He never came to Reading without thinking of Vic. She had grown up here, gone to school here, and as he'd entered the city from the north, he made a quick detour down the street where her parents had lived. The suburb boasted comfortable semi-detached houses and well-tended gardens, with an occasional garden gnome peeping tastefully from behind a hedge. He had found the neighbourhood dreadful then, and he discovered that time had done nothing to soften his opinion.

Easing the car to a halt, he let the engine idle while he studied the house. So unaltered did it appear that he wondered if it had been held in some sort of stasis while time eddied around it, and he had changed and aged. He saw it as he'd seen it the first time Vic took him home to meet her parents, down to the determined shine on the brass letterbox. They had looked upon him with well-bred disapproval, dismayed that their beautiful and scholarly daughter should have taken up with a policeman, and with a stab of discomfort he remembered that he had felt faintly ashamed of his less-than-conventional family. His parents had always cared more for books and ideas than the acquisition of middle-class possessions, and his childhood in their rambling house in the Cheshire countryside had been far removed from this tidy, ordered world.

He slipped the Midget into first gear and eased out the clutch, listening to the engine's familiar sputtering response. Perhaps Vic had chosen someone more suitable for the second go-round. He, at least, was well out of it. With that thought came a sense of release and the welcome realization that he did, actually, finally, mean it.

The snarl of Reading traffic hadn't improved since his last visit, and as he sat drumming his fingers on the steering wheel in the queue for city-centre parking, he remembered how much he had always disliked the place. It combined the worst of modern architecture with bad city planning, and the results were enough to make anyone's blood pressure rise.

Once he'd parked the car he found the modern block of offices which housed the advertising agency without too much difficulty. A pretty receptionist greeted him with a smile as he entered the third-floor suite. 'Can I help you, sir?' she asked, and her voice held a hint of curiosity.

He knew she must be trying to catalogue him – not a familiar client or supplier, no briefcase or samples to mark him as a commercial traveller – and he couldn't resist teasing her a bit. Her short bobbed dark hair and heart-shaped face gave her an appealing innocence. 'Nice office,' he said, looking slowly around the reception area. Modular furniture, dramatic lighting, art-deco advertising prints carefully framed and placed – it added up, he thought, to clever use of limited funds.

'Yes, sir. Is there someone you wanted to see?' she asked a little more forcefully, her smile fading.

He removed his warrant card and handed her the open folder. 'Superintendent Duncan Kincaid, Scotland Yard. I'd like to speak to someone about Connor Swann.'

'Oh.' She looked from his face to the card and back again, then her brown eyes filled with tears. 'Isn't it just awful? We only heard this morning.'

'Really? Who notified you?' he asked, casually retrieving his card.

She sniffed. 'His father-in-law, Sir Gerald Asherton. He rang John – that's Mr Frye—'

A door opened in the hallway behind her desk and a man came out, shrugging into a sports jacket. 'Melissa, love, I'm off to the—' His hand up to tighten his tie, he stopped as he saw Kincaid.

'Here's Mr Frye now,' she said to Kincaid, then

added to her boss, 'A man from Scotland Yard, here about Connor, John.'

'Scotland Yard? Connor?' Frye repeated, and his momentary bewilderment gave Kincaid a chance to study him. He judged him to be about his own age, but short, dark, and already acquiring that extra layer of padding that comes with desk-bound affluence.

Kincaid introduced himself, and Frye recovered enough to shake hands. 'What can I do for you, Superintendent? I mean, from what Sir Gerald said, I didn't expect . . .'

Smiling disarmingly, Kincaid said, 'I just have a few routine questions about Mr Swann and his work.'

Frye seemed to relax a bit. 'Well, look, I was just going round to the pub for some lunch, and I've got a client meeting as soon as I get back. Could we talk and grab a bite at the same time?'

'Suits me.' Kincaid realized that he was ravenously hungry, a not unexpected side effect of attending a post-mortem, but the prospect of the culinary delights to be found in a Reading pub didn't fill him with anticipation.

As they walked the block to the pub, Kincaid glanced at his companion. Three-piece suit in charcoal grey, expensively cut, but the waistcoat strained its buttons; midday beard shadow; hair slicked back in the latest yuppie fashion; and as Kincaid matched his stride to the shorter man's, he caught the scent of musky aftershave. He thought Connor had given the same attention to his appearance – and advertising was, after all, a business of image.

They made desultory chitchat until they reached their destination, and as they entered the White Hart, Kincaid's spirits lifted considerably. Plain and clean, the pub had an extensive lunch menu chalked on a board and was filled with escapees from other offices, all busily eating and talking. He chose the plaice, with chips and salad, his stomach rumbling. Turning to Frye, he asked, 'What are you drinking?'

'Lemonade.' Frye grimaced apologetically. 'I'm slimming, I'm afraid. I love beer, but it goes straight to my middle.' He patted his waistcoat.

Kincaid bought him a lemonade and ordered a pint for himself, not feeling the least bit of guilt at giving his companion cause for envy. Carrying their drinks, they threaded their way to a small table near the window. 'Tell me about Connor Swann,' he said as they settled into their seats. 'How long had he worked for you?'

'A little over a year. Gordon and I needed someone to do the selling, you see. We're neither of us really good at it, and we'd acquired enough clients that we thought we could justify—'

'Gordon's your partner?' Kincaid interrupted. 'I thought there were three of you.' He sipped his pint and licked a bit of foam from his lip.

'I'm sorry. I'd better start at the beginning, hadn't I?' Frye sighed and went on. 'I'm *Frye*, of course, Gordon is *Gillock*, and there isn't a *Blackwell*. When we went out on our own three years ago, we thought Gillock and Frye sounded like a fishmongers'.' Frye smiled a little sheepishly. 'The Blackwell was just to add a bit of class. Anyway, I function as creative director and Gordon does the media buying and oversees production, so we were stretched pretty thin. When we heard through a friend that Connor might be interested in an account executive's position, we thought it was just the ticket.'

The barmaid appeared at their table with laden plates. Tall and blonde, she might have been a Valkyrie in jeans and sweater. She bestowed a ravishing smile upon them along with their lunch and made her way back through the crowd. 'That's Marian,' Frye said. 'We call her the Ice Maiden. Everyone's madly in love with her and she enjoys it immensely.'

'Does the adjective refer to her looks or her disposition?' Kincaid looked at Frye's plate of salad and tucked happily into his steaming fish and chips.

'I'm not allowed fried things, either,' Frye said, eyeing Kincaid's food wistfully. 'Marian's disposition is sunny enough, but she's not generous with her favours. Even Connor drew a blank.'

'Did he chat her up?'

'Does the sun rise every morning?' Frye asked sarcastically, pushing a sprig of watercress into the corner of his mouth with his little finger. 'Of course Con chatted her up. It was as natural to him as breathing–' He stopped, looking stricken. 'Oh Christ, that was tasteless. I'm sorry. It's just that I haven't quite taken it in yet.'

Kincaid squeezed a little more lemon on his excellent fish and asked, 'Did you like him? Personally, I mean.'

Frye looked thoughtful. 'Well yes, I suppose I did. But it's not that simple. We were quite chuffed to have him at first, as I said. Of course, we wondered why he would have left one of the best firms in London for us, but he said he'd been having domestic problems, wanted to be a bit closer to home, get out of the London rat race, that sort of thing.' He took another bite of salad and chewed deliberately.

Kincaid wondered if Frye's sorrowful expression reflected his opinion of his lunch or his feelings about Connor. 'And?' he prompted gently.

'I suppose it was naïve of us to have believed it. But Con could be very charming. Not just with women – men liked him, too. That was part of what made him a good salesman.'

'He was good at his job?'

'Oh yes, very. When he put his mind to it. But that was the problem. He was so full of enthusiasm at first – plans and ideas for everything – that I think Gordon and I were rather swept away.' Frye paused. 'Looking back on it, I can see that there was a kind of frantic quality to it, but I didn't realize it at the time.'

'Back up just a bit,' Kincaid said, his forkful of chips halted in mid-air. 'You said you were naïve to have believed Connor's reasons for coming to work for you – did you find they weren't true?'

'Let's say he left a good deal out,' Frye answered ruefully. 'A few months later we began hearing trickles through the grapevine about what had really happened.' He drew his brows together in a frown. 'Didn't his wife tell you? You have spoken to the wife?'

'Tell me what?' Kincaid avoided the question, trying to fit the vivid image of Julia in his mind into that neutral possessive. *The wife.*

Frye scraped ham and shredded carrot into a neat pile in the centre of his plate. 'Con's firm in London handled the ENO account. That's how he met her – at some reception or other. I suppose she must have attended with her family. So when she left him and he had a . . .' Looking rather embarrassed, Frye studied his plate and pushed his food around with his fork. 'I guess you'd call it an emotional breakdown. Apparently he went quite bonkers – broke down crying in front of clients, that sort of thing. The firm kept it all very hush-hush – I suppose they felt they couldn't risk offending the Ashertons by publicly turning him out on his ear.'

They had all been very discreet, Kincaid thought. Had compassion entered into it at all? 'The firm gave him a recommendation when he came to you?'

'We wouldn't have taken him on, otherwise,' Frye answered matter-of-factly.

'When did things begin to go wrong?'

An expression of guilt replaced the embarrassment on Frye's face. 'It's not that Con was a total wash-out – I didn't mean to give you that impression.'

'I'm sure you didn't,' Kincaid said soothingly, hoping to forestall Frye's *let's not speak ill of the dead* qualifications.

'It was a gradual thing. He missed appointments with clients – always with a good excuse, mind you, but after a few times even good excuses begin to wear thin. He promised things we couldn't deliver—' He shook his head in remembered dismay. 'That's a creative director's nightmare. And all those new accounts he was going to bring in, all those connections he had . . .'

'Didn't materialize?'

Frye shook his head regretfully. ''Fraid not.'

Kincaid pushed away his empty plate. 'Why did you keep him on, Mr Frye? It certainly sounds as if he became more of a liability than an asset.'

'Call me John,' Frye said. Leaning forward confidentially, he continued, 'The funny thing is, a few months ago Gordon and I had just about screwed ourselves up to give him the sack, but then things started to improve. Nothing earth-shaking, but he seemed to become a bit more dependable, a bit more interested.'

'Any idea what prompted the change?' Kincaid asked, thinking of Sharon and little Hayley.

Frye shrugged. 'Not a clue.'

'Did you know he had a girlfriend?'

'Girlfriends, you mean. Plural,' Frye said with emphasis. With the resigned air of the much-married, he added, 'Once my wife met him a few times, it was more than my life was worth to have a pint with him after work. She was sure he'd lead me into temptation.' He smiled. 'Fortunately, or unfortunately, depending on your point of view, I never had Connor's knack with women.'

The lunchtime crowd had thinned. Relieved from the crush at the bar, Marian came to collect their empty plates. 'Anything else, lads? A sweet? There's some smashing gâteau left—'

'Don't torment me, please.' Frye put his hands over his face with a moan.

Marian scooped up Kincaid's plate and gave him a most un-icy wink. Smothering a chuckle, he thought that Frye's wife needn't have worried about Connor's influence – her husband's weaknesses obviously lay in other directions. That train of thought reminded him of a particular weakness they hadn't addressed. 'Were you aware of Connor's gambling debts?'

'Debts?' Frye asked, draining the last drop of lemonade from his glass. 'I knew he liked a bit of racing, but I never knew it was that serious.'

'Ever hear of a chap called Kenneth Hicks?'

Frye wrinkled his brow for a moment, then shook his head. 'Can't say that I have.'

Kincaid pushed his chair back, then stopped as another question occurred to him. 'John, did you ever meet Connor's wife, Julia?'

Frye's reaction surprised him. After a moment of rather sheepish throat-clearing, he finally looked Kincaid in the eye. 'Well, um, I wouldn't say I exactly met her.'

Kincaid raised an eyebrow. 'How can you "not exactly" meet someone?'

'I saw her. That is, I went to see her, and I did.' At Kincaid's even more doubtful expression he coloured and said, 'Oh hell, I feel an idiot, a right prat. I was curious about her, after all I'd heard, so when I saw the notice in the paper of her show in Henley . . .'

'You went to the opening?'

'My wife was away at her mum's for the night, and I thought, well, why not, there's no harm in it.'

'Why should there have been?' Kincaid asked, puzzled.

'I want to paint,' Frye said simply. 'That's why I studied art in the first place. My wife thinks it's frivolous of me – two kids to support and all that—'

'—and artists are bad influences?' Kincaid finished for him.

'Something like that.' He smiled ruefully. 'She does get a bit carried away sometimes. Thinks I'd bugger off and leave them to starve, I suppose, if someone waggled a paintbrush under my nose.'

'What happened at the opening, then? Did you meet Julia?'

Frye gazed dreamily past Kincaid's shoulder. 'She's quite striking, isn't she? And her paintings . . . well, if I could paint like that, I wouldn't spend my life doing print layouts for White's Plumbing Supply and Carpetland.' He gave a self-deprecating grimace. 'But I can't.' Focusing again on Kincaid, he added, 'I didn't meet her, but not from lack of trying. I'd drunk my cheap champagne – not without a good bit of it knocked down my shirt-front by careless elbows – and had almost made my way through the mob to her when she slipped out of the front door.'

'Did you follow her?'

'Eventually I elbowed my way to the door, thinking I'd at least pay my respects on my way out.'

'And?' Kincaid prompted impatiently.

'She was nowhere in sight.'

Chapter Nine

The trees arched overhead, their branches interlocking like twined fingers, squeezing tighter and tighter – Gemma blew a wisp of hair from her face and said, 'Silly goose.' The words seemed to bounce back at her, then it was quiet again inside the car except for an occasional squeaking as the twigs and rootlets protruding from the banks brushed against the windows. The sound reminded her of fingernails on chalkboard. London and Tommy Godwin's urbane civility seemed a world away, and for a moment she wished she'd insisted on attending the post-mortem with Kincaid. He had left a message for her at the Yard, summing up the rather inconclusive results.

She shifted down into second gear as the gradient grew steeper. Kincaid had been with her when she'd driven this way the first time, his presence forestalling any lurking claustrophobia. It was all quite silly, really, she chided herself. It was just a narrow road, after all, and some of her discomfort could surely be put down to her London-bred distrust of the country.

Nevertheless, she spied the turning for Badger's End with some relief, and soon bumped to a stop in the clearing before the house. She got out of the car and stood for a moment. Even in the chill air, the damp scent of leaf mould reached her nose, rich as autumn distilled.

In the stillness she heard the same curious, high-pitched humming sound she and Kincaid had noticed before. She looked up, searching for power lines, but saw only more leaves and a patch of uniformly grey sky. Perhaps it was some sort of generator or transformer, or – she smiled, her temper improving by the moment – UFOS. She'd try that one on the guv.

Her lips still curved in the hint of a smile as she rang the bell. Vivian Plumley opened the door, as she had before, but this time she smiled as she recognized Gemma. 'Sergeant. Please come in.'

'I'd like a word with Dame Caroline, Mrs Plumley,' Gemma responded as she stepped into the flagged hall. 'Is she in?'

'She is, but she's teaching just now.'

Gemma heard the piano begin, then a soprano voice singing a quick, lilting line. Words she couldn't distinguish interrupted the singing, then a second voice repeated the line. Darker and more complex than the first voice, it possessed an indefinable uniqueness. Even through the closed sitting room door, Gemma recognized it instantly. 'That's Dame Caroline.'

Vivian Plumley regarded her with interest. 'You have a good ear, my dear. Where have you heard her?'

'On a tape,' Gemma said shortly, suddenly reluctant to confess her interest.

Vivian glanced at her watch. 'Come and have a cuppa. She should be finished shortly.'

'What are they singing?' Gemma asked as she followed Vivian down the hall.

'Rossini. One of Rosina's arias from *The Barber of Seville*. In Italian, thank goodness.' She smiled over her shoulder at Gemma as she pushed open the door into the kitchen. 'Although in this household that's not the most politically correct thing to say.'

'Because of the ENO's policy?'

'Exactly. Sir Gerald is quite firm in agreeing with their position. I think Caro has always preferred singing an opera in its original language, but she doesn't express her opinion too forcefully.' Vivian smiled again, affectionately. The disagreement was obviously a long-standing family tradition.

'Something smells heavenly,' Gemma said, taking a deep breath. After her previous visit, the kitchen seemed as comforting and familiar as home. The red Aga radiated heat like a cast-iron heart, and on its surface two brown loaves rested on a cooling rack.

'Bread's just out of the oven,' Vivian said as she assembled mugs and a stoneware teapot on a tray. On the Aga a copper kettle stood gently steaming.

'You don't use an electric one?' Gemma asked curiously.

'I'm a dinosaur, I suppose. I've never cared for gadgets.' Turning her attention fully on Gemma, Vivian added, 'You will have some hot bread, won't you? It's getting on for teatime.'

'I had some lunch before I left London,' Gemma said, remembering the cold and greasy sausage roll hastily snatched from the Yard canteen after her interview at LB House. 'But yes, I'd love some, thanks.' She went nearer as Vivian poured boiling water into the pot and began slicing the bread. 'Wholemeal?'

'Yes. Do you like it?' Vivian looked pleased. 'It's my trademark, I'm afraid, and my therapy. It's kneaded twice, and takes three risings, but it puffs up in the oven like a dream.' She gave Gemma a humorous glance. 'And it's hard to stay frustrated with life when you've done that much pounding.'

As they seated themselves at the scarred oak table, Gemma confided, 'I grew up in a bakery. My parents have a small shop in Leyton. Almost everything's done by machine, of course, but Mum could usually be persuaded to let us get our hands in the dough.'

'It sounds a good upbringing,' Vivian said approvingly as she poured tea into Gemma's mug.

A flowery cloud of steam enveloped Gemma's face. 'Earl Grey?'

'You do like it, I hope? I should have asked. It's a habit – that's what I always have in the afternoons.'

'Yes, thank you,' Gemma answered demurely, thinking that if she were to make a practice of taking afternoon tea in houses like this, she had bloody well better learn to like it.

She ate her bread and butter in appreciative silence, wiping the last crumbs from the plate with her fingertip. 'Mrs Plumley—'

'Everyone calls me Plummy,' Vivian said in invitation. 'The children started it when they were tots, and it stuck. I've rather grown to like it.'

'All right, then. Plummy.' Gemma thought the name suited her. Even dressed as she was today, in a brightly coloured running suit and co-ordinating turtleneck, Vivian Plumley had about her an aura of old-fashioned comfort. Noticing that the other woman still wore her wedding ring, Gemma half-consciously rubbed the bare finger on her left hand.

They sat quietly, drinking their tea, and in the relaxed, almost sleepy atmosphere, Gemma found that a question came as easily as if she had been talking to friend. 'Didn't you find it odd that Connor stayed on such close terms with the family after he and Julia separated? Especially with no children involved . . .'

'But he knew them first, you see, Caro and Gerald. He'd met them through his job, and cultivated them quite actively. I remember thinking at the time that he seemed quite smitten with Caro, but then she's always collected admirers the way other people collect butterflies.'

Although Plummy had uttered this without the least hint of censure, Gemma had a sudden vision of a struggling insect pinned ruthlessly to a board. 'Ugh,' she said, wrinkling her nose in distaste. 'I could never stand the thought.'

'What?' asked Plummy. 'Oh, butterflies, you mean. Well, perhaps it was an unkind comparison, but men always seem to flutter so helplessly around her. They think she needs looking after, but the truth of it is that she's quite capable of looking after herself. Personally, I can't imagine it.' She smiled at Gemma. 'I don't think I've ever inspired that desire in anyone.'

Gemma thought of Rob's automatic assumption that she would provide for his every need, both physical and emotional. It had never occurred to him that she might have a few of her own. She said, 'I never thought of it quite like that, but men haven't fallen over themselves trying to look after me, either.' Sipping her tea, she continued, 'About Dame Caroline – you said you were at school together. Did she always want to sing?'

Plummy laughed. 'Caro was front and centre from the day she was born. At school she sang the leading part in every programme. Most of the other girls quite despised her, but she never seemed to notice. She might as well have worn blinkers – she knew what she wanted and she never gave a thought to anything else.'

'She launched her career quite early for a singer, didn't she?' Gemma asked, remembering the snippets she'd heard from Alison Douglas.

'That was partly Gerald's doing. He plucked her out of the chorus and put her centre-stage, and she had the drive and ambition to meet the challenge, if not the experience.' She reached out and broke a corner from a slice of the bread she'd set on the table, then took an experimental nibble. 'Just checking,' she said, smiling at Gemma. 'Quality control.' Taking a sip of her tea, she continued, 'But you realize that this all happened more than thirty years ago, and there are only a few of us who remember Gerald and Caro before they were leading lights.'

Gemma contemplated this for a moment, following Plummy's example and reaching for another slice of bread. 'Do they like being reminded that they were ordinary once?'

'I think there is a certain comfort in it.'

What had it been like for Julia, Gemma wondered, growing up in her parents' shadow? It was difficult enough under any circumstances to shake off one's parents' influence and become a self-governing individual. She washed down a bite of bread with tea before asking, 'And that's how Julia met Connor? Through her parents?'

After a moment's thought, Plummy said, 'I believe it was an ENO fund-raising reception. In those days Julia still occasionally attended musical functions. She was just beginning to make her mark as an artist, and she hadn't completely left her parents' orbit.' She shook her head. 'It took me by surprise from the start – Julia had always preferred the sort of intellectual and arty types, and Con was about as far removed from that as one could imagine. I tried talking to her, but she wouldn't hear a word of it.'

'And were they as ill-matched as you thought?'

'Oh yes,' she answered with a sigh, swirling the tea in the bottom of her mug. 'More so.'

When Plummy didn't elaborate, Gemma asked, 'Did you know that Connor had been seeing someone?'

She looked up in surprise. 'Recently, you mean? A girlfriend?'

'A young woman with a small daughter.'

'No. No, I didn't.' With the compassion Gemma had begun to expect of her, Plummy added, 'Oh, the poor thing. I suppose she will have taken his death quite badly.'

The words *unlike Julia* seemed to hang unspoken between them. 'She's moved back, you know,' said Plummy. 'Julia. Into the flat. I told her I didn't think it looked well at all, but she said it was her flat, after all, and she had the right to do whatever she liked with it.'

Gemma thought of the upstairs studio, empty of Julia Swann's disturbing presence, and felt an unaccountable sense of relief. 'When did she go?'

'This morning, early. She has missed her studio, poor love – I never understood why she let Con stay on in the house. But there's no reasoning with her once she's made up her mind about something.'

The exasperated affection in Plummy's voice reminded Gemma of her own mum, who swore that her red-haired daughter had been born stubborn. Not that Vi Walters was one to talk, Gemma thought with a smile. 'Was Julia always so headstrong?'

Plummy regarded her steadily for a long moment, then said, 'No, not always.' She glanced at her watch. 'Have you finished your tea, dear? Caro should be free by now, and she has another student coming this afternoon, so we'd better sandwich you in between.'

'Caro, this is Sergeant James,' Plummy announced as she ushered Gemma into the sitting room. Then she withdrew, and Gemma felt the draught of cool air as the door clicked shut.

Caroline Stowe stood with her back to the fire, as had her husband when Gemma and Kincaid had interviewed him two days earlier. She stepped towards Gemma with her hand outstretched. 'How nice to meet you, Sergeant. How can I help you?'

Her hand felt small and cool in Gemma's, as soft as a child's. Involuntarily, Gemma glanced at the photograph on the piano. While it had given her a hint of the woman's feminine delicacy, it hadn't begun to express her vitality. 'It's just a routine follow-up on the report you gave Thames Valley CID, Dame Caroline,' said Gemma, and her own voice sounded harsh in her ears.

'Sit down, please.' Dame Caroline moved to the sofa and patted the cushion invitingly. Over white wool trousers she wore a long garnet-coloured sweater. The soft cowl neck framed her face, its colour the perfect foil for her pale skin and dark hair.

Gemma, who had dressed with particular care that morning, suddenly found her favourite olive silk skirt and blouse as drab as camouflage, and as she sat down she felt awkward and clumsy. A flush of embarrassment warmed her cheeks and she said quickly, 'Dame Caroline, I understand from your initial statement that you were at home last Thursday evening. Can you tell me what you did?'

'Of course, Sergeant, if you find it necessary,' Caroline said with an air of gracious resignation. 'I had dinner with Plummy – that's Vivian Plumley – then we watched something on the telly, I'm afraid I can't remember what. Does it matter?'

'Then what did you do?'

'Plummy made us some cocoa, that must have been around ten o'clock. We talked for a bit, then went to bed.' Apologetically, she added, 'It was a very ordinary evening, Sergeant.'

'Do you remember what time your husband came in?'

'I'm afraid not. I sleep quite soundly, and we have separate beds, so he seldom disturbs me when he comes in late after a performance.'

'And your daughter didn't disturb you when she returned in the early hours of the morning?' Gemma asked, wanting to shake Caroline's polished complacency just a bit.

'She did not. My daughter is a grown woman and comes and goes as she pleases. I'm not in the habit of keeping tabs on her whereabouts.'

Bull's-eye, thought Gemma. She'd hit a sensitive spot. 'I understand from Mrs Plumley that your daughter has gone back to the flat she shared with Connor. Did you approve of her being on her own again so soon, considering the circumstances?'

Caroline seemed to bite back a response, then sighed. 'I thought it rather ill-advised, but then my approval has never had much effect on Julia's actions. And she has behaved very badly over Connor's death from the first.' Looking suddenly tired, Caroline rubbed her fingers over her cheekbones, but Gemma noticed that she didn't stretch the skin.

'In what way?' Gemma asked, although she'd had proof enough that Julia wasn't playing the grieving widow to perfection.

Shrugging, Caroline said, 'There are things that must be done, and people have certain expectations . . . Julia has simply not met her obligations.'

Gemma wondered if Julia would have done what was necessary if she hadn't been sure her parents would step in and take care of everything. The fact that Julia seemed to resent them doing so only served to illustrate the perversity of human nature, and Gemma had begun to think that their relationship might be more perverse than most. She turned a page in her small notebook, running through her questions in her mind. 'I believe Connor came here for lunch last Thursday?' At Caroline's nod, she continued, 'Did you notice anything unusual about his behaviour that day?'

Smiling, Caroline said, 'Con was very entertaining, but there was nothing unusual about that.'

'Do you remember what you talked about?' Gemma asked, and as she watched Caroline ponder the question, she realized she'd never before seen a woman capable of furrowing her brow prettily.

'Oh, nothing memorable or weighty, Sergeant. Local gossip, Gerald's performance that night—'

'So Connor knew your husband would be in London?'

Looking perplexed, Caroline answered, 'Well, of course Con knew Gerald would be in London.'

'Do you know why Connor would have visited the Coliseum that same afternoon?'

'I can't imagine. He certainly didn't say anything to us about going to London – are you saying he visited the theatre?'

'According to the porter's sign-in sheet, but no one else admits to seeing him.'

'How very odd,' Caroline said slowly, and for the first time Gemma sensed her departing from a comfortably rehearsed script. 'Of course, he did leave in rather a tiz—'

'What happened?' Gemma felt a prickle of excitement. 'You said he hadn't done anything out of the ordinary.'

'I don't know that I'd describe it as out of the ordinary. Con was never very much good at sitting still. He excused himself for a moment while Gerald and I were having our coffee. He said he meant to give Plummy a hand in the kitchen, and that's the last we saw of him. A few minutes later we heard his car start up.'

'And you thought something had upset him?'

'Well, I suppose we did think it a bit odd that he hadn't said goodbye.'

Gemma turned carefully back through the pages of her notebook, then looked up at Caroline. 'Mrs Plumley said she did the washing up alone. She didn't see Connor again after she left the dining room. Do you think he went upstairs to see Julia? And perhaps they had a row?'

Caroline clasped her hands in her lap, and the shadows shifted on the garnet sweater as she took a breath. 'I can't say, Sergeant. If that were the case I'm sure Julia would have said something.'

Gemma didn't share her sentiments. 'Did you know that Connor had a girlfriend, Dame Caroline? Technically, I suppose she would have been his mistress, since he and Julia were still married.'

'A girlfriend? Con?' Caroline said quietly, then as she looked into the fire she added more softly still, 'He never said.'

Remembering what Kincaid had told her, Gemma said, 'Her name is Sharon Doyle, and she has a four-year-old daughter. Apparently it was a fairly serious relationship, and he . . . um, entertained her quite often at the flat.'

'A child?' Caroline returned her gaze to Gemma. Her dark eyes had dilated and Gemma saw the fire reflected in their liquid and luminous surface.

The afternoon had drawn in as they talked, and now the fire and the lamps cast a noticeable glow in the quiet room. Gemma could imagine serene hours spent here with music and conversation, or time whiled away on the comfortably worn chintz sofa with a book, but never voices raised in anger. 'What if Julia found out about Sharon? Would they have argued over it? Would Julia have liked Connor having another woman in her flat?'

After a long moment, Caroline said, 'Julia is often a law unto herself, Sergeant. I can't begin to guess how she would react to a given situation. And why does it matter anyway?' she added wearily. 'Surely you don't think Julia had anything to do with Con's death?'

'We're trying to find an explanation for Connor's behaviour that last afternoon and evening. He made an unexpected visit to the theatre. He also met someone later that evening, after he'd returned to Henley, but we don't yet know who it was.'

'What *do* you know?' Caroline straightened her back and regarded Gemma directly.

'The results of the post-mortem didn't tell us much. We're still waiting on some of the forensic reports – all we can do until then is gather information.'

'Sergeant, I think you're being deliberately vague,' said Caroline, teasing her a little.

Unwilling to be drawn any further, Gemma focused on the first thing that came to mind. She'd been absently examining the paintings Kincaid and Julia had talked about – what had Julia said the painter was called? Flynn? No, Flint. That was it. The rosy bare-breasted women were voluptuous, somehow innocent and slightly decadent at the same time, and the sheen of their satin gowns made Gemma think of the costume fabrics she'd seen that morning at LB House. 'I met an old friend of yours today, Dame Caroline. Tommy Godwin.'

'Tommy? Good God, what on earth could you possibly want with Tommy?'

'He's very clever, isn't he?' Gemma settled back more comfortably on the sofa and tucked her notebook into her bag. 'He told me a lot about the early days, when you were all starting out with the Opera. It must have been terribly exciting.'

Caroline's expression softened. She gazed absently into the fire, and after a moment said, 'It was glorious. But, of course, I didn't realize quite how special it was, because I had nothing to compare it to. I thought that life could only get better, that everything I touched would turn to gold.' She met Gemma's eyes again. 'Well, that's the way of it, isn't it, Sergeant? You learn that the charmed times can't last.'

The words held an echo of such sorrow that Gemma felt their weight upon her chest. The photographs on the piano pulled at her insistently, but she kept her eyes on Caroline's face. She had no need to look at them – Matthew Asherton's smiling image had burned itself upon her memory. Taking a breath, she said, with a daring born out of her own fear, 'How do you manage to go on?'

'You protect what you have,' Caroline said quietly, vehemently. Then she laughed, breaking the spell. 'Tommy wasn't quite so elegant in those days, though you wouldn't think it to look at him now. He shed his background like a snake sloughing off its skin, but he hadn't completed the process. There were still a few rough edges.'

Gemma said, 'I can't imagine,' and they both laughed.

'Tommy was never less than amusing, even at his least polished. We did have some lovely times . . . and we had such vision. Gerald and Tommy and I –

we were going to change the face of opera.' Caroline smiled fondly.

How could you bear to give it up? thought Gemma. Aloud, she said, 'I've heard you sing. I bought a tape of *Traviata*. It's marvellous.'

Caroline folded her arms loosely under her breasts and stretched her dainty feet towards the fire. 'It is, isn't it? I've always loved singing Verdi. His heroines have a spiritual quality that you don't find in Puccini, and they allow you more room for interpretation. Puccini you must sing exactly as it's written or it becomes vulgar – with Verdi you must find the heroine's heart.'

'That's what I felt when I listened to Violetta,' Gemma said with delight. Caroline had given definition to her own vaguely formed impressions.

'Do you know the history of *Traviata*?' When Gemma shook her head, Caroline continued, 'In Paris in the 1840s there lived a young courtesan named Marie Duplessis. She died on the second of February, 1846, just nineteen days after her twenty-second birthday. Among her numerous lovers in her last year were Franz Liszt and Alexandre Dumas, *fils*. Dumas wrote a play based on Marie's life called *La Dame aux Camélias*, or *Camille*—'

'And Verdi adapted the play as *Traviata*.'

'You've been swotting,' said Caroline in mock disappointment.

'Not really, just reading the liner notes. And I didn't know that Violetta was based on a real person.'

'Little Marie is buried in the cemetery at Montmartre,

just below the church of Sacre Coeur. You can visit her grave.'

Gemma found herself unable to ask if Caroline herself had made such a pilgrimage – it came too near the forbidden territory of Matthew's death. She shivered a little at the thought of such waste. Marie Duplessis must have held on to her life with all the passion Verdi wrote into Violetta's music.

A bell rang, echoing in the passage outside the sitting room. The front door – Plummy had said Caroline had another student coming. 'I'm sorry, Dame Caroline. I've kept you too long.' Gemma slid the strap of her handbag over her shoulder and stood up. 'Thank you for your time. You've been very patient.'

Caroline rose and once again offered Gemma her hand. 'Goodbye, Sergeant.'

As Gemma neared the sitting room door, Plummy opened it and said, 'Cecily's here, Caro.'

As Gemma passed the girl in the hall, she had a brief impression of dark skin and eyes and a flashing shy smile, then Plummy ushered her gently out into the dusk. The door closed and Gemma stood breathing the cool, damp air. She shook her head to clear it, but that made the dawning realization no less uncomfortable.

She had been seduced.

'A message for you, Mr Kincaid,' Tony called out cheerfully from the bar as Kincaid entered the

Chequers. 'And your room's ready for you.' Tony seemed to do everything around the place, and all with the same unflagging good nature. Now he fished a message slip from beneath the bar and handed it to Kincaid.

'Jack Makepeace called?'

'You've just missed him by a few minutes. Use the phone in the lounge if you like.' Tony gestured towards the small sitting area opposite the bar.

Kincaid rang High Wycombe CID and shortly Makepeace came on the line. 'We've run down a possible lead on your Kenneth Hicks, Superintendent. Rumour from some racing sources has it that he does his drinking in a pub in Henley called the Fox and Hounds. It's on the far side of town, off the Reading road.'

Kincaid had just come through Henley on his way from Reading, and would now have to turn round and go back. He swore under his breath but didn't criticize Makepeace for not contacting him by bleeper or car phone – it wasn't worth the loss of good will. 'Anything known about him?'

'No record to speak of – a few juvenile offences. He's a petty villain from the sound of it, not a serious one. Hand in the till here and there, that sort of thing.'

'Description?'

'Five foot eight or nine, nine stone, fairish hair, blue eyes. No available address. If you want to talk to him I guess you'll have to do a spot of drinking at the Fox and Hounds.'

Kincaid sighed with resignation at the prospect. 'Thanks, Sergeant.'

Unlike the pub where he'd lunched in Reading, the Fox and Hounds turned out to be every bit as dreary as he'd imagined. The sparse late afternoon activity centred around the snooker table in the back room, but Kincaid choose the public bar, seating himself at an inadequately wiped plastic-topped table with his back against the wall. Compared to the other customers, he felt conspicuously well groomed in jeans and a fisherman's jersey. He sipped the foam from his pint of Brakspear's bitter and settled back to wait.

He'd killed half the pint as slowly as he could when a man came in who fitted Kenneth Hicks's general description. Kincaid watched as he leaned on the bar and said a few low words to the barman, then accepted a pint of lager. He wore expensive-looking clothes badly on his slight frame, and his narrow face had a pinched look that spoke of a malnourished childhood. Kincaid watched over the rim of his pint as the man glanced nervously around the bar, then took a seat at a table near the door.

The sneaky bugger's paranoia would have given him away even if his looks hadn't, thought Kincaid, and he smiled in satisfaction. He drank a little more of his beer, then stood and casually carried his glass across to the other man's table. 'Mind if I join you?' he said as he pulled up a stool and sat down.

'What if I do?' the man answered, shrinking back and holding his glass before his body like a shield.

Kincaid could see specks of dandruff mixed with the styling cream that darkened the fair hair. 'If you're Kenneth Hicks, you're out of luck, because I want a word with you.'

'What if I am? Why should I talk to you?' His eyes shifted from one side of Kincaid's body to the other, but Kincaid had sat between him and the door. The grey light from the front windows illuminated the imperfections of Hicks's face – a patch of pale stubble missed, the dark spot of a shaving cut on his chin.

'Because I asked you nicely,' Kincaid said as he pulled his warrant card from his hip pocket and held it open in front of Hicks's face. 'Let me see some identification, if you don't mind.'

A sheen of perspiration appeared on Hicks's upper lip. 'Don't have to. Harassment, that's what that is.'

'Oh, I don't think it's harassment at all,' Kincaid said softly, 'but if you like we'll call in the local lads and have our little chat in the Henley nick.'

For a moment he thought Hicks would bolt, and he balanced himself a little better on the stool, his muscles tensing. Then Hicks set his glass down on the plastic table with a thump and wordlessly handed Kincaid his driving licence.

'A Clapham address?' Kincaid asked, after he had examined it for a moment.

'It's me mum's,' Hicks said sullenly.

'But you stay here in Henley, don't you?' Kincaid

shook his head. 'You really should keep these things current, you know. We like to know where to find you when we want you.' He pulled a notebook and pen from his pocket and slid them across the table. 'Why don't you write down your address for me before we forget? Make sure you get it right, now,' he added as Hicks reluctantly picked up the pen.

'What's it to you?' Hicks asked as he scribbled a few lines on the paper and shoved it back.

Kincaid held out his hand for the pen. 'Well, I have a vested interest in staying in touch with you. I'm looking into Connor Swann's death, and I think you know a good deal about Connor Swann. It would be very odd if you didn't, considering the amount of money he paid you every month.' Kincaid drank another half-inch of his pint and smiled at Hicks, whose sallow skin had faded almost to green at the mention of Connor's name.

'I don't know what you're talking about,' Hicks managed to squeak, and now Kincaid could smell his fear.

'Oh, I think you do. The way I heard it is that you do some unofficial collecting for a bookie here in town, and that Connor was in over his head—'

'Who told you that? If it was that little tart of his, I'll fix her—'

'You'll not touch Sharon Doyle.' Kincaid leaned forward, abandoning his amiable pretence. 'And you'd better hope she's not accident prone, because I'll hold you responsible if she so much as breaks a little finger.

Have you got that, sunshine?' He waited until Hicks nodded, then said, 'Good. I knew you were a bright boy. Now unfortunately, Connor didn't discuss his financial problems with Sharon, so you're going to have to help me out. If Connor owed money to your boss, why did he pay you directly?'

Hicks took a long pull on his lager and fumbled in his jacket pocket until he found a crumpled packet of Benson & Hedges. He lit one with a book of matches bearing the pub's name, and seemed to gather courage as he drew in the smoke. 'Don't know what you're talkin' about, and you can't—'

'Connor may not have taken very good care of some parts of his life, but in others he was quite meticulous. He recorded every cheque he wrote – did you know that, Kenneth? You don't mind if I call you Kenneth, do you?' Kincaid added, all politeness again. When Hicks didn't reply, he continued. 'He paid you large amounts on a very regular basis. I'd be curious to see how those amounts tally with what he owed your boss—'

'You leave him out of this!' Hicks almost shouted, sloshing beer on the table. He looked round to see if anyone else had heard, then leaned forward and lowered his voice to a hiss. 'I'm telling you, you leave him—'

'What were you doing, Kenneth? A little loan-sharking on the side? Carrying Con's debts with interest? Somehow I don't think your boss would take too kindly to your skimming his clients like that.'

'We had a private arrangement, Con and me. I helped him out when he was in trouble, same as he'd have done for me, same as any mates.'

'Oh, mates, was it? Well, that puts a different complexion on it entirely. I'm sure in that case Connor didn't mind you making money off his debts.' Kincaid leaned forward, hands on the edge of the table, resisting the urge to grab Hicks by the lapels of his leather bomber jacket and shake him until his brains rattled. 'You're a bloodsucker, Kenneth, and with mates like you nobody needs enemies. I want to know when you saw Connor last, and I want to know exactly what you talked about, because I'm beginning to think Con got tired of paying your cut. Maybe he threatened to go to your boss – is that what happened, Kenneth? Then maybe the two of you had a little scuffle and you pushed him in the river. What do you think, sunshine? Is that how it happened?'

The bar had begun to fill and Hicks had to raise his voice a little to make himself heard over the increasing babble. 'No, I'm telling you, man, it wasn't like that at all.'

'What *was* it like?' Kincaid said reasonably. 'Tell me about it, then.'

'Con had a couple of really stiff losses, close together, couldn't come up with the ready. I was flush at the time so I covered him. After that it just got to be sort of a habit.'

'A nasty habit, just like gambling, and one I'll bet Con got fed up with pretty quickly. Con hadn't written you a cheque the last few weeks before he died. Was he balking, Kenneth? Had he had enough?'

Perspiration beaded on Hicks's upper lip and he wiped it with the back of his hand. 'No, man, the horses had been good to him the last couple of weeks, for a change. He paid off what he owed – we were square, I swear we were.'

'That's really heart-warming, just like good little Boy Scouts. I'll bet you shook hands on it, too.' Kincaid sipped from his glass again, then said conversationally, 'Nice local beer, don't you think?' Before Hicks could reply he leaned across the little table until he was inches from the man's face. 'Even if I believed you, which I don't, I think you'd look for some other way to soak him. You seem to know a lot about his personal life, considering your *business* arrangement. Looking for another foothold, were you, Ken? Did you find something out about Connor that he didn't want anyone else to know?'

Hicks shrank back. 'Don't know what you're talkin' about, man,' he said, then wiped spittle from his lower lip. 'Why don't you ask that slut of his what she knows? Maybe she found out hell'd freeze over before he'd marry her.' He smiled, showing nicotine-stained teeth, and Kincaid found it no improvement over his sneer. 'Maybe she shoved him in the river – did you ever think about that one, Mr Bloody Know-it-all?'

'What makes you think he wouldn't have married Sharon?'

'Why should he? Get himself stuck with a stupid

little cow like that – take on some other bugger's bleedin' kid? Not on your nelly.' Sniggering, Hicks pulled another cigarette from the packet and lit it from the butt of the first. 'And her with a gob like a fishwife.'

'You're a real prince, Kenneth,' Kincaid said generously. 'How do you know Sharon thought Con intended to marry her? Did she tell you?'

'Too right, she did. Said, "He'll get shut of you then, Kenneth Hicks. I'll make sure of it." Stupid—'

'You know, Kenneth, if you'd been the one found floating face-down in the Thames, I don't think we'd have had to look far for a motive.'

'You threatening me, man? You can't do that – that's—'

'Harassment, I know. No, Kenneth, I'm not threatening you, just making an observation.' Kincaid smiled. 'I'm sure you had Connor's best interests at heart.'

'He used to tell me things, when he'd had a few, like.' Hicks lowered his voice confidentially. 'Wife had him by the balls. She crooked her little finger, he'd come running with his tail between his legs. He'd had a hell of a row with her that day, the bitch—'

'What day, Kenneth?' Kincaid said very distinctly, very quietly.

Cigarette frozen halfway to his lips, Hicks stared at Kincaid like a rat surprised by a ferret. 'Don't know. You can't prove nothing.'

'It was the day he died, wasn't it, Kenneth? You saw Connor the day he died. Where?'

Hicks's close-set eyes shifted nervously away from Kincaid's face and he drew sharply on the cigarette.

'Spit it out, Kenneth. I'll find out, you know. I'll start by asking these nice people here.' Kincaid nodded towards the bar. 'Don't you think that's a good idea?'

'So what if I did have a couple of pints with him? How was I to know it was different from any other day?'

'Where and when?'

'Here, same as always. Don't know what time,' Hicks said evasively, then added as he saw Kincaid's expression, 'Twoish, maybe.'

After lunch, Kincaid thought. Con had come straight here from Badger's End. 'He told you he'd had a row with Julia? What about?'

'Don't know, do I? Nothin' to do with me.' Hicks clamped his mouth shut so decisively that Kincaid changed tack.

'What else did you talk about?'

'Nothin'. We just had a friendly pint, like. Not against the law, is it, havin' a friendly drink with a mate?' Hicks asked, voice rising if he might be working himself up to hysteria.

'Did you see Connor again after that?'

'No, I never. Not after he left here.' He took a last drag on his cigarette and ground it out in the ashtray.

'Where were you that night, Kenneth? From eight o'clock or so on?'

Shaking his head, Hicks said, 'None of your friggin' business, is it? I've had enough of your bleedin' harassment. I ain't done nothin', fuckin' filth got no right to keep after me.' He shoved his empty glass away and pushed back on his stool, watching Kincaid, the whites of his eyes showing beneath the irises.

Kincaid debated the benefit of pushing him any further, and decided against it. 'All right, Kenneth, have it your way. But stay around where I can find you, just in case we need to have another little chat.' Hicks's stool screeched against the floor as he stood up. As he pushed past, Kincaid reached up and sank his fingers into the sleeve of his leather jacket. 'If you even think about disappearing, boyo, I'll have the lads after you so fast you won't be able to find a hole big enough to hide your skinny backside. Do we understand each other, mate?'

After a long moment, Hicks nodded and Kincaid smiled and let him go. 'There's a good boy, Ken. See you around.'

Kincaid turned and watched Hicks scuttle out of the door into the street, then he carefully wiped his fingers against his jeans.

Chapter Ten

Not one to let good beer go to waste, Kincaid drained the last drop of his pint. He considered briefly having another, but the pub's atmosphere didn't encourage lingering.

Out in the street, he sniffed the air curiously. He'd noticed the smell when he arrived in town, but it seemed stronger now. Familiar but elusive . . . tomatoes cooking, perhaps? Finding his car free of sprayed graffiti and still in possession of its hub caps, Kincaid stood still for a moment and closed his eyes. Hops. Of course, it was hops – it was Monday and the brewery was in full operation. The wind must have shifted since he'd arrived at the pub, bringing the rich smell with it. The brewery would be closing soon, as well as most of the shops, he thought as he glanced at his watch – rush hour, such as it was, had begun in Henley.

He'd navigated his way onto the Reading road, intent on exchanging the day's findings with Gemma back at the Chequers, when the signpost for the Station Road carpark caught his eye. Almost without thinking he found himself making the turn and pulling into a vacant slot. From there it was only a few hundred yards' walk down Station Road to the river. On his right lay the boathouse flats, serene behind their iron fence in the dusk.

Something had been niggling at him – he couldn't swear to the date of the last cheque Connor had written Kenneth. Kincaid had never finished his interrupted search of Con's desk, and now he let himself into the flat with the key he'd used earlier, intending to have another look at the cheque book.

He stopped just inside the door. Looking around, he tried to pinpoint why the flat felt different. Warmth, for one thing. The central heating had been switched on. Con's shoes had disappeared from beneath the settee. The untidy stack of newspapers on the end table had gone as well, but something even less definable spoke of recent human occupation. He sniffed, trying to place the faint scent in the air. Something tugged at the fringes of his mind, then vanished as he heard a noise above.

He held his breath, listening, then moved quietly towards the stairs. A scrape came, then a thump. Someone moving furniture? He'd only been a few minutes behind Kenneth leaving the pub – had the little sod beaten him here, bent on destroying evidence? Or had Sharon come back, after all?

Both doors on the first landing had been pulled to, but before he could investigate, the noise came again from above. He climbed the last flight of steps, carefully keeping his feet to the edge of the treads. The studio door stood open a few inches, not enough to give him a clear view into the room. Taking a breath, he used his fist to slam the door open. He charged into the room as the door bounced against the wall.

Julia Swann dropped the stack of canvases she held in her hands.

'Jesus, Julia, you gave me a fright! What the hell are you doing here?' He stood breathing hard, adrenaline still rushing through his body.

'*I* gave *you* a fright!' She stared at him wide-eyed, holding her balled hand to her chest and flattening her black sweater between her breasts. 'You probably just cost me ten years off my life, Superintendent, not to mention damage to my property.' She bent to retrieve her paintings. 'I might ask you the same question – what are you doing in my flat?'

'It's still under our jurisdiction. I'm sorry I frightened you. I had no idea you were here.' Trying to regain a semblance of authority, he added, 'You should have notified the police.'

'Why should I feel obliged to let the police know I'd come back to my own flat?' She sat on the rolled arm of the chair she used for a prop in her paintings and looked at him challengingly.

'Your husband's death is still under investigation, Mrs Swann, and he did live here, in case you'd forgotten.' He came nearer to her and sat on the only other available piece of furniture, her worktable. His feet dangled a few inches above the floor and he crossed his ankles to stop them swinging.

'You called me Julia before.'

'Did I?' Then, it had been instinctive, involuntary.

Now he used it deliberately. 'Okay, Julia.' He drew the syllables out. 'So what are you doing here?'

'I should think that would be rather obvious.' She gestured around her and he turned, examining the room. Paintings, both the small flower studies and the larger portraits, had been stacked against the walls, and a few had been hung. Dust had vanished from the visible surfaces, and some of the paints and paper familiar to him from her workroom at Badger's End had appeared on the table. She had brought in a large pot plant and placed it near the blue velvet chair – those, along with the faded Persian rug and the brightly coloured books in the case behind the chair, formed the still-life tableau he'd seen in several of the paintings at the gallery.

The room felt alive once more, and he finally identified the scent that had eluded him downstairs. It was Julia's perfume.

She had slid down into the depths of the chair and sat quietly smoking with her legs stretched out, and as he looked at her he saw that her eyes were shadowed with fatigue. 'Why did you give this up, Julia? It doesn't make any sense.'

Studying him, she said, 'You look different out of your proper policeman's kit. Nice. Human, even. I'd like to draw you.' She stood suddenly and touched her fingers to the angle of his jaw, turning his head. 'I don't usually do men, but you have an interesting face, good bones that catch the light well.' Just as quickly, she sank into the chair again and regarded him.

He still felt the imprint of her fingers against his

skin. Resisting the urge to touch his jaw, he said, 'You haven't answered me.'

Sighing, she ground the half-smoked cigarette into a pottery ashtray. 'I don't know if I can.'

'Try me.'

'You would have to know how things were with us, towards the end.' Idly, she rubbed the nap on the chair arm the wrong way. Kincaid waited, watching her. She looked up and met his eyes. 'He couldn't pin me down. The more he tried the more frustrated he got, until finally he started imagining things.'

Fastening on the first part, Kincaid asked, 'What do you mean, he couldn't pin you down?'

'I was never there for him, not in the way he wanted, not when he wanted . . .' She crossed her arms as if suddenly cold and rubbed her thumbs against the fabric of her sweater. 'Have you ever had anyone suck you dry, Superintendent?' Before he could answer, she added, 'I can't go on calling you Super-bloody-intendent. Your name's Duncan, isn't it?' She gave his name a slight stress on the first syllable, so that he heard in it a Scots echo.

'What kind of things did Connor imagine, Julia?'

Her mouth turned down at the corners and she shrugged. 'Oh, you know. Lovers, secret trysts, that sort of thing.'

'And they weren't true?'

'Not then.' She lifted her eyebrows and gave him a little flirtatious smile, challenging him.

'You're telling me that Connor was jealous of *you*?'

Julia laughed, and the smile that transformed her

thin face moved him in a way he couldn't explain. 'It's so ironic, isn't it? What a joke. Connor Swann, everyone's favourite Lothario, afraid his own wife might be messing him about.' Kincaid's consternation must have shown, because she smiled again and said, 'Did you think I didn't know Con's reputation? I would have to have been deaf, dumb and blind not to.' Her mirth faded and she added softly, 'Of course, the more I slipped away, the more women he notched on his braces. Was he punishing me? Or was he just looking for what I couldn't give him?' She stared past Kincaid at the window he knew must be darkening.

'You still haven't answered my question,' he said again, but this time gently.

'What?' She came back to him from her reverie. 'Oh, the flat. I was exhausted, in the end. I ran away. It was easier.' They looked at each other in silence for a moment, then she said, 'You can see that, can't you, Duncan?'

The words 'ran away' echoed in his mind and he had a sudden vision of himself, packing up only the most necessary of possessions, leaving Vic in the flat they had chosen with such care. It had been easier, easier to start again with nothing to remind him of his failure, or of her. 'What about your studio?' he said, shutting off the flow of memory.

'I've missed it, but I can paint anywhere, if I must.' She leaned back in the chair, watching him.

Kincaid thought back to his earlier interviews with her, trying to put a finger on the change he sensed. She was still sharp and quick, her intelligence always evident, but the brittle nervousness had left her. 'It wasn't easy for you, was it, those months you spent at Badger's End?' She stared back at him, her lips parted, and he felt again that frisson along his spine that came with knowing her in a way more intimate than words.

'You're very perceptive, Duncan.'

'What about Trevor Simons? Were you seeing him then?'

'I told you, no. There wasn't anyone.'

'And now? Do you love him?' A necessary question, he told himself, but the words seemed to leave his lips of their own accord.

'Love, Duncan?' Julia laughed. 'Do you want to split philosophical hairs over the nature of love and friendship?' She continued more seriously, 'Trev and I are friends, yes, but if you mean am I in love with him, the answer is no. Does it matter?'

'I don't know,' Kincaid answered truthfully. 'Would he lie for you? You did leave the opening that night, you know. I have an independent witness who saw you go.'

'Did I?' She looked away from him, fumbling for the cigarette packet that had slipped under the chair. 'I suppose I did, for a bit. It was rather a crush. I don't like to admit it, but sometimes things like that make me feel a little claustrophobic.'

'You're still smoking too much,' he said as she found the packet and lit another cigarette.

'How much is too much? You're splitting hairs again.' Her smile held a hint of mischief.

'Where did you go, when you left the gallery?'

Julia stood up and went to the window, and he twisted around, watching her as she closed the blinds against the charcoal sky. Still with her back to Kincaid, she said, 'I don't like bare windows, once it's dark. Silly, I know, but even up here I always feel someone might be watching me.' She turned to him again. 'I walked along the River Terrace for a bit, had a breath of air, that's all.'

'Did you see Connor?'

'No, I didn't,' she answered, coming back to her chair. This time she curled herself into it with her legs drawn up, and as she moved the bell of her hair swung against her neck. 'And I doubt I was gone more than five or ten minutes.'

'But you saw him earlier that day, didn't you? At Badger's End, after lunch, and you had a row.'

He saw her chest move with the quick intake of breath, as if she might deny it, but she only watched him quietly for a moment before answering, 'It was such a stupid thing, really, such a petty little end note. I was ashamed.

'He came upstairs after lunch, bounding in like a great overgrown puppy, and I lit into him. I'd had a letter that morning from the building society – he'd not made a payment in two months. That was our arrangement, you see,' she explained to Kincaid, 'that he could stay in the flat as long as he kept up the payments. Well, we argued, as you can imagine, and I told him he had to come up with the money.' Pausing, she put out the cigarette she'd left burning in the ashtray, then took another little breath. 'I also told him he needed to think about making other arrangements. It was too worrying, about the payments, I mean . . . and things were difficult for me at home.'

'And he didn't take that well?' Kincaid asked. She shook her head, her lips pressed together. 'Did you give him a time limit?'

'No, but surely he could see that we couldn't go on like that for ever . . .'

Kincaid asked the question that had been bothering him from the beginning. 'Why didn't you just divorce him, Julia? Get it over with, make a clean break. This was no trial separation – you knew when you left him that it couldn't be mended.'

She smiled at him, teasing. 'You of all people should know the law, Duncan. Especially having been through it yourself.'

Surprised, he said, 'Ancient history. Are my scars still visible?'

Julia shrugged. 'A lucky guess. Did your wife file against you?' When he nodded, she continued, 'Did you agree to her petition?'

'Well, of course. There was no point going on.'

'Do you know what would have happened if you had refused?'

He shook his head. 'I never thought about it.'

'She would've had to wait two years. That's how long it takes to prove a contested divorce.'

'Are you saying that Connor refused to let you divorce him?'

'Got it in one, dear Superintendent.' She watched him as he digested this, then said softly, 'Was she very beautiful?'

'Who?'

'Your wife, of course.'

Kincaid contrasted the image of Vic's delicate, pale prettiness with the woman sitting before him. Julia's face seemed to float between the blackness of her turtlenecked jersey and her dark hair, almost disembodied, and in the lamplight the lines of pain and experience stood out sharply. 'I suppose you would say she was beautiful. I don't know. It's been a long time.'

Realizing that his rear had gone numb from sitting on the hard table edge, he pushed off with his hands, stretched and lowered himself to the Persian rug. He wrapped his arms around his knees and looked up at Julia, noticing how the difference in perspective altered the planes and shadows of her face. 'Did you know about Con's gambling when you married him?'

She shook her head. 'No, only that he liked to go racing, and that was rather a lark for me. I'd never been—' She laughed at his expression. 'No, really. You think I had this very sophisticated and cosmopolitan upbringing, don't you? What you don't understand is that my parents don't do anything unless it's connected with music.' She sighed, then said reflectively, 'I loved the colours and the movement, the horses' grace and perfect form. It was only gradually that I began to see that it wasn't just fun for Con, not in the sense it was for me. He'd sweat during the race, and sometimes I'd see his hands tremble. And then I began to realize he was lying to me about how much he'd bet.' Shrugging, she added, 'After a bit I stopped going.'

'But Con kept betting.'

'Of course we had rows. "A harmless pastime" he called it. One he deserved after the pressures at work. But it was only towards the end that it became really frightening.'

'Did you bail him out, pay his debts?'

Julia looked away from him, resting her chin on her hand. 'For a long time, yes. It was my reputation, too, after all.'

'So this row you had last Thursday was old business, in a sense?'

She managed a small smile. 'Put that way, yes, I suppose it was. It's so frustrating when you hear yourself saying things you've said a hundred times before – you know it's useless but you can't seem to stop.'

'Did he say anything different when he left you? Anything that varied from the normal pattern of these arguments?'

'No, not that I can remember.'

And yet he had gone straight to Kenneth. Had he meant to borrow the money for the mortgage? 'Did he say anything to you about going to London that afternoon, to the Coliseum?'

Julia lifted her head from her hand, her dark eyes widening in surprise. 'London? No. No, I'm sure he didn't. Why should he have gone to the Coli? He'd just seen Mummy and Daddy.'

The childish diminutives sounded odd on her lips, and she seemed suddenly young and very vulnerable. 'I'd hoped you might tell me,' he said softly. 'Did you ever hear Connor mention someone called Hicks? Kenneth Hicks?' He watched her carefully, but she only shook her head, looking genuinely puzzled.

'No. Why? Is he a friend?'

'He works for a local bookie, does some collecting for him, among other things. He's also a nasty piece of work, and Connor paid him large amounts of money on a regular basis. That's why I came back, to have another look at Connor's cheque book.'

'I never thought of looking through Con's things,' Julia said slowly. 'I've not even been in the study.' She dropped her head in both hands and said through her splayed fingers, 'I suppose I was putting off the inevitable.' After a moment she raised her head and looked at him, her lips twisting with a mixture of embarrassment and bravado. 'I did find some woman's things in the bedroom and in the bath. I've packed them up in a box – I didn't know what else to do with them.'

So Sharon had not come back. 'Give them to me. I think I can return them to their rightful owner.' Although he read the question in her expression, she didn't speak, and they regarded one another in silence. He sat near enough to touch her, and the desire came to him to raise his hand and lay the backs of his fingers against the hollow of her cheek.

Instead, he said gently, 'He was seeing someone, you know. A quite steady arrangement, from the sound of it. She has a four-year-old daughter, and Con told her that he would marry her and look after them both, just as soon as you'd let him have a divorce.'

For a long moment Julia's face went blank, wiped as clean of expression as a mannequin's, then she gave a strangled laugh. 'Oh, poor Con,' she said. 'The poor, silly bastard.'

For the first time since Kincaid had met her, he saw her eyes fill with tears.

Gemma finished her second packet of peanuts and licked the salt from the tips of her fingers. Looking up, she saw Tony watching her and smiled a little shamefacedly. 'Starving,' she said by way of apology.

'Let me have the kitchen fix you something.' Tony seemed to have adopted her as his own personal responsibility and was even more solicitous than usual. 'We've got lovely pork chops tonight, and a vegetarian lasagne.'

Surreptitiously, Gemma glanced at her watch beneath the level of the bar. 'I'll wait a bit longer. Thanks, Tony.' After leaving Dame Caroline, she had driven to the pub and carried her case upstairs. Suddenly overcome by a wave of exhaustion, she'd stretched out on top of the duvet in her good clothes and slept deeply and dreamlessly for an hour. She'd awakened feeling cold and a little stiff, but refreshed. After a good wash and brush, she'd changed into her favourite jeans and sweater and gone down to wait for Kincaid.

Tony, polishing glasses at the far end of the bar,

still kept an anxious eye on the level of cider in her glass. She had almost decided to let him refill it when he looked towards the door and said, 'There's your boss now, love.'

Kincaid slid onto the stool beside her. 'Has Tony been plying you with drink?' He went on without waiting for an answer, 'Good, because I'm going to ply you with food. Sharon Doyle told me that Connor favoured the Red Lion in Wargrave – only place the food was up to his standards. I think we should suss it out for ourselves.'

'Will you be having a drink before you go, Mr Kincaid?' asked Tony.

Kincaid looked at Gemma. 'Hungry?'

'Famished.'

'Then we had better go straight on, Tony.'

Tony flapped his dishcloth at them. 'Cheerio. Though if you don't mind my saying so,' he added in a slightly affronted tone, 'their food's no better than ours.'

Having lavished reassurances upon Tony, they escaped to the car and drove to Wargrave in silence.

Only when they had settled at a table in the cheerful atmosphere of the Red Lion did Gemma say, 'Tony said you had a message from Sergeant Makepeace. What did he want? Where have you been?'

Kincaid, intent on his menu, said, 'Let's order first. Then I'll tell you. See anything you fancy? Gratin of haddock and smoked salmon? Prawns in garlic sauce? Chicken breast with red and green peppercorns?' He looked up at her, grinning, and she thought his eyes looked unusually bright. 'Con had it right – no shepherd's pie or bangers and mash to be found here.'

'Are you sure our expenses will run to this?' Gemma asked.

'Don't worry, Sergeant,' he said with exaggerated authority. 'I'll take care of it.'

Unconvinced, Gemma gave him a doubtful glance, but said, 'I'll have the chicken, then. And the tomato and basil soup for starters.'

'Going the whole hog?'

'Pudding, too, if I can find room for it.' She closed her menu and propped her chin on her hands. He had seated her with her back to the crackling fire and the warmth began to penetrate her sweater. 'I feel I deserve it.'

The barman came round to them, his pad ready. He had a dishcloth tucked into his belt, dark, curling hair restrained in a pony-tail, and an engaging smile. 'What will you have?'

Kincaid ordered the gratin for himself and added a bottle of American Fumé Blanc. When they had finished the young man said, 'Right, then. I'll just pass this to the kitchen.' As he slipped back behind the bar, he added, 'My name's David, by the way. Just give me a shout if you need anything else.'

Gemma and Kincaid looked at each other, brows raised, then she said, 'Do you suppose the service is always this good, or is it just because it's slow tonight?'

She looked around the room. Only one other table was occupied – in the far corner a couple sat, heads bent close together.

'I'll bet he has a good memory for customers. After we eat, we'll give it a go.'

When David had returned and filled their glasses with chilled wine, Kincaid said, 'Tell me.'

Gemma related her interview with Tommy Godwin, omitting her rather inglorious arrival. 'I'm not sure I buy the bit about his coming into the theatre from the front and standing up at the back of the stalls. Doesn't feel quite right.'

Their starters came, and as Kincaid tucked into his pâté, he said, 'And what about Dame Caroline? Any joy there?'

'It seems their lunch didn't go quite as smoothly as they claimed at first. Connor excused himself to help with the washing up, but Plummy says he never came into the kitchen, and he left without saying goodbye to Gerald and Caroline.' She scraped the last bit of soup from the cup. 'I think he must have gone upstairs to Julia.'

'He did, and they had a nasty row.'

Gemma felt her mouth drop open. She closed it with a snap, then said, 'How could you possibly know that?'

'Kenneth Hicks told me, then Julia herself.'

'All right, guv,' Gemma said, exasperated. 'You've got that cat-in-the-cream look. Give.'

By the time he'd recounted his day, their main courses had come and they both ate quietly for a few minutes. 'What I can't understand,' he said as he finished a bite of fish and sipped his wine, 'is how a yobbo like Kenneth Hicks managed to hook Connor so thoroughly.'

'Money can be a powerful incentive.' Gemma deliberated between more braised leeks or more roast potatoes, then took both. 'Why did Julia lie about the row with Connor? It seems innocent enough.'

Kincaid hesitated, then shrugged. 'I suppose she didn't think it significant. It certainly wasn't a new argument.'

Fork halfway to her mouth, Gemma said hotly, 'But this wasn't a case of failing to mention something that might or might not have been significant. She deliberately lied. And she lied about leaving the gallery as well.' She returned her fork with its speared chicken to her plate, and leaned towards Kincaid. 'It's not right the way she's behaved, refusing to take care of the funeral arrangements. What would she have done, let the county bury him?'

'I doubt that very much.' Kincaid pushed his plate aside and leaned back a little in his chair.

Although his tone had been mild enough, Gemma felt rebuked. Feeling a flush begin to stain her cheeks, she retrieved her fork, then put it down again as she realized she'd lost her appetite.

Watching her, Kincaid said, 'Finished already? What about that pudding?'

'I don't think I can possibly manage it.'

'Drink your wine, then,' he said, topping up her glass, 'and we'll have a word with David.'

Gemma bristled at this avuncular instruction, but before she could respond he caught the barman's eye.

'Ready for your sweets?' David said as he reached their table. 'The chocolate roulade is heavenly—' As they both shook their heads he continued with hardly a break in stride, 'No takers. Cheese, then? The cheese selection is quite good.'

'A question or two, actually.' Kincaid had opened his wallet. First he showed David his warrant card, then a snapshot of Connor he had begged from Julia. 'We understand this fellow was a regular customer of yours. Do you recognize him?'

'Of course I do,' answered David, puzzled. 'It's Mr Swann. What do you mean, "was"?'

'I'm afraid he's dead,' Kincaid said, using the standard formula. 'We're looking into the circumstances of his death.'

'Mr Swann – dead?' For a moment the young man looked so pale that Kincaid reached out and pulled up a chair from the next table.

'Sit down,' said Kincaid. 'The mob is not exactly queuing up for service at the bar.'

'What?' David folded into the proffered chair as if legless. 'Oh, I see what you mean.' He gave a wan attempt at a smile. 'It's just a bit of a shock, that's all. Seems like just the other night he was here, and he was always so . . . larger-than-life. Vital.' Reaching out, he touched the surface of the photograph with a tentative fingertip.

'Can you remember what night it was you saw him

last?' Kincaid asked quietly, but Gemma could sense his concentrated attention.

David drew his brows together, but said quickly enough, 'My girlfriend, Kelly, was working late on the checkout at Tesco's, didn't finish till half-past nine or thereabouts . . . Thursday. It must have been Thursday.' He glanced at them both, expecting approbation.

Kincaid met Gemma's eyes across the table and she saw the flash of victory, but he only said, 'Good man. Do you remember what time he came in on Thursday?'

'Late-ish. Must have been after eight.' Warming to his tale, David continued, 'Sometimes he came in by himself, but usually he was with people I thought must be clients of some sort. Not that I eavesdropped on purpose, mind you,' he added, looking a bit uncomfortable, 'but when you're a waiter sometimes you can't help but overhear, and they seemed to be talking business.'

'And that night?' Gemma prompted.

'I remember it particularly because it was different. He came in alone, and even then he didn't seem his usual self. He was short with me, for one thing. "Something's really got on his wick," I thought.' Remembering Gemma, he added, 'Sorry, miss.'

She smiled at him. 'Don't mind me.'

'Mr Swann, now, he could put it away with the best of them, but he was always jolly with it. Not like some.' David made a face and Gemma nodded sympathetically. As if that had reminded him of his other customers, he glanced at the table at the back, but its occupants were still too engrossed in each other to notice his lack of attention. 'Then this other bloke came in, and they took a table for dinner.'

'Did they know each other?' Kincaid asked.

'What did—' Gemma interjected, but Kincaid stopped her with a quickly lifted hand.

'Oh, I'm sure they must have done. Mr Swann stood up as soon as the other bloke came in the door. They went straight to their table after that, so I didn't hear what they said – custom was fairly good that night – but things seemed friendly enough at first.'

'And then?' Kincaid said into the moment's pause.

David looked from one to the other, less comfortable now. 'I guess you could say they had a heated discussion. Not a shouting match – they didn't really raise their voices, but you could tell they were arguing. And Mr Swann, well, he always enjoyed the food here, made a point to compliment the chef, that sort of thing.' He paused, as if making sure they fully understood the import of what he was about to say. 'He didn't even finish his dinner.'

'Do you remember what he had?' Kincaid asked, and Gemma knew he was thinking of the still incomplete lab report on the contents of Connor's stomach.

'Steak. Washed down with a good part of a bottle of Burgundy.'

Kincaid considered this, then asked, 'What happened after that?'

David shifted in his chair and scratched his nose. 'They paid their bills – separately – and left.'

'They left together?' Gemma asked, clarifying the point.

Nodding, David said, 'Still arguing, as far as I could tell.' He was fidgeting more obviously now, turning round in his chair to glance at the bar.

Gemma looked at Kincaid, and receiving an almost imperceptible nod, said, 'Just one more thing, David. The other man, what did he look like?'

David's smile lit his face. 'Very elegant, nice dresser, if you know what I mean. Tall, thin, fairish – ' he puckered his brow and thought for a moment – 'in his fifties, I should think, but he'd kept himself well.'

'Did he pay by credit card?' Kincaid asked hopefully.

Shaking his head and looking genuinely regretful, David said, 'Sorry. Cash.'

Making an effort to keep the excitement out of her voice, Gemma congratulated him. 'You're very observant, David. We seldom get a description half as good.'

'It's the job,' he said, smiling. 'You get in the habit. I put names with the faces when I can. People like to be recognized.' Pushing back his chair, he looked questioningly from one to the other. 'All right if I clear up now?'

Kincaid nodded and handed him a business card. 'You can ring us if you think of anything else.'

David had stood and deftly stacked their dirty dishes on his arm when he stopped and seemed to hesitate. 'What happened to him? Mr Swann. You never said.'

'To tell you the truth, we're not quite sure, but we are treating it as a suspicious death,' said Gemma. 'His body was found in the Thames.'

The plates rattled and David steadied them with his other hand. 'Not along here, surely?'

'No, at Hambleden Lock.' Gemma fancied she saw a shadow of relief cross the young man's face, but put it down to the normal human tendency to want trouble kept off one's own patch.

David reached for another dish, balancing it with nonchalant ease. 'When? When did it happen?'

'His body was found early Friday morning,' Kincaid said, watching David with a pleasant expression that Gemma recognized as meaning his interest was fully engaged.

'Friday morning?' David froze, and although Gemma couldn't be sure in the flickering reflection from the fire, she thought his face paled. 'You mean Thursday night . . .'

The front door opened and two middle-aged couples came in, faces rosy with the cold. David looked from them to the couple at the back, who were finally showing signs of restiveness. 'I'll have to go. Sorry.' With a flash of an apologetic smile and a rattle of crockery, he hurried to the bar.

Kincaid watched him for a moment, then shrugged and smiled at Gemma. 'Nice lad. Might make a good copper. Has the memory for it.'

'Listen.' Gemma leaned towards him, her voice urgent.

At that moment the two rosy-faced couples, having ordered drinks at the bar, sat down at the next table. They smiled at Gemma and Kincaid in a neighbourly fashion, then began a clearly audible conversation among themselves. 'Here, David's left us a bill,' said Kincaid. 'Let's settle up and be on our way.'

Not until they had stepped out into the street again was Gemma able to hiss at him, 'That was Tommy Godwin.' Seeing Kincaid's blank expression, she said, 'The man with Connor that night. I'm sure it was Tommy Godwin. That's what I kept trying to tell you,' she added testily.

They had stopped on the pavement just outside the pub and stood holding their coat collars up around their throats, a defence against the fog that had crept up from the river. 'How can you be certain?'

'I'm telling you, it had to be him.' She heard her voice rise in exasperation and made an attempt to level it. 'You said yourself that David was observant. His description was too accurate for it to be anyone but Tommy. It's beyond the bounds of probability.'

'Okay, okay.' Kincaid held up a hand in mock surrender. 'But what about the theatre? You'll have to recheck—'

The pub door flew open and David almost catapulted into them. 'Oh, sorry. I thought I might catch you. Look—' He stopped, as if his impetus had vanished. Still in shirtsleeves, he folded his arms across his torso and stamped his feet a little. 'Look – I had no way of knowing, did I? I thought it was just a bit of argy-bargy. I'd have felt a right prat interfering . . .'

'Tell us what happened, David,' said Kincaid. 'Do you want to go back inside?'

David glanced at the door. 'No, they'll be all right for a bit.' He looked back at them, swallowed and went on. 'A few minutes after Mr Swann and the other bloke left, I came out for a break. Kelly usually drops in for a drink when she gets off work, and I like to keep an eye open for her – a bird on her own at night, you know. It's not as safe as it used to be.' For a moment he paused, perhaps realizing just whom he was lecturing, and Gemma could feel his embarrassment intensify. 'Anyway, I was standing just about where we are now, having a smoke, when I heard a noise by the river.' He pointed down the gently sloping street. 'It was clear, not like tonight, and the river's only a hundred yards or so along.' Again he stopped, as if waiting to be drawn.

'Could you see anything?' Kincaid asked.

'The street lamp reflecting off fair hair, and a slightly smaller, darker figure. I think it must have been Mr Swann and the other bloke, but I couldn't swear to it.'

'They were fighting?' Gemma couldn't keep the disbelief from her voice. She found the idea of Tommy Godwin involved in a physical confrontation almost inconceivable.

'Scuffling. Like kids in a school playground.'

Kincaid glanced at Gemma, his eyebrows raised in surprise. 'What happened then, David?'

'I heard Kelly's car. Loose exhaust,' he added in explanation. 'You can hear the bloody thing for a mile. I went to meet her, and when we came back, they were gone.' He scanned their faces anxiously. 'You don't think . . . I never dreamed . . .'

'David,' said Kincaid, 'can you tell us what time this happened?'

He nodded. 'Quarter to ten, or near enough.'

'The other man,' put in Gemma, 'would you know him if you saw him again?'

She could see the gooseflesh on his arms from the cold, but he stood still, considering. 'Well, yes. I suppose I would. Surely, you don't think he—'

'We might want you to make an identification. Just a matter of routine,' Gemma added soothingly. 'Can we reach you here? You'd better give us your home address and telephone as well.' She passed her notebook to him and he scribbled in it, squinting in the orange glow of the street lamps. 'You'd better see to your customers,' she said when he'd finished, smiling at him. 'We'll be in touch if we need you.'

When David had gone, she turned to Kincaid. 'I know what you're thinking, but it's not possible! We know he was in London a few minutes after eleven—'

Kincaid touched his fingers to her shoulder, gently turning her. 'Let's have a look at the river.' As they walked the fog enveloped them, sneaking into their clothes, beading their skin, so that their faces glistened when caught by the light. The pavement ended and their footsteps scrunched on gravel, then they heard the lapping of water against shoreline. 'It must be close now,' said Kincaid. 'Can you smell it?'

The temperature had dropped noticeably as they neared the water, and Gemma shivered, hugging her coat around her. The darkness before them became denser, blacker, and they stopped, straining their eyes. 'What is this place?'

Kincaid shone his pocket torch on the gravel. 'You

can see the wheel ruts where cars have been parked. Forensic will love this.'

Gemma turned to him, clamping down on her chattering teeth. 'How could Tommy have done it? Even if he'd choked Connor and dumped him in the boot of his car, he would have to have driven like a demon to be in London before eleven o'clock. He couldn't possibly have driven to Hambleden and carried Con's body all that way.'

'But,' Kincaid began reasonably, 'he could have left the body in the boot, driven to London to establish an alibi, and dumped the body later.'

'That doesn't make sense. Why go to the theatre, the one place that would connect him with the Ashertons, and through them, with Connor? And if he wanted to establish an alibi, why not sign in with the porter? It was only chance that Alison Douglas saw him in Gerald's dressing room, and Gerald certainly hasn't mentioned it.' Having forgotten the cold and damp in the heat of her argument, Gemma drew breath for her final salvo. 'And even if the rest of it were true, how could he possibly have carried Con's body from the Hambleden carpark to the lock?'

Kincaid smiled his most infuriating smile, the one that meant he found her vehemence amusing. 'Well, I suppose we had better ask him, hadn't we?'

Chapter Eleven

Alison Douglas protested when Gemma rang her early the next day. 'But, Sergeant, how can I possibly ask the ushers to come in this morning when they worked last night? And some of them have other jobs or school.'

'Do the best you can. The alternative is having them down to the Yard, which I doubt most of them would be too keen on.' Gemma tried to keep the irritation out of her voice. A restless night and a drive back to London in the thick of the commuter traffic had left her feeling shirty, but that was no excuse for taking it out on Alison. And it was not the most reasonable of requests, after all. 'I'll be there before noon,' she told Alison, ringing off.

Replacing the receiver in its cradle, she surveyed with distaste the paperwork swamping Kincaid's desk. She felt none of her usual satisfaction in having appropriated his office, but rather the same discomfort that had kept her awake into the wee hours. Something had been different about Kincaid last night – at first she had only been aware of a rather feverish quality to his behaviour, but as she tossed and turned through the night she came to the conclusion that his responses to her had altered as well. Had she only imagined the easy companionship of the previous evening in London? He had sought her out. Had his delight in her flat and evident enjoyment of her company caused her to drop her barriers a dangerous notch too far?

She shrugged and rubbed her eyes, trying to massage away the fatigue, but she couldn't erase the fleeting thought that the change in Kincaid's manner had something to do with his visit to Julia Swann.

In the end, Alison managed to bring in four of the ushers, and they sat cramped together on folding chairs in her office, looking disgruntled but curious.

Gemma introduced herself, adding, 'I'll try not to keep you any longer than necessary. Do any of you know Tommy Godwin, the Wardrobe Manager? Tall, thin, fairish man, very well dressed?' Looking at them, she wasn't hopeful that sartorial elegance had a place in their vocabularies. The three young men were neat but ordinary, and the girl had managed what Gemma recognized as low-budget dressing with a bit of flair. 'I want to know if anyone saw him last Thursday evening.' The young men glanced sideways at one another from blank faces. Behind them Alison stood with arms crossed, leaning lightly against the wall, and Gemma saw her mouth open slightly in surprise.

Shaking her head slightly at Alison, Gemma waited, letting the silence stretch.

Finally, the girl spoke. 'I did, miss.' Her voice held a trace of West Indian cadence, probably acquired from parents or other family members who were first-generation immigrants, thought Gemma.

Letting out the breath she'd been unconsciously holding, Gemma said, 'Did you? You're sure it was Thursday evening, now? *Pelleas and Melisande*, right?' She hadn't really expected such a positive result, still didn't quite trust it.

'Yes, miss.' The girl smiled as if she found Gemma's doubt amusing. 'I see all the productions – I can tell which is which.'

'Good. I'm glad one of us can.' Gemma smiled, silently kicking herself for sounding patronizing. 'What's your name?'

'Patricia, miss. I'm a design student – I'm interested in costumes, so sometimes I help out a bit with Wardrobe. That's how I know Mr Godwin.'

'Can you tell me about Thursday evening?'

The girl glanced round at Alison as if seeking permission from the nearest authority. 'Go ahead, Patricia, tell the Sergeant. I'm sure it's quite all right,' responded Alison.

'Mr Godwin came into the foyer from the street doors. Usually I stand just inside the auditorium and listen to the performance, but I'd just come back from the Ladies' and was crossing the foyer myself. I called out to him, but he didn't hear me.'

Gemma didn't know whether she felt relief or disappointment – if Tommy had been telling the truth about watching the performance, he couldn't have been in Wargrave with Connor. 'What did he do then, did you see?'

'Went in the next aisle over. Roland's,' she added with a sideways glance at the best-looking of the young men.

'Did you see him?' asked Gemma, turning her attention to him. He smiled at her, comfortable with the sudden attention. 'I can't say for sure, miss, as I don't know him, but I don't remember seeing anyone of that description.'

At least he hadn't called her 'ma'am'. Gemma returned the smile and turned her attention back to Patricia. 'Once you'd gone back to your post in the auditorium, did you see him again?'

The girl shook her head. 'The mob started out just afterwards, and I had my hands full.'

'Interval so soon?' asked Gemma, puzzled.

'No.' Patricia shook her head more forcefully this time. 'Final curtain. I'd only realized I needed to go for a pee' – she sent a quelling glance at the young men – 'just in time.'

'Final curtain?' Gemma repeated faintly. 'I thought you meant he'd come in just after the performance began.'

'No, miss. Five minutes, maybe, before the end. Just before eleven o'clock.'

Gemma drew in a breath, collecting herself. So it might have been Tommy in the Red Lion after all. 'Did you see him later on, Patricia, when you were clearing up?'

'No, miss.' Having entered into the spirit of things,

she sounded as if she genuinely regretted having nothing more to offer.

'Okay, thanks, Patricia. You've been a great help.' Gemma looked at the men. 'Anyone else have anything to add?' Receiving the expected negatives, she said, 'All right, thank you.' Patricia trailed out last, looking back a little shyly. 'Bright girl,' said Gemma as the door closed.

'What is all this about Tommy, Sergeant?' asked Alison, coming to sit on the edge of her desk. She brushed absently at the wrinkles in her brown wool suit. The fabric was the same soft tone as her hair and eyes and made her look, thought Gemma, like a small brown wren.

'Are you quite sure you didn't see him until you went to Gerald's dressing room?'

'I'm positive. Why?'

'He told me he was here in the theatre during the entire performance that night. But Patricia's just contradicted that, and she seems a reliable witness.'

'Surely you don't think Tommy had anything to do with Connor's death? That's just not possible. Tommy is . . . well, everyone likes Tommy. And not just because he's witty and amusing,' Alison said as though Gemma had suggested it. 'That's not what I mean. He's kind when he doesn't have to be. I know you wouldn't think it from his manner, but he notices people. That girl, Patricia – I imagine he gave her some encouragement. When I first started here I tiptoed around everything, terrified of making a mistake, and he always had a kind word for me.'

'I'm sure you're right,' said Gemma, hoping to soothe Alison's hostility, 'but there is a discrepancy here, and I must follow it through.'

Alison sighed, looking suddenly weary. 'I suppose you must. What can I do to help?'

'Think back to those few minutes in Sir Gerald's dressing room. Did you notice anything at all unusual?'

'How can I tell?' asked Alison, her feathers ruffling again. 'How can I be sure my recollection's not distorted by what you've told me? That I'm not making something out of nothing?' When Gemma didn't respond, she went on more quietly. 'I have been thinking about it. They stopped talking when I came into the room. I felt as if I'd put my foot in – you know?' She looked at Gemma for confirmation. 'Then after that awkward bit, they seemed a bit too hearty, too jolly. I think now that's why I only stayed a minute, just long enough to offer the usual congratulations, although I didn't consciously realize it at the time.'

'Anything else?' Gemma asked, without too much anticipation.

'No. Sorry.'

'That's okay.' Smiling at Alison, Gemma made an effort to overcome the lethargy that seemed to be creeping into her limbs. 'I will have to talk to him again, and he's proving rather elusive. This morning I've tried his flat, LB House, and here, with no joy. Any suggestions?'

Alison shook her head. 'No, he ought to be around.'

Seeing the spark of concern in Alison's eyes,

Gemma said thoughtfully, 'I hope our Mr Godwin won't prove too difficult to find.'

High Wycombe CID had obligingly made room for Kincaid at an absent DI's desk, and there he had spent the morning, going through report after inconclusive report. He stretched, wondering if he should have another cup of dreadful coffee, or give it up and have some lunch.

Duty and coffee were grudgingly in the lead when Jack Makepeace put his head round the door. 'Anything?'

Kincaid pulled a face. 'Sod all. You've read them. Any word from the team in Wargrave?'

Makepeace grinned evilly. 'Two crushed lager cans, some foil gum wrappers, the remains of a dead bird and half a dozen used condoms.'

'A popular parking spot, is it?'

'It marks the beginning of a footpath that runs along the river for a bit, then loops around the churchyard. Parking there isn't strictly legal, but people do it anyway, and I dare say a spot of midnight necking goes on as well.' Makepeace fingered his moustache for a moment. 'The forensic lads say the gravel's much too soft and messed about for tyre casts.'

'I expected as much.' Kincaid regarded him thoughtfully. 'Jack, if the body went in the river at Wargrave, could it have drifted downstream to Hambleden by morning?'

Makepeace was shaking his head before Kincaid had finished. 'Not possible. River's too slow, for one thing, and there's Marsh Lock, just past Henley, for another.'

Thinking of Julia's brief escape from the gallery, he said, 'Then I suppose the same would be true of Henley, if he'd gone in along the River Terrace?'

Makepeace levered his bulk away from the door frame and walked over to the area map on the office wall. He pointed a stubby finger at the twisting blue ribbon representing the River Thames. 'Look at all these twists and turns, all making places where a body might catch.' Turning back to Kincaid, he added, 'I think your body went in within a few hundred yards of where it was found.'

Kincaid pushed back the creaky chair, stretched out his legs and laced his fingers behind his neck. 'I'm afraid you're right, Jack. I'm just clutching at straws. What about the houses along the river, above the lock? House-to-house turn up anything?'

'Either they were all sleeping like babies by ten o'clock,' Makepeace said sarcastically, laying his cheek against the back of his hand, 'or they see talking to us as an excuse to trot out their own pet phobias. Remember that flat conversion at the beginning of the weir walkway? Old biddy in one of the riverside flats says she heard voices some time after the late news finished. When she looked out of her window she saw a man and a boy on the walkway. "Poofters," she says. "Queers sinning against the Lord." And motorcycle hoodlums to boot.' Makepeace's eyes crinkled in amusement. 'It seems the boy had longish hair and wore leather, and that was good enough for her. Before my PC could get away, she asked him if he'd been saved by Jesus.'

Kincaid snorted. 'Doesn't make me miss my days on the beat. What about access from south of the river, then? Through the meadows.'

'Need a Land Rover, or something with a four-wheel drive. Ground's like glue after all this rain.' Makepeace studied Kincaid's face, then said sympathetically, 'Bad luck. Oh' – he patted the file tucked under his left arm – 'here's something might cheer you up – final report from pathology.' He handed it across to Kincaid. 'Spot of lunch?'

'Give me ten minutes,' Kincaid said with a wave, then dug into the file.

After a cursory read-through he picked up the phone and eventually managed to reach Dr Winstead in his lair. 'Doctor,' he said when he had identified himself, 'I know now what time Connor ate – nine, or shortly thereafter. Are you sure he couldn't have died as early as ten?'

'Meat and potatoes, was I right?'

'Steak, actually,' Kincaid admitted.

'I'd put it closer to midnight, unless the fellow had stomach acid that would've stripped paint.'

'Thanks, Dr Winnie.' Kincaid rang off and contemplated the scattered reports. After a moment he swept them into a pile, pulled up the knot on his tie and went in search of more pleasant prospects.

*

When Gemma returned to the Yard, she found a message on her desk that read simply, 'Tom Godwin called. Brown's Hotel, three o'clock.'

She went in search of the duty sergeant. 'Was that all, Bert? Are you sure?'

Affronted, he said, 'Have you ever known me to make a mistake with a message, Gemma?'

'No, of course not.' She patted his grizzled head affectionately. 'It's just odd, that's all.'

'That's what the gentleman said, verbatim,' said Bert, slightly mollified. 'The guv'nor wants to see you, by the way.'

'Oh, terrific,' she muttered under her breath, and received a sympathetic glance from Bert.

'He hasn't eaten anyone since lunch, love.'

'Ta, Bert,' said Gemma, grinning. 'That makes me feel ever so much better.'

Still, she went along the corridor in some trepidation. In truth, Chief Superintendent Denis Childs was known to be fair with his staff, but there was something in his pleasant and courteous manner that made her want to confess even imagined misdeeds. His door stood open, as was his policy, and Gemma tapped lightly before entering. 'You wanted to see me, sir?'

Childs looked up from a file. He had recently adopted granny-style reading glasses, and they looked so incongruous perched on his massive moon-shaped face that she had to bite her lip to stifle a giggle. Fortunately, he took them off and dangled them daintily from thumb and forefinger. 'Sit down, Sergeant. What have you and Kincaid been up to the past few days – tiddlywinks? I've had a prod from the assistant commissioner, wanting to know why we haven't produced the expected brilliant results. Apparently Sir Gerald Asherton has put quite a flea in his ear.'

'It's only been four days, sir,' Gemma said, stung. 'And the pathologist only got round to the PM yesterday. Anyway,' she added hurriedly, before Childs could trot out his dreaded maxim – *results, not excuses* – 'we have a suspect. I'm interviewing him this afternoon.'

'Any hard evidence?'

'No, sir, not yet.'

Childs folded his hands across his belly and Gemma marvelled, as she always did, that for all his bulk the man radiated such physical magnetism. As far as she knew, he was happily married and used his appeal for nothing more sinister than keeping the typists working to order.

'All the teams are out just now – we've had a regular rash of homicides. But as badly as I need the two of you, I don't think we want to let the AC down, do you, Sergeant? It's always in our best interest to keep the powers-that-be happy.' He smiled at her, his teeth blindingly white against his olive skin. 'Will you pass that along to Superintendent Kincaid when you talk to him?'

'Yes, sir,' Gemma answered, and, taking that as dismissal, beat a hasty and grateful retreat.

When Gemma returned to Kincaid's office, bars of sunlight slanted into the room. They looked solid enough to touch, the quality of the light almost viscous. Not quite trusting the phenomenon, she went to the window and peered through the blinds. The sky was indeed clear and as blue as it ever managed with the city smog. She looked from the window to the paperwork, lying haphazardly where she'd left it. The angle of the light across the desk revealed streaks of dust and several perfect fingerprints – smiling, Gemma walked over and wiped them away with a tissue. Remove the evidence – that was the first rule. Then she grabbed her bag from the coat stand and made for the lift before anyone could stop her.

She cut through St James's Park, walking quickly, taking in great breaths of the cool, clear air. The English have an instinct for sunshine, however brief its duration, she thought, like a radar early-warning system. The park was busy with others who had heeded the signal, some walking as quickly as she was, obviously on their way somewhere, others strolling or sitting on benches, and all looking oddly out of place in their business clothes. The trees, which in the past few days' drizzle had looked drab as old washing, showed remnants of red and gold in the sunlight, and pansies and late chrysanthemums made a brave showing in the beds.

She came out into the Mall, and by the time she'd made her way along St James's Street to Piccadilly she could feel her heart beating and warmth in her face. But it was only a few more blocks along Albemarle Street, and her head felt clear for the first time that day.

Although she had timed it accurately, arriving a few minutes early, Tommy Godwin was there before her. He waved at her, looking as much at home in the hotel's squashy armchair as he might in his own parlour. She made her way over to him, suddenly aware of her windblown hair and pink cheeks, and of her unfashionably sensible low-heeled shoes.

'Do have a seat, my dear. You look as if you've been exerting yourself unnecessarily. I've ordered for you – I hope you don't mind. Stuffy and old-fashioned as it is' – he nodded at the room, with its wood-panelled walls and crackling fire – 'they do a proper tea here.'

'Mr Godwin, this is not a social occasion,' Gemma said as severely as she could while sinking into the depths of her chair. 'Where have you been? I've been trying to reach you all day.'

'I paid a visit to my sister in Clapham this morning. A gruesome but regular family necessity, one which I fear most of us are subject to – unless one has had the good fortune to come into the world via test tube, and even that has ramifications that don't bear thinking of.'

Gemma tried to straighten her back against the chair's soft cushion. 'Please don't take me round the mulberry bush, Mr Godwin. I need some answers from you.'

'Can't we have tea first?' he asked plaintively. 'And call me Tommy, please.' Leaning toward her confidentially, he said, 'This hotel was the model for Agatha Christie's *At Bertram's Hotel* – did you know that,

Sergeant? I don't believe it's changed much since her day.'

Curious in spite of her best intentions, Gemma looked round the room. Some of the little old ladies seated nearby might have been Miss Marple's clones. The faded prints of their dresses (covered by sensibly woolly cardigans) harmonized with the faded blues and violets of their hair rinses, and their shoes – Gemma's comfortable flats weren't even in the same realm of sensibleness as their stout brogues.

What an odd place to appeal to Tommy Godwin, she thought, studying him covertly. She pegged today's navy jacket as cashmere, his shirt as immaculate pale grey broadcloth, his trousers charcoal and his silk tie a discreetly rich navy and red paisley.

As if reading her mind, he said, 'It's the pre-war aura I can't resist. The Golden Age of British manners – vanished now, much to our loss. I was born during the Blitz, but even during my childhood there were still traces of gentility in English life. Ah, here's our tea,' he said as the waiter brought a tray to their table. 'I've ordered Assam to go with the sandwiches – I hope that's all right – and a pot of Keemun later with the cakes.'

Tea in Gemma's family had run to Tetley's Finest teabags, stewed in a tin pot. Not liking to admit that she had never tasted either, she pounced on his previous remark. 'You only think that time must have been perfect because you didn't live it. I imagine the generation between the wars saw Edwardian England as the Golden Age, and probably the Edwardians felt the same way about the Victorians.'

'A good point, my dear,' he said seriously as he poured tea into her cup, 'but there was one great difference – the First World War. They had looked into the mouth of hell, and they knew how fragile our hold on civilization really is.' The waiter returned, placing a three-tiered tray on their small table. Tiny sandwiches filled the bottom tray, scones the middle, and cakes the top, the crowning touch. 'Have a sandwich, my dear,' said Tommy. 'The smoked salmon is particularly nice.'

He sipped his tea and continued his lecture, a cucumber sandwich poised in his fingers. 'It's fashionable these days to pooh-pooh the Golden Age crime novel as trivial and unrealistic, but that was not the case at all. It was their stand against chaos. The conflicts were intimate, rather than global, and justice, order and retribution always prevailed. They desperately needed that reassurance. Did you know that Britain lost nearly a third of its young men between 1914 and 1918? Yet that war didn't physically threaten us in the same way as the next – it stayed safely on the European Front.'

Pausing to down half the cucumber sandwich in one bite, he chewed for a moment, then said sadly, 'What a waste it must have seemed, the flower of Britain's manhood lost, with nothing to show for it but some newspaper headlines and politicians' speeches.' He smiled. 'But if you read Christie or Allingham or

Sayers, the detective always got his man. And you'll notice that the detective always operated outside the system – the stories expressed a comforting belief in the validity of individual action.'

'But weren't the murders always clean and bloodless?' Gemma asked rather impatiently through a mouthful of sandwich. She'd felt too tired and unsettled to eat lunch, and her walk had left her suddenly ravenous.

'Some of them were in fact quite diabolical. Christie was particularly fond of poisoning, and I can think of no less civilized way to commit murder.'

'Are you suggesting that there are civilized methods of murder?' *Such as drowning your victim in a convenient river*, she thought, wondering at the bizarre turn the conversation seemed to be taking.

'Of course not, my dear, only that I've always found the idea of poison especially abhorrent – such suffering and indignity for one person to inflict upon another.'

Gemma drank a little more of her tea. She rolled it around on her tongue, deciding she liked the rich, malty taste. 'So you prefer your murders quick and clean, do you, Tommy?'

'I don't prefer them any way at all, my dear,' he said, glancing up at her as he poured more tea into her cup. He was playing with her, teasing her, she could see it in the suppressed laughter in his eyes.

Time for a little dose of reality, she thought, licking a crumb from her fingertip. 'I've always thought drowning would be quite horrible myself. Giving in at last to that desperate need to draw air into the lungs, then choking, struggling, until unconsciousness comes as a blessed relief.'

Tommy Godwin sat quite still, watching her, his hands relaxed on the tabletop. What beautiful hands he had, thought Gemma, the fingers long and slender, the nails perfectly kept. She found quite inconceivable the idea of him fighting like a common ruffian, using those hands to choke and squeeze, or perhaps to hold a thrashing body under water.

'You're quite right, my dear,' he said softly. 'It was tasteless of me to go on that way, but crime novels are rather a hobby of mine.' He picked up a watercress sandwich and looked at it a moment before returning it to the plate. The eyes that met hers were a surprisingly dark blue, and guileless. 'Do you think poor Connor suffered?'

'We don't know. The pathologist didn't find evidence indicating he'd inhaled river water, but that doesn't rule it out.' She let the silence stretch for a heartbeat, then added, 'I was hoping you might tell me.'

His eyes widened. 'Oh, come now, Sergeant. You can't think—'

'You lied to me about attending the opera that night. One of the ushers saw you come in from the street just minutes before the performance ended. And I have a witness who can place you in a pub in Wargrave, having a not-too-friendly dinner with Connor Swann,' she said, tendering her bluff with all the authority she could manage.

For the first time since she had met him, Tommy Godwin seemed at a loss for words. As she studied his still face, she saw that most of his attractiveness lay not in his individual features, but in the expression of alert, humorous inquisitiveness that usually animated them. Finally, he sighed and pushed away his empty plate. 'I should have known it was no use. Even as a child I was never any good at lying. I had meant to attend the performance that night – that much at least was true. Then I had an urgent message from Connor on my answerphone, saying he needed to see me. I suppose he must have been looking for me when he came to the theatre that afternoon.'

'He asked you to meet him at the Red Lion?'

As Tommy nodded the waiter brought their second pot of tea. Lifting the pot, Tommy said, 'You must try the Keemun, my dear. What would you like with it?'

Gemma had started to shake her head when he said, 'Please, Sergeant, do have something. This was to be a special treat for you – I thought hardworking policewomen probably didn't have too many opportunities to take afternoon tea.'

She heard Allson's words again, and she found that no matter what else Tommy might have done, she couldn't reject this small act of kindness. 'I'll have a scone then, please.'

Having taken a scone for himself, he poured tea into her cup from the fresh pot. 'Taste your tea. You can put milk in it if you like, but I'd advise you not to.'

Gemma did as instructed, then looked up at him in surprise. 'It's sweet.'

He looked pleased. 'Do you like it? It's a north China Congou. The best of the China blacks, I think.'

'Tell me about Connor,' Gemma said, spreading clotted cream and strawberry jam on her scone.

'There's not much to tell, really. I met him at the Red Lion, as you said, and from the beginning he behaved quite oddly. I'd never seen him like that, although I'd heard stories about the weeks after he and Julia first separated. He had been drinking, but I didn't think he'd had enough to account for his manner. It was . . . I don't know . . . almost hysterical, really.'

'Why did he want to see you?'

Tommy washed down a bite of scone with tea. 'I found out soon enough. He said he'd decided he wanted his old job back – that he'd had enough of dealing with two-bit, small-town accounts, and he wanted me to intercede for him.'

'Could you have done it?' asked Gemma in some surprise.

'Well, yes, I suppose so. I've known the firm's senior partner for years. In fact, it was I who encouraged him to go after the ENO account in the first place.' He looked at Gemma over the cup he held cradled in both hands. 'It's unfortunate that we can't foresee the consequences of our actions. If I had not done that, Connor would never have met Gerald and Caro, and through them, Julia.

'But you refused Connor's request.'

'Politely at first. I told him that my reputation would ride on his performance, and that considering his previous conduct, I didn't feel I could risk it. The truth of the matter is,' he added, setting down his cup and looking away from Gemma, 'I never liked him. Not the thing to say when one is suspected of foul play, is it, dear Sergeant?' He smiled, teasing her once more, then said reflectively, 'I can remember their wedding day quite clearly. It was a June wedding, in the garden at Badger's End – I know you won't have seen it, but it can be quite lovely at that time of year. All Plummy's doing, although Julia used to help her quite a bit when she had the time.

'Everyone said how perfect Julia and Connor looked together, and I have to admit they did make a handsome couple, but when I looked at them I saw only disaster. They were completely, utterly unsuited for one another.'

'Do stick to the point, Tommy, please,' said Gemma, wondering how she could impress the gravity of the situation upon him with her mouth full of scone.

He sighed. 'We argued. He became more and more abusive, until finally I told him I'd had enough. I left. That's all.'

Moving her plate out of the way, Gemma leaned towards him. 'That's not all, Tommy. The barman came out just after you and Connor left the pub. He says he saw you fighting down by the river.'

Although she wouldn't have believed that a man with Tommy Godwin's poise and experience could blush, she could have sworn his face turned pink with embarrassment.

There was a moment's pause as he refused to meet her eyes. Finally, he said, 'I've not done anything like that since I was at school, and even then I considered any form of physical violence both undignified and uncivilized. It was the accepted way to get on in the world, beating what one wanted out of someone else, and I made a deliberate choice to live my life differently. It got me labelled a pansy and a poofter, of course,' he added with a hint of the familiar, charming smile, 'but I could live with that. What I couldn't live with was the thought of abandoning my principles.

'When I found myself locked in a ridiculous schoolboy scuffle with Connor, I simply stopped and walked away.'

'And he let you?'

Tommy nodded. 'I think he'd run out of steam himself by that time.'

Had you parked your car on the gravel by the river?'

'No, I'd found a spot on the street, a block or two up from the pub. Someone may have seen it,' he added hopefully. 'It's a classic Jaguar, red, quite distinctive.'

'And then, after you'd returned to your car?'

'I drove to London. Having agreed to see Con, against my better judgement, I'd spoiled my evening, and I felt he'd made rather a fool of me. I thought I'd try to salvage as much of my original plan as I could.'

'Five minutes' worth?' asked Gemma, sceptically.

He smiled. 'Well, I did my best.'

'And you didn't make a point of stopping by Sir Gerald's dressing room in order to establish an alibi?'

Patiently, he said, 'I wanted to congratulate him, as I told you before, Sergeant.'

'Even though you hadn't actually seen the performance?'

'I could tell by the audience's response that it had been particularly good.'

She searched his face, and he returned her gaze steadily. 'You're right, you know, Tommy,' she said at last. 'You are an awful liar. I suppose you went straight home from the theatre.

'I did, as a matter of fact.'

'Is there anyone who can vouch for you?'

'No, my dear. I'm afraid not. And I parked at the back of my building and went up in the service lift, so I didn't see anyone at all. I'm sorry,' he added, as if it distressed him to disappoint her.

'I'm sorry, too, Tommy.' Gemma sighed. Feeling suddenly weary, she said, 'You could have put Connor's body in the boot of your car, then driven back to Hambleden after the performance and dumped him in the lock.'

'Really? What an extraordinarily imaginative idea.' Tommy sounded amused.

Exasperated, she said, 'You do realize that we'll have to impound your car so that the forensics team can go over it. And we'll have to search your flat for evidence. And you will have to come down to the Yard with me now and make a formal statement.'

He lifted the delicate porcelain teapot and smiled at her. 'Well, then you had better finish your tea, my dear Sergeant.'

Chapter Twelve

Lunch with Jack Makepeace improved Kincaid's outlook on life considerably. Replete with cheese, pickle and pints of Greene King ale, they blinked as they came out into the street from the dim interior of a pub near the High Wycombe nick. 'That's a surprise,' said Makepeace, turning his face up to the sun. 'And I doubt it'll last long – the forecast is for cats and dogs.'

The perfect antidote to a morning spent wheel-spinning, thought Kincaid as he felt the faint warmth of the sun against his face, was a good walk. 'I think I'll take advantage of it,' he said to Makepeace as they reached the station. 'You can reach me if anything comes up.'

'Some people have all the luck,' Makepeace answered good-naturedly. 'It's back to the salt mines for the likes of me.' He waved and disappeared through the glass doors.

Kincaid made the short drive from High Wycombe to Fingest, and on reaching the village he hesitated for a moment before turning into the pub's carpark. Although the vicarage looked mellow and inviting in the afternoon sun and the vicar was certainly the authority on local walks, he decided it was much too likely he'd end up spending the rest of the afternoon being comfortably entertained in the vicar's study.

In the end, Tony proved as useful and accommodating on the matter of walks as he had about everything else. 'I've just the thing,' he said, retrieving a book from the mysterious recesses under the bar. 'Local pub walks. Three and a half miles too much for you?' He eyed Kincaid measuringly.

'I think I can just about manage that,' Kincaid said, grinning.

'Fingest, Skirmett, Turville, and back to Fingest. All three villages are in their own valleys, but this particular walk avoids the steepest hill. You might get a bit mucky, though.'

'Thanks, Tony. I promise not to trample mud over your carpets. I'll just go and change.'

'Take my compass,' Tony called out as Kincaid turned away, producing it from the palm of his hand like a conjuror. 'It'll come in handy.'

At the top of the first long climb, some thoughtful citizen had placed a bench on which the winded walker could sit and enjoy the view. Kincaid took brief advantage of it, then toiled on, through woods and fields and over stiles. At first the vicar's brief history rolled through his mind, and as he walked he imagined the progression of Celts, Romans, Saxons and Normans settling these hills, all leaving their own particular imprint upon the land.

After a while the combination of fresh air, exercise and solitude worked its magic, and his mind returned freely to the question of Connor Swann's death, sorting the facts and impressions that he had gathered so far. The pathologist's evidence made it highly unlikely that Tommy Godwin had killed Connor outside the Red Lion in Wargrave. He might, of course, have knocked Connor unconscious and killed him a couple of hours later after returning from London – but, like Gemma, Kincaid could come up with no logical scenario for the later removal of the body from the car to the lock.

Dr Winstead's report also meant that Julia could not have killed Con during her brief absence from the gallery, and David's statement placing Connor in Wargrave until at least ten o'clock made it impossible for her to have met him along the River Terrace and made an assignation for later. Kincaid shied away from the feeling of relief that this conclusion brought him, and forced himself to consider the next possibility – that she had met Connor much later and that Trevor Simons had lied to protect her.

So caught up was he in these ruminations that he failed to see the cowpat until he had put his foot in it. Swearing, he wiped his trainer as best he could on the grass. Motive was like that, he mused as he walked on more carefully – sometimes you just couldn't see it until you fell into it. Hard as he tried, he couldn't come up with a likely reason why Julia would have wanted to kill Con, nor did he believe that having had one row with him that day, she would have agreed to meet him later in order to have another.

Had that lunchtime argument with Julia been the trigger for Connor's increasingly odd behaviour during the rest of that day? Yet it was only after he had left Kenneth that Con had visibly deviated from an expected pattern. And that brought Kincaid to Kenneth – where had Kenneth been on Thursday evening, and why had asking him about his movements sent him from reluctant co-operation into complete and obstinate withdrawal? As he pictured Kenneth, huddled in his bomber jacket as if it were armour, he remembered the female witness Makepeace had mentioned. 'A boy in leather,' she'd said . . . Kenneth was slightly built and Makepeace had described him as five foot eight or nine. Next to Connor he might easily have been mistaken for a boy. It was certainly a possibility worth pursuing.

The woods enclosed him again as he left Skirmett. He walked in a dim and soundless world, his footfalls absorbed by the leaf mould. Not even birdsong broke the stillness, and when he stopped, staring after a flash of white that might have been a deer bounding away, he could hear the rush of his own blood in his ears.

Kincaid walked on, following the next tendril that shot out from the amoebic mass of speculation. If Connor had driven away from the Red Lion after his scuffle with Tommy Godwin, where had he gone? Sharon Doyle's face came into his mind – she, like Kenneth, had become belligerent when Kincaid had pushed her about her movements later that evening.

As he came into Turville he looked northwest, towards Northend, up the hill where Badger's End lay hidden under the dark canopy of the beeches. What had brought Julia back to that house, as if drawn by an unseen umbilical cord?

He stopped at the Northend turning and frowned. Some thread ran through this case that he couldn't quite grasp – he felt it move away whenever he approached it too closely, like some dark underwater creature always swimming just out of reach.

Nestled among Turville's cluster of cottages, the Bull and Butcher beckoned, but Kincaid declared himself immune to the temptation of Brakspear's ales and pushed on into the fields again.

He soon came out onto the road that led to Fingest. The sun had dropped beneath the tops of the trees, and the light slanted through the boles, illuminating dust motes and flickering on his clothes like a faulty film projector.

By the time the now-familiar twin-gabled tower of Fingest church came into view, Kincaid found he had made two decisions. He would ask Thames Valley to pick up Kenneth Hicks, and then they'd see how well Hicks's bravado held up in an interview room in the local nick.

And he would pay another visit to Sharon Doyle.

When Kincaid returned to the Chequers, a bit muddy as Tony had predicted and feeling pleasantly tired from his walk, there was still no word from Gemma regarding her progress with Tommy Godwin. He rang the Yard and left a message for her with the duty sergeant. As soon as she finished in London she was to join him again. He wanted her in on the interview with Hicks. And considering Kenneth's obvious dislike of women, Kincaid thought with a smile, maybe she should conduct it.

In Henley, Kincaid left the car near the police station and walked down Hart Street, his eyes on the tower of the church of St Mary the Virgin.

Square and substantial, it anchored the town around it like the hub of a wheel. Church Avenue lay neatly tucked in the tower's shadow, facing the churchyard as if it were its own private garden. A plaque set into the stonework informed him that the row of almshouses had been endowed by John Longland, Bishop of Lincoln, in 1547, and rebuilt in 1830.

The cottages were unexpectedly charming, built of a very pale green-washed stucco, with bright blue doors and lace curtains in every window. Kincaid knocked at the number Sharon Doyle had given him. He heard the sound of the television, and faintly, the high voice of a child.

He had raised his hand to knock again when Sharon opened the door. Except for the unmistakable golden corkscrew curls, he would hardly have recognized her. She wore no makeup, not even lipstick, and her bare face looked young and unprotected. The tarted-up clothes and high heels were gone – replaced by a faded sweatshirt, jeans and dirty trainers, and in the few days since he had seen her she seemed visibly thinner. To his surprise, she also seemed rather pathetically glad to see him.

'Superintendent! What are you doing here?' A sticky and dishevelled version of the child in the wallet photo Kincaid had seen slipped up beside Sharon and wrapped herself around her mother's leg.

'Hullo, Hayley,' said Kincaid, squatting at her eye level. He looked up at Sharon and added, 'I came to see how you were getting on.'

'Oh, come in,' she said, as if making an effort to recall her manners, and she stepped back, hobbled by the child clinging to her like a limpet. 'Hayley was just having her tea, weren't you, love? In the kitchen with Gran.' Now that she had Kincaid in the sitting room, she seemed to have no idea what to do with him, and simply stood there stroking the child's tangle of fair curls.

Kincaid looked around the small room with interest. Doilies and dark furniture, fringed lampshades and the smell of lavender wax, all as neat and clean as if they had been preserved in a museum. The sound of the television was only a bit louder than it had been when he stood outside, and he surmised that the cottage's interior walls must be constructed of thick plaster.

'Gran likes the telly in the kitchen,' Sharon said into the silence. 'It's cosier to sit in there, close by the range.'

The front room might have been the scene of some long-ago courtship, thought Kincaid. He imagined young lovers sitting stiltedly on the horsehair chairs, then remembered that these cottages had been built for pensioners, and any wooing must have been done by those old enough to know better. He wondered if Connor had ever come here.

Diplomatically, he said, 'If Hayley would like to go in with Gran and finish her tea, perhaps you and I could go outside and have a chat.'

Sharon gave Kincaid a grateful glance and bent down to her daughter. 'Did you hear what the superintendent said, love? He needs to have a word with me, so you go along in with Gran and finish your tea. If you eat up all your beans and toast, you can have a biscuit,' she added cajolingly.

Hayley studied her mum as if gauging the sincerity of this pledge.

'I promise,' said Sharon, turning her and giving her a pat on the bottom. 'Go on now. Tell Gran I'll be along in a bit.' She watched the little girl disappear through the door in the back of the room, then said to Kincaid, 'Just let me get a cardy.'

The cardy turned out to be a man's brown wool cardigan, a bit moth-eaten, and ironically reminiscent of the one Sir Gerald Asherton had worn the night Kincaid met him. Seeing Kincaid's glance, Sharon smiled and said, 'It was my granddad's. Gran keeps it for wearing about the house.' As she followed Kincaid out into the churchyard, she continued, 'Actually, she's my great-gran, but I never knew my real gran. She died when my mum was a baby.'

Although the sun had set in the few minutes Kincaid had been inside the house, the churchyard looked even more inviting in the soft twilight. They walked to a bench across the way from the cottages, and as they sat down Kincaid said, 'Is Hayley always so shy?'

'She's always chattered like a magpie, from the day she learned to talk, even with strangers.' Sharon's hands lay loosely in her lap, palms turned up. They might have been disembodied, so unanimated were they, and Kincaid noticed that since he'd seen her last, the small pink nails had been bitten to the quick. 'It's only since I told her about Con that she's been like this.' She looked up at Kincaid in appeal. 'I had to tell her, didn't I, Mr Kincaid? I couldn't let her think he just scarpered, could I? I couldn't let her think he didn't care about us.'

Kincaid gave the question careful consideration before answering. 'I think you did the right thing, Sharon. It would be hard or her now, regardless, and in the long run I'm sure it's better to tell the truth. Children sense when you're lying, and then they have that betrayal to deal with as well as the loss.'

Sharon listened intently, then nodded once when he'd finished. She studied her hands for a moment. 'Now she wants to know why we can't see him. My auntie Pearl died last year and Gran took her to the viewing before the funeral.'

'What did you tell her?'

Shrugging, Sharon said, 'Different people do things different ways, that's all. What else could I say?'

'I imagine she wants some concrete evidence that Con is really gone. Perhaps you could take her to see his grave, afterwards.' He gestured at the graves laid out so neatly in the green grass of the churchyard. 'That should seem familiar enough to her.'

She turned to him again, her hands clenching convulsively.

'There's not been anyone to talk to, see? Gran doesn't want to know about it – she disapproved of him anyway—'

'Why was that?' asked Kincaid, surprised that the woman would not have been pleased at a better prospect for her great-granddaughter.

'Marriage is marriage in the eyes of the Lord,' mimicked Sharon, and Kincaid had a sudden clear vision of the old lady. 'Gran's very firm in her beliefs. It made no difference that Con wasn't living with *her*. And as long as Con was married I had no rights, Gran said. Turned out she knew what she was on about, didn't she?'

'You must have girlfriends you can talk with,' said Kincaid, as there seemed no helpful answer to the last question.

'They don't want to know, either. You'd think I'd got leprosy or something all of a sudden – they act like they're afraid it might rub off on them and spoil their fun.' Sharon sniffed, then added more softly, 'I don't want to talk to them about Con, anyway. What we had was between us, and it doesn't seem right to air it like last week's washing.'

'No, I can see that.'

They sat quietly for a few minutes as the lights

began to come on in the cottages. Indistinct shapes moved behind the net curtains, and every so often a pensioner would pop out from one door and then another, putting out milk bottles or picking up papers. It made Kincaid think of those elaborate German clocks, the kind in which the little people bob cheerfully in-and-out as the hour chimes. He looked at the girl beside him, her head again bent over her hands. 'I'll see you get your things back, Sharon. *She* would want you—' Bloody hell, now he was doing it. 'Mrs Swann would like you to have them,' he corrected himself.

Her response, when it came, surprised him. 'Those things I said, the other night . . . well, I've been thinking.' In the fading light he caught a quick flash of her eyes before she looked away from him again. 'It wasn't right, what I said. You know. About her . . .

'About Julia having killed Connor, is that what you mean?'

She nodded, picking idly at a spot on the front of her sweatshirt. 'I don't know why I said it. I wanted to hit at someone, I suppose.' After a moment she continued in a tone of discovery, 'I think I wanted to believe she was as awful as Con said. It made me feel better. Safer.'

'And now?' Kincaid asked, and when she didn't answer he continued, 'You had no reason for making those accusations? Con never said anything that made you think Julia might have threatened him?'

Shaking her head, she said so softly that he had to

lean close to catch it, 'No.' She smelled of Pears soap, and the good, clean ordinariness of it suddenly squeezed at his throat.

The twilight deepened, and from some of the cottage windows came the blue flicker of televisions. Kincaid imagined the pensioners, all women that he had seen, having their evening meals early so that they could settle down in front of the box, uninterrupted, isolated from themselves as well as one another. He gave a tiny shudder, shaking off the wave of melancholy that threatened him, like a dog coming out of water. Why should he begrudge them their comfort, after all?

Beside him, Sharon stirred and pulled the cardigan a little closer about her. Rubbing his hands together to warm them, he turned to her, saying briskly, 'One more thing, Sharon, and then you'd better go in before you catch a chill. We have a witness who's certain he saw Connor at the Red Lion in Wargrave after he left you that night. Con met a man who fits the description of Tommy Godwin, an old friend of the Ashertons. Do you know him, or did you ever hear Con mention him?'

He could almost hear her thinking as she sat beside him in the dark, and he thought that if he looked closely enough he would see her brow furrowed in concentration. 'No,' she said eventually, 'I never did.' She turned to him, pulling her knee up on the bench so that she could face him directly. 'Did they . . . were they having a row?'

'According to the witness, it was not a particularly friendly meeting. Why?'

She put her hand to her mouth, nibbling at the nail of her index finger. Nail-biting was a form of self-mutilation that had never tempted Kincaid, and it always made him wince for the damaged flesh. He waited, lacing his own fingers together to stop himself from pulling her hand away from her mouth.

'I thought it was me made him angry,' she said in a rush. 'He came back that night. He wasn't pleased to see me – he wanted to know why hadn't I gone back to Gran's, like I said.' She touched Kincaid's sleeve. 'That's why I didn't say anything before. I felt such a bloody fool.'

Kincaid patted her hand. 'Why hadn't you gone home?'

'Oh, I did. But Gran's bridge finished early – one of the old ladies felt a bit ill – so I came back. I was sorry I'd left in a huff before. I thought he'd be glad to see me and we could—' She gulped, unable to go on, but what she had hoped was painfully clear to Kincaid without any further elaboration.

'Was he drunk?'

'He'd had a few, but he wasn't proper pissed, not really.'

'And he didn't tell you where he'd been or who he'd seen?'

Sharon shook her head. ''E said, "What are you doing here?" and walked past me like I was a piece of bloody furniture or something.'

'Then what? Tell me bit by bit, everything you can remember.'

Closing her eyes, she thought for a moment, then began obediently, 'He went into the kitchen and fixed himself a drink—'

'Not to the drinks trolley?' asked Kincaid, remembering the plethora of bottles.

'Oh, that was just for show. Company. Con drank whisky and he always kept a bottle on the kitchen counter,' she said, then continued more slowly. 'He came back into the sitting room and I noticed he kept rubbing at his throat. "Are you all right?" I asked him. "You're not feeling ill, love?" But he didn't answer. He went upstairs into the study and closed the door.'

'Did you follow him?' Kincaid asked when she lapsed into silence.

'I didn't know what to do. I'd started up the stairs when I heard him talking – he must have rung someone.' She looked at Kincaid and even in the dim reflected light he could see her distress. 'He was laughing. That's what I couldn't understand. Why would he laugh when he'd hardly said boo to me?

'When he came downstairs again, he said, "I'm going out, Shar. Lock up when you leave." Well, I'd had enough by that time, I can tell you. I told him to lock his own bloody door – I wasn't hanging about to be treated like a bloody tart, was I? I told him if he wanted to see me he could pick up the sodding phone and ring me, and I'd think about it if I hadn't anything better to do.'

'What did Connor say to that?'

''E just stood there, his face all blank, like he hadn't heard a word I said.'

Kincaid had heard Sharon in full fury, and he thought Connor must have been very preoccupied indeed. 'And did you? Leave, I mean?'

'Well, I had to, didn't I? What else was I to do?'

'The scene definitely called for a grand exit,' said Kincaid, smiling.

Sharon smiled back a little reluctantly. 'I slammed the bloody door so hard I ripped my nail right off. Hurt like hell, too.'

'So you didn't actually see him leave the flat?'

'No. I stood about for a minute. I guess I still hoped he'd come after me, say he was sorry. Silly cow,' she added bitterly.

'You weren't silly at all. You had no way of explaining Con's behaviour – in your place I think I'd have done exactly the same.'

She took a moment to absorb this, then said haltingly, 'Mr Kincaid, do you know why Con said those things . . . why he treated me like that?'

Wishing he had some comfort to give her, he said, 'No,' then added with more certainty than he felt, 'but I'm going to find out. Come on, let's get you inside. Your gran'll have the police out after you.'

Her smile was as weak as his little joke, and manufactured simply to please him, he felt sure. As they reached the cottage door, he asked, 'What time was it when you left Con, Sharon? Do you remember?'

She nodded at the massive tower behind them. 'Church clock struck eleven just as I came round the Angel.'

After he left Sharon, it seemed the most natural thing in the world to Kincaid that he should continue down the hill and along the river to Julia's flat. He would collect Sharon's things while he was thinking of it, and while he was there he'd question Julia again about her movements after the gallery closed that night.

Or so said the rational, logical part of his mind. Some other part stood back and watched the machinations of the first, an amused and taunting spectator. Why didn't he admit he hoped he might sit with her, watching the warm lamplight reflect from the shining curve of her hair? Or admit that he wanted to see again the way her lips curved up at the corners when she found something he said amusing? Or that his skin still remembered the touch of her fingers against his face?

'Bollocks!' Kincaid said aloud, banishing the spectator to the recesses of his mind. He needed to clear up a few points, that was all, and his interest in Julia Swann was purely professional.

The wind that earlier cleared the sky had died at sunset, leaving the evening still and hushed, waiting expectantly. Lights reflecting on the water's surface made it look ice-solid, and as he passed the Angel pub and walked along the embankment, he felt the chill air hovering over the river like a cloud.

As he came opposite Trevor Simons's gallery, he

saw Simons come out of the door. Hurriedly crossing the street, Kincaid found him still bent over the latch. He touched his arm. 'Mr Simons. Having a bit of trouble with your lock?'

Simons jumped, dropping the heavy key-ring he'd held in his hand. 'Christ, Superintendent, you gave me a fright.' He stooped to retrieve the keys and added, 'It does stick a bit, I'm afraid, but I've done it now.'

'On your way home?' Kincaid said pleasantly, wondering even as he asked if Simons's itinerary included a visit to Julia. Now that she was reinstalled in the flat just down the road, they would have no more need of furtive meetings in the workshop behind the gallery.

Simons stood a little awkwardly, holding his keys in one hand and a portfolio in the other. 'Yes, actually. Did you need to see me?'

'There were one or two things,' Kincaid answered, making a decision as he spoke. 'Why don't we go across the road and have a drink?'

'It won't take more than half an hour, will it?' Simons looked at his watch. 'We're going out for a meal tonight. My wife's sent the children to friends – it's more than my life's worth to be late.'

Kincaid hastened to reassure him. 'We'll just nip across to the Angel. I promise we won't be long.'

They found the pub busy, but it was a sedate crowd – made up, judged Kincaid, mostly of professional people having a quick drink before making their way home after work.

'Nice place,' Kincaid said, as they settled comfortably at a table by one of the windows overlooking the river. 'Cheers. I admit I've developed rather a taste for Brakspear's Special.' Tasting his beer, he watched his companion curiously. Simons had sounded a bit embarrassed about his dinner engagement, yet it had the ring of truth. 'Sounds as though you and your wife have quite a romantic evening planned,' Kincaid said, fishing.

Simons looked away, his earlier discomfort more evident. The silver in his thick brown hair caught the light as he ran a hand through it. 'Well, Superintendent, you know what women are like. She'll be very disappointed if I don't participate with enthusiasm.'

A boat motored slowly under the Henley Bridge, its port and starboard lights gleaming steadily. Kincaid idly pushed his beer mat back and forth with one finger, then looked up at Simons. 'Did you know that Julia's moved back into her flat?'

'Yes. Yes, I did. She rang me yesterday.' Before Kincaid could respond, Simons said more forcefully, 'Look, Superintendent. I took your advice the other day. I told my wife about . . . what happened with Julia.' Simons's fine-boned face looked drawn with exhaustion, and as he sipped his whisky and water, his hand trembled slightly.

'And?' Kincaid said when he didn't continue.

'She was shocked. And hurt, as you can imagine,' Simons said quietly. 'I think that the damage won't be easy to repair. We've had a good marriage, probably better than most. I should never have been so careless with it.'

'You sound as though you don't mean to continue things with Julia,' Kincaid said, knowing it was none of his business, and that his investigation hardly justified crossing the boundary of good manners.

Simons shook his head. 'I can't. Not if I mean to mend things with my wife. I've told Julia.'

'How did she take it?'

'Oh, she'll be all right.' Simons smiled with the same gentle, self-deprecating humour Kincaid had seen before. 'I was never more than a passing fancy to Julia, I'm afraid. I've probably saved her the bother of having to say, "Sorry, old dear, but it was only a bit of a lark."'

It occurred to Kincaid that Simons, like Sharon Doyle, was probably glad of a non-partisan ear, and he pushed his advantage. 'Were you in love with her?'

'I'm not sure "love" and "Julia" exist in the same vocabulary, Mr Kincaid. I've been married almost twenty years – to me love means darned socks and "Whose turn is it to take out the rubbish, darling?"' Grinning, he drank a little more of his whisky. 'It may not be exciting, but you know where you are—' He sobered suddenly. 'Or at least you should, unless one of you behaves like an ass.

'I was infatuated with Julia, fascinated, entranced; but I'm not sure one could ever get close enough to love her.'

As much as Kincaid disliked the necessity, he dug in, his voice suddenly harsh. 'Were you infatuated enough to lie for her? Are you sure she didn't leave the gallery when the party finished that night? Did she tell you that she had to see someone? That she'd be back in an hour or two?'

The pleasant humour vanished from Trevor Simons's face. He finished his whisky and set his glass down deliberately, carefully, in the exact centre of its mat. 'She did not.

'I may be an adulterer, Superintendent, but I'm not a liar. And if you think Julia had anything to do with Connor's death, I can tell you you're barking up the wrong tree. She was with me from the time we closed up the gallery until daybreak. And having burned my bridges, so to speak, by confessing to my wife, I'll testify to that in court if I must.'

Chapter Thirteen

Kincaid rang the bell and waited. He rang again, shifting his weight a bit from foot to foot and whistling under his breath. No sound came from inside the flat, and he turned away, feeling an unexpected stab of disappointment.

The sound of the door opening stopped him. When he turned back he found Julia looking at him silently, registering neither pleasure nor dismay at his presence. She lifted the wineglass she held in a mock salute. 'Superintendent. Is this a social call? You can't join me if you're going to play the heavy.'

'My, my,' he said, taking in the faded red jersey she wore over black leggings, 'an outbreak of colour. Is this significant?'

'Sometimes one has to abandon one's principles when one hasn't done laundry,' she answered rather owlishly. 'Do come in – what will you think of my manners? Of course,' she added as she stepped back into the sitting room, 'it might be my concession to mourning.'

'A reverse statement?' Kincaid asked, following her into the kitchen.

'Something like that. I'll get you a glass. The wine's upstairs.' She opened a cupboard and stood up on her toes, stretching to reach a shelf. Kincaid noticed that she wore thick socks but no shoes, and her feet looked small and unprotected. 'Con arranged everything in the kitchen to suit himself,' she said, snagging a glass. 'And it seems whenever I want anything it's always just out of reach.'

Kincaid felt as if he'd barged in on a party in progress. 'Were you expecting someone? There's no need for me to interrupt – I only wanted a quick word with you, and I thought I'd pick up Sharon Doyle's things as well.'

Julia turned round and stood with her back against the counter, looking up at him, holding both glasses against her chest. 'I wasn't expecting a soul, Superintendent. There's not a soul to expect.' She chuckled a little at her own humour. 'Come on. We had graduated from "Superintendent", hadn't we?' she added over her shoulder as she led him back through the sitting room. 'I suppose I'm the one backsliding.'

She wasn't more than a bit tipsy, Kincaid decided as he climbed the stairs after her. Her balance and co-ordination were still good, although she moved a little more carefully than usual. As they passed the first landing he glimpsed the tumbled, unmade bed through the bedroom's open doorway, but the study door still stood tightly shut.

When they reached the studio he saw that the lamps were lit and the blinds drawn, and it seemed to him that the room had acquired another layer of Julia's personality in the twenty-four hours since he'd seen it last. She had been working and a partially finished painting was pinned to the board on her worktable. Kincaid recognized the plant from the rambles of his Cheshire boyhood – speedwell, the gentian-blue flowers along the pathside that were said to 'speed you well' upon your journey. He also remembered his dismay in discovering that its beauty could not be held captive – the delicate blooms wilted and died within minutes of picking.

The rest of the table's surface held open botanical texts, crumpled papers and several used glasses. The room smelled of cigarette smoke, and very faintly of Julia's perfume.

She padded across the Persian carpet and sank to the floor in front of the armchair, which she used as a backrest. Beside the chair were Julia's ashtray, close to overflowing, and an ice bucket holding a bottle of white wine. She filled Kincaid's glass. 'Sit down, for heaven's sake, Duncan. You can't hold a funeral celebration standing up.'

Kincaid lowered himself to the floor and accepted his drink. 'Is that what we're doing?'

'With a bloody good Cap d'Antibes, too. Con would have liked a wake, don't you think? He was all for Irish tradition.' Tasting what remained of her wine, she made a face. 'Warm.' She refilled her glass, then lit a cigarette. 'I'm going to cut down, I promise,' she said in anticipation of Kincaid's protest, smiling.

'What are you doing, barricading yourself up here like this, Julia? The rest of the house doesn't look like anyone's been in it.' He examined her face, deciding that the shadows under her eyes were more pronounced than they had been the day before. 'Have you eaten anything?'

Shrugging, she said, 'There were still some bits and pieces in the fridge. Con's sort of bits, of course. I would have settled for bread and jam. I suppose I hadn't realized – ' she paused to draw on her cigarette – 'that it would have become Con's house. Not mine. Yesterday I spent most of the day cleaning, but it didn't seem to make any difference – he's everywhere.' She made a circular gesture with her head, indicating the studio. 'Except here. If he ever came up here, he left no traces.'

'What makes you want to eradicate him so thoroughly?'

'I told you before, didn't I?' She knitted her brow and gazed at him over the rim of her glass, as if she couldn't quite remember. 'Con was a first-class shit,' she said, without heat. 'A drinker, a gambler, a womanizer, a lout with a load of Irish blarney that he thought would get him anything he wanted – why would I want to be reminded of him?'

Kincaid raised a sceptical eyebrow and sipped his wine. 'Can we attribute this to Con, too?' he asked, tasting its crisp delicacy against the roof of his mouth.

'He had good taste, and he was surprisingly adept at finding a bargain,' Julia admitted. 'A legacy of his upbringing, I would imagine.'

Kincaid wondered if Connor's attraction to Sharon Doyle stemmed from his upbringing as well – a spoiled only son of a doting mum might have considered devotion his due. He hoped that Con had also seen her value.

Uncannily echoing his thoughts, Julia said, 'The mistress – what did you say she's called?'

'Sharon. Sharon Doyle.'

Julia nodded, as if it fit an image in her mind. 'Blonde and a little plump, young, not very sophisticated?'

'Have you seen her?' Kincaid asked, surprised.

'Didn't need to.' Julia's smile was rueful. 'I only imagined my antithesis,' she said, having a little difficulty with the consonants. 'Look at me.'

Kincaid found it all too easy to oblige. Framed in the dark bell of her hair, her face revealed humour and intelligence in equal measure. He said, teasing her, 'I'll only follow your hypothesis so far. Are you suggesting I should regard you as ancient and world-weary?'

'Well, not quite.' This time she gave him the full benefit of her grin, and Kincaid thought again how odd it seemed to see Sir Gerald's smile translated so directly onto her thin face. 'But you do see what I mean?'

'Why should Connor have wanted someone as unlike you as he could find?'

She hesitated a moment, then shook her head, shying away from it. 'This girl – Sharon – how is she taking it?'

'I'd say she's coping, just.'

'Do you think it would help if I spoke to her?' She

ground out her cigarette and added more lightly, 'I've never quite been sure of the proper protocol in these situations.'

Kincaid sensed how vulnerable Sharon would feel in Julia's presence, and yet she had no one with whom she could share her grief. He had seen stranger alliances formed. 'I don't know, Julia. I think she'd like to attend Connor's funeral. I'll tell her she's welcome, if you like. But I wouldn't expect too much.'

'Con will have told her horror tales about me, I'm sure,' Julia said, nodding. 'It's only natural.'

Regarding her quizzically, Kincaid said, 'You're certainly feeling magnanimous tonight. Is it something in the air? I just had a word with Trevor Simons and he was in the same frame of mind.' He paused, swallowing a little more of his wine, and when Julia didn't respond, he went on, 'He's says he's willing to swear under oath that you were together the entire night, regardless of the damage to his marriage.'

She sighed. 'Trev's a decent sort. Surely it won't come to that?' Wrapping her arms around her calves, she rested her chin on her knees and looked at Kincaid steadily. 'You can't really think I killed poor Con, can you?' When Kincaid didn't answer she lifted her head and said, '*You* don't think that, do you, Duncan?'

Kincaid ran the evidence through his mind. Connor had died between the closing of the gallery show and the very early hours of the morning, the time for which Trevor Simons had given Julia a cast-iron alibi. Simons was a decent sort, as Julia had so aptly put it, and Kincaid had disliked goading him, but he felt more certain now than ever that he would not have compromised himself by lying for Julia.

But even as he set out these facts, he knew that they had little to do with what he felt. He studied her face. Could one see guilt, if one had the right skills, the right information? He had sensed it often enough, and his rational mind told him the assessment must be based on a combination of subliminal cues – body language, smell, shadings in the voice. But he also knew that there was an element to it that transcended the rational – call it a hunch, or a feeling, it didn't matter. It was based on an innate and inexplicable knowledge of another human being, and his knowledge of Julia went bone-deep. He was as certain of her innocence as of his own.

Slowly, he shook his head. 'No. I don't think you killed Connor. But someone did, and I'm not sure we're getting any closer to it.' His back had begun to ache and he stretched, recrossing his legs. 'Do you know why Connor would have had dinner with Tommy Godwin the night he died?'

Julia sat up straight, her eyes widening in astonishment. 'Tommy? Our Tommy? I've known Tommy since I was this high.' She held out a hand, toddler height. 'I can't imagine anything less likely than the two of them having a social get-together. Tommy never quite approved of Con, and I'm sure he made it clear. Very politely, of course,' she added fondly. 'If Con had meant to see Tommy, surely he would have said?'

'According to Godwin, Con wanted his old job back, and thought he might help.'

Julia shook her head. 'That's piffle. Con had a screaming nervous breakdown. The firm wouldn't have considered it.' Her eyes were peat-dark, and guileless.

Kincaid closed his eyes for a moment, in the hope that removing her face from his sight would allow him to gather his thoughts. When he opened them again he found her watching him. 'What did Connor say that day, Julia? It seems to me that his behaviour only became out of the ordinary after he left you at lunchtime. I think you've not quite told me the whole truth.'

She looked away from him, fumbling for her cigarettes, then pushed the packet away and stood up, as graceful as a dancer. Moving to the table, she unscrewed the top of a paint tube and squeezed a drop of deep blue colour onto her palette. Choosing a fine brush, she dabbed a little of the colour onto the painting. 'Can't seem to get the bloody thing quite right, and I'm tired of looking at it. Maybe if I—'

'Julia.'

She stopped, paintbrush frozen in mid-air. After a long moment, she rinsed the brush and placed it carefully beside the drawing, then turned to him. 'It began ordinarily enough, just the way I told you. A little row about money, about the flat.' She came back to the arm of the chair.

'Then what happened?' He moved closer to her and touched her hand, urging her on.

Julia captured his hand between her palms and held it tightly. She looked down, rubbing the back of his hand with her fingertips. 'He begged me,' she said so softly Kincaid had to strain to hear. 'He literally got down on his knees and begged me. Begged me to take him back, begged me to love him. I don't know what set him off that day. I'd thought he had pretty well accepted things.'

'What did you tell him?'

'That it was no use. That I meant to divorce him as soon as the two-year limit had passed, if he still refused to co-operate.' She met Kincaid's eyes. 'I was perfectly beastly to him, and it wasn't his fault. None of it was.'

'What are you talking about?' Kincaid said, startled enough to forget for a moment the sensation of her fingers against his skin.

'It was all my fault, from the very beginning. I should never have married Con. I knew it wasn't fair, but I was in love with the idea of getting married, and I suppose I thought we'd muddle through somehow.' She laughed, letting go his hand. 'But the more he loved me, the more he needed, the less I had to give. In the end there was nothing at all.' Softly, she added, 'Except pity.'

'Julia,' Kincaid said sharply, 'you were not responsible for Connor's needs. There are people who will suck you dry, no matter how much you give. You couldn't—'

'You don't understand.' She slipped from the arm of the chair, moving restlessly away from him, then turned back as she reached the worktable. 'I knew when I married Con I couldn't love him. Not him, not anyone, not even Trev, who hasn't asked for much except honesty and affection. I can't, do you see? I'm not capable.'

'Don't be absurd, Julia,' Kincaid said, pushing to his feet. 'Of course you—'

'No.' She stopped him with the one flat word. 'I can't. Because of Matty.'

The despair in her voice banished his anger as quickly as it had come. He went to her and drew her gently to him, stroking her hair as she laid her head against his shoulder. Her slender body fitted into the curve of his arms as easily as if it had always been there, and her hair felt as silky as feathers against the palm of his hand. She smelled faintly, unexpectedly, of lilac. Kincaid took a breath, steadying himself against the wave of dizziness that swept over him, forcing himself to concentrate on the matter at hand. 'What has Matty to do with it, Julia?'

'Everything. I loved him, too, you see, but that never seemed to occur to anyone . . . except Plummy, I suppose. She knew. I was ill, you know . . . afterwards. But it gave me time to think, and it was then I decided that nothing would ever hurt me like that again.' She pulled away from him just enough to look up into his face. 'It's not worth it. Nothing is.'

'But surely the alternative – lifetime of emotional isolation – is worse?'

She came back into his arms, resting her cheek in the hollow of his shoulder. 'It's bearable, at least,' she said, her voice muffled, and he felt her breath, warm through the fabric of his shirt. 'I tried to explain it to Con that day – why I could never give him what he wanted . . . a family, children. I had nothing to go by, you see, no blueprint for an ordinary life. And a child

– I could never take that risk. You do you see that, don't you?'

He saw himself with uncomfortable clarity, curling up like a wounded hedgehog after Vic had shattered his safe and comfortable existence. He had protected himself from risk as surely as Julia. But she, at least, had been honest with herself, while he had used work, with the convenient demands of a cop's life, as an excuse for not making emotional commitments. 'I do see it,' he said softly, 'but I don't agree with it.'

He rubbed her back, gently kneading the knotted muscles, and her shoulder blades felt sharp under his hands. 'Did Connor understand?'

'It only made him more angry. It was then I was beastly to him. I said—' She stopped, shaking her head, and her hair tickled Kincaid's nose. 'Horrid things, really horrid. I'm so ashamed.' Harshly, she added, 'It's my fault he's dead. I don't know what he did after he left Badger's End that day, but if I hadn't sent him away so cruelly—' She was crying now, her words coming in hiccuping gulps.

Kincaid took her face in his hands and wiped the tears from her cheeks with his thumbs. 'Julia, Julia. You don't know that. You can't know that. You were not responsible for Connor's behaviour, or for his death.' He looked down at her, and in her tousled hair and tear-streaked face he saw again the child of his vision, alone with her grief in the narrow white bed. After a moment he said, 'Nor were you responsible for Matthew's death. Look at me, Julia. Do you hear me?'

'How can you know that?' she asked fiercely.

'Everyone thought . . . Mummy and Daddy never forgave—'

'Those who knew and loved you never held you responsible, Julia. I've spoken to Plummy. And the vicar. You're the one who has never forgiven yourself. That's too heavy a burden for anyone to carry for twenty years. Let it go.'

For a long moment she held his gaze, then he felt the tension drain from her body. She returned her head to his shoulder, slipped her arms round his waist and leaned against him, letting him support her weight.

Thus they stood, quietly, until Kincaid became aware of every point where their bodies made contact. For all her slenderness, her body seemed suddenly, undeniably solid against his, and her breasts pressed firmly against his chest. He could hear his blood pounding in his ears.

Julia gave a hiccuping sigh and raised her head a little. 'I've gone and made your shirt all soggy,' she said, rubbing at the damp patch on his shoulder. Then she tilted her head so that she could look into his face and added, her voice husky with suppressed laughter, 'Does Scotland Yard always render its services so . . . enthusiastically?'

He stepped back, flushing with embarrassment, wishing he had worn less-revealing jeans rather than slacks. 'I'm sorry. I didn't mean—'

'It's all right,' she said, drawing him to her again. 'I don't mind. I don't mind at all.'

Chapter Fourteen

He woke to the sound of Tony's voice. 'Morning tea, Mr Kincaid,' he said as he tapped on the door and entered. 'And a message for you from Sergeant Makepeace at High Wycombe. Something about catching the bird you wanted?'

Kincaid sat up and ran a hand through his hair, then accepted the cup. 'Thanks, Tony,' he said to Tony's departing back. So they had found Kenneth Hicks and brought him in. They wouldn't be able to hold him long without cause. He should have checked in last night – hot tea sloshed onto his hand as awareness came flooding into his still groggy brain.

Last night. Julia. Oh, bloody hell. What have I done? How could he have been so unprofessional? With the thought came the memory of Trevor Simons's words, 'I never meant to do it. It was just . . . Julia,' and of his own rather supercilious comments about the man's loss of judgement.

He closed his eyes. Never, in all his years in the force, had he crossed that line, hadn't even thought, really, that he needed to protect himself from the temptation. Yet even in his self-reproach he found that there was a part of him that felt no remorse, for their union had been clean and healing, a solace for old wounds and a destruction of barriers too long held.

It was not until he entered the Chequers' dining room and saw Gemma seated alone at a table that he remembered the message he'd left for her yesterday. When had she arrived, and how long had she waited for him?

Sitting down across from her, he said, 'You're an early bird,' with as much aplomb as he could manage. 'We'll need to get on to High Wycombe as soon as we can. They're holding Kenneth Hicks for questioning.'

Gemma answered him without a trace of her usual morning cheeriness. 'I know. I've spoken to Jack Makepeace already.'

'Are you all right, Gemma?'

'Headache.' She nibbled without much enthusiasm on a piece of dry toast.

'Tony pour you one drink too many?' he said, attempting to humour her, but she merely shrugged. 'Look,' he said, wondering if the flush of guilt he felt were visible, 'I'm sorry about last night. I was . . . delayed.' She must have rushed here from London and waited for him, might even have been worried about him, and he had sent no word. 'I should have rung you. It was thoughtless of me.' Tilting his head, he studied her, measuring her mood. 'Shall I grovel some more? Would a bed of hot coals do?'

This time she smiled and he gave an inward sigh of relief. Searching for a change of subject, he said, 'Tell me about Tommy Godwin.' Just then his breakfast arrived, and he tucked into eggs and bacon while Gemma briefly recounted her interview.

'I took a statement, and I've had the forensics lads go over his flat and car.'

'I saw Sharon Doyle again, and Trevor Simons,' he said through a mouthful of toast. 'And Julia. Connor went home again after his scuffle with Tommy, Gemma. It looks as though Tommy Godwin's out of the frame unless we can prove he met Con again later. He did ring someone from the flat, though – problem is, we've no earthly idea who it was.'

Julia. There had been a familiarity, an unconscious intimacy, in the way Kincaid said her name. Gemma tried to concentrate on her driving, tried to ignore the certainty that was growing in the pit of her stomach. Surely she was imagining things? And what if it were true? Why should it matter so much to her if Duncan Kincaid had formed a less-than-professional relationship with a suspect in a murder investigation? It was common enough – she'd seen it happen with other officers – and she'd never thought he was infallible. Had she?

'Grow up, Gemma,' she said under her breath. He was human, and male, and she should never have forgotten that even gods sometimes have feet of clay.

But those reminders made her feel no less miserable, and she was thankful when the High Wycombe roundabouts claimed all her attention.

'I've had Hicks warming up nicely for you the last half-hour,' Jack Makepeace said in greeting when they found him in his office. He shook their hands, and Gemma thought he gave hers an extra little squeeze. 'Thought it would do him a world of good. Too bad he didn't quite manage to finish his breakfast.' Makepeace winked at Gemma. 'He's made his phone call – his mum, or so he says – but the cavalry's not come to the rescue.'

Having been briefed earlier on the telephone by Makepeace, Kincaid had brought Gemma up to date in the car and suggested that she begin the interview. 'He doesn't care for women,' Kincaid said as Makepeace left them at the nondescript door of Room A. 'I want you to upset his balance a bit, prime him for me.'

One interview room seldom differed much from another – they could be expected to meet some variation of small and square, and to smell of stale cigarette smoke and human sweat, but when Gemma entered the room she swallowed convulsively, fighting the instinctive urge to cover her nose. Unshaven and all too obviously unbathed, Kenneth Hicks reeked of fear.

'Christ,' Kincaid muttered in Gemma's ear as he came in behind her. 'We should've brought masks.' He coughed, then added at full volume as he pulled out a chair for Gemma, 'Hullo, Kenneth. Like the accommodation? Not quite up to the Hilton, I'm afraid, but then what can you do?'

'Go fuck yourself,' Hicks said succinctly. His voice was nasal, and Gemma pegged his accent as South London.

Kincaid shook his head as he sat down beside Gemma, facing Hicks across the narrow laminated table. 'I'm disappointed in you, Kenneth. I thought you had better manners. We'll just record our little conversation,' he said, pushing the switch on the tape recorder. 'If you don't mind, of course. You don't mind, do you, Kenneth?'

Gemma studied Kenneth Hicks while Kincaid nattered pleasantly on and fiddled with the recorder. Hicks's narrow, acne-spotted face seemed permanently stamped with a surly expression. In spite of the warmth of the room, he had kept on a black leather bomber jacket, and he rubbed nervously at his nose and chin as Kincaid's patter continued. There seemed something vaguely familiar about him, and Gemma frowned with frustration as it hovered on the fringe of her mind.

'Sergeant James will be asking you a few questions,' Kincaid said, pushing his chair back from the table a bit. He folded his arms and stretched out his legs, as if he might catnap through the interview.

'Kenneth,' she said pleasantly, when they had completed the recorded preliminaries, 'why don't you make it easy for everyone and tell us exactly what you were doing the night Connor Swann was killed?'

Hicks darted a glance at Kincaid. 'I already told the

other bloke, the one as brought me in here. Big ginger-haired berk.'

'You told Sergeant Makepeace that you were drinking with friends at the Fox and Hounds in Henley until closing, after which you continued the party in the friends' flat,' said Gemma, and the sound of her voice brought Hicks's eyes back to her. 'Is that right?' she added a little more forcefully.

'Yeah, that's right. That's just like I told him.' Hicks seemed to gain a little confidence from her recital. He relaxed in his chair and stared at Gemma, letting his eyes rest for a long moment on her breasts.

She smiled sweetly at him and made a show of consulting her notebook. 'Thames Valley CID took statements last night from the friends you named, Kenneth, and unfortunately none of them seems to remember you being there at all.'

Hicks's skin turned the colour of the room's nicotine-stained walls as the blood drained from his face. 'I'll kill 'em, the friggin' little shits. They're lying their bloody heads off.' He looked from Gemma to Kincaid, and, apparently finding no reassurance in their expressions, said a little more frantically, 'You can't do me for this. I never saw Con after we had that drink at the Fox. I swear I didn't.'

Gemma flipped another page in her notebook. 'You may have to, unless you can come up with a little better accounting of your movements after half-past ten. Connor made a telephone call from his flat around then, and afterwards said he meant to go out.'

'Who says he did?' asked Hicks, with more shrewdness than Gemma had credited him.

'Never mind that. Do you want to know what I think, Kenneth?' Gemma asked, leaning towards him and lowering her voice confidentially. 'I think Connor rang you and asked you to meet him at the lock. You argued and Connor fell in. It could happen to anybody, couldn't it, Ken? Did you try to help him, or were you afraid of the water?' Her tone said she understood and would forgive him anything.

'I never!' Hicks pushed his chair back from the table. 'That's a bleedin' lie. And how the bleedin' hell am I supposed to have got there without a car?'

'Connor picked you up in his car,' Gemma said reasonably, 'and afterwards you hitched a ride back to Henley.'

'I didn't, I tell you, and you can't prove I did.'

Unfortunately, Gemma knew from Thames Valley's reports that he was correct – Connor's car had been freshly washed and vacuumed and forensics had found no significant traces. 'Then where were you? Tell the truth this time.'

'I've told you already. I was at the Fox, then at this bloke's. Jackie – he's called Jackie Fawcett.'

Kincaid recrossed his ankles lazily and spoke for the first time since Gemma had begun. 'Then why wouldn't your mates give you a nice, tidy alibi, Kenneth? I can see two possibilities – the first is that you're lying, and the second is that they don't like you, and I must say I don't know which I think is the more likely.

Did you help out other friends the same way you helped Connor?'

'Don't know what you're on about.' Hicks pulled a battered cigarette pack from the pocket of his jacket. He shook it, then probed inside it with thumb and forefinger before crumpling it in disgust.

Gemma took up the thread again. 'That's what you argued about, isn't it, Kenneth? When you met Con after lunch, did you tell him he had to pay up? Did he agree to meet you later that evening? Then when he turned up without the money, you fought with him.' She embroidered as she went along.

An element of pleading crept into Hicks's voice. 'He didn't owe me nothin', I told you.' He kept his eyes fixed anxiously on Kincaid, and Gemma wondered what Kincaid had done to put the wind up him like that.

Straightening up in his chair, Kincaid said, 'So you're telling me that Con paid you off, and yet I happen to know that Con was so hard up he couldn't make the mortgage on the flat. I think you're lying. I think you said something to Connor over that little social pint at the Fox that sent him over the edge. What was it, Kenneth? Did you threaten to have your boss call out his muscle?' He stood up and leaned forward with his hands on the table.

'I never threatened him. It wasn't like that,' Hicks squeaked, shrinking away from Kincaid.

'But he did still owe you money?'

Hicks looked at them, sweat beading on his upper lip, and Gemma could see him calculating which way to turn next. *Rat in a trap*, she thought, and pressed her lips together to conceal her satisfaction. They waited in silence, until finally Hicks said, 'Maybe he did. So what? I never threatened him like you said.'

Moving restlessly back and forth in the small space before the table, Kincaid said, 'I don't believe you. Your boss was going to take it out of your skin if you didn't come up with the ready – I don't believe you didn't use a little persuasion.' He smiled at Hicks as he came near him again. 'And the trouble with persuasion is that sometimes it gets out of hand. Isn't that so, Kenneth?'

'No. I don't know. I mean—'

'Are you saying that it wasn't an accident? That you intended to kill him?'

'That's not what I meant.' Hicks swallowed and wiped his hands on his thighs. 'I only made him a suggestion, a proposition, like.'

Kincaid stopped pacing and stood very still with his hands in his pockets, watching Hicks. 'That sounds very interesting, Kenneth. What sort of proposition?'

Gemma held her breath as Hicks teetered on the edge of confession, afraid any move might nudge him in the wrong direction. Listening to the ragged cadence of his breathing, she offered up a silent little incantation to the god of interviews.

Hicks spoke finally, with the rush of release, and his words were venomous. 'I knew about him from the first, him and his hoity-toity Ashertons. You would've thought they were the bleedin' Royals, the way he talked, but I knew better. That Dame Caroline's just a jumped-up tart, no better than she should be. And all the fuss they made over that kid what drowned, well, he wasn't even Sir Gerald's kid, was he, just a bleedin' little bastard.' Matty. He was talking about Matty, Gemma thought, trying to make sense of it.

Kincaid sat down again, pulling his chair up until he could rest his elbows on the table. 'Let's start again from the beginning, shall we, Kenneth?' he said very quietly, very evenly, and Gemma shivered. 'You told Connor that Matthew Asherton was illegitimate, have I got that right?'

Hicks's Adam's apple bobbed in his skinny throat as he swallowed and nodded, then looked in appeal at Gemma. He'd got more than he bargained for, she thought, wondering suddenly what Kincaid might have done if she hadn't been in the room and the tape recorder running.

'How could you possibly know that?' Kincaid asked, still soft as velvet.

''Cause my uncle Tommy was his bleedin' dad, that's how.'

In the silence that followed, Kenneth Hicks's ragged, adenoidal breathing sounded loud in Gemma's ears. She opened her mouth, but found she couldn't quite formulate any words.

'Your uncle Tommy? Do you mean Tommy Godwin?' Kincaid said finally, not quite managing to control his surprise.

Gemma felt as if a giant hand were squeezing her

diaphragm. She saw again the silver-framed photograph of Matthew Asherton – the blond hair and the impish grin on his friendly face. She remembered Tommy's voice as he spoke of Caroline, and she wondered why she had not seen it before.

'I heard him telling me mum about it when the kid drowned,' said Hicks. He must have interpreted the shock in their faces as disbelief, because he added on a rising note of panic, 'I swear. I never said nothin', but after I met Con and he went on about them, I remembered the names.'

Gemma felt a wave of nausea sweep over her as the corollary sank in. 'I don't believe you. You can't be Tommy Godwin's nephew, it's just not possible,' she said hotly, thinking of Tommy's elegance, and of his courteous patience as she'd taken him through his statement at the Yard, but even as she resisted the idea, she felt again that odd sense of familiarity. Could it be something in the line of the nose, or the set of the jaw?

'You go to Clapham and ask me mum, then. She'll tell you soon enough—'

'You said you made Connor a proposition,' Kincaid dropped the words into Hicks's protest like stones in a pool. 'Just what was it, exactly?'

Hicks rubbed his nose and sniffed, shifting away from eye contact with them.

'Come on, sunshine, you can tell us all about it,' Kincaid urged him. 'Spit it out.'

'Well, the Ashertons have got to be pretty stinking with it, haven't they, what with their titles and all.

Always in the newspapers, in the gossip sections. So I figured they'd not like it put about that their kid was wrong side of the blanket, like.'

The intensity of Kincaid's anger seemed to have abated. 'Do I take it that you suggested to Connor that he should blackmail his own in-laws?' he asked, regarding Hicks with cool amusement. 'What about your own family? Did it occur to you that this might damage your uncle and your mother?'

'He wasn't to say I was the one told him,' Hicks said, as if that absolved him of any culpability.

'In other words, you didn't care how it might affect your uncle as long as it couldn't be traced back to you.' Kincaid smiled. 'Very noble of you, Kenneth. And how did Connor react to your little proposition?'

'He didn't believe me,' said Hicks, sounding aggrieved. 'Not right away. Then he thought about it a bit and he started to get all strung up. He said how much money was I thinking about, and when I told him "start with fifty-thousand quid and we'd split it, we could always ask for more later," he bloody laughed at me. Told me to shut my friggin' face and if I ever said another word about it, he'd kill me.' Hicks blinked his pale lashes and added, as if he still couldn't quite believe it, 'After everything I did for him!'

'He really didn't understand why Connor was angry with him,' Kincaid said to Gemma as they stood at the zebra crossing separating High Wycombe Station from the carpark where they had left Gemma's Escort. 'He's more than a few bricks short of a load in the morals department, is our Kenneth. I imagine it's only the fact that he's such a "timorous wee beastie" that's kept him to petty villainy – although I think the comparison does an injustice to the poor mouse,' he added, brushing at the sleeve of his jacket.

It was one of his favourites, Gemma noticed with the detachment that had overtaken her, a fine blue-and-grey wool that brought out the colour of his eyes. Why was he waffling on as if he'd never come across a small-time crook before?

The oncoming traffic came to a halt and they crossed on the stripes. Kincaid glanced at his watch as they reached the opposite pavement. 'I think we can manage a word with Tommy Godwin before lunch if we drive like the hounds of hell are after us. In fact,' he said as they reached the car and Gemma dug the Escort's keys out of her bag, 'since it looks as though we may not need to come back here, we'd better pick up our things and get my car back to London as well.'

Without a word, Gemma started the engine as he slid in beside her. She felt as though a kaleidoscope inside her head had shifted, jumbling the pieces so that they no longer made a recognizable pattern.

Kincaid touched her arm. 'Gemma, what is it? You've been like this since breakfast. If you really don't feel well—'

She turned towards him, tasting salt where she had bitten the inside of her lip. 'Did you believe him?'

'Who, Kenneth?' asked Kincaid, sounding a bit puzzled. 'Well, you have to admit, it does make sense of things that—'

'You haven't met Tommy. Oh, I can believe that Tommy was Matthew's dad,' she conceded, 'but not the rest of it. It's a cock-and-bull story if I ever—'

'Just improbable enough to be true, I'm afraid,' said Kincaid. 'And how else could he have found out about Tommy and Matthew? It gives us the missing piece, Gemma – motive. Connor confronted Tommy over dinner that night with what he'd found out, and Tommy killed him to keep him quiet.'

'I don't believe it,' Gemma said stubbornly, but even as she spoke little slivers of doubt crept into her mind. Tommy loved Caro, and Julia. You could see that. And Gerald he spoke of with respect and affection. Had protecting them been enough reason for murder? But even if she could swallow that premise, the rest still didn't make sense to her. 'Why would Connor have agreed to meet him at the lock?'

'Tommy promised to bring him money.'

Gemma stared blindly at the drizzle that had begun to coat the windscreen. 'Somehow I don't think that Connor wanted money,' she said with quiet certainty. 'And that doesn't explain why Tommy went to London to see Gerald. It can't have been to establish an alibi, not if Connor was still alive.'

'I think you're letting your liking for Tommy Godwin affect your judgement, Gemma. No one else has a shred of motive. Surely you can see—'

The anger that had been building in her all morning broke like a flash flood. 'You're the one that's blind,' she shouted at him. 'You're so besotted with Julia Swann that you won't consider that she might be implicated in Connor's death, when you know as well as I do that the husband or wife is most likely to be involved in a spouse's murder. How can you be sure Trevor Simons isn't lying to protect her? How do you know she didn't meet Connor before his dinner with Tommy, before the gallery opening, and arrange to meet him later that night? Maybe she thought a scandal involving her family would damage her career. Maybe she wanted to protect her parents. Maybe . . .' She ran down, her fury quickly spent, and sat waiting desolately for the inevitable backlash. This time she had really crossed over the line.

But instead of giving her the dressing-down she expected, Kincaid looked away. In the silence that followed she could hear the swishing of tyres on the damp road, and a faint ticking that seemed to be inside her own head. 'Perhaps you're right,' he said finally. 'Perhaps my judgement can't be trusted. But unless we come up with concrete physical evidence, it's all I have to go on with.'

They made the journey back to London in separate cars, meeting again at Kincaid's flat as they had arranged. The drizzle had followed them, and Kincaid drew the cover over the Midget before locking it. As he climbed into Gemma's car he said, 'You really must do something about your tyres, Gemma. The right rear is as bald as my grandad's head.' It was an often-repeated nag, and when she didn't rise to the bait, he sighed and continued, 'I rang LB House on the mobile phone. Tommy Godwin didn't come in today, said he was unwell. Didn't you say his flat was in Highgate?'

Gemma nodded. 'I have the address in my note-book. It's quite near here, I think.' A formless anxiety settled over her as she drove, and it was with relief that she spotted the block of flats. She left the car in the circular drive and hopped out, jiggling her foot in impatience as she waited for Kincaid to lock his side of the car and catch her up at the building's entrance.

'Christ, Gemma, is there a fire no one bothered to tell me about?' he said, but she ignored the barb and pushed through the frosted-glass doors. When they presented their identification to the doorman, he scowled and grudgingly directed them to take the lift to the fourth floor.

'Nice building,' Kincaid said as they rose creakingly in the lift. 'It's been well maintained, but not overly modernized.' The fourth-floor landing, tiled in a highly polished black-and-white geometric design, bore him out. 'Deco, if I'm not mistaken.'

Gemma, searching for the flat number, had only been listening with half an ear. 'What?' she asked, knocking at 4C.

'Art Deco. The building must date from between—'

The door swung open and Tommy Godwin regarded them quizzically. 'Mike rang me and said the Bill were paying another call. Very disapproving he was, too. I think he must have had unfortunate dealings with the law in a previous existence.' Godwin wore a paisley silk dressing gown and slippers, and his usually immaculate blond hair stood on end. 'You must be Superintendent Kincaid,' he said as he ushered them into the flat.

Having assured herself that Tommy hadn't gone and put his head in the oven or something equally silly, Gemma felt irrationally angry with him for having worried her. She followed slowly behind the men, looking about her. A small, sleek kitchen lay to her left, done in the same black and white as the landing. To her right, the sitting room carried on the theme, and through its bank of windows she could see a grey London spread before her. All the lines of the furniture were curved, but without fussiness, and the monochromatic color scheme was accented by a collection of pink frosted glass. Gemma found the room restful, and saw that its gentle order fitted Tommy like a second suit of clothes.

A Siamese cat posed on a chair beneath the window. Paws tucked under her chest, she regarded them with unblinking sapphire eyes.

'You're quite right, Superintendent,' Tommy said as she joined them, 'these flats were built in the early thirties, and they were the ultimate in advanced design for their day. They've held up remarkably well, unlike most of the post-war monstrosities. Sit down, please,' he added as he seated himself in a fan-shaped chair that complemented the swirling design on his dressing gown. 'Although I must say, I think it must have been a bit nerve-racking during the war, as high above the city as we are. You'd have felt like a sitting duck when the German bombers came over. A chink in the blackout and—'

'Tommy,' Gemma interrupted severely, 'they said at LB House that you weren't well. What is it?'

He ran a hand through his hair, and in the clear grey light Gemma saw the skin beginning to pouch a little under his eyes. 'Just a bit under the weather, Sergeant. I must admit that yesterday rather took its toll.' He stood and went to the drinks cabinet against the wall. 'Will you have a little sherry? It's appropriately near lunchtime, and I'm sure Rory Alleyn always accepted a sherry when he was interrogating suspects.'

'Tommy, this isn't a detective novel, for heaven's sake,' said Gemma, unable to contain her exasperation.

He turned to look at her, sherry decanter poised in one hand. 'I know, my dear. But it's my way of whistling in the dark.' The gentleness of his tone told her that he acknowledged her concern and was touched by it.

'I won't refuse a small one,' said Kincaid, and Tommy placed three glasses and the decanter on a small cocktail tray. The glasses were sensuously scalloped in the same delicate frosted pink as the fluted lampshades and vases Gemma had already noticed, and when she tasted the sherry it seemed to dissolve on her tongue like butter.

'After all,' said Tommy as he filled his own glass and returned to his chair, 'if I'm to take the blame for a crime I didn't commit, I might as well do it with good grace.'

'Yesterday you told me you'd been to Clapham to visit your sister.' Gemma paused to lick a trace of sherry from her lip, then went on more slowly. 'You didn't tell me about Kenneth.'

'Ah.' Tommy leaned against the chair back and closed his eyes. The light etched lines of exhaustion around his mouth and nose, delineated the pulse ticking in his throat. Gemma wondered why she hadn't seen the grey mixed in with the gold at his temples. 'Would you admit to Kenneth, given a choice?' Tommy said, without moving. 'No, don't answer that.' He opened his eyes and gave Gemma a valiant attempt at a smile. 'I take it you've met him?'

Gemma nodded.

'Then I can also assume that the whole sordid cat is out of the bag.'

'I think so, yes. You lied to me about your dinner with Connor. There wasn't any question of him going back to his old job. He confronted you with what Kenneth had told him.' This seemed to be her day for making accusations, she thought, finding that she took Tommy's deception personally, as if she'd been betrayed by a friend.

'A mere taradiddle, my dear—' Catching Gemma's expression he stopped and sighed. 'I'm sorry, Sergeant. You're quite right. What do you want to know?'

'Start from the beginning. Tell us about Caroline.'

'Ah, you mean from the very beginning.' Tommy swirled the sherry in his glass, watching it reflectively. 'I loved Caro, you see, with all the blind, single-minded recklessness of youth. Or perhaps age has nothing to do with it . . . I don't know. Our affair ended with Matthew's conception. I wanted her to leave Gerald and marry me. I would have loved Julia as my own child.' Pausing, he finished his sherry and returned the glass to the tray with deliberate care. 'It was a fantasy, of course. Caro was beginning a promising career, she was comfortably ensconced at Badger's End with the backing of the Asherton name and money. What had I to offer her? And there was Gerald, who has never behaved less than honourably in all the years I've known him.

'One makes what adjustments one must,' he said, smiling at Gemma. 'I've come to the conclusion that great tragedies are created by those who don't make it through the adjustment stage. We went on. As "Uncle Tommy" I was allowed to watch Matty grow up, and no one knew the truth except Caro and me.

'Then Matty died.'

Kincaid set his empty glass on the cocktail tray, and the click of glass against wood sounded loud as a shot in the silent room. Gemma gave him a startled glance – so focused had she been on Tommy that for a moment she had forgotten his presence. Neither of them spoke, and after a moment, Tommy continued.

'They shut me out. Closed ranks. In their grief Caro and Gerald had no room for anyone else's. As much as I loved Matty, I also saw that he was an ordinary little boy, with an ordinary little boy's faults and graces. The fact that he was also extraordinarily gifted meant no more to him than if he'd had an extra finger or been able to do lightning calculus in his head. Not so, Gerald and Caro. Do you understand that? Matty was the embodiment of their dreams, a gift God had sent them to mould in their own image.'

'So how did Kenneth come into this?' asked Gemma.

'My sister is not a bad sort. We all have our crosses – Kenneth is hers. She was still at school when our mother died. I was barely making ends meet at the time and wasn't able to do much for her, so I think she married Kenneth's dad out of desperation. As it turned out, he stayed around just long enough to produce his son and heir, then scarpered, leaving her with a baby to look after as well as herself.'

Gemma saw an echo of her own marriage in Tommy's account of his sister, and she shuddered at the thought that in spite of all her efforts, her own little son might turn out to be like Kenneth. It didn't bear thinking of. She finished her sherry in one long swallow, and as the warmth spread to her stomach and suffused her face, she remembered she'd gone without breakfast that morning.

Tommy shifted in his chair and smoothed the fold of his dressing gown across his lap. The cat seemed to take that as an invitation, leaping easily up and settling herself under his hands. His long, slender fingers stroked her chocolate-and-cream fur, and Gemma found she could not force herself to see those hands wrapped around Connor's throat. She looked up and met Tommy's eyes.

'After Matty died,' he said, 'I went to my sister and poured out the whole story. There was no one else.'

Clearing his throat, he reached for the decanter and poured himself a little more sherry. 'I don't remember that time very clearly, you understand, and I've just been piecing things together myself. Kenneth can't have been more than eight or nine, but I think he was born a sneak – possessive of his mother, always hiding and eavesdropping on adult conversations. I had no idea he was even in the house that day. Can you imagine how shocked I was when Connor told me what he had heard, and who had told him?'

'Why did Connor come to you?' asked Kincaid. 'Did he ask for money?'

'I don't think Connor knew what he wanted. He seemed to have got it into his head that Julia would have loved him if it hadn't been for Matty's death, and that if Julia had known the truth about Matty, things would have been different between them. I'm afraid he wasn't very coherent. "Bloody liars," he kept saying, "They're all bloody hypocrites."' Tommy laced his fingers together and sighed. 'I think Con had bought the Asherton family image lock, stock and barrel, and he couldn't bear the disillusionment. Or perhaps he just needed someone to blame for his own failure. They had hurt him and he had been powerless, unable to nick even their armour. Kenneth put the perfect weapon into his waiting hands.'

'Couldn't you have stopped him?' Kincaid asked.

Tommy smiled at him, undeceived by the casual tone. 'Not in the way you mean. I begged him, pleaded with him to keep quiet, for Gerald's and Caro's sake, and for Julia's, but that only seemed to make him angrier. In the end I even tussled with him, much to my shame.

'When I walked away from Connor I had made up my mind what to do. The lies had gone on long enough. Connor was right, in a sense – the deception had warped all our lives, whether we realized it or not.'

'I don't understand,' said Kincaid. 'Why did you think killing Connor would put an end to the deception?'

'But I didn't kill Connor, Superintendent,' Tommy said flatly, weariness evident in the set of his mouth. 'I told Gerald the truth.'

Chapter Fifteen

Gemma started the Escort's engine and let it idle while Kincaid buckled himself into the passenger seat. She had been silent all the way from Tommy's flat down to the car. Kincaid glanced at her, feeling utterly baffled. He thought of the usual free give-and-take of their working relationship, and of dinner at her flat just a few nights ago, when they had shared such easy intimacy. At some level he had been aware of her special talent for forming bonds with people, but he had never quite formulated it. She had welcomed him into her warm circle, made him feel comfortable with himself as well as her, and he had taken it for granted. Now, having seen the rapport she'd developed with Tommy Godwin, he felt suddenly envious, like a child shut out in the cold.

She swatted at a spiralling wisp that had escaped her plait and turned to him. 'What now, guv?' she said, without inflection.

He wanted urgently to repair the damage between them, but he didn't quite know how to proceed, and other matters needed his immediate attention. 'Hold on a tick,' he said, and dialled the Yard on the mobile phone. He asked a brief question and rang off. 'According to forensics, Tommy Godwin's flat and car were as clean as a whistle.' Feeling his way tentatively, he said, 'Perhaps I was a bit hasty in my conclusions about Tommy. That's more your style,' he added with a smile, but Gemma merely went on regarding him with a frustratingly neutral expression. He sighed and rubbed his face. 'I think we'll have to see Sir Gerald again, but first let's have something to eat and see where we are.'

As Gemma drove he closed his eyes, wondering how he might mend their relationship, and why the solution to this case continued to elude him.

They stopped at a café in Golders Green for a late lunch, having rung Badger's End and made sure that Sir Gerald would see them whenever they arrived.

Much to Kincaid's satisfaction, Gemma ate her way steadily through a tuna sandwich without any of the reluctance she'd shown at breakfast. He finished his ham-and-cheese, then sipped his coffee and watched Gemma as she polished off a bag of crisps. 'I can't make sense of it,' he said when she had reached the finger-licking stage. 'It can't have been Gerald whom Con phoned from the flat. According to Sharon, Con made that call at a little after half-past ten, when Gerald was busy conducting a full orchestra.'

'He might have left a message,' said Gemma, wiping her fingertips with a paper napkin.

'With whom? Your porter would have remembered. Alison what's-her-name would have remembered.'

'True.' Gemma tasted her coffee and made a face. 'Cold. Ugh.' She pushed her cup away and folded her arms on the tabletop. 'It would make much more sense if Sir Gerald rang Con after Tommy had left.'

According to Tommy, Gerald had expressed neither shock nor outrage at his revelation. He gave Tommy a drink, as if nothing out of the ordinary had occurred, then said as if to himself, 'The worm ate Arthur's empire from the inside, too, as he always knew it would.' Tommy had left him sitting slumped in his makeup chair, glass in hand.

'What if the call Sharon overheard had nothing to do with Connor's murder? We have no proof that it did.' Kincaid drew speculative circles on the tabletop with the damp end of his spoon. 'What if Con didn't follow Sharon out of the flat? He didn't tell her he meant to leave right away.'

'You mean that if Gerald had rung him after Tommy left, he might still have been there? And he might have agreed to meet him at the lock?' continued Gemma with a spark of interest.

'But we've no proof,' said Kincaid. 'We've no proof of anything. This entire mess is like a pudding – as soon as you sink your teeth into it, it slides away.'

Gemma laughed, and Kincaid gave thanks for even a small sign of a thaw.

By the time they reached Badger's End, the drizzle had evolved into a slow and steady rain. They sat for a moment in the car, listening to the rhythmic patter on roof and bonnet. Lamps were already lit in the house, and they saw a flick of the curtain at the sitting room window.

'The light will be gone soon,' said Gemma. 'The evenings draw in so early in this weather.' As Kincaid reached for the door handle, she touched his arm. 'Guv, if Sir Gerald killed Connor, why did he want us in on it?'

Kincaid turned back to her. 'Maybe Caroline insisted. Maybe his friend, the assistant commissioner, volunteered us, and he didn't think he should protest.' Sensing her discomfort, he touched her fingers and added, 'I don't like this, either, Gemma, but we have to follow it through.'

They dashed for the house under the cover of one umbrella, and stood huddled together on the doorstep. They heard the short double ring as Kincaid pushed the bell, but before he could lift his finger, Sir Gerald opened the door himself. 'Come in by the fire,' he said. 'Here, take your wet things off. It's beastly out, I'm afraid, and not likely to get any better.' He shepherded them into the sitting room, where a fire blazed in the grate, and Kincaid had a moment's fancy that it was never allowed to go out.

'You'll need something to warm you inside as well as out,' said Sir Gerald when they were established with their backs to the fire. 'Plummy's making us some tea.'

'Sir Gerald, we must talk to you,' said Kincaid, making a stand against the tide of social convention.

'I'm sorry Caroline's out,' said Gerald, continuing

in his hearty, friendly way as if there were nothing the least bit odd about their conversation. 'She and Julia are making the final arrangements for Connor's funeral.'

'Julia's helping with the funeral?' asked Kincaid, surprised enough to be distracted from his agenda.

Sir Gerald ran a hand through his sparse hair, and sat down on the sofa. It was his spot, obviously, as the cushions had depressions that exactly matched his bulk, like a dog's favourite old bed. Today he wore another variation of the moth-eaten sweater, this time in olive green, and what seemed to be the same baggy corduroys Kincaid had seen before. 'Yes. She seems to have had a change of heart. I don't know why, and I'm too thankful to question it,' he said, and gave them his engaging smile. 'She came in like a whirlwind after lunch and said she'd made up her mind what should be done for Con, and she's been putting us through our paces ever since.'

It would seem that Julia had made peace with Con's ghost. Kincaid pushed the thought of her aside and concentrated on Gerald. 'It's you we wanted to see, sir.'

'Have you found something?' He sat forward a bit and scanned their faces anxiously. 'Tell me, please. I don't want Caroline and Julia upset.'

'We've just come from Tommy Godwin, Sir Gerald. We know why Tommy came to see you at the theatre the night Connor died.' As Kincaid watched, Gerald sank back into the sofa, his face suddenly shuttered. Remembering the comment Sir Gerald had made to

Tommy, Kincaid added, 'You knew that Tommy was Matthew's father all along, didn't you, sir?'

Gerald Asherton closed his eyes. Under the jut of his eyebrows, his face looked impassive, remote and ancient as a biblical prophet's. 'Of course I knew. I may be a fool, Mr Kincaid, but I'm not a blind fool. Have you any idea how beautiful they were together, Tommy and Caroline?' Opening his eyes, he continued, 'Grace, elegance, talent – you would have thought they'd been made for one another. I spent my days in terror that she would leave me, wondering how I would anchor my existence without her. When things seemed to fizzle out between them with Matty's conception, I thanked the gods for restoring her to me. The rest didn't matter. And Matty . . . Matty was everything we could have wanted.'

'You never told Caroline you knew?' put in Gemma, disbelief evident in her tone.

'How could we have gone on, if I had?'

It had started, thought Kincaid, not with outright lies but with a denial of the truth, and that denial had become woven into the very fabric of their lives. 'But Connor meant to wreck it all, didn't he, Sir Gerald? You must have felt some relief when you heard the next morning that he was dead.' Kincaid caught Gemma's quick, surprised glance, then she moved quietly to stand by the piano, examining the photographs. He left the fire and sat in the armchair opposite Gerald.

'I must admit I felt some sense of reprieve. It shamed me, and made me all the more determined to get to the bottom of things. He was my son-in-law, and in spite of his sometimes rather hysterical behaviour, I cared for him.' Gerald clasped his hands and leaned forward. 'Please, Superintendent, surely it can't benefit Connor for all this past history to be raked over. Can't we spare Caroline that?'

'Sir Gerald—'

The sitting room door opened and Caroline came in, followed by Julia. 'What a perfectly horrid day,' said Caroline, shaking fine drops of water from her dark hair. 'Superintendent. Sergeant. Plummy's just coming with some tea. I'm sure we could all do with some.' She slipped out of her leather jacket and tossed it wrong-side-out over the sofa back, before sitting beside her husband. The deep red silk of the jacket's lining rippled like blood in the glow from the fire.

Kincaid met Julia's eyes and saw pleasure mixed with wariness. It was the first time he had seen her with her mother, and he marvelled at the combination of contrast and similarity. It seemed to him as if Julia were Caroline stretched and reforged, edges sharpened and refined, with the unmistakable stamp of her father's smile. And in spite of her tough mannerisms, her face was as transparent to him as his own, while he found Caroline's unreadable.

'We've been to Fingest church,' said Julia, speaking to him as if there were no one else in the room. 'Con's mum would have insisted on a Catholic funeral and burial, with all the trappings, but it didn't matter the least bit to Con, so I mean to do what seems right to me.' She crossed the room to warm her hands by the fire. Dressed for the outdoors, she wore a heavy oiled-wool sweater still beaded with moisture, and her cheeks were faintly pink from the cold. 'I've been round the churchyard with the vicar, and I've picked a gravesite within a stone's throw of Matty's. Perhaps they'll like being neighbours.'

'Julia, don't be irreverent,' said Caroline sharply. Turning to Kincaid, she added, 'To what do we owe the pleasure of your company, Superintendent?'

'I've just been telling Sir Gerald—'

The door swung open again as Plummy came through with a laden tea tray. Julia went immediately to her aid, and together they arranged the tea things on the low table before the fire. 'Mr Kincaid, Sergeant James.' Plummy smiled at Gemma, looking genuinely pleased to see her. 'I've made extra, in case you've not had a proper lunch again.' She busied herself pouring, this time into china cups and saucers rather than the comfortable stoneware mugs they'd used in the kitchen.

Refusing the offer of freshly toasted bread, Kincaid accepted tea reluctantly. He looked directly at Gerald. 'I'm sorry, sir, but I'm afraid we must go on with this.'

'Go on with what, Mr Kincaid?' said Caroline. She had taken her cup from Plummy and returned to perch on the arm of the sofa, so that in spite of her small stature she seemed to hover protectively over her husband.

Kincaid wet his lips with a sip of tea. 'The night Connor died, Dame Caroline, Tommy Godwin visited your husband in his dressing room at the Coliseum. He told Sir Gerald that he had just had a very unpleasant encounter with Connor. Although Connor was a little drunk and not terribly coherent, it eventually became clear that he had discovered the truth about Matthew's parentage, and was threatening to make his knowledge public with as much attendant scandal as possible.' Kincaid paused, watching their faces. 'Connor had discovered, in fact, that Matthew was Tommy's son, not Gerald's.'

Sir Gerald had sunk into the sofa cushions again, eyes closed, his hand only loosely balancing the cup on his knee.

'Tommy and Mummy?' said Julia. 'But that means Matty . . .' She subsided, her eyes wide and dark with shock. Kincaid wished he could have softened it for her somehow, wished he could comfort her as he had yesterday.

Vivian Plumley also watched the others, and Kincaid saw in her the perpetual observer, always on the edge of the family but not privy to its deepest secrets. She nodded once and compressed her lips, but Kincaid couldn't tell if her expression indicated distress or satisfaction.

'What utter nonsense, Superintendent,' said Caroline. She laid her hand lightly on Gerald's shoulder. 'I won't have it. You've overstepped the bounds of good manners as well as—'

'I am sorry if it distresses you, Dame Caroline, but I'm afraid it is necessary. Sir Gerald, will you tell me exactly what you did after Connor left you that night?'

Gerald touched his wife's hand. 'It's all right, Caro. There can't be any harm in it.' He roused himself, sitting forward a little and draining his teacup before he began. 'There's not much to tell, really. I'd had quite a stiff drink with Tommy, and I'm afraid I kept on after he left. By the time I left the theatre I was well over the limit. Shouldn't have been driving, of course, very irresponsible of me, but I managed without mishap.' He smiled, showing healthy pink gums above his upper teeth. 'Well, almost without mishap. I had a bit of a run-in with Caro's car as I was parking mine. It seems my memory misled me by a foot or so as to its position, and I gave the paintwork a little scrape on the near side. It must have been close on one o'clock when I wobbled my way up to bed. Caro was asleep. I knew Julia was still out, of course, as I hadn't seen her car in the drive, but she's long past having a curfew.' He gave his daughter an affectionate look.

'But I thought I heard you come in around midnight,' said Plummy. She shook her head. 'I just opened my eyes and squinted at the clock – perhaps I misread it.'

Caroline slipped from the arm of the sofa and went to stand with her back to the fire. 'I really don't see the point of this, Superintendent. Just because Connor was obviously disturbed does not mean we should be subjected to some sort of fascist grilling. We've already been over this once – that should be enough. I hope you realize that your assistant commissioner will hear about your irrational behaviour.'

She stood with her hands clasped behind her back and her feet slightly apart. In her black turtleneck, with fitted trousers tucked inside soft leather riding boots, she looked as though she might have been playing a trouser role in an opera. With her chin-length dark hair and in those clothes, she could easily pass for a boy on the verge of manhood. Her colour was a little high, as befitted the hero/heroine under trying circumstances, but her voice, as always, was perfectly controlled.

'Dame Caroline,' said Kincaid, 'Connor may have been emotionally distraught, but he was also telling the truth. Tommy admitted it, and Sir Gerald has confirmed it as well. I think it's time—' He caught a movement out of the corner of his eye. Caroline's jacket slid from the back of the sofa to the cushion with a rustling sound, the soft black leather as fluid as running water.

An odd sensation came over him, as if he had suddenly receded down a tunnel, distorting both his hearing and his vision. Blinking, he turned again to Caroline. Rearrange a few insignificant pieces in the pattern, and the whole thing shifted, turning on itself and popping into focus, clear and sharp and irrefutable. It amazed him now that he hadn't seen it all from the beginning.

They were all watching him with various degrees of concern. Smiling at Gemma, who had frozen with her cup poised midway in the air, he set his own empty cup firmly upon the table. 'It wasn't the doorbell you heard that night, Mrs Plumley, it was the telephone. And it wasn't Gerald you heard coming in a few minutes after midnight, but Caroline.

'Connor rang this number from the flat a little before eleven o'clock. I think it likely that he was looking for Julia, but it was Caroline who answered the phone.' Kincaid rose and went to stand against the piano, so that he could face Caroline directly. 'He couldn't resist baiting you, could he, Caroline? You were the architect of the deception he felt had cost him his happiness, after all.

'You thought you could calm him down, make him see reason, so you said you'd meet him. But you didn't want him making a scene in a public place, so you suggested somewhere you wouldn't be overheard – what could have been more natural than your favourite walk along Hambleden Lock?

'You dressed quickly, I imagine in something quite similar to the things you're wearing just now, and put on your leather jacket. The night was cold and damp, and it's a good brisk walk from the carpark to the river. You slipped quietly out of the house, making sure not to wake Plummy, and when you reached the river you waited for Con at the beginning of the weir.'

He shifted his position a bit, putting his hands in his trouser pockets. They all watched him, as mesmerized as if he were a conjuror about to pull a rabbit from a hat. Julia's eyes looked glazed, as if she were unable to assimilate a second shock so soon after the first.

'What happened then, Caroline?' he asked. Closing his eyes, he pictured the scene as he spoke. 'You walked along the weir, and you argued. The more you tried to reason with Con, the more difficult he became. You reached the lock, crossing over it to the far side, and there the paved path ends.' He opened his eyes again and watched Caroline's still, composed face. 'So you stood with Connor on the little concrete apron just upstream of the sluicegate. Did you suggest turning back? But Con was out of control by that time, and the argument disintegrated into—'

'Please, Superintendent,' said Sir Gerald, 'you really have gone too far. This is all absurd. Caro couldn't kill anyone. She's not physically capable – just look at her. And Con was over six feet tall and well built . . .'

'She's also an actress, Sir Gerald, trained to use her body on the stage. It may have been something as simple as stepping aside when he rushed at her. We'll probably never be certain of that, or know what actually killed Connor. From the results of the post-mortem I think it likely he had a laryngospasm – his throat closed from the shock of hitting the water, and he died from suffocation without ever drawing water into his lungs.

'What we do know,' he said, turning back to Caroline, 'is that help was less than fifty yards away. The lock-keeper was at home, he had the necessary equipment and expertise. And even had he not been available, there were other houses just a bit further along the opposite bank of the river.

'Whether Connor's fall into the river was an accident, or self-defence, or a deliberate act of violence, the fact remains that you are culpable, Dame Caroline. You might have saved him. Did you wait what seemed a reasonable time for him to come up again? When he didn't surface, you walked away, drove home and climbed back into bed, where Gerald found you sleeping peacefully. Only you were a bit more flustered than you thought, and didn't quite manage to leave your car exactly as it had been.'

Caroline smiled at him. 'That's quite an amusing fiction, Mr Kincaid. I'm sure the chief constable and your assistant commissioner will find it most entertaining as well. You have nothing but circumstantial evidence and an overactive imagination.'

'That may be true, Dame Caroline. We will have forensics go over your car and your clothes, however, and there's the matter of the witness who saw a man and, she assumed, a boy wearing a leather jacket on the weir walkway – she may recognize you in an identity parade.

'Whether or not we can build a case against you that will hold up in court, those of us here today will know the truth.'

'Truth?' said Caroline, at last allowing her voice to rise in anger. 'You wouldn't know truth if it came up and bit you, Mr Kincaid. The truth is that this family will stand together, as we always have, and you can't touch us. You're a fool to think—'

'Stop it! Just stop it, all of you.' Julia rose from the sofa and stood shaking, her hands clenched and her face drained of colour. 'This has gone on long enough. How can you be such a hypocrite, Mummy? No wonder Con was furious. He'd bought your load of rubbish and taken on my share of it, too.' She paused for a breath, then said more evenly, 'I grew up hating myself because I never quite fitted into your ideal circle, thinking that if I'd only been different, better somehow, you would have loved me more. And it was all a lie, the perfect family was a lie. You warped my life with it, and you would have warped Matty's, too, if you'd been given a chance.'

'Julia, you mustn't say these things.' Sir Gerald's voice held more anguish than when he'd defended his wife. 'You've no right to desecrate Matthew's memory.'

'Don't talk to me about Matty's memory. I'm the only one who really grieved for Matty, the little boy who could be rude and silly, and sometimes had to sleep with his light on because he was frightened of his dreams. You only lost what you wanted him to be.' Julia looked at Plummy, who still sat quietly on the edge of her seat, her back straight as a staff. 'I'm sorry, Plummy, that's unfair to you. You loved him – you loved both of us, and honestly.

'And Tommy – as ill as I was I remember Tommy coming to the house, and now I can understand what I only sensed then. He sat with me, offering what solace he could, but you were the only one who might have comforted him, Mummy, and you wouldn't see him. You were too busy making high drama of your grief. He deserved better.'

In two lightning steps, Caroline crossed the space that separated her from Julia. She raised her open hand and slapped her daughter across the face. 'Don't you dare speak to me like that. You don't know anything. You're making a fool of yourself with this ridiculous scene. You're making fools of us all, and I won't have it in my house.'

Julia stood her ground. Even though her eyes filled with tears, she neither spoke nor lifted a hand to touch the white imprint on her cheek.

Vivian Plumley went to her and put an arm gently around her shoulders. She said, 'Maybe it's time someone made a scene, Caro. Who knows what might have been avoided if some of these things had been said long ago?'

Caroline stepped back. 'I only meant to protect you, Julia, always. And you, Gerald,' she added, turning to him.

Wearily, Julia said, 'You've protected yourself, from the very beginning.'

'We were all right as we were,' said Caroline. 'Why should anything change?'

'It's too late, Mummy,' said Julia, and Kincaid heard an unexpected note of compassion. 'Can't you see that?'

Caroline turned to her husband, hand out in a gesture of supplication. 'Gerald—'

He looked away.

In the silence that followed, a gust of wind blew a spatter of rain against the window, and the fire flared up in response. Kincaid met Gemma's eyes. He nodded slightly and she came to stand beside him. He said, 'I'm sorry, Dame Caroline, but I'm afraid you'll need to come with us to High Wycombe and make a formal statement. You can come in your own car, if you like, Sir Gerald, and wait for her.'

Julia looked at her parents. What judgement would she pass on them, wondered Kincaid, now that they had revealed themselves as all too fallibly human, and flawed?

For the first time Julia's hand strayed to her cheek. She went to Gerald and briefly touched his arm. 'I'll wait for you here, Daddy,' she said. Then she turned away and left the room without another glance at her mother.

When they had rung High Wycombe and organized the preliminaries, Kincaid excused himself and slipped out of the sitting room. By the time he reached the top landing he had to catch his breath, and he felt a welcome ache in his calves. He tapped lightly on the door of Julia's studio and opened it.

She stood in the centre of the room, holding an open box in her arms and looking about her. 'Plummy's cleaned up after me, can you tell?' she said as he came in.

It did look uncharacteristically clean and lifeless, as if the removal of Julia's attendant clutter had stripped it of its heart.

'There's nothing left I need, really. I suppose what I wanted was to say goodbye.' She gestured around the room with her chin. The mark of her mother's hand stood out clearly now, fiery against the pale skin of her cheek. 'I won't be back here again. Not in the same way. This was a child's refuge.'

'Yes,' said Kincaid. She would move on now, into her own life. 'You'll be all right.'

'I know.' They looked at one another and he

understood that he would not see her again, that their coming together had served its purpose. He would move on now as well, perhaps take a leaf from Gemma's book – she had been hurt, as he had, but she had put it behind her with the forthright practicality he so admired.

After a moment, Julia said, 'What will happen to my mother?'

'I don't know. It depends on the forensic evidence, but even if we turned up something fairly concrete, I doubt we'll make anything stiffer than involuntary manslaughter stick.'

She nodded.

Near to the eaves as they were, the sound of the rain beating against the roof came clearly, and the wind rattled the windows like a beast seeking entrance. 'Julia, I'm sorry.'

'You mustn't be. You only did your job, and what you knew was right. You couldn't violate your integrity to protect me, or my family. There's been enough of that in this house,' she said firmly. 'Are you sorry about what happened with us, as well?' she added, with a trace of a smile.

Was he sorry? For ten years he had kept his emotions safely, tightly reined, until he had almost forgotten how it felt to give another person access. Julia had forced his hand, made him see himself in the mirror of her isolation, and what he found frightened him. But probing beyond the fear, he felt a new and unexpected sense of freedom, even of anticipation.

He smiled back at Julia. 'No.'

Chapter Sixteen

'We should have taken the Midget,' Kincaid said testily as Gemma pulled up the Escort in front of the Carlingford Road flat.

'You know as well as I do that the bloody thing leaks in the rain,' she retorted, glaring at him. She felt as miserable and bedraggled as a cat forced into the bath, and he wasn't much of an improvement. As she watched, a rivulet of water trickled down his forehead from his matted hair.

He wiped it away with the back of his hand, then burst out laughing. 'Gemma, look at us. How can you be so stubborn?'

After what seemed an interminable session at High Wycombe, they had started back to London on the M40, only to have a puncture before they reached the North Circular Road. Gemma had pulled over to the verge and plunged out into the driving rain, refusing his help in changing the tyre. He had stood in the rain, arguing with her while she worked, so that in the end they were both soaked to the skin.

'It's too late to collect Toby tonight,' he said. 'Come in and get some dry things on before you catch your death, and have something proper to eat. Please.'

After a moment, she said, 'All right,' but the words she'd meant to be acquiescent came out grudging and sullen. Her bad temper seemed to be out of control, feeding on itself, and she didn't know how to break the cycle.

They didn't bother with umbrellas as they crossed the road to Kincaid's building – how could they get any more wet, after all? – and the pellets of water stung against her skin.

When they reached the flat, Kincaid went straight to the kitchen, leaving a dripping trail on the carpet. He pulled an already uncorked bottle of white wine from the fridge and poured two glasses. Handing her one, he said, 'Start on this. It will warm you up from the inside. Sorry I haven't anything stronger. And in the meantime I'll get you something dry to put on.'

He left her standing in the sitting room holding her glass, too wet to sit down, too exhausted to sort out her own feelings. Was she angry with him because of Julia? She had felt a communion between them, an understanding that excluded her, and the strength of her reaction dismayed her.

She tasted the wine, then drank half the glass. Chill in her mouth, it did seem to generate some warmth in her middle.

Or was she angry with Caroline Stowe for having taken her in, and Kincaid merely happened to be the nearest available target?

Perhaps it was just the waste of it all that made her feel like chucking something.

Sid uncurled himself from his nest on the sofa, stretching, and came to her. He elongated his sleek body as he rubbed around her ankles and butted his head against her legs. She bent to scratch him in the soft spot under his chin, and his throat began to vibrate under her fingertips. 'Hullo, Sid. You've got the right idea tonight – warm and dry. We should all be so lucky.'

She looked around the familiar and comfortable room. Light from the lamps Kincaid had switched on spilled out in warm pools, illuminating his collection of brightly coloured London transport posters. The coffee table held a haphazard pile of books and an empty mug, and the sofa a crumpled afghan rug. Gemma felt a sudden pang of longing. She wanted to feel at home here, wanted to feel safe.

'I didn't know about underthings,' said Kincaid, returning from the bedroom carrying a stack of folded clothes with a big fluffy towel on the top. 'I suppose you'll have to make do.' He deposited the jeans and sweatshirt on the sofa and draped the towel around her shoulders. 'Oh, and socks. I forgot socks.'

Wiping her facc with one end of the towel, Gemma began fumbling with her sodden plait. Her fingers were too numb with cold to work properly, and she felt tears of frustration smart behind her eyelids.

'Let me help,' he said gently. He turned her around and deftly worked her hair loose, combing it out with his fingers. 'Now.' Rotating her until she faced him again, he began rubbing her head with the towel. His hair stood on end where he had scrubbed at it, and his skin smelled warm and damp.

The weight of his hands against her head seemed to crumble her defences, and she felt her legs go limp and boneless, as if they could no longer support her weight. She closed her eyes against the faintness, thinking *too much wine, too quickly*, but the sensation didn't pass. Reaching up, she put a hand over his, and a buzz ran through her like electric current as their skin made contact.

He stopped his towelling of her hair, looking at her with concern. 'Sorry,' he said. 'Did I get carried away?'

When she managed to shake her head, he let the towel slide to her shoulders and began gently rubbing her neck and the back of her head. She thought disjointedly of Rob – he had never looked after her like this. No one had. And nowhere in her calculations had she reckoned with the power of tenderness, irresistible as gravity.

The pressure of his hand on the back of her head brought her a stumbling step forward, against him, and she gasped with shock as his weight pressed her icy clothes to her skin. She turned her face up, and of its own volition her hand reached for him, cupping the back of his damp head, pulling his mouth down to meet hers.

Drowsily, Gemma raised herself on one elbow and looked at him, realizing she'd never seen him asleep.

His relaxed face seemed younger, softer, and the fan of his eyelashes made dark shadows on his cheeks. His eyelids fluttered for an instant, as if he were dreaming, and the corners of his mouth turned up in the hint of a smile.

She reached out to smooth the unruly chestnut hair from his brow and froze. Suddenly, in that small act of intimacy, she saw the enormity, the absurdity, of what she had done.

She drew her hand back as if stung. Oh dear God, what had she been thinking of? What on earth had possessed her? How could she face him at work in the morning, say, 'Yes, guv, no, guv, right-oh, guv,' as if nothing had happened between them?

Her heart racing, she slid carefully from the bed. They'd left a trail of wet clothes across the bedroom, and as she disentangled hers from the jumble she felt tears fill her eyes. She swore under her breath. *Silly, bloody fool.* She never cried. Even when Rob had left her, she hadn't cried. Shivering, she pulled on damp pants, slipped her soggy jumper over her head.

She had done what she'd sworn she'd never do. As hard as she'd worked to earn her position, to be considered an equal, a colleague, she'd shown herself no better than any tart who slept her way up the ladder. A wave of dizziness swept over her as she stepped into her skirt and she swayed.

What could she do now? Ask for a transfer? Everyone would know why – she might as well wear a sign and save them speculating. Resign? Give up her dreams, let all her hard work turn to dust in her fingers? How could she bear it? Oh, she would have sympathy and a plausible excuse – too hard a life for a single mum, a need to spend more time with her son – but she would know how badly she had failed.

Kincaid stirred and turned, freeing an arm from the covers. Staring at him, she tried to memorize the curve of his shoulder, the angle of his cheek, and her heart contracted with longing and desire. She turned away, afraid of her own weakness.

In the sitting room she squelched her bare feet into her shoes and gathered up her coat and bag. The dry jeans and sweater he'd brought her still lay neatly folded on the sofa, and the towel he'd used to dry her hair lay crumpled on the floor. She picked it up and held its soft nap against her cheek, imagining that it smelled faintly of shaving soap. With exaggerated care she folded it and placed it beside the clothes, then let herself quietly out of the flat.

When Gemma reached the street door, she found the rain still coming down in relentless sheets, a solid wall of water. She stood for a moment, watching it. In her traitorous mind she imagined running back up the stairs and into the flat, shedding her clothes and climbing back into bed beside his sleeping form.

She pushed open the door, stepped slowly out into the rain and crossed the road, making no effort to shield herself. The dim outline of the Escort was familiar, comforting even. Scrabbling for the handle as if she were blind, she wrenched the door open and half fell into the driver's seat. She wiped her streaming face with her hands and started the engine.

The radio blared into life and instead of hitting the off switch, she reflexively jammed a tape into the player. Caroline Stowe's voice filled the car as Violetta sang her last aria, begging for life, for love, for the physical strength to match her courageous will.

Gemma put her head down against the steering wheel and wept.

After a moment she mopped her face with some tissues and put the car into gear, and when the music finished the only sound was the drumming of the rain against the roof.

The soft click of a door penetrated Kincaid's consciousness. He struggled towards the surface of sleep, but it clung to him tenaciously, dragging him down again into its cotton-wool depths. His body felt boneless, warmly lethargic, and his eyelids seemed to have acquired surplus weight. Rousing himself enough to tuck his exposed arm under the covers, he felt the sheet cool and empty beside him. He blinked. Gemma. She must have gone to the loo – women always had to go to the loo – or perhaps to the kitchen for a glass of water.

He smiled a little at his own stupidity. What he wanted, needed, had been right under his nose all along and he'd been too blind to see it. Now he felt as if his life had come round full circle, complete, and he imagined the pattern of their days together. Work, then home, and at day's end he would find sanctuary beside her, entangling himself in the curtain of her coppery hair.

Kincaid stretched his arm across her pillow, ready to enfold her when she returned. The rain beat steadily against the windowpane, counterpoint to the warmth of the room. With a sigh of contentment, he drifted once again into sleep.

Deborah Crombie

Mourn Not Your Dead

What follows is the first chapter of the latest Duncan Kincaid/Gemma James mystery, *Mourn Not Your Dead*.

It is available in hardback from Macmillan in January 1997, priced £15.99.

Chapter One

His office seemed to shrink as he paced. The walls drew in, their angles distorted by the elongated shadows cast from the swivel lamp on his desk. The Yard always felt a bit eerie at night, as if the very emptiness of the rooms had a presence. He stopped at the bookcases and ran his finger along the spines of the well-thumbed books on the top shelf. Archaeology, art . . . canals . . . crime reference . . . Many of them were gifts from his mother, sent in her continual quest to remedy what she considered his lack of a proper education. Although he'd tried to group them alphabetically by subject, there were a few inevitable strays. Kincaid shook his head – would that he could order his life even half as well as he did his books.

He glanced at his watch for the tenth time in as many minutes, then crossed to his desk and sat down very deliberately. The call that had brought him in had been urgent – a high-ranking police officer found murdered – and if Gemma didn't arrive soon he'd have to go on to the crime scene without her. She'd not been in to work since she had left his flat on Friday evening. And although she had called in and requested leave from the Chief Superintendent, she had not answered Kincaid's increasingly frantic calls over the past five days. Tonight Kincaid had asked the duty sergeant to contact her and she'd responded.

Unable to contain his restlessness, he rose again and had reached to pull his jacket from the coat stand when he heard the soft click of the latch. He turned and saw her standing with her back to the door, watching him, and a foolish grin spread across his face. 'Gemma!'

'Hello, Guv.'

'I've tried and tried to ring you. I thought something must have happened—'

She was already shaking her head. 'I went to my sister's for a few days. I needed some time—'

'We have to talk.' He moved a step nearer and stopped, examining her. She looked exhausted, her pale face almost transparent against the copper of her hair, and the skin beneath her eyes held faint purple shadows. 'Gemma—'

'There's nothing to say.' She slumped, resting her shoulders against the door as if she needed its support. 'It was all a dreadful mistake. You can see that, can't you?'

He stared at her, astonishment freezing his tongue. 'A mistake?' he managed finally, then wiped a hand across his suddenly dry lips. 'Gemma, I don't understand.'

'It never happened.' She took a step towards him, entreating, then stopped as if afraid of his physical proximity.

'It did happen. You can't change that, and I don't want to.' He went to her then and put his hands on her shoulders, trying to draw her to him. 'Gemma, please, listen to me.' For an instant he thought she might tilt her head into the hollow of his shoulder, relax against him. Then he felt her shoulders tense under his fingers and she pulled away.

'Look at us. Look at where we bloody are,' she said, thumping a fist against the door at her back. 'We can't do this. I've compromised myself enough already.' She took a ragged breath and added, spacing the words out as if to emphasize their weight, 'I can't afford it. I've my career to think of . . . and Toby.'

The phone rang, its short double *brrr* echoing loudly in the small room. He stepped back towards his desk and fumbled for the receiver, bringing it to his ear. 'Kincaid,' he said shortly, then listened for a moment. 'Right, thanks.' Replacing the handset in the cradle, he looked at Gemma. 'Car's waiting.' Sentences formed and dissolved in his mind, each sounding more futile than the last. This was not the time or the place to discuss it, and he would only embarrass them both by going on about it now.

Finally, he turned away and slipped into his jacket, using the moment to swallow his disappointment and compose his features in as neutral an expression as he could manage. Facing her again, he said, 'Ready, Sergeant?'

Big Ben struck ten o'clock as the car sped south across Westminster Bridge, and in the back seat beside Gemma, Kincaid watched the lights shimmer on the

Thames. They sat in silence as the car zigzagged on through South London, inching its way towards Surrey. Even their driver, a usually chatty young PC called Williams, seemed to have caught their mood, remaining hunched in taciturn concentration over the wheel.

Clapham had vanished behind them when Gemma spoke. 'You'd better fill me in on this one, Guv.'

Kincaid saw the flash of Williams's eyes as he cast a surprised glance at them in the rearview mirror. Gemma should have been briefed, of course, and he roused himself to answer as ordinarily as possible. Gossip in the ranks would do neither of them any good. 'Little village near Guildford. What's it called, Williams?'

'Holmbury St Mary, sir.'

'Right. Alastair Gilbert, the division commander at Notting Dale, found in his kitchen with his head bashed in.'

He heard Gemma draw a sharp breath, then she said with the first spark of interest he'd heard all evening, 'Commander Gilbert? Jesus. Any leads?'

'Not that I've been told, but it's early days yet,' Kincaid said, turning to study her.

She shook her head. 'There will be an unholy stink over this one, then. And aren't we the lucky coppers, having it land in our laps?' When Kincaid snorted in wry agreement, she glanced at him and added, 'You must have known him.'

Shrugging, he said, 'Didn't everyone?' He was unwilling to elaborate in front of Williams.

Gemma settled back into her seat. After a moment

she said, 'The local lads will have been there before us. Hope they haven't messed about with the body.'

Kincaid smiled in the dark. Gemma's possessiveness over bodies always amused him. From the beginning of a case, she considered the corpse her personal property and she didn't take unnecessary interference kindly. Tonight, however, her prickliness brought him a sense of relief. It meant she had engaged herself in the case, and it allowed him to hope that their working relationship, at least, was not beyond salvage. 'They've promised to leave it until we've had a chance to see things *in situ*.'

Gemma nodded in satisfaction. 'Good. Do we know who found him?'

'Wife and daughter.'

'Ugh.' She wrinkled her nose. 'Not at all nice.'

'At least they'll have a WPC to do the hand-holding,' Kincaid said, making a half-hearted attempt to tease her. 'Lets you off the hook.' Gemma often complained that female officers were good for more than breaking bad news to victims' families and offering comforting shoulders, but when the task fell to her she did it exceptionally well.

'I should hope so,' she answered and looked away towards her window, but not before he thought he saw her lips curve in a smile.

A half-hour later they left the A road at Abinger Hammer, and after a few miles of twisting and turning down a narrow lane, they entered the sleepy village of Holmbury St Mary. Williams pulled on to the verge and consulted a scribbled sheet of directions under the map light. 'When the road curves left we stay straight on, just to the right of the pub,' he muttered as he put the car into gear again.

'There,' said Kincaid, wiping condensation from his window with the sleeve of his coat. 'This must be it.'

Turning to look out of her window, Gemma said, 'Look. I've never seen that particular sign before.' He heard the pleasure in her voice.

Kincaid leaned across her just in time to catch a glimpse of a swinging pub sign showing two lovers silhouetted against a smiling moon. Then he felt Gemma's breath against his cheek and caught the faint scent of peaches that always seemed to hover about her. He sat back quickly and turned his attention ahead.

The lane narrowed past the pub, and the blue flashing of the panda cars' lights lit the scene with an eerie radiance. Williams brought their car to a halt several yards back from the last car and almost against the hedge on the right, making allowance, Kincaid guessed, for the passing of the coroner's van. They slid from the car, stretching their cramped legs and huddling closer into their coats as the November chill struck them. A low mist hung in the still air, and plumes of condensation formed in front of their faces as they breathed.

A constable materialized before them in the lane, Cheshire Cat-like, the white checks on his hatband creating a dog-toothed smile. Kincaid identified them, then peered through the gate from which the constable had come, trying to make out features in the dark bulk of the house.

'Chief Inspector Deveney is waiting for you in the

kitchen, sir,' said the constable. The gate moved silently as he opened it and led them through. 'There's a path just here that goes round the back. The scene-of-crime lads will have some lamps rigged up shortly.'

'No sign of forced entry?'

'No, sir, nor any tracks that we've been able to see. We've been careful to keep to the stones.'

Kincaid nodded in approval. When his eyes adjusted to the dimness within the precincts of the garden wall, he could see that the house was large and stolidly Tudor. Red brick, he thought, squinting, and above that black-and-white half timbering. Not the real thing, surely – more likely Victorian, a representation of the first migration of the well off into suburbia. A faint light shone through the leaded panes in the front door, echoed by faint glints from the upstairs windows.

Carefully he knelt and touched the grass. The lawn that separated them from the house felt as smooth and dense as black velvet. It seemed that Alastair Gilbert had lived very well.

The flagged path indicated by the constable took them along the right side of the house, then curved around to meet light spilling out from an open door. Beyond it Kincaid thought he could see the outline of a conservatory.

A silhouette appeared against the light, and a man came down the steps towards them. 'Superintendent?' He extended his hand and grasped Kincaid's firmly. 'I'm Nick Deveney.' An inch or so shy of Kincaid's height and near his age, Deveney flashed them a friendly smile. 'You're just in time to have a word with the pathologist.' He stepped aside, allowing Kincaid, Gemma and the still-silent Williams to enter the house before him.

Kincaid passed through a cloakroom, registering a few pairs of neatly aligned wellies on the floor and mackintoshes hanging from hooks. Then he stepped through into the kitchen proper and halted, the others piling up at his back.

The kitchen had been white. White ceramic floors, white ceramic walls, set off by cabinets of a pale wood. A detached part of his mind recognized the cabinets as something he had seen when planning the refitting of his own kitchen – they were freestanding, made by a small English firm, and quite expensive. The other part of his mind focused on the body of Alastair Gilbert, sprawled face down near a door on the far side of the room.

In life, Gilbert had been a small, neat man known for the perfection of his tailoring, the precision of his haircuts, the gloss upon his shoes. There was nothing neat about him now. The metallic smell of blood seemed to lodge at the back of Kincaid's nose. Blood matted Gilbert's dark hair. Blood had splattered, and smeared, and run in scarlet rivulets across the pristine white floor.

A small sound, almost a whisper, came from behind Kincaid. Turning, he was just in time to see a pasty-faced Williams push his way out through the door, followed by the faint sound of retching. Kincaid raised an eyebrow at Gemma, who nodded and slipped out after Williams.

A woman in surgical overalls knelt beside the body, her profile obscured by a shoulder-length fall of straight, black hair. She hadn't looked up or paused in her work when they had entered the room, but now she sat back on her heels and regarded Kincaid. He came nearer and squatted, just out of the blood's path.

'Kate Ling,' she said, holding up her gloved hands. 'You won't mind if I don't shake?'

Kincaid thought he detected a trace of humour in her oval face. 'Not at all.'

Gemma returned and dropped down beside him. 'He'll be all right,' she said softly. 'I've sent him along to the duty constable for a cuppa.'

'Can't tell you much,' Dr Ling said as she began stripping off her gloves. 'Blood's not congealing, as you can see.' She gestured at the body with the deflated latex fingers of an empty glove. 'Possibly taking some sort of anticoagulant. From the body temperature I'd say he's been dead four or five hours, give or take an hour or two.' Her eyelid drooped in a ghost of a wink. 'But look at this,' she added, pointing with a slender index finger. 'I think the weapon has left several crescent-shaped depressions, but I'll know more when I get him cleaned up.'

Looking closely, Kincaid thought he detected fragments of skull in the blood-matted hair, but no crescent shapes. 'I'll take your word for it, Doctor. Any defence wounds?'

'Not that I've found so far. All right with you if I have him moved now? The sooner I get him on the table, the more we'll know.'

'It's your call, Doc.' Kincaid stood up.

'The photographer and the scene-of-crime lads would like to move the live bodies out as well,' said Deveney, 'so they can get on with things.'

'Right.' Kincaid turned to him. 'Can you fill me in on what you've got so far? Then I'd like to see the family.'

'Claire Gilbert and her daughter came home around half-past seven. They'd been away several hours, doing some shopping in Guildford. Mrs Gilbert parked the car in the garage as usual, but as they came across the back garden towards the house they saw that the back door stood open. When they entered the kitchen they found the Commander.' Deveney nodded towards the body. 'Once she'd ascertained there wasn't a pulse, Mrs Gilbert called us.'

'In a nutshell,' said Kincaid, and Deveney smiled. 'So what's the theory? Did the wife do it?'

'There's nothing to suggest they had a fight – nothing broken, no marks on her. And the daughter says they were shopping. Besides—' Deveney paused. 'Well, wait till you meet her. I've had her check the house, and she says she can't find a few items of jewellery. There have been a few thefts reported in the area recently. Petty things.'

'No suspects in the thefts?'

Deveney shook his head.

'All right, then. Where are the Gilberts?'

'I've a constable with them in the sitting room. I'll take you through.'

Pausing in the doorway for a final glimpse of the body, Kincaid thought of Alastair Gilbert as he had seen him last – lecturing from a podium, extolling the virtues of order, discipline, and logical thinking in police work – and he felt an unexpected stirring of pity.

Deborah Crombie

A Share in Death

Pan Books £5.99

'The lights glowed softly in the windows of Followdale House, as welcoming as death . . .'

A week's holiday is just what Detective Superintendent Duncan Kincaid of Scotland Yard needs after wrapping up a gruelling murder case. And Followdale House, a timeshare hotel on the rolling Yorkshire Moors, offers peace, relaxation, an odd assortment of fellow guests as company – even the chance of romance in the shape of the alluring scientist Hannah Alcock.

Unfortunately, by day two Followdale House also offers a dead body, floating naked in the hotel pool . . .

His vacation over before it has barely begun, Kincaid finds himself in the middle of a deadly game of cat-and-mouse, as a ruthless killer stalks Followdale's next victim . . .

Deborah Crombie

All Shall Be Well

Pan Books £5.99

'Jasmine Dent let her head fall back against the pillows and closed her eyes. Morphine coats the mind like fuzz on a peach, she thought sleepily . . .'

Superintendent Duncan Kincaid is deeply saddened to discover that his terminally ill neighbour, Jasmine Dent, has died. And when the autopsy reveals a lethal dose of morphine, everyone assumes suicide.

Everyone except Duncan Kincaid, that is. Jasmine had asked a friend to help her overdose, but she had abandoned that plan at the last minute. And why were there no empty morphine bottles in her flat? *And* no suicide note?

With the help of Jasmine's own journals, Kincaid explores his neighbour's life, from her childhood in India to the final months of her illness, discovering a hauntingly beautiful young woman, secretive and ambitious. Somewhere in her past lies the key to her murder . . .

All Pan Books are available at your local bookshop or newsagent, or can be ordered direct from the publisher. Indicate the number of copies required and fill in the form below.

Send to: Macmillan General Books C.S.
Book Service By Post
PO Box 29, Douglas I-O-M
IM99 1BQ

or phone: 01624 675137, quoting title, author and credit card number.

or fax: 01624 670923, quoting title, author, and credit card number.

or Internet: http://www.bookpost.co.uk

Please enclose a remittance* to the value of the cover price plus 75 pence per book for post and packing. Overseas customers please allow £1.00 per copy for post and packing.

*Payment may be made in sterling by UK personal cheque, Eurocheque, postal order, sterling draft or international money order, made payable to Book Service By Post.

Alternatively by Access/Visa/MasterCard

Card No. | | | | | | | | | | | | | | | | |

Expiry Date | | | | | | | | | | | | | | | | |

Signature ______________________________

Applicable only in the UK and BFPO addresses.

While every effort is made to keep prices low, it is sometimes necessary to increase prices at short notice. Pan Books reserve the right to show on covers and charge new retail prices which may differ from those advertised in the text or elsewhere.

NAME AND ADDRESS IN BLOCK CAPITAL LETTERS PLEASE

Name ______________________________

Address ______________________________

____

____

____

8/95

Please allow 28 days for delivery.
Please tick box if you do not wish to receive any additional information. ☐

Hot Money

Dick Francis has written thirty-nine international bestsellers and is widely acclaimed as one of the world's finest thriller writers. His awards include the Crime Writers' Association's Cartier Diamond Dagger for his outstanding contribution to the crime genre, and an honorary Doctorate of Humane Letters from Tufts University of Boston. In 1996 Dick Francis was made a Mystery Writers of America Grand Master for a lifetime's achievement.

Also by Dick Francis in Pan Books

DEAD CERT
NERVE
FOR KICKS
ODDS AGAINST
FLYING FINISH
BLOOD SPORT
FORFEIT
ENQUIRY
RAT RACE
BONECRACK
SMOKESCREEN
SLAY-RIDE
KNOCK DOWN
HIGH STAKES
IN THE FRAME
RISK
TRIAL RUN
WHIP HAND
REFLEX
TWICE SHY
BANKER
THE DANGER
PROOF
BREAK IN
BOLT
THE EDGE
STRAIGHT

LONGSHOT
COMEBACK
DRIVING FORCE
DECIDER
WILD HORSES
COME TO GRIEF
TO THE HILT
10lb PENALTY
FIELD OF THIRTEEN
SECOND WIND
SHATTERED

THE SPORT OF QUEENS
(autobiography)

LESTER:The Official
Biography

DICK FRANCIS
OMNIBUS ONE:
Long Shot, Straight, High
Stakes

DICK FRANCIS
OMNIBUS TWO:
Forfeit, Risk,
Reflex

Dick Francis

HOT MONEY

PAN BOOKS

First published 1987 by Michael Joseph Ltd

This edition first published 1988 by Pan Books
an imprint of Pan Macmillan Ltd
Pan Macmillan, 20 New Wharf Road, London N1 9RR
Basingstoke and Oxford
Associated companies throughout the world
www.panmacmillan.com

ISBN 0 330 30505 0

33 35 37 39 38 36 34

A CIP catalogue record for this book is available from the British Library.

Printed and bound in Great Britain by
Mackays of Chatham plc, Chatham, Kent

With love and thanks as usual

to

MERRICK and FELIX

THE PEMBROKES

MALCOLM PEMBROKE

HIS WIVES	1	**Vivien**
	2	**Joyce**
	3	**Alicia**
	4	**Coochie**
	5	**Moira**
VIVIEN'S CHILDREN	1	**Donald**, married to Helen
	2	**Lucy**, married to Edwin
	3	**Thomas**, married to Berenice
JOYCE'S CHILD	1	**Ian**, unmarried
ALICIA'S CHILDREN	1	**Gervase**, married to Ursula
	2	**Ferdinand**, married to Debs
	3	**Serena**, unmarried
COOCHIE'S CHLDREN	1	**Robin**
	2	**Peter**, dead

CHAPTER ONE

I intensely disliked my father's fifth wife, but not to the point of murder.

I, the fruit of his second ill-considered gallop up the aisle, had gone dutifully to the next two of his subsequent nuptials, the changes of 'mother' punctuating my life at six and fourteen.

At thirty however I'd revolted: wild horses couldn't have dragged me to witness his wedding to the sharp-eyed honey-tongued Moira, his fifth choice. Moira had been the subject of the bitterest quarrel my father and I ever had and the direct cause of a non-speaking wilderness which had lasted three years.

After Moira was murdered, the police came bristling with suspicion to my door, and it was by the merest fluke that I could prove I'd been geographically elsewhere when her grasping little soul had left her carefully tended body. I didn't go to her funeral, but I wasn't alone in that. My father didn't go either.

A month after her death he telephoned me, and it

was so long since I'd heard his voice that it seemed that of a stranger.

'Ian?'

'Yes,' I said.

'Malcolm.'

'Hello,' I said.

'Are you doing anything?'

'Reading the price of gold.'

'No, dammit,' he said testily. 'In general, are you busy?'

'In general,' I said, 'fairly.'

The newspaper lay on my lap, an empty wine glass at my elbow. It was late evening, after eleven, growing cold. I had that day quit my job and put on idleness like a comfortable coat.

He sighed down the line. 'I suppose you know about Moira?'

'Front page news,' I agreed. 'The price of gold is on . . . er . . . page thirty-two.'

'If you want me to apologize,' he said, 'I'm not going to.'

His image stood sharp and clear in my mind: a stocky, grey-haired man with bright blue eyes and a fizzing vitality that flowed from him in sparks of static electricity in cold weather. He was to my mind stubborn, opinionated, rash and often stupid. He was also financially canny, intuitive, quick-brained and courageous, and hadn't been nicknamed Midas for nothing.

'Are you still there?' he demanded.

'Yes.'

'Well . . . I need your help.'

He said it as if it were an everyday requirement, but I couldn't remember his asking anyone for help ever before, certainly not me.

'Er . . .' I said uncertainly. 'What sort of help?'

'I'll tell you when you get here.'

'Where is "here"?'

'Newmarket,' he said. 'Come to the sales tomorrow afternoon.'

There was a note in his voice which couldn't be called entreaty but was far from a direct order, and I was accustomed only to orders.

'All right,' I said slowly.

'Good.'

He disconnected immediately, letting me ask no questions: and I thought of the last time I'd seen him, when I'd tried to dissuade him from marrying Moira, describing her progressively, in the face of his implacable purpose, as a bad misjudgement on his part and as a skilful, untruthful manipulator and, finally, as a rapacious blood-sucking tramp. He'd knocked me down to the floor with one fast, dreadful blow, which he'd been quite capable of at sixty-five, three years ago. Striding furiously away, he'd left me lying dazed on my carpet and had afterwards behaved as if I no longer existed, packing into boxes everything I'd left in my old room in his house and sending them by public carrier to my flat.

Time had proved me right about Moira, but the unforgivable words had remained unforgiven to her death and, it had seemed, beyond. On this October evening, though, perhaps they were provisionally on ice.

I, Ian Pembroke, the fourth of my father's nine children, had from the mists of infancy loved him blindly through thunderous years of domestic in-fighting which had left me permanently impervious to fortissimo voices and slammed doors. In a totally confused chaotic upbringing, I'd spent scattered unhappy periods with my bitter mother but had mostly been passed from wife to wife in my father's house as part of the furniture and fittings, treated by him throughout with the same random but genuine affection he gave to his dogs.

Only with the advent of Coochie, his fourth wife, had there been peace, but by the time she took over I was fourteen and world-weary, cynically expecting a resumption of hostilities within a year of the honeymoon.

Coochie, however, had been different. Coochie of all of them had been my only real mother, the only one who'd given me a sense of worth and identity, who'd listened and encouraged and offered good advice. Coochie produced twin boys, my half-brothers Robin and Peter, and it had seemed that at last Malcolm Pembroke had achieved a friendly family unit, albeit a sort of sunny clearing surrounded by jungle thickets of ex-wives and discontented siblings.

I grew up and left home but went back often, never feeling excluded. Coochie would have seen Malcolm into a happy old age but, when she was forty and the twins eleven, a hit-and-run driver swerved her car off the road and downhill onto rocks. Coochie and Peter had been killed outright. Robin, the elder twin, suffered brain damage. I had been away. Malcolm was in his office: a policeman went to him to tell him, and he let me know soon after. I'd learned the meaning of grief on that drizzly afternoon, and still mourned them all, their loss irreparable.

On the October evening of Malcolm's telephone call, I glanced at them as usual as I went to bed, their three bright faces grinning out from a silver frame on my chest of drawers. Robin lived – just – in serene twilight in a nursing home. I went to see him now and again. He no longer looked like the boy in the photograph, but was five years older, growing tall, empty-eyed.

I wondered what Malcolm could possibly want. He was rich enough to buy anything he needed, maybe – only maybe – excluding the whole of Fort Knox. I couldn't think of anything I could do for him that he couldn't get from anyone else.

Newmarket, I thought. The sales.

Newmarket was all very well for me because I'd been working as an assistant to a racehorse trainer. But Newmarket for Malcolm? Malcolm never gambled on horses, only on gold. Malcolm had made several immense consecutive fortunes from buying and selling the hard yellow stuff, and had years ago reacted to my stated choice of occupation by saying merely, ‘Horses? Racing? Good Lord! Well, if that’s what you want, my boy, off you go. But don’t expect me to know the first thing about anything.’ And, as far as I knew, he was still as ignorant of the subject as he’d been all along.

Malcolm and Newmarket bloodstock sales simply didn’t mix. Not the Malcolm I’d known, anyway.

I drove the next day to the isolated Suffolk town whose major industry was the sport of kings, and among the scattered purposeful crowd found my father standing bareheaded in the area outside the sale-ring building, eyes intently focused on a catalogue.

He looked just the same. Brushed grey hair, smooth brown vicuna knee-length overcoat, charcoal business suit, silk tie, polished black shoes; confidently bringing his City presence into the casual sophistication of the country.

It was a golden day, crisp and clear, the sky a cold cloudless blue. I walked across to him in my own brand of working clothes: cavalry twill trousers, checked wool shirt, padded olive-green jacket, tweed cap. A surface contrast that went personality deep.

‘Good afternoon,’ I said neutrally.

He raised his eyes and gave me a stare as blue as the sky.

'So you came.'

'Well . . . yes.'

He nodded vaguely, looking me over. 'You look older,' he said.

'Three years.'

'Three years and a crooked nose.' He observed it dispassionately. 'I suppose you broke that falling off a horse?'

'No . . . You broke it.'

'Did I?' He seemed only mildly surprised. 'You deserved it.'

I didn't answer. He shrugged. 'Do you want some coffee?'

'OK.'

We hadn't touched each other, I thought. Not a hug, not a handshake, not a passing pat on the arm. Three years' silence couldn't easily be bridged.

He set off not in the direction of the regular refreshment room, but towards one of the private rooms set aside for the privileged. I followed in his footsteps, remembering wryly that it took him roughly two minutes any time to talk himself into the plushest recesses, wherever.

The Newmarket sales building was in the form of an amphitheatre, sloping banks of seats rising all round from the ground-level ring where each horse was led round while being auctioned. Underneath the seating and in a large adjacent building were rooms used as offices by auctioneers and bloodstock agents, and as entertainment rooms by commercial firms, such as Ebury Jewellers, Malcolm's present willing hosts.

I was used only to the basic concrete boxes of the bloodstock agents' offices. Ebury's space was decorated in contrast as an expensive showroom, with well-lit glass display cases round three walls shining with silver and sparkling with baubles, everything locked away safely but temptingly visible. Down the centre of the room, on brown wall-to-wall carpeting, stood a long polished table surrounded with armed, leather-covered dining chairs. Before each chair was neatly laid a leather-edged blotter alongside a gold-tooled tub containing pens, suggesting that all any client needed to provide here was his cheque book.

A smooth young gentleman welcomed Malcolm with enthusiastic tact and offered drinks and goodies from the well-stocked buffet table which filled most of the fourth wall. Lunch, it seemed, was an all-day affair. Malcolm and I took cups of coffee and sat at the table, I, at any rate, feeling awkward. Malcolm fiddled with his spoon. A large loud lady came in and began talking to the smooth young man about having one of her dogs modelled in silver. Malcolm raised his eyes to them briefly and then looked down again at his cup.

'What sort of help?' I said.

I suppose I expected him to say he wanted help in

some way with horses, in view of the venue he'd chosen, but it seemed to be nothing as straightforward.

'I want you beside me,' he said.

I frowned, puzzled. 'How do you mean?'

'Beside me,' he said. 'All the time.'

'I don't understand.'

'I don't suppose you do,' he said. He looked up at my face. 'I'm going to travel a bit. I want you with me.'

I made no fast reply and he said abruptly, explosively, 'Dammit, Ian, I'm not asking the world. A bit of your time, a bit of your attention, that's all.'

'Why now, and why me?'

'You're my son.' He stopped fiddling with the spoon and dropped it onto the blotter where it left a round stain. He leaned back in his chair. 'I trust you.' He paused. 'I need someone I can trust.'

'Why?'

He didn't tell me why. He said, 'Can't you get some time off from work? Have a holiday?'

I thought of the trainer I'd just left, whose daughter had made my job untenable because she wanted it for her fiancé. There was no immediate need for me to find another place, save for paying the rent. At thirty-three, I'd worked for three different trainers, and had lately come to feel I was growing too old to carry on as anyone's assistant. The natural progression was towards becoming a trainer myself, a dicey course without money.

'What are you thinking?' Malcolm asked.

'Roughly whether you would lend me half a million quid.'

'No,' he said.

I smiled. 'That's what I thought.'

'I'll pay your fares and your hotel bills.'

Across the room the loud lady was giving the smooth young man her address. A waitress had arrived and was busy unpacking fresh sandwiches and more alcohol onto the white-clothed table. I watched her idly for a few seconds, then looked back to Malcolm's face, and surprised there an expression that could only be interpreted as anxiety.

I was unexpectedly moved. I'd never wanted to quarrel with him: I'd wanted him to see Moira as I did, as a calculating, sweet-talking honeypot who was after his money, and who had used the devastation of Coochie's death to insinuate herself with him, turning up constantly with sympathy and offers to cook. Malcolm, deep in grief, had been helpless and grateful and seemed hardly to notice when she began threading her arm through his in company, and saying 'we'. I had for the whole three silent years wanted peace with my father, but I couldn't bear to go to his house and see Moira smirking in Coochie's place, even if he would have let me in through the door.

Now that Moira was dead, peace was maybe possible, and it seemed now as though he really wanted it also. I thought fleetingly that peace wasn't his prime object, that peace was only a preliminary necessary for some other purpose, but all the same it was enough.

'Yes,' I said, 'all right. I can take time off.'

His relief was visible. 'Good! Good! Come along then, I may as well buy a horse.' He stood up, full of sudden energy, waving his catalogue. 'Which do you suggest?'

'Why on earth do you want a horse?'

'To race, of course.'

'But you've never been interested . . .'

'Everyone should have a hobby,' he said briskly, though he'd never had one in his life. 'Mine is racing.' And, as an afterthought, he added, 'Henceforth,' and began to walk to the door.

The smooth young man detached himself from the dog lady and begged Malcolm to come back any time. Malcolm assured him he would, then wheeled round away from him again and marched across to one of the display cabinets.

'While I was waiting for you, I bought a cup,' he said to me over his shoulder. 'Want to see? One rather like that.' He pointed. 'It's being engraved.'

The cup in question was a highly-decorated and graceful elongated jug, eighteen inches tall and made undoubtedly of sterling silver.

'What's it for?' I asked.

'I don't know yet. Haven't made up my mind.'

'But . . . the engraving?'

'Mm. The Coochie Pembroke Memorial Challenge Trophy. Rather good, don't you think?'

'Yes,' I said.

He gave me a sidelong glance. 'I thought you'd think so.' He retraced his steps to the door. 'Right, then, a horse.'

Just like old times, I thought with half-forgotten pleasure. The sudden impulses which might or might not turn out to be thoroughly sensible, the intemperate enthusiasms needing instant gratification . . . and sometimes, afterwards, the abandoning of a débâcle as if it didn't exist. The Coochie Pembroke Memorial Challenge Trophy might achieve worldwide stature in competition or tarnish unpresented in an attic: with Malcolm it was always a toss-up.

I called him Malcolm, as all his children did, on his own instructions, and had grown up thinking it natural. Other boys might have Dad: I had my father, Malcolm.

Outside Ebury's room, he said, 'What's the procedure, then? How do we set about it?'

'Er . . .' I said. 'This is the first day of the Highflyer Sales.'

'Well?' he demanded as I paused. 'Go on.'

'I just thought you ought to know . . . the minimum opening bid today is twenty thousand guineas.'

It rocked him only slightly. 'Opening bid? What do they sell them for?'

'Anything from a hundred thousand up. You'll be lucky today to get a top-class yearling for under a quarter of a million. This is generally the most expensive day of the year.'

He wasn't noticeably deterred. He smiled. 'Come on, then,' he said. 'Let's go and start bidding.'

'You need to look up the breeding first,' I said. 'And then look at the animals, to see if you like them, and then get the help and advice of an agent . . .'

'Ian,' he said with mock sorrow, 'I don't know anything about the breeding, I can just about tell if a thing's got four legs, and I don't trust agents. So let's get on and bid.'

It sounded crazy to me, but it was his money. We went into the sale-ring itself where the auction was already in progress, and Malcolm asked me where the richest bidders could be found, the ones that really meant business.

'In those banks of seats on the left of the auctioneers, or here, in the entrance, or just round there to the left . . .'

He looked and listened and then led the way up to a section of seats from where we could watch the places I'd pointed out. The amphitheatre was already more than three-quarters full, and would later at times be crammed, especially whenever a tip-top lot came next.

'The very highest prices will probably be bid this evening,' I said, half teasing him, but all he said was, 'Perhaps we should wait, then.'

'If you buy ten yearlings,' I said, 'six might get to a

racecourse, three might win a race and one might be pretty good. If you're lucky.'

'Cautious Ian.'

'You,' I said, 'are cautious with gold.'

He looked at me with half-shut eyes. 'Not many people say that.'

'You're fast and flamboyant,' I said, 'but you sit and wait for the moment.'

He merely grunted and began paying attention to the matter in hand, intently focusing not on the merchandise but on the bidders on the far side of the ring. The auctioneers in the box to our left were relaxed and polished, the one currently at the microphone elaborately unimpressed by the fortunes passing. 'Fifty thousand, thank you, sir; sixty thousand, seventy . . . eighty? Shall I say eighty? Eighty, thank you, sir. Against you, sir. Ninety? Ninety. One hundred thousand. Selling now. I'm selling now. Against you, sir? No? All done? All done?' A pause for a sweep round to make sure no new bidder was frantically waving. 'Done, then. Sold to Mr Siddons. One hundred thousand guineas. The next lot . . .'

'Selling now,' Malcolm said. 'I suppose that means there was a reserve on it?'

I nodded.

'So until the fellow says "selling now", it's safe to bid, knowing you won't have to buy?'

'Yours might be the bid that reaches the reserve.'

He nodded. 'Russian roulette.'

We watched the sales for the rest of the afternoon, but he aimed no bullets at his own head. He asked who people were. 'Who is that Mr Siddons? That's the fourth horse he's bought.'

'He works for a bloodstock agency. He's buying for other people.'

'And that man in navy, scowling. Who's he?'

'Max Jones. He owns a lot of horses.'

'Every time that old woman bids, he bids against her.'

'It's a well-known feud.'

He sniffed. 'It must cost them fortunes.' He looked around the amphitheatre at the constantly changing audience of breeders, trainers, owners and the simply interested. 'Whose judgement would you trust most?'

I mentioned several trainers and the agents who might be acting on their behalf, and he told me to tell him when someone with good judgement was bidding, and to point them out. I did so many times, and he listened and passed no comment.

After a while, we went out for a break, an Ebury scotch, a sandwich and fresh air.

'I suppose you know,' Malcolm said casually, watching yearlings skittering past in the grasp of their handlers, 'that Moira and I were divorcing?'

'Yes, I heard.'

'And that she was demanding the house and half my possessions?'

'Mm.'

'And half my future earnings?'

'Could she?'

'She was going to fight for it.'

I refrained from saying that whoever had murdered Moira had done Malcolm a big favour, but I'd thought it several times.

I said instead, 'Still no clues?'

'No, nothing new.'

He spoke without regret. His disenchantment with Moira, according to his acid second wife, my own mother Joyce, had begun as soon as he'd stopped missing Coochie; and as Joyce was as percipient as she was catty, I believed it.

'The police tried damned hard to prove I did it,' Malcolm said.

'Yes, so I heard.'

'Who from? Who's your grapevine?'

'All of them,' I said.

'The three witches?'

I couldn't help smiling. He meant his three living ex-wives, Vivien, Joyce and Alicia.

'Yes, them. And all of the family.'

He shrugged.

'They were all worried that you might have,' I said.

'And were you worried?' he asked.

'I was glad you weren't arrested.'

He grunted noncommittally. 'I suppose you do know that most of your brothers and sisters, not to mention the witches, told the police you hated Moira?'

'They told me they'd told,' I agreed. 'But then, I did.'

'Lot of stinkers I've fathered,' he said gloomily.

Malcolm's personal alibi for Moira's death had been as unassailable as my own, as he'd been in Paris for the day when someone had pushed Moira's retroussé little nose into a bag of potting compost and held it there until it was certain she would take no more geranium cuttings. I could have wished her a better death, but it had been quick, everyone said. The police still clung to the belief that Malcolm had arranged for an assassin, but even Joyce knew that that was nonsense. Malcolm was a creature of tempest and volatility, but he'd never been calculatingly cruel.

His lack of interest in the horses themselves didn't extend to anything else at the sales: inside the sale-ring he had been particularly attentive to the flickering electronic board which lit up with the amount as each bid was made, and lit up not only in English currency but in dollars, yen, francs, lire and Irish punts at the current exchange rates. He'd always been fascinated by the workings of money, and had once far more than doubled a million pounds simply by banking it in the United States at two dollars forty cents to the pound, waiting five years, and bringing it back when the rate stood at one dollar twenty cents, which neatly gave him twice the capital he'd started with and the interest besides. He thought of the money market, after gold, as a sort of help-yourself cornucopia.

None of his children had inherited his instinct for timing and trends, a lack he couldn't understand. He'd told me directly once or twice to buy this or sell that, and he'd been right, but I couldn't make money the way he did without his guidance.

He considered that the best years of his talent had been wasted: all the years when, for political reasons, the free movement of capital had been restricted and when gold bullion couldn't be bought by private Britons. Always large, Malcolm's income, once the controls were lifted, went up like a hot air balloon, and it was at the beginning of that period, when he'd woken to the possibilities and bought his first crock of gold for sixty pounds an ounce to sell it presently for over a hundred, that he'd first been called Midas.

Since then, he'd ridden the yellow roller-coaster several times, unerringly buying when the price sank ever lower, selling as it soared, but before the bubble burst, always seeming to spot the wobbling moment when the market approached trough or peak.

Coochie had appeared wearing ever larger diamonds. The three witches, Vivien, Joyce and Alicia, each with a nice divorce settlement agreed in less sparkling days, unavailingly consulted their lawyers.

There was a second electronic board outside the sale-ring showing the state of the sale inside. Malcolm concentrated on the flickering figures until they began to shine more brightly in the fading daylight, but he still paid no close attention to the merchandise itself.

'They all look very small,' he said reprovingly, watching a narrow colt pass on its way from stable to sale-ring.

'Well, they're yearlings.'

'One year old, literally?'

'Eighteen months, twenty months: about that. They race next year, when they're two.'

He nodded and decided to return to the scene of the action, and again found us seats opposite the big-money crowd. The amphitheatre had filled almost to capacity while we'd been outside, and soon, with every seat taken, people shoved close-packed into the entrance and the standing-room sections: the blood of Northern Dancer and Nijinsky and of Secretariat and Lyphard was on its regal way to the ring.

A hush fell in the building at the entrance of the first of the legend-bred youngsters, the breath-held expectant hush of the knowledgeable awaiting a battle among financial giants. A fat cheque on this sales evening could secure a Derby winner and found a dynasty, and it happened often enough to tempt belief each time that this . . . *this* . . . was the one.

The auctioneer cleared his throat and managed the introduction without a quiver. 'Ladies and gentlemen, we now have Lot No 76, a bay colt by Nijinsky . . .' He recited the magical breeding as if bored, and asked for an opening bid.

Malcolm sat quiet and watched while the numbers flew high on the scoreboard, the price rising in jumps of fifty thousand; watched while the auctioneer scanned the bidding faces for the drop of an eyelid, the twitch of a head, the tiny acknowledgements of intent.

'... against you, sir. No more, then? All done?' The auctioneer's eyebrows rose with his gavel, remained poised in elevation, came smoothly, conclusively down. 'Sold for one million seven hundred thousand guineas to Mr Siddons ...'

The crowd sighed, expelling collective breath like a single organism. Then came rustling of catalogues, movement, murmuring and rewound expectation.

Malcolm said, 'It's a spectator sport.'

'Addictive,' I agreed.

He glanced at me sideways. 'For one million ... five million ... there's no guarantee the colt will ever race, isn't that what you said? One could be throwing one's cash down the drain?'

'That's right.'

'It's a perfectly blameless way of getting rid of a lot of money very fast, wouldn't you say?'

'Well ...' I said slowly, 'is that what you're at?'

'Do you disapprove?'

'It's your money. You made it. You spend it.'

He smiled almost secretively at his catalogue and said, 'I can hear the "but" in your voice.'

'Mm. If you want to enjoy yourself, buy ten next-best horses instead of one super-colt, and get interested in them.'

'And pay ten training fees instead of one?'

I nodded. 'Ten would drain the exchequer nicely.'

He laughed in his throat and watched the next half-grown blue-blood reach three million guineas before Mr Siddons shook his head. ' . . . sold for three million and fifty thousand guineas to Mrs Terazzini . . .'

'Who's she?' Malcolm asked.

'She owns a worldwide bloodstock empire.'

He reflected. 'Like Robert Sangster?'

'Yep. Like him.'

He made a noise of understanding. 'An industry.'

'Yes.'

The following lot, a filly, fetched a more moderate sum, but the hush of expectancy returned for the next offering. Malcolm, keenly tuned by now to the atmosphere, watched the bidders as usual, not the nervous chestnut colt.

The upward impetus stopped at a fraction over two million and the auctioneer's eyebrows and gavel rose. 'All done?'

Malcolm raised his catalogue.

The movement caught the eye of the auctioneer, who paused with the gavel raised, using his eyebrows as a question, looking at Malcolm with surprise. Malcolm sat in what could be called the audience, not with the usual actors.

'You want to bid, sir?' asked the auctioneer.

'And fifty,' Malcolm said clearly, nodding.

There was a fluttering in the dovecot of auctioneers as head bent to head among themselves, consulting. All round the ring, necks stretched to see who had spoken, and down in the entrance-way the man who'd bid last before Malcolm shrugged, shook his head and turned his back to the auctioneer. His last increase had been for twenty thousand only: a last small raise over two million, which appeared to have been his intended limit.

The auctioneer himself seemed less than happy. 'All done, then?' he asked again, and with no further replies, said, 'Done then. Sold for two million and seventy thousand guineas to . . . er . . . the bidder opposite.'

The auctioneer consulted with his colleagues again and one of them left the box, carrying a clipboard. He hurried down and round the ring to join a minion on our side, both of them with their gaze fastened on Malcolm.

'Those two auctioneers won't let you out of their sight,' I observed. 'They suffered badly from a vanishing bidder not so long ago.'

'They look as if they're coming to arrest me,' Malcolm said cheerfully; and both of the auctioneers indeed made their way right to his side, handing him the clipboard and politely requiring him to sign their bill of sale, in triplicate and without delay. They retired to ground level but were still waiting for us with steely intent when, after three further sales had gone through as expected, we made our way down.

They invited Malcolm civilly to the quieter end of their large office, and we went. They computed what he owed and deferentially presented the total. Malcolm wrote them a cheque.

They politely suggested proof of identity and a reference. Malcolm gave them an American Express card and the telephone number of his bank manager. They took the cheque gingerly and said that although Mr . . . er . . . Pembroke should if he wished arrange insurance on his purchase at once, the colt would not be available for removal until . . . er . . . tomorrow.

Malcolm took no offence. He wouldn't have let anyone he didn't know drive off with a horsebox full of gold. He said tomorrow would be fine, and in high good spirits told me I could ferry him back to his Cambridge hotel, from where he'd come that morning in a taxi, and we would have dinner together.

After we'd called in at an insurance agent's office and he'd signed some more papers and another cheque, we accordingly walked together to the car park from where people were beginning to drift home. Night had fallen, but there were lights enough to see which car was which, and as we went I pointed out the row ahead where my wheels stood.

'Where are you going to send your colt?' I asked, walking.

'Where would you say?'

'I should think,' I said . . . but I never finished the answer, or not at that actual moment.

A car coming towards us between two rows of parked cars suddenly emitted two headlight beams, blinding us; and at the same moment it seemed to accelerate fiercely, swerving straight towards Malcolm.

I leaped . . . flung myself . . . at my father, my flying weight spinning him off balance, carrying him off his feet, knocking him down. I fell on top of him, knowing that the pale speeding bulk of the car had caught me, but not sure to what extent. There was just a bang and a lot of lights curving like arcs, and a whirling view of gleams on metal, and a fast crunch into darkness.

We were on the ground then between two silent parked cars, our bodies heavy with shock and disorientation, in a sort of inertia.

After a moment, Malcolm began struggling to free himself from under my weight, and I rolled awkwardly onto my knees and thankfully thought of little but bruises. Malcolm pushed himself up until he was sitting with his back against a car's wheel, collecting his wits but looking as shaken as I felt.

'That car,' he said eventually, between deep breaths, 'was aiming . . . to kill me.'

I nodded speechlessly. My trousers were torn, thigh grazed and bleeding.

'You always had . . . quick reactions,' he said. 'So now . . . now you know . . . why I want you beside me . . . all the time.'

CHAPTER TWO

It was the second time someone had tried to kill him, he said.

I was driving towards Cambridge a shade more slowly than usual, searching anxiously in the rear-view mirror for satanically-minded followers but so far thankfully without success. My right leg was stiffening depressingly from the impact of twenty minutes ago, but I was in truth fairly used to that level of buffet through having ridden over the years in three or four hundred jump races, incurring consequent collisions with the ground.

Malcolm didn't like driving for reasons Coochie had deftly diagnosed as impatience. Coochie hadn't liked his driving either, for reasons (she said) of plain fear, and had taken over as family chauffeur. I too had been used to driving Malcolm from the day I gained my licence: I would need to have been delirious to ask him to take the wheel just because of some grazed skin.

The second time someone had tried to kill him . . .

'When was the first time?' I asked.

'Last Friday.'

It was currently Tuesday evening. 'What happened?' I said.

He took a while over answering. When he did there was more sadness in his voice than anger, and I listened to his tone behind the words and slowly understood his deepest fears.

'One moment I was walking the dogs . . . well, I think I was, but that's it, I don't really remember.' He paused. 'I think I had a bang on the head . . . Anyway, the last thing I remember is calling the dogs and opening the kitchen door. I meant to take them through the garden to that field with the stream and the willows. I don't know how far I went. I shouldn't think far. Anyway, I woke up in Moira's car in the garage . . . it's still there . . . and it's damn lucky I woke up at all . . . the engine was running . . .' He stopped for a few moments. 'It's funny how the mind works. I knew absolutely at once that I had to switch off the engine. Extraordinary. Like a flash. I was in the back seat, sort of tumbled . . . toppled over . . . half lying. I got up and practically fell through between the front seats to reach the key in the ignition, and when the engine stopped I just lay there, you know, thinking that I was bloody uncomfortable but not having any more energy to move.'

'Did anyone come?' I said, when he paused.

'No . . . I felt better after a while. I stumbled out of the car and was sick.'

'Did you tell the police?'

'Sure, I told them.' His voice sounded weary at the recollection. 'It must have been about five when I set off with the dogs. Maybe seven by the time I called the police. I'd had a couple of stiff drinks by then and stopped shaking. They asked me why I hadn't called them sooner. Bloody silly. And it was the same lot who came after Moira. They think I did it, you know. Had her killed.'

'I know.'

'Did the witches tell you that too?'

'Joyce did. She said you couldn't have. She said you might have . . . er . . .' I baulked from repeating my mother's actual words, which were 'throttled the little bitch in a rage', and substituted more moderately, ' . . . been capable of killing her yourself, but not of paying someone else to do it.'

He made a satisfied noise but no comment, and I added, 'That seems to be the family concensus.'

He sighed. 'It's not the police concensus. Far from it. I don't think they believed anyone had tried to kill me. They made a lot of notes and took samples . . . I ask you . . . of my vomit, and dusted over Moira's car for fingerprints, but it was obvious they were choked with doubts. I think they thought I'd been going to commit suicide and thought better of it . . . or else that I'd staged it in the hope people would believe I couldn't have killed Moira if someone was trying to kill *me* . . .'

He shook his head. 'I'm sorry I told them at all, and that's why we're not reporting tonight's attempt either.'

He had been adamant, in the sales car park, that we shouldn't.

'What about the bump on your head?' I asked.

'I had a swelling above my ear. Very tender, but not very big. The word I heard the police use about that was "inconclusive".'

'And if you'd died . . .' I said thoughtfully.

He nodded. 'If I'd died, it would have wrapped things up nicely for them. Suicide. Remorse. Implicit admission of guilt.'

I drove carefully towards Cambridge, appalled and also angry. Moira's death hadn't touched me in the slightest, but the attacks on my father showed me I'd been wrong. Moira had had a right to live. There should have been rage, too, on her behalf.

'What happened to the dogs?' I said.

'What? Oh, the dogs. They came back . . . they were whining at the kitchen door. I let them in while I was waiting for the police. They were muddy . . . heaven knows where they'd been. They were tired anyway. I fed them and they went straight to their baskets and went to sleep.'

'Pity they couldn't talk.'

'What? Yes, I suppose so. Yes.' He fell into silence, sighing occasionally as I thought over what he'd told me.

'Who,' I said eventually, 'knew you were going to Newmarket Sales?'

'Who?' He sounded surprised at the question, and then understood it. 'I don't know.' He was puzzled. 'I've no idea. I didn't know myself until yesterday.'

'Well, what have you been doing since the police left you last Friday night?'

'Thinking.' And the thoughts, it was clear, had been melancholic: the thoughts now saddening his voice.

'Mm,' I said, 'along the lines of why was Moira killed?'

'Along those lines.'

I said it plainly. 'To stop her taking half your possessions?'

He said unwillingly, 'Yes.'

'And the people who had a chief interest in stopping her were your likely heirs. Your children.'

He was silent.

I said, 'Also perhaps their husbands and wives, also perhaps even the witches.'

'I don't want to believe it,' he said. 'How could I have put a murderer into the world.'

'People do,' I said.

'*Ian!*'

The truth was that, apart from poor Robin, I didn't know my half-brothers and half-sisters well enough to have any certainty about any of them. I was usually on speaking terms with them all, but didn't seek them out. There had been too much fighting, too many rows:

Vivien's children disliked Alicia's, Alicia's disliked them and me, Vivien hated Joyce and Joyce hated Alicia very bitterly indeed. Under Coochie's reign, the whole lot had been banned from sleeping in the house, if not from single-day visits, with the result that a storm of collective resentment had been directed at me whom she had kept and treated as her own.

'Apart from thinking,' I said, 'what have you been doing since Friday night?'

'When the police had gone, I . . . I . . .' he stopped.

'The shakes came back?' I suggested.

'Yes. Do you understand that?'

'I'd have been scared silly,' I said. 'Stupid not to be. I'd have felt that whoever had tried to kill me was prowling about in the dark waiting for me to be alone so he could have another go.'

Malcolm audibly swallowed. 'I telephoned to the hire firm I use now and told them to send a car to fetch me. Do you know what panic feels like?'

'Not that sort, I guess.'

'I was sweating, and it was cold. I could feel my heart thumping . . . banging away at a terrible rate. It was awful. I packed some things . . . I couldn't concentrate.'

He shifted in his seat as the outskirts of Cambridge came up in the headlights and began to give me directions to the hotel where he said he'd spent the previous four nights.

'Does anyone know where you're staying?' I asked,

turning corners. 'Have you seen any of your old chums?'

Malcolm knew Cambridge well, had been at university there and still had friends at high tables. It must have seemed to him a safe city to bolt to, but it was where I would have gone looking for him, if not much else failed.

'Of course I have,' he said in answer to my question. 'I spent Sunday with the Rackersons, dined with old Digger in Trinity last night . . . it's nonsense to think they could be involved.'

'Yes,' I agreed, pulling up outside his hotel. 'All the same, go and pack and check out of here, and we'll go somewhere else.'

'It's not necessary,' he protested.

'You appointed me as minder, so I'm minding,' I said.

He gave me a long look in the dim light inside the car. The doorman of the hotel stepped forward and opened the door beside me, an invitation to step out.

'Come with me,' my father said.

I was both astounded by his fear and thought it warranted. I asked the doorman where I should park, and turned at his suggestion through an arch into the hotel's inner courtway. From there, through a back door and comfortable old-fashioned hallways, Malcolm and I went up one flight of red-carpeted stairs to a lengthy winding corridor. Several people we passed glanced down at my torn trouser-leg with the dried-blood scenery inside, but no one said anything: was it still British politeness, I wondered, or the new creed of not getting involved? Malcolm, it seemed, had forgotten the problem existed.

He brought his room key out of his pocket and, with it raised, said abruptly, 'I suppose *you* didn't tell anyone I would be at the sales.'

'No, I didn't.'

'But you knew.' He paused. 'Only you knew.'

He was staring at me with the blue eyes and I saw all the sudden fear-driven question marks rioting through his mind.

'Go inside,' I said. 'The corridor isn't the place for this.'

He looked at the key, he looked wildly up and down the now empty corridor, poised, almost, to run.

I turned my back on him and walked purposefully away in the direction of the stairs.

'*Ian*,' he shouted.

I stopped and turned round.

'Come back,' he said.

I went back slowly. 'You said you trusted me,' I said.

'I haven't seen you for three years . . . and I broke your nose . . .'

I took the key out of his hand and unlocked the door. I supposed I might have been suspicious of me if I'd been attacked twice in five days, considering I came into the high-probability category of son. I switched on the light and went forward into the room which was free from lurking murderers that time at least.

Malcolm followed, only tentatively reassured, closing the door slowly behind him. I drew the heavy striped curtains across the two windows and briefly surveyed the spacious but old-fashioned accommodation: reproduction antique furniture, twin beds, pair of armchairs, door to bathroom.

No murderer in the bathroom.

'Ian . . .' Malcolm said.

'Did you bring any scotch?' I asked. In the old days, he'd never travelled without it.

He waved a hand towards a chest of drawers where I found a half-full bottle nestling among a large number of socks. I fetched a glass from the bathroom and poured him enough to tranquillize an elephant.

'For God's sake . . .' he said.

'Sit down and drink it.'

'You're bloody arrogant.'

He did sit down, though, and tried not to let the glass clatter against his teeth from the shaking of his hand.

With much less force, I said, 'If I'd wanted you dead, I'd have let that car hit you tonight. I'd have jumped the other way . . . out of trouble.'

He seemed to notice clearly for the first time that there had been any physical consequences to our escape.

'Your leg,' he said, 'must be all right?'

'Leg is. Trousers . . . can I borrow a pair of yours?'

He pointed to a cupboard where I found a second suit almost identical to the one he was wearing. I was three inches taller than he and a good deal thinner but, belted and slung round the hips, whole cloth was better than holey.

He silently watched me change and made no objection when I telephoned down to the reception desk and asked them to get his bill ready for his departure. He drank more of the scotch, but nowhere was he relaxed.

'Shall I pack for you?' I asked.

He nodded, and watched some more while I fetched his suitcase, opened it on one of the beds and began collecting his belongings. The things he'd brought spoke eloquently of his state of mind when he'd packed them: about ten pairs of socks but no other underwear, a dozen shirts, no pyjamas, two towelling bath-robes, no extra shoes. The clearly new electric razor in the bathroom still bore a stick-on price tag, but he had brought his antique gold-and-silver-backed brushes, all eight of them, including two clothes brushes. I put everything into the case, and closed it.

'Ian,' he said.

'Mm?'

'People can pay assassins . . . You could have decided not to go through with it tonight . . . at the last moment . . .'

'It wasn't like that,' I protested. Saving him had been utterly instinctive, without calculation or counting of risks: I'd been lucky to get off with a graze.

He said almost beseechingly, with difficulty, 'It wasn't you, was it, who had Moira . . . Or me, in the garage . . .? Say it wasn't you.'

I didn't know really how to convince him. He'd known me better, lived with me longer than with any of his other children, and if his trust was this fragile then there wasn't much future between us.

'I didn't have Moira killed,' I said. 'If you believe it of me, you could believe it of yourself.' I paused. 'I don't want you dead, I want you alive. I could never do you harm.'

It struck me that he really needed to hear me say I loved him, so although he might scoff at the actual words, and despite the conditioned inhibitions of my upbringing, I said, feeling that desperate situations needed desperate remedies, 'You're a great father . . . and . . . er . . . I love you.'

He blinked. Such a declaration pierced him, one could see. I'd probably overdone it, I thought, but his distrust had been a wound for me too.

I said much more lightly, 'I swear on the Coochie Pembroke Memorial Challenge Trophy that I would never touch a hair on your head . . . nor Moira's either, though I did indeed loathe her.'

I lifted the suitcase off the bed.

'Do I go on with you or not?' I said. 'If you don't trust me, I'm going home.'

He was looking at me searchingly, as if I were a stranger, which I suppose in some ways I was. He had never before, I guessed, had to think of me not as a son but as a man, as a person who had led a life separate from his, with a different outlook, different desires, different values. Sons grew from little boys into their own adult selves: fathers tended not to see the change clearly. Malcolm, I was certain, thought of me basically as still having the half-formed personality I'd had at fifteen.

'You're different,' he said.

'I am the same. Trust your instinct.'

Some of the tension at last slackened in his muscles. His instinct had been trust, an instinct strong enough to carry him to the telephone after three silent years. He finished the scotch and stood up, filling his lungs with a deep breath as if making resolves.

'Come with me, then,' he said.

I nodded.

He went over to the chest of drawers and from the bottom drawer, which I hadn't checked, produced a briefcase. I might have guessed it would be there somewhere: even in the direst panic, he wouldn't have left behind the lists of his gold shares or his currency exchange calculator. He started with the briefcase to the door, leaving me to bring the suitcase, but on impulse I went over again to the telephone and asked for a taxi to be ready for us.

'But your car's here,' Malcolm said.

'Mm. I think I'll leave it here, for now.'

'But why?'

'Because if I didn't tell anyone you were going to Newmarket Sales, and nor did you, then it's probable you were followed there, from . . . er . . . here. If you think about it . . . the car that tried to kill you was waiting in the sales car park, but you didn't have a car. You went there by taxi. Whoever drove at you must have seen you and me together, and known who I was, and guessed you might leave with me, so although I didn't see anyone following us tonight from Newmarket, whoever-it-was probably knew we would come here, to this hotel, so . . . well . . . so they might be hanging about in the courtyard where we parked, where it's nice and dark outside the back door, waiting to see if we come out again.'

'My God!'

'It's possible,' I said. 'So we'll leave through the front with the doorman in attendance, don't you think?'

'If you say so,' he said weakly.

'From now on,' I said, 'we take every exaggerated precaution we can think of.'

'Well, where are we going in this taxi?'

'How about somewhere where we can rent a car?'

The taxi-driver, however, once we'd set off without incident from the hotel, bill paid, luggage loaded, doorman tipped, informed us doubtfully that nine o'clock on a Tuesday night wasn't going to be easy. All the car-hire firms' offices would be closed.

'Chauffeur-driven car, then,' Malcolm said. 'Fellows who do weddings, that sort of thing. Twenty quid in it for you if you fix it.'

Galvanized by this offer, the taxi-driver drove us down some back streets, stopped outside an unpromising little terraced house and banged on the door. It opened, shining out a melon-slice of light, and gathered the taxi-driver inside.

'We're going to be mugged,' Malcolm said.

The taxi-driver returned harmlessly, however, accompanied by a larger man buttoning the jacket of a chauffeur's uniform and carrying a reassuring peaked cap.

'The firm my brother-in-law works for does mostly weddings and funerals,' the taxi-driver said. 'He wants to know where you want to go.'

'London,' I said.

London appeared to be no problem at all. The driver and his brother-in-law climbed into the front of the taxi which started off, went round a corner or two, and pulled up again outside a lock-up garage. We sat in the taxi as asked while the two drivers opened the garage, disclosing its contents. Which was how Malcolm and I proceeded to London in a very large, highly-polished black Rolls-Royce, the moonlighting chauffeur separated from us discreetly by a glass partition.

'Why did you go to the sales at all?' I asked Malcolm. 'I mean, why Newmarket? Why the sales?'

Malcolm frowned. 'Because of Ebury's, I suppose.'

'The jewellers?'

'Yes . . . well . . . I knew they were going to have a showroom there. They told me so last week when I went to see them about Coochie's jewellery. I mean, I know them pretty well, I bought most of her things from there. I was admiring a silver horse they had, and they said they were exhibiting this week at Newmarket Sales. So then yesterday when I was wondering what would fetch you . . . where you would meet me . . . I remembered the sales were so close to Cambridge, and I decided on it not long before I rang you.'

I pondered a bit. 'How would you set about finding where someone was, if you wanted to, so to speak?'

To my surprise he had a ready answer. 'Get the fellow I had for tailing Moira.'

'Tailing . . .'

'My lawyer said to do it. It might save me something, he said, if Moira was having a bit on the side, see what I mean?'

'I do indeed,' I agreed dryly. 'But I suppose she wasn't?'

'No such luck.' He glanced at me. 'What do you have in mind?'

'Well . . . I just wondered if he could check where everyone in the family was last Friday and tonight.'

'Everyone!' Malcolm exclaimed. 'It would take weeks.'

'It would put your mind at rest.'

He shook his head gloomily. 'You forget about assassins.'

'Assassins aren't so frightfully easy to find, not for ordinary people. How would you set about it, for instance, if you wanted someone killed? Put an ad in *The Times*?'

He didn't seem to see such a problem as I did, but he agreed that 'the fellow who tailed Moira' should be offered the job of checking the family.

We discussed where we should stay that night: in which hotel, in fact, as neither of us felt like returning home. Home, currently, to me, was a rather dull suburban flat in Epsom, not far from the stable I'd been working for. Home for Malcolm was still the house where I'd been raised, from which Moira had apparently driven him, but to which he had returned immediately after her death. 'Home' for all the family was that big house in Berkshire which had seen all five wives come and go: Malcolm himself had been brought up there, and I could scarcely imagine what he must have felt at the prospect of losing it.

'What happened between you and Moira?' I said.

'None of your goddam business.'

We travelled ten miles in silence. Then he shifted, sighed, and said, 'She wanted Coochie's jewellery and I wouldn't give it to her. She kept on and on about it, rabbit, rabbit. Annoyed me, do you see? And then . . . well . . .' he shrugged, 'she caught me out.'

'With another woman?' I said without surprise.

He nodded, unashamed. He'd never been monogamous and couldn't understand why it should be expected. The terrible rows in my childhood had all been centred on his affairs: while he'd been married to Vivien and then to Joyce, he had maintained Alicia all the time as his mistress. Alicia bore him two children while he was married to Vivien and Joyce, and also one subsequently, when he'd made a fairly honest woman of her, at her insistence.

I liked to think he had been faithful finally to Coochie, but on the whole it was improbable, and I was never going to ask.

Malcolm favoured our staying at the Dorchester, but I persuaded him he was too well known there, and we settled finally on the Savoy.

'A suite,' Malcolm said at the reception desk. 'Two bedrooms, two bathrooms and a sitting room, and send up some Bollinger right away.'

I didn't feel like drinking champagne, but Malcolm did. He also ordered scrambled eggs and smoked salmon for us both from room service, with a bottle of Hine Antique brandy and a box of Havana cigars for comforts.

Idly I totted up the expenses of his day: one solid silver trophy, one two-million-guinea thoroughbred, insurance for same, Cambridge hotel bill, tip for the taxi-driver, chauffeured Rolls-Royce, jumbo suite at the Savoy with trimmings. I wondered how much he was really worth, and whether he intended to spend the lot.

We ate the food and drank the brandy still not totally in accord with each other. The three years' division had been, it seemed, a chasm not as easy to cross as I'd thought. I felt that although I'd meant it when I said I loved him, it was probably the long memories of him that I really loved, not his physical presence here and now, and I could see that if I was going to stay close to him, as I'd promised, I would be learning him again and from a different viewpoint; that each of us, in fact, would newly get to know the other.

'Any day now,' Malcolm said, carefully dislodging ash from his cigar, 'we're going to Australia.'

I absorbed the news and said, 'Are we?'

He nodded. 'We'll need visas. Where's your passport?'

'In my flat. Where's yours?'

'In the house.'

'Then I'll get them both tomorrow,' I said, 'and you stay here.' I paused. 'Are we going to Australia for any special reason?'

'To look at gold mines,' he said. 'And kangaroos.'

After a short silence, I said, 'We don't just have to escape. We do have to find out who's trying to kill you, in order to stop them succeeding.'

'Escape is more attractive,' he said. 'How about a week in Singapore on the way?'

'Anything you say. Only . . . I'm supposed to ride in a race at Sandown on Friday.'

'I've never understood why you like it. All those cold wet days. All those falls.'

'You get your rush from gold,' I said.

'Danger?' His eyebrows rose. 'Quiet, well-behaved, cautious Ian? Life is a bore without risk, is that it?'

'It's not so extraordinary,' I said.

I'd ridden always as an amateur, unpaid, because something finally held me back from the total dedication needed for turning professional. Race riding was my deepest pleasure, but not my entire life, and in consequence I'd never developed the competitive drive necessary for climbing the pro ladder. I was happy with the rides I got, with the camaraderie of the changing room, with the wide skies and the horses themselves, and yes, one had to admit it, with the risk.

'Staying near me,' Malcolm said, 'as you've already found out, isn't enormously safe.'

'That's why I'm staying,' I said.

He stared. He said, 'My God,' and he laughed. 'I thought I knew you. Seems I don't.'

He finished his brandy, stubbed out his cigar and decided on bed; and in the morning he was up before me, sitting on a sofa in one of the bathrobes and reading the *Sporting Life* when I ambled out in the underpants and shirt I'd slept in.

'I've ordered breakfast,' he said. 'And I'm in the paper – how about that?'

I looked where he pointed. His name was certainly there, somewhere near the end of the detailed lists of yesterday's sales. 'Lot 79, ch. colt, 2,070,000 gns. Malcolm Pembroke'.

He put down the paper, well pleased. 'Now, what do we do today?'

'We summon your private eye, we fix a trainer for the colt, I fetch our passports and some clothes, and you stay here.'

Slightly to my surprise, he raised no arguments except to tell me not to be away too long. He was looking rather thoughtfully at the healing graze down my right thigh and the red beginnings of bruising around it.

'The trouble is,' he said, 'I don't have the private eye's phone number. Not with me.'

'We'll get another agency, then, from the yellow pages.'

'Your mother knows it, of course. Joyce knows it.'

'How does she know it?'

'She used him,' he said airily, 'to follow me and Alicia.'

There was nothing, I supposed, which should ever surprise me about my parents.

'When the lawyer fellow said to have Moira tailed, I got the private eye's name from Joyce. After all, he'd done a good job on me and Alicia all those years ago. Too bloody good, when you think of it. So get through to Joyce, Ian, and ask her for the number.'

Bemused, I did as he said.

'Darling,' my mother shrieked down the line. 'Where's your father?'

'I don't know,' I said.

'Darling, do you know what he's bloody *done*?'

'No . . . what?'

'He's given a *fortune*, darling, I mean literally *hundreds* of *thousands*, to some wretched little film company to make some absolutely *ghastly* film about tadpoles or something. Some bloody fool of a man telephoned to find out where your father was, because it seems he promised them even *more* money which they'd like to have . . . I ask you! I know you and Malcolm aren't talking, but you've got to do something to stop him.'

'Well,' I said, 'it's his money.'

'Darling, don't be so *naive.* Someone's going to inherit it, and if only you'd swallow all that bloody pride, as I've told you over and over, it would be *yours.* If you go on and on with this bloody quarrel, he'll leave it all to Alicia's beastly brood, and I cannot *bear* the prospect of her gloating for ever more. So make it up with Malcolm *at once*, darling, and get him to see sense.'

'Calm down,' I said. 'I have.'

'*What?*'

'Made it up with him.'

'Thank God, at *last*!' my mother shrieked. 'Then, darling, what are you waiting for? Get onto him *straight* away and stop him spending your inheritance.'

CHAPTER THREE

Malcolm's house, after three years of Moira's occupancy, had greatly changed.

Malcolm's Victorian house was known as 'Quantum' because of the Latin inscription carved into the lintel over the front door. QUANTUM IN ME FUIT – roughly, 'I did the best I could.'

I went there remembering the comfortable casualness that Coochie had left and not actually expecting that things would be different: and I should have known better, as each wife in turn, Coochie included, had done her best to eradicate all signs of her predecessor. Marrying Malcolm had, for each wife, involved moving into his house, but he had indulged them all, I now understood, in the matter of ambience.

I let myself in through the kitchen door with Malcolm's keys and thought wildly for a moment that I'd come to the wrong place. Coochie's pinewood and red-tiled homeliness had been swept away in favour of glossy yellow walls, glittering white appliances and shelves crowded with scarlet and deep pink geraniums cascading from white pots.

Faintly stunned, I looked back through time to the era before Coochie, to Alicia's fluffy occupancy of broderie anglaise frills on shimmering white curtains with pale blue work-tops and white floor tiles; and back further still to the starker olive and milk-coffee angularities chosen by Joyce. I remembered the day the workmen had torn out my mother's kitchen, and how I'd gone howling to Malcolm: he'd packed me off to Joyce immediately for a month, which I didn't like either, and when I returned I'd found the white frills installed, and the pale blue cupboards, and I thought them all sissy, but I'd learned not to say so.

For the first time ever, I wondered what the kitchen had looked like in Vivien's time, when forty-five or so years ago young Malcolm had brought her there as his first bride. Vivien had been dispossessed and resentful by the time I was born, and I'd seldom seen her smiling. She seemed to me the least positive of the five wives and the least intelligent but, according to her photographs, she had been in her youth by streets the most beautiful. The dark sweep of her eyebrows and the high cheekbones remained, but the thick black hair had thinned now in greying, and entrenched bitterness had soured the once sweet mouth. Vivien's marriage, I'd guessed, had died through Malcolm's boredom with her, and although they now still met occasionally at events to do with their mutual children and grandchildren, they were more apt to turn their backs than to kiss.

Vivien disliked and was plaintively critical of almost everybody while at the same time unerringly interpreting the most innocent general remarks of others as being criticism of herself. It was impossible to please her often or for long, and I, like almost all the extended family, had long ago stopped trying. She had indoctrinated her three offspring with her own dissatisfactions to the point where they were nastily disparaging of Malcolm behind his back, though not to his face, hypocrites that they were.

Malcolm had steadfastly maintained them through young adulthood and then cast them loose, each with a trust fund that would prevent them from actually starving. He had treated all seven of his normally surviving children in the same way; his eighth child, Robin, would be looked after for ever. None of us seven could have any complaints: he had given us all whatever vocational training we'd chosen and afterwards the cushion against penury, and at that point in each of our lives had considered his work done. Whatever became of us in the future, he said, had to be in our own hands.

With the family powerfully in mind, I went from the kitchen into the hall where I found that Moira had had the oak panelling painted white. Increasingly amused, I thought of the distant days when Alicia had painstakingly bleached all the old wood, only to have Coochie stain it dark again: and I supposed that perhaps Malcolm enjoyed change around him in many ways, not just in women.

His own private room, always called the office although more like a comfortable cluttered sitting room, seemed to have escaped the latest refit except in the matter of gold velvet curtains replacing the old green. Otherwise, the room as always seemed filled with his strong personality, the walls covered with dozens of framed photographs, the deep cupboards bulging with files, the bookshelves crammed, every surface bearing mementoes of his journeyings and achievements, nothing very tidy.

I went over to the desk to find his passport and half-expected to hear his voice at any minute even though I'd left him forty miles away persuasively telephoning to 'the fellow who tailed Moira'.

His passport, he'd said, was in the second drawer down on the right-hand side, and so it was, among a large clutter of bygone travel arrangements and expired medical insurances. Malcolm seldom threw much away, merely building another cupboard for files. His filing system was such that no one but he had the slightest idea where any paper or information could be found, but he himself could put his finger on things unerringly. His method, he'd told me once long ago, was always to put everything where he would first think of looking for it; and as a child, I'd seen such sense in that that I had copied him ever since.

Looking around again, it struck me that although

the room was crammed with objects, several familiar ones were missing. The gold dolphin, for instance, and the gold tree bearing amethysts, and the Georgian silver candelabras. Perhaps at last, I thought, he had stored them prudently in the bank.

Carrying the passport, I went upstairs to fetch clothes to add to his sketchy packing and out of irresistible curiosity detoured into the room which had been mine. I expected a bright Moira-style transformation, but in fact nothing at all had been changed, except that nothing of me remained.

The room was without soul; barren. The single bed, stripped, showed a bare mattress. There were no cobwebs, no dust, no smell of neglect, but the message was clear: the son who had slept there no longer existed.

Shivering slightly, I closed the door and wondered whether the absolute rejection had been Malcolm's or Moira's and, shrugging, decided I didn't now mind which.

Moira's idea of the perfect bedroom turned out to be plum and pink with louvred doors everywhere possible. Malcolm's dressing room next door had received the same treatment, as had their joint bathroom, and I set about collecting his belongings with a strong feeling of intruding upon strangers.

I found Moira's portrait only because I kicked it while searching for pyjamas: it was underneath Malcolm's chest of drawers in the dressing room. Looking to see what I'd damaged, I pulled out a square gold frame which fitted a discoloured patch on the wall and, turning it over, found the horrible Moira smiling at me with all her insufferable complacency.

I had forgotten how young she had been, and how pretty. Thirty years younger than Malcolm; thirty-five when she'd married him and, in the painting anyway, unlined. Reddish-gold hair, pale unfreckled skin, pointed chin, delicate neck. The artist seemed to me to have caught the calculation in her eyes with disconcerting clarity, and when I glanced at the name scrawled at the bottom I understood why. Malcolm might not have given her diamonds, but her portrait had been painted by the best.

I put her back face down under the chest of drawers as I'd found her, where Malcolm, I was sure, had consigned her.

Fetching a suitcase from the boxroom (no decor changes there), I packed Malcolm's things and went downstairs, and in the hall came face to face with a smallish man carrying a large shotgun, the business end pointing my way.

I stopped abruptly, as one would.

'Put your hands up,' he said hoarsely.

I set the suitcase on the floor and did as he bid. He wore earth-stained dark trousers and had mud on his hands, and I asked him immediately, 'Are you the gardener?'

'What if I am? What are you doing here?'

'Collecting clothes for my father . . . er . . . Mr Pembroke. I'm his son.'

'I don't know you. I'm getting the police.' His voice was belligerent but quavery, the shotgun none too steady in his hands.

'All right,' I said.

He was faced then with the problem of how to telephone while aiming my way.

I said, seeing his hesitation, 'I can prove I'm Mr Pembroke's son, and I'll open the suitcase to show you I'm not stealing anything. Would that help?'

After a pause, he nodded. 'You stay over there, though,' he said.

I judged that if I alarmed him there would be a further death in my father's house, so I very slowly and carefully opened the suitcase, removed the underpants and the rest, and laid them out on the hall floor. After that, I equally slowly took my own wallet out of my pocket, opened it, removed a credit card and laid it on the floor face upwards. Then I retreated backwards from the exhibits, ending with my back against the closed and locked front door.

The elderly gardener came suspiciously forward and inspected the show, dropping his eyes only in split seconds, raising them quickly, giving me no chance to jump him.

'That's his passport,' he said accusingly.

'He asked me to fetch it.'

'Where is he?' he said. 'Where's he gone?'

'I have to meet him with his passport. I don't know where he's going.' I paused. 'I really am his son. You must be new here. I haven't seen you before.'

'Two years,' he said defensively. 'I've worked here two years.' He seemed to come quite suddenly to a decision to believe me, and almost apologetically lowered the gun. 'This house is supposed to be locked up,' he said. 'Then I see you moving about upstairs.'

'Upsetting,' I agreed.

He gestured to Malcolm's things. 'You'd better pack them again.'

I began to do so under his still watchful eye.

'It was brave of you to come in here,' I said, 'if you thought I was a burglar.'

He braced his shoulders in an old automatic movement. 'I was in the army once.' He relaxed and shrugged. 'Tell you the truth, I was coming in quietly-like to phone the police, then you started down the stairs.'

'And . . . the gun?'

'Brought it with me just in case. I go after rabbits . . . I keep the gun handy.'

I nodded. It was the gardener's own gun, I thought. Malcolm had never owned one, as far as I knew.

'Has my father paid you for the week?' I said.

His eyes at once brightened hopefully. 'He paid me last Friday, same as usual. Then Saturday morning he phoned my house to tell me to come round here to see to the dogs. Take them home with me, same as I always do when he's away. So I did. But he was gone off the line before I could ask him how long he'd be wanting me to have them.'

I pulled out my cheque-book and wrote him a cheque for the amount he specified. Arthur Bellbrook, he said his name was. I tore out the cheque and gave it to him and asked him if there was anyone else who needed wages.

He shook his head. 'The cleaner left when Mrs Pembroke was done in . . . er . . . murdered. Said she didn't fancy the place any more.'

'Where exactly was Mrs Pembroke . . . er . . . murdered?'

'I'll show you if you like.' He stored the cheque away in a pocket. 'Outside in the greenhouse.'

He took me, however, not as I'd imagined to the rickety old familiar greenhouse sagging against a mellowed wall in the kitchen garden, but to a bright white octagonal wrought-iron construction like a fancy birdcage set as a summer-house on a secluded patch of lawn. From far outside, one could clearly see the flourishing geraniums within.

'Well, well,' I said.

Arthur Bellbrook uttered 'Huh' as expressing his disapproval and opened the metal-and-glass door.

'Cost a fortune to heat, will this place,' he observed. 'And it got too hot in the summer. The only thing as will survive in it is geraniums. Mrs Pembroke's passion, geraniums.'

An almost full sack of potting compost lay along one of the work surfaces, the top side of it slit from end to end to make the soil mixture easy to reach. A box of small pots stood nearby, some of them occupied by cuttings.

I looked at the compost with revulsion. 'Is that where . . .?' I began.

'Yes,' he said. 'Poor lady. There's no one ought to die like that, however difficult they could be.'

'No,' I agreed. A thought struck me. 'It was you who found her, wasn't it?'

'I went home like always at four o'clock, but I was out for a stroll about seven, and I thought I would just come in to see what state she'd left the place in. See, she played at gardening. Never cleaned the tools, things like that.' He looked at the boarded floor as if still seeing her there. 'She was lying face down, and I turned her over. She was dead all right. She was white like always but she had these little pink dots in her skin. They say you get those dots from asphyxiation. They found potting compost in her lungs, poor lady.' He had undoubtedly been shocked and moved at the time, but there was an echo of countless repetitions in his voice now and precious little feeling.

'Thank you for showing me,' I said.

He nodded and we both went out, shutting the door behind us.

'I don't think Mr Pembroke liked this place much,' he said unexpectedly. 'Last spring, when she chose it, he said she could have it only if he couldn't see it from the house. Otherwise he wouldn't pay the bill. I wasn't supposed to hear, of course, but there you are, I did. They'd got to shouting, you see.'

'Yes,' I said, 'I do see.' Shouting, slammed doors, the lot.

'They were all lovey-dovey when I first came here,' he said, 'but then I reckon her little ways got to him, like, and you could see it all going downhill like a runaway train. I'm here all day long, see, and in and out of the house, and you couldn't miss it.'

'What little ways?' I asked casually.

He glanced at me sideways with reawakening suspicions. 'I thought you were his son. You must have known her.'

'I didn't come here. I didn't like her.'

He seemed to find that easily believable.

'She could be as sweet as sugar . . .' He paused, remembering. 'I don't know what you'd call it, really, what she was. But for instance last year, as well as the ordinary vegetables for the house, I grew a special little patch separately . . . fed them, and so on . . . to enter in the local show. Just runner beans, carrots and onions, for one of the produce classes. I'm good at that, see? Well, Mrs Pembroke happened to spot them a day or two before I was ready to harvest. On the Thursday, with the show on the Saturday. "What huge vegetables," she says, and I tell her I'm going to exhibit them on Saturday. And she looks at me sweet as syrup and says, "Oh no, Arthur. Mr Pembroke and I both like vegetables, as you know. We'll have some of these for dinner tomorrow and I'll freeze the rest. They are *our* vegetables, aren't they, Arthur? If you want to grow vegetables to show, you must do it in your own garden in your own time." And blow me, when I came to work the next morning, the whole little patch had been picked over, beans, carrots, onions, the lot. She'd taken them, right enough. Pounds and pounds of them, all the best ones. Maybe they ate some, but she never did bother with the freezing. On the Monday, I found a load of the beans in the dustbin.'

'Charming,' I said.

He shrugged. 'That was her sort of way. Mean, but within her rights.'

'I wonder you stayed,' I said.

'It's a nice garden, and I get on all right with Mr Pembroke.'

'But after he left?'

'He asked me to stay on to keep the place decent. He paid me extra, so I did.'

Walking slowly, we arrived back at the kitchen door. He smelled faintly of compost and old leaves and the warm fertility of loam, like the gardener who'd reigned in this place in my childhood.

'I grew up here,' I said, feeling nostalgia.

He gave me a considering stare. 'Are you the one who built the secret room?'

Startled, I said, ‘It’s not really a room. Just a sort of triangular-shaped space.’

‘How do you open it?’

‘You don’t.’

‘I could use it,’ he said obstinately, ‘for an apple store.’

I shook my head. ‘It’s too small. It’s not ventilated. It’s useless, really. How do you know of it?’

He pursed his lips and looked knowing. ‘I could see the kitchen garden wall looked far too thick from the back down at the bottom corner and I asked old Fred about it, who used to be gardener here before he retired. He said Mr Pembroke’s son once built a sort of shed there. But there’s no door, I told him. He said it was the son’s business, he didn’t know anything about it himself, except that he thought it had been bricked up years ago. So if it was you who built it, how do you get in?’

‘You can’t now,’ I said. ‘I did brick it up soon after I built it to stop one of my half-brothers going in there and leaving dead rats for me to find.’

‘Oh.’ He looked disappointed. ‘I’ve often wondered what was in there.’

‘Dead rats, dead spiders, a lot of muck.’

He shrugged. ‘Oh well, then.’

‘You’ve been very helpful,’ I said. ‘I’ll tell my father.’

His lined face showed satisfaction. ‘You tell him I’ll keep the dogs and everything in good nick until he comes back.’

'He'll be grateful.'

I picked up the suitcase from inside the kitchen door, gave a last look at Moira's brilliant geraniums, vibrantly alive, shook the grubby hand of Arthur Bellbrook, and (in the car hired that morning in London) drove away towards Epsom.

Collecting my own things from my impersonal suburban flat took half the time. Unlike Malcolm, I liked things bare and orderly and, meaning always to move to somewhere better but somehow never going out to search, I hadn't decked the sitting room or the two small bedrooms with anything brighter than new patterned curtains and a Snaffles print of Sergeant Murphy winning the 1923 Grand National.

I changed from Malcolm's trousers into some of my own, packed a suitcase and picked up my passport. I had no animals to arrange for, nor any bills pressing. Nothing anywhere to detain me.

The telephone answering machine's button glowed red, announcing messages taken. I rewound the tape and listened to the disembodied voices while I picked out of the fridge anything that would go furry and disgusting before my return.

Something, since I'd left the day before, had galvanized the family into feverish activity, like stirring an anthill with a stick.

A girlish voice came first, breathless, a shade anxious. 'Ian, this is Serena. Why are you always out? Don't you sleep at home? Mummy wants to know where Daddy is. She knows you and he aren't speaking, she's utterly thick to expect you to know, but anyway she insisted I ask you. So if you know, give me a ring back, OK?'

Serena, my half-sister, daughter of Alicia, the one child born to Alicia in wedlock. Serena, seven years my junior, lay in my distant memory chiefly as a small fair-haired charmer who'd followed me about like a shadow, which had flattered my twelve-year-old ego disgracefully. She liked best to sit on Malcolm's lap, his arms protectively around her, and from him, it had seemed to me, she could conjure a smile when he was angry and pretty dresses when she had a cupboardful.

Alicia, in sweeping out of the house when Serena was six, taking with her not only Serena but her two older boys, had left me alone in the suddenly quiet house, alone in the frilly kitchen, alone and untormented in the garden. There had been a time then when I would positively have welcomed back Gervase, the older boy, despite his dead rats and other rotten tricks; and it had actually been in the vacuum after his departure that I contrived the bricking up of my kitchen-wall room, not while he was there to jeer at it.

Grown up, Gervase still displayed the insignia of a natural bully: mean tightening of the mouth, jabbing forefinger, cold patronizing stare down the nose, visible enjoyment of others' discomfiture. Serena, now tall and slim, taught aerobic dancing for a living, bought clothes still by the cartload and spoke to me only when she wanted something done.

'Mummy wants to know where Daddy is . . .' The childish terms sat oddly in the ear, somehow, coming from someone now twenty-six; and she alone of all his children had resisted calling Malcolm, Malcolm.

The next caller was Gervase himself. He started crossly, 'I don't like these message contraptions. I tried to get you all evening yesterday and I hear nothing but your priggish voice telling me to leave my name and telephone number, so this time I'm doing it, but under protest. This is your brother Gervase, as no doubt you realize, and it is imperative we find Malcolm at once. He has gone completely off his rocker. It's in your own interest to find him, Ian. We must all bury our differences and stop him spending the family money in this reckless way.' He paused briefly. 'I suppose you do know he has given half a million . . . *half a million* . . . to a busload of retarded children? I got a phone call from some stupid gushing female who said, "Oh Mr Pembroke, however can we thank you?" and when I asked her what for, she said wasn't I *the* Mr Pembroke who had solved all their problems, Mr Malcolm Pembroke? Madam, I said, what are you talking about? So she told me. *Half a million pounds.* Are you listening, Ian? He's irresponsible. It's out of proportion. He's got to be prevented from giving way to such ridiculous impulses. If you ask me, it's the beginning of senility. You must find him and tell us where he's got to, because so far as I can discover he hasn't answered his telephone since last Friday morning when I rang him to say Alicia's alimony had not been increased by the rate of inflation in this last quarter. I expect to hear from you without delay.'

His voice stopped abruptly on the peremptory order and I pictured him as he was now, not the muscular thick-set black-haired boy but the flabbier, overweight thirty-five-year-old stockbroker, over-bearingly pompous beyond his years. In a world increasingly awash with illegitimate children, he increasingly resented his own illegitimacy, referring to it ill-temperedly on inappropriate occasions and denigrating the father who, for all his haste into bed with Alicia, had accepted Gervase publicly always as his son, and given him his surname with legal adoption.

Gervase had nonetheless been taunted early on by cruel schoolmates, developing an amorphous hatred then which later focused itself on me, Ian, the half-brother who scarcely valued or understood the distinction between his birth and mine. One could understand why he'd lashed out in those raw adolescent days, but it was a matter of regret, I thought, that he'd never outgrown his bitterness. It remained with him, festering, colouring his whole personality, causing people often to wriggle away from his company, erupting in didactic outbursts and wretched unjustified jealousies.

Yet his wife appeared to love him forgivingly, and had produced two children, both girls, the first of them appearing a good three years after the well-attended marriage. Gervase had said a little too often that he himself would never in any circumstances have burdened a child with what he had suffered. Gervase, to my mind, would spend his last-ever moments worrying that the word 'illegitimate' would appear on his death certificate.

Ferdinand, his brother, was quite different, taking illegitimacy as of little importance, a matter of paperwork, no more.

Three years younger than Gervase, a year younger than myself, Ferdinand looked more like Malcolm than any of us, a living testimony to his parentage. Along with the features, he'd inherited the financial agility but lacking Malcolm's essential panache had carved himself a niche in an insurance company, not a multi-million fortune.

Ferdinand and I had been friends while we both lived in the house as children, but Alicia had thoroughly soured all that when she'd taken him away, dripping into all her children's ears the relentless spite of her dispossession. Ferdinand now looked at me with puzzlement as if he couldn't quite remember why he disliked me, and then Alicia would remind him sharply that if he wasn't careful I would get my clutches on his, Gervase's and Serena's rightful shares of Malcolm's money, and his face would darken again into unfriendliness.

It was a real pity about Ferdinand, I thought, but I never did much about it.

After Gervase on my answering machine came my mother, Joyce, very nearly incoherent with rage. Someone, it appeared, had already brought the *Sporting Life* to her notice. She couldn't *believe* it, she said. Words failed her. (They obviously didn't.) How *could* I have done anything as stupid as taking Malcolm to Newmarket Sales, because obviously I would have been there with him, it wasn't his scene otherwise, and why had I been so *deceitful* that morning when I'd talked to her, and would I without fail ring her *immediately*, this was a *crisis*, Malcolm had got to be stopped.

The fourth and last message, calmer after Joyce's hysteria, was from my half-brother Thomas, the third of Malcolm's children, born to his first wife, Vivien.

Thomas, rising forty, prematurely bald, pale skinned, sporting a gingerish moustache, had married a woman who acidly belittled him every time she opened her mouth. ('Of course, Thomas is absolutely useless when it comes to . . .' [practically anything] and 'if only poor Thomas was capable of commanding a suitable salary' and 'Dear Thomas is one of life's failures, aren't you, darling?') Thomas bore it all with hardly a wince, though after years of it I observed him grow less effective and less decisive, not more, almost as if he had come to believe in and to act out his Berenice's opinion of him.

'Ian,' Thomas said in a depressed voice, 'this is

Thomas. I've been trying to reach you since yesterday lunchtime but you seem to be away. When you've read my letter, please will you ring me up.'

I'd picked up his letter from my front doormat but hadn't yet opened it. I slit the envelope then and found that he too had a problem. I read:

Dear Ian,

Berenice is seriously concerned about Malcolm's wicked selfishness. She, well, to be honest, she keeps on and on about the amounts he's throwing away these days, and to be honest the only thing which has pacified her for a long time now is the thought of my eventual share of Malcolm's money, and if he goes on spending at this rate, well my life is going to be pretty *intolerable*, and I wouldn't be telling you this if you weren't my brother and the best of the bunch, which I suppose I've never said until now, but sometimes I think you're the only sane one in the family even if you do ride in those dangerous races, and, well, can you do anything to reason with Malcolm, as you're the only one he's likely to listen to, even though you haven't been talking for ages, which is unbelievable considering how you used to be with each other, and I blame that money-grubbing Moira, I really do, though Berenice used to think that anything or anyone who came between you and Malcolm could only be to my benefit, because Malcolm might with luck cut you out of his will.

Well, I didn't mean to say that, old chap, but it's what Berenice thought, to be honest, until Moira was going to take half of everything in the divorce settlement, and I really thought Berenice would have a seizure when she heard that, she was so furious. It really would save my sanity, Ian, if you could make Malcolm see that we all *NEED* that money. I don't know what will happen if he goes on spending it at this rate. I do *BEG* you, old chap, to stop him.

Your brother Thomas.

I looked at the letter's general incoherence and at the depth of the plea in the last few sentences with their heavily underlined words and thought of the non-stop barrage of Berenice's disgruntlement, and felt more brotherly towards Thomas than ever before. True, I still thought he should tell his wife to swallow her bile, not spill it all out on him, corroding his self-confidence and undermining his prestige with everyone within earshot; but I did at least and perhaps at last see how he could put up with it, by soothing her with the syrup of prosperity ahead.

I understood vaguely why he didn't simply ditch her and decamp: he couldn't face doing what Malcolm had done, forsaking wife and children when the going got rough. He had been taught from a very young age to despise Malcolm's inconstancy. He stayed grimly glued to Berenice and their two cheeky offspring and suffered for his virtue; and it was from fear of making the same calamitous mistake, I acknowledged, that I had married no one at all.

Thomas's was the last message on the tape. I took it out of the machine and put it in my pocket, inserting a fresh tape for future messages. I also, after a bit of thought, sorted through a boxful of family photographs, picking out groups and single pictures until I had a pretty comprehensive gallery of Pembrokes. These went into my suitcase along with a small cassette player and my best camera.

I did think of answering some of the messages, but decided against it. The arguments would all have been futile. I did truly believe in Malcolm's absolute right to do what he liked with the money he had made by his own skill and diligence. If he chose to give it in the end to his children, that was our good luck. We had no rights to it; none at all. I would have had difficulty in explaining that concept to Thomas or Joyce or Gervase or Serena, and apart from not wanting to, I hadn't the time.

I put my suitcase in the car, along with my racing saddle, helmet, whip and boots and drove back to the Savoy, being relieved to find Malcolm still there, unattacked and unharmed.

He was sitting deep in an armchair, dressed again as for the City, drinking champagne and smoking an oversize cigar. Opposite him, perched on the front edge of an identical armchair, sat a thin man of much Malcolm's age but with none of his presence.

'Norman West,' Malcolm said to me, waving the cigar vaguely at his visitor; and to the visitor he said, 'My son, Ian.'

Norman West rose to his feet and shook my hand briefly. I had never so far as I knew met a private detective before, and it wouldn't have been the occupation I would have fitted to this damp-handed nervous threadbare individual. Of medium height, he had streaky grey hair overdue for a wash, dark-circled brown eyes, greyish unhealthy skin and a day's growth of greying beard. His grey suit looked old and uncared for and his shoes had forgotten about polish. He looked as much at home in a suite in the Savoy as a punk rocker in the Vatican.

As if unerringly reading my mind he said, 'As I was just explaining to Mr Pembroke, I came straight here from an all-night observation job, as he was most insistent that it was urgent. This rig fitted my observation point. It isn't my normal gear.'

'Clothes for all seasons?' I suggested.

'Yes, that's right.'

His accent was the standard English of bygone radio announcers, slightly plummy and too good to be true. I gestured to him to sit down again, which he did as before, leaning forward from the front edge of the seat cushion and looking enquiringly at Malcolm.

'Mr West had just arrived when you came,'

Malcolm said. 'Perhaps you'd better explain to him what we want.'

I sat on the spindly little sofa and said to Norman West that we wanted him to find out where every single member of our extended family had been on the previous Friday from, say, four o'clock in the afternoon onwards, and also on Tuesday, yesterday, all day.

Norman West looked from one to the other of us in obvious dismay.

'If it's too big a job,' Malcolm said, 'bring in some help.'

'It's not really *that*,' Norman West said unhappily. 'But I'm afraid there may be a conflict of interest.'

'What conflict of interest?' Malcolm demanded.

Norman West hesitated, cleared his throat and hummed a little. Then he said, 'Last Saturday morning I was hired by one of your family to find *you*, Mr Pembroke. I've already been working, you see, for one of your family. Now you want me to check up on *them*. I don't think I should, in all conscience, accept your proposition.'

'*Which* member of my family?' Malcolm demanded.

Norman West drummed his fingers on his knee, but decided after inner debate to answer.

'Mrs Pembroke,' he said.

CHAPTER FOUR

Malcolm blinked. 'Which one?' he asked.

'Mrs Pembroke,' Norman West repeated, puzzled.

'There are nine of them,' I said. 'So which one?'

The detective looked uncomfortable. 'I spoke to her only on the telephone. I thought . . . I assumed . . . it was the Mrs Malcolm Pembroke for whom I worked once before, long ago. She referred me to that case, and asked for present help. I looked up my records . . .' He shrugged helplessly. 'I imagined it was the same lady.'

'Did you find Mr Pembroke,' I asked, 'when you were looking for him?'

Almost unwillingly, West nodded. 'In Cambridge. Not too difficult.'

'And you reported back to Mrs Pembroke?'

'I really don't think I should be discussing this any further.'

'At least, tell us how you got back in touch with Mrs Pembroke to tell her of your success.'

'I didn't,' he said. 'She rang me two or three times

a day, asking for progress reports. Finally on Monday evening, I had news for her. After that, I proceeded with my next investigation, which I have now concluded. This left me free for anything Mr Pembroke might want.'

'I want you to find out which Mrs Pembroke wanted to know where I was.'

Norman West regretfully shook his unkempt head. 'A client's trust . . .' he murmured.

'A client's trust, poppycock!' Malcolm exploded. 'Someone who knew where to find me damn near killed me.'

Our detective looked shocked but rallied quickly. 'I found you, sir, by asking Mrs Pembroke for a list of places you felt at home in, as in my experience missing people often go to those places, and she gave me a list of five such possibilities, of which Cambridge was number three. I didn't even go to that city looking for you. As a preliminary, I was prepared to telephone to all the hotels in Cambridge asking for you, but I tried the larger hotels first, as being more likely to appeal to you, sir, and from only the third I got a positive response. If it was as easy as that for me to find you, it was equally easy for anyone else. And, sir, if I may say so, you made things easy by registering under your own name. People who want to stay lost shouldn't do that.'

He spoke with a touching air of dignity ill-matched to his seedy appearance and for the first time I thought he might be better at his job than he looked. He must have been pretty efficient, I supposed, to have stayed in the business so long, even if catching Malcolm with his trousers off couldn't have taxed him sorely years ago.

He finished off the glass of champagne that Malcolm had given him before my arrival, and refused a refill.

'How is Mrs Pembroke paying you?' I asked.

'She said she would send a cheque.'

'When it comes,' I said, 'you'll know which Mrs Pembroke.'

'So I will.'

'I don't see why you should worry about a conflict of interests,' I said. 'After all, you've worked pretty comprehensively for various Pembrokes. You worked for my mother, Joyce Pembroke, to catch my father with the lady who gave her grounds for divorce. You worked for my father, to try to catch his fifth wife having a similar fling. You worked for the unspecified Mrs Pembroke to trace my father's whereabouts. So now he wants you to find out where all his family were last Friday and yesterday so as to be sure it was none of his close relatives who tried to kill him, as it would make him very unhappy if it were. If you can't square that with your conscience, of course with great regret he'll have to retain the services of someone else.'

Norman West eyed me with a disillusionment which again encouraged me to think him not as dim as he looked. Malcolm was glimmer-eyed with amusement.

'Pay you well, of course,' he said.

'Danger money,' I said, nodding.

Malcolm said, 'What?'

'We don't want him to step on a rattlesnake, but in fairness he has to know he might.'

Norman West looked at his short and grimy nails. He didn't seem unduly put out, nor on the other hand eager.

'Isn't this a police job?' he asked.

'Certainly,' I said. 'My father called them in when someone tried to kill him last Friday, and he'll tell you all about it. And you have to bear in mind that they're also enquiring into the murder of Moira Pembroke, whom you followed through blameless days. But you would be working for my father, not for the police, if you take his cash.'

'Pretty decisive, aren't you, sir?' he said uneasily.

'Bossy,' Malcolm agreed, 'in his quiet way.'

All those years, I thought, of getting things done in a racing stable, walking a tightrope between usurping the power of the head lad on one hand and the trainer himself on the other, like a lieutenant between a sergeant-major and a colonel. I'd had a lot of practice, one way and another, at being quietly bossy.

Malcolm unemotionally told West about his abortive walk with the dogs and the brush with carbon monoxide, and after that described also the near-miss at Newmarket.

Norman West listened attentively with slowly

blinking eyes and at the end said, 'The car at Newmarket could have been accidental. Driver looking about for cigarettes, say. Not paying enough attention. Seeing you both at the last minute . . . swerving desperately.'

Malcolm looked at me. 'Did it seem like that to you?'

'No.'

'Why not?' West asked.

'The rate of acceleration, I suppose.'

'Foot on accelerator going down absent-mindedly during search for cigarettes?'

'Headlights, full beam,' I said.

'A sloppy driver? Had a few drinks?'

'Maybe.' I shook my head. 'The real problem is that if the car *had* hit us – or Malcolm – there might have been witnesses. The driver might have been stopped before he could leave the sales area. The car number might have been taken.'

West smiled sorrowfully. 'It's been done successfully before now, in broad daylight in a crowded street.'

'Are you saying,' Malcolm demanded of me, 'that the car *wasn't* trying to kill me?'

'No, only that the driver took a frightful risk.'

'Did any witnesses rush to pick us up?' Malcolm asked forcefully. 'Did anyone so much as pass a sympathetic remark? No, they damned well didn't. Did anyone try to stop the driver or take his number? The hell they did.'

'All the same,' West said, 'your son is right. Hit-and-run in a public place has its risks. If it was tried here, and, sirs, I'm not saying it wasn't, the putative gain must have outweighed the risk, or, er, in other words – '

'In other words,' Malcolm interrupted with gloom, 'Ian is right to think they'll try again.'

Norman West momentarily looked infinitely weary, as if the sins of the world were simply too much to contemplate. He had seen, I supposed, as all investigators must, a lifetime's procession of sinners and victims; and, moreover, he looked roughly seventy and hadn't slept all night.

'I'll take your job,' he said without enthusiasm, radiating minimum confidence, and I glanced at Malcolm to see if he really thought this was the best we could do in detectives, signs of intelligence or not. Malcolm appeared to have no doubts, however, and spent the next five minutes discussing fees which seemed ominously moderate to me.

'And I'll need a list,' West said finally, 'of the people you want checked. Names and addresses and normal habits.'

Malcolm showed unexpected discomfort, as if checking that amorphous entity 'the family' was different from checking each individual separately, and it was I who found a piece of Savoy writing paper to draw up the list.

'OK,' I said, 'first of all there's Vivien, my father's first wife. Mrs Vivien Pembroke.'

'Not her,' Malcolm objected. 'It's ridiculous.'

'Everyone,' I said firmly. 'No exceptions. That makes it fair on everyone . . . because there are going to be some extremely angry relations when they all realize what's happening.'

'They won't find out,' Malcolm said.

Fat chance, I thought.

To West, I said, 'They all telephone each other all the time, not by any means always out of friendship but quite often out of spite. They won't gang up against you because they seldom form alliances among themselves. Some of them are pretty good liars. Don't believe everything they say about each other.'

'*Ian*!' Malcolm said protestingly.

'I'm one of them, and I know,' I said.

After Vivien's name on the list I wrote the names of her children:

Donald

Lucy

Thomas

'Thomas,' I said, 'is married to Berenice.' I added her name beside his. 'He is easy to deal with, she is not.'

'She's a five-star cow,' Malcolm said.

West merely nodded.

'Lucy,' I said, 'married a man called Edwin Bugg. She didn't like that surname, and persuaded him to change it to hers, and she is consequently herself a Mrs Pembroke.'

West nodded.

'Lucy is a poet,' I said. 'People who know about poetry say her stuff is the real thing. She makes a big production of unworldliness which Edwin, I think, has grown to find tiresome.'

'Huh,' Malcolm said. 'Edwin's an out-and-out materialist, always tapping me for a loan.'

'Do you give them to him?' I said interestedly.

'Not often. He never pays me back.'

'Short of money, are they?' West asked.

'Edwin Bugg,' Malcolm said, 'married Lucy years ago because he thought she was an heiress, and they've scraped along ever since on the small income she gets from a trust fund I set up for her. Edwin's never done a stroke of work in his parasitic life and I can't stand the fellow.'

'They have one teenage schoolboy son,' I said, smiling, 'who asked me the last time I saw him how to set about emigrating to Australia.'

West looked at the list and said to Malcolm, 'What about Donald, your eldest?'

'Donald,' said his father, 'married a replica of his mother, beautiful and brainless. A girl called Helen. They live an utterly boring virtuous life in Henley-on-Thames and are still billing and cooing like newlyweds although Donald must be nearly forty-five, I suppose.'

No one commented. Malcolm himself, rising sixty-nine, could bill and coo with the best, and with a suppressed shiver I found myself thinking for the first time about the *sixth* marriage, because certainly, in the future, if Malcolm survived, there would be one. He had never in the past lived long alone. He liked rows better than solitude.

'Children?' Norman West asked into the pause.

'Three,' Malcolm said. 'Pompous little asses.'

West glanced at me questioningly, and yawned.

'Are you too tired to take all this in?' I asked.

'No, go ahead.'

'Two of Donald's children are too young to drive a car. The eldest, a girl at art school, is five foot two and fragile, and I cannot imagine her being physically capable of knocking Malcolm out and carrying his body from garden to garage and inserting him into Moira's car.'

'She hasn't the courage either,' Malcolm said.

'You can't say that,' I disagreed. 'Courage can pop up anywhere and surprise you.'

West gave me a noncommittal look. 'Well,' he said, taking the list himself and adding to it, 'this is what we have so far. Wife number one: Vivien Pembroke. Her children: Donald (44), wife Helen, three offspring. Lucy, husband Edwin (née Bugg), school-age son. Thomas, wife Berenice . . .?'

'Two young daughters.'

'Two young daughters,' he repeated, writing.

'My grandchildren,' Malcolm protested, 'are all too young to have murdered anybody.'

'Psychopaths start in the nursery,' West said laconically. 'Any sign in any of them of abnormal violent behaviour? Excessive cruelty, that sort of thing? Obsessive hatreds?'

Malcolm and I both shook our heads but with a touch of uncertainty; his maybe because of something he did know, mine because of all I didn't know, because of all the things that could be hidden.

'Does greed, too, begin in the nursery?' I said.

'I wouldn't say so, would you?' West answered.

I shook my head again. 'I'd say it was nastily adult and grows with opportunity. The more there is to grab, the greedier people get.'

Malcolm said, only half as a question, 'My fortune corrupts . . . geometrically?'

'You're not alone,' I said dryly. 'Just think of all those multi-billionaire families where the children have already had millions settled on them and still fight like cats over the pickings when their father dies.'

'Bring it down to thousands,' West said unexpectedly. 'Or to hundreds. I've seen shocking spite over hundreds. And the lawyers rub their hands and syphon off the cream.' He sighed, half disillusionment, half weariness. 'Wife number two?' he asked, and answered his own question, 'Mrs Joyce Pembroke.'

'Right,' I said. 'I'm her son. She had no other children. And I'm not married.'

West methodically wrote me down.

'Last Friday evening,' I said, 'I was at work in a racing stable at five o'clock with about thirty people as witnesses, and last night I was certainly not driving the car that nearly ran us over.'

West said stolidly, 'I'll write you down as being cleared of primary involvement. That's all I can do with any of your family, Mr Pembroke.' He finished the sentence looking at Malcolm who said, 'Hired assassin' between his teeth, and West nodded. 'If any of them hired a good professional, I doubt if I'll discover it.'

'I thought good assassins used rifles,' I said.

'Some do. Most don't. They pick their own way. Some use knives. Some garotte. I knew of one who used to wait at traffic lights along his victim's usual route to work. One day, the lights would be red, the victim would stop. The assassin tapped on the window, asking a question . . . or so it's supposed. The victim wound down the window and the assassin shot him point blank in the head. By the time the lights turned green and the cars behind started tooting their horns, the assassin had long gone.'

'Did they ever catch him?' I asked.

West shook his head. 'Eight prominent businessmen were killed that way within two years. Then it stopped. No one knows why. My guess is the assassin lost his nerve. It happens in every profession.'

I thought of jump jockeys to whom it had happened

almost overnight, and I supposed it occurred in stockbrokers also. Any profession, as he said.

'Or someone bumped him off because he knew too much,' Malcolm said.

'That too is possible.' West looked at the list. 'After Mrs Joyce?'

Malcolm said sourly, 'The lady you so artfully photographed me with at the instigation of, as you call her, Mrs Joyce.'

The West eyebrows slowly rose. 'Miss Alicia Sandways? With, if I remember, two little boys?'

'The little boys are now thirty-five and thirty-two,' I said.

'Yes.' He sighed. 'As I said, I recently dug out that file. I didn't realize that . . . er . . . Well, so we have wife number three, Mrs Alicia Pembroke. And her children?'

Malcolm said, 'The two boys, Gervase and Ferdinand. I formally adopted them when I married their mother, and changed their surname to Pembroke. Then we had little Serena,' his face softened, 'and it was for her I put up with Alicia's tantrums the last few years we were together. Alicia was a great mistress but a rotten wife. Don't ask me why. I indulged her all the time, let her do what she liked with my house, and in the end nothing would please her.' He shrugged. 'I gave her a generous divorce settlement, but she was very bitter. I wanted to keep little Serena . . . and Alicia screamed that she supposed I didn't want the boys because they were illegitimate. She fought in the courts for Serena, and she won . . . She filled all her children's heads with bad feelings for me.' The old hurt plainly showed. 'Serena did suggest coming back to look after me when Coochie was killed, but it wasn't necessary because Moira was there. When Moira was killed, she offered again. It was kind of Serena. She's a nice girl, really, but Alicia tries to set her against me.'

West, in a pause that might or might not have been sympathetic, wrote after Alicia's name:

Gervase. Illegitimate at birth, subsequently adopted

Ferdinand. The same

Serena. Legitimate

'Are they married?' he asked.

'Gervase has a wife called Ursula,' I said. 'I don't know her well, because when I see them they're usually together and it's always Gervase who does the talking. They too, like Thomas, have two little girls.'

West wrote it down.

'Ferdinand,' I said, 'has married two raving beauties in rapid succession. The first, American, has gone back to the States. The second one, Deborah, known as Debs, is still in residence. So far, no children.'

West wrote.

'Serena,' I said, 'is unmarried.'

West completed that section of the list. 'So we have wife number three, Mrs Alicia Pembroke. Her children are Gervase, wife Ursula, two small daughters.

Ferdinand, current wife Debs, no children. Serena, unmarried . . . er . . . a fiancé, perhaps? Live-in-lover?'

'I don't know of one,' I said, and Malcolm said he didn't know either.

'Right,' West said. 'Wife number four?'

There was a small silence. Then I said, 'Coochie. She's dead. She had twin sons. One was killed with her in a car crash, the other is brain-damaged and lives in a nursing home.'

'Oh.' The sound carried definite sympathy this time. 'And wife number five, Mrs Moira Pembroke, did she perhaps have any children from a previous marriage?'

'No,' Malcolm said. 'No previous marriage, no children.'

'Right.' West counted up his list. 'That's three ex-wives . . . er, by the way, did any of them remarry?'

I answered with a faint smile, 'They would lose their alimony if they did. Malcolm was pretty generous in their settlements. None of them has seen any financial sense in remarrying.'

'They all should have done,' Malcolm grumbled. 'They wouldn't be so warped.'

West said merely, 'Right. Then, er, six sons, two daughters. Four current daughters-in-law, one son-in-law. Grandchildren . . . too young. So, er, discounting the invalid son and Mr Ian here, there are fourteen adults to be checked. That will take me a week at least. Probably more.'

'As fast as you can,' I said.

He looked actually as if he had barely enough strength or confidence to get himself out of the door let alone embark on what was clearly an arduous task.

'Can I tell them all why I'm making these enquiries?' he asked.

'Yes, you damned well can,' Malcolm said positively. 'If it's one of them, and I hope to God it isn't, it might put the wind up them and frighten them off. Just don't tell them where to find me.'

I looked down at the list. I couldn't visualize any of them as being criminally lethal, but then greed affected otherwise rational people in irrational ways. All sorts of people . . . I knew of a case when two male relatives had gone into a house where an old woman had been reported newly dead, and taken the bedroom carpet off the floor, rolling it up and making off with it and leaving her lying alone in her bed above bare boards, all to seize her prize possession before the rest of the family could get there. Unbelievable, I'd thought it. The old woman's niece, who cleaned my flat every week, had been most indignant, but not on her aunt's account. 'It was the only good carpet in the house,' she vigorously complained. 'Nearly new. The only thing worth having. It should have come to me, by rights. Now I'll never get it.'

'I'll need all their addresses,' West said.

Malcolm waved a hand. 'Ian can tell you. Get him to write them down.'

Obediently I opened my suitcase, took out my

address book and wrote the whole list, with telephone numbers. Then I got out the pack of photographs and showed them to West.

'Would they help you?' I asked. 'If they would, I'll lend them to you, but I want them back.'

West looked through them one by one, and I knew that he could see, if he were any detective at all, all the basic characters of the subjects. I liked taking photographs and preferred portraits, and somehow taking a camera along gave me something positive to do whenever the family met. I didn't like talking to some of them; photography gave me a convincing reason for disengagements and drifting around.

If there was one common factor in many of the faces it was discontent, which I thought was sad. Only in Ferdinand could one see real lightheartedness, and even in him, as I knew, it could come and go; and Debs, his second wife, was a stunning blonde, taller than her husband, looking out at the world quizzically as if she couldn't quite believe her eyes, not yet soured by disappointment.

I'd caught Gervase giving his best grade-one bullying down-the-nose stare, and saw no good purpose in ever showing him the reflection of his soul. Ursula merely looked indeterminate and droopy and somehow guilty, as if she thought she shouldn't even have her photo taken without Gervase's permission.

Berenice, Thomas's wife, was the exact opposite, staring disapprovingly straight into the lens, bold and sarcastic, unerringly destructive every time she uttered. And Thomas, a step behind her, looking harried and anxious. Another of Thomas alone, smiling uneasily, defeat in the sag of his shoulders, desperation in his eyes.

Vivien, Joyce and Alicia, the three witches, dissimilar in features but alike in expression, had been caught when they weren't aware of the camera, each of them watching someone else with disfavour.

Alicia, fluffy and frilly, still wore her hair brought youthfully high to a ribbon bow on the crown, from where rich brown curls tumbled in a cascade to her shoulders. Nearly sixty, she looked in essence younger than her son Gervase, and she would still have been pretty but for the pinched hardness of her mouth.

She had been a fair sort of mother to me for the seven years of her reign, seeing to my ordinary needs like food and new clothes and treating me no different from Gervase and Ferdinand, but I'd never felt like going to her for advice or comfort. She hadn't loved me, nor I her, and after the divorce we had neither felt any grief in separation. I'd detested what she'd done afterwards to Gervase, Ferdinand and Serena, twisting their minds with her own spite. I would positively have liked to have had friendly brothers and sisters as much as Malcolm would have valued friendly children. After nearly twenty years, Alicia's intense hurt still spread suffering outward in ripples.

Serena's picture showed her as she had been a year

earlier, before aerobic dancing had slimmed her further to a sexless-looking leanness. The fair hair of childhood had slightly darkened, and was stylishly cut in a short becoming cap-shape which made her look young for her twenty-six years. A leggy Peter Pan, I thought, not wanting to grow up: a girl-woman with a girlish voice saying 'Mummy and Daddy', and an insatiable appetite for clothes. I wondered briefly whether she were still a virgin and felt faintly surprised to find that I simply didn't know and, moreover, couldn't tell.

'These are very interesting,' West said, glancing at me. 'I should certainly like to borrow them.' He shuffled them around and sorted them out. 'Who are these? You haven't put their names on the back, like the others.'

'That's Lucy and Edwin, and that's Donald and Helen.'

'Thanks.' He wrote the identification carefully in small neat letters.

Malcolm stretched out a hand for the photographs which West gave him. Malcolm looked through them attentively and finally gave them back.

'I don't remember seeing any of these before,' he said.

'They're all less than three years old.'

His mouth opened and shut again. He gave me a brooding look, as if I'd just stabbed him unfairly in the ribs.

'What do you think of them?' I asked.

'A pity children grow up.'

West smiled tiredly and collected the lists and photographs together.

'Right, Mr Pembroke. I'll get started.' He stood up and swayed slightly, but when I took a step forward to steady him he waved me away. 'Just lack of sleep.' On his feet, he looked even nearer to exhaustion, as if the outer greyness had penetrated inwards to the core. 'First thing in the morning, I'll be checking the Pembrokes.'

It would have been churlish to expect him to start that afternoon, but I can't say I liked the delay. I offered him another drink and a reviving lunch, which he declined, so I took him to the hotel's front door and saw him safely into a taxi, watching him sink like a collapsing scarecrow into the seat cushions.

Returning to the suite, I found Malcolm ordering vodka and Beluga caviar from room service with the abandon to which I was becoming accustomed. That done, he smoothed out the *Sporting Life* and pointed to one section of it.

'It says the Arc de Triomphe race is due to be run this Sunday in Paris.'

'Yes, that's right.'

'Then let's go.'

'All right,' I said.

Malcolm laughed. 'We may as well have some fun. There's a list here of the runners.'

I looked where he pointed. It was a bookmaker's advertisement showing the ante-post prices on offer.

'What are the chances,' Malcolm said, 'of my buying one of these horses?'

'Er,' I said. 'Today, do you mean?'

'Of course. No good buying one *after* the race, is there?'

'Well . . .'

'No, of course not. The winner will be worth millions and the others peanuts. *Before* the race, that's the thing.'

'I don't suppose anyone will sell,' I said, 'but we can try. How high do you want to go? The favourite won the Epsom Derby and is reported to be going to be syndicated for ten million pounds. You'd have to offer a good deal more than that before they'd consider selling him now.'

'Hm,' Malcolm said. 'What do you think of him as a horse?'

I smothered a gasp or two and said with a deadpan face, 'He's a very good horse but he had an exceptionally exhausting race last time out. I don't think he's had enough time to recover, and I wouldn't back him this time.'

'Have you backed him before?' Malcolm asked curiously.

'Yes, when he won the Derby, but he was favourite for that, too.'

'What do you think will win the Arc de Triomphe, then?'

'Seriously?' I said.

'Of course seriously.'

'One of the French horses, Meilleurs Voeux.'

'Can we buy him?'

'Not a hope. His owner loves his horses, loves winning more than profit and is immensely rich.'

'So am I,' Malcolm said simply. 'I can't help making money. It used to be a passion, now it's a habit. But this business about Moira jolted me, you know. It struck me that I may not have a hell of a lot of time left, not with enough health and strength to enjoy life. I've spent all these years amassing the stuff, and for what? For my goddam children to murder me for it? Sod that for a sad story. You buy me a good horse in this race on Sunday and we'll go and yell it home, boy, at the top of our lungs.'

It took all afternoon and early evening to get even a tinge of interest from anyone. I telephoned to the trainers of the English – or Irish – runners, asking if they thought their owners might sell. I promised each trainer that he would go on training the horse, and that my father would send him also the two-million-guinea colt he'd bought yesterday. Some of the trainers were at the Newmarket Sales and had to be tracked down to hotels, and once tracked, had to track and consult with their owners. Some simply said no, forget it.

Finally, at seven forty-five, a trainer from Newmarket rang back to say his owner would sell a half-share if his price was met. I relayed the news and the price to Malcolm.

'What do you think?' he said.

'Um . . . the horse is quite good, the price is on the high side, the trainer's in the top league.'

'OK.' Malcolm said. 'Deal.'

'My father accepts,' I said. 'And, er, the colt is still in the sales stables. Can you fetch it tomorrow, if we clear it with the auctioneers?'

Indeed he could. He sounded quite cheerful altogether. He would complete his paperwork immediately if Malcolm could transfer the money directly to his bloodstock account, bank and account number supplied. I wrote the numbers to his dictation. Malcolm waved a hand and said, 'No problem. First thing in the morning. He'll have it by afternoon.'

'Well,' I said, breathing out as I put the receiver down, 'you now own half of Blue Clancy.'

'Let's drink to it,' Malcolm said. 'Order some Bollinger.'

I ordered it from room service, and while we waited for it to arrive I told him about my encounter with his gardener, Arthur Bellbrook.

'Decent chap,' Malcolm said, nodding. 'Damned good gardener.'

I told him wryly about Moira and the prize vegetables, which he knew nothing about.

'Silly bitch,' he said. 'Arthur lives in a terrace house

with a pocket handkerchief garden facing north. You couldn't grow prize stuff there. If she'd asked me I'd have told her that, and told her to leave him alone. Good gardeners are worth every perk they get.'

'He seemed pretty philosophical,' I said, 'and, incidentally, pretty bright. He'd spotted that the kitchen garden wall is thicker than it should be at the corner. He'd asked old Fred, and heard about the room I built there. He wanted to know how to get in, so he could use it as an apple store.'

Malcolm practically ejected from his armchair, alarm widening his eyes, his voice coming out strangled and hoarse. 'My God, you didn't tell him, did you?'

'No, I didn't,' I said slowly. 'I told him it was empty and was bricked up twenty years ago.' I paused. 'What have you put in there?'

Malcolm subsided into his chair, not altogether relieved of anxiety.

'Never you mind,' he said.

'You forget that I could go and look.'

'I don't forget it.'

He stared at me. He'd been interested, all those summers ago, when I'd designed and built the pivoting brick door. He'd come down the garden day after day to watch, and had patted me often on the shoulder, and smiled at the secret. The resulting wall looked solid, felt solid, *was* solid. But at one point there was a thick vertical steel rod within it, stretching from a concrete underground foundation up into the beam supporting the roof. Before I'd put the new roof on, I'd patiently drilled round holes in bricks (breaking many) and slid them into the rod, and arranged and mortared the door in neat courses, so that the edges of it dovetailed into the fixed sections next to it.

To open the room, when I'd finished everything, one had first to remove the wedge-like wooden sill which gave extra support to the bottom course of the door when it was closed, and then to activate the spring latch on the inner side by poking a thin wire through a tiny hole in the mortar at what had been my thirteen-year-old waist height. The design of the latch hadn't been my own, but something I'd read in a book: at any rate, when I'd installed it, it worked obligingly at once.

It had pleased me intensely to build a door that Gervase would never find. No more dead rats. No more live birds, shut in and fluttering with fright. No more invasions of my own private place.

Gervase had never found the door and nor had anyone else and, as the years passed, grass grew long in front of the wall, and nettles, and although I'd meant to give the secret to Robin and Peter some day, I hadn't done so by the time of the crash. Only Malcolm knew how to get in – and Malcolm had used the knowledge.

'What's in there?' I repeated.

He put on his airiest expression. 'Just some things I didn't want Moira to get her hands on.'

I remembered sharply the objects missing from his study.

'The gold dolphin, the amethyst tree, the silver candelabra . . . those?'

'You've been looking,' he accused.

I shook my head. 'I noticed they were gone.'

The few precious objects, all the same, hardly accounted for the severity of his first alarm.

'What else is in there?' I said.

'Actually,' he said, calmly now, 'quite a lot of gold.'

CHAPTER FIVE

'Some people buy and sell gold without ever seeing it,' he said. 'But I like possessing the actual stuff. There's no fun in paper transactions. Gold is beautiful on its own account, and I like to see it and feel it. But it's not all that easy to store it in banks or safety deposits. Too heavy and bulky. And insurance is astronomical. Takes too much of the profit. I never insure it.'

'You're storing it there in the wall . . . waiting for the price to rise?'

'You know me, don't you?' He smiled. 'Buy low, bide your time, sell high. Wait a couple of years, not often more. The price of gold itself swings like a pendulum, but there's nothing, really, like gold shares. When gold prices rise, gold shares often rise by two or three times as much. I sell the gold first and the shares a couple of months later. Psychological phenomenon, you know, that people go on investing in gold mines, pushing the price up, when the price of gold itself is static or beginning to drop. Illogical, but invaluable to people like me.'

He sat looking at me with the vivid blue eyes, teaching his child.

'Strategic Minerals, now. There never was anything like the Strategic Minerals Corporation of Australia. This year, the price of gold itself rose twenty-five per cent, but Strats – shares in Strategic Minerals – rose nearly a thousand per cent before they dropped off the top. Incredible, I got in near the beginning of those and sold at nine hundred and fifty per cent profit. But don't be fooled, Strats happen only once or twice in a lifetime.'

'How much,' I said, fascinated, 'did you invest in Strats?'

After a brief pause he said, 'Five million. I had a feeling about them . . . they just smelled right. I don't often go in so deep, and I didn't expect them to fly so high, no one could, but there you are, all gold shares rose this year, and Strats rose like a skylark.'

'How are they doing now?' I asked.

'Don't know. I'm concerned with the present. Gold mines, you see, don't go on for ever. They have a life: exploration, development, production, exhaustion. I get in, wait a while, take a profit, forget them. Never stay too long with a rising gold share. Fortunes are lost by selling too late.'

He did truly trust me, I thought. If he'd doubted me still, he wouldn't have told me there was gold behind the brick door, nor that even after tax he had made approximately thirty million pounds on one deal. I stopped worrying that he was overstretching himself in buying the colt and a half-share in Blue Clancy. I stopped worrying about practically everything except how to keep him alive and spending.

I'd talked to someone once whose father had died when she was barely twenty. She regretted that she hadn't ever known him adult to adult, and wished she could meet him again, just to talk. Watching Malcolm, it struck me that in a way I'd been given her wish: that the three years' silence had been a sort of death, and that I could talk to him now adult to adult, and know him as a man, not as a father.

We spent a peaceful evening together in the suite, talking about what we'd each done during the hiatus, and it was difficult to imagine that outside, somewhere, a predator might be searching for the prey.

At one point I said, 'You gave Joyce's telephone number on purpose to the film man, didn't you? And Gervase's number to the retarded-children lady? You wanted me with you to see you buy the colt . . . You made sure that the family knew all about your monster outlays as soon as possible, didn't you?'

'Huh,' he said briefly, which after a moment I took as admission. One misdirected telephone call had been fairly possible: two stretched credibility too far.

'Thomas and Berenice,' I said, 'were pretty frantic over some little adventure of yours. What did you do to stir *them* up?'

'How the hell do you know all this?'

I smiled and fetched the cassette player, and re-ran for him the message tape from my telephone. He listened grimly but with an undercurrent of amusement to Serena, Gervase and Joyce and then read Thomas's letter, and when he reached Thomas's intense closing appeal I waited for explosions.

They didn't come. He said wryly, 'I suppose they're what I made them.'

'No,' I said.

'Why not?'

'Personality is mysterious, but it's born in you, not made.'

'But it can be brainwashed.'

'Yes, OK,' I said. 'But you didn't do it.'

'Vivien and Alicia did . . . because of me.'

'Don't wallow in guilt so much. It isn't like you.'

He grinned. 'I don't feel guilty, actually.'

Joyce, I thought, had at least played fair. A screaming fury she might have been on the subject of Alicia, but she'd never tried to set me against Malcolm. She had agreed in the divorce settlement when I was six that he should have custody of me: she wasn't basically maternal, and infrequent visits from her growing son were all she required. She'd never made great efforts to bind me to her, and it had always been clear to me that she was relieved every time at my departure. Her life consisted of playing, teaching, and writing about bridge, a game she played to international tournament standard, and she was often abroad. My visits had always disrupted the acute concentration she needed for winning, and as winning gave her the prestige essential for lecture tours and magazine articles, I had more often raised impatience in her than comradeship, a feeling she had dutifully tried to stifle.

She had given me unending packs of cards to play with and had taught me a dozen card games, but I'd never had her razor memory of any and every card played in any and every game, a perpetual disappointment to her and a matter for impatience in itself. When I veered off to make my life in a totally different branch of the entertainment industry, she had been astonished at my choice and at first scornful, but had soon come round to checking the racing pages during the steeplechase season to see if I was listed as riding.

'What did you tell Thomas and Berenice?' I asked Malcolm again, after a pause.

With satisfaction he said, 'I absentmindedly gave their telephone number to a wine merchant who was to let me know the total I owed him for the fifty or so cases of 1979 Pol Roger he was collecting for me to drink.'

'And, er, roughly how much would that cost?'

'The 1979, the Winston Churchill vintage, is quite exceptional, you know.'

'Of course it would be,' I said.

'Roughly twenty-five thousand pounds, then, for fifty cases.'

Poor Thomas, I thought.

'I also made sure that Alicia knew I'd given about a quarter of a million pounds to fund scholarships for bright girls at the school Serena went to. Alicia and I haven't been talking recently. I suppose she's furious I gave it to the school and not to Serena herself.'

'Well, why did you?'

He looked surprised. 'You know my views. You must all carve your own way. To make you all rich too young would rob you of incentive.'

I certainly did know his views, but I wasn't sure I always agreed with them. I would have had bags of incentive to make a success of being a racehorse trainer if he'd lent, advanced or given me enough to start, but I also knew that if he did, he'd have to do as much for the others (being ordinarily a fair man), and he didn't believe in it, as he said.

'Why did you want them all to know how much you've been spending?' I asked. 'Because of course they all will know by now. The telephone wires will have been red hot.'

'I suppose I thought . . . um . . . if they believed I was getting rid of most of it there would be less point in killing me . . . do you see?'

I stared at him. 'You must be crazy,' I said. 'It sounds to me like an invitation to be murdered without delay.'

'Ah well, that too has occurred to me of late.' He smiled vividly. 'But I have you with me now to prevent that.'

After a speechless moment I said, 'I may not always be able to see the speeding car.'

'I'll trust your eyesight.'

I pondered. 'What else have you spent a bundle on, that I haven't heard about?'

He drank some champagne and frowned, and I guessed that he was trying to decide whether or not to tell me. Finally he sighed and said, 'This is for your ears only. I didn't do it for the same reason, and I did it earlier . . . several weeks ago, in fact, before Moira was murdered.' He paused. 'She was angry about it, though she'd no right to be. It wasn't her money. She hated me to give anything to anyone else. She wanted everything for herself.' He sighed. 'I don't know how you knew right from the beginning what she was like.'

'Her calculator eyes,' I said.

He smiled ruefully. He must have seen that look perpetually, by the end.

'The nursing home where Robin is,' he said unexpectedly, 'needed repairs. So I paid for them.'

He wasn't talking, I gathered, in terms of a couple of replaced window-frames.

'Of course, you know it's a private nursing home?' he said. 'A family business, basically.'

'Yes.'

'They needed a new roof. New wiring. A dozen urgent upgradings. They tried raising the residential fees too high and lost patients, familiar story. They asked my advice about fund-raising. I told them not to bother. I'd get estimates, and all I'd want in return was that they'd listen to a good business consultant who I'd send them.' He shifted comfortably in his armchair. 'Robin's settled there. Calm. Any change upsets him, as you know. If the whole place closed and went out of business, which was all too likely, I'd have to find somewhere else for him, and he's lost enough . . .'

His voice tapered off. He had delighted in Robin and Peter when they'd been small, playing with them on the carpet like a young father, proud of them as if they were his first children, not his eighth and ninth. Good memories: worth a new roof.

'I know you still go to visit him,' he said. 'The nurses tell me. So you must have seen the place growing threadbare.'

I nodded, thinking about it. 'They used to have huge vases of fresh flowers everywhere.'

'They used to have top quality everything, but they've had to compromise to patch up the building. Country houses are open money drains when they age. I can't see the place outliving Robin, really. You will look after him, when I've gone?'

'Yes,' I said.

He nodded, taking it for granted. 'I appointed you his trustee when I set up the fund for him, do you remember? I've not altered it.'

I was glad that he hadn't. At least, somewhere, obscurely, things had remained the same between us.

'Why don't we go and see him tomorrow?' he said. 'No one will kill me there.'

'All right,' I agreed: so we went in the hired car in the morning, stopping in the local town to buy presents of chocolate and simple toys designed for three-year-olds, and I added a packet of balloons to the pile while Malcolm paid.

'Does he like balloons?' he asked, his eyebrows rising.

'He gets frustrated sometimes. I blow the balloons up, and he bursts them.'

Malcolm looked surprised and in some ways disturbed. 'I didn't know he could feel frustration.'

'It seems like that. As if sometimes he half remembers us . . . but can't quite.'

'Poor boy.'

We drove soberly onwards and up the drive of the still splendid-looking Georgian house which lay mellow and symmetrical in the autumn sunshine. Inside, its near fifty rooms had been adapted and transformed in the heyday of private medicine into a highly comfortable hospital for mostly chronic, mostly old, mostly rich patients. Short-stay patients came and went, usually convalescing after major operations performed elsewhere, but in general one saw the same faces month after month: the same faces ageing, suffering, waiting for release. Dreadfully depressing, I found it, but for Robin, it was true, it seemed the perfect haven, arrived at after two unsuccessful stays in more apparently suitable homes involving other children, bright colours, breezy nurses and jollying atmospheres. Robin seemed better with peace, quiet and no demands, and Malcolm had finally acted against professional advice to give them to him.

Robin had a large room on the ground floor with French doors opening on to a walled garden. He seldom went out into the garden, but he preferred the doors open in all weathers, including snow-storms. Apart from that, he was docile and easy to deal with, and if anyone had speculated on the upheavals that might happen soon if puberty took its natural course, they hadn't mentioned it in my hearing.

He looked at us blankly, as usual. He seldom spoke, though he did retain the ability to make words: it was just that he seemed to have few thoughts to utter. Brain damage of that magnitude was idiosyncratic, we'd been told, resulting in behaviour individual to each victim. Robin spoke rarely and then only to himself, in private, when he didn't expect to be overheard: the nurses sometimes heard him, and had told us, but said he stopped as soon as he saw them.

I'd asked them what he said, but they didn't know, except for words like 'shoes' and 'bread' and 'floor': ordinary words. They didn't know why he wouldn't speak at other times. They were sure, though, that he understood a fair amount of what others said, even if in a haze.

We gave him some pieces of chocolate which he ate,

and unwrapped the toys for him which he fingered but didn't play with. He looked at the balloon packet without emotion. It wasn't a frustration day: on those, he looked at the packet and made blowing noises with his mouth.

We sat with him for quite a while, talking, telling him who we were while he wandered around the room. He looked at our faces from time to time, and touched my nose once with his finger as if exploring that I was really there, but there was no connection with our minds. He looked healthy, good looking, a fine boy: heart-breaking, as always.

A nurse came in the end, middle-aged, kind-faced, to take him to a dining room for lunch, and Malcolm and I transferred to the office where my father was given a saviour's welcome and offered a reviving scotch.

'Your son, slow progress, I'm afraid.' Earnest, dedicated people.

Malcolm nodded. No progress would have been more accurate.

'We do our best for him always.'

'Yes, I know.' Malcolm drank the scotch, shook their hands, made our farewells. We left, as I always left, in sadness, silence and regret.

'So bloody unfair,' Malcolm said halfway back to London. 'He ought to be laughing, talking, roaring through life.'

'Yes.'

'I can't bear to see him, and I can't bear not to. I'd give all my money to have him well again.'

'And make a new fortune afterwards,' I said.

'Well, yeah, why not?' He laughed, but still with gloom. 'It would have been better if he'd died with the others. Life's a bugger, sometimes, isn't it?'

The gloom lasted back to the Savoy and through the next bottle of Bollinger, but by afternoon Malcolm was complaining of the inactivity I'd thrust upon him and wanting to visit cronies in the City. Unpredictability be our shield, I prayed, and kept my eyes open for speeding cars; but we saw the day out safely in offices, bars, clubs and a restaurant, during which time Malcolm increased his wealth by gambling a tenner at evens on the day's closing price of gold which fell by two pounds when the trend was upwards. 'It'll shoot right up next year, you watch.'

On Friday, despite my pleas for sanity, he insisted on accompanying me to Sandown Park races.

'You'll be safer here,' I protested, 'in the suite.'

'I shan't *feel* safer.'

'At the races, I can't stay beside you.'

'Who's to know I'll be there?'

I gazed at him. 'Anyone who guesses we are now together could know. They'll know how to find *me*, if they look in the papers.'

'Then don't go.'

'I'm going. You stay here.'

I saw, however, that the deep underlying apprehension which he tried to suppress most of the time would erupt into acute nervous anxiety if I left him alone in the suite for several hours, and that he might, out of boredom, do something much sillier than going to the races, like convincing himself that anyone in his family would keep a secret if he asked it.

Accordingly I drove him south of London and took him through the jockeys' entrance gate to the weighing room area where he made his afternoon a lot safer by meeting yet another crony and being instantly invited to lunch in the holy of holies.

'Do you have cronies all over the world?' I asked.

'Certainly,' he said, smiling broadly. 'Anyone I've known for five minutes is a crony, if I get on with them.'

I believed him. Malcolm wasn't easy to forget, nor was he hard to like. I saw the genuine pleasure in his immediate host's face as they walked away together, talking, and reflected that Malcolm would have been a success in whatever career he had chosen, that success was part of his character, like generosity, like headlong rashness.

I was due to ride in the second race, a steeplechase for amateurs, and as usual had arrived two prudent hours in advance. I turned away from watching Malcolm and looked around for the owner of the horse I was about to partner, and found my path blocked by a substantial lady in a wide brown cape. Of all the members of the family, she was the last I would have expected to see on a racecourse.

'Ian,' she said accusingly, almost as if I'd been pretending to be someone else.

'Hello.'

'Where have you been? Why don't you answer your telephone?'

Lucy, my elder half-sister. Lucy, the poet.

Lucy's husband Edwin was, as always, to be found at her side, rather as if he had no separate life. The leech, Malcolm had called him unkindly in the past. From a Bugg to a leech.

Lucy was blessed with an unselfconsciousness about her weight which stemmed both from unworldliness and an overbelief in health foods. 'But nuts and raisins are *good* for you,' she would say, eating them by the kilo. 'Bodily vanity, like intellectual arrogance, is a sickness of the soul.'

She was forty-two, my sister, with thick straight brown hair uncompromisingly cut, large brown eyes, her mother's high cheek-bones and her father's strong nose. She was as noticeable in her own way as Malcolm was himself, and not only because of her shapeless clothes and dedicated absence of cosmetics. Malcolm's vitality ran in her too, though in different directions, expressing itself in vigour of thought and language.

I had often, in the past, wondered why someone as talented and strongminded as she shouldn't have made a marriage of equal minds, but in recent years had come to think she had settled for a nonentity like Edwin because the very absence of competition freed her to be wholly herself.

'Edwin is concerned,' she said, 'that Malcolm is leaving his senses.'

For Edwin, read Lucy, I thought. She had a trick of ascribing her own thoughts to her husband if she thought they would be unwelcome to her audience.

Edwin stared at me uneasily. He was a good-looking man in many ways, but mean spirited, which if one were tolerant one would excuse because of the perpetual knife-edge state of his and Lucy's finances. I wasn't certain any more whether it was he who had actually failed to achieve employment, or whether Lucy had in some way stopped him from trying. In any event, she earned more prestige than lucre for her writing, and Edwin had grown tired of camouflaging the frayed elbows of his jackets with oval patches of thin leather badly sewn on.

Edwin's concern, it seemed, was real enough although if it had been his alone they wouldn't have come.

'It isn't fair of him,' he said, meaning Malcolm. 'Lucy's trust fund was set up years ago before inflation and doesn't stretch as far as it used to. He really ought to put that right. I've told him so several times, and he simply ignores me. And now he's throwing his money away in this profligate way as if his heirs had no rights at all.' Indignation shook in his voice, along with, I could see, a very definite fear of a rocky future if the fortune he'd counted on for so long should be snatched away in the last furlong, so to speak.

I sighed and refrained from saying that I thought that Malcolm's heirs had no rights while he was alive. I said merely, soothingly, 'I'm sure he won't let you starve.'

'That's not the point,' Edwin said with thin fury. 'The point is that he's given an *immense* amount of money to Lucy's old college to establish post-graduate scholarships for poets.'

I looked from his pinch-lipped agitated mouth to Lucy's face and saw shame where there should perhaps have been pride. Shame, I thought, because she found herself sharing Edwin's views when they ran so contrary to her normal disdain for materialism. Perhaps even Lucy, I thought, had been looking forward to a comfortably off old age.

'You should be honoured,' I said.

She nodded unhappily. 'I am.'

'No,' Edwin said. 'It's disgraceful.'

'The Lucy Pembroke Scholarships,' I said slowly.

'Yes. How did you know?' Lucy asked.

And there would be the Serena Pembroke Scholarships, of course. And the Coochie Pembroke Memorial Challenge Trophy . . .

'What are you smiling at?' Lucy demanded. 'You can't say you've made much of a success of your life so far, can you? If Malcolm leaves us all nothing, you'll end up carting horse-muck until you drop from senility.'

'There are worse jobs,' I said mildly.

There were horses around us, and racecourse noises, and a skyful of gusty fresh air. I could happily spend my life, I knew, in almost any capacity that took me to places like Sandown Park.

'You've wasted every talent you have,' Lucy said.

'My only talent is riding horses.'

'You're blind and stupid. You're the only male Pembroke with decent brains and you're too lazy to use them.'

'Well, thanks,' I said.

'It's not a compliment.'

'No, so I gathered.'

'Joyce says you're sure to know where Malcolm is as you've finally made up your quarrel, though you'll lie about it as a matter of course,' Lucy said. 'Joyce said you would be here today on this spot at this time, if I wanted to reach you.'

'Which you did, rather badly.'

'Don't be so obtuse. You've got to stop him. You're the only one who can, and Joyce says you're probably the only one who won't try . . . and you *must* try, Ian, and succeed, if not for yourself, then for the rest of the family.'

'For you?' I asked.

'Well . . .' She couldn't openly abandon her principles, but they were bending, it seemed. 'For the others,' she said stalwartly.

I looked at her with new affection. 'You're a hypocrite, my dear sister,' I said.

In smarting retaliation, she said sharply, 'Vivien thinks you're trying to cut the rest of us out and ingratiate yourself again with Malcolm.'

'I expect she would,' I said. 'I expect Alicia will think it also, when Vivien has fed it to her.'

'You really are a bastard.'

'No,' I said, my lips twitching, 'that's Gervase.'

'*Ian!*'

I laughed. 'I'll tell Malcolm you're concerned. I promise I will, somehow. And now I've got to change my clothes and ride in a race. Are you staying?'

Lucy hesitated but Edwin said, 'Will you win?'

'I don't think so. Save your money.'

'You're not taking it seriously,' Lucy said.

I looked straight at her eyes. 'Believe me,' I said, 'I take it very seriously indeed. No one had a right to murder Moira to stop her taking half Malcolm's money. No one has a right to murder Malcolm to stop him spending it. He is fair. He will leave us all provided for, when the time comes, which I hope may be twenty years from now. You tell them all to stop fretting, to ease off, to have faith. Malcolm is teasing you all and I think it's dangerous, but he is dismayed by everyone's greed, and is determined to teach us a lesson. So you tell them, Lucy, tell Joyce and Vivien and everyone, that the more we try to grab, the less we will get. The more we protest, the more he will spend.'

She looked back silently. Eventually she said, 'I am ashamed of myself.'

'Rubbish,' Edwin said to me vehemently. 'You must stop Malcolm. You must.'

Lucy shook her head. 'Ian's right.'

'Do you mean Ian won't even try?' Edwin demanded incredulously.

'I'm positive he won't,' Lucy said. 'Didn't you hear what he said? Weren't you listening?'

'It was all rubbish.'

Lucy patted my arm. 'We may as well see you race, while we're here. Go and get changed.'

It was a more sisterly gesture and tone than I was used to, and I reflected with a shade of guilt that I'd paid scant attention to her own career for a couple of years.

'How is the poetry going?' I asked. 'What are you working on?'

The question caught her unprepared. Her face went momentarily blank and then filled with what seemed to be an odd mixture of sadness and panic.

'Nothing just now,' she said. 'Nothing for quite a while,' and I nodded almost apologetically as if I had intruded, and went into the weighing room and through to the changing room reflecting that poets, like mathematicians, mostly did their best work when young. Lucy wasn't writing; had maybe stopped altogether.

And perhaps, I thought, the frugality she had for so long embraced had begun to seem less worthy and less worth it, if she were losing the inner sustaining comfort of creative inspiration.

Poor Lucy, I thought. Life could be a bugger, as Malcolm said. She had already begun to value the affluence she had long despised or she wouldn't have come on her mission to Sandown Park, and I could only guess at the turmoil in her spiritual life. Like a nun losing her faith, I thought. But no, not a nun. Lucy, who had written explicitly of sex in a way I could never believe had anything to do with Edwin (though one could be wrong), wouldn't ever have been a nun.

With such random thoughts, I took off my ordinary clothes and put on white breeches and a scarlet jersey with blue stripes on the sleeves, and felt the usual battened-down excitement which made me breathe deeply and feel intensely happy. I rode in about fifty races a year, if I was lucky . . . and I would have to get another job fairly soon, I reflected, if I were to ride exercise regularly and stay fit enough to do any good.

Going outside, I talked for a while to the trainer and owner of the horse I was to ride, a husband and wife who had themselves ridden until twenty years earlier in point-to-point races and who liked to re-live it all vicariously through me. The husband, George, was now a public trainer on a fairly grand scale, but the wife, Jo, still preferred to run her own horses in amateur races. She currently owned three steeplechasers, all pretty good. It did me no harm at all to be seen on them and to be associated in racing minds with that stable.

'Young Higgins is jumping out of his skin,' Jo said.

Young Higgins was the name of that day's horse. Young Higgins was thirteen, a venerable gentleman out to disprove rumours of retirement. We all interpreted 'jumping out of his skin' as meaning fit, sound and pricking his ears with enthusiasm, and at his age one couldn't ask for much more. Older horses than he had won the Grand National, but Young Higgins and I had fallen in the great race the only time we'd tried it, and to my regret Jo had decided on no more attempts.

'We'll see you in the parade ring, then, Ian, before the race,' George said, and Jo added, 'And give the old boy a good time.'

I nodded, smiling. Giving all of us a good time was the point of the proceedings. Young Higgins was definitely included.

The minute George and Jo turned away to go off towards the grandstands, someone tapped me on the back of the shoulder. I turned round to see who it was and to my total astonishment found myself face to face with Lucy's older brother, Malcolm's first child, my half-brother Donald.

'Good heavens,' I said. 'You've never been to the races in your life.'

He often told me he hadn't, saying rather superciliously that he didn't approve of the sordid gambling.

'I haven't come for the races,' he said crossly. 'I've come to see you about Malcolm's taking leave of his senses.'

'How . . . er . . .?' I stopped. 'Did Joyce send you?' I said.

'What if she did? We are all concerned. She told us where to find you, certainly.'

'Did she tell the whole family?' I asked blankly.

'How do I know? She telephoned us. I daresay she telephoned everyone she could get hold of. You know what she's like. She's your mother, after all.'

Even so late in his life, he couldn't keep out of his voice the old resentments, and perhaps also, I reflected, they were intensifying with age. My mother had supplanted his, he was saying, and any indiscretion my mother ever committed was in some way my fault. He had thought in that illogical way for as long as I'd been aware of him, and nothing had changed.

Donald was, in the family's opinion, the brother nearest in looks to myself, and I wasn't sure I liked it. Irrefutably, he was the same height and had blue eyes less intense in colour than Malcolm's. Agreed, Donald had middling brown curly hair and shoulders wider than his hips. I didn't wear a bushy moustache though, and I just hoped I didn't walk with what I thought of as a self-important strut; and I sometimes tried to make sure, after I'd been in Donald's company, that I absolutely didn't.

Donald's life had been so disrupted when Malcolm

had ousted Vivien, Donald always told us, that he had never been able to decide properly on a career. It couldn't have been easy, I knew, to survive such an upheaval, but Donald had only been nine at the time, a bit early for life decisions. In any event, as an adult he had drifted from job to job in hotels, coming to harbour at length as secretary of a prestigious golf club near Henley-on-Thames, a post which I gathered had proved ultimately satisfactory in social standing, which was very important to his self-esteem.

I didn't either like or dislike Donald particularly. He was eleven years older than I was. He was *there.*

'Everyone insists you stop Malcolm squandering the family money,' he said, predictably.

'It's *his* money, not the family's,' I said.

'What?' Donald found the idea ridiculous. 'What you've got to do is explain that he owes it to us to keep the family fortune intact until we inherit it. Unfortunately we know he won't listen to any of us except you, and now that you appear to have made up your quarrel with him, you are elected to be our spokesman. Joyce thinks we have to convince you first of the need to stop Malcolm, but I told her it was ridiculous. You don't need convincing, you want to be well off one day just the same as the rest of us, of course you do, it's only natural.'

I was saved from both soul-searching and untrue disclaimers by the arrival of Helen, Donald's wife, who had apparently been buying a racecard.

'We're not staying,' Donald said disapprovingly, eyeing it.

She gave him a vague smile. 'You never know,' she said.

Beautiful and brainless, Malcolm had said of her, and perhaps he was right. Tall and thin, she moved with natural style and made cheap clothes look expensive: I knew they were cheap because she had a habit of saying where they'd come from and how much she'd paid for them, inviting admiration of her thriftiness. Donald always tried to shut her up.

'Do tell us where to watch the races from,' she said.

'We're not here for that,' Donald said.

'No, dear, we're here because we need money now that the boys have started at Eton.'

'No, dear,' Donald said sharply.

'But you know we can't afford . . .'

'Do be quiet, dear,' Donald said.

'Eton costs a bomb,' I said mildly, knowing that Donald's income would hardly stretch to one son there, let alone two. Donald had twin boys, which seemed to run in the family.

'Of course it does,' Helen said, 'but Donald puts such store by it. "My sons are at Eton," that sort of thing. Gives him *standing* with the people he deals with in the golf club.'

'Helen, dear, do be quiet.' Donald's embarrassment showed, but she was undoubtedly right.

'We thought Donald might have inherited before the

boys reached thirteen,' she said intensely. 'As he hasn't, we're borrowing every penny we can to pay the fees, the same as we borrowed for the prep school and a lot of other things. But we've borrowed against Donald's expectations . . . so you see it's essential for us that there really is plenty to inherit, as there are so many people to share it with. We'll be literally bankrupt if Malcolm throws too much away . . . and I don't think Donald could face it.'

I opened my mouth to answer her but no sound came out. I felt as if I'd been thrust into a farce over which I had no control.

Walking purposefully to join us came Serena, Ferdinand and Debs.

CHAPTER SIX

'Stay right here,' I said to all of them. 'I have to go into the weighing room to deal with a technicality. Stay right here until I come out.'

They nodded with various frowns, and I dived into privacy in a desperate search for a sheet of paper and an envelope.

I wrote to Malcolm:

> Half the family have turned up here, sent by Joyce. For God's sake stay where you are, keep out of sight and wait until I come to fetch you.

I stuck the note into the envelope, wrote Malcolm's name on the outside, and sought out an official who had enough rank to send someone to deliver it.

'My father is lunching in the Directors' dining room,' I said. 'And it's essential that he gets this note immediately.'

The official was obliging. He was going up to the Stewards' room anyway, he said, and he would take it himself. With gratitude and only a minor lessening of despair – because it would be just like Malcolm to come down contrarily to confront the whole bunch – I went out again into the sunlight and found the five of them still faithfully waiting exactly where I'd left them.

'I say,' Debs said, half mocking, 'you do look dashing in all that kit.'

Donald looked at her in surprise, and I had a vivid impression of his saying soon in his golf club, 'My brother, the amateur jockey . . .' knowing that if I'd been a professional he would have hushed it up if he could. A real snob, Donald: but there were worse sins.

Debs, Ferdinand's second wife, had come to the races in a black leather coat belted at the waist, with shoulder-length blonde hair above and long black boots below. Her eyelids were purple, like her fingernails. The innocence I'd photographed in her a year ago was in danger of disappearing.

Ferdinand, shorter than Debs and more like Malcolm than ever, appeared to be in his usual indecision over whether I was to be loved or hated. I smiled at him cheerfully and asked what sort of a journey he'd had.

'A lot of traffic,' he said lamely.

'We didn't come here to talk about traffic,' Serena said forbiddingly. 'We want to know where Daddy is.'

Malcolm's little Serena, now taller than he, was dressed that day in royal blue with white frills at neck and wrists, a white woollen hat with a pompom on top covering her cap of fair hair. She looked a leggy sixteen, not ten years older. Her age showed only in the coldness of her manner towards me, which gave no sign of thawing.

In her high-pitched, girlish voice she said, 'We want him to settle very substantial sums on us all right now. Then he can go to blazes with the rest.'

I blinked. 'Who are you quoting?' I asked.

'Myself,' she said loftily, and then more probably added, 'Mummy too. And Gervase.'

It had Gervase's thuggish style stamped all over it.

Donald and Helen looked distinctly interested in the proposal. Ferdinand and Debs had of course heard it before.

'Gervase thinks it's the best solution,' Ferdinand said, nodding.

I doubted very much that Malcolm would agree, but said only, 'I'll pass on your message next time he gets in touch with me.'

'But Joyce is sure you know where he is,' Donald objected.

'Not exactly,' I said. 'Do you know that Lucy and Edwin are here too?'

They were satisfactorily diverted, looking over their shoulders to see if they could spot them in the growing crowds.

'Didn't Joyce tell you she was sending so many of you here?' I asked generally, and it was Ferdinand, sideways, his face turned away, who answered.

'She told Serena to come here. She told Serena to tell me, which she did, so we came together. I didn't know about Donald and Helen or Lucy and Edwin. I expect she wanted to embarrass you.'

His eyes swivelled momentarily to my face, wanting to see my reaction. I don't suppose my face showed any. Joyce might call me 'darling' with regularity but could be woundingly unkind at the same time, and I'd had a lifetime to grow armour.

Ferdinand happened to be standing next to me. I said on impulse into his ear, 'Ferdinand, who killed Moira?'

He stopped looking for Lucy and Edwin and transferred his attention abruptly and wholly to me. I could see calculations going on in the pause before he answered, but I had no decoder for his thoughts. He was the most naturally congenial to me of all my brothers, yet the others were open books compared with him. He was secretive, as perhaps I was myself. He had wanted to build his own kitchen-wall hidey-hole when I'd built mine, only Malcolm had said we must share, that one was enough. Ferdinand had sulked and shunned me for a while, and smirked at Gervase's dead rats. I wondered to what extent people remained the same as they'd been when very young: whether it was safe to assume they hadn't basically changed, to believe that if one could peel back the layers of living one would come to the known child. I wanted Ferdinand to be as I had known him at ten, eleven, twelve

– a boy dedicated to riding a bicycle while standing on his head on the saddle – and not in a million years a murderer.

'I don't know who killed Moira,' he said finally. 'Alicia says you did. She told the police it *had* to be you.'

'I couldn't have.'

'She says the police could break your alibi if they really tried.'

I knew that they had really tried: they'd checked every separate five minutes of my day, and their manner and their suspicions had been disturbing.

'And what do *you* think?' I asked curiously.

His eyelids flickered. 'Alicia says . . .'

I said abruptly, 'Your mother says too damned much. Can't you think for yourself?'

He was offended, as he would be. He hooked his arms through those of Debs and Serena and made an announcement. 'We three are going to have a drink and a sandwich. If you fall off and kill yourself, no one will miss you.'

I smiled at him, though his tone had held no joke.

'And don't be so bloody forgiving,' he said.

He whirled the girls away from me and marched them off. I wondered how he'd got the day off from work, though I supposed most people could if they tried. He was a statistician, studying to be an actuary in his insurance company. What were the probabilities, I wondered, of a thirty-two-year-old statistician whose wife had purple fingernails being present when his brother broke his neck at Sandown Park?

Donald and Helen said that they too would run a sandwich to earth (Donald's words) and Helen added earnestly that *she* would care that I finished the race safely, whatever Ferdinand said.

'Thanks,' I said, hoping I could believe her, and went back into the changing room for an interval of thought.

Lucy and Edwin might leave before the end of the afternoon, and so might Donald and Helen, but Ferdinand wouldn't. He liked going racing. He'd said on one mellow occasion that he'd have been quite happy being a bookmaker; he was lightning fast at working out relative odds.

The problem of how to extract Malcolm unseen from the racecourse didn't end, either, with those members of the family I'd talked to. If they were all so certain I knew where Malcolm was, one of the others, more cunning, could be hiding behind trees, waiting to follow me when I left.

There were hundreds of trees in Sandown Park.

The first race came and went, and in due course I went out to partner Young Higgins in the second.

Jo as usual had red cheeks from pleasure and hope. George was being gruffly businesslike, also as usual, telling me to be especially careful at the difficult first fence and to go easy up the hill past the stands the first time.

I put Malcolm out of my mind, and also murder,

and it wasn't difficult. The sky was a clear distant blue, the air crisp with the coming of autumn. The leaves on all those trees were yellowing, and the track lay waiting, green and springy, with the wide fences beckoning to be flown. Simple things; and out there one came starkly face to face with oneself, which I mostly found more exhilarating than frightening. So far, anyway.

Jo said, 'Only eight runners, just a perfect number,' and George said, as he always did, 'Don't lie too far back coming round the last long bend.'

I said I would try not to.

Jo's eyes were sparkling like a child's in her sixty-year-old face, and I marvelled that she had never in all that time lost the thrill of expectation in moments like these. There might be villains at every level in horse racing, but there were also people like Jo and George whose goodness and goodwill shone out like search-lights, who made the sport overall good fun and wholesome.

Life and death might be serious in the real world, but life and death on a fast steeplechaser on a Friday afternoon in the autumn sunshine was a lighthearted toss-up, an act of health on a sick planet.

I fastened the strap of my helmet, was thrown up on Young Higgins and rode him out onto the track. Perhaps if I'd been a professional and ridden up to ten times as often I would have lost the swelling joy that that moment always gave me: one couldn't grin like a maniac, even to oneself, at a procession of bread-and-butter rides on cold days, sharp tracks, bad horses.

Young Higgins was living up to his name, bouncing on his toes and tossing his head in high spirits. We lined up with the seven others, all of whose riders I happened to know from many past similar occasions. Amateurs came in all guises: there was a mother, an aunt and a grandfather riding that afternoon, besides a journalist, an earl's son, a lieutenant colonel, a showjumper and myself. From the stands, only a keen eye could have told one from the other without the guidance of our colours, and that was what amateur racing was all about: the equality, the levelling anonymity of the starting gate.

The tapes went up and we set off with three miles to go, almost two whole circuits, twenty-two jumps and an uphill run to the winning post.

The aunt's horse, too strong for her, took hold of the proceedings and opened up an emphatic lead, which no one else bothered to cut down. The aunt's horse rushed into the difficult downhill first fence and blundered over it, which taught him a lesson and let his rider recover control, and for about a mile after that there were no dramatic excitements. The first race I'd ever ridden in had seemed to pass in a whirling heaving flurry leaving me breathless and exhausted, but time had stretched out with experience until one could watch and think and even talk.

'Give me room, blast you,' shouted the lieutenant colonel on one side of me.

'Nice day,' said the earl's son chattily on the other, always a clown who enlivened his surroundings.

'Shift your *arse*!' yelled the mother to her horse, giving him a crack round that part of his anatomy. She was a good rider, hated slow horses, hated not to win, weighed a muscular ten stone and was scornful of the showjumper, whom she had accused often of incompetence.

The showjumper, it was true, liked to set his horse right carefully before jumps, as in the show ring, and hadn't managed to speed up in the several steeplechase races he'd ridden so far. He wasn't in consequence someone to follow into a fence and I avoided him whenever possible.

The journalist was the best jockey in the race, a professional in all but status, and the grandfather was the worst but full of splendid reckless courage. More or less in a bunch, the whole lot of us came round the bottom bend and tackled the last three jumps of the first circuit. The aunt was still in front, then came the lieutenant colonel, myself and the earl's son in a row, then the mother just behind, with the showjumper and the grandfather beside her. I couldn't see the journalist: somewhere in the rear, no doubt, biding his wily time.

The lieutenant colonel's mount made a proper hash of the last of the three fences, jogging both of his rider's feet out of the irons and tipping the military backside into the air somewhere in the region of the horse's mane. Landing alongside and gathering my reins, I saw that the lieutenant colonel's balance was hopelessly progressing down the horse's galloping shoulder as he fought without success to pull himself back into the saddle.

I put out an arm, grasped his jersey and yanked him upwards and backwards, shifting his disastrous centre of gravity into a more manageable place and leaving him slowing and bumping in my wake as he sat down solidly in the saddle, trying to put his feet back into his flying stirrups, which was never very easy at thirty miles an hour.

He had breathing space to collect things going up the hill, though, as we all did, and we swept round the top bend and down to the difficult fence again with not much change in order from the first time.

Someone had once long ago pulled me back into the saddle in that same way: it was fairly common in jump racing. Someone had also once tipped me straight into the air with an upward wrench of my heel, but that was another story. The lieutenant colonel was saying 'Thanks' and also 'Move over, you're crowding me,' more or less in the same breath.

After crossing the water jump for the second time over on the far side of the track, the showjumper made a spurt to the front and then slowed almost to a standstill on landing over the next fence, having jumped especially pedantically, and the aunt crashed into the back of him with some singularly un-aunt-like language.

'Lovely lady,' said the earl's son, appreciatively, as we passed the débâcle. 'How are you going yourself?'

'Not bad,' I said. 'How are you?'

We jumped the last of the seven far-side fences together and in front, and put all our energies into staying there round the long last bend and over the three last fences. I could hear horses thudding behind me and the mother's voice exhorting her slowcoach. Approaching the Pond fence, I could sense the earl's son's horse beginning to tire, I could see that precious winning post far ahead and the way to it clear, and for at least a few moments I thought I might win. But then the lieutenant colonel reappeared fast at my elbow, still shouting for room, and between the last two fences, as I'd feared he would, the journalist materialized from the outback and made it look easy, and Young Higgins tired into Middle-Aged Higgins on the hill.

He and I finished third, which wasn't too bad, with the earl's son, persevering, not far away fourth.

'A nice afternoon out,' he said happily as we trotted back together, and I looked at the lights in his eyes and saw it was the same for him as for me, a high that one couldn't put into words, an adventure of body and spirit that made of dismounting and walking on the ground a literal coming down to earth.

Jo was pleased enough, patting Young Higgins hard.

'Ran a great race, didn't you, old boy? Jumped like a stag.'

'You'd have been second,' said George, who had good binoculars, 'if you'd let the lieutenant colonel fall off.'

'Yeah, well,' I said, unbuckling the girths, 'there were a lot of hooves down there.'

George smiled. 'Don't forget to weigh in.' (He said it every time.) 'Come for a drink in the Owners' bar when you've changed.'

I accepted. It was part of the ritual, part of the bargain. They liked to re-live Young Higgins' outing fence for fence in return for having given me the ride. They were still standing in the unsaddling enclosure talking to friends when I went out again in street clothes, and with welcoming smiles waved me into their group. None of my own family being in sight, I went with them without problems and, over glasses of Jo's favourite brandy and ginger ale, earned my afternoon's fun by describing it.

I returned to the weighing room area afterwards and found that not only were all the same family members still on the racecourse, but that they had coalesced into an angry swarm and had been joined by one of the queen bees herself, my mother Joyce.

Joyce, in fur and a green hat, was a rinsed blonde with greenish eyes behind contact lenses which seldom missed a trick in life as in cards. Dismayed but blank-faced, I gave her a dutiful peck on her smooth cheek which, it seemed, she was in no mood to receive.

'Darling,' she said, the syllables sizzling with displeasure, 'did you or did you not send that weasel Norman West to check up on my whereabouts last Friday?'

'Er,' I said.

'Did you or did you not send him sniffing round Vivien on the same errand?'

'Well,' I said, half smiling, 'I wouldn't have put it as crudely, but I suppose so, yes.'

The battery of eyes from the others was as friendly as napalm.

'Why?' Joyce snapped.

'Didn't Norman West tell you?'

She said impatiently, 'He said something nonsensical about Malcolm being attacked. I told him if Malcolm had been attacked, I would have heard of it.'

'Malcolm was very nearly killed,' I said flatly. 'He and I asked Norman West to make sure that none of you could have done it.'

Joyce demanded to be told what had happened to Malcolm, and I told her. She and all the others listened with open mouths and every evidence of shock, and if there was knowledge, not ignorance, behind any of the horrified eyes, I couldn't discern it.

'Poor Daddy!' Serena exclaimed. 'How *beastly.*'

'A matter for the police,' Donald said forcefully.

'I agree,' I said. 'I'm surprised they haven't been to see all of you already, as they did when Moira died.'

Edwin said, with a shake of the head, 'How near, how near,' and then, hearing the regret in his voice as clearly as I did, added hurriedly, 'What a blessing he woke up.'

'When the police make their enquiries,' I said, 'they don't exactly report the results to Malcolm. He wants to make sure for himself that none of the family was at Quantum last Friday afternoon. If you cooperate with Norman West when he gets to you, you'll set Malcolm's mind at rest.'

'And what if we can't prove where we were?' Debs asked.

'Or even remember?' Lucy said.

'Malcolm will have to live with it,' Joyce said crisply.

'Living with it would present him less problem,' I said dryly. 'It's dying he wants to avoid.'

They stared at me in silence. The reality of Moira's murder had been to them, I guessed, as to me, a slow-burning fuse, with seemingly no bad consequences at first, but with accelerating worries as time passed. Perhaps they, as I had done, had clung to the motive-less-intruder-from-outside theory at first because the alternative was surely unthinkable, but in the weeks since then, they must at least have begun to wonder. The fuse would heat soon into active suspicions, I saw, which might tear apart and finally scatter for ever the fragile family fabric.

Would I mind, I thought? Not if I still had Malcolm . . . and perhaps Ferdinand . . . and Joyce . . . and maybe Lucy, or Thomas . . . Serena . . . would I care if I never again laid eyes on Gervase?

The answer, surprisingly enough, was yes, I would mind. Imperfect, quarrelsome, ramshackle as it was, the family were origins and framework, the geography of living. Moira, ungrieved, was already rewriting that map, and if her murderer remained for ever undiscovered, if Malcolm himself – I couldn't think of it – were killed, there would be no healing, no reforming, no telephone network for information, no contact, just a lot of severed galaxies moving inexorably apart.

The big bang, I thought, still lay ahead. The trick was to smother the fuse before the explosion, and that was all very well, but where was the burning point, and how long had we got?

'Buy me a drink, darling,' Joyce commanded. 'We're in deep trouble.'

She began to move off, but the others showed no signs of following. I looked at the seven faces all expressing varying degrees of anxiety and saw them already begin to move slightly away from each other, not one cohesive group, but Donald and Helen as a couple, Lucy and Edwin, a pair, and Ferdinand, Debs and Serena, the youngest trio.

'I'll tell Malcolm your fears,' I said. 'And your needs.'

'Oh yes, please do,' Helen said intensely.

'And Gervase's plan,' Ferdinand added.

'Do come on, darling,' Joyce said peremptorily over her shoulder. 'Which way is the bar?'

'Run along, little brother,' Lucy said with irony. Serena said, 'Mumsie's waiting,' and Debs fairly tittered. I thought of sticking my toes in and making Joyce come back, but what did it matter? I could put up with the jibes, I'd survived them for years, and I understood what prompted them. I shrugged ruefully and went after Joyce, and could feel the pitying smiles on the back of my neck.

I steered Joyce into the busy Members' bar which had a buffet table along one side with salads and breads and a large man in chef's clothes carving from turkeys, haunches of beef and hams on the bone. I was hungry after riding and offered Joyce food, but she waved away the suggestion as frivolity. I bought her instead a large vodka and tonic with a plain ginger ale for myself, and we found spare seats at a table in a far corner where, after the merest glance around to make sure she wouldn't be overheard among the general hubbub, she leaned forward until the brim of the green hat was practically touching my forehead and launched into her inquisition.

'Where is your father?' she said.

'When did you last see your father?' I amended.

'What on earth are you talking about?'

'That picture by Orchardson.'

'Stop playing games. Where is Malcolm?'

'I don't know,' I said.

'You're lying.'

'Why do you want to find him?'

'*Why?*' She was astonished. 'Because he's out of his mind.' She dug into her capacious handbag and brought out an envelope, which she thrust towards me. 'Read that.'

I opened the envelope and found a small piece of newspaper inside, a snipped paragraph without headline or provenance.

It said:

> Second-string British contender is Blue Clancy, second in last year's Derby and winner this year of Royal Ascot's King Edward VII Stakes. Owner Ramsey Osborn yesterday hedged his Arc bets by selling a half-share in his four-year-old colt to arbitrageur Malcolm Pembroke, who launched into bloodstock only this week with a two million guineas yearling at the Premium Sales.

Ouch, I thought.

'Where did it come from?' I asked.

'What does it matter where it came from? That new "Racing Patter" column in the *Daily Towncrier*, as a matter of fact. I was drinking coffee this morning when I read it and nearly choked. The point is, is it true?'

'Yes,' I said.

'*What*?'

'Yes,' I said again. 'Malcolm bought half of Blue Clancy. Why shouldn't he?'

'Sometimes,' my mother said forcefully, 'you are so stupid I could hit you.' She paused for breath. 'And what exactly is an arbitrageur?'

'A guy who makes money by buying low and selling high.'

'Oh. Gold.'

'And foreign currencies. And shares. And maybe racehorses.'

She was unmollified. 'You know perfectly well he's just throwing his money away to spite everybody.'

'He didn't like Moira being killed. He didn't like being attacked himself. I shouldn't think he'll stop spending until he knows whether we have or haven't a murderer in the family, and even then . . .' I smiled, 'he's getting a taste for it.'

Joyce stared. 'Moira was murdered by an intruder,' she said.

I didn't answer.

She took a large swallow of her vodka and tonic and looked at me bleakly. She had been barely twenty when I was born, barely nineteen when Malcolm had whisked her headlong from an antique shop in Kensington and within a month installed her in his house with a new wedding ring and too little to do.

Malcolm, telling me now and again about those days, had said, 'She understood figures, you see. And she could beat me at cards. And she looked so damned demure. So young. Not bossy at all, like she was later. Her people thought me an upstart, did you know? Their ancestors traced back to Charles II, mine traced back to a Victorian knife-grinder. But her people weren't rich, you know. More breeding than boodle. It was an impulse, marrying Joyce. There you are, I admit it. Turned out she didn't like sex much, more's the pity. Some women are like that. No hormones. So I went on seeing Alicia. Well, I would, wouldn't I? Joyce and I got on all right, pretty polite to each other and so on, until she found out about Alicia. Then we had fireworks, all hell let loose for months on end, do you remember? Don't suppose you remember, you were only four or five.'

'Five and six, actually.'

'Really? Joyce liked being mistress of the house, you know. She learned about power. Grew up, I suppose. She took up bridge seriously, and started voluntary work. She hated leaving all that, didn't much mind leaving me. She said Alicia had robbed her of her self-esteem and ruined her position in the local community. She's never forgiven her, has she?'

Joyce had returned to the small Surrey town where her parents had lived and later died, their social mantle falling neatly onto her able shoulders. She bullied the local people into good works, made continual bridge-tournament forays, earned herself a measure of celebrity, and no, had never forgiven Alicia.

In the bar at Sandown she was dressed, as always,

with a type of businesslike luxury: mink jacket over grey tailored suit, neat white silk shirt, long strings of pearls, high-heeled shoes, green felt hat, polished calf handbag. 'A well-dressed, well-bred, brassy blonde' Alicia had once called her, which was both accurate and unfair, as was Joyce's tart tit-for-tat opinion of Alicia as 'White meat of chicken aboard the gravy train'.

Joyce drank most of the rest of her vodka and said, 'Do you really think one of the family is capable of murder?'

'I don't know.'

'But *who*?'

'That's the question.'

'It isn't possible,' she insisted.

'Well,' I said. 'Take them one by one. Tell me why it's impossible in each individual case, according to each person's character. Start at the beginning, with Vivien.'

'No, Ian,' she protested.

'Yes,' I said. 'Help me. Help Malcolm. Help us all.'

She gave me a long worried look, oblivious to the movement and noise going on all around us. The next race was already in progress but without noticeable thinning of the crowd who were watching it on closed circuit television above our heads.

'Vivien,' I prompted.

'Impossible, just impossible. She's practically dim-witted. If she was ever going to murder anybody, it would have been long ago and it would have been Alicia. Alicia ruined Vivien's marriage, just like mine. Vivien's a sniffler, full of self-pity. And why would she do it? For those three wimpish offspring?'

'Perhaps,' I said. 'They all need money. She hasn't enough herself to bail them out of their holes.'

'It's still impossible.'

'All right,' I said. 'How about Donald? And Helen?'

Donald had been ten, more than half Joyce's age, when she had married Malcolm, and he had been in and out of Quantum, as had Lucy and Thomas, whenever Malcolm had exercised his joint-custody rights and had them to stay. Joyce's lack of interest in children had definitely extended to her step-children, whom she'd found noisy, bad tempered and foul mannered, though Malcolm disagreed.

'Donald's a pompous, snobbish ass,' she said now, 'and as insecure as hell under the bluster. Malcolm thinks Helen's as brainless as she's pretty, but I'd say you don't need brains to murder, rather the opposite. I'd think Helen would fight like a fury to save her cubs from physical harm. But Moira wasn't threatening her cubs, not directly. I'd think Helen could be only a hot-blood killer, but so could most people, driven hard enough to defend themselves or their young.'

I wondered if she knew about the school-fees crisis: if they hadn't directly told her, she had got them remarkably right.

'Lucy?' I said.

'Lucy thinks everyone is inferior to herself, especially if they have more money.'

Poor Lucy, I thought. 'And Edwin?' I said.

Joyce frowned. 'Edwin . . .'

'Edwin isn't impossible?' I asked.

'He never gets time off from running errands. Not enough time anyway for waiting around to catch Moira alone in her glass house.'

'But in character?'

'I don't know enough about him,' Joyce confessed. 'He yearns for money, that's for sure, and he's earned it, picking up after Lucy all these years. I don't know his impatience level.'

'All right then,' I said, 'what about Thomas?'

'Thomas!' Joyce's face looked almost sad. 'He wasn't as insufferable as Donald and Lucy when he was little. I liked him best of the three. But that damned Vivien screwed him up properly, didn't she? God knows why he married Berenice. She'll badger him into the grave before he inherits, and then where will she be?'

Joyce finished the vodka and said, 'I don't like doing this, Ian, and I'm stopping right here.'

Thomas, I thought. She wasn't sure about Thomas, and she doesn't want to say so. The analysis had all of a sudden come to an unwelcome, perhaps unexpected, abyss.

'Another drink?' I suggested.

'Yes. Gervase is drinking, did you know?'

'He always drinks.'

'Ursula telephoned me to ask for advice.'

'Did she really?' I was surprised. 'Why didn't she ask Alicia?'

'Ursula detests her mother-in-law,' Joyce said. 'We have that in common. Ursula and I have become quite good friends.'

Amazing, I thought, and stood up to fetch the refills.

Joyce's eyes suddenly widened in disbelief, looking beyond me.

'I knew you were lying,' she said bitterly. 'There's Malcolm.'

CHAPTER SEVEN

I turned, not knowing whether to be frightened or merely irritated.

Malcolm hadn't seen Joyce, and he wasn't looking for her or for me but solely for a drink. I made my way to the bar to meet him there and took him by the arm.

'Why aren't you bloody upstairs?' I said.

'I was outstaying my welcome, old chap. It was getting very awkward. They had an ambassador to entertain. I've been up there three bloody hours. Why didn't you come and fetch me?'

'Joyce,' I said grimly, 'is sitting over there in the corner. I am buying her a drink, and she saw you come in.'

'Joyce!' He turned round and spotted her as she looked balefully in our direction. 'Damn it.'

'Prowling around outside we also have Donald and Helen, Lucy and Edwin, Ferdinand and Debs, and Serena.'

'Christ,' he said. 'Hunting in pairs.'

'You may joke,' I said, 'and you may be right.'

'I couldn't stay up there. They were waiting for me to leave, too polite to tell me to go.'

He looked apprehensive, as well he might.

'Will Joyce tell them all that I'm here?'

'We'll see if we can stop it,' I said. 'What do you want to drink? Scotch?'

He nodded and I squeezed through the throng by the bar and eventually got served. He helped me carry the glasses and bottles back to the table, and sat where I'd been sitting, facing Joyce. I fetched another chair from nearby and joined my ever non-loving parents.

'Before you start shouting at each other,' I said, 'can we just take two things for granted? Joyce wants Malcolm to stop scattering largesse, Malcolm wants to go on living. Both ends are more likely to be achieved if we discover who murdered Moira, in case it is Moira's murderer who wishes also to kill Malcolm.' I paused. 'OK for logic?'

They both looked at me with the sort of surprise parents reserve for unexpected utterances from their young.

Malcolm said, 'Surely it's axiomatic that it's Moira's murderer who's trying to kill me?'

I shook my head. 'Ever heard of copycat crime?'

'My God,' he said blankly. 'One possible murderer in the family is tragedy. Two would be . . .'

'Statistically improbable,' Joyce said.

Malcolm and I looked at her with respect.

'She's right,' Malcolm said, sounding relieved, as if one killer were somehow more manageable than two.

'OK,' I agreed, wondering what the statistical probabilities really were, wondering whether Ferdinand could work them out, 'OK, the police failed to find Moira's murderer although they tried very hard and are presumably still trying . . .'

'Trying to link me with an assassin,' muttered Malcolm darkly.

'We might, as a family,' I said, 'have been able to overcome Moira's murder by making ourselves believe in the motiveless unknown outside-intruder theory . . .'

'Of course we believe it,' Joyce said faintly.

'Not now, we can't. Two unknown outside-intruder motiveless murders – because Malcolm was meant to die – are so statistically improbable as to be out of sight. The police haven't found Moira's murderer, but we have now got to try to do it ourselves. It's no longer safe not to, which is why we engaged Norman West.' I looked directly at Joyce. 'Stop fussing over what Malcolm is spending and start thinking of ways to save his life, if only so that he can make more money, which he can do, but only if he's alive.'

'Ian . . .' She was shocked.

'You roused the whole family this morning on the telephone, telling them where to find me, and now seven of them that we know of are here, and others may be who've kept out of sight. Much though we hate the idea, Moira's murderer may be here.'

'No, no,' Joyce exclaimed.

'Yes,' I said. 'Malcolm's primary defence against being murdered is staying out of reach of lethal instruments, which means people not knowing where to find him. Well, you, my darling mother, brought the whole pack here to the races, so now you'd better help Malcolm to leave before they catch him.'

'I didn't know he'd be here,' she protested.

'No, but he is. It's time to be practical.'

No one pointed out that if she *had* known he'd be there, she would have sent everyone with even more zeal.

'Do you have any ideas?' Malcolm asked me hopefully.

'Yes, I do. But we have to have Joyce's help, plus her promise of silence.'

My mother was looking less than her normal commanding self and gave assurances almost meekly.

'This is not a private bar,' I said, 'and if any of the family have bought Club passes, they may turn up in here at any moment, so we'd best lose no time. I'm going to leave you both here for a few minutes, but I'll be back. Stay in this corner. Whatever happens, stay right here. If the family find you, still stay here. OK?'

They both nodded, and I left them sitting and looking warily at each other in the first tête-à-tête they'd shared for many a long year.

I went in search of the overall catering director whom I knew quite well because one of his daughters rode against me regularly in amateur races, and found him by sending urgent messages via the manager of the Members' bar.

'Ian,' he said ten slow minutes later, coming to the bar from the back, where the bottles were, 'what's the trouble?'

He was a company director, head of a catering division, a capable man in his fifties, sprung from suburbia, upwardly mobile from merit, grown worldly wise.

I said the trouble was private, and he led me away from the crowds, through the back of the bar and into a small area of comparative quiet, out of sight of the customers.

My father, I told him, badly needed an immediate inconspicuous exit from the racecourse and wanted to know if a case of vintage Bollinger would ease his passage.

'Not skipping his bookie, I hope?' the caterer said laconically.

'No, he wants to elope with my mother, his ex-wife, from under the eyes of his family.'

The caterer, amused, agreed that Bollinger might be nice. He also laughed at my plan, told me to put it into operation, he would see it went well, and to look after his Rosemary whenever she raced.

I went back through the bar to collect Malcolm and to ask Joyce to fetch her car and to drive it to where the caterers parked their vans, giving her directions. The two of them were still sitting alone at the table, not exactly gazing into each other's eyes with rapture but at least not drawn apart in frost. They both seemed relieved at my reappearance, though, and Joyce picked up her handbag with alacrity to go to fetch her car.

'If you see any of the others,' I said, 'just say you're going home.'

'I wasn't born yesterday, darling,' she replied with reviving sarcasm. 'Run along and play games, and let me do my part.'

The game was the same one I'd thought of earlier in the changing-room, modified only by starting from a different point. It was just possible that the wrong eyes had spotted Malcolm in his brief passage outside from the exit door of the Directors' rooms to the entrance door of the bar, but even if so, I thought we could fool them.

In the quiet private space at the rear of the bar, the catering director was watching the large chef remove his white coat and tall hat.

'A case of vintage Bollinger for the caterer, a handout for the chef,' I murmured in Malcolm's ear. 'Get Joyce to drop you at a railway station, and I'll see you in the Savoy. Don't move until I get there.'

Malcolm, looking slightly dazed, put on the chef's coat and hat and pulled out his wallet. The chef looked delighted with the result and went back to slicing his turkeys in temporary shirtsleeves. Malcolm and the catering director left through the bar's rear door and set off together through the racecourse buildings to go outside to the area where the caterers' vans were parked. I waited quite a long anxious time in the bar, but eventually the catering director returned, carrying the white disguise, which he restored to its owner.

'Your father got off safely,' he assured me. 'He didn't see anyone he knew. What was it all about? Not really an elopement, was it?'

'He wanted to avoid being assassinated by his disapproving children.'

The caterer smiled, of course not believing it. I asked where he would like the fizz sent and he took out a business card, writing his private address on the back.

'Your father lunched with the Directors, didn't he?' he said. 'I thought I saw him up there.' His voice implied that doing favours for people who lunched with the Directors was doubly vouched for, like backing up a cheque with a credit card, and I did my best to reinforce further his perception of virtue.

'He's just bought a half share in an Arc de Triomphe runner,' I said. 'We're going over for the race.'

'Lucky you,' he said, giving me his card. He frowned suddenly, trying to remember. 'Didn't Rosemary tell me something about your father's present wife being pointlessly murdered some weeks ago? His late wife, I suppose I should say. Dreadful for him, dreadful.'

'Yes,' I said. 'Well . . . some people connected with

her turned up here today unexpectedly, and he wanted to escape meeting them.'

'Ah,' he said with satisfied understanding. 'In that case, I'm glad to have been of help.' He chuckled. 'They didn't really look like elopers.'

He shook my hand and went away, and with a couple of deep breaths I left the Members' bar and walked back to the weighing room to pick up my gear. There was still one more race to be run but it already felt like a long afternoon.

George and Jo were there when I came out carrying saddle, helmet, whip and holdall, saying they'd thought they'd catch me before I left.

'We've decided to run Young Higgins again two weeks tomorrow at Kempton,' Jo said. 'You'll be free for that, won't you?'

'Yes, indeed.'

'And Park Railings, don't forget, at Cheltenham next Thursday.'

'Any time, any place,' I said, and they laughed, conspirators in addiction.

It occurred to me as they walked away, looking back and waving, that perhaps I'd be in Singapore, Australia or Timbuktu next week or the week after; life was uncertain, and that was its seduction.

I saw none of the family on my way to the exit gate, and none between there and my car. With a frank sigh of relief, I stowed my gear in the boot and without much hurry set off towards Epsom, a detour of barely ten miles, thinking I might as well pick up my mail and listen to messages.

The telephone answering machine did have a faculty for listening to messages from afar, but it had never worked well, and I'd been too lazy to replace the remote controller which, no doubt, needed new batteries anyway.

With equally random thoughts I drove inattentively onwards, and it wasn't until I'd gone a fair distance that I realized that every time I glanced in the rear-view mirror I could see the same car two or three cars back. Some cars passed me: it never did, nor closed a gap to catch up.

I sat up, figuratively and literally, and thought, 'What do you know?' and felt my heart beat as at the starting gate.

What I didn't know was whose car it was. It looked much like the hired one I was driving, a middle-rank four-door in underwashed cream; ordinary, inconspicuous, no threat to Formula One.

Perhaps, I thought sensibly, the driver was merely going to Epsom, at my own pace, so at the next traffic lights I turned left into unknown residential territory, and kept on turning left at each crossroads thereafter, reasoning that in the end I would complete the circle and end up facing where I wanted to go. I didn't hurry nor continually look in the rear-view mirror, but when I was back again on a road – a different one – with signposts to Epsom, the similar car was still somewhere on my tail, glimpsed tucked in behind a van.

If he had only a minimal sense of direction, I thought, he would realize what I had done and guess I now knew he was following. On the other hand, the back roads between Sandown Park and Epsom were a maze, like most Surrey roads, and he might possibly not have noticed, or thought I was lost, or . . .

Catching at straws, I thought. Face facts. I knew he was there and he knew I knew and what should I do next?

We were already on the outskirts of Epsom and almost automatically I threaded my way round corners, going towards my flat. I had no reason not to, I thought. I wasn't leading my follower to Malcolm, if that was what he had in mind. I also wanted to find out who he was, and thought I might outsmart him through knowing some ingenious short cuts round about where I lived.

Many of the houses in that area, having been built in the thirties without garages, had cars parked permanently on both sides of the streets. Only purpose-built places, like my block of flats, had adequate parking, except for two or three larger houses converted to flats which had cars where once there had been lawns.

I drove on past my home down the narrow roadway and twirled fast into the driveway of one of the large houses opposite. That particular house had a narrow exit drive also into the next tree-lined avenue: I drove straight through fast, turned quickly, raced round two more corners and returned to my own road to come up behind the car which had been following me.

He was there, stopped, awkwardly half-parked in too small a space with his nose to the kerb, rear sticking out, brake lights still shining: indecision showing all over the place. I drew to a halt right behind him, blocking his retreat, put on my brakes, climbed out, took three or four swift strides and opened the door on the driver's side.

There was a stark moment of silence.

Then I said, 'Well, well, well,' and after that I nodded up towards my flat and said, 'Come on in,' and after that I said, 'If I'd known you were coming, I'd have baked a cake.'

Debs giggled. Ferdinand, who had been driving, looked sheepish. Serena, unrepentant, said, 'Is Daddy here?'

They came up to my flat where they could see pretty clearly that no, Daddy wasn't. Ferdinand looked down from the sitting room window to where his car was now parked beside mine in neat privacy, and then up at the backs of houses opposite over a nearby fence.

'Not much of a view,' he said disparagingly.

'I'm not here much.'

'You knew I was following you, didn't you?'

'Yes,' I said. 'Like a drink?'

'Well . . . scotch?'

I nodded and poured him some from a bottle in the cupboard.

'No ice,' he said, taking the glass. 'After that drive, I'll take it neat.'

'I didn't go fast,' I said, surprised.

'Your idea of fast and mine round those goddam twisty roads are about ten miles an hour different.'

The two girls were poking about in the kitchen and bedrooms and I could hear someone, Serena no doubt, opening doors and drawers in a search for residues of Malcolm.

Ferdinand shrugged, seeing my unconcern. 'He hasn't been here at all, has he?' he said.

'Not for three years.'

'Where is he?'

I didn't answer.

'We'll have to torture you into telling,' said Ferdinand. It was a frivolous threat we'd used often in our childhood for anything from 'Where are the cornflakes?' to 'What is the time?' and Ferdinand himself looked surprised that it had surfaced.

'Mm,' I said. 'As in the tool shed?'

'Shit,' Ferdinand said. 'I didn't mean . . .'

'I should absolutely hope not.'

We both remembered, though, the rainy afternoon when Gervase had put the threat into operation, trying to make me tell him where I'd hidden my new cricket bat which he coveted. I hadn't told him, out of cussedness. Ferdinand had been there, too frightened of

Gervase to protest, and also Serena, barely four, wide-eyed and uncomprehending.

'I thought you'd forgotten,' Ferdinand said. 'You've never mentioned it.'

'Boys will be bullies.'

'Gervase still is.'

Which of us, I thought, was not as we had been in the green garden? Donald, Lucy, Thomas, Gervase, Ferdinand, Serena – all playing there long ago, children's voices calling through the bushes, the adults we would become already forming in the gangling limbs, smooth faces, groping minds. None of those children . . . *none of us* . . . I thought protestingly, could have killed.

Serena came into the sitting room carrying a white lace negligée and looking oddly shocked.

'You've had a woman here!' she said.

'There's no law against it.'

Debs, following her, showed a more normal reaction. 'Size ten, good perfume, expensive tastes, classy lady,' she said. 'How am I doing?'

'Not bad.'

'Her face cream's in the bathroom,' Serena said. 'You didn't tell us you had a . . . a . . .'

'Girlfriend,' I said. 'And do you have . . . a boy-friend?'

She made an involuntary face of distaste and shook her head. Debs put a sisterly arm round Serena's shoulders and said, 'I keep telling her to go to a sex therapist or she'll end up a dry old stick, but she won't listen, will you love?'

Serena wriggled free of Debs' arm and strode off with the negligée towards the bedrooms.

'Has anyone ever assaulted her?' I asked Ferdinand. 'She has that look.'

'Not that I know of.' He raised his eyebrows. 'She's never said so.'

'She's just scared of sex,' Debs said blithely. 'You wouldn't think anyone would be, these days. Ferdinand's not, are you, bunny?'

Ferdinand didn't react, but said, 'We've finished here, I think.' He drained his scotch, put down his glass and gave me a cold stare as if to announce that any semi-thaw I might have perceived during the afternoon's exchanges was now at an end. The ice-curtain had come down again with a clang.

'If you cut us out with Malcolm,' he said, 'you'll live to regret it.'

Hurt, despite myself, and with a touch of acid, I asked, 'Is that again what Alicia says?'

'Damn you, Ian,' he said angrily, and made for the door, calling, 'Serena, we're going,' giving her no choice but to follow.

Debs gave me a mock gruesome look as she went in their wake. 'You're Alicia's number one villain, too bad, lovey. You keep your hooks off Malcolm's money or you won't know what hit you.'

There was a fierce last-minute threat in her final

words, and I saw, as the jokey manner slipped, that it was merely a façade which hid the same fears and furies of all the others, and her eyes, as she went, were just as unfriendly.

With regret, I watched from the window as the three of them climbed into Ferdinand's car and drove away. It was an illusion to think one could go back to the uncorrupted emotions of childhood, and I would have to stop wishing for it. I turned away, rinsed out Ferdinand's glass, and went into my bedroom to see how Serena had left it.

The white negligée was lying on my bed. I picked it up and hung it in its cupboard, rubbing my cheek in the fabric and smelling the faint sweet scent of the lady who came occasionally for lighthearted interludes away from a husband who was all but impotent but nevertheless loved. We suited each other well: perfectly happy in ephemeral passion, with no intention of commitment.

I checked round the flat, opened a few letters and listened to the answering machine: there was nothing of note. I spent a while thinking about cars. I had arranged on the telephone two days earlier that the hotel in Cambridge would allow my own car to remain in their park for a daily fee until I collected it, but I couldn't leave it there for ever. If I took a taxi to Epsom station, I thought, I could go up to London by train. In the morning, I would go by train to Cambridge, fetch my car, drive back to the flat, change to the hired car and drive that back to London. It might even be a shade safer, I thought, considering that Ferdinand, and through him the others, would know its colour, make and number, to turn that car in and hire a different one.

The telephone rang. I picked up the receiver and heard a familiar voice, warm and husky, coming to the point without delay.

'How about now?' she said. 'We could have an hour.'

I could seldom resist her. Seldom tried.

'An hour would be great. I was just thinking of you.'

'Good,' she said. 'See you.'

I stopped worrying about cars and thought of the white lace negligée instead; more enticing altogether. I put two wine glasses on the table by the sofa and looked at my watch. Malcolm would scarcely have reached the Savoy, I thought, but it was worth a try; and in fact he picked up the telephone saying he had that minute walked into the suite.

'I'm glad you're safely back,' I said. 'I've been a bit detained. I'll be two or three hours yet. Don't get lost.'

'Your mother is a cat,' he said.

'She saved your skin.'

'She called me a raddled old roué done up like a fifth-rate pastrycook.'

I laughed and could hear his scowl down the line.

'What do you want after caviar,' he said, 'if I order dinner?'

'Chef's special.'

'God rot you, you're as bad as your mother.'

I put the receiver down with amusement and waited through the twenty minutes it would take until the doorbell rang.

'Hello,' she said, as I let her in. 'How did the races go?'

I kissed her. 'Finished third.'

'Well done.'

She was older than I by ten or twelve years, also slender, auburn-haired and unselfconscious. I fetched the always-waiting champagne from the refrigerator, popped off the cork and poured our drinks. They were a ritual preliminary, really, as we'd never yet finished the bottle and, as usual, after half a glass, there was no point in sitting around on the sofa making small talk.

She exclaimed over the long black bruise down my thigh. 'Did you fall off a horse?'

'No, hit a car.'

'How careless.'

I drew the bedroom curtains to dim the setting western sun and lay with her naked between the sheets. We were practised lovers and comfortable with each other, philosophical over the fact that the coupling was usually better for one than the other, rarely earth-moving for both simultaneously. That day, like the time before, it turned out ecstatic for her, less so for me, and I thought the pleasure of giving such pleasure enough in itself.

'Was it all right for you?' she said finally.

'Yes, of course.'

'Not one of your great times.'

'They don't come to order. Not your turn, my turn. It's luck.'

'A matter of friction and angles,' she teased me, repeating what I'd once said. 'Who's showering first?'

She liked to return clean to her husband, acknowledging the washing to be symbolic. I showered and dressed, and waited for her in the sitting room. She was an essential part of my life, a comfort to the body, a contentment in the mind, a bulwark against loneliness. I usually said goodbye with regret, knowing she would return, but on that particular afternoon I said, 'Stay,' knowing all the same that she couldn't.

'What's the matter?' she said.

'Nothing.'

'You shivered.'

'Premonition.'

'What of?' She was preparing to go, standing by the door.

'That this will be the last time.'

'Don't be silly,' she said. 'I'll be back.'

She kissed me with what I knew was gratitude, the way I too kissed her. She smiled into my eyes. 'I'll be back.'

I opened the door for her and she went away lightheartedly, and I knew that the premonition had been not for her, but for myself.

*

I ferried the cars in the morning, going from London to Cambridge and Epsom and back to the hire firm, and no one followed me anywhere, as far as I could see.

When I'd departed, Malcolm had been full of rampaging indignation over the non-availability of first-class seats on any flight going to Paris the following day for the Arc de Triomphe.

'Go economy,' I said, 'it's only half an hour.'

It appeared that there were no economy seats either. I left him frowning but returned to find peace. He had chartered a private jet.

He told me that snippet later, because he was currently engaged with Norman West who had called to give a progress report. The detective still seemed alarmingly frail but the grey on-the-point-of-death look had abated to fawn. The dustbin clothes had been replaced by an ordinary dark suit, and the greasy hair, washed, was revealed as almost white and neatly brushed.

I shook his hand: damp, as before.

'Feeling better, Mr West?' I asked.

'Thank you, yes.'

'Tell my son what you've just said,' Malcolm commanded. 'Give him the bad news.'

West gave me a small apologetic smile and then looked down at the notepad on his knee.

'Mrs Vivien Pembroke can't remember what she did on the Friday,' he said. 'And she spent Tuesday alone at home sorting through piles of old magazines.'

'What's bad news about that?' I asked.

'Don't be obtuse,' Malcolm said impatiently. 'She hasn't an alibi. None of the whole damn bunch has an alibi.'

'Have you checked them all?' I said, surprised. 'You surely haven't had time.'

'I haven't,' he agreed.

'Figure of speech.' Malcolm waved a hand. 'Go on telling him, Mr West.'

'I called on Mrs Berenice Pembroke.' West sighed expressively. 'She found me unwelcome.'

Malcolm chuckled sourly. 'Tongue like a rhinoceros-hide whip.'

West made a small squirming movement as if still feeling the lash, but said merely, with restraint, 'She was completely uncooperative.'

'Was Thomas there, when you called?' I asked.

'No, sir, he wasn't. Mrs Pembroke said he was at work. I later telephoned his office, to the number you gave me, hoping he could tell me where both his wife and himself had been at the relevant times, and a young lady there said that Mr Pembroke left the firm several weeks ago, and she knew nothing of his present whereabouts.'

'Well,' I said, stumped. 'I didn't know.'

'I telephoned Mrs Pembroke again to ask where her husband worked now, and she told me to . . . er . . . drop dead.'

Thomas, I thought, had worked for the same firm of

biscuit makers from the day he'd finished a course in bookkeeping and accountancy. Berenice referred disparagingly to his occupation as 'storekeeping' but Thomas said he was a quantity surveyor whose job it was to estimate the raw materials needed for each large contract, and cost them, and pass the information to the management. Thomas's promotions within the firm had been minor, such as from second assistant to first assistant, and at forty he could see, I supposed, that he would never be boardroom material. How bleak, I thought, to have to face his mid-life limitations with Berenice cramming them down his throat at every turn. Poor old Thomas . . .

'Mrs Joyce Pembroke,' West said, 'is the only one who is definite about her movements. On each relevant day, she was playing bridge. She didn't like me snooping, as she called it, and she wouldn't say who she was playing bridge with as she didn't want those people bothered.'

'You can leave Mrs Joyce Pembroke out,' I said.

'Huh?' Malcolm said.

'You know perfectly well,' I told him, 'that Joyce wouldn't kill you. If you'd had any doubts, you wouldn't have gone off in a car with her yesterday.'

'All right, all right,' he said, grumbling. 'Cross Joyce off.'

I nodded to West, and he put a line through Joyce.

'Yesterday I called on Mrs Alicia Pembroke and then later on Mrs Ursula Pembroke.' West's face showed no joy over the encounters. 'Mrs Alicia Pembroke told me to mind my own business, and Mrs Ursula Pembroke had been crying and wouldn't speak to me.' He lifted his hands out in a gesture of helplessness. 'I couldn't persuade either of them of the advantage of establishing alibis.'

'Did you get any impression,' I asked, 'that the police had been there before you, asking the same questions?'

'None at all.'

'I told you,' Malcolm said. 'They didn't believe I was attacked. They thought I'd just staged the whole thing.'

'Even so . . .'

'They checked everyone out over Moira, as you no doubt remember, and came up with a load of clean slates. They're just not bothering to do it again.'

'Do you happen to have their telephone number with you?'

'Yes I do,' he said, bringing a diary out of an inner pocket and flicking over the pages. 'But they won't tell you anything. It's like talking to a steel door.'

I dialled the number all the same and asked for the superintendent.

'In what connection, sir?'

'About the attempted murder of Mr Malcolm Pembroke a week ago yesterday.'

'One moment, sir.'

Time passed, and a different voice came on the line, plain and impersonal.

'Can I help you, sir?'

'About the attempted murder of Mr Malcolm Pembroke . . .'

'Who are you, sir?'

'His son.'

'Er . . . which one?'

'Ian.'

There was a brief rustling of paper.

'Could you tell me your birth date, as proof of identity?' Surprised, I gave it.

Then the voice said, 'Do you wish to give information, sir?'

'I wanted to find out how the investigation was going.'

'It isn't our custom to discuss that.'

'But . . .'

'But I can tell you, sir, that investigations into the alleged attack are being conducted with thoroughness.'

'*Alleged!*' I said.

'That's right, sir. We can find no evidence at all that there was another party involved.'

'I don't believe it.'

With slightly exaggerated patience but also a first flicker of sympathy, he said, 'I can tell you, sir, that there was no evidence of Mr Pembroke being dragged from the garden to the garage, which he alleged must have happened. No marks on the path. No scrapes on the heels of Mr Pembroke's shoes, which we examined at the time. There were no fingerprints except his own on the door handles of the car, no fingerprints except his anywhere. He showed no signs of carbon monoxide poisoning, which he explained was because he had delayed calling us. We examined the scene thoroughly the following morning, after Mr Pembroke had left home, and we found nothing at all to indicate the presence of an assailant. You can be sure we are not closing the case, but we are not at this time able to find grounds for suspicion of any other person.'

'He was nearly killed,' I said blankly.

'Yes, sir, well I'm sorry, sir, but that's how things stand.' He paused briefly. 'I can understand your disbelief, sir. It can't be easy for you.' He sounded quite human, offering comfort.

'Thank you at least for talking to me,' I said.

'Right, sir. Goodbye.'

'Goodbye,' I said slowly, but he had already gone.

'*Now* what's the matter?' Malcolm asked, watching my face.

I repeated what I'd just heard.

'Impossible!' Malcolm said explosively.

'No.'

'What then?'

'Clever.'

CHAPTER EIGHT

'Which door did you go out of, with the dogs?' I asked.

'The kitchen door, like I always do.'

'The kitchen door is about five steps along that covered way from the rear door into the garage.'

'Yes, of course it is,' Malcolm said testily.

'You told me that you set off down the garden with the dogs, and I suppose you told the police the same thing?'

'Yes, of course I did.'

'But you can't really remember actually going. You remember that you meant to, isn't that what you told me?'

He frowned. 'I suppose it is.'

'So what if you never made it to the garden, but were knocked out right there by the kitchen door? And what if you weren't dragged from there into the garage, but *carried*?'

His mouth opened. 'But I'm . . .'

'You're not too heavy,' I said. 'I could carry you easily in a fireman's lift.'

He was five foot seven, stocky but not fat. He weighed ten stone something, I would have guessed.

'And the fingerprints?' Norman West asked.

'In a fireman's lift,' I said, 'you sling the person you want to carry over your left shoulder, don't you, with his head hanging down your back. Then you grasp his knees with your left arm, and hold his right wrist in your own right hand, to stop him slipping off?'

They both nodded.

'So if you're holding someone's wrist, you can put his hand easily onto any surface you like, including car door handles . . . particularly,' I said, thinking, 'if you've opened the doors yourself first with gloves on, so that your victim's prints will be on top of any smudges you have made.'

'You should have been an assassin,' Malcolm said. 'You'd have been good at it.'

'So now we have Malcolm slumped in the back seat, half lying, like you said. So next you switch on the engine and leave the doors open so that all the nice fumes pour into the car quickly.'

'Doors?' Malcolm interrupted.

'The driver's door and one of the rear doors, at the least.'

'Oh, yes.'

'And then you have,' I said, 'a suicide.'

'And when I woke up,' Malcolm said gloomily, 'I put my prints all over the place. On the ignition key . . . everywhere.'

'No one could have counted on that.'

'It just looked bad to the police.'

We contemplated the scenario.

'If it happened like that,' West said, 'as indeed it could have done, whoever attacked you had to know that you would go out of the kitchen door at around that time.'

Malcolm said bleakly, 'If I'm at home, I always go for a walk with the dogs about then. Take them out, bring them back, give them their dinners, pour myself a drink. Routine.'

'And . . . er . . . is there anyone in your family who doesn't know when you walk the dogs?'

'Done it all my life, at that time,' Malcolm said.

There was a short silence, then I said, 'I wish I'd known all this when that car nearly killed us at Newmarket. We really ought to have told the police.'

'I was fed up with them,' Malcolm said. 'I've spent hours and hours with the suspicious buggers since Moira's death. I'm allergic to them. They bring me out in a rash.'

'You can't blame them, sir. Most murdered wives are killed by their husbands,' West said. 'And frankly, you appeared to have an extremely strong motive.'

'Rubbish,' Malcolm said. 'I don't see how people can kill people they've loved.'

'Unfortunately it's common.' West paused. 'Do you want me to continue with your family, sir, considering how little progress I've been able to make with them?'

'Yes,' Malcolm said heavily. 'Carry on. I'll get Joyce to tell them all to answer your questions. She seems to be able to get them to do what she wants.'

To get them to do what *they* want, I thought. She couldn't stir them into courses they didn't like.

Norman West put his notebook into his jacket pocket and shifted his weight forward on his chair.

'Before you go,' I said, 'I thought you might like to know that I asked the telephonist of the Cambridge hotel if anyone besides yourself had asked if a Mr Pembroke was staying there last weekend. She said they'd definitely had at least three calls asking for Mr Pembroke, two men and a woman, and she remembered because she thought it odd that no one wanted to talk to him, or would leave a message; they only wanted to know if he was there.'

'*Three!*' Malcolm exclaimed.

'One would be Mr West,' I pointed out. To West, I said, 'In view of that, could you tell us who asked you to find my father?'

West hesitated. 'I don't positively know which Mrs Pembroke it was. And . . . er . . . even if I became sure during these investigations, well, no sir, I don't think I could.'

'Professional ethics,' Malcolm said, nodding.

'I did warn you, sir,' West said to me, 'about a conflict of interests.'

'So you did. Hasn't she paid you yet, then? No name on any cheque?'

'No, sir, not yet.'

He rose to his feet, no one's idea of Atlas, though world-weary all the same. He shook my hand damply, and Malcolm's, and said he would be in touch. When he'd gone, Malcolm sighed heavily and told me to pour him some scotch.

'Don't you want some?' he said, when I gave him the glass.

'Not right now.'

'What did you think of Mr West?'

'He's past it.'

'You're too young. He's experienced.'

'And no match for the female Pembrokes.'

Malcolm smiled with irony. 'Few are,' he said.

We flew to Paris in the morning in the utmost luxury and were met by a chauffeured limousine which took its place with regal slowness in the solid traffic jam moving as one entity towards Longchamp.

The French racecourse; aflutter with flags, seemed to be swallowing *tout le monde* with insatiable appetite, until no one could walk in a straight line through the public areas where the crowds were heavy with guttural vowels and garlic.

Malcolm's jet/limousine package also included, I found, an invitation from the French Jockey Club, passes to everywhere and a Lucullan lunch appointment with the co-owner of Blue Clancy, Mr Ramsey Osborn.

Ramsey Osborn, alight with the *joie de vivre* gripping the whole place, turned out to be a very large sixtyish American who towered over Malcolm and took to him at once. Malcolm seemed to see the same immediate signals. They were cronies within two minutes.

'My son, Ian,' Malcolm said eventually, introducing me.

'Glad to know you.' He shook my hand vigorously. 'The one who fixed the sale, right?' His eyes were light grey and direct. 'Tell you the truth, there's a colt and a filly I want to buy for next year's Classics, and this way Blue Clancy will finance them very nicely.'

'But if Blue Clancy wins the Arc?' I said.

'No regrets, son.' He turned to Malcolm. 'You've a cautious boy, here.'

'Yeah,' Malcolm said. 'Cautious like an astronaut.'

The Osborn grey eyes swivelled back my way. 'Is that so? Do you bet?'

'Cautiously, sir.'

He laughed, but it wasn't unalloyed good humour. Malcolm, I thought, was much more to his liking. I left them sitting down at table together and, confident enough that no assassin would penetrate past the eagle-eyed doorkeepers of the upper citadel of the French Jockey Club, went down myself to ground level, happier to be with the action.

I had been racing in France a good deal, having for

some years been assistant to a trainer who sent horses across the Channel as insouciantly as to York. Paris and Deauville were nearer anyway, he used to say, despatching me from Epsom via nearby Gatwick airport whenever he felt disinclined to go himself. I knew in consequence a smattering of racecourse French and where to find what I wanted, essential assets in the vast stands bulging with hurrying, vociferous, uninhibited French racegoers.

I loved the noise, the smell, the movement, the quick angers, the gesticulations, the extravagance of ground-level French racing. British jockeys tended to think French racegoers madly aggressive, and certainly once I'd actually had to defend with my fists a jockey who'd lost on a favourite I'd brought over. Jockeys in general had been insulted and battered to the extent that they no longer had to walk through crowds when going out or back from races at many tracks, and at Longchamp made the journey from weighing room to horse by going up an escalator enclosed with plastic walls like a tunnel, across a bridge, and down a similar plastic-tunnel escalator on the other side.

I wandered around, greeting a few people, watching the first race from the trainers' stand, tearing up my losing pari-mutuel ticket, wandering some more, and feeling finally, without any work to do, without any horse to saddle, purposeless. It was an odd feeling. I couldn't remember when I'd last gone racing without being actively involved. Racing wasn't my playground, it was my work; without work it felt hollow.

Vaguely depressed, I returned to Malcolm's eyrie and found him blossoming in his new role as racehorse owner. He was referring to Le Prix de l'Arc de Triomphe familiarly as 'the Arc' as if it hadn't swum into his consciousness a bare half-week earlier, and discussing Blue Clancy's future with Ramsey Osborn as if he knew what he was talking about.

'We're thinking of the Breeders' Cup,' he said to me, and I interpreted the glint in his eyes as a frantic question as well as an instant decision.

'If he runs well today,' Osborn put in, qualifying it.

'It's a long way to California,' I said, agreeing with him. 'To the world championships, one might say.'

Malcolm was grateful for the information and far from dismayed by it. Pretty well the opposite, I saw. It would be to California we would go on the way to Australia, I guessed, rather than Singapore.

Lunch seemed to be continuing all afternoon, in the way French lunches do, with tidy circles of chateaubriand appearing, the empty plates to be cleared before small bundles of beans and carrots were served, followed by fresh little cheeses rolled in chopped nuts, and tiny strawberry tartlets with vanilla coulis. According to the menu, I had through my absence missed the *écrevisses*, the consommé, the *crêpes de volaille*, the *salade verte* and the sorbet. Just as well, I thought, eyeing the *friandises* which arrived with the coffee. Even amateur jockeys had to live by the scales.

Malcolm and Ramsey Osborn passed mellowly to cognac and cigars and watched the races on television. No one was in a hurry: the Arc was scheduled for five o'clock and digestion could proceed until four-thirty.

Ramsey Osborn told us he came from Stamford, Connecticut, and had made his money by selling sports clothes. 'Baseball caps by the million,' he said expansively. 'I get them made, I sell them to retail outlets. And shoes, shirts, jogging suits, whatever goes. Health is big business, we'd be nowhere without exercise.'

Ramsey looked as if he didn't exercise too much himself, having pads of fat round his eyes, a heavy double chin and a swelling stomach. He radiated goodwill, however, and listened with kind condescension as Malcolm said reciprocally that he himself dealt modestly in currency and metal.

Ramsey wasn't grasping Malcolm's meaning, I thought, but then for all his occasional flamboyance Malcolm never drew general attention to his wealth. Quantum was a large comfortable Victorian family house, but it wasn't a mansion: when Malcolm had reached mansion financial status, he'd shown no signs of wanting to move. I wondered briefly whether that would change in future, now that he'd tasted prodigality.

In due course, the three of us went down to the saddling boxes and met both Blue Clancy and his trainer. Blue Clancy looked aristocratic, his trainer more so. Malcolm was visibly impressed with the trainer, as indeed was reasonable, as he was a bright young star, now rising forty, who had already trained six Classic winners and made it look easy.

Blue Clancy was restless, his nostrils quivering. We watched the saddling ritual and the final touches; flick of oil to shine the hooves, sponging of nose and mouth to clean and gloss, tweaking of forelock and tack to achieve perfection. We followed him into the parade ring and were joined by his English jockey who was wearing Ramsey's white, green and crimson colours and looking unexcited.

Malcolm was taking with alacrity to his first taste of big-time ownership. The electricity was fairly sparking. He caught my eye, saw what I was thinking, and laughed.

'I used to think you a fool to choose racing,' he said. 'Couldn't understand what you saw in it.'

'It's better still when you ride.'

'Yes . . . I saw that at Sandown. And about time, I suppose.'

Ramsey and the trainer claimed his attention to discuss tactics with the jockey, and I thought of the summer holidays when we were children, when Gervase, Ferdinand and I had all learned to ride. We'd learned on riding-school ponies, cycling to the nearby stables and spending time there grooming, feeding and mucking out. We'd entered local gymkhanas, and booted the poor animals in pop-the-balloon races. We'd ridden them backwards, bareback and with our knees on the saddle, and Ferdinand, the specialist, standing briefly on his head. The ponies had been docile and no doubt tired to death, but for two or three years we had been circus virtuosi: and Malcolm had paid the bills uncomplainingly, but had never come to watch us. Then Gervase and Ferdinand had been whisked away by Alicia, and in the lonely vacuum afterwards I'd ridden almost every possible morning, laying down a skill without meaning it seriously, not realizing, in the flurry of academic school examinations, that it was the holiday pastime that would beckon me for life.

Blue Clancy looked as well as any of the others, I thought, watching the runners walk round, and the trainer was displaying more confidence than uncertainty. He thanked me for fixing the sale (from which he'd made a commission) and assured me that the two-million-guinea yearling was now settled snugly in a prime box in his yard. He'd known me vaguely until then as another trainer's assistant, a dogsbody, but as son and go-between of a new owner showing all signs of being severely hooked by the sport, I was now worth cultivation.

I was amused and far from minding. Life was like that. I might as well make the most of Malcolm's coat-tails while I was on them, I thought. I asked if I could see round the trainer's yard next time I was in Newmarket, and he said sure, he'd like it, and almost seemed to mean it.

'I'm sometimes there with George and Jo,' I said. 'Schooling their few jumpers. I ride them in amateur 'chases.' Everyone in Newmarket knew who George and Jo were: they were the equivalent of minor royalty.

'Oh, that's you, is it?' He put a few things together. 'Didn't realize that was you.'

'Mm.'

'Then come any time.' He sounded warmer, more positive. 'I mean it,' he said.

The way upwards in racing, I thought, ironic at myself, could lead along devious paths. I thanked him without effusiveness, and said 'Soon.'

Blue Clancy went out to the parade and the rest of us moved to the owners' and trainers' stand, which was near the core of things and buzzing with other similar groups locked in identical tensions.

'What chance has he got?' Malcolm demanded of me. 'Seriously.' His eyes searched my face as if for truth, which wasn't what I thought he wanted to hear.

'A bit better than he had on Thursday, since the second favourite has been scratched.' He wanted me to tell him more, however unrealistic, so I said, 'He's got a good chance of being placed. Anything can happen. He could win.'

Malcolm nodded, not knowing whether or not to believe me, but wanting to. Well and truly hooked, I thought, and felt fond of him.

I thought in my heart of hearts that the horse would finish sixth or seventh, not disgraced but not in the money. I'd backed him on the pari-mutuel but only out of loyalty: I'd backed the French horse Meilleurs Voeux out of conviction.

Blue Clancy moved well going down to the start. This was always the best time for owners, I thought, while the heart beat with expectation and while the excuses, explanations, disappointments were still ten minutes away. Malcolm lifted my binoculars to his eyes with hands that were actually trembling.

The trainer himself was strung up, I saw, however he might try to disguise it. There was only one 'Arc' in a year, of course, and too few years in a lifetime.

The horses seemed to circle for an interminable time at the gate but were finally fed into the slots to everyone's satisfaction. The gates crashed open, the thundering rainbow poured out, and twenty-six of Europe's best thoroughbreds were out on the right-hand circuit straining to be the fastest, strongest, bravest over one and a half miles of grass.

'Do you want your binoculars?' Malcolm said, hoping not.

'No. Keep them, I can see.'

I could see Ramsey Osborn's colours on the rails halfway back in the field, the horse moving easily, as were all the others at that point of the race. In the 'Arc', the essentials were simple: to be in the first ten coming round the last long right-hand bend, not to swing too wide into the straight and, according to the horse's stamina, pile on the pressure and head for home. Sometimes in a slow-starting 'Arc', one jockey would slip the field on the bend and hang on to his lead; in others, there would be war throughout to a whisker verdict. Blue Clancy's 'Arc' seemed to be run at give-no-quarter speed, and he came into the finishing straight in a bunch of flying horses, lying sixth or eighth, as far as I could see.

Malcolm shouted 'Come on,' explosively as if air had backed up in his lungs from not breathing, and the ladies around us in silk dresses and hats, and the men in grey morning suits, infected by the same urgency, yelled and urged and cursed in polyglot babel. Malcolm put down the raceglasses and yelled louder, totally involved, rapt, living through his eyes.

Blue Clancy was doing his bit, I thought. He hadn't blown up. In fact, he was hanging on to fifth place. Going faster. Fourth . . .

The trainer, more restrained than owners, was now saying, 'Come on, come *on*' compulsively under his breath, but two of the horses already in front suddenly came on faster than Blue Clancy and drew away from the field, and the real hope died in the trainer with a sigh and a sag to the shoulders.

The finish the crowd watched was a humdinger which only a photograph could decide. The finish Malcolm, Ramsey, the trainer and I watched was two lengths further back, where Blue Clancy and his jockey, never giving up, were fighting all out to the very end, flashing across the line absolutely level with their nearest rival, only the horse's nose in front taking his place on the nod.

'On the nod,' the trainer said, echoing my thought.

'What does that mean?' Malcolm demanded. He was high with excitement, flushed, his eyes blazing. 'Were we third? Say we were third.'

'I think so,' the trainer said. 'There'll be a photograph.'

We hurried down from the stand to get to the unsaddling enclosure, Malcolm still short of breath and slightly dazed. 'What does on the nod mean?' he asked me.

'A galloping horse pokes his head out forward with each stride in a sort of rhythm, forward, back, forward, back. If two horses are as close as they were, and one horse's nose is forward when it passes the finishing line, and the other horse's happens to be back . . . well, that's on the nod.'

'Just luck, you mean?'

'Luck.'

'My God,' he said, 'I never thought I'd feel like that. I never thought I'd *care*. I only did it for a jaunt.'

He looked almost with wonderment at my face, as if I'd been before him into a far country and he'd now discovered the mystery for himself.

Ramsey Osborn, who had roared with the best, beamed with pleasure when an announcement confirmed Blue Clancy's third place, saying he was sure glad the half-share sale had turned out fine. There were congratulations all round, with Malcolm and Ramsey being introduced to the owners of the winner, who were Italian and didn't understand Ramsey's drawl. Press photographers flashed like popping suns. There were television cameras, enquiring journalists, speeches, presentations. Malcolm looked envious of the Italian owners: third was fine but winning was better.

The four of us went for a celebratory drink; champagne, of course.

'Let's go for it,' Ramsey said. 'The Breeders' Cup. All the way.'

'We'll have to see how he is after today,' the trainer said warningly. 'He had a hard race.'

'He'll be all right,' Ramsey said with hearty confidence. 'Did you see the distance? Two lengths behind the winner. That's world class and no kidding.'

The trainer looked thoughtful but didn't argue. The favourite, undeniably world class, had finished second, victory snatched away no doubt by his earlier exhausting outing. He might not come back at all after his gruelling 'Arc'. The French favourite (and mine), Meilleurs Voeux, had finished fifth which made Blue Clancy better than I'd thought. Maybe he wouldn't be disgraced in the Breeders' Cup, if we went. I hoped we would go, but I was wary of hope.

The afternoon trickled away with the champagne, and Malcolm, almost as tired as his horse, sank euphorically into the limousine going back to the airport and closed his eyes in the jet.

'My first ever runner,' he said sleepily. 'Third in the "Arc". Not bad, eh?'

'Not bad.'

'I'm going to call the yearling Chrysos.'

'Why Chrysos?' I said.

He smiled without opening his eyes. 'It's Greek for gold.'

Malcolm was feeling caged in the Savoy.

On Sunday night, when we returned from Paris, he'd hardly had the energy to undress. By Monday morning, he was pacing the carpet with revitalized energy and complaining that another week in the suite would drive him bonkers.

'I'm going back to Quantum,' he said. 'I miss the dogs.'

I said with foreboding, 'It would take the family half a day at most to find out you were there.'

'I can't help it. I can't hide for ever. You can come and stay close to me there.'

'Don't go,' I said. 'You're safe here.'

'Keep me safe at Quantum.'

He was adamant and began packing, and short of roping him to the bedstead, I couldn't stop him.

Just before we left, I telephoned Norman West and found him at home – which didn't bode well for the investigations. He was happy to tell me, he said, that it was now certain Mrs Deborah Pembroke, Ferdinand's wife, couldn't have been at Newmarket Bloodstock Sales, as on that day she had done a photo-modelling session. He had checked up with the magazine that morning, as Mrs Deborah had told him he could, and they had provided proof.

'Right,' I said. 'What about Ferdinand himself?'

'Mr Ferdinand was away from his office on both those days. Working at home on the Friday. The next week, he attended a course on the statistical possibilities of insurance fraud. He says that after registration on the Monday, they kept no record of attendance. I checked there too, and no one clearly remembers, they're all half strangers to each other.'

I sighed. 'Well . . . my father and I are going back to Quantum.'

'That's not wise, surely.'

'He's tired of imprisonment. Report to us there, will you?'

He said he would, when he had more news.

Cross off Debs, I thought. Bully for Debs.

I drove us down to Berkshire, stopping at Arthur Bellbrook's house in the village to collect the dogs. The two full-grown Dobermanns greeted Malcolm like puppies, prancing around him and rubbing against his legs as he slapped and fondled them. Real love on both sides, I saw. Uncomplicated by greed, envy or rejection.

Malcolm looked up and saw me watching him.

'You should get a dog,' he said. 'You need something to love.'

He could really hit home, I thought.

He bent back to his friends, playing with their muzzles, letting them try to snap at his fingers, knowing they wouldn't bite. They weren't guard dogs as such: he liked Dobermanns for their muscular agility, for their exuberance. I'd been brought up with relays of them around me, but it wasn't the affection of dogs I wanted, and I'd never asked for one of my own.

I thought of the afternoon he'd let them out of the kitchen and then been hit on the head. The dogs must have seen or sensed someone there. Though not guard dogs, they should still have warned Malcolm.

'Do those two dogs bark when strangers call?' I asked.

'Yes, of course.' Malcolm straightened, still smiling, letting the lithe bodies press against his knees. 'Why?'

'Did they bark a week last Friday, when you set out to walk them?'

The smile died out of his face. With almost despair he said, 'No. I don't think so. I don't remember. No . . . not especially. They were pleased to be going out.'

'How many of the family do they know well?' I said.

'Everyone's been to the house several times since Moira died. All except you. I thought at first it was to support me, but . . .' he shrugged with disillusion, 'they were all busy making sure none of the others ingratiated themselves with me and cut them out.'

Every possibility led back to the certainty we couldn't accept.

Malcolm shuddered and said he would walk through the village with the dogs. He would meet people he knew on the way, and there were people in that village who'd been close friends with Vivien, Alicia and Joyce and had sided with them, and had since fed them inflammatory half-lies about Malcolm's doings.

'You know the village grapevine is faster than telex,' I said. 'Put the dogs in the car.'

He wouldn't listen. It was only six days since the second time someone had tried to kill him, but he was already beginning to believe there would be no more attempts. Well, no more that morning, I supposed. He walked a mile and a half with the dogs, and I drove slowly ahead, looking back, making sure at each turn that he was coming into sight. When he reached the house safely, he said I was being over-protective.

'I thought that was what you wanted,' I said.

'It is and it isn't.'

Surprisingly, I understood him. He was afraid and ashamed of it, and in consequence felt urged to bravado. Plain straightforward fear, I thought, would have been easier to deal with. At least I got him to wait outside with the dogs for company while I went into the house to reconnoitre, but no one had been there laying booby traps, no one was hiding behind doors with raised blunt instruments, no one had sent parcel bombs in the post.

I fetched him, and we unpacked. We both took it for granted I would sleep in my old room, and I made up the bed there. I had bought provisions in London to the extent of bread, milk, lemons, smoked salmon and caviar, a diet both of us now considered normal. There was champagne in the cellar and a freezer full of post-Moira TV dinners in cardboard boxes. We weren't going to starve, I thought, inspecting them, though we might get indigestion.

Malcolm spent the afternoon in his office opening letters and talking to his stockbroker on the telephone, and at the routine time proposed to give the dogs their pre-dinner walk.

'I'll come with you,' I said.

He nodded without comment, and in the crisp early October air we set off down the garden, through the gate into the field, and across to the willow-lined stream he had been aiming for ten days earlier.

We had all sailed toy boats down that stream when we'd been children, and picked watercress there, and got thoroughly wet and muddy as a matter of course. Alicia had made us strip, more than once, before she would let us into her bridal-white kitchen.

'Last Monday,' Malcolm said casually, watching the dogs sniff for water rats round the tree roots, 'I made a new will.'

'Did you?'

'I did. In Cambridge. I thought I might as well. The old one left a lot to Moira. And then, after that

Friday . . . well, I wanted to put things in order, in case . . . just in case.'

'What did you do with it?' I asked.

He seemed amused. 'The natural question is surely, "What's in it? What have you left to *me*?" '

'Mm,' I said dryly. 'I'm not asking that, ever. What I'm asking is more practical.'

'I left it with the solicitor in Cambridge.'

We were wandering slowly along towards the stream, the dogs quartering busily. The willow leaves, yellowing, would fall in droves in the next gale, and there was bonfire smoke drifting somewhere in the still air.

'Who knows where your will is?' I asked.

'I do. And the solicitor.'

'Who's the solicitor?'

'I saw his name on a brass plate outside his office and went in on impulse. I've got his card somewhere. We discussed what I wanted, he had it typed up, and I signed it with witnesses in his office and left it there for safekeeping.'

'For a brilliant man,' I said peaceably, 'you're as thick as two planks.'

CHAPTER NINE

Malcolm said explosively, 'You're bloody rude,' and, after a pause, 'In what way am I thick? A new will was essential.'

'Suppose you died without telling me or anybody else you'd made it, or where it could be found?'

'Oh.' He was dismayed, then brightened. 'The solicitor would have produced it.'

'If he knew you by reputation, if he had any idea of the sums involved, if he heard you were dead, if he were conscientious, and if he knew who to get in touch with. If he were lazy, he might not bother, he's under no obligation. Within a month, unless you boasted a bit about your wealth, he'll have forgotten your will's in his files.'

'You seem to know an awful lot about it.'

'Joyce worked for years for the Citizens Advice Bureau, do you remember? I used to hear lurid tales of family squabbles because no one knew where to find a will they were sure had been made. And equally lurid tales of family members knowing where the will was and burning it before anyone else could find it, if they didn't like what was in it.'

'That's why I left it in safekeeping,' Malcolm said. 'Precisely because of that.'

We reached the far boundary of the field. The stream ran on through the neighbour's land, but at that point we turned back.

'What should I do then?' he asked. 'Any ideas?'

'Send it to the probate office at Somerset House.'

'How do you mean?'

'Joyce told me about it, one time. You put your will in a special envelope they'll send you if you apply for it, then you take it or send it to the central probate office. They register your will there and keep it safe. When anyone dies and any solicitor anywhere applies for probate, the central probate office routinely checks its files. If it has ever registered a will for that person, that's the envelope that will be opened, and that's the will that will be proved.'

He thought it over. 'Do you mean, if I registered a will with the probate office, and then changed my mind and wrote a new one, it wouldn't be any good?'

'You'd have to retrieve the old will and re-register the new one. Otherwise the old will would be the one adhered to.'

'Good God. I didn't know any of this.'

'Joyce says not enough people know. She says if people would only register their wills, they couldn't be pressured into changing them when they're gaga or frightened or on their deathbeds. Or at least, wills made like that would be useless.'

'I used to laugh, rather, at Joyce's voluntary work. Felt indulgent.' He sighed. 'Seems it had its uses.'

The Citizens Advice Bureau, staffed by knowledgeable armies of Joyces, could steer one from the cradle to the grave, from marriage to divorce to probate, from child allowance to old age supplements. I'd not always listened attentively to Joyce's tales, but I'd been taken several times to the Bureau, and I seemed to have absorbed more than I'd realized.

'I kept a copy of my new will,' Malcolm said. 'I'll show it to you when we go in.'

'You don't need to.'

'You'd better see it,' he said.

I didn't argue. He whistled to the dogs who left the stream reluctantly, and we made our way back to the gate into the garden.

'Just wait out here while I check the house,' I said.

He was astonished. 'We've only been out for half an hour. And we locked the doors.'

'You regularly go out for half an hour at this time. And how many of the family still have keys to the house?'

He was silent. All of the people who had ever lived there could have kept their keys to the house, and there had never been any need, before now, to change the locks.

'Stay here, then?' I asked, and he nodded sadly.

The kitchen door was still locked. I let myself in and went all through the house again, but it was quiet and undisturbed, and doors that I'd set open at certain angles were still as I'd left them.

I called Malcolm and he came into the kitchen and began getting the food for the dogs.

'Are you going through this checking rigmarole every single time we leave the house?' he said, sounding as if he didn't like it.

'Yes, until we get the locks changed.'

He didn't like that either, but expressed his disapproval only in a frown and a rather too vigorous scraping of dog food out of a tin.

'Fill the water bowls,' he said rather crossly, and I did that and set them down again on the floor.

'It isn't so easy to change the locks,' he said. 'They're all mortice locks, as you know, set into the doors. The one on the front door is antique.'

The front door keys were six inches long and ornate, and there had never been more than three of them, as far as I knew.

'All right,' I said. 'If we keep the front door bolted and the keys in your safe, we won't change that one.'

A little pacified, he put the filled dinner bowls on the floor, wiped his fingers and said it was time for a noggin. I bolted the kitchen door on the inside and then followed him through the hall to the office, where he poured scotch into two glasses and asked if I wanted to desecrate mine with ice. I said yes and went back to the kitchen to fetch some. When I returned, he had taken some sheets of paper from his open briefcase and was reading them.

'Here you are. Here's my will,' he said, and passed the papers over.

He had made the will, I reflected, before he had telephoned me to put an end to our quarrel, and I expected not to figure in it in consequence, but I'd done him an injustice. Sitting in an armchair and sipping the whisky, I read through all the minor bequests to people like Arthur Bellbrook, and all the lawyerly gobbledegook 'upon trust' and without commas, and came finally to the plain language.

'To each of my three divorced wives Vivien Joyce and Alicia I bequeath the sum of five hundred thousand pounds.

'My son Robin being provided for I direct that the residue of my estate shall be divided equally among my children Donald Lucy Thomas Gervase Ian Ferdinand and Serena.'

A long clause followed with provisions for 'if any of my children shall pre-decease me', leaving 'his or her share' to the grandchildren.

Finally came two short sentences:

'I bequeath to my son Ian the piece of thin wire to be found on my desk. He knows what he can do with it.'

Surprised and more moved than I could say, I looked up from the last page and saw the smile in Malcolm's eyes deepen to a throaty chuckle.

'The lawyer chap thought the last sentence quite obscene. He said I shouldn't put that sort of thing in a will.'

I laughed. 'I didn't expect to be in your will at all.'

'Well . . .' He shrugged. 'I'd never have left you out. I've regretted for a long while . . . hitting you . . . everything.'

'Guess I deserved it.'

'Yes, at the time.'

I turned back to the beginning of the document and re-read one of the preliminary paragraphs. In it, he had named me as his sole executor, when I was only his fifth child. 'Why me?' I said.

'Don't you want to?'

'Yes. I'm honoured.'

'The lawyer said to name someone I trusted.' He smiled lopsidedly. 'You got elected.'

He stretched out an arm and picked up from his desk a leather pot holding pens and pencils. From it, he pulled a wire about ten inches long and about double the thickness of the sort used by florists for stiffening flower stalks.

'If this one should get lost,' he said, 'just find another.'

'Yes. All right.'

'Good.' He put the wire back in the pot and the pot back on the desk.

'By the time you pop off,' I said, 'the price of gold

might have risen out of sight and all I'd find in the wall would be spiders.'

'Yeah, too bad.'

I felt more at one with him than at any time since he'd telephoned, and perhaps he with me. I hoped it would be a very long time before I would have to execute his will.

'Gervase,' I said, 'suggests that you should distribute some of your money now, to . . . er . . . reduce the estate tax.'

'Does he? And what do you think?'

'I think,' I said, 'that giving it to the family instead of to scholarships and film companies and so on might save your life.'

The blue eyes opened wide. 'That's immoral.'

'Pragmatic.'

'I'll think about it.'

We dined on the caviar, but the fun seemed to have gone out of it.

'Let's have shepherd's pie tomorrow,' Malcolm said. 'There's plenty in the freezer.'

We spent the next two days uneventfully at Quantum being careful, but with no proof that care was needed.

Late on Tuesday afternoon, out with the dogs and having made certain that Arthur Bellbrook had gone home, we walked round behind the kitchen wall and came to the treasure house.

A veritable sea of nettles guarded the door. Malcolm looked at them blankly. 'The damn things grow overnight.'

I pulled my socks over the bottoms of my trousers and assayed the traverse; stamped down an area by the bottom of the door and with fingers all the same stinging felt along to one end of the wooden sill and with some effort tugged it out. Malcolm leaned forward and gave me the piece of wire, and watched while I stood up and located the almost invisible hole. The wire slid through the tiny tube built into the mortar and, under pressure, the latch inside operated as smoothly as it had when I'd installed it. The wire dislodged a metal rod out of a slot, allowing the latch to spring open.

'I oiled it,' Malcolm said. 'The first time I tried, it was as rusty as hell.'

I pushed the edge of the heavy narrow door and it opened inwards, its crenellated edges disengaging from the brick courses on each side with faint grating noises but with no pieces breaking off.

'You built it well,' Malcolm said. 'Good mortar.'

'You told me how to mix the mortar, if you remember.'

I stepped into the small brick room which was barely four feet across at the far end and about eight feet long, narrowing in a wedge-shape towards the door which was set into one of the long walls. The wider end wall was stacked to waist height with flat wooden boxes like those used for château-bottled wines. In front, there were two large cardboard boxes with heavily taped-down tops. I stepped further in and tried to open one of the wine-type boxes, but those were nailed shut. I turned round and took a couple of steps back and stood in the doorway, looking out.

'Gold at the back, treasures in front,' Malcolm said, watching me with interest.

'I'll take your word for it.'

The air in the triangular room smelled faintly musty. There was no ventilation, as I'd told Arthur Bellbrook, and no damp course, either. I reset the rod into the latch on the inside, as it wouldn't shut unless one did, and stepped outside. My teenage design limitations meant that one had to go down on one's knees to close the door the last few inches, hooking one's fingers into a hollow under the bottom row of bricks and pulling hard. The door and walls fitted together again like pieces of jigsaw, and the latch inside clicked into place. I replaced the sill under the door, kicking it home, and tried to encourage the crushed nettles to stand up again.

'They'll be flourishing again by morning,' Malcolm said. 'Rotten things.'

'Those cardboard boxes are too big to come out through the door,' I observed, rubbing stings on my hands and wrists.

'Oh, sure. I took them in empty and flat, then set them up, and filled them bit by bit.'

'You could take those things out again now.'

There was a pause, then he said, 'I'll wait. As things are at present, they might as well stay there.'

I nodded. He whistled to the dogs and we went on with the walk. We had given up referring explicitly to fear of the family, but it still hung around us like grief. On our return from the field, Malcolm waited outside without comment until I checked through the house, and prosaically began feeding the dogs on my report of all clear.

Neither of us discussed how long all the precautions were going to have to go on. Norman West's latest report had been as inconclusive as his first, and by Wednesday evening the pitiful summary I'd been making of his results read as follows:

DONALD:	busy about the golf club. Cannot pinpoint any times.
HELEN:	working at home making Henley souvenirs.
LUCY:	reading, walking, writing, meditating.
EDWIN:	housework, shopping for groceries, going to public library.
THOMAS:	looking for new job, suffering headaches.
BERENICE:	housekeeping, looking after children, uncooperative.
GERVASE:	commuting to London, in and out of his office, home late.

URSULA: looking after daughters, unhappy.
FERDINAND: on statistics course, no attendance records.
DEBS: photo-session vouched for on Newmarket Sales day.
SERENA: teaching aerobics mornings and most evenings, shopping for clothes afternoons.
VIVIEN: pottering about, can't remember.
ALICIA: probably the same, unhelpful.
JOYCE: playing bridge.

All one could say, I thought, was that no one had made any effort to produce alibis for either relevant time. Only Debs had a firm one, which had been arranged and vouched for by others. All the rest of the family had been moving about without timing their exits and entrances: normal behaviour for innocent people.

Only Joyce and I lived beyond half an hour's drive from Quantum. All of the others, from Donald at Henley to Gervase at Maidenhead, from Thomas near Reading to Lucy near Marlow, from Ferdinand in Wokingham to Serena in Bracknell, and even Vivien in Twyford and Alicia near Windsor, all of them seemed to have put down roots in a ring round the parent house like thistledown blown on the wind and reseeding.

The police had remarked on it when investigating

Moira's murder, and had checked school runs and train timetables until they'd been giddy. They had apparently caught no one lying, but that seemed to me inconclusive in a family which had had a lot of practice in misrepresentation. The fact had been, and still was, that anybody could have got to Quantum and home again without being missed.

I spent a short part of that Wednesday wandering around Moira's greenhouse, thinking about her death.

The greenhouse was invisible from the house, as Arthur Bellbrook had said, set on a side lawn which was bordered with shrubs. I wondered whether Moira had been alarmed to see her killer approach. Probably not. Quite likely, she had herself arranged the meeting, stating time and place. Malcolm had once mentioned that she didn't like casual callers, preferring them to telephone first. Perhaps it had been an unforeseen killing, an opportunity seized. Perhaps there had been a quarrel. Perhaps a request denied. Perhaps one of Moira's specials in acid-sweet triumphs, like picking Arthur Bellbrook's vegetables.

Moira in possession of Quantum, about to take half of everything Malcolm owned. Moira smugly satisfied, oblivious to her danger. I doubted if she had believed in her nightmare death even while it was happening.

Malcolm spent the day reading the *Financial Times* and making phone calls: yen, it appeared from snatches I overheard, were behaving gruesomely from Malcolm's point of view.

Although making calls outward, neither of us was keen to answer inward calls since that morning, when Malcolm had been drenched by a shower of recriminations from Vivien, all on the subject of meanness. He had listened with wry pain and given me a resumé once Vivien had run out of steam.

'One of the cats in the village told her we were here, so now the whole family will know,' he said gloomily. 'She says Donald is bankrupt, Lucy is starving and Thomas got the sack and can't deal with unemployment. Is it all true? It can't be. She says I should give them twenty thousand pounds each immediately.'

'It wouldn't hurt,' I said. 'It's Gervase's idea watered down.'

'But I don't believe in it.'

I explained about Donald's school fees crisis, Lucy's crumbling certainties, Thomas with Berenice chipping away at his foundations. He said their troubles lay in their own characters, which was true enough. He said if he gave those three a hand-out, he would have to do it for us all, or there would be a shooting civil war among Vivien, Joyce and Alicia. He made a joke of it, but he was stubborn. He had provided for us through our trust funds. The rest was up to us. He hadn't changed his mind. He'd thought over Vivien's suggestion, and the answer was no.

He telephoned back to Vivien and to her fury told her so. I could hear her voice calling him wicked, mean, cruel, vindictive, petty, sadistic, tyrannical and evil. He took offence, shouted at her to shut up, shut up, and finally slammed down the receiver while she was still in full flood.

All Vivien had achieved, I thought, was to make him dig his toes in further.

I thought him pig-headed, I thought him asking to be murdered. I looked at the unrelenting blue eyes daring me to argue, and wondered if he thought giving in would be weakness, if he thought baling out his children would diminish his own self-respect.

I said nothing at all. I was in a bad position to plead for the others, as I stood to gain myself. I hoped for many reasons that he would be able to change his mind, but it had to come from inside. I went out to Moira's greenhouse to give him time to calm down, and when I returned neither of us mentioned what had passed.

On the dogs' walk that afternoon, I reminded him that I was due to ride at Cheltenham the following day, and asked if he had any cronies in that direction with whom he could spend the time.

'I'd like to see you ride again,' he said.

He constantly surprised me.

'What if the family come too?'

'I'll dress up as another chef.'

I didn't know that it was wise, but again he had his own way, and I persuaded myself he would come to no harm on a racecourse. When we got there, I introduced him to George and Jo who congratulated him on Blue Clancy and took him off to lunch.

I looked around apprehensively all afternoon for brothers, sisters, mother and step-mothers, but saw none. The day was cold and windy with everyone turning up collars and hunching shoulders to keep warm, with hats on every head, felt, tweed, wool and fur. If anyone had wanted to hide inside their clothes, the weather was great for it.

Park Railings gave me a splendid ride and finished fourth, less tired than his jockey, who hadn't sat on a horse for six days. George and Jo were pleased enough, and Malcolm, who had been down the track with them to watch one of the other steeplechases from beside one of the jumps, was thoughtful.

'I didn't realize you went so fast,' he said, going home. 'Such speed over those jumps.'

'About thirty miles an hour.'

'I suppose I could buy a steeplechaser,' he said, 'if you'd ride it.'

'You'd better not. It would be favouritism.'

'Huh.'

We went thirty miles towards Berkshire and came to a hostelry he liked where we stopped for the late afternoon noggins (Arthur Bellbrook was taking the dogs home with him for the night) and waited lazily until dinner.

We talked about racing, or rather Malcolm asked questions and I answered them. His interest seemed inexhaustible, and I wondered if it would die as fast as it had sprung up. He couldn't wait to find out what Chrysos might do next year.

We ate without hurrying, lingering over coffee, and went on home, pulling up yawning outside the garage, sleepy from fresh air and French wine.

'I'll check the house,' I said without enthusiasm.

'Oh, don't bother, it's late.'

'I'd better check it. Honk the horn if you see something you don't like.'

I left him in the car, let myself into the kitchen and switched on the lights. The door to the hall was closed as usual, to keep the dogs, when they were there, from roaming through the house. I opened the door to the hall and switched on the hall lights.

I stopped there briefly, looking round.

Everything looked quiet and peaceful, but my skin began to crawl just the same, and my chest felt tight from suddenly suspended breath.

The door to the office and the door to the sitting room were not as I had left them. The door to the office was more than half open, the door to the sitting room all but closed; neither standing at the precise narrow angle at which I'd set them every time we'd been out.

I tried to remember whether I'd actually set the doors before leaving that morning, or whether I'd forgotten. But I *had* set them. I knew I had. I'd picked up my saddle and other gear in the hall after doing it, and shut the hall-to-kitchen door, and locked the outside door, leaving the dogs with Arthur Bellbrook in the garden.

I hadn't until then thought of myself as a coward, but I felt dead afraid of going further into the house. It was so large, so full of dark corners. There were two cellars, and the several unlit attic bedrooms of long-gone domestic servants, and the boxroom deep with shadows. There were copious cupboards everywhere and big empty wardrobes. I'd been round them all three or four times during the past few days, but not at night, and not with the signals standing at danger.

With an effort, I took a few steps into the hall, listening. I had no weapon. I felt nakedly vulnerable. My heart thumped uncomfortably. The house was silent.

The heavy front door, locked and bolted like a fortress, had not been touched. I went over to the office, reached in with an arm, switched on the light and pushed the half-open door wider.

There was no one in there. Everything was as Malcolm had left it in the morning. The windows shone blackly, like threats. Taking a deep breath, I repeated the procedure with the sitting room, but also checking the bolts on the French windows, and after that with the dining room, and the downstairs cloakroom, and then with worse trepidation went down the passage beside the stairs to the big room that had been our playroom when we were children and a billiard room in times long past.

The door was shut. Telling myself to go on with it, I opened the door, switched on the light, pushed the door open.

There was no one there. It wasn't really a relief, because I would have to go on looking. I checked the storeroom opposite, where there were stacks of garden furniture, and also the door at the end of the passage, which led out into the garden: securely bolted on the inside. I went back to the hall and stood at the bottom of the stairs, looking upward.

It was stupid to be so afraid, I thought. It was home, the house I'd been brought up in. One couldn't be frightened by home.

One was.

I swallowed. I went up the stairs. There was no one in my bedroom. No one in five other bedrooms, nor in the boxroom, no one in the bathrooms, no one in the plum and pink lushness of Malcolm's own suite. By the end, I was still as scared as I'd been at the beginning, and I hadn't started on cellars or attics or small hiding places.

I hadn't looked under the beds. Demons could be waiting anywhere to jump out on me, yelling. Giving in, I switched off all the upstairs lights and went cravenly back to the hall.

Everything was still quiet, mocking me.

I was a fool, I thought.

Leaving the hall and kitchen lights on, I went back to Malcolm who started to get out of the car when he saw me coming. I waved him back and slid in beside him, behind the driving wheel.

'What's the matter?' he said.

'Someone may be here.'

'What do you mean?'

I explained about the doors.

'You're imagining things.'

'No. Someone has used their key.'

We hadn't yet been able to have the locks changed, although the carpenter was due to be bringing replacements the following morning. He'd had difficulty finding good new locks to fit into such old doors, he'd said, and had promised them for Thursday, but I'd put him off until Friday because of Cheltenham.

'We can't stay out here all night,' Malcolm protested. 'It's bound to be the wind or something that moved the doors. Let's go to bed, I'm whacked.'

I looked at my hands. They weren't actually shaking. I thought for a while until Malcolm grew restless.

'I'm getting cold,' he said. 'Let's go in, for God's sake.'

'No . . . we're not sleeping here.'

'What? You can't mean it.'

'I'll lock the house, and we'll go and get a room somewhere else.'

'At this time of night?'

'Yes.' I made to get out of the car and he put a hand on my arm to catch my attention.

'Fetch some pyjamas, then, and washing things.'

I hesitated. 'No, I don't think it's safe.' I didn't say I couldn't face it, but I couldn't.

'Ian, all this is crazy.'

'It would be crazier still to be murdered in our beds.'

'But just because two doors . . .'

'Yes. Because.'

He seemed to catch some of my own uneasiness because he made no more demur, but when I was headed again for the kitchen he called after me, 'At least bring my briefcase from the office, will you?'

I made it through the hall again with only a minor tremble in the gut; switched on the office light, fetched his briefcase without incident and set the office door again at its usual precise angle. I did the same to the sitting room door. Perhaps they would tell us in the morning, I thought, whether or not we had had a visitor who had hidden from my approach.

I went back through the hall, switched the lights off, shut the hall-to-kitchen door, let myself out, left the house dark and locked and put the briefcase on the car's back seat.

On the basis that it would be easiest to find a room in London, particularly at midnight, for people without luggage, I drove up the M4 and on Malcolm's instructions pulled up at the Ritz. We might be refugees, he said, but we would be staying in no camp, and he explained to the Ritz that he'd decided to stay overnight in London as he'd been delayed late on business.

'Our name is Watson,' I said impulsively, thinking suddenly of Norman West's advice and picking out of the air the first name I could think of. 'We will pay with travellers' cheques.'

Malcolm opened his mouth, closed it again, and kept blessedly quiet. One could write whatever name one wanted onto travellers' cheques.

The Ritz batted no eyelids, offered us connecting rooms (no double suites available) and promised razors, toothbrushes and a bottle of scotch.

Malcolm had been silent for most of the journey, and so had I, feeling with every heart-calming mile that I had probably over-reacted, that maybe I hadn't set the doors, that if any of the family had let themselves into the house while we were out, they'd been gone long before we returned. We had come back hours later than anyone could have expected, if they were judging the time it would take us to drive from Cheltenham.

I could have sat at the telephone in the house and methodically checked with all the family to make sure they were in their own homes. I hadn't thought of it, and I doubted if I could have done it, feeling as I had.

Malcolm, who held that sleeping pills came a poor second to scotch, put his nightcap theory to the test and was soon softly snoring. I quietly closed the door between our two rooms and climbed between my own sheets, but for a long time lay awake. I was ashamed of my fear in the house which I now thought must have been empty. I had risked my neck without a qualm over big fences that afternoon: I'd been petrified in the house that someone would jump out on me from the dark. The two faces of courage, I thought mordantly: turn one face to the wall.

We went back to Berkshire in the morning and couldn't reach Quantum by car because the whole village, it seemed, was out and blocking the road. Cars and people everywhere: cars parked along the roadsides, people walking in droves towards the house.

'What on earth's going on?' Malcolm said.

'Heaven knows.'

In the end I had to stop the car, and we finished the last bit of the journey on foot.

We had to push through crowds and were unpopular until people recognized Malcolm, and made way for him, and finally we reached the entrance to the drive . . . and there literally rocked to a stop.

To start with there was a rope stretched across it, barring our way, with a policeman guarding it. In front of the house, there were ambulances, police cars, fire engines . . . swarms of people in uniform moving purposefully about.

Malcolm swayed with shock, and I felt unreal,

disconnected from my feet. Our eyes told us: our brains couldn't believe.

There was an immense jagged gaping hole in the centre of Quantum.

People standing near us in the gateway, round-eyed, said, 'They say it was the gas.'

CHAPTER TEN

We were in front of the house, talking to policemen. I couldn't remember walking up the drive.

Our appearance on the scene had been a shock to the assembled forces, but a welcome one. They had been searching for our remains in the rubble.

They told us that the explosion had happened at four-thirty in the morning, the *wumph* and reverberation of it waking half the village, the shockwaves breaking windows and setting dogs howling. Several people had called the police, but when the force had reached the village, everything had seemed quiet. No one knew where the explosion had occurred. The police drove round the extended neighbourhood until daylight, and it was only then that anyone saw what had happened to Quantum.

The front wall of the hall, the antique front door with it, had been blown out flat onto the drive, and the centre part of the upper storey had collapsed into the hall. The glass in all the windows had disappeared.

'I'm afraid it's worse at the back,' a policeman said

phlegmatically. 'Perhaps you'd come round there, sir. We can at least tell everyone there are no bodies.'

Malcolm nodded mechanically and we followed the policeman round to the left, between the kitchen and garage, through to the garden and along past the dining-room wall. The shock when we rounded onto the terrace was, for all the warning, horrific and sickening.

Where the sitting room had been, there was a mountain of jumbled dusty bricks, plaster, beams and smashed furniture spilling outwards onto the grass. Malcolm's suite, which had been above the sitting room, had vanished, had become part of the chaos. Those of the attic rooms that had been above his head had come down too. The roof, which had looked almost intact from the front, had at the rear been stripped of tiles, the old sturdy rafters standing out against the sky like picked ribs.

My own bedroom had been on one side of Malcolm's bedroom: all that remained of it were some shattered spikes of floorboards, a strip of plaster cornice and a drunken mantle clinging to a cracked wall overlooking a void.

Malcolm began to shake. I took off my jacket and put it round his shoulders.

'We don't have gas,' he said to the policeman. 'My mother had it disconnected sixty years ago because she was afraid of it.'

There was a slight spasmodic wind blowing, enough

to lift Malcolm's hair and leave it awry. He looked suddenly frail, as if the swirling air would knock him over.

'He needs a chair,' I said.

The policeman gestured helplessly to the mess. No chairs left.

'I'll get one from the kitchen. You look after him.'

'I'm quite all right,' Malcolm said faintly.

'The outside kitchen door is locked, sir, and we can't allow you to go in through the hall.'

I produced the key, showed it to him, and went along and in through the door before he could stop me. In the kitchen, the shiny yellow walls themselves were still standing, but the door from the hall had blown open, letting in a glacier tongue of bricks and dust. Dust everywhere, like a veil. Lumps of plaster had fallen from the ceiling. Everything glass, everything china in the room had cracked apart. Moira's geraniums, fallen from their shelves, lay in red farewell profusion over her all-electric domain.

I picked up Malcolm's pine armchair, the one thing he had insisted on keeping through all the changes, and carried it out to where I'd left him. He sank into it without seeming to notice it and put his hand over his mouth.

There were firemen and other people tugging at movable parts of the ruins, but the tempo of their work had slowed since they'd seen we were alive. Several of them came over to Malcolm, offering sympathy, but mostly wanting information, such as were we certain there had been no one else in the house?

As certain as we could be.

Had we been storing any gas in the house? Bottled gas? Butane? Propane? Ether?

No.

Why ether?

It could be used for making cocaine.

We looked at them blankly.

They had already discovered, it seemed, that there had been no mains gas connected. They were asking about other possibilities because it nevertheless looked like a gas explosion.

We'd had no gas of any sort.

Had we been storing any explosive substances whatsoever?

No.

Time seemed disjointed.

Women from the village, as in all disasters, had brought hot tea in thermos flasks for the men working. They gave some to Malcolm and me, and found a red blanket for Malcolm so that I could have my jacket back in the chill gusty air. There was grey sheet cloud overhead: the light was grey, like the dust.

A thick ring of people from the village stood in the garden round the edges of the lawn, with more arriving every minute across the fields and through the garden gate. No one chased them away. Many were taking photographs. Two of the photographers looked like Press.

A police car approached, its siren wailing ever louder as it made slow progress along the crowded road. It wailed right up the drive, and fell silent, and presently a senior-looking man not in uniform came round to the back of the house and took charge.

First, he stopped all work on the rubble. Then he made observations and wrote in a notebook. Then he talked to the chief of the firemen. Finally he came over to Malcolm and me.

Burly and black moustached, he said, as to an old acquaintance, 'Mr Pembroke.'

Malcolm similarly said, 'Superintendent,' and everyone could hear the shake he couldn't keep out of his voice. The wind died away for a while, though Malcolm's shakes continued within the blanket.

'And you, sir?' the superintendent asked me.

'Ian Pembroke.'

He pursed his mouth below the moustache, considering me. He was the man I'd spoken to on the telephone, I thought.

'Where were you last night, sir?'

'With my father in London,' I said. 'We've just . . . returned.'

I looked at him steadily. There were a great many things to be said, but I wasn't going to rush into them.

He said noncommittally, 'We will have to call in explosive experts as the damage here on preliminary inspection, and in the absence of any gas, seems to have been caused by an explosive device.'

Why didn't he say bomb, I thought irritably. Why shy away from the word? If he'd expected any reaction from Malcolm or me, he probably got none as both of us had come to the same conclusion from the moment we'd walked up the drive.

If the house had merely been burning, Malcolm would have been dashing about, giving instructions, saving what he could, dismayed but full of vigour. It was the implications behind a bomb which had knocked him into shivering lassitude: the implications and the reality that if he'd slept in his own bed, he wouldn't have risen to bath, read the *Sporting Life*, go to his bank for travellers' cheques and eat breakfast at the Ritz.

And nor, for that matter, would I.

'I can see you're both shocked,' the superintendent said unemotionally. 'It's clearly impossible to talk here, so I suggest you might come to the police station.' He spoke carefully, giving us at least theoretically the freedom of refusing.

'What about the house?' I said. 'It's open to the four winds. Apart from this great hole, all the windows are broken everywhere else. There's a lot of stuff still inside . . . silver . . . my father's papers in his office . . . some of the furniture.'

'We will keep a patrol here,' he said. 'If you'll give the instructions, we'll suggest someone to board up the windows, and we'll contact a construction firm with a tarpaulin large enough for the roof.'

'Send me the bill,' Malcolm said limply.

'The firms concerned will no doubt present their accounts.'

'Thanks anyway,' I said.

The superintendent nodded.

A funeral for Quantum, I thought. Coffin windows, pall roof. Lowering the remains into the ground would probably follow. Even if any of the fabric of the house should prove sound enough, would Malcolm have the stamina to rebuild, and live there, and remember?

He stood up, the blanket clutched around him, looking infinitely older than his years, a sag of defeat in the cheeks. Slowly, in deference to the shaky state of his legs, Malcolm, the superintendent and I made our way along past the kitchen and out into the front drive.

The ambulances had departed, also one of the fire engines, but the rope across the gateway had been overwhelmed, and the front garden was full of people, one young constable still trying vainly to hold them back.

A bunch in front of the rest started running in our direction as soon as we appeared, and with a feeling of unreality I saw they were Ferdinand, Gervase, Alicia, Berenice, Vivien, Donald, Helen . . . I lost count.

'Malcolm,' Gervase said loudly, coming to a halt in front of us, so that we too had to stop. 'You're alive!'

A tiny flicker of humour appeared in Malcolm's eyes at this most obvious of statements, but he had no chance of answering as the others set up a clamour of questions.

Vivien said, 'I heard from the village that Quantum had blown up and you were both dead.' Her strained voice held a complaint about having been given erroneous news.

'So did I,' Alicia said. 'Three people telephoned . . . so I came at once, after I'd told Gervase and the others, of course.' She looked deeply shocked, but then they all did, mirroring no doubt what they could see on my own face but also suffering from the double upset of misinformation.

'Then when we all get here,' Vivien said, 'we find you *aren't* dead.' She sounded as if that too were wrong.

'What did happen?' Ferdinand asked. 'Just look at Quantum.'

Berenice said, 'Where were you both, then, when it exploded?'

'We thought you were dead,' Donald said, looking bewildered.

More figures pushed through the crowd, horror opening their mouths. Lucy, Edwin and Serena, running, stumbling, looking alternately from the wounded house to me and Malcolm.

Lucy was crying, 'You're alive, you're alive!' Tears ran down her cheeks. 'Vivien said you were dead.'

'I was told they were dead,' Vivien said defensively. Dim-witted . . . Joyce's judgement came back.

Serena was swaying, pale as pale. Ferdinand put an arm round her and hugged her. 'It's all right, girl, they're not dead after all. The old house's a bit knocked about, eh?' He squeezed her affectionately.

'I don't feel well,' she said faintly. 'What happened?'

'Too soon to say for certain,' Gervase said assertively. 'But I'd say one can't rule out a bomb.'

They repudiated the word, shaking their heads, covering their ears. Bombs were for wars, for wicked schemes in aeroplanes, for bus stations in far places, for cold-hearted terrorists . . . for other people. Bombs weren't for a family house outside a Berkshire village, a house surrounded by quiet green fields, lived in by an ordinary family.

Except that we weren't an ordinary family. Ordinary families didn't have fifth wives murdered while planting geraniums. I looked around at the familiar faces and couldn't see on any of them either malice or dismay that Malcolm had escaped. They were all beginning to recover from the shock of the wrongly reported death and also beginning to realize how much damage had been done to the house.

Gervase grew angry. 'Whoever did this shall pay for it!' He sounded pompous more than effective.

'Where's Thomas?' I asked.

Berenice shrugged waspishly. 'Dear Thomas went out early on one of his useless job-hunting missions.

I've no idea where he was going. Vivien telephoned after he'd left.'

Edwin said, 'Is the house insured against bombs, Malcolm?'

Malcolm looked at him with dislike and didn't answer.

Gervase said masterfully, 'You'd better come home with me, Malcolm. Ursula will look after you.'

None of the others liked that. They all instantly made counter-proposals. The superintendent, who had been listening with attentive eyes, said at this point that plans to take Malcolm home would have to be shelved for a few hours.

'Oh, really?' Gervase stared down his nose. 'And who are you?'

'Detective Superintendent Yale, sir.'

Gervase raised his eyebrows but didn't back down. 'Malcolm's done nothing wrong.'

'I want to talk to the superintendent myself,' Malcolm said. 'I want him to find out who tried to destroy my house.'

'Surely it was an accident,' Serena said, very upset.

Ferdinand still had his arm round her. 'Face facts, girl.' He hesitated, looking at me. 'Vivien and Alicia told everyone you were both living here again . . . so how come you escaped being hurt?'

'Yes,' Berenice said. 'That's what I asked.'

'We went to London for a night out and stayed there,' I said.

'Very lucky,' Donald said heartily, and Helen, who stood at his elbow and hadn't spoken so far at all, nodded a shade too enthusiastically and said, 'Yes, yes.'

'But if we'd been in the office,' I said, 'we would have been all right.'

They looked along the front of the house to the far corner where the office windows were broken but the walls still stood.

'You wouldn't be in the office at four-thirty in the morning,' Alicia said crossly. 'Why should you be?'

Malcolm was growing tired of them. Not one had hugged him, kissed him, or made warm gestures over his survival. Lucy's tears, if they were genuine, had come nearest. The family obviously could have accommodated his death easily, murmuring regrets at his graveside, maybe even meaning them, but looking forward also with well-hidden pleasure to a safely affluent future. Malcolm dead could spend no more. Malcolm dead would free them to spend instead.

'Let's go,' he said to the superintendent, 'I'm cold.'

An unwelcome thought struck me. 'Did any of you,' I asked the family, 'tell Joyce . . . about the house?'

Donald cleared his throat. 'Yes, I . . . er . . . broke it to her.'

His meaning was clear. 'You told her we were dead?'

'Vivien said you were dead,' he said, sounding as defensive as she had. 'She said I should tell Joyce, so I did.'

'My God,' I said to the superintendent, 'Joyce is my mother. I'll have to phone her at once.'

I turned instinctively back to the house, but the superintendent stopped me, saying the telephones weren't working.

He, I and Malcolm began to move towards the gate, but we had gone only halfway when Joyce herself pushed through the crowd and ran forward, frantically, fearfully distraught.

She stopped when she saw us. Her face went white and she swayed as Serena had done, and I sprinted three or four long strides and caught her upright before she fell.

'It's all right,' I said, holding her. 'It's all right. We're alive.'

'Malcolm . . .'

'Yes, we're both fine.'

'Oh, I thought . . . Donald said . . . I've been crying all the way here, I couldn't see the road . . .' She put her face against my jacket and cried again with a few deep gulps, then pushed herself off determinedly and began searching her tailored pockets for a handkerchief. She found a tissue and blew her nose. 'Well, darling,' she said, 'as you're alive, what the hell's been going on?'

She looked behind Malcolm and me and her eyes widened.

'The whole bloody tribe come to the wake?' To

Malcolm she said, 'You've the luck of the devil, you old bugger.'

Malcolm grinned at her, a distinct sign of revival.

The three ex-wives eyed each other warily. Any mushy idea that the near-death of the man they'd all married and the near-destruction of the house they'd all managed might have brought them to sisterly sympathy was a total non-starter.

'Malcolm can come and stay with me,' Joyce said.

'Certainly not,' Alicia said instantly, clearly alarmed. 'You can take your precious Ian. Malcolm can go with Gervase.'

'I won't have it,' Vivien said sharply. 'If Malcolm's going anywhere, it's fitting he should stay with Donald, his eldest son.'

Malcolm looked as if he didn't know whether to laugh or scream.

'He's staying with me,' I said. 'If he wants to.'

'In your flat?' Ferdinand asked.

I had an appalling vision of my flat disintegrating like Quantum but, unlike Quantum, killing people above and below.

'No, not there,' I said.

'Then where, darling?' Joyce asked.

'Wherever we happen to be.'

Lucy smiled. It was the sort of thing she was happy with. She pulled her big brown cloak closer round her large form and said that it sounded a thoroughly sensible proposal. The others looked at her as if she were retarded instead of the brains of the tribe.

'I'll go wherever I want to,' Malcolm said flatly, 'and with Ian.'

I collected a battery of baleful glares, all of them as ever afraid I would scoop their shares of the pool: all except Joyce, who wanted me to.

'As that's settled,' she said with a hint of maternal smugness which infuriated all the others, 'I want to see just how bad the damage is to the house.' She looked at me briefly. 'Come along, darling, you can show me.'

'Run along, mummy's boy,' Gervase said spitefully, smarting from having been spurned by Malcolm.

'Poor dear Ian, tied to mummy's apron strings.' Berenice's effort came out thick with detestation. 'Greedy little Ian.'

'It isn't fair,' Serena said plaintively. 'Ian gets everything, always. I think it's beastly.'

'Come on, darling,' Joyce said. 'I'm waiting.'

I felt rebellious, tried to smother it, and sought for a different solution.

'You can all come,' I said to them. 'Come and see what really happened here.'

The superintendent had in no way tried to break up the family party but had listened quietly throughout. I happened to catch his eye at that point, and he nodded briefly and walked back beside Malcolm as everyone slowly moved round to the rear of the house.

The extent and violence of the damage there

silenced even Gervase. All of the mouths gaped: in all eyes, horrified awe.

The chief fireman came over and with a certain professional relish began in a strong Berkshire accent to point out the facts.

'Blast travels along the lines of least resistance,' he said. 'This is a good strong old house, which I reckon is why so much of it is still standing. The blast, see, travelled outwards, front and back from a point somewhere near the centre of the main upper storey. Some of the blast went upwards into the roof, bringing down some of those little attic bedrooms, and a good bit of blast, I'd reckon, blew downwards, making a hole that the upper storey and part of the attic just collapsed into, see what I mean?'

Everyone saw.

'There's this wall here,' he pointed to the one between what had been the sitting room and what was still the dining room, 'this wall here, with the chimney built into it, this is one of the main load-bearing walls. It goes right up to the roof. Same the other side, more or less. Those two thick walls stopped the blast travelling sideways, except a bit through the doorways.' He turned directly to Malcolm. 'I've seen a lot of wrecked buildings, sir, mostly burned, it's true, but some gas explosions, and I'd say, and mind you, you'd have to get a proper survey done, but I'd say, on looking at this house, that although it got a good shaking you could think of rebuilding it. Good solid Victorian house, otherwise it would have folded up like a pack of cards.'

'Thank you,' Malcolm said faintly.

The fireman nodded. 'Don't you let any fancy demolition man tell you different, sir. I don't like people being taken advantage of when they're overcome by disasters. I've seen too much of that, and it riles me. What I'm telling you is a straight opinion. I've nothing to gain one way or the other.'

'We're all grateful,' I said.

He nodded, satisfied, and Gervase finally found his voice.

'What sort of bomb was it?' he asked.

'As to that, sir, I wouldn't know. You'd have to wait for the experts.' The fireman turned to the superintendent. 'We shut off the electricity at the meter switch in the garage when we got here, and likewise turned off the mains water under a man-hole cover out by the gate. The storage tank in the roof had emptied through the broken pipes upstairs and water was still running when we got here, and all that water's now underneath the rubble. There's nothing I can see can start a fire. If you want to go into the upper storey at the sides, you'll need ladders, the staircase is blocked. I can't vouch for the dividing walls up there, we looked through the windows but we haven't been inside, you'd have to go carefully. We didn't go up to the attic much, bar a quick look from up the ladder. But down here, you should be all right in the dining room and in that big room the other side of this mess, and also in the kitchen and the front room on the far side.'

'My office,' Malcolm said.

The superintendent nodded, and I reflected that he already knew the layout of the house well from earlier repeated visits.

'We've done as much as we can here,' the fireman said. 'All right if we shove off now?'

The superintendent, agreeing, went a few steps aside with him in private consultation and the family began to come back from suspended animation.

The Press photographers moved in closer, and took haphazard pictures of us, and a man and a woman from different papers approached with insistent questions. Only Gervase seemed to find those tolerable and did all the answering. Malcolm sat down again on the pine chair, which was still there, and gathered his blanket around him, retreating into it up to his eyes like a Red Indian.

Vivien, spotting him, went over and told him she was tired of standing and needed to sit down and it was typically selfish of him to take the only seat, and an insult to her, as she was the senior woman present. Glancing at her with distaste, Malcolm got to his feet and moved a good distance away, allowing her to take his place with a self-satisfied smirk. My dislike of Vivien rose as high as her cheekbones and felt as shrewish as her mouth.

Alicia, recovered, was doing her fluttery feminine act

for the reporters, laying out charm thickly and eclipsing Serena's little-girl ploy. Seeing them together, I thought that it must be hard for Serena to have a mother who refused to mature, who in her late fifties still dressed and behaved like an eighteen-year-old, who for years had blocked her daughter's natural road to adulthood. Girls needed a motherly mother, I'd been told, and Serena didn't have one. Boys needed one too, and Joyce wasn't one, but I'd had a father all the time and in the end I'd also had Coochie, and Serena hadn't had either, and there lay all the difference in the world.

Edwin was having as hard a time as Donald in putting on a show of rejoicing over Malcolm's deliverance.

'It's all very well for you,' he said to me bitterly, catching my ironic look in his direction. 'Malcolm despises me – and don't bother to deny it, he makes it plain enough – and I don't see why I should care much for him. Of course, I wouldn't wish him dead . . .'

'Of course not,' I murmured.

'. . . but, well, if it had happened . . .' he stopped, not actually having the guts to say it straight out.

'You'd have been glad?' I said.

'No.' He cleared his throat. 'I could have faced it,' he said.

I almost laughed. 'Bully for you, Edwin,' I said. 'Hang in there, fellow.'

'I could have faced your death, too,' he said stuffily.

Oh well, I thought. I asked for that.

'How much do you know about bombs?' I asked.

'That's a ridiculous question,' he said, and walked off, and I reflected that Norman West had reported Edwin as spending an hour most days in the public library, and I betted one could find out how to make bombs there, if one persevered.

Berenice said to me angrily, 'It's all your fault Thomas is out of work.'

I blinked. 'How do you make that out?'

'He's been so worried about Malcolm's behaviour that he couldn't concentrate and he made mistakes. He says you could get Malcolm to help us, but of course I tell him you won't, why should you, you're Malcolm's pet.' She fairly spat the last word, the rage seething also in her eyes and tightening all the cords in her neck.

'You told Thomas that?' I said.

'It's true,' she said furiously. 'Vivien says you've always been Malcolm's favourite and he's never been fair to Thomas.'

'He's always been fair to all of us,' I said positively, but of course she didn't believe it.

She was older than Thomas by four or five years and had married him when she was well over thirty and (Joyce had said cattily) desperate for any husband that offered. Ten years ago, when I'd been to their wedding, she had been a thin, moderately attractive woman lit up by happiness. Thomas had been proud of himself and proprietary. They had looked, if not an exciting couple, stable and full of promise, embarking on a good adventure.

Ten years and two daughters later, Berenice had put on weight and outward sophistication and lost whatever illusions she'd had about marriage. I'd long supposed it was basic disappointment which had made her so destructive of Thomas, but hadn't bothered to wonder about the cause of it. Time I did, I thought. Time I understood the whole lot of them, because perhaps in that way we might come to know who could and who couldn't murder.

To search through character and history, not through alibis. To listen to what they said and didn't say, to learn what they could control, and what they couldn't.

I knew, as I stood there looking at the bunch of them, that only someone in the family itself could go that route, and that if I didn't do it, no one else would.

Norman West and Superintendent Yale could dig into facts. I would dig into the people. And the problem with that, I thought, mocking my own pretension, was that the people would do anything to keep me out.

I had to recognize that what I was going to do could produce more trouble than results. Spotting the capability of murder could elude highly-trained psychiatrists, who had been known to advise freedom for reformed characters only to have them go straight out and kill. A highly-trained psychiatrist I was not. Just someone who could remember how we *had* been, and could learn how we were now.

I looked at the monstrously gutted house and shivered. We had returned unexpectedly on Monday; today was Friday. The speed of planning and execution was itself alarming. Never again were we likely to be lucky. Malcolm had survived three attacks by sheer good fortune, but Ferdinand wouldn't have produced healthy statistics about a fourth. The family looked peacefully normal talking to the reporters, and I was filled with a sense of urgency and foreboding.

CHAPTER ELEVEN

One of Malcolm's dogs came bounding across the grass towards him, followed a few seconds later by the other. Malcolm put a hand out of his blanket and patted them, but with more absentmindedness than welcome. After them came Arthur Bellbrook with a face of consternation and concern which lightened considerably when he set eyes on Malcolm. In his grubby trousers and ancient tweed jacket, he came at a hobbling run in old army boots and fetched up very out of breath at Malcolm's side.

'Sir! You're alive! I went to Twyford to fetch some weedkiller. When I got back, they told me in the village . . .'

'Gross exaggeration,' Malcolm said, nodding.

Arthur Bellbrook turned to me, panting. 'They said you were both dead. I couldn't get down the road . . . had to come across the fields. Look at the house!'

I explained about our going to London, and asked him what time he'd gone home the previous day.

'Four o'clock, same as always. Say three-forty, then.

About then.' He was beginning to get his breath back, his eyes round with disbelief as he stared at the damage.

Nearer to three-thirty, I privately reckoned, if he was admitting to going home early at all.

'Did you go in the house at any time during the day?' I asked.

He switched his gaze from the ruins to me and sounded aggrieved. 'No, I didn't. You know I couldn't have. You've been locking the place like it's a fortress since you came back, and I didn't have a key. Where could I have got a key from?'

I said placatingly, 'It's just that we're anxious . . . someone got in, they must have.'

'Not me.' He was slightly mollified. 'I was working in the kitchen garden all day, digging potatoes and such like. I had the two dogs with me, tied up on their leads. If anyone had tried to get in the house, they'd have barked for sure, but they didn't.'

Malcolm said, 'Arthur, could you keep the dogs with you for another day or two?'

'Yes, I . . .' He looked helplessly at the heap of rubble spilling out across the terrace and onto the lawn. 'What do you want me to do about the garden?'

'Just . . . carry on,' Malcolm said. 'Keep it tidy.' It didn't seem incongruous to him to polish the setting, though I thought that perhaps, left to its own, nature would scatter leaves and grow longer grass and soften the raw brutality of the jagged edges.

The superintendent, seeing Arthur Bellbrook, came

across to him and askcd the same questions that I had. Again, they seemed to know each other well, undoubtedly from Moira's investigations, and if there didn't seem to be friendship, there was clearly a mutual respect.

The reporters, having sucked the nectar from Gervase, advanced on Malcolm and on the gardener and the superintendent. I moved away, leaving them to it, and tried to talk to Ferdinand.

He was unfriendly and answered with shrugs and monosyllables.

'I suppose,' I said bitterly, 'you would rather I was lying in shreds and bloody tatters under all that lot.'

He looked at the tons of fallen masonry. 'Not really,' he said coolly.

'That's something.'

'You can't expect us to like it that you've an inside edge with Malcolm.'

'You had three years,' I pointed out, 'during which he wouldn't speak to me. Why did you waste them? Why didn't you get an inside edge yourself?'

'We couldn't get past Moira.'

I half smiled. 'Nor could I.'

'It's now we're talking about,' he said. He looked greatly like Malcolm, right down to the stubbornness in the eyes.

'What do you want me to do, walk away and let him be murdered?' I said.

'Walk away . . .?'

'That's why he wants me with him, to try to keep him safe. He asked me to be his bodyguard, and I accepted.'

Ferdinand stared. 'Alicia said . . .'

'Alicia is crazy,' I interrupted fiercely. 'So are you. Take a look at yourself. Greed, jealousy and spite, you've let them all in. I won't cut you out with Malcolm, I'd never attempt it. Try believing that instead, brother, and save yourself a lot of anxiety.'

I turned away from him in frustration. They were all illogical, I thought. They had almost begged me to use any influence I had with Malcolm to stop him spending and bale them out, and at the same time they believed I would ditch them to my own advantage. But then people had always been able to hold firmly to two contradictory ideas at the same time, as when once, in racing's past, Stewards, Press and public alike had vilified one brilliant trainer as 'most crooked', and elected one great jockey as 'most honest', blindly and incredibly ignoring that it was the self-same trusted jockey who for almost all of his career rode the brilliant trainer's horses. I'd seen a cartoon once that summed it up neatly: 'Entrenched belief is never altered by the facts.'

I wished I hadn't lashed out at Ferdinand. My idea of detection from the inside wasn't going to be a riotous success if I let my own feelings get in the way so easily. I might think the family unjust, they might think me conniving: OK, I told myself, accept all that and forget it. I'd had to put up with their various resentments for much of my life and it was high time I developed immunity.

Easier said than done, of course.

Superintendent Yale had had enough of the reporters. The family had by this time divided into two larger clumps, Vivien's and Alicia's, with Joyce and I hovering between them, belonging to neither. The superintendent went from group to group asking that everyone should adjourn to the police station. 'As you are all here,' he was saying, 'we may as well take your statements straight away, to save you being bothered later.'

'Statements?' Gervase said, eyebrows rising.

'Your movements yesterday and last night, sir.'

'Good God,' Gervase said. 'You don't think any of us would have done this, do you?'

'That's what we have to find out.'

'It's preposterous.'

None of the others said anything, not even Joyce.

The superintendent conferred with a uniformed colleague who was busy stationing his men round the house so that the ever-increasing spectators shouldn't get too close. The word must have spread, I thought. The free peepshow was attracting the next villages, if not Twyford itself.

Much of the family, including Malcolm, Joyce and myself, packed into the three police cars standing in the front drive, and Gervase, Ferdinand and Serena set off on foot to go back to the transport they had come in.

'I wouldn't put it past Alicia,' Joyce said darkly to the superintendent as we drove past them towards the gate, 'to have incited that brood of hers to blow up Quantum.'

'Do you have any grounds for that statement, Mrs Pembroke?'

'Statement? It's an opinion. She's a bitch.'

In the front passenger seat, Yale's shoulders rose and fell in a sigh.

The road outside was still congested with cars, with still more people coming on foot. Yale's driver stopped beside Joyce's car, which she'd left in the centre of the road in her haste, and helped to clear room for her to turn in. With her following, we came next to the hired car Malcolm and I had arrived in, but as it was hopelessly shut in on three sides by other locked vehicles, we left it there and went on in the police car.

In his large modern police station with its bullet-proofed glass enquiry desk, the superintendent ushered us through riot-proofed doors to his office and detailed a policewoman to take Joyce off for some tea. Joyce went protestingly, and Yale with another sigh sat us down in his bare-looking Scandinavian-type place of business.

He looked at us broodingly from behind a large desk. He looked at his nails. He cleared his throat. Finally he said to Malcolm, 'All right. You don't have to say it. I do not believe you would blow up your house just to make me believe that someone is trying to kill you.'

There was a long pause.

'That being so,' he said, as we both sat without speaking, 'we must take the attack in the garage more seriously.'

He was having a hard time, I thought. He ran a finger and thumb down his large black moustache and waited for comments from us that still didn't come.

He cleared his throat again. 'We will redouble our efforts to find Mrs Moira Pembroke's killer.'

Malcolm finally stirred, brought out his cigar case, put a cigar in his mouth and patted his pockets to find matches. There was a plastic notice on Yale's desk saying NO SMOKING. Malcolm, his glance resting on it momentarily, lit the match and sucked the flame into the tobacco.

Yale decided on no protest and produced a glass ashtray from a lower drawer in his desk.

'I would be dead twice over,' Malcolm said, 'if it weren't for Ian.'

He told Yale about the car roaring straight at us at Newmarket.

'Why didn't you report this, sir?' Yale said, frowning.

'Why do you think?'

Yale groomed his moustache and didn't answer.

Malcolm nodded. 'I was tired of being disbelieved.'

'And . . . er . . . last night?' Yale asked.

Malcolm told him about our day at Cheltenham, and

about Quantum's inner doors. 'I wanted to sleep in my own bed. I was tired. Ian absolutely wouldn't have it, and drove us to London.'

Yale looked at me steadily. 'Did you have a premonition?'

'No, I don't think so.' I hadn't felt a shiver, as I had in my flat. Perhaps the premonition in the flat had been for the house. 'I was just . . . frightened,' I said.

Malcolm glanced at me with interest.

Yale said, 'What of?'

'Not of bombs,' I said. 'I never considered that. Frightened there was someone in the house. I couldn't have slept there, that's all.' I paused. 'I saw the way the car drove at my father at Newmarket – it hit my leg, after all – and I believed him, of course, about being attacked and gassed in the garage. I knew he wouldn't have murdered Moira, or have had her murdered by anyone else. I believe absolutely in his extreme danger. We've been moving around, letting no one know where to find us, until this week.'

'My fault,' Malcolm said gloomily. 'I insisted on coming back here. Ian didn't want to.'

'When the doors were moved,' I said, 'it was time to go.'

Yale thought it over without comment for a while and then said, 'When you were in the house looking round, did you see anything unusual except for the doors?'

'No, nothing.'

'Nothing where it shouldn't be? Or absent from where it should have been?'

I thought back to that breathless heart-thumping search. Whoever had moved the doors must at least have looked into the office and the sitting room. I hadn't bothered with the position of any of the other doors except closing the one from the kitchen to the hall. Someone could have looked into all the rooms in the house, for all I knew.

'No,' I said in the end. 'Nothing else seemed out of place.'

Yale sighed again. He sighed a lot, it seemed to me. 'If you think of anything later, let me know.'

'Yes, all right.'

'The time-frame we're looking at,' he said, 'is between about three-forty p.m., when the gardener went home taking the dogs, and ten-thirty p.m., when you returned from Cheltenham.' He pursed his lips. 'If you hadn't stayed out to dinner, what time would you have been home?'

'We meant to stay out to dinner,' Malcolm said. 'That's why Arthur had the dogs.'

'Yes, but if . . .'

'About six-thirty,' I said. 'If we'd gone straight home after the last race.'

'We had a drink at the racecourse after the last race,' Malcolm said. 'I had scotch, Ian had some sort of fizzy gut-rot.' He tapped ash into the ashtray. He was enjoying having Yale believe him at last, and seemed to be feeling expansive.

'Ian thinks,' he said, 'that I was probably knocked out just outside the kitchen door that day, and that I was carried from there straight into the garage, not dragged, and that it was someone the dogs knew, as they didn't bark. They were jumping up and down by the kitchen door, I can remember that, as they do if someone they know has come. But they do that anyway when it's time for their walk, and I didn't give it a thought.' He inhaled a lot of smoke and let it out into the superintendent's erstwhile clean air. 'Oh yes, and about the fingerprints . . .' He repeated what I'd said about firemen's lifts.

Yale looked at me neutrally and polished his moustache. He was difficult to read, I thought, chiefly because he didn't want to be read. All policemen, I supposed, raised barriers and, like doctors and lawyers, tended not to trust what they were told, which could be bitterly infuriating to the truthful.

He must have been forty or forty-five, I supposed, and had to be competent to have reached that rank. He looked as if he habitually had too little exercise and too many sandwiches, and gave no impression of wallowing in his own power. Perhaps now he'd dropped his over-smart suspicions of Malcolm, he could actually solve his case, though I'd heard the vast majority of criminals were in jail because of having been informed on, not detected. I did very much want him to succeed.

I wished he could spontaneously bring himself to share what he was thinking, but I supposed he'd been trained not to. He kept his counsel anyway on that occasion, and I kept mine, and perhaps it was a pity.

A policewoman came in and said, looking harassed, that she didn't know where to put the Pembroke family.

Yale thought briefly and told her to show them all to his office. Malcolm said, 'Oh God,' and dragged on his cigar, and presently the whole troop arrived.

I got to my feet and Alicia immediately sat on my chair. Vivien and Joyce both glared at Malcolm, still seated, willing him to rise, which he didn't. Which of them could he possibly give his chair to, I thought, stifling laughter, without causing exmarital bloodshed?

With a straight face, Yale asked the policewoman to fetch two more chairs, and I couldn't even tell if he were amused or simply practical. When Vivien and Joyce were suitably enthroned, he looked around and counted us all: thirteen.

'Who's missing?' he asked.

He got various answers: 'My wife, Debs', 'Thomas, my husband', 'Ursula, of course.'

'Very well. Now, if any of you know anything or guess anything about the explosion at Quantum House, I want to hear about it.'

'Terrorists,' Vivien said vaguely.

Everyone ignored her and no one else made any suggestion.

'While you are here,' Yale said, 'I'll ask you all to

answer certain questions. I'll have my personnel write down your answers, and of course after that you can leave. The questions are, what were you doing yesterday between three in the afternoon and midnight, what were you doing a week last Tuesday between the same hours, and what were you doing two weeks ago today, Friday, also between three p.m. and midnight?'

Edwin said crossly, 'We've already answered most of those questions for that wretched man, West. It's too much to go over it all again.'

Several of the others nodded.

Yale looked blank. 'Who is West?'

'A detective,' Berenice said. 'I sent him away with a flea in his ear, I can tell you.'

'He was awfully persistent,' Helen said, not liking the memory. 'I told him I couldn't possibly remember exactly, but he went on prying.'

'Dreadful little man,' Serena said.

'He said I was illegitimate,' Gervase complained sourly. 'It's thanks to Joyce that he knew.'

Yale's mouth opened and closed again and he took a deep breath. 'Who is West?' he asked intensely.

'Fellow I hired,' Malcolm said. 'Private detective. Hired him to find out who was trying to kill me, as I reckoned the police weren't getting anywhere.'

Yale's composure remained more or less intact. 'All the same,' he said, 'please answer the questions again. And those of you without husband and wife here, please answer for them as best you can.' He looked around at all the faces, and I would have sworn he was puzzled. I looked to see what he had seen, and I saw the faces of ordinary people, not murderers. Ordinary people with problems and hang-ups, with quirks and grievances. People anxious and disturbed by the blasting of the house that most had lived in and all had visited. Not one of them could possibly be a murderer, I thought. It had after all to be someone from outside.

I felt a lot of relief at this conclusion until I realized I was raising any excuse not to have to find a murderer among ourselves; yet we did have to find one, if Malcolm were to live. The dilemma was permanent.

'That's all for now,' Yale said, rising to his feet. 'My staff will take your statements in the interview rooms. And Mr Pembroke senior, will you stay here a moment? And Mr Ian Pembroke also? There are the arrangements to be made about the house.'

The family left me behind with bad grace. 'It's my job, not Ian's, to see to things. I am the eldest.' That was Donald. 'You need someone with know-how.' That was Gervase, heavily. 'It's not Ian's house.' Petulance from Edwin.

Yale managed however to shovel them all out, and immediately the door had closed, I said, 'While they're all in the interview rooms, I'm taking my father out of here.'

'The house . . .' Malcolm began.

'I'll see to the house later. We're leaving here now,

this minute. If Superintendent Yale will lend us a police car, fine; otherwise we'll catch buses or taxis.'

'You can have a police car within reason,' Yale said.

'Great. Then . . . um . . . just take my father to the railway station. I'll stay here.'

'All right.'

To Malcolm, I said, 'Go to London. Go to where we were last night. Use the same name. Don't telephone anyone. Don't for God's sake let anyone know where you are.'

'You're bloody arrogant.'

'Yes. This time, listen to me.'

Malcolm gave me a blue glare, stubbed out his cigar, stood up and let the red blanket drop from his shoulders to the floor.

'Where will you be?' Yale asked him.

'Don't answer,' I said brusquely.

Malcolm looked at me, then at the superintendent. 'Ian will know where I am. If he doesn't want to tell you, he won't. Gervase tried to burn some information out of him once, and didn't succeed. He still has the scars . . .' he turned to me ' . . . don't you?'

'Malcolm!' I protested.

Malcolm said to Yale, 'I gave Gervase a beating he'll never forget.'

'And he's never forgiven me,' I said.

'Forgiven you? For what? You didn't snitch to me. Serena did. She was so young she didn't really understand what she'd been seeing. Gervase could be a proper bully.'

'Come on,' I said, 'we're wasting time.'

Superintendent Yale followed us out of his office and detailed a driver to take Malcolm.

'I'll come in the car, once I can move it,' I said to him. 'Don't go shopping, I'll buy us some things later. Do be sensible, I beg you.'

'I promise,' he said; but promises with Malcolm weren't necessarily binding. He went out with the driver and I stood on the police station steps watching his departure and making sure none of the family had seen him or could follow.

Yale made no comment but waved me back to his office. Here he gave me a short list of reputable building contractors and the use of his telephone. I chose one of the firms at random and explained what was needed, and Yale took the receiver himself and insisted that they were to do minimum weather-proofing only, and were to move none of the rubble until the police gave clearance.

'When the driver returns from taking your father,' he said to me, disconnecting, 'we can spare him to ferry you back to your car.'

'Thank you.'

'I'm trusting you, you know, to maintain communications between me and your father.'

'I'll telephone here every morning, if you like.'

'I'd much rather know where he is.'

I shook my head. 'The fewer people know, the safer.'

He couldn't exactly accuse me of taking unreasonable precautions, so he left it, and asked instead, 'What did your half-brother burn you with?'

'A cigarette. Nothing fancy.'

'And what information did he want?'

'Where I'd hidden my new cricket bat,' I answered: but it hadn't been about cricket bats, it had been about illegitimacy, which I hadn't known at the time but had come to understand since.

'How old were you both?'

'I was eleven. Gervase must have been thirteen.'

'Why didn't you give him the bat?' Yale asked.

'It wasn't the bat I wouldn't give him. It was the satisfaction. Is this part of your enquiries?'

'Everything is,' he said laconically.

The hired car was movable when I got back to it and as it was pointing in that direction I drove it along to Quantum. There were still amazing numbers of people there, and I couldn't get past the now more substantial barrier across the drive until the policeman guarding it had checked with Superintendent Yale by radio.

'Sorry, sir,' one of them said, finally letting me in. 'The superintendent's orders.'

I nodded and drove on, parking in front of the house beside two police cars which had presumably returned from taking the many family members to their various cars.

I had already grown accustomed to the sight of the house; it still looked as horrific but held no more shocks. Another policeman walked purposefully towards me as I got out of the car and asked what I wanted. To look through the downstairs windows, I said.

He checked by radio. The superintendent replied that I could look through the windows as long as the constable remained at my side, and as long as I would point out to him anything I thought looked wrong. I readily agreed to that. With the constable beside me, I walked towards the place where the hall could still be discerned, skirting the heavy front door, which had been blown outwards, frame and all, when the brick-work on either side of it had given way.

QUANTUM IN ME FUIT lay face downwards on the gravel. I did the best I could. Someone's best, I thought, grateful to be alive, hadn't quite been good enough.

'Don't go in, sir,' the young constable said warningly. 'There's more could come down.'

I didn't try to go in. The hall was full of ceilings and floors and walls from upstairs, though one could see daylight over the top of the heap, the daylight from the back garden. Somewhere in the heap were all of Malcolm's clothes except the ones he'd worn to Cheltenham, all his vicuna coats and handmade shoes, all of the gold-and-silver brushes he'd packed on his flight to Cambridge, and somewhere, too, the portrait of Moira.

Jagged arrows of furniture stuck up from the devastation like the arms of the drowning, and pieces of dusty unrecognizable fabric flapped forlornly when a gust of wind took them. Tangled there, too, was everything I'd brought with me from my flat, save only my racing kit – saddle, helmet and holdall – which was still in the boot of the car along with Malcolm's briefcase. Everything was replaceable, I supposed; and I felt incredibly glad I hadn't thought of bringing the silver-framed picture of Coochie and the boys.

There was glass everywhere along the front of the house, fallen from the shattered windows. With the constable in tow, I crunched along towards the office, passing the ruins of the downstairs cloakroom on the way, where a half-demolished wall had put paid to the plumbing.

The office walls themselves, like those of the kitchen, were intact, but the office door that I'd set at such a careful angle was wide open with another brick and plaster glacier spilling through it. The shockwave that must have passed through the room to smash its way out through the windows had lifted every unweighted sheet of paper and redistributed it on the floor. Most of the pictures and countless small objects were down there also, including, I noticed, the pen pot holding the piece of wire. Apart from the ancient bevelled glass of a splendid breakfront bookcase which stood along one wall, everything major looked restorable, though getting rid of the dust would be a problem in itself.

I spent a good deal of time gazing through the open spaces of the office windows, but in the end had to admit defeat. The positions of too much had been altered for me to see anything inexplicably wrong. I'd seen nothing significant in there the previous evening when I'd fetched Malcolm's briefcase, when I'd been wide awake with alarm to such things.

Shaking my head I moved on round the house, passing the still shut and solidly bolted garden door which marked the end of the indoor passage. The blast hadn't shifted it, had dissipated on nearer targets. Past it lay the long creeper-covered north wall of the old playroom, and I walked along there and round into the rear garden.

The police had driven stakes into the lawn and tied ropes to them, making a line for no one to cross. Behind the rope the crowd persisted, open-eyed, chattering, pointing, coming to look and moving away to trail back over the fields. Among them Arthur Bellbrook, the dogs at his side, was holding a mini-court in a semi-circle of respectful listeners. The reporters and Press photographers seemed to have vanished but other cameras still clicked in a barrage. There was a certain restrained orderliness about everything which struck me hard as incongruous.

Turning my back to the gawpers, I looked through

the playroom window, seeing it, like the office, from the opposite angle to the previous night. Apart from the boxroom and my bedroom, it was the only room unmetamorphosed by Moira, and it still looked what it had been for forty years, the private domain of children.

The old battered armchairs were still there, and the big table that with a little imagination had been fort, boat, spaceship and dungeon in its time. The long shelves down the north wall still bore generations of train sets, building sets, board games and stuffed toys. Robin and Peter's shiny new bicycles were still propped there, that had been the joy of their lives in the week before the crash. There were posters of pop groups pinned to the walls and a bookcase bulging with reprehensible tastes.

The explosion on the other side of the thick load-bearing wall had done less damage to the playroom than to anywhere else I'd seen; only the broken windows and the ubiquitous dust, which had flooded in from the passage, showed that anything had happened. A couple of teddy bears had tumbled off the shelves, but the bicycles were still standing.

Anything there that shouldn't be there, anything not there that should be, Yale had said. I hadn't seen anything the night before in those categories, and I still couldn't.

With a frustrated shrug, I skirted the poured-out guts of the house and on the far side looked through the dining-room windows. Like the playroom, the dining room was relatively undamaged, though here the blast had blown in directly from the hall, leaving the now familiar tongue of rubble and covering everything with a thick grey film. For ever after, I would equate explosions with dust.

The long table, primly surrounded by high-backed chairs, stood unmoved. Some display plates held in wires on the wall had broken and fallen off. The sideboard was bare, but then it had been before. Malcolm had said the room had hardly been used since he and Moira had taken to shouting.

I continued round to the kitchen and went in through the door, to the agitation of the constable. I told him I'd been in there earlier to fetch the pine chair, which someone had since brought back, and he relaxed a very little.

'That door,' I said, pointing to one in a corner, 'leads to the cellars. Do you know if anyone's been down there?'

He didn't think so. He was pretty sure not. He hadn't heard anyone mention cellars.

The two underground rooms lay below the kitchen and dining room, and without electric lights I wasn't keen to go down there. Still . . . what excuse did I have not to?

Malcolm kept some claret in racks there, enough to grieve him if the bottles were broken. Coochie had used the cellars romantically for candlelit parties with red-checked tablecloths and gypsy music, and the folding tables and chairs were still stacked there, along with the motley junk of ages that was no longer used but too valuable to throw away.

'Do you have a torch, constable?' I asked.

No, he hadn't. I went to fetch the one I'd installed by habit in the hired car and, in spite of his disapproval, investigated downstairs. He followed me, to do him justice.

To start with, the cellars were dry, which was a relief as I'd been afraid the water from the storage tank and the broken pipes would have drained down and flooded them.

None of Malcolm's bottles was broken. The chimney wall, continuing downwards as sturdy foundations, had sheltered everything on its outer side as stalwartly below as it had above.

The dire old clutter of pensioned-off standard lamps, rocking chair, pictures, tin trunk, tiger skin, bed head-board, tea trolley, all took brief life in the torchlight and faded back to shadow. Same old junk, undisturbed.

All that one could say again was that nothing seemed to be there in the cellar that shouldn't be, and nothing not there that should. Shrugging resignedly, I led the way upstairs and closed the door.

Outside again, I looked into the garage, which seemed completely untouched, and walked round behind it to the kitchen garden. The glass in the old greenhouse was broken, and I supposed Moira's little folly, away on the far side of the garden, would have suffered the same fate.

I dearly wanted to go down to the far end of the kitchen garden to make sure the gold store was safe, but was deterred by the number of interested eyes already swivelled my way, and particularly by Arthur Bellbrook's.

The wall itself looked solid enough. The crowds were nowhere near it, as it was away to the left, while they were coming in from the fields on the right.

The constable stood by my side, ready to accompany me everywhere.

Shrugging, I retreated. Have faith, I thought, and drove away to London.

CHAPTER TWELVE

Malcolm had achieved a double suite at the Ritz with views of Green Park. He had lunched on Strasbourg pâté and Dover sole, according to the remains on the white-clothed room-service table, and had reached the lower half of a bottle of Krug.

'How are the shakes?' I said, putting his briefcase down beside him.

'Were you followed here?' he asked.

'I was not.'

He was doing his best to pretend he had regained total command of himself, yet I guessed the train journey had been an anxious and lonely ordeal. It was difficult for me to imagine the escalating trauma within him. How could anyone be the target of deadly unrelenting virulence and not in the end break down? I'd got to invent something better for him, I thought, than cooping him up in millionaire cells. Make him safe, give him back his lightheartedness, set him free.

'Um,' I said. 'I hope your passport's still in your briefcase.'

'Yes, it is.' He had taken it in his briefcase to Paris.

'Good.'

An unfortunate thought struck him. 'Where's yours?' Malcolm asked.

'In the rubble. Don't worry, I'll get a replacement. Do you have a visa for America?'

'Yes. I also had one for Australia once, but they only last a year. If we go, we'll have to get new visas from Australia House.'

'How about if you go to America tomorrow?' I said.

'*Tomorrow*? How can I?'

'I'll take you safely to Heathrow and see you off.'

'Dammit, that's not what I meant.'

'No,' I said. 'Well . . . the Breeders' Cup races are three weeks tomorrow at Santa Anita. Why don't we phone Ramsey Osborn? Why don't we phone Blue Clancy's trainer? Why don't you fly to Los Angeles tomorrow and have a fine old time at the races for three weeks? They have racing every day on the same track. If I know you, you'll be cronies with the racetrack committee immediately. Ramsey Osborn will send introductions. You can stay where the Breeders' Cup organizers do, at the Beverly Wilshire hotel which I've heard is right at the end of Rodeo Drive where there's a man's shop so expensive you have to make an appointment to be let in. Buy a few shirts there, it'll make a nice dent in your bankroll. Forget Quantum. Forget the bloody family. They won't know where you are and they'll never find you.'

I stopped only a fraction for breath, not long enough for him to raise objections. 'On the Tuesday after the Breeders' Cup, they're running the Melbourne Cup in Melbourne, Australia. That's their biggest race. The whole country stops for it. A lot of the people from the Breeders' Cup will go on to Australia. You'll have made cronies among them by the dozen. I've heard it's all marvellous. I've never been, and I'd love to. I'll join you as soon as my passport's renewed and I'll go on minding your back – if you still want me to.'

He had listened at first with apathy, but by the end he was smiling. I'd proposed the sort of impulsive behaviour that had greatly appealed to him in the past, and it still did, I was grateful to see.

'A damn sight better than rotting at the Ritz,' he announced.

'Great,' I said. 'Get out your diary for the numbers.'

It was soon settled. Blue Clancy would go over for the Breeders' Cup as long as he was fit. Ramsey Osborn, booming away in Stamford, Connecticut, promised introductions galore to a score of very dear friends he'd met a couple of times out West. Why didn't Malcolm stop off at Lexington on the way and feast his eyes on some real bloodstock? Ramsey had some very good friends in Lexington who would be delighted to have Malcolm stay with them. Ramsey would call them and fix it. Stay by the phone, you guys, he said. He would fix it and call back. It was breakfast time in Connecticut, he said. It would be an hour earlier in Lexington. He would see if the lazy so and so's were out of bed.

Whether they were or they weren't, Ramsey phoned back within twenty minutes. As before, Malcolm talked on the sitting-room telephone, I on the extension in my bedroom.

'All set,' Ramsey said. 'They're expecting you, Malcolm, tomorrow, and I'm flying down Sunday. They're real sweet guys, you'll love them. Dave and Sally Cander. Dogwood Drift Farm, outside of Lexington.' He read out the telephone number. 'You got that?'

Malcolm had got it.

Ramsey asked where Malcolm was planning to stay for the Breeders' Cup. 'Beverly Wilshire? Couldn't be better. Centre of the universe. I'll make reservations right away.'

Malcolm explained he needed a two-bedroom suite for himself and me. Sure thing, Ramsey agreed. No problem. See you, he said. We had made his day, he said, and to have a good one.

The sitting room seemed smaller and quieter when he'd gone off the line, but Malcolm had revitalized remarkably. We went at once by taxi to Australia House where Malcolm got his visa without delay, and on the way back stopped first at his bank for more travellers' cheques and then in Piccadilly a little short of the Ritz to shop in Simpson's for replacement clothes from the skin up, not forgetting suitcases to pack them in.

Malcolm paid for all of mine with his credit card, which was a relief. I hardly liked to ask him outright for my fare to California, but he'd thought of my other finances himself already and that evening gave me a bumper cheque to cover several additional destinations.

'Your fare and so on. Pay Arthur Bellbrook. Pay Norman West. Pay the contractors for weatherproofing Quantum. Pay for the hired car. Pay your own expenses. Anything else?'

'Tickets to Australia?'

'We'll get those in the morning. I'll pay for them here, with mine to Lexington. If we can get you a Los Angeles ticket without a date on, I can pay for that too.'

We made plans about telephone calls. He was not to phone me, I would phone him.

We dined in good spirits, the dreadful morning at least overlaid. He raised his glass: 'To Blue Clancy' and 'To racing' and 'To life.'

'To life,' I said.

I drove him to Heathrow in the morning safely as promised, and saw him on his way to Lexington via New York and Cincinnati. He was fizzing at least at half strength and gave me a long blue look before he departed.

'Don't think I don't know what I owe you,' he said.

'You owe me nothing.'

'Bloody Moira,' he said uncxpcctcdly, and looked back and waved as he went.

Feeling good about him, I telephoned from the airport to Superintendent Yale but got one of his assistants: his chief was out at Quantum and had left a message that if I phoned I was to be asked if I could join him. Yes, I could, I agreed, and arrived in the village about forty minutes later.

The road to the house wasn't as congested as the day before, but fresh waves of sightseers still came and went continuously. I drove up to the gate and after radio consultation the constable there let me pass. Another policeman was at my side the moment I stopped in front of the house. Different men, both of them, from the day before.

Superintendent Yale appeared from the direction of the kitchen, having been alerted by the gateman, I surmised.

'How is Mr Pembroke?' he asked, shaking hands with every sign of having adopted humanity as a policy.

'Shaken,' I said.

He nodded understandingly. He was wearing an overcoat and looked cold in the face, as if he'd been out of doors for some time. The mild wind of yesterday had intensified rawly and the clouds looked more threatening, as if it would rain. Yale glanced with anxiety at the heavens and asked me to go round with him to the back garden.

The front of the house looked sad and blind, with

light brown plywood hammered over all the windows and a heavy black tarpaulin hanging from under the roof to hide the hole in the centre. At the rear, the windows were shuttered and the bare roof rafters were covered but the devastated centre was still open to the elements. Several men in hard hats and overalls were working there, slowly picking up pieces from the huge jumble and carrying them to throw them into a rubbish skip which stood a short distance away across the lawn.

'Do they propose to move all that by hand?' I asked.

'As much as is necessary,' Yale said. 'We've got a surprise for you.' He waved to a man in beige overalls with a blue hard hat who came over to us and asked me my name.

'Ian Pembroke,' I said obligingly.

He unzipped the front of his overalls, put a hand inside and drew out a battered navy-blue object which he held out to me with a small satisfied smile. 'You may need this,' he said.

Never a truer word. It was my passport.

'Where on earth did you find it?' I said, delighted.

He shrugged and pointed to the mess. 'We always come across a few things unharmed. We're making a pile of them for you, but don't get your hopes up.'

I zipped the passport into my new Simpson's Barbour and thought gratefully that I wouldn't have to trail around getting a new one.

'Have you found any gold-and-silver-backed brushes?' I asked.

'Not so far.'

'They're my father's favourite things.'

'We'll look out for them,' he said. 'Now, we'd like you to help us in return.'

'Anything I can.'

He was a lean, highly professional sort of man, late forties I guessed, giving an impression of army. He said his name was Smith. He was an explosives expert.

'When you first came here yesterday morning,' he said, 'did you smell anything?'

I was surprised. I thought back.

'Brick dust,' I said. 'The wind was stirring it up. It was in my throat.'

He grunted. 'This looks like a gas explosion, but you're quite certain, aren't you, that there was no gas in the house?'

'Absolutely certain.'

'Do you know what cordite smells like?' he asked.

'Cordite? Like after a gun's been fired, do you mean?'

'That's right.'

'Well, yes, I know what it smells like.'

'And you didn't smell that here yesterday morning?'

I looked at him, puzzled. 'No one was shot,' I said.

He smiled briefly. 'Do you know what cordite is?' he asked.

'Not really.'

'It was used very commonly as a general explosive,' he said, 'before Nobel invented dynamite in 1867. It's less fierce than dynamite. It's sort of high-grade gunpowder, and it's still used in some types of quarries. It explodes comparatively slowly, at about two thousand five hundred metres per second, or a little over. It explodes like a gas. It doesn't punch small holes through walls like a battering ram. It's rather like an expanding balloon that knocks them flat.'

I looked at the house.

'Yes, like that,' Smith said.

'Cordite . . .' I frowned. 'It means nothing.'

'Its strong smell lingers,' he said.

'Well . . . we didn't get here until ten, and the explosion was at four-thirty in the morning, and it was fairly windy, though not as rough as today. I should think any smell had blown away.' I paused. 'What about all the people who were here before us? What do they say?'

'They're not here today,' Smith said succinctly. 'I haven't asked them.'

'No one said anything to me about a smell,' I said.

Smith shrugged. 'We'll do microscopic tests. We would do, anyway. But it looks to me as if cordite is a strong possibility.'

'Can you buy cordite?' I asked vaguely. 'Can anyone?'

'No, they definitely can't,' Smith said with decision. 'Twenty years or so ago, maybe, but not now. Since terrorism became a part of life, most sorts of explosives are highly regulated. It's extremely difficult for the general public to get hold of them. There are a few explosive substances on the open market, but detonators to set them off are not.'

I found I was thinking of cordite in terms of the small quantities used in firearms, whereas to knock down half a house . . .

'How much cordite would that have taken?' I asked, gesturing to the results.

'I haven't yet worked it out. A good deal.'

'What would it have been in?'

'Anything.'

'What does it look like? Is it like jelly?'

'No, you're thinking of high-explosive TNT. That's liquid when it's fed into bomb cases, then it gels inside. Bombs dropped from aircraft are that sort. Cordite is loose grains, like gunpowder. To get a useful result, you have to compress it. Confine it. Then you need heat to start off the chemical reaction, which proceeds at such a rate that the ingredients appear to explode.'

'Appear!' I said, and added hastily, 'OK, I take your word for it, don't explain.'

He gave me a slightly pitying look but let up on the lecture and went back to searching in the ruins. Superintendent Yale asked if any of the Pembrokes had ever had any connection whatever with quarries. None that I knew of, I said. It was most improbable.

'Or had friends who had quarries, or who worked in quarries?'

I didn't know. I'd never heard of any.

My gaze wandered away from Smith and his fellow diggers after truth, and I became more aware of the audience beyond the rope in the garden. There weren't anything like as many as the day before, but clearly the work in progress was a draw in itself.

Arthur Bellbrook was there again, talking away. He must enjoy the celebrity, I thought. He'd been the one who'd found Moira, and now there was the house . . . Arthur was talking as if he owned the news, rocking back on his heels and sticking his stomach out. The dogs on their leads patiently waited. It didn't matter to them, I supposed, that Arthur was into maybe the twentieth account of life and death with the Pembrokes.

A stray piece of memory connected Arthur to the smell of cordite, and I couldn't think why that should be until I remembered him carrying his shotgun into the house on the day he'd thought I was a burglar.

I cast the stray thought out but it sauntered back, telling me it was nothing to do with Arthur and shotguns.

What then?

I frowned, trying to remember.

'What's the matter?' Yale said, watching me.

'Nothing, really.'

'You've thought of something. One of your family does have a quarry connection, is that it?'

'Oh no,' I half laughed. 'Not that. The smell of cordite . . .'

The smell of cordite on a misty morning, and the gardener . . . not Arthur, but old Fred before him . . . telling us children to keep out of the way, to go right back out of the field, he didn't want our heads blown off . . .

I remembered abruptly, like a whole scene springing to life on a film screen. I walked across to where Smith in his hard blue hat bent to his task and said, without preamble, 'Does cordite have another name?'

He straightened, with a piece of brick and plaster in his hand.

'I suppose so,' he said. 'It's commonly called "black powder".'

Black powder.

'Why?' he said.

'Well, we had some here once. But long ago, when we were children. Twenty years ago at least, probably more. But I suppose . . . some of the family could have remembered . . . as I just have.'

Yale, who had followed me to listen, said, 'Remember what?'

'There used to be four or five great old willow trees down by the stream, across the field.' I pointed. 'Those you can see now are only twenty years old or so. They grow very fast . . . they were planted after they took the old trees down. They were splendid old trees, huge, magnificent.'

Yale made hurrying-up motions with his hands, as if to say the state of long-gone willows, however patrician, was immaterial.

'They were at the end of their lives,' I said. 'If there was a gale, huge branches would crack off. Old Fred, who was the gardener for years here before Arthur, told my father they weren't safe and they'd have to come down, so he got some foresters to come and fell them. It was dreadful seeing them come down . . .' I didn't think I'd tell Yale that half the family had been in tears. The trees had been friends, playground, climbing frames, deepest purple imaginary rain forests: and, afterwards, there was too much daylight and the dead bodies being sawn up for firewood and burned on bonfires. The stream hadn't looked the same when open to bright sunshine; rather ordinary, not running through dappled mysterious shade.

'Go on,' Yale said with half-stifled impatience. 'What's all this about trees?'

'The stumps,' I said. 'The tree men sawed the trees off close to the ground but left the stumps, and no one could get them out. A tractor came from a nearby farm and tried . . .' We'd had a great time then, having rides all day. 'Anyway, it failed. Nothing else would move the stumps, and Fred didn't want to leave them there to rot, so he decided to blow them up . . . with black powder.'

'Ah,' Yale said.

Black powder had sounded, somehow, as if it ought

to belong to pirates. We'd been most impressed. Fred had got his powder and he'd dug a hole down below the stubborn roots of the first stump, and filled it and set off one enormous explosion. It was just as well he'd cleared us out of the field first because the blast had knocked Fred himself flat although he'd been about a hundred feet away. The first tree stump had come popping out of the ground looking like a cross between an elephant and an octopus, but Malcolm, who came running in great alarm to see what had happened, forbade Fred to blow up the others.

As I told the gist of this to Yale and Smith, the second reel of the film was already unrolling in my mind, and I stopped fairly abruptly when I realized what I was remembering.

'Fred,' I said, 'carried the box of black powder back to the tool shed and told us never to touch it. We were pretty foolish but not that crazy. We left it strictly alone. And there the box stayed until it got covered over with other junk and we didn't notice it or think of it any more . . .' I paused, then said, 'Wouldn't any explosive be useless after all this time?'

'Dynamite wouldn't last much more than a year in a tool shed,' Smith said. 'One hot summer would ruin it. But black powder – cordite – is very stable, and twenty years is immaterial.'

'What are we waiting for?' Yale said, and walked towards the tool shed which lay behind the garage on the near side of the kitchen garden.

The tool shed was a place I hadn't thought of looking into the day before: but even if I had, I doubted if I would have remembered the black powder. Its memory had been too deep.

'Where is this box?' Yale asked.

I looked at the contents of the tool shed in perplexity. I hadn't been in there for years, and in that time it had passed from Fred to Arthur. Fred had had an upturned orange box to sit on while he waited through heavy showers: Arthur had an old fireside chair. Fred had had a tray with a cracked mug and a box of sugar cubes and had come indoors to fetch his tea: Arthur had an electric kettle. Fred had tended old tools lovingly: Arthur had shiny new ones with paint still on the handles.

Beyond the tools and the chair, in the centre section of the spacious shed, were things like mowers, chainsaws and hedgeclippers and, at the furthest shadowy end, the flotsam by-passed by time, like the stuff in the cellar, stood in forgotten untidy heaps.

It all looked unpromisingly undisturbed, but Yale called up a pair of young policemen and told them to take everything out of the tool shed and lay each object separately on the ground. Smith went back to the rubble, but Yale and I watched the policemen and so did Arthur Bellbrook, who came hurrying across the moment he saw what was happening.

'What's going on?' he said suspiciously.

'When did you last clean out the tool shed?' Yale asked.

Arthur was put out and beginning to bridle.

'Just say,' I said to him. 'We just want to know.'

'I've been meaning to,' he said defensively. 'That's Fred's old rubbish, all that at the back.'

The superintendent nodded, and we all watched the outgoing procession of ancient, rusting, broken and neglected tat. Eventually one of the men came out with a dirty wooden box which I didn't recognize at first because it was smaller than I'd seen in my memory. He put it on the ground beside other things, and I said doubtfully, 'I think that's it.'

'Mr Smith,' Yale called.

Mr Smith came. Yale pointed at the box, which was about the size of crates used for soft drink bottles, and Smith squatted beside it.

The lid was nailed shut. With an old chisel, Smith prised it open and peeled back the yellowish paper which was revealed. Inside the paper, half-filling the box, there was indeed black powder.

Smith smelled it and poked it around. 'It's cordite, all right, and in good condition. But as it's here, it obviously hasn't been used. And anyway, there wouldn't have been anything like enough in this box to have caused that much damage to the house.'

'Well,' I said weakly, 'it was only an idea.'

'Nothing wrong with the idea,' Smith said. He looked

around at the growing collection of discards. 'Did you find any detonators?'

He had everyone open every single packet and tin: a lot of rusty staples and nails saw daylight, and old padlocks without keys and rotting batteries, but nothing he could identify as a substance likely to set off an explosion.

'Inconclusive,' he said, shrugging, and returned to his rubble.

Yale told Arthur to leave the cordite where it was and do what he liked with the rest, and Arthur began throwing the decaying rubbish into the skip.

I tried to apologize for all the waste of time, but the superintendent stopped me.

'When you saw the tree stump blown up, which of your brothers and sisters were there?'

I sighed, but it had to be faced. 'Gervase, Ferdinand and I were always together at that time, but some of the older ones were there too. They used to come for weekends still after they were grown up. Vivien used to make them, so that Malcolm wouldn't cut them out. Alicia hated it. Anyway, I know Lucy was there, because she wrote a poem about roots shrieking blindly to the sky.'

Yale looked sceptical.

'She's a poet.' I said lamely. 'Published.'

'The roots poem was published?'

'Yes.'

'All right, then. She was there. Who else?'

'Someone was carrying Serena on his shoulders when we had to leave the field for the explosion. I think it must have been Thomas. He used to make her laugh.'

'How old were you all at that time?' Yale asked.

'I don't know exactly.' I thought back. Alicia had swept out not very long after. 'Perhaps I was thirteen. Gervase is two years older, Ferdinand one year younger. Lucy would have been . . . um . . . twenty-two, about, and Thomas nineteen. Serena must have been six, at that rate, and Donald . . . I don't know if he was there or not . . . he would have been twenty-four.'

Yale thoughtfully pulled out his notebook and asked me to repeat the ages, starting with Donald.

'Donald twenty-four, Lucy twenty-two, Thomas nineteen, Gervase fifteen, myself thirteen, Ferdinand twelve, Serena six.'

'Right,' he said, putting a full-stop.

'But what does it matter, if the cordite is still here?' I said.

'They all saw the force of the explosion,' he said. 'They all saw it knock the gardener over from a hundred feet away, isn't that what you said?'

I looked at the shattered house and said forlornly, 'None of them could have done it.'

Yale put his notebook away. 'You might be right,' he said.

Smith again came over to join us. 'You've given me an idea,' he said to me. 'You and your tree roots. Can you draw me a plan of where the rooms were, exactly, especially those upstairs?'

I said I thought so, and the three of us went into the garage out of the wind, where I laid a piece of paper on the bonnet of Moira's car and did my best.

'The sitting room stretched all the way between the two thick walls, as you know,' I said. 'About thirty feet. Above that . . .' I sketched, 'there was my room, about eight feet wide, twelve deep, with a window on the short side looking out to the garden. Malcolm's bedroom came next, I suppose about fifteen feet wide and much deeper than mine. The passage outside bent round it . . . and then his bathroom, also looking out to the garden, with a sort of dressing room at the back of it which also led out of the bedroom . . .' I drew it. 'Malcolm's whole suite would have been about twenty-two feet wide facing the garden, by about seventeen or eighteen feet deep.'

Yale studied the drawing. 'Your room and the suite together were more or less identical with the sitting room, then?'

'Yes, I should think so.'

'A big house,' he commented.

'It used to be bigger. The kitchen was once a morning room, and where the garage is now there were kitchens and servants' halls. And on the other side, where the passage now goes out into the garden, there were gun rooms and flower rooms and music rooms, a bit of a rabbit warren. I never actually saw the wings, only photographs of them. Malcolm had them pulled down when he inherited the house, to make it easier to deal with without the droves of servants his mother had.'

'Hm,' he said. 'That explains why there are no sideways-facing windows on the ground floor.'

'Yes,' I agreed.

He borrowed my pen and did some calculations and frowned.

'Where exactly was your father's bed?'

I drew it in. 'The bed was against the wall between his room and the large landing, which was a sort of upstairs place to sit in, over the hall.'

'And your bed?'

'Against the wall between my room and Malcolm's.'

Smith considered the plan for some time and then said, 'I think the charge here was placed centrally. Did your father by any chance have a chest, or anything, at the foot of his bed?'

'Yes, he did,' I said, surprised. 'A long box with a padded top for a seat. He kept his tennis things in it, when he used to play.'

'Then I'd think that would be where the explosion occurred. Or under your father's bed. But if there was a box at the foot, I'd bet on that.' Smith borrowed the pen again for some further calculations and looked finally undecided.

'What's the matter?' I asked.

'Mm . . . well, because of your tree roots, I was

thinking of an explosive that farmers and landowners use sometimes which is safer than cordite. They blow up tree trunks, clear blocked ditches, that sort of thing. You can buy the ingredients anywhere without restrictions and mix it yourself.'

'That sounds extraordinary,' I said.

He smiled slightly. 'It's not so easy to get the detonators to set it off.'

'What is it, then?' I asked.

Yale, too, was listening with great interest.

'Fertilizer and diesel oil,' Smith said.

'What?' I sounded disappointed and Smith's smile expanded.

'Ammonium nitrate,' he said. 'You can buy it in fine granules from seed merchants and garden centres, places like that. Mix it with fuel oil. Dead simple. As far as I remember, but I'd have to look it up to be sure, it would be sixteen parts fertilizer to one part oil. The only problem is,' he scratched his nose, 'I think you'd need a good deal of it to do the sort of damage we have here. I mean, again I'd have to look it up, but I seem to remember it'll be volume in cubic metres over three, answer in kilos.'

'What volume?' I asked.

'The volume of the space you want cleared by the explosion.'

He looked at the mixed emotions I could feel on my face and dealt at least with the ignorance.

'Say you want effective destruction of everything

within a space three metres by three metres by three metres. Twenty-seven cubic metres, OK? Volume of your bedroom, near enough. Divide by three, equals nine. Nine kilos of explosive needed.'

'Is that,' I said slowly, 'why reports of terrorist attacks are often so definite about the weight of the bomb used?'

'Absolutely. The area cleared directly relates to the size of the . . . er . . . bomb. If you can analyse the type of explosive and measure the area affected, you can tell how much explosive was needed.'

Superintendent Yale was nodding as if he knew all that.

'But you don't think this bomb went off in my bedroom,' I said.

'No, I don't. Nine kilos of ammonium nitrate in your bedroom would have annihilated it and made a nasty hole all round, but I wouldn't have thought it would bring half a house down. So if we locate the device in that foot-of-the-bed box, we are looking at something in the region of . . .' he did some more calculations ' . . . say at least seventy-five cubic metres for your father's bedroom . . . that's twenty-five kilos of explosive.'

'That's heavy,' I said blankly.

'Yes. A large suitcaseful. But then you'd need a suitcaseful also if you were using cordite. For demolishing this whole house, you'd have needed four times that amount, placed in about four places on the ground floor right against the thickest walls. People often think a small amount of explosive will do a tremendous lot of damage, but it doesn't.'

'What sets it off, then?' I asked.

'Ah.' He smiled the professional smile that wasn't about to give away its secrets. 'Let's just say fulminate of mercury, plus, I should say, an electrical circuit.'

'Please do explain,' I said.

He hesitated, then shrugged. 'ANFO won't explode on its own, it's very stable.'

'What's ANFO?' I interrupted.

'Ammonium nitrate fuel oil. The first letters. ANFO for short.'

'Oh yes. Sorry.'

'So you stick into it a package of something that explodes fast: the detonator, in fact. Then you arrange to heat the detonating substance, either with a burning fuse, or by an electrical circuit which can be achieved by ordinary batteries. The heat sets off the detonator, the detonator detonates the ANFO. And bingo . . .'

'Bang, you're dead.'

'Quite right.'

'At four-thirty in the morning,' I said, 'it would probably be a time-bomb, wouldn't it?'

Mr Smith nodded happily. 'That's what we're looking for. If it was an alarm clock, for instance, we'll probably find the pieces. We usually do if we look hard enough. They don't vaporize in the explosion, they scatter.'

CHAPTER THIRTEEN

I drove unhurriedly to Epsom but as soon as I let myself into my flat, I knew I wouldn't stay there. It was too negative, too empty, too boring. I wouldn't live there much longer, I thought.

There were a few letters, a few bills, a few messages on the answering machine, but nothing of great interest. If I'd been blown up at Quantum along with Malcolm, it wouldn't have made any vital difference to anybody, and I didn't like that thought very much.

I went into the bedroom to see what I'd got left in the way of clothes and came to the white lace negligée. Well, maybe *she* would have been sorry for a while. I wished I could phone her, but it was forbidden: her husband would answer as he had once before when I'd tried, and too many 'sorry, I've got the wrong number' messages would raise the suspicions of the dimmest of men, which he reputedly wasn't.

Apart from her, I thought, making a mental inventory, I mostly knew a lot of racing people on the borderline between acquaintance and friend. Enough to be asked to parties, enough for contentment at work. I knew I wasn't in general unpopular. It was enough, I guessed. Or it had seemed enough, up to now.

I had enjoyed being with Malcolm more than I'd realized. I missed him already, and in the twelve days I'd spent with him, I'd developed a taste for spontaneity which made sitting around in my flat impossible. I packed a pair of breeches and a sweater, added some limp old shirts to the new ones in the Simpson's suitcase, closed up the flat and went down to the car park.

My own car stood there, but I took the hired one again, meaning to turn it in some time and return for my own by train. First stop was at the bank to drop through the letter box an envelope containing Malcolm's cheque, with a paying-in slip to lodge it in my account. After that, I set off again in the overall direction of Quantum, but without really knowing where I was going.

I felt an awful aversion to the task of searching the psyches of the family, but I ended up in a place from where visiting them all would be easy, taking by impulse a turn onto the road to the village of Cookham and booking a room there in an old inn friendly with dark oak beams and log fires.

Norman West was out. I phoned him on the hour at four and five and reached him at six. He said apologetically that he had stopped working on the Pembroke case, there was nothing else he could do. He was sorry he hadn't been able to solve the . . . er . . . problem, and should he send his account to Mr Pembroke at the Savoy, or at Quantum House?

'Neither,' I said. 'We'd like you to carry on working.' And I told him what had happened to Quantum and very nearly to ourselves.

'Dear me,' he said.

I laughed internally, but I supposed 'dear me' was as apt a comment as any.

'So would you mind traipsing all the way round again to ask what everyone was doing the day before yesterday between three p.m. and midnight?'

He was silent for an appreciable interval. Then, he said, 'I don't know that it would be useful, you know. Your family were unhelpful before. They would be doubly unhelpful again. Surely this time the police will make exhaustive enquiries? I think I must leave it to them.'

I was more dismayed than I expected. 'Please do reconsider,' I said. 'If the police go asking the family their movements, and then you do also, I agree they won't like it. But if after that I too go and ask, they may be upset enough or angry enough to let out things that could tell us . . . one way or another.' I paused. 'I suppose I'm not making much sense.'

'Do you remember what you said to me about stepping on a rattlesnake?' he said.

'Well, yes.'

'You're proposing to stir up one with a stick.'

'We absolutely have to know who the rattlesnake is.'

I heard him sigh and could feel his disinclination.

'Look,' I said, 'could you just meet me somewhere? You gave my father and me summaries of what all the family were doing on those two days we asked about, but there must be much more you could tell me. If you don't want to visit them again, could you just . . . help me?'

'I don't mind doing that,' he said. 'When?'

'Tonight? Tomorrow?'

Tonight he was already working. Tomorrow he was taking his wife to visit their grandchildren all day as it was Sunday, but his evening would be free. He knew the pub I was staying in, he would come there, he said; he would meet me in the bar at seven.

I thanked him for that anyway, and next telephoned two stables along on the Downs to ask the trainers if I could ride exercise on their horses for several mornings, if it would be useful to them. The first said no, the second said yes, he was a couple of lads short and he'd be glad of the free help. Start Monday, first lot, pull out at seven-thirty, could I be there by seven-fifteen?

'Yes,' I said appreciatively.

'Stay to breakfast.'

Sanity lay in racing stables, I thought, thanking him. Their brand of insanity was my sort of health. I couldn't stay away for long. I felt unfit, not riding.

I spent the evening in the bar in the pub, mostly listening to a lonely man who felt guilty because his wife was in hospital having her guts rearranged. I never did discover the reason for the guilt but while he grew slowly drunk, I learned a lot about their financial troubles and about his anxieties over her illness. Not a riotously amusing evening for me, though he said he felt better himself from being able to tell a perfect stranger all the things he'd been bottling up. Was there anyone at all, I wondered, going to bed, who went through life feeling happy?

I dawdled Sunday away pleasurably enough, and Norman West, true to his word, appeared at seven.

His age was again very apparent from the grey-white hair downwards, and when I remarked that he looked tired, he said he'd been up most of the previous night but not to worry, he was used to it. Had he been to see his grandchildren? Yes, he had: lively bunch. He accepted a double scotch with water and, under its reviving influence, opened the large envelope he was carrying and pulled out some papers.

'Your photographs of the family are in here,' he said, patting the envelope, 'and I've also brought these copies of all my notes.' He laid the notes on the small table between us. 'You can have them to keep. The originals are in my files. Funny thing,' he smiled fleetingly, 'I used to think that one day I'd write a book about all my cases, but there they are, all those years of work, sitting in their files, and there they'll stay.'

'Why don't you write it?' I asked.

'I'm better at following people.'

I reflected that following people was what he'd been

good at when Joyce had first employed him, and that probably we'd expected too much of him, setting him to unravel attempted murders.

He said, 'You'll find there's a definite pattern about the movements of your family, and at the same time an absence of pattern. The murder of Mrs Moira and the gassing of Mr Pembroke both took place at about five in the evening, and at five almost all your family are habitually on the move. Mind you, so is most of the working population. It's a time of day when it's easy to lose an hour or so without anyone noticing. Traffic jams, left work late, stopped for a drink, watched television in shop windows . . . I've heard all those from erring husbands. The list is limitless of things people think up as excuses for getting home late. With a family like yours, where practically no one has a set time for leaving a place of work, it's even easier. That's why it's been almost hopeless establishing alibis, and I'm pretty sure the police found the same thing over Mrs Moira. When there's no expectation of anyone arriving at a regular time, no one looks at the clock.'

'I do understand,' I said thoughtfully.

'Newmarket was a bit different,' he said, 'because it meant someone being away from their normal environment for a whole day, assuming that Mr Pembroke was followed from his hotel when he left at lunchtime for Newmarket. And one has to assume that a follower would be in position much earlier than that, because he wouldn't know when Mr Pembroke would leave, or where he would go.' Hc cleared his throat and sipped his whisky. 'I thought it would be simple in those circumstances to discover which family member had been away all of that Tuesday, but in fact it wasn't, as you'll read. Now, if the explosive device was planted in Quantum House between four when the gardener usually left and six, when you might have returned from the races, we're back to the . . . er . . .'

'Five o'clock shadow,' I said.

He looked mildly shocked. It wasn't a laughing matter. 'I've no doubt the same pattern will be found,' he said. 'No one will be able, or willing, to say exactly where they were or where anyone else was during that period.'

'We may be lucky,' I said.

He said maybe, and looked unconvinced.

'Couldn't you please tell me,' I said, 'which Mrs Pembroke got you to find Malcolm? I know all about your ethics, but after this bomb . . . can't you? Whose name was on the cheque?'

He considered, staring at his drink as if to find wisdom in the depths. He sighed heavily, and shrugged.

'I didn't get paid,' he said. 'The cheque never came. I'm not sure, but I think . . . I think it was the voice of Mrs Alicia Pembroke.' He shook his head. 'I asked her if it was her, when I interviewed her. She said it wasn't but I think she was lying. But two other people found out on their own account, don't forget, by doing exactly as I did, telephoning around.'

'I won't forget.'

He looked at me sombrely. 'I hope Mr Pembroke can't be found as easily at this moment.'

'I don't think so,' I said.

'Can I give you some advice?'

'Please do.'

'Carry a weapon with you.'

'Mr West!'

'Even if it's only a pot of pepper,' he said, 'or a can of spray paint. There's a good deal of enmity towards you in your family because of your favoured status with Mr Pembroke. You were supposed to die with him in the house, I should imagine. So don't go unprepared.'

I swallowed and thanked him. He nodded and prosaically produced a smaller envelope from an inner pocket, which contained his account. I wrote him his cheque. He took it, inspected it, and put it away.

He rose wearily to his feet and shook my hand. 'Any time you want to,' he said, 'phone me. I don't mind talking, if it will help.'

I thanked him again and he went greyly away, leaving me on my own with his notes and a feeling of nakedness.

I began reading the notes. It so happened that he had reversed his original working order, or perhaps the order had become reversed during the copying: in any event, the eldest-to-youngest progression had been transposed, and it was Serena's notes which came first.

Norman West had written all his notes in longhand

with aides-mémoire to himself, and I could almost hear his radio-announcer voice in my head as I read.

Miss Serena Pembroke (26) unmarried, lives at 14 Mossborough Court, Bracknell, a block of flats just off the Easthampstead Road, turn left by the pub. Flats built during Bracknell's new-town expansion, middle-income, business people tenants, keep themselves to themselves. Pretty girl, one of the neighbours said (No. 12) but don't know her name. Miss S. has lived there three months. One bedroom, one sitting room, kit, bath, all small.

Miss S. works at Deanna's Dance and Aerobics Studio, High Street, Bracknell, teaching aerobics. Private business, sloppily run (my opinion), owned by Mrs Deanna Richmond (45?) whose mind is on a younger gent with a hairy chest, gold chain showing, rubbish.

Miss S. works mornings Monday to Friday 8.00 to 1.30 pm, taking classes, first office workers, then housewives. Miss S. and another girl (Sammy Higgs) work in rotation, half hour on, half off. Miss S.'s times are 8–8.30, 9–9.30, 10–10.30, 11–11.30, 12–12.30, 1–1.30 most days.

Miss S. and Sammy H. are both good workers. The clients I spoke to said classes v. good. Continuous, therefore popular. A girl can drop in on way to office, on way home after taking children to school, etc. Sign in, pay on way out. Clients come from all over – large clientele.

Evening classes, Monday to Friday, 7 pm–8.30 only. Miss S. does these alone. (S. Higgs does afternoons 1.30–4 pm.) Evenings quite social – rests for clients' drinks etc. Well attended.

Miss S. has bad menstrual cramps every month. Can't dance or exercise. Always two days off. The Tuesday of Newmarket Sales was one of these days – the second. Miss S. called in Monday morning in pain, didn't work, no one expected her Tuesday, she returned Wednesday. Mrs Deanna Richmond's daughter stands in on these occasions and also if either girl especially asks for time off otherwise. No records kept of these times.

Miss S. leads sober, hard-working, regulated life.

Likes pretty clothes, a bit immature (my opinion), has few friends. Goes to her brother's house (Mr Ferdinand) a good deal at weekends, or to her mother's (Mrs Alicia).

No ascertainable love life.

Miss S. likes shopping and window-shopping. On the Friday of attack on Mr Pembroke she says she bought food and frilly white blouse at Marks and Spencers, she thinks. (Not sure of the day.) She buys something to wear about four times a week probably – tights, leotards, sweaters, etc. 'Has to look nice for her clients.'

Miss S. owns two-year-old grey/silver Ford Escort,

but usually jogs one mile to work to warm up. Drives only if cold or wet. Car clean from automatic car wash: Miss S. goes through same car wash approx every two weeks. Car wash people corroborate, but can't remember exact dates.

Miss S. says Mr Ian must have killed Mrs Moira because she (Mrs Moira) took away both Mr Pembroke and his (Mr Ian's) inheritance, and he hated her. She says Mr Ian must have tried to kill Mr Pembroke for the money. The police are fools not to arrest him, she says. I told her Mr Ian couldn't have killed Moira or attacked his father as he was seeing round a racehorse training stable forty miles away at both times, with thirty or more witnesses. I said he obviously hadn't been driving the car which nearly ran him down. She says he could have arranged it. In my opinion, Miss S. doesn't want to be convinced of Mr Ian's innocence. She wants the killer to be Mr Ian because she doesn't want to find any others in her family guilty. If it is Mr Ian, she can bear it, she says, because it would serve him right for being Daddy's pet. (Muddled thinking!)

End of enquiry.

The three pages of notes on Serena were held together with a paperclip. I shuffled Serena to the bottom of the pack and came to the next paperclip, holding notes on Debs and Ferdinand.

Norman West used grey paperclips, not silver. Most appropriate, I thought.

The first page read:

Mrs Deborah Pembroke (27) second wife of Mr Ferdinand, lives with him at Gables Cottage, Reading Road, Wokingham, Berkshire.

Mrs Deborah works as a photographic model chiefly for mail-order catalogues, and was engaged in London on the Tuesday of Newmarket Sales modelling a succession of swimsuits. There were two other models there, also a photographer and two assistants, also a dresser, a representative of the mail-order firm and a notetaker. The swimsuit session went on until 6 pm. Mrs D. was there until the end. Vouched for without possibility of doubt. Mrs Debs has no firm alibi for the previous Friday evening. She finished work early in London at 3.30 (corroborated by mail-order people) and drove home. No witness to arrival (Mr Ferdinand was out).

Owing to her Tuesday engagement Mrs Debs could not have been at Newmarket. Friday, inconclusive.

Mrs Debs drives her own car, a scarlet Lancia. When I inspected it, it was dusty overall, with no sign of contact with Mr Ian.

Mrs Debs appeared undisturbed in the main by my questions and gave the following answers. She says her husband is the only good one in the

Pembroke family, the only one with any sense of humour. She says he listens to his mother too much, but she'll change that in time. She says they'll be well off one day as long as Mr Ian doesn't queer their pitch. She said that she was happy enough and is in no hurry to have children. She objected to my asking about such a personal matter.

End of enquiry.

I turned over the page and on the next one found:

Mr Ferdinand Pembroke (32) married to Deborah (2nd wife), lives at Gables Cottage, Reading Road, Wokingham, Berks.

Mr Ferdinand is a statistician/actuary for the Merchant General Insurance Company, head office in Reading, Berks. He works about a third of the time at home, where he has a computer with a link to the one in the insurance company offices. Both he and his company like the arrangement which means he can do exacting work without constant interruption. In addition, his company arranged for him to go on an anti-fraud course, as they are pleased with his ability.

I visited his office and explained to his boss that Mr Pembroke senior wanted to prove his children couldn't have been implicated in attacking him. Mr Ferdinand's boss wanted to be helpful, but in the end couldn't satisfy me.

Mr F. was not in the office on Friday afternoon, nor on the following Tuesday. On the Friday he'd worked at home, on Tuesday he was on the course.

I checked with the course at the Bingham Business Institute, City of London. Mr F. signed in on the first day, Monday, but after that no stringent attendance records were kept. Mr F. couldn't suggest anyone on the course who knew him well enough to swear he was there on Tuesday. I asked if he had made notes on the lectures. He said he didn't take any: the Tuesday lectures were about statistical probabilities and how to calculate them; basic stuff which he knew about. I checked this on the course schedule. The Tuesday lectures were as he said.

Mr Ferdinand drives a cream/grey Audi. It was clean when I saw it. Mr F. says he washes it himself with a brush on a hose (he showed it to me) and he does it frequently. He says he likes things to be clean.

Although he was working at home on the Friday afternoon, he was not in when Mrs Debs arrived from London. He says he had finished the job he'd been working on and decided to drive over to Henley and feed the ducks on the Thames. He found it peaceful. He liked the fresh air. He often did it, had done all his life, he said. He didn't know Mrs Debs was finishing work as early as 3.30 that day, but he said that wouldn't have stopped him going out. They were independent people and not accountable to each other for every minute.

I stopped reading and lifted my head. It was true that Ferdinand had always been attracted to the ducks. I couldn't count the number of times we'd walked along the Henley towpath, scattering bread and listening to the rude laughter of the mallards. Malcolm was the one who took us, whenever Alicia started throwing plates. She squawked rather like the ducks, I'd thought, and had had enough sense not to say so.

I went on reading:

Mr Ferdinand is hard working and successful, going to be more so. (My opinion and his boss's.) He has planning ability and energy. He is physically like his father, stocky and strong. (I remember Mr Pembroke 28 years ago. He threatened to throw me over his car when he found out I'd been following him, and I believed he could do it. Mr Ferdinand is the same.)

Mr F. can be very funny and good company, but his moods change to black disconcertingly fast. He is casual with his wife, not possessive. He is protective of his sister Serena. He is attentive to his mother, Mrs Alicia. He seems to have ambivalent feelings about Mr Pembroke and Mr Ian; I gathered from his inconsistent attitude that he liked them both in the past but no longer trusts them. Mr F. is capable of hate, I think.

End of enquiry.

I put Debs and Ferdinand to the back of the pile but had no mental stamina left for the next section on Ursula and Gervase. I put all the notes into the envelope and ate some pub steak instead and decided I would see the family in the age-reversed order Norman West had handed me, taking the easy ones first. Where was the bravado that had led me to tell Malcolm at Cambridge that I would stay with him just because it was dangerous?

Where indeed.

Somewhere under the rubble of Quantum.

In the morning, I rode out on the windy Downs, grateful for the simplicity of horses and for the physical pleasure of using one's muscles in the way they were trained for. Vigour seemed to flow of its own accord in my arms and legs, and I thought that maybe it was the same for a pianist sitting down after a few days to play; there was no need to work out what to do with one's fingers, it was easy, it was embedded in one's brain, the music came without thought.

I thanked my host sincerely after breakfast and drove towards Quantum thinking of the telephone call I'd made to Malcolm the evening before. It had been nearly midnight for me: nearly six, early evening, for him.

He had arrived safely, he said, and Dave and Sally Cander were true blue cronies. Ramsey Osborn had flown down. The Canders were giving a party, starting in five minutes. He'd seen some good horses. He'd had some great new ideas for spending money (wicked chuckle). How were things in England?

He sounded satisfactorily carefree, having shed depression with the miles, and I said things were the same as when he left except that the house was wrapped up in tarpaulins. The state of the house troubled him for roughly ten seconds, and after that he said he and Ramsey might be leaving Lexington on Tuesday or Wednesday; he wasn't sure.

'Wherever you go,' I said, 'will you please give the Canders a telephone number where I can reach you?'

'I promise,' he said blithely. 'Hurry up with your passport, and come over.'

'Soon.'

'I've got used to you being with me. Keep looking round for you. Odd. Must be senile.'

'Yes, you sound it.'

He laughed. 'It's a different world here, and I like it.'

He said goodbye and disconnected, and I wondered how many horses he would have bought by the time I reached him.

Back at the pub in Cookham, I changed out of riding clothes and dutifully telephoned Superintendent Yale.

He had nothing to tell me, nor I to tell him: the call was short.

'Where is your father?' he asked conversationally.

'Safe.'

He grunted. 'Phone me,' he said, and I said, 'Yes.'

With a heavy lack of enthusiasm I returned to the car and pointed its nose towards Bracknell, parking in one of the large featureless car parks and walking through to the High Street.

The High Street, long before, had been the main road through a minor country town; now it was a pedestrian backwater surrounded by the factories, offices and convoluted ring roads of mushroom progress. 'Deanna's Dance and Aerobics Studio' looked like a wide shop front flanked by a bright new shiny newsagent on one side and on the other a photographic shop whose window display seemed to consist chiefly of postcard-sized yellow fluorescent labels with prices on, mostly announcing '20% OFF'.

Deanna's studio consisted firstly of a reception area with a staircase on one side leading upwards. A young girl sitting behind the reception desk looked up and brightened when I pushed open the glass entrance door and stepped onto some thick grey carpet, but lost interest when I asked for Serena, explaining I was her brother.

'Back there,' she said. 'She's taking class at the moment.'

Back there was through white-painted double doors.

I went through and found myself in a windowless but brightly lit and attractive area of small tables and chairs, where several women sat drinking from polystyrene cups. The air vibrated with the pulse of music being played somewhere else, and when I again asked for Serena and was directed onwards, I came to its source.

The studio itself ran deeply back to end in a wall of windows overlooking a small strip of garden. The floor was of polished wood, sprung somehow so that it almost bounced underfoot. The walls were white except for the long left-hand one, which was entirely of looking-glass. The music, warm and insistent, invited rhythmic response.

Serena herself danced with her back to the mirror. Facing her, in three spread-out rows, was a collection of clients, all female, bouncing in unison on springy ankles, arms and legs swinging in circles and kicks. On every face, concentration and sweat. 'Go for the burn,' Serena commanded, looking happy, and her class with an increase of already frenetic energy, presumably went.

'Great, ladies, that's great,' Serena said eventually, stopping jumping and switching off the music machine which stood in a corner near where I'd come in. She gave me an unfriendly glance but turned with radiance back to the customers. 'If any of you want to continue, Sammy will be here within a minute. Take a rest, ladies.'

A few of the bodies stayed. Most looked at the

clock on the wall and filed panting into a door marked 'changing rooms'.

Serena said, 'What do you want?'

'Talk.'

She looked colourful but discouraging. She wore a bright pink long-sleeved body stocking with white bouncing shoes, pink and white leg-warmers and a scarlet garment like a chopped off vest. 'I'll give you five minutes,' she said.

She was hardly out of breath. A girl who was apparently Sammy Higgs came in in electric blue and started taking charge, and Serena with bad grace led me back through the refreshment area and the entrance hall and up the stairs.

'There are no classes up here just now. Say what you've come for and then go.'

Upstairs, according to a notice on the wall, Deanna offered ballroom dancing tuition, also 'ballet and posture'. Serena stood with her hands on her skinny pink hips and waited.

'Malcolm wants me to find out who bombed Quantum,' I said.

She glowered at me. 'Well, I didn't.'

'Do you remember the day old Fred blew up the tree stump?'

'No,' she said. She didn't bother to think, hadn't tried to remember.

'Thomas gave you a ride on his shoulders out of the

field, and the blast of the explosion knocked old Fred over.'

'I don't know what you're talking about.'

'Why are you so hostile?'

'I'm not. Where's Daddy?'

'With friends,' I said. 'It saddens him that you're hostile.'

She said bitterly, 'That's a laugh. He's rejected all of us except you. And I'll bet you killed Moira.'

'He hasn't rejected you,' I said. 'And I didn't.'

'He kicked us all out. I loved him when I was little.' Tears appeared suddenly in her eyes and she shook them angrily away. 'He couldn't wait to get rid of me.'

'He tried to keep you, but Alicia wouldn't have it. She fought him in the courts for custody, and won.'

'He didn't want me,' she said fiercely. 'He only said so to spite Mummy, to make her suffer. I know all about it.'

'Alicia told you?'

'Of course she did. Daddy couldn't wait to get rid of us, to get rid of Mummy, to get married again, to . . . to . . . throw everything about us out of the house, to tear out all the pretty rooms . . . blot us out.'

She was deeply passionate with the old feelings, still smouldering after twenty years. I remembered how upset I'd been when Alicia tore out my own mother's kitchen, how I'd felt betrayed and dispossessed. I had been six, as Serena had been, and I still remembered it clearly.

'Give him a chance,' I suggested.

'I did give him a chance. I offered to help him after Moira died and he still didn't want me. And look at the way he's behaving,' she said. 'Throwing money away. If he thinks I care a tuppenny damn about his stupid scholarships, he's a fool. You can toady up to him all you like, but I'm not going to. He can keep his damned money. I can manage without it.'

She looked hard-eyed and determinedly stubborn. The old man in all of us, I thought.

'You've had your five minutes,' she said. She side-stepped me in swift movements and made for the stairs. 'See you at the funeral.'

'Whose funeral?' I asked, following her.

'Anyone's,' she said darkly, and ran weightlessly down the stairs as if skimming were more normal than walking.

When I reached the entrance hall, she was vanishing through the white double doors. It was pointless to pursue her. I left Deanna's studio feeling I had achieved nothing, and with leaden spirits went back to the car and drove to Wokingham to call on Ferdinand.

I half-hoped he wouldn't be in, but he was. He came to the door frowning because I had interrupted him at his computer, and grudgingly let me in.

'We've nothing to say,' he said, but he sounded more resigned than forbidding; half-relaxed, as he'd been in my flat.

He led the way into the front room of the bungalow

he and Debs had bought on the road to Reading. The front room was his office, a perfectly natural arrangement to Ferdinand, since Malcolm's office had always been at home.

The rest of the bungalow, which I'd visited two or three times before, was furnished sparsely in accordance with Debs' and Ferdinand's joint dislike of dirt and clutter. One of the three bedrooms was completely empty, one held a single bed and a chest of drawers (for Serena's visits), and in the third, the couple's own, there was a mattress on a platform and a wall of cupboards and enclosed shelves that Ferdinand had put together himself. The sitting room held two chairs, a standard lamp, a lot of floor cushions and a television set. In the tidy kitchen, there was a table with four stools. All visible life was in the office, though even there, in direct contrast to Malcolm's comfortable shambles, a spartan order of neatness ruled.

Ferdinand's computer bore a screenful of graphics. He glanced at it and then looked with some impatience back to me.

'What do you want?' he asked. 'I've a lot to do after being away on a course.'

'Can't you save all that,' I gestured to the screen, 'or whatever it is you do? Record it, and come out to a pub for lunch.'

He shook his head and looked at his watch. Then, in indecision, said, 'I suppose I have to eat,' and fiddled about with the computer. 'All right. Half an hour, max.'

I drove us to the town centre and he pointed out a pub with a car park. The bar was full of business people similarly out for lunch breaks, and I bought scotch and sandwiches after a good deal of polite elbowing. Ferdinand had secured a table from which he was clearing the past customer's detritus with a finicky expression.

'Look,' I said, handing him his drink as we sat down, 'Malcolm wants me to find out who's trying to kill him.'

'It isn't me,' he said. He took a swallow, unconcerned.

'Do you remember old Fred blowing up the tree roots, that time? When we were about twelve or thirteen? When the blast blew old Fred flat?'

He stared. 'Yes, I do,' he said slowly, 'but that's years ago. It can't have anything to do with the house.'

'Why not?' I asked. 'That bang made a big impression on us. Memories last more or less for ever, they just need digging up. The explosives expert working at Quantum asked if I knew what cordite was, and I remembered old Fred.'

Ferdinand did his own digging. 'Black powder . . . in a box.'

'Yes, it's still there in the tool shed. Still viable, but not used on the house. They're working now on its being a homemade explosive called ANFO.'

Ferdinand was visibly shaken and after a minute said, 'I suppose I hadn't considered . . . what it was.'

'Do you know what ANFO is?' I asked.

He said no uncertainly, and I thought he wasn't being truthful. Perhaps he felt that knowing could be considered guilt. I needed to jolt him into being more positive. Into being an ally, if I could.

'Malcolm's made a new will,' I said.

'And left you the lot, I suppose,' he sneered bitterly.

'No,' I said. 'If he dies from normal causes, we all inherit equally.' I paused, and added an invention. 'If someone murders him, it all goes to charities. So how about you getting on the telephone and telling the whole tribe to help me find out who's trying to do them out of their future?'

CHAPTER FOURTEEN

In my room at Cookham in the evening, I read Norman West's notes on Gervase and Ursula.

Gervase first:

Mr Gervase Pembroke (35) lives with Mrs Ursula at 14 Grant St, Maidenhead, a detached house with a quarter-acre garden in good residential neighbourhood. They have been married for 11 years and have 2 daughters (8 and 6) both attending a private school.

Mr G. is a stockbroker who commutes to the City firm of Wells, Gibson & Cathcart. (Wells, Gibson and Cathcart have all died or retired long ago, but the respected name is kept.) Mr Gervase works for his own commission within the firm: each partner does. He has flexible working hours; he's his own boss to a great extent. He used to work harder than he does now but has become erratic of late, according to the firm's lady receptionist. She didn't like to say outright, but I gathered Mr G. sometimes returns from lunch the worse for drink, and sometimes doesn't return at all.

She didn't of course note down such times. She said she'd heard two of the other partners discussing Mr G., saying he'd lost his nerve and was selling his clients only gilts. They thought that too much playing safe was bad stockbroking. She had no qualms in denigrating Mr G., who she said has a filthy temper when things don't go his way, and never appreciates how hard she works (!)

I requested to interview Mr G. at his place of work. I was shown into his office and explained who I was. He said he knew. I said as a preliminary that I understood he was the illegitimate son of Mrs Alicia Pembroke, and the interview ended immediately. He physically hustled me out (bruise on left arm). He said I'd insulted him. Perhaps I did! I managed to say that if he could produce office records – letters written, brokerage transactions – for the Tuesday in question, he would be in the clear. He said to consult his secretary, which I did. Mr G. went into the office that morning, she confirmed, and dictated two letters. Mr G. told her he was going to see a new client, and left at 10.30 am. She didn't know who the client was, he was not listed on Mr G.'s office diary. It was more usual for new clients to come to the office, but not invariable. Mr G. didn't return to the office that day, but returned Wednesday in bad mood (with a hangover?).

Mr G. left the office the previous Friday (secretary's notes) at midday, didn't return. (Mr G. worked normally all day Monday.)

Mr G. commutes by train, leaves off-white Rover in station car park. His car clean and unmarked when I saw it.

Visited Mr G. at his home to ask about the client on Tuesday re solid alibi. Mr G. said none of my business. Guess: client was either a mistress or a bottle, or else Mr G. wants me to believe that.

Mr G.'s alcohol problem is serious (my opinion) but not incapacitating. He has strong masterful manner, but must have insecurities (illegitimacy??) to make him drink and treat people badly. (His secretary does not love him.) Mr G. appears to make good income, no sign of financial straits.

Attentive to Mrs Alicia. Bossy and possessive with his wife and children. Jealous of Mr Ian and (my judgement) fears him. (I don't know why this is. Something in the past? Mr Pembroke's preference?) Despises but also fears Mr Pembroke. (A lot of bluster when he talked of him.)

Mr G. is physically strong but getting less so, I'd think. Takes little exercise, somewhat overweight. Difficult personality. A bully.

End of enquiry.

I paperclipped Gervase together with a sigh. Norman West, for all his ineffective appearance, had a way of getting to the heart of things pretty smartly.

What had he made of Ursula, I wondered. Ursula, the quiet wife, who had talked in tears to Joyce. Pretty enough in an insipid way, she was like an unfinished painting, without highlights. Pleasant enough to me whenever Gervase allowed, she had never told me her thoughts. I turned with unexpected interest to the West view of Gervase's wife.

> Mrs Ursula Pembroke (35) wife of Mr Gervase, lives with him at 14 Grant St, Maidenhead. She has no employment beyond looking after children and household. A cleaner comes in Monday to Friday mornings, 9 am to 1 pm, stays Tuesdays and Thursdays until 4 pm, also babysits whenever asked. (I had to make two visits to Mrs U. On the first occasion she had been crying and wouldn't talk. On the second she was cooperative.)
>
> The daughters' school is at the other end of Maidenhead. Mrs U. shares the school run with a family nearby; Mrs U.'s mornings are Tuesday and Thursday; afternoons Mon., Wed. and Fri. Mrs U.'s car is a cream Austin. Clean.
>
> On the Friday of the attack on Mr Pembroke, the daughters were invited to tea by the other school run family (the mother corroborates). Mrs U. left

the daughters there after school (4 pm). Picked them up about 6.30.

On the following Tuesday, Mrs U. arranged for the cleaner to stay and give the daughters their tea as she wanted a day out in London. The cleaner told me Mrs U. did the school run, came back and changed, and drove away to the station to catch the train. She (Mrs U.) said she would be back late as she would go to the cinema after she'd done her shopping. Mrs U. has done this several times lately. She returned at 10 pm. Cleaner went home. (Mrs U. gave me permission to consult the cleaner.) Mrs U. says she didn't go to the cinema, she didn't like the look of the films, she just had dinner in a steak house. She also said she had been into a church to pray. She hadn't bought anything (nothing fitted).

Mrs U. nervous and evasive about trip to London. Did she go to Newmarket? Possible (my opinion) that she goes to London to meet someone, doesn't want cleaner or husband to know. Who? Lover? Not possible, she hasn't the air, they can't hide that inner excitement. Priest? Friend unacceptable to Mr G.? Doctor? Some sort of solace, I would say.

Mrs U. unhappy woman but wouldn't unbutton. Loyal. Any wife of Mr G. liable to be unhappy (my opinion). Mrs U. doesn't like having the cleaner around for so long. Mr G. insists on cleanliness. Mrs U. gets tired of the cleaner's incessant chatter. All adds to Mrs U.'s stress. Mrs U. would like a job or to do voluntary work. Mr G. won't have it. 'The children come first.' (Mrs U. obviously very fond of the children.)

Mrs U. wishes Mr Pembroke would give all the family a lot of money now so that they would stop griping about it. She sees nothing wrong in Mr Ian, but her husband won't let her talk to him. She could like Mr Pembroke, she thinks he's funny and generous, but her husband ditto. She can't go against her husband. She has no money of her own, I'd say. She's in a trap. (Can't support children herself, couldn't leave without them.)

Does she believe killing Mr Pembroke could solve her problems? Does she believe if Mr G. becomes richer it will make things right? I could tell her it won't.

End of enquiry.

Poor Mrs U. Poor Ursula. Could she have blown up Quantum? Perhaps, if she'd wanted to. She sounded desperate enough for anything, but if she had any sense, her desperation should drive her to beg from Malcolm, not to kill him.

I clipped Ursula behind Gervase: forever in his shadow.

I wondered why she'd married him, but then I'd attended their wedding also, and if one hadn't in the past been on the wrong end of his glowing cigarette, one could have taken him as he seemed on the surface, confident, good looking, positive and strong. A rising young stockbroker. A catch.

I put Gervase and Ursula back in the envelope but they wouldn't stay there, they stuck like burrs in my mind.

There must be thousands, hundreds of thousands of sad marriages like that, I thought, where the unhappiness came from inside. Probably one could more easily withstand disasters that came from without, survive wars, poverty, illness, grief. Much harder to find any good way forward when personality disintegrated. Each of them was disintegrating, Ursula because of Gervase, Gervase because of . . .

Because of Malcolm? Because of Malcolm's boredom with Vivien, his affair with Alicia, his quick marriage to Joyce? Because of illegitimacy? But Ferdinand had been a product of the same process, and Ferdinand was whole.

There were questions without answers. The most likely answers were often wrong. I didn't know why Gervase was disintegrating: I thought only that the process had already begun when we both lived at Quantum; had maybe begun in the womb.

I slept with troubled dreams and went to ride the next morning as if for therapy and release. Solace, Norman West's word, met the case. The raw morning, the moving horses, the filthy language and the crude jokes, a daily fix of the sort of reality I'd chosen at eighteen. I didn't know why I'd liked horses so much.

Choice sprang from deep needs, but where did the needs come from?

I wasn't accustomed to thinking in that way. I usually coasted along, not worrying much, doing my job, enjoying riding in races, making love without strings. Lazy in many respects, I dared say, but uncomplicated. An opt-out that had come to an abrupt end with meeting Malcolm at Newmarket.

It was Tuesday.

Ursula's cleaner, I thought, driving back to Cookham, would currently be chatting away with no respite for Ursula until the girls got back from school. I wondered if Ursula was quietly going bananas at 14 Grant St, Maidenhead. I changed into ordinary clothes and went along there to find out.

The cleaner came to the door; middle-aged, in a flowered overall, with an inquisitive face. Mrs Pembroke was lying down with a headache, she said, and yes, perhaps she could go upstairs and ask her if her brother-in-law might take her out to lunch. Perhaps I would like to wait in the hall.

I waited, and presently Ursula came downstairs looking wan and wearing a coat and gloves.

'Oh!' she said faintly when she saw me. 'I thought it was Ferdinand.'

I'd hoped she would. I said, 'Where would you best like to go?'

'Oh.' She was irresolute. She looked back up the stairs and saw the cleaner watching interestedly from the landing. If she didn't come out with me, she'd be stuck with explaining.

'Come on,' I said persuasively. 'The car's warm.'

It sounded a silly thing to say, but I suppose she listened to the intention, not the words. She continued across the hall and came with me out of the front door, closing it behind us.

'Gervase won't like this,' she said.

'Why should he know?'

'She'll find a way of telling him.' She gestured back to the house, to the cleaner. 'She likes to make trouble. It brightens up her life.'

'Why do you keep her?'

She shrugged. 'I hate housework. If I sack her, I'd have to do it. Gervase thinks she's thorough, and he pays her. He said he wouldn't pay anyone else.'

She spoke matter-of-factly, but I was startled by the picture of domestic tyranny. We got into the car and I drove out of the town and towards the village of Bray, and twice more on the way she said, 'Gervase won't like this.' We stopped at a small roadside restaurant and she chose homemade soup and moussaka, several times looking over her shoulder as if her husband would materialize and pounce.

I ordered a carafe of red wine. Not for her, she protested, but when it came she drank it almost absent-mindedly. She had removed the coat and gloves to reveal a well-worn grey skirt topped by a blue sweater with a cream shirt underneath. She wore a string of pearls. Her dark hair was held back at one side by a tortoiseshell slide, and there was no lipstick on her pale mouth. The sort of appearance, I supposed, that Gervase demanded.

When the soup came, she said, 'Ferdinand phoned last night and told Gervase that Malcolm had made a new will, according to you.'

'Yes, he made one,' I agreed. 'He showed it to me.'

'Gervase didn't tell me,' she said. 'He phoned Alicia and told her, and I listened. That's what usually happens. He doesn't tell me things, he tells his mother.'

'How do you get on with Alicia?' I asked.

She very carefully drank the soup already in her spoon. She spoke as if picking her way through a minefield.

'My mother-in-law,' she said intensely, 'has caused more trouble than anyone since Eve. I can't talk about her. Drink your soup.'

I had the impression that if she once started talking about Alicia, she would never stop. I wondered how to start her, but when I tentatively asked what she meant about trouble, she shook her head vehemently.

'Not here,' she said.

I left it. She talked about her children, which she could do without strain, looking almost animated, which saw us through to the moussaka.

'What do you do on your trips to London?' I asked casually.

She looked amazed, then said, 'Oh yes, that

wretched Mr West. Gervase was furious with him. Then Gervase was annoyed with me also, and wanted to know where I'd been. I'd been wandering around, that's all.' She ate her moussaka methodically. 'Ferdinand told Gervase and Gervase told Alicia something about a tree stump. What was that all about?'

I explained about the cordite.

She nodded. 'Gervase told Alicia he'd had a good laugh when old Fred was knocked flat.'

She seemed undisturbed by the thought of explosives. We finished the lunch, I paid the bill, and we set off on the short road back to Maidenhead. A little way along there, I stopped the car in a lay-by and switched off the engine.

She didn't ask why we'd stopped. After a pause she said, 'Alicia is ruining our marriage, I suppose you know that?'

I murmured an assent.

'I'd known Gervase for only four months when we got married. I didn't realize . . . She's twisted him from birth, hasn't she? With her awful lies and spite. She sets him against you all the time. Gervase says terrible things about you sometimes . . . I mean, violent . . . I hate it. I try to tell him not to, but he doesn't listen to me, he listens to her. She says you sneer at him, you think you're much superior, because you're legitimate. I know you don't. Gervase believes her though. She tells him over and over that Malcolm threw them out and never loved them. She's wicked. And look what she's done to Serena. Gervase says she was a bright girl, but Alicia wouldn't let her stay on at school, Alicia wanted her to be a little girl, not to grow up. And Serena hates all men, and it's Alicia's fault. The only men Serena will let touch her are Ferdinand and Gervase. It's such a waste. Alicia got rid of Ferdinand's first wife, did you know? Went on and on at her until she couldn't stand it and left. I don't know how Debs puts up with her. It's driving me insane, you know, her drip, drip, drip. She's the worst enemy you'll ever have. If it was you that had been murdered, she would have done it.'

'She wasn't always like that,' I said, as she paused. 'When she lived at Quantum, she treated me the same as Ferdinand and Gervase.'

'Then it must have started when Malcolm kept you there on your own, and as she's got older it's got worse. She's much worse now than she was when we got married, and she was bad enough then. She hated Coochie, you know, and Coochie was nice, wasn't she? I was sorry when Coochie died. But Coochie banned all the family from staying in the house except you, and I should think that's when Alicia turned against you. Or let it all out. I bet it was there inside all the time. Like Gervase keeps things in and lets them out violently . . . so does Serena, and Ferdinand too . . . they're all like that. I wish Alicia would die. I can understand people wanting to kill. I would like to kill Alicia.'

She stopped abruptly, the raw truth quivering in her voice.

'Drive me home,' she said. 'I shouldn't have said that.'

I didn't immediately restart the engine. I said, 'Is it Alicia that's causing Gervase to drink?'

'Oh!' Ursula gulped, the flow of anger ending, the misery flooding back. 'It's just . . . everything. I can see he's unhappy, but he won't let me help him, he won't talk to me, he just talks to *her*, and she makes it worse.'

I sighed and set off towards Grant Street. Alicia hadn't quite reached sixty: the worst of the witches could outlive them all.

'I shouldn't have told you all this,' Ursula said, when I stopped at the door. 'Gervase won't like it.'

'Gervase won't know what you've said.'

She fished a handkerchief out of her handbag and blew her nose.

'Thank you for the lunch. Did your mother tell you we've had lunch a few times in London, she and I? She gives me good advice. I can't tell Gervase, he'd be furious.'

I nodded. 'Joyce told me you were friends.'

'She's awfully catty about Alicia. It cheers me up no end.' She gave me a wan smile and got out of the car. She waved as she opened her front door: I waved back and drove away, and covered the few miles to Cookham.

I thought it might be interesting to see what Norman West had made of Alicia, and I searched through the notes until I came to her.

West had written:

Mrs Alicia Pembroke (59) refused to speak to me at all on my first visit and was ungracious and edgy on my second.

Mrs Alicia lives at 25 Lions Court, London Road, Windsor, a block of flats. She still maintains she can't remember what she was doing on the Friday or the Tuesday: she was pottering about, she says. 'One day is much like another.' I think she's being obstructive for the sake of it.

Mrs A. drives a big silver/grey Fiat. Clean, no damage.

Mrs A. antagonistic to me personally because of my following her in Mrs Joyce's divorce case, although in the end she benefited.

Twenty-eight years ago! She remembers every detail of that time. Can't remember last Tuesday . . .

I asked her if she had ever engaged me to work for her. She said no. (?)

Mrs A. has changed from the Miss A. I followed. Miss A. was full of giggles, very little-girl. Mrs A. still dresses very young, acts young, but is embittered. Odd how some women flower in love affairs and wither in marriage. Seen it often. Seems as if the spice of secrecy and naughtiness is what they love, not the man himself.

Mrs A. very bitter on subject of Mr Pembroke spending money. Mr Ian's name brought angry looks. Mrs A. turned me out.

End of enquiry.

Short and unsweet, I thought.

I couldn't face going to see Alicia at that moment. I didn't think her physically capable of carrying Malcolm while he was unconscious, and I didn't think her efficient enough to construct a bomb: good enough reasons for avoiding something I wanted to do as much as jump into a crocodile-infested swamp.

I didn't want to talk to Gervase either, but that couldn't be as easily avoided.

I drove back to Grant Street in the early evening and parked along the road from No 14 waiting for the master to return. It wasn't until I was sitting there that I remembered Norman West's advice about defence. Pepper . . . paint . . . I couldn't see myself throwing either in Gervase's eyes, or anyone else's for that matter. Gervase was, goddammit, my brother. Half-brother. Cain killed Abel. Abel hadn't had his pepper ready, or his paint.

Upon that sober reflection, Gervase came home.

His Rover turned into his house's short driveway and pulled up outside the garage. Gervase, carrying a briefcase, let himself in through the front door. Five minutes later, I walked along the road and rang the bell.

The door was opened by one of the children, who called over her shoulder, 'It's Ian.'

Gervase, still in his City suit, came immediately into the hall from his sitting room, looking inhospitable and carrying a cut-glass tumbler half filled with what I expected was scotch.

'Ferdinand phoned me,' he said authoritatively. 'It's the police's business to look into the bombing of Quantum, not yours.'

'Malcolm asked me to,' I said.

'You'd better come in, I suppose.' He was grudging, but pointed me to the room he'd left. 'Do you want a drink?'

'Yes, please.'

He poured from the scotch bottle into a duplicate tumbler, and handed me the glass, gesturing to the matching jug of water which stood on a silver tray. I diluted my drink and sipped it, and said, 'Thanks.'

He nodded, busy with his own.

There was no sign of Ursula, but I could hear the two girls' high voices in the kitchen and supposed she was with them. They would tell her I had come, and she would be worrying about her lunch.

'Ferdinand told me about Malcolm's new will,' Gervase said with annoyance. 'It's ridiculous putting in that clause about being murdered. What if some random mugger bumps him off? Do we all lose our inheritance?'

'Some random mugger is unlikely. A paid assassin might not be.'

Gervase stared. 'That's rubbish.'

'Who killed Moira?' I said. 'Who's tried three times to kill Malcolm?'

'How should I know?'

'I think you should put your mind to it.'

'No. It's for the police to do that.' He drank. 'Where is he now?'

'Staying with friends.'

'I offered him a bed here,' he said angrily, 'but I'm not good enough, I suppose.'

'He wanted to be away from the family,' I said neutrally.

'But he's with you.'

'No, not any more.'

He seemed to relax a little at the news. 'Did you quarrel again?' he said hopefully.

We were still standing in the centre of the room, as the offer of a drink hadn't extended to a chair also. There were fat chintz-covered armchairs in a stylized flower pattern on a mottled grey carpet, heavy red curtains and a brick fireplace with a newly-lit fire burning. I'd been in his house about as seldom as in Ferdinand's, and I'd never been upstairs.

'We haven't quarrelled,' I said. 'Do you remember when old Fred blew up the tree stump?'

He found no difficulty in the change of subject.

'Ferdinand said you'd asked that,' he said. 'Yes, of course I remember.'

'Did Fred show you how he set off the explosive?'

'No, he damn well didn't. You're not trying to make out that I blew up the house, are you?' His anger, always near the surface, stoked up a couple of notches.

'No,' I said calmly. 'I should have said, did Fred show you or anyone else how he set off the explosive.'

'I can only speak for myself,' he said distinctly, 'and the answer is no.'

Gervase was heavy and, I thought, getting heavier. His suit looked filled. I had never quite grown to his height. He was the tallest and biggest of all Malcolm's children and easily the most forceful. He looked a strong successful man, and he was cracking up for lack of a piece of paper that no one gave a damn about except himself.

Perhaps, I thought, there was something of that obsessiveness in us all. In some it was healthy, in others destructive, but the gene that had given Malcolm his Midas obsession with gold had been a dominant strain.

Gervase said, 'Will Malcolm ante up anything before he dies?'

His voice was as usual loud and domineering, but I looked at him speculatively over my glass. There had been an odd sub-note of desperation, as if it weren't just of academic interest to him, but essential. Norman West's notes recycled themselves: '. . . lost his nerve and was selling only gilts. Too much playing safe was bad stockbroking . . .' Gervase, who had seemed comfortably fixed, might all of a sudden not be.

I answered the words of the question, not the implications. 'I did ask him to. He said he would think about it.'

'Bloody old fool,' Gervase said violently. 'He's playing bloody games with us. Chucking the stuff away just to spite us. Buying bloody *horses.* I could strangle him.' He stopped as if shocked at what he'd more or less shouted with conviction. 'Figure of speech,' he said, hard-eyed.

'I'll try again,' I said, ignoring it, 'but Vivien tried, and rubbed him up the wrong way so that he stuck his toes in. Malcolm's obstinate, the way we all are, and the more anyone tries to push him, the harder he'll resist.'

'It's you that got him to buy horses. He wouldn't have thought of it on his own.' He was glaring at me. 'Two million pounds for a bloody *colt.* Do you realize what two million pounds means? Have you any idea? *Two million pounds* for a four-legged nothing? He's raving mad. Two million pounds invested in any one of us would give us freedom from worry for the rest of our lives, and he goes and spends it on a *horse.* Retarded children are bad enough, half a million for retarded children . . . but that's not enough for him, is it? Oh no. He buys that bloody horse Blue Clancy, and how many more millions did that cost him? How many?' He was insistent, belligerent, demanding, his chin thrust aggressively forward.

'He can afford it,' I said. 'I think he's very rich.'

'Think!' Gervase grew even angrier. 'How do you know he isn't flinging away every penny? I'll find a way of stopping him. He's *got* to be stopped.'

He suddenly stretched out his free hand and plucked my half-full glass from my grasp.

'Go on, get out of here,' he said. 'I've had enough.'

I didn't move. I said, 'Throwing me out won't solve any problems.'

'It'll make a bloody good start.' He put both glasses on the table and looked ready to put thought into action.

'When Malcolm fled to Cambridge,' I said, 'did Alicia tell you where he was?'

'What?' It stopped him momentarily. 'I don't know what you're talking about. Go on, get out.'

'Did you telephone to Malcolm's hotel in Cambridge?'

He hardly listened. He embarked on a heartfelt tirade. 'I'm fed up with your sneers and your airs and graces. You think you're better than me, you always have, and you're *not*. You've always weaselled into Malcolm's good books and set him against us and he's blind and stupid about you . . . and get out.' He stepped forward threateningly, one hand in a fist.

'But you still want me to plead your case,' I said, standing still.

His mouth opened but no words came out.

'Alicia tells you I sneer at you,' I said, 'but I don't. She tells you lies, you believe them. I've never set Malcolm against you. You hit me now, and I might think of it. If you want me to try to get him to cough up, you'll put that fist down and give me my scotch back, and I'll drink it and go.'

After a long staring pause, he turned his back on me. I took it as agreement to the terms and picked up one of the glasses, not sure whether it was mine or his.

It was his. The drink was much stronger, hardly any water in it at all. I put it down and picked up the other. He didn't turn round, didn't notice.

'Gervase,' I said dispassionately, 'try a psychiatrist.'

'Mind your own bloody business.'

I drank a mouthful of scotch but as a token only, and put the glass down again.

'Goodbye,' I said.

He still showed me his back, and was silent. I shrugged wryly and went out into the hall. Ursula and the two girls stood in the kitchen doorway looking anxious. I smiled at them lopsidedly and said to Ursula, 'We'll get through it somehow.'

'I hope so.' Forlorn hope, she was saying.

'I'll be back,' I said, not knowing if I meant it, but meaning anyway that anything I could do to help her or Gervase, I would do.

I let myself out of the front door quietly, and back

at Cookham telephoned to the Canders in Lexington. I talked to Mrs Cander; Sally.

Malcolm had gone to Stamford, Connecticut with Ramsey, she said. She thought they were fixing some kind of deal. She and Dave had really enjoyed Malcolm's visit and Malcolm had just loved the horse farms. Yes, of course she had Ramsey's phone number, he was an old friend. She read it out to me. I thanked her and she said sure thing and to have a nice day.

Ramsey and Malcolm were out. A woman who answered said to try at five-thirty. I tried at five-thirty Connecticut time and they were still out. The woman said Mr Osborn was a busy man and would I like to leave a message. I asked her to tell Mr Pembroke that his son Ian had phoned, but that there was no special news. She would do that, she said.

I went to bed and in the morning rode out on the Downs, and afterwards, from the house of the trainer whose horses I was riding, got through to Superintendent Yale's police station. He was there and came on the line.

'Where are you?'

'At the moment in a racing stable near Lambourn.'

'And your father?'

'I don't know.'

He made a disbelieving grunt. 'What time could you meet me at Quantum House?'

I looked at my watch. 'In riding clothes,' I said, 'in

forty-five minutes. If you want me to change, add on an hour.'

'Come as you are,' he said. 'Mr Smith says there's something to see.'

CHAPTER FIFTEEN

At Quantum, the heap of rubble had reduced to merely a mess.

I walked round to the back of the house and found two men in hard hats barely ankle deep as they methodically removed debris brick by brick from house to rubbish skip. The wind had abated and the clouds had relented to the extent that a pale sunshine washed the scene, making it to my eyes more of a wasteland than ever.

Superintendent Yale stood beside a trestle table that had been erected on the lawn, with the explosives expert Smith in his beige overalls and blue hat standing close beside him, heads bent in conference. There were no spectators any more on the far side of the rope across the lawn, not even Arthur Bellbrook. I walked over to the experts and said good morning.

'Good morning,' they said, looking up. 'Glad you came,' Smith said.

He stretched out a casual hand and picked up an object from the table, holding it out to me.

'We've found this,' he said. 'What do you think?'

I took the thing from him. It had been a coil of thin plastic-coated wire, but the coils had been stretched so that the wire was straighter, but still curled. It was about eighteen inches long. The plastic coating had been white, I thought. About an inch of bare wire stuck out of the plastic at each end. Onto the plastic, near one end, someone had bonded a hand from a clock. The hand pointed to the bare wire, so that the wire was an extension of the hand.

I looked at it with despair, though not with shock. I'd been fearing and hoping . . . trying not to believe it possible.

When I didn't ask what it was, Yale said with awakening suspicion, 'Does your silence mean that you know what it is?'

I looked up at the two men. They hadn't expected me to know, were surprised by my reaction, even astonished.

'Yes,' I said drearily. 'I do know. Did you find any other bits?'

Smith pointed to a spot on the table. I took a step sideways and stared down. There were some pieces of metal and plastic, but not those I'd expected. No cogwheels or springs. A grey plastic disc with a small hole in the centre.

'Was this a clock?' I said dubiously.

'A battery-driven clock,' Smith said. 'There's the coil from the electric motor.'

The coil was tiny, about a centimetre in diameter.

'How did you find it in all this rubbish?' I asked.

'We found various remains of the padded box which used to stand at the foot of Mr Pembroke's bed. These small pieces became embedded in the lid when the box blew apart. The wire with the clock's hand on it, and this . . .' he picked up the flat plastic disc ' . . . were in the same area.' He turned the plastic disc over to reveal a clock face on the other side. 'There should also be at least one other piece of wire somewhere, and some of the clock case and a battery or two, but we haven't found those yet. This was not actually an alarm clock, I don't think. We've found no sign of an alarm mechanism.'

'No, it won't have been an alarm clock,' I said.

The superintendent had been growing restive during Smith's account and could contain himself no longer.

'Will you please explain your familiarity with this device,' he said formidably. 'Did the gardener use this sort of thing for blowing up the tree trunk?'

'No, I don't think so. This device wasn't meant for setting off bombs. It was a toy.'

'What sort of toy?'

'Well . . . it was for switching things on. Torch bulbs, mostly. Like the lights we had on a station in a train set. A buzzer, sometimes. It was incredibly simple.'

'Explain,' Yale commanded.

I glanced at Smith. He was nodding resignedly.

'You get an old or cheap clock,' I said. 'We had

wind-up clocks, not a battery clock. You fix a length of wire to one of the hands, like this, so that a bare bit of wire sticks out and makes the hand much longer.'

'The hands are still on the clock, I take it?'

'Oh yes. Though sometimes we'd pull the minute hand off and just use the hour hand, because it's stronger, even though it's shorter. All you need is for the bare wire to reach out beyond the edge of the clock face. We used glue to stick the wire to the hand. Then you have a long bit of wire coming out from the centre of the front of the clock, and you fasten the free end of that to a battery. One of those nine-volt batteries with things like press-studs at the end.'

Smith was still nodding. Yale looked very much as if I shouldn't know such things.

'We made quite a lot of other gadgets,' I said, hearing the defensiveness in my voice. 'Buzzers for morse codes. Rudimentary telephones. Not just time switches. I made a lock once which could only be operated with a straight piece of wire.' And it still worked fine, although I wasn't going to show him.

Yale sighed. 'So in this case, we've got the wire fixed to the clock's hand at one end and to a battery at the other, right? Go on from there.'

'You need two more lengths of wire. One goes from the battery to whatever you want to activate. In our case, it was usually a torch bulb screwed into a metal holder. We fastened a bare end of wire to the metal holder. Then the third wire went back from the metal holder to the clock. We fixed this wire with glue to the clock case itself, not to the hands, in such a way that the bare end of wire was pointing out forwards, towards you if you were facing the clock like this.' I demonstrated with the clock face. 'We usually stuck it on over the number twelve, at the top, but you could fix it anywhere you liked. Then you wind up the clock and set the hand with the wire where you want it, and just wait. The wired hand travels round towards the jutting out wire and eventually hits against it at right angles. The circuit is thus complete from the clock wires to the battery to the light and back to the clock, so the light goes on. The clock hand keeps on trying to go round and the jutting wire keeps stopping it, so the light stays on. Well . . .' I finished lamely, 'that's what happened when we made them.'

'Them?' Yale said with apprehension.

'They were easy to make. They were interesting. I don't know how many we had, but quite a few.'

'My God.'

'There might be one still in the playroom,' I said. 'The old train sets are there.'

Yale looked at me balefully. 'How many of your family saw these devices?' he asked.

'Everyone.'

'Who made them?'

'I did, Gervase did, and Ferdinand. Thomas did. I don't remember who else.'

'But your whole family knows how to make a simple time switch?'

'Yes, I should think so.'

'And why,' he said, 'haven't you mentioned this before?'

I sighed and twisted the wired clock hand round in my fingers. 'Because,' I said, 'for starters I didn't think of it until after I'd left here the other day. After we'd been digging out the black powder and so on, and I'd been looking back to the past. I didn't want you to find this. I wanted you to find something sophisticated, that no one in the family could have thought up.'

'Hm,' he said, seeming to accept it. 'How many people outside your family knew about these clocks?'

'Several did, I suppose, but it was such a long time ago. No one would remember, would they?'

'They might.' Yale turned to Smith. 'This toy, is this really what set off the bomb?'

Smith nodded. 'It sounds just right. Wire in a detonator where the Pembroke children had a torch bulb . . .' He spread his hands. 'It wouldn't need more current than that.'

Not surprisingly, they decided to take a look in the playroom. They picked their way cautiously across the ankle-twisting rubble and headed for the passage which was comparatively clear by this time. The playroom, when we reached it, was shadowy inside, with the windows boarded up. Light of sorts seeped in through the door, but it took a few minutes for eyes to acclimatize, during which Yale bumped into the bicycles, knocking them over. I helped him pick them up. He wanted to know whose they were, and I told him about Peter and Robin.

He made no especial comment but watched while I went over to the shelves and began peering into boxes. I hadn't been in the room at all since the twins had gone, and their own playthings had overlaid those outgrown and abandoned by their elder brothers and sisters so that most of what I was looking at was unfamiliar and seemed to belong to strangers. It took several minutes to locate the box I thought I wanted, and to pick it off the shelves and put it on the table.

Someone, Coochie I dared say, had packed the trains away for good after Gervase and Ferdinand had left and I'd been busy with school and horses. At one time, the tracks had run permanently round half the room, but Peter and Robin had been television-watchers more than the rest of us, and hadn't dragged them out again. I opened the box and found the old treasures undisturbed, looking more battered than I'd thought, with rust on the much-used wheels.

I lifted out a couple of engines and some coaches, then followed them with a tunnel, a signal box with green and red bulbs and a brown plastic railway station adorned with empty bulb-holders among the advertisement stickers. I suppose to any adult, his childhood's rediscovered toys look smaller, deader, less appealing than he remembers. The trains were dusty and sad, relics ready for the skip outside, melancholic. The little lights had long gone out.

I took everything out of the box, but there were no clocks.

'Sorry,' I said. 'They could be in anything, really. If they're here.'

Smith began looking into any box whose contents weren't easily identifiable by the picture on top. Yale, with a no-hope expression, followed suit. I packed the trains back into oblivion with regret.

'Well, just look here,' Smith said suddenly. 'Gold mine.'

He had produced from a jumble of Lego constructions a bright new-looking clock with a Mickey Mouse face in unfaded technicolour. Mickey's hands in fat white gloves were the hands of the clock. To the minute hand was fixed a coil of white plastic-covered wire. A second white coil was stuck to the scarlet clock casing, its bared end jutting out over noon. When Smith held it all up, the white coils stretched out and down like curling streamers.

I looked at it blankly.

'I've never seen that one before,' I said. 'We didn't make them decorative. Ours were . . .' I sought for the word ' . . . utilitarian.'

Smith picked away among the Lego. 'Can't find a battery,' he reported. 'Nor a torch bulb, for that matter.' A pause. 'Wait a minute . . .' He rattled around and, finally, triumphantly produced a red and white Lego tower with a bulb-holder lodged inside near the top.

'A lighthouse, wouldn't you say?' he asked, standing it upright. 'Neat.'

'Someone made this for your twin brothers,' Yale said. 'Are you sure you never saw it?'

I shook my head. 'I didn't live here then, only visited. The twins had a short attention span, anyway. They tired of new toys pretty quickly. Always wanted to get on with the next thing.'

'I'll find out who made it,' Yale said. 'Can you sort out a box to put it in? I'll give you a receipt, of course.'

Smith found him an empty Lego box and into it they packed the bright co-star of an act that had brought half the house down. There was room in the box for the lighthouse, so they took that, too. Yale solemnly wrote a receipt on a page of his notebook and gave it to me, and with him carrying the box we went out into the daylight, blinking as our eyes adjusted after the gloom.

As we walked back in the general direction of the trestle table, Smith said, 'We've put all the clothes we've found on a table in the garage. I'm afraid they're mostly torn and unwearable, but you might want to see. All the personal things we've salvaged are in a cardboard carton. Do you want to take those today, or wait until we're finished?'

'Look now, take later,' I said.

Smith half smiled. 'They're in that box under the table.'

I squatted down beside the brown cardboard carton and opened the top flaps. Inside there was quite a good collection of dusty bits and pieces, more than I would have imagined. I picked out one of Malcolm's precious brushes and ran my finger over the gold and silver chased backing. The dust came off and the metal shone in the sunlight. He would be pleased, I thought.

'We've found five of those,' Smith observed. 'Two are badly dented, the others look all right.'

'There were eight,' I said. 'In his dressing room.'

He shrugged. 'We might find more.'

I turned over a few things in the box. Mostly they were uninteresting, like a bottle of aspirins from the bathroom. At the bottom, I came across one or two things of my own – an empty spongebag and the tape recorder.

I lifted the recorder out, straightened up and put it on the table. Pressed the start button. Absence of results.

'It was just a chance you might want it,' Smith said philosophically. 'It doesn't work as it is, but you might want to get it mended.'

'Probably cheaper to buy a new one,' I said. I pressed the rewind and fast-forward buttons pointlessly, and then the eject button, which worked. The plastic lid staggered open, revealing a tape within. I had to think for a minute which tape it was and then remembered it was only the one from my answering machine; nothing interesting. I shut the lid and put the recorder back in the box under the table.

'If you find my camera, now that would be good news,' I said, straightening again.

Yale had lost interest and was preparing to leave.

'Was it yours?' said Mr Smith. 'It's in the skip, I'm afraid. Badly smashed.'

'Oh well . . .'

'Were you insured?'

I shook my head. 'Never thought of it.'

Smith made sympathetic gestures and went back to the rubble. The superintendent said I should telephone him the following morning without fail. He ran his thumb and finger down his moustache and asked me if I now knew who had bombed the house.

'No,' I said. 'I don't. Do you?'

He wouldn't say he didn't, but he didn't. He picked up the Lego box and marched off with it, and I went to look at the clothes in the garage.

Nothing was worth saving, I thought. All highly depressing. My jodhpur boots with the toes flattened, Malcolm's vicuna coats with triangular tears. I left it all as it lay and started out on a quick hike round the garden to make sure all was well with the gold, and came upon Arthur Bellbrook digging potatoes within six feet of it. My heart jumped a bit. His was undisturbed.

We exchanged good mornings and remarks about

the weather. He asked what he should do with the potatoes and I told him to take them home. He nodded his thanks. He complained that the pick-up trucks for the rubbish skips were ruining the lawn. He said souvenir hunters had stripped Mrs Pembroke's fancy greenhouse of every single geranium, including the cuttings, but not to worry, without glass in the windows they would have died in the first frost. It had been a mild autumn, but frost would come soon.

He looked along the length of the kitchen garden, his back towards the end wall. He would dig everything over, he said, ready for winter.

I left him bending again to his task, not sure whether he was a guardian of the gold or a threat to it. Malcolm had a nerve, I thought, hiding his stockpile in that place and seeing Arthur work close to it day after day. Malcolm had more nerve than was good for him.

I drove to the pub in Cookham, where they were getting used to my hours, took a bath, put on trousers, shirt and jersey and, accompanied by Norman West's notes, went down to the bar for a drink before lunch. I read:

> Mr Thomas Pembroke (39) lives with his wife Berenice at 6 Arden Haciendas, Sonning, Nr. Reading, in the strip of new townhouses where old Arden House used to be. Two daughters (9 and 7) go to comprehensive school.
>
> Mr T. used to work as quantity surveyor for

Reading firm of biscuit makers, Shutleworth Digby Ltd. He got sacked for wrong estimates several weeks ago. I was told unofficially at the firm that he'd cost them thousands by ordering six times the glacé cherries needed for a run of 'dotted pinks'. (Had to laugh!) No laughing matter when tons of sliced almonds turned up after 'nut fluffs' had been discontinued. Mr T. didn't contest sacking, just left. Firm very relieved. Mr T. had been getting more and more useless, but had long service.

Mr T. didn't tell his wife he'd lost his job, but went off as if to work every day. (Common reaction.) On Newmarket Sales Tuesday he was 'walking about', same as the previous Friday. Pressed, he says he probably went to the public library in Reading, he did that most days; also sat around wherever there were seats, doing nothing. He read the job-offer pages in newspapers, but apparently did little to find work. No heart. (My opinion.)

Mr T. on brink of nervous breakdown (my opinion). I interviewed him in coffee shop. His hands trembled half the time, rattling cup against teeth, and he's not yet forty. Alcohol? Don't think so. Nerves shot to hell.

Mr T. drives old grey Austin 1100. Has slight dent in front wing. Mr T. says it's been there weeks. Car dirty, could do with wash, Mr T. says he has no energy for things like that.

Mr T.'s opinion of Mr Ian is very muddled (like

the rest of him). Mr Ian is 'best of bunch, really', but also Mr T. says Mr Ian is Mr Pembroke's favourite and it isn't fair. (!)

End of enquiry.

With a sigh, I put Thomas to the back and read about Berenice; no happy tale.

Mrs Berenice Pembroke (44 according to Mrs Joyce), wife of Mr Thomas, lives at 6 Arden Haciendas. No job. Looks after daughters, spends her days doing housework and reading trashy romances (according to Mrs Joyce again!).

Mrs B. very hard to interview. First visit, nothing. Second visit, a little, not much. She couldn't produce alibi for either day.

I asked about children and school journeys. Mrs B. doesn't drive them, they go by bus. They walk alone along pavement in residential side road to and from bus stop, which is about one-third of mile away, on the main thoroughfare. Mrs B.'s mother lives actually on the bus route. The girls get off the bus there most afternoons and go to their grandmother's for tea.

Interviewed Mrs B.'s mother. Not helpful. Agreed girls go there most days. Sometimes (if cold, wet or dark) she drives them home at about 7 pm. Other days, they finish journey by bus. I asked why they go there for tea so often and stay so late. Told to mind my own business. Younger girl said Granny makes better teas, Mummy gets cross. Told to shut up by older girl. Mrs B.'s mother showed me out.

Mrs B. drives old white Morris Maxi, clean, no marks on it.

Mrs B. gave no opinion of Mr Ian when asked, but looked as if she could spit. Says Mr Pembroke is wicked. Mrs B. slammed her front door (she hadn't asked me in!).

End of enquiry.

I put Berenice, too, back in the packet, and cheered myself up just a fraction with a slice of pork pie and a game of darts.

From the outside, Arden Haciendas were dreadful: tiny houses of dark brown-red brick set at odd angles to each other, with dark-framed windows at odd heights and dark front doors leading from walled front gardens one could cross in one stride. Nevertheless, Arden Haciendas, as Joyce had informed me a year earlier when Thomas had moved there, were socially the in thing, as they had won a prize for the architect.

God help architecture, I thought, ringing the bell of No 6. I hadn't been to this house before: had associated Thomas and Berenice always with the rather ordinary bungalow they'd bought at the time of their wedding.

Berenice opened the door and tried to close it again

when she saw me, but I pushed from my side and put my shoe over the threshold, and finally, with ill grace, she stepped back.

'We don't want to see you,' she said. 'Dear Thomas isn't well. You've no right to shove your way in here. I hate you.'

'Well, hate or not, I want to talk to Thomas.'

She couldn't say he wasn't there, because I could see him. Inside, the Haciendas were open plan with rooms at odd angles to each other, which explained the odd-angled exteriors. The front door led into an angled off-shoot of the main room, which had no ceiling where one would expect it, but soared to the rafters. Windows one couldn't see out of let daylight in at random points in the walls. Horrible, I thought, but that was only, as Mr West would say, my opinion.

Thomas rose to his feet from one of the heavily-stuffed armchairs brought from the bungalow, old comfortable chairs looking incongruous in all the aggressive modernity. There was no carpet on the woodblock floor; Thomas's shoes squeaked on it when he moved.

'Come in, old chap,' he said.

'We don't want him,' Berenice objected.

Thomas was looking haggard and I was shocked. I hadn't seen him, I realized, for quite a long time. All youth had left him, and I thought of him as he had been at eighteen or nineteen, laughing and good-humoured, coming for weekends and making Serena giggle.

Twenty years on, he looked middle-aged, the head balder than when I'd last taken his photograph, the ginger moustache less well tended, the desperation all-pervading. Norman West's assessment of early breakdown seemed conservative. It looked to me as if it had already happened. Thomas was a lot further down the line to disintegration than Gervase.

Ferdinand, he confirmed in answer to my question, had told him about Malcolm's will and about Malcolm's wish that I should try to find out who wanted to kill him. Thomas couldn't help, he said.

I reminded him of the day old Fred blew up the tree stump. Ferdinand had mentioned that too, he said. Thomas had been there. He remembered it clearly. He had carried Serena on his shoulders, and Fred had been blown flat.

'And do you remember the time switches we used to make, with wire on the clocks' hands?'

He stared, his eyes gaunt. After a long pause, he said, 'Yes.'

'Thomas, after Gervase and Ferdinand left Quantum, did you or they make any more of them?'

Berenice interrupted, 'Dear Thomas couldn't make a time switch to save his life, could you, darling?' Her voice was pitying, sneering, unkind. Thomas sent her a haunted look but no protest.

'Someone gave Robin and Peter a Mickey Mouse clock with white plastic-covered wires stuck on it,' I said. 'Very bright and attractive.'

Thomas shook his head helplessly.

'In the rubble at Quantum, they've found a clock hand stuck onto some white plastic-covered wire.'

'Oh, my God,' Thomas said miserably.

'So what?' Berenice demanded. 'Dear Thomas does overact so.'

'So,' I said, 'someone who knew how to make these time switches blew up Quantum.'

'What of it?' she said. 'I can't see Thomas doing it. Not enough nerve, have you, darling?'

Thomas said to me, 'Have a drink?'

Berenice looked disconcerted. Asking me to have a drink had been for Thomas an act of rebellion against her wishes. There hadn't been many of them, I guessed. I accepted with thanks, although it was barely five-thirty and to my mind too early. I'd chosen the hour on purpose, hoping both that Thomas would have returned from his day's wanderings and that the daughters would stop at their grandmother's house on their way home from school.

Thomas squeaked across the floor to the kitchen, which was divided from the main room only by a waist-high counter, and began opening cupboards. He produced three tumblers which he put clumsily on the counter, and then sought in the fridge interminably for mixers. Berenice watched him with her face screwed into an expression of long-suffering impatience and made no move to help.

'We have some gin somewhere,' he said vaguely,

having at last found the tonic. 'I don't know where Berenice puts things. She moves them about.'

'Dear Thomas couldn't find a book in a library.'

Thomas gave her a look of black enmity which she either didn't see or chose to ignore. He opened another cupboard, and another, and in his wife's continued unhelpful silence finally found a nearly full bottle of Gordon's gin. He came round into the main room and poured from the bottle into three glasses, topping up inadequately from a single bottle of tonic.

He handed me a glass. I didn't much care for gin, but it was no time to say so.

He held out the second glass to Berenice.

'I don't want any,' she said.

Thomas's hand was trembling. He made an awkward motion as if to raise the glass to his own lips, then put it down with a bang on the counter, and in an uncoordinated movement accidentally knocked the gin bottle over so that it fell to the floor, smashing into green shiny pieces, the liquid spreading in a pool.

Thomas bent down to pick up the bits. Berenice didn't help.

She said, 'Thomas can't get anything right, can you, darling?' The words were no worse than others, but the acid sarcasm in her voice had gone beyond scathing to unbearable.

Thomas straightened with a face filled with passionate hatred, the worm turning at last, and by the neck he held the top part of the green bottle, the broken edges jagged as teeth.

He came up fast with his hand rising. Berenice, cushioned in complacency, wasn't even looking at him and seemed not to begin to understand her danger.

Malcolm said I had fast reactions . . . I dropped my own drink, grasped Berenice by both arms and swung her violently round and out of the slicing track of the razor-sharp weapon. She was furiously indignant, protesting incredulously, sprawling across the floor where I'd almost thrown her, still unaware of what had been happening.

Thomas looked at the damage he'd done to me for a long blank second, then he dropped the fearsome bottle and turned to stumble off blindly towards his front door. I took two strides and caught him by the arm.

'Let me go . . .' He struggled, and I held on. 'Let me go . . . I can't do anything right . . . she's right.'

'She's bloody wrong.'

I was stronger than he. I practically dragged him across the room and flung him into one of the armchairs.

'I've cut you,' he said.

'Yes, well, never mind. You listen to me. You both listen to me. You're over the edge. You're going to have to face some straight facts.'

Berenice had finally realized how close she'd come to needing stitches. She looked with anger at the point of my left shoulder where jersey and shirt had been ripped away, where a couple of cuts were bleeding. She turned to Thomas with a bitterly accusing face and opened her mouth.

'Shut up,' I said roughly. 'If you're going to tell him he's incompetent, don't do it. If you're going to complain that he could have cut you instead, yes he could, he was trying to. Sit down and *shut up*.'

'Trying to?' She couldn't believe it. She sat down weakly, her hair awry, her body slack, eyes shocked.

'You goaded him too far. Don't you understand what you've been doing to him? Putting him down, picking him to pieces every time you open your mouth? You have now completely succeeded. He can't function any more.'

'Dear Thomas – ' she began.

'Don't say that. You don't mean it.'

She stared.

'If he were your dear Thomas,' I said, 'you would help him and encourage him, not sneer.'

'I'm not listening to this.'

'You just think what you stirred up in Thomas today, and if I were you, I'd be careful.' I turned to Thomas, 'And it's not all her fault. You've let her do it, let her carp all this time. You should have stopped her years ago. You should have walked out. You've been loyal to her beyond reason and she's driven you to want to kill her, because that's what I saw in your face.'

Thomas put a hand over his eyes.

'You were dead lucky you didn't connect with her mouth or her throat or whatever you were going for. There would have been no going back. You just think what would have happened, both of you. The consequences to yourselves, and to your girls. *Think!*' I paused. 'Well, it's beyond facing.'

'I didn't mean it,' Thomas mumbled.

'I'm afraid you did,' I said.

'He couldn't have done,' Berenice said.

'He did mean it,' I said to her. 'It takes quite a force to tear away so much woollen jersey. Your only hope is to believe to the depths of your soul that he put all his goaded infuriated strength behind that blow. I'll tell you, I was lucky too. I was moving away fast trying to avoid being cut, and it can have been only the points of the glass that reached my skin, but I'll remember the speed of them . . .' I broke off, not knowing how else to convince her. I didn't want to say, 'It bloody hurts,' but it did.

Thomas put his head in his hands.

'Come on,' I said to him, 'I'm taking you out of here. On your feet, brother.'

'Don't be ridiculous,' Berenice said.

'If I leave him here, will you cuddle him?'

The negative answer filled her whole face. She wouldn't have thought of it. She was aggrieved. It would have taken little time for her to stoke up the recriminations.

'When the firemen have gone,' I said, 'fires often start again from the heat in the embers.'

I went over to Thomas. 'Come on. There's still life ahead.'

Without looking up, he said in a dull sort of agony, 'You don't know . . . It's too late.'

I said 'No' without great conviction, and then the front door opened with a bang to let in the two girls.

'Hello,' they said noisily, bringing in swirls of outside air. 'Granny turned us out early. What's going on? What's all this glass on the floor? What's all the blood on your arm?'

'A bottle got broken,' I said, 'and I fell on it.'

The young one looked at the bowed head of her father, and in a voice that was a devastating mimic of her mother's, vibrating with venom and contempt, she said, 'I'll bet it was Dear Thomas who broke it.'

Berenice heard for herself what she'd been doing to her husband. Heard what she was implanting in her own children. The revelation seemed to overwhelm her, and she sought for excuses.

'If we had more money . . . If only Malcolm . . . It's not fair . . .'

But they had two cars, thanks to their trust fund, and a newly-built townhouse, and Thomas's unemployment had brought no immediate financial disaster: money wasn't their trouble, nor would it cure it.

'Why didn't you get a job?' I said. 'What did you

ever expect of Thomas? That he'd set the world alight? He did the best he could.'

Quantum in me fuit . . .

'I wanted a son,' she said flatly. 'Thomas got a vasectomy. He said two children were enough, we couldn't afford any more. It wasn't fair. Malcolm should have given us more money. *I always wanted a son.*'

Dear God, I thought: flat simple words at the absolute heart of things, the suppurating disappointment that she had allowed to poison their lives. Just like Gervase, I thought. So much unhappiness from wanting the unobtainable, so much self-damage.

I could think of nothing to say. Nothing of help. It was too late.

I went across to Thomas and touched him on the shoulder. He stood up. He didn't look at his family, or at me. I put my hand lightly under his elbow and steered him to the front door, and in unbroken silence we left the wasteland of his marriage.

CHAPTER SIXTEEN

I took Thomas to Lucy's house.

It seemed to me, as I drove away from the pretentious Haciendas, that Lucy's particular brand of peace might be just what Thomas needed. I couldn't take him to Vivien, who would demolish him further, and Joyce, who was fond of him, would be insufferably bracing. I frankly didn't want him with me in Cookham; and Donald, influenced by Berenice, tended to despise him.

Lucy was in, to my relief, and opened the front door of the farm cottage where she and Edwin led the simple life near Marlow.

She stared at us. At my red arm. At Thomas's hanging head.

'Sister, dear,' I said cheerfully. 'Two brothers needing succour come knocking at thy gate. Any chance of hot sweet tea? Loving looks? A sticking plaster?'

Edwin appeared behind her, looking peevish. 'What's going on?'

To Lucy, I said, 'We cracked a bottle of gin, and I fell on it.'

'Are you drunk?' she said.

'Not really.'

'You'd better come in.'

'Ferdinand has been on the telephone,' Edwin said without welcome, staring with distaste at my blood as we stepped over his threshold. 'He warned us you'd be turning up some time. You might have had the courtesy to let us know in advance.'

'Sorry,' I said dryly.

Lucy glanced swiftly at my face. 'This is trouble?'

'Just a spot.'

She took Thomas by the arm and led him out of the tiny entrance hall into her book-filled sitting room. Edwin's and Lucy's cottage consisted of two rooms downstairs, which had been partly knocked into one, with a modern bathroom tacked on at the back. The stairs, which were hidden behind a latched door, led up to three rooms where one had to inch round the beds, bending one's head so as not to knock it on the eaves. Laura Ashley wallpaper everywhere covered uneven old plaster, and rag rugs provided warmth underfoot. Lucy's books were stacked in columns on the floor along one wall in the sitting room, having overflowed the bookcases, and in the kitchen there were wooden bowls, pestles and mortar, dried herbs hanging.

Lucy's home was unselfconscious, not folksy. Lucy herself, large in dark trousers and thick handknitted sweater, sat Thomas in an armchair and in a very short time thrust a mug of hot liquid into his unwilling hand.

'Drink it, Thomas,' I said. 'How about some gin in it?' I asked Lucy.

'It's in.'

I smiled at her.

'Do you want some yourself?' she said.

'Just with milk.' I followed her into the kitchen. 'Have you got any tissues I could put over this mess?'

She looked at my shoulder. 'Are tissues enough?'

'Aspirins?'

'I don't believe in them.'

'Ah.'

I drank the hot tea. Better than nothing. She had precious few tissues, when it came to the point, and far too small for the job. I said I would leave it and go along to the hospital later to get it cleaned up. She didn't argue.

She said, 'What's all this about?' and dipped into a half-empty packet of raisins and then offered me some, which I ate.

'Thomas has left Berenice. He's in need of a bed.'

'Not here,' she protested. 'Take him with you.'

'I will if you won't keep him, but he'd be better off here.'

She said her son, my nephew, was up in his bedroom doing his homework.

'Thomas won't disturb him,' I said.

She looked at me doubtfully. 'There's something you're not telling me.'

'The last straw,' I said, 'has just broken Thomas. If someone doesn't treat him kindly, he'll end up in the nut house or the suicide statistics and I am not, repeat not, joking.'

'Well . . .'

'That's my girl.'

'I'm not your girl,' she said tartly. 'Perhaps I'm Thomas's.' Her face softened slightly. 'All right, he can stay.'

She ate another handful of raisins and went back to the sitting room, and I again followed. Edwin had taken the second armchair. Lucy lowered her bulk onto a leather stool beside Thomas, which left me on my feet looking around. There were no other seats. Resignedly I sat on the floor and rested my back against a wall. Neither Lucy nor Edwin commented. Neither had invited me to sit.

'As I'm here,' I said, 'I may as well ask the questions I was going to come and ask tomorrow.'

'We don't want to answer,' Edwin said. 'And if you get blood on the wallpaper you can pay for redecorating.'

'The police will come,' I said, twisting slightly out of harm's way. 'Why not practise on me? They'll ask about the timing device that set off the bomb at Quantum.'

Thomas stirred. 'I made it, you know. The Mickey Mouse clock.'

It was the first time he'd spoken since we'd left his house. Lucy looked as if she thought him delirious, then raised her eyebrows and started to concentrate.

'Not that,' she said, troubled.

'Do you remember those clocks?' I asked.

'Of course I do. We've got one upstairs, that Thomas made for our son.'

'What sort of face has it got?'

'A sailing ship. Did the Mickey Mouse clock explode . . .?'

'No,' I said. 'The one actually used had a grey plastic dial with white numbers. The Mickey Mouse clock was intact, in the playroom.'

Thomas said dully, 'I haven't made one for years.'

'When did you make the Mickey Mouse for Robin and Peter?' I asked.

'I didn't make it for them. I made it a long time ago for Serena. She must have given it to them. It made her laugh, when I made it.'

'You were a nice boy, Thomas,' Lucy said. 'Funny and kind.'

Edwin said restlessly, 'I would have thought any timing device would have been blown to unrecognizable fragments by such a big bomb.'

'It seems they often find pieces,' I said.

'Do you mean,' he demanded, 'that they've actually sifted through all those tons of rubbish?'

'More or less. They know it was a battery clock. They found part of the motor.'

'It serves Malcolm right the house was blown up,' Edwin said with barely suppressed violence. 'Flinging money about on ridiculous scholarships. Keeping us poor. I suppose *you're* all right, aren't you?' There was a sneer there for me, openly. 'He's never been fair to Lucy. You've always been in the way, smarming him up, taking the lion's share. He gives you whatever you ask for while we have to struggle along on a pittance.'

'Is that the authentic voice of Vivien?' I asked.

'It's the truth!'

'No,' I said. 'It's what you have been told over and over again, but it's not the truth. Most people believe a lie if they're told it often enough. It's easy enough after all to believe a lie if you've heard it only once. Especially if you want to believe it.'

Lucy looked at me intently. 'You care about this, don't you?'

'About being cast perpetually as the family villain? Yes, I dare say I do. But I was thinking also of Thomas. He's been told ad infinitum that he's useless, and now he believes it. I'm going now, Lucy.' I stood up without haste. 'You tell Thomas over and over that he's a worthwhile person, and maybe he'll begin to believe that instead. You have to believe in yourself to get anywhere.'

'Oh yes,' she said quietly. 'You do.'

'What you've written,' I said, 'is for ever.'

Her eyes widened. 'How do you know . . . that I've lost . . .'

'I guessed.' I bent and kissed her cheek, to her surprise. 'Are you seriously in need?'

'Financially?' She was startled. 'No worse than usual.'

'Of course we are,' Edwin said to her waspishly. 'You're earning almost nothing now and you still spend a fortune on books.'

Lucy looked only mildly embarrassed, as if she'd heard that often before.

'If I held the purse-strings,' Edwin complained, 'you'd use the public library, as I do.'

'Why don't you work, Edwin?' I asked.

'Lucy doesn't like bustle.' He seemed to think it explanation enough. 'We'd be perfectly happy if Malcolm trebled Lucy's trust fund, as he ought to. He has millions, we live in a hovel. It's not fair.'

'Doesn't Lucy despise money?' I asked. 'And people who have it? Do you want her to become what she despises?'

Edwin glared.

Lucy looked at me blandly. 'There's no such state as perfection,' she said.

I drove back to Reading, to the hospital that had an emergency room open all evening, and there got my shoulder and upper arm cleaned and stitched. There were three cuts, it seemed, variously deep but nothing frightful, and they had long stopped bleeding: with the stitches, they would heal almost instantly. The staff advised pain-killers pro tem. I thanked them and eventually drove to Cookham feeling more than slightly tired but chiefly hungry, and having remedied both conditions satisfactorily, set off again next morning to ride. There was no problem there with the stitches: they were tender to the touch and stiff when I lifted my arm, but that was all.

Restored yet again in spirit by the dose of fresh air, I took a lazy day off from the emotional battering of the family and went to London to get my American and Australian visas. It was only a week since I'd ridden Park Railings at Cheltenham and it felt like eternity. I bought a new sweater and had my hair cut and thought about Ursula 'wandering about' through days of escape. One could wander for hours in London, thinking one's thoughts.

On an impulse, I telephoned Joyce, not expecting her to be in.

'Darling,' she yelled. 'I'm going out. Bridge. Where are you?'

'In a phone box.'

'Where's your father?'

'I don't know.'

'Darling, you're *infuriating*. What did you ring for?'

'I suppose . . . just to hear your voice.'

It seemed to stump her entirely. 'Are you out of your head? You tell that old bugger . . . tell him . . .' She choked on it.

'That you're glad he's alive?' I suggested.

'Don't let the old sod get blown up.'

'No,' I said.

'Must rush, darling. Don't break your neck. 'Bye . . .'

''Bye now,' I said.

I wondered if she ever talked on the telephone except at the top of her voice. The decibels were comforting, somehow. At least she never sounded bored. I would rather infuriate her than bore her, I thought.

I went unhurriedly back to Cookham and in the evening bent again to Norman West's notes.

Of Edwin, he had said:

> Mr Edwin Pembroke (53) née Bugg, lives with his wife Lucy in No 3 Wrothsay Farm Cottages, near Marlow. One son (15), attends state school, bicycles to school, has latchkey, gets his own tea, goes upstairs, does homework, working for exams, conscientious, doesn't know if his parents were around on the Friday or Tuesday at specified hours, doesn't expect so. He comes downstairs about 8 or 9 pm, they all eat vegetarian meal then. (No TV!) Mrs L. cooks in a wok. Mr E. washes up.
>
> Mr E. does the housework (not much) and shopping, mostly vegetables. He spends hours reading in public library (librarians agree). Goes to pub, spends more hours over one beer (barman indignant). Takes laundry to laundromat. Listens to radio.

Spends hours doing crossword puzzles. (The garden's untidy. Mr E. doesn't like gardening. They grow only runner beans, they're easy.)

Mr E. and Mrs L. share an old Hillman, which Mr E. mostly drives. (Mrs L. has licence.) Car dusty and rusty, no dents.

Mr E. good-looking man, complete drone (my opinion). Idle life suits him. Mr E.'s idle life seems to suit Mrs L. also – no accounting for people. She does less than he does, come to think. Mr E. has sharp sarcastic manner on occasions. Detests Mr Ian, curses Mr Pembroke but at same time wants money from him (!). Definitely thinks of Mr Pembroke's money too much, broods on it, talked about it all the time.

End of enquiry.

Of Lucy, among other things, he had written:

Mrs L. spends large parts of the day unaware of what's going on around her (my opinion). I had to repeat several questions. It seemed she didn't hear me, but nothing wrong with her ears. She listens to things going on in her own head (can't put it very well). Has no alibis for Friday or Tuesday. Can't remember where she was. (I believe it.) Goes for rambling walks. Mrs L. very troubled over something, but wouldn't say what. She ate a tinful of peanuts while I was there, looked surprised when they'd gone.

So much for Lucy and Edwin, I thought. What about Donald and Helen?

Donald Pembroke (44) eldest of Mr Pembroke's offspring, lives at Marblehill House, detached chalet-style house which goes with his job, Secretary, Marblehill Golf Club (rich club, high fees) near Henley-on-Thames. Long waiting list for membership, rich members.

Mr D. has staff (green keeper, club steward, etc). He himself oversees and runs the whole place, is said to be good at it, members like him, say he gets things done, runs tight ship, decent bar, club rooms, tournaments etc, always listens to and deals with complaints, seen as friend, authority figure, social equal. Mr D. likes his work. His social standing extremely important to him (my opinion). Keeps up high appearances.

As to alibis for the Friday and Tuesday in question: no alibis ascertainable. Is always 'round the place', never at any place at set hours except first thing in the mornings (9 am) to see to post with office staff. Has Mondays off, works Saturdays and Sundays.

Walks to work (barely 100 yds). Usually returns home at 7 pm (much earlier in winter), sometimes stays until bar closes. Often walks round later to see all is well everywhere. Dedicated.

Mr D. has daughter in art school, high fees. Also twin sons who have started this term at Eton, previously at good prep. school. (How does he afford it?)

Mr D. drives silver Mercedes, 2 years old. Clean. No marks of collision with Mr Ian.

Mr D. thinks it's very bad news Mr Ian is back in Mr Pembroke's favour. Certain to mean less inheritance for him (Mr D.). He's angry about that. But he also thinks Mr Ian the only one who can persuade Mr Pembroke to distribute some wealth now. Sees no inconsistency in these beliefs. (He'll use Mr Ian, doesn't have to trust him, he said.) Thinks Mr Pembroke's recent expenditure unreasonable, 'insane' (!). Says he's senile.

Mr D. gave me rapid answers; busy. Says his financial affairs were none of my business, edgy on subject. Is he in debt? (My opinion, considering his expenses, probably.) Champagne lifestyle.

End of enquiry.

And Helen?

Mrs Helen Pembroke (43) wife of Mr D. Very good-looking lady. Very worried, wouldn't say what about.

I interviewed her in Marblehill House – big name

for fairly ordinary-sized three-bedroom, nice sitting room, though, over-looking golf course. Good furniture, appearance of wealth.

Mrs H. works at home (on dustsheet in dining room) painting views of Henley by hand onto plates, jugs, boxes; all china. Very quick, very good (to my eyes), nice pictures. They go off to be glazed, she said, then sell in local shops. Reasonably paid, she says. (What's reasonable? She says her work was to be seen as a hobby. Mr D. refers to it in that way.)

Mrs H. works alone nearly every day, no alibis for Friday or Tuesday. Sometimes drives into Henley to shop, no regular pattern. Mrs H. has white Cavalier, clean, no dents.

No children at home. Daughter shares flat with friends near art school (more expense).

Mrs H. ultra-loyal to Mr D. Says my enquiries unnecessary. Says it's ridiculous to suppose Mr D. would attack his father. Out of the question. (My opinion, she wasn't too sure.) They need more cash badly (my opinion).

Mrs H. mostly shares Mr D.'s opinion of Mr Ian, but doesn't seem to dislike him personally.

End of enquiry.

On Friday morning, I called in on a public library and looked up 'explosives' in encyclopaedias. Ammonium nitrate was there, also the proportion of fertilizer to diesel oil needed, also the formula for relating volume to kilos. The knowledge was available to anyone who sought it.

On Friday after lunch I went to the Marblehill Golf Club and found Donald in the clubroom placating a foursome who had arrived late and missed their game.

'Go over to the house,' he said when he saw me. 'I can't talk here.' He turned decisively back to the problem in hand and I did what I was told, like a good little brother.

Helen was resigned more than annoyed to see me. 'Ferdinand said you would come, and we had the police here yesterday. Not that we could tell them anything, or you either.'

She was wearing a painter's smock over jeans and looked dressed by Dior. She took me into the sitting room and pointed to a chair, and with unconscious grace sat herself half-on, half-off a polished table, raising her wrists to keep her paint-smudged hands away from the furniture.

Donald came bustling in, telling me he could give me ten minutes. 'Don't see what you can do,' he said. 'Leave it to the police.'

'What did they ask you?'

'About Fred blowing up the tree stump. I said yes, of course we'd been there. Helen and I weren't then married. It was the first time she'd met Malcolm, she was staying the weekend.'

'Saturday morning,' she said, nodding. 'The gardener came in specially to blow up the tree trunks. Not something one would forget, seeing him knocked flat. I took a photograph of the tree roots afterwards. It's still in one of our albums.'

'And the time switch clocks, do you remember those?' I asked.

'Naturally,' Donald said.

Helen added, 'Dear Thomas made two for our boys for their birthday once, when they could just tell the time.' She had said Dear Thomas, I noticed, as if she had meant it, not as Berenice said it. 'They got lost in one of our moves.'

'Where's Malcolm?' Donald asked brusquely.

'I don't know.'

'You're lying,' he said, but for once I wasn't. Malcolm and Ramsey Osborn had left the Osborn residence, according to the female voice on the line the evening before, and had given her no number at which they could be reached. I could try again tomorrow, she said. Mr Osborn should have let her know by then; he usually did.

'Did either of you,' I asked, 'trace Malcolm to Cambridge the weekend he was put in the car?'

I hadn't expected any answer but negative, but the question came at them unexpectedly and Helen practically jumped.

'Did you?' I said to her.

'No, of course not,' Donald said quickly. 'We had no

way of knowing he would go to Newmarket Sales, if that's what you're inferring.'

'The hotel at Cambridge said three people – two men and a woman – had asked if Malcolm was staying there,' I said. 'One was Norman West, who were the others? I'm not saying you went to Newmarket Sales, just did one of you trace Malcolm?'

They looked at me glumly. Then Helen said, 'I suppose so.'

'Why?' I asked.

Donald cleared his throat. 'I needed his signature on a guarantee.'

'Go on, what guarantee?'

'For a temporary bank loan.' He swallowed. 'I thought he might . . .'

'We had to have the money in a hurry,' Helen said. 'The bank manager told Donald we could borrow it if Malcolm would guarantee it. Then we couldn't get hold of Malcolm. We had to think where he might be, and he's always going to Cambridge. Donald and I just talked about it, guessing, wondering . . . And then, well, Donald went over to the club house and I just picked up the AA book and found those hotels in Cambridge, and without really believing in it I tried two . . . only two . . . and he was there, at the second. When Donald came home I told him and the extraordinary thing was, he'd had the same idea and got the same result.' She paused. 'We were pretty desperate, you see.'

'Don't say that,' Donald said. ' "Desperate" gives the wrong picture.'

'What did you need the money for?' I asked.

They looked at each other, foreheads wrinkled in worry. Finally, reluctantly, but as if coming to a decision, Donald said, 'We had some interest to pay unexpectedly. I had negotiated three months' deferment of interest on a loan, or at least I thought I had, and then I got a threatening demand. I had to pay at once or they'd start proceedings.' The desperation he said wasn't there, definitely had been; it still echoed in his voice. 'I couldn't have it getting around the golf club, could I?' he demanded. 'No one in the family could lend me a large sum in a hurry. Our ordinary bank overdraft is always at maximum. The finance company was inflexible. I knew Malcolm wouldn't *give* me the money, he has those stupid warped views, but I did think he might guarantee . . . just for a short while . . .'

To save the whole pack of cards collapsing, perhaps he might. Malcolm wasn't cruel. He'd lent Edwin money sometimes in the past. Donald, I thought, had stood a good chance.

'But when you'd found where he was, you didn't get in touch with him, did you?'

'No,' Donald said. 'I didn't relish telling Malcolm our troubles. I didn't want to look a fool, and Helen thought of a different way out.'

I looked at her enquiringly.

'Popped my baubles,' she said with a brave attempt

at lightness. ‘Took them to London. All my lovely rocks.’ She held her head high, refusing to cry.

‘Pawned them?’ I said.

‘We’ll get them back,’ she said valiantly, trying to believe it.

‘What day did you pop them?’

‘Wednesday. Donald took the money in cash to the finance company, and that gives us a three-months’ breather.’

Wednesday, I thought. The day after someone had failed to kill Malcolm at Newmarket.

‘When did the finance company start threatening you?’

‘The Thursday before,’ Helen said. ‘They gave us a week. They were utterly beastly, Donald said.’

‘Vivien tried to get Malcolm to give us some money,’ Donald said with resentment, ‘and he flatly refused.’

‘Well,’ I said, half-smiling, ‘she called him an evil, wicked, vindictive tyrant, and that’s not the best way in the world to persuade Malcolm to be generous. If she’d used honey, she might have succeeded.’

Helen said, ‘You’re the only one he’ll listen to. I don’t care if you get millions more than us. All the others are furious about it, they don’t believe it about equal shares in his will, but I don’t care. If you could just . . . I mean . . .’

‘I’ll try,’ I promised, ‘but the equal shares are true.’

It fell on deaf ears. They believed what they believed, the whole lot of them, feeding and reinforcing their fears every time they consulted.

I left Donald and Helen among their antique furniture and behind their shaky façade and trundled along to Quantum to see how things were developing.

Not fast, was the answer. The place was abandoned except for a solitary uniformed policeman sitting in a police car outside what had been the front door. One could see right through the house now. The tarpaulin that had hung from the roof had come down. The policeman was the one who had accompanied me on my tour of peering in through the windows, and I gathered he was pleased to have a visitor to enliven a monotonous stint.

He picked up his car radio and spoke into it to the effect that Mr Ian Pembroke had come by. A request came back, which he relayed to me: would Mr Pembroke please drop in at the police station when he left? Mr Pembroke would.

The policeman and I walked round to the back of the house. Mr Smith had gone, also his helpers. The last of the rubble was away from the house and overflowing a skip. A flat black plastic sheet, the sort used for roofing hayricks, lay where a week ago the walls of my bedroom had come tumbling down. The interior doors had been sealed with plywood, like the windows, to deter looters, and the broken end of the staircase had been barred off. A house with its centre torn out; a thirty-foot yawn between surviving flanks.

'It looks terrible,' I said, and the policeman agreed.

Arthur Bellbrook was cleaning his spades, getting

ready to leave. I gave him a cheque for his wages for that week and the next, and added a chunk for the care of the dogs. He gave me dignified thanks. He hoped Mr Pembroke was all right, poor man, and I said I thought so.

'I had my picture in the paper,' he said. 'Did you see it?'

I said I was sorry I hadn't.

'Oh, well. I did.' He shrugged disappointedly and set off homewards, and I walked down to where he'd earlier been digging potatoes, and then further, to check that the nettles were still untrampled on the far side of the wall.

The green sea looked dusty and ageing but upright. They too, I supposed, would die with the frost.

The policeman was watching me incuriously. I stopped and stared at the house from a distance, giving the impression that that's why I had gone as far as I had, and then walked back and took my leave. The house from a distance looked just as bad, if not worse.

Superintendent Yale shook my hand. Things were almost friendly at the police station but they were no nearer discovering who had planted the bomb. Enquiries were proceeding, the superintendent said and perhaps I could help.

'Fire away,' I said.

'We interviewed the former gardener, Fred Perkins,' Yale said. 'We asked him about the tree stump and what he used to blow it up. Besides cordite, that is. What sort of a fuse.'

I was interested. 'What did he say? Does he remember?'

'He said he'd got the black powder and some detonators and some fuse cord from a quarryman friend of his. The black powder was in the box which we saw, the detonators were in a separate tin with the cord and the instructions.'

'The instructions!' I repeated incredulously.

'Yes.' He sighed. 'Fred Perkins says he followed the instructions because he'd never blown anything up before. He said he used a bit of extra black powder just to make sure.'

'It was quite an explosion.'

'Yes. We asked him what he'd done with the other detonators. He says Mr Pembroke took them away from him that morning, when he came running out of the house. We need to ask Mr Pembroke what he did with them, so . . . er . . . where is he?'

'I really don't know,' I said slowly, 'and that's the truth. I can probably find him, but it'll take a day or two.' I thought for a moment, then said, 'Surely he would have thrown away those detonators years ago.'

'If he had any sense he wouldn't have thrown them anywhere,' Yale said. 'Mr Smith says you handle detonators with extreme caution if you don't want to lose a finger or an eye. They can explode if you knock or drop them or make them too warm. Mr Pembroke's correct course would have been to turn them over to the police.'

'Maybe he did,' I said.

'We'd like to find out.'

'But would detonators still detonate after twenty years?' I asked.

'Mr Smith thinks it possible, perhaps likely. He wouldn't take any liberties, he said.'

'What does a detonator look like?' I asked.

He hesitated, but said, 'Mr Smith said we might be looking for a small aluminium tube about the thickness of a pencil or slightly less, about six centimetres long. He says that's what the army used. He used to be in the Royal Engineers. He says the tube contains fulminate of mercury, and the word "fulminate" means to flash like lightning.'

'He should know.'

'Fred Perkins can't clearly remember what his detonators looked like. He remembers he had to fasten the cord into the end of the tube with pliers. Crimp it in. Mr Smith says civilians who touch explosives should be certified.'

I reflected. 'Did Mr Smith find out exactly what the Quantum bomb was made of?'

'Yes. ANFO, as he thought. He said the whole thing was amateur in the extreme.'

'Amateurs,' I said dryly, 'run faster than anyone else.'

As an amateur, I went to Kempton Park the next day and on Young Higgins beat the hell out of a lot of professionals.

I didn't know what possessed me. It seemed that I rode on a different plane. I knew it was the horse who had to be fast enough; the jockey, however determined, couldn't do it on his own. Young Higgins seemed inspired and against more formidable opponents than at Sandown produced a totally different race.

There were no aunts riding this time, no lieutenant colonels falling off. No earl's son to chat to. No journalist to make it look easy. For some reason, George and Jo had entered Young Higgins in a high-class open three-mile steeplechase, and I was the only amateur in sight.

I'd ridden against an all-professional field of top jockeys a few times before, and it was usually a humbling experience. I had the basic skills and a good deal of touch. I could get horses settled and balanced. I liked speed, I liked the stretch of one's spirit: but there was always a point against top professionals at which that wasn't enough.

George and Jo were unfussed. Young Higgins was fitter than at Sandown, they thought, and at Kempton there was no hill to tire him. They were bright-eyed and enthusiastic, but not especially hopeful. 'We didn't want to change you for a professional,' they said in explanation. 'It wouldn't have been fair.'

Maybe not fair, but prudent, I thought. The top pros raced with sharper eyes, better tactics, more strength, quicker reactions. Theirs was an intenser determination, a fiercer concentration. Humour was for before and after, not during. Race-riding was their business, besides their pleasure, and some of them thought of amateur opponents as frivolous unfit nuisances who caused accidents and endangered lives.

Perhaps because of an arrogant desire to prove them wrong, perhaps because of the insights and realities I'd faced in a traumatic week, perhaps because of Young Higgins himself: I rode anyway with a new sharp revelationary perception of what was needed for winning, and the horse and I came home in front by four lengths to a fairly stunned silence from the people on the stands who'd backed everything else on the card but us.

George and Jo were vindicated and ecstatic. Young Higgins tossed his head at the modest plaudits. A newspaperman labelled the result as a fluke.

I'd cracked it, I thought. I'd graduated. That had been real professional riding. Satisfactory. But I was already thirty-three. I'd discovered far too late the difference between enjoyment and fire. I'd needed to know it at nineteen or twenty. I'd idled it away.

'This is no time,' Jo said laughing, 'to look sad.'

CHAPTER SEVENTEEN

I flew to New York two days later, still not knowing where to find Malcolm.

The voice at Stamford, Connecticut, always helpful but uninformed, had thought, the previous evening, that the gentlemen might have gone back to Kentucky: they'd been talking of buying a horse that they'd seen there a week earlier. Another horse, not the one they'd bought yesterday.

It was just as well, I thought, that Donald and Helen and Thomas and Berenice and Edwin and Lucy and Vivien and Joyce didn't know. That Gervase, Ursula, Alicia, Ferdinand, Debs and Serena hadn't heard. All fourteen of them would have fallen upon Malcolm and torn him apart.

I chose New York for the twin reasons that Stamford, Connecticut, was barely an hour and a half's drive away (information from the voice) and that everyone should see New York some time. My journeys before that had been only in Europe, to places like Paris,

Rome, Athens and Oslo. Beaches and race-meetings and temples. Horses and gods.

I was heading for a hotel on 54th Street, Manhattan, that the voice had recommended: she would tell Mr Pembroke I would be there, as soon as she knew where Mr Pembroke was. It seemed as good an arrangement as any.

Superintendent Yale didn't know I'd left England, nor did any of the family. I sighed with deep relief on the aeroplane and thought about the visits I'd made the day before to Alicia and Vivien. Neither had wanted to see me and both had been abrasive, Alicia in the morning, Vivien in the afternoon.

Alicia's flat outside Windsor was spacious and overlooked the Thames, neither of which pleasures seemed to please her. She did reluctantly let me in, but was unplacated by my admiration of her view.

She was, in fact, looking youthfully pretty in a white wool dress and silver beads. Her hair was pulled high in a velvet bow on the crown, and her neat figure spoke of luck or dieting. She had a visitor with her already when I called, a fortyish substantial-looking man introduced coquettishly as Paul, who behaved with unmistakable lordliness, the master in his domain. How long, I wondered, had this been going on?

'You might have said you were coming,' Alicia complained. 'Ferdinand said you would, some time. I told him to tell you not to.'

'It seemed best to see everyone,' I said neutrally.

'Then hurry up,' she said. 'We're going out to lunch.'

'Did Ferdinand tell you about Malcolm's new will?'

'He did, and I don't believe a word of it. You've always been Malcolm's wretched little pet. He should have sent you back to Joyce when I left. I told him to. But would he listen? No, he wouldn't.'

'That was twenty years ago,' I protested.

'And nothing's changed. He does what he likes. He's utterly selfish.'

Paul listened to the conversation without stirring and with scant apparent interest but he did, it seemed, have his influence. With an arch look at him, Alicia said, 'Paul says Gervase should force Malcolm to give him power of attorney.'

I couldn't offhand think of anything less likely to happen.

'Have you two known each other long?' I asked.

'No,' Alicia said, and the look she gave Paul was that of a flirt of sixteen.

I asked her if she remembered the tree stump. 'Of course. I was furious with Malcolm for letting Fred do anything so ridiculous. The boys might have been hurt.'

And did she remember the switches? How could she forget them, she said, they'd been all over the house. Not only that, Thomas had made another one for Serena some time later. It had sat in her room gathering dust. Those clocks had all been a pest.

'You were good to me in those old days,' I said.

She stared. There was almost a softening round her

eyes, but it was transitory. 'I had to be,' she said acidly. 'Malcolm insisted.'

'Weren't you ever happy?' I asked.

'Oh, yes.' Her mouth curled in a malicious smile. 'When Malcolm came to see me, when he was married to Joyce. Before that weaselly detective spoiled it.'

I asked her if she had engaged Norman West to find Malcolm in Cambridge.

She looked at me with wide empty eyes and said blandly, 'No, I didn't. Why would I want to? I didn't care where he was.'

'Almost everyone wanted to find him to stop him spending his money.'

'He's insane,' she said. 'Paranoid. He should hand control over to Gervase, and make sure that frightful Ursula isn't included. She's the wrong wife for Gervase, as I've frequently told him.'

'But you didn't ask Norman West to find Malcolm?'

'No, I didn't,' she said very sharply. 'Stop asking that stupid question.' She turned away from me restlessly. 'It's high time you went.'

I thought so too, on the whole. I speculated that perhaps the presence of Paul had inhibited her from saying directly to my face the poison she'd been spreading behind my back. They would dissect me when I'd gone. He nodded coolly to me as I left. No friend of mine, I thought.

If my visit to Alicia had been unfruitful, my call on Vivien was less so. Norman West's notes had been minimal: name, address, sorting magazines, no alibis. She wouldn't answer any of my questions either, or discuss any possibilities. She said several times that Malcolm was a fiend who was determined to destroy his children, and that I was the devil incarnate helping him. She hoped we would both rot in hell. (I thought devils and fiends might flourish there, actually.)

Meanwhile, I said, had she employed Norman West to find Malcolm in Cambridge? Certainly not. She wanted nothing to do with that terrible little man. If I didn't remove myself from her doorstep she would call in the police.

'It can't be much fun,' I said, 'living with so much hatred in your head.'

She was affronted. 'What do you mean?'

'No peace. All anger. Very exhausting. Bad for your health.'

'Go away,' she said, and I obliged her.

I drove back to Cookham and spent a good deal of the evening on the telephone, talking to Lucy about Thomas and to Ferdinand about Gervase. 'We are all our brothers' keepers,' Lucy said, and reported that Thomas was spending most of the time asleep. 'Retreating,' Lucy said.

Lucy had spoken to Berenice. 'Whatever did you say to her, Ian? She sounds quite different. Subdued.

Can't see it lasting long, can you? I told her Thomas was all right and she started blubbing.'

Lucy said she would keep Thomas for a while, but not for his natural span.

Ferdinand, when he heard my voice, said, 'Where the hell have you been? All I get is your answering machine. Did you find out who killed Moira?' There was anxiety, possibly, in his voice.

'I found out a few who didn't,' I said.

'That's not what I asked.'

'Well,' I said, 'like you with your computer, I've fed in a lot of data.'

'And the result?'

'The wheels are turning.'

'Computers don't have wheels. Come to think of it, though, I suppose they do. Anyway, you've left a whole trail of disasters behind you, haven't you? I hear Thomas has left Berenice, and as for Gervase, he wants your guts for taking Ursula out to lunch. Did you do that? Whatever for? You know how possessive he is. There's a hell of a row going on.'

'If you want to hang on to Debs,' I said, 'don't listen to Alicia.'

'What the hell's that got to do with Gervase and Ursula having a row?' he demanded.

'Everything.'

He was furious. 'You've always got it in for Alicia.'

'The other way round. She's a dedicated trouble-maker who's cost you one wife already.' He didn't immediately answer. I said, 'Gervase is knocking back a fortune in scotch.'

'What's that got to do with anything?'

'How do you cope so well with illegitimacy?'

'*What?*'

'Everything's linked. So long, pal. See you.' I put the receiver down with a sigh, and ate dinner, and packed.

In the morning, having paid a few bills, I took the hired car to Heathrow and turned it in there and, with a feeling of shackles dropping off, hopped into the air.

I spent four nights in New York before I found Malcolm; or before he found me, to be more precise.

In daily consultations, the Stamford voice assured me that I wasn't forgotten, that the message would one day get through. I had a vision of native bearers beating through jungles, but it wasn't like that, it transpired. Malcolm and Ramsey had simply been moving from horse farm to horse farm through deepest Kentucky, and it was from there he finally phoned at eight-ten in the morning.

'What are you doing in New York?' he demanded.

'Looking at skyscrapers,' I said.

'I thought we were meeting in California.'

'Well, we are,' I said. 'When?'

'What's today?'

'Friday.'

'Hang on.'

I heard him talking in the background, then he returned. 'We're just going out to see some horses breeze. Ramsey reserved the rooms from tomorrow through Saturday at the Beverly Wilshire, he says, but he and I are going to spend a few more days here now. You go to California tomorrow and I'll join you, say, on Wednesday.'

'Couldn't you please make it sooner? I do need to talk to you.'

'Did you find something out?' His voice suddenly changed gear, as if he'd remembered almost with shock the world of terrors he'd left behind.

'A few things.'

'Tell me.'

'Not on the telephone. Not in a hurry. Go and see the horses breeze and meet me tomorrow.' I paused. 'There are horses in California. Thousands of them.'

He was quiet for a few moments, then he said, 'I owe it to you. I'll be there,' and disconnected.

I arranged my air ticket and spent the rest of the day as I'd spent all the others in New York, wandering around, filling eyes and ears with the city . . . thinking painful private thoughts and coming to dreadful conclusions.

Malcolm kept his word and, to my relief, came without Ramsey who had decided Stamford needed him if Connecticut were to survive. Ramsey, Malcolm said, would be over on Wednesday, we would all have three days at the races and go to Australia on Saturday night.

He was crackling with energy, the eyes intensely blue. He and Ramsey had bought four more horses in partnership, he said in the first three minutes, and were joining a syndicate to own some others down under.

A forest fire out of control, I thought, and had sympathy for my poor brothers.

The Beverly Wilshire gave us a suite with brilliant red flocked wallpaper in the sitting room and vivid pink and orange flowers on a turquoise background in the bedrooms. There were ornate crimson curtains, filmy cream inner curtains, a suspicion of lace, an air of Edwardian roguishness brought up to date. Rooms to laugh in, I thought. And with little wrought-iron balconies outside the bowed windows looking down on a pool with a fountain and gardens and orange trees, not much to complain of.

We dined downstairs in a bar that had tables at one end and music, and Malcolm said I looked thinner.

'Tell me about the horses,' I said; and heard about them through the smoked salmon, the salad, the veal and the coffee.

'Don't worry,' he said, near the beginning. 'They're not all as expensive as Blue Clancy and Chrysos. We got all four for under a million dollars, total, and they're two-year-olds ready to run. Good breeding; the best. One's by Alydar, even.'

I listened, amused and impressed. He knew the

breeding of all his purchases back three generations, and phrases like 'won a stakes race' and 'his dam's already produced Group I winners' came off his tongue as if he'd been saying them all his life.

'Do you mind if I ask you something?' I said eventually.

'I won't know until you ask.'

'No . . . um . . . just how rich *are* you?'

He laughed. 'Did Joyce put you up to that question?'

'No. I wanted to know for myself.'

'Hm.' He thought. 'I can't tell you to the nearest million. It changes every day. At a rough estimate, about a hundred million pounds. It would grow now of its own accord at the rate of five million a year if I never lifted a finger again, but you know me, that would be boring, I'd be dead in a month.'

'After tax?' I said.

'Sure.' He smiled. 'Capital gains tax usually. I've spent a year's investment income after tax on the horses, that's all. Not as much as that on all those other projects that the family were going bananas about. I'm not raving mad. There'll be plenty for everyone when I pop off. More than there is now. I just have to live longer. You tell them that.'

'I told them you'd said in your will that if you were murdered, it would all go to charity.'

'Why didn't I think of that?'

'Did you think any more of letting the family have some of the lucre before you . . . er . . . pop off?'

'You know my views on that.'

'Yes, I do.'

'And you don't approve.'

'I don't disapprove in theory. The trust funds were generous when they were set up. Many fathers don't do as much. But your children aren't perfect and some of them have got into messes. If someone were bleeding, would you buy them a bandage?'

He sat back in his chair and stared moodily at his coffee.

'Have they sent you here to plead for them?' he asked.

'No. I'll tell you what's been happening, then you can do what you like.'

'Fair enough,' he said, 'but not tonight.'

'All right.' I paused. 'I won a race at Kempton, did you know?'

'Did you really?' He was instantly alive with interest, asking for every detail. He didn't want to hear about his squabbling family with its latent murderer. He was tired of being vilified while at the same time badgered to be bountiful. He felt safe in California although he had, I'd been interested to discover, signed us into the hotel as Watson and Watson.

'Well, you never know, do you?' he'd said. 'It may say in the British papers that Blue Clancy's coming over, and Ramsey says this hotel is the centre for the Breeders' Cup organizers. They're having reception rooms here, and buffets. By Wednesday, he says, this place will be teeming with the international racing crowd. So where, if someone wanted to find me, do you think they'd look first?'

'I think Norman West gave us good advice.'

'So do I.'

The Watsons, father and son, breakfasted the following morning out in the warm air by the pool, sitting in white chairs beside a white table under a yellow sun umbrella, watching the oranges ripen amid dark green leaves, talking of horrors.

I asked him casually enough if he remembered Fred and the tree roots.

'Of course I do,' he said at once. 'Bloody fool could have killed himself.' He frowned. 'What's that got to do with the bomb at Quantum?'

'Superintendent Yale thinks it may have given someone the idea.'

He considered it. 'I suppose it might.'

'The superintendent, or some of his men, asked old Fred what he'd used to set off the cordite . . .' I told Malcolm about the cordite still lying around in the tool shed ' . . . and Fred said he had some detonators, but after that first bang, you came out and took them away.'

'Good Lord, I'd forgotten that. Yes, so I did. You were all there, weren't you? Pretty well the whole family?'

'Yes, it was one of those weekends. Helen says it

was the first time she met you, she was there too, before she was married to Donald.'

He thought back. 'I don't remember that. I just remember there being a lot of you.'

'The superintendent wonders if you remember what happened to the detonators after you'd taken them away.'

He stared. 'It's twenty years ago, must be,' he protested.

'It might be the sort of thing you wouldn't forget.'

He shook his head doubtfully.

'Did you turn them over to the police?'

'No.' He was definite about that, anyway. 'Old Fred had no business to have them, but I wouldn't have got him into trouble, or the friend he got them from, either. I'll bet they were nicked.'

'Do you remember what they looked like?' I asked.

'Well, yes, I suppose so.' He frowned, thinking, pouring out more coffee. 'There was a row of them in a tin, laid out carefully in cotton wool so that they shouldn't roll about. Small silverish tubes, about two and a half inches long.'

'Fred says they had instructions with them.'

He laughed. 'Did he? A do-it-yourself bomb kit?' He sobered suddenly. 'I suppose it was just that. I don't remember the instructions, but I dare say they were there.'

'You did realize they were dangerous, didn't you?'

'I probably did, but all those years ago ordinary

people didn't know so much about bombs. I mean, not terrorist bombs. We'd been bombed from the air, but that was different. I should think I took the detonators away from Fred so he shouldn't set off any more explosions, not because they were dangerous in themselves, if you see what I mean?'

'Mm. But you did know you shouldn't drop them?'

'You mean if I'd dropped them, I wouldn't be here talking about it?'

'According to the explosives expert working at Quantum, quite likely not.'

'I never worked with explosives, being an adjutant.' He buttered a piece of croissant, added marmalade and ate it. His service as a young officer in his war had been spent in arranging details of troop movements and as assistant to camp commanders, often near enough to the enemy but not seeing the whites of their eyes. He never spoke of it much: it had been history before I was born.

'I remembered where the cordite was, even after all this time,' I said. 'If you imagine yourself going into the house with this tin of detonators, where would you be likely to put it? You'd put it where you would think of looking for it first, wouldn't you?'

'Yes,' he nodded, 'always my system.' A faraway unfocused look appeared in his eyes, then he suddenly sat bolt upright.

'I know where they are! I saw the tin not so very long ago, when I was looking for something else. I didn't pay much attention. It didn't even register what was in it, but I'm pretty sure now that that's what it was. It's a sort of sweet tin, not very big, with a picture on top.'

'Where was it, and how long ago?'

'Surely,' he said, troubled, 'they'd be duds by this time?'

'Quite likely not.'

'They're in the office.' He shrugged self-excusingly. 'You know I never tidy that place up. I'd never find anything ever again. I'm always having to stop people tidying it.'

'Like Moira?'

'She could hardly bear to keep her hands off.'

'Where in the office?' I remembered the jumble in his desk drawer when I'd fetched his passport. The whole place was similar.

'On top of some of the books in the breakfront bookcase. Bottom row, right over on the right-hand side, more or less out of sight when the door's closed. On top of the Dickens.' His face suddenly split into a huge grin. 'I remember now, by God. I put it there because the picture on the tin's lid was The Old Curiosity Shop.'

I rubbed my hand over my face, trying not to laugh. Superintendent Yale was going to love it.

'They're safe enough there,' Malcolm said reasonably, 'behind glass. I mean, no one can pick them up accidentally, can they? That's where they are.'

I thought it highly likely that that's where they weren't, but I didn't bother to say so. 'The glass in the breakfront is broken,' I said.

He was sorry about that. It had been his mother's, he said, like all the books.

'When did you see the tin there?' I asked.

'Haven't a clue. Not all that long ago, I wouldn't have thought, but time goes so quickly.'

'Since Moira died?'

He wrinkled his forehead. 'No, probably not. Then, before that, I was away from the house for a week or ten days when I couldn't stand being in the same place with her and she obdurately wouldn't budge. Before that, I was looking for something in a book. Not in Dickens, a shelf or two higher. Can't remember what book, though I suppose I might if I went back and stood in front of them and looked at the titles. Altogether, over three months ago, I should say.'

I reflected a bit and drank my coffee. 'I suppose the bookcase must have been moved now and then for redecorating. The books taken out . . .'

'Don't be ridiculous,' Malcolm interrupted with amusement. 'It weighs more than a ton. The books stay inside it. Redecorating goes on around it, and not at all if I can help it. Moira tried to make me take everything out so she could paint the whole office dark green. I stuck my toes in. She had the rest of the house. That room is mine.'

I nodded lazily. It was pleasant in the sunshine. A

few people were sunbathing, a child was swimming, a waiter in a white jacket came along with someone else's breakfast. All a long way away from the ruins of Quantum.

From that quiet Sunday morning and on until Wednesday, Malcolm and I led the same remote existence, being driven round Los Angeles and Hollywood and Beverly Hills in a stretch-limousine Malcolm seemed to have hired by the yard, neck-twisting like tourists, going out to Santa Anita racetrack in the afternoons, dining in restaurants like Le Chardonnay.

I gradually told him what was happening in the family, never pressing, never heated, never too much at one time, stopping at once if he started showing impatience.

'Donald and Helen should send their children to state schools,' he said moderately.

'Maybe they should. But you sent Donald to Marlborough, and you went there yourself. Donald wants the best for his boys. He's suffering to give them what you gave him effortlessly.'

'He's a snob to choose Eton.'

'Maybe, but the Marlborough fees aren't much less.'

'What if it was Donald and Helen who've been trying to kill me?'

'If they had plenty of money they wouldn't be tempted.'

'You've said that before, or something like it.'

'Nothing has changed.'

Malcolm looked out of the long car's window as we were driven up through the hills of Bel Air on the way to the racetrack.

'Do you see those houses perched on the cliffs, hanging out over space? People must be mad to live like that, on the edge.'

I smiled. 'You do,' I said.

He liked Santa Anita racetrack immediately and so did I; it would have been difficult not to. Royal palms near the entrances stretched a hundred feet upward, all bare trunks except for the crowning tufts, green fronds against the blue sky. The buildings were towered and turreted, sea-green in colour, with metal tracery of stylized palm leaves along the balconies and golden shutters over rear-facing windows. It looked more like a château than a racecourse, at first sight.

Ramsey Osborn had given Malcolm fistfuls of instructions and introductions and, as always, Malcolm was welcomed as a kindred spirit upstairs in the Club. He was at home from the first minute, belonging to the scene as if he'd been born there. I envied him his ease and didn't know how to acquire it. Maybe time would do it. Maybe millions. Maybe a sense of achievement.

While he talked easily to almost strangers (soon to be cronies) about the mixing of European and American bloodlines in thoroughbreds, I thought of the phone call I'd made at dawn on Monday morning to Superintendent Yale. Because of the eight-hour time difference, it was already afternoon with him, and I thought it unlikely I would reach him at first try. He was there, however, and came on the line with unstifled annoyance.

'It's a week since you telephoned.'

'Yes, sorry.'

'Where are you?'

'Around,' I said. His voice sounded as clear to me as if he were in the next room, and presumably mine to him, as he didn't at all guess I wasn't in England. 'I found my father,' I said.

'Oh. Good.'

I told him where Malcolm had stored the detonators. 'On top of *The Old Curiosity Shop*, as appropriate.'

There was a shattered silence. 'I don't believe it,' he said.

'The books are all old and leatherbound classics standing in full editions. Poets, philosophers, novelists, all bought years ago by my grandmother. We were all allowed to borrow a book occasionally to read, but we had to put it back. My father had us well trained.'

'Are you saying that anyone who borrowed a book from that bookcase could have seen the detonators?'

'Yes, I suppose so, if they've been there for twenty years.'

'Did you know they were there?'

'No. I didn't read those sort of books much. Spent my time riding.'

Lucy, I thought, had in her teens plunged into poets as a fish into its native sea, but twenty years ago she had been twenty-two and writing her own immortality. None of the rest of us had been scholars. Some of grandmother's books had never been opened.

'It is incredible that when someone thought of making a bomb, the detonators were to hand,' Yale complained.

'Other way round, wouldn't you think?' I said. 'The availability of the detonators suggested the bomb.'

'The pool of common knowledge in your family is infuriating,' he said. 'No one can be proved to have special access to explosives. No one has a reliable alibi . . . except Mrs Ferdinand . . . Everyone can make a timing device and nearly all of you have a motive.'

'Irritating,' I agreed.

'That's the wrong word,' he said sourly. 'Where's your father?'

'Safe.'

'You can't stay in hiding for ever.'

'Don't expect to see us for a week or two. What chance is there of your solving the case?'

Enquiries were proceeding, he said with starch. If I came across any further information, I would please give it to him.

Indeed, I said, I would.

'When I was younger,' he said to my surprise, 'I used to think I had a nose for a villain, that I could always tell. But since then, I've met embezzlers I would have trusted my savings to, and murderers I'd have let marry my daughter. Murderers can look like harmless ordinary people.' He paused. 'Does your family know who killed Moira Pembroke?'

'I don't think so.'

'Please enlarge,' he said.

'One or two may suspect they know, but they're not telling. I went to see everyone. No one was even guessing. No one accusing. They don't want to know, don't want to face it, don't want the misery.'

'And you?'

'I don't want the misery either, but I also don't want my father killed, or myself.'

'Do you think you're in danger?'

'Oh, yes,' I said. '*In loco* Moira.'

'As chief beneficiary?'

'Something like that. Only I'm not chief, I'm equal. My father made a new will saying so. I've told the family but they don't believe it.'

'Produce the will. Show it to them.'

'Good idea,' I said. 'Thank you.'

'And you,' he paused, 'do you know, yourself?'

'I don't know.'

'Guess, then.'

'Guessing is one thing, proof is another.'

'I might remind you it's your duty . . .'

'It's not my duty,' I interrupted without heat, 'to go off half-cocked. My duty to my family is to get it right or do nothing.'

I said goodbye to him rather firmly and concluded, from his tone as much as his words, that the police had no more information than I had, and perhaps less: that they hadn't managed (if they'd tried) to find out where the grey plastic clock had come from or who had bought it, which was their only lead as far as I could see and a pretty hopeless proposition. It had been a cheap mass-production clock, probably on sale in droves.

Malcolm said on one of our car journeys, after I'd been telling him about Berenice, 'Vivien, you know, had this thing about sons.'

'But she had a boy first. She had two.'

'Yes, but before Donald was born, she said she wouldn't look at the baby if it was a girl. I couldn't understand it. I'd have liked a girl. Vivien's self-esteem utterly depended on having a boy. She was obsessed with it. You'd have thought she'd come from some dreadful tribe where it really mattered.'

'It did matter,' I said. 'And it matters to Berenice. All obsessions matter because of their results.'

'Vivien never loved Lucy, you know,' he said thoughtfully. 'She shoved her away from her. I always thought that was why Lucy got fat and retreated into poetic fantasies.'

'Berenice shoves off her daughters onto her mother as much as she can.'

'Do you think Berenice murdered Moira?' he said doubtfully.

'I think she thinks that having more money would make her happier, which it probably would. If you were going to think of any . . . er . . . distribution, I'd give it to the wives as well as the husbands. Separately, I mean. So they had independence.'

'Why?' he said.

'Gervase might value Ursula more if she didn't need him financially.'

'Ursula's a mouse.'

'She's desperate.'

'They're all desperate,' he said with irritation. 'It's all their own faults. The fault, dear Brutus, is not in our stars but in ourselves, that we are underlings.'

'I dare say,' I said.

'The bell captain at the hotel gave me a tip for the fourth race.'

Back to horses.

Another day, another journey.

Malcolm said, 'What did Serena say, when you saw her?'

'She said you could stuff your money, or words to that effect.'

Malcolm laughed.

'She also said,' I went on, 'that Alicia told her you'd only tried to get custody of her that time so as to be cruel to Alicia.'

'Alicia's a real bitch.'

'She's got a lover, did you know?' I said.

He was thunderstruck. 'Who is he?'

'Someone else's husband, I should think. That's what she likes, isn't it?'

'Don't be so bloody accurate.'

Further down the road we were talking about the time switch clocks, which had been an unwelcome piece of news to him also.

'Thomas was best at making them, wasn't he?' Malcolm said. 'He could do them in a jiffy. They were his idea originally, I think. Serena brought one over for Robin and Peter which Thomas had made for her years ago.'

I nodded. 'A Mickey Mouse clock. It's still there in the playroom.'

'Serena made them a lighthouse of Lego to go with it, I remember.' He sighed deeply. 'I miss Coochie still, you know. The crash happened not long after that.' He shook his head to rid it of sadness. 'What race shall we choose for the Coochie Memorial Trophy? What do you think?'

On another day, I asked why Ferdinand didn't mind being illegitimate when Gervase did, to the brink of breakdown.

'I don't know,' Malcolm said. 'Gervase always thinks people are sneering and laughing, even now. Someone rubbed his nose in it when he was young, you know. Told him he was rubbish, a mistake, should have been aborted. Boys can be bloody cruel. Gervase got aggressive to compensate, I suppose. Nothing ever worried Ferdinand very much. He's like me in more than looks.'

'Only two wives so far,' I said incautiously.

'Why don't you get married?' he asked.

I was flippant. 'Haven't met the one and only. Don't want five.'

'Don't you trust yourself?' he said.

Christ, I thought, that was sharp, that was penetrating. That was unfair. It was because of him that I didn't trust myself: because in inconstancy, I felt I was very much his son.

His imprint, for better or worse, was on us all.

CHAPTER EIGHTEEN

On Wednesday, the Beverly Wilshire came alive as Ramsey had prophesied and Ramsey himself blew in with gusto and plans. We would go to parties. We would go round the horse barns. We would go to a Hollywood Gala Ball.

The Breeders' Cup organizers opened their reception room where everyone concerned with the races could have breakfast and cocktails (together if they liked) and talk about horses, could arrange cars and tickets and talk about horses, could meet the people they'd met at Epsom and Longchamp and talk about horses. Well-mannered people in good suits and silk dresses, owners whose enthusiasm prompted and funded the sport. Big bucks, big business, big fun.

Malcolm adored it. So did I. Life in high gear. Early on Friday, we went out to the racecourse to see Blue Clancy in his barn and watch him breeze round the track in his last warm-up before the big one. His English trainer was with him, and his English lad. There was heady excitement, a lot of anxiety. The orderly bustle of stable life, the smells, the swear words, the earthy humour, the pride, the affection, the jealousies, the injustices, the dead disappointments, all the same the world over.

Blue Clancy looked fine, worked well, threw Malcolm and Ramsey into back-slapping ecstasies. 'Wait until tomorrow,' the trainer said cautiously, watching them. 'We're taking on the best in the world, don't forget. The hot money is for a California-bred horse.'

'What's hot money?' Malcolm demanded.

'The bets made by people in the know. People with inside information.'

Who cared, Malcolm said. He couldn't remember ever having more fun in his life: and I thought his euphoria was at least partly due to his three close approaches to losing it.

Along with a thousand others, we went to the ball, though in the stretch-limo, not a converted pumpkin, and in the vast sound stage which had lately held a split-open aeroplane for filming cabin dramas, Malcolm danced with several ladies he'd known well for two days. He spent his time laughing. He was infectious. Everyone around him lit up like nightlights, banishing gloom.

We slept, we ate breakfast, we went to the races. The smog that all week had covered the mountains everyone swore were there on the far side of the track, relented and evaporated and disclosed a sunlit rocky backdrop worthy of the occasion. Tables with tablecloths had appeared overnight throughout the Club stands, and overworked black-coated waiters sweated under huge trays of food, threading through ever-moving racegoers, never dropping the lot.

There were seven Breeders' Cup races; various distances, variously aged horses. The first five each offered a total purse (for first, second, third and so on) of one million dollars. Blue Clancy's race, the one-and-a-half-mile Turf, had a purse of two million, and the climactic event, the Breeders' Cup Classic, promised three. They weren't racing for peanuts. The owner of the winner of Blue Clancy's race would be personally richer by six hundred and twenty-nine thousand dollars, enough to keep him in Bollinger for weeks.

We cheered home the first five winners. We went down to the saddling stalls and saw Blue Clancy prepared. We went up to the stands and bit our nails.

Five of the seven races were run on the dirt track, two on grass, of which this was the second; and most of the European horses were running on grass, the green stuff of home. Blue Clancy was taking on the Epsom Derby winner, the Arc de Triomphe winner and the winner of the Italian Derby. On paper, he looked to have an outside chance of coming fourth. In Malcolm's and Ramsey's eyes, he was a shoo-in. (Malcolm had learned the local jargon.)

Blue Clancy broke cleanly from the gate away on the far side of the course and his English jockey held him handily in sixth place all down the far side. Ramsey and Malcolm were looking through binoculars and muttering encouragements. Blue Clancy, not hearing them, swung into the long left-hand bottom bend in no better position and was still lying sixth when the field crossed the dirt track as they turned for home. Malcolm's muttering grew louder. 'Come on, you bugger. Come on.'

There was no clear leader. Three horses raced together in front, followed by a pair together, then Blue Clancy alone. Too much to do, I thought: and the agile colt immediately proved me wrong. His jockey swung him wide of the others to allow him a clear run and gave him unmistakable signals that now was the time that mattered, now, this half-minute, if never again.

Blue Clancy accelerated. Malcolm was shouting, Ramsey was speechless. Blue Clancy in third place, all the crowds roaring. Blue Clancy still faster, second now. Malcolm silent, mouth open, eyes staring. The incredible was happening, awesome, breathtaking . . . and Blue Clancy had definitely, indubitably won.

Malcolm's eyes were like sapphires lit from inside. He still couldn't speak. Ramsey grabbed him by the arm and pulled him, and the two of them ran, almost dancing, weaving through slowcoaches, making their way down to greet their champion's return. I followed close on their heels, marvelling. Some owners were always lucky, some owners always weren't; it was an inexplicable fact of racing life. Malcolm's luck was stupendous. It always had been, in everything except wives. I should have known, I supposed, that it would come with him onto the track. King Midas had touched him, and Blue Clancy was his latest gold.

I wondered ironically what the family would say. The fortune he'd flung away on horses had already come back: Blue Clancy was worth at least double what he'd been before the Arc.

Chrysos, I daydreamed, would win the Derby. The tadpole film (about sharks actually, Malcolm had told me) would win at Cannes. The Pol Roger would appreciate. Everyone would see the point of not murdering the golden goose (Wrong sex, never mind. It was a lightheaded day.) We could return home to welcomes and safety.

Only it wasn't like that. We would return home to an unassessable danger, and it was essential to be aware of it, and to plan.

Sobered as always by what lay ahead, I nevertheless went to a post-race party in fine spirits, and after that to Los Angeles airport to fly through the night to Australia. The party, the people came with us. Melbourne took up the impetus, pressing forward to its own Cup, always held on the first Tuesday in November. Everything, they told us there, stopped for the race. Schoolchildren had a holiday and the Melbourne shops closed. The Hyatt Hotel, where we stayed (Watson and Watson), had a lobby criss-crossed by people known better in Newmarket, all with the ready grins of kids out of school.

Ramsey had surpassed himself in the matter of reservations. Even to reach our floor, we had to use a special key in the elevator, and there was a private lounge up there for cocktails and breakfast (but separately). Malcolm appreciated it, took it all in his stride, ordered champagne, breathed Melbourne air and became an instant Australian.

Out at Flemington racecourse (no château), there was less sophistication than at Santa Anita, just as much enthusiasm, very good food, a much better parade ring. Malcolm found the day's racing less compulsive than Paris or California through not owning a runner. He'd tried to remedy this on arrival, but no one would sell one of the top bunch, and he wanted nothing less. Instead, he set about gambling with method but only in tens and soon tired of it, win or lose. I left him and Ramsey in the Committee rooms and wandered down to the crowd as in Paris, and wondered how many in the throng struggled with intractable problems in their shirtsleeves, no shirts, carnival hats. When the party was over, Malcolm would grow restless and want to move on, and I wasn't ready. Under the shade of trees, surrounded by beer cans, listening to the vigorous down-under language, I searched for the solution that would cause us least grief.

There was no truly easy way out. No overlooking or dodging what had been done to Moira. But if someone could plead guilty and plead diminished responsibility owing to stress, there might be a quiet trial and a lifetime for us of visiting a sort of hospital instead of a rigorous prison. Either way, any way, there were tears in our future.

On top of that I had to be right, and I had to convince Malcolm beyond any doubt that I was. Had to convince all the family, and the police, without any mistake. Had to find a way of doing it that was peaceful and simple, for all our sakes.

I watched the Melbourne Cup from ground level, which meant in effect that I didn't see much of it because of the other thousands doing the same. On the other hand, I was closer to the horses before and after, watching them walk, listening to comments, mostly unflattering, from knowledgeable elbowers striving for a view.

The Melbourne Cup runners were older and more rugged than stars back home. Some were eight or nine. All raced far more often, once a week not being unusual. The favourite for that day's race had won on the course three days earlier.

They were racing for a purse of a million Australian dollars, of which sixty-five per cent went to the winner, besides a handsome gold cup. Thwarted this year, Malcolm, I imagined, would be back next year. He'd met in Paris and California several of the owners now standing in the parade ring and I could guess the envy he was feeling. No one was as passionate as a new convert.

When the race was finally off, I couldn't hear the commentary for the exhortations around me, but it didn't much matter: the winner was owned by one of the international owners and afterwards I found Malcolm beside the winner's enclosure looking broody and thinking expensive thoughts.

'Next year,' he said.

'You're addicted.'

He didn't deny it. He and Ramsey slapped each other on the back, shook hands and promised like blood brothers to meet regularly on every major race-course in the world. Ramsey, the bulky manufacturer of millions of baseball caps, had somewhere along the line realized what 'metal' really meant in Malcolm's vocabulary and from cronies they had become comfortable friends, neither feeling at an advantage over the other.

They discussed staying on in Australia but Ramsey said the baseball caps needed guidance. Malcolm wavered about going to see some gold mines in Kalgoorlie but decided on a gold share broker in Melbourne instead. We spent Melbourne Cup night in a farewell dinner, and when Ramsey had departed in the morning and left us alone in the quiet breakfast room upstairs, Malcolm looked at me as if coming down to earth for the first time since we'd left England. With a touch of despondency, he asked for how long he was to be exiled for safety's sake.

'But you've enjoyed it,' I said.

'God, yes.' The remembrance flashed in his eyes. 'But it's not real life. We have to go back. I know I've avoided talking about it, it's all dreadful. I know you've been thinking about it all this time. I could see it in your face.'

'I've come to know them all so much better,' I said, 'my brothers and my sisters. I didn't care for them all that much, you know, before Moira died. We've always met of course from time to time, but I'd forgotten to a great extent what we had been like as children.' I paused for a bit, but he didn't comment. 'Since the bomb went off at Quantum,' I said, 'a great deal of the past has come back. And I've seen, you know, how the present has grown out of that past. How my sisters-in-law and my brother-in-law have been affected by it. How people easily believe lies, old and new. How destructive it is to yearn for the unobtainable, to be unsatisfied by anything else. How obsessions don't go away, they get worse.'

He was silent for a while, then said, 'Bleak.' Then he sighed and said, 'How much do they need, then? How much should I give them? I don't believe in it, but I see it's necessary. Their obsessions have got worse as I've grown richer. If the money wasn't there, they'd have sorted themselves out better. Is that what you're saying?'

'Yes, partly.' It hadn't been, entirely, but as it had

produced a reaction I'd wanted but hadn't expected, I kept quiet.

'All right, then,' he said. 'I've had a bloody good holiday and I'm feeling generous, so draw up a list of who's to get what.'

'All equal,' I said.

He began to protest, but sighed instead. 'What about you, then?'

'I don't know. We'll decide about that later.'

'I thought you wanted half a million to set up as a trainer.'

'I've changed my mind. For now, anyway. There's something else I want to do first.'

'What's that?'

I hesitated. I'd barely admitted it to myself, had certainly told no one else.

'Go on,' he urged.

'Be a jockey. Turn professional.'

'Good Lord,' he said, astonished, 'haven't you left it too late?'

'Maybe. We'll see. I'll have three or four years, perhaps. Better than not trying.'

'You amaze me.' He reflected. 'Come to think of it, you've constantly amazed me since you came to Newmarket Sales. It seems I hardly knew you before.'

'That's how I feel about you,' I said, 'and about all of the family.'

*

We set off homewards later the same day, travelling west via Singapore. Malcolm's gold share broker happened to be going there at the same time, so I changed places with him on the aeroplane and let the two of them say things like 'percussion and rotary air blast drilling to get a first idea' and 'diamond core drilling is necessary for estimating reserves accurately', which seemed to entertain them for hours.

I thought meantime about invitations. About invitations like meat over bear pits. The right invitation would bring the right visitor. The problem was how to make the invitation believable.

Part of the trouble was time. When we reached England, Malcolm would have been out of harm's way for four weeks, and I for almost three. We'd been safe, and I'd had time to reflect: those on the plus side. On the minus, as far as the invitation was concerned, was the fact that it would be six weeks since Malcolm had survived in the garage, and ten since Moira had died. Would a classic trap invitation work after so long an interval? Only one thing to do: try it and see.

Malcolm's voice was saying, '. . . a section assaying five point eight grams per tonne' and a bit later, '. . . Big Bell's plant milling oxide and soft rock', and '. . . the future is good in Queensland, with those epithermal gold zones at Woolgar'. The broker listened and nodded and looked impressed. My old man, I thought, really knows his stuff. He'd told me at one point on our journeyings that there were roughly twenty-five hundred active gold mines in Australia and that it would soon rival or even surpass Canada as a producer. I hadn't known gold was big in Canada. I was ignorant, he said. Canada had so far come regularly second to South Africa in the non-communist world.

We'd taught each other quite a lot, I thought, in one way and another.

I would need someone to deliver the invitation. Couldn't do it myself.

'Market capitalization per ounce . . .' I heard the broker saying in snatches, and ' . . . in situ reserves based on geological interpretation . . .'

I knew who could deliver the invitation. The perfect person.

'As open-cut mining cost as little as two hundred Australian dollars an ounce . . .'

Bully for open-cut mining, I thought, and drifted to sleep.

We left spring behind in Australia on Wednesday and came home to winter on Friday in England. Malcolm and I went back to the Ritz as Mr and Mr Watson and he promised with utmost sincerity that he wouldn't telephone anyone, not even his London broker. I went shopping in the afternoon and then confounded him at the brandy and cigar stage late that evening by getting through to Joyce.

'But you said . . .' he hissed as he heard her voice jump as usual out of the receiver.

'Listen,' I hissed back. 'Hello, Joyce.'

'Darling! Where are you? What are you doing? Where's your father?'

'In Australia,' I said.

'*What?*' she yelled.

'Looking at gold mines,' I said.

It made sense to her, as it would make sense to them all.

'He went to California, I saw it in the paper,' she said. 'Blue Clancy won a race.'

'We went to Australia afterwards.'

'*We?* Darling, where are you now?'

'It doesn't matter where I am,' I said. 'To make it safe for us to come home, will you help to find out who killed Moira?'

'But darling, the police have been trying for weeks . . . and anyway, Ferdinand says it has to be Arthur Bellbrook.'

'It's not Arthur Bellbrook,' I said.

'Why not?' She sounded argumentative, still wanting it to be Arthur, wanting it to be the intruder from outside. 'He could have done it easily. Ferdinand says he could have done everything. It has to be him. He had a shotgun, Ferdinand says.'

I said, 'Arthur didn't use his shotgun. More importantly, he wouldn't have made a timing device exactly like we'd made as children, and he hadn't a motive.'

'He could have detested Moira.'

'Absolutely,' I said, 'but why should he want to kill Malcolm, whom he liked? I saw his face when he found Malcolm was alive that morning after the bomb, and he was genuinely glad.'

'Everyone wants it to be Arthur Bellbrook,' she said obstinately. 'He found her body.'

'If the police thought he'd done it, they wouldn't have been so suspicious of Malcolm.'

'You've got an answer for everything,' she complained.

I had myself for a while wished it to be Arthur. After all, there had been the affair of the prize vegetables (but he'd sounded philosophical about them, and would anyone kill for so little?) and he'd been in the army and might know about explosives. But he stood to lose rather than gain from Malcolm's death, and it was beyond believing that he would trace Malcolm to Cambridge, follow him to Newmarket Sales and try to run him down. That was the work of obsession. Arthur placidly digging potatoes; Arthur enjoying the temporary fame; Arthur looking after the dogs. Arthur had been the personification of stolid, sensible balance.

Besides, whoever had tried to run Malcolm down at Newmarket had guessed Malcolm would leave the sales with me and would come to the car park, and at that point Arthur would have had no reason to think so. He didn't know me. Hadn't met me until he came into the house with his shotgun, thinking I was a burglar. I'd had to exclude Arthur, although with regret.

Joyce said, 'Darling, how do you expect to succeed where the police have failed?'

'The police can't do what we can do.'

'What do you mean? What can we do?'

I told her. Malcolm's mouth opened and there was a long silence from Joyce.

'Let me get this straight,' she said eventually. 'You want me to telephone to everyone in the family . . .'

'*Everyone*,' I said emphatically. 'If a husband answers, tell him, then ask to speak to the wife, and tell her too. And vice versa.'

'Yes,' she said. 'I'm to say you're in Australia, both of you. Right?'

'Yes.'

'I'm to gush. Dreadful word, where *did* you learn it? I'm to let all this drip out as if it were of absolutely no importance but something I've just thought of? Darling, you can't mean I have to ring up *Alicia*?'

'Especially Alicia. Tell her I told you she has a boy-friend. That should stir her up nicely.'

'Darling, you don't mean it!'

'Ask her. And . . . er . . . do you know if the police are still guarding Quantum?'

'They told Donald that if he wanted constant guards, he'd have to get his own now. No one in the family wants to spend the money, so the police just have it on their occasional surveillance list, apparently.'

'And has anything else much happened in the family since we've been away?'

'No, nothing new. Thomas left Berenice, did you know that?'

'Yes . . . Is he still with Lucy?'

'Yes, darling, I think so. Do you want me to tell him too?'

'You might as well.'

'I'm to think of something to phone them about and gossip a bit, and then I'm to say that I don't really care who killed Moira, but I don't think the police were thorough. Is that right? They never thought of looking for her notepad, the one she used to keep in the kitchen, in one of the drawers of those dazzling white cabinets. When anyone telephoned when she was in the kitchen, which was a lot of the time, she doodled their names with stars and things round it and wrote notes like "Donald, Sunday, noon" when people were coming to visit. I'm to say the police could never have found it but I've just remembered it, and I wonder if it's still there. I'm thinking of telling the police about it after the weekend. Is that right?'

'That's right,' I said.

'And I'm to say, what if she wrote down the name of her murderer?'

'Yes,' I said.

'Darling, why do you think her murderer telephoned? To make an appointment to kill her? You don't mean that, do you?'

'To make an appointment to see her, yes. To kill her, I don't know.'

'But why, darling? Why do you think the killer telephoned?'

'Because Malcolm told me she didn't like people just dropping in,' I said. 'She preferred people to telephone first. And because Moira's greenhouse can't be seen from the road, the drive, or from any windows of Quantum. Malcolm made her put it where it was well out of sight on that patch of lawn surrounded by shrubs, because he didn't like it. If anyone had come to see Moira unannounced that evening, they'd have found the house empty. If they'd telephoned first, she'd have said to come round to the greenhouse, that's where she'd be.'

'I suppose that's logical, darling. The police always did say she knew her killer, but I didn't want to believe it unless it was Arthur Bellbrook. He knew her. He fits all round, darling.'

'If Arthur had killed her, why would he go back later and find her body?'

'Darling, are you *sure* it wasn't Arthur Bellbrook?'

'Positive.'

'Oh dear. All right then, darling. You want me to start those phone calls tomorrow but definitely not before ten o'clock, and to go on all day until I've reached everyone? You do realize, I hope, that I'm playing in a sort of exhibition bridge game tomorrow evening?'

'Just keep plugging along.'

'What if they're out, or away?'

'Same thing. If nothing happens and we get no results, I'll phone you on Monday evening.'

'Darling, let me go to Quantum with you.'

'No, definitely not.' I was alarmed. 'Joyce, promise me you'll stay in Surrey. Promise!'

'Darling, don't be so vehement. All right, I promise,' She paused. 'Was that old bugger in good nick when you last saw him?'

'In excellent nick,' I said.

'Can't help being fond of him, darling, but don't bloody tell him I said so. Can't go back, of course. But well, darling, if there's one thing I regret in my life it's getting that frightful man West to catch him with Alicia. If I'd had any bloody *sense*, darling, I'd have turned a blind eye and let him have his bit on the side. But there it is, I was too young to know any better.'

She said goodbye cheerfully, however, promising to do all the phone calls in the morning, and I put the receiver down slowly.

'Did you hear any of that last bit?' I asked Malcolm.

'Not a lot. Something about if she'd had any sense, she wouldn't have done something or other.'

'Wouldn't have divorced you,' I said.

He stared incredulously. 'She insisted on it.'

'Twenty-seven years later, she's changed her mind.'

He laughed. 'Poor old Joyce.' He spent no more

thought on it. 'Moira didn't doodle on notepads that I know of.'

'I dare say she didn't. But if you were a murderer, would you bet on it?'

He imagined it briefly. 'I'd be very worried to hear from Joyce. I would think long and hard about going to Quantum to search for the notepad before she told the police.'

'And would you go? Or would you think, if the police didn't find it when Moira was first murdered, then it isn't there? Or if it is there, there's nothing incriminating on it?'

'I don't know if I would risk it. I think I would go. If it turned out to be a silly trap of Joyce's, I could say I'd just come to see how the house was doing.' He looked at me questioningly. 'Are we both going down there?'

'Yes, but not until morning. I'm jet-lagged. Don't know about you. I need a good sleep.'

He nodded. 'Same for me.'

'And that shopping you were doing?' he eyed the several Fortnum & Mason carrier bags with tall parcels inside. 'Essential supplies?'

'Everything I could think of. We'll go down by train and . . .'

He waved his cigar in a negative gesture. 'Car and chauffeur.' He fished out his diary with the phone numbers. 'What time here?'

Accordingly, we went in the morning in great comfort and approached Quantum circumspectly from the far side, not past the eyes of the village.

The chauffeur goggled a bit at the sight of the house, with its missing centre section and boarded-up windows and large new sign saying: 'Keep out. Building unsafe.'

'Reconstructions,' Malcolm said.

The chauffeur nodded and left, and we carried the Fortnum & Mason bags across the windy central expanse and down the passage on the far side of the staircase, going towards the playroom.

Black plastic sheeting still covered all the exposed floor space, not taut and pegged down, but wrinkled and slack. Our feet made soft crunching noises on the grit under the plastic and there were small puddles here and there as if rain had blown in. The boarded-up doors and the barred stairs looked desolate, and far above, over the roof, the second black plastic sheet flapped like sails between the rafters.

Sad, sad house. Malcolm hadn't seen it like that, and was deeply depressed. He looked at the very solid job the police had made of hammering the plywood to the door frame of the playroom and asked me politely how I proposed to get in.

'With your fingernails?' he suggested.

I produced a few tools from one of the bags. 'There are other shops in Piccadilly,' I said. 'Boy scouts come prepared.'

I'd thought it likely that I wouldn't be able to get

the plywood off easily as I understood they'd used four-inch nails, so I'd brought a hammer and chisel and a saw, and before Malcolm's astonished gaze proceeded to dig a hole through the plywood and cut out a head-high, body-wide section instead. Much quicker, less sweat.

'You didn't think of all this since yesterday, did you?' he asked.

'No. On the plane. There were a lot of hours then.'

I freed the cut-out section and put it to one side, and we went into the playroom. Nothing had changed in there. Malcolm fingered the bicycles when his eyes had adjusted to the partial light, and I could see the sorrow in his body.

It was by that time nine-thirty. If Joyce by any chance phoned the right person first, the earliest we could have a visitor was about half past ten. After that, anything was possible. Or nothing.

Malcolm had wanted to know what we would do if someone came.

'All the family have keys to the outside kitchen door,' I said. 'We never had the locks changed, remember? Our visitor will go into the kitchen that way and we will go round and . . . er . . .'

'Lock him in,' Malcolm said.

'Roughly, yes. And then talk about confessing. Talk about what to do with the future.'

I went round myself to the kitchen door and made sure it did still unlock normally, which it did. I locked it again after a brief look inside. Still a mess in there, unswept.

I returned to the playroom and from the bags produced two stick-on mirrors, each about eight inches by ten.

'I thought you'd brought champagne,' Malcolm grumbled. 'Not saws and bloody looking-glasses.'

'The champagne's there. No ice.'

'It's cold enough without any bloody ice.' He wandered aimlessly round the playroom, finally slumping into one of the armchairs. We had both worn layers of the warmest clothes we had, leaving the suitcases in the Ritz, but the raw November air looked as if it would be a match for the Simpson's vicuna overcoat and my new Barbour, and the gloves I had bought for us in the same shop the day before. We were at least out of the wind which swirled round and through the house, but there was no heat but our own.

I stuck one of the mirrors onto the cut-out piece of plywood, and the other at the same height onto the wall which faced the playroom door, the side wall of the staircase: stuck it not exactly opposite the door but a little further along towards the hall.

'What are you doing?' Malcolm asked.

'Just making it possible for us to see anyone come up the drive without showing ourselves. Would you mind sitting in the other chair, and telling me when the mirrors are at the right angle? Look into the one on the stair wall. I'll move the other. OK?'

He rose and sat in the other chair as I'd asked, and I moved the plywood along and angled it slightly until he said, 'Stop. That's it. I can see a good patch of drive.'

I went and took his place and had a look for myself. It would have been better if the mirrors had been bigger, but they served the purpose. Anyone who came to the house that way would be visible.

If they came across the fields we'd have to rely on our ears.

By eleven, Malcolm was bored. By eleven-thirty, we'd temporarily unbolted and unlocked the door at the end of the passage and been out into the bushes to solve the problem posed by no plumbing. By twelve, we were into Bollinger in disposable glasses (disgusting, Malcolm said) and at twelve-thirty ate biscuits and pâté.

No one came. It seemed to get colder. Malcolm huddled inside his overcoat in the armchair and said it had been a rotten idea in the first place.

I had had to promise him that we wouldn't stay overnight. I thought it unlikely anyway that someone would choose darkness rather than daylight for searching for a small piece of paper that could be anywhere in a fairly large room, and I'd agreed to the chauffeur returning to pick us up at about six. Left to myself, I might have waited all night, but the whole point of the exercise was that Malcolm himself should be there. We would return in the morning by daybreak.

He said, 'This person we're waiting for . . . you know who it is, don't you?'

'Well . . . I think so.'

'How sure are you, expressed as a percentage?'

'Um . . . ninety-five.'

'That's not enough.'

'No, that's why we're here.'

'Edwin,' he said. 'It's Edwin, isn't it?'

I glanced across at him, taking my gaze momentarily off the mirrors. He wanted it to be Edwin. He could bear it to be Edwin. In Edwin's own words, he could have faced it. Edwin might possibly have been capable of killing Moira, I thought: an unplanned killing, shoving her head into the potting compost because the open bag of it gave him the idea. I didn't think he had the driving force, the imagination or the guts to have attempted the rest.

When I didn't contradict him, Malcolm began saying, 'If Edwin comes . . .' and it was easier to leave it that way.

Time crept on. It was cold. By two-thirty, to stoke our internal fires, we were eating rich dark fruit cake and drinking claret. (Heresy, Malcolm said. We should have had the claret with the pâté and the champagne with the cake. As at weddings? I asked. God damn you, he said.)

I didn't feel much like laughing. It was a vigil to which there could be no good end. Malcolm knew as well as I did that he might be going to learn something he fervently didn't want to know. He didn't deep down want anyone to come. And I wanted it profoundly.

By three-thirty, he was restless. 'You don't really mean to go through all this again tomorrow, do you?'

I watched the drive. No change, as before. 'The Ritz might give us a packed lunch.'

'And Monday? Not Monday as well.' He'd agreed on three days before we'd started. The actuality was proving too much.

'We'll give up on Monday when it gets dark,' I said.

'You're so bloody persistent.'

I watched the mirrors. Come, I thought. *Come.*

'Joyce might have forgotten the phone calls,' Malcolm said.

'She wouldn't forget.'

'Edwin might have been out.'

'That's more likely.'

A light-coloured car rolled up the drive, suddenly there.

No attempt at concealment. No creeping about, looking suspicious. All confidence. Not a thought given to entrapment.

I sat still, breathing deeply.

She stood up out of the car, tall and strong. She went round to the passenger side, opened the door, and lifted out a brown cardboard box which she held in front of her, with both arms round it, as one holds groceries. I'd expected her to go straight round to the kitchen door, but she didn't do that, she walked a few steps into the central chasm, looking up and around her as if with awe.

Malcolm noticed my extreme concentration, rose to his feet and put himself between me and the mirrors so that he could see what I was looking at. I thought he would be stunned and miserably silent, but he was not in the least.

'Oh, no,' he said with annoyance. 'What's *she* doing here?'

Before I could stop him, he shot straight out of the playroom and said, 'Serena, do go away, you're spoiling the whole thing.'

I was on his heels, furious with him. Serena whirled round when she heard his voice. She saw him appear in the passage. I glimpsed her face, wide-eyed and scared. She took a step backwards, and tripped on a fold of the black plastic floor covering, and let go of the box. She tried to catch it . . . touched it . . . knocked it forward.

I saw the panic on her face. I had an instantaneous understanding of what she'd brought.

I yanked Malcolm back with an arm round his neck, twisting and flinging us both to find shelter behind the wall of the staircase.

We were both still falling when the world blew apart.

CHAPTER NINETEEN

I lay short of the playroom door trying to breathe. My lungs felt collapsed. My head rang from the appalling noise, and the smell of the explosive remained as a taste as if my mouth were full of it.

Malcolm, on his stomach a few feet away, was unconscious.

The air was thick with dust and seemed to be still reverberating, though it was probably my concussion. I felt pulped. I felt utterly without strength. I felt very lucky indeed.

The house around us was still standing. We weren't under tons of new rubble. The tough old load-bearing walls that had survived the first bomb had survived the second – which hadn't anyway been the size of a suitcase.

My chest gave a heave, and breath came back. I moved, struggled to get up, tried things out. I felt bruised and unwell, but there were no broken bones; no blood. I rolled to my knees and went on them to Malcolm. He was alive, he was breathing, he was not bleeding from ears or nose: at that moment, it was enough.

I got slowly, weakly, to my feet, and walked shakily into the wide centre space. I could wish to shut my eyes, but one couldn't blot it out. One had to live through terrible things if they came one's way.

At the point where the bomb had exploded, the black floor covering had been ripped right away, and the rest was doubled over and convoluted in large torn pieces. Serena – the things that had been Serena – lay among and half under the black folds of plastic: things in emerald and frilly white clothes, pale blue leg-warmers, dark blue tights; torn edges of flesh, scarlet splashes . . . a scarlet pool.

I went round covering the parts of her completely with the black folds, hiding the harrowing truth from anyone coming there unprepared. I felt ill. I felt as if my head were full of air. I was trembling uncontrollably. I thought of people who dealt often with such horrors and wondered if they ever got hardened.

Malcolm groaned in the passage. I went back to him fast. He was trying to sit up, to push himself off the floor. There was a large area already beginning to swell on his forehead, and I wondered if he'd simply been knocked out through hitting the wood floor at high speed.

'God,' he said in anguish. 'Serena . . . oh dear God.'

I helped him to his groggy feet and took him out into the garden through the side door, and round past the office to the front of the house. I eased him into the passenger seat of Serena's car.

Malcolm put his head in his hands and wept for his daughter. I stood with my arms on top of the car and my head on those, and felt wretched and sick and unutterably old.

I'd hardly begun to wonder what to do next when a police car came into the drive and rolled slowly, as if tentatively, towards us.

The policeman I'd looked through the windows with stopped the car and stepped out. He looked young, years younger than I was.

'Someone in the village reported another explosion . . .' He looked from us to the house questioningly.

'Don't go in there,' I said. 'Get word to the superintendent. Another bomb has gone off here, and this time someone's been killed.'

Dreadful days followed, full of questions, formalities, explanations, regrets. Malcolm and I went back to the Ritz where he grieved for the lost child who had tried hard to kill him.

'But you said . . . she didn't care about my money. *Why* . . . why did she do it all?'

'She wanted . . .' I said. 'To put it at its simplest, I think she wanted to live at Quantum with you. That's what she's longed for since she was six, when Alicia took her away. She might perhaps have grown up sweet and normal if the courts had given you custody, but courts favour mothers, of course. She wanted to have back what had been wrenched away from her. I saw her cry about it, not long ago. It was still sharp and real to her. She wanted to be your little girl again. She refused to grow up. She dressed very often like a child.'

He was listening with stretched eyes, as if seeing familiar country haunted by devils.

'Alicia was no help to her,' I said. 'She filled her with stories of how you'd rejected her, and she actively discouraged her from maturing, because of her own little-girl act.'

'Poor Serena.' He looked tormented. 'She didn't have much luck.'

'No, she didn't.'

'But Moira . . .?' he said.

'I think Serena made herself believe that if she got rid of Moira, you would go back to Quantum and she would live there with you and look after you, and her dream would come true.'

'It doesn't make sense . . .'

'Murder has nothing to do with sense. It has to do with obsession. With compulsion, irresistible impulse, morbid drive. An act beyond reason.'

He shook his head helplessly.

'It's impossible to know,' I said, 'whether she intended to kill Moira on that day. I wish we could know, but we can't . . . she can't have meant to kill her the way she did, because no one could know there'd be a slit-open nearly full sack of potting compost waiting there, handy. If she meant to kill Moira that day, she'd have taken some sort of weapon. I've been wondering, you know, if she meant to hit her over the head and put her in the car, the way she did you.'

'God . . .'

'Anyway, after Moira was out of the way, Serena offered to live with you at Quantum and look after you, but you wouldn't have it.'

'But it wouldn't have worked, you know. I didn't even consider it seriously. It was nice of her, I thought, but I didn't want her, it's true.'

'And I expect you made it clear in a fairly testy way?'

He thought about it. 'I suppose in the end I did. She kept on about it, you see. Asked me several times. Came to Quantum to beg me. I got tired of it and said no pretty definitely. I told her not to keep bothering me . . .' He looked shattered. 'She began to hate me then, do you think?'

I nodded unhappily. 'I'd think so. I think she finally believed she would never have what she craved for. You could have given it to her, and you wouldn't. The rejection was ultimate. Absolute. Extreme. She believed it, as she'd never really believed it before. She told me she'd given you a chance, but you'd turned her down.'

He put a hand over his eyes.

'So shc set out to kill you, and finally to kill the house as well . . . to destroy what she couldn't have.'

I still wondered, as I'd wondered in New York, whether it was because I, Ian, had gone back to live at Quantum with Malcolm that she'd come to that great violent protest. I had too often had what she'd yearned for. The bomb had been meant as much for me as for Malcolm, I thought.

'Do you remember that morning when she found we weren't dead?' I asked. 'She practically fainted. Everyone supposed it was from relief, but I'll bet it wasn't. She'd tried three times to kill you and it must have seemed intolerable to her that you were still alive.'

'She must have been . . . well . . . insane.'

Obsessed . . . insane. Sometimes there wasn't much difference.

Malcolm had given up champagne and gone back to scotch. The constant bubbles, I saw, had been a sort of gesture, two fingers held up defiantly in the face of danger, a gallant crutch against fear. He poured a new drink of the old stuff and stood by the window looking over Green Park.

'You knew it was Serena . . . who would come.'

'If anyone did.'

'How did you know?'

'I saw everyone, as you know. I saw what's wrong with their lives. Saw their desperations. Donald and Helen are desperate for money, but they were coping the best way they could. Bravely, really, pawning her jewellery. They thought you might help them with guaranteeing a loan, if they could find you. That's a long way from wanting to kill you.'

Malcolm nodded and drank, and watched life proceeding outside.

'Lucy,' I said, 'may have lost her inspiration but not her marbles. Edwin is petulant but not a planner, not dynamic. Thomas . . .' I paused. 'Thomas was absolutely desperate, but for peace in his house, not for the money itself. Berenice has made him deeply ineffective. He's got a long way to go, to climb back. He seemed to me incapable almost of tying his shoelaces, let alone making a time bomb, even if he did invent the wired-up clocks.'

'Go on,' Malcolm said.

'Berenice is obsessed with herself and her desires, but her grudge is against Thomas. Money would make her quieter, but it's not money she really wants, it's a son. Killing Moira and you wouldn't achieve that.'

'And Gervase?'

'He's destroying himself. It takes all his energies. He hasn't enough left to go around killing people for money. He's lost his nerve. He drinks. You have to be courageous and sober to mess with explosives. Ursula's desperation takes her to churches and to lunches with Joyce.'

He grunted in his throat, not quite a chuckle.

Joyce had been thanked by us on the telephone on the Saturday night when we'd come back exhausted.

She'd been devastated to the point of silence about what had happened and had put the phone down in tears. We phoned her again in the morning. 'I got Serena first,' she said sorrowfully. 'She must have gone out and bought all the stuff . . . I can't bear it. That dear little girl, so sweet when she was little, even though I hated her mother. So *awful.*'

'Go on, then,' Malcolm said. 'You keep stopping.'

'It couldn't have been Alicia or Vivien, they're not strong enough to carry you. Alicia's new boyfriend would be, but why should he think Alicia would be better off with you dead? And I couldn't imagine any of them constructing a bomb.'

'And Ferdinand?'

'I really couldn't see it, could you? He has no particular worries. He's good at his job. He's easy-going most of the time. Not him. Not Debs. That's the lot.'

'So did you come to Serena just by elimination?' He turned from the window, searching my face.

'No,' I said slowly. 'I thought of them all together, all their troubles and heart-aches. To begin with, when Moira died, I thought, like everyone else did, that she was killed to stop her taking half your money. I thought the attacks on you were for money, too. It was the obvious thing. And then, when I'd seen them all, when I understood all the turmoils going on under apparently normal exteriors, I began to wonder whether the money really mattered at all . . . And when I was in New York,

I was thinking of them all again but taking the money out . . . and with Serena . . . everything fitted.'

He stirred restlessly and went to sit down.

'It wouldn't have convinced the police,' he said.

'Nor you either,' I agreed. 'You had to see for yourself.' We fell silent, thinking what in fact he had seen, his daughter come to blast out the kitchen rather than search it for a notepad.

'But didn't you have any proof?' he said eventually. 'I mean, any real reason to think it was her? Something you could put your finger on.'

'Not really. Nothing that would stand up in court. Except that I think it was Serena who got Norman West to find you in Cambridge, not Alicia, as West himself thought.'

He stared. 'Why do you think that?'

'Alicia said she hadn't done it. Both West and I thought she was lying, but I think now she was telling the truth. Do you remember the tape from my telephone answering machine? Do you remember Serena's voice? "Mummy wants to know where Daddy is. I told her you wouldn't know, but she insisted I ask." That's what she said. Alicia told me positively that she herself hadn't wanted to know where you were. If Alicia's telling the truth, it was *Serena* who wanted to know, and she wanted to know because she'd lost us after failing to run you over. Lost us because of us scooting up to London in the Rolls.'

'My God,' he said. 'What happened to the tape? I suppose it got lost in the rubble.'

'No, it's in a box in the garage at Quantum. A few things were saved. Several of your gold-and-silver brushes are there too.'

He waved the thought away, although he was pleased enough. 'I suppose Serena did sound like Alicia on the telephone. I sometimes thought it was Alicia, when she phoned. Breathless and girlish. You know. Norman West just got it wrong.'

'She did call herself Mrs Pembroke,' I pointed out. 'Just to confuse matters. Or maybe she said Ms and he didn't hear clearly.'

'It doesn't much matter.' He was quiet for a while. 'Although it was terrible yesterday, it was the best thing, really. We'll grieve and get over this. She couldn't have borne to be locked up, could she, not with all that energy . . . not in drab clothes.'

On that Sunday morning also, we began telephoning to the family to tell them what had happened. I expected to find that Joyce had already told them, but she hadn't. She'd talked to them all the day before, they said, but that was all.

We left a lot of stunned silences behind us. A lot of unstoppable tears.

Malcolm told Alicia first, and asked if she'd like him to come to see her, to comfort her. When she could speak, she said no. She said Serena didn't kill Moira, Ian did. Everything was Ian's fault. Malcolm put the receiver down slowly, rubbed his hand over his face, and told me what she'd said.

'It's very hard,' he said, excusing her, 'to face that you've given birth to a murderer.'

'She helped to make her a murderer,' I said.

I spoke to my four brothers and to Lucy. Malcolm told Vivien last.

They all asked where we were: Joyce had told them we were in Australia. In London, we said, but didn't add where. Malcolm said he couldn't face having them all descend on him before he was ready. By the end, I was dropping with fatigue and Malcolm had finished off half a bottle. Long before bedtime, we were asleep.

We went back to Quantum on Monday, as we'd promised the police, and found Mr Smith poking around like old times.

All physical signs of Serena had mercifully been taken away, and all that remained were the torn flaps of black plastic that hadn't been near her.

Mr Smith shook hands with us dustily and after a few commiserating platitudes came out with his true opinions.

'Anyone who carries a fully-wired explosive device from place to place is raving mad. You don't connect the battery until the device is where you want it to go off. If you're me, you don't insert the detonator, either. You keep them separate.'

'I don't suppose she meant to drop it,' I said.

'Mind you, she was also unlucky,' Mr Smith said judiciously. 'It is possible, but I myself wouldn't risk it, to drop ANFO with a detonator in it and have it not explode. But maybe dropping it caused the clock wires to touch.'

'Have you found the clock?' I asked.

'Patience,' he said, and went back to looking.

A policeman fending away a few sensation seekers told us that Superintendent Yale had been detained, and couldn't meet us there: please would we go to the police station. We went, and found him in his office.

He shook hands. He offered sympathy.

He asked if we knew why Serena had gone to Quantum with a second bomb, and we told him. Asked if we knew why she should have killed Moira and tried to kill Malcolm. We told him my theories. He listened broodingly.

'There will be an inquest,' he said. 'Mr Ian can formally identify the remains. You won't need to see them . . . her . . . again, though. The coroner's verdict will be death by misadventure, I've no doubt. You may be needed to give an account of what happened. You'll be informed of all that in due course.' He paused. 'Yesterday, we went to Miss Pembroke's flat and conducted a search. We found a few items of interest. I am going to show you some objects and I'd be glad if you'd say whether you can identify them or not.'

He reached into a carton very like the one Serena had been carrying, which stood on his desk. He brought out a pile of twenty or thirty exercise books with spiral bindings and blue covers and after that a tin large enough to contain a pound of sweets, with a picture on top.

'*The Old Curiosity Shop*,' Malcolm said sadly.

'No possibility of doubt,' Yale nodded. 'The title's printed across the bottom of the picture.'

'Are there any detonators in it?' I asked.

'No, just cotton wool. Mr Smith wonders if she used more than one detonator for each bomb, just to make sure. He says amateurs are mad enough to try anything.'

I picked up one of the notebooks and opened it.

'Have you seen those before, sirs?' Yale asked.

'No,' I said, and Malcolm shook his head.

In Serena's looping handwriting, I read:

'Daddy and I had such fun in the garden this morning. He was teaching the dogs to fetch sticks and I was throwing the sticks. We picked a lot of beautiful daffodils and when we went indoors I put them all in vases in all the rooms. I cooked some lamb chops for lunch and made mint sauce and peas and roast potatoes and gravy and for pudding we had ice cream and peaches. Daddy is going to buy me some white boots with zips and silver tassels.

He calls me his princess, isn't that lovely? In the afternoon, we went down to the stream and picked some watercress for tea. Daddy took his socks off and rolled up his trousers and the boys *no* the boys weren't there I won't have them in my stories it was Daddy who picked the watercress and we washed it and ate it with brown bread. This evening I will sit on his lap and he will stroke my hair and call me his little princess, his little darling, and it will be lovely.'

I flicked through the pages. The whole book was full. Speechlessly I handed it to Malcolm, open where I'd read.

'All the notebooks are like that,' Yale said. 'We've had them all read right through. She's been writing them for years, I would say.'

'But you don't mean . . . they're recent?' I said.

'Some of them are, certainly. I've seen several sets of books like these in my career. Compulsive writing, I believe it's called. These of your sister's are wholesome and innocent by comparison. You can't imagine the pornography and brutality I've read. They make you despair.'

Malcolm, plainly moved, flicking over pages, said, 'She says I bought her a pretty red dress . . . a white sweater with blue flowers on it . . . a bright yellow leotard – I hardly know what a leotard is. Poor girl. Poor girl.'

'She bought them herself,' I said. 'Three or four times a week.'

Yale tilted the stack of notebooks up, brought out the bottom one and handed it to me. 'This is the latest. It changes at the end. You may find it interesting.'

I turned to the last entries in the book and with sorrow read:

'Daddy is going away from me and I don't want him any more. I think perhaps I will kill him. It isn't so difficult. I've done it before.'

There was a space on the page after that, and then, lower down: 'Ian is back with Daddy.'

Another space, and then,

'IAN IS AT QUANTUM WITH DADDY. I CAN'T BEAR IT.'

After yet another space, she had written my name again in larger-still capitals 'IAN' and surrounded it with a circle of little lines radiating outwards: an explosion with my name in the centre.

That was the end. The rest of the notebook was empty.

Malcolm read the page over my arm and sighed deeply. 'Can I have them?' he said to Yale. 'You don't need them, do you? There won't be a trial.'

Yale hesitated but said he saw no reason to retain them. He pushed the pile of books towards Malcolm and put the sweet tin on top.

'And the lighthouse and clock,' I said. 'Could we have those?'

He produced the Lego box from a cupboard, wrote

a list of what we were taking on an official-looking receipt and got Malcolm to sign it.

'All very upsetting, Mr Pembroke,' he said, again shaking hands, 'but we can mark our case closed.'

We took the sad trophies back to the Ritz, and that afternoon Malcolm wrote and posted cheques that would solve every financial problem in the Pembrokes' repertoire.

'What about the witches?' he said. 'If Helen and that dreadful Edwin and Berenice and Ursula and Debs are all having their own share, what about those other three?'

'Up to you,' I said. 'They're your wives.'

'*Ex*-wives.' He shrugged and wrote cheques for them also. 'Easy come, easy go,' he said. 'Bloody Alicia doesn't deserve it.'

'Engines work better with a little oil,' I said.

'Greasing their palms, you mean.' He still didn't believe in it. Still felt he was corrupting them by giving them wealth. Still thinking that *he* could stay sane and reasonably sensible when he had millions, but nobody else could.

He wrote a final cheque and gave it to me. I felt awkward taking it, which he found interesting.

'You should have had double,' he said.

I shook my head, reeling at noughts. 'You've post-dated it,' I said.

'Of course I have. I've post-dated all of them. I don't have that much in readies lying around in the bank.

Have to sell a few shares. The family can have the promise now and the cash in a month.'

He licked the envelopes. Not a cruel man, I thought.

On Tuesday, because I wished it, we went to see Robin.

'He won't remember Serena,' Malcolm said.

'No, I don't expect so.'

We went in the car I'd hired the day before for going to Quantum, and on the way stopped again to buy toys and chocolate and a packet of balloons.

I had taken with us the Lego lighthouse and the Mickey Mouse clock, thinking they might interest Robin, over which Malcolm shook his head.

'He won't be able to make them work, you know.'

'He might remember them. You never know. They used to be his and Peter's, after all. Serena gave them the clock and made them the lighthouse.'

Robin's room was very cold because of the open French windows. Malcolm tentatively went across and closed them, and Robin at once flung them open. Malcolm patted Robin's shoulder and moved away from the area, and Robin looked at him searchingly, in puzzlement, and at me the same way, as he sometimes did: trying, it seemed, to remember, and never quite getting there.

We gave him the new toys which he looked at and put down again, and after a while I opened the Lego box and brought out the old ones.

He looked at them for only a moment and then went on a long wander round and round the room, several times. Then he came to me, pointed at the packet of balloons and made a puffing noise.

'Good Lord,' Malcolm said.

I opened the packet and blew up several balloons, tying knots in the necks, as I always did. Robin went on making puffing noises until I'd blown up every balloon in the packet. His face looked agitated. He puffed harder to make me go faster.

When they were all scattered round the room, red, yellow, blue, green and white, bobbing about in stray air currents, shiny and festive, he went round bursting them with furious vigour, sticking his forefinger straight into some, pinching others, squashing the last one against the wall with the palm of his hand, letting out the anger he couldn't express.

Most times, after this ritual, he was released and at peace, and would retreat into a corner and sit staring into space or huddled up, rocking.

This time, however, he went over to the table, picked up the lighthouse, pulled it roughly apart into four or five pieces and threw them forcefully out of the wide-open window. Then he picked up the clock and with violence yanked the wires off, including the Mickey Mouse hands.

Malcolm was aghast. Docile Robin's rage shouted out of his mute body. His strength was a revelation.

He took the clock in his hand and walked round the

room smashing it against the wall at each step. Step, *smash*, step, *smash*, step, *smash*.

'Stop him,' Malcolm said in distress.

'No . . . he's talking,' I said.

'He's not talking.'

'He's telling us . . .'

Robin reached the window and threw the mangled clock far and high into the garden. Then he started shouting, roaring without words, his voice rough from disuse and hoarse with the change taking place from boy into man. The sound seemed to excite him until his body was reverberating, pouring out sound, the dam of silence swept away. 'Aaah . . . aaah . . . aaah . . .' and then real words, 'No . . . No . . . No . . . Serena . . . No . . . Serena . . . No . . . Serena . . . No . . .' He shouted to the skies, to the fates, to the wicked unfairness of the fog in his brain. Shouted in fury and frenzy. 'Serena . . . No . . . Serena . . . No . . .' and on and on until it became mindless, without meaning, just words.

I stepped close beside him in the end and yelled in his ear, 'Serena's dead.'

He stopped shouting immediately. 'Serena's dead,' I repeated. 'Like the clock. Smashed. Finished. Dead.'

He turned and looked at me vaguely, his mouth open, no sound coming out, the sudden silence as unnerving as the shouting had been.

'Serena-is-dead,' I said, making each word separate, giving it weight.

'He doesn't understand,' Malcolm said: and Robin went away and sat in a corner with his arms round his knees and his head down, and began rocking.

'The nurses think he understands quite a lot,' I said. 'Whether he understands that Serena is dead, I don't know. But at least we've tried to tell him.' Robin went on rocking as if we weren't there.

'What does it matter?' Malcolm said helplessly.

'It matters because if he does understand, it may give him rest. I brought the lighthouse and the clock because I wondered if Robin remembered anything at all. I thought it worth trying . . . didn't expect quite these results . . . but I think he smashed the clock Serena gave him because it reminded him of her, because she gave it to him and Peter shortly before the car crash. Somewhere in that woolly head, things sometimes connect.'

Malcolm nodded, puzzled and instinctively alarmed.

'One could almost think it was that afternoon,' I said, 'seeing the twins happy at Quantum where she hungered to be, seeing you there with them, loving them; perhaps it was that afternoon which finally tipped her over into the insanity of trying to make her fantasy come true. It didn't come true . . . you met Moira . . . but I'm certain she tried.'

Malcolm was staring saying 'No! Don't say it! *Don't!*'

I said it anyway. 'I think Robin saw the hit-and-run driver who forced their car off the road. In whatever mangled dreamlike way, he knows who it was. No

Serena, no Serena, no . . . You heard him. I've thought ever since New York that it could possibly have happened that way. Serena's obsession was full-blown a long time ago, long before she got rid of Moira. I think she killed Peter . . . and Coochie.'

EPILOGUE

We all went back to Quantum a year later for the Grand Reopening Ceremony, the house bedecked with garlands and champagne corks popping.

After much soul-searching, Malcolm had decided to rebuild. Without Quantum as its centre, the family would have fallen apart, and he didn't want that to happen. When he told everyone of his intention, there was great communal relief, and he saw without question that it was the right thing to do.

The rancour level lessened dramatically after the arrival of the cheques and the production of his will for inspection, and I was suddenly not everyone's villain, though still and forever Alicia's. Malcolm, having deleted Serena by codicil, sent his will to the Central Probate Office for registration and let everyone know it.

Malcolm still felt that he had pampered and corrupted his children, but he had to admit they were happier because of it. Dramatically happier in some cases, like Donald and Helen whose problems had all been financial. Helen redeemed her baubles and stopped painting china, and Donald paid off the finance company and the bank and ran the golf club with a light heart.

A few weeks after Serena's death, Helen asked me over to Marblehill House. 'A drink before dinner,' she said. I went on a freezing evening in December and she surprised me by kissing me in greeting. Donald was standing with his back to a roaring fire, looking contentedly pompous.

'We wanted to thank you,' Helen said. 'And I suppose . . . to apologize.'

'There's no need.'

'Oh, yes. We all know there is. Not everyone will say so, but they know.'

'How's Malcolm?' Donald asked.

'He's fine.'

Donald nodded. Even the fact that Malcolm and I were still together seemed no longer to worry him, and later, when we'd sat round the fire drinking for a while, he asked me to stay on for dinner. I stayed, and although we were never going to be in and out of each other's houses every five minutes, at least on that evening we reached a peaceful plateau as brothers.

Some time later, I went to see Lucy. She and Edwin had made no changes to their cottage and had no plans to move, much to Edwin's disgust.

'We should live somewhere more *suitable*,' he said

to her crossly. 'I never thought we would stay here when you inherited.'

Lucy looked at him with affection. 'If you want to leave, Edwin, you can, now that you have money of your own.'

He was disconcerted; open mouthed. 'I don't want to leave,' he said, and it was clearly the truth.

Lucy said to me, 'I'll find a good use for my money: keep the capital, give away most of the income. We have no anxieties now, and that's a relief, I agree, but I haven't changed altogether. I don't believe in luxurious living. It's bad for the soul. I'm staying here.' She ate a handful of raisins determinedly, the old man looking out of her eyes.

Thomas was no longer her guest. Thomas, against all advice, had gone back to Berenice.

I called at Arden Haciendas one dark cold afternoon and Thomas opened the front door himself, looking blank when he saw me.

'Berenice is out,' he said, letting me in.

'I came to see you. How are you doing?'

'Not so bad,' he said, but he still looked defeated.

He gave me a drink. He knew where the gin was, and the tonic. He said Berenice and he had been going to marriage guidance sessions, but he didn't know that they were doing much good.

'You can get vasectomies reversed sometimes,' I said.

'Yes, but I don't really want to. Suppose I did, and

we had another girl? Unless Berenice can get over not having sons, I'm going to leave her again. I told her.'

I gazed at him, awestruck. 'What did she say?'

'Nothing much. I think she's afraid of me, really.'

As long as it didn't go to his head, I thought that might not be at all a bad thing.

I went to see Gervase and Ursula soon after. The change in Ursula, who let me in, was like unwrapping a brown paper parcel and finding Christmas inside. The old skirt, shirt, pullover and pearls had vanished. She wore narrow scarlet trousers, a huge white sweater and a baroque gold chain. She smiled at me like a shy conspirator and came with me into the sitting room. Gervase, if not overpoweringly friendly, seemed ready for neutrality and a truce.

'I told Gervase,' Ursula said sweetly, 'that now that I can afford to leave him and take the girls with me, I'm staying because I want to, not because I have to. I'm staying as long as he gets help with this ridiculous fixation about his birth. Who *cares* that Malcolm wasn't married to Alicia at the time? I certainly don't. No one does. Ferdinand doesn't. Ferdinand's been very good, he's been over here several times giving Gervase advice.'

Gervase, who in the past would have shouted her down, listened almost with gratitude. The bear that had run himself into a thicket was being led out by compassionate hands.

Ferdinand, when I called, was in rocketing good

spirits. He and Debs had moved immediately from their small bare bungalow into a large bare bungalow with a tennis court, a swimming pool and a three-car garage. Affluence was fun, he said; but one of the new house's rooms was also his office. He was going on with his job.

'I took your remarks to heart, you know,' he said. 'Took a look at what Alicia had done to us. I don't listen to her any more. She won't get rid of Debs and she won't get rid of Ursula. Have you seen Ursula? Transformation! I've told Gervase he has a wife in a million and a mother who's nothing but trouble. I've been talking to him about illegitimacy . . . isn't that what you wanted?' He punched my arm lightly. 'Stay to dinner?' he said.

I didn't go to see either Alicia or Vivien. I stayed a few nights with Joyce.

'Darling, how's that old fool getting along?'

'He spends a lot of time at Quantum with the builders.'

'Don't let him catch pneumonia. It's bitter outside.'

'He does what he likes,' I said.

'Darling, when did he not?'

Joyce rushed busily away to a bridge tournament in Paris, kissing my cheek, patting me with approval, telling me to be careful not to break my neck in those frightful races I insisted on riding.

I gave her the assurances and went back to Lambourn, now my home instead of Epsom. I'd asked the trainer I'd been riding exercise for if he knew of anyone needing a second-string stable jockey, if I should take the giant step of turning professional.

He stared. 'I heard you don't need to. Didn't you come into money?'

'Forget the money. What chance would I have?'

'I saw you win that race at Kempton,' he said. 'If you turn pro, if you come to Lambourn, I'll give you plenty of rides.'

He was as good as his word, and George and Jo, astonished but happy, entered their few horses to fit in.

I bought a house in Lambourn and Malcolm came to live in it while Quantum was rebuilt. Malcolm loved Lambourn. He went often up to the Downs with the trainer I was riding for to watch the horses work, and far from losing interest in racing, grew more and more involved. When I won my first professional race, the Bollinger ran through Lambourn like a river.

By the day the following November that we all went to the house for the Grand Reopening (with embossed invitation cards and an army of caterers), everyone's lives had settled into the new patterns.

Malcolm had been to the 'Arc' again, and round the world with Ramsey Osborn. Chrysos had won the Futurity at Doncaster and was tipped for the next year's Derby. Blue Clancy had gone to stud, syndicated for millions.

I had ended my first professional season with a respectable score and at the start of my second had become the chief retained jockey for the stable. I would be a trainer in the end, I supposed. Meantime, I felt alive and fulfilled as never before.

Lucy and Edwin were still eating healthily in the cottage. Lucy, coming to terms with not writing more poetry herself, had started on a scholarly biography and commentary on the Life and Work of Thomas Stearns Eliot. Edwin was still doing the shopping.

Donald and Helen, arm in arm, wandered round the garden like lovers.

Ferdinand fussed over Debs, who was pregnant.

Gervase had recovered most of his bullishness, which seemed to reassure Ursula rather than cow her. She came in a mink coat, laughing with pleasure.

In Berenice, the fire had gone out: in Thomas, it had been faintly rekindled. No longer needing a job, he was learning to play golf. Berenice was house-hunting, with Thomas's approval.

Alicia came looking girlish, trilling away in a voice like an echo of Serena's, and everyone made polite remarks to her with closed teeth.

Vivien complained that Malcolm had re-done the house too much in Coochie's taste. Joyce made diplomatic friends with the married couple he had engaged to look after him. He – and they – had been living in the house for a week.

All of the grandchildren were there, re-exploring the place: children's voices again in the garden. Robin, far away, had fallen silent once more and had never since that violent day wanted me to blow up balloons.

Malcolm and I walked out through the new sitting-room windows and from the lawn looked up at the house. It felt whole again, not just physically, but at peace.

'I don't feel Serena's here, do you?' Malcolm said.

'No, she isn't.'

'I was afraid she might be. I'm glad she's not.'

We went further down the lawn.

'Did you notice I'd taken the golden dolphin and the amethyst tree and so on out of the wall and put them in the sitting room?' he asked casually.

'Yes, I did.'

'I sold the gold too.'

I glanced at him. He looked quizzically back.

'The price rose sharply this year, as I thought it would. I took the profit. There's nothing in the wall now except spiders and dust.'

'Never mind.'

'I'm leaving the clause in the will though.' The family had been curious about his leaving me the piece of wire, and he'd refused to explain. 'I'll buy more gold, and sell it. Buy and sell. Forward and backward. One of these days . . .' his blue eyes gleamed '. . . you may win on the nod.'

All Pan Books are available at your local bookshop or newsagent, or can be ordered direct from the publisher. Indicate the number of copies required and fill in the form below.

Send to: Macmillan General Books C.S.
Book Service By Post
PO Box 29, Douglas I-O-M
IM99 1BQ

or phone: 01624 675137, quoting title, author and credit card number.

or fax: 01624 670923, quoting title, author, and credit card number.

or Internet: http://www.bookpost.co.uk

Please enclose a remittance* to the value of the cover price plus 75 pence per book for post and packing. Overseas customers please allow £1.00 per copy for post and packing.

*Payment may be made in sterling by UK personal cheque, Eurocheque, postal order, sterling draft or international money order, made payable to Book Service By Post.

Alternatively by Access/Visa/MasterCard

Card No. | | | | | | | | | | | | | | | | |

Expiry Date | | | | | | | | | | | | | | | | |

Signature ______________________________

Applicable only in the UK and BFPO addresses.

While every effort is made to keep prices low, it is sometimes necessary to increase prices at short notice. Pan Books reserve the right to show on covers and charge new retail prices which may differ from those advertised in the text or elsewhere.

NAME AND ADDRESS IN BLOCK CAPITAL LETTERS PLEASE

Name ______________________________

Address ______________________________

____

____

____

8/95

Please allow 28 days for delivery.
Please tick box if you do not wish to receive any additional information. ☐

Hack

By the same author

Snap

Non-fiction (with Peter Mason)

Criminal Blunders

Trouble and Strife

John Burns

Hack

PAN BOOKS

First published 1996 by Masquerade Publications

This edition first published 1998 by Pan Books
an imprint of Pan Macmillan Ltd
Pan Macmillan, 20 New Wharf Road, London N1 9RR
Basingstoke and Oxford
Associated companies throughout the world
www.panmacmillan.com

ISBN 0 330 35488 4

3 5 7 9 8 6 4 2

A CIP catalogue record for this book is available from the British Library.

Typeset by Intype London Ltd
Printed and bound in Great Britain by
Mackays of Chatham plc, Chatham, Kent

The characters depicted within have no resemblance whatsoever to anyone living or dead or yet to be born. Anyone who sees himself/herself in these pages should lay off the drink for a while. The events and characters are marginally less factual than the *Sunday Sport*'s exclusive, 'World War II Bomber Found on Moon'.

To Rita, whose idea this all was

Chapter One

Only one public-spirited citizen bothered to phone in and report the body, though at least a dozen must have seen the thing. Thirteen if you count whoever put it there.

I was just around the corner in Magpie Court when the tip-off came. Good as gold, Inspector McIvor gave me a bleep. It read: 'Maxwell lookalike found bobbing – Mac.' I called him back. He was in Hampton's, no doubt already blowing his twenty quid tip-off fee on a doxy or two. 'Good evening, you ageing lounge lizard,' I said sweetly. Mac loves it when I talk dirty. 'You rang?'

He said, 'Might have one for you. The river police have a corpse floating around in St Katharine's Dock. Could be a tourist, pushed in by one of our local muggers. Who knows?'

I was not exactly enthusiastic. 'Who knows, indeed. Might be a drunk who tripped and fell, might be a suicide, might be a heart case, a headcase, whatever. Might even be a police officer doing the world a favour.'

Mac said, 'Oh well, thought you'd like to know.'

He rang off and returned to his fleurie and his floosies, for Mac is a man of simple needs.

I was in Ross Gavney's flat, pouring fat tumblers of twenty-year-old Scotch down my throat at an unprecedented rate of knots. Ross and I go all the way back to Holly Hill comprehensive but we keep up the old ties despite everything. He thinks there is something richly hilarious in my being a crime hack, nay, the chief crime correspondent for a national red top. Ross does complicated things with bonds and futures, thereby earning himself more money than is humanly decent.

I am happy for Ross, especially when he calls me up and invites me to empty his decanters. Generally we sit around and rubbish each other's football loyalties. He, God help him, is an Arsenal man.

In the old days Ross was a yuppy, one of Thatcher's favoured children. He still has all the trappings, city slicker suits, fluffed out hair, docklands flat.

We were in the aforesaid apartment, arguing the toss over England's chances against Poland when Mac bleeped. While I did my ace reporter bit, Ross poured me another half gallon of single malt.

'What next?' he asked, after I had finished with Mac.

'Next?' I was puzzled. 'Nothing. I wait till the police haul him out, dry him down and then pronounce him dead. They're sticklers for that sort of thing.'

He said, 'How do you know it's a man?'

I flopped a languid wrist. 'It's either one or the other.'

Ross sipped thoughtfully. He persisted: 'When do you know if it's a story? I mean, this could be another Calvi case. All you crime reporters got that one wrong.'

This was unkind but true, which in my experience is usually the same thing. Roberto Calvi, aka God's Banker, aka head of the Banco Ambrosiano, where the Pope lodges his pay cheque, was found swinging under Blackfriars Bridge in the eighties. Suicide, we all cried, conveniently ignoring every fact which screamed murder.

I sighed. It was a sigh custom-built to say, 'Listen, dear friend of my youth, I have in my left hand a glass of Glenfarclas, and in my right, a cigar worthy of my deepest appreciation. Why bother me with trifles?'

Ross is not a man who listens to sighs. He said, 'So, you boys wait until the police tell you what they've found and you just put it into English?'

This was a vile slur on my profession. I have never knowingly put anything into English. Tabloid-speak, yes, journalese if I'm pissed. But if ever a phrase in English pops up in my copy, we have trained sub-editors to throw it out.

I lowered my glass and looked Ross dead in the eye. I said, 'This is the picture. A body, male or female, is found floating in the dock. Today all over London, bodies have been found in bed – sometimes their own – under a bus, in hospital corridors, in Cardboard City, wherever. A few – only a tiny few – are tastefully decorated with bullets, needles or knives. The rest have been topped by the Great Serial Killer in the Sky. In short, no story.'

'What's the betting?'

'Eh?'

Ross said, 'I'll bet there's a story in it.'

'Balls.'

After this it developed into a sordid argument about the size of the bet (my fiver against a bottle of his whisky) and then I did the biz. Just to impress Ross, I even rang Scotland Yard's press bureau to see if they had anything on the story. I wasn't expecting anything from them. Usually they don't know what day it is.

'Good evening. It's Thursday,' I said helpfully.

'Oh, it's you. What do you want?' asked a young lady. Ruthie or Zeintab.

I said, 'You know perfectly well what I want but we've no time for that malarkey now. Just tell me if you have anything on a wet corpse in St Katharine's Dock.'

'Nope.'

'You have been ever so helpful. Thank you.'

As I switched off the mobile, I was alarmed to see Ross breeze into the room, a belted Burberry over the navy pinstripes. 'Ready?' he asked brightly.

I kissed my glass goodbye and donned my hack mac. Outside the May monsoon scythed in off the Thames, running through the gutters and putting halos around the street lamps.

'Let me make a few more phone calls,' I begged. But Ross strode off and I splashed away in his wake.

As I said, Magpie Court is hardly a kick in the pants off the dock, but by the time we got there I was drenched through. Under his golf umbrella Ross was dry and debonair.

We rounded a corner by a snotty wine bar and ran smack into the police tapes. Beyond them was a clutch of sodden coppers gazing into the dock for enlightenment. A police river launch was parked in the middle with its spotlight aimed at the pointy end of a white yacht. You couldn't make out its name. You couldn't see anything, what with all that rain between us and the action.

A beefy figure swam out of the waterfall. It was Pennycuik, my friend H, a detective inspector of the old school. He'd tell me all about it. 'Hello, Harry,' I said warmly.

'Piss off,' he responded.

'Good evening, officer,' said Ross from about a foot above my head.

Pennycuik wiped his eyes and looked up at him. Clearly this stranger was not one of your scumbag reporters. Too distinguished for that. I could hear Harry's brain cell charging around in perplexity.

I said smoothly, 'Inspector Pennycuik, I don't believe you have met the Right Honourable Lewis Trefoyle, the junior Home Office minister.'

Ross didn't blink. He put out a nice dry pink hand and gave H a nice dry pink smile.

Harry said, 'Oh,' and stuck out a hand like a drowned fish.

'And what have we here?' asked Ross. His voice was just the right blend of fruity pomposity and blind ignorance we have come to expect from our political masters.

Our heroic D.I. favoured him with a yellow smile. 'It's a body, sir,' he said, displaying the lightning intelligence of London's finest.

'Suspicious?' I asked him.

Harry pretended I was dead. He addressed Ross. 'We got a call, about eight thirty, from a punter, ah, one of the customers.' He pointed towards the snooty wine bar.

'I cannot see the body,' said Ross peevishly. 'How could he?'

Harry said, 'It was before the rain. This just came on. The call was passed on to the river police and they located the body.'

'Man or woman?' This was me again.

He spoke to Ross again. 'We believe it to be a male, but it is lying face down in the water so we cannot ascertain exactly.'

Ascertain! I love the way coppers talk when they are in the presence of their superiors, which is mostly all the time.

'They're taking their time hauling it ashore,' I observed.

Ross looked at his Longines. 'Yes, it's gone nine.'

Harry shook the rain from his brow. 'It snagged itself in the cable of that boat. It shouldn't be long now.'

At which point there came a distant sound, as of a waterlogged stiff being hauled into a rubber dinghy.

'There it is,' said H happily.

Ross looked down his nostrils at him. 'Is this, inspector, what one would term a suspicious death?'

Harry shifted his feet in a puddle. 'The caller said

he heard sounds of an altercation shortly prior to the incident and then there was a splash.'

'That would probably be the guy hitting the water,' I said sagely.

H glared at me but let it pass. On the dockside a quartet of young coppers were falling over each other to unload the late lamented, now gift-wrapped in rubber sheeting.

The corpse, a skinny specimen, was manhandled past us, still face down. He was wearing a Casablanca trenchcoat, its white newness marred by ugly black oil weals from the yacht's hawser. Behind us there was a waiting ambulance. As the bearers reached it, they turned their dripping burden over. And everyone did a double take. The stiff was not a he, or anything like one. These were the mortal remains of a beautiful and, guessing by the bumps in the rubber sheet, shapely young woman. Her dead white face was fringed with jet black hair and her huge dark eyes gazed back at us in dumb surprise. Her carmine lips were slightly open and her eyelashes were matted with rain.

And slap bang in the middle of her forehead was the neatest little bullet hole you ever did see.

'My God!' gasped Ross. 'It's Claudine!'

And so it was.

Chapter Two

Claudine. Claudine Tournier. Not looking her freshly minted, rip-roaringly happy customary self.

The pert lovable face which grinned out on the Great British eating public from a billion freezer packs was for once unsmiling and a shade on the grey side. Never more would we see her pout provocatively from the nation's TV screens, urging all and sundry to sample her frozen haricots bearnais or apple chartreuse. Nor would we hear her husky promise: 'I could be so good for you.'

All that healthy eating hadn't done much for her. But it had been a slick show while it lasted. The fair Claudine blended the two vital ingredients of our age – sex and green living – to sell her wares to those who deem it wrong to eat bits of animals.

She even made a virtue of such bizarre beliefs. Every pack of Claudine's wares carries a little sticker, saying that 2p or 5p of the cost goes towards conservation issues – saving the blubber-mouthed whale, keeping the Opeydopey tribe in clean loin cloths, that sort of thing.

Very praiseworthy, and very lucrative by all accounts. But nobody was bitching about that, not with Claudine spending half her life scooting off to what us hacks call the world's killing fields to plant couscous or reap noodles.

Naturally these endeavours made her something of a saint, marginally behind the Queen Mum and Mother Teresa in Britain's league of the great and good.

All these thoughts went clippety clop through my brain as I grabbed the mobile from my pocket and punched in the office number.

'News Desk,' announced a sad and bitter voice. Vic.

'Vic. It's Max. Ring the bells on Back Bench, we've got a belter here. Claudine Tournier's been murdered. Nobody else has it, so tag it exclusive.'

'What?'

Even Vic sounded interested. He probably ate her stuff.

I said, 'Yep. Shot in the head. Tell the monkey bench to get out her snaps and put me through to Copy.'

Vic said, 'When was she killed?'

'About forty minutes ago. I'm going to dictate straight on, but you'd better get someone there to dig out her cuttings and fill in the biog.'

'Wait a minute.' Vic put the phone to one side and I pictured him trundling across to Back Bench and dolefully breaking the news to the night editor and his bunch of ne'er-do-wells. I effed and blinded to myself in impatience.

Vic returned. 'Give us all you've got.'

This is honestly the way people on News Desk

talk. They think you would leave out all the good bits unless they reminded you.

He switched me through to Copy. It was Deaf Daphne in the final throes of terminal boredom.

'Hi Daff. It's Max Chard. This one's for News Desk.'

'Catchline?' I told her to call the story GONER and began dictating off the top of my head at about 500 words per min.

Green queen Claudine Tournier was gunned down last night and her body tossed in the Thames after a secret date with a mystery man.

'How are you spelling Claudine?'

A stifled scream from my end. I told her how, and spelt out Tournier too. By some great good fortune she knew how to spell Thames. Anyway, after a fifteen minute spelling bee, I got the story through. It ran on like this:

The sexy chef who put the ooh-la-la into instant meals was shot between the eyes from point blank range after a blazing row.

French-born Claudine (insert age) *was dumped into St Katharine's Dock in the shadow of London's Tower Bridge – a well known meeting place for lovers.*

Claudine was married to top City money man Sir James Tomlin. Police were last night seeking him to break the tragic news.

Her young killer, who used a revolver fitted with a silencer, fled as drinkers in the trendy wine bar Port O' Call raised the alarm.

One man said, 'I heard a couple arguing furiously just outside and I thought it was a lover's tiff.

'Then there was a splash. It is horrifying to think I had just heard a murder.'

Claudine's body drifted under a luxury yacht moored in the upmarket marina and it took police 30 minutes to free it.

The chic chef was still in her trademark designer suit and dressed for a night on the town.

Detectives are baffled by the ruthless killing. A senior officer said, 'Miss Tournier was a very beautiful and much admired young woman.

'We cannot confirm whether her attacker was a boyfriend. She was not sexually assaulted and we cannot tell if she was robbed.'

Police are also investigating whether the killing was an underworld hit. One officer admitted the shooting had the signature of a professional hit man.

Claudine was slain by a single shot from a small calibre hand gun. She was dead before her body hit the water.

Police frogmen will scour the yacht basin for the murder weapon from first light today.

The smouldering French beauty used provocative TV ads to build an international empire with her Claudine's Cuisine range of freezer foods.

She ploughed hundreds of thousands of pounds back into helping the world's poor and saving animals facing extinction.

Her tireless work earned her the MBE in the Queen's birthday honours and . . .

And blah blah and yet more blah. Not exactly deathless prose but sufficient for the IQ of our readers. I expect by now you're wondering where all that stuff came from. The hand gun and so on. Elementary. If it had been a Uzi submachinegun or a Kalashnikov, the guy in the bar would have heard it.

Small calibre? Well, it was a neat little hole. The quotes? That's what Harry and the drinker would have told me if they'd been feeling chatty. The line that her killer was a young man? He legged it before the alarm was raised. You don't do that if you're knocking on sixty.

OK, so when last seen she was wearing a rubber sheet, but underneath, you can bet your boots, she was not togged up in a shell suit. Hence my dressed to kill description. And that bit hinting the gunman was her secret lover? – well, you've got to make the reader sit up and go 'Cor!', haven't you?

Daphne put me back on to Vic. He was whingeing. 'You didn't tell me exactly where this happened. Pictures want to send a man.'

I said, 'No percentage. All they'll get is a grainy snap of the dock. The police have whisked her off.'

'You could have told us earlier,' he accused.

This again is how desk people think. If you found Lord Lucan holed up in Wagga Wagga they'd complain that he wasn't riding Shergar.

I just said, 'All right, if it makes them any happier, tell them to send a monkey to the wine bar. It's on the starboard corner of the dock, coming from the Tower Hotel. I'll be inside asking if anyone's got any nice shots of Claudine getting her head blown off.'

We parted on terms of mutual hatred. I switched off and turned to Ross who was a strangely silent man.

'Drink?' I suggested, pointing to the tastefully

frosted door of the bar. He tagged along. We plunged in and ordered a bottle that said it came all the way from Jacob's Creek. I shrugged off my mac and pretended the Austin Reed check two-piece was meant to cling moistly to my slender frame. The Law was much in evidence, asking decent drunks what they had heard/seen/suspected about tonight's merriment. I eavesdropped.

'Not a thing,' proclaimed a city gent jovially. Why are people always so damn happy to tell us they know nothing? The ones who do know are generally miserable.

I espied a secretary type who was sitting alone and looking as if she had just found a dead platypus in her ration of Jacob's Creek. I flashed the press pass. Her fuzzy blue eyes ignored it. I gabbled some gibberish about Claudine's little contretemps and asked what she knew. She was silent for so long I felt like introducing her to Ross.

After a slurp or two she finally said, 'I was supposed to meet Miss Tournier here.'

I patted myself on the back. 'You're her secretary?'

She shook her head no.

'You work for her?'

Another shake.

This could go on all night. Who was she to Claudine? Her next-door neighbour, her kid sister, her colonic irrigationist?

My voice was as soft as a pigeon's coo. 'So what do you do?'

'I work for Sir James.'

'Ahh.' This wasn't helping.

She clammed up and looked set to stay that way unless I did something. Here is where your trained hack suddenly appears to lose all interest in his hard-nosed probing. He changes the game. The trick is to get your quarry totally distracted from your evil aims.

So, with studied deliberation, I laid my packet of Bensons flat down in the middle of our little round table. I pulled out a single cigarette and placed it on top of the pack. She wasn't looking, but she would. Next, I pulled back my sleeves, thus exposing my manly wrists. I fetched a penknife from my jacket pocket, pulled out the blade and studied it earnestly. Now she was looking. My every fibre seemed absorbed with the strange ceremony of the penknife and the cigarette. I ignored her eyes. I took the knife and in slow motion I bisected the cigarette dead centre. Then I picked up the non-filter stub and carelessly tossed it on the floor. She goggled. I folded the penknife, replaced it, put the dwarf cigarette in my mouth and lit it.

I looked at her po-faced. I said, 'I'm trying to cut down.'

She blinked and gave a little giggle. But the show wasn't over yet, folks. I raised my glass, held it towards the light, and spoke almost to myself. 'You know, I was in Jacob's Creek last year . . .' Pause. ' . . . and it wasn't this bloody colour.'

Another giggle, this time deeper in her throat. We're almost there. I aimed a finger at her glass. I said, 'You don't seem to be enjoying it either. Can I get you something different?'

She glanced down, hesitated, then came: 'Just a mineral water, please.'

I detected an ever so slight thank you smile. Two minutes later the secretary bird was a new woman. I must try water some day.

Her name was Shirley. No second name. She dressed like a TV weather girl, all buttons and lapels. She came from Loughton. She worked in Freleng-Bourke, where Sir James earned his crust. She knew the late lamented who apparently was a frequent visitor to the offices. Shirley's baby eyes took on something of a glow when she spoke of Sir Jas. But it was hard to tell whether she loved or hated the man.

'So you had a message from him to Claudine?' I prompted.

Shirley went all dumb again.

'Not exactly,' she whispered at last.

I ran my finger round the rim of the glass, lit a cigarette, leered at a blonde, counted my fingers and waited. I had just embarked on a filthy limerick about a young lady called Shirley, who liked to be rogered most rarely, when she broke surface again.

'It was a message from me,' she said, nostrils flaring.

These kids watch too many soap operas.

'From you?'

A half nod. 'Yes. I had to tell her about Sir James.'

'And what about Sir James?'

She took a deep breath and looked at me with misery flooding her eyes.

'He's run off with his secretary,' she said.

Chapter Three

News Desk woke me sometime gone three. 'Got a pen handy?' Vic demanded.

Sure Vic. I always go to bed with a biro stuck up my nostril. I rummaged round a bit, swearing and grunting just to make him feel bad. He probably felt better.

'Okay, Vic. Shoot.'

'You're on the 7.30 to Geneva. BA flight 401. The tickets are at the information desk. You pick them up thirty minutes before the flight. Pictures are sending Frank Frost. All right?'

I said, 'Would you care to tell me which sodding airport?'

'Oh. Heathrow. Terminal One.'

I said, 'That helps. You got a hotel booked? Is the hire car fixed? You got some money for me?'

'There's five hundred with your tickets.'

Five hundred quid! That might just buy me a cheese fondue. And he hadn't fixed the car, or the hotel. Thank you Shirley for tipping me off that Sir James was in Geneva. I growled myself back to sleep.

Four hours and forty-five minutes later I was in a window seat of an Airbus ripping holes through the clouds. On my right was Mad Frankie Frost who is roughly seventeen foot tall and not the best of travelling companions. He was saying: 'Then on the way back from Tokyo I got upgraded to First and there was plenty of room to stretch out in, but when we were chasing Fergie in Bali we were on an old Boeing and you couldn't . . .'

I was too tired to listen, what with the hurly-burly of the night before. I could still hear Shirley grassing on her boss. Great stuff altogether, but it meant I had to file a whole new update for the final. And after that, of course, I needed a largish gin or seven and things went downhill from there. Hence the present headache and feeling of impending death. Actually, a gin would come in handy right now. I flagged down a passing stewardess and outlined my requirements. She screwed up her freckled face and intoned, 'The drinks trolley will be circulating soon.'

Meanwhile Frankie was still rabbiting on about leg-space on long-haul. I had half a mind to fetch out my penknife and saw him off around the knees.

Freckles returned with a plastic tray containing objects heavily bandaged in clingfilm. 'Breakfast,' she announced.

I looked at the tray. 'Do you have any food instead?' I asked.

She frowned and wafted off in considerable dudgeon.

By the time we hit Geneva I had breakfasted off three gins. I only wanted one, maybe two. I ordered the third just to see Freckles wrinkle her nose up at me again.

Frankie went to the Hertz desk and got us a Volvo. Yes, a Volvo. I told him, 'You should have got a BMW or a Merc. This thing's a bloody tank.'

'Yes,' said he, 'but it's got more leg room.'

We took the Lausanne Road with Lake Geneva looking sullen on our right. A bullyboy wind was kicking the heads off the waves. Shirley, God bless her, had all the details. The lovebirds were roosting in a village called Morges. Rather apt, considering Claudine's present whereabouts.

My chauffeur had us there coming up lunchtime. We drove down a narrow street where everyone had the same taste in windowboxes. Red geraniums bloomed from every orifice. Maybe they get a subsidy for growing them.

We fetched up outside a bijou villa. Very romantic. Frankie whistled. 'This must have cost him a packet.'

Monkeys always want to know how much things cost. It is strange because monkeys do not like spending money.

I lit a cigarette and hung around while Frankie dressed himself from head to toe in motor drives, zoom lenses, filters, sureshots, flash units and all his other toys.

I walked up the front drive past a Peugeot the size of a shoebox. Frankie clattered and clanked behind me like Robocop. Just as I reached the front door it opened. A happy moment. There is nothing so stultifyingly boring as doorstepping a house where the inmates refuse to open up.

A young woman appeared. She was pretty, but not stunning. Good grey blue eyes, auburn hair, small mouth. She seemed surprised to see us, but that might just have been because Frankie was darting hither and thither, banging off pix.

Her mouth opened and she blinked in time with the motordrive. There was no sign of her paramour.

'Miss Pearson?' I said brightly. 'Good morning. I have just come from London to see you.'

She pondered this for a moment. 'Me?' she asked nervously, her gaze fixed on Frankie.

'It's all right,' I reassured. 'He's more frightened of you than vice versa.'

Her lips pursed up. 'Who are you?'

A trace of hostility there. Time for appeasement. I turned on Frankie and said snottily, 'Stop that right now. You're upsetting Miss Pearson.'

Frankie got the idea. He let his cameras dangle. I turned back on Emma Pearson and smiled. 'Now that's better, isn't it?'

Her stiffness eased a fraction. 'Who are you?' she persisted. Still no sign of Sunny Jim.

'I'm Max. Max Chard. And this is my friend Frankie Frost.'

'You're newspaper reporters,' she accused.

It is something I have never understood, but hacks always get pissed off when someone says: 'You're a reporter.' I wonder do double glazing salesmen, Ku Klux Klan pinheads and Arsenal fans get similarly narked when people suss them out. Maybe we're just more sensitive.

I looked hurt. I asked, 'May we come in?'

'Why?' Hands on hips.

She wasn't quite sure whether to display icy

disdain or blazing anger, so she came across sort of tepid. I gave Sir James's little rascal a long look, taking in the dove grey blouse, slim, short navy skirt, high heels. Chic on the outside, not so fantastic when unwrapped, I guessed. Maybe she was a nymphomaniac. I have heard there are such things.

I said carefully, 'I have something very important to say to you and I cannot really say it in the street.'

This is a useful hack trick because the reaction affords you a glimpse of your victim's nature. If their eyes glitter, it's because they think it might have something to do with the National Lottery; if they invite you in, they're bored and desirous of boring you; if they say nothing, they're as guilty as hell.

She said nothing.

I smiled a sharp sardonic smile. Or it might have been ironic. I couldn't see it. I said, 'You may think you know why we're here, but you're way off target.'

She gave a sort of 'Oh yeah?' snort.

Behind me I could hear Frankie getting restless. Any minute now he'd whip out the Canon and blow the whole thing. I had to do something drastic.

'You think my office has gone to all the expense of sending us here just to expose your affair with Sir James. Frankly, we don't give a damn,' I lied.

Emma Pearson made a sound somewhere between a gulp and an argggh. She reeled back in the doorway. I said 'thank you' and breezed past her into the villa.

I was three yards down the hall and still breezing before she twigged it. By then Frankie was halfway through the door and it was too late. She followed me dumbly into the lounge, a sort of Laura Ashley meets World of Leather affair. If the roguish James was around, he wasn't showing it.

I sat down. 'Mind if we sit?' I asked.

She hung around standing for a while then plonked herself on a distant sofa, straightening her skirt. She had nice legs. Her back was towards the open doorway leading from the hall.

Her voice was controlled and even. 'I have no idea why you are harassing us.'

Us. So the Great Lover was still in the neighbourhood. I spoke softly and lovingly. 'Perhaps you have not heard the news, Miss Pearson. Claudine Tournier has been murdered.'

Not a blink. Not a scream. Not even a joyful whoop.

'Murdered?'

'Murdered.'

She went through the who/what/where/when/why rigmarole and I told her everything but the who and why. I even pointed to the middle of my forehead to show where the bullet went in. Still no reaction.

'Is Sir James at home?' I asked gesturing around.

She said he wasn't but didn't feel like expanding on the subject.

'Naturally I would like to speak to him.'

'Well you can't.'

'It's all right dear,' said a disembodied voice. The hair on the back of my neck stood up. It took me a moment to spot the owner. A scale model human being, standing behind a shrub in a tub which in turn was behind the sofa. Sir James Tomlin in the flesh, all five foot nothing of him. He must have slipped in while I was eyeballing his beloved. He came forward and stared at me through darkened lenses. I stared back. He was fitted out in a double-breasted blazer. A tragic sartorial mistake.

There was silence, but for Frankie panting in the corner.

Sir James demanded, 'How did you find us?' Nothing about Claudine, please note.

I said, 'We took the Lausanne road out of Geneva and turned left at the signpost.'

He said, 'You know what I mean.'

Why do small men bark? I lit a cigarette without asking him kindly and puffed a lazy puff before answering.

'We know you and Miss Pearson have been having an affair for three months,' I began crisply.

'We know you took her on holiday to Antigua in March, while Claudine was off doing good turns. In April you occupied a suite together at the Sherry Netherlands in New York. This month it's Switzerland.

'We know you often overnight at 32C Drummond Lane, Maida Vale, which is Miss Pearson's flat. We know the lot.'

He balled his little fists. 'Who told you?'

I said, 'I can't remember. Anyways, it doesn't matter. My interest is why your wife was murdered last night.'

Tomlin said, 'You are accusing me? How dare you impugn my integrity.'

I turned to Frankie. 'Did I impugn?' Frankie said

he didn't think so and made a mental note to ask me later what impugn meant.

Sir James glowered. 'Emma – Miss Pearson and I arrived here yesterday morning. I could not have killed my wife.'

'You'd have to be one hell of a shot,' I conceded.

I wasn't bothered about upsetting him in his first day of widowerhood: he couldn't have cared much for Claudine if he was playing house with La Pearson. Just then a telephone rang in the hallway. Sir James the Lover reverted to Sir James the Captain of Industry. 'Answer that please, Miss Pearson.'

She went off. Her boyfriend sat down on a chair facing me and began breathing heavily. Both of us were trying hard to hear what was being said.

It went along these lines. She said, 'We know.' A long silence, then: 'No. Sir James wants it cancelled. It cannot go ahead now.'

From my seat I could just see her back. She was as stiff as a stick insect with hypertension.

More silence. Our Emma was not the chattiest of girls. After a while I heard: 'The complete package is off. Sir James doesn't care how many . . .'

Then her voice shot up an octave. 'Candy!' she exclaimed. 'Oh no! Candy must be stopped . . . yes, instantly.'

Opposite me Sir James went all rigid and porridge faced. He was the same size sitting down as standing up.

Out in the hall Emma was going ballistic. 'Candy must be stopped,' she repeated. 'I don't care how.'

Sir James popped up out of the cushions. He

bellowed, and that is really the only way to describe it: 'Emma! Not now! We'll call back.'

Her voice wound down to its usual alto pitch. She mumbled a sentence or two and put down the phone. As she returned to the lounge her boyfriend gave her the sort of glare he had previously reserved for me. She looked shaken and stirred.

I said, 'Interesting times we live in, eh?'

Sir James said tightly, 'Get out. Get out this very minute or I'll call the police.'

I rose languidly and made for the door, taking care not to get between the merry couple and Frankie who was going zap-zap-zap. Sir James chivvied him down the hall like a pygmy in hot pursuit of a giraffe.

The door slammed behind us and we were back on the street of a thousand geraniums.

'Strong drink is called for,' I said, and Frankie happily concurred, knowing I'd be buying.

So who the hell was Candy? And what mischief was she up to? And why was it so important to stop her?

These pretty puzzles occupied me while Frankie found us a bar. We sat outside in the fitful sunshine, drinking pissy beer that cost as much as the down payment on a studio flat.

'I am a bewildered man,' I told my monkey. My monkey furrowed his brow in sympathy.

'If we broke the sad tidings,' I continued, 'neither of them seemed the slightest surprised. They were more concerned with how we found out about their legover situation.'

'She's a bit of a dog,' Frankie said, conveniently forgetting the old slappers he hangs around with.

'And why is Candy in trouble?' I asked.

'Candy?'

'Yes. Emma Pearson said Candy has to be stopped.'

'I didn't hear her. Let's eat.'

Monkeys are the most primitive form of human life. Give them free drink, a meal on expenses and a bauble for their camera and they are happy little souls. We call them monkeys because they scamper about, chattering all the while. They call us blunts. This has nothing to do with our blunt pens. It has a lot to do with cockney rhyming slang. And there you have it in one single syllable word – the collected wit and wisdom of monkeys.

I abandoned the Candy conundrum and started thinking instead of what on earth I would write for the day's story. After an omelette which had more in common with a Michelin tyre than a Michelin star, I got through on the freephone to the Mother Inferior, to wit, Angela Whipple. Angela is News Editor. She was once a reporter and the battle-hardened veteran of a dozen Naomi Campbell picture captions, therefore she is uniquely equipped to tell us rough tough reporters our job.

'Ah, there you are,' she sang out, as if she'd spent a lifetime tracking me down.

I could not lie. 'Yes, here I am.'

I told her of the day's events. She asked me what the story was so I outlined something like: *Exclusive: I break news of Claudine's murder to runaway husband in Alpine love nest.*

'Great,' she enthused. 'Now go back and ask Tomlin if he's planning to marry his secretary, and who does he think killed his wife.'

Yes, you know and I know that Sir James was in no mood to unburden himself to me, but news editors lead sheltered lives. I said that was a terrific idea and I was on my way.

Angela added, 'And we need copy early. There's a colour spread on our bingo millionaire so all copy must be off stone by six.'

One of these days World War Three will break out and we won't have the story because we're running an eight-page sex survey showing that four out of three people bonk on their heads.

I rooted out Frankie who was charming the grizzled waiter into writing out false receipts for lunch. We returned to the scene of our crime. The Peugeot had gone from the driveway and no-one answered our knock. I sauntered round to the back garden and peered through the window. Nothing moved. Frankie fired off another hundred shots and back we went to the bar.

My story was on the thin side though there were some interesting and extremely questionable quotes from Sir James and his young lady. I didn't mention Candy.

Back to Angela. 'They fled while I was filing,' I said. 'Looks like they're flying back to London tonight.'

This was her cue to say, 'Hop on the next plane.' Instead she asked, 'You got a car?'

I checked over my shoulder. 'No. We've got a Volvo.'

'What? Anyway, I want you to see Claudine's mother. Maybe she knows something.'

I had a small query. 'Isn't her mum somewhere in France?'

Angela said, 'Yes. It's a place called Quimper.' She pronounced it Quimper.

She turned from the phone and shouted to our esteemed Foreign Editor. I could hear him thumbing through his Ottoman Empire atlas. Eventually Angela said, 'Yes, France.'

'Angie,' I reminded her, 'we are in Switzerland.'

'Well, Switzerland's next door to France.'

I gently pointed out that Quimper is a damn sight closer to London than we were to Quimper. Angela was not to be swayed. She knows that all these foreign places are in Europe, and that's where I was.

I said, 'We'll not get there until very late tonight. Maybe tomorrow.'

She tried to cheer me up. 'It doesn't matter. There's a great story breaking about a *Blind Date* guest accused of rape.'

In short, Claudine's murder was yesterday's news. You could wrap your chips in it. I'd be lucky if my story made a top on page nine.

I broke it to Frankie who was so upset he bought a round. We hired a room so he could wire his pix and then set off into the tail end of the afternoon.

I had maligned our hackmobile. It sang lustily all the way through to Macon, then over to Orleans and up to Rouen where we pulled in for the night at a place which looked cheap and cheerful but lied on both counts.

It was gone midnight and we were bordering on collapse. A bottle of wine apiece restored our sang-froid. We regaled each other with harrowing yarns of incompetent news/picture editors and Frankie, the shameless old tart, spoke of his many sexual conquests.

He was in rib-tickling form and I laughed 'til my nose ran. Frankie is a boon companion at times like these, not that I would ever tell him that.

Come the dawn, we breakfasted off croissants and bits of clammy ham and set forth again. Quimper, when we eventually got there, was wet and grey. We stopped and had a monster meal, picked up a couple of blank receipts and drove the final stretch to the humble abode of Madame Tournier. And pretty humble it was too. Picture a low grey stone farmhouse with puddles round the door and a bunch of bolshy-looking cows peering over the hedge, and there you have it.

The door was answered by a young wolf. Well, he didn't open the door, he just started ripping it to pieces when he heard our footsteps. The actual opener was a woman in her sixties with round healthy cheeks and big brown eyes. She was a fine looking woman for her age and would have looked even finer if she'd dried her tears.

I asked her if she spoke English and she did, which was a blessing as my French is fit to be taken out and shot. She said, 'You are journalists?' and I wasn't the slightest offended.

I went through the sorry-to-upset-you-at-such-a-distressing-time palaver and she summoned a brave smile and invited us into her maison. Frankie peeked around apprehensively. I think he expected to see English lambs ablaze on the table.

Madame Tournier asked if we'd like coffee and we said you bet and off she went to the kitchen while I took in the room. I can never figure out how the French are renowned for their style yet they live surrounded by all that is naff and hideous. The Tournier family seat was typical of the species. A good garage sale would have done it a power of good. Huge dark wooden dressers, tables built by Swan Hunter, knick-knacks, bric-à-brac, gimcrack whatnots adorning everything stationary. No doubt if the homicidal dog were not constantly on the prowl they would have stuck a carriage clock on his bonce.

There were pictures galore. Claudine at four, with a little girl half her age, squinting into the sun. They were obviously sisters. The whole family (Papa had a moustache) gathered proudly around a car. Some elderly French buffers cradling the infants. Claudine and the mini-Claudine with calves down on the farm. A wedding with the girls, now teenagers, in pink. Claudine in university gear. The other one in a bikini. A rather fanciable one that. Then shot after shot of Claudine up the Niger, down the Ganges, over the hills and far away. The biggest by far was of Claudine in power business suit, displaying her MBE. Not a single solitary shot of Sir James.

Madame Tournier returned just as the brutish dog began taking an unhealthy interest in the delicate area of my trousers. 'Sophie!' she admonished.

And the dirty bitch slunk off.

We sat down in big overstuffed chairs while Madame Tournier fetched out her hankie and blew a concealed trumpet into it.

She said in garlic-flavoured English, 'You know Claudine?'

I shook my head. Madame Tournier sighed and looked around the mugs' gallery on the dresser. She was a million miles off, somewhere I hope I never get to.

I said quietly, 'I saw Sir James yesterday.'

As conversation openers go, it was a real bummer. Madame Tournier flicked a contemptuous eyelid but said nothing. I gathered her son-in-law was not Mr Popular hereabouts. 'He's in Switzerland,' I said, just to start a fire going.

'He can stay there.' Through gritted teeth.

Half a dozen clocks tick-tocked to each other in French. Otherwise a heavy air of silence enveloped the proceedings. I let it hang there, knowing she would break first. She looked at me full face.

'Claudine told me such things about him . . . did you know she was planning to leave him?'

I arched my eyebrows obligingly.

'She had taken enough, enough of his . . .' Madame Tournier tailed off and peered into her coffee cup.

I oozed sympathy. 'Yes, I had heard about his . . .' I said, not having the faintest idea what she was talking about.

Madame Tournier fired me a fierce look. 'Maybe it will come out now?' she asked.

I tried a Gallic shrug. 'Maybe. But we need proof.'

'Proof! If you know, you just write and put it in your newspaper.'

It's amazing how little the French know of our libel laws. I looked away and said, 'I have just written a story about him and his girlfriend.'

A bitter laugh from her corner. 'That means nothing. Perhaps the English journals are too frightened to tell the real story.'

So it was something naughtier than Sir James's hanky-panky. What then?

Madame Tournier was inside her own head. 'I talked to Claudine on Tuesday and she was so looking forward to tomorrow.'

'Tomorrow?'

'Yes, she loves Asia so much.'

I guessed that meant Claudine was off on her travels again, or would have been if someone hadn't stopped her dead in her tracks.

I said, 'Where was she going?'

'She told me India, Sri Lanka, Cambodia and Laos. Her first time in Laos. She had so many plans. She adored her children.'

'Your daughter did not have any of her own,' I said.

This was a roundabout way of asking why the union of Tomlin and Claudine was not blessed with progeny.

Madame Tournier regarded me like I was some sort of dotard.

'Of course not.' She said it in French.

I was none the wiser. I said, 'No one in England can understand why Claudine was killed.'

Another acid laugh. 'Ask James Tomlin.'

I said, 'He denied having anything to do with it.'

Madame Tournier sniffed and said he would. So what was the point of me asking him then? I switched direction.

'You have lots of photographs,' I said stupidly. Claudine's mum took a dekko at the dresser and started off crying. Frankie and I exchanged glances and waited.

She dried up after a couple of minutes. I would have said sorry but that might have set her going again. Instead I pointed at one happy snap and said, 'You have another daughter?'

God knows where my brain was today. That was like saying to a man who has just lost his right leg that you see his left one is still hanging on in there. Madame Tournier just nodded.

She sipped on her coffee and said, 'Natalie is coming back from England with Claudine.'

Frankie eyed the pic of Natalie in her bikini. 'She's a real belter,' he said. Thank you, Frankie.

Madame said, 'She is just like Claudine. They are very close. Like twins almost.' She still spoke of her ex-daughter in the present tense.

I returned to the chase. 'Why should anyone want to kill her?'

She wandered around the question, inspecting it from here and there before answering.

'Maybe it was to do with the Foundation.'

The WorldCare Foundation was Claudine's baby. It administered her pet projects through a board of directors which included MPs, showbiz stars and sundry undesirables.

'You think it was someone in the Foundation?' I asked in a fairly desperate bid to get a story out of the interview.

Madame Tournier hesitated. 'Yes.'

God Bless you ma'am. 'Why?'

More dithering. 'Last month Claudine was here and she said there was a scandal. I do not know what scandal but my daughter was very upset.'

'Money?' I probed.

'No. I do not think so. It was something bigger.'

Bigger than money? Let's be realistic here.

'She was very angry. She said it would look bad. There were important people, Claudine said.'

Zip-a-dee-dooh-dah. I had a story. Readers might consider my reaction a mite cold-blooded. Sadly, this is the way we are. I remember once being in Ulster during the heady days of sectarian assassination when a Catholic teenager vanished. We all trawled round to see his granny. What do you think has happened? we asked her. She said, 'I'm dreading that my wee Tommy's lying shot down in a gutter somewhere with his dear life blood running out of him.' To which one of my colleagues responded, 'Great!' The idiot hack was only saying what everyone was thinking: what a great quote. But it fairly made granny blink.

Back to the present. 'What else could the scandal be?'

'I do not know,' she repeated. 'But Claudine said it would shock many people.'

'And destroy their reputations?' I asked, teasing quotes out of her. Madame Tournier looked vague but said that was about it.

For my own curiosity I asked, 'Did Claudine ever mention anyone called Candy?'

'Candy?' A quick flip through the memory banks. 'No, I have not heard of Candy. Who is she?'

I admitted my knowledge of Candy was on a par with hers, then I sat back to savour my lukewarm chicory while Frankie got on with his panchromatic artistry.

She showed us to the door. As I said goodbye I looked into a face that was fashioned for smiling but now was creased from crying. I felt sorry someone had popped Claudine. Or I felt sorry for her mum anyway.

Back in the Volvo I said to Frankie, 'Drink?'

'Yup.'

The story wrote itself:

SULTRY murder victim Claudine Tournier was gunned down to stop her exposing a high society scandal, her mother revealed last night.

Lovers of the English language might argue that Claudine was not the victim of a sultry murder. Fortunately my dear news editor Angela Whipple is not a lover of the English language.

'Nice one, Max,' she said when I rang through. 'Now what are you doing?'

I told her I was teaching French girls to English kiss.

She said, 'All right, as long as you're back tonight. You have a lot to follow up this end.'

I asked her what had happened to the Blind Date rapist. She sounded glum.

'They dropped the charge,' she said.

That's how it goes in newspapers. The Lord giveth, the Lord taketh away.

Chapter Four

Home to Rosie.

Every girl I've ever met called Rose is sweet and placid, plain and simple. Every Rosemary is much the same, maybe with aspirations as A Thinker. You picture them reading the boring bits in the Sunday heavies just for the hell of it. Why is it then that every girl called Rosie is a stark raving nutter? Such is mine. She once stabbed me with a corkscrew for nothing. Something to do with another girl, I think.

She has what the poofs in our features department like to call a pre-Raphaelite face. What, incidentally, is a post-Raphaelite face?

No matter. Back to Rosie Bannister. She's got long gypsy ringlets, smoky eyes, a dirty voice, a shape that disturbs a man and a very nice flat in Battersea. Thence I sallied with a bottle of Oscar de la Renta and a litre of duty-free Gordons.

She was pleased to see me. She shut the door in my face.

'Rosie,' I begged the door. ''Tis I! Your darlin' Max.'

She said something rude. I looked through the letterbox at her legs. By God, they go on a bit. I wasn't worried. It was Saturday night so she was probably out of drink. I clinked the bottles together for encouragement. The door opened a sliver.

'What do you want?' a corner of her mouth asked. They come up with some dumb questions.

I said I wanted to soothe her fretful brow and bring laughter to her lips.

'Ha!'

'You see, it's working already.'

Rosie let me in. I wrapped her in my arms and nuzzled her neck. She examined the ceiling. It was a lovely neck. It really suited her. At length we parted and got down to the preliminaries.

'You didn't phone,' she accused, fetching ice, tonic and glasses. She was out of lemon.

'I couldn't. I was up to my ears chasing Claudine Tournier's old man and her family across half Europe.'

Her lips formed a gorgeous pout. They entreated: come and kiss me. So I did. Rosie said, 'Stop that. I'm cross with you.'

It took a couple of stiffish gins before she ran through her catechism of complaint. I looked repentant and we were friends again. We got on to her day. She had flogged some of her lizard designs to a fashion house and was feeling chipper. Rosie is artistic. She draws things, usually lizards, and makes fearsome iguanas to stick on your coffee table. I often think Rosie eyes me as base clay from which she will fashion something fabulous. One of these days I'm going to wake up covered in scales with my tongue poking out.

She was curled in one corner of the white settee, draped in a woolly smock thing, the colour of overripe strawberries, with leggings a touch lighter and bluer than charcoal. Every now and then she flicked away a rogue curl with an unvarnished hand. You could call her beautiful, but that wouldn't be doing her justice. Women mesmerise me. They just walk across a room, or flick the hair out of their eyes and I am in thrall. They don't even know they're doing it. Rosie has a million such tricks. The only thing is you get so enchanted by them that you forget everything else that's going on.

Rosie was saying, 'So, do you fancy going?'

I kick started my brain. 'Sorry, love. I was just thinking about the Tournier story. What were you saying?'

She clicked her teeth in annoyance. They're great teeth. She said, 'Kim and Dan are having a party tonight; shall we go?'

Kim and Dan Young were originally my friends but, like so much else in my life, have been shanghaied by Rosie. Dan is a lobby reporter and Kim a lady monkey, so it was a mixed marriage and no one gave it a chance. But after a year together they're still lovey-dovey which just goes to show something or other. When I introduced Rosie to the happy couple she giggled. Later I asked her why. She said, 'Kim and Dan Young. They sound like a Vietnam war atrocity.'

I roared too. Then we went on to invent suitable imaginary kids for them. We came up with Sam, Ben, Hugh. Oh how we laughed. I suppose you had to be there.

Returning to Rosie's question, my first instinct

was to say bugger Kim and Dan, let's stay home with the TV off, but I said, 'It's your call.'

Rosie looked sour. 'Why can't you make up your mind?' she asked, ignoring the fact she couldn't make a decision either.

We batted it back and forth for a gin or two and then we voted to go, which was what she wanted all along.

It was very much a hacks' party, though some desk people had slunk in when no one was looking. My fond news editor whooped with joy when she saw me, kissed me smudgily and said sweet things about my Tournier exclusive. She never can hold her drink.

By her side was her ever-loving Arfur. Arfur is a down table sports sub on the *Mail* so by rights we should have slung him out on his ear, but we are a bunch of big softies, us hacks.

Someone clapped her hands over my eyes and breathed throatily in my left ear: 'Guess who?' It was Dania, my favourite typographical error. Dania and I were hot stuff together not so very long ago. Come to think of it, it was because of Dania that I now have a corkscrew scar on my shoulder. She has since surrendered herself to Jonathon (sic) Elwood, though what she sees in the lout is beyond me. Jonathon waved a cheery glass in my direction and yelled, 'Great story!' which I took to mean: you're a God-awful writer but the story was good. I smiled between my teeth.

Of Rosie there was never a sign. Whenever we grace these thrashes she invariably goes off to talk to strange men, leaving me in the most dubious of company, like that of my mate Tommy from the

Express who had just discovered a new dive in Belgravia where the drink is cheap and the women cheaper still.

Next I fell among thieves, various riff-raff from the News of the Screws. The Wildebeest was there, one arm wrapped around a bottle, the other clutching a brace of hackettes. The Wildebeest is an appalling man whose company is shunned by every right-thinking member of society. We are bosom buddies. We fell in love during the hunt for the Biggleswade Bigamist when the Wildebeest bailed me out of a Danish nick after a sad misunderstanding at a strip club. He was regaling us with his latest atrocity, involving his paper's Prize Pets contest, where he ran over the winner, formerly a handsome tabby cat. And so the idle hours rolled by until Rosie appeared by my side. It was her sweet way of saying: 'They're down to the white wine. Any second now they'll open the aftershave. Let's get the hell out of here.' And get the hell we did.

Back in Battersea I rang my own flat to see if my answerphone had missed me. It had. There was one message, from a Miss Ham. It took me a moment to remember Miss Ham was our Shirley, the girl who blew the gaff on Sir James Tomlin. She wanted me to ring her at her Essex domicile. I promised the answerphone I would, but not right now, for Rosie had just drifted into vision minus her smock and leggings. That's another one of her tricks.

*

The Sundays carried run of the mill stories on Claudine's killing. Nothing new there, though the Indy hinted at financial headaches at Freleng-Bourke, Sir James's firm.

Rosie and I went down to Richmond and drank gin and ginger beer with lime and ice whilst enjoying the sunshine outside a ye olde riverfront pub frequented by king-size American tourists. Gazing at Old Father Thames rolling muddily along I remembered I was supposed to ring Shirley.

For the first time I talked about the story to Rosie who was fresh and minty in green and white stripes. She reckoned it was Sir James what done it. Furthermore, she indicated that any man who is unfaithful to his woman should be chopped into small pieces. I took this as a coded warning.

I left my call to Shirley until the evening, reasoning she would be out on such a glorious May afternoon, spotting Ford Capris or whatever it is Essex people get up to in their off hours.

The phone answered after one ring. 'Yes?' said a plaintive voice. Shirley herself.

I lied a bit about having just got back from French France and asked her what's new. Sir James, she said, was in London, had scrubbed his schedule and was spending a lot of time with cronies behind closed doors.

Well, hold the front page girls, I thought. She wanted to know when she would see the grand I promised her for all the inside stuff on Sir James's love life. I told her soon. She didn't appear to have much to say for herself. I diagnosed newsitis. This is a distressing psychological ailment afflicting those who want to prolong their fifteen minutes of fame. You get their story, run it, and move on to the next one. But some people are not content with a one-off splash and colour spread. So they pester you for months, even years afterwards with every trivial event in their grey day in the fond hope you'll bung them another wad of tenners and make them a media star again.

I said I had a busy time at the Old Bailey next week and I would get back to her after it. She said okay, but didn't sound too happy.

I asked her if she knew a girl called Candy. She sucked on it for a moment and said, 'I don't know. It sort of rings a bell.'

So does my local innkeeper, but I don't write a story about it. Shirley said she would ask around. I made her promise. Then she said, 'Do you pay for other stories?'

I was wary. 'It depends if they make the paper and what sort of show they get.'

'It's not about the murder.'

What was it then? A crash on the Southend arterial? A three-in-a-bed in Theydon Bois?

I said, 'Shirley, I just do crime stuff. But if it's any good, I'll put you on to our News Desk.' Which is shorthand for I'm having a rare day off, so why don't you go and bother somebody else?

I could hear her chewing her lip as she mulled it over. She said, 'Maybe you could tell me if it's worth anything?'

I gave in. 'What is it?'

She said, 'You know Leon Knapp?'

'Leon Knapp? Oh, the pop singer.'

She said, 'He's vanished.'

I pictured the wrinkly rocker vanishing from the chat show circuit forever. It was a happy prospect.

I said, 'What do you mean, vanished?'

She said, 'Everyone's tearing their hair out looking for him. They're all worried frantic.'

'Who they?'

'His manager. His PR man. Sir James.'

I said, 'Sir James? Sir James! What's his connection with Leon Knapp?'

She said, 'Leon was going to be on the Asian tour with Claudine – well part of it. But they can't find him to tell him it's off.'

'I still don't get it,' I said trying to imagine Leon Knapp taking time off from his ego trip to give the Third World a helping hand. No, not the Leon we know and loathe.

'And,' said Shirley, 'he's one of the Foundation's trustees.'

'Aaaah!' A much more believable image popped up. Leon, his pockets stuffed with stolen Foundation money, topping up his plastic tan on some tropical island with a sugar bowl of cocaine for company. Rumour has it he's funny that way.

'Is it any good?' asked Shirley, meaning was the story worth a few bob.

I told her it might be. We'd have to check it out. He might just be chewing the wallpaper in some funny farm. Or plotting another comeback.

She was disappointed but she said she'd trust me, which almost qualified her for a story of her own.

We said bye bye to each other and I put the phone down. I looked in the mirror. There were deep lines of thought etched across my brow. I shook my head and they went away.

Monday. Off to the Old Bailey for the winding up of the Silence of the Crams murder. By rights it should have been a straight up and downer. Everyone knew the unspeakable Crams had done in their Kurdish au pair and grilled her on the barbecue. But the couple were on legal aid and their brief was determined to give us a run for our money. This morning, with the jury out, he was arguing that a drunken orgy pic of the Crams in the *Star* showed his clients in a bad light and was prejudicial and so forth. He looked like he had lots more nonsense where this came from. We fell into a dreamless slumber while he took his time to get to the point, namely that the pre-trial publicity meant his clients were denied a fair hearing, therefore the two loonies should be let loose forthwith. Mr Justice Seamley tittered and said he'd adjourn and think about it over a bottle of port, though he didn't mention the port out loud. He billowed out scratching his curls. We took his exit as a heaven-sent sign to head for the bar.

Nobody was feeling very talkative so with nothing better to do I glanced through our final edition. I had passed on Shirley's tip about the vanishing Leon Knapp to our showbiz man with his finger on the pulse of pop. He had furnished his usual glittering prose:

Mystery last night surrounded the whereabouts of legendary rock idol Leon Knapp . . .' it began. I read no further. If ever you see a newspaper story which begins: 'Mystery surrounded . . .' it means the reporter hasn't the faintest idea what's happening so there's no point reading on. I was also unimpressed with the word 'whereabouts'. This is far too long for our readers. By the time they get to the end of it they've forgotten how it started.

I cast our great organ aside and rang News Desk. I got Nigel. He's the guy with the friendly smile who sits beside Angela sharpening a stiletto and waiting for her to turn her back. He sounded really glad to hear from me. He was less chummy when I warned him there might be no show from the Crams today.

'Oh,' he said. I knew what he was thinking. News Desk people the land over are convinced that every morning the bigwigs of British justice and all the raggedy-arsed reporters get together to conspire against them.

Nige said, 'Leave it to Agency and come back.'

I said I needed more background stuff on Marjorie Cram and I was meeting contacts. He gave a grudging okay, knowing what I was really up to but unable to prove it.

Half an hour later we were still guzzling away when Big Ben, the hacks' friend, reeled in. Ben Ashbee is a detective super and a super detective. That is to say he talks to us hacks and tells us things. Well, he talks to me anyway. I asked him why he was hanging around the Bailey and he said he was just watching a bunch of druggies getting sent down.

Nothing to write home about there. I asked what else was doing. He said he was fronting the Claudine Tournier investigation which was nice for me.

'Any moves?' I asked, buying him drink and luring him to a secluded cloister of the bar.

He said the betting was Sir James was the guilty party; that it looked like a contract hit as Sir James had a most convenient alibi. The murder weapon a .32. Motive? Probably money. All very trite and tiresome.

'Can you pin it on him?' I asked. Ben, a melancholy man at the best of times, turned his mouth down, which I took to mean not a hope in hell.

We talked about the WorldCare Foundation and the singular absence of Knapp. He put the last item down to dissolute living. I asked whether a girl called Candy figured anywhere in the investigation. He said no and looked so forlorn I bought him a bag of smoky bacon crisps.

Tired out by all the excitement, I eddied back to the office. Things were even quieter there. I got out my black book and started ringing people so they could share my boredom. I caught Mac McIvor, my deep throat police inspector, just before he sneaked off to the pub. He said, 'My tip about Claudine's body must be a nice little earner,' signalling that he expected £500 at least.

I pointed out that he had not tipped me off about Claudine: all he had said was there was a corpse littering St Katharine's Dock. But I didn't really argue the point. It wasn't my money.

Mac said Sir James had been interviewed a couple

of times, with a smarty pants lawyer holding his hand. The Serious Fraud Office were taking a quiet interest in Freleng-Bourke. Otherwise Claudine's death was just like Leon Knapp's vanishing trick. Mystery surrounded it.

On a sudden whim I rang Freleng-Bourke and got through to Sir James Tomlin's private office. A male voice answered. Someone younger and doubtless taller than the passionate pygmy.

No, Sir James was not available, and who was calling please? He was polite but guarded.

I said, 'May I speak to Candy?'

A sharp intake of breath. 'Who is calling please?'

I came clean: 'This is Max Chard.'

'Oh!' followed by silence.

'I am the chief crime correspondent of—'

'I know who you are, Mister Chard,' he cut in. He was still guarded but had forgotten to be polite.

Chief crime correspondents accept this as their lot in life. I lit a Bensons and waited for him to tell me to eff off. Instead he said, 'Candy? Would you care to tell me what this is about?'

I said I would prefer to speak to Candy. He hesitated and said, 'One moment.'

I waited five moments. He came back on. 'I am afraid there is no one here who can help you.' He was lying but I didn't know what he was lying about.

'Is Miss Pearson there?' I tried.

He didn't bother looking. 'No.'

'And I suppose she won't be there all day?'

'That is correct.' He switched to patronising public

school twerp mode. 'I suggest if you have any queries about Freleng-Bourke you call our press office and—'

'And will they tell me about Candy?' I snapped.

Splutter of outrage and the phone went down.

It had been fun while it lasted, not that it told me anything. I returned to my Bensons and my little black book. I got all the way through to the Rs before I found anyone else worth annoying. Ross Gavney.

'I owe you a fiver,' I said by way of introduction.

'What? Oh, yes.' Ross sounded preoccupied.

'Are you preoccupied?' I asked.

'No. Not really. Well, actually, yes, just, yes, a little.'

Ross does not normally stick a comma after every word. I thought about it and said, 'You want me to go away?'

'Well, yes. Sorry, Max, but things are rather . . .'

I said that's okay, I'd catch him again, and if he cared to invite me round to slaughter his whisky, I'd gladly pay up on the bet. Ross said right, terrific, fine. And that was that. I replaced the phone and pondered on my old chum. The sunshine was somehow gone from his voice. Probably some awful mid-life crisis, like should he swop the Saab turbo for an XJS. I felt deeply perplexed and concerned. Maybe I was thirsty.

After lunch I got down to the serious business of the day. Expenses. If you've ever wondered why newspapers are singularly devoid of any imaginative spark, it's because the poor hacks devote every last ounce of creativity to doing their exes. As works of fiction they rival Dickens, the crime statistics and the *Sunday Sport* at their best.

I had returned from France with £350 in traveller's cheques, what was left of my £500 advance. There is a holy commandment in newspapers that you must never, never, never, *ever* return a single penny the office has advanced you: that you must show you spent it all in the pursuit of the story. My task for the afternoon was to launder the loose £350. My exes duly reflected that I paid forty quid for an interpreter in Switzerland, fifty for one in France. I bought route maps, newspapers, a bottle of champagne for Sir James, and a few outrageously expensive meals for myself. I also got the worst exchange rate in francs known to man. Grand total: £527, not counting hotel and car.

I was gazing on my handiwork with admiration when the phone rang. Shirley Ham on the other end. She bubbled and babbled incomprehensibly. There was a horrendous racket going on in the background. She was either calling from a Cairo street market or a British Rail station. I told her to calm down and start again. After a few breaths she got it together. She said, 'You remember you asked me to find out about Candy?'

I said I did. She said, 'I've got lots of news for you; you're going to be really surprised.'

I said that was nice, and what was the news?

She went all coy. 'Not on the phone,' she said, as if I were asking her to confess her sexual fantasies.

'Where then?' I asked.

'Are you free tonight?'

Steady on, Shirl. I'm not that sort of man. I

admitted I was free and happy to meet her anywhere, as long as it wasn't in Essex.

She thought about it and came up with a pub, the Scimitar on Mile End Road, which was a fair compromise as it was in no man's land, between the City and the wilderness.

I said seven o'clock. She said eight. She wanted to see someone first, she explained. She was about to ring off when she dropped me a teaser. 'You've got it all wrong about Candy.'

'What have I got wrong?'

A giggle. 'You'll find out tonight.'

Be still my beating heart. But I managed to survive the intervening hours without tearing my hair out. A black cab dropped me outside the Scimitar ten minutes off eight. I ordered a Gordons and took in the scenery.

In the old days this was a watering hole for the Krays and their hired help. Every Friday night the twins used to muscle in, put the frighteners on everybody, relieve the landlord of fifty quid, and muscle out again, pausing only to duff up stray drinkers. Since then the place had gone to hell. Now it was a theme pub and the theme was crooks. But not the local real life rootin' tootin' shootin' bad boys: the sepia prints on the walls featured Al Capone, Bugsy Siegel and Legs Diamond. Or maybe it was John Dillinger. I never can tell those two apart. For my money, the biggest crook on view was the barman, running a nice extortion racket with his prices. He was wearing a butcher-style apron, a clip on moustache, and he had his slicked-back hair parted dead centre. He did not seem embarrassed.

The wallpaper was doing its best to pretend it was bricks, bricks punctuated here and there with ragged edged bullet holes, designed to make you feel you were enjoying your pint of London bitter at the scene of the St Valentine's Day Massacre. Just the sort of place for a romantic date. Off the bar there were little wooden alcoves. I inspected the contents. No Shirley. The clientele were youngish, moneyed and not visibly gifted with taste. The men favoured shiny double-breasteds with ties as muted as Hiroshima. Their treble-voiced partners were blondes with Grand Canyon cleavages and Tenerife tans.

Back to the bar area where the barman was doing something awful to a shot of good gin with blue curacao and creme de menthe. I averted my eyes. The piano rag music came courtesy of Scott Joplin. I settled into another Gordons and pretended I didn't mind. When The Entertainer popped up for the third time, I was getting restless. Where was Shirley in this my hour of need? I started playing the fruit machine, a sure sign of desperation. I was down a fiver before I gave up and asked the barman for his phone. I didn't want to use my own mobile because all the poseurs in the place were flashing theirs. I got through to a grumpy old geezer who told me Shirley wasn't home; that she'd gone out to see a man called Mike or something.

'Max?' I suggested.

'Yer, that's it,' he graciously conceded.

I fed the phone another 50p while Shirl's dad took

his time about finding a pen and writing down my bleep number. I made him repeat it just as the money ran out. By now it was coming up 9.30 and if Shirley had walked in the door I would have been a shade tetchy with her. But she didn't. I gave the barman a message just in case she called in. I licked my glass dry and wandered out on to Mile End Road to hunt a taxi. They were all heading the wrong way, back to Ongar or Bow or wherever it is cabbies go to rest their mouths. I walked a good half mile, passing at least three pubs, before a cab rescued me. My bleep went off as I clambered aboard. It said, 'Call call call – Mac Mac Mac'.

I took this to mean McIvor wanted me to call him urgently, or three times, or possibly both.

'Where to, mate?' asked my driver.

'To London,' said I, pointing west.

Chapter Five

I suppose it's about time I gave you the SP on Mac. His full name is Terence something McIvor and he's Irish, or Ulsterish, to be precise. He talks funny. In his youth, a year or so back, he was a rising star in the Royal Ulster Constabulary, a fine body of men who decided they could do without him after all. Mac prefers to draw a veil over exactly how and why he and the RUC parted company. But I gather a certain detective inspector and his missus are no longer calling each other snookyookums.

Mac came to England and naturally gravitated to the Met, who welcome all the riff-raff they can clap their hands on. It's a bit like the Foreign Legion only less picky. In the Met's ranks Mac looked like a choirboy with the brains of Einstein's smarter brother. They made him up to inspector but stuck him in internal investigations, the police department which turns over naughty plods and reports back to itself. One of these days someone will refer it to the Monopolies Commission. Mac didn't like the job, not through any moral scruple or sense of decency. Good God, no. He just found it boring. So he looked around for some amusing sideline to while away the tedious hours.

He was still looking when we first met, in the aftermath of the Milky Bar Killer storm. There was a school of thought in softy papers like the *Guardian* that the police were a mite over-zealous in shooting dead the young thug when he was (a) out of his tree on crack, (b) unarmed, and (c) asleep. Scotland Yard's heroic defence was: 'Our officers fired, believing they were about to be fired upon.' Though quite how they came to believe they were in danger from a snoring zonked out tearaway was never quite explained. In all the brouhaha over the killings it was sometimes overlooked that the Milky Bar Kid, a pasty-faced, four-eyed little runt, had already murdered a building society clerk. Our thoughtful leader writer redressed the balance. He inclined to the view that the Law had done us all a favour in putting Milky down. And seeing he was shot while he was sleeping, he didn't feel a thing. A sort of mercy killing, our Voice of Sanity argued. But the Grauniad and a posse of headline hunting MPs started fulminating about Gun Law, shoot-to-kill policies, that sort of tosh. Nobody said anything about stupidity.

Mac was on the squad set up to investigate the antics of the armed desperadoes from the Met's firearms unit. We bumped into each other in a bar down Richmond way, fell to talking about the Rugby World Cup, the price of drink, the shape of the barmaid and so on. I wasn't cultivating him: we just hit it off naturally. I suppose it was a case of opposites attract.

Somewhere in the course of our yattering Mac let slip that one of the Yard's gunslingers had a spot of previous. He was involved in the shooting of another unarmed villain when he was with Avon and Somerset. It gave me an exclusive splash with picture by-line and all. And that, I thought, was that.

But next morning, bright and early, I got a call from Mac, suggesting it might be a nice gesture on my part to bung him some readies. I got him £300 and he was my friend for life. Also he had found his true vocation, assisting us gentlemen of the Fourth Estate in our tireless pursuit of truth and justice. Since then he's built himself a network of like-minded coppers who tip him off when something's doing. He gives them 25 per cent of what we pay him and trousers the rest. I reckon he lifts forty grand a year, and that's not counting his police pay. We launder our payments through some addresses in Belfast and Donegal so the Met can't trace leaks back to him.

Mac is sallow and skeletal, has a long foxy face and wide foxy eyes. Women tell me he's attractive, but I can't see it. He likes dark suits, dark shirts and bold monochrome ties. Picture a jazz musician with an unhealthy interest in white powders and you have a photofit of Mac. He has never learned to tie anything other than a Windsor knot. His hair is mousy brown, lank, and flops over one eye. When he's not at his desk digging up stuff to sell, he hangs around Hampton's, a wine bar of dubious taste. I have never looked more than twice at a pretty woman there, because the odds are she's already been the victim of a Mac Attack. I would guess Hampton's pick up about five grand of the money Mac makes from us, for he is an alarmingly generous man.

Back to where we were: I called Hampton's from the cab. Yes, Mac was there, said Louise, just a minute, she'd get him. I listened to the background shrieks and guffaws that pass for civilised conversation in the dive. Mac came on.

'How's about ye?' he said in that quaint Frank Carson-ish way of his.

I told him I was in the jacuzzi with Michelle Pfeiffer and went Gluggle-bubble-giggle to prove it.

Up front the taxi driver said, 'You all right, guv?'

I ignored him. 'What've you got for me?'

Mac said, 'You're not going to believe this.'

I promised I wouldn't but said he could tell me anyway.

He licked his lips and said, 'They've found another body, another woman, in St Katharine's Dock . . .'

I said, 'Stone me!' Or something similar.

' . . . and at the exact same spot where Claudine Tournier was dumped. What about that, hey?'

He didn't know anything else, whether the latest victim had jumped or was pushed, what her name was and all the rest. I told him to line up a bottle for me and I'd be there within the hour, after I dropped by the dock.

'Just as long as you don't drop into it,' he cackled and was gone.

I told Big Ears, the cabbie, 'Change of plan. Take me to St Katharine's Dock.'

He had earwigged enough of the conversation to grasp there was another body in the Thames. He said, 'Are you a reporter, squire?'

I said no: that I worked for the Port of London Authority, and it was my sad duty in life to chart floating women who posed a danger to shipping. He said, 'Wot?' and gave me a funny look in his rear view mirror.

We trundled on through the gloom grey canyons of E1 until we found London's favourite bathing spot for fashionable young ladies. It was deja vu all over again. Daisy chains of police blue and white cordon tapes ringed the dock approach. On the quayside a motley gang of fourteen-year-old Plods were saying useful things like: 'Move along there' and 'There's nothing to see.'

For once they were telling the truth. The ambulance had been and gone. A fleet of yachts paddled in the ebb tide and all was serene, apart from the forensic civvies snapping souvenir shots and scribbling in their big blue folders in joined up writing.

I disembarked from my cab and was instantly confronted by my old mate, Harry, the defective inspector last seen hanging about these parts on the night of Claudine's splashdown. He was not a happy bobby.

'How did you know there was something going on here?' he demanded belligerently.

'I think it's a gift, Harry,' I said.

He stuck his finger in my chest. 'I've got a crow to pick with you,' he said in an interesting use of English.

I told him to pick away. He ordered me to think back to our last meeting. I thought.

'You introduced me to a bloke you said was Lewis Trefoyle from the Home Office.'

'Junior Minister at the Home Office,' I said, ever a stickler for accuracy.

H said, 'Well, I was watching *Newsnight* last night and Lewis Trefoyle was on and it wasn't him at all. He's about ten years older than your pal, bald as an egg and fat.'

My pupils dilated in shock, horror, outrage. 'Not him! But he told me he was Trefoyle and I believed him. I even bought him drink.'

Harry snorted and sneered.

I said, 'There is another alternative you might consider, Harry. Maybe the bloke who was on *Newsnight* was only pretending to be Lewis Trefoyle, and the one with me was the genuine article. The Beeb can get things wrong, you know.'

He stomped off a few yards and stomped back a few yards, muttering to himself. I lit a cigarette and offered the packet. For a moment he looked as if he might throw it, and me, into the dock. There was a long fraught silence.

I broke it, saying I was sorry about my phoney Trefoyle; that I was under the cosh to get the story in time for the edition, hence my shameful subterfuge; that I owed him a large scotch; that I felt bad about my trickery, grovel, grovel, grovel, lick, lick, lick. Harry peered at me intently and he could see I was sincere.

He said, 'Don't ever try anything like that again, Chard.'

I swore blind I wouldn't and moved briskly on to this evening's cabaret. Who was the victim?

Harry looked sly. He said, 'You can call her Unlucky.'

I said I could call her downright unfortunate. But what was her name?

'Unlucky,' Harry said. He had a silly grin slicked across his mug.

I narrowed my eyes and looked cross. Harry said happily, 'That's what Thames Division call her.' He nodded at a couple of bods from the river police.

I exhaled a long controlled jet of smoke. I said, 'And why do they call her Unlucky, H?'

He was practically in hysterics. 'Because they've got her listed as DB 13.'

'DB 13?'

'DB 13,' said Harry. 'Every time they find a body in the Thames they give it a number. DB stands for dead body. This is DB 13 – their thirteenth dead body this year. Unlucky 13. What would you call her?'

I let him have his little laugh. I said, 'What else?'

He said, 'All I can say is there's a connection.'

'With Claudine Tournier's murder?'

'That's what I said.'

I said, 'A copycat job? Shot in the head?'

Harry dithered over how much he would tell me. 'No, this one was strangled.'

I blinked. Our murderer shoots one woman and strangles another. I said, 'I don't get it. What's the connection?'

'Who the victim is, that's the connection.' He was enjoying himself.

'And you won't tell me that?'

'That's right.'

For a moment I thought I might chuck him in the dock. My steely self-resolve held. I said, 'Obviously Victim Number Two was dead before she hit the water, that's why you say she was strangled. She couldn't have told you who she was, or how she was linked with Claudine. So she must have had something on her that gave you the lead.'

Harry said, 'That's all you get.'

And he would have been right but for the sudden appearance of a pimply youth dressed up as a copper. He addressed his boss. 'The rest of Miss Ham's things have been sent to the incident room, sir.'

Miss Ham!

'Christ!' I said out loud. 'It's Shirley.'

Harry goggled and bulged. 'What do you know about her?' he yelped.

I flicked my cigarette into the dock. I bestowed a seraphic smile on H and said, 'She's called Shirley Ham. And that's all you get.'

It is never pleasant watching a middle aged nitwit go bananas. I closed my eyes and blocked my ears. Harry ranted through his repertoire of swear words, made up a couple more, vowed to rip up my Scotland Yard press pass, recklessly accused me of inventing quotes, and threatened to report me to the Press Association. I think he meant the Press Complaints Commission.

After a while he ran out of puff so he just stood there sweating and steaming.

I said in tones of sweet reason, 'Can we make a deal?'

'A deal!' More rude words.

I said, 'Just listen to me.' He grumbled but went quiet. I said, 'Let me buy you a drink and then I'll show you mine if you show me yours.'

I led him unprotesting to the Port O' Call, where I first clapped eyes on Shirley. He grunted that okay, he'd listen. And he'd have a glass of red. He didn't say please.

I parked him at the very same table where Shirley and I had sat and elbowed my way through the suits at the bar. A fluffy Kiwi barmaid gave me a welcoming wink and I winked right back. I can be ever so bold when Rosie's not around. I ordered a cheeky little sauvignon from the sunny side of the Andes and returned to Harry who didn't look as if he'd missed me.

We each had a hearty slurp and I got down to it. I filled him in on my supposed meet with Shirley, her job at Freleng-Bourke, her gossip about Sir James.

Harry nodded at each point but he wasn't impressed. I took a deep breath, hesitated, then told him about the mysterious Candy and how Shirley had called to say she had the info but was topped before she could tell me.

That made Harry's little pink ears stick out. He even dragged out a notebook and scribbled in it.

I said, 'That's the whole deal, H. Everything I know. Now, what made you link Shirley with Claudine?'

He waffled something about the papers she was

carrying but shut up. I topped up the glass to ease his lockjaw.

He guzzled a mouthful before he unbent. He said, 'Her handbag was lying on the dockside. She had credit cards, cheque book, a tube season ticket with her picture on it. That's how I know who she was.'

I said, 'Yes, but where's the Claudine connection?'

Harry patted his pocket. 'Papers,' he said.

It took a third glass of sauvignon before he allowed me a peek. The only interesting stuff was bumf on the WorldCare Foundation, a copy of a letter to the trustees, outlining Claudine's planned schlep around Asia. It listed all those to whom copies had been sent. I spotted Leon Knapp's name, and Proudhoe Veizey, the silver-locked thespian. The itinerary was longer than the Great Wall of China – Calcutta, Bombay, Dacca, Madras, Colombo, Kandy, Bangkok, Chiang Mai, Vientiane, Phnom Penh, and back to Blighty. There was a list of dates and functions, opening birth control clinics, meeting people with five syllable names, and so on.

I said, 'Shirley didn't work for the Foundation. Why does she have this letter?'

Harry said, 'No idea. But you can see there's a connection.'

I handed the letter back to him and we lapsed into silence. There was something tugging away at the back of my brain. Something about the letter.

I said, 'Let's see it again, H.'

I started reading from the very top and got halfway down the second page before it hit me – the bit where it said '. . . Madras, Colombo, Kandy, Bangkok . . .'

There it was, in letters a hundred foot high. Kandy! That was Shirley's big surprise for me. There never had been a mystery woman called Candy. But there was something funny going on in Kandy. I smiled to myself.

But of course I never said a word to Harry.

Nothing ever gets done in newspapers until after morning conference. In the meantime, news editors like to pretend they call the shots by despatching reporters to doorsteps and shouting into telephones and running around with bits of paper. This goes on for a couple of lunatic hours before conference begins in the Editor's office and a companionable hush falls upon the newsroom. Reporters lounge around telling lies and trading hooky meal receipts.

Meanwhile, behind the mock mahogany doors of the Editor's suite, the big boys and girls are getting down to the things that really matter. The Editor reveals he spent the previous evening watching a re-run of *Hancock's Half Hour* and everyone agrees it was a hoot, though not a single one of them saw it. He tells the Features Editor to do a piece on the Beeb's treasure trove of comedy, which we've already done twice this year. The Features Editor says: 'Good thinking' into his beard. The Regional Editor, an ageing harridan who thinks she's a sixteen-year-old sexpot, agrees it's a knock-'em-dead idea and goes on to waffle about how footballers' legs give her a kick. The Sports

Editor guffaws heartily bccause he and the Regional Editor are currently enjoying a secret affair, a secret known only to the entire office. The City Editor, a woman of some intellect, says she doesn't think footballers are the slightest bit sexy, but hasn't the England fly half got a terrific bum? The Features Editor glares at her and intimates that only a frustrated old boot could find anything sexy in a rugby player. The Leader Writer, still thinking about *Hancock's Half Hour*, recalls a particularly hilarious episode. Nobody laughs because the Leader Writer is universally and justly loathed. The Foreign Editor regales the company by telling him how he almost cut his toes off with the lawnmower yesterday. That reminds the Editor of the time he closed the Mercedes door on his thumb. Everyone coos in sympathy. The Pictures Editor, fresh back from a freebie to Acapulco, informs the gathering of the right way to drink tequila. The Executive Editor says that personally he's never liked tequila, but seeing he has never professed to liking anything, no one is at all surprised. The Diary Editor fondles his tie and lets slip a totally fabricated indiscretion about a minor royal and a rent boy. The News Editor says the *Mirror* buy-up of the polo groupie hooker ('How I Made A Mint From Polo!') was a waste of sixty grand. The entire company gives her a dirty look; she has just reminded them they're supposed to be talking about newspapers. The Editor sighs and says: 'Okay, what have we got today?' One by one his lieutenants produce their menus and argue about why such and such is a great story. The Editor, who is not fit to edit the *Beano*, wibbles and wobbles and makes his ruling. No one argues, for the Editor's indecision is final, and they can see his eyes straying to the mock mahogany mini bar in the corner. The assorted lackeys gather up their papers and return to their desks in varying states of dudgeon. So it was this morning.

I ambushed Angela Whipple as she wafted past, shedding fragrances like a travelling Body Shop. I said, 'Angie, I've got a lead on the Tournier story, but it means a foreign.'

Angela was wary because foreigns cost money. 'Where to?'

'Sri Lanka. To Kandy.'

I could see she was perplexed. Until now, Angela thought Sri Lanka was the leader of a yoga cult.

'You know, off India,' I said.

'India! Why do you want to go to India?'

Using only small words I explained all the stuff about Candy and Kandy, and how Shirley had been murdered investigating it. My exclusive story was in our London final edition, but I hadn't expected Angie to have read it all the way through.

She didn't like the idea, asked me what I hoped to find, and I had to admit I didn't know. She said she would talk about it to the Piltdown Man, executive editor Tony Belker. That meant I wasn't going. Belker and I share a deep and abiding hatred. Every now and then he tries to have me fired for landing us with a libel writ or getting blotto. The man has no sense of humour.

I aimed a mental kick at my backside, acknowledging I'd blown Sri Lanka. What I should have done was to have taken Angie out for a liquid lunch, told her the Kandy line, hinted that the *Sun* might be on the same track and then feigned boredom. After an hour or two she'd piece the whole thing together, suggest I shoot off to Kandy and think what a clever little news editor she was.

Angie bustled off to Belker's festering lair and I treated myself to a cup of yellow tea from the machine. She returned before my first grimace and said no, and forgot me. I ambled round to our library which is manned by the biggest bunch of amnesiacs since I can't remember when. After half an hour's hunting they dug out a book on Sri Lanka that was so old it called the place Ceylon. I flipped to the section on Kandy to see what I was missing. Kandy, it said, was the former capital, much beloved by English colonists and still redolent of the Empire's glory days with its architecture and unhurried ways. It was home to the Temple of the Tooth, which housed one of the Buddha's molars. There was much to see and do in Kandy's leafy environs, the book said, like watching spectacular festivals where elephants trundle around town tarted up like Danny La Rue. In a throwaway line, my guide to the pearl of the Indian Ocean happened to mention that once a month there is a Poya Day holiday, when 'all places of public entertainment are closed and the sale of alcohol is forbidden'. I closed the manual, reflecting that maybe I wasn't missing so much after all.

Back at my desk I found a brief from Angela to do up an early page story on gun-happy teenagers. I trawled through cuttings, invented a horrified senior police officer, got him to say something outlandish, and hammered out 500 words. I was about to sneak off for a livener when the phone went. D.I. Harry Pennycuik wanted me to drift down to the Tournier incident room and make a statement. I said I'd a dental appointment and he said balls.

The statement took ten minutes. Harry didn't have any intelligent questions to ask, though he made base insinuations about the nature of the affair between Shirl and me. On the desk in the incident room was the WorldCare Foundation letter he had lifted from Shirley's bag. I tried to read it again upside down. I was thus engaged when a woodentop entered the room and said the boss wanted H. for a mo. He waddled out. I grabbed the letter, stuck it in a convenient photocopier, and dashed myself off a copy before he waddled back in. I meandered home to the office by way of Scribes and El Vino's, the letter rubbing shoulders with my chequebook.

Maybe it was missing out on Sri Lanka or maybe it was just plain ennui. Whatever, I felt mischievous. I dug out the number for Sir James's private office and gave it a call. The same man answered. I didn't bother to introduce myself. I said, 'The next time anybody asks you about Kandy, tell them it's a place in Sri Lanka.'

'What!'

'It is a place in Sri Lanka,' I said, putting big spaces between each word.

Silence at his end. 'What we used to call Ceylon,' I added helpfully.

Another stretch of silence. Then: 'That is Max Chard?'

'That is I.'

'Why are you calling? What are you saying?' His voice was higher than normal.

'I'm saying that Kandy must be stopped,' I said.

'I do not understand . . .'

I said, 'Ask Sir James. He'll explain it. Or better still, ask his beloved Emma Pearson. She said in my presence, "Kandy must be stopped – I don't care how".'

He took a breath and got himself back together. He said, 'Mister Chard, no one here has anything to say to you. I suggest you stop harassing Sir James or we shall be obliged to complain to your editor.'

I said, 'Never mind. See you in Kandy.'

He was saying 'What!' again, only in capital letters, when I put the phone down.

I edged across to News Desk when no one was looking and nicked their *Evening Standard* to see what it had about Shirley's murder. I think it was only then I began to feel anything about it. There was a small pic, taken three or four years back, of Shirley, with her hair in flyaway style. Probably tinted. There was a bigger shot of her grieving mum and dad, a middle-aged party with too much beef. The story was the usual flat tabloidese, not a patch on mine. But reading between the lines you got an idea of the ghastliness of her killing. Shirley was their only child. She lived for ice skating, and, somewhat surprisingly, was a whizz at ballroom dancing. I tried to picture Shirley all dolled up in sequins, doing the fandango with a big lipsticky smile. I couldn't. Where the story got to me was her parents' total bewilderment. Why should anyone want to kill Shirley? they asked. I'd asked myself the same question the night before and come to the conclusion she was murdered to shut her up. Possible? yes. Probable? yes. But it seemed a lame excuse for killing a girl of barely 25. She had a boy-friend, Darren, her fandango partner. They were planning a September wedding, a fortnight's honey-moon in Corfu and they'd even bought themselves a flat in Epping. Darren said the ordinary trite things about being in shock, broken-hearted, how much they loved each other. People are always trite when faced with a tragedy beyond their comprehension. They look for hard-edged words to convey their terrible loss, but all they can find is the commonplace currency of everyday life. Yet often it is the very trivia of what they say that brings it home. Her mum said Shirley bought her wedding dress on Saturday and now it hung in the wardrobe, never to be worn. I saw a bedroom, pastel pink and littered with idiot stuffed animals, and, in a corner, a wardrobe, its door ajar to reveal a fussy, frilly bridal gown, hanging there silent and accusing like an Elizabethan ghost.

The Law had weighed in with banal quotes about 'a brutal killing', 'a girl with so much to live for.'

And so little to die for. What was the awful secret that made someone murder Shirley? I flipped through my mental list of suspects. It was a short list. Sir James Tomlin. Not very likely. He would have to stand on a chair to strangle her. Anyway, why should he want her dead – because she'd discovered he had his hand in the till? Hardly. Half the financiers in the City are up to their ears in jiggery pokery as a matter of principle.

And why was Claudine Tournier tipped in the Thames? Because she had a secret lover? Because Sir James was sick of veggie meals? I realised how little I knew of the romantic financier. I studied his form in *Who's Who*, where he listed his hobbies as skiing and reading, though not simultaneously. His unlisted hobby was collecting wives. There were three of them. First one deceased. Third one likewise. But the one in the middle, a Margaret Delsey Ford, had so far bucked the trend. There was also a son by Wife One, Henry Michael James, b. July 3, 1959. Where are they now? I mused.

There were evening drinkies at the Yard for a deputy assistant commissioner who was packing it in and going straight. He kindly invited the crime hacks to join him, and as the Met were buying, we could hardly refuse. It was an amiable do, lots of foul jokes and recollections of drunken debauchery. Sometimes us crime hacks and the Old Bill have a lot in common. The difference is we get paid to drink with them.

Among the gathering was Big Ben Ashbee, the superintendent in the Tournier case. In a moment of bonhomie, brought on by free drink, I told him about the Kandy connection. Ben tugged at an imaginary moustache, brooded, and said big deal. I sniffed and said that was the last juicy titbit I brought him. Ben said he hoped so and told me the latest from his side of the divide. Shirley, he said, was topped somewhere else at least an hour before her body was dumped in the dock. She was strangled with a thin rope and the killer had not been too clever about how he did it. There were burn marks around her chin and upper neck, suggesting he bungled it first time round, or maybe she put up a fight. So far motiveless. They'd found her bag and everything, except one shoe, a low, white open-toed affair, for the record. Big Ben lapsed into the doldrums and I asked instead about the Tournier case. A bad move. I thought he was going to cry, so obviously nothing doing there. I wandered off before he could borrow my hankie.

By this time the party was getting perilously near the fall-down drunk stage and a uniformed killjoy was busy detaching guests from their bottles. A bunch of us wandered off in search of curry and lager, though not necessarily in that order. Somewhere between the tandoori tikka and the chicken passanda my bleep started yelping. 'Call me,' it commanded. Apart from me, the only other me I know has smoky eyes and a dirty laugh. Yep, Rosie.

It was gone one when I finally rang, from the back of a taxi steaming south. She said, 'You're pissed.'

I couldn't disagree because I dropped the mobile. When I picked it up she was saying, '. . . and it's too late now, so go home.'

'It's not too late, Rosie,' I said, using far too many esses.

'It bloody well is. You should have called me earlier.'

'I prefer to call you Rosie.'

She said, 'I'm asleep. Call me in the morning – if you wake up.'

I tried my usual ploy of swearing undying love and obedience, and Rosie delivered her usual rebuff. But she did say, 'Okay, me too', before switching me off.

Back in my lonely garret, actually a basement apartment off Pilbeam Gardens, I was greeted by a ringing telephone. Aha! So Rosie's changed her mind, thought I.

But it was not Rosie. Whoever it was didn't introduce himself. His voice was distorted, as if he was speaking through a fog. He sounded a perfect stranger, well, an obviously imperfect stranger, for he did not like me one little bit.

'We've got your number, Chard,' he said.

'So it would appear.'

'And we know where you live. We can get to you anytime.'

I said, 'Is this a threatening call or are you emergency plumbers?'

He said, 'Call it a warning – the only one you'll get. Leave the Claudine Tournier story alone.'

'Or else?'

'Remember what happened to the last snooper.'

I said, 'Oh, you must be the gentleman who's not very good at strangling people.'

He laughed. It wasn't one of those wicked bloodcurdling laughs that makes your toes curl. It was a straightforward ordinary laugh. It made my toes curl.

He slapped the phone down. I immediately punched out 1471 and got a sing song machine to tell me where Mister Menace had rung from. It was a 730 number, somewhere in Victoria. It kept ringing for a couple of minutes before someone answered it. A man.

'Yus?' he said.

I said, 'My name is Chard. Someone there has just called me.'

'Wasn't me, mate.'

I said, 'I know. But has someone else called?'

'Don't know, mate.'

'Is that a private number?'

'Wot, this?'

I said, 'Yes – this.'

'No mate.'

I said, 'Where am I calling?'

'It's Victoria Station. It's a call box.'

I said, 'Thanks, anyway. Sorry to bother you.' We both hung up and I stood stock still for a long time thinking. I was as sober as a teetotal judge. More so.

Chapter Six

It is never a smart move to tell a newshound to push off. It only makes him want to push on. This is a basic lesson which trouser-dropping celebs and dodgy Cabinet Ministers fail to grasp. They hide themselves from us and bleat about invasions of privacy. The upshot is we bivouac on their doorsteps for weeks and root around for further scandals in their tawdry lives. And we find 'em. What they should do, as soon as the story breaks, is invite the hacks in, offer them cups of tea – nothing stronger – and say: 'It's a fair cop. I've been a naughty boy.' Ten minutes later it's all over. You see, if they invite us to invade their privacy, it's no fun anymore. It's like telling a schoolboy to come scrump your apples. Besides, we love being hated.

Another thing people should know is threats don't scare us. We reserve all our fear and deep dread terror for News Desk. News Desk has the power to do terrible things to us, like bounce our exes or give us the boot. We wake in the night, a cold sweat upon us, hearing the voice of the Desk demand: 'How come the *Mail* got the mother?' Such is the nightmare of every true hack.

Therefore I was not all that worried about my

mystery caller. The one thing that bothered me was how he got my number, for I'm ex-directory. Not only am I ex-d, but I'm ex-d in my sister's married name, and I'm very choosy about whom I give my number. I was intrigued about why my caller felt it necessary to warn me off. I must be getting close to something and I wanted to get a damn sight closer. Close enough to understand what was going on.

I thought about my caller's voice. It was not one of those cor blimey smash-yer-face-in types which are such a lively feature of Old Bailey reporting. This bloke sounded middle class, educated, in control of his faculties, if a mite melodramatic. He had not denied choking our Shirley, but then he might just have wanted me to believe he was capable of murder. I gave up and clambered into my welcoming bed.

In the morning, after a gallon or two of tea, I rang the Tournier incident room, got Harry and told him someone was threatening to do me in. I heard him shout round the room: 'Did any of you phone Max Chard last night?' which is the closest Harry has ever come to cracking a joke. He took the details anyway, laughed heartlessly and suggested my caller might be Shirley's jealous boyfriend. H was in sparkling form this morning.

I was not so effervescent. I hung around the Bailey, knocked off a piece on a fine upstanding pillar of the community who went out and knifed three coppers. Despite the fact that the incident was witnessed by half of west London, it took the jury two hours to make their minds up.

Afterwards there was nothing else to do so I

headed back to the office and, inspired by my late night caller, started sifting through cuttings on Sir James, Claudine and the Foundation. In Tomlin's file there was a diary item about his divorce from Wife Two, an unpleasant affair by the sound of it. A year before that there was a cosy women's section interview with Wife Two at her home in Virginia Water. She was big on charity and small on talking about herself, though that might just be the interviewer's ineptitude. I tried directory inquiries. No, they didn't have any listings for a Tomlin in Virginia Water. Maybe she'd gone back to her maiden name. I phoned directory again. Yes, there were two M. Fords, both ex-d. I said, 'Oh dear, this is her son's year tutor. I must speak to her urgently about his school trip. There has been an accident . . .'

The operator was sympathetic but refused to play. I said, 'Perhaps I'd better drive round to her house. Do you have a Ford in Fairham or Fairburn Way?'

The operator forgot herself. 'No. One's in Primrose Avenue, the other in Badger View.'

Which was all I wanted. At the back of our library is a stack of reverse directories which are strictly illegal. They cost us a bundle. I turned to North Surrey and Primrose Avenue. At number 72 there dwelt an M. W. Ford. Not my Margaret Delsey. I tried Badger View. Yes, there she blew. M.D. Ford at number 26.

I told News Desk what I was up to and ventured by train and taxi to darkest Surrey. It was a balmy May afternoon with a playful breeze rippling through the cherry trees or whatever they were. Badger View gave off the scent of freshly-mown money. Big houses, big cars, big burglar alarms. Here and there the hired help toiled manfully in perfect gardens. Otherwise there wasn't a soul for miles around. I didn't view any badgers either. I tiptoed up the garden path so as not to wake the neighbours and pushed the bell on a front door big enough to cover a garage. In the middle of the door there was a bobbly glass panel. Presently a face swam into view behind it. It was hard to tell if it was Quasimodo or just the distortion of the glass. On my side I wasted a perfectly good smile. The door opened about a foot. 'Yes?' she said. She was Margaret Delsey Ford, as was, Margaret Tomlin, as she became, and was now right back to Margaret Delsey Ford again.

I said she didn't know me, which was true, showed her my press pass and asked if I could talk to her about James Tomlin.

She said, 'Come in.'

I was barely over the threshold, my brain still reeling from the shock, when she said, 'Drink?'

I think I needed brandy, but I settled for gin & tonic. She dished it up in a glass vase. She was equally kind to herself. She threw herself with enthusiasm into an adjoining chair and hoisted her vase. 'Cheers!' she said in Australian. That explained things. I knocked back a goodly sip and looked around. A big airy room, with billowy chairs and sofas, yellow wallpaper and yellow wood tables. The Tudor beams were all wrong. My eyes came back to her. I don't know what Sir James's secret allure was, but he could certainly catch 'em. He must have a certain je ne sais quoi, or what the French would call I don't know what. This version was tall and dark. In a couple of years her hair would be just brushed with grey. She had an open vivacious face and a smile that lurked on the brink of laughter. She had a toothsome overbite. She said, 'Call me Margie. Now, what can I tell you about the little ratbag?'

A woman after my own heart. I owned up and said I didn't know what I wanted to hear about Tomlin, so, could she just chatter on and we'd see what came out. She said great, and let rip a muscular laugh.

'First of all,' she said when she'd recovered herself, 'Sir Jimmy Tomlin is a snake, though that's not fair to snakes. He's a money-grubbing, egotistical, smarmy, little bastard. Those are his good points.'

If I wasn't already promised to Rosie Bannister, I would have run off with Margie Ford right there and then. I looked at her frankly. She was decked out in an outsize bright blue casual shirt with baggy beige pants. No shoes. I said, 'There's something that really puzzles me: how does Tomlin do it?'

'Beg pardon?'

'What do girls like you see in him?'

Margie drank deep of her gin and pondered this. She said, 'Have you ever read Graham Greene?'

'Not so as you'd notice.'

She said, 'Greene says when two people are in love, each is in love with the other's image of himself or herself.'

I said, 'Greene says that?'

She shook her hair at me. 'You don't get it. Let me give you a fr'instance. Fr'instance an Ozzie secretary arrives in London still wet behind the ears and lands a job with a fabulously wealthy man. Well, fabulously wealthy by Brisbane standards. Before she knows it, he's inviting her out to dinner where he spends more on the wine than she earns in a month. The little squirt looks into her eyes and tells her she's the greatest thing out of Oz since Dame Nellie Melba. He buys her flowers – fields of roses. He takes her to Ascot. Miss Nobody from Nowhere gets within spitting distance of the Queen. They go skiing. St Moritz, would you believe. They fly Concorde to the States. Wherever they go, there are people fawning and drooling over him. And her. He keeps giving her all this claptrap about how wonderful she is. Then one day he takes her to Maxim's, the Paris one, and he gives her a little box. "Will you marry me?" he says. And she says, "Just give me a sec to change my briefs." And that's what happened. I fell in love with his image of myself, just like Graham Greene says.'

I said, 'Maybe this explains Jack Nicholson's success.'

She said, 'Maybe he's got something else.'

I said, 'Yours was a whirlwind romance?'

Margie nodded. She snatched my vase and made free with the gin again. She was a shade mean in the tonic department.

She said over her shoulder, 'But we didn't live happily ever after. Two, three years at best. In the meantime I went home to mum who was pretty sick. I think it was then Jimmy started playing around.'

'With Claudine?'

Margie settled down again. 'No way. She was

absolute yonks after that. He was well in with a bunch of creeps and wowsers like Lewis Trefoyle.'

Well, well, well. Lewis Trefoyle. Isn't life funny?

Margie was saying, 'And there was that ginger guy who's a big cheese in the Jockey Club.'

'Clernthorpe?'

'Yes, Gus Clernthorpe. Now there's another weirdo for you.'

Margie sunk herself in her gin and brooded over past wounds. She said, 'Next thing I know is Jimmy's in the sack with Clernthorpe's ex. In that mob everyone was playing doctors with everyone else. And it didn't matter what sex they were.'

I said, 'Is Sir James a bit bi?'

'No, not him. But all the rest of them were at it like knives. Every time I see that smug bastard Trefoyle on the telly, I laugh so much I nearly spill my drink.'

I said, 'When you heard what Tomlin was up to, you kicked him out?'

'Flat on his skinny little backside,' she said with relish.

I said, 'You have a son.'

Margie went very still. She picked the words as if she was picking nettles. 'I had a stepson,' she said. 'He was at boarding school. He seemed an okay kid then. After uni he got a job with his father. I don't see him anymore.'

'Is that sad?'

Margie fidgeted with her cushion, looked into her glass, tugged at her sleeve and generally made it known she didn't want to talk about it. That was tough because I did. I hung back waiting.

The words came in a rush. 'It's no loss, Maxie. I don't want to see him either. If anything, he's worse than his father, and that's saying it all.'

'How?' I pushed.

'It doesn't matter how. He's weird.'

'Like Lewis Trefoyle is weird?'

Margie nodded her head but was silent. The silence lingered.

I said, 'Do you mean gay?'

'Hell, no. There's nothing weird about that these days.'

I said, 'Well, what do you mean by weird?'

She tossed her head back. She said, 'Look, let's leave this. I don't want to talk about it. They're just weird.'

So what do these geezers do? I mused. Drink lemonade or something? I backed off. I said, 'The police suspect Tomlin of having Claudine murdered.'

She was amused. 'They've got that one wrong. He's too sneaky for that. He'd just let her divorce him, pay up and move on to the next girl with beans for brains.'

I said, 'What if he had money troubles and couldn't afford to pay up?'

'Jimmy never has money troubles. That gang he hangs around with look after each other. Fleas on a dog's tail, they are. I reckon they've all got something on each other from when they were at Winchester or Eton or one of those dumps.'

I said, 'What about someone else in the pack killing Claudine?'

'Sure. They're capable of it. But why bother?'

Margie uncoiled to liberate the gin and I reviewed the story so far. She'd given me some lively stuff, but I couldn't see what use I could make of it.

I said, 'Do you know Leon Knapp?'

'What, old Crap Knapp? Yeah, he's one of the deadbeats too.'

I said I didn't see him as the public school pinstripe type. Margie said, 'No, it's funny that. Maybe they liked his singing.' We both had a good laugh over that one.

But she didn't laugh when I threw into the conversation the story of my dead of night caller. Her big happy bunny smile vanished like snow off a ditch. She said, 'You better watch out.'

I said, 'That's what he said.'

She frowned. 'No, I'm serious. That bunch are capable of anything. I ain't joking.'

I promised to lock my doors and never to take sweets from strange men. That didn't seem to reassure her. So I said, 'Tell me about Brisbane', and the sun shone again. She chattered on for a while until I consulted my fake Rolex which said ten past five. By now I knew more about Brisbane than was necessary. I thanked Margie. She said no sweat, she'd enjoyed it, and if I fancied another drink . . .

I looked at her and she looked at me a second longer than was polite. There were flecks of brown in her green eyes. She was smiling. Then a vision of Rosie with a corkscrew came between us. I made my excuses and left.

I caught a cruddy little train where they wouldn't let me smoke but it was belting out great clouds of diesel. I phoned Rosie to let her know her loving man was homeward bound. It was a grievous blunder. It gave her time to prepare a meal. My normal practice is to pop up unannounced. That way we get to sample the international cuisine on offer down Woolaton Road. One night it's afelia with roast potatoes, the next it's spring rolls and something in chilli black bean sauce, or cod and chips. All good healthy wholesome stuff. Rosie's home cooking is a different kettle of fish altogether. She's more a gardener than a cook. Everything is green. She eats more spinach than Popeye. Tonight's bill of fare was salad with olives and the smallest plaice fillet ever caught in British waters. There was also a heap of baldy little new potatoes. Rosie tucked in and professed herself well satisfied. I lied and opened a bottle of frascati to drown the taste.

We reviewed our respective days as we hid the plates in the dishwasher: she had lunched with a Selfridge's buyer who showed interest in her lizards. She promised me a treat if the deal came through. I suggested dinner out. I told her about my meeting with the Brisbane Belle. When I'd finished, she said, 'Bloody typical.'

I said, 'What is?'

She said, 'Claudine's Foundation.'

'Eh?'

Rosie said, 'Claudine gets the idea for the Foundation to help the sick and poor; but look who runs it – her crummy husband and his old school tie pals.'

I said, 'Maybe that's because they can count, or they can con their rich friends into handing over large sums.'

Rosie said, 'Phooey', or something worse.

I said, 'How dare you impugn Sir James.'

We were sitting down now on the sofa so her punch didn't hit home. She poured the rest of the frascati into her glass. A dirty trick.

I said, 'Jimmy and his weirdos club together to give Mrs Jimmy a helping hand with her pet project. What's wrong with that?'

A snort from the south end of the sofa. Rosie said, 'I bet you all the money in the WorldCare Foundation is controlled by him. If he wanted to embezzle it, she'd never know.'

I thought about it and had to concede she might be right. It's probably all that spinach she packs away. I reached in my pocket and picked out the Foundation letter I'd copied when I gave Harry Pennycuik my statement. The heading listed the trustees. Tomlin himself, Proudhoe Veizey the alleged actor, Martin Crowley, whoever he might be, Leon Knapp wherever he might be, Gus Clernthorpe the Jockey Club joker, and one H. M. J. Tomlin. The hon. press was our old friend Lewis Trefoyle MP, PC, QC etc. Every man jack of them a bosom buddy of Sir James, unless Martin Crowley was a decent soul. I didn't think so.

Rosie draped herself across me to read the letterhead. She said, 'Told you so.'

I said, 'Who, and if so, why, is Martin Crowley?'

'The round the world man.'

It came back to me. Crowley was the toff who circumnavigated the globe in a sieve or something. It was an eight day wonder in the heavies. Having won her argument, Rosie was bored. She said, 'There's damn all on TV.'

I suggested an early night. She messed up my hair. And so the two of us rumpled the cushions for a while. Suddenly she sprung free and held me at bay with a finger stuck in my chest. She announced, 'Hey, I've found a great deal for the Maldives.'

I said, 'And who are they when they're at home?'

She said, 'You know, the Maldives. The islands. You're due for a holiday and you promised we'd go somewhere special.'

'Do they have bars in the Maldives?' I asked, wary after reading that bit about Poya Days in Sri Lanka.

'Stacks of them. Every street corner has one.'

I said, 'I don't fancy it anyway. We'd end up lying on our bum staring at the sun all day long.'

Rosie pictured herself lying on her bum staring at the sun. 'So?'

We were deep in argument when the phone broke in. Night Desk and the ever cheery voice of Vic.

'Have you seen the *Mirror*?' he demanded.

Considering his edition was hot off the presses, I considered this pretty dumb. But I just said no.

Vic said, 'We need to catch up on their splash.'

'Which is?'

He read it to me in tones which would never win him any prizes for elocution. The great thing about the *Mirror* is their stories are as short as ours, so he finished it before I could fall asleep. He said, 'We need copy in ten minutes top whack.'

I said it was a load of bilge but if he wanted it, he'd get it. The story concerned a former copper in the

Royal Protection Squad who had put a senorita in the family way when he was supposed to be guarding Prince Charles during a Spanish holiday. Gripping stuff, you'll agree.

How, you might ask, can I get the story from cold in ten mins? Fortunately there is honour among thieves. The age-old practice among hacks is to let a story run as an exclusive in your own first edition and then share it around the pack. I rang Geordie, my opposite number at the *Mirror*, and bawled at him for not telling me. He said oops, he thought it wasn't worth passing on. I had to agree. I said, 'Is it kosher?' He said as kosher as gefilte fish, which was a pleasant change from his usual drink-inspired copy. The *Mirror*'s stringer in Madrid had even spoken to Senorita Con Infanta herself. So I put the phone down, rephrased the *Mirror* stuff, for Geordie is not the most literate of men, and let Vic have it. He didn't say thanks.

Rosie was still off sunning herself in the Maldives. She spoke eloquently of azure seas and tropical palms nodding their sleepy heads in the noonday sun. I said not a word, but my silence was every bit as eloquent.

'You're a selfish git,' she said, and wrecked my hair again.

The police called a morning press conf. at Leman Street nick. Big Ben Ashbee was the master of ceremonies. He looked even sadder than usual. I put it down to a deserved hangover from last night's thrash. Ben kicked off the proceedings, saying the murder squad required the public's help in retracing Claudine's movements on the night of her shooting. A polite way of saying they hadn't a clue. For the purposes of the exercise they had a WPC with fat legs kitted out in a white mac. She was supposed to resemble Claudine. I look more like Claudine. I don't have a moustache.

We all hoofed it down to St Katharine's Dock where the pretend Claudine sauntered up and down smiling for the monkeys. Big Ben said she would strut her stuff again at 8 pm in the fond hope it would jog the memory of the evening drinkers. I suggested he got another WPC, wrap a rope round her neck and chuck her in the dock in the fond hope someone might remember Shirley's last minutes. Ben told me to go away.

I went off to the Tower hotel where I sat with a pint knocking out a picture caption.

Dressed to kill . . . a plucky police girl walks the lonely quayside where sexy socialite Claudine Tournier was slain.

WPC Anne Scott bravely volunteered for the tragic role because of her uncanny resemblance to the murdered woman.

She wore an identical designer mac for her grim mission at the Thames marina where . . .

And so on. You don't really want to hear it. But that line about the marina had given me an idea. I quit the hotel and navigated round to the Port O'Call where the Kiwi barmaid greeted me with dancing eyes. I reciprocated by ordering a glass of New Zealand pinot noir. The place was calm as they hadn't uncaged the city gents for their lunch yet. I inspected the walls which featured yachts the size of the *QE2* and weather-grained veterans of the briny deep. I pointed to one old buffer and said, 'I suppose you get lots of these in here?'

She said, 'The ancient mariners? Oh yeah.'

I mentioned a few names, dropping Crowley's into the pot. She didn't know half of them, which was hardly surprising as I just made them up. But Crowley she did know. He pops in every now and then. Seems a nice guy. Doesn't drink much. Her knowledge of nice guys is somewhat narrow.

And has he been in recently? I asked, as if I was making light conversation. She said no. She thought it over. She said yes. He'd been in last week. I said I'd bought his book and would love him to autograph it for me. Was he in the night I was there? And what night was that? she asked. I ordered another glass of what folks drink in New Zealand when they're feeling frisky. I pretended to think about it.

'Oh, I know,' I said brightly. 'It was the night that woman was murdered.'

'Which one?'

I'd forgotten that murdering women was a nightly sport in these parts. I said, 'I think it must have been the first one.'

'Who? Claudine Tournier?'

'Yes, her.'

The barmaid said, 'God, wasn't that awful? I mean, when you think of all the great work she's been doing in Africa and India, I mean, who would want to murder her?'

I nodded my head in sad agreement. First, Claudine gets holed in the temporal lobe, then Poland stuffs England three-nil. What is the world coming to?

Miss Kiwi was raving on about Claudine's beauty, her riches, her generosity. I called her to heel. 'Was he in that night?'

'Was who in?'

'Martin Crowley.'

She said, 'Oh, him. Yeah, I think he was. Him and another guy.'

'Another ancient mariner?'

'Naoow. The other one was a business type.'

I said, 'Maybe a weekend sailor?'

She said, 'Too soft for that. Why all the interest in Martin Crowley, anyway?'

I repeated my feeble excuse about wanting him to autograph his boring book. She said, 'Oh yeah', but didn't look convinced. I said cheerio and she winked a fond farewell. It was probably something indecent in morse code.

The Piltdown Man wanted to see me. Why? I asked Angie. She got busy with her bits of paper, averted her eyes and muttered something about exes. I straightened my tie and went in search of Tony Belker, regretting there wasn't time to equip myself with a silver crucifix, a Holy Bible and maybe a sharpened wooden stake.

He had his blinds drawn because he was watching TV golf. He immediately clicked to CeeFax when I entered. 'Siddown!' he commanded. He stood up. I suppose this is a trick they learn on power management courses. Lesson One: How to make your staff fcel inferior. I took a look at his paunch and felt infinitely superior. I sat, one leg hooked over the othcr, and switched on a 100-watt smile. He frowned at his bitten fingernails. Belker is living proof that man and warthog must never again mate. He's got little piggy eyes set deep beneath a chevron of bushy brows. There's maybe an inch of forehead before the hairline begins. He's florid, fat, fifty and, with a bit of luck, should keel over with a heart attack any day now. I sat there thinking what I would write on his wreath while he rummaged in a drawer. He produced my expenses, slapped a paw on them and said, 'How do you account for these?'

I said, 'Ah, I'm glad you mentioned them. I forgot to charge for phone calls.'

He said, 'You've charged for everything else you could think of.'

He didn't mean it as a compliment but I nodded gracious acknowledgement. Belker picked up the exes, turned his back on me, and shook them in a fury. He never looks you in the eye. He said, 'Extortionate claims like these set my teeth on edge.'

I said, 'Oh yes. I forgot the toothbrush. And the toothpaste.'

'What?' A porcine squeal.

I said, 'It was a rush job. I didn't have time to pack. I had to buy a toothbrush.'

Belker's shoulders trembled in Neanderthal rage. He still had his back turned, affording me a wide panorama of his backside. Fat-assed men should wear overcoats at all times. He said, 'I will not tolerate expenses fiddles. You have charged for two interpreters.'

I said, 'Noblesse oblige.'

'What?'

I explained my French was not up to coping with the heady accents of Geneva or Brittany. Belker flung a glare over his shoulder. He sucked air through his teeth and tried to regain his bestial composure. He returned to the fray.

'I accept foreign exes can be high, but they are not there for reporters to defraud the paper out of hundreds of pounds. This sort of claim rips the arse out of exes.'

I said, 'And Y-Fronts. I forgot to claim for underwear.'

Belker goggled in outrage. He flapped his arms wildly, bounced off the wall and pointed at the door. I uncrossed my legs, smiled at him again and quit the world of the undead. Behind me, Belker got his voice back. He yelled, 'You've really blown it this time, Chard. You'll regret ever daring to submit these exes.'

And he was probably right. I resolved to keep my nose clean and sleep with a string of garlic around my neck.

Chapter Seven

Next morning the bunch of dysfunctionals which passes as an Old Bailey jury retired to consider their verdict in the Silence of the Crams case. Half an hour later they were back, in solid agreement that Stan Cram and his haggish wife Vi were guilty of the murder of their au pair. I think it was the fact Stan used to be an estate agent that swung things.

Mr Justice Seamley got on his high horse and described the couple as wicked, villainous, and generally a bad lot. Stan got life with a recommended minimum of 20 years. Vi got life, which meant she could be out barbecuing au pairs again in seven years. Justice was seen to be done.

The gentlemen of the Press adjourned to Harry's Bar to look at their notebooks. Most time our shorthand is so atrocious that we get together and make up quotes, but today there was a hackette from the *Telegraph* who had a verbatim note of the proceedings. The snag was that it took her half the morning to go through her brimming notebook and dig out the lively stuff. It wasn't as good as the quotes we make up.

Armed at last with all the guff and a gin, I sat down to compose. Reporters, the tabloid hacks especially, work to a rigid formula. We take a news event and revamp it as a piece of soap opera. We are basically playwrights. We have a set cast of characters and a simple plot. General news reporters are luckier than crime people because they get to play with a slightly larger cast. Our playlets feature a baddie, a goodie and a victim. Sometimes, as when a have-a-go hero gets himself killed, the goodie and victim are rolled into one, leaving us with a cast of two. We sift through the wearisome hours of courtroom blarney to furnish our actors with their lines. We re-enact the dirty deed, editing out the humdrum bits, and there you have it. A tale of murder most foul told in 500 words, not counting the by-line.

In the Cram case we had a couple of ace baddies. The tabloid crime journo's favourite word, evil, fitted them like a wetsuit. Plus, he was a furtive, oily, little weasel, while Vi Cram had all the native charm of a meter maid. The victim was another great character – a 21-year-old Kurdish refugee who had fled Saddam's waves of war only to be grilled on a Surbiton patio. She would have been better still had she not looked like Mahatma Gandhi, right down to the specs.

The Crams deserved more than the standard 500 golden words. They got about five times that. The gruesome twosome had belted their au pair with a claw hammer last Whitsun for reasons unknown, but it was widely assumed she was threatening to tell the police that Stan had raped her. Afterwards Vi chopped her in chunks and burned her on the barbie. In custody they never once coughed or said oops, despite hours of Plod interrogation – so that gave us the Silence of the Crams motif.

Besides my lead story, featuring Mr Justice Seamley's 'heartless and horrific' crack, I supplied a handful of pre-written background pieces on the killer king and queen of Stirton Close. We unearthed an ex-wife – 'Stan had mad, staring eyes', and Vi's broken-hearted mother – 'I Hope my Daughter Rots in Hell', and a clutch of neighbours – 'The Monsters Next Door'. Neighbours often serve as sort of spear carriers in our dramas. They march on stage, deliver their asides, and get to hell off so that we can concentrate on the real stars. The victim's family were unable to come up with any good lines, largely because they didn't speak English. That didn't stop us attributing the odd red-blooded quote to them. Dad apparently said he'd give the world for a blunt breadknife and five minutes alone with Stan Cram. Mum said Vi was more cruel than Saddam. It made a rattling good yarn, just the thing our readers like served up with their cornflakes.

I phoned my copy through and asked to be put on to News Desk. I got Norbert, our dithering foreign editor, which meant that Angela Whipple and all the other empty vessels were off somewhere getting tanked up.

I told Norbert I was seeing contacts but would keep in touch. Norbert said he wished he could join me. I said yes, that's too bad, but I'd have a drink for him anyway. We were running out of pleasantries when he remembered he wanted to tell me something.

He said, 'You know your friend, Leon Knapp?'

I said he wasn't my friend, but what about him?

Norbert said, 'He's turned up.'

'Dead?' I asked hopefully.

Norbert treated me to a tolerant chortle. 'No, no, no. He's alive, but not terribly well.'

'That's bad,' I said, inspecting my empty glass. 'I'll hear about it later. Where was he?'

Norbert couldn't remember. Somewhere in the Middle East. Oh yes, Amman.

I bade him bye bye and pondered. Amman. What on earth was Knapp doing there? Jordan is hardly renowned as a mecca for coke snorters. Maybe he was doing a Cat Stevens and turning Moslem. The hackette from the *Telegraph* tapped me on the shoulder and said it was her round. I forgot Leon Mustafa Knapp.

I made it back to the office some time late in the afternoon. No one wanted me and I needed a cup of boot black coffee with extra sugar before I remembered why I had bothered to show. The case of the unvanishing Knapp. I switched on my console, typed in my password, *crippen*, and began ploughing through the tapes. It wasn't on staff copy, freelance, foreign stringers or Reuters. I finally ran it to ground on Associated Press who didn't think the story particularly riveting. Their staffer in Oman – not Amman – had filed as follows:

OMAN, Friday – The former English pop singer,

Leon Knapp, was admitted to the American Hospital here today, said to be suffering from acute stomach pains.

A medical spokesman at the hospital said that Knapp required emergency treatment but his condition was not listed as serious. The 48-year-old singer, an overnight celebrity in the Seventies, was en route to London when he was taken ill.

An ambulance met his plane at Oman International Airport, and paramedics carried Knapp to a waiting ambulance. He was said to have been travelling alone.

In London, England there has been recent concern for the singer's welfare following reports that he had failed to fulfil several long-standing commitments.

In the Seventies, Knapp, from Birmingham, England sold millions of records worldwide. His most famous song, 'Bananas For You', was simultaneously a number one hit in Britain and the United States.

And that was it. Not a word about where the lonely Leon had picked up his bellyache, no mention of drugs.

I'd like to say I had a hack's hunch. But I cannot lie. I just had a sudden whim. I rang AP's London office, said we were doing up the Knapp story, and could I have the number for their man in Oman. I certainly could. I phoned the sunny sheikhdom and got a lady who was on the first disc of her Berlioz course in English. 'Jus' mommem pliz,' she instructed. A mommem later on came the author himself. Nope, sorry, he knew nothing more of our Leon. The plane was a KLM 747, winging home to Amsterdam. I said fine, but where did it come from.

Even before he opened his mouth, I knew what was coming.

Sri Lanka.

Call it a hack's hunch.

Hotfoot and panting, I charged up to News Desk and broke the glad tidings to Angie. She was in the middle of dictating her schedule for evening conference so she was not pleased to see me. She made it clear she cared as much about where Knapp had been hiding himself as she did about European sugar beet subsidies. Talk to me later, she said, hoping I'd go off, have a drink and forget about it.

I was not to be put off. Angela sighed and said, 'All right. Go and talk to Belker and see if he falls for it.'

I began to regret yesterday's tête à tête with The Man With Two Bums, but I summoned up my nerve and battered on his door. He was peeved at having his TV golf interrupted again. When he saw it was me, he was even less delighted. I spelt out the story for him, mentioning Kandy every third word.

He let me run through my whole spiel. Then he smiled. It was not a 'Great idea, Max!' smile; more of a 'You are a worm beneath my feet, Chard, and you haven't got a hope' smile.

He made me wait for his answer. He reached in his top drawer and withdrew my exes claim. He poked it with a sausage finger. He said, 'You are a luxury we cannot afford. If I was sending to Sri Lanka, which I'm not, I would not send you. I wouldn't send you as far as Clapham Common – not after this.'

He hoisted my exes aloft and let them fall, fluttering forlorn to the floor. I said we might be missing a great story. Belker said he could live with that. I said he was a loathsome, fat, foul-breathed, pompous imbecile with the news judgement of a baboon. But I said it to myself so he kept on smiling. I closed the door on his smile and trooped back to my corner of the news room. Around me merry hacks hammered out stories, pausing only to ask questions of each other: 'Who's the Prime Minister?' 'How many v's in evil?'

For once I did not help them out. I rang The Stone dive bar, told them to set me up a pint and I was gone like a thief in the night.

I got home early and mooched around the place with nothing to do. I stuck a Bob Marley disc in the player but it made me think of sunny places: places like Sri Lanka. I pressed eject. I was debating whether to slit my wrists or overdose on milk when the phone warbled. Rosie. 'Coming round?' she asked.

'We eat out?'

'You paying?'

'Why not?'

We settled for Thai. Beef in green curry sauce for me, oodles of noodles for her. She listened to my tale of woe and called Belker a few things I hadn't thought of. I had just got round to thinking what a wise and wonderful woman Rosie is when, ever so casually, she slipped it in. She said, 'Thought any more about the Maldives?'

I told her I had thought considerably less about the Maldives. She pouted at her noodles and said a holiday was just what I needed to stop me turning into an old grump. She dived into her bag and whipped out a travel brochure. It represented the Maldives as paradise minus the bad bits. Sun, sand, sea, snorkelling and lots of other things beginning with S, though it didn't mention sex, sunburn or scotch.

'It doesn't say anything about bars,' I said.

Rosie pointed at a mixed quarter of nutters grinning out of the page. 'They're drinking,' she said.

'It might be water.'

She clicked her tongue. 'Honestly, drink is all you ever think about.'

'Not entirely all.'

She turned on the famous dirty laugh and an adjacent voyeur poured lemon grass soup down his shirt. Rosie said, 'Are you staying with me tonight?'

We have a very simple arrangement which I do not understand. Three, sometimes four nights a week she lets me share the duvet down in Battersea. The rest of the time she chooses to live alone. Alone, apart from her toffee-nosed cat, Blue, who eyes me askance and shimmies his backside at me. At least I have the satisfaction of knowing that all my private parts are where they ought to be.

Rosie never explains why half the time she doesn't want me around the place. I don't think she and I could ever marry, because I'd have to spend every other night kipping in a bus shelter. There is no forward planning to our arrangement. She simply says, 'Are you staying tonight?' and I stay.

As always, I told her I'd be there to hold her hand through the long night watches, but first I had to leg it back to my place for a fresh supply of clothes. I paid the bill, persuaded a reluctant Thai into parting with a couple of blank receipts, kissed Rosie au revoir and semaphored a cab.

My place is surprisingly neat. I like clothes, so I hang my suits up every night, regardless of what state I'm in. Similarly, I unknot my ties, drape them on the rack, consign my grubby shirts etc. to the laundry bin. I even have a few pairs of shoe trees for my Loakes. I don't spend a lot of time in my flat, regarding it rather as a hotel bedroom with a kitchen tacked on. There is also the lounge and beyond it a patch of mouldy grass where one might sit enjoying the sun. Two might find it a bit of a squeeze. Inside, the overall mood is a pensive grey, which I find least distressing in the mornings. There's little in the way of decoration. Rosie says that's because I haven't bonded with the flat and don't feel like sharing my identity with it. I said she might be right because I don't share my drink with it either. But apparently that's different.

When I got home I tuned in the answerphone. Tommy, my partner in crime from the *Express*, reported he had tickets for the England visit to Landsdowne Road, and did I fancy a drunken weekend by the banks of the Liffey with a rugby match to boot. Indeed I did. I made a mental note to call him soonest. There was also a rather subdued call from Ross Gavney, saying he wanted to talk to me urgently. I glanced at my watch and phoned his Magpie Court flat. I heard seven rings before his answer phone chipped in to tell me he was not available at present but would I leave my message after the beep and he would get back to me. I told him I was the competitions manager of the *Reader's Digest* and I was calling him, Mister Ross Gavney, as a valued customer, to let him know he hadn't won a thing. Just on the off chance, I called his office. The phone rang on and on unheard.

It was getting late now, and Rosie becomes fractious when I'm late. I shot off to the bedroom, unhooked a lightweight black and grey two-piece, a Sea Island cotton shirt with a hint of apricot, a Paco Rabanne tie of misty blue. I keep an overnight bag stocked to the gills with socks, underpants, notebooks, pens, a tape recorder, batteries and aspirin. I was dragging it off the shelf when something disturbed me. It wasn't a noise. It was more a movement in the air. I paused and cocked an ear. Nothing, apart from the usual background sounds of all-in sumo wrestling from the flat upstairs. I stood still and wound back my memory, wondering whether I had locked the Chubb security before I went out this morning. Us crime reporters are all too aware of the burglary statistics in London. We are even more aware of Plod's manifest ineptitude at catching burglars.

I pictured myself returning to the flat. No. I had just used the Yale key to get in. So there might be someone else in the vicinity. I eased off my shoes, wrapped my keys around my hand like a knuckleduster and went exploring on tiptoe. The lounge was asleep and empty. I parted the curtains across the patio doors. No lurkers out there. But there was still a vague sense of something wrong, that someone else was sharing my space. I tried the bathroom and peered into the shower cubicle. Not a soul. If I had an intruder, it wasn't Psycho. I was padding down the narrow hallway towards the kitchen when my super-sensory perception detected something which did not belong. A faint but distinct whiff of petrol. I do not have a car. I stopped in mid-stride and considered the petrol motif. If someone is planning to torch your flat, there is a set procedure to the way they go about it. The routine is they lift the letterbox, squirt a jet of petrol through it, light a match and retire to a safe distance. That's the way they do it. Secure in such knowledge, I wheeled about, tramped back up the hallway to the front door and got down on my hands and knees for a good sniff. Alas, the petrol merchant was not au fait with the rules on torching people's flats. For even as I knelt there, snorting at the berber, he sneaked up behind me and smacked me on the head with a refrigerator. My teeth bit the carpet.

My brain said, 'Sod this for a game of soldiers' and did a runner. I dragged it back and got my eyes working. They couldn't see much because they were flat against the floor, but they registered that the beige pile was turning reddy brown. Meanwhile, to my rear all was quiet, causing me to wonder whether her upstairs had fallen on me. My ears had gone on the blink and what feeling I had was concentrated on a great lump of crimson pain in the back of my head. If my sense of smell was operating, it had nothing to contribute to the proceedings. I waggled my tongue about and tasted that heady mix of salt and copper which doctors call blood.

After a while decked out in the hallway, I heard a groan, a long, aching, Gawd-help-us groan. It came from me. Apart from the pain in the head I felt warm and cosy and ever so sleepy. I was even getting to like lying there. Then something grabbed me by the ankles and I began to be towed backwards towards the lounge. My chin bumped along the floor leaving a muddy wake through the tufts. My shoulders, arms and hands stayed where they were. After a while they got the general idea and followed suit. It was a boring journey with not much in the way of scenery. I nodded off.

When I awoke I found myself sprawled in my Conran lounger. The world was a shade gloomy and black round the edges. I let my pupils sidle from side to side. Just off camera there was a fuzzy noise which I eventually worked out was the opening and closing of doors. A man appeared before me. I didn't know him from Adam, apart from the fact I don't believe Adam wore a ski mask. I gave the stranger my deepest concentration. He was of average height, average build and had a more than average penchant for black clothing. Sweater, trousers, gloves, the lot. I didn't think he had slipped in to give me a box of Cadbury's Milk Tray because the Milk Tray man doesn't wander around with a wheel brace in his mitt. I eliminated as suspects most of the men and some of the women I knew. My brain started playing Smart Alec. 'Aha!' it said. 'This geezer has just applied that wheel brace to your cranium.' I said thank you brain. I'd already figured that out myself. I studied him hard to see if there were any Clues I could pass on to the rozzers. I couldn't tell whether the wheel brace came from a BMW or a JCB. There wasn't even a Marks & Sparks tag sticking out the back of his jumper.

Burglar Bill paced around the lounge with average sized paces, poking in my nooks and crannies. He had a lot to learn about good housekeeping. He scattered books and tapes willy-nilly in his path. I moaned again, possibly thinking about all the mess I'd have to clean up. His head pivoted round and he glared at me. I'm guessing it was a glare. He disappeared from view and returned clutching a Clue – a black sports bag emblazoned with the legend Adidididadadadadasas. I subbed it down to Adidas. He ripped back the zipper and began stowing all the loot inside. It was about now that I realised my visitor was not the usual breed of burglar. He ignored the video and CDs galore, opting instead for every scrap of paper he could find. He was doing his burglar business when the telephone pealed out. He froze. I froze. Or at least I just sprawled there like a squid on a rock.

Brrriinnnng-brrriinnng! went the telephone. He let it. After a due interval I heard my tinny recorded voice inform the caller: 'I'm not here at the moment, or if I am, I'm in no state to talk to you. But feel free to chat to my machine.' The burglar and I listened to the message all the way through. So did the caller. Then he/she hung up without saying a word. Don't you just hate it when people do that? My burglar didn't like it either. He ripped the phone off the wall and trussed me to the chair with the cable. I thought it was time we got acquainted.

I said, 'The cheque's in the post.' My voice had a built-in echo.

No response from my captor. So he wasn't from American Express.

I had another go. 'I've never met your wife, and anyway, she seduced me.'

The burglar was as chatty as a dumb Trappist monk with laryngitis. I was not getting through here. A sudden flash of inspiration hit me like a wheel brace. I said, 'You are the Kandy Man and I claim my five pounds.'

That worked. He smacked me across the shins with his favourite toy. Through the pain I heard him say, 'You were warned.' His voice was blurred, or it might have been my hearing. He returned to his labours. He opened my briefcase and decanted its entire contents into his bag. I watched aghast as dozens of dodgy taxi bills and dinner receipts vanished from sight. I wondered briefly if he was a fellow hack with a lot of expenses to do. He paused to flip through a notebook full of my pidgin shorthand and about as readable as a Booker Prize winner.

He was not in any hurry. Every now and then he nipped off to scour the neighbourhood for hidey holes. At length he zipped up the bag and stood before me. I suspected he was about to clunk me with the wheel brace again, but no, he disappeared kitchenwards and returned clutching a gallon can of petrol. Or it might have been five litres.

He unscrewed the cap and began splashing it over

me and the chair. Oh hell, I thought. He slipped from vision again and I heard the cheery sploshing of four-star unleaded all over the place. I tested my bonds. There was some give. I squirmed a little and estimated I could wriggle free without much problem. But there was a big black question mark over whether I had the strength to stand up. I discussed tactics with myself. My brain suggested I feign unconsciousness, wait until my visitor had cleared off and then flee like the wind. I didn't argue.

When next my burglar flitted into view, I followed his movements through knitted eyelashes. My mouth was drooped open in vapid stupor. My breath came light and slow. He stood barely a yard away. I saw his arm swing back and he gave me another playful slap on the bean with his wheel brace. It didn't hurt at all. I wasn't being brave or anything – I just passed out. I passed back in, in time to see him scoop up the holdall. He was halfway out of the room when he remembered the wheel brace. He came back for it, presumably in case his JCB sprung a puncture on the way home.

I waited until I heard him fiddle at the front door before I began wrestling off the telephone cord. Then I heard a noise which put the fear of God into me. The rattle of a matchbox. I was out of the chair and on the floor even as he struck the match. The front door slammed and there was a Whooosh! from the hallway.

As feared, my legs refused to play and I pitched forward on my face to the floor. The sweet treacherous stench of petrol hung over everything, me especially. I forced my arms into action and scrabbled my way towards the patio doors. I think I ripped the curtain down because I got snagged up in it. The glass reflected a wall of flame behind me. I freed the bottom bolt and pushed. The door gave an inch. The top bolt said if you want this bloody door open, you're going to have to deal with me first. I gazed up at it in anguish. I could feel the heat now. I pushed at the door again. It stayed put. I looked around for something to smash the glass. The only weapon to hand was a paperback. Probably *Bonfire of the Vanities*. I gritted my teeth, closed my eyes, forced myself upright against the wall and grabbed that damn bolt. The agony was bloodcurdling. For a moment the door refused to budge and then it flew open, throwing me onto the patio. I clawed to the middle of the lawn, at which point there was a great hollow Booom! behind me and all the glass in the doors shot out.

I fought out of my petrol-soaked jacket and trousers and didn't bother to hang them up. There were little licks of flame racing across the lawn towards me, following my tracks. I salvaged the mobile from my pocket and dialled 999. The operator, a chatty type, asked me which service I required – fire, police or ambulance. I was feeling reckless. I ordered all three.

I squirmed back to the fence, tore off my shirt and waited for the sirens. I thought of the intruder and what he had done to my suits, my silks, my legs, my poor head. 'You bastard!' I screamed at the night. 'You filthy lump of dog turd. You vicious, stinking shit.' There was lots more of this. After a while I calmed down and started thinking about what I should do next. I could hardly wander the world in Y-Fronts and spotted socks. Fortunately Rosie allows me to keep a small stash of casual gear at her place. I thought about Rosie. I'd better tell her why I was late for the date. I called her number.

'I've been tied up,' I said wittily.

'You bastard,' she said wittily. And hung up.

Chapter Eight

That night I slept in the stiff sheets of St Thomas's hospital. Doctors have a rule: if anyone ever bangs their head and loses consciousness, even for a fraction of a second, whoever owns the head must spend the night at the mercy of the National Health Service. I enjoyed myself.

They carted me off half naked to Casualty, my stretcher accompanied by a bulky Boy in Blue. He came in handy, explaining to the paramedics that I was not the victim of a foiled suicide attempt. I was, he told them, the skin-of-the-teeth survivor of a fire bombing. The nurses looked at me with awe and I reciprocated. I was wheeled down fifty miles of squeaking corridors where somebody zipped off x-rays, another white coat embroidered my skull, a third took my blood pressure (normal), a fourth applied cooking alcohol to my legs. I wasn't up to licking it off. A nurse with breasts like zeppelins slipped a thermometer under my tongue, nearly suffocating me in the process. My temperature was surprisingly normal. I put it down to shock.

They wheeled me backwards and forwards for an hour until they found a bed which was not already occupied. They gave me something vile to drink, possibly water, and a lethal cocktail of painkillers and sedatives.

They all went off to play with somebody else and I used the interlude to give Rosie another call. I had a hard job getting her to shut up and listen. It was worth the effort. In the end she came over all tearful and contrite. She was rotten and selfish, she told me, and that was a first. How could I forgive her? She'd make it up to me. I lay there on the crackling sheets having a whale of a time.

Rosie said, 'Are you badly hurt, love?'

I put on a stiff upper lip and moaned, 'Yes.'

Rosie wailed, 'I'll be right over.'

I whispered 'Okay' in a way that suggested she'd better hurry if she wanted to see her darling Max before St Peter did.

I also rang News Desk. Vic answered. So that's one suspect down the Swanee. He wanted to know every nasty little detail about my ordeal. I had a sneaking suspicion he was rooting for the burglar. He made me dictate a first person story: 'Our Crimebuster Beats Hellfire Murder Bid.' It's odd, reporting about yourself. It's also a bundle of fun. I lied about my age, and invented loads of exciting tosh that made the copytaker go 'Wow!' I verballed the burglar. He said he'd fry me like a slice of bacon. I dreamed up a few heroic quotes for myself. I spat defiance and told him to change his deodorant and where to stick his car jack. A pop-eyed sergeant sat by the bedside while I was dictating. After I'd done he got me to make a statement. And after that he was a disappointed man.

'So you didn't kick him in the groin?' he asked, ballpoint hovering.

'No.'

'But you just said . . .'

'Don't believe everything you read in the papers,' I said.

'And that bit about trying to rip off his mask?'

'Ditto.'

The sergeant looked as if he wished I'd gone whooof! in a blaze of glory instead of lying here making up porkies. I asked him if he had any drink concealed about his person. He said no. He probably had half a bottle of vodka tucked down his trousers, but he wasn't going to share it with some phoney hero. He cleared off, leaving me with a taciturn woodentop for company. I was grateful for his silence. It gave me time to think about the evening's adventure.

I had no doubt that Burglar Bill was up to his eye teeth in the Claudine Tournier affair. Why else should he belt me for mentioning Kandy? But why did he break in? His final intention was clear enough. He planned to torch the flat. Intruders don't cruise the streets of our city with jerrycans of petrol unless such is their intention. But then why was he tooled up with a wheel brace? Maybe that was in case he bumped into anyone. And why did he nick all my papers? There was nothing in the flat that would land anyone in trouble, apart from me. I keep a lot of info in my head. My contact book was in my pocket. The pocket of the jacket untidily discarded on my singed back lawn. I ticked myself off for leaving it behind. A hack's contact book is absolutely vital to him. For starters, that's where he keeps his pin number for the hole-in-the-wall beer token dispensers. Mine also contained hundreds of names and numbers, some of them very sensitive indeed. For instance, there's a man who used to be in Special Branch but now earns his keep in MI5 and who sometimes . . . maybe we'd better not go into that.

I thought about what else was in my jacket. My passport. Not so long ago a passport was an essential accessory for every proper hack. If you turned up in the office without it, you could be fired on the spot. And justly so. The principle was that if the office wanted to send you somewhere at a moment's notice you had to be ready. That was in the days when newspapers had news in them. You also need a second passport, one without a Tel Aviv entry, in case you're sent to Beirut, Damascus or one of those places where evidence of a visit to Israel is proof you are a Zionist spy. What else had I left on the lawn? Chequebook, credit cards, at least a hundred quid in readies, the Thai restaurant receipt. Oh yes, the WorldCare Foundation letter. Christ, I had to get that back before the Old Bill spotted it. I reflected that my burglar was downright careless in not frisking me. It suggested that Plan A was merely to toast the flat.

The questions chased each other down the back alleys of my mind until I heard the skippety-skip of heels heralding the arrival of Rosie. She was as fragrant as a meadow at dawn, flushed and fantastic. She leaned over me and poured kisses of sweet bounty on my fevered brow. I forgot the nurse with the zeppelins. Rosie kissed me on the lips, which was bloody painful as my teeth had gone halfway through them when the burglar bashed me. Every couple of seconds she broke off to tell me how much she loved me and that I was a poor thing and she would take care of me and cater to my every whim and how much she wanted me to bc home with her. She was warming to her theme and I thought any minute now she's going to hop into bed beside me. I wished the nurse had left a couple of spare sedatives.

She lifted her hair out of my face and gave me a look of heart-tugging sympathy. I said, 'Have you brought a first aid kit?'

She bobbed her head, fished in her bag, and produced three miniatures of whisky. That would do for a start. She propped them on my bedside locker and added forty Bensons to the pile.

'You're a treasure,' I said, deeply moved.

I unscrewed one of the dinky little bottles and reached for a glass. I heard a loud 'Harrummph!' from the other side of the bed. The silent policeman had given voice. Maybe he wanted a tincture himself.

He pointed at the golden bottle. 'You're not supposed to touch that.'

I said, 'What?'

He said, 'It's dangerous to drink after taking sedatives.'

Rosie said belligerently, 'Are you a doctor or something?'

My bodyguard conceded he wasn't a doctor, but he had Experience of This Sort of Thing. Rosie said it was none of his business, and why wasn't he out catching the man who thumped me? PC 49 got to his feet and yelled, 'Nurse!'

Before I had time to stash my scotch under the pillow, a ministering angel appeared and trousered the lot. She wagged a finger at me. 'Sedatives and alcohol don't mix,' she said. 'And smoking is forbidden.'

I wanted to be home, or better still, at Rosie's place. I wagged a finger back at her. 'If you'd given me whisky, I wouldn't need sedation.'

She brushed an imaginary germ from the sheets and said, 'You've also had some very strong painkillers.'

'They're not working.'

Rosie did her Florence Nightingale bit. 'Are you very sore?'

I grimaced. 'All over. My head, my shins, my knees, my tonsils.'

The Angel of Death fluffed up my pillows. She said, 'What you need is a good night's sleep. That'll cure your aches and pains. You'll wake up feeling much, much better. Won't he officer?'

PC Spoilsport said that's right, sleep cures everything. It doesn't do much for sleeping sickness, I said, but I was too tired to argue the point.

The nurse turned on Rosie. 'Now, Mrs Chard. It's time you left. Your husband has just been through a great deal. I think we should let him rest, don't you?'

I don't think Rosie liked being called Mrs Chard, and I'm not sure she liked having me described as her husband. At any rate she nodded in dumb obedience. I wish I could get her to do that.

She flung her arms around my aching head, planted another juicy one on my lips and off she went. I watched her trim little bottom wiggle away and half of me went chasing after her.

Now she was gone I felt bloody awful. Wracked with pain is the expression that came to mind.

The nurse was scribbling something on the chart at the foot of my bed.

'How am I?' I asked.

'You're all right. You're not in any danger, if that's what you're thinking.'

I winced away a tidal wave of pain. I said, 'When people ring the hospital, what condition do you tell them I'm in?'

She smiled the smile of the truly insane.

'We tell them you're comfortable.'

They woke me at dawn with tea from the office machine, shovelled pills into me, and asked me how I was. I told them. They smiled in tender sorrow and went on to the next unfortunate. It was a small ward, about a dozen patients in varying states of decay. One man had a bandage like a turban all round his head. Another was encased in plaster and hanging from the ceiling. I didn't even have a strip of Elastoplast to show for my troubles. I felt aggrieved. My silent partner of the night before had gone, taking his considerable medical lore with him. If there was still a copper guarding me, he was either dolled up as a nurse or swathed in bandages.

I closed my eyes and sought sanctuary in sleep. A

nurse prodded me awake by popping a thermometer through my broken lips.

'My, my. You're quite a celebrity,' she said.

'Mmpphh?'

'Don't talk until I've taken your temperature. Yes,' she continued. 'I've been reading all about you in the paper.'

'Ooofwhumphuh?'

'Mouth closed, please. You can see it yourself in a minute. Read it over breakfast. You'll like that.'

I nodded vigorously. The back of my head fell off. She saw my agony and gave a cheery laugh like the tinkle of falling bedpans. She patted my lifeless wrist. 'Don't worry. We'll soon have you up and about.'

I said to myself, 'You bet. As soon as the pubs are open.'

She lied about me enjoying breakfast. I pushed it away so that it didn't put me off the paper. There was a short on page one about our ace crime reporter escaping death by a whisker. Full story: see page five. I saw page five. I beamed back at myself from a two column pic. I certainly didn't look like someone who had been almost frazzled. I read my glittering account. It was not bad, but for the fact that some halfwitted sub had seen fit to embellish my quotes, the ones I'd invented in the first place. I read: The raider smirked and said, 'Right, Chard, you know what happens to nosey parkers – they end up on a slab.' What he actually said was, 'Burn, baby, burn.' And I never said he smirked. How could I tell what his face was up to under the ski mask? It really pisses me off when newspapers get things wrong. I tossed the paper aside in disgust.

The morning dragged on like a *Sunday Express* intro. Occasionally someone would come up and have a butcher's at my legs or head, scrawl on the chart, and wander off. The main man and his posse of juniors spent a good 20 seconds peering at the chart. I don't think they noticed me.

I was slipping into slumber when my first visitor hove into view. Big Ben Ashbee, the super. He gave me his undertaker's smile and a bunch of grapes.

I said, 'I usually get my grapes from a bottle.'

In my story I was careful not to mention the Kandy line. I didn't want to tip off the rest of Fleet Street. I hinted instead that my attacker was linked to a drugs racket and had been sent by that well known baddie, Mr Big. But I told Ben the full bit. He tugged his ear and said, 'Umm humm', which I took to mean he thought it a sensational item.

I told him not to bother lining up an identity parade because one geezer in a ski mask looks much like any other geezer in a ski mask. Ben said forensics had taken a look at the ashes and found nothing significant. Now they had a couple of men doing door-to-door stuff. So far no one had seen, heard, suspected anything until my flat lit up the neighbourhood. Ben remembered he had some bits and pieces for me. He handed over a Tesco's carrier bearing my once beautiful suit. I took a peek inside and it didn't look as if Ben had nicked anything. My suit still reeked of petrol and for the first time I thought there might be something in the hospital's no smoking rule.

Ben asked me if I knew anyone who might want to do me in. I said yes, there's Tony Belker, and one of the monkeys, and a certain sub, and an old girlfriend, and the neo-Nazi in our library, and . . .

Ben said Umm humm again and away he went.

The battery on my mobile was dead but I coaxed the ward sister into wheeling up a pay phone. I rang the world to let it know I would live to write again. The world was unimpressed. I got Mac on the golf course, practising his cheating.

'Are you well there, boy?' he asked.

Holding my own, I assured him. He said I'd go blind. Ah, the old ones are the best. He said, 'I hear tell you've changed your name from Chard.'

I fell for it. I said, 'What's it now?'

'Max Charred.' He spelt it out. It still wasn't funny.

I put the phone down on his cackle and lay back to await the Seventh Cavalry. They showed up around lunchtime while the locals were packing away grub that looked as if it had already been eaten. Angela Whipple led the charge, bearing a hamper as big as a wardrobe. I whisked it open and there, ripe green and glorious, was a bottle of Moët. She prised the cork out, giving Tutankhamun in the bed next door a minor heart attack. We knocked it back like cossacks and rooted around for more goodies. The hamper was a get-well-soon prezzie from the Editor. Angie coughed up with a bottle of Gordons. The NHS doesn't stretch to providing tonic so we drank it with borrowed Lucozade. After a while you get used to it.

Meanwhile other hacks showed up like ghouls at a plane crash. Cigars, cigarettes, bottles and flasks built up on my locker. I could have opened an off-licence. Everyone was most concerned, particularly the ward sister who kept trying to throw out my beloved brethren as they were giving the casualty ward a bad name. I was sitting up, chewing a chicken and quaffing red biddy, when the dear noisy crew suddenly hushed. The Editor himself had arrived. Now this was an honour. Not as good as a pay rise, but an honour just the same. The foot soldiers slipped away like wraiths and I was left grinning at the boss. Normally he doesn't speak to me. He brushes past in the corridor, evincing a deep interest in his shoelaces. But newspapers are funny things. Most of the time editors and the rest of the executive rabble spend their days dreaming up ways to make life miserable for you. They're pretty good at it too. I've seen them drive droves of hacks to the looney bin or the bottle. Sometimes both. I could rattle off the names of a dozen good men who died before their due, thanks to editors and their ilk. Those who survive the daily round are tortured souls with shattered marriages and jangling nerves. You can hear the Valium rattle as they pass. Editors look on the destruction they've wreaked and they are well pleased. It's their way of exercising power.

But if someone else does something nasty to one of their hacks, by God, they're for it. And the abused hack finds himself on the receiving end of a generosity that would make the prodigal son feel hard done by. So it was with me. The Editor asked after my limbs, my head, my happiness. He said the paper was putting up a five grand reward for info leading to the arrest of The Petrol Can Kid. I blushed and nearly spilled my wine. Furthermore, said the Editor, I was to take time off, as much time as I wanted. And when I was fit enough, say in a month, the paper would send me somewhere nice and sunny for a holiday.

'With my girlfriend?' I asked.

Only the slightest hesitation. Yes, with my girlfriend. The Editor recommended the Caribbean or Bali, places with which he is uncommonly well acquainted. He folded up his half moons, told me if there was anything, anything, I needed, I just had to call his secretary. He departed, leaving me to think I must thank my burglar, if ever they caught him.

Rosie interrupted my kindly thoughts. She swooped, dived, hugged, kissed, caressed and mauled my mangled body. The ward's bandaged peeping toms stopped licking their wounds and began fighting for a ringside seat. We were forced to draw the curtains. Alone at last we grinned at each other like a pair of idiots. Beyond the screen the zimmer frame brigade listened to a chorus of ooohs, yumms and the occasional Arrrrghh! when she hugged too hard. We were rudely interrupted by a staff monkey who wanted an up-to-the-minute shot of me. He also persuaded Rosie to pout provocatively over my injured skull. And who can blame him?

After he'd gone, we took time out to talk. I was careful not to say a word about the Editor's freebie holiday for I knew what Rosie would say. The Maldives. She poked around in my hamper and finished off the glazed fruits while I told her of the lazy days of recuperation ahead. She said super, she would help me shop for a new wardrobe. Oh no you won't, I thought. But I said that would be nice and I would lodge in her flat and help her draw lizards. Rosie said, 'Oh no you won't.' We breezed away the afternoon until a nurse parted the curtains and turfed Rosie out on her ear.

The next day I was set free. They were glad to help me on my way. I exchanged the hospital shroud for a pair of jeans and an Elvis Costello tour tee shirt and limped around Rosie's place with an air of heroic suffering. Rosie insisted I stay and I got the impression that meant permanently, or at least until I was fit to walk the streets.

The Law paid me a couple of visits but we didn't have much to say to each other. They were getting nowhere on the Claudine Tournier/Shirley Ham killings and I think they'd lost interest in my pyromaniac. The paper ran a shortish follow-up on my status, with a pic of Rosie and me, and some hamfisted quotes. Friends popped up every few minutes, largely because it was a great excuse to get out of the office. Whenever things went quiet Rosie would feed me an improving book. She reads some weird stuff. I started at A for Allende (Isabelle), hurriedly moved on to B for Brookner (Anita), and by the time I hit C for Colette (no first name) I must have read at least a dozen pages and my head was hurting. I surrendered myself instead to the pleasures of daytime TV. There is much to be said for the medium. It does not require your intellectual participation. Therefore I was able to watch *Neighbours* while thinking of something else altogether, which the actors were also doing. Mostly I thought about The Man in Black. He had left me with a pair of multi-coloured shins and lips like Mick Jagger's. What manner of man was this, I mused, who could callously incinerate two dozen exquisite suits and God knows how many shirts? What did I know that made me worth burning?

I pondered while Rosie played with her crayons. All was domestically blissful apart from the grub. Whole fields of spinach were laid waste for my delectation. It didn't make me any smarter. Rosie said it was chock full of iron. I soon had metal fatigue.

On the third night of convalescence the phone shrilled while she was doing something nasty with bean sprouts. I was hoping it was meals on wheels. It was Vic on Night Desk. He didn't ask after my welfare. He said, 'A bloke's been on three times to get your new number. I've told him we don't give out personal details, but he keeps on ringing. He also wants your new address.'

I said, 'Does he call himself the Masked Marauder?'

'No, he calls himself . . .' Vic broke off and went on a paper chase around the desk. He picked up the phone again. 'He says his name is Gitney or something.'

I didn't know any Gitneys. I said, 'Might it be Gavney?'

Vic said it might be. He couldn't read his notes. I said it was very kind of Vic to ring me and he said that's okay, he was doing nothing anyway.

I rang Ross Gavney at his Magpie Court number and he snatched up the phone.

'Yes?' he demanded.

I said, 'You're supposed to say: "This is the Gavney residence; how might I be of assistance?" '

'Max!'

I said, 'A lucky guess.'

There was what they call a pregnant pause. I reflected this was a shade odd. He was supposed to be dying to talk to me. He cleared his throat and said, 'I've been trying to get your number but the paper wouldn't let me have it.'

I said, 'I know.'

A three beat silence. He said, 'I feel very bad about this.'

'I feel a hell of a lot worse,' I said. I asked him why he felt bad.

Ross said, 'Well, it's my fault really. If I hadn't made that stupid bet, you'd be okay.'

I said, 'I don't think I'll ever forgive you. But if you were to buy me a large steak I might just weaken.'

Ross laughed. It was a tense little heh-heh. A laugh you could do without smiling. He said, 'You haven't eaten yet?'

I said, 'I don't eat any more. I graze.'

Another snippet of laughter. Ross said, 'Well, I'm doing nothing tonight. If you like, I'll pick you up and treat you to dinner.'

I said, 'I'm beginning to forgive you already.'

His voice picked up pace. He said, 'Tell me where you're living now and I'll collect you.'

For some curious reason I didn't feel like giving

him Rosie's address. I rolled over the question and said, 'Don't bother – it's just as easy for me to pop round to Magpie Court.'

'Half an hour, say?'

'Half an hour.'

Ross said, 'Great. Look forward to seeing you.' He didn't sound as if he meant it.

I cast an appraising eye over the few garments in my cache at Rosie's place. The nearest thing I had to proper clothes was an ecru linen jacket and a pair of navy slacks. I tried on a faded lavender shirt and I looked too precious for my own good. I settled for a navy crew neck, slipped on my black loafers and kissed Rosie goodbye.

I got to Magpie Court fifteen minutes later than promised. Ross was on the phone to Tokyo or Wall Street, checking up on his pork scratchings futures. I was welcomed instead by his idiot brother, Euan. I have never felt too fond of Euan ever since he nearly took my eye out with a homemade air pistol when I was fourteen. He must have been all of twelve. He's still mad keen on shooters though these days he prefers potting pheasants to people. Tonight he pretended the Great Eye Incident had never happened. I fingered an imaginary scar over my left eye to remind him. He said hello and stuck a whisky in my hand so maybe he's improving. I limped towards a nearby chair, taking care not to spill a single drop. Euan is another of those City types who consider it a wasted day if he hasn't knocked up a million before breakfast.

He's got a mansion in the shires with all the adornments, including a wife who could steal your breath away and twin daughters who look like they belong in the Hitler Youth kindergarten. But Euan's old lady has recently told him to pack his pyjamas and clear off. A fling with a floozy, I gather. Now he's cluttering up Ross's guest bedroom and looking very down on his luck indeed. We didn't have a lot to say to each other.

Ross got off the phone and said, 'Here's to the Great Escaper.'

The Great Escaper smiled bravely and stuck his nose in his glass. Euan mumbled his best wishes and sloped off. Ross said, 'How do you feel?'

I said, 'Like I look. Only worse.'

He said, 'You don't look too bad. A bit pale maybe.'

He was looking a trifle peakish himself, and edgy with it. I had the feeling he wanted to confide in me but couldn't make up his mind.

I said, 'Where are we going?'

Ross said, 'I thought perhaps John Dory's.'

I said, 'But that's a fish restaurant.'

'Where, then?'

I said, 'I have a desperate craving for roast beef and Yorkshire pudding without the Yorkshire pudding. Maybe I'm pregnant.'

Ross laughed and this time he was more relaxed about it. He suggested a place by the Tower and we drained our whiskies and went. The restaurant was knee deep in Japanese tourists, thirsting for Merrie Englande at very unmerrie prices. Judging by their dress, they evidently thought the place had a golf course upstairs. I didn't feel so bad about my outfit.

I waited until we got to the port and Stilton stage before I asked, 'What's on your mind?'

Ross swallowed a nugget of cheese and went into a coughing fit. I topped up my glass and passed the port to the left. Ross got his larynx working again.

'Mind? Nothing. I was just very worried about you. I felt responsible, and . . .'

'And balls,' I said. Ross blinked but didn't say anything. I took my time lighting a cigar and admiring its glow. I started. I spoke in flat, undramatic tones, all the while locking my eyes on his. I said, 'You and I, Ross, go back to the birth of time. You've copied my English homework, I've copied your maths. You've bled my nose and I've punched your head. You wrecked my bike, and I stole your girlfriend. You've got drunk with me, I've chased women with you. What's yours is mine, and vice versa. If ever I marry, you'd be my best man, and if ever you have children, I'll dandle them upon my knee. We are as close as brothers. We don't have secrets.'

I paused. Ross was listening intently, but not giving anything away. I said, 'And now we have a secret.'

'A secret?' he said warily.

'A secret. It begins the night you bet me there was a story behind a stiff in the Thames.'

He said, 'I didn't know—'

I stopped him. 'No, you didn't know it was Claudine Tournier. None of us knew until we saw her face. I thought: "Hello, it's Claudine Tournier." The Old Bill thought: "Hello, hello, hello, it's Claudine Tournier." But you didn't.'

'I didn't?'

'You didn't. You said, "My God, it's Claudine!" Just Claudine. As if there was only one Claudine in the whole wide world.'

I stopped to see if Ross wanted to say anything. He didn't. I said, 'You also started acting like a zombie. You stopped talking. When we went to that wine bar you stood there knocking it back and staring at the wall. If I hadn't been so busy I would have got it out of you there and then. It was only later I thought about it. You said, "It's Claudine." That meant you were on first name terms with La Tournier. Nothing wrong with that. But you didn't want me to know about it.'

I took a lazy draw on the cigar. I said, 'So, you see, Ross, we have a secret.'

He was looking down at the table, rolling a crumb of Stilton across the linen folds.

I said, 'But that was only the start of the secret.'

He glanced up. 'The start?'

I said, 'Oh yes, there's more. We'll pass over the day I rang you, when you couldn't stick a sensible sentence together, and we'll move on to tonight.'

'Tonight?' It was like talking to a parrot.

I said, 'This very eve. You were desperate to get hold of me. Why? Because you felt guilty about me nearly getting fried alive. Because you knew that it was all tied up with the killing of Claudine. You said, and I quote: "It's all my fault. If I hadn't made that stupid bet you'd be okay".'

I took in a centilitre of port. Ross sat hunched over the table, his eyes hooded. He didn't seem inclined to talk. I exhaled a blue billow of cigar smoke. I said,

'Now that was a very interesting thing to say. And it puzzles me. You see, when I wrote the story on my arsonist, I deliberately implied he was an underworld villain, a straightforward gangster. I never for one moment suggested he had anything to do with Claudine's murder.

'But I knew he was up to his balaclava in it because of something he said at the flat. I know that, he knows that, and nobody else knows that. Nobody except you. I haven't the faintest idea how you know. That is your big secret, Ross, and I'd like you to share it with me.'

I sat back. I hadn't blinked an eye throughout my little monologue and I was still intent on every reflex, every nuance from my good old mate. The cigar smoke made pretty spirals in the air, otherwise we were frozen. I waited a long time. When he spoke, he didn't look at me. His voice was so low I had to lean forward to hear him.

He said, 'I can't.'

I said, 'You can't tell me the secret?'

He made a sort of shrug which could have meant anything but added up to no.

I said softly, 'Ross, I very nearly died in there. I don't even know why.'

He said, 'I'm sorry . . .'

I was silent, forcing him to go on.

He tasted his port and looked across the glass at me. He said, 'Max, it's not what you think. It's different. It's something I want to tell you, but I can't.'

I felt betrayed and vicious and I still didn't know

what was going on. I said, 'You're full of crap. Maybe you'll tell the police.'

He said, 'The police!'

I said, 'Yes, those blokes in the funny hats.'

He said, 'Christ, Max, don't involve them. Please.'

I laughed without humour. I said, 'Maybe you'd prefer it if I stopped nosing round this whole affair.'

His eyes told me he would like that very much.

I said, 'Well that's tough, Ross. I'm sticking with this one all the way through. I want you to tell your friends that. Tell them I'm going to turn them over and wring them dry.'

He said, 'Look, it's over. Just trust me. I just can't . . .'

I said, 'Why don't you pick up the bill and get out of here. And any time you feel like calling me – don't.'

He sat for a few minutes. His face was pointy. Then he stood up slowly and gave me a last look of entreaty. My eyes were cold as death. He turned and walked away. We didn't say goodbye.

I stayed on with the port and a new cigar until I couldn't stand the taste any more. I got them to call me a taxi and I returned to the land of the living.

Chapter Nine

First thing next morning I moved house again. It was my fourth address in a week. I felt like giving Salman Rushdie a ring and comparing notes. This time I hid myself away in the Barbican. My brainy brother Dominic keeps a second-floor flat there. But as he prefers to earn his living in Vancouver, teaching the natives all they need to know about social anthropology, the flat lies vacant ten months a year. I phoned his log cabin in the middle of the black Canadian night, got Dominic out of bed and told him my sorry tale. Supportive as ever, he grouched, 'You deserved it.' But he got on to the Barbican concierge and arranged for me to squat. I liked the thought of the Barbican. Its name means a fortified tower, and a fortified tower suited me down to the ground right now. I tried to persuade Rosie to pack up her lizards and move in. She said, 'Has it got a studio?' I lied and said the flat had its own art gallery, get-slim gym and beach. Rosie doubted my word and stayed put in Battersea, borough of my dreams. I think I was secretly glad she wasn't sharing my bolthole.

I gave Rosie and nobody else my address and number. I told the office if they wanted me they just had to bleep my pager. I didn't want News Desk knowing where I was in case the Black Blazer phoned and some loon gave him the details. It's happened before. I armed myself with a couple of extra batteries for the mobile phone and pulled up the drawbridge. It was a clean, well-lighted place with soft hued walls and a stack of golden pine furniture. Dominic had left behind a rainbow of grey suits which were presumably too bohemian for the backwoods of Canada. They fitted me after a fashion. His taste in ties was atrocious, as was his musical inclination. I thumbed through CDs by Simple Minds, Mike Oldfield and Jean Michel Jarre before I found a Bonnie Raitt album. I stuck it on the player, helped myself to Dominic's gin and put my feet up on the dwarfish table. I was home and dryish.

There's not much to do in the Barbican, unless you're lucky enough to have a flat facing out on the local roads, where you can sit counting taxis. Dominic's faced inwards. I counted five trees. His books made Rosie's look like a rattling good read. I survived until Bonnie Raitt stopped warbling. Any more of this and I'll start talking to myself, I said. I picked up the mobile and called News Desk. Angela Whipple was sweet and solicitous. I said, 'Can you get me a laptop, Angie?'

'No problem. Where do you want it sent?'

I thought about it and remembered a bar behind Smithfield. I told her to give me half an hour and I'd be there to meet the messenger. She was feeling perky. She said, 'How will he recognise you?'

I said, 'Tell him to look for the man with his flies undone.'

I was on my second G&T when a young freelance who does shifts for us shambled in looking bemused. Maybe it was his first time in a bar. I waved a mitt and he sighed with relief. He handed over the laptop and I offered him a drink. But he wanted a half of lager shandy instead. Signs of a grievously misspent youth.

I got myself home, brewed up a jug of coffee and kickstarted the laptop. I keyed in DLIBFILE, which in English means our electronic library. I wasn't sure what I was looking for and I wasn't particularly hopeful. The real editor of a newspaper is often its lawyer, which is why you rarely get to read the dirty stuff. Oh, the stories I could tell you would make your eyes whizz round like Catherine Wheels.

My general idea was to splash around in the backwaters of all the leading characters and see what rippled the surface. I locked on to the little green screen and embarked on my task.

There is a convention among cops and crime reporters: they don't write stories, we don't investigate murders. Possibly an awful lot more murderers might be caught if it were the other way around, but then your newspapers would be extremely boring. This is the price you pay for your daily tabloid.

There are occasions when we do play Plod. Imagine, for instance, that a top spook at Cheltenham spy centre is found dead, wearing nothing but a suspender belt and a silly smile. Naturally the public has a right to know what's been going on here, especially as Those In Authority have not the faintest intention of telling them. So us hacks beetle off to Gloucs. and start acting all steely-eyed. After a few hours of this most of us get bored, write some guff about a sinister conspiracy and repair to the bar. You do get the occasional oddball who makes the career his lifelong vocation. He usually works for the *Observer* or one of the other tomfool heavies. Months, even years after the event, he still churns out great reams of impenetrable copy. Still, it keeps him off the streets.

When it comes to common or garden murder, such as Claudine's or Shirley's, we all stand back and leave it to the Old Bill. That's what I should have been doing. But I was a bitter and twisted man. Besides, I wasn't entirely convinced that the Law would ever collar the man with the itchy matchbox finger.

But even before the bonfire I had been acting the super sleuth. It took me a while to work out why. It was all Ross's fault. He'd bet me the unknown corpse in St Katharine's Dock was a story. So he'd won the bet. But I wanted to prove I could get a bigger and better story than he ever imagined. I suppose it comes down to ego. I needed to show off, to demonstrate that I'm smarter than the average hack. It's pathetic but it's true. So that was why I was acting like a gin-fuelled Miss Marple. As well as that, I was enjoying myself.

I had a list and I worked my way systematically through it from Cowley to Veizey via Tomlin. I worked all afternoon, pausing only for the occasional screen break and coffee. I appropriated a sheaf of creamy notepaper and made notes in a large, clear longhand so I didn't have to decipher them afterwards. Thc clock on the bookshelf winked out 18.37 when I at last switched off the laptop. I made myself a proper drink. Dominic favours Plymouth gin, but I'm not picky. It was a grey evening towards the fag end of May, so I lit the chairside lamp before I settled down to read my findings. They didn't impress. I felt I'd missed *Neighbours* and *Home And Away* for nothing. I read:

LEWIS TREFOYLE: 51, Junior minister at Home Office, previously junior min. Welsh Office. MP for Butterley since '84. Marginal seat. Political leanings more Con than Lab. Keen on hanging and forced repatriation of immigrants, providing they're black. Outside interests: non-executive director Chalencidon Properties, also minor consultancies. Rumoured holiday home in Cyprus, the illegal part. Wealthy but not openly so. Married once, divorced once. Viewed by his colleagues as a cold fish.

LEON KNAPP: aged 47/49/52. Born Leo Knapowlski. Founder member of Rotors teenybop band. Made and squandered a fortune. *Sunday People* bought up roadie's tale of drugs and depravity – 'Road to Ruin'. He didn't sue. *Mirror* earlier paid ex-wife for 'Life with Leon the Louse'. Seems he liked blacking her eyes and wearing her knickers.

PROUDHOE VEIZEY: 53. Born Proudhoe Veizey. Ham actor typecast in string of Brit films as pompous duffer. Overacts even in kids' panto – 'Veizey's Widow Twankey is nothing like a Dame' – *Evening Standard.*

Confirmed bachelor, as the diary writers say. Oft seen in the Garrick molesting stray Tories in fond hope of a knighthood.

MARTIN CROWLEY: 46. Ex-marine commando and Falklands veteran, possibly with Special Boat Service. Messes about with boats and not much else. Briefly linked to woman golfer. Affair bunkered after he kept sailing off into the sunset. Tough and tetchy.

GEORGE 'GUS' CLERNTHORPE: 51. Big light in Jockey Club until unseated over links with fugitive tycoon. Lavish party thrower. Less lavish about where the money comes from. Hints of shady property deals. His ginger locks said to be a rug. Gossip writers call him Gorgeous Gussie, but don't say why. Lawyers no doubt.

SIR JAMES TOMLIN: 50. Low profile City moneybags. Hangs around with Square Mile's premier division. Likes women and firing people. Has son, Henry Michael James. Nothing known. Whispers of cash flow problems for Sir J. Educ. Harrow & Cambridge.

I read through my research and tacked another name to the list. I didn't have to dial up our library.

ROSS GAVNEY: 36. Educ. St John's PE, Littlemere, Holly Hill comp. Exeter college. PPE. Dapper bond dealer. Enjoys his money. Occasional girlfriend,

Chloe. Mixes well and widely. Skis and golfs. Secretive bugger.

I sat back, thought about that one, and added, 'Arsenal fan.'

I poured myself another stiff one and read through it all again. Now, I said, spot the man who murdered Claudine and poor Shirley. More to the point, find the evil monster who set fire to my suits. The only one who fitted that description was the unlovely Martin Crowley who used to be paid to kill people. I recalled that my matchbox man had a blurred voice, as if he were trying to disguise it. That meant he was someone I knew. I wouldn't know Martin Crowley if he sailed through the door. Then I recalled that my hearing was not too clever at the time. So maybe his voice wasn't disguised. That left me nowhere.

Sir James was in Geneva when Claudine was topped, Knapp probably in Sri Lanka for all three events. I couldn't picture the flabby pink Trefoyle getting his hands dirty. Proudhoe Veizey would faint clean away at the scent of petrol. I didn't know enough about Gus Clernthorpe. I pencilled a question mark against him. Ross had a surefire alibi for Claudine, thanks to me. I think he was taller than my arsonist. I scratched my tummy and cogitated. There was always the possibility that a couple of them had clubbed together and hired themselves a hitman. Why? Because of a common threat. I ran through the suspects. What did they have in common? Barring

Ross, they were all close mates. Nothing sinister in that. I was about to chuck my notes in the bin when I remembered. They were all linked to the WorldCare Foundation. Whatever mischief they're up to, I reasoned, it involves Claudine's pet project. But Ross has nothing to do with it. Or has he? Ross has a secret, and a big one to boot. It must be a lulu if he's prepared to spike a 20-year friendship.

All this thinking made me hungry. There was no point in calling Rosie because she had shot up north to Huddersfield or Halifax or some place beginning with H to flaunt herself at a textile exhibition. I didn't know they still had textiles up there.

I showered and picked out a suit that made me look like an insurance salesman minus the charisma. I sashayed round to a sushi place off Broad Street. I ordered up a plate of raw fish. I'd gone off roast beef. I was fiddling with my chopsticks when the bleep went off. CALL TROPPER, it said. Who he? I said. I gave Night Desk a ring. 'Have you just bleeped me, Vic?'

'Um hum. A bloke called Tropper wants you to give him a bell.'

I said, 'Did he leave a number?'

Vic did his usual Mogadon-inflamed rumple around the desk and came up with an 0181 number. Somewhere in the outer darkness. I rang it. 'Mister Tropper?' I said.

'Trotter,' he corrected.

'My name's Chard: you want to talk to me.'

He said, 'Yes. It's about Shirl. Shirley Ham.'

He spoke in Estuary English, sticking an r in yes

and dropping the t in about. Maybe he was a trendy TV talk show host. I asked him what about Shirley. He said, 'I'm Darren. I'm her boyfriend.'

Not any more you're not. I waited for him to elaborate. He said, 'Hello? You still there, Mike?'

'Max,' I corrected.

'Oh yes, well, I was thinking, like maybe we could get together and talk about it.'

I said, 'And what do you want to talk about?'

He said, 'Well, I knew what she was up to, working for you, didn't I? I mean, I'm her fiancé, so she told me things.'

I remembered the *Evening Standard* story. Darren was the man who skipped the light fandango with her. I said, 'You've talked to the police?'

'Yes, well that's the problem, innit? They think I did it. I need to talk to somebody because Shirl's been murdered, and I don't know what it's about.'

I asked him where he was. 'Dagenham.'

Dagenham! If south Essex is the backside of England, Dagenham is the pimple on its unlovely bum. I said warily, 'Where do you want to meet?'

'Here's okay with me. How about you?'

Not bloody likely. I sent my brain on a pub crawl. It remembered the Scimitar down the Mile End Road. No, that would be tasteless, considering Shirley was bumped off just before we were due to meet there.

'The Scimitar,' I said, and told him where it was. He wanted to know how he could recognise me. I told him I'd be the one standing by the snapshot of Al Capone. That satisfied him.

I was there by nine. Judging by the mood of the

customers, I must have hit the unhappy hour. Darren arrived along with my first drink. He was much as expected. A crinkly-haired specimen in jeans and tee shirt. His leather jacket was too new so it looked plastic. Maybe it was plastic. He asked for a pint of bitter. We found ourselves an empty snug and sat facing each other. He was nervous and tugged at his fingers.

I said, 'You have something to talk about?'

He said, 'Well, yes, Shirl told me she was pulling this job for you.'

I said, 'She offered information to my newspaper.'

He said, 'She was trying to dig up the dirt at Claudine Turner's place.'

'Tournier.'

He said, 'Yes, well, her. Shirl phoned me that day and said she'd got some great stuff that'd be worth a bundle.'

I said, 'Did she tell you what?'

'No. I thought, well, you'd know.'

I said, 'She was supposed to meet me here but never showed.'

Darren looked around as if he expected Shirley to pop up grinning. He said morosely, 'The police think I murdered Shirley because they don't believe where I was.'

'Where were you?'

He said, 'I was at home. On my own, watching telly. The first thing I know was them knocking on the door and telling me she was dead. They just came out with it. I was choked.'

Not half as much as Shirley. He took in a huge

gulp of beer. I said, 'Did she give you any idea what information she had?'

'No, she got it from someone she knew at the Foundation. She was all excited because we needed the money. We was getting married in September, you know.'

I bought him another pint. He brooded aloud: 'I was doing overtime and all. I was looking forward to getting married even though my mum said I was wrong. I didn't mind about it.'

'Didn't mind about what, Darren?'

He looked embarrassed. 'Well, Shirl was pregnant, like.'

I said, 'Christ! That's really tough for you.'

Darren said, 'No, no. It wasn't my kid or nothing.'

I offered him a cigarette and said casually, 'Who was the dad, then?'

He said, 'Shirl never told me, she said it was all over – with him, I mean. She never said his name but I think it was somebody in her office.'

I said, 'When was the baby due?'

'November. That's why we was getting married this year.'

I counted backwards. 'So she must have met the father only a month or so back.'

Darren said, 'Yes, well, we was split up then. We'd had a real up and downer at Easter and didn't see each other for a few weeks. It happened then. It was nothing serious or nothing. She just got pissed one night . . .'

'You planned to keep the baby.' I made it a statement.

'Oh yes, sure we was going to keep it all right.'

I said, 'And the real father would never know.' Another statement inviting confirmation.

Darren looked shifty. He took in a mouthful and wiped his lips. He said, 'Maybe not.'

'Maybe not?' I pushed the words back across the table. You've got to do better than that, Darren.

He tucked his chin in like a boxer and started pulling his fingers again. I sighed. 'You might as well tell me.'

He owned up. 'Well, Shirl had a plan, see. She was going to go to him when the baby was born and make him pay up. She reckoned she could sting him hard. And he couldn't do nothing about it because she could always go to the Child Support Agency and make him pay.'

I said, 'Did he know Shirley was pregnant?'

'I don't know, do I? It don't matter anyhow. Shirl's dead.'

I said, 'And maybe he killed her.'

I left Darren mulling this one over. It hadn't occurred to him before. I was in desperate need of company. I flagged a cab and told the driver to take me to Hampton's. I was that desperate.

The bar was thronged with Fleet Street's hopeless cases. They welcomed me back to their bosom, asked after my injuries and made tasteless cracks about legovers. I smiled with a touching fortitude and limped to the corner where Mac was chatting up the new barmaid. He gave me his Mafia kiss and ordered up a glass.

He said, 'Jesus, boy, you've got a face on you as long as a Lurgan spade.'

I took his word for it. I said, 'I'm bored with my own company.'

'I always said you were a boring old fart.'

I raised my glass in gracious salute. I said, 'What's new with the world?'

He said, 'Not a lot, apart from that barmaid. She's Finnish, you know. She could finish me off any day.'

Mac has a way with words. I said, 'She probably will. Underneath that blonde wig is a bald man.'

He cackled, 'Sure they're all the same in the dark.'

The conversation made its usual headlong plunge into the abyss and the glasses kept coming. Half way down the second bottle Mac interrupted his own obscene observations to say, 'Here, have you seen they've found the murder weapon?'

'What murder weapon?'

'Claudine Tournier's, you eejit. It was caught up in some fella's anchor chain or something. He was pulling up the chain this morning when the gun fell out.'

I said, 'What was it?'

'A wee toy thing. A thirty-two,' Mac said.

Or what we in the trade like to call a ladies' gun. Czech-made, evidence of our burgeoning trade links with our old Commie foes. It had bits of a makeshift silencer still stuck to the barrel. The rest was blown away. There were no prints, no track record of any prior hits.

At this point the door to Hampton's shot open and the Wildebeest shambled in leading a conga of like-minded reprobates. All hope of sensible conversation was gone. I didn't mind. I'd been sensible all day long. It was too long for a grown man.

I settled into my castle keep with ease. There was an open-all-hours mini-mart within limping distance and I stocked myself up with instant meals, cigarettes and the other essentials of life. It was Thursday lunchtime and I was eating Bird's Eye cod mornay and tender sliced baby lamb plus hot 'n' spicy rice. That's the only trouble with instant meals. You need five of them before you feel a thing. I had my feet up and was deeply engrossed in *Coronation Street* videoed from the night before. I was thinking what a God-awful boozer the Rover's Return is when a wisp of a question drifted across my mind. Why, it whispered, don't you ring the Foundation and ask them straight out what they've got going in Kandy? This was the sort of question that any proper hack would have asked on Day One. I watched *Coronation Street* all the way through – by heck, lad, there's some reet ugly lasses oop north – before I called the Foundation. I wanted to get them before their lunchtime drinkies wore off. That's a tip to aspiring journalists. Between 2.30 and 3.30 is the best time to catch them unguarded. Get on first name terms as fast as you can. That way they forget themselves and think they're still talking to a mate in the bar. The only snag about this cunning ploy is you have to interrupt your own lunch break to do it, so it's useful only if you are a teetotaller or you're trying to impress the boss.

I got them to put me through to the Foundation's press office where a five-year-old girl squeaked a hello. I donned a Scottish accent, Edinburghian, I think it was. I said my name was Max Bygraves. I was a freelance journo who'd been commissioned by the *Big Issue* to do a bit on Claudine's Legacy of Love, and how the Foundation was functioning on, even though its founder had foundered.

The child identified herself as Jo Earley – 'But call me Jo.' She said super, and what did I want to know? She sounded too young to drink, so I abandoned my bar room mate approach. I went at Kandy from an oblique angle, starting off in Mozambique, shooting up to the Sudan and winging way out east to Vientiane. Jo kept up a running travelogue. I pretended to be taking notes, asking her to spell out place names or expand on a particular item. We travelled on. I guided Jo India-wards. Her voice went off the scale into bat-speak as she enthused over a street clinic in Bombay. She'd been there! She'd seen it for herself! It was true! Gosh!!! And I could have written a book about the Foundation's literacy programme in Bangladesh.

I asked in that laid back way of mine: 'Anything else on the Indian sub-continent?'

I had to explain what that meant. Yes indeed, said Jo. Much more. Self-help projects in Uttar Pradesh, ante natal care in the Punjab, birth control education all over the shop. I marvelled at the sheer scale of Claudine's empire and wondered how she ever found the time to go and get herself murdered.

Jo had run out of places and she still hadn't said a thing about Kandy. I directed our footsteps further south. 'Haven't you got something in Colombo too?'

A fluffy-headed pause. 'Where's Colombo?'

I said, 'In Sri Lanka.'

'Oh, there! No, we've nothing in Colombo, but there's a project in Kandy and I think that's in Sri Lanka.'

I sounded as if I didn't much care either. 'What you got there?'

Jo said, 'I'm not up to date on that one. I've never been there. But my boss has been to it several times. He could tell you all about it but he's out of the office right now. I'll just see what I've got on it.'

She was flipping through papers. 'Ah, here it is!' she yipped. 'It's a handicraft centre. That's all it says. Wait a minute, you're in luck. I can see my boss coming back now so you can talk to him, Mister Bygraves.'

'And what's his name, Jo?'

She said, 'Tomlin. Michael Tomlin.'

Well, well, well. You could have knocked me down with an 11-stone feather. I said, 'Sorry, Jo. I'll have to call him back. There's a call from New York holding on the other line.'

I brewed myself a Douwe Egberts decaff and did a think. A handicrafts centre? I couldn't picture Leon the Louse scooting off to the far reaches to buy himself a wooden elephant. Maybe the place turns out terrific saris. But none of this explained the panic in the Tomlin camp every time someone mentioned Kandy. Well, let's see what else the handicraft centre might keep under the counter. Drugs? Highly possible. Colombo is a handy stopover port for clippers plying their nefarious trade in unprocessed poppy juice from the Gulf of Bangkok. What else? Elephant tusks? Exotic but unlikely. I didn't know if Sri Lanka had any tigers worth bumping off and grinding up as aphrodisiacs for Chinese gents who have never heard of Kir Royale. Money laundering? For all I know, in Kandy they wash your dirty money in the street and pin it up to dry. But why bother going all the way to Sri Lanka? There are enough shysters within half a mile of the Barbican, tripping over each other to offer you their discreet services. There are even a couple of companies who make a bomb out of laundering IRA funds.

So what was so special about Kandy? I knew there wasn't much point in ringing up Sir Jimmy, inviting him out for a pint and asking him the score. If I tried Lewis Trefoyle, he'd probably get MI5 to lace my gin with an Undetectable Poison. I wandered around the flat kicking the chairs. When some stranger dressed like Zorro pours petrol down your trouser front you have a natural inclination to ask why. The answer to that one, I knew, lay way down there in Kandy.

I had a vague suggestion of an idea nibbling away at the back of my hand-crocheted head. I know the exact moment it slipped in. It was that afternoon when the Editor sat down by my hospital bedside, peeled himself a grape and suggested I take my wearisome bones off to Bali or some other place full of sunshine and drink at 5p a gallon. Surely, I reasoned, Sri Lanka was such a spot.

I hauled out the mobile and phoned our Travel Ed, Rick, a seasoned traveller who gets car sick on the way to work.

He said, 'Hi, Max. I was wondering when I'd hear from you. I've got a nice surprise.'

It was a surprise, and it was very, very nice, but not for me. A fortnight for two shacked up in a Barbados pleasure palace where the blue Caribbean licked the private beach clean every morning. A privileged resort where one could bask, bathe, scuba dive and walk on the water.

I said, 'Sounds magic, Rick. But to tell you the truth, I'd really love to go east.'

Rick sounded hurt and baffled. He said, 'Everything's built in on this one. Eat all you want, drink all you want. You don't have to pay a penny.'

I admit I was tempted, but my inner resolve held. The things I do for love. I said, 'You've gone to a lot of trouble setting it up, and thanks a million, Rick. It's my fault really. I should have let you know before, but I didn't feel well enough to ring.'

This was designed to have a triple-pronged effect: to stroke his ego, tell him I was an idiot who didn't know a gift horse when he saw one, and to elicit his sympathy. It hit the target on all three.

'No, I understand,' said Rick. 'I kept this one for you because it's such a gem, but if you don't want to go to Barbados, that's that. Now tell me where you are thinking about and I'll see what I can do. Thailand? Bali?'

I said, 'Sri Lanka, actually.'

He muted his surprise. 'Sri Lanka? You know

they're still having trouble with the Tamil Tigers? Tourists aren't allowed in the north.'

I said I knew, but crazy little fool that I was, I had my heart set on it. Rick thought aloud: 'I don't think the Sri Lanka tourist people lay on any press trips. Maybe Air Lanka does. Or some of the better package holiday companies. You want a trip for two, don't you?'

I said I did. He said he'd try. I put the phone away feeling a right little clever clogs.

Normally I don't care a fig for freebies. There's a grave danger you might end up on a trip with the agony aunt of the *Basildon Bugle*, wittering on about the grub. I'd best explain how freebies work. Travel companies, airlines, cruise lines and so on deluge newspaper travel eds with offers of free holidays. In the office the prime trips are shared out among those the Editor loves. That leaves me out for a start. It's a sobering thought that I had to get myself nearly flambéd before I was allowed to join the club. The Editor's pet pets get all the top junkets – *QE2* cruises, China, bloody Bali etc. Then you come down to the middle rankers who get to roast their bums in Kenya or freeze their tootsies off in Iceland. Lower still, the office toadies clamour for a gîte in the Dordogne or a week off-season in a farmhouse in Tuscany. At the bottom of the pile are the menial minions who are content with a weekend in the West Country. Self catering.

All of these souls, be they a night editor golfing in Augusta, or a features sub caravanning in Wales, are charged with the same awesome responsibility: they have to write a travel feature – anything up to 800 words of unmitigated claptrap. Naturally it's in everyone's interest to keep the freebies rolling in, therefore if you had your wallet nicked in Naples or developed full-blown dysentery in the Dominican Republic, you tend to brush that aside and write about the friendly folk and the delicious food.

Freebies come with several strings attached. Often the donor company invites a group of journos. This is the Press Trip. If, as so often happens, you find yourself saddled with a bunch of social lepers, you get homesick pretty quickly. Sometimes you end up in the company of travel writers who are even worse. Many years back I did a story which the Editor actually liked. He sent me off to Malta for revenge. My fellow travellers were all travel writers. All the day long they talked of nothing else but last year in Marienbad or the jaunt to Aspen, Ho Chi Minh city, wherever. They went to bed at ten with Agatha Christie books. I don't think they even knew which continent we were in. Tour companies aren't bright enough to invite a bunch of horny-handed hacks together, so you don't have any drinking mates. I became an expert on Malta's singles bars.

When you're safely home in England and receiving medication, then you start thinking about the 800 words you have to write. The best way into it is through an anecdote, usually invented. Here's how it goes:

It is not often you stroll along a sea-kissed beach, scented by frangipani, and chance upon a golden doubloon.

I came across several, one too many in fact, and had to retire to my hammock in the shade of the whispering palms to regain my bearings.

For on Bloggoland, the idyllic isle where Captains Blood and Blackbeard once buried their booty, a golden doubloon is not what it used to be.

These days it's the name of a swashbuckling cocktail – a large jigger of rum with a generous drop of brandy, topped off with grenadine and lime.

If Blackbeard were still holding court in Bloggoland's pretty harbour, I'm sure he would happily exchange his golden doubloons for the 20th century version . . .

Now all you need is a linking sentence, say something along the lines of – *The buccaneering tradition of this enchanted Caribbean paradise lives on in its lively carnivals and street parties.*

After that you pick up the tour company's brochure and tap in whole chunks of it, right down to the stuff about the island's happy, innocent ways. You conveniently forget that Bloggoland is the Numero Uno refuelling point for planes weighed down with Colombian cocaine.

That's the way you do it. Pick up any tabloid on Saturday and you read whole pages of sheer garbage that would set your teeth on edge.

But then maybe I'm just ethical.

Chapter Ten

I was ferreting around in my brother's drawers looking for salacious stuff (the nearest I came was a pair of lilac boxer shorts with big pink hearts) when my bleep let me know it was still working. News Desk desired concourse. It was Nigel, Angela Whipple's deputy.

'Nothing important, Max. Just thought you'd be interested – Leon Knapp is back in Britain.'

I said, 'He must have come via Lourdes. Last I heard he was sick as a pig.'

A matey laugh from Nige. 'Seems he had a bleeding ulcer.'

I said, 'I've got a bleeding headache but I don't make a song and dance about it.'

More sounds of hilarity. I said, 'What's he got to say for himself?'

Nigel said, 'He's not talking. He got into Heathrow and they drove him away airside.'

Airside is the private bit. Hacks aren't allowed into it except by special arrangement.

Nigel said, 'His manager came out with a statement. Let's see. Where is it? Ah, here we are: "Leon, as everyone knows, is a true professional and he is very upset that he missed engagements. He hopes to resume his career in the very near future. He has returned to his home and we ask that the Press respect his privacy until he is fully recovered".'

I said, 'The manager's not saying what Leon was up to in Sri Lanka.'

Nigel said, 'No, but showbiz asked him if Leon had a nervous breakdown.'

'And?'

I could hear the shrug. 'He just said the ulcer was brought on by stress.'

I had an idea. I was having a great day for ideas. I said, 'Nige, put me through to showbiz.'

I got on to the luvvies, let them know it was me and asked for Knapp's home number. 'Why?'

They can be ever so precious, showbiz reporters. I told them I was a Leon fan from way back. They didn't believe me. I pulled rank and said it was none of their business. They squealed and fluttered but they gave me a number. Somewhere way out in the Berkshire badlands.

I gave it a call. Brriinng-brinnngg, brriinng-brriinnngg it went without answer. I switched off the mobile and thought about it. Maybe he was there, but didn't feel like talking to strangers. But how did he know it was a stranger calling? I remembered ex-Sir Anthony Blunt, former keeper of the Queen's pictures and well known traitor. When the story broke about him Blunt stayed in his flat, refusing to answer the phone. Yet we knew his chums had been able to get through. Finally one of us, not me this time, had a brainwave. He called Blunt, let the phone ring out three times and he put it down again. Then he called back immediately. Blunt picked it up immediately. 'Hello,' he said. And the hack got a quote or two.

It's a wheeze I've used many a time since. It works once in twenty times. I used it today on Leon Knapp, alias Leo Knapowski.

'Hello,' he said in fluent Brummie.

I positively gushed, 'Leon! You're home! Thank God for that!'

He said, 'Who's that?' There was a thin edge to his voice. Tension or native dialect. I couldn't tell which.

I elbowed the question aside and pushed on, showering exclamation marks down the phone. 'We were so worried! Poor you! It must have been such a shock! I was absolutely horrified when I heard you were in hospital!'

'Is that Ted?' The edge was sharper.

I rushed on heedless. 'I've been talking to my dad and he had ulcer trouble some years back. He said what really did the trick for him was yoghurt. Not ordinary yoghurt, but that lovely, thick, creamy Greek yoghurt. You can get it from any Waitrose or Sainsburys. You get a tub of that, stir in a big, big spoonful of honey, the clear honey, and it does you the world of good, and . . .'

It didn't sound as if I was doing Leon's ulcer any good at all. He cut across me tetchily: 'Who are you? Why are you calling?'

'Me?' You could see my eyebrows arch in astonishment. 'This is Bobby. Bobby Maxwell. I know Sir

James. That's how I got your number. But as I was saying, it's great to know you'll soon be up and about . . .'

Our Leon was a suspicious cove. He accused: 'I don't know you. What did you say your name was?'

I chimed a peal of laughter. 'Of course you don't know me. It's Bobby. Just ask Sir James about me. By the way, I was at his place in Switzerland recently and I had *a great* time. You should ask him for the loan of it. You could get yourself fighting fit there, and the great charm of it is it's very private, well away from all those snooping reporters.'

Knapp said, 'Look, Bobby, whoever you are, it's kind of you to call, but I'm trying to get some rest. Goodbye.'

I jumped in before he could get the phone down. I said, 'You've been eating too many Kandy curries.'

I had his attention again. He said warily, 'What about Kandy?'

'Kandy? I'm going there next week.'

He poked at the statement with his toe. He said, 'That's funny. I've never heard anyone mention any Bobby.'

I lit a Bensons and puzzled over what to say next. When I answered I sounded even more guarded than him. I said, 'You know the form, Leon. We've all got to be discreet.'

He didn't answer but he was still listening. He needed something more. I said, 'There were plans to close Kandy down, you know.'

An edgy 'Yeah?' Nothing else. But I was headed the right direction. I thought back to that moment in

Switzerland when Sir James and I glared at each other while his little piece of mischief, Miss Emma Pearson, went haywire on the hall phone.

I said, 'I was in Switzerland with Jimmy and Emma when the balloon went up. He was livid.'

'Yeah.' Stripped of any nuance.

I took a shot in the murk. 'You weren't flavour of the month, Leon. But I expect you know that.'

I held my breath waiting for him. I was turning purple round the ears when he finally said, 'I'm out of it.'

Out of what? Out of his minuscule mind on coke? Out of the white slave trade? Out of clean underwear?

I said, 'That's a shame, Leon. I was hoping you could give me a few traveller's tips on Kandy and the handicraft centre.'

'The what?'

Hellfire and damnation. I'd said the wrong thing. We were right back to his impersonation of a brick wall with paranoia. I tried an all-mates-together laugh. 'You know what I mean. The set-up.'

Leon said, 'Who are you?'

That was the third time he'd asked me, and the third time I didn't feel inclined to tell him. I said, 'I know we've never met, but just call me a friend.'

I think he wanted to call me something altogether different. He said, 'I've told you: I'm out of it. If you want to know something, ask the others.'

And the phone went down with a clatter and a clunk.

I slid off to the shower to think things over. Big brother Dominic pampers himself in the hygiene department. I splashed myself all over with Givenchy bath oil and plastered my locks with lashings of creamy lanolin. I smelt so sweet I could almost fancy myself. All the while the high-powered shower battered me senseless. I emerged fresh and pink and somewhat eroded. I wrapped my fragrant form in Dominic's robe, uncorked the Booths and draped myself across a chair.

The ulcerous Leon is the talkative type by nature. His every sentence begins with a capital I and carries a me or two, with the odd myself thrown in, just in case the listener forgets who the star is around here. But he'd been curiously reticent during our little chat. He'd doled out a few dozen words at most. Strange. Taken on their own, Leon's utterings were about as meaningful as anything he ever sang. But when I dovetailed them into what little I knew, he had blabbed his head off.

First, whatever was going on in Kandy it was not the sort of thing you talked about in front of the children. Second, Sir James and the 'others' were embroiled in it. Third, there had been a major flap, and Leon was the cause of it. He was no longer a part of the Kandy club. I guessed he hadn't left of his own accord. He'd sounded miffed when he said, 'I'm out of it.'

My paisley patterned shins poked out of the paisley patterned robe. I frowned at them. I wanted to be on the next plane to Sri Lanka. But not on pins like these. And certainly not togged up like Noel Coward. I started my preparations anyway. I spent the next hour ransacking Dominic's wardrobe for suitable gear.

He had a couple of lightweights and a drawerful of casual stuff. I made my selection, packed a baby Samsonite, adding razors, soap etc. Big Brother didn't have a camera, or if he did, he was off somewhere snapping beavers with it. I said, 'Never mind, you can always buy yourself an Olympus in duty free.' And then I said, 'Balls, you're not a monkey.' I got on the phone again, this time to ace lensman Frankie Frost. I know precisely what makes Frankie happy. I said, 'Fancy a little trip to a land of dusky maidens and curry galore?'

'Wot – Bradford?'

Sometimes you despair. I told him. He gibbered with delight and climbed a nearby wall.

'Frankie,' I said, when he'd got himself down again, 'this is real secret squirrel stuff. You mustn't tell anyone in the office.'

He had difficulty taking that one in. I tried again. 'No one must know. Nobody. Not even your girlfriend.'

He seemed to latch on. I don't think he tells her much anyway. I briefed him to get himself a visa, to grab my spare passport from Foreign Desk and do likewise. Frankie said, 'Done. Why all the secrecy?'

I said, 'Walls have ears.'

He said, 'You all right, Max?'

I felt out the bump on my head with tender searching fingers. It was still in the same place. 'Yes, I'm hunky-dory. Do me a favour and meet me tonight in the Ball and Chain. About eight.'

Frankie assumed the monkey's traditional role of penniless artiste. He mumbled, 'I'm broke.'

I said, 'I'm buying them.'

That did the trick.

I had a reason for pouring drink down his throat. I knew Frankie would dearly love to pack up his gizmos and come play with me in Sri Lanka. But I also knew he would want to do that only if the office was picking up the bill. If he thought he might have to reach in his own laden pockets he'd have conniptions. I had to hit him when his resistance was low.

We met up in the Ball and Chain. By day it's awash with lawyers, the Old Bill, hacks, murderers' alibi witnesses and similar scum. In the evening it is a quiet, half-civilised place where they even wash the glasses sometimes.

Frankie handed me a stack of mail. Get-well-never cards, I suspected. I pushed the pile aside and asked him about his week. He was in fine fettle. He'd had a good one. Monday he was at Gatwick, snapping the girl whose boyfriend got shot on their New Orleans honeymoon. The *Mail* had bought her up so she wouldn't be posing for any pix. But all the papers sent people just to give the *Mail* minders a hard time of it. We do that a lot. It's great fun.

Frankie started a rumpus in the arrivals lounge, punched a *Mirror* hack on the nose and sent the tearful widow sprawling. This might be seen as a touch heartless, seeing the poor girl had just lost her bridegroom. Normally we would be more considerate. But once someone sells their story to another paper, they become a legitimate target for all the others.

Those are the rules. And she was a star player in the game. If she didn't like it, she could always give the *Mail* their twenty grand back and the hacks would behave like the proper little gentlemen we are.

She was still sobbing as the *Mail* boys hustled her out of the terminal and threw her in the back of a limo. They'd blown it there because they forgot to get one with tinted glass. The widow wanted to sit up but the *Mail* heavies kept nailing her to the floor so no one else could get a shot of her. Every now and then she fought free to stick her head out the window and hurl obscenities at the pursuing pack. Then the *Mail* muscle would sit on her again. The upshot was everybody got a pic, and a far better pic than the *Mail*'s. The three-day bride made a four-column show on all the tabloid front pages next day, looking hysterical, haggard and ravaged by tears. Everyone stuck made up quotes on top of the snatched pic. 'Bring Back My Billy' (*Mirror*). 'Our Honeymoon Hell' (*Star*). 'Bill Bonked My Bridesmaid' (*Sun*). 'Man Has Cabbage Heart Transplant' (*Sport*). The only losers were the *Mail* who showed the ex-bride all noble and grieving, a single tear trickling mascara down her chops. They had sent one of their Sybil Fawlty weepie writers who penned 1,500 words of slush.

Anyway, back to the Ball & Chain and Frankie. I let him spin out his over-egged account of the day, ensuring his glass was never empty. He finished his ripping yarn and remembered me. 'What's this hush-hush trip about, then?'

I checked the bar for eavesdroppers, bugs and lip readers just to impress him and led him to a corner table. I told him the score. All he and I stood to gain from it was a couple of free flights, I said. After that we paid our own way. If we got a story, we could rip off the office hand over fist in exes. If not, we had each sacrificed a week's holiday and whatever it cost us in food and lodgings. I didn't mention drink. Frankie knew I'd take care of that.

When I'd finished he looked a stricken man. I didn't blame him. Now that I'd spelt out the deal it didn't sound that attractive to me either. I woke the barman and got another two drinks in. Frankie gulped a gollop of London Pride. He slid me a nervous glance. I could hear his little monkey brain thinking. It was thinking: 'Max is mad. It must be that bump on the beam.'

I said, 'You think I'm crazy.'

He didn't even try to humour me. He said, 'You're bloody bananas. Why should we fund the office on a story? What do you expect to get anyway?'

Two unanswerable questions. I force-fed him a cigarette to shut him up. I said, 'Frankie, you know you're the best snapper we've got. That's why I'm asking you. If anyone can get the story, it's you.'

Frankie is by no means our best monkey. There are at least three up the tree ahead of him. But he's a good foot-in-the-door man, and he's easily led. Not this time. He gave a sour laugh. 'That sod Belker knocked a hundred off my French exes. And you're saying we should do a foreign for free. No way.'

I argued this way and that. Frankie was unmoving. In desperation I hinted he might even win an award if he landed the story. Hacks and monkeys alike go all funny whenever anyone mentions awards. Our official line is: 'Awards? Who cares about them?' Unofficially we live in the pathetic hope that we might land one. And if our dreams are realised, we say: 'This silly old thing? I never wanted it. The Editor forced me to enter.' I remember the quote from a gnarled hack who late in his years finally bagged one: 'Awards are like piles. Sooner or later every bum gets them.' Only he didn't say bum.

Thus far Frankie had not even picked up a Highly Commended. No doubt this irked. I let him chew on the idea that Sri Lanka might eventually fill that gap on the lavatory wall while I ripped into my mail. American Express had sent me a wrist-slapping billet doux over the matter of an unpaid £1,264. The next missive was more interesting. It read:

> Hello Max,
>
> I'm really sorry you feel I'm holding out on you. I am holding out, because it's something I cannot bring myself to tell you. I don't know if I ever shall.
>
> I did not have anything to do with the attempt on your life. That is truly unthinkable. Whether you like it or not, I still regard you as my nearest and dearest friend.
>
> You may be in danger, but most certainly NOT from me. If you need my help in any way, just call.

The big scrawl at the bottom of the page said Ross. I laughed. It was one of those hollow jobs. Across the table Frankie looked up. 'All right, one for the strasse,' he said proffering his empty glass.

I tottered over to the bar where I was greeted without enthusiasm. I eyed myself in the mirror while the barman jiggled the optic. My face didn't look happy and it felt the same. Frankie was not falling for my wizard wheeze. I was still at the bar, double-checking my change, when I heard an amazing Whisssh-bisssh-BOOOF! From the corner. I swung around and there was Frankie running for cover. The middle of the table where we had been sitting was ablaze. Either American Express was doing a new line in blistering reminders or my private mail had self-combusted. I snatched up a water jug, shot over to the corner and splashed it on the bonfire. It blazed on. Frankie poked his head up by the fruit machine and started yelling for a fire extinguisher.

The barman rolled out from behind the counter armed with another jug. An interested bystander thoughtfully kicked the burning pile off the table, thereby almost setting the whole place alight. Frankie joined in the fun, jumping up and down on anything that glowed. Together, splashing and stamping, we beat the hell out of the fire, and mightily proud of ourselves we were too. The barman went off to phone the Law while Frankie and I fished ash out of our drinks. I turned over the charred debris with a delicate toe. The guilty party was a manila Jiffy bag, or what used to be a manila Jiffy bag. Now only a couple of singed corners remained. Them and a scorched contraption with wires protruding.

'What the hell's that?' asked Frankie, keeping his distance.

'That,' I said, 'is a warning.'

'What warning?'

'A warning to keep away from Sri Lanka.'

Frankie licked a burn mark the size of an amoeba on his hand. He was not used to letter bombs going off mid-drink. The experience made him a truculent and vengeful monkey. He gave the letter bomb a boot.

I flicked burnt paper from my sleeve. 'That settles it,' I said.

'Settles what?'

I said, 'There's no way I can ask you to go to Kandy if you could get hurt.'

Frankie said, 'Bollocks. Try keeping me away.'

'But, Frankie,' I said in angelic tones, 'I could never forgive myself if something happened to you. These buggers aren't kidding about, you know.'

He pointed at his invisible scar. 'See that? Nobody does that to Frank Frost.'

I murmured a weak protestation. He steam-rollered it down. He stuck his uninjured hand in a bulging pocket. He said, 'Right, let's have a drink and talk about Sri Lanka.'

We were savouring the first sips when an idea suddenly struck a match in his beady eyes.

'You know something?' he said. 'This is the kind of story that wins awards.'

We had to wait a week before Rick the Travel Ed came up with the trip. I fretted and kicked my heels, or Dominic's heels anyway. I needed something else to fill my waking hour. Which was why I fled the fortress one fine morning to seek stimulus at East London coroner's court. On the menu today was the item of Shirley Patricia Ham, late of Loughton, in the county of Essex. It was just the formal opening. Normally hacks don't bother to cover these. They don't provide copy. What happens is a copper gets up and says the corpse of the deceased was found at such and such a spot and identification was made by so and so. I was the sole hack present and the coroner gave me a fishy look. I heard a subbed down version of the autopsy. Shirley died from asphyxiation, the coroner's clerk read out. I blinked. A portly middle-aged man with a scrubby moustache paddled in, followed closely by a woman who looked just like him, minus the whiskers. I recognised them as Shirley's mum and dad. You don't usually get family at inquest openings. They sat very close to each other at the back of the room while D.I. Harold Pennycuik got up on his hind legs and said inquiries were continuing. The coroner said thanks a lot folks and adjourned the inquest until July 23.

I grabbed Shirley's dad as he emerged blinking in the sunshine. He was dry-eyed, but you could see he was not quite with us. I poked my hand out. I said who I was and how sorry I was. Mr Ham stepped back and looked me up and down. He was considering whether I might have murdered his only child. After a moment's careful appraisal he declared me not guilty.

He said, 'Shirley didn't meet you that night.'

I said no, that's why I'd called him. I asked if she'd told him what she planned to tell me. He hesitated, trying to get it right. 'No. She just said, see you later, I'm just going to see Mike about something.'

'Max,' I corrected automatically.

'Max,' he said.

I said, 'But she never hinted what her information was?'

Mr Ham waggled his head. He said, 'I can't remember. But she was expecting to get something from you.'

Yes, large wads of fivers, I thought. I said, 'Shirley had been selling us stories.'

Mr Ham looked at me hard. 'I hope my daughter was not murdered just for helping you get a cheap story,' he said.

And off he walked, leaving me feeling like whoever it was who killed Cock Robin.

I was in a bar in Cheapside, trying to convince myself I wasn't such a bad sort after all, when my bleep bleep-bleeped. At first I didn't know it was mine. The place was stacked to the rafters with City white collar criminals, each armed with mobile phones, pagers, parking alarms. There was also the electronic trill of the till plus the microwave timer adding to the gaiety of the moment. When my pager gave voice, half a dozen adjoining drinkers dived into their pockets. It took me a moment to suss out I was the wanted man. My neighbours glared at me. I pressed the message button and said, 'Jesus Christ!' Right out loud. I read the message again. It still said the same thing: 'PSE CALL SIR JAMES TOMLIN SOONEST – NEWS DESK'. I didn't. I ordered another gin soonest and did a spot of pondering. Why should the mighty midget feel the pressing need for my conversation? Maybe they'd watered the gin, or else they'd beefed up the tonic, because I didn't come up with any answers. I sought out the gents, locked myself in a cubicle and dialled the Tomlin number. My old chum, the snotty twerp in Sir James's private office, answered. He recognised my voice too. He asked me where I was calling from and I told him precisely where. I don't think he believed me but he was ever so polite. He said, 'If it is convenient for you, Mister Chard, Sir James would very much like to see you.'

'Why?'

'I believe he wishes to have a conversation with you.'

'Where?'

'Wherever is suitable for you.'

I said, 'Maybe he would like to meet me at my convenience.' It wasn't a great joke, but it deserved at least a ripple. He ignored it.

He said, 'Sir James is free now. He's here, of course.'

I said, 'Where's here of course?'

He gave me an address in Victoria Street, a ten minute limp from my present address. I said I was having a drink with a murder squad detective and would be there shortly. This was a subtle way of saying that if my body turned up in the Thames, the Old Bill would know where to point the finger.

I took my time ambling round to the premises of Freleng-Bourke. It was a slabby office block with mauve windows. It looked like it had liver trouble. A sallow individual, decked out as a security guard, shepherded me to reception, where a Miss Jamaica lookalike turned on a smile that warmed the cockles of my heart and much more besides. She led me like a puppy down a flecked marble corridor to a flecked marble lift. We were alone. Miss Jamaica hit the top button. She was cool and spicy and delicious. I was none of these. I joked feebly: 'You're going all the way with me?'

She gave an easy languid laugh. 'All the way.'

By the time we hit the penthouse floor I was a grinning imbecile. She didn't seem to notice. Off she tripped down another marble corridor, pink this time, with me panting a yard or so in arrears. She knocked on an acre of pink tinted ash. A voice commanded: 'Come in.'

We came in. She said, 'Mister Chard to see you, Sir James.' And she was gone. I felt as if someone had turned off the sun.

Tomlin said, 'Won't you sit down, Mister Chard?' He indicated a fragile settee with spindly little legs. I eased myself down. He was already seated, but he got up from behind his desk and opened a cupboard knee deep in bottles and glasses.

'Care for a drink?'

I said I cared for a gin. He did the business and helped himself to a thimble of sherry. He handed over the glass and pulled up an ancient chair to face me. It was higher off the ground than my chi-chi settee so our eyes were level. But his were half hidden behind his tinted specs. They went with the mauve windows.

I sampled the gin and inspected the privileges of high office. Floor to ceiling roman blinds across a panoramic window. Bland walls, dotted here and there with shots of bods in dinner jackets smirking at each other. Squidgy buff carpet littered with antique chairs and sideboards. It didn't look much like an office.

'Care for a cigar?' he pushed a silver box my way. I shook my head.

'A cigarette?' Another silver box.

I was wondering what he was going to offer me next. Miss Jamaica? I accepted a cigarette and eyed him through the smoke. He said, 'I'm sure you're wondering why I asked you here.'

I indicated that a certain perplexity had crossed my mind. He had his lips set in a benign smile. The sort of smile that doctors in looney bins wear to work. He tacked one leg over the other and regarded me fondly. He said, 'I believe we started off on the wrong foot, Mister Chard, or may I call you Max?'

I said, 'Okay, Jimmy.'

The smile slipped off the edge of his mouth. He said, 'When we met in Switzerland, I was understandably upset. My wife had just been murdered and I suspected that you were a muck-raking reporter.'

He got that one right. I nursed my gin and didn't say a thing.

Tomlin said, 'So I hope you will forgive my brusqueness at our first meeting. I am not by nature a discourteous man.'

I thought that one deserved a smile.

He pushed on. 'I have subsequently learned that you are a highly respected crime journalist and that you were engaged in the legitimate pursuit of a news story. I know you have since tried to contact me and have been, ah, fobbed off. I'll be honest with you, Max. I was still upset about the incident in Switzerland.'

I tipped my cigarette in an ashtray the size of a soup tureen. I said, 'So what's changed?'

He flipped over the palm of a hand. 'I felt I was being unreasonable. I have asked you here so that we can speak without rancour. I believe you wish to ask me some questions about my late wife's work. I understand this. You are involved in reporting a story: my only interest is to see my wife's killer brought to justice. The two are not incompatible. I have already spoken at length to the police. However, I feel your persistence is to be welcomed. Investigative journalists can sometimes succeed where the proper authorities have failed.'

It was a lengthy speech. It made me feel thirsty. I peered into my empty glass. He took the hint and gave the gin bottle another squeeze. He sat himself down again, switched on the smile and said, 'Now, what do you want to talk about?'

I said, 'Kandy.'

His voice drifted up a semi-tone. 'Kandy? I gather you are referring to my wife's WorldCare work?'

I said he had gathered correctly. He eased back in his chair and studied the distant ceiling.

'Kandy,' he said, 'is the location for one of her many projects.'

So far he hadn't even stuck a name on Claudine. I said, 'And what's so special about it?'

A light cocktail party laugh. He treated himself to a little sigh. He said, 'You see, I am perplexed, because to be totally frank, the Sri Lankan operation is a very minor part of the Foundation's programme.'

I sipped my gin.

Tomlin said, 'In various parts of the Third World, the Foundation has specific projects which are intended to focus on self help. For example, in Mozambique there is a rural farming project . . .'

I said, 'And in Kandy?'

'In Kandy there is a cultural crafts centre. Its aim is to encourage local skills by producing and selling traditional handiwork. Batiks, hand-woven silks, jewellery. The island is rich in gem stones, you know. The centre sells its products to tourists and the money helps to fund other local activities.'

I said, 'It's a souvenir shop.'

'If you like, yes.'

I said, 'But what makes it so popular?'

Tomlin frowned. 'I'm afraid I don't quite understand.'

I said, 'Leon Knapp speaks highly of it.'

He said sharply, 'You've spoken to him?'

I said, 'Oh yes. At length. I got him when he came home and we had a good natter about what goes on in Kandy.'

Tomlin forgot to smile. He sat rock still, his specs scanning my face.

I said carelessly, 'Seems like Leon had a great old time of it in Kandy. But he didn't say much about arts and crafts.'

Tomlin sat there holding his glass tightly. He got up and toddled off to the drinks bar to top up his sherry. He called, 'Care for another drink?'

People should never say: 'Care for another drink?' It makes you sound like an alco. They should say: 'Let me top you up', or, better still, just snatch your glass and splosh drink into it. I overcame my distaste. 'Thanks.'

Tomlin said, 'What did Leon say?' He still had his back to me. The words came out as hard as little stones.

I went coy. 'I'd rather not go into that.'

He returned with a gin, a miserly sample this time. He attempted a laugh. 'Leon can be quite a joker.'

'He said some very funny things.'

Tomlin was working out how to follow this when there was a brisk knock on the door. It sailed open before he had a chance to say come in. A man in his late twenties entered. He eyed me suspiciously.

'My son,' said Tomlin.

He grunted. 'Pleasedtomeetyou.' I knew the voice. This was the stroppy herbert who answered my calls. He didn't offer to shake hands.

Little Tomlin senior said to big Tomlin junior, 'We were talking about the Kandy project.'

Junior looked baleful but didn't speak. Tomlin turned back to me. He said, 'I think that's all I can tell you. If you have any further queries, please don't hesitate to call. Michael and I would be delighted to help.'

I felt all hurt. Sir James didn't want me around any more. I emptied my glass and stood up. I said, 'Thanks, but I'll get all I want when I'm out there.'

'Out there?' This from Tomlin junior.

I said, 'Yes. Didn't I say? I'm going to Kandy next week.'

I showed myself out. The Tomlins had suddenly developed rigor mortis.

On the way out of the building, Miss Jamaica and I dazzled each other with our smiles.

Chapter Eleven

We caught an early One-Eleven out of Heathrow. It was the first of June but it looked like the thirty-first of January. Neither of us felt like talking. We met up in the departure lounge, had a beer apiece and opened our papers. I was reading a fun-filled story about a gym mistress who had run off with her star pupil. Her star girl pupil. But my mind wasn't on it. I don't quite know where it was. Sometimes it was back with Rosie who wasn't speaking to me any more ('You rotten sod – we were supposed to be going on holiday to the Maldives'). Sometimes it was with the Old Bill and the letter bomb ('Seems like somebody else doesn't like you' – D.I. Harry 'Horselaughs' Pennycuik). Occasionally it strayed to that glorious moment in the office, the day I dropped in to pick up my exes. I'd been zipping down the corridor when the bog door popped open and out bulged the evil Belker. He put on a slimy smile and asked after my health. I said I was feeling wonderful, just to piss him off. He said that was great, but what was I doing in the office? Was I back in harness already? Oh no, I responded. It was much, much too soon for that. I gave him the sunniest of smiles and said the Editor had insisted I go on a nice freebie. And whither was I bound? he inquired, in the fond hope it was someplace renowned for its malarial mosquitoes and rabid bats. I said, 'Do you remember that time I asked you to send me to Kandy?'

He nodded dumbly, his lizard eyes sick with premonition.

I said, 'Well, I'm off to Sri Lanka in the morning.'

The Beast Belker paled beneath his pallor. His eyes went squiffy and his jaw froze. I stood there beaming at him, watching his lips grind out: 'Have a nice time.'

'I will,' I assured him. 'I will.'

And off I swung down the corridor, whistling a breezy tune.

It was a happy memory. Less happy was the memory of my flaming hate mail. They'd called in the anti-terrorist gang to see if the letter bomb had the stamp of the Animal Liberation Front, the IRA or similar headbangers. It didn't. It was a homemade affair with a couple of ounces of gunpowder, a battery and a crude trigger. The general principle was for it to go pop as soon as I ripped open the envelope. Fate didn't like the idea. It had a better plan which involved Frankie pushing the envelope into a beer puddle while I was off buying yet more drink. The beer soaked through the envelope, short circuited the electrics and set the thing off.

I asked the anti-terrorist ace what would have happened if I had opened it as planned. He said at worst I might have lost my typing finger. So it was just a nuisance bomb, a way of letting me know the baddies still hadn't forgotten me. I went through the whole Claudine Tournier/Shirley Ham story with them. The anti-terrorist blokes got bored and went off to practise drilling holes in cardboard men. Big Ben Ashbee, the super fronting the murder inquiry, listened sadly and told me to watch my step. His cliché, not mine. I suggested he lock up Sir James Tomlin and his brigands for my protection. Nothing doing. But did I want someone riding shotgun on me in London? I pictured a large Plod sharing my Barbican retreat and boring me senseless with his colourful memoirs of booking desperado motorists who hadn't paid their road tax. I said no thank you, Ben. I'd just sleep with a loaded ballpoint under the pillow. He seemed to think that would do the trick.

The airport speaker went bing bong and a girl who had gone to elocution lessons announced the departure of KLM 338 to Amsterdam. Would passengers kindly get off their backsides and scurry along to Gate Thirty-six. Frankie and I were in devilish mood so we hung on for the final call.

The flight was half empty. Our fellow fliers were business types with personal organisers and stripey ties. They took the *FT* or *Der Telegraaf* from the courtesy trolley. The flash ones took both. None of the suits looked capable of anything more violent than slapping the temp's rump.

I wasn't really in the mood, but I had a Dutch gin, noblesse oblige and I read the duty free tariff with the fascination of a connoisseur. Frankie fell asleep with his mouth open and his legs across the aisle. We skimmed down into Schipol, taking care to avoid the high-rise flats. It was coming up their lunchtime. Just gone my breakfastime.

Frankie and I legged it over to the long haul terminal where he found a kiddies' room littered with space invader machines. He pushed a couple of blond infants out of the way and started blowing green blobs to purple bits. I'm not sure if he was even looking at the screen. He just wanted to press buttons. Monkeys are suckers for that sort of thing. A blissful smile wrapped itself halfway around his face. The machines were for free. There was also a video cartoon channel, but that was probably beyond his attention span.

I left him playing in the kindergarten while I converted some of my pounds into guilders and cruised the duty free mall. Schipol has a great reputation as a happy shopping ground, but I've never figured out why. If ever I feel like blowing seventy quid on an Armani tie, there's a friendly psychiatrist I know.

We had three hours to kill before the Colombo flight. I treated myself to some muddy coffee, a hunk of rubber cheese and croissants which tasted marginally less interesting than balsa wood. I had an Amstel beer to placate my aggrieved palate. Ten quid, thank you werry much. Our flight flashed up on the departures board. I went and detached Frankie from his machine. His pupils were scooting around like space invaders on warp factor five.

There was a double security check, which meant everyone bound for Sri Lanka had to stand by clicking their tongues for five minutes while Frankie demonstrated that his various geegaws were not ingeniously disguised bombs. I don't know why they bothered.

Anybody could see he was too tall to be a Tamil Tiger. A Tamil Camel, maybe.

On the plane our seats were about three inches from the in-flight movie screen. Besides which my earphones didn't work. I explained our predicament to a blonde concealing her naked body in the blue uniform of a KLM stewardess. She laughed gaily and said tough titty. Hacks do not take kindly to being treated without due respect. We started a row. She called up reinforcements in the shape of her twin sisters. They roped in the head steward who was hiding in the galley. Pretty soon the whole plane was in uproar as they scoured it for alternative seats. We rejected their first suggestions out of hand. They were in the no smoking ghetto. We eventually got what we wanted, a pair of seats near the galley, so that we could summon up refreshments more easily. It's a terrible thing to admit, but hacks get a buzz out of starting petty rows like these. It keeps our adrenalin on stream.

The 747 swung out wide over Amsterdam and hid itself in a cloud a thousand miles long. I'd exhausted the papers. The only thing to do was follow our progress on the screen map. They waited an hour and stuck on a movie. It was some candyfloss effort about a sexy pizza girl who teams up with a lunatic chef to bilk the Mafia out of fifty zillion dollars. She kept her clothes on, otherwise I might have enjoyed it. Six miles beneath us Greece slumbered while I snoozed. Frankie went into a coma. I woke up in Oman in brazen sunshine. So this was where Leon Knapp was stretchered off. It didn't look a jolly place to have a bleeding ulcer, or even a head cold. Frankie slept on.

Off we flew again, out across the Persian Gulf and tacking south east over the Indian Ocean. Sri Lanka finally put in an appearance. I gazed down on a green and sunny isle and wondered what dark secret lurked beneath its leafy canopy. I was feeling melodramatic.

They poured us off at Colombo about ten in the morning. Everyone seemed delighted to see us. We flashed our cheesiest smiles and charmed through immigration. I sent Frankie to change £1,000 into coin of the realm while I sought out a taxi. The cab bosses lived in a cubby hole by the information desk.

I said to one: 'Mount Lavinia.'

He gave me a dirty look. I wondered whether he had a sister called Lavinia. Another driver came to the rescue. 'No Mount Lavinia, sir,' he said happily.

I had a brochure in my pocket which promised paradise at 'the magical Mount Lavinia hotel'. I also had two ocean-front rooms booked there. I showed them the brochure.

'Ah, Mount Lavinia,' said bloke one.

'It's closed,' said bloke two.

'Yes. Closed,' said the first bloke. 'But we have very good hotel in Colombo.'

'Much better than Mount Lavinia. Special price for you,' said the second one.

Frankie loomed over my shoulder. 'What the hell's going on?'

I made the introductions. 'Frankie, these are a couple of con artists; con artists, meet Frankie.'

They flashed their teeth at the pleasure of

meeting him. I said, 'Now, I want you to take us to the Mount Lavinia. We always stay at closed hotels.'

Number one glanced at number two. Number two glanced back. Number one said, 'It is very far away, sir.'

'Very far,' I agreed. 'Eight miles south of Colombo. That far.' I had read my brochure.

Frankie cut in, 'How much?'

More silent communion as they weighed up how much they could skim us for. Number one said, 'Forty American dollars. Thirty English pounds. Air conditioned taxi, sirs.'

Frankie and I laughed hysterically. I said, 'Let's call it five pounds.'

Now it was their turn to roll about in merriment. We haggled on amid convulsions of outraged laughter until they agreed to do the biz for fifteen quid. It was still a rip off but we were getting thirsty. We bounced off in the back of a dusty Datsun towards the chaos that calls itself Colombo. The chief industry hereabouts is the making of noise, and very good they are at it too. Tuk-tuks parped, trucks blared, bikes and trikes ting-a-linged and in the shade of whopping great trees buddhist monks tinkled their bells so as not to be left out of things. We bumped around for an hour until we fetched up outside a hotel of sparkling brilliance. 'Mount Lavinia,' said our driver, as if he'd built it himself. It was open and it had welcome writ large on the mat.

We checked in, ordered a brace of Goldbrews and stretched ourselves on the terrace. Far below, boisterous waves slapped the rocks about.

'This is the life,' said Frankie.

'I wonder what the poor are doing,' I mused.

'Drinking better beer than this,' said Frankie.

But he forced himself to down a couple more Goldbrews before shambling off to his room, returning in a pair of Bermuda shorts of rare and hideous design. He said, 'I'm going for a swim', just in case I got the wrong idea and thought he was offering himself up for seduction.

I retired to my room and began poring over maps, brochures and guidebooks. Kandy came highly recommended. There was a botanical garden with 4,000 plants, and there was a huge lake, a colourful bazaar and the celebrated Tooth Temple. It was up in the hills, 70 miles north of Colombo, and the most interesting way of getting there was by train. The brochures suggested first class in the observation car of the Intercity express. That was the way to do it. I've always been a sucker for trains, especially those kitted out with buffets. Such was the Intercity express. I wandered down to reception where a Miss de Silva made all the bookings. I was about to head for the bar when a sudden thought assailed me. I said, 'Is it a Poya day tomorrow?'

Miss de Silva assured me it wasn't. I drifted off again. I got five yards when she called after me: 'Even if it was, you could still drink in the hotel.'

Clever girl, that Miss de Silva.

Frankie and I went walkies in the evening. He had burned his shoulders basking by the pool. The pain was hellish, he said. I said, 'Is it as bad as the time you got burned by the letter bomb?' He didn't speak to me for half an hour.

We found a restaurant before he died and tucked into a motley assortment of things. At least I did. Frankie had a pizza. We embarked on the local fire-water which was alcoholic and drinkable, which, I suppose, is the same thing. But I was glad of my bottle of duty free Glenfiddich back at the hotel. The bill for our excursion was on the nice side of £10. Frankie was delighted. I wasn't so tickled. The owner refused to hand over any blank receipts.

Back in my room Frankie kindly helped me with the Glenfiddich. I told him the plan. At the crack of ten we were to get up, breakfast and voyage north to Kandy on the famous express. He didn't like the idea.

'Why don't we hire a car and drive there?' he demanded.

Because I wasn't going to risk my life with all those jay-walking buffaloes around, that's why. He grumbled a bit but bowed to my superior wisdom.

Life moves at a different pace in the tropics. Things are slower there. Nowhere is this more true than on the Intercity express train from Colombo to Kandy and vice versa. If there'd been a copper on the track he would have booked us all for loitering. We sat in the observation car, watching myopic butterflies bat into the rear window. 'Great way to travel,' snorted Frankie. And the buffet car wasn't quite what I had in mind. It offered chipped blue cups of milky tea. There were also unidentifiable things to eat, but it seemed a shame to disturb the flies. Otherwise it was a jolly outing. We were surrounded by amiable Sri Lankans, determined to make us enjoy ourselves. They pressed their services as bearers, guides, interpreters. I said, great, we were Serbo-Croat. They shut up.

One man, who had been sitting silently watching us, broke into a laugh. He came across, dipped his head in a bow and said, 'Hello, I'm Varun.' He was about thirty, slimmish, neat and looked just like anybody else. We said hello Varun and returned to watching the jungle unfold inch by inch. Varun was not to be put off. He squeezed in beside us and launched into a long catechism of his remarkable talents. He could drive, guide, translate, show us the best bars, the plushest hotels, the most complaisant young women. Somewhere along the line I got interested. And what would his inestimable services cost us?

He measured us out carefully. 'Fifty pounds a day.'

I said, 'Call it thirty.'

We called it forty and shook hands. When the train finally clawed its way into Kandy, Varun snatched our luggage and told us to follow. He stormed his way through the reception committee of vendors and beggars, telling them to bugger off. Varun had us sussed. He led us directly to a leafy cafe, ordered up a couple of Singha beers and left to get a car. He returned ten minutes later with something that looked suspiciously like our battered Datsun of the day before. Varun thought it the bee's knees.

He said, 'I will do all driving. You must have very special knowledge to drive in Sri Lanka.'

This very special knowledge was apparently attained with the help of a large shot of arrak.

Varun scoffed a couple and then said, 'Now you want very special hotel with all amenity. I take you to MacDuff hotel. There is everything you desire. Swimming pool, very fine restaurant. Very clean. All rooms Ay Cee.'

I said, 'What's Ay Cee?'

'Air condition. Everywhere air condition. It is a hotel for gentlemen.'

We didn't like the sound of that. Frankie said, 'How much?'

Not very much at all – twenty-five quid for a double room, with a view over the lake thrown in. We parked our stuff and went walkabout. On first acquaintance Kandy seemed to live up to its advance hype. A civilised but colourful burgh, peopled by snake charmers, monks, fortune tellers, musicians and individuals selling things made from coconuts – mats, carved masks, arrak, mandolins, cures for impotence, money boxes, pots, coconut treacle, coconut pickle. The less imaginative simply flogged coconuts.

Varun, a man who liked his arrak, called a drink stop. We took our ease and watched the rich tapestry of Kandyian society unscroll around us. There were plenty of shysters and knaves on view, but I've seen worse in Rio. I've seen a damn sight worse in Oxford Street. But I didn't see a soul who looked as if he might have a hand in Sir James Tomlin's funny business, whatever it might be.

Varun, dipping into his third arrak, felt it was time

he earned his keep. He said, 'Now I show you how to save the fifty pounds a day you pay me.'

'Forty pounds.'

'Okay, forty pounds. First you ask for the bill and I show you the five-card trick which people play on the tourists.'

He had our undivided attention. We got the bill, presented inside a leather-look folder. Varun produced a pair of specs with one arm missing and perused it.

'First card is they charge you too much,' he said. 'Then they put on the bill something you do not have. Third card is they add it up wrong. Fourth card, they give you wrong change.'

He stopped. I said, 'And the fifth card?'

He smiled slyly. 'You see in a minute.'

It took about fifteen times that. In the meantime he got the prices knocked down, wiped three mystery brandies off the bill, corrected the waiter's arithmetic and made him cough up the right small change.

'Now,' said Varun, still looking like a fox, 'you tell me if everything is okay.'

It all looked kosher. Then I counted up the big 100 rupee notes the waiter had placed on top of the bill. There should have been eight. There were seven. I summoned the waiter. Where's the other note? I demanded. After all, it was worth seven quid. The waiter's face was a study in outraged innocence. He picked up the bill, and there lying under it in the folder was the missing 100 rupees.

'I gave you right money,' he shouted and stumped off in a huff.

Varun said, 'That is the fifth trick. He was hoping you pick up the money on top of the bill and walk away. That way you never know he has stolen 100 rupees. That's the biggest trick of all. You see? Pretty soon I earn my fifty pounds a day.'

'Forty pounds.'

'Forty pounds.'

We had a guide, we had transport, we had lodgings. What more could a man want? Well he could do with a decent meal for a start. Dish of the day at the MacDuff was not a decent meal for man or beast. It was billed as special curry. I asked a deliriously happy waiter what was so special about it.

'Wenison,' said he.

'Wenison?'

He spread his fingers and poked them out like antlers above each ear. 'Wenison.'

If they could build cars from deer they'd last forever. I pushed Bambi's remains around my plate and picked at the rice. What I would have given for a decent Ruby Murray down Soho.

Later in the lounge we settled ourselves in vast clubbable armchairs and lit into the arrak. Varun insisted on the Polgoda Walauwa premium version, at a price to match. 'What every gentleman drinks,' he said. Just for the novelty of it, we decided to be gentlemen. The arrak was peppery and sweet at the same time, but thinned out with soda you could almost get to like it. Varun was an expert on liquor. He told me something I had never known before.

'Inside every barrel of White Horse Scottish whisky they put the head of a white horse,' he vouchsafed. 'That is why it has a very fine taste. That is why they call it White Horse.'

I absorbed this information. I said, 'So, when they're making Johnny Walker do they go around looking for blokes called Johnny Walker to stick in it?'

Varun regarded me as if I were an idiot. He changed the subject. 'Tomorrow I show you all the famous sights in Kandy. I take you to the Tooth Temple and we go to watch the elephants in the river.'

Frankie said, 'What are the elephants doing in the river?'

'They are getting washed, of course,' said Varun, regarding Frankie as if he were an idiot.

It was time to let our trusty guide in on what we were up to in Kandy. I didn't fill in all the fine detail but I said there was mischief afoot. Varun dropped his smile. He listened with his head cocked and his gaze steady on me. When I had done he said, 'There are many things in Sri Lanka which people do not speak of.'

But he was prepared to speak of them. There were the mothers who twist the feet of their newborn babes to provide them, the doting mums, with a living begging bowl. It paid well until the kid was about seven or eight, by which time the mother had usually produced another crippled little earner. There were drug dealers in the south, rent boys and prostitutes on every beach. And then there were the baby farms. The government had rooted out most of them but they were still operating in the backwoods. The farms were big money, said Varun. A country girl could earn herself £200 just by giving birth. Her child vanished into a flaky orphanage while middlemen scouted out likely buyers. The biggest market was among childless Scandinavian couples.

Varun said, 'They come here and see the child. They want it. They say to the middlemen: "Okay, we give you two thousand pounds." Everybody says that is fine. They give the child a western name, so now she is not called Saliya. She is called Mary. They go home, but they do not take Mary with them. When they are home they put her name on their passport. They have papers which say it is a legal adoption. They come back to get their baby. When they are leaving Sweden or Denmark no one says to them: "Where is your baby?" Many tourists leave their baby at home. When they come here, the baby sellers play their five-card trick. They say the price is now two thousand more. The man and woman pay because they want their baby. But the sellers say they must pay for medicine because she has been sick. And they must pay for her clothes. Now they have their baby and they are happy. But the seller plays his last card. He says he needs to bribe immigration fellows. He needs another two thousand. They are desperate, but they want to go home with their baby very quick. They give him the money. Total bill is seven thousand, not two thousand. Next day they fly to Sweden with little Mary. When they come to immigration in Sweden, the officer looks at their passport and sees her name. Everything seems okay. He lets Mary in. That's how it's done.'

'Wow!' said Frankie.

Varun helped himself to my cigarettes. He was

enjoying his role as racket buster. He said, 'Maybe you do not believe me? If you want to see, you just go to airport and watch for white couples with a brown baby. You ask them how they got their baby. They don't talk to you.'

I said, 'Does the baby trade go on in Kandy?'

Varun shrugged. 'Maybe. I don't know. I will ask for you.'

I thought of the various low lifes associated with Tomlin and tried to picture them flogging hot babies. Morally they were capable of anything but realistically this wasn't their style. There had been nothing in our files on any of them being the proud possessor of a heavily tanned son or daughter. And the financial rewards were small beer. Varun might see £7,000 as megabucks, but Tomlin dealt in millions. There was something more to it than imported infants.

Frankie was thinking along the same lines. He said, 'Maybe they get the kids to swallow bags of heroin.'

Eh? I said, 'Yes, Frankie, and maybe they stuff their nappies with stolen elephants.'

'Don't be bloody stupid.'

'I won't if you won't,' I promised.

Frankie was aggrieved. 'All right, maybe it's not heroin. But they could hide a stack of diamonds in the nappies.'

Diamonds. I hadn't thought of that. I asked Varun if there was a thriving trade in under-the-counter sparklers.

'Most certainly yes, Mister Max,' he said, reaching for his arrak. 'There is illegal trade in everything. In diamonds, in drugs, in gold. You name it and there is smuggling. Anything. Absolutely anything.'

'Coconuts?' queried Frankie.

And thus ended that particular meeting of the Brains' Trust.

Chapter Twelve

The Alahaka arts and culture centre perched itself on a hill road just outside of town. To get there you drove through trees the height of skyscrapers, their branches bowed down with chittering macaque monkeys. The arts centre was in a cleft cut into the hillside. Behind it there was dense jungle. Beneath it, a spectacular fall to Kandy. You got a great view of the much-vaunted lake and the Mahaveli river – 'The longest river in Sri Lanka,' boasted Varun. This is like a Dutchman singing the praises of the highest hillock in Holland, but we did the decent thing and gaped with awe.

Frankie had gone overboard with his camera gear and looked like he had mugged a coachload of Japanese tourists. I was Mr Cool in my borrowed suit. I had a tape recorder with a hidden mike tucked under my watch strap. I also had a small notebook and pen. That's all I needed.

We were the first visitors of the day to the centre and were greeted like kings by a bevy of lissom lovelies with fluttery eyelashes. They pointed out brass lamps and perfume sprays, silk scarves and ties, the many and several products of the good old coconut palm, filigree silver and pretty-pretty gems, squat little boxes of tea, rugs to stick on your floor, rugs to hang on your wall, saris, wood carvings and all manner of things. I bought Rosie a postcard depicting a fresco of a topless beauty with a thirtyeight double-D frontage. On the back of the card was an apposite poem. I quote:

Ladies like you,
Make men pour out their hearts,
And you also,
Have thrilled the body,
Making its hair stiffen with desire

I wrote the message: Wish you were Her, and handed it to a salesgirl with a peek-a-boo sari. She licked a stamp with a delicate pink tongue. That fairly made my hair stiffen. I don't think Frankie had noticed a single artefact on display. He was just standing there leering at the girls. Varun was wandering around picking up doodahs, examining the prices and saying: 'Oh dear me, no,' with a rueful laugh and a scrunched up face. I went for a long browse through the shelves, shadowed by a girl with a hole in the back of her frock. Whenever I paused to look at something she would dart forward and assure me, 'Very good price. Extremely popular with all our customers.' She had lovely eyes so I believed her, despite Varun's derisory hoots.

I asked her name. Malini. I said, 'The centre is a charity, yes?'

Malini bobbed her head, yes, then shook her head,

no. 'It is self help. It promotes Sri Lankan traditional craftsmen.'

I said, 'So the money goes to them?'

Another bit of bobbing and shaking. 'Some yes. Not all. Much is raised to help the local community.'

I said, 'What does it help?'

Malini frowned in concentration. She said, 'You wait here.' She skipped off. I waited holding a pink wooden elephant in my hand. It gave me a sour look.

'Can I help you Mister Charrod?'

I turned around to find a slim, dapper man standing two inches behind me.

'It's Chard,' I said.

'Yes, Mister Charrod. How might I be of assistance?'

I said for a kick-off I'd like to know how he knew my name, or an approximation thereof. He flashed a double-decker smile.

'I was told to expect you, Mister Charrod. Mister Tomlin said you are coming.'

I said, 'And you are . . .?'

'I am Mister Hector Samarsinghe,' he said. 'I am very pleased to meet you.'

The feeling was not mutual. Mister Hector Samarsinghe looked the type you wouldn't buy a new car from. He had funny eyes, a mix of nutty brown and sea green. This might sound a happy blend. It wasn't. You didn't really notice the brown bit. What you did notice were the green centres, as cold, as empty, as dead as a stuffed snake's. He was dressed according to the fashion of the isle, that is in a pastel shirt with trousers which looked as if their matching jacket was hung up elsewhere. He was suave and at ease. He stuck out a ring-bedecked hand and waved at his wares.

'You like our centre, Mister Charrod?'

I said I was speechless with admiration. My soul thirsted for every detail of its operation. Samarsinghe invited us all to his office for a chat. It was a spacious room, decorated in a mix of the mysterious east and the moneyed west. Our host ordered Malini to get cracking with the teapot. He took up residence in a swivel chair behind the desk. He was facing me head on. I was in a rattan chair with no arms. Varun in another off to my left. Frankie was drifting about somewhere in the background.

Samarsinghe pressed his fingertips together and dipped his head in a sketchy bow. He said, 'Now, what would you like to know, Mister Charrod?'

I didn't answer immediately. I looked around. Here is another tip to those lost souls who hanker to become hacks: You can sit the long day through, interviewing someone who blocks your every query with a no comment, yet all the while his surroundings scream out to be heard. They tell you more about the man than he knows himself. By the props on view I could see that Mister Hector Samarsinghe was one rather in love with his bathroom mirror. On the desk was a twelve by ten snap of him presenting or accepting something from Claudine Tournier. The left wall was given over to a whole album of such shots. Hector looked exactly the same in each. Only his partners were different. Here he was gladhanding Sir James Tomlin's snotty son, there another with Leon

Knapp. The goldfish mug of Lewis Trefoyle goggled out of a third, Proudhoe Veizey in a fourth, and so on. There were also about half a dozen heads whom I did not recognise. I flicked a glance out of the corner of my eye at Frankie and he flicked one back. We had just said to each other: 'We must snatch shots of these.'

Malini swayed in with the teapot. Samarsinghe slung her out and started playing mummy. I waited until the spoons had ceased stirring. I produced my notebook, unsheathed the Bic and poised it an inch above the virgin page.

I asked him how he spelt his name and I wrote it down in whopping great letters. I laid the notebook on the desk so he could read it upside down. I asked him was he the manager? No, the director. And how old was he? For the record he was 44. His first lie. And when did the Foundation become involved? Two years back. And where did he come from? Dambulla, wherever that might be. And how do you spell that? You could spell it with an H on the end or leave the H off, said Hector. It's amazing the sort of thing we journos pick up. And what did the arts centre promote? He went into his spiel and I wrote bits down, still in huge infantile letters. I sensed that Varun was rapidly losing faith in my skills as an ace investigator. But how was he to know I was up to my very favourite trick. It is one of such simplicity and beauty that I commend it to all. What you do is stick your notebook – and every single word you write – on plain view. The victim reads exactly what you have written and he thinks: 'We've got a right thicko here.' This is what you want him to think. Every now and then he inadvertently lets slip something interesting. You do not write it down. You lay your pen aside, feign disinterest and move on to some other blockbuster question, like is he married? Gradually he becomes emboldened. He lets a little more slip. Sometimes the victim does this just to test what a dummy you are. He's even having fun at your expense. Or so he thinks. What he doesn't know is that the little bug under your wrist strap is picking up everything he says.

Thus it was with Hector Samarsinghe. I asked him where the coconuts came from, did Leon enjoy his visit, how many hours a week was the centre open, were the sales girls his daughters, how often did Tomlin drop in, what was the most popular item, did the Tamil Tigers deter tourists, was Proudhoe Veizey a customer, could I buy cheap glasses locally, who were those other geezers in the photo gallery, were the four-legged monkeys dangerous, how much profit did the shop clear, was the Tooth Temple worth a visit, how did he feel about Claudine's murder, would he care for a cigarette, why did so many big shots visit him, could I have another cup, please, did his wife work at the centre and more. Much, much more.

I wrote it all down, except the bits about the Tomlin fraternity. Frankie meanwhile knew precisely what I was up to and he sat in the corner with a look of utter boredom wrapped round his face. Varun was still in the dark. His eyes sliced from me to Samarsinghe and back to me as if he was watching a Wimbledon final.

I was almost through with the questions, but I broke off to pull a little stunt. I said, 'Hector, you've got something on sale I wanted to ask you about. Do you mind having a look at it?'

Samarsinghe fired a glance at Frankie. Frankie was deeply engrossed in a leaflet about silkworms. Samarsinghe said, 'Now?'

I stood up as if he had already agreed. He followed. We left the other two in the office. I knew that the moment we walked out the door Frankie would be banging off snaps of all the pictures on the wall.

I looked around for something interesting. I saw a pith helmet in a fetching pinkish shade. 'Ah, this is it,' I declared. 'I was wondering if this was an antique, you know, something left over from the days of the Raj?'

Samarsinghe laughed in his sorrow. 'I am sorry. No. This is modern, made just this year. You like it?'

'Yes, I do. How much is it, Hector?'

He turned on a generous display of his molars. 'For you it is free. It is a gift from me, Mister Charrod.'

I squeaked in protestation. He insisted. I took it. I lingered over a shelf of ghastly shell ornaments just to give Frankie time to do his dirty work. Samarsinghe was anxious to get back to his office. I said conversationally, 'I love this pith helmet – was it made locally?'

'Yes. Our children at the orphanage.'

He turned away and said quickly, 'There is a Missus Charrod perhaps?' He stuck out his hand at a rack of scarves. 'Or perhaps you have a lady friend?'

The great salesman won me over. Rosie might

indeed like one of these wrapped round her neck. I patted him fondly on the arm. I said, 'This time I'm paying for it, Hector. It's money in a good cause.'

He eased up. We argued amiably over the price. I was trying to pay the full whack and he was insisting I pay less. An unusual experience in Sri Lanka. After a brief struggle I won the day. I also chipped in about £20 towards his Good Works. By God, there are times when I make me want to throw up.

Samarsinghe had a glitter in his hard little eyes. As far as he was concerned, our interview had been bland, boring and totally unrevealing. We strolled back to the office, each laughing up his sleeve at the other. Frankie was still comatose in his corner. Varun was playing with his car keys. I asked a few more daft questions and Frankie took a sunny shot of us together, then one of Hector looking heroic. We took our leave, but not until Samarsinghe made me promise to call him if there was anything more I needed. I promised, for I am ever anxious to make others happy.

Frankie, Varun and I didn't speak until we were back in the Datsun. Varun said, 'He is a crook, Mister Max. He is not telling the truth to you.'

Frankie said, 'Got the pix. Let's get a drink.'

As we were cruising down the hill, I showed Frankie my purchases.

'What's that?' he said, poking a finger at my hat.

'That is a pith helmet.'

'What do you want that for?' he asked.

'To wear when I'm pithed.'

Varun drove us past a hotel. We bollocked him and

made him reverse us right back to it. We had our drinks by the poolside, where a couple of Parisian housewives displayed that bikini tops are being worn off the bust this season. Frankie poured beer down his chin and licked his lips. Varun, normally the life and soul of things, was gloomy. He thought I'd come away empty handed. Well, let's just see what we got.

The cluster of unknowns on the office wall were mostly City money men. They came, they saw, they contributed. Samarsinghe had described Michael Tomlin as 'a dear friend'. The implication was he was a frequent visitor. Leon Knapp likewise. Samarsinghe had shot off into the undergrowth when I tossed his name into the pot. Martin Crowley had been there twice, going home each time with buddhist figurines. Them and something else, I bet. The florid thespian Proudhoe Veizey and the Right Hon. Lewis Trefoyle showed their all-abiding interest in the Third World by banging on the centre's door every now and then. But at least the natives had been largely spared Sir James Tomlin. He had been here only once.

According to Tomlin, Kandy was but a dot in the WorldCare Foundation empire. Let us pretend that is true. Let us also remember that the Foundation press officer hardly knew it existed. Here we have some insignificant offshoot of Claudine's labours. How then do you explain why all these money-crazed City slackers are so damn keen on going there? It couldn't just be the repro pith helmets.

But hold a moment. They didn't come to see the centre. When I'd mentioned it to Knapp, he'd gone cold on me. They came for something else, some place else.

Samarsinghe had told me the box office takings were doled out among local needy causes. A maternity unit, craft workshops, a paediatric clinic and all that. So what. Where's the funny stuff?

The waiter wheeled up with another round and I counted my change like a clever boy, for I knew all about the five-card trick. BONG! The brain lit up. The old five-card trick. That's what Samarsinghe had tried to pull. He told me more than I ever wished to know about sundry deserving causes. All but for one. The big note was lying under the bill of goods. And I knew just what it was.

An orphanage. I remembered that one brief moment when he forgot himself and broke cover. He said, 'our children at the orphanage.' And then he changed the subject so suddenly it jarred. For he knew he had mentioned the unmentionable.

I lay back in my lounger and patted myself on the back. They can't outfox Max. I'd hit it smack on the head. The orphanage. That's the scene of sin and shame.

I looked at the topless sunbathers, they looked at me. Then I looked at their faces. They smiled, I smiled. A man could be happy here.

My innocent reverie was broken by a shout from Frankie who was looking over the fence at the world outside. He seemed excited, as if he had just discovered a nudist colony serving free drink. I traipsed over for a peek. The prospect was unspectacular, a view of the road we had just descended. You could see the Alahaka arts centre on top of the hill. You could also see the fair Malini stepping daintily forth. We watched her shimmer down the road in our direction for a couple of hundred yards. She fetched up under a giant tree. She stood there as if she was waiting for a bus.

'She's waiting for a bus,' said Frankie.

I said, 'Stay here. I want to talk to her.'

I hoofed off with the sun burning a hole in my head. When I got to Malini I was hot and sticky and pink behind the ears. She was as cool as an ice cube in an Eskimo's freezer in winter. She bowed her head and showed her teeth which looked like they'd been made from the white bits of coconut. She was pleased to see me.

I said, 'Hi, Malini. There's something I forgot to ask Hector; I wonder if you could tell me.'

Her eyes said, 'Come be my lover and we will dwell in paradise all our days.' Her lips said, 'Of course. If I can help you.'

I said, 'I didn't get the address of the orphanage. Can you give me it?'

Her eyes flashed, her chin wobbled, her nostrils flared. 'The orphanage! Go away! Go back to England! I do not want to speak to you.'

I got the impression I'd said something wrong. I tried again. 'I just want to visit it, to see how it's run.'

'Ha!'

In just two letters she managed to convey that I was lower than a submarine's bum, that I should be horsewhipped, boiled in oil and forced to listen to Barry Manilow records.

I said, 'What's wrong with me seeing the orphanage?'

She didn't spit in my face, but the thought went through her mind. She said, 'You're like the rest of them. I thought you were nice men. Go away!'

I might have tried to press my credentials as a nice man but for the noisy arrival of a rusty, dusty bus. She hopped aboard, throwing a venomous glance back. The driver tooted his horn and off she went, hotly pursued by a dust storm.

I didn't mind. I ambled back down the road whistling to myself. My next stop was the orphanage. That's where whoever it was was getting up to whatever it was.

Chapter Thirteen

The guidebooks are strangely silent on the subject of Kandyian orphanages. We were forced to boot Varun out onto the street to quiz the locals. He came back tired, thirsty, but with a big self-satisfied smirk. He'd earned his thirty quid for the day.

We were now back in the hotel MacDuff and deeply engrossed in our bright red feet. This is something else the guidebooks don't think worth mentioning: in Sri Lanka they smear hotel corridors and steps with an inch of vermilion polish each new morning. Whole armies of lackeys are engaged upon this ritual, and it is very enjoyable watching them at their task whilst you sip a Singha. The effect of their labours is pleasing to the eye, and, for all I know, keeps at bay ants, Bengal tigers and yuppie flu. There is alas a slight drawback. If you pad barefoot from your room to the pool, as we had just done, your feet look as if they have a terminal case of scarlet fever. So there we were in the lee of the poolside palm, examining our flaming tootsies when Varun panted into view. He handed us a list. Kandy, it appears, has orphanages the way Switzerland has mountains.

There was one each for the Protestant and Roman

Catholic foundlings, one for Hindus, another for Moslems, a third for Buddhist babes. I didn't spot any for atheists. There were also various private affairs. These looked the most likely. We still had a couple of hours to go to dinner, so we got ourselves dressed and went knocking on doors. I had a carefully thought-out strategy. It involved me saying, 'Hi, we're friends of Sir James Tomlin' and seeing how things went from there.

'Who?' said the bewildered matron at the first orphanage.

'Who?' said the suspicious manager at the second.

Soon the entire countryside was saying 'Who?' like a bunch of owls in an echo chamber. The wearisome day wore on and our driver stopped speaking to us. But Frankie and I know that stories are like passionate women. They don't drop in your lap and say, 'Take me, big boy. I'm yours.' You have to go wooing them. We kept on knocking. Frankie, minus his beloved necklace of cameras, looked almost human. But I could see his hand hovering over the pocket holding his little Olympus idiot-proof shooter.

It was the seventh, maybe the eighth place we visited. The Perelawaya Children's Refuge. I said to the fat lady in the front office that I was a chum of Sir James. She said who? I turned and started trekking back to the car. 'Hello! Hello!' someone yammered behind me. I turned right round again. A weedy bloke with a malnourished moustache sought my attention.

'Yes?' I asked.

'You are a friend of Sir James?'

We'd hit it. This was the spot. Dig here. Out of my

left ear I could hear Frankie uncoiling from the car. I advanced on the small man. I said, 'You must be . . .'

'Niaz.'

'Niaz! Of course. Leon Knapp told me all about you, Niaz.'

'Ah, Mister Leon,' Niaz sprung a joyful smile. 'He is very much liked here. I don't think so in England perhaps?'

News travels fast in these parts. I said, 'Perhaps.' We both laughed, though God knows why. I gave him a full up and downer. If he'd been six inches taller he'd have been a six footer. He was in his early forties but he fidgeted like an adolescent. His thick black hair was plastered with thick black grease. He was ever so anxious to please. So far I'd got away with my bluff, but I reckoned I might have ten minutes at most before he wised up and told us to naff off.

I said, 'Martin Crowley was right: this is a beautiful spot.'

Niaz said, 'You know Mister Martin?'

I said, 'Know him? We went through commando training together.'

Frankie rolled his eyes. But Niaz believed me. We had a good chuckle about Martin Crowley too. Just when I was thinking Niaz must be on the old nitrous oxide, he stopped beaming. A nasty, suspicious look started descending from his hairline.

He said, 'Mister Samarsinghe did not say you were coming.'

I had taken the precaution of arming myself with Frankie's duty free litre of Glenfiddich. The bugger had made me pay him for it too. I whipped out the bottle, stuffed it in Niaz's hand and said, 'I know. I should have called you first. But we just got into town and thought we'd pay you a visit.'

Niaz ogled the Glenfiddich. I'd done something right for a change. He said, 'I do not know your names.'

I said, 'We're business partners of Sir James. I'm Sebastian du Maurier and this is my friend, Joe Soap.'

Frankie glowered. Niaz presented a welcoming hand. 'Come, come,' he urged. 'I am very pleased to welcome any friends of Sir James.'

He shepherded us to a bungalow half screened by trees. It looked out on the main block, another bungalow, but one that sent out shoots in all directions. Niaz told us to make ourselves comfortable in his lounge. It had a TV set, cane furniture and a grubby air of bachelorhood. No pictures.

'Drink?' offered Niaz.

'Yes please,' said Frankie, eyeing his former whisky.

Niaz disappeared behind a curtain, returning with three glasses of arrak. It wasn't even the premium version. We toasted each other and did some more laughing.

'Sir James has been very good to us,' said Niaz. 'He sends many friends to visit us.'

I said, 'The refuge is very dear to his heart. He wanted to come with us but he couldn't spare the time. You know what it's like in big business.'

Niaz nodded sadly. We sipped a while and pondered the heavy sacrifices one must make in big business. He brightened up. 'Never mind, Mister

Sebastian, I want to ask what I can do to make you and Mister Joe happy.'

Tell me what's going on, that's what.

I said, 'My friend, Lewis, you know Lewis Trefoyle, said he had a very interesting time here. But of course we had to come to see for ourselves.'

Niaz said, 'Ah yes, Mister Lewis. He is a very kind man.'

I took that to mean Trefoyle made free with his wallet. I hauled mine out. Niaz was aghast. 'No! No, please, Mister Sebastian. Sir James always pays for his friends.'

Does he now? And what exactly does he pay for?

I said, 'We were hoping to have a quick look round the refuge first. Unless that is inconvenient.'

I still had my wallet on show. I fished out a chunk of Sri Lankan rupees, around two hundred pounds in orange and blue notes. It was way over the top and it was meant to be. I said, 'I know Sir James pays, but I'd like to make a small private donation, and I wouldn't want you to tell anyone.'

Niaz snapped up the money like a magpie. I got the impression the orphans wouldn't see much of it. He said, 'It is late, but we have a little time to show you our refuge.'

We said nice things about each other and raised our glasses in warm tributes. Frankie was a mite fretful and I knew what was knocking around in his monkey mind: the light was going. If he wanted snaps, he'd soon have to shoot flash and that way everybody would know what he was doing.

I said casually, 'How many children do you have in the refuge?'

Niaz counted them up. 'We have nine. We had ten, but there was an accident.'

'An accident?'

He didn't like that question. He just repeated, 'An accident.'

I said, 'How old are they?'

Niaz had it off by heart. 'The youngest is Ajit: he's seven. Lalin is the biggest. He's twelve, so he will be going soon.'

Going where and why? I rolled the arrak around like mouth-wash, puzzling over what to say next. If I hit one wrong button, he'd tell me to sling my hook, and I wouldn't get my money back either. I had to pick on something seemingly innocent. I waved my glass at the walls. I said, 'You don't have any pictures.'

That was the wrong button. 'Pictures? What pictures? Photographs are not allowed – you must know that.' Our host was very narked indeed.

Frankie got there before me. He said, 'No, not photographs, pictures. You know, pictures. Everywhere we've been, there are all these lovely paintings of Sri Lanka.'

Niaz let his jaw muscles droop in a smile. 'Ah, paintings. I thought you meant photographs.' He laughed at his own foolishness and we joined in heartily. He said, 'Of course I do have photographs of the children here – I took them myself, with my own camera.'

'Oh yes?' Frankie again. A little too keenly.

Niaz stuck out an arm, flipped open a chairside

cupboard and produced his prize. It was an eight by ten of a bunch of kids squinting in the sun. They were all boys. They didn't look as if they were having the time of their lives. I said, 'They look very happy children.'

'Oh yes,' enthused Niaz. 'All very good. All speak good English.'

I wanted to know which one was the 'accident' victim. I said, 'And they're all here now?'

Niaz shook his head. 'This boy, Janath, is not here. The accident.'

'Of course.' I studied the child he had pointed out. He looked about seven, or maybe an underdeveloped nine-year-old. He was the least happy of a hapless bunch. His face was at odds with his grinning Mickey Mouse tee shirt. I passed the snap to Frankie, my index finger pinned on Janath. I tipped back the last of my drink.

Niaz said, 'Would you like one?'

I thought what the hell and held out my glass. Niaz had a fit. He chortled and roared and whinnied while Frankie and I looked at each other, trying to figure out the joke. 'No, not an arrak, Mister Sebastian,' he said between convulsions, 'No, no, no. I mean a boy.' And off he went roaring again.

Dear God in heaven.

All along I had known there was something nasty about Kandy, but not exactly what. Now here was this little man, spelling it out callously, as carelessly as if he were selling cheap lighters. Frankie, still holding the picture, popped his eyes. If Niaz had not been wiping away tears of laughter he would have seen our horror. It took me half a minute to get my breathing back in synch.

I said, 'A boy? Why not?'

Niaz said, 'Okay Mister Sebastian. You pick a boy. You too Mister Joe.'

Frankie was still not quite with us. I took the photograph from him and pointed to the oldest looking boy. Frankie, after a little pause, chose another, a child of maybe six or seven. We were both operating by instinct. I was going for the boy who'd give me the best words, Frankie for the one who'd make the best shot. Niaz congratulated us on our discernment. He said, 'Now you finish your drinks and we go and see them.'

Frankie said he'd had enough arrak. He was still white. I whopped my glass back. Niaz said, 'We go now.'

I remember entering a room that was part dormitory, part playroom. Every single child looked up when we entered. None of them smiled. I remember that very clearly. The room was clean, but you felt the children were somehow neglected, as if each had to make his own way in the world. I cannot remember much of what Niaz said. I just recall him prattling on and on and urging the boys to look pleased to see their visitors. They didn't.

Then I was alone in a room with a skinny sad-eyed boy. He said, 'Do you have batteries for my Nintendo? Do you have any Mario games?'

I shook my head. He lost interest and began scratching the back of his leg. I took the tape recorder from my pocket and turned the cassette over. I said, 'What is your name?'

'Lalin. You call me Lal.' He didn't look up.

I didn't recognise my voice, it was so quiet, so edgy. I said, 'How old are you, Lal?'

'Eleven.' He did not want to talk to me.

I said, 'Men come to see you, Lal. What do they do?' He was a strange mix of resentfulness and submissiveness.

I said, 'I do not want to do anything to you. I just want you to tell me about the men.'

He glanced at me sharply but did not speak. I let him think about it. I inspected the room. The walls were whitewashed and bare. There was a big bed in the corner, a settee, a drinks bar and a TV set with a video. A door led off to a bathroom. The fittings were simple yet after the children's room they looked lavish.

I said, 'Are you happy here?'

Lal studied his trainers. I said, 'Where are you from?' His mouth was set in childish stubbornness.

I said, 'Lal, I am not like the other men.'

He shot me another glance. We were both standing. I was by the door, he beside the bed. I did not move closer. A terrible sadness overwhelmed me. I thought of this room and the awful things that had happened here. I looked at this child, as slim as a fish, with eyes as old as the world.

I said in hardly even a whisper, 'Sweet Jesus Christ, what have they done to you?'

And he told me. He gave me their names. Mister Martin and Mister Mike – Michael Tomlin, Knapp,

Trefoyle and all the rest of that sordid freemasonry. He told me of the 'accident', that a man – he didn't know who – had suffocated his friend, Janath. Janath was ten. Soon he, Lal, would have to leave the refuge. And go where? He shook his head. Maybe Galle, for the tourist men. Maybe Negombo. Niaz had other places for boys when the men here tired of them.

I said, 'Soon my friend Frankie is going to come in here and take a photograph of you.'

Lal shook his head vehemently. 'No. You are not allowed photographs. Mister Leon took photographs and they were very angry.'

I said, 'Listen to me. I am a journalist. You understand? I write for newspapers. I want to write about what these men are doing. I want to stop them.'

He gave me the merest glimmer of a smile. 'You will say they are bad? You will say they killed Janath?'

I said, 'I will say they are very, very bad. Maybe they will go to jail. But they will never come here again.'

Lal shrugged his shoulders carelessly. 'Okay. You take my picture.'

Something was tugging at the hem of my conscience and shouting, 'Oi!' I listened to it. It was the rarely-heard voice of decency which told me that I too was using Lal, abusing him after my own fashion. He was just a story for me, a great big bold by-line, something to make all my Fleet Street peers say: 'Nice one, Max.' I told my conscience to stay out of it.

I said, 'Lal, you must not say anything to anyone about this. Not even your best pal. If you do, Mister

Niaz will hear of it. You will be in danger, very serious danger.'

Lal absorbed this with eyes that had already seen so much wickedness. He understood.

I said, 'When I am gone you must say I asked you questions but you refused to tell me anything. You got that?'

He nodded. I said, 'Now, when the bad men leave, what do they do? Do they give you a present? Do they give you money?'

I had my wallet out and was rifling through the notes. Lal said, 'Yes, they give me money. Sometimes ten rupees. We give all the money to Niaz.'

Ten rupees. Just seventy pence. And they took even that away from him.

He said, 'Perhaps you will give me more? I will say I did not tell you about the tourist men. I'll pretend you were angry with me because I did not say. Do you want to beat me?'

He just stood there and said it. I said, 'God Almighty, no. Just say you told me nothing.'

There was a light, urgent tapping on the door. I edged it open and Frankie squeezed in. He was yellow in the 40-watt hall light. He said, 'I'm going to kill those bastards.'

I said, 'Later, Frankie, later. Say hello and goodbye to Lal. Take his snap and let's get out of here. We'd better move it before Niaz catches on.'

I whipped the blankets off the bed and rigged them over the thin curtains to keep Frankie's flash from showing outside. He knocked off half a dozen shots. Lal sat on the edge of the bed in his white shirt and shorts. His face was dark and sombre. He made a great pic. We re-made the bed, took a deep breath and ventured out into the corridor. Behind us Lal sat where he was, holding a 100 rupee note. I said, 'I promise, I'll do everything I can for you and your friends.'

A sad smile turned the corners of his lips. He said, 'Okay.' I don't think he believed me.

Frankie grabbed my shoulder. 'Quick, Max, here's Niaz.'

He was skipping down the corridor towards us, his face split in a grin. He was actually happy in that place. Beside me I could hear Frankie's teeth grind. He was trying to return the smile.

Niaz said, 'Good? Yes?'

I said, 'Very good, Niaz. I couldn't believe it.'

He was pleased with himself. He said, 'When you come back tomorrow you must bring small gifts for the boys. Just a little toy or a pen. They always like pens. That is all you need.'

He guided us back down the corridor. We passed the open doorway where the other boys played. There was something eerie about them. I think it was their silence. Their passive eyes regarded us as we passed and they returned to their wordless games. They never smiled.

Niaz kept up the patter all the way back to his bungalow. I don't remember much about it, except him extolling the honesty and happiness of his children. Then he said, 'Soon they will have new friends.'

I said, 'Oh?'

'Yes. Sir James says some of his friends prefer the girls, the young girls.'

It is hard to act conversational when you're talking to someone you'd like to see strung up by the neck. I managed it somehow. I said, 'Really? And where do the girls come from?'

Niaz pointed towards the window. 'From north of Trincomalee. Orphans from the Tamil Tigers.'

So the waifs of war who had lost their mums and dads to terrorists now stood to lose their last shreds of innocence and hope to European paedophiles. I wanted to be away from there. I gave an elaborate yawn. I said, 'You must forgive me, Niaz. We had a long flight in and I'm rather tired.'

He was kind and thoughtful, which made things worse. He said, 'I am sorry. I talk too much. When I see you tomorrow, I will be more quiet. You are staying at the Citadel of course?'

I said, 'Yes, the Citadel.'

Niaz said, 'Good. It is a splendid hotel. You and Mister Joe have a nice meal and then you sleep.'

He made a pillow with his hands and laid his head on it, just in case I didn't get the idea. He guided us out via the front office. The fat woman had gone. Niaz clutched my hand and shook it. It would be nice to report that his grip was slithery and slimy. It was a good firm honest-to-God handshake. It had no place here.

We made it back out to the car. Varun was bouncing up and down with excitement. He said, 'You got your story, Mister Max?'

I nodded. I didn't feel like talking to anyone.

'And you got your photos, Mister Frank?'

Frankie said, 'I did. And I pinched this one too.' He pulled out the group shot of the boys taken by Niaz. Varun was horrified. 'You stole the photo? That is very bad.'

'That's nothing,' said Frankie, reaching into his jacket. 'I nicked our whisky back and all.'

It was a subdued little trio that sat around table thirteen in the MacDuff hotel. Frankie was fretting over what to do with his snaps – whether to have them processed here or air-freight the film back to London or just go back with the roll in his camera bag. Varun was waiting to be arrested for aiding and abetting a pair of international thieves and con men. I was trying to wash away the taste of the day and working out how the whole thing – the murders, the child abuse – fitted together. The answers took their time in coming. But after a few hours of largely silent contemplation I thought I had it worked out. It went like this:

Claudine was not party to the deal. She had found out about it. Her mother had told me there was a big scandal – 'bigger than money' – about to break in the WorldCare Foundation. That's why she was topped. Shirley had gone a little too far down the same track. That's why she got a rope round her neck. The killer/killers feared she'd passed the stuff on to me, hence the attempt to cook me. Hence the letter bomb – a warning to keep what I had to myself.

Sir James Tomlin was not a paedophile. He'd made just one visit here. But he seemed to be behind the whole deal. Why? To cater for the whims of his deviant mates. And why should he do that? For money, most likely. His ex-wife, the one down in Virginia Water, had told me Tomlin would never have any money worries; his chums would always bail him out. The Kandy racket gave him powerful leverage with his City playmates, and a way of making all sorts of influential friends. People like the foul Lewis Trefoyle. Plus, according to Lal, Tomlin's son and heir, Michael, was a perv.

So what did I have as a story? Not a lot. I could not sit down and go through that tape again, not then – the awfulness of things was still in the quick of my mind. But I could dispassionately review the show so far. Any right-thinking member of society will agree that the Tomlins and all their ilk should be exposed to the world and then consigned to sew mailbags for life in E-wing max-security Durham. Those who are more right-thinking than most might prefer them to be hung, drawn and quartered. It is sad but true that newspaper lawyers are not right-thinking members of society. They would far, far rather let a mass murderer wander the streets than land the paper with a penny in libel damages. I imagined how Royce, our monocular lawyer, would react to my story.

Who is your source?

An eleven-year-old orphan, locked away in Sri Lanka.

Do you have his sworn affidavit?

No, but I've got him on tape.

Inadmissible. Does he know what an affidavit is?

Sure, Royce. The boys in the orphanage talk of nothing else.

Do you have a secondary source?

Yes. A six-year-old boy.

And he is too young—

—To know what an affidavit is. I know.

Did you see at the orphanage any of the people whom you have named?

No. But the creep who runs the place said they visited. Frankie heard him too.

Would the manager testify in court?

Yes. Against us. He'd say I made it all up.

Did you speak to anyone else who has seen the men named at the orphanage?

No.

Do you have any photographs confirming that Tomlin or anyone else has visited the boys?

No. Photographs are banned.

Do you have any evidence that they are engaging in similar acts against children within the United Kingdom?

Nary a whit.

What is our defence if they issue a writ for libel?

That it's true: that we're exposing it because it is in the public interest.

How do we justify in a British court that an alleged incident in Sri Lanka allegedly involving Sri Lankan children is within the British public interest?

I don't know, Royce. You're the lawyer.

Do you have any forensic evidence that the children have in fact been abused?

No.

So our entire case rests upon the wholly unsubstantiated word of an eleven-year-old child?

And the six-year-old.

Shut the door on your way out.

Even if I got the story nailed down, there was still a slight problem. To give it maximum bite, we would have to use big pix of Lal and the other boy, Ajit, staring dead-eyed at you out of the paper. The bigger the pix the better. We would also identify the boys by name, just to convince our sceptical readers we hadn't made the whole thing up. Sometimes they think that, you know.

So we would be identifying very clearly the child victims of a sex ring. If the boys involved were from Tunbridge Wells, our editor would end up in chokey, sharing the bedpan with Frankie and me, and the paper would be fined millions. Judges get very prickly about newspapers naming minors in cases like these. But because our boys were Sri Lankan, and they were abused there, we could stick their names, their faces, their fingerprints, their sock sizes in the paper and nobody could say boo. All right, our paper isn't exactly a soaraway seller in Sri Lanka, so you might think no one locally would ever link the boys. Up to a point. The story itself would be too big to ignore, therefore all the Sri Lankan press would leap on it. They'd contact our syndication people and buy Frankie's pix and my copy. End result: everyone in the entire island would know the boys' names and could point them out in the street. I could argue that this would be the responsibility of local editors, so don't blame me, guv. But when you come down to it, the boys' public exposure would be courtesy of that well known pair of social workers, Max and Frankie. And knowing all that, I would still name them.

We wiped out the Glenfiddich and went to bed. There was a fresh bowl of mangoes and papayas in my room. There was a minibar cram full of cheap drink. The coverlet of my bed was turned down and crisp clean sheets beckoned. Tomorrow I would wake to honeyed sunshine. I looked on all this and wished like hell I was somewhere else.

The sun was shooting shards of brilliance off the lake as we breakfasted. We discussed tactics. We'd already got the dirty stuff. Now we needed the ordinary foot-in-the-door pix and quotes from Samarsinghe and Niaz.

We hit the gift shop first. I strode right up to the sales counter. Behind me Frankie was going zip-a-dee-do-dah with all the cameras he possessed. It was good to see him back in his monkey suit.

You could tell that the beauteous Malini wanted me to drop dead on the spot, but the customer is always right, so she had to grit her teeth and ask how she could help me.

I said we'd been to the orphanage, and no doubt her boss might like to know it was a front for a child sex ring. Drag him hither, I commanded. Malini gave me an odd look. It said that she had ordered the jury out to have a re-think on the question of my guilt.

She fetched Samarsinghe. Gone was the big-hearted shopkeeper of yesterday. In his place was a spitting, eye-rolling nutter. 'Out! Out! Out!' he yelled, pointing helpfully to the door. I stayed In! In! In!

I said, 'Mister Samarsinghe, are you aware that your English friends are using children as young as six for sex? That money from this centre is used to supply the victims? That—'

I didn't get much further because he grabbed up a walking cane (price 150 rupees) and began thumping me around the head. Frankie had retired to a safe distance and was popping away. You could hear him go zzzip-zzzip-zzzip, then Samarsinghe's whack! then zzzip-zzzip-zzzip, and so on. I was glad Samarsinghe wasn't fitted with a motordrive. I backed all the way out with these two lunatics running amok around me. In the background I could see Malini's anxious eyes. I like to think she was worried about me. Samarsinghe followed me out onto the steps, still whacking like billy-oh. There was better light out here for Frankie so I obligingly stood there, letting Samarsinghe beat the living Bejasus out of me. I kept on firing off questions, like: 'Do you rape the boys?' and 'How many have you murdered?' and 'How much do you charge for your own sons?' – questions framed to make him go berserk, thereby providing us with tastier pix. He responded with whacks! and a string of cuss words you just could not print in a decent newspaper. The *Guardian*, yes, but not a God-fearing tabloid. None of what he said was particularly enlightening but it didn't worry me. I'd just verbal Samarsinghe and get him to say some shocking things when I was writing up the story. After all, I had a witness. He didn't. Frankie was taking his time over the snaps. I had the uncalled for suspicion he might be enjoying the spectacle. Our noble driver, Varun, threatened to come to my rescue but Frankie waved him out of shot. I'd had enough. I grabbed the stick from Samarsinghe and said, 'If you hit me one more time, I'll rip your lungs out.' That gave him pause. It also gave us enough time to bundle into the Datsun and scoot off. I was bloodied but unbowed. Frankie was cock-a-hoop, whatever that means.

He said, 'I got some great smudges.'

I said, 'I got some great bruises.'

Varun said, 'I break that man's back, yes?'

No. I tried to explain the tabloid hack's code of ethics. It was a bit like trying to explain the jokes in Kafka.

Three miles down the road we rumbled up outside the Perelawaya Children's Refuge and the whole jolly game started again. Frankie skimmed off half a dozen exteriors. He got a terrific shot of a couple of cowed boys looking out the window. He had switched his attentions to the smaller bungalow before Niaz steamed up. And steamed was the word. His language was much the same as Samarsinghe's, only without the clean bits. If my mother had been there she would have boxed his ears for the things he said about her.

I had a hidden agenda in coming back to the orphanage – to pretend that the boys had told me nothing. It was my feeble strategy for trying to protect the children we had seen. I let Frankie get his grainy snaps and then I pinned Niaz against the wall. I said, 'Why are the boys here too frightened to talk to me?'

He said something nasty so I banged his head off the wall. It made a pleasant boom.

I said, 'Why did the two boys refuse to tell us who comes here?'

Niaz said he was going to have us arrested. I tested his head again. It still boomed.

I said, 'I already know who visits – Leon Knapp gave me their names. But why won't the boys talk?'

Niaz was torn between the desire to spit in my eyes and to keep his head off the concrete. His head won. He went mutinously quiet.

I said, 'How did one boy die?'

He wasn't saying. I shook him around a bit more. Frankie thoughtfully offered to help but I said he might get his hands dirty. Varun wanted to floss his teeth with the car jack. I was sorely tempted.

In the end I let Niaz go. But before we left, I grabbed his grubby little ear and told it, 'Those boys were scared stiff, they're too frightened even to help themselves. But I'm going to help them. And if I find you've as much as slapped their wrist when I'm gone, I'll break your bloody neck.'

'We'll tear your head off,' Frankie contributed.

'We will kill you,' Varun said, clashing his teeth together.

We drove off in the general direction of beer. Behind us Niaz gulped and felt his bumps.

*

The raven-haired receptionist at the MacDuff was a girl of many talents. She spoke English to the English, French to the Frenchish, Japanese to the rich. If there'd been any Americans around, doubtless she would have spoken broken English too. She saw me loping across the lobby and sang out, 'Good afternoon, Mister Chard. You had a caller a few minutes ago.'

'Who?'

She said, 'I'm afraid the gentleman would not leave his name.'

Note the use of the conditional tense.

I said, 'Was there any message?'

'No. He just wished to know if you were staying here.'

Frankie and I looked at each other. Varun looked at the bar. Frankie said, 'You know what this means?'

I knew. Frankie said it anyway. 'It means they've tracked us down here. We'd better move it.'

We left Varun watering in the bar while we packed. Sri Lanka is a place of beauty with beauties all over the place, but we wanted to be far gone from it. Just say, for instance, that Niaz made up some totally Mickey Mouse story about me threatening to kill him and ran screaming to the cops. You're never quite sure how the Old Bill will behave in foreign lands. Are they addled and raddled with corruption? Are they the type likely to throw two honest journos in the slammer? Would they believe the word of some local sleazebag instead of two upright gents from Her Majesty's Press?

The best answer I could come up with was yes, they damn well would. This, I'm sure, is grossly unfair to the Sri Lankan constabulary, but having been banged up by their brothers in Denmark, Nigeria, Sweden and Kenya inter alia, I tend to lean on the paranoid side. Therefore I packed with haste. We still had three days on the island before KLM sent in a 747 to get us out. If we had to hang around in Sri Lanka for the next seventy-two hours, at least we could hang around somewhere less risky. Mount Lavinia beckoned.

Chapter Fourteen

There aren't many roads out of Kandy. That made it easier for them.

We tootled off southerly and westerly, banging along at fifty miles an hour. It doesn't sound much, but with buffaloes, goats and escaped mental patients on bikes lurking behind every corner, it felt like a hell-for-leather burn-up. En route Varun embarked on a long family saga, involving uncles in Trincomalee, aunts in Saudi, brothers in poverty, etc. Catherine Cookson could have knocked out a dozen block-busters from his ramblings. I have a very low tolerance threshold to stories about other people's families; my own are bad enough. So I looked at the scenery. It was mostly green with here and there a pretty hamlet, just to keep your eyes on the job. The overall effect was one of pastoral tranquillity. My eyelids drooped.

We were five miles out of Kandy when the bandits struck. I woke to find Varun leaning on the brake.

'Wotsit?' I said.

What it was, was a couple of Sri Lankan young-sters, each about ten foot tall. For a nanosecond I thought it must have been something I'd drunk, then

I realised they were on stilts. They wobbled about in the middle of the road, blocking our progress.

I asked Varun what the blankety-blank they were doing. He was grinning. He said, 'It's okay, Mister Max. It's a local custom. In the south we have fishermen on poles and they get money from the tourists for taking their photographs. Here the children do it on stilts.'

'What? We're supposed to give them money for pissing about in the middle of the road?' I was cross. These ten-year-old Dick Turpins had just wrecked a perfectly pleasant memory of Rosie misbehaving herself. I told Varun to tell them to sling their hooks. He gave a ripe chuckle and did nothing of the sort.

He said, 'Admit it, Mister Max. You have been caught in the children's net. Let Mister Frankie take their photo, you give the children a few rupees and we go on. Everybody happy.'

I wasn't. I didn't see why I should pay for Frankie's holiday snaps. I was grumbling along these lines until it occurred to me that the pic might come in handy when I eventually got round to writing my travel feature. It would take up space and cut down the amount of junk I'd have to write. Plus the stilt highwayboys gave me just the right sort of daft anecdote for the intro. I pushed Frankie out with instructions to smudge. I had to give him the money before he would get out. Varun and I puffed on our Bensons while Frankie laboured under the tropical sun. The children wobbled all over the shop. They weren't very good at it. We watched Frankie fiddle with his f stops and shutter speeds. He was all hot and moist. It was good fun watching him work. He didn't think much of it. He wasn't smiling. Nor were the boys. Not even a tiny grin.

They weren't smiling.

I sat forward and stared through the windscreen grime. Christ! I'd seen these faces, these unsmiling eyes before. Only last night these dead eyes had stared out at us from the orphanage playroom.

I shrieked, 'Run, Frankie! Run!'

He ran. He didn't know what was up, but he ran. He's been in far too many hairy places before to hang about. I thumped Varun on the shoulder. 'Get us out of here! Move it!'

The next bit took forever. Varun turned his bewildered gaze towards me in slo-mo. I remember him saying, 'What's wrong, Mister Frankie? Why are we going?'

I thumped him again. 'Go! Damn you! Go!'

Frankie was back in the car. The rear door was hanging open. He screamed, 'Back! Back! Back!' He was in the middle of the second Back! when they opened up. You just heard the bangs as the bullets socked into the Datsun. Varun's mouth was opening and closing without words.

I screamed, 'For Christ's sake, Varun! Panic!'

The two kids were still in front of us. He smacked the gearstick into reverse and kicked the accelerator. The engine roared and the tyres screeched like a bunch of stabbed sopranos. We rocketed back accompanied by the pong of burning rubber and the cracks of bullets. Frankie slammed the door and ducked down behind his camera gear in the back seat.

I was in the front passenger well, arms around my head. Our idiot driver was sitting up, one arm casually thrown across the top of my seat and looking back down the road to make sure we didn't hit any goats. I yelled at him, 'Get down!'

In the back Frankie said, 'Oh God! Oh God!'

I poked my head up. 'Have you been hit?'

'No.'

At which point the windscreen shattered and I had safety glass all over me like dandruff. Varun was still sitting up, spitting out glass. I'll say this for him. He could drive a hell of a lot faster going back than going forward. The bullets kept coming but whoever was firing them wasn't Annie Oakley. They were zinging past a yard or so abeam. Varun yelled, 'Don't hit my car!'

That did it for Frankie and me. We just started rolling about with laughter. It was the sheer surrealism of it all. The Datsun slewed round a right hand bend, nearly impaling us on an advancing truck, but we were out of the line of fire. Varun took his hoof off the accelerator. That stopped our roars. 'Keep going!' I bellowed.

'Faster!' shouted Frankie.

We must have done the best part of a mile before we let him ease up. Varun said, 'We'll call the Army.'

'Eh?'

'Tamil Tigers,' he explained.

I said, 'Since when have the Tamil Tigers been hiring local orphans to stage ambushes?'

Frankie said, 'We call an emergency underwear shop.'

That's one of the things that endears him to me. He can joke after nearly copping a bullet in his aperture setting. We wanted to inspect just how close we had come to a three-paragraph obit, but I wasn't happy hanging around. For all I knew, the gunslingers had a Maserati Bora parked up a banana tree and were about to give chase. I told Varun to forget Colombo and take to the hills. He interpreted this literally. He strongly recommended Nuwara Eliya where terraces of tea bushes perch on the high-rise countryside. He found himself a track and off we bumped, the sweet sunkissed air blasting through where the windscreen used to live. We examined the car's interior. The bullet which knocked the screen out had exited through the roof, indicating to a trained crime hack that the marksman was either a dwarf or he was firing from the ground. The exit hole was on the righthand rear passenger side, a spot normally occupied by Frankie's head. If I'd been sitting up, I'd have caught it somewhere around the left ear. Frankie whipped out the Olympus and started popping. He said, 'How many do you think there were?'

Varun said, 'Dozens.'

I said, 'We're talking about snipers, not bullets. I say there was at least one.'

Frankie said, 'I reckon two. One either side. We'll see when we get out.'

We stopped half an hour down the track. Judging by the holes in both sides, there'd been two hot shots. Or one with a gun that fired in stereo. The driver's mirror was gone. There were four deep gouges down the left wing. We'd lost both lights and half the number plate. They missed the tyres.

Frankie said, 'Looks like semi-automatic fire.' Monkeys like saying things like this. It makes them sound almost smart. I thought we'd been hit with hand guns, and not very macho ones at that. Otherwise the shots that peppered the wing would have continued on their wicked way and turned me into a tea bag.

Varun didn't care whether it was a bazooka or a water pistol. He wailed, 'Who will pay for my car?'

'We will,' said Frankie, meaning me.

That made Varun happy again. He smiled. 'No worries. Now I take you somewhere safe.'

I was proud of our little gofer. Most drivers in this situation would throw a fit or join the enemy. Not our Varun. He'd literally saved our lives and all he wanted in return was a new windscreen and a bit of bodywork. I felt a wave of reckless affection sweep over me. 'Varun,' I instructed, 'take us somewhere I can buy you a very tall, very special bottle of arrak. You deserve a drink.'

Mind you, I felt I deserved a few too.

We overnighted in the foothills of Nuwara. We had to stop early because the tropical night was coming down like thunder and we were minus lights. Also, Varun was less sober than the back road demanded. There was a hotel, a rickety old thing, knocked up in the days when they built the Empire. Varun stowed the air-conditioned Datsun out the back and we checked in using German names. I was Michael Schmeichel, Frankie Helmut Becker. We paid up front so the manager would not demand to see our passports. I said to him, 'Ver ist der bar?' And he answered in ripe German. Fortunately he also pointed to it. Many years ago the bar had been decorated in cream, possibly even white. Now it was yellow with nicotine and dead things. The central fan didn't work. The beer was warm. Somebody had murdered all the sofas and stuffing spilled out of the stab wounds. But we weren't bitching. We sat around a table mounted on an elephant's foot and pondered our past, present and immediate future. We all agreed that Samarsinghe and his dacoits had tried to do us in. Presumably they'd hoped we'd both get out of the car so they could pick us off at leisure. We diverged on what we thought they might do next. Frankie had them creeping through our windows at deep dead of night with oriental daggers chomped between their teeth. I guessed they would run for cover, fearing we had called in Plod and the British High Commission. But I also suspected there was more mischief lurking in the undergrowth. Varun went along with that one. He cheerfully asserted they would get Frankie and me at Colombo airport on our way home. There was logic behind this. Right now, Samarsinghe & Co were probably unaware of our hideout and we could stay hidden until it was time to fly away. But the only way out was via Colombo's Katunayake airport. The villains could easily bribe somebody there to keep them supplied with passenger flight manifests. They might even know already that we were scheduled to depart at noon on Friday. I rubbed a worried brow and ordered more drink.

There were other ways off the island, Varun informed. We could sneak down to Galle and catch a boat to the Maldives and fly home from there. Frankie liked the sound of that one. I didn't. It would take too long. But at least it offered the prospect of getting home alive. Frankie might have won the argument but for Varun remarking, 'Of course, the Maldives are Moslem.'

'So?' I said.

'So they do not have alcohol.'

So that knocked the Maldives off the map. We were back to Colombo airport and the prospect of an untimely end. We ordered more drink. I invited Varun to use all his skill and judgement and pick the spot where we would be most likely to fall bleeding. Without hesitation he chose the main hall. I recalled my first impressions of a rave party for half of Asia with people stampeding this way and that and back again. No one would notice a couple of hired killers mingling with the mob. Varun warmed to his theme. They could get us in the toilets, in the crowded cafe, in the press around the money changers.

'In the duty free shop?' Frankie asked.

Varun said that was unlikely and why bother asking anyway because we'd be murdered long before we got within sniffing distance of the tax free liquor counter.

I was intrigued. Why should we be safe there? Varun laughed at my ignorance. Because the killers would have to go through security, he explained.

They'd be frisked for guns, knives, what-have-you. And once you got into the departure lounge, there wasn't the same heaving mass of humanity.

I brooded. Frankie brooded. Varun hummed a mournful air. We could always ring the bells, I mused. A single call to the office would get them jumping on the Foreign Office. They'd get us protective custody. If I wanted, they'd send in a pack of minders to cover our backs. They'd lay on a private plane, if we needed. And they'd want to know what the bloody hell was going on. And I didn't want to tell them. Not until I had the whole shebang written up and tied with a bow.

Frankie was thinking aloud. He said, 'Is there an airport here?'

Indeed there was, said Varun. But that wasn't much use. It flew you to Galle, Trinco, Batticaloa and other sundry spots. All within the island.

'Yes,' pursued Frankie. 'And Colombo?'

And Colombo. I suddenly saw what was stirring in the candlelit corners of Frankie's brain. It was an idea of rare beauty.

I said, 'And in Colombo we can get an airside transfer to the KLM flight without having to check in.'

We'd lost Varun along the way. I let Frankie explain. 'We check in at Nuwara Eliya and tell them we're catching the Schipol flight out of Colombo. They transfer us to KLM at Colombo. We're already through security. We just wait around in the departure lounge until it's time to go.'

I said, 'And meanwhile the baddies are waiting for us to check in on the main concourse.'

A slow slice of a smile split Varun's face. 'That is very clever, Mister Frankie,' he said. 'I knew Mister Max was clever but I see you are just as smart.'

Mister Frankie, the smart ass, was so tickled he bought us all a drink.

We stayed put in Nuwara Eliya. I spent all of the next day drinking the local tea and writing up my notes. I didn't bother turning them into: *A child sex storm last night rocked the Government and big business* . . . That would come later. I got myself a wad of hotel note-paper, sepia with years of storage, and wrote everything out in a legible longhand. This wasn't an insurance policy. It was a last will and testament. If they were going to get me I was damn sure I'd get them. I wrote the whole yarn, right back to Claudine's mum predicting shock horror scandal in the World-Care Foundation, right up to our present plight. When I was done I read it in one solid sitting, checking for grammar and spelling bloomers. The last thing I wanted was some down table sub standing by my grave muttering, 'The bugger couldn't spell his name: we just made him look good.'

I did a proper job of it. I didn't even invent a single quote. This was the St James Version. But by the time I finished I felt about as happy as a sandboy facing a tidal wave. That was down to the tapes. It was grim work sitting there in that dusty room listening to the thin voice of Lal, describing without emotion the orphan boys' hideous life. Afterwards I yearned for company. But Frankie was hunting around for somewhere to develop his film and Varun had gone to check flights out of Nuwara Eliya. I wandered down to reception and got the directions for a shop with a photocopier. I ran off four copies and moved on to the next stop, a shop selling stamps and big envelopes. I posted one copy to Rosie, another to my sister in Yeovil. I thought about it for at least five minutes, then I addressed a third to Mr Ross Gavney, 27 Magpie Court. I thought about it some more and tore up that envelope. I wrote on the first page of each: 'By the time you receive this, I should be back in Blighty. If not, please forward these notes to Suptd. Ben Ashbee', with the relevant address. I still had two copies. I wanted to post them from some other place, just in case the local post office caught fire. I also had my original notes next to my heart.

Varun got back around six. I yipped a warm 'Hello!' because I was drinking alone in the gloom-laden bar and was beginning to view suicide in a fonder light. He was just as tickled to see me. He hadn't had a drink all day. But it had been worth it. He had two tickets for Friday's early bird flight into Colombo. I'd given him a whole heap of money. I didn't press him for the change. Frankie limped in dripping perspiration and joined the party. He had processed one roll and run off a string of contact prints. He must have used the Olympus because they were in focus. They mostly showed Ajit, the six-year-old, with a single shot of Lal. They were absolute knock-outs. Frankie said, 'I've got both on other films, but I'm posting these back now, just in case things get iffy.'

He wanted Varun to wire them out of AP in Colombo but I argued him out of it, pointing out that our Pic Desk would go spare if they knew he was in Sri Lanka and hadn't told them. Also, I didn't want AP nosing round my story.

Anyway, we had our escape mapped out, our tickets bought, my notes written and his smudges in our hands. It was time to enjoy ourselves.

We enjoyed ourselves for two solid days. I woke on the morning of the third to a sky as pink as Blackpool rock and to the chitter of grey monkeys armed with loud hailers. The room rocked when I walked. I tiptoed downstairs so as not to wake my hangover and forced myself to down a couple of hoppers – pancakes as thin as a butterfly's wing, with a fried egg plonked in the middle. Frankie had already gorged himself and was in hearty form. Snappers are too thick to get hangovers.

Varun stumbled around the place collecting our luggage. I was pleased to see his eyes had turned red in the night. We had a twenty minute drive to the airport. I thought at first it was a cricket pitch, until Varun pointed out a windsock, limp in the breezeless air. We checked in. We were the only passengers. Peering out of the terminal I could see why. Our plane was a 17th century single-decker bus with a rough approximation of a wing clapped on top. Somebody yelled out something in Sinhalese and Varun said, 'Your flight is ready.'

We said our farewells. It was a strangely subdued moment. Varun had been a good old mate through all the fun and games, getting shot at and getting ossified just like us. We shook each other warmly by the hand and swore undying friendship. Varun was still a shade subdued. Ooops. I'd forgotten to pay him. I hauled out my now slender wallet and did some mental arithmetic. Forty quid a day over five days was, what, two hundred. What the hell. Let's make it fifty a day, I doled the notes out in his hand. He counted them again. He said, 'For hire car there is also ten pounds a day insurance.'

I gazed into his crimson eyeballs. I said, 'Don't try your five-card trick on me, Varun.'

He laughed. 'Just keeping in practice, that is all.'

I planned to sleep all the way to Colombo but the pilot had a better idea. He saw the trip as one long fun-filled roller coaster ride, zooming up the crest of every thermal and plummeting like a shot parrot down the other side. Frankie loved it.

Colombo was wide awake and kicking up a stink when we juddered to a halt. In the front seat Baron von Richtofen got on the wireless and summoned up a mini minibus which ferried us over to international. There were too many people around in the departure lounge for us to feel comfortable. We sat there back-to-back, seeing a suicide bomber, a crazed knifeman in every passing Sri Lankan. We had about fifty pence left in rupees so there was nothing to do but sit there and imagine things. By the time they called our flight Frankie was Grade A Broadmoor material. We didn't speak until KLM 481 was a mile above Sri Lanka and we could smell the drinks trolley.

London arrived next day. A big grey island of concrete, blotched with parks and unexplained holes. It looked beautiful. As our dashing pilot, Captain van Transit, aimed for Heathrow, I made a momentous decision.'

I said, 'Frankie, I want you to live with me.'

He was horrified. Maybe not as horrified as me, but still shaken. I explained my thinking. Before Sri Lanka, I'd been the villains' only hate figure. But once Frankie started clicking in Kandy he became a target too. They had it in for both of us. We still had a chunk of scribbling and snapping to do, so why didn't Frankie share my hideaway until it was safe to stagger the streets again?

Frankie thought of the free food and drink in my bunker and he saw it made sense. 'Okay,' he said.

Five minutes after we got back to the Barbican I saw it wasn't okay. Our relationship made David and Goliath look the closest of mates.

'Clear that mess off the table,' I snarled, indicating half a ton of cameras.

'What mess?'

'That mess.'

'Where am I supposed to put them?' asked Frankie peevishly.

'I don't know. Under a bed. In a cupboard. Out of the way.'

My brother's flat was built for a bachelor, a tidy, clean, unencumbered bachelor.

'There's no room under the bed. He's got books and things there,' Frankie complained after a brief exploration.

'Try the wardrobe.'

In the end we pulled the settee away from the wall

and stuck everything there. We moved on to the next phase of the war. I said, 'Right, let's get the ground rules clear from the start. I sleep on the bed, you can kip on the floor.'

'Why should you get the bed?'

I said, 'Because it's my flat.'

He said, 'No it's not. It's your brother's.'

I said, 'Oh for God's sake, Frankie. Do you think my brother would want you in his bed?'

He saw the logic in this but he was still moody. I said, 'Okay, that's settled. Now meals. I do the cooking, you do the washing up.'

Frankie railed, 'Why should you get the easy bit?'

I thought of the endless minutes slaving over a hot microwave. I said, 'Because it's my flat.'

He said, 'And I'm your guest. Do you usually ask your guests to do the dishes?'

'Yes.'

Frankie muttered and went off to pour himself an outrageous whisky. I pretended not to notice. We haggled on about who should tidy the lounge, who did the shopping, who had the TV remote control. I let him have the buttons and he brightened up. The next battle caught me unawares. He picked up the phone and began picking out a number.

I said, 'Who are you calling?' I wasn't being nosy or anything. Just interested.

He said, 'A girl.'

I said, 'I'd better ring Rosie too.'

Frankie said, 'Yes, great. We can have them both round for a party tonight.'

Something went 'Uh-Oh' in my head. I said cautiously, 'Who is she?'

'Who? Mine? Just a girl I know.'

'Who?'

'Tara-lynn.'

Tara-lynn! May all the saints preserve us. Tara-lynn Throw-up-in-the-back-of-the-taxi Beavis. I said, 'You can't have her here. She'll wreck the place.'

Frankie said bitterly, 'I get it. It's okay for you to have Rosie round but I can't invite my girl. Why not?'

'Because, Frankie, the last time I saw Tara-lynn she was pouring a pint over some bloke's head because she thought he was somebody else; because she is the only person in recorded history to be barred from Hampton's; because she dances on tables after a small vodka.'

His eyes misted over with happy memories. He said, 'Yes, she does.'

'Well I don't want her dancing on any tables around here,' I said.

Frankie was scandalised. 'She wouldn't do a thing like that. She's changed now.'

I wondered if that meant she had started wearing knickers but I didn't say anything. I suppose I realised it was unfair to keep Frankie and the object of his sweaty passions parted. But I made him swear he'd pay for the damage and he'd kick her out as soon as she got boisterous.

There followed a happy hour of peace while we waded through the whisky and planned our next steps in the Tomlin affair. I'd already done a bit of thinking. I knew neither Tomlin nor his son would cough up.

Nor would Lewis Trefoyle. These days you need nothing less than a fork-lift truck to prise a sleazy politician out of office. Martin Crowley would break my neck if I asked him the time of day. Proudhoe Veizey would run bleating to his lawyers. Gus Clernthorpe would have us horsewhipped. And then there was Leon Knapp.

He was frightened and he was friendless. They'd blackballed him from the Kandy club so he might also be feeling hard done by. All that plus the verbal evidence from Sri Lanka. And even his own mother would have to admit Leon is not of the great thinkers of the day. If we leaned on him hard enough who knows what he might divulge. I outlined the master plan to Frankie and I think he caught enough of it to know what I had in mind. He was all set to go collect his motor and get snapping. I said this wasn't too clever. If the traffic plods stopped us they were liable to get alcohol poisoning from his breath. So he watched *Emmerdale* while I rang around to say honey, I'm home.

At least Rosie sounded pleased about it. She wanted to come round right there and then. I told her I had Frankie as an unpaying guest. She didn't want to come anywhere near the place. It took all my skills as a trained negotiator to make her change her mind. If I'd said anything about Tara-lynn's scheduled visit, she'd have left town.

Next, the office. I called Angela Whipple. She was busy, but not too busy to drop in a cheap crack. She said, 'While you were off sunning yourself, Jed

Kennedy picked up a nice little exclusive on the Tournier murder.'

Angie must have been under the cosh. It's not her style to snipe, especially about anything Kennedy might have written. He's a freelance who is better known as Cape Kennedy because of all the fliers he puts up. A flier is a news story which is the sole invention of the reporter. It has the merit of sounding as if it might be true. It has the demerit of being utter balls. I don't mind that. What I object to is being told to follow up a flier. It is useless to point out to a news editor that the whole thing is rubbish. What matters to a news editor is that it got a good show in the *People*, the *Mail* or wherever. It looked good. And that's all that counts.

I got Angie to put me through to Dinesh, a down table hack who owes me a favour and a tenner. He called up Kennedy's story from the library and read it out with many a chuckle.

Murder squad detectives probing the killing of beautiful business tycoon Claudine Tournier say the name of her killer could be in her little black book.

That's 25 words in the intro. Do they not have any subs over there? I read on:

The curvaceous 34-year-old was found shot dead last month and her body tossed into the Thames in London.

I don't think Cape Kennedy has quite caught the gist of things. Her body was not tossed into the Thames after they found it. Even the Old Bill draw the line at that. Cape burbled on:

Suspicion first pointed at an underworld hitman, known to be operating from a penthouse flat in Mayfair.

But 'tecs grilling her jet set friends now believe

Claudine, the wife of financier Sir James Tomlin, was leading a secret double life.

A senior officer said, 'She was a passionate woman with a string of devoted male admirers.

'We want to interview them all and we're going through her little black book. But many of them are married and we are meeting a wall of silence.'

I said, 'Balls, balls, balls.'

Dinesh said cheerfully, 'It gets worse.'

A close confidante of the dead woman who would not give her name said last night, 'Claudine had a list of lovers. She told me she couldn't resist young men with tight bottoms.

'It was an obsession for her. But she said she was frightened of one of them. She would not tell me who he was.

'I warned her to stay away but she couldn't help herself. It was a fatal attraction.'

The woman friend broke down in tears as she added, 'I'm sure she was killed by her jealous boyfriend when she tried to ditch him.'

Sir James Tomlin was too shaken to comment on the revelations last night but a City source said, 'This has come as a dreadful blow to him.

'He believed she was happy with him. He has been shocked to discover she was conducting affairs when he was out of town on high-pressure business trips . . .'

'Enough!' I told Dinesh. 'If you read any more I'll be sick.'

Now let us examine Cape Kennedy's world-beating exclusive. Its whole inspiration, I knew, came from iffy hints that I had stuck in my original copy the night of the murder. His story appeared in Monday's paper and he doesn't work Sundays. Therefore it was knocked up on Friday as a Sunday-for-Monday. We often do this. If there's not a lot in the diary for Sunday, the weekend news editor gets the hacks to write up all sorts of tosh on Friday. He has it in the bag. Come Sunday, he sends it to the subs, and they have half Monday's first edition sewn up before a single reporter has tapped a key. This is why Monday's tabloids always carry half-baked surveys – Do Girls Make Passes at Men Who Wear Glasses?/ Britain's Favourite Fantasy Harem/How to Squander A Million In A Day.

Getting back to the subject: whenever you see terms like 'senior officer' in a story, allow yourself a chuckle and turn to the horoscopes. You'll find them more factual. There is no such animal as the senior officer. He is on a par with the 'Buckingham Palace insider', the 'Cabinet colleague' and the unicorn. So, when you take the mythical animals' quotes out of Jed Kennedy's stuff you see it's nonsense with a capital S.

I rang the famous flier anyway for he is a mate.

'How goes it with the unemployed?' he asked impertinently.

I said, 'I was thinking of writing a great work of fiction and then I read your story.'

'Which one?' The man has no shame.

I said, 'The one about Claudine Tournier's little black book.'

He laughed. 'Great show, wasn't it? Anyway, it was nearly true.'

I said, 'Which word was that? I must have missed it.'

Kennedy said, 'No, seriously. Some guy called us last week. Wouldn't leave his name. A casual took the call. The bloke just asked us if we knew Claudine was putting it about. Our man asked who was she putting it about with. The bloke just said married men. Nothing else. End of story.'

I said, 'What do the murder squad say about it?'

'Don't know. Didn't ask.'

On such rock solid foundations many a page lead is built.

Chapter Fifteen

The girls came round that night. I feared we might have a cat fight on our hands. Frankie hoped we would. But everyone was on their best behaviour, by our standards anyway. Rosie engorged me with hugs and kisses and I didn't do much to dissuade her. She was tickled with her souvenirs of Sri Lanka. She was even more taken with my pith helmet. I rather liked it too. But I am a generous soul. I said, 'You have it.' More demonstrations of extreme affection. I wished I'd bought a dozen of the things.

Tara-lynn battered on the door with enough Chinese takeaways to feed Beijing. She was seven tenths sober, so she didn't eff and blind and, for all I know, she was wearing knickers. The four of us tucked into the grub and the laughter came easy.

Much later, in the refuge of Dominic's bedroom, Rosie got serious. She said, 'What next?'

'Next? I unbutton your blouse with my teeth. You've read the script.'

She pushed me away. She said, 'You know what I mean. So far you've been nearly murdered twice. If you get up their nose again they might make it third time lucky.'

I didn't want to talk about it. It was a news story. It was my province and she didn't know how things worked there. Hacks don't talk about their trade except to other hacks. We're not alone in this anti-social behaviour. Many feel the same. For instance, I can't imagine a brain surgeon coming home and saying to his wife: 'I've got a tricky ippydippyochtomy on tomorrow. What should I do?' Mind you, if he was married to Rosie, she'd probably tell him.

I said the Claudine Tournier story was mine, all mine. I wasn't going to walk away from it. The whole thing was set to blow to bits and I wanted to be there to watch it. Rosie threw a wobbly. She said, 'You're being irresponsible. Leave it to the police. You think a big story with your name on it is the most important thing in the world.'

I do think this, because I know it to be true. She went into a mile-long catalogue of my sins. I got home late. I drank too much. I never phoned her. I kept bad company. I frittered my money on riotous living. Until then I was unaware there was anything else you could do with money. And I never turned up when promised. And, and, and . . .

And I tried to jolly her out of it. Oh, and that was another thing: I patronised her all the time. I said, 'Has Tomlin hired you to monster me to death?'

Rosie went into a sulk. She knows I can't stand that. I surrendered. 'All right, all right. First thing tomorrow I go to Ben Ashbee and ask for protection. And I won't do any more snooping around.'

'Promise?'

'Promise.'

'Cross your heart and hope to die?'

'Cross my heart and hope to die a horrible death.'

Rosie looked me searchingly in the eyes. They were candid and unclouded by lies or trickery. She believed me.

But how was she to know I'd my fingers crossed behind my back.

Tara-lynn was first up. She'd polished off the last of the milk and skedaddled before either Frankie or I awoke. I left Rosie still in the arms of slumber and penned a note: 'Gone to give myself up. Call you later. Gallons of love.'

I didn't want to hang around in case she felt like escorting me to the cops, so Frankie and I slipped off to a greasy spoon and dined like kings. We got a taxi up to Muswell Hill, collected his office car and pointed it due west. I used the mobile en route to get the office to trace Leon Knapp's address. It was a house called Chantelle in the village of Barden, just the far side of Newbury. I remembered Chantelle was the name of a hit record for Leon in the days when young girls used to burst through reinforced concrete to kiss his jowls. I had a song in my heart too. It was a June morning of the type we used to make before we went European. Old England looked in pretty good nick as it flicked past us at 90mph on the M4. Even Frankie was moved to poetry: 'Nice, innit?'

And so we wended our blithesome way, in careless ignorance of the havoc we were about to wreak.

The house which called itself Chantelle looked as

if it had just been nicked from Acacia Avenue, Alicante. There was a spanking brilliance to the white stucco, set off by sun-baked red tiles and mysterious shadows in the cloisters. This is something else I never understand. Why do English people with wall-to-wall money build themselves houses which belong somewhere else? Take a trip along the upper reaches of the Thames and you are surrounded by Mexican haciendas and Disneyland castles. They don't half look daft in the English rain.

We parked the motor outside Maison Chantelle and gave it our scrutiny. A Japanese four-wheel-drive job tethered by the porch jarred with the Spanish motif. The Knapp mansion displayed a freshly nibbled acre of lawn and a bunch of bushes that looked as if they went to church twice on Sundays. A creeper of some sort had begun inching up the wall. Chantelle was spelled out in wrought iron at our end of the driveway and again on the wall of the house for the benefit of absent-minded postmen. The front door was woody and gnarled and black, as if it had narrowly survived the Spanish Inquisition. There wasn't a doorbell, just a chunk of pig iron serving as a knocker. I gave it a blatter and stood back. Frankie was silent but I could hear him thinking: 'This must have cost a packet.'

We waited ages until the mediaeval door sprung open to reveal a mediaeval figure in a red and white striped towelling robe.

'Yus?' said the figure. Knapp himself. This was the first time I'd ever seen him up close. I never knew he wore a rug. He'd just come from the shower so the hair over his ears was clinging wet. The rug was dull and dry.

I said, 'Good morning, Leon. I am Max Chard, and this is my photographer, Mister Frankie Frost.'

Frankie's Canon went click in my ear and the door went bang in my face.

I said, 'Hello, door.'

The door was the strong and silent type. I talked to it anyway. I said, 'Sorry to bother you door, we really want to see your master. You see, we've just come from Kandy.'

No response. I said, 'And everyone at the Perelawaya Children's Refuge sends Leon their greetings. They miss him. They send you their fondest wishes too, door.'

Nothing. I continued, 'Yes, and Lal and Ajit told me all sorts of things. But I suppose if you're not going to open up, you'll just have to read all about them in the paper.'

I left that one simmering quietly for a full minute. Still not a murmur.

I sighed. 'It's sad, door. Jimmy and Martin and the boys are pinning everything on Leon. They say he's the only one involved. Dearie me, the things they say he got up to . . . but I suppose if you're not going to let me in, I'll just have to take their word for it.'

The door opened its letterbox. 'It's lies. I'll sue you for every penny if you print a word.'

I said, 'Oh no you won't. Sir James Tomlin has given me twenty-four carat evidence. He's told me how Leon went to a bona fide orphanage and abused the boys. How he took snaps of them. How he has banned Leon from ever visiting the children again.'

The letterbox gulped. It said, 'Jimmy said that?'

'Indeed he did. And Martin Crowley and Lewis Trefoyle. And all the rest. If Leon sues my paper, we'll subpoena every one of them to testify against him.'

The letterbox flapped wordlessly for a moment, then it said, 'What do you want?'

I said, 'It's what Leon wants that counts. He needs damage limitation in spades. I am his only hope. Turn me away door, and your boss is stuffed.'

The letterbox threatened to call its lawyer.

I said, 'Do that. While you're at it, call the Sri Lankan High Commissioner, the Foreign Office and Detective Superintendent Benjamin Ashbee.'

'The police?' squeaked the letterbox.

I said, 'Not yet. But if you don't open up, you leave me with no alternative but to hand my dossier to Scotland Yard.'

The door gave me a black look and opened. Leon was a shade older, paler and uglier than when last seen.

He said, 'I'll talk to you. But no pictures.'

I cordially lied that we wouldn't take any snaps and we were in. The hallway was a chequerboard of black and cream tiles. A couple of shady nooks played home to darkly Spanish guitars. It was a dead ringer for Old Seville, though old Sevillians were most likely averse to stapling platinum discs to the walls. Leon, barefoot, padded down the hall and right out into a Spanish back garden, encrusted with a swimming pool. The pool was in the shape of a record, or maybe it was just round. He perched on the edge of a sun lounger, his eyes swivelling from Frankie to me. He didn't know whom to watch. I dropped into one of those swinging chair things and lit a cigarette. I said, 'They've hung you out to dry, Leon.'

'What?' One hand massaging one knee.

I said, 'You're the scapegoat.'

He said, 'I don't know what you're talking about.'

I furrowed my brow at him. 'Oh, come on, Leon. I've got Trefoyle – a Government minister – rubbishing you. Imagine how that will look if you sue us. Want to hear what he says?'

Knapp nodded dumbly. Both hands massaging both knees.

I ruffled through the back pages of my notebook and imagined Trefoyle's orotund English. I said, 'Here it is. Trefoyle says, "The orphanage has the highest criteria for the care and welfare of its young inmates. Its staff are of course aware that many have been traumatised by their previous experiences through the civil conflict. The director's primary objective is to ensure that these traumas are not exacerbated, that indeed they are mitigated by the work of the centre. Mister Niaz was most concerned when some of his charges began manifesting symptoms of distress. Naturally he called upon the expertise of a qualified child psychologist who inferred from the children's statements that they had been molested in a sexual manner. Mister Niaz instituted a most rigorous inquiry and informed the trustees of the WorldCare Foundation of his concern. The children were subject to diligent medical examinations and further counselling. These established that the children had in fact been abused. Each child so molested cited Mister Leon Knapp, a Foundation trustee, as the perpetrator. Mister Niaz obtained conclusive evidence of this when Mister Knapp was apprehended taking photographs of the boys whilst engaging in obscene and unnatural practices . . ." '

Leon had started to emit a strange whuffling sound. I said, 'Tough stuff, wouldn't you say? Do you want to hear Martin Crowley on the same subject?'

He didn't say no, so I flipped to another page. I read: 'I know Leon Knapp through my work on the Foundation. He always struck me as an oddball, a bit too full of his own ego. You know the type, he was famous for fifteen minutes once and he never learned to cope with the real world. The Foundation just used him as a minor celebrity. It was good for fund-raising. None of us had the faintest idea he was a pervert. If I could get my hands on him, I'd . . .'

'A minor celebrity?' Leon was hurt. Too hurt to notice Frankie squeezing off shots.

I said, 'They've screwed you to the wall. You'll never be anybody's king again.' This was a below-the-belt reference to one of his mawkish ballads which went: 'I wanna be your king, and you be my queen forever, Ooooh yeaah.'

It was in the mid-seventies out there by the pool but Knapp was hugging himself for comfort. A more civilised man might have taken pity on the wretch. I enjoy blood sports.

I said, 'The other trustees are holding a meet this weekend to which you're not invited. They will vote to kick you out. Then they'll go public. That's the story we're going to run all over page one, with the boys' pix and quotes across the centre spread on Monday. Unless you have a better idea.'

A pin prick of light shone briefly in his muddied brown eyes. 'What sort of idea?'

I said, 'You tell me all about the others' involvement and I'll play down your naughtiness. Call it plea bargaining.'

He gave a nervous laugh. He said, 'I call it blackmail.'

I said, 'Blackmail is an ugly word. Call it a dirty great threat.'

He said, 'You want me to talk about people like Tomlin? You want me to incriminate myself? You must be nuts. No deal.'

I stood up, closed my notebook and stuck it in my pocket. I said, 'Come on, Frankie. The man doesn't want to listen.'

I turned and began to walk away. I got five and a half steps before he tried another laugh. It was more of a jeer but it was ragged around the edges. He said, 'You're making it all up. I've done nothing. You can't print anything.'

I turned around slowly. I put on what I hoped was a thin cruel smile. I said, 'Pick up your paper on Monday and this is what you'll read: "Seventies rock idol Leon Knapp was last night branded an evil sex monster who preys on helpless orphans." Stop. New par. "The has-been singer exploits boys as young as six to gratify his depraved lust." Stop. New par.'

I'm not sure which bit got to him. I think it was

that crack about the has-been singer. At any rate, he buckled up and started feeling sorry for himself. I stood patiently waiting. Frankie banged off a whole roll. We let him bleat away to himself. I carried on with my imaginary news story: 'Bachelor Knapp broke down and wept when confronted with his shameful secret . . .'

He wiped a runny nose on the towelling robe. He said, 'Don't say any more. What do you want?'

I returned to the swing chair. I said, 'First of all I'd like a large gin and tonic while I think up a way to get you out of this mess.'

He actually looked grateful. He scuttled off, returning with ice bucket, bottle of Gordons, the lot. I took my time pouring the drink. You have to watch it with the tonic. I settled back and said, 'Right, Leon. First of all you should know I'm not all that interested in a tacky little sex scandal halfway across the world.'

I'm one hell of a liar. A flicker of relief chased across his eyes. I said, 'I'm a chief crime correspondent, which means I'm picky about the sort of stories that deserve my talents. This isn't one of them. Who cares what happens to a couple of Third World kids?'

More unconfined joy from the child molester. I said, 'What interests me is big stuff – drug barons, Mister Big gangsters, brutal killers, that sort of thing. Which is why I'm giving you a bad time.'

He said, 'I'm not with you . . .'

I was patient. I said, 'Claudine Tournier got herself murdered last month. So did a girl called Shirley

Ham. I'm betting it's because they found out about Kandy and—'

'—It wasn't me!'

I said, 'No. You had the perfect alibi. You were off in Sri Lanka abusing children. So who did it?'

He gripped the edge of his chair and leaned forward. 'You're not going to involve me?'

I said I wasn't. The fibs you have to tell in this job. His thin lips spread in a half smile. He said, 'I haven't a clue.'

I said, 'That's it, Leon. You've blown the deal.' And I stood up again. It took all the warmth of his lovable personality and an earnest promise to tell the truth before I consented to have another gin. Knapp's was a sordid and trite story. Once upon a time in old Amsterdam there was a club catering for paedophiles. It was there he first met the likes of Michael Tomlin and Gus Clernthorpe. They formed themselves into a seedy group, calling themselves the Young Boys Network. Knapp recruited his chum, Proudhoe Veizey. Tomlin added Trefoyle and Crowley. A couple of blue chip City types joined the fraternity. Happy times were had by all until the Dutch Old Bill took an interest. The Network tried Denmark but that was risky too. Then Claudine Tournier embarked on the WorldCare Foundation, with husband Sir James Tomlin and stepson Michael looking after the business side of things. Michael went to Sri Lanka to set up the Kandy project and found child sex on tap. Then Sir James took an interest.

He knew all about Michael's little peccadilloes. He also knew the Network numbered various influential types. He wasn't interested in paedophilia. But he was most anxious to have the City men and Trefoyle as business allies. He set up boys for them, they set up deals for him. It was his idea to launch the orphanage. This way the Network could run their own show without fear of leaks. He had the members made Foundation trustees, which gave them perfect cover for sex jaunts. They could even claim their travel expenses against tax. The local Law thought they were do-gooders and smiled on them. What could go wrong?

What went wrong was Claudine. She began asking questions about why Kandy was such a popular spot. Then, back in Britain, Michael nearly got done for indecently assaulting a schoolboy. Claudine made the connection. She blew up and tackled Sir James, threatening all sorts of mischief. She was hellbent on exposing his pals, thereby derailing his gravy train. He was less than enthusiastic about the idea.

Therefore Sir James had his wife murdered? Knapp thought that was it. And Shirley Ham? I had to explain to him who the late Shirl was. Yes, Tomlin probably topped her too. There was something that didn't fit, I said. Why was Tomlin so anxious that 'Kandy must be stopped' after Claudine's death. That was easy, said Knapp. The Network imposed a blanket ban on visits to the orphanage as soon as Claudine sussed what was really going on. Tomlin was frightened she might have private investigators turning it over. The whole operation went into cold storage until the trustees felt it was safe again.

But Leon broke the ban. And he took pix, which

was absolutely taboo. The boys told Niaz, he told Mike – Michael Tomlin – and he got Crowley to visit Knapp, offering to string him up unless he handed over the prints and the negs. Knapp handed them over.

And who was the merry matchman who nearly incinerated me? Knapp didn't know. Crowley most likely. Knapp was never privy to the Network's innermost council. Why did they ever admit him to their company anyway? The answer was the little plastic bags of cocaine he provided for Michael Tomlin. And there you have the whole story. Knapp sat back.

I said, 'Would you testify to all this in court?'

His eyes went slideabout. I produced my tape. I squawked it back a couple of revs and let him hear the sound of his own voice. He looked disappointed with me. I said, 'You'll testify?'

He said yes in a very small voice.

He didn't wave goodbye as we booted off home. But then we didn't wave to him either. When last seen he was a little red and striped thing standing alone in the cloisters.

I saw the light on the road to Hammersmith. I was sifting through my notes to take my mind off Frankie's driving. I was puzzling over one line of fractured shorthand when all of a sudden it hit me. KERPOW! I said, 'Jesus!' Frankie didn't blink. It's probably something all his passengers say.

I sat there savouring the moment. I said, 'I know who the killer is.'

'Oh yes? Who?'

'Michael Tomlin.'

Frankie said, 'How do you know it was him?'

I explained. The line of notes I'd been decoding read: 'He was a friend of Mike's.' I at first deciphered it as 'a friend of Max'. It's easily done – the shorthand outline for Mike's and Max are the same. The names are very similar. They can easily be confused in conversation. On the telephone for instance. A distant doorbell chimed in my brain. And that's when an idea walked in and turned the light on.

Frankie said, 'What are you raving about?'

I told him of the night Shirley was killed. Her dad had told me she'd gone to see Mike, and I, egotistical dimwit that I am, told him no, no, no – she'd gone to see me, Max. And while we were arguing about it, Mike Tomlin was wrapping a rope around her neck and slinging her in the Thames.

Frankie said, 'It might have been a different Mike.'

I said, 'Yeah. And maybe it was a different Adolf Hitler.'

Royce, our lawyer, listened to the tape and threw a fit. 'No corroboration. You've used menace. Knapp will withdraw everything he said. We'd be wide open to libel writs from every single one of them.'

I said, 'Apart from that, how do you like the story?'

He hated it. Newspaper lawyers hate anything true. They wander around muttering, 'The greater the truth, the greater the libel.' They also hate bald statements of fact. Here is an ideal intro in their world: 'An alleged man, in premises purporting to be a law court, was said to have been found guilty by person or persons unknown of driving under the influence of drink or drugs to such an extent as to impair his driving, as laid down under Section 37 of the Road Transport Act.' Riveting stuff, isn't it?

I saw I was getting nowhere with Royce so I roped in Angela Whipple and we cornered the Editor gazing out the window and scratching his backside. He looked allegedly guilty.

I went through the story at a gentle amble, for it was after lunch and his faculties were not at their sharpest. When I had done, he chewed his lip for half a minute. He said, 'Write what you've got and I'll have a look at it.' This was him saying, 'I haven't understood a word you said. I'll read your story when I sober up.'

I returned to my desk and hammered it out. Eighteen hundred words, which is an awful lot for a tabloid. I was checking it for spelling when I smelt something disgusting on the left flank.

Belker said, 'In my office. Now!'

It was a brief yet sunny conversation. He accused me of disobeying him by going to Kandy. I said it was my R&R leave and I was unaware certain countries were banned. He charged me with high treason for not telling the office what I was up to. I said that as a loyal hack I had forgone my hols to provide the paper with an exclusive. He stumped up and down, glaring at the ceiling and firing accusations over his shoulder. I let him. I have a theory: The Chard Theory of Relative Sobriety. You always hear people saying things like: 'You've got to forgive Charlie for throwing up in your bidet – he was drunk', or, 'I wouldn't have stuck the corkscrew in your shoulder if I'd been sober.' But this is wrong. In my experience, people are generally a whole lot more civilised when they're rat-arsed. Therefore, what we should say is: 'You can't blame Belker for running amok. He hasn't had a drink all day.'

I find that if you apply my theory to life, you are more tolerant of others' misbehaviour. So it was with Belker. I smiled sorrowfully at him. It didn't help. He booted me out of his office. And then he went off to do his damnedest to spike my story.

Between him and the scaredy-pants lawyer, they did a good job of it. All references to the Tomlin clique were excised. I ended up with this:

Wrinkly rocker Leon Knapp last night confessed he uses orphan boys to gratify his evil sex lust.

And he claimed a sinister paedophile ring murdered cuisine queen Claudine Tournier.

She was gunned down and her body thrown in the Thames after she stumbled on their sordid secret.

The perverts – who style themselves the Young Boys' Network – include a senior politician and top tycoons.

They abuse helpless children as young as six – rewarding them with cheap plastic toys or gaudy crayons. And Seventies' star Knapp says the ring also ordered the murder of secretary Shirley Ham when she learned of their depraved activities.

Knapp broke down and confessed to his role after we confronted him with evidence of systematic child sex abuse.

He stressed he played no part in the double murder, but admitted he was a frequent visitor to the phoney orphanage where the boys are caged.

We tracked down the Network's activities to a refuge for war waifs in Sri Lanka.

But when our chief crime correspondent Max Chard and ace lensman Frank Frost tried to see the boys, they were ambushed and shot at by hired gunmen working for the Network.

There was much more in like vein, with paragraphs beginning with And, For and But. Words like vile, seedy and sinister littered the copy like currants in a cake. I believe the posher schools tend to frown on tabloidese. It ain't good English, they sneer. Well maybe they should get Marcel Proust to write up the story of the call girl, the curate and the carrot. That would shut them up.

My story was set for Saturday's splash, with the Kandy pix and interviews on the centre spread. But some berk in West Lothian murdered his ex-wife because she won custody of their stupid white rabbit. Also, sports desk bagged the spread for a Wimbledon preview. My stuff was rejigged for a single column on page one, with the rest scrunched up at the back of the book. Then they had an even better idea. Why not hold it as a Sunday-for-Monday? That meant they'd slot it away in the twilight zone between the woman's pages and the bingo. The Chard Theory of Relative Sobriety failed me. I was fit to be tied. But then I was relatively sober myself.

I lassoed Frankie and we plunged into The Stone dive bar. We set off on a kamikaze drinking mission, pausing only to badmouth Belker, the Editor, the lawyer, and anyone else we could think of. Coming up eight, I had a window of sobriety. I remembered I'd better tell Ben Ashbee the score before the story hit the paper. I left Frankie congealing on a stool while I cabbed it to the nick. Big Ben said hello, and he'd nothing new to tell me, so would I kindly go and clutter up somewhere else. I said all right then, he could read all about it on Monday morning, right after he'd got his bollocking from the Commissioner. Ben invited me to sit.

It took an hour to tell, and a civilian clerk with nice legs wrote down every word of it. Ben listened to my brilliant theory about the Mike/Max conundrum and didn't laugh. D.I. Harry Pennycuik came in halfway through and started making smart remarks. Ben told him to rustle up some tea and that got rid of him. When I'd finished, Big Ben did a strange thing. He smiled. It rocked me. Then he said, 'Thanks, Max.' That knocked me off my chair.

Ben said, 'You've given me the excuse I needed.'

'What for?'

He said, 'To turn that lot over. They've been as tight as a duck's arse. Nobody's said a thing. Of course, you haven't got anything on the murders. On the basis of what you say, I can't even pull them in for questioning about the murders.'

Something here was passing me by. I said, 'So why are you so happy?'

Ben cleared his throat and said, 'Because I have reasonable suspicion that Michael Tomlin might be involved in the peddling of sex tours, in contravention of–'

'I know,' I said testily. 'But how does that help your murder inquiry?'

Big Ben smiled again. 'Because I have reasonable suspicion that pornographic literature or material might be—'

I caught on. 'A search warrant!'

'Several search warrants,' said Ben. 'And we'll look under every speck of dust.'

I said, 'When?'

Ben said, 'As soon as I get a sworn statement from Leon Knapp.'

He ordered the clerk to rush off and type him a transcript. He said he needed it right away. I didn't like the way things were going. I could see my story going out the window. I said, 'Are you seeing Knapp tonight?'

'Yes.' He reached for the phone.

I said, 'Ben, you owe me a favour. Don't lift Knapp, Tomlin or anyone until after my story's in Monday's paper.'

He said, 'Why not?'

I said, 'Because the Yard's press bureau will tell everyone you've got him and it will be in all the Sundays. Our lawyer will spike my story, saying it's sub judice.'

Ben looked uncertain. I said, 'Think of it. People read on Sunday that Tomlin has been lifted for running a child sex ring. Then on Monday they read my stuff that Claudine Tournier was murdered by a child sex ring. They'll say, "Just fancy that – it was her stepson what done it." I'd cop the lot for libel, contempt of court, the works.'

Ben's hand floated above the phone but he didn't pick it up. He said, 'Don't you ever tell a soul I did this: I'm giving you until Monday morning, after your paper is on the streets.'

I said, 'And then a dawn swoop?'

Ben said, 'And then we get the bugger out of bed.'

I rolled off into the night a happier man. I now had just the push I needed to force the Editor to give my story a decent show. News stories have a very limited shelf life because news executives have very limited intelligence. What happens is they read your raw copy one day and they say great, terrific stuff, let's run with it. But for one reason or another it doesn't make the paper – usually because advertising department have suddenly sold another three pages. So next day you put the story up again. The execs dimly remember having read it before. They say: 'It's old. It's already been done.' And no matter how sensational the story, they spike it. Until my interview with Ben, I feared my Kandy exposé was doomed to such a fate. They also had one insurmountable objection to it: they hadn't thought up the idea themselves, and that rankled.

But now I could go back to the Editor, tell him the Old Bill were nicking Mike Tomlin as a result of our exclusive, and he'd have to run the story. Then, after the jury found Tomlin guilty of something or other, we could run a big backgrounder on how our fearless investigation put him behind bars. The Editor would get to write one of his celebrated leaders on Why The Press Must Not Be Muzzled (Except When It Might Do The Tories A Mischief).

I tooled up back at the Barbican sometime in the early hours to find Rosie in residence. Asleep. There followed a brief but pathetic attempt to get her to make wild, abandoned love. She told me to go asleep: that she'd love me in the morning. Though how you can preplan wild, abandoned love is beyond me.

When the first faint fingertips of noon propped my eyes open, I felt more like a wild, abandoned funeral. I'm getting too old for this drinking business. I turned on Radio Four and listened to the heads. All foreign, apart from the traditional Friday night council house blaze in Jockland. Rosie was out. Her note told me that. I cranked up the coffee maker and leafed listlessly through the rivals. They offered standard Saturday morning fare – too many Royals, too many telly stars in love split mysteries. I thought what things would have been like if we'd run my story. All across Britain people would be going 'Strike a light!', 'Flaming 'eck!' and 'Och Aye the Noo!' Instead we offered them the stupid rabbit story under the head: 'LOOK BACK IN ANGORA – Hubby blasts ex in bunny battle.' No wonder the Press gets a bad name.

Rosie returned full of bounce. She'd nicked her sister's little blue Metro and was all set to take me for a whirl. I needed an outing, said Rosie, a qualified doctor in her spare time. Now, where should we go? I suggested Hampton's. She prescribed somewhere further afield. I said let's stop at Hampton's for a livener. Only for one, she said. Only for one. I agreed, hoping she might fall under the spell of Hampton's ageless ambience.

There were a few hacks from the Sundays leaning

on the bar for support. We swopped the usual vile slanders on our absent colleagues and ran through the current repertoire of jokes. I saw Rosie looking at her watch. She was on Buxton mineral water, so I suppose she wasn't enjoying herself as much as the rest of us. I waited until she slipped out to the loo and I ordered in another round. They charged £1.50 for the water. I know bars where you can get a decent pint for that. I was paying for her spendthrift ways when Gerry, the barman/owner, said, 'Did you meet your friend?'

I said, 'What friend?'

Gerry helped himself to a fistful of stale peanuts. He said, 'The bloke who was in here this morning.'

I pointed out that (a) I had many friends, and (b) I had not been in the dump in the morning. Therefore I didn't know who the hell he was talking about. He didn't know either. The man wasn't a hack. Gerry thought he was casually dressed, but he couldn't be sure. Was the man green, purple, orange, black, white? He hadn't asked him. Did Mr Mystery leave a message? Just said he'd catch me later. If Gerry had been the deep throat in Watergate, Nixon would still be president. I congratulated him on his observation skills, he said no problem, and off he rolled to rook another customer.

Rosie dragged me screaming and tearful out into the sunshine and tucked me into the passenger seat. She stuck Mozart or something like that on the tape and off we went to mix it with the weekend drivers. I fell asleep. When I awoke there was green all around me. Green trees, green fields, green hedges. I felt car sick. I said, 'Where are we?'

Rosie had no idea. Somewhere in Sussex, she guessed. Wasn't it glorious? It wasn't, but I didn't want to shatter her illusions.

She found us a country pub with roses fighting each other outside the door and a sign saying Bar Meals Served All Day. That meant they served drink all day. Inside it was one of those cosy welcoming inns so dear to our hearts. Everywhere you looked there were signs saying No Credit, No Denims, No Singing, No Dogs, No Dancing On Tables Without Your Drawers On. They hadn't got around to banning drink yet.

Rosie said, 'When I am a rich and famous designer, I'll buy a cottage in the country and keep chickens.' She had rationed herself to a weakish glass of white wine so she wasn't thinking straight.

I said, 'Will you come and visit me at weekends?'

She chirruped, 'No. You can have a summer house in the garden where you can sit and write famous books. In the evenings, we'll stroll down to the village pub and listen to the local gossip.'

I cocked an ear to the present local gossip. They were talking about double-glazing and grain subsidies. I told Rosie, 'I'll come to your cottage when I die. You can use my ashes to fertilise your roses.'

We drove back north along lanes that dipped and dived by rivers and pig farms. Rosie crooned soothing pastoral music. By the time we got back to London she had mellowed enough to unchain me for another bite at Hampton's. She went off to see a mate, promising to collect me later, for she was staying the night at the Barbican.

My mysterious friend had been in again but Gerry still hadn't bothered to ask his name. I wondered if it was a minion from the Law, seeking my assistance in solving the rest of the country's crime. Then I forgot all about it as I caroused with the Wildebeest and a herd of hacks from the *People.* It was five minutes off kicking out time when Gerry sang out, 'Car for Mister Chard. Max, your driver awaits without.'

I made my farewells and picked up a few receipts for my exes. It had been a night well spent. We set off for the Barbican by way of Battersea; an unusual route. But it allowed Rosie to pick up her toothbrush and sundries. She tossed them in the back and we headed back across the city along dark and drear back streets, following one of her mystic short cuts. We were tootling along merrily when she said with exasperation, 'For God's sake, pass.'

'What?'

She said, 'Not you. It's that silver car behind. It's stuck on my bumper.'

I craned round the headrest for a peek. The silver car was a top of the range BMW. I believe one should be considerate to fellow motorists, no matter how stinking rich they are. I said, 'Pull over and let him through.'

Rosie slowed to twenty. So did the Beemer. I said, 'Pull in to the side. He's frightened of scratching his new toy. Or maybe it's a woman driver.'

Rosie trundled up by the kerb. So did the Beemer. I sat up and had another look. The BMW had a tinted screen so you couldn't see anything inside. Also, it had lamps like Eddystone Lighthouse. I said, 'He might just be lonely.'

My chauffeuse said, 'Maybe he's looking for somewhere. Should we stop?'

I said, 'Where are we anyway?'

She said, 'I'm not sure.'

I said, 'Oh that's okay then. For a minute I thought we were lost.'

Rosie slapped the Metro down a gear and pumped the accelerator. We shot off like a nervous greyhound. The G force nearly knocked my head off. She said, 'I don't like it. I'm going to find somewhere less lonely.'

It was a good idea and it might have worked if the Beemer had behaved itself. Instead, it swung out behind us, accelerated and roared past, coming to a shrieking halt half way down the deserted street. Its front doors flew open simultaneously and two men stepped out.

Rosie started braking. I shouted, 'Don't stop, Rosie. Go!'

For I had noticed something she hadn't. The BMW's numberplate. It was MT something. As in Michael Tomlin something. Rosie found her right foot again and we scraped past, causing the driver to jump out of the way. I saw Tomlin's startled angry face flicker in our lights.

Rosie said, 'What's going on? Do you know him?'

Yes, I said. The bloke whose little toe she'd just pulped was Tomlin junior.

'The one you think murdered Claudine Tournier?'

'And Shirley Ham. That one.'

She said, 'Oh God, what does he want?'

I thought about it. I didn't feel he was looking for directions to the nearest doner kebab. I said, 'Don't talk. Just drive like the wind.'

I twisted round again. Tomlin and partner were back in their car and in hot pursuit. Rosie took the words out of my mouth. 'Oh shit!'

I was trying to think fast and not having much success. I said, 'Listen, Rosie. You've got nothing to do with me. You're a minicab driver for London and City. Okay? You're just driving me home. I'll get out right here and you scoot off. Find the nearest phone and ring nine-nine-nine.'

She said, 'No. I'm staying with you.'

'No. Drop me quick.'

'No.'

The Beemer was back licking our bumper. I said, 'Stick to this road. There's lights up ahead.'

Rosie promptly hurtled left into the darkest street in Christendom. Tomlin overshot. I heard the roar of his engine as he whizzed back and had another go at the corner.

The Metro's headlamps picked up empty buildings and sightless windows stretching all the way down the street to a brick wall. A brick wall ten feet high, straddling the roadway like the rock of ages. We didn't get close enough to inspect the graffiti. Rosie clipped a passing lamppost instead and we slewed round, coming to an untidy halt in the path of the pursuing Beemer. 'Double shit,' said Rosie.

We sat in our dented Metro watching the enemy. They pulled up ten or so yards away. Tomlin killed the lights and stepped out. He was in no hurry.

'Remember you're a minicab driver,' I told Rosie.

'No I'm not.'

'Please.'

She said, 'That's the last time I pick you up from Hampton's.'

'You may, alas, be right.'

Tomlin's pal had got out too. He stood leaning against the BMW and looking our way. We couldn't see his face, but I knew he wasn't the Good Samaritan. Tomlin arrived at the driver's side. He said, 'Good evening, Miss Bannister.'

So bang went my plan to pretend Rosie was a cabbie. He had both his hands in his pockets. He sounded chummy and relaxed. He strolled round to my side, stopping to admire the crumpled wing en route. He said, 'Had a bit of a bash, have we?'

I said, 'Just a pint of shandy, offisher.'

He thought that was funny. He smiled anyway. He leaned down to my level and said, 'Might I have a word with you, Max – in private?'

I unfurled myself and stepped out. I leaned through the window and whispered to Rosie. Get the engine started. There's just enough room for you to zip past his car and get away.'

She looked as if she hadn't heard me. I turned to face Tomlin. He was still sporting his used car salesman smile. He said, 'Let's talk by my car.'

I followed him like the faithful little puppy dog I am. I didn't speak. I was too busy negotiating with the Almighty his terms for letting us out of there alive. They were pretty steep. We reached the BMW and I saw Tomlin's passenger. It was Martin Crowley, well known thug of this parish. He smiled with the warmth of the big bad wolf. The Almighty's terms shot up.

Tomlin looked upon my parchment face and trembling limbs and somehow guessed my unease. He found it amusing. He said, 'Don't look so frightened – we just want to talk to you.'

As long as he did the talking. My lips weren't up to it. I looked back over my shoulder and saw Rosie frozen in the Metro. Tomlin pulled a paw from his pocket and made an urbane gesture. He said, 'I apologise if all this seems a shade melodramatic. I'm afraid Miss Bannister drove off from her flat before we could talk to you.'

So they'd been watching Rosie's place. I said through locked teeth, 'How did you get her address?'

Tomlin thought that was hilarious too. He said, 'Elementary, my dear Watson. When someone attacked you in your flat your paper carried a couple of stories about you. In one you were pictured with your girlfriend. The paper named her as Rosie Bannister. Did you know, that's how she lists herself in the phone book. Rosie Bannister. Martin tried to contact you at Hampton's today. When you didn't show there, we tried your girlfriend's flat. Simple, really.'

I tugged this about. If they were set on doing me a mischief, Crowley wouldn't have shown his face in Hampton's. What were they up to then?

Tomlin kindly explained. His voice was still as sweet as Muscadet. He said, 'We believe you have been to Kandy and we believe you might be contemplating writing a story for your paper.'

I said the thought had occurred. Tomlin pretended I hadn't said that. He said, 'Naturally, we are very concerned. Our work in Kandy has been blameless and if you were to put a slur on it, you might cause irreparable harm to the WorldCare Foundation. And, by implication, you might harm the reputations of the individual trustees.'

He gave me a moment to swallow this drivel. He said, 'Of course, we would be obliged to issue writs for defamation. Your newspaper would be faced with massive damages. Your own reputation as a respected journalist would also suffer.'

I said, 'You're saying I've got it wrong?'

Tomlin took his time. He said, 'The facts are these. One trustee, and we believe you may already have interviewed him, is alone responsible for an abuse of the trust we placed in him. We have subsequently dealt with him. He is no longer connected to the Foundation. His offences took place in a foreign country where Britain is unable to prosecute a case against him. We assure you that had these incidents taken place within the United Kingdom, we would have reported the matter to the police.'

I glanced back towards Rosie who showed all the animation of a robot in a Volvo ad.

Tomlin was still enthralled by the sound of his own voice. He said, 'We acknowledge you have gone to considerable efforts in your pursuit of this false story. We are prepared to make substantial recompense, providing you agree not to publish the story.'

I said, 'How substantial?'

He said, 'One hundred thousand pounds.'

He said it just like that. No emphasis. No rolling eyeballs. I leaned against the Beemer and counted up the noughts. There were five of them.

Martin Crowley chipped in from across the bonnet, 'It's a lot of money for what was it your newspaper called it – a few smacks with a wheel brace.'

Tomlin jumped in hastily: 'Not that we were party to that. I give you my word we were not involved. The sum I have mentioned is for your time and your discretion.'

I said, 'Discretion is my middle name.'

Tomlin said, 'Please don't misunderstand us. This is not what one might call hush money. We are simply anxious that the work of the Foundation is not jeopardised by baseless allegations.'

I peered up and down our dead-end street. This was the street that time forgot. Not even a scavenging mongrel, far less a busload of bobbies. I said, 'What happens if I say no?'

Crowley laughed. Tomlin didn't. He said, 'As I mentioned, we would be forced to seek legal redress against you, your editor and your newspaper.'

I said, 'And that's it?'

Tomlin seemed perplexed. 'I don't quite gather—'

I said, 'If I say no, do I end up in St Katharine's Dock with a bullet through the frontal lobe?'

The very idea caused him intense distress. 'Good heavens, no. I take it you are referring to the murder of my stepmother. I swear I had nothing to do with that.'

Tomlin had nothing to do with an awful lot of

things. I acted as if I was thinking the deal over. Tabloid journalists have one hidden weakness. Everyone thinks we're capable of anything dastardly. True, we're capable of anything in getting a story. But we're hopelessly incapable of forgetting a story.

I said, 'When would I get the money?'

He smiled again. 'That depends on you. Might I suggest you provide us first of all with your notebooks and photographs, then perhaps—'

I didn't hear what came next because Rosie suddenly woke up and started hooting the horn. It brayed through the street's black canyon, bouncing off the walls. I saw Crowley detach himself from the BMW's left wing and start running towards her, I jumped in front of him and he knocked me flat on my backside. He was fast. The horn stopped blaring before I picked myself up. There followed a slap like a thunderclap. I screamed, 'Rosie!' and legged it towards her. I needn't have worried. Martin Crowley was standing well back from the Metro and rubbing his jaw.

'Leave her alone, you bastard!' I yelled in a brief blaze of bravery.

Crowley turned. He was not particularly tall, but he had the sort of build you see in Staffordshire bull terriers and Panzer tanks. He said, 'If the bitch hits me again I'll drop her.'

Fortunately Rosie stayed put in the driver's seat, otherwise I would have been forced to tear his head off. We stood there glaring at each other until Tomlin steamed up and rescued him. He said, 'Let's be calm, Martin. There's a deal on the table and I would like to know how Max feels about it.'

I said, 'Max likes it.'

He beamed. 'Good, good. Perhaps you can let us have the material tomorrow?'

I was getting braver by the second. I pointed at Crowley. 'Just as long as he isn't around. Chain him up somewhere.'

Crowley squared off his eyebrows at me. Tomlin said, 'It's cool. Martin needn't be there.'

I said, 'Where's there?'

He gave me an address in Primrose Hill. I scribbled it on the back of my chequebook, along with his phone number. My writing was a touch fraught. Tomlin said, 'Fine. Everything's settled. I look forward to seeing you then, say around eleven?'

I said, 'When do I get the hundred grand?'

Tomlin was soothing. 'Let's say we'll give you part tomorrow, as an act of good faith.'

'How much?' I demanded in my craven mercenary way.

'Let's say twenty-five per cent.'

'Let's say fifty per cent.'

He rippled a laugh. 'All right. You win. Perhaps you should have been a businessman instead of a journalist.'

And he should have been a human being. I hammed it up, whingeing on about when he would hand over the rest. He said when he was satisfied I'd kept to my side of the bargain. He stuck out his hand and, so help me, I shook it cordially. So everyone was happy. Apart from Rosie and Crowley. Tomlin ambled back to the BMW. Crowley hung around looking thoughtfully at the Metro for a moment.

'Nice little car,' he said. And he stepped back and gave it the most savage kick right in the headlamp.

Then he looked at Rosie and he said in exactly the same tone, 'Nice little girlfriend.'

We trembled in our socks. He sneered a last bleak smile and rejoined Tomlin. We watched wordlessly as they reversed out of our street and were gone. I said, 'Jesus!'

Rosie began to cry.

Chapter Sixteen

She wanted me to go for the money. We were back in the flat and she'd dried her cheeks. Her eyes were still a bit snappy and she talked too fast, so I poured out a quadruple whisky and stuck it in her hand. She flopped herself over me on the sofa. It might have been an ordinary night except we don't ordinarily sit around talking about a stray one hundred thousand pounds. She said, 'That's twice what you make in a year. Grab it.'

She didn't really want the money. She just wanted me to let go of the story. That way we might be able to drive around London again without being shot, set alight, menaced or otherwise inconvenienced. I let her ramble on because she had to talk it out. I said yes and no at all the appropriate points but all the time I was thinking about what I did next. I was on what we weavers of words call the horns of a sodding huge dilemma. If I went to the Law and told them the score, they'd haul in Tomlin and Crowley, charge them with general nastiness, and lock them up. This had the advantage of stopping them from killing Rosie or me. It had the disadvantage of spiking my exclusive. Once the two loons were on a charge I couldn't write an unkind word about them. I was rather fond of my story. And what a great story it was turning out to be – Honest Crime Hack Offered Massive Bung To Stay Schtum About Child Sex Ring. Even the lawyer couldn't kill that. So I ruled out calling Plod.

I examined the other horn of the dilemma. It indicated that Rosie and I would end up with tags on our toes unless I surrendered the notes and negatives to Tomlin. Which again meant spiking my story. So that was out too.

I cast around for an alternative. I came up with it about three in the morning, with Rosie snoring in my ear. I put her to bed, set the alarm for seven, brushed my teeth and said my prayers.

Anyone who is not in the hack trade has already hit on a simple alternative: take the money and live. But I wouldn't be a hack if I did that. If this sounds very high-falutin' and sick making, I'm sorry. But it's true. Hacks willingly risk their lives just for the sake of a story. Sometimes they lose. Dozens of journos have been killed in what we used to call Yugoslavia. And why? For the sake of the story and the by-line, that's why. The victims weren't on danger money or a special bonus. Some newspapers were so mean they wouldn't even buy flak jackets for their boys. And when a hack gets home he is greeted by the likes of Belker, bollocking him for his expenses. Yet wander into any newspaper office and ask the assembled drunks would they like to go to Beirut/Sarajevo/Rwanda. You'd get trampled to death in the rush. It has nothing to do with courage. I suppose in the end it's all down to vanity. Reporters lucky enough to run for their lives through Sarajevo's Sniper's Alley are the envy of their mates. Yet what do they have to show for it? – a couple of picture by-lines and a story or two. That's the prize. And what a glorious prize it is.

The alarm buzzed like a bee with a stammer, waking me from a dream in which I was patiently explaining to Big Ben Ashbee how I knew that Martin Crowley was the git who incinerated all my worldly goods.

I shot up like a Saturn Five. I did know that. I knew for absolute stone cold certain that Crowley was the mad matchman. But how did I know? I sat there lacing together the torn shreds of my dream. And then it came to me. In our dead-end street meet, he'd said the hundred grand was not bad money for 'a few smacks with a wheel brace'.

Okay, so he might have read my story about the fire. But I remember I'd made a mistake when I was dictating copy that night from the hospital. I'd said the attacker bashed me with a car jack. Only the Law, my shins, and the man in black knew it was a wheel brace.

Something inside me said, 'Okay, so now you know Crowley is the villain, you must ring the Old Bill forthwith.' But I ignored it, recognising it as just a piece of brainwashing by Rosie.

I arose, brewed myself a coffee that would kill a horse and set to work. I found a virgin notebook, dug out the Sri Lankan original and began copying it. I scrawled off a few righthand pages in blue Biro, then a single one in red, a couple in black, back to blue, and so on. I altered the slope of the characters so that some looked scribbled, others leisurely. I jotted down fictitious phone numbers and names on facing pages. Hotel Demerara 216–333. Kandy Hire Cars 217–001. That sort of thing. I didn't write anything about the boy victims, Lal and Ajit. When I'd finished the notebook looked almost convincing. I sploshed coffee into a saucer and dipped the back cover in it. I got a bottle of Bud from the fridge and sprinkled it on the occasional page. Then a dash of whisky mixed with cigarette ash. I found a couple of 50 rupee notes and gummed them in towards the back with a mix of sugary coffee. Now it looked so much like the original notebook I had difficulty telling them apart. My strategy to keep Rosie and me and the story alive was progressing apace.

Next I phoned the Editor. It was nine thirty-three on a hazy Sunday morning. I know that because he asked me what time it was. He did not like being disturbed. He wanted to know why a menial such as I dared rouse him from his scratcher. I said I urgently needed his help. He didn't seem to want to help. I changed the angle. I said, 'Michael Tomlin and Martin Crowley have offered me one hundred thousand pounds if I don't let you see my story. Or they'll kill me for free.'

That shook him. He likes to think he's the only one around here with the right to kill me.

I added, 'If you run the story, they'll also kill my girlfriend.' All right, maybe I was pushing it a bit, but I had to keep him on the hook.

He said, 'Have you rung the police?'

I said no, and I explained why not – that my story

would collapse as soon as Tomlin was charged. The Editor was impressed. He said, 'We'll kill the story.'

I said another no. I'd like the story to run, the bigger the better. What gives Tomlin the right to censor our paper? 'You're the Editor.'

That one got all the way home. The Editor said, 'Right. Let's have every word of it – the threats, the child sex, the murders. We'll splash it and throw out the centre spread. Forget the lawyer. We'll take our chances. No one tells me what I can or cannot put in my paper.'

At the nice end of the phone I hopped around like a gleeful chimpanzee. Something occurred belatedly to the Editor. He said, 'Of course, my first concern is for you, and indeed, your girlfriend. We'd better move you somewhere Tomlin wouldn't suspect. Just for tonight anyway. You're sure he'll be arrested in the morning?'

As sure as bones. He'll be clapped in irons five minutes after my story breaks, I promised. And the police will play football with any bail application.

The Editor thought Rosie and I should go to ground in a quiet hotel outside London. I said what a clever idea, but where could we go? The Editor had the very place in mind: Standingbrooke Hall Hotel, a leafy mile or so from Tring, Herts. Very expensive, very exclusive, very discreet. He knows this because every six months the office hires out the entire west wing of Standingbrooke and invites the execs to what are laughingly called Think Tanks. Anyways, he ordered me to book ourselves a modest suite there and hide from the forces of darkness. This gleeful chimpanzee was half way up the wall by now.

The Editor told me to get there pronto. I said I had one more teensy weensy bit to do. I wanted to see Tomlin and reassure him I was still in his pocket. That might get me a few more good quotes. The Editor was awed by my quiet heroism in visiting the lair of the evil monster. Actually I was too. He didn't offer me half of his kingdom and his daughter's hand in marriage, which is just as well, for she's got a bum the size of Russia. But he did say: 'Good man', and, it was a great story. Congratulations. I blushed and said it was all thanks to his editorial leadership and he went away believing that.

So phase two of the master plan was up and away. On now to the tricky part. I shaved, showered and encased myself in the best suit on the premises. The green and yellow striped tie was not quite up to the occasion. I inspected myself in the mirror. I looked more serious than usual. Sober was the word. It was all wrong. I wanted to look greedy and gullible. But big brother didn't have anything filed in that section. I settled for a green polo shirt, blue sports jacket, grey trousers and brown Oxfords. By God, it was hideous, even for a Sunday. I wanted to fit myself up with the tape and hidden mike, but I suspected Tomlin might be on the lookout for tricks. I packed a spare notebook out of habit and blew a cheerio kiss to a sleeping Rosie. I went out, letting the door close with the softest of clicks.

London's entire black cab population was off somewhere eating bacon sarnies and I ended up having to call a minicab on the mobile. By one of those weird coincidences which Life puts into our humdrum day, the driver turned out to be Sri Lankan. He told me where I should have gone for cheap silk shirts, jewellery, glasses. I wrote it all down – it gave me authentic detail if I ever got round to writing that travel feature.

We purred up outside Mike Tomlin's gaff, a three-storey Georgian model with a garden the size of a beer mat. As I rattled the knocker, a solitary shaft of sunlight pierced the haze and landed on my head. A happy omen, I decided.

The door flew open as if he'd been waiting behind it. 'You came,' he declared with that ready perception that demonstrates the value of a good public school education.

'I came,' I agreed.

Tomlin ushered me indoors. He was togged out in a faded rugby shirt, worn jeans and scuffed trainers. He looked a lot better dressed than me.

I went straight for it. 'I haven't got the negatives yet. My snapper is up in Blackpool on the Sunday school sex lessons story.'

His face went down.

I said, 'But I have my notebooks. And the photographer should be back by Tuesday, so I'll get the pix then.'

His face went up again. He said, 'Just a moment.'

He walked off, leaving me to admire the red flock wallpaper of the hallway. It looked like he'd nicked it from a Chinese takeaway. He returned with Crowley snapping at his heels.

I feigned dismay. It was easy. I said, 'You promised me he wouldn't be here.'

Tomlin gave a smile that meant anything you wanted it to mean. He said, 'Just a precaution, Max. He'll be gone in a moment.'

Crowley stepped forth and produced a bug detector. He ran it up and down my outraged limbs. Nothing blooped or bleeped. But he was a cautious man, our Martin. Next he frisked me in a most intimate manner. He found my cigarettes. I had to show him they were ordinary Bensons. I even offered him one. He examined my lighter, my pens, my notebook. I half expected him to produce a sniffer dog out of his hip pocket. But that was it. He stepped back, nodded okay to Tomlin, and muscled off to the back of the house.

Tomlin led me into the lounge, another fine example of Chow Mein neo-Gothic, and invited me to make myself at home. I opted for centre seat on a sofa sprawled along the door wall. He played the genial host, offering me first a sherry and then a decent drink.

I swigged hard and said, 'You got the money?'

'First the notebook.'

I handed it over. Tomlin found himself a seat by the window and started reading. Half the stuff was in shorthand so he needed me to decipher it. I explained the basic symbols of Mr Pitman's shorthand system and after a while Tomlin was making inspired guesses at whole words. I told him he was very clever and he thought so too.

I said, 'There's nothing much in the pix – just a

few shots of the orphanage sign, a head and shoulders of Samarsinghe. Things like that. The real stuff is there, in the notes. But I'll have to give the photographer half the money to keep him quiet.'

Tomlin tapped the notebook against even white teeth, smelt the stench of assorted beverages, and thought better of it. He didn't make any move towards a safe or even a wallet. I said, 'You promised me half today.'

Tomlin laughed. Not a proper laugh. More the plastic sympathy chuckle of an insurance salesman telling you that you should have read the small print first. He said, 'You'll recall our deal was for the notes and the photographs. I have only the notes, or what you claim are the notes.'

I dripped out a craven smile. 'Yes, but you can see that's everything I've got. I'm honouring the deal. You should stick to your side of it.'

He didn't think so. He reckoned pay day came when the whole package was handed over. I got stroppy and said, okay, give me back my notes until I can deliver the pix too. Tomlin said quietly, 'I don't think Martin would agree to that, do you?'

I let my face play about at being narked, shocked, wounded, insulted. It enjoyed itself. I said, 'You mean I don't see a penny until you have the snaps?'

Tomlin said that was about the size of it. This would never do. I'd come here for money and I wasn't going away until I had filled my fevered little fist with fivers. I had a sulk.

He said, 'Don't worry, Max. You'll get the money. You say your photographer will be back by Tuesday?'

'At the latest.'

He said, 'Well then, you just have to wait until Tuesday and you'll get the money.'

I said, 'I won't.' It was a flat statement, without an ounce of defiance.

His eyebrows did a few press ups. 'You won't?'

I fiddled with my loose change. 'I mean I can't.'

'Why not?' Ah, this was more like the Michael Tomlin we have come to know and hate. A whisper of menace there.

'I mean I can't.' I elaborated, looking deadpan. 'Frankie – that's my monkey – won't hand over his smudges unless I bring something to the party.'

'What?'

I translated. Tomlin caught the gist. He said, 'You're saying you'll have to show him some money first?'

I nodded, speechless with admiration at his raging intellect. Now it was his turn to act furtive and mercenary. He said, 'How much will it take to convince him?'

I waved an extravagant arm. 'Ten thousand, anyway. We each spent about five grand on the trip – the office wasn't paying.'

Tomlin found his mock chuckle. 'I am not paying serious money until I have everything in my hands. However, I appreciate your situation. Let's say a goodwill payment of one hundred pounds each might help.'

Yelps of horror from the settee. He pushed it up a couple of notches. An encore of outrage. I was getting good at this. Tomlin got up, wandered around and looked at himself in the mirror above a black marble fireplace. I whinged away amid the cushions. At last he reached a decision. I could tell that because of the masterful way he breathed out his nose. He said, 'I'm still not satisfied that you are telling the truth. I am not satisfied that these are your notes in their entirety. I still need to be convinced. However, I am prepared to pay you one thousand pounds as a gesture in good faith. That's all.'

I licked my lips and said, oh all right then, give me the money. He reached for his pocket and fished out a wad of £50 notes. He counted them. They added up to £1,000. Exactly. So that's what he estimated paying out all along. But he'd made a big enough song and dance about it. He hesitated before stuffing them in my outstretched fingers. He said, 'I trust you will honour your end.'

He didn't say otherwise I'll knock your block off, but my telepathic powers picked up the message. He handed over the notes. I counted them again. Twice. I whined, 'I just hope this is enough to convince my photographer.'

Tomlin suddenly remembered he had a pressing engagement, so would I kindly hop it. He didn't shake my hand on the way out and I thought that was nice of him.

I called the Barbican from the mini cab and ordered up Blue Mountain coffee, eggs benedict, freshly squeezed papaya juice and a bowl of Rice Crispies. Rosie said she'd lost the map to the kitchen, and anyway, what was I doing, and, and, and. She was still pelting questions down the phone when I opened the door and said hello. I made the coffee because I had a mystery guest on the way. He turned out to be Dec somebody or other, a freelance monkey. In the meantime, I turfed Rosie's things off the bedside table and, wearing a pair of blue kitchen gloves so as not to mess up Tomlin's fingerprints, replaced them with his £1,000. It looked a pretty show. Dec confined himself to saying, 'Cor!' because he thought there was a lady present. He banged off a few flash shots inside, then on the balcony, where I was obliged to look grimly into camera whilst holding five hundred smackers in each blue-gloved hand. The notes didn't look much, but at least they were real, with Tomlin's whorls all over them. What lawyers call evidence.

Dec clattered off and I got down to rewriting my original copy. It would have been a lot easier if the Editor hadn't kept ringing me up to ask daft questions. Here is one of his more inspired: What, he asked, do the deviants eat when they're in Sri Lanka? I said curry. He said aaah, as if a great light had shone upon him. I tapped the story up on the laptop. Marcel Proust might have made a better job of it, but there you go. I hammered out the first few pars:

> Pin-striped perverts yesterday offered me a £100,000 bribe to hush up a squalid child sex ring.
>
> They vowed to murder me – and my girlfriend – if I refused their sleazy slush money.
>
> But today I name the top tycoons who use children as young as six in their barbaric orgies.

And I can reveal that:

* Provocative millionairess Claudine Tournier was ruthlessly gunned down when she stumbled on their secret.

* Wrinkly rocker Leon Knapp preys on helpless orphans for kinky sex.

* A squeaky clean politician is among the sinister group of paedophiles who style themselves The Young Boys Network.

I wasn't bothered about libels. The night lawyer could weed them out. He gets paid a lot more than me and I didn't want to deprive him of job satisfaction.

After I'd knocked it out – 2,500 words top whack – and sent the copy through the modem there was a long, long silence from the office. This often happens but you still get nervous about it. You picture teams of trouser-wetting lawyers tearing the stuff to pieces. What's really happening is they're sticking 'alleged' between all the interesting bits. Yes, theirs is a dirty job.

While I waited and fretted, Rosie did the sensible thing and packed us a pair of overnight bags. For once I had more clothes than her. She was skipping about the flat singing something from Beethoven or Tchaikovsky. It worried me. Only last night, awash with tears, she had begged me to drop the story and hide under the bed. Why this new-found chipperness? I wrapped her fondly around the waist and she said not until we get to the hideaway hotel. I explained that I just wanted to know what prompted her sunshine. After all, hadn't I ignored her heartfelt cry and written a story that endangered her life?

She said, and she smiled a loving smile when she said it. 'Oh, I always knew you'd write the story anyway. I was only telling you how I felt.'

Wasn't that nice? I swung her towards me to say something soppy and the phone rang just in time. The Editor with a verbal herogram. Great, terrific, super. Makes you sit up. Sells papers. Now, flee to the hidey hole, Chard, and get cracking on a follow-up. Oh, and love to Ruby.

I told Ruby who didn't like being thus called.

We grabbed our bags and the dented Metro and jogged up the A1 towards where they've stuck Tring. Every now and then I looked over my shoulder to check we were not towing a silver BMW. But we were as lacking in tails as a Manx cat. We were trickling along a country byway when Standingbrooke House Hotel jumped out of the hedges at us. It's a big, creamy white chunk of a place, half hidden by porticoes, battlements and assorted extravagances. Our rumpled Metro looked as if it belonged at the tradesmen's entrance, but the retainers who rushed to open the doors didn't say a word about it. Nor did the receptionist blink her violet lashes when I announced, 'I'm Oki Mboya of the Anglo-Nigerian Oil Corporation. You have my reservation.'

She tossed a welcome smile at Rosie. 'And you must be Mister Ndoke Emogu.'

Rosie affirmed that she was. I always use the Mboya alias when I'm hiding out in a hotel. That way if the opposition runs a check on the guest list they never think O. Mboya might be their old chum Max. They're looking for Smith or Brown or Jones.

We were ushered to a suite twice the size of Dominic's flat. A silver-haired porter with the demeanour of Our Man in Washington suggested we might like a drink to recover from our travels and we heard the clank of the Dom Perignon bucket before Rosie kicked a shoe off. We parked ourselves on the balcony and admired the back garden.

'We should do this more often,' said Rosie, appraising the scenery through a champagne flute.

At three hundred quid a night that wasn't the smartest idea she ever had, but I said yes, and ordered up another bottle. I felt it was the done thing. The hours glided past but not so as you'd notice. We tried out the circular bath tub, playing footsie under five fathoms, to the clink of crystal. I could see why the Editor held his Think Tanks here. It gave you all sorts of ideas.

Coming up dinner time I gave Ben Ashbee a ring. He was at home, staking up his beans, he said, which I thought was a euphemism for all sorts of high jinks. But he didn't appear to mind being disturbed.

I made sure he hadn't done anything silly, like feel Michael Tomlin's collar before my story appeared. He said no, but come the dawn, he'd have Tomlin as planned. I said, 'While you're at it, you'd better pinch Martin Crowley too.'

Ben prefers to make his own decisions. He grouched, 'And why should I do that?'

I told him of the hundred grand and the threat to

Rosie and me, laying it on with a shovel. Ben whistled, nearly breaking my eardrum. He was all set for lifting the pair of them right there and then. I had to remind him of his promise to hold back. I also swore I'd be a nice tame little prosecution witness for him. That reminded him. Last night they'd binged on Lonesome Leon's bell. He talked them half to death without the stimulus of rubber truncheons. They had a signed statement in the bag – enough to justify a search warrant at half a dozen homes. Add my complaint about the death threats – I'd gone a bit over the top there – and the Old Bill had just cause to make a nuisance of itself.

So much for the good news. The bad news was that Leon hadn't the faintest idea who popped Claudine and Shirley. I said never mind, the search warrant might turn up something. But Ben went back to his beans in melancholy.

In Suite 20, Rosie was making merry with the complimentary perfumes and powders. They even had stuff to spray on your armpits, though it was hard to imagine the usual denizens of Suite 20 having body odours. Maybe that was just for our Think Tank weekends.

A distant dinner gong rang in our tummies and we descended to dine. We were hardly dressed for the occasion. At least I wasn't. Rosie elected to wear a red silk shirt as an outrageously short frock which took the other guests' eyes off the Jocasta Innes green and silver decor. The maitre d' said 'Good evening' to Rosie's legs and propped her in a chair where he could keep a good eye on them. I don't think he noticed me.

The room was full of big beefy pillars so that each table found itself in an alcove, like a candlelit clearing in the forest. Behind each pillar there lurked wandering bands of waiters. One staggered up with a menu the size of Encyclopedia Britannica: another came burdened down with the burgundy-jacketed wine list. Everything cost a bomb. You knew that because they'd left the prices out.

It was probably sometime around when I was dithering whether to guzzle the Sancerre or the Meursault that Leon Knapp prised open his front door and stepped into the night. He didn't bother closing the door behind him. He walked down the portico and round the corner to the aircraft hangar which served as his garage. He used the gizmo on his key ring to raise the door. He went inside and turned on the light. This time he shut the door.

A waiter hove to off my left shoulder, brandishing what purported to be Celeriac Remoulade and I took his word for it. Rosie was already in possession of a pink soup. We hoisted our glasses and offered each other elaborate toasts.

And while we laughed, Leon was sitting in his sky blue Porsche with both courtesy lights on and a notepad on his lap. He began to write.

The Standingbrooke House chefs do not believe in stuffing their guests to the gills. Two forkfuls, and the celeriac was but a pleasant memory. A fresh covey of waiters whipped away the plates, and the wine wizard made another guest appearance. A Chateau de Malle arrived suffering from hypothermia. On came my crevettes. Rosie laid waste to a baby brill in black butter.

Leon kept writing. He had a lot to say and not much time to say it.

We cold-shouldered the game course and pushed on to the entrée. Roast lamb in the manner of Shrewsbury for me, fillet of beef teriyaki for her. She'd forgotten she was a vegetarian. A bottle of Aloxe-Corton helped ease the pain.

Leon finished his letter. He put it in an envelope, sealed it and propped it on the dashboard. He turned on the ignition. He was crying.

We breezed onwards through the desserts and cheese and vintage port, our conversation becoming jollier by the moment. The waiters suspected we were newly-wed. By God, how they hated me. We whistled up the coffee and Rosie stuck her nose in a goldfish bowl of brandy. I settled on a noble scotch. Our innocent glee bounced off the pillars and sang in our ears.

In the garage Leon stopped coughing. His head slumped forward on the steering wheel. That's the way they would find him, crumpled up with his wig uncombed.

Rosie and I made it back to Suite 20, pursued by a wagonload of tinkling bottles. She fiddled with the stereo while I gave Night Desk a call. Vic took it. He sounded as if he was having a rotten night. I told him about our evening, just to make things worse. Green venomous envy seeped down the phone. I made him tell me all about our first edition. I had the splash and a double-column WOB by-line. A WOB is when they print your name in white on black to make it look important. He read out the first half dozen pars. It was more or less as written. I had the centre spread too, with pic bylines for both Frankie and me, Vic said. Now would I piss off and leave him to news edit. I said I was so moved by his sweet nature that I would bring him a souvenir shower cap so his baldy head wouldn't get wet if he ever thought of having a shower. He banged the phone down.

Rosie poured me a bumper whisky and joined me on the chair. Dire Straits hummed out of the stereo. I had a great story in the paper, a lovely woman in my arms, music in my ears and the scent of Speyside in my nostrils. What more could a man want? Rosie thought of something.

Chapter Seventeen

A dawn as light as a kitten's purr was tickling the trees on Primrose Hill when they rat-tat-tat-tatted on Michael Tomlin's door. He was a heavy sleeper. They tattooed again with greater gusto. A window shot up. 'Whaddyawant?' he yelled.

They told him who they were, just in case he hadn't noticed the flashing lights and the funny uniforms. He asked them if they knew what time it was. They did. It was five-thirty. He grumbled awhile but he let them in. When he saw the search warrant he screamed blue murder. They gave him five minutes to dress, under the watchful eye of a D.C. with a nasty suspicious mind. Then they squeezed him in the back of the car between two Plods and off they drove.

I learned of all this several hours later while Rosie and I breakfasted in bed without our clothes on. I'd phoned Ben Ashbee to check that Tomlin was definitely in the nick. Oh yes, he said, but did I want the bad news or the bad news? I said I'd have the bad news first.

Ben said, 'Leon Knapp topped himself last night.'

I said, 'That's bad news?'

It was rotten news, said Ben. Leon was to be his

star witness if they found any child porn stashed in Tomlin's drum. Now their only hope was that his statement would be treated like a deathbed confession and admitted as evidence.

I said, 'Is it definitely an own goal? Tomlin didn't lace his cocaine with rat poison or anything?'

Ben said, 'No. Straightforward suicide. Shut himself in the garage and turned on the motor.'

I said, 'Any famous last words?'

Ben said, 'About twenty pages of them. You'll be pleased to hear he blamed press harassment and mentions you. He didn't say anything about the two murders.'

I said, 'What's the other bad news?'

They'd lost Crowley. He'd got away, largely thanks to them kicking in the door of the flat beneath his and scaring the drawers off a respectable old lady of Italian extraction. 'Who-a are-a you-a?' she cried, to which one of their number replied, 'Old Bill.' She said, 'Old-a Bill-a live-a uppa-da-stair-a.' By the time they'd sorted it all out, Crowley had taken to his toes.

I said, 'Ben, this is terrible news,' realising that Rosie and I would have to spend another night incarcerated in Standingbrooke Hall.

He promised to send a sympathetic plain clothes bloke to take our statement about the death threats. I told him to wait until I'd had my sauna and Rosie her facial. He said it should be the other way around.

I called the Editor. He still loved me. I said the police had warned me Crowley was on the loose and hunting for me. The Editor said oh dear, stay there until they catch him. I said whatever he thought best.

He reported that everyone was raving about my story. I don't think he'd canvassed Crowley's opinion. But I made all the right noises and praised him again for his campaigning leadership.

Rosie skipped off in the afternoon and looted a boutique or two while I cobbled together a follow up to the tune of:

Shamed rock star Leon Knapp killed himself yesterday, hours after he was branded a pervert.

His body was found in the fume-filled garage of his £1m Berkshire mansion.

His dead hand was still clutching a pathetic note telling how he chose to die rather than face the scandal over his life as a child molester.

Seventies teenybopper favourite Knapp was exposed by us as a ruthless paedophile who preyed on helpless orphans.

He was a leading member of a sinister group of deviants, calling themselves the Young Boys Network.

In a dawn swoop yesterday detectives investigating the sex ring arrested Knapp's pal, City whizz kid Mike Tomlin.

And they are seeking round-the-world yachtsman Martin Crowley. All three are trustees of the WorldCare Foundation, which Knapp admitted was used as a cover for child sex orgies.

Both Tomlin and Crowley had offered me a £100,000 bribe to stop me exposing the scandal.

Last month Foundation boss Claudine Tournier – Tomlin's stepmother – was mysteriously slain.

Bachelor Tomlin was arrested at his palatial London townhouse . . .

And so forth. I knew the Law wouldn't charge Tomlin until Tuesday morning so I could still get away with having a pop at him. I let the copy run to about 30 pars, leaving it up to the agencies and showbiz to fill in the backgrounder on Knapp. I looked at my watch. It was high time for high tea.

I had a lot of faith in our bobbies. I was banking on them failing to catch Crowley for at least six months, during which Rosie and I could continue to whoop it up at Standingbrooke Hall.

Therefore it came as a nasty surprise when on Thursday morning Big Ben rang to say they'd found him. This was not exactly true. He found them. And they'd tried to lose him again. Armed with his brief, Crowley had turned himself in at Whetstone nick, where the desk woodentop assured him nobody wanted him. In the end he had to go out to a phone box and ring Ben Ashbee who in turn called the nick and told them that if Crowley reappeared they'd better hold on to him. He did and they did.

But Ben had even bigger news to impart. In the process of turning over Mike Tomlin's gaff they came across a navy blazer with strands of stuff on the lapels. The forensic boys wheeled out their magnifying glass and discovered (a) fragments of the rope of the type used to throttle Shirley Ham, and (b) several dirty fair hairs of the type worn by Shirley Ham. They'd got him.

So far he hadn't coughed to murdering either her or his stepmother, but they expected him to stick his hands up any day now. They left Lewis Trefoyle alone because that's what you do with government ministers. Besides, they knew we were out to get him, and we are a thousand times worse than anything the Old Bailey can sling at you.

They charged Tomlin with Shirley's murder after Crowley grassed on him. They grabbed Gus Clernthorpe and he promptly fingered Crowley as the man with the matchbox. But they didn't charge him with that yet. They just hit them all for criminal conspiracy. They pulled in Proudhoe Veizey who cast himself in the role of supergrass. He came up with a motive for Claudine's killing. Two motives in fact. Yes, she had rumbled the orphanage racket and was threatening to blow it, along with every deviant on the Foundation's board. Veizey also revealed that Claudine was a girl with a libido which needed taking out for exercise every now and then. She was particularly partial to married men. And the hubbies, it seemed, were happy to oblige. Sir James Tomlin was well aware of his wife's horizontal hobbies, but he didn't care; he was twice as bad. So the betting was still that Claudine was murdered, probably by her loving stepson, to hush her up.

The office took me off the story because it was all wrapped up and anyway, as a prosecution witness in the threats case, the Law warned me to stay out of it. I was bored. Rosie had gone home to mum for a week's counselling. I returned to the Barbican, a squalid slum after Suite 20, and tuned in to *Neighbours* again. But it was no good. I'd lost the thread.

There were occasional moments to enliven the

dull days. The Sri Lankan press attaché invited me out for a lively lunch and told me what a great man I was. Out in Kandy they'd grabbed Samarsinghe, his mate Niaz, and a handful of other undesirables. They moved the boys to a pukka orphanage and were teaching them how to smile. And all because of my story.

It sent many a ripple around Fleet Street. The *Sunday Times* dep. ed. took me out for drinkies and dangled a job before me, but I said no, I preferred working for a newspaper. End of drink.

Chapter Eighteen

I began spending too much time and money stopping Hampton's from going broke. They were rowdy nights to be sure but I suppose I was still on a come down from the big story. I remembered Wellington's quote after duffing up Napoleon at Waterloo: Nothing is half so desolate as a battle lost, except a battle won. Something like that. Well that's the way I felt.

The Law eventually got around to charging Martin Crowley with attempting to set me alight. I got my picture in the paper again, but no by-line.

That night my bleep went when I was in the middle of telling a joke to Hampton's regulars. I rang Vic. He said Ross Gavney had phoned to pass on congrats and ask if we might meet sometime.

I thought about it for at least half a bottle. Even then I wasn't sure how I felt. The way I remembered it, my mate Ross had failed me in my hour of need. He had known something about the people who were out to get me, yet he'd refused to tell. Not the behaviour of your average tried and trusted ally. In just ten minutes he had shredded a friendship built on years. He knew he was doing it, but he still said tough luck, Max, you're on your own. And I'd said piss off and I never did like your rotten whisky anyway. So whatever way you looked at it, the old friends act was out the window. Why then should Ross start acting chummy again, knowing damn well he had broken Clause One, Para One of the Mates Charter? I didn't have an answer to that. And why now?

In the end I rang Magpie Court. I suppose it was more out of curiosity than anything. Ross picked it up on the third briiinnng. I said, 'Hello Ross.'

'Max!'

I took it he was glad I called. He said, 'I've phoned your office several times, but you're never in.'

I said, 'I'm always out.'

He laughed. I didn't.

There was a gap. He said, 'I've read your stuff on Tomlin – it's a fantastic story.'

I said, 'No, it's not fantastic. It's real. There's a difference.'

He started off trying to laugh but changed his mind. He said, 'We have unfinished business. At least I have. I owe you an explanation.'

I said, 'If you feel bad about something, you'd better work it out yourself. It's your problem.'

He said, 'I said I owe you an explanation, not an apology. There's a difference.'

I didn't feel like picking that one up. Ross said, 'It's your call, Max. We can get together and talk or we can hang up.'

I said, 'You mean you'll talk now they've locked Tomlin up? And Crowley? That's big of you.'

Ross said evenly, 'Yes, I'll talk, now they've got them.'

I laughed. I couldn't help myself. I said, 'Christ, Ross, you've got some weird ideas about friendship.'

He said, 'Do I take it that means we get together or we hang up?'

Hanging up seemed a good idea but my curiosity argued against it. He didn't regret keeping me in the dark. The way he saw it, he'd done it for a reason. A good reason. And he still felt that he was right. So what was the reason?

In the end I said okay. That I'd meet him.

Ross asked, 'Where? Here?'

I'd already made my mind up. I said, 'The Port O' Call.'

He said, 'Where's that?'

I said, 'It's the place where you first didn't tell me what you knew.'

The laugh didn't even have a smile on its face. He said, 'You have an over-developed sense of irony.'

I said, 'I know. I'll get rust one of these days.'

The taxi dropped me outside the Tower Hotel and I trickled around to St Katharine's Dock. I was in no particular hurry. There were spots of rain in the wind and a wall of smoky cloud was pushing across the river from Southwark. People walking by had their collars up and heads down. When I got to the dockside I had a look at the water, from force of habit. All you could see were boats and buoys.

It was a Wednesday evening and the Port O' Call was three-quarters empty. Ross had a table in the far corner where he could see the door. On the table was a bottle of red with a full glass for him and an empty one waiting for me. There was not much left in the bottle.

I sat down and lit myself a cigarette.

He said, 'Drink?'

I nodded. He poured it half way up, the way they do in restaurants. I sipped and smoked. I had nothing useful to say so I left it to him. He made a big play of lighting his cigar and checking the smoke was coming from the right end before he spoke. Ross said, 'First of all, Max, that was an ace job you did on the Claudine Tournier story, though I'm sure your fellow journalists have already told you so.'

I said, 'They have. But don't let it bother you.'

He turned on a chuckle. He said, 'I see. You want to give me a bad time.'

I had another sip. The wine tasted of cigarette. Ross said, 'What I did – what I did in not telling you the little I knew – I did out of honour.'

That deserved a crooked smile. I said, 'I always knew you were an honourable man. Brutus was an honourable man.'

He shrugged. 'Okay. Let's be dramatic about it. What do you know about honour? No, not honour – loyalty?'

My eyes said I knew a whole heap more than him. He put his glass down so that it made a loud clack. I leaned back and fluted smoke at a fibreglass anchor. I wondered what Rosie was doing tonight, and what was she wearing, how were her eyes.

Ross said, 'I'll talk about loyalty then. You have a loyalty to your paper, a loyalty to Rosie, a loyalty to your family, your friends. But most of all you have a loyalty to your paper.'

Close enough. I didn't interrupt.

He said, 'You fix your own priorities on loyalty. Everybody has to. You demanded total loyalty from me – not for yourself, but for your bloody newspaper. Jesus Christ, Max, you're more loyal to the paper than you are to yourself. You don't even see that. And I can't understand it.'

I said, 'Let me make it easy for you. I'm faithful to my story. I don't give a toss which paper carries it.'

He sorted this out while I flagged for another bottle. I filled my glass. He could look after himself.

'Okay,' he said, 'this isn't getting through. Let's go back to the night you reckoned I was keeping something from you. I admit it. I was.'

I drawled, 'Well, ain't that a surprise, folks?'

He ignored it. 'You wanted to know about Claudine Tournier. Let me tell you about her. She was a vicious, destructive, cold-hearted bitch, and she should have been drowned at birth.'

I said, 'Doesn't mean she was a bad person.'

He said, 'If you had known her you would have felt the same. Her marriage to Jim Tomlin was a sham, just to give her the social cachet and access to the money tree. His connections, his money got Claudine's Cuisine up and running. She needed him. She also knew a damn sight more about his stooges on the Foundation than you guessed. Remember, some of them funded her at the start.'

I said, 'So why would she expose them?'

Ross ground out a laugh. 'She would never have

done that. She just wanted to ruin Mike Tomlin. She tried to seduce him, you know. She didn't know he was a paedophile.'

I said, 'I want to get this right. Wicked stepmother is told to eff off by perverted stepson whereupon she vows to expose his sordid sex life whereupon he shoots her brains out?'

His mouth was still down at the corners but he managed a sort of smile. 'That's it.'

I watched Ross pour himself a glass. His hand didn't shake. His gaze didn't waver.

I said, 'So why are you still lying?'

He looked up with wide candid eyes. 'Lying?'

'Telling porkies. Being economical with the truth. That sort of lying.'

His face said he didn't understand. He said, 'I swear to you, it's all true.'

I said, 'No, Ross. It may be true, but it isn't all.'

He pushed his glass round and round and round on the table. Then he did it again anti-clockwise. I watched him through the smoke. He was arguing with himself. I don't know which side won.

He said, 'We're back at the beginning. We're talking about loyalties again.'

I said, 'I'm too tired for the game. If you want to tell me the full bit, go ahead. If you don't, then don't bother lying about it. We could both be somewhere else and liking it.'

He started doodling with the glass again. I looked around. The barmaid snapped a bright overbite at me. Yes, I could easily be somewhere else.

Ross opened up with a question. 'What would you

do to get a story? No, I don't mean that. I mean what would you *not* do?'

He thought he had the answer so I let him tell me. He said, 'I think there's nothing you wouldn't do, Max. I think if Rosie came in here now and said she'd been gang-banged by Cliff Richard and the Archbishop of Canterbury, you'd be on the phone to the paper before you even dried her tears.'

I smiled thinly. 'It's a great story,' I said.

He said, 'Yes, it is a great story. You'd get your name all over it. That's what I was trying to talk about. Your loyalty to the paper gets in the way of everything else. The story is all that counts.'

I said, 'And that's why you still won't tell me how you knew Claudine.'

'What?' He was wary.

I said it again slowly. He'd heard me all right the first time. He was just sorting out how to answer. He looked around first, as if to check for eavesdroppers. Then he leaned forward and his voice was as soft as prayer. He said, 'I met Claudine Tournier just before Christmas.'

He stopped and took a sip. Then he had a breath. He said, 'It was a charity do at the Mansion House and she was with a friend of mine, David. Lots of guests had celebrity partners because it was that sort of affair, but I was surprised to see David with Claudine Tournier. He has a real honey of a wife who usually goes everywhere with him.

'At one point in the evening I asked David about Babs. That's his wife. He winked at me. That's when I knew he was up to something with Tournier. I thought he was crazy. Though Claudine was a very sexy piece of business. I've got to say that.'

My glass was empty but I did not refill it. I was as still as last night's beer.

Ross said, 'I guessed right away that she was trouble. There was something hard about her, despite all the pouting and French accent. But I thought maybe it was a one night stand so I didn't say anything.'

He sipped again. 'Then just after the New Year, David told me he was in love with her. It was idiotic. He and Babs were the dream team. They have a young daughter and he dotes on her too. I told him to stop playing silly buggers but he was too far gone.'

Ross brooded on some memory. His face was set and sombre. He said, 'We'd planned a foursome ski trip – him and Babs, Chloe and me. I rented out a chalet in Champery for early February. David joined us the second week. With Claudine Tournier. He was like a sixteen-year-old in love for the first time. She loved every minute of it. She got her kicks out of making him obey her every whim. That really gave her a buzz. If she wanted a drink, she said go fetch, and he did. If she wanted to go shopping in Evian instead of skiing, that's what he wanted too.'

Ross leaned closer. He said, 'It was pathetic. It might even have been comic. But there was a real tragedy behind it. By this time Babs knew the score and she was devastated, totally shattered. She overdosed on barbiturates and they got her just in time. Babs was in a private psychiatric unit when we got back. He didn't go to see her. She farmed their daughter out to her mum. I don't think David even picked up the phone to ask how they were.'

I said, 'Does this story go somewhere?'

Ross gave me a look as bleak as winter. 'Oh yes, it goes somewhere. It goes to the end of March. That's when Claudine Tournier got tired of David and told him to find himself another girlfriend. For she'd just got herself a new boyfriend. He was a lot like David. Younger than her, wealthy, amusing. And married. I think that was an important plus. Claudine Tournier was a serial marriage wrecker.'

I said, 'So David jumped off Beachy Head?'

Ross said, 'He felt that way. And then he felt something different. He was angry and bitter and hurt. Claudine Tournier wrecked his life and he wanted her to know how it felt. He'd lost his home, his wife, his daughter. And she'd enjoyed watching him lose it all.'

I said, 'Cut to the bit where they fish her out of the dock.'

He gave a sliver of a smile. 'Yes. That night they found her. As soon as I saw her I thought: "Christ! David has killed her".'

I said, 'Which is why you didn't tell me?'

He nodded. 'Max, I know you. It was a story, a great story of sex, betrayal, murder. You couldn't have resisted it. You wouldn't care what Claudine Tournier had done to him. You would have splashed David all over the paper. That's why I kept quiet.'

I topped up both glasses and lit a cigarette. There were things coming back to me, little things, like a home-made silencer and the empty look on a certain man's face. I studied Ross. The tension lines around his mouth had eased. He thought he had finished. He had hardly started.

I said carefully, 'You showed remarkable loyalty to your friend David. What is his real name, by the way?'

He shook his head. 'No way. You might still turn him over.'

I said, 'You asked him if he'd killed her?'

'Yes. He denied it. But I wasn't certain.'

I said, 'And you doubted him all the way until the Old Bill lifted Mike Tomlin for the killing?'

Almost a nod.

I said, 'So you think it's safe to talk to me now they've got their hands on the alleged murderer?'

He didn't nod this time. He looked at me and you could see a dark question in his eyes. He said, 'The alleged murderer?'

I flicked ash off my cuff. I said, 'Yes, alleged. You know the quaint tradition of these isles: a man is innocent unless the jury says he's not. That goes for all of us, even Mike Tomlin, child molester and part-time murderer.'

Ross said, 'I don't know what you're saying, Max.'

I said, 'Mike Tomlin has coughed to just about every crime since somebody nicked an apple in the Garden of Eden. He says he abused little children, that he aided and abetted his cronies in doing likewise, that he's implicated in the attempted murder of one Max Chard, plus he was party to sending him an explosive love letter. He's banged to rights for the murder of Shirley Ham. They've got him screwed. He's going down for life. Maybe longer.'

My old mate was watching me, hardly breathing. I

canted my glass against the light. I said, 'But here's the strange thing, Ross. Never once, not even for a split second, has he ever admitted to topping Claudine.'

Ross said in a grey voice, 'But they've charged him . . .'

I said, 'Yes. They got carried away. But by the time he does his turn at the Bailey, they'll have dropped it, on the nitpicking grounds that he didn't do it.'

Ross echoed, 'He didn't do it?'

I said, 'So you see, you should have waited before you contacted me again.'

He didn't say anything but I knew what he was thinking. I gave him ten seconds and then I said, 'But I know why you rang me today. And today was the first time you rang.'

He said, 'No. I called you sev—'

I cut the lie in half. 'No, Ross. Today was the first time. And today was special because the papers told you Martin Crowley had been charged with attempting to murder me.'

He had his mouth open, still in the middle of his broken sentence. I said, 'And all along you thought it was your dear friend David who had tried to burn me alive.'

He shook his head slowly from side to side. The wine was acid on my tongue. I said, 'It wasn't David. It was Crowley. Isn't that funny, Ross?'

He didn't laugh.

I said, 'But you were right about Claudine – David murdered her. That's funny too.'

He slid his eyes away from me. He had nothing

more to say. I watched him and I waited. I waited until all the world was silent. I waited until he lifted his eyes once more.

I said, 'By the way, how's your lodger?'

'What?'

I said, 'Your brother. Euan. You know the bloke. He's the one who nearly took my eye out with a home-made gun. He's the bloke who's having to shack up with you because his old lady threw him out. He's the one who looks like an advert for Mogadon. The man who lost his wife and twin sons – two kids by the way, not a daughter – all for a rumple in the duvet with his French mistress. The man who put a bullet through her head. Bang!'

His face was gaunt and old and unhappy. When he finally spoke his voice was edged with entreaty. He said, 'Max, leave it. Please leave it.'

I said, 'I can't. You said it yourself. It's a great story of sex, betrayal, murder. I don't walk away from that. I even have the backgrounder – Brother Tells of Besotted City Whizz Kid's Fatal Attraction.'

I pulled back my sleeve and showed him the little black mike under my watch strap and the wire snaking up my arm. I said, 'I've got it all here.'

He gabbled for words. 'Jesus, Max, he's my brother. You can't do this to him. To me. Believe me, Claudine deserved it. She took his whole life away. Let him go.'

I sat there with the tape still running. He said, 'He's paid for it. He's still paying. What is Euan for you anyway? He's just another story, another by-line. But he's my brother. I mean, where do you stop, Max?

Would you turn over Rosie's family? Would you tear your own brother apart for a story?'

All of a sudden I felt very tired and lifeless. I stood up. I looked down at my old friend. One of us was a stranger.

He said it again. 'Where do you stop?'

I said, 'I don't know, Ross. Honest to God, I don't know.'

John Burns

Snap

Chapter One

It snowed in the night and the place where they found her body was now all white and winter wonderlandish. You could have stuck the scene on a Christmas card. It would have looked even better if Plod hadn't plonked a great yellow tent over her mortal remains. Also, there were dirty-grey patches of slush where the uniforms had parked their hooves.

So far we knew nearly nothing. They'd roped off the area and were keeping us at bay until they got a press officer out of bed to say no comment.

But the betting was that under the big top lay the corpse of one Joni Poelma, last seen, as they say, leaving a disco in Dulwich. Until then none of us knew that Dulwich had a disco. That was a week ago. Since then there had been the usual hullabaloo – TV appeals, posters, back checks on miles of video tape, the full bit. But Joni Poelma had stubbornly refused to reappear.

In the meantime nobody else was reported missing in Dulwich, therefore our lightning brains deduced that Joni had finally turned up.

It is not my usual practice to hang around in the snow waiting for the Old Bill to identify a missing

Dutch au pair. But February had been a thinnish month for news, and we'd run two splashes and three page leads on the story so far. Plus, in a surfeit of red biddy, our deranged Editor had stuck up a five-grand reward for information leading to Joni's whereabouts. He'd forgotten the proviso that we wanted her alive.

Unless he managed to worm his way out of it my bet was that the loot would go to the geezer with the frostbitten poodle nattering away to the Law on their side of the cordon tapes. We were perched on what in sunnier seasons you would call a grassy knoll so we had a ringside seat to all the action, not that there was any action to write home about. Below us the park fell away sharply before rolling into a little dip and finally running out of steam against a row of Victorian railings. The ironwork had a fine tracery of snow. Very chichi. It looked like it belonged in Dulwich.

Centre stage in all of this was the big yellow tent. We had nothing else to look at so we watched it. Every now and then the walls rippled as some Herbert inside biffed his head against them. They were either looking for clues or playing Twister.

The air was brittle and you could hear the forensic boys panting away in there. Nobody was saying anything. Outside the tent was the lumpish shape of Chief Inspector Tom Skelly in a red and white ski jacket. He and the tent clashed. He was standing by the bloke with the dog but they weren't talking. The dog was playing dumb too. Skelly had got all he wanted from the bodyfinder and pooch. He was just making sure we got nowhere near the man. Every now and then Skelly pitched us a baleful look.

I suppose if I was him I would have felt likewise. If we hadn't all made such a fuss about the vanishing Joni Poelma, a mere Detective Inspector would be chilling his toes out there in the park while Skelly sat in the station canteen, scoffing bacon sarnies and having the *Mirror* cartoons explained to him.

We weren't feeling too happy either. Everybody was out of fags so we just puffed out white plumes of air and pretended we were smoking. It was still too early for the pubs. Anyway, we had to hang around in the outlandish hope that Skelly or the press liaison officer might say something interesting. We shuffled our feet and looked bored. It wasn't hard.

Down below, a new character trekked into shot. A low moan of dismay escaped us. 'Oddjob!'

He heard it but he acted as if he didn't. Bob Jobley is a Scotland Yard press liaison officer. He is not a copper. He is a civilian only minus the brains for that task. Liaison officers know nothing, except what few crumbs the detective in charge bothers to tell them. Oddjob always knows less than nothing, hence our dismay.

Skelly somehow restrained himself from clasping Oddjob to his bosom and telling him all. They had maybe twenty seconds of chit-chat, then the liaison officer turned to face us. This was our signal to slalom downhill and pick his brains.

'Morning, Oddjob,' I greeted him.

He has no pride. 'Morning, Max.'

An agency hack fired the first question: 'Is it Joni Poelma?'

Oddjob simultaneously shrugged, strangled a

yawn, squeezed up his eyes and shook his head. The man's a polymath.

'It's not Joni?'

We got a repeat performance.

I said, 'Is that on the record?'

Over his shoulder I could see the great pink ham of Skelly's face. He was grinning. The only time Plods like him smirk at us like that is when they have something to smirk about, such as finally tripping over Joni Poelma's body. Or having somebody else doing the tripping over bit for them.

You could see that Skelly had no intention of telling us anything. That's why he was happy. You could also see that they'd found Joni. If it was some other stiff he'd be back down the nick scratching his chilblains by now.

Oddjob said: 'It is a body.' Thereby dispelling any suspicions that the tent might be harbouring Scotland Yard's camping club.

'Male or female?' This from someone behind me.

'It's too early to say,' lied Oddjob.

We ignored that. 'How was she murdered?'

Oddjob waved his mittens about. That meant our guess was as good as his. Better.

'Has she been here long?'

Oddjob said, 'That has yet to be established.'

After that there was a snowball fight of questions. I refrained from taking part and let the kids enjoy themselves. Anyway, I'm a minimalist. I find the less you know about a story the easier it is to write. For starters, you don't find awkward facts getting in the way. Nor do you get useless chunks of information cluttering up the narrative. I mean, right now a local radio hackette was asking Oddjob the name of the dog of the geezer who'd found Joni Poelma. Do the Great British Public really want to know what the dog was called? Indeed not. But just for the record, its name was Jack.

The alleged press briefing wound down to the point where even the bloke from the local weekly had run out of questions. Oddjob promised to meet us all at Dulwich nick around oneish when he should have yet more red-hot news for us. We grunted and shambled off as the pubs had opened. I looked back over my shoulder. Oddjob was standing at the cordon with his mitts sticking out, a forlorn figure that nobody wanted to talk to.

In the nearest bar I was on my second Gordon's and halfway through a slanderous story about my News Editor when my bleeper went off. It told me that the very same News Editor wanted me to ring her URGENTLY. I finished the story, listened to someone else's lies, ordered in a new round, and gave her a bell.

'Lo, Angie,' I said. 'You're missing me?'

She wasn't in the mood for banter. 'Yes, I bloody well am. I'm just about to go into conference and I need a schedule line on Joni Poelma. Is it her?'

'Yup.'

She said, 'Scotland Yard have confirmed it?'

'Nope.'

'But you're sure it's her?'

'Yup.'

She said, 'So what's the schedule line?'

I said, '*Gazette* Reader Finds Murdered Joni.'

Angela's a stickler for facts. 'Does he read our paper?'

I said, 'Probably not, but by the time I get to him, even his dog will be a lifelong reader.'

She said, 'OK, that'll do for conference. But before you slope off to the bar, I've got a job for you.'

I didn't like the sound of that. I said warily, 'Oh?'

Angie went all breezy which meant it was a crummy job. She said, 'I want you to go and see the Cardigans and set up an exclusive interview for features.'

'Who's doing the interview?'

She said, 'Beverley Nephews. She'll be down—'

Beverley Nephews! Otherwise known in the trade as Beverley Hills, for two very good reasons. I hauled my mind back to what Angie was saying. '. . . so we need you to stick your foot in the door and keep everybody else away from the Cardigans until Beverley gets there. OK?'

The Cardigans were the couple who until last week employed Joni to ride shotgun for their children. I remembered that he was big in chemicals and they played happy families in something marginally smaller than Buck House.

Angela said, 'They might need some convincing so we'll go for a buy up.'

And what nutter thought that one up? I just said, 'How much?'

'You can go up to a thousand.'

I said, 'Angie, the Cardigans spend that on dental

floss. They probably help the Sultan of Brunei when he's a bit strapped for readies.'

She sighed. 'All right, go to two thou, but no more.'

I holstered my mobile and returned to the bar. There are times when this game is just too silly for its own good.

Meriel, a hackette from the *Mail*, was thinking along the same lines. 'You'll never guess what News Desk have asked me to do,' she said.

I had a very good idea of precisely what but I listened politely.

She said, 'They've asked me to try and buy up the Cardigans.'

I chortled merrily. I said, 'Don't they read the papers? Wedge Cardigan uses fivers for wallpaper. How much are you offering them?'

Meriel stuck her nose in a glass of house white and said, 'Twenty.'

'Twenty thousand?'

She nodded. Now this was serious. The Cardigans might just bite on that. I put on my gravest face. I said, 'I don't think that's a very wise idea.' There was a strange undercurrent in my voice.

She darted me a curious look from under her Shetland pony fringe. 'What do you mean?'

I took a mouthful of gin and lit a Benson's before I bothered to answer. I simply repeated, 'It's not a wise idea.' This time my tones were so laden with sinister nuances that I sounded as if I was talking in slo-mo.

Meriel's fringe eyed me intently. 'Why?'

I took another swig and had a shufti around to

make sure no one was eavesdropping. I said, 'Because the police are going to lift Wedge Cardigan.'

The fringe swished hither and thither. 'What!'

I said, 'Keep your voice down. I've just had a tip from a detective mate. Don't tell anyone else.'

Meriel squeaked, 'They think he did it?'

'Sssh. Yes, he's in the frame, so you'd better forget trying to buy him up. Wait for the one o'clock briefing. They'll probably announce it then. But don't do anything in the meantime.'

The fringe trembled with a pitiful gratitude. She said: 'Thanks, Max. I owe you one.'

Those of you of a more squeamish disposition, that is to say who are not reporters, might regard this as a scumbag trick on my part. But look at it my way: the *Mail* has great buckets of cash to sling at any passing story. We don't. Yet my News Desk requires, no, *demands*, that I deliver the story, regardless of the *Mail*'s megabucks. If I fail, then I am seen to be a lesser hack than Meriel Fringe-face, and that would never do. Therefore I had to use an evil ruse. Besides, it's more fun playing dirty.

I licked my glass clean and said I had to hotfoot it back to the office. Meriel squeezed my arm and gave me a conspiratorial goodbye wink. I winked right back.

JOHN BURNS

Snap

Macmillan £16.99

When millionaire's au pair Joni Poelma goes missing after leaving a late-night club Max Chard's newspaper puts out a reward for information. Unfortunately they forget to mention that they want her found alive. And now Joni has turned up – very dead – in a snow-covered park in Dulwich.

In pursuit of the inside story, Max offers Gabriella Cardigan, Joni's employer, two grand for the lowdown. But the gorgeous Gabriella has a better idea: she offers Chard two grand instead.

Snap.

The deal is he takes Gabriella's son Jason, a would-be journalist, under his wing. Much to Max's surprise, Jason proves rather useful, for he has more than a passing knowledge of drugs. And the story is that Joni was killed because of her predilection for strange substances.

Snap.

But was she? Chard and his motor-mouth, motor-drive photographer, Frankie, go banging on doors and making nuisances of themselves. And that's when Max gets the bigger picture.

Snap.

Shut Eye

Adam Baron lives in Brighton and is a writer and comedian. As one-third of the comedy act The Baron Brothers, he has appeared on MTV, *The Paul Ross Show* and *The Lenny Beige Show.*

Shut Eye is his first novel.

Adam Baron

Shut Eye

PAN BOOKS

First published 1999 by Pan Books
an imprint of Pan Macmillan Ltd
Pan Macmillan, 20 New Wharf Road, London N1 9RR
Basingstoke and Oxford
Associated companies throughout the world
www.panmacmillan.com

ISBN 0 330 37063 4

3 5 7 9 8 6 4

A CIP catalogue record for this book is available from
the British Library.

Phototypeset by Intype London Ltd
Printed by Mackays of Chatham plc, Chatham, Kent

For my father, Charles Baron

the time of no reply
is calling me to stay
there's no hello and no goodbye
to leave, there is no way

NICK DRAKE

Acknowledgements

This book was written with the help of Jason Baron, Marcus Baron, Beverley Cousins, Naomi Delap, Dr William Drake, Lisanne Radice and Andrew Watts. General and essential encouragement came from the rest of my family, as well as from Lucy Barker, Jane Gregory, Alan Samson, Vicky Tennant and a girl I met on a beach in Portugal. Heartfelt thanks to one and all.

When I see it, this is what I see.

Teddy stretched his legs and followed the stewardesses off the plane. He joked about overtime payments with his co-pilot as he picked up his bags and headed through the blue channel. He asked Mike if he wanted to catch one before hitting the traffic, but the flight had been late and Mike begged off. Teddy wasn't surprised – Mike was a real family man. There was a time once when all Teddy had wanted to do was get out of the airport and go home too. But not tonight. He patted Mike on the back, told him goodnight, waved at the stewardesses, and headed for the bar.

Teddy could have gone and sat in the first-class lounge but for some reason he chose the espresso bar the public use, which serves a good cocktail as well as the coffee. He took off his cap, ordered a Scotch and soda, and thought of the caiporenias *he had drunk three nights ago in Rio. He looked around the sterile, white airport and then he checked himself out in the bar mirror. He ran a hand through hair which was still full but turning slowly from sandy to grey. He was OK. He looked just like an airline pilot. He stretched out his face to try to lose some of the lines around his eyes, smiled to himself at the stupidity of it, and relaxed.*

In the mirror Teddy noticed that a youngish man in a baseball cap, sitting three stools down, had seen him mugging to himself and he was embarrassed for a second until the man gave him a broad smile as if to say it's all right, I've done that. Teddy smiled back and took a long hit from the drink that had been placed in front of him. He yawned. He took another drink. When he glanced back up at the bar mirror a minute or so later, he noticed that the man in the baseball hat was looking straight at him.

Teddy and the man in the baseball hat chatted for thirty minutes or so, mostly about Teddy's job, because the younger man seemed quite reticent. Interested but reticent. All Teddy could get out of him was that he had just got back from a week in Paris and his friend was late picking him up. Two hours late by now; he was going to have to get the train. Teddy asked him if he lived in London and when the man said he did, and it was only ten minutes from Canonbury where Teddy lived, Teddy told him he was welcome to a lift if he wanted. The man shrugged his shoulders and said, 'Sure, why not?' but didn't look too grateful. He hadn't looked too grateful when Teddy had bought him a beer either.

Teddy finished his second Scotch and soda and stood down from the stool. The younger man followed suit. The barman watched the two men walk off together at about ten-thirty, Teddy putting his cap back on, the other man swinging a medium-sized black leather grip over his shoulder. The barman knew it was around then because that was when the night barman came in. He remembered the bag because he liked it and needed one himself, although he didn't think he could afford one like it. He told the police that he had never seen either of the men before but that it wasn't all that uncommon for some of the flight staff to stop off at his bar and offer lifts home to stray passengers, if they knew what he meant.

Teddy chatted as he drove, casually mentioning that his

wife was away on business, saying how much he hated going home to an empty house after a long trip. The man just nodded now and then and said yes or it must be, and then why not? when Teddy asked him if he wanted to come in and do some damage to a case of champagne he had won in a raffle. Teddy said great and he laughed out of nervousness. It was the first time he had done this, invite a stranger into his home, and he still wasn't sure if he was doing it or not or what was going to happen. He pulled into the forecourt of his building, drove through it and round the back, and pressed a button on a remote control device which activated a door to rise slowly in front of his car. Then he scraped the wing of his Rover as he put it in the garage and, laughing it off, blamed his wife for parking her Golf convertible too far over on his side.

Teddy was talking a lot now, about anything and nothing. He thought about his brother. The man in the baseball hat followed him through the garage and the back door, into the stylish, modern, spacious, two-bedroom flat, which Teddy shared with the wife who parked in so selfish a manner, and with whom the touching of car wings was as intimate as Teddy and she had been in almost six months. He turned to face the man behind him.

'So!' he said, rubbing his hands enthusiastically. 'Champagne!'

Teddy went to the fridge to fetch a bottle.

When Teddy's wife came home next morning, four hours earlier than expected, she found it, two-thirds full, standing next to one half empty glass, and one full glass, on the side of the American-style hot tub they'd had installed in the white tiled bathroom. It had gone flat. In the master bedroom, where she had gone after calling out her husband's name, she found another bottle of champagne and she found Teddy.

Teddy was on the bed, naked. The champagne bottle, or at least the top half of it, was protruding, like the funnel of an ocean liner, from Teddy's abdomen. The rest of it was scattered in pieces across his torso. Teddy's face had been smashed in, and a long spike of glass stuck out of what had once been his upper jaw but was now a crumpled hole encompassing both his mouth and his nose. Even someone as unqualified in medical matters as Teddy's wife could see that he was dead. Very. Mrs Morgan screamed, ran into the living room, and called the police who got a couple of flatfoots round there in minutes.

The two policemen found a woman who was obviously in shock, and a day-old corpse covered in broken glass. Later, at the morgue, another police officer found more glass fragments as well as a quantity of semen, and some of Teddy's blood, a long way up Teddy's anal canal. While it is true that nothing should be taken for granted in cases such as these, it can probably be assumed that the semen had arrived there first.

PART ONE

Chapter One

I don't really know what got me into boxing. I never did it when I was a kid, or at college, or when I was still on the force. I had occasion, a year or two back, to ask some questions at a gym that was beneath a pub behind King's Cross station, and I got to know the manager. She helped me to find out the answers to my questions, and a week or so later I went back to work out and train. After a couple of visits the manager talked me in to doing some sparring and, if you can excuse the pun, I was hooked. The only reason I can think of for my attachment to it is that standing across from a man whose express purpose is to punch your lights out in the shortest possible time available to him, does tend to relegate any other problems you might have to the recesses of the head which you are trying so hard to protect. Even if it is only for an hour or so.

The gym I go to is not a professional one, or rather, it is run for profit but no professionals train there. It is more of a fitness centre and club, attracting a lot of young kids who have seen Eubank or Benn on the TV, and the kind of cars they drive, and who want to see if they've got what it takes themselves. If they do they soon leave for bigger set-ups and if they don't they either give up or carry on coming for the love of it. Sal doesn't mind that. She took the place over when her husband was killed and I think she keeps it as a way of feeling close to him as much as anything else. She knows she's no Frank Warren and anyway she has another source of income which makes her boxing gym something of a sideline.

I like Sal's gym as much as I like Sal. Most Wednesday nights find me down there if nothing else comes up and I generally try to slip in another night as well. I get a sweat up, punch the bag, and then I either go home or stick around for a pint with Sal and some of the guys. A few of them may feel a bit funny about what I do for a living, and about the fact that I used to be in the Filth, as they put it, but they respect Sal, and seeing as I'm OK with her, they respect me. Or at least they pretend they do. One or two of them, I swear it, genuinely like me.

A lot of affluent media types around my age go to gyms to do what they call boxercise. They train and work out, do everything a boxer does except the actual boxing. It's a very good way to get fit. My gym, however, would never permit such a thing. Not because they think that if you train like a boxer you should use what you've learnt in the ring, but because they don't want to attract the affluent media types.

I parked my car in a delivery bay opposite The George, locked it, and crossed the street. I usually walk, or ride my bike down there, but it had been raining all day and autumn was beginning to give into a Big City Winter, so I'd decided on the Mazda. It was quarter past seven, dark as the streetlamps let it get. When I got downstairs I was late and Sal had already started the circuit training, putting fifteen or so guys through an experience close to absolute misery the first time you did it, and which never seemed to get easier any time after that. I decided to skip it. I got changed and headed straight to the weights room.

I stretched, worked out for half an hour in the slightly cramped, brightly lit room, and then I went in with Mountain Pete, a huge black guy who doesn't move around a whole lot, but who has a sizeable enough punch on the end of a long reach to make up for that. We waltzed for a round and a half and then I got under his guard a couple of times and he covered up before going to pieces a little. I backed him up in the corner, ducking and swinging round the side when he came out after me. I got a couple in under his jab. At the end of the third we broke off and stepped out. Mountain Pete could have created a sea with all the sweat running off him.

'You're getting good, Rucker,' he said to me, shaking his head, breathing hard. 'I'm fucked if I didn't used to be able to bounce your pretty white arse round this ring like a yo-yo. I'm going to have to start trying against you.' His face disappeared completely beneath a small white towel.

'Don't try too hard, Pete,' I said. 'You'll flood the place.'

'Fuck off, you cheeky cunt!' the towel said. I laughed and went to find Sal.

Sal was in the weights room herself now, teaching three new kids how to use the machines. I waited while she showed them the correct way to perform a bench press. Sal is around the forty mark, taller than most women, with a good, muscular figure and dark curly hair she only lets down outside the gym. She has a firm chin, a strong nose which she constantly reminds herself is too big, and soft, mahogany eyes which sometimes give the lie to her tough, no-nonsense exterior. Her cheeks are beginning to show the first broken capillaries of a woman who has never made friends with a bottle of whiskey because the bottle has never stayed round long enough. She is the sort of woman who never wears much make-up but who can transform herself from tough boxing coach into alluring modern woman with a silk blouse and a touch of lipstick.

When she saw me watching her, Sal left the kids, walked across to a table in the corner, and picked up the photograph I'd given her a week or so before. The photograph had a man's face on one side and my name and number on the back. I'd been showing it around for two weeks now, trying to find Edward Morgan's killer, a confusing experience which made me relish the focused simplicity to be found in Sal's gym. When Sal came over to me she was shaking her head.

'No,' she said, holding it in her hand, looking down at it. 'I thought it rang a bell when you gave it me but it's not clear enough, you can't see enough of his face.' She stared hard at the picture in her hand, trying to pull something familiar out of it. She shook her head again. 'No. I wish I could help you, Bill. I've handed out the rest you gave me but I wouldn't expect much if I were you.'

'I don't,' I said. 'It doesn't hurt though, passing out photos. It's the sort of thing that eats at you if you don't do it.'

'Yeah. People round here are not what you'd call talkative though, at the best of times.'

'I know.'

'Good luck with it though, Bill. He needs catching, he does.'

Sal walked over and put the picture back on the table. The three kids were standing by the rower, waiting for her.

'Thanks anyway, Sal.'

'Don't mention it, Masher,' she said, winking at me. I smiled at the tag and went back into the training room.

The reason Sal calls me the Masher has nothing to do with boxing, although it does sound like it might. Iron Mike, Smokin' Jo Frazier, Billy the Masher Rucker. A Masher, so Sal explains to me, is an old East End word for a man who dresses in a manner designed to attract young, impressionable women. She calls me this because two of the boys from the gym saw me going into a very swanky club one night and thought I looked just a little poncy. Telling them that I was on a case, and that you have to dress right to gain access to the places where you are trying to further your investigations, had little effect. I was a Masher.

'We'd have let you in no matter what you had on,' Tommy said. They were on the door. In my opinion, with their frilly blue dress shirts and floppy bow ties, they looked a lot more poncy than I did.

That piece of work turned out well. I had been looking for a girl who had run away from home in Sheffield and had found her working as a waitress in a place that did not require her to wear a shirt as she served the tables. I had persuaded her to call home and her family were relieved and I was five hundred pounds better off. The case I was on now was not going so well. In fact, it wasn't going at all. I had no clues, no idea where I could find any clues, and that day, after wandering aimlessly around half of north London, I had just about decided to give up on it. All I had was an unlimited supply of copies of a blown-up, grainy, indistinct photograph of a man's face, taken from the side. Not a lot. Ten detectives from Islington police station had worked their arses off for six months getting absolutely nowhere on it and it had taken me two and a half weeks of dull, solid graft to catch up with them.

The case had left me not only frustrated but deadened and exhausted. It was the biggest thing I'd had to do since leaving the force, and every day that passed meant that some poor bastard somewhere was a day closer to a very miserable death. This time of year was a killer anyway, dull slate-grey skies, ever shorter days, stained ugly buildings, and drizzle. It probably would have been a good idea to, but I didn't feel like climbing into the ring again so instead I stood watching a sixteen-year-old kid called Sanjay, who had only been coming a month or so, but who Sal thought might have something.

Sanjay was a lithe, good-looking lad, with snake-like muscles moving beneath smooth, caramel skin, and a natural cocky grace that was good to watch. His stomach was a cheese grater, the sort of thing no amount of training can give you once you've skipped past thirty. Ah, youth. He was quick too, with both his fists and his feet. Sal, however, stood shaking her head, her lips pursed and her arms folded.

'The problem,' she explained, looking straight ahead as the kid picked apart another Asian lad of about the same age, 'is The Prince. Sure, they see him, and that's what gets them into it, which is great, but then they try to fight like him. Look at this nonce.' She pointed at Sanjay and shook her head again, weary as a stallholder at Brick Lane when you're trying to save a few pounds. 'Where's the guard I taught him? What sort of a punch is that from down there? Anyone decent would beat the shit out of him.' She said this as Sanjay gave his friend a minute or two off, his gloves by his sides, dodging and smiling as his friend tried to connect. 'Christ!' Sal exclaimed. 'He'll do a fucking handstand in a minute!'

I laughed.

'The Prince is good though, Sal.'

'Good? He's a fucking genius! That's the thing. If he wasn't he'd get his teeth knocked in fighting like that.'

'And if he wasn't so cool these kids wouldn't be here.'

'I know. I've never had any Asian kids in here before the last eighteen months. Beats working in their old man's corner fucking shop, doesn't it now?'

Sal got into the ring and started swearing. Sanjay looked nonplussed, like a kid who gets yelled at for burning the kitchen down when he only wanted to help his mother. I told myself that it probably did beat working in a corner shop, but not by much, and I went to get changed.

On my way to the locker room I saw the three new kids, who were standing together watching what was going on in the ring. They were all black, fourteen or fifteen years old, equally free from concerns of weight and muscle tone. One of them was holding a bright orange object which could have been a coat or a small sleeping bag and which he obviously valued too highly to let out of his sight. He looked at me as I passed him and I thought he was going to say something but he didn't. He looked a little scared. I wondered why for a second before realizing that it's a strange thing to do, getting up on a little stage in front of twenty or so other guys, trying to hit someone and stop him hitting you. And not look stupid. I gave him a sympathetic glance but he looked away quickly. I took my things out of the locker and got under the shower.

I left the gym just as two of the black kids were

climbing through the ropes with Sal. They weren't much to watch and everyone else was milling around, starting more exercises, working on the bag. I turned at the door to wave to Mountain Pete who was skipping, trying to get some speed into those flat iron feet of his.

'Catch you next time, Mash!' he called out, getting the rope caught round his shins. I waved to Sal in the ring and she waved back as she showed the two kids how to face each other and begin. The kid who had looked scared darted his eyes over to me as Sal spoke to him. He looked even more nervous than he had before.

Outside, the temperature had taken a dive, and even though it is only half a centimetre long my hair let me know that I hadn't dried it properly. Hat time soon, I thought. The old brown Mazda started eventually but somehow it refused to drive me home, and took me to The Old Ludensian instead, a bar I frequent down on St John Street near to Smithfield. I stayed there for an hour and a half, sitting at the bar, talking to some of the regulars. I had three or four, flirted with the waitress who I always flirt with the waitress, and then went home.

Nicky, who owns The Old Ludensian, had suggested making a night of it down at The Titanic but I put him off. I didn't think I deserved a night of carousing and these days I can't enjoy it that way when I don't think I've earned it. I wouldn't have been able to stop thinking about a guy with a broad smile who was never going to smile again. Also, Nicky was probably the best-looking and most charming man I had ever met, and a night out with him often entailed drumming my fingers on the bar top while he chatted away to some impossibly gorgeous woman. Not tonight, Josephine.

'Soon though, Billy,' Nicky said. 'I don't see enough of you.' He had walked me to the door and was shaking my hand.

'You would if you let me pay for my drinks,' I told him. 'I get embarrassed.'

'After what you did for me, never.'

'OK, Nicky,' I said, shaking his hand. 'I'll see you. Probably when I've sorted this shit out, one way or another.'

'Make it soon, Billy, soon.' He slapped me on the back and I walked outside.

Nicky was referring to the time when, with the help of Mountain Pete, I had talked a certain gentleman into allowing him to remain alive. The gentleman was a mid-ranking member of an East End security association, and while Nicky had constantly refused to give the gentleman what he wanted whenever he had called at Nicky's bar, my friend had not been so ungenerous with the gentleman's wife. I did the talking while Mountain Pete showed the man how much the butt end of a twelve-gauge sawn-off shotgun can hurt somebody's head. I assured him that the butt was not the end Mountain Pete would be using next time, and the problem was solved. Mountain Pete is a member of a security association of his own, run out of Westbourne Park. Nicky was relieved and thankful, and since then neither Pete nor I had ever been allowed to part with a penny at the bar of The Old Ludensian. The incident shook Nicky up so much he didn't sleep with another married woman for at least a week.

I gunned my dream machine into life and this time it did take me back to my flat, which is above an old print shop behind Exmouth Market in Clerkenwell. No messages. I showered, poured myself a whiskey and took it to bed, drifting off into sleep with one of Nick Drake's stark mellow tunes on the stereo.

At two fifteen the phone woke me and I let the machine get it. The room seemed empty without the music, which had turned itself off. A big, angry voice said it knew I was there and told me to pick up. It was quite insistent. Why not? I did. The voice then told me that if I wanted to find the man whose face was in the photograph I had been showing around like I was a Catholic priest and it was a piece of Jesus's fucking toothbrush or some shit, I should go and stand in the entrance to the freight depot halfway down York Way as soon as I could get there. I was to wait and be sure to bring along some money – five hundred would be ample. Any less would not be. The voice said soon or don't bother, and then it became the dialling tone.

I sat up in bed and turned the lamp on.

I ran my hands over my head and yawned again, trying to bring myself to some level of decision-making consciousness. I thought about it. Standing around York Way in the middle of the night with a pocket full of money, waiting for a man who probably had, instead of information, a very big knife in his pocket, was not something I'd ever advise anyone else to do. The guy probably saw my name on the back of the photo somewhere or other and thought he was on to an easy mugging. York Way is not what you would call a safe place to hang out at the best of times, but even less so when it's two fifteen in the morning and someone knows you're going to be there. But what the hell. It was the first thing approaching a lead that I'd had and I was awake now anyway as the joke goes. I wanted to *do* something, even if that something was something very stupid.

It took me two and a half minutes to climb into jeans and a sweatshirt, pull on my Red Wings, and grab a jacket. I saw my wallet lying on the kitchen table. I left it there.

Outside there was no one about and I shivered myself awake as I lowered myself on to the torn driving seat of the Mazda. I checked my watch and pulled the belt on. I inserted the key into the ignition and turned it, expecting a fight. Luckily the car started first time.

Luckily?

Chapter Two

I don't normally take cases that the police are already working flat out on. I usually spend my time looking for runaway kids, teenagers or younger, who are a low priority to my ex-colleagues on the Met but a high priority to the families they have left behind. In most other matters the Met have me beaten. They have more resources, and more powers of surveillance, entry, and arrest. They do, however, tend to stand out like sore thumbs in bars and clubs and casinos in either cheap suits or tacky undercover leather jackets, and this makes room for me. The bars and the clubs are the sorts of places where I generally find my teenagers because they are often part of the reason the teenager comes to London in the first place. The Big City, provider of action and anonymity. I don't look like a copper, I don't even look like an ex-copper, and having spent the first fourteen years of my life in Toronto I can make sure that I don't sound like one either. I can go to the places I have to go to and not have half the kitchen staff legging it out of the back door before I've even managed a sip of my Canadian Club. Also, thanks to a vicious old man I haven't seen in twelve years, I know what it feels like to be a kid and to hate your life so much that anywhere, *anywhere*, is better than home. I do OK at what I do, but I usually leave the big stuff to my previous employers.

The message I found on my machine one bright Monday morning in mid October, however, intrigued me. I had just opened up the small, sparsely furnished office that I keep in a business unit up behind Highbury Fields. A plummy middle-aged male voice informed me that it belonged to one Sir Peter Morgan, and it asked if I could please call it back as soon as I was able. The voice was nervous and far too restrained, as if the owner of the voice was afraid of what the voice might say, and held it tightly in check like a pit bull on a leash in a Montessori Centre.

The name intrigued me. It had been in the news a lot recently, although it had been sidelined in the last couple of weeks by the state of Sarah Ferguson's thighs and the health, or lack of health, of the Russian President. I have a good memory for names, though, and even if I hadn't I could hardly have forgotten it. Sir Peter Morgan was a Conservative Member of Parliament, a (now) Shadow Minister at the Treasury. He was a leading Euro-sceptic and senior member of the 1922 Committee. He was a regular guest on *Question Time*, *Any Questions*, and those political programmes you turn off immediately when carving the Sunday roast. His name was especially familiar, however, for the fact that his younger brother Edward, an airline pilot, had recently been brutally murdered in the flat he shared with his wife of six years, by person or persons unknown wielding a broken champagne bottle. I wrote down the number he gave and sat for a second, wondering why he was calling me.

There were three other messages on my machine and I dealt with those first. One was from Joe Nineteen, a regular provider of information concerning the whereabouts of errant children, and one was from a woman whose son I had located six months ago; she wanted me to locate him again. The other was from Sharon. I called Joe and told him that his tip of the day before had been spot on and that I would be round to see him soon. I called the number the woman – a Mrs Lewes – had given, and left a message on her machine stating that I would be happy to help her and that I would be in touch when I knew more. I didn't call Sharon because the message was from yesterday and I had already arranged to have dinner with her after she'd reached me at home. I sat for a second, thinking, and then dialled the number the MP had given.

A secretary put me on hold for a minute and I was just about to hang up, redial, and leave a message when Sir Peter came on the line.

'Mr Rucker?' he asked.

'Yes. Sir Peter Morgan? I'm just returning your call.'

'Thank you. I . . .' He thought for a second. 'I was wondering if you are free for lunch today. Your services were recently recommended to me and I have something I would like to discuss with you.'

The MP's voice wasn't so restrained as it had been on the machine. The pit bull wasn't on its leash any more; it was dressed up like a poodle.

'May I enquire who you spoke with?' I asked. My usual customer survey.

'I really would rather do this in person if you don't mind, Mr Rucker. Could you meet me at one today? Do you know where the Portman Club is?'

I waited a second. I don't like talking to people who give orders by asking questions, or whose tone of voice indicates that they cannot conceive of ever not getting their way.

'Sir Peter,' I said, 'I have an idea as to what you might want to talk to me about. If it is what I think it is, I really don't think that I can be of much help to you. I'm not a big organization, I don't have anyone else working for me. I usually look for missing teenagers.'

'I am aware of that,' he answered. 'My information is, however, that you are very good at your job, and that it would be worth speaking to you.'

'All the same,' I went on, 'I don't want to waste any of your time.' Or mine, I thought. 'It would be pointless to come all the way down to your club to tell you exactly what I could tell you now.'

'Nevertheless, Mr Rucker, I would like to meet you. I will of course pay for your time, whatever the outcome, and I can assure you of a most excellent lunch.'

'I . . .'

'Please, Mr Rucker. It would save me the trouble of hunting you out. If you have an idea as to why I want to speak to you then you might understand how much it means to me that I should.'

The ex-Minister stopped speaking abruptly. The leash on his voice was back and ready to snap. I thought about it for a second. Something inside me sighed wearily.

'Crème brûlé?' I asked.

'I'm sorry?'

'On the menu. At your club.'

'Oh,' he said, thinking. 'Of course. The finest west of Paris.' He managed a short laugh.

'All right,' I said, 'I'll be there.'

He laughed again, stiffly. 'Thank you.' Then he added,

'I don't want to sound patronizing but the club insists that visitors should wear a jacket.'

'I'll buy one on the way, sir.'

'And a tie, I'm afraid.'

'Right. What about trousers?' I asked. I took the address from him and then hung up.

It was perfect. Mine is as good but I don't have a blowtorch to get the top perfectly crisp while leaving the underneath firm. I make do with a grill.

I had made a few calls, looked at the file I had on the missing Dominic Lewes, and decided that I would work on him either that evening or else the next day. I had drunk some coffee in the café that serves the business units, and then gone back to my flat and donned the Paul Smith suit that I had bought for my brother's wedding but never had a chance to wear. I'd chosen an antique Ralph Lauren from the seventy or so ties in my cupboard, which I collect, but which I seldom get a chance to wear.

We were sitting across from one another in the Portman Club's dining room, a huge, high-ceilinged room, with the requisite wood panelling, oil paintings of sea battles, and huge chandeliers. Sir Peter Morgan was a tall man of forty-seven/forty-eight, elegant in a conservative way, with a greying, full head of hair, which would make him look very distinguished in a few years' time. He had a high forehead above a narrow face, with striking blue eyes and a nose that seemed just a little too small compared with his other features, making him look slightly boyish. A pair of reading glasses hung on a delicate silver chain around his neck.

Throughout the three courses we made polite conversation. I asked him how he was normally addressed and he said that Sir Peter was fine. He didn't like being called Mr Morgan but he never complained when people made the mistake because it sounded very petty to do so. He told me a little about his job, I told him a little about mine. At one point I thought he was going to get into politics but luckily he didn't. It might have been the end of a very beautiful friendship. We ate, we chatted, he nodded at the odd acquaintance, and I noted his perfect Windsor knot over a starched Hilditch and Key blue striped shirt, with matching handkerchief poking cautiously out of the pocket of an exquisitely tailored single-breasted pinstripe. He showed few signs of his recent loss beyond an unwillingness to engage any of the people who passed the table in any conversation beyond the usual pleasantries. His table manners and posture demonstrated a man who was used to being in control of himself. He was like an uncle who invites you to lunch during your final year at Cambridge in order to dissuade you from going to live on a commune in Goa, recommend a tailor, and enquire as to which City firm you would like him to get you a job at when you graduated.

When the waitress took away our dessert plates Sir Peter told her that we would take our coffee upstairs. We stood up and I followed him through the dining room and up a broad circular staircase, covered in a deep red carpet held down by bold brass rods. The walls were similarly covered in oils, but most of these were of stern old men whose faces gave the impression that, unlike me, they hadn't found the crème brûlé at all satisfactory. We walked past them and along a broad corridor, towards a heavily polished oak door which Sir Peter pushed open. It didn't make a sound. On the other side of it was a large room, filled with armchairs that were mostly vacant, next to low coffee tables liberally covered in broadsheet newspapers. I say liberally: they were either the *Telegraph*, *The Times* or the *FT*. Sir Peter led me through the speckled columns of light charging through large arch windows on the opposite wall, across to the furthest corner of the room where we sat facing each other, both of us encased in green leather.

Sir Peter shifted uncomfortably in his seat, looking for a way to begin. I waited while he sipped his coffee, listening to the faint hum of traffic on Piccadilly. I noted that he had the same colour Turk's Head cufflinks as I had found in the pockets of a second-hand Gieves and Hawkes suit I'd bought on Portabello Road a year ago.

'Mr Rucker,' he began finally. 'I find this quite difficult. I've never needed the services of a private investigator before. I . . .' He stopped speaking and gazed out of the window.

'You want me to find the person who murdered your brother,' I said. Well, I didn't have all day.

'Yes. It's as simple as that I suppose. Yes. Yes I do.' He looked at me, relieved that the ice had been broken. He seemed scared too, scared of going over what had happened, of seeing it again.

'In that case I'm afraid that this has been a waste of time,' I said. 'Except for the crème brûlée. You are aware of the amount of manpower the police are already putting in to this? Especially now.'

'I am aware that the police are doing what they can.'

'I happen to know one of the officers on the case. He's good. I don't think that there is any doubt that they'll find whoever it is who's behind these killings.' Sir Peter seemed to wince, to shy away from what I was saying. I carried on.

'The first one hardly got into the news as far as I can remember. It certainly didn't make the TV. A lorry driver found dead in the sleeping area of his cab. Stabbed with a broken beer bottle and all his cash taken. Kids probably, crackheads who needed fifty quid bad enough at certain times that they'll quite cheerfully kill a man to get it. Without breaking a sweat. No sign of sexual activity, a simple robbery that possibly went wrong.' I leant forward for my coffee cup. Sir Peter was perfectly still, his expression blank, looking straight at me.

'The second one did make the headlines. A rent boy in Brixton, only fourteen, still at school, halfway through his GCSEs. This time there was sexual activity, although it's impossible to state in this case whether or not any of the four brands of sperm found in various areas of the corpse actually belonged to the perpetrator. Again a bottle, this time Lucozade I believe, was used to pierce the victim's abdomen. Pieces of glass were discovered in the boy's anal canal, which was severely lacerated.'

Sir Peter shifted in his seat and looked at me in a way which suggested he was used to being treated with just a touch more deference.

'You seem to know what you are talking about,' he said coldly.

'I read the newspaper. I also called DI Gold after I spoke to you earlier. The officer who recommended me to you. I trained with him at Hendon, he filled me in. With the MO similar to the motorway killing a link was established and background work done on the driver. It appears that he was a homosexual, or a bi-sexual bearing in mind that he was married with three children. The pathologist still insists that there was no evidence of sexual contact the night he died, but several men were found who admitted sexual encounters with him, some of them in his lorry. It's curious. Apparently the driver's wife was more distressed when an officer was forced to relay this information to her, than she had been when she'd been informed that her husband had been killed.'

I sat back and waited for a response but Sir Peter didn't say anything. I took a big sip of my coffee before it went cold. I hate cold coffee.

'The police don't like serial killers,' I continued. 'Even if it's only arse bandits as I can assure you they refer to gay men who are the target. They put a lot of people on it. That number was doubled when your brother was killed. It would have been increased anyway, but the fact that you are a prominent politician won't have hurt things. Anything I could do would be a drop in the ocean compared to what is already happening.'

I relaxed into my armchair and threaded my fingers together. The waitress walked over with a coffee jug and refilled my cup. I should have known, in a place like that. As she refilled Sir Peter's I gave myself a little ticking off. I was not being very kind. Something about him, his reserve perhaps, or simply his position as powerful politician, reversed to bereaved supplicant, made me want to be brutal with him. It seemed to be working; his face had a deeper, more introverted quality than his previous gravity. He smiled weakly at the waitress and then waited until she was quite a way off, serving a crumpled old man who looked suspiciously like Winston Churchill.

'It isn't that I doubt the police, Mr Rucker.' There was a certain impatience in his voice. 'I have visited the operations room, I have seen what they are doing.'

'Then you must know how ineffective I would be. They have officers out asking every possible question in thousands of different places. More importantly they have forensics, DNA tests. That's how this guy, assuming it is a guy, will be caught. Unfortunately you may have to wait until he does it again, maybe two or three times, but he'll make a mistake before too long. They always do.'

'I don't doubt you, Mr Rucker.' The irritation and impatience in his voice was overlaid by an increased imperative. 'But you see, from my point of view, it doesn't really matter what the police are doing. Edward was my brother. It matters to me what *I* am doing about it. I can't just sit back, I have to do something. I can't do nothing.' The MP's hands turned palm up and suddenly there was an appeal in his eyes, an honesty that I had not seen before.

'I can understand that, sir. But if you already know that employing me is really a way of easing your conscience, of trying to do something, then you know how pointless it is because you haven't done anything wrong and catching criminals is not your line. You're a politician, not a detective. It was not your fault, how could it have been? Also, from my point of view, I really don't want to spend my time on a fool's errand because you feel helpless. I sympathize with you but I'm sorry, there really isn't anything I can do.'

I stood up to go, but the MP let out a long sigh and pursed his lips against a swell of emotion.

'Mr Rucker,' he said. He was firm, his voice raised a little too loud. It stopped me. I sat back down again, resigned to hearing him out. I leant back in the armchair as he clasped his hands together and stared over his knuckles at me. I could see him around a table in a television studio, waiting for the jeers of a studio audience to die down.

'Mr Rucker. There is something. Something else. The police listened when I mentioned it but I could tell they were just being polite, they didn't believe me.' He hesitated. 'Mr Rucker, I heard what happened to my brother. I know the details. I was told there was evidence of sexual activity. With a man. My brother had been buggered before he was killed. I am well aware of this. But, Mr Rucker,' he looked right at me, 'one thing is wrong. I know that my brother was not a homosexual.'

His voice was lower now. He had regained control and was staring at me intently, his blue eyes not appealing to me but measured and precise, cold as an empty house. I suddenly lost all sympathy with him. So that's what he cares about, just like the lorry driver's wife.

'Sir Peter,' I said, 'it may be difficult for you—'

'I know what you are going to say, Mr Rucker; that I am an old Tory bigot who can't stand the fact that his brother was gay, who refuses to accept what the evidence so clearly displays. But you are wrong.'

'I didn't say—'

He cut me off. He leant forward towards me. 'You are not gay,' he said. He stated it flatly, like a logician beginning with a simple premise. 'You're not, are you?'

I looked at him, surprised, trying to work out where he was going.

'No,' I answered, 'I'm not, but . . .'

'And my brother was not either. He would not have slept with a man. He was not a homosexual.'

I didn't say anything. He could finish, then I could thank him for lunch, get up and leave.

'Do you know how I can tell?' he asked, his eyes fixing me now, sensing my irritation. I shrugged.

'I can tell, Mr Rucker, because I am.'

The MP sat back and smiled to himself ruefully. The room was suddenly silent except for the ticking of a grandfather clock which I hadn't noticed before. Sir Peter seemed to be lost within himself for a second, seeing things which I couldn't, things which seemed to bring him pleasure along with a dark, overshadowing wistfulness.

'Do you know, Mr Rucker, you are only the third person I have ever told that particular piece of information to. I didn't want to but somehow, ever since Edward was killed, being secretive doesn't seem to matter any more. Finding out who killed him does.' He smiled at me. 'It is amazing how simple it is to say it. Before I told my wife it was much worse. And before I told Edward I was a wreck. I was almost forty years old and I was so terrified of what he would say I couldn't eat for a week.' He laughed sadly and waited for me to say something. I didn't really know what.

'How did he take it?' I found myself asking.

'Oh, brilliantly. He said he'd been waiting for me to tell him ever since he was sixteen and I was nineteen. He was relieved that I had.'

'That must have meant a lot to you.'

'It did. My wife, quite understandably, was not so generous. We had already begun to lead separate lives within the same house but she was scared that I would "come out", as I believe they say, and it would humiliate her. She enjoys being the wife of a Minister you see, even an

Opposition Minister as she puts it.' He hesitated, and I waited for him to go on. 'Diana told me never to mention it again. To anybody. But I did decide to tell Edward. After I had told him I was then able to confide in him, to tell him of my feelings. We had long chats about it and it made the burden a lot easier to bear, knowing I could talk about how I felt, that he understood me and I would never have to worry that he would tell anybody. It was a great relief. For some reason I found that I hardly ever needed to do anything about it after that, I didn't need to take so many of the risks I was taking.'

The MP stopped for a second as the waitress came back over. She was either naturally very diligent or a member of the KGB. In the gap it afforded him the former Minister restored some of his reserve and when she was gone he said, 'The point, you see, is that I know he wasn't gay. We spoke about it and he told me he had never even thought about it for a second. He wasn't lying to me, he had no reason to. He had no problem with my sexual preference and would not have had if it were his own. Edward was a lot more open, far more relaxed about life than I am.'

'And you think it strange that he should be murdered by a serial killer specializing in homosexuals?'

'I do. Even if it was the same man I feel that the police are blinkering themselves by insisting that my brother was gay, and that this one fits a neat pattern.' I nodded my head reluctantly. The police do like things to be neat. They even go so far as making things neat when that is the last thing that they are. I'd done a fair bit of neatening myself in my time.

'You told them Edward wasn't gay?' I asked.

'I did, but I didn't tell them how I knew. They were

polite enough but I know they didn't take any notice. They think I just want to lessen the political embarrassment of what happened.'

I'd thought that myself earlier. I still wasn't sure if that wasn't the case.

'So, what you want is to employ somebody to explore the possibilities that you believe the police are overlooking.'

'Yes.'

'And you don't want a big organization because a big organization would just do what the police are doing. And they might not be, what you would call, discreet.'

'Yes. I told DI Gold that I wanted to hire someone, an individual to help me. I didn't expect to meet the resistance I am getting from you. DI Gold tried to talk me out of it, like you did, but when I told him I was determined, and would simply look in the Yellow Pages if he didn't recommend someone, he came up with your name. I am aware that it may turn out to be a waste of my money, but while there is a chance that I may be able to contribute, I will. DI Gold told me that you usually find missing children at a flat fee, but that I might be able to engage you by the day.'

'You might,' I said.

And I thought about it.

There was a chance it would be worthwhile, a chance I could dig something up, although it wasn't likely. It certainly wouldn't hurt my bank balance to try and I could probably fit in my other work around it. Also, it was a challenge, a piece of real work. I didn't know what to do, I was still shocked by what he had told me, or, rather, by the fact that he had told me it at all, here in this dusty, establishment boys' club where such a revelation was completely incongruous. I found myself saying that I would do my best for him until I'd either found something interesting or couldn't think of anything else to do. I told him he was almost definitely wasting his money and my time, but he seemed pleased. We discussed terms and then we stood up.

'Mr Rucker,' Sir Peter said, taking my hand. 'Thank you. I trust that anything I have told you will be treated in confidence.' He looked uneasy. 'My wife, you see.'

I told him that he had nothing to worry about. He nodded his thanks. Then he snapped back into Uncle mode and told me some of the history of the club, as he showed me out of the room and back down the broad staircase, which looked even more impressive on the way down. He pointed out a portrait of the club founder, and one of his own grandfather, and he told me what their motto meant: diligence and discretion.

At the bottom of the staircase we passed the waitress with another jug of fresh coffee in her hand. I could have sworn she looked disappointed to see us leaving.

Chapter Three

The drive back to my office was about half an hour longer than the drive there and I vowed once again to leave my car at home and use the bus more. Or walk, that would have been just as quick. I finally made it back to Highbury Corner and drove along Highbury Grove with the park on my left. Through the naked trees I could see the last rash of tennis players battling bravely on the faded red courts. I turned right, into the forecourt of the Lindaeur Buildings, and after waving into the security booth I parked next to the front entrance. As was often the case the huge, stately building, put up in the thirties, reminded me of an ocean liner. I locked up the car and, ignoring the waiting lift, I jogged up the four flights.

When I opened up my office it was glaringly bright, the sun having just reached round far enough to beam straight in through the huge windows. I let the straw blind down to about halfway, which subdued it and gave the small room a strange, almost tropical ambience. My machine informed me that the time was two thirty-six, and that I had one message. It was Andy Gold, wondering if I had agreed to help the MP, and would I like to talk to him about it? I called him back at the station and arranged to meet him in The Albion at four. He sounded stressed. In the background I could hear the clatter of typewriters, the other phone lines going, and what sounded like a very irate old woman telling somebody that her little boy could not possibly have done anything like that. They'd framed him the first time, I heard her say, and now they wanted to do it again. I smiled to myself grimly at the memory of day upon day upon day spent sitting in that room, feeling just as harassed as Andy did now. I told him not to work too hard and hung up before getting his reply.

I'd jotted down a few notes earlier, at The Portman, in a small hardback notebook, and I took it out on my desk and made some more. I had been engaged by a Tory MP with more money than sense (a complaint common amongst Tory MPs) to find out who had killed his brother, because the MP did not believe the police were exploring every angle open to them. The murder seemed to be the work of a serial killer with a distaste, or a very strange taste, for homosexuals. But the MP did not believe his brother would have had any contact with a homosexual so it seemed strange to him that his brother should be a target for this person. The police did not think it strange. I was to look into the possibility that his brother was murdered by someone other than the apparent serial killer, or else that the serial killer did not confine himself to homosexuals at all. Simple enough. I wrote a list of things to do, and then went through to the café for a cup of coffee.

The café is run by Ally, a very bright, attractive Italian girl, and her English boyfriend Mike. The unit is about twice the size of mine, with four small tables and more potted plants than the place really has room for. From a small, adjoining kitchen, they knock out sandwiches, hot meals and espresso to people in the other units, and they also deliver to nearby businesses. They both work a lot harder than I do but always manage to be cheerful to their customers and to each other – no mean feat considering that they share a flat as well as a business. The café is very convenient for me, being only three doors along, and I'll often leave a note on my door telling clients to wait in there for me if there's a chance that I'll be late. I have a spare coffee machine at my flat which I could bring along to my office if I wanted to, but I like Ally and Mike, so I don't. I like the fact that they are there, and it doesn't cost me much to contribute to their staying. Also, last Christmas, they had bought me my very own mug to use. It's bigger than their normal ones and it has a picture of Kojak on the side, though whether this is a reference to my profession, or to my hairline, was not made clear to me.

I had Kojak in my hand as I approached the counter. Mike was in the kitchen washing up while Ally was clearing a table from the last of the lunch rush. Mike called out hi through the open door.

'Been to see your bank manager, Bill?' he asked, looking at my suit.

'No, the Shadow Treasury Minister actually,' I replied.

'Blimey,' he said, 'your overdraft must be bigger than mine, mate!'

Ally put down the dirty plates she was carrying and smiled hello, before going round to the machine to pour me a black coffee.

Ally has the sort of smile that makes you wish sudden and calamitous death on her boyfriend, or at least that you didn't like him so much. She also has the shiniest black curly hair, and huge bottomless eyes, dark as olives. She handed Kojak back to me and made a tick in her tally book. I took the coffee gingerly by the rim, and went to sit at the table she had just cleared.

I had an hour to kill before meeting Andy Gold. I spent it sipping the coffee and staring at Kojak's everlasting lollipop, thinking about the seven years I had spent as a detective with the Islington Police. I had liked the job to begin with, and as I got higher up there always seemed some new aspect of the work to keep me interested. But then I got to the point where I seemed to be constantly battering my head against a mixture of a lack of resources to deal with the kind of criminals I wanted to deal with, and a lack of time to investigate anything properly. I came slowly to the conclusion that I was not employed to solve crimes and arrest their perpetrators, but as part of a political tool, a tool used to spread whitewash over the city so that the graffiti would not show through. At local election time the councillors would panic, and after a few words were whispered at the right cocktail parties there would be us, engaged in yet another useless crackdown on begging or street prostitution. Clean out an area, Harlesden say, by arresting a lot of very minor people, who get out after spending a night inside, to set up somewhere else. All it ever did was piss off your snitches, and make it harder to find them when you needed information about anything really important. And we never got to deal with the biggest reason the homeless or the whores inhabit any particular spot of God's green earth in any number; the pushers selling them crack pellets in Yorkie Bar foil, which they work all day and night scratching money together to buy. These guys would just disappear for a day or two and then they'd be back, leaning against shopfronts and lampposts, keeping on chewing, giving us the smile as we walked past. And the kids kept on selling themselves and the wheels kept on turning. After seven years I found myself both cynical and bored, with a mounting feeling of frustration.

I probably would have stuck it out though. I was still only in my late twenties, and at the time the feelings which I can articulate now usually just manifested themselves in a liking for the bottle and the kind of Need for Speed which was not the sort that Tom Cruise could have related to. I would probably have gone on for years, just like Andy Gold had done, getting more and more miserable about it, tied in by a mortgage and the hope of that next step up the ladder, getting further and further away from the reasons I joined up in the first place. You could say that my brother Luke saved me from that. I owe him my new status as a happy, well-adjusted, self-employed detective, with my own office and company vehicle. And I owe him a great deal more than that, so much more that if I try to think of a way to repay him it sends me insane.

Luke risked his life for me. For various reasons too long to go into a man I'd tried to put away wanted me dead and Luke found out about it. Luke knew the man was coming for me and though he was aware it was dangerous he drove across town to warn me. Because we look alike, and because Luke was driving my car, the man thought my brother was me and he tried to kill him. Some would say he succeeded. Luke risked his life for me and because he did that I knew I could not go on living the life I had been living. That life hadn't really been much, certainly not worth doing what Luke did to save it. Not worth spending the rest of *his* life – if you can call it that – lying in a hospital bed, unable to move even his eyelashes, kept alive by a constant stream of liquid nourishment fed through a plastic tube in his stomach, sitting helpless inside himself, a prison cell which, I was assured, he would never be released from. Not into this world, anyway.

I sipped Ally's coffee and traced my finger around the flower pattern on the vinyl tablecloth. I was sinking back into feelings of guilt, and a vein-searing impotence, shrunk by the image of Luke's inert body in the wreckage of my car, remembering the helplessness I felt, until time took me by the scruff of the neck and kept me from drowning. It was quarter to four. I shook off the thoughts I'd been having, like water from a raincoat. I got up and asked Ally for two portions of her unbelievable tiramisu to take home with me.

Ally cut one portion, placed it carefully in a cardboard carton, and then went to cut another.

'And if you could just give me the recipe as well, Ally, I'll be on my way.'

'Never!' she laughed. A long, elegant middle finger rested lightly on the top of the second piece, stopping it falling off the cake slicer. I'd been on at her for years about her tiramisu recipe.

'Why would you ever buy it from me if you could make it yourself?' she asked.

'Oh,' I said, 'I don't want to make it, I want to sell it!'

She laughed again and put the carton in a plastic bag.

'And who,' she asked, 'is the lucky girl?'

'Sorry?'

'Which privileged female will be sharing my tiramisu after you have cooked one of your famous meals for her?' Ally's eyebrows stood up into two neat arches.

'You should be a detective,' I said. 'Maybe I just think I'll be hungry later.'

'No,' she said, 'you exercise too much. There's definitely a second party involved here.'

I held up my hands.

'OK,' I admitted, 'you've got me bang to rights. But it's only Sharon.'

'Only Sharon,' she said meaningfully. 'Hmmm.'

I ignored the archness of Ally's tone, as well as that of her eyebrows, and took the bag from her.

'Actually,' I said, 'you wouldn't make a very good detective at all. Your method of interrogation is far too intimidating.'

We both laughed, and then I left, calling out bye to Mike who was still up to his elbows in soapsuds.

If you work all day looking for missing people in the squats or doorways of Camden, King's Cross, Dalston and Hackney, getting sworn at, spat at, threatened, and generally abused, then walking through the front door of The Albion, in Barnsbury, feels like St Peter has held open the door for you. It is an old, ivy-covered haven, with a wooden floor, sofas, horse brasses which somehow manage not to look kitsch, and no jukebox. It has the immediate effect of making you think that you have just been transported into the tranquil heart of the countryside and the one detective you would not be surprised to see there would be Miss Marple. I had a quick skirt around for Andy, ordered a Perrier, and sat at a small, gnarled table, with my eye on the door.

Andy Gold ducked in ten minutes after I had, at twenty past four, and he seemed to bring his day in with him. I waved off his offer of a drink, and he stood at the bar while the barmaid served him a pint of lager and a double whiskey, straight, no ice, which he drank off before coming over to sit down. He needed his other hand to hold his briefcase.

Andy is only about five-eight, qualifying for the Met a year after they lowered the height requirement. He has dark brown hair which he keeps constantly slicked back with its own natural grease, and he has the sort of face which looks like it could do with a damn good shave, immediately after it has been given a damn good shave. Like me his mother was Jewish and his father Anglo-Saxon, but his features are more Semitic than mine, his skin that Mediterranean non-brown, his nose prominent, his thick, bunched eyebrows giving a correct impression of over-anxious intensity. He's the same age as I am, give or take a couple of months, but he could easily pass for ten years older on a bad day. This, it seemed, was a bad day.

Andy sat down and took a long pull on his beer. He looked a wreck. His suit was creased to shit and his eyes were two boiled eggs in a dish of ketchup. He loosened his already loosened tie, sat forward in his chair, pushed his head forward and ran his nails hard over his scalp. Then he sat back and yawned, not bothering to cover up the fact that he had had a tonsillectomy at one point in his life, and had eaten too many sweets as a teenager. He drank his pint down to about an inch before taking any notice of me. I waited.

'So,' he said eventually, 'the MP doesn't think his bro was a homo.'

'No,' I said.

I reached into the back pocket of my trousers and pulled out two fifty-pound notes, which I let Andy see before slipping them quietly into the side pocket of his jacket. Andy nodded almost imperceptibly. Then he reached down for his briefcase which he placed on his knee and snapped the clasps on. He took out a brown folder which he laid on the table in front of me.

'You never saw this,' he said, as my hand reached out to open it.

Chapter Four

I pan-fried the sausages very quickly to brown the skins, and then I put them in the Le Creuset which Sharon had bought me last Christmas. I'd picked the sausages up from Molise's on the Farringdon Road, along with a couple of tins of Italian tomatoes, the ones that don't have acetic acid or any sugar added, and the smell of which makes you think of Tuscany, whether or not you've actually been there. I opened the tins and tipped the contents over the sausages, along with a large glug of extra virgin, six crushed cloves of garlic, a little white wine, a splash of Lea and Perrins, and two small dried Indian chilli peppers. I mashed the tomatoes up with a wooden spoon, remembered the tablespoon of honey, and then put the pot on to bubble for an hour. I made up some polenta, mixed it with two chopped, steamed leeks, and put that on to bake. Then I sat down on the sofa with some photocopies of material from the file which Andy Gold had been kind enough to show me.

It was clear that my friend and his colleagues had no doubt about Edward Morgan's murder being part of the series of gay slashings which the tabloids had taken such great delight in over the past six months. Teddy's details were in there alongside the details of the other two deaths.

John Evans was killed in the cab of his lorry. He was parked in a lay-by on the A1, just south of Stamford, and current theory believed that his assailant was probably a hitchhiker who he had propositioned, and who reacted with greater energy than the usual yes or no. Two severe contusions just above the hairline show that Evans was rendered immobile with what forensic scientists are certain was his own ten-pound hand wrench. Evans was then attacked with a broken bottle, receiving abdominal and chest injuries, which caused internal laceration severe enough to cause his heart to fail before he had time to bleed to death. The absence of any glass fragments in Evans' cab, to match those found in his body, led to the conclusion that the attack was to a large degree premeditated, because the assailant clearly had the weapon ready before he got into the lorry. Why a bottle was used in this way instead of a knife, is not known. These days, seriously effective knives are just as easy to get hold of as beer bottles. If the attackers were teenagers, then a knife would actually have been *easier* to obtain than a beer bottle.

As for motive, the report stated that a theory of simple violent robbery was hard to sustain. While it is true that John Evans was robbed of what is believed to be about a hundred pounds, Evans had no defence wounds on his arms and hands, nothing to show that he had tried, as would be natural, to stop whoever it was from stabbing him to death. He was, therefore, unconscious, or at least completely defenceless *before* he received the wounds to his stomach area which killed him. A mugger would usually have taken what he wanted after immobilizing his victim, and then left him unconscious. He would avoid murder if he could help it, and in this case it seems that he definitely could have done.

But he didn't.

The police appealed for witnesses, posting pictures of the driver in service stations and truck stops up and down the A1, and they interviewed all of Evans' friends and workmates. But nobody came forward with anything useful. The murder was privately put down to a crack-head getting carried away, and while the usual amount of manpower was still spent on it, it was assumed that the perpetrator would get caught sooner or later for doing something else. At this stage of the investigation no homosexual link was established.

I turned the page.

A young lad with smooth light brown skin and a big, goofy grin stared out at me from an A4 blow-up of a studio photograph. I could just make out a blue shirt, and a red and green striped school tie. I looked at the shot for a second or two, not really wanting to turn the page again. Then I put the picture aside.

James Waldock worked as a male prostitute, probably controlled by a Brixton outfit called the 22 Crew. The 22 are an enterprising bunch of dudes who hang out in a café on the Railton Road, and are gradually maturing into an efficient whores and scores team, expanding operations as far as the Yardies will let them and as long as they give them a big enough piece of the action. For a male prostitute in the City of London and its boroughs James was a couple of years older than the estimated average. He was fourteen.

James Waldock came from what the report politely termed a deprived background. Free of any fatherly influence, his mother was a user, and it was probably she who introduced him to her own profession, anxious that at his age he should begin to pay his way. His form teacher's report, which was in the file, stated that he was a quiet, surprisingly bright kid who, when he did attend school, was always attentive and liked to ask questions. He was, however, easily led by older boys, and he often tried to hide his intelligence behind an assumed bravado which didn't seem to come naturally to him. This happens a lot to young black males, so the teacher reported. White males too, I thought. I see it all the time. The peculiarly harsh way in which some boys aged fourteen or so rebuke the child in them, as if they hate the naivety within themselves, a naivety which has conned them into some sort of hope which they begin to see can only cause them frustration and disappointment. I remembered it myself, how I'd once challenged my father to a fight, just him and me, after he'd used his belt on Luke for coming home ten minutes late. How he had kicked the shit out of me. This tacked-on manfulness can look ugly and be dangerous, but it usually passes. If the kid is left alive long enough to grow out of it.

James was conscious through most of what happened to him. His body was found in the basement of a condemned block of council flats which is being taken down slowly, floor by floor from the top. Police believe that he was being buggered in a standing position, and that during or immediately after this, his head was battered hard against the wall he was being pushed up against. His nose was broken and scrapes of dry paint were found on his skin and in his mouth. Nonoxynol, the chemical used to lubricate certain brands of condoms, was found inside his anal canal, as well as two types of semen, along with the two types found in his stomach. The presence of the semen suggests that James was not exactly Aids aware, and that the Nonoxynol came from his attacker, the wearing of the condom being his attacker's idea; a way of avoiding DNA profiling. The condom was not found.

Cuts on both the inside and outside of James' wrists, and on his hands, show that he tried to defend himself against the Lucozade bottle which was repeatedly thrust into his chest, face and neck, and eventually left embedded deep in his stomach. The amount of cuts James received suggest that it took him some time to die, although it is impossible to say how many of them he received after he was actually dead. Once again, no trace of the bottom of the bottle, or the lid, were found. Like Evans, James was also robbed. It was clear that he had had at least four other clients that night, but there was no money on his body when it was found. The police, however, couldn't say for definite that it was his assailant who took the money. There are people who will rob a corpse, even if the corpse is that of a fourteen-year-old boy lying in a dismal basement, on top of enough blood to fill a bathtub. Some of these people, I thought, as I went to turn the heat down from under my Le Creuset, are police officers.

The picture they had of Edward Morgan, or Teddy, as his brother had referred to him when we parted from each other, and he urged me to do all I could to find out who killed him, could have been lifted straight out of the BA catalogue. Teddy was tan, fortyish, squared-jawed and blue-eyed. I could see no resemblance to his older brother. Teddy looked just the man to get you down safely when they had trouble with an engine, or calm your nerves during turbulence with a joke about rollercoaster rides. Perfect white teeth. I'd always wanted teeth like that. It seemed strange to think of such a confident, strong-looking person as a victim, someone weakened, viciously humiliated. Murdered. Looking at his clear, open face, I tried to decide whether or not I thought he was gay. The picture didn't tell me anything.

I read what had happened to him, what had been done to him. Already my mind was trying to see it, to see it happening as if it were a scene from a film. I read the statements given by the co-pilots, the stewardesses, the barman at the airport and then I read the scene of crime report. I read how his wife had discovered his body and a statement from her saying that she had no idea that her husband was involved in homosexual activity. Possible images of death flitted into my head like the ghosts of pinned butterflies. I was just getting to the forensic report when the door buzzer sounded.

It was very good to see Sharon. I was surprised by how well she was looking, and how delighted I was to see her standing in my doorway with a bottle of wine in her hand. We kissed hello. I took the bottle from her and she followed me into the kitchen, towards the smell which she was already congratulating me on.

I'd done a quick tidying-up job and my place didn't look too bad. I live in a converted photo-studio with black blinds, a small open-plan kitchen and floorboards which I haven't got round to sanding yet. Sharon has often promised to come round and help me do the place up a bit, and to this end she bought me a framed Salgado print for my birthday which is the only thing breaking the purity of the whitish walls. Every time she comes over she tells me my flat looks like I've just moved into it. She uses the words shelving, cupboards, uplighting and Ikea a lot.

I poured Sharon a glass of the Rosso di Montalcino she'd brought with her and then put some broccoli on to steam. As we sat on the sofa chatting I couldn't help thinking of how I had met her, and the thing that bound us to each other. The reason we have dinner once a month or so, go to the theatre or the movies every so often. The reason why sometimes she is the only person I can, or want, to talk to, or why I spend ages looking for her Christmas present. Why, once in a while, on a particular date perhaps, she calls me in the middle of the night, her voiçe breaking, and asks me to drive over.

I never used to get on particularly well with Sharon but in the last few years that has changed. Sharon was my brother Luke's fiancée. As a matter of fact she still is, technically. She certainly hasn't actually broken it off with him. It has been nearly four years since Luke was injured and if I think about it I know that Sharon must have seen somebody else in that time. But on the occasions that we meet she is discreet enough not to mention anything. I still see her as Luke's girl, though I would completely understand if one day she turned up at my flat with a nervous-looking man who she would like me to meet. It might be strange, but I would understand.

Luke and I were sharing a flat at the time he met Sharon, and as soon as he started to tell me about her I could tell it was something special. Luke was working in a bar on Camden High Street at the time, having yet to establish himself as the new star of the British stage, and Sharon had come in for a coffee. Luke said that when he saw her he just knew, and he was so nervous that he spilled her cappuccino all over the table. He wasn't too nervous to make sure he had a chat with her and find out her name though. Sharon, a law student. Sharon was immediately embarrassed about her name and assured Luke that she wasn't the stiletto sort and that her parents had been into the Bible; the Rose of Sharon. In that case, Luke said, it suits you. When Sharon got up to leave he told her to make sure that she came in again soon, and Luke put himself on the rota practically every hour the place was open over the coming week to make sure that he didn't miss her. He needn't have bothered, however; she came in again next day.

When I first met Sharon I was pretty sceptical. I couldn't believe that all the hyperbolic nonsense issuing from my lovestruck little brother's mouth was actually true. I just didn't venerate women the way he did. I'd asked Luke what it was about her and he'd spent hours trying to tell me. It wasn't so much that she was drop dead beautiful, he said, but that she had a constant, radiating warmth inside her, a kind of simple, mesmerizing energy which made him feel slightly childish. She also had a steely quality that kept Luke spellbound when, over dinner in our flat, she told us about what she wanted to do with her life, how most people went into the law to make money, or because they couldn't think of anything else to do. I thought it sounded just a little prissy, but when Sharon told how she wanted to make a difference, to use the legal system to help people, it actually was quietly inspiring. She asked me if that was what I felt about being a policeman, which I still was at the time. I remember feeling uncomfortable under her earnest glare, unable to match Sharon's fervour but then telling her yes, it actually was, and being happy and surprised to know that I was actually telling her the truth. Then.

Luke and Sharon soon started seeing each other seriously and his view of her never tempered. He agreed with almost everything she said, and I could see him trying to change to match up to her. This surprised me because Luke had always been flighty and noncommittal about most things, especially women. But even though Sharon was two or three years younger than Luke, she seemed to mature him. He took himself much more seriously. He worked a lot harder at his acting, going to evening classes at the Actor's Centre, sending out CVs all the time, and I have to admit things did start to go well for him. He got a good role at the Kings Head, and then a couple of bit-parts in the West End, and some TV. Luke had always written poetry, which he never showed anyone, not even me, and Sharon persuaded him not only to show it to her, but to work on it and send it off to magazines. He did, and after a while his stuff began to appear in the *Rialto*, *Stand Magazine*, and once *Poetry Review*. In general Luke began to approach things the same way that Sharon did, with a determined, though quiet confidence which was impressive but, I thought, somewhat forced and even unnatural. He became a graver, more weighty person and I wasn't sure I really knew him any more.

When Luke and Sharon told me that they were getting married I remember having mixed feelings. Luke was twenty-six, Sharon twenty-three, and I thought they were too young. I thought that Luke was perhaps growing old too soon, that he had completely shunted aside the child in him in an effort to keep up with Sharon. Sharon seemed to monopolize my brother and the times when they were in company she could never quite relax, giving the impression of marking time until she could get him alone again. I knew, however, that this was probably jealousy. I missed Luke's infantile sense of humour, and realized that it was Sharon's distrust of any sort of frivolity which bugged me. I had begun to miss my brother (and the aspiring actresses he used to introduce me to). I was pissed off that Luke never seemed up for a big night any more, or that he suddenly started getting a ridiculously sour expression on his face when I cut up a line on the coffee table. Fuck it – I was the Fuzz, for God's sake! I thought he was taking things too seriously, something which, ever since Luke could talk, he was constantly accusing me of.

I didn't think that Luke should marry Sharon, not yet at least, but my reservations would have only caused a rift between us so I put them aside. I kissed them both and told them they were stupid and that I would happily be best man at the divorce as well. Sharon kissed me back and told me, with that unnerving certainty of hers, that it wouldn't come to that. And she was right. It didn't come to a wedding either.

After we had finished the sausages, Sharon asked me what I was working on at the moment. I told her about the usual runaways, and then I told her about the MP. I told her what the MP had told me. He wouldn't have liked it but he didn't know Sharon. She wouldn't tell anybody.

'Peter Morgan is gay?' she asked, surprised.

'*Sir* Peter Morgan.'

'He doesn't look it,' she said. 'Does he?'

'I don't know,' I answered. 'I have no way of telling. Unless it's obvious of course.'

'Like when someone is all in leather, with a Freddie Mercury moustache?'

'I suppose,' I said. 'But it doesn't have to be that obvious. I know it's a cliché, but some people just look gay.'

'Maybe that's because they choose to look gay,' Sharon said, 'in whatever they're wearing. If they chose not to then you would never be able to guess, not even if they were in the leather. Peter Morgan chooses not to. It's still surprising though. I wonder how he voted on the age of consent debate?'

'Probably against, especially as he's keen that none of his political colleagues know about his orientation.'

'Damn hypocrite.'

'I know. But in a strange way I actually feel sorry for him.'

Sharon put down her wineglass.

'For being gay? And being a Tory at the same time!'

'No,' I said. 'Because he's realized that the way he's been living his life is wrong. All the intrigues and lies, the pretence, it all seems pointless to him after what has happened to his brother. But he's too far immersed in it to break out.'

'To return is as tedious as to go over?'

'Something like that. He knows that it doesn't matter, not really, if people know he's gay. He knows that it would probably make him happier if they did know. But he won't ever let it out. His wife, his position. He's stuck.'

Sharon sat back in her chair. 'It sounds like you quite liked him,' she said, with more than a hint of disapproval.

'I did,' I admitted, 'after a while. After he told me he was gay. It took courage to do that to a complete stranger. I could tell that he cares, or cared, about his brother.'

'So does Michael Howard I should think,' Sharon said. 'If he's got one.'

'Then maybe I'd like him too,' I said. I shrugged my shoulders. 'I don't know, there was just something about Morgan that I liked. Something intangible. He has a kind of wistful, removed quality about him.'

Sharon laughed. 'He doesn't on *Question Time*.'

'No,' I answered, thinking about it. 'You're right. He definitely doesn't look wistful on *Question Time*.'

I served the tiramisu, and after we'd devoured it with the animalistic relish which it deserved, Sharon told me what she had been doing recently. Sharon finished her pupillage two years ago, and works as a barrister for the Refugee Legal Centre, defending asylum seekers against deportation orders. It's a difficult, dispiriting job, given the current attitude towards refugees, or burdens on the state as they are portrayed. Sharon's success rate is a little higher than the average at about six per cent. She spends a lot of time in miserable detention centres, talking to people who are scared and desperate. They tell her about Nigerian prisons, Turkish punishment squads, and they show her bruises and scars from cigarette burns or knife cuts, which Sharon can never prove they did not inflict upon themselves. She watches their faces when she fails to win their last appeal, and then she imagines their faces when they are sent back to their country of origin, and she never hears from them again.

Sometimes though, there are lighter moments, and Sharon is the first to admit that some people do try it on. I sat listening to her tell me about a woman whose boyfriend was applying for asylum on some invented grounds of abuse, and who wrote to his girlfriend in Albania telling her exactly what to say at the airport when she came to England to join him. Customs officials found the letter in her bag, which not only blew her claim but her boyfriend's as well. I watched Sharon as she told the story. Her lipstick had dissolved into thin lines, which exaggerated the fullness of her mouth. She systematically pushed an errant strand of her dark blond hair back behind her left ear, as it kept repeating its offence of escape. Her teeth were stained by the wine, her eyes so clear and green you could see why unimaginative people often asked her if she wore those coloured contact lenses. I thought about Luke, and remembered the time he told me about them. How he had described those eyes just like they were, and I didn't believe him, thinking he was just a love-sick fool.

I laughed at Sharon's story, and apropos of nothing I suddenly told her that I was glad she had been able to come, and that it always meant a lot to me to see her. She smiled, and we looked at each other for a second. Neither of us said anything. Neither of us were self-conscious, we just sat there looking and smiling at each other. I don't know why. Then her smile took on the faintest, most distant tinge of sadness, like caramel which has just begun to burn. I looked down at the table, at a small stain of red from a drop of wine which had missed the glass. I saw Sharon's hand, resting on the table a few inches from mine. Her engagement ring. I didn't know she still wore it. I looked at the simple ring, one small diamond set into the gold band, for several seconds. I had lent Luke the money to buy it. He still owed me seven hundred quid, the bastard. I put both my hands on the table, pushed myself up without looking at Sharon, and went to make coffee.

In fact, I had no coffee. I had stood talking to the

youngest Molise boy in the deli for a full ten minutes while I tried to remember the thing which I knew I had to get. But it never came to me. I apologized to Sharon, a little too much. She said she didn't mind though. She looked a little nervous, but then she smiled at me again, softly. I looked away from her. All of a sudden I didn't want to be in my warm, cosy flat with Sharon. I was beginning to feel claustrophobic and heavy.

I clapped my hands together, trying to make the atmosphere disappear like a magician with a fake bunch of flowers. I had an idea.

'Do you want to see the famous William H. Rucker, Private Eye, scourge of the evil and corrupt, in action?' I asked her.

'You bet,' she answered with surprise, picking up quickly on my lightening of the mood.

'Are we going to catch a killer?' she asked.

'Nothing so exciting,' I told her.

The drive down to King's Cross only took five minutes. I parked the Mazda and then took Sharon, and my second-hand Nikon, into the twenty-four-hour-café at the bottom of the Pentonville Road. As usual, the café looked shabby and the tables were all dirty. The waitress came over but she didn't bother to wipe up from the people before us. We ordered *cafés au lait*. I took the camera out of my bag and rested it on the seat beside me. Remembering a very embarrassing time earlier in my career, I made sure that the film was in it. I smiled at Sharon and kept one eye on a group of teenage lads who were standing around on the corner of the Pentonville Road and Calshot Street.

'You take me to the loveliest places, Bill Rucker,'

Sharon said, using her serviette to create a stain-free square of Formica for herself.

I was looking for Dominic Lewes, whom I had found once before. His mother didn't want me to tell her where he was, which I would not have done anyway, she just wanted to know that he was alive, and what sort of state he was in. I didn't really expect to find him. It had been eight months since I had discovered him in this very spot, and I'd learnt over the past ten years that absolutely anything can happen in eight months to a young boy from Grimsby who's run away from home. Cold, hunger, death to name but the obvious and there are plenty of things which occur that are far from predictable even to someone who has seen a lot of it before. It would send you mad to think of all the things that can happen, that *are* happening right this second, to all of those young Odysseuses who have broken free from the ties that bound them and come to the damp rooms and stinking alleys that make up their London. Any number of things could have been done to Dominic in any number of places but still, it didn't hurt looking in the place I had found him before. We had wanted coffee anyway.

The coffees arrived, and Sharon and I sipped them, chatting, while I kept an eye out on the street.

'One thing though, Billy,' Sharon said, resting her elbows on the table and leaning forward. 'You never tell the parents where their kids are. I still don't really understand.'

'It's simple,' I told her. 'Kids run away for a reason. The kids who are happy don't run away. The kids who are quite miserable don't run away. It's the kids who are very miserable that run away. They wouldn't view what they had to go through here as acceptable unless the alternative was worse. When I first started I found this girl, twelve or thirteen, and took the dad down to this squat in Streatham where she was living. I thought I had just reunited a misunderstood teenager with her worried and non-recriminating family, and saved her from all sorts of bad shit. But you should have seen the poor kid's face when her loving dad showed up. The sheer terror. I thought she was going to vomit. And the dad's face. There was no relief, no joy. His face just sort of set when he saw her, hard as granite, and I knew immediately what I had sent the girl back to. He didn't say anything, he just pulled her into his car. Of course, not all the parents would be like this, but how can I know? I never tell them. Sometimes I tell the Bill, who tell social services, if the kid is very young and into some bad shit. But I'm not sending some poor kid back to a dad who thinks he's Nigel Benn, or an uncle who can't keep his cock in his drawers.'

I took a sip of coffee. It was surprisingly good. Outside, a car drew up and one of the lads on the corner pushed himself off the wall and walked over to it. He leant into the passenger side window for a second or two and then got in. The car drove away.

'But,' Sharon continued, 'and I don't mean to be rude about your abilities as an investigator, Mr Rucker, but if you won't tell the parents where their kid is, then why do they hire you? Most other agencies don't have your scruples, I shouldn't think.'

'They don't hire me at first,' I said. 'I usually get used when some agency or other, made up of overweight failed ex-cops pushing sixty, fails to find the kid, or when they've run away so many times that the parents know there's no point bringing them back again. It's the mothers usually, who hire me. Often I'm told only to contact them, that the father doesn't know about me. Some of the mothers, I swear, are glad that their son or daughter has escaped what they haven't been able to. They don't want them to go back, they just want to know that they are OK.'

'I see,' Sharon said, putting her long glass down on the saucer. 'I bet you still lose money though, doing it the way you do.'

'Yes,' I said, 'I probably do.'

At that moment, a boy in white jeans and a black MA1 walked around the corner and started talking to the other lads. The boy had short, bleached blond hair, but I was pretty certain it was Dominic. I pushed aside my coffee.

'Bingo,' I said.

I reached for my bag and pulled out a copy of the photo I'd taken of him last time. I looked at it, then at the boy on the street and yes, in spite of the hair, which had been long and dark, it was him. I grabbed hold of the Nikon.

'Wow,' Sharon whispered, 'action!'

I focused in on Dominic Lewes, but he was in shadow. Even with the lens I had I knew I could only get him if he stepped out into the light of the lamppost. I wasn't worried about it. By the look of him, the way the other lads treated him, I could tell that he came here often. If I couldn't get him tonight I could easily come back. I was amazed once again how easy my job sometimes was. I put the camera down on the chair beside me, and smiled broadly at an old lady who was looking very nervously at my distinctly suspicious behaviour. She turned away.

I kept an eye on the street, and we sat drinking coffee until Sharon said that she had to leave. She had a case to prepare for the morning. I put three pound coins on the table before she could do anything herself, and then gave her a look which told her that I didn't want a fight about it. As we were standing up she suddenly thought of something and delved into the postman's bag she always carries. She pulled out a slim blue A4 file.

'I don't know if you've seen all these,' she said, holding the file out to me. 'I went through Luke's books again a couple of weeks ago and collected together most of his poems. I also found some that he'd hidden in his acting notes.'

I took the file and looked at the sky-blue card. I didn't open it.

'Thanks,' I said, after a second or two. I felt that I should say something more but I didn't know what. I held the file gingerly for a second and then I opened my bag and put the file inside, careful not to bend it. Luke's poems, his private thoughts about Sharon, about me. About our father. I put the Nikon in next to them. I picked up the bag and walked over to the door with Sharon.

'Aren't you going to wait and take his picture?' Sharon asked, surprised that I was leaving, nodding over towards the corner where Dominic Lewes stood with his colleagues.

'It's too dark,' I said, 'but I know where he is. And it gives me yet another excuse to visit this delightful establishment.' I waved goodbye to the waitress, and pointed to our table to indicate that we weren't doing a runner. Sharon opened the door for me and we walked out into the sharp October air, redolent with eau-de-kebab and carbon monoxide.

I offered Sharon a lift home but she refused and hailed a cab before I could begin to persuade her. I opened the door for her, kissed her goodbye, and then closed it after she had climbed inside, in the ungraceful fashion only a London cab can enforce on you. Sharon slid the window down and thanked me for the evening. She said it was good to go out and just be together without mulling over the past like we were prone to doing. I said yes, it was. I wanted to fix up a day when we could both go and see Luke together, but just as I started speaking I noticed that Dominic Lewes was walking away from his pitch. With a man.

The man was taller than Dominic and from the side looked to be a lot older. He had a travel bag in his hand – probably just got off the train. I told Sharon I would phone her, then kissed her goodbye again hurriedly, feeling her cold hand on the side of my face. The cab U-turned and just made the lights before heading along the Euston Road towards the Westway. I waved. Then I walked off after Dominic Lewes and the man to whom he was about to purvey the delights of his fifteen-year-old body.

Chapter Five

Next morning I woke up at eight, got up at quarter past, and showered. I hadn't had more than half a bottle of wine and three or four slugs of John Power's last night and Mr Hangover (unlike Mr Phone Bill) had not decided to pay me a visit. I wrapped a towel round my waist and, ignoring the washing up, made a cafetière of light Colombian and two slices of toast with Lincolnshire honey. I set the pot down on a tile on my table, next to the file with Luke's poems in it, which I'd taken out of my bag last night but hadn't read yet. I thought about going through them now. I stared at the file lying on the table next to my ever-dying orange plant. Poetry – before 9 a.m.? Later.

After I'd left Sharon I'd followed Dominic Lewes and friend to a row of Victorian houses only two minutes walk away, some of which looked ready to fall down and others which had yellow alarm boxes on the walls and which wouldn't have looked out of place in Highgate Village. Dominic showed his friend into number 23 Elm Drive which, it wasn't difficult to see, was a squat. The man seemed to look nervously at the run-down hole he was about to enter, hesitating on the doorstep and running his tongue over his lips. But his needs were obviously stronger than his fear of cockroaches and mildew because he soon went in. I wrote the house number down and then smiled to myself. The old Mazda was showing signs that my investigative prowess was rubbing off on it. It was sat directly outside.

I moved the car and parked it further down the street towards King's Cross, but facing the house. I sat in the front seat, waiting, listening to the late book on Radio 4, which at any time would have been too early. After fifteen minutes the man who had gone into number 23 emerged – but without Dominic. I saw him walking towards the car and I had the sudden urge to jump out, tell him I was vice squad and scare the shit out of him. I let the urge pass.

He walked by without noticing that I was inside the Mazda and headed back the way he had come, no doubt to a wife and kids who by the look of him could well have been about Dominic's age. He was in his fifties, tallish, well dressed but not in the Peter Morgan bracket. He looked like he'd just been away for a few days on business and had decided to make the most of his last few hours of solitary anonymity. He looked pleased with himself. I had the sudden urge to jump out of the Mazda and kick the living shit out of him. I let the urge pass.

I thought about going home. I didn't know if Dominic would come out again and even if he did I was pretty sure I wouldn't be able to get a picture of him. Hell, I knew where he lived, I could easily come back in the daylight. And I was tired. Dominic, however, came out five minutes later, while I was still deciding. He didn't walk back towards his pitch though, but turned right out of his house and then right again at the top of the street, walking quickly. I hopped out the car and followed him, just catching sight of him as he crossed the street and headed towards a medium-sized tower block which announced the beginning of the Russell Estate. Concrete forest perhaps, if not quite concrete jungle.

Two figures waited by a fire exit at the bottom of the old, stained building, wearing dark puffas and B-hats. When Dominic walked up to them they both pushed themselves off the wall and stood in front of him. It didn't take long for Dominic to reassure them, however, probably because they recognized him, or if they didn't, with a password or the name of The Man. They let him through and held the fire exit open for him as he walked in quickly. I strolled past the building with my hands in my pockets until I was out of sight of the two doormen, and then I pretended to use a payphone across the road which didn't have a receiver on it.

Dominic was out again in less than ten minutes. I let him get round the corner before going after him. I watched him cross the road, turn left, and then insert his key into the door of 23 Elm Drive once again. I walked by back to the car.

In less than thirty minutes Dominic had picked up a john, sucked him off or let him fuck him, and then scored what was almost certainly twenty or forty quids' worth of crack or horse. And in the same amount of time I had ascertained these facts and in doing so had revealed the salient points about Dominic Lewes' life at that point in time. He was a smackhead who was young enough to sell his arse rather than go housebreaking which, for all I knew, he probably did as well. He'd come a long way since I'd first seen him – here he was jiving with the guys on the corner, gaining entry to secret, exclusive places. I was pretty sure he hadn't been a user when I'd seen him eight months ago, looking bewildered and lonely, asking any man that passed if they wanted to take him home with them. Even asking me. He had come a long way all right, and I'd found him in exactly the same place he'd started from. I got back into the car, turned the key and drove home.

I finished my breakfast and made two or three calls. It was a bright, clear morning, summer making one last stand in mid-October, and I was eager to get up and out into it. Probably the caffeine. I put on a dark Aquascutum suit which had been my uncle's, a white Pinks shirt without a tie, and a pair of old brogues I could see my face in while I was tying the laces. I ran my hand over my chin and regretted that I'd been too lazy to shave that morning. Too late. I turned the machine on, left a message to unknown callers that I would be on my office number from around lunchtime, and skipped downstairs into the street.

It was still only nineish and Exmouth Market was busy with people on their way to work, or looking through the four or five stalls which give the street its name (just). Workmen were busy ripping out the old Spar minimarket which was about to become another restaurant and a group of bleached trendies who didn't seem to have gone to bed yet sat outside Fred's Café, drinking cappuccinos, probably waiting for The Face to open. I walked past them, waved at Alberto through the window and bought a paper from the shop next door to Zak's Snacks. Walking back past my flat to the Mazda I flipped over to the sports pages and saw that Arsenal had lost last night at home to

Forest. 2–0. Campbell and Thomas. It put a spring in my step. What an absolutely perfect way to start the day.

I sat outside 23 Elm Drive for ten minutes but it was far too early and I gave up. I drove through the back streets which run horizontal to the Euston Road until I reached Harley Street and then I joined the main drag. It took me twenty minutes to drive the quarter of a mile further to the Westway, and once on it I didn't move very much faster until well past Ladbroke Grove. I didn't want to use the Westway, I never wanted to use it, but there was no choice really. I listened to ten minutes of *Call Nick Ross* and then switched over to Robert Elms on GLR. He was quite funny as usual and quite interesting as usual. But there was something about him which annoyed me. As usual.

And then I came to the place. The railing had been repaired long ago and the wrenching skid marks on the tarmac were also a thing of the past. Nobody would have been able to guess what had happened there because there was no evidence left, there was nothing to see any more; it was just a normal stretch of the flyover. But there was a lot for me to see and though I tried not to I saw it all. The gaping hole in the smashed barrier, the mess the car made after it had nosedived down on to the street below. I saw the rain and the flashing lights and the crowd of firemen and medics crowding round my wrecked car as I ran up to it and pushed my way through, through to the body they were cutting out of it, covered in blood, his face blank as if he wasn't even there. The way he just hung in their arms. And then hearing the sound of someone else begging to be let through the cordon and turning round to see Sharon arguing with the officers, who wouldn't let her through. And I was glad that they wouldn't let her through.

In the short-term car park at Heathrow I looked through my case to see that I had everything. Teddy's broad face grinned at me again. He still looked cheerful and in control. Alive. I hadn't mentioned any specific time to the barman so I went through his file again to make sure there wasn't anything I'd missed, any question that I would have liked to have asked and would feel annoyed about if I thought of it later. I didn't think I was going to get anywhere on this thing but at least I'd know that I'd done what I could. I took out the pathologist's report and quickly had another run through it.

Teddy Morgan died of a massive coronary thrombosis caused by severe lacerations to the abdomen and stomach lining which induced massive stress on the heart. He had been battered unconscious by a champagne bottle which caused a lot of structural damage to his face and which broke on impact. It was then used to cause the injuries to his stomach area which proved fatal.

A quantity of semen was found in Teddy's anal canal, and the police are unsure as to when it arrived there. While it was at first assumed that Teddy had been buggered before any attack was made on him, it is possible that this may have occurred after he was bludgeoned unconscious. The lack of any significant bloodstains directly under Teddy's body ruled out the theory that he was buggered while dead: the assailant would have had to turn the body over on to its front, and this would have soaked the sheets beneath his torso.

Fragments of glass were also found a long way up Teddy's anus. The police pathologist believed this to be one of the last things that had happened to Teddy, and that he could not have known anything about it. One of the larger fragments was matched to a long sliver of glass which had broken from the main body of the bottle, probably on initial impact with Teddy's skull, and the lacerations to Teddy's anal canal indicated that they were caused by a long, slender piece of glass rather than the main body of the bottle itself. The use of the shard of glass (as well as the lack of any alien fingerprints anywhere in the flat) suggested that the killer was, at that moment at least, wearing gloves. The rest of the shard was found jammed into what was left of Teddy's face.

The last thing that happened to Teddy was that whoever used the champagne bottle on him then stuck the top half of it into his gaping abdomen, wedging it between his hip and rib bones, where it stayed until Teddy's body was discovered by his wife. This struck me as the cruellest, most cynical thing his assailant had done – an insult to someone whom he had already humiliated, a two-finger salute stuck up to whoever found him, a salute which would never leave the memory. Even I could see it and I hadn't been there, and I wondered at the mind which would take pleasure in such an act. I suddenly had the strange realization which I used to get on the force, that the person I was thinking of was out there somewhere, out and about talking to people, laughing with them, sitting at a bar with them maybe. The police psychologist reported that the perpetrator's last action with the bottle meant that he was likely to have a highly developed, ironic sense of humour. That he liked a joke. Right, I thought, as I put the file back in my case. Ha ha ha.

It was now after ten and the airport wasn't that busy. The business flights were gone and it was not the time of the week or year when us Brits can't take it any more and rush off to other parts of the Continent we are so sceptical about. I wandered through the white halls avoiding the odd bag-laden trolley and looked for the Pavilion Bar.

The bar itself was a semi-circle surrounded by aluminium stools, none of which was occupied. I took one to the left side and ordered a Perrier from the only barman, the man I had come to see. He was tall, late twenties, with long light brown hair which was receding slightly at the sides, leaving him a full, back-combed widow's peak. He was clean-shaven with smooth, even-coloured skin, a large flat mole on his left cheek, and very dark, blue eyes. He was wearing wire-rim glasses which did not undercut the loose, rather lackadaisical style he had about him. As he took my order I noticed a hint of Australian in his accent, but it was difficult to tell which way round it was, whether he was English and had been there recently, or an Australian who'd been living here for ages. Perhaps it was neither. Perhaps there's an accent which people pick up simply from working in airports too long. Whatever it was it made me think of the time when Luke and I had gone backpacking in Queensland for a month, just before Luke had met Sharon.

The barman picked up a small bottle of Perrier from a row behind him, twirled it round in his hand with a very professional absent-mindedness, and then set it down in front of me next to a glass full of ice and a wedge of lemon. His movements were cool but not showy, a natural affinity with objects he touched every day, and they seemed to strike a cord with me as if I'd seen the man before. I was sure I hadn't. I took the wedge out of the glass, put it in an ashtray and poured the water over the ice. Then I watched the barman as he served another customer. I looked at the chairs standing up against the polished wooden sides of the bar like men in a firing squad, and wondered which of them Teddy had sat on. Which the other man, the man he had met. Maybe I was sitting on it. I thought about all the people who must come every day and sit on the stool recently used by someone who was going around London mutilating homosexuals. And never knew it. I took a sip of my drink and then caught the barman's eye.

The barman got the manager to cover him, took off his apron and came round the bar to join me. He told me that his name was Alex Mitchell, which I already knew, and then he said that he'd told the police everything he could remember but was happy to help me anyway. I gave him my card.

'He came up and sat down,' the barman said. 'The other guy was already here, he had been for quite a while. The pilot had a drink on his own and then the next time I looked the other guy was sat next to him and the pilot ordered a drink for both of them. I was too busy to hear what they were talking about. They stayed about half an hour more and then left. That's it.'

The barman shrugged his shoulders and sat back on his stool. He gave me a sort of hopeless look, as if to apologize for wasting my time coming all the way out there. I opened my case, took out a pad and looked down at some notes I had made. The file with Edward's murder in it stared at me and I closed my case quickly as though something, his screams perhaps, were going to escape from it.

'The man had a bag,' I said, 'which you noticed.'

'Yeah. It was leather, slung over his shoulder. I remembered because I needed one. I told the police that.'

'I know,' I said. I thought about it.

'Did it look empty or full?' I asked.

'Oh,' said Alex, 'I dunno really. Empty. Yeah, it looked pretty empty. Is that significant?'

'I don't know,' I admitted. 'It could be. It gives an indication that he hadn't travelled anywhere, that he only had a few things in it. Things he would need in the immediate future only.'

'Like murder things?' Alex asked.

'Maybe,' I said.

Alex reached over the bar and filled a glass with water from the soda gun. He took a sip from the glass and then set it down on the bar top.

'Tell me about the man,' I said.

He thought for a second. 'Well, it's hard,' he said, frowning. 'I already sat with the police on this computer imager thing, but all we got was the baseball hat really. I suppose that's why he wore it. He was white. Well built. Young.'

'Good-looking?'

'What?' he asked. 'I don't know. He didn't seem to be. I don't know.'

'As good-looking as Teddy? As Edward Morgan?'

Alex bit his thumbnail and then looked either side of me.

'I don't know. No. I don't think so, I don't know.'

'OK. Now,' I said, changing the subject, 'if you were to guess, what do you think he did? What was his job?'

Alex seemed surprised at the question.

'How would I know?' he asked.

'Well, for instance, you said he was well-built. He had on jeans and a leather jacket, trainers. Did he look like he wore these things all the time? Or did he look the sort who had changed into them from a suit after work, say?'

'No,' the barman said, getting into it a bit more, surprised that he was able to answer the question. 'No. He didn't look like he wore a suit or nothing. I don't know why I think that but he didn't. I can't imagine him in a suit. He sat sort of slouched, maybe that's why.'

'So if you had to guess, what did he look like he did? Manual work? Building work?'

'No.' Alex shook his head. 'He didn't seem like a bricky or something like that either.'

'Well, did he look like a student then?'

'Oh no. Not that I know why. He was more . . . weighty. In himself. In charge. He looked, I don't know . . .' I waited.

'Go on,' I said. 'It doesn't matter if it sounds stupid or it's just a guess. All I want to know is the impression you had of him.'

'He looked,' Alex went on, 'like someone with important things going on in his head. Real world things, not like a student looks. But I can't see him doing anything for a living. Strange though, his bag looked expensive, that's why I remembered it . . .'

'Right,' I said.

'But I can't think of him doing any sort of job.'

'Fine,' I said. 'That's fine.' I took a sip of water and then put my glass down on the bar. I looked at the barman and asked, 'Did Edward Morgan look gay to you?'

'Oh.' Alex hesitated for a second. 'Well, I didn't even think about it when he came up.' He ran a hand back through his hair. 'Not at all. Not that I'm an expert. But when he sat with the other guy, and then they left, well, I just assumed. Not that they touched or anything. But it was pretty obvious.'

'And the other man,' I went on, trying to keep him with it, 'when you served him initially, did he seem gay?'

He thought about it. He bit hard at his bottom lip.

'I don't know. Yeah, he did. Or, rather, he seemed *something*. Definitely something. Then when I saw the two of them leaving I knew what it was. Or, rather, when I found out what he did. What happened to the pilot. I can remember what he made me feel like when I served him, what he gave off. It was nasty. Like he knew stuff which wasn't nice. Not nice at all.' Alex seemed to have gone somewhere, but he came back and laughed. He shrugged his shoulders.

'It's funny,' he said. 'I can remember all that, now that you ask me. What he *seemed* like and stuff. But for the life of me I can't remember his face. I can't remember what the bastard looked like.'

I asked Alex a few more questions, without any great feats of reasoning standing in wait behind them. For some reason I didn't want to leave yet, as though there was a question that I wasn't asking but should be. When he said he'd been working at the airport for a couple of months I realized that my accent theory was wrong. He was an Australian, from the west coast, but he'd lived in Britain for the last two years.

'Thought I'd escape the crime and violence in Perth by coming to live with you genteel Poms.' I asked him if he was sure he hadn't heard anything more that the two men were saying and he replied he thought he heard Teddy asking the other guy if he wanted a lift. He remembered that Teddy had paid for all of the drinks.

After a while the bar manager began to give me significantly pissed-off looks – probably because she was actually having to do some work herself for a change. I smiled at her sweetly. I thanked the barman for his time and asked him to phone me if he remembered anything which he thought might be useful. He looked down at the card in his hand and said he would do. Then he slid the card into the pocket of his shirt as he walked back round to his usual side of the bar. I offered to pay Alex for the Perrier, but he told me to forget about it, and expertly flipped the empty bottle into the bin. This really annoyed his manager who pursed her lips into a tight O at the profligate liberty taken by one of her minions. I thanked Alex again, smiled to myself, and walked back to my car.

The drive back to Islington only took forty minutes. As I was cruising along the now deserted Westway I thought about what the barman had told me. I tried to conjure up a picture of a man, a man who seemed to have things on his mind. A man who slouched but seemed important, who knew nasty things. None came. I drove past the place again but this time very quickly and the only thing I was worried about was a traffic camera. I drove along the Euston Road and up to the Angel. I turned off Upper Street behind a 38 bus and stopped at the bottom of Cross Street in a red zone.

I made a quick visit to the library just across from the fish shop. I have a friend there who lets me take out back copies of newspapers even though this is not strictly permissible. I always take them back, often the same day. I just like sitting in my office with them, near the phone. I dumped an armful on to the back seat, got into the car again, and drove up Highbury Grove to the Studios. I parked and walked up to my office.

When I got up to the fourth floor I found Andy Gold sitting in the café, drinking coffee and quite obviously eyeing up Ally.

And looking pleased with himself.

Chapter Six

We were in my office. I couldn't put Ally through any more of Mr Gold's smoulderingly sensual glances and anyway the place had started to fill up for lunch. Andy was seated across from me and was taking a file out of his briefcase. I noticed that there were a couple of messages on my machine but I didn't think about playing them. Playing your answerphone messages with a policeman in the room is not what I'd call a good idea.

Andy placed an A5-size photograph on my desk. It was obviously taken from a security video – it was a slight downshot and the definition was poor. It wasn't a reproduction of the whole frame, it was a blow-up of one section, but the date and time could still be seen in the bottom left corner. It showed a man's face, in profile. Alongside but obscured by him, was another man wearing what looked to be, or at least could have been, an airline pilot's hat.

'That's our man,' Andy said, turning the picture round towards me.

I looked at the picture some more. It wasn't very clear, not clear at all, but it was a person. Only one person. It was a profile which somebody might recognize. I asked Andy when he had got hold of it.

'Last night,' he replied. Andy was happy. I got the

feeling that he was about to tell me something which illustrated how clever he was.

'We'd been through all the airport security vids and we did get a shot but from directly above. No use, you couldn't even see hair colour. Then we went through the ones from the stores with open fronts but there was no sign of our Edward or if there was it was too crowded to make him out. We went through those vids frame by frame for days but didn't get anything. I even took some copies home with me and you know how I like to leave my work at the office. We gave up on the vids weeks ago but yesterday, after I'd seen you, it suddenly struck me that our Mr Ed might have stopped off for something in one of the stores that are completely contained, for some mints or some johnnies or something.'

He broke off to take a sip of the coffee he had brought through with him and also, I suspected, for me to take in the magnitude of his investigative prowess.

'Well, we checked, but naturally enough Edward and friend didn't stop for refreshments, they had other things on their minds I presume. But they did walk pretty close to the Body Shop.' Andy leant forward with a smile on his face.

'Want to know how I know?'

I sighed. I wished I had a book in the office. Andy's chirpiness depressed me; as usual it had nothing to do with catching a killer and everything to do with being the one who did it.

'Watkins and Dawson were going through the tapes, fast-forwarding to see if anyone in a baseball cap, or Ed himself, came in. I suddenly realized that whenever anybody opened the door to go in or out, which they did a lot because the place was really busy, the camera got a peek at the concourse. At the people walking by. We knew the time Edward and his new pal left the bar so we went through the tape real slow at around that time and Houpla! Edward and his chutney chum.'

'Brilliant,' I said, 'you should be a detective.'

'Lucky, I know, but we nearly missed it. We got the still made last night and then had it cut and blown up.' He put his finger down on the middle of the man's face, and pushed the picture towards me.

'That's our bastard,' Andy said.

I picked the picture up and studied it.

'Have you given this to the beat boys yet?' I asked.

'Being done now.'

'What about media? Are you going to do a *Crimewatch* or anything?'

Andy sat back in his chair and sighed.

'Now that, my dear Bill, is the prob. The Governor, in his infinite, does not believe the picture is clear enough.'

'He has a point,' I said.

'He thinks that if we put it out we'll get every old dear from Skye to Southend calling in whenever they catch a peek of a bloke in a baseball cap through the sitting-room nets. He wasn't even sure about giving it to the plods.'

I was surprised. 'Why not?'

'Well, it's not so distinct that you could clock someone with it. On the street. More like if you already knew the guy you might put his face to it. And, for some reason, the Governor doesn't think that any of our Blue Boys socialize with crazed homicidal fags.'

'No,' I said. 'And perhaps he's even right about that. So what are you going to do?'

'Use it in evidence when we catch the cunt, and until then give it to the plods but tell them not to get too carried away. And give it to the plain-clothes team who are on the thing. They'll wave it around in the right places and who knows?' Andy paused for a second and smirked. 'The Gov didn't even mind you having a go with it.'

I smiled at the memory of a fat Scotsman with a perpetual look of disgust on his face, encased in a cloud of cigar smoke, Glenfidich and Aramis.

'Still remembers me then?' I asked.

'Oh, sure he does. Said he always had suspicions about you, especially when you quit. He thinks you couldn't take being around so many beefy men all the time. Said it was a good idea giving you the picture because you probably go to all those bender bars and might even know the geezer yourself.' Andy Gold laughed.

'Charming,' I said, and I took out an A4 manila envelope from my desk drawer, and slid the picture into it.

Andy told me he was going to troll the picture round to all the people he had interviewed already and that he'd let me know if anything came of it. He said he didn't hold out much hope really, and that his team were pretty well resigned to waiting for the next one. He said we were about due bearing in mind the length of time between the other murders. He left me with two copies of the photograph and I walked him down the hall to the lift. He popped into the café to take his coffee cup back and when he came out he was smiling again, having set aside thoughts of serial killers as easily as an onboard magazine when the flight attendant comes by.

'You know,' he said, as he stepped into the waiting lift, without even the faintest trace of irony, 'I think that Italian piece fancies me.'

*

Back in my office I made a call to the courier company I use and told them that I had a pick-up. Then I called Carl at the Repro place near my flat and told him that I would be biking over a picture that I wanted doing in postcard size. Two hundred to start with. I said I'd pick the copies up later, just before he shut.

'Oh, you mean *today*, Mr Rucker?' Carl replied wearily. I told him he was beautiful, and hung up.

One of the messages was from Sharon. She said she had been given a couple of tickets for a flamenco dance show at Sadler's Wells on Friday night and would I like to go. What was today? Wednesday. Cool, why not? I called her at work and arranged it. The other message was from Mrs Charlotte Morgan. She was just returning my call. She left a work number I could reach her on if I needed to speak to her today, or I could contact her at home that evening after seven. I called the work number and Mrs Morgan agreed, somewhat reluctantly, to meet me the following morning.

After I'd given the envelope with the photo in to the biker I spent the rest of the afternoon going through the newspapers I'd picked up from the library. As I read what the press had to say about the three murders, the image of the man's face was ever present in my mind. This face was out there somewhere, and it was highly likely that its owner was thinking of ways to provide the papers with even more copy.

I started with the lorry driver and the rent boy and then I went through everything there was about Edward Morgan. What I wanted to try and see was if they *felt* the same, not the way they were reported but the events themselves. There was something about them which seemed to me to be familiar in some way, as if I had read of something like them before but didn't know where. Probably in one of those pseudo-Victorian true crime books that always used to be kicking around the station house. For some reason my brother came to mind, as if he had mentioned something like this to me.

I wondered if the man in the picture had seen to Waldock and Evans as well as Teddy Morgan. The newspapers were in no doubt as to the link between the killings. Newspapers like to serialize everything; they sell more copies that way. While they couldn't print many of the details of how the murders were committed, they were allowed to mention the use of the bottles, which they all did with varying degrees of enthusiasm. The broadsheets were quite restrained but I was shocked once again by the dramatization given by all the tabloids. Their tone was one of horrified moral outrage at the murders, but underlined with a joyous 'we've got a great story' air. The very reporters who wondered as to who could possibly perpetrate such heinous crimes were the same ones who hounded the relatives of the dead for quotes. In one rag there was even a big exclusive which purported to be by the mother of James Waldock. It was about the sordid acts which her life of poverty and drug dependency had reduced her too: theft, deceit and prostitution. And, I thought to myself, talking to tabloid news journalists. I remembered the first time I had ever encountered such bullish insensitivity, picking up some rag in a Melbourne bus station. It was a graphic report about some other vicious killings, including pictures, splashed all over the first few pages. At the time I'd thought it unbelievable, even over there. Now it's commonplace, even here.

As I went through the lurid tales in the papers it struck me that if Teddy Morgan had been killed by the same man who killed Evans and Waldock, the killer had definitely broken his pattern to a certain degree. The question was whether or not Teddy's murder was pre-planned or opportunistic. Either way there was a discrepancy between that and the other murders: even given the baseball cap, the killer had, unlike the previous two times, given people a chance to see him. If it was just a 'lucky' chance – if the killer had been at the airport anyway and just happened to meet a gay airline pilot at the bar who offered him a lift home – then it would mean he had just got a little careless. He couldn't resist his urge to do what he does, even though he knew that he had been in a public place prior to the killing. If, however, the killer had planned to go to the airport in order to find a victim then he wasn't being careless; he was being over-confident. He didn't care if he was seen because he either thought that his hat was sufficient disguise or he didn't take into account the security cameras.

Irritatingly enough, neither the chance nor planned option seemed completely credible to me. I thought about the chance idea. The other crimes were obviously pre-planned; the bottle in each case appeared to have been prepared in advance and the perp made sure that there was no one else around, or if there was then they weren't the sort to go chatting to the Bill about the activities of a recently murdered boy-prostitute. Bearing in mind his previous meticulousness it seemed difficult to believe that the killer had just happened to be in the airport and had met Edward and decided to kill him. Also, his bag looked empty. What would a person who had to be at the airport anyway be doing with an empty bag? And how did he know that he would be able to use a bottle on Teddy if he had just met him? Because Teddy told him about the champagne he had? Maybe. But even so I found it hard to believe it was chance. The barman said that the man in the hat had been at the bar for a while. Why would he sit there, in an airport, if he wasn't hoping something was going to happen?

I suddenly realized that I hadn't asked the barman if he had noticed the guy before, on other days, checking the place out. Idiot. He probably wouldn't remember, and he would have told the police if he did remember seeing the guy previously, but even so. I might have been able to get him to remember, and if I did it would prove that the whole thing was intentional – he had gone there to find a victim. I made a mental note to call the airport first thing in the morning.

I didn't think it was a chance thing but the idea that it was planned also had me doubting. Why was he so deliberately careless? There are many ways to kill people you don't know without doing so after you have been seen chatting to them in a well-lit airport bar. Agreed, a killer of gay men does have to meet his victims and this will have to be in a public place (unless of course the victim is a prostitute or a lorry driver). Maybe the guy wanted to spread more panic – make it dangerous for men to pick each other up in public as well as dangerous to give them lifts or sell them sexual favours. But then why didn't he use a bar or a gay club? Too obvious? Perhaps. Male flight staff do have a reputation for homosexuality but was he really likely to meet one in a public area? Apparently, according to the barman, he was; Alex Mitchell said that some of the gay staff came to his bar. But that still leaves him with the problem of the cameras and the fact that Teddy's uniform would make his last movements particularly memorable to potential witnesses.

I tried to think how I would select my victims if I was in the habit of murdering homosexuals. While I did think that his first two strikes made sense, I really did not think that I would go to the airport. It would take me too long to meet somebody, by which time I would have become a regular feature in the place. Unless I lucked out first or second time. Not worth it. But then again, I thought, maybe the killer isn't very bright. It isn't written anywhere that serial killers should be, that's just in the movies. Or maybe it's me that's not very bright and Teddy's murder was excellently planned.

Well, nobody's caught him yet.

I felt that the discrepancies I'd found did increase the chance that Sir Peter Morgan was right, that the murder could have been a copycat set-up. But set up by whom? There was, however, one other option to consider if the killer was the same for all three murders. Not only had the murderer planned on murdering someone he met at the airport, he had planned who it was going to be. He knew Edward Morgan and had decided that he would be next. This option presented a myriad of different possible scenarios based on who Edward knew and where he went, none of which I knew anything about. Yet. Hacking away at that option would be fruitless at the moment and anyway my head felt pretty full of different takes on the thing as it was. I decided to leave all the stuff I had put into my brain to sift itself. I packed up the newspapers, turned on the machine, and went down to my car.

As I passed the café Ally saw me through the door and called out to me.

'Hey, Billy,' she laughed, 'such nice friends you've got!'

Chapter Seven

I had half an hour before my pictures would be done so I drove down to King's Cross and parked a few doors down from the squat inhabited by, among others, Dominic Lewes. It was still light but it wouldn't be for ever so I tried to think of a way to precipitate Dominic's appearance at his front door. Bomb scare? Too drastic. Eventually I just decided to walk right up and ring the doorbell.

'Yeah?'

It was a girl. I couldn't see much of her because the door was only open as far as the chain would let it. What I could see was that she wasn't one to get overly influenced by a Timotei ad or go overboard on fake tanning cream.

'I'm looking for Dominic,' I said.

'Who?'

'Dom.' Her face didn't register that she knew anyone of that name. 'Smallish kid,' I said. 'Bleached blond crop and brown eyes. He lives here?'

The girl hesitated for a second. A male voice behind her called out, 'Who is it?'

'Someone for Mikey,' the girl told him, turning round and moving away from the door.

The owner of the voice came up and took the chain off the door. He was a tall black guy, about the thirty mark, dressed in a black V-necked T-shirt and camel-colour jeans.

'What you want here?'

'Mikey,' I said, 'is Mikey home?'

'He called him Dominic before,' the girl said helpfully.

'Fuck off!'

The door was slammed in my face so hard I thought the glass would jump out.

Oh well.

I picked up the pictures from Carl and sat in my flat listening to PM and attaching a small sticker with my name and number on to the back of each one. When I had done that it was nearly eight so I made a quick bowl of pasta with Molise's red pesto. I packed up a small bag and, remembering to put a bunch of the repros in the side pocket, headed out the door. I picked up my bike from the hallway and carried it down the stairs.

Down at the gym I went through the circuit training, worked out, and then sparred four rounds with a wiry old bruiser called Archie. He must have been about fifty but he was a tough old bastard and certainly didn't expect any favours. So I didn't do him any. After getting under the shower I asked Sal if she could spare a minute.

I stood next to her while she looked at the photograph under the light of her office desk lamp. She nodded her head to herself and then shook it in irritation.

'You know what, I think I've seen this guy,' she said. 'Just for the moment though, don't ask me where.' She stared at the picture so hard I thought she'd wear it out.

'What's he done, this one?'

I told her what the police wanted him for.

'Well, you know me, Bill, the further you can keep me from the Boys in Blue the happier I am but I'll tell you, if I remember where I've seen this nonce I'll get on to you straight.'

'Thanks, Sal,' I said.

'And I'll show it round the gym, see if anyone else has any idea.'

'Thanks,' I said again. I gave Sal a cheque for some subs that I owed her and reached in my bag for my bike key.

There's a gay pub called The Centre quite near Sal's gym and I stopped off there on my way home and chatted to some of the clientele. They had all heard of the murders and were interested in the photograph I had. No one could place the man, however, though one nervous-looking sixtyish teacher type did look at the picture a little longer than necessary and was just a touch too vehement in his denial. When I mentioned this to him he said that he had had a rough day, that's all, and the last thing he wanted to think about was a serial killer. I told him that if he wasn't careful that would be the last thing he ever did think about.

Back in my flat the washing-up stared at me like an angry lover. I plunged into it and felt good when it was done. I lay on my futon and looked through some more of the newspaper articles but didn't get anywhere. The beginning of an investigation is always the most frustrating; you want to make connections but you haven't got anything to make them with. I put the papers aside and then remembered that I still hadn't read Luke's poems, the ones which Sharon had given me. I got up and fetched them from the kitchen table. I sat looking at the blue folder Sharon had put them in for a long time without taking the poems out. I didn't know why. The folder was made by a company called Avery and the style was a

Guidex Bradford® BLUE 21113. I stared at it a few minutes more and was about to open it up when the phone rang.

It was Nicky, wanting me to go down to The Old Ludensian.

'I can't tonight, mate,' I told him, looking at the folder, 'I've got something I should do.'

'Should?' Nicky laughed. 'Billy! I thought you were self-employed. Didn't they tell you when you got your Schedule D number that there was no such thing as should any more?'

'I think I missed that bit of the form.'

'Come on down,' Nicky insisted. 'There's no one in the bar, it's quiet. Come and keep me company.'

'Nicky . . .'

'Come *on*!'

I let Nicky talk me into it and I drove down and joined him. The place was jumping. I thought perhaps that he'd just got a rush on, but when I finally managed to push my way through the crush to the far end of the bar where Nicky always sits I realized I'd been had. He was with two friends. New friends. Hi, hi. Hi, hi. I ended up with the blonde one and a nose full of hooter in a flat off the Fulham Road. I didn't get back to Exmouth Market until well after seven the next morning. The blonde didn't seem too upset that her friend had got Nicky, and her me, or if she was she was polite enough not to show it. Her name was Trish and she was in Advertising.

When you have a hangover and haven't slept more than a couple of hours and generally feel like a piece of sun-dried shit, the best thing to do is shave, shine your shoes, put a tie round the collar of a bright white shirt and all in all look a lot smarter than you usually do. Then, not only will you feel more together, but if you happen to run into anyone you know the first thing they'll tell you is how good you're looking these days.

I did all these things and got to my office around ten. The temperature had fallen from the day before and the cold perked me up a bit. I didn't actually feel that bad but I wasn't so foolish as to think I'd got away with it. I knew it would hit me later. I ducked into the café for a coffee and because Mike was still out making deliveries Ally was there on her own. She looked me up and down as she handed me Kojak, and smiled.

'You know, Billy,' she said, 'it's not a bad effort but you should get some of that stuff which whitens the eyes. You know, takes away the little veins?'

I looked in the mirror behind her; blood-red cobwebs.

'Any time you want to give this job up just tell me, Ally, just say the word.'

I did my accounts, paid a few bills, and wrote a couple of letters reminding people that they had actually employed me in a professional capacity and that because of such I would be very grateful if they would send me some money. I had another look at Andy Gold's file and read the notes on Charlotte Morgan. At thirty-eight Charlotte was four years younger than Edward and had been married to him for seven years. She worked for a PR firm and had met her husband when her company won the BA account and decided to boost the profile of the airline's actual staff in their corporate identity. A sort of upgrade for the pilots. They had married after a courtship of only six months and moved into the Highbury apartment in which Edward's body had been found, often spending weekends at Mrs Morgan's family home in Pevensey,

Sussex, which she had inherited on the death of her father a year earlier. Neighbours reported them to be a quiet couple who were amiable enough but kept mostly to themselves. I had to smile at this. As a DC I had been given this description many times by people anxious to keep out of the picture or protect themselves against charges that they should have reported their neighbours' activities long ago. It didn't mean anything; the Morgans could have been holding sado-masochistic sex parties which included sacrificing chickens to voodoo gods and the description would have been the same. Quiet, kept to themselves.

The police had routinely ruled out any hint that Mrs Morgan was involved in her husband's murder. The only suspicious fact was that she had been away at the time, something which could look just a little convenient if there was anything else pointing to her. But there wasn't. The two PCs who had responded to her 999 call reported that her shock and trauma were genuine on discovering her husband lying dead with a champagne bottle jutting out of him. DI Drake, who was the first to interview her, also testified to her very real grief and shock. Everything pointed to the homosexual slasher idea, and when semen was discovered inside the corpse it was generally agreed that Mrs Morgan wasn't the one who put it there.

The semen. That made me think. Had they cross-checked it with that found on James Waldock? I called Andy quickly and managed to catch him. Of course they had checked it, what sort of prat did I take him for? There was no match. Another change then – the killer had been even more careless: he'd wiped his prints but left his DNA.

So. Mrs Charlotte Morgan wasn't a suspect and had no

idea that her husband was, or even might have been, a homosexual. She hadn't seen anyone suspicious hanging around in the area before she went away on business, and when she spoke to her husband on the phone from New York she didn't notice anything different about his mood or his tone of voice. In fact, she knew nothing, nothing that was any help to the police. But maybe, like Alex Mitchell, I would be able to get her to remember things she didn't even suspect she knew.

I'd arranged to meet Charlotte Morgan at twelve, in the small coffee lounge of Agnieszka's, the Polish expat club on Exhibition Road, South Ken. I'd thought of it because it is always very quiet, especially in the mornings, and is only five minutes' walk from where Mrs Morgan told me she worked. When I suggested it I was surprised that she actually knew where it was and had even been there. Nobody else I'd ever mentioned it to had.

I parked on a meter near Imperial College and got to Agnieszka's about ten minutes early for my meeting. From the outside the club looks like a house. There is only a very small plaque on the large black door to announce its identity to the world, as well as a small sign which asks that visitors ring the bell. I did so. The doorman, a small elderly man in a dark suit and tie, opened the door and showed me into the hallway.

'Hello, hello again!' the man said, bobbing the top half of his body up and down, his mouth breaking into a huge, cracked smile. I had no idea if he remembered me or whether this was simply his standard greeting. The man looked disapproving, upset even, when he saw that I didn't have a coat to hand him. I informed him that I was here for coffee and he showed me through to the lounge.

As he sat me down on one of the broad sofas I handed him my card and I told him that I was waiting for a woman to join me, and would he show her through when she arrived. His grave nod told me that he took it on himself as a great personal responsibility to do so, and he left me to my thoughts.

The coffee lounge in Agnieszka's takes up one end of the dining room, and as I waited for Mrs Morgan I let my eyes wander to the far end of the room. The impression is one of an old faded salon. The ceilings are high and the walls are almost completely hidden behind hundreds of oil paintings, their tops jutting forward slightly from the wall as if they are all competing for attention. The paintings are passionate, dramatic, especially the portraits of beautiful, dispossessed countesses, their eyes burning, their gaze set towards distant and lost horizons. What wallpaper that can be seen beneath the pictures is a dull, yellowy-cream colour that is torn in places and hasn't been changed in years. Dinner there is reasonably cheap and can be surprisingly good, but it isn't the food that I go there for. I go because the tableclothes aren't paper, the cutlery is silver, and because, in contrast to those found at The Portman Club, the manners there demonstrate genuine warmth rather than stiff English formality.

There was no one else in the lounge so I had only Bartók to disturb me. A waiter came over and asked me if I wanted please to tea or to coffee. I said that I wanted thankyou to coffee, and to mineral water also if it was possible. He said it was. Just as he was setting the tray down on the low table in front of me the door opened and Mrs Morgan was shown in by the doorman. I stood up and greeted her.

'William Rucker,' I said, shaking her hand.

'Charlotte,' the woman replied.

After the waiter had brought her coffee and she had taken a sip of it Charlotte Morgan folded her hands in her lap and looked at me. She looked very composed as she sat there and I was reminded of Sir Peter, the control he had shown. Two people with an ever-present pain inside them which they carried through their daily lives like a tumour. I looked for a sign which might give away her current emotional state but I couldn't see one.

'Well,' she said.

I met her gaze for a second and thought how I should begin with her. Charlotte Morgan was a tall woman with black, full-bodied hair and a firm, lightly tanned face which I couldn't imagine looked any more beautiful when she was younger than it did now. Her eyes were an amber-brown like those on a toy bear and set between them was a firm, slightly square nose which she probably hated, but which actually stopped her good looks from being simply the bland glossy-magazine sort. She had slim, long hands which she kept almost unnaturally still. They ended in Rioja-coloured nail varnish and I noticed that her left hand still bore a wedding ring. She was dressed in a fitted charcoal skirt-suit and a cream silk blouse, a thin gold chain flirting with the first closed button. I smiled politely into those deep eyes and I told her I was very grateful that she had been able to spare the time to see me.

'May I ask who employed you?' Mrs Morgan said. Her voice was light and more feminine than I would have imagined. I detected a purpose behind it, however, that made me imagine her shouting at one of her assistants who was taking too long over something.

'I'm sorry,' I replied, shaking my head slightly. 'You'll understand that I won't be able to tell you that.'

'No, I suppose not,' she conceded. She didn't press me. I think she had guessed it was Sir Peter. I wondered what she thought about that.

'I called DI Gold after you left your first message,' she told me. 'I wanted to know if it was all right for me to talk to you. He said it was. He said you used to work with him.'

'That's right,' I said. 'I did.' I smiled again.

'Why did you resign?' she asked.

What is this, *The Prisoner*?

'I didn't want to end up fat, overworked and cynical,' I explained, thinking of the Chief Inspector. I thought about Luke.

'No chance of that I shouldn't think,' Charlotte Morgan said, as she ran her hands back through her hair. I found myself blushing slightly. Was she flirting with me? No. She was just trying to act natural, to keep the black event which clouded her life from gaining sway. Or was it the PR lady, trying to get me onside, wanting to deal with me as effortlessly as possible?

I reached down for my coffee and took a sip of it, thinking that it was a good job I didn't go to Agnieszka's for that either.

'I'd just like to go over a few things with you if that's OK.' I tried to sound like I understood, that I wasn't a threat to her. Like an old male friend she could tell things to.

'Fire away,' she said.

Mrs Morgan took a deep breath and got herself together. I reached down for my briefcase and clicked the latch. It's an old brown leather manuscript case which I like to think makes me look arty.

'Have the police shown you this yet?' I asked. I pulled out a copy of the picture which Andy Gold had given me, and handed it to her.

'No,' she said, taking it from me. Mrs Morgan's voice was surprised and tentative. 'No.' She looked at the post-card askance, frowning, holding it between her thumb and index finger as if it were radioactive. I saw her taking the picture in, seeing Edward behind the man.

'I spoke to them yesterday,' she managed to say, 'and they said they would come to the flat, where I'm staying, later tonight. They said they had a picture but no, no I . . . I haven't seen it.'

Mrs Morgan looked at the picture that was shaking very slightly in her hand. I suddenly realized how difficult and shocking this must be to her, to look at a picture of the man who had very probably murdered her husband, a picture taken only hours before he did so. For some reason I had assumed that Andy Gold would have got round to her straight away. Then I realized that he was in no hurry for her to see it. Edward's wife was hardly likely to recognize some guy her husband had picked up in an airport bar and taken home for sex while she was away.

Charlotte Morgan looked at the picture. Her gaze had changed and she was just staring at it blankly.

'I can't believe . . .' she said. 'It's so . . .'

I waited.

'I'm sorry, Mrs Morgan,' I said, when she didn't go on. 'Do you think you've ever seen that man?'

'No,' she said. A wistful look came over her face which betrayed a bewildered hurt.

'It seems so bizarre,' she went on, 'to think of my

husband. With a man. This man.' She put the photograph down on the table. 'And to think of what this man did to him. It's . . .' She looked for the word. 'It's surreal,' she said. She shrugged her shoulders in a way which suggested that once she thought she knew about things, but she didn't know anything about anything any more.

'You never suspected?' I asked quietly. 'I mean, that Edward may have been interested in men?'

Her face set.

'No,' she said. 'I didn't.'

'Never?'

She let out a breath. 'There was one time when we talked about it, I mean the whole gay thing, but every couple must do that at some time or other.'

'Yes,' I agreed. 'But why did you talk about it? I mean, how did it come up?'

'What?' Mrs Morgan looked a little shocked. I was sure that Edward had told her about his brother being gay. Why shouldn't he have, they were married after all? I could see her wondering why I asked the question, wondering if I could possibly know as well.

'You know,' she said dismissively, 'one of those talks.'

'And what did Edward say?'

'Well, he just said that it wasn't for him. He thought it was OK for other people but not for him.'

'And you believed him?'

'Yes. Why shouldn't I believe him?'

'I don't know. If you suspected he might be gay, for instance. Is that why you brought the matter up, because you did have an idea he might have feelings towards men?'

'No!'

Mrs Morgan was getting flustered. On the police we

were taught that when this happens the interviewee is generally hiding something. What was Charlotte hiding? I told her that I was sorry I had to ask questions like that but I was only doing it to find out who killed her husband.

'You see, Mrs Morgan,' I explained, 'it doesn't really make any sense if your husband wasn't at least bisexual. If he wasn't, then it doesn't seem likely that he would be lured to his death by a man posing as a potential partner. Either that or the sexual activity that occurred was not consensual. That would mean that the killer had deviated a great deal. Also, the police have evidence which suggests that Edward went with the man in the picture there quite willingly.'

I sat back in my chair and tried to make the expression on my face as benevolent as possible. I reminded myself of a casino bouncer who had orders to beat me up once but who, I could tell, didn't really want to. He'd looked just like that before he'd kicked the shit out of me.

Mrs Morgan pondered the facts that I had given her, trying to find a way round them but unable to.

'He must have been,' she said finally. 'I suppose he must have been but I never even thought it. I—'

I cut her off.

'Mrs Morgan, how were sexual relations between yourself and your husband at that time?'

She looked up at me. Her lips tensed and her eyes opened. I knew the police had asked her this question. I wanted to see how she reacted when I asked it. From her expression I knew what she was going to say. She was no longer flustered, she had got hold of it. She knew my tack and had set up a wall against me. She was going to protect her marriage, not let some tin-pot investigator with see-through sincerity take away her memories after a lunatic had taken away her husband. The look on her face told me that she had no idea how her life had arrived at a point wherein a stranger would be grilling her in a café, however pleasant, about the quality of the sex she had had with her recently murdered husband.

'They were fine,' she said firmly, almost daring me to go on.

I left it there.

I hadn't enjoyed asking Charlotte the questions I had. The woman had enough to worry about as it was without raking over already dead grass to satisfy the whim of a guilt-stricken Tory MP. There was something she wasn't telling me though, I knew it. It may have been something mundane and irrelevant but there was something nevertheless. I wanted to know what it was but I had no right to badger her. I could tell it wouldn't have done me any good anyway. If there was something about this woman I needed to know, then I'd have to find out what it was myself.

I moved into safer waters, asking her if she knew the names of any of Edward's friends who she thought might be out of the ordinary. She said that most of the friends they had, they had in common. Except for work friends. She didn't remember Edward mentioning anyone more than anyone else, except for his regular co-pilots and the odd stewardess he used to tease her about. How they were always looking for pilots to marry and he'd loved to have met one who would have retired immediately to the family home and bred him a hoard of kids and not gone swanning off round the world on business all the time. She smiled without any humour in her face, remembering her husband's jokes.

She said, 'Maybe he should have; he couldn't have been killed then, could he?'

I ran out of questions and thanked Mrs Morgan for her time. I asked her how she was coping. She said that her company were being very understanding and that she wasn't having to deal with clients at the moment, which was a relief. She seemed glad to be off the subject of her husband and we chatted for a minute or two before she took a long look at her watch. I asked the waiter for the bill.

Mrs Morgan excused herself to go to the bathroom. When she came out she had applied some lipstick and done her eyelashes. She looked very beautiful and not a lot older than me. I caught a hint of eau de Issey as she walked past me into the hall, recognizing the scent because it was what Trish in Advertising had been wearing. As we entered the hallway the little bobbing doorman went into overdrive and had Mrs Morgan's mac on in no time. He told us that it was always a pleasure to see us there and that he hoped we would visit again soon. He held his hands together and beamed at us and I thought he was going to enquire about the kids. I smiled to myself, pressed a pound coin into his hand and followed Mrs Morgan on to the street.

Outside it had got even colder and an ominous cloud hovered over the stately buildings of Exhibition Road like a Zeppelin. I thanked Mrs Morgan again and gave her one of my cards. We shook hands and she walked off in the direction of Kensington Gore. I walked the other way, back to my car.

I wondered if she and her husband *had* been happy in bed together and decided that no, they hadn't. Her not wanting to discuss it was more than coyness. Maybe, like

Sir Peter, she didn't want to fail Edward, let him down by admitting that there had been a failure in his life, something which she thought was irrelevant, and nobody's business but hers. Perhaps she even blamed herself for Edward's murder, driving him to men after she hadn't been able to arouse him herself, and her denial of any marital problems was her way of pushing aside her own sense of blame. Maybe she was even involved in what happened to Edward, and she didn't want anyone to think that her marriage had been anything other than idyllic.

Or perhaps they had been blissfully happy and had had a wonderful love life.

But then I had another thought, one which wasn't particularly logical, and of which I was a little ashamed because it was based on an assumption which I didn't want to make. It went along these lines: why would a woman whose husband had been dead for just under three months make up her face, dab perfume behind her earlobes and walk in the opposite direction to her office at twelve fifteen on a grey morning in late October? I turned round and walked in the direction of Kensington Gore, doing up my jacket and digging my hands into my pockets. Because she always wore make-up? She hadn't with me. I broke into a light jog. Because she had an important meeting? She told me she wasn't seeing clients at the moment. I jogged faster until I was almost running.

When I got to the main road I caught sight of Charlotte Morgan walking on the other side of it, towards Knightsbridge. Almost immediately she turned into Kensington Gardens. I crossed over and kept fifty yards behind her as she walked past the round pond and across the park towards the Bayswater Road. I was worried she'd see me but she didn't look back. Crossing the Bayswater Road, she walked up Leinster Road and then turned into a small street on her right. I sprinted to the top of the street and took a very careful look round the corner. Leinster Mews. I was just in time to see one of the cottage doors being held open for her and Mrs Morgan step inside.

I sprinted back across Kensington Gardens and stuck my key into the door of the Mazda. I tried the ignition – nothing. Again – very little. Once again – more this time but my impatience made me pump the accelerator and I nearly flooded the engine. I waited. I made myself count to a hundred. I tried again. The engine took with the depth and enthusiasm of a man dragged out of a river who finally responds to the kiss of life. I pulled it out of the side street, cut into the traffic, much to the annoyance of a cab driver with a surprising command of old Saxon English, and sped past the Albert Hall. I drove through the park, back into Bayswater and turned up Leinster Road.

I sat in the Mazda at the far end of Leinster Mews keeping an eye on number 8. I booted up the camera and hoped I hadn't missed her. I waited about an hour, the camera on the dashboard, thinking that perhaps she had just popped in to collect a girlfriend for lunch or something and I was simply a sleazebag who was wasting his time.

But then the door opened.

A man stepped out. A man in a suit with a briefcase in his hand. I got a shot of him. The man looked around the mid-forties mark, maybe younger. Yes, a little younger. He had full, dark brown hair and large, steel-rimmed glasses. I thought he was just going to leave but he turned back into the doorway and a woman in a dressing gown met him halfway and kissed him. I got that too. The man kissed her back, hard, biting into her bottom lip, holding her head in his hands like he was going to shoot a basket. He grinned, a full, confident grin which told of pleasure recently enjoyed and already anticipated. The woman pulled him to her again but he broke off from her. Then he turned and walked over to a dark blue Jaguar parked at the top end of the Mews, which he got into, tossing the briefcase on the passenger seat beside him. I wrote down the plate number.

I had no idea who the man was.

The woman was Charlotte Morgan.

The door of the cottage shut. I put my camera down on the passenger seat. The Jag pulled off and I followed it out on to Leinster Road. I followed it along Bayswater and down Park Lane. I kept three or four cars back even though I didn't have to be careful because this man had no idea who I was. We drove down Grosvenor Place, past Victoria and along Birdcage Walk. Then the Jag turned into Parliament Square and skirted round St Stephen's Tower. After another right it turned into a gate which announced that it was private, with no access to members of the public. A barrier was raised in front of it and then the Jag disappeared. I stopped at a red light and looked at the gateway into which the car had gone.

It was the car park used by Members of Parliament.

PART TWO

Chapter Eight

I called Andy Gold from a phone box but I couldn't get hold of him and there was no one else I could think of who would be willing to run a vehicle registration check for me. I wasn't too concerned; I was pretty sure I could find out who the man in the Jag was on my own. I hung up and dialled the daytime number Sir Peter Morgan had given me.

Sir Peter wasn't at the Treasury, he was at Westminster today. I called the number I was given and reached his secretary and eventually convinced her that her boss would want to talk to me. I then arranged to see Sir Peter in his office in thirty-five minutes. He suggested a later time but I impressed upon him the need to see him soon, and he agreed. I hung up and then walked round to the entrance gate the Jag had driven through.

'Excuse me, sir,' I said, in broad Texan to the uniformed man on the gate. 'Could you help me?'

'If I can, sir,' the man replied. He had been sitting in his booth reading the *Sun* but he stood up and approached the window.

'I was just having an argument with my wife,' I explained. 'Shirley-Anne. You see I could have sworn I just saw the Prime Minister drive in here, in a blue-coloured Jaguar car, but she says it wasn't him.'

'And I'm afraid she'd be right, sir,' the guard said. 'Although Mr Lloyd might make it one day. No, the Prime Minister has a driver in any case.'

'So you're sure it wasn't John Major?'

'That was Graham Lloyd, sir, right Party, wrong man. And anyway, sir, John Major hasn't been PM for . . .'

'Was that who that was? Damn!' I leant forward. 'Do me a favour,' I said, taking a quick look back over my shoulder. 'Don't tell that to Shirley-Anne.'

I could feel the hangover now. It was catching me like a favourite in a steeplechase making its way through the field. I fed six twenty-pence pieces into the meter which was guarding my car and looked around for somewhere to get a quick bite to eat. I found a coffee bar and drank one of those Californian multi-vit drinks that really did make me feel a bit better – for the moment. I ate a samosa and then had one of those little Portuguese custard tart things with an espresso. London, a hundred different countries packed into one traffic jam. As I ate I wondered what the hell was going on in the life of Charlotte Morgan. I had mixed feelings about having caught her out; I was glad the case had started to move but it didn't make me happy to have my grubby suspicions confirmed. I didn't like to think of her having anything to do with her husband's death.

And then I had another thought. Sir Peter. Was I being made a fool of? I was soon to find out. I looked at a copy of the *Telegraph* which somebody had left behind, and read that Boris Yeltsin had had another heart attack and that a man with an unpronounceable name who I had never heard of before was in charge of the country. This worried me. A country with a lot of nuclear weapons should be run by someone you've heard of. I paid for my lunch and decided to leave the *Telegraph* where I'd found it. I didn't want to give Sir Peter the wrong idea.

'You're resigning?' the MP said, his mouth opening a little to demonstrate his surprise. We were sitting in his office, him in his discreet power chair backed by a panorama of the Thames and St Thomas's Hospital, and me opposite, my left foot sitting on my right knee. 'But you've only being working for two or three days!'

Sir Peter was shocked, and annoyed with me. But that was OK.

'I like knowing what I'm doing,' I told him. 'I don't like playing to someone else's agenda. I got enough of that on the force.' I settled back into the chair but didn't get too comfortable.

'I don't know what you mean!' Sir Peter's fingers spread wide apart and his head moved forward towards me, leaving his shoulders where they were.

'Fine,' I said. And I got up to go.

'Please,' Sir Peter stood up with me, 'won't you at least tell me what this is about?'

'No,' I replied. 'I don't want to tell you because you didn't hire me for that, and if you had told me that is what you wanted me to do I would never have agreed to work for you. That sort of thing isn't my line. Does that make any sense?'

'No,' Sir Peter protested.

'Fine,' I said again. 'But I don't believe you.'

This time I made it to the office door but Sir Peter took my arm before I got it open.

'All right,' he said, his voice now void of any false hurt.

'All right. I know what you're talking about but, please, let me explain.'

I sighed.

'Please,' Sir Peter said.

'I didn't hire you to snoop on my political enemies.' We were back at the desk. 'Anyway, Graham's one of us. Not that that means a damn thing these days.'

'Then why didn't you tell me about him?'

'Because I wasn't sure about it. I thought I was just being paranoid, but that if you came up with anything, well, so be it. I'm amazed it only took this long.'

'It was a fluke,' I said. 'How did you find out about it?'

'Well,' Sir Peter said, 'I introduced them. At one of those diplomatic things Ministers have to go to and hate, but which their friends and family adore. Edward was away on long haul and I ran into Charlotte in one of those ghastly restaurants in Notting Hill and asked her if she wanted to come along to the Portuguese embassy with my wife and myself.'

'And she met him there?'

'Yes. It was about eight months ago. They hit it off but I didn't think anything of it. Who wouldn't hit it off with Charlotte? She's a beautiful woman and she works in PR. Hitting it off with people is her job.'

'So why did you suspect they were seeing each other?'

'Coincidence, I suppose. Teddy and I met for lunch one day, about six weeks before he was killed. He told me that he and Charlotte were having problems. He didn't seem to think they were too serious, but he did say that she seemed quite off with him. I said that every marriage must be like that at some point.'

'I'm sure they are.'

'Yes. Anyway, it just happened that in a cab on the way back to the Treasury I saw Graham and Charlotte together on the Mall and Edward's words struck me. Oh, they weren't doing anything, they were just walking along. They could have run into each other and remembered meeting before, or Charlotte could have got Graham's number and phoned him on a work basis. But there was something about them. It was nothing blatant but it was something. Graham Lloyd is married, you know?'

'I had assumed that he was.'

'I have become adept at reading body language over the years. I've had to. It helped, of course, that Charlotte and Graham didn't know that anyone was watching them – not that they were doing anything to give themselves away. I just had the feeling.'

'So when your brother was murdered, why didn't you tell the police?'

'For the same reason I didn't tell you, only more so. I wasn't sure he was having an affair with Charlotte. I didn't want them bothering him if I was only imagining it. Even if I was sure it doesn't necessarily mean anything, and if the papers had got hold of it – Christ! I couldn't tell them and I didn't want to tell you. I wanted to see if you came up with it yourself.'

I sighed. I really love chasing around finding out things that my clients could have told me before I even started.

'There seems to be a lot of things you can't tell me. Can I be certain that's the lot?'

'Yes,' he said, relieved. 'And I'm sorry, I really am.'

'So. Are you going to tell the police about it now?'

'I suppose I'll have to.'

'Which won't hurt your corner at all,' I said. 'Will it?'

'I'm sorry?'

'Him being a pro-European, and you being as sceptical about Europe as Ian Paisley is about a united Ireland . . .'

'Now look here!' Sir Peter stood up. 'If you think for one minute that where the murder of my brother is concerned I would attempt to gain any sort of political advantage, then you couldn't be more wrong. How dare you?'

'Just to see what you'd say,' I admitted. 'You can see how I might think it. Get me to catch Lloyd in the act, maybe get some pictures off me which get leaked to the *Mail*. They're on your side, aren't they, on Europe?'

Sir Peter tried hard to suppress his outrage at my suggestion.

'If that was the case I could just have told the police of my suspicions first off, couldn't I? They would have revealed the truth just as you did, and I wouldn't have had to leak it to the papers, the police would have done it for me themselves. No?'

He had a point. Also, his anger did seem genuine. All in all I was inclined to believe that he wasn't using me in his bid to keep the jewel of Britain firmly entrenched behind her silver sea, away from nasty foreign hands. I decided not to tell him about the film I had though.

'Well,' I said, 'I apologize for doubting your motives. But if you had told me of your suspicions we wouldn't have had to have this conversation. Now, do you want to go to the police with this?'

'Yes. I think. Isn't that what you think?'

'No,' I said, 'it isn't. Like you said, the police are sure

that your brother's murder was part of a series of gay killings. For them, this will just confirm the pattern. Of course she was getting it somewhere else, she wasn't getting it at home, was she? But they will make trouble – just to do it – and somebody will almost certainly use his desk phone to call one of the tabloids and make himself a few quid. Nothing would be gained by that.'

'It disgusts me, you know, that police officers do that kind of thing.'

'You should have got Mr Howard to pay them more then.'

'It would happen anyway.'

'Yes,' I admitted, 'it probably would. I don't think telling the police would do much good in terms of finding out who killed your brother. Even if it was his wife and her lover.'

'So, what, we just leave it?'

'I'll see what I can come up with,' I said. 'If I do find anything more concrete, then we'll give it to the police. In the meantime, we can spare a few blushes.'

Sir Peter seemed relieved, either at retaining the services of yours truly or avoiding further conversations with the police. I asked him if he liked his sister-in-law and he said that yes, actually, he did. He said he would find it very difficult to believe that Charlotte had anything to do with Edward's death.

I handed Sir Peter a copy of the picture, knowing that Andy Gold had already shown it to him, and that he hadn't been able to tell him anything. Sir Peter gazed at the picture ruefully and then put it down on his desk, with a look which said that finding the man in it wouldn't actually do much for him. He wanted the man caught but it wouldn't make him happier. He sucked on his teeth, picked the photograph up again, and slid it into a drawer.

I stood up and shook Sir Peter's hand. As he walked me across his office I had a thought and I stopped at the door.

'What's Graham Lloyd like, by the way?' I asked.

Sir Peter stood holding the door handle and he looked me straight in the eye. His expression was measured and still, that very strange mixture of the deadly serious, and a wry smile, which I have only ever seen on upper-class Englishmen.

'Oh, Graham's a bastard,' Sir Peter said.

On the way back to my car I remembered that I wanted to speak to the barman at the airport so I stopped at a phone box. I called the number and a harassed woman told me that Alex hadn't come in today and no she didn't know when he would be there because he hadn't phoned her to tell her he wasn't coming, which was most unlike him and was that all because she had a bar full of customers? I smiled at the thought of the assistant manager with her polished nails cranking out cappuccinos and swearing under her breath at her errant subordinate. Thank you, I told her, that's all. It wasn't really that important. I hung up and walked around the corner to my car, beating a traffic warden to it by seconds.

Charlotte Morgan hadn't gone back to work that day. She might have nipped out after I'd seen her because she was no longer in her dressing gown when I got to the flat on Leinster Mews that she had either rented or was borrowing and she opened the door to me. As well as the clothes I had seen her in earlier she wore a look of not very pleasant surprise.

'Yes?' she said. 'What do you want?'

'To talk a little more,' I replied quietly.

'How did you get my address?' she demanded, one hand going to her hip.

'I followed you here.'

'What?'

'Earlier. I followed you here.'

I let Charlotte Morgan think about that for a second. Then I held up a roll of film. 'Now,' I said, 'are you going to let me in or should I just take this straight round to my friend Giles at the *News of the World*?'

She looked at me with horror, and at the small plastic case in my hand. I could almost see the pieces falling together in her mind and I tapped my feet until they were all in place. After a second or two Charlotte Morgan bit her bottom lip, took a step backward and opened the door.

It was a very nice place. Far too polished and expensively cluttered for my taste but then I'm the sort of person who never could see the point of buying over-priced generic articles from the Conran Shop that you don't exactly need. Charlotte Morgan, quite obviously, could see the point of that.

She was sat stiffly on the edge of a small Chesterfield while I had turned a high-backed French dining chair around and was straddling that facing her. She looked defensive, tense like a cornered cat. I looked at her and a rush of contempt filled me as I saw Lloyd again, kissing her the way he had. I calmed it down with the knowledge that I didn't have all the facts yet. I handed her the role of film which she took hesitantly, surprised to be given it.

'I'm not a sleaze hunter,' I told her. 'I want to find out

who killed your husband. I'm not going to tell anyone about the affair that you're having unless I think that it reflects upon that. The only way I can assess that is if you tell me about it. All about it. If you refuse then I'll assume you're hiding something and I'll go to the police. Do you understand?'

'Yes,' she said eventually.

'And if I go to the police, which believe me I should, then the newspapers are sure to get on to it. So. Once again, did you enjoy a happy sex life with your husband?'

She paused for a second until I let out a sigh of irritation.

'No,' she said, looking down at her lap.

'And you didn't tell anyone this because you didn't want people looking into your private life?'

'I suppose. We hadn't made love for some time but I couldn't see how that fact was in any way relevant to my husband's murder.'

'All right. Why weren't you and your husband making love?'

She looked up again. 'Because I didn't want to. It wasn't really a big thing for me. I still loved Edward. I think that I realized that it had never really been a sex thing for me. Edward was just such a lovely person so I said yes when he asked me to marry him.'

'When did you realize this?'

'Oh,' she said, and hesitated. 'When . . . when I met . . .'

'When you met Graham Lloyd.'

Mrs Morgan's mouth opened in surprise.

'Did you tell Edward about him?'

'No,' she said quickly. 'I mean, I was going to. Graham and I were both going to. He was going to tell his wife and we were going to divorce and get married. If you know what I mean. We still are.'

'Yes?'

'Yes. But it's difficult now. Graham, he doesn't need this kind of publicity, Christ knows what people might think. And Edward, he hasn't been dead long, I mean, it wouldn't be right, I . . .'

Mrs Morgan stopped speaking and began to cry. She put her head in her hands very neatly and cried quietly for a long time. She cried like she was doing something, a chore perhaps, which she had to get over before she could talk to me again. I watched her crying, the top of her head moving ever so slightly, and the animosity between us seemed to dissolve into the air. I felt sorry for her. When she stopped it was very suddenly and she sat up straight like she had before, and smiled a smile which said I'm drowning but I don't much care, and I'll do what I can before I disappear. I returned her smile and looked her in the eye.

'How did he take it? Edward? This lack of desire for him?'

'I don't really know,' she replied, thinking about it and pushing aside the remnants of a tear. 'He never said anything. Everything else between us seemed so normal. It seemed normal for me to be with Edward and living and sleeping next to him, but making love to another man. It wasn't like I didn't want to be with him, but my sex was somewhere else. This didn't seem too strange because it had never really been there with him.'

I nodded.

'But did he try to have sex with you?'

'A few times. He held me in that way, you know? In bed? But I didn't respond and he never pressed me.'

'Did he have a strong sex drive? For you?'

'I don't know. I kept thinking about that when everyone asked me if I thought he was gay. He certainly wanted to make love to me often enough but it was never like . . .' Charlotte took a breath. 'It was never like fucking. Not just that. It was more of a way to be together and communicate our affection.' She turned to the side, thinking of something, and I thought she was going to cry again.

'What is it?' I asked.

'I don't know. I still loved him. All that I ever had. But I didn't tell him, and I didn't show him, because the way that I had shown him before suddenly meant something different to me. I didn't want to fuck him. I never had and I couldn't. I wanted to find some other way to show him but it was too late then, it was too late because he was . . . He probably died thinking I didn't love him.'

Mrs Morgan looked down at her lap, where her rust-coloured fingernails were picking at the gold ring on her left hand. Her voice became small and hopeless.

'That's all I can think about,' she said. 'That's the only thing I can think about, that and what it must have been like for Teddy. When . . .'

Mrs Morgan tried very hard to stop them but her words broke up into sobs again. She pressed her fists into her face and her elbows into her sides to stop her grief shaking its way out of her. The sound she made wasn't loud, but the pain coming out of her seared the air like something tearing apart along a seam which didn't exist. I had never seen anyone cry from such a central place as Charlotte Morgan was crying. I saw my hand move up from my knee towards her, and I watched it hover for a second above the Alice band which held her hair in place.

I drew it back towards me and let it rest on the top of the chair.

I watched Charlotte Morgan crying for a long time, and I knew that I had a lot of questions that I should ask her. About Graham Lloyd. And jealousy. And her finances. And about what Edward would have done had she told him. And had she actually told him already. I knew that I should wait until she had finished her crying and ask her these things. That is what Andy Gold would have done and he would have been right to. This woman had lied to the police, she was a recently bereaved widow who, it transpired, had a secret lover. Andy would have waited and that is what I would have done too, if I was still bound by an oath which said I had to be dispassionate and clinical while exercising my duties in the pay of the public and in the public's interest.

Instead I stood up, set the chair gently aside and walked through the kitchen, and then out on to the street, with the sound of Charlotte Morgan's bewildered grief following me like a lost bird. I turned and closed the door quietly.

Chapter Nine

I drove home and changed into jeans and a work jacket which I bought years ago but which now makes me look fashionable, especially since it's faded to cream from a dark brown. As I dressed I thought about Charlotte and her lover as possibles for Edward Morgan's murder. I saw the way Charlotte had held on to Lloyd outside her cottage. I didn't let Charlotte's tears put me off; they were genuine but that didn't mean anything. Grief can be huge, but when it's joined by remorse it gets even bigger.

I pulled my boots on and checked the medicine cabinet for Advil. None. I put my camera into a bag and went downstairs to the chemist to get some.

The chemist was actually a pharmacy and one day someone will tell me what the difference is. Like optician and optometrist. Alberto saw me coming out of the pharmacy and walked out of Fred's towards me. We said hello and then he told me that someone had been asking after me.

'A young kid,' Alberto said. 'He asked if Billy Rucker ever came in here.'

'What did he look like?' I asked, thinking it might have been Dominic Lewes come to tell me to leave him alone.

'Oh,' Alberto said, 'he was black, only about fourteen.

All nerves and attitude. Said he needed to see you. I told him to call you but he said he had.'

'Well, I dare say he'll catch up with me. Thanks though, Alberto.'

'Hey,' he shrugged, 'it's nothing.'

He lit up a cigarette and I left him and walked to the car.

Another dirty table and another coffee that was surprisingly good in the café at the bottom of Calshot Street. This time it was daytime though and I was determined not to miss Dominic Lewes again. I wanted to get him out of the way so I could concentrate on Edward Morgan. I bought a copy of the *Standard* and read the back pages, my mind drifting away to gay MPs and their murdered brothers, young boys lying dead in damp basements and a woman who was tied up in intricate knots of pure misery, knots she may have tied for herself. And how unlikely it was that I'd be able to do anything about any of it. I was glad I had Dominic; something simple and easy to occupy me, nothing to do but wait and watch, and press a button.

Dominic walked up after forty minutes and stood on the other side of the street joining another lad of about the same age. I framed him and got full body shots and then close-ups of his face. He was wearing his MA1 and he looked cold, the zip right up to his chin. He leant against the window of a derelict kebab shop and then sat down on the window ledge and rubbed his hands together, before taking out a pack of cigarettes and lighting one. It seemed ironic that he was still too young to smoke. What would his mother say? I left one pound fifty on the table for the waitress who was looking my way but not indicating that she had any plans to come to the table.

Dominic didn't see me as I walked past King's Cross station and crossed the road up by St Pancras. I cut back down towards him and turned right into his road where my car was parked again. I put the bag in the boot, hoping that my camera would be safe in there for a few minutes. For some reason though, I had the feeling, which I get once in a while, that someone was watching me. I'd go back in half an hour and find either no Mazda, or a Mazda with no contents of any value inside and a broken quarter-light. I looked around, up and down the street. I didn't see anyone but the feeling wouldn't go away. I knew I was being irrational, that boots seldom got broken into in broad daylight, but I couldn't help it. I turned the key in the lock again, took out my bag and slung it back over my shoulder. I walked down the street towards the Cross, glancing over my shoulder once or twice, feeling like an idiot.

'Have you got the time, mate?'

I'd stopped in front of Dominic Lewes and the other lad. I was speaking to Dominic.

'Yeah,' Dominic replied, pushing up the sleeve of his jacket. 'It's ten to six.' He showed me his watch at the same time as telling me what the time was and I wondered why people did that. Did he think I wouldn't believe him?

'Thanks,' I said, turning to go. But then I stopped. 'Hey. Haven't I met you before?'

Dominic put both hands on the windowsill beneath

him and looked at me, squinting for a second. I could tell he thought he recognized me. He shook his head.

'I don't think so, mate.'

'Yes, we have.' I put my bag down on the pavement. 'It was right here!' I sounded pleased with myself for remembering. 'I bought you a sandwich, you didn't have any money, remember?'

'I'm not sure, mate, maybe.' Dominic laughed.

'It was a while ago. I'm really good with faces, though I can't even remember names the next day.' I smiled.

'It's Mikey.'

'Yeah, that's it.' I pointed at him and shook my head. 'You look different but I don't know why.'

At this point a car drew up and the other boy walked over to it and got in without saying anything to the driver. The driver was looking the other way as if nothing was happening. A regular. The car – a big, shapeless Ford saloon – drew off and headed up the Pentonville Road towards the Angel.

Dominic looked me in the eyes and stood up from the ledge. His lips pursed very slightly. He opened his mouth and his tongue ran over his teeth, as he took a small step towards me.

'I'll suck you for twenty,' he told me.

'God,' I said laughing, 'no. Thanks. No. But I'll buy you a sandwich and a cup of tea if you like, if you're hungry?'

'That's all right, mate.' Dominic paused. 'No johnny. Just my mouth and your cock.'

Dominic's eyes ran over my body and he stood even closer to me.

'No, no. Really.' I took a step back. 'Thanks all the same. But what about that tea, hey? You look freezing.'

I rubbed my hands together briskly. I wanted

Dominic to come with me because I wanted to persuade him to call his mother. I had last time and he'd done it, and she'd told me what it meant to her. He didn't bother answering me this time though, he just turned his head to the side and sucked his cheeks in, letting out a mocking hmm as he did so. The conversation was over. He obviously didn't need cups of tea any more, he was in control of his life now. He kept staring towards King's Cross as though something incredible had just captured his attention, thereby telling me to get lost. Oh well, I thought, I've got the pictures. I looked at the side of Dominic's face and neck and at his cropped hair, the colour of vanilla ice cream on a summer holiday.

'Your roots need doing,' I told him, picking up my bag. Then, 'Call your mother.'

Dominic's face changed for a second but he still didn't look at me. I moved off.

I had been walking away from my car when I stopped to talk to Dominic, and I kept on going that way so as not to make him think I was looking for him. I was a little pissed off. I'd done my job and would get my money, but I hadn't done everything I could have. I knew what a phone call would mean to Mrs Lewes. Maybe Bob Hoskins wasn't such a prick after all.

There was an alley on the right which I could duck down, saving me from walking all the way round the block to my car. I turned into it, stepping over a comatose drunk with an empty bottle of Imperial sherry clasped to his chest like a baby. It was beginning to get dark now and the high walls either side of me intensified the gloom, as though a dimmer switch had been turned down a notch. I walked up the alley, inhaling a wave of stale piss, kicking aside a couple of old needles and an uneaten chocolate bar. In huge red letters on the wall somebody had spray painted the words 'FUCK PIGS'. I had a sudden image of a disaffected youth committing bestiality with a Gloucester Old Spot. I smiled to myself and stuck my hands into my coat pockets.

The man stepped out in front of me when I was about five yards from the end of the alley, and he blocked the exit. He stood with his arms folded and one leg pointing further forward than the other. He looked straight at me with his head thrown back, dressed in biker boots, black Levis, a tight T-shirt and an expensive blazer jacket. One roll-up on the sleeves. He looked at me with a disgusted menace, and when I checked my stride and stopped he took a step forward. I recognized him immediately; I really am good with faces. He was the guy who came to the door on Elm Drive when I'd gone looking for Dominic.

'Who the fuck are you?'

He had unfolded his arms and was standing square in front of me. His voice was big, and it echoed off the alley walls with a metallic sound. I took my hands out of my pockets. I let my bag slide down my arm on to the ground beside me, keeping hold of the strap.

'I said, who the fuck are *you*?'

He was angry but in control. Confident. I could tell immediately that trying to bullshit this man wouldn't get me very far. So I didn't try. I didn't say anything.

'What you been taking pictures of my boys for? Why you been coming round? What you want?'

His boys.

'I'm talking to you, tosser.' A long finger stretched out towards me. 'If you're the Bill you're dead.'

'If I'm the Bill,' I replied quietly, 'you're nicked.'

He didn't like that.

'Gimme your bag. Now. Give it here.' He snapped his fingers.

I let go of the strap, keeping the bag behind me.

'Listen,' I said, fanning out my hands, taking a couple of small steps forward. 'I don't want any trouble. I'm just working for someone who wants to know that their son is still alive, that's all.' I tried a smile.

'You deaf, tosser? Are you? Well? I *said* . . .'

I hit him with a straight right arm with a lot of shoulder behind it. Unfortunately he saw it; late but he saw it. He'd begun to twist left, taking a lot of the weight out but it still sent him spinning against the wall. Before I could hit him again he came out and charged at me, grabbing my lapels, but I managed to use his weight to take him past me and into the other wall. He still had my lapels and he butted me hard below my left ear, holding on tight to me. It hurt.

I couldn't get an arm free to hit him so I rammed him hard up against the brickwork. And again. He was shaken and I did manage to get a hand free, but he lunged out at me with all that he had before I could swing at him. We both went sprawling, landing on the wet concrete side by side. We struggled, trying to get on top of each other. I heard fabric tearing. I thought that, even if he wins this fight, my opponent was going to have to lose another four hundred quid in Emporium. I managed to wedge my foot against a wall and, pushing hard, I got on top of him. His arms went up to my neck but I ignored them. I held him by his jacket and his T-shirt and I belted the shit out him, right after right after right, until his arms were on the floor beside him. I heard his nose break. I felt his top front teeth bite into my knuckles as they broke up and snapped out of the bone. I saw his eyes change their focus, from me, to his own pain, and then to something I couldn't know.

When the man wasn't moving any more and his head got heavy I stopped hitting him. I let him drop down to the floor. I pushed myself up from the ground and got to my feet, breathing hard, steadying myself against a head spin. Dominic's pimp was lying back, almost conscious. I waited, getting my breath back. His focus returned and he lay there looking at me. Blinking. His neck and T-shirt were soaked in blood and I saw that the ripping sound I heard had been the top pocket of his jacket; it was hanging on by a couple of threads. I took a breath. Then, for some reason, I leant over to pull the pocket off. Just as I reached it his hand went up to stop me and he winced. I held the limp piece of fabric in my hands. He looked devastated. I hadn't had to fight this guy at all, I should have just grabbed hold of his pocket and threatened to rip it off if he didn't get out of my way.

I pulled the pocket off and stood over the guy looking down at him. I wanted to say something to him, something cool and final. But I couldn't think of anything. Instead, something he had said to me came into my head. *My boys.*

I looked up the alley towards where Dominic was standing and I thought I saw another figure getting into a car. Another kid whose home had not been a home, who had come to find somewhere else to belong and had ended up belonging to this man here. A kid whose life was made up of so much shit that if you took it away from him he'd be lost, he wouldn't know what the fuck was going on.

'*My* boys.'

The pimp didn't move anything except his eyelids, which fluttered like two half-dead moths pinned to a board. I took a step back. I steadied myself. I looked into his soft brown eyes for a second and the fluttering stopped as he met my gaze. An appeal burst into his eyes like hold-up men in a bank, but I ignored it. Then I repeatedly kicked the man with all those boys as hard as I could in the groin until his soft eyes clouded over and he blacked out.

I stepped over the wino again. He was still smooching with the angels. I hitched my bag up over my shoulder and walked out on to the Pentonville Road. Night had fallen quickly and it was almost dark now. Dominic was gone. I felt cold all of a sudden and I shivered. I crossed the road and walked back into the café. The waitress who had served me the last two times I had been there and had seen me with my camera, looked shocked to see me. She stepped back against the counter, holding her hands by her sides. It said it all. It wasn't the blood on my face that she was surprised to see. It was me. Standing up. I threw the liberated pocket on to the counter.

'Your boyfriend'll want this,' I said to her. 'He'll need his jacket stitching.' The girl looked across at it and then quickly back at me. She narrowed her eyes. 'Come to think of it,' I added, 'he might need his face stitching too.' The girl's mouth opened into a small Oh, and her eyes widened, but she didn't say anything.

Chapter Ten

I fell asleep in the bath. I woke up when the water was cold and I got that feeling again, which I used to get when I was a child, of not knowing where I was. The eerie silence that seemed to hover in the air of my flat was not dispersed by the fact that I could actually hear things; the lazy rumble of traffic and a child crying somewhere for its mother. I lay in the water for a few minutes, getting colder and colder, staring at the toilet chain which seemed unnaturally still. I was still too, my body lying inert beneath the now grey water covering it like a shroud. I stood up, glad to break the still surface, glad of the noise the water made running off me and back into the bath. I leant across to the radiator for a towel.

It was my gym night but I decided that I had fulfilled my pugilistic requirements for the day. I turned the thermostat up and the answerphone on, and I lay on my sofa with a glass of John Powers on the floor beside me, which I immediately forgot about. I tried to go over what I knew about my case but I couldn't push the image of Dominic's pimp out of my mind. Thinking about what I'd done to him, my bones felt hollow; whatever he was there was no excuse for it. He could have been dead for all I knew. I wondered what it was that made me lose it the way I had. I kept hearing the words *my boys* over and over and then I made the connection. It was what my father had called Luke and me. *My boys* are useless. *My boys* are lazy. *My boys* are ungrateful.

No one tells me how I should treat *my boys.*

I was restless but I wasn't in the mood to do the rounds with the photo and there wasn't anything else of any use I could do until tomorrow. I thought about looking at Luke's poems but it had been a taxing day and I didn't think I could do justice to them. Instead I used the remote for my stereo to tune in to a match on 5-Live which was just entering the second half. It was Birmingham against Luton, two sides I don't have the slightest interest in, but I listened to it gladly, and to the post-match interviews. I switched to *The World Tonight* on Radio 4 and heard some politicians pretending to be stand-up comedians in, I supposed, an effort to hide the fact that they didn't have an awful lot to say. At about ten-thirty there was a click from my machine but no message followed as I had turned the volume to nil.

I turned the radio off and the TV on, sitting all the way through a film in which Keanu Reeves made great strides with his surfing technique, helped hold up banks and jumped out of aeroplanes without the reassurance of a parachute. It seemed that old Keanu had his days all filled up too. At about twelve-thirty I went to bed and tried to sleep but there were too many gatecrashers in my head making too much noise, so I took one of the Seconals that I'd asked a friend of mine to send over from New York where she was working. The Seconal felt like a spider spinning silk around my body, tighter and tighter until finally I was paralysed. When I was bound so tight, but so softly, that I couldn't move at all, the spider finished with her thread and bent down slowly to bite into me. Her poison was languorous and calming, and as her shadow covered me and blocked out the light completely I disappeared.

I woke up at eleven feeling empty and strangely removed after my flat, artificial sleep. I lay in bed for ten minutes looking calmly at the events of yesterday, from my conversations with Morgan and Charlotte to the face the waitress made when she realized what I'd done to her boyfriend. Yesterday seemed a long way away, and the faces I had seen there unreal, as if they were an implanted memory of a time I hadn't actually lived. I sat up against the wall and took a hold of myself, deciding not to take any more of those rhino pills before I went to bed. I ran through what I had to do today. Then I pushed aside the curtains to see that the day was a dull cold grey with no shadows anywhere. I got up and lumbered across the room to the telephone.

The message on the machine was from a certain Graham Lloyd. He must have tried my office last night and then looked me up in the phone book when he hadn't got me there. There was another message on from him as well, left, so the machine informed me, at 7.49 a.m. precisely. My, I thought, as I signally failed to phone him back with the urgency he requested, aren't we in a bit of a hurry today?

I had coffee and half a slice of toast and then called my office to get the messages off the work machine. Graham Lloyd had indeed left me a message at my office, not sounding quite so impatient as he had tried to reach me there first. There was also a message from Mrs Lewes asking if I'd got any news about Dominic. She asked me not to phone her, saying that she'd try me again. The final message was from Andy Gold, saying it was nothing urgent but that maybe he ought to come over and thrash out some ideas. I was surprised that he was giving any credence at all to any other theories than the one he was pursuing; gay slasher strikes again. It all seemed a lot to deal with. I thought I'd leave Andy to get in touch if he wanted to, and the MP could stew for a little while longer.

Not much longer. I was heading towards the shower when the phone rang. I picked it up with a pretty good idea who'd be on the other end. I was right.

'Rucker? Is that Rucker?'

My second ever phone conversation with a Tory MP. This was a pit bull in a Montessori Centre too but there was no leash anywhere.

'William Rucker speaking,' I said.

'Rucker. I don't know who the hell you are, but . . .' I cut him off.

'Can you hold, please.'

I put the phone down without waiting for his reply and opened my pocket diary. I'd arranged to meet Sharon later and I couldn't remember the exact time, whether it was half-six for some food before the show, or seven-thirty and we'd get something after. It was half-six. I leant over the table and picked up the phone again.

'Now then. Who do I have the pleasure of addressing?'

'Rucker,' the MP began again, 'you know damn well who this is. Now—'

'I'm sorry,' I said cutting him off again. I ran a hand over my head and tried to shake off the weary feeling I still had in spite of two cups of coffee. 'I'm sorry, but before we continue this conversation, can I ask you a question? Do you recall ever watching Ilie Nastase play tennis at all?'

That got him.

'Well, if you do,' I continued, 'you might remember him reminding an umpire to call him Mr Nastase. Not Nastase. *Mr* Nastase. It's the same for private detectives, I'm afraid.' I yawned.

'Look here—'

'No, Mr Lloyd, for I presume you are he. I will not look there. You call me, you want to speak to me. Far more, I imagine, than I want to speak to you. So I am William to restaurant owners, Billy to my friends and a firm Mr Rucker to you. Got it?'

'Don't you get—'

'I said got it, *lover boy?*'

There was a silence on the other end of the line which had the strange effect of waking me up a lot. Then, as if the first part of our conversation had never happened, Lloyd said, quite calmly, 'Mr Rucker. I think we should meet. Come to my office. No, on second thoughts don't come anywhere near my office. I'll meet you for lunch. Do you know The Flag on Carlisle Street?'

'No,' I said. 'Nor will I be there for lunch. I will, however, be sitting in The Colt on Stroud Green Road at exactly five p.m. If you'd like to join me.'

'I can't. Not at that time. Be in—'

'Fine,' I said. I tucked the receiver under my chin and took another swig of the now lukewarm coffee. 'In that case give my regards to a certain Andrew Gold when you see him. He's a police officer. He'll call on you at about six o'clock with a couple of boys in blue in tow if I'm not sitting in The Colt on Stroud Green Road at five, looking across a table at you with a G and T in your hand. All right?'

I put the receiver down and strolled into the bathroom, feeling the engines beginning to kick in now. There's nothing like being rude to someone in power when the caffeine isn't working. The phone went almost immediately but I let it ring and pulled aside the shower curtain. While I was getting drenched I wondered if all MPs had a secretary. If they did I felt sorry for Lloyd's; she probably wasn't having a very nice day today.

I walked down to the repro shop and gave Carl the film I'd shot of Dominic Lewes. Carl looked exhausted, like he'd been down in the lab all night. I felt some sympathy for him and told him that the pictures weren't that urgent and that he could take his time over them if he had to. He looked up quickly from the chit he was filling in.

'Who are you?' he said aghast. 'What have you done with the real Billy Rucker!'

After that I drove over to my office and sat behind my desk with Kojak and a bacon roll. I thought about Lloyd. I tried to work a scenario in which he could be placed. He wasn't the man in the picture but he could have hired him. I wondered if Edward had found out about the affair and had refused a divorce. Would that make Lloyd want to kill him? No, not these days, not unless Lloyd was really, *really* jealous and couldn't bear to think of Charlotte with Edward a second longer. Later on I'd meet Lloyd and maybe find out what kind of person he was.

I looked at the file and picked up the phone but was once again informed that Alex hadn't shown up for his shift that day and had not rung in with an excuse. The manager's voice was tight as a tripwire and I could hear a very persistent American woman in the background saying, 'Excuse me! Excuse me!' The manager put the phone down abruptly, without any goodbye. I couldn't really blame her.

I flicked over a few more pages until I found the statement given by Edward Morgan's co-pilot. I read how Michael James Chalkley had known Edward Morgan for two years and had often flown with him. He said he had no idea that Edward was gay. Chalkley himself was married with three young children, and had witnesses who saw him say goodbye to Edward shortly after exiting customs. One of the stewardesses also saw him get into his Saab in the car park and was then stuck behind him in traffic on the motorway, driving into London.

Originally I had decided that I wasn't going to bother with Chalkley. I didn't think for a minute that he was involved, and I couldn't imagine what I could get out of him beyond the report he gave Andy. I'd changed my mind though, because I wanted to know what sort of mood Edward was in before he was killed. If, for instance, he was miserable because he either suspected or knew for sure that Charlotte was seeing another man. I called the number Chalkley had listed, expecting a wife or a message but I got the man himself. He was in all day and yes he was happy to talk to me that afternoon if I wanted. I said that I definitely did and asked him what time would suit him. He said whenever; he was on guard duty and he wasn't going out. The screams of what sounded like a whole classroom of kids in the background told me what he meant by that.

I was glad I could get Chalkley out of the way today. I'd thought of hitting some gay bars with the pictures I had but there wasn't that much time before I had to meet Lloyd and it would be better if I had a clear time ahead to do that. Doing the rounds was still the most likely way that the guy was going to be caught, but often, when you're showing a picture round, someone will say 'Sure, he comes in here' and you have to wait until the place shuts to see if he does or not. You can't leave a message for the person to wait for you until you've finished some other business.

I copied down Chalkley's address in my diary and stood up to go. Before I could get to the door, however, it opened.

'Don't you ever bloody knock?' I asked.

'Only when I'm arresting someone,' Andy Gold said. 'And then, very very loudly.'

I sat back down and Andy must have telepathically heard me offer him a seat because he sat down too.

'Well,' he said, 'what you got?'

I told Andy that I didn't have anything more than he did.

'Nothing?' he asked, opening one eye wider than the other, not sounding like he entirely believed me. 'Not a sausage?'

'Not even a chipolata, mate.'

Andy didn't have much to give me either. He and his team had shown the picture round to everyone they'd interviewed before and no one had been able to tell them anything.

'I saw the widow,' he said, folding his arms. 'Not bad, not bad at all. Most blokes would have been more than content poking that every night, don't you think?'

I shrugged.

'If they were straight. Very nervous though, when I saw her. More so than before.'

'Probably the picture,' I said.

'Maybe. You'd already shown her it though, hadn't you?'

'Yes.'

'Funny thing,' Andy said, pretending to think. 'She never mentioned that you'd been to see her.' He folded his arms and sat back a little. 'It was me who brought it up, right at the end.'

'So?'

'So nothing. Just a little odd, that's all. Wouldn't you say? It was only a couple of hours after you spoke to her. I thought she might have said something.'

'Instantly forgettable,' I explained, 'that's me. Always been my problem that has.' Andy made a hmm sound but I didn't let him pursue it. I told him that if there wasn't anything very pressing then I had to go out. I stood up and he followed me out of my office into the corridor.

Michael Chalkley lived in a smallish terraced house in a back street two minutes away from the B-movie alien spacecraft which is Southgate tube station. He opened the door to me and led me into a small sitting room which had no carpet, and was crowded with yellow packing crates.

'We're moving,' he told me. 'Tomorrow. You were lucky to catch me.' He made some space on a sofa, and invited me to sit down.

Chalkley was a pleasant-looking man in his early forties. He had an elongated, rather sad face and had long since finished balding on top. Three toddlers, two of which I could see were twins, clung to his legs like vines and he had perfected that most impressive of feats: splitting his consciousness in two. He was paying a great deal of attention to me, as well as noting and responding to his kids' every movement and mood swing. He took his harassment, both from the kids and from myself, with an admirably stoic equanimity.

'The twins,' Chalkley explained, indicating the packing cases. 'We need a bigger place. And I want to be closer to the airport. Marion's mother doesn't want us to go, she lives round the corner, but we've decided.' He pulled the eldest child, a girl of four, on to his lap.

'Where are you off to?' I asked, suppressing a yawn. I felt slightly nauseous and detached from myself.

'Hayward's Heath,' he said. 'I've been transferred to Gatwick. I made pilot last month.'

I must have reacted to this remark because Chalkley smiled.

'It was fixed a long time before Edward was killed,' he said. 'Anyway, I don't think it works like that. You can't murder your way up the BA ladder as far as I'm aware, although it wouldn't surprise me to find out that some of our executives had done it that way. No, I've been on all the courses, this has been fixed for some time.'

I asked Chalkley what kind of man Edward was. He told me that he had really liked him, that Edward was kind and always very appreciative of those working under him.

'Some pilots can be arrogant,' he said, 'especially those who've been in the forces. Edward wasn't. The flight attendants got on with him especially well. A lot of them were very upset by what happened to him. One of the men, Jeff Downs, is gay and he felt very bad. He told me that he often went to that bar after work. He would have gone there that night but he had a date in town.'

While Chalkley sorted out the odd argument, filled some beakers with apple juice and performed minor first aid, he told me that he hadn't thought Edward was gay and was surprised to find out that he was. It didn't make him think any less of him.

'What about that last trip?' I asked. 'What mood was he in?'

'He was quite subdued,' Chalkley said, nodding slightly. 'As if there was something on his mind.'

I pictured Edward, brooding about his wife.

'He seemed better on the flight back though, and he seemed quite cheerful when I left him, although, thinking about it, there might have been something forced about it. I wanted to get home otherwise I might have gone for a quick drink with him. We often did that before braving the traffic.'

'So I understand.'

'Yes. I wish I had.' Chalkley let out a breath. 'I hardly need to say that I very much wish I had gone for a drink with him that night.'

That was all I wanted to know really, although I lingered a little while with Chalkley, asking questions I already knew the answer to or which I didn't really need answering. I accepted the coffee he offered me, and played with his kids while he made it. His eldest, Natasha, was very bright, and as pretty a child as you could imagine. We drank our coffees and then Chalkley showed me to the door. As I thanked him for his time I thought about the 'if onlys' which feature in almost every case I have ever dealt with. The 'if onlys' which haunt those who are left when someone is killed. I shook Chalkley's hand.

'Out of curiosity,' I said, 'and if it's OK to ask, why didn't you stick around for a drink with Edward that night?'

'Oh, the flight was late in. Head winds over Biscay. I wanted to get back.'

'I see. How late were you?'

'Half an hour,' he said. 'Forty minutes maybe.'

'Right. Right.'

I left Chalkley on his doorstep and walked up the garden path. I turned to shut the gate and then waved back at Natasha, who had climbed up on to the windowsill in the living room.

Lloyd lit a cigarette, blew the smoke across the table at me and took a sip from his orange juice. I'd told him it had to be a gin and tonic but I was willing to overlook the point. If I had thought more carefully when I was trying to find out who he was from the security guard at the House of Commons, I wouldn't have asked if he was John Major. He didn't look much like him. It would have been a lot more credible to have pegged him for the current Chancellor, Gordon Brown. He had a squarish, set face, full dark hair, and a head which seemed slightly too large for his body. His eyes were as dark as his suit and his teeth were as bright as the crisp white shirt which seemed a little tight round his neck. He put his lighter down beside his glass and looked at me.

'Right,' he said. 'What can I do for you?'

I'd left Michael Chalkley and driven down to see Joe Nineteen to give him a finder's fee I owed him from the week before. Joe is a West Indian former bus conductor of a very advanced though indeterminate age, who lives by the bus station at Finsbury Park. Joe often uses his connections on the London bus network to spot missing kids for me, and when he does so I visit him, which is always a pleasure, and give him an amount of money commensurate with how difficult it was for his contacts to locate a particular fugitive. He lives on his own, sitting on a stool outside his front door in any weather but rain, and he always has a pot of goat curry on his stove. Always. It's all he ever eats, and if I could make it as well as he can it would be all I ever ate too.

After a small bowlful of the stuff, I bought a copy of the *Standard* and walked up Stroud Green Road. I sat in a corner of The Colt on red velveteen and flicked through the paper keeping an eye on the door. Then I took out the picture and did a few sums. The security video had a digital clock on it. The plane had been late in and the time on the photo was only thirty-five minutes after the plane had landed, which meant that Edward couldn't have been sitting at the bar for very long before he left. The barman had seemed to imply that Edward had been there longer but this didn't really mean anything. I was annoyed that I hadn't been able to get to him before the police had. If a lazy cop thinks he knows what happened in a situation it isn't difficult to get a witness to agree, especially when you're talking marginally different time scales. It meant, however, that if the man in the hat had picked Edward up, he was a pretty fast worker. Or that he knew him. He was his lover and had arranged to meet him there.

Graham Lloyd came in a few minutes after five and looked around, presumably for me. Since he didn't know what I looked like he wasn't going to see me until I wanted him to. I watched him walk up to the bar, buy his drink and take it to a small round table in the back of the large room. He sat down and immediately lit a cigarette, pulling on it impatiently. I wondered if I was looking at a killer, at a man who had paid for the murder of a colleague's brother and made it look like part of a series. Once again I saw the lascivious, teasing way he had kissed the dead man's wife. I wanted it to be him.

Lloyd dragged on his cigarette so hard he definitely had something on his mind. I let him finish it before going over and introducing myself.

I sat down opposite, he lit up another cigarette and blew smoke in my face.

'Is it money?' he asked me with a smile. His tone was friendly. 'Is that it? Think you can make a few quid out of me? Mmm? Well, you're wrong, I'm afraid.'

I sighed.

'And I wouldn't bother going to the press if I were you. Beside the fact that none of the Tory sheets'd touch it right now, you don't *have* anything.' His smile said he thought I was extremely dim. 'Very silly giving away the film like that. Very silly indeed.'

He sipped his orange juice. He reminded me of a headmaster I once had, who would tut at you and shake his head for ages before getting his strap out.

'I would just like to ask you a few questions,' I said.

'As for the police,' he continued, 'I happen to know the Boss. And I don't mean some paltry detective or even a Chief Inspector, I mean the Boss. I don't really think they're going to pick me up on the say-so of some failed cop who had a breakdown, do you?'

Lloyd seemed to be enjoying himself. He gave a short laugh, shook his head at my incompetence and took a last drag on his cigarette. There was a certain overconfidence in his gestures, ingrained, I suspected, by years of easing his way nicely through life. I hadn't heard anything which required a response.

'I've done my homework on you, *Mr* Rucker. I'm pleased to say that you don't have anything on me.'

'Then you don't have anything to worry about, do you?' I said. 'I'm surprised you even came.'

'I'm not worried. I simply came to tell you that if you suggest anywhere, *anywhere*, that I am having an affair with *anybody*, I will not only sue you but you might find problems getting your licence renewed. Is that clear?' He was a little more serious now.

'Yes,' I said quietly, matching his earlier smile. 'I think so. You're threatening me. Thank you for being so frank.' I moved the ashtray he was using towards him. 'However, let's not get carried away. If I tell the police about your affair with Charlotte Morgan, they will go and talk to her about it. She admitted it to me, she will to them. You will then be interviewed by certain police officers. The Queen could not prevent this; I know the officers. The crime desks of various papers will find out about this. They will know which case these officers are working on, and will be very interested in the fact that these officers are talking to you. They'll put two and two together and the answer will be one. Page one. Let me see now; "Whizzkid MP Quizzed in Gay Slasher Case". That sounds quite tasty, doesn't it?'

Lloyd was silent, biting his bottom lip. I thought I could detect a hint of grudging admiration in his eye. He shrugged. I finished my mineral water.

'As for my licence, do what you like. It's about time I got out of this racket anyway. I don't like the company.'

I stood up and walked over to the bar, giving him time to think about it. When I got back, this time with a ginger ale, he didn't look so relaxed.

'Now,' I said. 'I'm not going to the papers. Yet. Or the

police. Tell me where you were on the sixth of July, a Friday, in the evening.'

He had thought ahead. As I was speaking he took an electronic organizer from his jacket pocket. He pressed some buttons and then turned the tiny screen round to show me.

'As you can see, I was out of the country. On a fact-finding trip. Keeping some Home Office morons in order if you must know.'

'That's what it says there.'

'That is what it would say anywhere. Because it happens to be true.'

'All right,' I said.

I reached into my pocket and pulled out one of the pictures. I tossed it on to the table and watched Lloyd's face as he picked it up and glanced at it dismissively. His face told me that he had never seen the man before or was a natural liar. I didn't know which one was more likely.

'Who's this?' he said.

'You tell me.'

'I can't. I have no idea who this man is.' He put the picture down. I put my finger on it.

'He's the man who met your mistress's husband at Heathrow airport,' I said. 'And very probably stuck a broken bottle into him. Several times. Either because that's the sort of thing he enjoys, or someone paid him to.'

'Then you'd better get out there and find him, if that is what *you* are being paid to do, and stop wasting your time on me.' The veneer on his voice had now completely rubbed off. He leant forward and pointed his finger at my chest. 'I had nothing to do with this, and you don't have anything to suggest I do beyond what you thought you saw when, like the grubby little man you obviously are, you were spying on myself and the friend I was trying to comfort in a time of obvious distress for her.'

'You were being very thorough.'

'Watch it. I'll repeat what I told you just so you get it straight. It would be very foolish of you to involve me any further in this business. Very foolish indeed.'

Lloyd finished his spiel and then did something which I don't think he meant me to see. He glanced, very quickly at the door. The glance was barely perceptible but it was there. Then he focused on me, looking at me like he was the chief whip and I was a backbencher about to abstain. I sat for a second thinking about his little glance. Then I excused myself, saying I would be back in a second, and I walked into the back of the pub towards the toilet.

I walked down the narrow corridor but instead of turning left into the toilet I went straight on and pushed open a fire door leading out of the back of the pub. I was in a small yard with a circular drain in the middle and crates of empty bottles stacked against two walls. I shut the door behind me. I looked around. Unfortunately, the only way out was an alley leading up to Stroud Green Road. I didn't much want to take it but I had no choice. I walked up it and emerged on to the street as nonchalantly as I could, immediately crossing the road without turning my head. Once on the other side I stepped into a doorway and looked back over at the pub.

A heavily built man in a long, single-breasted blue coat was standing by the door of The Colt, seemingly immersed in the *Standard*. Maybe he was immersed in it. I thought about waiting for Lloyd, to see if the man said anything to him when he came out but realized that, whoever the man was, he wouldn't speak to the MP. I thought about waiting around until they both realized I was gone, and then tailing the man in the coat if he went anywhere. No good, he probably knew my car by now. Or he didn't know anything about me and was waiting for his wife to finish using the toilet. I didn't know what to do. I certainly didn't want this man tailing me, if that was his intention. I was going to meet Sharon and I didn't want her getting involved in anything. Making the decision, I stepped out of the doorway and walked back across the road.

'Have you got a light?' I asked the man, having tapped him on the shoulder. He had turned round and was looking at me impassively. Slowly, he nodded.

'Thanks,' I said.

The man reached into his coat pocket without taking his eyes off me. A thick moustache bristled above a mouth with no lips. He held up a Zippo, popped it open and struck it. I didn't move. I didn't produce a cigarette for him to light either. I don't smoke. After a second I made a small turn to the left.

'You see that car,' I said, pointing towards the Mazda parked on the other side of the road, twenty or so yards down towards Finsbury Park. 'It's mine.'

'Is it?'

'Yes,' I said, 'it is. And I'm going to get in it and drive it away now.'

The man stared.

'Are you?'

'Yes,' I said, 'I am.'

'So?'

'So nothing.' I smiled. 'Just thought I'd let you know, that's all.'

The man didn't say anything. I walked away from him and crossed the road, turning back to look at him. He kept his eyes on me and didn't move. He hadn't moved by the time I'd got the engine started either, or pulled away from the kerb. He could tell I was still watching him. I just made an amber light and as I pulled away I saw him in the wing mirror. He folded up his paper, stuck it under his arm and walked into the pub. I made another amber light at Finsbury Park, and headed up the Blackstock Road.

Chapter Eleven

As far as I could tell I wasn't tailed as I drove back to Clerkenwell. I went home, showered, and then met Sharon at The Falcon on Farringdon Road where we both had the grilled sardines. I still felt strange from the morning, and more than a little edgy from the afternoon, and I had to make a conscious effort to engage with Sharon and shake myself into the evening. I kept drifting in and out of the conversation like a hologram on half power. I couldn't help thinking about Lloyd, and as we ate I found myself wishing that I hadn't arranged to go out with Sharon that night. I always found it impossible to enjoy myself when I was in the middle of something important; I just wanted to get out and find something Lloyd wouldn't be able to smirk at. I told myself it was too late now and not to ruin Sharon's evening by being sullen with her.

We got to Sadler's Wells fifteen minutes early, bought a programme and had a quick drink at the bar. The flamenco show lasted two hours, during which I was able to pull out all the thoughts which were nagging at me and stretch them in different directions. There were a lot of directions but none was any easier to move the events along than any other. Lloyd. Was he rattled because he had something to hide, or just because he didn't want his political career to take a nosedive before it was more than ten feet off the ground? I didn't know. I thought about it and paid some attention to the show, and when it was finished Sharon and I walked over to the pub opposite. The Shakespeare, or something.

'Well?' Sharon asked, after she had set the drinks on the table and sat down beside me. I took a sip of whiskey.

'I can see why you wanted to see that,' I said.

'Oh,' she replied, smiling. 'Can you now?'

'Yes,' I said. 'You appreciate the beauty of space and movement.'

'I do?'

'Yes. Especially when enacted by a man wearing nothing but baby oil, and trousers so tight you are immediately made aware of a certain decision made by his parents soon after he was born.'

Sharon laughed. 'He's a dancer,' she said. She shrugged her shoulders, doing a good impression of one of those earnest women on the *Late Review*. 'It has to be easy to see his body. It's his medium of expression.'

'I don't think medium would be the word I'd use,' I said.

'He really was brilliant though,' Sharon said. 'Wasn't he?'

'Yes,' I said. 'He was. And just the man to have around when you've got problems with cockroaches.'

As we hunched over our little table, Sharon asked me how the case was coming. I thought of an angry MP and a man with a moustache.

'Developments,' I said.

'Really? That's great.'

'Developments which probably don't mean anything,' I was sorry to add.

Above the hubbub of a busy Friday night I told Sharon about Charlotte Morgan and Graham Lloyd, and about how I had met up with the MP. I didn't tell her about the man outside The Colt though; I didn't want her to worry about me. Or burst out laughing at my paranoia.

'Do you think Lloyd did it?' Sharon asked.

'I know he didn't,' I said. 'He told me that he was in America at the time it happened. I'm going to check that out but I don't think he'd have come up with it if it was an out and out lie.'

'Then he's in the clear?'

'No, I don't think so. He could have had it done. Paid someone.'

Sharon looked doubtful. 'Do you really think so? How would an MP know how to hire a hit man? How would he know where to go?'

I laughed, 'It's not as hard as you'd think. Or as expensive.'

'So he might have hired someone, and told them exactly how to do it, to make it look like those other ones?'

'Yes,' I said, 'he could have. I was very dubious about that when Morgan told me that's what *he* thought had happened. You see, the police don't release all the details. It would be too horrifying to read over the cornflakes. There are things which happened in Teddy's killing which also happened when the lorry driver and the schoolboy were killed, but which very few people would have known about.'

'Such as?'

'Well, the police told the press that a bottle had been used in each case, but they didn't tell them that, both times, it had been deliberately left inside the body. Thrust in so it would stay there. That happened the third time too which made me think it had to be the same man.'

'And doesn't it still have to be?'

'Probably,' I admitted. 'But a well-placed MP could find out about the details of a case if he wanted to.'

'Really?'

'If he pretended he wasn't looking, sure.' I had a thought. 'And if he knew someone high up in the Metropolitan Police then that would make it even easier.'

'OK,' Sharon said, 'he could have done it. Or paid someone to do it. But why would he? I mean, it is a bit extreme, isn't it?'

'More than a bit. But there are millions of reasons why people kill each other. In this case there's the obvious. Jealousy. He couldn't stand the fact that his mistress was sleeping with another man, even if that man was her husband.'

'Except she wasn't sleeping with him, was she? Not in the biblical sense.'

'No, but he wasn't to know that. And if he was an obsessive, a real whacko, he might have been compelled to have Teddy killed.'

'Sounds plausible. I mean that he should be a whacko.'

'Mmm. Not sure I buy it though. Charlotte told me they were both getting divorced. Divorce would be an easier way of keeping her away from her husband.'

'Yes, but we all know what middle-aged men say about divorces when they fancy someone.'

'Good point,' I said. 'But I'm still doubtful. Killers possessed by jealousy tend to do the job themselves, in fits of heightened rage which outweigh any rational sense. They don't plan it meticulously like that, getting someone else to do it in a specific way.'

'So why else would he kill him?' Sharon asked.

'The most obvious reason of all,' I said. 'Money. But I don't know anything about that yet. He might need money, or he could be as flush as the Duke of Westminster for all I know.'

'Please,' Sharon said, holding her hands out towards me. 'Don't get me on the subject of the Duke of Westminster.'

Sharon sat back in her chair and smiled.

'Teddy,' she said.

'What?'

'You called him Teddy.'

'That's what his brother knew him as,' I said.

'It sounded like you knew him. Like you cared about him.'

I thought about Teddy and I nodded. 'I do feel like I knew him. At least a little. It's strange. Speaking to his wife, his brother and his colleague, I've picked up things about him. I can tell what a good guy he was. That he had a sense of humour and was generous and thoughtful. And I see his face, every day. I have this picture of him smiling into the camera. I look at the picture and can almost see him talking to me. He looks very confident in it. Empowered, you might say. I can imagine going out for a drink with him, like his co-pilot used to do. Then I try and figure out who left him carved to pieces with his face smashed in and then rammed a broken champagne bottle in his guts.'

The pub shut, and the bar staff went from quite friendly to extremely objectionable in the space of just twenty minutes. Only in England. After the stools had been taken from under us I could just as well have called it a night but Sharon said she didn't want to go home yet and she asked me to take her to the Old Ludensian, Nicky's bar, where she had never been. I agreed without much enthusiasm and we walked down there. Friday night is never a good time to go; the place is full of suits with foghorn voices barging their way to the bar as though they're still on the floor of the Stock Exchange. Nicky was out and we couldn't find a seat and a bull-necked rugby type with a red face and his tie pulled open decided that it would be a good idea to spill half his pint down my jacket and not feel any need to apologize. Sharon told me not to do anything about it. I became irritable, and was just waiting for the next idiot to fuck me off. I should have realized that it just wasn't right for me to be out that night, and gone home. I was tired and I had too much to think about. But then Nicky came in and got us a table and flirted with Sharon so we had to stay. I compensated for my tiredness and my increasingly foul mood by drinking too much of my friend's vodka.

The upshot was that when Nicky went to help out the barmen, Sharon and I got into a fight. Sharon asked me if I'd read Luke's poems and when I said I hadn't had time she looked at me like a schoolteacher. She said she wanted to send all the poems to a publisher and the suggestion really shocked me. Automatically, I didn't like the idea. She'd gone through all his private papers to find them and now she wanted to spread his private thoughts out for all the world to see. I told her that I knew what would happen, that the papers would get into it, Luke being in a coma and all that, and then Esther fucking Rantzen would be on the phone. The whole idea was mawkish. The publishing companies would only want to do it for the publicity, not the poems, and anyway we didn't have Luke's consent.

'Maybe one day he'll do it himself,' I told her, 'but until then I just don't think we have the right.'

When I said this to her, Sharon just shook her head and looked away from me. I could tell that she had something which she wanted to say but whatever it was she thought better of it. She looked upset for a minute and it pissed me off that she should be like that just because she wasn't getting her way. I was reminded of the feelings I used to have for her, my distrust of her motives concerning my brother. I was suspicious of her again, of the way she seemed to take everything upon herself. She tried to persuade me again but I just said that I didn't like the idea. Sharon said I was being irrational, that Luke had always intended publishing a book, that it was one of his real ambitions. I didn't listen to her. If you can't understand why not, I said, then there's no use me telling you. We were on the verge of shouting at each other when Nicky came back and the subject was changed. Sharon smiled brightly and told him all about the show we'd seen. I concentrated on the vodka, each shot of which seemed to harden me inside like a varnish.

After a while Sharon went home. I managed a smile but she didn't kiss me goodnight, telling me that I didn't have to wait outside for the cab with her. She said she would call me and I nodded. When she'd gone Nicky asked me what I was so pissed off about but I told him it was nothing. He said he really liked Sharon and I was surprised by my own reaction; it was an almost physical sensation of threat. I may have taken my brother's youth away from him but I didn't have to let one of my friends take his girlfriend. Now I *knew* I was being irrational, but I couldn't help it.

'Not this one, Nicky,' I slurred. 'OK?'

'Ah,' he said, holding his hands up. 'I get it. Sorry. No wonder you didn't call Trish back. She liked you by the way.'

'It's not like that,' I said, 'you don't understand.'

Puzzled, Nicky didn't pursue it.

I stayed late, propping up the bar long after Nicky had locked the door. I was still there when the kitchen staff left and the barmen, and when Jamie said goodnight too. I sat there feeling pissed and tired and fucked off with Sharon and not really knowing why, but getting more so with each glass of smooth clear vodka. Carla, the waitress I always flirt with, saw me sitting there and asked me if I needed a lift home. I sat up a bit and said yes. Nicky interrupted to say that he'd drive me if I wanted, giving me a serious look as he did so, but I said no, it was OK. I walked outside with Carla. I said something funny and she laughed and said something funnier back. I laughed. Then, as we got into her Beetle, Carla asked me where I lived. I told her but I needn't have bothered because we didn't go there.

Chapter Twelve

The journey out to the hospital usually takes about an hour and a half but I made good time because it was Sunday. It was another overcast day, a little warmer than it had been of late, though the forecast had predicted rain for later. It was good to drive through the quiet streets, usually so jammed with angry people in their hermetically sealed shells. The city looked strangely vulnerable. It was about two thirty when I turned into the entrance of the hospital, and parked where I usually do, over in the corner near the artificial lake. I locked up the Mazda, and then Sharon and I walked towards the forbidding Victorian building where my brother had been living for the last three years.

On Saturday I'd woken up at around ten, exhausted from high resolution dreams, in a bed that I wasn't familiar with. After the inevitable brittle goodbyes I walked out on to the street, which was in Hackney, and found a minicab office. I felt like shit, and the way the guy drove the cab didn't make me feel any better. When I got home I sat in Fred's for a while, seeing if I could spot anyone taking an undue interest in the street that led to my flat. There was no one. I went upstairs and I dialled the airport, and this time managed to get through to the barman. I was oddly relieved, having had the thought that the man in the hat may have wanted to cut down on any potential witnesses against him. Alex answered the phone and said yeah, of course he remembered me. He wanted to know how he could help. I asked him if he had seen the man in the hat any time prior to the night of the murder. He said he hadn't. He did remember that the man had been there a while before Edward had shown up. I got him to estimate the time and he guessed at around three-quarters of an hour. He asked if that was important and I told him that I wasn't sure whether it was or not. It could mean that he went there on purpose to find someone. He agreed. He told me that in an airport the passengers don't normally stay at the bar for too long unless they were early for their flights. And he wasn't taking one, was he? No, I said. I asked him if he was sure that Edward and the man had sat at the bar for a long time, and explained what the clock on the security video had said. Alex laughed.

'Jesus,' he protested, 'I didn't really remember all that much. It was you guys who all told me how much I remembered. Maybe they were there for twenty minutes not forty. How the fuck should I know? If I'd known he was going to waste the guy I'd have paid more attention, but I didn't, did I? I'd have put a stopwatch on him.'

Alex had a point. I apologized for bothering him again.

There was nothing I could find out about Graham Lloyd's financial status until Monday. I wrote the rest of the morning off and gazed out the window at the dome of St Paul's, a stranger on the skyline. I spent the afternoon mooching around, unable to focus on anything. At four I went for a long walk into Soho and bought some Levis from a place in Seven Dials. I sat in a gay pub on Argyle Street and handed out a few photographs, but everyone seemed to be a tourist. I'd do better during the week, when the regulars were in. It meant that the weekend was dead as far as my current assignment was concerned. I took the bus home and then went down to the gym to work out. I couldn't put much enthusiasm into it and left early, blaming a headache which later on turned out to be a prophesy. I ate fish and chips from the Golden Fry, drank half a bottle of a cheap Chilean, and fell asleep on the sofa.

Sharon and I hadn't said too much on the journey. Sharon seemed wary of me, and I was a little nervous too. Neither of us mentioned Friday night. I turned Radio 3 on and got some very grave organ music which really underlined the heaviness of the season. Sharon was wearing jeans and an enormous sweater, with her shortish hair pulled back in a ponytail. She'd brought along some exotic-looking flowers which lay in their paper on the back seat, their sweet powerful scent like another presence in the car with us. Sharon always takes along the most pungent flowers in the shop when she goes to the hospital, reasoning that though he can't see them, Luke must be able to breathe in their aroma.

Luke lay where he always lay, in the same position, with the same expression on his face. He is in a small ward with a curtain on two sides of his bed, the foot facing the door through which we had walked. His bed is really a big, electronic lilo, which inflates and deflates automatically in given areas. It does this to prevent pressure sores, critical occlusions of the blood vessels closest to the surface of the skin, by rotating the weight on any given part of Luke's body. Luke lay with his limbs in a pronounced contraction. Due to the lack of exercise, and in spite of the daily massages he receives, Luke's body has gradually taken on more and more of a spastic appearance, his legs, arms and hands drawing closer into him as his muscles lose the habit of stretching out. It looks as though he is afraid, and is constantly trying to protect himself from something awful, but I have been assured that the position of his limbs is simply a physical reaction to his muscles' inertia. It is completely separate from his mental state.

Sharon and I took chairs either side of his bed and Hazel, one of the nurses who looks after my brother, went to find a vase for Sharon's flowers. I had actually brought along a vase a couple of years ago, one which was a lot nicer than the hospital ones, but the nurses didn't realize it was Luke's and gave it to other patients as well as him. I'd noticed it today when we'd walked in, above the bed of a frail old lady. I never saw the point of saying anything about it.

Hazel came back with a vase and asked us how we were. We both said we were fine. Hazel is a tall, very thin black woman in her early thirties. I am always pleased to see that it is her on duty when I come because I can tell that she cares a great deal about Luke. The other nurses are very good as well, but Hazel has a special quality which is hard to define. I like the way she talks to Luke, without sounding patronizing, and the filthy jokes she makes under her breath about the doctors and the ward sister. Luke would have liked that if he could have heard her. Maybe he could hear her.

Hazel put the flowers on the windowsill at the head of the bed and left us alone. Sharon smiled at Luke and took hold of his right hand which, needless to say, rested in hers without making any sort of response. Slowly, she stretched out his fingers one by one, and gradually straightened out his wrist. Luke was wearing his blue pyjamas, with the rounded collars and black piping, which I had bought for him last Christmas. The top and bottom buttons were done up, the rest open to give room to Luke's gastrostomy tube, the artificial umbilical cord which has been inserted into his stomach through an opening made a couple of inches below his breastbone. The tube feeds Luke a constant supply of amino acids in liquid form, and is preferable to a drip because a drip would send nourishment straight into his bloodstream. Luke's gut is in perfect working order and the gastrostomy tube means that it has work to do, and so doesn't suffer the wastage inflicted on other parts of his body.

The colour of the pyjamas the nurses fit him into is one of the few things that ever change about my brother. The others are the length of his hair, or the light stubble which sits on his chin from time to time. It always strikes me as strange that his hair and beard should keep growing the way they do, as if some part of Luke is unaware that the rest of him has stopped, and carries on functioning regardless, like a striker who hasn't heard the whistle. When I'd first started coming I'd asked Hazel if I could shave Luke and she had allowed it, and now I do that if he happens to need it when I'm there.

Luke didn't need shaving today though so I was redundant in that capacity. Sharon held Luke's hand, which I always feel strange about doing, and she ran her other hand through his hair and chatted to him. She told him about work, and the various things she'd been doing with her spare time. She behaved with a patience and an efficiency which made me feel clumsy and unimaginative. I thought it was good the way she was with him, and I wondered what she talked to him about when I wasn't there. We both focused our attention on Luke, and Sharon did most of the talking. I could talk quite well when I was on my own with Luke, but was happy enough for Sharon to be in charge while I was there with her. I'm sure he would much rather listen to her.

As Sharon chatted away I studied Luke's face, and tried to decide if he was looking any older since he had been here. He looked thinner certainly, drawn, and his skin was very pale, but I wasn't sure if I could see any age on him. As often happens when I sit there watching him, I couldn't help imagining him in ten years' time. Twenty, thirty. Lying there as time passed him by, growing slowly into the body of an old man, a slower body, a body which had grown weary without having done anything to tire it. I couldn't imagine it. I couldn't imagine coming here every week or so for the rest of Luke's or my life, bringing along the baggage I had acquired, the sights and sounds and experiences, the children maybe; all the things Luke may never have, because he put himself in a position of danger so that I would not be in it. I couldn't imagine growing older, and watching Luke's parody of ageing growing older alongside me.

Sharon chatted on and I said the odd thing now and then. The ward was warm and Sharon pulled her sweater over her head, her full breasts pressing upwards against a fitted, ribbed T-shirt. The contrast between the young, vivacious woman and her inert fiancé was startling, and I had to make myself remember what they had looked like before, fighting together on the sofa, or dancing salsa at the Mambo Inn. Imagining that made me think of that night and I asked Sharon if she remembered it, how Luke and I were too English to ask anyone other than her to dance, and how we had had to keep whisking her away from overly amorous Latinos. Sharon said of course she remembered. And then a private memory crossed her mind and she looked back down at Luke. A wistful breeze blew across her features and she squeezed Luke's hand harder. As she set his hand down, however, the wistfulness was blown away by something stronger. She sat back in her chair, letting out a long, slow breath.

Sharon seemed to have gone somewhere and so I started to tell Luke about my case. I didn't tell him any of the details, just that it was paying well and that I might be able to get away sometime, do some skiing after Christmas. I told him how Forest were doing, and how he had better get well because they needed all the support they could get at the moment. I talked about going back to Australia with him, up to the Northern Territories this time. I told him that Sharon had recently made me go to see a Spanish porn show with her, and then told him that his acting agent had phoned recently to ask how he was doing. Apparently, she still got the odd enquiry after him. I told Luke that it really was about time that he got off his arse and started working again; his public were demanding it.

While I was speaking I hadn't really noticed Sharon. I turned towards her and saw that she wasn't looking at Luke but at me. Her expression was blank, her eyes narrowed slightly and her mouth open as though she couldn't quite believe something. I thought she was going to speak to me but suddenly she stood up and walked out of the door without a word. She didn't look round, at either Luke or myself. I called after her but she had already gone. Hearing me call Sharon's name, Hazel gave me a quizzical look from the other end of the ward.

I stayed with Luke another ten minutes. I didn't know what Sharon's problem was but soon became restless thinking about her. I tried to imagine how this all must be for her but because it was completely different for her than it was for me I couldn't. In some respects it was far easier for me. I wondered if Sharon had met somebody recently, a man she couldn't bring herself to go out with, or who she was going out with but was feeling very guilty about. Maybe that explained it. The thought was unpleasant to me, more so than it ever had been and I wondered why. It was probably seeing Luke lying there in his featureless limbo, imagining Sharon with another man. I thought about Sharon and the other man going out for a long time. Getting married maybe. Coming here together to see Luke. Or maybe Sharon would make the decision that she couldn't come at all any more.

I said goodbye to Luke, and found Hazel to say goodbye to her too. I went to look for Sharon in the cafeteria, but it was empty except for a young man in a white coat reading a fat paperback over a cup of coffee. I found her on a bench by the lake. Her hands were folded into the sleeves of her sweater. I sat next to her and prised one of her hands out, holding it between mine, rubbing it. I'd wanted to cheer her up but it wasn't sadness that I saw on her face. It was more like contempt. Contempt mixed with anger. I let go of her hand, which was as cold and unresponsive as Luke's had been on the few occasions I had ever taken hold of it.

'You OK?' I said, after a second or two.

'Yes.'

'Yes?'

Sharon let out a breath and turned her head away, towards a muffled-up old man who was being led slowly around the lake by a middle-aged woman.

'Sharon,' I asked her, 'is there something you want to tell me? I mean, if there is, you can. In fact, I want you to.'

Sharon turned, and looked at me.

'I mean it,' I assured her. 'You can. Really.'

She nodded to herself. She thought for a second and then looked at me with hard, measured eyes.

'Billy,' she said, 'what do the doctors say about Luke?'

The question threw me. She knew what they said.

'They say he's in a PVS.'

'And what does that mean?'

'Well, they say that he has no control of any of his physical faculties, but that they are uncertain as to any level—'

'Billy,' Sharon said, cutting me off. There was an edge to her voice. 'What do they say about recovery? About the chances of Luke waking up again?'

It was my turn to look away. 'The whole subject is open to debate,' I said. 'I've read about it. Occasionally someone is misdiagnosed and—'

'How occasionally? How occasionally is that, Billy?'

'Christ,' I said, 'I don't know. But it happens. And the doctor says that Luke isn't suffering at all. Not at all. So I see no reason why they shouldn't keep him alive, just in case, you know. It happens, it does . . .'

'Oh Billy,' Sharon said, her voice full of anger, 'I can't stand it! I can't stand it when you talk to Luke as if he's going to get better. I can't bear it!'

'Sharon . . .'

'Trips to Australia, going to see the football, oh God, Billy, it's so stupid of you! It's so stupid! He's never going to go away with you, or act again, or watch Nottingham bloody Forest. He's not. I wish you wouldn't speak like that. Every time you do it's like a wall is put up in front of me. It's killing me, Billy! It really is.'

I was shocked. Sharon was looking at me with something approaching hatred. Her eyes filled and her mouth trembled but she held on to it. I didn't know what to say.

'I don't understand . . .'

'Billy,' Sharon went on, ignoring me. 'You don't have to turn his machines off. You don't.' She took a breath. 'Because he's dead. Luke's dead. He is. He is. He's dead now and you just keep on pretending he isn't. We meet up all the time and you just pretend Luke couldn't make it, that he'll be along next time, that he's got a cold or something! But he hasn't got a cold. He's dead.'

Sharon's eyes filled up completely this time and I put a hand on her shoulder, but she shrugged it away as though it was painful to her. She moved further down the bench. I moved closer to her but she pushed herself off from the bench and ran into the trees. I saw her stop on the other side of the man-made lake and sit against a tree with her head in her hands. I couldn't hear her crying but it was only a small tree Sharon was leaning against and the rocking motion she was making disturbed the last of the flame-coloured leaves clinging to the thin, dark branches, leading several of them to lose their hold and float down to the floor around her. I turned my eyes away from her, to the ducks diving in the dirty brown water.

My brother wasn't dead. I understood why Sharon said what she had but she was wrong. I wasn't going to get mad with her, or think badly of her, but I couldn't help her either, not if that was the way she was choosing to deal with it. I felt sure now that someone else was involved. I was disappointed that killing Luke in her mind was the only way Sharon could deal with his presence in her life.

But then, I had always known how practical a person she was, how she dealt with things decisively before they took control of her. It was her way of getting on with her life, of not allowing what happened to Luke to claim her as well. I knew that. But I saw her as ruthless, the way she could decide to end something like that, to shut out my brother. I pictured her set face as she had walked out of the ward, not even turning to look at Luke.

I found myself thinking of Peter Morgan. I wondered if he had told his wife about employing me. I wondered what she had said. Leave it. Just accept it. Accept what happened, however bad it was. Don't make it worse for yourself by living in the past, raking over things you can't change. Maybe that's why I felt such sympathy for him, because he couldn't do this. Because he had lost his brother like I had and all he was left with was an image. The only difference was that the image he had was of blood, and sharp glass, and semen, while mine was of a greying young man who was still alive but equally motionless, whole but completely severed from himself. Present, a hundred yards away, but lost. Lost as a kid on a street corner.

When she was calmer Sharon walked back towards me. Her face was set hard again. We got into the car. We drove back into London with a pregnant silence joining the remnant of scent left from Luke's flowers. The roads were busier now, and it was slower going. As night fell I realized that I hadn't put the clock in my car back the night before. I did it with one hand as I drove along, feeling sad that it would be dark so early from now on. I made that point to Sharon but she didn't answer me. I turned the radio on, but every channel sounded tinny and annoying so I gave up on it. Once or twice, I glanced at Sharon in the passenger seat, but she kept her gaze fixed at nothing through her side window and wouldn't look at me. After the third time, I didn't look over again.

I pulled up outside Sharon's flat in Ladbroke Grove. It was residents' parking but as it was Sunday I was fine. I didn't have to leave the car there long however. When I went to undo my seat belt Sharon reached out a hand to stop me.

'I think I want to be on my own.'

'Right,' I said. 'Right.'

Sharon waited for a second. She looked at me for a long time, studying my face. Her look was one of complete self-control, the way you look when you've made a decision no one can talk you out of. A decision which has made itself.

'Billy,' she said, in a measured voice. 'I'm sorry for shouting at you. But I have to change things. We both have to. We keep going round the same circle. I need . . .' Her voice tailed off.

I didn't say anything. Sharon took my silence as a rebuke and said, by way of a wounded justification, emphasizing each word:

'I'm not very happy, Billy.'

Her voice accused me. I started to speak but Sharon was out of the car before I could say anything. I fumbled for my seat belt but I was already too late to catch her. I gave up and watched her run over to the block of converted flats she lived in, then fumble for her door key. *I'm not very happy*. What the fuck did she think I *was*? I watched her open the door hurriedly and let it swing behind her, keeping sight of her as she ran towards the stairs, until the door closed. I wondered how long it would be before I saw her again. When the door clicked shut I stared at it for a second and then I was aware, suddenly, of the lingering scent from the flowers which had been on the back seat and were now in a cheap plastic vase a foot above my brother Luke's head. The scent was cloying, insistent. I opened my window to get rid of it.

So, I thought, I'm dead too.

A light came on in her flat. A figure walked towards the window and drew the heavy curtains against the oncoming night. And me. I reversed up and pulled the car out into the street. I managed to scrape the side of a BMW parked too far out from the kerb, and its alarm went off, an outraged scream like a chisel rammed into my head. Fuck it. I drove back across London to Clerkenwell.

My flat was empty and I didn't want to be there. I went down to the Old Ludensian, and Nicky shut the place early because I was the only customer and why waste the electricity? We sat at the bar, the tables stacked high with chairs casting twisted shadows from the streetlights on the pillars and the whitewashed brick walls. Nicky didn't ask me about Carla so I didn't tell him. We drank a few beers. I'd meant to tell him about what had happened at the hospital but found myself not wanting to. I wound up telling him all about Teddy Morgan and then about Dominic Lewes.

We got talking about the whole gay thing. Nicky confessed to me that he had actually had a fling with a guy on Rhodes, where he'd gone after breaking up with a girlfriend. I was surprised; Nicky had the most heterosexual life of anyone I knew. He told me that he had never felt that way about any other man, but still found himself thinking about the tall American from Kansas whom he had fallen for. He said that the whole thing had confused him at the time and still did, especially when he started getting serious about a girl. He looked troubled, and suddenly embarrassed.

'You needn't worry, by the way,' he assured me. 'He was blond.'

I laughed and told Nicky that I was shocked and offended that he had never considered me as a sexual partner. Then I wondered if I would ever, *ever* meet anyone whose life was simple and straightforward, who could live happily in mind and body. I wished that we could somehow find a way to circumvent the body, the power it has over us to make us miserable. To trap us, like Luke was trapped, or Peter Morgan was; unable to live in his body, making only brief, clandestine sorties. What it would be like if we could either be free of the body or else free of the guilt we feel at some of the demands the body makes. I wondered what it meant that I spent hours in the gym, causing myself pain, trying to get my body to obey my commands. I wondered what it would be like to have the need to do that, not to yourself, but to others. To have power over other bodies.

Nicky and I drank another beer and sat in silence for a while. A car drove by, sending the shadows from the stacked chairs running across the walls like a hoard of demons. I left Nicky to his thoughts and went home to mine.

Chapter Thirteen

On Monday I got to my office before nine, had two slices of toast with coffee and waited for the mail. There was a time when the mail came before you even thought about getting out of bed in the morning. Now you have to wait for it.

I wrote a list of things to do. I left two messages for Sir Peter to call me and then typed out a letter to Mrs Lewes. I told her that her son was physically fit and seemed to be living in a house which had electricity and was heated. I told her that he had dyed his hair, which would explain his appearance in the pictures I was sending. I didn't want her thinking I was sending her photographs of somebody else's child. I slid the letter into a hardback A4 envelope, addressed it, and resolved to pick the pictures up from Carl later in the day. I wrote a letter to a man who owed me some money but then tore it up when a cheque from him was included in the mail, which arrived at about half past nine. It was accompanied by a letter addressed to a Mr J. Brinsford, the previous occupant of my office who, I knew for a fact, had emigrated to Sydney four years ago. It was from the Renault people who valued him highly as a customer and wanted to offer him the chance to test-drive the new Renault Megane. The only other letter was a bill for business rates which, unfortunately, was addressed to me.

Once I had dealt with the mail, thoughts of Sharon drifted into my head. They made me feel weighted down and slow, as though someone had replaced my blood with mercury. I began to run through the events of the previous day, pausing and rewinding, seeing her set face, feeling her shrug away under my hand, hearing the sound she made as her tears fought with her words for space. I had just got to the point when she ran off towards her flat when the shrill tone of the phone brought me back to the present. It was Morgan. He sounded excited and worried at the same time until I assured him that I hadn't called him for anything important.

'I need a favour,' I told him.

'Anything,' the MP replied. People seldom mean that.

'It's not a lot but you're the only person in the Commons I know.'

'I'm not in the Commons today, I'm afraid, I'm at the Treasury.'

'That doesn't matter,' I said. 'What I need to know is how to get hold of the register of Members' outside interests.'

'Ah,' the MP said, raising the pitch of his voice, 'you want to see if I'm involved in the arms trade. Or if I earn so much you can put your fee up. Well, I'm sorry to disappoint you but once you get to be a Minister you have to give up any other jobs you might do, and since our great humbling I haven't had time to line up any plum directorships. Yet. Come back in six months.'

There was a lightness to his tone which I hadn't heard before. I liked it. 'Sorry to disappoint,' I said. 'But it's not you I'm interested in, I'm afraid.'

Sir Peter said that it would be easier if he got his assistant at the Commons to photocopy the relevant page for me; I could pick it up from his office there rather than going rooting through the register myself. I also asked if he knew Graham Lloyd's address and he said he didn't but that it wouldn't be too difficult to find out. He would get his assistant to include it with the photocopy I was to pick up. I wondered if that was a good idea, letting his assistant see how much I was interested in Graham Lloyd's background, but Sir Peter laughed.

'No,' he assured me. 'It's all right. Thomasina's not what you'd call quick on the uptake. No, and to be perfectly frank I've never had a parliamentary assistant who was. I get them foisted on me by my constituency association. They tend to be the daughters of the ladies who organize the garden party fund-raisers which keep us afloat, the ladies who can get me thrown out on my ear any time they like. Pretty girls, all MPs' wives before they're twenty-five. It's perfectly all right, I assure you.' He stopped to think for a second. 'I'd worry if I was on the other side though. The Labour lot get brilliant assistants, LSE interns on their way to the *Guardian* or *The Economist*. He laughed. 'They're normally a damn sight quicker on the uptake than the idiot MP they're working for.'

I picked up a sealed brown envelope from Thomasina, who was indeed very pretty and dressed in a Chanel suit which must have cost about twice her monthly salary. Somehow, I didn't think her current job was her chief source of income. I walked back to my car and sat behind the steering wheel, using my nail to tear the envelope open, and then emptied the contents out on to the passenger seat.

Under Graham Lloyd's name was a list of three companies, none of which meant anything to me. They soon would though. At the bottom of the sheet was an address only five minutes' drive away over Vauxhall Bridge. As Lloyd had a London constituency I assumed that this was his only house but I made a mental note to check. I stuffed the sheet back into the envelope and pulled out into the traffic.

I actually drove over Westminster not Vauxhall Bridge and then down the Kennington Road. The square Lloyd lived in was on the left and I pulled into it and cruised round looking at the house numbers. The square was a little Georgian oasis in a dismal area of high-rises and big trunk roads wheezing carbon monoxide over small utility shops protected by steel meshes. Planted straight inside it, and ignoring the insistent groan of traffic, you might have thought you were in the middle of a prosperous town in the shires; the square was tree-lined, full of Volvos and Mercedes, and there was a rustic-looking pub in the corner. It seemed an ideal place for an MP to live.

The houses all had big, smartly painted doors with large brass knobs on, the kind that sit in the middle of the door and which you use to pull the door shut after you. The doors were either red, blue, or in the case of number 12, bright yellow. I stopped the Mazda outside number 12 and looked at the house for a second. Lloyd seemed to be doing all right if he could afford to live there. The house had three floors and wasn't broken up into flats as far as I could see, and there would be a sizeable garden out the back. I wondered if Lloyd's wife was in. I wondered what she would say if she knew that the man sitting in the conspicuously old and dirty car in the street outside was investigating the possibility that her husband, who was definitely involved with another woman, was also involved in the brutal murder of a fellow MP's brother. She'd hold her Marigolds up in horror.

I decided that it would serve no purpose telling Mrs Lloyd who I was. I'd only come because it was close, and I wanted to see the style to which Lloyd had become accustomed to living in. I pulled away from the house and drove back round to the Kennington Road, which was the only way in or out of the square. As I waited for a gap in the traffic I noticed the street name bolted to a brick wall, and only then appreciated the irony of Lloyd's address. He lived on Cleaver Square. Close. Close enough.

I drove back up the Kennington Road but didn't turn off towards Westminster. I eventually crossed over Southwark Bridge and headed up past Bank. The IRA have made this area virtually impossible to park in but I knew of an extortionate car park near Spitalfields Market where I left the Mazda, very glad I was on expenses. Thinking of the feeling that I'd had the other day at King's Cross I made sure it was all locked up and then walked up past Liverpool Street station to the City Road.

Company's House is a big building but not as impressive as you might think it should be, bearing in mind that within it are details of every business in the land. I had been there several times before and went straight to the reference section where I chose a table. I sat down and pulled the various pieces of paper from the envelope Thomasina had given me, laying the top one down on the table and putting the others back. I pushed the envelope aside and looked at the parliamentary register's entry for Graham Lloyd MP.

Carlson Holdings. Consultant. Part time.

Chalmers and Broge. Parliamentary Consultant. Part time.

The Buckner Group. Directorship.

On the table I was sitting at were two terminals. I moved in front of the nearest one to me and gazed at the screen which was displaying a menu of options. I moved the blinking green icon down the list to 'Company Search' and pressed 'Enter'. I then typed in 'Carlson Holdings' and hit 'Enter' again. The screen changed to one headed by the title 'Carlson Holdings PLC', with a list of information underneath.

Carlson Holdings was a very big company dealing in bonds and derivatives. It had a turnover greater than that of some small countries but only employed a hundred and fifty people. I took down the address and the phone number. I repeated the procedure for Chalmers and Broge and was told that it was basically a lobbyist company. They had only twelve full-time employees and their turnover was infinitesimal compared to that of the holdings company. Then I typed in 'Buckner Group'. The Buckner Group was also a small company, but it was involved in what the computer very unhelpfully termed 'Investments'. It didn't say what sort. The company was less than two years old and no figure was given for its annual turnover. It was based in Maidstone and the computer didn't tell me how many people worked there. I took the address and phone number down and then packed up my envelope and headed back to the lobby, where there was a public telephone in a conveniently soundproof booth.

'Hello, Personnel.' The voice, a young woman's with a bad cold, sounded bored. 'Juliet speaking.'

'Yes, hi there, Juliet,' I said, 'it's Fulton here from Accounts.'

'Who?'

'John Fulton, I'm sure we've met.'

'Oh, hello, Mr Fulton, sorry, I was a bit confused. The switchboard said it was an external call.'

'Christ, are the phones still doing that? Wondered what that noise was. Anyway, we're having a problem with some invoices. MP fellow, name of Lloyd. Graham. Wants to know why we haven't paid him for some work he did, when we think we already have.'

'Bloody cheek!' Juliet was quite appalled. 'Should spend more time running the country if you ask me rather than working on the side all the time the way they do.'

'Now then, Juliet. Anyway, can you give me a list of the days he's worked since this time last year, then we can clear this up.'

'OK, Mr Fulton. I'll phone you back. It'll take me a while, I'm not used to this new system yet.'

'I'd rather hold if you don't mind, Juliet, got to get this sorted.'

'Righto.'

I waited five minutes and I was afraid I was going to run out of change for the phone, but Juliet eventually came back on the line.

'Right,' she said, sniffing. 'He worked a total of thirty-six days since November the first last year. OK?'

'Wonderful. Thanks, Juliet.'

'Thanks, Mr Fulton.' She paused a little nervously. 'See you on the third.'

'The third?'

'At the ball, silly.' She giggled delightfully.

'Of course! Save the last dance for me.'

I went out for more change.

'Accounts. Alan speaking.'

Alan sounded like he also had a virus. Must be something going round the office.

'Yes, hello, Alan, Fulton here, Personnel. Got put through the switchboard for some reason.'

'Sorry, who?'

'Fulton. Now listen, Alan, Juliet and I are having a spot of bother down here.'

'Oh,' Alan said, 'how is Juliet?'

'Fine, Alan, she's fine. Except the Chief's in a stink, wants to cut back on freelance expenditure. So, we need to know some wage figures before he can decide which consultants to call in for the budget thing.'

The budget thing?

'All right, who were you thinking of?'

'Lloyd, Graham. MP I think. Your new system tell you that, can it?'

'Don't talk to me about this piece of shit.'

'Now then, Alan.'

'Just a mo there.'

Alan was a whiz with the new system whatever his reservations about it. He was back in no more than a minute.

'Seven-fifty the day,' he said.

'Thanks, Al. Most helpful. See you on the third.'

'The third?'

'The ball, stupid.'

'Oh God, yes. Yes.'

He paused for a second and lowered his voice.

'Fulton, you wouldn't happen to know if Juliet was going, would you?'

So, Lloyd was earning twenty-five grand p.a. from Carlson Holdings. I couldn't get anything out of the secretary I spoke to at Chalmers and Broge who immediately asked me if I was a journalist, and when I tried the Buckner Group all I got was an answerphone. It didn't matter. The twenty-five from Carlson plus whatever thanks a lobby firm give to a well-placed politician, *and* however much he made investing through the Buckner Group meant that Graham Lloyd was well enough off. There was also the salary I was helping to pay. He wasn't quite the Duke of Westminster but he was doing all right. It was disappointing but I hadn't realistically thought that I'd stumble on a motive as obvious as that. Graham Lloyd certainly didn't need to kill anyone for their wife's money. Oh well.

So he had nothing to do with it. I didn't totally dismiss the idea, but I could no longer see a reason why Lloyd should kill Teddy Morgan. The affair was just a coincidence which for various reasons neither he nor Charlotte Morgan wanted to let on about. Teddy may have known about the affair but he didn't sound like the sort of man who would stand in the way if his wife wanted a divorce, and so need removing. Lloyd had no motive and was in the States at the time of the murder. The man outside The Colt must just have been a man outside The Colt.

Even if he wasn't, the fact that Lloyd had hired a man to keep watch on a detective cum blackmailer who was very possibly out to fuck his life up, didn't make him a murderer.

The killer had to be the man in the baseball hat but I was still bothered by the idea. I just couldn't figure why he had let people at the airport see him, let alone stroll in front of a security camera with the victim. It just didn't seem very clever compared with the other murders. It meant that Sir Peter could still be right about a copycat killer riding the fame of another man, but the cat was not Graham Lloyd.

I ate lunch at a nearby Prêt à Manger and read the sign which said you could call either of the two bosses any time if you had any complaints. I had none, so I didn't, but I thought it was good that you could do that if you wanted to. I wondered how many calls they actually got. I wished you could do the same thing with British Telecom. Or British Rail. Phone the Chief Executive when your phone was cut off after you've paid the bill, or there was engineering work on the line when you'd been specifically told there wouldn't be. They'd get a few calls. I also wished you could phone whoever it is that organizes things so that airline pilots get carved up in their own homes, by someone who was looking increasingly likely to get away with it. Or who decides that people should have lovers in comas and not be able to deal with it any more. Or deal with the person who reminded them of it. It would be good to talk to that person. Very good. Or, rather, it would be good to talk to that person and for them to give you some answers.

I drove home and picked up the pictures of Dominic Lewes from Carl. I sent them off to his mother. I changed out of the suit I was in. I pulled on a pair of jeans, a T-shirt and my work jacket, and I spent the rest of the day walking round pubs asking if anyone had seen either of the men in the two photographs I was carrying.

Chapter Fourteen

In fact, I spent the rest of the week doing that. It was all there was left to do, and if it weren't for Graham Lloyd I would have got on to it much earlier. I went from pub to café to pub. When you're working on your own you just have to keep searching in the most likely places, hoping that the right person shows up. You have to leave a trail of messages for someone who may never see them, or want to contact you even if they did. There was a man out there looking for gay men and I had to go to the places he was likely to find them and hope our paths crossed. I could almost feel him out there and I wondered if he could feel me, my presence, searching for him. I hoped he could. I wondered all the time if I had already spoken to someone who knew what was going on. It annoyed me to think that I had very possibly been as close as two feet to the truth, that it resided in the thoughts of someone I had interviewed, right there, locked away behind a mere inch of skin and skull. I thought how far away and inaccessible people can be, even when you're sitting next to them. I remembered being a child, thinking that everyone must surely be able to see my secrets, the dark things I wanted.

I made a list and walked up and down various parts of London with the two photographs in my pocket. One was of Edward Morgan and the other was of the man who had probably killed him. I started in Islington, at the Edward VI near the Angel, and The Hart in Canonbury. In each pub I left a copy of the video-still behind the bar. I went to The Moorland Tavern and across Highbury Fields to The Cooper's Arms off the Blackstock Road. These were the gay pubs nearest to Edward's house and I tried them to find out if he had popped in any of them recently, either because he was a regular or because he was curious. Much to the chagrin of several of the men I talked to, he hadn't been seen in any of these places. Neither had the man in the baseball cap.

This kind of work can be very boring indeed but the fact that it was pubs I had to go and sit in meant it wasn't so bad. I'd chat to the barman for a while and then ask him if either Edward or the other man ever came in there. Others around the bar would notice the pictures the barman was peering at, and they would often come over to have a look at them themselves. If not, I took the pictures round. Once I had assured them that I was not the Old Bill come to arrest them for kissing in public (yes, it happens) they were usually very co-operative, and happy to help me.

In every pub I went to, at least some of the people recognized the picture of Edward, but it was only from the newspapers which carried the same one a few months ago. You would normally expect news stories, however lurid, to fade from the memory, but the people I was talking to had a very good reason to remember Edward's face. There was a respectful, even reverential hush whenever a group of men gathered round to take a look at the pictures. I could see them imagining what it must have been like for Edward, many of them knowing that it could have been a picture of them that a private detective was showing around the gay pubs and bars of London. One man, sitting in a chrome-filled café on Camden High Street, even said it, and seemed to age ten years as he did so: there but for the grace of God go I.

For the first three days I walked into a lot of pubs, met a lot of people but didn't get anywhere. It was frustrating, but patience is the primary requisite of my job and I didn't mind it too much. I know it's a bit of a cliché but gay bars are almost always a lot more friendly and easy to be in than most of the regular ones. People were polite and helpful and I believed them when they told me, either from behind a bar or in front of it, that they would keep an eye out for the man in the hat and would phone me if they saw him.

One guy said, 'He's like a virus amongst us, something which will kill you if you don't look out. He preys on loneliness and youth, the need to be with someone, feel another person's skin next to yours. You need to give love and he's waiting until you do it so that he can take your life. He's like AIDS. Except how will I know how to protect myself against him?'

I gave him a copy of the picture to keep.

'Remember his face,' I said. 'That's how.'

'And you're sure that's him?' the man asked hopefully.

'No,' I admitted. 'No, I'm not sure.'

'Well then,' the man said. He took the picture anyway.

Because I couldn't think of any other way of exploring the option that Edward had been killed by someone trying to fit it into the pattern of the other murders, I plugged away with the photo. My job had become as simple as it normally is: I had a face to find and all I had to do was look. I went to Clapham, Hampstead, Brixton, Westbourne Park, Notting Hill Gate. I spent hours sipping pints and chatting to people. I got hit on a few times and whenever I did I couldn't help thinking of Nicky and his American. I revisited places I had already been to and I had to get Carl to run me off some more copies of the picture, I had handed out so many. Some people said that the police had been round already. They laughed amongst themselves, remembering obviously uncomfortable coppers who they could just tell felt like mice in a snake's nest. They were easy to spot because they couldn't even bring themselves to pretend they were gay. I found it sad to think that they cared more about being mistaken for a poof than they did about finding a maniac before he could kill someone else.

I worked hard but only got one hit. A middle-aged man, in a pub on Old Compton Street, said he thought he may have seen the man, but then changed his mind quickly. I thought he might have changed it on purpose, in fact I was pretty sure he had, and I got quite excited. I asked the man if he was sure. Yes, he was. He told me he had to use the toilet and when he didn't come back after five minutes I could have kicked myself. He'd done exactly what I'd done to Lloyd. The fire escape was open and when I chased out of it on to Dean Street all I could see was a few hardy souls sitting outside a café and a waiter sneaking a fag break in a doorway. I wondered why he had legged it, why recognizing the man had caused him to panic. Was he scared? He didn't look it. Ashamed maybe? I made a mental note of his face in case I ran in to him again. I never did. None of the other patrons of the pub had seen him before.

Sitting in various pubs, bars and cafés I sometimes thought about Lloyd, and tried again to see if there was anything I'd missed out concerning the charming MP. I racked my brains for a way to get to him, to connect him with the man in the hat. I couldn't think of a way. I could, of course, let the police know about his affair, and I did resolve to do that when I ran out of anything else to do. It was, after all, the only thing of note I had managed to find out. It wouldn't do much good though, I knew. If he was innocent it would just cause a lot of embarrassment and if he was guilty it wasn't really much in the way of evidence against him. All it would do was cause him grief, which I wasn't too concerned about, but it would cause Edward's widow a whole lot too.

I called Sir Peter, having forgotten to check up on Lloyd's alibi, and he confirmed that Lloyd had been away when Edward was killed. Sir Peter's cheerfulness had vanished, a temporary blip on a downward slope, and my lack of progress didn't cheer him up any. I told him what I'd done and he insisted that I had to go on until there really was nothing more I could think of doing. I felt there was something masochistic about his fervour, as though he was punishing himself. I told him that I needed another cheque if I was to continue and he was more than willing to send me one. He sounded very depressed and I got the feeling that finding his brother's killer was all that he could think about now. He then told me something which proved that I was right. Sir Peter Morgan was resigning from the Tory front bench and retreating to the relative safety, as he put it, of the back benches. He might even chuck it all in completely, he said.

Spurred on by Sir Peter's unsettling determination I took a day off from the bars and pubs and interviewed some of the stewardesses Edward had flown with. Apart from glowing descriptions and in one case a flood of tears, I didn't get anything out of them. I spoke to the steward

Michael Chalkley had told me about and he said that he did go to the Pavilion Bar now and then, and he sometimes met men there. That meant that it could well have featured as a potential pick-up place for the killer, even though it was risky. But how, I wondered, would he have known about it? It certainly wasn't in the *Time Out Guide to Gay London*.

I thought about talking to Charlotte Morgan again but I knew it wouldn't lead anywhere, not if I couldn't find the man in the hat. One lunchtime I got a call from Andy Gold, and he met me at Mike and Ally's café for lunch.

Andy looked very tired, and unusually subdued. He picked at his sandwich and only made a half-hearted attempt to get me to tell him the information he suspected I was keeping from him. We chatted about old times, cases we had worked on together. He told me that he was sick of police work. He had been taken off the gay killer case and reassigned to something even more nasty, if that was possible. Somebody, other than their parents, was meeting young girls from school, apparently offering them modelling contracts, and then taking them for photo shoots. He may have taken some pictures for all the police knew but what he did then was almost too disgusting to imagine. There had been two so far and one lucky escape.

Andy said, 'It's not the bodies. They don't get me any more, they really don't. It's the family. The dad looking bewildered, the mother hysterical, a little sister who'll stay lost in the middle of her head for ever. The photo on the mantelpiece. And worse, we never learn. Something happens and we fix it and then there's something else that happens which we haven't thought of. There's always something else, some new way some poor fuck's going to cop it. Thinking ahead is too expensive, it pisses too many people off without apparent just cause. All we do is clean up after the shit's already been shat, then spray pretty-sounding words around to kill the smell. What's the fucking point of it?'

'Don't ask me,' I said. 'I left, remember?'

Andy gave me a set of keys to the Morgans' flat in Canonbury, and that night I took the short drive over there. Teddy's Rover was still in the garage, as was Charlotte's car. She hadn't been able to bring herself to go back there, even for that. I noted the scrapes of paint on the Rover's wheel arch and the slight dent in the side of the Golf. I walked through the garage and into the apartment the way I assumed Teddy and his guest had gone. The apartment was dark but for the orange light of a lamppost spreading in through the open curtains. I closed the curtains, flicked a switch and walked into the middle of the living room.

The flat was very large for two people. The floor was Norwegian pine and the walls were an off-white broken up by modern prints and the odd original. There was a Chesterfield sofa, a coffee table and two armchairs. The place was far more to my taste than Charlotte's mews cottage had been and I wondered if actually she was borrowing that from a friend, or had rented it complete. I liked the simplicity of the place, the roomy feel to it. I felt perhaps that my flat could look like a miniature version of it, if I ever got round to making that trip to Ikea.

I checked out the bathroom and then the bedroom. The forensics people had taken away the bedroom carpet, the bed, and all the sheeting so there was no sign of the events which had taken place there. There was a faint smell though: someone had closed the windows a little too early, and it's not the sort of smell you could ever forget once you'd encountered it. It was faint, the tart iron of blood mixed with that of old sex, and excrement, and something else, something indefinable but very present nevertheless. It was the smell, not just of death, but of violent death.

I stayed in the flat for a while, poking around, opening cupboards, not really knowing what I was looking for. I found a box containing four bottles of champagne and thought of the forensics report I'd read. I listened to the silence which seemed to ring from the walls, the indiscernible echoes of vicious blows and terrible screams. I sat back on the sofa and closed my eyes and tried to picture what had happened to Edward, patching together everything I knew about him and his last day alive, filling in the gaps with movements that I thought were the most probable.

I saw him at the airport. I saw him at the bar and then on the way home. I saw him smile. I saw him sitting where I was sitting now, with another man by his side. I managed to put together a scenario, complete with dialogue, one which I knew was plausible enough but could never be exactly right. Even if I had got the broad facts, and put them in roughly the right order, what I saw was only guesswork, a model which I had built simply to help me. Only two people ever knew what really happened in this flat. Only they really saw it. I was looking for one man so that I could ask him, but even if I found him he was hardly likely to tell me. And as for the other, I was sure that he would have been more than willing to speak to me if he could, but he would never be able to tell me. This flat, which was so full of his things, his clothes in the closets, half-empty bottles of after-shave, a brand new tennis racket, seemed so full of him I felt like saying, 'Teddy, who killed you, who was it?' The clothes and the scent and the tennis racket could make no answer to me.

I knew that sitting there moving different figures through my mind was just a fiction, but for some reason it seemed to help. It struck me that Edward's killer, in spite of the apparent frenzy of his actions, was someone perfectly in control of himself. He had waited until he was in the bedroom. Going into the bedroom is the last thing you do with someone. It was the last thing Edward had done. They had apparently been in the bath together, the man must have been itching to kill Edward then but he hadn't. He was a man with composure, a man able to deny himself something until the exact moment when it would give him most pleasure. It was this, I knew, which was making it so difficult for either the police or myself to find him.

Sitting in Edward's flat, and thinking of the person I felt I now knew, depressed me immeasurably. This easy-going man had, as far as I could tell, inspired only affection in all the people I had spoken to. I thought about his killer again and got a physical pang of hatred for him, for his cynicism, for his shrivelled and petrified heart. I wanted to catch him far more than I had done before, talking to his brother over the crème brûlée. I left the flat and knocked on the doors of some of the neighbouring flats and houses. I spoke to a few people who had nothing to tell me, no suddenly recalled flashes they hadn't relayed to the police. No one had seen anything or heard anything. The people were all unwilling to talk to me, annoyed that I had come round to remind them that they lived next door to the house where such a horrible thing had happened. One old man even looked at me suspiciously. He made the point that murderers often came back to the scene of their crimes. He closed the door a little once he had thought of this, and glanced back into his hallway. I got the feeling that as soon as I had gone he would phone the police. I didn't want to get Andy into trouble for giving me the flat keys so I got in my car and drove home before I could find out.

I dropped the keys off to Andy and went back to my round of the pubs with renewed determination. All that week and then the weekend too, and then Monday and Tuesday. I didn't do anything else or see anyone. Elbowing themselves into the spaces between the thoughts I was having about Edward Morgan and his death, were thoughts of Sharon. I hadn't seen or spoken to her. I left her a message which she didn't return, and I stopped myself at the last minute from leaving several more. It was obvious she didn't want to see me. I asked myself how I hadn't seen this coming, and then realized that I had in a way. It had been ages since we had been to see Luke together. Sharon never wanted to, saying it was better if we went on our own because that way he got more visits. It was me who suggested we drive out there together last Sunday. I kept seeing Sharon's face, remembering the times we had gone to the movies together or she had sat across from me at my table sipping wine, her teeth stained, her hair the colour of old Condrieu. I thought about going round to her flat, talking to her, trying to find out exactly what she thought, trying to make her see that she didn't have to abandon any hope that Luke would recover in order to get on with her life. I didn't go. I worked hard instead. I didn't really know what to say to her. I probably wanted to tell her she should live her life as a celibate, tragic heroine, stoic at the bedside of her fallen lover, waiting for the magic day when he would wake from his sleep and finally marry her. I couldn't say that so I didn't say anything.

To keep myself from brooding I hiked round London trying to catch a killer. The weather had turned from irritable to petulant, and then from that to sullen and miserable. It seemed dark all the time and London was dull and quiet, the streets clenched as people braced themselves for three months of freezing winter. The last of the tables disappeared from outside the cafés, the tennis courts and parks were emptying. The doorways which had held recognizable, sleeping forms in the summer, were now filled with mounds of old clothes and blankets which could have covered any number of people, or no one. Faces were tighter, bodies more tense, and there were less people hanging around to ask questions of. London itself seemed to hold on to its secrets tighter.

I had grown colder too. I kept myself to myself and got more and more depressed about both Sharon and Edward Morgan. I tried not to admit it but the case was going nowhere. No one had seen the man in the picture and in any case by now he had almost definitely changed his appearance completely. It was especially frustrating because I had become convinced, for no concrete reason that I could think of, that there was more to this than simply the latest instalment in a series of never-to-be-understood acts of savagery. There was, I knew it, but getting close to it was like trying to hold the shadow of a man who's left the room. I had nearly gone through the entire section of the *Time Out Guide to Gay London*, and once I had finished that I knew that there wasn't going to be anything else I could do to quell the doubts which were nagging at me like an ulcer. I trudged on, telling myself to think of the money, but after two and a half weeks of increasingly dull and aimless leg-work I had just about decided to give up on it.

But then one night I took the car down to the gym and did some training. Sal told me that she definitely hadn't seen the man in the picture I had given her a week and a half earlier. I went in with Mountain Pete. I watched a cocky boy who thought he was Naseem Hamed and noticed a look of fear on the face of another boy holding a big orange coat, who wasn't sure if he wanted to get into the ring with either of his friends, who were both a bit bigger than he was. I got in my car. I went to see Nicky, who I'd not seen for nearly two weeks, and then I went home to my bed, drifting off into sleep to the bitter honey of Nick Drake's ballads of death and longing.

And then a voice on my answerphone woke me from my dreams and I went to stand in the cold outside a freight depot behind King's Cross station, where the owner of the voice joined me and pointed a sawn-off shotgun at my head.

PART THREE

Chapter Fifteen

He was not, as far as I could tell, someone I'd met before. But he could have been. He'd stepped out from behind a trailer and I could barely make him out. What I could see was that he was tall, with a right arm strong enough to hold the weapon steady in one hand at arm's length. He was wearing what seemed to be jeans and a waist-length leather jacket.

And a baseball hat.

I didn't move. The night was very cold but suddenly I couldn't feel it. The man was backed by the blackened brickwork of the Victorian freight depot. He held the weapon steady as he took a step forward, his left foot dragging slightly as he did so.

'What the fuck do you want?'

It was the second time somebody had asked me that question recently. I still didn't have much of an answer to it. I was thinking what sort of a chance I'd have if I tried to bluff him out and get the gun off him. Not much.

He didn't seem upset that I hadn't answered his question. As he took another step forward his foot dragged again on the wet tarmac.

'Turn round.'

I didn't move. Turning round didn't seem like a wise

thing to do. I tried to find some spittle in the back of my throat.

'Listen,' I said, trying to sound casual, 'there's no need for this . . .'

'Shut the fuck up and turn around!' The voice was angry, nervous, not the sort you want with a finger behind it pressed against a trigger. I decided I may as well do what he said. He was standing far enough away that if I lunged for him he'd just blow my chest apart before I could reach him, and near enough that if I turned and made a pattern he couldn't easily miss if he wanted to blow a hole in my back.

Slowly, I edged round to the right until he was out of my frame of vision. I moved round some more and focused on the streetlight fifty yards across the road on York Way. I remembered speaking to a prostitute once, standing underneath that very lamppost. Why the fuck wasn't she there now? Why was there no one on the street at all? My throat was completely dry; I thought about it, but I couldn't have begged him if I wanted to. I did want to, and I would have if I'd thought it would have done any good. Why the hell not? But it wouldn't. I wondered if I would hear the shot. I wondered if I would even feel it. My stomach began to lurch, and then to tremble like there was a sparrow stuck in there. I suddenly became aware of an odour, a strong smell of aftershave. I couldn't tell which type. Through my fear I remember thinking, hey, that doesn't smell too bad.

I heard the foot scrape again. Then the entire freight depot fell on my head and the streetlight multiplied and spun around my eyes for a dazzling moment until everything was blackness.

*

When I came to I was inside.

Somehow I could tell this even though a thick canvas bag had been placed over my head and tied tightly round my neck with what I took to be a short length of rope. My hands were tied too, behind my back but not secured to anything. I was on a cold concrete floor. My head rang and I nearly threw up, which would have been a mistake given the bag. I could feel a cut on the back of my head where the butt of his gun had connected. I tried not to move, seeing if I could hear anything before my assailant knew I had woken up. He must have been watching me though and there's really nothing you can do to prevent the change in your body when you come into consciousness. I heard him stand up and push a steel chair aside violently which shrieked to a halt across the floor and then tipped over. I found myself pushing my feet against the floor, backing away from the sound that was coming towards me.

A hand grabbed my jacket and pulled me up. It then pushed me back and was replaced by two hands which jarred my back against the wall hard, three times in a row. I didn't resist except to try to keep my head from connecting. On the third time I was winded and started to cough violently. I was released and I kicked out, trying to get lucky where I thought his groin would be. I think I got the side of his leg and received a heavy, steel-capped toe in the ribs for my trouble. I curled up in pain, closing my arms on my sides, expecting more.

I heard the man step back and then take a few steps. There was a metallic sound and then another one much closer to me as the chair was set down and the man sat on it. There was silence for a second.

'I didn't think you were too bright. If you try anything else I'll blow your fucking bollocks off one by one.'

His voice was more controlled now, and mocking. It came to me muffled through the bag and my headache. I thought I caught a trace of North in it, Leeds maybe, from a long time ago. It was a white voice.

'Now then, Mr Rucker, I'm not very happy with you.'

'I guessed that.'

'Showing such a terrible photo of me around. It's a very poor likeness. I don't look very good at all.'

'You could let me have another one.'

'No. I've decided you're not going to be handing out any more photos.'

I heard the snap of a shotgun barrel as it was opened and shut again quickly.

'Not bad what you did to that flash coon Rollo though, I must say. I heard that some dentist somewhere is gonna make a nice few quid out of him. He'd wet his knickers if he knew I had you like this. He'd stick this fucking thing up your arse and you'd die with a smile on your face.'

The chair moved backwards and he came towards me.

'Me, I'm far more conventional.'

He gripped my jaw and forced the end of the gun barrel hard into my left eye, pushing my head back against the wall.

'What you know about me, hey?'

'Nothing.'

'No?'

'If I did I wouldn't be here like this, would I?'

'Maybe not. Maybe I'd be inside, hey, Rucker?'

'Maybe.'

'See, I know your name. Do you know mine?'

'Yeah, it's Cliff fucking Richard.'

He put his free hand round my neck, pushing it back and closing his fingers at the same time. I struggled for breath. I tried not to move too much, not knowing how much of a hair he kept his trigger on.

'It would be so easy,' he said. 'No one saw me come here, no one will see me leave.'

'My answerphone,' I said. 'Your voice is on it.'

'Clever. But it's not as if it'd make any difference if they did catch hold of me, would it?'

I didn't answer. He was right. He could kill ten more people and if they caught him for it he'd go away for exactly the same amount of time as if they caught him now.

'What have the Bill got?'

'Nothing,' I said. 'No one has anything.'

'Except the picture. You been pretty free with that, haven't you?'

I didn't answer that either. I tried to get my hands free without attracting his attention to the fact, but he'd done a pretty good job with them. I felt the grip on my throat relax and his body move back a little. The gun was still in my cheek and he pressed it in harder. I heard an assured click as he pulled the hammer back. I waited. I wouldn't hear the shot. I wouldn't feel it either.

We stayed like that for a long minute, the inside of the bag heating up more and more, the silence cut only by my own breathing and the small movements of the thick canvas. I wondered why he didn't just get it over with.

'Scared, Rucker?'

I was.

'Wish you'd stayed at home?'

I did.

'Wish you'd not gone round getting a bunch of shirts all excited with my pretty picture.'

I wished that too.

'Well, it's too fucking late, mate.'

He didn't say anything for a long time. I stayed in the present, I didn't think about anything profound. My mind didn't go anywhere. It turned off. All I could feel was fear, and pain great enough to force a way through it. I felt his hand round my neck again, this time at the back, pulling the rope tighter. I began to choke and I tried to struggle, realizing that he was going to do it that way. No noise. My struggling wasn't very effective but nevertheless he released the rope a bit, still holding it tight.

'No more pictures,' he said. 'Understand?' I was surprised. I tried to nod. He pushed the barrel even harder into my face. 'You're very lucky,' he said, in a voice that told me he was shaking his head. 'Very lucky indeed. I've heard you know certain people. If I hadn't heard that I wouldn't be telling you this. You'd have your brains splashed against this wall like some piece of modern fucking art.'

The way he was ramming the back of my head against the wall it felt like half my brain was smeared against it as it was. Sal, I thought, bless your cotton sweatpants. But surely she wasn't enough to stop him, was she? I didn't know. Right then I didn't care.

He still had hold of my jaw. He dug his fingers in and I could tell that his face was only a few inches away from mine. The face which had smiled at Edward Morgan, which had fooled a lorry driver, which had stood above the body of a schoolboy before its owner had ground a broken bottle into the remnants of the face it was looking down at. I got the strange sensation that somehow I had been in the state I was in now ever since I had started this case, ever since I had started handing out those pictures. The face was right in front of me but there was something in the way of me seeing it.

His hands relaxed and he moved away.

'You won't be lucky twice,' was all I heard him say.

Then the freight depot came down again.

I lay for a long time without trying to move. I had no idea how long I had been out this time but my whole body ached. I was dizzy with the thundering pain which was straining to burst my skull open and this time I did throw up. I gasped for air, finding it difficult to get the pieces of vomit out of my mouth, the thick canvas of the bag being sucked in every time I took a breath. I coughed and retched madly for a bit, panicked that I was going to suffocate, and then I made myself calm down and breathe through my nose. I listened for any sounds other than the ones I was making myself. I couldn't hear anything other than the slow movement of a car cruising down York Way. I lay still for a second, straining to hear if he was still there, waiting for me to try and get up. The place had an empty feel and I decided he'd left.

I was lying on my front, and I tried to turn over on to my side so that I could hook my hands under my feet. I winced at the pain in my side where he had kicked me and decided that he must have broken a rib or two. I rolled over on to the other side and managed to get my hands in front of me.

I undid the rope around my neck first and pulled the bag over my head, getting vomit in my eyes and in my hair. The air tasted good. I looked into the darkness and then scrunched the bag up and used the outside of it to wipe myself down quickly. I then moved my hands back and forth to create some slack and managed to pick at the many knots enough to be able to pull my left hand out. I loosed the slack on my right hand, threw it aside, and rubbed my wrists with the flats of my palms. Then I looked for a way out. I struggled to stand up, did it too quickly, and threw up again, a heave of bile which sent darts of agony spearing through my ribs. This time it was on the floor in front of me.

There wasn't much light in the place. I was surrounded by huge shapes which I took to be piles of boxes and container crates. I leant against one, waiting to make sure that I wasn't going to heave again. My stomach calmed down. I still couldn't see much. I fumbled around for a light switch without success. I bumped into the chair which the guy had been sitting on and realized that he must have been using a torch. He wouldn't have wanted any light to show from outside. The bag he'd used on me was heavy-duty canvas and I wouldn't have been able to tell if he'd been keeping me in broad daylight.

Eventually I found the door and managed to slide it open. I couldn't stop it making a loud, wrenching noise. I could see a huge, broken padlock hanging off it where he'd broken in. I stepped out cautiously into a courtyard. I was at the back of a building, with a dim security bulb casting deep shadows. I was nervous. I pulled up my sleeve and could just make out that it was now almost five thirty. There was no sign of the sun. I hesitated a second or two but reasoned to myself that if my attacker had wanted to kill me he wouldn't have waited until I was outside, with room to move, but would have done it when he had me tied up and blindfolded. Nevertheless, I looked cautiously round the corner before moving out into the space at the front of the depot. A sudden throb of pain in my head nearly took my legs away and I had to use the wall for support. Fuck it, a Brownie could have taken me out now if she'd wanted to. I pushed myself off the wall and walked awkwardly into the open space, towards the trailer which the man in the baseball hat had been hiding behind.

The trailer held no more unpleasant surprises for me. I passed it and walked out towards the street. The street-light was still there but this time there *was* a girl standing beneath it. I walked towards her, holding my head, and she must have thought I was a drunk the way I was moving.

'You got any money?'

She was frail and rather old. She wasn't attractive in any sense I could see. But then again, I wasn't exactly in the mood, no matter what she looked like. There would be men who were.

'Did you see a man,' I asked, pointing behind me, 'come out of there. Wearing a hat?'

'Fuck off,' the girl told me. I was too tired to argue with her.

My car was still where I'd left it. When I got to it I suddenly panicked, worried that he might have gone through my pockets for either my car keys or the money he'd told me to bring. The keys were still there but there was no money of course as I hadn't taken any with me. I wondered if he'd had a look and been disappointed. I didn't care. I just wanted to get home.

For a second I considered not driving. Two bangs on the head would rule me out as far as any medical expert would have been concerned, but there was no way I'd get a taxi anywhere. I got in and turned the key and nothing happened. I nearly began to cry. I waited and nothing happened again. I was about to stumble out, open the bonnet and take a look when I realized that I was on a slight incline, facing down towards King's Cross. I put the Mazda in gear, used both hands to release the handbrake and let her move forward. When she had picked up a bit of speed I pulled my foot off the clutch and the engine fired. I drove home very carefully, feeling like someone had installed the most powerful stereo in my car and turned the volume up to maximum. It was all bass, and my head was the only speaker.

I couldn't think about this. I just wanted to get into bed. As I drove along, pictures and sentences kept surfacing in my brain, but I just focused on the red lights and the road ahead and making sure I used the indicator when I turned right or left. I didn't want to get stopped. I got home slowly but without any trouble only to find that someone had taken my parking space. I parked in a delivery bay two streets away. I locked the car and walked down Exmouth Market to my flat. It was cold again and I shivered into a tunnel of wind, pulling my coat tight round me. I was tired, and as I got used to the throbbing in my skull my cheekbone began to hurt where the gun had been rammed into it. That pain was sharper and more defined and strangely comforting. The image of my bed was almost too much to bear now and I hurried myself along, holding one hand up to the cut on my cheek. It was wet with blood and I was surprised by that. My bed called to me; the sheets were still twisted round my form, the pillows packed together with a nest for my head. I'd take three Advils, get in, and all this would be a very bad dream.

My outside door was open. It was an inch ajar. Did I forget to lock it? I didn't think so but then I wasn't in the best frame of mind to remember a detail like that. I had been in a hurry. But when I looked closer I saw the lock had been forced. There was splintering on both the jamb and the door itself.

I pushed the door open a slice and peered up the stairs. Darkness. My hand moved towards the hall switch but I pulled it away. I listened. Nothing. I couldn't believe I'd been burgled. Maybe the man in the hat had set it up with some kids as a further warning that he could get to me. Maybe it was a fluke, a bizarre off-chance. What about Lloyd's goon? I stood, looking up the stairs, holding my breath, trying to figure out what was going on. I was vaguely aware that I was doing it to put off going up there. What if he'd changed his mind? What if he was up in my flat, sitting on my bed with his sawn-off shotgun in his hand? I still didn't really know why a man who had shown absolutely no compunction in killing at least three other men had let me go. What if he'd decided he didn't care who I knew?

I pushed the door open some more and stepped into the short, narrow hallway. I tried to remember if any of the stairs creaked at all. I stood at the bottom deciding what to do. Call the police? I didn't know. He couldn't have been up there, an idiot could have seen the state the door was in. What if nothing had been taken, what if he'd just done the door, done it himself after leaving me unconscious to show that he knew where I lived and he could break in when he felt like it? I'd look stupid if I called the police. I'd feel stupid.

I put a foot on the bottom stair. It didn't make any very loud noise and neither did any of the steps above it.

At the top of the stairs I saw that the door to my flat-proper had received the same treatment as the street door, only this door wasn't ajar but wide open.

I stopped again, peering into the darkness and up the stairs inside the door, which lead up to the studio. Again I couldn't hear anything. Again I had the same doubts and questions. I was afraid. No rationalization of the circumstances could quench the childish terror in me and my stomach started to flutter once more. I stepped forward and gripped the handrail, preparing myself for another meeting with a murderer, or the kind of mess I had witnessed in a lot of houses but never my own. Furniture everywhere, spray-can graffiti, drawers out, a turd or two among the debris. I walked up the stairs slowly.

I stopped in the doorway.

There wasn't a murderer in my flat. By the light of the anglepoise lamp by my bed, which I had left on, I could see that no one had ransacked it either. Or taken anything. My flat was exactly the same as I had left it, the drawers in, the furniture upright, and the walls still clear, with only the numbered Salgado print to decorate them. The only thing different was my bed.

On my bed lay a young man. He was naked, on his back. His arms were stretched up behind his head as though begging someone not to shoot him. He was covered in welts, cuts and bruises, and his stomach had been torn open. He had had his penis severed, and it lay on his chest, shrivelled up small, covered in blood like a newborn rat.

Chapter Sixteen

I stood in the silence of my room, my eyes pulled down to the body on my bed. I had a sudden flash of my brother, lying in what was left of my car, covered in blood. All of the pain I felt melted away and I found that I could neither move, nor take my eyes from the sight which had stopped me far more suddenly than any bang on the head. I felt a constriction in my chest and realized that I had stopped breathing, not wanting time to advance another second from where it stood now. I could taste the bile at the back of my throat and, when I did draw breath, the air was sickly sweet and so thick I could almost feel it against my tongue.

The boy was lying on top of my duvet with his face covered by a pillow. The duvet was drenched with his blood, especially beneath his belly, which was gouged open to its innards, with the skin pulled back to show his organs like an anatomical model. His torso and both his legs had been hacked at too, deep wounds running down the insides of his thighs from his groin to both of his knees.

The boy was a mess. I forced myself to take a step forward. And another. I found it difficult to take in what I was seeing. The smell grew stronger. The centre of my chest burned. I walked round and stood to the side of the raised futon. The lamp burned away happily. On the floor there was the bottom half of a wine bottle lying parallel to the boy's head. From the label I could see it was one of mine; it was the Grange, the Grange '86 which had cost a fortune and I'd been saving. The rug was stained deep red beneath it. I bent down to look closer but I didn't touch the bottle.

The top half of the bottle was rammed into the boy's throat. It was wedged in place between his chin and his breastbone. The pillow covering the boy's head was resting on top of it. The boy's head was propped forward by other pillows to create the pressure sufficient to hold the bottle in place. I could see behind the sides of the pillow; an ear, the side of a head. I put my hand on the pillow.

I didn't want to do this. I took my hand away and then I put it back. I took a breath before pulling the pillow off and setting it down on the floor next to the wine bottle. Then I turned my head back slowly and deliberately to look at the top of the bed.

I saw what I expected to see.

The boy was staring at a place high up above the door I had come through. His eyes were open but his mouth was shut, like he was watching a film at the cinema. He looked calm and unconcerned about what had happened to him. Only a little surprised. He looked casually unaware that he had half a broken bottle stuck in his throat, like a bank manager with his tie in his pint. His face was untouched. It was completely unmarked, the clear, simple features contrasting with the rest of his body which was covered in either slash wounds or the blood from them. I looked down at the face for some time, the full lips, the strong, dark eyebrows. He was looking away from me and I remembered how he had turned and looked away from me before. I bit into my bottom lip. On impulse I bent over and I ran my hand through the short, cheap vanilla ice-cream coloured hair. The vanilla went straight to the roots. I closed his staring eyes and walked over to the telephone.

I picked up the receiver and dialled three nines. I started to tell the girl that I needed the police but stopped when I heard a sound. It was the petulant whine of a siren, backed by an engine working too hard. It was close. It was getting closer. I told the girl to hold on, put the receiver on the table by the phone and walked over to the window. I made a hole in the blind. I was in time to see a squad car turn hard into my street and then I heard it screech to a stop outside my building. I heard two doors slam and hurried footsteps. I heard the footsteps stop at the bottom of the stairs.

I was in a flat with a corpse and I was covered in blood and vomit. Someone must have seen something going on, one of the postal workers from Mount Pleasant maybe, and called it in. Or else . . . I turned to the door and was suddenly confronted by Dominic. That thing on his chest. I wanted to cover him, take that bottle out of his throat, but I knew I couldn't do that. I waited for the sound of feet on the stairs and wasn't long in getting it.

I wanted to speak to them before they came running in and saw what there was to see in my flat. I hurried over to the door and got halfway down the first flight of stairs. I stopped before they turned into the door at the bottom, so that they wouldn't think I was trying to leg it. I wanted to tell the officers what they were going to see, to make sure they were rational and controlled about it. I wanted to tell them before they found it themselves. I wanted that to be on record.

I called out.

'Up here.'

A tall figure appeared at the door.

'There's a switch, just to your left. On the wall.'

A hand reached out and pushed the timer and the small bulb popped on. There were two of them, both about my age, a man and a woman, both staring up at me. I told them what was up in the flat behind me and that I had come home to find it. They both looked shocked, nervous. I told them they had nothing to worry about from me and that I wouldn't make any trouble. The WPC broke the silence by telling me to step back into the flat. She took a step towards me. I didn't much want to go back in there but I agreed.

I sat in the far corner, at the table, while the WPC made a brief examination of the body. The PC stood square in the doorway, glancing round anxiously at the windows in the front and the skylight to his right; any possible exits. Both of the officers were very efficient and neither of them made a scene or produced the torrents of vomit I have witnessed on similar, far less gruesome occasions. The PC was almost immediately on his radio reporting what he had found, asking for assistance, and I knew that very soon there wouldn't be a whole lot of room in my flat. By now, both officers were glaring at me, trying to decide if I really was going to cooperate with them and not try anything. Their faces told me that they didn't have any doubt as to what had happened here before they'd arrived.

I held my head, which was starting to thud again, the

contents of my room threatening to move on their own, to spin and merge into one another.

'You found him like this, is that what you're saying?'

Involuntarily, I followed her glance to my futon. It brought me back a little. 'Yes,' I said.

'And did you touch anything?' The WPC went to stand halfway between myself and Dominic. She should have called me Sir. But I understood the extenuating circumstances.

'No,' I said. 'Nothing. The pillow, I pulled it off his face.'

'Why?'

'Wouldn't you have?'

'And you live here you say?'

'Yes.'

'Where had you been before you came back?'

That was all the small talk I could manage. I held my head in my hands and ignored the question and then the others they pummelled me with. They gave up and the WPC asked her colleague whether or not we shouldn't all be waiting outside. The PC said better not but didn't give a reason. The three of us waited the ten minutes it took before anyone else arrived. I spent it keeping my eyes away from Dominic, fingering the blue folder my brother's poems were in, which had lain on the table for almost a week. I even pondered taking them out but the WPC looked nervous.

'Please don't touch anything,' she said, with an edge in her voice which she didn't bother trying to conceal.

'Sir,' I mumbled. I put the file down.

When the next car drew up and cut its siren the PC walked down and did the same thing I had, briefing the officers on the way up. There were two of them, both plainclothes, one very big, almost a kid. The other was a man I vaguely recognized, a tall, thin man with a very small head and a face which was so pinched it looked like a clay model. The elder one looked shaken but the younger one tried his best to look cynical and unconcerned, disgusted by the moral implications of the events only. They were followed in by four uniforms, each one taken aback like a row of dominoes. The elder plainclothes sat down opposite me and asked me a few simple questions which I answered, and then some harder ones which I did not. He cuffed me and then he led me past Dominic Lewes, who would soon be photographed by someone other than myself, and down into the street, by which time there was a total of four marked and two unmarked cars blocking the road outside my flat. I could see a space, a space in the row of cars where mine had been parked, but which had been occupied when I'd come back from the depot. I tried to remember the make of the car that had been there. An Escort. I thought it was an Escort.

I was pushed through a small, official crowd of sullen faces, all full of either curiosity or contempt, towards the top of the street. The morning was still dark and there was only the odd postman about to see me taken past the newly erected cordon and bundled into the back of one of the marked cars. It took less than five minutes before the car had arrived at the station on Carlisle Street.

Chapter Seventeen

It had been a long night. It turned out to be a long morning too. It was obvious that I was exhausted and having difficulty focusing but they didn't let me sleep. I wouldn't have done either. I was left to stew for twenty minutes and then the officer who had cuffed me came in with his younger colleague. The colleague looked like a big farm boy, strong enough to pull a tractor, and I hoped it didn't get nasty. I was feeling bad enough already.

A medical officer came in and took scrapings from underneath my fingernails as well as hair samples for matching and possible DNA profiling. I was asked to remove all my clothes and these were taken from me. They would be analysed for blood and semen traces, as well as for stray hairs or pieces of skin which did not belong to me. The medical officer then examined my body for cuts, scratching and bruises; plenty of which could be found. He paid particular attention to my groin area, taking swabs from my penis and removing more hair. The two officers sat in disgusted though joyful silence throughout, both with their arms folded in front of them. I was given a pair of jeans and a sweatshirt to wear but no shoes, socks, shorts or any underpants.

The medical officer expressed the opinion that I should see a doctor, both for the superficial wounds to my face and head, but also for suspected broken ribs and concussion.

'Let the bastard suffer,' the young man opined, but the doctor was sent for.

I asked for a lawyer and gave the uniformed officer minding the door Mike Williams' number.

'Shame his office isn't open yet, isn't it?' The older man stood up and brought his chair over to face me at the desk. 'Don't mind if we start without him, do you?'

It didn't matter what I minded. In fact, I was glad to get on with it; I wanted them to get an officer round to the freight depot on York Way to find evidence of what had happened to me there. With any luck there would still be the bag with my blood in it. That's if they got there before some idiot chucked it out. They might even get some prints off it if I was lucky.

I went through the events of the evening from going to the gym, and seeing Nicky, to getting the phone call and what had happened after that. I didn't know whether or not to mention the fact that I'd known Dominic Lewes but decided I should. There were files in my office that could link me to him. I told them how I had photographed him and beaten up his pimp who was apparently known as Rollo. I told them that the man who had beaten me up had mentioned his name. I told them that a Ford Escort, five or six years old, had been parked outside my flat but had gone by the time the police arrived. It was my opinion that its owner had killed Dominic, left his body in my flat and then waited outside for me to come home before making a call to the police. All of this was noted with clearly displayed scepticism.

I was beyond tired and it was now my ribs which were giving me the most trouble. Discovering Dominic's body in my flat had taken my mind off the painkillers I had intended taking and I asked if I could have some.

'The doctor will be here soon, sir,' the older man said with a smile.

The doctor didn't come for another hour, and only then because I refused to answer any more questions until he did, and took to groaning quietly. Not wanting a cell mortality on their records the two officers let the doctor into the room and he bandaged my head and my ribs and put a dressing on my face. He sent for a nurse and an hour later they stitched up the wound on the back of my head. The front of the head is harder, the doctor informed me. He was told not to give me anything that would send me to sleep. He didn't give me anything.

All I had to do was sit it out. Both the pain and the interrogation. I was nervous, but the physical evidence would say that I had been at York Way as I had claimed, and the police would find no forensic evidence on Dominic Lewes to say I had killed or indeed been anywhere near him. The ravings of the two officers, taking it in turns to play bad cop and bad cop, sailed over me. I gazed round at the dull grey walls, at the flimsy table, perfect for sweeping aside in dramatic temper tantrums by detectives who have seen too many reruns of *The Sweeney*. I drank three cups of lukewarm gun oil and as the tiny window announced the coming day, I waited for the appearance of my friend the Chief Inspector. The Chief liked to take a personal interest in the bigger cases, and I'd have to go through it all with him anyway so there was no point saying a great deal to these two. I tried to make some sort of sense out of what had happened, how everything had got tangled up together, but I could hardly make the table sit still let alone figure something which seemed totally incomprehensible. What did Dominic Lewes have to do with what I was doing for Sir Peter Morgan?

The Chief didn't come at all that day. They let me have two hours' sleep and Mike Williams came at around ten. He wasn't a criminal lawyer but he was glad to help and would know who to get in if it looked like I was going to need anyone special. I told him that I didn't need him around for the interrogations. He asked me if he should demand that I be sent to a hospital but I said no, it would only slow things down. I kept expecting Andy Gold to show up but then remembered he'd been taken off the case. I kept expecting him to show up anyway, because we were supposed to be friends, but then remembered that friendship can be an embarrassing concept for a police officer, especially if the friend in question is a suspect, a likely candidate for serial killer.

Milson and Clarke went at me all afternoon but I didn't tell them anything that I hadn't before. They tried to pick holes in my story, especially the York Way episode which I had no witnesses to, but when what you are telling is the truth your story tends to stand up – if you ignore the deviations and stick to the facts. It pissed them off, I could tell, but they still thought they probably had me. They asked me where I was the night John Evans was killed, where I was when James Waldock had been butchered and what I had been doing the night Edward Morgan had taken a man back to his flat. I couldn't tell them of course, not without looking at my diary, and they got a lot of pleasure out of that. They even sent for a baseball hat, which they put on my head, gazing at me in profile with copies of the picture I had been showing round in their hands. They photographed me and I assumed that they would be showing my picture round to the people they had interviewed already.

I tried to remember how long forensics people took. I was more than three years out of date but I did know that a case like this would get top billing. I figured that if the Chief wasn't here then the report wasn't ready yet; he wouldn't waste his time if there was a chance that forensic evidence would prove it one way or another. Milson and Clarke were just to soften me up, to keep me awake and my head hurting. I remembered what a good detective the Chief had been, what a calculating, heartless, vindictive bastard. Even if he knew I had nothing to do with it he'd have let Milson and Clarke have a go at me, to see if I knew anything else which might be useful to him.

At seven that night I was taken from the holding cell to an interview room and was eventually joined by Ken Clay, the Chief Inspector of Islington Police. He came into the room quickly, accompanied by a humourless, sour-faced DC I had never seen before. He pulled the chair opposite me and sat on it, his thighs running over the sides like a cake rising out of a tin.

'Well, Billy boy, we have been busy, haven't we?'

Clay's face was a huge, fleshy maze of broken vessels and his hands were too; matching mounds of unbleached tripe. He had placed a folder on top of the table and he pulled the contents out of it. He leafed through the fifteen or so pages briskly, his fingers clumsy, not built for such close work. He put them down and then smiled, giving me a flash of lurid red gums above yellow teeth stained with black.

'All of it. From the beginning. Don't leave anything out.'

I took a breath and went through it, from first meeting the MP, to trying to get a picture of Dominic Lewes, to the night before last when I'd been beaten up and come home to find a corpse in my bed. I didn't tell him about Charlotte and Lloyd but not for any other reason than belligerence. I'd let him have it if it looked like he was going to guess there was something missing. Clay's face was a livid mask.

When I'd finished, he sat back.

'You beat up a pimp and then the boy you're after winds up starkers, without his cock, in your bed, after someone sees you threatening a young lad with a knife and forcing him into your doorway.'

'What knife? That's crap, that's absolute crap.'

Clay laughed. 'Glad I'm not you, Billy.'

'I took his point but tried to ignore the mocking, self-satisfied tone. 'Who is he, the caller?'

'The caller preferred to remain anonymous.'

'What about the pimp? Have you found *him* yet?'

'He's relaxing downstairs.' Clay was pretending to be affable. I was surprised he was letting me ask him questions.

'He's still got a bit of a face on him. Claims he was mugged, doesn't know anything about any boy prostitutes or private detectives.'

'He was in Dominic's house, I saw him.'

'I know, I know. I believe you there, Billy. There. Just giving him rope to hang himself. You know the score.'

He fumbled for the top sheet of paper on the table and managed to pick it up. The DC sat up a bit.

'Now then,' he said. 'What have we got?' Clay's

sarcasm was stronger than his aftershave. 'A corpse in your flat, not *only* that of a boy you were looking for but *also* connected to a job you've been doing for a bereaved MP; exactly the same MO as that used by a serial killer the MP had paid you to look for. Curious. We've then got a flat door which has been broken into, very probably by your good self to make it look like someone else did it. Not very convincing. And . . .' Clay looked over at the DC and then at me. 'Thanks to Dr Burg at the forensics lab, we've got something a jury would be very interested in. *Very* interested in indeed.'

Clay leant forward. The DC sneered. They both stared at me with a look I recognized; that of detectives who had something. What? What forensic evidence? I began to get an uncomfortable feeling in the pit of my stomach. Did he mean fingerprints? It was my flat for God's sake. Blood on my clothes? Maybe, but it was mine and I had already accounted for it. Hadn't they checked the freight depot? What else could they have? I figured they were just fishing, but I didn't like the look on them.

I waited for it. Clay cleared his throat and read from the page.

' "On examination of the back passage no semen was found although traces of Nonoxynol were evident as were two hairs which, under examination, did not match those of the victim. They probably arrived there during the anal intercourse which accounts for the presence of the Nonoxynol. The hairs are both compatible with those usually found in the groin region." ' Clay paused and the DC sat up even straighter than he had been doing. Clay pointed his chin at me.

' "Microscope analysis of the hairs, and of those taken from the suspect in custody, shows that the hairs are of the same colour, width and type as the suspect's pubic hair, though only a DNA match could prove they came from the same person. At this stage I would *guess* at a likely positive outcome. The samples have been sent to Cambridge and I will advise when the results are in." JM Burg MD.'

Clay put the paper aside and raised his eyebrows. A muscle twitched in my jaw which could have been seen a mile away. I looked Clay in the eye.

'They were in my bed.'

Clay shook his head slowly. He spoke softly. 'They were up his arse you mean. They were way up there.'

'He shoved them up there, he . . .' I stopped speaking. There was no point, I was just falling into his trap, getting angry. A well of doubt rose from my bowels.

'They were found on my bed,' I said as calmly as I could. 'They were found by the killer and placed in the corpse to deflect suspicion from him on to me. The whole thing is a set-up to do that.' I tried to sound sure but Clay was right; evidence like that was always compelling in the hands of the right prosecution brief. Crying 'frame-up' always sounds like clutching at straws. Clay didn't say anything, waiting for me.

'I would hardly be likely to do him in my own flat, would I?'

'You could have got carried away. Butchering young boys isn't exactly logical, wherever you do it.'

'What about time of death?' I said.

'A couple of hours previous to discovery, maybe three. You could have done it easily.'

I turned my head away. A dead kid in my bed with my pubic hair inside his body. Caught red-handed, on the scene, after a tip-off. Mike Williams, I thought, I hope you know someone good.

'I wasn't there, I told you.'

'Yes, yes, York Way and the Big Bad Wolf.'

'Did you check it?'

'You were there, Billy, I'll give you that. Prints on the door handle like you said and a bag full of puke. Some blood. But there's nothing to say at what *time* you were there. What I think is you went there earlier, before picking up the arse and—'

'A girl, a whore on the road. I spoke to her . . .'

'Got a name? An address? Might be difficult to find her.'

Clay put down the sheet and picked up another. He started to read it, not seeming particularly interested in me. He was strangely subdued and I didn't know why. He would usually have gone after something this good like a bull through a gate in springtime. My mouth was dust. Clay let out a sigh. Then he shook his head and smiled.

'Such a shame,' he said, turning to the DC. 'It would have been very convenient.' He looked back at me. 'Not that I would have wanted to see a distinguished ex-colleague like yourself go down, mind you. No.' He paused and glanced back at the A4 sheet before putting it down. 'I fibbed about the time of death I'm afraid. It was earlier. Burg is sure it wasn't much after seven and it can't have been earlier than six-thirty because the boy was seen going into the Mcdonald's in King's Cross at that time. He was a regular and a lassie there recognized him.'

I took that on board. I was in the gym. Pete. Sal. Witnesses.

'Why did you check the Mcdonald's?' I asked. I was

relieved, curiosity moving into the space being vacated by panic.

'You've to thank Burg for it. If I were you I'd send him a bunch of flowers.' Clay pushed the pile of papers towards me and I picked up the top one and looked at it. 'There was a Big Mac in his stomach, or at least a small part of one. Burg patched it from the mayonnaise. You'd already told us the lad worked the King's Cross area so we checked the restaurant.'

I scanned the page trying to find the part I wanted. I couldn't. 'Where was the rest of it?' I asked. 'The burger?' I had a horrible feeling that I knew what the answer would be. Clay's smile made me feel slightly sick.

'Removed,' he said.

I saw a gaping hole of blood and intestines. Clay read from the sheet again.

' "Only a small part of the food was found, which had been chewed but had not begun to be digested, indicating that it cannot have been present for more than an hour at most. It is my opinion that the rest of the burger, assuming that all of it was consumed by the victim, was removed by the perpetrator to avoid an accurate assessment of the time of death. This theory is compatible with other evidence, specifically the slashing open of the stomach and the disturbance of other local organs." ' Clay pursed his lips and nodded to himself again. 'Clever fellow. Burg too. I'm not sure every stiff stitcher would have spotted that. He says he suspected something like it when he saw how the stomach had been carved up, and that's why he looked so closely for the food. There wasn't much of it left by all accounts.'

I caught a picture of two bloody hands scraping the contents out of Dominic Lewes' stomach.

'It means, of course, that your movements can be accounted for.'

I shut the picture out.

'Like I said. And the hair, I mean, he put it there. You can accept that, can't you?'

'Maybe. Or you could have fucked him before he met his maker. We might do you for that. Sex with a minor.'

I ignored that. 'But how did he get the kid into my flat? I'd gone back after the gym, he wasn't there then, after Burg says he was killed.'

'You're sure of that?'

'I'd have noticed,' I said.

Clay paused. He liked having me on the hook. He didn't want to let me go lightly, simply because I was the wrong fish.

'He was killed somewhere else,' he admitted finally. 'The body was moved. He'd been strangled. There was very little shit on your sheets which would not have been the case had he been done there. The blood patterns were wrong too, the major arteries didn't spurt the way they should have if his heart was beating. The boy kind of just leaked. All that gory stuff in your place was cosmetic. He carried the boy up there and *then* had his home anatomy lesson.'

'He was hoping I was out.'

'Or he was waiting outside till you *went* out.'

I thought for a second.

'Or he knew I was unconscious and he did it then,' I said. 'He was having a go at me and all the time Dominic's body was in the boot of his car.'

'Possible,' Clay admitted. 'Possibly so.'

Clay looked wistful. I'd seen him look that way before. It was the distant, all but faded ghost of compassion, conjured up by a vision of Dominic Lewes. He shook it off with a laugh.

'By the way, we had a look in your office, to see if we couldn't link you with the lorry driver or the other rent boy. Or Morgan. We found the keys in your flat. Your office diary said you were in the clear but we checked anyway. Some dodgy bar owner we weren't sure about and then a lawyer bird called Sharon. She backed you up.' Clay laughed again. 'Your office is not what you'd call impressive, is it? You doing well in the private sector, Rucker?'

Having established that I was no longer in the frame Clay asked me questions about the man in the hat. I told him that he might be from the North, and that he had practically admitted being the killer. He'd said it didn't matter if he killed me, he would go away for the same stretch anyway. Clay asked me if I'd seen enough of him to add to the picture image; apparently there's now a computer program that can do stuff like that. I told him that, unfortunately, I had not. I told Clay about the Escort. Whoever it was had obviously been waiting in it, and when I came back he called in a report about a young kid and a man with a knife. Clay said he'd already put it out on the wire.

I sat back in the chair and stretched. An hour or so had passed. Clay asked me about Rollo and I told him what had happened, that the Morgan thing and looking for Dominic were completely unconnected.

'They're not any more,' Clay said.

I asked if Clay had grilled Rollo on the man in the hat. Clay said he had but he'd pleaded ignorance. They were going to have another go at him. Clay said he thought that was the best bet for now, the closest they were to him;

Rollo was someone he knew of even if Rollo didn't know him.

I relaxed some more, allowing latent exhaustion to begin to spread into my bones. I was waiting for Clay to tell me I could go home. But he didn't. He put the sheets of A4 back into the file and sent the duty officer out for tea. He also turned the tape recorder off.

'Right then, Rucker.' Clay made a movement with his hips and his whole enormous frame shivered forward in the chair. 'What have you got?' I was about to reply but I was cut off. 'And don't give me any shit. You're close. The guy in the picture picked on you and then this bumboy winds up in your bed after you've had a go at his daddy. Not for the first time he's been there I don't imagine but this time he's dead. You're close, I know it. So give it to me.'

I shrugged my shoulders. He'd done this the wrong way round. If he'd said this when I thought I would be facing twelve indignant citizens having to explain what my pubic hairs were doing in the anal passage of a murdered fifteen-year-old rent boy I might have tried to answer. Now, I didn't have to say a thing.

'Tell me about Lloyd.'

That surprised me. How did he know?

'Lloyd?' I said.

'I've had Mother Teresa on my back. He says that a certain former detective from my division had been harassing a prominent and respected MP.'

'A different matter,' I said.

'Like fuck it is!'

'And harassment is a bit strong. I just wanted to chat.'

'About what? What did you want to chat about?'

I shrugged.

'TELL ME WHAT YOU *CHATTED* ABOUT!'

Clay continued to ask me that question, or tributaries of it, for the next hour, at a steady increase in volume. He also wanted to know what Dominic Lewes had to do with Morgan and simply would not believe that I was working on two things at once. He mentioned terrifying terms such as 'withholding evidence' and 'perverting the course of justice', but I knew the law. I didn't know the link between the two things myself, and I still couldn't think of a reason to tell him about Lloyd and Charlotte. There wasn't much the police could do other than lean on Lloyd and hope for a very unlikely confession. They had to catch the man who had beaten me up. Without him they didn't have anything.

He got tired eventually.

'You better find out what's going on, Rucker, and you'd better tell me when you know, or I'll make some big shit for you. We're checking that gym story of yours again and if it looks like you might not have been there exactly when you said, you'll be back in here quicker than piss down a drain. Hear me?'

Clay left in as much of a hurry as he'd arrived. A sergeant came in. My clothes were returned to me and I put them on; all except my shirt which would have to go in the nearest bin. I was allowed to keep the sweatshirt they had given me. I was made to sign for everything and was offered a lift home, which I initially declined. I didn't know whether or not I wanted to go home. I wanted to think about it over a curry but then I realized that I had no money on me. I changed my mind about the lift and told the sergeant on the front desk that. He said I should take a seat and wait.

It was now ten thirty and I was shafted. The adrenalin

which had kept my system in operation for the last thirty-six hours had drained away and all that was left was a deep lake of fatigue, along with a diminishing pain in my head and on my face, and an increasing pain in my ribs. I didn't rate the chance of sleep too highly though. It would have to be on the sofa in my flat, or on the sofabed in my office, and anyway the whirl of questions which had been stirred by the events of the last day and a half, but kept in the back of my brain, had begun to spin right out into the front of it.

Who broke into my flat? How did Dominic fit in? Lloyd, was Lloyd involved? It seemed ludicrous to think so but I couldn't think of anything more plausible. But if he was, why carry on after doing Edward? To fit me up? Really? Or *was* it all the same guy? How had the man got the picture with my address on the back? Was he in one of the pubs I went to? Did I speak to him? Had I spoken to the killer, been friendly, given him information to help him find me? Find Dominic?

And how the hell was I going to find any of this out?

When the boy in blue came to give me my ride he was plainly pissed off at having to do so. It was a course in crime detection he'd done, not the Knowledge. I ignored his attitude and told him where I lived. I'd decided to go home because I had some cash there which I could pick up and then cab it down to the twenty-four-hour greasy spoon on Theobald's Road before deciding where to sleep. At least I hoped I had some cash. My flat had been broken into by a psychopath *and* given the once-over by a team of detectives. Was it likely? At least I could change out of these clothes and pick up my cash card or a chequebook.

The car stopped at the top of Exmouth Market. I

walked down towards my flat, wondering if the police had left it open or fixed the door jamb for me. I wasn't looking forward to going in there. I wondered how much clearing up they'd done. I was tired, hungry, and in no small amount of pain. As I got closer I saw the light from Fred's Café on the right and I wondered if it was still open. It was quarter past eleven and I knew it would be but there wouldn't be any food on. They'd probably do me a sandwich if I pleaded but I wanted something hot. I walked past the café and was about to turn down towards my flat when I heard the door swing open. I glanced round as a figure hurried out of the door towards me. My heart bucked in my chest on impulse and I turned, backing away, pulling my hands out of my pockets.

'Billy!'

Sharon stood in front of me. I let out a breath. She went to put her arms around me, but stopped when I winced. She looked at me for a second, holding on to my arm, and then held a hand up to my face, lightly touching the bruising beneath my left eye.

'Oh, Billy,' Sharon said. Her voice was a mixture of worry and relief. It sounded good. Her eyes reached up for mine. Sharon rested her hand on my shoulder.

'They called me,' she said. 'I came but they wouldn't let me see you. I've been here all day. I was so worried.' Sharon's hand moved across my bruising again. She moved her body closer to me. The pain I was feeling, and the exhaustion and the latent fear, all seemed to rise up and out of me like the soul from a dead man's body. All the misunderstandings, the problems we'd had, went too. There wasn't anything left, nothing but the face in front of me, and the pleasure I felt seeing it there. I moved forward, filling the small gap between us, and Sharon's fingers closed round my neck.

'Oh, Billy,' Sharon said.

And then there was fear greater than when a shotgun had been pointed at my head.

'I love you. I love you so much.'

Chapter Eighteen

We stood in the street and we kissed for a long time. After that we just stood holding on to each other. I didn't want to let her go. I didn't want to not be holding her, I didn't want to deal with what we were doing or what would happen next. I felt hollow and weak. Eventually Sharon started to shiver with the cold and I released her and watched her run back into Fred's for her coat which she had left on the back of a chair.

Later, in her flat, we made love, gently at first because of my ribs, but then with a fervour which brooked no mitigation for pain or injury. Sharon was so familiar to me but her body was so strange; I found it odd that the woman I knew should have this great store of sexuality, a physicality which was as much herself as the Sharon I had known had been. Her full breasts, her nipples, her belly, her sex, the flushed look on her face when I entered her. This was not a woman I had known, not a woman I had even suspected. It was as though, when I helped her undo the buttons of her blouse, I hadn't expected to find anything underneath. What I did find was exhilarating, a nakedness so complete I was winded by it, a fist clenching desperate fingers round my heart.

I hadn't thought about anything, not even in the taxi over to West London during which we had sat, hands tight together, not speaking a word. Neither of us had said what was going to happen or spoken about the future. Sharon had led me up to her flat and then into her bedroom where we'd kissed for a long time before Sharon pulled away, her face solemn, her hands going to the bottom of my T-shirt which we pulled over my head. My ribs were bandaged and Sharon carefully undid them and then kissed the bruising there and held her cheek against it. When we were both naked we just sat looking at each other, the slightest sad smile on her lips, my bones light but my stomach heavy. I felt like I was about to throw up. Sharon moved under her duvet and I joined her beneath it, merging into the warmth and a smell which was so familiar but richer than I had ever experienced it. We held on to each other and Sharon drew me inside her almost immediately, her hand cold on my cock, her sex full and so wet I moved straight into her. We made love slowly, hardly moving, unwilling to surrender our skin to even the shortest moment of not touching. We came with our mouths locked together, Sharon's teeth biting into my lower lip.

We had both been completely silent, and now we lay together, Sharon clinging to the side of my torso which wasn't bruised, both my arms around her neck and shoulders. We still didn't speak, and there were still no thoughts in my head. There was just the smell of her and the feeling of her body next to me. Time was a closed warm space, a static world, a pressure cooker of sensation and emotion. It didn't have an outside to it; nowhere it had come from, nowhere it was going to.

We made love again and this time it was wild and uncontrolled as we let our emotions unleash themselves. I bit into her beautiful skin, making marks which would stay on her, and she did the same to me. The pain I felt seemed part of a greater, more powerful sensation, a tunnel of feelings which I'd never known I needed but I needed more than anything. We didn't speak to each other, not like we had spoken in my flat, or over dinner or in a bar. But there were words. Embarrassing words, sex words not love words. We tore at each other and pulled the other back close, we moved into different positions, our hands never satisfied, clawing, prying, our mouths moving constantly in an effort at completeness. I wanted to touch all of her with all of me, I wanted to have her in every possible position all at the same time, to turn her inside out and fuck her that way too. I wanted to do something which could never be undone, something which could never be just explained away, causing a slight blushing or a looking to the side. Something close to terrifying. I held on to her and scoured her body with my three-day beard. I felt her nails in my back, her teeth in my bottom lip, more, harder, my cheek, my stomach. I couldn't tell where my body ended and Sharon's began. It was stunning and uncontrollable and I never wanted it to end.

But it did end. We lay together, exhausted, feeding madly on air, our tears running down each other's faces. I moved on to my back and we lay side by side, Sharon's hand covering mine. Almost immediately I was asleep, but it was a sleep in which I was cut off from though aware of the room I was in and the body I was lying next to. My body just went somewhere, to a place of rest and perfect calm, where it lay detached from me in an ambient limbo. It felt like bathing in an enchanted pool. And then I floated back to a more connected sort of consciousness, a greater presence in the room, with Sharon there lying on her back with her eyes closed, her breasts rising and falling in a steady motion.

The duvet had long since fallen on to the floor and Sharon was naked. I could not accept or fully believe the actual fact of that. I looked at her body and found myself feeling guilty about doing so, as though I shouldn't be looking at her. I desperately wanted to touch her breasts, to hold them and run my hands down over her belly and entwine my fingers into the golden triangle of her pubic hair. But I was scared to, I was afraid of being so familiar. I didn't know why, given what we had just done, but the feeling would not go away. With her eyes closed I felt like a voyeur, seeing something I shouldn't, but I just couldn't keep my eyes from running all over her, boring into the places they had never had access to before. It was exhilarating. Had I always wanted to do this? I was suddenly aware of my own nakedness. I was naked. I was lying in a bed, naked, next to Sharon.

Sharon's eyelids pulled open and fluttered slowly like a moth's first wings. When she saw me watching her, her face creased into a smile which caused tears to well behind my eyes. I felt so good. So good. I looked into her eyes but couldn't stop my eyes darting back to her body. She saw this and we laughed together and she did it too, very obviously looking at me, checking me out. Beneath her gaze I began to grow hard again, but I wanted to be calm for a while. I used a fingernail to push some damp strands of hair from her cheek and moved closer to her. I ran my fingertips over her face and she closed her eyes and smiled. I stroked the side of her neck and then her shoulders. The feeling of her skin was tattooed on my fingers. I ran my hand over her left breast and then the right.

When my thumb began to play with Sharon's right nipple she moved away a little and, bringing her left hand up to her breast she covered it. She looked uncertain. Sharon's right nipple had an extra curve to it, a half moon added beneath the aureole. The half moon was raised from the skin and was just the same texture but separate from the rest of the nipple. It was as though someone had double stamped the nipple on to her, and the second time had been slightly out of kilter with the first. I was surprised that she had moved away from me.

'God,' Sharon said. She blushed, trying to pass it off. I was looking at her but she broke my gaze. 'I forgot about that.'

Sharon's voice was now the one I was used to hearing but it sounded strange, wrong; it didn't seem to belong here, where we were now.

'It doesn't matter,' I said.

'It's like an extra nipple. Not a whole one but kind of.' Now Sharon sounded self-conscious, either because she was nervous about what she was saying, or because she was finding it odd to be talking at all. 'I've had it since I was a child.'

'I like it.'

She shook her head.

'You don't have to say that.'

'I know. I like it. It's magical. It makes you . . . unique.' I smiled and moved closer. I didn't want to talk.

'It makes me self-conscious.' Sharon looked away for a second. 'It's why I don't go topless at the beach; people can't help looking at it.'

'That's not what they're looking at.'

'Ha. It is though. It's why I didn't that time when we went away. I could tell Lisa thought I was being square.'

She meant the time Luke, Sharon, myself and the girl I was kind of seeing at the time had gone to Crete for a week.

'I thought it was because of me.'

Sharon reddened a little more.

'Maybe that too,' she said.

I moved closer to Sharon and gently pulled her hand away. She didn't want to let me. I moved even closer until my face was right next to her breast. I stroked her nipple again and kissed it. Slowly I ran the tip of my finger all round it and kissed it again, tugging softly at it with my teeth.

'It's beautiful,' I said, and I meant it. It was fascinating. It felt good in my mouth. Sharon didn't answer. 'I'm not saying it to make you feel better. You don't believe me anyway, I can tell. But I mean it.'

'I should have told you though,' she said. 'I have done in the past. But I didn't think.'

'I'm glad you didn't think.'

'It must have been a bit of a surprise though.'

'No,' I said, 'it wasn't.'

'Billy . . .'

'It wasn't a surprise, Sharon. I mean it. I . . .' I moved up the bed and looked into her face. The next words came out of my mouth without me thinking about them. I immediately wished I hadn't said what I did but if I hadn't it would have only been putting off the inevitable.

'I knew about it,' I said. 'I mean it wasn't a surprise. And I like it, I do.'

Pain moved swiftly over Sharon's face like the shadow of a hawk. She smiled seriously at me and kissed me, running her thumb along my eyebrow, but something in the air seemed to change. The room grew suddenly colder. I tried to find a word to say but there wasn't one.

I wanted to tell Sharon that Luke hadn't told me about it in a bad way, a guys' way, he had just mentioned it once. I wanted to reassure her of that. I think she would have known it though. She wasn't upset that he'd told me, I was sure she didn't begrudge the things which Luke had spoken to me about. Including her. It was just the lurch in the stomach as time jerked back into gear. The space was broken. It was Luke. It was the fact of him.

Sharon bent over and retrieved the duvet and I helped her pull it over us. She turned her bedside lamp off. We lay together and kissed occasionally and tried to smooth away the thoughts that were rising back up to the surface of both of our minds. We both knew what they were. We lay there in the semi-dark and I pretended to be asleep but my eyes were open, staring blankly at the long, cream-coloured curtains covering the Georgian windows. I wasn't tired any more. My body, though without proper sleep or food for days, and carrying the signs of a beating, felt heavy and good, but my mind nagged at me to turn to it, to consider the living knot of thoughts which twisted inside.

I pushed the thoughts aside but I couldn't sleep. Sharon's head was resting on my chest and I tried not to move but she could tell I wasn't relaxed and her eyes opened to mine. Even though I could barely make out her face I could read there everything Sharon might have wanted to say to me. I looked into her darkened eyes for a second or two and then sat up a fraction.

I couldn't stay there. Sharon lifted her head and I moved from beneath her and pushed myself up from the bed. I slid over to the edge and stood up, immediately crouching down to my trousers, my sweatshirt and the rest of my clothes. I sat down again and dressed slowly with my back to Sharon, balling up the bandage and stuffing it into the back pocket of my jeans. When I was finished I turned back to her.

Sharon looked at me for a while without speaking. Then:

'Must you?'

I nodded. Sharon's face was unreadable as she turned slightly and nodded back, looking down at the duvet.

'I understand,' she said. I tried to smile. 'It's weird for me too.'

'I know it is.'

I left a second and then I leant over to kiss the top of her forehead. I'd meant a gentle kiss, but she took hold of my head and pressed her lips hard against me, surprising me with the frankness of her passion. It was a message, a clear statement. It was scary and I could feel an edge of hardness in her kiss which set a corresponding one up within me. I pressed my lips back against her before breaking off. I stood up again from the bed and looked down at her. She started to get up but I told her not to worry. I knew my way.

'There's some money in my purse,' Sharon said. 'On the table in the living room.'

'Thanks,' I said.

I walked into the living room and found the purse. I borrowed some money from it and called a cab. It didn't come for twenty minutes, during which time I sat in the living room on the edge of the sofa, staring at the carpet. When the door buzzer sounded I looked up at the entry phone and then at the closed bedroom door. I could almost feel Sharon's body, fitting into mine, her wrist resting on my hip bone. I thought about ignoring the cab and going back in there but suddenly the idea of being with Sharon, there, in her bed, filled me with an incomprehension which was something close to horror. Kissing her. Fucking her. Her sucking me, my tongue moving down between her legs. It was too much, it was way too much. I stood up, pulled the front door open, and walked into the hallway.

Chapter Nineteen

I woke to the sound of someone's voice, far away, a voice which sounded like my own voice but how could it be my voice? I was here, not somewhere else. I was confused. I rolled over, pushing aside the pillow that my head was under.

It was my voice. My answerphone was telling somebody that I wasn't in my office at the present time. The message ended and there was a long series of blips, followed by a woman's voice.

'Mr Rucker, this is Charlotte Morgan. I was wondering if you could call me. I would very much like to speak to you . . .'

I managed to prop myself up on the sofabed and reach over the table to the phone before Charlotte had finished speaking. My ribs bade me a fond good morning as I picked up the receiver.

'Mrs Morgan,' I said, 'hello. Yes. William Rucker.'

I pressed my elbow into my side. There was silence on the other end of the line for a second, before Charlotte Morgan spoke.

'Can you come and see me?' she said. 'At home? I've taken the day off but we could do it this evening if you wanted.' Now that I was more fully awake I realized that there was a bitter tinge to her voice. She sounded chastened and small.

'I'll be an hour,' I told her.

I stood up from the bed and kept my left arm close against my ribcage. I felt groggy and slow, and my head ached. My muscles had all closed in on me, like I was wearing a straitjacket which was a good size too small. The floor of my office was cold. I wondered what time it was and turned the clock on my desk round. Midday. I heard footsteps in the hall and the distant sound of a typewriter. I pulled the sheets from the bed and stuffed them into a cupboard which had always smelled of turps and paint and still did. Careful of my ribs, I put the bed up, pulled my jeans on, and found a clean T-shirt in the bottom drawer of my filing cabinet. I scratched my head, touched the stitches there and opened my office door. I wandered out into the corridor.

Ally's face dropped in horror when she saw me. In the mirror behind the counter I could see that the left side of my face was a sick yellow colour, sitting on a sweet purple like the skin of a swede.

'I know,' I said, acknowledging her shock. 'I didn't shave this morning.'

Ally poured me a coffee and held her hand out to my face. Women did that; what the hell good did they think it would do?

'The police were here,' she said. 'They asked me questions and they were in your office.'

'I know.'

'I made them let me watch them, so they didn't take anything.'

'Thank you,' I said. I was surprised at Ally's concern for my property.

'They used your phone a lot.'

'I'll send them the bill,' I said.

Ally asked what was going on. I told her that when I found out she'd be the first to know. I asked her if anyone else had been round.

'No,' she replied. 'Only that other policeman, the one who was here before. Your friend. He came a couple of hours after the other ones.'

The way Ally told me this made me think she was hiding something; probably the fact that Andy had made an embarrassing pass and she didn't want to say what a tosser he was because she thought I was tight with him. I suddenly remembered Andy's strange willingness to come over to my office to discuss Edward Morgan rather than meeting in his natural habitat, the pub.

'What did he want?' I asked. It can't have been me, he knew where I was.

'He wanted to know if anyone had been looking for you.'

'Right,' I said.

I carried the cup into my office and sat down at my desk with it. I wanted some space, a little time in which to think, but the number on the answerphone bugged at me. I took a pen and then pressed the play button. Five messages. The first was from the day before yesterday; a man enquiring about my services. I wrote the number down but didn't think I'd be calling him. I had a little too much on. Then Nicky wanting to know if I was out yet and what was going on. Sharon, the same thing, her voice concerned but efficient. The fourth person who'd called me didn't leave a name, but it was a voice I recognized.

'Rucker. I hope you get this message. I hope you got the

message I was trying to give you the other night. I hope I made myself clear because if you didn't get the message I'll have to come back and make sure you do. All right?'

It shocked me to hear his voice. I wanted to keep the message, to save it, as if having that would bring me closer to him. His voice sounded tangible, like I could hold it. Like I could hold his voice to account.

The final message was from Charlotte Morgan, and it cut out suddenly where I'd picked the phone up.

There was a pile of letters which I had ignored last night as well as the messages. I picked them up and went through them. The Direct Line people wanted to know if I, Julian Brinsford, wanted to see how much money I could save on motor insurance. The *National Geographic*, a rates reminder, and a white envelope with neat handwriting and a Doncaster postmark. I tore it open without thinking and pulled out a single piece of blue notepaper stapled to which was a cheque drawn on a building society account. The letter was dated 10 November and it must have been posted the day before I had gone on my fool's errand to York Way.

Dear Mr Rucker,

Thank you for the pictures you sent me of my son. It is such a great relief to know that he is all right. I'm afraid to say that he has not called me, but there was a call the day before yesterday which my husband answered but the caller rang off. It may have been him. If you see him again, please could you ask him to call me.

A cheque is enclosed. Thank you once again.

Yours sincerely,

Diane Lewes

I read the letter over and then looked at the cheque, pulling it free. I left the letter on the desk and dropped the cheque into the waste-paper bin. I couldn't really cash it, could I? Certainly, I had found her son, and sent the pictures of him to her which the contract between us had required. But then I'd killed him. I'd killed him by finding him. I'd killed him by taking a murder case and not clearing my backlog first, by involving him in something he should never have been anywhere near. I didn't know how I had done this, but I didn't have any doubt that I had.

I looked at the address Mrs Lewes had written in the top right-hand corner of her letter. There was a phone number with it. My hand reached over to the telephone but I knew I wasn't going to call her. The police would have told her that Dominic had been murdered. They wouldn't have told her where his body was found, not yet, not without charging me. I wasn't going to call her; what the hell would I have to say? I pulled open a drawer of my filing cabinet and looked for Dominic Lewes' file but it wasn't there. The police must have taken it. I dropped the letter into the drawer and pushed it shut.

I tried to think how Dominic had become involved. Someone had seen me taking his picture or talking to him. Who? Rollo. The other kid. The waitress. A little old lady. The girl in his house when I went to call there and asked if he was in. She'd called him Mikey. Who told someone about it? Which one of them? And who did they tell, the man in the hat? Lloyd? I didn't know. Anything was possible, but nothing seemed anywhere near likely. Had Lloyd tried to fit me up? Maybe, but if he had he must have known I would have fingered him; it was no way of keeping his name out of the papers. And why would he? What then? Was it part of the man in the hat's warning, knowing that I wasn't likely to go away for it? Perhaps. It was risky though. Wouldn't he have just tried giving me a kicking first to see what effect that had? If he was willing to take the risk of killing Dominic and leaving him in my flat, surely he would have risked just killing me. I scoured my mind for answers and for small pieces of information, something I knew or had seen but had overlooked. There was something, I was sure of it. A picture which had struck me. I remembered a feeling I'd had, when I'd gone to see Dominic, a feeling that someone was watching my car. There was that but there was something else too, I knew it. But I couldn't dredge it up.

The phone rang. I picked up and it was Sir Peter Morgan. He sounded tentative and apologetic. He'd heard what had happened to me but he didn't know all the details. He knew that I'd been beaten up and arrested, that a boy had been murdered and left in my apartment. One of the officers had phoned him and warned him off employing me.

'I understand,' I said. 'And don't blame yourself. When you take a case you have to accept what might come with it.'

I thought that would be all but Sir Peter said that in spite of the police he still wanted me to carry on.

'You're close,' he said. 'You must be. To whoever killed Edward. I'm very sorry about the boy but nevertheless it shows that you had found something out. Getting attacked and then having someone try to frame you. You must carry on.'

Again, there was an obsessive quality to Sir Peter's voice. I told him I'd think about it. I had some people to talk to and I'd decide what to do after that. I didn't want to carry on. I wanted to go and lie on a beach. I rang off and thought about what Morgan had said. Clay thought it too; I was close. I didn't feel close. I felt like I was playing blind man's buff and I kept bumping into the furniture.

I pulled on my jacket. Apart from the fact that I'd been officially warned off, I was in no state to go and see anyone; the T-shirt I was wearing had a tear in it and I hadn't showered, shaved or eaten properly for days. Apart from the food though, I didn't care. The way my face was arranged a suit would not have made me look any better, and a shave would have been as cosmetically effective as a window polish on a written-off Renault Megane. I would still look fucked. I called a cab, asked them to give me twenty minutes, locked my office and walked to the café.

Ally made me a sandwich which I ate quickly, washing it down with more coffee. I walked down to the forecourt and waited for the taxi by the front gate. The taxi took me down past Regent's Park and along the Marylebone Road before eventually pulling into Leinster Mews. When I got out to pay him the driver couldn't help himself.

'That's some shiner, mate.'

'Yeah.'

'Don't tell me; I should see the other guy, right?' He laughed.

'If you do,' I said, 'call the police. He's a serial killer.'

The cab pulled off and I walked down into the small street. I could see Lloyd, kissing Charlotte goodbye, getting into his car. The day was surprisingly warm for mid November. I saw that it had rained last night. Small stones gave a little under the soles of my boots and a freshness blew across from the park.

Before my hand could reach the door knocker of number 8, the door opened to reveal Charlotte Morgan. She was standing in a pair of jeans and a fitted black sweater which looked to be cashmere. She didn't have any make-up on and the difference between the way she looked now and the way she had before, in Agnieska's, was startling. She didn't look any worse, just different. She reminded me of Helen Mirren when she's playing a housewife rather than a successful career woman. She did look older though, and tired.

'Mr Rucker,' she said. 'Thank you for coming.'

Charlotte Morgan showed me into the small kitchen and invited me to sit at the table while she poured us both some coffee. I took a sip and waited as she took a chair herself. She studied my face.

'It wasn't the police?' she asked. 'Who did that?'

'No,' I said. 'Not them.'

'They were here.'

'I imagined they would be.'

'They showed me a picture of you. I told them that you had been to see me. They wanted to know if I had ever seen you before but I said that I hadn't. They wanted to know what we talked about.'

Charlotte looked nervous.

'Did you tell them?'

'No,' she said, 'I didn't. Not everything, no.'

She took a sip from her coffee and then looked down into the steam. I watched her and I remembered watching her before, in the other room. But this time she wasn't crying. There was a cast to her face which told me that whatever pain she felt was now enclosed within herself, locked up well away from the surface. She looked thoughtful and determined. Her look was a more effective cover than any amount of make-up.

Eventually, a bitter smile broke into her features and she glanced up at me.

'I want to thank you,' she said.

'Thank me?'

'For not telling the police. I thought you had when they phoned yesterday. I thought that's what they wanted. But it wasn't.'

'I still might have to tell them. I probably will.'

Charlotte Morgan nodded.

'I understand,' she said. 'But it doesn't matter now. I might even tell them myself.'

Charlotte put her cup down and leant forward on her elbows. Her eyes were looking at me but they were focused on her own thoughts. Luke had once told me of an acting exercise where you have to split your level of awareness into different layers: the distance, the immediate surroundings and then to a place no further than your own mind. That's where Charlotte Morgan was now.

'I saw Graham last night.'

I'd guessed this was coming.

'After the police were here. I'd been trying to see him for days but he was always too busy or something just came up. I knew what was going on but I wouldn't let myself believe it.'

I waited. I think she wanted me to say it. 'And he ended your relationship?'

'He said that it was too complicated, that things had changed. He said his wife was ill. He said all kinds of things. I didn't really listen to him. I didn't respond very well, I'm afraid.'

'I'm not surprised. It hasn't been easy for you.'

'Yes it has!' I was surprised by the ferocity of Charlotte's denial. 'It has been *so* easy for me. I wasn't killed. I didn't have a wife who was being unfaithful, unfaithful with a worthless bastard. I didn't have a wife who went to her lover the night she found her husband's body.'

Charlotte's focus had changed. It was levelled directly at me now. She finished off her thought: 'I didn't have a wife who was cold, who drove him to try and get some affection somewhere else.'

I let Charlotte take hold of herself. There was no point contradicting her. She ran her hands back through her hair and pushed them together in front of her like she was praying. Her hands touched her chin.

'Charlotte,' I said, 'why are you telling me this?'

She had regained her composure very quickly. I could see her censuring herself, reminding herself to keep it in. There was a notepad on the table beside her which she took hold of, and opened to the first page. She took a breath.

'A few weeks ago,' she said, looking down at the pad, 'Graham wanted me to invest in a concern of his.' My mind went to a computer screen in Company House. 'It was called the Buckner Group. Basically it's a vineyard in Sussex.'

'And did you?'

'Well, I was very interested to begin with. I am a very wealthy woman as you may already know, and it sounded like a good idea. Last summer was the best one ever, and with new techniques and cross-bred varieties of grape, England is becoming a viable place to produce wine.'

'Then why change your mind?'

'Well, it was my accountant really. He was always against the idea. He told me that investing in a vineyard is the best way to become a millionaire; if you're a billionaire.'

'Nice.'

'Yes. I brushed him off but he did some research which I hadn't asked him to do. He was my father's accountant. He's my godfather actually.'

'And he came up with some dubious figures.'

'Yes. Not in the vineyard in question but in two others that the Buckner Group owned. They're close to bankruptcy as a matter of fact. They owe over a hundred and fifty thousand to various people.'

'And you told Lloyd this?'

'Yes. He tried to whitewash me but I am a businesswoman after all. I told him that it just didn't make sense. Not for either of us. It would just be throwing good money after bad.'

'And did he get angry?'

'Yes, he did. It was our first argument. That was three weeks ago. Since then his passion for me . . . well, shall we say it began to cool a little.'

The bitter smile returned, but it was accompanied again by the look of determination. She shifted in her seat.

'Last night,' she continued, 'when he finally ended it, it got me thinking. He obviously wanted my money all along but did he want it so badly that he had my husband killed to get it?'

I looked hard at her. What was this, jealousy? Revenge?

'Divorce would have done that though,' I said. 'He would still have got your money.'

'Yes, he would, though it would have taken longer. Maybe too long, *and* he would have had to marry me. More importantly, there wouldn't have been as much. I collected a substantial sum from the life assurance policy Edward had taken out.'

'I see. He may also have figured that a recently bereaved widow would not be too financially aware, not too careful about investing her money with the lover who had promised to marry her.'

'Yes,' Charlotte Morgan agreed, 'he may very well have thought that. When he put the idea to me I was initially thrilled. For some reason I thought it was his way of committing to me, as if we were joining up all of our eggs into the same basket. And if that *was* his thinking he was right. If Miles hadn't been my accountant and willing to go the extra mile for me I'd have willingly given Graham my money. Even before we were married.'

Charlotte sat back. She picked up her cup but didn't drink out of it, holding it in her left hand with her right hand supporting her elbow.

'Do you want to tell this to the police?'

'I don't know. For some reason I wanted to tell you first. I want you to talk to him about it. I want you to let him know that I'm aware of what he was trying to do. Whether or not he killed my husband. Will you see him? I'd gladly pay you.'

'I have a client. Besides, why should he meet me? He's already warned me off once. What have I got on him?'

Charlotte stood up without answering me and walked into the living room. When she came back into the kitchen there was a packet in her hand. She set it down in front of me. On the front of the packet were the words QUICK PRINT'. I pulled the flap open and took out a set of negatives and seven black and white photographs.

'I had them developed,' Charlotte explained. 'At a one-hour place. Risky, I know. But I was curious. Graham told me to throw the film away and I told him that I had but I didn't. I didn't have a photograph of him, you see. Not even one. I didn't have one of us together. I know it's not the usual shot of a happy couple, and I hated you for taking it, but I wanted to keep it.'

I laid the pictures out on the table. Two were of the car, clearly showing the number plate, and one was of the front door of the house. Another showed Lloyd coming out of the door while another showed him in Charlotte's arms, kissing her, his hand up to her forehead. There was no doubt as to who the man in the picture was, and there was no doubt as to the nature of the kiss. The final two photographs pictured Lloyd walking to his Jag and then getting into it.

Charlotte put her finger on the picture of her and Lloyd.

'It's funny,' she said, straightening it out towards her. 'It's such an intimate picture. It's touching. It's odd to think it was taken by a snoop. No offence meant.'

'None taken.'

'It reminds me of that photo in Paris, you know, of the lovers.'

'Robert Doisneau. It's on every schoolgirl's wall.'

'That's the one. "The Kiss". Look at Graham,' she said. 'He looks like such a tender man. He looks so concerned, so involved.'

'Yes,' I agreed, 'he does.' She was right. It was a

surprisingly good shot and it really did convey a youthful, uncomplicated passion.

'To look at this,' Charlotte said, her lip curling down in disgust, 'and then to think of him. The way he has been on the phone, evasive, slippery, and the way he was last night. I was just trouble, an annoyance to be brushed aside without any fuss. You wouldn't know it was the same man. Here he looks, well, he looks like he's in love.'

'The camera always lies,' I said. 'That Doisneau shot was a set-up.'

I asked Charlotte if she wanted to go to the police. She said she didn't know. She didn't know if she could handle the publicity which we both knew would follow.

'At work,' she said, 'it would be impossible. I'm in PR. It would hardly help the image of the company.'

'Do you care?'

'I don't know. But I do know what the tabloids would do to me.'

I could see the story myself. They would crucify her, or at least the ones she hadn't sold her story to would, out of spite if nothing else. The Widow and the MP. Suspect MP and the pilot's wife. If Morgan was in the frame someone would be bound to speculate about whether she was in there with him. If he was innocent the mud would still stick to her for her infidelity, and if he was guilty no one would ever be completely sure she wasn't a part of it.

'I think I want you to handle it. Please. If it was Graham who did it then I don't care, I'll tell it all. But if he didn't I can't see the point. Can you?'

'No,' I agreed. 'Except the police will roast you if they find you've been holding out on this.'

'I don't care,' she said. 'And I won't hold out, not if you

think they'll be able to do anything you can't. But can you try first?'

'Yes,' I said.

I thought about showing Lloyd the photographs. I would enjoy that.

'And, Mr Rucker,' Charlotte said. 'I really do want them to catch whoever killed Edward. You know that, don't you?'

I looked at her.

'Yes,' I said.

I scooped up the photographs and handed Charlotte the negatives.

'Keep them somewhere safe,' I said.

She showed me to the door and walked me to the end of the mews, on to Leinster Road.

'Charlotte,' I said, as I held my arm out for a cab. I wanted to ask her the same question I'd asked Sir Peter Morgan about her. 'Do you really think that Graham Lloyd can have had anything to do with what happened to Edward?'

'I don't know,' Charlotte replied. 'It sounds so outlandish. But then if you'd told me two months ago that he was screwing me for my money and would drop me as soon as he either did or didn't get it, I wouldn't have believed that either.'

Chapter Twenty

Cleaver Square was quiet. I sat in the pub, by the window, with a pint of bitter which tasted so good I had to stop myself having another, which would have led me to needing to stop myself having another one after that. I was sitting in the corner, by the window, and I stayed there until I saw a blue Jaguar drive past slowly and then park. No other car followed it. I waited another five minutes, stood up and took my empty pint pot back to the bar. Then I walked out into the street.

I'd called Graham Lloyd from the phone in the back of the pub. I was pretty sure he wouldn't want to talk to me so I told his secretary I was a policeman and gave her an imaginary warrant card number which was in fact the phone number of a woman called Sue, which someone else had written in biro on a beer mat next to the phone. When he realized it was me on the line Lloyd was very unhappy indeed and proceeded to mouth off some legal-sounding invective until I told him about the photographs I had. He shut up. I informed him that I would be going to his house on Cleaver Square and would be there in about an hour. I was then going to show the photographs I had to whoever opened the door; whether that was Lloyd himself, or his wife, was his choice.

I crossed the square thinking that, apart from its

location, I couldn't imagine many more elegant spots in the whole capital. I walked past a green door and then a red door and up to a yellow door. The door, when I approached it, looked to be newly painted and I wondered if actually it had been a red door originally but with Lloyd hoping to rise in the Party he'd thought it politic to change it. No. In that case it would have been blue. Daft theory.

A young girl opened the door. With her Scandinavian accent and the fact that a small child was hammering both of his fists against her legs I assumed she was the au pair. Would she be interested in the photos? I didn't get a chance to find out. Graham Lloyd appeared from a side room.

'Ah,' he said, moving his hands like a lollipop man to indicate which room I was to go into. 'Please, this way.'

The child, surprised and pleased to see his father at such an unusual time, made a beeline for the door in front of me.

'Not *now*, Thomas. Go with Kristen.' Kristen picked the boy up and he had just begun a sustained bout of wailing at the fact when Lloyd closed the door behind me, shutting the noise out.

Lloyd made no comment about the state of my face. Maybe that's why the kid had started crying; he thought I was Frankenstein's monster come to kill his daddy.

'Please, Mr Rucker. Have a seat.'

We were in a large room which looked like the cross between an office and a study. It was all old-school Chesterfields but there were two computer terminals that I could see, as well as a fax machine and a small photocopier. I relaxed into an armchair. Lloyd hesitated above me. He seemed uncertain of what line to take, how to deal with me. He was friendly, but brusque at the same time.

Looking at him, in his public schoolboy only ever been to one tailor in his life outfit, I couldn't help wondering what it was that a stylish woman like Charlotte Morgan had seen in him. There must have been something though, and it wasn't necessarily on show for me to see. Maybe if he took his glasses off. His glasses were not stylish. He can't have been high enough up yet to warrant the attention of the spin doctors.

It was after 3 p.m. and a pale winter sun was sloping through the Georgian windows, resting on an empty wineglass like a broken yolk. Lloyd plunged his hands into his trouser pockets and rocked back on his heels.

'So,' he said. 'I am to understand that Charlotte kept the pictures you took. Yes? Or you had another set?'

I shrugged. 'What does it matter?'

'No. You're right. It matters that you have them. You won't mind me asking to check that, I presume.'

I fished in my coat pocket and handed him the packet. He stood back from me and leafed through the pictures quickly. His face clouded but then he smiled.

'She really is very beautiful, don't you think?'

Again I shrugged.

'You can understand why I fell for her, can't you? Anyone could. But you must also understand why I had to end it. After what happened.'

' "What happened"?'

'Yes.' Lloyd shook his head. 'Damned unfortunate. I know Morgan of course. Fine man. Very fine indeed.'

Lloyd walked over to the far wall. I was surprised by his relaxed manner. He hadn't mentioned our previous meeting, our hostility to each other, me and my swift exit. It was like a mad aunt, walled up in a room downstairs somewhere.

Lloyd stood thinking. He opened a small cabinet and drew out a bottle of malt and two tumblers. He walked over and sat opposite me, resting the bottle and the glasses on a low coffee table.

'I suppose she hates me,' he said. 'I don't blame her. But how was I supposed to know all this was going to happen? A discreet affair, that's what I thought was going on.'

'Charlotte says you talked about marriage.'

Lloyd looked uneasy. 'Well, I won't deny it. I was blown away, to begin with at least. That never happened to you?'

Oh yes, it had happened to me.

'But then I realized that it couldn't go on.'

'No?'

'No. It wasn't fair on her as much as anything. She was beginning to need me, I was a crutch to her. I knew I couldn't keep it up for ever so I broke it sooner rather than later. Before she couldn't do without it. I don't blame Charlotte if she's feeling bad. She really is having a very awful time.'

Without asking me if I wanted one, Lloyd poured me out a good measure of Scotch, and pushed the glass along the table towards me. He then filled the other glass but didn't pick it up. He sat back in his chair, still holding the bottle, stroking the body of it as though it were a big, fluffy cat, and he was Donald Pleasance. His hands looked like two, independent creatures, and for a second I was almost mesmerized by them. Reluctantly, I took my eyes from his hands, and the bottle they were lovingly caressing, and rested them on the MP's face.

Lloyd was trying the reasonable approach. His bullying sarcasm hadn't worked on me before so he thought he'd try to get me on-side with a bit of discreet male 'you know how it is' bandinage. I picked up the tumbler and took a sip.

'Scotch OK for you?'

'Actually,' I said, looking up, 'I'd prefer wine. If you have any.'

Lloyd looked mildly irritated but went to stand up. 'Of course. Red or white?'

'Either,' I replied. 'As long as it's English.'

Lloyd stopped, and sat back down. He bit into the side of his cheek and looked at me. He nodded to himself, as though he'd just worked something out.

'You don't care about infidelity, do you?' he stated.

'Not a lot.'

'No, I didn't think so. When you first approached Charlotte I thought you worked for a newspaper. I thought I'd have to write you a little cheque in the end. But then you told me you didn't have any evidence.'

'I didn't.'

'No. And now you do, but you don't care about our affair. It's not a cheque you want, is it?'

'No.'

'Not even if it were a rather large cheque?'

'It wouldn't make any difference. It isn't me who has the evidence, it's Mrs Morgan.'

'Yes, but she's not going to expose herself, is she?'

'Maybe not. I don't care either way. As you say, I'm not really interested in infidelity. I just want to know who killed an MP's brother. Oh, that and who left a boy prostitute on my bed, with his cock cut off, gutted like a trout at Billingsgate Market. And made it look like it was me who did it. I really am interested in finding out who did that.'

Lloyd put the bottle down on the table and picked up his glass without drinking from it. He certainly was a man who liked to build up to things.

'In that case, why are you here?'

I laughed.

'You want me to explain? You were having an affair with a rich woman whose husband was murdered. The company you own is up shit creek and as soon as the woman decides not to give you any money you dump her. Tell me, where the hell else should I be?'

'Looking for a killer. Do I look like one?'

I thought about what a worried gay guy had told me, sitting in a Soho coffee house.

'As much as any killer I've ever met,' I told him.

'OK,' he said. 'I dispute the facts you have given me. My company is not up shit creek, and neither did I either begin or end my relationship with Charlotte Morgan because of money. But if that is what you think I can understand your interest in me. Tell me what I can do to assure you of my innocence.'

'Show me your diary,' I said.

Lloyd reached into his pocket for his electronic organizer.

'No,' I said, 'the one on the desk.'

Lloyd stood up and walked over to the heavy oak desk where the fax machine sat next to some loose papers and a large black book with 1998 written on it in gold letters. I stood up too and took the book off him when he turned round. I walked over to the photocopier.

'Now wait a minute.'

'Fine,' I said, dropping the lid of the machine back down. 'Then I'll take it with me.'

'You have no right . . .'

'None at all,' I agreed. 'All I've got is pictures.'

Lloyd let me take copies of his diary. I thought about asking him for his company records but I was pretty sure that Charlotte Morgan's accountant would be able to tell me everything I wanted to know about them. As I used the machine I could feel Lloyd bridling next to me. He was finding it hard to stick to the tack he had chosen. He wanted to get rid of me, to stamp on me like a cockroach on the floor of a Cibar kitchen.

'Is that all?' Lloyd said, when I had finished collating the pages and handed him back his diary.

'For now. Unless you can think of anything else you can do to show me how innocent you are.'

'Shouldn't it be the other way round?'

'Usually,' I replied, 'but not in this case. The more you can tell me, the less you'll have to tell the police.'

'There's nothing more,' he said. 'Really.'

'That's a shame,' I told him. 'Because if I don't find anything else to either put you away or keep your nose out of it, then not even Mother Teresa will be able to keep your name out of the papers.'

'Mother Teresa?'

'Forget it,' I said.

There wasn't any more I could ask him. I walked over to the door and opened it. Lloyd followed me to the front door and got to the handle before me.

'Don't you want these?' he asked, handing me the photographs. The sarcasm had crept back into his voice, making him sound no older than his son.

'They're only copies,' I said.

'Nevertheless.' He handed them to me like they were hard-core porn snaps and I was trying to sell them to him. 'I don't want them lying around.'

'No. I don't imagine that you do.'

He held the door open and at that moment his son flew down the stairs, crying 'Daddy! Daddy!' and holding his arms out to Lloyd. The child grabbed hold of Lloyd's trouser leg but the MP ignored him.

'For God's sake, Kristen! How many times must I tell you? Keep Thomas upstairs during the day! How many times?'

I walked through the door and down the steps. I didn't wait for Lloyd to finish reprimanding his domestic staff to say goodbye to him.

Chapter Twenty-One

The taxi was already on the Clerkenwell Road before I realized where it was that I was going. Back to my flat. I hadn't been there for three days and I didn't know what I would find there. The cab got snarled up in traffic on the Farringdon Road so I got out and walked up past Carl's Repro shop, with a feeling of trepidation which I couldn't explain. It wasn't as if I was likely to find any more mutilated bodies lying on my bed. I could not, however, dispel a certain edginess as I walked into the small road and fished my spare keys out of my pocket.

The outside door had been mended, but this didn't surprise me because I shared it with another flat. There were only small signs that it had recently been broken into. The key turned in the lock quite normally and the door opened.

I stepped into the hallway and turned on the light even though I could see well enough. I walked up the stairs. When I got to the top of the first flight I could see that my door had not been mended. Nor was there any no-entry tape or police-aware stickers to indicate a police presence. The door was slightly ajar and I thought great, why don't you let the whole fucking world into my flat. I not only wondered if I'd still have the cash I had, I wondered if I'd still possess a stereo and a TV. I walked up the stairs into my living room.

Only the futon was gone. The space where it would have been yawned with its absence. The wine stain on the rug next to the space was larger than I remembered it, and more distinct now that it was in the daylight. Why the hell had he chosen my Grange, the finest wine ever made in Oz, one of the top ten made anywhere? What was wrong with the Sainsbury's Côte du Rhône? I wondered why the police hadn't taken the rug. They should have, they might have found something in it, a fingernail or a small piece of dirt from a shoe. I knew then that Ken Clay hadn't visited the scene; he would not have overlooked it. I folded the rug carefully and found a bag from the deli to put it in. I'd call Clay and tell him, and then enjoy the thought of what he would then say to the two alleged detectives who had been in charge of searching the place.

I spent about an hour in the bath, refilling with hot when the water started to go cold. I let stress and pain seep out of my body, and I let thoughts and questions seep into my mind. I tried to let them in slowly, one at a time, so that they wouldn't merge into one another.

There wasn't anything else Lloyd could have told me, except that he was the perp and he was hardly likely to do that. Was he desperate enough to be involved in this? It seemed, from what Charlotte Morgan had told me, that he was very good at hiding his real reasons, painting a coat of veneer over what he really wanted. If I was the police what could I do which would help me get to him? I could talk to his colleagues in the Commons, see if they remembered any changes of mood in him, if he had ever mentioned his financial troubles. I could talk to his partner in the Buckner Group. Both those things would probably only reveal motive, which I already had. Money. Someone might however have seen Lloyd with an unusual person, someone not dressed in a suit. Wearing a baseball hat maybe. It wasn't likely, I didn't peg Lloyd for being that stupid, but if he was a first-time employer of contract muscle then he just *might* have been careless.

Other thoughts came to me, which I processed and mainly discarded. Then some other thoughts came which could not be separated, but whirled around in no sort of order. They concerned Sharon, and what we had done in her flat, the significance of it and what markers and signs we had set for the future. What, if anything, it had determined. I wondered if what we had done meant what I had not even dared think it would mean, when I was so caught up in the painfully brilliant moment of her that there was no way I *could* think. Simply, I wondered if what we had done was right or wrong, if it was the future or something to be shocked at, appalled, something to be buried in the dark bog that we call experience. A scary place, full of sprites and foul gases, never to be returned to. I lay in the bath, staring at the ceiling, lying still, not even moving my eyelids.

I got out of the bath and dried myself gingerly. I pulled on some jeans, a T-shirt and sweatshirt. I sat at the table and made a few calls. The first was to Ken Clay and I got his machine. I told him that it might be worth sending some men round to the Commons with the picture, to do a discreet bit of canvassing. I said that it was unlikely but that someone there *may* have seen the man. I called a futon shop that I'd seen on Calthorpe Street and asked them for some prices and whether they delivered. I couldn't be bothered hunting around for anywhere cheaper so I asked them to send me one in the middle of their range. To my surprise they said they could do it before six, if I was at home. I told them to go ahead. I gave them my credit card number and wondered if I could charge the whole thing to Sir Peter Morgan, claiming it on expenses.

I put the phone down and took another look at my flat. Apart from the futon there was something else wrong with it, something else changed or missing. I looked around but all the major things were still there: my TV, my stereo, the four bottles of wine in my rack. My Salgado print. I even checked my loose cash and bank cards and was surprised to find that they were all where and as I had left them. I sat back down at the table. Maybe I was imagining it. I brushed my doubt aside and went to put the kettle on. Then I realized. I went back to the table again but the blue folder containing my brother's poems was not there.

I'd gone to open it when I was waiting for the cavalry, and the WPC had told me to leave it. They must have thought it was important and taken it in. That would have been on her suggestion; if the two idiots who'd been round earlier hadn't thought fit to remove a rug stained in the course of the crime they were hardly likely to seize on a collection of verse the suspect had casually turned to. I wanted the folder back, and was suddenly panicked. Was it the only copy or did Sharon have another? I hadn't even looked inside it. What if they'd lost it, or thrown it out? I dialled Clay's number again. I expected his machine but this time I got the man himself.

'Only if you give me what you have,' he said, after I'd told him what I wanted. 'Otherwise I'll keep them here and use them to bring a little culture to the place.'

I hesitated a second. A little bit couldn't hurt.

'Graham Lloyd,' I said. 'I sort of like him for it. Or, rather, I like him more than anyone else.'

'The one Mother Teresa . . .'

'A *maybe* maybe,' I said. 'But only for Edward Morgan. Maybe Dominic Lewes.'

'And?'

'And that's it. That's all I have. Really. That's why I suggested you take that picture to the Commons.'

'On what grounds do you suggest? Your say-so?'

'Make some up,' I said. 'Tell them he's been mugging MPs on their way home. That'll make them remember if they've seen him or not.'

Clay paused. 'I'll think about it.'

'Right. What about the folder?'

'Oh, that. I had DC Milson go through that with as fine a toothed comb as his mind can supply. I don't think he got much out of the experience. I didn't know you were so creative, Rucker.'

'I'm not,' I said. 'Are you going to let me have them? They're not important, I promise you. You can take copies if you're not sure and give me those.'

Clay thought for a second.

'OK, Rucker, they'll be on the front desk.'

'Thanks,' I said. 'Oh, and Ken, don't be too hard on Milson and the other chap.'

'Clarke.'

'Yeah, Clarke, that's it.'

'Not hard on them for what?' Clay asked.

'You'll see.' I put the phone down.

I was relieved. I thought about the folder and wondered how come I had never got round to looking in it. Didn't I want to read Luke's poems? Of course I did.

Didn't I? I'd have got round to them sooner or later if events hadn't got in the way first.

I spent the next hour going through Lloyd's diary. I looked at the dates on and around the day Teddy Morgan had been murdered. They didn't tell me much. There was an appointment with a man called Harvey, although whether that was a Christian or surname it didn't say. I wrote the name down and made a note to check it. I wrote down a few more names as well, knowing that Lloyd wasn't the type to write 'Contract killer, 11 a.m.' in his desk diary. I'd get him to tell me who the names referred to, check up on them, and then if there was a name that didn't match – who knows.

The futon came. Two guys carried it up the stairs and to my surprise it was fully constructed. When I remarked on this I was told that it was a showroom model, the only one they had in stock. I was glad. The two men wanted to know where they should put it and I told them to set it down where the other one had been. They did so and I thanked them and they left.

The futon was pretty much the same as the old one, with a black cover and an easy-fold mechanism. The actual mattress seemed to be thicker but I put this down to lack of use. I stared at it for a second and then tried out the mechanism to see how smooth it was. It was fine, and the sofa-shaped object changed easily into a bed. I stared down at it. Dominic Lewes stared back at me. I changed it into a sofa again.

I looked round my flat. The futon had always been where the futon was and the table had always been where the table was and the wardrobe where I keep most of my clothes had always been where that was. Was there any reason for it? Maybe if I moved the table to where the cupboard was, and I moved the cupboard to where my old futon had been, I could put the new futon where the table was now. There was a small enclave that fitted the table quite well but it would fit the futon even better. And having the wardrobe over there made sense because where it was now seemed to dominate the room and who wants to look at a wardrobe? If I moved the table there it would get more light and that way I could use the plug socket to the left of the wardrobe and it would also mean I wouldn't need the extension lead to the phone which stretched right across the middle of the floor.

And I wouldn't have to share my bed with the ghost of Dominic Lewes. His blood soaking down into me, his face saying that he wasn't at all surprised that he had been strangled and torn open, not after the life he had had, not after some of the other things which various people had done to him.

I changed the flat round. By the time I had finished it was dark. I kicked myself for forgetting to phone a lock-smith. I turned the stereo on, quite loud, and turned most of the lights in my flat on too. I left and walked down to my car and was amazed to find it without a clamp even though it was still in the delivery bay where I had left it three nights ago. I'd have to remember that. It started nonchalantly, as though I'd only been out of it five minutes to buy a newspaper, and it took me to the station where I had recently been incarcerated. I picked up the folder, left Clay the rug with a note, and got back in. I pulled off and swung the car round the one-way system, intending to go back to my round of the pubs. Old Compton Street, where the man had recognized the picture.

Instead I thought of something else. The one-way

system took me closer to King's Cross. I parked on one of the streets behind it. Elm Drive. I parked outside number 23. There were no lights on. I got out of the car and locked it. I walked up to the door and knocked. There was no answer. I pushed open the letter box and looked through it but I couldn't see anything.

I walked up to the top of the street and then back down a small alley, counting off the houses. When I got to number 23 I had a quick look round and then hopped over the fence and into the back garden. The garden was a small yard, with an overflowing dustbin which, by the smell of it, had been there some time. I walked up to the back door.

The door pushed open beneath my hand. I found a switch and was surprised when light came out of a single bulb dangling from the ceiling. I listened, but couldn't hear anything other than a leaking tap. I walked around the house. It was obvious that no one was living there. The whole house was miserable and cold with huge blotches of damp in the corners of the bedroom walls like sweat-stained nylon. Strange smells brushed past me like malignant ghosts. In one bedroom I found, lying on the floor next to an old mattress, a train timetable. Apart from the mattress it was all that was left in the room. His clothes and his other effects must already have been bagged and sent to his parents. They wouldn't have wanted a train timetable. I picked it up and saw that it showed times from London King's Cross to Newark North Gate and then connections from there to, among other places, Grimsby Town. A young man thinking about going home. He hadn't been thinking it for some time though; the timetable was out of date.

I flicked through the pages. Maybe the timetable had

just lain around for months and Dominic hadn't bothered to chuck it out. Perhaps he didn't realize he still had it. Or maybe he kept it on purpose, and looked at it now and then, when his head was somehow higher than the shit which surrounded him usually and which was slowly pulling him down into it. Maybe he looked at it now and then and wondered if one day he would ever make use of it. It was like a St Christopher, a small, desperate, useless talisman of hope. I decided that one day soon I really did have to speak with his mother, and when I did I would tell her about it. It might provide some kind of comfort to her to know that once in a while her son did think of home.

I had another idea. I left the car where it was and walked towards the Cross. I turned right. I walked past the spot where I had spoken to Dominic, past the alley Rollo had stopped me in. I crossed the road and peered through the window of the café at the bottom of Calshot Street, and then walked round the back. A gate was open. I glanced in and saw a small backyard with an old Biffa skip and some stacked crates. The back door of the café was ajar and I could see into the kitchen where a pair of dark hands was chopping a shiny mound of liver. I slipped into the yard and stood in shadow behind the skip, with my eye on the door. I waited.

She came out after about forty minutes, with a cigarette already in her mouth and a Bic going up to light it. I moved behind her slowly and pushed the door shut, making as little noise as possible. She turned at the sound.

'What . . .'

I didn't let her get any further. I grabbed hold of her wrist and pushed her backwards into the hard wood of the fence which surrounded the yard. A streetlight lit her face and I saw her recognize me. She tried to scream but I forced her back further by grabbing hold of her neck.

'Who else did you tell?'

She shook her head desperately but she didn't make any noise.

'Who the hell else did you tell about me watching Dominic?'

I loosened my grip a bit.

'I don't know Dominic.'

'Mikey. Mikey. Who did you tell?'

'No one . . .'

'You told Rollo. You told him and he was waiting for me. Someone else knew. Who the fuck was it, who did you tell?'

'No one. I swear. I never. Please.'

'Where's the girl who lived with Mikey?'

'I don't know. I never went there.'

'Didn't Rollo live there?'

'No, he just went for the money. Please, you're hurting me.'

I pressed my thumb harder, up into her chin.

'Who did you tell?'

'I didn't, I swear I didn't.'

I let go of her throat and put my hand over her mouth. I fished into my pocket and pulled out one of the pictures that were still in there.

'Who's this?'

'I don't know. I can't see it.'

I held the picture more into the light.

'I've never seen him, I . . .'

'Tell me about Rollo. How long have you been seeing him?'

'I'm not, I'm not! He just used to come in.'

'You knew what he did?'

'Not at first. Oh, listen, I screwed him a couple of times. He's got a really nice place, that's how I know he didn't live with those kids. When I heard about that boy it was terrible. He used to come in for Coke.'

'And the girl he lived with?'

'Yes, sometimes.'

'What was her name?'

'I don't–'

'What was her fucking name!'

My hands went up to her throat again.

'Emma, I think her name was Emma.'

I released her. I stood back. Her hands went straight up to her neck, and she rubbed it, breathing deeply. Her eyes narrowed and I could tell that she was scared. But not of me.

'You bastard,' she said. Her voice was small and full of hate. I left her there and walked back to the station.

I spoke to Ken Clay, who made a point not to mention the rug I'd left him, and I sat with a guy on their computer imager. I gave a description of Emma and he pressed the right buttons until something close to the face I had seen through a crack in the door of number 23 Elm Drive appeared on the screen. It's amazing what a memory the mind has for faces, if someone is trained to give it a hand. Clay said he'd get the picture and the name to the boys in blue first thing and it wouldn't be long before Emma turned up. I didn't ask him if he would give me a copy of it. I'd had enough of showing pictures around.

Clay wasn't angry with me any more, not now I was giving him stuff.

'What about the waitress?' he asked me.

'Pick her up,' I said. 'She might tell you who the bastard is eventually. I don't think she knows though.'

'Rollo neither,' Clay said. 'We've got him on a dealing charge, raided his place and found the usual.' There was a glint in Clay's eye which told me that 'found' might not be the right word. 'We've offered to forget about it if he'll give up the man in the picture and I can tell he wants to. He's either scared or hasn't got it.'

'The man said he knew him. Or at least knew who he was.'

'Everybody knows Rollo. He's a flash one, spreads it about. This other chap keeps himself to himself it seems.'

'Yes, but if he knew Rollo, maybe he's in the same line of business.'

'Maybe,' Clay said.

I left Clay to it and walked back to my car. I was glad I'd thought of the girl in the house Dominic was living in. Emma. She might know something. I'd let the police find her though. I didn't think it would take them long. I wondered if she'd tell them anything, or just clam up like Rollo. I remembered her sick face and her flat eyes.

I was exhausted. I thought of but immediately canned the idea of going down to Nicky's for a beer and drove home instead, to my newly arranged flat and to my newly installed futon.

Chapter Twenty-Two

In the next few days I went through the names in Lloyd's diary. I got him to tell me who they all were and each one of them checked out the way he had said they would. Other MPs, colleagues at both the lobby company and the Holdings firm as well as a couple of old friends and his brother. Harvey turned out to be Harvey Lawrence, Lloyd's only partner in the Buckner Group. I called him and pretended to be a potential investor. He seemed very pleased to hear from me and didn't even ask where I'd got hold of his name. I arranged to meet him in two days' time which would give me a chance to set up a meeting with Charlotte Morgan's accountant first.

But I never got the chance to meet either of them.

I wanted to talk to Dominic's other friends, the other kids on his patch. One of them must have seen him go off with the man in the hat that night. Andy phoned to tell me that the police had found Emma but she hadn't seen Dominic since the night before he was killed. I wanted to speak to the kid I'd seen Dominic with the night I'd had the run-in with Rollo. I was pretty sure I'd recognize him. I'd seen him and Dominic talking; they looked like friends. I set myself up in a pub this time, on the Pentonville Road itself, which was not as near as the café was but close enough that I could still tell if there was anyone standing about for business without having to get my zoom out and make a show of myself. The pub was dark and smoky and smelled of piss. It had a smallish stage which was occupied by a bored stream of readers' wives style strippers. The pub's clientele was made up exclusively of men but I wasn't the only one not bothering to pay attention.

The spot across the street was completely empty for the first day that I sat there watching it. I guessed this was due to what happened to Dominic, which the other kids would have heard about and felt that the best way to protect themselves was to go and stand on a different corner. They would always come back though; knowing that they would lose regular custom, their pimps would have told them they had to. Another possible reason for their absence was that the police had steamed in with pictures of Dominic and scared them all off. In that case they would still return, but it might take longer. Fear of the police was stronger in boy junkies than fear of serial killers. I sat in the pub all of that day and for most of the evening.

During the morning of the second day, a couple of lads showed up. I was glad. I didn't want to go traipsing all over Dalston and out to Stoke Newington to find the place they'd decamped to. I waited in the pub. When the number had risen to four by midday I took a stroll past to see if any of them was the boy I had seen with Dominic. No luck. I thought about asking them anyway but decided against. The word might get round and the place would be dead again. I went back to the pub.

It was difficult to see but by late afternoon I thought the boy had arrived. I put my bag over my shoulder again and walked out on to the street. I walked past the twenty-four-hour store and crossed over the road. I passed the Thameslink station and walked up towards the derelict kebab shop where the boys were waiting for pick-ups. There were three of them, standing together in tight jeans and bomber jackets. They looked just like any three teenagers, hanging out, trying to be cool, either chewing gum or smoking. Other people walked by, most not noticing them. A young girl checked one of them out. An old lady's face drew up into a frown when one of the kids spat on the pavement, not seeing her, forcing her to make a small diversion in her path.

When I was twenty feet or so away from them, I could tell that the boy was not there. None of them was him. I was disappointed but this time I did decide to speak to the others anyway as I was quite confident that I could do it without spooking them. I approached the nearest one, but spoke so that all of them could hear me.

'Listen, guys,' I said. 'I don't want to get you all nervous. I'm not the Bill or anything. I was just wondering if any of you knew that kid Mikey. He used to work from here.'

The three of them looked suspicious but not overly worried or defensive. The one nearest said, 'No, mate. Never knew him. Heard of him though. You sure you're not Bill?'

'I'm positive.'

'What are you then?'

I never got a chance to answer. I was stood facing towards the Cross, and I was about to speak when another boy walked around the corner towards us. He was black, about fourteen years old, and he was dressed in a bright orange puffa jacket and a blue cap which he had on backwards. The boy's face was bruised some, the damage hidden to a large degree by the natural colour of his skin, but evident nevertheless. He was walking with his hands in his pockets, his face a sullen mask of worry, and as he approached us one of the boys I was talking to looked up in a way which told me that he knew him. He nodded slightly and the black boy nodded back. I thought the black boy was going to say something, to make some sort of greeting but he didn't. He slowed down suddenly and came to a stop.

He came to a stop because of me.

Given warning, a second or two to get a hold of himself, the kid might just have bluffed it out and said hi to his mates and kept walking. But the surprise at seeing me was instant and as his gaze automatically locked into mine, his expression gave him away. He was afraid that I was there looking for *him*. Even then he could have shaken it off, if it were not for the fact that he could tell I had seen it. Seen his surprise. I stared into his eyes, trying to place him. I could feel recognition cogs wheeling into place and I knew that I'd have him in a matter of seconds.

Then I did have him.

The boy looked away from me and turned around immediately. He began to walk.

'Excuse me,' I said. He turned round very briefly but didn't stop. 'Excuse me,' I said again.

He was off.

How he wasn't killed by a cab accelerating away from the lights up towards the Angel I will never know. The shock and terror on the driver's face as he swerved straight into the goods van in the other lane was like a Munch sketch in motion. I ignored the havoc and the car horns and followed the kid over the road, keeping sight of his orange jacket as he ran and jostled through the crowd of pedestrians going to and from King's Cross. He ran towards the station and I just about kept up with him, fifteen or twenty yards behind him as he burned past the *Standard* vendors and the winos and the bus queues and the suits standing in line by the taxi rank. I ran after him, hampered by my hold-all which thudded against my hip with every second stride I took. I lost him as he turned right and ran up towards the Pancras Road.

Why the fuck was he running from me? I saw his face, nervous in the gym, just before he started sparring. Holding his coat. And earlier, just stood there, after I'd come out of the weights room. He'd come looking for me too, it must have been him Alberto saw in the café. Why was he . . . I thought of his bruises. Sal would never have let that happen to him in her gym. No way. Where did he get them? Why did I make him so terrified? No point worrying. He was running. He'd seen me and he was running.

I was on to him again as soon as I'd turned the way he had. He cut a right down a small road behind King's Cross station itself. I cut an earlier right and managed to beat him to the end, seeing him run out up ahead of me. He turned left and kept running and I followed, my side breaking as my ribs pulled apart where the cracks were beginning to knit. I pounded on, knowing that if he kept his pace up I was going to lose him. A boxing gym? He should have been at Crystal frigging Palace.

He took another right and I had an idea as to where he might be going. Again there was an earlier right, an old, cobbled mechanic's yard, and I took it, stopping myself before I flew out of the end of it. I held on to the wall and peered around the corner, just catching sight of a blur of orange as it came out ahead of me. I ducked back in and then heard the sound of his feet coming to a stop. Then there was the scuff sound of a quick sprint which stopped again, abruptly.

I pushed my ribs into my side and tried not to let my lungs pull in so much of the air it so desperately needed. Each breath was the ghost of the size tens I'd received at York Way. I left it a second and looked round the corner again, still breathing heavily. The kid was nowhere. I jogged up the street, up to the cast-iron fence-cum-wall at the top of it. I looked left and right but couldn't see the kid in either direction. I looked at the wall again and jumped up on to it, holding myself steady as I peered over the top.

The area I was looking into was land owned by British Rail. It was big, perhaps as big as two football pitches. I'd read somewhere that the land had been offered as part of a sweetener deal for companies interested in buying into the network when it was privatized. The land was central, perfect for high-rent office blocks and designer security homes. This hadn't happened yet though. The land was derelict, patched with the remains of abandoned fires lit by kids or the homeless, out for fun or heat. I could see rusting shopping trolleys and a punctured football, pieces of old carpet and a scorched three-piece suite.

And I could see a young boy in an orange puffa running directly away from where I was perched. He was running more slowly than he had been before, his head moving left and right as he looked around for me. As he moved his head and shoulders all the way round to take a look behind him, I dropped back out of sight.

After leaving a couple of seconds I pulled myself up again, this time getting a better hold so that I could duck down without coming off the wall completely. I looked over. I could see the boy jogging towards an old caravan, still looking all around him. The van was a hundred yards away. It was old and knackered, resting on six piles of bricks. I watched as the boy approached the van, reached up and knocked on the door. He pulled the door open. I ducked down again, knowing that he'd have one last look behind before stepping into the van. I came up to see the door closing. I took out my camera and zoomed in. I tried to see through the stained plastic windows but they were covered by brown curtains. I couldn't make out any movement behind them.

I focused on the door and was surprised when, after five minutes, it was thrown open. I caught a pair of hands, pushing the same boy out of the van on to the concrete. The door of the van shut and the boy got up. He held his knee where he'd fallen on it and then put his hand up to his face. Through the lens I could see that his nose was bleeding. The kid then hobbled off, one hand on his damaged knee, the other palm down, trying to staunch the flow of blood from his nose, wiping some on to the sleeve of his coat and then trying to wipe that off with his hand.

The boy walked off at a right angle to where I was sitting, towards a derelict building protected by wire meshing. He could probably get through there on to the street. It may even be where he slept. I looked up from the viewfinder and then put the camera back in my bag, still watching to make sure no one came out of the van.

I had it now. The gym. He wasn't scared of fighting. That wasn't why that doubt had come into his face when he saw me there. This kid looked like he got into fights quite often, and never came out of them too well. No. He was frightened of me. He was frightened of the picture that he'd seen me showing to Sal; it had been lying on the table in the weights room. He must have seen it. He was frightened because he knew the man in the picture and even more frightened of what might happen to him if he told me who the man was. I got the impression, thinking about it, that what frightened him most of all was that he really did want to tell me. He was terrified that that was exactly what he was going to do. That would have been fine if nothing could link me to him, but when he'd seen me on the corner with his colleagues he was sure he was in big trouble. If they knew he'd been looking for me, to tell me who the man in the picture was, they'd tell the man and he'd be as good as dead.

But now he had told me. I knew who was in there.

I jogged towards the van, trying to keep in line with the corner, away from the window. I thought about calling Ken Clay, but I wanted this guy for myself. I studied the curtains of the van but they didn't move. When I'd covered the distance from the wall I stood at the corner of the van and thought how to do it. From inside I could hear the sound of an efficient boom box tuned in to Radio One. Mark Radcliffe was assuring his listeners that he was very sorry indeed that his show was over for another day. I was glad of the noise; it would be a distraction. I waited until the next DJ had come on and assured his listeners of how glad he was to be with them for the next two hours. Still, I waited. Then the DJ announced that the next track would be a huge house-jungle crossover smash and was bound to break into the charts on Sunday. I wasn't ready to give an opinion on his prophetic statement but there was one thing I did know. The track was loud. I set my bag down on the ground beside me.

I walked round to the side of the caravan, where the door was, keeping my head below the level of the windows. I stood outside the door and reached for the handle. The kid had knocked but opened the door straight after he'd done so. It hadn't been locked. Was it now? I was about to find out. I pulled the handle.

I was inside the van. He was on the left, lying on a bed. He was propped up on some cushions and was just putting a beer down next to a half-empty litre bottle of cheap vodka on a small, built-in table to the right of the bed. At the foot of the bed, nearer to me than him, was a sawn-off shotgun, presumably the same one he had aimed at my head only a few days previously. In the split second before all hell let loose our eyes met.

He wasn't wearing a baseball hat now, and it was then that I realized what a perfect disguise his hat had been, why nobody had recognized him from the picture I'd been showing round; why he could know Rollo but Rollo didn't recognize him. The man was balding, with long, black greasy strands of hair hanging down from the sides of his head and down over his shoulders. On the top of his head, running down from the centre, and making a sharp turn to the left just above the brow, was a scar which dominated not only his head but his whole face. It was like a brand, the scar tissue old but still livid, something your eyes could not avoid, something which seemed to define him. I didn't know the cause of the scar, whether it was surgical, accidental or given to him on purpose, but I did know that with a hat on he was a different person. His hat was lying on the bed next to him.

He came forward towards the gun but I beat him to it. I was turning it on him when he took hold of the barrel with both of his hands and forced me back. For a split second the gun was pointing straight into his chest but I didn't pull the trigger. His momentum had taken him up into a standing position on the bed and it forced me backwards as he came off it and on to me. I backed into something, hard, and the gun went off, blowing a hole in the ceiling of the van and sending down a shower of debris. I pulled the trigger again, deliberately this time, blowing out one of the plastic windows. Knowing the gun was empty he released a hand from it and went for a straight right but I managed to get my head out of the way of his fist and it smacked into the plywood behind me. I got the butt of the gun into the side of his face. It straightened him up and before he could swing again I jabbed the end of the gun full into his face with as much of my weight behind it as I could get. It sent him the two feet towards the bed and he tripped backwards, thanks more to the contact with the bed than to what I'd done to him.

His face was pulsing blood. I wasn't sure how much he could see. He should have taken the count then but he didn't. He came up at me but before he could get to his feet I used the gun again. He went back further this time and his hand went for the nearest of the two bottles by the side of the bed which, to my relief, was the one that held the Becks. His fingers curled around the green glass and with one last effort he threw it with all his force, coming in after it, screaming like a stuck pig. I was showered with beer but the bottle missed me. I stepped to the side and the man missed me too; he crashed into the plywood which his fist had gone into. I used the gun again. He put his hands out to keep himself upright. I hit him again. Even then there was something left in him. It was like trying to fell a tree. I used the gun again and then one more time and then he didn't have anything left. I stood back from him and he slid down the wall of the van, settling on to the floor as gently as a lift in a four-star hotel.

The Spice Girls. I'll never forget that it was the Spice Girls which was all I could hear. I reached over and turned the sound off. I wanted it off because something else was trying to make me hear it. Or see it. I'd expected feelings of relief, even euphoria at finding the man who was now unconscious at my feet but all of a sudden it seemed trivial. There was something else, something bigger. My eyes went towards the unit at the top of the bed. My thoughts were racing ahead of me. The bottle. As he'd gone for the Becks bottle he'd knocked the litre bottle of vodka on to its side. It was still there. Even as he had done so it had started to come to me, though I didn't know what it was. Now I stared at the bottle. I got an uncomfortable feeling. I felt a racing in my stomach to match that in my head. There was a picture, a picture that I'd missed, something I'd seen but which hadn't registered. A bottle. A hand, the way it held . . . The vodka in the litre bottle swayed slightly, looking for equilibrium. It looked gentle, unconcerned. I stared at it.

I saw a man holding a bottle, holding it in a way which at the time had called out to me but I had failed to hear it. His hand on the bottle. Certain, calm, smiling. Holding it like . . . like he had some sort of affinity with it. I saw a bottle rammed into a young boy's throat. Other bottles. The pictures were becoming sharper. A boy, a truck driver. I felt the horror that comes from realization and the need to act, now, not wait another second, act before it all went out of focus. I didn't know how I knew what I did but I did know. I was certain. I *knew*. I could see it. It was the way he had held that bottle. I'd sat across from him as he smiled at me, and I'd been struck by it at the time but not struck hard enough. But now I knew what I knew and suddenly I knew how I could prove it. All of the inconsistencies, all of the elements which I couldn't fit into my scenario of what had happened to Edward, all suddenly made sense. Why I wasn't killed at York Way, why the killer didn't care about the video, why Teddy was preoccupied, how Dominic had become involved. The knowledge that had just come to me slid into the events easy as Cinderella's left foot. I snapped my eyes away from the vodka bottle and looked quickly round the caravan.

The man was lying on his side, curled up like he was asleep. Now I knew why he hadn't killed me; it was because he had never killed anyone. Not him. I searched for his mobile. I knew he'd have one, he was a pimp, wasn't he, at the very least? I tore the place apart until I finally found it in the pocket of a black leather jacket and used it to call Andy Gold. He wasn't there so I asked for Ken Clay. He came on the line and I told him that I was in a caravan on old BR land behind King's Cross.

'If you want the man in the hat,' I said, 'you better get here soon. He's unconscious but I don't know how long he'll be out.'

'Stay there,' Clay said. 'Don't fucking leave him.'

'I can't,' I said. 'Just get here.'

I was in a hurry. It wasn't a logical hurry, but it was speeding through me so fast I had to go with it.

'Just get here,' I said.

I could hear his protestations as I looked for the button to turn the thing off. I put the phone on the bed and took out my wallet. Andy Gold had given me a card which his bleeper company had issued and which had his number on it. I called it and told the woman the message I would like to leave. She wanted me to read it back to her.

'Just send the fucking thing!'

I dropped the phone and pushed open the door of the caravan. I grabbed my bag and ran to my car. There was a face in front of my eyes and as I ran I felt that I was running straight into it, my fists clenched, and I was about to smash a big hole in the confident smile that played on its broad lips.

I didn't feel the pain in my ribs any more.

When I got to Andy Gold's flat in Camden I double-parked and jumped out. He was already there, just getting out of his Astra. He locked it, and walked towards me, digging his flat keys out of his pocket. He looked puzzled.

'You've got the video?'

'Yes,' he said, 'it's inside. I never got round to taking it back. But I already gave you the picture.'

'Come on,' I said, 'quickly. I need to see it.'

We went inside. I asked Andy to find the place on the tape where he'd found Teddy, and the man in the hat. It didn't take him long.

'I already went through this about . . .'

I took the remote from him and hit the fast-forward button. I went back and forward over the next section of tape, going fast, and then slowing the tape right down. I couldn't see anything, but maybe it was because the door of the shop kept closing. I asked Andy to do the same thing with the other tape, the one from the concourse, which had shown Teddy and the man but had been useless due to the man's baseball cap. Again I hit the forward button, but this time the slow-mo. Andy sat beside me, not particularly engrossed in the screen, not knowing what to look for. The crowd of people inched past like a wave of zombies. Slowly. Slowly. My eyes flicked around them. I watched for five minutes, until I was almost ready to give up. Suddenly it didn't seem so obvious to me. Maybe I was wrong, maybe I had left the real villain lying unconscious in a caravan behind King's Cross. Andy started to fidget. Once again he told me that the tape was useless, you couldn't see enough of him. He wanted to know why I was looking at the time *after* Teddy and the man had gone by. He made a crack about wasting police time.

And then I saw him.

I hit pause on the remote and a hundred people stopped still. I looked at him, just catching the front of his face as he walked into the frame. No hat. Not a clear picture but a definite one. I stared at him. I'd stopped him, just like he'd stopped at least three people. The fuzzy V-hold on the screen made him shake like a fly caught in a web.

I put my finger on the screen. It took Andy a second to recognize him and another to realize why I was pointing him out. His breath stopped, as his mind processed the myriad objections to what my finger was telling him. He didn't say anything. He moved closer to the tiny shivering face in the top left corner of the screen. I could see him scouring his mind for a reason, a reason why it couldn't be him. Another second passed. Then Andy's eyes moved away from the screen and into space.

Suddenly, he made a grab for the telephone.

*

When I got to the airport it was busier than the last time I'd been there but it still wasn't crowded. I stood amongst the sparsely filled tables of the Pavilion Bar looking at a tall, slim figure who was chopping lemons at the bar. Alex Mitchell had his back to me but he must have felt my eyes on him because he stopped what he was doing and turned round to face me. He smiled but his smile disappeared immediately when he saw that I wasn't smiling. His face turned to chalk. Almost immediately he moved along the bar and turned to walk away but stopped when he saw Andy Gold blocking his exit. He backed up and hurried to the other end of the bar only to find an airport cop, complete with automatic rifle, standing square on to him, blocking his path that way too. It was then that he looked past me and saw the other six airport cops, all of whom Andy Gold had briefed, surrounding his bar.

Alex Mitchell should have given up then. But he didn't. He raised the knife he was still carrying high above his head and ran straight at the nearest cop. The bullet hit him almost exactly in the middle of his forehead.

PART FOUR

Chapter Twenty-Three

The smoking room of the Portman Club was no more crowded than it had been the last time I was there. This much was different though: the man sitting opposite me was no longer a Shadow Minister in Her Majesty's Opposition and would not even be an MP for that much longer. Sir Peter Morgan had recently announced his intention to stand down at the next election, a decision which was greeted by both the press and his colleagues with a great deal of respect and understanding. The press coverage which his announcement had received was shocking only in its restraint.

I hadn't wanted to meet Sir Peter at the Portman Club. I'd suggested we go to a café somewhere, or to my office, but Sir Peter had insisted and since he was paying me it was up to him. I'd turned down lunch though, not wanting to sit through another hour of small-talk before we got to the real meat. The crème brûlée was tempting but this time I let it pass. I arrived at the club just after two and was immediately shown upstairs and led through the polished mahogany door which swung open silently before me.

Sir Peter Morgan wanted me to tell him about it. He knew, as indeed the whole world knew, that the man who had murdered his brother had been shot dead by the police. He knew the name of that man but he didn't know a lot else. It was only a couple of days since Alex Mitchell had been confronted at Heathrow airport and the police had not yet revealed any more details about him or how he had committed his crimes. Not even to Sir Peter.

After I had joined the MP a different girl brought us coffee with the same good manners and diligence as her colleague had shown. We sat in the same seats we had used before and we were dressed about the same and there was the same hum of traffic from the street below as well as the same ticking of the grandfather clock which this time I noticed as soon as I entered the room.

Sir Peter looked older than he had done, almost frail. He seemed relaxed enough though but I still couldn't tell if the slight tension he demonstrated in his posture was due to the circumstances or was just the way he always sat. I'd never met him under what you would call normal conditions so I couldn't tell. Before he did anything else, Sir Peter reached into his breast pocket and pulled out a chequebook. He took out a fountain pen and scribbled on the cheque before snapping it off and setting it down on the table between us. It was face down so I couldn't see the amount Sir Peter had written it out for but I wasn't worried about that. I left the cheque there.

We both took sips from our coffee. A silence hung heavy between us which eventually the MP sought to break.

'Before you say anything,' Sir Peter began. 'I want to thank you.'

I put my cup down. 'There's no need.'

'I know. But . . .' He hesitated, his thoughts hovering. 'I want to thank you,' he reiterated. He took a deep breath and put his cup down on the table.

'So,' he said, clasping his hands together in his lap. 'So it was the barman who killed all those people.'

'Yes,' I said. 'It was. Alex Mitchell.'

'He was from Australia I understand.'

'Manly, I believe. A small district just across the bay from Sydney.'

Sir Peter thought for a second. 'I've never been there, to Australia. Too far away. Have you ever?'

'Yes,' I said, 'as a matter of fact I have. I went there with my brother, a few years ago.'

'Oh, I didn't know you had a brother too.'

'Yes,' I said, 'I do.'

'So this Mitchell man came over to work and started attacking innocent men.'

'Well no,' I said. 'No actually. He didn't start here.' I pulled a piece of paper out of my trouser pocket which I had collected from Andy Gold that morning. It was a fax from a detective with the Sydney PD, listing six names, two with question marks against them and the other four with ticks.

I looked at the fax and then handed it to Sir Peter.

'These men were all killed in Australia between four and seven years ago. Most were homosexuals and all but two had been murdered after having sex with someone it is believed they had never met before.'

'And he killed them? The same man killed all these men?'

Morgan was stunned. He held on to his glasses as he looked down at the sheet.

'I don't know,' I said. 'And neither do the police, but they're looking into it. Each of those men was killed with either a knife or a bottle and Alex Mitchell was resident in Australia at the time. All the killings took place within a hundred mile radius of where he was working. I think he was probably responsible for some of them.'

'Christ!' The MP sat back in his chair. 'How on earth did they connect them?'

'I remembered the cases,' I said, 'from when I was there. I even remembered them when I was at the airport two weeks ago, interviewing Alex Mitchell. I told Andy Gold about them the day before yesterday. They were all over the Sydney papers as I recall and even when I'm on holiday I tend to notice things like that.'

'*Deformation professionelle.*'

'Sorry?'

'It's what the French say when you can't escape your job even when you're not doing it. I think you have a bad case of that.'

'I think you're right,' I nodded. 'I do.'

Sir Peter looked at me and pursed his lips softly.

'How did you know?' he asked. 'That it was Mitchell?'

'It just came to me,' I said. 'I just suddenly knew it was him. I just knew it.'

'And that was all?'

'No,' I said. 'Once I'd realized, when I'd connected the use of the bottles with his job as a barman and the way I'd seen him handle bottles, I went round to DI Gold's house. We went through the airport videos. The police had only bothered to scrutinize them for the moments before and during the time when Edward actually left the bar. It was natural, I suppose, given that they already had a pretty obvious suspect.'

'But you looked further on.'

'Yes.'

'And you were looking for Mitchell.'

'That's right. I remembered him saying that the night

barman had just come on. That meant that *his* shift was over. And there he was, following Edward. He was only a few minutes behind. He didn't need to keep too close because he knew where Edward was going.'

'To the car park?'

'Yes. They have a separate area for the airport staff. He may have heard Edward talk about his car or just guessed that he had one. Either way he knew where to go.'

'But what happened? I mean, had Edward arranged to meet him?'

'No,' I said. 'My guess is no. I think he followed him there and then begged a lift off him. He may have said that his car had broken down or something, and then pretended to suddenly recognize him from the bar where Edward had been sitting. Edward won't have been too concerned about taking him. Why should he be? The man was friendly enough behind the bar, he won't have asked Edward to drive out of his way. Edward was a kind man, he would have taken him.'

'And then . . .' Morgan's words tailed off. I left a second and studied Morgan's face. He wanted me to go through it all.

'Well, I think that Mitchell just assumed your brother was gay, having seen him chatting to a man and then leaving with him. Apparently, some gay flight staff did visit his bar. Maybe he thought he could kill both of them, and this new twist was too good to pass up. But the other man had gone, so he begged a lift and then instead of Edward dropping him off somewhere he took him home. To his house.'

'And . . .'

'And then they shared a bath, and had intercourse and . . .'

'No!' the MP said. 'Not Edward! I just can't see it. I just can't. He wasn't gay, he *wasn't*.'

'Mr Morgan,' I said. I leant forward in my chair and lowered my voice. 'He didn't have to be. You, for instance. You *are* gay, yet you're married.'

'Yes, but that's different. I didn't know, not for a long time . . .'

'But if you had known, would you not have ever thought of sleeping with a woman? Wouldn't you have been curious to know what it would have been like, to do that?'

The MP looked confused. 'I don't know. No. Yes. Yes, maybe I would. I see what you mean.'

'You don't have to be certain you're gay or even really think it to wonder. Edward wondered. And I suppose Mitchell came on to him in the car. And Edward's wife was away, and they hadn't been getting on too well. Edward just thought he'd try it. You yourself said he was very open about things like that, and there was no reason anyone would find out. So he did what he did and then he was unlucky. Very unlucky. Just like Mitchell's other victims.'

'God,' the MP said. 'It's all so . . . God.'

I let him take in what I had told him. There really wasn't any doubt about it. The police had found something in Alex Mitchell's flat which could only have come from Edward. I didn't tell Morgan about that yet though. I watched him as a look of incomprehension came over his face.

'How could a man do such horrible things?' the MP asked, as if I could tell him. 'I mean, how on earth? To Edward, and all these other people?'

'It's impossible to say,' I told him. 'No doubt there'll be

some lawyers who'll come up with reasons, and some faux psychiatrist-cum-hack writer who'll put a book out blaming it all on his childhood. But no one will ever really know. Not really. I doubt he knew himself. If he had he might not have felt the need to do it. My own theory is that it's all about power.'

'Power? In what sense?'

'The most basic sense of all. Something about him told him he had no power in his life. Maybe he came from a very straight background and hated the power his sexual feelings had over him. He tried to pretend he had power over them by murdering homosexuals, these men who he saw sometimes and couldn't help feeling attracted to. This also had the effect of making him feel empowered because, as soon as he had begun, he could feel the power that he had over the police, who couldn't catch him. It made him feel strong, like he mattered.'

Sir Peter nodded. 'And the boy in your flat. More of the same?'

'Probably,' I said. 'Mitchell had nothing on me. I think it irked him. I think, when I spoke to him at the airport, that I gave the impression of being in control, of not being fazed by what he was doing. What I was really feeling was that I was wasting my time, that I was just going through the motions investigating it for you. I was blasé because I thought I was on an easy way to pay the phone bill. I think he wanted to bring me into it, to involve me in his actions, to make me really feel them.'

'And he saw you talking to the boy?'

'Yes,' I said, 'he was following me. I'd given him my card which had my office address on and he hooked me there and then tailed me to my flat. He followed me to King's Cross and saw me talk to Dominic Lewes. I remember sensing that someone was watching me but I thought it was just kids out to rip off my stereo. But it wasn't. I'd actually tried to reach Mitchell at the airport a couple of times, but he wasn't there; he was keeping tabs on me. I'd even made the mistake of worrying about him, thinking of him only as a potential witness the killer may have wanted to eliminate.

'A couple of days later he killed Dominic and then sat outside my flat waiting for me to leave. He may have planned a ruse to get me out of there himself but if he had he didn't need it. He got lucky; someone else got me out of bed, and I ran off on a fool's errand to York Way, giving him time to leave the body on my bed and put me in the frame for it. My road is quiet, it's an alley really, no one would have seen him. Later, when he'd seen me come home, he called the police and said he'd seen something strange, a man with a knife, and they arrived to find me there.'

Sir Peter sat back in his chair. Behind him, across the room, the door opened and a man stepped in and stood by the side of it, waiting quietly with his hands clasped in front of him. Sir Peter let out a long breath.

'It was my fault,' he said. He was serious. His voice came up from a deep well of regret and impotence. 'It was me. I never should have spoken to Edward, never. About the way I felt. I put it into his head. If it wasn't for me he wouldn't have gone with that man. He told me that he'd never even considered it, not ever. It was my fault.'

'No,' I said. 'He didn't go with a man because you suggested it. That simply isn't what happened. It wasn't as if he'd never heard of gay sex. It wasn't that that killed him.' I was telling this to Morgan because it was true. I wasn't trying to make him feel better. He didn't argue.

'Whatever you say.' Sir Peter smiled. He was a long way off. 'It doesn't make a lot of difference now though, does it?'

'No,' I said.

'It's over. It's over now.'

Sir Peter shifted forward in his chair and went to pick up the cheque, no doubt to hand it to me. His hand stopped in mid-air, however, when I said, 'No, Sir Peter, it's not. It's not quite over yet I'm afraid.'

The waitress came over with the coffee jug. As she poured, Sir Peter Morgan didn't take his eyes off me. When she had gone I reached into the side pocket of my jacket and drew out a photograph. I reached over to hand it to Sir Peter and he took it from me. He didn't have to use his glasses to see what it showed. The blood fled from his cheeks like ants from a burning nest.

'The police found it,' I told him. 'In Alex Mitchell's flat. He took it from Edward. There are more but the police have those. This kind of sums up the general mood though.'

Morgan was completely still, unable to take his eyes off the picture.

'I made some mistakes,' I told him. 'I got all ravelled up in Graham Lloyd. You're right about him being a bastard by the way, though it was never likely that he was involved, not really. But it was only a short while after I'd quizzed him that I got beaten up by the man in the video still. I was sure that Lloyd was paying him but if he was, what for? He certainly wouldn't have employed him to be a serial killer but he may have paid him to kill Edward. He had a motive. Yet Lloyd surely couldn't have been stupid enough to get the man he'd hired before to have a go at me after he knew I was interested in him. He would more likely have shut up tight and covered his tracks.'

Morgan was sitting very still, his eyes on me now. He still had the photograph in his hand.

'I knew this, and I had actually discounted Lloyd, but when I found Dominic Lewes' body in my flat it really threw me. I knew then that the same person had killed all of the men, just as the police had known all along. But I tried to make myself believe otherwise, to tie Lloyd in, largely because I didn't like him but mainly because it was the only way I could figure it. You see, I couldn't square the man in the baseball hat with his presence in the airport video. He would only have been there if he was the killer, but the killer had been meticulous and controlled and to a large degree very careful. There were only a few occasions when Mitchell had taken any real risks, and killing Edward was one of them. Except it wasn't much of a risk in retrospect because he knew that if he killed Edward everyone would think it was the man in the hat, who he'd been seen drinking with. And he was right, we all did think that. You were probably the only one who knew it wasn't him. Which is why you hired me. The killer had been careful and here was this guy getting caught on camera, meeting me but not finishing me off, letting me hear his voice, telling me who he knew. I couldn't square it so I hung on to Lloyd and hoped he was the answer.'

Sir Peter didn't say anything. I didn't have to go on. He knew what I was going to tell him. But he had asked me to come here and tell it to him and that is exactly what I was going to do.

'I made another mistake,' I said. 'A small one but

important, something I didn't check. The officer who initially interviewed Edward's co-pilot reported that Edward had asked him to go for a drink when the flight landed but that wasn't true. They sometimes did go for a drink together but Chalkley begged off that night without even being asked. He remembered that when I phoned him this morning and said he hadn't meant to give any other impression.'

'Does it matter?'

'Not now,' I said. 'But it gave the impression that Edward wanted Chalkley along when he certainly did not. It would have made it a lot easier for me if Chalkley *had* wanted to go because he would then have remembered how Edward put him off.'

'What does this show?'

'I'm sorry, Sir Peter, it really doesn't show that much. Call it my *deformation professionelle.* All it shows is that Edward knew he was going to meet someone. He was going to meet the man in the hat. The man who got me out of bed and proceeded to kick the shit out of me. A pimp, a petty hood and blackmailer. The very man who took the photograph you're looking at.'

But Sir Peter Morgan wasn't looking at it any more. It dropped from his fingers and fell down on to the table right next to the cheque Morgan had written out for me. Morgan held his hands up to his face and began to sob quietly, streams of water coming through his fingers almost immediately, like water through the sluice-gates of a dam.

'You said it was your fault,' I said, though I couldn't be sure he heard me. 'And it was. Not for making him want to know what it was like to sleep with a man, no. But it was your fault that Edward went to sit at that bar.'

'I'm sorry. I'm so sorry.'

I didn't say anything. He wasn't speaking to me.

'I told Teddy I wanted to go. I told him. I never should have mentioned the man, never. If I'd gone to meet him instead it would have been me the barman met. I'd have taken him home. Home or somewhere. It would have been me, not Edward.'

Sir Peter couldn't get any more out. He was sobbing, his shoulders jerking with the effort like one of those small wooden toys whose joints are sprung with string.

I glanced down at the table where the photograph lay. It was face up. It was a colour photograph, taken from behind a curtain which explained the blurring round the edges. The rest of the shot was clear enough though. It showed the inside of a small room. It showed a boom box, the same one that I'd seen in the caravan two days ago. I imagined it was there to mask the sound of the camera shutter as it captured the events taking place. It also showed a young black boy bent over a table, naked except for his socks. He was the boy I had first seen at Sal's gym and who had later run away from me. I cannot describe the expression on his face except to say that it conveyed far more than the immediate pain he was feeling. Behind the boy was a tall, rather thin white man who was also naked. The man was quite clearly Peter Morgan and it was also quite clear what he was doing.

Morgan was hunched over in his hands. I looked past him to see that Andy Gold was getting impatient. I turned back to Morgan and went through the rest of it quickly.

'The boy's brave,' I said. 'He's going to testify, against both you and the man who was pimping him. He hated what you did to him. He recognized you on the news one day and pegged you for one of his regulars. He told his pimp, a guy called Smile, to please him. You see, this Smile was seeing the boy's mother. He beat all shit out of her and only promised to lay off the boy's kid sister if the boy went to work for him. He wanted to get in Smile's good books because though he hated him hc thought it would help keep his sister safe. That didn't work too well though. Apparently Smile was keeping the sister for his own enjoyment.

'Smile was glad of what he heard though. About you being a prominent politician.' I picked up the photograph. 'He set this little show up and then started to hit you for cash. You panicked and told your brother, and he agreed to help you. Maybe he insisted, like you said, or maybe you begged him to go and meet the guy for you. I'll go with your version of that as it happens. Edward was a good guy; I think he would have insisted on helping.'

Morgan was nodding his head. His tears had dried up but his shoulders kept heaving up and down.

'He had the cash in the boot of his Rover, and after meeting up with Smile at the bar, and making sure who he was, he went off to the car park with him. Mitchell said they stuck around for thirty minutes before leaving but that was bullshit; he wanted to make it seem like Edward had never met the man in the hat before and was being picked up by him at the bar. That would make it seem more like Smile was the perpetrator, because the perpetrator had never previously known any of his victims beforehand. Telling the police that the two men sat at the bar for a while made a pick-up more plausible than if they had only been there two minutes.

'When they got to the car Edward gave the cash to Smile in exchange for the pictures and the negatives, which were found at Mitchell's place. Other copies were found in the caravan Smile used. He wasn't going to rest at one payoff; blackmailers never do. He'd have been back and you'd have had to do it all over again. Everything went OK this time though, it all went smoothly. Smile got the money and drove off. But that's when Alex Mitchell decided to show up. He went home with Edward and killed him, knowing that the guy he'd seen Edward with would be the prime suspect. And he was. Smile saw the video-still I was showing round, and he knew in what context he was wanted. He knew he'd likely go away for murder if I found him so he came after me to warn me off.'

Morgan was quite still now but his hands remained covering his face. I left a second and then said, 'You shouldn't feel guilty about what happened to your brother. Not about that really. But you should feel guilty.'

Andy Gold couldn't wait any longer. He walked across the room towards us, followed by two uniforms who had been standing out in the corridor. Without standing up I removed the wire I'd been wearing inside my jacket and handed it to him. Gold already had the pictures but wanted to catch Morgan talking about it in case the kid didn't come through. I knew it wasn't necessary, feeling pretty sure that Morgan would confess to it all on his own, but I couldn't see what harm it could do. Andy read Sir Peter Morgan his rights. One of the uniforms put some cuffs on him and stood him up. Morgan didn't look at me. His eyes were closed and he was mouthing something. I think it was the word 'sorry' repeated over and over again but the movement of his lips was so small I couldn't really be sure.

As the two officers walked the MP over to the door, Andy stopped and asked me if I was coming.

'No,' I said. 'Not yet.'

Andy shrugged and followed the two officers as they escorted Sir Peter Morgan from the room.

I sat back in the armchair and gazed at the elegant array of old leather furniture. Shafts of sunlight cut through the residual haze of homeless dust and old tobacco smoke. The clock ticked. I reached for my coffee before it went cold.

I'd wait there ten minutes and then slip out. I didn't have any desire to see Sir Peter Morgan being led out of his club by the police, past the grave portraits of his predecessors and the horrified eyes of his fellow members. I'd never wanted to meet him here anyway. I felt a curious heaviness, not the sort of feeling I associated with the other times I'd helped put away someone who preyed on people more helpless than themselves. I felt strangely rueful, and wondered why I should feel like that.

It was because he must have known. When he'd hired me he must have known what would happen to him if I was successful in pursuing my investigations. And plenty *would* happen to him, so much that I doubted whether he would be able to handle it. He had known who the man in the hat was and what I would find out if I found him. I guessed that was why he'd already announced his retirement, to cause as little embarrassment as he could. Putting his affairs in order like a Samurai before he falls on his sword. I remembered his fervour when he was urging me to go on with the case. It seemed strange to me now, that fervour, as though he did want to end it all but he needed me to help him; he couldn't plunge the blade in on his own. I had to admit that I felt a certain amount of pity for Sir Peter Morgan. I couldn't condone what he'd done with that boy and I didn't want to, but he knew that what he'd done was disgusting and it was his actions subsequently which led to his paying for it. No one would have known otherwise. He really didn't care what happened to himself, he didn't care at all. He just wanted to catch the bastard who killed his brother no matter what the consequences were. He loved his brother and wanted, in the end, to do right by him.

I could sympathize with that. I knew how that felt.

Chapter Twenty-Four

I left the Portman Club with Sir Peter Morgan's cheque in my pocket. I didn't have any qualms about taking it; I'd done what he'd asked me to do which, after I thought about it, was a more important service than I'd initially realized. I'd helped him to atone. I deserved the money. I banked it and did some sums and figured that I could afford to take a couple of weeks off.

During those two weeks I avoided buying a paper and I turned the radio off whenever the news came on. There was only one story, which I knew only too well, and even if the press had got all the facts, which I doubted, it would never be anything more than that; a story. No matter what words you use to describe a thing, words that are measured or those that are lurid and sensationalist, all you really have is words. Pictures don't help either; they're fictions too. I had entertained so many scenarios in my head about what had occurred with Edward Morgan and his brother that I didn't trust the final one, the one the world was busy putting together. I didn't read the papers just as I wouldn't go to a public execution. I now knew what the order of events had been without needing to be told again, and what did even they tell you about what really went on inside people? It was all just speculation, with varying degrees of malicious joy. I didn't need it.

The weather was cold and clear. I walked in the park and got over my cracked ribs and saw my face slowly reappearing in the mirror. I had a few drinks with Nicky but I never stayed late. I went to the gym, driving down there past the kids who were still on the corner like carp rising for the bait seconds after one of their number has been yanked away. At the gym I took it slowly, working out lightly and spending some time on the bike. Each time I went down there I saw the young boy, who never acknowledged my presence nor ever chatted to anyone else in the gym. He just concentrated on his business, whether it was curling a dumbbell or working with the rope. Sal told me that he was coming along well. He was focused, she said, and committed. Watching his set face and his narrowed eyes as he laid hell into the bag, I think I knew what he was focusing on.

I watched the dust grow on my answerphone and left the machine on. Sharon called me a couple of times but I didn't know what to say to her so I didn't pick up. Charlotte Morgan called to tell me that she was not going to go to the papers about her affair with Lloyd now that she knew he wasn't involved in her husband's murder. I'd guessed that she wouldn't and as much as I would have liked to see Lloyd's career take a serious knock I was relieved for her. Charlotte told me that she had, however, decided to invest in the vineyard Lloyd had mentioned though not in partnership with the MP, but with her accountant, who thought the investment very sound now that it wasn't tied to a failing concern. Lloyd was close, apparently, to putting a deal together himself, and was apoplectic to discover that he'd been gazumped by his former mistress. Revenge, it seems, is a dish best taken with a glass or two of English table wine.

I plucked up enough courage one morning to call Dominic Lewes' mother and arranged to meet her in Grimsby the next day. I drove up and we had coffee in a Little Chef on the outskirts of the city. She wouldn't hear of me apologizing for my part in her son's death, even though she now knew exactly what had happened.

'You didn't make him hate himself enough to go out and sell himself for drugs,' she told me. 'I know who did that.'

I told her about the times I'd seen her son and also the timetable I'd found in his room after he'd been killed. It didn't even begin to penetrate the cloak of sorrow she wore round herself.

'There is one thing though,' she said, as we were getting ready to leave. 'One thing which I like to think of. The police told me that this animal was due to strike again, that it was longer between murders than before. I like to think of the young man who he didn't kill because he got my Dominic. I like to think of a normal young boy with something to live for. I picture him sometimes, laughing with his mates or holding hands with someone special. He's a nice boy with a happy life. He doesn't live the sort of life Dominic did. When I imagine him sometimes I'm even glad it happened to my Dominic and not to him. He goes home and sees his parents at the weekend. He's happy. Dominic was never happy.'

I still didn't call Sharon. I just didn't know what to say to her. Every time I thought of her the images which played out in my mind were too much and I shut them down as soon as I realized I was thinking of her. After the first week the images were almost constant and I either walked them off or tried to dissolve them in Irish whiskey. One evening the phone rang and it was Trish, the woman I'd met at Nicky's when he'd conned me into going down to meet him. She asked me if I wanted dinner and I thought it might take my mind off things so I said yes, and we went to a new place on the Liverpool Road. Trish was a vivacious, attractive woman and we got on well together. She was also very interesting to talk to, something which I had completely failed to notice the first time I had seen her.

We chatted about this and that until the conversation eventually came round to families. I found myself telling Trish all about mine, about Luke and what had happened to him. I think I was a little drunk and I wound up telling her all about Sharon too and the night we had spent together. How bad I felt about it but how I couldn't stop a million different thoughts rushing round in my head. Trish nodded to herself as though something I was saying made sense.

'I could tell there was someone,' Trish said. 'When we were together. I could tell you weren't really into it.' I started to protest but she shook her head and laughed. 'It's OK,' she said. 'I don't mind. It was just that I could tell you weren't really up for it, but you couldn't think of a polite way to say no.'

Trish asked me what I was going to do about all of it. I told her that I didn't know. We had a long talk and at the end of it, after we'd left the restaurant and I'd walked her back to her car, she looked at me and smiled. She got in but before she drove off she wound her window down.

'I think you know what to do,' Trish said.

And suddenly, I did.

I stayed up that night and read all the poems that were in the file Sharon had given to me. I still hadn't looked at them. I couldn't stand the idea of knowing what my brother's thoughts were. Not after what had happened between me and his fiancée. Even before. Something in me had been aware for some time of feelings towards Sharon which were out of place, and it was horrified of them and scared of how my brother would feel if he knew. So I had avoided his thoughts and tried to view him as simply an inert piece of flesh, the subject of pity and remorse, to be visited and sanctified. I'd been far more cowardly than Sharon had. I'd talked about football matches and skiing as a way of avoiding the truth of what was going on. She had confronted her feelings and decided to be brave enough to go with them, to admit what we both knew: that we had become very close to each other. I couldn't face up to that because if I did I would also have to admit that Luke was irrevocably gone, that my brother was alive in name only. I could only ever love Sharon if I could first accept what she already had accepted and I had always turned away from knowing. That Luke was dead.

In the morning I drove out to the hospital. I sat next to Luke for ages, all day in fact, and I spoke for hours non-stop, telling him everything I felt about him and everything I felt about Sharon. I held his hand, pressing his grey knuckles hard against my forehead, occasionally soaking his palms and his wrists with my tears, the first time I had ever done so. I told Luke how sorry I was about what had happened to him. It was not the first time I had told him this, and I never did it from a knowledge of rational blame, but this time I felt more sorry than I ever had done before. I was now aware of what Luke's life had been like before he was attacked. I knew what he had given up. He had not only cast off his own life so that I could keep on living, he had also given that life to me. I held on to Luke's hand and begged for some sort of sign from him, a word to show that he understood what I was about to do. I waited for a long time before realizing that, though I had the chance in my life to know a happiness greater than I had felt possible since that night four years ago on the Westway, there was one thing I would have to do without for ever. I could ask for my brother's blessing until I was blue in the face, but he would never be able to answer, or to give it to me. Not now, not ever.

Eventually I kissed Luke's cold dry lips and said goodbye to him, and then to Hazel, who smiled at me fondly. I smiled back, feeling strangely elated. I drove back into London, all the way nursing a smile which seemed to be growing within myself, opening out inside my body like a huge orchid. A latent sense of guilt fought to stem it but the flower was too strong. I drove quickly, amazed and self-conscious about the way I was feeling, until the car was parked outside Sharon's building in Ladbroke Grove. It was dark by now and when I looked up I could see a light behind the curtains of Sharon's flat.

I hadn't told her I was coming. I sat in the car for five minutes, enjoying the expectation, the almost physical knowledge that I was about to see her. Her face was alive before my eyes but there was nothing I could do about that now, even if I wanted to. The orchid inside me had grown so huge it was trying to break through my ribcage. I wondered what Sharon was doing up there: reading a law report or *Marie Claire*. Or maybe she was with another man, the lover I had suspected. I didn't care. I was going up there, whatever the outcome was.

Simple as that.

As I reached for the door handle a poem came into my head; one of Luke's poems. The poem was about Sharon. It was about how Luke couldn't write about her, because she destroyed his centre, made him feel like a child, how his faculties had dissolved into a rush of sentiment he couldn't express without sounding ridiculous. But how, at the same time, he couldn't stop writing about her, even if he knew he was sounding stupid. It was one of my favourites in the collection because it was so fresh and honest. I remembered the ending:

She's sweet as a wish
and soft as a prayer
and the sun hides out in her golden hair

when the moon saw her face
he decided to take early retirement

and I love her more
than a sailboat loves the water.

I couldn't argue with that.

CRITICAL ACCLAIM FOR

Colin Dexter

The Remorseful Day

'Morse's last case is a virtuoso piece of plotting . . . by quitting the game on the top of his form [Dexter] has set his fellow crime-writers an example they will find it hard to emulate.'

Sunday Times

Death is Now My Neighbour

'Dexter has created a giant among fictional detectives and has never short-changed his readers.'

The Times

The Daughters of Cain

'This is Colin Dexter at his most excitingly devious.'

Daily Telegraph

The Wench is Dead

'Dextrously ingenious.'

Guardian

The Secret of Annexe 3

'A plot of classical cunning and intricacy.'

Times Literary Supplement

The Way Through the Woods

'Morse and his faithful Watson, Sergeant Lewis, in supreme form . . . Hallelujah.'

Observer

The Jewel That Was Ours

'Traditional crime writing at its best; the kind of book without which no armchair is complete.'

Sunday Times

The Riddle of the Third Mile

'Runs the gamut of brain-racking unputdownability.'

Observer

The Dead of Jericho

'The writing is highly intelligent, the atmosphere melancholy, the effect haunting.'

Daily Telegraph

Service of All the Dead

'A brilliantly plotted detective story.'

Evening Standard

The Silent World of Nicholas Quinn

'Morse's superman status is reinforced by an ending which no ordinary mortal could have possibly unravelled.'

Financial Times

Last Seen Wearing

'Brilliant characterization in original whodunnit.'

Sunday Telegraph

Last Bus to Woodstock

'Let those who lament the decline of the English detective story reach for Colin Dexter.'

Guardian

[illegible]

[illegible] 1975. There are now [illegible] novels in the series, of which [illegible] the last.

[illegible] won many awards for his novels, including the CWA Silver Dagger twice, and the CWA Gold Dagger for *The Wench is Dead* and *The Way Through the Woods*. In 1997 he was presented with the CWA Diamond Dagger for outstanding services to crime literature and in 2000 was awarded the OBE in the Queen's Birthday Honours List.

[illegible] Central Television, starring John Thaw and Kevin Whately.

THE REMORSEFUL DAY

Colin Dexter graduated from Cambridge University in 1953 and has lived in Oxford since 1966. His first novel, *Last Bus to Woodstock*, was published in 1975. There are now thirteen novels in the series, of which *The Remorseful Day* is, sadly, the last.

Colin Dexter has won many awards for his novels, including the CWA Silver Dagger twice, and the CWA Gold Dagger for *The Wench is Dead* and *The Way Through the Woods*. In 1997 he was presented with the CWA Diamond Dagger for outstanding services to crime literature, and in 2000 was awarded the OBE in the Queen's Birthday Honours List.

The Inspector Morse novels have, of course, been adapted for the small screen with huge success by Carlton/Central Television, starring John Thaw and Kevin Whately.

The Inspector Morse Novels

LAST BUS TO WOODSTOCK
LAST SEEN WEARING
THE SILENT WORLD OF NICHOLAS QUINN
SERVICE OF ALL THE DEAD
THE DEAD OF JERICHO
THE RIDDLE OF THE THIRD MILE
THE SECRET OF ANNEXE 3
THE WENCH IS DEAD
THE JEWEL THAT WAS OURS
THE WAY THROUGH THE WOODS
THE DAUGHTERS OF CAIN
DEATH IS NOW MY NEIGHBOUR
THE REMORSEFUL DAY

Also available in Pan Books

MORSE'S GREATEST MYSTERY AND OTHER STORIES
THE FIRST INSPECTOR MORSE OMNIBUS
THE SECOND INSPECTOR MORSE OMNIBUS
THE THIRD INSPECTOR MORSE OMNIBUS
THE FOURTH INSPECTOR MORSE OMNIBUS

COLIN DEXTER

THE REMORSEFUL DAY

PAN BOOKS

First published 1999 by Macmillan

This edition published 2000 by Pan Books
an imprint of Pan Macmillan Ltd
Pan Macmillan, 20 New Wharf Road, London N1 9RR
Basingstoke and Oxford
Associated companies throughout the world
www.panmacmillan.com

ISBN 0 330 37639 X

14 16 18 19 17 15

A CIP catalogue record for this book is available from the British Library.

Typeset by SetSystems Ltd, Saffron Walden, Essex
Printed and bound in Great Britain by
Mackays of Chatham plc, Chatham, Kent

For
George, Hilary, Maria, and Beverley
(Please note the Oxford comma)

Acknowledgements

[illegible] with large [illegible] [illegible] [illegible] for [illegible] [illegible] Africa [illegible] [illegible] some of the [illegible] and [illegible] of the many [illegible] on [illegible] and [illegible]

The author and publishers wish to thank the following [illegible] for permission to [illegible]

Extract from [illegible] [illegible] [illegible] are reproduced by permission of [illegible] Authors as the [illegible] [illegible]

Extract from [illegible] by David [illegible] are reproduced by permission of the author.

Extract from translation of [illegible] by Basil [illegible] reproduced by permission of the author.

Extract from [illegible] *Strange Holy Man* by [illegible]

Acknowledgements

My special thanks are due, imprimis to Terry Benczik from New Jersey, for sending me so many apposite quotations; to Cyndi Cook from Hawaii, for singing to me as I wrote these chapters; to Allison Dexter, for sharing with me her expertise on coronary care; to Eddie Andrews, one of my former pupils, for initiating me (at last!) into some of the mysteries of the SOCOs; and to Chris Burt, producer of so many Morse episodes on TV, for his constant support and encouragement.

The author and publishers wish to thank the following who have kindly given permission for use of copyright materials:

Extracts from *More Poems* XLI, *More Poems* XVI and *A Shropshire Lad* by A. E. Housman are reproduced by permission of The Society of Authors as the literary representative of the Estate of A. E. Housman.

Extract from *On the Dole in Darlington* by David Mackenzie reproduced by permission of the author.

Extract from translation of *An Die Musik* by Basil Swift reproduced by permission of the author.

Extract from *I'm a Stranger Here Myself* by Ogden Nash

(from the collection *Candy is Dandy*, Andre Deutsch Ltd, Copyright © 1938 by Ogden Nash, Renewed) is reprinted by permission of Curtis Brown Ltd, Andre Deutsch Ltd and Little, Brown and Company, Inc.

Extract from *Catch-22* by Joseph Heller is reproduced by permission of the author.

Extract from *The Fiddler of Dooney* by W. B. Yeats is reproduced by permission of A. P. Watt Ltd on behalf of Michael B. Yeats, and Simon & Schuster Inc.

Extract from *Come to Think of It* by G. K. Chesterton is reproduced by kind permission of A. P. Watt Limited on behalf of the Royal Literary Fund.

Extract from *Oxford* by Jan Morris is reproduced by permission of Oxford University Press.

Extract from *Lovelace Bleeding* by Roy Dean reproduced by permission of the author.

Extract from *Nightwood* by Djuna Barnes is reproduced by permission of the author and Faber and Faber Ltd.

Every effort has been made to trace all copyright holders but if any has been inadvertently overlooked, the author and publishers will be pleased to make the necessary arrangement at the first opportunity.

Ensanguining the skies
How heavily it dies
  Into the west away;
Past touch and sight and sound
Not further to be found
How hopeless under ground
  Falls the remorseful day.

(A. E. Housman,
More Poems, XVI)

When I wrote my 1997 letter I thought I had little to look forward to in 1998, but it turns out that I was stupidly optimistic

(David Mackenzie,
On the Dole in Darlington)

PROLEGOMENON

As o'er me now thou lean'st thy breast,
With launder'd bodice crisply pressed,
Lief I'd prolong my grievous ill –
Wert thou my guardian angel still
(Edmund Raikes, 1537–65,
The Nurse)

'So I OFTEN hook my foot over the side of the mattress.'

'You *what*?'

'Sort of anchors me to my side of the bed.'

'Double bed?'

'Not unknown is it, for a married couple? People can share the same bed but not the same thoughts – old Chinese saying.'

'Still makes me jealous.'

'Idiot!'

'Everybody gets a bit jealous sometimes.'

'Not everybody.'

'Not you, nurse?'

'I've just learned not to show it, that's all. And it's none of your business in any case.'

'Sorry.'

'How I hate men who say "sorry"!'

'I promise not to say it again, miss.'

'And will you promise me something else? To

be a bit more honest with yourself – and with me?'

'Scout's honour!'

'I can't believe you were ever in the Scouts.'

'Well, no, but . . .'

'Shall I test you?'

'Test me?'

'Would you like me to jump into bed with you *now*?'

'Yes!'

'You're quick on the buzzer.'

'Next question?'

'Do you think *I'd* like to jump into bed with *you*?'

'I'd like to think so.'

'What about the other patients?'

'You could draw the curtains.'

'What excuse . . . ?'

'You could always take my blood pressure.'

'*Again?*'

'Why not?'

'We know all about your blood pressure. High – very high – especially when I'm around.'

'It's those black stockings of yours.'

'You're a stocking-tops man!'

'Nice word, isn't it – stocking-tops?'

'If only you weren't stuck in this bloody ward!'

'I can always discharge myself.'

'Not a wise move, good sir – not in your case.'

'What time are you off duty?'

'Half-eight.'

'What'll you do then?'

'Off home. I'm expecting a phone call.'

'You're trying to make me jealous again.'

'After that, I suppose I'll just poke the thingummy, you know, around the four channels.'

'Five, now.'

'We don't get the new one.'

'What about Sky?'

'In *our* village, satellite dishes are most *definitely* discouraged.'

'You could always take a video home.'

'No need. We've got lots of videos. You should see some of them – you know, the sex ones.'

'You watch that sort of thing?'

'When I'm in the mood.'

'When's that?'

'Most of the time.'

'And even if you aren't in the mood?'

'Oh yes! They soon turn anybody on. Haven't you seen some of these Amsterdam videos? All sorts of bizarre things they get up to.'

'I haven't seen them, no.'

'Would you like to?'

'I'm not quite sure I would, no.'

'Not even if you watched them with me?'

'Please, nurse, am I allowed to change my mind?'

'We could arrange a joint viewing.'

'How – how bizarre's bizarre?'

'Well, in one of 'em there's this woman – about my age – lovely figure – wrists tied to the top of the four-poster bed – ankles tied to the bottom . . .'

'Go on.'

'Well, there's these two young studs – one black, one white – '

'No racial discrimination, then?'

' – and they just take turns, you know.'

'Raping her . . .'

'You're so *naive*, aren't you? She wouldn't have *been* in the bloody video, would she, if she didn't want to be? There *are* some people like her, you know. The only real sexual thrill they get is from some sort of submission – you know, that sort of thing.'

'Odd sort of women!'

'Odd? Unusual, perhaps, but . . .'

'How come you know so much about this?'

'When we were in Amsterdam, they invited me to do some porno-filming. Frank didn't mind. They made a pretty good offer.'

'So you negotiated a fee?'

'Hold on! I only said this particular woman was *about* my age – '

' – and had a lovely figure.'

'Would you like to see if it *was* me?'

'One condition.'

'What's that?'

'If I come, you mustn't hook your foot over the side of the mattress.'

'Not much danger of that.'

'Stay with me a bit longer!'

'No. You're not my only patient, and some of these poor devils'll be here long after *you've* gone.'

'Will you come and give me a chaste little kiss before you go off duty?'

'No. I'm shooting straight back to Lower Swinstead. I told you: I'm expecting a phone call.'

'From . . . your husband?'

'You must be kidding! Frank's in Switzerland for a few days. He's far too mean to call me from there – even on the cheap rates.'

'Another man in your life?'

'Jesus! You don't take me for a dyke, do you?'

'You're an amazing girl.'

'Girl? I'll be forty-eight this Thursday.'

'Can I take you out? Make a birthday fuss of you?'

'No chance. According to your notes, you're going to be in at least till the end of the week.'

'You know, in a way, I wish I *could* stay in. Indefinitely.'

'Well, I promise one thing: as soon as you're out, I'll be in touch.'

'Please! If you can.'

'And you'll come and see me?'

'If you invite me.'

'I'm inviting you now.'

Chapter One

[illegible]

Schubert's [illegible] on the [illegible] evening of Wednesday 15 July [illegible] – a bedroom [illegible] found in his North Oxford [illegible]

[illegible] had never [illegible] to explore the remoter corners even of his native land; and this, principally, because he could not imagine few if any places closer to his heart than Oxford – the city which, though not his natural mother, had for so many years performed the duties

Chapter One

You holy Art, when all my hope is shaken,
And through life's raging tempest I am drawn,
You make my heart with warmest love to waken,
As if into a better world reborn

(From *An Die Musik*, translated by
Basil Swift)

Apart (of course) from Wagner, apart from Mozart's compositions for the clarinet, Schubert was one of the select composers who could occasionally transport him to the frontier of tears. And it was Schubert's turn in the early evening of Wednesday, 15 July 1998, when – *The Archers* over – a bedroom-slippered Chief Inspector Morse was to be found in his North Oxford bachelor flat, sitting at his ease in Zion and listening to a Lieder recital on Radio 3, an amply filled tumbler of pale Glenfiddich beside him. And why not? He was on a few days' furlough that had so far proved quite unexpectedly pleasurable.

Morse had never enrolled in the itchy-footed regiment of truly adventurous souls, feeling (as he did) little temptation to explore the remoter corners even of his native land; and this, principally, because he could now imagine few if any places closer to his heart than Oxford – the city which, though not his natural mother, had for so many years performed the duties of a loving foster-parent. As for foreign travel, long faded were his boyhood dreams that roamed the sands round Samarkand; and a lifelong pterophobia still precluded any airline bookings to Bayreuth, Salzburg, Vienna – the trio of cities he sometimes thought he ought to see.

Vienna . . .

The city Schubert had so rarely left; the city in which he'd gained so little recognition; where he'd died of typhoid fever – only thirty-one.

Not much of an innings, was it – thirty-one?

Morse leaned back, listened, and looked semi-contentedly through the french window. In *The Ballad of Reading Gaol*, Oscar Wilde had spoken of that little tent of blue that prisoners call the sky; and Morse now contemplated that little tent of green that owners of North Oxford flats are wont to call the garden. Flowers had always meant something to Morse, even from his schooldays. Yet in truth it was more the nomenclature of the several species, and their context in the works of the great poets, that had compelled his imagination: fast-fading violets, the globèd peonies, the fields of asphodel . . . Indeed Morse was fully aware of the etymology and the mythological associations of the asphodel, although quite certainly he would never have recognized one of its kind had it flashed across a Technicolor screen.

It was still true though: as men grew older (so Morse told himself) the delights of the natural world grew ever more important. Not just the flowers, either. What about the birds?

Morse had reached the conclusion that if he were to be reincarnated (a prospect which seemed to him most blessedly remote) he would register as a part-time Quaker, and devote a sizeable quota of his leisure hours to ornithology. This latter decision was consequent upon his realization, however late in the day, that life would be significantly impoverished should the birds no longer sing. And it was for this reason that, the previous week, he had taken out a year's subscription to *Birdwatching*; taken out a copy of the RSPB's *Birdwatchers' Guide* from the Summertown Library; and purchased a second-hand pair of 8/50mm binoculars (£9.90) that he'd spotted in the window of the Oxfam Shop just down the Banbury Road. And to complete his programme he had called in at the Summertown Pet Store and taken home a small wired cylinder packed with peanuts – a cylinder now suspended from a branch overhanging his garden. From *the* branch overhanging his garden.

He reached for the binoculars now and focused on an interesting specimen pecking away at the grass below the peanuts: a small bird, with a greyish crown, dark-brown bars across the dingy russet of its back, and paler underparts. As he watched, he sought earnestly to memorize this remarkable bird's characteristics, so as to be able to match its variegated plumage against the appropriate illustration in the *Guide*.

Plenty of time for that though.

He leaned back once more and rejoiced in the radiant warmth of Schwarzkopf's voice, following the

English text that lay open on his lap: 'You holy Art, when all my hope is shaken . . .'

When, too, a few moments later, his mood of pleasurable melancholy was shaken by three confident bursts on a front-door bell that to several of his neighbours sounded considerably over-decibelled, even for the hard-of-hearing.

Chapter Two

When Napoleon's eagle eye flashed down the list of officers proposed for promotion, he was wont to scribble in the margin against any particular name: 'Is he *lucky*, though?'

(Felix Kirkmarkham, *The Genius of Napoleon*)

'Not disturbing you?'

Morse made no direct reply, but his resigned look would have been sufficiently eloquent for most people.

Most people.

He opened the door widely – perforce needed so to do – in order to accommodate his unexpected visitor within the comparatively narrow entrance.

'I *am* disturbing you.'

'No, no! It's just that . . .'

'Look, matey!' (Chief Superintendent Strange cocked an ear towards the lounge.) 'I don't give a dam if I'm disturbing *you*; pity about disturbing old Schubert, though.'

For the dozenth time in their acquaintance, Morse found himself quietly re-appraising the man who first beached and then readjusted his vast bulk in an armchair, with a series of expiratory grunts.

Morse had long known better than to ask Strange whether he wanted a drink, alcoholic or non-alcoholic.

If Strange wanted a drink, of either variety, he would ask for it, immediately and unambiguously. But Morse did allow himself one question:

'You know you just said you didn't give a dam. Do you know how you spell "dam"?'

'You spell it "d – a – m". Tiny Indian coin – that's what a dam is. Surely you knew that?'

For the thirteenth time in their acquaintance . . .

'Is that a single malt you're drinking there, Morse?'

It was only after Morse had filled, then refilled, his visitor's glass that Strange came to the point of his evening call.

'The papers – even the tabloids – have been doing me proud. You read *The Times* yesterday?'

'I never read *The Times*.'

'What? The bloody paper's there – there! – on the coffee table.'

'Just for the Crossword – and the Letters page.'

'You don't read the obituaries?'

'Well, perhaps just a glance sometimes.'

'To see if you're there?'

'To see if some of them are younger than me.'

'I don't follow you.'

'If they *are* younger, so a statistician once told me, I've got a slightly better chance of living on beyond the norm.'

'Mm.' Strange nodded vaguely. 'You frightened of death?'

'A bit.'

Strange suddenly picked up his second half-full

tumbler of Scotch and tossed it back at a draught like a visitor downing an initiatory vodka at the Russian Embassy.

'What about the telly, Morse? Did you watch *Newsroom South-East* last night?'

'I've got a TV – video as well. But I don't seem to get round to watching anything and I can't work the video very well.'

'Really? And how do you expect to understand what's going on in the great big world out there? You're supposed to *know* what's going on. You're a police officer, Morse!'

'I listen to the wireless—'

'*Wireless?* Where've you got to in life, matey? "Radio" – that's what they've been calling it these last thirty years.'

It was Morse's turn to nod vaguely as Strange continued:

'Good job I got *this* done for you, then.'

Sorry, sir. Perhaps I am a bit behind the times – as well as *The Times.*

But Morse gave no voice to these latter thoughts as he slowly read the photocopied article that Strange had handed to him.

Morse always read slowly.

MURDER POLICE SEEK ANONYMOUS CALLER

A MAN HAS rung the police anonymously with information that could help identify the killer of Mrs Yvonne Harrison who was found handcuffed and battered to death a year ago.

Detectives yesterday appealed for the caller to make contact again. No clear motive has ever been established for the murder of the 48-year-old nurse who was alone in her home in the Oxfordshire village of Lower Swinstead when her killer broke in through a ground-floor window.

Detective Chief Superintendent Strange of Thames Valley CID said that a man had rung twice: "We are very anxious to hear from this caller again as soon as possible. He can contact us in the strictest confidence. We don't believe the calls are a hoax and we don't believe the caller himself is the killer. But we think that he can give us more information to substantially further our enquiries into this brutal murder."

At the time of the murder Mrs Harrison's husband Frank was in London where he works for the Swiss Helvetia Bank. Their son Simon works at the Daedalus Press in Oxford; their daughter Sarah is a junior consultant in the Diabetes Centre at the Radcliffe Infirmary in Oxford.

Had Morse's eyes narrowed slightly as he read the last few lines? If they had, he made no reference to whatever might have puzzled or interested him there.

'I trust it wasn't you who split the infinitive, sir?'

'You never suspected that, surely? We're all used to sloppy reporting, aren't we?'

Morse nodded as he handed back the photocopied article.

'No! Keep it, Morse – I've got the original.'

'Very kind of you, sir, but . . .'

'But it interested you, perhaps?'

'Only the bit at the end, about the Radcliffe.'

'Why's that?'

'Well, as you know, I was in there myself – after I was diagnosed.'

'Christ! You make it sound as if you're the only one who's ever been bloody diagnosed!'

Morse held his peace, for his memory needed no jogging: Strange himself had been a patient in the self-same Radcliffe Infirmary a year or so before his own hospitalization. No one had known much about Strange's troubles. There had been hushed rumours about 'endocrinological dysfunction'; but not everyone at Police HQ was happy about spelling or pronouncing or identifying such a polysyllabic ailment.

'You know why I brought that cutting, Morse?'

'No! And to be honest with you, I don't much care. I'm on furlough, you know that. The quack tells me I'm run down – blood sugar far too high – blood pressure far too high. Says I need to have a quiet little rest-cure and try to forget the great big world out there, as you call it.'

'Some of us can't forget it though, can we?' Strange spoke the words very softly, and Morse got to his feet and turned off the CD player.

'Not one of your greatest triumphs that case, was it?'

'One of the few – very few, Morse – I got no-bloody-where with. And it wasn't exactly mine, either, as you know. But it was my responsibility, that's all. Still is.'

'What's all this got to do with me?'

Strange further expanded his Gargantuan girth as he further expounded:

'I thought, you know, with the wife . . . and all that . . . I thought it'd help to stay in the Force another year. But . . .'

Morse nodded sympathetically. Strange's wife had died very suddenly a year previously, victim of a coronary thrombosis which should surely never have afflicted one so slim, so cautious, so physically fit. She'd been an unlovely woman, Mrs Strange – outwardly timid and inwardly bullying; yet a woman to whom by all accounts Strange had been deeply attached. Friends had spoken of a 'tight' marriage; and most agreed that the widower would have been wholly lost on his own, at least for some while, had he jacked things in (as he'd intended) the previous September. And in the end he'd been persuaded to reconsider his position – and to continue for a further year. But he'd been uneasy back at HQ: a sort of supernumerary Super, feeling like a retired schoolmaster returning to a Common Room. A mistake. Morse knew it. Strange knew it.

'I still don't see what it's got to do with me, sir.'

'I want the case re-opened – not that it's ever been closed, of course. It worries me, you see. We should have got further than we did.'

'I still—'

'I'd like you to look at the case again. If anyone can crack it, *you* can. Know why? Because you're just plain bloody lucky, Morse, that's why! *And I want this case solved.*'

Chapter Three

Which of you shall have a friend and shall go unto him at midnight and say unto him, Friend, lend me three loaves. And he from within shall answer and say, Trouble me not: the door is now shut; I cannot rise and give thee. I say unto you, though he will not rise and give him, because he is his friend, yet because of his importunity he will rise and give him as many as he needeth

(*St Luke*, ch. XI, vv. 5–8)

Lucky?

Morse had always believed that luck played a bigger part in life than was acknowledged by many people – certainly by those distinguished personages who saw their personal merit as the only cause of their appropriate eminence. Yet as he looked back over his own life and career Morse had never considered his own lot a particularly lucky one, not at least in what folk referred to as the affairs of the heart. Strange may have had a point though, for without doubt his record with the Thames Valley CID was the envy of most of his colleagues – his success-rate the result, as Morse analysed the matter, of all sorts of factors: a curious combination of hard thinking, hard drinking (the two, for Morse, being synonymous), hard work (usually undertaken by Sergeant Lewis), and, yes, a sprinkling here and there of good fortune. The Romans had poured their libations not only to Jupiter and Venus and their associate deities in the Pantheon; but also to Fortuna, the goddess of good luck.

Lucky, then?

Well, a bit.

It was high time Morse said something:

'Why the Lower Swinstead murder? What's wrong with the Hampton Poyle murder, the Cowley murder . . . ?'

'Nothing to do with me, either of 'em.'

'That's the only reason then? Just to leave a clean slate behind you?'

For a few moments Strange appeared uncomfortable: 'It's partly that, yes, but . . .'

'The Chief Constable wouldn't look at any new investigation – not a serious investigation.'

'Not unless we had some new evidence.'

'Which in our case, as the poet said, we have not got.'

'This fellow that rang – '

'No end of people ring. We both know that, sir.'

' – rang twice. He knows something. I'm sure of it.'

'Did you speak to him yourself?'

'No. He spoke to the girl on the switchboard. Didn't want to be put through to anybody, he said. Just wanted to leave a message.'

'For you?'

'Yes.'

'A "he", you say?'

'Not much doubt about that.'

'Surely from the recordings . . . ?'

'We can't record every crazy sod who rings up and asks what the bloody time is, you know that!'

'Not much to go on.'

'*Twice*, Morse? The first time on the anniversary of the murder? Come off it! We've got a moral duty to re-open the case. Can't you understand that?'

Morse shook his head. 'Two anonymous phone calls? Just isn't worth the candle.'

And suddenly – why was this? – Strange seemed at ease again as he sank back even further in his chair:

'You're right, of course you are. The case wouldn't be worth re-opening – *unless*' (Strange paused for effect, his voice now affable and bland) 'unless our caller – identity cloaked in anonymity, Morse – had presented us with some . . . some new *evidence*. *And*, after my appeal, my nationally reported appeal, we're going to get some more! I'm not just thinking of another telephone call from our friend either, though I'm hopeful about that. I'm thinking of information from members of the public, people who thought the case was forgotten, people whose memories have had a jog, people who were a bit reluctant, a bit afraid, to come forward earlier on.'

'It happens,' conceded Morse.

The armchair creaked as Strange leaned forward once more, smiling semi-benignly, and holding out his empty tumbler: 'Lovely!'

After refilling the glasses, Morse asked the obvious question:

'Tell me this, sir. You had two DIs on the case originally – '

'Three.'

' – several DSs, God knows how many DCs and PCs and WPCs—'

'No such thing now. All the women are PCs – no sex discrimination these days. By the way, you were never guilty of sexual harassment, were you?'

'Seldom. The other way round, if anything.'

Strange grinned as he sipped his Scotch. 'Go on!'

'As I say, you had all those people on the case. They studied it. They lived with it. They—'

'Got nowhere with it.'

'Perhaps it wasn't altogether their fault. We're never going to solve everything. It's taken these mathematicians over three hundred years to solve Fermat's Last Theorem.'

'Mm.' Strange waggled his tumbler in front of him, holding it up towards the light, like a judge at the Beer Festival at Olympia.

'Just like the colour of my urine specimens at the Radcliffe.'

'Tastes better, though.'

'Listen. I'm not a crossword wizard like you. Sometimes I can't even finish the *Mirror* coffee-break thing. But I know one thing for sure. If you get stuck over a clue – '

'As occasionally even the best of us do.'

' – there's only one way to solve it. You go away, you leave it, you forget it, you think of the teenage Brigitte Bardot, and then you go back to it and – Eureka! It's like trying to remember a name: the more you think about it the more the bloody thing sinks below the horizon. But once you forget about it, once you come to it a second time, fresh—'

'I've never come to it a *first* time, apart from those early couple of days – you know that. I was on another case! And not particularly in the pink either, was I? Not all that long out of hospital myself.'

'Morse! I've *got* to re-open this case. You know why.'

'Try someone else!'

'I want you to think about it.'

'Look.' A note of exasperation had crept into Morse's voice. 'I'm on furlough – I'm tired – I'm sleeping badly – I drink too much – I'm beholden to no one – I've no relatives left – I can't see all that much purpose in life – '

'You'll have me in tears in a minute.'

'I'm only trying to say one thing, sir. Count me out!'

'You won't even *think* about it?'

'No.'

'You do realize that I don't *need* to plead with you about this? I don't want to pull rank on you, Morse, but just remember that I *can*. All right?'

'Try someone else, sir, as I say.'

'OK. Forget what I just said. Let's put it this way. It's a favour I'm asking, Morse – a personal favour.'

'What makes you think I'll still be here?'

'What's that supposed to mean?'

But Morse, it appeared, was barely listening as he stared out of the window on to his little patch of greenery where a small bird with a grey crown and darkish-brown bars across its back had settled beneath the diminishing column of peanuts.

'Look!' (He handed the binoculars to Strange.) 'Few nuts – and some of these rare species decide to take up special residence. I shall have to check up on the plumage but . . .'

Strange had already focused the binoculars with, as it seemed to Morse, a practised familiarity.

'Know anything about bird-watching, sir?'

'More than you, I shouldn't wonder.'

'Beautiful little fellow, isn't he?'

'She!'

'Pardon?'

'Immature female of the species.'

'*What* species?'

'*Passer domesticus*, Morse. Can't you recognize a bloody house-sparrow when you see one?'

For the fourteenth time Morse found himself re-appraising the quirkily contradictory character that was Chief Superintendent Strange.

'And you'll at least *think* about things? You can promise me that, surely?'

Morse nodded weakly.

And Strange smiled comfortably. 'I'm glad about that. And you'll be pleased about one thing. You'll have Sergeant Lewis along with you. I . . . did have a word with him, just before I came here, and he's—'

'You mean you've already . . .'

Strange flicked a stubby finger against his empty, expensive, cut-glass tumbler: 'A little celebration, perhaps?'

Chapter Four

He and the sombre, silent Spirit met –
They knew each other both for good and ill;
Such was their power, that neither could forget
His former friend and future foe; but still
There was a high, immortal, proud regret
In either's eye, as if 'twere less their will
Than destiny to make the eternal years
Their date of war, and their 'Champ Clos' the spheres
(Byron, *The Vision of Judgment*, XXXII)

It is possible for persons to be friendly towards each other without being friends. It is also possible for persons to be friends without being friendly towards each other. The relationship between Morse and Strange had always been in the latter category.

'Read through this as well!' Strange's tone was semi-peremptory as he thrust a folded sheet of ruled A4 across at Morse, in the process knocking his glass on to the parquet flooring. Where it broke into many pieces.

'Ah! Sorry about that!'

Morse rose reluctantly to fetch brush and pan from the kitchen.

'Could have been worse, though,' continued Strange. 'Could have been full, eh?'

As Morse carefully swept up the slivers of the cut-glass tumbler – originally one of a set of six (now three) which his mother had left him – he experienced an irrational anger and hatred wholly disproportionate to the small accident which had occurred. But he counted up to twenty; and was gradually feeling better, even as Strange extolled the bargain he'd seen in the Covered Market recently: glasses for only 50p apiece.

'Better not have any more Scotch, I suppose.'

'Not if you're driving, sir.'

'Which I'm bloody *not*. I'm being driven. And if I may say so, it's a bit rich expecting me to take lessons in drink-driving from you! But you're right, we've had enough.'

A further count, though this time only to ten, prolonged Morse's invariably slow reading of the two handwritten paragraphs, and he said nothing as he finally put the sheet aside.

It was Strange who spoke:

'Perhaps, you know, on second thoughts, we might, er . . . anither wee dram?'

'Not for me, sir.'

'That was meant to be the "royal we", Morse.'

Morse decided that a U-turn was merely a rational readjustment of a previously mistaken course, and he obliged accordingly – for both of them, with Strange's measure poured into one of the cheap-looking wine glasses he'd bought a few weeks earlier from the Covered Market, for only 50p apiece.

'Is this' (Morse pointed to the paper) 'what our dutiful duty-sergeant transcribed from the phone calls?'

'Well, not quite, no.' (Strange seemed curiously hesitant.) 'That's what *I* wrote down, as far as I – we – could fix the exact words. Very difficult business when you get things second-hand, garbled—'

Morse interrupted. 'No problem, surely? We *do* record everything that comes into HQ.'

'Not so easy as that. Some of these recordings are poor-quality reception; and when, you know, when somebody's speaking quietly, muffled sort of voice . . .'

Morse smiled thinly as he looked directly across at his superior officer. 'What you're telling me is that the recording equipment packed up, and there's no trace.'

'Anything mechanical packs up occasionally.'

'*Both* occasions?'

'Both occasions.'

'So all you've got to rely on is the duty-sergeant.'

'Right.'

'Atkinson, was that?'

'Er, yes.'

'Isn't he the one who's been taken off active duties?'

'Er, yes.'

'Because he's become half-deaf, I heard.'

'It's not a *joke*, Morse! Terrible affliction, deafness.'

'Would you like me to have a word with him myself?' For some reason Morse's smile was broader now.

'I've already, er . . .'

'Were you at home, sir, when this anonymous caller rang you?'

Strange shifted uncomfortably in the chair, finally nodding slowly.

'I thought you were ex-directory, sir.'

'You thought right.'

'How did he know your number then?'

' 'Ow the 'ell do I know!'

'The only people who'd know would be your close friends, family . . . ?'

'And people at HQ,' added Strange.

'What are you suggesting?'

'Well, for starters . . . have *you* got my telephone number?'

Morse walked out into the entrance hall and returned with a white-plastic telephone index, on which he pressed the letter 'S', then pushed the list of names and numbers there under the half-lenses now perched on Strange's nose.

'Not changed, has it?'

'Got an extra "five" in front of it. But you'd know that, wouldn't you?' The eyes over the top of the lenses looked shrewdly and steadily up at Morse.

'Yes. It's just the same with my number.'

'Do you think I should get a tap on my phone?'

'Wouldn't do any harm, if he rings again.'

'*When* he rings again.'

'Hoaxer! Sure to be.'

'Well-informed hoaxer, then.' Strange pointed to the paper still on the arm of Morse's chair. 'A bit in the know, wouldn't you say? Someone on the inside, perhaps? You couldn't have found one or two things referred to there in any of the press reports. Only the police'd know.'

'And the murderer,' added Morse.

'And the murderer,' repeated Strange.

Morse looked down once more at the notes Strange had made in his appropriately outsized, spidery handwriting:

Call One

That Lower Swinstead woman – nickers up and down like a yo-yo – a lot of paying clients and a few non-paying clients like me. Got nowhere much with the case did you – incompetant lot. For starters you wondered if it was one of the locals, didn't you? Then for the main course you wasted most of your time with the husband. Then you didn't have any sweet because you'd run out of money. Am I right? Idiots, the lot of you. No! Don't interrupt!
(Line suddenly dead.)

Call Two

Now *don't* interrupt this time, see? Don't say a dicky-bird! Like I said, that woman had more pricks than a second-hand dart-board, mine included, but it's not me who had anything to do with it. Want a clue? There's somebody coming out of the clammer in a fortnight – listen! He's one of your locals, isn't he? See what I mean? You cocked it all up before and you're lucky bastards to have another chance.
(Line suddenly dead.)

Morse looked up to find himself the object of Strange's steady gaze.

'It's incompet*ent*, sir, with an "e".'

'Thank you very much!'

'And most people put a "k" on "knickers".'

Strange smiled grimly. 'And Yvonne Harrison put an embargo on knickers, however you spell 'em!'

He struggled to his feet. 'My office Monday morning – first thing!'

'Eight o'clock?'

'Nine-thirty?'

'Nine-thirty.'

'Now get back to your Schubert – though I'm surprised you weren't listening to Wagner. Just the job, *The Ring*, for a long holiday, you know. Especially the Solti recording.'

Morse watched his visitor waddling somewhat unsteadily towards the police car parked confidently in the 'Resident's Only' parking area. (Yes! Morse had mentioned the apostrophe to the Chairman of the Residents' Welfare Committee.)

He closed the front door and for a few moments stood there motionless, acknowledging with a series of almost imperceptible nods the simple truth about the latest encounter between two men who knew each other well, both for good and ill:

Game, Set, Match, to Strange.

Or was it?

For there was something about what he had just learned, something he had not yet even begun to analyse, that was perplexing him slightly.

The following Sunday was a pleasant summer's day; and along with three-quarters of the population of

Hampshire, Morse decided to go down to Bournemouth. It took him over an hour to park the Jaguar; and it was a further half-hour before he reached the seafront where car-loads and bus-loads of formidable families were negotiating rights to a couple of square metres of Lebensraum. But moving away from the ice-cream emporia, Morse found progressively fewer and fewer day-trippers as he walked towards the further reaches of the shore-line. He'd always told himself he enjoyed the changing moods of Homer's deep-sounding sea. And he did so now.

Soon, he found himself standing alongside the slowly lapping water, debating with himself whether the tide was just coming in or just going out, and staring down at the glass-like circular configuration of a jellyfish.

'Is it dead?'

Until she spoke, Morse had been unaware of the auburn-haired young woman who now stood beside him, almost wearing a bikini.

'I don't know. But in the absence of anything better to do, I'm going to stand here till the tide comes in and find out.'

'But the tide's going *out*, surely?'

Morse nodded somewhat wistfully. 'You may be right.'

'Poor jellyfish!'

'Mm!' Morse looked down again at the apparently doomed, transparent creature at his feet: 'How very sad to be a jellyfish!'

He'd sounded a comparatively interesting man, and

the woman would have liked to stay there awhile. But she forced herself to forget the intensely blue eyes which momentarily had held her own; and walked away without a further word, for she felt a sudden, slight suspicion concerning the sanity of the man who stood there staring at the ground.

Chapter Five

In the country of the blind, the one-eyed man is King
(Afghan proverb)

It was on Tuesday the 14th, the day *before* Strange's visit to Morse, that Lewis had presented himself at the Chief Superintendent's office in Thames Valley Police HQ, in punctual obedience to the internal phone call.

'Something for you, Lewis. Remember the Lower Swinstead murder?'

'Well, vaguely, yes. And I've seen the bits in the paper, you know, about the calls. I was never really on the case myself though. We were on another—'

'Well, you're on it now – from next Monday morning, that is – once Morse gets back from Bermuda.'

'He hasn't left Oxford, has he?'

'*Joke*, Lewis.' Strange beamed with bonhomie, settling his chin into his others.

'The Chief Inspector's agreed?'

'Not much option, had he? And you enjoy working with the old sod. I know you do.'

'Not always.'

'Well, he always enjoys working with *you*.'

A strangely gratified Lewis made no reply.

'So?'

'Well, if it's OK with Morse . . .'

'Which it is.'

'I'll give him a ring.'

'No, you won't. He's tired, isn't he? Needs a rest. Give him a bit of time to himself – you know, crosswords, booze . . .'

'Wagner, sir. Don't forget his precious Wagner. He's just bought *another* recording of that *Ring Cycle* stuff, so he told me.'

'Which recording's that?'

'Conductor called "Sholty", I think.'

'Mm . . .' Strange pointed to three bulging green box-files stacked on the side of his desk. 'Little bit of reading there. All right? Chance for you to get a few moves ahead of Morse.'

Lewis got to his feet, picked up the files, and held them awkwardly in front of him, his chin clamping the top one firm.

'I've never been even *one* move in front of him, sir.'

'No? Don't you under-estimate yourself, Lewis! Let others do it for you.'

Lewis managed a good-natured grin. 'Not many people manage to get a move ahead of Morse.'

'Oh, really? Just a minute! Let me hold the door for you . . . And you're not quite right about what you just said, you know. There *are* one or two people who just occasionally manage it.'

'Perhaps you're right, sir. I've just not met one of 'em, that's all.'

'You have though,' said Strange quietly.

Lewis's eyes turned quizzically as he manoeuvred his triple burden through the door.

That same evening, Lewis had just finished his eggs and chips, had trawled the last slice of brown bread across the residual HP sauce, and was swallowing the last mouthful of full-cream cold milk, when he heard the call from above:

'Dad? Da – ad?'

Lewis looked down at the (presumably problematical) first sentence of his son's A-level French Prose Composition: 'Another bottle of this excellent wine, waiter!'

'Easy enough, that, isn't it?'

'What gender's "bottle"?'

'How am I supposed to know? What do you think I bought you that dictionary for?'

'Left it at school, didn't I!'

'So?'

'So you mean you don't know?'

'You're brighter than I thought, son.'

'Can't you guess?'

'Either masculine or feminine, sure to be.'

'That's *great.*'

'Feminine, say? So it's, er, "*Garçon! Une autre bouteille de cette—*"'

'No! You're useless, Dad! If you say "*Une autre bouteille*", you mean a *different* bottle of wine.'

'Oh.'

'You say "*Encore une bouteille de*" whatever it is.'

'Why do you ever ask me to help you?'

'Agh! Forget it! Like I say, you're bloody useless.'

Lewis had never himself read *Little Dorrit*, and unlike Morse would not have known the soothing secret of counting up to however-many. And in truth he felt angry and belittled as he walked silently down the stairs, picked up the box-files from the table in the entrance hall, walked past the living room, where Mrs Lewis sat deeply submerged in a TV soap, and settled himself down at the kitchen table, where he began to acquaint himself with the strangely assorted members of the Harrison family – wife, husband, daughter, son – four of the principal players in the Lower Swinstead case.

He concentrated as well as he could, in spite of those cruel words still echoing in his brain. And after a while he found himself progressively engaged in the earlier, more grievous agonies of other people: of Frank, the husband; of Sarah, the daughter; of Simon, the son; and of Yvonne, the mother, who had been murdered so brutally in the Cotswold village of Lower Swinstead, Oxon.

Chapter Six

The English country gentleman galloping after a fox
– the unspeakable in full pursuit of the uneatable
(Oscar Wilde)

AT FIRST HE'D felt some reluctance about an immediate interview with her. But finally he decided that earlier rather than later was probably best; and in tones considerably less peremptory than those in which Strange had summoned Lewis three days earlier, he called her to his office at 4.30 p.m.

At which time she stood silent and still for a few seconds at the door before knocking softly, feeling like a schoolgirl outside the headmistress's study.

'Come in!'

She entered and sat, as directed, in the chair opposite him, across the desk.

Professor Turner was a fair-complexioned, mild-mannered medic, in his early sixties – the internationally renowned chief-guru of the Radcliffe Infirmary's Diabetes Centre in Oxford.

'You wanted to see me, sir?'

Yes, he wanted to see her; but he also wanted to put her rather more at ease.

'Look, we're probably going to be together at lots of do's these next few months – years, perhaps – so, please, let's forget this "Sir" business, shall we? Please call me "Robert".'

Sarah Harrison, a slimly attractive, brown-eyed brunette in her late twenties, felt her shoulder muscles relax a little.

Not for long.

'I've sat in with you once or twice, haven't I?'

'Three times.'

'And I think you're going to be good, going to be up to it, you know what I mean?'

'Thank you.'

'But you're not quite good enough yet.'

'I'd hoped I was improving.'

'Certainly. But you're still strangely naive, I'm sorry to say. You seem to believe everything your patients tell you!'

'There's not much else to go on, is there?'

'Oh, but there is! There's a certain healthy and necessary scepticism; and then there's experience. You'll soon realize all this. What I'm saying is that you might as well learn it now rather than later.'

'Is there anything particular . . . ?'

'Things, plural. I'm thinking of what they tell you about their blood-sugar records, about their sexual competence, about their diet, about their alcohol-intake. You see, the only thing they can't fool you about is their *weight.*'

'And their blood pressure.'

Turner smiled gently at his pupil. 'I haven't got *quite* as much faith as you in our measurements of blood pressure.'

'But they don't all of them make their answers up.'

'Not *all* of them, no. It's just that we all like to pretend a bit. We all tend to say we're fine, even if we're feeling lousy. Don't we?'

'I suppose so.'

'And *our* main job' (Turner spoke with a quiet authority) 'is to give *information* – and to exert some sort of *influence* – about the way our patients cope with what, as you know, is potentially a very serious illness.'

Sarah said nothing. Just sat there. A little humiliated.

And he continued: 'There are a good many patients here who are professional liars. Some of them I've known for years, and they've known me. We tell each other lies, all right. But it doesn't matter – because we *know* we're telling each other lies . . . Anyway, that's enough about that.' (Turner looked down at her folder.) 'I see you've got Mr David Mackenzie on your list next Monday. I'll sit in with you on him. I think he did once tell me his date of birth correctly, but he makes everything else up as he goes along. You'll enjoy him!'

Again Sarah said nothing. And she was preparing to leave when Turner changed the subject abruptly, and in an unexpected direction.

Or *was* it unexpected?

'I couldn't help seeing the articles in the newspapers . . . and the department was talking about them.'

Sarah nodded.

'Would it mean a lot to you if they found who murdered your mother?'

'What do *you* think?' The tone of her voice bordered almost on the insolent, but Turner interpreted her reply tolerantly, for it was (he knew) hardly the most intelligent question he'd ever formulated.

'Let's just wish them better luck,' he said.

'Better brains, too!'

'Perhaps they'll put Morse on to it this time.'

Sarah's eyes locked steadily on his.

'Morse?'

'You don't know him?'

'No.'

'Heard of him, perhaps?' Turner's eyes grew suddenly shrewd on hers, and she hesitated before answering:

'Didn't my mother mention she'd nursed him somewhere?'

'Would you like to meet him, next time he comes in?'

'Pardon?'

'You didn't know he was diabetic?'

'We've got an awful lot of diabetics here.'

'Not too many like him, thank the Lord! Four hefty injections a day, and he informs me that he's devised a carefully calibrated dosage that exactly counterbalances his considerable daily intake of alcohol. And when I say considerable . . . Quite a dab hand, too, is Morse, at extrapolating his blood-sugar readings – backwards!'

'Isn't he worried about . . . about what he's doing to himself?'

'Why not ask him? I'll put him on your list.'

'Only if you promise to come along to monitor me.'

'With *you* around? Oh, no! Morse wouldn't like that.'

'How old is he?'

'Too old for you.'

'Single.'

'Gracious, yes! Far too independent a spirit for marriage . . . Anyway, have a good weekend! Anything exciting on?'

'Important, perhaps, rather than exciting. We've got a meeting up at Hook Norton tomorrow at the Pear Tree Inn. We're organizing another Countryside March.'

'That's the "rural pursuits" thing, isn't it? Fox-hunting—'

'Among other things.'

'The "toffs and the serfs".'

Sarah shook her head with annoyance. 'That's just the sort of comment we get from the urban chattering-classes!'

'Sorry!' Turner held up his right hand in surrender. 'You're quite right. I know next to nothing about fox-hunting, and I'm sure there must be things to be said in favour of it. But – please! – don't go and tell Morse about them. We just happened to be talking about fox-hunting the last time he was here – it was in the news – and I can't help remembering what he said.'

'Which was?' she asked coldly.

'First, he said he'd never thought much of the argument that the fox enjoys being chased and being pulled to little pieces by the hounds.'

'Does he think the chickens enjoy being pulled to little pieces by the fox?'

'Second, that the sort of people who hunt do considerably more harm to themselves than they do to the animals they hunt. He said they run a big risk of brutalizing themselves . . . dehumanizing themselves.'

The two of them, master and pupil, looked at each other over the desk for an awkward while; and the Professor of Diabetes Studies thought he may have seen a flash of something approaching fury in the dark-brown eyes of his probationary consultant.

It was the latter who spoke first:

'Mind if I say something?'

'Of course not.'

'I'm surprised, that's all. I fully, *almost* fully, accept your criticisms of my professional manner and my strategy with patients. But from what you've just said *you* sometimes seem to talk to your patients about other things than diabetes.'

'Touché.'

'But you're right . . . Robert. I've been getting too chatty, I realize that. And I promise that when I see Mr Morse I'll try very hard, as you suggest, to instil some sort of disciplined regimen into his daily life.'

Turner said nothing in reply. It was a good thing for her to have the last word: she'd feel so much better when she came to think back on the interview. As she would, he knew that. Many times. But he allowed himself a few quietly spoken words after the door had closed behind her:

'Oh Lady in Pink – Oh lovely Lady in Pink! There is very, very little chance of a disciplined regimen in Morse's life.'

Chapter Seven

Whoever could possibly confuse 'Traffic Lights' and 'Driving Licence'? *You* could! Just stand in front of your mirror tonight and mouth those two phrases silently to yourself

(Lynne Dubin, *The Limitations of Lip-reading*)

DISABILITIES, like many sad concomitants of life, are often cloaked in euphemism. Thus it is that the 'blind' and the 'impotent' and the 'deaf' are happily no longer amongst us. Instead, in their respective clinics, we know our fellow out-patients as those affected by impaired vision; as victims of chronic erectile dysfunction; as citizens with a serious hearing-impediment. The individual members of such groups, however, know perfectly well what their troubles are. And in the latter category, they tend to prefer the monosyllabic 'deaf', although they realize that there are varying degrees of deafness; realize that some are very deaf indeed.

Like Simon Harrison.

He had been a six-year-old (it was 1978) attending a village school in Gloucestershire when an inexplicably localized outbreak of meningitis had given cause for most serious concern in the immediate vicinity. And in particular to two families there: to the Palmer family in High Street, whose only daughter had tragically died; and to the Harrison family in Church Lane, whose son had slowly recovered in hospital after three weeks of intensive care, but with irreversible long-term deafness: twenty-five per cent residual hearing in the left ear; and almost nothing in the right.

Thereafter, for Simon, social and academic progress had been seriously curtailed and compromised: like an athlete being timed for the hundred-metres sprint over sand-dunes wearing army boots; like a pupil, with thick wadges of cotton-wool in each ear, seeking to follow instructions vouchsafed by a tutor from behind a thickly panelled door.

Oh God! Being deaf was such a dispiriting business.

But Simon was a fighter, and he'd tried hard to make the best of things. Tried so hard to master the skills of lip-reading; to learn the complementary language of 'signing' with movements of fingers and hands; to present a wholly bogus facial expression of comprehension in the company of others; above all, to come to terms with the fact that silence, for those who are deaf, is not merely an absence of noise, but is a wholly *passive* silence, in which the potential vibrancy of active silence can never again be appreciated. Deafness is not the brief pregnant silence on the radio when the listener awaits the Greenwich time-signal; deafness is a radio-set that is defunct, its batteries dead and non-renewable.

Few people in Simon's life had understood such things; and in his early teens, when the audiographical readings had begun to dip even more alarmingly, fewer and fewer people had been overly sympathetic.

Except his mother, perhaps.

And the reason for such lack of interest in the boy had not been difficult to fathom. He was an unattractive, skinny-limbed lad, with rather protuberant ears, and a whiny, nasal manner of enunciating his words, as though his disability were not so much one of hearing as one of speaking.

Yet it would be an exaggeration to portray the young Harrison as a hapless adolescent, so often mishearing, so often misunderstood. His school fellows were not a gang of unmitigated bullies; nor were his teachers an uncaring crew. No. It was just that no one seemed to like him much; certainly no one seemed to love him. Except his mother, perhaps.

But Simon did have some residual hearing, as we have seen; and the powerful hearing-aids he wore were themselves far more valuable than any sympathy the world could ever offer. And when, after many a struggle, he left school with two A-level certificates (a C in English and a D in History) he very soon had a job.

Still had a job.

In the early 1990s, Oxfordshire's potential facilities for business and industry had attracted many leading national and international companies. During those years, the county could boast the largest concentration of printing and publishing companies outside the metropolis; and it was to one of these, the Daedalus Press in North Oxford, that on leaving school Simon had applied for the post of apprentice proofreader. And had been successful, principally (let it be admitted) because of the employers' legal obligation to appoint a small percentage of semi-disabled applicants. Yet the 'apprentice' appellation was very soon to be deleted from Simon's job description, for he was proving to be surprisingly and encouragingly competent: accurate, careful, neat – a fair combination of qualities required in a proof-reader. And with any luck (so it was thought) experience would gradually bring with it that needful extra dimension of tedious pedanticism.

On the morning of Friday, 17 July, he found on his desk a photocopied extract from some unspecified tabloid which some unspecified colleague had left, and which he read through with keen attention; then read through a second time, with less interest in its content, it appeared, than in its form, since his proof-reading pen applied itself at five points in the article.

NEW CLUE TO OLD MURDER

Information received by Thames Valley Police seems likely to prompt renewed enquireis into the bizzarre murder of Mrs Yvonne Harrison just over a year ago.

Residents of the small hamlet of Lower Swinstead in Oxfordshire are bracing themselves for further statements and a fresh upsurge of media interest in the ghastley murder of their former neighbour

Tom Biffen, landlord of the Maidens Arms, remains philosophical however 'You can't blame people, can you? Exactly the same as Jack the Ripper. Nobody knows who he was. That's why he's so interesting. Same with who done Mrs Harrison in. Nobody knows who he was. Or she was.'

It's difficult to disagree. Would we still be reading about the Ripper if we knew who it was who murdered and mutilated a succession of prostitutes in the East End of London in the 1870s? As it is, his idetnity remains unknown, just like that of Yvonne's murderer.

The villagers themselves are less than forthcoming, and seem dubious about any new breakthrough in the case. 'Let's just wish the police a bit better luck this time round,' says Mrs May Kennedy, who runs the surprisingly well-stocked village shop.

And so say all of us. All of us, that is, except the murderer.

Chief Inspector Morse had not as yet encountered Simon Harrison; but he would have been reasonably impressed by the proof-reader's competence. Only reasonably, of course, since he himself was a man who somewhere, somehow, had acquired the aforementioned dimension of 'tedious pedanticism', and would have made three further amendments. *And*, of course, would have corrected that gross anachronism, since historical accuracy had engaged him from the age of ten, when he had taken it upon himself to memorize the sequence of the American presidents, and the dates of the kings and queens of England.

Chapter Eight

Bankers are just like anybody else,
Except richer
(Ogden Nash,
I'm a Stranger Here Myself)

The London offices of the Swiss Helvetia Bank are tucked away discreetly just behind Sloane Square. The brass plaque pin-pointing visitors to these premises, albeit highly polished, is perhaps disproportionately small. Yet in truth the Bank has little need to impress its potential clients. On the contrary. Such clients have every need to impress the Bank.

Just after 4 p.m. on Friday, 17 July, a smartly suited man in his late forties waved farewell to the uniformed guard at the security desk and walked out into the sunshine of a glorious summer's day. Traffic was already heavy; but that was of no concern to Frank Harrison, one of six Portfolio and Investment Managers of SHB (London). His company flat was only a few minutes' walk away in Pavilion Road.

Earlier in the day he'd been very much what they paid him so handsomely for being – shrewd, superior, trustworthy – when his secretary had poured coffee for a small, grey-haired man and for his larger, much younger, cosmetically exquisite wife.

'You realize that SHB deals principally with portfolio

investments of, well, let's say, over a million dollars? Is that, er . . .?'

The self-made citizen from South Carolina nodded. 'I think you can feel assured, sir, that we shall be able to meet that figure – ah! – *fairly* easily, shan't we, honey?'

He'd taken his wife's heavily diamonded left hand in his own and smiled, smiled rather sweetly, as Harrison thought.

And he himself had smiled, too – rather sweetly, as he hoped – as mentally he calculated the likely commission from his latest client.

Almost managed a smile again now, as he stopped outside Sloane Square Underground Station and bought a copy of the *Evening Standard*, flicking through the sheets, almost immediately finding the only item that appeared to interest him, then swiftly scanning the brief article before depositing the paper in the nearest litter bin. Had he been at all interested in horse-racing, he might have noticed that Carolina Cutie was running in the 4.30 at Kempton Park. But it had been many years since he had placed a bet with any bookie – instead now spending many hours of each working day studying on his office's computer-screens the odds displayed from the London, New York, and Tokyo stock exchanges.

Considerably safer.

And recently he'd been rather lucky in the management of his clients' investments.

And the bonuses were good.

He let himself into his flat, tapped in the numbers

on the burglar alarm, and walked into the kitchen, where he poured himself a large gin with a good deal of ice and very little tonic. But he'd never had any drinking problem himself. Unlike his wife. His murdered wife.

Lauren had promised to be along about 6 p.m., and she'd never been late. He would call a taxi . . . well, perhaps they'd spend an hour or so between the sheets first, although (if truth were told) he was not quite so keenly aware of her sexual magnetism as he had been a few months earlier. Passion was coming off the boil. It usually happened. On both sides, too. It had happened with Yvonne, with whom he'd scaled the heights of sexual ecstasy, especially in the first few months of their marriage. Yet even during those kingfisher days he had been intermittently unfaithful to her; had woken with heart-aching guilt in the small hours of so many worryful nights – until, that is, he had discovered what he *had* discovered about her; and until he had fallen in love with a woman who was living so invitingly close to him in Lower Swinstead.

The front-door bell rang at 5.50 p.m. Ten minutes early. Good sign! He felt sexually ready for her now; tossed back the last mouthful of his second gin; and went to greet her.

'You're in the paper again!' she blurted, almost accusingly, brandishing the relevant page of the *Evening Standard* in front of his face after the door was closed behind them.

'Really?'

For the second time Harrison looked down at the

headline, NEW CLUE TO OLD MURDER; and pretended to read the article through.

'Well?' she asked.

'Well, what?'

'What have you got to tell me?'

'I'm going to take you out for a meal and then I'm going to take you upstairs to bed – or maybe the other way round.'

'I didn't mean that. You know I didn't.'

'What are you talking about?'

'I want you to tell me what *happened*. You've never spoken about it, have you? Not to me. And I want to know!' Her upper lip was suddenly tremulous. 'So before we do anything else, you'd better—'

'Better what?' He snapped the words and his voice seemed that of a different man. 'Listen, my sweetheart! The day you tell me what to do, that's the day we finish, OK? And if you don't get that message loud and clear' (paradoxically the voice had dropped to a whisper) 'you'd better bugger off and forget we ever met.'

There were no tears in her eyes as she replied: 'I can't do that, Frank. But there's one thing I *can* do: I'm going, as you so delicately put it, to bugger off!'

In full control of herself she turned the catch on the Yale lock, and the door closed quietly behind her.

Chapter Nine

He looked at me with eyes I thought
I was not like to find
(A. E. Housman,
More Poems, XLI)

IT HAD BEEN the previous day, Thursday, when after collecting her boss's mail Barbara Dean had walked along the corridor, white blouse as ever perfectly pressed, flicking through the eleven envelopes held in her left hand. And looking with particular attention (again!) at the one addressed with a scarlet felt-pen, in outsize capital letters, to:

STRANGE (SUPER!)
POLICE
KIDLINGTON
OXFORD

The execution of this lettering gave her the impression of its being neither the work of a particularly educated nor of a particularly uneducated correspondent. Yet the lower-case legend along the top-left of the envelope – 'Private and Confidencial' (*sic*) – would perhaps suggest the latter. Whatever the case though, the envelope was always going to be *noticed* – by whomsoever. It was like someone entering a lucky-dip postal competition with multicoloured sketches adorning the periphery of the envelope; or like a lover mailing off a vastly outsize Valentine.

What would her boss make of it?

Barbara had been working at Police HQ for almost six years now, and had enjoyed her time there – especially these past three years working as the personal secretary of Chief Superintendent Strange; and she was very sad that he would be leaving at the end of the summer. 'Strange by name and strange by nature' – that's what she often said when friends had asked about him: an oddly contradictory man, that was for sure. He was a heavyweight, in every sense of the word; yet there were times when he handled things with a lightness of touch which was as pleasing as it was unexpected. His was the reputation of a blunt, no-nonsense copper who had not been born with quite the IQ of an Aristotle or an Isaac Newton; yet (in Barbara's experience) he could on occasion exhibit a remarkably compassionate insight into personal problems, including her own. All right (yes!) he was a big, blundering, awkward teddy-bear of a man: a bit (a lot?) hen-pecked at home – until recently of course; a man much respected, if not particularly liked, by his fellow officers; and (from Barbara's point of view) a man who had never, hardly ever, sought to take the slightest advantage of her . . . well, of her womanhood. Just that once, perhaps?

It had been at the height of the summer heat-wave of 1995. One day when she had been wearing the skimpiest outfit the Force could ever officially tolerate, she had seen in Strange's eyes what she thought (and almost hoped?) were the signs of some mild, erotic fantasy.

'You look very desirable, my girl!'

That's all he'd said.

Was that what people meant by 'sexual harassment'?

Not that she'd mentioned it to anyone; but the phrase was much in the headlines that long, hot summer, and she'd heard some of the girls talking in the canteen about it.

'*I* could do with a bi' o' that sexual harássment!' confessed Sharon, the latest and youngest tyro in the typing pool.

That was the occasion when one of the senior CID officers seated at the far end of the table had got to his feet, drained his coffee, and come across to lay a gentle hand on Sharon's sun-tanned shoulder.

'You mean sexual hárassment, I think. As you know, we usually exercise the recessive accent in English; and much as I admire our American friends, we shouldn't let them prostitute our pronunciation, young lady!'

He had spoken quietly but a little cruelly; and the uncomprehending Sharon was visibly hurt.

'Pompous prick! Who the hell does he think he is?' she'd asked when he was gone.

So Barbara told her.

Not that she knew him personally, although his blue eyes invariably smiled into hers, a little wearily sometimes but ever interestedly, whenever the two of them passed each other in the corridors; and when she sometimes fancied that he looked at her as though he knew what she was thinking.

God forbid!

It was not of Morse, though, but of Strange that she was thinking that morning when she tapped the customary twice on his office door and entered. Sometimes, when he sat there behind his desk – tie slightly askew, a light shower of dandruff over the shoulders of his jacket, hairs growing a little too prominently from his ears and from his nostrils, white shirt rather less than white and less than smoothly ironed – it was then, yes, that she wished to mother him. She – Barbara! – less than half his age.

That he'd never had such a complicated effect on other women, she felt completely convinced.

Well, no; not *completely* convinced . . .

CHAPTER TEN

He was a self-made man who owed his lack of success to nobody

(Joseph Heller, *Catch-22*)

'PROBABLY SOME NUTTER!' growled Strange as he slipped a paper-knife inside the top of the envelope, and unfolded the single, thin sheet of paper contained therein. And for a while frowned mightily; then smiled.

'Have a look at that, Babs!' he said proudly, making as if to hand the sheet across the desk. 'May well be what we've been waiting for – from my appeal, you know.'

'Won't there be some fingerprints on it?' she asked tentatively.

'Ah!'

'You can *get* fingerprints from paper?'

'Get almost anything from anything these days,' mumbled Strange. 'And what with DNA, forensics, psychological profiling – soon be no need for us detectives any more!'

But in truth he appeared a little abashed as he held the top of the sheet between his thumb and forefinger and leaned forward over the desk; and Barbara Dean leaned forward herself, and read the undated letter, typed on a patently antiquated machine through a red/black ribbon long past its operative sell-by date, with each keyed character unpredictably produced in either colour.

```
   You got it right when you said the
calls wsan't from the person that done it
because that wsa me, see! I made them
calls. But you got it wrong when you
didn't look a bit longer in the village,
Mister Strange. So you want some help so
there's a fellow due out of Bullingdon
Friday next week 24th OK. WATCH HIM
CAREFULLY!
   The Ringer.
   PS You can buy me a pint of Bass in the
Maidens if you recognize me.
```

'Bit illiterate?' suggested Strange.

'I wonder if he really is,' said Barbara, replacing her spectacles in their case.

'You should wear 'em more often. You've got just the face for specs, you know. Hasn't anyone ever told you that?'

No one ever had, and Barbara hoped she wasn't blushing.

'Thank you.'

'Well?'

'I'm not in the Crime Squad, sir.'

'But you don't think he'd last long in the typing-pool?'

'You fairly sure it's a "he"?'

'Sounds like it to me.'

Barbara nodded.

'Not much of a typist, like I say.'

'Spelling's OK – "recognize", and so on.'

'Can't spell "was".'

'That's not really spelling though, is it? You sometimes get typists who are sort of dyslexic with some words. They try to type "was", say, and they hit the "s" before the "a". Do things like that regularly but they don't seem to notice.'

'Ah!'

'Grammar's not so hot, I agree. Probably good enough to pass GCSE, I suppose, sir.'

'Does anyone ever *fail* GCSE?'

'Could do with a bit more punctuation too, couldn't it?'

'Dunno. Not as much as Morse'd put in.'

'Who do you think "The Ringer" is?'

'Ringer? One who rings, isn't it? Chap who's been ringing us up, like as not.'

'Does the postmark help?'

'Oxford. Not that that means anything. It could have been posted anywhere in our patch of the Cotswolds . . . Carterton! Yes. That's where they take the collections and do the sorting before bringing everything to Oxford.'

'Scores of villages though, sir.'

'Go and fetch Sergeant Dixon!'

'Know where he is?'

'Give you three guesses.'

'In the canteen?'

'In the canteen.'

'Eating a doughnut?'

'Doughnuts, plural.'

It was like some of the responses she'd learned so well from the Litany.

'I'll go and find him.'

'And send him straight to me.'

'The Lord be with you.'

'And with thy spirit.'

'You *do* go to church, sir!'

'Only for funerals.'

Sergeant Dixon was not so corpulent as Chief Superintendent Strange. But there was not all that much in it; and the pair of them would have made uncomfortable co-passengers in economy-class seating on an airline. Plenty of room, though, as Dixon drove out alone to Carterton in a marked police car. He'd arranged a meeting with the manager of the sorting office there. A manageress, as it happened, who quickly and competently answered his questions about the system operating in West Oxfordshire.

Yes, since the Burford office had been closed, Carterton had assumed postal responsibility for a pretty wide area. Dixon was handed a printed list of the Oxon districts now covered; was informed how many postmen were involved; where the collection points were, and how frequently the boxes were emptied; how and when the accumulated bags of mail were brought back to Carterton, and how they were there duly sorted and categorized – but not franked – before being sent on to Oxford.

'Any way a particular letter can be traced to a particular post-box?'

'No, none.'

'Traced to a particular village?'

'No.'

Dixon was not an officer of any great intellectual capacity; indeed Morse had once cruelly described him as 'the lowest-watt bulb in the Thames Valley Force'. He had only five years to go before retirement, and he knew that his recent elevation to the rank of sergeant was as high as he could ever hope to climb. Not too bad, though, for a man who had been given little encouragement either from home or from school: if he'd made something of himself he'd made something of himself *himself*, as he'd once put things. Not the most elegant of sentences. But 'elegance' had never been a word associated with Sergeant Dixon.

And yet, as he looked down at his outsize black boots, buffed and bulled, he was thinking as hard as he'd thought for many a moon. He was fully aware of the importance of his present enquiries, and he felt gratified to have been given the job. How good it would be if he could impress his superiors – something (he knew) he'd seldom done in his heretofore somewhat nondescript career.

So he took his time as he sat in that small postal office; took his time as he wrote down a few words in his black notebook; then another few words; then asked another question; then another . . .

When finally he drove back to Oxford, Sergeant Dixon was feeling rather pleased with himself.

That letter-cum-envelope was still exercising Strange's mind to its limits; but there seemed no cause for excitement. In late morning he had driven down to the Fingerprint Department at St Aldate's in Oxford – only to learn that there was little prospect of further enlightenment. The faint, over-smeared prints offered no hope: the envelope itself must have been handled by the original correspondent, by the collecting postman, by the sorter, by the delivering postman, by a member of the HQ post department, by Strange's secretary, by Strange himself – and probably by a few extra intermediary persons to boot. How many fingers there, pray?

Forget it?

Forget it!

Handwriting? Only those red-felt capitals on the cover. Was it worth getting in some under-employed graphologist to estimate the correspondent's potential criminality? To seek possible signs of his (?) childhood neglect, parental abuse, sexual perversion, drugs . . . ?

Forget it?

Forget it!

The typewriter? God! How many typewriters were there to be found in Oxfordshire? In any case, Strange held the view that in the early years of the new millennium the streets of the UK's major cities would be lined with past-sell-by-date typewriters and VDUs and computers and the rest. And how was he to find an obviously *ancient* typewriter for God's sake, one with a tired and overworked ribbon of red and black? He might as well try to trace the animal-inventory from the Ark.

Forget it?

Forget it!

What Strange needed now was new ideas.

What Strange needed now was Morse to be around.

Chapter Eleven

Take notice, lords, he has a loyal breast,
For you have seen him open 't. Read o'er this;
And after, this: and then to breakfast with
What appetite you have

(Shakespeare, *Henry VIII*)

Detective Sergeant Lewis of the Thames Valley CID kept himself pretty fit – very fit, really – in spite of a diet clogged daily with cholesterol. Quite simply, he had long held the view that some things went with other things. He had often heard, for example, that caviare was best washed down with iced champagne, although in truth his personal experience had occurred somewhat lower down the culinary ladder – with fried eggs necessarily complemented with chips and HP sauce; and (at breakfast time) with bacon, buttered mushrooms, well-grilled tomatoes, and soft fried bread. And, indeed, such was the breakfast that Mrs Lewis had prepared at 7.15 a.m. on Monday, 20 July 1998.

It will be of no surprise therefore for the reader to learn that Sergeant Lewis felt pleasingly replete when, just before 8 a.m., he drove from Headington down the Ring Road to the Cutteslowe roundabout, where he turned north up to Police HQ at Kidlington. No problems. All the traffic was going the other way, down to Oxford City.

He was looking forward to the day.

He'd known that working with Morse was never going to be easy, but he couldn't disguise the fact that his own service in the CID had been enriched immeasurably because of his close association, over so many years now, with his curmudgeonly, miserly, oddly vulnerable chief.

And now? There was the prospect of another case: a big, fat, juicy puzzle – like the first page of an Agatha Christie novel.

Most conscientiously therefore (after Strange had spoken to him) Lewis had read through as much of the archive material as he could profitably assimilate; and as he drove along that bright summer's morning he had a reasonably clear picture of the facts of the case, and of the hitherto ineffectual glosses put upon those facts by the CID's former investigating officers.

From the very start (as Lewis learned) several theories, including of course burglary, had been entertained, although none of such theories had made anywhere near complete sense. There had been no observable signs of any struggle, for example. And although Yvonne Harrison was found naked, handcuffed, and gagged, she had apparently not been raped or tortured. In addition, it appeared most unlikely that she had been forcibly stripped of the clothes she'd been wearing, since the skimpy lace bra, the equally skimpy lace knickers, the black blouse, and the minimal white skirt, were found neatly folded beside her bed.

Had she been lying there completely unclothed when some intruder had disturbed her? Surely it was an unusually early hour for her to be a-bed; and if she *had* been abed then, and if she had heard the front-door bell, or heard something, it seemed quite improbable that she would have confronted any burglar or (unknown?) caller without first putting something on to cover a body fully acknowledged to be beautiful. Such considerations had led the police to speculate on the likelihood of the murderer being well known to Mrs Harrison; and indeed to speculate on the possibility of the murderer living in the immediate and very circumscribed vicinity, and of being rather *too* well known to Mrs Harrison. Her husband was away from home a good deal, and few of the (strangely uncooperative?) villagers would have been too surprised, it seemed, if his wife conveniently forgot her marriage vows occasionally. In fact it had not been difficult to guess that most of the villagers, though loth to be signatories to any specific allegations, were fairly strongly in favour of some sort of 'lover-theory'. Yet although the Harrisons often appeared more than merely geographically distanced, no evidence was found of likely divorce proceedings.

Once Mr Frank Harrison, with a very solid (if very unusual) alibi, had been eliminated from the enquiries, painstakingly strenuous investigations had produced (as one of the final reports admitted) no sustainable line of positive enquiry . . .

As he pulled off right, into Thames Valley Police HQ, Lewis was smiling quietly to himself. Morse would very soon have established some 'sustainable line of positive enquiry'. Even if it was a wrong line.

So what?
Morse was very often wrong – at the start.
So what?
Morse was almost always right – at the finish.

CHAPTER TWELVE

Yet ev'n these bones from insult to protect
Some frail memorial still erected nigh,
With uncouth rhimes and shapeless sculpture deck'd,
Implores the passing tribute of a sigh
(Thomas Gray, *Elegy Written in a Country Churchyard*)

THE FOLLOWING IS an extract from *The Times*, Monday 20 July 1998:

A VILLAGE MURDER

TWO PSYCHICS AND a hypnotist have already been involved in the case. It has caught the attention of the *Still a Mystery* series on ITV, although it has yet to be promoted to the Premier Division of such classical unsolved cases as the disappearance of Lord Lucan, the fate of the racehorse Shergar, or the quest for the Holy Grail itself.

Although the murder of Yvonne Harrison has long been out of the immediate headlines, we are led to believe that the box-files concerning the case, stacked on the shelves at Thames Valley Police HQ, are definitely not accumulating layer upon layer of undisturbed dust. After all it is only just over a year since the body of Mrs Harrison was discovered in the bedroom of her Grade-II-listed Georgian house, set in four acres of wooded ground in the Cotswold village of Lower Swinstead. The home, 'The Windhovers', was sold for £350,000 fairly soon after the murder, and the family have long since left the quiet leafy village – all except Yvonne, of course, who is buried in the small, neatly mown churchyard of St Mary's, where, in the form of a Christian cross, a low, wooden stake is the only memorial to the body reposing beneath it:

Perhaps, when the ground is sufficiently settled, the murdered woman will have some worthier monument. But for the present the grave shows little if any sign of tender loving care, and flowers no longer adorn this semi-neglected spot.

Yvonne Harrison, a fully qualified nurse, had resumed work in Oxford after her two children had left home, and on the evening of her murder had returned to an empty house, her husband Frank, as normally during the week, spending his time in his London apartment. 'The Windhovers' had been broken into a few years earlier, when TV sets, video-equipment, radios, a computer, and sundry electrical items had been stolen. As a result, the Harrisons had installed a fairly sophisticated burglar alarm, with 'panic-buttons' in the main bedroom and beside the main entrance door; had enlisted in the local Neighbourhood Watch group; and had acquired a Rottweiler puppy, christened Rodney, who had subsequently displayed a healthier taste for Walkers Crisps than for any unwelcome visitors, and who had sadly been run over a few months previously.

With the smashed rear window, the burglary theory was at first the favourite, although there was no apparent theft of several readily displayed items of silverware and non-too-subtly concealed pieces of jewellery. What was far more obvious to those who entered the house later that night was a body – the body of Yvonne Harrison, lying on the bed in the main bedroom: naked, handcuffed, and gagged. And dead.

What immediately caught public interest was the fact that the man who discovered the body was none other than the murdered woman's husband.

A somewhat delayed post-mortem established that Yvonne Harrison had probably been murdered by some sort of 'tubular metal rod' two or three hours before her body was discovered at 11.20 p.m., and fairly certainly not after 9.30 p.m. Independent evidence corroborated the pathologist's findings. A local builder, Mr John Barron, had rung Mrs Harrison at 9 p.m. – on the dot, as instructed. But he had heard only the 'engaged' signal. At about 9.30 p.m. he had rung again; but although he had persisted there had been no reply. The phone was quite certainly ringing at the other end. Either the Ansaphone had not been activated . . . or else the lady of the house was not alive to take the call.

Another call however had been made more successfully that evening. An extraordinarily puzzling call. At just after 9 p.m. Yvonne's husband picked up his phone in Pavilion Road, London, to hear a man's voice informing him that his wife was in trouble and that he ought to get out there immediately. Normally he would have driven home post-haste in his BMW. But with the car in for repairs, he took a taxi to Paddington where he caught the 9.48 train to Oxford, arriving at 10.50, where he took another taxi for the ten-mile journey out to Lower Swinstead.

Late-night traffic was thin, and when Mr Patrick Flynn braked his Radio Taxi outside 'The Windhovers' at 11.20 p.m. he saw a village mansion ablaze with lights turned on in almost every room, and the burglar-alarm box emitting sharp blue flashes and a continuous ringing. The front door stood open . . . and the rest is history.

Or it **was** history until a fortnight ago, when two anonymous phone calls were received at Thames Valley Police HQ, where it is the view of Chief Superintendent Strange that promising new lines of enquiry may soon be opened.

It is surely universally to be hoped that the identity of Yvonne Harrison's murderer will finally be revealed; and that on some more permanent memorial in St Mary's churchyard the name of the murdered woman will be spelt correctly.

Chapter Thirteen

Ponderanda sunt testimonia, non numeranda
(All testimonies aggregate
Not by their number, but their weight)
(Latin proverb)

Most of the Thames Valley Police personnel were ever wont to pounce quickly upon any newspaper clipping concerning their competence, or alleged lack of competence. And that morning Lewis had been almost immediately apprised of the article in *The Times* – which he'd read and assimilated swiftly; far more swiftly (he suspected) than Morse would read it when he took it along at 8.30 a.m. The Chief was a notoriously slow reader, except of crossword clues.

Lewis remembered the case well enough; certainly remembered the frustration and disappointment that many of his CID colleagues had felt when lead after lead had appeared to peter out. Yes, he'd often experienced frustration himself, but seldom any prolonged disappointment; for which he was grateful – profoundly grateful – to Morse.

Most usually (Lewis knew it well) a murder investigation revolved around corroborated suspicion. A clue was pursued; a suspect targeted; an alibi checked; a motive weighed in the balances; a response to questioning interpreted as surly, cocky, devious, frightened

. . . It was all cumulative – that was the word! – a series of pieces in the jigsaw that seemed to form a coherent pattern sufficiently convincing for a formal charge to be brought; for a dossier to be sent to the DPP; for a period of remand, further questioning, sometimes further evidence, with nothing cropping up in the interim to vitiate the central police hypothesis: that in all probability the arrested suspect was guilty as hell.

That was the usual pattern.

Not with Morse though.

For some reason Morse often shunned the standard heap-of-evidence approach. In fact Lewis had seldom if ever observed him, through distaste or idleness perhaps, riffle through any heap of dutifully transcribed statements, claiming (as Morse did) that since he could seldom remember what he'd been doing himself the previous evening, he found it difficult to give much credence to people who claimed to recall anything from a week last Wednesday – unless, of course, it was watching *Coronation Street* or listening to *The Archers*, or some similar regularly timetabled ritual.

No, Morse seldom worked that way.

The opposite, more often than not.

With most prime suspects, if female, youngish, and even moderately attractive, Morse normally managed to fall in love, sometimes only for a brief term, yet sometimes throughout Michaelmas and Hilary and Trinity. Towards some other prime suspects, if men, Morse occasionally appeared surprisingly sympathetic, especially if he suspected that the quality of their lives had hardly been enhanced by getting hitched to some potential tart who had temporarily managed to camouflage her basic bitchiness . . .

Lewis had a quick look at the *Mirror*, drained his coffee, and looked at his watch: 8.25 a.m. Time he got moving.

As he walked out of the canteen, he (literally) bumped into the stout figure of Sergeant Dixon – 'Dixon-delighting-in-doughnuts' as Homer would have dubbed him.

'You see the thing on the Lower Swinstead thing?' (Variety was not a feature of Dixon's vocabulary.)

Lewis nodded, and Dixon continued:

'I was with him on that for a while. Poor ol' Strange. He thought he knew who done it, but he couldn't prove it, could he? Poor ol' Strange. Like I say, I was with him on that thing.'

Lewis nodded again; then climbed the stairs, wondering how that Monday morning would turn out – knowing how Morse hated holidays; how little he normally enjoyed the company of others; how very much he enjoyed a very regular allotment of alcohol; how he avoided almost all forms of physical exercise. And knowing such things, Lewis realized that in all probability he would fairly soon be driving Morse out to the muzak-free pub at Thrupp where a couple of pints of real ale would leave the Chief marginally mellower and where a couple of orange juices would leave the chauffeur (him!) unexcitedly unintoxicated.

Chapter Fourteen

The man who says to one, go, and he goeth, and to another, come, and he cometh, has, in most cases, more sense of restraint and difficulty than the man who obeys him

(John Ruskin, *The Stones of Venice*)

Lewis knocked deferentially on Morse's door before entering.

'Welcome home, sir! Nice break?'

'No!'

'You don't sound very—'

'Sh!'

So Lewis sat down obediently in the chair opposite, as his chief contemplated the last clue: 'Stiff examination (7)' A – T – P – Y; then immediately wrote in the answer, and consulted his wristwatch.

'Not bad, Lewis. Ten and a half minutes. Still it's usually a bit easier on Mondays.'

'Well done.'

'Have you done it, by the way?'

'Pardon?'

'That *is* a copy of today's *Times* you've got with you?'

'They showed it to me in the canteen—'

'Does Mrs Lewis know that the first place you head for after breakfast is the canteen?'

'Only for a coffee.'

'Not a crime, I suppose.'

'It's this article, sir – about the Harrison case.'

'So?'

'So you're not interested?'

'No!'

'But we're supposed to be re-opening the case, sir – you and me.'

'You and *I*, Lewis. And we are not.'

'But the Super said you'd agreed.'

'*When* am I supposed to have agreed?'

'Last week – Tuesday.'

'Last week – Wednesday! He came to see me on *Wednesday.*'

'You mean . . . he hadn't seen you *before* he saw me?'

'You're bright as a button this morning, Lewis.'

'But you must have agreed, surely?'

'In a way.'

'So what's biting you?'

Morse's blue eyes flashed across the desk. 'I'd had too much Scotch, that's what! I'd been trying to enjoy myself. I was on a week's furlough, remember?'

'But why start the week off in such a foul mood?'

'Why *not*, pray?'

'I don't know. It's just that, you know – another case for us to solve perhaps? Gives you a good feeling, that.'

Morse nodded reluctantly.

'So why agree to it, if you've no stomach for it?'

Morse looked down at the threadbare carpet – a carpet stopping regularly six inches from the skirting boards. 'I'll tell you why. Strange's carpet goes right up to the wall – you've noticed that? So if you ever get up to Super status, which I very much doubt, you just make sure you get a carpet that covers the whole floor – and a personal parking space while you're at it!'

'At least you've got your name on the door.'

'Remember that fellow in Holy Writ, Lewis? "I also am a man set under authority." I'm just like him – *under* authority. Strange doesn't *ask* me to do something: he tells me.'

'You could always have said no.'

'Stop sermonizing me! That case stinks of duplicity and corruption: the family, the locals, the police – shifty and thrifty with the truth, the whole bloody lot of them.'

'You sound as if you know quite a bit about it already.'

'Why shouldn't I? About a local murder like that? I do occasionally pick up a few things from my fellow officers, all right? And if you remember I *was* on the case right at the beginning, if only for a very short while. And why was that? Because we were on *another* case. Were we not?'

Lewis nodded. 'Another murder case.'

'Murder's always been our business.'

'So why—?'

'Because the case is old and tired, that's why.'

'Who'll take it on if we don't?'

'They'll find another pair of idiots.'

'So you're going to tell the Super . . .?'

'I've already *told* you. Give it a rest!'

'Why are you so sharp about it all?'

'Because I'm like the case, Lewis. I'm old and tired myself.'

The ringing of the telephone on Morse's desk cut across the tetchy stichomythia.

'Morse?'

'Sir?'

'You ready?'

'Half-past nine, you said.'

'So what?'

'It's only—'

'So what?'

'Shall I bring Sergeant Lewis along?'

'Please yourself.'

The phone was dead.

'That was Strange.'

'I could hear.'

'I'd like you to come along. All right with you?'

Lewis nodded. 'I'm a man under authority too.'

'*Lew*-is! Quote it accurately: "a man *set* under authority".'

'Sorry!'

But Morse was continuing with the text, as if the well-remembered words brought some momentary respite to his peevishness: '"Having under me soldiers, and I say unto one, Go and he goeth; and to another, Come and he cometh".'

'Lewis cometh,' said Lewis quietly.

Chapter Fifteen

I have received no more than one or two letters in my life that were worth the postage

(Henry Thoreau)

'C'm in! C'm in!'

It was 8.45 a.m.

'Ah! Morse. Lewis.'

Perhaps, in all good faith, Strange had intended to sound brisk rather than brusque; yet, judging from Morse's silence as he sat down, the Chief Superintendent had not effected a particularly good start. He contrived to beam expansively at his two subordinates, and especially at Morse.

'What does "The Ringer" mean to you?'

'Story by Edgar Wallace. I read it in my youth.'

Morse had spoken in clipped, formal tones; and Lewis, with a millimetre rise of the eyebrows, glanced quickly at his impassive face.

Something was wrong.

'What about you, Sergeant? You ever read Edgar Wallace?'

'Me?' Lewis grinned weakly. 'No, sir. I was a *Beano*-boy myself.'

'Anything else, Morse?'

'A campanologist?'

'Could be.'

Morse sat silently on.

'Anything else?'

'It's a horse that's raced under the name of a different horse – a practice, so they tell me, occasionally employed by unscrupulous owners.'

'How does it work?'

Morse shook his head. 'I've seldom donated any money to the bookmakers.'

'Or anyone else for that matter.'

Morse sat silently on.

'Anything else?'

'I can think of nothing else.'

'Well, let me tell *you* something. In Oz, it's what you call the quickest fellow in a sheep-shearing competition. What about that?'

'Useful thing to know, sir.'

'What about a "dead ringer"?'

'Somebody almost identical with somebody else.'

'Good! You're coming on nicely, Morse.'

'No, I'm not. I've stopped.'

Strange shook his massive head and smiled bleakly. 'You're an odd sod. You never seem to see anything that's staring you in the face. You have to look round half a dozen corners first, when all you've really got to do is to look straight up the bloody street in front of you!'

Lewis, as he sat beside his chief, knew that such a criticism was marginally undeserved; and he would have wished to set the record aright. But he didn't, or couldn't. As for Morse, he seemed quietly unconcerned about the situation: in fact (or was Lewis misunderstanding things?) even a little pleased.

'What about this, then?' Suddenly, confidently, Strange thrust the letter across the desk; and after what seemed to both the other men an unnecessarily prolonged perusal, the slow-reading Morse handed it back. Without comment.

'Well?'

'"The Ringer", you mean? You think it's the fellow who decided to ring you—'

'Ring me *twice*!'

'It's a possibility.'

'Where do you think it was posted?'

'Dunno. You'll have to show me the envelope.'

'Guess!'

'You're expecting me to say Lower Swinstead.'

'No. Just waiting for your answer.'

'Lower Swinstead.'

'Explain *that*, then!' Strange produced a white envelope on which, above the lurid red capitals, the pewter-gold first-class stamp was cancelled with a circular franking:

'All right,' conceded Morse. 'I'll try another guess. What about Oxford?'

'Hm! What about the writing on the envelope?'

'Probably an A-level examiner using up one of his red pens. His scripts were sending him bananas and he happened to see your invitation in one of the newspapers. He just wondered why it was only the candidates who were allowed to make things up, so he decided to have a go for himself. He's a nutter, sir. A harmless nutter. We always get them – you know that.'

'Oh, thank you, Morse!'

'No fingerprints, sir?' asked Lewis diffidently.

'Ah, no. No fingerprints. Good question, though!'

'Best forget it, then,' counselled Morse.

'Rea-lly?' Strange allowed the disyllable to linger ominously. 'When I was a lad, Morse, I once wrote off an entry for a Walt Disney competition and I drew a picture of Mickey Mouse on the front of the envelope.'

'Did you win?'

'No, I didn't. But let me just tell you one thing, matey: I'd like to bet you that somebody noticed it! That's the whole point, isn't it?'

'You've lost me, sir.'

Strange leaned back expansively. 'When I asked Sergeant Dixon where *he* thought the letter was posted, he agreed with you: Lower Swinstead. And when I showed him the postmark he said it might *still* have been posted there, because he knew that some of the letters from that part of the Cotswolds were brought to Oxford for franking. So he went out and did a bit of leg-work, and he traced the fellow who did the collections last week; and the postman remembered the envelope! There'd only been three letters that day in the box, and he'd noticed one of 'em in particular. Not surprising, eh? So Dixon decided to test things, just for his own satisfaction. He addressed an envelope to himself and posted it at Lower Swinstead.'

Strange now produced a white unopened envelope and passed it across the desk. It was addressed in red Biro to Sergeant Dixon at Police HQ Kidlington, the pewter-gold first-class stamp cancelled with the same circular franking:

Strange paused for effect. 'Perhaps you ought to start eating doughnuts, Morse.'

'They won't let me have any sugar these days, sir.'

'There's no sugar in beer, you're saying?'

Lewis was expecting some semi-flippant, semi-prepared answer from his chief – something about balancing his intake of alcohol with his intake of insulin. But Morse said nothing; just sat there staring at the intricate design upon the carpet.

'One of these days, perhaps,' persisted Strange quietly, 'you might revise your opinion of Dixon.'

'Why not put him in charge of the case? If you're still determined—'

'Steady on, Morse! That's enough of that. Just remember who you're talking to. And I'll tell you exactly why I'm not putting that idiot Dixon in charge. Because I've already put somebody else in charge – you and Lewis! Remember?'

'Lewis maybe, sir, but I can't do it.'

Feeling most uncomfortable during these exchanges, Lewis watched the colour rise in Strange's cheeks as several times his mouth opened and closed like that of a stranded goldfish.

'You do realize you've got little say in this matter, Chief Inspector? I am *not* pleading with you to undertake an investigation for Thames Valley CID. What I *am* doing, as your superior officer, is telling you that you've been assigned to a particular duty. That's all. And that's enough.'

'No. It's not enough.'

For several minutes the conversation continued in similar vein before Strange delivered his diktat:

'I see . . . Well, in that case . . . you give me no option, do you? I shall have to report this interview to the Chief Constable. And you know what that'll mean.'

Morse rose slowly to his feet, signalling Lewis to do the same. 'I don't think you're going to report this interview to the Chief Constable or to the Assistant Chief Constable or to anyone else, for that matter, are you, Superintendent Strange?'

Chapter Sixteen

The vilest deeds like poison weeds
Bloom well in prison-air,
It is only what is good in Man
That wastes and withers there:
Pale Anguish keeps the heavy gate,
And the warder is Despair
(Oscar Wilde,
The Ballad of Reading Gaol)

Until comparatively recently, Harry Repp had associated the word 'porridge' chiefly with the title of the TV comedy series and not with oatmeal stirred in boiling water. For as long as he could remember, his breakfasts had consisted of Corn Flakes covered successively (as his beer-gut had ballooned) with full, semi-skimmed, and finally the thinly insipid fully skimmed varieties of milk. It was his common-law wife, Debbie, who'd insisted: 'You keep pouring booze into your belly every night and it's low-fat milk for breakfast! Understood?' So there'd been little choice, had there? Until almost a year ago, when he had come to realize that the TV title was wholly appropriate, with porridge (occasionally ill-stirred in luke-warm water) providing the basic breakfast diet for prison inmates.

Normally Repp would have accepted the proffered dollop of porridge; but he asked only for two sausages and a spoonful of baked beans as he and his co-prisoners from A Wing stood queuing at the food counter at 8 a.m. He had read that prisoners in the condemned cell were always given the breakfast of their choice; but he felt he could himself have eaten little in such circumstances – with the twin spectres of death and terror so very close behind him. And even now, back in his cell, he managed only one mouthful of beans before pushing his plate away from him. He felt agitated and apprehensive, although he found it difficult to account for such emotions. After all, he wasn't awaiting the Governor and the flunkey from the Home Office and the Prison Chaplain . . . and the Hangman. Far from it. It was that day, Friday 24 July, that was set for his release from HM Prison, Bullingdon.

At 8.35 a.m., still in his prison clothing, he heard steps outside the cell, heard his name called, and was on his feet immediately, picking up the carrier bag in which he'd already placed his personal belongings: a battered-looking radio, a few letters still in their grubby envelopes, and a 'sexy-western' paperback that had clearly commanded regular re-reading. 'Let's hope we don't meet again, mate!' one of the prison officers had volunteered as the double doors were unlocked and Repp was escorted for the last time from the spur of A Wing.

At 8.50 a.m., after changing into his personal civvies, he was admitted into a bench-lined holding-cell, where another prisoner, a thin sallow-faced man in his forties, was already seated. Their exchange of conversation was brief and unmemorable:

'Not much more o' this shit, mate.'

'No,' said Repp.

At 9.05 a.m. his name was again called, and he was taken along to a reception desk where one of the Principal Officers took him through the forms pertaining to his release: identity check, behaviour and health records, details of destination and accommodation. It seemed to Repp somewhat reminiscent of a check-in at Heathrow or Gatwick. Except that this, as he kept reminding himself, wasn't a check-in at all. It was a check-out.

He signed his name to several documents without bothering too much what they were. But before signing one form he was asked to read some relevant words aloud: 'I understand that I am not allowed to possess or have anything to do with firearms or ammunition of any description . . .' It didn't matter anyway. In all probability there'd be no need to use the gun; and apart from himself only Debbie knew its whereabouts.

Almost finished now.

He took possession of an order issued under the Criminal Justice Act re Supervision in the Community, specifying the Oxford Probation Service in Park End Street as the office to which he was required to report regularly. Then he completed the Discharge Certificate itself, with a series of initials against Travel Warrant (Bullingdon to Oxford), Personal Property (as itemized), Personal Cash (£24.50), Discharge Grant (£45), Discharge Clothing (offered but not issued). And, finally, one further full signature, dated and countersigned by the Principal Officer, underneath the unambiguous assertion: I HAVE NO OUTSTANDING COMPLAINTS. And indeed Harry Repp had nothing much to complain about. At least, not about Bullingdon – except perhaps that any residual good in him had wasted and had withered there.

He was escorted across the prison yard to the main gates, where he reported to the Senior Officer, citing his full name and prison number to be checked against the Discharge List. And that was it. The heavy gates were opened, and Harry Repp stepped out of prison. A free man.

He looked at his wristwatch, repeatedly glancing around him as if he might be expecting someone to meet him. But there seemed to be no one. According to the bus timetable they'd given him, there would be a wait of ten minutes or so; and he walked slowly down the paved path which led from the Central Reception Area to the road. There he turned and looked back at the high concreted walls, lightish beige with perhaps a hint of some pinkish coloration, lamp-posts stationed at regular intervals in front of them, sturdily vertical until, at their tops, they leaned towards the prison, like guardsmen inclining their heads around a catafalque.

Harry Repp turned his back on the prison for the last time, and walked more briskly towards the bus stop and towards freedom.

Chapter Seventeen

What is it that roareth thus?
Can it be a Motor Bus?
All this noise and hideous hum
Indicat Motorem Bum
(A. D. Godley)

SEATED AT THE front window of the Central Reception Area, Sergeant Lewis had been a vigilant observer of the final events recorded in the previous chapter, immediately ducking down when the newly released man had turned to look back at the prison complex. Needlessly so, for the two men were quite unknown to each other.

This was hardly the trickiest assignment he'd ever been given, Lewis knew that; and in truth he could see little justification for the trouble being taken. Except in Superintendent Strange's (not usually fanciful) imagination, there seemed only a tenuous connection between the Harrison murder and Harry Repp – the latter sentenced to fifteen months' imprisonment, and now released early on parole on grounds of exemplary behaviour. And in any case, Strange's instructions (not Morse's) had been vague in the extreme: 'Keep an eye on him, see where he goes, who he meets, and, er, generally, you know . . . well, no need to tell an experienced officer like you.'

And yet (Lewis considered the point afresh) had Strange's motivation been *all* that fanciful? Repp was known to have been active in the vicinity at the relevant period, and had in fact been under limited police surveillance for some time, although not of course on the night of the murder. And then there was the letter to Strange – a letter which, whilst pointing a finger only vaguely at the general locality of Lower Swinstead, had quite specifically pointed towards the man now being released from prison.

As Repp walked away Lewis got to his feet and shook hands with the prison officer who had communicated to him as much as anyone at Bullingdon was ever likely to know about the man just released: aged 37; height 5′ 10″; weight 13 stone 4 pounds; hair dark-brown, balding; complexion medium; tattoo (naval design) covering left forearm; sentenced for the receipt and sale of stolen goods; at the time of arrest cohabiting with Debbie Richardson, of 15 Chaucer Lane, Burford.

After driving the unmarked police car from the crowded staff car park, Lewis stopped on the main road, moving round the car as he slowly checked his tyre pressures, all the while keeping watch on the bus stop, only fifty yards away, where two men, Repp and a slimmer ferrety-looking fellow, stood waiting; from where Lewis could hear so very clearly the frequently vociferated plaints from the ferret: 'Where the fuckin' 'ell's the fuckin' bus got to?'

In fact, the fuckin' bus was well on its way; and a few minutes later the two men boarded a virtually empty bus, and uncommunicatively took their separate seats.

Lewis moved smoothly into gear and followed discreetly, not at all unhappy when another (rather posh) car interposed itself between him and the bus. (Another posh car behind him, for that matter.) Any minor worry that Repp might unexpectedly get off at some stage between Bullingdon and Bicester was taking care of itself very nicely, since the bus made no stop whatsoever until reaching the Bure Place bus station in Bicester, where the ferret straightaway alighted (and straightaway disappeared); and where Repp, the immediate quarry, walked up the line of bus shelters to the 27 OXFORD (Direct) bay, promptly boarding the bus already standing there.

Repp was not the only one who had done his homework on the Bicester–Oxford timetable. For Lewis, knowing there would be a full ten-minute wait before departure, and leaving his car in the capacious car park opposite, walked quickly through the short passageway to Sheep Street, passing the public toilets on his left, where at Forbuoys Newsagent's he bought the *Mirror*. Even if there was a bit of a queue, so what? He would rather enjoy not following but chasing the 27 to Oxford. But the bus was still there, filling up quite quickly, as he got back into his car.

After the implementation of the Beeching Report of the mid-sixties, passengers between Oxford and Bicester had perforce to use their own cars. But the former railway line had now been re-opened; and the deregulated bus companies were trying their best, and sometimes succeeding, in tempting passengers back to public transport. There were no traffic jams on the rail; and a newly designated bus lane from Kidlington gave a comparatively fast-track entry into Oxford. So perhaps (Lewis pondered the matter) it was hardly surprising that Repp had not been picked up at Bullingdon by a friend, or by a relative, or by his common-law wife. Yet it would surely have been so much easier, quicker, more convenient that way?

At 10.10 a.m. the 27 pulled out of the bus station and headed towards Oxford, in due course crossing over the M40 junction and making appropriately good speed along the A34, before turning off through Kidlington and then over the A40 down towards Oxford City Centre.

And again Lewis was fortunate, for no one had got off the bus along the route until the upper reaches of the Banbury Road.

Easy!

Driving at a safe and courteous distance behind the bus, Lewis had ample opportunity for reflecting once more on the slightly disturbing developments of the previous few days . . .

Morse had been as good as his word that Monday morning, when the latter part of their audience with Strange had turned almost inexplicably bitter. No, Morse could not agree to any involvement in the reopening of the Harrison enquiries. Yes, Morse realized ('Fully, sir!') the possible implications of his non-compliance with the decision of a superior officer. Yet oddly enough, it had been Strange who had seemed the more unsure of himself during those final exchanges; and Lewis had found himself puzzled, and suspecting that there were certain aspects of the case of which he himself was wholly unaware.

Could it be . . . ?

Could it be perhaps . . . ?

Could it be perhaps that Morse had some reason for keeping his head above the turbid waters still swirling around the unsolved murder of Yvonne Harrison? Some *personal* reason, say? Some connection with the major participants in the case? Some connection (Lewis was thinking the unthinkable) with *the* major participant: with the murdered woman herself? For there must be *some* reason . . .

Some reason, too, for Morse's (virtually unprecedented) absence from HQ on those two following days, the Tuesday and the Wednesday? To be fair, he had rung Lewis (at home) early on the Tuesday morning, saying that he was feeling unwell, and in truth *sounding* unwell. He'd be grateful, he'd said, if Lewis could apologize to all concerned; perhaps for the following day as well. Lewis had rung Morse that Tuesday evening, but there was no answer; had rung again on the Wednesday evening – again with no answer.

Was Morse ill?

Not all that ill, anyway, because he'd appeared on the Thursday morning at his usual, comparatively early hour. And said nothing about his absence. Or about his row with Strange. Or about his health, for that matter. But Morse seldom mentioned his health . . .

Just below the Cutteslowe roundabout, the bus stopped and four passengers alighted – but not Repp.

At the Martyrs' Memorial, the majority of the passengers alighted – but not Repp.

At the Gloucester Green terminus, the last few passengers alighted – but not Repp.

The 27 bus was now empty.

Chapter Eighteen

Any fool can tell the truth; but it requires a man of some sense to know how to lie well

(Samuel Butler)

Lewis knew what he must do as soon as he saw Morse's maroon Jaguar parked in its wonted place.

'Still feeling better, sir?'

'Better than what?'

'Can you spare a minute?'

'Si' down!'

Seated opposite, in his own wonted place, Lewis said his piece.

'You're in a bit of a mess,' said Morse, at the end of the sorry story.

'That's not much help, is it?'

'Remember the Sherlock Holmes story, *Case of Identity*? A fellow gets in one side of a hansom cab, and gets out through the opposite side.'

'Doors on buses are always on the *same* side.'

'Really?'

'You never go on a bus.'

'But you weren't watching *either* side. You were queuing for coffee.'

'Buying a paper.'

'Listen!' Morse looked and sounded strained and

weary. 'I thought you were asking for my advice. Do you want to hear it?'

There was a brief silence before Morse continued: 'It's not really a question of your own competence or incompetence – probably the latter, I'm afraid. The main concern is what's happened to your man, Repp. Agreed?'

Lewis nodded joylessly.

'Well, the situation's fairly simple. You just lost contact with him in the middle of things, that's all. No great shakes, is it? He's fine, believe me! Absolutely fine. At this very second he's probably got his bottom on the top sheet with that common-law missus of his. She picked him up somewhere – that's for certain. Most of these people released from the nick have somebody to pick 'em up.'

'Except she doesn't drive a car.'

'All right. She arranged for somebody *else* to pick him up.'

'Why did he ask for a travel warrant, then?'

Morse looked less than happy. 'He got on the bus at Bicester and while he was sitting there somebody saw him and tapped on the window and offered him a lift to Oxford or wherever he was going – and we know where that is, don't we? *Home.* Which is exactly where he is now, you can put your bank balance on that! It's a racing certainty. And if you don't believe me, go and see for yourself!'

Lewis considered what he had just heard. 'It must have been somebody unexpected, sir. Like I say, he'd asked for a warrant.'

'You're right, yes. Well, partly right. Either unexpected – or not really expected . . . Perhaps not really welcome, either,' added Morse slowly, a weak smile playing on his lips as though for the first time that morning his brain was possibly engaged in some serious thinking.

'You reckon that's what happened?'

'Lewis! *Something* happened, didn't it? If you think your man decided to dematerialize, you've been watching too many space videos.'

'I don't watch—'

'Look! Remember what I've always told you when we've been on a case together – unlike this one! There's always, without exception, some wholly explicable, wholly logical causation for any chain of events, in any situation. In this case, you've just got to ask yourself where the link broke, then how it broke, then why it broke – and nothing in that sequence of events is going to be anything but simple and commonplace.'

Lewis looked the troubled man he was. 'I just can't see how . . .'

Morse's question was quietly spoken. 'You remember that car, the one you said somehow squeezed in between you and the bus from Bullingdon?'

Lewis looked across the desk in pained surprise. 'You don't think . . .'

'What do you remember about it?'

'Dark colour – black, I think – pretty recent Reg – one person in it – man, I think – pretty sure it was a man.'

'Not very observant – '

'I was looking at the *bus* all the time, for God's sake!'

' – and not much help, if you want the truth.'

No, it wasn't, Lewis knew that. 'What do I tell the Super, though?'

'If I were you? I certainly wouldn't tell him the truth. Not a very wise thing, you know, going through life telling nothing but the truth. So in this case, I'd tell him I'd followed the bus to Bicester, then followed the bus to Oxford, then seen Repp get off outside The Randolph, get picked up there in a car, and get driven off in the general direction of Chaucer Lane, Burford. Easy!'

Uneasy, however, was Lewis's minimal nod.

'But I'm *not* you, Lewis, am I? I'm a very accomplished liar myself, but I've never rated you too highly in that department.'

A puzzled look suddenly came over Lewis's brow. 'How come you know where Repp lives?'

'Great man Chaucer, born in 1343, it's thought—'

'You're not answering my question!'

'I know a lot of things, Lewis – far more than you think.'

'You've still not told me what I'm supposed to say to the Super.'

'Cut your losses and tell him the truth.'

'He'll tear me apart.'

'You may well be surprised.'

But, as he rose to his feet, Lewis appeared far from convinced.

'Well, I suppose I'd better—'

'Hold your horses!' (Morse looked at his wristwatch.) 'It may just be that I can help you.'

Lewis's eyebrows lifted a little as Morse continued:

'*You* promise to buy me a couple of drinks, and *I'll* promise to give you a big, fat juicy clue.'

'If you say so, sir.'

'Off we go then.'

'What's this big, fat—?'

'I'll give you the Registration Number of the car that you followed from Bullingdon to Bicester! Bargain, is it?'

Lewis's eyebrows lifted a lot. 'No kidding?'

Morse rechecked his wristwatch. 'First things first, though. They've already been open five minutes.'

Chapter Nineteen

It's good to hope; it's the waiting that spoils it
(Yiddish proverb)

With increasing impatience and with incipient disquiet, lighting one cigarette from another, drinking cup after cup of instant coffee, Deborah Richardson had been watching from the front-room window, on and off from 10.30 a.m., on and off from 11.30 a.m., and virtually on and on from midday and thereafter – at first with that curiously pleasing *expectation* of happy events which Jane Austen would have swapped for happiness itself. Not that Debbie had ever read Jane Austen. Heard of her, though, most recently from that elderly Oxford don (well, wasn't fifty-eight elderly?) with whom she'd spent the night at the Cotswold Hotel in Burford . . .

It wasn't that she was keenly anticipating any renewal of sexual congress with her newly liberated partner. Although she felt gratified that physically he'd always been so demanding of her, it had often occurred to her that he was probably enjoying the sex more for its own sake than because he was having it with *her*. And perhaps that was why only occasionally did she experience that 'intercrural effusion' of which she'd read in one of the women's magazines . . .

Nor was she looking forward to the regular resumption of cooking and washing and ironing that had monopolized her time in the years prior to his arrest . . .

Nor – she ought to be honest with herself! – was she at all anxious to witness his eating habits again, especially at breakfast, when he would regularly offer some trite and ill-informed commentary on whatever article he was reading in the *Sun*, and openly displaying thereby a semi-masticated mouthful of whatever . . .

And – oh, most definitely! – she would never never ever tolerate again the demands his erstwhile criminal dealings had made upon the space, *her* space, in the quite unpleasantly appointed little semi he'd bought three years earlier at rock-bottom price during the slump in the housing market. After which, at almost any given time, every conceivable square foot of space had been jam-packed with crates of gin and whisky, cartons of cigarettes, car radios, video recorders, cameras, computers, and Hi-Fi equipment. No! There'd have to be an end to all that stolen-property lark; and surely (now!) there'd be little further risk of Harry himself taking part in any of the actual burglaries. For he *had* taken part occasionally, Debbie knew that, although the police hadn't seemed to know, or perhaps just couldn't find sufficient evidence to prosecute. Certainly Harry had never asked for any further offences to be taken into consideration. He'd made only the one plea in mitigation of his sentence: he might have known the possible provenance of the miscellaneous merchandise he'd acquired; *might* have known, if only he'd asked – but he'd just never asked.

He was in business, that was all. He knew a few clients who wanted to buy things at less than market price. Who didn't? 'Just like yer duty-frees, innit? Everybody's always looking round for a bargain, officer' . . .

So?

So why was she still standing there at the window, staring up and down the quiet road? The answer was simple: she just wanted a man *around* the place. Without Harry she felt isolated, lonely, unshared. She'd lost her man; and there was no man there to talk to, to talk to others about, to grumble at, to argue with, even to walk out on – because you couldn't walk out on a man who wasn't there to start with, now could you?

Where was he? What had happened? . . .

Not that her grass-widowhood had been entirely minus men. There'd been that nice little affair with the young plasterer who'd come in to patch up a crack in the kitchen wall. And that civilized little liaison with the Oxford don (so undemanding, so appreciative) she'd met in a Burford pub. But in each case, and on every occasion, she'd been so very, very careful . . .

Only once had she had *that* dreadful worry, after buying a Home Pregnancy Kit from Boots, when she'd just had to tell Harry, and when he'd been surprisingly sympathetic. If they did have a kid, it'd be good for him (him!) to have a mum *and* a dad. Yeah! He'd hated both his mum and his dad – but he'd hated his mum *less*, and it was proper to have a choice. Something else too: you know, when the poor little bugger went to school and one of the other kids said what's your name or what's your dad do – well, it was probably old-fashioned to think like that but, yeah!, better to have two of them, two parents. So she ought to change her name to his, but no need for any of all that nuptial stuff! Just for the kid's sake, mind – nothing to do with any social worker!

But she'd be 'Debbie Repp', then; and that would be too close to 'demirep' (a word she'd met in the 'intercrural' article), which she'd looked up in the biggest dictionary she could find in the Burford Public Library: 'a person, esp. a woman, of dubious and libidinous disposition'. Her name, she'd decided, would henceforth remain 'Richardson'. And in any case the subsequent messy miscarriage had settled *that* domestic crisis.

At 12.50 p.m. she left her vigil for the kitchen, where she felt the neck of the champagne bottle, standing beside two glasses on the table there. Inappropriately *chambré* she decided (another recent addition to her vocabulary), and she put it back in the fridge. Not Premier Division stuff: £8.99 from the supermarket, although in truth she'd begrudged even that. Money! God, how important that was in life! They had enough money – what's more, money temporarily held in her own name. But that was Harry's money, and she would never dare to touch more of it than the reasonably generous allowance he'd authorized.

She'd taken some occasional office-cleaning jobs in Burford, usually from 6 p.m. to 8 p.m. But £4.75 per hour was hardly the rate of remuneration to support any reasonable lifestyle; certainly not the style she'd begun to get accustomed to with Harry. So did she find herself *almost* hoping that he might pick up again on some of those very shady but very profitable activities?

No! No! No!

At 1.15 p.m. she rang Bullingdon Prison, learning that Harry Repp had left on schedule that morning with a bus warrant for Oxford. Nothing further they could tell her: no longer their responsibility, was he? She could ring the Probation Office in Oxford – that might have been his first port-of-call. Which number she was about to dial when she noticed a car pulling up outside – an R-Reg., dark blue, expensive-looking model; and a man she'd never seen before getting out of it, and walking towards her up the narrow, amateurishly cemented front-path.

Chapter Twenty

Then said the Jews unto him, Thou art not yet fifty years old, and hast thou seen Abraham? Jesus said unto them, Verily, verily, I say unto you, Before Abraham was, I am

(*St John*, ch. VIII, vv. 57–58)

Already, an hour or so before driving out to see Debbie Richardson, it had been an unusual morning for Sergeant Lewis.

Morse had insisted on buying the second round in the Woodstock Arms, albeit one consisting only of one pint of Morrell's Best Bitter for himself, since as yet Lewis was only halfway down his obligatory orange juice.

Unusual? Yes. And quite certainly surprising.

'Do you really mean it – about the car number, sir?'

'Just be patient!'

'What do you think I *am* being?'

'You say the car was darkish, newish, toppish range?'

'Like I said, I was really concentrating on the bus.'

'Be more *specific*, man! Go for it. Back your hunches!'

'All right: black; R-reg; twenty thou.'

'That's better.'

Lewis smiled dubiously. 'Thank you.'

'And how many people in that car of yours? One? Two? Three?'

'Certainly one, sir.'

'We'll make a detective of you yet,' mumbled Morse, leaning forward as he buried his nose in the froth.

'Could've been two, I suppose. I can't really remember but . . . you know, it was a bit like one of those cars going off on a family holiday, you know what I mean?'

'No.'

'Well, you know—'

'For Christ's sake stop saying "you know"!'

'Well, you've got things packed everywhere, haven't you? Not just cases and things but nappies, bedding, towels, boots, wellingtons, thermoses, carrier bags – all piled up so you can hardly see out of the back window.'

'What sort of bags?'

Lewis was trying hard to re-visualize the scene, and fortunately Morse had picked on the one thing that finally jogged his fading memory. Bags! Yes, there'd been bags in the back of that car: bags you could stick all sorts of things inside. And suddenly the picture had grown clearer:

'Black bags!'

'You think he was off to the rubbish dump?'

'Could've been. "Waste Reception Area", by the way, sir.'

'Where's the biggest rubbish dump in Oxfordshire?'

'Or in Oxford, perhaps?' Lewis's face had brightened. 'Redbridge. People go there from all over the county – straight down the A34 – then turn off—' But Lewis stopped. 'Forget it, sir. From Bullingdon you'd turn on to the A41, and then straight on to the A34. You wouldn't go into Bicester at all.'

'And you're quite sure the car went into Bicester?'

'That's one thing I am sure about.'

'If only you'd concentrated on that car, Lewis, and forgotten all about the bus!'

'I just don't understand why you're so interested in the car. Repp was on the *bus*.'

'So you keep saying,' said Morse quietly. 'But you're not right, are you? Repp *wasn't* on the bus.'

'Not when he got to Oxford, no.'

'You lost him. You might as well face it.'

Lewis drained his orange juice. 'Yep! I agree. I lost him. And that's exactly why I need a bit of help.'

'Like the number of that car, you mean?'

'I think you're having me on about that.'

'Oh no. And if you think it'll help . . .'

Morse took out his pen and pushed his empty glass across the table: 'Your round! And pass me your notebook.'

A minute later, Lewis stared down at Morse's small, neat handwriting:

R456 LJB

And incredulity vied with amazement in his face as Morse continued quietly: 'You know, you weren't your usual sharp self this morning, were you? You failed to observe the car in *front* of you – and you failed to observe the car *behind* you.'

'You – you don't mean . . .?'

'I do mean, yes. *I* was right behind you this morning. But being the law-abiding citizen I am, I instructed my driver to keep an appropriately safe distance from the vehicle in front.'

'I just don't believe this. I just don't understand.'

'Easy, really. I thought it wouldn't be a bad idea to keep an eye on our Mr Repp, just like Strange did. So I rang up the prison Governor, an old friend of mine, and told him what I was intending to do; and he said there was no need because he'd had a call from Strange setting up *your* surveillance. So I just told him to forget it – told him we'd got some crossed wires – came out in an unmarked car, like you did – parked in the visitors' area – listened to Mahler's Eighth – and watched and waited. *And* took a flask of coffee – yes, *coffee*, Lewis – and the rest is history.'

'You're having me on!'

'Oh no! How the hell do you think I could give you that car number unless I'd *seen* the bloody thing? You don't think I'm psychic or something, do you?'

Lewis reflected on this extraordinary new development. Then slowly formulated his thoughts aloud. 'You saw the car in front of me. You saw who was in it and what was in it – '

'Black plastic bags, yes. You were right.'

' – and you saw the Registration Number.'

'Only just. You know, I'll have to see an optician soon.'

'You told me off for saying "you know",' snapped Lewis.

Morse curled his right hand lovingly round his beer glass. 'Sometimes, you don't fully appreciate my help, you know.'

Lewis let it go. 'And you knew the car went into Bicester, to the bus station. You knew it all the time.'

'Yes.'

'So when I went to get a paper you saw Repp get out of the bus and get into the car. But you didn't tell *me* – oh no! You just left me to go on a wild goose chase after the bus. Well, thank you *very* much.'

For a while Morse was silent. Then: 'How many times have I been to the Gents this morning?'

'Twice since you've been here.'

'Six times in all, Lewis! And the reason for such embarrassingly frequent retirements is not any lack of bladder-control. It's those diuretic pills they've put me on.'

The light slowly dawned; and Sergeant Lewis suddenly looked a happy man. 'The thermos, sir? Three cups of coffee in that, say?'

Morse nodded. Not a happy man.

'So when you got to Bicester bus station you were dying for a leak and you saw the Gents' loo there, and when you came out – the car was gone. Right?'

Reluctantly Morse nodded once more. 'And we followed you, you and the bus, back to Oxford.'

A gleeful Lewis looked as if he'd won the Lottery.

'You really should have kept your eyes on that car, sir!'

'You mean the black R-reg Peugeot, Lewis? You were right, by the way: £19,950 licensed and on the road, so they inform me. Not far off, were you?'

'And the owner?'

'Some insurance-broker in Gerrard's Cross reported it missing two days ago.'

Chapter Twenty-One

BURMA (Be Undressed Ready My Angel)
(An acronym frequently printed on the backs of envelopes posted to sweethearts by servicemen about to go on leave, or by prisoners about to be released)

Unlike the (equally unknown) man who had called upon her the previous evening, he held up his ID for several seconds in front of her face, like a conjurer holding up a playing card towards an audience.

But she didn't really look at it; didn't even notice his name. He seemed a decent, honest-looking sort of fellow – not one of those spooky pseuds who occasionally sought her company. And she was hardly too bothered if he *wasn't* one of those decent, honest-looking sort of fellows.

'Deborah Richardson?' (He sounded rather shy.)

'Yes.'

'Sergeant Lewis, Thames Valley CID.'

'He's not here, yet. It *was* Harry you wanted?'

'Can I come in?'

'Be my guest!'

As she sat opposite him at the Formica-topped table, Lewis saw a woman in her mid-thirties, of medium build, with short blonde hair, and wearing a white dress, polka-dotted in a gaudy green, that reached halfway down (or was it halfway up?) a pair of thighs now comfortably crossed in that uncomfortable kitchen. She was not by any standards a beautiful woman; certainly not a pretty one. Yet Lewis had little doubt that many men, including Morse perhaps, would have called her quietly (or loudly) attractive.

She lit a cigarette and smiled rather nervously, the pleasingly regular teeth unpleasingly coated with nicotine.

'He's OK, isn't he?'

'I'm sure he is, yes.'

'It's just – well, I was expectin' him a bit before now.'

'You didn't arrange to meet him at the prison?'

'No. We've got a car, in the garage, but I never got on too well with drivin'.'

'Perhaps one of his mates . . .?'

'Dunno, really. Expect so. He just said he'd be here as soon as he could.'

'He might have rung you.'

'Havin' a few beers, I should think. Only natural, innit? The champagne's back in the fridge anyway.'

Lewis looked at his watch, surprised how quickly the latter part of the morning had sped by. 'Only half-past one.'

'So? So why have you called then, Sergeant?'

Lewis played his less than promising hand with some care. 'It's just that we've received some . . . information, unconfirmed information, that Harry might have . . . well, there might be some slight connection between him and the murder of Mrs Harrison.'

'Harry never had nothin' to do with that murder!'

'You obviously remember the case.'

'Course I do! Everybody does. Biggest thing ever happened round here.'

'So as far as you know Harry had nothing—'

'You reckon I'd be tellin' you if he *had*?'

'But you say he hadn't?'

'Course he hadn't!'

'You see, all I'm saying is that Harry's a burglar – '

'*Was* a burglar.'

' – and there was some evidence that there could have been a burglary that night that might have gone a bit wrong perhaps.'

'What? Her lyin' on the bed there with her legs wide open? Funny bloody burglary!'

'How did you know that? How she was found?'

'Come off it! How the hell do any of us know anythin'? Common knowledge, wasn't it? Common gossip, anyway.'

'Where did you hear it?'

'Pub, I should think.'

'Maiden's Arms?'

'Shouldn't be surprised. Everybody talks about everythin' there. The landlord, 'specially. Still, that's what landlords—'

'Is he still there?'

'Tom? Oh, yes. Tom Biffen. Keeps about the best pint of bitter in Oxfordshire, so Harry said.' (Lewis made a mental note, for Morse would be interested.)

'You know him fairly well, the landlord?'

She lit another cigarette, her eyes widening as she leaned forward a little. '*Fairly* well, yes, Sergeant.'

Lewis changed tack. 'You saw Harry pretty regularly while he was inside?'

'Once a week, usually.'

'How did you get there?'

'Friends, mostly.'

'Awkward place to get to.'

'Yep.'

'When did you last see him?'

'Week ago.'

'What did you take him?'

'Bit o' cake. Few cigs. No booze, no drugs – nothin' like that. You can't get away with much there.'

'Can you get away with *anything* there?'

She leaned forward again and smiled as she drew deeply on her cigarette. 'Perhaps I could have done if I'd tried.'

'Could he give *you* anything? To take out?'

'Well, nothin' he shouldn't. Just as strict about that as the other way round. We all sat at tables, you know, and they were watchin' us all the time – all the screws. You'd be lucky to get away with anythin'.'

But Lewis knew that it was all a little too pat, this easy interchange. Things got in, and things got out – every prison was the same; and everybody knew it. Including this woman. And for the first time Lewis sensed that Strange was probably right: that the letter received by Thames Valley Police had been written by Harry Repp at Bullingdon Prison, handed to one of his visitors, and posted somewhere outside – at Lower Swinstead, say.

For whatever reason.

But as yet Lewis couldn't identify such a reason.

'*Did* Harry ever ask you to take anything out of prison?'

'Come off it! What'd he got in there to take *out*?'

'Letters perhaps?' suggested Lewis quietly.

'If he'd forgotten some address. Not often, though.'

'To some of his old cronies?'

'Crooks, you mean?'

'That's what I'm asking you, I suppose.'

'Few letters, yes. He didn't want them people in there lookin' through everythin' he wrote. Nobody would.'

'So you occasionally took one away?'

'Not difficult, was it? Just slip it in your handbag.'

'What was the last one you took out?'

'Can't remember.'

'I think you can.' Lewis was surprised with the firm tone of his own voice.

'No, I can't. Just told you, didn't I?' (Yet another cigarette.)

'Please don't lie to me. You see, I *know* you posted a letter at Lower Swinstead. Harry'd asked you to post it there because he thought – he was wrong as it turned out – that it would be postmarked from there.'

For the first time in the interview, Debbie Richardson seemed unsure of herself, and Lewis pressed home his perceptible advantages.

'How did you get to Lower Swinstead, by the way?'

'Only three or four miles—'

'You walked?'

'No, I drove—' She stopped herself. But the words, in Homeric phrase, had escaped the barrier of her teeth.

'Didn't you say you couldn't drive?'

'Lied to you, didn't I?'

'Why? Why lie to me?'

'I get used to it, that's why.' She leaned forward across the table. And Lewis saw for certain what he had already suspected for semi-certain – that she wore no bra beneath her dress; probably no knickers, either.

'How often do you go to the pub there, the Maiden's Arms?'

'Often as I can.'

'Not in the car, I hope?'

'Sometimes get a lift there – you know, if somebody rings.'

'When were you there last?'

'When I posted the letter.'

'Open all day, is it?'

'What's all this quizzin' about?'

'Just that my boss'll be interested, that's all.'

'You're all alike, you bloody coppers!'

It seemed a strange reply, and Lewis looked puzzled.

'Pardon?'

'What you just asked me – about the pub bein' open all day. Exactly what the other fellow asked.'

'What other fellow?'

'Can't remember his name. So what? Can't remember yours, come to that.'

'When was this?'

'Last night. Asked me out for a drink, didn't he? I reckon he fancied me a little bit. But I was already—'

'From the *police*, you say?'

'That's what he said.'

'You didn't check?'

Debbie Richardson shrugged her shoulders. 'Nice he was – sort o' well educated. Know what I mean?'

'You can't recall his name?'

'No, sorry. Tell you one thing though, Sergeant, er . . .'

'Lewis.'

'Had a lovely car, he did. Been nice it would – ridin' round in that. A Jag – maroon-coloured Jag.'

Chapter Twenty-Two

> . . . a mountain range of Rubbish, like an old volcano, and its geological foundation was Dust. Coal-dust, vegetable-dust, bone-dust, crockery-dust, rough dust, and sifted dust – all manner of Dust in the accumulated Rubbish
>
> (Dickens, *Our Mutual Friend*)

'Not for scrap, is she?' Stan Cox nodded towards the Jag parked in the no-parking area outside his office window in the Redbridge Waste Disposal Centre.

'Getting on a bit,' conceded Morse, 'like all of us. You know, windscreen wipers packing up, gear-box starting to jam, no heat . . .'

'Sounds a bit like the missus!'

'Pardon?'

'Joke, sir.'

'Ah, yes.' Morse's smile was even weaker than the witticism as he looked round the cramped office, his eyes catching a girlie calendar in the corner, from which a provocatively bare-breasted bimbo, with short blonde hair, stared back at him.

'Nice, ain't she!'

Morse nodded. 'Past her sell-by date, though. She's the May girl.'

'Remember the ol' song, sir – "From May to September"?'

'You just like having her around.'

It was Cox's turn to nod: 'Drives me mad, she does. Keeps me sane at the same time though, if you follows me meaning.'

Morse wasn't at all sure that he did, but he was conscious that he'd drunk too much beer that lunchtime; that he should never have driven himself out to Redbridge; that what he'd earlier seen as a clear-cut outline had now grown blurred around the periphery. In the pub, with Lewis, he'd felt convinced he could see a cause, a sequence, a structure, to the crime.

Perhaps two crimes now.

It was the same old tantalizing challenge to puzzles that had faced him ever since he was a boy. It was the certain knowledge that something *had* happened in the past – happened in an ordered, logical, very specific way. And the challenge had been, and still was, to gather the disparate elements of the puzzle together and to try to reconstruct that 'very specific way'.

Not too successfully now, though. For here, at Redbridge, there seemed a great gulf fixed between the fanciful hypothesis he'd so recently formulated, and the humdrum reality of a rubbish dump.

Is that what Cox was trying to say?

'How d'you mean? Keeps you sane?'

'Well, it's not exactly your Botanical Gardens here, is it? Just all the filth and useless stuff people want shut of. So there's not much good to look at, 'cept her, bless her heart! Pearl in a pigsty – that's what she is.'

'Why don't you write her a fan-letter?'

'Think she'd read it?'

'No.'

'So what can we do for you, Chief?'

Morse told him, making most of it up as he went along.

And when he'd finished, Cox nodded. 'No problem. We'd better just let the County Authorities know.'

'Already done,' lied Morse. And refusing a cup of coffee, he left the office and walked unaccompanied around the site, only a few hundred yards from the southern stretch of Oxford's Ring Road, thinking about the things he'd learned from Cox . . .

'Do you reckon,' he'd asked, 'you could dispose of a body here, in one of your, er . . . ?'

'Only in one of the compactor bins – that'd be the best bet. You'll be able to see for yourself, though. The others are a bit too open, really.'

'Black bag, say? Put a body in it? Just chuck it in?'

'You'd need a big bag.'

'Well, let's say we've got a big bag.'

'Heavy things, bodies. Ten, twelve stone, say? You couldn't just . . . well, unless you had two people, I suppose.'

'Or cut the body in half, perhaps.'

'Mm. Still a bit awkward, wouldn't you think? Unless it were stiff, of course.'

'Yes . . .'

'*Was* it stiff, this body of yours?'

'Er, no. No, I don't think it was.'

'Or unless it was a pretty small body. *Was* it small, this body of yours?'

'Er, no. No. I don't think it was.'

'Well, as I say . . .'

'How would *you* get rid of a body here?'

'Well, if it were a littl'un, like I said, I'd go for a compactor bin. They got ramps that go back and forrard reg'lar like, and everything soon gets pushed through into the back o' the bin. Doubt anybody'd notice it really – not *this* end, anyway.'

'There's *another* end?'

'Sutton Courtenay, yes, out near Didcot. The bins get driven out there, to the landfill-site. Somebody might notice summat there, I suppose.'

'Funny, isn't it? Dustmen always seem to notice some things, don't they?'

'You mean our Waste Disposal Operatives.'

'They refused to take my little bag of grass cuttings last week.'

'Ah, now you're talking business, sir.'

'Put a human head in the bottom of the bag though – '

' – and you'd probably get away with it? Right! But I shouldn't try your grass cuttings again, Inspector.'

As he walked around, Morse was impressed by the layout and the management of the large area designated there to the various categories of Oxford's disposable debris: car batteries; can bank; engine-oil cans; paper bank; clothing bank; tools; bottles (green, brown, white); bulky items; scrap metal; fridges and freezers; garden waste (green); garden waste (other) . . .

Only the vast 'Bulky Items' bins seemed to offer any scope so far; and even there a body would have lain uncomfortably and conspicuously amid the jagged edges of broken tables, awkwardly angled cupboards, tilted mattresses.

Then Morse stood still for many minutes inspecting what he'd been waiting to see: the compactor bins – twelve of them in a row. Each bin (Morse attempted a none-too-scientific analysis) was a 12-ton, 6 ft. × 20 ft., white-bodied metal container, a broad green stripe painted horizontally along its middle, with a grilled covering at the receiving end which customers could easily lift before depositing their car-booted detritus there; and where a ramp was ever moving forward and back, forward and back, and pushing the divers deposits from the bin's mouth through into some unseen, unsavoury interior. On the side of each bin were 'start/stop' and 'red/green' buttons and switches which appeared to control the complex operation; and even as Morse watched, a site-workman came alongside, somehow interpreting the evidence and (presumably?) deciding whether any particular bin was sufficiently stuffed to get lifted on to one of the great lorries lumbering around, and to get carted off to – where was it? – Sutton Courtenay.

Morse tackled the young pony-tailed operative as he was tapping one of the bins, rather like a man tapping the upturned hull of some stricken submarine to see if there were any signs of life.

'How long's it take to fill one of these things?'

'Depends. Holidays and weekends? Pretty quick – only a day, sometimes. Usually though? Two, three days. Depends, like I said.'

'How many bins have gone today?'

'Two? No, three, I think.'

'You didn't, er, notice anything unusual about . . . about anything?'

'What sort o' thing, mate?'

'Forget it, son! And, by the way, I wasn't aware I *was* one of your mates.'

'An' I wasn't aware you was me fuckin' father, neither!' spat the spotty-faced youth, as an outsmarted Morse walked unhappily away.

It had not been a particularly productive afternoon. Morse hadn't even had the nous to bring his little bag of grass cuttings along, to be tossed, with full official blessing, into the garden waste (green) depository.

Back in Cox's office Morse was (for him) comparatively generous with his gratitude for the help he'd been provided with. And before leaving, he took a last look at the month of May's lascivious self-offering to all who looked and longed and lusted after her. People like Stanley Cox; like Cox's fellow Waste Disposal Operatives; like Chief Inspector Morse, who stood in front of her again and thought she reminded him of another woman – a woman he'd met so very recently.

Reminded him of Debbie Richardson.

Chapter Twenty-Three

> A novel, like a beggar, should always be kept 'moving on'. Nobody knew this better than Fielding, whose novels, like most good ones, are full of inns
>
> (Augustine Birrell, *The Office of Literature*)

IT WAS STILL only 2.30 p.m. that same day when Lewis pulled into the small car park of the Maiden's Arms, a low-roofed building of Cotswold stone which was Lower Swinstead's only public house. A notice beside the entrance announced the opening hours for Friday as 12 noon–3 p.m., 6.30–11 p.m.

At a table by the sole window of the small bar sat two aged villagers drinking beer from straight pint glasses, smoking Woodbines, and playing cribbage. Only one other customer: a pale-faced, ear-pierced, greasy-haired youth, who stood feeding coin after coin into an unresponsive fruit machine. When Lewis asked for the landlord, the man behind the bar introduced himself as no less a personage.

'What can I get you, sir?'

Lewis showed his ID. 'Can we talk?'

Tom Biffen was a square of a man, small of stature and wide of body, his weather-beaten features framed with a grizzly beard, a pair of humorous eyes, and a single ear-ring in the left lobe. A dark-blue T-shirt paraded 'The Maidens Arms' across a deep chest.

Lewis came to the point without preamble: 'You know a woman called Deborah – Deborah Richardson?'

'Debbie? Oh yeah. Everybody knows Debbie.' He spoke with a West Country burr, and clearly neither of the card-players was hard-of-hearing, for had Lewis had occasion to turn round at that moment he would have noted a half-smiling nod of agreement on each of their faces.

Lewis continued: 'Her partner's been released from prison this morning. You know Harry Repp?'

'Harry? Oh yeah! Everybody knows Harry.' (The fingers of the card-players froze momentarily, and each had stopped smiling.)

'He's not been in this morning?'

'I'd've seen him if he had, wouldn't I?'

'It's just that he's not been home yet, that's all. And we want to make sure he's OK.'

'Having a noggin or two somewhere, I shouldn't wonder. That's what I'd be doing.'

'How long have you been landlord here?'

'Let's see now . . .'

'Seven year come September, Biff,' came an answer from behind.

'Thank you, Bert!' Biff turned his attention back to Lewis as he held a proprietorially polished glass up to the light like a radiographer examining an X-ray. 'You're going to ask me about the murder – I know that. There's been things in the papers, and we're all interested. Can't pretend we're not. Biggest thing ever happened round here.'

'Lots of rumours, weren't there? You know, about Mrs Harrison. Having a bit on the side, perhaps?'

'Well, it weren't me! And Alf and Bert here, they're both a bit past it now.'

('Speak for yourself!' – from one of the septuagenarians.)

'Did she ever come in here with any men?'

Biff shook his head indeterminately: 'Simon, the boy? Only occasionally though. Deaf, see! I 'spect it was a bit dull for him – not being able to hear the sparkling repartee of my regulars, like Alf and Bert here.'

('Used to drink Coca-Cola – ' from Alf, or was it Bert?)

'What about the daughter?'

'Sarah? Nice pair o' legs, Sarah.'

('Not the only nice pair o' things!' – *sotto voce* from behind.)

'With a boyfriend in tow, was it?'

'Sometimes.'

'With her mum?'

'Nah! Wouldn't have wanted *her* around, would she?'

'Why not?'

'Well . . . attractive, wasn't she, Sarah? It was her mum had the real sex-appeal, though. Could have had most fellahs round here, if they'd had a jar or two.'

('Even if they hadn't!' – from Bert, or was it Alf?)

'Did you ever come up with any names?'

'Names? Nah! Like I said . . .'

'Must have been rumours though?'

'Never heard any meself.' Biff looked over Lewis's shoulder: 'You ever hear any rumours, lads?'

'Not me,' said Bert.

'Nor me,' said Alf.

Lewis felt certain that all three of them were lying. And, according to the report, the police on the original enquiry had felt very much the same: that the villagers were quite willing to hint that Yvonne Harrison had not exactly been the high priestess of marital fidelity; but that when it came to naming names, they'd decided to clamp up. En bloc.

'Drink on the house, sir?'

Lewis declined, and bade his farewell, nodding to the card-players as he walked to the door, where he stopped and turned back towards the landlord, pointing to the T-shirt:

'Shouldn't there be an apostrophe before the "s"?'

Biff grinned. 'Funny you should say that. Fellow in here last night asked me exactly the same thing!'

Lewis walked slowly round to the car park, noting the plaque on the side-wall:

Parking strictly for customers.
Other vehicles will be clamped.
Release fee £25

Need more than that, thought Lewis, to un-clamp a small community which was so clearly still maintaining its conspiracy of silence.

But Lewis was wrong.

As he took out his car-keys, he saw the youth who had just been feeding the fruits of his labours into the fruit machine. Waiting for him. Beside the car.

'Police, aincha?'

'Yes?'

'You was asking about things in there.'

'I'm always asking about things.'

'Just that somebody else was asking them same sort o' questions, see? Couldn't help hearing, could I? And this fellah – he was asking *me* a few things. About Mrs Harrison. About if I'd ever seen her with any fellah in the pub. But I couldn't quite remember. Not at the time.'

'You remember now, though?'

'Right on the nail, copper. Told me to give 'im a buzz if I suddenly remembered something. Said, you know, it might be worthwhile like.'

'Why didn't you ring him?'

'That's just it, though. I'd seen her with the fellah that *asked* me, see? Same bleedin fellah!'

'You mean . . . it was *him* you'd seen with Mrs Harrison?'

'Right on the nail, copper.'

'What did he look like, this fellow?'

'Well, sort of . . . I can't really . . .'

'He gave you his name?'

'No. Gave me 'is phone number though, like I said.'

The youth produced a circular beer-mat from his pocket.

Lewis looked down at a telephone number written above the red *Bass* triangle, written in the small, neat hand he knew so well: the personal ex-directory telephone number of Chief Inspector Morse.

Chapter Twenty-Four

In many an Oxfordshire Ale-house the horseshoe is hung upside-down, in the form that is of an Arch or an Omega. This age-old custom (I have been convincingly informed) is not to allow the Luck to run out but to prevent the Devil building up a nest therein.

(D. Small, *A Most Complete Guide to the Hostelries of the Cotswolds*)

As he stood amid the wilderness of waste, a High Viz jacket over his summer shirt and a red safety helmet on his head, Chief Inspector Morse realized that he had miscalculated rather badly. But he'd had to check it up.

It had always been the same with him. Whenever as a young boy reading under his bedside lamp he'd come across an unfamiliar word, he'd known with certainty that he could never look forward to sleep until he'd traced the newcomer's credentials and etymology in *Chambers' Dictionary*, the book that stood alongside *The Family Doctor* (1910), *A Pictorial History of the Great War*, and *The Life of Captain Cook*, on the single short shelf that comprised his parents' library.

His father (sadly, almost tragically) had been a clandestine gambler. And Morse was fully aware that this time he himself had put his money on a rank outsider: the possibility that someone had murdered Harry Repp; had disposed of his body in the Redbridge Waste Disposal Centre; had disposed of this hypothetical body in a particular part of that Centre – specifically in one of the compactor bins perhaps: further, that the said and equally hypothetical bin had been, was being, or was about to be, driven out in a hypothetical black bag to Sutton Courtenay. And, above all, that somebody might have *observed* such a hypothetical deposit. Ridiculous! William Hill or Ladbrokes would probably have offered odds of 1,000,000–1 against any such eventuality.

On impulse Morse had driven down the A34, thence along the A4130, to the land-fill site on the outskirts of Sutton Courtenay. Where, after a series of telephone calls from the temporary (permanent) Portakabins, the management had finally acknowledged the *bona fides* of their dubious visitor.

It was in a Land-rover that (finally) Morse had been driven out to the tipping area, where virtually continuous convoys of lorries from the whole of Oxfordshire were raising the telescopic legs of container-cargoes to some 45 degrees as they began to tip their loads; moving forward in disjunctive jerks as they ensured the contents were fully discharged, and leaving behind a distinctive trail of their own particular type of rubbish. As a rather dispirited Morse watched these operations, he imagined that perhaps when viewed from some hovering helicopter each truck would seem like an artist's brush, with the trail of the gradually extending rubbish like a stroke of variegated paint being smeared across the canvas of the landscape. But Morse accepted the more prosaic truth of the situation immediately: the truck drivers themselves would very seldom, if ever, have occasion to notice, let alone to examine, the contents of the loads they were emptying.

He voiced his thoughts. 'If a driver dumped a body . . . well, he wouldn't really know much about it, would he?'

Colin Rice, the site manager, hesitated awhile before replying – not because he had the slightest doubt about the answer to this question, but because he felt reluctant immediately to disappoint his somewhat melancholic inquisitor.

'No.'

'How many of those compactor bins do you get from Redbridge every day?'

'Depends.'

'Today?'

'Four or five? I could check.'

'No. No need.'

Morse watched as the yellow-painted BOMAG tractors were once again setting about their dismal business, the metal teeth of their giant wheels compacting the recently deposited mounds; and then, with a fair-weather frontage reminiscent of a snowplough, pushing forward the levelled rubbish towards its burial ground.

For the moment Morse said nothing more, suddenly

and strangely aware that, if he half-closed his eyes, the piles of refuse around him could almost appear like some wondrously woven multi-coloured quilt, black and white mostly, but interspersed with vivid little patches of blue and red and yellow.

It was Rice who spoke: 'If anybody'd see anything it'd be those chaps on the levellers. They're looking forward at all the rubbish, see? Your normal truck driver, he's not even looking backwards at it.'

'You wouldn't be able to pin-point the place where any lorry-loads from Redbridge . . . ?'

The site manager shook his head. 'No chance.'

'If you had enough personnel though?'

'How many?'

'Five or six?'

'Five or six hundred, you mean?'

Morse decided to quit the unequal struggle. He kicked a hole in one of the black plastic bags at his feet, and briefly surveyed the nauseating mixture of spaghetti and tomatoes that oozed therefrom, like the innards of a road-squashed rabbit.

'If you'd like to stay?' suggested Rice, without enthusiasm. 'You never know. We had a load of brand-new cameras dumped here once.'

'I've never had a camera myself,' admitted Morse. 'I just hope you appropriated one for yourself.'

Rice smiled, forgivingly. 'You don't really know much about the rules in a place like this, do you, sir?'

Morse lifted his eyes from the ground towards the

giant cooling-towers of Didcot Power Station which stood sentinel on the immediate landscape, only a few hundred yards away.

'No, I don't,' he said quietly.

As he drove back along the A34 into Oxford, Morse doubted he'd expressed adequate thanks to Greenways Waste Management. He was (he acknowledged the fact) never a man renowned for voicing much gratitude. He'd even dismissed, and that cursorily, Rice's thoughtful offer of issuing a memo to everyone working either permanently or temporarily on the site, acquainting them with the situation.

But Morse felt unable to feel too self-critical, because he knew there *was* no 'situation'. And he repeated to himself this recently corroborated conviction as he turned on the car radio, and listened again to the slow movement of Bruckner's Seventh.

When later that same afternoon Lewis arrived back at Kidlington HQ, he felt more pleased, more excited, and (yes!) more confident in himself than he'd been for a long, long while. In almost all previous cases he'd usually reached first base only to find that Morse was already sprinting off to second base; and so on, and so on, all round the baseball pitch. So now he decided to do a little sprinting for himself.

First, he rang Redbridge – only to discover that Morse had already visited the site.

Second, he rang Sutton Courtenay – only to discover that Morse had already visited the site, and where he'd pronounced that any search of said site was quite certainly foredoomed to failure.

So Lewis had coolly countermanded these instructions.

It was as if he – Lewis – was taking charge of the case.

Well, he was, wasn't he?'

CHAPTER TWENTY-FIVE

Sometimes it is that searchers spot
The kind of thing they'd rather not
(Lessing, *Nathan der Weise*)

DURING 'JAMMIE' JARNOLD'S twenty-two years' service on the Sutton Courtenay site, he'd seen most things. Not everything. For example, he'd never caught a glimpse of that sack of notes the Metropolitan Police were certain had been deposited in one of the trucks on that long train which arrived in the early hours of each morning from Brentford, via a branchline from Didcot, with its thousands of tons of the capital's refuse. Four hundred and fifty thousand pounds, they'd said, in fivers and tenners. Yes, Jammie had kept his eyes wide open on that occasion; had occasionally climbed down from his cab to prod anything that seemed even minimally promising.

If, on balance, it was a steady old job, it was also a job that was unmemorable and predictably monotonous. For this reason, neither Jammie nor his colleagues in the team of BOMAC tractor-operators had dismissed as so much negligible bumf the single Xeroxed sheet which had been handed out that Saturday morning, both to permanent on-site personnel and to every dumper-truck driver entering the site from the far quarters of Oxfordshire.

MEMO FROM SITE MANAGER

Thames Valley Police have advised of the possibility of a human body, probably bagged, being recently conveyed from the Redbridge Centre in Oxford. Everyone is asked to be extra vigilant and to report anything unusual (or usual, provided its a body).

(Morse himself would have been pleased to write such a succinct note – though inserting, of course, an apostrophe in the humorous parenthesis.)

Just after the start of the shift, a colleague shouted across at Jammie, waving a copy of the memo.

'Better keep your eyes open!'

'What's the reward?'

'Night with Sophia Loren in the Savoy.'

'Bit young for me.'

'I still reckon you'll keep your eyes open.'

'Yeah! I reckon.'

'Like looking for a needle in an 'aystack though.'

'Like finding a shadow in the black-out, as me ol' mum used to say.'

'I like that, Jammie. Sort o' poetic, like.'

Jarnold braked his tractor at 10.05 a.m. and jumped down from his cab on to the semi-levelled, semi-compacted mound of recently deposited rubbish. It was not that the specific item he'd spotted was unusual in any way. In fact, any pair of shoes was a very common sight: thousands of pairs were ever to be observed on every part of the site, worn down, worn out, worn beyond any possible repair. But there were unusual aspects about this particular pair of shoes. For a start, they looked comparatively new and were clearly of good quality; then, they were the only objects sticking out of a large black bag; what's more, they seemed strangely reluctant to drop *out* of that large black bag, as if (perhaps?) they might be attached, permanently, to something *inside* that large black bag.

Jarnold shouted over to a colleague.

'Come over 'ere a sec!'

But already he had half-torn one side of the plastic.

'Christ!'

He turned away to vomit full-throatedly over a piece of conveniently positioned carpeting.

Had he been dining with Miss Loren at the Savoy, this would have caused considerable consternation. Not here, though. Not at the land-fill site at Sutton Courtenay in Oxfordshire.

Chapter Twenty-Six

Undergraduate:	But you're blowing up the wrong tyre, sir. It's the back one that's flat.
Don:	Goodness me! You mean the two of them are not connected?

(Freshman seeking to assist his tutor outside Trinity College, Oxford)

Morse (for some reason) was in that Saturday morning when Lewis knocked on his office door just after ten.

'Spare a few minutes, sir?'

'C'm in! I've finished the crossword.'

'How long?'

'Let's just say the brain is deteriorating.'

'Thirty thousand brain-cells a day we lose after thirty, so you told me once.'

Morse nodded morosely. 'I just thought I was the exception, that's all. Si' down!'

Lewis did so, and took a deep breath. 'I've been following you, sir.'

Morse looked across at his sergeant uncomprehendingly.

'You were at Debbie Richardson's house – before me; you were at the Maiden's Arms – before me; you were at Bullingdon – before me; you were at Redbridge – before me; you were out at Sutton Courtenay – before me. You've been one move ahead of me all the time.'

'Only *one*?'

'Why couldn't you just *tell* me?'

'Tell you what?' asked Morse. 'And don't forget that time when it was *me* following *you*: from Bullingdon. At exactly the distance recommended in the Highway Code.'

'Which is?'

'Next question?'

'You will be taking on the case, won't you?'

'Next question?'

'Why not?'

'Pass.'

'You're getting people's backs up here, you know that?'

'Nothing new about that.'

'But surely—?'

'Listen!' Unblinking blue eyes glared across the desk. 'I am not taking on the Harrison case.'

'I was just hoping you'd help me, that's all.'

'Yes?'

'Well, do you mind me asking you if . . . if you've got any personal interest in all of this?'

'Nil.' If there had been a quick flicker of unease in Morse's eyes, it was as quickly gone.

'But you know a lot about it, don't you? So you must have some idea about what happened on the night she was murdered?'

'Ideas – plural.'

'There was a logical sequence of events, as you would say.'

'There was a concatenation of events, yes, with each link of the chain causally connected to its predecessor.'

'What do you think happened that night?'

'Not much argument about that, is there?'

'You'd agree with this, then?' Lewis produced a sheet of A4 on which he had typed a timetable for the day of the murder:

7 a.m.–1 p.m.	Yvonne on early shift at JR2 Ward 7C
1.15–2 p.m.	Lunches in staff canteen
2.15–4 p.m. (?)	Drives down to Oxford shopping at M&S and Austin Reed
4.00(?)–4.30 p.m.	Drives home avoiding main traffic exodus
6–7 p.m.	Evening meal of mushroom omelette
9.00 p.m.	Local builder rings – number engaged or phone off hook
9.10 p.m.	Frank H gets phone call and catches 21.48 Paddington to Oxford train
9.30 p.m.	Builder rings again – ringing-tone but no reply
11.00 p.m.	F H gets taxi to Lower Swinstead
11.20 p.m.	Discovers wife naked, gagged, handcuffed and dead

Morse glanced at the sheet in perfunctory fashion. 'You ought to use the Oxford comma more.'

'Pardon?'

'The presumption was – is – that somewhere between nine and half-past . . .'

'Pathologist's report seemed to confirm that.'

'Would I had your faith in pathologists!'

'Not just that though, is it? The whole thing hangs together. Pretty well everything there's confirmed: statements from the hospital; receipts from the two shops; post-mortem details on the meal; phone calls checked out—'

'Nonsense! The builder? First time the number's engaged? Second time nobody answers? How the hell do you check that?'

'You can't check absolutely everything—'

'What about the husband? Odd sort of call, wasn't it? Drop whatever you're doing and get here double-quick! So who was it who rang him?'

'That's what I'm asking you, sir.'

'His number couldn't have been too well known. He was renting a flat, wasn't he?'

'Still is.'

'But somebody knew it – and rang him. Did we check the phone records of the suspects?'

'What suspects?'

'The two children?'

'They *weren't* suspects. And if they were, why shouldn't they ring their dad occasionally?'

'How did he pay for his train journey?'

'No credit-card record – must have paid cash. *And*

for the taxi ride. Anyway, he'd got the best alibi of anybody: taxi driver remembers the time exactly. He was just listening to the 11 o'clock news-headlines.'

'Was the train a bit late that night? If it's the one I sometimes catch, it's due in at 22.53.'

'Too late to find out, sir.'

'Rubbish! Too difficult, possibly. But they keep all these times of arrivals: they make statistical tables out of 'em, for heaven's sake.'

'Must've been on time, surely?'

'What? Seven minutes for somebody in one helluva rush? From Platform 2 to the taxi-rank? It'd only take a geriatric like me a couple of minutes.'

'Perhaps there was a queue.'

'*Was* there a queue?'

'Dunno. Perhaps he nipped into the snack-bar.'

'Closed.'

'I don't quite see what you're getting at.'

'What is essential, Lewis, is usually invisible to the outward eye.'

'Which doesn't help *me* much, does it?'

'All right. Get back to your facts.'

'She was burgled. At some point that evening the back patio window was smashed in from the outside and somebody was after something. The TV was unplugged – '

'But not taken.'

' – so he was probably disturbed. He must have thought the place was empty. Probably none of the lights would have been on – not then anyway. Midsummer, wasn't it? Sunset was about a quarter-past nine –

I looked it up.' (Morse nodded approvingly.) 'I know some people always leave one or two lights on anyway when they go out—'

'But she *didn't* go out.'

'No. So as I say the burglar must have thought the coast was clear, and must have been prepared for the alarm to ring – it's quite a way to the next house – while he grabbed a few of the valuables, smartish like.'

'The alarm was ringing when Harrison got there, wasn't it? Twenty-past eleven.'

Lewis nodded. 'Two hours or so after she was murdered.'

'And the alarm would cut out automatically after twenty minutes' ringing?'

'Yes.'

'So?'

'I dunno, sir. But it seems we didn't discount the theory that the murderer might have set it off himself.'

'You mean two hours *later*?'

'I don't know what I mean.'

'Pretty little puzzle.'

'You're not trying to help me, are you? You've usually got some theory or other of your own.'

Morse smiled amiably. 'The obvious one. Mrs H surprised a burglar and the burglar panicked and murdered her. Or perhaps . . .' (the smile had faded) '. . . perhaps she was entertaining one of her lovers that night and things went wrong – things went sadly wrong. That's all I've got to offer: the burglar theory and the lover theory. What else is there?'

'Maybe a bit of both, sir? Say she was in bed with

some fellow when she heard the window being smashed in and . . .'

'Could well be.'

'You see, she'd *not* had sex that night, sir – certainly not been raped or tortured or physically assaulted. Clothes all neatly folded by the side of the bed.'

'Couldn't the murderer have folded them? Doesn't take me long to fold a pair of pyjamas.'

Lewis shook his head slowly. 'Naked, gagged, handcuffed . . .'

'Yes,' agreed Morse. 'Don't forget the handcuffs.'

'Not much good remembering them, either.'

'No. I recall they were, er, not to be found later on.'

'But all the proper procedures were gone through. Left on her wrists till the PM, and the path people did all the usual checks – blood, fibres, hairs. Couldn't come up with anything though, could they? *And* they checked them for prints – job they'd normally leave to the SOCOs. Bit of a muddle, by the sound of it. Probably that's how they came to be lost.'

'Temporarily misplaced, Lewis.'

'Not the only things that went missing, were they? There was a file of personal letters . . .'

'I doubt they'd ever have been much help.'

'We still didn't do a very good job.'

'Bloody awful job.'

'If only we knew who rang Frank Harrison in London that night!'

'One of his children, the builder, the burglar, the lover, the candlestick-maker? I'm like you: I don't know. But unlike you I'm not concerned with the case.'

Lewis looked shrewdly into Morse's face. 'You're *interested* though, I think.'

Morse got to his feet. 'Just give me a lift down to Oddbins. I'm out of Glenfiddich.'

The phone rang as they were leaving.

'Morse?' (Strange's unmistakable voice.)

'Sir?'

'Listen to this!'

'Not me, sir. It just so happens that Sergeant Lewis—'

'MORSE!' But the receiver had already been transferred; and although aware of the explosions at the other end of the line, Morse walked out into the corridor and along to the Gentlemen's loo.

On his return, the telephone conversation had concluded.

'They've found a body. Out at Sutton Courtenay.'

'Just like I said.'

'No, sir. Not just like you said. *You* told the people there not to worry any more. It was *me* who told them to keep looking.'

'Well done! You were right and I was wrong. I *thought* Repp was due for his come-uppance, and probably he thought so too. But I just didn't follow it through. That letter he wrote from prison was a cry for help in a way, asking us to keep a protective eye on him. Which we did, of course. Or rather which we didn't.'

Suddenly he gave his chest a vigorous massage with his right hand.

'OK, sir?'

'Bit of indigestion.'

'You sure?'

'They've found the body, you say?'

'Half an hour ago.'

'You'd better get off then.'

'Will you come along?'

'Certainly not. I'm not worried about him any longer. He was a cheap crook, a part-time burglar, a nasty piece of work – should have been rumbled years ago. Good riddance, Harry Repp!'

Chapter Twenty-Seven

In the afternoon they came unto a land
In which it seemèd always afternoon,
All round the coast the languid air did swoon,
Breathing like one that hath a weary dream
(Tennyson, *The Lotos-eaters*)

After an excited, if somewhat dispirited, Lewis had dropped him off at Oddbins, Morse picked up two bottles of single-malt Glenfiddich ('£4 Off When Two Are Purchased'); then walked further down the Summertown shops to Boots, where he bought two large boxes of Alka-Seltzer (sixty tablets in all) and two packets of extra-strength BiSoDoL (sixty tablets in all), reckoning that such additional medicaments might keep him comparatively fit for a further fortnight. But in truth his acid-indigestion and heartburn were getting even worse. All right, it was a family affliction; but it gave little comfort to know that father and paternal grandfather had both endured agonies from hiatus hernia – a condition not desperately serious perhaps, but certainly far more painful than it sounded. The cure – so simple! – had been repeatedly advocated by his GP: 'Just pack up the booze!' And indeed Morse had occasionally followed such advice for a couple of days or so; only to assume, upon the temporary disappearance of the symptoms, that a permanent cure had been effected; and that a resumption of his erstwhile modus vivendi was thenceforth justified.

He would try again soon.

Not today, though.

He walked down South Parade to the Woodstock Road, turned right, and soon found himself at the Woodstock Arms, where the landlord rightly prided himself on a particularly fine pint of Morrell's Bitter – of which Morse took liberal advantage that early Saturday lunchtime. The printed menu and the chalked-up specials on the board were strong temptations to many a man. But not to Morse. These past two decades he had almost invariably taken his lunchtime calories in liquid form; and he did so now. Most of the habitués he knew by sight, if not by name; but after a few perfunctory nods he settled himself in a corner of the wall-seating, and thought of many things . . .

Instinctively (or so he told himself) he'd known that Harry Repp was doomed to die from the moment he'd left Bullingdon. Harry had known too much. Harry had been a bit-player – a bit more than a bit-player in the drama that had been enacted on the evening Yvonne Harrison was murdered. But Harry had decided to remain silent. And the reason for such silence was probably the reason for many a silence – money. Someone had ensured that Harry's discreet silence had been profitably rewarded. On his release Harry had probably decided that the goose could soon be persuaded to change the golden eggs from medium to large. But he'd miscalculated: something had happened – probably there'd been some communication during the last few weeks of his imprisonment – that had cast a cloud of fear over his impending release; justifiable fear, since he now lay stiff and cold amidst the trash and the filth of Sutton Courtenay.

It seemed a predictable outcome though far from an inevitable one, and Morse felt no real cause for any self-recrimination. Lewis would go along there – was probably there already; would join the SOCOs and supervise the necessary procedures; would draw a few tentative, temporary conclusions; would report to Strange; and all in all would probably do as good a job as any other member of the Thames Valley CID in seeking the motive for Repp's murder.

He ordered himself a third pint, conscious that the world seemed a considerably kindlier place than heretofore. He even found himself listening to the topics of conversation around him: darts, bar-billiards, Aunt Sally, push-penny . . . and perhaps (he thought) his own life might have been marginally enriched by such innocent divertissements.

Perhaps not, though.

Leaving the Woodstock Arms, he slowly walked the few hundred yards north to Squitchey Lane, where he turned right towards his bachelor flat.

No messages on the Ansafone; no letters or notes pushed through the letter-box. A free afternoon! – for which, in his believing days, he would have given thanks to the Almighty. His dark-blue Oxford University diary was beside the phone, and he looked through the following week's engagements. Not much there either, really: just that diabetes review at the Radcliffe

Infirmary at 9 a.m. on Monday. Only an hour or so that; but the imminent appointment disturbed him slightly. He had promised his consultant, and promised himself, that he would present a faithful record of his blood-sugar measurements over the previous fortnight. But he had failed to do so, and there was little he could now do to remedy the situation except to take half a dozen such measurements in the remaining interval of thirty-six hours and to extrapolate backwards therefrom, in order to present a neatly tabulated series of satisfactory readings. He'd done it before and he would do it again.

Kein Problem.

He half-filled a tumbler with Glenfiddich, then topped it up with commensurate tap-water. Such dilution (a recent innovation) would, as Morse knew, mark him out in the eyes of many a Scot as a sacrilegious Sassenach. But according to his GP, the liver preferred things that way; and Morse's liver (according to the same source) was in need of a bit of tender loving care, along with his heart, kidneys, stomach, pancreas, lungs.

Lungs . . .

Well, at least he'd finally managed to pack up smoking, a filthy habit, as he now recognized; but one which had given him almost as much pleasure as any other vice in life. And he knew that were he privy to the date and time of an early Judgement Day (the following Monday, say) he would set off immediately to the nearest newsagent's to buy in a store of cigarettes. And he almost did so now, as if he could already hear the trumpets sounding on the other side.

In the living room, he selected Bruno Walter's early recording of *Die Walküre*, with Lauritz Melchior and Lotte Lehmann singing the rôles of Siegmund and Sieglinde. Wonderful! So Morse turned the volume-control to maximum as he listened to the anagnorisis at the end of Act I, and heard neither of the telephone calls made to his ex-directory number that afternoon, conscious only that he was falling deliciously asleep as the benighted brother and sister rushed off into the forest to beget Siegfried . . .

It was coming up to 2.45 p.m. when Morse jerked abruptly awake, disappointed that his semi-erotic dream was prematurely terminated: a dream of a woman seated intimately close to him – a dream of Debbie Richardson, with legs provocatively crossed, the texture of the cheap black stockings tautly stretched along her upper thighs.

Wonderful!

But even as she'd leaned towards him, he'd voiced his deep anxiety: 'Aren't you frightened someone will come in?'

'No one'll come in. Harry won't be comin' back. Ever. I'll get you another drink. Just – stay – where – you – are.'

So Morse had stayed where he was, awaiting her return with impatience, and with an empty glass beside him. And when he awoke, he was still sitting there alone, awaiting her return with impatience, and with an empty glass beside him.

Wagner had long since run his course, and finally Morse got to his feet and turned off the CD player. He felt tired, hot, thirsty – and a sharp pain in his chest betokened another bout of indigestion. In the bathroom, he cleaned his teeth and dropped three Alka-Seltzer tablets into a glass of water; then he filled up the wash-basin and thrice dipped his head into the cold water. The tablets had fizzed and dissolved and he downed the dosage at a single draught. Thence to his bedroom, where he took his blood-sugar level: 24.8 – almost off the scale. His own fault, since he'd forgotten to inject himself at lunchtime – making up for it now, though, with an extra four units of Actrapid insulin. Just to be on the safe side. Back in the bathroom, he drank two further glasses of cold water, acknowledging how surprisingly pleasing was its taste, since water had seldom figured prominently in his drinking habits. Finally he decided that a couple of Paracetamol would be appropriate. So he shook out the tablets on to his palm; shook out three in fact – and decided to take the three. Just to be on the safe side.

Suddenly he was feeling much better, his faith in this curious combination of assorted medicaments seemingly justified once more. Suddenly, too, he decided to follow his consultant's somewhat despairing exhortation to take a bit of exercise occasionally. Why not? It was a warm and gentle summer's day.

In the small entrance hall, he noticed the figure '2' on the window of his Ansafone. Pressing 'Play' he listened to the first message:

Morse? Janet! Ten-past one Saturday afternoon. Good news! I hope to be back in Oxford on the 14th. So you'll be able to take me somewhere? To bed perhaps? Give me a ring – soon. Bye!

Any semi-remembrance of Debbie Richardson was lingering no longer, and Morse smiled happily to himself. He would ring immediately. But the second message had followed without a pause, and he was destined not to ring Sister McQueen that afternoon.

Instead he dialled HQ and finally got through to the young PC who had driven him out to Bullingdon the previous morning in an unmarked police car.

'Get the same car, Kershaw – nice, comfy seats – and pick me up from home *quam celerrime*.'

'Pardon?'

'Smartish!'

'Sir, I was just going off duty when you rang and I've—'

'Make it five minutes!'

Deeply puzzled, Morse walked back into the sitting-room where he sat in the black-leather armchair; and where his right hand reached for whisky once more as mentally he rehearsed that second, quite extraordinary message on the Ansafone:

Sir? Lewis here – half-past one, nearly – I'm out at Sutton Courtenay. Please come along as soon as you can – for my sake if nobody else's. I think you should get here before we move the body. You see, sir, it isn't the body of Harry Repp.

Chapter Twenty-Eight

Alas, poor Yorick! – I knew him, Horatio
(Shakespeare, *Hamlet*)

It was just after 4 p.m. that same Saturday afternoon when Morse and Lewis finally sat down together in the requisitioned office of the site manager.

'Straightaway I knew it wasn't him, sir, when I saw his arms. Harry Repp had this tattoo: all twisted chains and anchors, you know – a sort of . . .' Lewis undulated his hands vertically, as if tracing a woman's willowy figure.

'Convoluted involvement,' suggested Morse gently.

'Well, this fellow's not got any, has he? Anyway he's much smaller, only – what? – five-four, five-five. Doesn't weigh much either – eight, nine stone? No more.'

Morse nodded. 'And he's got different coloured hair, and he's got a port-wine stain on his neck, and he's not wearing Repp's clothes, and his shoes are three sizes smaller—'

'All right. I wasn't expecting the Queen's Medal!'

At which Eddie Andrews, the 2i/c senior SOCO, knocked on the door and entered the office, at once uncertain whether to address himself to Morse or to Lewis. He decided on the former:

'Safe, I reckon, to move him now? Dr Hobson says there's not much else she can do here.'

Morse shrugged. 'You'd better ask Sergeant Lewis. He's in charge.'

And Lewis rose to the occasion. 'Yes, move him. Thank you.'

As he was about to leave, Andrews noticed the TV set.

'Mind if I just see how Northants are getting on in the cricket?'

'Important to you, is it?' queried Morse mildly.

Andrews was digitally discovering Sport (Cricket) on Ceefax when the office door burst open to admit a florid-faced Chief Superintendent Strange, an officer resolutely determined to retain the appellation 'Chief', whatever most of his collateral colleagues in the Force were doing.

'You've ruined my afternoon's golf, Lewis! You know that?'

Surprisingly, the words were spoken with little sign of animus. But before Lewis could respond in any way, Strange was addressing Morse in considerably sharper tones:

'And how exactly do *you* come to be here?'

'Same as you really, sir. Ruined my day, too. I was just indulging in a little Egyptian PT – '

'After indulging in a lot of Scottish whisky by the smell of it!'

' – when Lewis here rang and asked me to come along. Well, he's been a faithful soul most of the time, so . . .'

'So you just came along as a sort of personal favour?'

'That's about it.' (Andrews sidled silently from the room.)

'Well let me tell you one thing, matey. You won't be staying *on* as a personal favour – is that clear? You'll be staying on because you're in charge of *this* case – because that's an *order*. You may have had some excuse as far as the Harrison case was concerned: I could just about understand that.' (Strange's voice had momentarily dropped to a semi-sympathetic register.) 'But you've no bloody excuse now. And if you decide to get on your high horse again and start arguing the toss with me, you'll be up before the Chief Constable first thing Monday morning!'

'The Chief's on furlough,' interposed a brave Lewis.

'Shut up, Lewis! And he'll have your guts for garters, Morse. So that's settled. All you've got to do is sober up and put your thinking-cap on.'

'I usually think better when—' But Morse's disquisition on his personal style of ratiocination was cut short by a further knock, with Dr Hobson's pretty head appearing round the door.

'Oh, sorry! It's just—'

'Come in!' growled Strange, his jowls still wobbling.

'Just thought I'd check. We've got him outside and Andrews says it's OK if—'

'Who *is* he?' asked Strange.

'Don't know. I had a tentative feel round his pockets. No wallet, though, no cards—'

'He's pretty easily recognizable though?'

'Oh, yes. His face is fine. It's his stomach that's all a gory mess where the knife or whatever it was went in.'

'At least we've got a good mug-shot of him then.'

'Probably identify him straightaway. I got this from his trouser-pocket.'

Strange looked down at a white 'Cardholder's Copy' receipt from Oddbins of Banbury Road, itemizing the purchase of a crate of Guinness, the number of the Visa credit card printed below in a faded indigo.

'There we are, Lewis! Shouldn't be too difficult, should it?' He handed over the receipt with an unconvincing smile. 'Unless you manage to lose *that*, of course.'

It was a hurtful dig. But the patient Lewis briefly examined the evidence himself, and sought to put a finger on the fairly obvious:

'Not much chance this afternoon, sir. Saturday? The banks'll all be shut.'

'What? For Christ's sake, man! We've put someone on the moon, remember? And you say we can't trace a credit-card number because it's a bloody *Saturday*! Is that what you're telling me?'

Morse had remained silent during these exchanges; and remained so now, his brain already galloping several furlongs ahead of the field. And Lewis, after such a withering rebuke, also remained silent, holding the receipt tightly, like a punter clutching a winning betting-slip. Only Strange, it appeared, was willing to break the awkward silence as he turned again to Dr Hobson.

'They're just carting him off, you say?'

'Yes.'

'Well, let us know – let Chief Inspector Morse know – what you come up with. Sooner the quicker. Understood?'

'Of course.'

The assembled personages rose to their feet; and matters at Sutton Courtenay were seemingly now at an end.

But not so; not quite.

It was Morse, at last, who made his brief though extraordinarily significant contribution to the afternoon's developments.

'Sir, I think you ought to have a look at him.'

'I don't like dead bodies any more than you do, Morse.'

'I know that, but . . .'

'But *what*?'

'. . . but you ought to have a look at him.' Morse spoke his words slowly and quietly. 'You see, I think it's quite possible that you'll recognize him.'

Frequently afterwards, in the post-Morse years, would Sergeant Lewis recall that afternoon at the fill-in site in Oxfordshire: when Chief Superintendent Strange had looked at the bloodless face of a murdered man; and when his erstwhile ruddy cheeks had paled to chalky white.

'Bloody 'ell! I knew him, Morse. I interviewed him twice in the Harrison murder enquiry.'

When the top brass had finally dispersed, Eddie

Andrews let himself back into the now deserted office, turned on the TV, found Sport (Cricket) on Ceefax and noted with quiet satisfaction that Northamptonshire were really doing rather well that day.

Chapter Twenty-Nine

Caliph:	And now how shall we employ the time of waiting for our deliverance?
Jafar:	I shall meditate upon the mutability of human affairs
Masrur:	And I shall sharpen my sword upon my thigh
Hassan:	And I shall study the pattern of this carpet
Caliph:	Hassan, I will join thee: Thou art a man of taste

(James Elroy Flecker, *Hassan*)

Most patiently – no, most impatiently – had PC Kershaw been waiting for his passenger to emerge from the closeted consultations. Like some starry-eyed teenager he had been looking forward so much to his first date with Susan Ho, a delightful, delicately featured Chinese girl, a researcher at Oxford's Criminological Department; and although he had been able to contact her after Morse's diktat, neither he nor she had been particularly pleased.

He opened the passenger door as Morse approached.

'It's all right, Kershaw. Sergeant Lewis'll be taking me back to Oxford.'

'You mean—?'

'I mean you can bugger off, yes.'

'Couldn't you have told me earlier, sir? I've been . . .'

But his voice trailed off as he found Morse's blue eyes looking straight at him; uncomprehending, cold.

Lewis was grinning wryly as he pushed the police car into first gear. 'You never treated even me as bad as that.'

'Cocky young sod! University graduate, God help us!'

'What's he doing with us?'

'Dunno. Learning how to make a cup o' tea, I shouldn't wonder.'

'Exactly where I started.'

'I hope he's better than you were.'

'Isn't it about time you told—'

'I just don't believe this!' said Morse as he picked up the single cassette that lay in the tray beside the gear-lever, inserted it into the player, and subsequently sank back into his seat with the look of a man sublimely satisfied with life.

'Just find out who usually drives this car, Lewis. He's a man after my own heart. I never realized we had such sensitivity in the Force. There's not much of it out there, you know.'

For a moment it seemed that Lewis was going to speak. But clearly he thought better of it; and as he drove way above the speed limit down the A34 to Oxford, he listened, with considerable enjoyment himself, to the Prelude to Wagner's *Parsifal*, convinced that Morse was soundly albeit unsnoringly asleep.

'Turn off here, Lewis.'

'Next exit's best, sir – avoid the city traffic that way.'

'Turn off *here*!'

So Lewis turned off there, driving sedately now, up the Abingdon Road, past Christ Church, straight over through Cornmarket and Magdalen Street, where (as bidden) he turned left at the lights by the Martyrs' Memorial and duly stopped (as bidden) on the double-yellows beneath the canopy of the Randolph, above which the Union Jack and the flag of the EC drooped languorously that late afternoon.

Lewis was still in brave mood. 'Like the Super said, don't you think you ought—'

'*Think*? That's exactly why I'm here – to think! I can't think unless I'm given the chance to think. You don't imagine I drink just for the *pleasure* of it, do you?'

Morse sat back with his pint of bitter and stared serenely at the Ashmolean Museum just opposite in Beaumont Street. 'If there's a bar anywhere in Britain with a better view than this . . .'

Lewis hesitated awhile over his orange juice. 'You ready to tell me how you knew it was Paddy Flynn?'

'I didn't really *know*. Just that I always wondered about him a bit. Key witness, agreed? Picked up Frank Harrison from the railway station, then parked outside the house just when the burglar alarm was ringing.'

Lewis nodded. 'Only person to give Harrison a convincing alibi.'

It was Morse's turn to nod. 'That's why Strange interviewed him.'

'Interviewed him twice.'

'Suspicious mind, that man's got!'

'But you're still not telling me how you guessed it was *him*.'

'Full of guesses, what we do, isn't it? After the first couple of days, I only read about the case at second hand – '

'Like me.'

' – but I remember thinking I'd have put an each-way bet on some of the outsiders in the race: the builder – he gave himself and several others an alibi; the landlord at the Maiden's Arms – he's got the testosterone level of a randy billy-goat; and then there was the taxi driver . . .'

'Why *him*, though?'

'Put yourself in his position. You pick up your fare outside the station and drive him out to Lower Swinstead; and there you're asked if you want to earn a bit – a lot – of extra money. You don't really have to do much at all. Fellow says he's going into the house – *his* house, anyway – and the burglar alarm is going to ring. All you've got to do is to say, if you're questioned about things, that you heard the alarm ringing while you were parked outside. Not too difficult? The alarm *was* ringing by then. And you're offered – what? I dunno – twenty or thirty quid, two or three hundred quid? But the key point is that Flynn never fully realized how vital his testimony was going to be.'

'Are you making it all up?'

'Yes! So allow me to continue making it all up. Flynn's got little idea of why he's getting such a bonus for doing virtually bugger-all. But then he starts to read a few press-reports; and unlike our boys he puts two and two together, and he smiles to himself because he knows the answer. And pretty soon he realizes he's sold himself stupidly cheap, and he decides he'll balance the books a bit better.'

'Are you saying what I think you're saying? He's been trying to blackmail Frank Harrison?'

Morse drained his pint. 'Not sure. But I'd like to bet that someone that night was more than ready to pay his way out of trouble.'

'Or her way.'

'Could be, yes.' Morse contemplated an empty glass. 'Is it your round or mine, by the way?'

'Yours.'

Morse consulted his wristwatch. 'Good gracious me! Time you drove me home. I need a shot of insulin, Lewis. You should've reminded me.'

'You still haven't told me why you thought it was Flynn,' complained Lewis as he drove north through the Summertown shopping area.

'Small man – that's why.'

'So's the landlord of the Maiden's Arms.'

'Ah, but Flynn was very fond of Guinness.'

'What the hell's *that* got to do with anything?'

'I forget. I'm, er, I'm getting muddled.'

Lewis pulled up outside Morse's flat.

'Anything . . . anything I can do for you, sir?'

'Certainly not. It's just that I'm beginning to feel exquisitely sleepy, that's all. The day's still comparatively young, I grant you. But don't ring me – not tonight – not unless anything dramatic happens.'

'You mean' (Lewis's heart rose within him) 'you mean you *are* going to take on the case?'

'Different ball-game, isn't it? As they say in Chicago or somewhere.'

'Shall I let the Super know?'

'I've already told him – when we were at the rubbish tip.'

Lewis shook his head in benign bewilderment as Morse made to get out of the car.

'And I'll take possession of this – just temporarily, of course. And if you can find out whose it is . . .'

He pocketed the *Parsifal* cassette and was walking towards his front door when Lewis wound down the car window.

'You can keep it as long as you like, sir. But let me have it back when you've finished with it. They said at Blackwell's it's the top recording – by a fellow called Napperbush.'

'You mean . . .?'

Lewis nodded happily.

'Thou art a man of taste.'

'I thought you'd be pleased, sir.'

'By the way, Lewis, we pronounce him "K-napper-t-s-busch",' amended the Chief Inspector, pedantically separating the consonantal clusters.

Chapter Thirty

> Often would the deaf man know the answers had he but the faculty of hearing the questions. Likewise would the unimaginative man guess wisely at the answers had he but the wit of posing to himself the appropriate questions
>
> (Viscount Mumbles, from *Essays on the Imagination*)

As Lewis drove up to HQ, one particular thought was troubling him – as it often had: the marked inferiority of his own mental processes compared with those of the man he had just left; the man who was doubtless now sleeping off the effects of what had been (even for Morse) a hyper-alcoholic afternoon. It wasn't that his own processes were necessarily all that much slower; just that they seemed always to leave the starting-blocks way after Morse had sprinted on ahead. Obviously (Lewis knew it!) innate intelligence was a big factor in everything: the speed of perception and understanding, the analysis of data, the linkage of things. But there was something else: the knack of *prospective* thinking, of looking ahead and asking oneself the right questions, as well as the wrong questions, about what was likely to happen in the future; and then of coming up with some answers, be they right or wrong.

So frequently in previous cases had Morse led him along, and by prompting the right questions evinced the right sort of answers. 'Socratic dialectic', Morse had called it, recounting how Socrates had managed to elicit from a totally untutored slave-boy the basic principles of plane geometry – just by asking the right questions.

So.

So, in his office that early evening, Lewis visualized himself seated opposite Morse – opposite Socrates, rather.

You've got to find the car, haven't you? The car that dumped the body? Where will you find it?

I don't know.

Where would you *have driven that car?*

I don't know. Anywhere, I suppose.

Isn't there blood everywhere? Blood all over your clothes?

Yes.

Haven't you got to change your clothes then?

Yes.

So you couldn't just leave the car anywhere, *could you? You couldn't walk too far all covered in blood?*

No.

So where would you go?

I'd go home, like as not.

Before, or after, you'd ditched the car?

Before, probably, although . . .

Go on!

Might be a bit risky. Neighbours would probably

notice the strange car. Might even notice the blood-stained clothes.

What's the alternative for you?

Well, get someone to meet me somewhere and bring me a full change of clothes.

Where would you meet?

Anywhere. How do I know. Except . . .

Go on!

If we met in a lay-by, say, I'd have to leave the car there, wouldn't I? I couldn't get back in and get the new clothes almost as blood-stained as the old. And the car would pretty certainly get reported almost immediately. So . . .

So?

So I'd have somebody to meet me. Friend? Wife, perhaps?

Where do you meet?

I don't know.

You do *know. You know the Chesterton story – I've often mentioned it.*

Remind me.

Where do you hide a leaf?

Ah, yes. In the forest.

Where do you hide a pebble?

On the shore.

Where do you hide a corpse?

On the battle-field.

And where do you hide a car?

In a car park.

Which car park?

I don't know.

The bigger the better?

Yes.

In Oxford?

Probably.

How many car parks are there in Oxford?

Dozens.

If you'd committed a murder near Oxford what would you want to do above all?

Get the hell out of the place.

How?

Drive away.

You haven't got a car now, have you?

Bus?

Where's the bus station?

Gloucester Green.

Isn't there a car park opposite?

Yes.

And you could catch a train?

Yes.

Isn't there a station car park opposite?

Yes . . .

As he drove down towards Oxford, Lewis felt pleased with himself, and just after he'd negotiated the Cutteslowe roundabout he was tempted to call in on Morse. But he put the temptation behind him. He felt fairly certain that the great man would be asleep.

And on this occasion he was right.

Instead, he decided to continue the Socratic dialogue, though this time installing *himself* as Chief

Inquisitor, and making the far bolder hypothesis that if only the blurred outlines of the anonymous murderer could be adjusted more sharply, it was Harry Repp who would come into focus.

Don't you think it would be easier, sir, for Debbie Richardson to take a change of clothes to *him*? Wouldn't it be dangerous for him to go out to Lower Swinstead?

I don't know, Lewis.

I asked you *two* questions.

I don't know. I don't know.

What do *you* think Harry Repp did?

I just don't know.

What about the car? Where's that? Come on! Back your hunch!

The car? Oh, I know where the car is, Lewis. It's parked at the back of Oxford Railway Station.

Chapter Thirty-One

His voice was angry: 'What time do you call *this*?'

She stood penitently on the doorstep: 'Sorry!'

'Where've you parked?' (It was the decade's commonest question in Oxford.)

'*Exactly*. I just couldn't find a parking space anywhere.'

(Terry Benczik, *Still Life with Absinthe*)

Lucky Lewis!

He was walking up the steps to the station when the automatic doors opened in front of him, and Sergeant Dick Evans of the British Transport Police came towards him. Old friends, they greeted each other with appropriate cordiality.

'Know anything about a stolen car – R456 LJB?'

'Parked here?'

'Dunno,' Lewis admitted.

'Well, not as far as I know. I've been in Reading all day, though. Just got back. Bob Mitchell'd know, perhaps. He's on duty here.'

'I'd better go and wake him up then.'

'He's not in the office. I looked in a couple of minutes ago – door's locked. Probably called out on some trouble somewhere. Saturday! Football yobbos and all that.'

'But it's not the football season,' protested Lewis.

'What's that got to do with it?'

'You straight off home?'

'Well, yes. It's getting late. If I can do anything to help an old mucker though . . . What's the trouble?'

Lewis told him; and the two men walked down the steps and across to the station car park.

It had been more than a year since Lewis had visited the station complex; and he was immediately surprised to find that the previously fairly extensive car-parking space had been drastically reduced: the northern section had been taken over by 'Another Prestigious Development' – a series of Victorian-style town-houses, built in attractive terra-cotta bricks, with white stuccoed lower storeys; 'spacious and luxurious' as the site-board guaranteed.

'Year or two back,' volunteered Evans, 'I'd've parked up there if I'd wanted to keep out of sight for a while. Used to be a bit dark and creepy late at night, if you got back late from Paddington on the milk float.'

Lewis nodded, but without comment. Late-night returns from concerts and operas in the capital had never figured large in the lifestyle of the Lewises. But now, in sunny daylight, the area seemed wholly benign, and still almost packed with cars marshalled there in semi-legitimate rows.

'What if you come,' asked Lewis, 'and you just can't find a space?'

'Not easy, is it? You can always try Gloucester Green' (Evans pointed vaguely across towards Hythe Bridge Street) 'or one of the side roads.'

The two sergeants walked together to the northern area of the park, away from the main road where, with any choice in the matter, any murderous villain (as well as Sergeant Evans) would surely have headed with an incriminating car. But things had changed. Parading the site, tall stanchions now stood there, topped with video-cameras and floodlights. No guarantee of complete security perhaps, but a sufficient deterrent for casual car thieves.

'You could still squeeze one or two more cars in?' suggested Lewis (himself a wizard at vehicular manoeuvring) pointing to a few square metres amid heaps of sand and piles of jagged half-bricks and broken tiles.

'Not if you're worried about your suspension.'

'Which he wasn't, Dick.'

'No sign of it though, is there?'

They walked systematically through the lines of cars down to the southern end of the car park, bounded by the Botley Road.

Again, nothing.

And the questions that had already worried Morse were worrying his sergeant now. *Was* there any sign of criminal activity here? Were they on some profitless pursuit of a questionable quarry?

Morse!

Top-of-the-head Morse!

Things just didn't happen like that.

At bottom, any police investigation was a matter of pretty firm facts; of accumulating such facts; and of aggregating them into a hard core of evidence, on which suspicion could be progressively corroborated, until an arrest could be made, a charge brought, a prosecution formulated, and finally a case heard in a court of law. That's how things happened.

A dispirited Lewis stood with Evans for only a few seconds longer before walking up to the exit-booth, where a red-and-white striped barrier was being intermittently raised as a few patrons returning early to Oxford inserted their parking-tokens, and where a uniformed Transport Policeman, clearly not at the peak of physical condition, came running towards them:

'What the 'ell are you doing here, Dick?'

'Just back from Reading, Bob. And what the 'ell's up with you? You know Sergeant Lewis here from HQ?'

Mitchell had regained some of his breath. 'HQ? Huh! That's exactly what's up. Chap who said he was from HQ. Rang about a car – said it was parked here at the station . . .'

Evans finished the sentence for him. 'But it wasn't.'

'No. But I thought I'd look around a bit. This chap'd sounded pretty positive, like. So I went over to Gloucester Green – and Bingo! Just behind the Irish pub there.'

'You've got this chap's number?' asked Lewis.

'In the office, yes. He said he couldn't get here himself. Said he was tired. Huh!'

'He must have given his name?'

' "Moss", I think it was. Look, I'll just . . .'

A temporarily rejuvenated Mitchell was bounding

up the station steps three at a time as Evans turned to Lewis:

'Reckon he misheard a bit.'

'Just a bit,' said Lewis, with quiet resignation.

Chapter Thirty-Two

Should any young or old officer experience incipient or actual signs of vomiting at the sight of some particularly harrowing scene of crime the said person should not necessarily attribute such nausea to some psychological vulnerability, but rather to the virtually universal reflex-reactions of the upper intestine

(*The SOCO Handbook*, Revised 1999)

Barry Edwards was another of the SOCO personnel called out that busy Saturday. In fact, simply because he lived only a short distance away along the Botley Road, he was the first of the team to arrive at the scene of the crime. A well-set, dark-haired man in his late twenties, he had a pair of diffident brown eyes that seemed to some of his colleagues strangely naive, as if he would ever be surprised by the scenes that would inevitably confront him in his new career.

His SOCO training had been completed only a few months previously, and now he was a fully fledged (civilian) officer, employed by the Thames Valley Police. Furthermore, thus far, he was enjoying his job. After leaving school, with a comparatively successful performance in the comparatively undemanding field of GCSE, he had worked as a supermarket shelf-filler, hospital porter, barman, and ironmonger's shop-assistant, before finally completing a police recruitment questionnaire and duly learning of the opportunities in his present profession. He had taken his chance; and he was enjoying his choice. He felt quite important sometimes, especially when he dealt off his own bat with some fairly minor affair, when (as he knew) he *was* important. And he'd looked forward to the time when he would be called out to a big job, to some major incident. Like murder. Like now – as he sensed immediately when he drove his van into the Gloucester Green Car Park. The full complement of the team would have been called in, and almost certainly he would witness, for the first time, the operation of those basic principles – preservation of the scene, continuity and non-contamination of evidence – which had guided his training in photography, fingerprinting, forensic labelling, and the meticulous procedure vital to all in-situ investigations.

Edwards had introduced himself immediately to the plain-clothed Sergeant Lewis, obviously the man in charge: yet perhaps only temporarily in charge, since (as Edwards guessed) it would only be a matter of time before some more senior-ranking officer would put in an appearance – just as he himself was awaiting Bill Flowers, the senior SOCO, a man who had seen everything in life. As he, Barry Edwards, hadn't. Not yet. For the moment, however, the appropriate procedure had been applied, with blue-and-white police ribbon cordoning off an area containing three cars, noses all to the wall: R 456 LJB; to its left, a grey H-Reg Citroën; to its right a dark-blue P-Reg Rover – the owner of the latter (just arrived) making a statement to one of two uniformed PCs summoned from the St Aldate's Station. No effort had as yet been made to disperse the growing band of curious onlookers who stood in silent, hopeful expectation of some gruesome discovery. Things were happening, though. Flowers arrived just before the other two SOCOs; and soon everything would be ready, once they got the word from someone. Doubtless the same someone awaited by Sergeant Lewis, the latter a man with 'under authority' written all over his honest and slightly worried features.

But there was a frustrating twenty-minute wait before the 'authority' put in his appearance, stepping from the back of a marked police car with a marked unsuppleness of limb, the slate-grey suit decidedly rumpled, the tell-tale crease around the waistband betokening an increase in girth over recent months. A white-haired man, of medium height, his face of a pale-olive colour, as if perhaps he had spent a holiday of less than uninterrupted sunshine in Torremolinos, or was suffering from incipient jaundice. But his voice was that of someone who demanded immediate attention – like another voice that Edwards once had known, that of his old Latin master.

Vox auctoritatis.

Lewis had approached the newcomer, and the two were in brief conversation before coming over to the others. Chief Inspector Morse (for such was he) appeared to recognize the other SOCOs, and nodded briefly as he was introduced to the youngest member of the team.

'Hello, Edwards!' He'd said nothing more, and Edwards gathered that the Chief Inspector was not a convert to the currently widespread practice of everyone addressing everyone – superiors, equals, and subordinates alike – by their Christian names. Yet he seemed a pleasant enough fellow, now surveying the scene with a keen if somewhat melancholy eye, while the SOCO team began to put on their green boilersuits and overboots.

'Anyone touched anything?'

'No more than we needed to, sir.' (It was Lewis who replied.)

Morse looked again at the car for some lingering while – the car he'd followed when Harry Repp had turned his back on Bullingdon. Then he lifted his eyes, and looked, again for some lingering while, at the pub sign of the Rosie O'Grady.

Bill Flowers was standing beside him.

'All yours!' pronounced Morse.

'Car's locked.'

'How do you know?'

'Door catches all in the locked position.'

Morse pressed a hand down on the nearside front handle.

'Don't—!' But Flowers checked his admonition in mid-voice.

'You're right. Any of your lads here ever a juvenile car thief?'

'I know somebody who was.'

'Where's he live?'

'Silverstone.'

Morse turned to Lewis. 'Give Johnson a ring.'

'Know his number?'

'Saturday afternoon? He'll be in the Summertown bookie's.'

'It's long gone afternoon, sir.'

'Ah!'

'There'll be a Local Directory in the pub.'

'You won't find him listed. They've cut his phone off.'

'So how—?'

'He'll be in the Dew Drop if he's won a few quid.'

'Perhaps he's not won a few quid.'

'He'll still be in the Dew Drop.'

'Do you know the number?'

'Get me a mobile!' snapped Morse.

Edwards watched as Morse turned his back on his colleagues, tapped out a number, and spoke *sotto voce* into the mouthpiece for a while, before blasting out *fortissimo*:

'Well, just tell him to get here on the bloody *bus* and get here bloody *quick*!'

Yet this order was not obeyed with either accuracy or immediacy, since there was a further twenty-minute wait before a rusting A-Reg Ford pulled up on the main road outside the Rosie O'Grady, whence emerged from the passenger seat a sparely built, nondescript man, in his late forties, a self-rolled cigarette dangling from a thin mouth that even from a few yards exuded the reek of strong, excessive alcohol.

'Mr Morse?'

The latter pointed to the car.

'Fee, is there?'

'Just open it, Malcolm!' (Edwards was surprised with the Christian-name address.)

The key-wizard made no further remonstration as he winched a bunch of skeleton-keys and bits of wire from his right-hand trouser-pocket. Then, turning his back on his expectant audience, he surveyed the problem synoptically. Like Capablanca contemplating his next move in the World Chess Championship.

'It's central-locking,' volunteered Flowers.

But Johnson said nothing, responding only for a semi-second with a look of contemptuous ingratitude.

As far as Edwards could make out, Morse had enjoyed that moment, since more than a semi-smile formed around his mouth when fifteen seconds later there was a quiet 'clunk' as the catches on the four doors sprang upwards in simultaneous freedom.

R456 LJB was open for inspection.

After pulling on a pair of green-latex gloves, Flowers now opened the two offside doors; and Morse glanced over the front seats, before contemplating for a good deal longer the darkly glutinous covering of blood that stained the seats and flooring in the back. With a softly spoken 'OK', he was walking away towards the Rosie O'Grady when Johnson tapped him on the shoulder.

'You mentioned expenses, Mr Morse?'

'I did. You're right.'

'Well, there's that taxi I came in – eight quid – two quid tip – ten quid – here and back. Twenny, I make that.'

'Since when's Snotty Joe been running a taxi business?'

'Well, you know, more a sort of . . . private hire, like.'

Morse felt in his pockets and pulled out a handful of coins. '85p, isn't it, the bus fare to St Giles'? And, you're right, you've got to get back.'

He handed Johnson two £1 coins. 'Keep the change. You can buy a copy of *The Times* to read on the ride back.'

'Wrong, aincha, Mr Morse! *Times* is 50p Sat'days.'

Unsmiling, Morse handed over a further 20p, and the pair parted without any further word. And Edwards, who had witnessed the brief scene, found himself wondering what exactly were the favours each had bestowed upon the other in the prosecution and pursuance of crime in North Oxford over recent years.

Morse was a few steps ahead of Lewis as he made his way to the pub entrance. 'We'd better leave 'em for half an hour or so. They won't want us breathing down their necks . . . By the way, you'd better lend me a fiver, Lewis. I've just parted with the only—'

Morse stopped. Turned round. Stepped back to the scene of the crime. Ordered Flowers to open the boot.

Not himself knowing the identity of the body he now saw curled up in foetal configuration there, young Edwards was to remember that particular moment with an oddly inappropriate sense of gratitude, for he saw the colour of Morse's cheeks fade by swiftly developing degrees from dingy yellow to sickly white, and watched as of a sudden the great man turned away and vomited violently over the recently renovated tarmac. It was like a fledgling actor appearing on stage with Sir John Gielgud and seeing *that* great man fluffing the friendliest of lines in rehearsal, and thereby giving some unexpected encouragement to the rest of the cast, all of them now less terrified of fluffing their own.

Chapter Thirty-Three

For the good are always the merry,
Save by an evil chance,
And the merry love the fiddle,
And the merry love to dance:

And when the folk there spy me,
They will all come up to me,
With 'Here is the fiddler of Dooney!'
And dance like a wave of the sea.

(W. B. Yeats,
The Fiddler of Dooney)

Morse, after disappearing into the Gents for several long minutes, now sat looking slightly more his wonted self as he sank his nose into the deep head on the Guinness.

'Just the stuff if you've got a foul taste in the throat!'

Giving his chief a little while to recover some measure of dignity, Lewis gazed around him. Everything was wooden there: the bar, the wall-settles, the floor, the table at which they sat – all good solid if somewhat battered wood, with any once-applied stain long since worn off. The walls and ceilings had originally been painted in yellow and orange, but now were coated over with the nicotine of countless cigarettes. The friezes of the walls were adorned with the dicta of several great Irishmen, their words attractively set in black-lettered Gaelic script. One in particular had already caught Lewis's eye:

> *Where is the use of calling it a lend*
> *when I know I will never see it again?*

Good question! But a question not so pressing as the one he now put to Morse:

'Was it a surprise to you?'

'Was *what* a surprise?'

'Finding Harry Repp's body in the boot?'

Morse nodded as he wiped away a white moustache.

'This morning I thought I had a fair idea about what we were dealing with. But now that I'm perfectly sure that I've none . . .' He pointed up at the wall to their right. 'Bit like Oscar Wilde, really.'

Lewis looked up at the words written there:

> *I was working on the proof of my poems all this morning and took out a comma. In the afternoon I put it back again.*

For Lewis it was a sombre moment and he sipped his orange juice with little joy; even less joy as he saw the outline of Chief Superintendent Strange looming large in the doorway, then waddling awkwardly to their table, where he sat down, wiping his moistened brow with a vast handkerchief.

'Pretty kettle o' fish you've got us into now, Morse!'

Then, turning to Lewis: 'You in the chair?'

'Well—'

'Good! Good man! I'll have the same as the Chief Inspector here.'

'Pint, sir?'

'The *same* as the Chief Inspector – that's what I said, Sergeant.'

Lewis repaired to the bar once more and listened to the comparatively quiet background music that was as Irish as the pub was Irish, all flutes and fiddles, and wondered how long Morse would stick the noise before calling for a few less decibels.

After taking a deep draught, Strange turned to Morse. 'You do realize, don't you, that you and Lewis have dragged me away from the golf course twice!'

'I'd've thought you'd be glad, especially if you were losing.'

Strange grinned wryly. 'I don't often win these days, you're right.'

'None of us gets much better as we get older.'

'Only two things we can be sure of, Morse – death and taxes. Some US President said that.'

'Benjamin Franklin,' supplied Lewis, to whom each of the two senior officers turned with some surprise, though without enquiry into the provenance of such splendid knowledge.

'What do you make of all this?' continued Strange quietly.

Morse shook his head. 'You may have been having a lousy round of golf. I was having a lovely sleep myself.'

'That's no answer.'

'Dr Hobson'll be here soon.'

'Already here.'

'Nothing we can do till we get some reports, results of the post-mortems—'

'Somebody once told me the plural should be post-mortes.'

'Bloody pedant!'

'It was *you* actually, Morse.'

'Ah!'

'You've got a good team of SOCOs.'

Morse nodded. 'So we'll wait to hear about all the bits and bobs they'll be bagging up and labelling and sending off to forensics. And all the fingerprints they'll be taking from windows and side-mirrors and body-work and seat-belt buckles and cassettes and . . .' Morse had run out of potential surfaces.

'That's it!' Strange sounded somewhat heartened. 'All you've got to do is eliminate ninety-five per cent of the dabs, and then you've got your man.'

'Unless he was wearing gloves,' suggested Lewis.

'It's all tied up with that bloody Lower Swinstead business!' blurted out Strange.

'You're probably right,' said Morse.

'And don't forget the simplest answer is usually the correct answer! Spur o' the moment stuff, most homicides. You know that.'

'Perhaps so,' admitted Morse, beckoning the landlord over. 'Open all day?'

'All night too should you wish it, sorr.'

And yes, of course the police could make use of one of the bars for the evening; of course the police could make use of whatever the Rosie O'Grady had to offer: telephone, washing and toilet facilities, bar facilities . . .

'And perhaps . . . ?' The landlord pointed to the two empty glasses. 'On the house – the pleasure's all mine.'

'Well, perhaps, er . . .' said Strange.

'You're twisting my arm,' said Morse.

'Make it *three* pints of Guinness,' said Lewis.

Morse glanced across at his sergeant with a look of astonishment; the landlord departed; and Strange got down to business.

'Logistics, Morse. Let's talk logistics. How many men do you want?'

'If you gave me a hundred, I wouldn't know what to do with one of them – not yet.'

'Now come off it, matey! Couldn't you perhaps have a look at when and how and what and why your bloody corpses were doing? See their relatives, friends, enemies, wives, for God's sake?'

'Flynn hadn't got a wife,' interposed Lewis.

'*Repp* had!'

'No, sir,' corrected Lewis bravely. 'He'd got a partner—'

'Well go and see *her*!' snapped Strange.

'No,' said Morse. 'I'll go to see her myself.'

'Why's that?'

'I have my reasons.'

The landlord had returned with the drinks. 'As I said – on the house, gentlemen!'

Morse thanked him and made a request: 'You know this, er, music you're playing here – this Irish music . . . ?'

'Perhaps you'd like it . . . ?'

'Yes. If you could turn it up just a bit?'

Lewis glanced across at the Chief Inspector with a

look of astonishment; the landlord departed; and Strange leaned back with an expression of contentment. 'You know, Morse, I'm glad you said that. The missus . . . we had a couple of days in Cork and we did a bit of Irish dancing together . . . me and the missus . . . or I suppose you'd say the missus and me.'

'The missus and I, sir.'

But further grammatical preferences were curtailed by the arrival of Dr Laura Hobson.

'Everything all right, Doctor?' shouted Strange, above the background music that had suddenly lunged to the foreground.

'No, everything's all wrong! I can*not* cope with things as they are out there. I want the car moved out to the lab with the body kept in the boot. How on earth you think—?'

'Done!' Strange held up the great slab that was his right hand. 'Lewis will arrange it immediately, once he's finished his drink. Si' down, Doctor. Just give me a minute or two.' He sat back in his chair, beaming like a benign old uncle.

'Takes you back, Morse, doesn't it?'

'Remember the old poem, sir?

"When I play on my fiddle in Dooney,
Folk dance like a wave of the sea . . ."'

'Yes! Yes, I do,' said Strange gently.

And for a while Sergeant Lewis and Dr Hobson remained silent, as if they knew they should be treading softly; as if they might be treading on other people's dreams.

Chapter Thirty-Four

Sunt lacrimae rerum et mentem mortalia tangunt
(Always in life are there tears being shed for things,
and human suffering ever touches the heart)
(Virgil, *Aeneid*, I, l. 462)

As she opened the door, the recently re-applied blonde dye showed little or no trace of the hair's brunette inheritance.

'Oh, hullo.' The greeting was less than enthusiastic.

'May I come in?' asked Morse.

Apart from the minimal towel held in front of her body, she was naked: 'Just wait there a sec – I'll just . . .'

She re-closed the door and Morse stood, as she had bidden, on the threshold. Stood there for a couple of minutes. And when she re-opened the door and re-appeared, it puzzled him that in such a comparatively long time she had done little other than to exchange the white towel for an equally minimal white dressing gown.

They sat opposite each other in the kitchen.

'Drink?' she ventured.

'No. I've had a busy day on the drink.'

'That good or bad?'

'Bit of both.'

'Mind if I have one?'

'Can you wait? Just a minute?'

'It's about Harry, isn't it?'

'Yes.'

'He's dead, isn't he?'

'He's been murdered,' said Morse flatly.

Debbie Richardson leaned forward on her elbows, the long fingers with their crimson nails vertically veiling her features. Then after a while she got to her feet and turned to the sink, where she moulded her hands into a shallow receptacle under the cold tap.

As they had spoken at the kitchen table, Morse had observed (how otherwise?) that whatever else Debbie Richardson had done behind the closed front door she had certainly not been searching for a bra; and now, as she leaned forward and held her face in the water, he observed (how otherwise?) that she'd had no thought for any knickers either. A provocative prick-teaser, that was what she was. Morse knew it; had known it when they'd met that once before. But for the moment his mind was many furlongs from fornication . . .

He felt fairly sure that she'd been upstairs when he'd rung the bell, for the light had been on in the front bedroom with the night now drawing in. Yet she'd answered the door very quickly, almost immediately in fact. Whoever the caller was, had she wished to give the impression to someone that she'd been downstairs all the while? It seemed a bit odd. After all, he could well have been a Jehovah's Witness or an equally dreaded member of the Mormons or a charity-worker bearing an envelope. Quite certainly though she hadn't rushed down the stairs from a bath, since about her was none of that freshly scented aura of a woman recently risen from her toilet. Rather perhaps (although Morse was no connoisseur in such matters) it was the musky odour of sex that lingered around her.

Whilst she had stood silently at the sink, he had strained his ears as acutely as any astronomer waiting for the faintest bleep from outer space. But of any other presence in the house there had been no sound at all; no sight at all either, except for the two unwashed wine glasses that stood on the draining board, a heel-tap of red in each of them. And Morse guessed that Debbie Richardson would never have taken the slightest risk of Claret and intercourse that day with anyone – unless it were with Harry Repp. And it *couldn't* have been with Harry Repp . . . Yet she may well have been tempted, this flaunting, raunchy woman who now dried her face and turned back to Morse; could certainly have been tempted if one of her admirers had called that evening for whatever reason – and if she had already known that Harry Repp was dead.

Morse watched her almost disinterestedly as she returned to the table.

'Shall I pour you that drink now?' he asked.

'Only if you'll join me.'

Quite extraordinarily, Morse gave the impression that he was quite extraordinarily sober; and he poured their drinks – gin (hers), whisky (his) – with only a carefully camouflaged shake of the right hand.

Quietly, as gently as he could, he told her almost as much as he knew of what had happened that day; and of the help that immediately awaited her should she so need it: advice, comfort, counselling . . .

But she shook her head. She'd be better off with sleepin' pills than with all that stuff. She needed nothin' of that. She'd be copin' OK, given a chance. Independent, see? Never wanted to share any worryin' with anyone. Loner most of her life, she'd been; ever since she'd been a teenager . . .

A tear ran hurriedly down her right cheek, and Morse handed her a handkerchief he'd washed and ironed himself.

'We ought to ring your GP: it's the usual thing.'

She blew her nose noisily and wiped the moisture from her eyes. 'You go now. I'll be fine.'

'We'll need a statement from you soon.'

'Course.'

'You'll stay here . . .?'

Before she could reply the phone rang, and she moved into the hallway to answer it.

'Hello?'

. . .

'You've got the wrong number.'

. . .

'You've got the *wrong number.*'

Had she replaced the receiver with needless haste? Morse didn't know.

'Not one of those obscene calls?'

'No.'

'Best to be on the safe side, though.' Giving her no chance to obstruct his sudden move, Morse picked up the receiver, dialled 1471, and duly noted the number given.

She had said nothing during this brief interlude,

but now proceeded to give her views on one of the most recent developments in telephonic technology: 'It'll soon be a tricky ol' thing conductin' some illicit liaison over the phone.'

Morse smiled, feeling delight and surprise in such elegant vocabulary. 'As I was saying, you'll stay here?'

She looked at him unblinking, eye to eye. 'You could always call occasionally to make sure, Inspector.'

For some little while they stood together on the inner side of the front door.

'You know . . . It doesn't hit you for a start, does it? You just don't take it in. But it's true, isn't it? He's dead. Harry's *dead*.'

Morse nodded. 'You'll be all right, though. Like you said, you can cope. You're a tough girl.'

'Oh God! He kept talkin' and talkin' about gettin' in bed with me again. Been a long time for him – and for me.'

'I understand.'

'You really think you *do*?'

Her cheeks were dry now, unfurrowed by a single tear. Yet Morse knew that she probably understood as much as he did about those Virgilian 'tears of things'. And for that moment he felt a deep compassion, as with the gentlest touch he laid his right hand briefly on her shoulder, before walking slowly along that amateurishly concreted path that led towards the road.

Once in the car, Morse turned to Sergeant Dixon:

'Well?'

'Light went off upstairs soon as you rung the bell, sir.'

'Sure of that?'

'Gospel.'

'Anyone leave, do you think?'

'Must a' been out the back if they did.'

'What about the cars parked here?'

'I took a list, like you said. Mostly local residents. I've checked with HQ.'

'Mostly?'

'There was an old D-reg Volvo parked at the far end there. Not there any longer though.'

'*And?*'

Dixon grinned as happily as if he were contemplating a plate of doughnuts. 'Car owned by someone from Lower Swinstead. You'll never guess who. Landlord o' the Maiden's Arms!'

Morse, appearing to assimilate this new intelligence without undue surprise, handed over the telephone number of the (hitherto) untraced caller who had just rung Debbie Richardson; and could hear each end of the conversation perfectly clearly as Dixon spoke with HQ once more.

The call had been made from Lower Swinstead.

From the Maiden's Arms.

Chapter Thirty-Five

The trouble about always trying to preserve the health of the body is that it is so difficult to do without destroying the health of the mind

(G. K. Chesterton)

At 9.20 a.m. on Monday, 27 July, as he sat in the out-patients' lounge at the Oxford Diabetes Centre at the Radcliffe Infirmary, Morse reflected on the unco-ordinated, hectic enquiries which had occupied many of his colleagues for the whole of the previous day. He had himself made no contribution whatsoever to the accumulating data thus garnered, suffering as he was from one long horrendous hangover. Because of this, he had most solemnly abjured all alcohol for the rest of his life; and indeed had made a splendid start to such long-term abstinence until early evening, when his brain told him that he was never going to cope with the present case without recourse, in moderate quantities, to his faithful Glenfiddich.

Several key facts now seemed reasonably settled. Paddy Flynn had been knifed to death at around noon the previous Friday; Harry Repp had died in very similar fashion about two or three hours later. Flynn had probably died instantaneously. Repp had met a slower end, almost certainly dying from the outpouring of blood that so copiously had covered the earlier blood in the back of the car, and quite certainly had been dead when someone, somewhere, had lugged the messy corpse into the boot of the same car. No sign of any weapon; only blood blood blood. And, of course, prints galore – far too many of them – subimposed, imposed, and superimposed everywhere. The vehicle's owner had allowed his second wife and his three step-children regular access to his latest supercharged model, and fingerprint elimination was going to be a lengthy business. Even lengthier perhaps would be the analysis by boffins back at Forensics of the hairs and threads collected on the sticky strips the SOCOs had taped over every square centimetre of the vehicle's upholstery.

Yet in spite of so many potential leads, Morse felt dubious (as did Dr Hobson) about their actual value. Too many cooks could spoil the broth, and too many crooks could easily spoil an investigation. For the moment, it was a question of waiting.

As Morse was waiting in the waiting room now . . .

On the day before, the Sunday, Morse had woken up, literally and metaphorically, to the fact that he should have been keeping an accurate record of his blood-sugar levels for the previous month. Thus it was that he had taken four such readings that day: 12.2; 9.9; 22.6; 16.4. Although realizing that he could never hope for an average anywhere near the 4–5 range normal for non-diabetic people, he was nevertheless somewhat disturbed by his findings, and immediately halved that very high third reading to 11.3. Then he'd extrapolated backwards as intelligently as he could for the previous six days, with the result that a reasonably satisfactory set of readings, neatly tabulated in his small handwriting, was now folded inside his blue appointment-card.

He was ready.

He had finally managed to produce a 'specimen', although inaccuracy of aim had resulted in a puddle on the unisex-loo's floor; and the dreaded weighing-in was over.

And so was the waiting.

'Mr Morse?'

The white-coated, slimly attractive brunette led the way to a consulting room, her name, black lettering on a white card, on the door: DR SARAH HARRISON.

'You knew my mother a bit, I believe,' she said as she opened a buff-coloured folder.

Morse nodded, but made no comment.

A quarter of an hour later the medical side of matters was over. Morse had not attempted to be overly clever. Just short and reasonably honest in his replies.

'These readings – are they genuine?'

'Partly, yes.'

'You could lose a stone or two, you know.'

'I agree.'

'But you won't.'

'Probably not.'

'How's the drink going?'

'Rather too quickly.'

'It's *your* liver, you know.'

'Yes.'

'Any problems with sex?'

'I've always had problems with sex.'

'You know what I mean – sex-drive . . . ?'

'I'm a bachelor.'

'What's that got to do with it?'

'Just that I lead a reasonably celibate life.'

'It *is* my job to *ask* these questions, you understand that.'

The dark-brown eyes were growing progressively less angry as she examined his feet, and then his eyes. She had in fact virtually finished with him when a nurse knocked and entered the room, explaining swiftly that an out-patient had just fainted in Reception; and since for the minute Dr Harrison was the only consultant there . . .

After she had left, Morse stepped quickly over to the desk and opened his own folder. On top lay a brief handwritten note:

> Don't be intimidated, Sarah! He's hugely economical with the truth, but he's really a softie at heart (I think).
> Robert (sic!)

And underneath it, a copy of a letter (Strictly Confidential) sent to the Summertown Health Centre and dated 18 May 1998.

Re Annual Review: E. Morse.

Dear Dr Roblin,

Haemoglobin A lc (as you'll see) is higher than we would like at 11.5%. I've instructed him to increase each of his four daily insulin doses by 2 units – up to 10, 6, 12, 36. In addition, his cholesterol level is getting rather worrying. It's pointless to ask him to cut his intake of alcohol, so please add to his prescribed medicines Atorvastatin 10 mg tablets nocte.

Eyes are remarkably good. Blood pressure is still too high. No problems with feet.

His general condition gives me no real cause for immediate anxiety, but I shall be glad if you can insist on a regular monthly review, at least for the rest of the year. I enclose the relevant clinical data.

Regards to your family.

With best wishes,
Professor R C Turner
Honorary Consultant Physician

P.S. He tells me he's stopped smoking! And he's certainly stopped listening to me.

Morse was sitting, slowly pulling on his socks, when Sarah Harrison returned.

'I'll tell you one thing: you've got quite nice feet.'

'I'm glad bits of me are OK.'

Whilst tying his shoelaces, Morse had missed the look of quick intelligence in the large brown eyes.

'Bit sneaky, wasn't it?' she held up the file.

Morse nodded. 'Don't worry, though. Professor Turner sent me a copy of that last letter.'

'Well, in that case, there's not really much more . . .' She got to her feet.

'Please!' Morse signalled to the chair, and obediently she sat down again. 'Why haven't you mentioned the murders, Doctor? They're all over the national papers.'

'I bought *six* of them yesterday, if you must know.'

'Your father? Your brother – Simon, isn't it? Do they know?'

'I've not seen Simon recently.'

'You could have phoned him.'

'Simon is *not* the sort of person you phone. He's deaf, *very* deaf – as you probably know anyway.'

'And your father?' repeated Morse.

'I . . . whether or not . . . Oddly enough I saw him last week. He came to stay with me for a couple of nights.'

'Which nights?'

'Wednesday and Thursday. He went back to London on Friday.'

'What time?'

'Is this the Inquisition?'

'It *is* my job to *ask* these questions, you understand that.'

'Touché! He caught the train – I'm not sure which one. He didn't bring the car – nowhere to park in Oxford, is there?'

'Why didn't you see him off?'

'I couldn't.'

'Were you working?'

'No. I'd arranged to have Thursday and Friday off myself. Like Dad, I'd a few days' holiday to make up.'

'So why not see him off?'

The eyes were fiery now. 'I'll tell you why. Because he took me out the previous night to Le Petit Blanc in Walton Street and we had a super meal *and* we had far too much booze – before, during, and after, all right? And I got as pissed as a tailed amphibian and tried to sleep things off with enough pills to frighten even you! And when I finally staggered downstairs – eleven? half-eleven? – I saw this note on the kitchen table: "Off back to London. Didn't want to wake you. Love Dad" – something like that.'

'Any time on the note?'

'Don't think so.'

'Have you kept it?'

'Course I've not kept it! Hardly a specimen of purple prose, was it?'

'Don't be cross with me,' said Morse gently as he got to his feet, and left the consulting room – with two blue cards for more immediate and urgent blood tests, and with instructions to fix up a further appointment for eight weeks' time.

After the door had closed behind him, Sarah dialled 9 for an outside line on the phone there; then called a number.

'Hullo? Hullo? Could you put me through to Simon Harrison, please?'

Chapter Thirty-Six

> Dr Franklin shewed me that the flames of two candles joined give a much stronger light than both of them separate; as is made very evident by a person holding the two candles near his face, first separate, and then joined in one
>
> (Joseph Priestley, *Optiks*)

As he sat awaiting his turn outside the cubicle reserved for blood-testing, Morse found himself wondering whether, wondering *how*, if at all, Sarah Harrison could have had any rôle to play in the appalling events of the weekend just passed. There *were* possibilities, of course (there were always possibilities in Morse's mind) and for a few minutes his brain accelerated sweetly and swiftly into that extra fifth gear. But stop a while! Strange had surely been right to remind him that the easiest answer was more often than not the correct one. What *was* the easiest answer, though? Lewis would know, of course; and it was at times like these that Morse needed Lewis's cautious 30 mph approach to life, if not to any stretch of road in front of him. Two heads were better than one, even though one of them was Lewis's. Yet what a cruel thought that was! And so unworthy . . .

'Mr Morse?'

A nurse led him behind the blood-letting curtain;

and as she wiped the inside of his right arm with a sterilizing swab of cotton wool before inserting a needle, Morse found himself thinking of Dr Sarah Harrison . . . wondering exactly what she was thinking (doing?) at that very moment.

'Hullo? Simon Harrison here.'

'Simon? Sarah! Are you hearing OK?'

'Where else? Course I'm here in the UK.'

'Are you *hearing* me all right?'

'Oh, sorry! Yes. Fantastic this new phone-system. You know that.'

'Are you on your own, Simon?' She was speaking softly.

'Yes. But you can never count on it, sis. You know that.'

'Now listen! I've only got a minute or so. I've just been talking to Chief Inspector Morse—'

'Who?'

'Morse! He's with the Thames Valley Police and he's just become one of my patients.'

'He wasn't on Mum's case.'

'Well, he's on *this* one.'

'So?'

'So we've got to be careful, Simon.'

'You told him Dad was here?'

'Had to! He'd have soon found out.'

'What's *wrong*, sis?'

'*Nothing*'s wrong. But I'm a bit frightened of him, and when he sees you—'

'Seizure? What? Say it again.'

'If he *sees* you, Simon, you did *not* come round last Wednesday. *You did not come—*'

'I *heard* you! I stayed at home and watched the telly. What was on, by the way?'

'Look it up in the *Radio Times*! And stop being—!'

A knock on the consulting-room door caused Sarah to replace the receiver hurriedly, almost hoping that another out-patient had passed out in Reception. But the knock was only a polite reminder that Dr Harrison's a.m. schedule was now running over half an hour late.

Yet even as the next out-patient was ushered in, Dr Sarah Harrison found herself wondering exactly what Chief Inspector Morse was thinking (doing?) at that very moment.

Turning right from the front entrance of the Radcliffe Infirmary, Morse began walking slowly down towards St Giles', noting that the time was 10.40 – twenty minutes before the pubs were due to open. Yet since drink was now definitely out for the duration, such an observation was of little moment.

The Oratory was on his right, a building he'd seldom paid attention to before, although he must have walked past it so many, many times. But apart from that wonderful line of cathedrals down the eastern side of England – Durham, York, Lincoln, Peterborough, Ely – the architecture of ecclesiastical edifices had never meant as much as they should have done to

Morse; and the reason why he now checked his step remains inexplicable.

He entered and looked around him: all surprisingly large and imposing, with a faint, seductive smell of incense, and statues of assorted saints around him, with tiers of candles lit beside their sandalled, holy feet.

A youngish woman had come in behind him, a Marks and Spencer carrier bag in her left hand. She dipped her right hand into the little font of blessed water there, then crossed herself and knelt in one of the rear pews. Morse envied her, for she looked so much at home there: looked as if she knew herself and her Lord so well, and was wholly familiar with all the trappings of prayer and the promises of forgiveness. She didn't stay long, and Morse guessed that the cause of her brief sojourn was probably the paucity of any sins worthy of confession. As she left, Morse could see some of the contents of the carrier bag: a Hovis loaf and a bottle of red plonk.

Bread and wine.

The door clicked to behind her, and Morse stepped over to meet St Anthony, wondering whence had sprung that oddly intrusive 'h'. According to the textual blurb at the base of the statue, this great and good man was clearly capable of performing quite incredible miracles for those who almost had sufficient faith. Morse picked up a candle from the box there and stuck it in an empty socket on the top row. At which point (it appeared) most worshippers would have prayed fervently for a miracle. But Morse wasn't at all sure what miracle he wanted. Nevertheless the elegant, elongated candle was of importance to him; and on some semi-irrational impulse he took a second candle and placed it beside the first. Together, side by side, they seemed to give a much stronger light than both of them separate.

A notice suggested an appropriate donation per candle, and Morse pushed a £1 coin into the slot in the wall behind St Anthony. Half of bitter. Then, remembering that he'd doubled his investment, the reluctant hagiolater pushed in a second £1 coin. A whole pint.

As he walked down to St Giles', the man who had virtually no faith in the Almighty and even less in miracles noted that the past few minutes had slipped by quickly. It was now just after 11 a.m.; and when he came in sight of the Bird and Baby on his right, he saw that the front door was open.

He went in.

Chapter Thirty-Seven

Careless talk costs lives

(Second World War slogan)

I think men who have a pierced ear are better prepared for marriage. They've experienced pain and bought jewelry

(Rita Rudner)

Five days after Morse had declined the free draw for a miracle at the Oratory, at noon, at Lower Swinstead, at the bar of the Maiden's Arms, Tom Biffen stood leaning forward on his tattooed arms. Very quiet so far for a Saturday. Just the two hardy perennials, horns already locked over their continuous cribbage; and the pale-faced, ear-pierced, greasy-haired youth already squaring up to the fruit machine.

It was twenty minutes later that the fourth customer arrived.

'Usual?'

The newcomer nodded and placed the requisite monies on the counter. The white van in the car park economically proclaimed the newcomer's profession: 'J. Barron, Builder'.

'Not out at Debbie's today, John?'

'What do you think? The day after the funeral?'

'No. Have you seen her since Harry . . .?'

'No. Well, I wouldn't have gone last weekend anyway, would I? Thought they'd like being on their own, like – you know, the day after they'd let him out and all that.'

'No.'

The youth was standing beside them, a £10-note folded lengthways between the index and middle fingers of his right hand.

'You're taking all me change,' complained Biffen as he exchanged the note for ten £1 coins from the till.

'You'll have bugger all left for the honeymoon,' ventured the builder; but the youth, unhearing or uncaring, had already walked back to what was perhaps the first great love of his life.

At the bar a few low-voiced confidences were being exchanged.

'When's the wedding, Biff?'

'Five weeks today.'

'Nice bit o' skirt?'

'Yeah. Dental receptionist down in Oxford somewhere.'

'Glad *one* of 'em's earning!' The builder half-turned towards the unremunerative machine. 'Nobody earns much of a living on them things.'

'Except the Company,' corrected the landlord.

'Except Tom Biffen,' corrected one of the cribbagers.

The landlord grunted.

Odd really. Most men in their latish seventies would ever have been susceptible to deafness, arthritis, baldness, sciatica, haemorrhoids, incontinence, impotence, cataracts, dementia, and all the rest. And perhaps (for all the landlord knew) the two old codgers suffered from every single one of them – except quite certainly the first.

Biffen lowered his voice: 'Did you get to the crematorium?'

'No. *Family*, wasn't it? I wasn't exactly a friend of the family.'

'I thought you builders and plumbers were friends of everybody, especially a strapping young fellow like you?'

'Young?'

But the landlord had a point. John Barron, tall and well built, with dark close-cropped hair and clean-cut features, certainly looked younger than his forty-one years; and what appeared a genuinely open smile appealed to all the local ladies – except his wife, who had been known occasionally to feel jealous.

'What exactly are you doing for Debbie?'

'In the back passage, off the kitchen – you know, the old coal-shed and the old loo. Knocking 'em into one so she can get her washing machine in – re-tiling the floor – re-plastering the walls – new electrical sockets – usual sort of thing.'

'Just at weekends?'

'Yeah, well . . .'

'Bit o' moonlighting? Cash payment?'

For a second or two Barron's mouth tightened distastefully, but he made no direct reply. 'I was hoping to finish it off before Harry was out.'

'Poor sod! Bet he was looking forward . . . you know. Attractive woman, our Debbie!'

'Yeah.' The builder took a deep draught of his bitter. 'Did you go – to the crem?'

'No. Like you said . . .'

'Have you seen her at all since . . . ?'

'No. Like you said . . .'

'The police've been round, they tell me.'

'Yeah. Came in – when was it? – Tuesday.'

'What'd they want?'

Doubtless the builder would have been enlightened immediately had not two further customers entered at that point: an elderly, back-packing, stoutly booted couple.

'Two glasses of orange juice, please!'

'Coming up, sir.'

'Beautiful little village you've got here. So quiet. So peaceful. "Far from the madding crowd" – you'll know the quotation?'

The landlord nodded unconvincingly as he passed over the drinks.

'And you serve meals as well!'

The couple walked over to the corner furthest from the fruit machine: she consulting the hostelry's menu; he plotting a possible p.m. itinerary from *Family Walks in the Cotswolds.*

'Quiet and peaceful!' mumbled the landlord, as one of the elders stepped forward with two empty straight glasses. Words were clearly superfluous.

'You were saying?' resumed the builder.

'Saying what?'

'About the police?'

'Ah, yes. That sergeant came in and asked some of us about Harry and Debbie.'

'But you hadn't seen either of them?'

'Right! But, I would've done, see – would've seen *her*, anyway, if it hadn't been for them – for the police. That Sat'day night I thought I'd just nip over and take 'em a bottle o' Shampers, like – give 'em both a bit of a celebration. Well, I'd just parked the car and I was just walking along when I saw this police car driving slowly round and the fellow inside making notes of Reg numbers by the look of it.'

'What'd you say?'

'Didn't say nothing, did I? Just waited till the coast was clear, then buggered off back here smartish. They'd seen the number, though. So not much point in . . .'

'Good story!'

'Bloody *true* story, mate!'

The builder finished his pint. 'Beer's in good nick, Biff.'

'Always in good nick!'

('Is it fuck!' came *sotto voce* from the region of the cribbage-board.)

'Summat else too,' continued the landlord as he pulled the builder a second pint. 'The police tell me there was a phone call for Debbie that Sat'day night – from the pay-phone here.'

'Could have been anybody.'

'Yeah.'

'Any ideas?'

'Sat'day nights? Come off it! Full up to the rafters, ain't we?'

The elderly lady now came to the bar and ordered gammon-and-pineapple with chips for two; and during this transaction the builder turned round and, with a fascination that is universal, watched the unequal struggle at the fruit machine.

From outside came the jingle of an ice-cream van – as happy a noise as any to the youngsters of Lower Swinstead that sunny lunchtime; almost as happy a noise as that clunk-clunk-clunk of coins falling into the winnings-tray of a fruit machine.

Conversation at the bar was temporarily suspended, since several noisy customers were now arriving, including three members of the highly unsuccessful Lower Swinstead Cricket Club. There was therefore a comparatively large audience for the seemingly endless music of the machine: clunk-clunk-clunk-clunk-clunk-clunk-clunk-clunk-clunk-clunk-clunk-clunk-clunk-clunk-clunk-clunk-clunk-clunk-clunk-clunk; and an even larger audience as the impassively faced youth pressed the 'Repeat' button – successfully – with a further twenty £1 coins duly clanking into the winnings-tray.

'Nearly enough for that honeymoon,' said the builder.

'Nonsense! He'll be putting it all back,' said one of the cricketers.

But he wasn't.

With a temporary lull in business, the landlord resumed the conversation. 'Business still pretty good, John?'

'Plenty o' work, yeah. Having to turn some things down.'

'What you got on at the minute?'

'Job in Burford in Sheep Street: bit o' roofing, bit o' pointing, bit o' painting.'

'High up, is it?'

'High enough. I'll need a coupla extensions on the ladder.'

Biffen screwed up his face and closed his eyes. 'You'd never get me up there.'

'You're OK, so long as things are firm.'

'Not if you get vertigo as bad as me.'

The coins bulged proudly in his trouser-pocket as the bride-groom designate walked out of the bar. Once in the passage that led to the toilets, he lifted the receiver from the pay-phone there, inserted 20p, and dialled a number.

But what he said, or to whom he spoke, not even the keen-eared elders could have known.

Chapter Thirty-Eight

> All persons are puzzles until at last we find in some word or act the key to the man, to the woman; straightway all their past words and actions lie in light before us
>
> (Emerson, *Journals*)

For much of the week Lewis had been working three-quarters of the way round the clock; but on Sunday, the day following the events described in the previous chapter, he felt refreshed after a good sleep and arrived at Kidlington Police HQ at 8.45 a.m. No sign of Morse. But that mattered little. It had been facts that were required. Not fancies. Not yet, anyway. And as he sat taking stock of the past week's activities, Lewis felt solidly satisfied – both with himself and with the performance of the personnel readily allocated to the case. There had been so much to cover . . .

Lewis had personally supervised the Monday and Tuesday enquiries into the activities of Paddy Flynn in the years, months, days – and morning – before his murder; and if the net result was perhaps somewhat disappointing, at least it had been thorough. Flynn had been living in an upstairs flat (converted a few years previously) in Morrell Avenue. He had been there for just over five months, paying £375 per calendar month for the privilege, and having virtually nothing to do with the tenant of the downstairs flat – a middle-aged accountant who, rain or shine, would walk each day down to St Clements, across Magdalen Bridge, and up the High to his firm's offices in King Alfred Street. He knew Flynn by sight, of course, but only exchanged words when occasionally they encountered each other in the narrow entrance hall. Of Flynn's lifestyle, he had no knowledge at all: no ideas about the activities in which his fellow-tenant might have been engaged. Well, just one little observation, perhaps, since not infrequently there was a car parked outside the semi – always a different car, and almost always gone the following morning. Lewis's notes had read: 'Has no knowledge of F's professional or leizure time activities'. But he'd consulted his dictionary, ever kept beside him, in case Morse decided to look at his notes, and quickly corrected the antepenultimate word.

By all accounts Flynn had led a pretty private, almost secretive life. He was quite frequently spotted in the local hostelries, quite frequently spotted in the local bookmakers, though never, apparently, the worse for excessive liquor or for excessive losses. His name figured nowhere in police records as even the pettiest of crooks, although he was mentioned in dispatches several times as the taxi driver who had picked up Frank Harrison from Oxford Railway Station on the night of Yvonne's murder. Radio Taxis had been his employer at the time; but he had been suspected of (possibly) fabricating fares for his own aggrandisement, and duly dismissed – without rancour, it appeared, and certainly without recourse to any industrial tribunal. Dismissed too, subsequently, by the proprietors of Maxim Removals, a firm of middle-distance hauliers, 'for attempted trickery with the tachometer'. (Lewis had spelled the last word correctly, having checked it earlier.) Since that time, five months previously, Flynn had reported regularly to the DSS office at the bottom of George Street. But lacking any testimonials to his competence and integrity, his attempts to secure further employment in any field of motor transport had been unsuccessful, his completed application forms seldom reaching even the slush-pile. It was all rather sad, as the woman regularly dealing with the Flynn file had testified.

He'd been thirty-two when, seven years earlier, he'd married Josie Newton, and duly fathered two daughters upon that lady – although (this the testimony of a brother in Belfast) the offspring had appeared so dissimilar in temperament, coloration, and mental ability, that there had been many doubts about their common paternity.

Josie Flynn had been unable or unwilling to offer much in the way of 'character-profiling' of her late husband (they'd never divorced); had scant interest in the manner of his murder; and, quite certainly, no interest in attending his 'last rites', whatever form these latter might take. Although he had treated her with ever-increasing indifference and contempt, he had never (she acknowledged it) abused her physically or sexually. In fact sex, even in the early months of their relationship, had never been a dominant factor in his life; nor, for that matter, had power or success or social acceptability or drink or even happiness. Just plain *money*. She'd not seen him for over two years; nor had her daughters – *she'd* seen to that. It was (again) all rather sad, according to Sergeant Dixon's report. Mr Paddy Flynn may not have been the ideal husband, but perhaps Ms Josephine Newton (now her preferred appellation) was hardly a paragon of rectitude in the marital relationship. 'Not exacly a saint herself?' as Dixon's handwritten addendum had suggested. And Lewis smiled to himself again, feeling a little superior.

It had been Lewis himself (no Morse beside him) who had visited Flynn's upstairs flat: smell of cigarette smoke everywhere; sheets on the single bed rather grubby; dirty cutlery and plates in the kitchen sink, but not too many of them; the top surface of the cooker in sore need of Mrs Lewis; soiled shirts, underpants, socks, handkerchiefs, in a neat pile behind the bathroom door; a minimal assemblage of trousers, jackets, shirts, underclothes, in a heavy wardrobe; a Corby trouser-press; eleven cans of Guinness in the otherwise sparsely stocked refrigerator; not a single book anywhere; two copies of the *Mirror* opened at the Racing pages; a TV set, but not even the statutory hard-core video; one CD, *Great Arias from Puccini*, but no CD player for Flynn to have gauged their magnitude; no pictures on the walls; no personal correspondence; and very little in the way of official communications, apart from Social Security forms: no sign of any bank account or credit facility.

Nothing much to go on.

And yet Lewis had sensed from the start that there was something missing. Sensed that he knew where that 'something missing' might well be.

And it was.

Most petty crooks had little in the way of imagination, having two or three favoured niches wherein to conceal their ill-gotten gains. And Paddy Flynn proved no exception. The small, brown-leather case was on the top shelf of the old mahogany wardrobe, tucked away on the far left, beneath a pair of faded-green blankets.

It took one DC just under twenty minutes to itemize the contents; a second DC just over thirty minutes to check the original itemization – a cache of legitimate bank-notes, in fifties, twenties, tens, and fives. The confirmed tally was £17,465 and Lewis knew that Morse would be interested.

And Morse, on being told, most decidedly *had* been interested.

A similarly painstaking review of Repp and Richardson had taken up the whole of the Wednesday. Little new had come to light except for the unexpected (?) discovery that an account with the Burford and Cheltenham Building Society showed a robust balance of £14,350 held in the name of Deborah Richardson, with regular monthly deposits (as was confidentially ascertained) always made in cash. Debbie Richardson had smilingly refused to answer Lewis's questions concerning the provenance of such comparatively substantial income, stating her belief that everybody – bishops, barmaids, presidents, prostitutes – all deserved some measure of privacy. Yes, Lewis had agreed; but he knew that Morse would be interested.

And Morse, on being told, most decidedly *had* been interested.

The Thursday and Friday had been taken up largely with a preliminary scrutiny and analysis of the scores of reports and statements taken from prison officers, bus drivers, rubbish-dump employees, car-park attendants, forensic boffins, and so on and so on – as well as from those members of the public who had responded to appeals for information. But so far there'd been little to show for the methodical police routine that Lewis had supervised. Vital, though! Criminal investigation was all about motives and relationships, about times and dates and alibis. It was all about building up a pattern from the pieces of a jigsaw. So many pieces, though. Some of them blue for the sky and the sea; some of them green and brown for the trees and the land; and sometimes, somewhere, one or two pieces of quirky coloration that seemed to fit in nowhere. And that, as Lewis knew, was where Morse would come in – as he invariably did. It was almost as if the Chief Inspector had the ability to cheat: to have sneaked some quick glimpse of the finished picture even before picking up the individual pieces.

Frequently when Lewis had seen him that week, Morse had been sitting in HQ, immobile and apparently immovable (apart from an hour or so over lunchtimes), occasionally and almost casually abstracting a page or two of a report, of a statement, of a letter, from one of the bulging box-files on his desk, YVONNE

HARRISON written large in black felt-tipped pen down each of the spines. Clearly (whatever else) Morse had come round to Strange's conviction that some causal connection between the cases had become overwhelmingly probable.

But that was no surprise to Lewis.

What had occasioned him puzzlement was the *number* of green box-files there, since he had himself earlier studied the same material when (he could swear it!) there had only been three.

Chapter Thirty-Nine

Q: Doctor, how many autopsies have you performed on dead people?
A: *All* of my autopsies are performed on dead people

(Reported in the *Massachusetts Lawyers' Journal*)

After (for him) an unprecedented early hour of retirement that same Sunday evening, at 9.30 p.m., Morse had awoken with a troublous headache. Assuming that the dawn was already breaking, he had confidently consulted his watch, to discover that it was still only 11.30 p.m. Thereafter he had woken up at regular ninety-minute intervals, in spite of equally regular doses of Alka-Seltzer and Paracetamol – his mind, even in the periods of intermittent slumber, riding the merry-go-round of disturbing dreams; his blood sugar ridiculously high; his feet suddenly hot and just as suddenly icy-cold; an indigestion pain that was occasionally excruciating.

Ovid (now almost becoming Morse's favourite Latin poet) had once begged the horses of the night to gallop slowly whenever some delightfully compliant mistress was lying beside him. But Morse had no such mistress beside him; and even if he had, he would still have wished those horses of the night to complete their course as quickly as they could possibly manage it.

He finally rose from the creased and crumpled sheets, and was shaving, just as rosy-fingered Dawn herself was rising over the Cutteslowe Council Estate.

At 6 a.m. he once more measured his blood-sugar level, now dipped dramatically from 24.4 at 1 a.m. to 2.8. Some decent breakfast was evidently required, and a lightly boiled egg with toast would fit the bill nicely. But Morse had no eggs; no slices of bread either. So, perforce, it had to be cereal. But Morse could find no milk, and there seemed no option but to resort to the solitary king-sized Mars bar which he always kept somewhere in the flat. For an emergency. *In rebus extremis*, like now. But he couldn't find it. Then – bless you St Anthony! – he discovered that the Co-op milkman had already called; and he had a great bowl of Corn Flakes, with a pleasingly cold pint of milk and several liberally heaped spoonsful of sugar. He felt wonderful.

Sometimes life was very good to him.

At 6.45 a.m. he considered (not too seriously) the possibility of walking up from his North Oxford flat to the A40 Ring Road, and thence down the gentle hill to Kidlington. About – what? – thirty-five to forty minutes to the HQ building. Not that he'd ever timed himself, for he'd never as yet attempted the walk.

Didn't attempt the walk that morning.

After administering his first insulin-dosage of the day, he drove up to Police HQ in the Jaguar.

Far quicker.

In his office, as he re-read the final findings of the two post-mortems (*sic*), Morse decided, as he usually did, that there was no point whatsoever in his trying to unjumble the physiological details of the lacerations inflicted on the visceral organs of each body. He had little interest in the stomach; had no stomach for the stomach. In fact he was more familiar with the nine-fold stomach of the bovine ilk (this because of cross-word puzzles) than with its mono-chambered human counterpart. Did it really matter much to know exactly how Messrs Flynn and Repp had met their ends? But yes, of course it did! If the technicalities pointed to a particular type of weapon; if the weapon could be accurately identified and then found; and if, finally, it could be traced to someone who was known to have had such a weapon and who had the opportunity of wielding it on the day of the murders . . .

Hold on though, Morse! Be fair! Amid a plethora of caveats, Dr Hobson *had* pointed to a fairly specific type of weapon, had she not? And he read again the paragraph headed 'Tentative Conclusions':

> The knife was quite probably not all that long, maybe no more than 6″–9″, since in each case the lacerations seem the result of forceful twisting, as if the murderer had gripped a handle that was short and firm, say perhaps not much more than 1″–1½″ in width. The knife-blade was fairly certainly short too (? 1½″), but very sharp, with its end shaped in triangular fashion (◺). It could have been something like a Stanley knife, the sort of thing commonly used in DIY household jobs, carpentry, building, that sort of thing.

Morse suddenly stopped reading, sat back in his chair, and placed his hands on his head, fingers interlinked, as he'd done so often at his teacher's bequest in his infant class. And what had been a faraway look in his eyes now gradually focused into an intense gaze as he considered the implications of the extraordinary idea which had suddenly occurred to him . . .

Very soon he was re-reading the whole report from Forensics, where almost all the earlier findings had been confirmed, although there remained much checking to be done. Prints of Flynn; prints of Repp; prints of the car-owner; and several other prints as yet to be identified. Doubtless some of these latter would turn out to be those of the car-owner's family. But (Morse read the last sentence of the report again): 'One set of fingerprints, repeated and fairly firm, may well prove to be of considerable interest'.

He leaned back again in his chair, pleasingly weary and really quite pleased with himself, because he knew whose fingerprints they were.

Oh yes!

Chapter Forty

Odd instances of strange coincidence are really not all that odd perhaps

(Queen Caroline's advocate, speaking in the House of Lords)

MORSE JERKED AWAKE as Lewis entered the office just before 8 a.m., wondering where he was, what time it was, what day it was. Yet it had been a wonderful little sleep, the deep and dreamless sleep that Socrates anticipated after swallowing the hemlock.

'No crossword this morning, sir?'

'Shop wasn't open.'

'Why don't you pay a paper-boy?'

'Because, Lewis, a little occasional exercise . . .'

Lewis sat down. 'Do you mind if I ask you something?'

Morse pointed to the reports laid out on the desk. 'You've read these?'

Lewis nodded. 'But, like I say, I've got something to ask you.'

'And I've got something to *tell* you. Is that all right, Lewis?' The voice was suddenly harsh. 'You'll remember from all our times together how coincidence occurs in life far more frequently than anyone – except me – is prepared to accept. Coincidence isn't unusual at all. It's the norm. Just like those consecutive numbers cropping up in the National Lottery every week. But in this case the coincidence is even odder than usual.'

(Lewis raised his eyebrows a little.)

'Let's go back to Yvonne Harrison's murder. She was a woman with exceptional sex-drive; but she certainly wasn't just the deaf-and-dumb nymphomaniac with a bedroom just above the public bar that many a man has fantasized about. Oh, no. She was highly intelligent, highly desirable, like the woman in the Larkin poem with the 'lash-wide stare', who in turn was attracted by a variety of men. A lot of men. So many men that over the years she inevitably came across a few paying clients with kinky preferences. I doubt she ever went in for S and M, but it looks very likely that a bit of bondage was on her list of services, probably with a hefty surcharge. It's well known that some men only find sexual satisfaction with women who put on a show of being utterly submissive and powerless. It gives these men the only sense of real power they're ever likely to experience in life, because the object of their desire is lying there defenceless, unstruggling, sometimes unspeaking, too. Not uncommon, that, Lewis. And you can read all about it in Krafft-Ebing's case-studies . . .'

(Lewis's eyebrows rose significantly.)

'. . . although, as you know, I'm no great expert in such matters. In fact, come to think of it, I can't even remember whether he's got one or two "b"s in his name. But it means there's a pretty obvious explanation of two of the items that puzzled our previous colleagues: a pair of handcuffs, and a gag not all that tightly tied. The woman offering such a specialist service is never going to answer back, never going to scratch your eyes out – and Yvonne Harrison had just about the longest fingernails . . .'

(Lewis's eyebrows rose a lot.)

'On the night of the murder she had a client in bed with her, and if ever there was a *locus classicus* for what they call *coitus interruptus* this was it, because someone interrupted the proceedings. Or at the very least, someone saw them there in bed together.'

'Harry Repp?'

'Repp was certainly there at some point. But I think he kept his cool and kept his distance that night. I think he realized there could well be something in it for himself. He was right, too. Because what he saw that night – what he later kept from the police – was going to prove very profitable, as you discovered, Lewis. Five hundred pounds a month *from someone* just for exercising his professional skills as a burglar in staying well out of sight and keeping his eyes wide open. Exactly what he saw, we shan't know, shall we? Unless he told Debbie Richardson, which I doubt.'

'What do *you* think he saw?'

'Pretty obvious, isn't it?'

'You mean he saw who murdered Mrs Harrison?'

Morse nodded.

'And you think you know who . . . ?'

Morse nodded.

But Lewis shook his head. 'It's all so wishy-washy, what you've just said. I don't know where to start. *When* was she murdered? *Who* rang her husband? *Who* set off the burglar alarm? *Who* – ?'

'Lewis! We, remember, are investigating something else. But if any study of the first case facilitates the solving of the second? So be it! And it does, as you'll agree.'

'I will?'

Morse nodded again. 'Three people were coincidentally involved in a clever and profitable deception that night, each of them able and willing to throw his individual spanner into any reconstruction the CID could reasonably come up with. First, there was Flynn, our *corpus primum*, who told as many lies as anybody: both about the time he picked Frank Harrison up from Oxford Station, and about what he noticed – or more probably the person he saw – when he got to Lower Swinstead. Second, there was Repp, our *corpus secundum*, who told us no lies at all, but only because he told us nothing at all. Third . . .'

Morse hesitated, and Lewis looked across the desk expectantly.

'There's this third man of ours, and a man most unlikely to become our *corpus tertium*. Once Repp was out of jail, the three of them – Repp himself, Flynn, and this third man – they all arranged to meet together. They'd done pretty well so far out of their conspiracy of silence, and they were all keen on continuing to squeeze the milch-cow even drier. So they *did* meet – a meeting where things went tragically wrong. Greed . . . jealousy . . . personal antipathies . . . whatever! Two of them had an almighty row in the car in which they were travelling together. And one of them, probably in a lay-by somewhere, knifed one of the others: one of them knifed Flynn. And the remaining two disposed of the body neatly enough at Redbridge – the rubbish bags proving very handy, I should think. So any profits no longer needed to be split three ways. And now the talk between the two of them must have been all about a fifty-fifty share-out of the spoils, and how it could be effected. But somewhere in the discussion there was one further almighty row; and this time it was Repp who had his innards ripped open.'

'You know who this "third" man was, you're saying?'

'So do you. We mentioned him when you produced that admirable schema of yours for the night of Yvonne's murder.'

'You're saying there was somebody else there that night?'

'There was *always* somebody else, Lewis, wasn't there? The man in bed with Yvonne Harrison.'

'If you say so, sir.'

'You see, the major problem our lads had was the *timing* of the murder. Her body wasn't examined until several hours later, and all the pathological guesswork had to be married with the evidence gleaned at the time, or gleaned later. For example, with the fact that *someone* was in bed with Yvonne at some specific time that night, although nobody really tried to discover who that person was – until I did. For example, again, with the fact that *someone* had tried to ring her twice that night, at 9 p.m. when the line was engaged, and again half an hour later when the phone rang unanswered. And if you add all this together, you'll find that the person who sorely misled the police, the person who was in bed with her, and the person who murdered both Paddy Flynn and Harry Repp – *was one and the same man.*'

There fell a silence between the two of them, broken finally by Lewis. 'You're *sure* about all this?'

'Only ninety-five per cent sure.'

'We'd better get our skates on then.'

'Hold your horses! One or two things I'd like you to check first, just to make it one hundred per cent.'

'So we've got a little while?'

'Oh, yes. No danger of anyone murdering *him* – not today, anyway. So this afternoon'll be fine. Get out to Lower Swinstead – take someone with you, mind! – and bring him back here. OK?'

'Fine. Only one thing, sir. You forgot to tell me his name.'

'Did I? Well, you've guessed it anyway. He's got a little business out there, hasn't he? A little building business. "J. Barron, Builder", as it says on his van.'

Chapter Forty-One

But when he once attains the utmost round,
He then unto the ladder turns his back,
Looks in the clouds, scorning the base degrees
By which he did ascend
(Shakespeare, *Julius Caesar*)

TWENTY MILES WEST of Oxford, twenty miles east of Cheltenham, lies the little Cotswold town of Burford. It owes its architectural attractiveness to the wealth of the wool-merchants in the fifteenth and sixteenth centuries; and up until the end of the eighteenth century the small community there continued to thrive, especially the coaching inns which regularly served the E–W travel. But the town was no longer expanding, with the final blow delivered in 1812, when the main London road, which crossed the High Street (the present-day Sheep Street and Witney Street), was rerouted to the southern side of the town (the present-day A40). But Burford remains an enchanting place, as summer tourists will happily testify as they turn off at the A40 roundabout. Picturesque tea shops, craft shops, public houses – all built in the locally quarried, pale-honey-coloured limestone – line the steeply curving sweep of the High Street that leads to the bridge at the bottom of the hill, under which runs the River Windrush, with all the birds and the bright meadows and cornfields around Oxfordshire.

Mrs Patricia Bayley, aged seventy, had lived for only three years in Sheep Street (*vide supra*), a pleasingly peaceful, tree-lined road, first left as one descended the hill. The house-date, 1687, had been carved (now almost illegibly) in the greyish and pitted stone above the front door of the three-storeyed, mullion-windowed building. Her husband, a distinguished anthropologist from University College, Oxford, had died (aged sixty-seven) only two months after his retirement; and only four months after buying the Sheep Street property. Often, since then, she had considered leaving the house and buying one of the older-persons' flats that had been springing up for the last decade all over North Oxford, for her present house was unnecessarily extensive and inappropriate for her solitary needs. Yet the children and the grandchildren (especially the latter) loved to stay there with her and to find themselves lost amid the random rooms. Only one real problem: she'd have to do something about the windows. There could be no Council permission for replacement windows; but the casements were quite literally falling apart. And the whole of the exterior just had to be repainted, from the gutterings along the top to the front door at the bottom. Should she get it all done? Three weeks earlier she'd stood and surveyed the scene. Could she ever find anywhere else so pleasingly attractive as this?

No! She'd stay.

She'd consulted the Yellow Pages and found *Barron,*

J, Builder and Decorator; not so far away, either – at Lower Swinstead. She'd rung him and he'd called round to survey the job. He'd seemed a personable sort of fellow; and when he'd quoted a reasonable (if slightly steep) estimate for both the restructuring and the repainting, she'd accepted.

He'd promised to be with her at 7.30 a.m. on Monday 3 August. And it was precisely at that time that he knocked in civilized manner on the front door of 'Collingwood', again admiring as he did so the drip-stone moulding above it.

Born in North Oxford, Mrs Bayley spoke her mind unapologetically: 'You look as if you've just come straight from the abattoir, Mr Barron!'

The builder (rather a handsome man, she thought) grinned wryly as he looked down at overalls bespattered with scarlet paint. 'Not my choice, Mrs B. I'm with *you*, all the way. If there's a better combination of colour than black and white and yellow, I don't know it.'

Mrs B felt gratified. 'Well, I'll let you get on then. I won't bother you – no one will bother you. It's all very quiet round here. Would you like some coffee later?'

'Tea, if you don't mind, Mrs B. Milk and two teaspoons of sugar, please. About ten? Smashing!'

From the ground-floor window she watched him as he removed the aluminium ladders from the top of the van, stood there for a few seconds looking up at the dormer window, then shaking out the first extension and, by means of a rope and pulley at the bottom, elongating the ladder to its fullest extent with a second, smaller extension. For a few seconds he stood there, holding the loftily assembled structure at right angles to the ground; then easing the pointed top of the third stage – most carefully, lovingly almost – into place against the casement of the dormer window some thirty feet above, before finally firming the bottom of the ladder on the compacted gravel of the pathway which divided the front of the houses there from the wide stretch of grass leading to the edge of Sheep Street, some four or five feet below.

For several minutes Mrs B stood by her front window on the ground floor, looking out a little anxiously to observe her builder's varied skills. Across the road, a solitary jogger in red trainers was running reasonably briskly past the Bay Tree Hotel, his tracksuit hood over his head, as if he were trying to work up a sweat; or just perhaps to keep his ears warm, since there was an unseasonal nip in the air that morning. Mrs B thought jogging a silly and dangerous way of keeping fit, though. She'd known the young North Oxford don who had written the hugely popular *Joys of Jogging*, and who had died aged twenty-seven, whilst on an early-morning not-so-joyful jog.

Jogging was a dangerous business.

Like climbing ladders.

And Mrs B's nerves could stand things no longer.

She would repair to the second-floor back-bedroom to continue with her quilting – as well as to quell the acute fear she felt for a man who (as she saw it) was risking his life at every second of his working day. But before doing so, she knew she had the moral duty to impart a few cautionary words of advice. And she opened the front door just as the builder was beginning his ascent, his left hand on a shoulder-high rung, his right hand grasping a narrowly serrated saw, a long chisel, and a red, short-handled Stanley knife.

'You *will* be careful, won't you? Please!'

The builder nodded, successively grasping each rung (each 'round' as the firemen say) at a point just above his shoulders as he climbed with measured step, professionally, confidently, to the top of the triple-length ladder. He'd always enjoyed being up high, ever since the vicar of St John the Baptist's in Burford had taken him and his fellow choirboys up to the top of the church. It was the first time in his young life he'd felt superior, felt powerful, as he traversed his way along the high places there with a strangely happy confidence, whilst the others inched their cautious way along the narrow ledges.

It was just the same now.

Once he had reached the top rung but three, he looked up and immediately decided he would be able to work at the top of the dormer without any trouble. Then he looked down, and saw that the ladder(s) beneath him, though sagging slightly in the middle (that was good), seemed perfectly straight and secure. Funny, really! Most people thought you were all right on heights just so long as you didn't look up or down. Rubbish! The only thing to avoid was looking laterally to left or right, when there really *was* the risk (at least for him) of losing all sense of the vertical and the horizontal. He dug his red Stanley knife into the upper lintel, then the lower sill; in each case, as he twisted the blade, finding the wooden texture crumble with ominous ease. Not surprising though, really, for he'd noticed the date above the door. He secured the top of the ladder to the gutterings – his normal practice – and began work.

At the appointed hour Mrs B boiled the kettle in the second-floor front (as her husband had called it); squeezed a Typhoo bag with the kitchen tongs; and stirred in two heaped spoonsful of sugar. Then, with the steaming cup and two digestive biscuits on a circular tray, she was about to make her way downstairs when something quite extraordinary flashed across her vision: she saw a pair of oblique parallel lines passing almost in slow motion across the oblong frame of the second-floor window. So sharply was that momentary configuration imprinted upon her retina that she was able to describe it so very precisely later that same afternoon; was able to recall that ear-splitting, skin-tingling shriek of terror as the man whose skull was about to be smashed to pieces fell headfirst on to the compacted pathway below, so very few yards from her own front door.

'Dead,' the senior paramedic had told her quietly, six minutes only after her panic-stricken call on 999. Incontrovertibly dead.

For the next hour or so Mrs Bayley wept almost uncontrollably. Partly from shock. Partly, too, from guilt, because (as she repeatedly reminded herself) it was *her* fault that he'd appeared upon the scene in the first place. She'd found his name among the local builders and house-renovators listed alphabetically in the Telephone Directory. In the Yellow Pages, in fact. Exactly where Sergeant Lewis, also, had discovered the address of J. Barron, Builder, together with a telephone number in Lower Swinstead.

Chapter Forty-Two

And what is the use of a book without pictures or conversations?

(Lewis Carroll, *Alice in Wonderland*)

Had he been left to himself, had he been without any knowledge of the context in which the apparent 'accident' had occurred, Lewis would not have suspected that it all amounted to murder. But it *had* been murder, he felt sure of that; and four hours earlier he had taken personal responsibility for initiating the whole apparatus of yet another murder enquiry. Same SOCOs as in the Sutton Courtenay murder, same pathologist, same everything; but with almost every sign of immediate activity over when, just before 3 p.m., Morse finally put in an appearance, very soon to be seating himself in Mrs Bayley's north-facing sitting room on the ground floor.

'Northamptonshire faring any better?' he asked the senior SOCO.

'Next year, perhaps,' said Eddie Andrews pessimistically.

'You'd be out of a job without me,' continued Morse. 'Just like Dr Hobson here.'

But the unsmiling pathologist could find little place in her heart for any banter and ignored the comment. As did Edwards.

The gloomy room was suddenly empty, apart from Sergeant Lewis. 'You said there wasn't any danger of *him* being murdered, sir.'

Morse could find no satisfactory answer, and stared silently out of the window until Mrs Bayley came in with (for Morse) wholly unwelcome cups of coffee and the same two digestive biscuits that Barron would have eaten with his over-sugared tea.

'You mentioned to Sergeant Lewis what you saw from the window? The one above this, wasn't it?'

She nodded. 'It made such a vivid imprint on the, er . . .'

'Retina?' suggested Lewis.

'Thank you, Sergeant. I *did* myself once work in the Oxford Eye Hospital.' She turned to Morse. 'You'll think me a silly old woman, but it reminded me of something I saw quite a few years ago now in one of the Sundays. There were these outline drawings sent in by readers and you had to guess what they were; and one of them always stuck in my, er . . .' (This time Lewis desisted.) She took a pencil and without permission made a quick little drawing in Lewis's notebook:

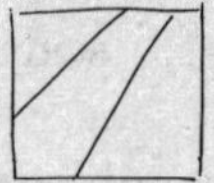

'Can't you guess, Inspector?' Her eyes twinkled.

Morse frowned, about to suggest something wildly inappropriate when the undeterred Lewis intervened:

'Giraffe walking past a window?'

'You clever man.'

'No!' Lewis smiled deprecatingly. 'I'd seen it before.'

He took a pencil and made an equally quick little drawing underneath:

'Aristocratic sardine in a tin!' she cried triumphantly.

'You clever woman!'

She shook her head. 'I'd seen it before.'

Morse sounded wearily impatient. 'I'm very sorry to interrupt the fun, Mrs Bayley, but . . .'

'Of course. Forgive me!'

'Which way was your, er, giraffe walking? Left to right? Right to left?'

'Left to right – exactly like I've drawn it, Inspector.'

'So if the ladder fell across the window from left to right, the bottom of the ladder must have slipped from right to left – that is, from your point of view here in the house, Mrs Bayley?'

'I'm not quite sure I follow you.'

'I mean, if someone had come along and given the ladder a hefty kick at the bottom, he'd probably have been coming from' (Morse pointed to the right) 'the centre of Burford, say, to' (Morse pointed vaguely to the left) 'wherever this road leads to?'

'Bourton on the Water.'

'Thank you, Lewis!'

'But we know that, sir – about the ladder, I mean. They found him six or seven yards to the right of the front door. That's from Mrs Bayley's point of view of course,' he added mischievously.

'Yes!' whispered the lady of the household, as so vividly she recalled that terrible sight, with the red Stanley knife lying there beside the shattered skull.

Morse was looking far from pleased. Even less so when a further cup of coffee was suggested. The room had become chillier, and he shivered slightly as he got to his feet. It was time for the clichés:

'If you *do* remember anything else – anything odd – anything unusual – anything at all . . .'

And suddenly she *had* remembered something. It was Morse's involuntarily shivering shoulders that had jogged – yes, *jogged* – her memory.

The jogger.

'There *was* something a bit unusual. We don't get many people jogging here – we're all a bit too old. But there was one this morning, about a quarter-to-eight. He'd pulled the hood of his tracksuit over his head as if he was feeling the cold a bit.'

'Or wasn't anxious to be recognized,' added Morse quietly.

'Perhaps *you* could recognize him though, Inspector. You see, he was wearing a very distinctive pair of training shoes. *Red*, they were.'

*

The two policemen left with appropriate expressions of gratitude; and with the two digestive biscuits still untouched on the circular tray, beside two cups, one of them full, of stone-cold coffee.

Chapter Forty-Three

For coping with even one quarter of that running course known as 'Marathon' – for coping without frequent halts for refreshment or periodic bouts of vomiting – a man has to dedicate one half of his youthful years to quite intolerable training and endurance. Such dedication is not for me

(Diogenes Small, 1797–1805, *The Joys of Occasional Idleness*)

After Lewis had turned right at the junction of Sheep Street and High Street and slipped the marked police car into the queue up to the A40 roundabout, Morse pointed peremptorily to the right, to the Cotswold Gateway Hotel.

Seated at a wall-settle in the bar, Morse tasted his pint of cask-conditioned ale and proclaimed it 'not so bad'. And Lewis, seated opposite, sipped his iced orange juice and said nothing.

Morse looked sourly out of sorts.

'Just nip and get me a packet of cigarettes, Lewis. Dunhill, if they've got them. I don't seem to . . .' In time-honoured fashion, he patted his trouser-pockets with little prospect, as it seemed, of finding any funds therein.

'I thought you'd stopped,' ventured Lewis, as minutes later Morse peeled off the cellophane.

'First today!' said Morse as with obvious gratification he inhaled deeply.

In turn, Lewis took a deep breath himself:

'You mustn't get cross with me if—'

'Certainly not.' Morse pushed his empty glass across the table.

Waiting at the bar, Lewis was rehearsing his carefully formulated sentence; was ready with it once he took his seat again.

'You mustn't be cross with me, sir, but—'

'Someone's been round to Mrs Barron? You've seen to that?'

'Dixon, yes. With WPC Towle – she's an experienced officer.'

'PC Towle, you mean. They're all PCs now, whatever the sex. Stands for Politically Correct.'

For the umpteenth time in his working life with Morse, Lewis knew that any potentially favourable wind had suddenly stopped blowing for him; and that it would be Morse who would now be sailing serenely on, whatever the state of the weather. As he did now:

'Something worrying you, Lewis?'

'Yes. Something *is*. We started off with two murders and you said you knew who the murderer was. And now this murderer of yours gets murdered himself and . . .'

'And there's not all that much point in sitting around in a pub all day just thinking about things. Is that what you're saying?'

'Yes! Why don't we sit back and look at what we've *got* – look at the *evidence*?'

'You're talking to me in italics, Lewis.'

'All right! But don't you think it *is* time – to start again – at the *beginning*?'

'No,' said Morse (no italics). 'Let's start with those red trainers.'

'All right. Good news that. There can't be more than a dozen people in Oxfordshire who've got a pair like that. Give us a few days. We'll find him. Guaranteed!'

'Let's hope you're right. Bit odd, though. Quarter-to-eight? And still running when Barron fell at ten-past-ten?'

'We're not all as unfit as you.'

'What? I could have run a marathon in that time. Once.'

Lewis smiled quietly to himself as Morse continued: 'You know, what worried me about the murders of Flynn and Repp was how anyone could have got away from that car without people noticing all the blood on his clothes. Then it struck me. Barron could have got away with it easily. His overalls were already covered in red – covered in the maroon paint from Debbie Richardson's out-house – *before* the murders. Nobody's going to worry about what he looks like, not in Lower Swinstead anyway. It's not exactly like spilling a bottle of Claret over your white tuxedo on the *QE2*. Is it now?'

'I wouldn't know, sir.'

'Being too clever, am I?'

'Perhaps.'

'You see, I thought *he* was clever, Barron. And in

spite of what some of these criminologists say, some criminals *are* clever.'

Lewis agreed. 'Pretty clever of our murderer to knock him off his ladder: no weapon, no fingerprints . . .'

'Mm.' Morse drained his beer and stood up. 'You will be glad to know that the brain is now considerably clearer, although I am still, if it's of interest to you, exceedingly puzzled as to why our murderer should decide to draw almost inevitable attention to himself by wearing such a conspicuous pair of plimsolls and running around Burford for two and a half hours.'

'Truth is, sir, some of 'em *aren't* all that clever. We both know that.'

By the time they were back at Kidlington HQ, the strangely disturbing news was already beginning to filter through.

Not that Morse himself was to be in his office that late Monday afternoon, for he had instructed Lewis to drop him off at his flat in North Oxford. He longed for some music: some Mozart (though not *Eine Kleine Nachtmusik*), some Wagner (though not the *Ride of the Valkyries*), some Vivaldi even (though not *The Four Seasons*), or some Vaughan Williams (though not *The Lark Ascending*).

Most especially not *The Lark Ascending*, since Morse (as we have seen) had already spent enough of his time with the dawn that day.

Chapter Forty-Four

CLINTON WINS ON BUDGET, BUT MORE LIES AHEAD

(From *USA's Best Newspaper Headlines*, 1997)

Sergeant Dixon swallowed the last of the jam-filled, sugar-coated doughnut: 'I'm beginning to think he's losing his marbles. First he says we go and bring Barron in – and the next thing is we're telling his missus he's croaked it.'

Sergeant Lewis looked up. 'How did she take it?'

'Not very well. Kate was very good with her but . . .'

'Her GP knows?'

'Yep. And she's got her mum and sister there, so . . . The kids though, innit? Poor little buggers: six and four.'

'Easier for them, I suppose.'

'Perhaps so. I just had the feeling though, you know, the marriage wasn't all that . . .' Dixon held out a shaky right hand, like that of a man with delirium tremens.

'What gave you that impression?'

Dixon tapped his right temple with a firmer finger. 'Experience, mate.'

He got up, walked over to the canteen counter, and looked hopefully along the glass shelves.

*

Lewis was summoned to Caesar's tent just after 5.30 p.m.

'Sorry state of affairs, Lewis, when a man can't even get a round of golf in on a Monday afternoon!'

'I just thought you ought to—'

'Winning I was. Two up at the turn. The swing really in the groove. And then . . .'

'I'm sorry, sir. But as I say I thought—'

'Where's Morse?'

'He, er, just went back home for a while.'

'Best place for him. Nothing but disaster since he took over things.'

'It was *you* wanted him,' said Lewis gently.

'Too clever – that's Morse's trouble! Time he jacked it in – like me. Make way for these bright young buggers checking in through the fast-track. It's all degrees these days, Lewis, and DNA, and . . .'

'Clipboards?'

Strange smiled sympathetically. 'Old Morse doesn't like clipboards much, does he?'

'No.'

'You'll miss him when he goes, won't you?'

'Is he going?'

'You'll be a richer man, for certain.'

Lewis made no reply.

'Did he have a couple of beers out at Burford?'

'Just the one.'

'Remarkable! And who paid for that, pray?'

'Oddly enough, *he* did.'

Strange looked across the desk shrewdly. 'Know

something, Lewis? You're nearly as big a liar as that American President.'

For the next ten minutes, and with no further lies, Lewis told the Chief Superintendent as much as he or anyone else (including Morse?) could know about the deliberate murder of J. Barron, Builder (and increasingly, as it appeared, Decorator) of Lower Swinstead.

'Mm!'

Strange contemplated the phone awhile; then rang Morse. But the ex-directory number was engaged. A minute later, he rang again; and, a minute later, again. Still engaged.

'Taken his phone off the bloody hook. Typical! He's supposed to be solving an assortment of murders.'

'He's a bit tired, sir. I don't think he's been sleeping very well.'

'Hardly surprising, is it? Having to get up for a pee every half hour?'

'I don't think it's *just* that.'

'What d'you mean?' Strange's voice was sharper.

'Well, nothing really.'

'*Out* with it, Lewis.'

'Just that sometimes perhaps it almost seems as if he doesn't really care all that much . . .'

'Interesting!'

For a while Strange pondered matters. Then decided: 'Go and knock him up!'

'Couldn't we give him a rest, just for today?' suggested a diffident Lewis. 'Not much *he* can do for the minute, is there? Not much *you* can do, either.'

'Mm. You could be right.'

'Why not get back to the golf course?'

'Because, Lewis – *because* I've let him off the hook. Three up at the turn . . .'

'I thought you said it was *two* up, sir.'

'Did I?'

Strange reached for the phone and rang Morse's number yet again.

Still engaged.

He stood up and repeated Lewis's words: 'Not much *you* can do, either. Why don't you just bugger off home. Eggs and chips, what?'

For a good deal of these exchanges between Strange and Lewis, Deborah Richardson had been standing, head tilted, in the narrow passageway at the back of the property, wondering whether she'd been sensible in choosing that particular shade of maroon for the newly established out-house. Two of the re-plastered walls had received their first coat – several weekends ago now – and they reminded her, according to the light, either of blackcurrant jam or of blood.

She thought she'd probably change things.

The phone rang.

She reached it at the sixth ring.

The arrangements, unusually involved, took a little while to get sorted out.

Once they were, she felt almost unprecedentedly excited.

Chapter Forty-Five

Nunquam ubi sub ubi!

After he had locked the door behind them she immediately, albeit a little nervously, commented upon the civilized appearance of the bachelor flat, listening with half an ear to a love-duet from one of the operas, although she had no idea which one; standing appreciatively for a while in front of a reproduction of *The Milkmaid*, although she had only just heard of Vermeer; looking wide-eyed along the shelves and shelves and shelves of books that lined three of the walls there; noticing too, although not herself a particularly house-proud woman, the thin layer of dust on the CD player and the thicker layer along the top of the skirting boards.

On the glass-topped coffee table there stood a chilled bottle of champagne, with two sparklingly bright glasses on their coasters beside it.

As quietly bidden, she sat down, the hem of the mini-dress riding more than halfway up her black-stockinged thighs as languidly she crossed her lengthy legs. Then, as he untwisted the wire at the top of the bottle, she turned away, holding the palms of her hands over her ears.

'No need for that,' he said. 'I'm an expert.'

Tilting the bottle to 45 degrees, he turned the cork

sharply, pulling only slightly – and that was it. Out! He filled the two glasses, sat opposite her, raised his glass, and said, 'Cheerio!'

It seemed to her a strange thing to say. 'Hello!' would surely have been more appropriate? It was obviously something he'd stored away in his verbal baggage from a period at least twenty-five years (she decided) earlier than her own.

Not that *that* mattered.

She sipped the champagne; sipped it again; and concluded, although she knew nothing whatever of Bruts and Crus, that it might well be fairly expensive stuff.

'Specially bought for the occasion?'

'No. I won it in a raffle.'

She took a further sip, then drank off the rest in a single draught. 'Lovely!'

He leaned forward and refilled her glass.

'Are you trying to get me drunk?'

'It might even things up a bit.'

'Mind if I smoke?'

'No. I'll join you.'

'You took a lot of trouble about gettin' me here – '

'Don't you like taxis?'

' – and I've never been told exactly what to wear before.'

He surveyed her vertically striped brown-and-white dress, and counted the button-holes: seven of them, the top three straining across her breasts.

'I like buttons. I've read that "unbuttoning" was Philip Larkin's favourite present participle.'

She let it go, fairly certain that she understood, and slowly unfastened the top button of her dress. 'I shall expect a fee, you know that.'

'Fee? You mean as well as the taxi and the champagne?'

She nodded, and pointed to the bottle. 'Will one be enough, do you think?'

'I won *two* in the raffle. The other one's cooling in the fridge.'

She drained her second glass, and sat back in the deeply comfortable settee, unfastening the second button as he again refilled her glass.

She patted the cushion beside her. 'Come and sit next to me.'

'In a little while. It's just that I'd like to get my fill of sitting here and lusting after you.'

She smiled. 'I wonder how we would have been together?'

'Know something? You've just quoted T. S. Eliot, virtually verbatim.'

She let it go, fairly certain that Eliot was a poet. But there wasn't much poetry out there – not in the world in which she moved. It all made her feel pleasingly important and decidedly sexy. Something more, too. As she tilted the third glass of champagne into her lipstick-moistened mouth; as she worked the third button of her dress loose; as she looked down at her bra-less breasts now almost fully exposed, she felt an animal sense of her own power – and she felt *good*.

He was right, though. She was enjoying teasing him, and he was enjoying being teased. No need for that rush to sexual congress the great majority of men (she knew full well) preferred.

'You know,' she said, 'I thought first of all when you rang that you wanted to ask me about the murders.'

'Afterwards, don't you think?'

She uncrossed her legs and leaned forward to light another cigarette. 'No. Let's get the inquisition over. Where's the bedroom, by the way?'

He pointed to a door on his left. 'Top sheet turned back in a very neat hypotenuse.'

She let it go, for her own mathematics had stopped well short of Pythagoras.

'I didn't ask you here for any grilling – you know that. But there *is* one thing I'd like you to tell me.'

'Fire away.'

'I think you've got a good idea who murdered Harry. And if you *have*, I'd like you to tell me.'

'But I don't – not for certain, I don't.' She recrossed the legs that a little earlier had been provocatively open.

'Go on!'

'It's just . . . well, I reckon perhaps it was Johnnie – *might* have been, anyway.'

'Why do you think that?'

'Somethin' he said and . . . well, you get the vibes sometimes.'

He seemed to know nothing of 'vibes' – interested only in strictly verbal significations.

'What exactly *did* he say?'

'Nothin' really. Nothin' I'm going to tell you, anyway.'

'When was this?'

'Sat'day night.'

'He was with you then?'

'Yes.'

'Did he often call round?'

'Quite often.'

'He'd been taking his time with your building alterations?' He drank the rest of the only glass of champagne he'd allowed himself – drank it swiftly, like a man in a pub who knows that if he stays any longer the next round will surely be his, and who therefore decides to depart.

'And you went to bed – quite often – with Barron?'

What the hell! If this fellow just so happened to be more gentle, more interesting, more articulate than some of her occasional partners – so bloody what!

'Yes!' She said it defiantly. 'Pretty good in bed he was, too!'

'I'm sorry,' he said slowly, 'but Mr Barron's dead.'

'You thought I didn't know?'

'How *did* you know?'

'Come off it! I wasn't born yesterday.'

He got to his feet and stepped over to sit beside her. For a while he held her right hand lightly in his; then, with his own right hand he refastened the top three buttons of the dress he'd specifically requested her to wear above no underwear.

Then he left the room and she heard his voice on the telephone: 'Radio Taxis? . . . One of your drivers, as soon as you can . . . to Burford . . . on my account, please . . . Morse.'

The two recently re-filled glasses of champagne – the one for her, and the one for him – remained untasted on the top of the coffee-table that had been polished so carefully before the arrival of Miss Debbie Richardson.

CHAPTER FORTY-SIX

> For the clash between the Classical and the Gothic revivals, visitors might go to the top end of Beaumont Street and compare the Greek glory of the Ashmolean on the left with the Gothic push of the Randolph Hotel on the right
>
> (Jan Morris, *Oxford*)

THE SPIRES RESTAURANT in the Randolph Hotel is an impressively elegant affair. A full complement of Oxford College crests is mounted in a frieze around the room, the regal ambience of the place relieved by the soft lighting of flambeaux on the brown-papered walls, and by two central chandeliers, holding similar flambeaux, that hang from the high-beamed ceiling. Twenty or so tables are spaciously arranged there, cross-draped with maroon tablecloths, and laid with gleaming silver-ware, sparkling wine glasses, and linen serviettes of a pale-ochre colour. The chairs, of uniform style, are upholstered in a material of bottle-green; and the colour combination of the room *in toto* has appealed to many (if not to all) as an unusually happy one. Two large windows on the room's northern side overlook Beaumont Street, with the Ashmolean Museum and the Taylorian Institute just across the way; whilst those seated beside three equally large windows on the eastern side look out on to the Martyrs'

Memorial, with St John's and Balliol Colleges beyond it, sharing with their fellow diners a vista of St Giles', the widest street in Oxford and visually one of the most attractive avenues in England.

At 7.15 that same evening, a man in the company of a much younger woman appeared to have eschewed either of these splendid views, for they had chosen a table (set for three) on the restaurant's west and windowless side, and now sat with their backs partly turned on the sprinkling of other early diners – like people who had no real objections to being seen, perhaps, but equally had no wish to draw attention to themselves.

At 7.25 p.m., the man was again consulting his wristwatch when a black-tied waiter asked if they would like a further drink while they waited.

Though expensive, the cocktail they had each been drinking was, in the young woman's judgement, 'absolutely yummy' – Cognac, Kümmel, Fraise Liqueur, topped with chilled champagne – and she nodded. Might just as well be happy about something.

'Same again,' said Frank Harrison. 'Ailish cocktails.' And when the waiter was gone: 'Where the hell's he got to? I've not got all bloody evening.'

'You've got to get back tonight, Dad?'

'That's got nothing to do with it. Seven-fifteen is seven-fifteen!'

'His hearing's not getting any better, you know. He probably thought you said seven-fifty.'

'Who's ever ordered a dinner for seven-fifty, for Christ's sake?'

For the moment Sarah said nothing further, looking

around her and enjoying the regal dignity of the restaurant. And in truth her father's tetchy impatience with Simon was not wholly displeasing to her. There had ever been a closer bond between herself and her father than with her mother; and, in turn, a very much closer bond between Simon and his mother than with his father. But such things were not spoken of freely in families; and it was better that way. Quite why she had always felt possessive about her father, she could not explain well even to herself. But she remembered clearly when she'd first been conscious of it: when she had crept silently downstairs late one night with a party in full swing below; and when, unseen herself, she'd watched her father kissing a young woman in the kitchen. She had cried herself to sleep that night. Only six, she'd been, but she could have murdered the woman. Disbelief? Shock? Outrage? All three mixed together, like a cocktail . . . like a cocktail topped up with a little chilled jealousy.

Simon appeared at 7.48. Like his father, not looking particularly in love with life.

'You're both early?' he ventured, as he took his seat. 'Seven-fifty, wasn't it?'

'Forget it!' His father passed over a menu.

'I could do with a drink first, Dad.'

'Just read the question-paper!'

Simon looked down at the succulent-sounding selections: *To Start . . . To Continue . . . Dessert . . . Beverages* – and felt a little happier, until Harrison père, brusquely ruling out starters, called over the waiter and put in their order for the main courses: Guinea Fowl; Calves'

Liver; Steak (medium). 'And a bottle of some decent Claret.'

'Just one?' queried Simon. 'Three of us?'

'Sarah's driving.'

'Aren't *you* driving, Dad?' asked Sarah.

'I don't really need my daughter to tell me what I can drink, thank you very much.'

Sarah put down her menu and stood up slowly. 'Excuse me a minute! I'm just off to . . .'

But before making her way to the Ladies' Powder Room, Sarah Harrison stopped at Reception.

'Can I ring one of your guests from here?'

'Of course.' The young girl smiled. 'Just ring the room number.' She pointed to the phone at the side of the desk.

'The name's Harrison – F. Harrison.'

'The receptionist tapped a few keys and looked at her video-screen.

'Yes. That's right.'

'Can you just give me the room number?'

'I'm sorry. I can't do that. It's strict company policy—'

'I'm his daughter, for God's sake!'

'Just a minute!' The girl moved away and the phone on the desk sprang to life when she returned: 'All yours.'

Sarah picked up the phone and listened, wondering what on earth she was going to say. But she needn't have bothered.

'Hellóho.' It was a female, husky, transatlantic voice.

Sarah put down the phone, a sudden glint of fury in her eyes.

She returned to the table to find father and brother,

heads close together, in what seemed a significant conversation. But there the exchanges stopped – whether because of her own return or the contemporaneous arrival of the main courses, Sarah was uncertain.

Thereafter the food was appreciatively consumed, the few transmensal exchanges wholly mundane and perfunctory, the bottle of Claret rapidly going and going and soon wholly gone.

'Another bottle, Dad?' suggested Simon.

'No!'

'I came on the *bus* – I'm going *back* on the bus.'

'But Dad's got to drive back to London, remember? Anyway I thought we were all supposed to keep sober tonight. Isn't that why we're here?'

'It *was*, yes. Just keep your voice down, will you? And read this. Simon's already seen it. Pretty quick off the mark, some of these local reporters.'

Sarah looked down at the copy of the *Oxford Mail* passed across to her, the lower half of the back page folded over to show the LATEST NEWS column:

> Thousands of families evacuated as Hurricane Georges lashes Florida Keys with torrential downpours and winds of over 120 m.p.h.
>
> Huge tailback on A40 as lorry carrying thousands of gallons of cows' blood overturns near Eynsham
>
> Local builder John Barron of Lower Swinstead pronounced dead on arrival at JR2 after falling from ladder in Sheep Street, Burford

Chapter Forty-Seven

Different things can add up in different ways whilst reaching an identical solution, just as 'eleven plus two' forms an anagram of 'twelve plus one'

(Margot Gleave, *A Classical Education*)

A WEALTH OF police personnel and well-targeted enquiries had borne swift if, here and there, unexpected evidence – evidence which Sergeant Lewis (alone in his office late that Monday evening) was able to shift and to categorize at his own pace. Thus far, the facts, and the glosses on the facts, formulated themselves as follows in Lewis's mind:

First. The shiny orange-red Stanley knife had been purchased, together with other items, from a hardware shop in Burford on the Saturday of the previous week (receipt unearthed in Barron's Expenses File). Barron could still have been a murderer – of course he could! – but quite certainly *not* with the knife he'd used that same morning as he stood almost atop the topmost section of the ladder and twisted the blade into the rotting, unresisting sill of the dormer window in Sheep Street.

Second. The stains on the overalls Barron had been wearing that morning had quite certainly *not* been human blood; but almost certainly smears of paint patented under the brand-name Cremosin, two-pint tins of which were found in Barron's garage, a space now used exclusively for building and decorating materials.

Third. On the morning of the Friday when Flynn and Repp had been murdered, Barron had left home around his usual time to spend some of the morning in Thame, where two properties were inviting tenders for renovation, for which Barron had been keen to submit his own estimates. Necessarily, of course, this evidence had been taken from Barron's wife, Linda; and yet (already) a dated parking ticket for four hours that morning (South Oxon DC, Cattle Market) had been found in Barron's van – evidence, if anything, to substantiate the claim that the builder had paid for a fairly extensive stay in the centre of Thame on July the 24th.

Fourth. There appeared, as yet, no evidence whatever that Barron had received any monies from anywhere to match the payments so regularly stashed into the balances of both Flynn and Repp. In short, *if* Barron had been the third man – *if* he had duly received his own share of the spoils for the conspiracy of silence – there was no sign of it, so far.

They were not in any way decisive, these findings and non-findings. The trouble was they all seemed to be pointing in the same direction.

Or were they?

For example (thought Lewis), it was surely to be expected that Barron would have got rid of the murder weapon and bought himself a new knife if in fact he *had* used the former for the murders.

For example (thought Lewis), it was most unlikely that Barron had only one pair of overalls. And if someone with an extravagantly fanciful mind (Morse!) could entertain the idea that a pair of white overalls covered with red paint was a good disguise for a soaking of blood . . . well, it *could* be, perhaps.

For example (thought Lewis), why buy a four-hour parking ticket in Thame on the day of the murders unless to create an alibi? Builders would usually have little difficulty in parking outside the properties in question. All right, parking was getting a nightmare everywhere, even for police cars, but . . .

For example (thought Lewis), why shouldn't Barron, like Flynn perhaps, have received his pay-offs in bank-notes, and kept them? No need to pay them into a bank or a building society. Why not put them in the loft? In the wardrobe? In a milk jug in the fridge? Like a few other self-employed builders, Barron might well be playing a canny little game with casual receipts, with ready-cash payments, with VAT evasions. And, if so, he would certainly not be over-anxious to account for any largish sums of money regularly entrusted to some official depository.

Lewis himself had felt pretty certain that Barron was their man; Morse was absolutely convinced. And yet the evidence thus far gathered seemed to be stacking up a little bit the wrong way. Lewis knew it. He had ever been a champion of the cumulative-evidence approach to crime: a piece-by-piece aggregation against a suspect that gradually mounted into an impressively documented pile that could be forwarded to the DPP. All right! Morse's method was occasionally very different. Yet many of the murders that the pair of them had solved together had been relatively uncomplicated: no real mystery, no real cunning, no real deviousness, no carefully woven web of deceit. Domestic stuff, next-door-neighbour stuff, most of it, with the husband returning home unexpectedly from work and finding his spouse abed with postman, milkman, gasman . . . builder?

But whichever way one looked at things, any direct evidence *against* the builder was proving surprisingly difficult to come by.

At 8.45 p.m., tired and hungry, Lewis decided that whatever further developments there were to be – and they were coming in all the time – he would have to take a break; and he drove home to Headington. But only after trying Morse's number once more. Ringing tone. No answer.

Morse came into HQ three-quarters of an hour later, and rang Lewis's home number immediately. Ringing tone. Answer.

Resignedly, about to start his eggs and chips, Lewis brought Morse up to date with the information received, suggesting that it was, at this point, all a bit ambivalent and equivocal, although in truth Lewis made use of neither of these epithets himself.

Morse sounded mildly interested, giving his own

verdict in somewhat pompous terms. He asserted that the character of the human condition was indeed 'ambiguity', the virtually inseparable mixture of the true and the false. But in the present case such apparent contradictions could be explained so very easily – in fact in exactly the way Lewis himself had just explained them. 'And,' continued Morse, 'you can be quite sure of one thing – no, two things: Barron murdered the pair of 'em; then somebody murdered Barron. Get that clear in your head, and we might make a bit of progress. OK? I'll see you in the morning.'

'Sir! Before you ring off. We tried to get you several times earlier but there was the engaged tone all the time.'

'That's funny. I only remember making the one call.'

'I thought perhaps – you know, you seemed a bit whacked . . .'

'You'd be wrong, Lewis. I *nearly* spent some time in bed. Not quite, though. Goodnight.'

The dramatic news came in at twenty minutes to midnight, as Morse sat at home making out a rough draft of his will. He'd no immediate relatives remaining, none at all; and therefore instructions for the post-mortem dissemination of all his worldly goods should not present too much of a complication. Nor did they. And he was writing out a fairish copy of a simple second draft – when the phone rang.

'What?'

. . .

'*What?*'

. . .

It was two minutes later before he spoke again: 'I'll be over straightaway.'

Chapter Forty-Eight

We trust we are not guilty of sacrilege in suggesting that the teaching of Religious Knowledge in some schools would pose an almighty challenge even for the Almighty Himself

(From the Introduction to *Religious Education in Secondary Schools: 1967–87*, HMSO)

Roy Holmes, aged fifteen, was a crudely disruptive pupil at school, a truculently unco-operative son in the Witney Street house he shared with his invalid mother, and a menace wherever he walked in the wider community. He took drugs; he was an inveterate and skilful shoplifter; he regularly snapped the stems of newly planted trees striving to establish themselves; he spat disgusting gobbets of phlegm on most of the pavements in Burford. In short, Roy Holmes was an appalling specimen of humankind. He deserved to have no real friends at all in life; and he had none.

Except one.

Ms Christine Coverley, aged twenty-seven, in her second year at Burford Secondary School, was not an impressive personage. A small, skinny, flat-chested, spotty-chinned, mousy-haired woman, she could scarcely have expected admirers anywhere – either among her fellow male members of staff, or among the motley collection of pupils, especially the boys, she was timetabled to teach. And, indeed, she had no such admirers.

Except one.

To complicate her incompetence as a teacher, she had been appointed *faute de mieux* to teach Religious Knowledge, a task wholly beyond her ability. Her classes taunted her mercilessly; and on more than one occasion such was the uproar in her classroom that teachers in adjacent rooms had barged in – only to find, with deep embarrassment, that a nominal teacher was already present there; and with even deeper embarrassment for Ms Coverley herself, resulting in fevered nightmares and anguish of soul that was often unbearable. One class, 4 Remove (Holmes's class), was even worse than the others – a group of pagan halfwits, of both sexes, whose interest in the pronouncements of major and minor prophets alike was nil. Over the year her hebdomadal clash with these monsters had been a terrifying ordeal; and the situation was quite hopeless. But no – not quite hopeless. Each night of term she would kneel in her bedsit and beseech the Almighty to grant her some deliverance from such despair. And one day her prayer had been answered.

In the middle of the summer term, at the end of one of her spectacularly disastrous lessons with 4 Remove, her eyes smarting with tears of humiliation, she had stopped the cocky, surly Holmes as he was about to leave the room:

'Roy! I know I'm useless. I *wouldn't* be though – if I got a bit of help, but I don't get any help from anyone.

I just want some help. And there's someone who *could* help me so easily if he wanted to. *You*, Roy!'

She turned away, wiped her moist cheeks, picked up her books, and left the empty classroom.

But Roy Holmes stood where he was, immobile. For the first time in his life someone had asked him for help – *him* – the despair of mother, vicar, social workers, headmaster, police; and suddenly he'd felt oddly, unprecedentedly moved, conscious somewhere deep inside himself of a compassion he'd never known and could scarcely recognize.

If, as Ms Coverley believed, her God sometimes moved in a mysterious way, it was not quite so dramatic as the way in which Roy Holmes was soon to move. In the next RK lesson one of the boys in the back row had been particularly foul-mouthed and disruptive, whilst Holmes had remained completely silent. After school that day, the youth in question returned home with a bleeding mouth, two broken teeth, and one bruised and hugely swollen eye. No one knew who was responsible. But then no one needed to know; since everyone knew who was responsible.

The nightmares were over, and Ms Coverley's last few weeks of the summer term were almost happy ones. Yet she knew that she was not the stuff that teachers are made of, and her resignation was received with relief by the headmaster. For the time being she decided to stay on in Burford, renewing the let on her ground-floor bedsit for a further two months.

The bell rang at 11.15 p.m. and Roy Holmes, somewhat the worse for drink or drugs or both, stood at the door when she opened it. His words were the words she had used to him, almost exactly so:

'I just want some help. And there's someone who can help me, if she wants to. You!'

It wasn't a lot he had to say; not a lot *she* had to say to the duty-sergeant, half an hour later, when she rang Burford Police Station; and not a lot when *he*, in turn, rang Thames Valley HQ, almost immediately put through to the home number of the man in charge of the enquiry into the death of J. Barron, Builder.

Roy Holmes, a pupil of Burford Secondary School, aged fifteen, living at 29A Witney Street, had been riding his mountain bike along the footway on the southern side of Sheep Street at approximately 10 a.m. that Monday, 3 August. By the youth's own admission he was showing off, expectorating regularly, terrorizing any pedestrians, riding no-handed – when he'd decided to defy all superstition and ride beneath the ladder he saw in front of him – when he'd badly misjudged whatever he'd misjudged – when he'd collided sharply with the bottom of the ladder – when the whole thing had jerked sideways – and when a man had toppled from the top of the ladder and landed on the compacted pathway outside 'Collingwood' . . .

Chapter Forty-Nine

'God save thee, ancient Mariner!
From the fiends, that plague thee thus! –
Why look'st thou so?' – 'With my cross-bow
I shot the Albatross.'

(Coleridge, *The Rime of the Ancient Mariner*)

THE FOLLOWING MORNING, Morse had been early summoned to the presence, summoned to Caesar's tent.

'Won't do, will it, Morse. Just won't do! You tell us to go and bring Barron in. And why? Because you say he's knifed Flynn and Repp. Fine! There's three of 'em, you say, originally involved in the cover-up over the Harrison murder, three of 'em prepared to stick to their stories – for a fee of course. Then suddenly we find two of 'em murdered, and somebody – *somebody*, Morse – thinks this'll be as good an opportunity as any to finish off number three. So whoever this somebody is, he decided he's been forking out way over the odds anyway, and he goes ahead with his plan. He's been living with three albatrosses round his neck, and suddenly he finds somebody else has cut the strings off *two* of 'em. Too good an opportunity to be missed. All adds up, doesn't it? Except, matey, for one thing: Barron's death turns out to be a bloody *accident*. Just some teenage lout . . .'

Strange took a breather, gulped down the last of his coffee, and stuck another chocolate biscuit in his mouth: 'Fancy a coffee?'

'No.'

'They'll be open in an hour, you mean?'

'Fifty minutes, actually.'

Strange suddenly sounded extremely pleased with himself: 'Did you actually say "actually", Morse?'

Oh dear.

It was Strange who broke the ensuing silence. 'Where are we, in all this?' he asked softly.

'I dunno. I felt convinced that the same fellow – Barron – had murdered both of them, both Flynn and Repp. I thought the motive was a pretty familiar one – money. You know, there's nothing much worse in life than people doing the same job and getting paid at different rates. It happens in every office, in every profession in the land. Anger . . . jealousy . . . bitterness . . . usually controllable but potentially dynamite. And I thought Barron had found out he wasn't doing half so well as his partners in crime.'

'And who exactly is this golden goose?'

'You know that as well as I do.'

'I do?'

'Oh, yes,' replied Morse quietly.

A knock at the door heralded PC Kershaw, the fast-track recruit with a First in History from Keble who'd driven Morse out to Sutton Courtenay, and whose duties for the present consisted mostly of supplying the Chief Superintendent with regular coffee and chocolate biscuits.

'Anything I can do for you, sir?'

'Yes,' growled Strange. 'Bugger off!' Then, turning back to Morse: 'Are you making *any* progress?'

'Early days. We've not even had the final path reports yet. Life's full of surprises.'

'And disappointments.'

'That too, yes.'

'Well if it *wasn't* Barron . . .'

'Dunno. But I'm sure the key figure in both cases is one and the same person – the man who was in bed with Yvonne Harrison the night she was murdered.'

'You don't think it was Repp?'

'No. As I see it, Repp had been recce-ing the property, maybe for several nights. It was going to be a gift for any professional burglar like him. And he knew pretty well all that went on that night—'

'Knew the fellow who was in bed with Yvonne?'

'Yes. But I don't think it was Repp or any other burglar who disturbed the bondage session that evening. I think that was somebody else. And I think it's most likely that our lover-boy knew that someone else.'

'And in your book Barron was the lover-boy?'

'Well, he was doing a job for her – hanging about the place quite a bit – strong, good-looking sort of fellow – the husband away a good deal of the time . . .'

'But I'll say it again – what if it *wasn't* Barron?'

'Plenty of other candidates, surely?'

'Oh yes?'

Morse measured his words carefully. 'I think that anyone meeting Yvonne Harrison, if she turned things on a bit – anyone, including me – would have given a month's beer money – '

'A week's in your case.'

' – for an hour or two between the sheets, or between the bedposts, or between anywhere else. By, er, by all accounts she was a . . . well, let's say she had the same effect on men as they tell me Viagra has on the impotent, or the victims of chronic erectile dysfunction, as they're known these days.'

'Really! So for all we know, this chap could have been a client from North Wales or somewhere.'

'More probably South Wales, sir.'

'And much more probably, somebody local.'

'Agreed.'

'Any ideas?'

'Well, the only fellow I've met in that little community who's topped up with surplus testosterone is the landlord of the Maiden's Arms.'

'You've interviewed him?'

'No.'

'Why not?'

'Because I'm still trying to come to terms with the fact that it *wasn't* Barron. You see I still think he's the key to all this ridiculously complex business. But complex only because those involved deliberately *made* it complex.'

'Barron's phone calls, you mean? No luck there?'

'No. Change of BT office, change of procedure, change of monitoring, files re-classified . . . no hope! Wouldn't help anyway. All Barron said was that he'd rung her and the number was engaged; and then rung her again and the call wasn't answered. Neat, wasn't it? No record of anything.'

'He was lying, you think?'

'Yes.'

'What about the burglar alarm?'

'Thunderstorm, possibly – that sets 'em off.'

'There wasn't a thunderstorm that night.'

'No? Probably a cat then – they set 'em off too.'

'They hadn't got a cat.'

'Oh.'

Strange lumbered to his feet. 'Look! You surely don't still think Barron's your man, do you?'

Morse smiled. '*Don't I?*'

Chapter Fifty

I can't tell a lie – not even when I hear one
(John Bangs, 1862–1922)

In the world of detective fiction, alibis are frequently concocted in order to mystify the reader. In what is called the 'real' world they usually provide an invaluable method of eliminating a few runners in an already limited field, thereby affording the police a better prospect of backing the likely winner. For (except in Morse's mind) an alibi is an alibi: if someone is seen in one place at one particular time, it seems highly improbable that this same someone may be seen in some other place at the *same* time. Yet it is sometimes difficult adequately to corroborate an alibi – viz, that plea of the criminal to have been in another place at the material time; and alibis may well be doubted, closely checked, and indeed, on occasion, be spectacularly broken.

This in various ways.

It is highly unlikely, for example, that a well-focused video camera will be in operation in that first particular place; and even if it is, some smart electronic alec may well be able to doctor the evidence. Almost always, therefore, corroboration will depend on the testimony of eyewitnesses who, even if honest, can be the victims of tricks of memory over times and sightings; *or*, on the testimony of witnesses who are dishonest, and are willing to fabricate falsehoods – for friends, perhaps, or for a fee. The alibi problem is further complicated by the confident assertion of some mystic sects that one *can*, in fact, be in two places simultaneously, although the police are grateful that such bizarre beliefs are currently not widely embraced.

Morse himself championed the view that all alibis should probably be ignored in the first instance, on the not illogical grounds that if just *one* of them were suspect, it was sensible to assume that all of them were . . .

Such views (with variants) Sergeant Lewis had heard several times before, and it was therefore with some diffidence that he broached the subject the following morning.

'Don't you reckon it would be a good idea to get all these alibis sorted out a bit clearer?'

'A bit more clearly, Lewis.'

'The night Mrs Harrison was murdered, the morning Flynn and Repp were murdered—'

'And don't forget Monday morning.'

'Barron, you mean? You surely don't still think—?'

Morse held up his right hand in surrender. 'You're right, perhaps. Let's make a list. Well, you make a list. Ready?'

He steepled his slim fingers in front of him and stared into the middle distance, though with little observable enthusiasm in his eyes:

'Frank Harrison
Simon Harrison
Sarah Harrison
Harry Repp
John Barron . . .'

'That's the short-list?'

Morse nodded.

'OK. First I'll recheck where they all were, or where they were all supposed to be, first when Mrs Harrison—'

'Already been done. You've read the files.'

'Weren't checked very thoroughly though, some of 'em.'

'Long time ago, Lewis. People forget or want to forget or pretend to forget.'

'A day like that though, when she was murdered? Biggest day in village history. Everybody remembers where they were, like when Kennedy was assassinated.'

'Nonsense, Lewis! People remember where they were and what they were doing at the time they *heard* of things like that. Agreed. But what else? Do you remember what you were doing for the rest of the day when Kennedy was shot? Do you?'

'No. I take your point, sir.'

'Who are you thinking of particularly?'

'Well the family got away with some pretty flimsy alibis, didn't they? Especially Simon and Sarah. No one seems to have checked them much at all.'

'Ye-es.'

'Simon said he got home from work about a quarter-past five, had a meal, then went down to the ABC cinema in George Street to see *The Full Monty*. Still had his ticket if I remember rightly.'

Morse nodded and Lewis continued:

'Sarah? She was at a Diabetes Conference in the Radcliffe Infirmary that day – no doubt about that. And after it had finished she went over the road to the Royal Oak for a drink with a few friends – no doubt about that either – and then left for her flat in Jericho at about a quarter-to-seven, where she listened to *The Archers*, had a long hot bath, watched the *Nine O'Clock News*, and then had an early night.'

'Making no mention in the course of her evidence that she had a phone call in the middle of the evening, as a result of which she tore down to the ABC Cinema, bought a ticket for *The Full Monty* – '

'Probably no seats left that night, sir.'

' – bought a ticket and promptly tore it across the middle and then tore out of the place – '

'Sir! Not so much of this tearing about all over the shop! She'd sprained her ankle just before then and she'd probably be hobbling—'

' – she hobbled out of the cinema with a very valuable little alibi in her pretty little hand.'

'Alibi for Simon, you mean?'

'Or for herself.'

'You're losing me again, sir.'

'I'm losing myself. Don't worry.'

'What about Frank Harrison?'

'You tell *me*!'

'Well, anyone who finds the body first is usually

going to be number one in your book, I know that. But there's no doubt about Paddy Flynn being on taxi-shift from 8 p.m. that night. He was seen on and off by his fellow-drivers as well as being contacted at regular intervals from base. No doubt either about him picking up Frank Harrison about eleven from Oxford railway station. But that's not to say – *is* it, sir? – that Harrison had just got off a train at the railway station. It would be the most natural thing in the world for anyone to *think* he had, but . . .'

Morse smiled. 'Could hardly have put it better myself. But somebody paid Flynn for something. So it was probably for something that happened after eleven o'clock. And there was only one person with Flynn then: Frank Harrison. And he's the only one of the whole bunch with the sort of money to buy Flynn off.'

'*And* buy Repp off, if we're right about him being there that night. Harrison must be earning, well . . .'

'A little more than you are, Lewis, yes. In fact he got a bonus – a *bonus* – of £85,000 last year. Seems he was sorting out his bank's involvement in the Nazi confiscation of Jewish assets, and his bosses were more than pleased with him.'

'How on earth do you know that?'

'Aren't we supposed to be detectives?'

Lewis pursued the matter no further. 'So, what do you think?'

'Waste of time as far as the children are concerned. But it might help to look at their father again.'

'You think it was Harrison who murdered his wife?'

'I dunno.'

'You think he murdered Flynn and Repp?'

'He had enough reason to. He couldn't go on forking out indefinitely.'

'So we'd better have a careful check on wherever *he* was that Friday morning.'

'Well, wherever else he was he wasn't in his London office.'

'How on earth—?'

'What else can I tell you?' asked Morse wearily.

'I've just asked you. Do you think he murdered Flynn and Repp?'

'He could have done. But somehow I don't believe he did.'

'So who . . .?'

'I keep telling you, Lewis. My modest bet is still on Barron.'

'Shouldn't we be looking a bit more into their backgrounds? Repp's? Flynn's? Barron's?'

'I don't think we're going to get anything more out of Debbie Richardson.'

'Why do you say that?'

'Just a feeling, Lewis. Just a feeling.'

'What about Flynn?'

Morse nodded. 'You're right. He was being paid for something. Exactly what, though . . . Yes. Leave that to me.'

'What about Barron? Shall I leave that to you, as well?'

'No, no! The less I have to do with the women in this case the better. You go along. And if you can find out more about where he was or where he was supposed to be on both those days . . . Yes, you do that!'

'All right. But don't you think we ought to widen the net, sir? Haven't we got any other suspects?'

'Tom Biffen, perhaps?'

Lewis's eyebrows shot up. 'You mean—?'

'The landlord of the Maiden's Arms, no less. We'll go out and interview him together once we get a chance. You'll be able to buy me a pint.'

'But wasn't it a Tuesday when Mrs Harrison was murdered?'

'You're right, yes.'

'Well, he always goes out fishing on Tuesdays, Biffen – dawn to dusk.'

'Really? How on earth do you know that?'

'Aren't we supposed to be detectives, sir?'

Chapter Fifty-One

Once cheated, wife or husband feels the same; and where there's marriage without love, there will be love without marriage

(Benjamin Franklin, *Poor Richard's Almanack*)

At 9.30 a.m. the following day, Mrs Linda Barron stepped back from the threshold, nodding rather wearily as Lewis produced his ID. In the kitchen, he accepted her offer of instant coffee.

She was a brunette of medium height, slightly overweight, with a small, cupid-lipped mouth, wearing a blue-striped kitchen apron over skirt and blouse.

Lewis decided she was coping with life, just about.

The smallish kitchen was cluttered with shelves and cupboards, the floor-space additionally limited by the usual appliances: cooker, dishwasher, fridge, microwave, washing machine. Lewis immediately noticed the damp patch of crumbling ceiling over the cooker. Same old story! Husband a plumber, and a tap-washer never gets fixed; husband a builder, and there's a two-year wait before a bit of re-plastering gets done . . . Difficult to say, offhand, whether the Barrons were better or worse off than they appeared.

From experience, Lewis had learned never to try his hand at commiseration or counselling; but when he questioned her, he did so in the kindly fashion that was his wont. He asked her tactfully about the times and places relevant to her husband's alibis; more tactfully about the family finances; most tactfully about the state of her marriage.

Alibis? On the two key dates she could be of little help. Mondays to Fridays he usually got home about 6 p.m., when she'd have a cooked meal ready for him. Between 8 and 9 p.m. he'd quite often go out for a pint or two, either down at the local or sometimes at a pub in Burford. But he wasn't a big drinker. She knew he'd rung up Mrs Harrison on the night of her murder – something about roofing tiles – but he'd not been able to get through. Tried twice – he'd told her so; the police knew all about that, though: it had been important evidence. On the second key date, the Friday, he'd gone off to Thame in the morning, she remembered that. He'd been asked for an estimate on some work there, and he'd gone over to size up the job. She didn't know – didn't ask – what he'd done after that; but he was back home at the usual sort of time. He always was on Fridays, because it was eggs-and-chips day – his favourite meal.

Mr J. Barron, Builder, was going up in Lewis's esteem.

Money? They were OK. For the past three years or so houses were selling fairly freely again; and mobility in the housing market always meant new owners wanting some renovation or structural changes: conservatories, extensions, garages, loft-conversions, patios. Yes, the past few years had been fairly good for them: she knew that better than he did. Her part in the business, for which she took a small official salary, was to look after the books: tax returns, invoices, VAT, expenses, bad debts – everything. If he was ever in the habit of accepting cash instead of the usual cheque-payments, she wasn't aware of it; and quite certainly neither of them was sufficiently bright in business-finance to be able to exploit any tax loopholes. She knew nothing about any regular payments in cash. ('What payments?') She'd have known if any envelopes had arrived through the post, because the mail was invariably delivered *after* he'd set off for work every morning. They had a joint account; and he had a separate private account, with an overdraft facility of £2,000.

Mr J. Barron, Builder, Lewis decided, was hardly in the Gates or the Soros brackets.

Marriage? It was only here that Linda Barron was less than fluent in her answers.

'Would you say the pair of you had a "tight" marriage?'

'. . . Perhaps not, no.'

'Was he ever unfaithful?'

'Aren't *most* men?'

'Not all of them,' said Lewis quietly.

She shrugged her shoulders.

'*Was* he?'

'. . . He may have been.'

'Do you think he ever had an affair with Mrs Harrison?'

'. . . No.'

'Would you have known?'

She smiled bleakly. 'Probably.'

'What about you, Mrs Barron? Were *you* ever unfaithful?'

'. . . Once or twice.'

'With Harry Repp?'

'God, no! I hardly knew him.'

'Tom Biffen?'

'. . . Once. He called one afternoon about eighteen months ago to bring a leg of lamb Johnnie won in the raffle. And . . .'

'What happened?'

'Do I *have* to tell you, Sergeant?'

'No. No, you don't, Mrs Barron.'

Wedlock for the Barrons (Lewis agreed with Dixon) did not appear to have been a wholly idyllic affair.

As he left, Lewis noticed on the wall in the hallway a framed photograph of a strong, fine-looking man in military uniform.

'Your husband?'

She nodded; and the rust-flecked hazel eyes were filmed with tears.

Chapter Fifty-Two

With a gen'rous ol' pal who will pick up the tab
It's always real cool in a nice taxi-cab
(J. Willington Spoole, *Mostly on the Dole*)

If Lewis's (Morse-initiated) interview had been a task of some fair difficulty, Morse's own (self-appointed) mission was wholly straightforward – the single problem being that of finding a parking-space in a car-cluttered Warwick Street, just off the Iffley Road.

In the outer office of Radio Taxis were seated two young ladies, their telephones, keyboards, and VDUs in front of them, with maps of Oxford, Oxfordshire, and the UK, pinned on the walls around. Morse was ushered through into the inner sanctum, where a six-foot, strongly built man of fifty or so, his short, dark hair greying at the temples, introduced himself:

'Jeff Measor, Company Secretary. How can I help?'

'Flynn, Paddy Flynn, he used to work for you – until you sacked him.'

Yes. Measor remembered him well enough. Flynn had worked for the company for just over a year. It was generally agreed that he'd been a competent driver, but he'd never fitted very happily into the team. There'd been several complaints from clients, including the reported 'Just help me get these bitches out of here!' request to the doorman at The Randolph, where three giggly and slightly unstable young ladies were attempting to alight. And, yes, a few other complaints about his less-than-sympathetic rejoinders to clients when sometimes (quite inevitably so) traffic-jams had caused his cab to be late. But Flynn had been a punctual man himself, invariably clocking in on time – one of those dedicated night-drivers who far preferred the 6 p.m.–2.30 a.m. shift. He'd known Oxford City and the surrounding area well – a big factor in taxi work; and there'd been no suspicion of his driving innocent clients on some roundabout route just to jump up the fare.

'Could he have fiddled a few quid here and there?'

'Not so easy these days. Everything's computerized in the cab. But I suppose . . .'

'How?'

'Well, let's say if he's cruising around the City Centre and gets a fare and doesn't clock it in. Just takes the cash and then goes back to cruising round as if he's been doing nothing else all the time . . .'

'Did he do that sort of thing?'

'Not that I know of.'

Morse was looking increasingly puzzled. 'He seems to have been a reasonably satisfactory sort of cabbie, then.'

'Well . . .'

'So why did you sack him?'

'Two things, really. As I said, he wasn't a good advertisement for the company. We always tell our drivers about the importance of friendliness and courtesy; but he wasn't quite . . . he always seemed a bit surly, and I doubt he ever swapped a few cheerful words with any of his passengers. Man of few words, Paddy Flynn. Not always though, by all accounts.'

'No?'

'No. Seems he used to do the rounds of the pubs and clubs – Oxford, Reading and so on – with a little group. Played the clarinet himself, and introduced things with a bit of Irish blarney. Quite popular for a while, I think, 'specially in those pubs guaranteeing music being played as loud as possible.'

Morse looked pained as Measor continued: 'Anyway, he just didn't fit in here. No one really liked him much. Simple as that!'

'*Two* things though, you said?' prompted Morse gently.

For the first time the articulately forthright Company Secretary was somewhat hesitant:

'It's a bit difficult to explain but . . . well, he never quite seemed up to coping with the radio side of the job. Still very important, the radio side is, in spite of all this latest technology. You know the sort of thing: we'll be phoning from the office here and asking one of the drivers if he's anywhere near Headington or Abingdon Road or wherever . . . Mind you, Inspector, the radio's not all *that* easy: distortion, interference, crackle, feedback, traffic-noise . . . You've certainly got to have your wits about you – and, well, he just couldn't quite cope with it well enough.'

'It doesn't seem all that much of a reason for sacking him, though.'

'It's not exactly like that, Inspector. You see, I don't myself employ drivers directly. They're contracted out to me. And so if I say to any owner of a taxi, or a group of taxis, "Look, there's no more work for you here" – well, that's it. It's like sub-contracting work on a building site. If I want to sack one of my staff here though, in the office, I'll have to give one verbal – recorded – and two written warnings.'

'No problems with Flynn, then?'

'Oh, no. And glad to see the back of him. Everybody was. One day he was here . . .'

'. . . and the next day he was gone,' added Morse slowly, as he thanked the Company Secretary – and felt that long familiar shiver of excitement along his shoulders.

Chapter Fifty-Three

At which period there were gentlemen and there were seamen in the navy. But the seamen were not gentlemen; and the gentlemen were not seamen

(Macaulay, *History of England*)

For Morse, that early evening followed much the same old pattern: same sort of bundle of ideas abounding in his brain; same impatience to reach that final, wonderfully satisfying, penny-dropping moment of insight; same old pessimism about the future of mankind; same old craving for a dram of Scotch that could make the world, at least for a while, a kindlier and a happier place; same old chauffeur – Lewis.

It was just after 6.30 p.m. when they were shown up a spiral flight of rickety stairs to the small office immediately above the bar of the Maiden's Arms. Around the walls, several framed diplomas paid tribute to the landlord's expertise and the cleanliness of his kitchen, although the untidy piles of letters and forms that littered the desk suggested a less than methodical approach to the hostelry's paperwork.

'Quick snifter, Inspector?'

'Later, perhaps.'

'Mind if I, er . . .?' Biffen reached behind him and poured out a liberal tot of Captain Morgan. 'You make me feel nervous!' Knocking back the neat rum in a single swallow, he smacked his lips crudely: 'Ahh!'

'Royal or Merchant?' asked Morse.

'Bit o' both.' But Biffen seemed disinclined to discuss his earlier years at sea, and came to the point immediately: 'How can I help you, gentlemen?'

So Morse told him: for the moment the village seemed to be at the centre of almost everything; and the pub was at the centre of village life and gossip; and the landlord was always going to be at the centre of the pub; so if . . .

For Lewis, Morse's subsequent interrogation seemed (indeed, was) aimless and desultory.

But Biffen had little to tell.

Of *course* the villagers had talked – still talked – talked all the time except when that media lot or the police came round. No secret, though, that the locals knew enough about Mrs H's occasional and more than occasional liaisons; no secret that they listened with prurient interest to the rumours, the wilder and wackier the better, concerning Mrs H's sexual predilections.

It was left to Lewis to cover the crucial questions concerning alibis.

The day of Mrs H's murder? Tuesday, that was. And Tuesday was always a special day – a sacrosanct sort of day. (He'd mentioned it earlier.) His one day off in the week when he refused to have anything at all to do with cellarage, bar-tending, pub-meals – fuck 'em all! Secretary of the Oxon Pike Anglers' Association, he was. Had been for the past five years. Labour of love! And every Tuesday during the fishing season he was out all day, dawn to dusk. Back late, almost always, though he couldn't say exactly when that day. No one had questioned him at the time. Why should they? He'd pretty certainly have met a few of his fellow-anglers but . . . what the hell was all this about anyway? Was he suddenly on the suspect-list? After all this time?

Thomas Biffen's eyes had hardened; and looking across at the brawny tattooed arms, the ex-boxer Sergeant Lewis found himself none too anxious ever to confront the landlord in a cul-de-sac.

Biffen was a family man? Well, yes and no, really. He'd been married – still was, in the legal sense. But his missus had gone off four years since, taking their two children with her: Joanna, aged three at the time, and Daniel, aged two. He still regularly gave her some financial support; always sent his kids something for their birthdays and Christmas. But that side of things had never been much of a problem. She was living with this fellow in Weston-super-Mare – fellow she'd known a long time – the same fellow in fact she'd buggered off with when they'd broken up.

'Whose fault was that?' asked Morse quietly.

Biffen shrugged. 'Bit o' both, usually, innit?'

'She'd been seeing someone else?'

Biffen nodded.

'Had *you* been seeing someone else?'

Biffen nodded.

'Someone local.'

'What's that got to do with it?'

It was Morse's turn to shrug.

'Well . . . Chap's got to get his oats occasionally, Inspector.'

'Mrs Harrison?'

Biffen shook his head. 'Wouldna minded, though!'

'Mrs Barron?'

'Linda? Huh! Not much chance there – with *him* around? SAS man, he was. Probably slice your prick off if he copped you mucking around with his missus.'

Lewis found himself recalling the photograph of the confident-looking young militiaman.

'Debbie Richardson?' suggested Morse.

'Most people've had a bit on the side with her.'

'You called yourself occasionally? While Harry was inside?'

'Once or twice.'

'Including the day after he was murdered.'

'Only to take a bottle – I told you that.'

'You fancied her?'

'Who wouldn't? Once she's got the hots on . . .'

Morse appeared to have lost his way, and it was Lewis who completed the questioning: 'Where were you earlier on the Friday when Flynn and Repp were murdered?'

'In the morning? Went into Oxford shopping. Not much luck, though. Tried to get a couple of birthday presents. You'd hardly credit it, but both o' my kids were born the same day – 3rd o' September.'

'Real coincidence.'

'Depends which way you look at it, Sergeant. Others'd call it precision screwing, wouldn't they?'

It was a crude remark, and Morse's face was a study

in distaste as Biffen continued: 'Couldn't find anything in the shops though, could I? So I sent their mum a cheque instead.'

Downstairs, it was far too early for any brisk activity; but three of the regulars were already foregathered there, to each of whom Biffen proffered a customary greeting.

'Evening, Mr Bagshaw! Evening, Mr Blewitt!'

One of the warring partners allowed himself a perfunctory nod, but the other was happily intoning a favourite passage from the cribbage litany: 'Fifteen-two; fifteen-four; two's six; three's nine; and three's twelve!'

With an 'Evening, Mr Thomas!' the landlord had completed his salutations.

In response, the youth pressed the start-button yet again, his eyes keenly registering the latest alignment of the symbols on the fruit machine.

'Now! What's it to be, gentlemen? On the house, of course.'

'Pint of bitter,' said Morse, 'and an orange juice. Want some ice in it, Lewis?'

A bored-looking barmaid folded up the *Mirror*, and pulled the hand-pump on the Burton Ale.

Chapter Fifty-Four

The time you won your town the race
We chaired you through the market-place;
Man and boy stood cheering by,
And home we brought you shoulder-high.

—

To-day, the road all runners come,
Shoulder-high we bring you home,
And set you at your threshold down,
Townsman of a stiller town

(A. E. Housman,
A Shropshire Lad, XIX)

It was just after 7.30 p.m. that same evening in the car park of the Maiden's Arms that Morse, after admitting to a very strange lapse of memory in missing *The Archers*, suddenly decided on a new line of enquiry that seemed to Lewis (if possible) even stranger: 'Drive me round to Holmes's place in Burford.'

'Why—?' began a weary Lewis.

'Get *on* with it!'

The ensuing conversation was brief. 'What did you make of Biffen, sir?'

'He decided to enlist in the ranks of the liars, like the rest of 'em.'

'Well, yes . . . if Mrs Barron was telling me the truth.'

'Probably not important anyway.'

Lewis waited a while. 'What *is* important, sir?'

'Barron! That's what's important. I'm still not absolutely sure I was on the wrong track but . . .'

'. . . but it looks as if you were.'

Morse nodded.

'What did you make of—?'

'Concentrate on the driving, Lewis! They're not used to Formula-One fanatics round here.'

A blurred shape slowly formed through the frosted glass of the front door, its green paint peeling or already peeled, which was finally opened by a pale-faced, wispily haired woman of some fifty-plus summers.

Lewis paraded his ID. 'Mrs Holmes?'

With hardly a glance at the documentation, the woman neatly reversed her wheelchair and led her visitors through the narrow, bare-floored, virtually bare-walled passageway – for indeed there was just the one framed memento of something on the wall to the left.

'I suppose it's about Roy?' She spoke with the dispirited nasal whine of a Birmingham City supporter whose team has just been defeated.

In the living room, in a much-frayed armchair, sat a youth smoking a cigarette, drinking directly from a can of Bass, a pair of black-stringed amplifiers stuck in his ears.

He vaguely reminded Morse of someone; but that was insufficient to stop him taking an intense and instant dislike to the boy, who had made no attempt to straighten his lounging sprawl, or to miss a single lyric from the latest rap record – until he saw Morse's lips speaking directly to him.

'Wha'?' Reluctantly Roy Holmes removed one of the ear-pieces.

'Why didn't you answer the door yourself, lad, and give your mum a break?'

The youth's eyes stared back with cold hostility. 'Couldn't 'ear it, could I? Not wi' this on.'

No Brummy accent there; instead, the Oxfordshire burr with its curly vowels.

His mother began to explain. 'It's the police, Roy—'

'Again? Bin there, 'aven't I. Made me statement. What more do they want? Accident, wonnit? I didn't try to 'ide nuthin. What the fuck?'

Morse responded quietly to the outburst. 'We appreciate your co-operation. But do you know what you've made of yourself in life so far? Shall I tell you, lad? You're about the most uncouth and loutish fourteen-year-old I've ever—'

'*Fifteen*-year-old,' interposed Mrs Holmes, more anxious, it seemed, to correct her son's natal credentials than to deny his innate crudity. 'Fifteen on March the 26th. Got it wrong in the papers, didn't they?'

'Well, well! Same birthday as Housman.'

Silence.

'*And*' (Morse now spoke directly to the mother) 'he'll be able to smoke in a year's time, and go to the pub for a pint a couple of years after that – if you give him some pocket-money, Mrs Holmes. Because I can't see him earning anything much himself, not in his present frame of mind.'

If Lewis had earlier noticed the tell-tale sign of drug dependency in the boy's eyes, he now saw a wider blaze of hatred there; and was sure that Morse was similarly and equally aware of both, as Mrs Holmes switched her wheelchair abruptly around and faced Morse aggressively:

'It was an accident – could happen to anybody – he didn't mean no trouble – like he *said* – like he *told* you . . . That's right, isn't it, Roy?'

'Leave me be!'

'Perhaps it wasn't you we came to Burford to see.'

For a few seconds there was a look of bewilderment, of anxiety almost, on Roy Holmes's face. Then, draining his can of beer, he got to his feet, and left the room.

Seconds later the front door slammed behind him with potentially glass-shattering force.

'What time will he be back?' asked Lewis.

She shrugged her narrow shoulders.

'You worry about him?'

'Everybody worries about him.'

'How long's he been on drugs?'

'Year – over a year.'

'How does he pay for them?'

'You tell *me*.'

'Not much of a son, is he?' said Morse.

She shook what once must have been a very pretty head with a gesture of desperation.

'Does he get the money from you?'

'I've got nothing to give him. He's not stupid. He knows that.'

'But . . .?' Morse pointed to the empty beer can; the empty packet of cigarettes.

'I dunno.'

Morse got to his feet. Lewis too.

'How long . . .?' Morse nodded to the wheelchair.

'Six years.'

Morse stopped in front of the one framed picture in the dingy hallway. Not a picture, though. A diploma.

> *Oxfordshire, Buckinghamshire, Berkshire Athletics Association*
>
> This is to certify that in the annual three-counties cross-country championships held in Cutteslowe Park, Oxford, on the 19th March, 1974, the winner of the ladies event from a field of seventy-two runners was:
>
> ELIZABETH JANE THOMAS
>
> Congratulations!
> Signed: *Monty Hillier* (Assn. Pres.)

For the second time that day Lewis noticed a film of tears in a woman's eyes; and for the second time that day Morse felt a shudder of excitement run along his shoulders.

Before they left, Morse turned to the erstwhile

athlete. 'The gods haven't smiled on you much, have they?'

'Not that I've noticed.'

'It's important for your son to do exactly what they've told him – with his Police Protection Order. You know that?'

'I suppose so.'

'And if you want cheering up a bit, Mrs Holmes, I'll tell you a big secret: I was about his age when I started drinking myself. A year younger, in fact.'

But the confession appeared to bring little comfort to the woman manoeuvring her wheelchair to the front door.

Morse gave her his card. 'One last thing. If there's anything you've forgotten to tell me? Anything you've not been willing to tell me . . . ?'

As the two detectives walked along the litter-strewn path up to a wooden front gate stripped of all but two of its vertical slats, Lewis's mind puzzled itself over those last few words. But Morse seemed deep in thought; and any questions for the moment, he knew, would be wholly inopportune.

Chapter Fifty-Five

Wherefore seeing we also are compassed about with so great a cloud of witnesses, let us lay aside every prejudice and error that doth so easily beset us

(*Letter to Hebrews*)

In his own way, Lewis was not unhappy that Morse had failed to put in his usual, comparatively early appearance the following morning. His own preferred programme of alibi-confirmation had earlier (as we have seen) been endorsed by Morse, albeit with muted enthusiasm; and Lewis was content to pursue such a programme solo.

It now appeared that Morse's simplistic hypothesis – that of casting Barron as a double murderer – was wholly discounted. It would have been convenient, certainly, if it *had* been Barron; and if Barron in turn had been murdered by whoever was behind . . . well, behind everything, really. Frank Harrison, say. And why *not* Frank Harrison? In Lewis's betting-book he was the one runner in the field with the requisite bank balance to fork out the regular dollops of hush-money. But with the potential collapse of global equity markets, such a bank balance might soon not be looking so healthy. And one of the laws of economics, as Lewis knew, was that people with pots of money could easily *lose* pots of money, including the person who hitherto had seen it as a matter of self-interest to divert some proportion of such monies to others: to Flynn, to Repp, perhaps to Barron. Then, almost miraculously, two of them had been crossed off the pay-roll; and if the third one . . .

Lewis could understand Morse's thinking perfectly well. But it had been wrong, as the great man had (virtually) admitted the previous evening. There had been that dramatic development in the case: Barron's death had been an accident. And the coincidence of Barron being knocked off a ladder *by accident* at virtually the same time someone else had planned to murder him *by criminal design* had clearly struck even Morse (a confirmed believer in coincidence) as quite extraordinarily improbable.

So what was needed now was a bit of old-fashioned procedure: some immediate phone calls; some speedy arrangements of interviews; some urgent checking of alibis. And so fortunate was Lewis that by 9.45 he had written down a firm timetable:

10.15 a.m. – interview with Simon Harrison (Jordan Hill)
11.15 a.m. – interview with Frank Harrison (Randolph)
12.15 p.m. – interview with Sarah Harrison (Ratcliffe Infirmary)

Back in HQ just after 2 p.m. (still no news from Morse) Lewis looked down, not without some satisfaction, at the notes he had made:

SIMON H

Friday 24 July: at his desk all a.m. – lunch in canteen – back at his desk till 4 p.m. when he took bus down to Summertown dentist (¾ hr). Home c. 6 p.m. Plenty of witnesses on and off all day, it seems.
Monday 3 Aug: (day off work) a.m. drove via M40 → Stokenchurch hoping for siting of red kite there – tried earlier in the year at Llandudno – both trips unsuccessful (keen bird-watcher). Back for lunch in White Hart (Wytham) – witnesses would include landlord etc.

Impossible for him to have been in on the Flynn/Repp murders. *Could* have pushed Barron off the ladder, if we wanted him for that, which we don't. Deafer than I thought and lip-reads a lot. Names a big problem: Flynn OK, but Repp and Barron hard for him – its something to do with the labial consonents (so he says). Intelligent, bit too *intense*, loner (?).

FRANK H

Friday 24 July: meeting in London office 10–11.45 a.m. with four colleagues. (Check!)
Monday 3 Aug: at Randolph (booked in the day before). Breakfast 7.50–8.40 a.m. (approx) with 'partner' (real honey acc. to Ailish at the bar.) Car apparently not moved from Resident's garage that day.

As suspect? Same as SH (see above). Smart business exec. type, pleasant enough, bit abrupt, not short of the pennies – asked me to join him in glass of champange (£7 a go!) Thinning on top, thickening in middle. Seems used to getting what he wants in life.

SARAH H

Friday 24 July: at BDA Conference in Manchester with boss – arr 12.30 p.m. ret 9.50 p.m. – rail both ways. Forget her!
Monday 3 Aug: consultant duties at Diabetes Centre in Ratcliffe Inf. Saw ten patients. Lunch in League of Fiends cafeteria. Forget her!

Attractive, clever, but perhaps hard streek somewhere?

Yes! Lewis felt pleased with his morning's work; and even more pleased with his afternoon's work, after he'd typed up the notes, correcting four of the six misspellings and tidying up one or two of the punctuational blemishes. There remained quite a bit of checking to be done, but none of it would be particularly onerous, and most of it probably unnecessary. The general upshot was unambiguous. None of the Harrison clan had murdered Flynn or Repp. Two of the three *could* have been on the scene when Barron was killed but neither of them had murdered him, because *no one* had murdered him. That was the only thing in the whole tragic business that now seemed wholly incontrovertible.

Chapter Fifty-Six

Have I Got News For You!
(TV programme title)

In nowise was Lewis surprised to meet Dixon in the police canteen.

'Busy day?'

'Well, yes and no really. Morse rang me up early—'

'He *what*?' spluttered Lewis.

'Well, early for me. Wanted me to check out on a few things, didn't he?'

'Such as?'

'Well, names of those going to lip-reading classes these last few years.'

'Simon Harrison, you mean?'

'Didn't say, did he? No problem, though. Just got the lists photocopied, didn't I?'

'What else?'

'Well, funny really. He wanted me to find out who Flynn's dentist was—'

'He *what*?'

'Well, easy that. Then to find out something about that Mrs Holmes – you know, before she was married . . . before she had her accident.'

Yes, Lewis could understand that.

'Then to ring that SOCO chap Andrews, the one who was out at Sutton Courtenay. Ask him to get a bit of a move on – you know, give him a kick up the arse, like, about the fingerprints. Morse got him to take Barron's, you knew that, didn't you?'

'Of course I knew that!' lied Lewis, euphoria fading fast.

'Well, there we are then. I suppose old Morse was just hoping, you know . . .'

Yes, Lewis knew exactly what Morse had been hoping.

'Has Andrews found anything?'

'Well, still working on it, isn't he? Messy old job, he said. Soon as he had any news though . . . Anyway I called round and stuck the stuff through the door. He was there, I reckon. The telly was on—'

'What?'

'Yeah, pretty certain of it. But he didn't come to the door. Odd sort of chap, isn't he?'

But the introductory 'Well's and the inquisitorial clausulae, (hallmarks of every Dixon sentence) had become too tiresome; and Lewis was glad when the canteen intercom cut across the conversation:

> 'Message for Chief Inspector Morse or Sergeant Lewis: Please ring Northampton SOCOs immediately. I repeat. Message for . . .'

Where are you, Dixon, in the hierarchy here? I'll tell you, mate. Nowhere – no bloody where – that's where!

Yet Lewis left such ungracious thoughts unspoken, jumping to his feet and leaving Dixon where he was, cheeks now jammed once more with a doughnut.

Two minutes later Lewis was through to an exultant Andrews, who wasted no time in breaking the dramatic news: there was a 'hit' – yippee! – a match of fingerprints! In the car. Two sets – definite, distinct. The prints of J. Barron, Builder of Lower Swinstead!

As he walked back to the canteen (Morse's phone still engaged) Lewis reflected on his brief exchange of views with Andrews. Morse had asked for any news to be communicated to him direct, and if necessary at his home number, though as both men knew there'd been little chance of that. Yet the situation was now perfectly clear; and Lewis freely conceded that Morse's early conviction that Barron had been involved in the murders seemed wholly vindicated. No room for more than three people in the cluttered stolen car, surely? And since neither Flynn nor Repp had stepped out of that car alive, the discovery of that third set of prints, Barron's, was of momentous significance: *Barron himself had been in the car.* The logic sounded pretty childish when it was put like that but . . .

Andrews's guess had been that Morse had suddenly fallen into some deep slumber after – well, after whatever; and Dixon's guess that he'd been watching TV with the volume too high. But the latter explanation seemed unlikely. Morse could (Lewis succumbed to his second unworthy thought that day) *could* have purchased some pornographic video; but would he have been able to master the operating instructions? Doubtful – especially having no children (better still, grandchildren) to explain things to him. Morse seldom watched TV anyway, or so he claimed. Just the news. Just occasionally.

Lewis finished his coffee, slowly coming to terms with the extraordinary news he'd just received: that Barron was a murderer – the second thing in the whole tragic business that now seemed wholly incontrovertible.

He rang Morse once again. If the call wasn't answered, he would drive down and see the situation for himself because he was getting a little worried.

The phone was ringing.

The call was answered.

Chapter Fifty-Seven

Ah, could thy grave, at Carthage, be!
Care not for that, and lay me where I fall!
Everywhere heard will be the judgement-call:
But at God's altar, oh! remember me
(Matthew Arnold)

Morse opened the front door. 'And there's me hoping for a rest day, like they tell me they have in the middle of test matches.'

But, in truth, he had not tried overhard to have much of a rest day . . .

Early that morning (as we have seen) he had rung Sergeant Dixon and given him a list of duties.

At 10 a.m. he had received a middle-aged, palely intelligent gentleman from Lloyds Bank, a guru on (inter alia) Wills, Dispositions, Codicils, and Covenants.

'From what you tell me, Mr Morse, you're not exactly going to bequeath a large fortune, are you? And with no relatives, no immediate dependants, no unmanageable debts – well, you might just as well write down a few things on half a page of A4. Save yourself money that way. Do it now, if you like. Just write a few simple sentences – "I leave the house to blank, the bank balance to blank, the books and records to blank, the residual estate to blank." That'll cover things for now – and you say you *do* want things covered? Just sign it, I'll witness it, and I'll see it's carried through, in case, you know . . . Then we can flesh it out a bit later.'

'No problems really then?'

'No. We shall, as a bank, charge a small commission of course. But you expected that.'

'Oh yes, Mr Daniel. I'd expected that,' said Morse.

At 11.15 a.m. he had taken the 2A bus down the Banbury Road as far as Keble Road, where he alighted and walked across the Woodstock Road to the Radcliffe Infirmary, where he was directed up to an office on the first floor.

'Yes? How can I help you?' The woman behind the desk seemed to be a fairly important personage with carefully coiffured grey hair and carefully clipped diction.

'I'm thinking of leaving my body to the hospital.'

'You've come to the right place.'

'What's the drill?'

She took a form from a drawer. 'Just fill this in.'

'Is that all?'

'Make sure you tell your wife and your children and your GP. You'll avoid quite a few problems that way.'

'Thank you.'

'Of course, I ought to tell you we may not *want* your body. The situation does, er, fluctuate. But you'd expected that.'

'Oh yes, I'd expected that,' said Morse.

'And you must make sure you die somewhere fairly locally. We can't come and collect you from Canada, you know.'

Perhaps it was a bleak joke.

'No, of course not.'

It had been a joyless experience for Morse, who now walked slowly down St Giles' towards The Randolph. He'd thought at the very least they'd have shown a little gratitude. Instead, he felt as though they were doing *him* a favour by agreeing (provisionally!) to accept a corpse that would surely be presenting apprentice anatomists and pathologists with some appreciably interesting items: liver, kidneys, lungs, pancreas, heart . . .

In the Chapters' Bar, Ailish Hurley, his favourite barmaid, greeted him in her delightful Irish brogue; and two pints of bitter later, as he walked round into Magdalen Street and almost immediately caught a bus back up to the top of the Banbury Road, he felt that the world was a happier place than it had been half an hour earlier.

Once home, he treated himself to a small(ish) Glenfiddich, deciding that his liquid intake of calories that lunchtime would nicely balance his dosage of insulin. Yes, things were looking up, and particularly so since the phone hadn't rung all day. What a wonderful thing it would be to go back to the days pre telephone (mobile and immobile alike), pre FAX, pre e-mail!

And, to cap it all, he'd bought himself a video – in front of which, in mid afternoon, he'd fallen fairly soundly asleep, though at some point half-hearing, as he thought, a slippery flop through the letter-box.

*

It was an hour later when he opened the envelope and read Dixon's notes on Simon Harrison; on Paddy Flynn; on Mrs Holmes.

Interesting!

Interesting!

Interesting!

And very much as he'd thought . . .

Only one thing was worrying him slightly. Why hadn't Lewis been in touch? He didn't want Lewis to get in touch but . . . perhaps he did want Lewis to get in touch. So he rang Lewis himself only to discover that the phone was out of order. Or was it? He banged the palm of his right hand against his forehead. He'd rung Dixon early that morning from the bedroom; then he'd had to go downstairs to check an address in the phone book, finishing the call there, and forgetting to replace the receiver in the bedroom. He'd done it before. And he'd do it again. It was not a matter of any great moment. He'd ring Lewis himself – not that he had anything much to say to him; not for the minute anyway.

He was about to pick up the phone when the doorbell rang.

CHAPTER FIFTY-EIGHT

It remains quite a problem to play the clarinet with false teeth, because there is great difficulty with the grip (this may even result in the plate being pulled out!). In addition there are problems with the breathing, because it is difficult to project a successful airstream

(Paul Harris, *Clarinet Basics*)

'BEEN TRYING TO get you all day, sir.'

'I've had other things to do, you know.'

'You just said you'd wanted a rest day.'

'Come in! Fancy a quick noggin?'

Lewis hesitated. 'Why not?'

'Ye gods! You must have had a bad day – or was it a good day?'

'I've had a *good* day, and so have you.'

Morse now listened quietly to the extraordinary news from Andrews, though without any sign of triumphalism.

Equally quietly he slowly read through Lewis's typed reports. Then read them a second time.

'Your orthography has come on enormously since they put that spell-check system into the word-processor.'

'Don't *you* have any problems with spellings – sometimes?'

'Only with "proceed".'

'Where does this all leave us, sir?'

'Things are moving fast.'

'We're getting near the end, you mean?'

'We were always near the end.'

'So what do you think happened?'

'Shan't ever know for certain, shall we? With all three of them dead, all three of them murdered—'

'Only *two*, surely?'

'If you say so, Lewis. If you say so.'

'You're not suggesting—?'

But Morse was not to be deflected:

'There were three people who had a vested interest in Yvonne Harrison's murder: Repp, Barron, and Flynn. Repp – because he'd been casing the property for a burglary; because he happened to be there on the night of the murder; and because he *knew who the murderer was.* Barron – a man with an SAS background, who'd found a woman who could gratify his sexual fantasies, and who also *knew who the murderer was* – because he was the fellow in bed with Yvonne that night. Flynn – the fellow who lied about the events that night and who, like the other two, *knew who the murderer was.* The three of them had got their clutches into the only person who could pay their price, the person who *did* pay their price: Frank Harrison. *He* was becoming a fatter and fatter cat in his banking business, so they thought – and, rightly it seems. So they were ready to up the stakes. And on the day Repp was released, they'd agreed to meet and co-ordinate some plan of action. But things went wrong. Pretty certainly they somehow discovered that they'd each been treated differently – *dangerously* differently; and bitterness, jealousy, rivalry, all surfaced, and there was one almighty row. I've said all this before! They'd stopped, perhaps in a lay-by along the A34 – take your pick! – and Barron got his Stanley knife out and threatened Flynn, the man who'd just happened to be at the taxi-rank that night, and who was now overplaying his hand. And soon it must have occurred to the other two that half a cake is considerably better than a third of one; and Flynn was murdered and dumped at Redbridge in those black bags, the ones the owner of the car was originally going to cart off to the rubbish dump.'

'Waste Disposal Centre.'

'After that? Who knows? But suddenly the situation was becoming more dangerous still. If half a cake is better than a third, what about a whole cake? So the two of them must have wrangled about the best way to capitalize on Flynn's beneficial departure . . . But how and why and when and where things went on from there, I've no more idea than you have – and that's not saying much, is it?'

'No,' said Lewis flatly.

Morse looked at his sergeant, and smiled wearily: 'You're annoyed, aren't you?'

'Annoyed? What about?'

'Dixon.'

'Why didn't you *tell* me?'

'You'd've accused me of wasting police resources. Do you know what I got him to do today?'

'Vaguely.'

'Well, let me tell you, specifically. First, I asked him to do a bit of fourth-grade clerical stuff at Oxpens, and get copies of those attending lip-reading classes these last five years. And he did it. Very efficiently. He found Simon Harrison's name there, for three years; and Paddy Flynn's there, for two years – overlapping. *Very* interesting that, because they must have known each other!

'Second, I asked Dixon to find out more about Flynn. Flynn was known as an amateur entertainer round the local pubs and clubs in Oxfordshire, playing the clarinet and compèring his little pop group. Till about three years ago, when things started to go wrong: he began to experience trouble with his hearing – something that later compromised his job with Radio Taxis; *and* at about the same time, according to the post-mortem details, he had a lot of dental trouble which meant he had to have all his top-front teeth extracted. And that's not a good thing for a clarinet-player.'

'It's not?'

'Well-known fact. Louis Armstrong had the same sort of trouble.'

'He was a *trumpet*-player!'

'Same *sort* of thing! Then I asked Dixon to look into Mrs Holmes's background. I had the impression when we spoke to her that she might have been a most attractive woman when she was younger; and I just wondered . . . I got Dixon to check up on her, that's all. Seems she used to live in Lower Swinstead before she moved to Burford and, well, look at things for yourself.'

Lewis read Dixon's notes:

Elizabeth Jane Thomas (b. 7.11.53)	
1976 (Feb.)	Son b. (Alan) illeg.
1983 (March)	Son b. (Roy) illeg.
1983 (Dec.)	m. Kenneth Holmes (Registry Office)
1991 (Sept.)	Husband killed in pile-up on A40 – same accident that caused all her trouble

'They don't call them "illegitimate" these days, and it should be "Register" Office.'

Morse nodded. 'You're missing the main point, though.'

'I am?'

'Remember when we were in the village pub? Remember Biffen greeting his customers?'

Yes. Lewis remembered that 'Evening, Mr Thomas': the young fellow forever playing the fruit machine, the young fellow who had spoken to him in the car park.

'You mean they're half-brothers? Roy Holmes and Alan Thomas?'

'Why not *full* brothers – with the same father? I knew there was something familiar about young Holmes . . . Anyway, there it is. Elizabeth Thomas was an unmarried mum in the village; Alan was already seven when his younger brother was born; and everybody knew him as Alan *Thomas.* So he kept the name when his mother married a few months later, and kept it when he went along with the family to live in Burford.'

'Interesting enough – but is it important?'

'I don't know,' said Morse slowly. 'I just don't know. But it throws up one or two new ideas.'

'If you say so, sir. Aren't you going to offer me another Scotch, by the way?'

What a strange day it had been! Even stranger, perhaps, in that Morse now left his own glass unreplenished.

'Shall I tell you something else, Lewis? You'd never believe it, but I've been watching the telly this afternoon. I picked up one of those RSPB videos.'

'You mean you know how to work the machine?'

'It's Strange's fault. Genuine bird-watcher, Strange! He told me the sparrow population in North Oxford's down by fifty per cent these last few years; and he told me the sparrow-hawks along Squitchey Lane are getting fatter. So I bought this video on birds of prey – you know, eagles, falcons, hobbies, merlins, red kites . . . did you hear me, Lewis? *Red kites.*'

Lewis looked puzzled. 'I'm not with you.'

'Your interview with Simon Harrison. He's a phoney bird-watcher, that fellow. Said he'd been off to Llandudno to try to spot a red kite. Llandudno! He meant *Llandovery,* Lewis – that was the only home of the red kite in the UK until they introduced a few near Stokenchurch.'

'I didn't know you were an expert—'

'I'm not. And nor is Simon Harrison. His alibi for

Monday morning's worthless. He wouldn't know a red kite from a red cabbage.'

Unaccustomedly relaxed, Lewis sipped his Glenfiddich and involuntarily repeated an earlier comment: 'Interesting enough – but is it *important*?'

'I just don't know,' said Morse slowly, himself now involuntarily repeating an earlier comment: 'But it throws up one or two new ideas . . .'

'Perhaps they've *all* been telling us a few lies, sir . . . except Mrs Barron, perhaps.'

Morse smiled. 'Don't you mean *especially* Mrs Barron?'

Chapter Fifty-Nine

Wherever God erects a house of prayer,
The Devil always builds a chapel there;
And 'twill be found, upon examination,
The latter has the largest congregation
(Daniel Defoe,
The True-born Englishman)

Mrs Linda Barron walked steadily up the aisle between the small assembly of mourners, her arm linked through that of her mother, both women dutifully dressed in bible-black suits . . .

On the whole, it hadn't been quite the ordeal she'd expected: in practical terms, the shock of it all continued to cocoon a good half of her conscious thoughts; whilst emotionally she had long since accepted that her love for her husband was as dead as the man who had been lying there in the coffin – until mercifully the curtains had closed, and the show was over. He would have enjoyed the hymn though, 'He Who Would Valiant Be', for he had been valiant enough (she'd learned that from his army friends) – as well as vain and domineering and unfaithful. Yes, she'd found herself moved by the hymn; and the tears ought to have come.

But they hadn't.

Outside, in the clear sunshine, she whispered

quickly into her mother's ear. 'Remember what I said. The kids are fine, if anybody asks. OK?'

But the grandmother made no reply. She was the very last person in the world to let the little ones down, especially the one of them. As for Linda, she girded up her loins in readiness for the chorus of commiseration she would have to cope with.

And indeed several of the family and friends of her late husband, J. Barron, Builder, had already emerged through the chapel doors, including Thomas Biffen, Landlord, whose creased white shirt was so tight around the neck that he had been forced to unfasten the top button beneath the black tie; including the perennial opponents, Alf and Bert, who had exchanged no words in the chapel, but whose thoughts were perhaps in tune during the service as each of them must have mused on their imminent mortality, and the prospects of encountering that great cribbage-player in the sky.

Including Frank Harrison.

Chief Superintendent Strange, who had been seated in the back row next to Morse, was the last but one to leave. His thoughts had roamed irreverently throughout the short service, and the superannuated minister's apparent confidence in the resurrection of the dead had filled him more with horror than with hope. He thought of his wife and of her death, and experienced that familiar sense of the guilt that still remained to be expiated. The hymn was all right, although he'd gone himself for 'Praise, My Soul, the King of Heaven' in the Instructions For My Funeral stapled to his last will and testament. But on the whole he dreaded church services almost as much as did the man seated beside him; and he could think of nothing more detestable than a funeral.

Morse himself had been sickened by the latest version (Series Something) of the Funeral Service. Gone were those resonant cadences of the AV and the Prayer Book: those passages about corruption putting on incorruptibility and the rest of it, which as a youth he'd found so poignant and powerful. They'd even had a cheerful hymn, for heaven's sake! Where was that wonderfully sad and sentimental hymn he'd chosen for his own farewell: 'O Love That Wilt Not Let Me Go'? Chosen, that is, before he'd recently decided to leave his body for medical science, although that decision itself was now in considerable doubt. In particular that little clause in sub-section 6 of Form D1 still stuck in his craw: 'Should your bequest be accepted . . .'

He pointedly avoided the priest who'd presided – a man (in Morse's view) excessively accoutred in ecclesiastical vestments, and wholly lacking in any sensitivity to the English language. But he did have a quick word of sympathy with the widow, shaking her black-gloved hand firmly before turning to her mother.

'Mrs Stokes?' he asked quietly.

'Yes?'

Morse introduced himself. 'My sergeant called to see your daughter – '

'Oh yes.'

' – when you were there looking after the children, I believe. Very kind of you. Must be a bit wearisome . . . I wouldn't know, though.'

'It's a pleasure really.'

'Who's looking after them today?'

'Oh they're, er . . . you know, a friend, a neighbour. Won't be for long anyway.'

'No.'

Morse turned away, following in Strange's steps towards the car park.

She was lying, of course – Morse knew that. There was only one of the Barron children at home that day; as there had been when Lewis had called. The elder of the two, Alice, was away somewhere. That much, though very little else, Lewis himself had been able to learn from the Barrons' GP the previous day. Morse thought he knew why, and another piece of the jigsaw had slipped into place.

'Hello! Chief Inspector Morse, isn't it? My daughter tells me she saw you recently. But perhaps you don't know me.'

'Let's say we've never been officially introduced, Mr Harrison.'

'Ah! You *do* know me. I know you, of course, and Sergeant Lewis has been to see me. You probably sent him.'

'As a matter of fact I did.'

'I realize you weren't yourself involved in my wife's murder case but, er . . .'

Harrison was by some three inches or so the taller of the two, and Morse felt slightly uncomfortable as a pair of pale-grey eyes, hard and unsmiling, looked slightly down on him.

'. . . but I'd heard about you. Yvonne spoke about you several times. She'd looked after you once when you were in hospital. Remember?'

Morse nodded.

'Quite taken by you, she was. "A sensitive soul" – I think that's what she called you; said you were interesting to talk to and had a nice voice. Told me she was going to invite you out to one of her, er, soirées. When I was away, of course.'

'I should hope so. Wouldn't have wanted any competition, would I?'

'*Did* you have any competition?'

'The only time I ever met Yvonne again was in the Maiden's Arms,' said Morse gently, unblinking blue eyes now looking slightly upward into the strong, clean-shaven face of Harrison senior.

As Strange struggled to squeeze his bulk between seat and steering wheel, Morse looked back and saw that the funeral guests were almost all departed. But Linda Barron stood there still, in close conversation with Frank Harrison – both of them now stepping aside a little as another black Daimler moved smoothly into place outside the chapel, with another light-brown, lily-bedecked coffin lying lengthways inside, the polished handles glinting in the sun.

Morse found himself pondering on the funeral. 'I wonder why *he* put in an appearance.'

'Who? Frank Harrison? Why shouldn't he? Lived in the same village – had him in to do those house repairs—'

'Knew his wife had been in bed with him.'

'Fasten your seat-belt, Morse!'

'Er, before we drive off, there's something—'

'Fasten your seat-belt! Know what that's an anagram of, by the way? "Truss neatly to be safe." Clever, eh? Somebody told me that once. You probably.'

For a few seconds Morse looked slightly puzzled.

'Couldn't have been me. It's got to be "belts". Otherwise there's one "s" short.'

'Just put the bloody thing on!'

But Morse left the bloody thing off as he looked directly ahead of him and completed his earlier sentence: 'Just before we drive off, sir, there's something I ought to mention. It's about Lewis. I'm fairly sure he's beginning to get some odd ideas about my being involved in some way with Yvonne Harrison.'

It was Strange's turn to look directly ahead of him.

'And you think I wasn't aware of that?' he asked quietly.

Chapter Sixty

Have respect unto the covenant: for the dark places of the earth are full of the habitations of cruelty
(*Psalm* 74, v. 20)

Once in Charlton Kings, a suburb on the eastern side of Cheltenham, Sergeant Lewis had followed the map directions carefully (he loved that sort of thing), turning right from the A40 through a maze of residential streets, and finally driving the unmarked police car past the sign on the white-washed wall beside the gateway – 'Sisters of the Covenant: Preparatory Boarding School for Girls' – and along the short gravelled drive that led to a large, detached Georgian house.

Destination reached; and purpose, shortly afterwards, fulfilled.

With a few extra suggestions from Morse, Lewis had found it comparatively easy to fill in most of the picture. The Barrons' GP had professional and wholly proper reasons for his guarded reticence. But other sources had been considerably less cautious with their help and information: the Burford Social Services, the NSPCC, the headmistress of the village primary school, the local Catholic priest, and, last of all, the middle-aged nun, dressed in a chocolate-brown habit and white wimple, who was expecting him and who found little difficulty in answering his brief, pointed questions.

Five nuns, all of them resident, looked after the school, which was specifically dedicated to the physical and spiritual well-being of girls between the ages of four and eleven (currently eighteen of them) who for varied reasons – poverty, indifference, criminality, cruelty – had been ill-used in their family homes. In spite of a modest benefaction, the school was a place of limited resources, at least in human terms; and was appropriately designated 'Private', with the majority of parents paying fees of between £1,000 and £1,500 per term.

Alice Barron, yes – now aged six – was one of the pupils there, referred to the school by her mother. She had been abused: not sexually, it seemed; but certainly physically; certainly psychologically.

No, Alice was not one of our Lord's brightest intellects; in fact she was in some ways a slow-witted child. This may have been the result of her home environment, but probably only partially so. Her younger sister (the teaching staff had learned) was as bright as the proverbial button; and such a circumstance could well have accounted to some degree for an impatient, expectant, aggressive parent to have . . .

'The father, you mean?'

'You're putting words into my mouth, Sergeant.'

'But if you were a betting woman – which I know you're not, of course . . .'

'What on earth makes you think that?' Her eyes momentarily glinted with humour. 'But if I *were*, I would not be putting much money on the mother, no.'

'How are the accounts for each term settled?'

'I looked that up, as you asked me. I can't be quite sure, but I suspect it's been in cash.'

'Isn't that unusual?'

'Yes, it is.'

'Does Alice know about her father's death?'

'Not yet, no.'

'Do you think this whole business is going to . . . ?'

'Difficult to tell, isn't it? She's improving, right enough. She's stopped wetting her bed, and she doesn't scream so loudly in the night.'

'But if you were going to have another bet?'

'If I were a bookmaker, I'd lay you even money on it.'

As he drove back up to the A40, Lewis felt fairly sure he knew only a quarter as much about horse-racing (and probably about life) as Sister Benedicta.

Chapter Sixty-One

character (n.) handwriting, style of writing: Shakes. *Meas. for M.* Here is the hand and seal of the Duke. You know the character, I doubt not

(Small's *Enlarged English Dict.* 18th ed.)

Back at HQ Lewis found a handwritten note for his personal attention:

> Well worthwhile going to the crem. One or two interesting conversations and one or two new ideas (or is it one?). Super and I off to have a jug (or is it two?). Tell anybody who wants me that I'm out to lunch and shan't be available till tomorrow morning – no Monday morning. M.

It was in Morse's hand, that small, neatly formed upright script that was recognizable anywhere; as indeed, for that matter, was Strange's hand – large, spidery, with a perpetual list to starboard, and often only semi-legible.

But Lewis was unconcerned. He would type up a report on his wholly satisfactory morning's work. And then he would sit back and let things slowly sink in, for it had now become clear that the Repp–Flynn–Barron mystery was solved. Completely solved now, with the knowledge that it was Linda Barron who had taken the hush-money; Linda Barron who must have insisted that if her husband ever thought of syphoning some of it off for himself she would expose him for the child-abuser that he was, and expose him to Social Services, to the police, to the folk in the village, to the Press. And she would have meant it, for she was past caring. My God, yes! And Barron had agreed.

Yes . . .

The big moments in the case were over; and he rang Mrs Lewis and asked her to have the chip-pan ready half an hour earlier than usual.

Yes . . .

In a strange kind of way, his confidence in himself had grown steadily throughout the present case, in spite of a few irritations like Dixon! *And* there was that one thing that had been interesting him and troubling him, in equal measure, for some considerable time now. Very soon he'd have to face up to telling Morse of his suspicions. But not just yet. He'd need to know a bit more about the Harrison murder first; especially about the contents of that fourth green box-file which had mysteriously added itself to the documents in the case, and which now sat alongside the other three on a shelf in Morse's office. Perhaps a bit later that afternoon, since Morse was unlikely to return.

What if he did, anyway?

Yes . . .

Lewis sat back after typing his report, his thoughts dwelling on the case that to all intents and purposes had now closed. He *was* right, wasn't he? But there were just one or two tiny items he hadn't as yet checked; and he knew that his conscience would be niggling him about them. No time like the present.

But not much luck. Still, those alibis for the Monday morning didn't much matter any longer. Or rather *non*-alibis, since neither Harrison Senior nor Harrison Junior had any alibi at all. And whilst Sarah Harrison did have an alibi, it still remained unchecked.

He rang the Diabetes Centre in the Radcliffe Infirmary, with almost immediate if unexpected success, since Professor Turner (clearly not a Monday–Friday medic) now confirmed everything that Miss Harrison herself had affirmed: 'In fact, Sergeant, she had to take over some of my patients mid-morning when I was summoned by my superiors—'

'Do you have any superiors, sir?'

On reflection, Lewis was more than a little pleased with that last question: just the sort of thing Morse would have asked. Was he, Lewis, just a little – after all this time – moving gradually nearer to Morsean wavelength?

At a quarter-past four he walked along the corridor to Morse's office, to cast a fresh eye (so he promised himself) on that bizarre, that puzzling, that haunting evening of Yvonne Harrison's murder – the source of so much trouble and tragedy.

Very soon he was virtually certain that he had seen none of the contents of that fourth box-file before; and had convinced himself that this was not merely a matter of some redistribution of the case-documents. The file contained the sort of personal items that many women, and doubtless many men, keep in one of the locked drawers of their desks or bureaux, often with some sense of guilt.

There were all the usual things that from experience Lewis had known so well: letters, many of them in their original envelopes, some from women, most of them from men; photographs, many of them of Yvonne herself (one topless) with a variety of men-friends; postcards from many a quarter of the globe, but mostly from Greece and Switzerland; three slim (unopened) bottles of perfume; various receipts for the purchase of ultra-expensive clothes and shoes. But for all the variety of material there, the box was scarcely half-full, and Lewis took his time. He looked at the photographs reasonably quickly (not quite so quickly at one of them, perhaps), before reading slowly (though not as slowly as Morse would have done) through the letters.

Then he saw it:

> that they would prefer to be ill in hospital and nursed by you than to be in full health and never see you again. I join them. You have monopolized my thoughts these last few days, ever since you promised – remember? – to get in touch once I was discharged. But no invitation, no phone call, no letter, nothing.

> If you have decided that it was all just a temporary infatuation, and if, on your part, it was nothing more than that – so be it. Just for a while longer though, let me look through my mail each morning in the hope

That was all. Just one small page of a longer letter. No date, no address, no salutation, no valediction, no name – nothing. And yet everything. Because the letter was written in that small, neatly formed upright script that was recognizable everywhere in the Thames Valley Police HQ.

As he re-read the page, Lewis was suddenly aware of another presence in the office; and looked up to find Chief Inspector Morse standing silently in the doorway.

Chapter Sixty-Two

Don't tell me, sweet, that I'm unkind
Each time I black your eye,
Or raise a weal on your behind –
I'm just a loving guy.

We both despise the gentle touch,
So cut out the pretence;
You wouldn't love it half as much
Without the violence
(Roy Dean, *Lovelace Bleeding*)

ANYONE WISHING TO take up Morse's earlier promise of being available the following Monday morning would have been disappointed, since he had put in no appearance by lunchtime. Yet he was not idle during those morning hours; and any visitor to the bachelor flat would have found him seated at his desk for much of the time; and for a fair proportion of that time found him writing quite busily and (as we have seen) very neatly. His old typewriter (with its defective 'e' and 't's) sat at his elbow; but he had never mastered the keyboard-skills with any real confidence, and he wrote now in long-hand with a medium-blue Biro.

For Priority Consideration

Several things have happened these last few days which have prompted me to put down in writing my own thoughts on the present state of play.

First, I've been waking up every day recently, after some nightmarish nights, with a premonition that some disaster is imminent. Whether death comes into such a category, I'm not sure. I can't agree with Socrates, though, that death is a blessing devoutly to be wished, even if it is (as I hope it is, as I believe it is) one long completely dreamless sleep. For the very fact of being alive is surely the best thing that's happened to (almost) all of us.

Second, the last murder case entrusted to the pair of us has been (one or two loose ends though) satisfactorily resolved. Repp and Flynn were murdered by Barron, and the murderer himself is now dead. So any further insight into the original Harrison murder from *their* angles is wholly precluded.

Third, I'm certain that Frank Harrison has been the paymaster. It's high time we brought him into HQ for intensive questioning, either directly about the murder of his wife, or at the very least about some culpable complicity of her murder.

Fourth, I'm also convinced that Yvonne H was murdered by one of her own family. Nothing else makes any sense at all, not to me anyway. That murder was not premeditated: few of them are. It was committed spontaneously, viciously, involuntarily perhaps, by whichever of the three it was who found Yvonne Harrison in a situation that was utterly unexpected – kinkiness, perversion, degradation, all rolled up into one.

On the face of it, the husband is the outsider of the three, so you will appreciate, Lewis, that in my book he's the favourite. It's the 'why' that worries me, though. He wasn't and isn't anybody's fool, and he must have known more than enough about his wife's tastes in bondage and possibly masochism. So I just can't see blazing jealousy as his motive, especially since, as I strongly suspect, he regularly experienced the (reported) joys of extra-marital sex himself.

A confession here.

Quite a few times I've found myself looking at the faces of people concerned with this case and thinking I'd seen them somewhere before. I thought it might be the result of interbreeding in a small community – no wonder some of the villagers are pretty tight-lipped! And I was right. That fruit-machine addict, for example: *Allen* Thomas. That's how you spell his name by the way, Lewis. I found it in the village-school records: Allen Alfred Thomas. Unusual these days, that spelling of 'Allen'. And 'Alfred' belongs more to the first half of the century, doesn't it? I also found out (well, Dixon found out) that the Christian names of Elizabeth Jane Thomas's father were 'Harold Alfred'; and that someone else in the village had a father with the Christian names 'Joseph Allen'. That someone else was Frank Harrison. And (believe me!) *he* was the father of the lad, and Elizabeth decided to give him a couple of

Christian names that, at least for herself, could confer some little pretence of legitimacy on her illegitimate son. (I wonder if his father gives him a fruit-machine allowance?)

Let's turn to the Harrison children.

Either of them *could* have murdered their mother. What would be the motive, though? I just can't see Sarah suddenly turning to murder because she finds her mother abed with one of her many lovers. What does it really matter to her that her mother enjoys a bit of biting and bondage occasionally? Shocked and disgusted? Yes, she'd certainly have been both. But driven to murder? No. There's something about her, though – something that tells me that she's up to her very smooth neck in things.

What about Simon Harrison? As we know he's always been a bit of a mummy's darling: a boy disadvantaged because of early deafness; a boy always needing extra understanding and extra love, and who found it (hardly surprisingly) from his mother. I'd guess myself that for Simon this relationship had always been very precious. Sacrosanct almost. I'd also guess that he had no notion whatsoever of his mother's idiosyncratic tastes in sexual gratification. Then one night, the night of the murder, he'd driven out to see her. And why not? Just to say hello, perhaps? Like his sister, he had a key to the front door, and he entered the house and disturbed the copulating couple – copulating in the most extraordinary circumstances; and he would have been shocked and disgusted (like his sister) but heartbroken, too, and disillusioned and betrayed. His mother performing those things with some plebeian local builder!

Where does all this lead us? First and foremost to an early, long-overdue, full-scale interview with Frank Harrison. Not too early though. Our colleagues got nowhere with him and we, Lewis, are a pair of bloodhounds very late on the scene, with the scent gone very cold.

Fifth, there's this business of the letter you found in the Harrison file. As I told you, I take full responsibility for the fact that some items originally discovered at the Harrison murder scene were subsequently, as they say, found to be missing. It was embarrassing for me to talk to you about this and I know that you in turn found it equally embarrassing to—

Morse laid down his pen and answered the phone: 'Lewis! What do you want?'

'You OK, sir?'

'Why shouldn't I be?'

'It's just that – well, you know that animal charity shop on the corner of South Parade and Middle Way . . .'

'I am *not* an animal-lover, Lewis.'

'Well, people leave things there, by the door, things for the shop to sell for charity—'

'Get *on* with it!'

'Guess what one of the shop assistants found when she got to work this morning?'

'Pair of handcuffs?'

'Pair of *something*, sir. Pair of red trainers! Almost brand new. This woman had read in the *Oxford Mail* about the Burford jogger and she thought . . .'

'You know something, Lewis? That's very interesting. Very interesting indeed. I'll be with you straightaway.'

Chapter Sixty-Three

With much talk will they tempt thee, and smiling upon thee will get out thy secrets
(*Ecclesiasticus*, ch. XIII, v. 11)

'You know, come to think of it, Lewis, we could do all of this now, couldn't we? Just the two of us.'

'No Dixon?'

'No Dixon.'

Lewis smiled outwardly and inwardly as he looked down at the action plan. It seemed to him a sensible and fair division of a good deal of labour. For example, he himself had spoken only very briefly with Sarah Harrison; Morse had not as yet spoken at all with Simon Harrison. Both matters now to be dealt with. And all leading up to the two of them, Morse and Lewis, meeting Frank Harrison a.s.a.p. after these and a few other checks and visits had been made. Harrison! – 'the corner-stone, the kingpin, the pivot', as Morse had asserted, before running out of synonyms. 'We've got plenty of time for all this – well, no, perhaps we haven't. So we can be pretty direct, but not sharp. Smile occasionally. No aggressiveness, no hostility, no belligerence,' Morse had asserted, before running out of synonyms again.

It all suited Lewis nicely. If Morse's philosophy in life was to aim high even if the target was altogether missed, he personally preferred to aim low in the hope at least of hitting something.

The voluntary (mornings only) help at the Oxford Animal Sanctuary Shop (Gifts Welcome) lived only a few hundred yards away in Osberton Road: a widow, a cat-lover, an intelligent witness – Mrs Gerrard. It was just that, as every weekday morning, she'd walked down to South Parade to buy the *Daily Telegraph*, about 8 o'clock before opening the shop, and she'd seen this –

'Yes?' Lewis smiled.

' – well, this youngish fellow – smartly dressed, suit and tie – and he put this Sainsbury's plastic bag in the doorway there. She couldn't describe him any better than that really; but she remembered his car, parked for a few seconds on the double-yellows alongside the shop. She wouldn't have noticed that either – except that it was the same make as hers, a Toyota Carina, P-Reg, a different colour though: hers was a turquoisy colour, his was silvery-grey. The trainers she had put carefully aside, under the counter in the shop.

No one in North Oxford with a Toyota was likely to drive unnecessarily far afield for any servicing and repairs, since there was a specialist garage in Summertown itself; and it took Lewis only a few minutes to learn that the owner of a silvery-grey P-Reg Carina was a regular and esteemed customer of the company, a man named Simon Harrison.

*

Simultaneously Morse was driving himself in the Jaguar through the low range of open hills that border Oxfordshire and Gloucestershire. His old pathologist friend, Max, had once told him that two pleasures grew ever deeper with advancing age, the pleasures of the belly and the pleasures of natural beauty. And Morse found himself concurring with the latter proposition as he turned right at the roundabout and drove down into Burford.

Christine Coverley was clearly surprised to see him, and clearly not happy.

'It's all a bit untidy—'

Morse smiled. 'Can I come in?'

'I haven't got long, I'm afraid.'

'It won't take long, I promise.'

'How can I . . .?'

'What were you doing last Monday morning? Between, say, nine and eleven?'

'Not the faintest, have I? Nobody could remember exactly—'

'Did you go out – for a newspaper, shopping, seeing someone?'

'I don't know. Like I say—'

'Can you have a look in your diary for me?'

'That wouldn't help.'

'What *would* help?'

'I don't know what you're getting at. Look, Inspector.' She glanced down at her wristwatch with what appeared incipient panic. 'Could we talk some other time, *please*? You see I've got—'

But it was too late.

There was the scratch of a key in the Yale lock and the front door was quickly opened and as quickly closed, and a youth entered from the narrow hallway to stand in the doorway of the single bed-sit room.

With staring eyes he looked first at Morse and then at Christine Coverley: 'What the fuck?'

'You haven't increased your word-power much since we last—' began Morse. But Roy Holmes had disappeared even more rapidly than he'd appeared.

In the stillness that followed the crash of the front door closing, Morse sat down in one of the armchairs, and gestured the speechless schoolmistress to seat herself in the other.

'Please tell me all about it,' he said, with no hint of aggressiveness or any of its synonyms. 'If you don't, I'm sorry but I shall have to take you down to Police HQ.'

After his twinkling Irish eyes had scrutinized Lewis's ID, Mr Tony Marrinan, the manager of The Randolph, was wholly co-operative; and very soon the outline of Frank Harrison's recent stay was revealed. Double-room booked with, as staff recalled her, a sultrily attractive if less than attractively mannered partner – late twenties, perhaps; meals taken together quite regularly in the Spires Restaurant – details available, if Sergeant Lewis wanted to see them.

As Sergeant Lewis did.

The pair had breakfasted together on each morning except the Monday, and Lewis was fairly soon looking at that day's Good Morning Breakfast chit, its details having been transferred immediately to the hotel's computer before being placed on a spike and then at the end of the day transferred to the accounts department upstairs for a limited period, as a check if any guest should query an entry on the final bill.

Interesting! Especially the bottom half of the chit:

Continental ☑	Full ☐
Date 3/8/98	Time 8.20
Table No. 7	Covers 1
Room No. 210	Waiter C.M.
Room Charge ☑	Other ☐
Guest Name: HARRISON	
Signature:	

'Covers', as Lewis learned, signified how many had been at the table: on the other chits it had the figure '2' beside it. But on the Monday morning just the one of them, and the restaurant manager remembered which one of them: 'It was the lady. I think Mr Harrison may have been feeling a little tired.'

Before he left the hotel, Lewis had a word with the chambermaid who had looked after Room 210, discovering that for much of the time over the period in question the DO NOT DISTURB notice had hung over the outside door-knob.

'And the bed looked as if it had been slept in each night?' (Lewis tried to smile knowingly.)

'Oh yes, sir. Oh yes.'

Perhaps the restaurant manager was right. Perhaps

Mr Harrison's stay in Oxford had been a busy and tiring one.

For one reason or another.

Before driving back to HQ, Morse called in at the Maiden's Arms, in the hope of finding Alf and Bert, Lower Swinstead's answer to 'Bill and Ben'. The time was now just after 2.30 p.m.; and Morse expected that they would be gone by then. But he was lucky; or at least half-lucky.

Bert, it seemed, had 'got the screws', and Alf was sitting alone by the window, slowly sipping the last of his beer, and readily accepting Morse's offer of 'one for the road'.

'Lost his nerve!' confided Alf. 'Lost the last five times we've a' been playing. Lost his nerve!'

'Like me to give you a quick game? Just the one?'

Morse had determined to lose the challenge in as swift and incompetent a manner as possible. But unfortunately the gods were smiling broadly on his hands; and very soon, *malgré lui*, he had won the single encounter by the proverbial street.

Unfortunately?

Oh no. For Alf appeared to recognize in his opponent a player of supreme skills; and instead of his wonted sullen silence on such occasions, he was soon speaking with unprecedented candour about life there in the village in general, and in particular about the Harrisons – with the result that after twenty minutes

Morse had learned more than any other police officer before him from any of the locals in Lower Swinstead.

'Did Frank ever come in the pub here with other women?'

'Never. In Lon'on most of his time, weren't he?'

'What about Simon?'

'He come in sometimes, but he never had no reg'lar girlfriend. Bit of a loner, Simon.'

'What about Sarah?'

'Lovely, she were – not seen her though this last coupla years. In fact, last time I seen her was here in the pub – sort of guest appearance singing with a pop group. Nice voice, she had, young Sarah.'

'Did she come in with any boyfriends?'

'Did she? I'll tell you summat – she did. Could've had anybody she wanted, I reckon.'

'Who did she want?'

Alf chuckled. 'Didn't want me – Bert neither! One or two was luckier though, mister.'

The light in Alf's old eyes suddenly sparked, like the coals on a fire that were almost ready to sink back to an ashen-grey; and he nodded his head – just as Bert, in his turn, would have nodded across the cribbage-board.

Enviously.

With the consulting rooms all taken up with a series of interviews for diabetes students, Lewis sat with Sarah Harrison behind a curtain in the Blood-Testing Room.

'Did you see your father while he was staying at the Randolph last week?'

'I always see my father when he comes to Oxford. In fact, I had a meal with him one evening.'

'So you get on well with him?'

Lewis's smile was not reciprocated, and she almost spat her reply at him: 'What the hell's *that* supposed to mean?'

'I'm not sure really. It's just that I've got a list of questions here from Chief Inspector Morse – by the way, I think you know him . . . ?'

'I've met him *once.*'

'Well he's asked me to ask you – not very well phrased, that – '

'What's he want to know?'

'What the relationships were like in your family.'

'I can't speak for Simon – you must ask *him.* If you mean did I have any preference? No. I loved Mum, and I loved, *love,* Dad. Some children love both their parents, you know.'

'You never felt that your mother loved Simon a bit more than she loved you – you know, because he was a bit handicapped, perhaps because he needed more affection than you did?'

There was a silence before Sarah answered the question; and as Lewis looked at her he realized how attractive she must have appeared to all the men and boys in the village; how attractive she was now, and would be for many years to come, in whatever place she found herself.

'You know I've never thought of it quite like that

before, but yes ... I suppose you could be right, Sergeant Lewis.'

After leaving the Maiden's Arms, where the fruit machine had stood unwontedly and unprofitably silent, Morse called on Allen (*sic*) Thomas at his home in Lower Swinstead. Alf had told him where to go: the lad was sure to be there. He'd not be at work, because he'd never done a hand's turn in his life.

And Alf was right.

The dingy room was untidy and undusted, with three empty cans on the top of the TV and a hugely piled ash-tray on the arm of the single armchair. But Thomas (the facial resemblance between him and Roy Holmes so very obvious to him now) was a paragon of civility compared with the crudity of that sibling of his, and Morse found himself feeling more pro than anti the unshaven youth in front of him.

'How often do you keep in touch with your dad?' began Morse.

The cigarette that had been dangling from Thomas's loose mouth fell to the carpet; and although it was swiftly retrieved the damage had been done. Thomas knew it. And Morse knew it. And fairly soon the truth, or what Morse took to be half of the truth, had started to surface.

Yes, Elizabeth Holmes was his natural mother.

Yes, Roy Holmes was his stepbrother – or his real brother – he'd never really known.

Yes, he kept in touch with his natural father, and his natural father kept in touch with him: Frank Harrison, yes – he'd always known that.

No. His father had never sent him what could loosely be called a fruit-machine allowance.

No. His father had never asked him to keep him regularly informed about any developments in the enquiries into Yvonne Harrison's murder.

No. He'd had no contact whatever recently either with his father or his mother or his brother.

Morse was half-smiling to himself as finally he drove back to Oxford, knowing beyond any peradventure that the No No No was in reality a Yes Yes Yes.

In the semi-co-ordinated strategy earlier agreed between the pair of them, Lewis's last allotted task had been some further enquiries into the balances and business activities of Mr Frank Harrison. Somewhat trickier than anticipated though. Yet far more exciting, as Lewis discovered after depositing (as agreed) the Sainsbury's bag, with contents, in Morse's office late that same afternoon, and ringing the London offices of the Swiss Helvetia Bank.

Reaching the senior manager surprisingly speedily.

Being informed that he, Lewis, ought really to get to London immediately and urgently.

Deciding to go.

Using the siren (one of Lewis's greatest joys) if he

found himself stuck, as he knew he would be, amidst the capital's inevitable gridlocks.

Morse took the red trainers from the bag and placed them on Simon Harrison's desk.

'These yours?'

'Pardon? What shorts?'

The interview wasn't going to be easy, Morse conceded that. Yet already the suspicion had crossed his mind that any deaf man, and especially a canny deaf man, might occasionally pretend to mis-hear in order to give himself a little more time to consider an awkward question.

'Your car, Mr Harrison? Toyota, P-Reg?'

'It ought to be what, Inspector?'

'Llandudno? Mean anything to you?'

'Did you know, you say? Didn't know?'

'The time for playing games is over, lad,' said Morse quietly. 'Let's start at the beginning again, shall we?' He pointed to the trainers. 'These yours?'

The truth, or what Morse took to be half of the truth, was fairly soon out.

The teenaged Simon had known Barron well enough because the builder had done a few things around the house, including a big structural job on the back patio. Frequently he'd found Barron in the kitchen having a mug of coffee with his mother, and he'd sensed that Barron fancied her. Jealous? Yes, he'd been jealous. Angry, too, because his mother had once confided in him that she found Barron a bit of a creep.

Then, so very recently, there'd been this upsurge of interest in his mother's murder, bringing with it a corresponding upsurge in his hatred of Barron.

Yes, he'd bought the trainers – £70! No, he'd not driven out to Stokenchurch that Monday morning. He'd driven out to Burford instead, where he knew that Barron was working.

Here Morse had interrupted. 'How did you know that?'

'Pardon?'

Was it a genuine plea? Morse was most doubtful, but he repeated the question with what he trusted was legible enunciation, conscious as he had been throughout of Simon's eyes upon his lips.

'He told me himself. You see, I wanted the outside of my flat, er . . . you know, the windows, doors . . . they were all getting a bit . . . Anyway, I asked him if he could do it and he said he'd come round and give me an estimate after he'd finished his next job. And I don't know why but he just happened to mention where it was, that's all.'

Morse nodded dubiously. Even if it wasn't the truth, it wasn't a bad answer. And Simon Harrison continued his unofficial statement:

He'd just felt – well, murderous. Simple as that. He'd always suspected that Barron was involved somehow in his mother's murder, and he was conscious of an ever-increasing hatred for the man. So he'd decided to go and see if Barron *was* there, in Sheep Street, balanced precariously (as he hoped) on the top of an extended ladder, painting the guttering or something. And he was.

Morse made a second interruption: 'So why didn't you . . .?'

Simon understood the inchoate query immediately, and for Morse his answer had the ring of truth about it:

'I wanted to make sure he *could* be pushed off. I'd noticed when he was doing Mum's roof that he used to anchor the top of his ladder to the troughing or chimney stack or something. And he'd done the same there, in Sheep Street – I could see it easily. So even if I'd had the guts to do it, the ladder wouldn't have fallen. *He* might have done, agreed, but . . . Anyway, I was a nervous wreck when I got back home; and when I read in the *Oxford Mail* that Mrs Somebody-or-other had mentioned seeing a jogger there wearing red trainers . . . I should have put them in the dustbin. Stupid, I was! But they'd cost me – well, I told you. And I've always loved animals, so . . . well, that's it really.'

Although less than convinced by what sounded a suspiciously shaky story, Morse was adequately impressed by the manner of the pleasantly spoken young man. Had he been as vain as Morse and many other mortals, he would probably have grown his hair fairly long over his temples in order to conceal his hearing-aids. But Harrison's dark hair was closely cropped, framing a clean-shaven face that seemed honest. Or reasonably so.

Asking Harrison to remind him of his home address and telephone number, Morse got to his feet and prepared to leave.

'You'll have to make an official statement, of course.'

'I realize that, yes.'

Morse pushed the trainers an inch or two further across the desk.

'You might as well keep them now. I only wish I were as fit as you.'

Was there a glint of humour in Simon's eyes as, in turn, he got to his feet?

'Fit a shoe, did you say, Inspector?'

Morse let it go. The man's hearing was very poor, little doubt of that. Which made it surprising perhaps that a mobile phone lay on the desk beside him.

On his second impulse that day, Morse drove down to North Oxford and stopped momentarily outside Simon Harrison's small property at 5 Grosvenor Street. The replacement windows with their aluminium frames had clearly been installed there fairly recently – frames whose glory (as advertised) was never to need any painting at all.

Courteously if somewhat cautiously received, Lewis listened carefully as one of the Bank's important personages spelled out the situation with (as was stressed) utter confidentiality, with appropriate delicacy, and with (for Lewis) a leavening of incomprehensible technicalities. In simple terms it amounted to this: Mr

Frank Harrison, currently on furlough, was currently also, if unofficially, on suspension from his duties with the Bank on suspicion, as yet unsubstantiated, of misappropriation of monies: viz. an unexplained black hole of some £520,000 in his department's Investment Portfolios.

CHAPTER SIXTY-FOUR

Refrain to-night
And that shall lend a kind of easiness
To the next abstinence: the next more easy;
For use almost can change the stamp of nature
(Shakespeare, *Hamlet*)

SLOANE SQUARE . . . GRIDLOCK . . . Siren . . . Gridlock . . . Siren . . .

It is not a matter for any surprise that car drivers occasionally contract one of the minor strains of the road-rage virus – even that patient man in the siren-assisted police car who finally pulled over on to the hard shoulder of the M40 and rang his chief.

'Been stuck in traffic, sir. Be with you in about an hour.'

'Lewis! Can't you hear the wireless? It's five-past seven – bang in the middle of *The Archers*. It can wait, surely!'

Lewis supposed it could; and would have said so. But the phone was dead.

Wireless! Huh! Everybody called it a 'radio' these days – well, everybody except Morse and one or two of the old 'uns, like Strange. Yes, come to think of it, Morse and Strange were the oldest of the HQ lot, with Strange six months the older, and due for retirement that next month.

The road was free and Lewis drove fast. It could wait – of course it could – the news about Harrison Senior. Perhaps it didn't matter all that much; and as Morse frequently reminded him nothing really mattered very much at all in the end. But he was looking forward to a swapping of notes. There had been some interesting developments, certainly on his own side; and he doubted not that Morse's researches that day had generated a few new ideas. Not that they needed any more high-flown ideas really, he decided, as a sudden torrential downpour called for more terrestrial concentration. He reduced his speed to 80 m.p.h.

At 7.20 p.m. Morse was sitting back in the black-leather armchair, knowing that only a few of the pieces in the jigsaw remained to be fitted. Earlier in the case the top half of the puzzle had presented itself as a monochrome blue, like the sky earlier that evening, although of late the weather had become sultry, as though a thunderstorm were brewing. But the jigsaw's undifferentiated blue had been duly broken by a solitary seagull or two, by a piece of soft-white cloud, and later perhaps (when Lewis arrived?) by what Housman so memorably had called 'the orange band of eve'. He felt almost happy. There was something else, too: he would quite certainly wait until that arrival before having his first drink of the day. It was quite easy really (as he told himself) to refrain from alcohol for a limited period.

The storm reached North Oxford fifty minutes later,

travelling from the south-west at a pace commensurate with Lewis's speed along the M40.

It may have had something to do with Wagner, but Morse enjoyed the intensity and the electricity of a thunderstorm, and he watched with deep pleasure the plashing rain and the dazzling flashes in the lightning-riven sky. From his viewpoint by the window of his flat, a slightly sagging telephone-wire cut the leaden heavens in two; and he watched as a succession of single drops of rain ran along the wire before finally falling off, reminding him of soldiers crossing a river on rope-harness, and finally dropping off on the other side. As he had once done himself.

Crossing the river . . .

His mother would never speak of 'dying': always of 'crossing the river'. It was a pleasing conceit; a pleasing metaphor. If he'd been a poet, he might have written a sonnet about that telephone-wire just outside. But Morse wasn't a poet. And the storm now ceased as suddenly as it had started.

And the front-door bell was ringing.

It was after 10 p.m. when, with Lewis now gone, Morse took stock of the situation – with renewed interest, though (truth to tell) with little great surprise. Lewis had declined the offer of alcohol, and Morse had decided to prolong his own virtually unprecedented abstinence. He felt tired, and at 10.30 p.m. decided that he would be early abed. So many times had he been counselled that beer made a lumpy mattress, that spirits made a hard pillow, and that in general alcohol was the stuff that nightmares were made of. So, if that were true, he could perhaps expect to be sleeping the sleep of the just that night. It would be a new experience.

He put on the RSPB video, and once again watched the wonderful albatross gliding effortlessly across the Antarctic wastes. So relaxing . . .

At 11.15 he switched off the bedroom light and turned as ever on to his right-hand side, conscious of a clear head, a freshness of mind, and a gently slumbrous lassitude.

Wonderful.

In spite of his occasional disillusionment about being cast up on to the shores of light in the first place, it would be wholly untrue to say that Morse was over-eager to embark upon that final journey to that further land. Indeed, like the majority of mortals, he was something of a hypochondriac; and that night he found himself becoming increasingly fearful about his own physical well-being. Or ill-being.

The illuminated green figures on the alarm clock showed 2.42 a.m. when he finally abandoned the unequal struggle. His mind was an uncontrollable whirligig at St Giles' Fair, and the indigestion-pains in his chest and in his arms were hard and unrelenting. He got up, poured himself a glass of Alka-Seltzer, poured himself a glass of the single malt, took up his medium-blue Parker pen, and resumed the exegesis he'd been writing when Lewis had interrupted him, deciding however to cross out the last (and uncompleted) sentence:

> 'It was embarrassing for me to talk to you about this and I know that you in turn found it equally embarrassing to—

There would be ample time to put that part of the record straight in the days ahead.

Tomorrow and tomorrow and tomorrow . . .

Chapter Sixty-Five

Jealousy is that pain which a man feels from the apprehension that he is not equally beloved by the person whom he entirely loves

(Addison, *The Spectator*)

Simon H is not a good liar, and I dragged some of the truth out of him. He is genuinely very deaf, and the telephone must always be a nightmare for him. So what's he got a mobile for? Even people with good hearing often have trouble with one. But, remember, even someone who's stone-deaf can communicate to some degree with someone on the other end, because he's always able to *speak* if not to hear.

Many people must have wanted Barron dead. And no one more so than Frank Harrison, who'd learned that Barron would soon be working up at some giddy height in a quietish street in Burford. The job had been mentioned, among other places no doubt, in the Maiden's Arms. And one person in that pub was in regular communication with Frank H: Allen Thomas, that soon-to-be-married youth who regularly wastes his substance on the fruit machine. How come? Like so many others in this case, he's dependent on Frank H – his father, remember! – who (rumour!) has just bought him a small flat in Bicester, and who has pretty certainly been making him a regular allowance for many years.

The plan had been a reasonably simple one – with one snag. Both the Harrisons, Senior and Junior, had some knowledge of Barron's ladder-technique from the several times he had worked at the family home: specifically his habit of tying the top of his ladders to something firm up there in the heights. It would seem likely that he'd do the same again, and there'd be little point in giving the ladder one great hefty push if it wouldn't topple to the ground. Some recce was therefore required; and Simon picked up his father that Monday morning in Oxford and drove him the twenty miles to Burford, leaving the car at the western end of Sheep Street, and then jogging up and down the opposite side of the street in tracksuit and trainers, noting that Barron was moving the ladder along every twelve minutes or so, and predictably re-roping the top each time. The only possibility then was to catch Barron after he'd *re*-climbed the ladder and was refixing the rope. A minute or so? Not much more. But enough. Simon's job was to phone his father, mobile to mobile, and just say 'Now!'. Nothing else. He hadn't the spunk he says (I believe him) to perform the deed himself; and it was his father, also in jogging kit, who would run along the pathway there and topple Barron to a death that in Simon's view was fully deserved and long overdue.

That was the plan. Something like it. So I believe.

But the countdown had been aborted because (Simon himself a witness) a bicycle, the front wheel jerked up repeatedly from the ground, was lurching its way along the path, and under the ladder, *and into* the ladder. Surplus to requirements therefore was the plan the Harrisons had plotted. Or so we are led to believe. Why such a proviso? Because I shall be surprised if any plan devised by the opportunistic Frank Harrison has ever come to a sorry nothing. Is it possible therefore that the accident of Barron's death was not quite so 'accidental' after all? Already Frank Harrison had accomplished something far more complex – his manipulation of the evidence surrounding his wife's murder, when it was imperative for him to establish one crucial fact: that no other living soul was present when he went into his house that night. But three other people knew this fact was untrue; and all three of them – whichever way intercommunication was effected – were subsequently rewarded for their roles in the conspiracy of complicity and silence.

Back to my proviso.

Can it be that Frank Harrison trawled his net even wider and dragged in the cyclist who sent Barron down to his death, the boy Holmes – the brother of Harrison's son Allen?

We turn now to the Harrison clan itself.

Our researchers have given us several pointers to the relationships within that family. The marriage itself had long been loveless: he with a string of mistresses in his Pavilion Road flat in London; she with a succession of straight or kinky but always besotted bedmates, with whom she fairly regularly dallied with mutual delight. And, doubtless, profit. Of the two children, Simon was clearly the mother's favourite – a boy who had battled bravely with his disability; a boy for whom his mother had found an affection considerably deeper than that for her daughter Sarah – a young lady who was very attractive physically, very bright academically, very talented musically, who from her early years had almost everything going for her, and who (unlike her brother) needed far less of her mother's tender loving care. Both children, as well as their parents, were probably fully aware of the imbalance here; and tacitly and tactfully accepted it.

At the time of their mother's murder, both the children had left home several years earlier. Sarah had already qualified as a doctor specializing with considerable distinction in the treatment of diabetes. And Simon had landed a surprisingly good job in publishing, and was now financially independent – if not emotionally independent, because he still yearned for that unique love his mother had always shown him; a love that had meant everything to him in those long years of an ever-struggling school-life in which he knew with joyous assurance that it was he – Simon! – who'd acquired the monopoly of a mother's love, more of it even than his father had ever had. He called to see her regularly, of course he did. But she probably always insisted that he rang her beforehand. No reason to ask why, surely? Simon was completely unaware of his mother's vespertinal divertissements.

But Frank certainly knew all about them, and they served as some sort of excuse and justification for his own adulterous liaisons. He didn't much care anyway. Perhaps he could shrug things off fairly easily. But Simon couldn't. Simon turned up unexpectedly one evening and found his mother lying on that very same bed where as a young boy (perhaps as an older boy?) he'd snuggled in beside her when his dad was away; and where he'd seen a man straddled across her on his elbows and his knees.

I doubt it had been exactly like that, though. More likely he'd seen a man bouncing down the stairs towards him, jerking up his trousers and fastening up his flies. A man he knew: Barron! Then he'd found his mother lying in the bedroom there: naked, gagged, handcuffed, with a pornographic video probably still running on the TV. Shell-shocked with disbelief and disillusionment, in the white heat of a furious jealousy – yes! – *he murdered his mother.*

Chapter Sixty-Six

We might now be stepping through a dark door with no bottom on the other side, and fall flat on our faces

(A member of the Honolulu City Council, quoted by the Press Corps)

Conscious that he was writing with increasing fluency, Morse poured himself another tumbler of single malt, and resumed his narrative:

With regard to events immediately thereafter, we can only guess. But at some point Simon rang his father in predictable panic. He had very few people he could call on. But he *could* call on his father – and there was a special loop-system on the telephone there. And Frank H got to the house as quickly as any man could have done that night. His BMW *was* in for servicing, that was checked; and I now believe (a bit late in the day) that the sequence of events was precisely as he claimed: taxi → Paddington; train → Oxford; Oxford (enter Flynn!) → Lower Swinstead.

Then? Probably we'll never really know. But five people, three of them now dead, *they* knew: Barron, who'd been disturbed *in medio coitu*; Flynn, the petty crook who just happened to be on hand; Repp, the burglar who'd been watching the property all evening; Frank H; and Simon H himself. Simon doesn't seem to me the calibre of fellow who could stay long at such a ghastly scene on his own; and I think it's more than likely that his father rang Sarah and told her to get along there post-haste, on the way buying a cinema ticket as an alibi for Simon. Certainly when I met Sarah I felt strongly that she probably knew who had murdered her mother. The trouble was that the three outsiders also knew: Repp and Barron, who were both local men – and Flynn, who'd met Simon in the lip-reading classes at Oxpens, and who must have seen him there that night.

What then was the family plan of campaign?

The two (or three) of them were determined to create the maximum amount of confusion – their only hope. The murder couldn't be concealed; but the waters around it could be made so muddied that any investigation was likely to shoot off into several blind alleys. We may postulate that a gag was tied around Yvonne's mouth (as I recall the report: 'no longer tight as if she had worked it looser in her desperation'); that a pair of handcuffs was snapped around her wrists; that one of the panes of the french window was smashed in from the outside. Why Yvonne's carefully folded clothes were not scattered all over the floor, I just don't know, because 'attempted rape' would have seemed a wholly probable explanation of the murder.

When and how the circling vultures closed in for

their shares of the kill – your guess, Lewis, is (almost) as good as mine. Some early liaison there must have been with Barron in order to establish the telephone alibi. Flynn probably just stayed around that night – a petty crook going through a bad patch, and naming his price immediately. I suspect that Repp, a real pro, held his hand for a couple of days or so before threatening to spill at least half the can of beans . . . unless he could be persuaded otherwise.

Whatever the case, financial arrangements were made, and as far as we know faithfully met. After the murder of his wife, much money was diverted from the assets of Frank H into other channels, although I'm still surprised to learn that there may well have been some serious misappropriation of funds at the Swiss Helvetia Bank.

All of which leaves one or two (or three!) points unresolved.

First, the burglar alarm. Now on his train-trip from London Frank H must have had thoughts galore. Several times he would have phoned home from the train, and *Sarah* must surely have been there to take the calls. And it was probably from the back of the taxi that Frank had the clever idea of ringing Sarah and telling her he would be ringing again, when the taxi was only half a minute or so from home, and asking her (Flynn wouldn't have heard, would he?) to turn on the burglar alarm. It *was* a clever idea, let's agree on that. It certainly and understandably caused huge confusion in the

> original police enquiry. The only person not wholly confused was Strange. It was he, from the word go, who suggested that the alarm might well have been set off deliberately by the murderer himself. (Never under-rate that man, Lewis!)

The time, as Morse saw, was 3.40 a.m., almost exactly one hour after he'd started writing. He was feeling pleasantly tired, and he knew he would slip into sleep so easily now. Yet he wanted to go (as Flecker had said) 'always that little further'; and perhaps more immediately to the point he wanted to pour himself a further Scotch – which he did before resuming.

> There is one more thing to consider, and it is of vital importance, as well as being (almost!) the only thing about which I was less than honest with you. That is, the extraordinary relationship between a drink-doped, drug-doped juvenile lout and an insignificant-looking little schoolma'am: between Roy Holmes and Christine Coverley. Something must have happened, probably at school, which had forged a wholly improbable but strangely strong bond between them – including a sexual relationship (she confessed as much). That's the reason she stayed on in Burford after the end of the summer term. Why is this important? Because we have been making one fundamental assumption in our enquiries which thus far has been completely unverified by any single independent witness. But truth will out! And first, and forthwith, we shall call in on Ms

Coverley for further questioning. How wise it was to hold our horses before facing Frank Harrison with a whole

(Here the narrative breaks off.)

Morse, who had been deeply asleep at his study desk, his head pillowed on folded arms, jerked awake just before 7.30 a.m., feeling wonderfully refreshed.

Life was a funny old business.

Chapter Sixty-Seven

To run away from trouble is a form of cowardice; and, whilst it is true that the suicide braves death, he does it not for some noble object but to escape some ill

(Aristotle, *Nicomachean Ethics*)

THE FOLLOWING MORNING Lewis was pleased with himself. Before Morse arrived, he'd turned to the *Police Gazette*'s 'Puzzle Corner', and easily solved the challenge there:

> What initially would an intelligent cyclist's thought be on studying the following list of operas by Verdi?
>
> *Tosca*
> *Aida*
> *Nabucco*
> *Don Carlos*
> *Ernani*
> *Macbeth*

'Initially' – that was the clue; and once you twigged it, the answer stared you in the face vertically.

Morse made an appearance at 9.10 a.m., looking (in Lewis's view) a little fitter than of late.

'Want to test your brain, sir?'

'Certainly not!'

Lewis pushed the puzzle across the desk, and Morse considered it, though for no more than a few seconds:

'Do *you* know the answer?'

'Easy! "Initially", sir – that's what you've got to think about. Just look at the first letters. Cyclist? Get it?'

'I thought the question was what would an *intelligent* cyclist's thought be.'

'I don't quite follow.'

'Not difficult surely, Lewis? You've just got the answer wrong, that's all. Any intelligent cyclist, any bright bus-driver – anyone! – would think exactly the same thing immediately.'

'They would?'

'The *question*'s phoney. Based on a false premise, isn't it? Based on the assumption that the facts you've been given are true.'

'You mean they're not?'

'*Tosca*? Written by *Verdi*?'

Oh dear! 'You were quick to spot that.'

Morse grinned. 'Not really. They often ask me to submit a little brain-teaser to the *Gazette*.'

'You mean—?'

Morse nodded. 'And talking of false premises, that's been a big part of our trouble. We've both been trying to check up on such a lot of things, haven't we? But there's *one* thing we've been prepared to accept without one ha'p'orth of evidence. So we'll get on to that without delay. Couple of cars we'll need. I'll just give Dixon a ring—'

Lewis got to his feet. 'I can deal with all that, sir.'

'Si' down, Lewis! I want to talk to you.'

Through the glass-panelled door Dixon finally saw the silhouette moving towards him: a woman in a wheelchair who brusquely informed him that she knew nothing of the whereabouts of her son. He had not been home the previous evening. He had a key. He was sometimes out all night, yes. No, she didn't know where. And if it was of any interest to the police, she didn't care – didn't bloody well *care*.

There was no reply to PC Kershaw's importunate ringing and knocking. But at last he was able to locate the mildly disgruntled middle-aged woman who looked after the two 'lets'; and who accompanied him back to the ground-floor flat. She appeared to have little affection for either of the two lessees, although when she opened the door she must have felt a horrified shock of sympathy with one of them.

Christine Coverley lay supine on a sheepskin rug in front of an unlit electric-fire. She was wearing a summery, sleeveless, salmon-pink dress, her arms very white, hands palm-upwards, with each of her wrists slashed deeply and neatly across. A black-handled kitchen-knife lay beside her left shoulder.

Young Kershaw was unused to such horrors; and over the next few days the visual image was to refigure repeatedly in his nightmares. Two patches on the rug were deeply steeped in blood; and Kershaw was reminded of the Welsh hill-farm where he'd once stayed and where the backs of each of the owner's sheep had been daubed with a dye of the deepest crimson.

No note was found by Kershaw; indeed no note was found by anyone afterwards. It was as if Christine had left this world with a despair she'd found incommunicable to anyone: even to her parents; even to the uncouth lout who penetrated her so pleasurably now, though at first against her will; even to the rather nice police inspector who'd seemed to her to understand so much about her. Far too much . . . including (she'd known it!) the fact that she had lied. Roy could never have been cycling along Sheep Street when Barron fell to his death because at that very moment he had been in bed with her . . .

Chapter Sixty-Eight

It is not the criminal things which are hardest to confess, but the ridiculous and the shameful

(Rousseau, *Confessions*)

Lewis had not been surprised – no, certainly not that. But disappointed? Yes. Oh yes! And Morse had been aware of his reaction, clearly anticipating it, yet saying nothing to lessen the impact of the revelation. The relationship between them would never be quite the same again, Lewis realized that. It wasn't at all the fact that Morse had driven out one evening (two evenings? ten evenings?) to meet a seductively attractive woman. Lewis had seen the sharply focused photographs of her body stretched out on the bed that night; and it could be no great wonder that many a man, young and old alike, had lusted after a woman such as that. No, it was something else. It was the out-of-character, under-hand way that Morse had allowed the dishonest subterfuge to linger on and on from the beginning of the case.

Indeed Morse had been less than wholly forthcoming in his confession even now, Lewis was fairly sure of it. Yes, Morse agreed, he *had* gained access to the file containing the intimate correspondence addressed to Y H. Yes, he *had* 'appropriated' the handcuffs, police handcuffs, with a number stamped on them that could easily be traced back to the officer issued with them, in this case to Morse himself. And yes (he readily admitted it) he *had* 'withdrawn' the relevant sheet of the issue-numbers kept at HQ. As far as the partial letter was concerned (Morse accepted immediately that it was in his own hand) Lewis had hoped, in an old-fashioned sort of way, that Morse had in fact *never* been invited to Lower Swinstead, in spite of his own plea for some communication from her; in spite of that almost schoolboyish business about looking through his mail every morning in the hope of finding something from her. And that was about it. Morse had wanted to cover up something of which he was rather ashamed and very embarrassed; just wanted his own name, previously his own good name, never to be associated with the life – and the death – of Yvonne Harrison. He'd been careless about leaving that single page of a longer letter but (as he asked Lewis to agree) it was hardly an incriminating piece of evidence. What Morse stoutly refused to accept was that what he had done, however cowardly and dishonest and foolish, had in any way jeopardized the course of the original enquiry, which he now had the nerve to assert had been conducted with almost unprecedented incompetence. Such arrogance was of course not all that unusual; yet in the present circumstances it seemed to Lewis quite gratuitously cheap.

Leaving all such considerations aside though, what stuck in Lewis's throat was that initial, duplicitous refusal on Morse's part to have anything to do with the original case. Agreed, once he had been drafted on to what seemed to both Lewis and Strange the second half of the *same* case, Morse had risen to his accustomed heights of logical analysis and depths of human understanding. Agreed, he had (as usual) been several furlongs ahead of the field – and, for once, on the right racecourse from the 'off'.

Who else but Morse could have put forward the quite extraordinary hypotheses made earlier that morning about the murder of J. Barron, Builder? The hypothesis (seemingly confirmed) that Roy Holmes – who'd do almost anything to *get* drugs and who'd do absolutely anything when he was *on* drugs – was having a sexual relationship with Christine Coverley; the hypothesis (seemingly confirmed) that the weirdly incongruous partnership had resulted from some incident or series of incidents at school; that the youth had agreed, for money, to make a statement to the police about a supposedly accidental collision with a high ladder – a statement that was wholly untrue, because Roy Holmes had been nowhere near Sheep Street that morning; the hypothesis (to *be* confirmed!) that it was Frank Harrison who had murdered Barron, and who had engineered an ingenious scheme whereby all suspicion would be diverted both from himself and from Simon – the scheme itself probably prompted by another son, by Allen Thomas, who regularly gathered a good deal of information from his vantage-point in the Maiden's Arms and who regularly passed it on to his father, the man at the centre of everything.

Lewis nodded to himself. No wonder Frank Harrison had gone to earth somewhere. Not for long though, surely. He had nowhere to go; nowhere to hide. Airports and seaports had been apprised of his passport number, and photographs would be on their way. Unless it was too late.

It was Morse's suggestion that the two of them together should interview Roy Holmes and Christine Coverley, with Lewis invited to do most of the talking with the youth. 'I detest him, Lewis! And you're better at that sort of things than I am.' It was flattering, but it didn't work. Morse was sadly wrong if he thought he could so easily re-establish some degree of integrity in the eyes of his sergeant.

In mid-morning, Lewis left the office without asking Morse if he would like a coffee. He knew that the omission would be noted; he knew that Morse would feel the hurt.

Not so.

When Lewis returned ten minutes later, he found Morse leaning back and beaming happily.

'Fetch me a coffee, will you, Lewis! No sugar – we diabetics, you know . . . Something to celebrate.' *The Times* was folded back in quarters in front of him, the crossword-grid completely filled in. 'Six and a half minutes! I've never done it quicker.'

'Shouldn't that be "more quickly"?'

'Good man! You're learning at last. You see it's a question, as I've told you, of the comparative adjective and the comparative adverb. If you say—'

The phone rang.

Dixon.

For the moment Roy Holmes was not to be found: he wasn't at home; he wasn't anywhere. Did Morse want him to keep looking?

'What the hell do you think?' Morse had snapped at him. 'You remember the old proverb? If at first you don't succeed, don't take up hang-gliding.'

The brief telephone conversation pleased Lewis, and for a few seconds he wondered if he was being a little unfair in his judgement on Morse. But only for a few seconds.

'Not the only one we can't find, sir.'

'Frank Harrison, you mean? Ye-es. I'm a bit puzzled about him. He might be a crook – he *is* a crook – but he's not a fool. He's an experienced, hard-nosed, single-minded, rich banker, and if you're all those things you don't suddenly put your fingers in the—'

The phone rang.

Kershaw.

Morse listened, saying nothing; but the eyes that lifted to look across the desk into Lewis's face, if not wholly surprised, seemed very disappointed and very sad. Much as two hours earlier Lewis's own eyes had looked.

In mid-afternoon (Morse was no longer at HQ) the phone rang.

Swiss Helvetia Bank.

'Could we speak to Superintendent Lewis, please?'

'Sergeant Lewis speaking.'

Chapter Sixty-Nine

SEC. OFF.: Antonio, I arrest thee at the suit of Count Orsino.
ANT.: You do mistake me, sir.
FIRST OFF.: No, sir, no jot.
(Shakespeare, *Twelfth Night*)

AT 5.20 P.M. he was still standing beside his minimal hand-luggage a few yards from the Euro-Class counter at Heathrow's Terminal 4, looking around him with as yet dismissable anxiety, but with gradually increasing impatience. 5.10 p.m. – that was when they'd agreed to meet, giving them ample time, once through the fast-track channel, to have some gentle relaxation together in the British Airways Lounge before boarding the 18.30 Flight 338.

Paris . . .

A long time ago he and Yvonne had gone to Paris on their honeymoon: lots of love, lots of sex, lots of sightseeing, lots of food and wine. A whole fortnight of it, although he'd known even then that just a week of it would have been rather better. It was not difficult (he already knew it well) to get bored even in the presence of a mistress; and he'd begun to realize on that occasion that it was perfectly possible to grow just a little wearied even in the company of a newly wed wife. There had been one or two incidents, too, when he'd thought Yvonne was experiencing similar thoughts . . . especially that time one evening when she'd quite obviously been exchanging long looks with a moustachioed Frenchman who looked exactly like Proust. He'd called her 'a flirtatious bitch' when they got to their hotel room; and when she'd glared back at him and told him they'd make a 'bloody good pair' one way or another . . .

There would be no trouble like that with Maxine: only two and a half days – just right, that! And she was a real honey, a law professor from Yale, aged forty-two, divorced, a little over-sexed, a little overweight, and hugely desirable.

She finally appeared, pulling an inordinately large suitcase on wheels.

'You're late!' His tone was a combination of anger and relief; and he immediately moved forward ahead of her to the back of the short queue at the First-Class counter.

'You didn't get my message, did you? I tried and tried—'

'Like I told you? On the mobile?'

'It wasn't working. I think you'd forgotten—'

'Christ!' Harrison took his mobile from an inside pocket, tapped a few digits, then another few; then repeated the blasphemy: 'Christ! I'd had enough of the bloody mobile recently and—'

'And you forgot that we'd agreed—'

'Sorry! Say you'll forgive me!'

He looked down at her squarish, slightly prognathic face, her dark-brown silky hair cut short in a fringe across her broad forehead and above the quietly gentle eyes that were becoming tearful now, perhaps from her hectic rush, perhaps from the undeserved brusqueness of his greeting, but perhaps above all from the knowledge that his love for her homodyned only with the waves of that physical lust which so often excited him. Yet the brief holiday had been *her* choice, and she knew that she wouldn't regret having made it. She enjoyed being with him: he was good fun and intelligent and well read and still handsome and still excellent in bed and – yes! – he was rich.

They moved nearer the counter, neither of them too anxious to speak – a phenomenon not uncommon with persons queuing, as if their concentration were required for the transactions ahead. But she volunteered some incidental information:

'Accident there was, near Stokenchurch, and I tried to—'

Gently he ran a hand through her silken hair. 'Sweetheart? Forget it!'

'It's just that we must have been stuck there half an hour and we saw – one of the other passengers pointed it out – a beautiful bird of prey there. A red kite.'

'Tell me later!'

There was now just the one business-suited man in front of them.

'Where have you booked us?'

'The best.'

'And the best air-tickets—?'

'Sh! Nothing but the best for you. Why not? Just think of me! No wife. No blackmailing kids. No problems at work. Nothing to spend money on for a day or two – except on you. I'm a rich man, sweetheart. I thought I'd told you.'

'Tickets, please?'

The smiling young lady scrutinized the perfectly valid tickets.

'Passports, please?'

The young lady scrutinized the perfectly valid passports.

'Smoking?'

'Non-smoking.'

'Window-centre? Centre-aisle?'

'Centre-aisle.'

'Luggage?'

Frank Harrison lugged the great case on to the trackway beside the desk.

'Only the one?'

'Yes.'

'You know where the club-lounge is?'

'Yes.'

'Enjoy your flight, sir, and enjoy your stay in Paris!'

He handed her a glass of champagne, and two glasses clinked. 'Here's to a wonderful little break together. Ritz – here we come!'

He leaned across and kissed her on the soft, unlipsticked mouth – a long, yearning kiss. His eyes closed. Her eyes closed.

'Mr Harrison?' A tap on the shoulder. 'Mr Frank Harrison?'

'What—?'

A uniformed police officer stood beside the small table: 'I'm sorry, sir, but we need to speak to you. Routine check.'

'Thames Valley Police, is this?'

'That's right, sir.'

'What exactly—?'

'It's not *just* that. Your employers want to speak to you as well.'

Harrison's eyes squinted in bewilderment.

'What the hell do *they* want? I'm on official furlough, for God's sake. They'll have to wait till I get back.'

'Will you come this way, sir? Please!'

A second uniformed policeman – young, dark-haired – stood just inside the entrance to the executive lounge; was still standing there a quarter of an hour later when Maxine, after drinking the one and then the other glass of champagne, went over to speak to him.

'Do you mind telling me, Officer, by whose authority—?'

'Not mine, miss,' said PC Kershaw. 'Please believe me. I also am a man *under* authority.'

'You haven't answered my question.'

'I'm from Thames Valley – we both are.'

'Who sent you here?'

'The CID.'

'Who?'

'Chief Inspector Morse.'

'Who's he when he's in his office?'

'He's an important man.'

'Very important?'

'Oh yes!' Kershaw nodded with a reverential smile.

'You talk as if he's God Almighty.'

'Some people think he is.'

'Do you?'

'Not always.'

'How long will you be keeping Mr Harrison?'

'I just don't know, Mrs Ridgway.'

Maxine poured herself a further glass of champagne, and pondered as she sat alone at the small table. They knew *her* name too . . .

He wasn't a particularly lucky man to associate with, Frank Harrison. The last time she'd been with him, over a year ago, he'd had that phone call from – well, he'd never said who from – to tell him that his wife had been murdered . . .

She was tempted to get up and – well, just leave. Just get out of there. Her case was on the plane by now though – suits, dresses, lingerie, shoes – but it *could* be returned perhaps? She still had her handbag with its far more important items: cards, keys, diary, money . . .

But she felt sure the PC at the door would never let her out. That's why he was there. Why else?

An announcement over the lounge Tannoy informed her that first-class passengers for British Airways Flight 338 to Paris should now proceed to Gate 3; and a dozen or so people were draining their drinks and gathering up their hand luggage. But for Maxine Ridgway it was now a feeling of deep sadness that had overtaken those earlier minutes of indecision and despair. She was no fool. She knew by heart the rôle she'd been asked to play in the Ritz; and she'd accepted the bargain, because it *would* have been a bargain.

She was not even bothering to wonder what she should do next when she heard the voice behind her: 'Come on, sweetheart! You heard the announcement. Gate 3.'

With her mind in a mingled state of amazement and relief, she picked up her hand luggage and followed him to the exit-doors, where there was now no sign of PC Kershaw, the man who had seemed to have a greater familiarity with Holy Writ than she had herself.

'Routine check, that's all,' asserted Frank Harrison. 'Just like the man said.'

Chapter Seventy

I cried for madder music and for stronger wine,
But when the feast is finished and the lamps expire,
Then falls thy shadow, Cynara! the night is thine;
And I am desolate and sick of an old passion,
Yea hungry for the lips of my desire:
I have been faithful to thee, Cynara! in my fashion

(Dowson, *Non Sum Qualis Eram Bonae Sub Regno Cynarae*)

'Let him go, Kershaw. Let him catch his flight.'

'You think that's wise, sir?'

'*What?*'

'I just wondered—'

'Look, lad! If I ever have to look to you as a fount of wisdom, it'll be the day you're dry behind the ears. Is that clear?'

'Sir!'

Morse put down the phone. It was 6.10 p.m.

'Do you think that was fair, sir?' asked Lewis.

'Probably not,' conceded Morse.

It had been Lewis, an hour earlier, who had received the call from the Bank: profound apology; embarrassing recantation; chagrin unspeakable! Over £500,000 indeed was still unaccountably missing; but not, *not* from Harrison's department. Enquiries subsequent to Lewis's visit had now established that any embezzlement or misappropriation of funds was most definitely not to be laid at the door of one of the Bank's most experienced, most trusted, most valued blah blah blah.

It was a call in which Morse was most interested, now repeating (with some self-congratulation) what he had earlier maintained: that Frank Harrison might well be, most likely *was,* capable of murder; but that it was quite out of character, definitely *infra dignitatem,* for him to stoop to cooking the books and fiddling the balance-and-loss ledgers.

'Do you think you may be wrong, sir?'

'Certainly not. He'll be back from Paris, believe me! There's no hiding-place for him. Not from me, there isn't.'

'You think he murdered his wife?'

'No. But he knows who did. *You* know who did. But we've got to get some evidence. We've been checking alibis – recent ones. But we've got to check those earlier alibis again.'

'Who are you thinking of?'

'Of whom am I thinking?' (Morse recalled the suspicion he'd voiced in his earlier notes.) 'I'm thinking of the only other person apart from Frank Harrison who had a sufficient motive to kill Yvonne.'

'You mean—?'

'Do you ever go to the pictures?'

'They don't call it the "pictures" any more.'

'I went to the pictures a year and a bit ago to see *The Full Monty.*'

'Surely not your sort of—?'

'*Exactly* my sort of thing. I laughed and I cried.'

'Oh yes.' (The penny had dropped.) 'Simon Harrison said he'd gone—'

' "Said", yes.'

'Said he'd gone with someone else, didn't he? A girlfriend.'

'Wasn't checked though, as far as I can see.'

'Understandable, isn't it? Nobody ever really thought of someone inside the family—'

'Oh yes they did. Frank Harrison was one of their first suspects.'

'But with those signs of burglary, the broken window, the burglar alarm . . .'

Morse nodded. 'At first almost everything pointed to an outside job. But then it slowly began to look like something else: a lover, a tryst, a sex-session, a quarrel, a murder . . .'

'And now we're coming back to the family, you say.'

'No one seems to have bothered to get a statement from the young lady Simon Harrison took to the pictures that evening.'

'Perhaps we could still trace her, sir?'

'Yes.'

'It's a long time ago though. She'd never remember—'

'Of course she would! It was all over the papers: "Woman Murdered" – and she'd been with that same woman's son the evening when it happened. She could never forget it!'

'It's still a long time—'

'Lewis! I don't eat all that much as you know. But when I'm cooking for myself – '

(Lewis's eyebrows rose.)

' – I always make sure the plate's hot. I can't abide eating off a cold plate.'

'You mean we could heat the plate up again?'

'The plate's already hot again. She's still around. She's a proud, married mum now living in Witney.'

'How do you know all that?'

'You can't do *everything* yourself, Lewis.'

'Dixon, you mean?'

'Good man, Dixon! So we're going to see her tonight. Just you and I.'

'You think Simon murdered his mum.'

'No doubt about that. Not any longer, Lewis,' said Morse quietly.

'Just because he found her in bed with someone . . .'

'With Barron. I *know* that, Lewis.'

Never before had Lewis been so hesitant in asking Morse a question:

'Did . . . did Mrs Harrison ever tell *you* that she was . . . seeing Barron?'

Morse hesitated – hesitated for far too long.

'No. No, she never told me that.'

Lewis waited a while, choosing his words carefully and speaking them slowly: 'If she *had* told you, would *you* have been as jealous as Simon Harrison?'

Again Morse hesitated. 'Jealousy is a dreadfully corrosive thing. The most powerful motive of all, in my view, for murder – more powerful than—'

The phone rang once more and Morse answered.

Kershaw.

'They'll soon be winging their way across the channel, sir. Anything more you want me to do?'

'Yes. Have a pint of beer, just the one, then bugger off home.'

Morse put down the phone.

'Good man, Kershaw! Bit of an old woman though. Reminds me of my Aunt Gladys in Alnwick, my last remaining relative. Well, she was. Dead now.'

'I think he'll do well, yes.'

'Kershaw? Should do. He got a First in History from Keble.'

'Bit more than me, sir.'

'Bit more than me, Lewis.'

The phone was ringing again.

Strange.

'Morse? You've let him out of the country, I hear?'

'Yes. We need a bit more time and a bit more evidence before we bring him in.'

'I agree,' said Strange, unexpectedly. 'No good just . . .'

'He'll be back for the day of reckoning.'

'You think so?'

'I know so.'

'And in the interim?'

'He'll be having a beano – kisses, wine, roses. "But when the feast is finished and the lamps expire . . ." You know the Dowson poem, sir?'

'Course I bloody do!'

'Well, I don't think he'll ever be really happy with any of these other women of his.'

'This one sounds like a bit of all right though.'

'I'd still like to bet he wakes up in the small hours sometimes and thinks back on the woman he loved more than any of them, feeling a bit desolate – '

' – and sick of an old passion.'

'Exactly.'

'Yvonne, you mean?'

'No, not Yvonne, sir. Elizabeth – Elizabeth Jane Thomas.'

Chapter Seventy-One

What more pleasant setting than the cinema for sweetly deodorized bodies to meet, unzip, and commune?

(Malcolm Muggeridge, *The Most of Malcolm Muggeridge*)

Sylvia Marsden (née Prentice) was temporarily living with her mother in a pleasantly appointed semi on a housing estate at Witney. And it was her mother (Lewis had phoned earlier) who had answered the door and shown the two detectives into the lounge where the buxom Sylvia, blouse open, was breast-feeding a very new baby – not in the slightest degree disconcerted to be thus interrupted in her maternal ministrations, one hand splayed across an engorged nipple, the fingers of the other playing lovingly around the lips of the suckling infant.

An awkwardly embarrassed Morse moved slowly round the room, simulating deep interest in the tasteless bric-a-brac that cluttered every surface and shelf in the brightly decorated room; whilst Lewis stood above the mother and child, smiling quasi-paternally and drawing the back of his right index-finger lightly across the cherubic cheek:

'Little treasure, isn't he? What's his name?'

'She's a she, actually – aren't you, Susie?'

'Ah yes, of course!'

Morse temporarily declined to take a seat but accepted, strangely enough, the offer of coffee, and began his questioning whilst looking through the window on to the neatly kept back garden.

'We're just having to make one or two further enquiries, Mrs Marsden—'

'Call me Sylvia!'

'It's about one of your former boyfriends—'

'Simon, yes, I know. That Sergeant Dixon told me. Nice man, isn't he? He got on ever so well with Mum.'

Morse nodded, aware of the probable reason. 'It's a long time ago now, I realize . . .'

'Not really. Not for me it isn't. The night Simon's mum was murdered? Can't forget something like that, can you?'

'That's good news, Sylvia. Now that night, that evening, the 9th—'

'Oh no! You've got it wrong. It was the 8th – the night Mrs Harrison was murdered. I'm quite sure of that. My birthday, wasn't it? Simon took me to the ABC in Oxford. Super film! All about these male strippers—'

'Did the police ever ask you about it?'

'No. Why should they?'

Sylvia rebuttoned her blouse, and as Morse turned at last to face her, Lewis could see the disappointment on his face.

Mrs Prentice (née Jones) who had clearly been listening keenly from the adjacent kitchen, now brought in two cups of coffee. 'I can remember that,' she volunteered. 'Like she says, that was your birthday, wasn't it, Sylv?'

'How did you find Simon, Mrs Prentice?' asked Lewis.

'I liked him. He used to come in sometimes but I think he felt a bit . . . you know, with his hearing.'

'He didn't come in that night?'

'No. I remember it well. Like Sylv says – well, not something you forget, is it? I saw him though, after he'd brought her back. And I heard the pair of 'em whispering on the doorstep. Nice boy, really. Could have done worse, couldn't you, Sylv?'

'I did *better*, Mum, OK?'

Clearly there was less than complete family agreement on the merits of baby Susie's official father and Morse swallowed his coffee quickly and, as ever, Lewis followed his chief's lead dutifully.

In the car outside they sat for some time in silence.

'You knew it was the 8th, sir. Why—?'

'Just to test her memory.'

There was another long silence.

'Looks as if we've been wrong, sir.'

'Looks as if *I've* been wrong.'

'Alibis don't come much better than that.'

'No.'

'You know when Mrs Whatshername said she heard the pair of 'em whispering outside, she probably heard more of the conversation than Simon ever did!'

Morse nodded with a wry grin. 'You don't think there's any chance that somebody bribed our Sylvia and Sylvia's mum . . . ?'

'Not the remotest. Do you?'

'No.'

'Where do we go from here, sir?'

'You can drop me off at the Woodstock Arms or . . .'

'No. I meant with the *case*, sir.'

'. . . or perhaps the Maiden's Arms.'

It seemed that Morse was hardly listening.

'I know you're disappointed, sir, but—'

'Disappointed? Nonsense!'

Some light-footed mouse had just scuttled across his scapulae; and when Lewis turned to look at him, it seemed as if someone had switched the electric current on behind his eyes.

'Yes, Lewis. Just drive me out to Lower Swinstead.'

Chapter Seventy-Two

Below me, there is the village, and looks how quiet and small!
And yet bubbles o'er like a city, with gossip, scandal, and spite

(Tennyson, *Maud*)

Unwontedly in a car, Morse was almost continuously talkative as they drove along: 'Do you know that lovely line of Thomson's about villages "embosomed soft in trees"?'

'Don't even know Thomson,' mumbled Lewis.

'Remarkable things! Strange, intimate little places where there's more going on than anybody ever dreams of. You get illicit liaisons, hopeless love affairs, illegitimate offspring, wife-swopping, interbreeding, neighbourly spite, class warfare – all that's for the insiders, though. If you're on the outside, they refuse to have anything to do with you. They clamp up. They present a united defensive front because they've got one thing in common, Lewis: the village itself. They're all members of the same football club. They may loathe each other's guts for most of the week, but come Saturday afternoon when they put on the same football shirts . . . Well, the next village better look out!'

'Except Lower Swinstead doesn't have a football team.'

'What are you talking about? They're *all* in the football team.'

Lewis drove down the Windrush Valley into Lower Swinstead.

'They don't all clamp up, anyway. Not to you, they don't. Compared with some of our lads you've squeezed a carton of juice out of 'em already.'

'But there's more squeezing to do, Lewis – just a little.'

Unwontedly in a pub, Morse had already taken out his wallet at the bar, and Lewis raised no objection.

'Pint of bitter – whatever's in the best nick.'

'It's all in the best nick,' began Biffen.

'And . . . orange or grapefruit, Lewis?'

The fruit machine stood idle and the cribbage-board was slotted away behind the bar. But the place was quite busy. Most of the customers were locals; most of them people who'd earlier been questioned about the Harrison murder; most of them members of the village team.

On the pub's noticeboard at the side of the bar, underneath 'Live Music Every Saturday', was an amateurishly printed yellow poster advertising the current week's entertainment:

8.30–11.30 p.m.

DON'T MISS IT

The widely acclaimed folk-singer

CYNDI COOK

with the ever popular
3 R's
Randy, Ray, Rick

'Popular?' asked Morse of the landlord.

'Packed out we are, every Sat'day.'

'Ever had Paddy Flynn and his group playing here?'

'Paddy who?'

'Flynn – the chap who was murdered.'

'Ah yes. Read about it, o'course. But I don't think he were ever here, Inspector. You know, fifty-odd groups a year and – how many years is it I've—'

'Forget it!' snapped Morse.

'The beer OK?'

'Fine. How's Bert, by the way? Any better?'

'Worse. Quack called to see him yesterday – just after we'd opened – told Bert's boy the old man oughta go in for a few days, like – but Bert told 'em he wasn't going to die in no hospital.'

For someone who knew almost nothing about some things, Thomas Biffen seemed to know an awful lot about others.

'Where does he live?' asked Morse.

*

It was Bert's son, a man already in his late fifties, who showed Morse up the narrow steepish steps to the bedroom where Bert himself lay, propped up against pillows, the backs of his hands, purple-veined and deeply foxed, resting on the top of the sheet.

'Missing the cribbage, I bet!' volunteered Morse.

The old face, yellowish and gaunt, lit up a little. 'Alf'll be glad of a rest. Hah!' He chuckled deeply in his throat. 'Lost these last five times, he has.'

'You're a bit under the weather, they tell me.'

'Still got me wits about me though. More'n Alf has sometimes.'

'Still got a good memory, you mean?'

'Allus had a good memory since I were at school.'

'Mind if I ask you a few things? About the village? You know . . . gossip, scandal . . . that sort of thing? I had a few words with Alf, but I reckon his memory's not as sharp as yours.'

'Never was, was it? Just you fire away, Inspector. Pleasure!'

Lewis, who had been left in the car, leaned across and opened the passenger door.

'Another member of the local football team?'

Morse smiled sadly and shook his head. 'I think he's in for a transfer.'

'What exactly did he—?'

'Get me home, Lewis.'

*

On the speedy journey back to Oxford, the pair spoke only once, and then in a fairly brief exchange:

'Listen, Lewis! We know exactly where Frank Harrison is; who's with him; how long he's booked in at his hotel; when his return flight is. So. I want you to make sure he's met at Heathrow.'

'If he comes back.'

'He'll be back. I want *you* to meet him. Charge him with anything you like, complicity in the murder of his missus; complicity in the murder of Barron – please yourself. Anything! But bring him back to me, all right? I've seldom looked forward—'

Morse suddenly rubbed his chest vigorously.

'You OK, sir?'

Morse made no reply immediately. But after a few miles had perked up considerably.

'Just drop me at the Woodstock Arms!'

'Do you think—?'

'And present my apologies to Mrs Lewis. As per usual.'

Lewis nodded as he turned right at the Woodstock Road roundabout.

As per usual.

In Paris, in the Ritz, later that same evening – a good deal later – Maxine Ridgway was finding it difficult to finish the lobster dish and almost impossible to drink another mouthful of the expensive white wine that looked to her exactly the colour and gravity of urine. She was tired; she was more than a little tipsy; she was slightly less than breathlessly eager for another bout of sexual frolicking on their king-size bed. And Frank, too, (she'd sensed it all evening) had been strangely reticent and surprisingly sober.

She braved the exchange: 'You're not quite your usual self tonight, Frank.'

'Why do you say that?'

'It's that business at Heathrow, isn't it?'

Frank leaned across the table and placed his right hand on her arm. 'I'll be OK soon, sweetheart. Don't worry! And I ought to tell you something: you're looking absolutely gorgeous!'

'You think so?'

'Why do you reckon all the waiters keep making detours round our table?'

'Tell me!'

'To have a look down the front of your dress.'

'Don't be silly!'

'You hadn't noticed?'

'Frank! It's been a long day – and I'm just so tired . . . so tired.'

'Not *too* tired, I hope? *Nicht zu müde*?'

'No, darling.'

'You don't want a sweet? A coffee?'

'No.'

'Well, you go up. I'll be with you soon. I've just got a couple of private phone calls to make. And I want to think for a little while – on my own, if you don't mind? And make sure you put that see-through thing on, all right? The one that'll send the garçon ga-ga when he brings our breakfast in the morning.'

'You've arranged that?'

Frank Harrison nodded; and watched the backs of her legs as she left the table.

Yes, he'd arranged for breakfast in their room.

He'd arranged everything.

Almost.

Chapter Seventy-Three

When I have fears that I may cease to be
Before my pen has glean'd my teeming brain . . .
(Keats, *Sonnet*)

Slowly Morse walked homeward from the Woodstock Arms, disappointed (as we have seen) if not wholly surprised, that the favourite in the Harrison Stakes had fallen (like Devon Loch) within sight of the winning-post. But now, at last (or so he told himself) Morse guessed the whole truth. And feeling pleasingly over-beered, he had earlier taken the unusual step of ordering a bar snack, and had enjoyed his liberally horse-radished beef sandwiches. He thought he would probably sleep well enough that night. After a while. Not just for a minute though. Truth was that he felt eager to continue (to finish off?) the notes he'd already been making on the Harrison murder, just in case something happened; just in case no one would be aware of the sweetly logical solution that had formulated itself in his mind that day.

Much earlier (Morse knew it) he should have paid far more attention to the thing that had puzzled him most about the Harrison murder: *motive.* Until now, Simon had fitted that bill pretty well, since Morse was sure that the mother–son relationship had been very close; much *too* close. Good thinking, that! Then, that very afternoon, a busty lusty lass sitting with Simon in the three-and-sixpennies had innocently scuppered his carefully considered scheme of things.

Once home, Morse poured himself a modestly liberal measure of Glenfiddich, and changed into a gaudily striped pair of pyjamas that blossomed in white and purple and red . . . before continuing, indeed completing, his written record.

This evening in Lower Swinstead I spoke at quite some length with Mr Bert Bagshaw. Why did I not follow my first instincts? Had I done so, I would have realized that any clues to that (most elusive) motivation for the murder of Yvonne Harrison would ever be likely to lie in the immediate locality itself, rather than in some external rape or alien burglary. Hardy's yokels usually knew all about the goings on in the Wessex villages; and their rôle is paralleled today by the likes of the Alfs and the Berts in the Cotswold public houses. Although I now know who murdered Yvonne Harrison, it will not be easy to prove the guilt of the accused party. I am reminded of the Greek philosopher Protagoras, who found it difficult to be dogmatic about the existence of the gods, partly because of the obscurity of the subject matter, and partly because of the brevity of human life.

But herewith I give my final thoughts on the murder of Yvonne Harrison, that crisply uniformed nurse who looked after me in hospital once (but once!) with such tempting, loving care . . .

He finished writing an hour later at 12.45 a.m.

Or perhaps, to be accurate, he wrote no more thereafter.

At which hour Lewis was somewhat uneasily asleep, not at all sure in his mind whether things were going well or going ill. Morse had insisted that it should be he, Lewis, who would be on hand when Frank Harrison and his lady passed through Arrivals at Heathrow. No problem there though. Still thirty-six hours to go before the scheduled British Airways flight was due to land, and Morse had been adamant that Harrison *would* be on that flight, and not flitting off to Kathmandu or the Cayman Islands. Yet one thing was ever troublously disturbing Lewis's thoughts: the real nature of the puzzling and secret relationship that had clearly existed between Morse and Yvonne Harrison.

CHAPTER SEVENTY-FOUR

We are adhering to life now with our last muscle – the heart

(Djuna Barnes, *Nightwood*)

MORSE AWOKE AT 2.15 a.m., his forehead wet with sweat, an excruciating ache along the whole of his left arm running up as far as his neck and jaw, a tightly constricting corselet of pain around his chest. He managed to reach the bathroom sink where he vomited copiously. Thence, in pathetically slow degrees, he negotiated the stairs, one by one – finally reaching the ground-floor telephone, where he dialled 999, and in a remarkably steady voice selected the first of the Ambulance Fire Police options. He was seated on the lime-green carpet beside the front door, its Yale lock and bolts now opened, when the ambulance arrived six minutes later.

It all happened so quickly.

After being attached to a portable heart-monitor, after a pain-killing injection, after chewing an aspirin, after having his blood pressure taken, Morse found himself lying, contentedly almost, eyes open, on a stretcher in the back of the ambulance.

Beside him a paramedic was looking down with well-disguised anxiety at the ghastly pallor of the face and the lips of a purple-blue: 'We'll just get the docs to have a look at you. We'll soon be there. Don't worry.'

Morse closed his eyes, conscious that life had always been a bit of a worry and seemed to have every likelihood of so continuing now . . .

He should perhaps have rung Lewis from upstairs – Lewis had a flat-key – instead of ringing 999.

But then, he realized, Lewis wouldn't have had all that medical equipment, now would he?

He'd been a little disappointed that he'd heard no ambulance siren.

But then, he realized, there wouldn't be all that much traffic, even in Oxford, at such an early hour, now would there?

Soon, he knew it, they'd be asking for his 'Religion'.

But then, he realized, it wouldn't take too long for him (or them) to write down 'None' in some appropriate box, now would it?

'Next of Kin', too. Trickier that though, because the penultimate member of the Morse clan had recently died, aged ninety-two.

But then it wouldn't take too long to write down 'None' again.

And there were more cheerful things to contemplate. Perhaps Nurse Harrison would be there in the ward again to sit by his bed in the small hours . . .

But then, he realized, Yvonne Harrison was now dead.

Perhaps Sister McQueen would be on duty to pull him through again?

But then, he realized, she was away for a month in far Carlisle, tending a frail, demanding mother.

The kindly paramedic held him down gently as he tried to sit up on the stretcher.

'Lewis! I must see Sergeant Lewis.'

'Of course. We'll make sure you see him as soon as they've had a quick look at you. We're nearly there.'

The night nurse in the 'goldfish-bowl', at the right of the Emergencies Entrance, watched as the automatic double-doors opened and the paramedics wheeled the latest casualty through, deciding immediately that Resuscitation Room B was the place for the newcomer. Quickly she bleeped the Senior House Officer.

The next ten minutes saw swift and methodical action: blood samples were promptly despatched somewhither; chest X-rays were taken; an electrocardiograph test had firmly established that the patient had suffered a hefty anterior myocardial infarct. But it was time for another move; and the activities of a young and kindly nurse with a clipboard, dutifully requesting details of medical history, next of kin, religion, and the like, were mercifully cut short by a specialist nurse who with all speed supervised an urgent transfer.

Morse had always delighted in sesquipedalian terminology, since his education in the Classics had given him much insight into the etymology of words more than a foot-and-a-half long. And now, as he lay in the Coronary Care Unit, he listened with interest to the words being spoken around him: thrombolysis;

tachycardia, strepto-something-something. One thing was certain: much was happening and was happening quickly again. As if there were little time to spare . . .

Were angels male or female? They'd started off life as male, surely? So there must have been a sort of trans-sexual interim when . . . Morse's mind was wondering . . . What gender was the Angel of Death then, whom he now saw standing at the right-hand side of his bed, with a nurse holding one gently restraining hand on a softly feathered wing, and the other hand on his own shoulder.

Morse awoke to full consciousness again, opened his eyes, and found Lewis's hand on his shoulder.

'Sorry to disturb you, sir.'

'You? What the 'ell are you doing here?'

'One o' the paras – knew who you were – and heard you say, you know . . .'

Morse nodded, and smiled.

'How you doing, sir?'

'Fine! It's just a case of mis-identity.'

'I mustn't be long. They've told me just a coupla minutes, you know.'

'Why's that?' asked Morse wearily.

'They say you need, you know, a lot of rest.'

'*Lew*-is! Why do you keep saying "you know" all the time?'

'Not said "actually" yet though, have I?'

'When you go up to bring Harrison in today—'

'Tomorrow, sir.'

'You sure?'

'Quite sure.'

'Don't forget! *I'm* doing the interviewing.'

Lewis turned to find Nurse Shelick standing behind him. 'Please!' her lips mouthed, as she looked down on Morse's intermittently closing eyes.

'Shan't be a second, nurse.'

He bent down and whispered: 'Anything I can do, sir?'

Morse's eyes were still closed, but he seemed to regain some of his earlier coherence.

'Yes. Second drawer down on the right. There's a Carlisle number for Sister McQueen. Give her a ring. Not today though . . . like you say, tomorrow. Just say I'm . . .'

Lewis prepared to go. 'Leave it to me, sir, and . . . keep a stout heart! Promise me that!'

Morse opened his eyes briefly. 'That's what my old father used to say.'

'So you *will*, won't you, sir?'

Morse nodded slowly. 'I'll try. I'll try ever so hard, my old friend.'

Lewis was checking back the tears as he walked away from the Coronary Care Unit, and failed to hear Nurse Shelick's quiet 'Goodbye'.

Chapter Seventy-Five

> The cart is shaken all to pieces, and the rugged road is very near its end
>
> (Dickens, *Bleak House*)

THAT SAME DAY was to be the longest and almost the unhappiest in Lewis's life. At 6.30 a.m. he drove out to Police HQ and sat quietly in Morse's office, the Harrison case the last thing that concerned him. At 7 a.m. he rang the JR2 and learned that Morse's condition was 'Critical but stable', although he had little real idea what that might signify on the Coronary Richter Scale.

Strange, early apprised of Morse's hospitalization, came in at 8 a.m., himself immediately ringing the JR2, and impatiently asking several questions – and being given the same answer as Lewis: 'Critical but stable'. As much was being done as humanly possible, Strange learned, and any visit was, at present, quite out of the question. For the minute it was all tests and further treatment. The ward had the police number of Sergeant Lewis, and would ring if . . . if there was any news.

Morse was fully conscious of what was going on around him. He felt fairly sure that he was dying, and pretended to himself that he would face death with at least some degree of dignity, if not with equanimity. He had been seated beside his old father when he'd died, and heard him reciting the Lord's Prayer, as if it were some sort of insurance policy. And Morse wondered whether his own self-interest might possibly be served by following suit. But if by any freak of chance there *was* an Almighty, well, He'd understand anyway; and since, in Morse's view, there wasn't, he'd be wasting his really (at this time) rather precious breath. No. The long day's task was almost done, and he knew that he must sleep . . .

At 1.30 p.m. the consultant looked down on the sleeping man. There had been no positive reaction from the comprehensive tests and treatments; no success from the diuretic dosages that should have cleared the fluid that was flooding the lungs; no cause for the slighest optimism from the echo-cardiogram.

He sat at the desk there and wrote:

> 'Clinical evidence that the heart is irreparably damaged; kidney failure already apparent. Without specific request from n.o.k. in my judgement inappropriate to resuscitate'

The nurse beside him read through what he had written.

'Nothing else we can do, is there?'

The consultant shook his head. 'Pray for a miracle,

that's about the only hope. So if he asks for anything, let him have it.'

'Even whisky?'

'Why do you say that?'

'He's already asked for a drop.'

'Something we don't stock in the pharmacy, I'm afraid.'

The nurse smiled gently to herself after the consultant had left, for someone had already slipped a couple of miniature Glenfiddichs into the top of Morse's bedside table; and there'd only been the one visitor.

Seated outside a café on the Champs Elysées, Maxine Ridgway clinked her glass across the table. It had been a splendid lunch and she felt almost happy.

'Thank you! You're a terrible, two-timing fellow – you know that. But you're giving me a wonderful time. You know that, too.'

'Yes, I do know. Trouble is the time's gone by so quickly.'

'No chance of staying another few days? Day or two? Day?'

'No. We're back in the morning as scheduled. I've got a meeting I've agreed to attend.'

'A board meeting?'

'No, no. Much more interesting. A meeting with a chief inspector of police. I've met him once before, only the once, at a funeral; and then only very briefly. But he's – well, he's a bit like me, in a way, I suppose.

He'd never run away from anyone, I reckon; and I'd never forgive myself if I ran away from him.'

Maxine looked over at Frank Harrison, and realized for the first time in their relationship that she was probably in love with the man. In those early heady days it had been all Daimlers and diamonds; but she would always have chosen the wine and the roses of these last forty-eight hours . . .

Suddenly she sensed that she was never going to see him again, and she yearned at that moment to be alone with him, and to give herself to him.

'Let's go back to the hotel, Frank.'

'What? On a beautiful sunny afternoon like this?'

'Yes!'

Frank Harrison leaned across and placed his right hand on her bare shoulder. 'Shall I tell you a secret, my darling? I was about to suggest exactly the same thing myself.'

It was a happy moment.

But a moment only.

Harrison got to his feet.

'I've just got to make a phone call first.'

'You can ring from the room.'

'No, it's a private call.'

'And you don't want me to—?'

'No, I don't.'

'If he asks for anything,' that's what the consultant said. And when Morse made his second request (the first already granted) the nurse rang Police HQ immediately. Lewis and Strange – Morse wanted to see them.

Perhaps she had given the two names in alphabetical order, but Lewis hoped it had been in order of preference – a hope though that had probably been unjustified, he thought, as he stood waiting at the back of the unit, since it had clearly been Strange who had been first on Morse's visiting list.

'Right old mess you've got yourself into, Morse!'

'Looks like it, I'm afraid.'

'You're in the best of hands, you know that.'

'I'm going to need a bit more than that.'

'Look, Morse. Don't you think it would be a good thing . . . don't you think I ought—?'

But Morse was shaking his head in some agitation.

'No! Please! If you really want to help . . .'

'Course! Course, I do!'

'Can you ask Lewis . . . ?'

'Course! Just you keep hold of the hooks, old mate! And that's an order. Don't forget I'm still your superior officer.'

'Lewis!' Morse spoke the name very quietly but quite clearly. His eyes were open, and his lips moved as if he were about to say something.

But if such were the case, he never said it; and Lewis decided to do what so many people have done beside a hospital bed; decided to speak a few comforting thoughts aloud:

'You've got the top load of quacks in Oxfordshire

looking after you, sir. All you've got to do – promise me! – is to do what they say and . . . And what I really want to say is thank-you for . . .'

But Lewis could get no further.

And in any case Morse had closed his eyes and turned his head away to face the pure-white wall.

Just a little word from Morse would have been enough.

But it wasn't to be.

A nurse was standing beside him, testing his lip-reading skills once more: 'I'm afraid we must ask you to go . . .'

At 4.20 p.m. Morse seemed to rally a little, and held his hand up for the nurse.

'I'm allowed a drop more Scotch?' he whispered.

She poured out the miserably small contents of the second miniature and held a jug of water over the glass.

'Yes?'

'No,' said Morse.

She put her arm around his shoulders, pulled him towards her, and held the glass to his lips. But he sipped so little that she wondered whether he'd drunk a single drop; and as he coughed and spluttered she took the glass away and for a few moments held him closely to her, and felt profoundly sad as finally she eased the white head back against the pillows.

For just a little while, Morse opened his eyes and looked up at her.

'Please thank Lewis for me . . .'

But so softly spoken were the words that she wasn't quite able to catch them.

The call came through to Sergeant Lewis just after 5 p.m.

Chapter Seventy-Six

Say, for what were hop-yards meant,
Or why was Burton built on Trent?
Oh many a peer of England brews
Livelier liquor than the Muse,
And malt does more than Milton can
To justify God's ways to man

(A. E. Housman,
A Shropshire Lad)

Before leaving for Heathrow, Lewis had informed Chief Superintendent Strange that it would not be at all sensible, in fact it would be wholly inappropriate, for him to continue as a protagonist, virtually *the* protagonist, in the Harrison case: he was exhausted mentally, physically, emotionally; and, well . . . he just begged for a rest. And Strange had granted his request.

'I'm going to put someone in charge who's considerably more competent than you and Morse ever were.'

'Yourself, sir?'

'That's it,' smiled Strange sadly. 'You have two or three days off – from tomorrow. You could take the missus to South Wales.'

'I said I needed a rest, sir! And there are one or two things that Morse . . .'

'Make a few calls you mean – yes. And go through his diary and see what dates . . .'

'I don't think there'll be many of those.'

'You don't?' asked Strange quietly.

'And I haven't got much of a clue how he was going to tackle Frank Harrison.'

Strange lumbered round the table and placed a vast hand on Lewis's shoulder. 'You've got a key?'

Lewis nodded.

'Just bring Harrison Senior straight to me. Then . . .'

Lewis nodded. He was full up to the eyes; and left without a further word.

On journeys concerned with potential criminals or criminal activity, CID personnel were never advised, and were seldom permitted, to travel alone. And the following morning Lewis was not wholly unhappy to be travelling alongside a familiar colleague, albeit alongside Sergeant Dixon. After the first few obligatory words, the pair of them had lapsed into silence.

There was never likely to be any risk of missing the returning couple at the Arrivals exit. Nor was there. And it was Lewis who read from his prepared notes, as unostentatiously as he could: 'Mr Frank Harrison, it is my duty as a police officer to inform you that I am authorized to remand you into temporary custody on two counts: first, on suspicion of the murder of Mr John Barron of Lower Swinstead on the 3rd of August, 1998; second, on suspicion of the murder of your wife,

Yvonne Harrison, on the 8th July 1997. It is also my duty to tell you—'

'Forget it, Sergeant. You told me what to expect. Just a couple of favours though, if that's all right? Won't take long.'

'What have you got in mind?' In truth, Lewis had neither the energy nor the enthusiasm to initiate any determined pursuit had Frank Harrison and partner decided to make a dash for it and vault the exit-barriers. But that was never going to happen. Nor did it.

'Well, it's the car, first of all. I left it—'

'All taken care of, sir. Or it will be.'

'Thank you. Second thing, then. You know the one thing I really missed in Paris? A pint of real ale, preferably brewed in Burton-on-Trent. The bars are open here and . . .'

'OK.'

Dixon stood beside him as Harrison ordered a pint of Bass and a large gin and tonic (and, of course, nothing else) whilst Lewis sat at a nearby table, momentarily alone with Maxine Ridgway.

'You know,' she said very firmly, 'you're quite wrong about one thing. I don't know too much about Frank's life, but it does just so happen I was with him the night that his wife was murdered. We were together in his London flat! I was there when the phone rang and when he ordered a taxi to Paddington—'

Frank Harrison was standing by the table now: 'Why don't you learn to keep your mouth shut, woman!' But his voice was resigned rather than angered, and if he had contemplated throwing the gin and tonic in her face, it was only for a second or two.

He sat down and drank his beer.

The damage had been done.

In the back of the police car as it returned to Oxford, Lewis realized, with an added sadness, that Morse had been wholly wrong, as it now transpired, in his final analysis of the Harrison murder. Frank Harrison, if his lady-friend were to be believed, just could *not* have murdered his wife that night; and the police must have been right, in the original enquiry, to cross him off their suspect list. It had all happened before, of course – many a time! – when Morse, after the revelation of some fatal flaw in his earlier reasoning, would find his mind leaping forward, suddenly, with inexplicable insight, towards the ultimate solution.

But those days had now gone.

It was not until the car was passing through the cutting in the Chilterns by Stokenchurch that Harrison spoke:

'Red kite country this is – now. Did you know that, Sergeant?'

'As a matter of fact I did, yes. I'm not into birds myself though. The wife puts some nuts out occasionally but . . .'

It may hardly be seen as a significant passage of conversation.

Harrison spoke again just after Dixon had turned off the M40 on to the A40 for Oxford.

'You know, I'm looking forward to seeing Morse again. I met him at Barron's funeral, but I don't think we got on very well . . . My daughter, Sarah, knows him though. He's one of her patients at the Radcliffe. She tells me he's a strange sort of fellow in some ways – interesting though, and *very* bright, but perhaps not taking all that good care of himself.'

Lewis remained silent.

'Why didn't he come up to Heathrow himself? Wasn't that the original idea?'

'Yes, I think it was.'

'Are we meeting at St Aldate's or Kidlington?'

'He won't be meeting you anywhere, sir. Chief Inspector Morse is dead.'

Chapter Seventy-Seven

Dear Sir/Madam

Please note that an entry on the Register of Electors in your name has been deleted for the following reason:

DEATH

If you have any objections, please notify me, in writing, before the 25th November, 1998, and state the grounds for your objection.

Yours faithfully

(Communication from Carlow County Council to an erstwhile elector)

After returning to HQ Lewis gave Strange an account of the quite extraordinary evidence so innocently (as it seemed) supplied by Maxine Ridgway.

But he could do no more.

For he had nothing more to give.

Unlike Morse, who had always professed enormous faith in pills – pills of all colours, shapes, and sizes – Lewis could hardly remember the last time he'd taken anything apart from the Vitamin C tablet he was bullied to swallow each breakfast-time. It had therefore been something of a surprise to learn that Mrs L kept such a copious supply of assorted medicaments; and retiring to bed unprecedentedly early that evening he had swallowed two Nurofen Plus tablets, and slept like the legendary log.

At 10 a.m. the following day he drove up to the mortuary at the JR2.

The eyes were closed, but the expression on the waxen face was hardly one of great serenity, for some hint of pain still lingered there. Like so many others contemplating a dead person, Lewis found himself pondering so many things as he thought of Morse's mind within the skull. Thought of that wonderful memory, of that sensitivity to music and literature, above all of that capacity for thinking laterally, vertically, diagonally – whateverwhichway that extraordinary brain should decide to go. But all gone now, for death had scattered that union of component atoms into the air, and Morse would never move or think or speak again.

Feeling slightly guilty, Lewis looked around him. But at least for the moment his only company was the dead. And bending down he put his lips to Morse's forehead and whispered just two final words: 'Good-bye, sir.'

Chapter Seventy-Eight

. . . & that I be not bury'd in consecrated ground
& that no sexton be asked to toll the bell
& that no murners walk behind me at my funeral
& that no flours be planted on my grave . . .

(Thomas Hardy, *The Mayor of Casterbridge*)

Morse had always been more closely attuned to life's adagios than its allegros; and his home reflected such a melancholic temperament. The pastel-coloured walls, haunted by the music of Wagner, Bruckner, and Mahler, were decorated with sombre-toned reproductions of Rembrandt, Vermeer, and Atkinson Grimshaw; and lined, in most rooms both upstairs and down, with long shelves of the poets and the novelists.

The whole place now seemed so very still as Lewis picked up two pints of semi-skimmed Co-op milk from the porch, picked up four letters from the doormat, and entered.

In the study upstairs there were several signs (as Lewis already knew) of a sunnier temperament: the room was decorated in a sun-bed tan, terracotta, and white, with a bright Matisse hanging on the only wall free of the ubiquitous books, CDs, and cassettes. A red angle-lamp stood on the desk with, beside it, a bottle of Glenfiddich, virtually empty, and a cut-glass tumbler, completely empty. Morse had timed his exit fairly satisfactorily.

Lewis sat down and quickly looked through the letters: BT; British Diabetic Association; Lloyds Bank; Oxford Brookes University. Nothing too personal perhaps in any of them, but he left them there unopened. He fully realized there would be quite a few details to be sorted out soon by someone. Not by him though. He had but the single mission there.

In the second drawer down on the right, he found six photographs and took them out. An old black-and-white snap of a middle-aged man and woman, the man showing facial lineaments similar to Morse's. A studio portrait of a fair-haired young woman, with a written message on the back: 'Like you I wish so much that things could have been different – love always – W'. Another smaller photograph, with a brief sentence in Morse's own hand: 'Sue Widdowson before she was arrested'. A holiday shot of a young couple on a beach somewhere, the dark-headed bronzed young woman in a white bikini smiling broadly, the young man's right arm around her shoulders, and (again) some writing on the back 'I only *look* happy. I miss you like crazy!!! Ellie'. Clipped to a photograph of a smartly attractive woman, in the uniform of a hospital sister, was a brief letter under a Carlisle address and telephone number: 'I understand. I just can't help wondering how we would have been together, that's all. *I'd* have had to sacrifice a bit of independence too you know! Always remember my love for you. J.' Only the one other photograph: that of Morse and Lewis standing next to each other beside the Jaguar, with no writing on the back at all.

Lewis tried the Carlisle number; with no success.

On the floor to the right of the desk lay a buff-coloured folder, its contents splayed out somewhat, as if perhaps it may have been knocked down accidentally; and he picked it up. On the front was written: 'For the attn. of Lewis'.

The top sheet was the printed FORM D1/D2, issued by the Department of Human Anatomy in South Parks Road, the second section duly signed by the donor; and countersigned by the same man who had witnessed the validity of the second single sheet of A4 to which Lewis now turned his attention:

MY WILL

I expressly forbid the holding of any religious service to mark my death. Nor do I wish any memorial service to be arranged thereafter. If any persons wish to remember me in any way, let it be in their thoughts.

If these handwritten paragraphs have any legal validity, as I am assured they do, my estate may be settled with little difficulty. I no longer have any direct next-of-kin, and even if I have, it makes no difference.

My worldly goods and chattels comprise: my flat (now clear of mortgage); its contents (including a good many rare first editions); two insurance policies; and the monies in my two accounts with Lloyds Bank. The total assets involved I take to be somewhere in the region of £150,000 at current rates and values.

It is my wish that the said estate, after appropriate charges, be divided (like Gaul) into three parts, in equal amounts (unlike Gaul) with the beneficiaries as follows:

(a) The British Diabetic Association

(b) Sister Janet McQueen (see address book)

(c) Sergeant Lewis, my colleague in the Thames Valley CID.

For several minutes, Lewis sat where he was, unmoving, but deeply moved. Why in heaven Morse should have shown such bitterness toward the Church, he couldn't know; and wouldn't know. And why on earth Morse had remembered *him* with such . . .

His thoughts still in confusion, Lewis tried the Carlisle number again; again without success.

He washed out the empty tumbler in the bathroom, and returned to the study, where he poured himself the last half-inch of Glenfiddich, sat down again, silently raised his glass, and drained it.

He looked down at the several sheets of paper remaining in the folder, marked on the first page 'Notes on the Harrison Case', and all written in Morse's hand, that same small upright script that Lewis had found in the Harrison files. He'd go through it all later though. For the moment he placed the other two single sheets on the top, and was preparing to leave, when he opened the second drawer down again, took out the photograph of the Jaguar, and slipped it into the folder – on top of everything else.

And noticed something else there, pushed to the back of the drawer.

A pair of handcuffs.

Chapter Seventy-Nine

Heaven has no rage like love to hatred turned,
Nor hell a fury like a woman scorned
(Congreve, *The Mourning Bride*)

If you're guilty, you'll have to prove it
(Groucho Marx)

Lewis finished reading through the folder early that same evening. Most of it he'd known about already. It was only when he'd come to the last three sheets that he was aware of the wholly new tenor of Morse's thinking.

> But herewith I give my final thoughts on the murder of Yvonne Harrison, that crisply uniformed nurse who looked after me in hospital once (but once!) with such tempting, loving care.
>
> From the start of this case, one person stood out high above the others in firmness of purpose, daring, and clarity of mind: Frank Harrison. He was still sexually attracted to Yvonne, but she was no longer attracted to him; indeed one night in hospital she told me that she used to hook her foot over her own side of the mattress to establish a sort of no-man's land between them. But she remained a woman obsessively interested in sex, both as prac-

tising participant and addicted voyeur. (She had mentioned to me some Amsterdam videos. But although I looked quite carefully through the scores of videos there, I could find nothing. I suspect they were innocently disguised under such labels as *The Jungle Book* or *Cooking with Herbs.*)

Now clearly Frank Harrison was – is – someone with a very strong sexual drive, and doubtless he claimed his marital rights on his spasmodic periods at home. But inevitably, when they were away from each other, Yvonne knew what he was up to, just as he knew what she was up to. And for that reason, I can find no compelling motive for Frank Harrison to have murdered his wife. There *might* have been the opportunity, for all we know. But his alibi was uncontested, since there seemed no reason to suspect the firm and explicit evidence of the man Flynn, who claimed to have picked him up from Oxford Station and driven him out to his home to Lower Swinstead.

It is now my view (I look forward to interviewing Frank H on the matter) that Flynn was not in fact paid for fixing his taxi-times for the purpose of Harrison's alibi. He was paid for something different.

Until so very recently I thought that Simon must have murdered his mother. He had ample motive if he found his beloved mum in bed with the local builder – God help us! And the other facts fitted that hypothesis neatly: he was known to Repp, the local shady character familiar to everyone around, as well as being a regular at the Maiden's Arms; known to Barron, of course; and also known to Flynn, because the pair of them had attended lip-reading classes together.

As you know, I was wrong.

But there was someone else who had an even more compelling motive, with the other facts fitting equally convincingly: Sarah Harrison. What motive could *she* have had? Simply this: that she and Barron had been secret lovers for a year or so before Yvonne's murder. I learned something about this from two most unlikely witnesses – from Alf and Bert, denizens of the Maiden's Arms. Particularly from Bert, who had seen the two of them together, both at the Three Pigeons in Witney and at the White Hart in Wolvercote, when he was playing away in the cribbage-league. I've little doubt that others in Lower Swinstead knew about it too, but they all kept their mouths shut. On that fateful evening, Sarah called home unexpectedly, and found her secret lover in bed with her mother – God help us! She was already known to Repp, as well as to Barron, of course. But where does that opportunistic fellow Flynn fit into the picture this time? There is now ample proof that he knew Sarah fairly well, because in the years before the murder the pair of them had performed in a pop group together in several pubs and clubs in West Oxfordshire (some details are known) although never as it happens at the Maiden's Arms.

And that's almost it, Lewis.

There remains just the one final matter to settle. The murder weapon was never found. But the path-report, as you'll recall, gave some indication of the type of weapon used. There were perhaps two blows only to Yvonne's head. The first rendered the right cheek-bone shattered and the bridge of the nose broken. The second, the more vicious and it seems the fatal blow, crashed across the base of the skull, doubtless as Yvonne tried to turn her head away in desperate self-defence. The suggestion made was that some sort of 'tubular metal rod' was in all probability the cause of such injuries.

An arm-crutch!

How do I know this? I don't. But I shall be inordinately surprised if I am not very close indeed to the truth. And – how many times has this happened? – it was you, Lewis, who did the trick for me again! Remember? You were reining back some fanciful notions of mine about Sarah tearing down to the cinema to buy a ticket, and you said that she wasn't going to be tearing about anywhere that night, because she'd sprained her ankle rather badly; and that if she were doing anything it would be *hobbling* about. Yes. Hobbling about on one of those metal arm-crutches they'd probably issued her with from the Physiotherapy Department. (Will you find out, Lewis, if and when the arm-crutch was returned?)

I realize that it won't be easy to establish Sarah's guilt, but we've got the long-awaited interview with her father to look forward to. He'll be a worthy opponent, I know that, but I'm beginning to suspect that even *he* has almost had enough by now. If I'm over-optimistic about such an outcome, there'll still be Sarah herself. It will be a surprise if the pair of them haven't been in close touch in recent days and weeks, and I've got a feeling that like her father she's almost ready herself to emerge from the hell she must have been going through for so long. Quite apart from judicial convictions and punishments, guilt brings its own moral retribution. We all know that.

One thing is certain. This will be – has been – my last case. I am now determined to retire and to take life a little more gently and sensibly. We've tackled so many cases together, old friend, and I'm very happy and very proud to have worked with you for so long.

That's it. The time is now 12.45 a.m., and suddenly I feel so very weary.

All the manuscript notes were with Strange within the half-hour.

And Lewis had nothing further to do with the investigation.

Chapter Eighty

I am retired. I am to be met with in trim gardens. I am already come to be known by my vacant face and careless gesture, perambulating at no fixed pace nor with any settled purpose. I walk about; not to and from

(Charles Lamb, *Last Essays of Elia*)

It seemed there was little to cloud the bright evening at the end of August, that same year, when Strange held his retirement party. The Chief Constable (no less!) had toasted his farewell from the Force, paying a fulsome tribute to his colleague's many years of distingished service in the Thames Valley CID, crowned, as it had been, with yet another significant triumph in the Yvonne Harrison murder case.

For his part, Strange had spoken reasonably wittily and blessedly briefly, and had included a personal tribute to Chief Inspector Morse:

'I don't think we're going to see his like again in a hurry, and people of lesser intellect like me should be grateful for that. And it's good to have with us here his faithful friend and, er, drinking-companion' (muted amusement) 'Sergeant Lewis' (Hear-Hear! all round). 'Morse had no funeral service and no memorial service, just as he wished; but I make no apology for remembering him here this evening because, quite simply, he had the most brilliant mind I ever encountered in the whole of my police career . . . Well now. All that remains for me is to thank you for coming along to see me off; to say thank you for the lawnmower and the book' (he held aloft a copy of Sir David Attenborough's *The Life of Birds*) 'and to remind you there's a splendid buffet next door, including a special plate of doughnuts for one of our number.' (Much laughter, and much subsequent applause.)

Lewis had clapped as much as the rest of them, but he had no wish to stay too long amid the back-slapping and the reminiscences; and soon made his way upstairs to the deserted canteen where he sat in a corner drinking an orange juice, wishing to be alone with his thoughts for a while . . .

The conclusion to the Harrison case had proved pretty much, though far from exactly, as Morse had predicted. Two hours after her father had been taken to HQ for questioning, Sarah Harrison (refusing to see her father) had presented herself voluntarily and made a full confession to the murder of her mother, making absolutely no apology for anything – except for causing her father (she knew it!) all that pain and agony of spirit. What would happen to her now, she said, would not really amount to imprisonment at all; but, in a curious sort of way, to a kind of liberation.

And perhaps it had been much the same, albeit rather later, for Frank Harrison himself, who (less eloquently than his daughter) had by degrees unburdened himself of his manifold sins and wickednesses, including the subsequent murder of his wife's lover, John Barron . . .

His actions, after receiving his daughter's frantic, frenetic phone call on the night of Yvonne's murder, had been straightforward. Train to Oxford; then taxi to Lower Swinstead, whence Barron had long since fled; and where Repp, though still around, remained unseen. Harrison had paid off Flynn, expecting him to drive away forthwith; thereafter very quickly dispatching his distraught daughter home. Coolly and ruthlessly he'd taken over. Confusion! – that was the only hope; and the only plan. Yvonne was already handcuffed, presumably for some bizarre bondage session, and what a blessing that had been! He'd tied a gag lightly around her mouth; gone on to the patio and smashed in the glass of the french window from the outside before unlocking it; he'd turned the lights on, every one of them, and yanked out the TV and the telephone leads, both upstairs and down; and finally, with illogical desperation, he'd decided to activate the burglar alarm, since even if no one heard it, it would be recorded (so he believed).

He'd done enough. Almost enough. Just the police now. He *had* to ring the police, immediately; and suddenly he realized he *couldn't* ring them – he'd just made sure of that himself. But there was his mobile, the mobile on which he'd already rung Sarah several times from the train and once from Flynn's taxi. He could always *lose* it though: and the longer he waited to ring for help, the better the chances for that confusion he'd tried so hard to effect. In detective stories he'd often read of the difficulties pathologists encountered in establishing the time parameters for any murder. Yes! He'd just go up to the main road and walk (run!) the half-mile or so to the next house. Which indeed he was doing when he heard the voice at the gate that led to the drive. He remembered Flynn's words exactly:

'I t'ink you moight be needin' a little help, sorr?' . . .

Epilogue

Certainly the gods are ironical: they always punish one for one's virtues rather than for one's sins

(Ernest Dowson, *Letters*)

'Didn't you want any food?'

'No thank you, sir. I've got a meal waiting at home.'

'Ah yes. Of course.'

'And I didn't particularly want to watch Dixon eating doughnuts.'

'No, I understand.' Strange lowered himself rather gingerly on to the inappropriately small chair opposite. 'Talking of eating, Lewis, what the hell's eating *you*, pray?'

As he'd requested (and as we have seen) Lewis had nothing further to do with the Harrison case. He had tried, and with some considerable success, to distance himself from the whole affair, even from thinking about it. There was just that one persistent, niggling worry that tugged away at his mind like some over-indulged infant tugging away at its mother's skirts in a supermarket: the knowledge that Morse, on his own admission, and for the first time in their collaboration, had acted dishonestly and dishonourably.

He looked up at Strange.

'What makes you think something's eating me?'

'Come *on*, Lewis! I wasn't born yesterday.'

So Lewis told him.

Told him of the unease he'd felt from the beginning of the case: that Morse had known far too little about it, and then again far too much; that Morse had originally voiced such vehement opposition to taking on the case, and yet had spent the last days of his life doing little else than trying to fathom its complexity.

'And that's all that's been bothering you?'

'*All*?'

'Look! Tell me! What's the very *worst* thing you think he could have done? There's this attractive nurse pulling him through a serious illness in hospital – a place where patients can get a bit low, and a bit vulnerable. Nurses, too, for that matter. And she fell for him a bit—'

'How do you know that?'

'She told me so. She told me one night in hospital when she was looking after *me*! Morse fell for *her* a bit, too – anybody would! – and after he's discharged he writes and asks her why she's not been in touch with him. But she doesn't write back, although she keeps his letter. Know why, Lewis? Because she doesn't really know how to cope with being in love herself.'

'How do you know *that*?'

'Does it matter? When she was murdered – well, you know the rest. Morse was on another case at the time – you were on it *with* him, for God's sake! And he said it was too much for the pair of you to take on another.'

'Only after he'd found his own letter.'

'Lewis!'

'Only after he'd recognized the handcuffs.'

'*Lewis!* Listen! Nothing Morse did then – *nothing* – affected that enquiry in the slightest way. Yvonne had kept some letters from her men-friends, the kinkies and the straights alike. She certainly didn't keep any from Barron. Maybe because he never wrote any, I dunno. Maybe because she just didn't want to.'

'Just the ones from her favourite clients.'

'You know that. You've seen them.'

'Some of them,' said Lewis slowly.

'Well I saw *all* the bloody letters!'

'Including the one from Morse.'

'Not a crime you know, writing a letter. It was immaterial anyway, as I keep trying to tell you.' Strange looked exasperated. 'It's just that it would have been awkward, wouldn't it? Bloody awkward! I wanted to protect the silly sod. You never thought he was a *saint*, did you?'

Lewis was silent for a while. No. He'd never thought of Morse as a possible candidate for sanctification.

But there was something wrong about what he'd just heard.

'So *you* saw the letter before *Morse* saw it, is that what you're saying?'

'Morse *never* saw the letter, not till you showed him that page of it. You see, Lewis, *I* took it – not Morse.'

'And you didn't check—'

'Couldn't have done, could I? It was a longish letter. But I didn't read it, so I wouldn't have spotted if there was any gap.'

'So it was you who kept some of the evidence separate?'

'Afraid so, yes. I was scared stiff one of *my* letters might be there, if you want the truth. And as things turned out it just became impossible for me to put that stuff back in the folder while the original enquiry was still going on.'

'So you got a new box-file when the case was re-opened . . .'

Strange nodded. 'Always felt guilty about it but—'

'Why didn't Morse spot the page you'd missed?'

'Perhaps he didn't look all that carefully. Not his way usually, was it? Perhaps he wasn't too interested in the literary shortcomings of her other admirers. Not very fond of spelling mistakes, now was he . . . ? or perhaps he just felt the letters were too private, like he'd hoped his own letter would be. How do *I* know? What I do know is that he wasn't looking for a list of lovers who might have been in bed with Yvonne that night. Somehow he was convinced he *knew* who the man was. He told me who it was; and he told you who it was. And he was right.'

Lewis nodded.

But the supermarket-brat was giving a final tug.

'Plenty of letters and none of them any help, I agree, sir. But just the one pair of handcuffs! And Morse realized there'd be no problem in tracing them, so he destroyed the issue-list. And we both know why, don't we, sir? *Because they were his.*'

'Come off it, Lewis! There's a hundred and one worse things in life than him giving some bloody cuffs he'd never used once in his life to some woman who'd asked him for them – whatever the reason.'

Slowly shaking his head, Lewis stared down at the canteen carpet disconsolately.

'It's just that he seems not quite the man . . .'

'And you can't forgive him for that.'

'Course I can forgive him! Just a bit of a jolt, that's all. Can't you understand that? After all those years we were together?'

'That's what's *really* eating you, isn't it? Be honest! It's just that you don't think as much of old Morse as you used to.'

'Not quite as much, no.'

Strange struggled to his feet. 'Must be off. Good to talk. I'd better get back downstairs.'

Lewis got to his feet. 'Mrs Lewis sends her very best wishes, sir.'

The two policemen shook hands, and the interesting exchange was apparently over.

But not so.

Halfway to the canteen exit, Strange suddenly turned round and came back to the table.

'Do you remember those issue-lists for handcuffs, Lewis?'

'It's a long time ago . . .'

'Well, they're just handwritten lists, kept up to date in a series of columns: date, name, rank, serial number. Just like this.' Strange took a folded sheet of A4 from an inside pocket. 'But you remember the serial-number on the pair you found in Morse's drawer?'

'Nine-two-two.'

He handed the sheet to Lewis. 'You've got a good memory!'

'Where did you get this?'

'Someone took it from HQ, Lewis. Morse did!'

Lewis looked down at the list, but could find no mention of Morse's name. Could see another name though – at the seventh entry down, along with the other details in the neatly ruled lines:

3 June '68	Strange	PC	734	922

'You mean. . .?'

'I *mean*, Lewis, that Morse knew I was having an affair with Yvonne Harrison. I don't know how he knew, but he always tended to know things, didn't he? He pinched that form, and he kept it till after the wife's funeral. Then he gave it to me. Said it would be useless without the cuffs, which he said *he* was going to keep anyway, just in case I ever did anything bloody stupid. And he said exactly what I said to you a few minutes ago: nothing – *nothing* – that happened then had affected the enquiry in the slightest way. Is that clear, Lewis?'

Yes it *was* clear. 'You're saying that all Morse did was to save you . . . and save Mrs Strange . . .'

'It would have broken her to pieces,' said Strange very quietly. 'And me. Would have broken both of us to pieces.'

'She never knew?'

'Never had the faintest idea. Thanks to Morse.'

Lewis was silent.

'Just like you, eh? About lots of things. You never had the faintest idea, for example, that I re-opened the Harrison case on the basis of a couple of bogus telephone calls, now did you?'

'You mean—?'

'I mean there *were* no telephone calls. I made 'em up myself. Both of 'em.'

'I just didn't realize . . .'

'Nobody did, except Morse of course. He guessed straightaway. But I'd like to bet he never told you! He just didn't want to let me down, that's all.'

'Why didn't he tell me all this though? It would have made such a lot of difference . . . at the end . . .'

'I dunno. Always an independent sod, wasn't he? And always had that great big streak of loyalty and integrity somewhere deep inside him. But you don't need me to tell you that. So he was never worried too much about what people thought of him. He certainly didn't give two monkeys what *I* thought of him, at least most of the time. In fact the only person he did want to think well of him was *you*, Lewis. So let me tell you something else. It's one helluva job having to live with guilt, as I've done. Almost everybody discovers the same, you know that. Frank Harrison did, didn't he? Sarah Harrison, too. It's something I hope you'll never have to go through yourself. Not that you ever will. Nor did Morse though. He once told me that the guiltiest he ever felt in his life was when a couple of the lads saw him flicking through a girlie magazine in the Summertown newsagent's. So . . . So just keep thinking well of him, Lewis – that's all I ask.'

The former Chief Superintendent lumbered across the still-deserted canteen to join the jollifications below.

But Lewis sat where he was.

Apart from the middle-aged woman at the counter reading the *Sun*, there seemed no one else there. And after looking around him as guiltily as Morse must have done in the Summertown newsagent's, for a little while, in his desolation, he wept silently.

No Birds Sing

Jo Bannister was born in Rochdale, Lancashire, and grew up in Birmingham, Nottingham and Bangor, Northern Ireland. After leaving school at sixteen, she joined the *County Down Spectator* as office junior, leaving as editor in 1988 to pursue her career as an author. She has won several awards for her writing, including recognition from the Royal Society of Arts and the British Press Awards. Her interests are riding and archaeology. She lives in Northern Ireland.

No Birds Sing is the fourth novel in her series of police novels set in Castlemere. The fifth novel, *Broken Lines*, is now available in Pan paperback and the sixth and most recent, *The Hireling's Tale,* is published in hardback by Macmillan.

'An exciting, well written novel.' *Sunday Times*

'Sensitive and intelligent writing produces a police procedural which ranks with the best of its kind . . . Highly recommended.' *Yorkshire Post*

'A sizzling crime story.' *Peterborough Evening Telegraph*

'Fresh, energetic, original plotting . . . The plot unwinds swiftly with surprises at every step.' *Jerusalem Post*

'Throbs with energy. The reader is absorbed from page one.' *Yorkshire Evening Press*

By the same author

The Matrix
The Winter Plain
A Cactus Garden
Striving with Gods
Mosaic
The Mason Codex
Gilgamesh
The Going Down of the Sun
Shards
Death and Other Lovers
A Bleeding of Innocents
Sins of the Heart
Burning Desires
The Lazarus Hotel
The Primrose Convention
Broken Lines
The Hireling's Tale

Jo Bannister

No Birds Sing

PAN BOOKS

First published 1996 by Macmillan

Papberback edition first published 1997 by Pan Books
an imprint of Pan Macmillan Ltd
Pan Macmillan, 20 New Wharf Road, London N1 9RR
Basingstoke and Oxford
Associated companies throughout the world
www.panmacmillan.com

Reissued 1999

ISBN 0 330 35044 7

3 5 7 9 8 6 4

A CIP catalogue record for this book is available from
the British Library.

Phototypeset by Intype London Ltd
Printed by Mackays of Chatham plc, Chatham, Kent

O what can ail thee, Knight-at-arms
Alone and palely loitering;
The sedge is wither'd from the lake,
And no birds sing.

'La Belle Dame sans Merci'
John Keats, 1795–1821

Part One

Chapter One

Strolling through Castlemere with Thomas Stirling on a Sunday morning made Mrs Cunningham feel like a young woman again.

Coming to town with Mr Cunningham was like taking part in military manoeuvres. So long for the drive in: mark. So long to find a parking space: mark. (They had a Ford Fiesta but Mr Cunningham drove as if it were a Chieftain tank.) So long to shop: 'Quickly, quickly, you 'orrible little woman, a Peruvian grandmother with gout could get round Tesco's faster than this,' or 'Look, we're three minutes behind schedule already! Better do Safeway's at the double.'

How different, then, walking these same streets with Thomas. He never hurried her, considered his time well spent if he had no more to show for it than the memory of her smile. They wandered, they chatted – mostly Marion Cunningham chatted, Thomas paying solemn attention to all her opinions. They paused to admire the sights – the castle crumbling on its hill above the diamond, the Georgian frontages below, the sparkle of canal water glimpsed through the Brick Lane entries, the boats in Mere Basin bright as bath-time toys.

Sometimes she reached out and touched him,

almost as if to prove that he was real. For reply his cornflower gaze adored her. When she was with Thomas she never gave Mr Cunningham a thought.

It didn't matter that the shops, except for the newsagent on the corner, were closed. They window-shopped. Mr Cunningham never window-shopped; but Thomas allowed himself to be steered from one display to the next and never cared what he was being invited to admire as long as it was pretty.

Today they stopped at the jeweller's. When Marion was a girl old Mr Reubenstein sold costume jewellery and alarm-clocks from a shop the size of a goat-house in one of the entries. His son Mr Reubenstein expanded into a proper shop in Castle Place selling better jewellery, silverware and a nice class of crystal, and *his* son Mr Reubenstein expanded into the shops on either side to create Rubens, a glittering array of jewellery, presentation-ware and *objets d'art*. It was all here: the precious, the semi-precious and the merely pleasing. Mr Reubenstein the latest was no snob when it came to selling. He agreed with Thomas: he'd put anything in his window if it was pretty and turned a profit.

Mrs Cunningham was looking at the rings. Some were new, others antique; several were a shade ostentatious for good taste but Mrs Cunningham didn't mind. She loved their fire, their sheer *joie de vivre*. 'Oh look, Thomas,' she said, pointing to a cluster of amethysts around a single diamond, 'that's a hundred years old. It was first worn by a lady when my grandma was in her pram.'

Thomas Stirling said, 'Ruggle,' and set about chewing the ear off his teddy; which Mrs Cunningham took to mean much the same as *tempus fugit*.

Thus preoccupied – Mrs Cunningham with the ring, her grandson with his bear – they did not for a moment notice that they had been joined at the glittering window by a third party; and indeed, to take the non-speciesist view, a fourth.

'Lovely, aren't they?'

Mrs Cunningham looked up, enthusiastic agreement on her lips; but she was so taken aback that all she could manage was a sort of non-committal moo.

Politely, the man showed no signs of having noticed. 'Every inch a gentleman,' thought Mrs Cunningham in mounting hysteria. But what did he expect? – standing there in his green felt fedora, his tartan muffler and his calf-length burgundy corduroy coat, like a man thrown out of a *Doctor Who* audition for being too peculiar.

It may have been the smear of lipstick that finally did for her, it may have been the puff of blusher; it may have been the brassy curls permed within an inch of their life peeping out from under the hat. Or it may have been the dog – if it was a dog and not a skinned rabbit – squatting on its naked rump at his feet. It wore a blue collar studded with rhinestones, and that was all. Its freckled fawn body was devoid of hair. There were tufts on its feet, a plume on its tail, an explosion of hair like a punk's Mohawk on its head, but its cat-sized torso was nude. It gave Mrs Cunningham a bored yawn revealing an absence of teeth.

She backed so hurriedly she almost fell off the kerb. 'Whoops,' said the strange man mildly. Flustered and embarrassed, Mrs Cunningham flashed him her most brilliant smile, wheeled the pram and set off across Castle Place like a galleon in full sail, her raincoat flapping round her. Her cheeks flamed.

She realized her behaviour was provincial but she'd been startled. Her willingness to live and let live was as well developed, she hoped, as in any middle-class woman of her generation – beside Mr Cunningham she seemed a dangerous libertarian – but her subconscious was honed by small-town mores fifty years before when an apparition in lipstick and a green fedora would have had insults, and worse, hurled at him in the street.

By the time she reached Dorinda Day's on the far side of the diamond she had regained enough self-possession to slow down and, under the guise of studying the latest thing in cruise wear, steal a backward glance at what the strange man was doing now. But in the time it took her to cross Castle Place he had disappeared, possibly into one of the shops, possibly up the steps to the castle. She gave a sigh that was mostly relief but just a little disappointed.

But she had little time to ponder who he'd been, where he'd come from and where he'd gone. In an instant the open space that all week was packed with parked cars and traffic and now held only a handful of strollers like herself, enjoying the April sunshine or fetching the Sunday papers, was filled with sound: an anarchic roar that drummed the ears and made Thomas Stirling drop his bear and howl in protest.

It came from the direction of Cambridge Road and filled Castle Place like water filling a bucket. Mrs Cunningham just had time to recognize the bellow of a high-powered car before it shot into sight, a big black

4×4 with bull-bars; and not enough time to complete the indignant thought, 'They'll cause an accident going at that speed!' before the behemoth slewed across the square where thirty seconds earlier she'd been pushing the pram. Then it mounted the pavement where, a few seconds before that, she and Thomas had been window-shopping. Mrs Cunningham gripped the handle of the pram until her knuckles turned white. In the instant that she realized what the vehicle was going to do, it did it.

There was toughened glass in the window of Rubens, and a grille designed to stop an opportunist brick without denying potential buyers a view of the goods. It might have been cellophane for all the resistance it offered. Safe in its cage the big dark bonnet smashed through glass and grille, spraying them and the wares they guarded in a rainbow arc of spinning, glittering, prism-scattered light.

By the time the air had cleared of stars Mrs Cunningham could see the monster entirely inside the shop, all five doors open, small dark figures – four of them, and perhaps they only seemed small beside the over-sized car – tossing in everything they could reach in a minute and a half. There was no time for discrimination, they took it all: gemstones and rhinestones and Christening mugs and charm-bracelets and watches.

At the end of ninety seconds they piled back in the car, the engine gunned – the sound drowning out the wail of the alarm – and the 4×4 lurched back through the wreckage of the window, spun on a rear tyre and shot off down Bedford Road at the foot of the diamond. First it disappeared from sight, Mrs Cunningham and half a dozen other stunned observers staring after it, then the fighter-plane roar of the engine faded into the distance.

For perhaps another minute only the shrill of the alarm, the broken glass tinselling the pavement and the gaping hole in Rubens' window display testified to what had happened. No one ran for the police. No one chased after the big dark car. The sheer speed of the episode, from a normal sleepy Sunday morning in Castle Place back to the same thing with burglar alarms, had paralysed them. Mrs Cunningham had one hand to her mouth: she couldn't have said why, but nor could she have moved it.

Then a new siren joined the first and a police car shot out of Market Lane, slewing to a halt in front of the ravished jeweller's. Two officers leapt out. The man dashed through the breach into the shop, the WPC – seeing Mrs Cunningham clinging to the pram – hurried over to check that she was all right. 'Did you see what happened?'

Mrs Cunningham nodded.

'You were standing here?'

Mrs Cunningham shook her head. 'Only a moment.' Her voice shook, too. 'Just before it happened we were over there. Right there. Right – there.'

WPC Wilson looked across the square and back to Mrs Cunningham, and frowned. It was a long way for a middle-aged woman to push a pram in a few seconds. 'Thank God you moved. Why did you – was there some kind of warning?'

'My guardian angel,' said Mrs Cunningham. She began to laugh. 'My guardian angel, constable, wears a green felt hat and make-up, and has a boiled rabbit on a lead.' Then the laughter turned to tears, and she lifted Thomas Stirling out of his pram and hugged him as if she meant never to let him go.

'Coincidence?' Detective Inspector Liz Graham pitched it precisely midway between a statement and a question. It didn't mean she had no opinion, rather that she wanted to hear Shapiro's first.

Detective Superintendent Frank Shapiro gave a morose shrug. 'What's the alternative? A ram-raider with a social conscience?' He glared at the papers littering his desk. It was the same desk he had had as Detective Chief Inspector. Most of the papers were the same too. It was Sunday afternoon.

'Could be. It's not in their interests to turn this into a murder inquiry.' She stood at the window gazing down at the canal, a tall woman who wore the CID uniform of tweed jacket, trousers and brogues with rather more style than most of her male colleagues. Long fair hair with an exuberent natural curl was tamed into a pleat for work, and her green eyes sparkled with intelligent good humour.

A persistent girlishness had somehow survived the bludgeoning effort of turning a job she had a talent for into a career until now, at forty, she had the rank she'd earned with a senior officer she liked and respected. People who'd known her through the struggle for acceptance reckoned she'd finally cracked the secret of dropping a year with each birthday. At last summer's Castlemere Horse Show she won a red rosette in the Pairs Jumping (Any Age) partnered by a seriously competitive seven-year-old on an Exmoor pony.

'So they sent a sweeper up ahead to clear the path?' Shapiro was unconvinced. 'Why not put out cones, or ask for a police escort?'

Liz grinned. She knew him well enough to recognize that gentle irony as the smoke-screen behind which he did his thinking. He was always open to rational argument, possibly because rational argument mostly proved him right. Yet coincidence tended to be the last thing they considered, when nothing else made sense. 'He was the look-out. It was his job to take a last look at the shop before they hit it, to make sure the area car hadn't just stopped for ice-creams at Cully's.'

Shapiro pictured the incident in his mind's eye. He was of an older generation than Liz, a thirty-year-man who wasn't the height of fashion when he started. He scraped through recruitment with question-marks against his height (modest), his bulk (immodest, even as a young man) and his manner (diffident going on vague). Only a note pointing out the wisdom of encouraging minorities got him a probationary posting. But the rest of the way to Detective Superintendent he made on merit, and the sheer ability that lay behind the broad amiable face and slightly disorganized manner had been a matter of public knowledge for so long now there was almost no one left who remembered what unpromising material he was once considered.

He nodded slowly. 'All right. They're not committed, they can change their minds right up to the moment they hit the window. There's a look-out on the street in case anything goes wrong at the last moment. If the area car *had* been doing the ice-cream run they'd have just kept driving.'

It was Liz's turn to look doubtful. 'Most look-outs

try to blend into the background. They don't dress up like something from an end-of-the-pier show.'

'Agreed,' said Shapiro. 'But that car was doing sixty when it hit Castle Place: the driver had just a few seconds to decide whether the raid was on or off. He hadn't time to hunt for the one chap who knew if it was safe to proceed. The look-out needs to be obvious from a speeding car a hundred yards away.'

They weren't arguing. They were trying to work it out, and that made sense. Liz thought it possible to push the hypothesis a little further. 'The woman with the pram said he vanished before the car arrived. So the plan is, if he's still there when they reach the target they keep going; if he isn't they do the job. That works. If the coast's clear and they do the raid the look-out's already offside so there's nothing to connect him to it. If he's still there, there's no raid.'

Shapiro was leafing through his papers. 'There's no mention of a Quentin Crisp look-alike at any of the earlier incidents.'

'I'm not convinced this is the Tynesiders at all.'

The Detective Superintendent elevated a shaggy eyebrow. 'Really?' He could invest a single word with enough polite disbelief to send most junior officers back-pedalling for their lives. But Liz mostly considered her opinions before expressing them, which made her harder to shift. Shapiro was forced to run to a second word. 'Why?'

She thought for a moment. 'Every police force in the country is watching out for a gang of ram-raiders who first struck in Middlesbrough five months ago and have reappeared at three- or four-week intervals in Harrogate, Barnsley, Mansfield, Nottingham and Leamington Spa. We're calling them the Tynesiders, though they could be from the Isle of Wight for all we know, because that's where they made their debut.' A strong forefinger tracked their progress down the map on the wall.

Usually Shapiro had a map of Cambridgeshire and Northamptonshire pinned up but today it was a larger map of England. It was not a new map. Either it was a very old map, that had had a lot of pins stuck in it tracing the course of a lot of criminal enterprises over the years, or it was the one that hung beside the dart-board in the canteen. To avoid perforating it further, Shapiro had tacked on stickers to represent the ram-raiders' activities. They described a wobbly but essentially vertical line down the centre of England.

'Logically,' said Liz, 'their next port of call is somewhere round Oxford and it shouldn't be for another week or more. They're fifty miles off course, and though I don't know why they follow that particular routine I can't see them changing it when it works so well.'

Shapiro shrugged. 'Perhaps they think it's time to throw in a wild card. Make it harder for us to second-guess them.'

Liz stared. 'Has anybody come close to second-guessing them?'

'Not that you'd notice,' admitted Shapiro.

Liz nodded. 'Then there's the look-out. Nobody's reported that before.'

'Nobody'd have reported it this time if Mrs Cunningham hadn't got talking to the Queen of the May. Anyway, it's obviously a disguise – even Quentin Crisp doesn't look *that* much like Quentin Crisp! As long as he's easily identifiable he doesn't have to stand out like a lighthouse. Maybe last time he was the one pushing the pram; or he was a jogger in a fluorescent shell-suit, or a blind man selling flags on the corner. Anything that the driver would spot in the couple of seconds he has to make his decision.' He picked up a couple of faxes, discarded them again. 'There's not enough detail in these. Get Scobie to phone round, see if that rings a bell with anyone.'

'We'll give it a shot by all means,' she agreed readily. 'But I still think it'll turn out to be another crew. Ram-raiding isn't that devastatingly original any more. And the Tynesiders have attracted enough attention in the last five months to inspire copy-cats.'

'Their timing's not that rigid – they've hit two towns in a fortnight before,' said Shapiro. He had an almost sentimental attachment to the idea. 'Yes, we're a bit off-line for them, but what's fifty miles on the motorway? Maybe one of them's got a granny in the area that it's time he visited. Ram-raiding may be old hat in the cities but it's a new departure for Castlemere. And—' He stopped.

'And?'

He scowled. '*And* I have a gut feeling about it. Fine, feel free to laugh – poor old Frank, used to be a decent detective until he started getting indigestion and thinking it was ESP. All I know is, some people can sense where there are underground streams and I get feelings about crooks. And my guts don't think these crooks are home-grown.'

'Well, we'll know when we catch them,' Liz said diplomatically.

'We'll know before that. If it's the Tynesiders, and

if they stick with their usual MO, they'll hit us again soon – maybe tomorrow, maybe Tuesday. I want to be ready. I'm staking our overtime budget that if we watch all the likely targets till then we'll catch them in the act.'

'You can't do a full surveillance of a dozen shops for two days! It'd cost a fortune.'

'It doesn't have to be all day.' Shapiro was working it out as he went along. 'They rely on surprise, on getting in and out again before we know what's happening. They don't want to get caught up in traffic, and they don't want to be roaring through town in the middle of the night when everyone within earshot will guess what they're up to. Sunday morning's good, they've used Sunday mornings before. Weekdays they come in before the morning rush – between six-thirty and seven-thirty – or twelve hours later, after the commuters are safely home and before they set out for a night on the tiles. If we do ninety minutes morning and evening for two days we'll get them.'

'Unless they're home-grown, in which case they'll go on a blinder and won't do it again until they've spent whatever they made this time.'

Shapiro glowered at her. He trusted his instincts, but not to the point of ignoring hers. If she was right his next request for overtime would be about as successful as Donovan's next promotion board. 'The lookout in the green fedora: isn't that a bit sophisticated for the home team?'

She smiled. 'Ask them when you catch them. If they recognize both the words "fedora" *and* "sophisticated", they're imports.'

In a way she hoped he was right. If it was the

Tynesiders it should be possible to predict their next move. Of course, police in Harrogate, Barnsley, Mansfield, Nottingham and Leamington had probably thought the same. But even knowing a crime was imminent you couldn't seal off a medium-sized town for days on end. It made sense to do two or three quick raids in an area before moving on. The homework – learning the road network, the emergency exists, the ways they could go if those ways were blocked – only needed doing once. If Castlemere had been on that same vertical line she'd have had no doubts. But why would whatever was drawing them south suddenly pull them fifty miles east? Why would the Tynesiders change anything about their MO when it had served them so well?

'All right,' Shapiro said as if he had the clincher, 'then think about this. The chap in the green hat could be a local in fancy-dress, but what about that dog? That's not a Jack Russell in drag. Have Donovan check the vets, see if any of them treats a Chinese Crested Dog.' He'd had the public library opened specially to lend him the *Observer Book of Dogs*. 'I'll bet you lunch at The Ginger Pig that they don't.'

'You're on,' said Liz. 'But it'll have to be Morgan – Donovan's in London, remember? We'll check the hotels too. If our friend isn't local, whether or not he's with the raiders, he's staying somewhere. He can disguise himself, but how do you set about disguising a naked dog? With a toupee?'

Shapiro grinned. Her sense of humour was one of the best things about Liz Graham. And her creativity, that had kick-started more stalled investigations than he could remember; and her willingness to do the groundwork while waiting for the lightning-stab of inspiration. A chauvinist, which Shapiro was not, would have gone on to note the aesthetic differences between the average DI and this tall handsome woman who shopped in London and Cambridge and not on the bargain rail at Suits Is Us in Viaduct Lane. She was a good detective, a good friend, good to have around.

The grin faded on Shapiro's face with the awareness that she probably wouldn't be around much longer. She was too good a detective to end her career as DI at a station the size of Queen's Street. She'd done work that would have won her promotion before now but for the glass ceiling. She'd broken through it to get here, and she'd break through it again; and Shapiro was too good a friend to hope they'd keep her waiting much longer.

But his heart sank wondering who they'd send him then. A dead-beat with no ambition to go any further, or a whizz-kid who couldn't wait to: Shapiro couldn't decide which he wanted least. There was no one of his own they'd promote into the job. Donovan would make a good DI in his own way; but he'd gone his own way too often in the past to expect another promotion. There was no one else.

'Frank?'

He blinked. 'Sorry. Just thinking.'

She smiled. 'Perhaps I should stop calling you Frank now you're a Superintendent.'

'And perhaps you shouldn't,' Shapiro glowered. 'Superintendent – what do you do with it? Chief Inspector you can shorten, but if people start calling me Super we'll have the place sounding like a finishing school.'

Not as long as Donovan works here, thought Liz. 'We were talking in the car,' she said. 'Donovan thought I should call you sir with a small S, he should call you sir with a capital S, and the constables should just grovel.'

Shapiro scowled. 'The next time Sergeant Donovan calls me sir with any sort of an S and it doesn't sound like a deliberate insult will be the first. Remind me: where is Castlemere's answer to Terry Wogan?'

Liz chuckled. Donovan had many good points, if you looked hard, but geniality wasn't one. 'Scotland Yard – the counter-terrorism course. That you and I both got out of going to? He'll be on the late train tomorrow night.'

'The train? Why didn't he take his bike?'

'I wondered that. He said he went to Scotland Yard in motorcycle gear once, and three different people tried to arrest him.'

Chapter Two

The train rattled through the dark. It was the last service of the evening, dubbed the Luvvies Train because of its popularity with patrons of the London theatres. But it took a particularly dedicated luvvy to travel beyond St Neots, especially on a Monday. Mostly those left in the emptying carriages were tired men and women who'd been in London on business that was a bit too much for one day and not quite enough for two.

Such a one was John Holloway, managing director of Holloway's (Boots & Shoes) of Castlemere. He'd been visiting the London retailers, listening to their views on why some lines sold like hot cakes and others like soggy sandwiches. But the conversational possibilities of soles, welts and toe-caps were exhausted by mid evening so he caught the last train home.

After it left the InterCity line and struck off across country there were only six people remaining in the first carriage: Holloway, a teenage girl in jeans and a woolly jacket, a woman of about fifty with a briefcase, a couple in their early twenties and a man in a black leather jacket slumped in the corner. He appeared to be asleep, except that once when Holloway glanced his way he caught the glint of a hawkish watchful eye under the heavy lid.

With nothing more to go on than that – the jacket might have made some people wary but Holloway had the greatest respect for black leather – he felt himself growing uneasy. He was a pragmatic man of fifty-nine: travelling late had never worried him before. That it was bothering him now made him wonder if perhaps subliminal danger signals were being broadcast, and though he wasn't sure what they meant he thought he knew where they were coming from.

For now he did nothing. But he decided to observe the order in which these people left the carriage. If the couple and one of the women left at Castlemere, and the man in the corner didn't, Holloway thought he'd travel further rather than leave the other woman alone with a man with those eyes.

But the dark miles poured steadily past the window, marked only by the lights of the occasional farmhouse, and nothing happened. The girl got up and walked through to the next carriage. The man in black watched her but made no attempt to follow. Holloway looked at his watch. A few more minutes and they'd be in Castlemere. He began to feel rather foolish. He thought he'd been wrong, that what had seemed like danger signs were only the disagreeable vibrations given off by a tired man at the end of a long day. He thought he was probably giving off some of his own.

Then, down the train, just close enough and loud enough to leave no doubt as to what it was, a girl screamed.

Holloway felt a sudden certainty, though he hadn't heard her speak, that it was the girl from his carriage.

But whatever had happened the man in black wasn't responsible; the cry had brought him from his seat and he was half way to the connecting door, a tall angular man who moved like an assassin.

The second carriage was as sparsely peopled as the first: a couple who might well have been to the theatre, two middle-aged women, two teenage boys. One of them went to get up but the man gestured him back like reprimanding a puppy. 'Stay here. I'll deal with it.' His voice was thick with purpose and an Irish accent.

There were more people in the third carriage: so many it seemed some were having to stand. One was the girl from the first carriage, and she'd have been screaming still but for a gloved hand clamped on her neck and the lancet point of a knife pricking the skin under her ear. Her face was creased up in terror, her mouth a ragged 'o', and she was shaking.

The man holding her had a ski-mask over his face. Beside the girl he seemed big, but not big enough to stand out of a line-up of ordinarily well-built men. Two other men wore the same uniform of dark ski-masks, gloves and jeans. Each had a rucksack that the passengers were filling with valuables.

The man holding the girl was in charge, yelling orders and menaces. 'You want to get home tonight? In one piece? Then do as you're told. Hold on to your rings and we'll cut your fingers off. Hold on to your earrings and we'll cut your ears. Give 'em up and we'll be on our way, but if anyone tries to stop us I'll kill her.' His hand jerked and the terrified girl, her face framed by a floss of fair hair, danced like a marionette. 'So nobody rushes us, nobody pulls the communication cord, nobody plays the hero. 'Cos if this turns nasty people are going to die, and one of them's going to be her.'

The sight of the knife stopped Detective Sergeant Donovan in his tracks. His instincts told him to go for it, that he could reach the man before he made the giant mental leap between threatening to kill someone and doing it. But it was too big a gamble for the sake of some jewellery. If he did nothing and no one got hurt, that would be enough. If he started a war that ended with a teenage girl getting her throat cut, it wouldn't matter who got their diamonds back and who did time: he'd be on Shapiro's carpet first thing tomorrow morning, and he'd deserve to be. He took a step back.

'You.' The man with the knife had seen him. 'Where are you going?' Under the throaty bellow there was an accent lurking but Donovan was no expert on English accents.

'I heard a yell, I thought I could help. I guess I was wrong.'

A ski-mask does more than hide large parts of the face. It emphasizes those parts that do show. When the man in this one smiled it was like the last ten minutes of *Jaws*. 'I like a man who can admit his mistakes. A man who knows when he's made one is less likely to make another, right?'

Donovan nodded silently.

'OK, back the way you came. You were at the front, yes? Well, go tell them what's happening. Tell them no one'll get hurt if they do as they're told. Stay where I can see you. Go on, do it.' He took the knife away from the girl's throat long enough to stab at the air.

'I'm going,' Donovan said quickly. He backed two

or three paces, then turned and jogged up the train.

When he reached the first carriage he stood in the doorway, blocking it. Hard and low he said, 'I'm a police officer. Listen to me and do as I say. There's a robbery going on. They'll be here in a minute. Don't argue, and don't go for the communication cord. Has anybody got a mobile phone?'

Emily Murchison nodded, her eyes round with alarm. She'd been jolted from a doze by the sudden flurry of activity; mentally she was still addressing a sales conference that had finished three hours before.

'Keep it out of sight, they're watching me. Dial this number,' – it was the front desk at Queen's Street, the only one he could be sure would be manned – 'then hold it in front of me. If you see them coming, ring off and kick it under the seats.'

Though Donovan looked like a Hell's Angel on his day off his voice could convey real authority when it had to. Miss Murchison did as he said.

When he heard the tone alter and the mutter of words – it might have been Sergeant Tulliver, who always muttered, or just the distance between the instrument and his ear – Donovan spoke his carefully chosen sentences. He spoke up, in the hope that Tulliver or whoever would hear and understand, and also so that he would be heard by the men in ski-masks.

'My name's Donovan,' he said. 'Everybody keep calm, but this train's being robbed. Steamers – three of them, they've taken a girl hostage, they're threatening to cut her throat. They started at the back of the train so they're almost through: when they've got our wallets they'll stop the train and disappear into The Levels. If everyone co-operates they'll be away from here in five minutes and we'll be in Castlemere in ten. So can we all just sit it out?'

'Good,' said the man behind him, and Donovan shied like a startled horse. He hadn't realized they were so close. But Miss Murchison had: she'd waited as long as she dared, then slid the phone out of sight under the table. It was too late to kick it away from her under the seats; instead she slipped it under the skirt of her coat.

'So let's everybody follow Mr Donovan's good advice,' said the big man, 'and keep calm and co-operate. You.' He pointed the knife at Miss Murchison, whose heart skipped a beat. 'That's a nice scarf you've got. Spread it on the floor, and everybody put on it everything they think we might want. Cash, watches, jewellery, plastic, cheque-books.'

Donovan couldn't risk parting with his wallet: his warrant card was in there. He made a show of emptying it on to the scarf – cash, credit card, everything the robbers would be looking for. They wouldn't be looking for a warrant card. Other policemen had difficulty believing Donovan was one.

'OK?' he asked bitterly when he was done.

'OK,' agreed the man with the knife. He looked at Miss Murchison. 'You next.'

The sales director of Castle Spa, bottlers of soft drinks and mineral waters, was proving equal to the occasion. She produced the mobile phone as if taking it from her pocket. 'I believe these have a certain second-hand value.'

Inside the mask, black wool hemmed with yellow, the thick-lipped mouth beamed. 'They do that. Stick it on the scarf.'

Donovan watched stony-faced, praying to a deity he only believed in for real emergencies. He thought his prayer had a good chance of being answered. The man with the knife couldn't pick the phone up without dropping either the weapon or the hostage, and when his colleagues arrived they'd be ready to leave. They'd shovel the contents of the scarf into a rucksack, pull the cord and jump out as the train stopped. There was neither time nor any reason for them to start playing with the buttons on a mobile phone. But if they do, Donovan was praying, please don't let them hit the last number redial button.

Also on to the scarf went Miss Murchison's purse, her ear-rings, a gold locket with pictures of her parents in it and three heavy gold rings from her right hand; and a wallet, purse and wedding rings in two different sizes from the young couple. At first the wife couldn't get hers off. The man with the knife growled, 'Take it off or I'll cut it off.'

She gave a little shriek and her hands knotted so that she couldn't have got a glove off, let alone a ring. Her husband gave up tugging at it and started to rise, putting his body between her and the knife.

Oh, God, thought Donovan in despair, this is where it goes from robbery with menaces to assault occasioning grievous bodily harm or maybe murder.

He edged in front of the knife, pressed the young man back to his seat, took the girl's hand in his own and raised it to his lips. ''Scuse me.' He put her finger in his mouth, made it slick with his saliva and drew off the ring with his teeth. He wiped it on his shirt and dropped it on to the pile.

All at once they were finished. The booty was bundled into a rucksack and the three men, their hostage still in tow, made for the door. One of them pulled the communication cord and they braced against the expected braking.

Nothing happened. The train continued oblivious through the darkness of the Castlemere Levels.

'Mustn't be working,' said Donovan, dead-pan. Or just possibly, he thought, somebody got a message to the police, who called the station, who called the driver on the radio and told him not to stop for anything.

'I'll make it bloody work. You.' The knife jabbed in Donovan's face. 'You lead the way.'

Stall, thought Donovan. Time's on our side – every minute brings us closer to home. 'The way where?'

'To the frigging driver!' For the first time perspiration was beading the skin round the man's eyes and there was alarm in his voice. 'He sits at the front, yes?'

Donovan did as he was told, led the way past notices threatening plague and mayhem on anyone disturbing the driver and tapped diffidently. 'Excuse me, but—'

A strong hand yanked him away. 'Bugger that!' The big man wrenched open the door and thrust the weapon inside.

The train began to slow. Filling the doorway, the man with the knife looked back at Donovan. If a ski-mask can look puzzled, this one did. Not a word had been spoken.

Donovan pushed past, looked into the cab. The driver was still in his seat, bent over his console, a finger hooked inside his tie. His face was white and running with sweat, his eyes stretched; choked sounds came from between clenched teeth.

'God help us!' With his hands under the driver's arms Donovan eased him out of the cab, leaving it empty. He sat the man on the floor, loosened his tie and belt, took off his own jacket to cover him. 'Try and breathe lightly. The worst'll pass in a couple of minutes.' One way or another, he thought parenthetically.

Behind him the man with the knife was staring at the vacant cab. 'Can you drive this thing?'

Donovan eyed him sourly. 'It doesn't need anyone to drive it, it'll stop itself. Have you never heard of a dead man's handle? Well, this is what it's for. Bursting in like that, you've given the poor sod a heart attack.'

Chapter Three

When the phone rang, the Grahams were busy. 'Let it *ring*!' gasped Liz. 'Do that. God, yes! Do it some more.'

But when it was still drilling its patient, insistent summons two minutes later she relented, pushed Brian off her and reached for it. By way of greeting she growled, 'This had better be good.'

'Oh, it is,' Shapiro said with conviction. 'Sorry to wake you' – the Detective Superintendent was divorced and lived alone – 'but you won't want to miss this. We have a train robbery in progress.'

'Good lord!'

They'd been married ten years, Brian Graham knew that tone: it meant that something more interesting than him had come along. He sighed, reached for his book.

'Where?'

'Coming in off The Levels,' said Shapiro. 'Somewhere about the Mile End Straight. I'm on my way there now.'

'Doesn't the driver know where he is?'

'He's not answering his radio.'

Liz didn't use the train much but it was an easy way to London so she'd done it the odd time. She ran a mental tape of the home straight. 'Which side of the tunnel?'

'All the signal box can say is that the train's come to a stop somewhere about the Mile End tunnel and the driver isn't answering his radio. We're not going to know any more till we get there.'

Liz frowned. 'If they can't talk to the driver, how do we know it's a robbery?'

'Ah,' said Shapiro heavily. 'You see the time? This is the last train we're talking about. Remember who was catching the last train?'

Premonition booted the air out of her. Trouble gravitated to Donovan like iron filings to a magnet. 'He got a message through?'

'Brief and garbled,' said Shapiro, 'but what's new?' Liz wasn't fooled: he was worried, too. 'Three men holding a girl at knife-point, relieving passengers of cash and valuables. At that point no one seemed to have been hurt but he rang off rather quickly.'

'He won't do anything rash,' Liz said quietly. 'He won't go to war for the sake of some money.'

Shapiro wasn't persuaded. 'Calling in was rash. If he was caught—' He avoided finishing the thought. 'He mustn't draw attention to himself. He doesn't want them knowing he's a policeman.'

'I don't expect he's planning to arrest them!'

'It's not what Donovan plans that you have to worry about,' Shapiro said grimly, 'it's what he does on the spur of the moment. If he thinks he can get the knife he'll go for it.'

'Maybe he'll get it. Maybe we'll get there and it'll all be over.'

'And maybe they'll kick his stupid head in.'

*

The reason for calling it the Mile End Straight was lost in the mists of time. The line ran straight for seven miles across the Castlemere Levels; the Mile End tunnel itself was half a mile long and three miles short of Castlemere.

The last train, braking steadily while its driver gasped and clutched his chest on the floor, made for the tunnel like a weary beast returning to its lair. There was something inevitable about it. Almost regardless of the emergency, a driver in control of his train would not have stopped in the tunnel. He would have stopped before if he could, continued through if he had to. Almost nothing that would go wrong on a train could get worse so fast that it made sense to try and deal with it inside a hill.

But this train had no driver, was incapable of making value judgements. All it knew was to bring itself to a halt as quickly as was consistent with passenger safety.

Before it was stationary the raiders had the door open. 'We're inside a frigging tunnel. Does it matter?'

'Won't have to,' decided the man with the knife. 'Go ahead, I'll cover you – me and Little Miss Pretty here.' She was still standing in the aisle, quaking and hugging herself, her face that was midway between child and woman streaked with tears. She let out a breathy little shriek as the man pushed her towards the door. 'Careful how you jump down, you don't want to hurt yourself.'

Donovan was calculating percentages. She was a young girl and they were three violent men high on crime and adrenalin. If he let them take her she might be all right, but she might not. If they had a car near here, and if there was no one to stop them, they would disappear with her into The Levels where rape was about the best she could hope for.

If he was going to intervene this was probably the only chance he'd get. When the girl jumped down, for a split second before the man followed she'd be out of range of the knife. If Donovan took him then she'd be safe. Even if they fought, even if he lost, there'd be time for her to hide in the darkness. The raider might have lost his knife by then, or be aware how much time was passing. If he grabbed a fresh hostage it could hardly be anyone more vulnerable.

He was going to do it. He filled his lungs, banished from his mind the likely consequences of failure and moved on to the balls of his feet, ready to jump as the girl jumped.

But the girl didn't jump. Instead she backed uncertainly from the door and a second later one of the ski-masks reappeared. 'There's torches up ahead.'

'So go the other way.' Precisely on cue, as they turned to look the length of the train, lights glittered in the portal behind them. 'Shit.'

Donovan said, 'Maybe you'd better give up the knife. Let the girl take it out: if they know you're not armed it'll take the heat out of the situation.'

'The knife?' The man looked at it as if he'd just noticed it. 'Yes, I could do that.' He held it out, left-handed, not to the girl but to Donovan. 'Here.'

Carefully Donovan reached for it. He was always careful around lethal weapons. But the man didn't change his mind and when Donovan's long fingers closed on the hilt he let it go. Donovan breathed out softly and looked up. 'Good—'

He was looking into the barrel of a small automatic pistol. 'After all,' said the man conversationally, 'I've still got this.'

It wasn't the first time Donovan had found himself looking up the muzzle of a gun but the sight never lost its ability to shock. He felt the strength drain from his muscles, the blood from his face. He breathed, 'You don't want to do that.'

'No,' agreed the man, 'but I will if I have to. I'm not going to jail for the sake of some costume jewellery and a mobile—' He stopped abruptly, mid-sentence, staring at Donovan through the yellow knitted rings. When he spoke again his voice was down to the bare bones of hatred. 'You *bastard*! That's how they got here so quickly – you called them. Now they've sealed the tunnel and they think we're trapped. But they don't know about this, do they?' He stabbed the gun at Donovan's eyes and Donovan recoiled. 'They think all they have to worry about is a knife. They might rush a knife but they won't rush this. All we have to do is find some way of letting them know we have it.'

Donovan had been a policeman for ten years. He knew a threat when he heard one.

The shot echoed round the tunnel like artillery. A thin blue line, marked by torches and rather spoiled by Shapiro's old tweed coat a little right of centre, had advanced a dozen metres under the hill when it sent them diving for the black brick wall.

'Anyone hurt?' rapped Shapiro, hoping no one could hear the rasp in his voice. Even these days it wasn't often that a Detective Superintendent got shot at. But no one had been hit and they fell back in disorder and relief.

Shapiro called Liz on the radio. 'I suppose you heard that.'

'Any damage?'

'No, thank God. Knives – Donovan said they had knives. He never said anything about guns!'

'I don't expect he knew,' Liz said reasonably. 'It's a wonder he got a message out at all, you can't blame him for not giving you chapter and verse.'

'You don't think—?'

'No, I don't,' she answered firmly. 'I think it was a warning. I think if they'd been going to kill him they'd have done it while they still had a chance of getting away. They must know by now they're not going anywhere, that they'll have to pay for anything they do. It may take time but in the end they'll come quietly because they have no choice. Hurting their hostages will only make matters worse.'

A less experienced officer might have believed her. But Shapiro knew not to expect too much sense from criminals with their backs to the wall. If Liz had been right, hostage dramas would always end peacefully, and they didn't. She knew that as well, of course. She was trying to reassure him. She must have forgotten all the times he'd sworn that if he'd had a gun he'd have shot Donovan himself.

'We're going to need support,' he said. 'I'll start the megaphone diplomacy, you get us some fire-power.'

The sound of the gunshot filled the front of the train. It made the girl clap her hands to her ears with a shrill little scream; it made Miss Murchison, who hadn't an hysterical bone in her body, grip the arms of her seat tightly; it penetrated the driver's private world of fear and pain.

Down the train came a series of softer bangs as the doors opened and hasty feet scrunched on cinders. One of the raiders flashed a torch down the tunnel. 'They're getting away!' It was a young man's voice, panic sharpening the native monotone of the lowland Scot.

The big man was older and more pragmatic. 'Let them go. We've got everybody we need right here.' Seven hostages were enough to control with one gun. If it came to a shoot-out, seven targets would be hard to miss.

Shapiro would be at one end of the tunnel, Donovan surmised, and Inspector Graham at the other. Neither would be pushed into doing something for the sake of being seen to. For one thing, they knew he was here, they'd be expecting him to do something clever. While they were waiting they'd try to open a dialogue. But however nasty this got they wouldn't let the robbers go. They wouldn't free men who'd do this to do it again.

A fog-horn croak battled up the long tunnel. 'My name's Frank Shapiro, it's my job to sort this out. You want to talk about how we do it?'

'They've got us. They've got us.' The boy was shaking his head like a caged bear.

'They *haven't* got us, and as long as I've got this they won't.' The big man hefted the gun; not extravagantly, just enough to make the point. That meant he was familiar with the weapon, knew what it could and couldn't do. It could punch holes in anything it was aimed at. It couldn't discriminate between intentional jerks on the trigger and accidental ones.

Had there been no other considerations Donovan would have waited. The longer these men had to think about their situation the more resigned they would become. Only the fact that their blood was up kept them from seeing there was nowhere left for them to go.

But the driver's condition injected a degree of urgency. Donovan was no doctor, couldn't distinguish between a heart spasm from which a man might recover without much help and a coronary attack in which every minute was vital. While he was softly softly catching monkeys a man could be dying. Reluctant as he was to draw attention to himself again, he said, 'You could use the phone to negotiate.'

The eyes burned in the holes of the ski-mask. 'Negotiate? They won't negotiate – they want us to put our hands up and I'm not going to do that. The only thing I have to say they know already: that I have hostages and a gun. That's all they need to know.'

In fact it wasn't. Shapiro also needed to know about the driver, and that so far none of the passengers had been injured. How he would use the information when half of it suggested there was time to resolve this peacefully and the other half that patience could cost a life Donovan had no idea, only that he'd want to know. But he didn't think he could say much more without giving himself away, and instinct warned that if these men knew he was a police officer his usefulness would come to an abrupt end.

He wasn't unafraid for his own safety – he'd been

hurt too often to have any illusions about plugging the holes in his body with a hanky while he got on with the job – but there was more to it than that. In reasonable working order he was the best thing the hostages had going for them. He knew how sieges worked, what the dangers were, how to keep the shit from hitting the fan. Shot, knocked out or bound and gagged he could do nothing. So it wasn't only self-regard that urged him to protect his identity. At least, he didn't think it was.

Hands spread he said soothingly, 'I'm only trying to help.' And in the moment of saying it, like a distant dawn breaking he got the first pale glimmer of how.

Chapter Four

When fishes flew and forests walked, Castlemere Levels was a marsh punctuated by islets. Even after the fens were drained the islets remained in the form of low hills with a distinct shrubby vegetation on top. Such was Mile End Hill. As late as the mid-nineteenth century the land was still so wet that it was easier to drive a tunnel through the hill than make a causeway strong enough to carry a train round it.

Shapiro met Liz on top; but she had to wait for him because she jogged while Shapiro trudged. As she waited, gazing round she saw a clutter of stones like a tumbledown cairn half-hidden by willow-scrub. By the time Shapiro arrived her eyes were aglow. 'I know what he's going to do!'

There was no judging how much time they had. Donovan would be trying to separate the raiders from their hostages but even once the means occurred to him the opportunity might prove elusive. He couldn't force the situation, not against men with guns. But Liz remembered him telling her about the shaft, felt sure he'd find some way of using it. Donovan's brain had the kind of boneless agility usually associated with ferrets in drainpipes.

It was Shapiro's decision but he respected Liz's

intuition. So often, coming at a problem from different angles, she and Donovan ended up in the same place. If she knew by the pricking of her thumbs what Donovan's next move would be, Shapiro wasn't going to say she was wrong. 'Prepare a welcoming committee,' he said. 'I'll get back on the loud-hailer, let them think we're trying to talk them out.'

'The old fool with the megaphone's trying again,' said the third man, easing the rucksack on his shoulders. 'Can't we shut him up?'

The man with the gun shook his head. 'I don't want to waste bullets till I know how many we're going to need.' His eyes, restlessly scanning the carriage, lit on Donovan and his voice hardened. 'What are you grinning at? I'll tell you one thing – if it comes to a shoot-out, you're the first. You brought them here; well, by God, you're not walking away.'

Donovan hadn't realized he was grinning; if he was, it was precipitate. He didn't need the gun to remind him how many ways this could go wrong. These were deeply dangerous men: only the hope that he'd found a way to deal with them played on his face like a shadow of a smile.

Cal Donovan was not a good-looking man. He went from wiry child to stringy teenager to stick-thin six-footer without passing through an attractive stage. The olive skin was drawn over the narrow bones of his face like a medieval icon while, sunk deep in bony pits, his dark eyes had an animal watchfulness that could flare to fevered intensity or sink to sullenness almost without warning. At thirty his self-command was better than it had been five years before but he still walked a tightrope between instinct and prudence, edgy as a cat with eight lives gone. Women, a few, glimpsed a certain tortured beauty; men reacted with the unease evoked by any powerful creature of unreliable temperament.

He spread long-fingered hands defensively. 'Don't shoot me, I'm your last best chance of getting out of here.'

The armed man leaned forward until Donovan was breathing gun-oil. 'Say what?'

By now Jody Perkins was a bright seventeen-year-old working on her Oxbridge entrance. But six years ago she was an active child with boundless curiosity and a Border Collie, and when she went missing on The Levels Donovan and a hundred other people turned out to search for her.

Which is how he knew about the ventilation shaft. They found her twenty feet down the corroded iron rungs set into its wall. Intrigued, she'd climbed that far and then panicked, clutching the ladder while the dog barked hysterically overhead. Constable Donovan was lowered on a rope and brought her up without further incident.

There were two things he didn't know about the shaft: whether the rungs went all the way down, and whether they would carry a man's weight. But this was a good time to find out. They couldn't force a dozen hostages up the pipe ahead of them, would have to make do with him.

Inspector Graham was out there somewhere. He'd told her about the lost child. Would she remember, guess what he'd do and be there to meet them when they emerged? Even if she didn't, men clambering off a dangerous ladder were at a disadvantage in the face of a hostage developing an unexpected hero complex. If they knew he was a copper they might be prepared; but if they thought he was—

'I work for Railtrack, maintenance section. There's an airshaft half-way through the tunnel. As far as I know you can still climb up on to the hill. From there you've got six hours of darkness and forty square miles of wilderness to get lost in.'

For a moment he thought they weren't going to buy it. Eyes hedged round by knitting raked him like claws. He felt their need for hope at war with their natural suspicion of anything that convenient.

Yet the shaft existed, he could show them. And whatever followed had to be better than being trapped in a tunnel. In the end, whether or not they trusted him, they'd go for it. It was probably the only chance they'd get.

They knew it. They also knew the risks. The muzzle of the gun under Donovan's jaw forced his head back. 'Jerk me around, flower, and you're dead. You go first; then if anybody falls it'll be you. First sign of trouble you're going to get buggered by a bullet.'

He bundled Donovan to the door. Then he gripped the girl's wrist.

Donovan took a deep breath. 'She can't come.'

The gun swung his way. 'Don't tell me what to do!'

'She's a wee girl, she couldn't climb on top of the train let alone fifty metres up an old shaft. Even if she doesn't fall she'll slow you up. And if she does fall she'll take everybody below her when she goes.'

He waited. He hoped he'd done enough to convince

them. If he hadn't he was prepared to fight for her, but he didn't expect to win.

After a moment the man with the gun nodded. 'OK.' He pushed the girl to a seat. 'OK, honey, you've done your bit. You stay here.' Speaking to all of them he went on: 'And let's not have an undignified rush for the exit. Stay where you are and wait. I don't know how long it'll take us to get up the shaft, and if I don't know you sure as hell don't. Anybody shows his face before we're gone, I'll put a hole in it.'

They wouldn't use the torch for fear of signalling their intentions. They dropped on to the track, the gunman pushing Donovan ahead of him, and walked back to the mid-point of the tunnel. 'OK, where's this shaft?'

Donovan found it by the down-draught of peaty air. There wasn't enough space between the roof of the train and the vaulting of the tunnel to stand up: he was on his hands and knees on top of the carriage when he felt the movement of air and his groping hand vanished into the void. 'Here.'

Perhaps two metres across, linking a black tunnel and a dark sky, the shaft received no natural light. Now the torch was essential. The last man wedged it in his top pocket so that it cast its beam up through the legs of those above. It gave a shaky fragmented light but enough to show where the rusty brackets were and, once, that the pinnings had gone on one side. Donovan stretched long limbs from the rung below to that above. For a moment he considered keeping quiet but wisdom prevailed. Probably the man with the gun would see it too and know Donovan had tried to kill him. If he didn't see it, as the thing came away from the wall the gun could go off, and Donovan knew where it was pointing.

'The next one's loose,' he said, and the man below said, 'Thanks' – as if he'd pointed out a dodgy paving-stone to a stranger in the street.

It was an arduous climb and, for them all in different ways, an anxious one. Even so, when Donovan reached for another rung and instead felt grass, for a moment he couldn't think what to do next. 'We're at the top.'

'Get out,' panted the man with the gun. They were all out of breath. 'Stay on your knees by the edge. Don't think you can run faster than I can climb these last couple of rungs.'

Donovan told himself he'd never intended to run, had always meant to wait and see if he had back-up before making his next move. If DI Graham was in position with an armed response unit he needed the three men out of the shaft before they realized. And if she wasn't, if no one had thought of the air-shaft, he had to be by the ladder as the man with the gun scrambled out.

It was an awkward manoeuvre with two free hands. If Donovan could catch him off balance and wrest the weapon from him, or send it spinning into the void, the thing would be over. They were two good reasons for behaving himself a little while longer. The effect of a bullet on the human body was a third.

After the oppressive darkness of the shaft the star-dusted sky over The Levels seemed vast. A couple of miles west the lights of Castlemere began; nearer, and also further out across the dark plain, were the scattered lights of farms. The curve of the hill hid from him the lights of the police down by the track and they would have no view of him. Unless the faint column of light from the torch was spotted . . .

'Turn the torch off,' said the man with the gun. 'You: back off a bit.'

Donovan had knelt by the top of the ladder, ostensibly obeying instructions, actually thinking that from there he could act too quickly to be stopped. The man below him must have thought so too. Reluctantly Donovan shuffled a metre sideways.

He looked round but there was nothing to see. No ring of armed police. No DI Graham with her fair hair spread on the breeze like a recruiting poster. No Superintendent Shapiro, broad face beaded with sweat from the climb, taking control in that reassuring, avuncular voice with just a touch of adenoidal accent. Not even a probationary constable or a school crossing patrol lady. He was on his own up here.

OK. So the priorities were to neutralize the gun and raise the alarm. Wee buns. But damn that woman, he thought bitterly: how come she always knew what he was planning right up to the moment he wanted her to?

If he went for the gun too soon the man would merely duck back into the shaft and shoot him from there; and if he waited too long he'd be on his feet and back in control. He waited . . . he waited . . . and then he dived.

He got it wrong. The extra metre made all the difference: instead of bowling the armed man across the turf, Donovan barely reached him, found himself clawing for the gun at full stretch. The man dodged him easily, came to his feet with the gun levelled at

Donovan's face. 'Bad move, flower.' The hatred in his voice was so profound it vibrated.

Donovan had heard of people freezing with fear. He'd assumed it was a figure of speech. He'd been frightened enough often enough that he'd have known if it had ever actually happened. He thought it was probably an excuse offered by people who knew they'd proved unequal to a situation; a sop to cowardice.

Flat on his back, the breath knocked from him, face to face with oblivion, it happened to Donovan now. He froze rigid. His muscles locked round the long bones and would not obey him. He needed to be up, twisting out of the line of fire, jinking for cover. In this light every metre he put between him and that gun halved the chance of a shot finding him, quartered its chance of killing him. He didn't have to get far, he didn't have to get out of range or out of sight, he just had to *get*. Anything he did now would improve the odds.

But he couldn't move. It was as if Lilliputians had swarmed over him with vines the moment he hit the ground. He felt his heart pound and his eyes round, and he couldn't raise a hand to defend himself. A detached part of his brain that was watching curiously, that clearly hadn't made the connection between his impending demise and its own, observed, If this was a novel the light would spring up now and DI Graham would leap into the ring shouting—

'Armed police officers! Drop your gun. Now! Do it now. Do it!'

Yes, reflected that wry remote portion of Donovan's brain watching him sprawl in the weeds moments from his own destruction, that's what she'd say. By the book.

Never mind blowing the bastard's head off while there was still time to save his. Do it by the book, then you never have to worry about justifying yourself. Only about breaking in a new detective sergeant.

For a second the man looked away. But the black eye of the gun remained fixed on Donovan's face, pinning him down, undistracted by the flare of torches, the shapes sprung into focus between them, the distinctive crouching attitudes of people aiming weapons. The man saw them; but stubbornly refusing to acknowledge the cordon and the certainty of capture it represented he turned back to the man at his feet.

Donovan whispered, 'Don't—'

The big man smiled. At least the fleshy lips spread; nothing resembling a smile reached the eyes. The gun twitched fractionally as his fore-finger took up the slack.

The crash of the shot rolled round the top of the hill. A woman's voice shouted, 'No!' into the echo. At last, and too late, Donovan tried to move, to throw himself those couple of metres that might make the difference between emergency surgery and the morgue. He managed to roll just once, then his long body slumped leadenly, face down this time, one arm about his head.

Before the smell of cordite cleared, two officers, one armed with a torch, the other with a gun, hurdled the broken wall and pin-pointed the two men still in the shaft. 'Let's be having you.'

Liz Graham bent over the fallen man, shook her head. It would take a doctor to make the death official but the fact of it was obvious. The bullet had entered above the left ear and taken the right ear with it.

'Damn, damn, damn. I didn't want that to happen.'

'Sorry, ma'am.' The man who fired was making his weapon safe. 'There was no option. He was going to shoot Sergeant Donovan.'

'Well, we couldn't have that, could we?' She sounded like someone putting a brave face on things. 'I suppose.' She looked round. 'Donovan? Where's he got to?'

He was on his knees beside the wall. It had taken him almost till then to realize it wasn't him who'd been shot. Simultaneous with the hammer-blow of sound he had felt, or thought he had, the shock of impact; his body had spasmed and gone weak and he'd felt his senses fade.

But instead of fading out he found himself taking in the smell of damp earth and listening to the conversation. Only then did he understand that he'd miscalculated. His initial reaction, before relief, was embarrassment. 'I'm here.'

'Are you all right?'

'Yeah.'

Liz smiled at the armed officer. 'That's Sergeant Donovan's idea of a full report. All right, let's see what we've got.' She bent again, carefully picked the remains of the ski-mask away from the remains of the face. 'I don't recognize him. Donovan?'

By then the others were out of the shaft, pulling off their own masks. A boy of about nineteen, a man in his early thirties: she hadn't seen either of them before. 'You're not from around here, are you?' They made no reply.

Liz turned back to her sergeant, to acknowledge his success. The expression in his eyes stopped her.

He was looking at the dead man on the grass. It wasn't a pretty sight but they were neither of them virgins: they'd seen uglier things, and much more upsetting ones, than an armed thug shot dead before he could kill someone else.

But Donovan was looking at him with neither hatred, triumph nor even relief, but as if he was seeing a ghost. His eyes were appalled.

'Donovan? Do you know him?'

'No,' he said hurriedly, accent thick as soda farls. 'No, I don't.' And it was the truth. But it wasn't the whole truth. He was looking at a man he'd never seen before; but the face he was seeing, white, half destroyed, the other half wry with the sheer unexpectedness of death, was his own.

Chapter Five

It was three-thirty on Tuesday morning before Shapiro gave up trying to interview the men in the cells. He'd sent Liz home an hour before, and Donovan an hour before that, as soon as he'd made a coherent report.

That took longer than it should have done. It was no wonder that a man who'd confronted his own mortality, who was alive now only because of a woman's intuition and the skill of a police marksman, had been unsettled by the experience. But Shapiro was surprised that Donovan, who habitually pushed his luck until it started pushing back, seemed so subdued. Reaction usually made him surly. Shapiro hoped that if the sergeant got some sleep in what remained of the night, by morning he would be himself again.

There were people, both at Queen's Street and Division, who would consider any change for the better. But Shapiro had known Donovan longer than most and recognized that his moods were the price to be paid for his commitment. He was difficult because he cared too much, because failure grieved him. A whole department of Donovans would have been impossible to command, but Shapiro had been glad of the one he'd got often enough to make allowances.

Unforthcomingness from Donovan he was accustomed to, but criminals under arrest were often oddly loquacious. When a man had been discovered half-way down a drainpipe with somebody else's silver-ware it was too late to be coy. Talking about it, sometimes angrily, often with a kind of dry humour, seemed to ease the stress of watching the next five years go up in smoke.

So he didn't understand why these two were set on silence. They had nothing to lose. They'd been taken in the act, there were dozens of witnesses, the third member of the gang died at the scene so there was no one to protect. Yet they refused to talk. They refused to give their names or addresses or accept the offer of legal representation. The older man spoke, when he spoke at all, with a Yorkshire accent, the younger was a Scot. They weren't violent, abusive or hysterical. Though the boy was clearly shaken, even without the support of his steadier colleague he could not be tricked or persuaded to reveal anything useful. In the end Shapiro had to concede that he wasn't going to make any progress unless their fingerprints were on record somewhere. He collected his coat to go home.

The woman was standing at the foot of the police station steps as he drove out of the yard. He almost didn't pause, never afterwards knew what made him take a second look, then stop and take a third.

A woman calling at Queen's Street at that hour of the morning was not so unusual in itself. As it was mostly men who got into trouble after the bars closed it was mostly women – wives, mothers, daughters – who got the job of collecting them when the paperwork was done. Also there was a small but dedicated band of female winos who, midway through the second bottle, remembered all the slights they'd suffered at the hands of the local constabulary and decided to have it out with them.

Somehow this woman, half-hidden in the shadows, matched neither template. She was hesitant, unsteady even, but he didn't think she was drunk. She was too tidy, too well-dressed for someone who spent half of every night propping up a lamp-post singing 'Nelly Dean'.

And women coming to collect errant male relatives were usually too angry to hover in Queen's Street. Some of them were angry with the police, others with their menfolk, but they'd all had disturbed nights and wanted to get home.

She could be worried about a missing person, a son or daughter who hadn't come home when they should have done. Shapiro put her at about forty, which was the right age to have children at the 'it's-my-life, I'll-stay-out-till-dawn-if-I-want-to' stage. Parents always assumed the worst the first time – Shapiro remembered, Shapiro had been through it. Not with Rachael, who was born sensible, or with David, who worked on the principle that if no one knew when to expect him no one would worry if he was late, so much as with the middle one. Sally looked so fragile and was actually the toughest of the three. A couple of times Shapiro had been worried enough about her to phone Queen's Street at three in the morning.

But that was the natural thing to do, wasn't it? – to phone, not to call in. So it was something more than anxiety that had brought her out in the middle of the night. Something had happened. She'd done something, or had something done to her; she wanted to report it now, not wait till morning, and she couldn't quite find the courage to climb those steps, walk up to the desk and make it official.

Shapiro stopped his car on the yellow lines and got out. She whirled at his tread and her eyes were afraid. Shapiro stopped a few feet from her, before his bulky presence could crowd her, and kept his hands in the pockets of his coat. Solemnly he introduced himself. 'Is there a problem? Can I help at all?'

She looked, wildly, from him to the lit door at the top of the steps. Framed by blonde hair in a shoulder-length bob she had a rather long, strong face whose lines suggested competence and a greater degree of self-confidence than she was currently exhibiting. She wore a camel coat over a cashmere sweater and tweed skirt. There were marks on the coat as if she'd been in an accident.

For a moment it seemed she was going to change her mind, hurry away with her story untold. She looked past him, saw the empty street beckoning, knew or guessed he had no power to detain her; the wrong word from him then and she would have taken to her heels. Her head rocked back, her face racked by indecision.

Shapiro said quietly, 'I *can* help, you know.'

She laughed at that, a single bark of desperate laughter that was no sooner out than turning to a sob. She bit her lips to bring it under control. Then she looked Shapiro in the eye – a gesture whose courage he only appreciated when he'd heard what she had to say – and her voice was intelligent and, in the circumstances, remarkably restrained. 'I do hope so, Superintendent, I could certainly use some help. You see, I've been raped.'

He spent the rest of the night with her. He offered to bring Liz in if she'd rather talk to another woman, but she declined.

Dr Greaves who examined her explained. 'When a woman's been abused by a man it can be enormously reassuring to be treated with respect by another one. In a way it's too easy to retreat into the compassion of women. Unless she's going to enter a nunnery she has to learn to deal with men again and the sooner she starts the easier it'll be. If she can talk to you, Superintendent, that's the best thing for her. She was fortunate it was you who saw her first.'

'Oh, yes,' growled Shapiro, 'it was certainly her lucky night.' He bit back his anger; none of this was the police surgeon's fault. 'What's he done to her?'

'Raped her,' Greaves confirmed. 'It's not the worst I've ever seen. He didn't beat up on her and he didn't do anything aberrant to her. The physical evidence is consistent with what she said – that he came up behind her, dragged her into the bushes, pushed her to the ground and raped her. I've got a good semen sample: you find him and it'll nail him.'

They were supposed to be installing a special interview room, something less clinical that could be used for occasions like this. But more urgent demands kept claiming the budget. Shapiro took her to his office, which if not exactly comfortable had never been accused of being clinical. WPC Wilson made coffee, and over it the woman told what happened. Shapiro offered the occasional prompt but hardly had to question her: she was remarkably professional about the whole business, knew what he needed to know and told him.

Her name was Helen Andrews, she was a divorcee and branch manager of a building society. She had a flat in a big Victorian house at the north end of town.

She'd been to a hen-night – one of her assistants was marrying a solicitor's clerk. They started off in The Ginger Pig and ended up at the bride's home in Castle Mews. When the party broke up, rather than call a taxi Mrs Andrews thought she'd enjoy the walk. It was only half a mile, it was a pleasant spring night and the road was well-lit all the way. She was not a timorous woman, it had not occurred to her to be afraid to walk the main streets of her own town at night.

At the foot of Castle Mount the road up to the ruins peeled away to the left. There was no traffic as Mrs Andrews went to cross. She heard no footsteps, had no intimation of danger; the first she knew was a hand closing over her mouth from behind, then she was hauled back up the kerb, across the pavement and into the broad sweep of shrubbery where the road circled up to the Mount. She was pushed to the ground and gagged with her own scarf.

'Did you see his face?'

The street was only a few strides away, lamplight penetrating the shrubbery in jagged fingers; if anyone had been passing she would have seen them though they would probably not have seen her. He had something white tied over his face, the hood of a sweatshirt over his head: all she could say for sure was that he was light-skinned rather than dark. He wasn't particularly big. He was stronger than her, but most men are stronger than most women. She wouldn't recognize him if he came to her for a mortgage.

She tried to throw him off but failed; after that she offered no resistance. She didn't want to be hurt. 'Was that wrong?'

Shapiro shook his head. 'There is no right or wrong. You survived. You did fine.'

'But the evidence. There'd have been more evidence, wouldn't there, if I'd made him work for it.'

He knew what she was saying. He put his hand on hers on the desk. 'Mrs Andrews, nobody is going to wonder if you're telling the truth because you weren't beaten to a pulp. No judge, no jury is going to wonder if a respectable professional woman walking home from a friend's house suddenly took it into her head to dive into the bushes with a man she didn't know and then scream rape. You behaved very sensibly. Thank God we're *not* conducting this interview in Castle General.'

She fixed him with sea-coloured blue-grey eyes, a cool intellectual gaze forcing itself through the shock and the grief. 'Mr Shapiro, are you saying you believe me?'

Dear God, she's strong, he thought in boundless admiration. She didn't have to come here. She was afraid how she'd be treated but she came anyway. She was willing to say all this, and be doubted, not because she has something to gain but because it's her duty: there's a dangerous man out there and we need to know about it. 'Mrs Andrews, I have no reason to doubt a single word you've said.'

At that, finally, she began to cry. Shapiro went on

holding her hand for a minute. Then he got up, poured her some more coffee, gave WPC Wilson a top-up and sat down again. 'Can you tell me what happened next?'

She sniffed and nodded, but there was little more to tell. The attack was completed quickly, efficiently, with minimal emotional investment: not so much a sex act as a smash and grab raid. He was finished, on his feet and away in the time it took her to get the scarf out of her mouth. She sat in the shrubbery for half an hour, clasping her knees and gently rocking, before she could bring herself to move.

Shapiro took her home. She lived alone: only a grey cat, indignant at being kept out all night, was waiting on the step. 'Is there someone I can call to come over?'

Mrs Andrews shook her head. 'I'd rather be alone.' The assault, and all that followed, had left her exhausted. Mentally she was numb; probably the morning would be harder than tonight.

Shapiro didn't like leaving her, but she wasn't hysterical and she had the right to be alone of she chose. He jotted his home number on her phone-pad. 'If you change your mind, call me. It doesn't matter when. I'll come myself, or send a WPC, or bring you a friend – whatever you want. Just don't sit here feeling desperate.' He thought a moment, useless compassion twisting his face. 'What happened – it wasn't about you, you know, it was about him. His inadequacies, his hang-ups. You're the same person you always were. Nothing someone like that could do to you would make you anything less.'

She wasn't really listening. She thanked him again, edged him towards the door. Reluctantly he went. 'One more thing. Is there anyone you'd like me to talk to? That you want to know about this and don't want to tell?' Telling people who mattered could be the worst part.

Again she shook her head. 'Don't think I'm not grateful, Superintendent. I appreciate everything you've done. When I'm ready to talk to people I will, but all I want to do now is sleep.'

So he left. There was no option: to press any more help on her would be to chisel away yet more of her autonomy, her freedom of choice, that had been the main casualty of the attack.

She hadn't been injured, no more than if she'd tripped on a kerb-stone. When she dusted the leaf-mould off her coat no physical signs would remain of what had happened. But that was no measure of the extent to which she had been hurt. What had been stolen from her was fundamental to who and what she was. It wasn't a vital organ, something she'd die without – the history of slavery proved how far a human being could be stripped of rights and still remain functional. But neither could it be replaced.

With strength and determination she would rebuild her life, but there was no way to excise this night's work. It was there for good. Her confidence, her self-esteem, would never again be what they were before. She knew now that however valuable she was as a human being – however good a friend, a lover, a businesswoman, however much money she earned, however pleasant the life she made for herself – almost any trash from the gutter, as long as he was a man and so physically stronger than her, could take it away.

It would probably never happen again. Rape was

still a rare occurrence, rape by a stranger in a public place rarest of all. But she would always know, from the womb out, what she had previously only acknowledged as a theoretical possibility: that half the population had the potential to reduce her to something of no consequence. That knowledge would shadow all the rest of her days.

Shapiro got home without further incident but he didn't get inside. There was something waiting on his path, something big and black and shapeless. He studied it from the safety of his car, debating whether he should call for assistance. But it didn't move, he couldn't hear it ticking, and he thought he'd investigate further before calling in the Bomb Squad. He wouldn't be the first policeman to launch a major terrorist alert because the laundry had left next door's washing in his porch.

Armed with the torch from his glove compartment he approached with caution. It almost could have been next door's laundry – something bulky bundled up in a bin-liner, the top tied with a bit of string. He knew better than to give it an experimental kick. Instead he used his penknife to make a nick in one of the folds. Nothing came out but a rather sweet heavy smell, just familiar enough to make his heart sink. He widened the nick and shone his torch inside.

Two minutes later he was on the phone to Queen's Street. 'I want SOCO, photographer, pathologist, the works. And screens. I don't want my neighbours watching while we reconstruct *A Student's Guide to Anatomy* with real pieces.

'No,' he added irritably, still shaken by what he'd seen, 'I don't know who it's likely to be inside. From the size, I doubt if it's all of anybody. But I've got a bin-bag full of meat sitting on my doorstep, and since my butcher doesn't do deliveries that makes it a murder inquiry.'

Chapter Six

Within the privacy of a tent erected in Shapiro's front garden, Dr Crowe slit the black bag open and carefully examined what it contained.

It's meat, Shapiro told himself when he felt his gorge rising, just meat. Whoever it once was, whatever their story, that's all it is now. If it was in the butcher's window I wouldn't give it a second look. Somehow that thought failed to appease his stomach.

When the forensic pathologist had finished piecing together the grisly jigsaw he straightened up, peeled off his rubber gloves and thrust his hands deep in his pockets. His plump face fell into thoughtful creases. 'I suppose you want a description.'

Shapiro looked in quiet horror at the shapeless mound on his path. 'Of that? You can tell me what *that* looked like?'

'Oh, yes,' said Dr Crowe, grimly confident; 'pretty much. But that wasn't what I meant. I can give you a fair description of the killer too.'

Startled, the superintendent's eyes flared at him. But though Dr Crowe was still a young man with a rather undergraduate sense of humour he didn't joke about murder. 'How?'

Crowe shrugged. 'It's my job. Do you want to make notes – for a Wanted poster?'

Impressed, Shapiro rooted for his notebook.

'All right,' said Crowe. 'It's a male you're looking for, of course – not very big but very powerful. Huge neck and shoulder muscles, big deep chest. Weight, maybe about eighty pounds. Interesting dentition: undershot jaw, the lower teeth projecting beyond the upper ones. The canine teeth are particularly prominent. Temper, *extremely* unreliable. Members of the public should not approach; even your officers ought to be armed. I suggest one of those poles with a noose at the end . . . '

'Hang on,' growled Shapiro, doubt turning to suspicion, 'hang on.' He hadn't written anything since the weight. He squinted at Crowe, who remained poker-faced; he looked at the remains on his path. 'Eighty pounds: what, five and a half stone? Most *victims* weigh more than that. Before I go on *News at Ten* appealing for calm and information, do you want to tell me what that – thing – is?'

An amiable grin from the pathologist acknowledged that the game was up. 'It *was* a pit-bull terrier.'

Understanding dawned. 'So the *murderer* . . .?'

Crowe nodded. 'Another pit-bull terrier, bigger or perhaps just meaner.'

Appalled, Shapiro stared at the carcase. 'A dog did that?'

'Oh, no,' Crowe said quickly, 'no. They fought to the death, the other dog ripped this one's throat out. Then somebody skinned it. To make it harder to identify.'

'And what was left he dumped on my path,' mused

Shapiro. 'Not even at Queen's Street, but my home. *Why?*'

'That's a bit outside the scope of forensics,' admitted Crowe. 'Have you been clamping down on dog-fighting recently?'

'I wasn't aware we had any to clamp down on.' Shapiro's expression was working through a range of possibilities, from shock to puzzlement to anger to resolution. 'So now we know better.'

Crowe was packing his gear. The body-bag hadn't been needed after all. 'Maybe they're warning you off.'

'I imagine they are,' said the superintendent bleakly. 'However, Shapiro's First Law of Getting Away With It advises against warning policemen off investigating things they didn't know needed investigating until someone warned them off.'

'The whole bloody town's gone mad,' Shapiro said with conviction. They'd gathered in his office at ten on Tuesday morning. He'd had no sleep, and judging from the shadows like bruises under Donovan's eyes neither had the sergeant. Liz alone seemed unaffected. She hadn't had as trying a night as the two men; even so, thought Shapiro irritably, she might have the grace to look tired. 'Ram-raiders,' he enumerated on thick fingers, 'train robbers, a rapist and now a dog-fighting ring. Whatever happened to stealing car radios and mugging old ladies on pension day?'

Even at the end of the twentieth century, Castlemere remained a provincial town with essentially provincial criminals. It wasn't the Vice Capital of anywhere, not even the fens. The local police had had their challenges but they usually came more widely spaced than this.

'How's Mrs Andrews?' asked Liz. She learned of the attack when she came in an hour earlier, still on a high from the success at Mile End. Seeing one of the raiders shot dead in front of her, knowing that her actions would be subject to scrutiny, in no way diminished the satisfaction she felt. But this did: that while she was keeping Brian awake with a blow-by-blow account of how clever she'd been, how clever Donovan had been, how lucky Castlemere was to have them, a decent woman walking home through the centre of town had been dragged under a bush and raped.

Shapiro gave an unhappy shrug. 'I don't know. She wasn't badly hurt; she said she'd be all right; I don't know how she really felt. I was going to ask you to see her sometime but God knows how you'll find the time now.'

Liz took his point. On sheer logistics they were going to be under pressure. 'How do you want to do this?'

'I don't want to pass Mrs Andrews on, even to you – she's had a tough enough time without being messed around now. Will you take the ram-raiders? And as dog-fighting's the sort of milieu in which DS Donovan will pass virtually unnoticed he can have the pit-bulls. All right so far?'

Liz nodded; Donovan said nothing. Standing by the door he matched Shapiro's bent-wood coat-stand for height, build and earnest attention to the proceedings. 'Sergeant?' the superintendent prompted gently.

Donovan blinked, came back from wherever his

mind had wandered. 'Oh – yeah. The dogs. I'll get on to it. What about the train?'

'What about it?'

'Who's dealing with that? We've two guys in the cells, another in the morgue, we've about thirty witness statements to collect – who's doing all that?'

'Me,' Shapiro said glumly. 'I've got Scobie taking statements, and unless the chaps in the cells change their minds they're not going to waste my time on inconsequential chit-chat. Once we get the all-clear over the shooting we can wrap it up. Yesterday's news, Donovan,' he added briskly, 'time to move on to fresh woods and pastures new.'

For a moment Donovan looked about to say something more; then he changed his mind. 'Dogs. I'm on it.'

When the door closed behind him Shapiro said, 'It's shaken him up, hasn't it?'

Liz raised an eyebrow. 'You're surprised? He was that close' – her fingers, all but touching. 'He did a good job there, Frank. I'd like to think those at Division who have him down as a loose cannon might recognize that last night he got a result nobody else here, including you and me, could have. How's the driver?'

'He'll be all right,' said Shapiro. 'It was his heart but they got him to intensive care in time.'

'Also thanks to Donovan.'

Shapiro smiled, the plump cheeks dimpling. 'Yes, all right, Inspector, I've got the message. Now, what about the ram-raiders? Any thoughts on them?'

She considered a moment. 'Well, they didn't show up last night and this morning also passed without incident. The Son of God might sanction another hour or two's surveillance if you ask nicely.' The senior officer at Queen's Street had always been known as God; the recent arrival of a much younger incumbent had somehow called for a new nickname.

Shapiro's expression was rueful. 'I tried already – got a very polite flea in my ear. In short, if I want any more stake-outs I can pay the overtime myself.' He scowled. 'I don't get it. They *should* have gone again by now. What's the problem, is it somebody's birthday?'

Liz refrained from repeating her doubts. 'What we really need is someone on the inside.'

Shapiro raised a quizzical eyebrow. 'Do you fancy your chances undercover, Inspector?'

Liz chuckled. 'If I knew where to find them I'd give it a shot. But I can't get any word on them. Maybe you're right, maybe it is the Tynesiders – that would explain the gossips in The Fen Tiger being as much in the dark as we are.' The hostelry was Castlemere's villains' pub long before the council gentrified the canal basin where it stood. Now weekend sailors brushed shoulders with the local Mafia and never understood the hush that fell when they used the pub phone to report the theft of their outboard motors.

'What about Donovan? Some of his snouts keep their ears pretty close to the ground.'

'Some of Donovan's snouts keep their entire bodies pretty close to the ground! But nobody seems to know much about this. I don't know what more we can do but wait for it to happen again and hope we can respond fast enough to catch them.' Her gaze had dropped disconsolately to the desk-top, lost beneath a week's worth of unfinished paperwork. Now it rose again, speculative. 'Unless we can find the chap in the green fedora. Just for the record, Frank, if we did, how would you feel about an undercover operation? If we could set one up?'

Shapiro was tired, but not tired enough to agree without thinking it through. His eyes narrowed. 'You?'

She shrugged. 'Whoever. In principle, would you approve?'

While he wrestled with it he pulled faces. He looked at Liz. He looked out of the window. He scratched his chin, missing the comfort of a beard to tug enjoyed by millennia of Shapiro men. Finally he said, 'I might. If we could do it cleanly so he wasn't a marked man from day one.'

'A marked man?' Her voice rose delicately on the question mark.

Shapiro smiled wearily. 'Definitely. A woman would stand out like a sore thumb in that sort of set-up. I'm sure there's nothing Donovan could do that you couldn't, but he's twice as likely to be accepted by the gang and four times as likely to be trusted with the sort of information we need. I'm sure you'd make a splendid ram-raider, Liz, but be realistic: your only way in would be as a gangster's moll and nobody'd talk times and routes in front of you.'

'*You* be realistic, Frank,' she retorted, amused, 'I'm fifteen years too old to be a gangster's moll! I take your point; but I wouldn't want Donovan doing it, not with last night still so fresh in his mind. You need a steady hand for undercover work: he needs time to get his nerve back. What about Scobie?'

Shapiro shook his head. 'You also need two brain-cells to rub together. How about Morgan?'

'Maybe. Oh, what's the point discussing it?' she said then impatiently. 'We don't know that the man in the green hat was their look-out, let alone where to find him or how to infiltrate a fifth columnist. Forget I asked; I just can't think what else to do.'

'If it was easy,' Shapiro said gently, 'they'd have got these people in Harrogate, Barnsley, Mansfield, Nottingham or Leamington. We may have to face the possibility that they're too bloody clever for us too.'

Liz was a pragmatist: she knew you couldn't win them all. She could live with that. What galled her was being unable to think up a plan of campaign. She looked away in irritation; when she looked back Shapiro had his eyes closed. 'Frank, you look like death warmed up. Get a few hours' sleep. I'll hold the fort.'

Shapiro opened his eyes and sniffed. 'The reason that senior posts are reserved for older personnel, Inspector, is that having your own office makes it easier to sleep on the job. A couple of hours' catching up on my paperwork and I'll be a new man.'

It was probably a joke, but anyway the chance didn't arise. As Liz was leaving the results on the fingerprints came through. The older of the two men downstairs was Edward Parker, sometime of Leeds; the younger was Martin Ginley of Motherwell; the dead man was Harry Black from Sunderland. Black and Parker had both done time for armed robbery, Ginley had convictions for theft and what used to be called joy-riding until it was noticed how often it led to funerals.

Shapiro scowled. 'Is there nothing left worth nicking in the north any more, that all their blaggers have to come down here?'

He thought that being confronted with their own records might encourage them to open up. But he learned nothing that Donovan hadn't already told him: what happened, who gave the orders, who had the weapons. On the face of it that might have been all there was to tell. But Shapiro knew men, particularly criminals; he knew when he was being lied to, and he knew when he was being told less than the truth. These two were holding something back, and he couldn't think what or why.

Until he was back in his own office, chewing his lip pensively, when Scobie knocked and came in with his arms full of papers and a puzzled expression gathered round his rugby-player's nose. 'Sir?'

'Constable?'

'The hostage, sir. The girl DS Donovan was worried about, who nearly got her throat cut.'

'What about her?'

'I can't find her, sir.'

Shapiro regarded him with more resignation than surprise. 'You mean you've lost her statement?'

'No, sir. She doesn't seem to have made a statement. I didn't take it, nor did Wilson or Morgan. Everyone on the train saw her but nobody remembers seeing her after they left the train. We don't even have a name and address for her.' Scobie watched the superintendent warily, waiting for the explosion.

Instead, slowly, Shapiro began to smile. 'The *cunning* so-and-sos! We all know that a well-prepared criminal is likely to be a successful criminal, but fancy being well enough prepared to bring your own hostage!'

DC Scobie was very good at running after escaping crooks, at bringing them down with a well-timed tackle and bringing tears to their eyes if they attempted to resist arrest. He wasn't as quick on the uptake. 'Sir?'

Shapiro spelled it out. 'She was one of them, Scobie. There weren't three of them, there were four. It was her job to be young, pretty and terrified, and not to struggle or try to escape the way a real hostage might. Black would need all his wits to handle a real hostage, but an accomplice would co-operate. She probably meant to go along when they left the train. But they couldn't take her up the shaft, not realistically; anyway there was no need. As we evacuated the train she slipped away in the dark and we didn't even miss her till now.' He chuckled. 'No wonder the lads downstairs didn't want to talk!'

Unsure what the joke was, Scobie didn't think he'd risk laughing too. 'What do you want me to do, sir?'

'Not a lot you can do, constable, is there? When Sergeant Donovan gets back you could get a full description from him. We'll circulate it, we might get lucky, but it's my guess we'll have to put her down as the one that got away. I doubt we'll see hide or hair of her again.'

Chapter Seven

They stared bellicosely at one another, nose to nose through the wire mesh.

One of them was mostly black with grey brindling on the nose, the broad chest and front legs. The skull was massive and rounded, ragged ears set low on each side. The baleful eyes were oddly triangular, with a prick of reddish light in each. The bolster of muscle that was the neck swelled into the barrel chest without any perceptible join, then narrowed to powerful loins and long, strong back legs. A ratty tail curved up like a scimitar. The grizzled lips fluttered like curtains over yellow tusks and from deep in the muscular throat came a low growl like distant thunder.

The other one said in an Irish accent, 'What do you call him?'

The constable at the kennels was deeply uneasy. He knew he was being pushed into doing something improper, and DS Donovan offering to take full responsibility wouldn't save him if there was trouble. If the dog got loose. If someone reported it. If, God forbid, it bit someone.

Sergeant Barraclough would have had none of it. But Barraclough was on his holidays and Constable Sutton, deputizing for him, laboured under two handicaps. One was the matter of rank. The other was that he owed Donovan a favour for helping him break up a feeding frenzy once when he left a pen unlatched. Others might have helped had they been about at the time but not many would have kept quiet about it afterwards. Donovan never said a word. When asked about the marks on his arms he said, dead-pan, 'Lovebites.'

'He's a stray,' explained Sutton, 'he's going to be put down. He doesn't have a name.'

'Brian Boru,' said Donovan with satisfaction.

Sutton unearthed a collar that would fit him, a lead that looked as if it might hold him and a muzzle big enough to accommodate those startling jaws. 'If anybody asks—' Donovan began; but he didn't finish the sentence.

'Yes?' the constable prompted anxiously.

Donovan thought for a moment longer. 'Lie,' he said then.

He took the dog to a lock-up behind Brick Lane. Then he fetched Billy Dunne out of the public bar of The Fen Tiger. 'Got something to show you.'

When Billy saw Brian Boru the scant natural colour – nocturnal for the most part, the little man didn't get a lot of sun on his skin – vanished from his tarnished cheek. 'Hell fire, Mr Donovan, what's that for?'

'What do you think? I want to match him.'

Billy was into a lot of things that weren't strictly legal. He could always find a ton of bricks that were surplus to requirements, a keg of beer that fell off the back of a lorry, a reconditioned video that the insurers had understood was past repair. He probably broke a law every day of the week, but as long as he kept his head down and his depredations minor he got away with most of them: police time could usually be spent more profitably than trying to trace Billy Dunne's breeze-blocks. It was more practical to use him than to charge him.

The little man backed the length of the lock-up as if the dog hadn't been chained. 'I don't know about that, Mr Donovan, I really don't.'

'Yes you do, Billy,' Donovan said patiently. 'There's dog-fighting going on round here and you know about it. And I want to know where to take him.'

'It's not *like* that, Mr Donovan,' pleaded Billy. 'It's like – a secret society, they don't admit just anyone. They get nasty if they think people are spying on them.'

'What do you think he's for,' snorted Donovan, indicating the dog, 'company? He's my passport. He's not neutered, he's not registered, if he's got a tattoo it's a skull and crossbones on his biceps. He's an illegal pit-bull and he makes me into a sporting man. They'll be happy to see me. Anyway, what's it to you? I'm not asking you to take me, just tell me where they are.'

'It's not *like* that,' Billy whined again. 'They don't advertise. They don't put a notice in the *Courier*.'

Donovan was running out of patience, which was not a thing he had in endless supply. 'If they did I wouldn't be wasting my time with you. If they did, I wouldn't have to remind you there's only a bit of a padlock holding the dog, I've got the key, and I don't know when he last had a square meal.'

Billy thought it was probably a joke. With any other officer of the law he'd have been sure; with Donovan he couldn't quite be. And he didn't have to risk it. 'OK!

OK, Mr Donovan, I'll tell you what I can. Not where they fight – I really don't know that. But I know where they exercise them. You can't give them a run in the park like a spaniel so they take them to the woods beside the river. You know the place? – there's a little car-park.' Donovan knew. 'I don't know if they're there every night, but I reckon if you went about eleven, with the dog, you'd likely meet someone could tell you what you want to know.'

After lunch Liz was at the Magistrate's Court giving evidence in a case of possessing cannabis resin. It wasn't a major drugs bust, eighteen-year-old Peter Cole had enough joints for himself and a few friends, and he'd been selling them on that basis for about what he paid for them. It wasn't an important matter at all, except in one respect. Peter Cole senior thought he could buy his son's acquittal.

He'd hired himself the smartest barrister in Castlemere, he'd lined up experts to testify to the defendant's intellectual and scholastic accomplishments, and he'd persuaded one of the group of friends to say that he'd bought the joints and was offering them to Cole. As a juvenile selling drugs to an adult the boy would get off more lightly than an adult convicted of selling to a juvenile.

The only obstacle to this convenient arrangement was that Liz had seen the exchange by the gates of Castle High when she'd been collecting her husband from school one afternoon. She saw who had the joints, who had the money, who ended up with what. Even if the subsequent deal suited both parties she was damned if she was going to watch one daft lad accept the lasting burden of another's conviction for the sake of a new mountain bike.

'Mr Fenton, I know what I saw,' she said calmly, for about the fourth time. 'I knew what I was seeing at the time, and nothing that the defendant, his father or anyone else has said since makes me doubt the evidence of my eyes. Peter was selling, the younger boy was buying.'

'Then you're saying that they're lying,' said Dan Fenton, the light of battle in his eyes – as if this were personal, as if he weren't merely saying what he was paid to, as if he and the police witness hadn't danced till the small hours at the Civic Ball last Christmas. 'That the witnesses who've come here to give evidence before His Worship are telling lies!'

'*Yes*, Mr Fenton,' she said in barely restrained exasperation, as if he were an inattentive pupil who'd just that moment grasped what she was saying.

'And can you suggest, Inspector Graham, why they should do such a thing?'

From the eminence of the witness box she looked down her nose at him. 'I can conceive of a reason, Mr Fenton, yes. But as I have no evidence, perhaps I should limit my testimony to those things I have seen with my own eyes.'

The Magistrates, at least, found her account convincing. She was leaving the court-house with a satisfied smile when she heard a quick tread on the steps behind her and turned. It was Gail Fisher from the *Castlemere Courier*, absent without leave from the Press table. So it was a matter of some urgency. 'I need a quick word – and for once it's me that wants to go off the record.'

Liz smiled. Castlemere police enjoyed a useful relationship with the local paper and the two women had much in common. They didn't agree on everything but rarely argued on important matters. 'How can I help?'

'I heard there was a rape in town last night.'

Caution dropped a veil in front of Liz's face. She considered the implications before saying anything. Then: 'Off the record? Yes. But we're not ready to say anything official yet. I'll call you as soon as we are.'

'Fair enough,' said Fisher. She was a few years younger than Liz, a dramatically attractive woman with a mass of curly dark hair and a liking for long dark gypsy skirts. Many reporters still working for provincial weeklies in their thirties have given up hope of getting anything better. But Gail Fisher had been to Fleet Street – Wapping, actually – didn't like it and came back. The *Courier* was lucky to have her. 'Really, I'm not wanting a story from you. I want to tell you one.'

'Go on.'

'It's not the first time. A friend of mine—' She looked up with a wide-mouthed grin. 'I know what that usually means, but honestly, it wasn't me, it was a friend of mine. She was working late in her office about a week ago. The place should have been empty, but as she locked up someone jumped her in the corridor.'

Liz was staring at her. 'Why don't I know anything about this?'

Fisher shrugged. 'Because that was how she wanted it. He had a scarf over his face, she couldn't even make an intelligent guess at his age. Grey sweats, white trainers, that's all she saw: she didn't see how you could find him from that and she couldn't have identified him if you did. She wasn't prepared to go through the extra trauma of a medical examination, police questioning, maybe her identity coming out, when she couldn't see how it would do any good. She picked herself up, went home, had a long bath and a stiff drink, and then she called me.'

'You could have called me.' Liz's tone was of mild reproof; inside she was fighting anger.

'No,' said Fisher. 'It was a matter of trust – I promised I wouldn't.'

'Then why are you telling me now? I can talk to her, but it's too late to do anything useful.'

'I don't want you to talk to her. I'm not going to tell you her name or where she works except that it's in the Mere Basin redevelopment. But if it's happened before it'll happen again. Once could be random, twice is a habit. I thought you needed to know that.'

'I needed to know a week ago! I needed to know when there was a chance of finding him before another woman got jumped. It's already too late for that.'

Fisher spread an apologetic hand. 'I didn't feel I had any choice. My friend had been raped once – forcing her to report it would be like raping her again.'

Liz nodded slowly, letting the anger go. 'Is she all right?'

Fisher gave an unhappy shrug. 'I don't know. She's on the pill, which is something to be grateful for. I want her to test for sexually transmitted diseases: she says she'll go in a day or two but keeps not doing. She's trying to pretend nothing happened; or rather, that what happened wasn't so terrible after all. She says she's had sex with men she didn't know much better, and she's had sex that hurt more. She says it doesn't matter. She was back at work the next day, but she's scared to death he'll corner her again.'

'Would she talk to me – like this, informally?'

'I don't know. I'll ask.'

'What's she like? No,' Liz added quickly, seeing Fisher about to shake her head, 'I'm not trying to work out who she is, only if there's something particular this man's looking for. The victim last night was early forties, fair, well built, single, a successful business-woman. Is your friend anything like that?'

The reporter's eyes widened. 'Inspector, my friend is *exactly* like that.'

Donovan borrowed a van, chained Brian Boru in the back. It was the only way he felt safe taking his eyes off the dog.

At eleven-fifteen that night the little car-park in the wood overlooking the water meadows of the River Arrow was not a hive of illicit activity. There were just two vehicles there. But that was two more than might have been expected, and neither of them was beating out the rhythm of the Lovers' Lane Rock. One was another van, the second a grey saloon with a small trailer attached.

With the dog on a long rope and a powerful torch in his other hand, Donovan followed the footpath into the trees. The utter darkness of the wood made the torch essential; otherwise he'd have brought a pick-axe handle.

They'd been wandering around for half an hour, wrapping the rope round trees and snarling at one another, and Donovan was about to head back and try another night when shadows moved at the edge of his sight and a man and a dog stepped on to the path in front of him.

A shudder of pure atavistic fear coursed through Donovan's body, as if the devil and his familiar were abroad in the wood that night. He couldn't tell how big the man was, only that he was solid with it; but the dog came halfway up his thigh, a swollen mass of bone and muscle under a coat that rippled in the torch-light. They stood immobile, blocking the path, while Donovan stared and Brian Boru drew himself up to his full impressive stature. The vibration of the challenge in his throat travelled the rope to Donovan's hand. He flicked the torch upwards.

The man covered his face, gestured peremptorily, and Donovan remembered his manners and dropped the beam. 'Sorry.'

''S all right,' the man said, amiably enough. 'Only, people get a bit twitchy, you know?'

'Not as twitchy as me,' growled Donovan. 'I keep expecting the frigging Dog Police to leap out of the trees.'

The man chuckled. 'You haven't been here before, have you?'

Donovan shook his head. 'The poor sod's been living in a lock-up. Somebody told me I could bring him here without being bothered.'

'Right enough. But that's no kind of exercise, dragging him round on a rope. Let him run, that's what I do. They can't do much damage out here.'

Looking again, Donovan realized the brute beside him had neither a lead nor a muzzle. He shivered. 'You don't know Brian. He's a desperate dog for a fight. He'll fight his own shadow if there's nothing else going. I like the dog, you know, but I wouldn't trust him an inch.'

'Brian?' The man laughed. 'That's not much of a name for a fighting dog.'

'Brian Boru,' said Donovan indignantly. 'How's your Irish history?'

'Bit of a sporting gent, was he?'

'There was nothing sporting about it. He killed Vikings, as many as he could, any way he could. Nowadays they'd call him the Butcher of Clontarf and take up a collection for disabled Norsemen. But when it's a matter of kill or be killed you have to admire the guy who does it best. It's like the dogs: you can't blame a dog for fighting when it's in his nature.'

'Right enough.' The man fell into step beside Donovan, his dog pacing silently at his heel. Donovan kept Brian's leash short. 'Dogs like these, a good scrap's the best exercise they can have. Did you ever think . . .?'

They walked back to the car-park. The van was gone; the other man put his dog into the trailer. 'Do you have a name?'

'Duggan,' said Donovan. 'Hugh Duggan.'

'First names are enough. 'I'm Mick.' He patted the trailer. 'And he's Thor. Listen. If I hear anything, should I let you know?'

'Oh, yeah,' said Donovan with conviction.

Chapter Eight

'Two rapes with a week between,' said Liz, stirring her coffee vengefully. 'That isn't a habit, it's a compulsion. It won't be long before he tries again.'

'I said that about the ram-raiders.' Shapiro sniffed. 'I'm still hiding round corners to avoid the Son of God.'

Superintendent Giles was not merely twelve years younger than his predecessor, he was a different kind of policeman. He had two degrees. He was computer literate. It was he who found the funding to stake out nine different premises when Shapiro was sure the ram-raiders would strike on Monday evening, and again when he revised that to Tuesday morning. Every time Shapiro met his cool blue gaze he saw pound signs clocking up.

Liz didn't feel like smiling. She wasn't angry with Shapiro: she was still angry with Gail Fisher and her friend, and even that was a kind of referred anger because she didn't know the man she was really angry with. She didn't subscribe to the Victorian view that it was a fate worse than death, but she had better reasons than sisterly solidarity for considering rape a peculiarly vicious offence.

It was a crime perpetrated exclusively by stronger people on weaker ones, as distasteful as a grown man beating a child or a strong one a cripple. Additionally, it tainted a special gift of joy. Like the Bad Fairy, the rapist waved a wand over something meant to be an abiding pleasure and turned it to gall. It wasn't like stealing a woman's purse. It was like stealing her purse, and coming back to steal it again every time she tried to open it for maybe the rest of her life. When it came to rape, Liz had no sense of humour.

'We have to find him,' she said flatly. 'Whatever it costs, we have to stop him.'

'I agree. But is money the answer? With unlimited funding, how would you have saved Mrs Andrews from being raped? You could turn Castlemere into a police state and still not be able to guarantee women's safety from molestation. Even a curfew wouldn't have saved the woman in the office block. It's easy to say that prevention's better than cure but mostly it can't be done. Usually the best we can do is catch those responsible for crimes and hope to restrict their opportunities to reoffend. There'll never be an entirely safe society; and what's more, there never was.'

Liz banged down her empty cup. 'No? Well, consider this. If there was anything out there as dangerous to men as men are to women, the army would be brought in to wipe it out.'

He understood her anger but Shapiro was concerned that it was clouding her judgement. He said quietly, 'And you think of this. The groups at greatest risk of violence in our society aren't women at all. Small children suffer the greatest number of attacks in the home, and young men the greatest number in the street. If you had a son of twenty and a daughter of twenty-one walking home late at night, the girl isn't the one you'd need to worry about.'

For a moment Liz went on eyeing him hotly; then she looked away. The annoying thing was, she knew he was right. 'You think I'm over-reacting.'

'No,' he said honestly. 'How can you over-react to something like this! But we need to focus on the right problem. It's nothing to do with sex. It's about dominance. Rapists are men attacking women because that's how the biology works. But the problem isn't that men can rape women, it's that a few men want to: that the urge to violence occasionally expresses itself that way. Rape isn't an excess of love but a burgeoning of hatred. Rapists don't want what they take, that's only an excuse; if there were no women to rape they'd victimize someone else. What they want is to hurt – physically, mentally, emotionally. All they really want from you is your pain.'

When she first worked for Shapiro, when he was a detective inspector and she a sergeant, Liz was always being made aware of how much he knew that she didn't. It happened less now, partly because she'd made a point of listening then, but still often enough to remind her that though she had her own strengths she didn't have his profound understanding of human nature. She still listened when Shapiro talked because there was still a lot he could teach her.

'All right,' she conceded with a flicker of grace, 'I'll try not to besmirch half the human race with the sins of a minority if you'll think of some way to catch the sod.'

'We're waiting for the results of the DNA test. That may come up trumps.'

Liz eyed him askance. 'If he's done it before, and been caught. But if he's done it before it was somewhere else, and if he's a local man he's only just started and won't be on file. DNA's a long shot.'

Shapiro felt the burden of her expectation. 'Without a description it's still probably the best we have. Unless . . .' On second thoughts he decided not to say it.

Liz finished for him, her lips tight. 'Unless he does it again, and this time he drops his driving licence. Frank, we could go through an awful lot of victims before he does something that stupid. We need to force the pace, push him into making a mistake. What about a decoy?'

Shapiro recoiled as if she'd offered him a bag of pork scratchings. 'To catch a rapist? You're on dangerous ground there, girl. This is a hit-and-run expert, remember. If there's anyone close enough to protect the decoy he won't strike. And if you move the cover back to where he isn't aware of them, he'll be in and out before they can reach her.' He winced. 'If you'll pardon the expression.'

'She'll have two massive advantages over the previous victims,' Liz pressed. 'She'll be ready for it, watching and listening for his first move. And she'll be a policewoman. We're better at self-defence than the average building society manageress.'

The pause meant Shapiro was considering it. He didn't like it but there weren't many options. Doing nothing but hoping for the best was one; this was the other. Finally he said, 'Even in a blonde wig, Wilson's too young and too small to fit the profile. Cathy Flynn would look the part but I don't know how she'd react if he took the bait. Besides, I don't think she'd volunteer, and I'm not ordering anyone to do that. Who's left? We're not exactly knee deep in good-looking blonde Whoopsies aged about forty who can handle themselves in a scrap.' Women Police Constables labour under a variety of nicknames up and down the country. 'Whoopsies' is one of the less pejorative.

'Who says it has to be a Whoopsie?'

'*Donovan* in a blonde wig?' The idea was enough to freeze the conversation in its tracks.

Liz recovered first, shaking the image out of her eyes like soapy water. '*Me,* Frank. I haven't met your Mrs Andrews but from your description, and Fisher's description of her friend, I'm the obvious choice. I'm the same age, build and colouring – if he went for them he'll go for me.'

But he wouldn't agree there and then. He wanted to think about it. Even if he were persuaded he'd need to get approval: Giles held the purse-strings. After the earlier fiascos, clutched might be a better word.

She got home a little after seven. Her husband was in the kitchen washing sugar-beet and flaked maize off his hands. Every morning Liz prepared three buckets of feed for her mare, and if she wasn't there at the appropriate times Brian would deliver them to the stable behind the house. It was the limit of his involvement with the horse, and it took Liz three years to persuade him to do that much.

It wasn't that he didn't like animals. He had a definite fondness for cats. But horses, with their unfathomable thought processes and instantaneous reactions, their iron feet and their sheer size, frightened him. It was in vain for Liz to point out that Polly was a middle-aged lady of sedate good manners, and that the appearance of a bucket was in any event a guarantee of good behaviour. Instead she bought a manger that hooked over the door and could be filled from outside the stable.

She put her arms round his middle and laid her cheek against his back, feeling his bones through his shirt. 'Good day at the chalk-face?'

'3b,' he said wearily, 'have just discovered nipples.' He taught art. Though his pupils ranged from eleven-year-olds to A-level students of nineteen it was always 3b that gave him trouble. Nipples, fig-leaves and those bits of voile, unexplained by the context, that floated in front of classical nudes at strategic moments. As 2b they were too shy to comment; as 4b they were too cool. But every year 3b stumbled on nipples with the thrill of Marilyn Monroe discovering updraughts. 'You?'

'Not very.' She turned him in the compass of her arms so that she could see his face. There was nothing remarkable about it. It was intelligent, kind and sensitive, and boasted a forehead that went most of the way back to his collar. Men who wouldn't have stood a chance if a freak nuclear accident in Market Harborough wiped out most of the male population couldn't see what a good-looking woman like Liz Graham saw in a balding art teacher; and wouldn't have believed that the answer was as simple as love if she'd told them. 'We need to talk about it. There's something I want to do, and I think maybe you have a right to be consulted.'

When he realized what she was proposing his first instinct was to stop her somehow. Not to forbid her, he knew he couldn't do that, he knew by trying he risked more than she was planning to, but by asking her, begging if he had to. His blood ran cold at the very idea.

But he'd been married to her for ten years, knew how important this was to her. She hadn't made detective inspector by pulling flashy stunts, she'd done it by hard work and professionalism. She hadn't dreamed this up on the drive home, she'd thought it through and believed it was the best way to trap a dangerous man who would otherwise remain free. That didn't put Graham's mind at rest, but it told him two things. That if she did it she'd do it properly, with all the support she needed. And that if she didn't do it, because of him, she'd think less of him.

He didn't dare ask how risky it could be. 'How safe can you make it?'

Proud of him, her smile was warm. 'Safer than points duty on market day; safer than clearing a pitch invasion after a four-one drubbing by Rochdale; about the same risk factor as going through Donovan's desk without wearing rubber gloves.'

But he didn't want humour, he wanted the truth. 'Seriously.'

Liz nodded, chastened. She owed him honesty. 'Pretty safe. I'll have a radio so I can have back-up within twenty seconds. If I can hold on to him for twenty seconds the thing's finished, he's behind bars, he can't harm anyone else.'

'What makes you think he'll go for it? I mean, why you? There must be dozens of attractive forty-year-old blondes in Castlemere. How do you catch his eye?'

'We look at what he's done already. Both times he

chose a semi-public place – if either woman had made enough noise she'd have been heard. So maybe the risk of being caught is part of the thrill. Also, he wants a certain type of victim, not just any woman who crosses his path. We can use that. I thought we'd start at Mere Basin. We don't know just where the first attack took place, but he was in one of the office blocks after normal hours so maybe he works there. If so he may notice another forty-year-old blonde coming and going late at night.'

'And if he takes the bait?'

'I yell, and Donovan and Scobie and Morgan dash up and sit on him.'

'You make it sound you couldn't possibly get hurt.'

She was holding his hand, her fingers woven with his. 'You can always get roughed up in this job, you know that. Mostly it's black eyes, occasionally a broken nose.' That took him back: she'd had a plaster over her nose the night he asked her to marry him. He hadn't meant to propose, not quite then, but that plaster brought out his nurturing instincts. 'It's pretty rare for anything to go further awry than that.'

'But it could happen.'

'With three large policemen watching my every move? No. We won't let it get that far out of hand.'

Brian Graham didn't like it any more than Shapiro had done, for some of the same reasons. He didn't give a damn about the overtime budget but he didn't want his wife putting herself in danger. Even a carefully controlled danger; even in a good cause.

On the other hand, every policeman's wife in the country saw him off to work feeling the same way, and Brian doubted if many of them were invited to say how many risks of what nature they should take in the course of their work. He appreciated being asked – she didn't have to do that, she could have said nothing until it was over.

'Donovan. And Scobie's the one with the nose?' His shudder was real enough. 'I don't know what effect they'll have on the enemy, but by God they frighten me.'

Quoting the Duke of Wellington was about the closest Brian came to machismo. His courage took quieter forms; like saying yes to something that filled him with dread when he could have said no. Liz's gaze on his face was fond. 'Brian Graham, you're a star.'

A few minutes later the phone went. When she came back anticipation was warring in her eyes with a little anxiety, and winning. 'That was Frank. We're on.'

Chapter Nine

That night, and again the following night, as the clock in Castle Place struck twelve, she drove under the iron archway and down the steep ramp into Mere Basin. Four canals met in the heart of Castlemere and a six-storey warehouse had been built over each of them on black brick vaults high enough to accommodate a narrowboat chimney and not much more. In recent years the Victorian warehouses had been redeveloped as shops, offices and apartments, and very pleasant it was when sunshine poured through the great square well of the buildings on to the peaty water and gaily-painted boats.

At midnight, however, the shops were shut and the offices were dark and all that could be seen of the two hundred people who lived there were cars parked in the basement garages and the glow of a few lights behind drawn curtains high up in the buildings. It wasn't quite enough to send shivers up the spine, but nor was it the obvious spot for a woman on her own to walk a dog.

In fact Liz was not on her own. Secreted about the Basin were DS Donovan and DCs Scobie and Morgan. Donovan was (of course) on a boat, Scobie was in a car and Morgan was in a little striped tent where the gas company had had the pipes up. To a casual eye the place was deserted.

Except for the tall fair woman with the little white dog who parked her car under The Barbican and walked unhurriedly beneath the building and out towards Broad Wharf. There were lights on the tow-path, but Broad Wharf was where they ended. Under the last of them she leaned against a bollard for a few minutes; then she turned round and wandered back. She did this on Tuesday night, and again on Wednesday night, by which time she was heartily sick of the little white dog she'd borrowed; and she didn't attract so much as a wolf-whistle.

On Thursday morning she found a summons from Superintendent Giles on her desk. She knew what he was going to say but she still didn't have an answer.

He was about her age, tall and slender and fair; like a recruiting sergeant for the Hitler Youth, someone remarked nastily when he first arrived. He greeted Liz politely and waited for her to take a seat before asking, 'Any luck at the Basin last night?'

There was only one reply possible. 'No, sir, not so far.'

His smile had a distant quality; not because he was an unkind man, more because the bias of his skills was administrational rather than personal. He liked the words 'organization' and 'method': it was impossible to swap a casual remark with him on the stairs without one or other coming into it. 'The thing is, Mrs Graham, we need results to justify the expenditure. I can't keep four detectives tied up for an hour every night when the only benefit is that Miss Tunstall gets her dog walked.' Miss Tunstall was his secretary.

'It's like any other kind of fishing,' Liz said apologetically. 'All you can do is bait the hook. You can't make the fish jump.'

'Do you know,' murmured Superintendent Giles, 'Mr Shapiro said exactly the same thing about his ram-raiders? Any sign of them yet?'

Liz exercised restraint. 'Not so far as I know, sir.'

'No,' he said thoughtfully. To be fair, he wasn't blaming her. He was responsible for making the best use of police resources, both human and financial: in his position she'd have been getting twitchy too. 'A difficult job, drawing out a rapist. When you've only a loose idea of where he might be and none at all of who he is. Well, you did your best, but I think we have to leave it there for now. Of course, if there's another incident and we have more to go on . . .'

Liz made a last effort, knowing as she did that it wouldn't sway him. 'Another incident means another victim. A woman who's been raped can't make good the loss with a cheque from the insurance company.'

'I do realize that,' Giles said, a shade frostily because it shouldn't have occurred to her that he needed telling. He was aware that he had yet to gain the full confidence of these people. They were polite enough, at least to his face, but somehow related to him as if he were not another police officer. As if he were an accountant. 'I don't think you've been wasting your time, Mrs Graham, I think you were right to try. But we can't go on forever. If we can narrow down some of the variables we'll try again.'

She wished she could argue, or even feel sure that he was wrong. Resignedly she nodded. 'Sir.'

Scobie and Morgan were plainly relieved though

they affected disappointment for Liz's sake. Donovan heard her in silence, his narrow face impervious. When she'd finished he looked idly out of the window and, apparently changing the subject, said, 'I've got a dog.'

Liz blinked. 'Have you? How nice.'

'Well, I'm looking after it. Mean big bastard; needs some walking.'

'Yes?'

'Thought I might start taking him up the tow-path every night. Say, about midnight, after everyone's gone home.'

Liz felt herself beginning to smile. 'Sounds a good idea. I quite like a walk about then myself. Perhaps I'll see you around.'

'Maybe not,' he said. 'But I'll be there.'

That evening when he went to feed Brian Boru he found a note under the garage door. It was short on detail but told him all he needed to know. 'Tonight, same time, same place.' There was no signature.

Donovan perched on the work-bench like a dyspeptic vulture, watching the dog. It ate as if against the clock, as if something even bigger and nastier might come along at any moment.

He was planning his next move. To keep the rendezvous, obviously; that was why he'd borrowed the dog in the first place. But alone? With back-up? – remembering that Shapiro wasn't yet aware of his line of inquiry? With the dog? – knowing that without him he'd probably be turned back but if he was there he might have to fight? Brian Boru was not a family pet, but being a thug didn't mean he could hold his own against professionals. His opponents would be fitter, better trained, expertly handled. Brian Boru had only his natural savagery, and in class company it wouldn't be enough. Donovan was aware that if he took him he might have to watch him torn apart. He wasn't a nice dog, but that was a bad end.

Ultimately though it didn't come down to how nice Brian was, or even how nice Donovan was. The dog was his entry to a vicious subculture. He was risking his own neck, and even if he'd liked the dog he wouldn't have prized its skin above his own. Without a dog he'd get nowhere. The animal faced destruction anyway: Donovan thought it likely, if there was any way to ask, that he'd sooner go down fighting than submit to the kindly humiliation of euthanasia.

But taking the dog meant going alone. What he was proposing was illegal. It might be possible to get clearance, in the way that Drugs Squad were allowed to use proscribed substances in their operations, but he couldn't get it before eleven. If he asked Shapiro he'd be told to wait.

Inspector Graham, on the other hand, owed him a favour. If he could cover her unofficial activities she could cover his. He went home to call her from the narrowboat where he lived on the canal.

Even as she answered, though, he thought better of it. Asking favours of a senior officer was a minefield. If she thought he was too far out of line she'd pull him up short. She had to: once she knew what he intended she had to either approve or forbid it. Better if she didn't know.

With an ease born of practice he moved into lie mode. 'Sorry to bother you at home, boss, but I'm going to be out late tonight – I don't know how late but probably till tomorrow. Can we walk the dogs some other time?'

She didn't suspect. 'Yes, fine. I wouldn't mind turning in at a decent hour for once.'

Donovan drove the van out into The Levels, making for the wood beside the river. The van was no more his than the dog was, but there's only one way to carry a dog on a motorcycle and he'd no intentions of stuffing Brian Boru inside his jacket. Before he got there two men in a car waved him over. 'Follow us.' Over the next several minutes they became a small convoy of vehicles, mostly large battered cars with a few large smart ones among them. Once when they paused someone walked back to check he had a dog. If he'd left Brian in the garage his inquiry would have ended in the ditch beside the road.

He tried to remember the way but they wove from lane to lane across The Levels and when they finally pulled into a yard beside a big barn they could have been anywhere inside a five-mile circle.

Mick strolled over, Thor beside him now restrained by a lead as thick as his thumb. He nodded at the back of Donovan's van. 'You brought him then.'

In these surroundings edginess came naturally. 'I don't know about this. Some of these dogs'd make light work of a buffalo!'

Pleased, Mick chuckled. 'Don't worry about the heavyweights – that's Thor's class, nobody'd expect a novice to face them. The freshers fight one another while they learn the game. If he's no taste for it you can take him home and no harm done.'

A shade reassured, Donovan patted Brian Boru's shoulder – twice, before Brian made it clear he should stop. 'He's a desperate dog but I wouldn't want to lose him.'

'No danger, not at this point. Dogs get killed in the big money matches, but to start with the only people interested are the owners and maybe a talent scout or two. If the dog handles himself you might get an offer for him.'

'I couldn't sell him,' Donovan said hastily; which was true enough because he didn't own him. 'Show me what happens.'

They pushed through the gathering crowd of men and dogs. Inside the barn were a number of wooden structures. At one end there were two of them, roped together from sheep hurdles – they could have been calf pens or any other small unit of agricultural containment. 'That's where they try the freshers,' said Mick.

'Freshers?'

'Freshmen – novices.' The man grinned. 'Stupid, isn't it? I don't know if they call them that everywhere.'

In the other half of the barn was a ring about four metres across, built like a section of a giant barrel, chest-high vertical lathes locked together by broad metal bands. Looking closer Donovan saw it was made in four pieces that bolted together – so it could be dismantled and taken between venues, he supposed. Any farmer could provide a few hurdles and a barn but the ring was custom-made and could have no other purpose. It was the pit that gave the pit-bull terrier its name.

Stout chains ran along the sides of the barn with shackles to which the dogs were being tied. Close-coupling prevented them from tearing one another apart for no profit, but nothing could stop them trading threats. As the barn filled the furious barking made conversation a matter of hands cupped round ears. But Donovan noticed an odd thing. The most noise came from the young dogs. The scarred old pros eyed each other in speculative silence, saving their energy for when it would do them most good.

Mick reappeared. 'Bring the dog, I've got him a match.'

Somehow, Donovan hadn't expected to have to go through with this. He'd thought he could use the dog as a passport but avoid fighting him. He'd expected to have a little time to see how things worked, maybe spot a few faces in the crowd, before having to commit himself. Being taken in hand like this was a stroke of luck for a genuine novice but the last thing that Donovan needed. 'Er . . .'

Mick gave his amiable grin again. 'Don't panic, I told you, he won't get hurt. Just a taste for both of you, see if you like it. Same for the other dog – it's his first night too. I've got a fiver on you for luck.'

If there'd been a way out he'd have taken it. But he couldn't leave for the chaos of vehicles in the yard, and a choice between fighting Brian on equal terms and having the crap kicked out of him by angry men faced with the loss of their money, their dogs and their freedom was no choice at all. 'What do we do?'

There was nothing squeamish about Cal Donovan. A childhood on a smallholding in a gritty little mid-Ulster town – it would have been called a village anywhere else in the British Isles – left him with few expectations and finding himself alone at the age of nineteen killed those too. He'd come to England with his brother in the early eighties after losing their parents and sister to a bomb in a chipshop. Within two years Padraig too was dead, taking second prize in a drag-race between a Metropolitan police car and a stolen Porsche. Padraig always wanted to be a policeman while Caolan seemed destined for other things. The Donovans were never mentioned in Glencurran now without someone observing that it's funny how things turn out and someone else muttering about dead men's shoes.

So Donovan had seen things most people hadn't and been involved in things most people only read about, and if they hadn't made him callous he had at least learned pragmatism. Fresh teeth-marks in Brian Boru's bull neck seemed a small enough price for safeguarding his own.

But he wasn't prepared for the undiluted savagery of the next several minutes.

The average dog-fight in the park over who found a bone first is high on sound, fury and flying fur and low on actual damage. By the time the terrified and embarrassed owners have prised the protagonists apart it can be quite hard to find who bit who where.

This was different. For one thing the handlers – not the owners but two men experienced in the job – far from breaking up the fight were encouraging it. Before they released them the animals were foaming with rage, their eyes bulging redly, their muscles knotted. When they were slipped, to a rumble of almost sexual excitement from the men gathered round, they met like clashing armies and the flash of their scimitar teeth through the flying spit, and a little later the flying blood, was like a battle with fixed bayonets.

For a short time neither contender had a clear advantage. They came together like Sumo wrestlers, their combined weight enough to snap a plank when they hit one of the hurdles. The vast jaws snapped and locked and disengaged and snapped again, and but for the fact that the other dog was fawn Donovan would have lost track of which head belonged to which.

After a few minutes' frenzied sparring the contest began to favour Brian Boru. He was no heavier than the other dog, might have been rather taller; mostly what he had was the desire to win. Match fighting, as distinct from the bare-knuckle stuff any dog high on testosterone can try his paw at in any back-alley, was a new experience. But he learned quickly and within minutes had the fawn dog on the defensive, an hysterical note creeping into its barking as it gave ground.

A minute after that a streak of blood appeared on its neck. 'That it then?' said Donovan tersely, readying the lead he could have moored his boat with.

'Not yet,' said Mick, amused. 'Got to give the other chap a chance to get his own back. He might just be a slow learner.'

In fact the fawn dog was a fast learner, had soon realized that being a hard man in the ginnels of The Jubilee didn't qualify him to go head to head with a genuine if untutored talent. He backed round the makeshift pit as quick as he could. Only the fear of exposing his flank stopped him turning tail.

'Ah, jeez,' said Donovan disgustedly, 'what more do you want? He's beat, take him home.'

Mick raised an eyebrow at the other owner. 'Is that what you want – to chuck in the towel? He might still come good.'

He was an older man than Donovan, shorter but powerfully built, a man who worked with his muscles and liked his dog to do the same. But he was as new to this as his animal. He eyed Mick uncertainly. 'You reckon?'

'Sure. He's not getting hurt – I'd give him a bit longer.'

'All right then,' said the man doubtfully.

It may have been the sound of his owner's voice that distracted the fawn dog. He turned aside, looking for a way out. Instead he gave Brian a way in. In an instant the black dog hurled him down, great jaws closing vice-like on flesh and bone, worrying it like worrying a shoe. The fawn dog screamed.

Donovan had Mick by the shirt-front. 'Stop it. Now.'

Mick's eyes flared. 'I'm not going in there!'

Donovan grabbed one of the handlers. The man was leaning on the hurdle, watching the mayhem with every sign of enjoyment. Blood sprayed in a fine arc, spattering his face. It also spattered Donovan's but there was no time to wipe it off. He dug his fingers hard into the man's arm and shouted over the baying of beasts and men. 'Break it up! Before he kills him!'

The man shook him off, unconcerned. He explained like explaining to a child: 'This is what it's about.'

Donovan had a great strength and a great weakness. His strength was that if something needed doing enough he would do it without thought for the possible consequences to himself. His weakness was the same. Almost before he'd decided to, certainly before he knew how or why, he had his leather jacket wrapped around his left arm. The thick lead doubled in his right hand like a truncheon, he vaulted the side of the pit. 'Brian, you bastard, that's enough!'

He expected the dog to round on him, hoped a mouthful of leather would hold him long enough to grab his collar. He hoped its owner would then have the guts to rescue the injured dog. He hoped he'd do it quickly because he didn't know how long he'd be able to hold the blood-crazed Brian Boru.

But Brian didn't go for him, was satisfied with the quarry he had. When Donovan tried to drag him off he found himself hauling at two dogs, the second gripped in the teeth of the first. The fawn dog was on his back now, wailing as Brian chewed on his throat.

In the end Donovan wrapped the short lead round Brian's neck and twisted, tightening it until Brian ran out of air and his eyes glazed. Even then it looked like he'd die with his teeth in his opponent's throat rather than let go. But the mist got into his eyes and his brain, and finally he gave a little choking grunt and shook his head, the fawn dog falling from his loosening jaws. Donovan wasted no time fussing over either of them. He had the muzzle on Brian's bloody face before the dog had a chance to recover his wits.

There was blood everywhere: on the fawn dog's throat and belly, on Brian's face and chest, on Donovan's hands and on his clothes. Deep scratches laced his wrists – not from Brian's teeth, but from the other dog's claws as it fought for its life. Its owner was in the pit now, trying to get his dog up. 'I think his leg's broke.'

'Then bloody well carry him,' Donovan panted savagely. 'And bloody well look after him, or I'll be round your place some night when you're not expecting it and I won't be alone.' He jerked the thick lead meaningfully.

It was an empty threat but the man didn't know that. He couldn't carry the dog alone. He organized some help to take it out to his car.

Donovan was still panting – with reaction, fury and deep humiliation at what he found himself party to – trying not to hate the strutting dog beside him who'd done no more than he'd been asked to, when a light tenor voice at his elbow said, 'I like that. I like a man who cares about the dogs. They're not machines, they deserve to be looked after, even in defeat. Did they hurt you?'

'I'm all right,' Donovan said wearily, turning to see who he was talking to. The man's face meant nothing to him, he didn't think they'd ever met. He was a slightly built individual with a pointed face and curly brown hair, probably rather older than he first appeared – mid forties maybe. A pleasant manner for such an unpleasant gathering. An owner? Or maybe a punter; he had a dog with him but it wasn't a fighting dog, not on that lead. Donovan's eyes followed the pale blue shoe-string down from the man's wrist to his pet.

And the little dog, naked except for an effusive topknot and a tassel at the end of its tail, gave Donovan a disdainful yawn, revealing toothless gums.

At seven on Friday morning Liz walked down to the stable, kissed Polly on the nose, then went into the adjoining storeroom to prepare the three buckets and two haynets that would fend off starvation for another day.

Fifteen minutes later she let herself quietly into the kitchen. Brian was still asleep upstairs and she trod softly to avoid disturbing him. She went to the phone and called Shapiro at home.

She must have woken him because he sounded woolly and disorganized for a moment. 'Liz? What time is it?'

'Seven-fifteen,' she said carefully. 'Frank, will you come over? Now?'

That got his brain moving. His voice over the phone was both sharp and concerned. 'What's the matter, Liz? What's happened?'

She didn't answer directly. 'And will you organize a team? SOCO, Dr Greaves – anyone you can think of. Oh,' she added as a fresh thought struck her, 'and did we ever get round to doing what the Son of God said and designating a rape victim support officer?' She began to laugh. At least, it was mostly laughter, though Shapiro could hear something like despair sobbing in the depths of it. 'Oh, Jesus, Frank – it wasn't me, was it?'

Part Two

Chapter Ten

It was four in the morning before the dog-match broke up. Donovan got Brian Boru back to the garage by half-past-five, swabbed both of them with disinfectant, then removed the muzzle and fed the dog. He tucked in like a new Lonsdale Belt taking breakfast for the cameras.

'Make the most of it, champ,' muttered Donovan, 'your fifteen minutes of fame have been and gone.' He intended Brian Boru would never set foot in a fighting pit again. He didn't have to: he'd already achieved all that was required of him. He left the dog to enjoy his victory meal, cutting through the entry that took him home.

At six o'clock it was too late to go to bed and still get to work at a decent hour; instead he made a hot drink and took it into *Tara*'s saloon. He kicked his shoes off and dropped on to one of the long couches to review the night's events. The next thing he knew it was ten o'clock and he had congealed cocoa among the bloodstains on his shirt.

Late or not, he was looking forward to seeing Shapiro. He parked his bike in the back yard and took the steps two at a time, so intent on his mission that he hardly noticed who was on duty downstairs. 'Chief in his office?'

The title was an anachronism now but everyone knew who he meant. 'No.'

Then the atmosphere hit Donovan like a forearm in the kidneys, making him break his step. His eyes filled with alarm. 'What's happened?'

Sergeant Tulliver was on the desk, a solidly constructed man on the run-in to retirement, a safe pair of hands and an unflappable manner expressed in the peaty old Fenland accent. 'Don't know, lad, we haven't been told. Not officially. Unofficially, I think your governor's been in a scrap.'

'DI Graham?' Before the words were out he knew what had happened. She'd gone ahead regardless. Without Scobie and Morgan, because the Son of God had pulled them, and without him because he'd gone dogfighting, she'd pressed on alone with a plan designed to draw out a rapist. It sounded as if she'd succeeded. But if she'd made an arrest the mood should be a lot lighter even if she got thumped in the process. 'Is she all right?'

Tulliver lifted mountainous shoulders. 'I don't know – honest. Dr Greaves has been to see her and Mr Shapiro's there now. But she's at home, not at the hospital. That must mean something.'

Marginally reassured, Donovan hesitated on the second step. Then he swung round and headed back the way he'd come. 'I'm going out there.'

But as he reached the back door Shapiro came in, and for a second as their eyes met Donovan was shocked to see a tired old man wearing his superintendent's overcoat and broad creased face.

Shapiro saw Donovan at the same moment, the dark eyes hollow with dread, the long sinews of his narrow body bow-string taut, the quick staccato movements. The hand which took Donovan's arm above the elbow felt a tremor of apprehension; he walked on without a word, taking the younger man with him. On the stairs, once they were alone, he said quietly, 'She's all right. Dr Greaves has looked her over and there's nothing to worry about. Come upstairs and I'll fill you in.'

Shapiro's office was at the top of the building, looking down on the Northampton canal. There were no boats moored here, the waterway was wide enough to keep traffic moving but not for it to stop. On summer weekends all this stretch was a two-way procession of cabin cruisers and narrowboats chugging along at a steady three miles an hour. But in the week, except at the height of the holiday season, there were only dourly determined anglers and small boys with dogs to disturb the stillness of the towpath.

Today Donovan wasn't interested in the view. 'What happened?'

There was no point talking round it. Shapiro parked his ample seat on the edge of his desk and gazed at his sergeant over folded arms. 'She was raped, lad. This morning, while she was feeding her horse. She's all right – I mean, she's not injured; a mild concussion, that's all. She sent you a message. This didn't happen because of anything you did or didn't do.'

It was the last thing she said before he left her alone with her husband. It made no sense and he put it down to the hysteria she'd held at bay so long, but when she explained he understood.

Donovan's Luck. Before she came to Castlemere it was a standing joke at Queen's Street; or not so much a joke as something they laughed at because it made them uncomfortable. Donovan was lucky in the sense that his share of bad luck fell on others. They used to say that if a maniac sprayed the canteen with a Sten gun, Donovan would catch the one dud round. Donovan's lucky, they used to say, but not for the people round him. He had no family left, and even the people he worked with got hurt. His last DI died of Donovan's Luck.

For two years Liz Graham had seemed immune; for most of that time Shapiro hadn't even heard the words. He expected to hear them again now. That was why she'd wanted the word put about. She'd been the victim of a vicious criminal, not Donovan's Luck. Yes, they'd had an arrangement; and yes, he'd cancelled it. But the attack on her wasn't a consequence of that. It would have happened whether they'd walked the dogs or not. Donovan hadn't let her down; in no sense was he responsible for what followed.

For the briefest of moments, gone so quickly that if he'd blinked Shapiro would have missed it, Donovan seemed to shrink. The blood drained from his face, his eyes glazed and he swayed; just once. A wordless moan slipped between his teeth. Then he sucked in a lungful of air so hard Shapiro heard the unsteady whistle in his throat, and blinked his eyes back into focus. '*Is* she all right?'

Shapiro pushed a chair towards him. 'Bit of a stunner, isn't it? Well, I've talked to her and I've talked to Greaves, and both of them say she wasn't hurt. A bit of a knock on the head, and then . . . But physically, nothing to worry about. Emotionally? – I imagine all right is a bit ambitious in the circumstances. But she's a survivor, she won't be beaten by this. For one thing she's got Brian; for another she's got us. Leave it today, but I think by tomorrow she'll be glad to see you.'

Incredulity drove from Donovan a snort half of laughter and half despair. 'Me? Christ Almighty, she won't want me within half a mile of her!'

Shapiro eyed him with compassion. 'This was nothing to do with you. She was in her own back yard.'

Donovan was shaking his head in a fractional, repetitive gesture of disbelief. 'How did it happen?'

When she'd fed Polly and made up the day's feeds she walked round to the lean-to where the hay was kept. She was reaching for a bale when movement flickered in the tail of her eye and, before she had time to react, a blow to the side of her head sent her sprawling in the litter.

Stars exploded between her and the faceless shape that bent over her. Her first vague notion, that she'd fallen and Brian had come to pick her up, foundered on two rocks: he slapped away the hands she raised to him, and he dropped heavily on top of her, hauling at her clothes and his own, in silence but for the fast rough breathing behind the white scarf tied over his face.

Too stunned for fear or horror, too stunned to resist, she felt his body against hers, his hand pinning her wrists, his swift penetration and mechanical rhythm as if she weren't there at all, as if he were doing this by himself. Before she had taken in the fact that she was being raped it was over: he was off her and gone.

For minutes longer she lay in the straw, separated from her emotions by an impervious transparency like plate glass. She could see through it but it cut her off from everything she knew. Beyond lay the common world of home and work, of people she loved and others she respected and who respected her; but the screen, for all that light went in and out, was solid and she could not do the same.

Then, as the mists began to clear, she worked out what she had to do and began doing it, mechanically, performing the actions though a sheet of glass separated her from the consequences. From habit she checked that the horse was all right. Then she went inside and called Frank Shapiro.

Donovan had some deep scratches on his left wrist. Unconsciously he traced them with the fingers of his other hand. As Shapiro talked, without knowing it he dug deeper with his nails, raking the long weals savagely until the blood started and Shapiro leaned forward and physically pulled his hands apart.

He looked up at the superintendent with his face flayed, the emotions pooling on the surface. 'It *was* my fault. If we'd been out till one o'clock she'd still have been in bed at seven!'

'Then he'd have waited,' Shapiro said patiently. 'There was nothing random about this: he knew who she was and where to find her, if he hadn't got her this morning he'd have got her another time. None of us could have anticipated or prevented this.'

On the face of it they had very little in common: men of different generations, races, perspectives and priorities. But they cared about the same things. It took something like this, and seeing the impotent fury in his own breast reflected in the turmoil in Donovan's eyes, to bring that home. 'But it still hurts, doesn't it?'

Shakily, Donovan nodded. His voice was low. 'I feel

like I want to break something.' Repressed violence surrounded him like an aura.

'Keep it together, lad,' growled Shapiro, 'for her sake. She needs to be able to rely on us. She does not need us under sedation in a back ward at Castle General.' After a moment Donovan nodded again.

'All right.' He gestured at Donovan's bloody wrists. 'Er – how did that happen?'

Donovan stared at him blankly. For a second he couldn't remember. Even when he did it seemed too trivial to dwell on. The morning's events had diluted his triumph to nothing and he threw away his hard-earned information in a couple of sentences. 'I was at a dog-fight last night. I've been offered a job driving for the ram-raiders.'

When everyone else had gone they sat side by side on the sofa, holding hands. Brian wanted to put his arm round her but instinct warned him now wasn't the time. The last man who held her gave her no choice. However kindly he meant it, however much they both needed it, he risked raising echoes of that trespass. He had to make himself wait until she was ready, until she came to him. He didn't know about the plate glass in her head but he knew there was something, some door that only had a handle on the inside.

He phoned to say he wouldn't be at school, didn't say why. He made coffee. He ran her another bath. She'd had one as soon as the doctor finished but she wanted another when they had the house to themselves. He hoped she'd ask him to stay, to help her, to wash her down like a weary horse as he had so often when she'd come home tired, sore and dispirited. But she said nothing. Neither did he; he left her to the steam and the smell of soap, and knew that in the privacy of the locked cell she would scrub the memory of her assailant off her skin but only deeper into her mind. He didn't know what to say or do to comfort her. He made more coffee.

They drank it side by side on the sofa. Her skin was pink and new, as if energetic use of the loofah could erase what had happened. She wasn't crying, hadn't cried from the start. First she was stunned, then shocked, then she was busy dealing with it; now what she felt was a hollow unreality. After a while she ventured, 'You know, this wasn't the worst that could have happened.'

'I know,' Brian said thickly, his hand gripping hers. 'I could have lost you.'

Liz smiled at him. Almost, she seemed the same as always. Almost, that was more shocking than anything else. 'Oh, no. Not for some little shit who can't keep his fly done up: it'll take more than that before you're rid of me.' She leaned against his long side, fitting into the curve of his body. He held his breath and let her settle there, let her drape his arm around her. 'No, I mean—' She struggled to express what she was feeling. 'It's supposed to be. It's supposed to be the most devastating thing that can happen to you – short of massive physical injury, or losing your wits, or losing your husband or child. Well, none of those things has happened to me so this should be the worst. But I don't feel devastated.

'I'm angry, oh yes, I'd like to smash his face in. I feel – soiled. And frustrated, because I had my hands on the bastard and I was too groggy to do anything about it. But I don't feel – diminished. I don't feel he's taken anything away, or even left anything behind that alters who I am. It's like the time I had my nose broken. Of course I resented it. It hurt, and the guy who did it had no right, and for a time it shook my confidence – it was visible proof that I'd failed to control the situation. I felt I'd failed professionally because I let his fist too near my nose.

'But nobody else thought that. There was some sympathy, a few jokes, and three months later my nose was fine and his was up against the bars for eighteen months. Well, this is the same. It's not my fault. I haven't done anything wrong. I was unlucky, but it doesn't say anything about *me*. It doesn't leave me with any fences to mend.

'I *won't* feel humiliated. What was taken from me has no value unless it's given freely. He's none the better for having it, I'm none the worse for losing it. The bruises will fade and I'll still be who I always was. I've coped with worse than this.' She sighed, a little shakily, sought out his eyes. 'Am I shocking you? I think a lot of people *would* be shocked. In a crazy way I almost feel relieved. Because it's over and I'm all right. Because this should be the worst and I know I can handle it.'

He didn't know how to respond. He didn't know if it was normal, even if the word 'normal' had any meaning in this context. Anyway, it wasn't how it seemed to him that mattered. If she'd found a way of dealing with it that didn't put her on the rack, that didn't reduce her to ashes from which she'd have to rebuild herself flake by flake, he wasn't going to argue. He wasn't going to complain because it should have torn her apart and hadn't. He held her against him. '*We* can deal with it. Together.'

She patted his hand where it lay across her belly. 'Mm.'

Brian tried to believe, almost convinced himself, that the tremor that ran through him then was a hybrid of love for her, terror at how near disaster had shaved them and an upsurge of the desire to protect her, though Liz was stronger and infinitely tougher than he. But that friendly pat, like patting her horse, far from bringing them together had driven the tip of a wedge between them. She hadn't rebuffed his support, she'd just put no value on it. She wanted to deal with what had happened alone, declined his involvement as kindly as if he were a child. He could feel her warm fresh skin, smell the soap mingled with the scent of her, but in every way that mattered they were on opposite sides of that handleless door. The shudder that ran through him was presentiment.

Chapter Eleven

Shapiro pursed his lips. 'What do you mean, you've been offered a job driving for the ram-raiders?'

Half an hour before, Donovan's head had been full of it. Between that and the dog-fight he'd had a good night – good enough to make up for some of the times he'd pushed his luck and his authority further than they were designed to stretch.

It was a gamble. The harder he pushed, the more chances he created. He staked his time, his reputation, often enough his neck and occasionally his job, and hoped for enough success to disarm his critics. As long as he came out ahead most of the time, blind eyes would be turned to his precise methods. He didn't compromise the integrity of investigations. He didn't trample suspects' rights and get cases thrown out of court. When a gamble failed he paid the price himself.

But he walked a perpetual tightrope between risks and results. He thought he hadn't enough liquidity to see him through a lean time, was only as good as his record. So two successes for the risk of one was a bonus. It meant he wouldn't face awkward questions about Brian Boru and why he didn't get prior approval for his actions. He'd looked forward to giving Shapiro his report. Now it hardly seemed worth the trouble of telling.

'Er – yeah. At the dog-fight. The guy with the skinned rabbit came over for a chat. Seems that's not his only dog – he's got a couple of bruisers he travels round the fights with. Seems there's a whole network of pits scattered across the country. Ours is new – that's why they came here instead of keep moving south, he wanted to try it out. I'm not sure where it was but given a bit of time to root around I'll find it.'

'And the job?'

'OK. So this guy's making small-talk, about the dogs mostly, but he keeps not going away. And I know who he is, of course, so I don't hurry him. He wants to know what I do for a living, and I tell him anything you don't have to pay tax on. He likes that, and soon afterwards we're talking about what he does for a living. Not in so many words, but he's happy enough for me to know it's not altogether legal. Well, everybody in that barn's into stuff that's not altogether legal.'

'You too,' murmured Shapiro, and Donovan eyed him warily and couldn't be sure if it was a joke.

'Right,' he agreed cautiously. 'Only he's down a driver. Don't know how – lost, stolen or strayed, walked out, got sacked or what. I know he didn't get arrested but I can hardly tell him that. Gates. That's what he calls himself – Tudor Gates.' That note of derision would have been more seemly, Shapiro thought, in someone who wasn't named Caolan. 'So he's looking for a driver and he wonders if I might be interested.'

'What did you say?'

A slow smile slid across Donovan's saturnine features. 'Ah, come on now, chief, what do you think? I told him I'd very likely be available.'

'Why you? For all he knows you can't drive to save your life, you stall at junctions and cry if somebody takes your parking place.' Shapiro's eyes narrowed. 'Or has he some reason to think differently?'

Donovan shrugged uncomfortably. 'I told him I'd done driving work before. As for bursting into tears . . .'

'Ye-es?'

Donovan sighed. 'He saw me stop the fight.' He explained what had happened.

'You got into a pit and separated two fighting dogs with your bare hands,' mused Shapiro. He paused for confirmation, one eyebrow raised, and Donovan gave a rueful nod. 'Now I understand. He's looking for madmen and he found one. What else?'

'The last driver must have split soon after the job at Rubens 'cos they've been sitting on their hands ever since and that's not how he works it. Mostly he hits a town two or three times in quick succession then gets the hell out. Losing his driver spiked that so he's still here. I think he wants to do another couple of raids, quick as you like, and then skip town.' He frowned. 'What?'

Shapiro was smiling; but it didn't last long. It wasn't Donovan he'd had this argument with, it was Liz, so there was scant satisfaction in being proved right. Just for the record though . . . 'Where's he from, your Mr Gates?'

Donovan shrugged. 'North, north-east? English accents all sound the same to me. Even without the green fedora and the curly wig he's as queer as a nine pound note, but he talks like a ship-builder.'

'The Tynesiders. They came here so Gates could fight his dogs, but after one raid they lost their driver. If they hadn't they'd have shown up Monday night or Tuesday morning and my name wouldn't be mud with the Son of God. Is Gates going to call you or what?'

'He wants to see me drive. I'm meeting him at the wood at midday.'

Shapiro looked at his watch. 'You haven't left us much time. Still, it won't take SO19 to arrest a ram-raider in a green felt hat. All right–'

'Er,' mumbled Donovan. 'Do you want to arrest them? Now, I mean.'

The superintendent dropped his nose to look at Donovan over glasses he didn't wear. 'Don't I?'

'If I'm on the inside we can get them in the act. The full crew, not just Gates, and no chance of them persuading a jury they were only recruiting stock-car drivers and I got it wrong.'

Shapiro was tempted. It had seemed a good idea when Liz suggested it but then there was no way in. Now the opportunity had presented itself almost like a gift. A man on the inside could learn more in a few hours than a skilled interrogator in days or weeks. Things dropped in casual conversation – earlier jobs, jobs being planned, contacts, fences. And a water-tight case. And really, not much risk, particularly with out-of-towners. People who knew him found it hard to believe Donovan was a policeman; someone who'd met him at a dog-fight wouldn't even wonder.

'If I said yes, how would you do it?'

Donovan grinned wolfishly. 'Go to the meet, scare them shitless with some handbrake turns, wait to hear from them and call you. Then drive them into an ambush.'

'You may not get the chance to call me. They won't be too trusting for your first outing.'

'I'll find some way to attract attention. Lights. I'll use the wrong lights – headlights if it's daytime, side-lights if it's dark. Chances are no one in the car'll notice. Put out the word that something big and fast and carrying the wrong lights is me – don't stop me, tail me and get on the radio.'

'You won't get carried away and ram somebody's shop-front? In the interests of authenticity, as it were.'

'Try not to,' Donovan promised solemnly.

'All right,' decided Shapiro, 'we'll do it. But look after yourself – these chaps are pros, put a foot wrong and they'll have you.'

'Yeah,' agreed Donovan, unconvinced. 'Funnily enough, he's not a bad sort. Weird, yes, but not – nasty. You know? It's almost as if he's in it more for the fun than the money. I think he gets a kick out of planning it, leaving us with egg on our faces.'

'Check the national computer, see if there's anything on him.'

'I will; but I don't think there will be. He told me with great pride the only time he was ever questioned by the police was when he witnessed a mugging. He was quite indignant – said he gave the best description he could, that lager-louts grabbing old ladies' pensions were the lowest of the low.'

'Honour among thieves,' Shapiro ruminated. 'There *is* such a thing, only don't count on it. Just because he has a soft spot for little old ladies doesn't mean he'll feel the same way about you if you blow your cover.'

'About the dogs—'

Shapiro had reached the same conclusion. 'We'll hold off till we have Gates under lock and key. I don't want to make him nervous: a man who enjoys intellectual challenges might put two and two together.'

'And Brian?'

Shapiro's mind went first to Brian Graham, the colour washed from his cheek, holding his wife's hand as a child holds the string of a balloon, for fear it will float away if he relaxes his grip. 'Oh – your dog.'

'I'll need to keep him for a bit. If they come to the garage and the dog's gone they'll wonder why.'

'All right. Try to keep him from killing anything.'

Awkwardly, Donovan said, 'And the boss?'

Shapiro vented a sigh. 'I don't think there's much we can do for her just now. But if we get this business wrapped up we can concentrate on finding her attacker.'

'Do you think she'll come back to work?'

'I don't know, lad. It's a hell of a thing to come to terms with, she may not want to work with people who know. Or maybe by the time she's got over the shock and the anger she'll be wanting her friends. The one thing I'm sure of is she'll have to set the pace herself. We mustn't impose on her our expectations of how she should feel.'

Donovan shook his head in a kind of brooding wonder. 'I can't begin to imagine how she feels. I don't know—' He stopped.

'What?'

Embarrassment made it hard to express himself. A sort of flagellatory urge drove him on. 'Maybe she shouldn't come back. I mean, how are any of us going to deal with that? How do we talk to her – what do we say? Do we act as if it never happened? Do we ask how she's feeling, as if she'd had flu? I don't know how to deal with it.'

'Exactly,' said Shapiro sharply. '*You* don't. This is your problem, Sergeant, you work out a solution. But I'm telling you now, let it become a problem to Inspector Graham and you'll have my reactions to worry about as well. Now.' He checked his watch again. 'Time you were off. And listen: be careful. However much of a card your Mr Gates is, these are not nice people and you're going to be out of touch for a lot of the time. Your first priority is to not get hurt. Don't play the hero. I don't want to find you dead in a ditch.'

Still stinging from the rebuke, Donovan said woodenly, 'Caution is my middle name' – a lie so outrageous that it left Shapiro temporarily speechless.

He went again to the little car-park above the water-meadows. As soon as he turned in among the trees he recognized the high-stepping 4×4 with its bull-bars and its black paint retouched at the front end. They'd been scrupulous about making repairs. Bull-bars or no, it was hard to believe those four headlamps had survived repeated encounters with security grilles; but anything broken had been replaced, anything dented had been knocked out and anything scratched had been repainted at the first opportunity. They weren't going to be stopped for a cracked headlight or because their vehicle appeared to have been in an unreported accident.

Donovan got out of his van, waited for Gates to do

the same. He didn't mind being thought a suspicious sod – in this line it was a good reputation to have.

The little dog got out first. Gates plainly took it everywhere. It reminded Donovan of one of those deeply sinister ventriloquist's dummies that seem smarter and more animated than the man operating them, leaving you to wonder who's pulling whose strings. Maybe the dog had Gates on the end of the pale blue lead.

Gates gave Donovan a smile of recognition that was probably no more than that. But Donovan was naive in many ways and uncomfortable around homosexuals. He relaxed only when the driver got out on the other side of the 4×4. He was about twenty-two, slim and fair, and the look Gates gave him was frankly proprietorial. Donovan mocked himself inwardly. If that was what Gates liked, Hugh Duggan's virtue should be as safe as houses.

Gates introduced them. 'Hugh, this is Andy.' The V-shaped smile on his pointed face broadened satirically. 'Hands off, he's mine. Andy'll be a good driver before long, but he still has some things to learn. Maybe you can teach him. I, on the other hand, drive like an old lady – but I know how I like to be driven.' A tilt of one eyebrow, so perfectly shaped it could have been plucked, invested the comment with sexual overtones. Donovan's expression made him chuckle.

Though they'd spent time together at the dog-fight this was Donovan's first chance to weigh up his prospective employer. For obvious reasons, the lighting in the barn was to show up the fighters, not the punters. Now the policeman made a conscious assessment of the man before him in terms that would mean something to other policemen.

Height, about five-eight; weight, somewhere under ten stone; age – probably mid forties though in the right light he could have passed for thirty. Light brown hair, cut just long enough to curl; high forehead but no sign of balding. Eyes, an odd pale hazel that at times looked almost amber. Face, a narrow heart-shape defined at the jaw by the V-shaped mouth and at the widest point by sculpted eyebrows. Voice – Shapiro was right, it was a well-modulated version of a Geordie patois, all the vowels sounded, many of the consonents slurred. Dress – depended how much he wanted to be noticed: green fedora and burgundy coat if he did, jacket and designer jeans if, like now, he didn't. Constant companion, a dog like a skinned rabbit. If he took it to a dog-fight and he brought it to test-drive a wheelman who might be all mouth, Donovan assumed it went everywhere.

With a patient air that reminded Donovan of Shapiro's, Gates said a second time, 'Hugh? You want to show us what you can do with this?'

Sulkily, the boy climbed into the back as Donovan took the wheel.

He'd done the Defensive Driving course. It hadn't taught him as much as a Lammas market in Glencurran, when herds of steers and tinker-boys on trotting horses could erupt from any side-street at any moment. But he had no great interest in cars – for pleasure he chose bikes every time – so in fact he wasn't well qualified for the job Gates wanted him for. All that got him through the audition was his ability to suspend his sense of self-preservation.

By taking corners at seventy that better drivers would have taken at sixty, and doing it with no sign of fear only a cold wolfish grin, he was able to fool Gates that he had control of the situation when in fact he was barely on nodding terms with it. The great old trees along the woodland rides came hurtling at him from unexpected directions and veered off just in time, mud and leaf-mould spraying from under the big tyres. High and heavy, the vehicle bucketed along the rough tracks leaping from rut to rut like a novice 'chaser. In the back the boy clung to whatever he could get his arms round, sucking his breath through his front teeth like draining a milk-shake.

In the front Gates hung on to his seat-belt with one hand and his dog with the other, his amber eyes flicking between Donovan's face and the track in mounting wonder. Momentarily he expected the car to lose its grip on the amorphous surface and roll, or side-swipe a tree, or hurtle over a thirty-foot cliff into one of the half-hidden sinkholes. But it kept not doing, and the more he studied the driver's face the more confident he grew that it would not. He knew more about men than cars, and a man who could enjoy himself in these circumstances, whose dark face betrayed only grim humour and determination, was a man you'd allow to drive you into hell because he'd probably manage to drive you out again. Had he but known it, Donovan had the job before he threw his first handbrake turn.

Had Gates but known it, Donovan had no idea what the car could and couldn't do. He'd read somewhere that 4×4s performed differently to road cars; in his ignorance he thought they were probably more stable. He knew what he could have done on two wheels, worked on the assumption that he should be able to do twice as much on four. If one of these trees didn't get out of his way in time he'd know better. The icy enjoyment that impressed Gates so much was a hybrid of detachment, because he needed to do this and couldn't have done it if he'd been thinking about the consequences, and real if faintly hysterical amusement because he did occasionally enjoy being frightened half to death.

At length, surprisingly calmly, Gates tapped him on the arm. 'You've made your point.'

As soon as the car stopped the back door opened and the boy swung out, his delicate face flushed with anger. 'You're not going to let him drive? He'll kill us all!'

Gates clucked gently. 'He knows what he's doing, Andy. There isn't a scratch on this car. Tell him, Hugh – you know what you're doing.'

'I know what I'm doing,' Donovan echoed obediently. His eyes swivelled back to Gates and sharpened. 'At least, I'm going to. I want to know exactly what I'm getting into. I've earned that.'

Gates considered for a moment, then nodded. 'All right. Let's go back to our place, I'll tell you what we do and how we do it. Only one thing, Hugh. If you come back with us now, you're in. Too many people have too much to lose for you to start getting cold feet.'

Donovan looked at Gates, at Andy, at the tops of the trees emerging from a nearby sinkhole. Then he nodded. 'I'm in.'

Chapter Twelve

Gates travelled in Donovan's van, the dog on his knee. Donovan didn't wish to seem inquisitive but even if he weren't a police spy there'd be things he'd want to know. 'How many are involved?'

'Six is the optimum figure,' Gates said willingly enough. 'We can do it with less but it takes too long. Any more and you start tripping over one another.'

'Six in the 4×4?' Donovan couldn't see it. It would take them but there'd be no room left for swag.

'Oh, no. We use two cars: the second to get me away – I'm the look-out – and for back-up if things go wrong. It hasn't happened yet, but I'm a Scout at heart, I like to be prepared. For the record, a breakdown would be considered your cock-up. I take it you're familiar with engines? Check that one over, make sure it's reliable.'

Donovan was better with engines than behind the wheel. He gave a brief affirmative nod. 'That what became of your last driver? He wasn't much of a mechanic?'

'He was an excellent mechanic,' Gates said sadly. 'What he wasn't so good at was taking orders. Above all I need to know that if I tell someone to do something, or to do nothing, that's what he'll do. Can I count on you that way, Hugh?'

Donovan met his sidelong gaze, saw the leprechaun twinkle, recognized that beneath it the man was in deadly earnest. 'I'll do what I'm paid for.'

Gates was satisfied with that. 'Fine.' He pointed a manicured forefinger. 'Turn right here, we're home.'

Lost at the end of a lane bounded by high banks was a cottage. A sign offering it for rent was propped against the side wall. When they left it would go up again.

'Cosy,' sniffed Donovan.

Gates smiled. 'We have to stay somewhere and we'd attract more notice in an hotel. As far as the estate agents know I'm alone here.' He gave the dog on his arm a quick hug, added coyly, 'Apart from Chang.'

'Where do you keep the big ones?' asked Donovan. 'I don't want to open the bog door and find myself eyeballing two pit-bulls.'

'There's a piggery at the back, I've got them in there.' An enthusiast, his pixie face brightened. 'Do you want to see them?'

'I already did.' The younger of Gates's dogs competed in a graduate match that left its opponent in much the same state as Brian Boru left his. The older dog made a kill.

Gates chuckled at the look on Donovan's face. 'I'm not sure you're cut out for the fighting game, Hugh.'

'Convince me,' grunted Donovan. 'I was only there because I met this guy in the wood and he took a shine to Brian. Which reminds me: I'll have to be back in town by six to feed him.'

'Move him down here with us. Andy'll come with

you, give you a hand, make sure you find your way back. You can collect your gear at the same time.' He climbed down from the van, headed for the back door of the cottage.

Donovan followed slowly. 'I wasn't thinking of moving in. I have somewhere to live.'

'Then think again,' Gates said pleasantly over his shoulder. 'I thought I made it clear: we're a team. We live together, work together, and when we're finished we move on together. What's the problem? You said you live alone, you've no commitments, there's only the dog to consider and he can come with us.'

Donovan had to remind himself that he was playing a part, he wouldn't have to do anything he agreed to. 'I'm used to being on my own, is all.'

The warmth in Gates's smile appeared to be genuine. 'So now you can get used to being part of a family.' He led the way inside.

If anything, the cottage was more run-down inside than out. Mostly the furniture was old and worn; where things had worn out entirely they'd been replaced with new cheap ones that were even nastier. The place smelled of neglect. Somebody's old mum had lived here, Donovan surmised, with a cat for company and somebody fetching her shopping once a week; enough to keep the old soul alive, not enough to keep the lane from getting overgrown. When she died, or went into a home, the cottage was rented while the family decided what to do with it.

'Go on through,' Gates said, 'say hello to Charlie while I give Chang his lunch.'

Charlie was a heavily-built man in his thirties shoehorned into a little-old-lady-sized chair, chewing on a pen and studying the back page of a newspaper. Donovan supposed he was picking racehorses, but what he was doing was the crossword.

'I'm the new driver,' Donovan offered, along with his assumed name. He looked round critically. 'There doesn't look to be room for six.'

'There isn't,' Charlie agreed in another of those impenetrable northern accents. 'There isn't room for six legless dwarves suffering from insomnia, let alone six working men who like to get some sleep from time to time. Don't go looking for a room, the best you'll do is a chair and a blanket. If there really were six of us you'd have to take turns at the chair.'

Donovan frowned. 'How many are we then?'

Charlie shrugged. 'You've met them. The coach, the boy and me. And you. And maybe Patsy, when the dust settles. For the moment Patsy's too scared to put in an appearance.'

Donovan tried to milk the information he needed without seeming nosy; it wasn't an easy task and he may not have wholly succeeded.

'The others left with your last driver, did they?'

Charlie gave a snort of grim humour. 'In a manner of speaking. He's dead, two of the lads are behind bars and Patsy's on the run.'

A terrible weight of foreboding settled on Donovan's head. He didn't want to ask; he didn't want to know. But he needed to, and besides too little curiosity would be as suspicious as too much. He said carefully, 'Last job go a bit wrong, did it?'

Charlie shook his head. 'Not the last one we did for the coach: don't worry on that score. Trouble was, he was away for the day – a dog-fight in East Anglia. All we had to do was stay out of trouble, and they couldn't even do that, the silly sods. Wanted a day in London, didn't they? You'll never guess what they did on the way back.'

Wanna bet? thought Donovan bleakly.

'A train robbery!' exclaimed Charlie, still unable to credit the absurdity of it. 'A goddamned frigging train robbery.'

Liz got as far as the bottom of the front steps and stopped, exactly where Mrs Andrews had and for much the same reason. She didn't want to do this. She didn't have to do it. All that had got her this far was the abstract notion that she ought to.

It would have been easier coming in the back way. If she headed straight for the stairs, with luck she would see no one who'd expect more than a polite nod until she was safe in CID at the top of the building. On the other hand, those she avoided meeting now she'd have to meet later. It would be nice to think that she'd taken all the hurdles she could at one outing, that after this she could come and go without either feeling or causing embarrassment. She had nothing to be ashamed of, was damned if she was going to tip-toe round the place as if she had.

So when she was ready she took a deep breath and marched up the steps into the front office like an Assistant Chief Constable paying a surprise visit in the hope of finding the Duty Sergeant asleep with his feet on the desk.

They'd have been less startled if she *had* been an Assistant Chief Constable – if she'd been an Assistant

Chief Constable in full ceremonial regalia complete with sword. There were three of them: Sergeant Tulliver, WPC Wilson and PC Stark who was bringing the Incident Book up to date. They did a matched set of double-takes, looking up as they heard the door, down again as they recognized her, then up once more in surprise at seeing her here and now.

Refusing to run, making herself face them, Liz sketched a smile. 'Bet the Incident Book makes good reading this week.'

For a moment none of them knew what to say. But she felt a wave, not of embarrassment nor even sympathy so much as respect, that gave her hope. The ice was cracked; soon it would break.

PC Stark said quietly, 'About the same as usual, ma'am. Some pain, some grief, and a lot of police officers doing work nobody could pay them enough for.'

Liz felt her heart swell. This wasn't going to be the torture she'd feared. She'd been right not to put it off. The support she needed, from people who knew about being hurt and humiliated and having to carry on regardless, was right here. She nodded. 'So what's new?' She headed for the stairs.

WPC Wilson came quickly round the counter, her face pink. 'Er—'

'Mm?'

But whatever the younger woman had wanted to say stuck in her throat. She coughed but couldn't clear it.

'The chief's upstairs,' said Tulliver, covering her confusion with his own. No one could get used to Shapiro's promotion. 'Shall I call him?'

'No, I'll stick my head in when I get up there.'

Wilson swallowed. 'Ma'am – what happened. If there's anything any of us can do, please say.'

Liz's smile broadened. 'I will. Thanks.' There was almost a spring in her step as she climbed. She was conscious of having emerged from an encounter she'd been dreading not merely unscathed but strengthened. More than just relief, she felt the stirrings of confidence.

Shapiro was in mortal combat with his paperwork. His expression was belligerent, his eyes slashing and stabbing like lethal weapons, his pen flashing spiky comments in margins and ending his signature with a vicious full stop. He flung the vanquished in a tray for a clerk to mail or file as appropriate. But still the foe waited in serried masses, an endless army of paper that grew even as he despatched it.

In fact this was nothing new. Shapiro's paperwork always mounted until either those waiting for it made a fuss or he couldn't find room on his desk for his elbows. What was different was the savagery with which he was attacking it, and that had less to do with the task than what he was using it as a diversion from.

Before she decided that twenty years as a policeman's wife was enough, Angela used to discourage him from working on Saturdays. She liked to have the family together for Shabbos, and though she appreciated that crime didn't keep kosher she would have raised a disapproving eyebrow at the triviality of his present occupation. Except that she'd have understood why he couldn't sit at home and think when anger was threatening to blow the top off his head. Paperwork wasn't an antidote, but the mindless tedium at least blunted the pain.

The step in the corridor outside his office was so familiar that for a moment he gave it no thought. A moment later his head jerked up and his eyes widened. 'Liz?' His voice rose as if he'd been cornered in his office on a Saturday morning by an axe-murderer.

From habit she tapped as she opened his door. 'On your own, Frank?'

Shapiro stumbled to his feet, ushered her in. She looked drawn, her skin pale and touched with grey. Even her bright hair had lost its glow. But in her eyes she was herself. A little bruised, a shade jet-lagged, but the authentic Liz Graham with her sharp mind and her cool head and her strong sense of purpose.

He spread a blunt hand at the littered desk. 'Paperwork,' he explained unnecessarily.

Liz nodded. 'The secret is to keep on top of it. As the bishop said—' She stopped. The unspoken punchline hung in the air between them, grey as ashes, heavy as lead.

'Oh, Liz.' Sorrow thickened Shapiro's throat.

She lifted her head abruptly and her eyes slapped him. Her tone was impatient; only someone who knew her as well as he did would have detected the tremor. 'For pity's sake, Frank, don't let's start analysing every word we say! I'm *not* going to have an attack of the vapours at every veiled reference to sex. I'm all right. Lots of unpleasant things happen in this world, and most of them happen to police officers. Pilots say it's not a bad landing if you walk away. Well, I'm walking, Frank. Tap-dancing may take a bit longer.'

Her courage struck him to the heart. Feeling his

eyes fill he blew his nose vigorously. In the course of a long and eventful career he'd met a wide variety of professional tragedies. He'd seen colleagues injured, maimed and killed; he'd seen them succumb to the stresses of the job and lose their nerve, their wits, their wives and everything they'd worked for. He'd known officers who had killed themselves and a few who'd killed other people.

But to the best of his knowledge he'd never known one who'd been raped. He tried to think of it as just another in the long list of injuries which criminals inflict on defenders of the law, but failed. It wasn't. You could laugh, ruefully, about the odd broken bone sustained in the course of duty; but the assault on Detective Inspector Graham couldn't be defused by a bit of healthy badinage.

The enormity of it left him rudderless. He'd known this woman for twelve years. They worked closely together, shared a deep respect as well as a genuine friendship that had survived various disagreements, conflicts of priority, even of principle. Now, because of a lightning attack behind her house, he'd no more idea what to say to her than Donovan had. Resentment at that seethed in his breast, only contained by the knowledge that he mustn't – absolutely must *not* – let her see that it made a difference. She'd never let him down, never once; he wasn't going to have her think that anything a barbarian could do to her could affect her relationships with friends and colleagues.

'Right,' he said briskly, stuffing his handkerchief in a trouser pocket. 'Now, what are you doing here?'

'Two things. Informing you that I'll be available for duty on Monday.' She gave a little self-deprecating smile. 'And making sure that when I arrive on Monday morning I won't get as far as the back door and bottle out.'

'Monday?' Shapiro was dismayed. 'Liz, that's too soon. Did Dr Greaves agree to that?'

'Dr Greaves gave me a thorough physical and the only damage he could find was a slight concussion. I've an appointment at the hospital later today, to make sure there aren't any souvenirs, and after that my diary's free. Now, I could sit at home feeling sorry for myself; I could go buy a wig and a long black coat like your granny wore so I could venture out in daylight without being recognized; I could spend the day with a counsellor and be reassured that it's perfectly normal to feel a whole lot of things I don't feel at all; or I could get on with my job. Which of these do *you* think'll make me feel most like a human being again?'

She wasn't as calm about this as she wanted him to think but perhaps that didn't matter. Perhaps pretending to be in control led to regaining control in fact. He had two concerns: whether she was competent to work, and whether the stress of trying would be harmful. On the first he had no doubts. She wouldn't be at her best and brightest, but Liz Graham in third gear still outperformed most people in top.

The second criterion was harder to judge. All his instincts told him she needed cosseting, needed time and space to rebuild in. He thought getting out in the sun with her horse, or on to a Greek beach with her husband, would speed the healing. But he couldn't trust her instincts on every issue but this one. He scrutinized his hands folded on the desk, gave a protracted sniff. 'My grandmother was a woman of impeccable fashion sense who owned a hat shop.'

Liz had known Shapiro as long as Shapiro had known Liz. She knew when she'd won an argument without him handing her a coconut. She vented an unsteady sigh. Girding herself for battle with him had stiffened sinews which softened with the victory. 'Monday then.'

'If you're sure it's what you want.' His gaze was compassionate but still troubled. 'Before you decide, think how you're going to deal with it when this becomes public knowledge. Because it will. You know this town: gossip'd get about somehow even if all the people moved out. I can tell you, the way I tell all rape victims, that every effort will be made to protect your identity, and I don't believe anyone at Queen's Street would betray that, but we have to be realistic. Because of who you are this isn't a normal rape case and you shouldn't count on anonymity. Sooner or later some sick sod you're in the process of arresting will throw it in your face. You need to know how you're going to react.'

She hadn't considered it. The rules to protect the privacy of rape victims worked so well she hadn't wondered if they'd work for her. But he was right: rumour was no respecter of law and the piquancy of a sex attack on the town's senior policewoman would lend it wings. By Monday all Castlemere's criminal fraternity would know what had happened. Most of them would have too much class to refer to it. But not all. It would happen; if not Monday, then soon.

She forced her voice on to a level. 'Professionally, I hope. You're right, sooner or later someone will. I'll try and think up a good put-down first. But how I deal with it is less important than the fact that I *will* deal with it. I have to, if I want to go on doing this job in this town. Whether it's Monday, a week on Monday or six months from now: it's not going to be any easier whenever it comes. That's why I'm here today. Some things get harder to do the longer you put them off. That's why I'd like to get back to work at once, even if it does give me some rough moments. I'll cope. You know that.'

He did; but it would still be like a knife turning in the wound. He wanted to protect her but he couldn't protect her forever. She wouldn't let him; apart from that it would be a bad idea. The rest of her career hung on what the next several days would bring.

But the next several days would be easier if the inquiry seemed to be making some progress. That meant discussing it. By her presence here Shapiro assumed she was ready to do that. 'You told me yesterday morning pretty much what happened. But you were still in shock. Has any more detail come back to you since?'

The thing was in her mind constantly, running and re-running before her eyes like a jerky, meaningless snatch of film. Yet focusing on it, thinking about it in a deliberate and coherent way, was unexpectedly hard. Liz made the effort, creases netting her eyes. But nothing new emerged. 'I really don't think so.'

Shapiro's face screwed up like an old apple. 'I need to get some sense of why *you*? Because you're another good-looking forty-year-old blonde professional woman? We know that's what he likes – is it just coincidence that he picked you? Has he seen you in your garden and thought "That'll do nicely"? Or was it more calculated than that? Did he know about the operation at the Basin – is that where he saw you, only he realized you had company then so he found out where and when he could get you alone?

'You see what I'm getting at? In the first case he's just a bastard, in the second he's a clever bastard. He knows who you are – precisely who, he knows you're involved in this investigation. He knows you tried to trap him, this was his reply. That makes the attack on you personal.

'Either he followed you home or found out where you live so he could ambush you when you least expected it. That's not just nasty, it's arrogant; and that means he's not doing this because of some primordial urge he can't resist, he's doing it for kicks. He's not at the mercy of his hormones, he won't be pushed into taking risks and making mistakes: he can wait until he can have what he wants at little or no danger to himself. He's going to be a sod to catch.'

'Well, Frank,' Liz exclaimed impatiently, 'I had actually worked that out. Something to do with the fact that he's already raped three women and we still don't know anything about him! I *know* it's going to be hard. It's always bloody hard. We've still got to bloody do it.'

'Of course we have,' he agreed mollifyingly, wanting to pat her shoulder and knowing she'd probably slap his hand away. 'And of course we will. I'm just looking for anything you can tell me that'll help. Every prison library is run by some clever bastard who thought he'd outwitted us. That's where this man's going to end up – stamping "Property of HM Prison Service" on cheap editions of Charles Dickens.'

Dropping her eyes Liz sketched an apologetic

shrug. 'I'm sorry, Frank, I don't mean to jump down your throat. I know it'll take time – God knows it always has when it's been me doing it! Don't feel you have to humour me: if I'm behaving like a silly mare you'd better tell me. By Monday I have to be back in full working order.'

'No,' he said gently, 'you don't.'

'Yes,' she said firmly, 'I do. And for what it's worth, I think he knew exactly who I was. To come to my house, to my own back yard – that's not like waylaying someone on the public street or in an office-block. That's as personal as it gets.'

'That's what I thought,' Shapiro admitted. 'Makes it worse, somehow, doesn't it?'

'Not for me it doesn't,' she gritted. 'So he knows where I live – I already knew that. Now let's track the bastard back to where *he* lives.'

Chapter Thirteen

All the time he was getting enough gear from his boat to look he was moving out, Donovan was waiting his chance to get word to Shapiro. But the boy shadowed him too closely. There was no time to use the phone, to pass a message to a neighbour or even drop a hint that might be acted on. Finally, in desperation, he wrote a note that he put in an envelope with the keys and dropped through the hatch of the *James Brindley* on the next mooring. What he wrote – 'Got a job offer, have to split, love to Liz' – would make no sense to Martin and Lucy Cole. But they knew where he worked, would have the wit to forward it to Queen's Street where Shapiro would understand what it meant.

Andy took a covetous look round *Tara* as they left. 'I can see why you don't want to muck in with us.'

Donovan shrugged. 'It's not mine, I've just been looking after it. Keeping the squatters out. Everything of mine's in the bags in the van.'

Brian Boru thought he was going fighting again: his eyes glowed with anticipation. Donovan didn't have to force him into the van, the dog dragged him out by the chain and clawed at the tailgate. He thought his life had improved immeasurably in the last few days.

Gates met them outside the cottage, greeted Donovan politely and Brian effusively – Brian's answer was to lift his lip just enough to show the tip of a fang – and had a quiet word with Andy while Donovan was unloading the van. He couldn't hear what they were saying but he could guess. 'Did he try to contact anyone?' 'He left a note when he dropped his key off. But I saw it, there was nothing in it.'

They settled Brian in the piggery – he couldn't see the other dogs, the exchange of threats and menaces as they heard one another didn't last – then went inside.

'There isn't much room,' Gates said wryly. 'If it's any comfort, we don't live like this all the time. It was the best I could do that was both handy and private.'

Coffee was simmering on the stove. Gates poured four cups and they joined Charlie in the little sitting-room. There were four chairs, which would have been enough if Chang hadn't claimed one of them. The nude dog and Donovan regarded each other with mutual dislike.

'Chang, Chang,' admonished Gates, patting his knee, 'come over here and let the nice gentleman sit down.' It was the first time in his life Donovan had been described as a nice gentleman. Either, in fact, let alone both.

'In the circumstances,' Gates went on, sipping his coffee, 'you'll forgive a certain reticence about who we are and where we're from. If this works out and you stay with us, I'll fill you in on all the details. For now, I expect what you really want to hear about is the next job.'

Donovan had to decide how much he knew about the last one. It was in the papers, of course, both the nationals and the *Castlemere Courier*, and as someone with a professional interest he would naturally have taken notice. On the other hand, he'd better not refer to facts which had come from SOCO or the national computer. He said, 'I take it that was you last Sunday?'

Gates nodded. 'Went like a charm. And next day everything fell apart because my driver fancied a trip to London and ripped off the other passengers on the way back.'

'Charlie said. Jeez,' whistled Donovan, 'I didn't think anybody robbed trains any more.'

'They don't,' Gates said succinctly. 'At least, not very successfully. I hope Charlie also said it was done without my knowledge and approval?'

'I did, coach,' said the big man obediently.

'So you understand the importance I place on rules,' said Gates. 'Because of what happens when people don't keep them. One man died and two are behind bars because they did their own thing. Well, I can do nothing about that except make sure it doesn't happen again. There are four of us now: it's enough if we pare the safety margin. I'll drive the second car, you three load the goods. But three isn't very many, and Andy's a bit new to it, and Hugh – have you done this before?'

'Driving. Not thieving.'

'You wouldn't have to do it this time if I had my way, I'd sooner keep you behind the wheel. But loading up would take forever with just two.'

'That's OK,' said Donovan, 'I'll leave the engine running, I can be back behind the wheel in a couple of seconds. What are we after – what do I concentrate on and what do I leave behind?'

'Electricals. Concentrate on the stuff in boxes at the back of the shop rather than the window display.' He flicked a little elfin grin. 'Ignore boxes printed with the word "toaster" and go for videos, TVs, stereos, electronic games. One advantage in going short-handed: we'll put you all on the front seat and drop the back one to make more room.'

'How do you work the look-out thing?'

Gates nodded his approval: the new driver was asking all the right questions. 'Me and Chang check out the area ten minutes before you arrive. If there's a clear run I'll get out of sight, back to my car. If there's a problem – a police patrol, too many people about, the council's ripped up our escape route to look for a gas leak – I'll take up a position where you can't miss seeing me and wait till you've passed.

'When you come in, Hugh, look for me. I'm obvious enough, if I'm there you'll see me, and if you do keep driving. Do nothing to attract attention, just carry on through town and make your way back here. If it was only a glitch we can try again later – later in the day, next morning, whenever. But I like everything in our favour before I commit us. I'd rather cancel a dozen times than have to shake off a police escort once.'

'I'll vote for that,' Donovan said with appropriate fervour. 'So where are we going, and when?'

'How long have you lived round here, Hugh?'

Donovan saw no point in lying. 'About eight years.'

'Then you know the town – where the various

shops are, the emergency exits and so on. What do you reckon to Stevens Electrical as a target?'

As the biggest electrical retailer in town, Stevens was the obvious choice. They would have state-of-the-art goods worth many thousands of pounds in stock every day of the year. Their shop window was wide and low enough for the 4x4, and there was room in the street to swing and hit it square on. However . . .

Donovan tried to explain his reservations tactfully to a man who took pride in his planning. 'Jagger Street's in the old part of town: turn off and you're into narrow streets as crooked as a dog's hind leg. There are only two exits on to decent roads – Castle Street, that comes back to the square, and Bedford Road. As soon as the alarm goes the cops'll block 'em both; and if we turn up a side street they'll have all bloody day to catch us.'

Gates watched him enigmatically. 'You mean I've got it wrong?'

Donovan shrugged. 'I'll do what you want. But you asked my opinion and that's it. Stevens is a good target in a bad place. If you don't like taking risks you'd best go somewhere else.'

'Such as?'

'Hell.' Donovan wondered if a police officer had ever before been asked to nominate a local business for a ram-raid. But there was no way out. 'What about Owens?'

'Owens in Bridgewater Street? That backs on to the by-pass?' He chuckled at Donovan's expression. 'Sorry, Hugh, I'm teasing. I came to the same conclusion. That's what we're doing. Owens.'

'When?'

'When we're ready.'

In the event it didn't take till Monday for the unpleasantness to start, and in the first instance it wasn't directed at Liz.

On Saturday afternoon Castlemere United were entertaining Norwich City in a match whose outcome was never in serious doubt. The three-one scoreline may have been ungenerous to United's share of play, but only those members of the sub-capacity crowd who were related to the home goalie felt they wuz robbed.

Football duty was popular with the policemen of Queen's Street, so it wasn't often that WPC Mary Wilson found herself directing fans in and out of the Rosedale ground. But an epidemic of spring flu threw the carefully worked out rosters back into the melting pot, and WPC Wilson accepted the task philosophically.

Right up to the moment when, separating two groups of opposing fans before their exchanges degenerated from friendly insults into something heavier, she found a pair of thick hands gripping her waist and a pair of thick lips pressed against her ear whispering, 'Was it you, darling? Good, was it? Want some more?'

She was so startled that she let her chance to identify the speaker escape. By the time she spun he'd already disappeared into a crowd of Castlemere supporters wearing United scarves and adolescent grins that, as men in their twenties and thirties, they should have outgrown by now.

'Who said that?' Her eyes flayed them. Most of

them had no idea what she was talking about; others chuckled knowingly and backed away, hands up, before her furious gaze. It could have been any of them. If no one owned up and no one pointed the finger she was helpless to proceed. Even if she'd identified the culprit she wasn't sure he'd committed an offence.

Except that he'd offended her. Anger spurred her on. The sensible thing would have been to let them away with no more than a withering stare. But the impertinence outraged her sense of decency and she was not prepared to let it pass. 'Go on, go home,' she sneered at them. 'Go home and tell your wives and your mums what a good afternoon you had. Be sure and tell them the best part, too. Only don't be surprised if they don't bray just as loud as you, you damned donkeys!'

By the time the ground was cleared, the away fans homeward bound and the police detail back at Queen's Street, Wilson had cooled down enough to regret her outburst. If Superintendent Giles had been in the station she'd have confessed to him. He wasn't, but Detective Superintendent Shapiro was.

He heard her out in silence, showing less emotion than he felt. When she was finished he said, 'Why are you telling me?'

She shrugged awkwardly. 'In case there's a complaint, so someone'll know what it was about.' She gave a wry smile. 'And because confession is good for the soul, sir.'

'Avoiding actions that need confessing is even better,' Shapiro said pontifically. Then the austerity melted. 'Don't worry about it, Constable, you sound as though you did all right. If they'd said it in front of Donovan he'd have decked them. Besides, who's going to come in here to complain? They must know we're itching to arrest someone.'

Happier, she started to leave; but then she turned in his doorway, her young face creased in bewilderment. 'Why would they do that, sir? Why would they make a joke of it? Whether or not they thought it was me.'

Shapiro sighed. 'Because they're young men, Constable Wilson, and young men have almost nothing in common with the rest of the human race. They'd been to a football match, yes? They'd spent all afternoon merrily bawling insults in one of the few situations where that's acceptable behaviour. They'd probably been drinking, and anyway they were high enough on wit and the sound of their own voices.

'So they came out of the ground looking for something else to shout about. One of them saw you and told his mates this rumour he heard about a policewoman getting raped. After that it was only a matter of time.

'It doesn't make them evil. It makes them stupid. It makes them childish. When they're together they lose about ten years apiece and revel in the kind of behaviour that any one of them, alone, would recognize as crass and be thoroughly ashamed of. They're probably ashamed of themselves now but it'll be another two or three years before they're mature enough to admit it. In the meantime it's easier to giggle than own up to being wrong.'

She nodded, and twitched a little grin, and left; but Shapiro felt like a man with a river lapping at his doorstep who thinks he hears the rumble of distant thunder.

It was WPC Flynn next, and she was altogether less resilient than Mary Wilson.

There'd been a Sunday morning market on Castle Mount since time immemorial. It enjoyed a reputation for roguery and shy dealing but it was hardly deserved. You were less likely to find stolen antiques than cheap clothes, mass produced ornaments, gaudy toys and cracked eggs.

It was a pleasant enough duty on a fine Sunday and WPC Flynn was wandering among the stalls looking for ideas for her mother's birthday present. A couple of regulars nodded a greeting and there was no indication of anything amiss until someone touched her elbow and said quietly, 'Check out the Undercover Agent.'

There is a glamorous side to underwear retailing, but it isn't the one seen on market stalls where string vests, combinations and really serviceable knickers may be found. The sight of winceyette nighties fluttering in the breeze reminded her passingly of her mother's birthday.

But what she saw as she pushed her way through an unexpected mass of winking, chuckling men made her forget again. Hoisted on a pole like a royal standard were a pair of voluminous navy-blue bloomers. A sign tacked to the pole announced: AS SUPPLIED TO CASTLEMERE POLICEWOMEN. SPECIAL OFFER: ONE PAIR ONLY.

With or without the law on her side WPC Wilson would have shut the stall down there and then. She'd have demanded receipts for every item displayed, queried the invoices, insisted on cross-checking with the supplier, and generally engaged in the sort of police harassment that lets everyone know just where the lines are drawn.

But WPC Flynn was a less robust sort of person and instead of wading in with righteous indignation she froze, staring at the placard in horror, and then blushed crimson. The chuckling turned to hoots of unrestrained hilarity. By the time PC Stark, who was checking out the motor supplies stall on the far side of the Mount, tracked down the rumpus she was fighting back tears.

'So what did you do, Constable?' Superintendent Giles asked him later.

'I confiscated them, sir,' Stark replied, staring stonily over his superior's head. 'To prevent a breach of the peace, and in case they were evidence. In order to do so without straining my back I considered it necessary to stand on the trestle holding the rest of his stock. Unfortunately' – the merest flicker of an expression – 'it broke, sir.'

Giles nodded slowly. 'That *was* unfortunate, Constable. I trust you didn't hurt your back after all?'

Beginning to suspect that the new superintendent might have hidden depths, Stark allowed himself the ghost of a smile. 'No, sir. Quite a soft landing, sir. Got a bit of mud on my uniform, but as luck would have it there was a lot of cloth lying around so I cleaned myself up with that.'

'Well done, Constable,' said Superintendent Giles.

Chapter Fourteen

Even if she refused to change her plans, which is what he expected, Shapiro thought Liz should know about the weekend's events before she turned up for work on Monday morning. On Sunday evening he called at her house.

She was ironing. Irrationally, he was surprised. He'd rather imagined that her clothes leapt out of the washing machine as well-ordered as the ideas springing from her head. Of course it was nonsense. Everyone's laundry, and everyone's thoughts, need knocking into shape before they're fit to be seen. The secret of good dressing, both sartorial and mental, is to do it in private.

But if there was nothing unusual about a woman ironing there was something distinctly odd about *what* she was ironing. She was ironing everything. Almost everything she owned was draped around the living-room, on the backs of chairs, on hangers hooked over doors. A couple of the shirts were Brian's, and there was a table-cloth and a dozen handkerchiefs, but otherwise the clothes were hers. She must have emptied every wardrobe and every drawer. She must have been stood here half the day to fill so many hangers.

Brian had showed him in. Now he retreated to the

kitchen with a helpless little shrug and no attempt to explain.

Shapiro realized, of course, that what Liz was doing had nothing to do with ensuring she had a tidy outfit for tomorrow. It was obsessive, ritualized cleaning. She could have chosen to clean the house from top to bottom, to paint the woodwork or to prune the roses within an inch of their lives: essentially it would have been the same. What she was doing was making a fresh start. The recent past was polluted by the actions of a stranger, and she with it; she was trying to draw a line under that by making the things with which she most nearly surrounded herself fresh and new. She couldn't sear the past out of her skin but she could sear it out of her clothes.

He said quietly, 'You want to tell me again how you're perfectly all right?'

The hand she waved at the room was not quite steady, nor was her laugh, but the effect was not of a psyche slipping out of control. She said, 'Don't misunderstand, Frank. This isn't madness, this is therapy.'

'I know.'

Her eyes were tired. 'You do? You want to try explaining it to Brian?'

'How is Brian?'

She put down the iron. After a moment she pulled the plug out, signalling the ritual complete. 'Hurt. Worse than me, I think. He wants things he can't have. He wants me to break down so he can gather me in his arms and console me. He wants me to behave like a woman wronged in a Victorian novel. But I'm not like that, Frank. I never was, he's no right to expect it. Brian's my husband, my lover and my best friend. But this is my problem. I have to tackle it the way that feels right to me; and it'll be done with when I feel it is. I'm not only not going to let it beat me, I'm not going to let it affect me any more than I can help.' She gave him a wan smile. 'I can't guarantee I won't succumb to occasional fits of strangeness – like this one – in the process; but hell, Frank, I could sing hymns on the interview tapes and still be less strange than some of the people we work with.'

'There are,' he agreed darkly, 'some very strange people about. Some of them aren't even policemen.' He told her about Wilson and Flynn.

She took it better than he'd expected, even managed a grim little chuckle at the placard pinned beneath the waving bloomers. 'Come on, Frank, you're not expecting me to be upset about that?'

'Cathy Flynn was.'

'Cathy Flynn's about as much use as a chocolate teapot. She ought never to be allowed out of the office.'

'She was upset on your behalf. They both were.'

'Well, they needn't be,' Liz said firmly. 'A week from now it'll be old news. Unless we make an arrest, in which case the joke's on him.'

Shapiro sighed. 'Liz, I have nothing but respect for the way you're coping with this. There's something very special about someone who can come through this kind of personal and professional trauma with their sense of proportion intact. So this is an observation, not a criticism. The effect this is going to have on policing this town is not exclusively in your hands.

'It's a matter of public knowledge now – God knows how it got out, we knew it would but I never guessed it'd be so soon – and as we might also have guessed there's a section of our citizenry that thinks it's funny. This may be only the start. If Superintendent Giles finds he can't deploy any of his women officers without starting a riot he may feel he has no choice but send you on leave till the dust settles.'

The way her hands fisted and her eyes sparked, he thought that if Liz had still been holding the iron she'd have thrown it at him. 'No, damn it!' she cried. 'If I can cope with the situation, so can Cathy Flynn and so can the Son of God. I will *not* be swept under the carpet to avoid embarrassing other people! I've done nothing wrong, Frank. I don't intend to be penalized for this.'

He had every sympathy; but he also recognized the realities of the situation. 'There's no question of that, Liz. But the bottom line is keeping the peace, and if that means sending you on leave you may have to go. We're not talking of retirement, we're talking of a week or two away while things settle down. Apart from anything else, it's tough for the Whoopsies to do their job while a bunch of little kids in men's clothing are ogling them and wondering if it was them.'

'Well, let's consider the Whoopsies by all means,' Liz said nastily. 'It's going to be pretty tough on me too – I just consider that it's part of my job. And part of theirs.' She frowned. 'Anyway, how does it help if I go to Bognor for a week? Or will you make a public announcement so nobody'll leer at the Whoopsies any more?'

'I know you're upset,' he chided her gently, 'but do try not to be crass. No, I'm not going on *Police Six* with it. What I might do is give Gail Fisher an interview confirming the basic facts and asking that anyone else who's been attacked and hasn't reported should come forward now. I could add that our officer who was attacked has taken some leave and gone away for a week. That should take the pressure off.'

Liz shook her head in bitter disbelief. 'Frank, I don't know why we're even discussing this. I'm fit to work, I want to work, I'm being paid to work – and you want to send me to the seaside because Cathy Flynn was upset by a pair of bloomers? Send *her* to Bognor, she needs it more than I do.'

Shapiro was inclined to agree. He felt himself starting to grin. 'Oh, Liz, why can't you be a lazy time-serving git like other coppers and take a free holiday when it's offered?'

But she wasn't smiling. 'You know why, Frank. Because after a week on the beach I'd need another. And after two I'd never get back.'

'So I should tell the Son of God you wouldn't welcome any such suggestion?'

She nodded incisively. 'Tell him I'd fight it tooth and nail.'

When Shapiro had gone she looked round the room, hung with clothes like ungainly Christmas decorations, in a kind of wonder and with the fragile beginnings of amusement. Whatever had she been thinking of? She put them away, keeping out only what she'd need for the morning.

Brian said, 'You're still going in, then?'

Again she nodded. 'I have to.'

'No,' he said carefully, 'you *want* to.'

She turned to him, held his gaze. His kind eyes were the best feature of an otherwise unremarkable face. She looked there for some understanding of how these events were affecting her, their implications for the medium and long-term future. Shapiro understood. He might not like how she wanted to handle it but he understood that her needs took priority over her inclinations. That she had to work backwards from where she wanted to be and make choices that would help her get there. She looked for some appreciation of that in Brian's eyes, and could not find it.

'I want,' she said fiercely, 'the same as you do – that this never happened. But that's not an option. As second choice, I want to have the damage repaired so that things are as good as they were before – between you and me, between me and my colleagues, between Queen's Street and the town. That *is* possible but it'll take hard work and it has to start with me. And I have to start tomorrow, before the cracks widen too far.'

The pain in his eyes was like another assault on her. 'Oh, Liz,' he said softly. 'I wish you'd tell me how you really feel.'

Despair flared in her like temper. 'I *have* told you!' she cried. 'You just don't listen.'

His sensitive hands reached for her shoulders but she shook him off impatiently. 'You see?' he murmured. His misery was like his soul, gentler than hers, not less passionate but less demonstrative. His heart would break with barely a crack. 'You're pushing me away. It's not *him* doing that, it's you. You seem to think I'm a detail you can sketch in when you've sorted out the important things with Frank Shapiro. But *I'm* important, Liz. I'm half of our marriage, you can't push me aside while you decide what to do. You owe me better than that. You owe us better.'

'And don't you owe me something?' she snapped back faster than thought. 'Support, maybe? Time and space? You must know how difficult this is for me. Why are we talking about *your* feelings when it's me that's been raped?'

She should have slapped his face: it would have been less hurtful. He recoiled, in fact, as if she had. He backed away. He knew he couldn't win a head-to-head with her when her hackles were up. He thought if he let it drop now, came back when she was calmer and they talked about it rationally, they might make some progress.

He was turning to leave the room when he suddenly saw himself through her eyes. That wasn't discretion, it was cowardice. If he let that be her last word it would never be erased; Damoclean, it would hang over them forever. He wheeled back, surprising her.

'How dare you accuse me of not supporting you?' he demanded in quiet fury. 'I have always backed you to the hilt. I've watched you do things, take risks, that knotted me up inside – things no man should have to watch his wife doing – rather than be accused of standing in your way. My career has always played second fiddle to yours. And you have the nerve to ask for my support!

'Can't you see I'm not a by-stander in this? I'm a victim too. Our marriage is the most important thing in my life, and what that animal did struck at its very heart. Of course I have feelings about it, and they matter, and if you're as blasé about all this as you pretend why can't you spare just a little interest and concern for them?'

'Blasé?' she shouted in outraged astonishment.

'Because I won't dissolve in tears on your manly bosom and let you decide what's best for me? Get a life, Brian! I'm running up a down escalator here, I don't know that I can reach the top, but I'm damn sure that if I don't give it all I've got I'll get dumped on the floor.

'I'm sorry if I haven't treated your feelings with due deference. I thought that since mine were having to get by on a lick and a promise yours could, too. But then I only had some man I don't know from Adam humping me. You had an animal strike at the very heart of the most important thing in your life. Hell, Brian, I'm really sorry I wasted all this time wondering what was right for me!'

They didn't go in for slanging matches. Disagreements between them were usually settled amicably. They had exchanged the odd cross word over the breakfast table, but nothing that needed forgiveness later. They had never had a real stand-up, drag-out fight before; perhaps, without something of this magnitude to prompt them, they never would have. They were two reasonable people, they didn't fight about things that could be settled sensibly.

But there were no reasonable answers this time, and neither was entirely rational. Nerves strung to top C, they hadn't enough composure for one, let alone to share.

'How can you even think you're fit to work?' Brian snorted derisively. 'If you can't exercise self-control in your own living-room, how the hell are you going to cope with a bunch of people who're full of their own woes and don't give a damn about yours?'

'With the support of my colleagues,' Liz shot back. 'Them I can count on.'

He sucked in a sharp breath at that, as if the barb were a physical one she'd struck into his flesh. 'I can't cope with this,' he admitted then, his voice trembling. 'I can't cope with you like this.'

'Then perhaps *you'd* better have a week at Bognor,' snarled Liz. 'Send me a postcard, let me know how your feelings are getting on.'

He had nothing more to say, nothing left to fight her with. He did what, in retrospect, he might have been wiser to do before – left the room, went upstairs.

Liz watched him go with a maelstrom of emotions in her breast. She felt anger, bitterness and a horrid kind of triumph because she'd stood her ground and he hadn't. But she also felt let down. She felt she'd let *him* down. She thought he'd said stupid, insensitive things; she thought *she'd* said some pretty unforgivable things too. She thought she should probably go after him. But she didn't.

Chapter Fifteen

There was nothing wrong with the 4x4. Donovan tinkered anyway, mainly for the pleasure of feeling oiled components slide under his fingers. He was a sensual man.

It was the oil that saved him.

When Donovan painted his boat he got so much paint on him that days later people would say, 'Green again this year? And yellow window frames?' When he changed a type-writer ribbon he looked like an extra on the *Black and White Minstrel Show.* And when he danced cheek-to-cheek with an engine he got oil all over his face.

Behind the cottage there was just room between the rusted outbuildings for the 4x4, Donovan's van and Gates's run-about. Washing against the back fence like a dark tide was a belt of woodland. There was no telling from here how deep it was or how far it went; it had a neglected look, surplus to requirements and forgotten. It was like a piece of primeval forest that had somehow escaped axe and plough, and would probably continue to do so having neither practical nor aesthetic value.

Donovan heard movement in the undergrowth and momentarily his heart quickened; but nothing in there was likely to give him a problem. The others might feel threatened by sounds of surreptitious movement in the bushes, but Donovan was fairly sure it wasn't a police dragnet closing in. Perhaps it was badgers – the woods round here were full of them.

It was neither policemen nor badgers. The green hem of the wood twitched as something pushed through and Donovan found a girl watching him over the remains of the fence. 'Who're you?' she demanded warily.

She'd stood close to him for long enough that she should have known. He recognized her, though the woolly jacket was torn and dirty now and the frizzy hair was tied back with a bandana. She looked older, not so squeaky-clean, not so likely to scream and shed terrified tears at the sight of a knife, but she was unmistakably the girl from the train.

But remembering faces is something policemen are trained for. Thieves tend not to look that closely at the people they're robbing. Also, Donovan had been clean then and wearing a collar and tie while Hugh Duggan's jeans, sweatshirt and person were all liberally anointed with oil.

The voice would be the hurdle. Donovan's accent, unremarkable in itself, was rare around Castlemere. Was it too late, he wondered, to assume a speech impediment? Probably, he'd talked to Gates for too long without. Maybe the best he could do was say as little as possible in front of the girl. 'Duggan,' he grunted. 'You?'

'Patsy,' she said. She waited for a reaction; when he didn't oblige she lost interest in him, her eyes sliding away across the yard. 'Tudor around?'

Donovan indicated the cottage.

The girl skipped over the fence, agile as a forest animal, passed him without a look. Preoccupied, she'd filed him in her mind as someone tall, taciturn and oily and left it at that. With luck, next time they met she'd remember him as the man from the yard, and after that as Hugh Duggan and nothing else. Donovan breathed a little easier.

He leaned on the bull-bars and eyed the wood. If this started getting nasty, that was the way he'd go. Five metres beyond the fence he'd be in deep gloom. In two minutes he could lose himself so completely it would take an army to find him.

But he didn't want to quit this close to success. The worst was over: she'd have remembered him by now if she was going to. Later she might get the nagging feeling of having seen him somewhere, not know where and decide he reminded her of someone on TV. Even if she did place him, all was not lost. So far as Patsy ever knew he was a railway engineer who knew about the air-shaft.

And in consequence led her companions into a police ambush, following which he swapped his job for one of the vacancies thus created. These people didn't stay free by believing in coincidence. They were cautious, suspicious. If the girl remembered him she'd tell Gates, and Gates would–

What? Beat the truth out of him? Not Gates; even if he'd been big enough it wasn't his style. Charlie was big enough but didn't seem the violent type either. No, if Patsy chanced to remember, and as a cautious man he felt the risk was too great, Gates would quit Castlemere as soon as he could pack. Donovan had the registration numbers of his cars but they were certainly false and would be changed at the first opportunity. To ensure a head start he'd probably shut Donovan in one of the outbuildings. It could take him hours to free himself, but he didn't think he risked anything worse.

So after a little while he stopped looking at the wood and went back to his engine. A while after that he went inside and cleaned up. But he didn't clean up too thoroughly.

Charlie was still puzzling over his crossword and didn't look up. 'Patsy's back.'

'I saw her outside.'

'Coach is pointing out the error of her ways. Best not to say anything.'

Donovan shrugged. 'None of my business.'

When he saw her next her face was rebellious, streaked with tears, and patched with hand-sized splashes of red that would darken into bruises. She threw herself into the chair beside Charlie's. 'Look what he's done to my face,' she said sulkily.

Charlie spared her no sympathy. 'Harry's dead and the boys are in jail, and you want me to worry about you getting your face smacked? Grow up, Patsy.'

'Don't blame me for what happened,' she said indignantly, 'it wasn't my idea.'

'No, it was Harry's. The flash ideas were *always* Harry's,' the big man said wearily. 'But he was a driver, ideas weren't his thing. If no one had gone along with his flash ideas he'd be alive now.'

The girl turned her back on him. The only other person in the room was Donovan. She regarded him critically for a while – too long, he felt his skin beginning to crawl. 'You any good then?' It sounded as if, whatever he said, she'd argue.

It was hard to equate this spiteful little witch with the terrified schoolgirl on the train. He'd risked his life to protect her; now he couldn't imagine how he'd been fooled. He shrugged. 'Ask the coach.'

'Ask the coach, tell the coach, kiss the coach's arse,' she mimicked bitterly. 'Does nobody round here have a thought in his head except what Tudor puts there?'

Finally Charlie looked at her. 'Yeah,' he said heavily. 'Harry did.'

The stairs creaked and Gates was watching them from halfway up, the light eyes astute, the small V-shaped smile speculative. When he had their full attention he said quietly, 'What about the 4x4, Hugh? Are you happy with it?'

'It'll do,' grunted Donovan, still rationing his words in front of Patsy.

Gates smiled. 'It had better – we need it first thing tomorrow. We hit the shop at seven. There'll be enough traffic about by then that we won't stand out, not enough to get in the way.'

Donovan felt a chill like a cool breath move up his spine. Twelve hours and this would be done. As long as she didn't remember for the next twelve hours it wouldn't matter what Patsy remembered after that.

Gates spelled out the plan in detail. Even so there wasn't a lot to remember. Andy in the run-about would drop him in Bridgewater Street at ten-to-seven. Eminently visible in white overalls with a paint brush in his pocket, Gates would linger outside Owens, ostensibly waiting for someone, actually checking for problems. At seven Donovan would arrive. If all was well

Gates would be out of sight by then, back in his car parked round the first corner, and he'd wait till the raid was complete. If the job went wrong, anyone who got there ahead of the police would get a lift; anyone else would be on his own. If it went well they'd meet back at the cottage.

'Whatever else you do, Hugh, don't bring the police. If you think you're being followed, lose them; if you can't lose them, lose the car and get away on foot. But if you are picked up, keep your mouth shut. You're on your own – I shan't be able to help you – but I'll keep your money for when you're able to spend it.'

He chuckled at Donovan's expression. 'I'm only saying if the worst comes to the worst. It won't, it never has yet, but I want you to understand what the priorities are. Not getting caught is first, together with keeping quiet if you're unlucky. The haul comes a poor third – what we miss one day we can make up another as long as we're all OK. But God help anyone who brings trouble to my door. I am *not* the price of your freedom. Betray me and somehow, some day, I'll make you pay.'

It wasn't the most lurid threat Donovan had ever heard but it may have been the most sincere. He gave a disdainful sniff. 'I don't grass.'

'Good. Because I don't make hollow threats.'

It was a long evening, with nothing for Donovan to do but avoid talking to Patsy, and a longer night in which the contours of the chair he sprawled in became ever more deeply impressed on his bones. He got no sleep until exhaustion finally claimed him about half an hour before Gates shook him awake. 'Time to move.'

He really was a very cautious man. Before he left the cottage he wanted to see everyone ready to go, dressed in their ram-raiding outfits and in the 4x4 with the back seat down and the engine on. 'I'm not going to twiddle my thumbs in town while you wrestle with the starter!' But the engine caught first time. 'Then let's do it. Good luck, everyone.' He waved a white arm from the window as Andy drove him away.

For ten minutes they sat in the front of the 4x4, listening to the throaty purr of the engine and growling at one another. All had cause to be on edge. Two of them were worried in case the police showed up, the third in case they didn't.

At six-fifty Donovan slammed the 4x4 into gear.

When they reached the by-pass, under the guise of washing fly-specks off the windscreen he turned on the lights. There were no police cars in sight but any of these drivers could be a policeman. Maybe the 4x4 had been spotted already; maybe he'd drive into an ambush. If not he'd have to kill a little time till help arrived. There was a telegraph pole set in the pavement not far from Owens, he didn't think Shapiro would mind him side-swiping that to jam the passenger door shut. He reckoned he could stop Charlie and the girl climbing out over him while Shapiro saw to Gates and the boy.

If Shapiro showed up. If somebody noticed these damn great headlights blazing away in the spring sunshine.

Even if they didn't, Queen's Street would quickly learn of a giant 4x4 wrapped round a telegraph pole in Bridgewater Street.

If they missed Gates at the scene they'd pick him

up at the cottage or fleeing the area. One way or another, Donovan thought it would work out.

Right up to the moment that he turned into Bridgewater Street and there was a knot of people on the pavement between the telegraph pole and Owens Electricals.

'Bloody hell,' said Charlie tersely.

They hadn't considered the possibility of something happening which would both prevent the raid and stop Gates warning them. Had some beat copper with his eye on a stripe used his initiative and stopped the small man in white overalls loitering outside the electrical store? Had Gates stepped back for a clearer view up the road and missed seeing a speeding van? Donovan thought he glimpsed blood splashed on the kerb.

'Slow down,' said Charlie, 'and keep going.'

There must have been a dozen people clustered outside the shop: men in suits, a couple of office cleaners and some schoolboys, craning forward and jostling as if something exciting had happened. Donovan could see nothing through the crush of them – no pointy hats, no white overalls – but if he'd been intending to drive through the window he couldn't have done it without killing someone.

Charlie reached across the girl and gave the wheel a fierce shake. 'Slow *down*, you stupid sod! You want them looking at us instead? Something's gone wrong, we'll work out what later. Slow down, stay calm, get back on the by-pass, and when you're sure we're not being followed head for the cottage. There's no need to panic – you haven't frigging done anything yet!'

The moment when he might have done something

had passed along with the telegraph pole. When he turned down the first side-street there was no sign of Gates's car. He made himself breathe again, eased the 4x4 back to a sensible speed; after a moment he fumbled the light-switch off. He didn't want anyone noticing now. 'What do you reckon went wrong?'

Charlie was still watching him mistrustfully. 'Anything – nothing – we'll hear soon enough. The main thing that went wrong was that you damn near blew it. I thought you said you'd done this before?'

Donovan's embarrassed shrug was by no means fabricated. 'I have, so. It's this business of looking out for people who may or may not be there that's new to me.'

There was no pursuit. He took the scenic route to be sure and reached the cottage around seven-thirty. The run-about was already in the yard.

Andy was in the kitchen. There was no sign of Gates.

'Well?' demanded Charlie.

The boy's delicate features twisted in disgust and something else which Donovan couldn't put a name to. 'The stupid bloody dog, wasn't it? Tudor would bring it with us. He tried to leave it in the car, it went to follow him and he shut the door on its foot.'

There was quite a long silence. Then Charlie said, not in a critical tone, more as if he wasn't sure he'd got it right, 'You mean, we scrubbed a job worth thousands of pounds because the dog caught its foot in the car door?'

Andy nodded, the fair hair flopping over his brow. There was a sort of grim amusement in his voice. 'There was blood everywhere. The dog was screaming, Tudor was crying, we were drawing a bigger crowd than a three-ring circus. All I could think of was to shovel them both back in the car and go looking for a vet. Tudor wouldn't leave the dog so I came on to tell you what happened. I'm going back in a couple of hours to pick them up.'

Charlie sighed. 'I can see the coach'd be upset. Still . . .'

'Stupid bloody dog,' Andy said again. Then Donovan realized what the odd inflection was. It was jealousy.

Donovan went outside and stood by the cars sucking fresh air deep into his lungs. He was thinking of those police officers who spent half their lives in this sort of situation, under cover, associating with people who'd crucify them if they found out. Donovan had been doing it for less than a day, risking not much more than a severe talking-to, and already he'd nearly blown it. He looked at the wood and wondered again about Plan B.

Fear of failure stopped him going. This was his idea, Shapiro went along because he said he could make it work. Circumstances beyond his control were one thing, if it got dangerous he'd cut and run with a clear conscience; but nothing had happened. He was in. Charlie was worried about his competence, not his bona fides. If he quit now there'd be no more chances. If he couldn't handle this he was just another small-town policeman and before long people would start expecting him to behave like one.

Donovan had always fancied his chances at undercover work. He looked the part, sounded it; he even moved like someone who was up to no good. But you also needed nerve to stay in deep cover when every instinct was telling you to up and run. Donovan had thought he had that, too; until that moment late on

Monday night when he delved deep into his reserves of courage and suddenly, unexpectedly, hit rock bottom.

The shock of that was as real now, as incredible and yet unavoidable, as in the instant when he froze on top of the Mile End Hill. He still couldn't believe he'd lost it so abruptly, so comprehensively. He could still taste the bone-sucking horror, the numb panic – he was going to die, he couldn't help himself, and *he wasn't ready*! In a moment the blithe assumption that he could take whatever fate dealt him, if not with equanimity at least with self-command, fell to dust. Fear unmanned him. If he wanted to go on doing this job he had to deal with it, and the only way he knew was head on. More hung on this than merely making an arrest. If he couldn't bridle his nerve now he'd have to rethink his entire career. He turned back to the cottage.

Patsy was standing at the kitchen door. He went to walk round her but she moved too, blocking his way.

'What?'

Her eyes searched his. She barely came up to his shoulder but she stood close, peering into his face. He could feel her scrutiny like claws in his skin. Her brows, almost colourless, were drawn together by the intensity of her stare. Behind her eyes there was a tense uncertainty, as if she knew something was wrong and didn't quite know what. Donovan didn't dare look away. He thought there was still a chance he could brazen it out. He said again, impatiently, '*What?*'

But as they stood toe to toe he saw the cores of her eyes change, the queries harden to exclamation marks as suspicion grew to conviction and the implications began to dawn on her. Her voice vibrated with accusation. 'You were on the train!'

Chapter Sixteen

Shapiro wondered if he should make an announcement about Liz's return, decided she'd resent the fuss. In retrospect, though, he wished he had. A word of warning to the Monday morning shift and the first thing she heard as she came up the back steps need not have been an argument between two constables as to whether she should resign.

DC Morgan was not an argumentative man. He came from the same fenland stock as Sergeant Tulliver, shared with him the native's peaty vowels and morose expression. People tended to ask what he was worrying about when he wasn't worried at all. He was an easy-going man who made sure of being good enough at his job but not so good that his superiors got any ideas about promoting him.

Another fenland trait that waxed strong in him was a clannish loyalty. He could be roused to a fierce protectiveness by an attack on his own.

It was a measure of Liz's success that she'd come into this insular community and within two years had its native sons considering her one of them. Her career had been an odd mixture of fighting for acceptance where it should have been automatic and finding friendship in unlikely places.

Morgan said gruffly, 'That's like saying anyone who gets his ribs kicked in had better quit because people know he can be beat. 'Course they bloody do. Nobody ever mistook me for Superman, never once, no more than they took you for Wonder Woman, Cathy Flynn! It isn't necessary, or even desirable, that they should. We need their support more than their adulation.' This may have been the longest statement ever volunteered by DC Morgan.

'That's easy for you to say, Dick Morgan,' snapped WPC Flynn, who was sufficiently ashamed of her performance the previous morning to be on the defensive. 'It's not you that's taking stick over it. Last time Donovan got himself pulped, did anyone put up witty posters about it? They did not. It's because she's a woman, and the attack a sexual one, that the men of this town think it's funny. As long as they know one of us was raped and don't know who, every policewoman in town is going to be fair game. If it was me I'd *want* a transfer: a fresh start somewhere it wasn't common knowledge. In everyone's interests.'

When no one replied, for a moment she thought she'd convinced them. Then she sensed Liz standing behind her and spun in a startled flurry of embarrassment.

'But mainly,' Liz said quietly, 'in the interests of those who can't deal with a bad joke without thinking it means the end of law enforcement as we know it.'

She didn't often pull rank on junior officers; she didn't often have to. She expected, and got, the respect of those ranked both below and above her. It had taken Queen's Street a little time to get used to the idea of a woman DI – a lot of sentences petered out in hums, hahs, mumbles and coughs until she specified, calmly but firmly, that the feminine form of Sir was Ma'am and the more they said it the easier it would come. Now they knew one another better she allowed some latitude – Donovan invariably called her Boss, which was meant as a compliment, and Guv was an institution among detectives. But it didn't extend to permitting a WPC who was reduced to hysterics by the sight of a pair of bloomers telling her where to work.

Flynn blushed scarlet. 'Sorry, ma'am. We weren't—'

'Expecting me? So I gather. You should know by now, I enjoy surprising people. And just for the record, I'm not going anywhere. Anyone who finds me an embarrassment had better learn to live with it.'

Half-way upstairs she heard a quick, heavy tread and Morgan fell into step behind her. He sounded contrite. 'Sorry, ma'am. We shouldn't even have been discussing it.'

Liz turned to face him. 'You weren't discussing it. You were doing what I expect of you – backing my judgement.' She flicked him a little grin in case he didn't know it was a joke. 'I like that line about needing support more than adulation. I must remember that, it'll look good in a report sometime.'

'Well, don't use it in front of the chief – I pinched it off him in the first place,' Morgan admitted. Chuckling, they climbed the last flight.

Liz barely had her diary out when Shapiro joined her, and by then he'd already spoken to Morgan. 'Well, that didn't take long.'

She gazed at him levelly. 'No; and it really upset me too. See that? I'm quivering like a jelly.' The hand she held out was steady as a rock.

Shapiro sniffed. 'Am I over-doing the Caring Workplace bit?'

She smiled. 'Just a smidgin.'

He nodded. 'So what are you doing today?'

Liz tapped her diary with a forefinger. 'I'm in the Crown Court at some point. Sharon Burke's applying for bail.'

'I could do that.'

'You could blow my nose for me as well, Frank, but I wouldn't thank you for that either. I want to do Burke because we've a better chance of keeping her in custody if I do. If you go it'll look like a big bad policeman oppressing a poor defenceless woman. If I do it, it won't.'

'Who's sitting?'

'Cushy Carnahan, he's a soft touch for a female defendant at the best of times. By the time Dan Fenton's piled on the agony about how this poor woman was bullied for most of her married life and only retaliated when she felt to be in mortal danger, he'll have lost sight of the fact that she drugged her husband's cocoa and set fire to his bed when he was too groggy to leave it. I'll remind him. I'll also remind him that she was arrested boarding a Channel ferry with her Italian toy-boy and her husband's nest-egg.'

'I take it you've not got a lot of sympathy for the notion of delayed self-defence, then.'

The look she gave him was scathing. 'Self-defence is when you have your back to the wall and no alternative. If Burke couldn't stop her setting fire to his pyjamas he also couldn't stop her packing her bags and starting a new life with the Latin lover of her choice. She didn't have to kill him. And if she gets bail we'll never see her again. I wonder if Mr Fenton's thought that if he's good today his fee may go on gondola rides?' Liz closed her diary and sat back. 'What else is new? Any progress on the rapes?'

He wished he had something to tell her. 'Not yet. I've got Scobie visiting known offenders but nobody's in the frame yet and to be honest the MO doesn't sound like any of our local perverts.'

Liz shook her head. 'I don't think this man's on record. Anywhere. I think it's something new with him. More than anyone else, sex offenders stick to a pattern, as if the pattern's more important than the sex. If a rapist had been targeting blonde middle-aged women anywhere in the country we'd know about it by now.'

'What's the alternative? That he's tried squash and golf and now he's taken up rape?' Shapiro wouldn't have joked about it, however wryly, with anyone else. But Liz was a colleague before she was a victim, and he'd already been warned about tip-toeing round her.

She grinned – a shade rueful but a definite grin. 'There's a first time for everything. Maybe he's just a beginner.'

Shapiro dropped his gaze apologetically. 'Sorry to get personal but you're the best witness we have. Would you say he was a youngster – a bit of a novice?'

She wasn't offended. She thought for a moment but had no doubts about the answer. 'Actually, no. He knew what he was doing. He wasn't a big man – I've told you all this, haven't I? – but there was a confidence about him. He didn't get violent because he didn't have to: he had surprise on his side. He knew what he wanted, he wasted no time, he took it and then he left.

Like a military operation. To me that doesn't seem like a kid still coming to terms with his sexuality. I got the feeling – no more than that, but it was a definite feeling – of someone about my age.'

'Old as that, eh?' Shapiro murmured sardonically.

'You know what I mean – past the first flush of youthful indiscretion, still this side of senility.'

'What about a psychiatric case?'

'No,' she said immediately, with a certainty she could not have explained. 'No, he was in control all right. Control was what it was all about.'

Shapiro nodded slowly. Then he looked at her. 'I will get him, you know. Whatever it takes. If the DNA's good enough I'll go for a mass screening.'

The hiss as she caught her breath was sharp enough to hear. 'Hell, Frank, I don't know if that's a good idea.'

'There's precedent.'

'Yes, but not all good. You can't supervise big numbers with total accuracy. Remember the time the culprit persuaded a friend to give a sample in his name? – confused the whole investigation.'

'So we're careful,' said Shapiro doggedly. 'And we could limit the numbers, if you're sure about his age. Men between thirty and fifty, say, excluding those above fourteen stone. He'd be in that group.'

'So would most of Queen's Street. So would Brian!'

'And most of Queen's Street, and Brian, would gladly give a blood sample to eliminate themselves from the inquiry. So will most other men. Then we take a closer look at the ones who don't – who're too busy, or too squeamish, or away on holiday – whatever.'

She stared at him, impressed and appalled in equal

measure. 'Have you any idea the man-hours you'd be getting into? You're talking of expenditure in excess of one hundred thousand pounds. You'll never get it approved.'

He raised one eyebrow. 'Have you any idea how stubborn I can be if the need arises?'

She had. She thought he could probably make it happen if he wanted it enough. 'There's a civil liberties aspect to this.'

'We're giving men the opportunity to clear themselves,' he said shortly. 'Where's the infringement of liberty in that? Besides, *rape* is a civil liberties issue.'

'Tell me about it.' For perhaps a minute Liz said nothing more; but Shapiro could see her thinking and knew the conversation wasn't over. Then she said, 'It's too big a sledge-hammer.'

'Three rapes inside three weeks is no nut!'

'It isn't Armageddon either. This is our town, Frank, I don't want to see it split. Making people take sides on this is too high a price even for catching a rapist.'

'We should wait for him to do it again? Or we could tell women to stay off the streets unless they travel in packs. Do you like what that'll do to the town?'

'Frank, I don't like any of this,' she said forcibly. 'But I don't think all-out war on half the population is the answer. Damn it, neither did you before Friday! I think the answer is detective work.'

'I have nothing to go on!' exclaimed Shapiro, bitter with frustration. 'The DNA'll help us put him away if we get him, but screening is the only way it'll help us find him.'

'What about a TV appeal? I doubt we'll persuade him to give himself up but we might reach someone who knows him. Women friends in particular might be anxious enough about their own safety to pick up the phone. We'll need a confidential line, this is too delicate to expect them to talk to an officer.

'But if we stress that we're just asking for ideas at this point, that we expect to get dozens of names and clear most of them right away, maybe women who've felt uneasy about a date will get to wondering and call us. After we've eliminated the improbables you could ask the others for blood samples.'

Shapiro had to concede she was right. Mass screening a town the size of Castlemere would be a logistical nightmare. It was a last resort, they weren't that desperate yet. He hadn't considered it after the rape of Mrs Andrews. He'd have to watch that. If Liz could keep the thing in perspective he had no excuse for not doing.

'Yes, all right, I'll see what I can set up. God, I hate going on telly!'

'Maybe I should do it,' said Liz.

Shapiro looked at her quickly but couldn't be quite sure that she was joking. He gave a disapproving sniff. 'You concentrate on keeping Sharon Burke behind bars. And catching my ram-raiders. I don't wish to gloat,' he added untruthfully, 'but it is the Tynesiders: Donovan made contact.'

She didn't begrudge him his small triumph. 'Where's Donovan now?'

Shapiro shrugged. 'I saw him on Friday when he was on his way to meet them. Saturday I got a message via his neighbours – coded, he must have been being watched when he wrote it, but saying there was another job in the offing. But it hasn't happened yet –

nobody's reported a big black 4x4 parked in their front window – so I assume he's still with them.'

'You don't think something could have gone wrong?' She meant, that he could be in trouble.

'I don't think so. They've no history of violence against the person. Remember Mrs Cunningham? They made sure she and the baby were safe before they went ahead. If Donovan makes a hash of it I think the worst that'll happen is that we'll lose them.'

Liz knew, because she knew him, that Shapiro was deliberately understating the risks involved to save her worry. 'Bunch of pussy-cats, hm? Only took up ram-raiding because the flower-arranging classes were full?'

'Listen,' he said in mock indignation, 'he's all right. It's making money they're interested in, not thumping coppers. They're businessmen. I'd rather deal with professional criminals any day than enthusiastic amateurs who learned the job from watching television. Like those madmen on the train. Like the sod who dumped a dead dog on my path. Did I tell you about that?'

'Yes, Frank.'

It made no difference. He told her again.

Chapter Seventeen

'Oh, no,' said Donovan with all the conviction he could muster. 'No, you're mistaken.'

But no doubt gathered in Patsy's bitter eyes to reward him. Her voice was flat with certainty. 'I *knew* I'd seen you before, and that's where. You were the guy on the train. The one who knew a way out.'

OK, Donovan thought rapidly, just because she knows that doesn't mean she knows everything. His voice dropped to a whine. 'Jesus, Patsy, don't tell the coach. I took this job in good faith. I didn't know it was you people on the train till after I got here. It was too late to back out so I kept my mouth shut. You'd have done the same.'

'I wouldn't have lied to Tudor. Not if I wanted to keep my face.' The bruises still rankled.

'I didn't lie. When he offered me the job I'd no reason to tell him, later I couldn't. It doesn't change anything. I was hired to drive, the fact I was on a train you robbed isn't relevant. I didn't try and stop you, I just tried to stop anyone getting hurt. Especially you. I thought you were in danger. I stuck my neck out for you.'

Moral blackmail was wasted on her. 'If you've nothing to hide, why can't I tell Tudor?'

Because he's brighter than you, Donovan thought grimly, he'll work it out and I'll spend the next six hours tunnelling out of a shed. 'Because it'll make everyone jumpy and cost me a job, and there's no need. What're you afraid of – that I'll tell the cops? Is that likely?'

'I don't know you,' Patsy said obstinately. 'How should I know what you're likely to do?'

'Well, I'm not going to do anything that'll put me in jail, now, am I? You can trust me that far.'

That may have been a mistake. Even at Patsy's age women have heard men say 'trust me' so often, and been let down, that the words automatically arouse suspicion. Her chin came up; it was the only way she could look down her nose at a man six foot tall. 'I don't have to trust you at all. Tudor can if he wants to.'

Donovan managed to shrug as if it didn't matter. 'OK. Then I'll get my cards and he'll get out of town. That'll cost him time and money, and he won't blame me: he'll blame the shambles on the train and the only one left from that is you.'

That reached her; he saw her waver. The icy certainty that would have sunk him began to crack. 'You said you worked for the railway.'

'So I did, till they laid me off. I didn't owe them any favours, that's why I helped your friends escape.'

'Did what?!'

'It's not my fault the Old Bill knew about the air-shaft as well! Be fair, I did my best to get them out.'

Patsy was trying to remember everything that had happened, everything that had been said. It was a week now and the details were fading. His explanation seemed to fit. 'Harry said you called the police. On that mobile phone.'

'Harry was wrong. The woman who owned it called them.'

'He was ready to beat your head in! Why didn't you say?'

'So he could beat her instead? Call me old-fashioned but I'd sooner not see guys beating up on women. I tried to help you, too. OK, you didn't need it but I didn't know that. I could've got hurt helping you.'

'Yes.' She was still thinking, still torn.

'Look,' he said reasonably, 'tell him if you're scared not to. Maybe it's for the best. But you'll be in trouble and I'll be down the road. Or you could forget we ever met. Who's to know? No one'd expect you to remember everybody on that train; you probably don't remember anyone else. For all our sakes, forget you remember me.'

Gates would have seen through it. But Patsy was thinking with her face and she was tempted. 'I don't know.' She turned abruptly back to the kitchen.

If Gates had been there she might have gone to him. But he wasn't, and she had an hour to think about it before he returned. An hour to anticipate his reaction. An hour for Donovan's suggestion to start sounding quite sensible.

Donovan was trading snarls with Brian Boru when he heard the car return. He stayed where he was. Patsy would screw him now or not at all. If she did, if Gates worked it out and opted to terminate his employment with a degree of prejudice, he could come looking for him.

But it wasn't Gates who came into the pig-sty, it was Charlie. 'Coach wants to talk to everyone inside.' Donovan scoured his face for subcurrents but found none. He followed the big man into the cottage.

Gates was still in his painter's whites, the front splashed with blood. He was pale and his cheeks carried the silvery tracks of dried tears but his voice was calm. Of the dog there was no sign.

'I want to apologize for this morning. My mistake put you all in danger. I don't accept sloppiness from you and you shouldn't have to take it from me. In the event all we've lost is time, but I let you down and I'm sorry. It won't happen again.'

There was an embarrassed silence before Charlie asked what they were all wondering. 'What about Chang, coach?'

Gates gave a watery smile. 'I shut the car door on his foot, all the little bones were broken. I told the vet it didn't matter what the treatment cost. But he said with so much damage you couldn't expect it to heal perfectly, that he'd always be lame. He thought it mightn't heal at all and he'd have to amputate. I didn't want that. Chang was special, I wanted to remember him at his best. I had the vet put him to sleep.'

A quiver of presentiment fluttered in Donovan's belly. Not that he had more than a passing interest in the fate of Gates's unpleasant little dog. But that was the point; it was *Gates's* unpleasant little dog, the man thought the sun shone out of its bare behind. But he destroyed it when it was no longer perfect. It was a timely reminder that Tudor Gates wasn't just an effeminate little man with a pleasant manner: he was the ring-leader of a criminal gang. His hobby was dog-fighting. He hurt people who let him down. He destroyed things that no longer pleased him.

Gates was regarding him oddly, puzzled that the dog's fate should affect him so. He looked quite touched. He patted Donovan's arm. 'He had a good life, you know. Now we have to look forward. How does everyone feel about having another go tonight, after the shops close?'

The Burke case was called before the Crown Court rose for lunch. Liz arrived with ten minutes to spare. She didn't need any more: she was familiar with the papers, knew how Mr Fenton would set out his stall and how she'd try to upset it. After that it was up to Cushy Carnahan, and he had as soft a spot for police-women as for female defendants.

She expected to win but it wouldn't break her heart to lose. As a fledgling detective she had taken defeats personally, as a reflection on her competence. But she'd grown out of that. She fought her cases but accepted that their resolution was in other hands. If Sharon Burke skipped the country it would be the system's failure, not hers.

So there was nothing about the case which would explain the sensation under her breastbone like a food processor chopping swedes. The case, the place and the people here were, with minor variations, the same as always. Even the defendants were depressingly familiar.

But if it wasn't any of them that was different then

it was Liz. She hadn't expected to feel so – exposed. So far as she knew, no one here was aware she'd been raped. There might be some speculation, but all Castlemere's policewomen were having to contend with that. If she couldn't cope she'd no right to criticize Cathy Flynn.

So she would cope, food processor or no food processor. How she felt wasn't branded on her forehead, any more than what she'd been subjected to. All she had to do was go through the motions. If she'd been going to panic she'd have done so before this. It was already too late for anything to go badly wrong.

A touch on her shoulder made her start but it was only the defending counsel in the Burke case, checking that she hadn't had a change of heart. 'I'm prepared to push for this woman. She's had a rough time, I don't think she ought to be treated like a criminal.'

'Murdering your husband is a criminal offence,' Liz reminded him gently.

'If it *was* murder.'

'It was murder unless it was self-defence, and it wasn't self-defence if she had an alternative. When Burke drank the Valium in his cocoa she had an alternative.'

Dan Fenton gave a tight smile. 'Let's not try it in the corridor, it offends the judge. I just wanted to be sure we're still at odds on this.'

'I'm afraid so, Mr Fenton, yes.'

He smiled again, more generously. 'Well, it's not the first time, I don't expect it'll be the last. I'd like to think we might still manage a twirl at the Civic Ball come Christmas.'

They'd cut a dash at the Town Hall last Christmas. Fenton was not a big man, neither as tall nor as broad as he seemed to think important lawyers ought to be. He compensated by assuming the attitudes and gestures of a big man, and attacking everything he did with gusto, whether defending a murderess or dancing the Gay Gordons. At the Town Hall he made a memorable figure in his white tuxedo and scarlet cummerbund, cheeks flushed with wine, thinning hair flying on the turns, as he danced the feet off every woman present who was sound in mind and limb and aged under sixty.

It was, thought Liz, the last determined expression of youth by a man who any day now would have to admit to being middle-aged. His wife had already crossed the threshold, watched from one of the little gilt chairs Davy May had set out with microscopic attention to nonchalance beside the dance-floor. Liz plopped down beside her when she made her escape. 'Mr Fenton's in good form,' she panted.

Amy Fenton nodded knowingly. 'I don't even try to keep up with him any more.' And she added, but somehow less as an afterthought than a summary: 'Dan likes to do everything well.'

All lawyers prefer winning cases to losing them, but Dan Fenton liked to win more than any barrister Liz knew. He did win most of the time. He deserved to – he put everything he had into it, time and effort and body and soul. Sharon Burke could hardly have put her defence in safer hands. Fenton and Cushy Carnahan together made a lethal cocktail.

Remand proceedings are about the shortest event in a court. Defendant's name is called, the prosecution asks for a continuing remand – a short one if he's in custody, a longer one if he's on bail – the defence agrees, the bench grants it and it's time for the next case. A couple of minutes apiece is usually sufficient.

A contested bail application takes longer. The prosecution outline their case in order to demonstrate the risk that witnesses may be interfered with or the accused do a runner. Defence counsel sets out to show what a decent citizen his client really is and how, but for the vagaries of fate, he'd be in line for beatification.

Finally it's the decision of the man on the bench, and he can't win. If he agrees to custody he risks jailing an innocent person. If he allows bail and witnesses are intimidated or the defendant repeats the offence or absconds, it's all his fault.

The responsibility had turned Cushy Carnahan into a wizened old man before he was sixty. He clutched the edge of the bench as if afraid that the tide of conflicting expectations would wash him away and followed sally and counter-attack from under brows drawn low by concentration, time and gravity.

Mr Fenton rose to make his application, thumbs lodged in the armholes of his waistcoat. Sharon Burke, he said, was an unhappy woman driven by circumstances to one terrible act of violence. Being ground to dust by a sadistic husband over a period of years had reduced her to such despair that she believed she was literally fighting for her life. There were no witnesses and no danger to anyone else. It would not be merely an act of mercy to release such a woman to the support of friends and family, said Mr Fenton, it would be an act of justice.

Liz opposed the application on the grounds that the fatal attack on Burke could not have occurred during a violent exchange as he had been rendered helpless by tranquillizers. Mrs Burke had an association with a foreign national and was arrested trying to leave the country, raising clear doubts as to whether she would remain within the jurisdiction of the court if granted bail.

Fenton rose to question her. 'Detective Inspector Graham, are you aware that my client suffered numerous attacks by her husband during the twenty-two years of their marriage, requiring hospital treatment on five occasions in the last three years?'

'I'm aware that Mrs Burke was treated by Accident and Emergency at Castle General for injuries which could have been caused deliberately. But she didn't make a complaint so we were unable to establish whether Mr Burke was responsible.'

'She told friends that her husband beat her.'

'But not us, sir. On the two occasions we asked about her injuries she said they were her own fault – that she was clumsy, she cut herself with the bread-knife; another time that she fell down the back step.'

'Inspector!' exclaimed Fenton derisively. 'You *believed* her?'

'Belief wasn't the issue. We couldn't act without a complaint.'

'So because you failed to gain Mrs Burke's confidence you consider there's no evidence of domestic violence, even though the poor woman was in A & E so often she knew the staff by name! And without a formal history of abuse you're unwilling to accept the painfully obvious truth that Sharon Burke was the victim of a violent marriage and suffered repeated episodes of mental, physical and sexual thuggery until she could take no more. Isn't that the truth, Inspector?'

'The truth is a matter for the jury to decide. My job is to ensure that they get the chance, and I believe Mrs Burke's release on bail could be prejudicial to that.'

Dan Fenton frowned. He'd known the police would object to bail but hadn't expected to have a fight on his hands. Most witnesses are made docile by their unfamiliarity with the situation. That's less of a factor with professional testimony, but he still wasn't used to losing arguments with people in the witness box.

It wasn't the first time DI Graham had given him trouble. He realized she was only doing her job, but if she wanted to make a name for herself he wished she'd do it some other way. He liked women, but better as secretaries and dancing partners and wives than opponents. His eyes hardened while his voice grew soft. The judge wouldn't like it but he too had a job to do.

'Inspector Graham, you seem to have a distorted picture of my client. She's not a bullion robber with an executive jet waiting. She doesn't have a numbered bank account in Switzerland. She's a woman of fifty who's known nothing but brutality all her married life. Yes, she killed her husband. She's never denied that. In immediate terror for her life, reeling from his latest assault, in a state of shock and despair she snatched at the chance to save herself further punishment.

'You say that once the attack on her was over she was no longer entitled to act in self-defence, and of course that's right. I'm sure you'd have handled it better. You'd have left the house, called your solicitor and the police, and begun proceedings to protect yourself from this violent bully you'd been unwise enough to marry.'

He was pushing both his luck and the rules of criminal pleading. Another member of the judiciary might have asked him to save these remarks for a more suitable occasion. But Fenton's reputation allowed him to get away with things for which a more junior barrister would have been taken to task.

But there was a limit to how much latitude he could expect so he kept moving, to say all he wanted to before he was stopped. 'But it's not you we're talking about, Inspector, it's Sharon Burke. Sharon has no financial independence. She left school at sixteen, married two years later. Her friends thought she'd done pretty well: Burke made a good living in the building trade, they had a nice house, took foreign holidays, ran a good car. It sounds a decent enough life, Inspector, doesn't it?'

His voice rose to a dramatic stridency. 'But then what can you – an intelligent, educated woman with a good job, social position, a decent home life – possibly know about humiliation? About being something for a man to wipe his feet on? Has she told you he raped her? Not occasionally, when he was drunk, but routinely, once or twice a week, any time he felt like it. His idea of foreplay, Inspector, was knocking her down.

'Can you imagine what that does to a woman's self-esteem? Can you imagine how hard it is to go on believing that you're an important human being with all the rights and privileges that go with that? Police, solicitors, court orders – these things exist for other people's benefit, not yours. Can you imagine how it must feel to be used like that?'

Afterwards Liz would say it happened too quickly for thought, that a moment came when the path divided and she had to choose with only instinct to guide her. In fact it wasn't like that. She seemed to have all the time in the world to weigh the alternatives, and decide what mattered to her. She'd had enough of discretion: it was more in her nature to fight back.

Even then she didn't rush. She glanced at the bench, where Judge Carnahan was red with indignation at what Fenton was doing but seemed somehow impotent to stop it. She glanced down at the Press table, saw Gail Fisher watching her with puzzlement growing to concern. She looked at the back of the court where the police officers, frozen in horror, didn't dare meet her gaze.

Then she looked back at the defending barrister. 'As a matter of fact, Mr Fenton,' she said, very calmly and quite without ambivalence, 'I know exactly how that feels.'

Part Three

Chapter Eighteen

Brian Graham had 3b for the first hour after lunch on Mondays. The lesson he'd prepared on design contained no nudes but the name of Charles Rennie Mackintosh was causing the usual hilarity when Mary McKenna put her head round his door and signalled him outside. 'Can we have a word in my office?' The same glance at the time-table that told her where he'd be also told her who he was teaching so she brought a student teacher to take over the class. The last time 3b were left alone for more than a few minutes they whitewashed the blackboard.

So this was going to take a little time. Puzzled, Brian followed the principal to her office and took the seat offered him. He'd left the door open; she closed it.

She had red hair and a forthright manner, and she came right to the point. 'Brian, you should have told me about Liz. We could have juggled the schedule, got you a bit of time off.'

He dropped his gaze as if she'd caught him out in some mischief. The colour rose in his throat. He mumbled, '*Me* take some time off? I couldn't get *her* to take some time off.'

'So I gather,' said Ms McKenna drily.

Brian caught the echo of import in that, made

himself look at her. He knew he was behaving stupidly, as if he had something to be ashamed of. But when he looked up McKenna's eyes were compassionate.

He didn't understand. 'How do you know about it?'

There were two questions there: the obvious one, to which the answer was that another teacher's husband was a witness in another case that morning, and the important one. McKenna had never flinched from dealing with difficult issues and now was no time to start. 'Brian, if you thought it was a secret I'd better tell you Liz made what amounts to a public statement in court this morning. I don't know any details, just that. Do you want to go home, see if she's all right?'

It was a kind offer but it went to his heart as straight as a well-aimed arrow. Liz wouldn't be at home, and she would be fine. He didn't need any details to know that this situation hadn't been forced on her. She hadn't been backed into a corner: Liz Graham didn't allow herself to be used like that. Liz Graham didn't do anything she didn't pretty well want to. She'd done this because she chose to: out of pride or anger or tactics, regardless of its effect on anyone else. On him. Liz would be all right: Liz was the strong one, the bruiser. She'd come through this with her head up, bloodied but triumphant, as she came through everything. Brian felt he'd had the legs cut from under him with a chainsaw.

He didn't trust himself to speak, just nodded. He collected his jacket and drove home. He sat by the phone for an hour before he picked it up.

*

'Well,' Superintendent Giles said manfully, 'you've put the cat among the pigeons now.'

'Yes,' agreed Liz. There was no point denying it.

'Can I ask why?'

She sketched a shrug. 'It seemed a good idea.'

'At the time.'

'Yes. And since.'

'Why?' He wasn't arguing, he genuinely wanted to understand.

'The situation was becoming impossible. Everyone in Castlemere knew a policewoman had been raped: until they found out who, the innuendo was going to affect every woman here, me included. The damage was done already; I thought if confidentiality was no longer possible the next best thing was to put the facts on record.'

'You thought all this,' Giles murmured astutely, 'between Fenton asking the question and you answering it?'

Liz conceded his point with a tiny grin. 'Not exactly. It was one of those seminal moments: I had either to tell the truth or lie. I suppose it made me think about how we were handling it. It seemed right then; I still think it was right.'

The superintendent pursed his lips. He had very clear eyes; now the blue in them was cool. 'If Fenton deliberately put you in that position to help his case I'll complain to the Bar Council.'

Liz shook her head. 'Coincidence, sir. There was no way he could have known; unless someone here told him and I don't believe that. I was damaging his case, he wanted to shut me up. He expected me to have to say no.' Again the little smile. 'It ruined his day when I said yes. Now he has to explain to Sharon Burke why she's going to be in custody for the next six months while the CPS gets its case together.'

'And' – Giles looked for words that made no assumptions – 'what are you going to do next?'

'You mean, will I tidy the place up by going into purdah for a while?' Her voice took on an edge. 'No, sir. I've done nothing to be ashamed of, I'm damned if I'm going into hiding.'

'How does your husband feel about it?'

Liz blinked. 'Brian?'

'Brian. He does know?'

'I shouldn't think so, not yet. He'll still be in school.'

Superintendent Giles regarded her thoughtfully. As policemen go he was a New Man: he valued the contribution of women officers to a police service which sometimes needed an infusion of compassion and sensitivity. He regretted that the only way women seemed able to get on the promotions ladder was by sacrificing those very virtues and starting to behave pretty much like men. He sighed. 'I shouldn't count on that, Inspector.'

Dead on cue, Miss Tunstall tapped and put her head round his door. 'Sorry to disturb you, sir. But I've got Detective Inspector Graham's husband on the phone, and he sounds rather upset.'

She found Brian at the kitchen table with three mugs in front of him, each half-full of the coffee he kept making but was too agitated to finish drinking.

She dropped into a chair opposite him, slinging her bag over the back. 'We'll have to make this quick, I'm needed back at the office.'

He literally gasped. She really had no idea what she'd done, what either of them was doing here. 'Liz, talk to me! Damn the office. Tell me what's going on. What happened, why you did it. What you were thinking of!'

She wasn't surprised he was upset. He was a private man, she could imagine how the news of this getting out would affect him. But there was nothing she could do to shield him. The situation was not of her making: she was sorry he was having problems but he'd have to rise above them just as she had. Now the facts were a matter of public record the gossip would soon wither and die.

She swallowed her impatience and told him how it had come about. 'It seemed the lesser of two evils. Things couldn't go on as they were. Every woman at Queen's Street was under pressure – I had to do something to protect them.'

'You didn't think maybe it's their job to protect you?'

Her eyes were wide with censure. 'No, Brian, I didn't. I'm the senior woman officer in Castlemere: I didn't get there by dumping my problems on my juniors.'

'Fine,' spat Brian, white-faced with fury. 'Well, we've established what's best for you and what's best for Queen's Street, and once we've got the traffic wardens' vote we can be quite sure all the legitimate interests have ben catered for. What about me, Liz? Do I figure *anywhere* in this? You must have asked yourself how going public was going to affect me. Didn't you? Please, Liz, you must have.'

The extent of his anger and distress amazed her.

She honestly didn't understand why he felt betrayed. Shapiro when she told him, and Giles when she told him, had been taken aback but respected her right to set the pace on this. It was a difficult situation, there were no perfect answers, but they were prepared to back her decisions simply because they *were* her decisions and no one else had a better right to make them. She didn't understand why her husband didn't feel the same way. 'Brian – *does* it affect you?'

It would be hard to find a gentler man than Brian Graham. It showed in everything he said and did, in the low voice, the self-effacing humour, even the way he walked. His virtues were the modest ones of kindness, dependability, generosity of spirit. Violence appalled him.

But he came as close then as he ever had to slapping her. His long hands fisted at his sides and it seemed to take an effort of will to keep them there. His bony skull rocked back, eyes shut as if in pain. His voice was a desperate whisper. 'Liz, what do you *mean*, does it affect me? Everything you do – everything that happens to you – affects me. You told a crowd of strangers that you'd been raped. You didn't ask me first. You didn't even tell me first. If Big Mac hadn't pulled me out of class I might have heard it from 3b!'

'It was going to come out sometime,' she said reasonably. 'It seemed better to pick my own moment.'

'But why didn't you *warn* me?'

'I didn't know what Dan Fenton was going to say! My only choice was between lying, glossing it over or telling the truth. I told the truth. I really don't see the problem.' The tragedy was, she really didn't.

His breathing was ragged. 'The problem? The problem is that tomorrow I'm going to have to face a bunch of kids who know my wife's been raped. Half of them are going to be embarrassed, the other half'll be over the moon. Christ almighty, they think they've put one over on you when they find out your first name! When they have this for ammunition they'll snipe and they'll snipe, and they won't stop until either I break down in front of them or I do some corrective dentistry on them with the board rubber. How can I teach like that? What if one of them knows who attacked you – an older brother, an uncle, a father even? Your honesty may have made your job easier but it's made mine damn near impossible.'

Unused to criticism from him she reacted with more speed than grace, leapt to her feet so quickly the chair spilled from under her. 'Brian,' she exclaimed in exasperation, 'don't be so pathetic! Of course it's difficult. Do you think it isn't difficult for me? But there's only two options: lie down under it or get up and kick back. You lie down if you want to but it's not my style. If the alternative to keeping my head down and telling fibs is everyone knowing, then so be it.

'I've been raped once. Well, my wits were fluttering round the eaves like a flock of starlings so I wasn't best able to prevent it. But I'm not concussed now, and I'm not submitting to any more violations. I won't be hustled out of sight by the kind of prejudice that expects the victim of a sex attack to pay the price – and pay it again and again for as long as anyone remembers. Women leave town to avoid that, but I'm not doing so. This wasn't my fault, not in any way at all, and I'm not going to act as if it was.

'Now you can deal with that, Brian,' she said

fiercely, 'or you can take that holiday in Bognor while the fuss blows over, but that's how it's going to be. I've earned the respect of this town, and I'm damn well going to have it. Not sympathy – I don't want sympathy – I want justice and respect. I'm going to stand up for my rights. Not just for me: for the other women who aren't strong enough to; and even for you, Brian, and all the other-halves who're worried about what the folk at work might say. And if you haven't the guts to stand with me, then God damn you!'

She didn't wait for a reply. She snatched up her bag and flung out to the car, and the wheels spat grit.

Half-way to Castlemere she found herself regretting some of that. Not what she'd said, because it was important and not just to her, but how she said it. She had a lot of anger to dispose of, she couldn't afford to do it at work, but Brian wasn't her enemy and he hadn't deserved what he got. She'd have to apologize. For two pins she'd have gone straight back and done it then. But she glanced at the clock on her dashboard and decided it could wait till this evening when they'd both be calmer and could perhaps move on from regrets to working out a compromise. She'd get away from work around five, they could talk properly then.

In fact she finished at seven, and when she got home Brian's car was gone from the drive and a drawerful of clothes from his chest. There was no note. She sat on the bed in stunned disbelief. She couldn't think where he might have gone. She couldn't think of anyone who might know. When she was forced to accept that she had no way of finding him, she cried – brokenly, desolately – for the first time since the attack.

Chapter Nineteen

DC Morgan was also in court on Monday morning, giving evidence before the magistrates in a case of handling stolen goods. The defence counsel asked for it to be called early to enable her to appear elsewhere in the afternoon; which would have been all right, Morgan thought morosely, if she'd reciprocated by getting on with the damn thing. Instead she challenged every word he said, and had her witnesses repeat themselves endlessly, with the result that Morgan was there from ten-twenty until noon. The eventual conviction was scant reward: no one was going to send a grandmother to prison for handling a frozen leg of lamb. Probation was the best Morgan had expected. Mrs Thelma Dickens, doyenne of petty crime in that sink of iniquity known as The Jubilee, gave him a wink as she left the court.

As a result Morgan wasn't at his desk when Keith Baker phoned at ten-thirty. The switchboard asked if anyone else could help but Baker said he'd call back later – it was nothing urgent, just something DC Morgan had been asking about. By the time Morgan got the message, however, Baker was half-way down a cow with a drenching tube. It was mid-afternoon before they finally made contact.

'That dog you were asking about,' said the vet. 'I treated it this morning.'

Morgan pricked up his ears. 'The Chinese thingy?'

'Crested Dog, yes. Painter brought it in. Shut its foot in a car door. Funny business.' Baker's answer to pressure of work was to talk like a telegram, omitting pronouns and conjunctions and anything else that didn't earn its space. 'Funny dog for a painter to have; but then he was funny sort of painter. More your interior decorator.'

'Did you fix it up?'

'Could have done. Would have done. Didn't want me to. Didn't want a lame dog. Had me put it down.'

Morgan frowned, disappointed. 'Then he'll not be back.'

'No – paid his bill before he left. Cash. Funny little sod – tried to tip me. Point is, though,' he went on, returning to the purpose of his phonecall, 'I got a look at the car that picked him up.'

Shapiro pushed the facts about like pushing cold food round a plate with a fork. 'They were on a raid this morning: the look-out was in white overalls for visibility. But his dog got hurt and he went to find a vet instead. So they're still here and still in business. We knew that, of course – Donovan would've been back if they'd left town.'

'Probably,' Morgan agreed cautiously.

'The car Baker saw – that's not the 4x4 so it's the look-out's car. That means it'll be in the target area for some minutes before the raiders arrive. We have the number, we know what the look-out looks like – pity about the dog but even without it he's pretty distinctive. We know the sort of goods they're interested in, and the times of day that suit them.'

He was thinking aloud. Morgan was good for thinking aloud to: he never interrupted, never got to the punchline first, but if questioned afterwards could repeat the salient points as proof that he hadn't nodded off half-way through.

Shapiro went on. 'Well, they missed their chance this morning. They must be getting anxious about hanging round here so long: my guess is they'll go straight to the next slot – tonight, an hour either side of seven – get it done and get out, hope for better luck elsewhere.'

He was convincing himself. He hoped he wasn't raising stout walls on marshmallow foundations. But Castlemere hadn't been good to them, even before the dog's accident they'd lost their driver somehow and had to waste time finding another. In fact they'd been unluckier than they knew, but hopefully they wouldn't realize that for a little while yet.

'All right,' he decided, 'I'll go see Mr Giles – grovel a bit, threaten a bit, whatever it takes to reinstate the stake-out. If we can watch those half dozen shops for two more hours we'll get them, I know we will.'

'If they go tonight,' said Morgan lugubriously. 'If nothing else goes wrong.'

After thirty years as a detective it took a lot to make Shapiro feel like an irrepressible optimist. Morgan was worth keeping around for that reason alone.

'Same time, same place,' said Gates, 'just the other end of the day. I'll be in place by ten-to-seven, you hit

Owens at seven. I'll go as a golfer – Andy, put the clubs and the big umbrella in the car.'

They went over the timings yet again. 'Two minutes,' insisted Gates. 'I don't care if they've got the Crown Jewels in there, you've only got two minutes so concentrate on the good stuff and get out when your time is up. Unless there's a police patrol nearby, two minutes isn't long enough for them to respond to the alarm. If it goes well, we'll meet back here at seven-thirty.'

When the time came they produced their ski-masks, Donovan started the 4x4 to prove it hadn't died during the day, then Andy drove Gates away. The raiders waited the statutory ten minutes then set off.

This time it went wrong before they reached the end of the lane. As Donovan went to turn out the little red car turned back in, flashing its lights waspishly. Donovan, reversing all the way to the cottage, had his attention fully occupied but Charlie could see that Gates was spitting tacks. He couldn't guess what had gone wrong this time but plainly something had, and this time Gates wasn't blaming himself. Charlie couldn't see how it could be his fault but he crossed his fingers just the same.

The cars pulled up side by side in the yard, disgorging all five occupants, tense and quarrelsome. Gates was ruddy with anger. 'Pack up, we're leaving.'

'What happened?' If Charlie hadn't asked Donovan would have had to.

'They were waiting for us! The town was full of coppers! They *thought* they were being discreet. They thought since they weren't in uniform no one could possibly know who they were. But there was no missing them. All the places we'd thought about hitting? – they were watching them. Electrical showrooms and jewellers. We did a quick tour, without getting too close, then we got out fast. They didn't spot us.'

'I don't understand,' said Charlie emptily. 'How could they be waiting for us?'

Gates was incandescent. 'How? Charlie, isn't it obvious? Somebody talked!'

Patsy took three quick steps back, out of range of his hands. Then her eyes flew to Donovan.

'Don't look at me,' he said rapidly, 'I've been chaperoned since I got here, the only way I could've talked to anyone is by telepathy.'

Gates stared at him, the elf eyes sharp as flint; then he nodded. 'I know that. I don't think it was you, or anyone here. Thanks to Harry and his bright ideas, two of our people are sitting in police cells right now. I imagine the pressure proved too much for one of them. Martin, probably – kids can't take it like a grown man.' He shook his head in angry disbelief. 'He can't have told them much or they'd be here. But he's said enough for them to watch the places we'd want to hit at the times we'd want to hit them.'

Charlie cleared his throat. 'Maybe not. We've done this a lot of times now – maybe they finally worked out how.'

He was too big to slap but Gates rounded on him with the same viciousness that Patsy provoked in him. 'You ever hear of police budgets, Charlie? You really think this one-horse town can afford to guard every shop we might be interested in? No, they were told.' His eyes circled the yard like cold fire, settled on the girl half behind the car. He started towards her and she shrank before him. His voice was a soft menacing monotone. 'I warned you what would happen if you let me down. I warned all of you.'

'Me, Tudor?' Her voice soared and cracked, and she stumbled backwards, trying to keep the vehicle between them. 'I haven't done nothing. I never told nobody.'

'You robbed that train. That's where our troubles began. But for that we'd have been finished here days ago. Harry'd be alive, nobody'd be in jail, nobody'd be talking to policemen.' His hands went to his narrow waist, tugging at the buckle of his belt.

Stripped of the social polish he was just another thug, cleverer than some, nastier than plenty. In the face of failure the elegant manner, the well-modulated voice, the air of gentle irony all deserted him and the man who bet on which dog could rip out another's throat was revealed.

'You've been trouble since I first clapped eyes on you,' hissed Gates, stalking her leopard-like between the cars. 'You were another of Harry's bright ideas: I should have told him to stick to driving then, if I had he'd still be here. But he wanted you in and I gave way. I thought, What harm can it do? But you poisoned him. Did you think I didn't know?' His voice turned to savage mimicry. ' "Oh, Harry, you're the best man here. Oh, Harry, you could be so much more than just a driver. Oh, Harry, why don't we do something of our own while Tudor's away? Do what I say, Harry, and I'll let you shove it up me some more!" '

The girl screamed at him in terror, 'That's not true! I *never* told him to go behind your back. Sure I liked him, but I was happy the way things were. The train was Harry's idea – I just went along for the laugh.'

'Then why aren't you laughing now?' Almost close enough to grab her, the little man moved on the balls of his feet like a dancer, the belt in his hand swinging free. 'Laugh, Patsy. Go on – laugh.'

It was as if no one else was there, just the two of them engaged in some sadistic game. Andy watched with a malevolent satisfaction that was clearly, if unconsciously, sexual. Charlie's broad face screwed up unhappily and he raised a hand in protest but somehow lacked the resolve to intervene.

Which left Donovan. Different rules apply under cover but he still didn't see how he could stand by while a vicious little crook flogged a young girl. OK, the girl was also a vicious little crook, but what she was mattered less than what Donovan was. All that crap about the King's Shilling: funny thing was, it mattered. You didn't take the money then make excuses not to do the job. You didn't do only those parts of the job that were easy and safe and got you home by six every night. You did, in so far as you were able, what needed doing, and accepted the long hours and the risks that came with the package.

And you didn't stand by and watch someone commit an assault occasioning grievous bodily harm. That was funny, too. He'd known the girl was a threat to him, thought it was because she remembered him from the train. But it would have made no difference if she'd forgotten him, had never seen him, if he'd never been on the train. What was going to betray him was his own sense of duty.

So he slipped behind Gates and reached over his

shoulder to catch his wrist as he raised his hand. 'Don't do that.'

Charlie stared at him in horror, Andy in resentment, Patsy in shock. Gates spun dervish-like, wresting his arm free, his face aglow with indignation. Coals sparked in the amber eyes. Like a foul-mouthed child he yelled at the top of his voice, 'Take your fucking hands off me!'

Donovan had just enough time to think, 'He really is mad. He's got no more control than a kid in a tantrum.' Then Gates's right arm whipped back, and the narrow strap split the air and opened Donovan's cheek to the bone.

Shock cushioned him from the pain. He was aware of the skin parting as under a blade; clapping his hand to it he met the start of blood. For a moment he could only stand and pant, fighting light-headedness. When that receded anger came. He fastened both hands in Gates's clothes and lifted him on to his toes. 'You little shit! Take my hands off you? I'll turn you over my knee and spank you.' He dropped him then, thrusting him away like week-old rubbish. 'Or I would if I didn't think you'd enjoy it.'

Charlie separated them, one big hand on Donovan's shoulder, stopping short of laying the other on Gates but interposing his solid body. 'Come on, now,' he rumbled mollifyingly. 'Let's cool it, shall we? Enough's gone wrong without us laying into one another.' He looked at Donovan's cheek, winced and groped in his pocket; but all he came up with was a used tissue and a toffee-paper.

Forced to stand back, Gates too was appalled at what he'd done. In his pocket was a newly laundered handkerchief. He took it out and proffered it. 'Hugh, I'm so sorry.' His voice had dropped a full octave from that banshee wail to a murmur of apparently sincere regret.

Donovan regarded him sourly for some moments but finally took the handkerchief. 'What, no lace?' he growled. When he touched it gingerly to his cheek it came away dyed in his blood.

The murderous rage had passed but Gates had not forgiven Patsy. His eyes on her were cold with hatred. 'This was your fault. Pack your gear and get out. If you show your face again I'll bury you.'

People come into crime in all sorts of ways – by design, carelessness or accident, for the money, for the kicks. Mostly it serves up more problems than solutions, but it fast becomes a way of life and the way out is not the way back. When Harry Black brought her in it was the nearest thing to a family Patsy could remember. Difficult as it was to imagine a way of life so bankrupt, so bereft of meaning, that dossing in tumbledown cottages between ram-raids was a step up, that was where Patsy had come from. And she didn't want to go back. So Gates's threat shook her in a way that his hands never had, that even the lash of his belt would not have done. Patsy couldn't face being alone again.

Whether it also shook loose a last chip of memory, like the last slate that hangs on for days after the storm before falling, or whether she remembered earlier and couldn't think what to do about it, there was no way of knowing. But her eyes flared at him and she shook her head urgently, the electric hair dancing. 'Tudor, no! You can't send me away. It's not my fault! I didn't grass you up, he did!'

Donovan looked up balefully over the bloody rag but there was no question about it: she'd finally decided where her loyalties lay. She was practically poking him in the eye.

Gates's gaze was caustic with disbelief. 'You – poison! He took that for you.' He jerked a hand at Donovan's cheek. 'That would have been your face if he hadn't stepped in.'

She shot back, 'He isn't who you think! You think that dog in the shed makes him one of us but he's not. He isn't even Hugh Duggan. His name's Donovan, he was on the train, and Harry reckoned it was him called the police.'

Chapter Twenty

So sure was she that it was Brian ringing the doorbell, Liz didn't even hurry to answer it. She wiped her face, composed her mind – a little, it would have taken too long to do the job properly – and fixed at the front of it what she wanted to say. She certainly owed him an apology, probably more than that, but something less than her soul. Where they went from here would have to be discussed, but whatever she'd said she didn't want to go alone. He was an ordinary man in many ways – too often she had put him aside while she dealt with urgent and important matters – but she was amazed at the size of the gap his absence left in her. That was the first thing she had to say.

It wasn't Brian. Gail Fisher of the *Courier* stood half sideways on the step as if expecting a rebuff. Liz blinked. She wasn't surprised that Fisher knew where she lived; she was astonished to see her here. 'I'm sorry, Gail, I've nothing to add to what I said in court.' A brittle note conveyed her displeasure.

'I'm sure.' Fisher nodded quickly. 'That isn't – exactly – why I'm here. Can we talk for a moment? I won't stay, I don't want to embarrass you, I just thought I ought to warn you about – well, what I've done.'

Liz sighed, took her to the living-room. 'I didn't just

come floating down the Arrow on a bubble, you know. I'm not going to be amazed to see what I said in open court quoted in Thursday's *Courier*.'

'Well, that's the point,' said Fisher. She seemed ill at ease, perched on the edge of the big sofa as if poised for flight. 'You won't have to wait till Thursday – I've given something to the dailies for tomorrow morning. I've also recorded a piece for the local radio: it'll be in their news magazine at nine tonight.'

If she'd thought about it Liz would have anticipated as much. She'd known she was crossing a Rubicon, hadn't expected or even wanted the reporter to shirk her obligations in order to protect her, like a child or an imbecile who couldn't take responsibility for her own actions. Once Liz had decided on her course, the sooner everybody knew the facts, the better.

She nodded slowly. 'Thanks for telling me. I'll call my father – he's the only person who matters who doesn't already know.'

Fisher swivelled quickly in her seat, her body bent forward. 'Inspector – Liz – I'm so sorry about what happened. The last thing I want to do is make things harder. I'm on your side: you do know that? Most people will be on your side. I don't think you'll regret what you did.'

Liz smiled tightly. 'Let's hope not.' The rape was different: that was a crime. She had no intention of discussing personal business, like the danger that what she'd done had destroyed her marriage.

As she was leaving, Fisher took her hand and held it a moment. Not a woman to whom casual intimacies came naturally, Liz was about to take it back; but the current of sympathy that travelled across the bridge stayed her a moment. She pressed the other woman's hand in reply. 'Thanks for coming. I know what to expect now.'

'Maybe; maybe not,' murmured Fisher.

Charlie lashed Donovan's hands to a pipe under the low roof of the byre. Agitated by the sudden flurry of activity the dogs could be heard whining and scratching at the wall of the adjoining pigsty.

Donovan didn't stand peaceably to be hung up like washing: he struggled and swore until Charlie knocked the fight out of him with a single punch under the ribs. He dropped doubled-up on the floor; Charlie lifted him and finished the job. His face close to Donovan's he murmured, 'You're in deep shit now, son.'

Gates was watching Donovan's face, waiting for the pain in his belly to be enough for him to worry what came next. When he saw the hurt in his eyes turn to fear, Gates began to speak. 'You're a policeman, aren't you?'

There was no point lying. He'd known Gates would work it out if he had anything to go on. Donovan nodded, setting off ripples of complaint in his wrists and midriff.

'And that's your name – Donovan?'

'Detective Sergeant Donovan. I'd show you my warrant card but I left it at home.' The ache under his ribs meant it took him two breaths to get it out.

Gates gave a tiny smile. 'I'll take your word. You work with Mr Shapiro then.'

Donovan was startled. 'You know him?'

'My homework includes weighing up the opposition. I've been to his house – I left him a souvenir.'

For an Irishman of Donovan's generation the words had only one meaning and it wasn't a pottery castle inscribed 'A Present From Portrush'. His racing heart missed a beat. 'A bomb?'

Gates laughed, a tinkling laugh merry with natural cruelty, like a child pulling the legs off a spider to see how many it needs to run away. 'Of course not. It may have been a bit of a bomb*shell* – you don't expect an anatomy lesson on your path first thing in the morning.'

'The skinned dog – that was you? *Why?*'

'I was cross with him. I got back from a dog-fight at three in the morning to find I'd no crew left – except for Charlie who was anxiously rehearsing ways of breaking the news! I wanted to hit back. I had Andy collect one of the night's losers and we took that round to him. I kind of hoped it might give him paws for thought.' The pun was wasted: no one so much as smiled. Gates gave a martyred little sigh.

Donovan was trying to think. 'You know he's looking for you? When he missed us in town he'd go back and talk to your friends again. He could be here any minute.'

'Yes, he could,' agreed Gates; 'if someone talked. But then, perhaps I did them an injustice. Perhaps all Mr Shapiro knows came from you.' He held his head on one side like an intelligent budgie. 'In which case, as long as he doesn't hear from you again we're safe.'

'He didn't hear from me this time. I'd no chance – damn it, you *know* that! It had to be someone else.' But Gates just smiled.

Donovan tugged but the belt securing his hands

only tightened. He glanced bitterly round the crew. Charlie wouldn't meet his eyes. In the doorway the girl sniffed and turned away. Andy leered at him with expectancy.

Gates seemed avuncular by comparison. The all-consuming rage had not returned, for which Donovan was glad: beside himself with fury he could kill as easily as spit. As long as he was in control he would put his long-term interests first.

But still Donovan didn't expect Gates to cut him down, help him put Brian Boru in the van and wave him goodbye. He'd thought if it got this far he might take a thumping before they made their escape. Well, no one had thumped him yet, not really. But somehow he wasn't reassured.

Gates said, 'Charlie, take Patsy and the car and get on your way. Head north up the motorway – they won't expect that. Me and Andy'll follow in the 4x4. We'll meet you at the second services. Get me a Danish and a *cappuccino* – we'll be there before it's cold.'

The big man looked quickly from Gates to Donovan and then at the floor. 'Um—'

Gates gave an understanding smile. 'Don't worry, we'll be right behind you. I just want to say goodbye to Sergeant Donovan.'

'He's getting rid of you, Charlie,' Donovan said, fast, before Gates could intervene or Charlie could leave and pretend he hadn't heard. 'He wants rid of you because you've got the wit to keep him off me. You're a thief, Charlie, that's all – if you'd been caught today that's all you'd have been charged with. If they catch you tomorrow the charge'll be the attempted murder of a police officer.'

'Shut up, Sergeant,' said Gates pleasantly.

'Or what?' snorted Donovan. 'You'll make me sorry? You're going to beat the shit out of me! I know that, you know it – Charlie knows it too, don't you? You don't like it, you don't need it, but unless you stop him now you're going to get a piece of it. When you're caught it'll make about four years' difference to your sentence.'

The big man raised unhappy eyes to Gates. He wasn't a fool, just a man who sometimes found it convenient to fool himself. He knew why Gates wanted him to leave. If he'd meant only to rough the policeman up he'd have done it in front of them all, as an example. If he wanted privacy it was because he meant to go further than that. 'Coach?'

Gates explained clearly and gently. 'He's a spy, Charlie. I can't let that pass and he knows it. He knows he's going to get hurt. He thinks he can split us by appealing to your better nature. You can't blame him: in the same circumstances anyone would lie. I want you to leave because showing him the error of his ways will take a few minutes and it'll be safest if you and Patsy go now.'

Charlie didn't need it to be true, only tolerably convincing. He didn't want a show-down with Gates: all he needed was a sop to his conscience and, if the worst happened, some ammunition for his brief. So he had every incentive to believe. Head down he shouldered past Gates and out into the yard.

Donovan saw his last best chance disappearing and yelled after him – 'Charlie!' – his voice soaring.

Gates murmured, 'Andy,' and the boy hit Donovan again where Charlie had. It wasn't a comparable blow but it was enough to take his breath away. By the time he had it back he could hear the car's engine dwindling down the lane.

'Just us now,' said Gates softly. 'And the dogs.'

Andy brought them from next door, a chain in each hand. Neither was muzzled, restrained only by collars like plough-harness, the chains making wild music as they pulled and tossed. But this wasn't a match situation, and though they were excited to be on the move the dogs weren't looking for a fight.

'And the other one,' said Gates.

Andy secured his brace to a handy bracket and left again. Donovan heard mingled snarls and shouts and hoped for the best, but Andy returned with Brian Boru.

Gates was watching Donovan's face. 'You've seen pit-bulls at work, you know what they can do to one another. I imagine you've also seen what they can do to people.'

Donovan's lip curled thinly but he said nothing, damned if he'd give Gates the satisfaction. He'd gone into this knowing he could get thumped; if he got bitten instead it might mean tetanus shots instead of X-rays but it would be the same freckled Irish nurse at Castle General dressing his wounds and lecturing him on his lifestyle. He thought he could take anything Gates could do to him.

Gates saw him think it and the V-shaped smile was brilliant. 'What – you think I'm *bluffing*? Winding you up for the pleasure of seeing you sweat? I'm sorry, Donovan, you were right the first time, when you told Charlie I was going to damn near murder you. Well, nearly right.'

He pivoted on his heel, gazing at the dogs. 'See

those, Donovan? Those are three of the best fighting dogs in Britain. I include your Brian because I know potential when I see it. I'd put serious money on any one of them to beat any other dog on the circuit.

'But anything palls eventually, even dog-fighting. And then you start wondering, is that all they can do? Dogs have been used to hunt elk, and lion, and bait bears and bulls. And hunt men. Could my dogs do that? Could they tackle the cleverest, most dangerous game of all?' Again he looked to Donovan for some reaction; again his only reward was the dew gathered on Donovan's lip.

He shrugged lightly. 'In theory they could. Dogs with no training at all have turned on and killed human beings so a trained fighting dog should have no problem. A quarry with no jaws to speak of, puny muscles, throat and belly exposed – it ought to be a foregone conclusion. But for the psychology. In their heads, dogs take the orders and men give them. Half their training has been about obedience, about accepting men as their pack leaders. Now I'm asking them to forget all that and kill a human being in cold blood.'

Donovan had been a policeman long enough to hear a lot of threats: if he'd taken them all seriously he'd have been a nervous wreck. Most threats were like a dog growling, an attempt to avoid rather than start a fight. Like dogs, people who wanted to hurt you didn't waste time on threats – they went straight for the throat.

'All right,' he said with a kind of world-weary nonchalance, 'What do you want?'

Gates blinked. 'Want?'

Donovan licked dry lips. 'What is it you want? My

chief could be here any time so you're not doing this for fun. There's something you want, something you think I can get for you. What is it? Tell me, let's see what we can do before one of them dogs gets loose and bites somebody.'

Gates was genuinely delighted. 'You do, don't you – you really think I'm saying this to frighten you! Why? For a safe passage? I don't need you for that, there's no one out there. Maybe Mr Shapiro will get here eventually; but I'll be long gone and so, I'm afraid, will you.'

Donovan shook his head, the black hair dancing in his face. 'Come on, Gates, talk to me. I know you're pissed off, I don't expect to get out of this scot-free. You want me to say I'm scared? OK, I'm scared. I'm going to get hurt here, I don't know how much; damn right I'm scared. But kill me? You don't need that any more than Charlie does. They get you for killing a copper, they throw away the key. You'd have a bad time in jail.'

'I'm not going to jail,' Gates said calmly. 'That's why you have to die, Donovan. If it was a question of punishment I could settle for less, but you're a danger to me as long as you live. From a wheelchair, from an iron lung, you'd tell Mr Shapiro things I don't want him to know.

'I'm sorry to be brutal but it's too late for us to start considering each other's feelings. I have to kill you; that being so, I intend to find out what these dogs can do. It's a chance I may never have again. I want to see how they solve the problem of killing a man.'

He gave an apologetic little shrug, as if he wasn't sure of the etiquette, the right thing to say next. 'It shouldn't take long. Supremacy isn't an issue: once they accept that you're fair game it'll be like killing a sheep – quicker, because you won't be running away. A few minutes should do it. The terminal wards are full of people who wish they could get it over that fast.'

Finally Donovan believed. Gates meant exactly what he said. He wasn't bluffing, he wasn't out to trade, he wasn't going to change his mind. This was where it ended: in screams and in blood. Donovan had seen it, knew what it was like when those jaws ripped into living flesh. A few minutes? – maybe. But minutes like those defied measurement on any clock.

His mouth was so dry he had trouble getting the words out. 'Untie me?'

'Don't be absurd.'

But Donovan wasn't thinking of escape, only of getting it over. He knew now that Gates wouldn't be satisfied with kicking his lights out, that he meant to kill him and to kill him this way. But Donovan didn't want to hang by his hands while the dogs leapt for him, tearing his flesh. With his hands free he still couldn't make a fight of it but on the ground he'd die quicker. 'For God's sake, man! How much do you reckon I owe you?'

Gates had no compassion. He didn't mind how long it took, how much trial and error. But he was concerned that the dogs might be inhibited by the fundamental difference between men and all their natural prey: that men go upright. If they could drag him down they would make their kill, but Gates was worried they would continue to consider the man taboo as long as he hung over them. This was a unique opportunity

– he couldn't try again if he got it wrong. He nodded slowly. 'All right.'

He needed to protect himself until the dogs took over. There were some tools just inside the door, rusted past identification except for a pitchfork. Distastefully brushing away the cobwebs he took it up. 'Cut him down, Andy. Leave his hands tied.'

Donovan staggered as the weight came off his arms but the pitchfork brought him up short. Numb with fear, it never occurred to him that the quickest way out of this was simply to keep going. He backed off, his bound hands before him, his eyes flickering between Gates and the puzzled fretful dogs. His breathing was ragged and under his clothes his body ran with sweat.

Accustomed to handling unreliable animals, Andy edged cautiously round him. Both he and Gates seemed to expect Donovan would *do* something. But fear disarmed him. All he could do was back away and hope to hang on to the contents of his stomach.

'All right,' Gates said softly from the door. 'Slip the dogs.'

'One at a time or all together?'

'All of them,' said Gates with a shudder. 'You won't want to go back in once the action starts.'

But Andy didn't share the older man's dread. He was a skilled handler, better than many men who'd been doing it longer, and he took pride in that. These dogs were part of him, their strength, their fury and their triumphs were all his. He wasn't afraid of anyone while he had such allies. He hooked the chains off the collars and the dogs milled round his legs. His lip curled disdainfully as Donovan stumbled back till the wall ended his retreat.

The dogs padded after Donovan with more curiosity than aggression, smelled his fear but couldn't work out what it meant. Sunk protectively in the fleshy folds of their faces, agleam with unexpected intelligence, their eyes pinned him to the wall.

Andy gave a chuckle. 'They don't know what to do. Come on, you useless lot, a man's nothing but a big rabbit standing on his back legs – he'll come apart just the same. Come on, do what you're trained for!' He aimed an encouraging boot at a muscular backside.

The shouts, the insults, the fear and excitement building in the byre struck a chord of familiarity in the dogs. Oh – *that* was what it was about, was it? They understood that, understood all about fighting – they just weren't sure what it was they were meant to fight. The milling became increasingly energetic and agitated, the animals snapping and snarling at each other in their confusion.

Then one, bolder or meaner than the others, reached a decision. Circling behind the pack he pirouetted on his back feet and launched himself into the air with all the strength of his powerful, agile body.

Fifty metres away in the darkness of the wood the badgers surfacing from their setts paused a moment in their business and raised their heads, startled by a man's screams echoing round the little cluster of buildings that had stood for so long silent.

Chapter Twenty-one

After she'd spoken to her father, Liz sat in the dark, debating whether she should listen to Gail Fisher's broadcast. She had no wish to. She knew Fisher wouldn't deliberately make things worse, but the bare facts were sensational enough. Liz had managed to keep her feelings under control thus far, but inside the edges remained steak-raw and even at her most optimistic she knew they must for the foreseeable future. Being talked about on the public airwaves would be an unpleasant experience.

But she thought she ought to listen. Inevitably the talk of the town tomorrow, she needed to know exactly what had been said and how much of the gossip was innocent exaggeration and how much malicious embroidery. She decided to grit her teeth and tune in. In a way, it was easier having the house to herself. She'd have hated someone listening along with her, sympathizing.

In the event the decision was taken out of her hands. As she was fiddling with the radio the phone rang; clicking her tongue impatiently she lifted it and said, 'Can you make this quick?' – and then her insides curled up with the fear that it might be Brian.

It was Shapiro. He sounded taken aback. 'Sorry?'

Liz sighed. 'Sorry, Frank, I was expecting – someone else. What is it, your ram-raiders struck again?'

'No, but they have been sighted. The car Keith Baker saw? – it's heading north on the motorway with Scobie maintaining a discreet surveillance. I thought you'd like to help me pull it in.'

Fleetingly she considered telling him about the broadcast; but it was too much like fate stepping in. She'd tell him later, when it was too late for either of them to listen. 'I'll pick you up at the office.'

By the time she'd collected Shapiro and the area car for back-up, Scobie was reporting developments. The vehicle he was following had pulled into a service area and the two occupants, a large man and a young girl, had gone into the café. Scobie had used his initiative, and the hoof-pick attachment on his Swiss Army knife, to immobilize their car before following.

When he saw a knot of people, half of them in uniform, coming purposefully across the concourse, Charlie knew the game was up. He finished his tea then spread his hands on the Formica table-top. 'Remember,' he said dully, 'you say nothing.'

But Patsy wasn't a career criminal, couldn't accept the risk of imprisonment with the same glum fatalism. She leapt up from the table, spilling her drink, and took off through the concourse like a hot prospect for The Oaks.

Liz could hardly have hoped for a better antidote to her own problems. Slapping her handbag against Shapiro's chest she said firmly, 'Mine,' and set off in pursuit.

A rack of paperbacks and a cardboard cut-out chef went flying as they scattered startled travellers. An amiable drunk was still trying to decide if he'd really been pushed aside by a snip of a girl moving like an express train when he was definitely pushed aside by a woman moving if anything faster.

They swept through the sweets and tobacco, through the souvenirs and novelties, on past the wash-rooms, between the slot-machines and children's rides. Beyond the rocking-horses and space-ships beckoned the black glass square of the back door. Once through it Patsy had the whole of the lorry park in which to lose herself. Insofar as she had a natural habitat, motorway lorry parks were it.

Not for the first time in racing history the prize was won in the last furlong by the best farrier. Patsy was wearing boots. Liz had on her lace-ups, and they felt like part of her. As Patsy snatched for the back door Liz grabbed a handful of frizzy fair hair and swung her in a crisp arc against the wall. With what breath she had left she gasped, 'You, my girl, are nicked.'

The expression Honour Among Thieves had never made much impression on Patsy. Her only motive was self-interest, and she was still just young enough to blame that on other people. Perhaps a decent up-bringing wouldn't have turned her into the Singing Nun, but now there was no way of knowing. Now she was the Planet Patsy surrounded only by hostile space, and she put herself first, last and everywhere in between because no one else gave her any priority at all.

She'd been there, just outside the door, when the policeman begged for Charlie's help. She'd said nothing because, then, she quite literally didn't care whether Donovan lived or died. The situation was different now. She needed something to bargain with. 'I can help you! You know a guy called Donovan? Tudor's going to kill him. You can stop it, but you'll never find them in time without me.'

Liz's racing breath caught in her throat. Scenarios flashed across her eyes. She loosed the girl's hair, fastened both hands in her lapels and lifted her until they were nose to nose. With infinite menace she growled, 'I've had a difficult week and I'm not in the mood for this. Why don't you tell me everything you know before I accidentally drop you head first into the Magic Roundabout?'

The time for discretion was over. The little convoy raced for the cottage with every light flashing, every siren wailing, every corner taken at speed and preferably on two wheels. Scobie adored it: *this* was what he joined the police for!

Even in the dark Patsy took them straight there, pointing out the byre as Liz stopped the car. The swinging headlights picked up the big dark 4×4 and, behind it, Donovan's van.

'Well, it's the right place,' said Liz. 'And they haven't left yet. Everybody watch out for those dogs: if they're on the loose we may have to wait for Armed Response to deal with them.' She'd let PC Stark drive, spent the short rough trip on the radio getting help. Gates and the boy she'd have tackled, but not the dogs. Patsy had left the cottage too soon to know how Gates intended to use them, but the mere fact of their presence here demanded caution despite the urgent need to find Donovan.

'Remember who brought you here,' whined the girl.

Liz turned on her an unforgiving stare. 'Don't worry, Patsy, nobody's going to forget your part in this.'

The prisoners were driven away then. Liz shouted after Scobie, 'I want Armed Response back here fastest. If they haven't left when you reach Queen's Street, put a bomb under them.'

Shapiro glowered. 'I should have thought of that sooner. I *knew* Gates had fighting dogs, I should have realized we'd need some way to neutralize them. Well, we'll just have to manage till the firearms get here. The uniforms have truncheons: you and I had better find something to carry.' He raised his voice. 'And if one of those things comes at you, beat its brains out first and we'll agree a story for the RSPCA later.'

There were five of them, the two detectives and three uniforms. It had been a matter of grabbing whoever they could without turning Queen's Street into the *Mary Celeste.*

Armed with a torch and a stout stick from the woodpile, Liz moved towards the byre. She knew the risks, but if she didn't go first then either a man nearing retirement or a junior officer would. And in an odd way recent events had not so much cowed her as made her reckless. She was just about ready to face another assailant: with her wits about her and a length of kindling she could begin getting her own back.

The door of the shed was ajar, hemmed with light. She listened a moment but heard nothing. She glanced back: the men with her were ready. 'If they're in here, try not to let them by. If they get as far as the wood we'll never find them.'

Someone ventured, 'Shouldn't we wait for the guns?'

'With DS Donovan in there?'

The hand on her arm was Shapiro's. He said quietly, 'Liz, if he is—'

She knew what he was saying, rounded on him furiously. 'I know. But certifying death is a doctor's job, and even they reckon on being in the same building when they do it! Now, *if* everyone's ready—?' She flung the door open.

No maelstrom of thick bodies, thick legs and snapping jaws hurled at her. The single dusty bulb hanging from the low roof, reinforced by the torches crowding the door, revealed no movement of any kind. But a sickly-sweet pungency hit her in the nostrils and there was something lying on the floor.

Prepared as she was, it took her a moment to be sure it was a man. The clothes were torn to rags, dark and heavy with blood. Through the rents gaped ragged flesh. He lay on his back, face destroyed, arms flung wide. Even through the shock that struck her as odd until she realized they'd done it – the dogs – grabbed at his flailing hands and tugged him between them like children fighting over a toy.

'Oh, dear God,' whispered Shapiro. Liz felt him sway against her.

'It isn't him,' she said hoarsely. 'Frank, look. Look at the head. Under the henna rinse that isn't black hair, it's blond. It isn't Donovan.'

When he made himself look closer Shapiro saw she was right. Donovan was six foot, this boy inches shorter. And he was only a boy, Shapiro thought; and now there was no chance of him ever being anything more.

'Then where is he?'

It was Liz. Shapiro looked at her blankly for a

moment, his mental processes numbed by what they had found. 'Hm?'

She shook his arm fiercely. 'Donovan. Where is he? What happened here? There were three of them, and three dogs. This must be – what did Patsy call him? – Andy. So where's Donovan, where's Gates, and where are those bloody dogs?'

Andy's mistake was in kicking not one of his own dogs, that associated him with nice things like food and walks, but Brian Boru, who didn't. It was an easy mistake to make – in a mill of agitated dogs one over-muscled backside looks much like another – but that moment's carelessness cost him his life. Brian had run the gauntlet of men's boots since he was a pup, didn't know there was such a thing as a friendly kick. Goaded to attack, he chose his own target.

Any one dog would probably have sunk its teeth somewhere soft, registered the resultant yell with a smirk and left it at that. But there were three of them, and three dogs is a pack. A pack doesn't behave in the same way as a single dog. It has no inhibitions, lacks that judicious combination of foresight and self-interest that serves dogs, and many people, as a conscience. It has no sense of fear.

A single dog will rarely bite because it feels about people the way most people feel about the police: they're strong, they have long memories and they never forgive. But the same dog in a pack situation is like a man on speed. Nothing scares him. He can't see that he's making trouble for himself: all he cares about is being in the thick of things, showing what he's made of. Mutual reinforcement escalates the situation until the pack has a nature and purpose of its own and all the well-trained, nice-mannered, thoroughly reliable dogs within it have shrugged off the trappings of civilization. By then it's out of control.

Brian's attack pressed the pack buttons in Gates's dogs. Swept away on a surge of adrenalin they forgot that the boy filling the air with screams and the scent of blood was their friend. As pack members their only allegiance was to each other. In the excitement of the moment instinct and training meshed so that they reacted as they always did to something struggling and shrieking and bleeding: they dragged him down and went for his throat.

Donovan cringed against the back wall, his eyes saucering, his forearms over his ears to muffle the sound. He made no attempt to intervene; nor would he have done had his hands been free; nor, he truly believed, had the victim been not a boy who'd tried to kill him but a casual bystander, even a friend. Afraid to his heart's core, he didn't think he could have waded into that frenzy to save his very soul.

He thought when they finished with Andy they'd turn on him, that his only hope was to get past while they were still fully occupied and before Gates shut the door. He dragged his eyes away from the mêlée and saw Gates watching too, gape-mouthed, through a six-inch gap, like a child watching something scary on TV from behind the couch.

There was a chance if Donovan moved now: if he left this corner running and hit the door before Gates could shoot the bolt.

The boy was quiet, dead or dying; though his body

still jerked under the dusty bulb, that was the dogs worrying at him. If they lost interest in him and looked round . . . But waiting could only make things worse. Donovan tore himself out of his corner and made a determined assault on the world sprint record.

Gates saw him a moment too late. He should have bolted the door as soon as Andy was beyond help. But the dog hadn't come near him, and by the time he realized the danger was not the animals, Donovan was two strides away. With a wordless howl he dropped his pitchfork and slammed the door.

But Donovan's shoulder hit it as it closed and he was travelling fast enough to burst it wide, flinging the smaller man half-way across the yard before he too stumbled and crashed in the dirt.

The vehicles. Inside one he'd be safe. The van was nearest: Donovan lurched to his feet and yanked at the door. But he'd locked it: he hadn't thought there was anything inside that could give him away but he didn't want anyone poking through it just in case. The 4x4 then.

He peered towards the shed. The weak light inside was enough to show him the broad-shouldered bulk of a dog standing in the doorway. He caught his breath and shrank back. But the frenzy was over, at least for now. It swaggered out like a boxer, unhurried, the big head swinging from side to side, scenting for him. The dark was no shield – it knew he was there, it would smell him out.

He didn't know where the other dogs were. But the longer he stayed here wondering, the more likely one of them was to find him. It didn't matter if they saw him as long as he reached the 4x4 first. He filled his lungs, cursed Gates's belt that he hadn't time to worry loose from his wrists, and ran.

Silhouetted against the light the dog's head came up as it saw him. Then it headed for him – not at speed, in a steady powerful lope. It could have caught him if it had tried but he reached the car with metres to spare and was already venting a relieved sigh as he reached for the nearside door.

It didn't move. He tried the handle again, anxiously – none of the dogs was more than a few seconds away – but still the door resisted him.

He scrambled round to the back – he hadn't realized how *long* the damn thing was! – and grabbed for the tailgate. The handle moved just enough for him to think he was safe, then stopped. Too scared now even to curse he kept going, down the long side to the driver's door.

A dog's head, raised in interest, appeared round the back of the vehicle.

Inside the light came on. For a fragment of a second Donovan thought it was because the door was opening. But someone inside had turned it on.

Gates had had the same idea; better luck or a sharper memory had brought him to the 4x4 first, and once inside he'd locked the doors. His elfin face was in profile; Donovan rattled the handle urgently but he didn't look round. He'd turned the light on only so Donovan could see that it was not luck that had defeated him. Then he turned it off again.

Donovan tugged at the door hard enough to rock the car, but he knew he was wasting time. A second dog joined the first at the rear of the vehicle, watching him. Breathing lightly, keeping his eye on them, he backed away round the bonnet. He threw a hunted glance towards the kitchen door, caught the hint of a stealthy movement. God, they had all his bolt-holes covered! Was it just luck or were they stalking him?

If he could reach the road, sooner or later a car would come. Sooner or later was too late. His eyes returned to the van. He must have had the keys: what happened to them? He patted his pockets, without success.

Still slowly backing he came against the broken fence and almost fell. One of the dogs bounded forward at that, just a single bounce that ended as Donovan righted himself. That would be the end. If he went down they'd have him.

He didn't want to go into the wood. Against other men he'd have held his own in there; against dogs he had no chance. But they were driving him that way. He didn't dare advance on them, they were bound to take that as a challenge. He picked his way carefully over the fence, still with his face to the dogs, and after a moment the green hem of the wood lifted for him.

He thought, I can climb – even with my hands tied I can climb six feet up a tree. They can't. If I can get higher than they can jump I'm safe, I can sit them out – for frigging days, if need be!

The last thing he meant to do was run. The dogs were curious about him, were trailing him at a distance – he could see the glint of eyes in the darkness – but there was no overt aggression about their movements yet. If he did nothing to make himself a target, like running, they might decide he was no fun and curl up for a snooze instead.

He backed steadily, and before the branches closed

round him he could see the distance between them stretching. The dogs were staying with the familiar smells of the cottage yard. The broken fence, that they could have sailed in an instant, seemed to mark the limit of their territory.

Another moment and he'd have been out of sight. But then one of the dogs seemed to realize he was escaping. It let out a sharp bark, hurdled the remains of the fence and bounded through the tangle of briars and long grass towards him, the others on its tail.

Donovan turned and fled. There was no sense in it – he didn't think he could outrun them, not in the open and not among the trees. But nor could he stand and wait for them. He ran as fast as he could, with the branches whipping his face and the black trunks looming out of the darkness almost, and sometimes entirely, too late for him to avoid them. Twice he fell, rolled and was on his feet and running again before the impetus of his flight was lost. He could hear the dogs crashing through the undergrowth, couldn't judge how close they were.

The third time he fell he knew it was over before he hit the ground. More than the pain, he heard his ankle break. He couldn't run any further, or climb, or defend himself. Andy's death had bought him a little time, nothing more. Instinct made him grope, on his hands and knees in the leaf-mould, for a tree to put at his back; when he found one he turned towards the sounds crashing towards him, just in time to catch the gleam of errant filtered moonlight off a sleak-coated, surging body sweeping down on him out of the blackness. He threw up his arms, and yelled once, and then it was on him.

Chapter Twenty-two

'Sir.' PC Stark was standing beside the 4×4, shining his torch inside. 'There's someone in here.'

Though he knew Donovan wouldn't be lurking in a darkened car, Shapiro found himself hurrying. There was no need: the man inside wasn't going anywhere. With the doors locked and the windows up, what he was sitting in wasn't so much a get-away car as a bunker. Despite the torches playing on his face he stared ahead almost without blinking, and Shapiro thought that if they hadn't come he'd probably have sat there until he starved.

'Shock?' asked Liz.

Shapiro nodded towards the shed. 'If I'd seen that happen I'd be pretty shocked, too.'

'Is it Gates?'

'I think so. He fits the description, plus he's the only one unaccounted for.' He tapped on the window. 'Mr Gates, you can come out now. It's quite safe.'

Gates looked at him then, his head turning slowly, mechanically. His eyes were glassy and he seemed quite disconnected from reality. He neither spoke nor reached for the door. After a few seconds his eyes slid forward again.

Stark said, 'Shall I open it, sir?'

Shapiro nodded. 'He can't stay in there forever.'

'Ask him about Donovan,' Liz said edgily, playing her torch round the yard while they waited. 'Better still, let me ask him.'

Shapiro's glance was faintly amused. 'You've been watching *Dirty Harry* films again. Calm down a minute. Let me talk to him. A minute won't make any difference at this stage.'

'No?' she shot back. 'Well, Donovan's missing and so are those dogs. If they're together, a minute could make all the difference in the world.'

Stark had the door open. Shapiro leaned his hand on the wheel. 'You're Tudor Gates, aren't you? Sergeant Donovan told me. And the boy inside is your friend Andy.'

At that, something flickered in the vacant eyes.

'There's an ambulance on its way,' Shapiro said gently, 'but I think he's dead. The dogs killed him, did they?'

That, finally, got a response. Puppet-like, Gates nodded. 'The dogs.' His voice was a broken whisper.

'Where are the dogs? Andy's in the shed but the dogs aren't there now. Where did they go?'

'Ask about *Donovan*,' hissed Liz.

Shapiro hissed back, 'I *am*!'

Gates whispered pathetically, 'My poor boy,' and a tear slid down beside his nose.

'They turned on him, didn't they?' Shapiro said softly. 'Then what? They took off? We have to find them before they attack someone else. Did Sergeant Donovan go after them?'

Gates blinked his eyes clear, intelligence creeping back; his head came up and the gaze that met the policeman's was haughty. 'No, Superintendent Shapiro, he did not.'

'Then where is he?'

Gates indicated the wood.

'And the dogs?'

'The same.'

Shapiro frowned. 'You said—'

Gates spat his hatred like venom. 'You think I'm lying? Why on earth would I bother lying to you? I said your spy didn't chase my dogs into the wood. You're the detective: you work it out.'

Liz already had. 'He wasn't chasing them,' she said briefly, already heading for the fence, 'they were chasing him.'

Shapiro wanted to lead the search. But someone had to stay with Gates, and pragmatically it had to be him. 'If things get hairy in there, seniority won't hold a candle to the ability to shin up a tree,' said Liz.

That earned a grim chuckle. 'I'll stay till the firearms get here and I can pass this' – he couldn't find a suitable word, shook a finger at Gates instead – 'on to someone else. Be careful, Liz. Stay close together. Don't even try to catch the dogs, just find Donovan. If he's hurt, stay with him and wait for us. We won't be far behind.'

Powerful torches turned the black wood into architecture, ranks of trunks receding into the shadows like columns, arching branches forming a vault like the undercroft of a great cathedral.

They spread out across a front thirty metres wide, close enough to bunch up if danger threatened, far enough apart to search a useful swathe of woodland. They weren't looking for a carelessly discarded cigarette butt, they were looking for a man, possibly injured, possibly worse. Speed was more important than precision. They moved at a pace between a strong walk and a jog, and they called and every thirty seconds they stopped and listened.

They'd been searching for a few minutes when Stark heard something. He didn't know what – a hoarse cry, the bark of a dog or fox, the grunt of a badger, maybe only an old tree groaning as the night grew cold. No one else heard it at all. But they wheeled in the direction he indicated. In the benighted wood one way was as good as another, and there was at least a chance that what Stark had heard was the missing man.

A minute later a shout came from that end of the line, and when she looked Liz saw that the beam of light from the furthest torch had stopped panning through the colonnade of trees to rest at the base of one of them. 'I think it's him, ma'am!'

Not until she was beside him could she see what Stark had seen. Grey on grey in the flat light of the torch, a shapeless heap among the roots of the tree, it didn't look much like a man. Her heart stumbled and she hurried down the track of Stark's torch.

'Ma'am!' The sharp note of warning brought her up short. From behind the bole of the tree another grey form was emerging. It moved deliberately, its massive head low. The light gleamed greenish off its baleful eyes. Less interested in her than in the man on the ground, it was already within one good bound of him. There was nothing they could do as quickly as the dog could reach Donovan.

Liz was breathing through parted lips. 'Everyone stay still, we don't want to alarm it.' Alarm it? Three divisions of Panzers wouldn't alarm that dog! 'Unless it goes for him, in which case we'll have to rush it.' Tightening her grip on the stave she edged forward. 'Come here, boy, come and talk to me. There's a good dog. Leave the nice man alone and come and talk to me.'

The average Labrador would have been putty in her hands, but this was no household pet. It made more sense to think of it as not a dog at all but a wild beast, savage and unpredictable. It responded to her blandishments by fluttering the lips over its scimitar teeth and emitted a growl like the starter-motor on a power-shovel.

She advanced a step at a time, her voice rhythmic, talking by turns to the dog and the men behind her. 'Good boy, take it easy. He doesn't like me this close. There's nothing to get excited about, old fellow, only me and this fence-post I'm going to beat your head in with. If he comes at me, somebody get to Donovan. Come on, there's a good boy, you don't want to take chunks out of the nasty policeman – he'll taste of engine-oil and antifouling.'

Finally, the heap under the tree stirred. A pale hand sketched a weary salute, and a voice thick with accent and frail with pain said, 'Boss – that's my dog.'

Liz sent two of the uniforms to find the paramedics; Stark stayed with her and Donovan. She sat by the tree and leaned the injured man against her, cushioning him. She took off her jacket and spread it over him. Stark took off his and put it round her shoulders.

She was content to wait for help, but Donovan couldn't rest. Wasted by pain and shock, awareness waxing and waning as if with fever, he couldn't let go of the horror, returning to it as if haunted. 'Did you see – in the byre?'

She nodded. But he couldn't see her face so she said aloud, 'Yes.'

'That should have been me.' With an effort he lifted his hands from his lap. Stark had untied him but they were swollen, clumsy and too painful with returning circulation to do whatever he had intended. He lowered them again, defeated. Under Liz's tweed jacket his thin body shivered.

She held him against her, sharing her warmth. 'Don't think about it. It's over.' By his side Brian Boru sat like a dog carved in jet.

'I can't stop seeing it,' said Donovan, his voice husky. 'Hearing him. They meant for that to be me. I was doing my job, and they wanted to see me torn apart for it.'

Anger stirred in Liz's breast – for him, for all of them. 'They're sick,' she gritted. 'They're sick, and they're vicious, and now one of them's dead and the others are going to prison. And you're going to be fine. Come on, Donovan, you've been hurt worse than this. Little old ladies of ninety-three get over broken ankles.'

That coaxed a fractional grin from him but it didn't last. 'Jesus, boss, I don't know. I think maybe this is the end. I don't think I can do it any more.'

Liz settled her arms about him firmly, holding him not like a lover, perhaps like a friend. 'What're you talking about? You'll be in plaster a couple of months, after that you'll just need to build up the strength. Footballers who break their legs are playing again before the end of the season.'

He shook his head weakly, insistently. His voice

was breathy as if his senses were slipping again, the words slurring. 'That's not what I mean. The leg'll mend. It's the rest of it. I don't think I can face – this – again.'

'This?' Her voice soared incredulously. 'You'll never have to face this again. This was one for the record books.'

'You're not *listening*,' Donovan whined fractiously, twisting against her, the pain of his broken ankle a hiss in his teeth. 'I'm scared, God damn it! I was never so scared in all my life. I was so bloody scared I didn't know what to do. I lost it. And I don't know how to get it back. I don't even know if I *want* it back.'

The breath caught in Liz's throat. Shocked as he was, clinging to reality by his fingernails, she knew what it cost him to say that. He was absolutely serious: for the first time in the two years she'd known him he seemed beaten. The ordeal of the last hours had been too much, psychologically and emotionally, and it had broken him.

Instinct warned that what she said now mattered.

By the time the professionals got hold of him the die would be cast: if he believed he couldn't function as a police officer any more they'd never convince him differently. But in the next few minutes, before the cavalry arrived with a stretcher and a bottle of nitrous oxide, she could do something for him. Not make things as they were: that was beyond her. And maybe not get him back to work. If he'd really had enough, she wouldn't even try.

What she could do was stop him sliding into a bad decision through being too exhausted to make a good one. She could get him back on the horse that threw him. After that, if he wanted to shoot the damn thing, stuff it and put it on castors, that was his choice. He had a right not to be a detective any more. But there were people who cared about him enough to want what was right for him, and it was his good fortune that one of them was here.

She said fervently, 'Donovan, of *course* you were scared! Do you think you shouldn't have been? Of course you freaked out! Do you think I'd have done any better? That the chief would? You can't win a situation like that, all you can do is get through somehow. It doesn't matter how. All that matters is surviving.

'And now you feel – flayed. Vivisected. It's not just the hurt, it's the helplessness. Something was done to you, something demeaning, that you were powerless to stop, and the humiliation is eating like acid into the bones of what you thought you were. A week ago you were a man with an important job, a good income, the respect of colleagues, the love of friends. Now that seems a world away. You're in a kind of limbo – alone and palely loitering in a place where no birds sing. Because something evil can crawl out of a nightmare and sink its claws in you, and use you in ways that make ashes of everything you've built.

'You know what that is, Donovan? That's rape; in every way that matters. It's not the physical assault that hurts, it's the loss of free will. We're not used to that, we thought we left it behind with childhood. Oh, we do lots of things we'd sooner not, but for adults there's always a choice. You can quit the job, end the relationship, whatever. Only the very young, maybe the very old and people in prison have no freedom and even they have rights. We assume that, between the extremes of dependency and providing we stay out of jail, we're in charge of our own lives.

'That's what the rapist destroys: the sense of autonomy. If anyone who's strong enough can dump all that about intrinsic human value and inalienable rights and use you any way he wants, the fabric between the nightmare and the real world has stretched so thin it seems it'll split wide any second and let the chaos in.'

He'd gone very still in the compass of her arms but Liz knew he was listening. Stark had gracefully withdrawn a little way, but she thought he was listening too. Only the dog, motionless at Donovan's side, holding her in its basilisk stare, was obviously listening and it couldn't understand a word.

She wanted to finish before they were interrupted. Her voice took it up again, soft but threaded through with a certainty that surprised even her. Crystallizing her thoughts for Donovan's benefit was sharpening her own understanding. 'What happened to us – both of us – was outside our control. We're not responsible, any more than if we'd been hit by a runaway truck. There was nothing to do except what we did: we endured.

'But now we have a choice. We can't pretend it never happened but we don't have to carry it through life like some great emotional burden. It happened, it's over; you got your ankle bust, I got away pretty lightly too. The scars will heal in time. It's what scars do – all they can do.' She took a deep breath that came out as a sigh. There was a kind of release in putting it into words. Her only regret was that she could talk like this to Donovan but hadn't managed to explain it to her husband.

'What I'm trying to say is that I'm not cut out to be a victim and I don't think you are either. After an air disaster, the victims are the ones who go to the funeral in boxes. The ones there on sticks are survivors.'

She was done. There was nothing she could usefully add; perhaps she'd said too much already. Among the dark trees wove the fireflies of distant torches.

Even though he'd been told the dog was Donovan's, the sight of it crouched over him made Shapiro's heart lurch. Constable Sutton edged towards it with a catching pole from the kennels. Brian Boru sat impassively to be lassoed, making them all feel rather foolish.

When it was done Shapiro hurried forward, anxiously taking in the white, strained face and shut eyes of the man on the ground. 'How is he?'

Liz looked up with a tired smile, made no effort to rise. 'He'll be all right. His ankle's broken, he's a bit battered – nothing more.'

'Does he know about—?' He gestured back towards the cottage.

Donovan raised one eyelid and squinted at him. 'Oh yeah.'

'You saw it happen?'

'I was a captive audience.' He flinched as the paramedics examined his leg.

'We've got all the people involved,' said Shapiro. 'How many of these killer dogs are we still looking for?'

Donovan had watched those dogs in action. He knew Andy would be alive now but for Brian's attack. But he'd be dead, and when he'd been defenceless with his back against this tree it had been Brian again who stood between him and carnage, snapping and snarling until Gates's dogs lost interest and moved off.

For a moment he appeared to consider Shapiro's question. Then he said, very firmly, 'Both of them.'

Chapter Twenty-three

It was the middle of the night before they finished. Though she had a backlog of work waiting, Liz thought she'd earned a lie-in: with no one but herself to consider – that's a joke, she thought bitterly, who else do I ever consider? – she threw Polly an extra slice of hay and set the alarm for an hour later than usual.

In the event she slept for perhaps an extra thirty minutes before wakening to the smell of coffee.

Before she was aware of knowing what it meant she was flying downstairs, dressed only in an oversized t-shirt bearing the legend 'Teachers do it AGAIN and AGAIN until they GET IT RIGHT!' and with her tangled hair streaming in a sunshine train behind her. Brian Graham just had time to put the tray down before she flung herself on him.

'You *bastard*!' she sobbed, clinging to him like a vine. 'How could you *do* that to me?'

'I'm sorry,' he murmured, holding her, feeling the rich warmth of her body through the thin cotton, breathing in the fresh-from-sleep smell. 'I – thought it was what you wanted.'

'Jesus, Brian,' she hissed down the neck of his shirt, 'How could I want that? I love you: don't you *know* that? I love you and I need you. There's other stuff that

I want, but the only thing I *need* is you. How could you think I wanted you to go?'

'Just because you said so,' said Brian mildly, shaking his head. 'Silly me.'

She pulled back and looked at him suspiciously; and yes, she was right, he was laughing at her. Or at them. And why not? They'd behaved like idiots, got hung up on words at a time when anyone could have told them the only reliable guide was instinct. 'Oh – come upstairs.'

'Shall I bring the tray?'

She stared at him. 'Are you mad?'

Afterwards he said pensively, 'We should have done that before.'

'I wanted to.'

'I wish you'd said. I thought it was the last thing you'd want. I thought maybe you'd never want it ever again.'

She put her head on one side. 'It?'

'It. This.' Brian gave a rueful grin. 'All right, sex. You know I had a sheltered upbringing: I was fifteen before I stopped saying "toilet" '.

Laced by his arms she giggled. Then her brow knit in the search for words that said exactly what she meant. 'The point is, Brian, this wasn't sex, this was making love. And what happened out there' – she nodded towards the yard – 'wasn't even sex. Not to me, probably not even to him. It was a mugging. Love is in the commitment and sex is in the joy; without either it's just a violation. They stick something up you when you go for a smear test, too, but nobody thinks of it as sex. It was a violent assault, neither more nor less. A forcible intrusion. Breaking and entering.'

Brian shook his head disbelievingly. 'Can it really mean so little to you? But what does that say—?' He heard himself reopening the argument, stopped abruptly. Nothing mattered to him as much as having her here.

But Liz wanted all the doubts resolved. 'About what?' Her eyes saucered with understanding. 'My God, Brian – what does it say about *us*? About us in bed? You think that because I'm not prepared to fall apart over this it means I put no value on what *we* do? That's it, isn't it? – that's what you think!'

Her astonished stare made him uncomfortable. He could have denied it, but they'd come close to the abyss by failing to make their feelings clear, lying was no way back. 'I suppose. Yes, that's what I was afraid of. Does that sound stupid?'

She rolled eel-like in his arms, came to rest on top of him, staring into his eyes from a range of inches. They were the blue of well-washed denim, and the hearts of them were warm but tucked in the corners she saw worry and fear. She'd done this to him. Not the man who raped her – Liz herself. He'd worried himself sick about a phantasm, something with no reality, a bad dream with no power to hurt them, and she hadn't seen it happening and stopped it. Perhaps he had been stupid, but she'd been cruel.

'Yes,' she said honestly, 'to me it does. But then, I know it isn't true. I can shrug this off – maybe not as easily as I make out, but I can put it out with the trash – because I know how pathetically ersatz a thing it was. And I know *that* because I have the real thing to compare it with. It doesn't touch us, Brian – it doesn't come anywhere *near* us.

'It's – like getting home and finding you've had burglars. It's a horrible feeling: somebody's been in your home, helping himself to things that belong to you, trespassing in a place where you'd always felt safe. Ask anyone who's been burgled: it's not what you lose that matters, it's the invasion. People spend weeks spring-cleaning to get rid of the feeling that the place where they live has been sullied.

'They say being burgled is a bit like being raped. It's not trivializing what happened to me to say that's how it felt. Vicious, dirty and offensive, and not like sex because sex is better than that. I'm hurt and angry, and when I'm angry I don't always hit the right targets – I don't know if you've ever noticed that? – but I swear to you, Brian, nothing that can be done in five minutes to a woman who had to be knocked out first can possibly affect a relationship she'd die for.'

When they'd had breakfast Brian said, 'Are you going into work now?' Liz nodded. 'Me too. Leave your car at home today.'

She frowned, puzzled. 'Why?'

He smiled. 'Because I want to drive my wife to work.'

So he was there to witness perhaps the strangest sight ever seen at Queen's Street, not excluding a Jewish Santa Claus at the Christmas party. Later Liz quizzed him closely, sure he must have known, but he hadn't. He'd just wanted people to see them together.

The police station was full of flowers. Bouquets wrapped in cellophane, bunches tied with wool, hyacinths in pots, a dozen long-stemmed red roses in a crystal vase, a clump of what looked like ragwort – it couldn't have been, it was too early in the year, perhaps it was a rare Japanese dahlia – and two boxed orchids. Additionally there were great mismatched armfuls of flowers that had arrived one at a time and been hurriedly introduced by a desk sergeant who was more concerned with clearing a corner of his work-space than running a match-making service for horticultural lonely hearts.

Liz stared at them open-mouthed from the back door. 'Somebody's birthday?'

WPC Wilson appeared from behind a small camellia. 'They're for you, ma'am.'

'*Me?*' Liz was genuinely staggered. 'Why should anyone send me flowers? Let alone' – she indicated the riot of colour with a stunned wave – 'Kew Gardens.'

'I take it you didn't hear the radio last night,' said Wilson diplomatically.

'Radio? Oh – that thing of Gail Fisher's? No, I was busy.' Her eyebrows, which had reached her hairline, fell suspiciously. 'Whatever did she say?'

Wilson shook her head blithely. 'Nothing special. Only what everyone here's been thinking for four days: that this town's lucky to have you, and instead of making cheap jokes it should send you flowers and then give you all the help and support it can. I think people took the flowers part more literally than she expected.'

'But—' Liz couldn't get her mind round it. She'd seen nothing similar in twenty years on the force. 'Who are they all *from?*'

'Some have cards attached, some haven't. A lot of

the single flowers were kids dropping them in on their way to school. Mostly the others were women.'

They'd hurried in red-faced, embarrassed by what they were doing, anxious to deliver their gift and get away; but aware at the same time of being part of something important, standing up to be counted on an issue that mattered. As the flowers mounted Wilson loved watching the women's faces change as they came in from the street, from the troubled certainty that they were making fools of themselves to delight at joining a groundswell of female solidarity, a regiment levied by a ten-minute radio slot rushing to the barricades armed with flowers.

Wilson indicated a bunch of parrot tulips. 'Those are from us. From Queen's Street.'

Sergeant Tulliver cleared his throat. 'There's a couple of empty cells, we could put them in there.'

Liz shook herself, got her brain back in gear. 'No, find me a van. Some I want to keep, and I think we should leave some on view here, and I'll take the others to the hospital. There's enough here to decorate the whole damn place.' She shook her head in wonder. The threat of tears pricked behind her eyes. 'Is Mr Shapiro in?'

Sergeant Tulliver nodded. 'Went up a few minutes ago.'

'At least, it was probably Mr Shapiro,' added Wilson with a grin. 'It could have been some carnations wearing his hat.'

He'd brought in a couple of vases as well. She found him in her office arranging the flowers with deep concentration and no skill. 'Did everybody hear this broadcast except me?'

His eyes avoided her. 'Somebody made a tape, I

listened to it after you'd gone home. I thought—' He made a shy gesture towards the carnations. 'I didn't expect everyone in town to have the same idea.' He drew her attention to a pot on the windowsill. 'Donovan sent that.'

She was past wondering how *he'd* heard the broadcast or managed to send her a plant from his hospital bed. She peered at it. 'What *is* it?'

'It's a Mother-in-law's Tongue,' said Shapiro. 'I told him it was a funny choice but he insisted.'

Liz thought it was funny too. After what had passed between them last night it was so funny they could hear her laughing all over the building.

When the phone rang it took her a moment to find it. It was Gail Fisher.

Liz said severely. 'I suppose I'vc you to thank for the fact that this police station looks like the Chelsea Flower Show.'

She could hear Fisher's delight. 'Really? I hoped somebody might take it up, but – well, I sent some narcissi just in case. They're not alone then?'

'Not exactly. If you can spare ten minutes, have a look before I take some of them to the hospital. It's enough to renew your faith in your fellow man. Or fellow woman, mostly.'

'Funny you should mention that,' said Fisher, her tone changing. 'I do want to see you, though not about the flowers. And not at Queen's Street. I have a friend who wants to talk to you. Could you meet me at her house?'

Liz sat up sharply, the flowers receding into a soft multi-coloured haze. 'Is this the same friend we were talking about before?'

'Yes. She – I think she feels she let the side down. She wants to help you find this man.'

The house was in Rosedale Avenue, a pleasant piece of stockbroker Tudor with a long front lawn running down to a stone bird-bath. You could tell you were in the nice part of town. In less salubrious areas people put their bird-baths in the back gardens; and there were places where they took them in at night, like washing.

Liz wasn't aware of having met Amanda Urquhart before but she seemed familiar: after a moment, queasily, she realized it was because they were as much alike as sisters. She was aged about forty, fair, well-built, tall, and a professional woman – an architect.

Liz said, 'I don't need to tell you that I understand how you feel. I'm glad you agreed to see me. Any way you want to handle this, that's what we do.'

Mrs Urquhart twitched a smile. 'However it'll do most good. I'm only sorry I couldn't get up the nerve to do it sooner. If it turns out the attack on you, or anyone else, could have been prevented—'

Liz interrupted. 'Don't even wonder, there's no way we'll ever know. If you help us find him now, that's the most we can ask for. Even if you can't help it's still the best you can do.'

Mrs Urquhart was a partner in the firm responsible for the Mere Basin redevelopment which had recycled the old warehouses as apartments, offices and cafés. Donovan called it 'yuppification' and threatened to cut his boat's warps if it got as far as Broad Wharf. But any such project would have been doomed to failure: with

The Jubilee only a spit away across Brick Lane the bulldozers would have been stolen. They didn't have bird-baths at all in The Jubilee, and at night they took the washing-*lines* inside.

She was attacked in the hallway as she left work late one evening. The firm had its offices in The Barbican. Like the other converted warehouses it was shops at ground level, offices on the first and second storeys and flats above that. Electronic access kept kids and drunks from wandering in but it wouldn't have stopped a professional burglar and anyone with business elsewhere in the building could have found his way to that corridor.

Mrs Urquhart finished about midnight, locked up and headed for the lift. Aware that she'd be late she'd deliberately parked her car beside the lifts in the basement garage.

She never reached the lift. A gloved hand reached over her shoulder and closed on her mouth, swinging her like a pendulum into the wall. 'I don't know now where he came from.' A slight tremor disturbed the even rhythm of her voice from time to time, and the toe of one court-shoe was tapping a beat of which she seemed unaware, but that was all. It was as if she was explaining why a flat roof she'd designed kept leaking rather than how her life flew apart one night. 'I must have walked right past him, but the first thing I knew was his hand over my face.'

'Could he have come from one of the offices?' asked Liz.

'I don't see how. There are two doors on my way to the lift, one on each side. But I know one of them was locked – it's the door to our back office but it isn't used, everyone goes through reception. The other office has never been let so it's locked, too. He must have squeezed into the doorway, but with the corridor light on I don't know how I missed him.'

'Could he have broken into the empty office?'

'I asked afterwards.' She gave a self-deprecating smile. 'Carefully, I'd already decided I wasn't going to report this, but I was confused and scared. I didn't know how it happened so I didn't know if it could happen again. I wanted to know how he'd surprised me like that. But there were no signs of a break-in.'

'Then he must have had a key.'

'Apparently not. I told the caretaker I'd heard someone in there late at night, and he checked and said there was no sign of a forced entry and, apart from the one at the estate agents, he had the only key. He obviously thought I'd imagined it. You know: hysterical middle-aged woman alone in the office late at night, frightening herself over nothing. I couldn't put him straight without saying more than I wanted to.'

'Could it have been the caretaker?' Liz asked.

Mrs Urquhart was sure. 'No. He's a tall man, particularly tall. The man who attacked me wasn't.'

'You got a good look at him?'

'Good enough, through the shooting stars. Not his face: he had a scarf over it. Absurd as it sounds, I think it was a white silk evening scarf. And soft leather gloves. A grey track-suit, the sort with a hood which he had pulled down. He was about my height, average build.'

'A young man, would you say?'

'He was fit enough: he went at it like going for a record. But—' She hesitated, thinking. 'Not very young. I don't know how I know that. My impression was of someone about my own age. Perhaps it was his voice.'

Liz's pulse skipped a beat. 'He *spoke* to you?'

'Yes; just a few words. But it wasn't a youngster's voice. He was an educated man, too.'

'What makes you say that?'

Amanda Urquhart's brow crinkled. 'It was something he said. What was it? You'd think it'd be branded in my memory, wouldn't you, but it was something – silly. It made no sense. And I was dizzy.'

'It could be important,' said Liz. She didn't want to put it any stronger than that for fear of scaring the memory away. 'Try and remember.'

Mrs Urquhart squeezed her eyes shut, trying to get it back. 'He bounced me off the wall, I banged my head; I staggered and he kicked the feet from under me. I went down on my hip. He grabbed my hands, pulled me on to my back and – did it. He didn't hurt me. If I'd been any more dazed I mightn't have noticed. I mean, we're not talking Guy the Gorilla here, all right?'

Liz grinned. 'Bit like a Chinese meal? – half an hour later you're ready for another?' They chuckled together, a conspiracy of women not diminishing the wrong done them so much as absorbing it, grinding the edges off in some emotional gizzard. The things that made them vulnerable also made them strong, and they felt that strength stir in their veins like the first twitch of a waking volcano.

Mrs Urquhart went back to what she was struggling with. 'I think he knew me. Well, he was waiting outside my office door, it was no great feat to read what was written on it; but it was more than that. Because he said—' Her eyes came up, startled, as the key finally found the right lock. 'He said, "*That's* what *I* call Deconstruction." Like that: as if it were the last word in an argument we'd had.'

Liz ran the words round her head but they didn't connect with anything. 'Do you know what he meant?'

'I know what Deconstruction is. I've no idea what he meant by it.'

'Um – what *is* Deconstruction?'

'Syncopated architecture,' said Mrs Urquhart with a terse grin. 'Deconstructionists like to pull the bits of a building apart and make them do something different. They think it's challenging. It never occurs to them that buildings evolved the way they did because that's what the people using them find most convenient.'

'You're not a Deconstructionist yourself, then.'

The architect shook her head. 'I'm a sort of Ante-Post-Modernist – I bet on certainties.'

'Then what was he saying?'

'I can't imagine. It's pretty esoteric stuff, and while people do get hot under the collar about modern architecture it's a hell of a distance from there to rape.'

'Perhaps it wasn't architecture he was talking about,' hazarded Liz. A ghost of a possibility hovered at the edge of her vision. 'He's an educated man, he knows what it means, he knows that as an architect it means something specific to you. What? – paradox? Turning things on their heads? Was he saying that when you met before you had the upper hand and this time it was different?'

Mrs Urquhart shrugged helplessly. 'It's possible.'

They were coming to the end of what the interview could usefully yield. Liz nodded slowly. 'All right. You know, you've told me quite a lot about this man that we didn't know before. That *I* didn't know. He's educated, he's probably quite well-off – the silk scarf, the leather gloves – and he's someone you've met and maybe slighted. Think about that. Try to picture a man of that type that you got the better of in some way. A competitor? That'd explain him knowing about Deconstruction. A dissatisfied client? If you start getting any feelings about who it could be, call me. It doesn't matter if you're wrong: we can check him out so discreetly he'll never know. If someone comes to mind, let me look into it.'

Liz rose to leave, and was about to do her usual parting speech about the courage of rape victims putting other women's interests first when the sheer fatuity of it hit her. She must have made it a dozen times and it had never struck her how bloody impertinent it was. Mumbling, she went to make her escape.

But something else occurred to Amanda Urquhart. 'I don't know if this'll be any help, but there was something odd about how he used his voice. He'd just committed rape in a building where people lived and worked: he should have been whispering – better still, he shouldn't have said anything at all. But he was so anxious for me to know how clever he was, how much cleverer than me, that he didn't just say it, he *declaimed* it. Do you know what I mean? He wasn't shouting, more – projecting. Like an actor. I even thought at the time: "This man's putting on a show." I half expected him to take a bow as the lift doors closed.'

'But he didn't?'

'No. He looked back up the corridor, and his eyes went through me as if I wasn't there.'

Chapter Twenty-four

'An actor?' exclaimed Shapiro. 'We're looking for a stage-struck rapist?' He'd been persuaded to adopt a couple of hyacinths for his desk. He peered between them like a startled badger.

It didn't sound too likely. Maybe in London or Cambridge, but Castlemere didn't have a great theatre tradition; hence the paucity of travellers on the Luvvies Train.

'Perhaps not an actor as such,' allowed Liz. 'How about an amateur? There's the Castlemere Players and the Gilbert & Sullivan Society; and some of the churches have drama groups.' Brian had helped out with the scenery.

Shapiro remained scathing. 'A church-going amateur Thespian rapist, then? Oh, yes, that's a question I can just see myself asking. "Tell me, vicar, that Wise Man in the Nativity Play – show any tendency to jump the angels, did he?" ' Then he remembered who he was talking to and his broad face softened with regret. 'I'm sorry, Liz. I keep forgetting–'

'Good,' she said briskly. 'Once we have the sod we can all forget.' Thinking about Brian set her on another track. 'He might not be an actor at all. What about a teacher or lecturer – someone who's used to addressing large groups of people? Or—' Running out of suggestions she sighed dispiritedly. 'We're really not making much progress, are we?'

Immediately Shapiro was contrite. He hadn't much to offer her, he could at least avoid undermining her hope. 'Yes we are: we know a lot about him that we didn't four days ago. Perhaps the most important thing is that he knew Amanda Urquhart before he attacked her. That makes it likely that he knew the other victims, too. Well enough to know where you lived and that you'd be out alone first thing in the morning. Well enough to know Mrs Andrews would be walking home late at night past Castle Mount.'

Liz hadn't thought of that. She hadn't thought that her attacker could be more than just a pervert with patience and an eye for detail: could be a man she knew, perhaps knew well. Before she could stop it the camera in her head began to reel fast-forward all the men she could think of – friends and colleagues and friends of colleagues and colleagues of friends and men who served in the greengrocer's and the butcher's – who fitted even part of the description. When she found herself contemplating Dick Morgan, who though he was not big as policemen go was still bigger than the man who raped her, she yanked herself up short with an audible gasp.

'What?' asked Shapiro, concerned.

'Nothing,' she said quickly. Then, slower, 'I hadn't thought that I might know this man. It's a bit of a shock, that's all. But it could help. If the three of us get together and discuss acquaintances we have in common—'

'It'll amount to most of the male population of

Castlemere,' said Shapiro wearily. 'You'll use the same shops, tradesmen, restaurants, pubs and sports clubs – there are only so many to go round, you're bound to use the same ones some of the time. Even your social circles will overlap. Damn it, he chose the three of you *because* you were of a type.'

Liz moved the hyacinths to one side of his desk to give her somewhere to rest her elbow. Her chin cupped in her hand, she thought.

Watching her, Shapiro saw the moment that the seed of an idea germinated and took root. Her eyes sharpened and narrowed as she scrutinized it, not in every detail but enough to decide that it was worth planting. When her gaze snapped up to meet his, he saw the old battle-light, that compound of determination, intelligence and hope, that put him in mind of a she-panther shaking out her serviette.

'What?'

'If Mrs Urquhart's right and she's not only met this man but argued with him on a professional matter, there should be some record of it. Maybe it goes back years, maybe he's nursed the grudge and it's only now he's turned to sexual violence that he saw the chance to avenge himself. But somewhere in a filing cabinet at Brewster & Urquhart there's an exchange of letters referring to Deconstruction. I'm going to call Mrs Urquhart and agree some cover-story so I can look through those files.'

Shapiro swivelled his chair to and fro, his gaze travelling between Liz and the view of the canal from his window. He pursed his lips. 'Aren't you forgetting something? This isn't your case. For very good reasons, this is definitely not your case.'

'I know that, Frank. But for the same very good reasons it had to be me who saw Mrs Urquhart and it has to be me who follows this up. I can't ask her to start dealing with someone else now.' She gave an apologetic shrug. 'You could tackle the caretaker at The Barbican. The attacker must have come from that empty office, and if there was no break-in he had a key.'

'All right,' agreed Shapiro, standing up, 'I'll go and see him. And you can start your paper-chase. But if it looks like leading anywhere, Liz, call me. I don't want you dealing with this man. For your sake – I know, you're fine, you don't need molly-coddling, but still – and also for the sake of the case. I don't want this man getting off on a technicality.'

'Like, being unable to plead on account of having had his head kicked in by a Detective Inspector?' She grinned tightly, though it may not have been a joke. 'Don't worry, Frank, I'll keep the secateurs out of sight.'

Shapiro went to Mere Basin. He'd been here often enough before, couldn't think why he suddenly felt so ill at ease. Then he understood. This was Donovan's backyard, he knew every cobble and stanchion on the waterfront. Shapiro couldn't remember the last time he was here without him.

Though in fact the bistros, boutiques, offices and apartments of the redevelopment were not his sergeant's natural habitat in the way the derelict wharves and crumbling warehouses further down the tow-path were. When Donovan died he'd come back as an alleycat. Unless he'd been the cat first.

The caretaker was as Mrs Urquhart described him – tall and unhelpful. He gave his name as Bibby: Shapiro assumed it was a surname and his first name was even sillier. He showed the way to the vacant office on the first floor, pointedly marking time while Shapiro looked round. He was a man of about thirty with the manners of an adolescent.

Shapiro fixed him with a cold eye. 'You said nobody was in here.'

'When?'

'A fortnight ago, when Mrs Urquhart told you she heard someone in this office late at night.' Bibby didn't ask why a detective superintendent was asking about so trivial a matter and Shapiro didn't offer a reason. He was ready to lie to protect the victim's privacy but for the moment it wasn't necessary. Bibby showed no curiosity about his presence, only a continuing resentment and the desire to see the back of him. 'You said she couldn't have, that no one had been in here.'

Bibby shrugged, unconcerned. 'That's right. I checked the door: there wasn't a mark on it.'

'Then you must have let him in.'

The caretaker regarded him with vulpine eyes. 'Get real, squire! I'm here to keep the burglars out, not to let them into the offices of their choice.'

'But you do have a key. You let people in here from time to time.'

'Sure I've let people in. The place is to rent, people come to see it, sometimes the estate agents show them round and sometimes I do. Then I show them out and lock up behind me.'

'When was the last time?'

Bibby had to think. 'A month maybe? There hasn't

been much interest – it's too small for most people who want to spend serious rent on an office.'

'And when did you last clean the place? I suppose you are meant to clean it occasionally?'

He was; but it wasn't a part of his job that he gave high priority to. He shrugged again. 'Probably about then.'

Shapiro crooked a forefinger and beckoned him. 'Then who's been perching his backside on this windowsill in the meantime?'

It wasn't a recent mark, fresh dust had fallen on the sill since it was made, but there was a definite bottom-sized depression where the older layers had been disturbed.

'I wouldn't claim to be a dust expert,' said Shapiro, 'but I don't think that's a month old. I'd guess it was made about the time Mrs Urquhart heard someone in here. He wasn't viewing the place, not that late at night. If you didn't let him in and he didn't break in then he had a key.'

Bibby shook his head. 'Not mine. These keys go nowhere without me.'

'You're sure of that?'

'Damn sure.'

'You never lend them to anyone?'

'More than my job's worth, squire.'

Reluctantly Shapiro accepted his word. He didn't like the man but he doubted Bibby was hiding anything. Too casual for a bad liar, not quite casual enough for a good one.

'The agents have their own keys?' Bibby nodded. 'Could they have shown someone round recently enough to make that mark?'

'Not that I know of.'

'Do they ever show people round without you knowing?'

Bibby scowled with justifiable irritation. 'You'd need to ask them, squire, wouldn't you?'

'I will,' promised Shapiro. 'I'll be sure to mention what an asset you are to them, too.'

They don't have irony where Bibby came from. For the first time his eyes warmed. 'Thanks, squire. 'Preciate it.'

Liz agreed with Amanda Urquhart an explanation of why the police needed access to the firm's correspondence files. They would say she'd received a threatening letter from someone who may have been a client at some time. But when she went to the office Mrs Urquhart said quietly, 'Never mind the cover story. I've told them.'

Liz tried not to let her eyes widen too noticeably. 'Everything?'

The other woman shrugged, only a little edgily. 'Yes. I'm damned if I'll let him make me a liar as well.'

'How were they – your colleagues?'

'Shocked. And angry, and kind. Like friends. I don't know what else I expected.'

'A bit of advice,' said Liz. 'Stock up on vases.'

They went through the correspondence disks on the firm's computer, working back from the date of the attack. Then they hunted through the filing-cabinet for anything relevant. They weren't sure what they were looking for. Ideally, a letter of complaint containing a veiled threat and the word Deconstruction. In reality, any communication from a man short of his dotage indicating real and sustained dissatisfaction. It was the nature of the business that there were more than a few of them.

There were several threats of legal action, a few of them aggressive on a personal level. But they all read as if they'd been written in anger and shouldn't be taken at face value. People who threaten to go to law rarely turn to violence as an alternative. And in all the letters they read, the only reference to Deconstruction was by a man who thought it was the same as demolition and was worried about an extension he'd built without planning permission.

There was one more possibility. Liz went through the more-than-slightly-dissatisfied list again, looking for a name she recognized. There were a few – as Shapiro had said, there were bound to be. None of them, so far as she could remember, were rather small men of about her own age with whom she'd crossed swords.

After two hours she sat back on her heels – running out of desk space they'd moved on to the carpet – and scowled. 'Damn. I thought we'd find something.'

Mrs Urquhart was frowning too. She looked as if she was trying to remember something. 'The man who thought Deconstruction was something you did with a bulldozer.'

Liz glanced around the confetti of papers. 'We didn't keep him. If you remember, you sorted him out and he was eternally grateful.'

'Yes,' said the architect pensively. 'But somebody else did that once – made that mistake, thought he was being clever by using technical jargon. Whoever was it? And why, and where?'

Mrs Urquhart's secretary was on the computer. 'The court case. That business of the swimming-pool roof that fell in. They tried to claim it was faulty design but it turned out the contractor had been using sub-standard materials.'

The architect's face cleared. 'That's what it was. About three, four years ago. We actually had to go to court over it. We won, but it was nasty enough for a while. I'd never been in court before.'

'Who brought the action?'

The secretary was busy with her disks again. 'Jason Fielder, 212 Cambridge Road.'

Mrs Urquhart nodded slowly, remembering. 'Yes. That was a very angry man – with every reason, if the roof had come down an hour earlier it would have killed his son.'

Liz felt the hairs standing up on her neck, like a terrier swelling at the sight of a rabbit. She didn't recognize the name but that might not mean they'd never met. 'What sort of a man is he – what does he do?'

'Something in the motor trade. He owns that big garage on the ring road.'

'A business which attracts its fair share of cowboys,' Liz observed pensively. 'What does he look like? How old is he?'

Mrs Urquhart shook her head decisively. 'He can't be our man. Yes, he's about the right age and build, and yes, he'd some reason to be bitter. But Inspector, it can't be him!'

'Why not?'

The architect didn't know whether to laugh or cry.

'Look, I know I didn't give you much of a description. His face was covered, his hands were covered, I only saw his eyes *and* I was stunned. I imagine it was the same with you?'

'So?'

'In spite of that,' said Amanda Urquhart, 'one of us would have noticed if he'd been black.'

Chapter Twenty-five

Four years on, Jason Fielder was still angry enough for his voice to quake when he described what happened. 'An hour earlier my son was in the pool. That Sunday all three of us spent half the morning in it. I could have lost my whole family, Inspector Graham – you wonder I wanted someone to pay for that?'

As Amanda Urquhart had said, he was not a big man. But what he lacked in stature he made up in sheer dynamism. He was never still: pacing the room he took Liz to, fiddling with the ornaments on the mantelpiece, opening and shutting the bureau. Liz thought at first that he was nervous, that she was finally on the right trail, that somehow she and the others had failed to notice that the man who attacked them was black.

But watching him prowl she realized he wasn't nervous at all: he just wasn't used to being awake and doing nothing. It was easy to see how a man with that sort of compulsive, unquenchable energy could come from a back-to-back in The Jubilee, skip school to work in a car-breaker's from the age of fifteen, and end up with a valuable business and a house in the best part of Cambridge Road.

'The court said you were blaming the wrong

people,' Liz reminded him. 'That the contractor cut corners, and Mrs Urquhart didn't know and wasn't in a position to know.'

'Oh, sure,' said Fielder savagely. 'Only the contractor had moved on without leaving a forwarding address by the time the pool roof damn near fell on my boy's head! All I know, Inspector, is that I paid a reputable firm for a swimming-pool extension and the first winter it fell down. If clever Mrs Urquhart didn't know what the contractor was doing she damn well should have done.'

'You're still angry with her.'

'Damn sure I'm angry! Wouldn't you be?'

'Probably,' admitted Liz. 'But I think I'd let it drop after a court told me I was being unreasonable.'

Fielder frowned, brows gathered over the fierce eyes. 'So did I. Is somebody saying different? The Urquhart woman – what's she saying about me?'

'Nothing,' Liz said honestly. 'She's – had a bit of trouble, but she isn't accusing you. Only something was said that reminded her of the court case. Does the word Deconstruction mean anything to you?'

He laughed aloud, a deep and still bitter laugh. 'What it doesn't mean,' he said, heavily ironic, 'is the roof falling into your swimming-pool. That was made quite clear to me.'

Liz allowed herself a wry smile. 'Extracting the Michael, was she?'

'That the same as taking the piss? Yeah, she did that all right. Left me feeling about so high.' The blunt fingers weren't even at full stretch. 'That was cheap. I wasn't trying to make a fool of her, only to make her take responsibility for her mistake – whether that was the design or the people she gave the contract to.'

'Have you seen her since?'

Fielder nodded. 'It's a small town, sooner or later you meet everyone.'

'What did you say to her?'

'Nothing. I crossed the street.'

There was nothing else to ask. Amanda Urquhart hadn't believed Jason Fielder raped her; Liz didn't believe it either. Using his hard-earned wealth to bring a legal action, that was his way. In certain circumstances she could imagine him shouting, waving his arms about, even slapping the woman he blamed for the near-tragedy. But stalking her, lying in wait and raping her to vent his fury? He'd have considered it beneath his dignity. It took him twenty years to make himself a man to be reckoned with. Liz couldn't see him resorting to a form of revenge that had been available to him when he was poor.

As he walked Liz to her car Jason Fielder gave a sudden deep chuckle. 'She didn't have it all her own way, though. The clever Mrs Urquhart. She might have made me feel like something she'd found in a bad bit of wood but my brief gave as good as he got. She didn't get any of those long words past him! Born with a silver dictionary in his mouth, that one.'

Liz smiled. 'Let me guess. Dan Fenton?'

Untroubled by false modesty, Fielder beamed. 'If you can afford the best, why settle for less?' Then he shook his head regretfully. 'We should have won. The work he put into it, we deserved to win. He said afterwards we would have done if it had been her partner's project. No offence, Inspector Graham, but he reckoned the jury would have expected a man to know whether or not the contractor was skimping on the materials. He reckoned they accepted a lower standard of competence because she was a woman.'

When Shapiro went to the building society which acted as agents for The Barbican he was astonished to find Helen Andrews behind the manager's desk.

A cocktail of hope and dread quickened her voice as she recognized him in return. 'Mr Shapiro! Is there some news?' She meant, had he found the man who raped her.

Recovering his composure he intoned reassuringly, 'We're making progress. Forgive me, I wasn't expecting to see you here. I came to ask about a vacant office at the Basin. You told me where you worked but I'd forgotten.'

She ushered him in, left word at the front desk that they shouldn't be disturbed. She wielded her seniority with grace: she knew she'd earned it and so did everyone round her. Like Liz Graham; like Amanda Urquhart. 'Then how can I help you?'

Shapiro had intended to fib, as Liz had to Jason Fielder, about the reason for his questions. Now there was no need. 'The man who attacked you also attacked a woman working late in The Barbican. She was his first victim, so far as we know, and he seems to have come out of an empty office that you have keys for. I need to know who has access to those keys.'

Mrs Andrews called up the information on her screen. 'That's the office on the first floor, opposite the architects.' A tremor shook her and she stared at him wide-eyed. 'It was Amanda Urquhart? Oh no. I know her, we were at school together. We were always called The Book-ends – we're the same age, height, build, colouring.' She blanched. 'Dear God, did he make a *mistake*? Was he looking for me that time, too?'

'No,' said Shapiro quickly, 'we've no reason to think that. My inspector fits the same description and he knew exactly who she was – he went to her home to rape her.'

'I heard what she did,' said Mrs Andrews softly. 'That took courage.'

'Yes,' agreed Shapiro. 'We're very proud of her.'

The woman gave a slow smile. 'Today's my first day back at work. I kept putting it off till I heard that thing on the radio. Then I thought, why am *I* hiding? I've done nothing wrong! I thought, as long as the victims hide their faces the perpetrators don't have to. So here I am.'

He wanted to say something encouraging, was afraid of offending her. Because he was a man and the victims were women the opportunities were legion, or felt to be if they were not. He settled for returning her smile. 'Good. So, the keys. They're kept here, are they?'

'In the safe. They're signed out if someone wants to view and in again afterwards. According to this' – she tapped the screen – 'they're there now, but I'll check.' She did, and they were.

'Who's had them out in the last six weeks?'

That information was there too. 'I have, four times. No one else.'

'To show people round? Who?'

'Different people. One was an accountant, one a barrister. Neither was interested after they'd seen the place: they liked the situation but both needed more room. Then there was a financial adviser – not a very good one, I don't think, he liked it but couldn't afford the rent – and a woman who runs a domestic service agency. She was the most recent, she's still thinking about it.'

'Apart from that your keys would have been here?'

'Yes.'

'Could members of your staff take them out without it appearing on the record?'

Mrs Andrews was taken aback but took time to consider it. 'I suppose so, but I can't imagine why they would. There's no one here I don't have total confidence in. Dealing with other people's properties you have to be sure of your staff.'

'Fair enough.' Shapiro was disappointed but not surprised. It would have been nice to get a positive response, something like: 'We've always wondered about Mr Wiggins, something about the way he dribbles around the female clients,' but that wasn't usually how it happened. Sometimes, if you were lucky, you got a snippet of information that looked like nothing until you put it together with snippets of information obtained elsewhere. Dutifully he jotted down the names and addresses of the people who'd viewed the office.

He arrived back at Queen's Street as Liz was parking her car; she waited and they went up together.

'Any luck?'

'Not that you'd notice. You?'

'A curiosity, but I don't think I'll call a Press conference yet.'

They went to Shapiro's office and he made some coffee. Living alone made him handy like that. This was the first posting Liz had had where it wasn't automatically assumed – until she put the record straight – that she'd do the catering for any group of officers which didn't include a WPC.

'The curiosity,' said Shapiro, hanging up his coat, 'is that the keys for the empty office are held by Helen Andrews.'

Liz stared at him. 'That *has* to mean something. So he could have met both of them there – Mrs Andrews was showing him round as Mrs Urquhart came out of her office.'

'I got the names of the people Mrs Andrews has taken there in the last six weeks. One's a woman, we can rule her out. The others are professional men, two financial wizards and a lawyer.'

'A lawyer.'

Shapiro thought she hadn't heard clearly so repeated it. 'Yes, a lawyer. A barrister.'

For several seconds, which is a long time for a pregnant silence, Liz said nothing. Her eyes were narrowed, calculating, and when she spoke again her tone carried an edge. 'We're looking for an educated man trained to use his voice, yes? That's a pretty good description of a barrister. Half his job is addressing large gatherings. And I know a lot of lawyers, so one viewing an office in The Barbican could easily have met all three of us. Who was it, Frank? Not Beanpole Barraclough, I hope, or Tubby Taylor?'

'No, it was Fairly Ordinary Fenton,' said Shapiro; and wondered why to all intents and purposes the world stopped turning. It was a modest enough joke by any standard. Usually he found he had to draw attention to his jokes; he couldn't remember the last time one had stopped a conversation dead. 'Liz, what is it?'

Her heart was thumping and she was fighting to keep her respiration under control. If he'd hit her with a wet sock wrapped round a gold brick she couldn't have looked more dumbfounded. 'Frank—'

'*What?*'

'I don't want to say it.'

'Say it anyway.'

She took a deep breath. 'About three years ago Dan Fenton and Amanda Urquhart crossed swords in court over the use of the word Deconstruction.'

Over the coffee they took a sober look at what they had. A man of the age and build described by the victims. A man who would own a silk evening scarf and soft leather gloves. A man for whom an unusual technical term had a peculiar significance. A man all three women had had dealings with.

'But – this is an important man we're talking about!' Liz said, doubt already creeping in. 'A respectable man. Would he really risk everything for the sake of a quick thrill in the hayshed?'

Shapiro shrugged ponderously. 'Perhaps he doesn't see it as a risk. It's the nature of his job to have more than a lay knowledge of rape: perhaps he thinks he can fox us. Perhaps that's what he's really after: not sex, he wasn't long enough to enjoy it, but the pleasure of seeing us every day and knowing we'd give our eye-teeth to collar him if we could only work it out.' His jaw tightened. 'That performance in court. That wasn't a wretched coincidence. You were in his way, he wanted to shut you up and he thought that would do it.'

'Amanda Urquhart got in his way when she got the judgement against his client,' Liz proposed slowly. 'Frank, is that who he targets – women who stand up to him, who cut him down to size? Call Helen Andrews, ask if she ever got the better of him.'

Mrs Andrews had no trouble remembering the man she showed round the office a fortnight before – just two days before the attack in the corridor. 'We'd met before. I was at another branch a couple of years ago and there was a misunderstanding. I showed someone a house, and while they were thinking about it I showed it to the Fentons. He made an offer, but the first couple came back and bettered it. I asked Mr Fenton if he wanted to reconsider. He obviously thought I was inventing the other buyer because he said that was his final offer and if it wasn't accepted promptly he'd withdraw it. So the sale went ahead.

'When he realized he'd lost it he got very shirty, threatened me with all sorts of legal action, but I'd done nothing improper and we both knew it. I stood my ground and there was nothing he could do. I was surprised when he phoned about the office in The Barbican, but not as surprised as him when I arrived to open up. We weren't five minutes before he said he wasn't interested. I don't know why he thought he might be – it's a fraction the size of the place they have now.'

'He never intended renting it,' Shapiro told Liz grimly. 'All he wanted was to get inside, so he could lay an ambush for Amanda Urquhart. She was top of his list: he'd watched her, he knew she worked late, he knew if he waited in the empty office two or three nights running she'd be alone when the rest of the floor was empty. He needed access to the office to fix the door so he could get back whenever he needed.'

'That's a lot of time to invest in a two-minute rape,' Liz objected; not because she thought he was wrong, more wanting to hear his argument.

'Yes. But these aren't casual attacks, they're planned like a military campaign. Like a legal battle. We know he's a perfectionist, he takes it personally if things go wrong: well, he commits rape the same way. He picks his target – a woman who's trodden on his toes anything up to four years previously – follows her round to learn her routine, when she'll be vulnerable; then he waits for the perfect moment when he can strike with minimal risk to himself.'

'That's what he did with me.' It was half a question, half a statement.

'Yes. He identified the half hour in the day when you always do the same thing, and you do it alone. You work some evenings and not others, you get around during the day, you go home different routes at different times. But almost always you get up at seven o'clock to feed the horse. Your fence runs alongside Belvedere Park – all he had to do was climb it and hide in the hayshed for ten minutes. It was the only time in your whole day he could be sure of getting you alone. Yes, to know that he must have watched you.'

'Then in God's name, Frank, why didn't I spot him? Why didn't I know I was being watched? I was *trying* to draw him out – if I knew I'd succeeded I could have stopped him there and then! He must have been laughing his leg off, watching me ponce up and down the waterfront with Miss Tunstall's powder-puff, knowing he was going to jump me when I was least expecting it. But I *should* have expected it! Damn it, it's my *job*!'

'Liz, stop this,' Shapiro said sharply, capturing between his own the hand she was tapping fiercely on his desk. 'Don't start looking for ways this could have been your fault. You didn't see him because he didn't want you to. This is a town of eighty thousand people and you have a job that takes you out among them: you're always in the public eye. You think being a police officer makes you psychic? It doesn't. You have the same faculties as everyone else. No blue lamp flashes in your head when you look at someone who's planning a crime. Damn it, I've had this conversation with Donovan before now but I never expected to have it with you!'

She gave a ragged sigh. 'I know that, Frank. Honestly, I'm not blaming myself. It's just, I can't help wondering if I'd done something different whether the result would have been the same. If I'd seen him watching me, could we have had him behind bars by now?'

Shapiro shook his head wearily. 'You'd just have thought, "Nosy sod" and got on with what you were doing. Same as I would, same as anyone. It doesn't work that way. We solve crimes; we don't often manage to prevent them.'

'All right,' said Liz, swallowing the sudden bile. 'Well, we knew he didn't pick his victims out of the phone-book. But there's more to it than just raping women who've annoyed him, isn't there? There has to be. Why do we all look alike? It can't be that every woman who ever crossed him looked the same. And why, in heaven's name, did he wait years to attack the first woman who offended him and then rape three in quick succession?'

'You've met his wife. What's she like?'

'Nice enough woman; bit on the quiet side, at least compared with him. She's—' She broke off. 'Ah.'

'About your age?' hazarded Shapiro. 'Fair, tall, well-built?'

'Four of a kind. What's going on, Frank? What does he think he's doing?'

Shapiro considered. 'Something's happened, in the last month or so, and I bet it involves her. Somehow she's both earned his fury and put herself out of reach. She's – I don't know, left him, got another man? Anyway, made him feel small. He hates that above all else. The most bitter moments of his life have been when strong women made him feel small. For whatever reason he can't do much about his wife, but he can start paying back some of the others. Beginning with those who remind him of her.'

There was a long pause before Liz spoke again. Then: 'Are we serious about this, Frank? It's not just an idea we're kicking round any more – we genuinely think Dan Fenton raped me and two other women? We don't have any proof. We have some circumstantial evidence but nothing' – she flashed a quick, tight grin – 'that a good lawyer couldn't kick out of court.'

'Forensics got a reasonable DNA sample. If it matches Fenton's, even he might have trouble explaining it away.'

'All right,' she conceded, 'it would convince you and it would convince me. But even DNA isn't the complete answer we used to be told it was. You can't use it *instead* of a case, you need a case as well. If we take liberties with Dan Fenton he'll tear us to shreds. This is a clever, clever man, remember, and this is his field as much as it is ours. He won't even run. He'll call in some favours, fix up some alibis, buy an expert witness to question the procedure for taking and analysing the samples, generally fog the issues so much no jury will convict him. We need something specific connecting him to one of the attacks.'

'A fingerprint would be nice,' Shapiro said wistfully. 'But you can't take them off rhododendrons and you can't take them off hay. The office is about the last chance. I'll have SOCO go over it with a magnifying glass.'

Even after a fortnight the Scenes Of Crime Officer found traces of adhesive clinging to the lock plate. 'Easiest trick in the book, that,' he said disgustedly. 'Only takes a few seconds; you could do it with someone a few feet away and they'd never know. You push the tongue back into the lock-case and hold it there with sticky tape – the clear sort, nobody'd notice unless they had their nose up against it. Then you shut the door and rattle it to show that it's locked. Only it isn't, it's just held by the latch. When you come back and turn the knob the door opens, you do what you've come for, you strip off the tape and leave, and this time the door locks behind you.'

He sniffed critically, a man in the pay of the law with the instincts of a criminal. 'In a perfect world you'd have a meths-impregnated tissue to wipe the lock-case afterwards; then if you smeared a bit of dust over it no one'd ever know. But that's maybe asking a lot of an amateur.'

'What makes you say he's an amateur?' asked Liz.

SOCO plainly thought she was being dim. 'He left something for us to find. When he didn't have to. And he left his bum-print on the windowsill while he was waiting. A professional would have dusted that off before he left. A *real* professional would have sat on the floor.'

Another phone-call to Helen Andrews pushed the case over the threshold of reasonable suspicion. 'Who left the office first? Well, he held the door for me if that's what you mean, then he shut it behind us. About the first piece of gentlemanly behaviour I ever had from him.' She wasn't a stupid woman, she knew this amount of interest in one of the four parties she'd shown round that office meant something. Her voice dropped and hardened. 'And, I take it, the last.'

Shapiro put the phone down, carefully, as if afraid it might break. 'I think,' he said, weighing his words, 'we have all we need to ask Mr Daniel Fenton for a blood sample. See if the DNA matches.'

'And if it doesn't?' asked Liz.

The superintendent looked thoughtfully at the ceiling, then at the backs of his hands. Then he scratched his chin and sniffed. Finally he said, 'Everybody has to retire sometime.'

Chapter Twenty-six

It was the habit of the Crown Court to rise as soon after four in the afternoon as was convenient. That is to say, a witness who was on the point of confessing to the crime himself would not be interrupted and told to come back in the morning, but no new witnesses would be sworn.

At a few minutes to four, therefore, Shapiro had the choice of intercepting Fenton as he left the court or meeting him as he returned to his office. The discreet thing would have been to go to his office. The slightly less discreet thing would have been to wait in the broad hall which served the four court-rooms as a mustering place, somewhere to give last-minute instructions, an arcade for the disbelieved to express their outrage to the agents of their disappointment.

Shapiro went into the court to wait. He found a seat at the front of the public gallery.

They knew one another, of course. Shapiro didn't give evidence as often now as he had a rank or two back, but police officers and lawyers in the same town inevitably know one another. That was almost the hardest thing for Shapiro to deal with: that this man knew Liz Graham, had traded pleasantries with her – outside in the hall, if they met in the street, at the

Civic Ball for pity's sake! – and after that he knocked her down and raped her. It was worse, much worse, than attacking a stranger.

So was what he did after that. In open court, knowing the answer, knowing the state her emotions must have been in even if she was making a supreme effort to hide it, he'd dared her to confess her own experience of sexual violence. A man swept away by a madness over which he had no control? No doubt that would be his defence; it might even be believed. But to Shapiro, sitting in the gallery watching the busy, self-important man dominate the front of the court even when the prosecuting counsel was on his feet, it looked more calculated than that. They were three uppity women that he wanted to take down a peg or two, and he did it that way because he wanted to and because he thought he could get away with it. Shapiro continued watching him with a dull deep anger, not savage but unforgiving, a sober and abiding enmity.

At first, Fenton barely registered his presence. From the corner of his eye he saw the slight disturbance as Shapiro took his seat – a bulky man, getting no more agile with the passage of time, he had never been able to slip through a crowd unnoticed; now he left a wake. Knowing the superintendent was not involved in the present case Fenton wondered briefly what his interest was, particularly at this point in the day, before returning his full attention to events outside The Fen Tiger on a Saturday evening last summer.

It was a critical moment for the defence. If the jury believed the two student nurses who were passing when someone got his face slashed with a broken bottle, Fenton's client had a new career opening up in the mail-bag industry. So it was vital to find the weakness in their story. Rising to cross-examine the second girl he fed the little inner flame that helped him to think of people who stood in his way as hostiles, wondering how he could trap her into undermining her own credibility.

So his mind was full of important thoughts, more than enough to eclipse a passing curiosity about a surplus detective superintendent. He had a difficult task, one which would have defeated many of his colleagues. Cometh the hour, he often thought with a certain inner smugness, cometh the Dan. He turned to the girl in the witness box with a smile as sincere as a crocodile's.

She was, he had to admit, a good witness, sure but not cocky, not deferential but polite. A lesser man might have despaired of shaking her. Fenton never despaired. But just when he needed his concentration most he began to feel Shapiro's eyes.

He tried to ignore them. The policeman had no business with him, was probably just filling time till the court rose. Even if he had something to say it couldn't be anything important; even if it were it would have to wait till this day's work was finished. There was no higher duty than that of a barrister to a client facing prison. He tried to put the sense of being watched – no, not that, he was constantly being watched, of being *scrutinized* – out of his mind while he got on with what he was being paid to do.

But Shapiro's gaze was steady – on his cheek as he faced the witness, on the back of his neck as he turned to the judge – its weight unvarying, its significance unavoidable, and Fenton found himself stumbling in his argument and omitting words from his sword-thrust submissions, like a comedian dying on his feet in a working-men's club.

He felt his cheek go ashy. He felt his command of the jury – of his audience, that he'd always played like a maestro – crumbling. He felt the judge watching him with puzzlement, then with concern, and the witness waiting tensely for the onslaught she'd been warned about and which had yet to materialize.

He didn't shake her story. He got through the cross-examination somehow but without making any dents in the nurse's account. A dew of sweat beaded his smooth face as he resumed his seat. Everyone had been expecting a rigorous review of the girl's testimony lasting an hour or more; now suddenly it was over and they could go home. The sense of anticlimax was palpable.

With a minuscule shrug, Judge Carnahan drew a line under his notes. 'Make a prompt start tomorrow, gentlemen, shall we? Ten-thirty suit?'

Fenton was looking at Shapiro, and Shapiro at Fenton. With difficulty the defending counsel dragged his eyes back to the bench. He rose slowly, as if smitten by a sudden palsy. He cleared his throat. Even then his voice was barely his own. 'I think it may be necessary, Your Honour, for the defence to seek an adjournment.'

'*Why?*' asked Shapiro.

It was no longer a question of If; even the blood sample taken by Dr Greaves was no more now than gilt on the gingerbread. Faced with a direct accusation,

Fenton had disdained to lie, had admitted – with hardly a flicker of guilt – the rape of Amanda Urquhart, Helen Andrews and Elizabeth Graham in Castlemere on sundry dates in March and April.

He sat in the interview room, the recording equipment on the table in front of him, a stony-faced constable by the door, Shapiro watching him as he might have watched Dr Jekyll turn into Mr Hyde, and marvelled that he wasn't afraid. He had no illusions about what this meant. It was the end of everything he'd worked for and enjoyed.

He felt it odd to be so little moved by the prospect. He'd known it could come to this but never expected it would, so it wasn't that he was prepared. Rather, he was detached from it – all of it, from what he'd done and from what would happen now. He shrugged negligently. 'Because I wanted to. Because it made me feel good.'

'Raping women made you *feel* good? Why?'

'Raping those women did. I don't really now why.'

'But—' Shapiro was unsettled by the surrealism of the situation. Not arresting a man he'd respected: he'd done that before, it wasn't a pleasant duty but he'd learned to step back and let professionalism take over. What he was finding hard to deal with was the lack of any emotional feedback from Dan Fenton.

It would have been easier if the man had denied it, so that the interview took a shape from the necessary direction of the questioning. But Fenton just sat there, meeting his gaze, answering his questions, making no attempt even to put a gloss on what he'd done; offering nothing that advanced in the least degree an understanding of what had happened.

Shapiro tried again. 'What you had, what you were in this town, that was all your own making. For damn near twenty years you put everything you had into building your career: time, energy, skill, commitment. And then – this. *Why*? Why does a man who's been a model citizen for twenty years suddenly rape three women? And not just any women: career women, women who've climbed the same greasy pole. Not for sex – you can buy that on the corner of Brick Lane any night of the week for less than what you'd charge to enter a plea for a careless driver.'

Fenton shook his head, once, precisely, the thinning fair hair stroking his brow. 'No, not sex.'

'Revenge, then. You were punishing them. Why that way, and why them?'

'Because—' He had to think about it, came up with an answer of a kind. 'Because they offended me. Because I found them offensive.'

'*Offended* you?' exclaimed Shapiro. 'What – laughed at your wig, made jokes about the Lord Chief Justice – what do you *mean*, they offended you?'

For almost the first time Fenton looked straight at him, eyes widening indignantly. 'Oh, come on, Superintendent, save the political correctness for someone who'll be impressed by it. It may be politic to pretend otherwise, and maybe you can't condone what I did, but don't tell me you like the way the girlies are muscling in any more than I do.'

'Muscling in?' Shapiro echoed faintly.

'Business, the professions – dear God, they're everywhere. The upper echelons of your world and mine are about the last remaining bastions: judges' chambers and the Association of Chief Constables are about the only places you can still walk without too much danger of tripping over a hat-box.'

'And that – bothers you?'

Fenton regarded him speculatively. Having nothing to hide and nothing to gain freed him to indulge the policeman's curiosity for just as long as it pleased him. For the moment he was willing to co-operate; when he got bored he would summon his own solicitor. He hadn't done so yet partly because he wasn't looking forward to meeting a colleague in these circumstances, and partly because he knew there was a limit to how much help a legal advisor could be. Also, he really didn't mind talking to Shapiro, as long as they kept it civilized. Shapiro was a civilized man. Shapiro remembered how things used to be.

'Don't misunderstand me,' Fenton said quickly, 'I like women. I enjoy their company, I like having them around. But I don't consider them my equal intellectually, and I resent being obliged to treat them as if they were. Positive discrimination: having to make room for them. If they were as good as they're supposed to be they'd make their own room.'

Shapiro scratched his nose pensively. 'It's a point of view. A lot of men share it; but most of them don't resort to rape. Why did you?'

Fenton smiled. 'I thought I could get away with it. Women who'd complain instantly of a smack in the eye hesitate to report rape. I thought Amanda Urquhart would prefer to lick her wounds in private. To start with, it was going to be just her. I owed her – you know that, do you? She treated my client with contempt because he misunderstood a piece of technical jargon. A man wouldn't have done that. The matter was of no consequence, she didn't have to make him feel he'd just stepped off a banana boat – whatever the pros and cons of the case, he was the victim, he was entitled to respect. A male defendant taking that attitude to a plaintiff would have been advised to mind his manners; and his pathetic little excuses for cocking up wouldn't have been accepted as an answer to the action. Against a man I'd have won that case.'

'So you waited four years and then raped her?'

His face closed, like a blind falling behind a window. He said stiffly, 'It wasn't – convenient – before.'

Shapiro made a mental note to pursue that later. 'But Mrs Urquhart did report it. It was her information that led us to you. You were so careful about everything else – why on earth did you speak to her? And something that specific: you might have known that could be traced back to you.'

Irritation flickered in Fenton's eyes. 'It's easy to be wise after the event, Mr Shapiro. Of course I should have kept quiet. But this was my first time, I was hyped up – somehow I wanted to put my signature on it. Anyone could have raped her: I think I wanted to mark it as my own work even though I hoped no one would ever unravel the cypher. I didn't think she'd remember, after four years. I didn't think she'd tell anyone even if she did.'

'You underestimated her. All of them. They were tougher than you thought, and they nailed you.'

'That's your interpretation,' Fenton said loftily. 'They were less modest than I expected, and that enabled you to nail me.'

Shapiro wanted nothing of his compliments. 'Why Helen Andrews?'

Fenton shrugged. 'I'd forgotten about her till she arrived to show me the office at The Barbican. After I'd finished with Urquhart I kept thinking about her. An absurd little co-incidence made it inevitable. A solicitor friend of mine was getting married and I was going to his stag night. It turned out the bride worked for the Andrews woman and *she* was going to be at the hen night. I knew where they'd end up and when – the happy couple agreed a two o'clock curfew to make sure we all got to the church sober. I made my excuses ten minutes early, drove to Castle Mount, changed my clothes – I had my tracksuit in the car – and waited for her. It was a clear night, she lives half a mile from the bride's home, she wasn't likely to drive home after a booze-up – yes, Superintendent, I did but then I knew I'd need to and rationed my drinking accordingly. I thought she'd be along within a few minutes and she was.'

'What if she'd had company? If she'd taken a taxi, or they'd organized lifts home?'

'Then I'd have haunted the rhododendrons till I got bored and went home. There's always another chance.' He gave a wry little smile. 'Until now, that is.'

Shapiro didn't return the smile. 'And Inspector Graham?'

The muscles either side of Fenton's mouth tightened, pursing his lips. 'She kept doing it, too. Making a fool of me. In court, in my own place. That's the trouble with women in the professions: you let them in and pretty soon they're trying to run things. I've worked hard for what I have: I don't expect to be pushed around by someone who's been fast-tracked to please the Equal Opportunities Commission. She pushed me, I pushed back.'

'You raped her! In her own back garden.'

'Well, I wasn't going to do it at the Basin with half CID looking on!'

Shapiro felt revulsion crawling up his skin. With difficulty he kept his voice even, measured. 'Were there any more, that we don't know about?'

'No.' The lawyer met the policeman's gaze with cool defiance. 'But there would have been.'

Shapiro considered that expressionlessly. It was one of the advantages, he'd found, of carrying some extra weight. A broad face could mask mental and emotional activity in a way a thin one never could. It was a real handicap to Donovan, for instance, that everything he felt showed in his face. He could never have sat here hating this man, wanting to tear him apart, concealing the fact right up to the moment that he could use it to best advantage.

Which, on mature reflection, he considered to be now. 'And what does Mrs Fenton think of the fact that you're going round raping clever women who look like her?'

That got a reaction, though it wasn't what Shapiro was expecting. Fenton said nothing and for long, long seconds did nothing either. Then he began to cry.

'Well, we were nearly right,' Shapiro told Liz afterwards. She'd waited in his office for him to complete the interview, containing her restlessness just barely. She didn't know what she was waiting for, what she hoped or expected to hear that would make her feel better. But she needed to know what there was to know about what happened, where the madness came from. 'We thought maybe she'd left him and so she did. She died, eight weeks ago. Cancer.'

It didn't make it any better. It didn't make it any more explicable. Perhaps it shaved a few grains off the knot of hatred gathered under her heart. 'How—? Why—?' She tried again. 'Why didn't we know? There must have been a funeral.'

'She was buried from her mother's house in Guildford. She died there – apparently Fenton couldn't cope with nursing her. He couldn't cope with her death, either. Nobody knew, not even the people he worked with – not even her friends in Castlemere.'

'Then – *is* he crazy? Diminished responsibility? Post-traumatic stress disorder?'

Shapiro couldn't tell from her tone how much of this was irony. He settled for answering as honestly as he could. 'No, I don't think so. It'll earn him some Brownie points with the judge but I don't think it'll be accepted as something beyond his control. Losing his wife was a catalyst, not a cause. He knew what he was doing. He isn't crazy, he's angry. She left him. She crossed him. He couldn't punish her so he took it out on you.'

'Because we crossed him too?'

'You were too good at your jobs. You each got the better of him in situations where his professional credibility was an issue. And you were still around after his wife was gone. Before it merely irritated him; after his wife died he couldn't bear to see you carrying on – wearing her face, as it were, and getting in his.'

'That *is* crazy,' swore Liz. She saw the prospect of a trial diminish, wasn't sure whether that would be easier or harder to deal with.

'Abnormal,' agreed Shapiro, 'not crazy. He could have stopped himself. He meant to stop after Mrs Urquhart. But by then he'd met Mrs Andrews again; and by the time he'd punished her you were getting up his nose. He knew about the decoy operation. We can guess how: somebody here let something slip, in all innocence, to one of the legal eagles and suddenly it's common knowledge in the robing room.' He squinted apologetically at her. 'If he'd any doubts about his next move, that decided him. I'm sorry, Liz. If I'd said no—'

She couldn't afford to think like that. She shook her head firmly. 'It might have taken him longer but he'd have got to me eventually. We'd locked horns too often, once he'd started down this road he'd have come to me sooner or later. And if it had taken longer he might have done more damage before we caught him.'

There was a lengthy silence, not because they were unsure what to say to each other but because there was nothing left to say. Finally Liz reached for her bag. 'Enough already.' She was hopeless at accents, even music-hall ones like Donovan's brogue and Shapiro's North London Jewish. Shapiro didn't in fact recognize the attempt. 'I've things to do. Believe it or not, I have to see a man about a dog.'

Chapter Twenty-seven

Liz drove. She got the van as close to the front of the clinic as she could, ignoring the No Parking signs, and Donovan manoeuvred himself out and on to his crutches. His plaster encased his leg from his toes to his knee and he hadn't got the knack of steering it yet. Liz watched him labour up the few shallow steps to the vet's front door.

There was no surgery: Keith Baker was doing his VAT. Donovan wasted no time on small talk. 'I want a certificate.'

Baker looked him up and down. 'You've got the wrong number of legs. You'll need one from a doctor.'

Donovan was not amused. 'Not for me. For Brian Boru.'

'Who—?'

'Doesn't matter what he is,' said Donovan firmly. 'What matters is that he's *not* a pit-bull terrier.'

The vet began to understand. 'And is he?'

'Oh, yes,' agreed Donovan readily. 'But I want a certificate saying he's something else.'

'You want me to lie.'

The policeman frowned. 'Is there not some disagreement as to what does and doesn't constitute a pit-bull?'

'Yes,' said Baker cautiously.

'And it comes down to someone's opinion, and if that person thinks he's a pit-bull he's put down and if they think he's a mongrel he isn't?'

'That's about the size of it,' admitted the vet.

'Well, this particular dog saved my neck. Not once but twice. He stopped a man who wanted to kill me and then he saw off some dogs that did. So I'm damned if I'm returning him to the kennels to be destroyed. I can keep him, and I can keep him out of trouble, if I can get him certified as something other than a pit-bull. There'll be no come-back. Everyone at Queen's Street knows what happened, nobody's gunning for him. If I get my piece of paper there'll be more blind eyes turned than at a convention of Nelson look-alikes.'

Baker considered. 'Can I see this dog?'

'He's in the van outside.'

The presence of Detective Inspector Graham at the wheel was not lost on Baker. Donovan was apparently telling the truth: there was a conspiracy to protect the dog from the consequences of its ancestry. He peered in at the back of the van. Brian Boru, one lip raised, stared back.

Baker sucked his teeth. 'I can see how people might think he was a pit-bull.'

Donovan gave a disdainful sniff. 'People *think* all sorts. I'm not interested in what people think, only in what can be proved. Can you make a definitive test that proves that dog there is a pit-bull terrier?'

'Well, no,' said Baker honestly.

'Right. Good. So what else could he be? Isn't he taller than your average pit-bull?'

There's no such thing as an average pit-bull, but

Baker knew what was expected of him. 'He could be, yes. I suppose he could be something like a bullmastiff.'

'Could he? Could he!' said Donovan with sharpened enthusiasm. 'And they're not dangerous, are they?'

'No, I believe the breed standard refers to high spirits and reliability. But he isn't pure-bred. He's too dark, for one thing, and his head isn't square enough.'

'OK. So if his daddy's a bullmastiff, what might his mammy be?'

'Dobermann pinscher?'

It was a shot from the hip. Donovan moved the target to make sure it struck gold. 'Dobermann pinscher, for sure! They're not dangerous either, are they?'

'They've been known to bite,' said Baker. 'Most breeds have. No, they're not required to be registered as a dangerous dog.'

'That's it then – he's a bullmastiff-Dobermann cross. For pity's sake, you only have to look at him! You'll put it on paper, will you?'

Baker considered, chewing his lip. 'What I will put on paper,' he said carefully, 'is that the owner understands the dog to be a bullmastiff-Dobermann cross and I see no reason to doubt it. That do?'

Donovan nodded slowly. Slowly a dark smile broke. 'Oh, yeah.'

Liz drove him home. So he wouldn't have far to hobble she drove down to Cornmarket and back up the tow-path. At one point she thought there was something wrong with the van, but it was Donovan whistling.

She parked beside *Tara*, accepted his invitation aboard for coffee. Then she glanced uneasily at Brian Boru. 'Um – is he going to want my biscuit?'

Donovan chuckled. 'I'll put him in the cable locker. He's used to being banished when I have callers.'

'You don't have any problem with him on your own?'

'No. He's not the sort of dog you get fond of, you know, but we've reached an understanding. He doesn't growl at me and I don't break his head with a tyre-iron.'

Of all those who were at the cottage, Brian Boru, armed with his certificate, was the only winner. Two of the original crew were dead, four were in custody, Gates was in a secure psychiatric unit and Donovan was in plaster. Gates's dogs were shot after one night's liberty by a farmer who found them couched on the carcase of a ewe. Even Chang was dead. Only Brian Boru, who had been marked for death and now had a chance for life, came out of the affair better than he went into it.

'What about your certificate?' asked Liz. 'When will you be back at work?'

'Next week, I hope. I can run a desk till this thing comes off.' He rapped the plaster.

She nodded slowly, relieved to hear him say it. She hadn't realized how much she relied on him until there was the chance he mightn't be there any more. There were other detective sergeants to be had, most of them easier on the nerves, but she felt about Donovan much as he felt about the dog: that they'd reached an understanding. Mutual respect was worth more to her than the uncritical fawning of a poodle. 'I wasn't sure you'd want to come back.'

He looked quickly up and down again, his narrow

face embarrassed. 'I – said some pretty stupid things. In the wood. It was a trying sort of a day.'

Liz laughed out loud. 'Yes, that's fair comment. But they weren't stupid things you said. Nobody could blame you if you decided not to get involved in anything like that again.'

He looked at her over his mug. 'Lots of people thought you'd have had enough after . . .' He left the sentence unfinished.

'After I was raped, Donovan,' she said shortly. 'You're a big boy now, you're allowed to use words like that. And yes, I dare say they did. Since it's what lots of people have been praying for since I got here, I expect they *did* hope this would be enough to see me off. Well, tough. It's a sod, but it's not enough of a sod to change my mind about what I want to do with the rest of my life. If I can deal with it, and Brian can – my Brian, not yours – then everyone else can too.'

Donovan was chewing his lip. There was something he wanted to say and he wasn't sure if he should. Liz rolled her eyes. 'Spit it out.'

After a moment, awkwardly, he did. 'I didn't know how to deal with it either. I didn't know – I still don't – how you're meant to face your boss when you know she's been raped. How you talk to her, what you say – if you say anything. It's too much. It goes beyond what we have the words for.

'If you'd been hit by a bus, now,' he hurried on, stammering in his discomfort, 'or shot even, however bad the damage, I'd have been there. I'd have *wanted* to be there, to see you, see how you were doing. Even if the news was all bad, I'd have wanted to be there. But you weren't shot, you were raped. I told the chief you wouldn't want to see me. What I meant was, I didn't want to see you. I couldn't face you. Jesus,' he swore disgustedly, 'this is pathetic!'

'Yes, it is,' she said frankly. 'But also pretty human. It's the same as avoiding someone who's been bereaved: you don't know what to say so you don't say anything. But anyone who's been there will tell you that *anything* you say, however clumsy, is better than nothing.'

He nodded slowly, the black hair lank in his face. He looked up from the coffee to meet her eyes; she saw him actually flinch. But he pressed on manfully. 'Then, I'm sorry. I'm sorry about what happened to you. I'm sorry if I made it worse. I wish I could've given you the sort of help you gave me. I owe you.'

There was something touching about such painful honesty from such a man. Liz smiled and shook her head. 'Donovan, you don't owe me a thing. You're good at your job. You only think you should be better because you're good enough to recognize what's possible and brave enough to measure yourself against it. But perfection isn't an option. Don't flay yourself because you make mistakes sometimes. Superman would make a terrible copper: humanity is an essential part of the job.'

He thought about that. 'If humanity means cocking up at regular intervals I could still make Chief Constable.'

'I'm talking about coppers,' Liz said reproachfully. 'Superman'd make a *wonderful* Chief Constable.'

That earned a black chuckle. But the eyes that met hers were finally clear, all the ghosts gone. 'What you said, about victims and survivors: I liked that. That's worth remembering.'

She elevated an eyebrow at him, disquietingly. Then abruptly she laughed. 'Tell me something. That stunt you pulled on the train, with the wedding-ring. You didn't learn that in Glencurran?'

'I did so,' he said, straight-faced. 'From my grandmother.'

'Your *grandmother?*' Liz's voice soared in wonder.

'My grandmother,' Donovan said solemnly, 'said I'd go straight to hell if I ever made love to a woman wearing a wedding-ring. And the little buggers can be the devil to shift.'

Soon after that Liz became aware that he was listening to something. He put his mug down and let his head tilt to one side.

'What is it?'

He shook his head, listened some more. Then he hauled himself to his feet, hopped to the window and pushed it wide. 'Come here. Do you hear it?'

She did. A slow smile spread across her face. She looked at him and nodded.

All along the canal, between the water and the tumbleweed wasteland of Cornmarket, the birds were singing.